Frederick Marryat,
Collection novels

In this book:
The Children of the New Forest
The Phantom Ship
Mr. Midshipman Easy
Peter Simple Vol. 1-2
The Three Cutters.

Captain Frederick Marryat (1792 – 1848) was a British Royal Navy officer, novelist, and a contemporary and acquaintance of Charles Dickens, noted today as an early pioneer of the sea story. He is now known particularly for the semi-autobiographical novel Mr Midshipman Easy and his children's novel The Children of the New Forest, and for a widely used system of maritime flag signalling, known as Marryat's Code.

In this book:
The Children of the New Forest……..Pag. 3
The Phantom Ship…………………Pag. 121
Mr. Midshipman Easy……….......Pag. 267
Peter Simple Vol. 1-2……………..Pag. 417
The Three Cutters…………..……..Pag. 606

The Children of the New Forest
Chapter One.

The circumstances which I am about to relate to my juvenile readers took place in the year 1647. By referring to the history of England of that date they will find that King Charles the First, against whom the Commons of England had rebelled, after a civil war of nearly five years, had been defeated, and was confined as a prisoner at Hampton Court. The Cavaliers, or the party who fought for King Charles, had all been dispersed, and the Parliamentary army under the command of Cromwell were beginning to control the Commons.

It was in the month of November in this year that King Charles, accompanied by Sir John Berkely Ashburnham and Legg, made his escape from Hampton Court, and rode as fast as the horses could carry them towards that part of Hampshire which led to the New Forest. The king expected that his friends had provided a vessel in which he might escape to France; but in this he was disappointed. There was no vessel ready, and after riding for some time along the shore he resolved to go to Titchfield, a seat belonging to the Earl of Southampton. After a long consultation with those who attended him, he yielded to their advice, which was, to trust to Colonel Hammond, who was governor of the Isle of Wight for the Parliament, but who was supposed to be friendly to the king. Whatever might be the feelings of commiseration of Colonel Hammond towards a king so unfortunately situated, he was firm in his duties towards his employers, and the consequence was that King Charles found himself again a prisoner in Carisbrook Castle.

But we must now leave the king, and retrace history to the commencement of the civil war. A short distance from the town of Lymington, which is not far from Titchfield, where the king took shelter, but on the other side of the Southampton Water, and south of the New Forest, to which it adjoins, was a property called Arnwood, which belonged to a Cavalier of the name of Beverley. It was at that time a property of considerable value, being very extensive, and the park ornamented with valuable timber; for it abutted on the New Forest, and might have been supposed to have been a continuation of it. This Colonel Beverley, as we must call him, for he rose to that rank in the king's army, was a valued friend and companion of Prince Rupert's, and commanded several troops of cavalry. He was ever at his side in the brilliant charges made by this gallant prince, and at last fell in his arms at the battle of Naseby. Colonel Beverley had married into the family of the Villiers, and the issue of his marriage was two sons and two daughters; but his zeal and sense of duty had induced him, at the commencement of the war, to leave his wife and family at Arnwood, and he was fated never to meet them again. The news of his death had such an effect upon Mrs Beverley, already worn with anxiety on her husband's account, that a few months afterwards she followed him to an early tomb, leaving the four children under the charge of an elderly relative till such time as the family of the Villiers could protect them; but, as will appear by our history, this was not at that period possible. The life of a king and many other lives were in jeopardy, and the orphans remained at Arnwood, still under the care of their elderly relation, at the time that our history commences.

The New Forest, my readers are perhaps aware, was first enclosed by William the Conqueror as a royal forest for his own amusement, for in those days most crowned heads were passionately fond of the chase; and they may also recollect that his successor, William Rufus, met his death in this forest by the glancing of an arrow shot by Sir Walter Tyrrell. Since that time to the present day it has continued a royal domain. At the period of which we are writing it had an establishment of verderers and keepers, paid by the Crown, amounting to some forty or fifty men. At the commencement of the civil war they remained at their posts, but soon found, in the disorganised state of the country, that their wages were no longer to be obtained; and then, when the king had decided upon raising an army, Beverley, who held a superior office in the forest, enrolled all the young and athletic men who were employed in the forest, and marched them away with him to join the king's army. Some few remained, their age not rendering their services of value, and among them was an old and attached servant of Beverley's, a man above sixty years of age, whose name was Jacob Armitage, and who had obtained the situation through Colonel Beverley's interest. Those who remained in the forest lived in cottages many miles asunder, and indemnified themselves for the non-payment of their salaries by killing the deer for sale and for their own subsistence.

The cottage of Jacob Armitage was situated on the skirts of the New Forest, about a mile and a half from the mansion of Arnwood; and when Colonel Beverley went to join the king's troops, feeling how little security there would be for his wife and children in those troubled times, he requested the old man, by his attachment to the family, not to lose sight of Arnwood, but to call there as often as possible to see if he could be of service to Mrs Beverley. The colonel would have persuaded Jacob to have altogether taken up his residence at the mansion; but to this the old man objected. He had been all his life under the greenwood tree, and could not bear to leave the forest. He promised the colonel that he would watch over his family, and ever be at hand when required; and he kept his word. The death of Colonel Beverley was a heavy blow to the old forester, and he watched over Mrs Beverley and the orphans with the greatest solicitude; but when Mrs Beverley followed her husband to the tomb he then redoubled his attentions, and was seldom more than a few hours at a time away from the mansion. The two boys were his inseparable companions, and he instructed them, young as they were, in all the secrets of his own calling. Such was the state of affairs at the time that King Charles made his escape from Hampton Court; and I now shall resume my narrative from where it was broken off.

As soon as the escape of Charles the First was made known to Cromwell and the Parliament, troops of horse were despatched in every direction to the southward, towards which the prints of the horses' hoofs proved that he had gone. As they found that he had proceeded in the direction of the New Forest, the troops were subdivided and ordered to scour the forest, in parties of twelve to twenty, while others hastened down to Southampton, Lymington, and every other seaport or part of the coast from which the king might be likely to embark. Old Jacob had been at Arnwood on the day before, but on this day he had made up his mind to procure some venison, that he might not go there again empty-handed; for Miss Judith Villiers was very partial to venison, and was not slow to remind Jacob if the larder was for many days deficient in that meat. Jacob had gone out accordingly; he had gained his leeward position of a fine buck, and was gradually nearing him by stealth, now behind a huge oak-tree, and then crawling through the high fern, so as to get within shot unperceived, when on a sudden the animal, which had been quietly feeding, bounded away and disappeared in the thicket. At the same time Jacob perceived a small body of horse galloping through the glen in which the buck had been feeding. Jacob had never yet seen the Parliamentary troops, for they had not during the war been sent into that part of the country, but their iron skull-caps, their buff accoutrements, and dark habiliments, assured him that such these must be; so very different were they from the gaily-equipped Cavalier cavalry commanded by Prince Rupert. At the time that they advanced, Jacob had been lying down in the fern near to some low black-thorn-bushes; not wishing to be perceived by them, he drew back between the bushes, intending to remain concealed until they should gallop out of sight; for Jacob thought, "I am a king's forester, and they may consider me as an enemy; and who knows how I may be treated by them?" But Jacob was disappointed in his expectations of the troops riding past him; on the contrary, as soon as they arrived at an oak-tree within twenty yards of where he was concealed, the order was given to halt and dismount; the sabres of the horsemen clattered in their iron sheaths as the order was obeyed, and the old man expected to be immediately discovered; but one of the thorn-bushes was directly between him and the troopers, and effectually concealed him. At last Jacob ventured to raise his head and peep through the bush; and he perceived that the men were loosening the girths of their black horses, or wiping away the perspiration from their sides with handfuls of fern.

A powerfully-framed man, who appeared to command the others, was standing with his hand upon the arched neck of his steed, which appeared as fresh and vigorous as ever, although covered with foam and perspiration. "Spare not to rub down, my men," said he, "for we have tried the mettle of our horses, and have now but one half-hour's breathing-time. We must be on, for the work of the Lord must be done."

"They say that this forest is many miles in length and breadth," observed another of the men, "and we may ride many a mile to no purpose; but here is James Southwold, who once was living in it as a verderer; nay, I think that he said that he was born and bred in these woods. Was it not so, James Southwold?"

"It is even as you say," replied an active-looking young man; "I was born and bred in this forest, and my father was a verderer before me."

Jacob Armitage, who listened to the conversation, immediately recognised the young man in question. He was one of those who had joined the king's army with the other verderers and keepers. It pained him much to perceive that one who had always been considered a frank, true-hearted young man, and who left the forest to fight in defence of his king, was now turned a traitor, and had joined the ranks of the enemy; and Jacob thought how much better it had been for James Southwold if he had never quitted the New Forest, and had not been corrupted by evil company: "He was a good lad," thought Jacob, "and now he is a traitor and a hypocrite."

"If born and bred in this forest, James Southwold," said the leader of the troop, "you must fain know all its mazes and paths. Now call to mind, are there no secret hiding-places in which people may remain concealed; no thickets which may cover both man and horse? Peradventure thou mayst point out the very spot where this man Charles may be hidden."

"I do know one dell, within a mile of Arnwood," replied James Southwold, "which might cover double our troop from the eyes of the most wary."

"We will ride there, then," replied the leader. "Arnwood, sayest thou? Is not that the property of the Malignant, Cavalier Beverley, who was shot down at Naseby?"

"Even so," replied Southwold; "and many is the time—that is, in the olden time, before I was regenerated—many is the day of revelry that I have passed there; many the cup of good ale that I have quaffed."

"And thou shalt quaff it again," replied the leader. "Good ale was not intended only for Malignants, but for those who serve diligently. After we have examined the dell which thou speakest of, we will direct our horses' heads towards Arnwood."

"Who knows but what the man Charles may be concealed in the Malignant's house?" observed another.

"In the day, I should say no," replied the leader; "but in the night the Cavaliers like to have a roof over their heads; and therefore at night, and not before, will we proceed thither."

"I have searched many of their abodes," observed another; "but search is almost in vain. What with their spring panels and secret doors, their false ceilings and double walls, one may ferret for ever and find nothing."

"Yes," replied the leader, "their abodes are full of these Popish abominations; but there is one way which is sure; and if the man Charles be concealed in any house, I venture to say that I will find him. Fire and smoke will bring him forth; and to every Malignant's house within twenty miles will I apply the torch; but it must be at night, for we are not sure of his being housed during the day. James Southwold, thou knowest well the mansion of Arnwood?"

"I know well my way to all the offices below—the buttery, the cellar, and the kitchen; but I cannot say that I have ever been into the apartments of the upper house."

"That it needeth not; if thou canst direct us to the lower entrance, it will be sufficient."

"That can I, Master Ingram," replied Southwold, "and to where the best ale used to be found."

"Enough, Southwold, enough; our work must be done, and diligently. Now, my men, tighten your girths; we will just ride to the dell: if it conceals not whom we seek, it shall conceal us till night, and then the country shall be lighted up with the flames of Arnwood, while we surround the house and prevent escape. Levellers, to horse!"

The troopers sprang upon their saddles, and went off at a hard trot, Southwold leading the way. Jacob remained among the fern until they were out of sight, and then rose up. He looked for a short time in the direction in which the troopers had gone, stooped down again to take up his gun, and then said, "There's providence in this; yes, and there's providence in my not having my dog with me, for he would not have remained quiet for so long a time. Who would ever have thought that James Southwold would have turned a traitor! More than traitor, for he is now ready to bite the hand that has fed him, to burn the house that has ever welcomed him. This is a bad world, and I thank heaven that I have lived in the woods. But there is no time to lose;" and the old forester threw his gun over his shoulder and hastened away in the direction of his own cottage.

"And so the king has escaped," thought Jacob, as he went along, "and he may be in the forest! Who knows but he may be at Arnwood, for he must hardly know where to go for shelter? I must haste and see Miss Judith immediately. 'Levellers, to horse!' the fellow said. What's a Leveller?" thought Jacob.

As perhaps my readers may ask the same question, they must know that a large proportion of the Parliamentary army had at this time assumed the name of Levellers, in consequence of having taken up the opinion that every man should be on an equality, and property should be equally divided. The hatred of these people to any one above them in rank or property, especially towards those of the king's party, which mostly consisted of men of rank and property, was unbounded, and they were merciless and cruel to the highest degree; throwing off much of hat fanatical bearing and language which had before distinguished the Puritans. Cromwell had great difficulty in eventually putting them down, which he did at last accomplish by hanging and slaughtering many. Of this Jacob knew nothing; all he knew was, that Arnwood was to be burnt down that night, and that it would be necessary to remove the family. As for obtaining assistance to oppose the troopers, that he knew to be impossible. As he thought of what must take place, he thanked God for having allowed him to gain the knowledge of what was to happen, and hastened on his way. He had been about eight miles from Arnwood when he had concealed himself in the fern. Jacob first went to his cottage to deposit his gun, saddled his forest pony, and set off for Arnwood. In less than two hours the old man was at the door of the mansion; it was then about three o'clock in the afternoon, and being in the month of November, there was not so much as two hours of daylight remaining. "I shall have a difficult job with the stiff old lady," thought Jacob, as he rang the bell; "I don't believe that she would rise out of her high chair for old Noll and his whole army at his back. But we shall see."

Chapter Two.

Before Jacob is admitted to the presence of Miss Judith Villiers, we must give some account of the establishment at Arnwood. With the exception of one male servant, who officiated in the house and stable as his services might be required, every man of the household of Colonel Beverley had followed the fortunes of their master, and as none had returned, they, in all probability, had shared his fate. Three female servants, with the man above mentioned, composed the whole household. Indeed, there was every reason for not increasing the establishment; for the rents were either paid in part or not paid at all. It was generally supposed that the property, now that the Parliament had gained the day, would be sequestrated, although such was not yet the case; and the tenants were unwilling to pay, to those who were not authorised to receive, the rents which they might be again called upon to make good. Miss Judith Villiers, therefore, found it difficult to maintain the present household; and although she did not tell Jacob Armitage that such was the case, the fact was, that very often the venison which he brought to the mansion was all the meat that was in the larder. The three female servants held the offices of cook, attendant upon Miss Villiers, and housemaid; the children being under the care of no particular servant, and left much to themselves. There had been a chaplain in the house, but he had quitted before the death of Mrs Beverley, and the vacancy had not been filled up; indeed, it could not well be, for the one who left had not received his salary for many months, and Miss Judith Villiers, expecting every day to be summoned by her relations to bring the children and join them, sat in her high chair waiting for the arrival of this summons, which, from the distracted state of the times, had never come.

As we have before said, the orphans were four in number; the two eldest were boys, and the youngest were girls. Edward, the eldest boy, was between thirteen and fourteen years old; Humphrey, the second, was twelve; Alice, eleven; and Edith, eight. As it is the history of these young persons which we are about to narrate, we shall say little about them at present, except that for many months they had been under little or no restraint, and less attended to. Their companions were Benjamin, the man who remained in the house, and old Jacob Armitage, who passed all the time he could spare with them. Benjamin was rather weak in intellect, and was a source of amusement rather than otherwise. As for the female servants, one was wholly occupied with her attendance on Miss Judith, who was very exacting, and had a high notion of her own consequence. The other two had more than sufficient employment; as, when there is no money to pay with, everything must be done at home. That, under such circumstances, the boys became boisterous and the little girls became romps, is not to be wondered at; but their having become so was the cause of Miss Judith seldom admitting them into her room. It is true that they were sent for once a day, to ascertain if they were in the house or in existence, but soon dismissed and left to their own resources. Such was the neglect to which these young orphans were exposed. It must, however, be admitted, that this very neglect made them independent and bold, full of health from constant activity, and more fitted for the change which was so soon to take place.

"Benjamin," said Jacob, as the other came to the door, "I must speak with the old lady."

"Have you brought any venison, Jacob?" said Benjamin, grinning; "else, I reckon, you'll not be over welcome."

"No, I have not; but it is an important business, so send Agatha to her directly."

"I will; and I'll not say anything about the venison."

In a few minutes Jacob was ushered up by Agatha into Miss Judith Villiers's apartment. The old lady was about fifty years of age, very prim and starched, sitting in a high-backed chair, with her feet upon a stool, and her hands crossed before her, her black mittens reposing upon her snow-white apron.

The old forester made his obeisance.

"You have important business with us, I am told," observed Miss Judith.

"Most important, madam," replied Jacob. "In the first place, it is right that you should be informed that his Majesty King Charles has escaped from Hampton Court."

"His majesty escaped!" replied the lady.

"Yes; and is supposed to be secreted somewhere in this neighbourhood. His majesty is not in this house, madam, I presume?"

"Jacob, his majesty is not in this house; if he were, I would suffer my tongue to be torn out sooner than I would confess it, even to you."

"But I have more for your private ear, madam."

"Agatha, retire; and Agatha, be mindful that you go downstairs, and do not remain outside the door."

Agatha, with this injunction, bounced out of the room, slamming-to the door so as to make Miss Judith start from her seat.

"Ill-mannered girl!" exclaimed Miss Judith. "Now, Jacob Armitage, you may proceed."

Jacob then entered into the detail of what he had overheard that morning, when he fell in with the troopers, concluding with the information that the mansion would be burnt down that very night. He then pointed out the necessity of immediately abandoning the house, as it would be impossible to oppose the troopers.

"And where am I to go to, Jacob?" said Miss Judith calmly.

"I hardly know, madam; there is my cottage, it is but a poor place, and not fit for one like you."

"So I should presume, Jacob Armitage; neither shall I accept your offer. It would ill befit the dignity of a Villiers to be frightened out of her abode by a party of rude soldiers. Happen what will, I shall not stir from this—no, not even from this chair. Neither do I consider the danger so great as you suppose. Let Benjamin saddle, and be prepared to ride over to Lymington immediately. I will give him a letter to the magistrate there, who will send us protection."

"But, madam, the children cannot remain here. I will not leave them here. I promised the colonel—"

"Will the children be in more danger than I shall be, Jacob Armitage?" replied the old lady stiffly. "They dare not ill-treat me—they may force the buttery and drink the ale—they may make merry with that and the venison which you have brought with you, I presume; but they will hardly venture to insult a lady of the house of Villiers."

"I fear they will venture anything, madam. At all events, they will frighten the children, and for one night they will be better in my cottage."

"Well, then, be it so; take them to your cottage, and take Martha to attend upon the Miss Beverleys. Go down now, and desire Agatha to come to me, and Benjamin to saddle as fast as he can."

Jacob left the room, satisfied with the permission to remove the children. He knew that it was useless to argue with Miss Judith, who was immovable when once she had declared her intentions. He was debating in his own mind whether he should acquaint the servants with the threatened danger; but he had no occasion to do so, for Agatha had remained at the door while Jacob was communicating the intelligence, and as soon as he had arrived at that portion of it by which she learnt that the mansion was to be burnt down that night, had run off to the kitchen to communicate the intelligence to the other servants.

"I'll not stay to be burnt to death," exclaimed the cook, as Jacob came in. "Well, Mr Armitage, this is pretty news you have brought. What does my lady say?"

"She desires that Benjamin saddles immediately, to carry a letter to Lymington; and you, Agatha, are to go upstairs to her."

"But what does she mean to do? Where are we to go?" exclaimed Agatha.

"Miss Judith intends to remain where she is."

"Then she will remain alone for me," exclaimed the housemaid, who was admired by Benjamin. "It's bad enough to have little victuals and no wages; but as for being burnt to death—Benjamin, put a pillion behind your saddle, and I'll go to Lymington with you. I won't be long in getting my bundle."

Benjamin, who was in the kitchen with the maids at the time that Jacob entered, made a sign significant of consent, and went away to the stable. Agatha went up to her mistress in a state of great perturbation, and the cook also hurried away to her bedroom.

"They'll all leave her," thought Jacob; "well, my duty is plain; I'll not leave the children in the house." Jacob then went in search of them, and found them playing in the garden. He called the two boys to him, and told them to follow him. "Now, Mr Edward," said he, "you must prove yourself your father's own son. We must leave this house immediately; come up with me to your rooms, and help me to pack up yours and your sisters' clothes, for we must go to my cottage this night. There is no time to be lost."

"But why, Jacob; I must know why?"

"Because the Parliamentary troopers will burn it down this night."

"Burn it down! Why, the house is mine, is it not? Who dares to burn down this house?"

"They will dare it, and will do it."

"But we will fight them, Jacob; we can bolt and bar; I can fire a gun, and hit too, as you know; then there's Benjamin and you."

"And what can you and two men do against a troop of horse, my dear boy? If we could defend the place against them, Jacob Armitage would be the first; but it is impossible, my dear boy. Recollect your sisters. Would you have them burnt to death, or shot by these wretches? No, no, Mr Edward; you must do as I say, and lose no time. Let us pack up what will be most useful, and load White Billy with the bundles; then you must all come to the cottage with me, and we will make it out how we can."

"That will be jolly!" said Humphrey; "come, Edward."

But Edward Beverley required more persuasion to abandon the house; at last old Jacob prevailed, and the clothes were put up in bundles as fast as they could collect them.

"Your aunt said Martha was to go with your sisters, but I doubt if she will," observed Jacob, "and I think we shall have no room for her, for the cottage is small enough."

"Oh no, we don't want her," said Humphrey; "Alice always dresses Edith and herself too, ever since mamma died."

"Now we will carry down the bundles, and you make them fast on the pony while I go for your sisters."

"But where does Aunt Judith go?" inquired Edward.

"She will not leave the house, Master Edward; she intends to stay and speak to the troopers."

"And so an old woman like her remains to face the enemy, while I run away from them!" replied Edward. "I will not go."

"Well, Master Edward," replied Jacob, "you must do as you please; but it will be cruel to leave your sisters here; they and Humphrey must come with me, and I cannot manage to get them to the cottage without you go with us; it is not far, and you can return in a very short time."

To this Edward consented. The pony was soon loaded, and the little girls, who were still playing in the garden, were called in by Humphrey. They were told that they were going to pass the night in the cottage, and were delighted at the idea.

"Now, Master Edward," said Jacob, "will you take your sisters by the hand and lead them to the cottage? Here is the key of the door; Master Humphrey can lead the pony; and Master Edward," continued Jacob, taking him aside, "I'll tell you one thing which I will not mention before your brother and sisters: the troopers are all about the New

Forest, for King Charles has escaped, and they are seeking for him. You must not, therefore, leave your brother and sisters till I return. Lock the cottage-door as soon as it is dark. You know where to get a light, over the cupboard; and my gun is loaded, and hangs above the mantelpiece. You must do your best, if they attempt to force an entrance; but above all, promise me not to leave them till I return. I will remain here to see what I can do with your aunt; and when I come back, we can then decide how to act."

This latter ruse of Jacob's succeeded. Edward promised that he would not leave his sisters, and it wanted but a few minutes of twilight when the little party quitted the mansion of Arnwood. As they went out of the gates, they were passed by Benjamin, who was trotting away with Martha behind him on a pillion, holding a bundle as large as herself. Not a word was exchanged, and Benjamin and Martha were soon out of sight.

"Why, where can Martha be going?" said Alice. "Will she be back when we come home to-morrow?"

Edward made no reply, but Humphrey said, "Well, she has taken plenty of clothes in that huge bundle, for one night, at least."

Jacob, as soon as he had seen the children on their way, returned to the kitchen, where he found Agatha and the cook collecting their property, evidently bent upon a hasty retreat.

"Have you seen Miss Judith, Agatha?"

"Yes; and she told me that she should remain, and that I should stand behind her chair, that she might receive the troopers with dignity; but I don't admire the plan. They might leave her alone, but I am sure that they will be rude to me."

"When did Benjamin say he would be back?"

"He don't intend coming back. He said he would not, at all events, till to-morrow morning, and then he would ride out this way, to ascertain if the report was false or true. But Martha has gone with him."

"I wish I could persuade the old lady to leave the house," said Jacob thoughtfully. "I fear they will not pay her the respect that she calculates upon. Go up, Agatha, and say I wish to speak with her."

"No, not I; I must be off, for it is dark already."

"And where are you going, then?"

"To Gossip Allwood's. It's a good mile, and I have to carry my things."

"Well, Agatha, if you'll take me up to the old lady, I'll carry your things for you."

Agatha consented, and as soon as she had taken up the lamp, for it was now quite dark, Jacob was once more introduced.

"I wish, madam," said Jacob, "you would be persuaded to leave the house for this night."

"Jacob Armitage, leave this house I will not, if it were filled with troopers; I have said so."

"But, madam—"

"No more, sir; you are too forward," replied the old lady haughtily.

"But, madam—"

"Leave my presence, Jacob Armitage, and never appear again. Quit the room, and send Agatha here."

"She has left, madam, and so has the cook, and Martha went away behind Benjamin; when I leave, you will be alone."

"They have dared to leave?"

"They dared not stay, madam."

"Leave me, Jacob Armitage, and shut the door when you go out." Jacob still hesitated. "Obey me instantly," said the old lady; and the forester, finding all remonstrance useless, went out, and obeyed her last commands by shutting the door after him.

Jacob found Agatha and the other maid in the courtyard; he took up their packages, and, as he promised, accompanied them to Gossip Allwood, who kept a small ale-house about a mile distant.

"But, mercy on us! What will become of the children?" said Agatha, as they walked along, her fears for herself having, up to this time, made her utterly forgetful of them. "Poor things! And Martha has left them."

"Yes, indeed; what will become of the dear babes?" said the cook, half-crying.

Now Jacob, knowing that the children of such a Malignant as Colonel Beverley would have sorry treatment if discovered, and knowing also that women were not always to be trusted, determined not to tell them how they were disposed of. He therefore replied:

"Who would hurt such young children as those? No, no, they are safe enough; even the troopers would protect them."

"I should hope so," replied Agatha.

"You may be sure of that; no man would hurt babies," replied Jacob. "The troopers will take them with them to Lymington, I suppose. I've no fear for them; it's the proud old lady whom they will be uncivil to."

The conversation here ended, and in due time they arrived at the inn. Jacob had just put the bundles down on the table when the clattering of horses' hoofs was heard. Shortly afterwards the troopers pulled their horses up at the door, and dismounted. Jacob recognised the party he had met in the forest, and among them Southwold. The troopers called for ale, and remained some time in the house, talking and laughing with the women, especially Agatha, who was a very good-looking girl. Jacob would have retreated quietly, but he found a sentinel posted at the door to prevent the egress of any person. He reseated himself, and while he was listening to the conversation of the troopers, he was recognised by Southwold, who accosted him. Jacob did not pretend not to know him, as it would have been useless; and Southwold put many questions to him as to who were resident at Arnwood. Jacob replied that the children were there, and a few servants, and he was about to mention Miss Judith Villiers, when a thought struck him,—he might save the old lady.

"You are going to Arnwood, I know," said Jacob, "and I have heard who you are in search of. Well, Southwold, I'll give you a hint. I may be wrong; but if you should fall in with an old lady, or something like one, when you go to Arnwood, mount her on your crupper, and away with her to Lymington as fast as you can ride. You understand me." Southwold nodded significantly, and squeezed Jacob's hand.

"One word, Jacob Armitage; if I succeed in the capture by your means, it is but fair that you should have something for your hint. Where can I find you the day after to-morrow?"

"I am leaving the country this night, and go I must. I am in trouble, that's the fact; when all is blown over, I will find you out. Don't speak to me any more just now." Southwold again squeezed Jacob's hand, and left him. Shortly afterwards the order was given to mount, and the troopers set off.

Armitage followed slowly and unobserved. They arrived at the mansion and surrounded it. Shortly afterwards he perceived the glare of torches, and in a quarter of an hour more thick smoke rose up in the dark but clear sky; at last the flames burst forth from the lower windows of the mansion, and soon afterwards they lighted up the country round to some distance.

"It is done," thought Jacob, and he turned to bend his hasty steps towards his own cottage, when he heard the galloping of a horse and violent screams; a minute afterwards James Southwold passed him with the old lady tied behind him, kicking and struggling as hard as she could. Jacob smiled, as he thought that he had by his little stratagem saved the old woman's life, for that Southwold imagined that she was King Charles dressed up as an old woman was evident; and he then returned as fast as he could to the cottage.

In half an hour Jacob had passed through the thick woods which were between the mansion and his own cottage, occasionally looking back, as the flames of the mansion rose higher and higher, throwing their light far and wide. He knocked at the cottage-door; Smoker, a large dog, cross-bred between the fox and bloodhound, growled till Jacob spoke to him, and then Edward opened the door.

"My sisters are in bed and fast asleep, Jacob," said Edward, "and Humphrey has been nodding this half-hour; had he not better go to bed before we go back?"

"Come out, Master Edward,"—replied Jacob, "and look." Edward beheld the flames and fierce light between the trees, and was silent.

"I told you that it would be so, and you would all have been burnt in your beds, for they did not enter the house to see who was in it, but fired it as soon as they had surrounded it."

"And my aunt!" exclaimed Edward, clasping his hands.

"Is safe, Master Edward, and by this time at Lymington."

"We will go to her to-morrow."

"I fear not; you must not risk so much, Master Edward. These Levellers spare nobody, and you had better let it be supposed that you are all burnt in the house."

"But my aunt knows the contrary, Jacob."

"Very true; I quite forgot that." And so Jacob had. He expected that the old woman would have been burnt, and then nobody would have known of the existence of the children; he forgot when he planned to save her, that she knew where the children were.

"Well, Master Edward, I will go to Lymington to-morrow and see the old lady; but you must remain here, and take charge of your sisters till I come back, and then we will consider what is to be done. The flames are not so bright as they were."

"No. It is my house that these Roundheads have burned down," said Edward, shaking his fist.

"It was your house, Master Edward, and it was your property; but how long it will be so remains to be seen. I fear it will be forfeited."

"Woe to the people who dare take possession of it," cried Edward; "I shall, if I live, be a man one of these days."

"Yes, Master Edward, and then you will reflect more than you do now, and not be rash. Let us go into the cottage, for it's no use remaining out in the cold; the frost is sharp to-night."

Edward slowly followed Jacob into the cottage. His little heart was full. He was a proud boy and a good boy, but the destruction of the mansion had raised up evil thoughts in his heart—hatred to the Covenanters, who had killed his father and now burnt the property—revenge upon them (how, he knew not); but his hand was ready to strike, young as he was. He lay down on the bed, but he could not sleep. He turned and turned again, and his brain was teeming with thoughts and plans of vengeance. Had he said his prayers that night, he would have been obliged to repeat, "Forgive us, as we forgive them who trespass against us." At last he fell fast asleep, but his dreams were wild, and he often called out during the night, and woke his brother and sisters.

Chapter Three.

The next morning, as soon as Jacob had given the children their breakfast, he set off towards Arnwood. He knew that Benjamin had stated his intention to return with the horse and see what had taken place, and he knew him well enough to feel sure that he would do so. He thought it better to see him, if possible, and ascertain the fate of Miss Judith. Jacob arrived at the still smoking ruins of the mansion, and found several people there, mostly residents within a few miles, some attracted by curiosity, others busy in collecting the heavy masses of lead which had been melted from the roof, and appropriating them to their own benefit; but much of it was still too hot to be touched, and they were throwing snow on it to cool it, for it had snowed during the night. At last Jacob perceived Benjamin on horseback riding leisurely towards him, and immediately went up to him.

"Well, Benjamin, this is a woeful sight. What is the news from Lymington?"

"Lymington is full of troopers, and they are not over civil," replied Benjamin.

"And the old lady—where is she?"

"Ah, that's a sad business," replied Benjamin, "and the poor children, too. Poor Master Edward! He would have made a brave gentleman."

"But the old lady is safe," rejoined Jacob. "Did you see her?"

"Yes, I saw her; they thought she *was* King Charles—poor old soul."

"But they have found out their mistake by this time?"

"Yes, and James Southwold has found it out too," replied Benjamin; "to think of the old lady breaking his neck!"

"Breaking his neck? You don't say so! How was it?"

"Why, it seems that Southwold thought that she was King Charles dressed up as an old woman, so he seized her and strapped her fast behind him, and galloped away with her to Lymington; but she struggled and kicked so manfully, that he could not hold on, and off they went together, and he broke his neck."

"Indeed!—a judgment—a judgment upon a traitor," said Jacob.

"They were picked up, strapped together as they were, by the other troopers, and carried to Lymington."

"Well, and where is the old lady, then? Did you see and speak to her?"

"I saw her, Jacob, but I did not speak to her. I forgot to say, that when she broke Southwold's neck, she broke her own too."

"Then the old lady is dead?"

"Yes, that she is," replied Benjamin; "but who cares about her? It's the poor children that I pity. Martha has been crying ever since."

"I don't wonder."

"I was at the 'Cavalier,' and the troopers were there, and they were boasting of what they had done, and called it a righteous work. I could not stand that, and I asked one of them if it were a righteous work to burn poor children in their beds? So he turned round, and struck his sword upon the floor, and asked me whether I was one of them—'Who are you then?' and I—all my courage went away, and I answered, I was a poor rat-catcher. 'A rat-catcher, are you? Well then, Mr Rat-catcher, when you are killing rats, if you find a nest of young ones, don't you kill them too? Or do you leave them to grow, and become mischievous, eh?'—'I kill the young ones, of course,' replied I. 'Well, so do we Malignants whenever we find them.' I didn't say a word more, so I went out of the house as fast as I could."

"Have you heard anything about the king?" inquired Jacob.

"No, nothing; but the troopers are all out again, and, I hear, are gone to the forest."

"Well, Benjamin, good-bye; I shall be off from this part of the country—it's no use my staying here. Where's Agatha and cook?"

"They came to Lymington early this morning."

"Wish them good-bye for me, Benjamin."

"Where are you going then?"

"I can't exactly say, but I think London way. I only stayed here to watch over the children; and now that they are gone, I shall leave Arnwood for ever."

Jacob, who was anxious, on account of the intelligence he had received of the troopers being in the forest, to return to the cottage, shook hands with Benjamin, and hastened away. "Well," thought Jacob, as he wended his way, "I'm sorry for the poor old lady; but still, perhaps, it's all for the best. Who knows what they might do with these children?—Destroy the nest as well as the rats, indeed:— they must find the nest first." And the old forester continued his journey in deep thought.

We may here observe that, bloodthirsty as many of the Levellers were, we do not think that Jacob Armitage had grounds for the fears which he expressed and felt that is to say, we believe that he might have made known the existence of the children to the Villiers family, and that they would never have been harmed by anybody. That by the burning of the mansion they might have perished in the flames, had they been in bed, as they would have been at that hour, had he not obtained intelligence of what was about to be done, is true; but that there was any danger to them on account of their father having been such a staunch supporter of the king's cause, is very unlikely, and not borne out by the history of the times; but the old forester thought otherwise; he had a hatred of the Puritans, and their deeds had been so exaggerated by rumour that he fully believed that the lives of the children were not safe. Under this conviction, and feeling himself bound by his promise to Colonel Beverley to protect them, Jacob resolved that they should live with him in the forest, and be brought up as his own grandchildren. He knew that there could be no better place for concealment; for, except the keepers, few people knew where his cottage was; and it was so out of the usual paths, and so embosomed in lofty trees, that there was little chance of its being seen, or being known to exist. He resolved, therefore, that they should remain with him till better times; and then he would make known their existence to the other branches of the family, but not before. "I can hunt for them, and provide for them," thought he, "and I have a little money, when it is required; and I will teach them to be useful; they must learn to provide for themselves. There's the garden, and the patch of land: in two or three years the boys will be able to do something. I can't teach them much; but I can teach them to fear God. We must get on how we can, and put our trust in Him who is a Father to the fatherless."

With such thoughts running in his head, Jacob arrived at the cottage, and found the children outside the door, watching for him. They all hastened to him, and the dog rushed before them, to welcome his master. "Down, Smoker, good dog. Well, Mr Edward, I have been as quick as I can. How have Mr Humphrey and your sisters behaved? But we must not remain outside to-day, for the troopers are scouring the forest, and may see you. Let us come in directly; for it would not do that they should come here."

"Will they burn the cottage down?" inquired Alice, as she took Jacob's hand.

"Yes, my dear, I think they would, if they found that you and your brothers were in it: but we must not let them see you."

They all entered the cottage, which consisted of one large room in front, and two back rooms for bedrooms. There was also a third bedroom, which was behind the other two, but which had not any furniture in it.

"Now let's see what we can have for dinner—there's venison left, I know," said Jacob: "come, we must all be useful. Who will be cook?"

"I will be cook," said Alice, "if you will show me how."

"So you shall, my dear," said Jacob, "and I will show you how. There's some potatoes in the basket in the corner—and some onions hanging on the string—we must have some water—who will fetch it?"

"I will," said Edward; who took up a pail and went out to the spring.

The potatoes were peeled and washed by the children—Jacob and Edward cut the venison into pieces—the iron pot was cleaned—and then the meat and potatoes put with water into the pot, and placed on the fire.

"Now I'll cut, up the onions, for they will make your eyes water."

"I don't care," said Humphrey; "I'll cut and cry at the same time."

And Humphrey took up a knife, and cut away most manfully, although he was obliged to wipe his eyes with his sleeve very often.

"You are a fine fellow, Humphrey," said Jacob. "Now we'll put the onions in, and let it all boil up together. Now, you see you have cooked your own dinner; ain't that pleasant?"

"Yes," cried they all; "and we will eat our own dinners as soon as it is ready."

"Then, Humphrey, you must get some of the platters down which are on the dresser; and Alice, you will find some knives in the drawer. And let me see, what can little Edith do? Oh, she can go to the cupboard and find the salt-cellar. Edward, just look-out, and if you see anybody coming or passing, let me know. We must put you on guard till the troopers leave the forest."

The children set about their tasks, and Humphrey cried out, as he very often did, "Now, this is jolly!"

While the dinner was cooking Jacob amused the children by showing them how to put things in order; the floor was swept, the hearth was made tidy. He showed Alice how to wash out a cloth, and Humphrey how to dust the chairs. They all worked merrily, while little Edith stood and clapped her hands.

But just before dinner was ready Edward came in and said, "Here are troopers galloping in the forest!" Jacob went out, and observed that they were coming in a direction that would lead near to the cottage.

He walked in, and after a moment's thought, he said, "My dear children, those men may come and search the cottage; you must do as I tell you, and mind that you are very quiet. Humphrey, you and your sisters must go to bed, and pretend to be very ill. Edward, take off your coat and put on this old hunting-frock of mine. You must be in the bedroom attending your sick brother and sisters. Come, Edith dear, you must play at going to bed, and have your dinner afterwards."

Jacob took the children into the bedroom, and removing the upper dress, which would have betrayed that they were not the children of poor people, put them in bed, and covered them up to the chins with the clothes Edward had put on the old hunting-shirt, which came below his knees, and stood with a mug of water in his hand by the bedside of the two girls. Jacob went to the outer room, to remove the platters laid out for dinner; and he had hardly done so, when he heard the noise of the troopers, and soon afterwards a knock at the cottage-door.

"Come in," said Jacob.

"Who are you, my friend?" said the leader of the troop, entering the door.

"A poor forester, sir," replied Jacob, "under great trouble."

"What trouble, my man?"

"I have the children all in bed with the smallpox."

"Nevertheless, we must search your cottage."

"You are welcome," replied Jacob; "only don't frighten the children if you can help it."

The man, who was now joined by others, commenced his search. Jacob opened all the doors of the rooms, and they passed through. Little Edith shrieked when she saw them; but Edward patted her, and told her not to be frightened. The troopers, however, took no notice of the children; they searched thoroughly, and then came back to the front room.

"It's no use remaining here," said one of the troopers. "Shall we be off? I'm tired and hungry with the ride."

"So am I; and there's something that smells well," said another. "What's this, my good man," continued he, taking off the lid of the pot.

"My dinner for a week," replied Jacob. "I have no one to cook for me now, and can't light a fire every day."

"Well, you appear to live well, if you have such a mess as that every day in the week. I should like to try a spoonful or two."

"And welcome, sir," replied Jacob; "I will cook some more for myself."

The troopers took him at his word; they sat down to the table, and very soon the whole contents of the kettle had disappeared. Having satisfied themselves, they got up, told him that his rations were so good that they hoped to call again; and, laughing heartily, they mounted their horses, and rode away.

"Well," said Jacob, "they are very welcome to the dinner; I little thought to get off so cheap." As soon as they were out of sight Jacob called to Edward and the children to get up again, which they soon did. Alice put on Edith's frock, Humphrey put on his jacket, and Edward pulled off the hunting-shirt.

"They're gone now," said Jacob, coming in from the door.

"And our dinners are gone," said Humphrey, looking at the empty pot and dirty platters.

"Yes; but we can cook another: and that will be more play, you know," said Jacob. "Edward, go for the water; Humphrey, cut the onions; Alice, wash the potatoes; and Edith, help everybody, while I cut up some more meat."

"I hope it will be as good," observed Humphrey; "that other did smell so nice!"

"Quite as good, if not better; for we shall improve by practice, and we shall have a better appetite to eat it with," said Jacob.

"Nasty men eat our dinner," said Edith. "Shan't have any more. Eat this ourselves."

And so they did as soon as it was cooked; but they were very hungry before they sat down.

"This is jolly!" said Humphrey, with his mouth full.

"Yes, Master Humphrey. I doubt if King Charles gets so good a dinner this day. Mr Edward, you are very grave and silent."

"Yes, I am, Jacob. Have I not cause? Oh! If I could but have mauled those troopers!"

"But you could not; so you must make the best of it. They say that every dog has his day, and who knows but King Charles may be on the throne again!"

There were no more visits to the cottage that day, and they all went to bed and slept soundly.

The next morning Jacob, who was most anxious to learn the news, saddled the pony, having first given his injunctions to Edward how to behave in case any troopers should come to the cottage. He told him to pretend that the children were in bed with the smallpox, as they had done the day before. Jacob then travelled to Gossip Allwood's, and he there learnt that King Charles had been taken prisoner, and was at the Isle of Wight, and that the troopers were all going back to London as fast as they came. Feeling that there was now no more danger to be apprehended from them, Jacob set off as fast as he could for Lymington. He went to one shop and purchased two peasant dresses which he thought would fit the two boys, and at another he bought similar apparel for the two girls.

Then with several other ready-made articles, and some other things which were required for the household, he made a large package, which he put upon the pony, and taking the bridle, set off home, and arrived in time to superintend the cooking of the dinner, which was this day venison-steaks fried in a pan, and boiled potatoes.

When dinner was over he opened his bundle, and told the little ones that now they were to live in a cottage they ought to wear cottage clothes, and that he had brought them some to put on, which they might rove about the woods in, and not mind tearing them. Alice and Edith went into the bedroom, and Alice dressed Edith and herself, and came out quite pleased with their change of dress. Humphrey and Edward put theirs on in the sitting-room, and they all fitted pretty well, and certainly were very becoming to the children.

"Now, recollect, you are all my grandchildren," said Jacob; "for I shall no longer call you Miss and Master—that we never do in a cottage. You understand me, Edward, of course?" added Jacob.

Edward nodded his head, and Jacob telling the children that they might now go out of the cottage and play, they all set off quite delighted with clothes which procured them their liberty.

We must now describe the cottage of Jacob Armitage, in which the children have in future to dwell. As we said before, it contained a large sitting-room, or kitchen, in which were a spacious hearth and chimney, table, stools, cupboards, and dressers; the two bedrooms which adjoined it were now appropriated, one for Jacob and the other for the two boys; the third, or inner bedroom, was arranged for the two girls, as being more retired and secure. But there were outhouses belonging to it: a stall, in which White Billy, the pony, lived during the winter; a shed and pigsty rudely constructed, with an enclosed yard attached to them; and it had, moreover, a piece of ground of more than an acre, well fenced in to keep out the deer and game, the largest portion of which was cultivated as a garden and potato-ground, and the other, which remained in grass, contained some fine old apple and pear trees. Such was the domicile; the pony, a few fowls, a sow and two young pigs, and the dog Smoker, were the animals on the establishment. Here Jacob Armitage had been born—for the cottage had been built by his grandfather—but he had not always remained at the cottage. When young, he felt an inclination to see more of the world, and had for several years served in the army. His father and brother had lived in the establishment at Arnwood, and he was constantly there as a boy. The chaplain of Arnwood had taken a fancy to him, and taught him to read—writing he had not acquired. As soon as he grew up he served, as we have said, in the troop commanded by Colonel Beverley's father; and after his death, Colonel Beverley had procured him the situation of forest ranger, which had been held by his father, who was then alive, but too aged to do the duty. Jacob Armitage married a good and devout young woman, with whom he lived several years, when she died, without bringing him any family; after which, his father being also dead, Jacob Armitage had lived alone until the period at which we have commenced this history.

Chapter Four.

The old forester lay awake the whole of this night, reflecting how he should act relative to the children; he felt the great responsibility that he had incurred, and was alarmed when he considered what might be the consequences if his days were shortened. What would become of them—living in so sequestered a spot that few knew even of its existence—totally shut out from the world, and left to their own resources? He had no fear, if his life was spared, that they would do well; but if he should be called away before they had grown up and were able to help themselves, they might perish. Edward was not fourteen years old; it was true that he was an active, brave boy, and thoughtful for his years; but he had not yet strength or skill sufficient for what would be required. Humphrey, the second, also promised well; but still they were all children. "I must bring them up to be useful—to depend upon themselves; there is not a moment to be lost, and not a moment shall be lost; I will do my best, and trust to God; I ask but two or three years, and by that time I trust that they will be able to do without me. They must commence to-morrow the life of foresters' children."

Acting upon this resolution, Jacob, as soon as the children were dressed and in the sitting-room, opened his Bible, which he had put on the table, and said:

"My dear children, you know that you must remain in this cottage, that the wicked troopers may not find you out; they killed your father, and if I had not taken you away, they would have burnt you in your beds. You must therefore live here as my children, and you must call yourselves by the name of Armitage, and not that of Beverley; and you must dress like children of the forest, as you do now, and you must do as children of the forest do; that is, you must do everything for yourselves, for you can have no servants to wait upon you. We must all work; but you will like to work if you all work together, for then the work will be nothing but play. Now, Edward is the oldest, and he must go out with me in the forest, and I must teach him to kill deer and other game for our support; and when he knows how, then Humphrey shall come out and learn how to shoot."

"Yes," said Humphrey, "I'll soon learn."

"But not yet, Humphrey, for you must do some work in the meantime; you must look after the pony and the pigs, and you must learn to dig in the garden with Edward and me when we do not go out to hunt; and sometimes I shall go by myself, and leave Edward to work with you when there is work to be done. Alice, dear, you must, with Humphrey, light the fire and clean the house in the morning. Humphrey will go to the spring for water, and do all the hard work; and you must learn to wash, my dear Alice—I will show you how; and you must learn to get dinner ready with Humphrey, who will assist you; and to make the beds. And little Edith shall take care of the fowls, and feed them every morning, and look for the eggs—will you, Edith?"

"Yes," replied Edith, "and feed all the little chickens when they are hatched, as I did at Arnwood."

"Yes, dear, and you'll be very useful. Now you know that you cannot do all this at once. You will have to try and try again; but very soon you will, and then it will be all play. I must teach you all, and every day you will do it better, till you want no teaching at all. And now, my dear children, as there is no chaplain here, we must read the Bible every morning. Edward can read, I know; can you, Humphrey?"

"Yes, all except the big words."

"Well, you will learn them by and by. And Edward and I will teach Alice and Edith to read in the evenings, when we have nothing to do. It will be an amusement. Now tell me, do you all like what I have told you?"

"Yes," they all replied; and then Jacob Armitage read a chapter in the Bible, after which they all knelt down and said the Lord's Prayer. As this was done every morning and every evening, I need not repeat it again. Jacob then showed them again how to clean the house, and Humphrey and Alice soon finished their work under his directions; and then they all sat down to breakfast, which was a very plain one, being generally cold meat, and cakes baked on the embers, at which Alice was soon very expert; and little Edith was very useful in watching them for her, while she busied herself about her other work. But the venison was nearly all gone; and after breakfast Jacob and Edward, with the dog Smoker, went out into the woods. Edward had no gun, as he only went out to be taught how to approach the game, which required great caution; indeed Jacob had no second gun to give him, if he had wished so to do.

"Now, Edward, we are going after a fine stag, if we can find him—which I doubt not—but the difficulty is to get within shot of him. Recollect that you must always be hid, for his sight is very quick; never be heard, for his ear is sharp; and never come down to him with the wind, for his scent is very fine. Then you must hunt according to the hour of the day. At this time he is feeding; two hours hence he will be lying down in the high fern. The dog is of no use unless the stag is badly wounded, when the dog will take him. Smoker knows his duty well, and will hide himself as close as we do. We are now going into the thick wood ahead of us, as there are many little spots of cleared ground in it where we may find the deer; but we must keep more to the left, for the wind is to the eastward, and we must walk up against it. And now that we are coming into the wood, recollect, not a word must be said, and you must walk as quietly as possible, keeping behind me. Smoker, to heel!" They proceeded through the wood for more than a mile, when Jacob made a sign to Edward, and dropped down into the fern, crawling along to an open spot, where, at some distance, were a stag and three deer grazing. The deer grazed quietly, but the stag was ever and anon raising up his head and snuffing the air as he looked round, evidently acting as a sentinel for the females.

The stag was perhaps a long quarter of a mile from where they had crouched down in the fern. Jacob remained immovable till the animal began to feed again, and then he advanced crawling through the fern, followed by Edward and the dog, who dragged himself on his stomach after Edward. This tedious approach was continued for some time, and they had neared the stag to within half the original distance, when the animal again lifted up his head and appeared uneasy. Jacob stopped and remained without motion. After a time the stag walked away, followed by the does, to the opposite side of the clear spot on which they had been feeding, and, to Edward's annoyance, the animal was now half a mile from them. Jacob turned round and crawled into the wood, and when he knew that they were concealed he rose on his feet and said:

"You see, Edward, that it requires patience to stalk a deer. What a princely fellow! But he has probably been alarmed this morning, and is very uneasy. Now we must go through the woods till we come to the lee of him on the other side of the dell. You see he has led the does close to the thicket, and we shall have a better chance when we get there, if we are only quiet and cautious."

"What startled him, do you think?" said Edward.

"I think, when you were crawling through the fern after me, you broke a piece of rotten stick that was under you, did you not?"

"Yes, but that made but little noise."

"Quite enough to startle a red deer, Edward, as you will find out before you have been long a forester. These checks will happen, and have happened to me a hundred times, and then all the work is to be done over again. Now then to make the circuit—we had better not say a word. If we get safe now to the other side we are sure of him."

They proceeded at a quick walk through the forest, and in half an hour had gained the side where the deer were feeding. When about three hundred yards from the game, Jacob again sank down on his hands and knees, crawling from bush to bush, stopping whenever the stag raised his head, and advancing again when it resumed feeding; at last they came to the fern at the side of the wood, and crawled through it as before, but still more cautiously as they approached the stag. In this manner they arrived at last to within eighty yards of the animal, and then Jacob advanced his gun ready to put it to his shoulder, and as he cocked the lock, raised himself to fire. The click occasioned by the cocking of the lock roused up the stag instantly, and he turned his head in the direction from whence the noise proceeded; as he did so Jacob fired, aiming behind the animal's shoulder: the stag made a bound, came down again, dropped on his knees, attempted to run, and fell dead, while the does fled away with the rapidity of the wind.

Edward started up on his legs with a shout of exultation. Jacob commenced reloading his gun, and stopped Edward as he was about to run up to where the animal lay.

"Edward, you must learn your craft," said Jacob; "never do that again; never shout in that way—on the contrary, you should have remained still in the fern."

"Why so? The stag is dead."

"Yes, my dear boy, that stag is dead; but how do you know but what there may be another lying down in the fern close to us, or at some distance from us, which you have alarmed by your shout? Suppose that we both had had guns, and that the report of mine had started another stag lying in the fern within shot, you would have been able to shoot it; or if a stag was lying at a distance, the report of the gun might have startled him so as to induce him to move his head without rising. I should have seen his antlers move and have marked his lair, and we should then have gone after him and stalked him too."

"I see," replied Edward, "I was wrong; but I shall know better another time."

"That's why I tell you, my boy," replied Jacob; "now let us go to our quarry. Ay, Edward, this is a noble beast. I thought that he was a hart royal, and so he is."

"What is a hart royal, Jacob?"

"Why, a stag is called a brocket until he is three years old; at four years he is a staggart; at five years a warrantable stag; and after five years he becomes a hart royal."

"And how do you know his age?"

"By his antlers: you see that this stag has nine antlers; now, a brocket has but two antlers, a staggart three, and a warrantable stag but four; at six years old, the antlers increase in number until they sometimes have twenty or thirty. This is a fine beast, and the venison is now getting very good. Now you must see me do the work of my craft."

Jacob then cut the throat of the animal, and afterwards cut off its head, and took out its bowels.

"Are you tired, Edward?" said Jacob, as he wiped his hunting-knife on the coat of the stag.

"No, not the least."

"Well, then, we are now, I should think, about four or five miles from the cottage. Could you find your way home? But that is of no consequence, Smoker will lead you home by the shortest path. I will stay here, and you can saddle White Billy and come back with him, for he must carry the venison back. It's more than we can manage—indeed, as much as we can manage with White Billy to help us. There's more than twenty stone of venison lying there, I can tell you."

Edward immediately assented, and Jacob desiring Smoker to go home, set about flaying and cutting up the animal for its more convenient transportation. In an hour and a half Edward, attended by Smoker, returned with the pony, on whose back the chief portion of the venison was packed. Jacob took a large piece on his own shoulders, and Edward carried another, and Smoker, after regaling himself with a portion of the inside of the animal, came after them. During the walk home Jacob initiated Edward into the terms of venery and many other points connected with deer-stalking, with which we shall not trouble our readers. As soon as they arrived at the cottage the venison was hung up, the pony put in the stable, and then they sat down to dinner with an excellent appetite after their long morning's walk. Alice and Humphrey had cooked the dinner themselves, and it was in the pot, smoking hot, when they returned; and Jacob declared he never ate a better mess in his life. Alice was not a little proud of this, and of the praises she received from Edward and the old forester. The next day Jacob stated his intention of going to Lymington to dispose of a large portion of the venison, and bring back a sack of oatmeal for their cakes. Edward asked to accompany him, but Jacob replied:

"Edward, you must not think of showing yourself at Lymington, or anywhere else, for a long while, until you are grown out of memory. It would be folly, and you would risk your sisters' and brother's lives, perhaps, as well as your own. Never mention it again: the time will come when it will be necessary, perhaps; if so, it cannot be helped. At present you would be known immediately. No, Edward, I tell you what I do mean to do: I have a little money left, and I intend to buy you a gun, that you may learn to stalk deer yourself without me: for recollect, if any accident should happen to me, who is there but you to provide for your brother and sisters? At Lymington I am known to many; but out of all who know me, there is not one who knows where my cottage is; they know that I live in the New Forest, and that I supply them venison, and purchase other articles in return. That is all that they know; and I may therefore go without fear. I shall sell the venison to-morrow, and bring you back a good gun; and Humphrey shall have the carpenters' tools which he wishes for—for I think, by what he does with his knife, that he has a turn that way, and it may be useful. I must also get some other tools for Humphrey and you, as we shall then be able to work all together; and some threads and needles for Alice, for she can sew a little, and practice will make her more perfect."

Jacob went off to Lymington as he had proposed, and returned late at night with White Billy well loaded; he had a sack of oatmeal, some spades and hoes, a saw and chisels, and other tools; two scythes and two three-pronged forks; and when Edward came to meet him he put into his hand a gun with a very long barrel.

"I believe, Edward, that you will find that a good one, for I know where it came from. It belonged to one of the rangers, who was reckoned the best shot in the forest. I know the gun, for I have seen it on his arm, and have taken it in my hand to examine it more than once. He was killed at Naseby, with your father, poor fellow! And his widow sold the gun to meet her wants."

"Well!" replied Edward, "I thank you much, Jacob, and I will try if I cannot kill as much venison as will pay back the purchase-money—I will, I assure you."

"I shall be glad if you do, Edward; not because I want the money back, but because then I shall be more easy in my mind about you all, if anything happens to me. As soon as you are perfect in your woodcraft, I shall take Humphrey in hand, for there is nothing like having two strings to your bow. To-morrow we will not go out: we have meat enough for three weeks or more; and now the frost has set in, it will keep well. You shall practise at a mark with your gun, that you may be accustomed to it: for all guns, even the best, require a little humouring."

Edward, who had often fired a gun before, proved the next morning that he had a very good eye; and after two or three hours' practice, hit the mark at a hundred yards almost every time.

"I wish you would let me go out by myself," said Edward, overjoyed at his success.

"You would bring home nothing, boy," replied Jacob. "No, no, you have a great deal to learn yet; but I tell you what you shall do: any time that we are not in great want of venison, you shall have the first fire."

"Well, that will do," replied Edward.

The winter now set in with great severity, and they remained almost altogether within doors. Jacob and the boys went out to get firewood, and dragged it home through the snow.

"I wish, Jacob," said Humphrey, "that I was able to build a cart, for it would be very useful, and White Bill would then have something to do; but I can't make the wheels, and there is no harness."

"That's not a bad idea of yours, Humphrey," replied Jacob; "we will think about it. If you can't build a cart, perhaps I can buy one. It would be useful if it were only to take the dung out of the yard on the potato-ground; for I have hitherto carried it out in baskets, and it's hard work."

"Yes, and we might saw the wood into billets, and carry it home in the cart instead of dragging it this way: my shoulder is quite sore with the rope, it cuts me so."

"Well, when the weather breaks up, I will see what I can do, Humphrey; but just now the roads are so blocked up, that I do not think we could get a cart from Lymington to the cottage, although we can a horse, perhaps."

But if they remained indoors during the inclement weather, they were not idle. Jacob took this opportunity to instruct the children in everything. Alice learnt how to wash and how to cook. It is true that sometimes she scalded herself a little, sometimes burnt her fingers; and other accidents did occur, from the articles employed being too heavy for them to lift by themselves; but practice and dexterity compensated for want of strength, and fewer accidents happened every day. Humphrey had his carpenters' tools; and although at first he had many failures, and wasted nails and wood, by degrees he learnt to use his tools with more dexterity, and made several little useful articles. Little Edith could now do something, for she made and baked all the oatmeal cakes, which saved Alice a good deal of time and trouble in watching them. It was astonishing how much the children could do, now that there was no one to do it for them; and they had daily instruction from Jacob. In the evening Alice sat down with her needle and thread to mend the clothes; at first they were not very well done; but she improved every day. Edith and Humphrey learnt to read while Alice worked, and then Alice learnt; and thus passed the winter away so rapidly, that although they had been five months at the cottage, it did not appear as if they had been there as many weeks. All were happy and contented, with the exception, perhaps, of Edward, who had fits of gloominess, and occasionally showed signs of impatience as to what was passing in the world, of which he remained in ignorance.

That Edward Beverley had fits of gloominess and impatience is not surprising. Edward had been brought up as the heir of Arnwood; and a boy at a very early age imbibes notions of his position, if it promises to be a high one. He was not two miles from that property which by right was his own. His own mansion had been reduced to ashes—he himself was hidden in the forest, and he could not but feel his position. He sighed for the time when the king's cause should be again triumphant, and his arrival at that age when he could in person support and uphold the cause. He longed to be in command as his father had been—to lead his men on to victory—to recover his property, and to revenge himself on those who had acted so cruelly towards him. This was human nature; and much as Jacob

Armitage would expostulate with him, and try to divert his feelings into other channels; long as he would preach to him about forgiveness of injuries, and patience until better times should come, Edward could not help brooding over these thoughts, and if ever there was a breast animated with intense hatred against the Puritans it was that of Edward Beverley. Although this was to be lamented, it could not create surprise or wonder in the old forester. All he could do was, as much as possible to reason with him, to soothe his irritated feelings, and by constant employment try to make him forget for a time the feelings of ill-will which he had conceived.

One thing was, however, sufficiently plain to Edward, which was, that whatever might be his wrongs, he had not the power at present to redress them; and this feeling, perhaps, more than any other, held him in some sort of check; and as the time when he might have an opportunity appeared far distant, even to his own sanguine imagination, so by degrees did he contrive to dismiss from his thoughts what it was no use to think about at present.

Chapter Five.

As we have before said, time passed rapidly; with the exception of one or two excursions after venison, they remained in the cottage, and Jacob never went to Lymington. The frost had broken up, the snow had long disappeared, and the trees began to bud. The sun became powerful, and in the month of May the forest began again to look green.

"And now, Edward," said Jacob Armitage, one day at breakfast, "we will try for venison again to sell at Lymington, for I must purchase Humphrey's cart and harness; so let us get our guns, and go out this fine morning. The stags are mostly by themselves at this season, for the does are with their young calves. We must find the slot of a deer, and track him to his lair, and you shall have the first shot if you like; but that, however, depends more upon the deer than upon me."

They had walked four or five miles when they came upon the slot or track of a deer, but Jacob's practised eye pointed out to Edward that it was the slot of a young one, and not worth following. He explained to Edward the difference in the hoof-marks and other signs by which this knowledge was gained, and they proceeded onwards until they found another slot, which Jacob declared to be that of a warrantable stag—that is, one old enough to kill and to be good venison.

"We must now track him to his lair, Edward."

This took them about a mile farther, when they arrived at a small thicket of thorns about an acre in extent.

"Here he is, you see, Edward; let me now see if he is harboured."

They walked round the thicket, and could not find any slot or track by which the stag had left the covert, and Jacob pronounced that the animal must be hid in it.

"Now, Edward, do you stay here while I go back to the lee side of the covert: I will enter it with Smoker, and the stag will, in all probability, when he is roused, come out to breast the wind. You will then have a good shot at him; recollect to fire so as to hit him behind the shoulder: if he is moving quick, fire a little before the shoulders; if slow, take aim accurately; but recollect, if I come upon him in the covert, I shall kill him if I can, for we want the venison, and then we will go after another to give you a chance."

Jacob then left Edward, and went down to the lee side of the covert, where he entered it with Smoker. Edward was stationed behind a thorn-bush, which grew a few yards clear of the covert, and he soon heard the creaking of the branches.

A short time elapsed, and a fine stag came out at a trot; he turned his head, and was just bounding away, when Edward fired, and the animal fell. Remembering the advice of Jacob, Edward remained where he was, in silence reloading his piece, and was soon afterwards joined by Jacob and the dog.

"Well done, Edward!" said the forester in a low voice, and covering his forehead to keep off the glare of the sun, he looked earnestly at a high brake between some thorn-trees, about half a mile to windward. "I think I see something there—look, Edward, your eyes are younger than mine. Is that the branch of a tree in the fern, or is it not?"

"I see what you mean," replied Edward. "It is not, it moves."

"I thought so, but my eyes are not so good as they once were. It's another stag, depend upon it; but how to get near him? We never can get across this patch of clear grass without being seen."

"No, we cannot get at him from this spot," replied Edward; "but if we were to fall back to leeward, and gain the forest again, I think that there are thorns sufficient from the forest to where he lies, to creep from behind one to the other, so as to get a shot at him; don't you?"

"It will require care and patience to manage that; but I think it might be done. I will try; it is my turn now, you know. You had better stay here with the dog, for only one can hide from thorn to thorn."

Jacob, ordering Smoker to remain, then set off. He had to make a circuit of three miles to get to the spot where the thorns extended from the forest, and Edward saw no more of him, although he strained his eyes, until the stag sprung out, and the gun was discharged. Edward perceived that the stag was not killed, but severely wounded, running towards the covert near which he was hid. "Down, Smoker," said he, as he cocked his gun. The stag came within shot, and was coming nearer when, seeing Edward, it turned. Edward fired, and then cheered on the dog, who sprang after the wounded animal, giving tongue, as he followed him. Edward, perceiving Jacob hastening towards him, waited for him.

"He's hard hit, Edward," cried Jacob, "and Smoker will have him; but we must follow as fast as we can."

They both caught up their guns and ran as fast as they could, when, as they entered the wood, they heard the dog at bay.

"We shan't have far to go, Edward; the animal is done up, Smoker has him at bay."

They hastened on another quarter of a mile, when they found that the stag had fallen on his knees, and had been seized by the throat by Smoker.

"Mind, Edward, now, how I go up to him, for the wound from the horn of the deer is very dangerous."

Jacob advanced from behind the stag, and cut his throat with his hunting-knife. "He is a fine beast, and we have done well to-day; but we shall have two journeys to make to get all this venison home. I could not get a fair shot at him—and see, I have hit him here in the flank."

"And here is my ball in his throat," said Edward.

"So it is. Then it was a good shot that you made, and you are master of the hunt this day, Edward. Now, I'll remain, and you go home for White Billy; Humphrey is right about the cart. If we had one, we could have carried all home at once; but I must go now and cut the throat of the other stag which you killed so cleverly. You will be a good hunter one of these days, Edward. A little more knowledge, and a little more practice, and I will leave it all to you, and hang my gun up over the chimney."

It was late in the evening before they had made their two trips and taken all the venison home, and very tired were they before it was all safely housed. Edward was delighted with his success, but not more so than was old Jacob. The next morning Jacob set off for Lymington, with the pony loaded with venison, which he sold, as well as two more loads which he promised to bring the next day, and the day after. He then looked out for a cart, and was fortunate in finding a small one just fitted to the size of the pony, who was not tall, but very strong, as all New Forest ponies are. He also procured harness, and then put Billy in the cart to draw him home; but Billy did not admire being put in a cart, and for some time was very restive, and backed and reared, and went every way but the right; but by dint of coaxing and leading, he at last submitted, and went straight on: but then the noise of the cart behind him frightened him, and he ran away. At last, having tired himself out, he thought that he might as well go quietly in harness, as he could not get out of it; and he did so, and arrived safe at the cottage. Humphrey was delighted at the sight of the cart, and said that now they should get on well. The next day Jacob contrived to put all the remainder of the venison in the cart, and White Billy made no more difficulty; he dragged it all to Lymington, and returned with the cart as quietly and cleverly as if he had been in harness all his life.

"Well, Edward, the venison paid for the cart, at all events," said Jacob, "and now, I will tell you all the news I collected while I was at Lymington. Captain Burly, who attempted to incite the people to rescue the king, has been hung, drawn, and quartered, as a traitor."

"They are traitors who condemned him," replied Edward in wrath.

"Yes, so they are; but there is better news, which is, that the Duke of York has escaped to Holland."

"Yes, that is good news; and the king?"

"He is still a prisoner in Carisbrook Castle. There are many rumours and talks, but no one knows what is true and what is false; but depend upon it, this cannot last long, and the king will have his rights yet."

Edward remained very grave for some time.

"I trust in heaven we all shall have our rights yet, Jacob," said he at last. "I wish I was a man!"

Here the conversation ended, and they went to bed.

This was now a busy time at the cottage. The manure had to be got out of the stable and pigsties, and carried out to the potato-ground and garden; the crops had to be put in; and the cart was now found valuable. After the manure had been carried out and spread, Edward and Humphrey helped Jacob to dig the ground, and then to put in the seed. The cabbage-plants of last year were then put out, and the turnips and carrots sown. Before the month was over the garden and potato-field were cropped, and Humphrey took upon himself to weed and keep it clean. Little Edith had also employment now; for the hens began to lay eggs, and as soon as she heard them cackling, she ran for the eggs and brought them in; and before the month was over Jacob had set four hens upon eggs. Billy, the pony, was now turned out to graze in the forest; he came home every night of his own accord.

"I'll tell you what we want," said Humphrey, who took the command altogether over the farm; "we want a cow."

"Oh yes, a cow," cried Alice; "I have plenty of time to milk her."

"Whose cows are those which I see in the forest sometimes?" said Humphrey to Jacob.

"If they belong to anybody, they belong to the king," replied Jacob; "but they are cattle which have strayed and found their way to the forest, and have remained here ever since. They are rather wild and savage, and you must be careful how you go too near them, as the bulls will run at you. They increase very fast: there were but six a few years ago, and now there are at least fifty in the herd."

"Well, I'll try and get one, if I can," said Humphrey.

"You will be puzzled to do that, boy," replied Jacob, "and as I said before, beware of the bulls."

"I don't want a bull," replied Humphrey; "but a cow would give us milk, and then we should have more manure for the garden. My garden will then grow more potatoes."

"Well, Humphrey, if you can catch a cow, no one will interfere; but I think you will not find it very easy, and you may find it very dangerous."

"I'll look-out for one," replied Humphrey, "anyhow. Alice, if we only had a cow, wouldn't that be jolly?"

The crops were now all up, and as the days began to be long, the work became comparatively light and easy. Humphrey was busy making a little wheelbarrow for Edith, that she might barrow away the weeds as he hoed them up; and at last this great performance was completed, much to the admiration of all, and much to his own satisfaction. Indeed, when it is recollected that Humphrey had only the hand-saw and axe, and that he had to cut down the tree, and then to saw it into plank, it must be acknowledged that it required great patience and perseverance even to make a wheelbarrow; but Humphrey was not only persevering, but was full of invention. He had built up a hen-house with fir poles, and made the nests for the hens to lay and hatch in, and they now had between forty and fifty chickens running about. He had also divided the pigsty, so that the sow might be kept apart from the other pigs; and they expected very soon to have a litter of young pigs. He had transplanted the wild strawberries from the forest, and had by manure made them large and good; and he had also a fine crop of onions in the garden, from seed which Jacob had bought at Lymington; now Humphrey was very busy cutting down some poles in the forest to make a cow-house, for he declared that he would have a cow somehow or another. June arrived, and it was time to mow down grass to make into hay for the winter, and Jacob had two scythes. He showed the boys how to use them, and they soon became expert; and as there was plenty of long grass at this time of the year, and they could mow when they pleased, they soon had White Billy in full employment carrying the hay home. The little girls helped to make it, for Humphrey had made them two rakes. Jacob thought that there was hay enough made, but Humphrey said that there was enough for the pony, but not enough for the cow.

"But where is the cow to come from, Humphrey?"

"Where the venison comes from," replied he,—"out of the forest."

So Humphrey continued to mow and make hay, while Edward and Jacob went out for venison. After all the hay was made and stacked, Humphrey found out a method of thatching with fern, which Jacob had never thought of; and when that was done, they commenced cutting down fern for fodder. Here again Humphrey would have twice as much as Jacob had ever cut before, because he wanted litter for the cow. At last it became quite a joke between him and Edward, who, when he brought home more venison than would keep in the hot weather, told Humphrey that the remainder was for the cow. Still Humphrey would not give up the point, and every morning and evening he would be certain to be absent an hour or two, and it was found out he was watching the herd of wild cattle who were feeding: sometimes they were very near, at others a long way off. He used to get up into the trees, and examine them as they passed under him, without perceiving him. One night Humphrey returned very late, and the next morning he was off before daylight. Breakfast was over, and Humphrey did not make his appearance, and they could not tell what was the matter. Jacob felt uneasy, but Edward laughed, and said:

"Oh, depend upon it, he'll come back and bring the cow with him."

Hardly had Edward said these words when in came Humphrey red with perspiration.

"Now then, Jacob and Edward, come with me; we must put Billy in the cart, and take Smoker and a rope with us. Take your guns too, for fear of accident."

"Why, what's the matter?"

"I'll tell you as we go along, but I must put Billy in the cart, for there is no time to be lost."

Humphrey disappeared, and Jacob said to Edward, "What can it be?"

"It can be nothing but the cow he is so mad about," replied Edward. "However, when he comes with the pony, we shall know; let us take our guns and the dog Smoker as he wishes."

Humphrey now drove up the pony and cart, and they set off.

"Well, I suppose you'll tell us now what we are going for?" said Edward.

"Yes, I will. You know I've been watching the cattle for a long while, because I wanted a cow. I have been in a tree when they have passed under me several times, and I observed that one or two of the heifers were very near calving. Yesterday evening I thought one could not help calving very soon indeed, and as I was watching I saw that she was uneasy, and that she at last left the herd and went into a little copse of wood. I remained three hours to see if she came out again, and she did not. It was dark when I came home, as you know. This morning I went before daylight and found the herd. She is very remarkable, being black and white spotted; and, after close examination, I found that she was not with the herd, so I am sure that she went into the copse to calve, and that she has calved before this."

"Well, that may be," replied Jacob; "but now I do not understand what we are to do."

"Nor I," replied Edward.

"Well then, I'll tell you what I hope to do. I have got the pony and cart to take the calf home with us, if we can get it—which I think we can. I have got Smoker to worry the heifer and keep her employed while we put the calf in the cart; a rope that we may tie the cow, if we can; and you with your guns must keep off the herd, if they come to her assistance. Now do you understand my plan?"

"Yes, and I think it very likely to succeed, Humphrey," replied Jacob, "and I give you credit for the scheme. We will help you all we can. Where is the copse?"

"Not half a mile farther," replied Humphrey. "We shall soon be there."

On their arrival they found that the herd were feeding at a considerable distance from the copse, which was perhaps as well.

"Now," said Jacob, "I and Edward will enter into the copse with Smoker, and you follow us, Humphrey. I will make Smoker seize the heifer if necessary; at all events, he will keep her at bay—that is, if she is here. First let us walk round the copse and find her *slot* as we call the track of a deer. See, here is her footing. Now let us go in."

They advanced cautiously into the thicket, following the track of the heifer, and at last came upon her. Apparently she had not calved more than an hour, and was licking the calf which was not yet on its legs. As soon as the animal perceived Jacob and Edward, she shook her head, and was about to run at them; but Jacob told Smoker to seize her, and the dog flew at her immediately. The attack of the dog drove back the heifer quite into the thicket, and as the dog bounded round her, springing this way and that way to escape her horns, the heifer was soon separated from the calf.

"Now then, Edward and Humphrey," said Jacob, advancing between the heifer and the calf, "lift up the calf between you and put it in the cart. Leave Smoker and me to manage the mother."

The boys put their arms under the stomach of the calf, and carried it away. The heifer was at first too busy defending herself against the dog to perceive that the calf was gone; when she did Jacob called Smoker to him, so as to bring him between the heifer and where the boys were going out of the thicket. At last the heifer gave a loud bellow, and rushed out of the thicket in pursuit of her calf checked by Smoker, who held on to her ear, and sometimes stopped her from advancing.

"Hold her, Smoker," said Jacob, who now went back to help the boys. "Hold her, boy. Is the calf in the cart?"

"Yes, and tied fast," replied Edward, "and we are in the cart too."

"That's right," replied Jacob. "Now I'll get in too, and let us drive off. She'll follow us, depend upon it. Here, Smoker! Smoker! Let her alone."

Smoker, at this command, came bounding out of the copse, followed by the heifer, lowing most anxiously. Her lowing was responded to by the calf in the cart, and she ran wildly up to it.

"Drive off, Humphrey," said Jacob; "I think I heard the lowing of the heifer answered by some of the herd, and the sooner we are off the better."

Humphrey, who had the reins, drove off; the heifer followed, at one time running at the dog, at another putting her head almost into the hind part of the cart; but the lowing of the heifer was now answered by deeper tones, and Jacob said:

"Edward, get your gun ready, for I think the herd is following. Do not fire, however, till I tell you. We must be governed by circumstances. It won't do to lose the pony, or to run any serious risk, for the sake of the heifer and calf. Drive fast, Humphrey."

A few minutes afterwards they perceived at about a quarter of a mile behind them, not the whole herd, but a single bull, who was coming up at a fast trot, with his tail in the air, and tossing his head, lowing deeply in answer to the heifer.

"There's only one, after all," said Jacob; "I suppose the heifer is his favourite. Well, we can manage him. Smoker, come in. Come in, sir, directly," cried Jacob, perceiving that the dog was about to attack the bull.

Smoker obeyed, and the bull advanced till he was within a hundred yards.

"Now, Edward, do you fire first—aim for his shoulder. Humphrey, pull up."

Humphrey stopped the pony, and the bull continued to advance, but seemed puzzled who to attack, unless it was the dog. As soon as the bull was within sixty yards, Edward fired, and the animal fell down on its knees, tearing the ground with its horns.

"That will do," said Jacob; "drive on again, Humphrey; we will have a look at that fellow by and by. At present we had better get home, as others may come. He's up again, but he is at a standstill. I have an idea that he is hit hard."

The cart drove on, followed by the heifer; but no more of the wild herd made their appearance, and they very soon gained the cottage.

"Now, then, what shall we do?" said Jacob. "Come, Humphrey, you have had all the ordering of this, and have done it well."

"Well, Jacob, we must now drive the cart into the yard, and shut the gate upon the cow, till I am ready."

"That's easy done, by setting Smoker at her," replied Jacob; "but, mercy on us, there's Alice and Edith running out!—the heifer may kill them. Go back, Alice, run quite into the cottage, and shut the door till we come."

Alice and Edith hearing this, and Edward also crying out to them, made a hasty retreat to the cottage. Humphrey then backed the cart against the paling of the yard, so as to enable Edward to get on the other side of it, ready to open the gate. Smoker was set at the heifer, and, as before, soon engaged her attention; so that the gate was opened and the cart drove in, and the gate closed again, before the heifer could follow.

"Well, Humphrey, what next?"

"Why, now lift the calf out and put it into the cow-house. I will go into the cow-house with a rope and a slip-knot at the end of it, get upon the beam above, and drop it over her horns as she's busy with the calf, which she will be as soon as you let her in. I shall pass the end of the rope outside, for you to haul up when I am ready, and then we shall have her fast, till we can secure her properly. When I call out 'ready,' do you open the gate and let her in. You can do that and jump into the cart afterwards, for fear she may run at you; but I don't think that she will, for it's the calf she wants, and not either of you."

As soon as Humphrey was ready with the rope he gave the word, and the gate was opened; the cow ran in immediately, and hearing her calf bleat, went into the cow-house, the door of which was shut upon her. A minute afterwards Humphrey cried out to them to haul upon the rope, which they did.

"That will do," said Humphrey from the inside; "now make the rope fast, and then you may come in."

They went in, and found the heifer drawn close to the side of the cow-house by the rope which was round her horns, and unable to move her head.

"Well, Humphrey, that's very clever; but now what's to be done?"

"First I'll saw off the tips of her horns, and then if she does run at us, she won't hurt us much. Wait till I go for the saw."

As soon as the ends of her horns were sawed off, Humphrey took another piece of rope, which he fastened securely round her horns, and then made the other end fast to the side of the building, so that the animal could move about a little and eat out of the crib.

"There," said Humphrey, "now time and patience must do the rest. We must coax her and handle her, and we soon shall tame her. At present let us leave her with the calf. She has a yard of rope, and that is enough for her to lick her calf, which is all that she requires at present. To-morrow we will cut some grass for her."

They then went out, shutting the cow-house door.

"Well, Humphrey, you've beat us after all, and have the laugh on your side now," said Jacob. "'Where there's a will, there's a way,' that's certain; and I assure you, that when you were making so much hay, and gathering so much litter, and building a cow-house, I had no more idea that we should have a cow than that we should have an elephant; and I will say that you deserve great credit for your way of obtaining it."

"That he certainly does," replied Edward. "You have more genius than I have, brother. But dinner must be ready, if Alice has done her duty. What think you, Jacob, shall we after dinner go and look after that bull?"

"Yes, by all means. He will not be had eating, and I can sell all I can carry in the cart at Lymington. Besides, the skin is worth money."

Chapter Six.

Alice and Edith were very anxious to see the cow, and especially to see the calf; but Humphrey told them that they must not go near till he went with them, and then they should see it. After dinner was over, Jacob and Edward took their guns, and Humphrey put Billy in the cart, and followed them. They found the bull where they left him, standing quite still; he tossed his head when they approached him, which they did carefully, but he did not attempt to run at them.

"It's my idea that he has nearly bled to death," said Jacob; "but there's nothing like making sure. Edward, put a bullet just three inches behind his shoulder, and that will make all safe."

Edward did so, and the animal fell dead. They went up to the carcass, which they estimated to weigh at least fifty stone.

"It is a noble beast," said Edward; "I wonder we never thought of killing one before."

"They ain't game, Edward," replied Jacob.

"No, they are not now, Jacob," said Humphrey; "as you and Edward claim all the game, I shall claim the cattle as my portion of the forest. Recollect, there are more, and I mean to have more of them yet."

"Well, Humphrey, I give you up all my rights, if I have any."

"And I all mine," added Edward.

"Be it so. Some day you'll see what I shall do," replied Humphrey. "Recollect, I am to sell the cattle for my own self-advantage until I buy a gun, and one or two things which I want."

"I agree to that too, Humphrey," replied Jacob; "and now to skin the beast."

The skinning and quartering took up the whole afternoon, and Billy was heavily laden when he drew his cart home. The next day Jacob went to Lymington to sell the bull and the skin, and returned home well satisfied with the profit he had made. He had procured, as Humphrey requested, some milk-pans, a small churn, and milk-pail, out of the proceeds, and had still money left. Humphrey told them that he had not been to see the heifer yet, as he thought it better not.

"She will be tame to-morrow morning, depend upon it," said he.

"But if you give her nothing to eat, will not the calf die?"

"Oh no, I should think not. I shall not starve her, but I will make her thankful for her food before she gets it. I shall cut her some grass to-morrow morning."

We may as well here say that the next morning Humphrey went in to the heifer. At first she tossed about and was very unruly. He gave her some grass, and patted her and coaxed her for a long while, till at last she allowed him to touch her gently. Every day for a fortnight he brought her her food, and she became quieter every day, till at last, if he went up to her, she never pushed with her horns. The calf became quite tame, and as the heifer perceived that the calf was quiet, she became more quiet herself. After the fortnight, Humphrey would not allow the heifer to receive anything except from the hand of Alice, that the animal might know her well; and when the calf was a month old, Humphrey made the first attempt to milk her. This was resisted at first by kicking, but in the course of ten days she gave down her milk. Humphrey then let her loose for a few days to run about the yard, still keeping the calf in the cow-house, and putting the heifer in to her at night, milking her before the calf was allowed to suck. After this, he adventured upon the last experiment, which was to turn her out of the yard to graze into the forest. She went away to some distance, and he was fearful that she would join the herd, but in the evening she came back again to her calf. After this he was satisfied, and turned her out every day, and they had no further trouble with her. He would not, however, wean the calf till the winter time, when she was shut up in the yard and fed on hay. He then weaned the calf, which was a cow-calf, and they had no more trouble with the mother. Alice soon learnt to milk her, and she became very tractable and good-tempered. Such was the commencement of the dairy at the cottage.

"Jacob," said Humphrey, "when do you go to Lymington again?"

"Why, I do not know. The end of August, as it is now, and the month of September, is not good for venison; and, therefore, I do not see what I shall have to go for."

"Well, I wish, when you do go, you would get something for Alice and something for me."

"And what is it that Alice wants?"

"She wants a kitten."

"Well, I think I may find that. And what do you want, Humphrey?"

"I want a dog. Smoker is yours altogether; I want a dog for myself, to bring up after my own fashion."

"Well, I ought to look-out for another dog: although Smoker is not old, yet one ought to have two dogs to one's gun, in case of accident."

"I think so too," replied Edward; "see if you can get two puppies, one for Humphrey, and one for myself."

"Well, I must not go to Lymington for them. I must cross the forest, to see some friends of mine whom I have not seen for a long while, and I may get some of the right sort of puppies there, just like Smoker. I'll do that at once, as I may have to wait for them, even if I do have the promise."

"May I go with you, Jacob?" said Edward.

"Why, I would rather not; they may ask questions."

"And so would I rather he would not, for he will shirk his work here."

"Why, what is there to do, Humphrey?"

"Plenty to do, and hard work, Edward; the acorns are fit for beating down, and we want a great many bushels for the pigs. We have to fatten three, and to feed the rest during the winter. I cannot get on well with only Alice and Edith; so if you are not very lazy, you will stay with us and help us."

"Humphrey, you think of nothing but your pigs and farm-yard."

"And you are too great a hunter to think of anything but a stag; but a bird in the hand's worth two in the bush, in my opinion; and I'll make more by my farm-yard than you ever will by the forest."

"Humphrey has nothing to do with the poultry and eggs, has he, Edward? They belong to Edith and me and Jacob shall take them to Lymington and sell them for us, and get us some new clothes for Sunday, for these begin to look rather worn—and no wonder."

"No, dearest, the poultry are yours, and I will sell them for you as soon as you please, and buy what you wish with the money," replied Jacob. "Let Humphrey make all the money he can with his pigs."

"Yes; and the butter belongs to me, if I make it," said Alice.

"No, no," replied Humphrey, "that's not fair; I find cows, and get nothing for them. We must go halves, Alice."

"Well, I have no objection to that," said Alice, "because you find the cows and feed them. I made a pound of butter yesterday, just to try what I could do; but it's not firm, Jacob. How is that?"

"I have seen the women make butter, and know how, Alice; so next time I will be with you. I suppose you did not wash your butter-milk well out, nor put any salt in it?"

"I did not put any salt in it."

"But you must, or the butter will not keep."

It was arranged that Edward should stay at home to assist in collecting the acorns for the pigs, and that Jacob should cross the forest alone to see after the puppies; and he set off the next morning. He was away two days, and then returned; said that he had a promise of two puppies, and that he had chosen them; they were of the same breed as Smoker, but they were only a fortnight old, and could not be taken from the mother yet awhile, so that he had arranged to call again when they were three or four months old, and able to follow him across the forest. Jacob also said that he was very near being hurt by a stag that had made at him—for at that season of the year the stags were very dangerous and fierce—but that he had fired, and struck off one of the animal's horns, which made it turn.

"You must be careful, Edward, how you go about the forest now."

"I have no wish to go," replied Edward; "as we cannot hunt, it is no use; but in November we shall begin again."

"Yes," replied Jacob, "that will be soon enough. To-morrow I will help you with the acorns, and the day afterwards, if I am spared, I will take Alice's poultry to Lymington for her."

"Yes, and when you come back you will help me to churn, for then I shall have a good deal of cream."

"And don't forget to buy the kitten, Jacob," said Edith.

"What's the good of a kitten?" said Humphrey, who was very busy making a bird-cage for Edith, having just finished one for Alice; "she will only steal your cream and eat up your birds."

"No, she won't; for we'll shut the door fast where the milk and cream is, and we'll hang the cages so high that Miss Puss won't be able to get at them."

"Well, then, a kitten will be useful," said Edward, "for she will teach you to be careful."

"My coat is a little the worse for wear, and so is yours, Edward. We must try if we cannot, like Alice, find means to pay for another."

"Humphrey," said Jacob, "I'll buy all you want, and trust to you for paying me again as soon as you can."

"That's just what I want," replied Humphrey. "Then you must buy me a gun and a new suit of clothes first; when I've paid for them I shall want some more tools, and some nails and screws, and two or three other things; but I will say nothing about them just now. Get me my gun, and I'll try what the forest will do for me—especially after I have my dog."

"Well, we shall see; perhaps you'll like to come out with me sometimes and learn woodcraft, for Edward knows as much as I do now, and can go out by himself."

"Of course I will, Jacob; I want to learn everything."

"Well, there's a little money left in the bag yet, and I will go to Lymington to-morrow. Now I think it is time that we went to bed; and if you are all as tired as I am, you will sleep soundly."

Jacob put into the cart the next day about forty of the chickens which Alice had reared; the others were kept to increase the number in the poultry-yard. They had cost little or nothing bringing up; for when quite young they only had a little oatmeal cake, and afterwards, with the potatoes which were left, they found themselves, as fowls can always do when they have a great range of ground to go over.

Jacob came back at sunset, with all the articles. He brought a new suit for Alice and Edith, with some needles and thread and worsted, and gave her some money which was left from the sale of the chickens, after he had made the purchases. He also bought a new suit for Edward and Humphrey, and a gun, which was much approved of by Humphrey, as it had a larger bore and carried a heavier bullet than either Jacob's or Edward's and there was a white kitten for Alice and Edith. There was no news, only that the Levellers had opposed Cromwell, and he had put them down with the other troops, and Jacob said that it appeared that they were all squabbling and fighting with each other.

Time passed; the month of November came on without anything to disturb the daily employments of the family in the forest: when one evening Jacob, who had returned from hunting with Edward (the first time they had been out since the season commenced), told Alice that she must do all she could to give them a good dinner the next day, as it was to be a feast.

"Why so, Jacob?"

"If you cannot guess, I won't tell you till the time comes," replied Jacob.

"Well then, Humphrey must help us," replied Alice, "and we will do what we can. I will try, now that we have some meat, to make a grand dinner."

Alice made all the preparations, and had for dinner the next day a piece of baked venison, a venison stew, a pair of roast chickens, and an apple-pie—which, for them, was a very grand dinner indeed. And it was very well-dressed; for Jacob had taught her to cook, and by degrees she improved upon Jacob's instruction. Humphrey was quite as clever at it as she was; and little Edith was very useful, as she plucked the fowls, and watched the things while they were cooking.

"And now I'll tell you," said Jacob, after saying grace, "why I asked you for a feast this day. It is because exactly on this day twelvemonth I brought you all to the cottage. Now you know."

"I did not know it certainly, but I daresay you are right," replied Edward.

"And now, children, tell me," said Jacob, "has not this year passed very quickly and very happily—quite as quickly and quite as happily as if you had been staying at Arnwood?"

"Yes, more so," replied Humphrey; "for then very often I did not know what to do to amuse myself, and since I have been here the days have always been too short."

"I agree with Humphrey," said Edward.

"And I am sure I do," replied Alice; "I'm always busy, and always happy, and I'm never scolded about dirtying my clothes or tearing them, as I used to be."

"And what does little Edith say?"

"I like to help Alice, and I like to play with the kitten," replied Edith.

"Well, my children," said Jacob, "depend upon it, you are most happy when your days pass quickest, and that is only the case when you have plenty to do. Here you are in peace and safety; and may it please God that you may continue so! We want very few things in this world—that is, we really want very few things, although we wish and sigh for many. You have health and spirits, which are the greatest blessings in life. Who would believe, to look at you all, that you were the same children that I brought away from Arnwood? You were then very different from what you are now. You are strong and healthy, rosy and brown, instead of being fair and delicate. Look at your sisters, Edward, do you think that any of your former friends—do you think that Martha, who had the care of them, would know them?"

Edward smiled and said, "Certainly not; especially in their present dresses."

"Nor would, I think, Humphrey be known again. You, Edward, were always a stout boy; and, except that you have grown very much, and are more brown, there is no great difference. You would be known again, even in your present forester's dress; but what I say is, that we ought to be thankful to the Almighty that you, instead of being burnt in your beds, have found health and happiness and security in a forester's hut; and I ought to be, and am, most thankful to heaven that it has pleased it to spare my life, and enable me to teach you all to the present how to gain your own livelihoods after I am called away. I have been able so far to fulfil my promise to your noble father; and you know not what a heavy load on my mind is every day lessened, as I see each day that you are more and more able to provide for yourselves. God bless you, dear children, and may you live to see many returns, and happy returns, of the day;" and Jacob was so much moved as he said this, that a tear was seen rolling down his furrowed cheek.

The second winter now came on. Jacob and Edward went out hunting usually about twice a week; for the old forester complained of stiffness and rheumatism, and not feeling so active as he used to be. Humphrey now accompanied Edward perhaps one day in the week, but not more, and they seldom returned without having procured venison, for Edward knew his business well, and no longer needed the advice of Jacob. As the winter advanced Jacob gave up going out altogether. He went to Lymington to sell the venison and procure what was necessary for the household; such as oatmeal and flour, which were the principal wants; but even these journeys fatigued him, and it was evident that the old man's constitution was breaking fast. Humphrey was always busy. One evening he was making something which puzzled them all. They asked him what it was for, but he would not tell them.

"It's an experiment that I am trying," said he, as he was bending a hazel stick. "If it answers, you shall know: if it does not, I've only had a little trouble for nothing. Jacob, I hope you will not forget the salt to-morrow when you go to Lymington, for my pigs are ready for killing, and we must salt the greatest part of the pork. After the legs and shoulders have lain long enough in salt, I mean to try if I cannot smoke them, and if I do, I'll then smoke some bacon. Won't that be jolly, Alice? Won't you like to have a great piece of bacon hanging up there, and only to have to get on a stool to cut off what you want, when Edward and I come home hungry and you've nothing to give us to eat?"

"I shall be very glad to have it, and I think so will you too, by the way you talk."

"I shall, I assure you. Jacob, didn't you say the ash-sticks were the best to smoke bacon with?"

"Yes, boy: when you are ready, I'll tell you how to manage. My poor mother used to smoke very well up this very chimney."

"I think that will do," said Humphrey, letting his hazel stick spring up, after he had bent it down, "but to-morrow I shall find out."

"But what is it for, Humphrey?" said Edith.

"Go away, puss, and play with your kitten," replied Humphrey, putting away his tools and his materials in a corner; "I've a great deal on my hands now, but I must kill my pigs before I think of anything else."

The next day Jacob took the venison into Lymington, and brought back the salt and other articles required. The pigs were then killed, and salted down under Jacob's directions; his rheumatism did not allow him to assist, but Humphrey and Edward rubbed in the salt, and Alice took the pieces of pork away to the tub when they were finished. Humphrey had been out the day before with the unknown article he had been so long about. The next morning he went out early before breakfast, and when he returned he brought a hare in his hand, which he laid on the table.

"There," said he, "my springe has answered, and this is the fruits of it. Now I'll make some more, and we will have something by way of a change for dinner."

They were very much pleased with Humphrey's success, and he was not a little proud of it.

"How did you find out how to make it?"

"Why, I read in the old book of travels which Jacob brought home with him last summer, of people catching rabbits and hares in some way like this; I could not make it out exactly, but it gave me the idea."

We ought to have told the reader that Jacob had more than once brought home an old book or two which he had picked up, or had given him, and that these had been occasionally looked into by Humphrey and Edward, but only now and then, as they had too much to do to find much time for reading, although sometimes in the evening they did take them up. When it is considered how young they were, and what a practical and busy life they led, this cannot be surprising.

Chapter Seven.

Humphrey was now after something else. He had made several traps, and brought in rabbits and hares almost every day. He had also made some bird traps, and had caught two gold-finches for Alice and Edith, which they put in the cages he had made for them. But, as we said, Humphrey was about something else; he was out early in the morning, and in the evening, when the moon was up, he came home late, long after they had all gone to bed; but they never knew why, nor would he tell them. A heavy fall of snow took place, and Humphrey was more out than ever. At last, about a week after the snow had lain on the ground, one morning he came in with a hare and rabbit in his hand, and said:

"Edward, I have caught something larger than a hare or a rabbit, and you must come and help me, and we must take our guns. Jacob, I suppose your rheumatism is too bad to let you come too?"

"No; I think I can manage. It's the damp that hurts me so much. This frosty air will do me good, perhaps. I have been much better since the snow fell. Now, then, let us see what you have caught."

"You will have to walk two miles," said Humphrey, as they went out.

"I can manage it, Humphrey; so lead the way."

Humphrey went on till they came close to a clump of large trees, and then brought them to a pit-fall which he had dug, about six feet wide and eight feet long, and nine feet deep.

"There's my large trap," said Humphrey, "and see what I have caught in it."

They looked down into the pit and perceived a young bull in it. Smoker, who was with them, began to bark furiously at it.

"Now, what are we to do? I don't think it is hurt. Can we get it out?" said Humphrey.

"No, not very well. If it was a calf we might; but it is too heavy; and if we were to get it out alive, we must kill it afterwards, so we had better shoot it at once."

"So I think," replied Humphrey.

"But how did you catch him?" said Edward.

"I read of it in the same book I did about the traps for hares," replied Humphrey. "I dug out the pit and covered it with brambles, and then put snow at the top. This is the thicket that the herd comes to chiefly in winter time; it is large and dry, and the large trees shelter it; so that is why I chose this spot. I took a large bundle of hay, put some on the snow about the pit, and then strewed some more about in small handfuls, so that the cattle must find it and pick it up, which I knew they would be glad to do, now that the snow is on the ground. And now, you see, I have succeeded."

"Well, Humphrey, you beat us, I will say," said Edward. "Shall I shoot him?"

"Yes, now that he is looking up."

Edward shot his ball through the forehead of the animal, which fell dead; but they were then obliged to go home for the pony and cart, and ropes to get the animal out of the pit, and a hard job they had of it too; but the pony helped them, and they did get it out at last.

"I will do it easier next time," said Humphrey. "I will make a windlass as soon as I can, and we will soon hoist out another, like they turn a bucket of water up from a well."

"It's nice young meat," said Jacob, who was skinning the bull, "not above eighteen months old, I should think. Had it been a full-grown one, like that we shot, it must have remained where it was, for we never could have got it out."

"Yes, Jacob, we should; for I should have gone down and cut it up in the pit, so that we would have handed it out by bits, if we could not have managed him whole."

They loaded the cart with the skin and quarters of the animal, and then drove home.

"This will go far to pay for the gun, Humphrey," said Jacob, "if it don't pay for more."

"I'm glad of it," said Humphrey; "but I hope it will not be the last which I take."

"That reminds me, Humphrey, of one thing; I think you must come back with the cart and carry away all the entrails of the beast, and remove all the blood which is on the snow, for I've observed that cattle are very scared with the smell and sight of blood. I found that out by once or twice seeing them come to where I have cut the throat of a stag, and as soon as they have put their noses down to where the blood was on the ground they have put their tails up and galloped away, bellowing at a terrible rate. Indeed I've heard say that if a murder has been committed in a wood, and you want to find the body, that a herd of cattle drove into it will serve you better than even a bloodhound."

"Thank you for telling me that, Jacob, for I should never have supposed it; and I'll tell you what I'll also do. I'll load the cart with fern litter, and put it at the bottom of the pit; so that if I could get a heifer or calf worth taking, it may not be hurt by the fall."

"It must have taken you a long while to dig that pit, Humphrey."

"Yes, it did, and as I got deeper the work was harder, and then I had to carry away all the earth and scatter it about. I was more than a month about it from the time that I began till it was finished, and I had a ladder to go up and down by at last, and carried the baskets of earth up, for it was too deep to throw it out."

"Nothing like patience and perseverance, Humphrey. You've more than I have."

"I'm sure he has more than I have, or shall ever have, I'm afraid," replied Edward.

During this winter, which passed rapidly away, very few circumstances of any consequence occurred. Old Jacob was more or less confined to the cottage by the rheumatism, and Edward hunted either by himself or occasionally with Humphrey. Humphrey was fortunate enough to take a bull and cow-calf in his pit-fall, both of them about a year or fifteen months old, and by a rude invention of his, by way of windlass, contrived, with the assistance of Edward, to hoist them uninjured out of the pit. They were put into the yard, and after having been starved till they were tamed, they followed the example of the heifer and calf, and became quite tame. These were an important addition to their stock, as may well be imagined. The only mishap under which they laboured was, old Jacob's confinement to the cottage, which, as the winter advanced, prevented him from going to Lymington; they could not therefore sell any venison, and Humphrey, by way of experiment, smoked some venison hams, which he hung up with the others. There was another point on which they felt anxiety, which was, that Jacob could not cross the forest to get the puppies which had been promised them, and the time was past, for it was now January, when he was to have called for them. Edward and Humphrey pressed the old man very hard to let one of them go; but the only answer they could obtain was, "that he'd be better soon." At last, finding that he got worse instead of better, he consented that Edward should go. He gave directions how to proceed, the way he was to take, and a description of the keeper's lodge; cautioned him to call himself by the name of Armitage, and describe himself as his grandson. Edward promised to obey Jacob's directions, and the next morning he set off, mounted upon White Billy, with a little money in his pocket, in case he should want it.

"I wish I was going with you," said Humphrey, as he walked by the side of the pony.

"I wish you were, Humphrey: for my part, I feel as if I were a slave set at liberty. I do justice to old Jacob's kindness and good-will, and acknowledge how much we are indebted to him; but still, to be housed up here in the forest, never seeing or speaking to any one, shut out from the world, does not suit Edward Beverley. Our father was a soldier, and a right good one; and if I were old enough I think even now I should escape and join the royal party, broken as it may be, and by all accounts is, at this moment. Deer-stalking is all very well, but I fly at higher game."

"I feel the same as you do," replied Humphrey; "but recollect, Edward, that the old man's very infirm, and what would become of our sisters if we were to leave them?"

"I know that well, Humphrey; I have no idea of leaving them, you may be sure; but I wish they were with our relations in safety, and then we should be free to act."

"Yes, we should, Edward; but recollect that we are not yet men, and boys of fifteen and thirteen cannot do much, although they may wish to do much."

"It's true that I am only fifteen," replied Edward, "but I am strong enough, and so are you. I think if I had a fair cut at a man's head, I would make him stagger under it, were he as big as a buffalo. As young as I have been to the wars, that I know well; and I recollect my father promising me that I should go with him as soon as I was fifteen."

"What puzzles me," replied Humphrey, "is the fear that old Jacob has of our being seen at Lymington."

"Why, what fear is there?"

"I cannot tell more than you; in my opinion, the rear is only in his own imagination. They surely would not hurt us (if we walked about without arms like other people), because our father had fought for the king? That they have beheaded some people is true; but then they were plotting in the king's favour, or in other ways opposed to Parliament. This I have gathered from Jacob: but I cannot see what we have to fear, if we remain quiet. But now comes the question, Edward; for Jacob has, I believe, said more to me on this one subject than he has to you. Suppose you were to leave the forest, what would be the first step which you would take?"

"I should of course state who I was, and take possession of my father's property at Arnwood, which is mine by descent."

"Exactly; so Jacob thinks, and he says that would be your ruin, for the property is sequestered, as they call it, or forfeited to the Parliament, in consequence of your father having fought against it on the king's side. It no longer belongs to you, and you would not be allowed to take it: on the contrary, you would in all probability be imprisoned, and who knows what might then take place? You see there is danger?"

"Did Jacob say this to you?"

"Yes, he did: he told me he dare not speak to you on the subject, you were so fiery; and if you heard that the property was confiscated you would certainly do some rash act, and that anything of the kind would be a pretence for laying hold of you; and then he said that he did not think that he would live long, for he was weaker every day; and that he only hoped his life would be spared another year or two, that he might keep you quiet till better times came. He said that if they supposed that we were all burnt in the house when it was fired, it would give them a fair opportunity of calling you an impostor, and treating you accordingly; and that there were so many anxious to have a gift of the property that you would have thousands of people compassing your death. He said that your making known yourself and claiming your property would be the very conduct that your enemies would wish you to follow, and would be attended with most fatal consequences; for he said, to prove that you were Edward Beverley, you must declare that I and your sisters were in the forest with him, and this disclosure would put the whole family in the power of their bitterest enemies; and what would become of your sisters, it would be impossible to say; but most likely they would be put under the charge of some Puritan family, who would have a pleasure in ill-treating and humiliating the daughters of such a man as Colonel Beverley."

"And why did he not tell me all this?"

"He was afraid to say anything to you; he thought that you would be so mad at the idea of this injustice that you would do something rash: and he said, 'I pray every night that my otherwise useless life may be spared; for, were I to die, I know that Edward would quit the forest.'"

"Never, while my sisters are under my protection," replied Edward; "were they safe, I would be out of it to-morrow."

"I think, Edward, that there is great truth in what Jacob says; you could do no good (for they would not restore your property), by making your seclusion known at present, and you might do a great deal of harm—'bide your time'—is good advice in such troubled times. I therefore think that I should be very wary if I were you; but I still think that there is no fear of either you or I going out of the forest in our present dresses and under the name of Armitage. No one would recognise us; you are grown tall, and so am I, and we are so tanned and sunburnt with air and exercise that we do look more like children of the forest than the sons of Colonel Beverley."

"Humphrey, you speak very sensibly, and I agree with you. I am not quite so fiery as the old man thinks; and if my bosom burns with indignation, at all events I have sufficient power to conceal my feelings when it is necessary. I can oppose art to art, if it becomes requisite, and which, from what you have said, I believe now is really so. One thing is certain, that while King Charles is a prisoner, as he now is, and his party dispersed or gone abroad, I can do nothing, and to make myself known would only be to injure myself and all of us. Keep quiet, therefore, I certainly shall, and also remain as I am now under a false name; but still I must and will mix up with other people, and know what is going on. I am willing to live in this forest and protect my sisters as long as it is necessary so to do; but although I will reside here, I will not be confined to the forest altogether."

"That's exactly what I think too, Edward, what I wish myself: but let us not be too hasty even in this. And now, I will wish you a pleasant ride; and, Edward, if you can, procure of the keepers some small shot for me; I much wish to have some."

"I will not forget; good-bye, brother."

Humphrey returned home to attend his farm-yard, while Edward continued his journey through the forest. Some estimate of the character of the two boys may be formed from the above conversation. Edward was courageous and impetuous—hasty in his resolves, but still open to conviction. Brought up as the heir to the property, he felt, more than Humphrey could be expected to do, the mortification of being left a pauper, after such high prospects in his early days: his vindictive feelings against the opposite party were therefore more keen, and his spirit mounted more under the conviction which he laboured. His disposition was naturally warlike, and this disposition had been fostered by his father when he was a child—still a kinder heart or a more generous lad never existed.

Humphrey was of a much more subdued and philosophical temperament, not perhaps so well calculated to lead as to advise; there was great prudence in him united with courage; but his was a passive courage rather than an active one—a courage which if assailed would defend itself valiantly, but would be wary and reflective before it would attack. Humphrey had not that spirit of chivalry possessed by Edward. He was a younger son, and had to earn, in a way, his own fortune, and he felt that his inclinations were more for peace than strife. Moreover, Humphrey had talents which Edward had not—a natural talent for mechanics, and an inquisitive research into science, as far as his limited education would permit him. He was more fitted for an engineer or an agriculturist than for a soldier, although there is no doubt that he would have made a very brave soldier, if such was to have become his avocation.

For kindness and generosity of nature he was equal to his brother, and this was the reason why an angry word never passed between them; for the question between them was, not which should have his way, but which should give up most to the wishes of the other. We hardly need say, that there never were two brothers who were more attached, and who so mutually respected each other.

Chapter Eight.

Edward put the pony to a trot, and in two hours was on the other side of the New Forest. The directions given to him by Jacob were not forgotten, and before it was noon he found himself at the gate of the keeper's house. Dismounting, and hanging the bridle of the pony over the rail he walked through a small garden, neatly kept but, so early in the year, not over gay, except that the crocus and snow drops were peeping. He rapped at the door with his knuckles, and a girl of about fourteen, very neatly dressed, answered the summons.

"Is Oswald Partridge at home, maiden?" said Edward.

"No, young man, he is not. He is in the forest."

"When will he return?"

"Towards the evening is his time, unless he is more than usually successful."

"I have come some distance to find him," replied Edward; "and it would vex me to return without seeing him. Has he a wife, or any one that I could speak to?"

"He has no wife; but I am willing to deliver a message."

"I am come about some dogs which he promised to Jacob Armitage, my relation; but the old man is too unwell, and has been for some time, to come himself for them, and he has sent me."

"There are dogs, young and old, large and small, in the kennels; so far do I know, and no more."

"I fear then I must wait till his return," replied Edward.

"I will speak to my father," replied the young girl, "if you will wait one moment."

In a minute or two the girl returned, saying that her father begged that he would walk in, and he would speak with him. Edward bowed, and followed the young girl, who led the way to a room, in which was seated a man dressed after the fashion of the Roundheads of the day. His steeple-crowned hat lay on the chair, with his sword beneath it. He was sitting at a table covered with papers.

"Here is the youth, father," said the girl; and having said this, she crossed the room and took a seat by the side of the fire. The man, or we should rather say gentleman—for he had the appearance of one, notwithstanding the sombre and peculiar dress he wore, continued to read a letter which he had just opened; and Edward, who feared himself the prisoner of a Roundhead when he only expected to meet a keeper, was further irritated by the neglect shown towards him by the party. Forgetting that he was, by his own assertion, not Edward Beverley, but the relative of one Jacob Armitage, he coloured up with anger as he stood at the door. Fortunately the time that it took the other party to read through the letter gave Edward also time for recollecting the disguise under which he appeared; the colour subsided from his cheeks, and he remained in silence, occasionally meeting the look of the little girl, who, when their eyes met, immediately withdrew her glance.

"What is your business, young man?" at last said the gentleman at the table.

"I came, sir, on private business with the keeper, Oswald Partridge, to obtain two young hounds, which he promised to my grandfather, Jacob Armitage."

"Armitage!" said the other party, referring to a list on the table; "Armitage—Jacob—yes—I see he is one of the verderers. Why has he not been here to call upon me?"

"For what reason should he call upon you, sir?" replied Edward.

"Simply, young man, because the New Forest is, by the Parliament, committed to my charge. Notice has been given for all those who were employed to come here, that they might be permitted to remain, or he discharged, as I may deem most advisable."

"Jacob Armitage has heard nothing of this, sir," replied Edward. "He was a keeper, appointed under the king; for two or three years his allowances have never been paid, and he has lived in his own cottage, which was left to him by his father, being his own property."

"And pray, may I ask, young man, do you live with Jacob Armitage?"

"I have done so for more than a year."

"And as your relation has received no pay and allowances, as you state, pray, by what means has he maintained himself?"

"How have the other keepers maintained themselves?" replied Edward.

"Do not put questions to me, sir," replied the gentleman; "but be pleased to reply to mine. What has been the means of subsistence of Jacob Armitage?"

"If you think he has no means of subsistence, sir, you are mistaken," replied Edward. "We have land of our own, which we cultivate; we have our pony and our cart; we have our pigs and our cows."

"And they have been sufficient?"

"Had the patriarchs more?" replied Edward.

"You are pithy at reply, young man; but I know something of Jacob Armitage, and we know," continued he, putting his finger close to some writing opposite the name on the list, "with whom he has been associated, and with whom he has served. Now allow me to put one question. You have come, you say, for two young hounds. Are their services required for your pigs and cows, and to what use are they to be put?"

"We have as good a dog as there is in the forest," replied Edward, "but we wish to have others, in case we should lose him."

"As good a dog as in the forest—good for what?"

"For hunting."

"Then you acknowledge that you do hunt?"

"I acknowledge nothing for Jacob Armitage, he may answer for himself," replied Edward; "but allow me to assure you that if he has killed venison no one can blame him."

"Perhaps you will explain why?"

"Nothing is more easy. Jacob Armitage served King Charles, who employed him as a verderer in the forest, and paid him his wages. Those who should not have done so rebelled against the king, took his authority from him, and the means of paying those he employed. They were still servants of the king, for they were not dismissed; and, having no other means of support, they considered that their good master would be but too happy that they should support themselves by killing, for their subsistence, that venison which they could no longer preserve for him without eating some themselves."

"Then you admit that Jacob Armitage has killed the deer in the forest?"

"I admit nothing for Jacob Armitage."

"You admit that you have killed it yourself."

"I shall not answer that question, sir; in the first place, I am not here to criminate myself; and, in the next, I must know by what authority you have the right to inquire."

"Young man," replied the other in a severe tone, "if you wish to know my authority, malapert as you are (at this remark Edward started, yet, recollecting himself he compressed his lips and stood still), this is my commission, appointing me the agent of Parliament to take charge and superintend the New Forest, with power to appoint and dismiss those whom I please. I presume you must take my word for it, as you cannot read and write."

Edward stepped up to the table, and very quietly took up the paper and read it. "You have stated what is correct, sir," said he, laying it down; "and the date of it is, I perceive, on the 20th of the last month of December. It is, therefore, but eighteen days old."

"And what inference would you draw from that, young man?" replied the gentleman, looking up to him with some astonishment.

"Simply this, sir—that Jacob Armitage has been laid up with the rheumatism for three months, during which time he certainly has not killed any venison. Now, sir, until the Parliament took the forest into their hands, it undoubtedly belonged to his majesty, if it does not now; therefore Jacob Armitage, for whatever slaughter he may have committed, is, up to the present, only answerable to his sovereign, King Charles."

"It is easy to perceive the school in which you have been brought up, young man, even if there was not evidence on this paper that your forefather served under the Cavalier Colonel Beverley, and has brought you up to his way of thinking."

"Sir, it is a base dog that bites the hand that feeds him," replied Edward with warmth. "Jacob Armitage, and his father before him, were retainers in the family of Colonel Beverley; they were indebted to him for the situation they now hold in the forest; indebted to him for everything; they revere his name, they uphold the cause for which he fell, as I *do*."

"Young man, if you do not speak advisedly, at all events you speak gratefully; neither have I a word of disrespect to offer to the memory of Colonel Beverley, who was a gallant man, and true to the cause which he espoused, although it was not a holy one; but in my position, I cannot, in justice to those whom I serve, give places and emolument to those who have been, and still are, as I may judge by your expressions, adverse to the present government."

"Sir," replied Edward, "your language, with respect to Colonel Beverley, has made me feel respect for you, which I confess I did not at first; what you say is very just; not that I think you harm Jacob Armitage; as, in the first place, I know that he would not serve under you; and, in the next, that he is too old and infirm to hold the situation; neither has he occasion for it, as his cottage and land are his own, and you cannot remove him."

"He has the title, I presume?" replied the gentleman.

"He has the title given to his grandfather, long before King Charles was born, and I presume the Parliament do not intend to invalidate the acts of former kings."

"May I inquire what relation you are to Jacob Armitage?"

"I believe, I have before said, his grandson."

"You live with him?"

"I do."

"And if the old man dies, will inherit his property?" Edward smiled, and looking at the young girl, said, "Now, I ask you, maiden, if your father does not presume upon his office?"

The young girl laughed, and said, "He is in authority."

"Not over me, certainly, and not over my grandfather, for he has dismissed him."

"Were you brought up at the cottage, young man?"

"No, sir, I was brought up at Arnwood. I was a playmate of the children of Colonel Beverley."

"Educated with them?"

"Yes, for, as far as my wilfulness would permit, the chaplain was always ready to give me instruction."

"Where were you when Arnwood was burnt down?"

"I was at the cottage at that time," replied Edward, grinding his teeth and looking wildly.

"Nay, nay, I can forgive any expression of feeling on your part, my young man, when that dreadful and disgraceful deed is brought to your memory. It was a stain that can never be effaced—a deed most diabolical, and what we thought would call down the vengeance of heaven. If prayers could avert, or did avert it, they were not wanting on our side."

Edward remained silent: this admission on the part of the Roundhead prevented an explosion on his part. He felt that all were not so bad as he had imagined. After a long pause, he said, "When I came here, sir, it was to seek Oswald Partridge, and obtain the hounds which he had promised us; but I presume that my journey is now useless."

"Why so?"

"Because you have the control of the forest, and will not permit dogs for the chase to be given away to those who are not employed by the powers that now govern."

"You have judged correctly, in so far that my duty is to prevent it; but as the promise was made previous to the date of my commission, I presume," said he, smiling, "you think I have no right to interfere, as it will be an *ex post facto* case, if I do: I shall not therefore interfere, only I must point out to you that the laws are still the same relative to those who take the deer in the forest by stealth—you understand me?"

"Yes, sir, I do; and if you will not be offended, I will give you a candid reply."

"Speak then."

"I consider that the deer in this forest belong to King Charles, who is my lawful sovereign, and I own no authority but from him. I hold myself answerable to him alone for any deer I may kill, and I feel sure of his permission and full forgiveness for what I may do."

"That may be your opinion, my good sir, but it will not be the opinion of the ruling powers; but if caught, you will be punished, and that by me, in pursuance of the authority vested in me."

"Well, sir; if so, so be it. You have dismissed the Armitages on account of their upholding the king, and you cannot, therefore, be surprised that they uphold him more than ever. Nor can you be surprised if a dismissed verderer becomes a poacher."

"Nor can you be surprised if a poacher is caught, that he incurs the penalty," replied the Roundhead. "So now there's an end of our argument. If you go into the kitchen, you will find wherewithal to refresh the outward man, and if you wish to remain till Oswald Partridge comes home, you are welcome."

Edward, who felt indignant at being dismissed to the kitchen, nodded his head and smiled upon the little girl, and left the room. "Well," thought he, as he went along the passage, "I came here for two puppies, and I have found a Roundhead. I don't know how it is, but I am not so angry with him as I thought I should be. That little girl had a nice smile—she was quite handsome when she smiled. Oh, this is the kitchen, to which," thought he, "the Lord of Arnwood is dismissed by a Covenanter and Roundhead, probably a tradesman or outlaw, who has served the cause. Well, be it so; as Humphrey says, 'I'll bide my time.' But there is no one here, so I'll try if there is a stable for White Billy, who is tired, I presume, of being at the gate."

Edward returned by the way he came, went out of the front door, and through the garden to where the pony was made fast, and led him away in search of a stable. He found one behind the house, and filling the rack with hay, returned to the house, and seated himself at a porch which was at the door which led to the back premises, for the keeper's house was large and commodious. Edward was in deep thought, when he was roused by the little girl, the daughter of the newly-appointed Intendant of the forest, who said:

"I am afraid, young sir, you have had but sorry welcome in the kitchen, as there was no one to receive you. I was not aware that Phoebe had gone out. If you will come with me, I may, perhaps, find you refreshment."

"Thanks, maiden, you are kind and considerate to an avowed poacher," replied Edward.

"Oh, but you will not poach, I'm sure; and if you do, I'll beg you off if I can," replied the girl, laughing.

Edward followed her into the kitchen, and she soon produced a cold fowl and a venison pasty, which she placed on the table; she then went out and returned with a jug of ale.

"There," said she, putting it on the table, "that is all that I can find."

"Your father's name is Heatherstone, I believe. It was so on the warrant."

"Yes, it is."

"And yours?"

"The same as my father's, I should presume."

"Yes, but your baptismal name?"

"You ask strange questions, young sir; but still I will answer you that: my baptismal name is Patience."

"I thank you for your condescension," replied Edward. "You live here?"

"For the present, good sir; and now I leave you."

"That's a nice little girl," thought Edward, "although she is the daughter of a Roundhead; and she calls me 'sir.' I cannot, therefore, look like Jacob's grandson, and must be careful." Edward then set to with a good appetite at the viands which had been placed before him, and had just finished a hearty meal when Patience Heatherstone again came in and said:

"Oswald Partridge is now coming home."

"I thank you, maiden," replied Edward. "May I ask a question of you? Where is the king now?"

"I have heard that he resides at Hurst Castle," replied the girl; "but," added she in a low tone, "all attempts to see him would be useless, and only hurt him and those who made the attempt." Having said this she left the room.

Chapter Nine.

Edward, having finished his meal, and had a good pull at the jug of ale, which was a liquor he had not tasted for a long while, rose from the table and went out of the back door and found there Oswald Partridge. He accosted him, stating the reason for his coming over to him. "I did not know that Jacob had a grandson; indeed, I never knew that he had a son. Have you been living with him long?"

"More than a year," replied Edward; "before that I was in the household at Arnwood."

"Then you are of the king's side, I presume?" replied Oswald.

"To death," replied Edward, "when the time comes."

"And I am also; that you may suppose, for never would I give a hound to any one that was not. But we had better go to the kennels; dogs may hear, but they can't repeat."

"I little thought to have met any one but you here when I came," said Edward; "and I will now tell you all that passed between me and the new Intendant." Edward then related the conversation.

"You have been bold," said Oswald—"but perhaps it is all the better—I am to retain my situation, and so are two others: but there are many new hands coming in as rangers. I know nothing of them but that they are little fitted for their places; and rail against the king all day long, which I suppose is their chief merit in the eyes of those who appoint them. However, one thing is certain, that if those fellows cannot stalk a deer themselves, they will do all they can to prevent others; so you must be on the alert, for the punishment is severe."

"I fear them not; the only difficulty is, that we shall not be able to find a sale for the venison now," replied Edward.

"Oh, never fear that; I will give you the names of those who will take all your venison off your hands without any risk on your part, except in the killing of it. They will meet you in the park, lay down ready money, and take it away. I don't know, but I have an idea that this new Intendant, or what you may call him, is not so severe as he pretends to be. Indeed, his permitting you to say what he did, and his own words relative to the colonel, convince me that I am right in the opinion that I formed."

"Do you know who he is?"

"Not much about him, but he is a great friend of General Cromwell's, and they say has done good service to the Parliamentary cause; but we shall meet again, for the forest is free, at all events."

"If you come here," continued Oswald, "do not carry your gun, and see that you are not watched home. There are the dogs for your grandfather. Why, how old must you be, for Jacob is not more than sixty, or thereabout?"

"I am fifteen past, nevertheless."

"I should have put you down for eighteen or nineteen at least. You are well grown indeed for that age. Well, nothing like a forest life to turn a boy into a man! Can you stalk a deer?"

"I seldom go out without bringing one down."

"Indeed! That Jacob is a master of his craft is certain. But you are young to have learnt it so soon. Can you tell the slot of a brocket from a stag?"

"Yes, and the slot of a brocket from a doe."

"Better still. We must go out together; and besides, I must know where the old man's cottage is (for I do not exactly); in the first place, because I may want to come to you, and in the next, that I may put others on a false scent.—Do you know the clump of large oaks, which they call the Clump Royal?"

"Yes, I do."

"Will you meet me there the day after to-morrow, at early dawn?"

"If I live and do well."

"That's enough. Take the dogs in the leashes, and go away now."

"Many thanks; but I must not leave the pony; he is in the stable."

The keeper nodded adieu to Edward, who left him to go to the stable for the pony. Edward saddled White Billy, and rode away across the forest with the dogs trotting at the pony's heels.

Edward had much to reflect upon as he rode back to the cottage. He felt that his position was one of more difficulty than before. That old Jacob Armitage would not last much longer he was convinced; even now the poor old man was shrunk away to a skeleton with pain and disease. That the livelihood to be procured from the forest would be attended with peril, now that order had been restored and the forest was no longer neglected, was certain; and he rejoiced that Humphrey had, by his assiduity and intelligence, made the farm so profitable as it promised to be. Indeed he felt that, if necessary, they could live upon the proceeds of the farm, and not run the risk of imprisonment by stalking the deer. But he had told the intendant that he considered the game as the king's property, and he was resolved that he would at all events run the risk, although he would no longer permit Humphrey so to do. "If anything happens to me," thought Edward, "Humphrey will still be at the cottage to take care of my sisters; and if I am obliged to fly the country, it will suit well my feelings, as I can then offer my services to those who still support the king." With these thoughts, and many others, he amused himself until, late in the evening, he arrived at the cottage. He found all in bed except Humphrey, who had waited for him, and to whom he narrated all that had passed. Humphrey said little in reply; he wished to think it over before he gave any opinion. He told Edward that Jacob had been very ill the whole of the day, and had requested Alice to read the Bible to him during the evening.

The next morning Edward went to Jacob, who for the last ten days had altogether kept his bed, and gave him the detail of what had happened at the keeper's lodge.

"You have been more bold than prudent, Edward," replied Jacob; "but I could not expect you to have spoken otherwise. You are too proud and too manly to tell a lie, and I am glad that it is so. As for your upholding the king, although he is now a prisoner in their hands, they cannot blame you or punish you for that, as long as you have not weapons in your hands; but now that they have taken the forest under their jurisdiction, you must be careful, for they are the ruling powers at present, and must be obeyed, or the forfeit must be paid. Still I do not ask you to promise me this or that; I only point out to you that your sisters will suffer by any imprudence on your part; and for their sakes be careful. I say this, Edward, because I feel that my days are numbered, and that in a short time I shall be called away. You will then have all the load on your shoulders which has been latterly on mine. I have no fear for the result, if you are prudent; these few months past, during which I have only been a burden to you, have proved that you and Humphrey can find a living here for yourselves and your sisters; and it is fortunate, now that the forest laws are about to be put in force, that you have made the farm so profitable. If I might advise, let your hunting in the forest be confined to the wild cattle; they are not game, and the forest laws do not extend to them, and the meat is as valuable as venison; that is to say, it does not sell so dear, but there is more of it; but stick to the farm as much as you can; for you see, Edward, you do not look like a low-born forester, nor ought you to do so; and the more quiet you keep, the better. As for Oswald Partridge, you may trust him; I know him well, and he will prove your friend for my sake, as soon as he hears that I am dead. Leave me now, I will talk to you again in the evening. Send Alice to me, my dear boy."

Edward was much distressed to perceive the change which had taken place in old Jacob. He was evidently much worse; but Edward had no idea how much worse he was. Edward assisted Humphrey in the farm, and in the evening again went to Jacob, and then told him of the arrangement he had made to meet Oswald Partridge on the following morning.

"Go, my boy," said Jacob; "be as intimate with him as you can, and make a friend of him—nay, if it should be necessary, you may tell him who you are; I did think of telling him myself, as it might be important to you one day as evidence. I think you had better bring him here to-morrow night, Edward; tell him I am dying, and wish to speak to him before I go. Alice will read the Bible to me now, and I will talk with you another time."

Early the next morning Edward set off to the appointed rendezvous with Oswald Partridge. The Clump Royal, as it was called, from the peculiar size and beauty of the oaks, was about seven miles from the cottage; and at the hour and time indicated Edward, with his gun in his hand, and Smoker lying beside him, was leaning against one of those monarchs of the forest. He did not wait long. Oswald Partridge, similarly provided, made his appearance, and Edward advanced to meet him.

"Welcome, Oswald," said Edward.

"And welcome to you also, my fine lad," replied Oswald. "I have been hard questioned about you since we parted—first, by the Roundhead Heatherstone, who plied me in all manner of ways to find out whether you are what you assert, the grandson of Jacob,—or some other person. I really believe that he fancies you are the Duke of York—but he could not get any more from me than what I knew. I told him that your grandfather's cottage was his own property, and a grant to his forefathers: that you were brought up at Arnwood, and had joined your grandfather after the death of the colonel, and the murderous burning of the house and all within it by his party. But the pretty little daughter was more curious still. She cross-questioned me in every way when her father was not present, and at last begged me as a favour to tell you not to take the deer, as her father was very strict in his duty, and, if caught, you would be imprisoned."

"Many thanks to her for her caution, but I hope to take one to-day, nevertheless," replied Edward; "a hart royal is not meat for Roundheads, although the king's servants may feast on them."

"That's truly said. Well, now I must see your woodcraft. You shall be the leader of the chase."

"Think you we can harbour a stag about here?"

"Yes, in this month, no doubt."

"Let us walk on," said Edward. "The wind is fresh from the eastern quarter: we will face it, if you please—or rather, keep it blowing on our right cheek for the present."

"'Tis well," replied Oswald; and they walked for about half an hour.

"This is the slot of a doe," said Edward, in a low voice, pointing to the marks; "yonder thicket is a likely harbour for the stag." They proceeded, and Edward pointed out to Oswald the slot of the stag into the thicket. They then walked round, and found no marks of the animal having left his lair.

"He is here," whispered Edward; and Oswald made a sign for Edward to enter the thicket, while he walked to the other side. Edward entered the thicket cautiously. In the centre he perceived, through the trees, a small cleared spot, covered with high fern, and felt certain that the stag was lying there. He forced his way on his knees till he had a better view of the place, and then cocked his gun. The noise induced the stag to move his antlers, and discover his lair. Edward could just perceive the eye of the animal through the heath; he waited till the beast settled again, took steady aim, and fired. At the report of the gun another stag sprung up and burst away. Oswald fired and wounded it, but the animal made off, followed by the dogs. Edward, who hardly knew whether he had missed or not, but felt almost certain that he had not, hastened out of the thicket to join in the chase; and, as he passed through the fern patch, perceived that his quarry lay dead. He then followed the chase, and, being very fleet of foot, soon came up with Oswald, and passed him without speaking. The stag made for a swampy ground, and finally took to the water beyond it, and stood at bay. Edward then waited for Oswald, who came up with him.

"He has soiled," said Edward, "and now you may go in and kill him."

Oswald, eager in the chase, hastened up to where the dogs and stag were in the water, and put a bullet through the animal's head.

Edward went to him, assisted him to drag the stag out of the water, and then Oswald cut its throat, and proceeded to perform the usual offices.

"How did you happen to miss him?" said Oswald, "for these are my shots?"

"Because I never fired at him," said Edward; "my quarry lies dead in the fern—and a fine fellow he is."

"This is a warrantable stag," said Oswald.

"Yes, but mine is a hart royal, as you will see when we go back."

As soon as Oswald had done his work, he hung the quarters of the animal on an oak-tree, and went back with Edward.

"Where did you hit him, Edward?" said Oswald, as they walked along.

"I could only see his eye through the fern, and I must have hit him thereabouts."

On their arrival at the spot Oswald found that Edward had put the ball right into the eye of the stag.

"Well," said he, "you made me suppose that you knew something of our craft, but I did not believe that you were so apt as you thought yourself to be. I now confess that you are a master, as far as I can see, in all branches of the craft. This is, indeed, a hart royal. Twenty-five antlers, as I live! Come, out with your knife, and let us finish; for if we are to go to the cottage we have no time to lose. It will be dark in half an hour." They hung all the quarters of the stag as before, and then set off for Jacob's cottage; Edward proposing that Oswald should take the cart and pony to carry the meat home the next morning, and that he would accompany him to bring it back.

"That will do capitally," said Oswald; "and here we are, if I recollect right, and I hope there is something to eat."

"No fear of that—Alice will be prepared for us," replied Edward.

Their dinner was ready for them; and Oswald praised the cooking. He was much surprised to find that Jacob had four grandchildren. After dinner he went into Jacob's room, and remained with him more than an hour. During this conference Jacob confided to Oswald that the four children were the sons and daughters of Colonel Beverley, supposed to have been burnt in the firing of Arnwood. Oswald came out, much surprised as well as pleased with the information, and with the confidence reposed in him. He saluted Edward and Humphrey respectfully, and said, "I was not aware with whom I was in company, sir, as you may well imagine; but the knowledge of it has made my heart glad."

"Nay, Oswald," replied Edward, "remember that I am still Edward Armitage, and that we are the grandchildren of old Jacob."

"Certainly, sir, I will, for your own sake, not forget that such is to be supposed to be the case. I assure you I think it very fortunate that Jacob has confided the secret to me, as it may be in my power to be useful. I little thought that I should ever have had my dinner cooked by a daughter of Colonel Beverley."

They then entered into a long conversation, during which Oswald expressed his opinion that the old man was sinking fast, and would not last more than three or four days. Oswald had a bed made up for him on the floor of the room where Edward and Humphrey slept, and the next morning they set off, at an early hour, with the pony and cart, loaded it with the venison, and took it across the forest to the keeper's lodge. It was so late when they arrived that Edward consented to pass the night there, and return home on the following morning. Oswald went into the sitting-room to speak with the Intendant of the forest, leaving Edward in the kitchen with Phoebe, the maidservant. He told the Intendant that he had brought home some fine venison, and wished his orders about it. He also stated that he had been assisted by Edward Armitage, who had brought the venison home for him in his cart, and who was now in the kitchen, as he would be obliged to pass the night there; and, on being questioned, he was lavish in his praises of Edward's skill and knowledge of woodcraft, which he declared to be superior to his own.

"It proves that the young man has had much practice, at all events," replied Mr Heatherstone, smiling. "He has been living at the king's expense, but he must not follow it up at the cost of the Parliament. It would be well to take this young man as a ranger if we could; for although he is opposed to us, yet, if he once took our service, he would be faithful, I am sure. You can propose it to him, Oswald. The haunches of that hart royal must be sent up to General Cromwell to-morrow: the remainder we will give directions for as soon as I have made up my mind how to dispose of it."

Oswald left the room, and came back to Edward. "General Cromwell is to have the haunches of your stag," said he to Edward, smiling; "and the Intendant proposes that you should take service as one of the rangers."

"I thank you," replied Edward, "but I've no fancy to find venison for General Cromwell and his Roundheads; and so you may tell the Intendant, with many thanks for his good-will towards me, nevertheless."

"I thought as much; but the man meant kindly, that I really think. Now, Phoebe, what can you give us to eat, for we are hungry?"

"You shall be served directly," replied Phoebe. "I have some steaks on the fire."

"And you must find a bed for my young friend here."

"I have none in the house, but there is plenty of good straw over the stables."

"That will do," replied Edward; "I'm not particular."

"I suppose not. Why should you be?" replied Phoebe, who was rather old and rather cross. "If you mount the ladder that you will see against the wall, you will find a good bed when you are at the top of it."

Oswald was about to remonstrate, but Edward held up his finger, and no more was said.

As soon as they had finished their supper Phoebe proposed that they should go to bed. It was late, and she would sit up no longer. Edward rose and went out, followed by Oswald, who had given up the keeper's house to the intendant and his daughter, and slept in the cottage of one of the rangers, about a quarter of a mile off. After some conversation they shook hands and parted, as Edward intended returning very early the next morning, being anxious about old Jacob.

Edward went up the ladder into the loft. There was no door to shut out the wind, which blew piercingly cold, and after a time he found himself so chilled that he could not sleep. He rose to see if he could not find some protection from the wind by getting more into a corner; for although Phoebe had told him that there was plenty of straw, it proved that there was very little indeed in the loft, barely enough to lie down upon. Edward, after a time, descended the ladder to walk in the yard, that by exercise he might recover the use of his limbs. At last, turning to and fro, he cast his eyes up to the window of the bedroom above the kitchen, where he perceived a light was still burning. He thought it was Phoebe, the maid, going to bed; and with no very gracious feelings towards her for having deprived him of his own night's rest, he was wishing that she might have the toothache or something else to keep her awake, when suddenly through the white window curtain he perceived a broad light in the room—it increased every moment—and he saw the figure of a female rush past it, and attempt to open the window—the drawing of the curtains showed him that the room was on fire. A moment's thought, and he ran for the ladder by which he had ascended to the loft, and placed it against the window. The flames were less bright, and he could not see the female who had been at the window when he went for the ladder. He ascended quickly, and burst open the casement—the smoke poured out in such volumes that it nearly suffocated him, but he went in; and as soon as he was inside, he stumbled against the body of the person who had attempted to open the window, but who had fallen down senseless. As he raised the body, the fire, which had been smothered from want of air when all the windows and doors were closed, now burst out, and he was scorched before he could get on the ladder again, with the body in his arms; but he succeeded in getting it down safe. Perceiving that the clothes were on fire, he held them till they were extinguished, and then, for the first time, discovered that he had brought down the daughter of the intendant of the forest. There was no time to be lost, so Edward carried her into the stable and left her there, still insensible, upon the straw, in a spare stall; while he hastened to alarm the house. The watering-butt for the horses was outside the stable; Edward caught up the pail, filled it, and hastening up the ladder, threw it into the room, and then descended for more.

By this time Edward's continual calls of "Fire! Fire!" had aroused the people of the house, and also of the cottages adjacent. Mr Heatherstone came out half dressed, and with horror on his countenance. Phoebe followed screaming, and the other people now hastened from the cottages.

"Save her! My daughter is in the room!" exclaimed Mr Heatherstone. "Oh, save her, or let me do so!" cried the poor man in agony; but the fire burst out of the window in such force, that any attempt would have been in vain.

"Oswald," cried Edward to him, "let the people pass the water up to me as fast as possible. They can do no good by looking on."

Oswald set the men to the work, and Edward was now supplied with water so fast that the fire began to diminish. The window was now approachable, and a few more buckets enabled him to put one foot into the room, and then every moment the flames and smoke decreased.

Meanwhile it would be impossible to describe the agony of the intendant, who would have rushed up the ladder into the flames had he not been held by some of the men. "My daughter! My child!—burnt—burnt to death!" exclaimed he, clasping his hands.

At that moment a voice in the crowd called out, "There were four burnt at Arnwood!"

"God of heaven!" exclaimed Mr Heatherstone, falling down into a swoon, in which state he was carried to a neighbouring cottage.

Meanwhile the supply of water enabled Edward to put out the fire altogether; the furniture of the room was burnt, but the fire had extended no farther; and when Edward was satisfied that there was no more danger, he descended the ladder, and left it to others to see that all was safe. He then called Oswald to him, and desired that he would accompany him to the stable.

"Oh sir," replied Oswald, "this is dreadful! And such a sweet young lady too."

"She is safe and well," replied Edward; "I think so, at least. I brought her down the ladder and put her in the stable before I attempted to put out the fire. See, there she is; she has not recovered yet from her swoon. Bring some water. She breathes! Thank God! There, that will do, Oswald, she is recovering. Now let us cover her up in your cloak, and carry her to your cottage. We will recover her there."

Oswald folded up the still unconscious girl in his cloak, and carried her away in his arms, followed by Edward.

As soon as they arrived at the cottage, the inmates of which were all busy at the keeper's lodge, they put her on a bed, and very soon restored her to consciousness.

"Where is my father?" cried Patience, as soon as she was sufficiently recovered.

"He is safe and well, miss," replied Oswald.

"Is the house burnt down?"

"No. The fire is all out again."

"Who saved me? Tell me."

"Young Armitage, miss."

"Who is he? Oh, I recollect now; but I must go to my father. Where is he?"

"In the other cottage, miss."

Patience attempted to stand, but found that she was too much exhausted, and she fell back again on the bed. "I can't stand," said she. "Bring my father to me."

"I will, miss," replied Oswald.

"Will you stay here, Edward?"

"Yes," replied Edward. He went out of the cottage-door, and remained there while Oswald went to Mr Heatherstone.

Oswald found him sensible, but in deep distress, as may be imagined. "The fire is all out, sir," said Oswald.

"I care not for that. My poor, poor child!"

"Your child is safe, sir," replied Oswald.

"Safe, did you say?" cried Mr Heatherstone, starting up. "Safe; where?"

"In my cottage. She has sent me for you."

Mr Heatherstone rushed out, passed by Edward, who was standing at the door of the other cottage, and was in his daughter's arms. Oswald came out to Edward, who then detailed to him the way in which he had saved the girl.

"Had it not been for the ill-nature of that girl Phoebe, in sending me to sleep where there was no straw, they would all have been burnt," observed Edward.

"She gave you an opportunity of rewarding good for evil," observed Oswald.

"Yes, but I am burnt very much in my arm," said Edward. "Have you anything that will be good for it?"

"Yes, I think I have: wait a moment."

Oswald went into the cottage and returned with some salve, with which he dressed Edward's arm, which proved to be very severely burnt.

"How grateful the Intendant ought to be—and will be, I have no doubt!" observed Oswald.

"And for that very reason I shall saddle my pony and ride home as fast as I can; and, do you hear, Oswald, do not show him where I live."

"I hardly know how I can refuse him, if he requires it."

"But you must not. He will be offering me a situation in the forest, by way of showing his gratitude; and I will accept of none. I have no objection to save his daughter, as I would save the daughter of my worst enemy, or my worst enemy himself, from such a dreadful death; but I do not want their thanks or offers of service. I will accept nothing from a Roundhead; and as for the venison in the forest, it belongs to the king, and I shall help myself whenever I think proper. Good-bye, Oswald, you will call and see us when you have time?"

"I will be with you before the week is out, depend upon it," replied Oswald.

Edward then asked Oswald to saddle his pony for him, as his arm prevented him from doing it himself, and as soon as it was done he rode away for the cottage.

Edward rode fast, for he was anxious to get home and ascertain the state of poor old Jacob; and, moreover, his burnt arm was very painful. He was met by Humphrey about a mile from the cottage, who told him that he did not think that the old man could last many hours, and that he was very anxious to see him. As the pony was quite tired with the fast pace that Edward had ridden, Edward pulled up to a walk, and as they went along acquainted Humphrey with what had passed.

"Is your arm very painful?"

"Yes, it is indeed," replied Edward; "but it can't be helped."

"No, of course not, but it may be made more easy. I know what will do it some good; for I recollect when Benjamin burnt his hand at Arnwood, what they applied to it, and it gave him great relief."

"Yes, very likely; but I am not aware that we have any drugs or medicine in the cottage. But here we are: will you take Billy to the stable, while I go on to old Jacob?"

"Thank God that you are come, Edward," said the old forester, "for I was anxious to see you before I die; and something tells me that I have but a short time to remain here."

"Why should you say so!—do you feel very ill?"

"No, not ill; but I feel that I am sinking fast. Recollect that I am an old man, Edward."

"Not so very old, Jacob; Oswald said that you were not more than sixty years old."

"Oswald knows nothing about it. I am past seventy six, Edward; and you know, Edward, the Bible says that the days of men are threescore years and ten; so that I am beyond the mark. And now, Edward, I have but few words to say. Be careful—if not for your own sake, at least for your little sisters'. You are young, but you are strong and powerful above your years, and can better protect them than I could. I see darker days yet coming—but it is His will, and who shall doubt that that is right? I pray you not to make your birth and lineage known as yet—it can do no good, and it may do harm—and if you can be persuaded to live in the cottage, and to live on the farm, which will now support you all, it will be better. Do not get into trouble about the venison, which they now claim as their own. You will find some money in the bag in my chest, sufficient to buy all you want for a long while—but take care of it; for there is no saying but you may require it. And now, Edward, call your brother and sisters to me, that I may bid them farewell. I am, as we all are, sinful, but I trust in the mercy of God through Jesus Christ. Edward, I have done my duty towards you, as well as I have been able; but promise me one thing—that you will read the Bible and prayers every morning and evening, as I have always done, after I am gone; promise me that, Edward."

"I promise you that it shall be done, Jacob," replied Edward, "and I will not forget your other advice."

"God bless you, Edward. Now call the children."

Edward summoned his sisters and Humphrey.

"Humphrey, my good boy," said Jacob, "recollect that in the midst of life we are in death; and that there is no security for young or old. You or your brother may be cut off in your youth; one may be taken, and the other left. Recollect, your sisters depend upon you, and do not therefore be rash: I fear that you will run too much risk after the wild cattle, for you are always scheming after taking them. Be careful, Humphrey, for you can ill be spared. Hold to the farm as it now is; it will support you all. My dear Alice and Edith, I am dying; very soon I shall be laid by your brothers in my grave. Be good children, and look up to your brothers for everything. And now, kiss me, Alice: you have been a great comfort to me, for you have read the Bible to me when I could no longer read myself. May your deathbed be as well attended as mine has been, and may you live happily, and die the death of a Christian! Good-bye, and may God bless you. Bless you, Edith; may you grow up as good and as innocent as you are now. Farewell, Humphrey—farewell, Edward—my eyes are dim—pray for me, children. O God of mercy—pardon my many sins, and receive my soul, through Jesus Christ. Amen, amen."

These were the last words spoken by the old forester. The children, who were kneeling by the side of the bed, praying as he had requested, when they rose up, found that he was dead. They all wept bitterly, for they dearly loved the good old man. Alice remained sobbing in Edward's arms, and Edith in Humphrey's, and it was long before the brothers could console them. Humphrey at last said to Alice, "You hurt poor Edward's arm—you don't know how painful it is! Come, dears, let us go into the other room, and get something to take the pain away."

These requests diverted the attention at the same time that it roused fresh sympathy in the little girls—they all went into the sitting-room. Humphrey gave his sisters some potatoes to scrape upon a piece of linen, while he took off Edward's coat, and turned up his shirt sleeves. The scraped potatoes were then laid on the burn, and Edward said they gave him great relief. Some more were then scraped by the little girls, who could not, however, repress their occasional sobs. Humphrey then told them that Edward had had nothing to eat, and that they must get him some supper. This again occupied them for some time; and when the supper was ready, they all sat down to it. They went to bed early, but not before Edward had read a chapter out of the Bible, and the prayers, as old Jacob had always done; and this again caused their tears to flow afresh.

"Come, Alice dear, you and Edith must go to bed," said Humphrey.

The little girls threw themselves into their brothers' arms; and having wept for some time, Alice raised herself, and taking Edith by the hand, led her away to the bedroom.

Chapter Ten.

"Humphrey," said Edward, "the sooner all this is over the better. As long as poor Jacob's body remains in the cottage there will be nothing but distress with the poor girls."

"I agree with you," replied Humphrey; "where shall we bury him?"

"Under the great oak-tree, at the back of the cottage," replied Edward. "One day the old man said to me that he should like to be buried under one of the oaks of the forest."

"Well then, I will go and dig his grave to-night," replied Humphrey; "the moon is bright, and I shall have it finished before morning."

"I am sorry that I cannot help you, Humphrey."

"I am sorry that you are hurt; but I want no help, Edward. If you will lie down a little, perhaps you will be able to sleep. Let us change the potato poultice before you go on."

Humphrey put the fresh dressing on Edward's arm; and Edward, who was very much exhausted, lay down in his clothes on the bed. Humphrey went out, and having found his tools, set to his task; he worked hard, and before morning had finished. He then went in, and took his place on the bed by the side of Edward, who was in a sound sleep. At daylight Humphrey rose, and waked Edward. "All is ready, Edward; but I fear you must help me to put poor Jacob in the cart; do you think you can?"

"Oh yes; my arm is much easier, and I feel very different from what I did last night. If you will go and get the cart I will see what I can do in the meantime."

When Humphrey returned he found Edward had selected a sheet to wind the body in, but could not do more till Humphrey came to help him. They then wrapped it round the body, and carried it out of the cottage, and put it into the cart.

"Now, Edward, shall we call our sisters?"

"No, not yet; let us have the body laid in the grave first, and then we will call them."

They dragged the body on the cart to the grave, and laid it in it, and then returned back and put the pony in the stable again.

"Are there not prayers proper for reading over the dead?" said Humphrey.

"I believe that there are, but they are not in the Bible; so we must read some portion of the Bible," said Edward.

"Yes, I think there is one of the Psalms which it would be right to read, Edward," said Humphrey, turning over the leaves; "here it is, the ninetieth, in which you recollect it says 'that the days of man are threescore years and ten.'"

"Yes," replied Edward, "and we will read this one also,—the 146th."

"Are our sisters risen, do you think?"

"I am sure that they are," replied Humphrey, "and I will go to them."

Humphrey went to the door, and said, "Alice—Alice and Edith—come out immediately." They were both ready dressed.

Edward took the Bible under his arm, and Alice by the hand. Humphrey led Edith until they arrived at the grave, when the two little girls saw the covered body of Jacob lying in it.

"Kneel down," said Edward, opening the Bible. And they all knelt down by the grave. Edward read the two Psalms, and then closed the book. The little girls took one last look at the body, and then turned away weeping to the cottage. Edward and Humphrey filled up the grave, and then followed their sisters home.

"I'm glad it's over," said Humphrey, wiping his eyes. "Poor old Jacob! I'll put a paling round his grave."

"Come in, Humphrey," said Edward.

Edward sat down upon old Jacob's chair, and took Alice and Edith to him. Putting his arm round each, he said:

"Alice and Edith, my dear little sisters, we have lost a good friend, and one to whose memory we cannot be too grateful. He saved us from perishing in the flames which burnt down our father's house, and has protected us here ever since. He is gone; for it has pleased God to summon him to Him, and we must bow to the will of Heaven; and here we are, brothers and sisters, orphans, and with no one to look to for protection but Heaven. Here we are, away from the rest of the world, living for one another. What then must we do? We must love one another dearly, and help one another. I will do my part, if my life is spared, and so will Humphrey, and so will you, my dear sisters. I can answer for all. Now it is no use to lament—we must all work, and work cheerfully; and we will pray every morning and every night that God will bless our endeavours, and enable us to provide for ourselves, and live here in peace and safety. Kiss me, dear Alice and Edith, and kiss Humphrey, and kiss one another. Let these kisses be the seals to our bond; and let us put our trust in Him who only is a father to the widow and the orphan. And now let us pray."

Edward and the children repeated the Lord's Prayer, and then rose up. They went to their respective employments, and the labour of the day soon made them composed, although then, for many days afterwards, it was but occasionally that a smile was seen upon their lips.

Thus passed a week, by which time Edward's arm was so far well that it gave him no pain, and he was able to assist Humphrey in the work on the farm. The snow had disappeared, and the spring, although it had been checked for a time, now made rapid advances. Constant occupation and the return of fine weather both had the effect of restoring the serenity of their minds; and while Humphrey was preparing the paling to fix round the grave of old

Jacob, Alice and Edith collected the wild violets which now peeped forth on sheltered spots, and planted the roots over the grave. Edward also procured all the early flowers he could collect, and assisted his sisters in their task; and thus, in planting it, and putting up the paling, the grave of the old man became their constant work-ground; and when their labour was done, they would still remain there and talk over his worth. The Sunday following the burial, the weather being fine and warm, Edward proposed that they should read the usual service, which had been selected by old Jacob, at the grave, and not in the cottage, as formerly; and this they continued afterwards to do, whenever the weather would permit; thus did old Jacob's resting-placing become their church, and overpower them with those feelings of love and devotion which give efficacy to prayer. As soon as the paling was finished Humphrey put up a board against the oak-tree, with the simple words carved on it, "Jacob Armitage."

Edward had every day expected that Oswald Partridge would have called upon him, as he had promised to do before the week was out; but Oswald had not made his appearance, much to Edward's surprise. A month passed away; Edward's arm was now quite well, and still Oswald came not. One morning Humphrey and Edward were conversing upon many points—the principal of which was upon Edward going to Lymington, for they were now in want of flour and meal—when Edward thought of what old Jacob had told him relative to the money that he would find in his chest. He went into Jacob's room and opened the chest, at the bottom of which, under the clothes, he found a leather bag, which he brought out to Humphrey; on opening it, they were much surprised to find in it more than sixty gold pieces, besides a great deal of silver coin.

"Surely this is a great sum of money," observed Humphrey. "I don't know what is the price of things but it appears to me that it ought to last us a long while."

"I think so too," replied Edward. "I wish Oswald Partridge would come, for I want to ask him many questions. I don't know the price of flour or anything else we have to purchase, nor do I know what ought to be paid for venison. I don't like to go to Lymington till I see him, for that reason. If he does not come soon I shall ride over and see what is the matter."

Edward then replaced the money in the chest, and he and Humphrey then went out to the farm-yard to go on with their work.

It was not until six weeks after the death of old Jacob that Oswald Partridge made his appearance.

"How is the old man, sir?" was his first question.

"He was buried a few days after you left," replied Edward.

"I expected as much," said the forester. "Peace be with him—he was a good man. And how is your arm?"

"Nearly well," replied Edward. "Now, sit down, Oswald, for I have a great deal to say to you; and first let me ask you what has detained you from coming here according to your promise?"

"Simply, and in few words—murder."

"Murder!" exclaimed Edward.

"Yes, deliberate murder, sir; in short, they have beheaded the king—beheaded King Charles, our sovereign."

"Have they dared to do it?"

"They have," replied Oswald. "We know little that is going on in the forest; but when I saw you last I heard that he was then in London, and was to be tried."

"Tried!" exclaimed Edward. "How could they try a king? By the laws of our country a man must be tried by his equals; and where were his equals?"

"Majesty becomes nought, I suppose," replied Oswald; "but still it is as I say. Two days after you left the Intendant hastened up to London; and from what I have understood, he was strongly opposed to the deed, and did all he could to prevent it, but it was of no use. When he left he gave me strict injunctions not to go away from the cottage for an hour, as his daughter was left alone, and as I promised, I could not come to you; but, nevertheless, Patience received letters from him, and told me what I tell you."

"You have not dined, Oswald?" said Edward.

"No, that I have not."

"Alice, dear, get some dinner, will you? And Oswald, while you dine, excuse me if I leave you for a while. Your intelligence has so astounded me that I can listen to nothing else till I have had a little while to commune with myself and subdue my feelings."

Edward was indeed in a state of mind which required calming down. He quitted the cottage and walked out for some distance into the forest in deep thought.

"Murdered at last!" exclaimed he. "Yes, well may it be called murder, and no one to save him—not a blow struck in his defence—not an arm raised. How much gallant blood has been shed in vain! Spirit of my fathers—didst thou leave none of thy mettle and thy honour behind thee? Or has all England become craven? Well, the time will come; and if I can no longer hope to fight for my king, at all events I can fight against those who have murdered him."

Such were Edward's thoughts as he wandered through the forest, and more than an hour elapsed before his impetuous blood could return to its usual flow; at last, more calm, he returned to the cottage, and listened to the details which Oswald now gave to him of what he had heard.

When Oswald had finished, Edward asked him whether the Intendant had returned.

"Yes, or I should not have been here," replied Oswald. "He came back yesterday, looking most disconsolate and grave, and I hear that he returns to London in a few days. Indeed, he told me so himself, for I requested permission to come over to see your grandfather. He said that I might go, but must return soon, as he must go back to London. I believe, from what Miss Patience told me, and what I have seen myself, that he is sincerely amazed and vexed at what has taken place; and so indeed are many more, who, although opposed to the king's method of government, never had an idea that things should have turned out as they have done. I have a message from him to you, which is, that he begs you will come to see him, that he may thank you for the preservation of his child."

"I will take his thanks from you, Oswald: that will do as well as if he gave them me in person."

"Yes, perhaps so; but I have another message from another party, which is, the young lady herself. She desires me to tell you that she will never be happy till she has seen you, and thanked you for your courage and kindness; and that you have no right to put her under such an obligation, and not give her an opportunity of expressing what she feels. Now, Mr Edward, I am certain that she is earnest in what she says, and she made me promise that I would persuade you to come. I could not refuse her, for she is a dear little creature; as her father will go to London in a few days, you may ride over and see her without any fear of being affronted by any offers which he may make to you."

"Well," replied Edward, "I have no great objection to see her again, for she was very kind to me; and as you say that the Intendant will not be there I perhaps may come. But now I must talk to you about other matters."

Edward then put many questions to Oswald relative to the value of various articles, and to the best method of disposing of his venison.

Oswald answered all his questions, and Edward took down notes and directions on paper.

Oswald remained with them for two days, and then bade them farewell, exacting a promise from Edward that he would come to the ranger's cottage as soon as he could. "Should the Intendant come back before he is expected, I will come over and let you know; but I think, from what I heard him say, he expected to be at least a month in London."

Edward promised that Oswald should see him in less than ten days, and Oswald set out on his journey.

"Humphrey," said Edward, as soon as Oswald was gone, "I have made up my mind to go to Lymington to-morrow. We must have some flour, and many other articles, which Alice says she can no longer do without."

"Why should we not both go, Edward?" replied Humphrey.

"No, not this time," replied Edward. "I have to find out many things and many people, and I had rather go by myself; besides, I cannot allow my sisters to be left alone. I do not consider there is any danger, I admit; but something might happen to them. I should never forgive myself. Still, it is necessary that you should go to Lymington with me some time or another, that you may know where to purchase and sell, if required. What I propose is, that I will ask Oswald to come and stay here a couple of days. We will then leave him in charge of our sisters, and go to Lymington together."

"You are right, Edward; that will be the best plan."

As Humphrey made this remark, Oswald re-entered the cottage.

"I will tell you why I have returned, Mr Edward," said Oswald. "It is of no consequence whether I return now or to-morrow. It is now early, and as you intend going to Lymington, it occurred to me that I had better go with you. I can then show you all you want, which will be much better than going by yourself."

"Thank you, Oswald, I am much obliged to you," said Edward.

"Humphrey, we will get the cart out immediately, or we shall be late. Will you get it, Humphrey? For I must go for some money, and speak to Alice."

Humphrey went immediately to put the pony in the cart, when Edward said:

"Oswald, you must not call me Mr Edward, even when we are alone; if you do, you will be calling me so before other people, and, therefore, recollect in future, it must be plain Edward."

"Since you wish it, certainly," replied Oswald; "indeed it would be better; for a slip of the tongue before other people might create suspicion."

The pony and cart were soon at the door, and Edward, having received further instructions from Alice, set off for Lymington, accompanied by Oswald.

Chapter Eleven.

"Could you have found your way to Lymington?" said Oswald, as the pony trotted along.

"Yes, I think so," replied Edward; "but I must have first gone to Arnwood. Indeed, had I been alone, I should have done so; but we have made a much shorter cut."

"I did not think that you would have liked to have seen the ruins of Arnwood," replied Oswald.

"Not a day passes without my thinking of them," replied Edward. "I should like to see them. I should like to see if any one has taken possession of the property; for they say it is confiscated."

"I heard that it was to be; but not that it was yet," said Oswald: "but we shall know more when we get to Lymington. I have not seen it for more than a year. I hardly think that any one will recognise you."

"I should think not; but I care little if they do. Indeed, who is there to know me?"

"Well, my introduction of you will save some surmises, probably; and I shall not take you among those who may be inclined to ask questions. See, there is the steeple; we have not more than a quarter of an hour's drive."

As soon as they arrived at Lymington, Oswald directed the way to a small hostelrie, to which the keepers and verderers usually resorted. In fact, the landlord was the party who took all the venison off their hands, and disposed of it. They drove into the yard, and, giving the pony and cart in charge of the hostler, went into the inn, where they found the landlord, and one or two other people, who were drinking.

"Well, Master Andrew, how fare you?" said Oswald.

"Let me see," said the corpulent landlord, throwing back his head, and putting out his stomach, as he peered at Oswald; "why, Oswald Partridge, as I am a born man. Where have you been this many a day?"

"In the forest, Master Andrew, where there are no few chops and changes."

"Yes, I heard you have a sort of Parliamentary keeper, I'm told; and who is this with you?"

"The grandson of an old friend of yours, now dead, poor old Jacob Armitage."

"Jacob dead, poor fellow! As true as flint was Jacob Armitage, as I'm a born man! And so he is dead! Well, we all owe heaven a death. Foresters and landlords, as well as kings, all must die!"

"I have brought Edward Armitage over here to introduce him to you, Master Andrew. Now that the old man is dead, you must look to him for forest meat."

"Oh, well, well, it is scarce now. I have not had any for some time. Old Jacob brought me the last. You are not one of the Parliamentary foresters, then, I presume?" continued the landlord, turning to Edward.

"No," replied Edward, "I kill no venison for Roundheads."

"Right, my sapling; right and well said. The Armitages were all good men and true, and followed the fortunes of the Beverleys; but there are no Beverleys to follow now. Cut off root and branch—more's the pity. That was a sad business. But come in; we must not talk here, for walls have ears, they say, and one never knows who one dares to speak before now."

Oswald and Edward then entered with the landlord, and arrangements were made between Master Andrew and the latter for a regular supply of venison during the season at a certain price; but as it would now be dangerous to bring it into the town, it was agreed that when there was any ready, Edward should come to Lymington and give notice, and the landlord would send out people to bring it in during the night. This bargain concluded, they took a glass with the landlord, and then went into the town to make the necessary purchases. Oswald took Edward to all the shops where the articles he required were to be purchased; some they carried away with them; others, which were too heavy, they left, to be called for with the cart as they went away. Among other articles, Edward required powder and lead, and they went to a gunsmith's where it was to be procured. While making his purchases, Edward perceived a sword, which he thought he had seen before, hanging up against the wall among other weapons.

"What sword is that?" said he to the man who was measuring out the powder.

"It's not my sword, exactly," replied the man; "and yet I cannot return it to its owner or to the family. It was brought me to be cleaned by one of Colonel Beverley's people, and before it was called for the house was burnt, and every soul perished. It was one of the colonel's swords, I am sure, as there is E.B. on a silver plate engraved on it. I have a bill owing me for work done at Arnwood, and I have no chance of its being paid now; so, whether I am to sell the sword, or what to do, I hardly know."

Edward remained silent for some little while, for he could not trust himself to speak; at last he replied: "To be candid with you, I am, and all my family have been, followers of the Beverley family, and I should be sorry if the colonel's sword was to fall into any other hands. I think, therefore, if I pay the bill which is due, you may safely let me hold the sword as a security for the money, with the express understanding that if it is ever claimed by the Beverley family, I am to give it up."

"Certainly," said Oswald; "nothing can be fairer or more clearly put."

"I think so, too, young man," replied the shopkeeper. "Of course, you will leave your name and address?"

"Yes; and my friend here will vouch for its being correct," replied Edward.

The shopkeeper then produced the account, which Edward paid; and giving on the paper the name of Edward Armitage, he took possession of the sword. He then paid for the powder and lead, which Oswald took charge of, and, hardly able to conceal his joy, hastened out of the shop.

"Oswald," cried Edward, "I would not part with it for thousands of pounds. I never will part with it but with my life."

"I believe so," replied Oswald; "and I believe more, that it will never be disgraced in your hands; but do not talk so loud, for there are listeners and spies everywhere. Is there anything else that you require?"

"No, I think not; the fact is that this sword has put everything out of my head. If there was anything else I have forgotten it. Let us go back to the inn, and we will harness the pony, and call for the flour and oatmeal."

When they arrived at the inn, Oswald went out to the yard to get the cart ready, while Edward went into the landlord's room to make inquiries as to the quantity of venison he would be able to take off his hands at a time. Oswald had taken the sword from Edward, and had put it in the cart while he was fastening the harness, when a man came up to the cart, and looked earnestly at the sword. He then examined it, and said to Oswald:

"Why, that was Colonel Beverley's, my old master's, sword. I knowed it again directly. I took it to Phillips, the gunmaker, to be cleaned."

"Indeed!" replied Oswald; "I pray what may be your name?"

"Benjamin White," replied the man; "I served at Arnwood till the night it was burned down; and I have been here ever since."

"And what are you doing now?"

"I'm tapster at the 'Commonwealth,' in Fish Street—not much of a place."

"Well, well, you stand by the pony, and look that nobody takes anything out of the cart, while I go in for some parcels."

"Yes, to be sure I will; but, I say, forester, how came you by that sword?"

"I will tell you when I come out again," replied Oswald.

Oswald then went in to Edward, and told him what had occurred.

"He will certainly know you, sir, and you must not come out till I can get him away," said he.

"You are right, Oswald; but before he goes, ask him what became of my aunt, and where she was buried, and also ask him where the other servants are—perhaps they are at Lymington as well as he."

"I will find it all out," replied Oswald, who then left Edward, and returned to the landlord and recommenced conversation.

Oswald, on his return, told Benjamin in what manner the sword had been procured from the shopman, by the grandson of old Armitage.

"I never knew that he had one," replied Benjamin; "nor did I know that old Jacob was dead."

"What became of all the women who were at Arnwood?" inquired Oswald.

"Why, Agatha married one of the troopers, and went away to London."

"And the others?"

"Why, cook went home to her friends, who live about ten miles from here, and I have never heard of her since."

"But there were three of them," said Oswald. "Oh yes; there was Phoebe," replied Benjamin, looking rather confused. "She married a trooper—the jilt!—and went off to London when Agatha did. If I'd have thought that she would have done so I would not have carried her away from Arnwood behind me on a pillion, as I did; she might have been burnt with the poor children, for all as I cared."

"Was not the old lady killed?"

"Yes; that is to say, she killed herself, rather than not kill Southwold."

"Where was she buried?"

"In the churchyard, at Saint Faith's, by the mayor and corporation; for there was not money enough found upon her person to pay the expenses of her burial."

"And so you are tapster at the 'Commonwealth.' Is it a good inn?"

"Can't say much for it. I shan't stay longer than I can help, I can tell you."

"Well, but you must have an easy place, if you can stay away so long as you do now."

"Won't I be mobbed when I go back! But that's always the case, make haste or not, so it's all one. However, I do think I must be a-going now, so good-bye, Mr Forester; and tell Jacob Armitage's grandson that I shall be glad to see him, for old Jacob's sake; and it's hard but I'll find him something to drink when he calls."

"I will: I shall see him to-morrow," replied Oswald, getting into the cart; "so good-bye, Benjamin," much to the satisfaction of Oswald, who thought that he would never go.

They went away at a rapid pace, to make up for lost time, and soon disappeared round the corner of the street. Oswald then got out again, summoned Edward, and having called for the flour and other heavy articles, they set off on their return.

During the drive Oswald made known to Edward the information which he had gained from Benjamin, and at a late hour they arrived safely at the cottage.

They staid up but a short time, as they were tired; and Oswald had resolved upon setting off before daylight on the following morning, which he did without disturbing any one; for Humphrey was up and dressed as soon as Oswald was, and gave him something to eat as he went along. All the others remained fast asleep. Humphrey walked about a mile with Oswald, and was returning to the farm, when he thought, as he had not examined his pit-fall for many days, that he might as well look at it, before he went back. He therefore struck in the direction in which it lay, and arrived there just as the day began to dawn.

It was the end of March, and the weather was mild for the season. Humphrey arrived at the pit, and it was sufficiently light for him to perceive that the covering had been broken in, and therefore, in all probability, something must have been trapped. He sat down and waited for daylight, but at times he thought he heard a heavy breathing, and once a low groan. This made him more anxious, and he again and again peered into the pit, but could not for a long while discover anything, until at last he thought that he could make out a human figure lying at the bottom. Humphrey called out, asking if there was any one there. A groan was the reply, and now Humphrey was horrified at the idea that somebody had fallen into the pit, and had perished, or was perishing for want of succour. Recollecting that the rough ladder which he had made to take the soil up out of the pit was against an oak-tree, close at hand, he ran for it, and put it down the pit, and then cautiously descended. On his arrival at the bottom, his fears were found to be verified, for he found the body of a lad half-clothed lying there. He turned it up, as it was lying with its face to the ground, and attempted to remove it and to ascertain if there was life in it, which he was delighted to find was the case. The lad groaned several times, and opened his eyes. Humphrey was afraid that he was not strong enough to lift it on his shoulders and carry it up the ladder; but on making the attempt, he found out, from exhaustion, the poor lad was light enough for him to carry him, which he did, and safely landed him by the side of the pit.

Recollecting that the watering-place of the herd of cattle was not far off, Humphrey then hastened to it, and filled his hat half full of water. The lad, although he could not speak, drank eagerly, and in a few minutes appeared much recovered. Humphrey gave him some more, and bathed his face and temples. The sun had now risen, and it was broad daylight. The lad attempted to speak, but what he did say was in so low a tone, and evidently in a foreign language, that Humphrey could not make him out. He therefore made signs to the lad that he was going away, and would be back soon; and having, as he thought, made the lad comprehend this, Humphrey ran away to the cottage as fast as he could; and as soon as he arrived he called for Edward, who came out, and when Humphrey told him in few words what had happened, Edward went into the cottage again for some milk and some cake, while Humphrey put the pony into the cart.

In a few moments they were off again, and soon arrived at the pit-fall, where they found the lad still lying where Humphrey had left him. They soaked the cake in the milk, and, as soon as it was soft, gave him some; after a time he swallowed pretty freely, and was so much recovered as to be able to sit up. They then lifted him into the cart, and drove gently home to their cottage.

"What do you think he is, Edward?" said Humphrey.

"Some poor beggar lad, who has been crossing the forest."

"No, not exactly; he appears to me to be one of the Zingaros or gipsies, as they call them: he is very dark, and has black eyes and white teeth, just like those I saw once near Arnwood, when I was out with Jacob. Jacob said that no one knew where they came from, but that they were all over the country, and that they were great thieves, and told fortunes, and played all manner of tricks."

"Perhaps it may be so; I do not think that he can speak English."

"I am most thankful to Heaven that I chanced this morning to visit the pit-fall. Only suppose that I had found the poor boy starved and dead! I should have been very unhappy, and never should have had any pleasure in looking at the cows, as they would always have reminded me of such a melancholy accident."

"Very true, Humphrey; but you have been saved that misfortune, and ought to be grateful to Heaven that such is the case. What shall we do with him now we have him?"

"Why, if he chooses to remain with us, he will be very useful in the cow-yard," said Humphrey.

"Of course," replied Edward, laughing, "as he was taken in the pit-fall, he must go into the yard with all he others who were captured in the same way."

"Well, Edward, let us get him all right again first, and then we will see what is to be done with him; perhaps he will refuse to remain with us."

As soon as they arrived at the cottage they lifted the lad out of the cart, and carried him into Jacob's room, and laid him on the bed, for he was too weak to stand.

Alice and Edith, who were much surprised at the new visitor, and the way in which he had been caught, hastened to get some gruel ready for him. As soon as it was ready they gave it to the boy, who then fell back on the bed with exhaustion, and was soon in a sound sleep. He slept soundly all that night; and the next morning, when he awoke, he appeared much better, although very hungry. This last complaint was easy to remedy, and then the lad got up and walked into the sitting-room.

"What's your name?" said Humphrey to the lad.

"Pablo," replied the lad.

"Can you speak English?"

"Yes, little," replied he.

"How did you happen to fall into the pit?"

"Not see hole."

"Are you a gipsy?"

"Yes, Gitano—same thing."

Humphrey put a great many more questions to the lad, and elicited from him, in his imperfect English, the following particulars.

That he was in company with several others of his race, going down to the sea-coast on one of their usual migrations, and that they had pitched their tents not far from the pit-fall. That during the night he had gone out to set some snares for rabbits, and going back to the tents, it being quite dark, he had fallen into the hole. That he had remained there three days and nights, having in vain attempted to get out. His mother was with the party of gipsies to which he belonged; but he had no father. He did not know where to follow the gang, as they had not said where they were going, farther than to the sea-coast. That it was no use looking for them; and that he did not care much about leaving them, as he was very unkindly treated. In reply to the question as to whether he would like to remain with them, and work with them on the farm, he replied that he should like it very much if they would be kind to him, and not make him work too hard; that he would cook the dinner, and catch them rabbits and birds, and make a great many things.

"Will you be honest, if we keep you, and not tell lies?" said Edward.

The lad thought a little while, and then nodded his head in the affirmative.

"Well, Pablo, we will try you, and if you are a good lad, we will do all we can to make you happy," said Edward; "but if you behave ill, we shall be obliged to turn you out of doors; do you understand?"

"Be as good as I can," replied Pablo; and here the conversation ended for the present.

Pablo was a very short-built lad, of apparently fifteen or sixteen years of age, very dark in complexion, but very handsome in features, with beautiful white teeth and large dark eyes; and there was certainly something in his intelligent countenance which recommended him, independent of his claim to their kindness from his having been left thus friendless in consequence of his misadventure. Humphrey was particularly pleased with and interested about him, as the lad had so nearly lost his life through his means.

"I really think, Edward," said Humphrey, as they were standing outside of the door of the cottage, "that the lad may be very useful to us, and I sincerely hope that he may prove honest and true. We must first get him into health and spirits, and then I will see what he can do."

"The fact is, my dear Humphrey, we can do no otherwise: he is separated from his friends, and does not know where to go. It would be inhuman, as we have been the cause of his misfortune, to turn him away; but although I feel this, I do not feel much security as to his good behaviour and being very useful. I have always been told that these gipsies were vagrants, who lived by stealing all they could lay their hands upon; and, if he has been brought up in that way, I fear that he will not easily be reformed. However, we can but try, and hope for the best."

"What you say is very just, Edward; at the same time, there is an honest look about this lad, although he is a gipsy, that makes me put a sort of confidence in him. Admitting that he has been taught to do wrong, do you not think that when told the contrary he may be persuaded to do right?"

"It is not impossible, certainly," replied Edward; "but, Humphrey, be on the safe side, and do not trust him too far, until you know more of him."

"That I most certainly will not," replied Humphrey. "When do you purpose going over to the keeper's cottage, Edward?"

"In a day or two; but I am not exactly in a humour now to be very civil to the Roundheads, although the one I have promised to visit is a lady, and a very amiable, pretty little girl into the bargain."

"Why, Edward, what has made you feel more opposed to them than usual?"

"In the first place, Humphrey, the murder of the king—for it was murder, and nothing better—I cannot get that out of my head; and yesterday I obtained what I consider as almost a gift from Heaven; and if it is so, it was not given but with the intention that I should make use of it."

"And what was that, Edward?"

"Our gallant father's sword, which he drew so nobly and so well in defence of his sovereign, Humphrey, and which I trust his son may one day wield with equal distinction, and, it may be, better fortune. Come in with me, and I will show it to you."

Edward and Humphrey went into the bedroom, and Edward brought out the sword, which he had placed by his side on the bed.

"See, Humphrey, this was our father's sword; and," continued Edward, kissing the weapon, "I trust I may be permitted to draw it to revenge his death, and the death of one whose life ever should have been sacred."

"I trust that you will, my dear brother," replied Humphrey; "you will have a strong arm and a good cause. Heaven grant that both may prosper! But tell me how you came by it."

Edward then related all that had passed during his visit with Oswald to Lymington, not forgetting to tell him of Benjamin's appearance, and the arrangements he had made relative to the sale of the venison.

As soon as dinner was over, Edward and Humphrey took down their guns, having agreed that they would go and hunt the wild cattle.

"Humphrey, have you any idea where the herd of cattle are feeding at this time?"

"I know where they were feeding yesterday and the day before, and I do not think that they will have changed their ground; for the grass is yet very young, and only grown on the southern aspects. Depend upon it we shall fall in with them not four miles from where we now are, if not nearer."

"We must stalk them as we do the deer, must we not? They won't allow us to approach within shot, Humphrey, will they?" said Edward.

"We have to take our chance, Edward; they will allow us to advance within shot, but the bulls will then advance upon us, while the herd increase their distance. On the other hand, if we stalk them, we may kill one, and then the report of the gun will frighten the others away. In the first instance there is a risk; in the second there is none, but there is more fatigue and trouble. Choose as you please, I will act as you decide."

"Well, Humphrey, since you give me the choice, I think that this time I shall take the bull by the horns, as the saying is; that is, if there are any trees near us, for if the herd are in an open place I would not run such a risk; but if we can fire upon them and fall back upon a tree in case of a bull charging, I will take them openly."

"With all my heart, Edward: I think it will be very hard, if, with our two guns and Smoker to back us, we do not manage to be masters of the field. However, we must survey well before we make our approach; and if we can get within shot without alarming or irritating them, we of course will do so."

"The bulls are very savage at this spring-time," observed Edward.

"They are so at all times, as far as I can see of them," replied Humphrey; "but we are near to them now, I should think—yes, there is the herd."

"There they are, sure enough," replied Edward: "now we have not to do with deer, and need not be so very cautious; but still the animals are wary, and keep a sharp look-out. We must approach them quietly, by slipping from tree to tree. Smoker, to heel!—down—quiet, Smoker—good dog!"

Edward and Humphrey stopped to load their guns, and then approached the herd in the manner which had been proposed, and were very soon within two hundred yards of the cattle, behind a large oak, when they stopped to reconnoitre. The herd contained about seventy head of cattle, of various sizes and ages. They were feeding in all directions, scattered, as the young grass was very short; but although the herd was spread over many acres of land, Edward pointed out to Humphrey that all the full-grown large bulls were on the outside, as if ready to defend the others in case of attack.

"Humphrey," said Edward, "one thing is clear—as the herd is placed at present, we must have a bull or nothing. It is impossible to get within shot of the others without passing a bull, and depend upon it our passage will be disputed; and moreover, the herd will take to flight, and we shall get nothing at all."

"Well," replied Humphrey, "beef is beef; and, as they say, beggars must not be choosers, so let it be a bull, if it must be so."

"Let us get nearer to them, and then we will decide what we shall do. Steady, Smoker!"

They advanced gradually, hiding from tree to tree, until they were within eighty yards of one of the bulls. The animal did not perceive them, and as they were now within range, they again stepped behind the tree to consult.

"Now, Edward, I think that it would be best to separate. You can fire from where we are, and I will crawl through the fern, and get behind another tree."

"Very well, do so," replied Edward: "if you can manage, get to that tree with the low branches, and then perhaps you will be within shot of the white bull, which is coming down in this direction. Smoker, lie down! He cannot go with you, Humphrey; it will not be safe."

The distance of the tree which Humphrey ventured to get to was about one hundred and fifty yards from where Edward was standing. Humphrey crawled along for some time in the fern, but at last he came to a bare spot of about ten yards wide, which they were not aware of, and where he could not be concealed. Humphrey hesitated, and at last decided upon attempting to cross it. Edward, who was one moment watching the motions of Humphrey, and at another that of the two animals nearest to them, perceived that the white bull farthest from him, but nearest to Humphrey, threw its head in the air, pawed with his foot, and then advanced with a roar to where Humphrey was on the ground, still crawling towards the tree, having passed the open spot, and being now not many yards from the tree. Perceiving the danger that his brother was in, and that, moreover, Humphrey himself was not aware of it, he hardly knew how to act. The bull was too far from him to fire at it with any chance of success; and how to let Humphrey know that the animal had discovered him and was making towards him, without calling out, he did not know. All this was the thought of a moment, and then Edward determined to fire at the bull nearest to him, which he had promised not to do till Humphrey was also ready to fire; and after firing to call Humphrey. He, therefore, for one moment, turned away from his brother, and, taking aim at the bull, fired his gun; but probably from his nerves being a little shaken at the idea of Humphrey being in danger, the wound was not mortal, and the bull galloped back to the herd, which formed a closed phalanx about a quarter of a mile distant. Edward then turned to where his brother was, and perceived that the bull had not made off with the rest of the cattle, but was within thirty yards of Humphrey, and advancing upon him, and that Humphrey was standing up beside the tree with his gun ready to fire. Humphrey fired, and, as it appeared, he also missed his aim; the animal made at him; but Humphrey, with great quickness, dropped his gun, and, swinging by the lower boughs, was into the tree, and out of the bull's reach, in a moment. Edward smiled when he perceived that Humphrey was safe; but still he was a prisoner, for the bull went round and round the tree roaring and looking up at Humphrey. Edward thought a minute, then loaded his gun and ordered Smoker to run in to the bull. The dog, who had only been restrained by Edward's keeping him down at his feet, sprang forward to the attack. Edward had intended, by calling to the dog, to induce the bull to follow it till within gunshot; but before the bull had been attacked, Edward observed that one or two more of the bulls had left the herd, and were coming at a rapid pace towards him. Under these circumstances, Edward perceived that his only chance was to climb into a tree himself, which he did, taking good care to take his gun and ammunition with him. Having safely fixed himself in a forked bough, Edward then surveyed the position of the parties. There was Humphrey in the tree, without his gun. The bull who had pursued Humphrey was now running at Smoker, who appeared to be aware that he was to decoy the bull towards Edward, for he kept retreating towards him. In the meantime the two other bulls were quite close at hand, mingling their bellowing and roaring with the first; and one of them as near to Edward as the first bull, which was engaged with Smoker. At last one of the advancing bulls stood still, pawing the ground as if disappointed at not finding an enemy, not forty yards from where Edward was perched. Edward took good aim, and when he fired the bull fell dead. Edward was reloading his piece when he heard a howl, and looking round saw Smoker flying up in the air, having been tossed by the first bull; and at the same time he observed that Humphrey had descended from the tree, recovered his gun, and was now safe again upon the lower bough. The first bull was advancing again to attack Smoker, who appeared incapable of getting away, so much was he injured by the fall, when the other bull, who apparently must have been an old antagonist of the first, roared and attacked him; and now the two boys were up in the tree, the two bulls fighting between them, and Smoker lying on the ground, panting and exhausted. As the bulls, with locked horns, were furiously pressing each other, both guns were discharged, and both animals fell. After waiting a little while to see if they rose again, or if any more of the herd came up, Edward and Humphrey descended from the trees and heartily shook hands.

Chapter Twelve.

"A narrow escape," said Edward, as he held his brother's hand.

"Yes, indeed we may thank Heaven for our preservation," replied Humphrey; "and poor Smoker! Let us see if he is much hurt."

"I trust not," said Edward, going up to the dog, who remained quite still on the ground, with his tongue out, and panting violently.

They examined poor Smoker all over very carefully, and found that there was no external wound; but on Edward pressing his side the animal gave a low howl.

"It is there where the horn of the bull took him," observed Humphrey.

"Yes," said Edward, pressing and feeling softly; "and he has two of his ribs broken. Humphrey, see if you can get him a little water, that will recover him more than anything else; the bull has knocked the breath out of his body. I think he will soon be well again, poor fellow."

Humphrey soon returned with some water from a neighbouring pool. He brought it in his hat and gave it to the dog, who lapped it slowly at first, but afterwards much faster, and wagging his tail.

"He will do now," said Edward; "we must give him time to recover himself. Now then, let us examine our quarry. Why, Humphrey, what a quantity of meat we have here! It will take three journeys to Lymington at least."

"Yes, and no time to lose, for the weather is getting warm already, Edward. Now what to do? Will you remain while I go home for the cart?"

"Yes, it's no use both going; I will stay here and watch poor Smoker, and take off the skins ready by the time you are back again. Leave me your knife as well as my own, for one will soon be blunt."

Humphrey gave his knife to Edward, and taking up his gun, set off for the cottage. Edward had skinned two of the bulls before Humphrey's return; and Smoker, although he evidently was in great pain, was on his legs again. As soon as they had finished and quartered the beasts, the cart was loaded, and they returned home; they had to return a second time, and both the pony and they were very tired before they sat down to supper. They found the gipsy boy very much recovered, and in good spirits. Alice said that he had been amusing Edith and her by tossing up three potatoes at a time, and playing them like balls; and that he had spun a platter upon an iron skewer and balanced it on his chin. They gave him some supper, which he ate in the chimney-corner, looking up and staring every now and then at Edith, to whom he appeared very much attached already.

"Is it good?" said Humphrey to the boy, giving him another venison-steak.

"Yes; not have so good supper in pit-hole," replied Pablo, laughing.

Early on the following morning Edward and Humphrey set off to Lymington with the cart laden with meat. Edward showed Humphrey all the shops and the streets they were in where the purchases were to be made—introduced him to the landlord of the hostelrie—and having sold their meat, they returned home. The rest of the meat was taken to Lymington and disposed of by Humphrey on the following day; and the day after that, the three skins were carried to the town and disposed of.

"We made a good day's work, Edward," said Humphrey, as he reckoned up the money they had made.

"We earned it with some risk, at all events," replied Edward; "and now, Humphrey, I think it is time that I keep my promise to Oswald, and go over to the Intendant's house and pay my visit to the young lady, as I presume she is—and certainly she has every appearance of being one. I want the visit to be over, as I want to be doing."

"How do you mean, Edward?"

"I mean that I want to go out and kill some deer; but I will not do it till after I have seen her: when my visit is over, I intend to defy the Intendant and all his verderers."

"But why should this visit prevent you going out this very day, if so inclined?"

"I don't know, but she may ask me if I have done so, and I do not want to tell her that I have; neither do I want to say that I have not if I have; and therefore I shall not commence till after I have seen her."

"When will you set off?"

"To-morrow morning; and I shall take my gun, although Oswald desired me not; but after the fight we had with the wild cattle the other day I don't think it prudent to be unarmed; indeed, I do not feel comfortable without I have my gun, at any time."

"Well, I shall have plenty to do when you are away—the potatoes must be hoed up, and I shall see what I can make of Master Pablo. He appears well enough, and he has played quite long enough; so I shall take him with me to the garden to-morrow, and set him to work. What a quantity of fruit there is a promise of in the orchard this year! And Edward, if this boy turns out of any use, and is a help to me, I think that I shall take all the orchard into garden, and then enclose another piece of ground, and see if we cannot grow some corn for ourselves. It is the greatest expense that we have at present, and I should like to take my own corn to the mill to be ground."

"But will not growing corn require plough and horses?" said Edward.

"No; we will till it by hand: two of us can dig a great deal at odd times, and we shall have a better crop with the spade than with the plough. We have now so much manure that we can afford it."

"Well, if it is to be done, it should be done at once, Humphrey, before the people from the other side of the forest come and find us out, or they will dispute our right to the enclosure."

"The forest belongs to the king, brother, and not to the Parliament: and we are the king's liegemen, and only look to him for permission," replied Humphrey; "but what you say is true, the sooner it is done the better, and I will about it at once."

"How much do you propose fencing in?"

"About two or three acres."

"But that is more than you can dig this year or the next."

"I know that; but I will manure it without digging, and the grass will grow so rich to what it will outside of the enclosure, that they will suppose it has been enclosed a long while."

"That's not a bad idea, Humphrey: but I advise you to look well after that boy, for he is of a bad race, and has not been brought up, I am afraid, with too strict notions of honesty. Be careful, and tell your sisters also to be cautious not to let him suppose that we have any money in the old chest, till we find out whether he is to be trusted or not."

"Better not let him know it under any circumstances," replied Humphrey; "he may continue honest, if not tempted by the knowledge that there is anything worth stealing."

"You are right, Humphrey; well, I will be off to-morrow morning and get this visit over. I hope to be able to get all the news from her, now that her father is away."

"I hope to get some work out of this Master Pablo," replied Humphrey; "how many things I could do if he would only work! Now, I'll tell you one thing—I will dig a saw-pit and get a saw, and then I can cut out boards, and build anything we want. The first time I go to Lymington I will buy a saw—I can afford it now; and I'll make a carpenter's bench for the first thing, and then, with some more tools, I shall get on; and then, Edward, I'll tell you what else I will do."

"Then, Humphrey," replied Edward, laughing, "you must tell me some other time, for it is now very late, and I must go to bed, as I have to rise early. I know you have so many projects in your mind that it would take half the night to listen to them."

"Well, I believe what you say is true," replied Humphrey, "and it will be better to do one thing at a time than to talk about doing a hundred; so we will, as you say, to bed."

At sunrise Edward and Humphrey were both up; Alice came out when they tapped at her door, as she would not let Edward go without his breakfast. Edith joined them, and they went to prayers. While they were so employed, Pablo came out and listened to what was said. When prayers were over, Humphrey asked Pablo if he knew what they had been doing.

"No, not much; suppose you pray sun to shine."

"No, Pablo," said Edith, "pray to God to make us good."

"You bad then?" said Pablo; "me not bad."

"Yes, Pablo, everybody very bad," said Alice; "but if we try to be good, God forgives us."

The conversation was then dropped, and as soon as Edward had had his breakfast, he kissed his sisters, bidding them and Humphrey farewell: he then threw his gun over his arm, and calling his puppy, which he had named Holdfast, set off on his journey across the forest.

Holdfast, as well as Humphrey's puppy, which had been named Watch, had grown very fine young animals. The first had been named Holdfast, because it would seize the pigs by the ears and lead them into the sty, and the other because it was so alert at the least noise: but, as Humphrey said, Watch ought to have learnt to lead the pigs, it being more in his line of business than Holdfast's, which was to be brought up for hunting in the forest, while Watch was being educated as a house and farm-yard dog.

Edward had refused to take the pony, as Humphrey required it for the farm-work, and the weather was so fine that he preferred walking; the more so, as it would enable him on his return across the forest to try for some venison, which he could not have done if he had been mounted on Billy's back. Edward walked quick, followed by his dog, which he had taught to keep to heel. He felt happy, as people do who have no cares, from the fine weather—the deep green of the verdure chequered by the flowers in bloom, and the majestic scenery which met his eye on every side. His heart was as buoyant as his steps, as he walked along, the light summer breeze fanning his face. His thoughts, however, which had been more of the chase than anything else, suddenly changed, and he became serious. For some time he had heard no political news of consequence, or what the Commons were doing with the king. This reverie naturally brought to his mind his father's death, the burning of his property, and its sequestration. His cheeks coloured with indignation, and his brow was moody. Then he built castles for the future. He imagined the king released from his prison, and leading an army against his oppressors; he fancied himself at the head of a troop of cavalry, charging the parliamentary horse. Victory was on his side. The king was again on his throne, and he was again in possession of the family estate. He was rebuilding the hall, and somehow or another it appeared to him that Patience was standing by his side, as he gave directions to the artificers—when his reverie was suddenly disturbed by Holdfast barking and springing forward in advance.

Edward, who had by this time got over more than half his journey, looked up, and perceived himself confronted by a powerful man, apparently about forty years of age, and dressed as a verderer of the forest. He thought at the time that he had seldom seen a person with a more sinister and forbidding countenance.

"How now, young fellow, what are you doing here?" said the man, walking up to him, and cocking the gun which he held in his hand as he advanced.

Edward quietly cocked his own gun, which was loaded, when he perceived that hostile preparation on the part of the other person, and then replied, "I am walking across the forest, as you may perceive."

"Yes, I perceive you are walking, and you are walking with a dog and a gun: you will now be pleased to walk with me. Deer-stealers are not any longer permitted to range this forest."

"I am no deer-stealer," replied Edward. "It will be quite sufficient to give me that title when you find me with venison in my possession; and as for going with you, that I certainly shall not. Sheer off or you may meet with harm."

"Why, you young good-for-nothing, if you have not venison, it is not from any will not to take it; you are out in pursuit of it, that is clear. Come, come, you've the wrong person to deal with: my orders are to take up all poachers, and take you I will."

"If you can," replied Edward; "but you must first prove that you are able so to do; my gun is as good and my aim is as sure as yours, whoever you may be. I tell you again, I am no poacher, nor have I come out to take the deer, but to cross over to the Intendant's cottage, whither I am now going. I tell you thus much, that you may not do anything foolish; and having said this, I advise you to think twice before you act once. Let me proceed in peace, or you may lose your place, if you do not by your own rashness lose your life."

There was something so cool and so determined in Edward's quiet manner, that the verderer hesitated. He perceived that any attempt to take Edward would be at the risk of his own life; and he knew that his orders were to apprehend all poachers, but not to shoot people. It was true that resistance with firearms would warrant his acting in self-defence; but admitting that he should succeed, which was doubtful, still Edward had not been caught in the act of killing venison, and he had no witnesses to prove what had occurred. He also knew that the Intendant had given very strict orders as to the shedding of blood, which he was most averse to under any circumstances; and there was something in Edward's appearance and manner so different from a common person, that he was puzzled. Moreover, Edward had stated that he was going to the Intendant's house. All things considered, as he found that bullying would not succeed, he thought it advisable to change his tone, and therefore said, "You tell me that you are going to the Intendant's house; you have business there, I presume? If I took you prisoner, it is there I should have conducted you; so, young man, you may now walk on before me."

"I thank you," replied Edward, "but walk on before you I will not: but if you choose to half-cock your gun again, and walk by my side, I will do the same. Those are my terms, and I will listen to no other; so be pleased to make up your mind, as I am in haste."

The verderer appeared very indignant at this reply, but after a time said, "Be it so."

Edward then uncocked his gun, with his eyes fixed upon the man, and the verderer did the same; and then they walked side by side, Edward keeping at the distance of three yards from him, in case of treachery.

After a few moments' silence, the verderer said, "You tell me you are going to the Intendant's house; he is not at home."

"But young Mistress Patience is, I presume," said Edward.

"Yes," replied the man, who, finding that Edward appeared to know so much about the Intendant's family, began to be more civil. "Yes, she is at home, for I saw her in the garden this morning."

"And Oswald, is he at home?" rejoined Edward.

"Yes, he is. You appear to know our people, young man; who may you be, if it is a fair question?"

"It would have been a fair question had you treated me fairly," replied Edward; "but as it is no concern of yours, I shall leave you to find it out."

This reply puzzled the man still more; and he now, from the tone of authority assumed by Edward, began to imagine that he had made some mistake, and that he was speaking to a superior, although clad in a forester's dress. He therefore answered humbly, observing that he had only been doing his duty.

Edward walked on without making any reply.

As they arrived within a hundred yards of the Intendant's house, Edward said:

"I have now arrived at my destination, and am going into that house, as I told you. Do you choose to enter it with me, or will you go to Oswald Partridge and tell him that you have met with Edward Armitage in me forest, and that I should be glad to see him? I believe you are under his orders, are you not?"

"Yes, I am," replied the verderer, "and as I suppose that all's right, I shall go and deliver your message."

Edward then turned away from the man, and went into the wicket-gate of the garden, and knocked at the door of the house. The door was opened by Patience Heatherstone herself, who said, "Oh, how glad I am to see you! Come in." Edward took off his hat and bowed; Patience led the way into her father's study, where Edward had been first received.

"And now," said Patience, extending her hand to Edward, "thanks, many thanks, for your preserving me from so dreadful a death. You don't know how unhappy I have been at not being able to give you my poor thanks for your courageous behaviour."

Her hand still remained in Edward's while she said this.

"You rate what I did too highly," replied Edward; "I would have done the same for any one in such distress: it was my duty as a—man," cavalier he was about to say, but he checked himself.

"Sit down," said Patience, taking a chair,—"nay, no ceremony; I cannot treat as an inferior one to whom I owe such a debt of gratitude."

Edward smiled as he took his seat.

"My father is as grateful to you as I am—I'm sure that he is; for I heard him when at prayer call down blessings on your head. What can he do for you? I begged Oswald Partridge to bring you here, that I might find out. Oh, sir, do pray let me know how we can show our gratitude by something more than words."

"You have shown it already, Mistress Patience," replied Edward; "have you not honoured a poor forester with your hand in friendship, and even admitted him to sit down before you?"

"He who has preserved my life at the risk of his own becomes to me as a brother—at least I feel as a sister towards him: a debt is still a debt, whether indebted to a king or to a—"

"Forester, Mistress Patience, that is the real word that you should not have hesitated to have used: do you imagine that I am ashamed of my calling?"

"To tell you candidly the truth, then," replied Patience, "I cannot believe that you are what you profess to be. I mean to say, that although a forester now, you were never brought up as such. My father has an opinion allied to mine."

"I thank you both for your good opinion of me, but I fear that I cannot raise myself above the condition of a forester; nay, from your father's coming down here, and the new regulations, I have every chance of sinking down to the lower grade of a deer-stealer and poacher; indeed, had it not been that I had my gun with me, I should have been seized as such this very day as I came over."

"But you were not shooting the deer, were you, sir?" inquired Patience.

"No, I was not; nor have I killed any since last I saw you."

"I am glad that I can say that to my father," replied Patience; "it will much please him. He said to me that he thought you capable of much higher employment than any that could be offered here, and only wished to know what you would accept. He has interest—great interest—although just now at variance with the rulers of this country, on account of the—"

"Murder of the king, you would or you should have said, Mistress Patience: I have heard how much he was opposed to that foul deed, and I honour him for it."

"How kind, how truly kind you are to say so!" said Patience, the tears starting in her eyes; "what pleasure to hear my father's conduct praised by you!"

"Why, of course, Mistress Patience, all of my way of thinking must praise him. Your father is in London, I hear?"

"Yes, he is; and that reminds me that you must want some refreshment after your walk. I will call Phoebe." So saying, Patience left the room.

The fact was, Mistress Patience was reminded that she had been sitting with a young man some time, and alone with him—which was not quite proper in those times, and when Phoebe appeared with the cold viands, she retreated out of hearing, but remained in the room.

Edward partook of the meal offered him in silence, Patience occupying herself with her work, and keeping her eyes fixed on it, unless when she gave a slight glance at the table to see if anything was required. When the meal was over, Phoebe removed the tray, and then Edward rose to take his leave.

"Nay, do not go yet—I have much to say first; let me again ask you how we can serve you."

"I never can take any office under the present rulers of the nation; so that question is at rest."

"I was afraid you would answer so," replied Patience gravely: "do not think I blame you; for many are there already who would gladly retrace their steps if it were possible. They little thought, when they opposed the king, that affairs would have ended as they have done. Where do you live, sir?"

"At the opposite side of the forest, in a house belonging to me now, but which was inherited by my grandfather."

"Do you live alone—surely not?"

"No, I do not."

"Nay, you may tell me anything, for I would never repeat what might hurt you, or you might not wish to have known."

"I live with my brother and two sisters, for my grandfather is lately dead."

"Is your brother younger than you are?"

"He is."

"And your sisters, what are their ages?"

"They are younger still."

"You told my father that you lived upon your farm?"

"We do."

"Is it a large farm?"

"No; very small."

"And does that support you?"

"That and killing wild cattle has lately."

"Yes, and killing deer also until lately?"

"You have guessed right."

"You were brought up at Arnwood, you told my father; did you not?"

"Yes, I was brought up there, and remained there until the death of Colonel Beverley."

"And you were educated, were you not?"

"Yes; the chaplain taught me what little I do know."

"Then, if you were brought up in the house and educated by the chaplain, surely Colonel Beverley never intended you for a forester?"

"He did not; I was to have been a soldier as soon as I was old enough to bear arms."

"Perhaps you are distantly related to the late Colonel Beverley?"

"No; I am not *distantly* related," replied Edward, who began to feel uneasy at this close cross-examination; "but still, had Colonel Beverley been alive, and the king still required his services, I have no doubt that I should have been serving under him at this time. And now, Mistress Patience, that I have answered so many questions of yours, may I be permitted to ask a little about yourself in return? Have you any brothers?"

"None; I am an only child."

"Have you only one parent alive?"

"Only one."

"What families are you connected with?"

Patience looked up with surprise at this last question—

"My mother's name was Cooper; she was sister to Sir Anthony Ashley Cooper, who is a person well-known."

"Indeed! Then you are of gentle blood?"

"I believe so," replied Patience, with surprise.

"Thank you for your condescension, Mistress Patience; and now, if you will permit me, I will take my leave."

"Before you go, let me once more thank you for saving a worthless life," said Patience: "well, you must come again when my father is here; he will be but too glad to have an opportunity of thanking one who has preserved his only child. Indeed, if you knew my father, you would feel as much regard for him as I do. He is very good, although he looks so stern and melancholy; but he has seldom smiled since my poor mother's death."

"As to your father, Mistress Patience, I will think as well as I can of one who is joined to a party which I hold in detestation: I can say no more."

"I must not say all that I know, or you would perhaps find out that he is not quite so wedded to that party as you suppose. Neither his brother-in-law nor he are great friends of Cromwell's, I can assure you; but this in confidence."

"That raises him in my estimation; but why then does he hold office?"

"He did not ask it; it was given to him, I really believe, because they wished him out of the way; and he accepted it because he was opposed to what was going on, and wished himself to be away. At least I infer so much from what I have learnt. It is not an office of power or trust which leagues him with the present Government."

"No; only one which opposes him to me and my mal-practices," replied Edward, laughing. "Well, Mistress Patience, you have shown great condescension to a poor forester, and I return you many thanks for your kindness towards me: I will now take my leave."

"And when will you come and see my father?"

"I cannot say; I fear that I shall not be able very soon to look in his injured face, and it will not be well for a poacher to come near him," replied Edward: "however, some day I may be taken and brought before you as a prisoner, you know, and then he is certain to see me."

"I will not tell you to kill deer," replied Patience; "but if you do kill them, no one shall harm you—or I know little of my power or my father's. Farewell then, sir; and once more, gratitude and thanks."

Patience held out her hand again to Edward, who this time, like a true cavalier, raised it respectfully to his lips. Patience coloured a little, but did not attempt to withdraw it, and Edward, with a low obeisance, quitted the room.

Chapter Thirteen.

As soon as he was out of the Intendant's house, Edward hastened to the cottage of Oswald Partridge, whom he found waiting for him; for the verderer had not failed to deliver his message.

"You have had a long talk with Mistress Patience," said Oswald, after the first greeting; "and I am glad of it, as it gives you consequence here. The Roundhead rascal whom you met was inclined to be very precise about doing his duty, and insisted that he was certain that you were on the look-out for deer; but I stopped his mouth by telling him that I often took you out with me, as you were the best shot in the whole forest, and that the Intendant knew that I did so. I think that if you were caught in the act of killing a deer you had better tell them that you killed it by my request, and I will bear you out, if they bring you to the Intendant, who will, I'm sure, thank me for saying so. You might kill all the deer in the forest after what you have done for him."

"Many thanks; but I do not think I can take advantage of your offer. Let them catch me if they can, and if they do catch me, let them take me if they can."

"I see, sir, that you will accept no favour from the Roundheads," replied Oswald; "however, as I am now head keeper, I shall take care that my men do not interfere with you, if I can help it; all I wish is to prevent any insult or indignity being offered to you: they not being aware who you are, as I am."

"Many thanks, Oswald; I must take my chance."

Edward then told Oswald of their having taken the gipsy boy in the pit, at which he appeared much amused.

"What is the name of the verderer whom I met in the forest?" inquired Edward.

"James Corbould; he was discharged from the army," replied Oswald.

"I do not like his appearance," said Edward.

"No; his face tells against him," replied Oswald; "but I know nothing of him; he has been here little more than a fortnight."

"Can you give me a corner to put my head in to-night, Oswald? For I shall not start till to-morrow morning."

"You may command all I have, sir," replied Oswald; "but I fear there is little more than a hearty welcome; I have no doubt that you could be lodged at the Intendant's house if you choose."

"No, Oswald, the young lady is alone, and I will not trust to Phoebe's accommodation again; I will stay here, if you will permit me."

"And welcome, sir: I will put your puppy in the kennel at once."

Edward remained that night at Oswald's, and at daylight he rose, and having taken a slight breakfast, throwing his gun over his shoulder, went to the kennel for Holdfast, and set off on his return home.

"That's a very nice little girl," were the words which Edward found himself constantly saying to himself as he walked along; "and she is of a grateful disposition, or she would not have behaved as she has done towards me—supposing me to be of mean birth;" and then he thought of what she had told him relative to her father, and Edward felt his animosity against a Roundhead wasting fast away. "I am not likely to see her again very soon," thought Edward, "unless, indeed, I am brought to the Intendant as a prisoner." Thus thinking upon one subject or another, Edward had gained above eight miles of his journey across the forest, when he thought that he was sufficiently far away to venture to look-out for some venison. Remembering there was a thicket not far from him, in which there was a clear pool of water, Edward thought it very likely that he might find a stag there cooling himself, for the weather was now very warm at noon-day. He therefore called Holdfast to him, and proceeded cautiously towards the thicket. As soon as he arrived at the spot, he crouched and crept silently through the underwood. At last he arrived close to the cleared spot by the pool. There was no stag there, but fast asleep upon the turf lay James Corbould, the sinister-looking verderer who had accosted him in the forest on the previous day. Holdfast was about to bark, when Edward silenced him, and then advanced to where the verderer was lying; and who having no dog with him to give notice of Edward's approach, still remained snoring with the sun shining on his face. Edward perceived that his gun was under him on the grass; he took it up, gently opened the pan and scattered the powder, and then laid it down again; for Edward said to himself, "That man has come out after me, that I am certain; and as there are no witnesses, he may be inclined to be mischievous, for a more wretched-looking person I never saw. Had he been deer-hunting, he would have brought his dog; but he is man-hunting, that is evident. Now I will leave him, and should he fall in with anything, he will not kill at first shot, that's certain; and if he follows me, I shall have the same chance of escape as anything else he may fire at." Edward then walked out of the covert, thinking that if ever there was a face which proclaimed a man to be a murderer it was that of James Corbould. As he was threading his way, he heard the howl of a dog, and on looking round, perceived that Holdfast was not with him. He turned back, and Holdfast came running to him. The fact was, that Holdfast had smelt some meat in the pocket of the verderer, and had been putting his nose in to ascertain what it was: in so doing he had wakened up Corbould, who had saluted him with a heavy blow on the head: this occasioned the puppy to give the howl, and also occasioned Corbould to seize his gun, and follow stealthily in the track of the dog, which he well knew to be the one he had seen the day before with Edward.

Edward waited for a short time, and not perceiving that Corbould made his appearance, continued on his way home, having now given up all thoughts of killing any venison. He walked fast, and was within six miles of the cottage, when he stopped to drink at a small rill of water, and then sat down to rest himself for a short time. While so doing, he fell into one of his usual reveries, and forgot how time passed away. He was, however, aroused by a low growl on the part of Holdfast, and it immediately occurred to him that Corbould must have followed him. Thinking it as well to be prepared, he quietly loaded his gun, and then rose up to reconnoitre. Holdfast sprang forward, and Edward looking in the direction, perceived Corbould partly hidden behind a tree, with his gun levelled at him. He heard the trigger pulled, and snap of the lock, but the gun did not go off; and then Corbould made his appearance, striking at Holdfast with the butt-end of his gun. Edward advanced to him and desired him to desist, or it would be the worse for him.

"Indeed, younker! It may be the worse for you," cried Corbould.

"It might have been if your gun had gone off," replied Edward.

"I did not aim at you. I aimed at the dog, and I will kill the brute, if I can."

"Not without danger to yourself; but it was not him that you aimed at—your gun was not pointed low enough to hit the dog—it was levelled at me, you sneaking wretch; and I have only to thank my own prudence and your sleepy head for having escaped with my life. I tell you candidly that I threw the powder out of your pan while you were asleep. If I served you as you deserve, I should now put my bullet into you, but I cannot kill a man who is defenceless—and that saves your life; but set off as fast as you can away from me, for if you follow me, I will show no more forbearance. Away with you directly," continued Edward, raising his gun to his shoulder and pointing it to Corbould; "if you do not be off, I'll fire."

Corbould saw that Edward was resolute, and thought proper to comply with his request: he walked away till he considered himself out of gunshot, and then commenced a torrent of oaths and abusive language, with which we shall not offend our readers. Before he went farther, he swore that he would have Edward's life before many days had passed, and then shaking his fist he went away. Edward remained where he was standing till the man was fairly out of sight, and then proceeded on his journey. It was now about four o'clock in the afternoon, and Edward, as he walked on, said to himself, "That man must be of a very wicked disposition, for I have offended him in nothing except in not submitting to be made his prisoner; and is that an offence to take a man's life for? He is a dangerous man, and will be more dangerous after being again foiled by me as he has been to-day. I doubt if he will go home; I am almost sure that he will turn and follow me when he thinks that he can without my seeing him; and if he does, he will find out where our cottage is—and who knows what mischief he may not do, and how he may alarm my little sisters? I'll not go home till dark; and I'll now walk in another direction, that I may mislead him." Edward then walked away more to the north, and every half-hour shifted his course, so as to be walking in a very different direction from where the cottage stood. In the meantime it grew gradually dark; and as it became so, every now and then when Edward passed a large tree he turned round behind it and looked to see if Corbould was following him. At last, just as it was dark, he perceived the figure of a man at no great distance from him, who was following him, running from tree to tree, so as to make his approach. "Oh, you are there!" thought Edward, "now will I give you a nice dance, and we will see whose legs are tired soonest. Let me see, where am I?" Edward looked round, and then perceived that he was close to the clump of trees where Humphrey had made his pit-fall for the cattle, and there was a clear spot of about a quarter of a mile between it and where he now stood. Edward made up his mind, and immediately walked out to cross the clearing, calling Holdfast to heel. It was now nearly dark, for there was only the light of the stars; but still there was sufficient light to see his way. As Edward crossed the cleared spot, he once looked round and perceived that Corbould was following him, and nearer than he was before, trusting probably to the increased darkness to hide his approach. "That will do," thought Edward, "come along, my fine fellow." And Edward walked on till he came to the pit-fall; there he stopped and looked round, and soon discovered the verderer at a hundred yards' distance. Edward held his dog by the mouth, that he should not growl or bark, and then went on in a direction so as to bring the pit-fall exactly between Corbould and himself. Having done so, he proceeded at a more rapid pace; and Corbould following him, also increased his, till he arrived at the pit-fall, which he could not perceive, and fell into it headlong; and as he fell into the pit, at the same time Edward heard the discharge of his gun, the crash of the small branches laid over it, and a cry on the part of Corbould. "That will do," thought Edward, "now you may lie there as long as the gipsy did, and that will cool your courage. Humphrey's pit-fall is full of adventure. In this case it has done me a service. Now I may turn and go home as fast as I can. Come, Holdfast, old boy, we both want our suppers. I can answer for one, for I could eat the whole of that pasty which Oswald set before me this morning." Edward walked at a rapid pace, quite delighted at the issue of the adventure. As he arrived near to the cottage he found Humphrey outside, with Pablo, on the look-out for him. He soon joined them, and soon after embraced Alice and Edith, who had been anxiously waiting for his return, and who had wondered at his being out so late. "Give me my supper, my dear girls," said Edward; "and then you shall know all about it."

As soon as Edward had satisfied his craving appetite—for he had not, as my readers must recollect, eaten anything since his departure early in the morning from the house of Oswald Partridge—he entered into a narrative of the events of the day. They all listened with great interest; and when Edward had finished, Pablo, the gipsy boy, jumped up, and said:

"Now he is in the pit, to-morrow morning I take gun and shoot him."

"No, no, Pablo, you must not do that," replied Edward, laughing.

"Pablo," said little Edith, "go and sit down; you must not shoot people."

"He shoot master then," said Pablo; "he very bad man."

"But if you shoot him, you will be a bad boy, Pablo," replied Edith, who appeared to have assumed an authority over him. Pablo did not appear to understand this, but he obeyed the order of his little mistress, and resumed his seat at the chimney-corner.

"But, Edward," said Humphrey, "what do you propose to do?"

"I hardly know; my idea was to let him remain there for a day or two, and then send to Oswald to let him know where the fellow was."

"The only objection to that is," replied Humphrey, "that you say his gun went off as he fell into the pit; it may be probable that he is wounded, and if so, he might die if he is left there."

"You are right, Humphrey, that is possible; and I would not have the life of a fellow-creature on my conscience."

"I think it would be advisable, Edward, that I should set off early to-morrow on the pony, and see Oswald, tell him all that has occurred, and show him where the pit-fall is."

"I believe that would be the best plan, Humphrey."

"Yes," said Alice, "it would be dreadful that a man should die in so wicked a state; let him be taken out, and perhaps he will repent."

"Won't God punish him, brother?" said Edith.

"Yes, my dear, sooner or later, the vengeance of Heaven overtakes the wicked. But I am very tired after so long a walk; let us go to prayers, and then to bed."

The danger that Edward had incurred that day was felt strongly by the whole party; and, with the exception of Pablo, there was earnest devotion and gratitude to Heaven when their orisons were offered up.

Humphrey was off before daybreak, and, at nine o'clock, had arrived at the cottage of Oswald, by whom he was warmly greeted before the cause of his unexpected arrival was made known. Oswald was greatly annoyed at Humphrey's narration, and appeared to be very much of the opinion of Pablo, which was, to leave the scoundrel where he was; but on the remonstrance of Humphrey, he set off, with two of the other verderers, and before nightfall Humphrey arrived at the pit-fall, where they heard Corbould groaning below.

"Who's there?" said Oswald, looking into the pit.

"It's me—it's Corbould," replied the man.

"Are you hurt?"

"Yes, badly," replied Corbould; "when I fell, my gun went off, and the ball has gone through my thigh. I have almost bled to death."

Humphrey went for the ladder, which was at hand, and, with much exertion on the part of the whole four of them, they contrived to drag out Corbould, who groaned heavily with pain. A handkerchief was tied tightly round his leg, to prevent any further bleeding, and they gave him some water, which revived him.

"Now, what's to be done?" said Oswald; "we can never get him home."

"I will tell you," said Humphrey, walking with him aside. "It will not do for any of these men to know our cottage, and we cannot take them there. Desire them to remain with the man, while you go for a cart to carry him home. We will go to the cottage, give Billy his supper, and then return with him in the cart, and bring your men something to eat. Then I will go with you, and bring the cart back again before daylight. It will be a night's walk, but it will be the safest plan."

"I think so too," replied Oswald, who desired the men to wait till his return, as he was going to borrow a cart; and then set off with Humphrey.

As soon as they arrived at the cottage, Humphrey gave the pony to Pablo to put into the stable and feed, and then communicated to Edward the state of Corbould.

"It's almost a pity that he had not killed himself out-right," observed Oswald; "it would have been justice to him for attempting your life without any cause; he is a bloodthirsty scoundrel, and I wish he was anywhere but where he is. However, the Intendant shall know of it, and I have no doubt that he will be discharged."

"Do nothing in a hurry, Oswald," replied Edward; "at present let him give his own version of the affair; for he may prove more dangerous when discharged than when under your control. Now sit down and take your supper. Billy must have an hour to get his, and therefore there is no hurry for you."

"That is your gipsy lad, Edward, is he not?" said Oswald.

"Yes."

"I like the boy's looks; but they are a queer race. You must not trust him too much," continued Oswald, in an under tone, "until you have tried him, and are satisfied of his fidelity. They are very excitable, and capable of strong attachment if well treated, that I know; for I did a gipsy a good turn once, and it proved to be the saving of my life afterwards."

"Oh, tell us how, Oswald," said Alice.

"It is too long a story now, my dear little lady," replied Oswald; "but I will another time. Whatever he may do, do not strike him; for they never forgive a blow, I am told by those who know them, and it never does them any good; as I said before, they are a queer race."

"He will not be beaten by us," replied Humphrey, "depend upon it, unless Edith slaps him; for she is the one who takes most pains with him, and I presume he would not care much about her little hand."

"No, no," replied Oswald, laughing, "Edith may do as she pleases. What does he do for you?"

"Oh, nothing as yet, for he is hardly recovered, poor fellow," replied Humphrey. "He follows Edith, and helps her to look for the eggs; and last night he set some springes after his own fashion, and certainly beat me, for he took three rabbits and a hare, while I, with all my traps, only took one rabbit."

"I think you had better leave that part of your livelihood entirely to him; he has been bred up to it, Humphrey, and it will be his amusement. You must not expect him to work very hard; they are not accustomed to it. They live a roving life, and never work if they can help it; still, if you make him fond of you, he may be very useful, for they are very clever and handy."

"I hope to make him useful," replied Humphrey, "but still I will not force him to do what he does not like. He is very fond of the pony already, and likes to take care of him."

"Bring him over to me, one of these days, so that he may know where to find me. It may prove of consequence if you have a message to send, and cannot come yourselves."

"That is very true," replied Edward; "I will not forget it. Humphrey, shall you or I go with the cart?"

"Humphrey, by all means; it will not do for them to suppose I had the cart from you, Edward; they do not know Humphrey, and he will be off again in the morning before they are up."

"Very true," replied Edward.

"And it is time for us to set off," replied Oswald. "Will Mistress Alice oblige me with something for my men to eat? For they have fasted the whole day."

"Yes," replied Alice, "I will have it ready before the pony is in the cart. Edith, dear, come with me."

Humphrey then went out to harness the pony, and when all was ready, he and Oswald set off again.

When they arrived at the pit-fall they found Corbould lying between the two other verderers, who were sitting by his side. Corbould was much recovered since his wound had been bound up, and he was raised up and put on the fodder which Humphrey had put into the cart, and they proceeded on their journey to the other side of the forest, the verderers eating what Humphrey had brought for them as they walked along. It was a tedious and painful journey for the wounded man, who shrieked out when the cart was jolted by the wheel getting into a rut or hole; but there was no help for it, and he was very much exhausted when they arrived, which was not till past midnight. Corbould was then taken to his cottage and put on the bed, and another verderer sent for a surgeon: those who had been with Oswald were glad to go to bed, for it had been a fatiguing day. Humphrey remained with Oswald for three hours, and then again returned with Billy, who, although he had crossed the forest three times in the twenty-four hours, appeared quite fresh and ready to go back again.

"I will let you know how he gets on, Humphrey, and what account he gives of his falling into the pit; but you must not expect me for a fortnight at least."

Humphrey wished Oswald good-bye; and Billy was so anxious to get back to his stable that Humphrey could not keep him at a quiet pace. "Horses, and all animals indeed, know that there is no place like home; it is a pity that men, who consider themselves much wiser, have not the same consideration," thought Humphrey as the pony trotted along. Humphrey thought a good deal about the danger that Edward had been subjected to, and said to himself, "I really think that I should be more comfortable if Edward was away. I am always in a fidget about him. I wish the new king, who is now in France, would raise an army and come over. It is better that Edward should be fighting in the field than remain here and risk being shot as a deer-stealer, or put in prison. The farm is sufficient for us all; and when I have taken in more ground it will be more than sufficient, even if I do not kill the wild cattle. I am fit for the farm, but Edward is not. He is thrown away, living in this obscurity, and he feels it. He will always be in hot water some way or another, that is certain. What a narrow escape he has had with that scoundrel, and yet how little he cares for it! He was intended for a soldier, that is evident; and if ever he is one, he will be in his element, and distinguish himself, if it pleases God to spare his life. I'll persuade him to stay at home a little while to help me to enclose the other piece of ground; and after that is done, I'll dig a saw-pit, and see if I can coax Pablo to saw with me. I must go to Lymington and buy a saw. If I once could get the trees sawed up into planks, what a quantity of things I could make, and how I could improve the place."

Thus thought Humphrey as he went along; he was all for the farm and improvements, and was always calculating when he should have another calf or a fresh litter of pigs. His first idea was, that he would make Pablo work hard; but the advice he had received from Oswald was not forgotten; and he now was thinking how he should coax Pablo into standing below in the saw-pit, which was not only hard work, but disagreeable, from the sawdust falling into the eyes. Humphrey's cogitations were interrupted by a halloo, and turning round in the direction of the voice, he perceived Edward, and turned the cart to join him.

"You're just come in time, Humphrey; I have some provision for Alice's larder. I took my gun and came out on the path which I knew you would return on, and I have killed a young buck. He is good meat, and we are scarce of provisions."

Humphrey helped Edward to put the venison in the cart, and they returned to the cottage, which was not more than three miles off. Humphrey told Edward the result of his journey, and then proposed that Edward should stop at home for a few days and help him with the new enclosure. To this Edward cheerfully consented; and as soon as they arrived at the cottage, and Humphrey had had his breakfast, they took their axes and went out to fell at a cluster of small spruce-firs about a mile off.

Chapter Fourteen.

"Now, Humphrey, what do you propose to do?"

"This," replied Humphrey: "I have marked out three acres or thereabouts of the land running in a straight line behind the garden. There is not a tree on it, and it is all good feeding-ground. What I intend to do is to enclose it with the spruce-fir posts and rails that we are about to cut down, and then set a hedge upon a low bank which I shall raise all round inside the rails. I know where there are thousands of seedling thorns, which I shall take up in the winter, or early in the spring, to put in, as the bank will be ready for them by that time."

"Well, that's all very good; but I fear it will be a long while before you have such a quantity of land dug up."

"Yes, of course it will; but, Edward, I have plenty of manure to spare, and I shall put it all over this land, and then it will become a rich pasture, and also an earlier pasture than what we can get from the forest, and will be very handy to turn the cows and the calves upon; or even Billy, if we want him in a hurry."

"All that is very true," replied Edward, "so that it will be useful, at all events, if you do not dig it up."

"Indeed it will," replied Humphrey; "I only wish it were six acres instead of three."

"I can't say I do," replied Edward, laughing; "you are too grand in your ideas; only think what a quantity of spruces we shall have to cut down on it, to post and rail what you just propose. Let it be three acres first, Humphrey; and when they are enclosed, you may begin to talk of three more."

"Well, perhaps you are right, Edward," said Humphrey.

"Why, here's Pablo coming after us: he's not coming to work, I presume, but to amuse himself by looking on."

"I don't think he is strong enough to do much hard work, Humphrey, although he appears very ingenious."

"No, I agree with you; and if he is to work, depend upon it it must not be by having work set out for him; he would take a disgust to it directly. I have another plan for him."

"And what is that, Humphrey?"

"I shall not set him anything to do, and shall make him believe that I do not think he is able to do anything. That will pique him, and I think by that means I shall get more work out of him than you would think, especially when, after he has done it, I express my wonder and give him praise."

"Not a bad idea, that; you will work upon his pride, which is probably stronger than his laziness."

"I do not think him lazy, but I think him unused to hard work, and, having lived a life of wandering and idleness, not very easy to be brought to constant and daily work, except by degrees, and by the means which I propose.—Here we are," continued Humphrey, throwing his axe and billhook down, and proceeding to take off his doublet: "now for an hour or two's fulfilment of the sentence of our first parents—to wit, 'the sweat of the brow.'"

Edward followed Humphrey's example in taking off his doublet; they selected the long thin trees most fitted for rails, and were hard at work when Pablo came up to them. More than a dozen trees had fallen, and lay one upon the other, before they stopped a while to recover themselves a little.

"Well, Pablo," said Humphrey, wiping his forehead, "I suppose you think looking on better than cutting down trees; and so it is."

"What cut down trees for?"

"To make posts and rails to fence in more ground. I shall not leave the boughs on."

"No, cut them off by and by, and then put poles on the cart and carry them home."

Edward and Humphrey then recommenced their labour, and worked for another half-hour, when they paused to recover their wind.

"Hard work, Pablo," said Humphrey.

"Yes, very hard work; Pablo not strong enough."

"Oh no, you are not able to do anything of this kind, I know. No work this for gipsies; they take birds' nests and catch rabbits."

"Yes," replied Pablo, nodding; "and you eat them."

"So he does, Pablo," said Edward; "so you are useful in your way; for if he had nothing to eat he would not be able to work. Strong man cut down trees, weak man catch rabbits."

"Both good," said Pablo.

"Yes, but strong man like work; not strong man not like work, Pablo. So now look on again, for we must have another spell."

"Strong man cut down trees, not strong man cut off branches," said Pablo, taking up the billhook and setting to work to cut off the boughs, which he did with great dexterity and rapidity.

Edward and Humphrey exchanged glances and smiles, and then worked away in silence till it was, as they supposed, dinner-time. They were not wrong in their supposition, although they had no other clock than their appetites, which, however, tell the time pretty correctly to those who work hard. Alice had the platters on the table, and was looking out to see if they were coming.

"Why, Pablo, have you been at work?" said Edith.

"Yes, little missy—work all the morning."

"Indeed he has, and has worked very well, and been very useful," said Edward.

"It has given you an appetite for your dinner, Pablo, has it not?" said Humphrey.

"Have that without work," replied the boy.

"Pablo, you are a very good gipsy boy," said Edith, patting his head with a patronising air; "I shall let you walk out with me and carry the basket to put the eggs in when you come home in the evening."

"That is a reward," said Humphrey, laughing.

After dinner they continued their labour, and by supper-time had so many trees cut down, that they determined to carry home the next day, and lay them along, to see how many more they would want. While they put the trees in the cart and took them home, Pablo contrived to lop off the boughs and prepare the poles for them to take away. As soon as they had cut down sufficient and carted them home, they then selected shorter trees for posts; and when Pablo had cleared them of the boughs, they sawed them out the proper lengths, and then carted them home. This occupied nearly the whole week, and then they proceeded to dig holes and set the posts in. The railing was then to be nailed to the posts, and that occupied them three days more; so that it was altogether a fortnight of hard work before the three acres were enclosed.

"There," said Humphrey, "that's a good job over; many thanks, Edward, for your assistance; and thank you too, Pablo, for you really have helped us very much indeed, and are a very useful, good boy. Now for raising the bank—that I must do when I can spare time; but my garden is overrun with weeds, and I must get Edith and Alice to help me there."

"If you don't want me any longer, Humphrey," said Edward, "I think I shall go over to see Oswald, and take Pablo with me. I want to know how that fellow Corbould is, and what he says; and whether the Intendant has come back; not that I shall go near him or his good little daughter, but I think I may as well go, and it will be a good opportunity of showing Pablo the way to Oswald's cottage."

"I think so too; and when you come back, Edward, one of us must go to Lymington; for I require some tools, and Pablo is very ragged. He must have some better clothes than these old ones of ours if he is to be sent messages. Don't you think so?"

"Certainly I do."

"And I want a thousand things," said Alice.

"Indeed, mistress, won't less than a thousand content you?"

"Yes, perhaps not quite a thousand, but I really do want a great many, and I will make you a list of them. I have not pans enough for my milk; I want salt; I want tubs; but I will make out a list, and you will find it a very long one."

"Well, I hope you have something to sell to pay for them?"

"Yes; I have plenty of butter salted down."

"What have you, Edith?"

"Oh, my chickens are not large enough yet: as soon as they are, Humphrey must get me some ducks and geese, for I mean to keep some; and by and by I will have some turkeys; but not yet. I must wait till Humphrey builds me the new house for them he has promised me."

"I think you are right, Edith, about the ducks and geese; they will do well on the water behind the yard, and I will dig you out a bigger pool for them."

"Edith, my dear, your little fingers are just made to weed my onions well, and I wish you would do it to-morrow morning, if you have time."

"*Yes*, Humphrey, but my little fingers won't smell very nice afterwards."

"Not till you have washed them, I guess; but there is soap and water, you know."

"Yes, I know there is; but if I weed the onions I cannot help Alice to make the butter; however, if Alice can do without me I will do it."

"I want some more seeds sadly," said Humphrey, "and I must make out my list. I must go to Lymington myself this time, Edward; for you will be puzzled with all our wants."

"Not if I know exactly what you do want; but as I really do not, and probably should make mistakes, I think it will be better if you do go. But it is bedtime, and as I shall start early, good-night, sisters; I beg you will let me have something to eat before I start. I shall try for some venison, as I come back, and shall take Smoker with me: he is quite well again, and his ribs are as stout as ever."

"And, Edward," said Alice, "I wish, when you kill any venison, that you would bring home some of those parts which you usually throw away, for I assure you, now that we have three dogs, I hardly know how to find enough for them to eat."

"I'll not fail, Alice," replied Edward, "and now once more good-night."

Early the next morning Edward took his gun, and, with Pablo and Smoker, set off for Oswald's cottage.

Edward talked a great deal with Pablo relative to his former life; and, by the answers which the boy gave him, was satisfied that, notwithstanding his doubtful way of bringing up, the lad was not corrupted, but was a well-minded boy. As they walked through a grove of trees, Edward still talking, Pablo stopped and put his hand before Edward's mouth, and then stooping down, at the same time seizing Smoker by the neck, he pointed with his finger. Edward at first could see nothing, but eventually he made out the horns of an animal just rising above a hillock. It was evidently one of the wild cattle. Edward cocked his gun and advanced cautiously, while Pablo remained where he was, holding Smoker. As soon as he was near enough to hit the head of the animal, Edward levelled and fired, and Pablo let Smoker loose, who bounded forward over the hillock. They followed the dog, and found him about to seize a calf which stood by a heifer that Edward had shot. Edward called him over and went up to the animal; it was a fine young heifer, and the calf was not more than a fortnight old.

"We cannot stop now, Pablo," said Edward. "Humphrey would like to have the calf, and we must take our chance of its remaining by its mother till we come back. I think it will for a day or two, so let us push on."

No further adventure happened, and they arrived a little after noon at Oswald's cottage. He was not at home; his wife saying that she believed that he was with the Intendant, who had come back from London the day before.

"But I will put on my hood and see," said the young woman.

In a few minutes she returned with Oswald.

"I am glad that you have come, sir," said Oswald, as Edward extended his hand, "as I have just seen the Intendant, and he has been asking many questions about you. I am certain he thinks that you are not the grandson of Jacob Armitage, and that he supposes I know who you are. He asked me where your cottage was, and whether I could not take him to it, as he wished to speak to you, and said that he felt great interest about you."

"And what did you say?"

"I said that your cottage was a good day's journey from here, and I was not certain that I knew the exact way, as I had been there but seldom; but that I knew where to find it, after I saw the forests of Arnwood. I told him about Corbould and his attempt upon you, and he was very wroth. I never saw him moved before; and young Mistress Patience, she was indeed angry and perplexed, and begged her father to send the assailant away as soon as he could be moved."

"Master Heatherstone replied, 'Leave it to me, my dear;' and then asked me what account Corbould gave of himself, and his falling into the pit. I told him that Corbould stated that he was following a deer, which he had severely wounded about noon-day, and having no dog with him, he could not overtake it, although he knew by its bleeding track that it could not hold out much longer. That he followed it until nightfall, and had it in view and close to him when he fell into the pit."

"Well, the story was not badly made up," said Edward, "only for a *stag* read *man*; and what did the Intendant say to that?"

"He said that he believed you, and that Corbould's story was false—as, if it had been a stag that he was following, no one would have known that he had fallen into the pit, and he would have remained there till now. I quite forgot to say, that when the Intendant said that he wished to call at your cottage, the young mistress said that she would go with him, as you had told her that you had two sisters living with you, and she wished very much to see them and make their acquaintance."

"I am afraid that we shall not be able to prevent this visit, Oswald," replied Edward. "He is in command here, and the forest is in his charge. We must see to it. I only should like, if possible, to have notice of his coming, that we may be prepared."

"You need no preparation, sir, if he should come," replied Oswald.

"Very true," said Edward; "we have nothing to conceal, and if he finds us in a pickle it is of no consequence."

"Rather the better, sir," replied Oswald. "Let your sisters be at the wash-tub, and you and your brother carting manure; he will then be more likely to have no suspicion of your being otherwise than what you assume to be."

"Have you heard any news from London, Oswald?"

"Not as yet. I was away yesterday evening, when Master Heatherstone came back, and I have not seen his man this morning. While you eat your dinner I will go into the kitchen; and if he is not there, Phoebe will be sure to tell me all that she has heard."

"Do not say that I am here, Oswald, as I do not wish to see the Intendant."

"Mum's the word, sir; but you must stay in the cottage, or others will see you, and it may come to his ears."

Oswald's wife then put before him a large pie, and some wheaten bread, with a biggin of good beer. Edward helped Pablo to a large allowance, and then filled his own platter; while thus occupied Oswald Partridge had left the cottage, as agreed.

"What do you say, Pablo? Do you think you can walk back to-night?"

"Yes. Like walking at night. My people always do; sleep in a daytime."

"Well, I think it will be better to go home: Oswald has only one bed, and I do not wish them to know that I am here; so Pablo, eat heartily, and then we shall not be so tired. I want to get home, that I may send Humphrey after the calf."

"One bed here; you stay," replied Pablo. "I go home and tell Master Humphrey."

"Do you think you would be able to find your way, Pablo?"

"Once go one way, always know same way again."

"You are a clever fellow, Pablo, and I have a mind to try you. Now drink some beer. I think, Pablo, you shall go home, and tell Humphrey that I and Smoker will be where the heifer lies dead, and have it skinned by nine o'clock to-morrow morning; so if he comes, he will find me there."

"Yes, I go now."

"No, not now, you must rest yourself a little more."

"Pablo not tired," replied the gipsy, getting up; "be back before supper. As I go along, look at calf and dead cow—see if calf stay with mother."

"Very well, then, if you wish it, you may go now," said Edward.

Pablo nodded his head, and disappeared.

A few minutes afterwards Oswald made his appearance.

"Is the boy gone?"

"Yes; he is gone back to the cottage;" and Edward then stated how he had killed the heifer, and wanted to obtain the calf.

"I've an idea that you will find that boy very useful, if he is properly managed."

"I think so too," replied Edward; "and I am glad to perceive that he is already attached to all of us. We treat him as ourselves."

"You are right; and now for the news that I have to tell you. The Duke Hamilton, the Earl of Holland, and Lord Capel have been tried, condemned, and executed."

Edward sighed. "More murder! But we must expect it from those who have murdered their king. Is that all?"

"No. King Charles the Second has been proclaimed in Scotland, and invited to come over."

"That is indeed news," replied Edward. "Where is he now?"

"At the Hague; but it was said that he was going to Paris."

"That is all that you have heard?"

"Yes; that was what was current when Master Heatherstone was in town. His man Sampson gave me the news; and he further said, 'That his master's journey to London was to oppose the execution of the three lords; but it was all in vain.'"

"Well," replied Edward, after a pause, "if the king does come over, there will be some work cut out for some of us, I expect. Your news has put me in a fever," continued Edward, taking up the biggin and drinking a large draught of beer.

"I thought it would," replied Oswald; "but until the time comes, the more quiet you keep the better."

"Yes, Oswald; but I can't talk any more; I must be left alone to think. I will go to bed, as I shall be off early in the morning. Is that fellow Corbould getting well?"

"Yes, sir; he is out of bed, and walks a little with a stick; but he is still very lame, and will be for some time."

"Good-night, Oswald; if I have anything to say I will write and send the boy. I do not want to be seen here any more."

"It will be best, sir. Good-night; I will put Smoker in the kennel to the right, as he will not be friendly with the other dogs."

Edward retired to bed, but not to sleep. The Scots had proclaimed the king, and invited him over. "He will surely come," thought Edward, "and he will have an army round him as soon as he lands." Edward made up his resolution to join the army as soon as he had heard that the king had landed; and what with considering how he should be able so to do, and afterwards building castles as to what he would do, it was long before he fell asleep; and when he did, he dreamt of battles and victory—he was charging at the head of his troops—he was surrounded by the dying and the dead. He was wounded, and he was somehow or another well again, as if by magic; and then the scene was changed, and he was rescuing Patience Heatherstone from his own lawless men, and preserving the life of her father, which was about to be sacrificed; and at last he awoke, and found that the daylight peeped through the windows, and that he had slept longer than he had intended to do. He arose and dressed himself quickly, and, not waiting for breakfast, went to the kennel, released Smoker from his durance, and set off on his return.

Before nine o'clock he had arrived at the spot where the heifer lay dead. He found the calf still by its side, bleating and walking round uneasily. As he approached with the dog, it went to a farther distance, and there remained. Edward took out his knife, and commenced skinning the heifer, and then took out the inside. The animal was quite fresh and good, but not very fat, as may be supposed. While thus occupied Smoker growled and then sprang forward, bounding away in the direction of the cottage, and Edward thought Humphrey was at hand. In a few minutes the pony and cart appeared between the trees, with Humphrey and Pablo in it, and Smoker leaping up at his friend Billy.

"Good-morning, Humphrey," said Edward, "I am almost ready for you; but the question is, how are we to take the calf? It is as wild as a deer."

"It will be a puzzler, without Smoker can run it down," said Humphrey.

"I take him, with Smoker," said Pablo.

"How will you take it, Pablo?"

Pablo went to the cart and took out a long small cord which Humphrey had brought with them, and made a noose at one end; he coiled the rope in his hand, and then threw it out to its full length, by way of trial. "This way I take him, suppose I get near enough. This way take bulls in Spain: call him lasso. Now come with me." Pablo had his rope again coiled in his hand, and then went round to the other side of the calf, which still remained lowing at about 200 yards' distance.

"Now tell Smoker," cried Pablo.

Humphrey set Smoker upon the calf, which retreated from the dog, presenting his head to run at it; and Pablo kept behind the animal, while Smoker attacked it, and drove it near to him.

As soon as the calf, which was so busy with the dog that it did not perceive Pablo, came sufficiently near to him, Pablo threw his rope, and caught the loop round the animal's neck. The calf set off galloping towards Humphrey, and dragging Pablo after him, for the latter was not strong enough to hold it.

Humphrey went to his assistance, and then Edward, and the calf was thrown down by Smoker, who seized it by the neck, and it was tied and put on the cart in a few minutes.

"Well done, Pablo! You are a clever fellow," said Edward, "and this calf shall be yours."

"It is a cow-calf," said Humphrey, "which I am glad of. Pablo, you did that well, and, as Edward says, the calf belongs to you."

Pablo looked pleased, but said nothing.

The meat and hide were put into the cart with some of the offal which Alice had asked for the dogs, and they set off on their return home.

Humphrey was very anxious to go to Lymington, and was not sorry that he had some meat to take with him: he determined to get off the next morning; and Edward proposed that he should take Pablo with him, that he might know the way there in case of any emergency, for they both felt that Pablo could be trusted. Edward said he would remain at home with his sisters, and see if he could be of any use to Alice; if not, there would be work in the garden. Humphrey and Pablo went away after breakfast, with Billy, and the meat and skin of the heifer in the cart. Humphrey had also a large basket of eggs and three dozen of chickens from Alice to be disposed of, and a list as long as the tail of a kite of articles which she and Edith required; fortunately there was nothing very expensive on the list, long as it was; but women in those day's required needles, pins, buttons, tapes, thread, worsted, and a hundred other little necessaries, as they do now. As soon as they were gone Edward, who was still castle-building instead of offering his services to Alice, brought out his father's sword and commenced cleaning it. When he had polished it up to his satisfaction, he felt less inclined than ever to do anything; so after dinner he took his gun and walked out into the forest, that he might indulge in his reveries. He walked on, quite unconscious of the direction in which he was going, and more than once finding his hat knocked off his head by the branch of a tree which he had not perceived—for the best of all possible reasons, because his eyes were cast on the ground—when his ears were saluted with the neighing of a horse. He looked up and perceived that he was near to a herd of forest ponies, the first that he had seen since he had lived in the forest.

This roused him, and he looked about him. "Where can I have been wandering to?" thought Edward: "I never fell in with any of the forest ponies before; I must therefore have walked in a direction quite contrary to what I usually do. I do not know where I am; the scenery is new to me. What a fool I am. It's lucky that nobody except Humphrey digs pitfalls, or I should probably have been in one by this time; and I've brought out my gun and left the dog at home. Well, I suppose I can find my way back." Edward then surveyed the whole herd of ponies, which were at no great distance from him. There was a fine horse or two among them, which appeared to be the leaders of the herd. They allowed Edward to approach to within two hundred yards, and then, with manes and tails streaming in the air, they darted off with the rapidity of the wind.

"Now I'll puzzle Humphrey when I go back," thought Edward. "He says that Billy is getting old, and that he wishes he could get another pony. I will tell him what a plenty there are, and propose that he should invent some way of catching one. That will be a poser for him; yet I'm sure that he'll try, for he is very ingenious. And now which way am I to turn to find my way home? I think it ought to be to the north; but which is north? For there is no sun out, and now I perceive it looks very like rain. I wonder how long I have been walking! I'm sure I don't know."

Edward then hurried in a direction which he considered might lead him homeward, and walked fast; but he once more fell into his habit of castle-building, and was talking to himself: "The king proclaimed in Scotland! He will come over of course: I will join his army—and then—"

Thus he went on, again absorbed in the news which he had gained from Oswald, till on a sudden he again recollected himself, and perceived that he had lost sight of the copse of trees on a high hill, to which he had been directing his steps. Where was it? He turned round and round, and at last found out that he had been walking away from it.

"I must dream no more," thought he; "or if I do indulge in any more day-dreams, I certainly shall neither sleep nor dream to-night. It is getting dark already, and here am I lost in the forest, and all through my own foolishness. If the stars do not shine, I shall not know how to direct my steps; indeed, if they do, I don't know whether I have walked south or north, and I am in a pretty pickle;—not that I care for being out in the forest on a night like this; but my sisters and Humphrey will be alarmed at my absence. The best thing I can do, is to decide upon taking some straight line, and continue in it: I must then get out of the forest at last, even if I walk right across it. That will be better than going backwards and forwards, or round and round, as I otherwise shall do, just like a puppy running after its own tail. So now shine out, stars."

Edward waited until he could make out Charles's Wain, which he well knew, and then the Polar Star. As soon as he was certain of that, he resolved to travel by it due north, and he did so, sometimes walking fast, and at others keeping up a steady trot for half a mile without stopping. As he was proceeding on his travels, he observed, under some trees ahead of him, a spark of fire emitted; he thought it was a glow-worm at first; but it was more like the striking of a flint against steel; and as he saw it a second time, he stopped, that he might ascertain what it might be before he advanced farther.

Chapter Fifteen.

It was now very dark, as there was no moon, and the stars were often obscured by the clouds, which were heavy, and borne along by the wind, which was very high. The light again appeared, and this time Edward heard the clash of the flint against the steel, and he was certain that it was somebody striking a light. He advanced very cautiously, and arrived at a large tree, behind which he remained to reconnoitre. The people, whoever they might be, were not more than thirty yards from him; a light spread its rays for a moment or two, and he could make out a figure kneeling and holding his hat to protect it from the wind; then it burnt brighter, and he saw that a lantern had been lighted, and then again, of a sudden, all was dark again: so Edward immediately satisfied himself that a dark lantern had been lighted and then closed. Who the parties might be he of course had no idea; but he was resolved that he would ascertain, if he could, before he accosted them and asked his way.

"They have no dog," thought Edward, "or it would have growled before this; and it's lucky that I have none either." Edward then crept softly nearer to them: the wind, which was strong, blew from where they were to where Edward stood, so that there was less chance of their hearing his approach.

Edward went on his hands and knees, and crawled through the fern until he gained another tree, and within ten yards of them, and from where he could hear what they might say. He was thus cautious, as he had been told by Oswald that there were many disbanded soldiers who had taken up their quarters in the forest, and had committed several depredations upon the houses adjacent to it, always returning to the forest as a rendezvous. Edward listened, and heard one say:

"It is not time yet! No, no: too soon by half an hour or more. The people from Lymington who buy him what he wants always bring it to him at night, that his retreat may not be discovered. They sometimes do not leave the cottage till two hours after dark, for they do not leave Lymington to go there till it is dark!"

"Do you know who it is who supplies him with food?"

"Yes, the people at the inn in Parliament Street—I forget the sign."

"Oh! I know. Yes, the landlord is a downright Malignant in his heart! We might squeeze him well, if we dared show ourselves in Lymington."

"Yes, but they would squeeze our necks tighter than would be agreeable, I expect," replied the other.

"Are you sure that he has money?"

"Quite sure; for I peeped through the chinks of the window-shutters, and I saw him pay for the things brought to him; it was from a canvas bag, and it was gold that he took out."

"And where did he put the bag after he had paid them?"

"That I can't tell, for as I knew that they would come out as soon as they were paid, I was obliged to beat a retreat, lest I should be seen."

"Well, then, how is it to be managed?"

"We must first tap at the door, and try if we can get in as benighted travellers: if that won't do, and I fear it will not, while you remain begging for admittance at the door, and keep him occupied, I will try the door behind, that leads into the garden; and if not the door, I will try the window. I have examined them both well, and have been outside when he has shut up his shutters, and I know the fastenings. With a pane out, I could open them immediately."

"Is there anybody else besides him in the cottage?"

"Yes, a lad who attends him, and goes to Lymington for him."

"No women?"

"Not one."

"But do you think we two are sufficient? Had we not better get more help? There is Broom, and Black, the gipsy, at the rendezvous. I can go for them, and be back in time: they are stout and true."

"Stout enough, but not true. No, no, I want no sharers in this business, and you know how ill they behaved in the last affair. I'll swear that they only produced half the swag. I like honour between gentlemen and soldiers; and that's why I have chosen you. I know I can trust you, Benjamin. It's time now—what do you say? We are two to one, for I count the boy as nothing. Shall we start?"

"I am with you. You say there's a bag of gold, and that's worth fighting for."

"Yes, Ben, and I'll tell you: with what I've got buried, and my share of that bag, I shall have enough, I think; and I'll start for the Low Countries, for England's getting rather too warm for me."

"Well, I shan't go yet," replied Benjamin; "I don't like your foreign parts; they have no good ale, and I can't understand their talk. I'd sooner remain in jolly old England with a halter twisted ready for me, than pass my life with such a set of chaps who drink nothing but Scheidam, and wear twenty pair of breeches. Come, let's be off: if we get the money, you shall go to the Low Countries, Will, and I'll start for the north, where they don't know me—for if you go, I won't stay here."

The two men then rose up; and the one whose name appeared to be Will, first examined if the candle in his dark lantern burnt well; and then they both set off, followed by Edward, who had heard quite enough to satisfy him that they were bent upon a burglary—if not murder. Edward followed them, so as to keep their forms indistinctly in sight, which was as much as he could do at twenty yards' distance: fortunately the wind was so high that they did not hear his footsteps, although he often trod upon a rotten stick, which snapped as it broke in twain. As near as Edward could guess, he had tracked them for about three miles, when they stopped, and he perceived that they were examining their pistols, which they took from their belts. They then went on again, and entered a small plantation of oak-trees, of about forty years' growth—very thick and very dark, with close underwood below. They followed each other through a narrow path, until they came to a cleared place in the middle of the plantation, in which there stood a low cottage, surrounded with covert on every side, with the exception of some thirty yards of land around it. All was still, and as dark as pitch; Edward remained behind the trees, and when the two men again stopped, he was not six feet from them. They consulted in a low tone, but the wind was so high that he could not distinguish what they said. At last they advanced to the cottage, and Edward, still keeping within the trees, shifted his position so that he should be opposite the gable end of the cottage. He observed one man to go up to the front door, while the other went round to the door behind, as had been agreed. Edward threw open the pan of the lock of the gun, and reprimed it, that he might be sure, and then waited for what was to follow. He heard the man Will at the front door, talking and asking for shelter in a plaintive but loud voice; and shortly afterwards he perceived a light through the chinks of the shutters—for Edward was continually altering his position to see what was going on in the front and in the back. At one time he thought of levelling his gun and killing one of the men at once; but he could not make up his mind to do that, as a burglary, although intended, had not yet been committed; so he remained passive until the attack was really made, when he resolved that he would come to the rescue. After some minutes of entreaty that they would open the door, the man in front commenced thumping and beating against it, as if he would make them open the door by force; but this was to attract the attention of those within, and divert it from the attempts that the other was making to get in behind. Edward was aware of this: he now kept his eye upon what was going on at the back. Advancing nearer, which he ventured to do now that both the men were so occupied, he perceived that the fellow had contrived to open the window close to the back door, and was remaining quite close to it with a pistol in his hand, apparently not wishing to run the risk of climbing in. Edward slipped under the eaves of the cottage, not six feet from the man, who remained with his back partly turned towards him. Edward then finding he had obtained this position unperceived, crouched down with his gun ready pointed.

As Edward remained in this position, he heard a shrill voice cry out, "They are getting in behind!" and a movement in the cottage. The man near him, who had his pistol in his hand, put his arm through the window and fired inside. A shriek was given, and Edward fired his gun into the body of the man, who immediately fell. Edward lost no time in reloading his gun, during which he heard the bursting open of the front door and the report of firearms; then all was silent for a moment, excepting the wailing of somebody within. As soon as his gun was reloaded Edward walked round to the front of the cottage, where he found the man who was called Ben lying across the threshold of the open door. He stepped across the body, and, looking into the room within, perceived a body stretched on the floor, and a young lad weeping over it.

"Don't be alarmed, I am a friend," said Edward, going in to where the body lay; and taking the light which was at the farther end of the chamber, he placed it on the floor, that he might examine the state of the person who was breathing heavily, and apparently badly wounded. "Rise up, my lad," said Edward, "and let me see if I can be of any use."

"Ah! No," cried the boy, throwing back his long hair from his temples, "he bleeds to death!"

"Bring me some water quick," said Edward, "there's a good lad, while I see where he is hurt."

The boy ran up to fetch the water, and Edward discovered that the ball had entered the neck, above the collar-bone, and that the blood poured out of the man's mouth, who was choking with the effusion. Although ignorant of surgery, Edward thought that such a wound must be mortal; but the man was not only alive but sensible, and although he could not utter a word, he spoke with his eyes and with signs. He raised his hand and pointed to himself first, and shook his head, as if to say that it was all over with him; and then he turned round his head, as if looking for the lad, who was now returning with the water. When the lad again knelt by his side, weeping bitterly, the man pointed to him, and gave such an imploring look that Edward immediately comprehended what he wished; it was to ask protection for the boy. It could not be misunderstood, and could Edward do otherwise than promise it to the dying man? His generous nature could not refuse it, and he said, "I understand you; you wish me to take care of your boy when you are gone. Is it not so?"

The man signified assent.

"I promise you I will do so. I will take him into my own family, and he shall share with us."

The man raised his hand again, and a gleam of joy passed over his features as he took the hand of the lad and put it into that of Edward. His eyes were then fixed upon Edward, as if to scrutinise into his character by his features, while the former bathed his temples and washed the blood from his mouth with the water brought by the boy, who appeared in a state of grief so violent as to paralyse his senses. After a minute or two another effusion of blood choked the wounded man, who, after a short struggle, fell back dead.

"He is gone!" thought Edward, "and now what is to be done? I must first ascertain whether the two villains are dead or not." Edward took a light and examined the body of Ben, lying over the threshold of the door; the man was quite dead, the ball having entered his brain. He was proceeding round the outside of the cottage to examine the state of the other man, whom he had shot himself; but the wind nearly blew out the light, and he therefore returned to the chamber and placed it on the floor, near to where the boy lay insensible over the corpse of the man who had died in the arms of Edward; and then went out without a light, and with his gun, to the other side of the cottage, where the other robber had fallen. As he approached the man, a faint voice was heard to say:

"Ben, Ben! Some water, for the love of God! Ben, I'm done for!"

Edward, without giving an answer, went back to the room for the water, which he took round to the man, and put it to his lips; he felt that he was bound by humanity so to do to a dying man, scoundrel though he might be. It was still dark, but not so dark as it had previously been, for the late moon was just rising.

The man drank the water eagerly, and said, "Ben, I can speak now, but I shan't long." He then pulled the basin towards him again, and after he had drunk, he said in broken sentences, "I feel—that I am bleeding to death—inside." Then he paused. "You know the oak—struck by lightning—a mile north—of this. Oh! I'm going fast. Three yards from it south—I buried all my—money; it's yours. Oh, another drink!" The man again attempted to drink out of the basin proffered by Edward; but as he made the attempt he fell back with a groan.

Edward, perceiving that he was dead, returned to the cottage to look after the lad, who still remained prostrate and embracing the corpse in the chamber. Edward then reflected upon what had best be done. After a time he decided upon dragging away the body of the robber named Ben outside of the threshold, and then securing the door. This, with some trouble, he effected, and he then made fast the window that had been forced open behind. Before he removed the boy, who lay with his face buried on the corpse, and appeared to be in a state of insensibility, Edward examined the corpse as it lay. Although plainly dressed, yet it was evident that it was not the body of a rustic; the features were fair, and the beard was carefully cut; the hands were white, and the fingers long, and evidently had never been employed in labour. That the body was that of some superior person disguised as a rustic, was evident, and this was corroborated by the conversation which took place between the two robbers. "Alas!" thought Edward, "the family of Arnwood appear not to be the only people who are in disguise in this forest. That poor boy! He must not remain there." Edward looked round, and perceived that there was a bed in the adjoining room, the door of which was open; he lifted up the boy, and carried him, still insensible, into the room, and laid him on the bed. He then went for some more water, which he found and threw into his face, and poured a little into his mouth. Gradually the boy stirred, and recovered from his stupor, and then Edward held the water to his mouth, and made him drink some, which he did, and then, suddenly aroused to a recollection of what had passed, the boy gave a shriek of woe, and burst into a paroxysm of tears. This ended in convulsive sobbings and low moanings. Edward felt that he could do no more at present, and that it would be better if he was left for a time to give vent to his grief. Edward sat down on a stool by the side of the orphan, and remained for some time in deep and melancholy thought. "How strange," thought he at last, "it is, that I should feel so little as I do now, surrounded by death, compared to what I did when good old Jacob Armitage died! Then I felt it deeply, and there was an awe in death. Now I no longer dread it. Is it because I loved the good old man, and felt that I had lost a friend? No, that cannot be the cause; I may have felt more grief but not awe or dread. Or is it because that was the first time that I had seen death, and it is the first sight of death which occasions awe? Or is it because that every day I have fancied myself on the battle-field, with hundreds lying dead and wounded around me, in my dreamings? I know not. Poor old Jacob died peaceably in his bed, like a good Christian, and trusting, after a blameless life, to find mercy through his Saviour. Two of these who are now dead, out of the three, have been summoned away in the height of their wickedness, and in the very commission of crime; the third has been foully murdered; and out of three lying dead, one has fallen by my own hand, and yet I feel not so much as when I attended the couch, and listened to the parting words of a dying Christian! I cannot account for it, or reason why; I only know that it is so, and I now look upon death unconcerned. Well, this is a kind of preparation for the wholesale murder and horrors of the battle-field, which I have so long sighed for—God forgive me if I am wrong! And this poor boy! I have promised to protect him, and I will. Could I fail my promise, I should imagine the spirit of his father (as I presume he was) looking down and upbraiding me. No, no, I will protect him. I and my brother and sisters have been preserved and protected, and I were indeed vile if I did not do to others as I have been done by. And now let me reflect what is to be done. I must not take the boy away, and bury the bodies; this person has friends at Lymington, and they will come here. The murder has taken place in the forest: then I must let the Intendant know what has occurred. I will send over to Oswald; Humphrey shall go. Poor fellow! What a state of anxiety must he and my little sisters be in at my not returning home! I had quite forgotten that; but it cannot be helped. I will wait till sunrise, and then see if the boy will be more himself, and probably from him I shall be able to find out what part of the forest I am in."

Edward took up the candle and went into the room in which he had laid the boy on the bed. He found him in a sound sleep. "Poor fellow," said Edward, "he has for a time forgotten his misery. What a beautiful boy he is! I long to know his history. Sleep on, my poor fellow! It will do you service."

Edward then returned to the other room, and recollected, or rather was reminded, that he had had no supper, and it was now nearly dawn of day. He looked into a cupboard and found plenty of provisions and some flasks of wine. "I have earned my supper," thought he, "and I will not, therefore, deny myself." So he brought out the viands and a flask of wine, and made a hearty meal. "It is long since I have tasted wine," thought he, "and it may be long ere I drink it again. I have little relish for it now; it is too fiery to the palate. I recollect, when a child, how my father used to have me at the table, and give me a stoup of claret, which I could hardly lift to my lips, to drink to the health of the king." The memory of the king raised other thoughts in Edward's mind, and he again sank into one of his reveries, which lasted till he fell into a slumber. When he woke up, it was at the voice of the boy, who in his sleep had cried out "Father!" Edward started up, and found that the sun was an hour high, and that he must have slept some time. He gently opened the cottage-door, looked at the bodies of the two men, and then walked out to survey the locality of the cottage, which he had but faintly made out during the night. He found that it was surrounded by a thicket of trees and underwood, so close and thick that there appeared to him no outlet in any direction. "What a place for concealment!" thought Edward, "but still these prowling thieves discovered it. Why, troops of horse might scour the forest for months, and never discover such a hiding-place." Edward walked round by the side of the thicket, to find out the track by which the robbers had entered when he followed them, and at last succeeded in doing so. He followed the path through the thicket until he was clear of it and again in the forest, but the scenery outside was unknown to him, and he had not an idea as to what part of the forest it was in. "I must question the boy," thought Edward. "I will go back and wake him up, for it is time that I was moving." As he was again turning into the thicket he heard a dog giving tongue, as if on a scent. It came nearer and nearer to him, and Edward remained to see what it might be. In a moment more he perceived his own dog, Smoker, come bounding out of a neighbouring copse, followed by Humphrey and Pablo. Edward hallooed. Smoker sprang towards him, leaping up, and loading him with caresses, and in another moment he was in Humphrey's arms.

"Oh, Edward, let me first thank God!" said Humphrey, as the tears started and rolled down his cheeks. "What a night we have passed! What has happened? That dear fellow Pablo thought of putting Smoker on the scent; he brought out your jacket and showed it to Smoker, and gave it him to smell, and then led him along till he was on your footsteps; and the dog followed him, it seems, although it has been round and round in every direction, till at last he has brought us to you."

Edward shook hands with Pablo, and thanked him. "How far are we from the cottage, Humphrey?"

"About eight miles, I should say, Edward; not more."

"Well, I have much to tell you, and I must tell it to you in few words before I go farther, and afterwards I will tell you all in detail."

Edward then gave a succinct narration of what had occurred, and, having thus prepared Humphrey and Pablo for what they were to see, led the way back through the thicket to the cottage inside of it. Humphrey and Pablo were much shocked at the scene of slaughter which presented itself to their eyes; and, after having viewed the bodies, they began to consult what had best be done.

The proposal of Edward, that Humphrey should go over and make known the circumstances to Oswald, that they might be communicated to the Intendant, was readily acceded to; and Pablo, it was agreed, should go home and tell Alice and Edith that Edward was safe.

"But now, Humphrey, about this boy; we cannot leave him here."

"Where is he?"

"He still sleeps, I believe. The question is, whether you should ride over with the pony or walk, and leave Pablo to return with the pony and cart; for I will not take the boy away or leave the house myself without removing the property which belongs to the boy, and of which I will make inquiry when he wakes. Besides, there is money, by what the robbers stated, which of course must be taken care of for him."

"I think it will be best for me to walk over, Edward. If I ride, I should arrive too late in the afternoon for anything to be done till next morning, and if I walk, I shall be in time enough, so that is settled. Besides, it will give you more time to remove the boy's property, which, as his father was in all probability a Malignant, and a denounced man, they might think right to secure for the government."

"Very true; then be it so. Do you start for the Intendant's; and Pablo, go home and fetch the pony and cart, while I remain here with the boy, and get everything ready."

Humphrey and Pablo both set off, and then Edward went to waken the boy, still lying on the bed.

"Come, you must get up now. You know that what's done cannot be undone; and if you are a good boy, and have read the Bible, you must know that we must submit to the will of God, who is our kind Father in heaven."

"Ah me!" said the boy, who was awake when Edward went to him, "I know well it is my duty, but it is a hard duty, and I am heart-broken. I have lost my father, the only friend I had in the world: who is there to love and to cherish me now? What will become of me?"

"I promised your father, before he died, that I would take care of you, my poor fellow; and a promise is sacred with me, even if it were not made to a dying man. I will do my best, depend upon it, for I have known myself what it is to want and to find a protector. You shall live with me and my brother and sisters, and you shall have all we have."

"Have you sisters, then?" replied the boy.

"Yes; I have sent for the cart to take you away from this, and to-night you shall be in our cottage; but now tell me—I do not ask who your father was, or why he was living here in secret, as I found it out by what I overheard the robbers say to one another—but how long have you lived here?"

"More than a year."

"Whose cottage is it?"

"My father bought it when he came, as he thought it safer so, that he might not be discovered or betrayed; for he had escaped from prison after having been condemned to death by the Parliament."

"Then he was a loyal man to his king?"

"Yes he was, and that was his only crime."

"Then fear not, my good boy; we are all loyal as well as he was, and will never be otherwise. I tell you this that you may safely trust to us. Now, if the cottage was his, the furniture and property were his also."

"Yes; all was his."

"And it is now yours, is it not?"

"I suppose so," said the boy, bursting into tears.

"Then listen to me;—your father is safe from all persecution now; he is, I trust, in heaven; and you they cannot touch, as you have done nothing to offend them; but still they will take possession of your father's property as soon as they know of his death, and find out who he was. This, for your sake, I wish to prevent them from doing, and have therefore sent for the cart, that I may remove to my cottage everything that is of value, that it may be held for your benefit; some day or another you may require it. The murder having been committed in the forest, and I having been a witness, and, moreover, having shot one of the robbers, I have considered it right to send over to the Intendant of the forest to give him notice of what has taken place within his jurisdiction. I do not think he is so bad a man as the rest; but still, when he comes here, he may consider it his duty to take possession of everything for the Parliament, as I have no doubt such are his orders, or will be when he communicates with the Parliament. Now this is a robbery which I wish to prevent, by carrying away your property before they come over, which they will to-morrow, and I propose that you shall accompany me, with all that you can take away, or that may be useful, this evening."

"You are very kind," replied the boy. "I will do all you wish; but I feel very weak, and very unwell."

"You must exert yourself for your own sake, my poor fellow. Come, now, sit up and put all your own clothes together. Collect everything in this room, while I look about the house. And tell me, had not your father some money? For the robbers said that they saw him counting it out of a sack, through the chinks of the shutters, and that was why they made the attack."

"Hateful money!" cried the boy. "Yes, he had, I believe, a great deal of money; but I cannot say how much."

"Now get up, and do as I request, my dear boy," said Edward, raising him up in his arms; "when your grief is lessened, you may have many happy days yet in store for you; you have a Father in heaven that you must put your trust in, and with Him you will find peace."

The boy rose up, and Edward closed the door of the chamber, that he might not see his father's corpse.

"I do put my trust in Heaven, good sir," replied the boy, "for it has already sent me a kind friend in my distress. You are good, I am sure; I see that in your face. Alas! How much more wretched would have been my condition if you had not fortunately come to our assistance! Too late, indeed, to save my poor father, but not too late to succour and console his child. I will go away with you, for I cannot stay here."

Chapter Sixteen.

Edward then took the counterpane off the bed, and went with it into the next room. He gently drew the body to the corner of the room, and covered it up with the counterpane, and then proceeded to examine the cupboards, etcetera. In one he found a good store of books, in another there was linen of all sorts, a great many curious arms, two suits of bright armour such as worn in those times, pistols and guns, and ammunition. On the floor of one of the cupboards was an iron chest about two feet by eighteen inches. It was locked. Edward immediately concluded that this chest held the money of the unfortunate man; but where was the key? Most likely about his person. He did not like to afflict the poor boy by putting the question to him, but he went to the body and examined the pockets of the clothes; he found a bunch of several keys, which he took, and then replaced the coverlid. He tried one of the keys, which appeared to be of the right size, to the lock of the iron chest, and found that it fitted it. Satisfied with this, he did not raise the lid of the chest, but dragged it out into the centre of the room. There were many things of value about the room; the candlesticks were silver, and there were goblets of the same metal. Edward collected all these articles, and a timepiece, and put them into a basket, of which there were two large ones at the end of the room, apparently used for holding firewood. Everything that he thought could be useful, or of value, he gathered together for the benefit of the poor orphan boy. He afterwards went into another small room, where he found sundry small trunks and cases locked-up. These he brought out without examining, as he presumed that they contained what was of value, or they would not be locked. When he had collected everything, he found that he had already more than the cart could carry in one trip; and he wanted to take some bedding with him, as he had not a spare bed in the cottage to give to the boy. Edward decided in his own mind that he would take the most valuable articles away that night, and return with the cart for the remainder early on the following morning. It was now past noon, and Edward took out of the cupboard what victuals were left, and then went into the chamber where the boy was, and begged that he would eat something. The poor boy said that he had no appetite; but Edward insisted, and at last prevailed upon him to eat some bread and drink a glass of wine, which proved of great service to him. The poor fellow shuddered as he saw the body covered up in the corner of the room, but said nothing. Edward was trying to make him eat a little more, when Pablo made his appearance at the door.

"Have you put up all that you want in the bed-chamber?" said Edward.

"Yes, I have put up everything."

"Then we will bring them out. Come, Pablo, you must help us."

Pablo made signs, and pointed to the door. Edward went out.

"First pull body away from this."

"Yes," replied Edward; "we must do so."

Edward and Pablo pulled the body of the robber on one side of the doorway, and threw over it some dried fern which lay by; they then backed the cart down to the door; the iron chest was first got in, then all the heavy articles, such as armour, guns, and books, etcetera, and by that time the cart was more than half-loaded. Edward then went into the chamber, and brought out the packages the boy had made up, and put them all in the cart until it was loaded high up; they brought out some blankets, and laid over all, to keep things steady; and then Edward told the boy that all was ready, and that they had better go.

"Yes, I am willing," replied he, with streaming eyes; "but let me see him once more."

"Come, then," said Edward, leading him to the corpse, and uncovering the face.

The boy knelt down, kissed the forehead and cold lips, covered up the face again, and then rose and wept bitterly on Edward's shoulder. Edward did not attempt to check his sorrow; he thought it better it should have vent; but, after a time, he led the boy by degrees till they were out of the cottage.

"Now, then," said Edward, "we must go, or we shall be late. My poor little sisters have been dreadfully alarmed at my not having come home last night, and I long to clasp them in my arms."

"Indeed you must," replied the boy, wiping away his tears, "and I am very selfish; let us go on."

"No room for cart to get through wood," said Pablo; "hard work, cart empty—more hard work, cart full."

And so it proved to be; and it required all the united efforts of Billy, Edward, and Pablo, to force a passage for the cart through the narrow pathway; but at last it was effected, and then they went on at a quick pace, and in less than two hours the cottage was in sight. When within two hundred yards of it, Edith, who had been on the watch, came bounding out, flew into Edward's arms, and covered him with kisses.

"You naughty Edward, to frighten us so!"

"Look, Edith, I have brought you a nice little play-fellow. Welcome him, dearest."

Edith extended her hand as she looked into the boy's face.

"He is a pretty boy, Edward, much prettier than Pablo."

"No, Missy Edith," said Pablo; "Pablo more man than he."

"Yes, you may be more man, Pablo; but you are not pretty."

"And where is Alice?"

"She was getting supper ready, and I did not tell her that I saw you coming, because I wanted first kiss."

"You little jealous thing! But here comes Alice. Dear Alice, you have been very uneasy, but it was not my fault," said Edward, kissing her. "If I had not been where I was this poor boy would have been killed as well as his father. Make him welcome, Alice, for he is an orphan now, and must live with us. I have brought many things in the cart, and to-morrow we will bring more, for we have no bed for him, and to-night he must sleep with me."

"We will make him as happy as we can, Edward; and we will be sisters to him," said Alice, looking at the boy, who was blushing deeply. "How old are you? And what is your name?"

"I am thirteen years old next January," replied the boy.

"And your Christian name?"

"I will tell you by and by," replied he, confused.

They arrived at the cottage, and Edward and Pablo were busy unpacking the cart, and putting all the contents into the inner chamber, where Pablo now slept, when Alice, who, with Edith, had been talking to the boy, came to Edward and said—"Edward, she's a girl!"

"A girl!" replied Edward, astonished.

"Yes, she has told me so, and wished me to tell you."

"But why does she wear boys' clothes?"

"It was her father's wish, as he was very often obliged to send her to Lymington to a friend's house, and he was afraid of her getting into trouble; but she has not told me her story as yet—she says that she will to-night."

"Well, then," replied Edward, "you must make up a bed for her in your room to-night. Take Pablo's bed, and he shall sleep with me. To-morrow morning I will bring some more bedding from her cottage."

"How Humphrey will be surprised when he comes back!" said Alice, laughing.

"Yes; she will make a nice little wife for him some years hence; and she may prove an heiress perhaps, for there is an iron chest with money in it."

Alice returned to her new companion, and Edward and Pablo continued to unload the cart.

"Well, Pablo, I suppose you will allow that, now that you know she is a girl, she is handsomer than you?"

"Oh yes," replied Pablo, "very handsome girl; but too much girl for handsome boy."

At last everything was out of the cart, the iron chest dragged into Pablo's room, and Billy put into his stable and given his supper, which he had well earned, for the cart had been very heavily loaded. They then all sat down to supper, Edward saying to their new acquaintance—

"So I find that I am to have another sister instead of another brother. Now you will tell me your name?"

"Yes; Clara is my name."

"And why did you not tell me that you are a girl?"

"I did not like, because I was in boys' clothes, and felt ashamed; indeed I was too unhappy to think about what I was. My poor dear father!" and she burst into tears.

Alice and Edith kissed her and consoled her, and she became calm again. After supper was over they busied themselves making arrangements for her sleeping in their room, and then they went to prayers.

"We have much to be thankful for, my dears," said Edward. "I am sure I feel that I have been in great danger, and I only wish that I had been more useful than I have been; but it has been the will of God, and we must not arraign His decrees. Let us return thanks for His great mercies, and bow in submission to His dispensations, and pray that He will give peace to poor little Clara, and soften her affliction."

And as Edward prayed, little Clara knelt and sobbed, while Alice caressed her with her arm round her waist, and at times stopped her prayer to kiss and console her. When they had finished, Alice led her away to her bedroom, followed by Edith, and they put her to bed. Edward and Pablo also retired, both worn out by the fatigue and excitement of the day.

They were up on the following morning at day-dawn, and, putting Billy in the cart, set off for the cottage of Clara. They found everything as they had left it, and, having loaded the cart with what had been left behind the day before, the bedding for two beds, with several articles of furniture which Edward thought might be useful, there being still a little room left, Edward packed up in a wooden case with dried fern all the wine that was in the cupboard; and, having assisted Pablo in forcing the cart once more through the path in the wood, he left him to return home with the cart, while he remained to wait the arrival of Humphrey, and whoever might come with him from the Intendant's. About ten o'clock, as he was watching outside of the wood, he perceived several people approaching him, and soon made out that Humphrey, the Intendant, and Oswald were among the number. When they came up to him Edward saluted the Intendant in a respectful manner, shook hands with Oswald, and then led the way by the narrow path through the wood to the cottage. The Intendant was on horseback, but all the rest were on foot.

The Intendant left his horse to the care of one of the verderers, and went through the wood on foot with the of the party, preceded by Edward. He appeared to be very grave and thoughtful, and Edward thought that there was a coolness in his manner towards himself,—for it must be recollected that Mr Heatherstone had not seen Edward since he had rendered him such service in saving the life of his daughter. The consequence was, that Edward felt somewhat indignant, but he did not express his feelings, by his looks even, but conveyed the party in silence to the cottage. On their arrival, Edward pointed to the body of the robber, which had been covered with fern, and the verderers exposed it.

"By whose hand did that man fall?" said the Intendant.

"By the hand of the party who lived in the cottage."

Edward then led the way round to the back of the cottage where the other robber lay—

"And this man was slain by my hand," replied Edward.

"We have one more body to see," continued Edward, leading the way into the cottage and uncovering the corpse of Clara's father.

Mr Heatherstone looked at the face and appeared much moved—"Cover it up," said he, turning away; and then sitting down on a chair close to the table—

"And how was this found?" he said.

"I neither saw this person killed nor the robber you first saw, but I heard the report of the firearms at almost the same moment, and I presume that they fell by each other's hands."

The Intendant called his clerk, who had accompanied him, and desired him to get ready his writing materials, and then said—

"Edward Armitage, we will now take down your deposition as to what has occurred."

Edward then commenced by stating "that he was out in the forest and had lost his way, and was seeking his way home—"

"You were out in the forest during the night?"

"Yes, sir, I was."

"With your gun?"

"I always carry my gun," replied Edward.

"In pursuit of game?"

"No, sir, I was not. I have never been out in pursuit of game during night-time in my life."

"What were you then about? You did not go out for nothing?"

"I went out to commune with my own thoughts: I was restless, and I wandered about without knowing where I went, and that is the reason why I lost my way."

"And pray what may have excited you?"

"I will tell you: I was over with Oswald Partridge the day before; you had just arrived from London, and he gave me the news that King Charles had been proclaimed in Scotland, and that news unsettled me."

"Well, proceed."

Edward met with no more interruption in his narrative. He stated briefly all that had taken place, from the time he fell in with the robbers till the winding up of the catastrophe.

The clerk took down all that Edward had stated, and then read it over to him, to ascertain if he had written it down correctly, and then inquired of Edward if he could read and write.

"I should hope so," replied Edward, taking the pen and signing his name.

The clerk stared, and then said, "People in your condition do not often know how to read and write, Mr Forester, and therefore you need not be offended at the question."

"Very true," replied Edward. "May I ask if my presence is considered any longer to be necessary?"

"You stated that there was a boy in the house, young man," said the Intendant: "what has become of him?"

"He is removed to my cottage."

"Why did you do so?"

"Because when his father died I promised to him that I would take care of his child; and I intend to keep my word."

"You had spoken with him, then, before he died?" said the Intendant.

"Not so; it was all carried on by signs on his part, but it was as intelligible as if he spoke, and what I replied he well understood; and I really think I removed a great anxiety off his mind by giving him the promise."

The Intendant paused, and then said, "I perceive that some articles have been removed—the bedding, for instance—have you taken anything away?"

"I have removed bedding, for I had no bed to offer to the lad, and he told me that the cottage and furniture belonged to his father; of course by his father's death it became his, and I felt that I was warranted in so doing."

"May I ask, did you remove any papers?"

"I cannot tell; the lad packed up his own things; there were some boxes removed, which were locked-up, and the contents are to me wholly unknown. I could not leave the boy here in this scene of death, and I could not well leave the property belonging to him to be at the mercy of any other plunderers of the forest. I did as I considered right for the benefit of the boy, and in accordance with the solemn promise which I made to his father."

"Still the property should not have been removed. The party who now lies dead there is a well-known Malignant."

"How do you know that, sir?" interrupted Edward; "did you recognise him when you saw the body?"

"I did not say that I did," replied the Intendant.

"You either must have so done, sir," replied Edward, "or you must have been aware that he was residing in this cottage: you have to choose between."

"You are bold, young man," replied the Intendant, "and I will reply to your observation. I did recognise the party when I saw his face, and I knew him to be one who was condemned to death, and who escaped from prison a few days before the one appointed for his execution. I heard search had been made for him, but in vain, and it was supposed that he had escaped beyond the seas. Now his papers may be the means of giving the Parliament information against others as well as himself."

"And enable them to commit a few more murders," added Edward.

"Silence, young man; the authorities must not be spoken of in so irreverent a manner. Are you aware that your language is treasonable?"

"According to Act of Parliament, as at present constituted, it may be," replied Edward; "but as a loyal subject of King Charles the Second, I deny it."

"I have no concern with your loyalty, young man, but I will not admit any language to be uttered in my presence against the ruling powers. The inquest is over. Let every one leave the house except Edward Armitage, to whom I would speak alone."

"Excuse me one moment, sir," said Edward, "and I will return."

Edward went out with the rest, and calling Humphrey aside, said to him, "Contrive to slip away unperceived; here are the keys; haste to the cottage as fast as you can; look for all the papers you can find in the packages taken there; bury them and the iron chest in the garden, or anywhere where they cannot be discovered."

Humphrey nodded, and turned away, and Edward re-entered the cottage.

He found the Intendant was standing over the corpse; he had removed the coverlid, and was looking mournfully down on the face disfigured with blood. Perceiving the entrance of Edward, he again took his seat at the table, and after a pause said—

"Edward Armitage, that you have been brought up very superior to your station in life is certain; and that you are loyal, bold, and resolute, is equally so; you have put me under an obligation which I never can repay, even if you allowed me to exert myself in your behalf. I take this opportunity of acknowledging it; and now allow me to say that for these times you are much too frank and impetuous. This is no time for people to give vent to their feelings and opinions. Even I am as much surrounded with spies as others, and am obliged to behave myself accordingly. Your avowed attachment to the king's cause has prevented me from showing that more than cordiality that I really feel for you, and to which you are in every way entitled."

"I cannot conceal my opinions, sir; I was brought up in the house of a loyal cavalier, and never will be otherwise."

"Granted—why should you be? But do you not yourself see that you do the cause more harm than good by thus avowing your opinions when such avowal is useless? If any other man in the county, who is of your opinion, was to express himself, now that your cause is hopeless, as you have done, the prisons would be crowded, the executions would be daily, and the cause would be in proportion weakened by the loss of the most daring. 'Bide your time' is a good motto, and I recommend it to you. You must feel that, however we may be at variance in our opinions, Edward Armitage, my hand and my authority never can be used against one to whom I am so indebted; and feeling this, you compel me in the presence of others to use a harshness and coldness towards you, contrary—wholly contrary—to what, you may believe me when I say it, I really feel for one who so nobly rescued my only child."

"I thank you, sir, for your advice, which I feel to be good, and for your good opinion, which I value."

"And which I feel that you deserve; and you shall have, young as you are, my confidence, which I know you will not abuse. I did know this man who now lies dead before us, and I did also know that he was concealed in this cottage: Major Ratcliffe was one of my earliest and dearest friends, and until this unhappy civil war, there never was any difference between us, and even afterwards only in politics, and the cause we each espoused. I knew, before I came down here as Intendant, where his place of concealment was, and have been most anxious for his safety."

"Excuse me, Mr Heatherstone, but each day I find more to make me like you than I did the day before: at first I felt most inimical; now I only wonder how you can be leagued with the party you now are."

"Edward Armitage, I will now answer for myself and thousands more. You are too young a man to have known the cause of the insurrection, or rather opposition to the unfortunate King Charles. He attempted to make himself absolute, and to wrest the liberties from the people of England; that his warmest adherents will admit. When I joined the party which opposed him, I little thought that matters would have been carried so far as they have been; I always considered it lawful to take up arms in defence of our liberties, but at the same time I equally felt that the person of the king was sacred."

"I have heard so, sir."

"Yes, and in truth; for never did any people strive more zealously to prevent the murder of the king—for murder it was—than my relative Ashley Cooper and myself. So much so, indeed, as to have incurred not only the suspicion but the ill-will of Cromwell, who, I fear, is now making rapid advances towards that absolute authority for which the king has suffered, and which he would now vest in his own person. I considered that our cause was just; and, had the power been left in the hands of those who would have exercised it with discretion and moderation, the king would even now have been on the throne, and the liberties of his subjects sacred; but it is easier to put a vast and powerful engine into motion than to stop it; and such has been the case in this unfortunate civil war. Thousands who took an active part against the king will, when the opportunity is ripe, retrace their steps; but I expect that we have much to suffer before that time will come. And now, Edward Armitage, I have said more to you than I have to any person breathing, except my own kinsman."

"I thank you for your confidence, sir, which not only will not be betrayed, but will act as a warning to guide my future conduct."

"I meant it should. Be no longer rash and careless in avowing your opinions. You can do no good to the cause, and may do yourself much harm. And now I must ask you another question, which I could not before the other people. You have surprised me by stating that Major Ratcliffe had a son here: there must be some mistake, or the boy must be an impostor. He had a daughter, an only daughter, as I have; but he never had a son."

"It is a mistake that I fell into, sir, by finding a boy here, as I stated to you at the inquest; and I considered it to be a boy until I brought her home, and she then discovered to my sisters that she was a girl dressed in boys' clothes. I did not give that as explanation at the inquest, as it was not necessary."

"I am right, then. I must relieve you of that charge, Edward Armitage; she shall be to me as a daughter, and I trust that you will agree with me, without any disparagement to your feelings, that my house will be a more fit residence for her than your cottage."

"I will not prevent her going, if she wishes it, after your explanation and confidence, Mr Heatherstone."

"One thing more. As I said to you before, Edward Armitage, I believe many of these verderers, all of whom have been selected from the army, are spies upon me: I must therefore be careful. You said that you were not aware that there were any papers?"

"I saw none, sir; but I suspect, from the many locked-up trunks and small boxes, that there may be; but when I went out with the others from the inquest, I despatched my brother Humphrey to the cottage, advising him to open all the locks and to remove any papers which he might find."

The Intendant smiled.

"Well, if such is the case, we have only to go to your cottage and make an examination. We shall find nothing, and I shall have performed my duty. I was not aware that your brother was here. I presume it was the young man who walked with Oswald Partridge."

"It was, sir."

"By his appearance, I presume that he also was brought up at Arnwood?"

"He was, sir, as well as I," replied Edward.

"Well, then, I have but one word more to say,—recollect, if I appear harsh and severe in the presence of others, it is only assumed towards you, and not real. You understand that?"

"I do, sir, and beg you will exercise your discretion."

The Intendant then went out and said to the party, "It appears from what I can extract from this lad Armitage, that there are boxes which he removed to his cottage; we will go there to see what they may contain. It is now noon. Have you any refreshment to offer us in your cottage, young man, when we arrive?"

"I keep no hostelrie, sir," replied Edward, somewhat gloomily; "my own labour, and my brother's, is sufficient for the support of my own family, but no more."

"Let us move on; and two of you keep your eye upon that young man," said the Intendant aside.

They then proceeded through the wood; the Intendant mounted his horse, and they set off for the cottage, where they arrived at about two o'clock in the afternoon.

Chapter Seventeen.

Humphrey came out as soon as he perceived the Intendant and his party approaching, and whispered to Edward that all was safe. The Intendant dismounted, and ordering everybody but his clerk to wait outside, was ushered into the cottage by Edward. Alice, Edith, and Pablo were in the room; the two girls were not a little flushed and frightened by the unusual appearance of so large a body of strangers.

"These are my sisters, sir," said Edward. "Where is Clara, Alice?"

"She is alarmed, and has gone into our bedroom."

"I hope you are not alarmed at my presence," said the Intendant, looking earnestly at the two girls. "It is my duty which obliges me to pay this visit; but you have nothing to fear. Now, Edward Armitage, you must produce all the boxes and packages which you took from the cottage."

"I will, sir," replied Edward, "and here are the keys. Humphrey, do you and Pablo bring them out."

The boxes were brought out, opened, and examined by the Intendant and his clerk, but of course no papers were found in them.

"I must now send in two of my people to search the house," said the Intendant. "Had you not better go to the little girl, that she may not be frightened?"

"I will go to her," said Alice.

Two of the people, assisted by the clerk, then searched the house; they found nothing worthy of notice, except the weapons and armour which Edward had removed, and which he stated to the Intendant that he took away as valuable property belonging to the little girl.

"It is sufficient," said the Intendant to his clerk—"undoubtedly there are no papers; but I must, before I go, interrogate this child, who has been removed thus; but she will be frightened, and I shall obtain no answer from her if we are so many, so let everybody leave the cottage while I speak to her."

The clerk and the others left the cottage, and the Intendant desired Edward to bring Clara from the bedroom. She came out, accompanied by and indeed clinging to Alice, for she was much alarmed.

"Come here, Clara," said the Intendant gently; "you do not know perhaps that I am your sincere friend; and now that your father is dead, I want you to come and live with my daughter, who will be delighted to have you as a companion. Will you go with me? And I will take care of you and be a father to you."

"I do not like to leave Alice and Edith; they treat me so kindly, and call me sister," replied Clara, sobbing.

"I am sure they do, and you must be fond of them already; but still it is your duty to come with me; and if your father could speak to you now he would tell you so. I will not force you away, but remember, you are born a lady, and must be brought up and educated as a lady, which cannot be the case in this cottage, although they are very kind to you, and very nice young people. You do not recollect me, Clara, but you have often sat on my knee when you were a little girl, and when your father lived in Dorsetshire. You recollect the great walnut-tree by the sitting-room window, which looked out in the garden, don't you?"

"Yes," replied Clara, with surprise.

"Yes, so do I too, and how you used to sit on my knee; and do you remember Jason, the big mastiff, and how you used to ride upon his back?"

"Yes," replied Clara, "I do; but he died a long while ago."

"He did, when you were not more than six years old. And now tell me, where did the old gardener bury him?"

"Under the mulberry-tree," replied Clara.

"Yes, so he did, and I was there when poor Jason was buried. You don't recollect me. But I will take off my hat, for I did not wear the same dress that I do now. Now look, Clara, and see if you remember me."

Clara, who was no longer alarmed, looked on the Intendant's face, and then said, "You called my father Philip, and he used to call you Charles."

"You are right, my sweet one," replied the Intendant pressing Clara to his bosom; "I did so, and we were great friends. Now, will you come with me? And I have a little girl, older than you by three or four years, who will be your companion and love you dearly."

"May I come and see Alice and Edith sometimes?"

"Yes, you shall; and she will come with you and make their acquaintance, if their brother will permit it. I will not take you away now, dearest; you shall remain here for a few days, and then we will come over and fetch you. I will send Oswald Partridge over to let you know the day, Edward Armitage, when we will come for her. Good-bye, dear Clara, and good-bye, my little girls. Humphrey Armitage, good-bye. Who is this lad you have there?"

"He is a gipsy whom Humphrey trapped in his pit-fall, sir, and we have soon tamed him," replied Edward.

"Well, then, Edward Armitage, good-bye," said the Intendant, extending his hand to him; "we must meet soon again."

The Intendant then went out of the cottage, and joined his people outside. Edward went out after him; and as the Intendant mounted his horse, he said very coldly to Edward, "I shall keep a sharp look-out on your proceedings, sir, depend upon it; I tell you so decidedly, so fare you well."

With these words the Intendant put the spurs to his horse, and rode away.

"What made him speak so sharply to you, Edward?" said Humphrey.

"Because he means kindly, but does not want other people to know it," replied Edward. "Come in, Humphrey; I have much to tell you and much to surprise you with."

"I have been surprised already," replied Humphrey. "How did this Roundhead know Clara's father so well?"

"I will explain all before we go to bed," replied Edward; "let us go in now."

The two brothers had a long conversation that evening, in which Edward made Humphrey acquainted with all that had passed between him and the Intendant.

"It's my opinion, Edward," said Humphrey, "that he thinks matters have been carried too far, and that he is sorry that he belongs to the Parliamentary party. He finds out, now that it is too late, that he has allied himself with those who have very different feelings and motives than his own, and has assisted to put power into the hands of those who have not the scruples which he has."

"Yes; and in ridding themselves of one tyranny, as they considered it, they have every prospect of falling into the hands of a greater tyrant than before; for, depend upon it, Cromwell will assume the sovereign power, and rule this kingdom with a rod of iron."

"Well, many more are, I have no doubt, or soon will be, of his opinion; and the time will come, be it sooner or later, when the king will have his own again. They have proclaimed him in Scotland already. Why does he not come over and show himself? His presence would, I think, induce thousands to flock to him,—I'm sure that it would me."

"I am very glad of this good intelligence with the Intendant, Edward, as it will not now be necessary for us to be so careful; we may go and come when we please. I almost wish you could be persuaded to accept any eligible offer he may make you. Many no doubt are in office, and serving the present government, who have the same feelings as the Intendant, or even feelings as strong as your own."

"I cannot bear the idea of accepting anything from them or their instruments, Humphrey; nor, indeed, could I leave my sisters."

"On that score you may make your mind easy;—Pablo and I are quite sufficient for the farm, or anything else we may want to do. If you can be more useful elsewhere, have no scruple in leaving us. If the king was to come over and raise an army, you would leave us, of course; and I see no reason why, if an eligible offer is made you, you should not do it now. You and your talents are thrown away in this forest, and you might serve the king and the king's cause better by going into the world and watching the times than you ever can by killing his venison."

"Certainly," replied Edward, laughing, "I do not much help his cause by killing his deer, that must be admitted; all I shall say is this,—if anything is offered to me which I can accept without injury to my feelings and my honour, I shall not decline it, provided that I may, by accepting it, prove of service to the king's cause."

"That is all I wish, Edward. And now I think we had better go to bed."

The next day they dug up the iron chest and the box into which Humphrey had put all the papers he had collected together. Edward opened the iron chest, and found in it a considerable quantity of gold in bags, and many trinkets and jewels which he did not know the value of. The papers he did not open, but resolved that they should be given to the Intendant, for Edward felt that he could trust in him. The other boxes and trunks were also opened and examined, and many other articles of apparent value discovered.

"I should think all these jewels worth a great deal of money, Humphrey," said Edward; "if so, all the better for poor little Clara. I am sorry to part with her, although we have known her so short a time; she appears to be such an amiable and affectionate child."

"That she is; and certainly the handsomest little girl I ever saw. What beautiful eyes! Do you know that on one of her journeys to Lymington she was very nearly taken by a party of gipsies? And by what Pablo can make out, it would appear that it was by the party which he belonged to."

"I wonder at her father's permitting her to go alone such a distance."

"Her father could not do otherwise. Necessity has no law. He could trust no other person, so he put her in boy's clothes that there might be less risk. Still, she must have been very intelligent to have done the office."

"She is thirteen years old, although she is small," replied Edward. "And intelligent she certainly is, as you may see by her countenance. Who would ever have imagined that our sisters would have been able to do what they are doing now? It's an old saying, 'We never know what we can do till we try.' By the bye, Humphrey, I met a famous herd of forest ponies the other day, and I said to myself, 'I wonder whether Humphrey will be clever enough to take one of them, as he has the wild cattle? For Billy is getting old, and we want a successor.'"

"We want more than a successor to Billy, Edward, we want two more to help him—and I have the means of maintaining two more ponies if I could catch them."

"I fear that you will never manage that, Humphrey," said Edward, laughing.

"I know well what you mean," replied Humphrey: "you wish to dare me to it—well, I won't be dared to anything, and I most certainly will try to catch a pony or two; but I must think about it first, and when I have arranged my plan in my mind I will then make the attempt."

"When I see the ponies in the yard I will believe it, Humphrey. They are as wild as deer and as fleet as the wind, and you cannot catch them in a pit-fall."

"I know that, good brother; but all I can say is, that I will try what I can do, and I can do no more—but not at present, for I am too busy."

Three days after this conversation Oswald Partridge made his appearance, having been sent by the Intendant to tell Edward that he should come over on the following day to take away little Clara.

"And how is she to go?" said Edward.

"He will bring a little nag for her, if she can ride—if she cannot, she must ride in the cart which will come for the baggage."

"Clara, can you ride a horse?"

"Yes," replied Clara, "if it does not jump about too much. I always rode one when I lived in Dorsetshire."

"This won't jump about, my little lady," said Oswald, "for he is thirty years old, I believe, and as steady as an old gentleman ought to be."

"I have had some conversation with Master Heatherstone," continued Oswald to Edward. "He is much pleased with you, I can tell you. He said, that in times like these he required young men like you about him; and that as you would not take the berth of verderer, he must find one better suited for you, for he said you were too good for such an office."

"Many thanks to him for his good opinion," replied Edward; "but I do not think that he has any office in his gift which I can accept."

"So I thought, but I said nothing. He again asked many questions relative to old Jacob Armitage, and he pressed me very hard. He said that Humphrey was as much above his position in appearance as you were; but as he was brought up at Arnwood he presumed that he had had the same advantages. And then he said—'But were his two sisters brought up at Arnwood also?' I replied that I believed not, although they were often there, and were allowed to play with the children of the house. He looked at me steadfastly, as if he would read my thoughts, and then went on writing. I cannot help thinking that he has a suspicion that you are not the grandchildren of old Jacob; but at the same time I do not think that he has an idea who you really are."

"You must keep our secret, Oswald," replied Edward. "I have a very good opinion of the Intendant, I acknowledge; but I will trust nobody."

"As I hope for future mercy, sir, I never will divulge it until you bid me," replied Oswald.

"I trust to you, Oswald, and so there's an end of the matter. But, tell me, Oswald, what do they say about his taking charge of this little girl?"

"Why, they did begin to talk about it; but when he gave out that it was the order of Parliament that the child should remain with him until further directions, of course they said nothing, for they dared not. It seems that the Ratcliffe property is sequestrated, but not yet granted to any one; and the Parliament will most likely, as soon as she is old enough, give her as a wife, with the property, to one of their party,—they have done it before now, as it secures the property under all changes."

"I perceive," replied Edward. "When did you hear that the little girl was to live with him?"

"Not till yesterday morning; and it was not till the evening that we knew it was the order of Parliament."

Edward did not think it right to tell Oswald what he knew, as it was a secret confided to him by the Intendant, and therefore merely observed, "I presumed that the child would not be left on our hands;" and then the conversation dropped.

As Oswald had informed them, the Intendant made his appearance in the forenoon of the following day, and was accompanied by his daughter, who rode by his side. A groom, on another horse, led a pony for Clara to ride; and a cart for the luggage followed at some distance. Edward went out to assist Miss Heatherstone to dismount, and she frankly extended her hand to him as she reached the ground. Edward was a little surprised as well as pleased at this condescension on her part towards a forester.

"You do me much honour, Mistress Patience," said he, bowing.

"I cannot forget that I owe my life to you, Master Armitage," replied Patience, "and I cannot be too grateful. May I request another favour of you?"

"Certainly, if it is in my power to do as you wish."

"It is this," said she, in a low voice: "that you will not hastily reject any overtures which may be made to you by my father; that is all. And now let me go in and see your sisters, for my father has praised them very much, and I wish to know them."

Edward led the way into the cottage, and Patience followed him, while the intendant was in conversation with Humphrey. Edward, having introduced his sisters and Clara, then went out to pay his respects to the Intendant, who, now they were alone, was very candid towards both him and Humphrey.

Edward then told the Intendant that there was an iron chest with a good deal of money in it, and jewels also, and many other articles of value in the other boxes.

"I fear, sir, that the cart will hardly hold all the goods."

"I do not intend to take away the heavy or more bulky articles, such as the bedding, armour, etc. I will only take Clara's own packages, and the valuables and papers. The remainder may stay here, as they can be of no use, till they are demanded from you. Where is Oswald Partridge?"

"In the stable with the horses, sir," replied Humphrey.

"Then, when the cart is loaded—and it had better be done by you while the men are in the stable—Oswald shall take charge of it, and take the things to my house."

"Here are the keys, sir," said Edward, presenting them.

"Good. And now, Edward Armitage, that we are alone, I want to have a little conversation with you. You are aware how much I feel indebted to you for the service you have rendered me, and how anxious I am to show my gratitude. You are born for better things than to remain an obscure forester, and perhaps a deer-stalker. I have now an offer to make to you, which I trust, upon reflection, you will not refuse—and I say reflection, because I do not wish you to give an answer till you have well reflected. I know that you will not accept anything under the present government, but a private situation you can raise no objection to; the more so as, so far from leaving your family, you will be more in a position to protect them. I am in want of a secretary, and I wish you to accept that office, to live entirely in my house, and to receive a handsome salary for your services, which will not, I trust, be too heavy. You will be near to your family here in the cottage, and be able to protect them and assist them; and what is more, you will mix with the world and know what is going on, as I am in the confidence of the government. Of course I put implicit confidence in you, or I would not offer the situation. But you will not be always down here: I have my correspondents and friends, to whom I shall have to send you occasionally on most trusty commissions. You, I am sure, will suit me in every respect, and I hope you will undertake the post which I now offer you. Give me no answer just now; consult with your brother, and give the offer due consideration, and when you have made up your mind you can let me know."

Edward bowed; and the Intendant went into the cottage.

Edward then assisted Humphrey and Pablo to get the iron chest on the cart, and covered it with the other packages and boxes, till the cart was well loaded. Leaving Pablo in charge till Oswald came from the stables, Edward and Humphrey then went into the cottage, where they found a very social party; Patience Heatherstone having succeeded in making great friends with the other three girls, and the Intendant, to Edward's surprise, laughing and joking with them. Alice and Edith had brought out some milk, biscuits, and all the fruit that was ripe, with some bread, a piece of cold salt beef, and a ham: and they were eating as well as talking.

"I have been praising your sisters' housekeeping, Armitage," said the Intendant. "Your farm appears to be very productive."

"Alice expected Miss Heatherstone, sir," replied Edward, "and made an unusual provision. You must not think that we live on such fare every day."

"No," replied the Intendant drily; "on other days I daresay you have other fare. I would almost make a bet that there is a pasty in the cupboard which you dare not show to the Intendant of the New Forest."

"You are mistaken, sir, for once," replied Humphrey. "Alice knows well how to make one, but she has not one just now."

"Well, I must believe you, Master Humphrey," replied the Intendant. "And now, my dear child, we must think of going, for it is a long ride, and the little girl is not used to a horse."

"Mistress Alice, many thanks for your hospitality; and now, farewell. Edith, good-bye, dear. Now, Clara, are you quite ready?"

They all went out of the cottage. The Intendant put Clara on the pony, after she had kissed Alice and Edith. Edward assisted Patience; and when she was mounted she said—

"I hope you will accept my father's offer—you will oblige me so much if you do."

"I will give it every consideration it deserves," replied Edward. "Indeed, it will depend more upon my brother than myself whether I accept it or not."

"Your brother is a very sensible young man, sir, therefore I have hopes," replied Patience.

"A quality which it appears you do not give me credit for, Miss Heatherstone."

"Not when pride or vindictive feelings obtain the mastery," replied she.

"Perhaps you will find that I am not quite so proud, or bear such ill-will, as I did when I first saw your father, Miss Heatherstone; and some allowance should be made, even if I did show such feelings, when you consider that I was brought up at Arnwood."

"True—most true, Master Armitage. I had no right to speak so boldly, especially to you, who risked your own life to save the daughter of one of those Roundheads who treated the family of your protector so cruelly. You must forgive me; and now, farewell!"

Edward bowed, and then turned to the Intendant, who had apparently been waiting while the conversation was going on. The Intendant bade him a cordial farewell; Edward shook Clara by the hand, and the cavalcade set off. They all remained outside of the cottage till the party were at some distance, and then Edward walked apart with Humphrey, to communicate to him the offer made by the Intendant, and ask his opinion.

"My opinion is made up, Edward; which is, that you should accept it immediately. You are under no obligation to the government, and you have already conferred such an obligation upon the Intendant that you have a right to expect a return. Why stay here, when you can safely mix with the world and know how things are going on? I do not require your assistance, now that I have Pablo, who is more useful every day. Do not lose such an opportunity of making a friend for yourself and all of us—a protector, I may say; and who is, by what he has confided to you, anything but approving of the conduct of the present government. He has paid you a deserved compliment by saying that he can and will trust you. You must not refuse the offer, Edward—it would really be folly if you did."

"I believe you are right, Humphrey; but I have been so accustomed to range the forest—I am so fond of the chase—I am so impatient of control or confinement, that I hardly know how to decide. A secretary's life is anything but pleasing to me, sitting at a table writing and reading all day long. The pen is but a poor exchange for the long-barrelled gun."

"It does more execution, nevertheless," replied Humphrey, "if what I have read is true. But you are not to suppose that your life will be such a sedentary one. Did he not say that he would have to trust you with missions of importance? Will you not, by going to London and other places, and mixing with people of importance, be preparing yourself for your proper station in life, which I trust that one day you will resume? And does it follow that because you are appointed a secretary you are not to go out in the forest and shoot a deer with Oswald, if you feel inclined—with this difference, that you may do it then without fear of being insulted or persecuted by such a wretch as that Corbould? Do not hesitate any longer, my dear brother; recollect that our sisters ought not to live this forest life as they advance in years—they were not born for it, although they have so well conformed to it. It depends upon you to release them eventually from their false position; and you can never have such an opening as is now offered you, by one whose gratitude alone will make him anxious to serve you."

"You are right, Humphrey, and I will accept the offer; I can but return to you if things do not go on well."

"I thank you sincerely for your decision, Edward," replied Humphrey. "What a sweet girl that Patience Heatherstone is!—I think I never saw such an enchanting smile!"

Edward thought of the smile she gave him when they parted but an hour ago, and agreed with Humphrey, but he replied—

"Why, brother, you are really in love with the Intendant's daughter."

"Not so, my dear fellow; but I am in love with her goodness and sweetness of disposition, and so are Alice and Edith, I can tell you. She has promised to come over and see them, and bring them flowers for their garden, and I hardly know what; and I am very glad of it, as my sisters have been buried here so long that they cannot but gain by her company now and then. No! I will leave Mistress Heatherstone for you; I am in love with little Clara."

"Not a bad choice, Humphrey: we both aspire high, for two young foresters, do we not? However, they say 'Every dog has his day,' and Cromwell and his parliament may have theirs. King Charles may be on his throne again now, long before—you catch a forest pony, Humphrey."

"I hope he will, Edward: but recollect how you laughed at the idea of my catching a cow—you may be surprised a second time. 'Where there is a will there is a way,' the saying is. But I must go and help Alice with the heifer; she is not very quiet yet, and I see her going out with her pail."

The brothers then parted, and Edward walked about, turning over in his mind the events of the day, and very often finding his thoughts broken in upon by sudden visions of Patience Heatherstone—and certainly the remembrance of her was to him the most satisfactory and pleasing portion of the prospect in his offered situation.

"I shall live with her, and be continually in her company," thought he. "Well, I would take a less pleasing office if only for that. She requested me to accept it to oblige her, and I will do so. How hasty we are in our conclusions! When I first saw her father, what an aversion I felt for him! Now, the more I know him, the more I like him, nay, more—respect him. He said that the king wished to be absolute, and wrest the liberties from his subjects, and that they were justified in opposing him; I never heard that when at Arnwood."

"If so, was it lawful so to do?"

"I think it was, but not to murder him; that I can never admit, nor does the Intendant: on the contrary, he holds his murderers in as great detestation as I do. Why, then, we do not think far apart from one another. At the commencement, the two parties were—those who supported him, not admitting that he was right, but too loyal to refuse to fight for their king—and those who opposed, hoping to force him to do right; the king for his supposed prerogatives, the people for their liberties. The king was obstinate, the people resolute, until virulent warfare inflamed both parties, and neither would listen to reason; and the people gained the upper hand, they wreaked their vengeance, instead of looking to the dictates of humanity and justice. How easy it had been to have deposed him, and have sent him beyond the seas! Instead of which they detained him a prisoner and then murdered him. The punishment was greater than the offence, and dictated by malice and revenge; it was a diabolical act, and will soil the page of our nation's history." So thought Edward, as he paced before the cottage, until he was summoned in by Pablo to their evening meal.

Chapter Eighteen.

"Edward," said Edith, "scold Pablo; he has been ill-treating my poor cat; he is a cruel boy." Pablo laughed. "See, Edward, he's laughing: put him in the pit-fall again, and let him stay there till he says he is sorry."

"I very sorry now Missy Edith, but cat bite me," said Pablo.

"Well, if pussy did, it didn't hurt you much; and what did I tell you this morning out of the Bible?—that you must forgive them who behave ill to you."

"Yes, Missy Edith, you tell me all that, and so I do; I forgive pussy 'cause she bite me, but I kick her for it."

"That's not forgiveness, is it, Edward? You should have forgiven it at once, and not kicked it at all."

"Miss Edith, when pussy bite me, pussy hurt me, make me angry, and I give her a kick; then I think what you tell me, and I do as you tell me. I forgive pussy with all my heart."

"I think you must forgive Pablo, Edith," said Edward, "if it is only to set him a good example."

"Well, I will this time; but if he kicks pussy again, he must be put in the pit-fall—mind that, Pablo."

"Yes, Missy Edith, I go into pit-fall, and then you cry, and ask Master Edward to take me out. When you have me put in pit-fall then you not good Christian, 'cause you not forgive; when you cry and take me out, then you good Christian once more."

By this conversation it will appear to the reader that they had been trying to impress Pablo with the principles of the Christian religion—and such was the case; Edith having been one of the most active in the endeavour, although very young for a missionary. However, Alice and Humphrey had been more successful, and Pablo was now beginning to comprehend what they had attempted to instil, and was really progressing every day.

Edward remained at the cottage, expecting to hear some message from the Intendant. He was right in his conjecture, for, on the third day, Oswald Partridge came over to say that the Intendant would be happy to see him, if he could make it convenient to go over; which Edward assented to do on the following day. Oswald had ridden over on a pony: Edward arranged to take Billy and return with him. They started early the next morning, and Edward asked Oswald if he knew why the Intendant had sent for him.

"Not exactly," replied Oswald; "but I think, from what I heard Miss Patience say, it is to offer you some situation, if you could be prevailed upon to accept it."

"Very true," replied Edward; "he offers me the post of secretary. What do you think?"

"Why, sir, I think I would accept it; at all events, I would take it on trial—there can be no harm done: if you do not like it you can only go back to the cottage again. One thing I am sure of, which is, that Master Heatherstone will make it as pleasant to you as he can, for he is most anxious to serve you."

"That I really believe," replied Edward; "and I have, pretty well, made up my mind to accept the office. It is a post of confidence, and I shall know all that is going on, which I cannot do while I am secluded in the forest; and depend upon it, we shall have stirring news."

"I suppose you think that the king will come over?" replied Oswald.

"I feel certain of it, Oswald; and that is the reason why I want to be where I can know all that is going on."

"Well, sir, it is my opinion that the king will come over, as well as yours; yet I think at present he stands but a poor chance; Master Heatherstone knows more on that score than any one, I should think; but he is very close."

The conversation then changed, and after a ride of eight hours they arrived at the Intendant's house. Edward gave Billy into Oswald's charge, and knocked at the door. Phoebe let him in, and asked him into the sitting-room, where he found the Intendant alone.

"Edward Armitage, I am glad to see you; and shall be still more so if I find that you have made up your mind to accept my proposition. What is your reply?"

"I am very thankful to you for the offer, sir," replied Edward; "and will accept it if you think that I am fitted for it, and if I find that I am equal to it: I can but give it a trial, and leave if I find it too arduous or too irksome."

"Too arduous it shall not be—that shall be my concern; and too irksome I hope you will not find it. My letters are not so many but that I could answer them myself, were it not that my eyes are getting weak, and I wish to save them as much as possible. You will therefore have to write chiefly what I shall dictate; but it is not only for that I require a person that I can confide in. I very often shall send you to London instead of going myself, and to that I presume you will have no objection?"

"Certainly none, sir."

"Well, then, it is no use saying any more just now; you will have a chamber in this house, and you will live with me, and at my table altogether. Neither shall I say anything just now about remuneration, as I am convinced that you will be satisfied. All that I require now, is to know the day that you will come, that everything may be ready."

"I suppose, sir, I must change my attire?" replied Edward, looking at his forester's dress; "that will hardly accord with the office of secretary."

"I agree with you that it will be better to keep that dress for your forest excursions, as I presume you will not altogether abandon them," replied the Intendant. "You can provide yourself with a suit at Lymington. I will furnish you the means."

"I thank you, sir, I have means, much more than sufficient," replied Edward, "although not quite so wealthy as little Clara appeared to be."

"Wealthy, indeed!" replied the Intendant. "I had no idea that poor Ratcliffe possessed so much ready money and jewels. Well, then, this is Wednesday; can you come over next Monday?"

"Yes, sir," replied Edward, "I see no reason to the contrary."

"Well, then, that is settled, and I suppose you would like to see your accommodation. Patience and Clara are in the next room. You can join them, and you will make my daughter very happy by telling her that you are to become a resident with us. You will of course dine with us to-day, and sleep here to-night."

Mr Heatherstone then opened the door, and saying to his daughter, "Patience, my dear, I leave you to entertain Edward Armitage till dinner-time," he ushered Edward in, and closed the door again. Clara ran up to Edward as soon as he went in; and having kissed him, Edward then took Patience's offered hand.

"Then you have consented?" said Patience inquiringly.

"Yes, I could not refuse such kindness," replied Edward.

"And when do you come?"

"On Monday night, if I can be ready by that time."

"Why, what have you to get ready?" said Clara.

"I must not appear in a forester's dress, my little Clara. I can wear that with a gun in my hand, but not with a pen: so I must go to Lymington and see what a tailor can do for me."

"You will feel as strange in a secretary's dress as I did in boys' clothes," said Clara.

"Perhaps I may," said Edward; although he felt that such would not be the case, having been accustomed to much better clothes when at Arnwood than what were usually worn by secretaries; and this remembrance brought back Arnwood in its train, and Edward became silent and pensive.

Patience observed it, and after a time said—"You will be able to watch over your sisters, Mr Armitage, as well here, almost, as if you were at the cottage. You do not return till to-morrow? How did you come over?"

"I rode the pony Billy, Mistress Patience."

"Why do you call her Mistress Patience, Edward?" said Clara. "You call me Clara: why not call her Patience?"

"You forget that I am only a forester, Clara," replied Edward, with a grave smile.

"No, you are a secretary *now*," replied Clara.

"Mistress Patience is older than you by several years. I call you Clara, because you are but a little girl; but I must not take that liberty with Mistress Heatherstone."

"Do you think so, Patience?" said Clara.

"I certainly do not think that it would be a liberty in a person, after being well acquainted with me, to call me Patience," replied she; "especially when that person lives in the house with us, eats and associates with us as one of the family, and is received on an equality; but I daresay, Clara, that Master Armitage will be guided by his own feelings, and act as he considers to be proper."

"But you give him leave, and then it is proper," replied Clara.

"Yes, if he gave himself leave, Clara," said Patience. "But we will now show him his own room, Clara," continued Patience, wishing to change the subject of conversation.

"Will you follow us, sir?" said Patience, with a little mock ceremony.

Edward did so without replying, and was ushered into a large airy room, very neatly furnished.

"This is your future lodging," said Patience; "I hope you will like it."

"Why, he never saw anything like it before," said Clara.

"Yes I have, Clara," replied Edward.

"Where did you?"

"At Arnwood; the apartments were on a much larger scale."

"Arnwood! Oh yes, I have heard my father speak of it," said Clara, with the tears starting in her eyes at his memory. "Yes, it was burnt down, and all the children burnt to death!"

"So they say, Clara; but I was not there when it was burnt."

"Where were you then?"

"I was at the cottage where I now live." Edward turned round to Patience, and perceived that her eyes were fixed upon him, as if she would have read his thoughts. Edward smiled, and said—

"Do you doubt what I say?"

"No, indeed!" said she, "I have no doubt that you were at the cottage at the time; but I was thinking that if the apartments at Arnwood were more splendid, those at your cottage are less comfortable. You have been used to better and to worse, and therefore will, I trust, be content with these."

"I trust I have shown no signs of discontent. I should indeed be difficult to please, if an apartment like this did not suit me. Besides, allow me to observe, that although I stated that the apartments at Arnwood were on a grander scale, I never said that I had ever been a possessor of one of them."

Patience smiled and made no reply.

"Now that you know your way to your apartment, Master Armitage, we will, if you please, go back to the sitting-room," said she. As they were going back into the sitting-room she said—"When you come over on Monday, you will, I presume, bring your clothes in a cart? I ask it, because I promised some flowers and other things to your sisters, which I can send back by the cart."

"You are very kind to think of them, Mistress Patience," replied Edward; "they are fond of flowers, and will be much pleased with possessing any."

"You sleep here to-night, I think my father said?" inquired Patience.

"He did make the proposal, and I shall gladly avail myself of it, as I am not to trust to Phoebe's ideas of comfort this time," said Edward, smiling.

"Yes, that was a cross action of Phoebe's; and I can tell you, Master Armitage, that she is ashamed to look you in the face ever since; but how fortunate for me that she was cross, and turned you out as she did! You must forgive her, as she was the means of your performing a noble action; and I must forgive her, as she was the means of my life being saved."

"I have no feeling except kindness towards Phoebe," replied Edward; "indeed I ought to feel grateful to her! For if she had not given me so bad a bed that night, I never should have been so comfortably lodged as it is proposed that I shall be now."

"I hope you are hungry, Edward," said Clara; "dinner is almost ready."

"I daresay I shall eat more than you do, Clara."

"So you ought, a great big man like you. How old are you, Edward?" said Clara; "I am thirteen; Patience is past sixteen: now how old are you?"

"I am not yet eighteen, Clara; so that I can hardly be called a man."

"Why, you are as tall as Mr Heatherstone."

"Yes, I believe I am."

"And can't you do everything that a man can do?"

"I really don't know; but I certainly shall always try so to do."

"Well, then, you must be a man."

"Clara, if it pleases you, I will be a man."

"Here comes Mr Heatherstone, so I know dinner is ready; is it not, sir?"

"Yes, my child, it is," replied Mr Heatherstone, kissing Clara; "so let us all go in."

Mr Heatherstone, as was usual at that time with the people to whose party he ostensibly belonged, said a grace before meat, of considerable length, and then they sat down to table. As soon as the repast was over Mr Heatherstone returned to his study, and Edward went out to find Oswald Partridge, with whom he remained the larger portion of the afternoon, going to the kennel and examining the dogs, and talking of matters connected with the chase.

"I have not two men that can stalk a deer," observed Oswald; "the men appointed here as verderers and keepers have not one of them been brought up to the business. Most of them are men who have been in the army, and I believe have been appointed to these situations to get rid of them, because they were troublesome; and they are anything but good characters; the consequence is, that we kill but few deer, for I have so much to attend to here, as none of them know their duties, that I can seldom take my own gun out. I stated so to the Intendant, and he said, that if you accepted an offer he had made you, and came over here, we should not want venison; so it is clear that he does not expect you to have your pen always in your hand."

"I am glad to hear that," replied Edward; "depend upon it his own table, at all events, shall be well supplied. Is not that the fellow Corbould, who is leaning against the wall?"

"Yes; he is to be discharged, as he cannot walk well, and the surgeon says he will always limp. He owes you a grudge, and I am glad that he is going away, for he is a dangerous man. But the sun is setting, Mr Edward, and supper will soon be on the table; you had better go back to the house."

Edward bade Oswald farewell, and returned to the Intendant's, and found that Oswald was correct, as supper was being placed on the table.

Soon after supper, Phoebe and the men-servants were summoned, and prayers offered up by the Intendant; after which Patience and Clara retired. Edward remained in conversation with the Intendant for about an hour, and then was conducted by him to his room, which had already been shown to him by Patience.

Edward did not sleep much that night. The novelty of his situation—the novelty of his prospects, and his speculations thereon, kept him awake till near morning; he was, however, up in good time, and having assisted at the morning prayers, and afterwards eaten a most substantial breakfast, he took his leave of the Intendant and the two girls, and set off on his return to the cottage, having renewed his promise of coming on the following Monday to take up his abode with them. Billy was fresh, and cantered gaily along, so that Edward was back early in the afternoon, and once more welcomed by his household. He stated to Humphrey all that had occurred, and Humphrey was much pleased at Edward having accepted the offer of the Intendant. Alice and Edith did not quite so much approve of it, and a few tears were shed at the idea of Edward leaving the cottage. The next day, Edward and Humphrey set off for Lymington, with Billy in the cart.

"Do you know, Edward," said Humphrey, "what I am going to try and purchase? I will tell you—as many kids as I can, or goats and kids, I don't care which."

"Why, have you not stock enough, already? You will this year have four cows in milk, and you have two cow calves bringing up."

"That is very true, but I do not intend to have goats for their milk, but simply for eating in lieu of mutton. Sheep I cannot manage, but goats, with a little hay in winter, will do well, and will find themselves in the forest all the year round. I won't kill any of the females for the first year or two, and after that I expect we shall have a flock sufficient to meet any demand upon it."

"It is not a bad idea, Humphrey; they will always come home, if you have hay for them during the winter."

"Yes, and a large shed for them to lie in when the snow is on the ground."

"Now I recollect, when we used to go to Lymington, I saw a great many goats, and I have no doubt that they are to be purchased. I will soon ascertain that for you, from the landlord of the hostelrie," replied Edward.

"We will drive there first, as I must ask him to recommend me a tailor."

On their arrival at Lymington, they went straight to the hostelrie, and found the landlord at home. He recommended a tailor to Edward, who sent for him to the inn, and was measured by him for a plain suit of dark cloth. Edward and Humphrey then went out, as Edward had to procure boots, and many other articles of dress to correspond with the one which he was about to assume.

"I am most puzzled about a hat, Humphrey," said Edward: "I hate those steeple-crowned hats, worn by the Roundheads; yet the hat and feather is not proper for a secretary."

"I would advise you to submit to wear the steeple-crowned hats, nevertheless," said Humphrey. "Your dress, as I consider, is a sort of disgrace to a cavalier born, and the heir of Arnwood; why not, therefore, take its hat as well? As secretary to the Intendant, you should dress like him; if not, you may occasion remarks, especially when you travel on his concerns."

"You are right, Humphrey, I must not do things by halves; and unless I wear the hat I might be suspected."

"I doubt if the Intendant wears it for any other reason," said Humphrey.

"At all events, I will not go to the height of the fashion," replied Edward, laughing. "Some of the hats are not quite so tall as the others."

"Here is the shop for the hat and for the sword-belt."

Edward chose a hat and a plain sword-belt, paid for them, and desired the man to carry them to the hostelrie.

While all these purchases on the part of Edward, and many others by Humphrey, such as nails, saws, tools, and various articles which Alice required for the household, were being gathered together, the landlord had sent out to inquire for the goats, and found out at what price they were to be procured. Humphrey left Edward to put away their goods into the cart, while he went out a second time, to see the goats; with the man who had them for sale he made an agreement for a male and three females with two kids each at their sides, and ten more female kids which had just been weaned. The man engaged to drive them from Lymington, as far as the road went into the forest, on the following day; when Humphrey would meet him, pay him his money, and drive them to the cottage, which would only be three miles from the place agreed upon. Having settled that satisfactorily, he returned to Edward, who was all ready, and they returned home.

"We have dipped somewhat into the bag to-day, Edward," said Humphrey; "but the money is well spent."

"I think so, Humphrey, but I have no doubt that I shall be able to replace the money very soon, as the Intendant will pay me for my services. The tailor has promised the clothes on Saturday without fail; so that you or I must go for them."

"I will go, Edward; my sisters will wish you to stay with them now, as you are so soon to leave them; and I will take Pablo with me, that he may know his way to the town; and I will show him where to buy things, in case he goes there by himself."

"It appears to me to have been a most fortunate thing your having caught Pablo as you did, Humphrey, for I do not well know how I could have left you if you had not."

"At all events I can do much better without you than I should have done," replied Humphrey; "although I think now that I could get on by myself; but still, Edward, you know we cannot tell what a day may bring forth, and I might fall sick, or something happen which might prevent my attending to anything; and then, without you or Pablo, everything might have gone to wrack and ruin. Certainly, when we think how we were left, by the death of old Jacob, to our own resources, we have much to thank God for in having got on so well."

"I agree with you, and also that it has pleased Heaven to grant us all such good health. However, I shall be close at hand if you want me, and Oswald will always call and see how you get on."

"I hope you will manage that he calls once a week."

"I will if I can, Humphrey, for I shall be just as anxious as you are to know if all goes on well. Indeed, I shall insist upon coming over to you once a fortnight; and I hardly think the Intendant will refuse me—indeed I am sure that he will not."

"So am I," replied Humphrey. "I am certain that he wishes us all well, and has, in a measure, taken us under his protection; but, Edward, recollect, I shall never kill any venison after this, and so you may tell the Intendant."

"I will, and that will be an excuse for him to send some over, if he pleases. Indeed, as I know I shall be permitted to go out with Oswald, it will be hard if a stray buck does not find its way to the cottage."

Thus did they continue talking over matters till they arrived at the cottage. Alice came out to them, saying to Humphrey—"Well, Humphrey, have you brought my geese and ducks?"

Humphrey had forgotten them, but he replied, "You must wait till I go to Lymington again on Saturday, Alice, and then I hope to bring them with me. As it is, look how poor Billy is loaded. Where's Pablo?"

"In the garden. He has been working there all day, and Edith is with him."

"Well then we will unload the cart, while you get us something to eat, Alice, for we are not a little hungry, I can tell you."

"I have some rabbit stew on the fire, Humphrey, all ready for you, and you will find it very good."

"Nothing I like better, my dear girl. Pablo won't thank me for bringing this home," continued Humphrey, taking the long saw out of the cart; "he will have to go to the bottom of the pit again, as soon as the pit is made."

The cart was soon unloaded, Billy taken out and turned out to feed, and then they went in to supper.

Humphrey was off the next morning, with Pablo, at an early hour, to meet the farmer of whom he had purchased the goats and kids. He found them punctual to the time, at the place agreed upon; and being satisfied with the lot, paid the farmer his money and drove them home through the forest.

"Goat very good, kid better; always eat kid in Spain," said Pablo.

"Were you born in Spain, Pablo?"

"Not sure, but I think so. First recollect myself in that country."

"Do you recollect your father?"

"No; never see him."

"Did your mother never talk about him?"

"Call her mother, but think no mother at all. Custom with Gitanas."

"Why did you call her mother?"

"'Cause she feed me when little, beat me when I get big."

"All mothers do that. What made you come to England?"

"I don't know, but I hear people say, Plenty of money in England—plenty to eat—plenty to drink; bring plenty money back to Spain."

"How long have you been in England?"

"One, two, three year; yes, three year and a bit."

"Which did you like best, England or Spain?"

"When with my people, like Spain best; warm sun—warm night. England, little sun, cold night, much rain, snow, and air always cold; but now I live with you, have warm bed, plenty victuals, like England best."

"But when you were with the gipsies, they stole everything, did they not?"

"Not steal everything," replied Pablo, laughing, "sometimes take and no pay when nobody there; farmer look very sharp—have big dog."

"Did you ever go out to steal?"

"Make me go out. Not bring back something, beat me very hard; suppose farmer catch me, beat hard too nothing but beat, beat, beat."

"Then they obliged you to steal?"

"Suppose bring nothing home, first beat, and then not have to eat for one, two, three days. How you like that, Master Humphrey? I think you steal after no victuals for three days?"

"I should hope not," replied Humphrey, "although I have never been so severely punished; and I hope, Pablo, you will never steal any more."

"Why steal any more?" replied Pablo. "I not like to steal; but because hungry I steal. Now I never hungry, always have plenty to eat; no one beat me now; sleep warm all night. Why I steal, then? No, Master Humphrey, I never steal more, 'cause I have no reason why, and 'cause Missy Alice and Missy Edith tell me how the good God up there say must not steal."

"I am glad to hear you give that as a reason, Pablo," replied Humphrey, "as it proves that my sisters have not been teaching you in vain."

"Like to hear Missy Alice talk; she talk grave. Missy Edith talk too, but she laugh very much; very fond Missy Edith, very happy little girl; jump about just like one of these kids we drive home; always merry. Hah! See cottage now; soon get home, Massa Humphrey. Missy Edith like see kids very much. Where we put them?"

Chapter Nineteen.

"We will put them into the yard for the present; I mean that Holdfast shall take charge of them by and by. I will soon teach him."

"Yes, he take charge of coat, or anything I tell him, why not take charge of goats? Clever dog, Holdfast. Massa Humphrey, you think Massa Edward take away both his dogs, Smoker and Watch? I say better not take puppy. Take Smoker, and leave puppy."

"I agree with you, Pablo. We ought to have two dogs here. I will speak to my brother. Now run forward and open the gate of the yard, and throw them some hay, Pablo, while I go and call my sisters."

The flock of goats was much admired, and the next morning was driven out into the forest to feed, attended by Pablo and Holdfast. When it was dinner-time, Pablo drove the flock near to the cottage, telling the dog to mind the goats. The sensible animal remained at once with them until Pablo's return from dinner; and it may be as well to observe here that in a few days the dog took charge of them altogether, driving them home to the yard every evening; and as soon as they were put into the yard the dog had his supper, and he took good care, therefore, not to be too late. To return to our narrative.

On Saturday Humphrey and Pablo went to Lymington to bring home Edward's clothes, and Humphrey made Pablo acquainted with all that he wanted him to know, in case it might be necessary to send him there alone.

Edward remained with his sisters, as he was to leave them on the Monday.

Sunday was passed as usual; they read the service at old Armitage's grave, and afterwards they walked in the forest; for Sunday was the only day on which Alice could find time to leave her duties in the cottage. They were not more grave than usual at the idea of Edward's leaving them, but they kept up their spirits, as they were aware that it was for the advantage of all.

On Monday morning, Edward, to please his sisters, put on his new clothes, and put his forester's dress in the bundle with his linen. Alice and Edith thought he looked very well in them, and said that it reminded them of the days of Arnwood. The fact was that Edward appeared as he was—a gentleman born; that could not well be concealed under a forester's dress, and in his present attire it was undeniable. After breakfast Billy was harnessed and brought to the cottage-door. Edward's linen was put in the cart, and, as he had agreed with Humphrey, he took only Smoker with him, leaving the puppy at the cottage. Pablo went with him to bring back the cart. Edward kissed his sisters, who wept at the idea of his leaving them, and shaking hands with Humphrey set off to cross the forest.

"Who would ever have believed this?" thought Edward, as he drove across the forest; "that I should put myself under the roof and under the protection of a Roundhead—one in outward appearance, and in the opinion of the world at least, if he is not so altogether in opinion. There is surely some spell upon me, and I almost feel as if I were a traitor to my principles. Why I know not, I feel a regard for that man, and a confidence in him. And why should I not? He knows my principles, my feelings against his party, and he respects them. Surely he cannot wish to gain me over to his party; that were indeed ridiculous—a young forester—a youth unknown. No, he would gain nothing by that, for I am nobody. It must be from good-will, and no other feeling. I have obliged him in the service I rendered his daughter, and he is grateful." Perhaps, had Edward put the question to himself, "Should I have been on such friendly terms with the Intendant—should I have accepted his offer, if there had been no Patience Heatherstone?" he might then have discovered what was the "spell upon him" which had rendered him so tractable; but of that he had no idea. He only felt that his situation would be rendered more comfortable by the society of an amiable and handsome girl, and he inquired no further.

His reverie was broken by Pablo, who appeared tired of holding his tongue, and said, "Massa Edward, you not like leave home—you think very much. Why you go there?"

"I certainly do not like to leave home, Pablo, for I am very fond of my brother and sisters; but we cannot always do as we wish in this world, and it is for their sakes, more than from my own inclinations, that I have done so."

"Can't see what good you do Missy Alice and Missy Edith 'cause you go away. How it possible do good, and not with them? Suppose bad accident, and you away, how you do good. Suppose bad accident, and you at cottage, then you do good. I think, Massa Edward, you very foolish."

Edward laughed at this blunt observation of Pablo's, and replied, "It is very true, Pablo, that I cannot watch over my sisters, and protect them in person when I am away; but there are reasons why I should go, nevertheless, and I may be more useful to them by going than by remaining with them. If I did not think so I would not leave them. They know nobody, and have no friends in the world. Suppose anything was to happen to me. Suppose both Humphrey and I were to die—for you know that we never know how soon that event may take place—who would there be to protect my poor sisters, and what would become of them? Is it not, therefore, wise that I should procure friends for them, in case of accident, who would look after them and protect them? And it is my hope, that by leaving them now, I shall make powerful and kind friends for them. Do you understand me?"

"Yes, I see now; you think more than me, Massa Edward. I say just now, you foolish; I say now, Pablo great fool."

"Besides, Pablo, recollect that I never would have left them as long as there was only Humphrey and me to look after them, because an accident might have happened to one of us; but when you came to live with us, and I found what a good clever boy you were, and that you were fond of us all, I then said, 'Now I can leave my sisters, for Pablo shall take my place, and assist Humphrey to do what is required, and to take care of them.' Am I not right, Pablo?"

"Yes, Massa Edward," replied Pablo, taking hold of Edward's wrist, "you quite right. Pablo does love Missy Alice, Missy Edith, Massa Humphrey, and you, Massa Edward; he love you all very much indeed; he love you so much that he die for you! Can do no more."

"That is what I really thought of you, Pablo, and yet I am glad to hear it from your own mouth. If you had not come to live with us, and had not proved so faithful, I could not have left to benefit my sisters; but you have induced me to leave, and they have to thank you if I am able to be of any service to them."

"Well, Massa Edward, you go; never mind us, we make plenty of work; do everything all the same as you."

"I think you will, Pablo, and that is the reason why I have agreed to go away. But, Pablo, Billy is growing old, and you will want some more ponies."

"Yes, Massa Edward, Massa Humphrey talk to me about ponies last night, and say, plenty in the forest. Ask me if I think us able catch them. I say yes, catch one, two, twenty, suppose want them."

"Ah! How will you do that, Pablo?"

"Massa Edward, you tell Massa Humphrey no possible, so I no tell you how," replied Pablo, laughing. "Some day you come see us, see five ponies in the stable. Massa Humphrey and I, we talk about, find out how; you see."

"Well, then, I shall ask no more questions, Pablo; and when I see the ponies in the stable then I'll believe it, and not before."

"Suppose you want big horse for ride, catch big horse, Massa Edward, you see. Massa Humphrey very clever, he catch cow."

"Catch gipsy," said Edward.

"Yes," said Pablo, laughing, "catch cow, catch gipsy, and by and by catch horse."

When Edward arrived at the Intendant's house, he was very kindly received by the Intendant and the two girls. Having deposited his wardrobe in his bedroom, he went out to Oswald and put Smoker in the kennel, and on his return found Pablo sitting on the carpet in the sitting-room, talking to Patience and Clara, and they all three appeared much amused. When Pablo and Billy had both had something to eat, the cart was filled with pots of flowers, and several other little things as presents from Patience Heatherstone, and Pablo set off on his return.

"Edward, you do look like a—," said Clara, stopping.

"Like a secretary, I hope," added Edward.

"Well, you don't look like a forester; does he, Patience?" continued Clara.

"You must not judge of people by their clothes, Clara."

"Nor do I," replied Clara. "Those clothes would not look well upon Oswald, or the other men, for they would not suit them; but they do suit you: don't they, Patience?"

Patience Heatherstone, however, did not make any answer to this second appeal made by Clara.

"Why don't you answer me, Patience?" said Clara.

"My dear Clara, it's not the custom for young maidens to make remarks upon people's attire. Little girls like you may do so."

"Why, did you not tell Pablo that he looked well in his new clothes?"

"Yes, but Pablo is not Mr Armitage, Clara. That is very different."

"Well, it may be, but still you might answer a question, if put to you, Patience; and I ask again, does not Edward look much better in the dress he has on than in that he generally has worn?"

"I think it a becoming dress, Clara, since you will have an answer."

"Fine feathers make fine birds, Clara," said Edward, laughing: "and so that is all we can say about it."

Edward then changed the conversation. Soon afterwards dinner was announced, and Clara again observed to Edward—"Why do you always call Patience, Mistress Heatherstone? Ought he not to call her Patience, sir?" said Clara, appealing to the Intendant.

"That must depend upon his own feelings, my dear Clara," replied Mr Heatherstone. "It is my intention to waive ceremony as much as possible. Edward Armitage has come to live with us as one of the family, and he will find himself treated by me as one of us. I shall, therefore, in future address him as Edward, and he has my full permission, and I may say it is my wish, that he should be on the same familiar terms with us all. When Edward feels inclined to address my daughter as he does you, by her name of baptism, he will, I daresay, now that he has heard my opinion, do so; and reserve 'Mistress Heatherstone' for the time when they have a quarrel."

"Then I hope he will never again address me that way," observed Patience; "for I am under too great obligations to him to bear even the idea of being on had terms with him."

"Do you hear that, Edward?" said Clara.

"Yes, I do, Clara; and after such a remark, you may be sure that I shall never address her in that way again."

In a few days Edward became quite at home. In the forenoon Mr Heatherstone dictated one or two letters to him, which he wrote; and after that his time was at his own disposal, and was chiefly passed in the company of Patience and Clara. With the first he had now become on the most intimate and brotherly footing; and when they addressed each other, Patience and Edward were the only appellations made use of. Once Mr Heatherstone asked Edward whether he would not like to go out with Oswald to kill a deer, which he did; but the venison was hardly yet in season. There was a fine horse in the stable at Edward's order, and he often rode out with Patience and Clara;

indeed his time passed so agreeably that he could hardly think it possible that a fortnight had passed away, when he asked permission to go over to the cottage and see his sisters.

With the Intendant's permission, Patience and Clara accompanied him; and the joy of Alice and Edith was great, when they made their appearance. Oswald had, by Edward's request, gone over a day or two before, to tell them that they were coming, that they might be prepared; and the consequence was that it was a holiday at the cottage. Alice had cooked her best dinner, and Humphrey and Pablo were at home to receive them.

"How pleasant it will be, if we are to see you and Clara whenever we see Edward!" said Alice to Patience. "So far from being sorry that Edward is with you I shall be quite glad of it."

"I water the flowers every day," said Edith, "and they make the garden look so gay."

"I will bring you plenty more in the autumn, Edith; but this is not the right time for transplanting flowers yet," replied Patience. "And now, Alice, you must take me to see your farm, for when I was here last I had no time; let us come now, and show me everything."

"But my dinner, Patience; I cannot leave it, or it will be spoiled, and that will never do. You must either go with Edith now, or wait till after dinner, when I can get away."

"Well, then, we will stay till after dinner, Alice, and we will help you to serve it up."

"Thank you, Pablo generally does that, for Edith cannot reach down the things. I don't know where he is."

"He went away with Edward and Humphrey, I think," said Edith. "I'll scold him when he comes back for being out of the way."

"Never mind, Edith, I can reach the dishes," said Patience, "and you and Clara can then take them, and the platters, and put them on the table for Alice."

And Patience did as she proposed, and the dinner was soon afterwards on the table. There was a ham, and two boiled fowls, and a piece of salted beef, and some roasted kid, besides potatoes and green peas; and when it is considered that such a dinner was set on the table by such young people, left entirely to their own exertions and industry, it must be admitted that it did them and their farm great credit.

In the meantime Edward and Humphrey, after the first greetings were over, had walked out to converse, while Pablo had taken the horses into the stable.

"Well, Humphrey, how do you get on?"

"Very well," replied Humphrey. "I have just finished a very tough job. I have dug out the saw-pit, and have sawed the slabs for the sides of the pit, and made it quite secure. The large fir-tree that was blown down is now at the pit, ready for sawing up into planks, and Pablo and I are to commence to-morrow. At first we made but a bad hand of sawing off the slabs, but before we had cut them all we got on pretty well. Pablo don't much like it, and indeed no more do I much, it is such mechanical work, and so tiring; but he does not complain. I do not intend that he shall saw more than two days in a week; that will be sufficient; we shall get on fast enough."

"You are right, Humphrey; it is an old saying, that you must not work a willing horse to death. Pablo is very willing, but hard work he is not accustomed to."

"Well, now you must come and look at my flock of goats, Edward, they are not far off. I have taught Holdfast to take care of them, and he never leaves them now, and brings them home at night. Watch always remains with me, and is an excellent dog, and very intelligent."

"You have indeed a fine flock, Humphrey!" said Edward.

"Yes, and they are improved in appearance already since they have been here. Alice has got her geese and ducks, and I have made a place large enough for them to wash in, until I have time to dig them out a pond."

"I thought we had gathered more hay than you required; but with this addition, I think you will find none to spare before the spring."

"So far from it, that I have been mowing down a great deal more, Edward, and it is almost ready to carry away. Poor Billy has had hard work of it, I assure you, since he came back, with one thing and another."

"Poor fellow, but it won't last long, Humphrey," said Edward, smiling; "the other horses will soon take his place."

"I trust they will," said Humphrey, "at all events by next spring; before that I do not expect that they will."

"By the bye, Humphrey, you recollect what I said to you that the robber I shot told me, just before he died?"

"Yes, I do recollect it now," replied Humphrey; "but I had quite forgot all about it till you mentioned it now, although I wrote it down, that we might not forget it."

"Well, I have been thinking all about it, Humphrey. The robber told me that the money was mine, taking me for another person; therefore I do not consider it was given to me, nor do I consider that it was his to give. I hardly know what to do about it, nor to whom the money can be said to belong."

"Well I think I can answer that question. The property of all malefactors belongs to the king; and therefore this money belongs to the king; and we may retain it for the king, or use it for his service."

"Yes, it would have belonged to the king had the man been condemned, and hung on the gallows as he deserved; but he was not, and therefore I think that it does not belong to the king."

"Then it belongs to whoever finds it, and who keeps it till it is claimed—which will never be."

"I think I must speak to the Intendant about it," replied Edward; "I should feel more comfortable."

"Then do so," replied Humphrey; "I think you are right to have no concealments from him."

"But, Humphrey," replied Edward, laughing, "what silly fellows we are! We do not yet know whether we shall find anything; we must first see if there is anything buried there; and when we have done so, then we will decide how to act. I shall, if it please God, be over again in a fortnight, and in the meantime, do you find out the place, and ascertain if what the fellow said is true."

"I will," replied Humphrey. "I will go to-morrow, with Billy and the cart, and take a spade and pick-axe with me. It may be a fool's errand, but still they say, and one would credit, for the honour of human nature, that the words of a dying man are those of truth. We had better go back now, for I think dinner must be ready."

Now that they had become so intimate with Patience Heatherstone—and I may add, so fond of her—there was no longer any restraint, and they had a very merry dinner-party; and after dinner, Patience went out with Alice and Edith, and looked over the garden and farm. She wished very much to ascertain if there was anything that they required, but she could discover but few things, and those only trifles; but she recollected them all, and sent them to the cottage a few days afterwards. But the hour of parting arrived, for it was a long ride back, and they could not stay any longer, if they wished to get home before dark, as Mr Heatherstone had requested Edward that they should do; so the horses were brought out, and wishing good-bye, they set off again, little Edith crying after them, "Come again soon! Patience, must come again soon!"

Chapter Twenty.

The summer had now advanced, when Oswald one day said to Edward—

"Have you heard the news, sir?"

"Nothing very particular," replied Edward; "I know that General Cromwell is over in Ireland, and they say very successful; but I have cared little for particulars."

"They say a great deal more, sir," replied Oswald; "they say that the king is in Scotland, and that the Scotch have raised an army for him."

"Indeed!" replied Edward, "that is news indeed! The Intendant has never mentioned it to me."

"I daresay not, sir; for he knows your feelings, and would be sorry to part with you."

"I will certainly speak to him on the subject," said Edward, "at the risk of his displeasure; and join the army I will, if I find what you say is true. I should hold myself a craven to remain here while the king is fighting for his own, and not to be at his side."

"Well, sir, I think it is true, for I heard that the Parliament had sent over for General Cromwell to leave Ireland, and lead the troops against the Scotch army."

"You drive me mad, Oswald! I will go to the Intendant immediately!"

Edward, much excited by the intelligence, went into the room where he usually sat with the Intendant. The latter, who was at his desk, looked up, and saw how flushed Edward was, and said very quietly—

"Edward, you are excited, I presume, from hearing the news which has arrived?"

"Yes, sir, I am very much so; and I regret very much that I should be the last to whom such important news is made known."

"It is, as you say, important news," replied the Intendant; "but if you will sit down, we will talk a little upon the subject."

Edward took a chair, and the Intendant said—

"I have no doubt that your present feeling is to go to Scotland, and join the army without delay?"

"Such is my intention, I candidly confess, sir. It is my duty."

"Perhaps you may be persuaded to the contrary before we part," replied the Intendant. "The first duty you owe is to your family in their present position; they depend upon you; and a false step on your part would be their ruin. How can you leave them, and leave my employ, without it being known for what purpose you are gone? It is impossible! I must myself make it known, and even then it would be very injurious to me, the very circumstance of my having one of your party in my service. I am suspected by many already, in consequence of the part I have taken against the murder of the late king, and also of the lords who have since suffered. But, Edward, I did not communicate this intelligence to you, for many reasons. I knew that it would soon come to your ears, and I thought it better that I should be more prepared to show you that you may do yourself and me harm, and can do no good to the king. I will now show you that I do put confidence in you; and if you will read these letters, they will prove to you that I am correct in what I assert."

The Intendant handed three letters to Edward, by which it was evident that all the king's friends in England were of opinion that the time was not ripe for the attempt, and that it would be only a sacrifice to stir in the matter; that the Scotch army raised was composed of those who were the greatest enemies to the king, and that the best thing that could happen for the king's interest would be that they were destroyed by Cromwell; that it was impossible for the English adherents of Charles to join them, and that the Scotch did not wish them so to do.

"You are no politician, Edward," said the Intendant smiling, as Edward laid the letters down on the table. "You must admit, that in showing you these letters I have put the utmost confidence in you?"

"You have indeed, sir; and thanking you for having so done, I hardly need add that your confidence will never be betrayed."

"That I am sure of; and I trust you will now agree with me and my friends that the best thing is to remain quiet?"

"Certainly, sir, and for the future I will be guided by you."

"That is all I require of you; and after that promise you shall hear all the news as soon as it arrives. There are thousands who are just as anxious to see the king on the throne again as you are, Edward—and you now know that I am one of them; but the time is not yet come, and we must bide our time. Depend upon it, that General Cromwell will scatter that army like chaff. He is on his march now. After what has passed between us this day, Edward, I shall talk unreservedly to you on what is going on."

"I thank you, sir, and I promise you faithfully, as I said before, not only to be guided by your advice but to be most secret in all that you may trust me with."

"I have confidence in you, Edward Armitage; and now we will drop the subject for the present: Patience and Clara want you to walk with them, so good-bye for a while."

Edward left the Intendant, much pleased with the interview. The Intendant kept his word, and concealed nothing from Edward. All turned out as the Intendant had foretold. The Scotch army was cut to pieces by Cromwell, and the king retreated to the Highlands; and Edward now felt satisfied that he could do no better than be guided by the Intendant in all his future undertakings.

We must now pass over some time in a few words. Edward continued at the Intendant's, and gave great satisfaction to Mr Heatherstone. He passed his time very agreeably, sometimes going out to shoot deer with Oswald, and often supplying venison to his brother and sisters. During the autumn, Patience very often went to the cottage, and occasionally Mr Heatherstone paid them a visit; but after the winter set in Edward came over by himself, shooting as he went; and when he and Smoker came, Billy always had a journey to go for the venison left in the forest. Patience sent Alice many little things for her own and Edith's use, and some very good books for them to read; and Humphrey, during the evenings, read with his sisters, that they might learn what he could teach them. Pablo also learnt to read and write. Humphrey and Pablo had worked at the saw-pit, and had sawed out a large quantity of boards and timber for building, but the work was put off till the spring.

The reader may recollect that Edward had proposed to Humphrey that he should ascertain whether what the robber had stated before his death, relative to his having concealed his ill-gotten wealth under the tree which was struck by lightning, was true. About ten days afterwards Humphrey set off on this expedition. He did not take Pablo with him, as, although he had a very good opinion of him, he agreed with Oswald that temptation should not be put in his way. Humphrey considered that it would be the best plan to go at once to Clara's cottage, and from that proceed to find the oak-tree mentioned by the robber. When he arrived at the thicket which surrounded the cottage, it occurred to him that he would just go through it and see if it was in the state which they had left it in; for after the Intendant had been there he had given directions to his men to remain and bury the bodies, and then to lock up the doors and bring the keys to him, which had been done. Humphrey tied Billy and the cart to a tree, and walked through the thicket. As he approached he heard voices; so he took care to advance very cautiously, for he had not brought his gun with him. He crouched down as he came to the opening before the cottage. The doors and windows were open, and there were two men sitting outside, cleaning their guns; and in one of them Humphrey recognised the man Corbould, who had been discharged by the Intendant as soon as his wound had been cured, and who was supposed to have gone to London. Humphrey was too far off to hear what they said: he remained there some time, and three more men came out of the cottage. Satisfied with what he had seen, Humphrey cautiously retreated, and gaining the outside of the thicket, led away Billy and the cart over the turf, that the noise of the wheels might not be heard.

"This bodes no good," thought Humphrey, as he went along, every now and then looking back to ascertain if the men had come out and seen him. "That Corbould, we know, has vowed vengeance against Edward and all of us, and has no doubt joined those robbers—for robbers they must be—that he may fulfil his vow. It is fortunate that I have made the discovery, and I will send over immediately to the Intendant." As soon as a clump of trees had shut out the thicket, and he had no longer any fear of being seen by these people, Humphrey went in the direction which the robber had mentioned, and soon afterwards he perceived the oak scathed with lightning, which stood by itself on a green spot of about twenty acres. It had been a noble tree before it had been destroyed; now it spread its long naked arms, covering a large space of ground, but without the least sign of vegetation or life remaining. The trunk was many feet in diameter, and was apparently quite sound, although the tree was dead. Humphrey left Billy to feed on the herbage close by, and then, from the position of the sun in the heavens, ascertained the point at which he was to dig. First looking around him to see that he was not overlooked, he took his spade and pick-axe out of the cart and began his task. There was a spot not quite so green as the rest, which Humphrey thought likely to be the very place that he should dig at, as probably it was not green from the soil having been removed. He commenced at this spot, and after a few moment's labour his pick-axe struck upon something hard, which, on clearing away the earth, he discovered to be the lid of a wooden box. Satisfied that he was right, Humphrey now worked hard, and in a few minutes he had cleared sufficient space to be able to lift out the box and place it on the turf. He was about to examine it, when he perceived, at about five hundred yards' distance, three men coming towards him. "They have discovered me," thought Humphrey; "and I must be off as soon as I can." He ran to Billy, who was close to him, and bringing the cart to where the box lay, he lifted it in. As he was getting in himself, with the reins in his hands, he perceived that the three men were running towards him as fast as they could, and that they all had guns in their hands. They were not more than a hundred and fifty yards from him when Humphrey set off, putting Billy to a full trot.

The three men observing this, called out to Humphrey to stop, or they would fire; but Humphrey's only reply was giving a lash to Billy, which set him off at a gallop. The men immediately fired, and the bullets whistled past Humphrey without doing any harm. Humphrey looked round, and finding that he had increased his distance, pulled up the pony, and went a more moderate pace. "You'll not catch me," thought Humphrey; "and your guns are not loaded, so I'll tantalise you a little." He made Billy walk, and turned round to see what the men were about; they had arrived at where he had dug out the box, and were standing round the hole, evidently aware that it was no use following him. "Now," thought Humphrey, as he went along at a faster pace, "those fellows will wonder what I have been digging up. The villains little think that I know where to find them, and they have proved what they are by firing at me. Now, what must I do? They may follow me to the cottage, for I have no doubt that they know where we live, and that Edward is at the Intendant's. They may come and attack us, and I dare not leave the cottage to-night, or send Pablo away, in case they should; but I will to-morrow morning." Humphrey considered as he went along all the circumstances and probabilities, and decided that he would act as he at first proposed to himself. In an hour he was at the cottage; and as soon as Alice had given him his dinner—for he was later than the usual dinner-hour—he told her what had taken place.

"Where is Pablo?"

"He has been working in the garden with Edith all the day," replied Alice.

"Well, dear, I hope they will not come to-night: to-morrow I will have them all in custody; but if they do come, we must do our best to beat them off. It is fortunate that Edward left the guns and pistols which he found in Clara's cottage, so we shall have no want of firearms; and we can barricade the doors and windows, so that they cannot get in in a hurry; but I must have Pablo to help me, for there is no time to be lost."

"But cannot I help you, Humphrey?" said Alice. "Surely I can do something?"

"We will see, Alice; but I think I can do without you. We have still plenty of daylight. I will take the box into your room."

Humphrey, who had only taken the box out of the cart and carried it within the threshold of the door, now took it into his sisters' bedroom, and then went out and called Pablo, who came running to him.

"Pablo," said Humphrey, "we must bring to the cottage some of the large pieces we sawed out for rafters; for I should not be surprised if the cottage were attacked this night." He then told Pablo what had taken place. "You see, Pablo, I dare not send to the Intendant to-night in case the robbers should come here."

"No, not send to-night," said Pablo; "stay here and fight them; first make door fast, then cut hole to fire through."

"Yes, that was my idea. You don't mind fighting them, Pablo?"

"No; fight hard for Missy Alice and Missy Edith," said Pablo; "fight for you too, Massa Humphrey, and fight for myself," added Pablo, laughing.

They then went for the pieces of squared timber, brought them from the saw-pit to the cottage, and very soon fitted them to the doors and windows, so as to prevent several men, with using all their strength, from forcing them open.

"That will do," said Humphrey; "and now get me the small saw, Pablo, and I will cut a hole or two to fire through."

It was dark before they had finished, and then they made all fast, and went to Pablo's room for the arms, which they got ready for service, and loaded.

"Now, we are all ready, Alice, so let us have our supper," said Humphrey. "We will make a fight for it, and they shall not get in so easily as they think."

After they had had their supper, Humphrey said the prayers, and told his sisters to go to bed.

"Yes, Humphrey, we will go to bed, but we will not undress; for if they come, I must be up to help you. I can load a gun, you know, and Edith can take them to you as fast as I load them. Won't you, Edith?"

"Yes, I will bring you the guns, Humphrey, and you shall shoot them," replied Edith.

Humphrey kissed his sisters, and they went to their room. He then put a light in the chimney, that he might not have to get one in case the robbers came, and then desired Pablo to go and lie down on his bed, as he intended to do the same. Humphrey remained awake till past three o'clock in the morning; but no robbers came. Pablo was snoring loud, and at last Humphrey fell asleep himself and did not awake till broad daylight. He got up, and found Alice and Edith were already in the sitting-room, lighting the fire.

"I would not wake you, Humphrey, as you had been sitting up so long. The robbers have not made their appearance, that is clear; shall you unbar the door and window-shutters now?"

"Yes, I think we may. Here, Pablo!"

"Yes," replied Pablo, coming out half asleep; "what the matter? Thief come?"

"No," replied Edith, "thief not come, but sun shine; and lazy Pablo not get up."

"Up now, Missy Edith."

"Yes, but not awake yet."

"Yes, Missy Edith, quite awake."

"Well then, help me to undo the door, Pablo."

They took down the barricades, and Humphrey opened the door cautiously, and looked out.

"They won't come now, at all events, I should think," observed Humphrey; "but there is no saying—they may be prowling about, and may think it easier to get in during daytime than at night. Go out, Pablo, and look about everywhere; take a pistol with you, and fire it off if there is any danger, and then come back as fast as you can."

Pablo took the pistol, and then Humphrey went out of the door and looked well round in front of the cottage, but he would not leave the door till he was assured that no one was there. Pablo returned soon after, saying that he had looked round everywhere, and into the cow-house and yard, and there was nobody to be seen. This satisfied Humphrey, and they returned to the cottage.

"Now, Pablo, get your breakfast, while I write the letter to the Intendant," said Humphrey; "and then you must saddle Billy and go over as fast as you can with the letter. You can tell him all I have not said in it. I shall expect you back at night, and some people with you."

"I see," said Pablo, who immediately busied himself with some cold meat which Alice put before him. Pablo had finished his breakfast and brought Billy to the door before Humphrey had finished his letter. As soon as it was written and folded Pablo set off as fast as Billy could go to the other side of the forest.

Humphrey continued on the look-out during the whole day, with his gun on his arm, and his two dogs by his side; for he knew the dogs would give notice of the approach of any one, long before he might see them; but nothing occurred during the whole day; and when the evening closed in he barricaded the doors and windows, and remained on the watch with the dogs, waiting for the coming of the robbers, or for the coming of the party which he expected would be sent by the Intendant to take them. Just as it was dark Pablo returned with a note from Edward saying that he would be over by ten o'clock, with a large party.

Humphrey had said in his letter that it would be better that any force sent by the Intendant should not arrive till after dark, as the robbers might be near and perceive them, and then they might escape; he did not therefore expect them to come till some time after dark. Humphrey was reading a book—Pablo was dozing in the chimney-corner—the two girls had retired into their room and had lain down on the bed in their clothes—when the dogs both gave a low growl.

"Somebody come," said Pablo, starting up.

Again the dogs growled, and Humphrey made a sign to Pablo to hold his tongue. A short time of anxious silence succeeded, for it was impossible to ascertain whether the parties were friends or enemies. The dogs now sprang up and barked furiously at the door, and as soon as Humphrey had silenced them, a voice was heard outside, begging for admission to a poor benighted traveller. This was sufficient: it could not be the party from the Intendant's, but the robbers who wished to induce them to open the door. Pablo put a gun into Humphrey's hand, and took another for himself; he then removed the light into the chimney, and on the application from outside being repeated, Humphrey answered—

"That he never opened the door at that hour of the night, and that it was useless their remaining."

No answer or repetition of the request was made, but, as Humphrey retreated with Pablo into the fireplace, a gun was fired into the lock of the door, which was blown off into the room, and had it not been for the barricades the door must have flown open. The robbers appeared surprised at such not being the case, and one of them inserted his arm into the hole made in the door to ascertain what might be the further obstacle to open it, when Pablo slipped past Humphrey, and gaining the door, discharged his gun under the arm which had been thrust into the hole in the door. The person, whoever it might have been, gave a loud cry, and fell at the threshold outside.

"I think that will do," said Humphrey; "we must not take more life than is necessary. I had rather that you had fired through his arm—it would have disabled him, and that would have sufficed."

"Kill much better," said Pablo. "Corbould shot through leg, come again to rob; suppose shot dead, never rob more."

The dogs now flew to the back of the cottage, evidently pointing out that the robbers were attempting that side. Humphrey put his gun through the hole in the door, and discharged it.

"Why you do that, Massa Humphrey, nobody there!"

"I know that, Pablo; but if the people are coming from the Intendant's they will see the flash and perhaps hear the report, and it will let them know what is going on."

"There is another gun loaded, Humphrey," said Alice, who with Edith had joined them without Humphrey observing it.

"Thanks, love; but you and Edith must not remain here: sit down on the hearth, and then you will be sheltered from any bullet which they may fire into the house. I have no fear of their getting in, and we shall have help directly, I have no doubt. Pablo, I shall fire through the back door; they must be there, for the dogs have their noses under it, and are so violent. Do you fire another gun, as a signal, through the hole in the front door."

Humphrey stood within four feet of the back door, and fired just above where the dogs held their noses and barked. Pablo discharged his gun as directed, and then returned to reload the guns. The dogs were now more quiet, and it appeared as if the robbers had retreated from the back door. Pablo blew out the light, which had been put more in the centre of the room, when Alice and Edith took possession of the fireplace.

"No fear, Missy Edith, I know where find everything," said Pablo, who now went and peered through the hole in the front door, to see if the robbers were coming to it again; but he could see and hear nothing for some time.

At last the attack was renewed; the dogs flew backwards and forwards, sometimes to one door and then to another, as if both were to be assailed: and at the same time a crash in Alice's bed-chamber told them that the robbers had burst in the small window in that room, which Humphrey had not paid any attention to, as it was so small that a man could hardly introduce his body through it. Humphrey immediately called Holdfast and opened the door of the room; for he thought that a man forcing his way in would be driven back or held by the dog, and he and Pablo dared not leave the two doors. Watch, the other dog, followed Holdfast into the bedroom; and oaths and curses, mingled with the savage yells of the dogs, told them that a conflict was going on. Both doors were now battered with heavy pieces of timber at the same time, and Pablo said—

"Great many robbers here."

A moment or more had passed, during which Pablo and Humphrey had both again fired their guns through the door, when, of a sudden, other sounds were heard—shots were fired outside, loud cries, and angry oaths and exclamations.

"The Intendant's people are come," said Humphrey, "I am sure of it."

Shortly afterwards Humphrey heard his name called by Edward, and he replied, and went to the door and undid the barricades.

"Get a light, Alice, dear," said Humphrey, "we are all safe now. I will open the door directly, Edward, but in the dark I cannot see the fastenings."

"Are you all safe, Humphrey?"

"Yes, all safe, Edward. Wait till Alice brings a light."

Alice soon brought one, and then the door was unfastened. Edward stepped over the body of a man which lay at the threshold, saying—

"You have settled somebody there, at all events," and then caught Edith and Alice in his arms.

He was followed by Oswald and some other men, leading in the prisoners.

"Bind that fellow fast, Oswald," said Edward. "Get another light, Pablo; let us see who it is that lies outside the door."

"First see who is in my bedroom, Edward," said Alice, "for the dogs are still there."

"In your bedroom, dearest? Well, then, let us go there first."

Edward went in with Humphrey, and found a man half in the window and half out, held by the throat and apparently suffocated by the two dogs. He took the dogs off; and desiring the men to secure the robber, and ascertain whether he was alive or not, he returned to the sitting-room, and then went to examine the body outside the door.

"Corbould, as I live!" cried Oswald.

"Yes," replied Edward; "he has gone to his account. God forgive him!"

On inquiry they found that of all the robbers, to the number of ten, not one had escaped—eight they had made prisoners, Corbould, and the man whom the dogs had seized, and who was found to be quite dead, made up the number. The robbers were all bound and guarded; and then, leaving them under the charge of Oswald and five of his men, Edward and Humphrey set off with seven more to Clara's cottage, to ascertain if there were any more to be found there. They arrived by two o'clock in the morning, and on knocking several times the door was opened and they seized another man, the only one who was found in it. They then went back to the cottage with their prisoner, and by the time that they had arrived it was daylight. As soon as the party sent by the Intendant had been supplied with breakfast, Edward bade farewell to Humphrey and his sisters, that he might return and deliver up his prisoners. Pablo went with him to bring back the cart which carried the two dead bodies. This capture cleared the forest of the robbers who had so long infested it, for they never had any more attempts made from that time.

Before Edward left, Humphrey and he examined the box which had been dug up from under the oak, and which had occasioned such danger to the inmates of the cottage; for one of the men stated to Edward that they suspected that the box which they had seen Humphrey dig out contained treasure, and that without they had seen him in possession of it, they never should have attacked the cottage, although Corbould had often persuaded them so to do; but as they knew that he was only seeking revenge—and they required money to stimulate them—they had refused, as they considered that there was nothing to be obtained in the cottage worth the risk, as they knew that the inmates had firearms and would defend themselves. On examination of its contents, they found in it a sum of forty pounds in gold, a bag of silver, and some other valuables in silver spoons, candlesticks, and ornaments for women. Edward took a list of the contents, and when he returned he stated to the Intendant all that had occurred, and requested to know what should be done with the money and other articles which Humphrey had found.

"I wish you had said nothing to me about it," said the Intendant, "although I am pleased with your open and fair dealing. I cannot say anything, except that you had better let Humphrey keep it till it is claimed—which, of course, it never will be. But, Edward, Humphrey must come over here and make his deposition, as I must report the capture of these robbers and send them to trial. You had better go with the clerk and take the depositions of Pablo and your sisters, while Humphrey comes here. You can stay till his return. Their depositions are not of so much consequence as Humphrey's, as they can only speak as to the attack, but Humphrey's I must take down myself."

When Patience and Clara heard that Edward was going over, they obtained leave to go with him to see Alice and Edith, and were to be escorted back by Humphrey. This the Intendant consented to, and they had a very merry party. Humphrey remained two days at the Intendant's house, and then returned to the cottage, where Edward had taken his place during his absence.

Chapter Twenty One.

The winter set in very severe, and the falls of snow were very heavy and frequent. It was fortunate Humphrey had been so provident in making so large a quantity of hay, or the stock would have been starved. The flock of goats, in great part, subsisted themselves on the bark of trees and moss; at night they had some hay given to them, and they did very well. It was hardly possible for Edward to come over to see his brother and sisters, for the snow was so deep as to render such a long journey too fatiguing for a horse. Twice or thrice after the snow fell he contrived to get over, but after that they knew that it was impossible, and they did not expect him. Humphrey and Pablo had little to do except attending to the stock, and cutting firewood to keep up their supply, for they now burnt it very fast. The snow lay several feet high round the cottage, being driven against it by the wind. They had kept a passage clear to the yard, and had kept the yard as clear as possible: they could do no more. A sharp frost and clear weather succeeded to the snow-storms, and there appeared no chance of the snow melting away. The nights were dark and long, and their oil for their lamp was getting low. Humphrey was anxious to go to Lymington, as they required many things; but it was impossible to go anywhere except on foot, and walking was, from the depth of the snow, a most fatiguing exercise. There was one thing, however, that Humphrey had not forgotten, which was, that he had told Edward that he would try and capture some of the forest ponies; and during the whole of the time since the heavy fall of snow had taken place he had been making his arrangements. The depth of the snow prevented the animals from obtaining any grass, and they were almost starved, as they could find nothing to subsist upon except the twigs and branches of trees which they could reach. Humphrey went out with Pablo and found the herd, which was about five miles from the cottage, and near to Clara's old home. He and Pablo brought with them as much hay as they could carry, and strewed it about, so as to draw the ponies nearer to them, and then Humphrey looked for a place which would answer his purpose. About three miles from the cottage he found what he thought would suit him; there was a sort of avenue between two thickets, about a hundred yards wide; and the wind blowing through this avenue, during the snow-storm, had drifted the snow at one end of it, and raised right across it a large mound several feet high. By strewing small bundles of hay he drew the herd of ponies into this avenue, and in it he left them a good quantity to feed upon every night for several nights, till at last the herd went there every morning.

"Now, Pablo, we must make a trial," said Humphrey. "You must get your lassos ready, in case they should be required. We must go to the avenue before daylight with the two dogs, tie one upon one side of the avenue and the other on the other, that they may bark and prevent the ponies from attempting to escape through the thicket. Then we must get the ponies between us and the drift of snow which lies across the avenue, and try if we cannot draw them into the drift. If so, they will plunge in so deep that some of them will not be able to get out before we have thrown the ropes round their necks."

"I see," said Pablo; "very good—soon catch them."

Before daylight they went with the dogs and a large bundle of hay, which they strewed nearer to the mound of drifted snow. They then tied the dogs up on each side, ordering them to lie down and be quiet. Then they walked through the thicket so as not to be perceived, until they considered that they were far enough from the snow-drift. About daylight the herd came to pick up the hay as usual, and after they had passed them Humphrey and Pablo followed in the thicket, not wishing to show themselves till the last moment. While the ponies were busy with the hay, they suddenly ran out into the avenue and separated, so as to prevent the ponies from attempting to gallop past them. Shouting as loud as they could, as they ran up to the ponies, and calling to the dogs, who immediately set up a barking on each side; the ponies, alarmed at the noise and the appearance of humphrey and Pablo, naturally set off in the only direction which appeared to them to be clear, and galloped away towards the mound of drifted snow, with their tails streaming, and snorting and plunging in the snow as they hurried along; but as soon as they arrived at the mound they plunged first up to their bellies, and afterwards, as they attempted to force their way where the snow was deeper, many of them stuck fast altogether, and struggled to clear themselves in vain. Humphrey and Pablo, who had followed them as fast as they could run, now came up with them and threw the lasso over the neck of one, and ropes with slip nooses over two more, which were floundering in the snow there together. The remainder of the herd, after great exertions, got clear off by turning round and galloping back—through the avenue. The three captured ponies made a furious struggle; but by drawing the ropes tight round their necks they were well-nigh choked, and soon unable to move. The lads then tied their fore-legs, and loosened the ropes round their necks that they might recover their breath.

"Got them now, Massa Humphrey," said Pablo.

"Yes, but our work is not yet over, Pablo; we must get them home; how shall we manage that?"

"Suppose they no eat to-day and to-morrow, get very tame."

"I believe that will be the best way; they cannot get loose again, do all they can."

"No, sir; but get one home to-day. This very fine pony; suppose we try him."

Pablo then put the halter on, and tied the end short to the fore-leg of the pony, so that it could not walk without keeping its head close to the ground—if it raised its head it was obliged to lift up its leg. Then he put the lasso round its neck to choke it if it was too unruly, and, having done that, he cast loose the ropes which had tied its fore-legs together.

"Now, Massa Humphrey, we get him home somehow. First I go loose the dogs; he 'fraid of the dogs, and run t'other way."

The pony, which was an iron-grey and very handsome, plunged furiously and kicked behind; but it could not do so without falling down, which it did several times before Pablo returned with the dogs. Humphrey held one part of the lasso on one side, and Pablo on the other, keeping the pony between them; and with the dogs barking at it behind, they contrived, with a great deal of exertion and trouble, to get the pony to the cottage. The poor animal, driven in this way on three legs, and every now and then choked with the lasso, was covered with foam before they arrived. Billy was turned out of his stable to make room for the newcomer, who was fastened securely to the manger and then left without food, that he might become tame. It was too late then, and they were too tired themselves to go for the other two ponies, so they were left lying on the snow all night, and the next morning they found them much tamer than they were at first, and during the day, following the same plan, they were both brought to the stable and secured alongside of the other. One was a bay pony with black legs, and the other a brown one. The bay pony was a mare, and the other two horses. Alice and Edith were delighted with the new ponies, and Humphrey was not a little pleased that he had succeeded in capturing them, after what had passed between Edward and himself. After two days' fasting, the poor animals were so tame that they ate out of Pablo's hand and submitted to be stroked and caressed; and before they were a fortnight in the stable. Alice and Edith could go up to them without danger. They were soon broken in; for the yard being full of muck, Pablo took them into it and mounted them. They plunged and kicked at first, and tried all they could to get rid of him, but they sank so deep into the muck that they were soon tired out; and after a month they were all three tolerably quiet to ride.

The snow was so deep all over the country that there was little communication with the metropolis. The Intendant's letter spoke of King Charles raising another army in Holland, and that his adherents in England were preparing to join him as soon as he marched southward.

"I think, Edward," said the Intendant, "that the king's affairs do now wear a more promising aspect, but there is plenty of time yet. I know your anxiety to serve your king, and I cannot blame it. I shall not prevent your going, although of course I must not be cognisant of your having so done. When the winter breaks up I shall send you to London. You will then be able better to judge of what is going on, and your absence will not create any suspicion; but you must be guided by me."

"I certainly will, sir," replied Edward. "I should indeed like to strike one blow for the king, come what will."

"All depends upon whether they manage affairs well in Scotland; but there is so much jealousy and pride, and I fear treachery also, that it is hard to say how matters may end."

It was soon after this conversation that a messenger arrived from London with letters, announcing that King Charles had been crowned in Scotland with great solemnity and magnificence.

"The plot thickens," said the Intendant; "and by this letter from my correspondent Ashley Cooper, I find that the king's army is well appointed, and that David Lesley is Lieutenant-General: Middleton commands the horse, and Wemyss the artillery. That Wemyss is certainly a good officer, but was not true to the late king:— may he behave better to the present! Now, Edward, I shall send you to London, and I will give you letters to those who will advise you how to proceed. You may take the black horse; he will bear you well. You will of course write to me, for Sampson will go with you, and you can send him back when you consider that you do not require or wish for his presence: there is no time to be lost, for, depend upon it, Cromwell, who is still at Edinburgh, will take the field as soon as he can. Are you ready to start to-morrow morning?"

"Yes, sir, quite ready."

"I fear that you cannot go over to the cottage to bid farewell to your sisters, but perhaps it is better that you should not."

"I think so too, sir," replied Edward; "now that the snow has nearly disappeared I did think of going over, having been so long absent, but I must send Oswald over instead."

"Well, then, leave me to write my letters, and do you prepare your saddle-bags. Patience and Clara will assist you. Tell Sampson to come to me."

Edward went to Patience and Clara, and told them that he was to set off for London on the following morning, and was about to make his preparations.

"How long do you remain, Edward?" inquired Patience.

"I cannot tell; Sampson goes with me, and I must of course be guided by your father. Do you know where the saddle-bags are, Patience?"

"Yes, Phoebe shall bring them to your room."

"And you and Clara must come and give me your assistance."

"Certainly we will, if you require it; but I did not know that your wardrobe was so extensive."

"You know that it is anything but extensive, Patience; but that is the reason why your assistance is more required. A small wardrobe ought at least to be in good order; and what I would require is, that you would look over the linen, and where it requires a little repair you will bestow upon it your charity."

"That we will do, Clara," replied Patience; "so get your needles and thread, and let us send him to London with whole linen. We will come when we are ready, sir."

"I don't like his going to London at all," said Clara; "we shall be so lonely when he has gone."

Edward had left the room, and having obtained the saddle-bags from Phoebe, had gone up to his chamber. The first thing that he laid hold of was his father's sword; he took it down, and having wiped it carefully, he kissed it, saying, "God grant that I may do credit to it, and prove as worthy to wield it as was my brave father!" He had uttered these words aloud; and again taking the sword, and laying it down on the bed, turned round, and perceived that Patience had, unknown to him, entered the room, and was standing close to him. Edward was not conscious that he had spoken aloud, and therefore merely said, "I was not aware of your presence, Patience. Your foot is so light."

"Whose sword is that, Edward?"

"It is mine; I bought it at Lymington."

"But what makes you have such an affection for that sword?"

"Affection for it?"

"Yes; as I came into the room you kissed it as fervently as—"

"As a lover would his mistress, I presume you would say," replied Edward.

"Nay, I meant not to use such vain words. I was about to say as a Catholic would a relic. I ask you again, why so? A sword is but a sword. You are about to leave this on a mission of my father's. You are not a soldier, about to engage in strife and war; if you were, why kiss your sword?"

"I will tell you. I do love this sword. I purchased it, as I told you, at Lymington, and they told me that it belonged to Colonel Beverley. It is for his sake that I love it. You know what obligations our family were under to him."

"This sword was then wielded by Colonel Beverley, the celebrated Cavalier, was it?" said Patience, taking it from off the bed and examining it.

"Yes, it was; and here, you see, are his initials upon the hilt."

"And why do you take it to London with you? Surely it is not the weapon which should be worn by a secretary, Edward: it is too large, and cumbrous, and out of character."

"Recollect, that till these last few months I have been a forester, Patience, and not a secretary. Indeed I feel that I am more fit for active life than the situation which your father's kindness has bestowed upon me. I was brought up, as you have heard, to follow to the wars, had my patron lived."

Patience made no reply. Clara now joined them, and they commenced the task of examining the linen; and Edward left the room, as he wished to speak with Oswald. They did not meet again till dinner-time. Edward's sudden departure had spread a gloom over them all,—even the Intendant was silent and thoughtful. In the evening he gave Edward the letters which he had written, and a considerable sum of money, telling him where he was to apply if he required more for his expenses. The Intendant cautioned him on his behaviour in many points, and also relative to his dress and carriage during his stay in the metropolis.

"If you should leave London there will be no occasion, nay, it would be dangerous to write to me. I shall take it for granted that you will retain Sampson till your departure, and when he returns here I shall presume that you have gone north. I will not detain you longer, Edward: may Heaven bless and protect you!"

So saying, the Intendant went away to his own room.

"Kind and generous man!" thought Edward; "how much did I mistake you when we first met!"

Taking up the letters and bag of money, which still remained on the table, Edward went to his room, and having placed the letters and money in the saddle-bag, he commended himself to the Divine Protector, and retired to rest.

Before daylight the sound of Sampson's heavy travelling boots below roused up Edward, and he was soon dressed. Taking his saddle-bags on his arm, he walked softly downstairs, that he might not disturb any of the family; but when he was passing the sitting-room he perceived that there was a light in it, and on looking in, that Patience was up and dressed. Edward looked surprised, and was about to speak, when Patience said—

"I rose early, Edward, because, when I took leave of you last night, I forgot a little parcel that I wanted to give you before you went. It will not take much room, and may beguile a weary hour. It is a little book of meditations. Will you accept it, and promise me to read it when you have time?"

"I certainly will, my dear Patience—if I may venture on the expression—read it, and think of you."

"Nay you must read it and think of what it contains," replied Patience.

"I will, then. I shall not need the book to remind me of Patience Heatherstone, I assure you."

"And now, Edward, I do not pretend to surmise the reason of your departure, nor would it be becoming in me to attempt to discover what my father thinks proper to be silent upon, but I must beg you to promise one thing."

"Name it, dear Patience," replied Edward; "my heart is so full at the thought of leaving you that I feel I can refuse you nothing."

"It is this,—I have a presentiment, I know not why, that you are about to encounter danger. If so, be prudent,—be prudent for the sake of your dear sisters—be prudent for the sake of all your friends, who would regret you—promise me that."

"I do promise you, most faithfully, Patience, that I will ever have my sisters and you in my thoughts, and will not be rash under any circumstances."

"Thank you, Edward; may God bless you and preserve you!"

Edward first kissed Patience's hand, that was held in his own; but perceiving the tears starting in her eyes, he kissed them off, without any remonstrance on her part, and then left the room. In a few moments more he was mounted on a fine powerful black horse, and followed by Sampson, on his road to London.

We will pass over the journey, which was accomplished without any event worthy of remark. Edward had, from the commencement, called Sampson to his side, that he might answer the questions he had to make upon all that he saw, and which the reader must be aware was quite new to one whose peregrinations had been confined to the New Forest and the town adjacent. Sampson was a very powerful man, of a cool and silent character, by no means deficient in intelligence, and trustworthy withal. He had long been a follower of the Intendant, and had served in the army. He was very devout; and generally, when not addressed, was singing hymns in a low voice.

On the evening of the second day they were close to the metropolis, and Sampson pointed out to Edward Saint Paul's Cathedral and Westminster Abbey, and other objects worthy of note.

"And where are we to lodge, Sampson?" inquired Edward.

"The best hotel that I know of for man and beast is the 'Swan with Three Necks,' in Holborn. It is not over frequented by roysterers, and you will there be quiet, and if your affairs demand it, unobserved."

"That will suit me, Sampson: I wish to observe, and not be observed, during my stay in London."

Before dark they had arrived at the hotel, and the horses were in the stable. Edward had procured an apartment to his satisfaction, and, feeling fatigued with his two days' travelling, had gone to bed.

The following morning he examined the letters which had been given to him by the Intendant, and inquired of Sampson if he could direct him on his way. Sampson knew London well: and Edward set out to Spring Gardens to deliver a letter, which the intendant informed him was confidential, to a person of the name of Langton. Edward knocked and was ushered in, Sampson taking a seat in the hall while Edward was shown into a handsomely-furnished library, where he found himself in the presence of a tall spare man, dressed after the fashion of the Roundheads of the time. He presented the letter. Mr Langton bowed and requested Edward to sit down; and after Edward had taken a chair, he then seated himself and opened the letter.

"You are right welcome, Master Armitage," said Mr Langton; "I find that, young as you appear to be, you are in the whole confidence of our mutual friend Mr Heatherstone. He hints at your being probably obliged to take a journey to the north, and that you will be glad to take charge of any letters which I may have to send in that direction. I will have them ready for you; and in case of need they will be such as will give a colouring to your proceeding, provided you may not choose to reveal your true object. How wears our good friend Heatherstone, and his daughter?"

"Quite well, sir."

"And he told me in one of his former letters that he had the daughter of our poor friend Ratcliffe with him. Is it not so?"

"It is, Mr Langton; and as gentle and pretty a child as you could wish to see."

"When did you arrive in London?"

"Yesterday evening, sir."

"And do you propose any stay?"

"That I cannot answer, sir; I must be guided by your advice. I have nought to do here, unless it be to deliver some three or four letters, given me by Mr Heatherstone."

"It is my opinion, Master Armitage, that the less you are seen in this city the better; there are hundreds employed to find out newcomers, and to discover from their people, or by other means, for what purpose they may have come; for you must be aware, Master Armitage, that the times are dangerous and people's minds are various. In attempting to free ourselves from what we considered despotism, we have created for ourselves a worse despotism, and one that is less endurable. It is to be hoped that what has passed will make not only kings, but subjects, wiser than they have been. Now what do you propose—to leave this instantly?"

"Certainly, if you think it advisable."

"My advice, then, is to leave London immediately. I will give you letters to some friends of mine in Lancashire and Yorkshire; in either county you can remain unnoticed, and make what preparations you think necessary. But do nothing in haste—consult well, and be guided by them, who will, if it is considered advisable and prudent, join with you in your project. I need say no more. Call upon me to-morrow morning an hour before noon, and I will have letters ready for you."

Edward rose to depart, and thanked Mr Langton for his kindness.

"Farewell, Master Armitage," said Langton; "to-morrow at the hour of eleven!"

Edward then quitted the house, and delivered the other letters of credence, the only one of importance at the moment was the one of credit; the others were to various members of the Parliament, desiring them to know Master Armitage as a confidential friend of the Intendant, and in case of need to exert their good offices in his behalf. The letter of credit was upon a Hamburgh merchant, who asked Edward if he required money. Edward replied that he did not at present, but that he had business to do for his employer in the north, and might require some when there, if it was possible to obtain it so far from London.

"When do you set out? And to what town do you go?"

"That I cannot well tell till to-morrow."

"Call before you leave this, and I will find some means of providing for you as you wish."

Edward then returned to the hotel. Before he went to bed he told Sampson that he found that he had to leave London on Mr Heatherstone's affairs, and might be absent some time; he concluded by observing that he did not consider it necessary to take him with him, as he could dispense with his services, and Mr Heatherstone would be glad to have him back.

"As you wish, sir," replied Sampson. "When am I to go back?"

"You may leave to-morrow as soon as you please. I have no letter to send. You may tell them that I am well, and will write as soon as I have anything positive to communicate."

Edward then made Sampson a present, and wished him a pleasant journey.

At the hour appointed on the following day Edward repaired to Mr Langton, who received him very cordially.

"I am all ready for you, Master Armitage: there is a letter to two Catholic ladies in Lancashire, who will take great care of you; and here is one to a friend of mine in Yorkshire. The ladies live about four miles from the town of Bolton, and my Yorkshire friend in the city of York. You may trust to either of them. And now, farewell; and, if possible, leave London before nightfall—the sooner the better. Where is your servant?"

"He has returned to Mr Heatherstone this morning."

"You have done right. Lose no time in leaving London; and don't be in a hurry in your future plans. You understand me. If any one accosts you on the road put no trust in any professions. You of course are going down to your relations in the north. Have you pistols?"

"Yes, sir; I have a pair which belonged to the unfortunate Mr Ratcliffe."

"Then they are good ones, I'll answer for it: no man was more particular about his weapons, or knew how to use them better. Farewell, Master Armitage, and may success attend you."

Mr Langton held out his hand to Edward, who respectfully took his leave.

Chapter Twenty Two.

Edward was certain that Mr Langton would not have advised him to leave London if he had not considered that it was dangerous to remain. He therefore first called upon the Hamburgh merchant, who, upon his explanation, gave him a letter of credit to a friend who resided in the city of York; and then returned to the hotel, packed up his saddle-bags, paid his reckoning, and, mounting his horse, set off on the northern road. As it was late in the afternoon before he was clear of the metropolis, he did not proceed farther than Barnet, where he pulled up at the inn. As soon as he had seen his horse attended to, Edward, with his saddle-bags on his arm, went into the room in the inn where all the travellers congregated. Having procured a bed and given his saddle-bags into the charge of the hostess, he sat down by the fire, which, although it was warm weather, was nevertheless kept alight.

Edward had made no alteration in the dress which he had worn since he had been received in the house of Mr Heatherstone. It was plain, although of good materials. He wore a high-crowned hat, and altogether would, from his attire, have been taken for one of the Roundhead party. His sword and shoulder-belt were indeed of more gay appearance than those usually worn by the Roundheads; but this was the only difference.

When Edward first entered the room there were three persons in it, whose appearance was not very prepossessing. They were dressed in what had once been very gay attire, but which now exhibited tarnished lace, stains of wine, and dust from travelling. They eyed him as he entered with his saddle-bags, and one of them said—

"That's a fine horse you were riding, sir. Has he much speed?"

"He has," replied Edward, as he turned away, and went into the bar to speak with the hostess, and give his property into her care.

"Going north, sir?" inquired the same person when Edward returned.

"Not exactly," replied Edward, walking to the window to avoid further conversation.

"The Roundhead is on the stilts," observed another of the party.

"Yes," replied the first; "it is easy to see that he has not been accustomed to be addressed by gentlemen; for half a pin I would slit his ears."

Edward did not choose to reply; he folded his arms and looked at the man with contempt.

The hostess, who had overheard the conversation, now called for her husband, and desired him to go into the room and prevent any further insults to the young gentleman who had just come in. The host, who knew the parties, entered the room, and said—

"Now you'll clear out of this as fast as you can; be off with you, and go to the stables, or I'll send for somebody whom you will not like."

The three men rose and swaggered, but obeyed the host's orders, and left the room.

"I am sorry, young Master, that these roysterers should have affronted you, as my wife tells me that they have. I did not know that they were in the house. We cannot well refuse to take in their horses; but we know well who they are, and, if you are travelling far, you had better ride in company."

"Thank you for your caution, my good host," replied Edward; "I thought that they were highwaymen, or something of that sort."

"You have made a good guess, sir; but nothing has yet been proved against them, or they would not be here. In these times we have strange customers, and hardly know who we take in. You have a good sword there, sir, I have no doubt; but I trust that you have other arms."

"I have," replied Edward, opening his doublet and showing his pistols.

"That's right, sir. Will you take anything before you go to bed?"

"Indeed I will, for I am hungry; anything will do, with a pint of wine."

As soon as he had supped Edward asked the hostess for his saddle-bags, and went up to his bed.

Early the next morning he rose and went to the stable to see his horse fed. The three men were in the stables, but they did not say anything to him. Edward returned to the inn, called for breakfast, and, as soon as he had finished, took out his pistols to renew the priming. While so occupied he happened to look up, and perceived one of the men with his face against the window, watching him. "Well, now you see what you have to expect, if you try your trade with me," thought Edward, "I am very glad that you have been spying." Having replaced his pistols, Edward paid his reckoning, and went to the stable desiring the ostler to saddle his horse and fix on his saddle-bags. As soon as this was done he mounted and rode off. Before he was well clear of the town the highwaymen cantered past him on three well-bred active horses. "I presume we shall meet again," thought Edward, who for some time cantered at a gentle rate, and then, as his horse was very fresh, he put him to a faster pace, intending to do a long day's work. He had ridden about fifteen miles, when he came to a heath, and, as he continued at a fast trot, he perceived the three highwaymen about a quarter of a mile in advance of him; they were descending a hill which was between them, and he soon lost sight of them again. Edward now pulled up his horse to let him recover his wind, and walked him gently up the hill. He had nearly gained the summit when he heard the report of firearms, and soon afterwards a man on horse back, in full speed, galloped over the hill towards him. He had a pistol in his hand, and his head turned back. The reason for this was soon evident, as immediately after him appeared the three highwaymen in pursuit. One fired his pistol at the man who fled, and missed him. The man then fired in return, and with true aim, as one of the highwaymen fell. All this was so sudden that Edward had hardly time to draw his pistol and put spurs to his horse before the parties were upon him, and were passing him. Edward levelled at the second highwayman as he passed him, and the man fell. The third highwayman, perceiving this, turned his horse to the side of the road, cleared a ditch, and galloped away across the heath. The man who had been attacked had pulled up his horse when Edward came to his assistance, and now rode up to him, saying—"I have to thank you, sir, for your timely aid; for these rascals were too many for me."

"You are not hurt, I trust, sir?" replied Edward.

"No, not the least; the fellow singed my curls though, as you may perceive. They attacked me but half a mile from here. I was proceeding north when I heard the clatter of hoofs behind me; I looked round, and saw at once what they were, and I sprung my horse out of the road to a thicket close to it, that they might not surround me. One of the three rode forward to stop my passage, and the other two rode round to the back of the thicket to get behind me. I then saw that I had separated them, and could gain a start upon them by riding back again, which I did as fast as I could, and they immediately gave chase. The result you saw. Between us we have broken up the gang; for both these fellows seem dead, or nearly so."

"What shall we do with them?"

"Leave them where they are," replied the stranger. "I am in a hurry to get on. I have important business at the city of York, and cannot waste my time in depositions, and such nonsense. It is only two scoundrels less in the world, and there's an end of the matter."

As Edward was equally anxious to proceed, he agreed with the stranger that it was best to do as he proposed.

"I am also going north," replied Edward, "and am anxious to get there as soon as I can."

"With your permission we will ride together," said the stranger. "I shall be the gainer, as I shall feel that I have one with me who is to be trusted to in case of any further attacks during our journey."

There was such a gentlemanlike, frank, and courteous air about the stranger, that Edward immediately assented to his proposal of their riding in company for mutual protection. He was a powerful, well-made man, of apparently about one or two and twenty, remarkably handsome in person, dressed richly, but not gaudily, in the cavalier fashion, and wore a hat with a feather. As they proceeded, they entered into conversation on indifferent matters for some time, neither party attempting by any question to discover who his companion might be. Edward had more than once, when the conversation flagged for a minute, considered what reply he should give in case his companion should ask him the cause of his journey, and at last had made up his mind what to say.

A little before noon they pulled up to bait their horses at a small village,—the stranger observing that he avoided Saint Alban's, and all other large towns, as he did not wish to satisfy the curiosity of people, or to have his motions watched; and therefore, if Edward had no objection, he knew the country so well that he could save time by allowing him to direct their path. Edward was, as may be supposed, very agreeable to this, and during their whole journey they never entered a town, except they rode through it after dark; and put up at humble inns on the roadside, where, if not quite so well attended to, at all events they were free from observation.

It was, however, impossible that this reserve could continue long, as they became more and more intimate every day. At last the stranger said—"Master Armitage, we have travelled together for some time, interchanging thoughts and feelings, but with due reserve as respects ourselves and our own plans. Is this to continue? If so, of course you have but to say so; but if you feel inclined to trust me, I have the same feeling towards you. By your dress I should imagine that you belonged to a party to which I am opposed; but your language and manners do not agree with your attire; and I think a hat and feathers would grace that head better than the steeple-crowned affair which now covers it. It may be that the dress is only assumed as a disguise: you know best. However, as I say, I feel confidence in you, to whatever party you may belong, and I give you credit for your prudence and reserve in these troubled times. I am a little older than you, and may advise you; and I am indebted to you, and cannot therefore betray you—at least I trust you believe so."

"I do believe it," replied Edward; "and I will so far answer you, Master Chaloner, that this attire of mine is not the one which I would wear if I had my choice."

"I believe that," replied Chaloner; "and I cannot help thinking you are bound north on the same business as myself, which is, I confess to you honestly, to strike a blow for the king. If you are on the same errand, I have two old relations in Lancashire who are stanch to the cause; and I am going to their house to remain until I can join the army. If you wish it, you shall come with me, and I will promise you kind treatment and safety while under their roof."

"And the names of these relatives of yours, Master Chaloner?" said Edward.

"Nay, you shall have them; for when I trust, I trust wholly. Their name is Conynghame."

Edward took his letters from out of his side-pocket, and handed one of them to his fellow-traveller. The address was, "To the worthy Mistress Conynghame, of Portlake, near Bolton, county of Lancaster."

"It is to that address that I am going myself," said Edward, smiling. "Whether it is the party you refer to you best know."

Chaloner burst out with a loud laugh.

"This is excellent! Two people meet, both bound on the same business, both going to the same rendezvous, and for three days do not venture to trust each other."

"The times require caution," replied Edward, as he replaced his letter.

"You are right," answered Chaloner, "and you are of my opinion. I know now that you have both prudence and courage. The first quality has been scarcer with us Cavaliers than the last; however, now all reserve is over, at least on my part."

"And on mine also," replied Edward.

Chaloner then talked about the chances of the war. He stated that King Charles's army was in a good state of discipline, and well found in everything; that there were hundreds in England who would join it, as soon as it had advanced far enough into England; and that everything wore a promising appearance.

"My father fell at the battle of Naseby, at the head of his retainers," said Chaloner, after a pause; "and they have contrived to fine the property, so that it has dwindled from thousands down to hundreds. Indeed, were it not for my good old aunts, who will leave me their estates, and who now supply me liberally, I should be but a poor gentleman."

"Your father fell at Naseby?" said Edward. "Were you there?"

"I was," replied Chaloner.

"My father also fell at Naseby," said Edward.

"Your father did?" replied Chaloner, "I do not recollect the name—Armitage—he was not in command there, was he?" continued Chaloner.

"Yes, he was," replied Edward.

"There was none of that name among the officers that I can recollect, young sir," replied Chaloner, with an air of distrust. "Surely you have been misinformed."

"I have spoken the truth," replied Edward; "and have now said so much that I must, to remove your suspicion, say more than perhaps I should have done. My name is not Armitage, although I have been so called for some time. You have set me the example of confidence, and I will follow it. My father was Colonel Beverley, of Prince Rupert's troop."

Chaloner started with astonishment.

"I'm sure that what you say is true," at last said he; "for I was thinking who it was that you reminded me of. You are the very picture of your father. Although a boy at the time, I knew him well, Master Beverley; a more gallant Cavalier never drew sword. Come, we must be sworn friends in life and death, Beverley," continued Chaloner, extending his hand, which was eagerly grasped by Edward, who then confided to Chaloner the history of his life.

When he had concluded, Chaloner said—"We all heard of the firing of Arnwood, and it is at this moment believed that all the children perished. It is one of the tales of woe that our nurses repeat to the children, and many a child has wept at your supposed deaths. But tell me, now, had you not fallen in with me, was it your intention to have joined the army under your assumed name of Armitage?"

"I hardly know what I intended to do. I wanted a friend to advise me."

"And you have found one, Beverley. I owe my life to you, and I will repay the debt as far as is in my power. You must not conceal your name to your sovereign; the very name of Beverley is a passport; but the son of Colonel Beverley will be indeed welcomed. Why, the very name will be considered as a harbinger of good fortune. Your father was the best and truest soldier that ever drew sword; and his memory stands unrivalled for loyalty and devotion. We are near to the end of our journey; yonder is the steeple of Bolton church. The old ladies will be out of their wits when they find that they have a Beverley under their roof."

Edward was much delighted at this tribute paid to his father's memory, and the tears more than once started into his eyes as Chaloner renewed his praise.

Late in the evening they arrived at Portlake, a grand old mansion, situated in a park crowded with fine old timber. Chaloner was recognised as they rode up the avenue by one of the keepers, who hastened forward to announce his arrival; and the domestics had opened the door for them before they arrived at it. In the hall they were met by the old ladies, who expressed their delight at seeing their nephew, as they had had great fear that something had happened to him.

"And something did very nearly happen to me," replied Chaloner, "had it not been for the timely assistance of my friend here, who, notwithstanding his Puritan attire, I hardly need tell you is a Cavalier devoted to the good cause, when I state that he is the son of Colonel Beverley, who fell at Naseby with my good father."

"No one can be more welcome, then," replied the old ladies, who extended their hands to Edward. They then went into a sitting-room, and supper was ordered to be sent up immediately.

"Our horses will be well attended to, Edward," said Chaloner; "we need not any longer look after them ourselves. And now, good aunts, have you no letters for me?"

"Yes, there are several; but you had better eat first."

"Not so; let me have the letters; we can read them before supper, and talk them over when at table."

One of the ladies produced the letters, which Chaloner, as he read them, handed over to Edward for his perusal. They were from General Middleton, and some other friends of Chaloner's who were with the army, giving him information as to what was going on, and what their prospects were supposed to be.

"You see that they have marched already," said Chaloner, "and I think the plan is a good one, and it has put General Cromwell in an awkward position. Our army is now between his and London, with three days march in advance. And we shall now be able to pick up our English adherents, who can join us without risk, as we go along. It has been a bold step, but a good one; and if they only continue as well as they have begun we shall succeed. The Parliamentary army is not equal to ours in numbers, as it is; and we shall add to ours daily. The king has sent to the Isle of Man for the Earl of Derby, who is expected to join to-morrow."

"And where is the army at this moment?" inquired Edward.

"They will be but a few miles from us to-night, their march is so rapid; to-morrow we will join if it pleases."

"Most willingly," replied Edward.

After an hour's more conversation, they were shown into their rooms, and retired for the night.

Chapter Twenty Three.

The next morning, before they had quitted their beds, a messenger arrived with letters from General Middleton, and from him they found that the king's army had encamped on the evening before not six miles from Portlake. As they hastily dressed themselves, Chaloner proposed to Edward that a little alteration in his dress would be necessary; and taking him to a wardrobe in which had been put aside some suits of his own, worn when he was a younger and slighter-made man than he now was, he requested Edward to make use of them. Edward, who was aware that Chaloner was right in his proposal, selected two suits of colours which pleased him most; and dressing in one, and changing his hat for one more befitting his new attire, was transformed into a handsome Cavalier. As soon as they had broken their fast they took leave of the old ladies, and, mounting their horses, set off for the camp. An hour's ride brought them to the outposts; and communicating with the officer on duty, they were conducted by an orderly to the tent of General Middleton, who received Chaloner with great warmth as an old friend, and was very courteous to Edward as soon as he heard that he was the son of Colonel Beverley.

"I have wanted you, Chaloner," said Middleton; "we are raising a troop of horse; the Duke of Buckingham commands it, but Massey will be the real leader of it; you have influence in this county, and will, I have no doubt, bring us many good hands."

"Where is the Earl of Derby?"

"Joined us this morning; we have marched so quick that we have not had time to pick our adherents up."

"And General Lesley?"

"Is by no means in good spirits: why I know not. We have too many ministers with his army, that is certain, and they do harm; but we cannot help ourselves. His majesty must be visible by this time; if you are ready I will introduce you; and when that is done we will talk matters over."

General Middleton then walked with them to the house in which the king had taken up his quarters for the night; and after a few minutes' waiting in the anteroom they were admitted into his presence.

"Allow me, your majesty," said General Middleton, after the first salutations, "to present to you Major Chaloner, whose father's name is not unknown to you."

"On the contrary, well-known to us," replied the king, "as a loyal and faithful subject, whose loss we must deplore. I have no doubt that his son inherits his courage and his fidelity."

The king held out his hand, and Chaloner bent his knee and kissed it.

"And now, your majesty will be surprised that I should present to you one of a house supposed to be extinct—the eldest son of Colonel Beverley."

"Indeed!" replied his majesty; "I heard that all his family perished at the ruthless burning of Arnwood. I hold myself fortunate, as a king, that even one son of so loyal and brave a gentleman as Colonel Beverley has escaped. You are welcome, young sir—most welcome to us; you must be near us; the very name of Beverley will be pleasing to our ears by night or day."

Edward knelt down and kissed his majesty's hand, and the king said—

"What can we do for a Beverley? Let us know, that we may show our feelings towards his father's memory?"

"All I request is, that your majesty will allow me to be near you in the hour of danger," replied Edward.

"A right Beverley reply," said the king, "and so we shall see to it, Middleton."

After a few more courteous words from his majesty they withdrew; but General Middleton was recalled by the king for a minute or two to receive his commands. When he rejoined Edward and Chaloner, he said to Edward—

"I have orders to send in for his majesty's signature your commission as captain of horse, and attached to the king's personal staff; it is a high compliment to the memory of your father, sir, and, I may add, your own personal appearance. Chaloner will see to your uniforms and accoutrements; you are well mounted, I believe you have no time to lose, as we march to-morrow for Warrington, in Cheshire."

"Has anything been heard of the Parliamentary army?"

"Yes; they are on the march towards London by the Yorkshire road, intending to cut us off if they can. And now, gentlemen, farewell; for I have no idle time, I assure you."

Edward was soon equipped, and now attended upon the king. When they arrived at Warrington they found a body of horse drawn up to oppose their passage onwards. These were charged, and fled with a trifling loss; and as they were known to be commanded by Lambert, one of Cromwell's best generals, there was great exultation in the king's army; but the fact was that Lambert had acted upon Cromwell's orders, which were, to harass and delay the march of the king as much as possible, but not to risk with his small force anything like an engagement. After this skirmish it was considered advisable to send back the Earl of Derby and many other officers of importance into Lancashire, that they might collect the king's adherents in that quarter and in Cheshire. Accordingly the earl, with about two hundred officers and gentlemen, left the army with that intention. It was then considered that it would be advisable to march the army direct to London; but the men were so fatigued with the rapidity of the march up to the present time, and the weather was so warm, that it was decided in the negative; and as Worcester was a town well affected to the king, and the country abounded with provisions, it was resolved that the army should march there, and wait for English reinforcements. This was done; the city opened the gates with every mark of satisfaction, and supplied the army with all that it required. The first bad news which reached them was the dispersion and defeat of the whole of the Earl of Derby's party by a regiment of militia, which had surprised them at Wigan during the night, when they were all asleep, and had no idea that any enemy was near to them. Although attacked at such a disadvantage, they defended themselves till a large portion of them were killed, and the remainder were taken prisoners, and most of them brutally put to death. The Earl of Derby was made a prisoner, but not put to death with the others.

"This is bad news, Chaloner," said Edward.

"Yes; it is more than bad," replied the latter; "we have lost our best officers, who never should have left the army; and now, the consequences of the defeat will be that we shall not have any people coming forward to join us. The winning side is the right side in this world; and there is more evil than that: the Duke of Buckingham has claimed the command of the army, which the king has refused; so that we are beginning to fight among ourselves. General Lesley is evidently dispirited, and thinks bad of the cause. Middleton is the only man who does his duty. Depend upon it we shall have Cromwell upon us before we are aware of it; and we are in a state of sad confusion—officers quarrelling, men disobedient, much talking, and little doing. Here we have been five days, and the works, which have been proposed to be thrown up as defences, not yet begun."

"I cannot but admire the patience of the king, with so much to harass and annoy him."

"He must be patient, perforce," replied Chaloner; "he plays for a crown, and it is a high stake; but he cannot command the minds of men, although he may the persons. I am no croaker, Beverley; but this I do say, that if we succeed with this army, as it is at present disorganised, we shall perform a miracle."

"We must hope for the best," replied Edward; "common danger may cement those who would otherwise be asunder; and when they have the army of Cromwell before them, they may be induced to forget their private quarrels and jealousies and unite in the good cause."

"I wish I could be of your opinion, Beverley," replied Chaloner; "but I have mixed with the world longer than you have, and I think otherwise."

Several more days passed, during which no defences were thrown up, and the confusion and quarrelling in the army continued to increase, until at last news arrived that Cromwell was within half a day's march of them, and that he had collected all the militia on his route, and was now in numbers nearly double to those in the king's army. All was amazement and confusion—nothing had been done—no arrangements had been made—and Chaloner told Edward that all was lost if immediate steps were not taken.

On the 3rd of October the army of Cromwell appeared in sight. Edward had been on horseback, attending the king, for the best part of the night; the disposition of the troops had been made as well as it could; and it was concluded, as Cromwell's army remained quiet, that no attempt would be made on that day. About noon the king returned to his lodging, to take some refreshment after his fatigue. Edward was with him; but before an hour had passed the alarm came that the armies were engaged. The king mounted his horse, which was ready saddled at the door; but before he could ride out of the city he was met and nearly beaten back by the whole body almost of his own cavalry, who came running on with such force that he could not stop them. His majesty called to several of the officers by name, but they paid no attention; and so great was the panic, that both the king, and his staff who attended him, were nearly overthrown and trampled under foot.

Cromwell had passed a large portion of his troops over the river without the knowledge of his opponents, and when the attack was made in so unexpected a quarter a panic ensued. Where General Middleton and the Duke of Hamilton commanded, a very brave resistance was made; but Middleton being wounded, and the Duke of Hamilton having had his leg taken off by a round shot, and many gentlemen having fallen, the troops, deserted by the remainder of the army, at last gave way, and the rout was general, the foot throwing away their muskets before they were discharged.

His majesty rode back into the town and found a body of horse, who had been persuaded by Chaloner to make a stand. "Follow me," said his majesty, "we will see what the enemy are about. I do not think they pursue, and if so, we may yet rally from this foolish panic."

His majesty, followed by Edward, Chaloner, and several of his personal staff, then galloped out to reconnoitre; but to his mortification he found that the troops had not followed him, but gone out of the town by the other gate, and that the enemy's cavalry in pursuit were actually in the town. Under such circumstances, by the advice of Chaloner and Edward, his majesty withdrew, and turning his horse's head he made all haste to leave Worcester. After several hours' riding, the king found himself in company of about 4000 of the cavalry who had so disgracefully fled; but they were still so panic-struck that he could put no confidence in them, and having advised with those about him he resolved to quit them. This he did without mentioning his intentions to any of his staff, not even Chaloner or Edward, leaving at night with two of his servants, whom he dismissed as soon as it was daylight, considering that his chance of escape would be greater if he was quite alone.

It was not till next morning that the troops discovered that the king had left them, and then they determined to separate, and as the major portion were from Scotland to make what haste they could back to that country. And now Chaloner and Edward consulted as to their plans.

"It appears to me," said Edward, laughing, "that the danger of this campaign of ours will consist in getting back again to our own homes; for I can most safely assert that I have not as yet struck a blow for the king."

"That is true enough, Beverley. When do you purpose going back to the New Forest? I think, if you will permit me, I will accompany you," said Chaloner. "All the pursuit will be to the northward to intercept and overtake the retreat into Scotland. I cannot therefore go to Lancashire; and indeed, as they know that I am out, they will be looking for me everywhere."

"Then come with me," said Edward; "I will find you protection till you can decide what to do. Let us ride on away from this, and we will talk over the matter as we go; but depend upon it, the farther south we get the safer we shall be; but still not safe, unless we can change our costume. There will be a strict search for the king to the south, as they will presume that he will try to get safe to France. Hark! What is that? I heard the report of arms. Let us ride up this hill and see what is going on."

They did so, and perceived that there was a skirmish between a party of Cavaliers and some of the Parliamentary cavalry at about a quarter of a mile distant.

"Come, Chaloner, let us at all events have one blow," said Edward.

"Agreed," replied Chaloner, spurring his horse; and down they went at full speed, and in a minute were in the *mêlée*, coming on the rear of the Parliamentary troops.

This sudden attack from behind decided the affair. The Parliamentary troopers, thinking that there were wore than two coming upon them, made off after another minute's combat, leaving five or six of their men on the ground.

"Thanks, Chaloner thanks, Beverley!" said a voice, which they immediately recognised. It was that of one of the king's pages. "These fellows with me were just about to run if you had not come to our aid. I will remain with them no longer, but join you if you will permit me."

"At all events remain here till they go away—I will send them off."

"My lads, you must all separate, or there will be no chance of escape. No more than two should ride together. Depend upon it we shall have more of the troops here directly."

The men, about fifteen in number, who had been in company with Grenville, considered that Chaloner's advice was good, and without ceremony set off with their horses' heads to the northward, leaving Chaloner, Edward, and Grenville together on the field of the affray. A dozen men were lying on the ground, either dead or severely wounded; seven of them were of the king's party, and the other five of the Parliamentary troops.

"Now what I propose," said Edward, "is this,—let us do what we can for those who are wounded, and then strip off the dresses and accoutrements of those Parliamentary dragoons who are dead, and dress ourselves in them, accoutrements and all. We can then pass through the country in safety, as we shall be supposed to be one of the parties looking for the king."

"That is a good idea," replied Chaloner, "and the sooner it is done the better."

"Well," said Edward, wiping his sword, which he still held drawn, and then sheathing it, "I will take the spoils of this fellow nearest to me: he fell by my hand, and I am entitled to them by all the laws of war and chivalry; but first let us dismount and look to the wounded."

They tied their horses to a tree, and having given what assistance they could to the wounded men, they proceeded to strip three of the Parliamentary troopers; and then, laying aside their own habiliments, they dressed themselves in the uniform of the enemy, and mounting their horses made all haste from the place. Having gained about twelve miles, they pulled up and rode at a more leisurely pace. It was now eight o'clock in the evening, but still not very dark; they therefore rode on another five miles, till they came to a small village, where they dismounted at an ale-house, and put their horses into the stable.

"We must be insolent and brutal in our manners, or we shall be suspected."

"Very true," said Grenville, giving the ostler a kick and telling him to bestir himself if he did not want his ears cropped.

They entered the ale-house, and soon found out they were held in great terror. They ordered everything of the best to be produced, and threatened to set fire to the house if it was not; they turned the man and his wife out of their bed, and all three went to sleep in it; and, in short, they behaved in such an arbitrary manner that nobody doubted that they were Cromwell's men. In the morning they set off again, by Chaloner's advice paying for nothing that they had ordered, although they had all of them plenty of money. They now rode fast, inquiring at the places which they passed through whether any fugitives had been seen, and if they came to a town, inquiring, before they entered, whether there were any Parliamentary troops. So well did they manage, that after four days they had gained the skirts of the New Forest, and concealed themselves in a thicket till night-time, when Edward proposed that he should conduct his fellow-travellers to the cottage, where he would leave them till his plans were arranged.

Edward had already arranged his plans. His great object was to ward off any suspicion of where he had been, and of course any idea that the Intendant had been a party to his acts; and the fortunate change of his dress enabled him now to do so with success. He had decided to conduct his two friends to the cottage that night, and the next morning to ride over in his Parliamentary costume to the Intendant's house, and bring the first news of the success of Cromwell and the defeat at Worcester; by which stratagem it would appear as if he had been with the Parliamentary, and not with the Royalist army.

As they had travelled along, they found that the news of Cromwell's success had not yet arrived: in those times there was not the rapidity of communication that we now have, and Edward thought it very probable that he would be the first to communicate the intelligence to the Intendant and those who resided near him.

As soon as it was dusk the three travellers left their retreat, and, guided by Edward, soon arrived at the cottage. Their appearance at first created no little consternation, for Humphrey and Pablo happened to be in the yard when they heard the clattering of the swords and accoutrements, and through the gloom observed, as they advanced, that the party were troopers. At first Humphrey was for running on and barring the door, but, on a second reflection, he felt that he could not do a more imprudent thing, if there was danger; and he therefore contented himself with hastily imparting the intelligence to his sisters, and then remaining at the threshold to meet the coming of the parties. The voice of Edward calling him by name dissipated all alarm, and in another minute he was in the arms of his brother and sisters.

"First let us take our horses to the stable, Humphrey," said Edward, after the first greeting was over, "and then we will come and partake of anything that Alice can prepare for us, for we have not fared over well for the last three days."

Accompanied by Humphrey and Pablo, they all went to the stables, and turned out the ponies to make room for the horses; and as soon as they were all fed and littered down they returned to the cottage, and Chaloner and Grenville were introduced. Supper was soon on the table, and they were too hungry to talk while they were eating, so but little information was gleaned from them that night. However, previous to Alice and Edith leaving the room to prepare beds for the newcomers, Humphrey ascertained that all was lost, and that they had escaped from the field. When the beds were ready, Chaloner and Grenville retired, and then Edward remained half an hour with Humphrey, to communicate to him what had passed. Of course he could not enter into detail; but told him that he would get information from their new guests after he had left, which he must do early in the morning.

"And now, Humphrey, my advice is this: My two friends cannot remain in this cottage, for many reasons; but we have the key of Clara's cottage, and they can take up their lodging there, and we can supply them with all they want until they find means of going abroad, which is their intention. I must be off to the Intendant's to-morrow, and the day after I will come over to you. In the meantime our guests can remain here, while you and Pablo prepare the cottage for them; and when I return everything shall be settled, and we will conduct them to it. I do not think there is much danger of their being discovered while they remain there, certainly not so much as if they were here; for we must expect parties of troops in every direction now, as they were when the king's father made his escape from Hampton Court. And now to bed, my good brother; and call me early, for I much fear that I shall not wake up, if you do not."

The brothers then parted for the night.

The next morning, long before their guests were awake, Edward had been called by Humphrey, and found Pablo at the door with his horse. Edward, who had put on his Parliamentary accoutrements, bade a hasty farewell to them, and set off across the forest to the house of the Intendant, where he arrived before they had left their bedrooms. The first person he encountered was, very fortunately, Oswald, who was at his cottage-door. Edward beckoned to him, being then about one hundred yards off; but Oswald did not recognise him at first, and advanced towards him in a very leisurely manner, to ascertain what the trooper might wish to inquire. But Edward called him Oswald, and that was sufficient. In few words Edward told him how all was lost, and how he had escaped by changing clothes with one of the enemy.

"I am now come to bring the news to the Intendant, Oswald. You understand me, of course?"

"Of course I do, Master Edward, and will take care that it is well-known that you have been fighting by the side of Cromwell all this time. I should recommend you to show yourself in this dress for the remainder of the day, and then every one will be satisfied. Shall I go to the Intendant's before you?"

"No, no, Oswald; the Intendant does not require me to be introduced to him, of course. I must now gallop up to his house and announce myself. Farewell for the present—I shall see you during the day."

Edward put spurs to his horse, and arrived at the Intendant's at full speed, making no small clattering in the yard below as he went in, much to the surprise of Sampson, who came out to ascertain what was the cause, and who was not a little surprised at perceiving Edward, who threw himself off the horse, and desiring Sampson to take it to the stable, entered the kitchen, and disturbed Phoebe, who was preparing breakfast. Without speaking to her, Edward passed on to the Intendant's room, and knocked.

"*Who* is there?" said the Intendant.

"Edward Armitage," was the reply, and the door was opened. The Intendant started back at the sight of Edward in the trooper's costume.

"My dear Edward, I am glad to see you in any dress; but this requires explanation. Sit down and tell me all."

"All is soon told, sir," replied Edward, taking off his iron skull-cap, and allowing his hair to fall down on his shoulders.

He then, in few words, stated what had happened, and by what means he had escaped, and the reason why he had kept on the trooper's accoutrements and made his appearance in them.

"You have done very prudently," replied the Intendant, "and you have probably saved me; at all events you have warded off all suspicion, and those who are spies upon me will now have nothing to report except to my favour. Your absence has been commented upon, and made known at high quarters, and suspicion has arisen in consequence. Your return as one of the Parliamentary forces will now put an end to all ill-natured remarks. My dear Edward, you have done me a service. As my secretary, and having been known to have been a follower of the Beverleys, your absence was considered strange, and it was intimated at high quarters that you had gone to join the king's forces, and that with my knowledge and consent. This I have from Langton; and it has in consequence injured me not a little: but now your appearance will make all right again. Now we will first to prayers, and then to breakfast; and after that we will have a more detailed account of what has taken place since your departure. Patience and Clara will not be sorry to recover their companion; but how they will like you in that dress I cannot pretend to say. However, I thank God that you have returned safe to us; and I shall be most happy to see you once more attend in the more peaceful garb of a secretary."

"I will, with your permission, sir, not quit this costume for one day, as it may be as well that I should be seen in it."

"You are right, Edward: for this day retain it; to-morrow you will resume your usual costume. Go down to the parlour; you will find Patience and Clara anxiously waiting for you, I have no doubt. I will join you there in ten minutes."

Edward left the room, and went downstairs. It hardly need be said how joyfully he was received by Patience and Clara. The former, however, expressed her joy in tears—the latter in wild mirth.

We will pass over the explanations and the narrative of what had occurred, which was given by Edward to Mr Heatherstone in his own room. The Intendant said, as he concluded—

"Edward, you must now perceive that, for the present, nothing more can be done; if it pleases the Lord, the time will come when the monarch will be reseated on his throne; at present, we must bow to the powers that be; and I tell you frankly it is my opinion that Cromwell aims at sovereignty, and will obtain it. Perhaps it may be better that we should suffer the infliction for a time, as for a time only can it be upheld, and it may be the cause of the king being more schooled and more fitted to reign than, by what you have told me in the course of your narrative, he at present appears to be."

"Perhaps so, sir," replied Edward. "I must say that the short campaign I have gone through has very much opened my eyes. I have seen but little true chivalric feeling, and much of interested motives, in those who have joined the king's forces. The army collected was composed of most discordant elements, and were so discontented, so full of jealousy and ill-will, that I am not surprised at the result. One thing is certain, that there must be a much better feeling existing between all parties, before such a man as Cromwell can ever be moved from his position; and, for the present, the cause may be considered as lost."

"You are right, Edward," replied the Intendant; "I would they were better; but, as they are, let us make the best of them. You have now seen enough to have subdued that fiery zeal for the cause which previously occupied your whole thoughts; now let us be prudent, and try if we cannot be happy."

Chapter Twenty Four.

It was only to Oswald that Edward made known what had occurred; he knew that he was to be trusted. The next day Edward resumed his forester's dress, while another one was preparing for him, and went over to the cottage; where, with the consent of the Intendant, he proposed remaining for a few days. Of course Edward had not failed to acquaint the Intendant with his proposed plans relative to Chaloner and Grenville, and received his consent; at the same time advising that they should gain the other side of the Channel as soon as they possibly could. Edward found them all very anxious for his arrival. Humphrey and Pablo had been to the cottage, which they had found undisturbed since the capture of the robbers, and made everything ready for the reception of the two Cavaliers, as on their first journey they took with them a cart-load of what they knew would be necessary. Chaloner and Grenville appeared to be quite at home already, and not very willing to shift their quarters. They, of course, still retained their troopers' clothes, as they had no other to wear until they could be procured from Lymington; but, as we have before mentioned, they were in no want of money. They, had been amusing the girls and Humphrey with a description of what had occurred during the campaign, and Edward found that he had but little to tell them, as Chaloner had commenced his narrative with an account of his first meeting with Edward when he had been attacked by the highwaymen. As soon as he could get away, Edward went out with Humphrey to have some conversation with him.

"Now, Humphrey, as you have pretty well heard all my adventures since our separation, let me hear what you have been doing."

"I have no such tales of stirring interest to narrate as Chaloner has been doing as your deputy, Edward," replied Humphrey. "All I can say is, that we have had no visitors—that we have longed for your return—and that we have not been idle since you quitted us."

"What horses were those in the stable," said Edward, "that you turned out to make room for ours when we arrived?"

Humphrey laughed, and then informed Edward of the manner in which they had succeeded in capturing them.

"Well, you really deserve credit, Humphrey, and certainly were not born to be secluded in this forest."

"I rather think that I have found that I was born for it," replied Humphrey, "although, I must confess, that since you have quitted us I have not felt so contented here as I did before. You have returned, and you have no idea what an alteration I see in you since you have mixed with the world, and have been a party in such stirring scenes."

"Perhaps so, Humphrey," replied Edward; "and yet do you know that, although I so ardently wished to mix with the world, and to follow the wars, I am anything but satisfied with what I have seen of it; and so far from feeling any inclination to return to it I rather feel more inclined to remain here, and remain in quiet and in peace. I have been disappointed, that is the truth. There is a great difference between the world such as we fancy it when we are pining for it, and the world when we actually are placed within the vortex, and perceive the secret springs of men's actions. I have gained a lesson, but not a satisfactory one, Humphrey; it may be told in a very few words. It is a most deceitful and hollow world! And that is all there is to be said."

"What very agreeable, pleasant young men are Masters Chaloner and Grenville," observed Humphrey.

"Chaloner I know well," replied Edward; "he is to be trusted, and he is the only one in whom I have been able to place confidence, and therefore I was most fortunate in falling in with him as I did on my first starting. Grenville I know little about; we met often, it is true, but it was in the presence of the king, being both of us on his staff; at the same time, I must acknowledge that I know nothing against him; and this I do know, which is, that he is brave."

Edward then narrated what had passed between the Intendant and himself since his return; and how well satisfied the Intendant had been with his *ruse* in returning to him in the dress of a trooper.

"Talking about that, Edward, do you not think it likely that we shall have the troopers down here in search of the king?"

"I wonder you have not had them already," replied Edward.

"And what shall we do if they arrive?"

"That is all prepared for," replied Edward; "although, till you mentioned it, I had quite forgotten it. The Intendant was talking with me on the subject last night, and here is an appointment for you as verderer, signed by him, which you are to use as you may find necessary; and here is another missive, ordering you to receive into your house two of the troopers who may be sent down here, and find them quarters and victuals, but not to be compelled to receive more. Until the search is over, Chaloner and Grenville must retain their accoutrements and remain with us: And, Humphrey, if you have not made any use of the clothes which I left here—I mean the first dress I had made when I was appointed secretary, and which I thought rather too faded to wear any longer—I will put it on now, as, should any military come here as scouters to the Intendant, I shall have some authority over them."

"It is in your chest, where you left it, Edward. The girls did propose to make two josephs out of it for winter wear; but they never have thought of it since, or have not had time. By the bye, you have not told me what you think of Alice and Edith after your long absence."

"I think they are both very much grown and very much improved," replied Edward, "but I must confess to you that I think it is high time that they were, if possible, removed from their present homely occupations, and instructed as young ladies should be."

"But how, Edward, is that to be?"

"That I cannot yet tell, and it grieves me that I cannot; but still I see the necessity of it, if ever we are to return to our position in society."

"And are we ever to return?"

"I don't know. I thought little of it before I went away and mixed in society; but since I have been in the world I have been compelled to feel that my dear sisters are not in their sphere, and I have resolved upon trying if I cannot find a more suitable position for them. Had we been successful I should have had no difficulty: but now I hardly know what to do."

"I have not inquired about Mrs Patience, brother; how is she?"

"She is as good and as handsome as ever, and very much grown; indeed, she is becoming quite womanly."

"And Clara?"

"Oh, I do not perceive any difference in her: I think she is grown, but I hardly observed her. Here comes Chaloner; we will tell him of our arrangements in case we are disturbed by the military parties."

"It is a most excellent arrangement," said Chaloner, when Edward had made the communication; "and it was a lucky day when I first fell in with you, Beverley."

"Not Beverley, I pray you; that name is to be forgotten; it was only revived for the occasion."

"Very true; then, Master Secretary Armitage, I think the arrangement excellent: the only point will be to find out what troops are sent down in this direction, as we must of course belong to some other regiment, and have been pursued from the field of battle. I should think that Lambert's squadrons will not be this way."

"We will soon ascertain that; let your horses be saddled and accoutred, so that should any of them make their appearance the horses may be at the door. It is my opinion that they will be here some time to-day."

"I fear that it will be almost impossible for the king to escape," observed Chaloner.

"I hardly know what to think of his leaving us in that way."

"I have reflected upon it," replied Edward, "and I think it was perhaps prudent: some were to be trusted, and some not; it was impossible to know who were and who were not—he therefore trusted nobody. Besides, his chance of escape, if quite alone, is greater than if in company."

"And yet I feel a little mortified that he did not trust me," continued Edward; "my life was at his service."

"He could no more read your heart than he could mine or others," observed Chaloner; "and any selection would have been invidious: on the whole, I think he acted wisely, and I trust that it will prove so. One thing is certain, which is, that all is over now, and that for a long while—we may let our swords rest in their scabbards. Indeed, I am sickened with it, after what I have seen, and would gladly live here with you, and help to till the land—away from the world and all its vexations. What say you, Edward; will you and your brother take me as a labourer after all is quiet again?"

"You would soon tire of it, Chaloner; you were made for active exertion and bustling in the world."

"Nevertheless, I think, under two such amiable and pretty mistresses, I could stay well contented here: it is almost Arcadian. But still it is selfish for me to talk in this way; indeed, my feelings are contrary to my words."

"How do you mean, Chaloner?"

"To be candid with you, Edward, I was thinking what a pity it is that two such sweet girls as your sisters should be employed here in domestic drudgery, and remain in such an uncultivated state—if I may be pardoned for speaking so freely—but I do so because I am convinced that, if in proper hands, they would grace a court; and you must feel that I am right."

"Do you not think that the same feelings have passed in my mind, Chaloner? Indeed, Humphrey will tell you that we were speaking on the same subject but an hour ago. You must, however, be aware of the difficulty I am in: were I in possession of Arnwood and its domain, then indeed—but that is all over now, and I presume I shall shortly see my own property, whose woods are now in sight of me, made over to some Roundhead, for good services against the Cavaliers at Worcester."

"Edward," replied Chaloner, "I have this to say to you, and I can say it because you know that I am indebted to you for my life, and that is a debt that nothing can cancel: If at any time you determine upon removing your sisters from this, recollect my maiden aunts at Portlake. They cannot be in better hands, and they cannot be in the hands of any person who will more religiously do their duty towards them, and be pleased with the trust confided to them. They are rich, in spite of exactions; but in these times women are not fined and plundered as men are, and they have been well able to afford all that has been taken from them, and all that they have voluntarily given to the assistance of our party. They are alone, and I really believe that nothing would make them more happy than to have the care of the two sisters of Edward Beverley—be sure of that. But I will be more sure of it, if you will find means of sending to them a letter, which I shall write to them. I tell you that you will do them a favour, and that if you do not accept the offer, you will sacrifice your sisters' welfare to your own pride,—which I do not think you would do."

"Most certainly I will not do that," replied Edward; "and I am fully sensible of your kind offer; but I can say no more until I hear what your good aunts may reply to your letter. You mistake me much, Chaloner, if you think that any sense of obligation would prevent me from seeing my sisters removed from a position so unworthy of them, but which circumstances have driven them to. That we are paupers is undeniable; but I never shall forget that my sisters are the daughters of Colonel Beverley."

"I am delighted with your reply, Edward, and I fear not that of my good aunts. It will be a great happiness to me when I am wandering abroad to know that your sisters are under their roof, and are being educated as they ought to be."

"What's the matter, Pablo?" said Humphrey to the former, who came running, out of breath.

"Soldiers," said Pablo; "plenty of them, gallop this way—gallop every way."

"Now, Chaloner, we must get ourselves out of this scrape; and I trust that afterwards all will be well," said Edward. "Bring the horses out to the door; and, Chaloner, you and Grenville must wait within: bring my horse out also, as it will appear as if I had just ridden over. I must in to change my dress. Humphrey, keep a look-out and let us know when they come."

Chaloner and Edward went in, and Edward put on his dress of secretary. Shortly afterwards a party of cavalry were seen galloping towards the cottage. They soon arrived there, and pulled up their horses. An officer who headed them addressed Humphrey in a haughty tone, and asked him who he was.

"I am one of the verderers of the forest, sir," replied Humphrey respectfully.

"And whose cottage is that? And who have you there?"

"The cottage is mine, sir; two of the horses at the door belong to two troopers who have come in quest of those who fled from Worcester; the other horse belongs to the secretary of the Intendant of the forest, Mr Heatherstone, who has come over with directions from the Intendant as to the capture of the rebels."

At this moment Edward came out and saluted the officer.

"This is the secretary, sir, Master Armitage," said Humphrey, falling back.

Edward saluted the officer, and said—

"Mr Heatherstone, the Intendant, has sent me over here to make arrangements for the capture of the rebels. This man is ordered to lodge two troopers as long as they are considered necessary to remain; and I have directions to tell any officer whom I may meet that Mr Heatherstone and his verderers will take good care that none of the rebels are harboured in this direction; and that it will be better that the troops scour the southern edge of the forest, as it is certain that the fugitives will try all that they can to embark for France."

"What regiment do the troopers belong to that you have here?"

"I believe to Lambert's troop, sir; but they shall come out and answer for themselves. Tell those men to come out," said Edward to Humphrey.

"Yes, sir; but they are hard to wake, for they have ridden from Worcester; but I will rouse them."

"Nay, I cannot wait," replied the officer. "I know none of Lambert's troops, and they have no information to give."

"Could you not take them with you, sir, and leave two of your men instead of them; for they are troublesome people to a poor man, and devour everything?" said Humphrey submissively.

"No, no," replied the officer, laughing, "we all know Lambert's people—a friend or enemy is much the same to them. I have no power over them, and you must make the best of it.—Forward! Men," continued the officer, saluting Edward as he passed on: and in a minute or two they were far in the distance.

"That's well over," observed Edward. "Chaloner and Grenville are too young-looking and too good-looking for Lambert's villains; and a sight of them might have occasioned suspicion. We must, however, expect more visits. Keep a good look-out, Pablo."

Edward and Humphrey then went in and joined the party inside the cottage, who were in a state of no little suspense during the colloquy outside.

"Why, Alice, dearest, you look quite pale," said Edward, as he came in.

"I feared for our guests, Edward. I'm sure that if they had come into the cottage, Master Chaloner and Master Grenville would never have been believed to be troopers."

"We thank you for the compliment, Mistress Alice," said Chaloner; "but I think, if necessary, I could ruffle and swear with the best, or rather the worst of them. We passed for troopers very well on the road here."

"Yes, but you did not meet any other troopers."

"That's very true, and shows your penetration. I acknowledge that with troopers there would have been more difficulty; but still, among so many thousands there must be many varieties, and it would be an awkward thing for an officer of one troop to arrest upon suspicion the men belonging to another. I think, when we are visited again, I shall sham intoxication—that will not be very suspicious."

"No, not on either side," replied Edward. "Come, Alice, we will eat what dinner you may have ready for us."

For three or four days the Parliamentary forces continued to scour the forest, and another visit or two was paid to the cottage, but without suspicion being created, in consequence of the presence of Edward, and his explanations. The parties were invariably sent in another direction. Edward wrote to the Intendant, informing him what had occurred, and requesting permission to remain a few days longer at the cottage; and Pablo, who took the letter, returned with one from the Intendant, acquainting him that the king had not yet been taken; and requesting the utmost vigilance on his part to ensure his capture, with directions to search various places, in company with the troopers who had been stationed at the cottage; or if he did not like to leave the cottage, to show the letter to any officer commanding parties in search, that they might act upon the suggestions contained in it. This letter Edward had an opportunity of showing to one or two officers commanding parties, who approached the cottage, and to whom Edward went out to communicate with, thereby preventing their stopping there.

At last, in about a fortnight, there was not a party in the forest, all of them having gone down to the sea-side, to look-out for the fugitives, several of whom were taken.

Humphrey took the cart to Lymington, to procure clothes for Chaloner and Grenville, and it was decided that they should assume those of verderers of the forest, which would enable them to carry a gun. As soon as Humphrey had obtained what was requisite, Chaloner and Grenville were conducted to Clara's cottage, and took possession,— of course never showing themselves outside the wood which surrounded it. Humphrey lent them Holdfast as a watch dog, and they took leave of Alice and Edith with much regret. Humphrey and Edward accompanied them to their new abode. It was arranged that the horses should remain under the care of Humphrey, as they had no stable at Clara's cottage.

On parting, Chaloner gave Edward the letter for his aunts; and then Edward once more bent his steps towards the Intendant's house, and found himself in the company of Patience and Clara.

Edward narrated to the Intendant all that had occurred, and the Intendant approved of what he had done; strongly advising that Chaloner and Grenville should not attempt to go to the continent till all pursuit was over.

"Here's a letter I have received from the Government, Edward, highly commending my vigilance and activity in pursuit of the fugitives. It appears that the officers you fell in with have written up to state what admirable dispositions we had made. It is a pity, is it not, Edward, that we are compelled to be thus deceitful in this world? Nothing but the times, and the wish to do good, could warrant it. We meet the wicked, and fight them with their own weapons; but although it is treating them as they deserve, our conscience must tell us that it is not right."

"Surely, sir, to save the lives of people who have committed no other fault except loyalty to their king, will warrant our so doing—at least, I hope so."

"According to the Scriptures, I fear it will not; but it is a difficult question for us to decide. Let us be guided by our own consciences; if they do not reproach us we cannot be far from right."

Edward then produced the letter he had received from Chaloner, requesting that the Intendant would have the kindness to forward it.

"I see," replied the Intendant; "I can forward these through Langton. I presume it is to obtain credit for money. It shall go on Thursday."

The conference was then broken up, and Edward went to see Oswald.

Chapter Twenty Five.

For several days Edward remained at home, anxiously awaiting every news which arrived; expecting every time that the capture of the king would be announced, and, with great joy, finding that hitherto all efforts had been unsuccessful. But there was a question which now arose in Edward's mind, and which was the cause of deep reflection. Since the proposal of sending his sisters away had been started, he felt the great inconvenience of his still representing himself to the Intendant as the grandson of Armitage. His sisters, if sent to the ladies at Portlake, must be sent without the knowledge of the Intendant; and if so, the discovery of their absence would soon take place, as Patience Heatherstone would be constantly going over to the cottage; and he now asked himself the question whether, after all the kindness and confidence which the Intendant had shown him, he was right in any longer concealing from him his birth and parentage. He felt that he was doing the Intendant an injustice in not showing to him that confidence which he deserved.

That he was justified in so doing at first, he felt; but since the joining the king's army, and the events which had followed, he considered that he was treating the Intendant ill, and he now resolved to take the first opportunity of making the confession. But to do it formally, and without some opportunity which might offer, he felt awkward. At last he thought that he would at once make the confession to Patience, under the promise of secrecy. That he might do at once; and, after he had done so, the Intendant could not tax him with want of confidence altogether. He had now analysed his feelings towards Patience; and he felt how dear she had become to him. During the time he was with the army she had seldom been out of his thoughts; and although he was often in the society of well-bred women, he saw not one that, in his opinion, could compare with Patience Heatherstone; but still, what chance had he of supporting a wife? At present, at the age of nineteen, it was preposterous. Thoughts like these ran in his mind, chasing each other, and followed by others as vague and unsatisfactory; and, in the end, Edward came to the conclusion that he was without a penny, and that being known as the heir of Beverley would be to his disadvantage; that he was in love with Patience Heatherstone, and had no chance at present of obtaining her; and that he had done well up to the present time in concealing who he was from the Intendant, who could safely attest that he knew not that he was protecting the son of so noted a Cavalier; and that he would confess to Patience who he was, and give as a reason for not telling her father, that he did not wish to commit him by letting him know who it was that was under his protection. How far the reader may be satisfied with the arguments which Edward was satisfied with, we cannot pretend to say; but Edward was young, and hardly knew how to extricate himself from the cloak which necessity had first compelled him to put on. Edward was already satisfied that he was not quite looked upon with indifference by Patience Heatherstone; and he was not yet certain whether it was not a grateful feeling that she had towards him more than any other; that she believed him to be beneath her in birth, he felt convinced, and therefore she could have no idea that he was Edward Beverley. It was not till several days after he had made up his mind that he had an opportunity of being with her alone, as Clara Ratcliffe was their constant companion. However, one evening Clara went out, and stayed out so long, carelessly wrapped up, that she caught cold; and the following evening she remained at home, leaving Edward and Patience to take their usual walk unaccompanied by her. They had walked for some minutes in silence, when Patience observed—

"You are very grave, Edward, and have been very grave ever since your return; have you anything to vex you beyond the failure of the attempt?"

"Yes, I have, Patience. I have much on my conscience, and do not know how to act. I want an adviser and a friend, and know not where to find one."

"Surely, Edward, my father is your sincere friend, and not a bad adviser."

"I grant it; but the question is between your father and me, and I cannot advise with him for that reason."

"Then advise with me, Edward, if it is not a secret of such moment that it is not to be trusted to a woman: at all events it will be the advice of a sincere friend; you will give me credit for that."

"Yes, and for much more; for I think I shall have good advice, and will therefore accept your offer. I feel, Patience, that although I was justified, on my first acquaintance with your father, in not making known to him a secret of some importance, yet now that he has put such implicit confidence in me, I am doing him and myself an injustice in not making the communication—that is, as far as confidence in him is concerned, I consider that he has a right to know all, and yet I feel that it would be prudent on my part that he should not know all, as the knowledge might implicate him with those with whom he is at present allied. A secret sometimes is dangerous; and if your father could not say that on his honour he knew not of the secret, it might harm him if the secret became afterwards known. Do you understand me?"

"I cannot say that I exactly do; you have a secret that you wish to make known to my father, and you think the knowledge of it may harm him. I cannot imagine what kind of secret that may be."

"Well, I can give you a case in point. Suppose now that I knew that King Charles was hidden in your stable-loft: such might be the case, and your father be ignorant of it, and his assertion of his ignorance would be believed; but if I were to tell your father that the king was there, and it was afterwards discovered, do you not see that by confiding such a secret to him I should do harm, and perhaps bring him into trouble?"

"I perceive now, Edward; do you mean to say that you know where the king is concealed? For if you do, I must beg of you not to let my father know anything about it. As you say, it would put him in a difficult position, and must eventually harm him much. There is a great difference between wishing well to a cause and supporting it in person. My father wishes the king well, I believe, but, at the same time, he will not take an active part, as you have already seen; at the same time, I am convinced that he would never betray the king if he knew where he was. I say, therefore, if that is your secret, keep it from him, for his sake and for mine, Edward, if you regard me."

"You know not how much I regard you, Patience. I saw many high-born women when I was away, but none could I see equal to Patience Heatherstone, in my opinion; and Patience was ever in my thoughts during my long absence."

"I thank you for your kind feelings towards me," replied Patience; "but, Master Armitage, we were talking about your secret."

"Master Armitage!" rejoined Edward; "how well you know how to remind me, by that expression, of my obscure birth and parentage, whenever I am apt to forget the distance which I ought to observe!"

"You are wrong!" replied Patience; "but you flattered me so grossly that I called you Master Armitage to show that I disliked flattery; that was all. I dislike flattery from those who are above me in rank, as well as those who are below me; and I should have done the same to any other person, whatever his condition might be. But forget what I said; I did not mean to vex you, only to punish you for thinking me so silly as to believe such nonsense."

"Your humility may construe that into flattery which was said by me in perfect sincerity and truth—that I cannot help," replied Edward. "I might have added much more, and yet have been sincere; if you had not reminded me of my not being of gentle birth I might have had the presumption to have told you much more; but I have been rebuked."

Edward finished speaking, and Patience made no reply: they walked on for several moments without exchanging another syllable. At last Patience said—

"I will not say who is wrong, Edward; but this I do know, that the one who first offers the olive-branch after a misunderstanding cannot but be right. I offer it now, and ask you whether we are to quarrel about one little word. Let me ask you, and give me a candid answer: Have I ever been so base as to treat as an inferior one to whom I have been so much obliged?"

"It is I who am in fault, Patience," replied Edward. "I have been dreaming for a long while, pleased with my dreams; and forgetting that they were dreams, and not likely to be realised. I must now speak plainly. I love you,

Patience; love you so much that to part from you would be misery—to know that my love was rejected, as bitter as death. That is the truth, and I can conceal it no longer. Now I admit you have a right to be angry."

"I see no cause for anger, Edward," replied Patience. "I have not thought of you but as a friend and benefactor; it would have been wrong to have done otherwise. I am but a young person, and must be guided by my father. I would not offend him by disobedience. I thank you for your good opinion of me, and yet I wish you had not said what you have."

"Am I to understand from your reply, that if your father raised no objection, my lowly birth would be none in your opinion?"

"Your birth has never come into my head, except when reminded of it by yourself."

"Then, Patience, let me return for the present to what I had to confide to you. I was—"

"Here comes my father, Edward," said Patience.

"Surely I have done wrong, for I feel afraid to meet him."

Mr Heatherstone now joined them, and said to Edward—

"I have been looking for you; I have news from London which has rejoiced me much. I have at last obtained what I have some time been trying for; and, indeed, I may say that your prudence and boldness in returning home as a trooper, added to your conduct in the forest, has greatly advanced, and ultimately obtained for me my suit. There was some suspense before that; but your conduct has removed it; and now we shall have plenty to do."

They walked to the house, and the Intendant, as soon as he had gained his own room, said to Edward—

"There is a grant to me of a property which I have long solicited for my services—read it." Edward took up the letter, in which the Parliament informed Mr Heatherstone that his application for the property of Arnwood had been acceded to, and signed by the Commissioners; and that he might take immediate possession. Edward turned pale as he laid the document down on the table.

"We will ride to-morrow, Edward, and look it over. I intend to rebuild the house."

Edward made no reply.

"Are you not well?" said the Intendant, with surprise.

"Yes, sir," replied Edward, "I am well, I believe, but I will confess to you that I am disappointed. I did not think that you would have accepted a property from such a source, and so unjustly sequestrated."

"I am sorry, Edward," replied the Intendant, "that I should have fallen in your good opinion; but allow me to observe that you are so far right, that I never would have accepted a property to which there were living claimants; but this is a different case. For instance, the Ratcliffe property belongs to little Clara and is sequestrated. Do you think I would accept it? Never! But here is a property without an heir; the whole family perished in the flames of Arnwood! There is no living claimant! It must be given to somebody, or remain with the Government. This property, therefore, and this property only, out of all sequestrated, I selected; as I felt that, in obtaining it, I did harm to no one. I have been offered others, but have refused them. I would accept of this, and this only; and that is the reason why my applications have hitherto been attended with no success. I trust you believe me, Edward, in what I assert?"

"First answer me one question, Mr Heatherstone. Suppose it were proved that the whole of the family did not, as it is supposed, perish at the conflagration of Arnwood? Suppose a rightful heir to it should at any time appear, would you then resign the property to him?"

"As I hope for heaven, Edward, I would!" replied the Intendant, solemnly raising his eyes upwards as he spoke. "I then should think that I had been an instrument to keep the property out of other hands less scrupulous, and should surrender it as a trust which had been confided to me for the time only."

"With such feelings, Mr Heatherstone, I can now congratulate you upon your having obtained possession of the property," replied Edward.

"And yet I do not deserve so much credit, as there is little chance of my sincerity being put to the test, Edward. There is no doubt that the family all perished; and Arnwood will become the dower of Patience Heatherstone."

Edward's heart beat quick. A moment's thought told him his situation. He had been prevented, by the interruption of Mr Heatherstone, from making his confession to Patience; and now he could not make it to anybody without a rupture with the Intendant, or a compromise, by asking what he so earnestly desired—the hand of Patience. Mr Heatherstone observing to Edward that he did not look so well, said supper was ready; and that they had better go into the next room. Edward mechanically followed. At supper he was tormented by the incessant inquiries of Clara, as to what was the matter with him. He did not venture to look at Patience, and made a hasty retreat to bed; complaining, as he well might do, of a severe headache.

Edward threw himself on his bed, but to sleep was impossible. He thought of the events of the day over and over again. Had he any reason to believe that Patience returned his affection? No: her reply was too calm, too composed, to make him suppose that; and now that she would be an heiress, there would be no want of pretenders to her hand; and he would lose her and his property at the same time. It was true that the Intendant had declared that he would renounce the property if the true heir appeared, but that was easy to say upon the conviction that no heir would appear; and even if he did renounce it, the Parliament would receive it again, rather than it should fall into the hands of a Beverley. "Oh that I had never left the cottage," thought Edward. "I might then at least have become resigned and contented with my lot. Now I am miserable, and, whichever way I turn, I see no prospect of being otherwise. One thing only I can decide upon, which is, that I will not remain any longer than I can help under this roof. I will go over and consult with Humphrey; and if I can only place my sisters as I want, Humphrey and I will seek our fortunes."

Edward rose at daylight, and, dressing himself, went down and saddled his horse. Desiring Sampson to tell the Intendant that he had gone over to the cottage, and would return by the evening, he rode across the forest, and arrived just as they were sitting down to breakfast. His attempts to be cheerful before his sisters did not succeed, and they were all grieved to see him look so pale and haggard. As soon as breakfast was over Edward made a sign, and he and Humphrey went out.

"What is the matter, my dear brother?" said Humphrey.

"I will tell you all. Listen to me," replied Edward, who then gave him the detail of all that had passed, from the time he had walked out with Patience Heatherstone till he went to bed. "Now, Humphrey, you know all; and what shall I do? Remain there I cannot!"

"If Patience Heatherstone had professed regard for you," replied Humphrey, "the affair would have been simple enough. Her father could have no objections to the match; and he would at the same time have acquitted his conscience as to the retaining of the property: but you say she showed none."

"She told me very calmly that she was sorry that I had said what I did."

"But do women always mean what they say, brother?" said Humphrey.

"She does, at all events," replied Edward; "she is truth itself. No, I cannot deceive myself. She feels a deep debt of gratitude for the service I rendered her; and that prevented her from being more harsh in her reply than what she was."

"But if she knew that you were Edward Beverley, do you not think it would make a difference in her?"

"And if it did, it would be too humiliating to think that I was only married for my rank and station."

"But, considering you of mean birth, may she not have checked those feelings which she considered under the circumstances improper to indulge?"

"Where there is such a sense of propriety there can be little affection."

"I know nothing about these things, Edward," replied Humphrey; "but I have been told that a woman's heart is not easily read; or if I have not been told it, I have read it or dreamt it."

"What do you propose to do?"

"What I fear you will not approve of, Humphrey; it is to break up our establishment altogether. If the answer is favourable from the Misses Conynghame, my sisters shall go to them; but that we had agreed upon already. Then for myself—I intend to go abroad, resume my name, and obtain employment in some foreign service. I will trust to the king for assisting me to that."

"That is the worst part of it, Edward; but if your peace of mind depends upon it, I will not oppose it."

"You, Humphrey, may come with me and share my fortunes, or do what you think more preferable."

"I think then, Edward, that I shall not decide rashly. I must have remained here with Pablo, if my sisters had gone to the Ladies Conynghame and you had remained with the Intendant; I shall, therefore, till I hear from you, remain where I am, and I shall be able to observe what is going on here, and let you know."

"Be it so," replied Edward; "let me only see my sisters well placed, and I shall be off the next day. It is misery to remain there now."

After some more conversation Edward mounted his horse and returned to the Intendant's. He did not arrive till late, for supper was on the table. The Intendant gave him a letter for Master Chaloner, which was enclosed in one from Mr Langton;—and further informed Edward that news had arrived of the king having made his escape to France.

"Thank God for that!" exclaimed Edward. "With your leave, sir, I will to-morrow deliver this letter to the party to whom it is addressed, as I know it to be of consequence."

The Intendant having given his consent, Edward retired without having exchanged a word with Patience or Clara beyond the usual civilities of the table.

The following morning Edward, who had not slept an hour during the night, set off for Clara's cottage, and found Chaloner and Grenville still in bed. At the sound of his voice the door was opened, and he gave Chaloner the letter; the latter read it and then handed it to Edward. The Misses Conynghame were delighted at the idea of receiving the two daughters of Colonel Beverley, and would treat them as their own; they requested that they might be sent to London immediately, where the coach would meet them to convey them down to Lancashire. They begged to be kindly remembered to Captain Beverley, and to assure him that his sisters should be well cared for.

"I am much indebted to you, Chaloner," said Edward; "I will send my brother off with my sisters as soon as possible. You will soon think of returning to France; and if you will permit me, I will accompany you."

"You, Edward! That will be delightful; but you had no idea of the kind when last we met. What has induced you to alter your mind?"

"I will tell you by and by; I do not think I shall be here again for some days. I must be a great deal at the cottage when Humphrey is away; for Pablo will have a great charge upon him—what with the dairy, and horses, and breed of goats, and other things—more than he can attend to; but as soon as Humphrey returns, I will come to you and make preparations for our departure. Till then farewell, both of you. We must see to provision you for three weeks or a month before Humphrey starts."

Edward bade them a hearty farewell, and then rode to the cottage.

Although Alice and Edith had been somewhat prepared for leaving the cottage, yet the time was so very uncertain, that the blow fell heavy upon them. They were to leave their brothers, whom they loved so dearly, to go to strangers; and when they understood that they were to leave in two days, and that they should not see Edward again, their grief was very great; but Edward reasoned with Alice and consoled her, although with Edith it was a more difficult task. She not only lamented her brothers, but her cow, her pony, and her kids; all the dumb animals were friends and favourites of Edith; and even the idea of parting with Pablo was the cause of a fresh burst of tears. Having made every arrangement with Humphrey, Edward once more took his leave, promising to come over and assist Pablo as soon as he could.

The next day Humphrey was busied in his preparations. They supplied the provisions to Clara's cottage; and when Pablo took them over in the cart, Humphrey rode to Lymington and provided a conveyance to London for the following day. We may as well observe that they set off at the hour appointed, and arrived safely at London in three days. There, at an address given in the letter, they found the coach waiting; and having given his sisters into the charge of an elderly waiting-woman, who had come up in the coach to take charge of them, they quitted him with many tears, and Humphrey hastened back to the New Forest.

On his return he found, to his surprise, that Edward had not called at the cottage as he had promised; and, with a mind foreboding evil, he mounted a horse and set off across the forest to ascertain the cause. As he was close to the Intendant's house he was met by Oswald, who informed him that Edward had been seized with a violent fever, and was in a very dangerous state, having been delirious for three or four days.

Humphrey hastened to dismount, and knocked at the door of the house; it was opened by Sampson, and Humphrey requested to be shown up to his brother's room. He found Edward in the state described by Oswald, and wholly unconscious of his presence; the maid, Phoebe, was by his bedside.

"You may leave," said Humphrey, rather abruptly; "I am his brother."

Phoebe retired, and Humphrey was alone with his brother.

"It was, indeed, an unhappy day when you came to this house," exclaimed Humphrey, as the tears rolled down his cheeks; "my poor, poor Edward."

Edward now began to talk incoherently, and attempted to rise from the bed, but his efforts were unavailing—he was too weak; but he raved of Patience Heatherstone, and he called himself Edward Beverley more than once, and he talked of his father and of Arnwood.

"If he has raved in this manner," thought Humphrey, "he has not many secrets left to disclose. I will not leave him, and will keep others away if I can."

Humphrey had been sitting an hour with his brother, when the surgeon came to see his patient. He felt his pulse, and asked Humphrey if he was nursing him.

"I am his brother, sir," replied Humphrey.

"Then, my good sir, if you perceive any signs of perspiration—and I think now that there is a little—keep the clothes on him and let him perspire freely. If so, his life will be saved."

The surgeon withdrew, saying that he would return again late in the evening.

Humphrey remained for another two hours at the bedside, and then feeling that there was a sign of perspiration, he obeyed the injunctions of the surgeon, and held on the clothes, against all Edward's endeavours to throw them off. For a short time the perspiration was profuse, and the restlessness of Edward subsided into a deep slumber.

"Thank Heaven! There are then hopes."

"Did you say there were hopes?" repeated a voice behind him.

Humphrey turned, and perceived Patience and Clara behind him, who had come in without his observing it.

"Yes," replied Humphrey, looking reproachfully at Patience, "there are hopes, by what the surgeon said to me—hopes that he may yet be able to quit this house, which he was so unfortunate as to enter."

This was a harsh and rude speech of Humphrey's; but he considered that Patience Heatherstone had been the cause of his brother's dangerous state, and that she had not behaved well to him.

Patience made no reply, but falling down on her knees by the bedside, prayed silently; and Humphrey's heart smote him for what he had said to her. "She cannot be so bad," thought Humphrey, as Patience and Clara quitted the room without the least noise.

Shortly afterwards the Intendant came up into the room, and offered his hand to Humphrey, who pretended not to see it, and did not take it.

"He has got Arnwood; that is enough for him," thought Humphrey; "but my hand in friendship he shall not receive."

The Intendant put his hand within the clothes, and feeling the high perspiration in which Edward was in, said—

"I thank thee, O God! For all Thy mercies, and that Thou hast been pleased to spare this valuable life."

"How are your sisters, Master Humphrey?" said the Intendant; "my daughter bade me inquire. I will send over to them and let them know that your brother is better, if you do not leave this for the cottage yourself after the surgeon has called again."

"My sisters are no longer at the cottage, Mr Heatherstone," replied Humphrey; "they have gone to some friends who have taken charge of them. I saw them safe to London myself, or I should have known of my brother's illness and have been here before this."

"You indeed tell me news, Master Humphrey," replied the Intendant. "With whom, may I ask, are your sisters placed, and in what capacity are they gone?"

This reply of the Intendant's reminded Humphrey that he had somewhat committed himself, as being supposed to be the daughters of a forester, it was not to be thought that they had gone up to be educated; and he therefore replied—

"They found it lonely in the forest, Mr Heatherstone, and wished to see London; so we have taken them there, and put them into the care of those who have promised that they shall be well placed."

The Intendant appeared to be much disturbed and surprised, but he said nothing, and soon afterwards quitted the room. He almost immediately returned with the surgeon, who, as soon as he felt Edward's pulse, declared that the crisis was over, and that when he awoke he would be quite sensible. Having given directions as to the drink of his patient, and some medicine which he was to take, the surgeon then left, stating that he should not call until the next evening, unless he was sent for, as he considered all danger over.

Edward continued in a quiet slumber for the major portion of the night. It was just break of day when he opened his eyes. Humphrey offered him some drink, which Edward took greedily; and seeing Humphrey, said—

"Oh, Humphrey, I had quite forgotten where I was—I'm so sleepy!" and with these words his head fell on the pillow, and he was again asleep.

When it was broad daylight Oswald came into the room—

"Master Humphrey, they say that all danger is over now, but that you have remained here all night. I will relieve you now, if you let me. Go and take a walk in the fresh air—it will revive you."

"I will, Oswald, and many thanks. My brother has woke up once, and, I thank God, quite sensible. He will know you when he wakes again, and then do you send for me."

Humphrey left the room, and was glad, after a night of close confinement in a sick-room, to feel the cool morning air fanning his cheeks. He had not been long out of the house before he perceived Clara coming towards him.

"How d'ye do, Humphrey?" said Clara; "and how is your brother this morning?"

"He is better, Clara, and I hope now out of danger."

"But, Humphrey," continued Clara; "when we came into the room last night, what made you say what you did?"

"I do not recollect that I said anything."

"Yes, you did; you said that there were now hopes that your brother would be able soon to quit this house, which he had been so unfortunate as to enter. Do you recollect?"

"I may have said so, Clara," replied Humphrey; "it was only speaking my thoughts aloud."

"But why do you think so, Humphrey? Why has Edward been unfortunate in entering this house? That is what I want to know. Patience cried so much after she left the room because you said that. Why did you say so? You did not think so a short time ago."

"No, my dear Clara, I did not, but I do now, and I cannot give you my reasons; so you must say no more about it."

Clara was silent for a time, and then said—

"Patience tells me that your sisters have gone away from the cottage. You told her father so."

"It is very true, they have gone."

"But why have they gone? What have they gone for? Who is to look after the cows and goats and poultry? Who is to cook your dinner, Humphrey? What can you do without them, and why did you send them away without letting me or Patience know that they were going, so that at least we might have bid them farewell?"

"My dear Clara," replied Humphrey—who, feeling no little difficulty in replying to all these questions, resolved to cut the matter short by appearing to be angry—"you know that you are the daughter of a gentleman, and so is Patience Heatherstone. You are both of gentle birth; but my sisters, you know, are only the daughters of a forester, and my brother Edward and I are no better. It does not become Mistress Patience and you to be intimate with such as we are, especially now that Mistress Patience is a great heiress: for her father has obtained the large property of Arnwood, and it will be hers after his death. It is not fit that the heiress of Arnwood should mix herself up with forester's daughters; and as we had friends near Lymington who offered to assist us, and take our sisters under their charge, we thought it better that they should go; for what would become of them, if any accident was to happen to Edward or to me? Now they will be provided for. After they have been taught, they will make very nice tire-women to some lady of quality," added Humphrey, with a sneer. "Don't you think they will, my pretty Clara?"

Clara burst into tears.

"You are very unkind, Humphrey," sobbed she. "You had no right to send away your sisters. I don't believe you—that's more!" and Clara ran away into the house.

Chapter Twenty Six.

Our readers may think that Humphrey was very unkind; but it was to avoid being questioned by Clara, who was evidently sent for the purpose, that he was so harsh. At the same time it must be admitted that Mr Heatherstone having obtained possession of Arnwood, rankled no doubt in the minds of both the brothers, and every act now, on the part of him or his family, was viewed in a false medium. But our feelings are not always at our control, and Edward was naturally impetuous, and Humphrey so much attached, and so much alarmed at his brother's danger, that he was even more excited. The blow fell doubly heavy, as it appeared that at the very same time Patience had rejected his brother and taken possession of their property, which had been held by the family for centuries. What made the case more annoying was, that explanation, if there was any to offer on either side, was, under present circumstances, almost impossible.

Soon after Clara left him Humphrey returned to his brother's room. He found him awake, and talking to Oswald. Ardently pressing his brother's hand, Edward said—

"My dear Humphrey, I shall soon be well now, and able, I trust, to quit this house. What I fear is, that some explanation will be asked for by the Intendant, not only relative to my sisters having left us, but also upon other points. This is what I wish to avoid, without giving offence. I do not think that the Intendant is so much to blame in having obtained my property, as he does not know that a Beverley existed, but I cannot bear to have any further intimacy with him, especially after what has taken place between me and his daughter. What I have to request is, that you will never quit this room while I am still here, unless you are relieved by Oswald; so that the Intendant or anybody else may have no opportunity of having any private communication with me, or forcing me to listen to what they may have to say. I made this known to Oswald before you came in."

"Depend upon it, it shall be so, Edward; for I am of your opinion. Clara came to me just now, and I had much trouble, and was compelled to be harsh, to get rid of her importunity."

When the surgeon called, he pronounced Edward out of danger, and that his attendance would be no longer necessary. Edward felt the truth of this. All that he required was strength; and that he trusted in a few days to obtain.

Oswald was sent over to the cottage to ascertain how Pablo was going on by himself. He found that everything was correct, and that Pablo, although he felt proud of his responsibility, was very anxious for Humphrey's return, as he found himself very lonely. During Oswald's absence on this day, Humphrey never quitted the room and although the Intendant came up several times he never could find an opportunity of speaking to Edward, which he evidently wished to do.

To inquiries made as to how he was, Edward always complained of great weakness, for a reason which will soon be understood. Several days elapsed, and Edward had often been out of bed during the night, when not likely to be intruded upon, and he now felt himself strong enough to be removed; and his object was to leave the Intendant's house without his knowledge, so as to avoid any explanation.

One evening Pablo came over with the horses after it was dark. Oswald put them into the stable; and the morning proving fine and clear, a little before break of day Edward came softly downstairs with Humphrey, and, mounting the horses, set off for the cottage, without any one in the Intendant's house being aware of their departure.

It must not be supposed, however, that Edward took this step without some degree of consideration as to the feelings of the Intendant. On the contrary, he left a letter with Oswald, to be delivered after his departure, in which he thanked the Intendant sincerely for all the kindness and compassion he had shown towards him assured him of his gratitude and kind feelings towards him and his daughter, but said that circumstances had occurred of which no explanation could be given without great pain to all parties, which rendered it advisable that he should take such an apparently unkind step as to leave without bidding them farewell in person; that he was about to embark immediately for the continent, to seek his fortune in the wars; and that he wished all prosperity to the family, which would ever have his kindest wishes and remembrances.

"Humphrey," said Edward, after they had ridden about two miles across the forest, and the sun had risen in an unclouded sky, "I feel like an emancipated slave. Thank God! My sickness has cured me of all my complaints, and all I want now is active employment. And now, Humphrey, Chaloner and Grenville are not a little tired of being inured up in their cottage, and I am as anxious as they are to be off. What will you do? Will you join us, or will you remain at the cottage?"

"I have reflected upon it, Edward, and I have come to the determination of remaining at the cottage. You will find it expensive enough to support one where you are going, and you must appear as a Beverley should do. We have plenty of money saved to equip you, and maintain you well for a year or so; but after that you may require more. Leave me here. I can make money, now that the farm is well stocked; and I have no doubt that I shall be able to send over a trifle every year to support the honour of the family. Besides, I do not wish to leave this for another reason. I want to know what is going on, and watch the motions of the Intendant and the heiress of Arnwood. I also do not wish to leave the country until I know how my sisters get on with the Ladies Conynghame: it is my duty to watch over them. I have made up my mind, so do not attempt to dissuade me."

"I shall not, my dear Humphrey, as I think you have decided properly; but I beg you will not think of laying by money for me—a very little will suffice for my wants."

"Not so, good brother; you must and shall, if I can help you, ruffle it with the best. You will be better received if you do; for, though poverty is no sin, as the saying is, it is scouted as sin should be, while sins are winked at. You know that I require no money, and therefore you must and shall, if you love me, take it all."

"As you will, my dear Humphrey. Now then, let us put our horses to speed, for, if possible, we will to-morrow morning leave the forest."

By this time all search for the fugitives from Worcester had long been over, and there was no difficulty in obtaining the means of embarkation. Early the next morning everything was ready, and Edward, Humphrey, Chaloner, Grenville, and Pablo set off for Southampton, one of the horses carrying the little baggage which they had with them. Edward, as we have before mentioned, with the money he had saved, and the store at the cottage, which had been greatly increased, was well supplied with cash; and that evening they embarked, with their horses, in a small sailing vessel, and, with a favourable light wind, arrived at a small port of France on the following day. Humphrey and Pablo returned to the cottage, we need hardly now say, very much out of spirits at the separation.

"Oh, Massa Humphrey," said Pablo, as they rode along, "Missy Alice and Missy Edith go away—I wish go with them. Massa Edward go away—I wish go with him. You stay at cottage—I wish stay with you. Pablo cannot be in three places."

"No, Pablo; all you can do is to stay where you can be most useful."

"Yes, I know that. You want me at cottage very much. Missy Alice and Edith and Massa Edward no want me; so I stay at cottage."

"Yes, Pablo, we will stay at the cottage, but we can't do everything now. I think we must give up the dairy, now that my sisters are gone. I'll tell you what I have been thinking of, Pablo. We will make a large enclosed place, to coax the ponies into during the winter, pick out as many as we think are good, and sell them at Lymington. That will be better than churning butter."

"Yes, I see; plenty of work for Pablo."

"And plenty for me, too, Pablo; but you know, when the enclosure is once made, it will last for a long while; and we will get the wild cattle into it if we can."

"Yes, I see," said Pablo. "I like that very much; only not like trouble to build place."

"We shan't have much trouble, Pablo: if we fell the trees inside the wood at each side, and let them lie one upon the other, the animals will never break through them."

"That very good idea—save trouble," said Pablo. "And what you do with cows, suppose no make butter?"

"Keep them, and sell their calves; keep them, to entice the wild cattle into the pen."

"Yes, that good. And turn out old Billy to 'tice ponies into pen," continued Pablo, laughing.

"Yes, we will try it."

We must now return to the Intendant's house. Oswald delivered the letter to the Intendant, who read it with much astonishment.

"Gone! Is he actually gone?" said Mr Heatherstone.

"Yes, sir, before daylight this morning."

"And why was I not informed of it?" said Mr Heatherstone; "why have you been a party to this proceeding, being my servant? May I inquire that?"

"I knew Master Edward before I knew you, sir," replied Oswald.

"Then you had better follow him," rejoined the Intendant, in an angry tone.

"Very well, sir," replied Oswald, who quitted the room. "Good Heaven! How all my plans have been frustrated!" exclaimed the Intendant, when he was alone. He then read the letter over more carefully than he had done at first. "'Circumstances had occurred of which no explanation could be given by him.' I do not comprehend that—I must see Patience."

Mr Heatherstone opened the door, and called to his daughter.

"Patience," said Mr Heatherstone, "Edward has left the house this morning; here is a letter which he has written to me. Read it, and let me know if you can explain some portion of it, which to me is incomprehensible. Sit down and read it attentively."

Patience, who was much agitated, gladly took the seat and perused Edward's letter. When she had done so she let it drop in her lap, and covered all her face, the tears trickling through her fingers. After a time the Intendant said—

"Patience, has anything passed between you and Edward Armitage?"

Patience made no reply, but sobbed aloud. She might not have shown so much emotion, but it must be remembered that for the last three weeks since Edward had spoken to her, and during his subsequent illness, she had been very unhappy. The reserve of Humphrey, the expressions he had made use of, his repulse of Clara, and her not having seen anything of Edward during his illness, added to his sudden and unexpected departure without a word to her, had broken her spirits, and she sank beneath the load of sorrow.

The Intendant left her to recover herself before he again addressed her. When she had ceased sobbing, her father spoke to her in a very kind voice, begging her that she would not conceal anything from him, as it was most important to him that the real facts should be known.

"Now tell me, my child, what passed between Edward and you?"

"He told me, just before you came up to us that evening, that he loved me."

"And what was your reply?"

"I hardly know, my dear father, what it was that I said. I did not like to be unkind to one who saved my life, and I did not choose to say what I thought, because—because—because he was of low birth; and how could I give encouragement to the son of a forester without your permission?"

"Then you rejected him?"

"I suppose I did, or that he considered that I did so. He had a secret of importance that he would have confided to me, had you not interrupted us."

"And now, Patience, I must request you to answer me one question candidly. I do not blame you for your conduct, which was correct under the circumstances. I also had a secret which I perhaps ought to have confided; but I did consider that the confidence and paternal kindness with which I treated Edward would have been sufficient to point out to you that I could not have been very averse to an union—indeed, the freedom of communication which I allowed between you must have told you so: but your sense of duty and propriety has made you act as you ought to have done, I grant, although contrary to my real wishes."

"Your wishes, my father?" said Patience. "Yes—my wishes; there is nothing that I so ardently desired as an union between you and Edward; but I wished you to love him for his own merits."

"I have done so, father," replied Patience, sobbing again, "although I did not tell him so."

The Intendant remained silent for some time, and then said—

"There is no cause for further concealment, Patience; I have only to regret that I was not more explicit sooner. I have long suspected, and have since been satisfied, that Edward Armitage is Edward Beverley, who, with his brother and sisters, were supposed to have been burnt to death at Arnwood."

Patience removed her handkerchief from her face, and looked at her father with astonishment.

"I tell you that I had a strong suspicion of it, my dear child, first, from the noble appearance, which no forest garb could disguise; but what gave me further conviction was, that when at Lymington I happened to fall in with one Benjamin, who had been a servant at Arnwood, and interrogated him closely. He really believed that the children were burnt; it is true that I asked him particularly relative to the appearance of the children—how many were boys and how many were girls, their ages, etcetera; but the strongest proof was, that the names of the four children corresponded with the names of the Children of the Forest, as well as their ages, and I went to the church register and extracted them. Now this was almost amounting to proof; for it was not likely that four children in the forest cottage should have the same ages and names as those of Arnwood. After I had ascertained this point, I engaged Edward, as you know, wishing to secure him; for I was once acquainted with his father, and at all events well acquainted with the Colonel's merits. You remained in the house together, and it was with pleasure that I watched the intimacy between you; and then I exerted myself to get Arnwood restored to him. I could not ask it for him, but I prevented it being given to any other, by laying claim to it myself. Had Edward remained with us, all might have succeeded as I wished; but he would join in the unfortunate insurrection, and I knew it useless to prevent him, so I let him go. I found that he took the name of Beverley during the time he was with the king's army, and when I was last in town I was told so by the commissioners, who wondered where he had come from; but the effect was, that it was now useless for me to request the estate for him, as I had wished to do—his having served in the royal army rendered it impossible. I therefore claimed it for myself, and succeeded. I had made up my mind that he was attached to you, and you were equally so to him; and as soon as I had the grant sent down, which was on the evening he addressed you, I made known to him that the property was given to me; and I added, on some dry questions being put to me by him, relative to the possibility of there being still existing an heir to the estate, that there was no chance of that, and that you would be the mistress of Arnwood. I threw it out as a hint to him, fancying that, as far as you were concerned, all would go well, and that I would explain to him my knowledge of who he was after he had made known his regard for you."

"Yes, I see it all now," replied Patience; "in one hour he is rejected by me, and in the next he is told that I have obtained possession of his property. No wonder that he is indignant, and looks upon us with scorn. And now he has left us: we have driven him into danger, and may never see him again. Oh, father! I am very, very miserable!"

"We must hope for the best, Patience. It is true that he has gone to the wars, but it does not therefore follow that he is to be killed. You are both very young—much too young to marry—and all may be explained. I must see Humphrey, and be candid with him."

"But Alice and Edith,—where are they gone, father?"

"That I can inform you. I have a letter from Langton on the subject, for I begged him to find out. He says that there are two young ladies of the name of Beverley, who have been placed under the charge of his friends the Ladies Conynghame, who is aunt to Major Chaloner, who has been for some time concealed in the forest. But I have letters to write, my dear Patience. To-morrow, if I live and do well, I will ride over to the cottage to see Humphrey Beverley."

The Intendant kissed his daughter; and she left the room.

Poor Patience! She was glad to be left to herself, and think over this strange communication. For many days she had felt how fond she had been of Edward, much more so than she had believed herself to be. "And now," she thought, "if he really loves me, and hears my father's explanation, he will come back again." By degrees, she recovered her serenity, and employed herself in her quiet domestic duties.

Mr Heatherstone rode over to the cottage the next day, where he found Humphrey busily employed as usual; and, what was very unusual, extremely grave. It was not a pleasant task for Mr Heatherstone to have to explain his conduct to so very young a man as Humphrey; but he felt that he could not be comfortable until the evil impression against him was removed, and he knew that Humphrey had a great deal of sterling good sense. His reception was cool; but when the explanation was made, Humphrey was more than satisfied, as it showed that the Intendant had been their best friend, and that it was from a delicacy on the part of Patience, rather than from any other cause, that the misunderstanding had occurred. Humphrey inquired if he had permission to communicate the substance of their conversation to his brother, and Mr Heatherstone stated that such was his wish and intention when he confided it to Humphrey. It is hardly necessary to say that Humphrey took the earliest opportunity of writing to Edward at the direction which Chaloner had left with him.

Chapter Twenty Seven.

But we must follow Edward for a time. On his arrival at Paris he was kindly received by King Charles, who promised to assist his views in joining the army.

"You have to choose between two generals, both great in the art of war—Condé and Turenne; I have no doubt that they will be opposed to each other soon—that will be the better for you, as you will learn tactics from such great players."

"Which would your majesty recommend me to follow?" inquired Edward.

"Condé is my favourite, and he will soon be opposed to this truculent and dishonest court, who have kept me here as an instrument to accomplish their own wishes, but who have never intended to keep their promises and place me on the English throne. I will give you letters to Condé and recollect that whatever general you take service under you will follow him, without pretending to calculate how far his movements may be right or wrong—that is not your affair. Condé is now just released from Vincennes; but, depend upon it, he will be in arms very soon."

As soon as he was furnished with the necessary credentials from the king Edward presented himself at the levée of the prince of Condé.

"You are here highly spoken of," said the prince, "for so young a man. So you were at the affair of Worcester? We will retain you, for your services will be wanted by and by. Can you procure any of your countrymen?"

"I know but of two that I can recommend from personal knowledge; but these two officers I can venture to pledge myself for."

"Any more?"

"That I cannot at present reply to your highness—but I should think it very possible."

"Bring me the officers to-morrow at this hour, Monsieur Beverley—*au revoir.*"

The prince of Condé then passed on to speak to other officers and gentlemen who were waiting to pay their respects.

Edward went to Chaloner and Grenville, who were delighted with the intelligence which he brought them. The next day they were at the prince's levée, and introduced by Edward.

"I am fortunate, gentlemen," said the prince, "in securing the services of such fine young men. You will oblige me by enlisting as many of your countrymen as you may consider likely to do good service, and then follow me to Guienne, to which province I am now about to depart. Be pleased to put yourself into communication with the parties named in this paper, and after my absence you will receive from them every assistance and necessary supplies which may be required."

A month after this interview, Condé, who had been joined by a great number of nobles, and had been reinforced by troops from Spain, set up the standard of revolt. Edward and his friends joined them, with about 300 English and Scotch, whom they had enlisted, and very soon afterwards Condé obtained the victory at Blenan, and in April 1652 advanced to Paris.

Turenne, who had taken the command of the French army, followed him, and a severe action was fought in the streets of the suburb D'Antoine, in which neither party had the advantage. But eventually Condé was beaten back by the superior force of Turenne; and not receiving the assistance he expected from the Spaniards, he fell back to the frontiers of Champagne.

Previous to his departure from Paris, Edward had received Humphrey's letter, explaining away the Intendant's conduct; and the contents removed a heavy load from Edward's mind; but he now thought of nothing but war, and although he cherished the idea of Patience Heatherstone, he was resolved to follow the fortunes of the prince as long as he could. He wrote a letter to the Intendant, thanking him for his kind feelings and intentions towards him, and he trusted that he might one day have the pleasure of seeing him again. He did not, however, think it advisable to mention the name of his daughter, except in inquiring after her health, and sending his respects. "It may be years before I see her again," thought Edward, "and who knows what may happen?"

The prince of Condé now had the command of the Spanish forces in the Netherlands; and Edward, with his friends, followed his fortunes, and gained his good-will: they were rapidly promoted.

Time flew on, and in the year 1654 the court of France concluded an alliance with Cromwell, and expelled King Charles from the French frontiers. The war was still carried on in the Netherlands. Turenne bore down Condé, who had gained every campaign; and the court of Spain, wearied with reverses, made overtures of peace, which were gladly accepted by the French.

During these wars Cromwell had been named Protector, and had shortly afterwards died.

Edward, who but rarely heard from Humphrey, was now anxious to quit the army and go to the king, who was in Spain; but to leave his colours while things were adverse was impossible.

After the peace and the pardon of Condé by the French king, the armies were disbanded, and the three adventurers were free. They took their leave of the prince, who thanked them for their long and meritorious services; and they then hastened to King Charles, who had left Spain and come to the Low Countries. At the time of their joining the king, Richard, the son of Cromwell, who had been nominated Protector, had resigned, and everything was ready for the Restoration.

On the 15th of May 1660 the news arrived that Charles had been proclaimed king on the 8th, and a large body of gentlemen went to invite him over. The king sailed from Scheveling, was met at Dover by General Monk, and conducted to London, which he entered amidst the acclamations of the people, on the 29th of the same month.

We may leave the reader to suppose that Edward, Chaloner, and Grenville were among the most favoured of those in his train. As the procession moved slowly along the Strand, through a countless multitude, the windows of all the houses were filled with well-dressed ladies, who waved their white kerchiefs to the king and his attendant suite. Chaloner, Edward, and Grenville, who rode side by side as gentlemen in waiting, were certainly the most distinguished among the king's retinue.

"Look, Edward," said Chaloner, "at those two lovely girls at yon window. Do you recognise them?"

"Indeed I do not. Are they any of our Paris beauties?"

"Why, thou insensible and unnatural animal! They are thy sisters, Alice and Edith: and do you not recognise behind them my good aunts Conynghame?"

"It is so, I believe," replied Edward. "Yes, now that Edith smiles, I'm sure it is they."

"Yes," replied Grenville, "there can be no doubt of that; but will they, think you, recognise us?"

"We shall see," replied Edward, as they now approached within a few yards of the window; for while they had been speaking the procession had stopped.

"Is it possible," thought Edward, "that these can be the two girls in russet gowns that I left at the cottage? And yet it must be. Well, Chaloner, to all appearance, your good aunts have done justice to their charge."

"Nature has done more, Edward. I never thought that they would have grown into such lovely girls as they have, although I always thought that they were handsome."

As they passed Edward caught the eye of Edith, and smiled.

"Alice, that's Edward!" said Edith, so loud as to be heard by the king, and all near him.

Alice and Edith rose and waved their handkerchiefs, but they were obliged to cease, and put them to their eyes.

"Are those your sisters, Edward?" said the king.

"They are, your majesty."

The king rose in his stirrups, and made a low obeisance to the window where they were standing.

"We shall have some court beauties, Beverley," said the king, looking at him over his shoulder.

As soon as the ceremonies were over, and they could escape from their attendance on the king's person, Edward and his two friends went to the house in which resided the Ladies Conynghame and his sisters.

We pass over the joy of this meeting after so many years' absence, and the pleasure which it gave to Edward to find his sisters grown such accomplished and elegant young women. That his two friends, who were, as the reader will recollect, old acquaintances of Alice and Edith, were warmly received, we hardly need say.

"Now, Edward, who do you think was here to-day—the reigning belle, and the toast of all the gentlemen?"

"Indeed! I must be careful of my heart. Dear Edith, who is she?"

"No less than one with whom you were formerly well acquainted, Edward—Patience Heatherstone."

"Patience Heatherstone," cried Edward, "the toast of all London!"

"Yes; and deservedly so, I can assure you: but she is as good as she is handsome, and, moreover, treats all the gay gallants with perfect indifference. She is staying with her uncle, Sir Ashley Cooper; and her father is also in town, for he called here with her to-day."

"When did you hear from Humphrey, Edith?"

"A few days back. He has left the cottage now, altogether."

"Indeed! Where does he reside then?"

"At Arnwood. The house has been rebuilt, and I understand is a very princely mansion. Humphrey has charge of it, until it is ascertained to whom it is to belong."

"It belongs to Mr Heatherstone, does it not?" replied Edward.

"How can you say so, Edward? You received Humphrey's letters a long while ago."

"Yes, I did; but let us not talk about it any more, my dear Edith. I am in great perplexity."

"Nay, dear brother, let us talk about it," said Alice, who had come up and overheard the latter portion of the conversation.

"What is your perplexity?"

"Well," replied Edward, "since it is to be so, let us sit down and talk over the matter. I acknowledge the kindness of Mr Heatherstone, and feel that all he asserted to Humphrey is true; still I do not like that I should be indebted to him for a property which is mine, and that he has no right to give. I acknowledge his generosity, but I do not acknowledge his right of possession. Nay, much as I admire, and I may say, fond as I am (for time has not effaced the feeling) of his daughter, it still appears to me that, although not said, it is expected that she is to be included in the transfer; and I will accept no wife on such conditions."

"That is to say, because all you wish for, your property and a woman you love, are offered you in one lot, you will not accept them; they must be divided, and handed over to you in two!" said Alice, smiling.

"You mistake, dearest; I am not so foolish; but I have a certain pride, which you cannot blame. Accepting the property from Mr Heatherstone is receiving a favour, were it given as a marriage portion with his daughter. Now, why should I accept as a favour what I can claim as a right? It is my intention of appealing to the king and demanding the restoration of my property. He cannot refuse it."

"Put not your trust in princes, brother," replied Alice. "I doubt if the king, or his council, will consider it advisable to make so many discontented as to restore property which has been so long held by others, and by so doing create a host of enemies. Recollect also that Mr Heatherstone and his brother-in-law Sir Ashley Cooper have done the king much more service than you ever have, or can do. They have been most important agents in his restoration, and the king's obligations to them are much greater than they are to you. Besides, merely for what may be called a point of honour, for it is no more, in what an unpleasant situation will you put his majesty! At all events, Edward, recollect you do not know what are the intentions of Mr Heatherstone; wait and see what he proffers first."

"But, my dear sister, it appears to me that his intentions are evident. Why has he rebuilt Arnwood? He is not going to surrender my property and make me a present of the house."

"The reason for rebuilding the mansion was good. You were at the wars; it was possible that you might or that you might not return. He said this to Humphrey, who has all along been acting as his factotum in the business; and recollect, at the time that Mr Heatherstone commenced the rebuilding of the mansion, what prospect was there of the restoration of the king, or of your ever being in a position to apply for the restoration of your property? I believe, however, that Humphrey knows more of Mr Heatherstone's intentions than he has made known to us; and I therefore say again, my dear Edward, make no application till you ascertain what Mr Heatherstone's intentions may be."

"Your advice is good, my dear Alice, and I will be guided by it," replied Edward.

"And now let me give you some advice for your friends, Masters Chaloner and Grenville. That much of their property has been taken away and put into other hands, I know; and probably they expect it will be restored upon their application to the king. Those who hold the property think so too, and so far it is fortunate. Now, from wiser heads than mine, I have been told that these applications will not be acceded to, as is supposed; but, at the same time, if they were to meet the parties, and close with them at once, before the king's intentions are known, they would recover their property at a third or a quarter of the value. Now is their time: even a few days' delay may make a difference. They can easily obtain a delay for the payment of the moneys. Impress that upon them, my dear Edward, and let them, if possible, be off to their estates to-morrow and make the arrangements."

"That is advice which must be followed," replied Edward. "We must go now, and I will not fail to communicate it to them this very night."

We may as well here inform the reader that the advice was immediately acted upon, and that Chaloner and Grenville recovered all their estates at about five years' purchase.

Edward remained at court several days. He had written to Humphrey, and had despatched a messenger with the letter, but the messenger had not yet returned. The court was now one continual scene of fêtes and gaiety. On the following day a drawing-room was to be held, and Edward's sisters were to be presented. Edward was standing, with many others of the suite, behind the chair of the king, amusing himself with the presentations as they took place, and waiting for the arrival of his sisters. Chaloner and Grenville were not with him, they had obtained leave to go into the country, for the object we have before referred to—when his eyes caught, advancing towards the king, Mr Heatherstone, who led his daughter Patience. That they had not perceived him was evident; indeed her eyes were not raised once, from the natural timidity felt by a young woman in the presence of royalty. Edward half concealed himself behind one of his companions, that he might gaze upon her without reserve. She was indeed a lovely young person, but little altered, except having grown taller and more rounded and perfect in her figure; and her court-dress displayed proportions which her humble costume at the New Forest had concealed, or which time had not matured. There was the same pensive sweet expression in her face, which had altered little; but the beautiful rounded arms, the symmetrical fall of the shoulders, and the proportion of the whole figure, was a surprise to him; and Edward, in his own mind, agreed that she might well be the reigning toast of the day.

Mr Heatherstone advanced and made his obeisance, and then his daughter was led forward, and introduced by a lady unknown to Edward. After he had saluted her, the king said, loud enough for Edward to hear—

"My obligations to your father are great. I trust that the daughter will often grace our court." Patience made no reply, but passed on; and, soon afterwards, Edward lost sight of her in the crowd. If there ever had been any check to Edward's feelings towards Patience—and time and absence have their effect upon the most ardent of lovers—the sight of her so resplendent in beauty acted upon him like magic; and he was uneasy till the ceremony was over, and he was enabled to go to his sisters.

When he entered the room he found himself in the arms of Humphrey, who had arrived with the messenger. After the greetings were over, Edward said—

"Alice, I have seen Patience, and I fear I must surrender at discretion. Mr Heatherstone may make his own terms; I must waive all pride rather than lose her. I thought that I had more control over myself; but I have seen her, and feel that my future happiness depends upon obtaining her as a wife. Let her father but give me her, and Arnwood will be but a trifle in addition!"

"With respect to the conditions upon which you are to possess Arnwood," said Humphrey, "I can inform you what they are. They are wholly unshackled, further than that you are to repay by instalments the money expended in the building of the house. This I am empowered to state to you, and I think you will allow that Mr Heatherstone has fully acted up to what he stated were his views when he first obtained a grant of the property."

"He has, indeed," replied Edward.

"As for his daughter, Edward, you have yet to 'win her and wear her,' as the saying is. Her father will resign the property to you as yours by right; but you have no property in his daughter, and I suspect that she will not be quite so easily handed over to you."

"But why should you say so, Humphrey? Have we not been attached from our youth?"

"Yes, it was a youthful passion, I grant; but recollect, nothing came of it, and years have passed away. It is now seven years since you quitted the forest, and in your letters to Mr Heatherstone you made no remark upon what had passed between you and Patience. Since that, you have never corresponded or sent any messages; and you can hardly expect that a girl, from the age of seventeen to twenty-four, will cherish the image of one who, to say the least, had treated her with indifference. That is my view of the matter, Edward. It may be wrong."

"And it may be true," replied Edward mournfully.

"Well, my view is different," replied Edith. "You know, Humphrey, how many offers Patience Heatherstone has had, and has every day, I may say. Why has she refused them all? In my opinion, because she has been constant to a proud brother of mine, who does not deserve her!"

"It may be so, Edith," replied Humphrey. "Women are riddles—I only argued upon the common sense of the thing."

"Much you know about women," replied Edith. "To be sure, you do not meet many in the New Forest, where you have lived all your life."

"Very true, my dear sister; perhaps that is the reason that the New Forest has had such charms for me."

"After that speech, sir, the sooner you get back again the better!" retorted Edith. But Edward made a sign to Humphrey, and they beat a retreat.

"Have you seen the Intendant, Humphrey?"

"No; I was about to call upon him, but I wanted to see you first."

"I will go with you. I have not done him justice," replied Edward, "and yet I hardly know how to explain to him—"

"Say nothing, but meet him cordially; that will be explanation sufficient."

"I shall meet him as one whom I shall always revere, and feel that I owe a deep debt of gratitude. What must he think of my not having called upon him?"

"Nothing. You hold a place at court. You may not have known that he was in London, as you have never met him; your coming with me will make it appear so. Tell him that I have just made known to you his noble and disinterested conduct."

"You are right—I will. I fear, however, Humphrey, that you are right, and Edith wrong, as regards his daughter."

"Nay, Edward, recollect that I have, as Edith observed, passed my life in the woods."

Edward was most kindly received by Mr Heatherstone. Edward, on Mr Heatherstone repeating to him his intentions relative to Arnwood, expressed his sense of that gentleman's conduct, simply adding—

"You may think me impetuous, sir; but I trust you will believe me grateful."

Patience coloured up and trembled when Edward first saw her. Edward did not refer to the past for some time after they had renewed their acquaintance. He wooed her again, and won her. Then all was explained.

About a year after the Restoration there was a fête at Hampton Court, given in honour of three marriages taking place—Edward Beverley to Patience Heatherstone, Chaloner to Alice, and Grenville to Edith; and, as his majesty himself said, as he gave away the brides, "Could loyalty be better rewarded?"

But our young readers will not be content if they do not hear some particulars about the other personages who have appeared in our little history. Humphrey must take the first place. His love of farming continued. Edward gave him a large farm, rent free; and in a few years Humphrey saved up sufficient to purchase a property for himself. He then married Clara Ratcliffe, who has not appeared lately on the scene, owing to her having been, about two years before the Restoration, claimed by an elderly relation, who lived in the country, and whose infirm state of health did not permit him to quit the house. He left his property to Clara, about a year after her marriage to Humphrey. The cottage in the New Forest was held by, and eventually made over to, Pablo, who became a very steady character, and in the course of time married a young girl from Arnwood, and had a houseful of young gipsies. Oswald, so soon as Edward came down to Arnwood, gave up his place in the New Forest, and lived entirely with Edward as his steward; and Phoebe also went to Arnwood, and lived to a good old age, in the capacity of housekeeper, her temper becoming rather worse than better as she advanced in years.

This is all that we have been able to collect relative to the several parties; and so now we must say farewell.

The Phantom Ship

Chapter One.

About the middle of the seventeenth century, in the outskirts of the small but fortified town of Terneuse, situated on the right bank of the Scheldt, and nearly opposite to the island of Walcheren, there was to be seen in advance of a few other even more humble tenements, a small but neat cottage, built according to the prevailing taste of the time. The outside front had, some years back, been painted of a deep orange, the windows and shutters of a vivid green. To about three feet above the surface of the earth, it was faced alternately with blue and white tiles. A small garden, of about two rods of our measure of land, surrounded the edifice; and this little plot was flanked by a low hedge of privet, and encircled by a moat full of water, too wide to be leaped with ease. Over that part of the moat which was in front of the cottage-door was a small and narrow bridge, with ornamented iron handrails, for the security of the passenger. But the colours, originally so bright, with which the cottage had been decorated, had now faded; symptoms of rapid decay were evident in the window-sills, the door-jambs, and other wooden parts of the tenement and many of the white and blue tiles had fallen down and had not been replaced. That much care had once been bestowed upon this little tenement, was as evident as that latterly it had been equally neglected.

The inside of the cottage, both on the basement and the floor above, was divided into two larger rooms in front, and two smaller behind; the rooms in front could only be called large in comparison with the other two, as they were little more than twelve feet square, with but one window to each. The upper floor was, as usual, appropriated to the bedrooms; on the lower, the two smaller rooms were now used only as a wash-house and a lumber-room; while one of the larger was fitted up as a kitchen, and furnished with dressers, on which the metal utensils for cookery shone clean and polished as silver. The room itself was scrupulously neat; but the furniture as well as the utensils, were scanty. The boards of the floor were of a pure white, and so clean that you might have laid anything down without fear of soiling it. A strong deal table, two wooden-seated chairs, and a small easy couch, which had been removed from one of the bedrooms upstairs, were all the moveables which this room contained. The other front room had been fitted up as a parlour; but what might be the style of its furniture was now unknown, for no eye had beheld the contents of that room for nearly seventeen years, during which it had been hermetically sealed, even to the inmates of the cottage.

The kitchen, which we have described, was occupied by two persons. One was a woman, apparently about forty years of age, but worn down by pain and suffering. She had evidently once possessed much beauty: there were still the regular outlines, the noble forehead, and the large dark eye; but there was a tenuity in her features, a wasted appearance, such as to render the flesh transparent; her brow, when she mused, would sink into deep wrinkles, premature though they were; and the occasional flashing of her eyes strongly impressed you with the idea of insanity. There appeared to be some deep-seated, irremoveable, hopeless cause of anguish, never for one moment permitted to be absent from her memory: a chronic oppression, fixed and graven there, only to be removed by death. She was dressed in the widow's coif of the time; but although clean and neat, her garments were faded from long wear. She was seated upon the small couch which we have mentioned, evidently brought down as a relief to her, in her declining state.

On the deal table in the centre of the room sat the other person, a stout, fair-haired, florid youth of nineteen or twenty years old. His features were handsome and bold, and his frame powerful to excess; his eye denoted courage and determination, and as he carelessly swung his legs, and whistled an air in an emphatic manner, it was impossible not to form the idea that he was a daring, adventurous, and reckless character.

"Do not go to sea, Philip; oh, promise me *that*, my dear child," said the female, clasping her hands.

"And why not go to sea, mother?" replied Philip; "what's the use of my staying here to starve?—for, by Heaven! it's little better, I must do something for myself and for you. And what else can I do? My uncle Van Brennen has offered to take me with him, and will give me good wages. Then I shall live happily on board, and my earnings will be sufficient for your support at home."

"Philip—Philip, hear me. I shall die if you leave me. Whom have I in the world but you? O my child, as you love me, and I know you *do* love me, Philip, don't leave me; but if you will, at all events do not go to sea."

Philip gave no immediate reply; he whistled for a few seconds, while his mother wept.

"Is it," said he at last, "because my father was drowned at sea that you beg so hard, mother?"

"Oh, no—no!" exclaimed the sobbing woman. "Would to God—"

"Would to God what, mother?"

"Nothing—nothing. Be merciful—be merciful, O God!" replied the mother, sliding from her seat on the couch, and kneeling by the side of it, in which attitude she remained for some time in fervent prayer. At last she resumed her seat, and her face wore an aspect of more composure.

Philip, who during this, had remained silent and thoughtful, again addressed his mother.

"Look ye, mother. You ask me to stay on shore with you, and starve,—rather hard conditions:— now hear what I have to say. That room opposite has been shut up ever since I can remember—why, you will never tell me; but once I heard you say, when we were without bread and with no prospect of my uncle's return—you were then half frantic, mother, as you know you sometimes are—"

"Well, Philip, what did you hear me say?" inquired his mother, with tremulous anxiety.

"You said, mother, that there was money in that room which would save us; and then you screamed and raved, and said that you preferred death. Now, mother, what is there in that chamber, and why has it been so long shut up? Either I know that, or I go to sea."

At the commencement of this address of Philip, his mother appeared to be transfixed, and motionless as a statue; gradually her lips separated, and her eyes glared; she seemed to have lost the power of reply; she put her hand to her right side, as if to compress it, then both her hands, as if to relieve herself from excruciating torture: at last she sank, with her head forward, and the blood poured out of her mouth.

Philip sprang from the table to her assistance, and prevented her from falling on the floor. He laid her on the couch, watching with alarm the continued effusion.

"Oh! mother—mother, what is this?" cried he, at last, in great distress.

For some time his mother could make him no reply; she turned further on her side, that she might not be suffocated by the discharge from the ruptured vessel, and the snow-white planks of the floor were soon crimsoned with her blood.

"Speak, dearest mother, if you can," repeated Philip in agony; "What shall I do?—what shall I give you? God Almighty! what is this?"

"Death, my child, death!" at length replied the poor woman, sinking into a state of unconsciousness.

Philip, now much alarmed, flew out of the cottage, and called the neighbours to his mother's assistance. Two or three hastened to the call; and as soon as Philip saw them occupied in restoring his mother, he ran as fast as he could to the house of a medical man, who lived about a mile off;—one Mynheer Poots, a little, miserable, avaricious wretch but known to be very skilful in his profession. Philip found Poots at home, and insisted upon his immediate attendance.

"I will come—yes, most certainly," replied Poots, who spoke the language but imperfectly; "but, Mynheer Vanderdecken, who will pay me?"

"Pay you! my uncle will, directly that he comes home."

"Your uncle, de Skipper Vanbrennen: no, he owe me four guilders, and he has owed me for a long time. Besides his ship may sink."

"He shall pay you the four guilders, and for this attendance also," replied Philip in a rage; "come directly,—while you are disputing, my mother may be dead."

"But, Mr Philip, I cannot come, now I recollect. I have to see the child of the Burgomaster at Terneuse," replied Mynheer Poots.

"Look you, Mynheer Poots," exclaimed Philip, red with passion; "you have but to choose,—will you go quietly, or must I take you there? You'll not trifle with me."

Here Mynheer Poots was under considerable alarm, for the character of Philip Vanderdecken was well known.

"I will come by-and-by, Mynheer Philip, if I can."

"You'll come now, you wretched old miser," exclaimed Philip, seizing hold of the little man by the collar, and pulling him out of his door.

"Murder! murder!" cried Poots, as he lost his legs, and was dragged along by the impetuous young man.

Philip stopped, for he perceived that Poots was black in the face.

"Must I then choke you, to make you go quietly? for, hear me, go you shall, alive or dead."

"Well, then," replied Poots, recovering himself, "I will go, but I'll have you in prison to-night: and, as for your mother, I'll not—no, that I will not—Mynheer Philip, depend upon it."

"Mark me, Mynheer Poots," replied Philip, "as sure as there is a God in heaven, if you do not come with me, I'll choke you now; and when you arrive, if you do not your best for my poor mother, I'll murder you there. You know that I always do what I say, so now take my advice, come along quietly, and you shall certainly be paid, and well paid—if I sell my coat."

This last observation of Philip, perhaps, had more effect than even his threats. Poots was a miserable little atom, and like a child in the powerful grasp of the young man. The doctor's tenement was isolated, and he could obtain no assistance until within a hundred yards of Vanderdecken's cottage; so Mynheer Poots decided that he would go—first, because Philip had promised to pay him, and secondly, because he could not help it.

This point being settled, Philip and Mynheer Poots made all haste to the cottage; and on their arrival, they found his mother still in the arms of two of her female neighbours, who were bathing her temples with vinegar. She was in a state of consciousness, but she could not speak; Poots ordered her to be carried up stairs and put to bed, and pouring some acids down her throat, hastened away with Philip to procure the necessary remedies.

"You will give your mother that directly, Mynheer Philip," said Poots, putting a phial into his hand; "I will now go to the child of the Burgomaster, and will afterwards come back to your cottage."

"Don't deceive me," said Philip, with a threatening look.

"No, no, Mynheer Philip, I would not trust to your uncle Vanbrennen for payment, but you have promised, and I know that you always keep your word. In one hour I will be with your mother; but you yourself must now be quick."

Philip hastened home. After the potion had been administered, the bleeding was wholly stopped; and in half an hour, his mother could express her wishes in a whisper. When the little doctor arrived, he carefully examined his patient, and then went down stairs with her son into the kitchen.

"Mynheer Philip," said Poots, "by Allah! I have done my best, but I must tell you that I have little hopes of your mother rising from her bed again. She may live one day or two days, but not more. It is not my fault, Mynheer Philip," continued Poots, in a deprecating tone.

"No, no; it is the will of Heaven," replied Philip, mournfully.

"And you will pay me, Mynheer Vanderdecken?" continued the doctor after a short pause.

"Yes," replied Philip in a voice of thunder, and starting from a reverie. After a moment's silence, the doctor recommenced:

"Shall I come to-morrow, Mynheer Philip? You know that will be a charge of another guilder: it is of no use to throw away money or time either."

"Come to-morrow, come every hour, charge what you please; you shall certainly be paid," replied Philip, curling his lip with contempt.

"Well, it is as you please. As soon as she is dead the cottage and the furniture will be yours, and you will sell them of course. Yes, I will come. You will have plenty of money. Mynheer Philip, I would like the first offer of the cottage, if it is to let."

Philip raised his arm in the air as if to crush Mynheer Poots, who retreated to the corner.

"I did not mean until your mother was buried," said Poots, in a coaxing tone.

"Go, wretch, go!" said Philip, covering his face with his hands, as he sank down upon the blood-stained couch.

After a short interval, Philip Vanderdecken returned to the bedside of his mother, whom he found much better; and the neighbours, having their own affairs to attend to, left them alone. Exhausted with the loss of blood, the poor woman slumbered for many hours, during which she never let go the hand of Philip, who watched her breathing in mournful meditation.

It was about one o'clock in the morning when the widow awoke. She had in a great degree recovered her voice, and thus she addressed her son:—

"My dear, my impetuous boy, and have I detained you here a prisoner so long?"

"My own inclination detained me, mother. I leave you not to others until you are up and well again."

"That, Philip, I shall never be. I feel that death claims me; and O my son, were it not for you, how should I quit this world rejoicing! I have long been dying, Philip,—and long, long have I prayed for death."

"And why so, mother?" replied Philip, bluntly; "I've done my best."

"You have, my child, you have: and may God bless you for it. Often have I seen you curb your fiery temper—restrain yourself when justified in wrath—to spare a mother's feelings. 'Tis now some days that even hunger has not persuaded you to disobey your mother. And, Philip, you must have thought me mad or foolish to insist so long, and yet to give no reason. I'll speak—again—directly."

The widow turned her head upon the pillow, and remained quiet for some minutes; then, as if revived, she resumed:

"I believe I have been mad at times—have I not, Philip? And God knows I have had a secret in my heart enough to drive a wife to frenzy. It has oppressed me day and night, worn my mind, impaired my reason, and now, at last, thank Heaven! it has overcome this mortal frame: the blow is struck, Philip—I'm sure it is. I wait but to tell you all,—and yet I would not,—'twill turn your brain as it has turned mine, Philip."

"Mother," replied Philip, earnestly, "I conjure you, let me hear this killing secret. Be heaven or hell mixed up with it, I fear not. Heaven will not hurt me and Satan I defy."

"I know thy bold, proud spirit, Philip,—thy strength of mind. If any one could bear the load of such a dreadful tale, thou couldst. My brain, alas! was far too weak for it; and I see it is my duty to tell it to thee."

The widow paused as her thoughts reverted to that which she had to confide; for a few minutes the tears rained down her hollow cheeks; she then appeared to have summoned resolution, and to have regained strength.

"Philip, it is of your father I would speak. It is supposed—that he was—drowned at sea."

"And was he not, mother?" replied Philip, with surprise.

"O no!"

"But he has long been dead, mother?"

"No,—yes,—and yet—no," said the widow, covering her eyes. Her brain wanders, thought Philip, but he spoke again:

"Then where is he, mother?"

The widow raised herself, and a tremor visibly ran through her whole frame, as she replied—

"In **Living Judgment**."

The poor woman then sank down again upon the pillow, and covered her head with the bedclothes, as if she would have hid herself from her own memory. Philip was so much perplexed and astounded, that he could make no reply. A silence of some minutes ensued when, no longer able to bear the agony of suspense, Philip faintly whispered—

"The secret, mother, the secret; quick, let me hear it."

"I can now tell all, Philip," replied his mother, in a solemn tone of voice. "Hear me, my son. Your father's disposition was but too like your own;—O may his cruel fate be a lesson to you, my dear, dear child! He was a bold, a daring, and, they say, a first-rate seaman. He was not born here, but in Amsterdam; but he would not live there, because he still adhered to the Catholic religion. The Dutch, you know, Philip, are heretics, according to our creed. It is now seventeen years or more that he sailed for India, in his fine ship the Amsterdammer, with a valuable cargo. It was his third voyage to India, Philip, and it was to have been, if it had so pleased God, his last, for he had purchased that good ship with only part of his earnings, and one more voyage would have made his fortune. O! how often did we talk over what we would do upon his return, and how these plans for the future consoled me at the idea of his absence, for I loved him dearly, Philip,—he was always good and kind to me! and after he had sailed, how I hoped for his return! The lot of a sailor's wife is not to be envied. Alone and solitary for so many months, watching the long wick of the candle and listening to the howling of the wind—foreboding evil and accident—wreck and widowhood. He had been gone about six months, Philip, and there was still a long dreary year to wait before I could expect him back. One night, you, my child, were fast asleep; you were my only solace—my comfort in my loneliness. I had been watching over you in your slumbers: you smiled and half pronounced the name of mother; and at last I kissed your unconscious lips, and I knelt and prayed—prayed for God's blessing on you, my child, and upon him too—little thinking, at the time, that he was so horribly, so fearfully *cursed*."

The widow paused for breath, and then resumed. Philip could not speak. His lips were sundered, and his eyes riveted upon his mother, as he devoured her words.

"I left you and went down stairs into that room, Philip, which since that dreadful night has never been re-opened. I sate me down and read, for the wind was strong, and when the gale blows, a sailor's wife can seldom sleep. It was past midnight, and the rain poured down. I felt unusual fear,—I knew not why, I rose from the couch and dipped my finger in the blessed water, and I crossed myself. A violent gust of wind roared round the house and alarmed me still more. I had a painful, horrible foreboding; when, of a sudden, the windows and window-shutters were all blown in, the light was extinguished, and I was left in utter darkness. I screamed with fright—but at last I recovered myself, and was proceeding towards the window that I might reclose it, when whom should I behold, slowly entering at the casement, but—your father,—Philip!—Yes, Philip,—it was your father!"

"Merciful God!" muttered Philip, in a low tone almost subdued into a whisper.

"I knew not what to think,—he was in the room; and although the darkness was intense, his form and features were as clear and as defined as if it were noon-day. Fear would have inclined me to recoil from,—his loved presence to fly towards him. I remained on the spot where I was, choked with agonising sensations. When he had entered the room, the windows and shutters closed of themselves, and the candle was relighted—then I thought it was his apparition, and I fainted on the floor.

"When I recovered I found myself on the couch, and perceived that a cold (O how cold!) and dripping hand was clasped in mine. This reassured me, and I forgot the supernatural signs which accompanied his appearance. I imagined that he had been unfortunate, and had returned home. I opened my eyes, and beheld my loved husband and threw myself into his arms. His clothes were saturated with the rain; I felt as if I had embraced ice—but nothing can check the warmth of woman's love, Philip. He received my caresses but he caressed not again: he spoke not, but looked thoughtful and unhappy. 'William—William,' cried I; 'speak, to your dear Catherine.'

"'I will,' replied he, solemnly, 'for my time is short.'

"'No, no, you must not go to sea again; you have lost your vessel but you are safe. Have I not you again?'

"'Alas! no—be not alarmed, but listen? for my time is short. I have not lost my vessel, Catherine, *but I have lost*!—Make no reply, but listen; I am not dead, nor yet am I alive. I hover between this world and the world of spirits. Mark me.'

"'For nine weeks did I try to force my passage against the elements round the stormy Cape, but without success; and I swore terribly. For nine weeks more did I carry sail against the adverse winds and currents, and yet could gain no ground and then I blasphemed,—ay, terribly blasphemed. Yet still I persevered. The crew, worn out with long fatigue, would have had me return to the Table Bay; but I refused; nay, more, I became a murderer—unintentionally, it is true, but still a murderer. The pilot opposed me, and persuaded the men to bind me, and in the excess of my fury, when he took me by the collar, I struck at him; he reeled; and, with the sudden lurch of the vessel, he fell overboard, and sank. Even this fearful death did not restrain me; and I swore by the fragment of the Holy Cross, preserved in that relic now hanging round your neck, that I would gain my point in defiance of storm and seas, of lightning, of heaven, or of hell, even if I should beat about until the Day of Judgment.'

"'My oath was registered in thunder, and in streams of sulphurous fire. The hurricane burst upon the ship, the canvass flew away in ribbons; mountains of seas swept over us, and in the centre of a deep o'erhanging cloud, which shrouded all in utter darkness, were written in letters of livid flame, these words—***Until the Day of Judgement.***'

"'Listen to me, Catherine, my time is short. *One hope* alone remains, and for this am I permitted to come here. Take this letter.' He put a sealed paper on the table. 'Read it, Catherine, dear, and try if you can assist me. Read it, and now farewell—my time is come.'

"Again the window and window-shutters burst open—again the light was extinguished, and the form of my husband was, as it were, wafted in the dark expanse. I started up and followed him with outstretched arms and frantic screams as he sailed through the window;—my glaring eyes beheld his form borne away like lightning on the wings of the wild gale, till it was lost as a speck of light, and then it disappeared. Again the windows closed, the light burned, and I was left alone!

"Heaven, have mercy! My brain!—my brain!—Philip!—Philip!" shrieked the poor woman; "don't leave me—don't—don't—pray don't!"

During these exclamations the frantic widow had raised herself from the bed, and, at the last, had fallen into the arms of her son. She remained there some minutes without motion. After a time Philip felt alarmed at her long quiescence; he laid her gently down upon the bed, and as he did so her head fell back—her eyes were turned—the widow Vanderdecken was no more.

Chapter Two.

Philip Vanderdecken, strong as he was in mental courage, was almost paralysed by the shock when he discovered that his mother's spirit had fled; and for some time he remained by the side of the bed, with his eyes fixed upon the corpse, and his mind in a state of vacuity. Gradually he recovered himself; he rose, smoothed down the pillow, closed her eyelids, and then clasping his hands, the tears trickled down his manly cheeks. He impressed a solemn kiss upon the pale white forehead of the departed, and drew the curtains round the bed.

"Poor mother!" said he, sorrowfully, as he completed his task, "at length thou hast found rest,—but thou hast left thy son a bitter legacy."

And as Philip's thoughts reverted to what had passed, the dreadful narrative whirled in his imagination and scathed his brain. He raised his hands to his temples, compressed them with force, and tried to collect his thoughts, that he might decide upon what measures he should take. He felt that he had no time to indulge his grief. His mother was in peace: but his father—where was he?

He recalled his mother's words—"One hope alone remained." Then there was hope. His father had laid a paper on the table—could it be there now? Yes, it must be—his mother had not had the courage to take it up. There was hope in that paper, and it had lain unopened for more than seventeen years.

Philip Vanderdecken resolved that he would examine the fatal chamber—at once he would know the worst. Should he do it now, or wait till daylight?—but the key, where was it? His eyes rested upon an old japanned cabinet in the room: he had never seen his mother open it in his presence: it was the only likely place of concealment that he was aware of. Prompt in all his decisions, he took up the candle, and proceeded to examine it. It was not locked; the doors swung open, and drawer after drawer was examined, but Philip discovered not the object of his search; again and again did he open the drawers, but they were all empty. It occurred to Philip that there might be secret drawers, and he examined for some time in vain. At last he took out all the drawers, and laid them on the floor, and lifting the cabinet off its stand he shook it. A rattling sound in one corner told him that in all probability the key was there concealed. He renewed his attempts to discover how to gain it, but in vain. Daylight now streamed through the casements, and Philip had not desisted from his attempts: at last, wearied out, he resolved to force the back panel of the cabinet; he descended to the kitchen, and returned with a small chopping-knife and hammer, and was on his knees busily employed forcing out the panel, when a hand was placed upon his shoulder.

Philip started: he had been so occupied with his search and his wild chasing thoughts, that he had not heard the sound of an approaching footstep. He looked up and beheld the Father Seysen, the priest of the little parish, with his eyes sternly fixed upon him. The good man had been informed of the dangerous state of the widow Vanderdecken, and had risen at daylight to visit and afford her spiritual comfort.

"How now, my son," said the priest: "fearest thou not to disturb thy mother's rest? and wouldst thou pilfer and purloin even before she is in her grave?"

"I fear not to disturb my mother's rest, good father," replied Philip, rising on his feet, "for she now rests with the blessed. Neither do I pilfer or purloin. It is not gold, I seek although if gold there were, that gold would now be mine. I seek but a key, long hidden, I believe, within this secret drawer, the opening of which is a mystery beyond my art."

"Thy mother is no more, sayest thou, my son? and dead without receiving the rites of our most holy church! Why didst thou not send for me?"

"She died, good father, suddenly, most suddenly, in these arms, about two hours ago. I fear not for her soul, although I can but grieve you were not at her side."

The priest gently opened the curtains, and looked upon the corpse. He sprinkled holy water on the bed, and for a short time his lips were seen to move in silent prayer. He then turned round to Philip.

"Why do I see thee thus employed? and why so anxious to obtain that key? A mother's death should call forth filial tears and prayers for her repose. Yet are thine eyes dry, and thou art employed upon an indifferent search while yet the tenement is warm which but now held her spirit. This is not seemly, Philip. What is the key thou seekest?"

"Father, I have no time for tears—no time to spare for grief or lamentation. I have much to do, and more to think of than thought can well embrace. That I loved my mother, you know well."

"But the key thou seekest, Philip?"

"Father, it is the key of a chamber which has not been unlocked for years, which I must—will open; even if—"

"If what, my son?"

"I was about to say what I should not have said. Forgive me, Father; I meant that I must search that chamber."

"I have long heard of that same chamber being closed: and that thy mother would not explain wherefore, I know well for I have asked her, and have been denied. Nay, when, as in duty bound, I pressed the question, I found her reason was disordered by my importunity, and, therefore, I abandoned the attempt. Some heavy weight was on thy mother's mind, my son, yet would she never confess or trust it with me. Tell me, before she died, hadst thou this secret from her?"

"I had, most holy father."

"Wouldst thou not feel comfort if thou didst confide to me, my son? I might advise, assist—"

"Father, I would indeed—I could confide it to thee, and ask for thy assistance—I know 'tis not from curious feeling thou wouldst have it, but from a better motive. But of that which has been told it is not yet manifest whether it is as my poor mother says, or but the phantom of a heated brain. Should it indeed be true, fain would I share the burthen with you—yet little you might thank me for the heavy load. But no—at least not now—it must not, cannot be revealed. I must do my work—enter that hated room alone."

"Fearest thou not?"

"Father, I fear nothing. I have a duty to perform—a dreadful one, I grant; but, I pray thee, ask no more; for like my poor mother, I feel as if the probing of the wound would half unseat my reason."

"I will not press thee further, Philip. The time may come when I may prove of service. Farewell, my child; but I pray thee to discontinue thy unseemly labour, for I must send in the neighbours to perform the duties to thy departed mother, whose soul I trust is with its God."

The priest looked at Philip; he perceived that his thoughts were elsewhere; there was a vacancy and appearance of mental stupefaction, and as he turned away, the good man shook his head.

"He is right," thought Philip, when once more alone; and he took up the cabinet, and placed it upon the stand. "A few hours more can make no difference: I will lay me down, for my head is giddy."

Philip went into the adjoining room, threw himself upon his bed, and in a few minutes was in a sleep as sound as that permitted to the wretch a few hours previous to his execution.

During his slumbers the neighbours had come in, and had prepared everything for the widow's interment. They had been careful not to wake the son, for they held as sacred the sleep of those who must wake up to sorrow. Among others, soon after the hour of noon, arrived Mynheer Poots; he had been informed of the death of the widow, but having a spare hour, he thought he might as well call, as it would raise his charges by another guilder. He first went into the room where the body lay, and from thence he proceeded to the chamber of Philip, and shook him by the shoulder.

Philip awoke, and, sitting up, perceived the doctor standing by him.

"Well, Mynheer Vanderdecken," commenced the unfeeling little man, "so it's all over. I knew it would be so; and recollect you owe me now another guilder, and you promised faithfully to pay me; altogether, with the potion, it will be three guilders and a half—that is, provided you return my phial."

Philip, who at first waking was confused, gradually recovered his senses during this address.

"You shall have your three guilders and a half, and your phial to boot, Mr Poots," replied he, as he rose from off the bed.

"Yes, yes; I know you mean to pay me—if you can. But look you, Mynheer Philip, it may be some time before you sell the cottage. You may not find a customer. Now, I never wish to be hard upon people who have no money, and I'll tell you what I'll do. There is a something on your mother's neck. It is of no value—none at all, but to a good Catholic. To help you in your strait I will take that thing, and then we shall be quits. You will have paid me, and there will be an end of it."

Philip listened calmly: he knew to what the little miser had referred,—the relic on his mother's neck; that very relic upon which his father swore the fatal oath. He felt that millions of guilders would not have induced him to part with it.

"Leave the house," answered he, abruptly. "Leave it immediately. Your money shall be paid."

Now Mynheer Poots, in the first place, knew that the setting of the relic, which was in a square frame of pure gold, was worth much more than the sum due to him: he also knew that a large price had been paid for the relic itself, and, as at that time such a relic was considered very valuable, he had no doubt but that it would again fetch a considerable sum. Tempted by the sight of it when he entered the chamber of death, he had taken it from the neck of the corpse, and it was then actually concealed in his bosom, so he replied,—"My offer is a good one, Mynheer Philip, and you had better take it. Of what use is such trash?"

"I tell you no," cried Philip, in a rage.

"Well, then, you will let me have it in my possession till I am paid, Mynheer Vanderdecken—that is but fair. I must not lose my money. When you bring me my three guilders and a half and the phial, I will return it to you."

Philip's indignation was now without bounds. He seized Mynheer Poots by the collar, and threw him out of the door. "Away immediately," cried he, "or by—"

There was no occasion for Philip to finish the imprecation. The doctor had hastened away with such alarm, that he fell down half the steps of the staircase, and was limping away across the bridge. He almost wished that the relic had not been in his possession; but his sudden retreat had prevented him, even if so inclined, from replacing it on the corpse.

The result of this conversation naturally turned Philip's thoughts to the relic, and he went into his mother's room to take possession of it. He opened the curtains—the corpse was laid out—he put forth his hand to untie the black ribbon. It was not there. "Gone!" exclaimed Philip. "They hardly would have removed it—never would. It must be that villain Poots—wretch! but I will have it, even if he has swallowed it, though I tear him limb from limb!"

Philip darted down the stairs, rushed out of the house, cleared the moat at one bound and, without coat or hat, flew away in the direction of the doctor's lonely residence. The neighbours saw him as he passed them like the wind; they wondered, and they shook their heads. Mynheer Poots was not more than half way to his home for he had hurt his ankle. Apprehensive of what might possibly take place, should his theft be discovered, he occasionally looked behind him; at length, to his horror, he beheld Philip Vanderdecken at a distance, bounding on in pursuit of him. Frightened almost out of his senses, the wretched pilferer hardly knew how to act; to stop and surrender up the stolen property was his first thought, but fear of Vanderdecken's violence prevented him; so he decided on taking to his heels, thus hoping to gain his house, and barricade himself in, by which means he would be in a condition to keep possession of what he had stolen, or at least to make some terms ere he restored it.

Mynheer Poots had need to run fast, and so he did, his thin legs bearing his shrivelled form rapidly over the ground; but Philip, who, when he witnessed the doctor's attempt to escape, was fully convinced that he was the culprit, redoubled his exertions, and rapidly came up with the chase. When within a hundred yards of his own door, Mynheer Poots heard the bounding steps of Philip gain upon him, and he sprang and leaped in his agony. Nearer and nearer still the step, until at last he heard the very breathing of his pursuer; and Poots shrieked in his fear, like the hare in the jaws of the greyhound. Philip was not a yard from him; his arm was outstretched when the miscreant dropped down paralysed with terror; and the impetus of Vanderdecken was so great, that he passed over his body, tripped and after trying in vain to recover his equilibrium, he fell and rolled over and over. This saved the little doctor; it was like the double of a hare. In a second he was again on his legs, and before Philip could rise and again exert his speed, Poots had entered his door and bolted it within. Philip was, however, determined to repossess the important treasure; and as he panted, he cast his eyes around to see if any means offered for his forcing his entrance into the house. But as the habitation of the doctor was lonely, every precaution had been taken by him to render it secure against robbery; the windows below were well barricaded and secured, and those on the upper story were too high for any one to obtain admittance by them.

We must here observe, that although Mynheer Poots was,—from his known abilities, in good practice, his reputation as a hard-hearted, unfeeling miser was well established. No one was ever permitted to enter his threshold, nor, indeed, did any one feel inclined. He was as isolated from his fellow-creatures as was his tenement, and was only to be seen in the chamber of disease and death. What his establishment consisted of no one knew. When he first settled in the neighbourhood, an old decrepit woman occasionally answered the knocks given at the door by those who required the doctor's services; but she had been buried some time, and ever since all calls at the door had been answered by Mynheer Poots in person, if he were at home, and if not, there was no reply to the most importunate summons. It was then surmised that the old man lived entirely by himself, being too niggardly to pay for any assistance. This Philip also imagined; and as soon as he had recovered his breath, he began to devise some scheme by which he would be enabled not only to recover the stolen property, but also to wreak a dire revenge.

The door was strong and not to be forced by any means which presented themselves to the eye of Vanderdecken. For a few minutes he paused to consider, and as he reflected, so did his anger cool down, and he decided that it would be sufficient to recover his relic without having recourse to violence. So he called out in a loud voice—

"Mynheer Poots, I know that you can hear me. Give me back what you have taken, and I will do you no hurt; but if you will not, you must take the consequence, for your life shall pay the forfeit before I leave this spot."

This speech was indeed very plainly heard by Mynheer Poots; but the little miser had recovered from his fright, and, thinking himself secure, could not make up his mind to surrender the relic without a struggle; so the doctor answered not, hoping that the patience of Philip would be exhausted, and that by some arrangement, such as the sacrifice of a few guilders, no small matter to one so needy as Philip, he would be able to secure what he was satisfied would sell at a high price.

Vanderdecken, finding that no answer was returned, indulged in strong invective, and then decided upon measures certainly in themselves by no means undecided.

There was part of a small stack of dry fodder standing not far from the house, and under the wall a pile of wood for firing. With these Vanderdecken resolved upon setting fire to the house, and thus, if he did not gain his relic, he would at least obtain ample revenge, he brought several armfuls of fodder and laid them at the door of the house, and upon that he piled the faggots and logs of wood, until the door was quite concealed by them. He then procured a light from the steel, flint, and tinder which every Dutchman carries in his pocket, and very soon he had fanned the pile into a flame. The smoke ascended in columns up to the rafters of the roof, while the fire raged below. The door was ignited, and was adding to the fury of the flames, and Philip shouted with joy at the success of his attempt.

"Now, miserable despoiler of the dead—now, wretched thief, now you shall feel my vengeance," cried Philip, with a loud voice. "If you remain within, you perish in the flames; if you attempt to come out, you shall die by my hands. Do you hear, Mynheer Poots—do you hear?"

Hardly had Philip concluded this address, when the window of the upper floor furthest from the burning door was thrown open.

"Ay,—you come now to beg and to entreat;—but no—no," cried Philip—who stopped as he beheld at the window what seemed to be an apparition, for instead of the wretched little miser, he beheld one of the loveliest forms Nature ever deigned to mould—an angelic creature, of about sixteen or seventeen, who appeared calm and resolute in the midst of the danger by which she was threatened. Her long black hair was braided and twined round her beautifully-formed head; her eyes were large, intensely dark, yet soft; her forehead high and white, her chin dimpled, her ruby lips arched and delicately fine, her nose small and straight. A lovelier face could not be well imagined; it reminded you of what the best of painters have sometimes, in their more fortunate moments, succeeded in embodying, when they would represent a beauteous saint. And as the flames wreathed and the smoke burst out in columns and swept past the window, so might she have reminded you in her calmness of demeanour of some martyr at the stake.

"What wouldst thou, violent young man? Why are the inmates of this house to suffer death by your means?" said the maiden, with composure.

For a few seconds Philip gazed, and could make no reply; then the thought seized him that in his vengeance, he was about to sacrifice so much loveliness. He forgot everything but her danger, and seizing one of the large poles which he had brought to feed the flame, he threw off and scattered in every direction the burning masses, until nothing was left which could hurt the building but the ignited door itself; and this, which as yet—for it was of thick oak plank—had not suffered very material injury, he soon reduced, by beating it, with clods of earth, to a smoking and harmless state. During these active measures on the part of Philip, the young maiden watched him in silence.

"All is safe now, young lady," said Philip. "God forgive me that I should have risked a life so precious. I thought but to wreak my vengeance upon Mynheer Poots."

"And what cause can Mynheer Poots have given for such dreadful vengeance?" replied the maiden, calmly.

"What cause, young lady? He came to my house—despoiled the dead—took from my mother's corpse a relic beyond price."

"Despoiled the dead!—he surely cannot—you must wrong him, young sir."

"No, no. It is the fact, lady,—and that relic—forgive me—but that relic I must have. You know not what depends upon it."

"Wait, young sir," replied the maiden; "I will soon return."

Philip waited several minutes, lost in thought and admiration: so fair a creature in the house of Mynheer Poots! Who could she be? While thus ruminating, he was accosted by the silver voice of the object of his reveries, who, leaning out of the window held in her hand the black ribbon to which was attached the article so dearly coveted.

"Here is your relic, sir," said the young female; "I regret much that my father should have done a deed which well might justify your anger: but here it is," continued she, dropping it down on the ground by Philip; "and now you may depart."

"Your father, maiden! can he be *your* father?" said Philip, forgetting to take up the relic which lay at his feet.

She would have retired from the window without reply, but Philip spoke a again—

"Stop, lady, stop one moment, until I beg your forgiveness for a wild, foolish act. I swear by this sacred relic," continued he, taking it from the ground and raising it to his lips, "that had I known that any unoffending person had been in this house, I would not have done the deed, and much do I rejoice that no harm hath happened. But there is still danger, lady; the door must be unbarred, and the jambs, which still are glowing, be extinguished, or the house may yet be burnt. Fear not for your father, maiden; for had he done me a thousand times more wrong, you will protect each hair upon his head. He knows me well enough to know I keep my word. Allow me to repair the injury I have occasioned, and then I will depart."

"No, no; don't trust him," said Mynheer Poots, from within the chamber.

"Yes, he may be trusted," replied the daughter; "and his services are much needed for what could a poor weak girl like me, and a still weaker father, do in this strait? Open the door, and let the house be made secure." The maiden then addressed Philip—"He shall open the door, sir, and I will thank you for your kind service. I trust entirely to your promise."

"I never yet was known to break my word, maiden," replied Philip; "but let him be quick, for the flames are bursting out again."

The door was opened by the trembling hands of Mynheer Poots, who then made a hasty retreat upstairs. The truth of what Philip had said was then apparent. Many were the buckets of water which he was obliged to fetch before the fire was quite subdued; but during his exertions neither the daughter nor the father made their appearance.

When all was safe, Philip closed the door, and again looked up at the window. The fair girl made her appearance, and Philip, with a low obeisance, assured her that there was then no danger.

"I thank you, sir," replied she—"I thank you much. Your conduct, although hasty at the first, has yet been most considerate."

"Assure your father, maiden, that all animosity on my part hath ceased, and that in a few days I will call and satisfy the demand he hath against me."

The window closed, and Philip, more excited but with feelings altogether different from those with which he had set out, looked at it for a minute, and then bent his steps to his own cottage.

Chapter Three.

The discovery of the beautiful daughter of Mynheer Poots had made a strong impression upon Philip Vanderdecken, and now he had another excitement to combine with those which already overcharged his bosom. He arrived at his own house, went upstairs, and threw himself on the bed from which he had been roused by Mynheer Poots. At first, he recalled to his mind the scene we have just described, painted in his imagination the portrait of the fair girl, her eyes, her expression, her silver voice, and the words which she had uttered; but her pleasing image was soon chased away by the recollection that his mother's corpse lay in the adjoining chamber, and that his father's secret was hidden in the room below.

The funeral was to take place the next morning, and Philip, who, since his meeting with the daughter of Mynheer Poots, appeared even to himself not so anxious for immediate examination of the room, resolved that he would not open it until after the melancholy ceremony. With this resolution he fell asleep; and, exhausted with bodily and mental excitement, he did not wake until the next morning, when he was summoned by the priest to assist at the funeral rites. In an hour all was over; the crowd dispersed, and Philip, returning to the cottage, bolted the door that he might not be interrupted, and felt happy that he was alone.

There is a feeling in our nature which will arise when we again find ourselves in the tenement where death has been, and all traces of it have been removed. It is a feeling of satisfaction and relief at having rid ourselves of the memento of mortality, the silent evidence of the futility of our pursuits and anticipations. We know that we must one day die, but we always wish to forget it. The continual remembrance would be too great a check upon our mundane desires and wishes; and, although we are told that we ever should have futurity in our thoughts, we find that life is not to be enjoyed if we are not permitted occasional forgetfulness. For who would plan what rarely he is permitted to execute, if each moment of the day he thought of death? We either hope that we may live longer than others, or we forget that we may not.

If this buoyant feeling had not been planted in our nature, how little would the world have been improved even from the Deluge! Philip walked into the room where his mother had lain one short hour before, and unwittingly felt relief. Taking down the cabinet, he now recommenced his task; the back panel was soon removed, and a secret drawer discovered; he drew it out, and it contained what he presumed to be the object of his search,—a large key with a slight coat of rust upon it, which came off upon its being handled. Under the key was a paper, the writing on which was somewhat discoloured; it was in his mother's hand, and ran as follows:—

"It is now two nights since a horrible event took place which has induced me to close the lower chamber, and my brain is still bursting with terror. Should I not, during my lifetime, reveal what occurred, still this key will be required, as at my death the room will be opened. When I rushed from it I hastened upstairs, and remained that night with my child; the next morning I summoned up sufficient courage, to go down, turn the key and bring it up into my chamber. It is now closed till I close my eyes in death. No privation, no suffering, shall induce me to open it, although in the iron cupboard under the buffet farthest from the window, there is money sufficient for all my wants; that money will remain there for my child, to whom, if I do not impart the fatal secret, he must be satisfied that it is one which it were better should be concealed,—one so horrible as to induce me to take the steps which I now do. The keys of the cupboards and buffets were, I think, lying on the table, or in my work-box, when I quitted the room. There is a letter on the table—at least I think so. It is sealed. Let not the seal be broken but by my son, and not by him unless he knows the secret. Let it be burnt by the priest,—for it is cursed;—and even should my son know all that I do, oh, let him pause,—let him reflect well before he breaks the seal,—for 'twere better he should know NO MORE!"

"Not know more!" thought Philip, as his eyes were still fixed upon the paper. "Yes, but I must and will know more, so forgive me dearest mother, if I waste no time in reflection. It would be but time thrown away, when one is resolved as I am."

Philip pressed his lips to his mother's signature, folded up the paper and put it into his pocket; then taking the key, he proceeded downstairs.

It was about noon when Philip descended to open the chamber; the sun shone bright, the sky was clear, and all without was cheerful and joyous. The front door of the cottage being closed, there was not much light in the passage when Philip put the key into the lock of the long-closed door, and with some difficulty turned it round. To say that when he pushed open the door he felt no alarm would not be correct; he did feel alarm, and his heart palpitated; but he felt more than was requisite of determination to conquer that alarm, and to conquer more, should more be created by what he should behold. He opened the door, but did not immediately enter the room: he paused where he stood, for he felt as if he was about to intrude into the retreat of a disembodied spirit, and that that spirit might reappear. He waited a minute, for the effort of opening the door had taken away his breath, and, as he recovered himself, he looked within.

He could but imperfectly distinguish the objects in the chamber, but through the joints of the shutters there were three brilliant beams of sunshine forcing their way across the room, which at first induced him to recoil as if from something supernatural; but a little reflection reassured him. After about a minute's pause, Philip went into the kitchen, lighted a candle, and, sighing deeply two or three times as if to relieve his heart, he summoned his resolution, and walked towards the fatal room. He first stopped at the threshold, and, by the light of the candle, took a hasty survey. All was still: and the table on which the letter had been left, being behind the door, was concealed by its being opened. It must be done, thought Philip: and why not at once? continued he, resuming his courage; and, with a firm step, he walked into the room and went to unfasten the shutters. If his hand trembled a little when he called to mind how supernaturally they had last been opened, it is not surprising. We are but mortal, and we shrink from contact with aught beyond this life. When the fastenings were removed and the shutters unfolded, a stream of light poured into the room so vivid as to dazzle his eyesight; strange to say, this very light of a brilliant day overthrew the resolution of Philip more than the previous gloom and darkness had done; and with the candle in his hand, he retreated hastily into the kitchen to re-summon his courage, and there he remained for some minutes with his face covered, and in deep thought.

It is singular that his reveries at last ended by reverting to the fair daughter of Mynheer Poots, and her first appearance at the window; and he felt as if the flood of light which had just driven him from the one, was not more impressive and startling than her enchanting form at the other. His mind dwelling upon this beauteous vision appeared to restore Philip's confidence; he now rose and boldly walked into the room. We shall not describe the objects it contained as they chanced to meet the eyes of Philip, but attempt a more lucid arrangement.

The room was about twelve or fourteen feet square, with but one window; opposite to the door stood the chimney and fireplace, with a high buffet of dark wood on each side. The floor of the room was not dirty, although about its upper parts spiders had run their cobwebs in every direction. In the centre of the ceiling hung a quicksilver globe, a common ornament in those days, but the major part of it had lost its brilliancy, the spiders' webs enclosing it like a shroud. Over the chimney-piece were hung two or three drawings, framed and glazed, but a dusty mildew was spotted over the glass, so that little of them could be distinguished. In the centre of the mantelpiece was an image of the Virgin Mary, of pure silver, in a shrine of the same metal, but it was tarnished to the colour of bronze or iron; some Indian figures stood on each side of it. The glass doors of the buffets on each side of the chimney-piece were also so dimmed that little of what was within could be distinguished: the light and heat which had been poured into the room, even for so short a time, had already gathered up the damp of many years, and it lay as a mist, and mingled with the dust upon the panes of glass: still here and there a glittering of silver vessels could be discerned, for the glass doors had protected them from turning black, although much dimmed in lustre.

On the wall facing the window were other prints, in frames equally veiled in damp and cobwebs and also two bird-cages. The bird-cages Philip approached, and looked into them. The occupants, of course, had long been dead; but at the bottom of the cages was a small heap of yellow feathers, through which the little white bones of the skeletons were to be seen, proving that they had been brought from the Canary Isles; and, at that period, such birds were highly valued. Philip appeared to wish to examine everything before he sought that which he most dreaded, yet most wished, to find. There were several chairs round the room: on one of them was some linen; he took it up. It was some that must have belonged to him when he was yet a child. At last, Philip turned his eyes to the wall not yet examined (that opposite the chimney piece), through which the door was pierced, and behind the door as it lay open, he was to find the table, the couch, the work-box, and the FATAL LETTER. As he turned round, his pulse, which had gradually recovered its regular motion, beat more quickly, but he made the effort, and it was over. At first he examined the walls, against which were hung swords and pistols of various sorts but chiefly Asiatic bows and arrows, and other implements of destruction. Philip's eyes gradually descended upon the table and little couch behind it, where his mother stated herself to have been seated when his father made his awful visit. The work-box and all its implements were on the table, just as she had left them. The keys she mentioned were also lying there, but Philip looked, and looked again; there was no letter, he now advanced nearer, examined closely—there was none that he could perceive, either on the couch or on the table—or on the floor. He lifted up the work-box to ascertain if it was beneath—but no. He examined among its contents, but no letter was there. He turned over the pillows of the couch, but still there was no letter to be found. And Philip felt as if there had been a heavy load removed from his panting chest. "Surely, then," thought he, as he leant against the wall, "this must have been the vision of a heated imagination. My poor mother must have fallen asleep, and dreamt this horrid tale. I thought it was impossible, at least I hoped so. It must have been as I suppose; the dream was too powerful, too like a fearful reality,—partially unseated my poor mother's reason." Philip reflected again, and was then satisfied that his suppositions were correct.

"Yes, it must have been so, poor dear mother! how much thou hast suffered; but thou art now rewarded, and with thy God."

After a few minutes (during which he surveyed the room again and again with more coolness, and perhaps some indifference, now that he regarded the supernatural history as not true), Philip took out of his pocket the written paper found with the key, and read it over,—"The iron cupboard under the buffet farthest from the window."

"'Tis well." He took the bunch of keys from off the table, and soon fitted one to the outside wooden doors which concealed the iron safe. A second key on the bunch opened the iron doors; and Philip found himself in possession of a considerable sum of money, amounting, as near as he could reckon, to ten thousand guilders, in little yellow sacks.

"My poor mother!" thought he; "and has a mere dream scared thee to penury and want, with all this wealth in thy possession?" Philip replaced the sacks, and locked up the cupboards, after having taken out of one, already half emptied, a few pieces for his immediate wants. His attention was next directed to the buffets above, which with one of the keys, he opened; he found that they contained china, and silver flagons, and cups of considerable value. The locks were again turned, and the bunch of keys thrown upon the table.

The sudden possession of so much wealth added to the conviction, to which Philip had now arrived that there had been no supernatural appearance, as supposed, by his mother, naturally revived and composed his spirits; and he felt a reaction which amounted almost to hilarity. Seating himself on the couch, he was soon in a reverie, and, as before reverted to the lovely daughter of Mynheer Poots indulging in various castle-buildings, all ending, as usual, when we choose for ourselves, in competence and felicity. In this pleasing occupation he remained for more than two hours, when his thoughts again reverted to his poor mother and her fearful death.

"Dearest, kindest mother!" apostrophised Philip aloud, as he rose from his leaning position, "here thou wert, tired with watching over my infant slumbers, thinking of my absent father and his dangers, working up thy mind and anticipating evil, till thy fevered sleep conjured up this apparition. Yes, it must have been so; for see here, lying on the floor, is the embroidery, as it fell from thy unconscious hands, and with that labour ceased thy happiness in this life. Dear, dear mother!" continued he; a tear rolling down his cheek as he stooped to pick up the piece of muslin, "how much hast thou suffered when—God of Heaven!" exclaimed Philip, as he lifted up the embroidery, starting back with violence, and overturning the table, "God of Heaven, and of Judgment, there is—there *is*," and Philip clasped his hands, and bowed his head in awe and anguish, as in a changed and fearful tone he muttered forth—"the LETTER!"

It was but too true,—underneath the embroidery on the floor had lain the fatal letter of Vanderdecken. Had Philip seen it on the table when he first went into the room, and was prepared to find it, he would have taken it up with some degree of composure: but to find it now, when he had persuaded himself that it was all an illusion on the part of his mother; when he had made up his mind that there had been no supernatural agency; after he had been indulging in visions of future bliss and repose, was a shock that transfixed him where he stood and for some time he remained in his attitude of surprise and terror. Down at once fell the airy fabric of happiness which he had built up during the last two hours; and as he gradually recovered from his alarm, his heart filled with melancholy forebodings. At last he dashed forward, seized the letter, and burst out of the fatal room.

"I cannot, dare not, read it here," exclaimed he: "no, no, it must be under the vault of high and offended Heaven, that the message must be received." Philip took his hat, and went out of the house; in calm despair he locked the door, took out the key, and walked he knew not whither.

Chapter Four.

If the reader can imagine the feelings of a man who, sentenced to death, and having resigned himself to his fate, finds himself unexpectedly reprieved; who, having recomposed his mind after the agitation arising from a renewal of those hopes and expectations which he had abandoned, once more dwells upon future prospects, and indulges in pleasing anticipations: we say, that if the reader can imagine this, and then what would be that man's feelings when he finds that the reprieve is revoked, and that he is to suffer, he may then form some idea of the state of Philip's mind when he quitted the cottage.

Long did he walk, careless in which direction, with the letter in his clenched hand, and his teeth firmly set. Gradually he became more composed: and out of breath with the rapidity of his motion, he sat down upon a bank, and there he long remained, with his eyes riveted upon the dreaded paper, which he held with both his hands upon his knees.

Mechanically he turned the letter over; the seal was black. Philip sighed:— "I cannot read it now," thought he, and he rose and continued his devious way.

For another half-hour did Philip keep in motion, and the sun was not many degrees above the horizon. Philip stopped and looked at it till his vision failed. "I could imagine that it was the eye of God," thought Philip, "and perhaps it may be. Why, then, merciful Creator, am I thus selected from so many millions to fulfil so dire a task?"

Philip looked about him for some spot where he might be concealed from observation—where he might break the seal, and read this mission from a world of spirits. A small copse of brushwood, in advance of a grove of trees, was not far from where he stood. He walked to it, and sat down, so as to be concealed from any passers by. Philip once more looked at the descending orb of day, and by degrees he became composed.

"It is thy will," exclaimed he; "it is my fate, and both must be accomplished."

Philip put his hand to the seal,—his blood thrilled when he called to mind that it had been delivered by no mortal hand, and that it contained the secret of one in judgment. He remembered that that one was his father; and that it was only in the letter that there was hope,—hope for his poor father, whose memory he had been taught to love, and who appealed for help.

"Coward that I am, to have lost so many hours!" exclaimed Philip; "yon sun appears as if waiting on the hill, to give me light to read."

Philip mused a short time; he was once more the daring Vanderdecken. Calmly he broke the seal, which bore the initials of his father's name, and read as follows:—

"To *Catherine*.

"One of those pitying spirits whose eyes rain tears for mortal crimes has been permitted to inform me by what means alone my dreadful doom may be averted.

"Could I but receive on the deck of my own ship the holy relic upon which I swore the fatal oath, kiss it in all humility, and shed one tear of deep contrition on the sacred wood, I then might rest in peace.

"How this may be effected, or by whom so fatal a task will be undertaken, I know not. O Catherine, we have a son—but, no, no, let him not hear of me. Pray for me, and now, farewell.

"*I. Vanderdecken.*"

"Then it is true, most horribly true," thought Philip; "and my father is even now **In Living Judgment**. And he points to me,—to whom else should he? Am I not his son, and is it not my duty?"

"Yes, father," exclaimed Philip aloud, falling on his knees, "you have not written these lines in vain. Let me peruse them once more."

Philip raised up his hand; but although it appeared to him that he had still hold of the letter, it was not there—he grasped nothing. He looked on the grass to see if it had fallen—but no, there was no letter, it had disappeared. Was it a vision?—no, no, he had read every word. "Then it must be to me, and me alone, that the mission was intended. I accept the sign.

"Hear me, dear father,—if thou art so permitted,—and deign to hear me, gracious Heaven—hear the son who, by this sacred relic, swears that he will avert your doom, or perish. To that will he devote his days; and having done his duty, he will die in hope and peace. Heaven, that recorded my rash father's oath, now register his son's upon the same sacred cross, and may perjury on my part be visited with punishment more dire than his! Receive it, Heaven, as at the last I trust that in thy mercy thou wilt receive the father and the son: and if too bold, O pardon my presumption."

Philip threw himself forward on his face, with his lips to the sacred symbol. The sun went down, and the twilight gradually disappeared; night had, for some time, shrouded all in darkness, and Philip yet remained in alternate prayer and meditation!

But he was disturbed by the voices of some men, who sat down upon the turf but a few yards from where he was concealed. The conversation he little heeded; but it had roused him and his first feeling was to return to the cottage, that he might reflect over his plans; but although the men spoke in a low tone, his attention was soon arrested by the subject of their conversation, when he heard the name mentioned of Mynheer Poots. He listened attentively, and discovered that they were four disbanded soldiers, who intended that night to attack the house of the little doctor, who had, they knew, much money in his possession.

"What I have proposed is the best," said one of them; "he has no one with him but his daughter."

"I value her more than his money," replied another; "so, recollect before we go, it is perfectly understood that she is to be my property."

"Yes, if you choose to purchase her, there's no objection," replied a third.

"Agreed; how much will you in conscience ask for a paling girl?"

"I say five hundred guilders," replied another.

"Well, be it so, but on this condition, that if my share of the booty does not amount to so much, I am to have her for my share, whatever it may be."

"That's very fair," replied the other: "but I'm much mistaken if we don't turn more than two thousand guilders out of the old man's chest."

"What do you two say—is it agreed—shall Baetens have her?"

"O yes," replied the others.

"Well, then," replied the one who had stipulated for Mynheer Poots's daughter, "now I am with you heart and soul. I loved that girl, and tried to get her,—I positively offered to marry her, but the old hunks refused me, an ensign, an officer; but now I'll have revenge. We must not spare him."

"No, no," replied the others.

"Shall we go now, or wait till it is later? In an hour or more the moon will be up,—we may be seen."

"Who is to see us? unless, indeed, some one is sent for him. The later the better, I say."

"How long will it take us to get there? Not half an hour if we walk. Suppose we start in half an hour hence, we shall just have the moon to count the guilders by."

"That's all right. In the meantime, I'll put a new flint in my lock, and have my carbine loaded. I can work in the dark."

"You are used to it, Jan."

"Yes, I am,—and I intend this ball to go through the old rascal's head."

"Well, I'd rather you should kill him than I," replied one of the others, "for he saved my life at Middleburgh, when every one made sure I'd die."

Philip did not wait to hear any more; he crawled behind the bushes until he gained the grove of trees, and passing through them, made a détour, so as not to be seen by these miscreants. That they were disbanded soldiers, many of whom were infesting the country, he knew well. All his thoughts were now to save the old doctor and his daughter from the danger which threatened them; and for a time he forgot his father, and the exciting revelations of the day. Although Philip had not been aware in what direction he had walked when he set off from the cottage, he knew the country well; and now that it was necessary to act, he remembered the direction in which he should find the lonely house of Mynheer Poots: with the utmost speed he made his way for it, and in less than twenty minutes he arrived there out of breath.

As usual, all was silent, and the door fastened. Philip knocked, but there was no reply. Again and again he knocked, and became impatient. Mynheer Poots must have been summoned, and was not in the house; Philip therefore called out so as to be heard within, "Maiden, if your father is out, as I presume he must be, listen to what I have to say—I am Philip Vanderdecken. But now I overheard four wretches, who have planned to murder your father, and rob him of his gold. In one hour, or less, they will be here, and I have hastened to warn and to protect you, if I may. I swear upon the relic that you delivered to me this morning, that what I state is true."

Philip waited a short time, but received no answer.

"Maiden," resumed he, "answer me, if you value that which is more dear to you than even your father's gold to him. Open the casement above, and listen to what I have to say. In so doing there is no risk; and even if it were not dark, already have I seen you."

A short time after this second address, the casement of the upper window was unbarred, and the slight form of the fair daughter of Mynheer Poots was to be distinguished by Philip through the gloom.

"What wouldst thou young sir, at this unseemly hour? and what is it thou wouldst impart, but imperfectly heard by me, when thou spokest this minute at the door?"

Philip then entered into a detail of all that he had overheard, and concluded by begging her to admit him, that he might defend her.

"Think, fair maiden, of what I have told you. You have been sold to one of those reprobates, whose name I think they mentioned was Baetens. The gold, I know, you value not; but think of thine own dear self—suffer me to enter the house, and think not for one moment that my story is feigned. I swear to thee, by the soul of my poor dear mother, now, I trust, in heaven, that every word is true."

"Baetens, did you say, sir?"

"If I mistook them not, such was the name; he said he loved you once."

"That name I have in memory—I know not what to do, or what to say: my father has been summoned to a birth, and may be yet away for many hours. Yet how can I ope the door to you—at night—he not at home—I alone? I ought not—cannot—yet do I believe you. You surely never could be so base as to invent this tale."

"No—upon my hopes of future bliss I could not, maiden! you must not trifle with your life and honour, but let me in."

"And if I did, what could you do against such numbers?"

"They are four to one—would soon overpower you, and one more life would be lost."

"Not if you have arms; and I think your father would not be left without them. I fear them not—you know that I am resolute."

"I do indeed—and now you'd risk your life for those you did assail. I thank you, thank you kindly, sir—but dare not ope the door."

"Then, maiden, if you'll not admit me, here will I now remain; without arms, and but ill able to contend with four armed villains; but still, here will I remain and prove my truth to one I will protect 'gainst any odds—yes, even here!"

"Then shall I be thy murderer!—but that must not be. Oh! sir—swear, swear by all that's holy, and by all that's pure, that—you do not deceive me."

"I swear by thyself, maiden, than all to me more sacred!"

The casement closed, and in a short time a light appeared above. In a minute or two more the door was opened to Philip by the fair daughter of Mynheer Poots. She stood with the candle in her right hand, the colour in her cheeks varying—now flushing red, and again deadly pale. Her left hand was down by her side, and in it she held a pistol half concealed. Philip perceived this precaution on her part, but took no notice of it; he wished to re-assure her.

"Maiden!" said he, not entering, "if you still have doubts—if you think you have been ill advised in giving me admission—there is yet time to close the door against me; but for your own sake I entreat you not. Before the moon is up, the robbers will be here. With my life I will protect you, if you will but trust me. Who indeed could injure one like you?"

She was indeed (as she stood irresolute and perplexed from the peculiarity of her situation, yet not wanting in courage when it was to be called forth) an object well worthy of gaze and admiration. Her features thrown into broad light and shade by the candle which at times was half extinguished by the wind—her symmetry of form and the gracefulness and singularity of her attire—were matter of astonishment to Philip. Her head was without covering, and her long hair fell in plaits behind her shoulders; her stature was rather under the middle size, but her form perfect; her dress was simple but becoming, and very different from that usually worn by the young women of the district. Not only her features but her dress would at once have indicated to a traveller that she was of Arab blood, as was the fact.

She looked in Philip's face as he spoke—earnestly, as if she would have penetrated into his inmost thoughts; but there was a frankness and honesty in his bearing, and a sincerity in his manly countenance, which re-assured her. After a moment's hesitation she replied—

"Come in, sir; I feel that I can trust you."

Philip entered. The door was then closed and made secure.

"We have no time to lose, maiden," said Philip: "but tell me your name, that I may address you as I ought."

"My name is Amine," replied she, retreating a little.

"I thank you for that little confidence; but I must not dally. What arms have you in the house, and have you ammunition?"

"Both. I wish that my father would come home."

"And so do I," replied Philip, "devoutedly wish he would, before these murderers come; but not, I trust, while the attack is making, for there's a carbine loaded expressly for his head, and if they make him prisoner, they will not spare his life, unless his gold and your person are given in ransom. But the arms, maiden—where are they?"

"Follow me," replied Amine, leading Philip to an inner room on the upper floor. It was the sanctum of her father, and was surrounded with shelves filled with bottles and boxes of drugs. In one corner was an iron chest, and over the mantelpiece were a brace of carbines and three pistols.

"They are all loaded," observed Amine, pointing to them, and laying on the table the one which she had held in her hand.

Philip took down the arms and examined all the primings. He then took up from the table the pistol which Amine had laid there, and threw open the pan. It was equally well prepared. Philip closed the pan, and with a smile observed:—

"So this was meant for me, Amine?"

"No—not for you—but for a traitor, had one gained admittance."

"Now, maiden," observed Philip, "I shall station myself at the casement which you opened, but without a light in the room. You may remain here, and can turn the key for your security."

"You little know me," replied Amine. "In that way at least I am not fearful: I must remain near you and reload the arms—a task in which I am well practised."

"No, no," replied Philip, "you might be hurt."

"I may. But think you I will remain here idly, when I can assist one who risks his life for me? I know my duty, sir, and I shall perform it."

"You must not risk your life, Amine," replied Philip; "my aim will not be steady if I know that you're in danger. But I must take the arms into the other chamber, for the time is come."

Philip, assisted by Amine, carried the carbines and pistols into the adjoining chamber; and Amine then left Philip, carrying with her the light. Philip, as soon as he was alone, opened the casement and looked out—there was no one to be seen; he listened, but all was silent. The moon was just rising above the distant hill, but her light was dimmed by fleecy clouds, and Philip watched for a few minutes; at length he heard a whispering below. He looked out, and could distinguish through the dark the four expected assailants, standing close to the door of the house. He walked away softly from the window, and went into the next room to Amine, whom he found busy preparing the ammunition.

"Amine, they are at the door, in consultation. You can see them now without risk. I thank them, for they will convince you that I have told the truth."

Amine, without reply, went into the front room and looked out of the window. She returned, and laying her hand upon Philip's arm, she said—"Grant me your pardon for my doubts. I fear nothing now but that my father may return too soon, and they seize him."

Philip left the room again, to make his reconnoissance. The robbers did not appear to have made up their mind—the strength of the door defied their utmost efforts, so they attempted stratagem. They knocked, and as there was no reply, they continued to knock louder and louder: not meeting with success, they held another consultation, and the muzzle of a carbine was then put to the keyhole, and the piece discharged. The lock of the door was blown off, but the iron bars which crossed the door within, above and below, still held it fast.

Although Philip would have been justified in firing upon the robbers when he first perceived them in consultation at the door, still there is that feeling in a generous mind which prevents the taking away of life, except from stern necessity; and this feeling made him withhold his fire until hostilities had actually commenced. He now levelled one of the carbines at the head of the robber nearest to the door, who was busy examining the effect which the discharge of the piece had made, and what further obstacles intervened. The aim was true, and the man fell dead, while the others started back with surprise at the unexpected retaliation. But in a second or two a pistol was discharged at Philip, who still remained leaning out of the casement, fortunately without effect; and the next moment he felt himself drawn away, so as to be protected from their fire. It was Amine, who, unknown to Philip, had been standing by his side.

"You must not expose yourself, Philip," said she, in a low tone.

"She called me Philip," thought he, but made no reply.

"They will be watching for you at the casement now," said Amine. "Take the other carbine, and go below in the passage. If the lock of the door is blown off, they may put their arms in, perhaps, and remove the bars. I do not think they can, but I'm not sure; at all events, it is there you should now be, as there they will not expect you."

"You are right," replied Philip, going down.

"But you must not fire more than once there; if another fall, there will be but two to deal with, and they cannot watch the casement and force admittance too. Go—I will reload the carbine."

Philip descended softly and without a light. He went up to the door, and perceived that one of the miscreants, with his arm through the hole where the lock was blown off, was working at the upper iron bar, which he could just reach. He presented his carbine, and was about to fire the whole charge into the body of the man under his raised arm, when there was a report of fire-arms from the robbers outside.

"Amine has exposed herself," thought Philip, "and may be hurt."

The desire of vengeance prompted him first to fire his piece through the man's body, and then he flew up the stairs to ascertain the state of Amine. She was not at the casement; he darted into the inner room, and found her deliberately loading the carbine.

"My God! how you frightened me, Amine. I thought by their firing that you had shown yourself at the window."

"Indeed I did not; but I thought that when you fired through the door they might return your fire, and you be hurt; so I went to the side of the casement and pushed out on a stick some of my father's clothes, and they who were watching for you fired immediately."

"Indeed, Amine! who could have expected such courage and such coolness in one so young and beautiful?" exclaimed Philip, with surprise.

"Are none but ill-favoured people brave, then?" replied Amine, smiling.

"I did not mean that, Amine—but I am losing time. I must to the door again. Give me that carbine, and reload this."

Philip crept down stairs that he might reconnoitre, but before he had gained the door he heard at a distance the voice of Mynheer Poots. Amine, who also heard it, was in a moment at his side with a loaded pistol in each hand.

"Fear not, Amine," said Philip, as he unbarred the door, "there are but two, and your father shall be saved."

The door was opened, and Philip, seizing his carbine, rushed out; he found Mynheer Poots on the ground between the two men, one of whom had raised his knife to plunge it into his body, when the ball of the carbine whizzed through his head. The last of the robbers closed with Philip, and a desperate struggle ensued—it was however, soon decided by Amine stepping forward and firing one of the pistols through the robber's body.

We must here inform our readers that Mynheer Poots, when coming home, had heard the report of fire-arms in the direction of his own house. The recollection of his daughter and of his money—for to do him justice he did love her best—had lent him wings; he forgot that he was a feeble old man and without arms; all he thought of was to gain his habitation. On he came, reckless, frantic, and shouting, and rushed into the arms of the two robbers, who seized and would have despatched him, had not Philip so opportunely come to his assistance.

As soon as the last robber fell, Philip disengaged himself and went to the assistance of Mynheer Poots, whom he raised up in his arms and carried into the house as if he were an infant. The old man was still in a state of delirium from fear and previous excitement.

In a few minutes, Mynheer Poots was more coherent.

"My daughter!" exclaimed he—"my daughter! where is she?"

"She is here father, and safe," replied Amine.

"Ah! my child is safe," said he, opening his eyes and staring. "Yes, it is even so—and my money—my money—where is my money?" continued he, starting up.

"Quite safe, father."

"Quite safe—you say quite safe—are you sure of it?—let me see."

"There it is, father, as you may perceive, quite safe—thanks to one whom you have not treated so well."

"Who—what do you mean?—Ah, yes, I see him now—'tis Philip Vanderdecken—he owes me three guilders and a half, and there is a phial—did he save you—and my money, child?"

"He did, indeed at the risk of his life."

"Well, well, I will forgive him the whole debt—yes, the whole of it; but—the phial is of no use to him—he must return that. Give me some water."

It was some time before the old man could regain his perfect reason. Philip left him with his daughter, and, taking a brace of loaded pistols, went out to ascertain the fate of the four assailants. The moon, having climbed above the bank of clouds which had obscured her, was now high in the heavens, shining bright, and he could distinguish clearly. The two men lying across the threshold of the door were quite dead. The others, who had seized upon Mynheer Poots, were still alive, but one was expiring and the other bled fast. Philip put a few questions to the latter, but he either would not or could not make any reply; he removed their weapons and returned to the house, where he found the old man attended by his daughter, in a state of comparative composure.

"I thank you, Philip Vanderdecken—I thank you much. You have saved my dear child, and my money—that is little, very little—for I am poor. May you live long and happily!"

Philip mused; the letter and his vow were, for the first time since he fell in with the robbers, recalled to his recollection, and a shade passed over his countenance.

"Long and happily—no, no," muttered he, with an involuntary shake of the head.

"And I must thank you," said Amine, looking inquiringly in Philip's face. "O, how much have I to thank you for!—and indeed I am grateful."

"Yes, yes, she is very grateful," interrupted the old man; "but we are poor—very poor. I talked about my money because I have so little, and I cannot afford to lose it; but you shall not pay me the three guilders and a half—I am content to lose that, Mr Philip."

"Why should you lose even that, Mynheer Poots?—I promised to pay you, and will keep my word. I have plenty of money—thousands of guilders, and know not what to do with them."

"You—you—thousands of guilders!" exclaimed Poots. "Pooh, nonsense, that won't do."

"I repeat to you, Amine," said Philip, "that I have thousands of guilders: you know I would not tell you a falsehood."

"I believed you when you said so to my father," replied Amine.

"Then, perhaps, as you have so much, and I am so very poor, Mr Vanderdecken—"

But Amine put her hand upon her father's lips, and the sentence was not finished.

"Father," said Amine, "it is time that we retire. You must leave us for to-night, Philip."

"I will not," replied Philip; "nor, you may depend upon it, will I sleep. You may both to bed in safety. It is indeed time that you retire—good night, Mynheer Poots. I will but ask a lamp, and then I leave you—Amine, good night."

"Good night," said Amine, extending her hand, "and many, many thanks."

"Thousands of guilders!" muttered the old man, as Philip left the room and went below.

Chapter Five.

Philip Vanderdecken sat down at the porch of the door; he swept his hair from his forehead, which he exposed to the fanning of the breeze; for the continued excitement of the last three days had left a fever on his brain which made him restless and confused. He longed for repose, but he knew that for him there was no rest. He had his forebodings—he perceived in the vista of futurity a long-continued chain of danger and disaster, even to death; yet he beheld it without emotion and without dread. He felt as if it were only three days that he had begun to exist; he was melancholy, but not unhappy. His thoughts were constantly recurring to the fatal letter—its strange supernatural disappearance seemed pointedly to establish its supernatural origin, and that the mission had been intended for him alone; and the relic in his possession more fully substantiated the fact.

"It is my fate, my duty," thought Philip. Having satisfactorily made up his mind to these conclusions, his thoughts reverted to the beauty, the courage, and presence of mind shown by Amine. "And," thought he, as he watched the moon soaring high in the heavens, "is this fair creature's destiny to be interwoven with mine? The events of the last three days would almost warrant the supposition. Heaven only knows, and Heaven's will be done. I have vowed, and my vow is registered, that I will devote my life to the release of my unfortunate father—but does that prevent my loving Amine?—No, no; the sailor on the Indian seas must pass months and months on shore before he can return to his duty. My search must be on the broad ocean, but how often may I return? and why am I to be debarred the solace of a smiling hearth?—and yet—do I right in winning the affections of one who, if she loves, would, I am convinced, love so dearly, fondly truly—ought I to persuade her to mate herself with one whose life will be so precarious?—but is not every sailor's life precarious, daring the angry waves, with but an inch of plank 'tween him and death? Besides, I am chosen to fulfil a task—and if so, what can hurt me, till in Heaven's own time it is accomplished? but then how soon, and how is it to end?—in death! I wish my blood were cooler, that I might reason better."

Such were the meditations of Philip Vanderdecken, and long did he revolve such chances in his mind. At last the day dawned, and as he perceived the blush upon the horizon, less careful of his watch he slumbered where he sat. A slight pressure on the shoulder made him start up and draw the pistol from his bosom. He turned round and beheld Amine.

"And that pistol was intended for me," said Amine, smiling, repeating Philip's words of the night before.

"For you, Amine?—yes, to defend you, if 'twere necessary, once more."

"I know it would—how kind of you to watch this tedious night after so much exertion and fatigue! but it is now broad day."

"Until I saw the dawn, Amine, I kept a faithful watch."

"But now retire and take some rest. My father is risen—you can lie down on his bed."

"I thank you, but I feel no wish for sleep. There is much to do. We must to the burgomaster and state the facts, and these bodies must remain where they are until the whole is known. Will your father go, Amine, or shall I?"

"My father surely is the more proper person, as the proprietor of the house. You must remain; and if you will not sleep, you must take some refreshment. I will go in and tell my father; he has already taken his morning's meal."

Amine went in, and soon returned with her father, who had consented to go to the burgomaster. He saluted Philip kindly as he came out; shuddered as he passed on one side to avoid stepping over the dead bodies, and went off at a quick pace to the adjacent town, where the burgomaster resided.

Amine desired Philip to follow her, and they went into her father's room, where, to his surprise, he found some coffee ready for him—at that time a rarity, and one which Philip did not expect to find in the house of the penurious Mynheer Poots; but it was a luxury which, from his former life, the old man could not dispense with.

Philip, who had not tasted food for nearly twenty-four hours, was not sorry to avail himself of what was placed before him. Amine sat down opposite to him, and was silent during his repast.

"Amine," said Philip at last, "I have had plenty of time for reflection during this night, as I watched at the door. May I speak freely?"

"Why not?" replied Amine. "I feel assured that you will say nothing that you should not say, or should not meet a maiden's ear."

"You do me justice, Amine. My thoughts have been upon you and your father. You cannot stay in this lone habitation."

"I feel it is too lonely; that is for his safety—perhaps for mine—but you know my father—the very loneliness suits him—the price paid for rent is little, and he is careful of his money."

"The man who would be careful of his money should place it in security—here it is not secure. Now, hear me, Amine. I have a cottage surrounded, as you may have heard, by many others, which mutually protect each other. That cottage I am about to leave—perhaps for ever; for I intend to sail by the first ship to the Indian seas."

"The Indian seas! why so?—did you not last night talk of thousands of guilders?"

"I did, and they are there; but, Amine, I must go—it is my duty. Ask me no more, but listen to what I now propose. Your father must live in my cottage; he must take care of it for me in my absence; he will do me a favour by consenting, and you must persuade him. You will there be safe. He must also take care of my money for me. I want it not at present—I cannot take it with me."

"My father is not to be trusted with the money of other people."

"Why does your father hoard? He cannot take his money with him when he is called away. It must be all for you—and is not then my money safe?"

"Leave it then in my charge, and it will be safe; but why need you go and risk your life upon the water, when you have such ample means?"

"Amine, ask not that question. It is my duty as a son, and more I cannot tell, at least at present."

"If it is your duty I ask no more. It was not womanish curiosity—no, no—it was a better feeling, I assure you, which prompted me to put the question."

"And what was that better feeling, Amine?"

"I hardly know—many good feelings perhaps mixed up together—gratitude, esteem, respect, confidence, good-will. Are not these sufficient?"

"Yes, indeed, Amine, and much to gain upon so short an acquaintance; but still I feel them all, and more, for you. If, then, you feel so much for me, do oblige me by persuading your father to leave this lonely house this day, and take up his abode in mine."

"And where do you intend to go yourself?"

"If your father will not admit me as a boarder for the short time I remain here, I will seek some shelter elsewhere; but if he will, I will indemnify him well—that is, if you raise no objection to my being for a few days in the house?"

"Why should I? Our habitation is no longer safe, and you offer us a shelter. It were, indeed, unjust and most ungrateful to turn you out from beneath your own roof."

"Then persuade him, Amine. I will accept of nothing, but take it as a favour; for I should depart in sorrow if I saw you not in safety.—Will you promise me?"

"I do promise to use my best endeavours—nay, I may as well say at once it shall be so; for I know my influence. Here is my hand upon it. Will that content you?"

Philip took the small hand extended towards him. His feelings overcame his discretion; he raised it to his lips. He looked up to see if Amine was displeased, and found her dark eye fixed upon him, as once before when she admitted him, as if she would see his thoughts—but the hand was not withdrawn.

"Indeed, Amine," said Philip, kissing her hand once more, "you may confide in me."

"I hope—I think—nay, I am sure I may," at last replied she.

Philip released her hand. Amine returned to her seat and for some time remained silent, and in a pensive attitude. Philip also had his own thoughts, and did not open his lips. At last Amine spoke.

"I think I have heard my father say that your mother was very poor—a little deranged; and that there was a chamber in the house which had been shut up for years."

"It was shut up till yesterday."

"And there you found your money? Did your mother not know of the money?"

"She did, for she spoke of it on her death-bed."

"There must have been some potent reasons for not opening the chamber."

"There were."

"What were they, Philip?" said Amine, in a soft and low tone of voice.

"I must not tell, at least I ought not. This must satisfy you—'twas the fear of an apparition."

"What apparition?"

"She said that my father had appeared to her."

"And did he, think you, Philip?"

"I have no doubt that he did. But I can answer no more questions, Amine. The chamber is open now, and there is no fear of his re-appearance."

"I fear not that," replied Amine, musing. "But," continued she, "is not this connected with your resolution of going to sea?"

"So far will I answer you, that it has decided me to go to sea; but I pray you ask no more. It is painful to refuse you, and my duty forbids me to speak further."

For some minutes they were both silent, when Amine resumed—

"You were so anxious to possess that relic, that I cannot help thinking it has connection with the mystery. Is it not so?"

"For the last time, Amine, I will answer your question—it has to do with it; but now no more."

Philip's blunt and almost rude manner of finishing his speech was not lost upon Amine, who replied:—

"You are so engrossed with other thoughts, that you have not felt the compliment shown you by my taking such interest about you, sir?"

"Yes, I do—I feel and thank you too, Amine. Forgive me, if I have been rude; but recollect, the secret is not mine—at least, I feel as if it were not. God knows, I wish I never had known it, for it has blasted all my hopes in life."

Philip was silent; and when he raised his eyes, he found that Amine's were fixed upon him.

"Would you read my thoughts, Amine, or my secret?"

"Your thoughts, perhaps—your secret I would not; yet do I grieve that it should oppress you so heavily as evidently it does. It must, indeed, be one of awe to bear down a mind like yours, Philip."

"Where did you learn to be so brave, Amine?" said Philip, changing the conversation.

"Circumstances make people brave or otherwise; those who are accustomed to difficulty and danger fear them not."

"And where have you met with them, Amine?"

"In the country where I was born, not in this dank and muddy land."

"Will you trust me with the story of your former life, Amine? I can be secret, if you wish."

"That you can be secret, perhaps, against my wish, you have already proved to me," replied Amine, smiling; "and you have a claim to know something of the life you have preserved. I cannot tell you much, but what I can will be sufficient. My father, when a lad, on board of a trading vessel, was taken by the Moors, and sold as a slave to a Hakim, or physician, of their country. Finding him very intelligent, the Moor brought him up as an assistant, and it was under this man that he obtained a knowledge of the art. In a few years he was equal to his master; but, as a slave, he worked not for himself. You know, indeed it cannot be concealed, my father's avarice. He sighed to become as wealthy as his master, and to obtain his freedom; he became a follower of Mahomet, after which he was free, and practised for himself. He took a wife from an Arab family, the daughter of a chief whom he had restored to health, and he settled in the country. I was born; he amassed wealth, and became much celebrated; but the son of a Bey dying under his hands was the excuse for persecuting him. His head was forfeited, but he escaped; not, however, without the loss of all his beloved wealth. My Mother and I went with him; he fled to the Bedouins, with whom we remained some years. There I was accustomed to rapid marches, wild and fierce attacks, defeat and flight, and oftentimes to indiscriminate slaughter. But the Bedouins paid not well for my father's services, and gold was his idol. Hearing that the Bey was dead, he returned to Cairo, where he again practised. He was allowed once more to amass until the heap was sufficient to excite the cupidity of the new Bey; but this time he was fortunately made acquainted with the intentions of the ruler. He again escaped, with a portion of his wealth, in a small vessel, and gained the Spanish coast; but he never has been able to retain his money long. Before he arrived in this country he had been robbed of almost all, and has now been for these three years laying up again. We were but one year at Middleburg, and from thence removed to this place. Such is the history of my life, Philip."

"And does your father still hold the Mahomedan faith, Amine?"

"I know not. I think he holds no faith whatever: at least he hath taught me none. His god is gold."

"And yours?"

"Is the God who made this beautiful world, and all which it contains—the God of nature—name him as you will. This I feel, Philip, but more I fain would know; there are so many faiths, but surely they must be but different paths leading alike to heaven. Yours is the Christian faith, Philip. Is it the true one? But every one calls his own the true one, whatever his creed may be."

"It is the true and only one, Amine. Could I but reveal—I have such dreadful proofs—"

"That your own faith is true: then is it not your duty to reveal these proofs? Tell me, are you bound by any solemn obligations never to reveal?"

"No, I am not; yet do I feel as if I were. But I hear voices—it must be your father and the authorities—I must go down and meet them."

Philip rose and went down stairs. Amine's eyes followed him as he went and she remained looking towards the door.

"Is it possible," said she, sweeping the hair from off her brow, "so soon,—yes, yes, 'tis even so. I feel that I would sooner share his hidden woe—his dangers—even death itself were preferable with him, than ease and happiness with any other. And it shall be strange indeed if I do not. This night my father shall move into his cottage; I will prepare at once."

The report of Philip and Mynheer Poots was taken down by the authorities, the bodies examined, and one or two of them recognised as well-known marauders. They were then removed by the order of the burgomaster. The authorities broke up their council, and Philip and Mynheer Poots were permitted to return to Amine. It will not be necessary to repeat the conversation which ensued: it will be sufficient to state that Poots yielded to the arguments employed by Amine and Philip, particularly the one of paying no rent. A conveyance for the furniture and medicines was procured, and in the afternoon most of the effects were taken away. It was not, however, till dusk that the strong box of the doctor was put into the cart, and Philip went with it as a protector. Amine also walked by the side of the vehicle, with her father. As it may be supposed, it was late that night before they had made their arrangements, and had retired to rest.

Chapter Six.

"This, then, is the chamber, which has so long been closed," said Amine, on entering it the next morning long before Philip had awakened from the sound sleep produced by the watching of the night before. "Yes, indeed, it has the air of having long been closed." Amine looked around her, and then examined the furniture. Her eyes were attracted to the birdcages: she looked into them:— "Poor little things!" continued she, "and here it was his father appeared unto his mother. Well, it may be so,—Philip saith that he hath proofs; and why should he not appear? Were Philip dead, I should rejoice to see his spirit,—at least it would be something. What am I saying—unfaithful lips, thus to betray my secret?—The table thrown over:— that looks like the work of fear; a workbox, with all its implements scattered,—only a woman's fear: a mouse might have caused all this; and yet there is something solemn in the simple fact that, for so many years, not a living being has crossed these boards. Even that a table thus overthrown could so remain for years seems scarcely natural, and therefore has its power on the mind. I wonder not that Philip feels there is so heavy a secret belonging to this room—but it must not remain in this condition—it must be occupied at once."

Amine, who had long been accustomed to attend upon her father, and perform the household duties, now commenced her intended labours.

Every part of the room, and every piece of furniture in it, were cleaned; even the cobwebs and dust were cleared away, and the sofa and table brought from the corner to the centre of the room; the melancholy little prisons were removed; and when Amine's work of neatness was complete, and the sun shone brightly into the opened window, the chamber wore the appearance of cheerfulness.

Amine had the intuitive good sense to feel that strong impressions wear away when the objects connected with them are removed. She resolved, then, to make Philip more at ease; for, with all the fire and warmth of blood inherent in her race, she had taken his image to her heart, and was determined to win him. Again and again did she resume her labour, until the pictures about the room, and every other article, looked fresh and clean.

Not only the birdcages, but the workbox and all the implements, were removed; and the piece of embroidery, the taking up of which had made Philip recoil as if he had touched an adder, was put away with the rest. Philip had left the keys on the floor. Amine opened the buffets, cleaned the glazed doors, and was busy rubbing up the silver flagons, when her father came into the room.

"Mercy on me!" exclaimed Mynheer Poots; "and is all that silver?—then it must be true, and he has thousands of guilders; but where are they?"

"Never do you mind, father; yours are now safe, and for that you have to thank Philip Vanderdecken."

"Yes, very true; but as he is to live here—does he eat much—what will he pay me? He ought to pay well, as he has so much money."

Amine's lips were curled with a contemptuous smile, but she made no reply.

"I wonder where he keeps his money; and he is going to sea as soon as he can get a ship? Who will have charge of his money when he goes?"

"I shall take charge of it, father," replied Amine.

"Ah—yes—well—we will take charge of it. The ship may be lost."

"No, *we* will not take charge of it, father: you will have nothing to do with it. Look after your own."

Amine placed the silver in the buffets, locked the doors, and took the keys with her when she went out to prepare breakfast, leaving the old man gazing through the glazed doors at the precious metal within. His eyes were rivetted upon it, and he could not remove them. Every minute he muttered, "Yes, all silver."

Philip came down stairs; and as he passed by the room, intending to go into the kitchen, he perceived Mynheer Poots at the buffet, and he walked into the room. He was surprised as well as pleased with the alteration. He felt why and by whom it was done, and he was grateful. Amine came in with the breakfast, and their eyes spoke more than their lips could have done; and Philip sat down to his meal with less of sorrow and gloom upon his brow.

"Mynheer Poots," said Philip, as soon as he had finished, "I intend to leave you in possession of my cottage, and I trust you will find yourself comfortable. What little arrangements are necessary, I will confide to your daughter previous to my departure."

"Then you leave us, Mr Philip, to go to sea? It must be pleasant to go and see strange countries—much better than staying at home. When do you go?"

"I shall leave this evening for Amsterdam," replied Philip, "to make my arrangements about a ship; but I shall return, I think, before I sail."

"Ah! you will return. Yes—you have your money and your goods to see to; you must count your money. We will take good care of it. Where is your money, Mr Vanderdecken?"

"That I will communicate to your daughter this forenoon, before I leave. In three weeks, at the furthest, you may expect me back."

"Father," said Amine, "you promised to go and see the child of the burgomaster; it is time you went."

"Yes, yes—by-and-by—all in good time; but I must wait the pleasure of Mr Philip first: he has much to tell me before he goes."

Philip could not help smiling when he remembered what had passed when he first summoned Mynheer Poots to the cottage; but the remembrance ended in sorrow and a clouded brow.

Amine, who knew what was passing in the minds of both her father and Philip, now brought her father's hat, and led him to the door of the cottage; and Mynheer Poots, very much against his inclination—but never disputing the will of his daughter—was obliged to depart.

"So soon, Philip?" said Amine, returning to the room.

"Yes, Amine, immediately; but I trust to be back once more before I sail; if not, you must now have my instructions. Give me the keys."

Philip opened the cupboard below the buffet, and the doors of the iron safe.

"There, Amine, is my money. We need not count it, as your father would propose. You see that I was right when I asserted that I had thousands of guilders. At present they are of no use to me, as I have to learn my profession. Should I return some day, they may help me to own a ship. I know not what my destiny may be."

"And should you not return?" replied Amine, gravely.

"Then they are yours, as well as all that is in this cottage, and the cottage itself."

"You have relations, have you not?"

"But one, who is rich—an uncle, who helped us but little in our distress, and who has no children. I owe him but little—and he wants nothing. There is but one being in this world who has created an interest in this heart, Amine, and it is you. I wish you to look upon me as a brother. I shall always love you as a dear sister."

Amine made no reply. Philip took some more money out of the bag which had been opened, for the expenses of his journey, and then locking up the safe and cupboard, gave the keys to Amine. He was about to address her when there was a slight knock at the door, and in entered Father Seysen, the priest.

"Save you my son; and you, my child, whom as yet I have not seen. You are, I suppose, the daughter of Mynheer Poots?"

Amine bowed her head.

"I perceive, Philip, that the room is now opened; and I have heard of all that has passed. I would now talk with thee, Philip, and must beg this maiden to leave us for a while alone."

Amine quitted the room; and the priest, sitting down on the couch, beckoned Philip to his side. The conversation which ensued was too long to repeat. The priest first questioned Philip relative to his secret; but on that point he could not obtain the information which he wished. Philip stated as much as he did to Amine, and no more. He also declared his intention of going to sea, and that, should he not return, he had bequeathed his property—the extent of which he did not make known—to the doctor and his daughter. The priest then made inquiries relative to Mynheer Poots, asking Philip whether he knew what his creed was, as he had never appeared at any church, and report said that he was an infidel. To this Philip, as usual, gave his frank answer, and intimated that the daughter, at least, was anxious to be enlightened, begging the priest to undertake a task to which he himself was not adequate. To this request Father Seysen, who perceived the state of Philip's mind with regard to Amine, readily consented. After a conversation of nearly two hours, they were interrupted by the return of Mynheer Poots, who darted out of the room the instant he perceived Father Seysen. Philip called Amine, and having begged her as a favour to receive the priest's visits, the good old man blessed them both and departed.

"You did not give him any money, Mr Philip?" said Mynheer Poots, when Father Seysen had left the room.

"I did not," replied Philip; "I wish I had thought of it."

"No, no—it is better not—for money is better than what he can give you; but he must not come here."

"Why not, father," replied Amine, "if Mr Philip wishes it? It is his own house."

"O yes, if Mr Philip wishes it; but you know he is going away."

"Well, and suppose he is—why should not the Father come here? He shall come here to see me."

"See you, my child!—what can he want with you? Well, then, if he comes, I will not give him one stiver—and then he'll soon go away."

Philip had no opportunity of further converse with Amine; indeed he had nothing more to say. In an hour he bade her farewell in presence of her father, who would not leave them, hoping to obtain from Philip some communication about the money which he was to leave behind him.

In two days Philip arrived at Amsterdam, and having made the necessary inquiries, found that there was no chance of vessels sailing for the East Indies for some months. The Dutch East India Company had long been formed, and all private trading was at an end. The Company's vessels left only at what was supposed to be the most favourable season for rounding the Cape of Storms, as the Cape of Good Hope was designated by the early adventurers. One of the ships which were to sail with the next fleet was the Ter Schilling, a three-masted vessel, now laid up and unrigged.

Philip found out the captain, and stated his wishes to sail with him, to learn his profession as a seaman; the captain was pleased with his appearance, and as Philip not only agreed to receive no wages during the voyage, but to pay a premium as an apprentice learning his duty, he was promised a berth on board as the second mate, to mess in the cabin; and he was told that he should be informed whenever the vessel was to sail. Philip having now done all that he could in obedience to his vow, determined to return to the cottage; and once more he was in the company of Amine.

We must now pass over two months, during which Mynheer Poots continued to labour at his vocation, and was seldom within doors, and our two young friends were left for hours together. Philip's love for Amine was fully equal to hers for him. It was more than love,—it was a devotion on both sides, each day increasing. Who indeed could be more charming, more attractive in all ways than the high-spirited, yet tender Amine? Occasionally the brow of Philip would be clouded when he reflected upon the dark prospect before him; but Amine's smile would chase away the gloom and as he gazed on her, all would be forgotten. Amine made no secret of her attachment; it was shown in every word, every look, and every gesture. When Philip would take her hand, or encircle her waist with his arm, or even when he pressed her coral lips, there was no pretence of coyness on her part. She was too noble, too confiding; she felt that her happiness was centred in his love, and she lived but in his presence. Two months had thus passed away, when Father Seysen, who often called, and had paid much attention to Amine's instruction, one day came in as Amine was encircled in Philip's arms.

"My children," said he, "I have watched you for some time:— this is not well. Philip, if you intend marriage, as I presume you do, still it is dangerous. I must join your hands."

Philip started up.

"Surely I am not deceived in thee, my son," continued the priest in a severe tone.

"No, no, good Father; but I pray you leave me now: to-morrow you may come, and all will be decided. But I must talk with Amine."

The priest quitted the room, and Amine and Philip were again alone. The colour in Amine's cheek varied and her heart beat, for she felt how much her happiness was at stake.

"The priest is right, Amine," said Philip sitting down by her. "This cannot last;—would that I could ever stay with you; how hard a fate is mine! You know I love the very ground you tread upon, yet I dare not ask thee to wed to misery."

"To wed with thee would not be wedding misery, Philip," replied Amine, with downcast eyes.

"'Twere not kindness on my part, Amine. I should indeed be selfish."

"I will speak plainly, Philip," replied Amine. "You say you love me,—I know not how men love,—but this I know, how I can love. I feel that to leave me now were indeed unkind and selfish on your part; for, Philip, I—I should die. You say that you must go away—that fate demands it,—and your fatal secret. Be it so;—but cannot I go with you?"

"Go with me, Amine—unto death?"

"Yes, death; for what is death but a release? I fear not death, Philip; I fear but losing thee. Nay, more; is not your life in the hands of Him who made all? then why so sure to die? You have hinted to me that you are chosen—selected for a task;—if chosen, there is less chance of death; for until the end be fulfilled, if chosen, you must live. I would I knew your secret, Philip: a woman's wit might serve you well: and if it did not serve you, is there no comfort, no pleasure in sharing sorrow as well as joy with one you say you dote upon?"

"Amine, dearest Amine, it is my love, my ardent love alone, which makes me pause; for, O Amine, what pleasure should I feel if we were this hour united? I hardly know what to say, or what to do. I could not withhold my secret from you if you were my wife, nor will I wed you till you know it. Well, Amine, I will cast my all upon the die. You shall know this secret, learn what a doomed wretch I am, though from no fault of mine, and then you yourself shall decide. But remember my oath is registered in heaven, and I must not be dissuaded from it: keep that in mind, and hear my tale,—then if you choose to wed with one whose prospects are so bitter, be it so,—a short-lived happiness will then be mine, but for you, Amine—"

"At once the secret, Philip," cried Amine, impatiently.

Philip then entered into a detail of what our readers are acquainted with. Amine listened in silence; not a change of feature was to be observed in her countenance during the narrative. Philip wound up with stating the oath which he had taken. "I have done," said Philip, mournfully.

"'Tis a strange story, Philip," replied Amine: "and now hear me;—but give me first that relic,—I wish to look upon it. And can there be such virtue—I had nigh said, such mischief—in this little thing? Strange; forgive me, Philip,—but I've still my doubts upon this tale of *Eblis*. You know I am not yet strong in the new belief which you and the good priest have lately taught me. I do not say that it *cannot* be true: but still, one so unsettled as I am may be allowed to waver. But, Philip, I'll assume that all is true. Then, if it be true, without the oath you would be doing but your duty; and think not so meanly of Amine as to suppose she would restrain you from what is right. No, Philip, seek your father, and, if you can, and he requires your aid, then save him. But, Philip do you imagine that a task like this, so high, is to be accomplished at one trial? O! no; if you have been so chosen to fulfil it, you will be preserved through difficulty and danger until you have worked out your end. You will be preserved and you will again and again return;—be comforted—consoled—be cherished—and be loved by Amine as your wife. And when it pleases Him to call you from this world, your memory, if she survive you, Philip, will equally be cherished in her bosom. Philip, you have given me to decide;—dearest Philip, I am thine."

Amine extended her arms, and Philip pressed her to his bosom. That evening Philip demanded his daughter of the father, and Mynheer Poots, as soon as Philip opened the iron safe and displayed the guilders, gave his immediate consent.

Father Seysen called the next day and received his answer—and three days afterwards, the bells of the little church of Terneuse were ringing a merry peal for the union of Amine Poots and Philip Vanderdecken.

Chapter Seven.

It was not until late in the autumn that Philip was roused from his dream of love (for what, alas! is every enjoyment of this life but a dream?) by a summons from the captain of the vessel with whom he had engaged to sail. Strange as it may appear, from the first day which put him in possession of his Amine, Philip had no longer brooded over his future destiny; occasionally it was recalled to his memory, but immediately rejected, and, for the time, forgotten. Sufficient he thought it, to fulfil his engagement when the time should come; and though the hours flew away, and day succeeded day, week week, and month month, with the rapidity accompanying a life of quiet and unvarying bliss, Philip forgot his vow in the arms of Amine, who was careful not to revert to a topic which would cloud the brow of her adored husband. Once, indeed, or twice, had old Poots raised the question of Philip's departure, but the indignant frown and the imperious command of Amine (who knew too well the sordid motives which actuated her father, and who, at such times, looked upon him with abhorrence) made him silent, and the old man would spend his leisure hours in walking up and down the parlour with his eyes riveted upon the buffets, where the silver tankards now beamed in all their pristine brightness.

One morning, in the month of October, there was a tapping with the knuckles at the cottage door. As this precaution implied a stranger, Amine obeyed the summons.

"I would speak with Master Philip Vanderdecken," said the stranger, in a half-whispering sort of voice.

The party who thus addressed Amine was a little meagre personage, dressed in the garb of the Dutch seaman of the time, with a cap made of badger-skin hanging over his brow. His features were sharp and diminutive, his face of a deadly white, his lips pale, and his hair of a mixture between red and white. He had very little show of beard—indeed, it was most difficult to say what his age might be. He might have been a sickly youth early sinking into decrepitude, or an old man, hale in constitution, yet carrying no flesh. But the most important feature, and that which immediately riveted the attention of Amine, was the eye of this peculiar personage—for he had but one; the right eye-lid was closed, and the ball within had evidently wasted away; but his left eye was, for the size of his face and head, of unusual dimensions, very protuberant, clear and watery, and most unpleasant to look upon, being relieved by no fringe of eyelash either above or below it. So remarkable was the feature, that when you looked at the man, you saw his eye and looked at nothing else. It was not a man with one eye, but one eye with a man attached to it; the body was but the tower of the lighthouse, of no further value, and commanding no further attention, than does the structure which holds up the beacon to the venturous mariner; and yet, upon examination, you would have perceived that the man, although small, was neatly made; that his hands were very different in texture and colour from those of common seamen; that his features in general, although sharp, were regular; and that there was an air of superiority even in the obsequious manner of the little personage, and an indescribable something about his whole appearance which almost impressed you with awe. Amine's dark eyes were for a moment fixed upon the visitor, and she felt a chill at her heart for which she could not account, as she requested that he would walk in.

Philip was greatly surprised at the appearance of the stranger, who, as soon as he entered the room, without saying a word sat down on the sofa by Philip in the place which Amine had just left. To Philip there was something ominous in this person taking Amine's seat; all that had passed rushed into his recollection and he felt that there was a summons from his short existence of enjoyment and repose to a life of future activity, danger, and suffering. What peculiarly struck Philip was, that when the little man sat beside him, a sensation of sudden cold ran through his whole frame. The colour fled from Philip's cheek, but he spoke not. For a minute or two there was a silence. The one-eyed visitor looked round him, and turning from the buffets, he fixed his eyes on the form of Amine, who stood before him; at last the silence was broken by a sort of giggle on the part of the stranger, which ended in—

"Philip Vanderdecken—he! he!—Philip Vanderdecken, you don't know me?"

"I do not," replied Philip, in a half angry tone.

The voice of the little man was most peculiar—it was a sort of subdued scream, the notes of which sounded in your ear long after he had ceased to speak.

"I am Schriften, one of the pilots of the Ter Schilling," continued the man; "and I'm come—he! he!"—and he looked hard at Amine—"to take you away from love,"—and looking at the buffets—"he! he! from comfort, and from this also," cried he, stamping his foot on the floor as he rose from the sofa—"from terra firma—he! he!—to a watery grave perhaps. Pleasant!" continued Schriften, with a giggle; and with a countenance full of meaning he fixed his one eye on Philip's face.

Philip's first impulse was to put his new visitor out of the door; but Amine, who read his thoughts, folded her arms as she stood before the little man, and eyed him with contempt, as she observed:—

"We all must meet our fate, good fellow; and, whether by land or sea, death will have his due. If death stare him in the face, the cheek of Philip Vanderdecken will never turn as white as yours is now."

"Indeed!" replied Schriften, evidently annoyed at this cool determination on the part of one so young and beautiful; and then fixing his eye upon the silver shrine of the Virgin on the mantelpiece—"You are a Catholic, I perceive—he!"

"I am a Catholic," replied Philip; "but does that concern you? When does the vessel sail?"

"In a week—he! he!—only a week for preparation—only seven days to leave all—short notice!"

"More than sufficient," replied Philip, rising up from the sofa. "You may tell your captain that I shall not fail. Come, Amine, we must lose no time."

"No, indeed," replied Amine, "and our first duty is hospitality: Mynheer, may we offer you refreshment after your walk?"

"This day week," said Schriften, addressing Philip, and without making a reply to Amine. Philip nodded his head, the little man turned on his heel and left the room, and in a short time was out of sight.

Amine sank down on the sofa. The breaking-up of her short hour of happiness had been too sudden, too abrupt, and too cruelly brought about for a fondly doting, although heroic woman. There was an evident malignity in the words and manner of the one-eyed messenger, an appearance as if he knew more than others, which awed and confused both Philip and herself. Amine wept not, but she covered her face with her hands as Philip, with no steady pace, walked up and down the small room. Again, with all the vividness of colouring, did the scenes half forgotten recur to his memory. Again did he penetrate the fatal chamber—again was it obscure. The embroidery lay at his feet, and once more he started as when the letter appeared upon the floor.

They had both awakened from a dream of present bliss, and shuddered at the awful future which presented itself. A few minutes was sufficient for Philip to resume his natural self-possession. He sat down by the side of his Amine, and clasped her in his arms. They remained silent. They knew too well each other's thoughts; and, excruciating as was the effort, they were both summoning up their courage to bear, and steeling their hearts against, the conviction that, in this world, they must now expect to be for a time, perhaps for ever, separated.

Amine was the first to speak: removing her arm; which had been wound round her husband, she first put his hand to her heart, as if to compress its painful throbbings, and then observed—

"Surely that was no earthly messenger, Philip! Did you not feel chilled to death when he sat by you? I did as he came in."

Philip, who had the same thought as Amine, but did not wish to alarm her, answered confusedly—

"Nay, Amine, you fancy—that is, the suddenness of his appearance and his strange conduct have made you imagine this; but I saw in him but a man who, from his peculiar deformity, has become an envious outcast of society—debarred from domestic happiness, from the smiles of the other sex; for what woman could smile upon such a creature? His bile raised at so much beauty in the arms of another, he enjoyed a malignant pleasure in giving a message which he felt would break upon those pleasures from which he is cut off. Be assured, my love, that it was nothing more."

"And even if my conjecture were correct, what does it matter?" replied Amine. "There can be nothing more, nothing which can render your position more awful, and more desperate. As your wife, Philip, I feel less courage than I did when I gave my willing hand. I knew not then what would be the extent of my loss; but fear not, much as I feel here," continued Amine, putting her hand to her heart—"I am prepared, and proud that he who is selected for such a task is my husband." Amine paused. "You cannot, surely, have been mistaken, Philip?"

"No! Amine, I have not been mistaken, either in the summons, or in my own courage, or in my selection of a wife," replied Philip, mournfully, as he embraced her. "It is the will of Heaven."

"Then may its will be done," replied Amine, rising from her seat. "The first pang is over. I feel better now, Philip. Your Amine knows her duty."

Philip made no reply; when, after a few moments, Amine continued—

"But one short week, Philip—"

"I would it had been but one day," replied he; "it would have been long enough. He has come too soon—the one-eyed monster."

"Nay, not so, Philip. I thank him for the week—'tis but a short time to wean myself from happiness. I grant you, that were I to teaze, to vex, to unman you with my tears, my prayers, or my upbraidings (as some wives would do, Philip), one day would be more than sufficient for such a scene of weakness on my part, and misery on yours. But, no, Philip, your Amine knows her duty better. You must go like some knight of old to perilous encounter, perhaps to death; but Amine will arm you, and show her love by closing carefully each rivet to protect you in your peril, and will see you depart full of hope and confidence, anticipating your return. A week is not too long, Philip, when employed as I trust I shall employ it—a week to interchange our sentiments, to hear your voice, to listen to your words (each of which will be engraven on my heart's memory), to ponder on them, and feed my love with them is your absence and in my solitude. No! no! Philip; I thank God that there is yet a week."

"And so do I, then, Amine! and, after all, we knew that this must come."

"Yes! but my love was so potent, that it banished memory."

"And yet, during our separation, your love must feed on memory, Amine."

Amine sighed. Here their conversation was interrupted by the entrance of Mynheer Poots, who, struck with the alteration in Amine's radiant features, exclaimed, "Holy prophet! what is the matter now?"

"Nothing more than what we all knew before," replied Philip; "I am about to leave you—the ship will sail in a week."

"Oh! you will sail in a week?"

There was a curious expression in the face of the old man as he endeavoured to suppress, before Amine and her husband, the joy which he felt at Philip's departure. Gradually he subdued his features into gravity, and said—

"That is very bad news, indeed."

No answer was made by Amine or Philip, who quitted the room together.

We must pass over this week, which was occupied in preparations for Philip's departure. We must pass over the heroism of Amine, who controlled her feelings, racked as she was with intense agony at the idea of separating from her adored husband. We cannot dwell upon the conflicting emotions in the breast of Philip, who left competence, happiness, and love, to encounter danger privation, and death. Now, at one time, he would almost resolve to remain, and then at others, as he took the relic from his bosom, and remembered his vow registered upon it, he was nearly as anxious to depart. Amine, too, as she fell asleep in her husband's arms, would count the few hours left them; or she would shudder, as she lay awake and the wind howled, at the prospect of what Philip would have to encounter. It was a long week to both of them, and, although they thought that time flew fast, it was almost a relief when the morning came that was to separate them; for, to their feelings, which, from regard to each other, had been pent up and controlled they could then give vent; their surcharged bosoms could be relieved; certainty had driven away suspense, and hope was still left to cheer them and brighten up the dark horizon of the future.

"Philip," said Amine, as they sat together with their hands entwined, "I shall not feel so much when you are gone. I do not forget that all this was told me before we were wed, and that for my love I took the hazard. My fond heart often tells me that you will return; but it may deceive me—return you *may*, but not in life. In this room I shall await you; on this removed to its former station, I shall sit; and if you cannot appear to me alive, O refuse me not, if it be possible, to appear to me when dead. I shall fear no storm, no bursting open of the window. O no! I shall hail the presence even of your spirit. Once more: let me but see you—let me be assured that you are dead—and then I shall know that I have no more to live for in this world, and shall hasten to join you in a world of bliss. Promise me, Philip."

"I promise all you ask, provided Heaven will so permit; but, Amine," and Philip's lips trembled, "I cannot—merciful God! I am indeed tried. Amine, I can stay no longer."

Amine's dark eyes were fixed upon her husband—she could not speak—her features were convulsed—nature could no longer hold up against her excess of feeling—she fell into his arms, and lay motionless. Philip, about to impress a last kiss upon her pale lips, perceived that she had fainted.

"She feels not now," said he, as he laid her upon the sofa; "it is better that it should be so—too soon will she awake to misery."

Summoning to the assistance of his daughter Mynheer Poots, who was in the adjoining room, Philip caught up his hat, imprinted one more fervent kiss upon her forehead, burst from the house, and was out of sight long before Amine had recovered from her swoon.

Chapter Eight.

Before we follow Philip Vanderdecken in his venturous career, it will be necessary to refresh the memory of our readers, by a succinct recapitulation of the circumstances that had directed the enterprise of the Dutch towards the country of the East, which was now proving to them a source of wealth, which they considered as inexhaustible.

Let us begin at the beginning. Charles the Fifth, after having possessed the major part of Europe, retired from the world for reasons best known to himself, and divided his kingdoms between Ferdinand and Philip. To Ferdinand he gave Austria and its dependencies; to Philip, Spain; but to make the division more equal and palatable to the latter, he threw the Low Countries, with the few millions vegetating upon them, into the bargain. Having thus disposed of his fellow-mortals much to his own satisfaction, he went into a convent, reserving for himself a small income, twelve men, and a pony. Whether he afterwards repented his hobby, or mounted his pony is not recorded; but this is certain—that in two years he died.

Philip thought (as many have thought before and since) that he had a right to do what he pleased with his own. He therefore took away from the Hollanders most of their liberties: to make amends, however, he gave them the Inquisition; but the Dutch grumbled, and Philip, to stop their grumbling, burnt a few of them. Upon which the Dutch, who are aquatic in their propensities, protested against a religion which was much too warm for their constitutions. In short, heresy made great progress; and the duke of Alva was despatched with a large army to prove to the Hollanders that the Inquisition was the very best of all possible arrangements, and that it was infinitely better that a man should be burnt for half an hour in this world than for an eternity in the next.

This slight difference of opinion was the occasion of a war which lasted about eighty years, and which, after having saved some hundreds of thousands the trouble of dying in their beds, at length ended in the Seven United Provinces being declared independent.—Now we must go back again.

For a century after Vasco de Gama had discovered the passage round the Cape of Good Hope, the Portuguese were interfered with by other nations. At last the adventurous spirit of the English nation was roused. The passage to India by the Cape had been claimed by the Portuguese as their sole right: they defended it by force. For a long time no private company ventured to oppose them, and the trade was not of that apparent value to induce any government to embark in a war upon the question. The English adventurers, therefore, turned their attention to the discovery of a north-west passage to India, with which the Portuguese could have no right to interfere, and in vain attempts to discover that passage the best part of the fifteenth century was employed. At last they abandoned their endeavours, and resolved no longer to be deterred by the Portuguese pretensions.

After one or two unsuccessful expeditions, an armament was fitted out and put under the orders of Drake. This courageous and successful navigator accomplished more than the most sanguine had anticipated. He returned to England in the month of May, 1580, after a voyage which occupied him nearly three years; bringing home with him great riches, and having made most favourable arrangements with the king of the Molucca Islands.

His success was followed up by Cavendish and others, in 1600. The English East India Company, in the meanwhile, received their first charter from the government and had now been with various success carrying on the trade for upwards of fifty years.

During the time that the Dutch were vassals to the crown of Spain, it was their custom to repair to Lisbon for the productions of the East, and afterwards to distribute them through Europe; but when they quarrelled with Philip, they were no longer admitted as retailers of his Indian produce: the consequence was that, while asserting and fighting for their independence, they had also fitted out expeditions to India. They were successful; and in 1602 the various speculators were, by the government, formed into a company, upon the same principles and arrangement as those which had been chartered in England.

At the time, therefore, to which we are reverting, the English and Dutch had been trading in the Indian seas for more than fifty years; and the Portuguese had lost nearly all their power, from the alliances and friendships which their rivals had formed with the potentates of the East, who had suffered from the Portuguese avarice and cruelty.

Whatever may have been the sum of obligation which the Dutch owed to the English for the assistance they received from them during their struggle for independence, it does not appear that their gratitude extended beyond the Cape; for, on the other side of it, the Portuguese, English, and Dutch fought and captured each other's vessels without ceremony; and there was no law but that of main force. The mother countries were occasionally called upon to interfere; but the interference up to the above time had produced nothing more than a paper war; it being very evident that all parties were in the wrong.

In 1650 Cromwell usurped the throne of England, and the year afterwards, having, among other points, vainly demanded of the Dutch satisfaction for the murder of his regicide ambassador, which took place in this year, and some compensation for the cruelties exercised on the English at Amboyne some thirty years before, he declared war with Holland. To prove that he was in earnest, he seized more than two hundred Dutch vessels and the Dutch then (very unwillingly) prepared for war. Blake and Van Tromp met, and the naval combats were most obstinate. In the "History of England" the victory is almost invariably given to the English, but in that of Holland to the Dutch.—By all accounts, these engagements were so obstinate, that in each case they were both well beaten. However, in 1654, peace was signed; the Dutchman promising "to take his hat off" whenever he should meet an Englishman on the high seas—a mere act of politeness, which Mynheer did not object to, as it *cost nothing*. And now, having detailed the state of things up to the time of Philip's embarkation, we shall proceed with our story.

As soon as Philip was clear of his own threshold he hastened away as though he were attempting to escape from his own painful thoughts. In two days he arrived at Amsterdam, where his first object was to procure a small, but strong, steel chain to replace the ribbon by which the relic had hitherto been secured round his neck. Having done this, he hastened to embark with his effects on board of the Ter Schilling. Philip had not forgotten to bring with him the money which he had agreed to pay the captain, in consideration of being received on board as an apprentice rather than a sailor. He had also furnished himself with a further sum for his own exigencies. It was late in the evening when he arrived on board of the Ter Schilling, which lay at single anchor, surrounded by the other vessels composing the Indian fleet. The captain, whose name was Kloots, received him with kindness, showed him his berth, and then went below in the hold to decide a question relative to the cargo, leaving Philip on deck to his own reflections.

And this, then, thought Philip, as he leaned against the taffrail and looked forward—this, then, is the vessel in which my first attempt is to be made. First and—perhaps last. How little do those with whom I am about to sail imagine the purport of my embarkation? How different are my views from those of others? Do *I* seek a fortune? No! Is it to satisfy curiosity and a truant spirit? No! I seek communion with the dead. Can I meet the dead without danger to myself and these who sail with me? I should think not, for I cannot join it but in death. Did they surmise my wishes and intentions, would they permit me to remain one hour on board? Superstitious as seamen are said to be, they might find a good excuse, if they knew my mission, not only for their superstition, but for ridding themselves of one on such an awful errand. Awful indeed! and how to be accomplished? Heaven alone, with perseverance on my part, can solve the mystery. And Philip's thoughts reverted to his Amine. He folded his arms, and entranced in meditation, with his eyes raised to the firmament, he appeared to watch the flying scud.

"Had you not better go below?" said a mild voice, which made Philip start from his reverie.

It was that of the first mate, whose name was Hillebrant, a short, well-set man of about thirty years of age. His hair was flaxen, and fell in long flakes upon his shoulders, his complexion fair, and his eyes of a soft blue: although there was little of the sailor in his appearance, few knew or did their duty better.

"I thank you," replied Philip; "I had, indeed, forgotten myself, and where I was: my thoughts were far away. Good night, and many thanks."

The Ter Schilling, like most of the vessels of that period, was very different in her build and fitting from those of the present day. She was ship-rigged, and of about four hundred tons burden. Her bottom was nearly flat, and her sides fell in (as she rose above the water), so that her upper decks were not half the width of the hold.

All the vessels employed by the Company being armed, she had her main deck clear of goods, and carried six nine-pounders on each broadside; her ports were small and oval. There was a great spring in all her decks,—that is to say, she ran with a curve forward and aft. On her forecastle another small deck ran from the knight-heads, which was called the top-gallant forecastle. Her quarter-deck was broken with a poop, which rose high out of the water. The bowsprit staved very much, and was to appearance almost as a fourth mast: the more so, as she carried a square spritsail and sprit-topsail. On her quarter-deck and poop-bulwarks were fixed in sockets implements of warfare now long in disuse, but what were then known by the names of cohorns and patteraroes; they turned round on a swivel, and were pointed by an iron handle fixed to the breech. The sail abaft the mizzen-mast (corresponding to the driver or spanker of the present day) was fixed upon a lateen-yard. It is hardly necessary to add (after this description) that the dangers of a long voyage were not a little increased by the peculiar structure of the vessels, which (although with such top hamper, and so much wood above water, they could make good way before a favourable breeze) could hold no wind, and had but little chance if caught upon a lee-shore.

The crew of the Ter Schilling was composed of the captain, two mates, two pilots, and forty-five men. The supercargo had not yet come on board. The cabin (under the poop) was appropriated to the supercargo; but the main-deck cabin to the captain and mates, who composed the whole of the cabin mess.

When Philip awoke the next morning, he found that the topsails were hoisted, and the anchor short-stay apeak. Some of the other vessels of the fleet were under weigh and standing out. The weather was fine and the water smooth? and the bustle and novelty of the scene were cheering to his spirits. The captain, Mynheer Kloots, was standing on the poop with a small telescope, made of pasteboard, to his eye, anxiously looking towards the town. Mynheer Kloots, as usual, had his pipe in his mouth, and the smoke which he puffed from it for time obscured the lenses of his telescope. Philip went up the poop ladder and saluted him.

Mynheer Kloots was a person of no moderate dimensions, and the quantity of garments which he wore added no little to his apparent bulk. The outer garments exposed to view were, a rough fox-skin cap upon his head, from under which appeared the edge of a red worsted nightcap; a red plush waistcoat, with large metal buttons; a jacket of green cloth, over which he wore another of larger dimensions of coarse blue cloth, which came down as low as what would be called a spencer. Below he had black plush breeches, light-blue worsted stockings, shoes, and broad silver buckles; round his waist was girded, with a broad belt, a canvas apron, which descended in thick folds nearly to his knee. In his belt was a large broad-bladed knife in a sheath of shark's skin. Such was the attire of Mynheer Kloots, captain of the Ter Schilling.

He was as tall as he was corpulent. His face was oval, and his features small in proportion to the size of his frame. His grizzly hair fluttered in the breeze, and his nose (although quite straight) was, at the tip, fiery red from frequent application to his bottle of schnapps, and the heat of a small pipe which seldom left his lips, except for *him* to give an order, or for *it* to be replenished.

"Good morning, my son," said the captain, taking his pipe out of his mouth for a moment. "We are detained by the supercargo, who appears not over-willing to come on board; the boat has been on shore this hour waiting for him, and we shall be last of the fleet under weigh. I wish the Company would let us sail without these *gentlemen*, who are (*in my opinion*) a great hinderance to business; but they think otherwise on shore."

"What is their duty on board?" replied Philip.

"Their duty is to look after the cargo and the traffic, and if they kept to that it would not be so bad; but they interfere with everything else and everybody, studying little except their own comforts; in fact, they play the king on board, knowing that we dare not affront them, as a word from them would prejudice the vessel when again to be chartered. The Company insist upon their being received with all honours. We salute with five guns on their arrival on board."

"Do you know anything of this one whom you expect?"

"Nothing, but from report. A brother captain of mine (with whom he has sailed) told me that he is most fearful of the dangers of the sea, and much taken up with his own importance."

"I wish he would come," replied Philip; "I am most anxious that we should sail."

"You must be of a wandering disposition, my son: I hear that you leave a comfortable home, and a pretty wife to boot."

"I am most anxious to see the world," replied Philip; "and I must learn to sail a ship before I purchase one, and try to make the fortune that I covet." (Alas! how different from my real wishes, thought Philip, as he made this reply.)

"Fortunes are made, and fortunes are swallowed up too, by the ocean," replied the captain. "If I could turn this good ship into a good house, with plenty of guilders to keep the house warm, you would not find me standing on this poop. I have doubled the Cape twice, which is often enough for any man; the third time may not be so lucky."

"Is it so dangerous, then?" said Philip.

"As dangerous as tides and currents, rocks and sand-banks, hard gales and heavy seas, can make it,—no more! Even when you anchor in the bay, on this side of the Cape, you ride in fear and trembling, for you may be blown away from your anchor to sea or be driven on shore among the savages, before the men can well put on their clothing. But when once you're well on the other side of the Cape, then the water dances to the beams of the sun as if it were merry, and you may sail for weeks with a cloudless sky and a following breeze, without starting tack or sheet, or having to take your pipe out of your mouth."

"What ports shall we go into, Mynheer?"

"Of that I can say but little. Gambroon, in the Gulf of Persia, will probably be the first rendezvous of the whole fleet. Then we shall separate: some will sail direct for Bantam, in the island of Java; others will have orders to trade down the Straits for camphor, gum, benzoin, and wax; they have also gold and the teeth of the elephant to barter with us: there (should we be sent thither) you must be careful with the natives, Mynheer Vanderdecken. They are fierce and treacherous, and their curved knives (or creeses, as they call them) are sharp and deadly poisoned. I have had hard fighting in those Straits both with Portuguese and English."

"But we are all at peace now."

"True, my son; but when round the Cape, we must not trust to papers signed at home; and the English press us hard, and tread upon our heels wherever we go. They must be checked; and I suspect our fleet is so large and well appointed in expectation of hostilities."

"How long do you expect your voyage may occupy us?"

"That's as may be: but I should say about two years;—nay, if not detained by the factors, as I expect we shall be, for some hostile service, it may be less."

"Two years," thought Philip, "two years from Amine!" and he sighed deeply, for he felt that their separation might be for ever.

"Nay, my son, two years is not so long," said Mynheer Kloots, who observed the passing cloud on Philip's brow. "I was once five years away, and was unfortunate, for I brought home nothing, not even my ship. I was sent to Chittagong, on the east side of the great Bay of Bengala, and lay for three months in the river. The chiefs of the country would detain me by force; they would not barter for my cargo, or permit me to seek another market. My powder had been landed and I could make no resistance. The worms ate through the bottom of my vessel and she sank at her anchors. They knew it would take place, and that then they would have my cargo at their own price. Another vessel brought us home. Had I not been so treacherously served, I should have had no need to sail this time; and now my gains are small, the Company forbidding all private trading. But here he comes at last; they have hoisted the ensign on the staff in the boat; there—they have shoved off. Mynheer Hillebrant, see the gunners ready with their linstocks to salvo the supercargo."

"What duty do you wish me to perform?" observed Philip. "In what can I be useful?"

"At present you can be of little use, except in those heavy gales in which every pair of hands is valuable. You must look and learn for some time yet; but you can make a fair copy of the journal kept for the inspection of the Company, and may assist me in various ways, as soon as the unpleasant nausea, felt by those who first embark, has subsided. As a remedy, I should propose that you gird a handkerchief tight round your body so as to compress the stomach, and make frequent application of my bottle of schnapps, which you will find always at your service. But now to receive the factor of the most puissant Company. Mynheer Hillebrant, let them discharge the cannon."

The guns were fired, and soon after the smoke had cleared away, the boat, with its long ensign trailing on the water, was pulled alongside. Philip watched the appearance of the supercargo—but he remained in the boat until several of the boxes with the initials and arms of the Company were first handed on the deck; at last the supercargo appeared.

He was a small, spare, wizen-faced man with a three-cornered cocked-hat, bound with broad gold lace, upon his head, under which appeared a full-bottomed flowing wig, the curls of which descended low upon his shoulders. His coat was of crimson velvet, with broad flaps: his waistcoat of white silk, worked in coloured flowers, and descending half-way down to his knees. His breeches were of black satin, and his legs were covered with white silk stockings. Add to this, gold buckles at his knees and in his shoes, lace ruffles to his wrists, and a silver-mounted cane in his hand, and the reader has the entire dress of Mynheer Jacob Janz Von Stroom, the supercargo of the Honourable Company, appointed to the good ship Ter Schilling.

As he looked round him, surrounded at a respectful distance, by the captain, officers, and men of the ship, with their caps in their hands, the reader might be reminded of the picture of the "Monkey who had seen the world," surrounded by his tribe. There was not, however, the least inclination on the part of the seamen to laugh, even at his flowing, full-bottomed wig: respect was at that period paid to dress; and although Mynheer Von Stroom could not be mistaken for a sailor, he was known to be the supercargo of the Company, and a very great man. He therefore received all the respect due to so important a personage.

Mynheer Von Stroom did not, however, appear very anxious to remain on deck. He requested to be shown into his cabin, and followed the captain aft, picking his way among the coils of ropes with which his path was encumbered. The door was opened, and the supercargo disappeared. The ship was then got under weigh, the men had left the windlass, the sails had been trimmed, and they were securing the anchor on board, when the bell of the poop-cabin (appropriated to the supercargo) was pulled with great violence.

"What can that be?" said Mynheer Kloots (who was forward), taking the pipe out of his mouth. "Mynheer Vanderdecken, will you see what is the matter?"

Philip went aft, as the pealing of the bell continued, and opening the cabin door, discovered the supercargo perched upon the table and pulling the bell-rope, which hung over its centre, with every mark of fear in his countenance. His wig was off, and his bare skull gave him an appearance peculiarly ridiculous.

"What is the matter, sir?" inquired Philip.

"Matter!" spluttered Mynheer Von Stroom—"call the troops in with their firelocks. Quick, sir. Am I to be murdered, torn to pieces, and devoured? For mercy's sake, sir, don't stare, but do something—look, it's coming to the table! O dear! O dear!" continued the supercargo, evidently terrified out of his wits.

Philip, whose eyes had been fixed on Mynheer Von Stroom, turned them in the direction pointed out, and much to his astonishment perceived a small bear upon the deck, who was amusing himself with the supercargo's flowing wig, which he held in his paws, tossing it about and now and then burying his muzzle in it. The unexpected sight of the animal was at first a shock to Philip; but a moment's consideration assured him that the animal must be harmless, or it never would have been permitted to remain loose in the vessel.

Nevertheless, Philip had no wish to approach the animal, whose disposition he was unacquainted with, when the appearance of Mynheer Kloots put an end to his difficulty.

"What is the matter, Mynheer?" said the captain. "O! I see: it is Johannes," continued the captain, going up to the bear, and saluting him with a kick, as he recovered the supercargo's wig. "Out of the cabin, Johannes! Out, sir!" cried Mynheer Kloots, kicking the breech of the bear till the animal had escaped through the door. "Mynheer Von Stroom, I am very sorry,—here is your wig. Shut the door, Mynheer Vanderdecken, or the beast may come back, for he is very fond of me."

As soon the door was shut between Mynheer Von Stroom and the object of his terror, the little man slid off the table to the high-backed chair near it, shook out the damaged curls of his wig, and replaced it on his head; pulled out his ruffles, and, assuming an air of magisterial importance, struck his cane on the deck, and then spoke.

"Mynheer Kloots, what is the meaning of this disrespect to the supercargo of the puissant Company?"

"God in Heaven! no disrespect, Mynheer;—the animal is a bear, as you see; he is very tame, even with strangers. He belongs to me. I have had him since he was three months old. It was all a mistake. The mate, Mynheer Hillebrant, put him in the cabin, that he might be out of the way while the duty was carrying on, and he quite forgot that he was here. I am very sorry, Mynheer Von Stroom; but he will not come here again, unless you wish to play with him."

"Play with him! I! supercargo to the Company, play with a bear! Mynheer Kloots, the animal must be thrown overboard immediately."

"Nay, nay; I cannot throw overboard an animal that I hold in much affection, Mynheer Von Stroom; but he shall not trouble you."

"Then, Captain Kloots, you will have to deal with the Company, to whom I shall represent this affair. Your charter will be cancelled, and your freight-money will be forfeited."

Kloots was, like most Dutchmen, not a little obstinate, and this imperative behaviour on the part of the supercargo raised his bile. "There is nothing in the charter that prevents my having an animal on board," replied Kloots.

"By the regulations of the Company," replied Von Stroom, falling back in his chair with an important air, and crossing his thin legs, "you are required to receive on board strange and curious animals, sent home by the governors and factors to be presented to crowned heads,—such as lions, tigers, elephants, and other productions of the East;—but in no instance is it permitted to the commanders of chartered ships to receive on board, on their own account, animals of any description, which must be considered under the head and offence of private trading."

"My bear is not for sale, Mynheer Von Stroom."

"It must immediately be sent out of the ship, Mynheer Kloots. I order you to send it away,—on your peril to refuse."

"Then we will drop the anchor again, Mynheer Von Stroom, and send on shore to head-quarters to decide the point. If the Company insists that the brute be put on shore, be it so; but recollect, Mynheer Von Stroom, we shall lose the protection of the fleet, and have to sail alone. Shall I drop the anchor, Mynheer?"

This observation softened down the pertinacity of the supercargo: he had no wish to sail alone, and the fear of this contingency was more powerful than the fear of the bear.

"Mynheer Kloots, I will not be too severe; if the animal is chained, so that it does not approach me, I will consent to its remaining on board."

"I will keep it out of your way as much as I can; but as for chaining up the poor animal, it will howl all day and night and you will have no sleep, Mynheer Von Stroom," replied Kloots.

The supercargo, who perceived that the captain was positive and that his threats were disregarded, did all that a man could do who could not help himself. He vowed vengeance in his own mind, and then, with an air of condescension, observed—"Upon those conditions, Mynheer Kloots, your animal may remain on board."

Mynheer Kloots and Philip then left the cabin; the former, who was in no very good humour, muttering as he walked away—"If the Company send their *monkeys* on board, I think I may well have my *bear*." And pleased with his joke, Mynheer Kloots recovered his good humour.

Chapter Nine.

We must allow the Indian fleet to pursue its way to the Cape with every variety of wind and weather. Some had parted company; but the rendezvous was Table Bay, from which they were again to start together.

Philip Vanderdecken was soon able to render some service on board. He studied his duty diligently, for employment prevented him from dwelling too much upon the cause of his embarkation, and he worked hard at the duties of the ship, for the exercise procured for him that sleep which otherwise would have been denied.

He was soon a favourite of the captain, and intimate with Hillebrant, the first mate; the second mate, Struys, was a morose young man, with whom he had little intercourse. As for the supercargo, Mynheer Jacob Janz Von Stroom, he seldom ventured out of his cabin. The bear, Johannes, was not confined, and therefore Mynheer Von Stroom confined himself; hardly a day passed that he did not look over a letter which he had framed upon the subject, all ready to forward to the Company; and each time that he perused it he made some alteration, which he considered would give additional force to his complaint, and would prove still more injurious to the interests of Captain Kloots.

In the mean time, in happy ignorance of all that was passing in the poop-cabin, Mynheer Kloots smoked his pipe, drank his schnapps, and played with Johannes. The animal had also contracted a great affection for Philip, and used to walk the watch with him.

There was another party in the ship whom we must not lose sight of—the one-eyed pilot, Schriften, who appeared to have imbibed a great animosity towards our hero, as well as to his dumb favourite the bear. As Philip held the rank of an officer, Schriften dared not openly affront, though he took every opportunity of annoying him, and was constantly inveighing against him before the ship's company. To the bear he was more openly inveterate, and seldom passed it without bestowing upon it a severe kick, accompanied with a horrid curse. Although no one on board appeared to be fond of this man, everybody appeared to be afraid of him, and he had obtained a control over the seamen which appeared unaccountable.

Such was the state of affairs on board the good ship Ter Schilling, when, in company with two others, she lay becalmed about two days' sail to the Cape. The weather was intensely hot, for it was the summer in those southern latitudes, and Philip, who had been lying down under the awning spread over the poop, was so overcome with the heat, that he had fallen asleep. He awoke with a shivering sensation of cold over his whole body, particularly at his chest, and, half-opening his eyes, he perceived the pilot, Schriften, leaning over him, and holding between his finger and his thumb a portion of the chain which had not been concealed, and to which was attached the sacred relic. Philip closed them again, to ascertain what were the man's intentions: he found that he gradually dragged out the chain, and, when the relic was clear, attempted to pass the whole over his head, evidently to gain possession of it. Upon this attempt Philip started up and seized him by the waist.

"Indeed!" cried Philip, with an indignant look, as he released the chain from the pilot's hand.

But Schriften appeared not in the least confused at being detected in his attempt: looking with his malicious one eye at Philip, he mockingly observed—

"Does that chain hold her picture?—he! he!"

Vanderdecken rose, pushed him away, and folded his arms.

"I advise you not to be quite so curious, Master Pilot, or you may repent it."

"Or perhaps," continued the pilot quite regardless of Philip's wrath, "it may be a child's caul, a sovereign remedy against drowning."

"Go forward to your duty, sir," cried Philip.

"Or, as you are a Catholic, the finger-nail of a saint; or, yes, I have it—a piece of the holy cross."

Philip started.

"That's it! that's it!" cried Schriften, who now went forward to where the seamen were standing at the gangway.

"News for you, my lads!" said he; "we've a bit of the holy cross aboard, and so we may defy the devil!"

Philip, hardly knowing why, had followed Schriften as he descended the poop-ladder, and was forward on the quarterdeck, when the pilot made this remark to the seamen.

"Ay! ay!" replied an old seaman to the pilot; "not only the devil, but the Flying Dutchman to boot."

"Flying Dutchman," thought Philip, "can that refer to—?" and Philip walked a step or two forward, so as to conceal himself behind the mainmast, hoping to obtain some information, should they continue the conversation. In this he was not disappointed.

"They say that to meet with him is worse than meeting with the devil," observed another of the crew.

"Who ever saw him?" said another.

"He has been seen, that's sartain, and just as sartain that ill luck follows the vessel that falls in with him."

"And where is he to be fallen in with?"

"O! they say that's not so sartain—but he cruises off the Cape."

"I should like to know the whole long and short of the story," said a third.

"I can only tell what I've heard. It's a doomed vessel; they were pirates, and cut the captain's throat, I believe."

"No! no!" cried Schriften, "the captain is in her now—and a villain he was. They say that, like somebody else on board of us now, he left a very pretty wife, and that he was very fond of her."

"How do they know that, pilot?"

"Because he always wants to send letters home when he boards vessels that he falls in with. But, woe to the vessel that takes charge of them!—she is sure to be lost, with every soul on board!"

"I wonder where you heard all this," said one of the men. "Did you ever see the vessel?"

"Yes, I did!" screamed Schriften; but, as if recovering himself, his scream subsided into his usual giggle, and he added, "but we need not fear her, boys; we've a bit of the true cross on board." Schriften then walked aft as if to avoid being questioned, when he perceived Philip by the mainmast.

"So, I'm not the only one curious?—he! he! Pray did you bring that on board, in case we should fall in with the Flying Dutchman?"

"I fear no Flying Dutchman," replied Philip, confused.

"Now I think of it, you are of the same name; at least they say that his name was Vanderdecken—eh?"

"There are many Vanderdeckens in the world besides me," replied Philip who had recovered his composure; and having made this reply, he walked away to the poop of the vessel.

"One would almost imagine this malignant one-eyed wretch was aware of the cause of my embarkation," mused Philip; "but no! that cannot be. Why do I feel such a chill whenever he approaches me? I wonder if others do; or whether it is a mere fancy on the part of Amine and myself. I dare ask no questions.—Strange, too, that the man should feel such malice towards me. I never injured him. What I have just overheard confirms all; but there needed no confirmation. Oh, Amine! Amine! but for thee, and I would rejoice to solve this riddle at the expense of life. God in mercy check the current of my brain," muttered Philip, "or my reason cannot hold its seat!"

In three days the Ter Schilling and her consorts arrived at Table Bay, where they found the remainder of the fleet at anchor waiting for them. Just at that period the Dutch had formed a settlement at the Cape of Good Hope, where the Indian fleets used to water and obtain cattle from the Hottentot tribes who lived on the coast, and who for a brass button or a large nail would willingly offer a fat bullock. A few days were occupied in completing the water of the squadron, and then the ships, having received from the Admiral their instructions as to rendezvous in case of parting company, and made every preparation for the bad weather which they anticipated, again weighed their anchors and proceeded on their voyage.

For three days they beat against light and baffling winds, making but little progress; on the third, the breeze sprang up strong from the southward, until it increased to a gale, and the fleet were blown down to the northward of the bay. On the seventh day the Ter Schilling found herself alone, but the weather had moderated. Sail was again made upon the vessel, and her head put to the eastward, that she might run in for the land.

"We are unfortunate in thus parting with all our consorts," observed Mynheer Kloots to Philip, as they were standing at the gangway; "but it must be near meridian, and the sun will enable me to discover our latitude. It is difficult to say how far we may have been swept by the gale and the currents to the northward. Boy, bring up my cross-staff, and be mindful that you do not strike it against anything as you come up."

The cross-staff at that time was the simple instrument used to discover the latitude, which it would give to a nice observer to within five or ten miles. Quadrants and sextants were the invention of a much later period. Indeed, considering that they had so little knowledge of navigation and the variation of the compass, and that their easting and westing could only be computed by dead reckoning, it is wonderful how our ancestors traversed the ocean in the way they did, with comparatively so few accidents.

"We are full three degrees to the northward of the Cape," observed Mynheer Kloots, after he had computed his latitude. "The currents must be running strong; the wind is going down fast, and we shall have a change, if I mistake not."

Towards the evening it fell calm, with a heavy swell setting towards the shore; shoals of seals appeared on the surface, following the vessel as she drove before the swell; the fish darted and leaped in every direction, and the ocean around them appeared to be full of life as the sun slowly descended to the horizon.

"What is that noise we hear?" observed Philip; "it sounds like distant thunder."

"I hear it," replied Mynheer Kloots. "Aloft there, do you see the land?"

"Yes," replied the man after a pause in ascending the topmast shrouds. "It is right ahead—low sand-hills, and the sea breaking high."

"Then that must be the noise we hear. We sweep in fast with this heavy ground-swell. I wish the breeze would spring up."

The sun was dipping under the horizon, and the calm still continued: the swell had driven the Ter Schilling so rapidly on the shore that now they could see the breakers which fell over with the noise of thunder.

"Do you know the coast, pilot?" observed the captain to Schriften, who stood by.

"Know it well," replied Schriften; "the sea breaks in twelve fathoms at least. In half an hour the good ship will be beaten into toothpicks, without a breeze to help us." And the little man giggled as if pleased at the idea.

The anxiety of Mynheer Kloots was not to be concealed; his pipe was every moment in and out of his mouth. The crew remained in groups on the forecastle and gangway, listening with dismay to the fearful roaring of the breakers. The sun had sunk down below the horizon, and the gloom of night was gradually adding to the alarm of the crew of the Ter Schilling.

"We must lower down the boats," said Mynheer Kloots to the first mate, "and try to tow her off. We cannot do much good, I'm afraid; but at all events the boats will be ready for the men to get into before she drives on shore. Get the tow ropes out and lower down the boats, while I go in to acquaint the supercargo."

Mynheer Von Stroom was sitting in all the dignity of his office, and, it being Sunday, had put on his very best wig. He was once more reading over the letter to the Company, relative to the bear, when Mynheer Kloots made his appearance, and informed him in a few words that they were in a situation of peculiar danger, and that in all probability the ship would be in pieces in less than half an hour. At this alarming intelligence, Mynheer Von Stroom jumped up from his chair, and in his hurry and fear knocked down the candle which had just been lighted.

"In danger! Mynheer Kloots!—why the water is smooth and the wind down! My hat—where is my hat and my cane? I will go on deck. Quick! A light—Mynheer Kloots, if you please to order a light to be brought; I can find nothing in the dark. Mynheer Kloots, why do you not answer? Mercy on me! he is gone and has left me."

Mynheer Kloots had gone to fetch a light, and now returned with it. Mynheer Von Stroom put on his hat, and walked out of the cabin. The boats were down, and the ship's head had been turned round from the land: but it was now quite dark and nothing was to be seen but the white line of foam created by the breakers as they dashed with an awful noise against the shore.

"Mynheer Kloots, if you please, I'll leave the ship directly. Let my boat come alongside—I must have the largest boat for the Honourable Company's service—for the papers and myself."

"I'm afraid not, Mynheer Von Stroom," replied Kloots; "our boats will hardly hold the men as it is, and every man's life is as valuable to himself as yours is to you."

"But, Mynheer, I am the Company's supercargo. I order you—I will have one—refuse if you dare."

"I dare, and do refuse," replied the captain, taking his pipe out of his mouth.

"Well, well," replied Mynheer Von Stroom, who now lost all presence of mind—"we will, sir—as soon as we arrive—Lord help us!—we are lost. O Lord! O Lord!" And here Mynheer Von Stroom, not knowing why, hurried down to the cabin, and in his haste tumbled over the bear Johannes, who crossed his path, and in his fall his hat and flowing wig parted company with his head.

"O! mercy! where am I? Help—help here! for the Honourable Company's supercargo!"

"Cast off there in the boats, and come on board," cried Mynheer Kloots, "we have no time to spare. Quick now, Philip, put in the compass, the water, and the biscuit; we must leave her in five minutes."

So appalling was the roar of the breakers, that it was with difficulty that the orders could be heard. In the mean time Mynheer Von Stroom lay upon the deck, kicking, sprawling, and crying for help.

"There is a light breeze off the shore," cried Philip, holding up his hand.

"There is, but I'm afraid it is too late. Hand the things into the boats, and be cool, my men. We have yet a chance of saving her, if the wind freshens."

They were now so near to the breakers that they felt the swell in which the vessel lay becalmed turned over here and there on its long line, but the breeze freshened and the vessel was stationary! The men were all in the boats, with the exception of Mynheer Kloots, the mates, and Mynheer Von Stroom.

"She goes through the water now," said Philip.

"Yes, I think we shall save her," replied the captain: "steady as you go, Hillebrant," continued he to the first mate, who was at the helm. "We leave the breakers now—only let the breeze hold ten minutes."

The breeze was steady, the Ter Schilling stood off from the land, again it fell calm, and again she was swept towards the breakers; at last the breeze came off strong, and the vessel cleaved through the water. The men were called out of the boats; Mynheer Von Stroom was picked up along with his hat and wig, carried into the cabin, and in less than an hour the Ter Schilling was out of danger.

"Now we will hoist up the boats," said Mynheer Kloots, "and let us all, before we lie down to sleep, thank God for our deliverance."

During that night the Ter Schilling made an offing of twenty miles, and then stood to the southward; towards the morning the wind again fell, and it was nearly calm.

Mynheer Kloots had been on deck about an hour, and had been talking with Hillebrant upon the danger of the evening, and the selfishness and pusillanimity of Mynheer Von Stroom, when a loud noise was heard in the poop-cabin.

"What can that be?" said the captain; "has the good man lost his senses from the fright? Why, he is knocking the cabin to pieces."

At this moment the servant of the supercargo ran out of the cabin.

"Mynheer Kloots, hasten in—help my master—he will be killed—the bear!—the bear!"

"The bear! what Johannes?" cried Mynheer Kloots. "Why, the animal is as tame as a dog. I will go and see."

But before Mynheer Kloots could walk into the cabin, out flew in his shirt the affrighted supercargo. "My God! my God! am I to be murdered?—eaten alive?" cried he, running forward, and attempting to climb the fore-rigging.

Mynheer Kloots followed the motions of Mynheer Von Stroom with surprise, and when he found him attempting to mount the rigging, he turned aft and walked into the cabin, when he found to his surprise that Johannes was indeed doing mischief.

The panelling of the state cabin of the supercargo had been beaten down, the wig boxes lay in fragments on the floor, the two spare wigs were lying by them, and upon them were strewed fragments of broken pots and masses of honey, which Johannes was licking up with peculiar gusto.

The fact was, that when the ship anchored at Table Bay, Mynheer Von Stroom, who was very partial to honey, had obtained some from the Hottentots. This honey his careful servant had stowed away in jars, which he had placed at the bottom of the two long boxes, ready for his master's use during the remainder of the voyage. That morning, the servant fancying that the wig of the previous night had suffered when his master tumbled over the bear, opened one of the boxes to take out another. Johannes happened to come near the door, and scented the honey. Now, partial as Mynheer Von Stroom was to honey, all bears are still more so, and will venture everything to obtain it. Johannes had yielded to the impulse of his species, and, following the scent, had come into the cabin, and was about to enter the sleeping berth of Mynheer Stroom, when the servant slammed the door in his face; whereupon Johannes beat in the panels, and found an entrance. He then attacked the wig-boxes, and, by showing a most formidable set of teeth, proved to the servant, who attempted to drive him off, that he would not be trifled with. In the meanwhile, Mynheer Von Stroom was in the utmost terror: not aware of the purport of the bear's visit, he imagined that the animal's object was to attack him. His servant took to his heels after a vain effort to save the last box, and Mynheer Von Stroom, then finding himself alone, at length sprang out of his bed-place, and escaped, as we have mentioned, to the forecastle, leaving Johannes master of the field, and luxuriating upon the *spolia opima*. Mynheer Kloots immediately perceived how the case stood. He went up to the bear and spoke to him, then kicked him, but the bear would not leave the honey, and growled furiously at the interruption. "This is a bad job for you, Johannes," observed Mynheer Kloots; "now you will leave the ship, for the supercargo has just grounds of complaint. Oh, well! you must eat the honey, because you will." So saying, Mynheer Kloots left the cabin, and went to look after the supercargo, who remained on the forecastle, with his bald head and meagre body, haranguing the men in his shirt, which fluttered in the breeze.

"I am very sorry, Mynheer Von Stroom," said Kloots, "but the bear shall be sent out of the vessel."

"Yes, yes, Mynheer Kloots; but this is an affair for the most puissant Company—the lives of their servants are not to be sacrificed to the folly of a sea-captain. I have nearly been torn to pieces."

"The animal did not want you; all he wanted was the honey," replied Kloots. "He has got it, and I myself cannot take it from him. There is no altering the nature of an animal. Will you be pleased to walk down into my cabin until the beast can be secured? He shall not go loose again."

Mynheer Von Stroom who considered his dignity at variance with his appearance, and who perhaps was aware that majesty deprived of its externals was only a jest, thought it advisable to accept the offer. After some trouble with the assistance of the seamen, the bear was secured and dragged away from the cabin, much against his will, for he had still some honey to lick off the curls of the full-bottomed wigs. He was put into durance vile, having been caught in the flagrant act of burglary on the high seas. This new adventure was the topic of the day, for it was again a dead calm, and the ship lay motionless on the glassy wave.

"The sun looks red as he sinks," observed Hillebrant to the captain, who with Philip was standing on the poop; "we shall have wind before to-morrow, if I mistake not."

"I am of your opinion," replied Mynheer Kloots. "It is strange that we do not fall in with any of the vessels of the fleet. They must all have been driven down here."

"Perhaps they have kept a wider offing."

"It had been as well if we had done the same," said Kloots. "That was a narrow escape last night. There is such a thing as having too little as well as having too much wind."

A confused noise was heard among the seamen, who were collected together and, looking in the direction of the vessel's quarter, "A ship! No—Yes, it is!" was repeated more than once.

"They think they see a ship," said Schriften, coming on the poop. "He! he!"

"Where?"

"There in the gloom!" said the pilot, pointing to the darkest quarter in the horizon, for the sun had set.

The captain, Hillebrant, and Philip directed their eyes to the quarter pointed out, and thought they could perceive something like a vessel. Gradually the gloom seemed to clear away, and a lambent pale blaze to light up that part of the horizon. Not a breath of wind was on the water—the sea was like a mirror—more and more distinct did the vessel appear, till her hull, masts, and yards were clearly visible. They looked and rubbed their eyes to help their vision, for scarcely could they believe that which they did see. In the centre of the pale light, which extended about fifteen degrees above the horizon, there was indeed a large ship about three miles distant; but although it was a perfect calm, she was to all appearance buffeting in a violent gale, plunging and lifting over a surface that was smooth as glass, now careening to her bearing, then recovering herself. Her topsails and mainsail were furled, and the yards pointed to the wind; she had no sail set, but a close-reefed foresail, a storm staysail, and trysail abaft. She made little way through the water, but apparently neared them fast, driven down by the force of the gale. Each minute she was plainer to the view. At last she was seen to wear, and in so doing, before she was brought to the wind on the other tack, she was so close to them that they could distinguish the men on board: they could see the foaming water as it was hurled from her bows; hear the shrill whistle of the boatswain's pipes, the creaking of the ship's timbers, and the complaining of her masts; and then the gloom gradually rose, and in a few seconds she had totally disappeared!

"God in heaven!" exclaimed Mynheer Kloots.

Philip felt a hand upon his shoulder, and the cold darted through his whole frame. He turned round and met the one eye of Schriften, who screamed in his ear—

"**Philip Vanderdecken**—that's the *Flying Dutchman*!"

Chapter Ten.

The sudden gloom which had succeeded to the pale light, had the effect of rendering every object still more indistinct to the astonished crew of the Ter Schilling. For a moment or more not a word was uttered by a soul on board. Some remained with their eyes still strained towards the point where the apparition had been seen, others turned away full of gloomy and foreboding thoughts. Hillebrant was the first who spoke: turning round to the eastern quarter, and observing a light on the horizon, he started, and seizing Philip by the arm, cried out, "What's that?"

"That is only the moon rising from the bank of clouds," replied Philip, mournfully.

"Well!" observed Mynheer Kloots wiping his forehead, which was damped with perspiration, "I *have* been told of this before, but I have mocked at the narration."

Philip made no reply. Aware of the reality of the vision, and how deeply it interested him, he felt as if he were a guilty person.

The moon had now risen above the clouds, and was pouring her mild pale light over the slumbering ocean. With a simultaneous impulse, every one directed his eyes to the spot where the strange vision had last been seen; and all was a dead, dead calm.

Since the apparition the pilot, Schriften, had remained on the poop; he now gradually approached Mynheer Kloots, and looking round, said—

"Mynheer Kloots, as pilot of this vessel, I tell you that you must prepare for very bad weather."

"Bad weather!" said Kloots, rousing himself from a deep reverie.

"Yes, bad weather, Mynheer Kloots. There never was a vessel which fell in with—what we have just seen but met with disaster soon afterwards. The very name of Vanderdecken is unlucky—He! he!"

Philip would have replied to this sarcasm, but he could not; his tongue was tied.

"What has the name of Vanderdecken to do with it?" observed Kloots.

"Have you not heard, then? The captain of that vessel we have just seen is a Mynheer Vanderdecken—he is the Flying Dutchman!"

"How know you that, pilot?" inquired Hillebrant.

"I know that, and much more, if I chose to tell," replied Schriften; "but never mind, I have warned you of bad weather, as is my duty;" and, with these words, Schriften went down the poop-ladder.

"God in heaven! I never was so puzzled and so frightened in my life," observed Kloots. "I don't know what to think or say.—What think you, Philip? was it not supernatural?"

"Yes," replied Philip, mournfully. "I have no doubt of it."

"I thought the days of miracles had passed," said the captain, "and that we were now left to our own exertions, and had no other warnings but those the appearance of the heavens gave us."

"And they warn us now," observed Hillebrant. "See how that bank of clouds has risen within these five minutes—the moon has escaped from it but it will soon catch her again—and see, there is a flash of lightning in the north-west."

"Well, my sons, I can brave the elements as well as any man, and do my best. I have cared little for gales or stress of weather; but I like not such a warning as we have had tonight. My heart's as heavy as lead, and that's the truth. Philip, send down for the bottle of schnapps, if it is only to clear my brain a little."

Philip was glad of an opportunity to quit the poop; he wished to have a few minutes to recover himself and collect his own thoughts. The appearance of the Phantom Ship had been to him a dreadful shock; not that he had not fully believed in its existence; but still, to have beheld, to have been so near that vessel—that vessel in which his father was fulfilling his awful doom—that vessel on board of which he felt sure that his own destiny was to be worked out—had given a whirl to his brain. When he had heard the sound of the boatswain's whistle on board of her, eagerly had he stretched his earing to catch the order given—and given, he was convinced, in his father's voice. Nor had his eyes been less called to aid in his attempt to discover the features and dress of those moving on her decks. As soon, then, as he had sent the boy up to Mynheer Kloots Philip hastened to his cabin and buried his face in the coverlid of his bed, and then he prayed—prayed until he had recovered his usual energy and courage, and brought his mind to that state of composure which could enable him to look forward calmly to danger and difficulty, and feel prepared to meet it with the heroism of a martyr.

Philip remained below not more than half an hour. On his return to the deck, what a change had taken place! He had left the vessel floating motionless on the still waters, with her lofty sails hanging down listlessly from the yards. The moon then soared aloft in her beauty, reflecting the masts and sails of the ship in extended lines upon the smooth sea. Now all was dark: the water rippled short and broke in foam; the smaller and lofty sails had been taken in, and the vessel was cleaving through the water; and the wind, in fitful gusts and angry moanings, proclaimed too surely that it had been awakened up to wrath, and was gathering its strength for destruction. The men were still busy reducing the sails, but they worked gloomily and discontentedly. What Schriften, the pilot, had said to them, Philip knew not; but that they avoided him and appeared to look upon him with feelings of ill-will, was evident. And each minute the gale increased.

"The wind is not steady," observed Hillebrant: "there is no saying from which quarter the storm may blow: it has already veered round five points. Philip, I don't much like the appearance of things, and I may say with the captain that my heart is heavy."

"And, indeed, so is mine," replied Philip; "but we are in the hands of a merciful Providence."

"Hard a-port! flatten in forward! brail up the trysail, my men! Be smart!" cried Kloots, as from the wind's chopping round to the northward and westward, the ship was taken aback, and careened low before it. The rain now came down in torrents, and it was so dark that it was with difficulty they could perceive each other on the deck.

"We must clew up the topsails while the men can get upon the yards. See to it forward, Mr Hillebrant."

The lightning now darted athwart the firmament, and the thunder pealed.

"Quick! quick, my men, let's furl all!"

The sailors shook the water from their streaming clothes, some worked, others took advantage of the night to hide themselves away, and commune with their own fears.

All canvass was now taken off the ship, except the fore-staysail, and she flew to the southward with the wind on her quarter. The sea had now risen, and roared as it curled in foam, the rain fell in torrents, the night was dark as Erebus, and the wet and frightened sailors sheltered themselves under the bulwarks. Although many had deserted from their duty, there was not one who ventured below that night. They did not collect together as usual—every man preferred solitude and his own thoughts. The Phantom Ship dwelt on their imaginations and oppressed their brains.

It was an interminably long and terrible night—they thought the day would never come. At last the darkness gradually changed to a settled sullen grey gloom—which was day. They looked at each other, but found no comfort in meeting each other's eyes. There was no one countenance in which a beam of hope could be found lurking. They were all doomed—they remained crouched where they had—sheltered themselves during the night, and said nothing.

The sea had now risen mountains high, and more than once had struck the ship abaft. Kloots was at the binnacle, Hillebrant and Philip at the helm, when a wave curled high over the quarter, and poured itself in resistless force upon the deck. The captain and his two mates were swept away, and dashed almost senseless against the bulwarks—the binnacle and compass were broken into fragments—no one ran to the helm—the vessel broached to—the seas broke clear over her, and the mainmast went by the board.

All was confusion. Captain Kloots was stunned, and it was with difficulty that Philip could persuade two of the men to assist him down below. Hillebrant had been more unfortunate—his right arm was broken, and he was otherwise severely bruised; Philip assisted him to his berth, and then went on deck again to try and restore order.

Philip Vanderdecken was not yet much of a seaman, but, at all events, he exercised that moral influence over the men which is ever possessed by resolution and courage. Obey willingly they did not, but they did obey, and in half an hour the vessel was clear of the wreck. Eased by the loss of her heavy mast, and steered by two of her best seamen, she again flew before the gale.

Where was Mynheer Von Stroom during all this work of destruction? In his bed-place, covered up with the clothes, trembling in every limb, and vowing that it ever again he put his foot on shore, not all the companies in the world should induce him to trust to salt-water again. It certainly was the best plan for the poor man.

But although for a time the men obeyed the orders of Philip, they were soon seen talking earnestly with the one-eyed pilot, and after a consultation of a quarter of an hour, they all left the deck, with the exception of the two at the helm. Their reasons for so doing were soon apparent—several returned with cans full of liquor, which they had obtained by forcing the hatches of the spirit-room. For about an hour Philip remained on deck, persuading the men not to intoxicate themselves, but in vain; the cans of grog offered to the men at the wheel were not refused, and, in a short time, the yawing of the vessel proved that the liquor had taken its effect. Philip then hastened down below to ascertain if Mynheer Kloots was sufficiently recovered to come on deck. He found him sunk into a deep sleep, and with difficulty it was that he roused him, and made him acquainted with the distressing intelligence. Mynheer Kloots followed Philip on deck; but he still suffered from his fail: his head was confused, and he reeled as he walked, as if he also had been making free with the liquor. When he had been on deck a few minutes, he sank down on one of the guns in a state of perfect helplessness; he had, in fact, received a severe concussion of the brain. Hillebrant was too severely injured to be able to move from his bed, and Philip was now aware of the helplessness of their situation. Daylight gradually disappeared, and as darkness came upon them, so did the scene become more appalling. The vessel still ran before the gale, but the men at the helm had evidently changed her course, as the wind that was on the starboard was now on the larboard quarter. But compass there was none on deck, and, even if there had been, the men in their drunken state would have refused to listen to Philip's orders or expostulations. "He," they said, "was no sailor, and was not to teach them how to steer the ship." The gale was now at its height. The rain had ceased, but the wind had increased, and it roared as it urged on the vessel, which, steered so wide by the drunken sailors, shipped seas over each gunnel; but the men laughed, and joined the chorus of their songs to the howling of the gale.

Schriften, the pilot, appeared to be the leader of the ship's company. With the can of liquor in his hand, he danced and sang, snapped his fingers, and, like a demon, peered with his one eye upon Philip; and then would he fall and roll with screams of laughter in the scuppers. More liquor was handed up as fast as it was called for. Oaths shrieks laughter, were mingled together; the men at the helm lashed it amid-ships, and hastened to join their companions and the Ter Schilling flew before the gale; the fore-staysail being the only sail set, checking her, as she yawed to starboard or to port. Philip remained on deck by the poop-ladder. Strange, thought he, that I should stand here, the only one left now capable of acting,—that I should be fated to look by myself upon this scene of horror and disgust—should here wait the severing of this vessel's timbers,—the loss of life which must accompany it—the only one calm and collected, or aware of what must soon take place. God forgive me, but I appear, useless and impotent as I am, to stand here like the master of the storm,—separated, as it were, from my brother mortals by my own peculiar destiny. It must be so. This wreck then must not be for me, I feel that it is not,—that I have a charmed life, or rather a protracted one, to fulfil the oath I registered in heaven. But the wind is not so loud, surely the water is not so rough: my forebodings may be wrong and all may yet be saved. Heaven grant it! For how melancholy, how lamentable is it to behold men created in God's own image, leaving the world, disgraced below the brute creation!

Philip was right in supposing that the wind was not so strong, nor the sea so high. The vessel, after running to the southward till past Table Bay, had, by the alteration made in her course, entered into False Bay, where, to a certain degree, she was sheltered from the violence of the winds and waves. But although the water was smoother, the waves were still more than sufficient to beat to pieces any vessel that might be driven on shore at the bottom of the bay, to which point the Ter Schilling was now running. The bay so far offered a fair chance of escape, as, instead of the rocky coast outside, against which, had the vessel run, a few seconds would have insured her destruction, there was a shelving beach of loose sand. But of this Philip could, of course, have no knowledge, for the land at the entrance of the bay had been passed unperceived in the darkness of the night. About twenty minutes more had elapsed, when Philip observed that the whole sea around them was one continued foam. He had hardly time for conjecture before the ship struck heavily on the sands, and the remaining masts fell by the board.

The crush of the falling masts, the heavy beating of the ship on the sands, which caused many of her timbers to part, with a whole sea which swept clean over the fated vessel, checked the songs and drunken revelry of the crew. Another minute, and the vessel was swung round on her broadside to the sea, and lay on her beam ends. Philip, who was to windward clung to the bulwark, while the intoxicated seamen floundered in the water to leeward, and attempted to gain the other side of the ship. Much to Philip's horror, he perceived the body of Mynheer Kloots sink down in the water (which now was several feet deep on the lee side of the deck), without any apparent effort on the part of the captain to save himself. He was then gone, and there were no hopes for him. Philip thought of Hillebrant, and hastened down below; he found him still in his bed-place, lying against the side. He lifted him out, and with difficulty climbed with him on deck, and laid him in the long-boat on the booms as the best chance of saving his life. To this boat the only one which could be made available, the crew had also repaired; but they repulsed Philip who would have got into her; and, as the sea made clean breakers over them, they cast loose the lashings which confined her. With the assistance of another heavy sea which lifted her from the chocks she was borne clear of the booms and dashed over the gunnel into the water, to leeward, which was comparatively smooth—not, however, without being filled nearly up to the thwarts. But this was little cared for by the intoxicated seamen, who, as soon as they were afloat, again raised their shouts and songs of revelry as they were borne away by the wind and sea towards the beach. Philip, who held on by the stump of the mainmast, watched them with an anxious eye, now perceiving them borne aloft on the foaming surf, now disappearing in the trough. More and more distant were the sounds of their mad voices, till, at last, he could hear them no more,—he beheld the boat balanced on an enormous rolling sea, and then he saw it not again.

Philip knew that now his only chance was to remain with the vessel, and attempt to save himself upon some fragment of the wreck. That the ship would long hold together he felt was impossible; already she had parted her upper decks, and each shock of the waves divided her more and more. At last, as he clung to the mast, he heard a noise abaft, and he then recollected that Mynheer Von Stroom was still in his cabin. Philip crawled aft, and found that the poop-ladder had been thrown against the cabin door, so as to prevent its being opened. He removed it and entered the cabin, where he found Mynheer Von Stroom clinging to windward with the grasp of death,—but it was not death, but the paralysis of fear. He spoke to him, but could obtain no reply, he attempted to move him, but it was impossible to make him let go the part of the bulk-head that he grasped. A loud noise and the rush of a mass of water told Philip that the vessel had parted amid-ships, and he unwillingly abandoned the poor supercargo to his fate, and went out of the cabin door. At the after-hatchway he observed something struggling,—it was Johannes the bear, who was swimming, but still fastened by a cord which prevented his escape. Philip took out his knife and released the poor animal, and hardly had he done this act of kindness, when a heavy sea turned over the after part of the vessel, which separated in many pieces, and Philip found himself struggling in the waves. He seized upon a part of the deck which supported him, and was borne away by the surf towards the beach. In a few minutes he was near to the land, and shortly afterwards the piece of planking to which he was clinging struck on the sand, and then, being turned over by the force of the running wave, Philip lost his hold, and was left to his own exertions. He struggled long, but, although so near to the shore, could not gain a footing; the returning wave dragged him back, and thus was he hurled to and fro until his strength was gone. He was sinking under the wave to rise no more when he felt something touch his hand. He seized it with the grasp of death. It was the shaggy hide of the bear Johannes, who was making for the shore, and who soon dragged him clear of the surf, so that he could gain a footing. Philip crawled up the beach above the reach of the waves, and, exhausted with fatigue, sank down in a swoon.

When Philip was recalled from his state of lethargy, his first feeling was intense pain in his still-closed eyes, arising from having been many hours exposed to the rays of an ardent sun. He opened them, but was obliged to close them immediately, for the light entered into them like the point of a knife. He turned over on his side, and covering them with his hand remained some time in that position, until, by degrees, he found that his eyesight was restored. He then rose, and, after a few seconds, could distinguish the scene around him. The sea was still rough, and tossed about in the surf fragments of the vessel; the whole sand was strewed with her cargo and contents. Near him was the body of Hillebrant, and the other bodies who were scattered on the beach told him that those who had taken to the boat had all perished.

It was, by the height of the sun, about three o'clock in the afternoon, as near as he could estimate; but Philip suffered such an oppression of mind, he felt so wearied, and in such pain, that he took but a slight survey. His brain was whirling, and all he demanded was repose. He walked away from the scene of destruction, and having found a sand-hill, behind which he was defended from the burning rays of the sun, he again lay down, and sank into a deep sleep, from which he did not wake until the ensuing morning.

Philip was roused a second time by the sensation of something pricking him on the chest. He started up, and beheld a figure standing over him. His eyes were still feeble, and his vision indistinct; he rubbed them for a time, for he first thought it was the bear Johannes, and again, that it was the supercargo Von Stroom, who had appeared before him; he looked again, and found that he was mistaken, although he had warrant for supposing it to be either, or both. A tall Hottentot, with an assaguay in his hand, stood by his side; over his shoulder he had thrown the fresh-severed skin of the poor bear, and on his head, with the curls descending to his waist, was one of the wigs of the supercargo Von Stroom. Such was the gravity of the black's appearance in this strange costume (for in every other respect he was naked), that, at any other time, Philip would have been induced to laugh heartily; but his feelings were now too acute. He rose upon his feet, and stood by the side of the Hottentot, who still continued immovable, but certainly without the slightest appearance of hostile intentions.

A sensation of overpowering thirst now seized upon Philip, and he made signs that he wished to drink. The Hottentot motioned to him to follow, and led over the sand-hills to the beach, where Philip discovered upwards of fifty men, who were busy selecting various articles from the scattered stores of the vessel. It was evident by the respect paid to Philip's conductor, that he was the chief of the kraal. A few words, uttered with the greatest solemnity, were sufficient to produce, though not exactly what Philip required, a small quantity of dirty water from a calabash, which, however, was to him delicious. His conductor then waved to him to take a seat on the sand.

It was a novel and appalling, and, nevertheless, a ludicrous scene: there was the white sand, rendered still more white by the strong glare of the sun, strewed with the fragments of the vessel, with casks, and bales of merchandise; there was the running surge with its foam, throwing about particles of the wreck: there were the bones of whales which had been driven on shore in some former gale and which, now half-buried in the sand, showed portions of huge skeletons; there were the mangled bodies of Philip's late companions, whose clothes, it appeared, had been untouched by the savages, with the exception of the buttons, which had been eagerly sought after; there were naked Hottentots (for it was summer time, and they wore not their sheepskin krosses) gravely stepping up and down the sand, picking up everything that was of no value, and leaving all that civilised people most coveted;—to crown all, there was the chief, sitting in the still bloody skin of Johannes, and the broad-bottomed wig of Mynheer Stroom, with all the gravity of a vice-chancellor in his countenance, and without the slightest idea that he was in any way ridiculous. The whole presented, perhaps, one of the most strange and chaotic tableaux that ever was witnessed.

Although, at that time, the Dutch had not very long formed their settlement at the Cape, a considerable traffic had been, for many years, carried on with the natives for skins and other African productions. The Hottentots were, therefore, no strangers to vessels, and, as hitherto they had been treated with kindness, were well-disposed towards Europeans. After a time, the Hottentots began to collect all the wood which appeared to have iron in it, made it up into several piles, and set them on fire. The chief then made a sign to Philip, to ask him if he was hungry; Philip replied in the affirmative, when his new acquaintance put his hand into a bag made of goat-skin, and pulled out a handful of very large beetles, and presented them to him. Philip refused them with marks of disgust, upon which, the chief very sedately cracked and ate them; and having finished the whole handful, rose, and made a sign to Philip to follow him. As Philip rose, he perceived floating on the surf, his own chest; he hastened to it, and made signs that it was his, took the key out of his pocket and opened it, and then made up a bundle of articles most useful, not forgetting a bag of guilders. His conductor made no objection, but calling to one of the men near, pointed out the lock and hinges to him, and then set off, followed by Philip, across the sand-hills. In about an hour they arrived at the kraal, consisting of low huts covered with skins, and were met by the women and children, who appeared to be in high admiration at their chief's new attire: the showed every kindness to Philip, bringing him milk, which he drank eagerly. Philip surveyed these daughters of Eve, and, as he turned from their offensive, greasy attire, their strange forms, and hideous features, he sighed and thought of his charming Amine.

The sun was now setting, and Philip still felt fatigued. He made signs that he wished to repose. They led him into a hut, and, though surrounded as he was with filth and his nose assailed by every variety of bad smell attacked, moreover, by insects, he laid his head on his bundle, and uttering a short prayer of thanksgiving, was soon in a sound sleep.

The next morning he was awakened by the chief of the kraal, accompanied by another man who spoke a little Dutch. He stated his wish to be taken to the settlement where the ships came and anchored, and was fully understood; but the man said that there were no ships in the bay at the time. Philip, nevertheless, requested he might be taken there, as he felt that his best chance of getting on board of any vessel would be by remaining at the settlement, and, at all events, he would be in the company of Europeans, until a vessel arrived. The distance, he discovered, was but one day's march, or less. After some little conversation with the chief, the man who spoke Dutch desired Philip to follow him and that he would take him there. Philip drank plentifully from a bowl of milk brought him by one of the women, and again refusing a handful of beetles offered by the chief, he took up his bundle, and followed his new acquaintance.

Towards evening they arrived at the hills, from which Philip had a view of Table Bay and the few houses erected by the Dutch. To his delight, he perceived that there was a vessel under sail in the offing. On his arrival at the beach, to which he hastened, he found that she had sent a boat on shore for fresh provisions. He accosted the people, told them who he was, told them also of the fatal wreck of the Ter Schilling, and of his wish to embark.

The officer in charge of the boat willingly consented to take him on board, and informed Philip that they were homeward bound. Philip's heart leaped at the intelligence. Had she been outward bound, he would have joined her; but now he had a prospect of again seeing his dear Amine before he re-embarked to follow out his peculiar destiny. He felt that there was still some happiness in store for him, that his life was to be chequered with alternate privation and repose, and that his future prospect was not to be one continued chain of suffering until death.

He was kindly received by the captain of the vessel, who freely gave him a passage home; and in three months, without any events worth narrating, Philip Vanderdecken found himself once more at anchor before the town of Amsterdam.

Chapter Eleven.

It need hardly be observed that Philip made all possible haste to his own little cottage, which contained all that he valued in this world. He promised to himself some months of happiness, for he had done his duty; and he felt that, however desirous of fulfilling his vow, he could not again leave home till the autumn, when the next fleet sailed, and it was now but the commencement of April. Much, too, as he regretted the loss of Mynheer Kloots and Hillebrant, as well as the deaths of the unfortunate crew, still there was some solace in the remembrance that he was for ever rid of the wretch Schriften, who had shared their fate; and besides he almost blessed the wreck, so fatal to others, which enabled him so soon to return to the arms of his Amine.

It was late in the evening; when Philip took a boat from Flushing, and went over to his cottage at Terneuse. It was a rough evening for the season of the year. The wind blew fresh, and the sky was covered with flaky clouds, fringed here and there with broad white edges, for the light of the moon was high in the heavens, and she was at her full. At times her light would be almost obscured by a dark cloud passing over her disk; at others, she would burst out in all her brightness. Philip landed, and, wrapping his cloak round him, hastened up to his cottage. As with a beating heart he approached, he perceived that the window of the parlour was open, and that there was a female figure leaning out. He knew that it could be no other than his Amine, and, after he crossed the little bridge, he proceeded to the window, instead of going to the door. Amine (for it was she who stood at the window) was so absorbed in contemplation of the heavens above her, and so deep in communion with her own thoughts, that she neither saw nor heard the approach of her husband. Philip perceived her abstraction, and paused when within four or five yards of her. He wished to gain the door without being observed, as he was afraid of alarming her by his too sudden appearance, for he remembered his promise, "that if dead he would, if permitted, visit her as his father had visited his mother." But while he thus stood in suspense, Amine's eyes were turned upon him: she beheld him; but a thick cloud now obscured the moon's disk, and the dim light gave to his form, indistinctly seen, an unearthly and shadowy appearance. She recognised her husband, but having no reason to expect his return, she recognised him as an inhabitant of the world of spirits. She started, parted the hair away from her forehead with both hands, and again earnestly gazed on him.

"It is I, Amine, do not be afraid," cried Philip, hastily.

"I am not afraid," replied Amine, pressing her hand to her heart. "It is over now. Spirit of my dear husband—for such I think thou art—I thank thee! Welcome, even in death, Philip—welcome!" and Amine waved her hand mournfully, inviting Philip to enter as she retired from the window.

"My God! she thinks me dead," thought Philip, and, hardly knowing how to act, he entered in at the window, and found her sitting on the sofa. Philip would have spoken; but Amine, whose eyes were fixed upon him as he entered, and who was fully convinced that he was but a supernatural appearance, exclaimed—

"So soon—so soon! O God! thy will be done: but it is hard to bear. Philip, beloved Philip, I feel that I soon shall follow you."

Philip was now more alarmed: he was fearful of any sudden reaction when Amine should discover that he was still alive.

"Amine, dear, hear me. I have appeared unexpectedly and at an unusual hour; but throw yourself into my arms, and you will find that your Philip is not dead."

"Not dead!" cried Amine, starting up.

"No, no, still warm in flesh and blood, Amine—still your fond and doting husband," replied Philip, catching her in his arms, and pressing her to his heart.

Amine sank from his embrace down upon the sofa, and fortunately was relieved by a burst of tears, while Philip, kneeling by her, supported her.

"O God! O God! I thank thee," relied Amine, at last. "I thought it was your spirit, Philip. O! I was glad to see even that," continued she, weeping on his shoulder.

"Can you listen to me, dearest?" said Philip, after a silence of a few moments.

"O speak—speak, love; I can listen for ever."

In a few words Philip then recounted what had taken place, and the occasion of his unexpected return, and felt himself more than repaid for all that he had suffered, by the fond endearments of his still agitated Amine.

"And your father, Amine?"

"He is well; we will talk of him to-morrow."

"Yes," thought Philip, as he awoke next morning, and dwelt upon the lovely features of his still slumbering wife; "yes, God is merciful. I feel that there is still happiness in store for me; nay, more, that that happiness also depends upon my due performance of my task, and that I should be punished if I were to forget my solemn vow. Be it so,—through danger and to death will I perform my duty, trusting to His mercy for a reward both here below and in heaven above. Am I not repaid for all that I have suffered? O yes more than repaid," thought Philip, as with a kiss he disturbed the slumber of his wife, and met her full dark eyes fixed upon him, beaming with love and joy.

Before Philip went down stairs, he inquired about Mynheer Poots.

"My father has indeed troubled me much," replied Amine. "I am obliged to lock the parlour when I leave it, for more than once I have found him attempting to force the locks of the buffets. His love of gold is insatiable: he dreams of nothing else, he has caused me much pain, insisting that I never should see you again, and that I should surrender to him all your wealth. But he fears me, and he fears your return much more."

"Is he well in health?"

"Not ill, but still evidently wasting away—like a candle burnt down to the socket, flitting and flaring alternately; at one time almost imbecile, at others, talking and planning as if he were in the vigour of his youth. O what a curse it must be—that love of money! I believe—I'm shocked to say so, Philip,—that that poor old man, now on the brink of a grave into which he can take nothing, would sacrifice your life and mine to have possession of those guilders, the whole of which I would barter for one kiss from thee."

"Indeed, Amine, has he then attempted anything in my absence?"

"I dare not speak my thoughts, Philip, nor will I venture upon surmises, which it were difficult to prove. I watch him carefully;—but talk no more about him. You will see him soon, and do not expect a hearty welcome, or believe that, if given, it is sincere, I will not tell him of your return, as I wish to mark the effect."

Amine then descended to prepare breakfast, and Philip walked out for a few minutes. On his return, he found Mynheer Poots sitting at the table with his daughter.

"Merciful Allah! am I right?" cried the old man: "is it you, Mynheer Vanderdecken?"

"Even so," replied Philip; "I returned last night."

"And you did not tell me, Amine."

"I wished that you should be surprised," replied Amine.

"I am surprised! When do you sail again, Mynheer Philip? very soon, I suppose? perhaps to-morrow?" said Mynheer Poots.

"Not for many months, I trust," replied Philip.

"Not for many months!—that is a long while to be idle. You must make money. Tell me, have you brought back plenty this time?"

"No," replied Philip; "I have been wrecked, and very nearly lost my life."

"But you will go again?"

"Yes, in good time I shall go again."

"Very well, we will take care of your house and your guilders."

"I shall perhaps save you the trouble of taking care of my guilders," replied Philip, to annoy the old man, "for I mean to take them with me."

"To take them with you! for what, pray?" replied Poots, in alarm.

"To purchase goods where I go, and make more money."

"But you may be wrecked again and then the money will be all lost. No, no; go yourself, Mynheer Philip; but you must not take your guilders."

"Indeed I will," replied Philip; "when I leave this, I shall take all my money with me."

During this conversation it occurred to Philip that, if Mynheer Poots could only be led to suppose that he took away his money with him, there would be more quiet for Amine who was now obliged, as she had informed him, to be constantly on the watch. He determined, therefore, when he next departed, to make the doctor believe that he had taken his wealth with him.

Mynheer Poots did not renew the conversation, but sank into gloomy thought. In a few minutes he left the parlour, and went up to his own room, when Philip stated to his wife what had induced him to make the old man believe that he should embark his property.

"It was thoughtful of you, Philip, and I thank you for your kind feeling towards me; but I wish you had said nothing on the subject. You do not know my father; I must now watch him as an enemy."

"We have little to fear from an infirm old man," replied Philip, laughing. But Amine thought otherwise, and was ever on her guard.

The spring and summer passed rapidly away, for they were happy. Many were the conversations between Philip and Amine, relative to what had passed—the supernatural appearance of his father's ship, and the fatal wreck.

Amine felt that more dangers and difficulty were preparing for her husband, but she never once attempted to dissuade him from renewing his attempts in fulfilment of his vow. Like him, she looked forward with hope and confidence, aware that, at some time, his fate must be accomplished, and trusting only that that hour would be long delayed.

At the close of the summer, Philip again went to Amsterdam, to procure for himself a berth in one of the vessels which were to sail at the approach of winter.

The wreck of the Ter Schilling was well known; and the circumstances attending it, with the exception of the appearance of the Phantom Ship, had been drawn up by Philip on his passage home, and communicated to the Court of Directors. Not only on account of the very creditable manner in which that report had been prepared, but in consideration of his peculiar sufferings and escape, he had been promised by the Company a berth, as second mate, on board of one of their vessels, should he be again inclined to sail to the East Indies.

Having called upon the Directors, he received his appointment to the Batavia, a fine vessel of about 400 tons burden. Having effected his purpose, Philip hastened back to Terneuse, and, in the presence of Mynheer Poots, informed Amine of what he had done.

"So you go to sea again?" observed Mynheer Poots.

"Yes, but not for two months, I expect," replied Philip.

"Ah!" replied Poots, "in two months!" and the old man muttered to himself.

How true it is that we can more easily bear up against a real evil than against suspense! Let it not be supposed that Amine fretted at the thought of her approaching separation from her husband; she lamented it, but feeling his departure to be an imperious duty, and having it ever in her mind, she bore up against her feelings, and submitted, without repining, to what could not be averted. There was, however, one circumstance, which caused her much uneasiness—that was the temper and conduct of her father. Amine, who knew his character well, perceived that he already secretly hated Philip, whom he regarded as an obstacle to his obtaining possession of the money in the house; for the old man was well aware that if Philip were dead, his daughter would care little who had possession of, or what became of it. The thought that Philip was about to take that money with him had almost turned the brain of the avaricious old man. He had been watched by Amine, and she had seen him walk for hours muttering to himself, and not, as usual, attending to his profession.

A few evenings after his return from Amsterdam, Philip, who had taken cold, complained of not being well.

"Not well!" cried the old man, starting up; "let me see—yes, your pulse is very quick. Amine, your poor husband is very ill. He must go to bed, and I will give him something which will do him good. I shall charge you nothing, Philip—nothing at all."

"I do not feel so very unwell, Mynheer Poots," replied Philip; "I have a bad headache certainly."

"Yes, and you have fever also, Philip, and prevention is better than cure; so go to bed, and take what I send you, and you will be well to-morrow."

Philip went up stairs, accompanied by Amine; and Mynheer Poots went into his own room to prepare the medicine. So soon as Philip was in bed, Amine went down stairs, and was met by her father, who put a powder into her hands to give to her husband, and then left the parlour.

"God forgive me if I wrong my father," thought Amine, "but I have my doubts. Philip is ill, more so than he will acknowledge; and if he does not take some remedies, he may be worse—but my heart misgives me—I have a foreboding. Yet surely he cannot be so diabolically wicked."

Amine examined the contents of the paper: it was a very small quantity of dark-brown powder, and, by the directions of Mynheer Poots, to be given in a tumbler of warm wine. Mynheer Poots had offered to heat the wine. His return from the kitchen broke Amine's meditations.

"Here is the wine, my child; now give him a whole tumbler of wine, and the powder, and let him be covered up warm, for the perspiration will soon burst out and it must not be checked. Watch him, Amine, and keep the clothes on, and he will be well to-morrow morning." And Mynheer Poots quitted the room, saying, "Good night, my child."

Amine poured out the powder into one of the silver mugs on the table, and then proceeded to mix it up with the wine. Her suspicions had, for the time been removed by the kind tone of her father's voice. To do him justice as a medical practitioner, he appeared always to be most careful of his patients. When Amine mixed the powder, she examined and perceived that there was no sediment, and the wine was as clear as before. This was unusual, and her suspicions revived.

"I like it not," said she; "I fear my father—God help me!—I hardly know what to do—I will not give it to Philip. The warm wine may produce perspiration sufficient."

Amine paused, and again reflected. She had mixed the powder with so small a portion of wine that it did not fill a quarter of the cup; she put it on one side, filled another up to the brim with the warm wine, and then went up to the bedroom.

On the landing-place she was met by her father, whom she supposed to have retired to rest.

"Take care you do not spill it, Amine. That is right, let him have a whole cupful. Stop, give it to me; I will take it to him myself."

Mynheer Poots took the cup from Amine's hands, and went into Philip's room.

"Here, my son, drink this off, and you will be well," said Mynheer Poots, whose hand trembled so that he spilt the wine on the coverlid. Amine, who watched her father, was more than ever pleased that she had not put the powder into the cup. Philip rose on his elbow, drank off the wine, and Mynheer Poots then wished him good night.

"Do not leave him, Amine, I will see all right," said Mynheer Poots, as he left the room. And Amine, who had intended to go down for the candle left in the parlour, remained with her husband, to whom she confided her feelings and also the fact that she had not given him the powder.

"I trust that you are mistaken, Amine," replied Philip; "indeed I feel sure that you must be. No man could be so bad as you suppose your father."

"You have not lived with him as I have—you have not seen what I have seen," replied Amine. "You know not what gold will tempt people to do in this world—but, however, I may be wrong. At all events, you must go to sleep, and I shall watch you, dearest. Pray do not speak—I feel I cannot sleep just now—I wish to read a little—I will lie down by-and-by."

Philip made no further objections, and was soon in a sound sleep, and Amine watched him in silence till midnight long had passed.

"He breathes heavily," thought Amine; "but had I given him that powder, who knows if he had ever awoke again? My father is so deeply skilled in the Eastern knowledge, that I fear him. Too often has he, I well know, for a purse well filled with gold, prepared the sleep of death. Another would shudder at the thought; but he, who has dealt out death at the will of his employers, would scruple little to do so even to the husband of his own daughter; and I have watched him in his moods and know his thoughts and wishes. What a foreboding of mishap has come over me this evening!—what a fear of evil! Philip is ill, 'tis true, but not so very ill. No! no! Besides his time is not yet come; he has his dreadful task to finish. I would it were morning. How soundly he sleeps!—and the dew is on his brow. I must cover him up warm, and watch that he remains so. Some one knocks at the entrance-door. Now will they wake him. 'Tis a summons for my father."

Amine left the room, and hastened down stairs. It was as she supposed, a summons for Mynheer Poots to a woman taken in labour. "He shall follow you directly," said Amine; "I will now call him up." Amine went up stairs to the room where her father slept, and knocked; hearing no answer, as usual, she knocked again.

"My father is not used to sleep in this way," thought Amine, when she found no answer to her second call. She opened the door and went in. To her surprise, her father was not in bed. "Strange," thought she; "but I do not recollect having heard his footsteps coming up after he went down to take away the lights." And Amine hastened to the parlour, where, stretched on the sofa, she discovered her father apparently fast asleep; but to her call he gave no answer. "Merciful Heaven! is he dead?" thought she, approaching the light to her father's face. Yes, it was so!—his eyes were fixed and glazed—his lower jaw had fallen.

For some minutes, Amine leant against the wall in a state of bewilderment; her brain whirled; at last she recovered herself.

"'Tis to be proved at once," thought she, as she went up to the table, and looked into the silver cup in which she had mixed the powder—it was empty! "The God of Righteousness hath punished him!" exclaimed Amine; "but O! that this man should have been my father! Yes! it is plain. Frightened at his own wicked, damned intentions, he poured out more wine from the flagon, to blunt his feelings of remorse, and not knowing that the powder was still in the cup, he filled it up and drank himself—the death he meant for another! For another!—and for whom? one wedded to his own daughter!—Philip! my husband! Wert thou not my father," continued Amine, looking at the dead body, "I would spit upon thee? and curse thee!—but thou art punished, and may God forgive thee! thou poor, weak, wicked creature!"

Amine then left the room and went up stairs, where she found Philip still fast asleep, and in a profuse perspiration.

Most women would have awakened their husbands, but Amine thought not of herself; Philip was ill, and Amine would not arouse him to agitate him. She sat down by the side of the bed, and with her hands pressed upon her forehead, and her elbows resting on her knees, she remained in deep thought until the sun had risen and poured his bright beams through the casement.

She was roused from her reflections by another summons at the door of the cottage. She hastened down to the entrance, but did not open the door.

"Mynheer Poots is required immediately," said the girl, who was the messenger.

"My good Therese," replied Amine, "my father has more need of assistance than the poor woman; for his travail in this world I fear, is well over. I found him very ill when I went to call him, and he has not been able to quit his bed. I must now entreat you to do my message, and desire Father Seysen to come hither; for my poor father is, I fear, in extremity."

"Mercy on me!" replied Therese. "Is it so? Fear not but I will do your bidding, Mistress Amine."

The second knocking had awakened Philip, who felt that he was much better, and his headache had left him. He perceived that Amine had not taken any rest that night, and he was about to expostulate with her, when she at once told him what had occurred.

"You must dress yourself, Philip," continued she, "and must assist me to carry up his body, and place it in his bed, before the arrival of the priest. God of mercy! had I given you that powder, my dearest Philip—but let us not talk about it. Be quick, for Father Seysen will be here soon."

Philip was soon dressed, and followed Amine down into the parlour. The sun shone bright, and its rays were darted upon the haggard face of the old man, whose fists were clenched, and his tongue fixed between the teeth on one side of his mouth.

"Alas! this room appears to be fatal. How many more scenes of horror are to pass within it?"

"None, I trust," replied Amine; "this is not, to my mind, the scene of horror. It was when that old man (now called away—and a victim to his own treachery) stood by your bed-side, and with every mark of interest and kindness, offered you the cup—*that* was the scene of horror," said Amine, shuddering—"one which long will haunt me."

"God forgive him! as I do," replied Philip, lifting up the body, and carrying it up the stairs to the room which had been occupied by Mynheer Poots.

"Let it at least be supposed that he died in his bed, and that his death was natural," said Amine. "My pride cannot bear that this should be known, or that I should be pointed at as the daughter of a murderer! O Philip!"

Amine sat down, and burst into tears.

Her husband was attempting to console her, when Father Seysen knocked at the door. Philip hastened down to open it.

"Good morning, my son. How is the sufferer?"

"He has ceased to suffer, father."

"Indeed!" replied the good priest, with sorrow in his countenance; "am I then too late? yet have I not tarried."

"He went off suddenly, father, in a convulsion," replied Philip, leading the way up stairs.

Father Seysen looked at the body and perceived that his offices were needless, and then turned to Amine, who had not yet checked her tears.

"Weep, my child, weep! for you have cause," said the priest. "The loss of a father's love must be a severe trial to a dutiful and affectionate child. But yield not too much to your grief, Amine; you have other duties, other ties, my child—you have your husband."

"I know it, father," replied Amine; "still must I weep, for I was *his* daughter."

"Did he not go to bed last night then that his clothes are still upon him? When did he first complain?"

"The last time that I saw him, father," replied Philip; "he came into my room and gave me some medicine, and then he wished me good night. Upon on a summons to attend a sick bed, my wife went to call him, and found him speechless."

"It has been sudden," replied the priest; "but he was an old man, and old men sink at once. Were you with him when he died?"

"I was not, sir," replied Philip; "before my wife had summoned me and I had dressed myself, he had left this world."

"I trust, my children, for a better." Amine shuddered. "Tell me Amine," continued the priest, "did he show signs of grace before he died? for you know full well that he has long been looked on as doubtful in his creed and little attentive to the rites of our holy church."

"There are times, holy father," replied Amine, "when even a sincere Christian can be excused, even if he give no sign. Look at his clenched hands, witness the agony of death on his face, and could you, in that state expect a sign?"

"Alas! 'tis but too true, my child: we must then hope for the best. Kneel with me, my children, and let us offer up a prayer for the soul of the departed."

Philip and Amine knelt with the priest, who prayed fervently; and as they rose, they exchanged a glance which fully revealed what was passing in the mind of each.

"I will send the people to do their offices for the dead, and prepare the body for interment," said Father Seysen; "but it were as well not to say that he was dead before I arrived, or to let it he supposed that he was called away without receiving the consolations of our holy creed."

Philip motioned his head in assent as he stood at the foot of the bed, and the priest departed. There had always been a strong feeling against Mynheer Poots in the village;—his neglect of all religious duties—the doubt whether he was even a member of the church—his avarice and extortion—had created for him a host of enemies; but, at the same time, his great medical skill, which was fully acknowledged, rendered him of importance. Had it been known that his creed (if he had any) was Mahomedan, and that he had died in attempting to poison his son-in-law, it is certain that Christian burial would have been refused him, and the finger of scorn would have been pointed at his daughter. But as Father Seysen, when questioned, said, in a mild voice, that "he had departed in peace," it was presumed that Mynheer Poots had died a good Christian although he had acted little up to the tenets of Christianity during his life. The next day the remains of the old man were consigned to the earth with the usual rites; and Philip and Amine were not a little relieved in their minds at everything having passed off so quietly.

It was not until after the funeral had taken place that Philip, in company with Amine, examined the chamber of his father-in-law. The key of the iron chest was found in his pocket; but Philip had not yet looked into this darling repository of the old man. The room was full of bottles and boxes of drugs, all of which were either thrown away, or, if the utility of them was known to Amine, removed to a spare room. His table contained many drawers, which were now examined, and among the heterogeneous contents were many writings in Arabic—probably prescriptions. Boxes and papers were also found, with Arabic characters written upon them; and in the box which they first took up was a powder similar to that which Mynheer Poots had given to Amine. There were many articles and writings, which made it appear that the old man had dabbled in the occult sciences, as they were practised at that period, and those they hastened to commit to the flames.

"Had all these been seen by Father Seysen!" observed Amine, mournfully. "But here are some printed papers, Philip!"

Philip examined them, and found that they were acknowledgments of shares in the Dutch East-India Company.

"No, Amine, these are money, or what is as good—these are eight shares in the Company's capital, which will yield us a handsome income every year. I had no idea that the old man made such use of his money. I had some intention of doing the same with a part of mine before I went away, instead of allowing it to remain idle."

The iron chest was now to be examined. When Philip first opened it; he imagined that it contained but little; for it was large and deep, and appeared to be almost empty; but when he put his hands down to the bottom, he pulled out thirty or forty small bags, the contents of which, instead of being silver guilders, were all coins of gold; there was only one large bag of silver money. But this was not all; several small boxes and packets were also discovered, which, when opened, were found to contain diamonds and other precious stones. When everything was collected, the treasure appeared to be of great value.

"Amine, my love, you have indeed brought me an unexpected dower," said Philip.

"You may well say *unexpected*," replied Amine. "These diamonds and jewels my father must have brought with him from Egypt. And yet how penuriously were we living until we came to this cottage! And with all this treasure he would have poisoned my Philip for more! God forgive him!"

Having counted the gold, which amounted to nearly fifty thousand guilders, the whole was replaced, and they left the room.

"I am a rich man," thought Philip, after Amine had left him; "but of what use are riches to me? I might purchase a ship and be my own captain, but would not the ship be lost? That certainly does not follow; but the chances are against the vessel; therefore I will have no ship. But is it right to sail in the vessels of others with this feeling?—I know not; this, however, I know, that I have a duty to perform, and that all our lives are in the hands of a kind Providence, which calls us away when it thinks fit. I will place most of my money in the shares of the Company, and if I sail in their vessels, and they come to misfortune by meeting with my poor father, at least I shall be a common sufferer with the rest. And now to make my Amine more comfortable."

Philip immediately made a great alteration in their style of living. Two female servants were hired: the rooms were more comfortably furnished; and in everything in which his wife's comfort and convenience were concerned, he spared no expense. He wrote to Amsterdam and purchased several shares in the Company's stock. The diamonds and his own money he still left in the hands of Amine. In making these arrangements the two months passed rapidly away; and everything was complete when Philip again received his summons, by letter, to desire that he would join his vessel. Amine would have wished Philip to go out as a passenger instead of going as an officer, but Philip preferred the latter, as otherwise he could give no reason for his voyage to India.

"I know not why," observed Philip, the evening before his departure, "but I do not feel as I did when I last went away; I have no foreboding of evil this time."

"Nor have I," replied Amine; "but I feel as if you would be long away from me, Philip; and is not that an evil to a fond and anxious wife?"

"Yes, love, it is; but—"

"O, yes, I know it is your duty, and you must go," replied Amine, burying her face in his bosom.

The next day Philip parted from his wife, who behaved with more fortitude than on their first separation. "*All* were lost but *he* was saved," thought Amine. "I feel that he will return to me. God of Heaven, Thy will be done!"

Philip soon arrived at Amsterdam; and having purchased many things which he thought might be advantageous to him in case of accident, to which he now looked forward as almost certain, he embarked on board the Batavia, which was lying at single anchor, and ready for sea.

Chapter Twelve.

Philip had not been long on board, ere he found that they were not likely to have a very comfortable passage; for the Batavia was chartered to convey a large detachment of troops to Ceylon and Java, for the purpose of recruiting and strengthening the Company's forces at those places. She was to quit the fleet off Madagascar, and run direct for the Island of Java; the number of soldiers on board being presumed sufficient to insure the ship against any attack or accidents from pirates or enemies' cruisers. The Batavia, moreover, mounted thirty guns, and had a crew of seventy-five men. Besides military stores, which formed the principal part of her cargo, she had on board a large quantity of specie for the Indian market. The detachment of soldiers was embarking when Philip went on board, and in a few minutes the decks were so crowded that it was hardly possible to move. Philip, who had not yet spoken to the captain, found out the first mate, and immediately entered upon his duty, with which, from his close application to it during his former voyage and passage home, he was much better acquainted than might have been imagined.

In a short time all traces of hurry and confusion began to disappear, the baggage of the troops was stowed away, and the soldiers having been told off in parties, and stationed with their messing utensils between the guns of the main deck, room was thus afforded for working the ship. Philip showed great activity as well as method in the arrangements proposed and the captain, during a pause in his own arduous duties, said to him—

"I thought you were taking it very easy, Mr Vanderdecken, in not joining the ship before, but, now you are on board, you are making up for lost time. You have done more during the forenoon than I could have expected. I am glad that you are come, though very sorry you were not here when we were stowing the hold, which, I am afraid, is not arranged quite so well as it might be. Mynheer Struys, the first mate, has had more to do than he could well give attention to."

"I am sorry that I should not have been here, sir," replied Philip; "but I came as soon as the Company sent me word."

"Yes, and as they know that you are a married man, and do not forget that you are a great shareholder, they would not trouble you too soon. I presume you will have the command of a vessel next voyage. In fact, you are certain of it, with the capital you have invested in their funds. I had a conversation with one of the senior accountants on the subject this very morning."

Philip was not very sorry that his money had been put out to such good interest, as to be the captain of a ship was what he earnestly desired. He replied, that "he certainly did hope to command a ship after the next voyage, when he trusted that he should feel himself quite competent to the charge."

"No doubt, no doubt, Mr Vanderdecken. I can see that clearly. You must be very fond of the sea."

"I am," replied Philip; "I doubt whether I shall ever give it up."

"*Never* give it up! You think so now. You are young, active, and full of hope; but you will tire of it by and bye, and be glad to lay by for the rest of your days."

"How many troops do we embark?" inquired Philip.

"Two hundred and forty-five rank and file, and six officers. Poor fellows! there are but few of them will ever return: nay, more than one-half will not see another birthday. It is a dreadful climate. I have landed three hundred men at that horrid hole, and in six months, even before I had sailed, there were not one hundred left alive."

"It is almost murder to send them there," observed Philip.

"Pshaw! they must die somewhere, and if they die a little sooner, what matter? Life is a commodity to be bought and sold like any other. We send out so much manufactured goods and so much money to barter for Indian commodities. We also send out so much life, and it gives a good return to the Company."

"But not to the poor soldiers, I am afraid."

"No; the Company buy it cheap and sell it dear," replied the captain, who walked forward.

True, thought Philip, they do purchase human life cheap, and make a rare profit of it, for without these poor fellows how could they hold their possessions in spite of native and foreign enemies? For what a paltry and cheap annuity do these men sell their lives? For what a miserable pittance do they dare all the horrors of a most deadly climate, without a chance, a hope of return to their native land, where they might haply repair their exhausted energies, and take a new lease of life! Good God! if these men may be thus heartlessly sacrificed to Mammon, why should I feel remorse if in the fulfilment of a sacred duty imposed on me by him who deals with us as He thinks meet, a few mortals perish? Not a sparrow fails to the ground without His knowledge, and it is for him to sacrifice or to save. I am but the creature of his will, and I but follow my duty,—but obey the commands of One whose ways are inscrutable. Still, if for my sake this ship be also doomed, I cannot but wish that I had been appointed to some other, in which the waste of human life might have been less.

It was not until a week after Philip arrived on board, that the Batavia and the remainder of the fleet were ready for sea.

It would be difficult to analyse the feelings of Philip Vanderdecken on this his second embarkation. His mind was so continually directed to the object of his voyage, that although he attended to his religious duty, yet the business of life passed before him as a dream. Assured of again meeting with the Phantom Ship, and almost equally assured that the meeting would be followed by some untoward event in all probability by the sacrifice of those who sailed with him, his thoughts preyed upon him, and wore him down to a shadow. He hardly ever spoke, except in the execution of his duty. He felt like a criminal; as one who, by embarking with them, had doomed all around him to death, disaster, and peril; and when *one* talked of his wife, and *another* of his children—when they would indulge in anticipations, and canvass happy projects, Philip would feel sick at heart, and would rise from the table and hasten to the solitude of the deck. At one time he would try to persuade himself that his senses had been worked upon in some moment of excitement, that he was the victim of an illusion; at another he would call to mind all the past—he would feel its terrible reality: and then the thought would suggest itself that with this supernatural vision Heaven had nothing to do; that it was but the work and jugglery of Satan. But then the relic—by such means the devil would not have worked. A few days after he had sailed, he bitterly repented that he had not stated the whole of his circumstances to Father Seysen, and taken his advice upon the propriety of following up his search; but it was now too late; already was the good ship Batavia more than a thousand miles from the port of Amsterdam, and his duty, whatever it might be, *must* be fulfilled.

As the fleet approached the Cape, his anxiety increased to such a degree that it was remarked by all who were on board. The captain and officers commanding the troops embarked, who all felt interested in him, vainly attempted to learn the cause of his anxiety. Philip would plead ill health; and his haggard countenance and sunken eyes silently proved that he was under acute suffering. The major part of the night he passed on deck, straining his eyes in every quarter, and watching each change in the horizon, in anticipation of the appearance of the Phantom Ship; and it was not till the day dawned that he sought a perturbed repose in his cabin. After a favourable passage, the fleet anchored to refresh at Table Bay, and Philip felt some small relief, that up to the present time the supernatural visitation had not again occurred.

As soon as the fleet had watered, they again made sail, and again did Philip's agitation become perceptible. With a favouring breeze, however, they rounded the Cape, passed by Madagascar, and arrived in the Indian Seas, when the Batavia parted company with the rest of the fleet, which steered to Cambroon and Ceylon. "And now," thought Philip, "will the Phantom Ship make her appearance? It has only waited till we should be left without a consort to assist us in distress." But the Batavia sailed in a smooth sea and under a cloudless sky, and nothing was seen. In a few weeks she arrived off Java, and previous to entering the splendid roads of Batavia, hove-to for the night. This was the last night they would be under sail, and Philip stirred not from the deck, but walked to and fro, anxiously waiting for the morning. The morning broke—the sun rose in splendour, and the Batavia steered into the roads. Before noon she was at anchor, and Philip, with his mind relieved, hastened down to his cabin, and took that repose which he so much required.

He awoke refreshed, for a great weight had been taken off his mind. "It does not follow, then," thought he, "that because I am on board the vessel that therefore the crew are doomed to perish; it does not follow that the Phantom Ship is to appear because I seek her. If so, I have no further weight upon my conscience. I seek her, it is true, and wish to meet with her; I stand, however, but the same chance as others; and it is no way certain, that, because I seek, I am sure to find. That she brings disaster upon all she meets, may be true, but not that I bring with me the disaster of meeting her. Heaven, I thank thee! Now can I prosecute my search without remorse."

Philip, restored to composure by these reflections, went on deck. The debarkation of the troops was already taking place, for they were as anxious to be relieved from their long confinement, as the seamen were to regain a little space and comfort. He surveyed the scene. The town of Batavia lay about one mile from them, low on the beach; from behind it rose a lofty chain of mountains, brilliant with verdure, and, here and there, peopled with country seats belonging to the residents, delightfully embosomed in forests of trees. The panorama was beautiful; the vegetation was luxuriant, and, from its vivid green, refreshing to the eye. Near to the town lay large and small vessels, a forest of masts; the water in the bay was of a bright blue, and rippled to a soft breeze; here and there small islets (like tufts of fresh verdure) broke the uniformity of the waterline; even the town itself was pleasing to the eye, the white colour of the houses being opposed to the dark foliage of the trees which grew in the gardens and lined the streets.

"Can it be possible," observed Philip to the captain of the Batavia, who stood by him, "that this beautiful spot can be so unhealthy? I should form a very different opinion from its appearance."

"Even," replied the captain, "as the venomous snakes of the country start up from among its flowers, so does Death stalk about in this beautiful and luxuriant landscape. Do you feel better, Mynheer Vanderdecken."

"Much better," replied Philip.

"Still, in your enfeebled state, I should recommend you to go on shore."

"I shall avail myself of your permission, with thanks. How long shall we stay here?"

"Not long, as we are ordered to run back. Our cargo is all ready for, us, and will be on board soon after we have discharged."

Philip took the advice of his captain; he had no difficulty in finding himself received by a hospitable merchant, who had a house at some distance from the town, and in a healthy situation. There he remained two months, during which he re-established his health, and then re-embarked a few days previous to the ship being ready for sea. The return voyage was fortunate, and in four months from the date of their quitting Batavia, they found themselves abreast of St. Helena; for vessels, at that period, generally made what is called the eastern passage, running down the coast of Africa, instead of keeping towards the American shores. Again they had passed the Cape without meeting with the Phantom Ship; and Philip was not only in excellent health, but in good spirits. As they lay becalmed, with the island in sight, they observed a boat pulling towards them, and in the course of three hours she arrived on board. The crew were much exhausted from having been two days in the boat, during which time they had never ceased pulling to gain the island. They stated themselves to be the crew of a small Dutch Indiaman, which had foundered, at sea two days before; she had started one of her planks, and filled so rapidly that the men had hardly time to save themselves. They consisted of the captain, mates, and twenty men belonging to the ship and an old Portuguese Catholic priest, who had been sent home by the Dutch governor, for having opposed the Dutch interests in the Island of Japan. He had lived with the natives, and been secreted by them for some time, as the Japanese government was equally desirous of capturing him with the intention of taking away his life. Eventually he found himself obliged to throw himself into the arms of the Dutch, as being the less cruel of his enemies.

The Dutch government decided that he should be sent away from the country; and he had, in consequence, been put on board of the Indiaman for a passage home. By the report of the captain and crew, one person only had been lost; but he was a person of consequence, having for many years held the situation of President in the Dutch factory in Japan. He was returning to Holland with the riches which he had amassed. By the evidence of the captain and crew, he had insisted, after he was put into the boat, upon going back to the ship to secure a casket of immense value, containing diamonds and other precious stones, which he had forgotten; they added, that while they were waiting for him the ship suddenly plunged her bowsprit under, and went down head foremost, and that it was with difficulty they had themselves escaped. They had waited for some time to ascertain if he would rise again to the surface, but he appeared no more.

"I knew that something would happen," observed the captain of the sunken vessel, after he had been sitting a short time in the cabin with Philip and the captain of the Batavia; "we saw the Fiend or Devil's Ship, as they call her, but three days before."

"What! the Flying Dutchman, as they name her?" asked Philip.

"Yes; that, I believe, is the name they give her," replied the captain. "I have often heard of her; but it never was my fate to fall in with her before, and I hope it never will be again, for I am a ruined man, and must begin the world afresh."

"I have heard of that vessel," observed the captain of the Batavia. "Pray, how did she appear to you?"

"Why, the fact is, I did not see anything but the loom of her hull," replied the other. "It was very strange; the night was fine, and the heavens clear; we were under top-gallant sails, for I do not carry on during the night, or else we might have put the royals on her; she would have carried them with the breeze. I had turned in, when about two o'clock in the morning, the mate called me to come on deck. I demanded what was the matter, and he replied he could hardly tell, but that the men were much frightened, and that there was a Ghost Ship, as the sailors termed it, in sight. I went on deck; all the horizon was clear, but on our quarter was a sort of fog, round as a ball, and not more than two cables' length from us. We were going about four knots and a half free, and yet we could not escape from this mist. 'Look there,' said the mate. 'Why, what the devil can it be?' said I, rubbing my eyes. 'No banks up to windward, and yet a fog in the middle of a clear sky, with a fresh breeze, and with water all around it;' for you see the fog did not cover more than half a dozen cables' length, as we could perceive by the horizon on each side of it. 'Hark, sir!' said the mate—'they are speaking again.' 'Speaking!' said I, and I listened; and from out this ball of fog I heard voices. At last, one cried out, 'Keep a sharp look out forward, d'ye hear?' 'Ay, ay, sir!' replied another voice. 'Ship on the starboard bow, sir.' 'Very well; strike the bell there forward.' And then we heard the bell toll. 'It must be a vessel,' said I to the mate. 'Not of this world, sir,' replied he. 'Hark!' 'A gun ready forward.' 'Ay, ay, sir!' was now heard out of the fog, which appeared to near us; 'all ready, sir.' 'Fire!' The report of the gun sounded in our ears like thunder, and then—"

"Well, and then?" said the captain of the Batavia, breathless.

"And then?" replied the other captain, solemnly, "the fog and all disappeared as if by magic, the whole horizon was clear and there was nothing to be seen."

"Is it possible?"

"There are twenty men on deck to tell the story," replied the captain, "and the old Catholic priest to boot, for he stood by me the whole time I was on deck. The men said that some accident would happen and in the morning watch, on sounding the well, we found four feet water. We took to the pumps, but it gained upon us, and we went down, as I have told you. The mate says that the vessel is well known—it is called the Flying Dutchman."

Philip made no remarks at the time, but he was much pleased at what he had heard. "If," thought he "the Phantom Ship of my poor father appears to others as well as to me, and they are sufferers, my being on board can make no difference. I do but take my chance of falling in with her, and do not risk the lives of those who sail in the same vessel with me. Now my mind is relieved, and I can prosecute my search with a quiet conscience."

The next day Philip took an opportunity of making the acquaintance of the Catholic priest, who spoke Dutch and other languages as well as he did Portuguese. He was a venerable old man, apparently about sixty years of age, with a white flowing beard, mild in his demeanour, and very pleasing in his conversation.

When Philip kept his watch that night, the old man walked with him, and it was then, after a long conversation, that Philip confided to him that he was of the Catholic persuasion.

"Indeed, my son, that is unusual in a Hollander."

"It is so," replied Philip; "nor is it known on board—not that I am ashamed of my religion, but I wish to avoid discussion."

"You are prudent, my son. Alas! if the reformed religion produces no better fruit than what I have witnessed in the East, it is little better than idolatry."

"Tell me, father," said Philip—"they talk of a miraculous vision—of a ship not manned by mortal men. Did you see it?"

"I saw what others saw," replied the priest; "and certainly, as far as my senses would enable me to judge, the appearance was most unusual—I may say supernatural; but I had heard of this Phantom Ship before, and moreover that its appearance was the precursor of disaster. So did it prove in our case, although, indeed, we had one on board, now no more, whose weight of guilt was more than sufficient to sink any vessel; one, the swallowing up of whom, with all that wealth from which he anticipated such enjoyment in his own country, has manifested that the

Almighty will, even in this world, sometimes wreak just and awful retribution on those who have merited His vengeance."

"You refer to the Dutch President, who went down with the ship when it sank."

"I do; but the tale of that man's crime is long; to-morrow night, I will walk with you, and narrate the whole. Peace be with you, my son, and good night."

The weather continued fine, and the Batavia hove-to in the evening, with the intention of anchoring the next morning in the roadstead of St. Helena. Philip, when he went on deck to keep the middle watch, found the old priest at the gangway waiting for him. In the ship all was quiet; the men slumbered between the guns, and Philip, with his new acquaintance, went aft, and seating themselves on a hencoop, the priest commenced as follows:—

"You are not, perhaps, aware that the Portuguese, although anxious to secure for themselves a country discovered by their enterprise and courage, and the possession of which, I fear, has cost them many crimes, have still never lost sight of one point dear to all good Catholics—that of spreading wide the true faith, and planting the banner of Christ in the regions of idolatry. Some of our countrymen having been wrecked on the coast, we were made acquainted with the islands of Japan; and seven years afterwards, our holy and blessed St. Francis, now with God, landed on the Island of Ximo, where he remained for two years and five months, during which he preached our religion and made many converts. He afterwards embarked for China, his original destination, but was not permitted to arrive there; he died on his passage, and thus closed his pure and holy life. After his death, notwithstanding the many obstacles thrown in our way by the priests of idolatry, and the persecutions with which they occasionally visited the members of our faith, the converts to our holy religion increased greatly in the Japanese islands. The religion spread fast, and many thousands worshipped the true God.

"After a time, the Dutch formed a settlement at Japan, and when they found that the Japanese Christians around the factories would deal only with the Portuguese, in whom they had confidence, they became our enemies; and the man of whom we have spoken, and who at that period was the head of the Dutch Factory, determined, in his lust for gold, to make the Christian religion a source of suspicion to the emperor of the country, and thus to ruin the Portuguese and their adherents. Such, my son, was the conduct of one who professed to have embraced the reformed religion as being of greater purity than our own.

"There was a Japanese lord of great wealth and influence, who lived near us, and who, with two of his sons, had embraced Christianity, and had been baptised. He had two other sons, who lived at the emperor's court. This lord had made us a present of a house for a college and school of instruction: on his death, however, his two sons at court, who were idolaters, insisted upon our quitting this property. We refused, and thus afforded the Dutch principal an opportunity of inflaming these young noblemen against us: by this means he persuaded the Japanese emperor that the Portuguese and Christians had formed a conspiracy against his life and throne for, be it observed, that when a Dutchman was asked if he was a Christian, he would reply, 'No; I am a Hollander.'

"The emperor, believing in this conspiracy, gave an immediate order for the extirpation of the Portuguese, and then of all the Japanese who had embraced the Christian faith: he raised an army for this purpose and gave the command of it to the young nobleman I have mentioned, the sons of the lord who had given us the college. The Christians, aware that resistance was their only chance, flew to arms, and chose as their generals the other two sons of the Japanese lord, who, with their father, had embraced Christianity. Thus were the two armies commanded by four brothers, two on the one side and two on the other.

"The Christian army amounted to more than 40,000 men, but of this the emperor was not aware, and he sent a force, of about 25,000 to conquer and exterminate them. The armies met, and after an obstinate combat (for the Japanese are very brave) the victory was on the part of the Christians, and, with the exception of a few who saved themselves in the boats, the army of the emperor was cut to pieces.

"This victory was the occasion of making more converts, and our army was soon increased to upwards of 50,000 men. On the other hand, the emperor, perceiving that his troops had been destroyed, ordered new levies and raised a force of 150,000 men, giving directions to his generals to give no quarter to the Christians, with the exception of the two young lords who commanded them, whom he wished to secure alive, that he might put them to death by slow torture. All offers of accommodation were refused, and the emperor took the field in person. The armies again met, and on the first day's battle the victory was on the part of the Christians; still they had to lament the loss of one of their generals, who was wounded and taken prisoner, and, no quarter having been given, their loss was severe.

"The second day's combat was fatal to the Christians. Their general was killed; they were overpowered by numbers, and fell to a man. The emperor then attacked the camp in the rear, and put to the sword every old man, woman, and child. On the field of battle, in the camp, and by subsequent torture, more than 60,000 Christians perished. But this was not all; a rigorous search for Christians was made throughout the Islands for many years; and they were, when found, put to death by the most cruel torture. It was not until fifteen years ago, that Christianity was entirely rooted out of the Japanese empire, and during a persecution of somewhat more than sixteen years, it is supposed that upwards of 400,000 Christians were destroyed; and all this slaughter, my son, was occasioned by the falsehood and avarice of that man who met his just punishment but a few days ago. The Dutch Company, pleased with his conduct, which procured for them such advantages, continued him for many years as the president of their factory in Japan. He was a young man when he first went there, but his hair was grey when he thought of returning to his own country. He had amassed immense wealth—immense, indeed, must it have been to have satisfied avarice such as his! All has now perished with him, and he has been summoned to his account. Reflect a little, my son. Is it not better to follow up our path of duty; to eschew the riches and pleasures of this world, and, at our summons hence, to feel that we have hopes of bliss hereafter?"

"Most true, holy father," replied Philip, musing.

"I have but a few years to live," continued the old man, "and God knows I shall quit this world without reluctance."

"And so could I," replied Philip.

"*You*, my son!—no. You are young, and should be full of hopes. You have still to do your duty in that station to which it shall please God to call you."

"I know that I have a duty to perform," replied Philip. "Father, the night air is too keen for one so aged as you. Retire to your bed, and leave me to my watch and my own thoughts."

"I will, my son; may Heaven guard you! Take an old man's blessing. Good night."

"Good night," replied Philip, glad to be alone. "Shall I confess all to him?" thought Philip. "I feel I could confess to him—but no. I would not to Father Seysen—why to him? I should put myself in his power, and he might order me—No, no! my secret is my own. I need no advisers." And Philip pulled out the relic from his bosom, and put it reverently to his lips.

The Batavia waited a few days at St. Helena, and then continued her voyage. In six weeks Philip again found himself at anchor in the Zuyder Zee, and having the captain's permission, he immediately set off for his own home, taking with him the old Portuguese priest, *Mathias*, with whom he had formed a great intimacy, and to whom he had offered his protection for the time he might wish to remain in the Low Countries.

Chapter Thirteen.

"Far be it from me to wish to annoy you, my son," said Father Mathias, as with difficulty he kept pace with the rapid strides of Philip, who was now within a quarter of a mile of his home; "but still, recollect that this is but a transitory world, and that much time has elapsed since you quitted this spot. For that reason, I would fain desire you, if possible, to check these bounding aspirations after happiness, these joyful anticipations in which you have indulged since we quitted the vessel. I hope and trust in the mercy of God, that all will be right, and that in a few minutes you will be in the arms of your much-loved wife; but still, in proportion as you allow your hopes to be raised, so will you inevitably have them crushed should disappointment cross your path. At Flushing we were told that there has been a dreadful visitation in this land, and death may not have spared even one so young and fair."

"Let us haste on father," replied Philip; "what you say is true, and suspense becomes most dreadful."

Philip increased his speed, leaving the old man to follow him: he arrived at the bridge with its wooden gate. It was then about seven o'clock in the morning, for they had crossed the Scheldt at the dawn of day.

Philip observed that the lower shutters were still closed.

"They might have been up and stirring before this," thought he, as he put his hand to the latch of the door. It was not fastened. Philip entered; there was a light burning in the kitchen; he pushed open the door, and beheld a maid-servant leaning back in her chair, in a profound sleep. Before he had time to go in and awaken her, he heard a voice at the top of the stairs, saying, "Marie, is that the doctor?"

Philip waited no longer; in three bounds he was on the landing-place above, and pushing by the person who had spoken, he opened the door of Amine's room.

A floating wick in a tumbler of oil gave but a faint and glimmering light; the curtains of the bed were drawn, and by the side of it was kneeling a figure which was well known to Philip—that of Father Seysen. Philip recoiled; the blood retreated to his heart; he could not speak: panting for breath, he supported himself against the wall, and at last vented his agony of feeling by a deep groan, which aroused the priest, who turned his head, and perceiving who it was, rose from his knees, and extended his hand in silence.

"She is dead, then!" at last exclaimed Philip.

"No! my son, not dead; there is yet hope. The crisis is at hand; in one more hour her fate will be decided: then, either will she be restored to your arms, or follow the many hundreds whom this fatal epidemic has consigned to the tomb."

Father Seysen then led Philip to the side of the bed, and withdrew the curtain. Amine lay insensible, but breathing heavily; her eyes were closed. Philip seized her burning hand, knelt down, pressed it to his lips, and burst into a paroxysm of tears. As soon as he had become somewhat composed, Father Seysen persuaded him to rise and sit with him by the side of the bed.

"This is a melancholy sight to witness at your return, Philip," said he; "and to you who are so ardent, so impetuous, it must be doubly so; but God's will be done. Remember, there is yet hope—not strong hope, I grant; but still, there is hope, for so told me the medical man who has attended her, and who will return, I expect, in a few minutes. Her disease is a typhus fever, which has swept off whole families within these last two months, and still rages violently; fortunate indeed, is the house which has to mourn but one victim. I would that you had not arrived just now, for it is a disease easily communicated. Many have fled from the country for security. To add to our misfortunes, we have suffered from the want of medical advice, for the physician and the patient have been swept away together."

The door was now slowly opened, and a tall, dark man, in a brown cloak, holding to his nose a sponge saturated with vinegar, entered the room. He bowed his head to Philip and the priest, and then went to the bedside. For a minute he held his fingers to the pulse of the sufferer, then laying down her arm, he put his hand to her forehead, and covered her up with the bedclothes. He handed to Philip the sponge and vinegar, making a sign that he should use it, and beckoned Father Seysen out of the room.

In a minute the priest returned. "I have received his directions, my son; he thinks that she may be saved. The clothes must be kept on her, and replaced if she should throw them off; but everything will depend upon quiet and calm after she recovers her senses."

"Surely, we can promise her that," replied Philip.

"It is not the knowledge of your return, or even the sight of you, which alarms me. Joy seldom kills, even when the shock is great, but there are other causes for uneasiness."

"What are they, holy Father?"

"Philip, it is now thirteen days that Amine has raved, and during that period I have seldom quitted her but to perform the duties of my office to others who required it. I have been afraid to leave her, Philip, for in her ravings she has told such a tale even unconnected as it has been, as has thrilled my soul with horror. It evidently has long lain heavily on her mind, and must retard her recovery. Philip Vanderdecken, you may remember that I would once have had the secret from you—the secret which forced your mother to her tomb, and which now may send your young wife to follow her, for it is evident that she knows all. Is it not true?"

"She does know all," replied Philip, mournfully.

"And she has in her delirium told all. Nay, I trust she has told more than all; but of that we will not speak now: watch her, Philip. I will return in half an hour, for by that time, the doctor tells me, the symptoms will decide whether she will return to reason, or be lost to you for ever."

Philip whispered to the priest that he had been accompanied by Father Mathias, who was to remain as his guest, and requested him to explain the circumstances of his present position to him, and see that he was attended to. Father Seysen then quitted the room, when Philip sat down by the bedside, and drew back the curtain.

Perhaps there is no situation in life so agonising to the feelings as that in which Philip was now placed. His joyful emotions, when expecting to embrace in health and beauty the object of his warmest affections, and of his continual thought during his long absence, suddenly checked by disappointment, anxiety and grief, at finding her lying emaciated, changed, corrupted with disease—her mind overthrown—her eyes unconscious of his presence—her existence hanging by a single hair—her frame prostrate before the king of terrors, who hovers over her with uplifted dart, and longs for the fiat which should permit him to pierce his unconscious victim.

"Alas!" thought Philip, "is it thus we meet, Amine? Truly did Father Mathias advise me, as I hurried so impetuously along, not (as I fondly thought) to happiness, but to misery. God of Heaven! be merciful, and forgive me. If I have loved this angelic creature of thy formation, even more than I have thee, spare her, good Heaven, spare her—or I am lost for ever."

Philip covered up his face, and remained for some time in prayer. He then bent over his Amine, and impressed a kiss upon her burning lips. They were burning hot; still there was moisture upon them, and Philip perceived that there was also moisture on her forehead. He felt her hand, and the palm of it was moist; and carefully covering her with the bedclothes, he watched her with anxiety and hope.

In a quarter of an hour he had the delight of perceiving that Amine was in a profuse perspiration; gradually her breathing became less heavy, and instead of the passive state in which she had remained, she moved, and became restless. Philip watched, and replaced the clothes as she threw them off, until she at last appeared to have fallen into a profound and sweet sleep. Shortly after, Father Seysen and the physician made their appearance. Philip stated, in few words, what had occurred. The doctor went to the bedside, and in half a minute returned.

"Your wife is spared to you, Mynheer, but it is not advisable that she should see you so unexpectedly; the shock may be too great in her weak state; she must be allowed to sleep as long as possible; on her waking she will have returned to reason. You must leave her then to Father Seysen."

"May I not remain in the room until she awakes? I will then hasten away unobserved."

"That will be useless; the disease is contagious, and you have been here too long already. Remain below; you must change your clothes, and see that they prepare a bed for her in another room, to which she must be transported as soon as you think she can bear it; and then let these windows be thrown open, that the room may be properly ventilated. It will not do to have a wife just rescued from the jaws of death run the risk of falling a sacrifice to the attentions necessary to a sick husband."

Philip perceived the prudence of this advice, and quitting the room with the medical man, he went and changed his clothes, and then joined Father Mathias, whom he found in the parlour below.

"You were right, Father," said Philip, throwing himself on the sofa.

"I am old and suspicious, you are young and buoyant, Philip; but I trust all may yet be well."

"I trust so too," replied Philip. He then remained silent and absorbed in thought, for now that the imminent danger was over, he was reflecting upon what Father Seysen had communicated to him, relative to Amine's having revealed the secret whilst in a state of mental aberration. The priest, perceiving that his mind was occupied, did not interrupt him. An hour had thus passed, when Father Seysen entered the room.

"Return thanks to Heaven, my son. Amine has awakened, and is perfectly sensible and collected. There is now little doubt of her recovery. She has taken the restorative ordered by the doctor though she was so anxious to repose once more, that she could hardly be persuaded to swallow it. She is now again fast asleep, and watched by one of the maidens, and in all probability will not move for many hours; but every moment of such sleep is precious, and she must not be disturbed. I will now see to some refreshment, which must be needful to us all. Philip, you have not introduced me to your companion, who, I perceive, is of my own calling."

"Forgive me, sir," replied Philip; "you will have great pleasure in making acquaintance with Father Mathias who has promised to reside with me, I trust, for some time. I will leave you together, and see to the breakfast being prepared; for the delay of which I trust Father Mathias will accept my apology."

Philip then left the room and went into the kitchen. Having ordered what was requisite to be taken into the parlour, he put on his hat and walked out of the house. He could not eat; his mind was in a state of confusion; the events of the morning had been too harassing and exciting, and he felt as if the fresh air was necessary to his existence.

As he proceeded, careless in which direction, he met many with whom he had been acquainted, and from whom he had received condolence at his supposed bereavement, and congratulations when they learnt from him that the danger was over; and from them he also learnt how fatal had been the pestilence.

Not one-third of the inhabitants of Terneuse and the surrounding country remained alive, and those who had recovered were in a state of exhaustion, which prevented them from returning to their accustomed occupations. They had combated disease, but remained the prey of misery and want; and Philip mentally vowed that he would appropriate all his savings to the relief of those around him. It was not until more than two hours had passed away that Philip returned to the cottage. On his arrival he found that Amine still slumbered, and the two priests were in conversation below.

"My son," said Father Seysen, "let us now have a little explanation. I have had a long conference with this good father, who hath much interested me with his account of the extension of our holy religion among the Pagans. He hath communicated to me much to rejoice at, and much to grieve for; but, among other questions put to him, I have (in consequence of what I have learnt during the mental alienation of your wife) interrogated him upon the point of a supernatural appearance of a vessel in the Eastern seas. You observe, Philip, that your secret is known to me, or I could not have put that question. To my surprise he hath stated a visitation of the kind to which he was eye-witness, and which cannot reasonably be accounted for, except by supernatural interposition. A strange and certainly most awful visitation! Philip, would it not be better (instead of leaving me in a maze of doubt) that you now confided to us both all the facts connected with this strange history, so that we may ponder on them, and give you the benefit of advice of those who are older than yourself, and who by their calling may be able to decide more correctly whether this supernatural power has been exercised by a good or evil intelligence?"

"The holy father speaks well, Philip Vanderdecken," observed Mathias.

"If it be the work of the Almighty, to whom should you confide, and by whom should you be guided, but by those who do his service on this earth? If of the evil one, to whom but to those whose duty and wish it is to counteract his baneful influence? And reflect, Philip, that this secret may sit heavily on the mind of your cherished wife, and may bow her to the grave, as it did your (I trust) sainted mother. With you, and supported by your presence, she may bear it well; but recollect how many are the lonely days and nights that she must pass during your absence, and how much she must require the consolation and help of others. A secret like this must be as a gnawing worm, and, strong as she may be in courage, must shorten her existence but for the support and the balm she may receive from the ministers of our faith. It was cruel and selfish of you, Philip, to leave her, a lone woman, to bear up against your absence, and at the same time oppressed with so fatal a knowledge."

"You have convinced me, holy father," replied Philip. "I feel that I should before this have made you acquainted with this strange history. I will now state the whole of the circumstances which have occurred, but with little hope your advice can help me in a case so difficult, and in a duty so peremptory, yet so perplexing."

Philip then entered into a minute detail of all that had passed, from the few days previous to his mother's death until the present time, and when he had concluded, he observed,—"You see father, that I have bound myself by a solemn vow—that that vow has been recorded and accepted, and it appears to me that I have nothing now to do but to follow my peculiar destiny."

"My son, you have told us strange and startling things—things not of this world—if you are not deceived. Leave us now. Father Mathias and I will consult upon this serious matter; and, when we are agreed, you shall know our decision."

Philip went upstairs to see Amine; she was still in a deep sleep. He dismissed the servant, and watched by the bedside. For nearly two hours did he remain there, when he was summoned down to meet the two priests.

"We have had a long conversation, my son," said Father Seysen, "upon this strange and perhaps supernatural occurrence. I say *perhaps*, for I would have rejected the frenzied communications of your mother as the imaginings of a heated brain; and for the same reason I should have been equally inclined to suppose that the high state of excitement that you were in at the time of her death may have disordered your intellect; but as Father Mathias positively asserts that a strange, if not supernatural, appearance of a vessel did take place, on his passage home, and which appearance tallies with and corroborates the legend—if so I may call it—to which you have given evidence, I say that it is not impossible but that it is supernatural."

"Recollect that the same appearance of the Phantom Ship has been permitted to me and to many others," replied Philip.

"Yes," replied Father Seysen; "but who is there alive of those who saw it but yourself? But that is of little importance. We will admit that the whole affair is not the work of man, but of a superior intelligence."

"Superior, indeed!" replied Philip. "It is the work of Heaven!"

"That is a point not so easily admitted; there is another power as well as that which is divine—that of the devil!—the arch-enemy of mankind! But as that power, inferior to the power of God, cannot act without his permission, we may indirectly admit that it is the will of Heaven that such sighs and portents should be allowed to be given on certain occasions."

"Then our opinions are the same, good Father."

"Nay, not exactly, my son. Elymas, the sorcerer, was permitted to practise his arts—gained from the devil—that it might be proved, by his overthrow and blindness, how inferior was his master to the Divine Ruler; but it does not therefore follow that sorcery generally was permitted. In this instance it may be true that the evil one has been permitted to exercise his power over the captain and crew of that ship, and, as a warning against such heavy offences, the supernatural appearance of the vessel may be permitted. So far we are justifiable in believing. But the great questions are, first, whether it be your father who is thus doomed? and, secondly, how far you are necessitated to follow up this mad pursuit, which, it appears to me—although it may end in your destruction—cannot possibly be the means of rescuing your father from his state of unhallowed abeyance? Do you understand me, Philip?"

"I certainly understand what you would say, Father; but—"

"Answer me not yet. It is the opinion of this holy Father as well as of myself, that, allowing the facts to be as you suppose, the revelations made to you are not from on high, but the suggestions of the devil to lead you into danger and ultimately to death; for if it were your task, as you suppose, why did not the vessel appear on this last voyage, and how can you (allowing that you met her fifty times) have communication with that, or with those which are but phantoms and shadows, things not of this world? Now, what we propose is, that you should spend a proportion of the money left by your father in masses for the repose of his soul, which your mother, in other circumstances, would certainly have done; and that, having so done, you should remain quietly on shore until some new sign should be given to you which may warrant our supposing that you are really chosen for this strange pursuit?"

"But my oath, Father—my recorded vow!"

"From that, my son, the holy Church hath power to absolve you; and that absolution you shall receive. You have put yourself into our hands, and by our decision you must be guided. If there be wrong, it is we, and not you, who are responsible; but, at present, let us say no more. I will now go up, and so soon as your wife awakens, prepare her for your meeting."

When Father Seysen had quitted the room, Father Mathias debated the matter with Philip. A long discussion ensued, in which similar arguments were made use of by the priest; and Philip, although not convinced, was at least doubtful and perplexed. He left the cottage.

"A new sign—a corroborative sign," thought Philip; "surely there have been signs and wonders enough. Still it may be true that masses for my father's soul may relieve him from his state of torture. At all events, if they decide for me I am not to blame. Well, then, let us wait for a new sign of the divine will—if so it must be;" and Philip walked on, occasionally thinking on the arguments of Father Seysen, and oftener thinking of Amine.

It was now evening, and the sun was fast descending. Philip wandered on, until at last he arrived at the very spot where he had knelt down and pronounced his solemn vow. He recognised it: he looked at the distant hills. The sun was just at the same height; the whole scene, the place, and the time were before him. Again Philip knelt down, took the relic from his bosom and kissed it. He watched the sun—he bowed himself to the earth. He waited for a sign, but the sun sank down, and the veil of night spread over the landscape. There was no sign; and Philip rose and walked home towards the cottage, more inclined than before to follow the suggestions of Father Seysen.

On his return, Philip went softly up stairs and entered the room of Amine, whom he found awake and in conversation with the priests. The curtain was closed, and he was not perceived. With a beating heart he remained near the wall at the head of the bed.

"Reason to believe that my husband has arrived!" said Amine, in a faint voice. "Oh tell me, why so?"

"His ship is arrived, we know; and one who had seen her said that all were well."

"And why is he not here, then? Who should bring the news of his return but himself? Father Seysen, either he has not arrived or he is here—I know he must be, if he is safe and well. I know my Philip too well. Say! is he not here? Fear not, if you say yes; but if you say no, you kill me!"

"He is here, Amine," replied Father Seysen—"here and well."

"O God! I thank you; but where is he? If he is here, he must be in this room, or else you deceive me. Oh, this suspense is death!"

"I am here," cried Philip, opening the curtains.

Amine rose with a shriek, held out her arms, and then fell senseless back. In a few seconds, however, she was restored, and proved the truth of the good Father's assertion, "that joy does not kill."

We must now pass over the few days during which Philip watched the couch of his Amine, who rapidly regained her strength. As soon as she was well enough to enter upon the subject, Philip narrated all that had passed since his departure; the confession which he had made to Father Seysen, and the result. Amine, too glad that Philip should remain with her, added her persuasions to those of the priests, and, for some little time, Philip talked no more of going to sea.

Chapter Fourteen.

Six weeks had flown away, and Amine, restored to health, wandered over the country, hanging on the arm of her adored Philip, or nestled by his side in their comfortable home. Father Mathias still remained their guest; the masses for the repose of the soul of Vanderdecken had been paid for, and more money had been confided to the care of Father Seysen to relieve the sufferings of the afflicted poor. It may be easily supposed that one of the chief topics of conversation between Philip and Amine, was the decision of the two priests, relative to the conduct of Philip. He had been absolved from his oath, but, at the same time that he submitted to his clerical advisers, he was by no means satisfied. His love for Amine, her wishes for his remaining at home, certainly added weight to the fiat of Father Seysen; but, although he in consequence obeyed it more willingly, his doubts of the propriety of his conduct remained the same. The arguments of Amine, who, now that she was supported by the opinion of the priests, had become opposed to Philip's departure; even her caresses, with which those arguments were mingled were effective but for the moment. No sooner was Philip left to himself no sooner was the question, for a time, dismissed, than he felt an inward accusation that he was neglecting a sacred duty. Amine perceived how often the cloud was upon his brow; she knew too well the cause, and constantly did she recommence her arguments and caresses, until Philip forgot that there was aught but Amine in the world.

One morning, as they were seated upon a green bank, picking the flowers that blossomed round them, and tossing them away in pure listlessness, Amine took the opportunity, that she had often waited for, to enter upon a subject hitherto unmentioned.

"Philip," said she, "do you believe in dreams? think you that we may have supernatural communications by such means?"

"Of course we may," replied Philip; "we have proof abundant of it in the holy writings."

"Why, then, do you not satisfy your scruples by a dream?"

"My dearest Amine, dreams come unbidden; we cannot command or prevent them."

"We can command them, Philip: say that you would dream upon the subject nearest to your heart, and you *shall*."

"I shall?"

"Yes! I have that power, Philip, although I have not spoken of it. I had it from my mother, with much more that of late I have never thought of. You know, Philip, I never say that which is not. I tell you, that, if you choose, you shall dream upon it."

"And to what good, Amine? If you have power to make me dream, that power must be from somewhere."

"It is, of course: there are agencies you little think of, which, in my country, are still called into use. I have a charm, Philip, which never fails."

"A charm, Amine! do you, then, deal in sorcery? for such powers cannot be from Heaven."

"I cannot tell. I only know the power is given."

"It must be from the devil, Amine."

"And why so, Philip? May I not use the argument of your own priests, who say, 'that the power of the devil is only permitted to be used by Divine intelligence, and that it cannot used without that permission?' Allow it then to be sorcery, or what you please, unless by Heaven permitted, it would fail. But I cannot see why we should suppose that it is from an evil source. We ask for a warning in a dream to guide our conduct in doubtful circumstances. Surely the evil one would rather lead us wrong than right!"

"Amine, we may be warned in a dream, as the patriarchs were of old; but to use mystic or unholy charms to procure a vision, is making a compact with the devil."

"Which compact the evil could not fulfil if not permitted by a higher power. Philip, your reasoning is false. We are told that, by certain means, duly observed, we may procure the dreams we wish. Our observance of these means is certainly the least we can attend to, to prove our sincerity. Forgive me, Philip, but are not observances as necessary in your religion—which I have embraced? Are we not told that the omission of the mere ceremony of water to the infant will turn all future chance of happiness to misery eternal."

Philip answered not for some time. "I am afraid, Amine," said he, at last, in a low tone; "I—"

"I fear nothing, Philip, when my intentions are good," replied Amine. "I follow certain means to obtain an end. What is that end? It is to find out (if possible) what may be the will of Heaven in this perplexing case. If it should be through the agency of the devil, what then? He becomes my servant, and not my master; he is permitted by Heaven to act against himself;" and Amine's eyes darted fire, as she thus boldly expressed herself.

"Did your mother often exercise her art?" inquired Philip, after a pause.

"Not to my knowledge; but it was said that she was most expert. She died young (as you know), or I should have known much more. Think you, Philip, that this world is solely peopled by such dross as we are?—things of clay—perishable and corruptible? Lords over beasts—and ourselves but little better. Have you not, from your own sacred writings, repeated acknowledgments and proofs of higher intelligences mixing up with mankind and acting here below? Why should what was then, not be now! and what more harm is there to apply for their aid now, than a few thousand years ago? Why should you suppose that they were permitted on the earth then—and not permitted now? What has become of them? Have they perished? have they been ordered back—to where—to heaven? If to heaven—the world and mankind have been left to the mercy of the devil and his agents. Do you suppose that we, poor mortals, have been thus abandoned? I tell you plainly, I think not. We no longer have the communications with those intelligences that we once had, because, as we become more enlightened, we become more proud, and seek them not: but that they still exist—a host of good against a host of evil, invisibly opposing each other—is my conviction. But, tell me, Philip, do you in your conscience believe that all that has been revealed to you is a mere dream of the imagination?"

"I do not believe so, Amine: you know well I wish I could."

"Then is my reasoning proved; for if such communications can be made to you, why cannot others? You cannot tell by what agency; your priests say it is that of the evil one; you think it is from on high. By the same rule who is to decide from whence the dream shall come?"

"'Tis true, Amine, but are you certain of your power?"

"Certain of this; but if it pleases superior intelligence to communicate with you, *that* communication may be relied upon. Either you will not dream, but pass away the hours in deep sleep, or what you dream will be connected with the question at issue."

"Then, Amine, I have made my mind up—I will dream: for at present my mind is racked by contending and perplexing doubts. I would know whether I am right or wrong. This night your art shall be employed."

"Not this night, nor yet to-morrow night, Philip. Think you one moment that, in proposing this, I serve you against my own wishes? I feel as if the dream will decide against me, and that you will be commanded to return to your duty; for I tell you honestly, I think not with the priests; but I am your wife, Philip, and it is my duty that you should not be deceived. Having the means, as I suppose, to decide your conduct, I offer them. Promise me that, if I do this, you will grant me a favour which I shall ask as my reward."

"It is promised, Amine, without its being known," replied Philip, rising from the turf; "and now let us go home."

We observed that Philip, previous to his sailing in the Batavia, had invested a large proportion of his funds in Dutch East India stock: the interest of the money was more than sufficient for the wants of Amine, and, on his return, he found that the funds left in her charge had accumulated. After paying to Father Seysen the sums for the masses, and for the relief of the poor, there was a considerable residue, and Philip had employed this in the purchase of more shares in the India Stock.

The subject of their conversation was not renewed. Philip was rather averse to Amine practising those mystical arts, which, if known to the priests, would have obtained for her in all probability the anathema of the Church. He could not but admire the boldness and power of Amine's reasonings, but still he was averse to reduce them into practice. The third day had passed away, and no more had been said upon the subject. Philip retired to bed, and was soon fast asleep; but Amine slept not. So soon as she was convinced that Philip would not be awakened, she slipped from the bed and dressed herself. She left the room, and in a quarter of an hour returned, bringing in her hand a small brazier of lighted charcoal, and two small pieces of parchment, rolled up and fixed by a knot to the centre of a narrow fillet. They exactly resembled the philacteries that were once worn by the Jewish nation, and were similarly applied. One of them she gently bound upon the forehead of her husband, and the other upon his left arm. She threw perfumes into the brazier, and as the form of her husband was becoming indistinct, from the smoke which filled the room, she muttered a few sentences, waved over him a small sprig of some shrub which she held in her white hand, and then closing the curtains and removing the brazier, she sat down by the side of the bed.

"If there be harm," thought Amine, "at least the deed is not his—'tis mine; they cannot say that he has practised arts that are unlawful and forbidden by his priests. On my head be it!" And there was a contemptuous curl on Amine's beautiful arched lip, which did not say much for her devotion to her new creed.

Morning dawned, and Philip still slumbered. "'Tis enough," said Amine, who had been watching the rising of the sun, as she beheld his upper limb a pear above the horizon. Again she waved her arm over Philip, holding the sprig in her hand, and cried, "Philip, awake!"

Philip started up, opened his eyes, and shut them again to avoid the glare of the broad daylight, rested upon his elbow, and appeared to be collecting his thoughts.

"Where am I?" exclaimed he. "In my own bed? Yes!" He passed his hand across his forehead, and felt the scroll.

"What is this," continued he, pulling it off and examining it. "And Amine, where is she? Good Heavens, what a dream! Another?" cried he, perceiving the scroll tied to his arm. "I see it now. Amine, this is your doing." And Philip threw himself down, and buried his face in the pillow.

Amine, in the mean time, had slipped into bed, and had taken her place by Philip's side. "Sleep, Philip, dear: sleep!" said she, putting her arms round him; "we will talk when we wake again."

"Are you there, Amine?" replied Philip, confused. "I thought I was alone; I have dreamed." And Philip again was fast asleep before he could complete his sentence. Amine, too, tired with watching, slumbered, and was happy.

Father Mathias had to wait a long while for his breakfast that morning; it was not till two hours later than usual that Philip and Amine made their appearance.

"Welcome my children," said he; "you are late."

"We are, Father," replied Amine; "for Philip slept, and I watched till break of day."

"He hath not been ill, I trust," replied the priest.

"No not ill; but I could not sleep," replied Amine.

"Then didst thou do well to pass the night—as I doubt not thou hast done, my child, in holy watchings."

Philip shuddered; he knew that the watching, had its cause been known, would have been, in the priest's opinion, anything but holy. Amine quickly replied—

"I have, indeed, communed with higher powers, as far as my poor intellect hath been able."

"The blessing of our holy Church upon thee, my child!" said the old man, putting his hand upon her head; "and on thee, too, Philip."

Philip, confused, sat down to the table; Amine was collected as ever. She spoke little, it is true, and appeared to commune with her own thoughts.

As soon as the repast was finished, the old priest took up his breviary, and Amine beckoning to Philip, they went out together. They walked in silence until they arrived at the green spot where Amine had first proposed to him that she should use her mystic power. She sat sown, an Philip, fully aware of her purpose, took his seat by her in silence.

"Philip," said Amine, taking his hand, and looking earnestly in his face, "last night you dreamed."

"I did indeed, Amine," replied Philip, gravely.

"Tell me your dream, for it will be for me to expound it."

"I fear it needs but little exposition, Amine. All I would know is, from what intelligence the dream has been received?"

"Tell me your dream," replied Amine, calmly.

"I thought," replied Philip, mournfully, "that I was sailing as captain of a vessel round the Cape; the sea was calm and the breeze light; I was abaft; the sun went down, and the stars were more than usually brilliant; the weather was warm, and I lay down on my cloak, with my face to the heavens, watching the gems twinkling in the sky and the occasionally falling meteors. I thought that I fell asleep, and awoke with a sensation as if sinking down. I looked around me; the masts; the rigging, the hull of the vessel—*all* had disappeared, and I was floating by myself upon a large, beautifully-shaped shell on the wide waste of waters. I was alarmed, and afraid to move, lest I should overturn my frail bark and perish. At last I perceived the fore-part of the shell pressed down, as if a weight were hanging to it; and soon afterwards, a small white hand, which grasped it. I remained motionless, and would have called out that my little bark would sink, but I could not. Gradually a figure raised itself from the waters and leaned with both arms over the fore-part of the shell, where I first had seen but the hand. It was a female, in form beautiful to excess; the skin was white as driven snow; her long loose hair covered her, and the ends floated in the water; her arms were rounded and like ivory; she said, in a soft sweet voice—

"'Philip Vanderdecken, what do you fear? Have you not a charmed life?'

"'I know not,' replied I, 'whether my life be charmed or not; but this I know, that it is in danger.'

"'In danger!' replied she; 'it might have been in danger when you were trusting to the frail works of men, which the waves love to rend to fragments—your *good* ships, as you call them, which but float about upon sufferance; but where can be the danger when in a mermaid's shell, which the mountain wave respects, and upon which the cresting surge dare not throw its spray? Philip Vanderdecken, you have come to seek your father!'

"'I have,' replied I; 'is it not the will of Heaven?'

"'It is your destiny—and destiny rules all above and below. Shall we seek him together? This shell is mine; you know not how to navigate it; shall I assist you?'

"'Will it bear us both?'

"'You will see,' replied she, laughing, as she sank down from the fore-part of the shell, and immediately afterwards appeared at the side, which was not more than three inches above the water. To my alarm, she raised herself up, and sat upon the edge, but her weight appeared to have no effect. As soon as she was seated in this way—for her feet still remained in the water—the shell moved rapidly along, and each moment increased its speed, with no other propelling power than that of her volition.

"'Do you fear now, Philip Vanderdecken?'

"'No!' replied I.

"She passed her hands across her forehead, threw aside the tresses which had partly concealed her face, and said—'Then look at me.'

"I looked, Amine, and I beheld you!"

"Me!" observed Amine, with a smile upon her lips.

"Yes, Amine, it was you. I called you by your name, and threw my arms round you. I felt that I could remain with you, and sail about the world for ever."

"Proceed, Philip," said Amine, calmly.

"I thought we ran thousands and thousands of miles—we passed by beautiful islands, set like gems on the ocean-bed; at one time bounding against the rippling current, at others close to the shore—skimming on the murmuring wave which rippled on the sand, whilst the cocoa-tree on the beach waved to the cooling breeze.

"'It is not in smooth seas that your father must be sought,' said she; 'we must try elsewhere.'

"By degrees the waves rose, until at last they were raging in their fury, and the shell was tossed by the tumultuous waters; but still not a drop entered, and we sailed in security over billows which would have swallowed up the proudest vessel.

"'Do you fear now, Philip?' said you to me.

"'No' replied I; 'with you, Amine, I fear nothing.'

"'We are now off the Cape again,' said she; 'and here you may find your father. Let us look well round us, for if we meet a ship it must be *his*. None but the Phantom Ship could swim in a gale like this.'

"Away we flew over the mountainous waves—skimming from crest to crest between them, our little bark sometimes wholly out of the water; now east, now west, north, south, in every quarter of the compass, changing our course each minute. We passed over hundreds of miles: at last we saw a vessel tossed by the furious gale.

"'There,' cried she, pointing with her finger, 'there is your father's vessel, Philip.'

"Rapidly did we approach—they saw us from on board, and brought the vessel to the wind. We were alongside—the gangway was clearing away—for though no boat could have boarded, our shell was safe. I looked up. I saw my father, Amine! Yes, saw him, and heard him as he gave his orders. I pulled the relic from my bosom, and held it out to him. He smiled as he stood on the gunnel, holding on by the main shrouds. I was just rising to mount on board, for they had handed to me the man-ropes, when there was a loud yell, and a man jumped from the gangway into the shell. You shrieked, slipped from the side and disappeared under the wave, and in a moment the shell, guided by the man who had taken your place, flew away from the vessel with the rapidity of thought. I felt a deadly chill pervade my frame. I turned round to look at my new companion—it was the pilot Schriften!—the one-eyed wretch who was drowned when we were wrecked in Table Bay!

"'No! no! not yet!' cried he.

"In an agony of despair and rage, I hurled him off his seat on the shell, and he floated on the wild waters.

"'Philip Vanderdecken,' said he, as he swam, 'we shall meet again!'

"I turned away my head in disgust, when a wave filled my bark, and down it sank. I was struggling under the water sinking still deeper and deeper, but without pain, when I awoke."

"Now, Amine," said Philip, after a pause, "what think you I of my dream?"

"Does it not point out that I am your friend, Philip, and that the pilot Schriften is your enemy?"

"I grant it; but he is dead."

"Is that so certain?"

"He hardly could have escaped without my knowledge."

"That is true, but the dream would imply otherwise. Philip, it is my opinion that the only way in which this dream is to be expounded is—that you remain on shore for the present. The advice is that of the priests. In either case you require some further intimation. In your dream *I* was your safe guide—be guided now by me again."

"Be it so, Amine. If your strange art be in opposition to our holy faith, you expound the dream in conformity with the advice of its ministers."

"I do. And now, Philip, let us dismiss the subject from our thoughts. Should the time come, your Amine will not persuade you from your duty; but recollect, you have promised to grant *one* favour when I ask it."

"I have: say, then, Amine what may be your wish?"

"O! nothing at present. I have no wish on earth but what is gratified. Have I not you, dear Philip?" replied Amine, fondly throwing herself on her husband's shoulder.

Chapter Fifteen.

It was about three months after this conversation that Amine and Philip were again seated upon the mossy bank which we have mentioned, and which had become their favourite resort. Father Mathias had contracted a great intimacy with Father Seysen, and the two priests were almost as inseparable as were Philip and Amine. Having determined to wait a summons previous to Philip's again entering upon his strange and fearful task; and, happy in the possession of each other, the subject was seldom revived. Philip, who had, on his return, expressed his wish to the Directors of the Company for immediate employment, and, if possible, to have the command of a vessel, had, since that period, taken no further steps, nor had had any communication with Amsterdam.

"I am fond of this bank, Philip," said Amine; "I appear to have formed an intimacy with it. It was here, if you recollect, that we debated the subject of the lawfulness of inducing dreams; and it was here, dear Philip, that you told me your dream, and that I expounded it."

"You did so, Amine; but if you ask the opinion of Father Seysen, you will find that he would give rather a strong decision against you—he would call it heretical and damnable."

"Let him, if he pleases. I have no objection to tell him."

"I pray not, Amine; let the secret remain with ourselves only."

"Think you Father Mathias would blame me?"

"I certainly do."

"Well, I do not; there is a kindness and liberality about the old man that I admire. I should like to argue the question with him."

As Amine spoke, Philip felt something touch his shoulder, and a sudden chill ran through his frame. In a moment his ideas reverted to the probable cause: he turned round his head, and, to his amazement, beheld the (supposed to be drowned) mate of the Ter Schilling, the one-eyed Schriften, who stood behind him with a letter in his hand. The sudden appearance of this malignant wretch induced Philip to exclaim, "Merciful Heaven! is it possible?"

Amine, who had turned her head round at the exclamation of Philip, covered up her face, and burst into tears. It was not I fear that caused this unusual emotion on her part, but the conviction that her husband was never to be at rest but in the grave.

"Philip Vanderdecken," said Schriften, "he! he! I've a letter for you—it is from the Company."

Philip took the letter, but, previous to opening it, he fixed his eyes upon Schriften. "I thought," said he, "that you were drowned when the ship was wrecked in False Bay. How did you escape?"

"How did I escape?" replied Schriften. "Allow me to ask, how did you escape?"

"I was thrown up by the waves," replied Philip; "but—"

"But," interrupted Schriften, "he! he! the waves ought *not* to have thrown me up."

"And why not, pray? I did not say that."

"No! but I presume you wish it had been so; but, on the contrary, I escaped in the same way that you did—I was thrown up by the waves—he! he! but I can't wait here. I have done my bidding."

"Stop," replied Philip; "answer me one question. Do you sail in the same vessel with me this time?"

"I'd rather be excused," replied Schriften; "I am not looking for the Phantom Ship, Mynheer Vanderdecken;" and, with this reply, the little man turned round, and went away at a rapid pace.

"Is not this a summons, Amine?" said Philip, after a pause, still holding the letter in his hand, with the seal unbroken.

"I will not deny it, dearest Philip. It is most surely so; the hateful messenger appears to have risen from the grave that he might deliver it. Forgive me, Philip; but I was taken by surprise. I will not again annoy you with a woman's weakness."

"My poor Amine," replied Philip, mournfully. "Alas! why did I not perform my pilgrimage alone? It was selfish of me to link you with so much wretchedness, and join you with me in bearing the fardel of never-ending anxiety and suspense."

"And who should bear it with you, my dearest Philip, if it is not the wife of your bosom? You little know my heart if you think I shrink from the duty. No, Philip, it is a pleasure, even in its most acute pangs; for I consider that I am, by partaking with, relieving you of a portion of your sorrow, and I am proud that I am the wife of one who has been selected to be so peculiarly tried. But, dearest, no more of this. You must read the letter."

Philip did not answer. He broke the seal, and found that the letter intimated to him that he was appointed as first mate to the Vrow Katerina, a vessel which sailed with the next fleet; and requesting he would join as quickly as possible, as she would soon be ready to receive her cargo. The letter, which was from the secretary, further informed him that, after this voyage, he might be certain of having the command of a vessel as captain, upon conditions which would be explained when he called upon the Board.

"I thought, Philip, that you had requested the command of a vessel for this voyage," observed Amine, mournfully.

"I did," replied Philip; "but not having followed up my application, it appears not to have been attended to. It has been my own fault."

"And now it is too late."

"Yes, dearest, most assuredly so: but it matters not; I would as willingly, perhaps rather, sail this voyage as first mate."

"Philip, I may as well speak now. That I am disappointed, I must confess; I fully expected that you would have had the command of a vessel, and you may remember that I exacted a promise from you on this very bank upon which we now sit, at the time that you told me your dream. That promise I shall still exact, and I now tell you what I had intended to ask. It was, my dear Philip, permission to sail with you. With you, I care for nothing. I can be happy under every privation or danger; but to be left alone for so long, brooding over my painful thoughts, devoured by suspense, impatient, restless, and incapable of applying to any one thing—that, dear Philip, is the height of misery, and that is what I feel when you are absent. Recollect, I have your promise, Philip. As captain, you have the means of receiving your wife on board. I am bitterly disappointed in being left this time; do, therefore, to a certain degree, console me by promising that I shall sail with you next voyage, if Heaven permit your return."

"I promise it, Amine, since you are so earnest. I can refuse you nothing; but I have a foreboding that yours and my happiness will be wrecked for ever. I am not a visionary, but it does appear to me that, strangely mixed up as I am, at once with this world and the next, some little portion of futurity is opened to me. I have given my promise, Amine, but from it I would fain be released."

"And if ill *do* come, Philip, it is our destiny. Who can avert fate?"

"Amine, we are free agents, and to a certain extent are permitted to direct our own destinies."

"Ay, so would Father Seysen fain have made me believe; but what he said in support of his assertion was to me incomprehensible. And yet he said that it was a part of the Catholic faith. It may be so—I am unable to understand many other points. I wish your faith were made more simple. As yet the good man—for good he really is—has only led me into doubt."

"Passing through doubt, you will arrive at conviction, Amine."

"Perhaps so," replied Amine; "but it appears to me that I am as yet but on the outset of my journey. But come, Philip; let us return. You must to Amsterdam, and I will go with you. After your labours of the day, at least until you sail, your Amine's smiles must still enliven you. Is it not so?"

"Yes, dearest, I would have proposed it. I wonder much how Schriften could come here. I did not see his body it is certain, but his escape is to me miraculous. Why did he not appear when saved? where could he have been? What think you, Amine?"

"What I have long thought, Philip. He is a Ghoul with evil eye, permitted for some cause to walk the earth in human form; and is certainly, in some way, connected with your strange destiny. If it requires anything to convince me of the truth of all that has passed, it is his appearance—the wretched Afrit! Oh, that I had my mother's powers!—but I forget, it displeases you, Philip, that I ever talk of such things, and I am silent."

Philip replied not; and, absorbed in their own meditations, they walked back in silence to the cottage. Although Philip had made up his own mind, he immediately sent the Portuguese priest to summon Father Seysen, that he might communicate with them and take their opinion as to the summons he had received. Having entered into a fresh detail of the supposed death of Schriften, and his reappearance as a messenger, he then left the two priests to consult together, and went upstairs to Amine. It was more than two hours before Philip was called down, and Father Seysen appeared to be in a state of great perplexity.

"My son," said he, "we are much perplexed. We had hoped that our ideas upon this strange communication were correct, and that, allowing all that you have obtained from your mother and have seen yourself to have been no deception, still that it was the work of the evil one, and, if so, our prayers and masses would have destroyed this power. We advised you to wait another summons, and you have received it. The letter itself is of course nothing, but the reappearance of the bearer of the letter is the question to be considered. Tell me, Philip, what is your opinion on this point? It is possible he might have been saved—why not as well as yourself?"

"I acknowledge the possibility, Father," replied Philip; "he may have been cast on shore and have wandered in another direction. It is possible, although anything but probable; but since you ask me my opinion, I must say candidly that I consider he is no earthly messenger—nay, I am sure of it. That he is mysteriously connected with my destiny is certain. But who he is, and what he is, of course I cannot tell."

"Then, my son, we have come to the determination, in this instance not to advise. You must act now upon your own responsibility and your own judgment. In what way soever you may decide, we shall not blame you. Our prayers shall be, that Heaven may still have you in its holy keeping."

"My decision, holy Father is to obey the summons."

"Be it so, my son; something may occur which may assist to work out the mystery,—a mystery which I acknowledge to be beyond my comprehension, and of too painful a nature for me to dwell upon."

Philip said no more, for he perceived that the priest was not at all inclined to converse. Father Mathias took this opportunity of thanking Philip for his hospitality and kindness, and stated his intention of returning to Lisbon by the first opportunity that might offer.

In a few days Amine and Philip took leave of the priests and quitted for Amsterdam—Father Seysen taking charge of the cottage until Amine's return. On his arrival, Philip called upon, the Directors of the Company, who promised him a ship on his return from the voyage he was about to enter upon, making a condition that he should become part owner of the vessel. To this Philip consented, and then went down to visit the Vrow Katerina, the ship to which he had been appointed as first mate. She was still unrigged, and the fleet was not expected to sail for two months. Only part of the crew were on board, and the captain, who lived in Dort, had not yet arrived.

So far as Philip could judge, the Vrow Katerina was a very inferior vessel; she was larger than many of the others, but old, and badly constructed; nevertheless, as she had been several voyages to the Indies, and had returned in safety, it was to be presumed that she could not have been taken up by the Company if they had not been satisfied as to her seaworthiness. Having given a few directions to the men who were on board, Philip returned to the hostelrie where he had secured apartments for himself and Amine.

The next day, as Philip was superintending the fitting of the rigging, the captain of the Vrow Katerina arrived, and stepping on board of her by the plank which communicated with the quay, the first thing that he did was to run to the mainmast and embrace it with both arms, although there was no small portion of tallow on it to smear the cloth of his coat. "Oh! my dear Vrow, my Katerina!" cried he, as if he were speaking to a female. "How do you do? I'm glad to see you again—you have been quite well, I hope? You do not like being laid up in this way. Never mind, my dear creature! you shall soon be handsome again."

The name of this personage who thus made love to his vessel was Wilhelm Barentz. He was a young man, apparently not thirty years of age, of diminutive stature and delicate proportions. His face was handsome, but womanish. His movements were rapid and restless, and there was that appearance in his eye which would have warranted the supposition that he was a little flighty, even if his conduct had not fully proved the fact.

No sooner were the ecstasies of the captain over, than Philip introduced himself to him, and informed him of his appointment. "Oh! you are the first mate of the Vrow Katerina Sir, you are a very fortunate man. Next to being captain of her, first mate is the most enviable situation in the world."

"Certainly not on account of her beauty," observed Philip; "she may have many other good qualities."

"Not on account of her beauty! Why, sir, I say (as my father has said before me, and it was his Vrow before it was mine) that she is the handsomest vessel in the world. At present you cannot judge; and besides being the handsomest vessel, she has every good quality under the sun."

"I am glad to hear it, sir," replied Philip; "it proves that one should never judge by appearances. But is she not very old?"

"Old! not more than twenty-eight years—just in her prime. Stop, my dear sir, till you see her dancing on the waters, and then you will do nothing all day but discourse with me upon her excellence, and I have no doubt that we shall have a very happy time together."

"Provided the subject be not exhausted," replied Philip.

"That it never will be on my part: and allow me to observe, Mr Vanderdecken, that any officer who finds fault with the Vrow Katerina quarrels with me. I am her knight, and I have already fought three men in her defence,—I trust I shall not have to fight a fourth."

Philip smiled: he thought that she was not worth fighting for; but he acted upon the suggestion, and, from that time forward, he never ventured to express an opinion against the beautiful Vrow Katerina.

The crew were soon complete, the vessel rigged, her sails bent, and she was anchored in the stream, surrounded by the other ships composing the fleet about to be despatched. The cargo was then received on board, and, as soon as her hold was full, there came, to Philip's great vexation, an order to receive on board 150 soldiers and other passengers, many of whom were accompanied by their wives and families. Philip worked hard, for the captain did nothing but praise the vessel, and at last they had embarked everything, and the fleet was ready to sail.

It was now time to part with Amine, who had remained at the hostelrie, and to whom Philip had dedicated every spare moment that he could obtain. The fleet was expected to sail in two days, and it was decided that on the morrow they should part. Amine was cool and collected. She felt convinced that she should see her husband again, and with that feeling she embraced him as they separated on the beach, and he stepped into the boat in which he was to be pulled on board.

"Yes," thought Amine, as she watched the form of her husband, as the distance between them increased—"yes, I know that we shall meet again. It is not this voyage which is to be fatal to you or me; but I have a dark foreboding that the next, in which I shall join you, will separate us for ever—in which way I know not—but it is destined. The priests talk of free will. Is it free-will which takes him away from me? Would he not rather remain on shore with me? Yes. But he is not permitted, for he must fulfil his destiny. Free-will? Why, if it were not destiny it were tyranny. I feel, and have felt, as if these priests are my enemies; but why I know not: they are both good men, and the creed they teach is good. Goodwill and charity love to all, forgiveness of injuries, not judging others. All this is good; and yet my heart whispers to me that—but the boat is alongside, and Philip is climbing up the vessel. Farewell, farewell, my dearest husband. I would I were a man! No, no! 'tis better as it is."

Amine watched till she could no longer perceive Philip, and then walked slowly to the hostelrie. The next day, when she arose, she found that the fleet had sailed at daylight, and the channel, which had been so crowded with vessels, was now untenanted.

"He is gone," muttered Amine; "now, for many months of patient, calm enduring,—I cannot say of living, for I exist but in his presence."

Chapter Sixteen.

We must leave Amine to her solitude, and follow the fortunes of Philip. The fleet had sailed with a flowing sheet, and bore gallantly down the Zuyder Zee; but they had not been under way an hour before the Vrow Katerina was left a mile or two astern. Mynheer Barentz found fault with the setting and trimming of the sails, and with the man at the helm, who was repeatedly changed; in short, with everything but his dear Vrow Katerina: but all would not do; she still dropped astern, and proved to be the worst-sailing vessel in the fleet.

"Mynheer Vanderdecken," said he, at last, "the Vrow, as my father used to say, is not so very *fast before* the wind. Vessels that are good on a wind seldom are; but this I will say, that, in every other point of sailing, there is no other vessel in the fleet equal to the Vrow Katerina."

"Besides," observed Philip, who perceived how anxious how captain was on the subject, "we are heavily laden, and have so many troops on deck."

The fleet cleared the sands and were then close-hauled, when the Vrow Katerina proved to sail even more slowly than before. "When we are so *very* close-hauled," observed Mynheer Barentz, "the Vrow does not do so well; but a point free, and then you will see how she will show her stern to the whole fleet. She is a fine vessel, Mynheer Vanderdecken, is she not?"

"A very fine, roomy vessel," replied Philip, which was all that in conscience, he could say.

The fleet sailed on, sometimes on a wind, sometimes free, but let the point of sailing be what it might, the Vrow Katerina was invariably astern, and the fleet had to heave-to at sunset to enable her to keep company; still, the captain continued to declare that the point of sailing on which they happened to be, was the only point in which the

Vrow Katerina was deficient. Unfortunately, the vessel had other points quite as bad as her sailing; she was crank, leaky, and did not answer the helm well, but Mynheer Barentz was not to be convinced. He adored his ship and like all men desperately in love he could see no fault in his mistress. But others were not so blind, and the admiral, finding the voyage so much delayed by the bad sailing of one vessel, determined to leave her to find her way by herself so soon as they had passed the Cape. He was, however, spared the cruelty of deserting her, for a heavy gale came on which dispersed the whole fleet, and on the second day the good ship Vrow Katerina found herself alone, labouring heavily in the trough of the sea, leaking so much as to require hands constantly at the pumps, and drifting before the gale as fast to leeward almost as she usually sailed. For a week the gale continued, and each day did her situation become more alarming. Crowded with troops, encumbered with heavy stores she groaned and laboured, while whole seas washed over her, and the men could hardly stand at the pumps. Philip was active, and exerted himself to the utmost, encouraging the worn-out men, securing where aught had given way, and little interfered with by the captain, who was himself no sailor.

"Well," observed the captain to Philip, as they held on by the belaying-pins, "you'll acknowledge that she is a fine weatherly vessel in a gale—is she not? Softly, my beauty, softly," continued he, speaking to the vessel, as she plunged heavily into the waves, and every timber groaned. "Softly, my dear, softly. How those poor devils in the other ships must be knocking about now. Heh! Mynheer Vanderdecken, we have the start of them this time: they must be a terrible long way down to leeward. Don't you think so?"

"I really cannot pretend to say," replied Philip, smiling.

"Why, there's not one of them in sight. Yes! by Heavens, there is! Look on our lee-beam. I see one now. Well, she must be a capital sailer, at all events: look there, a point abaft the beam. Mercy on me! how stiff she must be to carry such a press of canvass!"

Philip had already seen her. It was a large ship on a wind, and on the same tack as they were. In a gale, in which no vessel could carry the topsails, the Vrow Katerina being under close-reefed foresails and staysails, the ship seen to leeward was standing under a press of sail—topgallant-sail, royals, flying jib, and every stitch of canvass which could be set in a light breeze. The waves were running mountains high, bearing each minute the Vrow Katerina down to the gunwale: and the ship seen appeared not to be affected by the tumultuous waters, but sailed steadily and smoothly on an even keel. At once Philip knew it must be the Phantom Ship, in which his father's doom was being fulfilled.

"Very odd, is it not?" observed Mynheer Barentz.

Philip felt such an oppression on his chest that he could not reply. As he held on with one hand, he covered up his eyes with the other.

But the seamen had now seen the vessel, and the legend was too well known. Many of the troops had climbed on deck when the report was circulated, and all eyes were now fixed upon the supernatural vessel; when a heavy squall burst over the Vrow Katerina, accompanied with peals of thunder and heavy rain, rendering it so thick that nothing could be seen. In a quarter of an hour it cleared away, and, when they looked to leeward the stranger was no longer in sight.

"Merciful Heaven! she must have been upset, and has gone down in the squall," said Mynheer Barentz. "I thought as much, carrying such a press of sail. There never was a ship that could carry more than the Vrow Katerina. It was madness on the part of the captain of that vessel; but I suppose he wished to keep up with us. Heh, Mynheer Vanderdecken?"

Philip did not reply to these remarks, which fully proved the madness of his captain. He felt that his ship was doomed, and when he thought of the numbers on board who might be sacrificed, he shuddered. After a pause, he said—

"Mynheer Barentz, this gale is likely to continue, and the best ship that ever was built cannot, in my opinion, stand such weather. I should advise that we bear up, and run back to Table Bay to refit. Depend upon it, we shall find the whole fleet there before us."

"Never fear for the good ship, Vrow Katerina," replied the captain; "see what weather she makes of it."

"Cursed bad," observed one of the seamen, for the seamen had gathered near to Philip to hear what his advice might be. "If I had known that she was such an old, crazy beast, I never would have trusted myself on board. Mynheer Vanderdecken is right; we must back to Table Bay ere worse befall us. That ship to leeward has given us warning—she is not seen for nothing,—ask Mr Vanderdecken, captain; he knows that well, for he *is* a sailor."

This appeal to Philip made him start; it was, however, made without any knowledge of Philip's interest in the Phantom Ship.

"I must say," replied Philip, "that, whenever I have fallen in with that vessel, mischief has ever followed."

"Vessel! why, what was there in that vessel to frighten you? She carried too much sail, and she has gone down."

"She never goes down," replied one of the seamen.

"No! no!" exclaimed many voices; "but we shall, if we do not run back."

"Pooh! nonsense! Mynheer Vanderdecken, what say you?"

"I have already stated my opinion," replied Philip, who was anxious, if possible, to see the ship once more in port, "that the best thing we can do, is to bear up for Table Bay."

"And, captain," continued the old seaman who had just spoken, "we are all determined that it shall be so, whether you like it or not; so up with the helm, my hearty, and Mynheer Vanderdecken will trim the sails."

"Why! what is this?" cried Captain Barentz. "A mutiny on board of the Vrow Katerina? impossible! The Vrow Katerina! the best ship, the fastest in the whole fleet!"

"The dullest old rotten tub," cried one of the seamen.

"What!" cried the captain, "what do I hear? Mynheer Vanderdecken, confine that lying rascal for mutiny."

"Pooh! nonsense! he's mad," replied the old seaman. "Never mind him; come, Mynheer Vanderdecken, we will obey you; but the helm must be up immediately."

The captain stormed, but Philip, by acknowledging the superiority of his vessel, at the same time that he blamed the seamen for their panic, pointed out to him the necessity of compliance, and Mynheer Barentz at last consented. The helm was put up, the sails trimmed, and the Vrow Katerina rolled heavily before the gale. Towards the evening the weather moderated, and the sky cleared up; both sea and wind subsided fast; the leaking decreased, and Philip was in hopes that in a day or two they would arrive safely in the Bay.

As they steered their course, so did the wind gradually decrease, until at last it fell calm; nothing remained of the tempest but a long heavy swell which set to the westward, and before which the Vrow Katerina was gradually drifting. This was respite to the worn-out seamen, and also to the troops and passengers, who had been cooped below or drenched on the main-deck.

The upper deck was crowded; mothers basked in the warm sun with their children in their arms; the rigging was filled with the wet clothes, which were hung up to dry on every part of the shrouds; and the seamen were busily employed in repairing the injuries of the gale. By their reckoning, they were not more than fifty miles from Table Bay, and each moment they expected to see the land to the southward of it. All was again mirth, and every one on board, except Philip, considered that danger was no more to be apprehended.

The second mate, whose name was Krantz, was an active, good seaman, and a great favourite with Philip, who knew that he could trust to him, and it was on the afternoon of this day that he and Philip were walking together on the deck.

"What think you, Vanderdecken, of that strange vessel we saw?"

"I have seen her before, Krantz; and—"

"And what?"

"Whatever vessel I have been in when I have seen her, that vessel has never returned into port—others tell the same tale."

"Is she, then, the ghost of a vessel?"

"I am told so; and there are various stories afloat concerning her: but of this, I assure you—that I am fully persuaded that some accident will happen before we reach port, although everything at this moment appears so calm, and our port is so near at hand."

"You are superstitious," replied Krantz; "and yet, I must say, that, to me, the appearance was not like a reality. No vessel could carry such sail in the gale; but yet, there are madmen afloat who will sometimes attempt the most absurd things. If it was a vessel, she must have gone down, for when it cleared up she was not to be seen. I am not very credulous, and nothing but the occurrence of the consequences which you anticipate will make me believe that there was anything supernatural in the affair."

"Well! I shall not be sorry if the event proves me wrong," replied Philip; "but I have my forebodings—we are not in port yet."

"No! but we are but a trifling distance from it, and there is every prospect of a continuance of fine weather."

"There is no saying from what quarter the danger may come," replied Philip; "we have other things to fear than the violence of the gale."

"True," replied Krantz; "but, nevertheless, don't let us croak. Notwithstanding all you say, I prophesy that in two days, at the farthest, we are safely anchored in Table Bay."

The conversation here dropped, and Philip was glad to be left alone. A melancholy had seized him—a depression of spirits, even greater than he had ever felt before. He leant over the gangway and watched the heaving of the sea.

"Merciful Heaven!" ejaculated he, "be pleased to spare this vessel; let not the wail of women, the shrieks of the poor children, now embarked, be heard; the numerous body of men, trusting to her planks,—let not them be sacrificed for my father's crimes." And Philip mused. "The ways of Heaven are indeed mysterious," thought he. "Why should others suffer because my father has sinned? And yet, is it not so everywhere? How many thousands fall on the field of battle in a war occasioned by the ambition of a king, or the influence of a woman! How many millions have been destroyed for holding a different creed of faith! *He* works in his own way, leaving us to wonder and to doubt!"

The sun had set before Philip had quitted the gangway and gone down below. Commending himself, and those embarked with him, to the care of Providence, he at last fell asleep; but, before the bell was struck eight times, to announce midnight, he was awakened by a rude shove of the shoulder, and perceived Krantz, who had the first watch, standing by him.

"By the Heaven above us! Vanderdecken, you have prophesied right. Up—quick! *The ship's on fire!*"

"On fire!" exclaimed Vanderdecken, jumping out of his berth—'where?"

"The main-hold."

"I will up immediately, Krantz. In the mean time, keep the hatches on and rig the pumps."

In less than a minute Philip was on deck, where he found Captain Barentz, who had also been informed of the case by the second mate. In a few words all was explained by Krantz: there was a strong smell of fire proceeding from the main-hold; and, on removing one of the hatches, which he had done without calling for any assistance, from a knowledge of the panic it would create, he found that the hold was full of smoke; he had put it on again immediately, and had only made it known to Philip and the captain.

"Thanks for your presence of mind," replied Philip; "we have now time to reflect quietly on what is to be done. If the troops and the poor women and children knew their danger, their alarm would have much impeded us: but how could she have taken fire in the main-hold?"

"I never heard of the Vrow Katerina talking fire before," observed the captain; "I think it is impossible. It must be some mistake—she is—"

"I now recollect that we have in our cargo several cases of vitriol in bottles," interrupted Philip. "In the gale, they must have been disturbed and broken. I kept them above all, in case of accident: this rolling, gunwale under, for so long a time must have occasioned one of them to fetch way."

"That's it, depend upon it," observed Krantz.

"I did object to receive them, stating that they ought to go out in some vessel which was not so encumbered with troops, so that they might remain on the main-deck; but they replied, that the invoices were made out and could not be altered. But now to act. My idea is, to keep the hatches on, so as to smother it if possible."

"Yes," replied Krantz; "and, at the same time, cut a hole in the deck just large enough to admit the hose, and pump as much water as we can down into the hold."

"You are right, Krantz; send for the carpenter, and set him to work. I will turn the hands up, and speak to the men. I smell the fire now very strong; there is no time to lose. If we can only keep the troops and the women quiet we may do something."

The hands were turned up, and soon made their appearance on deck, wondering why they were summoned. The men had not perceived the state of the vessel, for, the hatches having been kept on, the little smoke that issued ascended the hatchway, and did not fill the lower deck.

"My lads," said Philip, "I am sorry to say that we have reason to suspect that there is some danger of fire in the main-hold."

"I smell it!" cried one of the seamen.

"So do I," cried several others, with every show of alarm, and moving away as if to go below.

"Silence, and remain where you are, my men. Listen to what I say: if you frighten the troops and passengers we shall do nothing; we must trust to ourselves; there is no time to be lost. Mr Krantz and the carpenter are doing all that can be done at present; and now, my men, do me the favour to sit down on the deck, every one of you, while I tell you what we must do."

This order of Philip's was obeyed, and the effect was excellent: it gave the men time to compose themselves after the first shock; for, perhaps, of all shocks to the human frame, there is none which creates a greater panic than the first intimation of fire on board of a vessel—a situation, indeed, pitiable, when it is considered that you have to choose between the two elements seeking your destruction. Philip did not speak for a minute or two. He then pointed out to the men the danger of their situation, what were the measures which he and Krantz had decided upon taking; and how necessary it was that all should be cool and collected. He also reminded them that they had but little powder in the magazine, which was far from the site of the fire, and could easily be removed and thrown overboard; and that, if the fire could not be extinguished, they had a quantity of spars on deck to form a raft, which, with the boats, would receive all on board, and that they were but a short distance from land.

Philip's address had the most beneficial effects; the men rose up when he ordered them; one portion went down to the magazine, and handed up the powder, which was passed along and thrown overboard; another went to the pumps; and Krantz, coming up, reported the hole to have been cut in the planking of the deck above the main-hold: the hoses were fixed, and a quantity of water soon poured down, but it was impossible that the danger could be kept secret. The troops were sleeping on the deck and the very employment of the seamen pointed out what had occurred, even if the smoke, which now increased very much, and filled the lower deck, had not betrayed it. In a few minutes the alarm of *Fire!* was heard throughout the vessel, and men, women, and children, were seen, some hurrying on their clothes, some running frightened about the decks, some shrieking, some praying, and the confusion and terror were hardly to be described.

The judicious conduct of Philip was then made evident: had the sailors been awakened by the appalling cry, they would have been equally incapable of acting as were the troops and passengers. All subordination would have ceased: some would have seized the boats, and left the majority to perish: others would have hastened to the spirit-room, and, by their drunkenness added to the confusion and horror of the scene: nothing would have been effected, and almost all would in all probability have perished miserably. But this had been prevented by the presence of mind shown by Philip and the second-mate, for the Captain was a cipher:— not wanting in courage certainly, but without conduct or a knowledge of his profession. The seamen continued steady to their duty, pushing the soldiers out of the way as they performed their allotted tasks: and Philip perceiving this, went down below, leaving Krantz in charge; and by reasoning with the most collected, by degrees he brought the majority of the troops to a state of comparative coolness.

The powder had been thrown overboard, and another hole having been cut in the deck on the other side, the other pump was rigged, and double the quantity of water poured into the hold; but it was evident to Philip that the combustion increased. The smoke and steam now burst through the interstices of the hatchways and the holes cut in the deck with a violence that proved the extent of the fire which raged below, and Philip thought it advisable to remove all the women and children to the poop and quarter-deck of the ship, desiring the husbands of the women to stay with them. It was a melancholy sight, and the tears stood in Philip's eyes as he looked upon the group of females—some weeping and straining their children to their bosoms; some more quiet and more collected than the men: the elder children mute or crying because their mothers cried, and the younger ones, unconscious of danger playing with the first object which attracted their attention, or smiling at their parents. The officers commanding the troops were two ensigns newly entered, and very young men, ignorant of their duty and without any authority—for men in cases of extreme danger will not obey those who are more ignorant than themselves—and, at Philip's request, they remained with and superintended the women and children.

So soon as Philip had given his orders that the women and children should be properly clothed (which many of them were not), he went again forward to superintend the labour of the seamen, who already began to show symptoms of fatigue, from the excess of their exertions; but many of the soldiers now offered to work at the pumps, and their services were willingly accepted. Their efforts were in vain. In about half an hour more, the hatches were blown up with a loud noise, and a column of intense and searching flame darted up perpendicularly from the hold, high as the lower mast-head. Then was heard the loud shriek of the women, who pressed their children in agony to their breasts, as the seamen and soldiers who had been working the pumps, in their precipitate retreat from the scorching flames, rushed aft, and fell among the huddled crowd.

"Be steady, my lads—steady, my good fellows," exclaimed Philip; "there is no danger yet. Recollect we have our boats and raft, and although we cannot subdue the fire, and save the vessel, still we may, if you are cool and collected, not only save ourselves, but every one—even the poor infants who now appeal to you as men to exert yourselves in their behalf. Come, come, my lads, let us do our duty—we have the means of escape in our power if we lose no time. Carpenter, get your axes, and cut away the boom-lashings. Now, my men, let us get our boats out, and make a raft for these poor women and children; we are not ten miles from the land. Krantz, see to the boats with the starboard watch: larboard watch with me, to launch over the booms. Gunners, take any of the cordage you can, ready for lashing. Come, my lads, there is no want of light—we can work without lanterns."

The men obeyed: as Philip, to encourage them, had almost jocularly remarked (for a joke is often well-timed, when apparently on the threshold of eternity) there was no want of light. The column of fire now ascended above the main-top—licking with its forky tongue the top-mast rigging—and embracing the main-mast in its folds: and the loud roar with which it ascended proved the violence and rapidity of the combustion below and how little time there was to be lost. The lower and main decks were now so filled with smoke that no one could remain there: some few poor fellows sick in their cots had long been smothered, for they had been forgotten. The swell had much subsided, and there was not a breath of wind: the smoke which rose from the hatchways ascended straight up in the air, which, as the vessel had lost all steerage way, was fortunate. The boats were soon in the water, and trusty men placed in them: the spars were launched over, arranged by the men in the boats and lashed together. All the gratings were then collected and firmly fixed upon the spars for the people to sit upon; and Philip's heart was glad at the prospect which he now had of saving the numbers which were embarked.

Chapter Seventeen.

But their difficulties were not surmounted—the fire now had communicated to the main-deck and burst out of the port-holes amid-ships—and the raft which had been forming alongside was obliged to be drifted astern where it was more exposed to the swell. This retarded their labour, and, in the mean time the fire was making rapid progress; the main-mast which had long been burning, fell over the side with the lurching of the vessel, and the flames out of the main-deck ports soon showed their points above the bulwarks, while volumes of smoke were poured in upon the upper-deck almost suffocating the numbers which were crowded there; for all communication with the fore-part of the ship had been for some time cut off by the flames, and every one had retreated aft. The women and children were now carried on to the poop; not only to remove them farther from the suffocating smoke, but that they might be lowered down to the raft from the stern.

It was about four o'clock in the morning when all was ready, and by the exertions of Philip and the seamen, notwithstanding the swell, the women and children were safely placed on the raft where it was considered that they would be less in the way, as the men could relieve each other in pulling when they were tired.

After the women and children had been lowered down, the troops were next ordered to descend by the ladders; some few were lost in the attempt, falling under the boat's bottom and not re-appearing; but two-thirds of them were safely put on the berths they were ordered to take by Krantz, who had gone down to superintend this important arrangement. Such had been the vigilance of Philip, who had requested Captain Barentz to stand over the spirit-room hatch, with pistols, until the smoke on the main-deck rendered the precaution unnecessary, that not a single person was intoxicated, and to this might be ascribed the order and regularity which had prevailed during this trying scene. But before one-third of the soldiers had descended by the stern ladder, the fire burst out of the stern windows with a violence that nothing could withstand; spouts of vivid flame extended several feet from the vessel, roaring with the force of a blowpipe; at the same time the flames burst through all the after-ports of the main-deck, and those remaining on board found themselves encircled with fire, and suffocated with smoke and heat. The stern ladders were consumed in a minute and dropped into the sea the boats which had been receiving the men were obliged also to back astern from the intense heat of the flames; even those on the raft shrieked as they found themselves scorched by the ignited fragments which fell on them as they were enveloped in an opaque cloud of smoke, which hid from them those who still remained on the deck of the vessel. Philip attempted to speak to those on board, but he was not heard. A scene of confusion took place which ended in great loss of life. The only object appeared to be who should first escape; though, except by jumping overboard, there was no escape. Had they waited, and (as Philip would have pointed out to them) have one by one thrown themselves into the sea, the men in the boats were fully prepared to pick them up; or had they climbed out to the end of the latteen mizen-yard which was lowered down, they might have descended safely by a rope, but the scorching of the flames which surrounded them, and the suffocation from the smoke was overpowering, and most of the soldiers sprang over the taffrail at once, or as nearly so as possible. The consequence was, that there were thirty or forty in the water at the same time, and the scene was as heart-rending as it was appalling; the sailors in the boats dragging them in as fast as they could—the women on the raft, throwing to them loose garments to haul them in; at one time a wife shrieking as she saw her husband struggling and sinking into eternity; at another, curses and execrations from the swimmer who was grappled with by the drowning man, and dragged with him under the surface. Of eighty men who were left of the troops on board at the time of the bursting out of the flames from the stern windows, but twenty-five were saved. There were but few seamen left on board with Philip, the major part having been employed in making the raft or manning the three boats; those who were on board remained by his side, regulating their motions by his. After allowing full time for the soldiers to be picked up, Philip ordered the men to climb out to the end of the latteen yard which hung on the taffrail, and either to lower themselves down on the raft if it was under, or to give notice to the boats to receive them. The raft had been dropped farther astern by the seamen, that those on board of it might not suffer from the smoke and heat; and the sailors one after another lowered themselves down and were received by the boats. Philip desired Captain Barentz to go before him, but the captain refused. He was too much choked with smoke to say why, but no doubt but that it would have been something in praise of the Vrow Katerina. Philip then climbed out; he was followed by the captain, and they were both received into one of the boats.

The rope, which had hitherto held the raft to the ship, was now cast off, and it was taken in by the boats; and in a short time the Vrow Katerina was borne to leeward of them; and Philip and Krantz now made arrangements for the better disposal of the people. The sailors were almost all put into boats that they might relieve one another in pulling; the remainder were placed on the raft, along with the soldiers, the women, and the children. Notwithstanding that the boats were all as much loaded as they could well bear, the numbers on the raft were so great, that it sunk nearly a foot under water, when the swell of the sea poured upon it; but stanchions and ropes to support those on board had been fixed and the men remained at the sides, while the women and children were crowded together in the middle.

As soon as these arrangements were made, the boats took the raft in tow, and just as the dawn of day appeared, pulled in the direction of the land.

The Vrow Katerina was, by this time, one volume of flame: she had drifted about half a mile to leeward, and Captain Barentz, who was watching as he sat in the boat with Philip, exclaimed—"Well, there goes a lovely ship, a ship that could do everything but speak—I'm sure that not a ship in the fleet would have made such a bonfire as she has—does she not burn beautifully—nobly? My poor Vrow Katerina! perfect to the last, we never shall see such a ship as you again! Well, I'm glad my father did not live to see this sight, for it would have broken his heart, poor man."

Philip made no reply; he felt a respect even for Captain Barentz's misplaced regard for the vessel. They made but little way, for the swell was rather against them, and the raft was deep in the water. The day dawned, and the appearance of the weather was not favourable; it promised a return of the gale. Already a breeze ruffled the surface of the water, and the swell appeared to increase rather than go down. The sky was overcast and the horizon thick. Philip looked out for the land, but could not perceive it, for there was a haze on the horizon, so that he could not see more than five miles. He felt that to gain the shore before the coming night was necessary for the preservation of so many individuals of whom more than sixty were women and children, who without any nourishment, were sitting on a frail raft, immersed in the water. No land in sight—a gale coming on, and in all probability, a heavy sea and dark night. The chance was indeed desperate, and Philip was miserable—most miserable—when he reflected that so many innocent beings might, before the next morning, be consigned to a watery tomb,—and why?—yes, there was the feeling—that although Philip could reason against—he never could conquer; for his own life he cared nothing—even the idea of his beloved Amine was nothing in the balance at these moments. The only point which sustained him, was the knowledge that he had his duty to perform, and, in the full exercise of his duty, he recovered himself.

"Land ahead!" was now cried out by Krantz, who was in the headmost boat, and the news was received with a shout of joy from the raft and the boats. The anticipation and the hope the news gave was like manna in the wilderness—and the poor women on the raft, drenched sometimes above the waist by the swell of the sea, clasped the children in their arms still closer, and cried—"My darling, you shall be saved."

Philip stood upon the stern-sheets to survey the land, and he had the satisfaction of finding that it was not five miles distant and a ray of hope warmed his heart. The breeze now had gradually increased, and rippled the water. The quarter from which the wind came was neither favourable nor adverse, being on the beam. Had they had sails for the boats, it would have been otherwise, but they had been stowed away, and could not be procured. The sight of land naturally rejoiced them all, and the seamen in the boat cheered, and double-banked the oars, to increase their way; but the towing of a large raft sunk under water was no easy task; and they could not, with all their exertions, advance more than half a mile an hour.

Until noon they continued their exertions not without success; they were not three miles from the land; but, as the sun passed the meridian a change took place; the breeze blew strong; the swell of the sea rose rapidly; and the raft was often so deeply immersed in the waves as to alarm them for the safety of those upon her. Their way was proportionably retarded, and by three o'clock they had not gained half a mile from where they had been at noon. The men not having had refreshment of any kind during the labour and excitement of so many hours, began to flag in their exertions. The wish for water was expressed by all—from the child who appealed to its mother, to the seaman who strained at the oar. Philip did all he could to encourage the men but finding themselves so near to the land, and so overcome with fatigue, and that the raft in tow would not allow them to approach their haven they murmured, and talked of the necessity of casting loose the raft and looking out for themselves. A feeling of self prevailed, and they were mutinous; but Philip expostulated with them, and out of respect for him, they continued their exertions for another hour, when a circumstance occurred which decided the question, upon which they had recommenced a debate.

The increased swell and the fresh breeze had so beat about and tossed the raft, that it was with difficulty, for some time, that its occupants could hold themselves on it. A loud shout, mingled with screams, attracted the attention of those in the boats, and Philip looking back, perceived that the lashings of the raft had yielded to the force of the waves, and that it had separated amidship. The scene was agonising; husbands were separated from their wives and children—each floating away from each other—for the part of the raft which was still towed by the boats had already left the other far astern. The women rose up and screamed, and held up their children; some, more frantic, dashed into the water between them, and attempted to gain the floating wreck upon which their husbands stood, and sank before they could be assisted. But the horror increased—one lashing having given way, all the rest soon followed; and, before the boats could turn and give assistance, the sea was strewed with the spars which composed the raft, with men, women, and children clinging to them. Loud were the yells of despair, and the shrieks of the women, as they embraced their offspring, and in attempting to save them were lost themselves. The spars of the raft still close together, were hurled one upon the other by the swell, and many found death by being jammed between them. Although all the boats hastened to their assistance, there was so much difficulty and danger in forcing them between the spars, that but few were saved, and even those few were more than the boats could well take in. The seamen and a few soldiers were picked up, but all the females and the children had sunk beneath the waves.

The effect of this catastrophe may be imagined, but hardly described. The seamen who had debated as to casting them adrift to perish, wept as they pulled towards the shore. Philip was overcome, he covered his face, and remained for some time without giving directions, and heedless of what passed.

It was now five o'clock in the evening; the boats had cast off the tow-lines and vied with each other in their exertions. Before the sun had set, they all had arrived at the beach, and were safely landed in the little sand bay into which they had steered; for the wind was off the shore and there was no surf. The boats were hauled up, and the exhausted men lay down on the sands, till warm with the heat of the sun, and forgetting that they had neither eaten nor drunk for so long a time, they were soon fast asleep. Captain Barentz, Philip, and Krantz; as soon as they had seen the boats secured, held a short consultation, and were then glad to follow the example of the seamen; harassed and worn out with the fatigue of the last twenty-four hours, their senses were soon drowned in oblivion.

For many hours they all slept soundly, dreamt of water, and awoke to the sad reality that they were tormented with thirst, and were on a sandy heath with the salt waves mocking them; but they reflected how many of their late companions had been swallowed up, and felt thankful that they had been spared. It was early dawn when they all rose from the forms which they had impressed on the yielding sand; and by the directions of Philip, they separated in every direction, to look for the means of quenching their agony of thirst. As they proceeded over sand-hills, they found growing in the sand a low spongy-leaf sort of shrub, something like what in our greenhouses is termed the ice-plant; the thick leaves of which were covered with large drops of dew. They sank down on their knees, and proceeded from one to the other licking off the moisture which was abundant, and soon felt a temporary relief. They continued their search till noon without success, and hunger was now added to their thirst; they then returned to the beach to ascertain if their companions had been more successful. They had also quenched their thirst with the dew of heaven but had found no water or means of subsistence; but some of them had eaten the leaves of the plant which had contained the dew in the morning, and had found them, although acid, full of watery sap and grateful to the palate. The plant in question is the one provided by bounteous Providence for the support of the camel and other beasts in the arid desert, only to be found there, and devoured by all ruminating animals with avidity. By the advice of Philip they collected a quantity of this plant and put it into the boats, and then launched.

They were not more than fifty miles from Table Bay; and although they had no sails, the wind was in their favour. Philip pointed out to them how useless it was to remain, when before morning they would, in all probability arrive at where they would obtain all they required. The advice was approved of and acted upon; the boats were shoved off and the oars resumed. So tired and exhausted were the men, that their oars dipped mechanically into the water, for there was no strength left to be applied; it was not until the next morning at daylight, that they had arrived opposite False Bay, and they had still many miles to pull. The wind in their favour had done almost all—the men could do little or nothing.

Encouraged, however, by the sight of land which they knew, they rallied; and about noon they pulled, exhausted, to the beach at the bottom of Table Bay, near to which were the houses, and the fort protecting the settlers, who had for some few years resided there. They landed close to where a broad rivulet at that season (but a torrent in the winter) poured its stream into the bay. At the sight of fresh water, some of the men dropped their oars, threw themselves into the sea when out of their depth—others when the water was above their waists—yet they did not arrive so soon as those who waited till the boat struck the beach and jumped out upon dry land. And then they threw themselves into the rivulet, which coursed over the shingle, about five or six inches in depth allowing the refreshing stream to pour into their mouths till they could receive no more, immersing their hot hands, and rolling in it with delight.

Despots and fanatics have exerted their ingenuity to invent torments for their victims—how useless—the rack, the boot, tire,—all that they have imagined are not to be compared to the torture of extreme thirst. In the extremity of agony the sufferers cry for water, and it is not refused: they might have spared themselves their refined ingenuity of torment, and the disgusting exhibition of it, had they only confined the prisoner in his cell, and refused him *water*.

As soon as they satisfied the most pressing of all wants, they rose dripping from the stream, and walked up to the houses of the factory; the inhabitants of which, perceiving that boats had landed when there was no vessel in the bay, naturally concluded that some disaster had happened, and were walking down to meet them. Their tragical history was soon told. The thirty-six men that stood before them were all that were left of nearly three hundred souls embarked, and they had been more than two days without food. At this intimation no further questions were asked by the considerate settlers, until the hunger of the sufferers had been appeased when the narrative of their sufferings was fully detailed by Philip and Krantz.

"I have an idea that I have seen you before," observed one of the settlers. "Did you come on shore when the fleet anchored?"

"I did not," replied Philip; "but I have been here."

"I recollect now," replied the man; "you were the only survivor of the Ter Schilling, which was lost in False Bay."

"Not the only survivor," replied Philip; "I thought so myself; but I afterwards met the pilot, a one-eyed man, of the name of Schriften, who was my shipmate: he must have arrived here after me. You saw him, of course?"

"No, I did not. No one belonging to the Ter Schilling ever came here after you; for I have been a settler here ever since, and it is not likely that I should forget such a circumstance."

"He must, then, have returned to Holland by some other means."

"I know not how. Our ships never go near the coast after they leave the bay; it is too dangerous."

"Nevertheless, I saw him," replied Philip, musing.

"If you saw him, that is sufficient; perhaps some vessel had been blown down to the eastern side, and picked him up; but the natives in that part are not likely to have spared the life of a European. The Caffres are a cruel people."

The information that Schriften had not been seen at the Cape was a subject of meditation to Philip. He had always had an idea as the reader knows, that there was something supernatural about the man; and this opinion was corroborated by the report of the settler.

We must pass over the space of two months during which the wrecked seamen were treated with kindness by the settlers, and at the expiration of which a small brig arrived at the bay, and took in refreshments: she was homeward bound, with a full cargo, and being chartered by the Company, could not refuse to receive on board the crew of the Vrow Katerina. Philip, Krantz, and the seamen embarked; but Captain Barentz remained behind to settle at the Cape.

"Should I go home," said he to Philip, who argued with him, "I have nothing in the world to return for. I have no wife—no children. I had but one dear object, my Vrow Katerina, who was my wife, my child, my everything;—she is gone, and I never shall find another vessel like her; and if I could, I should not love it as I did her. No, my affections are buried with her,—are entombed in the deep sea. How beautifully she burnt!—she went out of the world like a phoenix, as she was. No! no! I will be faithful to her—I will send for what little money I have, and live as near to her tomb as I can—I never shall forget her as long as I live. I shall mourn over her, and 'Vrow Katerina,' when I die, will be found engraven on my heart."

Philip could not help wishing that his affections had been fixed upon a more deserving object, as then, probably, the tragical loss had not taken place; but he changed the subject, feeling that, being no sailor, Captain Barentz was much better on shore than in the command of a vessel. They shook hands and parted—Philip promising to execute Barentz's commission, which was to turn his money into articles most useful to a settler, and have them sent out by the first fleet which should sail from the Zuyder Zee. But this commission it was not Philip's good fortune to execute. The brig, named the Wilhelmina sailed and soon arrived at St. Helena. After watering she proceeded on her voyage. They had made the Western Isles, and Philip was consoling himself with the anticipation of soon joining his Amine, when to the northward of the islands, they met with a furious gale before which they were obliged to scud for many days, with the vessel's head to the south-east; and as the wind abated, and they were able to haul to it, they fell in with a Dutch fleet of five vessels, commanded by an admiral, which had left Amsterdam more than two months, and had been buffeted about by contrary gales for the major part of that period. Cold, fatigue, and bad provisions, had brought on the scurvy; and the ships were so weakly manned, that they could hardly navigate them. When the captain of the Wilhelmina reported to the admiral that he had part of the crew of the Vrow Katerina on board, he was ordered to send them immediately to assist in navigating his crippled fleet. Remonstrance was useless. Philip had but time to write to Amine, acquainting her with his misfortunes and disappointment; and, confiding the letter to his wife, as well as his narrative of the loss of the Vrow Katerina for the directors, to the charge of the captain of the Wilhelmina, he hastened to pack up his effects, and repaired on board of the admiral's ship with Krantz and the crew. To them were added six of the men belonging to to Wilhelmina, whom the admiral insisted on retaining; and the brig, having received the admiral's despatches, was then permitted to continue her voyage.

Perhaps there is nothing more trying to the seaman's feelings than being unexpectedly forced to recommence another series of trials, at the very time when they anticipate repose from their former; yet how often does this happen! Philip was melancholy. "It is my destiny," thought he, using the words of Amine, "and why should I not submit?" Krantz was furious, and the seamen discontented and mutinous; but it was useless. Might is right on the vast ocean, where there is no appeal—no trial or injunction to be obtained.

But hard as their case appeared to them, the admiral was fully justified in his proceeding. His ships were almost unmanageable with the few hands who could still perform their duty; and this small increase of physical power might be the means of saving hundreds who lay helpless in their hammocks. In his own vessel, the Lion which was manned with two hundred and fifty men when she sailed from Amsterdam, there were not more than seventy capable of doing duty; and the other ships had suffered in proportion.

The first captain of the Lion was dead, the second captain in his hammock, and the admiral had no one to assist him but the mates of the vessel, some of whom crawled up to their duty more dead than alive. The ship of the second in command, the Dort, was even in a more deplorable plight. The commodore was dead; the first captain was still doing his duty; but he had but one more officer capable of remaining on deck.

The admiral sent for Philip into his cabin, and having heard his narrative of the loss of the Vrow Katerina, he ordered him to go on board the commodore's ship as captain, giving the rank of commodore to the captain at present on board of her; Krantz was retained on board his own vessel, as second captain; for by Philip's narrative, the admiral perceived at once that they were both good officers and brave men.

Chapter Eighteen.

The fleet under Admiral Rymelandt's command was ordered to proceed to the East Indies by the western route, through the Straits of Magellan into the Pacific Ocean—it being still imagined, notwithstanding previous failures, that this route offered facilities which might shorten the passage to the Spice Islands.

The vessels composing the fleet were the Lion of forty-four guns, bearing the admiral's flag; the Dort of thirty-six guns, with the commodore's pendant—to which Philip was appointed; the Zuyder Zee of twenty; the Young Frau of twelve, and a ketch of four guns, called the Schevelling.

The crew of the Vrow Katerina were divided between the two larger vessels; the others, being smaller, were easier worked with fewer hands. Every arrangement having been made, the boats were hoisted up, and the ships made sail. For ten days they were baffled by light winds, and the victims to the scurvy increased considerably on board of Philip's vessel. Many died and were thrown overboard, and others were carried down to their hammocks.

The newly-appointed commodore, whose name was Avenhorn, went on board of the admiral, to report the state of the vessel and to suggest, as Philip had proposed to him, that they should make the coast of South America, and endeavour by bribery or by force to obtain supplies either from the Spanish inhabitants or the natives. But to this the admiral would not listen. He was an imperious, bold, and obstinate man, not to be persuaded or convinced, and with little feeling for the sufferings of others. Tenacious of being advised, he immediately rejected a proposition which, had it originated with himself, would probably have been immediately acted upon; and the commodore returned on board his vessel, not only disappointed, but irritated by the language used towards him.

"What are we do, Captain Vanderdecken? you know too well our situation—it is impossible we can continue long at sea; if we do, the vessel will be drifting at the mercy of the waves, while the crew die a wretched death in their hammocks. At present we have forty men left; in ten days more we shall probably have but twenty; for as the labour becomes more severe, so do they drop down the faster. Is it not better to risk our lives in combat with the Spaniards, than die here like rotten sheep?"

"I perfectly agree with you, commodore," replied Philip;—"but still we must obey orders. The admiral is an inflexible man."

"And a cruel one. I have a great mind to part company in the night, and if he finds fault, I will justify myself to the Directors on my return."

"Do nothing rashly—perhaps, when day by day he finds his own ship's company more weakened, he will see the necessity, of following your advice."

A week had passed away after this conversation, and the fleet had made little progress. In each ship the ravages of the fatal disease became more serious, and, as the commodore had predicted, he had but twenty men really able to do duty. Nor had the admiral's ship and the other vessels suffered less. The commodore again went on board to reiterate his proposition.

Admiral Rymelandt was not only a stern, but a vindictive man. He was aware of the propriety of the suggestion made by his second in command, but having refused it, he would not acquiesce; and he felt revengeful against the commodore, whose counsel he must now either adopt, or by refusing it be prevented from taking the steps so necessary for the preservation of his crew, and the success of his voyage. Too proud to acknowledge himself in error, again did he decidedly refuse, and the commodore went back to his own ship. The fleet was then within three days of the coast, steering to the southward for the Straits of Magellan, and that night, after Philip had returned to his cot, the commodore went on deck and ordered the course of the vessel to be altered some points more to the westward. The night was very dark, and the Lion was the only ship which carried a poop-lantern, so that the parting company of the Dort was not perceived by the admiral and the other ships of the fleet. When Philip went on deck next morning, he found that their consorts were not in sight. He looked at the compass, and perceiving that the course was altered, inquired at what hour and by whose directions. Finding that it was by his superior officer, he of course said nothing. When the commodore came on deck, he stated to Philip that he felt himself warranted in not complying with the admiral's orders, as it would have been sacrificing the whole ship's company. This was, indeed, true.

In two days they made the land, and running into the shore, perceived a large town and Spaniards on the beach. Then anchored at the mouth of the river, and hoisted English colours, when a boat came on board to ask them who they were and what they required? The commodore replied that the vessel was English, for he knew that the hatred of the Spanish to the Dutch was so great that, if known to belong to that nation, he would have had no chance of procuring any supplies, except by force. He stated that he had fallen in with a Spanish vessel, a complete wreck, from the whole of the crew being afflicted with the scurvy; that he had taken the men out, who were now in their hammocks below, as he considered it cruel to leave so many of his fellow-creatures to perish, and that he had come out of his course to land them at the first Spanish fort he could reach. He requested that they would immediately send on board vegetables and fresh provisions for the sick men, whom it would be death to remove, until after a few days, when they would be a little restored; and added, that in return for their assisting the Spaniards, he trusted the governor would also send supplies for his own people.

This well made-up story was confirmed by the officer sent on board by the Spanish governor. Being requested to go down below and see the patients, the sight of so many poor fellows in the last stage of that horrid disease—their teeth fallen out, gums ulcerated, bodies full of tumours and sores—was quite sufficient; and hurrying up from the lower deck, as he would have done from a charnel-house, the officer hastened on shore and made his report.

In two hours a large boat was sent off with fresh beef and vegetables sufficient for three days' supply for the ship's company, and these were immediately distributed among the men. A letter of thanks was returned by the commodore, stating that his health was so indifferent as to prevent his coming on shore in person to thank the governor, and forwarding a pretended list of the Spaniards on board, in which he mentioned some officers and people of distinction, whom he imagined might be connected with the family of the governor, whose name and titles he had received from the messenger sent on board; for the Dutch knew full well the majority of the noble Spanish families—indeed, alliances had continually taken place between them, previous to their assertion of their independence. The commodore concluded his letter by expressing a hope that, in a day or two, he should be able to pay his respects, and make arrangements for the landing of the sick, as he was anxious to proceed on his voyage of discovery.

On the third day, a fresh supply of provisions was sent on board, and so soon as they were received the commodore, in an English uniform went on shore and called upon the governor, gave a long detail of the sufferings of the people he had rescued, and agreed that they should be sent on shore in two days, as they would by that time be well enough to be moved. After many compliments, he went on board, the governor having stated his intention to return his visit on the following day, if the weather were not too rough. Fortunately, the weather was rough for the next two days, and it was not until the third that the governor made his appearance. This was precisely what the commodore wished.

There is no disease, perhaps, so dreadful or so rapid in its effects upon the human frame, and at the same time so instantaneously checked, as the scurvy, if the remedy can be procured. A few days were sufficient to restore those, who were not able to turn in their hammocks, to their former vigour. In the course of the six days nearly all the crew of the Dort were convalescent, and able to go on deck; but still they were not cured. The commodore waited for the arrival of the governor, received him with all due honours, and then, so soon as he was in the cabin, told him very politely that he and all his officers with him were prisoners. That the vessel was a Dutch man-of-war, and that it was his own people, and not Spaniards, who had been dying of the scurvy. He consoled him, however, by pointing out that he had thought it preferable to obtain provisions by this *ruse*, than to sacrifice lives on both sides by taking them by force, and that his Excellency's captivity would endure no longer than until he had received on board a sufficient number of live bullocks and fresh vegetables to insure the recovery of the ship's company; and, in the mean time, not the least insult would be offered to him. Whereupon the Spanish governor first looked at the commodore and then at the file of armed men at the cabin-door, and then to his distance from the town; and then called to mind the possibility of his being taken out to sea. Weighing all these points in his mind, and the very moderate ransom demanded (for bullocks were not worth a dollar a piece in that country), he resolved, as he could not help himself, to comply with the commodore's terms. He called for pen and ink, and wrote an order to send on board immediately all that was demanded. Before sunset the bullocks and vegetables were brought off, and, so soon as they were alongside, the commodore, with many bows and many thanks, escorted the governor to the gangway, complimenting him with a salvo of great guns, as he had done before, on his arrival. The people on shore thought that his Excellency had paid a long visit, but, as he did not like to acknowledge that he had been deceived, nothing was said about it, at least in his hearing, although the facts were soon well known. As soon as the boats were cleared, the commodore weighed anchor and made sail well satisfied with having preserved his ship's company and as the Falkland Islands, in case of parting company, had been named as the rendezvous, he steered for them. In a fortnight he arrived, and found that his admiral was not yet there. His crew were now all recovered, and his fresh beef was not yet expended, when he perceived the admiral and the three other vessels in the offing.

It appeared that so soon as the Dort had parted company, the admiral had immediately acted upon the advice that the commodore had given him, and had run for the coast. Not being so fortunate in a *ruse* as his second in command, he had landed an armed force from the four vessels, and had succeeded in obtaining several head of cattle, at the expense of an equal number of men killed and wounded. But at the same time they had collected a large quantity of vegetables of one sort or another, which they had carried on board and distributed with great success to the sick, who were gradually recovering.

Immediately that the admiral had anchored, he made the signal for the commodore to repair on board, and taxed him with disobedience of orders in having left the fleet. The commodore did not deny that he had so done, but excused himself upon the plea of necessity, offering to lay the whole matter before the Court of Directors so soon as they returned; but the admiral was vested with most extensive powers, not only of the trial, but the *condemnation* and punishment of any person guilty of mutiny and insubordination in his fleet. In reply, he told the commodore that he was a prisoner, and to prove it, he confined him in irons under the half-deck.

A signal was then made for all the captains: they went on board, and of course Philip was of the number. On their arrival, the admiral held a summary court-martial, proving to them by his instructions that he was so warranted to do. The result of the court-martial could be but one—condemnation for a breach of discipline, to which Philip was obliged reluctantly to sign his name. The admiral then gave Philip the appointment of second in command, and the commodore's pendant, much to the annoyance of the captains commanding the other vessels; but in this the admiral proved his judgment, as there was no one of them so fit for the task as Philip. Having so done, he dismissed them. Philip would have spoken to the late commodore, but the sentry opposed it, as against his orders; and with a friendly nod, Philip was obliged to leave him without the desired communication.

The fleet remained three weeks at the Falkland Islands, to recruit the ships' companies. Although there was no fresh beef, there was plenty of scurvy-grass and penguins. These birds were in myriads on some parts of the island, which, from the propinquity of their nests, built of mud, went by the name of *towns*. There they sat close together (the whole area which they covered being bare of grass) hatching their eggs and rearing their young. The men had but to select as many eggs and birds as they pleased and so numerous were they, that when they had supplied themselves, there was no apparent diminution of the numbers. This food, although in a short time not very palatable to the seamen, had the effect of restoring them to health, and before the fleet sailed, there was not a man who was afflicted with the scurvy. In the mean time the commodore remained in irons, and many were the conjectures concerning his ultimate fate. The power of life and death was known to be in the admiral's hands, but no one thought that such power would be exerted up on a delinquent of so high a grade. The other captains kept aloof from Philip, and he knew little of what was the general idea. Occasionally when on board of the admiral's ship, he ventured to bring up the question, but was immediately silenced; and feeling that he might injure the late commodore (for whom he had a regard), he would risk nothing by importunity; and the fleet sailed for the Straits of Magellan without anybody being aware of what might be the result of the court-martial.

It was about a fortnight after they had left the Falkland Islands, that they entered the Straits. At first they had a leading wind which carried them half through, but this did not last, and they then had to contend not only against the wind, but against the current, and they daily lost ground. The crews of the ships also began to sicken from fatigue and cold. Whether the admiral had before made up his mind, or whether irritated by his fruitless endeavours to continue his voyage, it is impossible to say; but after three weeks' useless struggle against the wind and currents, he hove to and ordered the captains on board, when he proposed that the prisoner should receive his punishment— and that punishment was—*to be deserted*; that is, to be sent on shore with a day's food, where there was no means of obtaining support, so as to die miserably of hunger. This was a punishment frequently resorted to by the Dutch at that period, as will be seen by reading an account of their voyages; but at the same time seldom, if ever, awarded to one of so high a rank as that of commodore.

Philip immediately protested against it, and so did Krantz, although they were both aware, that by so doing, they would make the admiral their enemy; but the other captains, who viewed both of them with a jealous eye, and considered them as interlopers and interfering with their advancement, sided with the admiral. Notwithstanding this majority, Philip thought it his duty to expostulate.

"You know well, admiral," said he, "that I joined in his condemnation for a breach of discipline: but at the same time there was much in extenuation. He committed a breach of discipline to save his ship's company, but not an error in judgment, as you yourself proved, by taking the same measure to save your own men. Do not, therefore, visit an offence of so doubtful a nature with such cruelty. Let the Company decide the point when you send him home, which you can do so soon as you arrive in India. He is sufficiently punished by losing his command: to do what you propose will be ascribed to feelings of revenge more than to those of justice. What success can we deserve if we commit an act of such cruelty; and how can we expect a merciful Providence to protect us from the winds and waves, when we are thus barbarous towards each other?"

Philip's arguments were of no avail. The admiral ordered him to return on board his ship, and had he been able to find an excuse, he would have deprived him of his command. This he could not well do; but Philip was aware that the admiral was now his inveterate enemy. The commodore was taken out of irons and brought into the cabin, and his sentence was made known to him.

"Be it so, admiral," replied Avenhorn; "for to attempt to turn you from your purpose, I know would be unavailing. I am not punished for disobedience of orders, but for having, by my disobedience, pointed out to you your duty—a duty which you were forced to perform afterwards by necessity. Then be it so; let me perish on these black rocks, as I shall, and my bones be whitened by the chilly blasts which howl over their desolation. But mark me, cruel and vindictive man! I shall not be the only one whose bones will bleach there. I prophesy that many others will share my fate, and even you, admiral, *may* be of the number,—if I mistake not, we shall lie side by side."

The admiral made no reply, but gave a sign for the prisoner to be removed. He then had a conference with the captains of the three smaller vessels; and, as they had been all along retarded by the heavier sailing of his own ship, and the Dort commanded by Philip, he decided that they should part company, and proceed on as fast as they could to the Indies—sending on board of the two larger vessels all the provisions they could spare, as they already began to run short.

Philip had left the cabin with Krantz after the prisoner had been removed. He then wrote a few lines upon a slip of paper—"Do not leave the beach when you are put on shore, until the vessels are out of sight;" and requesting Krantz to find an opportunity to deliver this to the commodore, he returned on board of his own ship.

When the crew of the Dort heard of the punishment about to be inflicted upon their old commander, they were much excited. They felt that he had sacrificed himself to save them, and they murmured much at the cruelty of the admiral.

About an hour after Philip's return to his ship, the prisons was sent on shore and landed on the desolate and rocky coast, with a supply of provisions for two days. Not a single article of extra clothing, or the means of striking a light, was permitted him. When the boat's keel grazed the beach, ha was ordered out. The boat shoved off, and the men were not permitted even to bid him farewell.

The fleet, as Philip had expected, remained hove to shifting the provisions, and it was not till after dark that everything was arranged. This opportunity was not lost. Philip was aware that it would be considered a breach of discipline, but to that he was indifferent; neither did he think it likely that it would come to the ears of the admiral, as the crew of the Dort were partial both to the commodore and to him. He had desired a seaman whom he could trust, to put into one of the boats a couple of muskets, and a quantity of ammunition, several blankets, and various other articles, besides provisions for two or three months for one person; and as soon as it was dark the men pulled on shore with the boat, found the commodore on the beach waiting for them, and supplied him with all these necessaries. They then rejoined their ship, without the admiral's having the least suspicion of what had been done, and shortly after the fleet made sail on a wind, with their heads off shore. The next morning, the three smaller vessels parted company, and by sunset had gained many miles to windward, after which they were not again seen.

The admiral had sent for Philip to give him his instructions, which were very severe, and evidently framed so as to be able to afford him hereafter some excuse for depriving him of his command. Among others, his orders were, as the Dort drew much less water than the admiral's ship, to sail ahead of him during the night, that if they approached too near the land as they beat across the Channel, timely notice might be given to the admiral, if in too shallow water. This responsibility was the occasion of Philip's being always on deck when they approached the land on either side of the Straits. It was the second night after the fleet had separated that Philip had been summoned on deck as they were nearing the land of Terra del Fuego: he was watching the man in the chains heaving the head, when the officer of the watch reported to him that the admiral's ship was ahead of them instead of astern. Philip made inquiry as to when he passed, but could not discover; he went forward, and saw the admiral's ship with her poop-light, which, when the admiral was astern, was not visible. "What can be the admiral's reason for this?" thought Philip; "has he run ahead for purpose to make a charge against me of neglect of duty? It must be so. Well, let him do as he pleases; he must wait now till we arrive in India, for I shall not allow him to *desert* me; and with the Company, I have as much, and I rather think, as a large proprietor, more interest than he has. Well as he has thought proper to go ahead, I have nothing to do but to follow. 'You may come out of the chains there.'"

Philip went forward: they were now, as he imagined, very near to the land, but the night was dark and they could not distinguish it. For half an hour they continued their course, much to Philip's surprise, for he now thought he could make out the loom of the land, dark as it was. His eyes were constantly fixed upon the ship ahead, expecting every minute that she would go about; but no, she continued her course, and Philip followed with his own vessel.

"We are very close to the land, sir," observed Vander Hagen, the lieutenant, who was the officer of the watch.

"So it appears to me: but the admiral is closer and draws much more water than we do," replied Philip.

"I think I see the rocks on the beam to leeward, sir."

"I believe you are right," replied Philip: "I cannot understand this. Ready about, and get a gun ready—they must suppose us to be ahead of them, depend up on it."

Hardly had Philip given the order, when the vessel struck heavily on the rocks. Philip hastened aft; he found that the rudder had been unshipped, and the vessel was immovably fixed. His thoughts then reverted to the admiral. "Was he on shore?" He ran forward, and the admiral was still sailing on with his poop-light about two cables' length ahead of him.

"Fire the gun, there," cried Philip, perplexed beyond measure.

The gun was fired, and immediately followed up by the flash and report of another gun close astern of them. Philip looked with astonishment over the quarter, and perceived the admiral's ship close astern to him, and evidently on shore as well as his own.

"Merciful Heaven!" exclaimed Philip, rushing forward, "what can this be?" He beheld the other vessel, with her light ahead, still sailing on and leaving them. The day was now dawning, and there was sufficient light to make out the land. The Dort was on shore not fifty yards from the beach, and surrounded by the high and barren rocks; yet the vessel ahead was apparently sailing on over the land. The seamen crowded on the forecastle, watching this strange phenomenon; at last it vanished from their sight.

"That's the Flying Dutchman, by all that's holy!" cried one of the seamen, jumping off the gun.

Hardly had the man uttered these words when the vessel disappeared.

Philip felt convinced that it was so, and he walked away aft in a very perturbed state. It must have been his father's fatal ship which had decoyed them to probable destruction. He hardly knew how to act. The admiral's wrath he did not wish, just at that moment, to encounter. He sent for the officer of the watch, and having desired him to select a crew for the boat, out of those men who had been on deck, and could substantiate his assertions, ordered him to go on board of the admiral, and state what had happened.

As soon as the boat had shoved off, Philip turned his attention to the state of his own vessel. The daylight had increased and Philip perceived that they were surrounded by rocks, and had run on shore between two reefs, which extended half a mile from the mainland. He sounded round his vessel, and discovered that she was fixed from forward to aft, and that without lightening her, there was no chance of getting her off. He then turned to where the admiral's ship lay aground and found that, to all appearance, she was in even a worse plight, as the rocks to leeward of her were above the water, and she was much more exposed, should bad weather come on. Never, perhaps, was there a scene more cheerless and appalling: a dark wintry sea—a sky loaded with heavy clouds—the wind cold and piercing—the whole line of the coast one mass of barren rocks, without the slightest appearance of vegetation; the inland part of the country presented an equally sombre appearance, and the higher points were capped with snow, although it was not yet the winter season. Sweeping the coast with his eye, Philip perceived, not four miles to leeward of them (so little progress had they made), the spot where they had *deserted* the commodore.

"Surely this has been a judgment on him for his cruelty," thought Philip, "and the prophecy of poor Avenhorn will come true—more bones than his will bleach on those rocks." Philip, turned round again to where the admiral's ship was on shore, and started back, as he beheld a sight even more dreadful than all that he had viewed—the body of Vander Hagen, the officer sent on board of the admiral hanging at the main-yard-arm. "My God! is it possible?" exclaimed Philip, stamping with sorrow and indignation.

His boat was returning on board, and Philip awaited it with impatience. The men hastened up the side, and breathlessly informed Philip that the admiral, as soon as he had heard the lieutenant's report, and his acknowledgment that he was officer of the watch, had ordered him to be hung, and that he had sent them back with a summons for him to repair on board immediately, and that they had seen another rope preparing at the other yardarm.

"But not for you, sir," cried the men—"that shall never be—you shall not go on board—and we will defend you with our lives."

The whole ship's company joined in this resolution, and expressed their determination to resist the admiral. Philip thanked them kindly—stated his intention of not going on board, and requested that they would remain quiet, until it was ascertained what steps the admiral might take. He then went down to his cabin, to reflect upon what plan he should proceed. As he looked out of the stern windows, and perceived the body of the young man still swinging in the wind, he almost wished that he was in his place, for then there would be an end to his wayward fate: but he thought of Amine, and felt, that for her he wished to live. That the Phantom Ship should have decoyed him to destruction was also a source of much painful feeling, and Philip meditated, with his hands pressed to his temples. "It is my destiny," thought he at last, "and the will of Heaven must be done: we could not have been so deceived if Heaven had not permitted it." And then his thoughts reverted to his present situation.

That the admiral had exceeded his powers in taking the life of the officer was undeniable, as although his instructions gave him power of life and death, still it was only to be decided by the sentence of the court-martial held by the captains commanding the vessels of the fleet; he therefore felt himself justified in resistance. But Philip was troubled with the idea that such resistance might lead to much bloodshed; and he was still debating how to act, when they reported to him that there was a boat coming from the admiral's ship. Philip went upon deck to receive the officer, who stated that it was the admiral's order that he should immediately come on board, and that he must consider himself now under arrest and deliver up his sword.

"No! no!" exclaimed the ship's company of the Dort. "He shall not go on board. We will stand by our captain to the last."

"Silence, men! silence!" cried Philip. "You must be aware, sir," said he to the officer, "that in the cruel punishment of that innocent young man the admiral has exceeded his powers: and, much as I regret to see any symptoms of mutiny and insubordination, it must be remembered, that if those in command disobey the orders they have received, by exceeding them, they not only set the example, but give an excuse for those who otherwise would be bound to obey them, to do the same. Tell the admiral that his murder of that innocent man has determined me no longer to consider myself under his authority, and that I will hold myself as well as him answerable to the Company whom we serve, for our conduct. I do not intend to go on board and put myself in his power, that he might gratify his resentment by my ignominious death. It is a duty that I owe these men under my command to preserve my life, that I may, if possible, preserve theirs in this strait; and you may also add, that a little reflection must point out to him that this is no time for us to war with, but to assist each other with all our energies. We are here, shipwrecked on a barren coast, with provisions insufficient for any lengthened stay, no prospect of succour, and little of escape. As the commodore truly prophesied, many more are likely to perish as well as him—and even the admiral himself may be of the number. I shall wait his answer; if he choose to lay aside all animosity, and refer our conduct to a higher tribunal, I am willing to join with him in rendering that assistance to each other which our situation requires—if not, you must perceive, and of course will tell him, that I have those with me who will defend me against any attempt at force. You have my answer, sir, and may return on board."

The officer went to the gangway, but found that none of his crew, except the bowman were in the boat; they had gone up to gain from the men of the Dort the true history of what they but imperfectly heard: and before they were summoned to return, had received full intelligence. They coincided with the seamen of the Dort, that the appearance of the Phantom Ship, which had occasioned their present disaster, was a judgment upon the admiral, for his conduct in having so cruelly *deserted* the poor commodore.

Upon the return of the officer with Philip's answer, the rage of the admiral was beyond all bounds. He ordered the guns aft which would bear upon the Dort to be double-shotted, and fired into her; but Krantz pointed out to him that they could not bring more guns to bear upon the Dort, in their present situation, than the Dort could bring to bear upon them; that their superior force was thus neutralised, and that no advantage could result from taking such a step. The admiral immediately put Krantz under arrest, and proceeded to put into execution his insane intentions. In this he was, however, prevented by the seamen of the Lion, who neither wished to fire upon their consort, or to be fired at in return. The report of the boat's crew had been circulated through the ship, and the men felt too much ill-will against the admiral, an perceived at the same time the extreme difficulty of their situation, to wish to make it worse. They did not proceed to open mutiny, but they went down below, and when the officers ordered them up, they refused to go upon deck; and the officers, who were equally disgusted with the admiral's conduct, merely informed him of the state of the ship's company, without naming individuals so as to excite his resentment against any one in particular. Such was the state of affairs when the sun went down. Nothing had been done on board the admiral's ship, for Krantz was under arrest, and the admiral had retired in a state of fury to his cabin.

In the mean time, Philip and the ship's company had not been idle—they had laid an anchor out astern, and hove taut: they had started all the water, and were pumping it out, when a boat pulled alongside, and Krantz made his appearance on deck.

"Captain Vanderdecken, I have come to put myself under your orders, if you will receive me—if not, render me your protection; for, as sure as fate, I should have been hanged to-morrow morning, if I had remained in my own ship. The men in the boat have come with the same intention—that of joining you, if you will permit them."

Although Philip would have wished it had been otherwise, he could not well refuse to receive Krantz, under the circumstances of the case. He was very partial to him, and to save his life, which certainly was in danger, he would have done much more. He desired that the boat's crew should return; but when Krantz had stated to him what had occurred on board the Lion, and the crew earnestly begged him not to send them back to almost certain death, which their having effected the escape of Krantz would have assured, Philip reluctantly allowed them to remain.

The night was tempestuous, but the wind being now off shore, the water was not rough. The crew of the Dort, under the directions of Philip and Krantz, succeeded in lightening the vessel so much during the night, that the next morning they were able to haul her off, and found that her bottom had received no serious injury. It was fortunate for them that they had not discontinued their exertions, for the wind shifted a few hours before sunrise, and by the time that they had shipped their rudder, it came on to blow fresh down the Straits, the wind being accompanied with a heavy swell.

The admiral's ship still lay aground, and apparently no exertions were used to get her off. Philip was much puzzled how to act: leave the crew of the Lion he could not; nor indeed could he refuse, or did he wish to refuse the admiral, if he proposed coming on board; but he now made up his mind that it should only be as a passenger, and that he would himself retain the command. At present he contented himself with dropping his anchor outside, clear of the reef, where he was sheltered by a bluff cape, under which the water was smooth, about a mile distant from where the admiral's ship lay on shore; and he employed his crew in replenishing his water-casks from a rivulet close to where the ship was anchored. He waited to see if the other vessel got off, being convinced that if she did not, some communication must soon take place. As soon as the water was complete, he sent one of his boats to the place where the commodore had been landed, having resolved to take him on board, if they could find him; but the boat returned without having seen anything of him, although the men had clambered over the hills to a considerable distance.

On the second morning after Philip had hauled his vessel off, they observed that the boats of the admiral's ship were passing and repassing from the shore, landing her stores and provisions; and the next day, from the tents pitched on shore, it was evident that she was abandoned, although the boats were still employed in taking articles out of her. That night it blew fresh, and the sea was heavy; the next morning her masts were gone, and she turned on her broadside: she was evidently a wreck, and Philip now consulted with Krantz how to act. To leave the crew of the Lion on shore was impossible: they must all perish when the winter set in upon such a desolate coast. On the whole, it was considered advisable that the first communication should come from the other party, and Philip resolved to remain quietly at anchor.

It was very plain that there was no longer any subordination among the crew of the Lion, who were to be seen, in the day time, climbing over the rocks in every direction, and at night, when their large fires were lighted, carousing and drinking. This waste of provisions was a subject of much vexation to Philip. He had not more than sufficient for his own crew, and he took it for granted that, so soon as what they had taken on shore should be expended, the crew of the Lion would ask to be received on board of the Dort.

For more than a week did affairs continue in this state when one morning a boat was seen pulling towards the ship and in the stern-sheets Philip recognised the officer who had been sent on board to put him under arrest. When the officer came on deck he took off his hat to Philip.

"You do, then, acknowledge me as in command," observed Philip.

"Yes, sir, most certainly; you were second in command, but now you are first—for the admiral is dead."

"Dead!" exclaimed Philip—"and how?"

"He was found dead on the beach, under a high cliff, and the body of the commodore was in his arms; indeed, they were both grappled together. It is supposed, that in his walk up to the top of the hill, which he used to take every day, to see if any vessels might be in the Straits, he fell in with the commodore—that they had come to contention, and had both fallen over the precipice together. No one saw the meeting, but they must have fallen over the rocks, as the bodies are dreadfully mangled."

On inquiry, Philip ascertained that all chance of saving the Lion had been lost after the second night, when she had beat in her larboard streak, and six feet water in the hold; that the crew had been very insubordinate, and had consumed almost all the spirits; and that not only all the sick had already perished, but also many others who had either fallen over the rocks, when they were intoxicated, or had been found dead in the morning from their exposure during the night.

"Then the poor commodore's prophecy has been fulfilled!" observed Philip to Krantz. "Many others, and even the admiral himself, have perished with him—peace be with them! And now let us get away from this horrible place as soon as possible."

Philip then gave orders to the officer to collect his men, and the provisions that remained, for immediate embarkation. Krantz followed soon after with all the boats, and before night everything was on board. The bodies of the admiral and commodore were buried where they lay, and the next morning the Dort was under weigh, and with a slanting wind was laying a fair course through the Straits.

Chapter Nineteen.

It appeared as if their misfortunes were to cease, after the tragical death of the two commanders. In a few days, the Dort had passed through the Straits of Magellan, and was sailing in the Pacific Ocean with a blue sky and quiet sea. The ship's company recovered their health and spirits, and the vessel being now well manned, the duty was carried on with cheerfulness.

In about a fortnight, they had gained well up on the Spanish coast, but although they had seen many of the inhabitants on the beach, they had not fallen in with any vessels belonging to the Spaniards. Aware that if he met with a Spanish ship of superior force it would attack him, Philip had made every preparation, and had trained his men to the guns. He had now, with the joint crews of the vessels, a well-manned ship, and the anticipation of prize-money had made his men very eager to fall in with some Spaniard, which they knew that Philip would capture if he could. Light winds and calms detained them for a month on the coast, when Philip determined upon running for the Isle St. Marie, where, though he knew it was in possession of the Spaniards, he yet hoped to be able to procure refreshments for the ship's Company, either by fair means or by force. The Dort was, by their reckoning, about thirty miles from the island, and having run in until after dark, they had hove to till the next morning. Krantz was on deck; he leant over the side, and as the sails flapped to the masts, he attempted to define the line of the horizon. It was very dark, but as he watched, he thought that he perceived a light for a moment, and which then disappeared. Fixing his eyes on the spot, he soon made out a vessel, hove to, and not two cables' length distant. He hastened down to apprise Philip and procure a glass. By the time Philip was on deck the vessel had been distinctly made out to be a three-masted xebeque, very low in the water. After a short consultation it was agreed that the boats on the quarter should be lowered down, and manned and armed without noise, and that they should steal gently alongside and surprise her. The men were called up, silence enjoined, and in a few minutes the boat's crew had possession of the vessel; having boarded her and secured the hatches before the alarm could be given by the few who were on deck. More men were then taken on board by Krantz, who, as agreed upon, lay to under the lee of the Dort until the daylight made its appearance. The hatches were then taken off, and the prisoners sent on board of the Dort. There were sixty people on board,—a large number for a vessel of that description.

On being interrogated, two of the prisoners, who were well-dressed and gentlemanlike persons, stepped forward and stated that the vessel was from St. Mary's, bound to Lima, with a cargo of flour and passengers; that the crew and captain consisted of twenty-five men, and all the rest who were on board had taken that opportunity of going to Lima. That they themselves were among the passengers, and trusted that the vessel and cargo would be immediately released, as the two nations were not at war.

"Not at war at home, I grant," replied Philip, "but in these seas, the constant aggressions of your armed ships compel me to retaliate, and I shall therefore make a prize of your vessel and cargo. At the same time, as I have no wish to molest private individuals, I will land all the passengers and crew at St. Mary's, to which place I am bound in order to obtain refreshments, which now I shall expect will be given cheerfully as your ransom, so as to relieve me from resorting to force." The prisoners protested strongly against this, but without avail. They then requested leave to ransom the vessel and cargo, offering a larger sum than they both appeared to be worth: but Philip, being short of provisions refused to part with the cargo, and the Spaniards appeared much disappointed at the unsuccessful issue of their request. Finding that nothing would induce him to part with the provisions, they then begged hard to ransom the vessel; and to this, after a consultation with Krantz, Philip gave his assent. The two vessels then made sail, and steered on for the island, then about four leagues distant. Although Philip had not wished to retain the vessel, yet, as they stood in together, her superior speed became so manifest, that he almost repented that he had agreed to ransom her.

At noon, the Dort was anchored in the roads, out of gunshot, and a portion of the passengers allowed to go on shore and make arrangements for the ransom of the remainder, while the prize was hauled alongside, and her cargo hoisted into the ship. Towards evening, three large boats with livestock and vegetables, and the sum agreed upon for the ransom of the xebeque, came alongside; and as soon as one of the boats was cleared, the prisoners were permitted to go on shore in it, with the exception of the Spanish pilot, who, at the suggestion of Krantz, was retained, with a promise of being released directly the Dort was clear of the Spanish seas. A negro slave was also, at his own request, allowed to remain on board, much to the annoyance of the two passengers before mentioned, who claimed the man as their property, and insisted that it was an infraction of the agreement which had been entered into. "You prove my right by your own words," replied Philip; "I agreed to deliver up all the passengers, but no *property*; the slave will remain on board."

Finding their endeavours ineffectual, the Spaniards took a haughty leave. The Dort remained at anchor that night to examine her rigging, and the next morning they discovered that the xebeque had disappeared, having sailed unperceived by them during the night.

As soon as the anchor was up and sail made on the ship, Philip went down to his cabin with Krantz, to consult as to their best course. They were followed by the negro slave, who, shutting the door and looking watchfully round, said that he wished to speak with them. His information was most important, but given rather too late. The vessel which had been ransomed, was a government advice-boat, the fastest sailer the Spaniards possessed. The pretended two passengers were officers of the Spanish navy, and the others were the crew of the vessel. She had been sent down to collect the bullion and take it to Lima, and at the same time to watch for the arrival of the Dutch fleet, intelligence of whose sailing had been some time before received overland. When the Dutch fleet made its appearance, she was to return to Lima with the news, and a Spanish force would be detached against it. They further learnt that some of the supposed casks of flour contained 2,000 gold doubloons each, others bars of silver; this precaution having been taken in case of capture. That the vessel had now sailed for Lima there was no doubt. The reason why the Spaniards were so anxious not to leave the negro on board of the Dort, was, that they knew that he would disclose what he now had done. As for the pilot, he was a man whom the Spaniards knew they could trust, and for that reason they had better be careful of him, or he would lead the Dort into some difficulty.

Philip now repented that he had ransomed the vessel, as he would, in all probability, have to meet and cope with a superior force, before he could make his way clear out of these seas; but there was no help for it. He consulted with Krantz, and it was agreed that they should send for the ship's company and make them acquainted with these facts; arguing that a knowledge of the valuable capture which they had made, would induce the men to fight well, and stimulate them with the hopes of further success. The ship's company heard the intelligence with delight, professed themselves ready to meet double their force, and then by the directions of Philip, the casks were brought up on the quarter-deck, opened, and the bullion taken out. The whole, when collected, amounted to about half a million of dollars, as near as they could estimate it, and a distribution of the coined money was made from the capstan the very next day; the bars of metal being reserved until they could be sold, and their value ascertained.

For six weeks Philip worked his vessel up the coast, without falling in with any vessel under sail. Notice had been given by the advice-boat, as it appeared, and every craft large and small, was at anchor under the batteries. They had nearly run up the whole coast, and Philip had determined that the next day he would stretch across to Batavia, when a ship was seen in-shore under a press of sail, running towards Lima. Chase was immediately given, but the water shoaled, and the pilot was asked if they could stand on. He replied in the affirmative, stating that they were now in the shallowest water, and that it was deeper within. The leadsman was ordered into the chains, but at the first heave, the lead-line broke; another was sent for, and the Dort still carried on under a heavy press of sail. Just then, the negro slave went up to Philip, and told him that he had seen the pilot with his knife in the chains, and that he thought he must have cut the lead-line so far through, as to occasion its being carried away, and told Philip not to trust him. The helm was immediately put down; but as the ship went round she touched on the bank, dragged, and was again clear.—"Scoundrel!" cried Philip. "So you cut the lead-line? The negro saw you, and has saved us."

The Spaniard leaped down from off the gun, and, before he could be prevented, had buried his knife in the heart of the negro. "Maldetto! take that for your pains," cried he in a fury, grinding his teeth and flourishing his knife.

The negro fell dead. The pilot was seized and disarmed by the crew of the Dort, who were partial to the negro, as it was from his information that they had become rich.

"Let them do with him as they please," said Krantz to Philip.

"Yes," replied Philip, "summary justice."

The crew debated a few minutes, and then lashed the pilot to the negro, and carried him off to the taffrail. There was a heavy plunge, and he disappeared under the eddying waters in the wake of the vessel.

Philip now determined to shape his course for Batavia. He was within a few days' sail of Lima, and had every reason to believe that vessels had been sent out to intercept him. With a favourable wind he now stood away from the coast, and for three days made a rapid passage. On the fourth, at daylight, two vessels appeared to windward, bearing down upon him. That they were large armed vessels was evident; and the display of Spanish ensigns and pennants, as they rounded to, about a mile to windward, soon showed that they were enemies. They proved to be a frigate of a larger size than the Dort and a corvette of twenty-two guns.

The crew of the Dort showed no alarm at this disparity of force; they clinked their doubloons in their pockets, vowed not to return them to their lawful owners, if they could help it, and flew with alacrity to their guns. The Dutch ensign was displayed in defiance, and the two Spanish vessels again putting their heads towards the Dort, that they might lessen their distance, received some raking shot, which somewhat discomposed them, but they rounded to at a cable's length, and commenced the action with great spirit, the frigate lying on the beam, and the corvette on the bow of Philip's vessel. After half an hour's determined exchange of broadsides, the fore-mast of the Spanish frigate fell, carrying away with it the maintop-mast; and this accident impeded her firing. The Dort immediately made sail, stood on to the corvette, which she crippled with three or four broadsides, then tacked, and fetched alongside of the frigate, whose lee guns were still impeded with the wreck of the foremast. The two vessels now lay head and stern, within ten feet of each other, and the action recommenced to the disadvantage of the Spaniard. In a quarter of an hour the canvass, hanging overside, caught fire from the discharge of the guns, and very soon communicated to the ship, the Dort still pouring in a most destructive broadside, which could not be effectually returned. After every attempt to extinguish the flames, the captain of the Spanish vessel resolved that both vessels should share the same fate. He put his helm up, and running her on to the Dort, grappled with her, and attempted to secure the two vessels together. Then raged the conflict; the Spaniards attempting to pass their grappling-chains so as to prevent the escape of their enemy, and the Dutch endeavouring to frustrate their attempt. The chains and sides of hot vessels were crowded with men fighting desperately; those struck down falling between the two vessels, which the wreck of the foremast still prevented from coming into actual collision. During this conflict, Philip and Krantz were not idle. By squaring the after-yards, and putting all sail on forward they contrived that the Dort should pay off before the wind with her antagonist, and by this manoeuvre they cleared themselves of the smoke which so incommoded them; and having good way on the two vessels, they then rounded to so as to get on the other tack, and bring the Spaniard to leeward. This gave them a manifest advantage and soon terminated the conflict. The smoke and flames were beat back on the Spanish vessel—the fire which had communicated to the Dort was extinguished—the Spaniards were no longer able to prosecute their endeavours to fasten the two vessels together, and retreated to within the bulwarks of their own vessel; and after great exertions, the Dort was disengaged, and forged ahead of her opponent, who was soon enveloped in a sheet of flame. The corvette remained a few cables' length to windward, occasionally firing a gun. Philip poured in a broadside, and she hauled down her colours. The action might now be considered at an end, and the object was to save the crew of the burning frigate. The boats of the Dort were hoisted out, but only two of them would swim. One of them was immediately despatched to the corvette, with orders for her to send all her boats to the assistance of the frigate, which was done, and the major part of the surviving crew were saved. For two hours the guns of the frigate, as they were heated by the flames, discharged themselves; and then, the fire having communicated to the magazine she blew up, and the remainder of her hull sank slowly and disappeared. Among the prisoners, in the uniform of the Spanish service, Philip perceived the two pretended passengers; this proving the correctness of the negro's statement. The two men-of-war had been sent out of Lima on purpose to intercept him, anticipating, with such a preponderating force, an easy victory. After some consultation with Krantz, Philip agreed, that as the corvette was in such a crippled state, and the nations were not actually at war, it would be advisable to release her with all the prisoners. This was done, and the Dort again made sail for Batavia, and anchored in the roads three weeks after the combat had taken the place. He found the remainder of the fleet, which had been despatched before them, and had arrived there some weeks, had taken in their cargoes, and were ready to sail for Holland. Philip wrote his despatches in which he communicated to the Directors the events of the voyage; and then went on shore, to reside at the house of the merchant who had formerly received him, until the Dort could be freighted for her voyage home.

Chapter Twenty.

We must return to Amine, who is seated on the mossy bank where she and Philip conversed when they were interrupted by Schriften, the pilot. She is in deep thought, with her eyes cast down, as if trying to recall the past. "Alas! for my mother's power," exclaimed she; "but it is gone—gone for ever! This torment and suspense I cannot bear—those foolish priests too!" And Amine rose from the bank and walked towards her cottage.

Father Mathias had not returned to Lisbon. At first he had not found an opportunity, and afterwards, his debt of gratitude towards Philip induced him to remain by Amine, who appeared each day to hold more in aversion the tenets of the Christian faith. Many and many were the consultations with Father Seysen, many were the exhortations of both the good old men to Amine, who, at times, would listen without reply, and at others, argue boldly against them. It appeared to them, that she rejected their religion with an obstinacy as unpardonable as it was incomprehensible. But, to her, the case was more simple: she refused to believe, she said, that which she could not understand. She went so far as to acknowledge the beauty of the principles, the purity of the doctrine; but when the good priests would enter into the articles of their faith, Amine would either shake her head, or attempt to turn the conversation. This only increased the anxiety of the good Father Mathias to convert and save the soul of one so young and beautiful; and he now no longer thought of returning to Lisbon, but devoted his whole time to the instruction of Amine, who, wearied by his incessant importunities, almost loathed his presence.

Upon reflection, it will not appear surprising that Amine rejected a creed so dissonant to her wishes and intentions. The human mind is of that proud nature, that it requires all its humility to be called into action before it will bow, even to the Deity.

Amine knew that her mother had possessed superior knowledge, and an intimacy with unearthly intelligences. She had seen her practise her art with success, although so young at the time, that she could not now recall to mind the mystic preparations by which her mother had succeeded in her wishes; and it was now that her thoughts were wholly bent upon recovering what she had forgotten, that Father Mathias was exhorting her to a creed which positively forbade even the attempt. The peculiar and awful mission of her husband strengthened her opinion in the lawfulness of calling in the aid of supernatural agencies; and the arguments brought forward by these worthy, but not over-talented, professors of the Christian creed, had but little effect upon a mind so strong, and so decided, as that of Amine—a mind which, bent as it was upon one object, rejected with scorn tenets, in roof of which, they could offer no visible manifestation, and which would have bound her blindly to believe what appeared to her contrary to common sense. That her mother's art could bring evidence of *its* truth she had already shown, and satisfied herself in the effect of the dream which she had proved upon Philip;—but what proof could they bring forward?—Records—*which they would not permit her to read*!

"Oh! that I had my mother's art," repeated Amine once more as she entered the cottage; "then would I know where I was at this moment. Oh! for the black mirror, in which I used to peer at her command, and tell her what passed in array before me. How well do I remember that time—the time of my father's absence, when I looked into the liquid on the palm of my hand, and told her of the Bedouin camp—of the skirmish—the horse without a rider—and the turban on the sand!" And again Amine fell into deep thought. "Yes," cried she, after a time, "thou canst assist me, mother! Give me in a dream thy knowledge; thy daughter begs it as a boon. Let me think again. The word—what was the word? what was the name of the spirit—Turshoon? Yes, methinks it was Turshoon. Mother! mother! help your daughter."

"Dost thou call upon the Blessed Virgin, my child?" said Father Mathias, who had entered the room as she pronounced the last words. "If so, thou dost well, for she may appear to thee in thy dreams, and strengthen thee in the true faith."

"I called upon my own mother, who is in the land of spirits, good father," replied Amine.

"Yes; but as an infidel, not, I fear, in the land of the blessed spirits, my child."

"She hardly will be punished for following the creed of her fathers, living where she did, where no other creed was known?" replied Amine indignantly. "If the good on earth are blessed in the next world—if she had, as you assert she had, a soul to be saved—an immortal spirit—He who made that spirit will not destroy it because she worshipped as her fathers did. Her life was good: why should she be punished for ignorance of that creed which she never had an opportunity of rejecting?"

"Who shall dispute the will of Heaven, my child? Be thankful that you are permitted to be instructed, and to be received into the bosom of the holy church."

"I am thankful for many things, father; but I am weary, and must wish you a good night."

Amine retired to her room—but not to sleep. Once more did she attempt the ceremonies used by her mother, changing them each time, as doubtful of her success. Again the censer was lighted—the charms essayed; again the room was filled with smoke as she threw in the various herbs which she had knowledge of, for all the papers thrown aside at her father's death had been carefully collected, and on many were directions found as to the use of those herbs. "The word! the word! I have the first—the second word! Help me, mother!" cried Amine, as she sat by the side of the bed, in the room, which was now so full of smoke that nothing could be distinguished. "It is of no use," thought she, at last, letting her hands fall at her side; "I have forgotten the art. Mother! mother! help me in my dreams this night."

The smoke gradually cleared away, and, when Amine lifted up her eyes, she perceived a figure standing before her. At first she thought she had been successful in her charm; but, as the figure became more distinct, she perceived that it was Father Mathias, who was looking at her with a severe frown and contracted brow, his arms folded before him.

"Unholy child! what dost thou?"

Amine had roused the suspicions of the priests, not only by her conversation, but by several attempts which she had before made to recover her lost art; and on one occasion, in which she had defended it, both Father Mathias and Father Seysen had poured out the bitterest anathemas upon her, or any one who had resort to such practices. The smell of the fragrant herbs thrown into the censer, and the smoke, which afterwards had escaped through the door and ascended the stairs, had awakened the suspicious of Father Mathias, and he had crept up silently, and entered the room without her perceiving it. Amine at once perceived her danger. Had she been single, she would have dared the priest; but, for Philip's sake, she determined to mislead him.

"I do no wrong, father," replied she calmly, "but it appears to me not seemly that you should enter the chamber of a young woman during her husband's absence. I might have been in my bed. It is a strange intrusion."

"Thou canst not mean this, woman! My age—my profession—are a sufficient warranty," replied Father Mathias, somewhat confused at this unexpected attack.

"Not always, father, if what I have been told of monks and priests be true," replied Amine. "I ask again, why comest thou here into an unprotected woman's chamber?"

"Because I felt convinced that she was practising unholy arts."

"Unholy arts!—what mean you? Is the leech's skill unholy? Is it unholy to administer relief to those who suffer?—to charm the fever and the ague, which rack the limbs of those who live in this unwholesome climate?"

"All charms are most unholy."

"When I said charms, father, I meant not what you mean; I simply would have said a remedy. If a knowledge of certain powerful herbs, which, properly combined, will form a specific to ease the suffering wretch—an art well known unto my mother, and which I now would fain recall—if that knowledge, or a wish to regain that knowledge, be unholy, then are you correct."

"I heard thee call upon thy mother for her help."

"I did, for she well knew the ingredients; but I, I fear, have not the knowledge that she had. Is that sinful, good father?"

"'Tis, then, a remedy that you would find?" replied the priest; "I thought that thou didst practise that which is most unlawful."

"Can the burning of a few weeds be then unlawful? What did you expect to find? Look you, father, at these ashes—they may, with oil, be rubbed into the pores and give relief—but can they do more? What do you expect from them—a ghost?—a spirit?—like the prophet raised for the King of Israel?" And Amine laughed aloud.

"I am perplexed, but not convinced," replied the priest.

"I, too, am perplexed and not convinced," responded Amine, scornfully. "I cannot satisfy myself that a man of your discretion could really suppose that there was mischief in burning weeds; nor am I convinced that such was the occasion of your visit at this hour of the night to a lone woman's chamber. There may be natural charms more powerful than those you call supernatural. I pray you, father, leave this chamber. It is not seemly. Should you again presume, you leave the house. I thought better of you. In future, I will not be left at any time alone."

This attack of Amine's upon the reputation of the old priest was too severe. Father Mathias immediately quitted the room, saying, as he went out, "May God forgive you for your false suspicions and great injustice! I came here for the cause I have stated, and no more."

"Yes!" soliloquised Amine, as the door closed, "I know you did; but I must rid myself of your unwelcome company. I will have no spy upon my actions—no meddler to thwart me in my will. In your zeal you have committed yourself, and I will take the advantage you have given me. Is not the privacy of a woman's chamber to be held sacred by you sacred men! In return for assistance in distress—for food and shelter—you would become a spy. How grateful, and how worthy of the creed which you profess!" Amine opened her door as soon as she had removed the censer, and summoned one of the women of the house to stay that night in her room, stating that the priest had entered her chamber, and she did not like the intrusion.

"Holy father! is it possible?" replied the woman. Amine made no reply, but went to bed; but Father Mathias heard all that passed as he paced the room below. The next day he called upon Father Seysen, and communicated to him what had occurred and the false suspicions of Amine.

"You have acted hastily," replied Father Seysen, "to visit a woman's chamber at such an hour of the night."

"I had my suspicions, good Father Seysen."

"And she will have hers. She is young and beautiful."

"Now, by the blessed Virgin—"

"I absolve you, good Mathias," replied Father Seysen, "but still, if known, it would occasion much scandal to our church."

And known it soon was; for the woman who had been summoned by Amine did not fail to mention the circumstance and Father Mathias found himself everywhere so coldly received, and, besides, so ill at ease with himself, that he very soon afterwards quitted the country, and returned to Lisbon, angry with himself for his imprudence, but still more angry with Amine for her unjust suspicions.

Chapter Twenty One.

The cargo of the Dort was soon ready, and Philip sailed and arrived at Amsterdam without any further adventure. That he reached his cottage, and was received with delight by Amine need hardly be said. She had been expecting him; for the two ships of the squadron, which had sailed on his arrival at Batavia, and which had charge of his despatches, had, of course, carried letters to her from Philip, the first letters she had ever received from him during his voyages. Six weeks after the letters Philip himself made his appearance, and Amine was happy. The Directors were, of course, highly satisfied with Philip's conduct, and he was appointed to the command of a large armed ship, which was to proceed to India in the spring, one-third of which, according to agreement, was purchased by Philip out of the funds which he had in the hands of the Company. He had now five months of quiet and repose to pass away, previous to his once more trusting to the elements and this time, as it was agreed, he had to make arrangements on board for the reception of Amine.

Amine narrated to Philip what had occurred between her and the priest Mathias, and by what means she had rid herself of his unwished for surveillance.

"And were you practising your mother's arts, Amine?"

"Nay, not practising them, for I could not recall them, but I was trying to recover them."

"Why so, Amine? this must not be. It is, as the good father said, 'unholy.' Promise me you will abandon them now and for ever."

"If that act be unholy, Philip, so is your mission. You would deal and co-operate with the spirits of another world—I would do no more. Abandon your terrific mission—abandon your seeking after disembodied spirits, stay at home with you Amine, and she will cheerfully comply with your request."

"Mine is an awful summons from the Most High."

"Then the Most High permits your communion with those who are not of this world?"

"He does; you know even the priests do not gainsay it although they shudder at the very thought."

"If then He permits to one, He will to another; nay, ought that I can do is but with His permission."

"Yes, Amine, so does He permit evil to stalk on the earth but He countenances it not."

"He countenances your seeking after your doomed father, your attempts to meet him; nay, more He commands it. If you are thus permitted, why may not I be? I am your wife, a portion of yourself; and when I am left over a desolate hearth while you pursue your course of danger, may not I appeal also to the immaterial world to give me that intelligence which will soothe my sorrow, lighten my burden, and which, at the same time, can hurt no living creature? Did I attempt to practise these arts for evil purposes, it were just to deny them me, am wrong to continue them; but I would but follow in the step of my husband, and seek, as he seeks, with a good intent."

"But it is contrary to our faith."

"Have the priests declared your mission contrary to their faith? or, if they have, have they not been convinced to the contrary, and been awed to silence? But why argue, my dear Philip? Shall I not now be with you? and while with you I will attempt no more. You have my promise; but if separated I will not say but I shall then require of the invisible a knowledge of my husband's motions, when in search of the invisible also."

The winter passed rapidly away, for it was passed by Philip in quiet and happiness; the spring came on, the vessel was to be fitted out, and Philip and Amine repaired to Amsterdam.

The Utrecht was the name of the vessel to which he had been appointed, a ship of 400 tons, newly launched, and pierced for twenty-four guns. Two more months passed away, during which Philip superintended the fitting and loading of the vessel, assisted by his favourite Krantz, who served in her as first mate. Every convenience and comfort that Philip could think of was prepared for Amine; and in the month of May he started with orders to stop at Gambroon and Ceylon, run down the Straits of Sumatra, and from thence to force his way into the China seas, the Company having every reason to expect from the Portuguese the most determined opposition to the attempt. His ship's company was numerous, and he had a small detachment of soldiers on board to assist the supercargo, who carried out many thousand dollars to make purchases at ports in China, where their goods might not be appreciated. Every care had been taken in the equipment of the vessel, which was perhaps the finest, the best manned, and freighted with the most valuable cargo, which had ever been sent out by the India Company.

The Utrecht sailed with a flowing sheet, and was soon clear the English Channel; the voyage promised to be auspicious, favouring gales bore them without accident to within a few hundred miles of the Cape of Good Hope, when, for the first time, they were becalmed. Amine was delighted: in the evenings she would pace the deck with Philip; then all was silent, except the splash of the wave as it washed against the side of the vessel—all was in repose and beauty, as the bright southern constellations sparkled over their heads.

"Whose destinies can be in these stars, which appear not to those who inhabit the northern regions?" said Amine, as she cast her eyes above, and watched them in their brightness; "and what does that falling meteor portend? what causes its rapid descent from heaven?"

"Do you then put faith in stars, Amine?"

"In Araby we do; and why not? They were not spread over the sky to give light—for what then?"

"To beautify the world. They have their uses, too."

"Then you agree with me—they have their uses, and the destinies of men are there concealed. My mother was one of those who could read them well. Alas! for me they are a sealed book."

"Is it not better so, Amine?"

"Better!—say better to grovel on this earth with our selfish, humbled race, wandering in mystery and awe, and doubt, when we can communicate with the intelligences above! Does not the soul leap at her admission to confer with superior powers? Does not the proud heart bound at the feeling that its owner is one of those more gifted than the usual race of mortals? Is it not a noble ambition?"

"A dangerous one—most dangerous."

"And therefore most noble. They seem as if they would speak to me: look at you bright star—it beckons to me."

For some time, Amine's eyes were raised aloft; she spoke not, and Philip remained at her side. She walked to the gangway of the vessel, and looked down upon the placid wave, pierced by the moonbeams far below the surface.

"And does your imagination, Amine, conjure up a race of beings gifted to live beneath that deep blue wave, who sport amidst the coral rocks, and braid their hair with pearls?" said Philip, smiling.

"I know not, but it appears to me that it would be sweet to live there. You may call to mind your dream, Philip; I was then, according to your description, one of those same beings."

"You were," replied Philip, thoughtfully.

"And yet I feel as if water would reject me, even if the vessel were to sink. In what manner this mortal frame of mine may be resolved into its elements, I know not; but this I do feel, that it never will become the sport of, or be tossed by, the mocking waves. But come in, Philip, dearest; it is late, and the decks are wet with dew."

When the day dawned, the look-out man at the masthead reported that he perceived something floating on the still surface of the water, on the beam of the vessel. Krantz went up with his glass to examine, and made it out to be a small boat, probably cut adrift from some vessel. As there was no appearance of wind, Philip permitted a boat to be sent to examine it and after a long pull, the seamen returned on board, towing the small boat astern.

"There is a body of a man in it, sir," said the second mate to Krantz, as he gained the gangway; "but whether he is quite dead or not, I cannot tell."

Krantz reported this to Philip, who was, at that time sitting at breakfast with Amine, in the cabin, and then proceeded to the gangway, to where the body of the man had been already handed up by the seamen. The surgeon, who had been summoned, declared that life was not yet extinct, and was ordering him to be taken below, for recovery, when, to their astonishment, the man turned as he lay, sat up, and ultimately rose upon his feet and staggered to a gun, when, after a time, he appeared to be fully recovered. In reply to questions put to him, he said that he was in a vessel which had been upset in a squall, that he had time to cut away the small boat astern, and that all the rest of the crew had perished. He had hardly made this answer, when Philip, with Amine, came out of the cabin, and walked up to where the seamen were crowded round the man; the seamen retreated so as to make an opening, when Philip and Amine, to their astonishment and horror, recognised their old acquaintance, one-eyed pilot Schriften.

"He! he! Captain Vanderdecken I believe—glad to see you in command, and you too, fair lady."

Philip turned away with a chill at his heart; Amine's eye flashed as she surveyed the wasted form of the wretched creature. After a few seconds she turned round and followed Philip into the cabin, where she found him with his face buried in his hands.

"Courage, Philip, courage!" said Amine; "it was indeed a heavy shock, and I fear me, forebodes evil; but what then? it is our destiny."

"It is! it ought perhaps to be mine," replied Philip, raising his head; "but you, Amine, why should you be a partner—"

"I am your partner, Philip, in life and in death. I would not die first, Philip, because it would grieve you; but your death will be the signal for mine, and I will join you quickly."

"Surely, Amine, you would not hasten your own?"

"Yes! and require but one moment for this little steel to do its duty."

"Nay! Amine, that is not lawful—our religion forbids it."

"It may do so, but I cannot tell why. I came into this world without my own consent; surely I may leave it without asking the leave of priests! But let that pass for the present what will you do with that Schriften?"

"Put him on shore at the Cape—I cannot bear the odious wretch's presence. Did you not feel the chill, as before, when you approached him?"

"I did—I knew that he was there before I saw him; but still I know not why, I feel as if I would not send him away."

"Why not?"

"I believe it is because I am inclined to brave destiny, not to quail at it. The wretch can do no harm."

"Yes, he can—much: he can render the ship's company mutinous and disaffected; besides, he attempted to deprive me of my relic."

"I almost wish he had done so; then must you have discontinued this wild search."

"Nay, Amine, say not so; it is my duty, and I have taken my solemn oath—"

"But this Schriften—you cannot well put him ashore at the Cape; being a Company's officer, you might send him home if you found a ship there homeward bound; still were I you I would let destiny work. He is woven in with ours, that is certain. Courage, Philip, and let him remain."

"Perhaps you are right, Amine: I may retard, but cannot escape, whatever may be my intended fate."

"Let him remain, then, and let him do his worst. Treat him with kindness—who knows what we may gain from him?"

"True, true, Amine; he has been my enemy without cause. Who can tell?—perhaps he may become my friend."

"And if not, you will have done your duty. Send for him now."

"No, not now—to-morrow; in the mean time, I will order him every comfort."

"We are talking as if he were one of us, which I feel that he is not," replied Amine; "but still, mundane or not we cannot but offer mundane kindness, and what this world, or rather what this ship, affords. I long now to talk with him to see if I can produce any effect upon his ice-like frame. Shall I make love to the ghoul?" And Amine burst into a bitter laugh.

Here the conversation dropped, but its substance was not disregarded. The next morning, the surgeon having reported that Schriften was apparently quite recovered, he was summoned into the cabin. His frame was wasted away to a skeleton, but his motions and his language were as sharp and petulant as ever.

"I have sent for you, Schriften, to know if there is anything that I can do to make you more comfortable. Is there anything that you want?"

"Want?" replied Schriften, eyeing first Philip and then Amine. "He! he I think I want filling out a little."

"That you will, I trust, in good time; my steward has my orders to take care of you."

"Poor man," said Amine, with a look of pity, "how much he must have suffered! Is not this the man who brought you the letter from the Company, Philip?"

"He! he! yes! Not very welcome, was it, lady?"

"No, my good fellow; it's never a welcome message to a wife, that sends her husband away from her. But that was not your fault."

"If a husband will go to sea and leave a handsome wife when he has, as they say, plenty of money to live upon on shore, he! he!"

"Yes, indeed, you may well say that," replied Amine.

"Better give it up. All folly, all madness—eh, captain?"

"I must finish this voyage, at all events," replied Philip to Amine, "whatever I may do afterwards. I have suffered much, and so have you, Schriften. You have been twice wrecked; now tell me, what do you wish to do? Go home in the first ship, or go ashore at the Cape, or—"

"Or do anything, so I get out of this ship—he! he!"

"Not so. If you prefer sailing with me, as I know you are a good seaman, you shall have your rating and pay of pilot—that is, if you choose to follow my fortunes."

"Follow?—Must follow. Yes! I'll sail with you, Mynheer Vanderdecken, I wish to be always near you—he! he!"

"Be it so, then: as soon as you are strong again, you will go to your duty; till then, I will see that you want for nothing."

"Nor I, my good fellow. Come to me if you do, and I will be your help," said Amine. "You have suffered much; but we will do what we can to make you forget it."

"Very good!—very kind!" replied Schriften, surveying the lovely face and figure of Amine. After a times shrugging up his shoulders, he added—"A pity! Yes, it is! Must be, though."

"Farewell!" continued Amine, holding out her hand to Schriften.

The man took it, and a cold shudder went to her heart; but she, expecting such a result, would not appear to feel it. Schriften held her hand for a second or two in his own, looking at it earnestly, and then at Amine's face. "So fair—so good! Mynheer Vanderdecken, I thank you. Lady, may Heaven preserve you!" Then squeezing the hand of Amine, which he had not released, Schriften hastened out of the cabin.

So great was the sudden icy shock which passed through Amine's frame when Schriften pressed her hand, that when with difficulty she gained the sofa, she fell upon it. After remaining with her hand pressed against her heart for some time, during which Philip bent over her, she said, in a breathless voice, "That creature must be supernatural—I am sure of it—I am now convinced. Well," continued she, after a pause of some little while, "all the better, if we can make him a friend; and if I can I will."

"But think you, Amine, that those who are not of this world have feelings of kindness, gratitude, and ill-will, as we have? Can they be made subservient?"

"Most surely so. If they have ill-will—as we know they have—they must also be endowed with the better feelings. Why are there good and evil intelligences? They may have disencumbered themselves of their mortal clay, but the soul must be the same. A soul without feeling were no soul at all. The soul is active in this world, and must be so in the next. If angels can pity, they must feel like us. If demons can vex, they must feel like us. Our feelings change, then why not theirs? Without feelings, there were no heaven, no hell. Here our souls are confined, cribbed, and overladen—borne down by the heavy flesh by which they are, for the time, polluted; but the soul that has winged its flight from clay is, I think, not one jot more pure, more bright, or more perfect, than those within ourselves. Can they be made subservient, say you! Yes, they can; they can be forced, when mortals possess the means and power. The evil-inclined may be forced to good, as well as to evil. It is not the good and perfect spirits that we subject by art, but those that are inclined to wrong. It is over them that mortals have the power. Our arts have no power over the perfect spirits, but over those which are ever working evil, and which are bound to obey and do good, if those who master them require it."

"You still resort to forbidden arts, Amine. Is that right?"

"Right! If we have power given to us, it is right to use it."

"Yes, most certainly, for good; but not for evil."

"Mortals in power, possessing nothing but what is mundane, are answerable for the use of that power; so those gifted by superior means are answerable as they employ those means. Does the God above make a flower to grow, intending that it should not be gathered! No! neither does he allow supernatural aid to be given, if he did not intend that mortals should avail themselves of it."

As Amine's eyes beamed upon Philip's, he could not for the moment subdue the idea rising in his mind, that she was not like other mortals; and he calmly observed, "Am I sure, Amine, that I am wedded to one mortal as myself?"

"Yes! yes! Philip, compose yourself, I am but mortal; would to Heaven I were not. Would to Heaven I were one of those who could hover over you, watch you in all your perils, save and protect you in this your mad career but I am but a poor weak woman, whose heart beats fondly, devotedly for you—who for you would dare all and everything—who, changed in her nature, has become courageous and daring from her love—and who rejects all creeds which would prevent her from calling upon heaven, or earth, or hell, to assist her in retaining with her her soul's existence!"

"Nay! nay! Amine,—say not you reject the creed. Does not this,"—and Philip pulled from his bosom the holy relic,—"does not this, and the message sent by it, prove our creed is true?"

"I have thought much of it, Philip. At first it startled me almost into a belief; but even your own priests helped to undeceive me. They would not answer you; they would have left you to guide yourself; the message and the holy word, and the wonderful signs given, were not in unison with their creed, and they halted. May I not halt, if they did? The relic may be as mystic, as powerful as you describe; but the agencies may be false and wicked—the power given to it may have fallen into wrong hands; the power remains the same, but it is applied to uses not intended."

"The power, Amine, can only be exercised by those who are friends to Him who died upon it."

"Then is it no power at all or if a power, not half so great as that of the arch-fiend; for his can work for good and evil both. But on this point, dear Philip, we do not well agree, nor can we convince each other. You have been taught in one way, I another. That which our childhood has imbibed—which has grown up with our growth, and strengthened with our years—is not to be eradicated. I have seen my mother work great charms and succeed. You have knelt to priests. I blame not you!—blame not, then, your Amine. We both mean well—I trust do well."

"If a life of innocence and purity were all that were required, my Amine would be sure of future bliss."

"I think it is; and thinking so, it is my creed. There are many creeds: who shall say which is the true one? And what matters it?—they all have the same end in view—a future Heaven."

"True Amine, true," replied Philip, pacing the cabin thoughtfully; "and yet our priests say otherwise."

"What is the basis of their creed, Philip?"

"Charity and good-will."

"Does charity condemn to eternal misery those who have never heard this creed—who have lived and died worshipping the Great Being after their best endeavours, and little knowledge?"

"No, surely."

Amine made no further observations; and Philip, after pacing for a few minutes in deep thought, walked out of the cabin.

The Utrecht arrived at the Cape, watered, and proceeded on her voyage, and, after two months of difficult navigation, cast anchor off Gambroon. During this time Amine had been unceasing in her attempts to gain the good-will of Schriften. She had often conversed with him on deck, and had done him every kindness, and had overcome that fear which his near approach had generally occasioned. Schriften gradually appeared mindful of this kindness, and at last to be pleased with Amine's company. To Philip he was at times civil and courteous, but not always; but to Amine he was always deferent. His language was mystical,—she could not prevent his chuckling laugh, his occasional "He! he!" from breaking forth. But when they anchored at Gambroon, he was on such terms with her, that he would occasionally come into the cabin; and, although he would not sit down, would talk to Amine for a few minutes, and then depart. While the vessel lay at anchor at Gambroon, Schriften one evening walked up to Amine, who was sitting on the poop. "Lady," said he, after a pause, "yon ship sails for your own country in a few days."

"So I am told," replied Amine.

"Will you take the advice of one who wishes you well? Return in that vessel—go back to your own cottage, and stay there till your husband comes to you once more."

"Why is this advice given?"

"Because I forebode danger—nay, perhaps death, a cruel death—to one I would not harm."

"To me!" replied Amine, fixing her eyes upon Schriften, and meeting his piercing gaze.

"Yes, to you. Some people can see into futurity further than others."

"Not if they are mortal," replied Amine.

"Yes, if they are mortal. But, mortal or not, I do see that which I would avert. Tempt not destiny further."

"Who can avert it? If I take your counsel, still was it my destiny to take your counsel. If I take it not, still it was my destiny."

"Well, then, avoid what threatens you."

"I fear not, yet do I thank you. Tell me, Schriften, hast thou not thy fate some way interwoven with that of my husband? I feel that thou hast."

"Why think you so, lady?"

"For many reasons: twice you have summoned him—twice have you been wrecked, and miraculously reappeared and recovered. You know, too, of his mission—that is evident."

"But proves nothing."

"Yes! it proves much; for it proves that you knew what was supposed to be known but to him alone."

"It was known to you, and holy men debated on it," replied Schriften, with a sneer.

"How knew you that, again?"

"He! he!" replied Schriften. "Forgive me, lady; I meant not to affront you."

"You cannot deny that you are connected mysteriously and incomprehensibly with this mission of my husband's. Tell me, is it, as he believes, true and holy?"

"If he thinks that it is true and holy, it becomes so."

"Why, then, do you appear his enemy?"

"I am not *his* enemy, fair lady."

"You are not his enemy?—why, then, did you once attempt to deprive him of the mystic relic by which the mission is to be accomplished?"

"I would prevent his further search, for reasons which must not be told. Does that prove that I am his enemy? Would it not be better that he should remain on shore with competence and you, than be crossing the wild seas on this mad search? Without the relic it is not to be accomplished. It were a kindness, then, to take it from him."

Amine answered not, for she was lost in thought.

"Lady," continued Schriften, after a time, "I wish you well. For your husband I care not, yet do I wish him no harm. Now, hear me; if you wish for your future life to be one of ease and peace—if you wish to remain long in this world with the husband of your choice, of your first and warmest love—if you wish that he should die in his bed at a good old age, and that you should close his eyes, with children's tears lamenting, and their smiles reserved to cheer their mother—all this I see, and can promise is in futurity, if you will take that relic from his bosom and give it up to me. But if you would that he should suffer more than man has ever suffered, pass his whole life in doubt anxiety, and pain, until the deep wave receive his corpse, then let him keep it. If you would that your own days be shortened, and yet those remaining be long in human suffering—if you would be separated from him, and die a cruel death—then let him keep it. I can read futurity and such must be the destiny of both. Lady, consider well; I must leave you now. To-morrow I will have your answer."

Schriften walked away and left Amine to her own reflections. For a long while she repeated to herself the conversation and denunciations of the man, whom she was now convinced was not of this world, and was in some way or another deeply connected with her husband's fate. "To me he wishes well, no harm to my husband, and would prevent his search. Why would he?—that he will not tell. He has tempted me tempted me most strangely. How easy 'twere to take the relic whilst Philip sleeps upon my bosom—but how treacherous! And yet a life of competence and ease, a smiling family, a good old age; what offers to a fond and doting wife! And if not, toil, anxiety, and a watery grave; and for me! Pshaw! that's nothing. And yet to die separated from Philip, is that nothing? Oh, no, the thought is dreadful.—I do believe him. Yes he has foretold the future, and told it truly. Could I persuade Philip? No! I know him well; he has vowed, and is not to be changed. And yet, if the relic were taken without his knowledge, he would not have to blame himself. Who then would he blame? Could I deceive him? I, the wife of his bosom, tell a lie? No! no! it must not be. Come what will, it is our destiny, and I am resigned. I would that Schriften had not spoken! Alas! we search into futurity, and then would fain retrace our steps, and wish we had remained in ignorance."

"What makes you so pensive, Amine?" said Philip, who some time afterwards walked up to where she was seated.

Amine replied not at first. "Shall I tell him all?" thought she. "It is my only chance—I will." Amine repeated the conversation between her and Schriften. Philip made no reply; he sat down by Amine and took her hand. Amine dropped her head upon her husband's shoulder. "What think you, Amine?" said Philip, after a time.

"I could not steal your relic, Philip; perhaps you'll give it to me."

"And my father, Amine, my poor father—his dreadful doom to be eternal! He who appealed, was permitted to appeal to his son, that that dreadful doom might be averted. Does not the conversation of this man prove to you that my mission is not false? Does not his knowledge of it strengthen all? Yet, why would he prevent it?" continued Philip, musing.

"Why I cannot tell, Philip, but I would fain prevent it. I feel that he has power to read the future, and has read aright."

"Be it so; he has spoken, but not plainly. He has promised me what I have long been prepared for—what I vowed to Heaven to suffer. Already have I suffered much, and am prepared to suffer more. I have long looked upon this world as a pilgrimage, and (selected as I have been) trust that my reward will be in the other. But, Amine, you are not bound by oath to Heaven, you have made no compact. He advised you to go home. He talked of a cruel death. Follow his advice and avoid it."

"I am not bound by oath, Philip; but hear me; as I hope for future bliss, I now bind myself."

"Hold, Amine!"

"Nay, Philip, you cannot prevent me; for if you do now, I will repeat it when you are absent. A cruel death were a charity to me, for I shall not see you suffer. Then may I never expect future bliss, may eternal misery be my portion, if I leave you as long as fate permits us to be together. I am yours—your wife; my fortunes, my present, my future, my all, are embarked with you, and destiny may do its worst, for Amine will not quail. I have no recreant heart to turn aside from danger or from suffering. In that one point, Philip, at least, you chose, you wedded well."

Philip raised her hand to his lips in silence, and the conversation was not resumed. The next evening, Schriften came up again to Amine. "Well, lady?" said he.

"Schriften, it cannot be," replied Amine; "yet do I thank you much."

"Lady, if he must follow up his mission, why should you?"

"Schriften, I am his wife—as for ever, in this world, and the next. You cannot blame me."

"No," replied Schriften, "I do not blame, I admire you. I feel sorry. But, after all, what is death? Nothing. He! he!" and Schriften hastened away, and left Amine to herself.

Chapter Twenty Two.

The Utrecht sailed from Gambroon, touched at Ceylon, and proceeded on her voyage in the Eastern seas. Schriften still remained on board; but since his last conversation with Amine he had kept aloof, and appeared to avoid both her and Philip; still there was not, as before, any attempt to make the ship's company disaffected, nor did he indulge in his usual taunts and sneers. The communication he had made to Amine had also its effect upon her and Philip; they were more pensive and thoughtful; each attempted to conceal their gloom from the other; and when they embraced, it was with the mournful feeling that perhaps it was an indulgence they would soon be deprived of: at the same time, they steeled their hearts to endurance and prepared to meet the worst. Krantz wondered at the change, but of course could not account for it. The Utrecht was not far from the Andaman Isles, when Krantz, who had watched the barometer, came in early one morning and called Philip.

"We have every prospect of a typhoon, sir," said Krantz; "the glass and the weather are both threatening."

"Then we must make all snug. Send down top-gallant yards and small sails directly. We will strike top-gallant masts. I will be out in a minute."

Philip hastened on deck. The sea was smooth, but already the moaning of the wind gave notice of the approaching storm. The vacuum in the air was about to be filled up, and the convulsion would be terrible; a white haze gathered fast, thicker and thicker; the men were turned up, everything of weight was sent below, and the guns were secured. Now came a blast of wind which careened the ship, passed over, and in a minute she righted as before; then another and another, fiercer and fiercer still. The sea, although smooth, at last appeared white as a sheet with foam, as the typhoon swept along in its impetuous career; it burst upon the vessel, which bowed down to her gunnel and there remained; in a quarter of an hour the hurricane had passed over, and the vessel was relieved, but the sea had risen, and the wind was strong. In another hour the blast again came, more wild, more furious than the first, the waves were dashed into their faces, torrents of rain descended, the ship was thrown on her beam ends, and thus remained till the wild blast had passed away, to sweep destruction far beyond them, leaving behind it a tumultuous angry sea.

"It is nearly over, I believe, sir," said Krantz. "It is clearing up a little to windward."

"We have had the worst of it, I believe," said Philip.

"No! there is worse to come," said a low voice near to Philip. It was Schriften who spoke.

"A vessel to windward scudding before the gale," cried Krantz.

Philip looked to windward, and in the spot where the horizon was clearest, he saw a vessel under topsails and foresail, standing right down. "She is a large vessel; bring me my glass." The telescope was brought from the cabin, but before Philip could use it, a haze had again gathered up to windward, and the vessel was not to be seen.

"Thick again," observed Philip, as he shut in his telescope; "we must look out for that vessel, that she does not run too close to us."

"She has seen us, no doubt, sir," said Krantz.

After a few minutes the typhoon again raged, and the atmosphere was of a murky gloom. It seemed as if some heavy fog had been hurled along by the furious wind; nothing was to be distinguished except the white foam of the sea, and that not the distance of half a cable's length, where it was lost in one dark grey mist. The storm-stay-sail, yielding to the force of the wind, was rent into strips and flogged and cracked with a noise even louder than the gale. The furious blast again blew over, and the mist cleared up a little.

"Ship on the weather beam close aboard of us," cried one of the men.

Krantz and Philip sprang upon the gunwale, and beheld the large ship bearing right down upon them, not three cables' length distant.

"Helm up! she does not see us, and she will be aboard of us!" cried Philip. "Helm up, I say, hard up, quick!"

The helm was put up, as the men, perceiving their imminent danger, climbed upon the guns to look if the vessel altered her course; but no—down she came, and the head-sails of the Utrecht having been carried away, to their horror they perceived that she would not answer her helm, and pay off as they required.

"Ship ahoy!" roared Philip through his trumpet—but the gale drove the sound back.

"Ship ahoy!" cried Krantz on the gunwale, waving his hat. It was useless—down she came, with the waters foaming under her bows, and was now within pistol-shot of the Utrecht.

"Ship ahoy!" roared all the sailors, with a shout that must have been heard: it was not attended to: down came the vessel upon them, and now her cutwater was within ten yards of the Utrecht. The men of the Utrecht, who expected that their vessel would be severed in half by the concussion, climbed upon the weather gunwale, all ready to catch at the ropes of the other vessel, and climb on board of her. Amine, who had been surprised at the noise on deck, had come out, and had taken Philip by the arm.

"Trust to me—the shock—," said Philip. He said no more; the cutwater of the stranger touched their sides; one general cry was raised by the sailors of the Utrecht,—they sprang to catch at the rigging of the other vessel's bowsprit, which was now pointed between their masts—they caught at nothing—nothing—there was no shock—no concussion of the two vessels—the stranger appeared to cleave through them—her hull passed along in silence—no cracking of timbers—no falling of masts—the foreyard passed through their mainsail, yet the canvas was unrent—the whole vessel appeared to cut through the Utrecht, yet left no trace of injury—not fast, but slowly, as if she were really sawing through her by the heaving and tossing of the sea with her sharp prow. The stranger's forechains had passed their gunwale before Philip could recover himself. "Amine," cried he at last, "the Phantom Ship!—my father!"

The seamen of the Utrecht, more astounded by the marvellous result than by their former danger, threw themselves down upon deck; some hastened below, some prayed, others were dumb with astonishment and fear. Amine appeared more calm than any, not excepting Philip; she surveyed the vessel as it slowly forced its way through; she beheld the seamen on board of her coolly leaning over the gunwale, as if deriding the destruction they had occasioned; she looked for Vanderdecken himself, and on the poop of the vessel, with his trumpet under his arm she beheld the image of her Philip—the same hardy, strong build—the same features—about the same age apparently—there could be no doubt it was the *doomed* Vanderdecken.

"See, Philip," said she, "see your father!"

"Even so—Merciful Heaven! It is—it is!" and Philip, overpowered by his feelings, sank upon deck.

The vessel had now passed over the Utrecht; the form of the elder Vanderdecken was seen to walk aft and look over the taffrail; Amine perceived it to start and turn away suddenly—she looked down, and saw Schriften shaking his fist in defiance at the supernatural being! Again the Phantom Ship flew to leeward before the gale, and was soon lost in the mist but, before that, Amine had turned and perceived the situation of Philip. No one but herself and Schriften appeared able to act or move. She caught the pilot's eye, beckoned to him, and with his assistance Philip was led into the cabin.

Chapter Twenty Three.

"I have then seen him," said Philip, after he had lain down on the sofa in the cabin for some minutes to recover himself while Amine bent over him. "I have at last seen him, Amine! Can you doubt now?"

"No, Philip, I have now no doubt," replied Amine, mournfully; "but take courage, Philip."

"For myself, I want not courage—but for you, Amine—you know that his appearance portends a mischief that will surely come."

"Let it come," replied Amine, calmly; "I have long been prepared for it, and so have you."

"Yes, for my self; but not for you."

"You have been wrecked often, and have been saved—then why should not I?"

"But the sufferings!"

"Those suffer least who have most courage to bear up against them. I am but a woman weak and frail in body, but I trust I have that within me which will not make you feel ashamed of Amine. No, Philip, you will have no wailing; no expression of despair from Amine's lips; if she can console you she will; if she can assist you she will; but come what may, if she cannot serve you, at least she will prove no burden to you."

"Your presence in misfortune would unnerve me, Amine."

"It shall not; it shall add to your resolution. Let fate do its worst."

"Depend upon it, Amine, that will be ere long."

"Be it so," replied Amine; "but Philip, it were as well you showed yourself on deck; the men are frightened, and your absence will be observed."

"You are right," said Philip; and rising and embracing her, he left the cabin.

"It is but too true, then," thought Amine. "Now to prepare for disaster and death; the warning has come. I would I could know more. Oh! mother, mother, look down upon thy child, and in a dream reveal the mystic arts which I have forgotten,—then should I know more; but I have promised Philip, that unless separated—yes, that idea is worse than death, and I have a sad foreboding; my courage fails me only when I think of that!"

Philip, on his return to the deck, found the crew of the vessel in great consternation. Krantz himself appeared bewildered—he had not forgotten the appearance of the Phantom Ship off Desolation Harbour, and the vessels following her their destruction. This second appearance, more awful than the former, quite unmanned him; and when Philip came out of the cabin he was leaning in gloomy silence against the weather-bulkhead.

"We shall never reach port again, sir," said he to Philip, as he came up to him.

"Silence, silence; the men may hear you."

"It matters not; they think the same," replied Krantz.

"But they are wrong," replied Philip, turning to the seamen. "My lads! that some disaster may happen to us, after the appearance of this vessel is most probable; I have seen her before more than once, and disasters did then happen; but here I am, alive and well, therefore it does not prove that we cannot escape as I have before done. We must do our best, and trust in Heaven. The gale is breaking fast, and in a few hours we shall have fine weather. I have met this Phantom Ship before, and care not how often I meet it again. Mr Krantz, get up the spirits—the men have had hard work, and must be fatigued."

The very prospect of obtaining liquor appeared to give courage to the men; they hastened to obey the order, and the quantity served out was sufficient to give courage to the most tearful, and induce others to defy old Vanderdecken and his whole crew of imps. The next morning the weather was fine, the sea smooth, and the Utrecht went gaily on her voyage.

Many days of gentle breezes and favouring winds gradually wore off the panic occasioned by the supernatural appearance; and, if not forgotten, it was referred to either in jest or with indifference, he now had run through the straits of Malacca, and entered the Polynesian archipelago. Philip's orders were to refresh and call for instructions at the small island of Boton, then in possession of the Dutch. They arrived there in safety, and after remaining two days, again sailed on their voyage, intending to make their passage between the Celebes and the island of Galago. The weather was still clear and the wind light; they proceeded cautiously, on account of the reefs and currents, and with a careful watch for the piratical vessels, which have for centuries infested those seas; but they were not molested, and had gained well up among the islands to the north of Galago, when it fell calm, and the vessel was borne to the eastward of it by the current. The calm lasted several days, and they could procure no anchorage; at last they found themselves among the cluster of islands near to the northern coast of New Guinea.

The anchor was dropped, and the sails furled for the night; a drizzling small rain came on, the weather was thick, and watches were stationed in every part of the ship, that they might not be surprised by the pirate proas, for the current ran past the ship at the rate of eight or nine miles per hour, and these vessels, if hid among the islands, might sweep down upon them unperceived.

It was twelve o'clock at night, when Philip, who was in bed, was awakened by a shock; he thought it might be a proa running alongside, and he started from his bed and ran out. He found Krantz, who had been awakened by the same cause, running up undressed. Another shock succeeded, and the ship careened to port. Philip then knew that the ship was on shore.

The thickness of the night prevented them from ascertaining where the were, but the lead was thrown over the side, and they found that they were lying on shore on a sandbank, with not more than fourteen feet water on the deepest side, and that they were broadside on with a strong current pressing them further up on the bank; indeed the current ran like a mill-race, and each minute they were swept into shallow water.

On examination they found that the ship had dragged her anchor which, with the cable, was still taut from the starboard bow, but this did not appear to prevent the vessel from being swept further up on the bank. It was supposed that the anchor had parted at the shank, and another anchor was let go.

Nothing more could be done till daybreak, and impatiently did they wait till the next morning. As the sun rose, the mist cleared away, and they discovered that they were on shore on a sandbank, a small portion of which was above water, and round which the current ran with great impetuosity. About three miles from them was a cluster of small islands with cocoa-trees growing on them, but with no appearance of inhabitants.

"I fear we have little chance," observed Krantz to Philip. "If we lighten the vessel the anchor may not hold, and we shall be swept further on, and it is impossible to lay out an anchor against the force of this current."

"At all events we must try; but I grant that our situation is anything but satisfactory. Send all the hands aft."

The men came aft, gloomy and dispirited.

"My lads!" said Philip, "why are you disheartened?"

"We are doomed, sir; we knew it would be so."

"I thought it probable that the ship would be lost—I told you so; but the loss of the ship does not involve that of the ship's company—nay, it does not follow that the ship is to be lost, although she may be in great difficulty, as she is at present. What fear is there for us, my men?—the water is smooth—we have plenty of time before us—we can make a raft and take to our boats—it never blows among these islands, and we have land close under our lee. Let us first try what we can do with the ship; if we fail we must then take care of ourselves."

The men caught at the idea and went to work willingly; the water-casks were started, the pumps set going, and everything that could be spared was thrown over to lighten the ship; but the anchor still dragged, from the strength of the current and bad holding-ground; and Philip and Krantz perceived that they were swept further on the bank.

Night came on before they quitted their toil, and then a fresh breeze sprung up and created a swell, which occasioned the vessel to beat on the hard sand; thus did they continue until the next morning. At daylight the men resumed their labours, and the pumps were again manned to clear the vessel of the water which had been started, but after a time they pumped up sand. This told them that a plank had started and that their labours were useless; the men left their work, but Philip again encouraged them and pointed out that they could easily save themselves, and all that they had to do was to construct a raft which would hold provisions for them, and receive that portion of the crew who could not be taken into the boats.

After some repose the men again set to work; the top-sails were struck, the yards lowered down, and the raft was commenced under the lee of the vessel, where the strong current was checked. Philip, recollecting his former disaster took great pains in the construction of this raft, and aware that as the water and provisions were expended there would be no occasion to tow so heavy a mass, he constructed it in two parts, which might easily be severed, and thus the boats would have less to tow, as soon as circumstances would enable them to part with one of them.

Night again terminated their labours, and the men retired to rest the weather continuing fine, with very little wind. By noon the next day the raft was complete; water and provisions were safely stowed on board; a secure and dry place was fitted up for Amine in the centre of one portion; spare robes, sails, and everything which could prove useful in case of their being forced on shore, were put in. Muskets and ammunition were also provided, and everything was ready, when the men came aft and pointed out to Philip that there was plenty of money on board, which it was folly to leave, and that they wished to carry as much as they could away with them. As this intimation was given in a way that made it evident they intended that it should be complied with, Philip did not refuse; but resolved, in his own mind, that when they arrived at a place where he could exercise his authority, the money should be reclaimed for the Company to whom it belonged. The men went down below, and while Philip was making arrangements with Amine, handed the casks of dollars out of the hold, broke them open and helped themselves—quarrelling with each other for the first possession, as each cask was opened. At last every man had obtained as much as he could carry, and had placed his spoil on the raft with his baggage, or in the boat to which he had been appointed. All was now ready—Amine was lowered down, and took her station—the boats took in tow the raft which was cast off from the vessel, and away they went with the current, pulling with all their strength to avoid being stranded upon that part of the sandbank which appeared above water. This was the great danger which they had to encounter, and which they very narrowly escaped.

They numbered eighty-six souls in all: in the boats there were thirty-two; the rest were on the raft, which, being well-built and full of timber, floated high out of the water, now that the sea was so smooth. It had been agreed upon by Philip and Krantz, that one of them should remain on the raft and the other in one of the boats; but at the time the raft quitted the ship, they were both on the raft, as they wished to consult, as soon as they discovered the direction of the current, which would be the most advisable course for them to pursue. It appeared, that as soon as the current had passed the bank, it took a more southerly direction towards New Guinea. It was then debated between them whether they should or should not land on that island, the natives of which were known to be pusillanimous, yet treacherous. A long debate ensued, which ended, however, in their resolve not to decide as yet, but wait and see what might occur. In the mean time, the boats pulled to the westward, while the current set them fast down in a southerly direction.

Night came on and the boats dropped the grapnels with which they had been provided; and Philip was glad to find that the current was not near so strong, and the grapnels held both boats and raft. Covering themselves up with the spare sails with which they had provided themselves, and setting a watch, the tired seamen were soon fast asleep.

"Had I not better remain in one of the boats?" observed Krantz. "Suppose, to save themselves, the boats were to leave the raft."

"I have thought of that," replied Philip, "and have, therefore, not allowed any provisions or water in the boats; they will not leave us for that reason."

"True, I had forgotten that."

Krantz remained on watch, and Philip retired to the repose which he so much needed. Amine met him with open arms.

"I have no fear, Philip," said she; "I rather like this wild, adventurous change. We will go on shore and build our hut beneath the cocoa-trees, and I shall repine when the day comes which brings succour, and releases us from our desert isle. What do I require but you?"

"We are in the hands of One above, dear, who will act with us as He pleases. We have to be thankful that it is no worse," replied Philip. "But now to rest, for I shall soon be obliged to watch."

The morning dawned with a smooth sea and a bright blue sky; the raft had been borne to leeward of the cluster of uninhabited islands of which we spoke, and was now without hopes of reaching them; but to the westward were to be seen on the horizon the refracted heads and trunks of cocoa-nut trees, and in that direction it was resolved that they should tow the raft. The breakfast had been served out, and the men had taken to the oars, when they discovered a proa, full of men, sweeping after them from one of the islands to windward. That it was a pirate vessel there could be no doubt; but Philip and Krantz considered that their force was more than sufficient to repel them, should an attack be made. This was pointed out to the men; arms were distributed to all in the boats, as well as to those on the raft; and that the seamen might not be fatigued, they were ordered to lie on their oars, and await the coming up of the vessel.

As soon as the pirate was within range, having reconnoitred her antagonists, she ceased pulling, and commenced firing from a small piece of cannon, which was mounted on her bows. The grape and langridge which she poured upon, them wounded several of the men, although Philip had ordered them to lie down flat on the raft and in the boats. The pirate advanced nearer, and her fire became more destructive, without any opportunity of returning it by the Utrecht's people. At last it was proposed, as the only chance of escape, that the boats should attack the pirate. This was agreed to by Philip; more men were sent in the boats; Krantz took the command; the raft was cast off, and the boats pulled away. But scarcely had they cleared the raft, when, as by one sudden thought, they turned round, and pulled away in the opposite direction. Krantz's voice was heard by Philip, and his sword was seen to sash through the air; a moment afterwards he lunged into the sea, and swam to the raft. It appeared that the people in the boats, anxious to preserve the money which they had possession of, had agreed among themselves to pull away and leave the raft to its fate. The proposal for attacking the pirate had been suggested with that view, and as soon as they were clear of the raft, they put their intentions into execution. In vain had Krantz expostulated and threatened; they would have taken his life; and when he found that his efforts were of no avail he leaped from the boat. "Then are we lost, I fear," said Philip. "Our numbers are so reduced, that we cannot hope to hold out long. What think you, Schriften?" ventured Philip addressing the pilot who stood near to him.

"Lost—but not lost by the pirates—no harm there! He! he!"

The remark of Schriften was correct. The pirates, imagining that in taking to their boats the people had carried with them everything that was valuable, instead of firing at the raft immediately gave chase to the boats. The sweeps were now out and the proa flew over the smooth water, like a sea-bird, passed the raft, and was at first evidently gaining on the boats but their speed soon slackened, and as the day passed, the boats and then the pirate vessel disappeared in the southward; the distance between them being apparently much the same as at the commencement of the chase.

The raft being now at the mercy of the wind and waves Philip and Krantz collected the carpenter's tools which had been brought from the ship, and selecting two spars from the raft, they made every preparation for stepping a mast and setting sail by the next morning.

The morning dawned, and the first objects that met their view were the boats pulling back towards the raft, followed closely by the pirate. The men had pulled the whole night, and were worn out with fatigue It was presumed that a consultation had been held, in which it was agreed that they should make a sweep, so as to return to the raft, as, if they gained it, they would be able to defend themselves, and moreover obtain provisions and water, which they had not on board at the time of their desertion. But it was fated otherwise; gradually the men dropped from their oars, exhausted, into the bottom of the boat and the pirate vessel followed them with renewed ardour. The boats were captured one by one; the booty found was more than the pirates anticipated, and it hardly need be said that not one man was spared. All this took place within three miles of the raft, and Philip anticipated that the next movement of the vessel would be towards them, but he was mistaken. Satisfied with their booty, and imagining that there could be no more on the raft, the pirate pulled away to the eastward, towards the islands from amongst which she had first made her appearance. Thus were those who expected to escape, and who had deserted their companions, deservedly punished; whilst those who anticipated every disaster from this desertion discovered that it was the cause of their being saved.

The remaining people on board the raft amounted to about forty-five; Philip, Krantz, Schriften, Amine, the two mates, sixteen seamen, and twenty-four soldiers, who had been embarked at Amsterdam. Of provisions they had sufficient for three or four weeks; but of water they were very short, already not having sufficient for more than three days at the usual allowance. As soon as the mast had been stepped and rigged, and the sails set (although there was hardly a breath of wind), Philip explained to the men the necessity of reducing the quantity of water, and it was agreed that it should be served out so as to extend the supply to twelve days, the allowance being reduced to half a pint per day.

There was a debate at this time, as the raft was in two parts, whether it would not be better to cast off the smaller one and put all the people on board the other; but this proposal was overruled, as, in the first place, although the boats had deserted them, the number on the raft had not much diminished, and moreover, the raft would steer much better under sail, now that it had length, than it would do if they reduced its dimensions and altered its shape to a square mass of floating wood.

For three days it was a calm, the sun poured down his hot beams upon them, and the want of water was severely felt; those who continued to drink spirits suffered the most.

On the fourth day the breeze sprung up favourably, and the sail was filled; it was a relief to their burning brows and blistered backs; and as the raft sailed on at the rate of four miles an hour, the men were gay and full of hope. The land below the cocoa-nut trees was now distinguishable, and they anticipated that the next day they could land and procure the water which they now so craved for. All night they carried sail, but the next morning they discovered that the current was strong against them, and that what they gained when the breeze was fresh, they lost from the adverse current as soon as it went down; the breeze was always fresh in Use morning, but it fell calm in the evening. Thus did they continue for four days more, every noon being not ten miles from the land, but the next morning swept away to a distance, and having their ground to retrace. Eight days had now passed, and the men, worn out with the exposure to the burning sun, became discontented and mutinous. At one time they insisted that the raft should be divided, that they might gain the land with the other half; at another, that the provisions which they could no longer eat should be thrown overboard to lighten the raft. The difficulty under which they lay was the having no anchor or grapnel to the raft, the boats having carried away with them all that had been taken from the ship. Philip then proposed to the men that, as everyone of them had such a quantity of dollars, the money should be sewed up in canvas bags, each man's property separate; and that with this weight to the ropes they would probably be enabled to hold the raft against the current for one night, when they would be able the next day to gain shore; but this was refused—they would not risk their money. No, no—fools! they would sooner part with their lives by the most miserable of all deaths. Again and again was this proposed to them by Philip and Krantz, but without success.

In the mean time Amine had kept up her courage and her spirits, proving to Philip a valuable adviser and a comforter in his misfortunes. "Cheer up, Philip," would she say; "we shall yet build our cottage under the shade of those cocoa-nut trees, and pass a portion, if not the remainder of our lives in peace; for who indeed is there who would think to find us in these desolate and untrodden regions?"

Schriften was quiet and well-behaved; talked much with Amine, but with nobody else. Indeed, he appeared to have a stronger feeling in favour of Amine than he had ever shown before. He watched over her and attended her; and Amine would often look up after being silent and perceive Schriften's face wear an air of pity and melancholy which she had believed it impossible that he could have exhibited.

Another day passed; again they neared the land, and again did the breeze die away, and they were swept back by the current. The men now arose, and in spite of the endeavours of Philip and Krantz, they rolled into the sea all the provisions and stores, everything but one cask of spirits and the remaining stock of water; they then sat down at the upper end of the raft with gloomy, threatening looks and in close consultation.

Another night closed in; Philip was full of anxiety. Again he urged them to anchor with their money, but in vain; they ordered him away, and he returned to the after part of the raft, upon which Amine's secure retreat had been erected; he leant on it in deep thought and melancholy, for he imagined that Amine was asleep.

"What disturbs you, Philip?"

"What disturbs me? The avarice and folly of these men. They will die, rather than risk their hateful money. They have the means of saving themselves and us, and they will not. There is weight enough in bullion on the fore part of the raft to hold a dozen floating masses such as this, yet they will not risk it. Cursed love of gold, it makes men fools, madmen, villains! We have now but two days' water—doled out as it is drop by drop. Look at their emaciated, broken-down, wasted forms, and yet see how they cling to money, which probably they will never have occasion for, even if they gain the land. I am distracted!"

"You suffer, Philip, you suffer from privation, but I have been careful; I thought that this would come; I have saved both water and biscuit—I have here four bottles;—drink, Philip, and it will relieve you."

Philip drank; it did relieve him, for the excitement of the day had pressed heavily on him.

"Thanks, Amine—thanks, dearest! I feel better now.—Good Heaven! are they such fools as to value the dross of metal above one drop of water in a time of suffering and privation such as this?"

The night closed in as before; the stars shone bright, but there was no moon. Philip had risen at midnight to relieve Krantz from the steerage of the raft. Usually the men had lain about in every part of the raft, but this night the majority of them remained forward. Philip was communing with his own bitter thoughts, when he heard a scuffle forward? and the voice of Krantz crying out to him for help, he quitted the helm, and seizing his cutlass ran forward, where he found Krantz down, and the men securing him. He fought his way to him, but was himself seized and disarmed. "Cut away—cut away," was called out by those who held him; and, in a few seconds, Philip had the misery to behold the after part of the raft, with Amine upon it, drifted apart from the one on which he stood.

"For mercy's sake! my wife—my Amine—for Heaven's sake, save her!" cried Philip, struggling in vain to disengage himself. Amine also, who had run to the side of the raft held out her arms—it was in vain—they were separated more than a cable's length. Philip made one more desperate struggle, and then fell down deprived of sense and motion.

Chapter Twenty Four.

It was not until the day had dawned that Philip opened his eyes, and discovered Krantz kneeling at his side; at first his thoughts were scattered and confused; he felt that some dreadful calamity had happened to him, but he could not recall to mind what it was. At last it rushed upon him, and he buried his face in his hands.

"Take comfort," said Krantz; "we shall probably gain the shore to-day, and we will go in search of her as soon as we can."

"This, then, is the separation and the cruel death to her which that wretch Schriften prophesied to us," thought Philip; "cruel indeed to waste away to a skeleton, under a burning sun, without one drop of water left to cool her parched tongue; at the mercy of the winds and waves; drifting about—alone—all alone—separated from her husband, in whose arms she would have died without regret; maddened with suspense and with the thoughts of what I may be suffering, or what may have been my fate. Pilot, you are right; there can be no more cruel death to a fond and doting wife. Oh! my head reels! What has Philip Vanderdecken to live for now?"

Krantz offered such consolation as his friendship could suggest, but in vain. He then talked of revenge, and Philip raised his head. After a few minutes' thought, he rose us. "Yes," replied he, "revenge!—revenge upon these dastards and traitors! Tell me, Krantz how many can we trust?"

"Half of the men, I should think, at least. It was a surprise." A spar had been fitted as a rudder, and the raft had now gained nearer the shore than it ever had done before. The men were in high spirits at the prospect, and every man was sitting on his own store of dollars which in their eyes, increased in value in proportion as did their prospect of escape.

Philip discovered from Krantz, that it was the soldiers and the most indifferent seamen who had mutinied on the night before, and cut away the other raft; and that all the best men had remained neuter.

"And so they will be now, I imagine," continued Krantz; "the prospect of gaining the shore has, in a manner, reconciled them to the treachery of their companions."

"Probably," replied Philip, with a bitter laugh; "but I know what will rouse them. Send them here to me."

Philip talked to the seamen whom Krantz had sent over to him. He pointed out to them that the other men were traitors not to be relied upon; that they would sacrifice everything and everybody for their own gain; that they had already done so for money, and that they themselves would have no security, either on the raft or on shore, with such people; that they dare not sleep for fear of having their throats cut, and that it were better at once to get rid of those who could not be true to each other; that it would facilitate their escape, and that they could divide between themselves the money which the others had secured, and by which they would double their own shares. That it had been his intention, although he had said nothing to enforce the restoration of the money for the benefit of the

Company, as soon as they had gained a civilised port, where the authorities could interfere; but that, if they consented to join and aid him, he would now give them the whole of it for their own use.

What will not the desire of gain effect? Is it therefore to be wondered at, that these men, who were indeed but little better than those who were thus in his desire of retaliation, denounced by Philip, consented to his proposal? It was agreed, that if they did not gain the shore, the others should be attacked that very night, and tossed into the sea.

But the consultation with Philip had put the other party on the alert; they too held council, and kept their arms by their sides. As the breeze died away, they were not two miles from the land, and once more they drifted back into the ocean. Philip's mind was borne down with grief at the loss of Amine; but it recovered to a certain degree when he thought of revenge: that feeling stayed him up, and he often felt the edge of his cutlass, impatient for the moment of retribution.

It was a lovely night; the sea was now smooth as glass, and not a breath of air moved in the heavens; the sail of the raft hung listless down the mast, and was reflected upon the calm surface by the brilliancy of the starry night alone. It was a night for contemplation—for examination of oneself, and adoration of the Deity; and here, on's frail raft, were huddled together more than forty beings, ready for combat, for murder, and for spoil. Each party pretended to repose; yet each were quietly watching the motions of the other, with their hands upon their weapons. The signal was to be given by Philip: it was, to let go the halyards of the yard, so that the sail should fall down upon a portion of the other party, and entangle them. By Philip's directions, Schriften had taken the helm, and Krantz remained by his side.

The yard and sail fell clattering down, and then the work of death commenced; there was no parley, no suspense; each man started upon his feet and raised his sword. The voices of Philip and of Krantz alone were heard, and Philip's sword did its work. He was nerved to his revenge, and never could be satiated as long as one remained who had sacrificed his Amine. As Philip had expected, many had been covered up and entangled by the falling of the sail, and their work was thereby made easier.

Some fell where they stood: others reeled back, and sunk down under the smooth water; others were pierced as they floundered under the canvas. In a few minutes the work of carnage was complete. Schriften meanwhile looked on, and ever and anon gave vent to his chuckling laugh—his demoniacal "he! he!"

The strife was over, and Philip stood against the mast to recover his breath. "So far art thou revenged, my Amine," thought he; "but, oh! what are these paltry lives compared to thine?" And now that his revenge was satiated, and he could do no more, be covered his face up in his hands, and wept bitterly, while those who had assisted him were already collecting the money of the slain for distribution. These men, when they found that three only of their side had fallen lamented that there had not been more, as their own shares of the dollars would have been increased.

There were now but thirteen men besides Philip, Krantz, and Schriften, left upon the raft. As the day dawned, the breeze again sprung up, and they shared out the portions of water, which would have been the allowance of their companions who had fallen. Hunger they felt not; but the water revived their spirits.

Although Philip had had little to say to Schriften since the separation from Amine, it was very evident to him and to Krantz that all the pilot's former bitter feelings had returned. His chuckle, his sarcasms, his "He! he!" were incessant; and his eye was now as maliciously directed to Philip as it was when they first met. It was evident that Amine alone had for the time conquered his disposition; and that with her disappearance had vanished all the good will of Schriften towards her husband. For this Philip cared little; he had a much more serious weight on his heart—the loss of his dear Amine; and he felt reckless and indifferent concerning anything else.

The breeze now freshened, and they expected that in two hours, they would run on the beach, but they were disappointed; the step of the mast gave way from the force of the wind, and the sail fell upon the raft. This occasioned great delay; and before they could repair the mischief, the wind again subsided, and they were left about a mile from the beach. Tired and worn out with his feelings, Philip at last fell asleep by the side of Krantz, leaving Schriften at the helm. He slept soundly—he dreamt of Amine—he thought she was under a grove of cocoa-nuts, in a sweet sleep; that he stood by and watched her, and that she smiled in her sleep and murmured "Philip," when suddenly he was awakened by some unusual movement. Half dreaming still, he thought that Schriften, the pilot, had in his sleep been attempting to gain his relic, had passed the chain over his head, and was removing quietly from underneath his neck the portion of the chain which, in his reclining posture, he lay upon. Startled at the idea, he threw up his hand to seize the arm of the wretch, and found that he had really seized hold of Schriften, who was kneeling by him, and in possession of the chain and relic. The struggle was short, the relic was recovered, and the pilot lay at the mercy of Philip, who held him down with his knee on his chest. Philip replaced the relic on his bosom, and, excited to madness, rose from the body of the now breathless Schriften, caught it in his arms, and hurled it into the sea.

"Man or devil! I care not which," exclaimed Philip, breathless; "escape now, if you can!"

The struggle had already roused up Krantz and others, but not in time to prevent Philip from wreaking his vengeance upon Schriften. In few words, he told Krantz what had passed; as for the men, they cared not; they laid their heads down again, and, satisfied that their money was safe, inquired no further.

Philip watched to see if Schriften would rise up again, and try to regain the raft; but he did not make his appearance above water, and Philip felt satisfied.

Chapter Twenty Five.

What pen could portray the feelings of the fond and doting Amine, when she first discovered that she was separated from her husband? In a state of bewilderment, she watched the other raft as the distance between them increased. At last the shades of night hid it from her aching eyes, and she dropped down in mute despair.

Gradually she recovered herself, and turning round, she exclaimed, "Who's here?"

No answer.

"Who's here!" cried she in a louder voice; "alone—alone—and Philip gone. Mother, mother, look down upon your unhappy child!" and Amine frantically threw herself down so near to the edge of the raft, that her long hair, which had fallen down, floated on the wave.

"Ah me! where am I?" cried Amine, after remaining in a state of torpor for some hours. The sun glared fiercely upon her, and dazzled her eyes as she opened them—she cast them on the blue wave close by her, and beheld a large shark motionless by the side of the raft, waiting for his prey. Recoiling from the edge, she started up. She turned round and beheld the raft vacant, and the truth flashed on her. "Oh! Philip, Philip!" cried she, "then it is true and you are gone for ever! I thought it was only a dream: I recollect all now. Yes—all—all!" And Amine sank down again upon her cot which had been placed in the centre of the raft, and remained motionless for some time.

But the demand for water became imperious; she seized one of the bottles, and drank. "Yet why should I drink or eat? why should I wish to preserve life?" She rose, and looked round the horizon. "Sky and water, nothing more. Is this the death I am to die—the cruel death prophesied by Schriften—a lingering death under a burning sun, while my vitals are parched within? Be it so! Fate, I dare thee to thy worst—we can die but once—and without him, what care I to live? But yet I may see him again," continued Amine, hurriedly, after a pause. "Yes, I may—who knows? then welcome life; I'll nurse thee for that bare hope—bare indeed, with naught to feed on. Let me see—is it here still?" Amine looked at her zone, and perceived her dagger was still in it. "Well, then, I will live since death is at my command, and be guardful of life for my dear husband's sake." And Amine threw herself on her resting-place that she might forget every thing. She did: from that morning till the noon of the next day she remained in a state of torpor.

When she again rose, she was faint; again she looked round her—there was but sky and water to be seen.

"Oh! this solitude—it is horrible! death would be a release—but no, I must not die—I must live for Philip." She refreshed herself with water and a few pieces of biscuit, and folded her arms across her breast. "A few more days without relief, and all must be over. Was ever woman situated as I am, and yet I dare to indulge hope? Why, 'tis madness! And why am I thus singled out: because I have wedded with Philip? It may be so; if so, I welcome it. Wretches! who thus severed me from my husband; who to save their own lives, sacrificed a helpless woman! Nay! they might have saved me, if they had had the least pity;—but no, they never felt it. And these are Christians! The creed that the old priests would have had me—yes! that Philip would have had me embrace. Charity and good-will! They talk of it, but I have never seen them practise it! Loving one another!—forgiving one another!—say rather hating and preying upon one another! A creed never practised: why, if not practised of what value is it? Any creed were better—I abjure it, and if I be saved, will abjure it still for ever. Shade of my mother! is it that I have listened to these men—that I have to win my husband's love, tried to forget that which thou taughtest, even when a child at thy feet—that faith which our forefathers for thousands of years lived and died in—that creed proved by works, and obedience to the prophet's willis it for this that I am punished? Tell me, mother—oh! tell me in my dreams."

The night closed in, and with the gloom rose heavy clouds; the lightning darted through the firmament, ever and anon lighting up the raft. At last, the flashes were so rapid, not following each other—but darting down from every quarter at once, that the whole firmament appeared as if on fire, and the thunder rolled along the heavens, now near and loud, then rumbling in the distance. The breeze rose up fresh, and the waves tossed the raft, and washed occasionally even to Amine's feet, as she stood in the centre of it.

"I like this—this is far better than that calm and withering heat—this rouses me," said Amine as she cast her eyes up, and watched the forked lightning till her vision became obscured. "Yes, this is as it should be. Lightning, strike me if you please—waves, wash me off and bury me in a briny tomb—pour the wrath of the whole elements upon this devoted head—I care not, I laugh at, I defy it all. Thou canst but kill, this little steel can do as much. Let those who hoard up wealth—those who live in splendour—those that are happy—those who have husbands, children, aught to love—let them tremble; I have nothing. Elements! be ye fire, or water, or earth, or air, Amine defies you! And yet—no no, deceive not thyself. Amine, there is no hope; thus will I mount my funeral bier, and wait the will of destiny." And Amine regained the secure place which Philip had fitted up for her in the centre of the raft, threw herself down upon her bed and shut her eyes.

The thunder and lightning was followed up by torrents of heavy rain, which fell till daylight; the wind still continued fresh, but the sky cleared, and the sun shone out. Amine remained shivering in her wet garments: the heat of the sun proved too powerful for her exhausted state, and her brain wandered. She rose up in a sitting posture, looked around her, saw verdant fields in every direction, the cocoa-nuts waving to the wind—imagined even that she saw her own Philip in the distance hastening to her; she held out her arms strove to get up, and run to meet him, but her limbs refused their office; she called to him, she screamed, and sank back exhausted on her resting-place.

Chapter Twenty Six.

We must for a time return to Philip, and follow his strange destiny. A few hours after he had thrown the pilot into the sea they gained the shore, so long looked at with anxiety and suspense. The spars of the raft, jerked by the running swell undulated and rubbed against each other, as they rose and fell to the waves breaking on the beach. The breeze was fresh, but the surf was trifling, and the landing was without difficulty. The beach was shelving, of firm white sand, interspersed and strewed with various brilliant-coloured shells; and here and there, the bleached fragments and bones of some animal which had been forced out of its element to die. The island was, like all the others, covered with a thick wood of cocoa-nut trees, whose tops waved to the breeze, or bowed to the blast, producing a shade and a freshness which would have been duly appreciated by any other party than the present, with the exception only of Krantz; for Philip thought of nothing but his lost wife, and the seamen thought of nothing but of their sudden wealth. Krantz supported Philip to the beach, and led him to the shade; but after a minute he rose, and running down to the nearest point, looked anxiously for the portion of the raft which held Amine, which was now far, far away. Krantz had followed, aware that, now the first paroxysms were past, there was no fear of Philip's throwing away his life.

"Gone, gone for ever!" exclaimed Philip, pressing his hands to the balls of his eyes.

"Not so, Philip, the same providence which has preserved us, will certainly assist her. It is impossible that she can perish among so many islands many of which are inhabited; and a woman will be certain of kind treatment."

"If I could only think so," replied Philip.

"A little reflection may induce you to think that it is rather an advantage than otherwise, that she is thus separated—not from you, but from so many lawless companions whose united force we could not resist. Do you think that, after any lengthened sojourn on this island, these people with us would permit you to remain in quiet possession of your wife? No!—they would respect no laws; and Amine has, in my opinion, been miraculously preserved from shame and ill treatment, if not from death."

"They durst not, surely! Well, but Krantz, we must make a raft and follow her; we must not remain here—I will seek her through the wide world."

"Be it so, if you wish, Philip, and I will follow your fortunes," replied Krantz, glad to find that there was something, however wild the idea, for his mind to feed on. "But now let us return to the raft, seek the refreshment we so much require, and after that we will consider what may be the best plan to pursue."

To this, Philip, who was much exhausted, tacitly consented, and he followed Krantz to where the raft had been beached. The men had left it, and were each of them sitting apart from one another under the shade of his own chosen cocoa-nut tree. The articles which had been saved on the raft had not been landed, and Krantz called upon them to come and carry the things on shore—but no one would answer or obey. They each sat watching their money, and afraid to leave it, lest they should be dispossessed of it by the others. Now that their lives were, comparatively speaking, safe, the demon of avarice had taken full possession of their souls; there they sat, exhausted, pining for water, longing for sleep, and yet they dared not move,—they were fixed as if by the wand of the enchanter.

"It is the cursed dollars which have turned their brains," observed Krantz to Philip; "let us try if we cannot manage to remove what we most stand in need of, and then we will search for water."

Philip and Krantz collected the carpenter's tools, the best arms, and all the ammunition, as the possession of the latter would give them an advantage in case of necessity; they then dragged on shore the sail and some small spars, all of which they carried up to a clump of cocoa-nut trees, about a hundred yards from the beach.

In half an hour they had erected an humble tent, and put into it what they had brought with them, with the exception of the major part of the ammunition, which, as soon as he was screened by the tent, Krantz buried in a heap of dry sand behind it; he then, for their immediate wants, cut down with an axe a small cocoa-nut tree in full bearing. It must be for those who have suffered the agony of prolonged thirst, to know the extreme pleasure with which the milk of the nuts were one after the other poured down the parched throats of Krantz and Philip. The men witnessed their enjoyment in silence, and with gloating eyes. Every time that a fresh cocoa-nut was seized and its contents quaffed by their officers, more sharp and agonising was their own devouring thirst—still closer did their dry lips glue themselves together—yet they moved not, although they felt the tortures of the condemned.

Evening closed in; Philip had thrown himself down on the spare sails, and had fallen asleep, when Krantz set off to explore the island upon which they had been thrown. It was small, not exceeding three miles in length, and at no one part more than five hundred yards across. Water there was none, unless it were to be obtained by digging; fortunately, the young cocoa-nuts prevented the absolute necessity for it. On his return, Krantz passed the men in their respective stations. Each was awake, and raised himself on his elbow to ascertain if it were an assailant; but, perceiving Krantz, they again dropped down. Krantz passed the raft—the water was now quite smooth, for the wind had shifted off shore, and the spars which composed the raft hardly jostled each other. He stepped upon it, and, as the moon was bright in the heavens he took the precaution of collecting all the arms which had been left, and throwing them as far as he could into the sea. He then walked to the tent, where he found Philip still sleeping soundly, and in a few minutes he was reposing by his side. And Philip's dreams were of Amine; he thought that he saw the hated Schriften rise again from the waters, and, climbing up to the raft, seat himself by her side. He thought that he again heard his unearthly chuckle and his scornful laugh, as his unwelcome words fell upon her distracted ears. He thought that she fled into the sea to avoid Schriften, and that the waters appeared to reject her—she floated on the surface. The storm rose, and once more he beheld her in the sea-shell skimming over the waves. Again, she was in a furious surf on the beach, and her shell sank, and she was buried in the waves: and then he saw her walking on shore without fear and without harm, for the water which spared no one, appeared to spare her. Philip tried to join her, but was prevented by some unknown power, and Amine waved her hand and said, "We shall meet again, Philip; yes, once more on this earth shall we meet again."

The sun was high in the heavens and scorching in his heat, when Krantz first opened his eyes, and awakened Philip. The axe again procured for them their morning's meal. Philip was silent; he was ruminating upon his dreams, which had afforded him consolation. "We shall meet again!" thought he. "Yes, once more at least we shall meet again. Providence! I thank thee."

Krantz then stepped out to ascertain the condition of the men. He found them faint, and so exhausted, that they could not possibly survive much longer, yet still watching over their darling treasure. It was melancholy to witness such perversion of intellect, and Krantz thought of a plan which might save their lives. He proposed to them each separately, that they should bury their money so deep, that it was not to be recovered without time: this would prevent any one from attacking the treasure of the other, without its being perceived and the attempt frustrated, and would enable them to obtain their necessary food and refreshment without danger of being robbed.

To this plan they acceded. Krantz brought out of the tent the only shovel in their possession, and they, one by one, buried their dollars many feet deep in the yielding sand. When they had all secured their wealth, he brought them one of the axes, and the cocoa-nut trees fell, and they were restored to new life and vigour. Having satiated themselves, they then lay down upon the several spots under which they had buried their dollars, and were soon enjoying that repose which they all so much needed.

Philip and Krantz had now many serious consultations as to the means which should be taken for quitting the island, and going in search of Amine; for although Krantz thought the latter part of Philip's proposal useless, he did not venture to say so. To quit this island was necessary; and provided they gained one of those which were inhabited, it was all that they could expect. As for Amine, he considered that she was dead before this, either having been washed off the raft, or that her body was lying on it exposed to the decomposing heat of a torrid sun.

To cheer Philip, he expressed himself otherwise; and whenever they talked about leaving the island, it was not to save their own lives, but invariably to search after Philip's lost wife. The plan which they proposed and acted upon was, to construct a light raft, the centre to be composed of three water-casks, sawed in half, in a row behind each other, firmly fixed by cross pieces to two long spars on each side. This, under sail, would move quickly through the water, and be manageable so as to enable them to steer a course. The outside spars had been selected and hauled on shore, and the work was already in progress; but they were left alone in their work, for the seamen appeared to have no idea at present of quitting the island. Restored by food and repose, they were now not content with the money which they had—they were anxious for more. A portion of each party's wealth had been dug up, and they now gambled all day with pebbles, which they had collected on the beach, and with which they had invented a game. Another evil had crept among them: they had cut steps in the largest cocoa-nut trees, and with the activity of seamen had mounted them, and by tapping the top of the trees, and fixing empty cocoa-nuts underneath, had obtained the liquor, which in its first fermentation is termed toddy, and is afterwards distilled into arrack. But as toddy, it is quite sufficient to intoxicate; and every day the scenes of violence and intoxication, accompanied with oaths and execrations, became more and more dreadful. The losers tore their hair, and rushed like madmen upon those who had gained their dollars; but Krantz had fortunately thrown their weapons into the sea, and those he had saved, as well as the ammunition, he had secreted.

Blows and bloodshed, therefore, were continual, but loss of life there was none, as the contending parties were separated by the others, who were anxious that the play should not be interrupted. Such had been the state of affairs for now nearly a fortnight while the work of the raft had slowly proceeded. Some of the men had lost their all, and had, by the general consent of those who had won their wealth, been banished to a certain distance that they might not pilfer from them. These walked gloomily round the island, or on the beach, seeking some instrument by which they might avenge themselves, and obtain repossession of their money. Krantz and Philip had proposed to these men to join them and leave the island, but they had sullenly refused.

The axe was now never parted with by Krantz. He cut down what cocoa-nut trees they required for subsistence, and prevented the men from notching more trees to procure the means of inebriation. On the sixteenth day all the money had passed into the hands of three men, who had been more fortunate than the rest. The losers were now by far the more numerous party, and the consequence was, that the next morning these three men were found lying strangled on the beach; the money had been re-divided, and the gambling had re-commenced with more vigour than ever.

"How can this end?" exclaimed Philip to Krantz, as he looked upon the blackened countenances of the murdered men.

"In the death of all," replied Krantz. "We cannot prevent it. It is a judgment."

The raft was now ready; the sand had been dug from beneath it, so as to allow the water to flow in and float it, and it was now made fast to a stake and riding on the peaceful waters. A large store of cocoa-nuts, old and young, had been procured and put on board of her, and it was the intention of Philip and Krantz to have quitted the island the next day.

Unfortunately, one of the men, when bathing, had perceived the arms lying in the shallow water. He had dived down and procured a cutlass: others had followed his example, and all had armed themselves. This induced Philip and Krantz to sleep on board of the raft and keep watch; and that night, as the play was going on, a heavy loss on one side ended in a general fray. The combat was furious for all were more or less excited by intoxication. The result was melancholy, for only three were left alive. Philip, with Krantz watched the issue; every man who fell wounded was put to the sword, and the three left, who had been fighting on the same side, rested panting on their weapons. After a pause two of them communicated with each other, and the result was an attack upon the third man, who fell dead beneath their blows.

"Merciful Father! are these thy creatures?" exclaimed Philip.

"No," replied Krantz, "they worshipped the devil as Mammon. Do you imagine that those two, who could now divide more wealth than they could well spend if they return to their country—will consent to a division? Never—they must have all—yes, all!"

Krantz had hardly expressed his opinion, when one of the men, taking advantage of the other turning round a moment from him, passed his sword through his back. The man fell with a groan, and the sword was again passed through his body.

"Said I not so? But the treacherous villain shall not reap his reward," continued Krantz, levelling the musket which he held in his hand, and shooting him dead.

"You have done wrong, Krantz; you have saved him from the punishment he deserved. Left alone on the island, without the means of obtaining his subsistence, he must have perished miserably and by inches, with all his money round him; that would have been torture indeed!"

"Perhaps I was wrong. If so, may Providence forgive me, I could not help it. Let us go ashore, for we are now on this island alone. We must collect the treasure and bury it, so that it may be recovered; and, at the same time, take a portion with us; for who knows but that we may have occasion for it. Tomorrow we had better remain here, for we shall have enough to do in burying the bodies of these infatuated men, and the wealth which has caused their destruction."

Philip agreed to the propriety of the suggestion; the next day they buried the bodies where they lay; and the treasure was all collected in a deep trench, under a cocoa-nut tree, which they carefully marked with their axe. About five hundred pieces of gold were selected and taken on board of the raft with the intention of secreting them about their persons, and resorting to them in case of need.

The following morning they hoisted their sail and quitted the island. Need it be said in what direction they steered? As may be well imagined, in that quarter where they had last seen the raft with the isolated Amine.

Chapter Twenty Seven.

The raft was found to answer well, and although her progress through the water was not very rapid, she obeyed the helm and was under command. Both Philip and Krantz were very careful in taking such marks and observations of the island as should enable them, if necessary, to find it again. With the current to assist them they now proceeded rapidly to the southward, in order that they might examine a large island which lay in that direction. Their object, after seeking for Amine was to find out the direction of Ternate; the king of which they knew to be at variance with the Portuguese, who had a fort and factory at Tidore, not very far distant from it; and from thence to obtain a passage in one of the Chinese junks, which, on their way to Bantam, called at that island.

Towards evening they had neared the large island, and they soon ran down it close to the beach. Philip's eyes wandered in every direction to ascertain whether anything on the shore indicated the presence of Amine's raft, but he could perceive nothing of the kind, nor did he see any inhabitants.

That they might not pass the object of their search during the night, they ran their raft on shore, in a small cove where the waters were quite smooth, and remained there until the next morning, when they again made sail and prosecuted their voyage. Krantz was steering with the long sweep they had fitted for the purpose, when he observed Philip, who had been for some time silent, take from his breast the relic which he wore, and gaze attentively upon it.

"Is that your picture, Philip?" observed Krantz.

"Alas! no, it is my destiny," replied Philip, answering without reflection.

"Your destiny! What mean you?"

"Did I say my destiny? I hardly know what I said," replied Philip, replacing the relic in his bosom.

"I rather think you said more than you intended," replied Krantz; "but at the same time something near the truth. I have often perceived you with that trinket in your hand, and I have not forgotten how anxious Schriften was to obtain it and the consequences of his attempt upon it. Is there not some secret—some mystery attached to it? Surely, if so, you must now sufficiently know me as your friend to feel me worthy of your confidence."

"That you are my friend, Krantz, I feel; my sincere and much-valued friend, for we have shared much danger together and that is sufficient to make us friends; that I could trust you, I believe, but I feel as if I dare not trust any one. There is a mystery attached to this relic (for a relic it is), which as yet has been confided to my wife and holy men alone."

"And if trusted to holy men, surely it may be trusted to sincere friendship, than which nothing is more holy."

"But I have a presentiment that the knowledge of my secret would prove fatal to you. Why I feel such a presentiment I know not; but I feel it, Krantz; and I cannot afford to lose you, my valued friend."

"You will not then make use of my friendship, it appears," replied Krantz. "I have risked my life with you before now and I am not to be deterred from the duties of friendship by a childish foreboding on your part, the result of an agitated mind and a weakened body. Can anything be more absurd than to suppose that a secret confided to me can be pregnant with danger, unless it be, indeed, that my zeal to assist you may lead me into difficulties. I am not of a prying disposition; but we have been so long connected together, and are now so isolated from the rest of the world, that it appears to me it would be a solace to you, were you to confide in one whom you can trust, what evidently has long preyed upon your mind. The consolation and advice of a friend, Philip, are not to be despised, and you will feel relieved if able to talk over with him a subject which evidently oppresses you. If, therefore, you value my friendship, let me share with you in your sorrows."

There are few who have passed through life so quietly, as not to recollect how much grief has been assuaged by confiding its cause to, and listening to the counsels and consolations of some dear friend. It must not, therefore appear surprising that, situated as he was, and oppressed with the loss of Amine, Philip should regard Krantz as one to whom he might venture to confide his important secret. He commenced his narrative with no injunctions, for he felt that if Krantz could not respect his secret for his secret's sake, or from good will towards him, he was not likely to be bound by any promise; and as, during the day, the raft passed by the various small capes and headlands of the island, he poured into Krantz's ear the history which the reader is acquainted with. "Now you know all," said Philip, with a deep sigh, as the narrative was concluded. "What think you? Do you credit my strange tale, or do you imagine as some well would, that it is a mere phantom of a disordered brain?"

"That it is not so, Philip, I believe," replied Krantz; "for I too have had ocular proof of the correctness of a part of your history. Remember how often I have seen this Phantom Ship—and if your father is permitted to range over the seas, why should you not be selected and permitted to reverse his doom? I fully believe every word that you have told me, and since you have told me this, I can comprehend much that in your behaviour at times appeared unaccountable; there are many who would pity you, Philip, but I envy you."

"Envy me?" cried Philip.

"Yes! envy you: and gladly would I take the burden of your doom on my own shoulders, were it only possible. Is it not a splendid thought that you are summoned to so great a purpose,—that instead of roaming through the world as we all do in pursuit of wealth, which possibly we may lose after years of cost and hardship, by the venture of a day, and which, at all events, we must leave behind us,—you are selected to fulfil a great and glorious work—the work of angels, I may say—that of redeeming the soul of a father, *suffering* indeed for his human frailties, but not doomed to perish for eternity; you have, indeed, an object of pursuit worthy of all the hardships and dangers of a maritime life. If it ends in your death, what then? Where else ends our futile cravings, our continual toil, after nothing? We all must die—but how few—who, indeed, besides yourself—was ever permitted before his death to ransom the soul of the author of his existence! Yes, Philip, I envy you!"

"You think and speak like Amine. She, too, is of a wild and ardent soul, that would mingle with the beings of the other world, and hold intelligence with disembodied spirits."

"She is right," replied Krantz; "there are events in my life, or rather connected with my family, which have often fully convinced me that this is not only possible but permitted. Your story has only corroborated what I already believed."

"Indeed! Krantz?"

"Indeed, yes; but of that hereafter: the night is closing in we must again put our little bark in safety for the night, and there is a cove which I think appears suited for the purpose."

Before morning a strong breeze, right on shore, had sprung up, and the surf became so high as to endanger the raft; to continue their course was impossible; they could only haul up their raft, to prevent its being dashed to pieces by the force of the waves, as the seas broke on the shore. Philip's thoughts were, as usual, upon Amine; and as he watched the tossing waters, as the sunbeams lightened up their crests, he exclaimed, "Ocean, hast thou my Amine? If so, give up thy dead! What is that?" continued he, pointing to a speck on the horizon.

"The sail of a small craft of some description or another," replied Krantz; "and apparently coming down before the wind to shelter herself in the very nook we have selected."

"You are right; it is the sail of a vessel—of one of those peroquas which skim over these seas; how she rises on the swell! She is full of men apparently."

The peroqua rapidly approached, and was soon close to the beach; the sail was lowered, and she was backed in through the surf.

"Resistance is useless should they prove enemies," observed Philip. "We shall soon know our fate."

The people in the peroqua took no notice of them until the craft had been hauled up and secured; three of them then advanced towards Philip and Krantz, with spears in their hands, but evidently with no hostile intentions. One addressed them in Portuguese asking them who they were.

"We are Hollanders," replied Philip.

"A part of the crew of the vessel which was wrecked?" inquired he.

"Yes!"

"You have nothing to fear—you are enemies to the Portuguese, and so are we. We belong to the island of Ternate—our king is at war with the Portuguese, who are villains. Where are your companions? on which island?"

"They are all dead," replied Philip. "May I ask you whether you have fallen in with a woman, who was adrift on a part of the raft by herself: or have you heard of her?"

"We have heard that a woman was picked up on the beach to the southward, and carried away by the Tidore people to the Portuguese settlement, on the supposition that she was a Portuguese."

"Then God be thanked, she is saved," cried Philip. "Merciful Heaven! accept my thanks.—To Tidore you said?"

"Yes; we are at war with the Portuguese, we cannot take you there."

"No! but we shall meet again."

The person who accosted them was evidently of consequence. His dress was to a certain degree Mahometan, but mixed up with Malay; he carried arms in his girdle and a spear in his hand; his turban was of printed chintz; and his deportment like most persons of rank in that country, was courteous and dignified.

"We are now returning to Ternate, and will take you with us. Our king will be pleased to receive any Hollanders, especially as you are enemies to the Portuguese dogs. I forgot to tell you that we have one of your companions with us in the boat; we picked him up at sea much exhausted, but he is now doing well."

"Who can it be?" observed Krantz; "it must be some one belonging to some other vessel."

"No," replied Philip, shuddering, "it must be Schriften."

"Then my eyes must behold him before I believe it," replied Krantz.

"Then believe your eyes," replied Philip, pointing to the form of Schriften, who was now walking towards them.

"Mynheer Vanderdecken, glad to see you. Mynheer Krantz, I hope you are well. How lucky that we should all be saved. He! he!"

"The ocean has then, indeed, given up its dead, as I requested," thought Philip.

In the mean time, Schriften, without making any reference to the way in which they had so unceremoniously parted company, addressed Krantz with apparent good-humour, and some slight tinge of sarcasm. It was some time before Krantz could rid himself of him.

"What think you of him, Krantz?"

"That he is a part of the whole, and has his destiny to fulfil as well as you. He has his part to play in this wondrous mystery, and will remain until it is finished. Think not of him. Recollect, your Amine is safe."

"True," replied Philip, "the wretch is not worth a thought; we have now nothing to do but to embark with these people; hereafter we may rid ourselves of him, and strive then to rejoin my dearest Amine."

Chapter Twenty Eight.

When Amine again came to her senses, she found herself lying on the leaves of the palmetto, in a small hut. A hideous black child sat by her, brushing off the flies. Where was she?

The raft had been tossed about for two days, during which Amine remained in a state of alternate delirium and stupor. Driven by the current and the gale, it had been thrown on shore on the eastern end of the coast of New Guinea. She had been discovered by some of the natives, who happened to be on the beach trafficking with some of the Tidore people. At first they hastened to rid her of her garments, although they perceived that she was not dead; but before they had left her as naked as themselves, a diamond of great value, which had been given to her by Philip, attracted the attention of one of the savages; failing in his attempt to pull it off, he pulled out a rusty, blunt knife, and was busily sawing at the finger, when an old woman of authority interfered and bade him desist. The Tidore people also, who were friends with the Portuguese, pointed out that to save one of that nation would insure a reward; they stated moreover, that they would, on their return, inform the people of the Factory establishment that one of their countrywomen had been thrown on shore on a raft. To this Amine owed the care and attention that was paid to her; that part of New Guinea being somewhat civilised by occasional intercourse with the Tidore people, who came there to exchange European finery and trash for the more useful productions of the island.

The Papoose woman carried Amine into her hut, and there she lay for many days, wavering between life and death, carefully attended, but requiring little except the moistening of her parched lips with water, and the brushing off of the mosquitoes and flies.

When Amine opened her eyes, the little Papoose ran out to acquaint the woman, who followed her into the hut. She was of large size, very corpulent and unwieldy, with little covering on her body; her hair, which was woolly in its texture, was partly plaited, partly frizzled, a cloth round her waist, and a piece of faded yellow silk on her shoulders, was all her dress. A few silver rings, on her fat fingers, and a necklace of mother-of-pearl, were her ornaments. Her teeth were jet black, from the use of the betel-nut, and her whole appearance was such as to excite disgust in the breast of Amine.

She addressed Amine, but her words were unintelligible: and the sufferer, exhausted with the slight effort she had made, fell back into her former position, and closed her eyes. But if the woman was disgusting, she was kind, and by her attention and care Amine was able in the course of three weeks, to crawl out of the hut and enjoy the evening breeze. The natives of the island would at times surround her, but they treated her with respect, from fear of the old woman. Their woolly hair was frizzled or plaited, sometimes powdered white with chunam. A few palmetto-leaves round the waist and descending to the knee was their only attire; rings through the nose and ears, and feathers of birds, particularly the bird of paradise, were their ornaments; but their language was wholly unintelligible. Amine felt grateful for life; she sat under the shade of the trees, and watched the swift peroquas as they skimmed the blue sea which was expanded before her; but her thoughts were elsewhere—they were on Philip.

One morning Amine came out of the hut with joy on her countenance, and took her usual seat under the trees. "Yes, mother, dearest mother, I thank thee; thou hast appeared to me; thou hast recalled to me thy arts, which I had forgotten, and had I but the means of conversing with these people, even now would I know where my Philip might be."

For two months did Amine remain under the care of the Papoose woman. When the Tidore people returned, they had an order to bring the white woman, who had been cast on shore, to the Factory, and repay those who had taken charge of her. They made signs to Amine, who had now quite recovered her beauty, that she was to go with them. Any change was preferable to staying where she was, and Amine followed them down to a peroqua, on which she was securely fixed, and was soon darting through the water with her new companions; and, as they flew along the smooth seas, Amine thought of Philip's dream and the mermaid's shell.

By the evening they had arrived at the southern point of Galolo, where they landed for the night: the next day they gained the place of their destination, and Amine was led up to the Portuguese factory.

That the curiosity of those who were stationed there was roused, is not to be wondered at—the history given by the natives of Amine's escape appeared so miraculous. From the commandant to the lowest servant, every one was waiting to receive her. The beauty of Amine, her perfect form, astonished them. The commandant addressed a long compliment to her in Portuguese, and was astonished that she did not make a suitable reply—but as Amine did not understand a word that he said, it would have been more surprising if she had.

As Amine made signs that she could not understand the language, it was presumed that she was either English or Dutch, and an interpreter was sent for. She then explained that she was the wife of a Dutch captain, whose vessel had been wrecked, and that she did not know whether the crew had been saved or not. The Portuguese were very glad to hear that a Dutch vessel had been wrecked, and very glad that so lovely a creature as Amine had been saved. She was informed by the commandant that she was welcome, and that during her stay there everything should be done to make her comfortable; that in three months they expected a vessel from the Chinese seas, proceeding to Goa, and that, if inclined, she should have a passage to Goa in that vessel, and from that city she would easily find other vessels to take her wherever she might please to go; she was then conducted to an apartment, and left with a little negress to attend upon her.

The Portuguese commandant was a small, meagre, little man dried up to a chip, from long sojourning under a tropical sun. He had very large whiskers, and a very long sword: these were the two most remarkable features in his person and dress.

His attentions could not be misinterpreted; and Amine would have laughed at him, had she not been fearful that she might be detained. In a few weeks, by due attention, she gained the Portuguese language so far as to ask for what she required; and before she quitted the island of Tidore she could converse fluently. But her anxiety to leave, and to ascertain what had become of Philip, became greater every day; and at the expiration of the three months her eyes were continually bent to seaward, to catch the first glimpse of the vessel which was expected. At last it appeared; and as Amine watched the approach of the canvas from the west, the commandant fell on his knees, and declaring his passion, requested her not to think I of departure, but to unite her fate with his.

Amine was cautious in her reply, for she knew that she was in his power. "She must first receive intelligence of her husband's death, which was not yet certain; she would proceed to Goa, and if she discovered that she was single, she would write to him."

This answer, as it will be discovered, was the cause of great suffering to Philip. The commandant, fully assured that he could compass Philip's death, was satisfied—declared that, as soon as he had any positive intelligence, he would bring it to Goa himself, and made a thousand protestations of truth and fidelity.

"Fool!" thought Amine, as she watched the ship, which was now close to the anchorage.

In half an hour the vessel had anchored, and the people had landed. Amine observed a priest with them as they walked up to the fort. She shuddered—she knew not why. When they arrived, she found herself in the presence of Father Mathias.

Chapter Twenty Nine.

Both Amine and Father Mathias started, and drew back with surprise, at this unexpected meeting. Amine was the first to extend her hand; she had almost forgotten at the moment how they had parted, in the pleasure she experienced in meeting with a well-known face.

Father Mathias coldly took her hand, and laying his own upon her head, said; "May God bless thee, and forgive thee, my daughter, as I have long done." Then the recollection of what had passed rushed into Amine's mind, and she coloured deeply.

Had Father Mathias forgiven her? The event would show; but this is certain, he now treated her as an old friend, listened with interest to her history of the wreck, and agreed with her upon the propriety of her accompanying him to Goa.

In a few days the vessel sailed, and Amine quitted the factory and its enamoured commandant. They ran through the Archipelago in safety, and were crossing the mouth of the Bay of Bengal, without having had any interruption to fine weather.

Father Mathias had returned to Lisbon when he quitted Ternicore, and, tired of idleness, had again volunteered to proceed as a missionary to India. He had arrived at Formosa, and, shortly after his arrival, had received directions from his superior to return, on important business, to Goa; and thus it was that he fell in with Amine at Tidore.

It would be difficult to analyse the feelings of Father Mathias towards Amine—they varied so often. At one moment he would call to mind the kindness shown to him by her and Philip, the regard he had for the husband, and the many good qualities which he acknowledged that she possessed; and *now* he would recollect the disgrace, the unmerited disgrace, he had suffered through her means and he would then canvass whether she really did believe him an intruder in her chamber for other motives than those which actuated him or whether she had taken advantage of his indiscretion. These accounts were nearly balanced in his mind: he could have forgiven all if he had thought that Amine was a sincere convert to the Church; but his strong conviction that she was not only an unbeliever, but that she practised forbidden arts, turned the scale against her. He watched her narrowly and when in her conversation she showed any religious feeling, his heart warmed towards her: but when, on the contrary, any words escaped her lips which seemed to show that she thought lightly of his creed, then the full tide of indignation and vengeance poured into his bosom.

It was in crossing the Bay of Bengal, to pass round the southern cape of Ceylon, that they first met with bad weather; and when the storm increased, the superstitious seamen lighted candles before the small image of the saint which was shrined on deck. Amine observed it, and smiled with scorn; and as she did so, almost unwittingly, she perceived that the eye of Father Mathias was earnestly fixed upon her.

"The Papooses I have just left do no worse than worship their idols, and are termed idolaters," muttered Amine. "What, then, are these Christians?"

"Would you not be better below?" said Father Mathias, coming over to Amine. "This is no time for women to be on deck; they would be better employed in offering up prayers for safety."

"Nay, father, I can pray better here. I like this conflict of the elements; and as I view, I bow down in admiration of the Deity who rules the storm—who sends the winds forth in their wrath, or soothes them into peace."

"It is well said, my child," replied Father Mathias; "but the Almighty is not only to be worshipped in his works, but in the closet, with meditation, self-examination and faith. Hast thou followed up the precepts which thou hast been taught?—hast thou reverenced the sublime mysteries which have been unfolded to thee?"

"I have done my best, father," replied Amine, turning away her head, and watching the rolling wave.

"Hast thou called upon the Holy Virgin, and upon the saints—those intercessors for mortals erring like thyself?"

Amine made no answer; she did not wish to irritate the priest, neither would she tell an untruth.

"Answer me, child," continued the priest with severity.

"Father," replied Amine, "I have appealed to God alone—the God of the Christians—the God of the whole universe!"

"Who believes not everything, believes nothing, young woman. I thought as much! I saw thee smile with scorn just now. Why didst thou smile?"

"At my own thoughts, good father."

"Say rather at the true faith shown by others."

Amine made no answer.

"Thou art still an unbeliever and a heretic. Beware, young woman!—beware!"

"Beware of what, good father? Why should I beware? Are there not millions in these climes more unbelieving and more heretic, perhaps, than I? How many have you converted to your faith? What trouble, what toil, what dangers have you not undergone to propagate that creed; and why do you succeed so ill? Shall I tell you, father? It is because the people have already had a creed of their own—a creed taught to them from their infancy, and acknowledged by all who live about them. Am I not in the same position? I was brought up in another creed; and can you expect that that can be dismissed, and the prejudices of early years at once eradicated? I have thought much of what you have told me—have felt that much is true—that the tenets of your creed are godlike: is not that much? and yet you are not content. You would have blind acknowledgment, blind obedience: I were then an unworthy convert. We shall soon be in port: then teach me, and convince me, if you will. I am ready to examine and confess, but on conviction only. Have patience, good father, and the time may come when I *may* feel what now I *do not*—that yon bit of painted wood is a thing to bow down to and adore."

Notwithstanding this taunt at the close of this speech, there was so much truth in the observations of Amine, that Father Mathias felt their power. As the wife of a Catholic he had been accustomed to view Amine as one who had backslided from the Church of Rome—not as one who had been brought up in another creed. He now recalled to mind that she had never yet been received into the Church, for Father Seysen had not considered her as in a proper state to be admitted, and had deferred her baptism until he was satisfied of her full belief.

"You speak boldly; but you speak as you feel, my child," replied Father Mathias, after a pause. "We will, when we arrive at Goa, talk over these things, and, with the blessing of God, the new faith shall be made manifest to you."

"So be it," replied Amine.

Little did the priest imagine that Amine's thoughts were at that moment upon a dream she had had at New Guinea, in which her mother appeared, and revealed to her her magic arts, and that Amine was longing to arrive at Goa that she might practise them.

Every hour the gale increased, and the vessel laboured and leaked. The Portuguese sailors were frightened, and invoked their saints. Father Mathias and the other passengers gave themselves up for lost, for the pumps could not keep the vessel free; and their cheeks blanched as the waves washed furiously over the vessel: they prayed and trembled. Father Mathias gave them absolution. Some cried like children, some tore their hair, some cursed, and cursed the saints they had but the day before invoked. But Amine stood unmoved; and as she heard them curse, she smiled in scorn.

"My child," said Father Mathias, checking his tremulous voice, that he might not appear agitated before one whom he saw so calm and unmoved amidst the roaring of the elements—"my child, let not this hour of peril pass away. Before thou art summoned, let me receive thee into the bosom of our Church—give thee pardon for thy sins, and certainty of bliss hereafter."

"Good father, Amine is not to be frightened into belief, even if she feared the storm," replied she; "nor will she credit your power to forgive her sins merely because she says in fear that which in her calm reason she might reject. If ever fear could have subjected me, it was when I was alone upon the raft—that was, indeed a trial of my strength of mind, the bare recollection of which is, at this moment, more dreadful than the storm now raging, and the death which may await us. There is a God on high in whose mercy I trust—in whose love I confide—to whose will I bow. Let him do his will."

"Die not, my child, in unbelief."

"Father," replied Amine, pointing to the passengers and seamen, who were on the deck crying and wailing, "these are Christians—these men have been promised by you, but now, the inheritance of perfect bliss. What is their faith, that it does not give them strength to die like men? Why is it that a woman quails not, while they lie grovelling on the deck?"

"Life is sweet, my child—they leave their wives, their children, and they dread hereafter. Who is prepared to die?"

"I am," replied Amine. "I have no husband—at least, I fear I have no husband. For me life has no sweets; yet, one little hope remains—a straw to the sinking wretch. I fear not death, for I have nought to live for. Were Philip here, why, then indeed—but he is gone before me, and now, to follow him is all I ask."

"He died in the faith, my child—if you would meet him, do the same."

"He never died like these," replied Amine, looking with scorn at the passengers.

"Perhaps he lived not as they have lived," replied Father Mathias. "A good man dies in peace, and hath no fear."

"So die the good men of all creeds, father," replied Amine; "and in all creeds death is equally terrible to the wicked."

"I will pray for thee, my child," said Father Mathias, sinking on his knees.

"Many thanks—thy prayers will be heard, even though offered for one like me," replied Amine, who, clinging to the man-ropes, made her way up to the ladder, and gained the deck.

"Lost! signora, lost!" exclaimed the captain, wringing his hands as he crouched under the bulwark.

"No!" replied Amine, who had gained the weather side, and held on by a rope; "not lost this time."

"How say you, signora?" replied the captain, looking with admiration at Amine's calm and composed countenance. "How say you, signora?"

"Something tells me, good captain, that you will not be lost if you exert yourselves—something tells it to me here," and Amine laid her hand to her heart. Amine had a conviction that the vessel would not be lost, for it had not escaped her observation that the storm was less violent, although, in their terror, this had been unnoticed by the sailors.

The coolness of Amine, her beauty, perhaps, the unusual sight of a woman so young, calm and confiding, when all others were in despair, had its due effect upon the captain and sea men. Supposing her to be a Catholic, they imagined that she had had some warrant for her assertion, for credulity and superstition are close friends. They looked upon Amine with admiration and respect, recovered their energies, and applied to their duties. The pumps were again worked; the storm abated during the night, and the vessel was, as Amine had predicted, saved.

The crew and passengers looked upon her almost as a saint, and talked of her to Father Mathias, who was sadly perplexed. The courage which she had displayed was extraordinary; even when he trembled, she showed no sign of fear. He made no reply, but communed with his own mind, and the result was unfavourable to Amine. What had given her such coolness? What had given her the spirit of prophecy? Not the God of the Christians, for she was no believer. Who then? and Father Mathias thought of her chamber at Terneuse, and shook his head.

Chapter Thirty.

We must now again return to Philip and Krantz, who had a long conversation upon the strange reappearance of Schriften. All that they could agree upon was, that he should be carefully watched, and that they should dispense with his company as soon as possible. Krantz had interrogated him as to his escape, and Schriften had informed him, in his usual sneering manner, that one of the sweeps of the raft had been allowed to get adrift during the scuffle, and that he had floated on it, until he had gained a small island; that on seeing the peroqua he had once more launched it, and supported himself by it, until he was perceived and picked up. As there was nothing impossible, although much of the improbable, in this account, Krantz asked no more questions. The next morning, the wind having abated, they launched the peroqua, and made sail for the island of Ternate.

It was four days before they arrived, as every night they landed and hauled up their craft on the sandy beach. Philip's heart was relieved at the knowledge of Amine's safety, and he could have been happy at the prospect of again meeting her, had he not been so constantly fretted by the company of Schriften.

There was something so strange, so contrary to human nature, that the little man, though diabolical as he appeared to be in his disposition, should never hint at, or complain of, Philip's attempts upon his life. Had he complained—had he accused Philip of murder—had he vowed vengeance, and demanded justice on his return to the authorities, it had been different—but no—there he was, making his uncalled-for and impertinent observations with his eternal chuckle and sarcasm, as if he had not the least cause of anger or ill-will.

As soon as they arrived at the principal port and town of Ternate, they were conducted to a large cabin, built of palmetto leaves and bamboo, and requested not to leave it until their arrival had been announced to the king. The peculiar courtesy and good breeding of these islanders was the constant theme of remark of Philip and Krantz; their religion, as well as their dress, appeared to be a compound of the Mahometan and Malayan.

After a few hours, they were summoned to attend the audience of the king, held in the open air. The king was seated under a portico, attended by a numerous concourse of priests and soldiers. There was much company but little splendour. All who were about the king were robed in white, with white turbans, but he himself was without ornament. The first thing that struck Philip and Krantz, when they were ushered into the presence of the king, was the beautiful cleanliness which everywhere prevailed: every dress was spotless and white as the sun could bleach it.

Having followed the example of those who introduced them, and saluted the king after the Mahometan custom, they were requested to be seated; and through the Portuguese interpreters—for the former communication of the islanders with the Portuguese, who had been driven from the place, made the Portuguese language well known by many—a few questions were put by the king, who bade them welcome, and then requested to know how they had been wrecked.

Philip entered into a short detail, in which he stated that his wife had been separated from him, and was, he understood, in the hands of the Portuguese factory at Tidore. He requested to know if his majesty could assist him in obtaining her release, or in going to join her.

"It is well said," replied the king. "Let refreshments be brought in for the strangers, and the audience be broken up."

In a few minutes there remained of all the court but two or three of the king's confidential friends and advisers; and a collation of curries, fish, and a variety of other dishes, was served up. After it was over, the king then said, "The Portuguese are dogs, they are our enemies—will you assist us to fight them? We have large guns, but do not understand the use of them as well as you do. I will send a fleet against the Portuguese at Tidore, if you will assist me. Say, Hollanders, will you fight? You," addressing Philip, "will then recover your wife."

"I will give an answer to you to-morrow," replied Philip, "I must consult with my friend. As I told you before, I was the captain of the ship, and this was my second in command—we will consult together." Schriften, whom Philip had represented as a common seaman, had not been brought up into the presence of the king.

"It is good," replied the king; "to-morrow we will expect your reply."

Philip and Krantz took their leave, and, on their return to the cabin, found that the king had sent them, as a present, two complete Mahometan dresses, with turbans. These were welcome, for their own garments were sadly tattered, and very unfit for exposure to the burning sun of those climes. Their peaked hats, too, collected the rays of heat, which were intolerable; and they gladly exchanged them for the white turban. Secreting their money in the Malayan sash, which formed a part of the attire, they soon robed themselves in the native garments, the comfort of which was immediately acknowledged. After a long consultation, it was decided that they should accept the terms offered by the king, as this was the only feasible way by which Philip could hope to re-obtain possession of Amine. Their consent was communicated to the king on the following day, and every preparation was made for the expedition.

And now was to be beheld a scene of bustle and activity. Hundreds and hundreds of peroquas, of every dimension, floating close to the beach, side by side, formed a raft extending nearly half a mile on the smooth water of the bay, teeming with men, who were equipping them for the service: some were fitting the sails; others were carpentering where required; the major portion were sharpening their swords, and preparing the deadly poison of the pine-apple for their creeses. The beach was a scene of confusion: water in jars, bags of rice, vegetables, salt-fish, fowls in coops, were everywhere strewed about among the armed natives, who were obeying the orders of the chiefs, who themselves walked up and down, dressed in their gayest apparel, and glittering in their arms and ornaments. The king had six long brass four-pounders, a present from an Indian captain; these, with a proportionate quantity of shot and cartridges, were (under the direction of Philip and Krantz) fitted on some of the largest peroquas, and some of the natives were instructed how to use them. At first, the king, who fully expected the reduction of the Portuguese fort, stated his determination to go in person, but in this he was overruled by his confidential advisers, and by the request of Philip, who could not allow him to expose his valuable life. In ten days all was ready, and the fleet, manned by seven thousand men, made sail for the island of Tidore.

It was a beautiful sight, to behold the blue rippling sea, covered with nearly six hundred of these picturesque craft, all under sail, and darting through the water like dolphins in pursuit of prey; all crowded with natives, whose white dresses formed a lively contrast with the deep blue of the water. The large peroquas, in which were Philip and Krantz, with the native commanders, were gaily decorated with streamers and pennons of all colours, that flowed out and snapped with the fresh breeze. It appeared rather to be an expedition of mirth and merriment, than one which was proceeding to bloodshed and slaughter.

On the evening of the second day they had made the island of Tidore, and run down to within a few miles of the Portuguese factory and fort. The natives of the country, who disliked, though they feared to disobey, the Portuguese, had quitted their huts near the beach and retired into the woods. The fleet, therefore, anchored and lay near the beach, without molestation, during the night. The next morning, Philip and Krantz proceeded to reconnoitre.

The port and factory of Tidore were built upon the same principle as almost all the Portuguese defences in those seas. An outer fortification, consisting of a ditch, with strong palisades embedded in masonry, surrounded the factory and all the houses of the establishment. The gates of the outer wall were open all day for ingress and egress, and closed only at night. On the seaward side of this enclosure was what may be termed the citadel, or real fortification; it was built of solid masonry, with parapets, was surrounded by a deep ditch, and was only accessible by a drawbridge, mounted with cannon on every side. Its real strength, however, could not well be perceived, as it was hidden by the high palisading which surrounded the whole establishment. After a careful survey, Philip recommended that the large peroquas with the cannon should attack by sea, while the men of the small vessels should land and surround the fort, taking advantage of every shelter which was afforded them to cover themselves while they harassed the enemy with their matchlocks, arrows, and spears. This plan having been approved of, one hundred and fifty peroquas made sail; the others were hauled on the beach, and the men belonging to them proceeded by land.

But the Portuguese had been warned of their approach, and were fully prepared to receive them; the guns mounted to the seaward were of heavy calibre and well served. The guns of the peroquas, though rendered as effectual as they could be, under the direction of Philip, were small, and did little damage to the thick stone front of the fort. After an engagement of four hours, during which the Ternate people lost a great number of men, the peroquas, by the advice of Philip and Krantz, hauled off, and returned to where the remainder of the fleet was stationed; and another council of war was held. The force, which had surrounded the fort, on the land side, was, however, not withdrawn, as it cut off any supplies or assistance; and, at the same time, occasionally brought down any of the Portuguese who might expose themselves—a point of no small importance, as Philip well knew, with a garrison so small as that in the fort.

That they could not take the fort by means of their cannon was evident; on the sea side it was for them impregnable: their efforts must now be directed to the land. Krantz, after the native chiefs had done speaking, advised that they should wait until dark, and then proceed to the attack in the following way. When the breeze set along shore, which it would do in the evening, he proposed that the men should prepare large bundles of dry palmetto and cocoa-nut leaves; that they should carry their bundles and stack them against the palisades to windward, and then set fire to them. They would thus burn down the palisades, and gain an entrance into the outer fortification; after which they could ascertain in what manner they should next proceed. This advice was too judicious not to be followed. All the men who had not matchlocks were set to collect fagots; a large quantity of dry wood was soon got together, and before night they were ready for the second attack.

The white dresses of the Ternates were laid aside: with nothing on them but their belts, and scimitars, and creeses, and blue under-drawers, they silently crept up to the palisades, there deposited their fagots, and then again returned, again to perform the same journey. As the breastwork of fagots increased, so did they more boldly walk up, until the pile was completed; they then, with a loud shout, fired it in several places. The flames mounted, the cannon of the fort roared, and many fell under the discharges of grape and hand-grenade. But stifled by the smoke, which poured in volumes upon them, the people in the fort were soon compelled to quit the ramparts to avoid suffocation. The palisades were on fire, and the flames mounting in the air, swept over, and began to attack the factory and houses. No resistance was now offered, and the Ternates tore down the burning palisades, and forced their way into the intrenchment, and with their scimitars and creeses put to death all who had been so unfortunate as not to take refuge in the citadel. These were chiefly native servants, whom the attack had surprised, and for whose lives the

Portuguese seemed to care but little, for they paid no attention to their cries to lower the drawbridge, and admit them into the fort.

The factory, built of stone, and all the other houses, were on fire, and the island was lighted up for miles. The smoke had cleared away, and the defences of the fort were now plainly visible in the broad glare of the flames. "If we had scaling-ladders," cried Philip, "the fort would be ours; there is not a soul on the ramparts."

"True, true," replied Krantz, "but even as it is, the factory walls will prove an advantageous post for us after the fire is extinguished; if we occupy it, we can prevent them showing themselves while the ladders are constructing. To-morrow night we may have them ready, and having first smoked the fort with a few more fagots, we may afterwards mount the walls, and carry the place."

"That will do," replied Philip, as he walked away. He then joined the native chiefs, who were collected together outside of the intrenchment, and communicated to them his plans. When he had made known his views, and the chiefs had assented to them, Schriften, who had come with the expedition unknown to Philip, made his appearance.

"That won't do; you'll never take that fort, Philip Vanderdecken. He! he!" cried Schriften.

Hardly had he said the words when a tremendous explosion took place, and the air was filled with large stones, which flew and fell in every direction, killing and maiming hundreds. It was the factory which had blown up, for in its vaults there was a large quantity of gunpowder, to which the fire had communicated.

"So ends that scheme, Mynheer Vanderdecken. He! he!" screamed Schriften; "you'll never take that fort."

The loss of life and the confusion caused by this unexpected result occasioned a panic, and all the Ternate people fled down to the beach where their peroquas were lying.

It was in vain that Philip and their chiefs attempted to rally them. Unaccustomed to the terrible effects of gunpowder in any large quantities, they believed that something supernatural had occurred, and many of them jumped into the peroquas and made sail, while the remainder were confused, trembling, and panting, all huddled together, on the beach.

"You'll never take that fort, Mynheer Vanderdecken," screamed the well-known voice.

Philip raised his sword to cleave the little man in two, but he let it fall again. "I fear he tells an unwelcome truth," thought Philip; "but why should I take his life for that?"

Some few of the Ternate chiefs still kept up their courage, but the major part were as much alarmed as their people. After some consultation, it was agreed that the army should remain where it was till the next morning, when they should finally decide what to do.

When the day dawned, now that the Portuguese fort was no longer surrounded by the other buildings, they perceived that it was more formidable than they had at first supposed. The ramparts were filled with men, and they were bringing cannon to bear on the Ternate forces. Philip had a consultation with Krantz, and both acknowledged, that, with the present panic, nothing more could be done. The chiefs were of the same opinion, and orders were given for the return of the expedition, indeed, the Ternate chiefs were fully satisfied with their success; they had destroyed the large fort, the factory, and all the Portuguese buildings; a small fortification only was uninjured; that was built of stone, and inaccessible, and they knew that the report of what had been done would be taken and acknowledged by the king as a great victory. The order was therefore given for embarkation, and in two hours the whole fleet, after a loss of about seven hundred men, was again on its way to Ternate. Krantz and Philip this time embarked in the same peroqua, that they might have the pleasure of each other's conversation. They had not, however, sailed above three hours when it fell calm, and, towards the evening, there was every prospect of bad weather. When the breeze again sprung up, it was from an adverse quarter, but these vessels steer so close to the wind, that this was disregarded: by midnight however the wind had increased to a gale, and before they were clear of the N.E. headland of Tidore, it blew a hurricane and many were washed off into the sea from the different craft, and those who could not swim, sank, and were drowned. The sails were lowered, and the vessels lay at the mercy of the wind and waves, every sea washing over them. The fleet was drifting fast on the shore, and before morning dawned, the vessel in which were Philip and Krantz was among the rollers on the beach off the northern end of the island. In a short time she was dashed to pieces, and every one had to look out for himself. Philip and Krantz laid hold of one fragment, and were supported by it till they gained the shore; here they found about thirty more companions, who had suffered the same fate as themselves. When the day dawned, they perceived that the major part of the fleet had weathered the point, and that those who had not, would in all probability escape, as the wind had moderated.

The Ternate people proposed, that as they were well armed, they should, as soon as the weather moderated, launch some of the craft belonging to the islanders, and join the fleet but Philip, who had been consulting with Krantz, considered this a good opportunity for ascertaining the fate of Amine. As the Portuguese could prove nothing against them, they could either deny that they had been among the assailants, or might plead that they had been forced to join them. At all risks, Philip was determined to remain, and Krantz agreed to share his fate; and seeming to agree with them, they allowed the Ternate people to walk to the Tidore peroquas, and while they were launching them, Philip and Krantz fell back into the jungle and disappeared. The Portuguese had perceived the wreck of their enemies, and, irritated by the loss they had sustained, they had ordered the people of the island to go out and capture all who were driven on shore. Now that they were no longer assailed, the Tidore people obeyed them, and very soon fell in with Philip and Krantz, who had quietly sat down under the shade of a large tree, waiting the issue. They were led away to the fort, where they arrived by nightfall. They were ushered into the presence of the Commandant, the same little man who had made love to Amine, and as they were dressed in Mussulman's attire, he was about to order them to be hung, when Philip told him that they were Dutchmen, who had been wrecked, and forced by the king of Ternate to join his expedition; that they had taken the earliest opportunity of escaping, as was very evident, since those who had been thrown on shore with them had got off in the island boats, while they chose to remain. Whereupon the little Portuguese Commandant struck his sword firm down on the pavement of the ramparts, *looked* very big, and then ordered them to prison for further examination.

Chapter Thirty One.

As every one descants upon the want of comfort in a prison, it is to be presumed that there are no very comfortable ones. Certainly that to which Philip and Krantz were ushered, had anything rather than the air of an agreeable residence. It was under the fort, with a very small aperture looking towards the sea, for light and air. It was very hot and moreover destitute of all those little conveniences which add so much to one's happiness in modern houses and hotels. In fact, it consisted of four bare walls, and a stone floor, and that was all.

Philip, who wished to make some inquiries relative to Amine, addressed, in Portuguese, the soldier who brought them down.

"My good friend, I beg your pardon—"

"I beg yours," replied the soldier, going out of the door, and locking them in.

Philip leant gloomily against the wall; Krantz, more mercurial, walked up and down three steps each way and turn.

"Do you know what I am thinking of?" observed Krantz, after a pause in his walk. "It is very fortunate that (lowering his voice) we have all our doubloons about us; if they don't search us, we may yet get away by bribing."

"And I was thinking," rejoined Philip, "that I would sooner be here than in company with that wretch Schriften, whose sight is poison to me."

"I did not much admire the appearance of the Commandant; but I suppose we shall know more to-morrow."

Here they were interrupted by the turning of the key, and the entrance of a soldier with a chatty of water, and a large dish of boiled rice. He was not the man who had brought them to the dungeon, and Philip accosted him.

"You have had hard work within these last two days?"

"Yes, indeed! signor."

"The natives forced us to join the expedition, and we escaped."

"So I heard you say, signor."

"They lost nearly a thousand men," said Krantz.

"Holy St. Francis! I am glad of it."

"They will be careful how they attack Portuguese in a hurry, I expect," rejoined Krantz.

"I think so," replied the soldier.

"Did you lose many men?" ventured Philip, perceiving that the man was loquacious.

"Not ten of our own people. In the factory there were about a hundred of the natives, with some women and children; but that is of no consequence."

"You had a young European woman here, I understand," said Philip with anxiety; "one who was wrecked in a vessel—was she among those who were lost?"

"Young woman!—Holy St. Francis. Yes, now I recollect. Why the fact is—"

"Pedro!" called a voice from above; the man stopped, put his fingers to his lips, went out, and locked the door.

"God of Heaven! give me patience," cried Philip; "but this is too trying."

"He will be down here again to-morrow morning," observed Krantz.

"Yes! to-morrow morning but what an endless time will suspense make of the intervening hours."

"I feel for you," replied Krantz; "but what can be done? The hours must pass, though suspense draws them out into interminable years; but I hear footsteps."

Again the door was unlocked, and the first soldier made his appearance. "Follow me—the Commandant would speak with you."

This unexpected summons was cheerfully complied with by Philip and his companion. They walked up the narrow stone steps, and at last found themselves in a small room in presence of the Commandant, with whom our readers have been already made acquainted. He was lolling on a small sofa, his long sword lay on the table before him, and two young native women were fanning him, one at his head, and the other at his feet.

"Where did you get those dresses?" was the first interrogatory.

"The natives, when they brought us prisoners from the island on which we had saved ourselves, took away our clothes, and gave us these as a present from their king."

"And engaged you to serve in their fleet, in the attack of this fort?"

"They forced us," replied Krantz; "for, as there was no war between our nations, we objected to this service: notwithstanding which, they put us on board, to make the common people believe that they were assisted by Europeans."

"How am I to know the truth of this?"

"You have our word in the first place, and our escape from them in the second."

"You belonged to a Dutch East-Indiaman. Are you officers or common seamen?"

Krantz, who considered that they were less likely to be detained if they concealed their rank on board, gave Philip a slight touch with his finger as he replied, "We are inferior officers. I was third mate, and this man was pilot."

"And your captain, where is he?"

"I—I cannot say whether he is alive or dead."

"Had you no woman on board?"

"Yes! the captain had his wife."

"What has become of her?"

"She is supposed to have perished on a portion of the raft which broke a drift."

"Ha!" replied the Commandant, who remained silent for some time.

Philip looked at Krantz, as much as to say, "Why all this subterfuge;" but Krantz gave him a sign to leave him to speak.

"You say you don't know whether your captain is alive or dead?"

"I do."

"Now, suppose I was to give you your liberty, would you have any objection to sign a paper, stating his death, and swearing to the truth of it?"

Philip stared at the Commandant, and then at Krantz.

"I see no objection, exactly; except that if it were sent home to Holland we might get into trouble. May I ask, Signor Commandant, why you wish for such a paper?"

"No!" roared the little man, in a voice like thunder. "I will give no reason, but that I wish it; that is enough; take your choice—the dungeon, or liberty and a passage by the first vessel which calls."

"I don't doubt—in fact—I'm sure, he must be dead by this time," replied Krantz, drawling out the words in a musing manner. "Commandant, will you give us till to-morrow morning to make our calculations?"

"Yes, you may go."

"But not to the dungeon, Commandant," replied Krantz; "we are not prisoners certainly; and, if you wish us to do you a favour, surely you will not ill-treat us?"

"By your own acknowledgment you have taken up arms against the most Christian King; however, you may remain at liberty for the night—to-morrow morning will decide whether or no you are prisoners."

Philip and Krantz thanked the little Commandant for his kindness, and then hastened away to the ramparts. It was now dark, and the moon had not yet made her appearance. They sat there on the parapet enjoying the breeze, and feeling the delight of liberty even after their short incarceration; but, near to them, soldiers were either standing or lying, and they spoke but in whispers.

"What could he mean by requiring us to give a certificate of the captain's death; and why did you answer as you did?"

"Philip Vanderdecken, that I have often thought of the fate of your beautiful wife, you may imagine; and when I heard that she was brought here, I then trembled for her. What must she appear, lovely as she is, when placed in comparison with the women of this country? And that little Commandant—is he not the very person who would be taken with her charms? I denied our condition, because I thought he would be more likely to allow us our liberty as humble individuals, than as captain and first-mate; particularly as he suspects that we led on the Ternate people to the attack; and when he asked for a certificate of your death, I immediately imagined that he wanted it in order to induce Amine to marry him. But where is she? is the question. If we could only find out that soldier, we might gain some information."

"Depend upon it, she is here," replied Philip, clenching his hands.

"I am inclined to think so," said Krantz; "that she is alive, I feel assured."

The conversation was continued until the moon rose, and threw her beams over the tumbling waters. Philip and Krantz turned their faces toward the sea, and leant over the battlements in silence; after some time their reveries were disturbed by a person coming up to them with a "*Buenos noctes, signor*."

Krantz immediately recognised the Portuguese soldier, whose conversation with him had been interrupted.

"Good night, my friend! We thank Heaven that you have no longer to turn the key upon us."

"Yes, I'm surprised!" replied the soldier, in a low tone.—"Our Commandant is fond of exercising his power; he rules here without appeal, that I can tell you."

"He is not within hearing of us now," replied Krantz. "It is a lovely spot this to live in! How long have you been in this country?"

"Now thirteen years, signor, and I'm tired of it. I have a wife and children in Oporto—that is, I *had*—but whether they are alive or not, who can tell?"

"Do you not expect to return and see them?"

"Return—signor! no Portuguese soldier like me ever returns. We are enlisted for five years, and we lay our bones here."

"That is hard indeed."

"Hard, signor," replied the soldier in a low whisper; "it is cruel and treacherous. I have often thought of putting the muzzle of my arquebuse to my head; but while there's life there's hope."

"I pity you, my good fellow," rejoined Krantz; "look you, I have two gold pieces left—take one; you may be able to send it home to your poor wife."

"And here is one of mine, too, my good fellow," added Philip, putting another in his hand.

"Now may all the saints preserve you, signors," replied the soldier, "for it is the first act of kindness shown to me for many years—not that my wife and children have much chance of ever receiving it."

"You were speaking about a young European woman when we were in the dungeon," observed Krantz, after a pause.

"Yes, signor, she was a very beautiful creature. Our commandant was very much in love with her."

"Where is she now?"

"She went away to Goa, in company with a priest who knew her, Father Mathias, a good old man; he gave me absolution when he was here."

"Father Mathias!" exclaimed Philip; but a touch from Krantz checked him.

"You say the commandant loved her?"

"Oh yes: the little man was quite mad about her; and had it not been for the arrival of Father Mathias, he would never have let her go, that I'm sure of, although she was another man's wife."

"Sailed for Goa, you said?"

"Yes, in a ship which called here. She must have been very glad to have got away, for our little commandant persecuted her all day long, and she evidently was grieving for her husband. Do you know, signors, if her husband is alive?"

"No, we do not; we have heard nothing of him."

"Well, if he is, I hope he will not come here; for should the commandant have him in his power, it would go hard with him. He is a man who sticks at nothing. He is a brave little fellow, *that* cannot be denied; but to get possession of that lady, he would remove all obstacles at any risk—and a husband is a very serious one, signors. Well, signors," continued the soldier, after a pause, "I had better not be seen here too long—you may command me if you want anything; recollect, my name is Pedro—good night to you, and a thousand thanks," and the soldier walked away.

"We have made one friend, at all events," said Krantz, "and we have gained information of no little importance."

"Most important," replied Philip. "Amine then has sailed for Goa with Father Mathias! I feel that she is safe, and in good hands. He is an excellent man, that Father Mathias—my mind is relieved."

"Yes; but recollect you are in the power of your enemy. We must leave this place as quick as we can—to-morrow we must sign the paper. It is of little consequence, as we shall probably be at Goa before it arrives; and even if we are not, the news of your death would not occasion Amine to marry this withered piece of mortality."

"That I feel assured of; but it may cause her great suffering."

"Not worse than her present suspense, believe me, Philip; but it is useless canvassing the past—it must be done. I shall sign as Cornelius Richter, our third mate; you, as Jacob Vantreat—recollect that."

"Agreed," replied Philip, who then turned away, as if willing to be left to his own thoughts. Krantz perceived it, and lay down under the embrasure, and was soon fast asleep.

Chapter Thirty Two.

Tired out with the fatigue of the day before, Philip had laid himself down by Krantz and fallen asleep; early the next morning he was awakened by the sound of the commandant's voice, and his long sword rattling as usual upon the pavement. He rose, and found the little man rating the soldiers—threatening some with the dungeons, others with extra duty. Krantz was also on his feet before the commandant had finished his morning's lecture. At last, perceiving them, in a stern voice he ordered them to follow him into his apartment. They did so, and the commandant, throwing himself upon his sofa, inquired whether they were ready to sign the required paper, or go back to the dungeon. Krantz replied that they had been calculating chances and that they were in consequence so perfectly convinced of the death of the captain, that they were willing to sign any paper to that effect; at which reply, the commandant immediately became very gracious, and having called for materials, he wrote out the document, which was duly subscribed to by Krantz and Philip. As soon as they had signed it, and he had it in his possession, the little man was so pleased, that he requested them to partake of his breakfast.

During the repast, he promised that they should leave the island by the first opportunity. Although Philip was taciturn, yet, as Krantz made himself very agreeable, the commandant invited them to dinner. Krantz, as they became more familiar, informed him that they had each a few pieces of gold, and wished to be allowed a room where they could keep their table. Whether it was the want of society or the desire of obtaining the gold, probably both, the commandant offered that they should join his table, and pay their proportion of the expenses; a proposal which was gladly acceded to. The terms were arranged, and Krantz insisted upon putting down the first week's payment in advance. From that moment the commandant was the best of friends with them, and did nothing but caress them whom he had so politely shoved into a dungeon below water. It was on the evening of the third day, as they were smoking their Manilla cheroots that Krantz, perceiving the commandant in a peculiarly good humour, ventured to ask him why he was so anxious for a certificate of the captain's death; and in reply was informed, much to the astonishment of Philip, that Amine had agreed to marry him upon his producing such a document.

"Impossible!" cried Philip, starting from his seat.

"Impossible, signor,—and why impossible?" replied the commandant, curling his mustachios with his fingers, with a surprised and angry air.

"I should have said impossible too," interrupted Krantz, who perceived the consequences of Philip's indiscretion, "for had you seen, commandant, how that woman doated upon her husband, how she fondled him, you would with us have said, it was impossible that she could have transferred her affections so soon; but women are women, and soldiers have a great advantage over other people; perhaps she has some excuse, commandant.—Here's your health, and success to you."

"It is exactly what I would have said," added Philip, acting upon Krantz's plan: "but she has a great excuse, commandant, when I recollect her husband, and have you in my presence."

Soothed with the flattery, the commandant replied, "Why, yes, they say military men are very successful with the fair sex.—I presume it is because they look up to us for protections and where can they be better assured of it, than with a man who wears a sword at his thigh?—Come, signors we will drink her health. Here's to the beautiful Amine Vanderdecken."

"To the beautiful Amine Vanderdecken!" cried Krantz, tossing off his wine.

"To the beautiful Amine Vanderdecken," followed Philip. "But, commandant, are you not afraid to trust her at Goa, where there are so many enticements for a woman, so many allurements held out for her sex?"

"No, not in the least—I am convinced that she loves me—nay, between ourselves, that she doats upon me."

"Liar!" exclaimed Philip.

"How, signor! is that addressed to me?" cried the commandant, seizing his sword, which lay on the table.

"No, no," replied Philip, recovering himself; "it was addressed to her. I have heard her swear to her husband, that she would exist for no other but him."

"Ha! ha! Is that all?" replied the commandant; "my friend, you do not know women."

"No, nor is he very partial to them either," replied Krantz, who then leant over to the commandant and whispered, "He is always so when you talk of women. He was cruelly jilted once, and hates the whole sex."

"Then we must be merciful to him," replied the little officer: "suppose we change the subject."

When they repaired to their own room, Krantz pointed out to Philip the necessity for his commanding his feelings, as otherwise they would again be immured in the dungeon. Philip acknowledged his rashness, but pointed out to Krantz, that the circumstance of Amine having promised to marry the commandant, if he procured certain intelligence of his death, was the cause of his irritation. "Can it be so? Is it possible that she can have been so false?" exclaimed Philip; "yet his anxiety to procure that document seems to warrant the truth of his assertion."

"I think, Philip, that in all probability it is true," replied Krantz, carelessly; "but of this you may be assured, that she has been placed in a situation of great peril, and has only done so to save herself for your sake. When you meet, depend upon it she will fully prove to you that necessity had compelled her to deceive him in that way and that if she had not done so, she would, by this time, have fallen a prey to his violence."

"It may be so," replied Philip, gravely.

"It is so, Philip, my life upon it. Do not for a moment harbour a thought so injurious to one who lives but in your love. Suspect that fond and devoted creature! I blush for you, Philip Vanderdecken."

"You are right, and I beg her pardon for allowing such feelings or thoughts to have for one moment overpowered me," responded Philip; "but it is a hard case for a husband who loves as I do, to hear his wife's name bandied about, and her character assailed by a contemptible wretch like this commandant."

"It is, I grant; but still I prefer even that to a dungeon," replied Krantz, "and so, good night."

For three weeks they remained in the fort, every day becoming more intimate with the commandant, who often communicated with Krantz, when Philip was not present, turning the conversation upon his love for Amine and entering into a minute detail of all that had passed. Krantz perceived that he was right in his opinion, and that Amine had only been cajoling the commandant, that she might escape. But the time passed heavily away with Philip and Krantz, for no vessel made its appearance.

"When shall I see her again?" soliloquised Philip one morning, as he lolled over the parapet, in company with Krantz.

"See who?" said the commandant, who happened to be at his elbow.

Philip turned round and stammered something unintelligible.

"We were talking of his sister, commandant," said Krantz, taking his arm, and leading him away.—"Do not mention the subject to my friend, for it is a very painful one, and forms one reason why he is so inimical to the sex. She was married to his intimate friend and ran away from her husband: it was his only sister; and the disgrace broke his mother's heart, and has made him miserable. Take no notice of it, I beg."

"No, no, certainly not; I don't wonder at it: the honour of one's family is a serious affair," replied the commandant.—"Poor young man, what with his sister's conduct, and the falsehood of his own intended, I don't wonder at his being so grave and silent. Is he of good family, signor?"

"One of the noblest in all Holland," replied Krantz;—"he is heir to a large property, and independent by the fortune of his mother; but these two unfortunate events induced him to quit the States secretly, and he embarked for these countries that he might forget his grief."

"One of the noblest families?" replied the commandant;—"then he is under an assumed name—Jacob Vancheat is not his true name, of course."

"Oh, no," replied Krantz;—"that it is not, I assure you; but my lips are sealed on that point."

"Of course, except to a friend who can keep a secret. I will not ask it now. So he is really noble?"

"One of the highest families in the country, possessing great wealth and influence—allied to the Spanish nobility by marriage."

"Indeed!" rejoined the commandant, musing—"I dare say he knows many of the Portuguese as well."

"No doubt of it, they are all more or less connected."

"He must prove to you a most valuable friend, Signor Richter."

"I consider myself provided for for life as soon as we return home. He is of a very grateful, generous disposition, as he would prove to you, should you ever fall in with him."

"I have no doubt of it; and I can assure you that I am heartily tired of staying in this country. Here I shall remain probably for two years more before I am relieved, and then shall have to join my regiment at Goa, and not be able to obtain leave to return home without resigning my commission. But he is coming this way."

After this conversation with Krantz, the alteration in the manner of the Portuguese commandant, who had the highest respect for nobility, was most marked. He treated Philip with a respect which was observable to all in the fort; and which was, until Krantz had explained the cause, a source of astonishment to Philip himself. The commandant often introduced the subject to Krantz, and sounded him as to whether his conduct towards Philip had been such as to have made a favourable impression; for the little man now hoped, that through such an influential channel, he might reap some benefit.

Some days after this conversation, as they were all three seated at table, a corporal entered, and saluting the commandant, informed him that a Dutch sailor had arrived at fort, and wished to know whether he should be admitted. Both Philip and Krantz turned pale at this communication—they had a presentiment of evil but they said nothing. The sailor was ordered in, and in a few minutes, who should make his appearance but their tormentor, the one-eyed Schriften. On perceiving Philip and Krantz seated at the table, he immediately exclaimed, "Oh! Captain Philip Vanderdecken, and my good friend Mynheer Krantz, first mate of the good ship Utrecht, I am glad to meet you again."

"Captain Philip Vanderdecken!" roared the commandant, as he sprung from his chair.

"Yes, that is my captain, Mynheer Philip Vanderdecken and that is my first mate, Mynheer Krantz; both of the good ship Utrecht: we were wrecked together, were we not. Mynheer? He! he!"

"Sangue de—Vanderdecken! the husband! Corpo del diavolo—is it possible!" cried the commandant, panting for breath, as he seized his long sword with both hands and clenched it with fury.—"What, then, I have been deceived, cajoled, laughed at!" Then, after a pause—the veins of his forehead distending so as almost to burst—he continued, with a suppressed voice, "Most noble sir, I thank you; but now it is my turn.—What, ho! there! Corporal—men, here, instantly—quick!"

Philip and Krantz felt convinced that all denial was useless. Philip folded his arms and made no reply. Krantz merely observed, "A little reflection will prove to you, sir, that this indignation is not warranted."

"Not warranted!" rejoined the commandant with a sneer, "you have deceived me; but you are caught in your own trap. I have the paper signed, which I shall not fail to make use of. *You* are dead, you know, Captain; I have your own hand to it, and your wife will be glad to believe it."

"She has deceived you, commandant, to get out of your power, nothing more," said Vanderdecken. "She would spurn a contemptible withered wretch like yourself, were she as free as the wind."

"Go on, go on; it will be my turn soon. Corporal, throw these two men into the dungeon: a sentry at the door till further orders. Away with them! Most noble sir, perhaps your influential friends in Holland and Spain will enable you to get out again."

Philip and Krantz were led away by the soldiers, who were very much surprised at this change of treatment. Schriften followed them; and as they walked across the rampart to the stairs which led to their prison, Krantz, in his fury, burst from the soldiers, and bestowed a kick upon Schriften, which sent him several feet forward on his face.

"That was a good one—he! he!" cried Schriften, smiling and looking at Krantz as he regained his legs.

There was an eye, however, which met theirs with an intelligent glance, as they descended the stairs to the dungeon. It was that of the soldier Pedro. It told them that there was one friend upon whom they could rely, and who would spare no endeavour to assist them in their new difficulty. It was a consolation to them both; a ray of hope which cheered them as they once more descended the narrow steps, and heard the heavy key turned which again secured them in their dungeon.

Chapter Thirty Three.

"Thus are all our hopes wrecked," said Philip, mournfully; "what chance have we now of escaping from this little tyrant?"

"Chances turn up," replied Krantz; "at present, the prospect is not very cheering. Let us hope for the best. I have an idea in my head which may probably be turned to some account," continued Krantz, "as soon as the little man's fury is over."

"Which is?"

"That, much as he likes your wife, there is something which he likes quite as well—money. Now, as we know where all the treasure is concealed, I think he may be tempted to offer us our liberty, if we were to promise to put it into his possession."

"That is not impossible. Confound that little malignant wretch Schriften; he certainly is not, as you say, of this world. He has been my persecutor through life, and appears to act from an impulse not his own."

"Then must he be part and portion of your destiny. I'm thinking whether our noble commandant intends to leave us without anything to eat or drink."

"I should not be surprised; that he will attempt my life I am convinced, but not that he can take it; he may, however, add to its sufferings."

As soon as the commandant had recovered from his fury, he ordered Schriften in, to be examined more particularly; but, after every search made for him, Schriften was nowhere to be found. The sentry at the gate declared that he had not passed: and a new search was ordered, but in vain. Even the dungeons and galleries below were examined, but without success.

"Can he be locked up with the other prisoners?" thought the commandant: "impossible—but I will go and see."

He descended and opened the door of the dungeon, looked in, and was about to return without speaking, when Krantz said, "Well, signor, this is kind treatment, after having lived so long and so amicably together; to throw us into prison merely because a fellow declares that we are not what we represented ourselves to be; perhaps you will allow us a little water to drink?"

The commandant, confused by the extraordinary disappearance of Schriften hardly knew how to reply. He at last said in a milder tone than was to be anticipated, "I will order them to bring some, signor."

He then closed the door of the dungeon and disappeared.

"Strange," observed Philip, "he appears more pacified already." In a few minutes the door was again opened, and Pedro came in with a chatty of water.

"He has disappeared like magic, signors, and is nowhere to be found. We have searched everywhere, but in vain."

"Who?—the little old seaman?"

"Yes, he whom you kicked as you were led to prison. The people all say, that it must have been a ghost. The sentry declares that he never left the fort, nor came near him; so how he has got away is a riddle, which I perceive has frightened our commandant not a little."

Krantz gave a long whistle as he looked at Philip.

"Are you to have charge of us, Pedro?"

"I hope so."

"Well, tell the commandant that when he is ready to listen to me, I have something of importance to communicate."

Pedro went out.

"Now, Philip, I can frighten this little man into allowing us to go free, if you will consent to say that you are not the husband of Amine."

"That I cannot do, Krantz. I will not utter such a falsehood."

"I was afraid so, and yet it appears to me that we may avail ourselves of duplicity to meet cruelty and injustice. Unless you do as I propose, I hardly know how I can manage it; however, I will try what I can do."

"I will assist you in every way, except disclaiming my wife: that I never will do."

"Well, then, I will see if I can make up a story that will suit all parties: let me think."

Krantz continued musing as he walked up and down, and was still occupied with his own thoughts, when the door opened, and the commandant made his appearance.

"You have something to impart to me, I understand—what is it?"

"First, sir, bring that little wretch down here and confront him with us."

"I see no occasion for that," replied the commandant; "what, sir, may you have to say?"

"Do you know who you have in your company when you speak to that one-eyed deformity?"

"A Dutch sailor, I presume."

"No—a spirit—a demon—who occasioned the loss of the vessel; and who brings misfortune wherever he appears."

"Holy Virgin! what do you tell me, signor?"

"The fact, Signor Commandant. We are obliged to you for confining us here, while he is in the fort; but beware for yourself."

"You are laughing at me."

"I am not; bring him down here. This noble gentleman has power over him. I wonder, indeed, at his daring to stay while he is so near; he has on his heart that which will send him trembling away. Bring him down here, and you shall at once see him vanish with curses and screams."

"Heaven defend us!" cried the commandant, terrified.

"Send for him now, signor."

"He is gone—vanished—not to be found!"

"I thought as much," replied Philip, significantly.

"He is gone—vanished—you say. Then, commandant, you will probably apologise to this noble gentleman for your treatment of him, and permit us to return to our former apartments. I will there explain to you this most strange and interesting history."

The commandant, more confused than ever, hardly knew how to act. At last he bowed to Philip, and begged that he would consider himself at liberty; "and," continued he to Krantz, "I shall be most happy at an immediate explanation of this affair, for everything appears so contradictory."

"And must, until it is explained. I will follow you into your own room; a courtesy you must not expect from my noble friend, who is not a little indignant at your treatment of him."

The commandant went out, leaving the door open. Philip and Krantz followed: the former retiring to his own apartment; the latter, bending his steps after the commandant to his sitting-room. The confusion which whirled in the brain of the commandant made him appear most ridiculous. He hardly knew whether to be imperative or civil; whether he was really speaking to the first mate of the vessel, or to another party; or whether he had insulted a noble, or been cajoled by a captain of a vessel: he threw himself down on his sofa, and Krantz, taking his seat in a chair, stated as follows:—

"You have been partly deceived and partly not, commandant. When we first came here, not knowing what treatment we might receive, we concealed our rank; afterwards I made known to you the rank of my friend on shore; but did not think it worth while to say anything about his situation on board of the vessel. The fact is, as you may well suppose of a person of his dignity, he was owner of the fine ship which was lost through the intervention of that one-eyed wretch; but of that by-and-by. Now for the story. About ten years ago there was a great miser in Amsterdam; he lived in the most miserable way that a man could live in; wore nothing but rags; and having been formerly a seaman, his attire was generally of the description common to his class. He had one son, to whom he denied the necessaries of life, and whom he treated most cruelly. After vain attempts to possess a portion of his father's wealth, the devil instigated the son to murder the old man, who was one day found dead in his bed; but as there were no marks of violence which could be sworn to, although suspicion fell upon the son, the affair was hushed up, and the young man took possession of his father's wealth. It was fully expected that there would now be rioting and squandering on the part of the heir, as is usually the case; but, on the contrary, he never spent anything, but appeared to be as poor—even poorer—than he ever was. Instead of being gay and merry, he was, in appearance, the most miserable, downcast person in the world; and he wandered about, seeking a crust of bread wherever he could find it. Some said that he had been inoculated by his father, and was as great a miser as his father had been; others shook their heads, and said that all was not right. At last, after pining away for six or seven years, the young man died at an early age, without confession or absolution; in fact, he was found dead in his bed. Beside the bed there was a paper addressed to the authorities, in which he acknowledged that he had murdered his father for the sake of his wealth; and that when he went to take some of it for his expenses on the day afterwards, he found his father's spirit sitting on the bags of money, and menacing him with instant death, if he touched one piece. He returned again and again, and found his father a sentinel as before. At last, he gave up attempting to obtain it: his crime made him miserable, and he continued in possession, without daring to expend one sixpence of all the money. He requested that, as his end was approaching, the money should be given to the church of his patron saint, wherever that church might be found; if there was not one, then that a church might be built and endowed. Upon investigation, it appeared that there was no such church in either Holland or the Low Countries (for you know that there are not many Catholics there); and they applied to the Catholic countries, Lisbon and Spain, but there again they were at fault; and it was discovered, that the only church dedicated to that saint was one which had been erected by a Portuguese nobleman in the city of Goa, in the East Indies. The Catholic bishop determined that the money should be sent to Goa and, in consequence it was embarked on board of my patron's vessel, to be delivered up to the first Portuguese authorities he might fall in with.

"Well, signor, the money, for better security was put down into the captain's cabin, which, of course, was occupied by my noble friend, and when he went to bed the first night he was surprised to perceive a little one-eyed old man sitting on the boxes."

"Merciful Saviour!" exclaimed the commandant, "what, the very same little man who appeared here this day?"

"The very same," replied Krantz.

The commandant crossed himself, and Krantz proceeded:—

"My noble patron was, as you may imagine, rather alarmed; but he is very courageous in disposition, and he inquired of the old man who he was, and how he had come on board.

"'I came on board with my own money,' replied the spectre. 'It is all my own, and I shall keep it. The Church shall never have one stiver of it if I can help it.'

"Whereupon, my patron pulled out a famous relic, which he wears on his bosom, and held it towards him; at which the old man howled and screamed, and then most unwillingly disappeared. For two more nights the spectre was obstinate, but at the sight of the relic, he invariably went off howling, as if in great pain; every time that he went away, invariably crying out 'Lost—lost!'—and during the remainder of the voyage he did not trouble us any more.

"We thought, when our patron told us this, that he referred to the money being lost to him, but it appears he referred to the ship; indeed it was very inconsiderate to have taken the wealth of a parricide on board; we could not expect any good fortune with such a freight, and so it proved. When the ship was lost, our patron was very anxious to save the money; it was put on the raft, and when we landed, it was taken on shore and buried, that it might be restored and given to the church to which it had been bequeathed; but the men who buried it are all dead, and there is no one but my friend here, the patron, who knows the spot.—I forgot to say that as soon as the money was landed on the island and buried, the spectre appeared as before, and seated itself over the spot where the money was interred. I think, if this had not been the case, the seamen would have taken possession of it. But, by its appearance here this day, I presume it is tired, and has deserted its charge, or else has come here that the money might be sent for, though I cannot understand why."

"Strange—very strange! So there is a large treasure buried in the sand?"

"There is."

"I should think, by the spectre's coming here, that it has abandoned it."

"Of course it has, or it would not be here."

"What can you imagine to have been the cause of its coming?"

"Probably to announce its intention, and request my friend to have the treasure sent for; but you know it was interrupted."

"Very true; but it called your friend Vanderdecken."

"It was the name which he took on board of the ship."

"And it was the name of the lady."

"Very true. He fell in with her at the Cape of Good Hope, and brought her away with him."

"Then she is his wife?"

"I must not answer that question. It is quite sufficient that he treats her as his wife."

"Ah! indeed. But about this treasure. You say that no one knows where it is buried but the patron, as you call him?"

"No one."

"Will you express my regret at what has passed, and tell him I will have the pleasure of seeing him to-morrow."

"Certainly, signor," replied Krantz, rising from his chair, and wishing the commandant a good evening as he retired.

"I was after one thing, and have found another. A spectre that must have been; but he must be a bold spectre that can frighten me from doubloons; besides, I can call in the priests. Now, let me see: if I let this man go on condition that he reveals the site of the treasure to the authorities—that is to me—why then I need not lose the fair young woman. If I forward this paper to her, why then I gain her; but I must first get rid of him. Of the two, I prefer—yes!—the gold! But I cannot obtain both. At all events, let me obtain the money first. I want it more than the Church does; but if I do get the money, these two men can expose me. I must get rid of them—silence them for ever—and then perhaps I may obtain the fair Amine also. Yes, their death will be necessary to secure either; that is, after I have the first in my possession. Let me think."

For some minutes the commandant walked up and down the room, reflecting upon the best method of proceeding. "He says it was a spectre, and he has told a plausible story," thought he; "but I don't know—I have my doubts; they may be tricking me. Well, be it so. If the money is there, I will have it; and if not, I will have my revenge. Yes! I have it: not only must they be removed, but by degrees all the others too who assist in bringing the treasure away. Then—but—who's there, Pedro?"

"Yes, signor."

"How long have you been here?"

"But as you spoke, signor; I thought I heard you call."

"You may go—I want nothing."

Pedro departed; but he had been some time in the room, and had overheard the whole of the commandant's soliloquy.

Chapter Thirty Four.

It was a bright morning when the Portuguese vessel on which Amine was on board entered into the bay and roadstead of Goa. Goa was then at its zenith,—a proud, luxurious, superb, wealthy city—the capital of the East—a city of palaces whose viceroy reigned supreme. As they approached the river, the two mouths of which form the island upon which Goa is built, the passengers were all on deck; and the Portuguese captain, who had often been there, pointed out to Amine the most remarkable buildings. When they had passed the forts, they entered the river, the whole line of whose banks were covered with the country seats of the nobility and hidalgos—splendid buildings embosomed in groves of orange-trees, whose perfume scented the air.

"There, signora, is the country palace of the viceroy," said the captain, pointing to a building which covered nearly three acres of ground.

The ship sailed on until they arrived nearly abreast of the town, when Amine's eyes were directed to the lofty spires of the churches, and other public edifices; for Amine had seen but little of cities during her life, as may be perceived when her history is recollected.

"That is the Jesuits' church, with their establishment," said the captain, pointing to a magnificent pile. "In the church now opening upon us lie the canonised bones of the celebrated Saint Francisco, who sacrificed his life in his zeal for the propagation of the Gospel in these countries."

"I have heard of him from Father Mathias," replied Amine; "but what building is that?"

"The Augustine convent; and the other, to the right, is the Dominican."

"Splendid, indeed!" observed Amine.

"The building you see now, on the water-side, is the viceroy's palace; that to the right again, is the convent of the barefooted Carmelites; yon lofty spire is the cathedral of St. Catherine; and that beautiful and light piece of architecture is the church of our Lady of Pity. You observe there a building with a dome, rising behind the viceroy's palace?"

"I do," replied Amine.

"That is the Holy Inquisition."

Although Amine had heard Philip speak of the Inquisition, she knew little about its properties; but a sudden tremor passed through her frame as the name was mentioned, which she could not herself account for.

"Now we open upon the viceroy's palace, and you perceive what a beautiful building it is," continued the captain. "That large pile, a little above it, is the Custom-house, abreast of which we shall come to an anchor. I must leave you now, signora."

A few minutes afterwards the ship anchored opposite the Custom-house. The captain and passengers went on shore with the exception of Amine, who remained in the vessel while Father Mathias went in search of an eligible place of abode.

The next morning the priest returned on board the ship, with the intelligence that he had obtained a reception for Amine in the Ursuline convent, the abbess of which establishment he was acquainted with; and before Amine went on shore, he cautioned her that the lady-abbess was a strict woman, and would be pleased if she conformed as much as possible to the rules of the convent; that this convent only received young persons of the highest and most wealthy families, and he trusted that she would be happy there. He also promised to call upon her, and talk upon those subjects so dear to his heart, and so necessary to her salvation. The earnestness and kindness with which the old man spoke melted Amine to tears; and the holy father quitted her side to go down and collect her baggage with a warmth of feeling towards her which he had seldom felt before, and with greater hopes than ever that his endeavours to convert her would not ultimately be thrown away.

"He is a good man," thought Amine, as she descended—and Amine was right. Father Mathias was a good man; but, like all men, he was not perfect. A zealot in the cause of his religion, he would have cheerfully sacrificed his life as a martyr; but if opposed or thwarted in his views, he could then be cruel and unjust.

Father Mathias had many reasons for placing Amine in the Ursuline convent. He felt bound to offer her that protection which he had so long received under her roof; he wished her to be under the surveillance of the abbess, for he could not help imagining, although he had no proof, that she was still essaying or practising forbidden arts. He did not state this to the abbess, as he felt it would be unjust to raise suspicions; but he represented Amine as one who would do honour to their faith to which she was not yet quite converted. The very idea of effecting a conversion is to the tenants of a convent an object of surpassing interest, and the abbess was much better pleased to receive one who required her counsels and persuasions, than a really pious Christian, who would give her no trouble. Amine went on shore with Father Mathias; she refused the palanquin which had been prepared for her, and walked up to the convent. They landed between the Custom-house and the viceroy's palace, passed through the large square behind it, and then went up the Strada Diretta, or straight street, which led up to the Church of Pity, near to which the convent is situated. This street is the finest in Goa, and is called Strada Diretta from the singular fact that almost all the streets in Goa are quadrants or segments of circles. Amine was astonished. The houses were of stone, lofty and massive; at each story was thrown out a balcony of marble, elaborately carved; and over each door were the arms of the nobility, or hidalgos, to whom the houses belonged. The square behind the palace and the wide streets were filled with living beings; elephants with gorgeous trappings; led or mounted horses in superb housings; palanquins, carried by natives in splendid liveries; running footmen; syces; every variety of nation, from the proud Portuguese to the half-covered native; Mussulmans, Arabs, Hindoos, Armenians; officers and soldiers in their uniforms, all crowded and thronged together,—all was bustle and motion. Such was the wealth, the splendour, and luxury of the proud city of Goa—the Empress of the East at the time we are now describing.

In half an hour they forced their way through the crowd, and arrived at the convent, where Amine was well received by the abbess; and, after a few minutes' conversation, Father Mathias took his leave; upon which the abbess immediately set about her task of conversion. The first thing she did was to order some dried sweetmeats—not a bad beginning, as they were palatable; but as she happened to be very ignorant, and unaccustomed to theological disputes, her subsequent arguments did not go down as well as the fruit. After a rambling discourse of about an hour, the old lady felt tired, and felt as if she had done wonders. Amine was then introduced to the nuns, most of whom were young, and all of good family. Her dormitory was shown to her; and expressing a wish to be alone, she was followed into her chamber by only sixteen of them, which was about as many as the chamber could well hold.

We must pass over the two months during which Amine remained in the convent. Father Mathias had taken every step to ascertain if her husband had been saved upon any of the islands which were under the Portuguese dominions, but could gain no information. Amine was soon weary of the convent; she was persecuted by the harangues of the old abbess, but more disgusted at the conduct and conversation of the nuns. They all had secrets to confide to her—secrets which had been confided to the whole convent before: such secrets, such stories, so different from Amine's chaste ideas—such impurity of thought—that Amine was disgusted at them. But how could it be otherwise? The poor creatures had been taken from the world in the full bloom of youth, under a ripening sun, and had been immured in this unnatural manner to gratify the avarice and pride of their families. Its inmates being wholly composed of the best families, the rules of this convent were not so strict as others; licences were given—greater licences were taken—and Amine, to her surprise, found that in this society, devoted to Heaven, there were exhibited more of the bad passions of human nature than she had before met with. Constantly watched, never allowed a moment to herself, her existence became unbearable; and, after three months, she requested Father Mathias would find her some other place of refuge, telling him frankly that her residence in that place was not very likely to assist her conversion to the tenets of his faith. Father Mathias fully comprehended her, but replied, "I have no means."

"Here are means," replied Amine, taking the diamond ring from her finger. "This is worth eight hundred ducats in our country; here, I know not how much."

Father Mathias took the ring. "I will call upon you to-morrow morning, and let you know what I have done. I shall acquaint the lady abbess that you are going to your husband, for it would not be safe to let her suppose that you have reasons for quitting the convent. I have heard what you state mentioned before, but have treated it as scandal: but you, I know, are incapable of falsehood."

The next day Father Mathias returned, and had an interview with the abbess, who after a time sent for Amine, and told her that it was necessary that she should leave the convent. She consoled her as well as she could at leaving such a happy place, sent for some sweetmeats to make the parting less trying, gave her a blessing, and made her over to Father Mathias; who, when they were alone, informed Amine "that he had disposed of the ring for eighteen hundred dollars, and had procured apartments for her in the house of a widow lady, with whom she was to board."

Taking leave of the nuns, Amine quitted the convent with Father Mathias, and was soon installed in her new apartments, in a house which formed part of a spacious square called the Terra di Sabaio. After the introduction to her hostess, Father Mathias left her. Amine found her apartments fronting the square, airy and commodious. The landlady, who had escorted her to view them, not having left her, she inquired "what large church that was on the other side of the square?"

"It is the Ascension," replied the lady; "the music is very fine there; we will go and hear it to-morrow, if you please."

"And that massive building in face of us?"

"That is the Holy Inquisition," said the widow, crossing herself.

Amine again started, she knew not why. "Is that your child?" said Amine, as a boy of about twelve years old entered the room.

"Yes," replied the widow, "the only one that is left me. May God preserve him." The boy was handsome and intelligent, and Amine, for her own reasons, did everything she could to make friends with him, and was successful.

Chapter Thirty Five.

Amine had just returned from an afternoon's walk through the streets of Goa: she had made some purchases at different shops in the bazaar, and had brought them home under her mantilla. "Here, at last, thank Heaven, I am alone and not watched," thought Amine, as she threw herself on the couch. "Philip, Philip, where are you?" exclaimed she. "I have now the means, and I soon will know." Little Pedro, the son of the widow, entered the room, ran up to Amine and kissed her. "Tell me, Pedro, where is your mother."

"She is gone out to see her friends this evening, and we are alone. I will stay with you."

"Do so, dearest. Tell me, Pedro, can you keep a secret?"

"Yes, I will—tell it me."

"Nay, I have nothing to tell, but I wish to do something: I wish to make a play, and you shall see things in your hand."

"Oh! yes, show me, do show me."

"If you promise not to tell."

"No, by the Holy Virgin, I will not."

"Then you shall see."

Amine lighted some charcoal in a chafing-dish, and put it at her feet; she then took a reed pen, some ink from a small bottle, and a pair of scissors, and wrote down several characters on a paper singing, or rather chanting, words which were not intelligible to her young companion. Amine then threw frankincense and coriander seed into the chafing-dish, which threw out a strong aromatic smoke; and desiring Pedro to sit down by her on a small stool, she took the boy's right hand and held it in her own. She then drew upon the palm of his hand a square figure with characters on each side of it, and in the centre poured a small quantity of the ink, so as to form a black mirror of the size of half a crown.

"Now all is ready," said Amine; "look, Pedro, what see you in the ink?"

"My own face," replied the boy.

She threw more frankincense upon the chafing-dish, until the room was full of smoke, and then chaunted:—

"Turshoon, turyo-shoon—come down, come down.

"Be present, ye servants of these names.

"Remove the veil, and be correct."

The characters she had drawn upon the paper, she had divided with the scissors, and now taking one of the pieces, she dropped it into the chafing-dish still holding the boy's hand.

"Tell me now, Pedro, what do you see?"

"I see a man sweeping," replied Pedro, alarmed.

"Fear not, Pedro, you shall see more. Has he done sweeping?"

"Yes, he has."

And Amine muttered words, which were unintelligible, and threw into the chafing-dish the other half of the paper with the characters she had written down. "Say now, Pedro, 'Philip Vanderdecken, appear.'"

"Philip Vanderdecken appear!" responded the boy, trembling.

"Tell me what thou seest, Pedro—tell me true?" said Amine anxiously.

"I see a man lying down on the white sand—(I don't like this play)."

"Be not alarmed, Pedro, you shall have sweetmeats directly. Tell me what thou seest, how the man is dressed?"

"He has a short coat—he has white trowsers—he looks about him—he takes something out of his breast and kisses it."

"'Tis he, 'tis he! and he lives! Heaven, I thank thee. Look again, boy."

"He gets up—(I don't like this play; I am frightened; indeed I am)."

"Fear not."

"Oh, yes, I am—I cannot," replied Pedro, falling on his knees; "pray let me go."

Pedro had turned his hand, and spilt the ink, the charm was broken, and Amine could learn no more. She soothed the boy with presents, made him repeat his promise that he would not tell, and postponed further search into fate until the boy should appear to have recovered from his terror, and be willing to resume the ceremonies.

"My Philip lives—mother, dear mother, I thank you."

Amine did not allow Pedro to leave the room until he appeared to have quite recovered from his fright; for some days she did not say anything to him, except to remind him of his promise not to tell his mother, or any one else, and she loaded him with presents.

One afternoon when his mother was gone out Pedro came in and asked Amine "whether they should not have the play ever again!"

Amine, who was anxious to know more, was glad of the boy's request, and soon had everything prepared. Again was her chamber filled with the smoke of the frankincense: again was she muttering her incantations: the magic mirror was on the boy's hand, and once more had Pedro cried out, "Philip Vanderdecken, appear!" when the door burst open, and Father Mathias, the widow, and several other people made their appearance. Amine started up—Pedro screamed and ran to his mother.

"Then I was not mistaken at what I saw in the cottage at Terneuse," cried Father Mathias, with his arms folded over his breast, and with looks of indignation; "accursed sorceress! you are detected."

Amine returned his gaze with scorn, and coolly replied, "I am not of your creed—you know it. Eaves-dropping appears to be a portion of your religion. This is my chamber—it is not the first time I have had to request you to leave it—I do so now—you—and those who have come in with you."

"Take up all those implements of sorcery first," said Father Mathias to his companions. The chafing-dish, and other articles used by Amine, were taken away; and Father Mathias and the others quitting the room: Amine was left alone.

Amine had a foreboding that she was lost; she knew that magic was a crime of the highest degree in Catholic countries, and that she had been detected in the very act. "Well, well," thought Amine: "it is my destiny, and I can brave the worst."

To account for the appearance of Father Mathias and the witnesses, it must be observed, that the little boy Pedro had, the day after Amine's first attempt, forgotten his promise, and narrated to his mother all that had passed. The widow, frightened at what the boy had told her, thought it right to go to Father Mathias, and confide to him what her son had told her, as it was, in her opinion, sorcery. Father Mathias questioned Pedro closely, and, convinced that such was the case, determined to have witnesses to confront Amine. He, therefore, proposed that the boy should appear to be willing to try again, and had instructed him for the purpose, having previously arranged that they should break in upon Amine, as we have described.

About half an hour afterwards, two men dressed in black gowns came into Amine's room, and requested that she would follow them, or that force would be used. Amine made no resistance: they crossed the square: the gate of a large building was opened, they desired her to walk in, and, in a few seconds, Amine found herself in one of the dungeons of the Inquisition.

Chapter Thirty Six.

Previous to continuing our narrative, it may be as well to give our readers some little insight into the nature, ceremonies, and regulations of the Inquisition, and in describing that of Goa, we may be said to describe all others, with very trifling, if any, variation.

The Santa Casa, or Inquisition of Goa, is situated on one side of a large square, called the Terra di Sabaio. It is a massy handsome pile of stone buildings, with three doors in the front: the centre one is larger than the two lateral, and it is through the centre door that you go into the Hall of Judgment. The side-doors lead to spacious and handsome apartments for the Inquisitors, and officers attached to the establishment.

Behind these apartments are the cells and dungeons of the Inquisition; they are in two long galleries, with double doors to each, and are about ten feet square. There are about two hundred of them; some are much more comfortable than the others, as light and air are admitted into them: the others are wholly dark. In the galleries the keepers watch, and not a word or a sound can proceed from any cell without their being able to overhear it. The treatment of those confined is, as far as respects their food, very good: great care is taken that the nourishment is of that nature that the prisoners may not suffer from the indigestion arising from want of exercise. Surgical attendance is also permitted them; but unless on very particular occasions no priests are allowed to enter. Any consolation to be derived from religion, even the office of confessor and extreme unction, in case of dissolution, are denied them. Should they die during their confinement, whether proved guilty or not of the crime of which they are accused, they are buried without any funeral ceremony, and tried afterwards; if then found guilty, their bones are disinterred, and the execution of their sentence is passed upon their remains.

There are two Inquisitors at Goa: one the Grand Inquisitor, and the other his second, who are invariably chosen from the order of St. Dominique; these two are assisted in their judgment and examinations by a large number selected from the religious orders, who are termed deputies of the Holy Office, but who only attend when summoned: they have other officers, whose duty it is to examine all published books, and ascertain if there is anything in their pages contrary to the holy religion. There is also a public accuser, a procureur of the Inquisition, and lawyers, who are permitted to plead the case of the prisoners, but whose chief business and interest it is to obtain their secrets and betray them. What are termed *Familiars* of the Inquisition, are in fact, nothing but this description of people: but this disgraceful office is taken upon themselves by the highest nobility, who think it an honour, as well as a security, to be enrolled among the Familiars of the Inquisition, who are thus to be found dispersed throughout society; and every careless word, or expression, is certain to be repeated to the Holy Office. A summons to attend at the Inquisition is never opposed; if it were, the whole populace would rise and enforce it. Those who are confined in the dungeons of the Inquisition are kept separate; it is a very uncommon thing to put two together: it is only done when it is considered that the prolonged solitude of the dungeon has created such a depression of spirits as to endanger the life of the party. Perpetual silence is enjoined and strictly kept. Those who wail or weep, or even pray, in their utter darkness, are forced by blows to be quiet. The cries and shrieks of those who suffer from this chastisement, or from the torture, are carried along the whole length of the corridors, terrifying those who, in solitude and darkness, are anticipating the same fate.

The first question put to a person arrested by the Inquisition, is a demand, "What is his property?" He is desired to make an exact declaration of everything that he is worth, and swear to the truth of his assertions; being informed that, if there is any reservation on his part, (although he may be at that time innocent of the charges produced against him) he will, by his concealment, have incurred the wrath of the Inquisition; and that, if discharged for the crime he is accused of, he will again be arrested for having taken a false oath to the Inquisition; that, if innocent, his property will be safe, and not interfered with. It is not without reason that this demand is made. If a person accused confesses his crime, he is, in most cases, eventually allowed to go free, but all his property becomes confiscated.

By the rules of the Inquisition it is made to appear as if those condemned have the show of justice; for, although two witnesses are sufficient to warrant the apprehension of any individual, seven are necessary to convict him; but as the witnesses are never confronted with the prisoners, and torture is often applied to the witnesses, it is not difficult to obtain the number required. Many a life is falsely sworn away by the witness, that he may save his own.

The chief crimes which are noticed by the Inquisition are those of sorcery, heresy, blasphemy, and what is called *Judaism*.

To comprehend the meaning of this last crime, for which more people have suffered from the Inquisition than for any other, the reader must be informed, that when Ferdinand and Isabella of Castile drove all the Jews out of Spain, they fled to Portugal, where they were received on the sole condition that they should embrace Christianity: this they consented, or appeared to consent, to do; but these converts were despised by the Portuguese people, who did not believe them to be sincere. They obtained the title of *New* Christians, in contradistinction to that of *Old* Christians. After a time the two were occasionally intermingled in marriage; but when so, it was always a reproach to the old families; and descendants from these alliances were long termed, by way of reproach, as having a portion of the New Christians in them.

The descendants of the old families thus intermingled, not only lost *caste*, but, as the genealogy of every family was well known, they were looked upon with suspicion, and were always at the mercy of the Holy Office, when denounced for Judaism,—that is, for returning to the old Jewish practices of keeping the Passover, and the other ceremonies enforced by Moses.

Let us see how an accusation of this kind works in the hands of the Inquisition. A really sincere Catholic, descended from one of these unhappy families, is accused and arrested by the orders of the Inquisition; he is ordered to declare his property, which,—convinced of his innocence, and expecting soon to be released, he does without reservation. But hardly has the key of the dungeon turned upon him, when all his effects are seized and sold by public auction, it being well understood that they never will be restored to him. After some months' confinement, he is called into the Hall of Justice, and asked if he knows why he is in prison; they advise him earnestly to confess and to conceal nothing, as it is the only way by which he can obtain his liberty. He declares his ignorance and being sent for several times, persists in it. The period of the *auto-da-fé*, or act of faith, which takes place every two or three years, (that is, the public execution of those who have been found guilty by the Inquisition,) approaches. The public accuser then comes forward, stating that the prisoner has been accused by a number of witnesses of Judaism. They persuade him to acknowledge his guilt. He persists in his innocence; they then pass a sentence on him, which they term *Convicte Invotivo*, which means "found guilty, but will not confess his crime;" and he is sentenced to be burnt at the approaching celebration. After this they follow him to his cell, and exhort him to confess his guilt, and promise that if he does confess he shall be pardoned; and these appeals are continued until the evening of the day before his execution. Terrified at the idea of a painful death, the wretch, at last, to save his life, consents. He is called into the Hall of Judgment, confesses the crime that he has not committed, and imagines that he is now saved.—Alas! now he has entangled himself, and cannot escape.

"You acknowledge that you have been guilty of observing the laws of Moses. These ceremonies cannot be performed alone; you cannot have eaten the Paschal lamb *alone*; tell us immediately, who were those who assisted at those ceremonies, or your life is still forfeited, and the stake is prepared for you."

Thus has he accused himself without gaining anything, and if he wishes to save his life, he must accuse others; and who can be accused but his own friends and acquaintances? nay, in all probability, his own relations—his brothers, sisters, wife, sons, or daughters—for it is natural to suppose that, in all such practices, a man will trust only his own family. Whether a man confesses his guilt, or dies asserting his innocence, his worldly property is in either case confiscated; but it is of great consequence to the Inquisition that he should confess, as his act of confession, with his signature annexed, is publicly read, and serves to prove to the world that the Inquisition is impartial and just; nay, more, even merciful, as it pardons those who have been proved to be guilty.

At Goa the accusations of sorcery and magic were much more frequent than at the Inquisitions at other places, arising from the customs and ceremonies of the Hindoos being very much mixed up with absurd superstitions. These people, and the slaves from other parts, very often embraced Christianity to please their masters; but since, if they had been baptised and were afterwards convicted of any crime, they were sentenced to the punishment by fire; whereas if they had not been baptised, they were only punished by whipping, imprisonment, or the galleys; upon this ground alone many refused to embrace Christianity.

We have now detailed all that we consider, up to the present, necessary for the information of the reader; all that is omitted he will gather as we proceed with our history.

Chapter Thirty Seven.

A few hours after Amine had been in the dungeon, the jailors entered: without speaking to her they let down her soft silky hair, and cut it close off. Amine, with her lip curled in contempt, and without resistance and expostulation, allowed them to do their work. They finished, and she was again left to her solitude.

The next day the jailors entered her cell, and ordered her to bare her feet, and follow them. She looked at them, and they at her. "If you do not, we must," observed one of the men, who was moved by her youth and beauty. Amine did as she was desired, and was led into the Hall of Justice, where she found only the Grand Inquisitor and the Secretary.

The Hall of Justice was a long room with lofty windows on each side, and also at the end opposite to the door through which she had been led in. In the centre, on a raised daïs, was a long table covered with a cloth of alternate blue and fawn coloured stripes; and at the end opposite to where Amine was brought in, was raised an enormous crucifix, with a carved image of our Saviour. The jailor pointed to a small bench, and intimated to Amine that she was to sit down.

After a scrutiny of some moments, the secretary spoke:—

"What is your name?"

"Amine Vanderdecken."

"Of what country?"

"My husband is of the Low Countries; I am from the East."

"What is your husband?"

"The captain of a Dutch Indiaman."

"How came you here?"

"His vessel was wrecked, and we were separated."

"Whom do you know here?"

"Father Mathias."

"What property have you?"

"None; it is my husband's."

"Where is it?"

"In the custody of Father Mathias."

"Are you aware why you are brought here?"

"How should I be?" replied Amine, evasively; "tell me what I am accused of?"

"You must know whether you have done wrong or not. You had better confess all your conscience accuses you of."

"My conscience does not accuse me of doing anything."

"Then you will confess nothing?"

"By your own showing, I have nothing to confess."

"You say you are from the East: are you a Christian?"

"I reject your creed."

"You are married to a Catholic?"

"Yes a true Catholic."

"Who married you?"

"Father Seysen, a Catholic, priest."

"Did you enter into the bosom of the Church?—did he venture to marry you without your being baptised?"

"Some ceremony did take place which I consented to."

"It was baptism, was it not?"

"I believe it was so termed."

"And now you say that you reject the creed?"

"Since I have witnessed the conduct of those who profess it, I do. At the time of my marriage I was disposed towards it."

"What is the amount of your property in the Father Mathias's hands."

"Some hundreds of dollars—he knows exactly."

The Grand Inquisitor rang a bell; the jailors entered, and Amine was led back to her dungeon.

"Why should they ask so often about my money?" mused Amine; "if they require it, they may take it. What is their power? What would they do with me? Well, well, a few days will decide." A few days;—no, no, Amine; years, perhaps would have passed without decision, but that in our months from the date of your incarceration, the *auto-da-fé*, which had not been celebrated for upwards of three years, was to take place, and there was not a sufficient number of those who were to undergo the last punishment to render the ceremony imposing. A few more were required for the stake, or you would not have escaped from those dungeons so soon. As it was, a month of anxiety and suspense, almost insupportable, had to be passed away before Amine was again summoned to the Hall of Justice.

Amine, at the time we have specified, was again introduced to the Hall of Justice, and was again asked if she would confess. Irritated at her long confinement and the injustice of the proceedings, she replied, "I have told you once for all, that I have nothing to confess; do with me as you will, but be quick."

"Will torture oblige you to confess?"

"Try me," replied Amine, firmly, "try me, cruel men, and if you gain but one word from me, then call me craven. I am but a woman, but I dare you—I defy you."

It was seldom that such expressions fell upon the ears of her judges, and still more seldom that a countenance was lighted up with such determination. But the torture was never applied until after the accusation had been made and answered.

"We shall see," said the Grand Inquisitor; "take her away."

Amine was led back to her cell. In the mean time, Father Mathias had had several conferences with the Inquisitor. Although in his wrath he had accused Amine, and had procured the necessary witnesses against her, he now felt uneasy and perplexed. His long residence with her—her invariable kindness till the time of his dismissal—his knowledge that she had never embraced the faith—her boldness and courage—nay, her beauty and youth—all worked strongly in her favour. His only object now was to persuade her to confess that she was wrong, induce her to embrace the faiths, and save her. With this view he had obtained permission from the Holy Office to enter her dungeon and reason with her,—a special favour which, for many reasons, they could not well refuse him. It was on the third day after her second examination, that the bolts were removed at an unusual hour, and Father Mathias entered the cell, which was again barred, and he was left alone with Amine. "My child! my child!" exclaimed Father Mathias, with sorrow in his countenance.

"Nay, father, this is mockery. It is you who brought me here—leave me."

"I brought you here, 'tis true; but I would now remove you, if you will permit me, Amine."

"Most willingly; I'll follow you."

"Nay, nay; there is much to talk over, much to be done. This is not a dungeon from which people can escape so easily."

"Then tell me what have you to say; and what is it must be done?"

"I will."

"But stop; before you say one word, answer me one question as you hope for bliss. Have you heard aught of Philip?"

"Yes, I have. He is well."

"And where is he?"

"He will soon be here."

"God, I thank thee! shall I see him, father?"

"That must depend upon yourself."

"Upon myself? Then tell me, quickly, what would they have me do?"

"Confess your sins—your crimes."

"What sins?—what crimes?"

"Have you not dealt with evil beings, invoked the spirits, and gained the assistance of those who are not of this world?"

Amine made no reply.

"Answer me. Do you not confess?"

"I do not confess to have done anything wrong."

"This is useless. You were seen by me and others. What will avail your denial? Are you aware of the punishment which most surely awaits you, if you do not confess, and become a member of our Church?"

"Why am I to become a member of your Church? Do you then punish those who refuse?"

"No; had you not already consented to receive baptism, you would not have been asked to become so; but, having been baptised, you must now become a member, or be supposed to fall back into heresy."

"I knew not the nature of your baptism at that time."

"Granted; but you consented to it."

"Be it so. But pray, what may be the punishment, if I refuse?"

"You will be burnt alive at the stake; nothing can save you. Hear me, Amine Vanderdecken: when next summoned, you must confess all; and, asking pardon, request to be received into the Church; then will you be saved, and you will—"

"What?"

"Again be clasped in Philip's arms."

"My Philip—my Philip!—you indeed press me hard; but, father, if I confess I am wrong, when I feel that I am not—"

"Feel that you are not!"

"Yes. I invoked my mother's assistance; she gave it me in a dream. Would a mother have assisted her daughter if it were wrong?"

"It was not your mother, but a fiend who took the likeness."

"It was my mother. Again you ask me to say that I believe that which I cannot."

"That which you cannot! Amine Vanderdecken, be not obstinate."

"I am not obstinate, good father. Have you not offered me what is to me beyond all price, that I should again be in the arms of my husband? Can I degrade myself to a lie?—not for life, or liberty, or even for my Philip."

"Amine Vanderdecken, if you will confess your crime before you are accused, you will have done much; after your accusation has been made, it will be of little avail."

"It will not be done, either before or after, father. What I have done I have done, but a crime it is not to me and mine—with you it may be, but I am not of yours."

"Recollect also that you peril your husband, for having wedded with a sorceress. Forget not; to-morrow I will see you again."

"My mind is troubled," replied Amine. "Leave me, father, it will be a kindness."

Father Mathias quitted the cell, pleased with the last words of Amine. The idea of her husband's danger seemed to have startled her.

Amine threw herself down on the mattress in the corner of the cell, and hid her face.

"Burnt alive!" exclaimed she after a time, sitting up and passing her hands over her forehead. "Burnt alive! and these are Christians. This, then was the cruel death foretold by that creature, Schriften—foretold—yes, and therefore must be—it is my destiny—I cannot save myself. If I confess then, I confess that Philip is wedded to a sorceress, and he will be punished too. No, never—never; I can suffer; 'tis cruel—'tis horrible to think of,—but 'twill soon be over. God of my fathers, give me strength against these wicked men, and enable me to bear all, for my dear Philip's sake."

The next evening, Father Mathias again made his appearance. He found Amine calm and collected: she refused to listen to his advice or follow his injunctions. His last observation, that "her husband would be in peril if she was found guilty of sorcery," had steeled her heart, and she had determined that neither torture nor the stake should make her confess the act. The priest left the cell, sick at heart; he now felt miserable at the idea of Amine's perishing by so dreadful a death; accused himself of precipitation, and wished that he had never seen Amine, whose constancy and courage, although in error, excited his admiration and his pity. And then he thought of Philip, who had treated him so kindly—how could he meet him? And if he asked for his wife, what answer could he give?

Another fortnight passed, when Amine was again summoned to the Hall of Judgment, and again asked if she confessed her crimes. Upon her refusal, the accusations against her were read. She was accused by Father Mathias with practising forbidden arts, and the depositions of the boy Pedro and the other witnesses were read. In his zeal, Father Mathias also stated that he had found her guilty of the same practices at Terneuse; and, moreover, that in the violent storm, when all expected to perish, she had remained calm and courageous and told the captain that they would be saved; which could only have been known by an undue spirit of prophecy, given by evil spirits. Amine's lip curled in derision when she heard the last accusation. She was asked if she had any defence to make.

"What defence can be offered," replied she, "to such accusations as these? Witness the last—because I was not so craven as the Christians, I am accused of sorcery. The old dotard! but I will expose him. Tell me, if one knows that sorcery is used, and conceals or allows it, is he not a participator and equally guilty?"

"He is," replied the Inquisitor, anxiously awaiting the result.

"Then I denounce—" and Amine was about to reveal that Philip's mission was known, and not forbidden by Fathers Mathias and Seysen; when, recollecting that Philip would be implicated, she stopped.

"Denounce whom?" inquired the Inquisitor.

"No one," replied Amine, folding her arms and dropping her head.

"Speak, woman!"

Amine made no answer.

"The torture will make you speak."

"Never!" replied Amine. "Never! Torture me to death, if you choose; I prefer it to a public execution!"

The Inquisitor and the secretary consulted a short time. Convinced that Amine would adhere to her resolution and requiring her for public execution, they abandoned the idea of the torture.

"Do you confess?" inquired the Inquisitor.

"No," replied Amine, firmly.

"Then take her away."

The night before the *auto-da-fé*, Father Mathias again entered the cell of Amine, but all his endeavours to convert her were useless.

"To-morrow will end it all, father," replied Amine; "leave me—I would be alone."

Chapter Thirty Eight.

We must now return to Philip and Krantz. When the latter retired from the presence of the Portuguese Commandant, he communicated to Philip what had taken place, and the fabulous tale which he had invented to deceive the Commandant. "I said that you alone knew where the treasure was concealed," continued Krantz, "that you might be sent for, for in all probability he will keep me as a hostage: but never mind that, I must take my chance. Do you contrive to escape somehow or other, and rejoin Amine."

"Not so," rejoined Philip; "you must go with me, my friend: I feel that, should I part with you, happiness would no longer be in store for me."

"Nonsense—that is but an idle feeling: besides, I will evade him somehow or another."

"I will not show the treasure unless you go with me."

"Well, you may try it at all events."

A low tap at the door was heard. Philip rose and opened it (for they had retired to rest), and Pedro came in. Looking carefully round him, and then shutting the door softly, he put his finger on his lips, to enjoin them to silence. He then in a whisper told them what he had overheard. "Contrive, if possible, that I go with you," continued he; "I must leave you now; he still paces his room." And Pedro slipped out of the door, and crawled stealthily away along the ramparts.

"The treacherous little rascal! But we will circumvent him if possible," said Krantz, in a low tone. "Yes, Philip, you are right, we must both go, for you will require my assistance. I must persuade him to go himself. I'll think of it—so, Philip, good night."

The next morning Philip and Krantz were summoned to breakfast; the Commandant received them with smiles and urbanity. To Philip he was peculiarly courteous. As soon as the repast was over, he thus communicated to him his intentions and wishes:—

"Signor, I have been reflecting upon what your friend told me, and the appearance of the spectre yesterday, which created such confusion; it induced me to behave with a rashness for which I must now offer my most sincere apologies. The reflections which I have made, joined with the feelings of devotion which must be in the heart of every true Catholic, have determined me, with your assistance, to obtain this treasure dedicated to the holy church. It is my proposal that you should take a party of soldiers under your orders, proceed to the island on which it is deposited, and having obtained it, return here. I will detain any vessel which may in the mean time put into the roadstead, and you shall then be the bearers of the treasure and of my letters to Goa. This will give you an honourable introduction to the authorities, and enable you to pass away your time there in the most agreeable manner. You will, also, signor, be restored to your wife, whose charms had such an effect upon me; and for mention of whose name in the very unceremonious manner which I did, I must excuse myself upon the ground of total ignorance of who she was, or of her being in any way connected with your honourable person. If these measures suit you, signor, I shall be most happy to give orders to that effect."

"As a good Catholic myself," replied Philip, "I shall be most happy to point out the spot where the treasure is concealed, and restore it to the church. Your apologies relative to my wife I accept with pleasure, being aware that your conduct proceeded from ignorance of her situation and rank; but I do not exactly see my way clear. You propose a party of soldiers. Will they obey me? Are they to be trusted? I shall have only myself and friend against them, and will they be obedient?"

"No fear of that, signor, they are well disciplined; there is not even occasion for your friend to go with you. I wish to retain him with me, to keep me company during your absence."

"Nay! that I must object to," replied Philip; "I will not trust myself alone."

"Perhaps I may be allowed to give an opinion on this subject?" observed Krantz. "I see no reason, if my friend goes accompanied within a party of soldiers only, why I should not go with him; but I consider it would be unadvisable that he proceed in the way the commandant proposes, either with or without me. You must recollect, commandant, that it is no trifling sum which is to be carried away; that it will be open to view, and will meet the eyes of your men; that these men have been detained many years in this country, and are anxious to return home. When, therefore, they find themselves with only two strangers with them—away from your authority, and in possession of a large sum of money—will not the temptation be too strong? They will only have to run down the southern channel, gain the port of Bantam and they will be safe; having obtained both freedom and wealth. To send, therefore, my friend and me, would be to send us to almost certain death; but if you were to go, commandant, then the danger would no longer exist. Your presence and your authority would control them; and; whatever their wishes or thoughts might be, they would quail before the flash of your eye."

"Very true—very true," replied Philip—"all this did not occur to me."

Nor had it occurred to the commandant, but when pointed out, the force of these suggestions immediately struck him, and long before Krantz had finished speaking, he had resolved to go himself.

"Well, signors," replied he; "I am always ready to accede to your wishes; and since you consider my presence necessary and as I do not think there is any chance of another attack from the Ternate people just now, I will take upon myself the responsibility of leaving the fort for a few days under the charge of my lieutenant, while we do this service to holy Mother Church. I have already sent for one of the native vessels, which are large and commodious, and will, with your permission, embark to-morrow."

"Two vessels will be better," observed Krantz; "in the first place, in case of an accident; and next, because we can embark all the treasure in one with ourselves, and put a portion of the soldiers in the other; so that we may be in greater force, in case of the sight of so much wealth stimulating them to insubordination."

"True, signor," we will have two vessels; "your advice is good."

Everything was thus satisfactorily arranged, with the exception of their wish that Pedro should accompany them on their expedition. They were debating how this should be brought on the tapis, when the soldier came to them, and stated that the commandant had ordered him to be of the party, and that he was to offer his services to the two strangers.

On the ensuing day everything was prepared. Ten soldiers and a corporal had been selected by the commandant; and it required but little time to put into the vessels the provisions and other articles which were required. At daylight they embarked—the Commandant and Philip in one boat; Krantz, with the corporal and Pedro, in the other. The men, who had been kept in ignorance of the object of the expedition, were now made acquainted with it by Pedro, and a long whispering took place between them, much to the satisfaction of Krantz, who was aware that the mutiny would soon be excited, when it was understood that those who composed the expedition were to be sacrificed to the avarice of the commandant. The weather being fine they sailed on during the night; passed the island of Ternate at ten leagues' distance; and before morning were among the cluster of isles, the southernmost of which was the one on which the treasure had been buried. On the second night the vessels were beached upon a small island; and then, for the first time, a communication took place between the soldiers who had been in the boat with Pedro and Krantz, and those who had been embarked with the commandant. Philip and Krantz had also an opportunity of communicating apart for a short time.

When they made sail the next morning, Pedro spoke openly; he told Krantz that the soldiers in the boat had made up their minds, and that he had no doubt that the others would do so before night; although they had not decidedly agreed upon joining them in the morning when they had re-embarked. That they would despatch the commandant, and then proceed to Batavia, and from thence obtain a passage home to Europe.

"Cannot you accomplish your end without murder?"

"Yes, we could; but not our revenge. You do not know the treatment which we have received from his hands; and sweet as the money will be to us, his death will be even sweeter. Besides, has he not determined to murder us all in some way or another? It is but justice. No, no; if there was no other knife ready—mine is."

"And so are all ours!" cried the other soldiers, putting their hands to their weapons.

One more day's sail brought them within twenty miles of the island; for Philip knew his landmarks well. Again they handed, and all retired to rest, the commandant dreaming of wealth and revenge; while it was arranging that the digging up of the treasure which he coveted should be the signal for his death.

Once more did they embark, and the commandant heeded not the dark and lowering faces with which he was surrounded. He was all gaiety and politeness. Swiftly did they skim over the dark-blue sea, between the beautiful islands with which it was studded; and before the sun was three hours high, Philip recognised the one sought after, and pointed out to the commandant the notched cocoa-nut tree, which served as a guide to the spot where the money had been concealed. They landed on the sandy beach, and the shovels were ordered to be brought on shore by the impatient little officer; who little thought that every moment of time gained was but so much *time* lost to him, and that while he was smiling and meditating treachery, that others could do the same.

The party arrived under the tree—the shovels soon removed the light sand, and in a few minutes, the treasure was exposed to view. Bag after bag was handed up, and the loose dollars collected into heaps. Two of the soldiers had been sent to the vessels for sacks to put the loose dollars in, and the men had desisted from their labour; they laid aside their spades, looks were exchanged, and all were ready.

The commandant turned round to call to and hasten the movements of the men who had been sent for the sacks, when three or four knives simultaneously pierced him through the back; he fell, and was expostulating, when they were again buried in his bosom, and he lay a corpse. Philip and Krantz remained silent spectators—the knives were drawn out, wiped, and replaced in their sheaths.

"He has met his reward," said Krantz.

"Yes," exclaimed the Portuguese soldiers—"justice, nothing but justice."

"Signors, you shall have your share," observed Pedro; "shall they not, my men?"

"Yes! yes!"

"Not one dollar, my good friends," replied Philip; "take all the money, and may you be happy; all we ask, is your assistance to proceed on our way to where we are about to go. And now, before you divide your money, oblige me by burying the body of that unfortunate man."

The soldiers obeyed. Resuming their shovels, they soon scooped out a shallow grave: the commandant's body was thrown in, and covered up from sight.

Chapter Thirty Nine.

Scarcely had the soldiers performed their task, and thrown down their shovels, when they commenced an altercation. It appeared that this money was to be again the cause of slaughter and bloodshed. Philip and Krantz determined to sail immediately in one of the peroquas, and leave them to settle their disputes as they pleased. He asked permission of the soldiers to take from the provisions and water, of which there was ample supply, a larger proportion than was their share; stating, that he and Krantz had a long voyage and would require it, and pointing out to them that there were plenty of cocoa-nuts for their support. The soldiers, who thought of nothing but their newly-acquired wealth allowed him to do as he pleased; and, having hastily collected as many cocoa-nuts as they could, to add to their stock of provisions, before noon, Philip and Krantz had embarked and made sail in the peroqua, leaving the soldiers with their knives again drawn, and so busy in their angry altercation as to be heedless of their departure.

"There will be the same scene over again, I expect," observed Krantz, as the vessel parted swiftly from the shore.

"I have little doubt of it; observe, even now they are at blows and stabs."

"If I were to name that spot, it should be the '*Accursed Isle.*'"

"Would not any other be the same, with so much to inflame the passions of men?"

"Assuredly: what a curse is gold!"

"And what a blessing!" replied Krantz. "I am sorry Pedro is left with them."

"It is their destiny," replied Philip; "so let's think no more of them. Now what do you propose? With this vessel, small as she is, we may sail over these seas in safety, and we have, I imagine, provisions sufficient for more than a month."

"My idea is, to run into the track of the vessels going to the westward, and obtain a passage to Goa."

"And if we do not meet with any, we can, at all events, proceed up the Straits, as far as Pulo Penang without risk. There we may safely remain until a vessel passes."

"I agree with you; it is our best, nay our only, place; unless, indeed, we were to proceed to Cochin, where junks are always leaving for Goa."

"But that would be out of our way, and the junks cannot well pass us in the Straits, without their being seen by us."

They had no difficulty in steering their course; the islands by day, and the clear stars by night, were their compass. It is true that they did not follow the more direct track, but they followed the more secure, working up the smooth waters, and gaining to the northward more than to the west. Many times they were chased by the Malay proas which infested the islands, but the swiftness of their little peroqua was their security; indeed, the chase was, generally speaking, abandoned as soon as the smallness of the vessel was made out by the pirates, who expected that little or no booty was to be gained.

That Amine and Philip's mission was the constant theme of their discourse, may easily be imagined. One morning, as they were sailing between the isles, with less wind than usual, Philip observed:

"Krantz, you said that there were events in your own life, or connected with it, which would corroborate the mysterious tale I confided to you. Will you now tell me to what you referred?"

"Certainly," replied Krantz; "I've often thought of doing so, but one circumstance or another has hitherto prevented me; this is, however, a fitting opportunity. Prepare, therefore, to listen to a strange story, quite as strange, perhaps, as your own:—

"I take it for granted, that you have heard people speak of the Hartz Mountains," observed Krantz.

"I have never heard people speak of them, that I can recollect," replied Philip; "but I have read of them in some book, and of the strange things which have occurred there."

"It is indeed a wild region," rejoined Krantz, "and many strange tales are told of it; but strange as they are, I have good reason for believing them to be true. I have told you, Philip, that I fully believe in your communion with the other world—that I credit the history of your father, and the lawfulness of your mission; for that we are surrounded, impelled, and worked upon by beings different in their nature from ourselves, I have had full evidence, as you will acknowledge, when I state what has occurred in my own family. Why such malevolent beings as I am about to speak of should be permitted to interfere with us, and punish, I may say, comparatively unoffending mortals, is beyond my comprehension; but that they are so permitted is most certain."

"The great principle of all evil fulfils his work of evil; why, then, not the other minor spirits of the same class?" inquired Philip. "What matters it to us, whether we are tried by, and have to suffer from, the enmity of our fellow-mortals, or whether we are persecuted by beings more powerful and more malevolent than ourselves? We know that we have to work out our salvation, and that we shall be judged according to our strength; if then there be evil spirits who delight to oppress man, there surely must be, as Amine asserts, good spirits, whose delight is to do him service. Whether, then, we have to struggle against our passions only, or whether we have to struggle not only against our passions, but also the dire influence of unseen enemies we ever struggle with the same odds in our favour, as the good are stronger than the evil which we combat. In either case we are on the 'vantage ground, whether, as in the first, we fight the good cause single-handed, or as in the second, although opposed, we have the host of Heaven ranged on our side. Thus are the scales of Divine justice evenly balanced, and man is still a free agent, as his own virtuous or vicious propensities must ever decide whether he shall gain or lose the victory."

"Most true," replied Krantz, "and now to my history:—

"My father was not born, or originally a resident, in the Hartz Mountains; he was the serf of an Hungarian nobleman, of great possessions, in Transylvania; but, although a serf, he was not by any means a poor or illiterate man. In fact, he was rich and his intelligence and respectability were such, that he had been raised by his lord to the stewardship; but, whoever may happen to be born a serf, a serf must he remain, even though he become a wealthy man: and such was the condition of my father. My father had been married for about five years; and by his marriage had three children—my eldest brother Caesar, myself (Hermann), and a sister named Marcella. You know, Philip, that Latin is still the language spoken in that country; and that will account for our high-sounding names. My mother was a very beautiful woman, unfortunately more beautiful than virtuous: she was seen and admired by the lord of the soil; my father was sent away upon some mission; and, during his absence, my mother, flattered by the attentions, and won by the assiduities, of this nobleman yielded to his wishes. It so happened that my father returned very unexpectedly, and discovered the intrigue. The evidence of my mother's shame was positive; he surprised her in the company of her seducer! Carried away by the impetuosity of his feelings, he watched the opportunity of a meeting taking place between them, and murdered both his wife and her seducer. Conscious that, as a serf, not even the provocation which he had received would be allowed as a justification of his conduct he hastily collected together what money he could lay his hands upon, and, as we were then in the depth of winter, he put his horses to the sleigh, and taking his children with him, he set off in the middle of the night, and was far away before the tragical circumstance had transpired. Aware that he would be pursued, and that he had no chance of escape if he remained in any portion of his native country (in which the authorities could lay hold of him), he continued his flight without intermission until he had buried himself in the intricacies and seclusion of the Hartz Mountains. Of course, all that I have now told you I learned afterwards. My oldest recollections are knit to a rude, yet comfortable cottage, in which I lived with my father, brother, and sister. It was on the confines of one of those vast forests which cover the northern part of Germany; around it were a few acres of ground, which, during the summer months, my father cultivated, and which, though they yielded a doubtful harvest, were sufficient for our support. In the winter we remained much in doors, for, as my father followed the chase, we were left alone, and the wolves, during that season, incessantly prowled about. My father had purchased the cottage, and land about it of one of the rude foresters, who gain their livelihood partly by hunting, and partly by burning charcoal, for the purpose of smelting the ore from the neighbouring mines; it was distant about two miles from any other habitation. I can call to mind the whole landscape now: the tall pines which rose up on the mountain above us, and the wide expanse of forest beneath, on the topmost boughs and heads of whose trees we looked down from our cottage, as the mountain below us rapidly descended into the distant valley. In summer-time the prospect was beautiful: but during the severe winter, a more desolate scene could not well be imagined.

"I said that, in the winter, my father occupied himself with the chase; every day he left us, and often would he lock the door, that we might not leave the cottage. He had no one to assist him, or to take care of us—indeed, it was not easy to find a female servant who would live in such a solitude; but could he have found one, my father would nut have received her, for he had imbibed a horror of the sex, as the difference of his conduct towards us, his two boys, and my poor little sister, Marcella evidently proved. You may suppose we were sadly neglected; indeed, we suffered much, for my father, fearful that we might come to some harm, would not allow us fuel, when he left the cottage; and we were obliged, therefore, to creep under the heaps of bears' skins, and there to keep ourselves as warm as we could until he returned in the evening, when a blazing fire was our delight. That my father chose this restless sort of life may appear strange, but the fact was, that he could not remain quiet; whether from the remorse for having committed murder, or from the misery consequent on his change of situation, or from both combined, he was never happy unless he was in a state of activity. Children, however, when left much to themselves, acquire a thoughtfulness not common to their age. So it was with us; and during the short cold days of winter, we would sit silent, longing for the happy hours when the snow would melt and the leaves would burst out, and the birds begin their songs, and when we should again be set at liberty.

"Such was our peculiar and savage sort of life until my brother Caesar was nine, myself seven, and my sister five years old, when the circumstances occurred on which is based the extraordinary narrative which I am about to relate.

"One evening my father returned home rather later than usual; he had been unsuccessful, and, as the weather was very severe, and many feet of snow were upon the ground, he was not only very cold, but in a very bad humour. He had brought in wood, and we were all three gladly assisting each other in blowing on the embers to create the blaze, when he caught poor little Marcella by the arm and threw her aside; the child fell, struck her mouth, and bled very much. My brother ran to raise her up. Accustomed to ill-usage and afraid of my father, she did not dare to cry, but looked up in his face very piteously. My father drew his stool nearer to the hearth, muttered something in abuse of women, and busied himself with the fire, which both my brother and I had deserted when my sister was so unkindly treated. A cheerful blaze was soon the result of his exertions; but we did not, as usual, crowd round it. Marcella, still bleeding, retired to a corner, and my brother and I took our seats beside her, while my father hung over the fire gloomily and alone. Such had been our position for about half an hour, when the howl of a wolf, close under the window of the cottage, fell on our ears. My father started up, and seized his gun: the howl was repeated, he examined the priming, and then hastily left the cottage, shutting the door after him. We all waited (anxiously listening), for we thought that if he succeeded in shooting the wolf, he would return in a better humour; and, although he was harsh to all of us, and particularly so to our little sister, still we loved our father, and loved to see him cheerful and happy, for what else had we to look up to? And I may here observe, that perhaps there never were three children who were fonder of each other; we did not, like other children, fight and dispute together; and if, by chance, any disagreement did arise between my elder brother and me, little Marcella would run to us, and kissing us both, seal, through her entreaties, the peace between us. Marcella was a lovely, amiable child; I can recall her beautiful features even now—Alas! poor little Marcella."

"She is dead, then?" observed Philip.

"Dead! yes, dead!—but how did she die?—But I must not anticipate, Philip; let me tell my story.

"We waited or some time, but the report of the gun did not reach us, and my elder brother then said, 'Our father has followed the wolf, and will not be back for some time. Marcella, let us wash the blood from your mouth, and then we will leave this corner, and go to the fire and warm ourselves.'

"We did so, and remained there until near midnight, every minute wondering, as it grew later, why our father did not return. We had no idea that he was in any danger, but we thought that he must have chased the wolf for a very long time. 'I will look out and see if father is coming,' said my brother Caesar, going to the door. 'Take care,' said Marcella, 'the wolves must be about now, and we cannot kill them, brother.' My brother opened the door very cautiously, and but a few inches: he peeped out.—'I see nothing,' said he, after a time, and once more he joined us at the fire. 'We have had no supper,' said I, for my father usually cooked the meat as soon as he came home; and during his absence we had nothing but the fragments of the preceding day.

"'And if our father comes home after his hunt, Caesar,' said Marcella, 'he will be pleased to have some supper; let us cook it for him and for ourselves.' Caesar climbed upon the stool, and reached down some meat—I forget now whether it was venison or bear's meat; but we cut off the usual quantity, and proceeded to dress it, as we used to do under our father's superintendence. We were all busy putting it into the platters before the fire, to await his coming, when we heard the sound of a horn. We listened—there was a noise outside, and a minute afterwards my father entered, ushering in a young female, and a large dark man in a hunter's dress.

"Perhaps I had better now relate what was only known to me many years afterwards. When my father had left the cottage, he perceived a large white wolf about thirty yards from him; as soon as the animal saw my father, it retreated slowly growling and snarling. My father followed; the animal did not run, but always kept at some distance; and my father did not like to fire until he was pretty certain that his ball would take effect; thus they went on for some time, the wolf now leaving my father far behind, and then stopping and snarling defiance at him, and then, again, on his approach, setting off at speed.

"Anxious to shoot the animal (for the white wolf is very rare) my father continued the pursuit for several hours, during which he continually ascended the mountain.

"You must know, Philip, that there are peculiar spots on those mountains which are supposed, and, as my story will prove, truly supposed, to be inhabited by the evil influences: they are well known to the huntsmen, who invariably avoid them. Now, one of these spots, an open space in the pine forests above us, had been pointed out to my father as dangerous on that account. But, whether he disbelieved these wild stories or whether, in his eager pursuit of the chase, he disregarded them, I know not; certain, however, it is, that he was decoyed by the white wolf to this open space, when the animal appeared to slacken her speed. My father approached, came close up to her, raised his gun to his shoulder, and was about to fire, when the wolf suddenly disappeared. He thought that the snow on the ground must have dazzled his sight, and he let down his gun to look for the beast—but she was gone; how she could have escaped over the clearance, without his seeing her, was beyond his comprehension. Mortified at the ill success of his chase, he was about to retrace his steps, when he heard the distant sound of a horn. Astonishment at such a sound—at such an hour—in such a wilderness, made him forget for the moment his disappointment, and he remained riveted to the spot. In a minute the horn was blown a second time, and at no great distance; my father stood still, and listened: a third time it was blown. I forget the term used to express it, but it was the signal which, my father well knew, implied that the party was lost in the woods. In a few minutes more my father beheld a man on horseback, with a female seated on the crupper, enter the cleared space, and ride up to him. At first, my father called to mind the strange stories which he had heard of the supernatural beings who were said to frequent these mountains; but the nearer approach of the parties satisfied him that they were mortals like himself. As soon as they came up to him, the man who guided the horse accosted him. 'Friend Hunter, you are out late, the better fortune for us; we have ridden far, and are in fear of our lives which are eagerly sought after. These mountains have enabled us to elude our pursuers; but if we find not shelter and refreshment, that will avail us little, as we must perish from hunger and the inclemency of the night. My daughter, who rides behind me, is now more dead than alive—say, can you assist us in our difficulty?'

"'My cottage is some few miles distant,' replied my father, 'but I have little to offer you besides a shelter from the weather; to the little I have you are welcome. May I ask whence you come?'

"'Yes, friend, it is no secret now; we have escaped from Transylvania, where my daughter's honour and my life were equally in jeopardy!'

"This information was quite enough to raise an interest in my father's heart, he remembered his own escape; he remembered the loss of his wife's honour, and the tragedy by which it was wound up. He immediately, and warmly, offered all the assistance which he could afford them.

"'There is no time to be lost then, good sir,' observed the horseman; 'my daughter is chilled with the frost, and cannot hold out much longer against the severity of the weather.'

"'Follow me,' replied my father, leading the way towards his home.

"'I was lured away in pursuit of a large white wolf,' observed my father; 'it came to the very window of my hut, or I should not have been out at this time of night.'

"'The creature passed by us just as we came out of the wood,' said the female, in a silvery tone.

"'I was nearly discharging my piece at it,' observed the hunter; 'but since it did us such good service, I am glad I allowed it to escape.'

"In about an hour and a half, during which my father walked at a rapid pace, the party arrived at the cottage, and, as I said before, came in.

"'We are in good time, apparently,' observed the dark hunter, catching the smell of the roasted meat, as he walked to the fire and surveyed my brother and sister, and myself. 'You have young cooks here, Meinheer.' 'I am glad that we shall not have to wait,' replied my father. 'Come, mistress, seat yourself by the fire; you require warmth after your cold ride.' 'And where can I put up my horse, Meinheer?' observed the huntsman. 'I will take care of him,' replied my father, going out of the cottage door.

"The female must, however, be particularly described. She was young, and apparently twenty years of age. She was dressed in a travelling-dress, deeply bordered with white fur, and wore a cap of white ermine on her head. Her features were very beautiful, at least I thought so, and so my father has since declared. Her hair was flaxen, glossy, and shining, and bright as a mirror; and her mouth, although somewhat large when it was open, showed the most brilliant teeth I have ever beheld. But there was something about her eyes, bright as they were, which made us children afraid; they were so restless, so furtive; I could not at that time tell why, but I felt as if there was cruelty in her eye; and when she beckoned us to come to her, we approached her with fear and trembling. Still she was beautiful, very beautiful. She spoke kindly to my brother and myself, patted our heads and caressed us; but Marcella would not come near her; on the contrary, she slunk away, and hid herself in the bed, and would not wait for the supper, which half an hour before she had been so anxious for.

"My father, having put the horse into a close shed, soon returned, and supper was placed upon the table. When it was over, my father requested that the young lady would take possession of his bed, and he would remain at the fire, and sit up with her father. After some hesitation on her part, this arrangement was agreed to, and I and my brother crept into the other bed with Marcella, for we had as yet always slept together.

"But we could not sleep; there was something so unusual, not only in seeing strange people, but in having those people sleep at the cottage, that we were bewildered. As for poor little Marcella, she was quiet, but I perceived that she trembled during the whole night, and sometimes I thought that she was checking a sob. My father had brought out some spirits, which he rarely used, and he and the strange hunter remained drinking and talking before the fire. Our ears were ready to catch the slightest whisper—so much was our curiosity excited.

"'You said you came from Transylvania?' observed my father.

"'Even so, Meinheer,' replied the hunter. 'I was a serf to the noble house of —; my master would insist upon my surrendering up my fair girl to his wishes: it ended in my giving him a few inches of my hunting-knife.'

"'We are countrymen, and brothers in misfortune,' replied my father, taking the huntsman's hand, and pressing it warmly.

"'Indeed! Are you then from that country?'

"'Yes; and I too have fled for my life. But mine is a melancholy tale.'

"'Your name?' inquired the hunter.

"'Krantz.'

"'What! Krantz of —? I have heard your tale; you need not renew your grief by repeating it now. Welcome, most welcome, Meinheer, and, I may say, my worthy kinsman. I am your second cousin, Wilfred of Barnsdorf,' cried the hunter, rising up and embracing my father.

"They filled their horn-mugs to the brim, and drank to one another after the German fashion. The conversation was then carried on in a low tone; all that we could collect from it was that our new relative and his daughter were to take up their abode in our cottage, at least for the present. In about an hour they both fell back in their chairs and appeared to sleep.

"'Marcella, dear, did you hear?' said my brother, in a low tone.

"'Yes,' replied Marcella in a whisper, 'I heard all. Oh! brother, I cannot bear to look upon that woman—I feel so frightened.'

"My brother made no reply, and shortly afterwards we were all three fast asleep.

"When we awoke the next morning, we found that the hunter's daughter had risen before us. I thought she looked more beautiful than ever. She came up to little Marcella and caressed her: the child burst into tears, and sobbed as if her heart would break.

"But, not to detain you with too long a story, the huntsman and his daughter were accommodated in the cottage. My father and he went out hunting daily, leaving Christina with us. She performed all the household duties; was very kind to us children; and, gradually, the dislike even of little Marcella wore away. But a great change took place in my father; he appeared to have conquered his aversion to the sex, and was most attentive to Christina. Often, after her father and we were in bed would he sit up with her, conversing in a low tone by the fire. I ought to have mentioned that my father and the huntsman Wilfred, slept in another portion of the cottage, and that the bed which he formerly occupied, and which was in the same room as ours, had been given up to the use of Christina. These visitors had been about three weeks at the cottage, when, one night, after we children had been sent to bed, a consultation was held. My father had asked Christina in marriage, and had obtained both her own consent and that of Wilfred; after this, a conversation took place, which was, as nearly as I can recollect, as follows.

"'You may take my child, Meinheer Krantz, and my blessing with her, and I shall then leave you and seek some other habitation—it matters little where.'

"'Why not remain here, Wilfred?'

"'No, no, I am called elsewhere; let that suffice, and ask no more questions. You have my child.'

"'I thank you for her, and will duly value her; but there is one difficulty.'

"'I know what you would say; there is no priest here in this wild country: true; neither is there any law to bind; still must some ceremony pass between you, to satisfy a father. Will you consent to marry her after my fashion? if so, I will marry you directly.'

"'I will,' replied my father.

"'Then take her by the hand. Now, Meinheer, swear.'

"'I swear,' repeated my father.

"'By all the spirits of the Hartz mountains—'

"'Nay, why not by Heaven?' interrupted my father.

"'Because it is not my humour,' rejoined Wilfred; 'if I prefer that oath, less binding perhaps, than another, surely you will not thwart me.'

"'Well be it so then; have your humour. Will you make me swear by that in which I do not believe?'

"'Yet many do so, who in outward appearance are Christians,' rejoined Wilfred; 'say, will you be married, or shall I take my daughter away with me?'

"'Proceed,' replied my father, impatiently.

"'I swear by all the spirits of the Hartz mountains, by all their power for good or for evil, that I take Christina for my wedded wife; that I will ever protect her, cherish her, and love her; that my hand shall never be raised against her to harm her.'

"My father repeated the words after Wilfred.

"'And if I fail in this my vow, may all the vengeance of the spirits fall upon me and upon my children; may they perish by the vulture, by the wolf, or other beasts of the forest; may their flesh be torn from their limbs, and their bones blanch in the wilderness: all this I swear.'

"My father hesitated, as he repeated the last words; little Marcella could not restrain herself, and as my father repeated the last sentence, she burst into tears. This sudden interruption appeared to discompose the party, particularly my father; he spoke harshly to the child, who controlled her sobs, burying her face under the bed-clothes.

"Such was the second marriage of my father. The next morning, the hunter Wilfred mounted his horse, and rode away.

"My father resumed his bed, which was in the same room as ours; and things went on much as before the marriage, except that our new mother-in-law did not show any kindness towards us; indeed during my father's absence, she would often beat us, particularly little Marcella, and her eyes would flash fire, as she looked eagerly upon the fair and lovely child.

"One night, my sister awoke me and my brother.

"'What is the matter?' said Caesar.

"'She has gone out,' whispered Marcella.

"'Gone out!'

"'Yes, gone out at the door, in her night-clothes,' replied the child; 'I saw her get out of bed, look at my father to see if he slept, and then she went out at the door.'

"What could induce her to leave her bed, and all undressed to go out, in such bitter wintry weather, with the snow deep on the ground was to us incomprehensible; we lay awake, and in about an hour we heard the growl of a wolf, close under the window.

"'There is a wolf,' said Caesar. 'She will be torn to pieces.'

"'Oh no!' cried Marcella.

"In a few minutes afterwards our mother-in-law appeared; she was in her night-dress, as Marcella had stated. She let down the latch of the door, so as to make no noise, went to a pail of water, and washed her face and hands, and then slipped into the bed where my father lay.

"We all three trembled—we hardly knew why; but we resolved to watch the next night: we did so; and not only on the ensuing night, but on many others, and always at about the same hour, would our mother-in-law rise from her bed and leave the cottage; and after she was gone we invariably heard the growl of a wolf under our window, and always saw her, on her return, wash herself before she retired to bed. We observed also that she seldom sat down to meals, and that when she did she appeared to eat with dislike; but when the meat was taken down to be prepared for dinner, she would often furtively put a raw piece into her mouth.

"My brother Caesar was a courageous boy; he did not like to speak to my father until he knew more. He resolved that he would follow her out, and ascertain what she did. Marcella and I endeavoured to dissuade him from this project; but he would not be controlled; and the very next night he lay down in his clothes, and as soon as our mother-in-law had left the cottage he jumped up, took down my father's gun, and followed her.

"You may imagine in what a state of suspense Marcella and I remained during his absence. After a few minutes we heard the report of a gun. It did not awaken my father; and we lay trembling with anxiety. In a minute afterwards we saw our mother-in-law enter the cottage—her dress was bloody. I put my hand to Marcella's mouth to prevent her crying out, although I was myself in great alarm. Our mother-in-law approached my father's bed, looked to see if he was asleep, and then went to the chimney and blew up the embers into a blaze.

"'Who is there?' said my father, waking up.

"'Lie still, dearest,' replied my mother-in-law; 'it is only me; I have lighted the fire to warm some water; I am not quite well.'

"My father turned round, and was soon asleep; but we hatched our mother-in-law. She changed her linen, and threw the garments she had worn into the fire; and we then perceived that her right leg was bleeding profusely, as if from a gun-shot wound. She bandaged it up, and then dressing herself, remained before the fire until the break of day.

"Poor little Marcella, her heart beat quick as she pressed me to her side—so indeed did mine. Where was our brother Caesar? How did my mother-in-law receive the wound unless from his gun? At last my father rose, and then for the first time I spoke, saying, 'Father, where is my brother Caesar?'

"'Your brother!' exclaimed he; 'why, where can he be?'

"'Merciful Heaven! I thought, as lay very restless last night,' observed our mother-in-law, 'that I heard somebody open the latch of the door; and, dear me, husband, what has become of your gun?'

"My father cast his eyes up above the chimney, and perceived that his gun was missing. For a moment he looked perplexed; then, seizing a broad axe, he went out of the cottage without saying another word.

"He did not remain away from us long; in a few minutes he returned, bearing in his arms the mangled body of my poor brother; he laid it down, and covered up his face.

"My mother-in-law rose up, and looked at the body, while Marcella and I threw ourselves by its side, wailing and sobbing bitterly.

"'Go to bed again, children,' said she, sharply. 'Husband,' continued she, 'your boy must have taken the gun down, to shoot a wolf, and the animal has been too powerful for him. Poor boy! he has paid dearly for his rashness.'

"My father made no reply. I wished to speak—to tell all—but Marcella who perceived my intention, held me by the arm, and looked at me so imploringly, that I desisted.

"My father, therefore, was left in his error; but Marcella and I, although we could not comprehend it, were conscious that our mother-in-law was in some way connected with my brother's death.

"That day my father went out and dug a grave; and when he hid the body in the earth, he piled up stones over it so that the wolves should not be able to dig it up. The shock of this catastrophe was to my poor father very severe; for several days he never went to the chase, although at times he would utter bitter anathemas and vengeance against the wolves.

"But during this time of mourning on his part, my mother-in-law's nocturnal wanderings continued with the same regularity as before.

"At last my father took down his gun to repair to the forest; but he soon returned, and appeared much annoyed.

"'Would you believe it, Christina, that the wolves—perdition to the whole race—have actually contrived to dig up the body of my poor boy, and now there is nothing left of him but his bones?'

"'Indeed!' replied my mother-in-law. Marcella looked at me; and I saw in her intelligent eye all she would have uttered.

"'A wolf growls under our window every night, father,' said I.

"'Ay, indeed! Why did you not tell me, boy? Wake me the next time you hear it.'

"I saw my mother-in-law turn away; her eyes flashed fire, and she gnashed her teeth.

"My father went out again, and covered up with a larger pile of stones the little remnants of my poor brother which the wolves had spared. Such was the first act of the tragedy.

"The spring now came on; the snow disappeared, and we were permitted to leave the cottage; but never would I quit for one moment my dear little sister, to whom since the death of my brother, I was more ardently attached than ever; indeed, I was afraid to leave her alone with my mother-in-law, who appeared to have a particular pleasure in ill-treating the child. My father was now employed upon his little farm, and I was able to render him some assistance.

"Marcella used to sit by us while we were at work, leaving my mother-in-law alone in the cottage. I ought to observe that, as the spring advanced, so did my mother-in-law decrease her nocturnal rambles, and that we never heard the growl of the wolf under the window after I had spoken of it to my father.

"One day, when my father and I were in the field, Marcella being with us, my mother-in-law came out, saying that she was going into the forest to collect some herbs my father wanted, and that Marcella must go to the cottage and watch the dinner. Marcella went; and my mother-in-law soon disappeared in the forest, taking a direction quite contrary to that in which the cottage stood, and leaving my father and I, as it were, between her and Marcella.

"About an hour afterwards we were startled by shrieks from the cottage—evidently the shrieks of little Marcella. 'Marcella has burnt herself, father,' said I, throwing down my spade. My father threw down his, and we both hastened to the cottage. Before we could gain the door, out darted a large white wolf, which fled with the utmost celerity. My father had no weapon; he rushed into the cottage, and there saw poor little Marcella expiring. Her body was dreadfully mangled, and the blood pouring from it had formed a large pool on the cottage floor. My father's first intention had been to seize his gun and pursue; but he was checked by this horrid spectacle; he knelt down by his dying child, and burst into tears. Marcella could just look kindly on us for a few seconds, and then her eyes were closed in death.

"My father and I were still hanging over my poor sister's body, when my mother-in-law came in. At the dreadful sight she expressed much concern; but she did not appear to recoil from the sight of blood, as most women do.

"'Poor child!' said she, 'it must have been that great white wolf which passed me just now, and frightened me so. She's quite dead, Krantz.'

"'I know it—I know it!' cried my father, in agony.

"I thought my father would never recover from the effects of this second tragedy; he mourned bitterly over the body of his sweet child, and for several days would not consign it to its grave, although frequently requested by my mother-in-law to do so. At last he yielded, and dug a grave for her close by that of my poor brother, and took every precaution that the wolves should not violate her remains.

"I was now really miserable, as I lay alone in the bed which I had formerly shared with my brother and sister. I could not help thinking that my mother-in-law was implicated in both their deaths, although I could not account for the manner; but I no longer felt afraid of her; my little heart was full of hatred and revenge.

"The night after my sister had been buried, as I lay awake, I perceived my mother-in-law get up and go out of the cottage. I waited some time, then dressed myself, and looked out through the door, which I half opened. The moon shone bright and I could see the spot where my brother and my sister had been buried; and what was my horror when I perceived my mother-in-law busily removing the stones from Marcella's grave!

"She was in her white night-dress and the moon shone full upon her. She was digging with her hands, and throwing away the stones behind her with all the ferocity of a wild beast. It was some time before I could collect my senses, and decide what I should do. At last I perceived that she had arrived at the body, and raised it up to the side of the grave. I could bear it no longer, I ran to my father and awoke him.

"'Father, father!' cried I, 'dress yourself, and get your gun.'

"'What!' cried my father, 'the wolves are there, are they?'

"He jumped out of bed, threw on his clothes, and, in his anxiety, did not appear to perceive the absence of his wife. As soon as he was ready I opened the door; he went out, and I followed him.

"Imagine his horror, when (unprepared as he was for such a sight) he beheld, as he advanced towards the grave not a wolf, but his wife, in her night-dress, on her hands and knees, crouching by the body of my sister, and tearing off large pieces of the flesh, and devouring them with all the avidity of a wolf. She was too busy to be aware of our approach. My father dropped his gun; his hair stood on end, so did mine; he breathed heavily, and then his breath for a time stopped. I picked up the gun and put it into his hand. Suddenly he appeared as if concentrated rage had restored him to double vigour; he levelled his piece, fired, and with a loud shriek down fell the wretch whom he had fostered in his bosom.

"'God of Heaven!' cried my father, sinking down upon the earth in a swoon, as soon as he had discharged his gun.

"I remained some time by his side before he recovered. 'Where am I?' said he, 'what has happened? Oh!—yes, yes! I recollect now. Heaven forgive me!'

"He rose and we walked up to the grave; what again was our astonishment and horror to find that, instead of the dead body of my mother-in-law, as we expected, there was lying over the remains of my poor sister, a large white she-wolf.

"'The white wolf!' exclaimed my father, 'the white wolf which decoyed me into the forest—I see it all now—I have dealt with the spirits of the Hartz Mountains.'

"For some time my father remained in silence and deep thought. He then carefully lifted up the body of my sister, replaced it in the grave, an covered it over as before, having struck the head of the dead animal with the heel of his boot, and raving like a madman. He walked back to the cottage, shut the door, and threw himself on the bed; I did the same, for I was in a stupor of amazement.

"Early in the morning we were both roused by a loud knocking at the door, and in rushed the hunter Wilfred.

"'My daughter—man—my daughter!—where is my daughter?' cried he in a rage.

"'Where the wretch, the fiend, should be, I trust,' replied my father, starting up, and displaying equal choler; 'where she should be—in hell! Leave this cottage, or you may fare worse.'

"'Ha—ha!' replied the hunter, 'would you harm a potent spirit of the Hartz Mountains. Poor mortal, who must needs wed a were wolf.'

"'Out, demon! I defy thee and thy power.'

"'Yet shall you feel it; remember your oath—your solemn oath—never to raise your hand against her to harm her.'

"'I made no compact with evil spirits.'

"'You did, and if you failed in your vow, you were to meet the vengeance of the spirits. Your children were to perish by the vulture, the wolf—'

"'Out, out, demon!'

"'And their bones blanch in the wilderness. Ha!—ha!'

"My father, frantic with rage, seized his axe, and raised it over Wilfred's head to strike.

"'All this I swear,' continued the huntsman, mockingly.

"The axe descended; but it passed through the form of the hunter, and my father lost his balance, and tell heavily on the floor.

"'Mortal!' said the hunter, striding over my father's body, 'we have power over those only who have committed murder. You have been guilty of a double murder: you shall pay the penalty attached to your marriage vow. Two of your children are gone, the third is yet to follow—and follow them he will, for your oath is registered. Go—it were kindness to kill thee—your punishment is, that you live!'

"With these words the spirit disappeared. My father rose from the floor, embraced me tenderly, and knelt down in prayer.

"The next morning he quitted the cottage for ever. He took me with him, and bent his steps to Holland, where we safely arrived. He had some little money with him; but he had not been many days in Amsterdam before he was seized with a brain fever, and died raving mad. I was put into the asylum, and afterwards was sent to sea before the mast. You now know all my history. The question is, whether I am to pay the penalty of my father's oath? I am myself perfectly convinced that, in some way or another, I shall."

On the twenty-second day the high land of the south of Sumatra was in view: as there were no vessels in sight, they resolved to keep their course through the Straits, and run for Pulo Penang, which they expected, as their vessel lay so close to the wind, to reach in seven or eight days. By constant exposure Philip and Krantz were now so bronzed that with their long beards and Mussulman dresses, they might easily have passed off for natives. They had steered the whole of the days exposed to a burning sun; they had lain down and slept in the dew of the night; but their health had not suffered. But for several days, since he had confided the history of his family to Philip, Krantz had become silent and melancholy: his usual flow of spirits had vanished and Philip had often questioned him as to the cause. As they entered the Straits, Philip talked of what they should do upon their arrival at Goa; when Krantz gravely replied, "For some days, Philip, I have had a presentiment that I shall never see that city."

"You are out of health, Krantz," replied Philip.

"No, I am in sound health, body and mind. I have endeavoured to shake off the presentiment, but in vain; there is a warning voice that continually tells me that I shall not be long with you. Philip, will you oblige me by making me content on one point? I have gold about my person which may be useful to you; oblige me by taking it, and securing it on your own."

"What nonsense, Krantz."

"It is no nonsense, Philip. Have on not had your warnings? Why should I not have mine? You know that I have little fear in my composition, and that I care not about death; but I feel the presentiment which I speak of more strongly every hour. It is some kind spirit who would warn me to prepare for another world. Be it so. I have lived long enough in this world to leave it without regret; although to part with you and Amine, the only two now dear to me, is painful, I acknowledge."

"May not this arise from over-exertion and fatigue, Krantz? Consider how much excitement you have laboured under within these last four months. Is not that enough to create a corresponding depression? Depend upon it, my dear friend, such is the fact."

"I wish it were; but I feel otherwise, and there is a feeling of gladness connected with the idea that I am to leave this world arising from another presentiment, which equally occupies my mind."

"I hardly can tell you—but Amine and you are connected with it. In my dreams I have seen you meet again; but it has appeared to me as if a portion of your trial was purposely shut from my sight in dark clouds; and I have asked, 'May not I see what is there concealed?'—and an invisible has answered, 'No! 'twould make you wretched. Before these trials take place, you will be summoned away:' and then I have thanked Heaven, and felt resigned."

"These are the imaginings of a disturbed brain, Krantz; that I am destined to suffering may be true; but why Amine should suffer, or why you, young, in full health and vigour should not pass your days in peace, and live to a good old age, there is no cause for believing. You will be better tomorrow."

"Perhaps so," replied Krantz; "but still you must yield to my whim, and take the gold; If I am wrong, and we do arrive safe, you know, Philip, you can let me have it back," observed Krantz, with a faint smile—"but you forget, our water is nearly out, and we must look out for a rill on the coast to obtain a fresh supply."

"I was thinking of that when you commenced this unwelcome topic. We had better look out for the water before dark, and as soon as we have replenished our jars, we will make sail again."

At the time that this conversation took place, they were on the eastern side of the strait, about forty miles to the northward. The interior of the coast was rocky and mountainous; but it slowly descended to low land of alternate forest and jungles, which continued to the beach: the country appeared to be uninhabited. Keeping close in to the shore, they discovered, after two hours' run, a fresh stream which burst in a cascade from the mountains, and swept its devious course through the jungle, until it poured its tribute into the waters of the strait.

They ran close in to the mouth of the stream, lowered the sails, and pulled the peroqua against the current, until they had advanced far enough to assure them that the water was quite fresh. The jars were soon filled, and they were again thinking of pushing off; when, enticed by the beauty of the spot, the coolness of the fresh water, and wearied with their long confinement on board of the peroqua, they proposed to bathe—a luxury hardly to be appreciated by those who have not been in a similar situation. They threw off their Mussulman dresses, and plunged into the stream, where they remained for some time. Krantz was the first to get out: he complained of feeling chilled, and he walked on to the banks where their clothes had been laid. Philip also approached nearer to the beach intending to follow him.

"And now, Philip," said Krantz, "this will be a good opportunity for me to give you the money. I will open my sash and pour it out, and you can put it into your own before you put it on."

Philip was standing in the water, which was about level with his waist.

"Well, Krantz," said he, "I suppose if it must be so, it must—but it appears to me an idea so ridiculous—however, you shall have your own way."

Philip quitted the run, and sat down by Krantz, who was already busy in shaking the doubloons out of the folds of his sash. At last he said—

"I believe, Philip, you have got them all now?—I feel satisfied."

"What danger there can be to you, which I am not equally exposed to, I cannot conceive," replied Philip; "however—"

Hardly had he said these words, when there was a tremendous roar—a rush like a mighty wind through the air—a blow which threw him on his back—a loud cry—and a contention. Philip recovered himself, and perceived the naked form of Krantz carried off with the speed of an arrow by an enormous tiger through the jungle. He watched with distended eyeballs; in a few seconds the animal and Krantz had disappeared!

"God of Heaven! would that thou hadst spared me this," cried Philip, throwing himself down in agony on his face. "Oh! Krantz, my friend—my brother—too sure was your presentiment. Merciful God! have pity—but thy will be done;" and Philip burst into a flood of tears.

For more than an hour did he remain fixed upon the spot, careless and indifferent to the danger by which he was surrounded. At last, somewhat recovered, he rose, dressed himself, and then again sat down—his eyes fixed upon the clothes of Krantz, and the gold which a on the sand.

"He would give me that gold. He foretold his doom. Yes! yes! it was his destiny, and it has been fulfilled. *His bones will bleach in the wilderness*, and the spirit-hunter and his wolfish daughter are avenged."

The shades of evening now set in, and the low growling of the beasts of the forest recalled Philip to a sense of his own danger. He thought of Amine; and hastily making the clothes of Krantz and the doubloons into a package, he stepped into the peroqua, with difficulty shoved it off, and with a melancholy heart, and in silence, hoisted the sail, and pursued his course.

"Yes, Amine," thought Philip, as he watched the stars twinkling and coruscating; "yes, you are right, when you assert that the destinies of men are foreknown, and may by some be read. My destiny is, alas! that I should be severed from all I value upon earth? and die friendless and alone. Then welcome death, if such is to be the case; welcome—a thousand welcomes! what a relief wilt thou be to me! what joy to find myself summoned to where the weary are at rest! I have my task to fulfil. God grant that it may soon be accomplished, and let not my life be embittered by any more trials such as this."

Again did Philip weep, for Krantz had been his long-tried, valued friend? his partner in all his dangers and privations, from the period that they had met when the Dutch fleet attempted the passage round Cape Horn.

After seven days of painful watching and brooding over bitter thoughts, Philip arrived at Pulo Penang, where he found a vessel about to sail for the city to which he was destined. He ran his peroqua alongside of her, and found that she was a brig under the Portuguese flag, having, however, but two Portuguese on board, the rest of the crew being natives. Representing himself as am Englishman in the Portuguese service, who had been wrecked, and offering to pay for his passage, he was willingly received, and in a few days the vessel sailed.

Their voyage was prosperous; in six weeks they anchored in the roads of Goa; the next day they went up the river. The Portuguese captain informed Philip where he might obtain lodging; and passing him off as one of his crew, there was no difficulty raised as to his landing. Having located himself at his new lodging, Philip commenced some inquiries of his host relative to Amine, designating her merely as a young woman who had arrived there in a vessel some weeks before but he could obtain no information concerning her. "Signor," said the host, "to-morrow is the grand *auto-da-fé*; we can do nothing until that is over; afterwards, I will put you in the way to find out what you wish. In the mean time, you can walk about the town; to-morrow I will take you to where you can behold the grand procession, and then we will try what we can do to assist you in your search."

Philip went out, procured a suit of clothes, removed his beard, and then walked about the town, looking up at every window to see if he could perceive Amine. At a corner of one of the streets, he thought he recognised Father Mathias, and ran up to him; but the monk had drawn his cowl over his head, and when addressed by that name, made no reply.

"I was deceived," thought Philip; "but I really thought it was him." And Philip was right; it was Father Mathias, who thus screened himself from Philip's recognition.

Tired, at last he returned to his hotel, just before it was dark. The company there were numerous; everybody for miles distant had come to Goa to witness the *auto-da-fé*,—and everybody was discussing the ceremony.

"I will see this grand procession," said Philip to himself, as he threw himself on his bed. "It will drive thought from me for a time; and God knows how painful my thoughts have now become. Amine, dear Amine, may angels guard thee!"

Chapter Forty.

Although to-morrow was to end all Amine's hopes and fears—all her short happiness—her suspense and misery—yet Amine slept until her last slumber in this world was disturbed by the unlocking and unbarring of the doors of her cell, and the appearance of the head gaoler with a light. Amine started up—she had been dreaming of her husband—of happiness! She awoke to the sad reality. There stood the gaoler, with a dress in his hand, which he desired she would put on. He lighted a lamp for her, and left her alone. The dress was of black serge, with white stripes.

Amine put on the dress, and threw herself down on the bed, trying, if possible, to recall the dream from which she had been awakened, but in vain. Two hours passed away, and the gaoler again entered, and summoned her to follow him. Perhaps one of the most appalling customs of the Inquisition is, that after accusation, whether the accused parties confess their guilt or not, they return to their dungeons, without the least idea of what may have been their sentence, and when summoned on the morning of the execution they are equally kept in ignorance.

The prisoners were all summoned by the gaolers from the various dungeons, and led into a large hall, where they found their fellow-sufferers collected.

In this spacious, dimly-lighted hall, were to be seen about two hundred men, standing up, as if for support, against the walls, all dressed in the same black and white serge; so motionless, so terrified were they, that if it had not been for the rolling of their eyes, as they watched the gaolers, who passed and repassed, you might have imagined them to be petrified. It was the agony of suspense, worse than the agony of death. After a time, a wax candle, about five feet long, was put into the hands of each prisoner, and then some were ordered to put on over their dress the *Sanbenitos*—others the *Samarias*! Those who received these dresses, with flames painted on them, gave themselves up for lost; and it was dreadful to perceive the anguish of each individual as the dresses were, one by one brought forward, and with the heavy drops of perspiration on his brows, he watched with terror lest one should be presented to him. All was doubt, fear, and horror!

But the prisoners in this hall were not those who were to suffer death. Those who wore the Sanbenitos had to walk in the procession, and receive but slight punishment; those who wore the Samarias had been condemned, but had been saved from the consuming fire, by an acknowledgment of their offence; the flames painted on their dresses were *reversed*, and signified that they were not to suffer; but this the unfortunate wretches did not know, and the horrors of a cruel death stared them in the face!

Another hall, similar to the one in which the men had been collected, was occupied by female culprits. The same ceremonies were observed—the same doubt fear and agony, were depicted upon every countenance. But there was a third chamber, smaller than the other two, and this chamber was reserved for those who had been sentenced and who were to suffer at the stake. It was into this chamber that Amine was led, and there she found seven other prisoners, dressed in the same manner as herself: two only were Europeans, the other five were negro slaves. Each of these had his confessor with him, and was earnestly listening to his exhortation. A monk approached Amine, but she waved him away with her hand: he looked at her, spat on the floor, and cursed her. The head gaoler now made his appearance with the dresses for those who were in this chamber; these were Samarias, only different from the others, inasmuch as the flames were painted on them *upwards* instead of down. These dresses were of grey stuff, and loose, like a waggoner's frock; at the lower part of them, both before and behind, was painted the likeness of the wearer that is the face only, resting upon a burning fagot, and surrounded with flames and demons. Under the portrait was written the crime for which the party suffered. Sugar-loaf caps, with flames painted on them, were also brought and put on their heads, and the long wax candles were placed into their hands.

Amine, and the others condemned, being arrayed in these dresses, remained in the chambers for some hours before it was time for the procession to commence, for they had been all summoned up by the gaolers at about two o'clock in the morning.

The sun rose brilliantly, much to the joy of the members of the Holy Office, who would not have had the day obscured on which they were to vindicate the honour of the Church, and to prove how well they acted up to the mild doctrines of the Saviour—those of charity, good-will, forbearing one another forgiving one another. God of Heaven! And not only did those of the Holy Inquisition rejoice, but thousands and thousands more, who had flocked from all parts to witness the dreadful ceremony, and to hold a jubilee—many, indeed, actuated by fanatical superstition, but more attended from thoughtlessness and the love of pageantry. The streets and squares through which the procession was to pass were filled at an early hour. Silks, tapestries, and cloth of gold and silver, were hung over the balconies, and out of the windows, in honour of the procession. Every balcony and window was thronged with ladies and cavaliers in their gayest attire, all waiting anxiously to see the wretches paraded before they suffered; but the world is fond of excitement, and where is anything so exciting to a superstitious people as an *auto-da-fé*?

As the sun rose, the heavy bell of the cathedral tolled, and all the prisoners were led down to the grand hall, that the order of the procession might be arranged. At the large entrance-door, on a raised one sat the Grand Inquisitor, encircled by many of the most considerable nobility and gentry of Goa. By the Grand Inquisitor stood his secretary, and as the prisoners walked past the throne and their names were mentioned, the secretary, after each, called out the names of one of those gentlemen, who immediately stepped forward, and took his station by the prisoner. These people are termed god-fathers; their duty is to accompany and be answerable for the prisoner, who is under their charge, until the ceremony is over. It is reckoned a high honour conferred on those whom the Grand Inquisitor appoints to this office.

At last the procession commenced. First was raised on high the standard of the Dominican order of monks, for the Dominican order were the founders of the Inquisition, and claimed this privilege by prescriptive right. After the banner, the monks themselves followed, in two lines. And what was the motto of their banner?—"Justitia et Misericordia!" Then followed the culprits, to the number of three hundred, each with his godfather by his side, and his large wax candle lighted in his hand. Those whose offences have been most venial walk first; all are bareheaded and barefooted. After this portion; who wore only the dress of black and white serge, came those who carried the Sanbenitos; then those who wore the Samarias, with the flames reversed. Here there was a separation in the procession, caused by a large cross, with the carved image of our Saviour nailed to it, the face of the image carried forward. This was intended to signify, that those in advance of the crucifix, and upon whom the Saviour looked down, were not to suffer; and that those who were behind, and upon whom his back was turned, were cast away, to perish for ever, in this world and the next. Behind the crucifix followed the seven condemned; and, as the greatest criminal, Amine walked the last. But the procession did not close here. Behind Amine were five effigies, raised high on poles, clothed in the same dresses, painted with flames and demons. Behind each effigy was borne a coffin, containing a skeleton; the effigies were of those who had died in their dungeon, or expired under the torture, and who had been tried and condemned after their death, and sentenced to be burnt. These skeletons had been dug up and were to suffer the same sentence as, had they still been living beings, they would have undergone. The effigies were to be tied to the stakes, and the bones were to be consumed. Then followed the members of the Inquisition; the familiars, monks, priests, and hundreds of penitents in black dresses, which concealed their faces, all with the lighted tapers in their hands.

It was two hours before the procession, which had paraded through almost every important street in Goa, arrived at the cathedral in which the further ceremonies were to be gone through. The barefooted culprits could now scarcely walk, the small sharp flints having so wounded their feet, that their tracks up the steps of the cathedral were marked with blood.

The grand altar of the cathedral was hung with black cloth, and lighted up with thousands of tapers. On one side of it was a throne for the Grand Inquisitor, on the other, a raised platform for the Viceroy of Goa, and his suite. The centre aisle had benches for the prisoners and their godfathers; the other portions of the procession falling off to the right and left to the side aisles, and mixing for the time with the spectators. As the prisoners entered the cathedral, they were led into their seats, those least guilty sitting nearest to the altar, and those who were condemned to suffer at the stake being placed the farthest from it.

The bleeding Amine tottered to her seat, and longed for the hour which was to sever her from a Christian world. She thought not of herself, nor of what she was to suffer: she thought but of Philip; of his being safe from these merciless creatures—of the happiness of dying first, and of meeting him again in bliss.

Worn with long confinement, with suspense and anxiety, fatigued and suffering from her painful walk, and the exposure to the burning sun, after so many months' incarceration in a dungeon, she no longer shone radiant with beauty; but still there was something even more touching in her care-worn yet still perfect features. The object of universal gaze, she walked with her eyes cast down, and nearly closed; but occasionally, when she did look up, the fire that flashed from them spoke the proud soul within, and many feared and wondered, while more pitied that one so young, and still so lovely, should be doomed to such an awful fate. Amine had not taken her seat in the cathedral more than a few seconds, when, overpowered by her feelings and by fatigue she fell back in a swoon.

Did no one step forward to assist her? to raise her up, and offer her restoratives? No—not one. Hundreds would have done so, but they dared not: she was an outcast, excommunicated, abandoned, and lost; and should any one, moved by compassion for a suffering fellow-creature, have ventured to raise her up he would have been looked upon with suspicion, and most probably have been arraigned, and have had to settle the affair of conscience with the Holy Inquisition.

After a short time two of the officers of the Inquisition went to Amine and raised her again in her seat, and she recovered sufficiently to enable her to retain her posture.

A sermon was then preached by a Dominican monk, in which he portrayed the tender mercies, the paternal love of the Holy Office. He compared the Inquisition to the ark of Noah, out of which all the animals walked after the deluge, but with this difference highly in favour of the Holy Office, that the animals went forth from the ark no better than they went in, whereas those who had gone into the Inquisition with all the cruelty of disposition, and with the hearts of wolves, came out as mild and patient as lambs.

The public accuser then mounted the pulpit, and read from it all the crimes of those who had been condemned, and the punishments which they were to undergo. Each prisoner, as his sentence was read, was brought forward to the pulpit by the officers to hear it, standing up, with his wax candle lighted in his hand. As soon as the sentences of all those whose lives had been spared were read the Grand Inquisitor put on his priestly robes, and followed by several others, took off from them the ban of excommunication (which they were supposed to have fallen under), by throwing holy water on them with a small broom.

As soon as this portion of the ceremony was over, those who were condemned to suffer, and the effigies of those who had escaped by death, were brought up one by one, and their sentences read; the winding up of the condemnation of all was in the same words, "that the Holy Inquisition found it impossible, on account of the hardness of their hearts and the magnitude of their crimes, to pardon them. With great concern it handed them over to secular justice to undergo the penalty of the laws; exhorting the authorities at the same time to show clemency and mercy towards the unhappy wretches, and if they must suffer death, that at all events it might be without the *spilling of blood*." What mockery was this apparent intercession not to shied blood, when, to comply with their request, they substituted the torment and agony of the stake!

Amine was the last who was led forward to the pulpit, which was fixed against one of the massive columns of the centre aisle, close to the throne occupied by the Grand inquisitor. "You, Amine Vanderdecken," cried the public accuser. At this moment an unusual bustle was heard in the crowd under the pulpit, there was struggling and expostulation, and the officers raised their wands for silence and decorum—but it continued.

"You, Amine Vanderdecken, being accused—"

Another violent struggle; and from the crowd darted a young man, who rushed to where Amine was standing, and caught her in his arms.

"Philip! Philip!" screamed Amine falling on his bosom; as he caught her, the cap of flames fell off her head and rolled along the marble pavement. "My Amine—my wife—my adored one—is it thus we meet? My lord, she is innocent. Stand off, men," continued he to the officers of the Inquisition, who would have torn them asunder: "stand off, or your lives shall answer for it."

This threat to the officers, and the defiance of all rules, were not to be borne; the whole cathedral was in a state of commotion, and the solemnity of the ceremony was about to be compromised. The Viceroy and his followers had risen from their chairs to observe what was passing, and the crowd was pressing on, when the Grand Inquisitor gave his directions, and other officers hastened to the assistance of the two who had led Amine forward, and proceeded to disengage her from Philip's arms. The struggle was severe. Philip appeared to be endued with the strength of twenty men; and it was some minutes before they could succeed in separating him and when they had so done, his struggles were dreadful.

Amine, also, held by two of the familiars, shrieked, as she attempted once more, but in vain, to rush into her husband's arms. At last, by a tremendous effort, Philip released himself; but as soon as he was released, he sank down helpless on the pavement; the exertion had caused the bursting of a blood-vessel, and he lay without motion.

"Oh God! Oh God! they have killed him! monsters—murderers!—let me embrace him but once more!" cried Amine, frantically.

A priest now stepped forward—it was Father Mathias—with sorrow in his countenance; he desired some of the bystanders to carry out Philip Vanderdecken, and Philip, in a state of insensibility, was borne away from the sight of Amine, the blood streaming from his mouth.

Amine's sentence was read—she heard it not, her brain was bewildered. She was led back to her seat, and then it was that all her courage, all her constancy and fortitude gave way; and during the remainder of the ceremony, she filled the cathedral with her wild hysterical sobbing; all entreaties or threats being wholly lost upon her.

All was now over except the last and most tragical scene of the drama. The culprits who had been spared were led back to the Inquisition by their godfathers, and those who had been sentenced were taken down to the banks of the river to suffer. It was on a large open space, on the left of the custom-house, that this ceremony was to be gone through. As in the cathedral raised thrones were prepared for the Grand Inquisitor and the who, in state headed the procession, followed by an immense concourse of people. Thirteen stakes had been set up, eight for the living, or the dead. The executioners were sitting on, or standing by, the piles of wood and faggots, waiting for their victims. Amine could not walk she was at first supported by the familiars, and then carried by them, to the stake which had been assigned for her. When they put her on her feet opposite to it, her courage appeared to revive, she walked boldly up, folded her arms and leant against it.

The executioners now commenced their office: the chains were passed round Amine's body—the wood and faggots piled around her. The same preparations had been made with all the other culprits, and the confessors stood by the side of each victim. Amine waved her hand indignantly to those who approached her, when Father Mathias, almost breathless, made his appearance from the crowd, through which he had forced his way.

"Amine Vanderdecken—unhappy woman! had you been counselled by me this would not have been. Now it is too late, but not too late to save your soul. Away then with this obstinacy—this hardness of heart; call upon the blessed Saviour, that he may receive your spirit—call upon his wound's for mercy. It is the eleventh hour, but not too late. Amine," continued the old man with tears, "I implore you, I conjure you. At least, may this load of trouble be taken from my heart."

"'Unhappy woman!' you say?" replied she, "say rather, 'unhappy priest:' for Amine's sufferings will soon be over, while you must still endure the torments of the damned. Unhappy was the day when my husband rescued you from death. Still more unhappy the compassion which prompted him to offer you an asylum and a refuge. Unhappy the knowledge of you from the *first* day to the *last*. I leave you to your conscience—if conscience you retain—nor would I change this cruel death for the pangs which you in your future life will suffer. Leave me—*I die in the faith of my forefathers*, and scorn a creed that warrants such a scene as this."

"Amine Vanderdecken," cried the priest on his knees, clasping his hands in agony.

"Leave me, Father."

"There is but a minute left—for the love of God—"

"I tell you then, leave me—that minute is my own."

Father Mathias turned away in despair, and the tears coursed down the old man's cheeks. As Amine said, his misery was extreme.

The head executioner now inquired of the confessors whether the culprits died in the *true* faith? If answered in the affirmative, a rope was passed round their necks and twisted to the stake, so that they were strangled before the fire was kindled. All the other culprits had died in this manner; and the head executioner inquired of Father Mathias, whether Amine had a claim to so much mercy. The old priest answered not, but shook his head.

The executioner turned away. After a moment's pause, Father Mathias followed him, and seized him by the arm saying, in a faltering voice, "Let her not suffer long."

The Grand Inquisitor gave the signal, and the fires were all lighted at the same moment. In compliance with the request of the priest, the executioner had thrown a quantity of wet straw upon Amine's pile, which threw up a dense smoke before it burst into flames.

"Mother! mother! I come to thee!" were the last words heard from Amine's lips.

The flames soon raged furiously, ascending high above the top of the stake to which she had been chained. Gradually they sunk down; and only when the burning embers covered the ground, a few fragments of bones hanging on the chain were all that remained of the once peerless and high-minded Amine.

Chapter Forty One.

Years have passed away since we related Amine's sufferings and cruel death; and now once more we bring Philip Vanderdecken on the scene. And during this time, where has he been? A lunatic—at one time frantic, chained, coerced with blows; at others, mild and peaceable. Reason occasionally appeared to burst out again, as the sun on a cloudy day, and then it was again obscured. For many years there was one who watched him carefully, and lived in hope to witness his return to a sane mind; he watched in sorrow and remorse—he died without his desires being gratified. This was Father Mathias!

The cottage at Terneuse had long fallen into ruin; for many years it waited the return of its owners, and at last the heirs-at-law claimed and recovered the substance of Philip Vanderdecken. Even the fate of Amine had passed from the recollection of most people; although her portrait over burning coals, with her crime announced beneath it, still hangs—as is the custom in the church of the Inquisition—attracting from its expressive beauty, the attention of the most careless passers-by.

But many, many years have rolled away—Philip's hair is white—his once powerful frame is broken down—and he appears much older than he really is. He is now sane; but his vigour is gone. Weary of life, all he wishes for is to execute his mission—and then to welcome death.

The relic has never been taken from him: he has been discharged from the lunatic-asylum, and has been provided with the means of returning to his country. Alas! he has now no country—no home—nothing in the world to induce him to remain in it. All he asks is—to do his duty and to die.

The ship was ready to sail for Europe; and Philip Vanderdecken went on board—hardly caring whither he went. To return to Terneuse was not his object; he could not bear the idea of revisiting the scene of so much happiness and so much misery. Amine's form was engraven on his heart, and he looked forward with impatience to the time when he should be summoned to join her in the land of spirits.

He had awakened as from a dream, after so many years of aberration of intellect. He was no longer the sincere Catholic that he had been; for he never thought of religion without his Amine's cruel fate being brought to his recollection. Still he clung on to the relic—he believed in that—and that only. It was his god—his creed—his everything—the passport for himself and for his father into the next world—the means whereby he should join his Amine—and for hours would he remain holding in his hand that object so valued—gazing upon it—recalling every important event in his life, from the death of his poor mother, and his first sight of Amine, to the last dreadful scene. It was to him a journal of his existence, and on it were fixed all his hopes for the future.

"When! oh when is it to be accomplished?" was the constant subject of his reveries. "Blessed indeed will be the day when I leave this world of hate, and seek that other in which the weary are at rest."

The vessel on board of which Philip was embarked as a passenger was the Nostra Señora da Monte, a brig of three hundred tons, bound for Lisbon. The captain was an old Portuguese, full of superstition, and fond of arrack—a fondness rather unusual with the people of his nation. They sailed from Goa, and Philip was standing abaft, and sadly contemplating the spire of the cathedral, in which he had last parted with his wife, when his elbow was touched, and he turned round.

"Fellow-passenger, again!" said a well-known voice—it was that of the pilot Schriften.

There was no alteration in the man's appearance; he showed no marks of declining years; his one eye glared as keenly as ever.

Philip started, not only at the sight of the man, but at the reminiscences which his unexpected appearance brought to his mind. It was but for a second, and he was again calm and pensive.

"You here again, Schriften?" observed Philip. "I trust your appearance forebodes the accomplishment of my task."

"Perhaps it does," replied the pilot; "we both are weary."

Philip made no reply; he did not even ask Schriften in what manner he had escaped from the fort; he was indifferent about it; for he felt that the man had a charmed life.

"Many are the vessels that have been wrecked, Philip Vanderdecken, and many the souls summoned to their account by meeting with your father's ship, while you have been so long shut up," observed the pilot.

"May our next meeting with him be more fortunate—may it be the last!" replied Philip.

"No, no! rather may he fulfil his doom, and sail till the day of judgment!" replied the pilot, with emphasis.

"Vile caitiff! I have a foreboding that you will not have your detestable wish. Away!—leave me! or you shall find, that although this head is blanched by misery, this arm has still some power."

Schriften scowled as he walked away; he appeared to have some fear of Philip, although it was not equal to his hate. He now resumed his former attempts of stirring up the ship's company against Philip, declaring that he was a Jonah, who would occasion the loss of the ship, and that he was connected with the Flying Dutchman. Philip very soon observed that he was avoided; and he resorted to counter-statements, equally injurious to Schriften, whom he declared to be a demon. The appearance of Schriften was so much against him, while that of Philip, on the contrary, was so prepossessing, that the people on board hardly knew what to think. They were divided: some were on the side of Philip—some on that of Schriften; the captain and many others looking with equal horror upon both, and longing for the time when they could be sent out of the vessel.

The captain, as we have before observed, was very superstitious, and very fond of his bottle. In the morning he would be sober and pray; in the afternoon he would be drunk and swear at the very saints whose protection he had invoked but a few hours before.

"May holy Saint Antonio preserve us, and keep us from temptation," said he, on the morning after a conversation with the passengers about the Phantom Ship. "All the saints protect us from harm," continued he, taking off his hat reverentially and crossing himself. "Let me but rid myself of these two dangerous men without accident, and I will offer up a hundred wax candles, of three ounces each, to the shrine of the Virgin, upon my safe anchoring off the tower of Belem." In the evening he changed his language.

"Now, if that Maldetto Saint Antonio don't help us, may he feel the coals of hell yet! damn him, and his pigs too; if he has the courage to do his duty, all will be well; but he is a cowardly wretch, he cares for nobody, and will not help those who call upon him in trouble. Carambo, that for you!" exclaimed the captain, looking at the small shrine of the saint at the bittacle, and snapping his fingers at the image; "that for you, you useless wretch, who never help us in our trouble. The pope must canonise some better saints for us, for all we have now are worn out. They could do something formerly, but now I would not give two ounces of gold for the whole calendar; as for you, you lazy old scoundrel—" continued the captain, shaking his fist at poor Saint Antonio.

The ship had now gained off the southern coast of Africa, and was about one hundred miles from the Lagullas coast; the morning was beautiful, a slight ripple only turned over the waves, the breeze was light and steady, and the vessel was standing on a wind at the rate of about four miles an hour.

"Blessed be the holy saints," said the captain, who had just gained the deck; "another little slant in our favour, and we shall lay our course. Again, I say, blessed be the holy saints, and particularly our worthy patron, Saint Antonio, who has taken under his peculiar protection the Nostra Señora da Monte. We have a prospect of fine weather; come, signors, let us down to breakfast, and after breakfast, we enjoy our cigarros upon the deck."

But the scene was soon changed; a bank of clouds rose up from the eastward with a rapidity that to the seamen's eyes was unnatural, and it soon covered the whole firmament; the sun was obscured, and all was one deep and unnatural gloom; the wind subsided, and the ocean was hushed. It was not exactly dark, but the heavens were covered with one red haze, which gave an appearance as if the world was in a state of conflagration.

In the cabin the increased darkness was first observed by Philip, who went on deck; he was followed by the captain and passengers, who were in a state of amazement. It was unnatural and incomprehensible. "Now, holy Virgin, protect us!—what can this be?" exclaimed the captain in a fright "Holy Saint Antonio, protect us!—but this is awful."

"There—there!" shouted the sailors, pointing to the beam of the vessel. Every eye looked over the gunnel to witness what had occasioned such exclamations. Philip, Schriften, and the captain, were side by side. On the beam of the ship, not more than two cables' length distant, they beheld slowly rising out of the water the tapering masthead and spars of another vessel. She rose, and rose, gradually; her topmasts and topsail yards, with the sails set, next made their appearance; higher and higher she rose up from the element. Her lower masts and rigging, and, lastly, her hull showed itself above the surface. Still she rose up, till her ports, with her guns, and at last the whole of her floatage was above water and there she remained close to them, with her main yard squared, and hove-to.

"Holy Virgin!" exclaimed the captain, breathless; "I have known ships to *go down*, but never to *come up* before. Now will I give one thousand candles, of ten ounces each, to the shrine of the Virgin, to save us in this trouble. One thousand wax candles! Hear me, blessed lady, ten ounces each! Gentlemen," cried the captain to the passengers, who stood aghast; "why don't you promise?—promise, I say; *promise*, at all events."

"The Phantom Ship—the Flying Dutchman," shrieked Schriften; "I told you so, Philip Vanderdecken; there is your father—he, he!"

Philip's eyes had remained fixed on the vessel; he perceived that they were lowering down a boat from her quarter. "It is possible," thought he, "I shall now be permitted!" and Philip put his hand into his bosom and grasped the relic.

The gloom now increased, so that the strange vessel's hull could but just be discovered through the murky atmosphere. The seamen and passengers threw themselves down on their knees, and invoked their saints. The captain ran down for a candle, to light before the image of St. Antonio, which he took out of its shrine and kissed with much apparent affection and devotion, and then replaced.

Shortly afterwards the splash of oars was heard alongside, and a voice calling out, "I say, my good people, give us a rope from forward."

No one answered, or complied with the request. Schriften only went up to the captain, and told him that if they offered to send letters they must not be received, or the vessel would be doomed, and all would perish.

A man now made his appearance from over the gunnel, at the gangway. "You might as well have let me had a side-rope, my hearties," said he, as he stepped on deck; "where is the captain?"

"Here," replied the captain, trembling from head to foot. The man who accosted him appeared a weather-beaten seaman, dressed in a fur cap and canvas petticoats; he held some letters in his hand.

"What do you want?" at last screamed the captain.

"Yes—what do you want?" continued Schriften, "He! he!"

"What, you here, pilot?" observed the man—"well—I thought you had gone to Davy's locker, long enough ago."

"He! he!" replied Schriften, turning away.

"Why, the fact is, captain, we have had very foul weather and we wish to send letters home; I do believe that we shall never get round this cape."

"I can't take them," cried the captain.

"Can't take them! well, it's very odd; but every ship refuses to take our letters. It's very unkind; seamen should have a feeling for brother seamen, especially in distress. God knows, we wish to see our wives and families again; and it would be a matter of comfort to them if they only could hear from us."

"I cannot take your letters—the saints preserve us!" replied the captain.

"We have been a long while out," said the seaman, shaking his head.

"How long?" inquired the captain, not knowing what to say.

"We can't tell; our almanack was blown overboard, and we have lost our reckoning. We never have our latitude exact now, for we cannot tell the sun's declination for the right day."

"Let *me* see your letters," said Philip, advancing and taking them out of the seaman's hands.

"They must not be touched!" screamed Schriften.

"Out, monster!" replied Philip; "who dares interfere with me?"

"Doomed—doomed—doomed!" shrieked Schriften, running up and down the deck, and then breaking into a wild fit of laughter.

"Touch not the letters," said the captain, trembling as if in an ague fit.

Philip made no reply, but held his hand out for the letters.

"Here is one from our second mate to his wife at Amsterdam who lives on Waser Quay."

"Waser Quay has long been gone, my good friend; there is now a large dock for ships where it once was," replied Philip.

"Impossible!" replied the man; "here is another from the boatswain to his father, who lives in the old market-place."

"The old market-place has long been pulled down, and there now stands a church upon the spot."

"Impossible!" replied the seaman; "here is another from myself to my sweetheart, Vrow Ketser—with money to buy her a new brooch."

Philip shook his head. "I remember seeing an old lady of that name buried some thirty years ago."

"Impossible! I left her young and blooming. Here's one for the house of Slutz and Company, to whom the ship belongs."

"There's no such house now," replied Philip; "but I have heard that, many years ago, there was a firm of that name."

"Impossible! you must be laughing at me. Here is a letter from our captain to his son—"

"Give it me," cried Philip, seizing the letter. He was about to break the seal, when Schriften snatched it out of his hand and threw it over the lee gunnel.

"That's a scurvy trick for an old shipmate," observed the seaman. Schriften made no reply, but catching up the other letters which Philip had laid down on the capstan, he hurled them after the first.

The strange seaman shed tears, and walked again to the side. "It is very hard—very unkind," observed he, as he descended; "the time may come when you may wish that your family should know your situation." So saying, he disappeared. In a few seconds was heard the sound of the oars retreating from the ship.

"Holy St. Antonio!" exclaimed the captain. "I am lost in wonder and fright. Steward, bring me up the arrack."

The steward ran down for the bottle; being as much alarmed as his captain, he helped himself before he brought it up to his commander. "Now," said the captain, after keeping his mouth for two minutes to the bottle, and draining it to the bottom, "what is to be done next?"

"I'll tell you," said Schriften, going up to him: "that man there has a charm hung round his neck; take it from him and throw it overboard, and your ship will be saved; if not, it will be lost, with every soul on board."

"Yes yes, it's all right, depend upon it," cried the sailors.

"Fools," replied Philip, "do you believe that wretch? Did you not hear the man who came on board recognise him, and call him shipmate? He is the party whose presence on board will prove so unfortunate."

"Yes, yes," cried the sailors, "it's all right; the man did call him shipmate."

"I tell you it's all wrong," cried Schriften; "that is the man: let him give up the charm."

"Yes, yes; let him give up the charm," cried the sailors; and they rushed upon Philip.

Philip started back to where the captain stood. "Madmen, know ye what ye are about? It is the holy cross that I wear round my neck. Throw it overboard if you dare, and your souls are lost for ever;" and Philip took the relic from his bosom and showed it to the captain.

"No, no, men;" exclaimed the captain, who was now more settled in his nerves; "that won't do—the saints protect us."

The seamen, however, became clamorous; one portion were for throwing Schriften overboard, the other for throwing Philip; at last, the point was decided by the captain, who directed the small skiff hanging astern to be lowered down, and ordered both Philip and Schriften to get into it. The seamen approved of this arrangement, as it satisfied both parties. Philip made no objection; Schriften screamed and fought, but he was tossed into the boat. There he remained trembling in the stern-sheets, while Philip, who had seized the sculls, pulled away from the vessel in the direction of the Phantom Ship.

Chapter Forty Two.

In a few minutes the vessel which Philip and Schriften had left was no longer to be discerned through the thick haze; the Phantom Ship was still in sight, but at a much greater distance from them than she was before. Philip pulled hard towards her, but although hove to, she appeared to increase her distance from the boat. For a short time he paused on his oars, to regain his breath, when Schriften rose up and took his seat in the stern-sheets of the boat. "You may pull and pull, Philip Vanderdecken," observed Schriften; "but you will not gain that ship—no, no, that cannot be—we may have a long cruise together, but you will be as far from your object at the end of it, as you are now at the commencement.—Why don't you throw me overboard again? You would be all the lighter—He! he!"

"I threw you overboard in a state of phrenzy," replied Philip, "when you attempted to force from me my relic."

"And have I not endeavoured to make others take it from you this very day?—Have I not—He! he!"

"You have," rejoined Philip; "but I am now convinced that you are as unhappy as myself, and that in what you are doing, you are only following your destiny, as I am mine. Why and wherefore I cannot tell, but we are both engaged in the same mystery;—if the success of my endeavours depends upon guarding the relic, the success of yours depends upon your obtaining it, and defeating my purpose by so doing. In this matter we are both agents, and you have been, as far as my mission is concerned, my most active enemy. But, Schriften, I have not forgotten, and never will, that you kindly *did advise* my poor Amine; that you prophesied to her what would be her fate, if she did not listen to your counsel; that you were no enemy of hers, although you have been and are still mine. Although my enemy, for her sake I *forgive you*, and will not attempt to harm you."

"You do then *forgive your enemy*, Philip Vanderdecken?" replied Schriften, mournfully, "for such I acknowledge myself to be."

"I do, with *all my heart, with all my soul*," replied Philip.

"Then have you conquered me, Philip Vanderdecken; you have now made me your friend, and your wishes are about to be accomplished. You would know who I am. Listen:— When your father, defying the Almighty's will, in his rage took my life, he was vouchsafed a chance of his doom being cancelled, through the merits of his Son. I had also my appeal, which was for *vengeance*; it was granted that I should remain on earth, and thwart your will. That as long as we were enemies, you should not succeed; but that when you had conformed to the highest attribute of Christianity, proved on the holy cross, that of *forgiving your enemy*, your task should be fulfilled. Philip Vanderdecken, you have forgiven your enemy, and both our destinies are now accomplished."

As Schriften spoke, Philip's eyes were fixed upon him. He extended his hand to Philip—it was taken; and as it was pressed, the form of the pilot wasted as it were into the air, and Philip found himself alone.

"Father of Mercy, I thank thee," said Philip, "that my task is done, and that I again may meet my Amine."

Philip then pulled towards the Phantom Ship, and found that she no longer appeared to leave; on the contrary, every minute he was nearer and nearer and at last, he threw in his oars, climbed up her sides and gained her deck.

The crew of the vessel crowded round him.

"Your captain," said Philip; "I must speak with your captain."

"Who shall I say, sir?" demanded one, who appeared to be the first mate.

"Who?" replied Philip: "tell him his son would speak to him, his son, Philip Vanderdecken."

Shouts of laughter from the crew followed this answer of Philip's; and the mate, as soon as they ceased, observed with a smile.

"You forget, sir, perhaps you would say his father."

"Tell him his son, if you please," replied Philip; "take no note of grey hairs."

"Well, sir, here he is coming forward," replied the mate, stepping aside and pointing to the captain.

"What is all this?" inquired the captain.

"Are you Philip Vanderdecken, the captain of this vessel?"

"I am, sir," replied the other.

"You appear not to know me! But how can you? you saw me but when I was only three years old; yet may you remember a letter which you gave to your wife."

"Ha!" replied the captain; "and who, then, are you?"

"Time has stopped with you, but with those who live in the world he stops not; and for those who pass a life of misery, he hurries on still faster. In me behold your son, Philip Vanderdecken, who has obeyed your wishes; and, after a life of such peril and misery as few have passed, has at last fulfilled his vow, and now offers to his father the precious relic that he required to kiss."

Philip drew out the relic, and held it towards his father. As if a flash of lightning had passed through his mind, the captain of the vessel started back, clasped his hands, fell on his knees, and wept.

"My son, my son!" exclaimed he, rising and throwing himself into Philip's arms; "my eyes are opened—the Almighty knows how long they have been obscured." Embracing each other, they walked aft, away from the men, who were still crowded at the gangway.

"My son, my noble son, before the charm is broken—before we resolve, as we must, into the elements, oh! let me kneel in thanksgiving and contrition: my son, my noble son, receive a father's thanks," exclaimed Vanderdecken. Then with tears of joy and penitence he humbly addressed himself to that Being, whom he once so awfully defied.

The elder Vanderdecken knelt down: Philip did the same; still embracing each other with one arm, while they raised on high the other, and prayed.

For the last time the relic was taken from the bosom of Philip and handed to his father—and his father raised his eyes to heaven and kissed it. And, as he kissed it, the long tapering upper spars of the Phantom vessel, the yards and sails that were set, fell into dust, fluttered in the air, and sank upon the wave. The mainmast, foremast, bowsprit, everything above the deck, crumbled into atoms and disappeared.

Again he raised the relic to his lips and the work of destruction continued—the heavy iron guns sunk through the decks and disappeared; the crew of the vessel (who were looking on) crumbled down into skeletons, and dust, and fragments of ragged garments; and there were none left on board the vessel in the semblance of life but the father and son.

Once more did he put the sacred emblem to his lips, and the beams and timbers separated, the decks of the vessel slowly sank, and the remnants of the hull floated upon the water; and as the father and son—the one young and vigorous, the other old and decrepit—still kneeling, still embracing, with their hands raised to heaven, sank slowly under the deep blue wave, the lurid sky was for a moment illumined by a lightning cross. Then did the clouds which obscured the heavens roll away swift as thought—the sun again burst out in all his splendour—the rippling waves appeared to dance with joy. The screaming sea-gull again whirled in the air, and the scared albatross once more slumbered on the wing. The porpoise tumbled and tossed in his sportive play, the albicore and dolphin leaped from the sparkling sea.—All nature smiled as if it rejoiced that the charm was dissolved for ever, and that "***The Phantom Ship" Was No More***.

Mr. Midshipman Easy

Chapter One.
Which the reader will find very easy to read.

Mr Nicodemus Easy was a gentleman who lived down in Hampshire; he was a married man, and in very easy circumstances. Most couples find it very easy to have a family, but not always quite so easy to maintain them. Mr Easy was not at all uneasy on the latter score, as he had no children; but he was anxious to have them, as most people covet what they cannot obtain. After ten years, Mr Easy gave it up as a bad job. Philosophy is said to console a man under disappointment, although Shakespeare asserts that it is no remedy for toothache; so Mr Easy turned philosopher, the very best profession a man can take up, when he is fit for nothing else; he must be a very incapable person indeed who cannot talk nonsense. For some time, Mr Easy could not decide upon what description his nonsense should consist of; at last he fixed upon the rights of man, equality, and all that; how every person was born to inherit his share of the earth, a right at present only admitted to a certain length that is, about six feet, for we all inherit our graves, and are allowed to take possession without dispute. But no one would listen to Mr Easy's philosophy. The women would not acknowledge the rights of men, whom they declared always to be in the wrong; and, as the gentlemen who visited Mr Easy were all men of property, they could not perceive the advantages of sharing with those who had none. However, they allowed him to discuss the question, while they discussed his port wine. The wine was good, if the arguments were not, and we must take things as we find them in this world.

While Mr Easy talked philosophy, Mrs Easy played patience, and they were a happy couple, riding side by side on their hobbies, and never interfering with each other. Mr Easy knew his wife could not understand him, and therefore did not expect her to listen very attentively; and Mrs Easy did not care how much her husband talked, provided she was not put out in her game. Mutual forbearance will always ensure domestic felicity.

There was another cause for their agreeing so well. Upon any disputed question Mr Easy invariably gave it up to Mrs Easy, telling her that she should have her own way—and this pleased his wife; but, as Mr Easy always took care, when it came to the point, to have his way, he was pleased as well. It is true that Mrs Easy had long found out that she did not have her own way long; but she was of an easy disposition, and as, in nine cases out of ten, it was of very little consequence how things were done, she was quite satisfied with his submission during the heat of the argument. Mr Easy had admitted that she was right, and if like all men he would do wrong, why what could a poor woman do? With a lady of such a quiet disposition, it is easy to imagine that the domestic felicity of Mr Easy was not easily disturbed. But, as people have observed before, there is a mutability in human affairs. It was at the finale of the eleventh year of their marriage that Mrs Easy at first complained that she could not enjoy her breakfast. Mrs Easy had her own suspicions, everybody else considered it past doubt, all except Mr Easy; he little "thought, good easy man, that his greatness was ripening;" he had decided that to have an heir was no easy task, and it never came into his calculations that there could be a change in his wife's figure. You might have added to it, subtracted from it, divided it, or multiplied it, but as it was a zero, the result would be always the same. Mrs Easy also was not quite sure—she believed it might be the case, there was no saying; it might be a mistake, like that of Mrs Trunnion's in the novel, and, therefore, she said nothing to her husband about the matter. At last Mr Easy opened his eyes, and when, upon interrogating his wife, he found out the astounding truth, he opened his eyes still wider, and then he snapped his fingers, and danced, like a bear upon hot plates, with delight, thereby proving that different causes may produce similar effects in two instances at one and the same time. The bear dances from pain, Mr Easy from pleasure; and again, when we are indifferent, or do not care for anything, we snap our fingers at it, and when we are overjoyed and obtain what we most care for, we also snap our fingers. Two months after Mr Easy snapped his fingers, Mrs Easy felt no inclination to snap hers, either from indifference or pleasure. The fact was, that Mrs Easy's time was come, to undergo what Shakespeare pronounces "the pleasing punishment that women bear;" but Mrs Easy, like the rest of her sex, declared, "that all men were liars," and most particularly poets.

But while Mrs Easy was suffering, Mr Easy was in ecstasies. He laughed at pain, as all philosophers do when it is suffered by other people, and not by themselves.

In due course of time, Mrs Easy presented her husband with a fine boy, whom we present to the public as our hero.

Chapter Two.

In which Mrs Easy, as usual, has her own way.

It was the fourth day after Mrs Easy's confinement that Mr Easy, who was sitting by her bedside in an easy-chair, commenced as follows: "I have been thinking, my dear Mrs Easy, about the name I shall give this child."

"Name, Mr Easy! why, what name should you give it but your own?"

"Not so, my dear," replied Mr Easy; "they call all names proper names, but I think that mine is not. It is the very worst name in the calendar."

"Why, what's the matter with it, Mr Easy?"

"The matter affects me as well as the boy. Nicodemus is a long name to write at full length, and Nick is vulgar. Besides, as there will be two Nicks, they will naturally call my boy young Nick, and of course I shall be styled old Nick, which will be diabolical."

"Well, Mr Easy, at all events then let me choose the name."

"That you shall, my dear, and it was with this view that I have mentioned the subject so early."

"I think, Mr Easy, I will call the boy after my poor father—his name shall be Robert."

"Very well, my dear, if you wish it, it shall be Robert. You shall have your own way. But I think, my dear, upon a little consideration, you will acknowledge that there is a decided objection."

"An objection, Mr Easy?"

"Yes, my dear; Robert may be very well, but you must reflect upon the consequences; he is certain to be called Bob."

"Well, my dear, and suppose they do call him Bob?"

"I cannot bear even the supposition, my dear. You forget the county in which we are residing, the downs covered with sheep."

"Why, Mr Easy, what can sheep have to do with a Christian name?"

"There it is; women never look to consequences. My dear, they have a great deal to do with the name of Bob. I will appeal to any farmer in the county, if ninety-nine shepherds' dogs out of one hundred are not called Bob. Now observe, your child is out of doors somewhere in the fields or plantations; you want and you call him. Instead of your child, what do you find? Why, a dozen curs at least, who come running up to you, all answering to the name of Bob, and wagging their stumps of tails. You see, Mrs Easy, it is a dilemma not to be got over. You level your only son to the brute creation by giving him a Christian name which, from its peculiar brevity, has been monopolised by all the dogs in the county. Any other name you please, my dear, but in this one instance you must allow me to lay my positive veto."

"Well, then, let me see—but I'll think of it, Mr Easy; my head aches very much just now."

"I will think for you, my dear. What do you say to John?"

"Oh, no, Mr Easy, such a common name?"

"A proof of its popularity, my dear. It is scriptural—we have the apostle and the baptist—we have a dozen popes who were all Johns. It is royal—we have plenty of kings who were Johns—and, moreover, it is short, and sounds honest and manly."

"Yes, very true, my dear; but they will call him Jack."

"Well, we have had several celebrated characters who were Jacks. There was—let me see—Jack the Giant Killer, and Jack of the Bean Stalk—and Jack—Jack—"

"Jack Spratt," replied Mrs Easy.

"And Jack Cade, Mrs Easy, the great rebel—and three-fingered Jack, Mrs Easy, the celebrated negro—and, above all, Jack Falstaff, ma'am, Jack Falstaff—honest Jack Falstaff—witty Jack Falstaff—"

"I thought, Mr Easy, that I was to be permitted to choose the name."

"Well, so you shall, my dear; I give it up to you. Do just as you please; but depend upon it that John is the right name. Is it not now, my dear?"

"It's the way you always treat me, Mr Easy; you say that you give it up, and that I shall have my own way, but I never do have it. I am sure that the child will be christened John."

"Nay, my dear, it shall be just what you please. Now I recollect it, there were several Greek emperors who were Johns; but decide for yourself, my dear."

"No, no," replied Mrs Easy, who was ill, and unable to contend any longer, "I give it up, Mr Easy. I know how it will be, as it always is: you give me my own way as people give pieces of gold to children, it's their own money, but they must not spend it. Pray call him John."

"There, my dear, did not I tell you, you would be of my opinion upon reflection? I knew you would. I have given you your own way, and you tell me to call him John; so now we're both of the same mind, and that point is settled."

"I should like to go to sleep, Mr Easy; I feel far from well."

"You shall always do just as you like, my dear," replied the husband, "and have your own way in everything. It is the greatest pleasure I have when I yield to your wishes. I will walk in the garden. Good-bye, my dear."

Mrs Easy made no reply, and the philosopher quitted the room. As may easily be imagined, on the following day the boy was christened John.

Chapter Three.

In which our hero has to wait the issue of an argument.

The reader may observe that, in general, all my first chapters are very short, and increase in length as the work advances. I mention this as a proof of my modesty and diffidence. At first, I am like a young bird just out of its mother's nest, pluming my little feathers and taking short flights. By degrees I obtain more confidence, and wing my course over hill and dale.

It is very difficult to throw any interest into a chapter on childhood. There is the same uniformity in all children until they develop. We cannot, therefore, say much relative to Jack Easy's earliest days; he sucked and threw up his milk, while the nurse blessed it for a pretty dear, slept, and sucked again. He crowed in the morning like a cock, screamed when he was washed, stared at the candle, and made wry faces with the wind. Six months passed in these innocent amusements, and then he was put into shorts. But I ought here to have remarked, that Mrs Easy did not find herself equal to nursing her own infant, and it was necessary to look out for a substitute.

Now a commonplace person would have been satisfied with the recommendation of the medical man, who looks but to the one thing needful, which is a sufficient and wholesome supply of nourishment for the child; but Mr Easy was a philosopher, and had latterly taken to craniology, and he descanted very learnedly with the doctor upon the effect of his only son obtaining his nutriment from an unknown source. "Who knows," observed Mr Easy, "but that my son may not imbibe with his milk the very worst passions of human nature."

"I have examined her," replied the doctor, "and can safely recommend her."

"That examination is only preliminary to one more important," replied Mr Easy. "I must examine her."

"Examine who, Mr Easy?" exclaimed his wife, who had lain down again on the bed.

"The nurse, my dear."

"Examine what, Mr Easy?" continued the lady.

"Her head, my dear," replied the husband. "I must ascertain what her propensities are."

"I think you had better leave her alone, Mr Easy. She comes this evening, and I shall question her pretty severely. Dr Middleton, what do you know of this young person?"

"I know, madam, that she is very healthy and strong, or I should not have selected her."

"But is her character good?"

"Really, madam, I know little about her character; but you can make any inquiries you please. But at the same time I ought to observe, that if you are too particular in that point, you will have some difficulty in providing yourself."

"Well, I shall see," replied Mrs Easy.

"And I shall feel," rejoined the husband.

This parleying was interrupted by the arrival of the very person in question, who was announced by the housemaid, and was ushered in. She was a handsome, florid, healthy-looking girl, awkward and naïve in her manner, and apparently not overwise; there was more of the dove than of the serpent in her composition.

Mr Easy, who was very anxious to make his own discoveries, was the first who spoke. "Young woman, come this way, I wish to examine your head."

"Oh! dear me, sir, it's quite clean, I assure you," cried the girl, dropping a curtsey.

Dr Middleton, who sat between the bed and Mr Easy's chair, rubbed his hands and laughed.

In the meantime, Mr Easy had untied the string and taken off the cap of the young woman, and was very busy putting his fingers through her hair, during which the face of the young woman expressed fear and astonishment.

"I am glad to perceive that you have a large portion of benevolence."

"Yes," replied the young woman, dropping a curtsey.

"And veneration also."

"Thanky, sir."

"And the organ of modesty is strongly developed."

"Yes, sir," replied the girl, with a smile.

"That's quite a new organ," thought Dr Middleton.

"Philo-progenitiveness very powerful."

"If you please, sir, I don't know what that is," answered Sarah, with a curtsey.

"Nevertheless you have given us a practical illustration. Mrs Easy, I am satisfied. Have you any questions to ask? But it is quite unnecessary."

"To be sure, I have, Mr Easy. Pray, young woman, what is your name?"

"Sarah, if you please, ma'am."

"How long have you been married?"

"Married, ma'am?"

"Yes, married."

"If you please, ma'am, I had a misfortune, ma'am," replied the girl, casting down her eyes.

"What, have you not been married?"

"No, ma'am, not yet."

"Good heavens! Dr Middleton, what can you mean by bringing this person here?" exclaimed Mrs Easy. "Not a married woman, and she has a child!"

"If you please, ma'am," interrupted the young woman, dropping a curtsey, "it was a very little one."

"A very little one!" explained Mrs Easy.

"Yes, ma'am, very small indeed, and died soon after it was born."

"Oh, Dr Middleton!—what could you mean, Dr Middleton?"

"My dear madam," exclaimed the doctor, rising from his chair, "this is the only person that I could find suited to the wants of your child, and if you do not take her, I cannot answer for its life. It is true that a married woman might be procured; but married women who have a proper feeling will not desert their own children; and, as Mr Easy asserts, and you appear to imagine, the temper and disposition of your child may be affected by the nourishment it receives, I think it more likely to be injured by the milk of a married woman who will desert her own child for the sake of gain. The misfortune which has happened to this young woman is not always a proof of a bad heart, but of strong attachment, and the overweening confidence of simplicity."

"You are correct, doctor," replied Mr Easy, "and her head proves that she is a modest young woman, with strong religious feeling, kindness of disposition, and every other requisite."

"The head may prove it all for what I know, Mr Easy, but her conduct tells another tale."

"She is well fitted for the situation, ma'am," continued the doctor.

"And if you please, ma'am," rejoined Sarah, "it was *such a little one.*"

"Shall I try the baby, ma'am?" said the monthly nurse, who had listened in silence. "It is fretting so, poor thing, and has its dear little fist right down its throat."

Dr Middleton gave the signal of assent, and in a few seconds Master John Easy was fixed to Sarah as tight as a leech.

"Lord love it, how hungry it is—there, there, stop it a moment, it's choking, poor thing!"

Mrs Easy, who was lying on her bed, rose up, and went to the child. Her first feeling was that of envy, that another should have such a pleasure which was denied to herself, the next that of delight, at the satisfaction expressed by the infant. In a few minutes the child fell back in a deep sleep. Mrs Easy was satisfied; maternal feelings conquered all others, and Sarah was duly installed.

To make short work of it, we have said that Jack Easy in six months was in shorts. He soon afterwards began to crawl and show his legs; indeed, so indecorously, that it was evident that he had imbibed no modesty with Sarah's milk, neither did he appear to have gained veneration or benevolence, for he snatched at everything, squeezed the kitten to death, scratched his mother, and pulled his father by the hair; notwithstanding all which, both his father and mother and the whole household declared him to be the finest and sweetest child in the universe. But if we were to narrate all the wonderful events of Jack's childhood from the time of his birth up to the age of seven years, as chronicled by Sarah, who continued his dry nurse after he had been weaned, it would take at least three volumes folio. Jack was brought up in the way that every only child usually is—that is, he was allowed to have his own way.

Chapter Four.

In which the Doctor prescribes going to school as a remedy for a cut finger.

"Have you no idea of putting the boy to school, Mr Easy?" said Dr Middleton, who had been summoned by a groom with his horse in a foam to attend immediately at Forest Hill, the name of Mr Easy's mansion, and who, upon his arrival, had found that Master Easy had cut his thumb. One would have thought that he had cut his head off by the agitation pervading the whole household—Mr Easy walking up and down very uneasy, Mrs Easy with great difficulty prevented from syncope, and all the maids bustling and passing round Mrs Easy's chair. Everybody appeared excited except Master Jack Easy himself, who, with a rag round his finger, and his pinafore spotted with blood, was playing at bob-cherry, and cared nothing about the matter.

"Well, what's the matter, my little man?" said Dr Middleton, on entering, addressing himself to Jack, as the most sensible of the whole party.

"Oh, Dr Middleton," interrupted Mrs Easy, "he has cut his hand; I am sure that a nerve is divided, and then the lockjaw—"

The doctor made no reply, but examined the finger: Jack Easy continued to play bob-cherry with his right hand.

"Have you such a thing as a piece of sticking-plaster in the house, madam?" observed the doctor, after examination.

"Oh, yes—run, Mary—run, Sarah!" In a few seconds the maids appeared, Sarah bringing the sticking-plaster, and Mary following with the scissors.

"Make yourself quite easy, madam," said Dr Middleton, after he put on the plaster, "I will answer for no evil consequences."

"Had I not better take him upstairs, and let him lie down a little?" replied Mrs Easy, slipping a guinea into the doctor's hand.

"It is not absolutely requisite, madam," said the doctor; "but at all events he will be kept out of more mischief."

"Come, my dear, you hear what Dr Middleton says."

"Yes, I heard," replied Jack; "but I shan't go."

"My dear Johnny—come, love—now do, my dear Johnny."

Johnny played bob-cherry, and made no answer.

"Come, Master Johnny," said Sarah.

"Go away, Sarah," said Johnny, with a back-hander.

"Oh, fie, Master Johnny!" said Mary.

"Johnny, my love," said Mrs Easy, in a coaxing tone, "come now—will you go?"

"I'll go in the garden and get some more cherries," replied Master Johnny.

"Come, then, love, we will go into the garden." Master Johnny jumped off his chair, and took his mamma by the hand.

"What a dear, good, obedient child it is!" exclaimed Mrs Easy: "you may lead him with a thread."

"Yes, to pick cherries," thought Dr Middleton. Mrs Easy, and Johnny, and Sarah, and Mary went into the garden, leaving Dr Middleton alone with Mr Easy, who had been silent during this scene. Now Dr Middleton was a clever, sensible man, who had no wish to impose upon any one. As for his taking a guinea for putting on a piece of sticking-plaster, his conscience was very easy on that score. His time was equally valuable, whether he were employed for something or nothing; and, moreover, he attended the poor gratis. Constantly in the house, he had seen much of Mr John Easy, and perceived that he was a courageous, decided boy, of a naturally good disposition; but from the idiosyncrasy of the father and the doting folly of the mother, in a sure way of being spoiled. As soon, therefore, as the lady was out of hearing, he took a chair, and made the query at the commencement of the chapter, which we shall now repeat.

"Have you no idea of putting the boy to school, Mr Easy?"

Mr Easy crossed his legs, and clasped his hands together over his knees, as he always did when he was about to commence an argument.

"The great objection that I have to sending a boy to school, Dr Middleton, is, that I conceive that the discipline enforced is, not only contrary to the rights of man, but also in opposition to all sound sense and common judgment. Not content with punishment, which is in itself erroneous and an infringement of social justice, they even degrade the minds of the boys still more by applying punishment to the most degraded part, adding contumely to tyranny. Of course it is intended that a boy who is sent to school should gain by precept and example but is he to learn benevolence by the angry look and the flourish of the vindictive birch—or forbearance by the cruelty of the ushers—or patience, when the masters over him are out of all patience—or modesty, when his nether parts are exposed to general examination? Is he not daily reading a lesson at variance with that equality which we all possess, but of which we are unjustly deprived? Why should there be a distinction between the flogger and the flogged? Are they not both fashioned alike after God's image, endowed with the same reason, having an equal right to what the world offers, and which was intended by Providence to be equally distributed? Is it not that the sacred inheritance of all, which has tyrannously and impiously been ravished from the many for the benefit of the few, and which ravishment, from long custom of iniquity and inculcation of false precepts, has too long been basely submitted to? Is it not the duty of a father to preserve his only son from imbibing these dangerous and debasing errors, which will render him only one of a vile herd who are content to suffer, provided that they live? And yet are not these very errors inculcated at school, and impressed upon their mind inversely by the birch? Do not they there receive their first lesson in slavery with the first lesson in A B C; and are not their minds thereby prostrated, so as never to rise again, but ever to bow to despotism, to cringe to rank, to think and act by the precepts of others, and to tacitly disavow that sacred equality which is our birthright? No, sir, without they can teach without resorting to such a fundamental error as flogging, my boy shall never go to school."

And Mr Easy threw himself back in his chair, imagining, like all philosophers, that he had said something very clever.

Dr Middleton knew his man, and therefore patiently waited until he had exhausted his oratory.

"I will grant," said the doctor at last, "that all you say may have great truth in it; but, Mr Easy, do you not think that by not permitting a boy to be educated, you allow him to remain more open to that very error of which you speak? It is only education which will conquer prejudice, and enable a man to break through the trammels of custom. Now, allowing that the birch is used, yet it is at a period when the young mind is so elastic as to soon become indifferent; and after he has attained the usual rudiments of education, you will then find him prepared to receive those lessons which you can yourself instil."

"I will teach him everything myself," replied Mr Easy, folding his arms consequentially and determinedly.

"I do not doubt your capability, Mr Easy; but unfortunately you will always have a difficulty which you never can get over. Excuse me, I know what you are capable of, and the boy would indeed be happy with such a preceptor, but—if I must speak plain—you must be aware as well as I am, that the maternal fondness of Mrs Easy will always be a bar to your intention. He is already so spoiled by her, that he will not obey; and without obedience you cannot inculcate."

"I grant, my dear sir, that there is a difficulty on that point; but maternal weakness must then be overcome by paternal severity."

"May I ask how, Mr Easy, for it appears to be impossible?"

"Impossible! By heavens, I'll make him obey, or I'll—" Here Mr Easy stopped before the word "flog" was fairly out of his mouth—"I'll know the reason why, Dr Middleton."

Dr Middleton checked his inclination to laugh, and replied, "That you would hit upon some scheme, by which you would obtain the necessary power over him, I have no doubt; but what will be the consequence? The boy will consider his mother as a protector, and you as a tyrant. He will have an aversion to you, and with that aversion he will never pay respect and attention to your valuable precepts when he arrives at an age to understand them. Now it appears to me that this difficulty which you have raised may be got over. I know a very worthy clergyman who does not use the birch; but I will write, and put the direct question to him; and then if your boy is removed from the danger arising from Mrs Easy's over-indulgence, in a short time he will be ready for your more important tuition."

"I think," replied Mr Easy, after a pause, "that what you say merits consideration. I acknowledge that in consequence of Mrs Easy's nonsensical indulgence, the boy is unruly, and will not obey me at present; and if your friend does not apply the rod, I will think seriously of sending my son John to him to learn the elements."

The doctor had gained his point by flattering the philosopher.

In a day he returned with a letter from the pedagogue in answer to one supposed to be sent to him, in which the use of the birch was indignantly disclaimed, and Mr Easy announced to his wife, when they met that day at tea-time, his intentions with regard to his son John.

"To school, Mr Easy? what, send Johnny to school! a mere infant to school!"

"Surely, my dear, you must be aware that at nine years it is high time that he learned to read."

"Why he almost reads already, Mr Easy; surely I can teach him that. Does he not, Sarah?"

"Lord bless him, yes, ma'am, he was saying his letters yesterday."

"Oh, Mr Easy, what can have put this in your head? Johnny dear, come here—tell me now what's the letter A. You were singing it in the garden this morning."

"I want some sugar," replied Johnny, stretching his arm over the table to the sugar-basin, which was out of his reach.

"Well, my love, you shall have a great lump if you will tell me what's the letter A."

"A was an archer, and shot at a frog," replied Johnny, in a surly tone.

"There now, Mr Easy; and he can go through the whole alphabet—can't he, Sarah?"

"That he can, the dear—can't you, Johnny dear?"

"No," replied Johnny.

"Yes, you can, my love; you know what's the letter B. Now don't you?"

"Yes," replied Johnny.

"There, Mr Easy, you see what the boy knows, and how obedient he is too. Come, Johnny dear, tell us what was B."

"No, I won't," replied Johnny, "I want some more sugar;" and Johnny, who had climbed on a chair, spread himself over the table to reach it.

"Mercy! Sarah, pull him off—he'll upset the urn," screamed Mrs Easy. Sarah caught hold of Johnny by the loins to pull him back, but Johnny, resisting the interference, turned round on his back as he lay on the table, and kicked Sarah in the face, just as she made another desperate grasp at him. The rebound from the kick, given as he lay on a smooth mahogany table, brought Johnny's head in contact with the urn, which was upset in the opposite direction, and, notwithstanding a rapid movement on the part of Mr Easy, he received a sufficient portion of boiling liquid on his legs to scald him severely, and induce him to stamp and swear in a very unphilosophical way. In the meantime Sarah and Mrs Easy had caught up Johnny, and were both holding him at the same time, exclaiming and lamenting. The pain of the scald and the indifference shown towards him were too much for Mr Easy's temper to put up with. He snatched Johnny out of their arms, and, quite forgetting his equality and rights of man, belaboured him without mercy. Sarah flew in to interfere, and received a blow which not only made her see a thousand stars, but sent her reeling on the floor. Mrs Easy went off into hysterics, and Johnny howled so as to be heard at a quarter of a mile.

How long Mr Easy would have continued it is impossible to say; but the door opened, and Mr Easy looked up while still administering the punishment, and perceived Dr Middleton in mute astonishment. He had promised to come in to tea, and enforce Mr Easy's arguments, if it were necessary; but it certainly appeared to him that in the argument which Mr Easy was then enforcing, he required no assistance. However, at the entrance of Dr Middleton, Johnny was dropped, and lay roaring on the floor; Sarah, too, remained where she had been floored, Mrs Easy had rolled on the floor, the urn was also on the floor, and Mr Easy, although not floored, had not a leg to stand upon.

Never did a medical man look in more opportunely. Mr Easy at first was not certainly of that opinion, but his legs became so painful that he soon became a convert.

Dr Middleton, as in duty bound, first picked up Mrs Easy, and laid her on the sofa. Sarah rose, picked up Johnny, and carried him kicking and roaring out of the room; in return, for which attention she received sundry bites. The footman, who had announced the doctor, picked up the urn, that being all that was in his department. Mr Easy threw himself panting and in agony on the other sofa, and Dr Middleton was excessively embarrassed how to act: he perceived that Mr Easy required his assistance, and that Mrs Easy could do without it; but how to leave a lady who was half really and half pretendedly in hysterics, was difficult; for if he attempted to leave her, she kicked and flounced, and burst out the more. At last Dr Middleton rang the bell, which brought the footman, who summoned all the maids, who carried Mrs Easy upstairs, and then the doctor was able to attend to the only patient who really required his assistance. Mr Easy explained the affair in a few words broken into ejaculations from pain, as the doctor removed his stockings. From the applications of Dr Middleton, Mr Easy soon obtained bodily relief; but what annoyed him still more than his scalded legs, was the doctor having been a witness to his infringement of the equality and rights of man. Dr Middleton perceived this, and he knew also how to pour balm into that wound.

"My dear Mr Easy, I am very sorry that you have had this accident, for which you are indebted to Mrs Easy's foolish indulgence of the boy; but I am glad to perceive that you have taken up those parental duties which are inculcated by the Scriptures. Solomon says, 'that he who spares the rod, spoils the child,' thereby implying that it is the duty of a father to correct his children, and in a father, the so doing does not interfere with the rights of man, or any natural equality, for the son being a part or portion of the father, he is correcting his own self only; and the proof of it is, that a father, in punishing his own son, feels as much pain in so doing as if he were himself punished. It is, therefore, nothing but self-discipline, which is strictly enjoined us by the Scriptures."

"That is exactly my opinion," replied Mr Easy, comforted at the doctor having so logically got him out of the scrape. "But—he shall go to school tomorrow, that I'm determined on."

"He will have to thank Mrs Easy for that," replied the doctor.

"Exactly," replied Mr Easy. "Doctor, my legs are getting very hot again."

"Continue to bathe them with the vinegar and water, Mr Easy, until I send you an embrocation, which will give you immediate relief. I will call tomorrow. By-the-bye, I am to see a little patient at Mr Bonnycastle's: if it is any accommodation, I will take your son with me."

"It will be a great accommodation, doctor," replied Mr Easy.

"Then, my dear sir, I will just go up and see how Mrs Easy is, and to-morrow I will call at ten. I can wait an hour. Good-night."

"Good-night, doctor."

The doctor had his game to play with Mrs Easy. He magnified her husband's accident—he magnified his wrath, and advised her by no means to say one word, until he was well, and more pacified. The next day he repeated this dose, and, in spite of the ejaculations of Sarah, and the tears of Mrs Easy, who dared not venture to plead her cause, and the violent resistance of Master Johnny, who appeared to have a presentiment of what was to come, our hero was put into Dr Middleton's chariot, and with the exception of one plate of glass, which he kicked out of the window with his feet, and for which feat, the doctor, now that he had him all to himself, boxed his ears till he was nearly blind, he was, without any further eventful occurrence, carried by the doctor's footman into the parlour of Mr Bonnycastle.

Chapter Five.

Jack Easy is sent to a school at which there is no flogging.

Master Jack had been plumped down in a chair by the doctor's servant, who, as he quitted him, first looked at his own hands, from which the blood was drawn in several parts, and then at Master Jack, with his teeth closed and lips compressed, as much as to say, "If I only dared, would not I, that's all?" and then walked out of the room, repaired to the carriage at the front door, when he showed his hands to the coachman, who looked down from his box in great commiseration, at the same time fully sharing his fellow-servant's indignation. But we must repair to the parlour. Dr Middleton ran over a newspaper, while Johnny sat on the chair all of a heap, looking like a lump of sulks, with his feet on the upper front bar, and his knees almost up to his nose. He was a promising pupil, Jack.

Mr Bonnycastle made his appearance—a tall, well-built, handsome, fair man, with a fine powdered head, dressed in solemn black, and knee buckles; his linen beautifully clean, and with a peculiar bland expression of countenance. When he smiled he showed a row of teeth white as ivory, and his mild blue eye was the *ne plus ultra* of beneficence. He was the beau-idéal of a preceptor, and it was impossible to see him and hear his mild pleasing voice, without wishing that all your sons were under his protection. He was a ripe scholar, and a good one, and at the time we speak of had the care of upwards of one hundred boys. He was celebrated for turning them out well, and many of his pupils were rising fast in the senate, as well as distinguishing themselves in the higher professions.

Dr Middleton, who was on intimate terms with Bonnycastle, rose as he entered the room, and they shook hands. Middleton then turned to where Jack sat, and pointing to him, said, "Look there."

Bonnycastle smiled. "I cannot say that I have had worse, but I have almost as bad. I will apply the Promethean torch, and soon vivify that rude mass. Come, sit down, Middleton."

"But," said the doctor, as he resumed his chair, "tell me, Bonnycastle, how you will possibly manage to lick such a cub into shape, when you do not resort to flogging?"

"I have no opinion of flogging, and therefore I do not resort to it. The fact is, I was at Harrow myself, and was rather a pickle. I was called up as often as most boys in the school, and I perfectly recollect that eventually I cared nothing for a flogging. I had become case-hardened. It is the least effective part that you can touch a boy upon. It leaves nothing behind to refresh their memory."

"I should have thought otherwise."

"My dear Middleton, I can produce more effect by one caning than twenty floggings. Observe, you flog upon a part for the most part quiescent; but you cane upon all parts, from the head to the heels. Now, when once the first sting of the birch is over, then a dull sensation comes over the part, and the pain after that is nothing; whereas a good sound caning leaves sores and bruises in every part, and on all the parts which are required for muscular action. After a flogging, a boy may run out in the hours of recreation, and join his playmates as well as ever, but a good caning tells a very different tale; he cannot move one part of his body without being reminded for days by the pain of the punishment he has undergone, and he is very careful how he is called up again."

"My dear sir, I really had an idea that you were excessively lenient," replied Middleton, laughing; "I am glad that I am under a mistake."

"Look at that cub, doctor, sitting there more like a brute than a reasonable being; do you imagine that I could ever lick it into shape without strong measures? At the same time, allow me to say, that I consider my system by far the best. At the public schools, punishment is no check; it is so trifling that it is derided: with me punishment is punishment in the true sense of the word, and the consequence is, that it is much more seldom resorted to."

"You are a terrorist, Bonnycastle."

"The two strongest impulses in our nature are fear and love. In theory, acting upon the latter is very beautiful; but in practice, I never found it to answer,—and for the best of reasons, our self-love is stronger than our love for others. Now I never yet found fear to fail, for the very same reason that the other does, because with fear we act upon self-love, and nothing else."

"And yet we have many now who would introduce a system of schooling without correction; and who maintain that the present system is degrading."

"There are a great many fools in this world, doctor."

"That reminds me of this boy's father," replied Dr Middleton; who then detailed to the pedagogue the idiosyncrasy of Mr Easy, and all the circumstances attending Jack being sent to his school.

"There is no time to be lost then, doctor. I must conquer this young gentleman before his parents call to see him. Depend upon it, in a week I will have him obedient and well broke in."

Dr Middleton wished Jack good-bye, and told him to be a good boy. Jack did not vouchsafe to answer. "Never mind, doctor, he will be more polished next time you call here, depend upon it," and the doctor departed.

Although Mr Bonnycastle was severe, he was very judicious. Mischief of all kinds was visited but by slender punishment, such as being kept in at play hours, etcetera; and he seldom interfered with the boys for fighting, although he checked decided oppression. The great *sine quâ non* with him was attention to their studies. He soon discovered the capabilities of his pupils, and he forced them accordingly; but the idle boy, the bird who "could sing and wouldn't sing," received no mercy. The consequence was, that he turned out the cleverest boys, and his conduct was so uniform and unvarying in its tenor, that if he was feared when they were under his control, he was invariably liked by those whom he had instructed, and they continued his friends in after life.

Mr Bonnycastle at once perceived that it was no use coaxing our hero, and that fear was the only attribute by which he could be controlled. So, as soon as Dr Middleton had quitted the room, he addressed him in a commanding tone, "Now, boy, what is your name?"

Jack started; he looked up at his master, perceived his eye fixed upon him, and a countenance not to be played with. Jack was no fool, and somehow or another, the discipline he had received from his father had given him some intimation of what was to come. All this put together induced Jack to condescend to answer, with his forefinger between his teeth, "Johnny."

"And what is your other name, sir?"

Jack, who appeared to repent his condescension, did not at first answer, but he looked again in Mr Bonnycastle's face, and then round the room: there was no one to help him, and he could not help himself, so he replied "Easy."

"Do you know why you are sent to school?"

"Scalding father."

"No; you are sent to learn to read and write."

"But I won't read and write," replied Jack sulkily.

"Yes, you will and you are going to read your letters now directly."

Jack made no answer. Mr Bonnycastle opened a sort of book-case, and displayed to John's astonished view a series of canes, ranged up and down like billiard cues, and continued, "Do you know what those are for?"

Jack eyed them wistfully; he had some faint idea that he was sure to be better acquainted with them but he made no answer.

"They are to teach little boys to read and write, and now I am going to teach you. You'll soon learn. Look now here," continued Mr Bonnycastle, opening a book with large type, and taking a capital at the head of a chapter, about half an inch long. "Do you see that letter?"

"Yes," replied Johnny, turning his eyes away, and picking his fingers.

"Well, that is the letter B. Do you see it? Look at it, so that you may know it again. That's the letter B. Now tell me what that letter is."

Jack now determined to resist, so he made no answer.

"So you cannot tell; well, then, we will try what one of these little fellows will do," said Mr Bonnycastle, taking down a cane. "Observe, Johnny, that's the letter B. Now, what letter is that? Answer me directly."

"I won't learn to read and write."

Whack came the cane on Johnny's shoulders, who burst out into a roar as he writhed with pain.

Mr Bonnycastle waited a few seconds. "That's the letter B. Now tell me, sir, directly, what that letter is."

"I'll tell my *mar*." Whack! "O law! O law!"

"What letter is that?"

Johnny, with his mouth open, panting, and the tears on his cheeks, answered indignantly, "Stop till I tell Sarah."

Whack came the cane again, and a fresh burst from Johnny.

"What letter's that?"

"I won't tell," roared Johnny; "I won't tell—that I won't."

Whack—whack—whack, and a pause. "I told you before, that's the letter B. What letter is that? Tell me directly."

Johnny, by way of reply, made a snatch at the cane. Whack—he caught it, certainly, but not exactly as he would have wished. Johnny then snatched up the book, and dashed it to the corner of the room. Whack, whack. Johnny attempted to seize Mr Bonnycastle with his teeth. Whack, whack, whack, whack; and Johnny fell on the carpet, and roared with pain. Mr Bonnycastle then left him for a little while, to recover himself, and sat down.

At last Johnny's exclamations settled down in deep sobs, and then Mr Bonnycastle said to him, "Now, Johnny, you perceive that you must do as you are bid, or else you will have more beating. Get up immediately. Do you hear, sir?"

Somehow or another, Johnny, without intending it, stood upon his feet.

"That's a good boy; now you see, by getting up as you were bid, you have not been beaten. Now, Johnny, you must go and bring the book from where you threw it down. Do you hear, sir? bring it directly!"

Johnny looked at Mr Bonnycastle and the cane. With every intention to refuse, Johnny picked up the book and laid it on the table.

"That's a good boy; now we will find the letter B. Here it is: now, Johnny, tell me what that letter is."

Johnny made no answer.

"Tell me directly, sir," said Mr Bonnycastle, raising his cane up in the air. The appeal was too powerful. Johnny eyed the cane; it moved, it was coming. Breathlessly he shrieked out, "B!"

"Very well indeed, Johnny—very well. Now your first lesson is over, and you shall go to bed. You have learned more than you think for. To-morrow we will begin again. Now we'll put the cane by."

Mr Bonnycastle rang the bell, and desired Master Johnny to be put to bed, in a room by himself, and not to give him any supper, as hunger would, the next morning, much facilitate his studies. Pain and hunger alone will tame brutes, and the same remedy must be applied to conquer those passions in man which assimilate him with brutes. Johnny was conducted to bed, although it was but six o'clock. He was not only in pain, but his ideas were confused; and no wonder, after all his life having been humoured and indulged—never punished until the day before. After all the caresses of his mother and Sarah, which he never knew the value of—after stuffing himself all day long, and being tempted to eat till he turned away in satiety, to find himself without his mother, without Sarah, without supper—covered with weals, and, what was worse than all, without his own way. No wonder Johnny was confused; at the same time that he was subdued; and, as Mr Bonnycastle had truly told him, he had learned more than he had any idea of. And what would Mrs Easy have said, had she known all this—and Sarah too? And Mr Easy, with his rights of man? At the very time that Johnny was having the devil driven out of him, they were consoling themselves with the idea, that, at all events, there was no birch used at Mr Bonnycastle's, quite losing sight of the fact, that as there are more ways of killing a dog besides hanging him, so are there more ways of teaching than *à posteriori*. Happy in their ignorance, they all went fast asleep, little dreaming that Johnny was already so far advanced in knowledge as to have a tolerable comprehension of the *mystery of cane*. As for Johnny, he had cried himself to sleep at least six hours before them.

Chapter Six.

In which Jack makes essay of his father's sublime philosophy and arrives very near to truth at last.

The next morning Master Jack Easy was not only very sore but very hungry, and as Mr Bonnycastle informed him that he would not only have plenty of cane, but also no breakfast, if he did not learn his letters, Johnny had wisdom enough to say the whole alphabet, for which he received a great deal of praise, the which if he did not duly appreciate, he at all events infinitely preferred to beating. Mr Bonnycastle perceived that he had conquered the boy by one hour's well-timed severity. He therefore handed him over to the ushers in the school, and as they were equally empowered to administer the needful impulse, Johnny very soon became a very tractable boy.

It may be imagined that the absence of Johnny was severely felt at home, but such was not the case. In the first place, Dr Middleton had pointed out to Mrs Easy that there was no flogging at the school, and that the punishment received by Johnny from his father would very likely be repeated—and in the next, although Mrs Easy thought that she never could have survived the parting with her own son, she soon found out that she was much happier without him. A spoiled child is always a source of anxiety and worry, and after Johnny's departure, Mrs Easy found a quiet and repose much more suited to her disposition. Gradually she weaned herself from him, and, satisfied with seeing him occasionally and hearing the reports of Dr Middleton, she at last was quite reconciled to his being at school, and not coming back except during the holidays. John Easy made great progress; he had good natural abilities, and Mr Easy rubbed his hands when he saw the doctor, saying, "Yes, let them have him for a year or two longer, and then I'll finish him myself." Each vacation he had attempted to instil into Johnny's mind the equal rights of man. Johnny appeared to pay but little attention to his father's discourses, but evidently showed that they were not altogether thrown away, as he helped himself to everything he wanted, without asking leave. And thus was our hero educated until he arrived at the age of sixteen, when he was a stout, good-looking boy, with plenty to say for himself,—indeed, when it suited his purpose, he could outtalk his father.

Nothing pleased Mr Easy so much as Jack's loquacity.—"That's right; argue the point, Jack—argue the point, boy," would he say, as Jack disputed with his mother. And then he would turn to the doctor, rubbing his hands, and observe, "Depend upon it, Jack will be a great, a very great man." And then he would call Jack and give him a guinea for his cleverness; and at last Jack thought it a very clever thing to argue. He never would attempt to argue with Mr Bonnycastle, because he was aware that Mr Bonnycastle's arguments were too strong for him, but he argued with all the boys until it ended in a fight which decided the point; and he sometimes argued with the ushers. In short, at the time we now speak of, which was at the breaking up of the Midsummer holidays, Jack was as full of argument as he was fond of it. He would argue the point to the point of a needle, and he would divide that point into as many as there were days of the year, and argue upon each. In short, there was no end to Jack's arguing the point, although there seldom was point to his argument.

Jack had been fishing in the river, without any success, for a whole morning, and observed a large pond which had the appearance of being well stocked—he cleared the park palings, and threw in his line. He had pulled up several fine fish, when he was accosted by the proprietor, accompanied by a couple of keepers.

"May I request the pleasure of your name, young gentleman?" said the proprietor to Jack.

Now Jack was always urbane and polite.

"Certainly, sir; my name is Easy, very much at your service."

"And you appear to me to be taking it very easy," replied the gentleman. "Pray, sir, may I inquire whether you are aware that you are trespassing?"

"The word trespass, my dear sir," replied Jack, "will admit of much argument, and I will divide it into three heads. It implies, accordng to the conventional meaning, coming without permission upon the land or property of another. Now, sir, the question may all be resolved in the following. Was not the world made for all? and has any one, or any portion of its inhabitants an exclusive right to claim any part of it, as his property? If you please, I have laid down the proposition, and we will now argue the point."

The gentleman who accosted Jack had heard of Mr Easy and his arguments; he was a humorist, and more inclined to laugh than to be angry; at the same time he considered it necessary to show Jack that under existing circumstances they were not tenable.

"But, Mr Easy, allowing the trespass on the property to be venial, surely you do not mean to say that you are justified in taking my fish; I bought the fish, and stocked the pond, and have fed them ever since. You cannot deny but that they are private property, and that to take them is a theft?"

"That will again admit of much ratiocination, my dear sir," replied Jack; "but—I beg your pardon, I have a fish." Jack pulled up a large carp, much to the indignation of the keepers and to the amusement of their master, unhooked it, placed it in his basket, renewed his bait with the greatest *sang froid*, and then throwing in his line, resumed his discourse. "As I was observing, my dear sir," continued Jack, "that will admit of much ratiocination. All the creatures of the earth were given to man for his use—man means mankind—they were never intended to be made a monopoly of. Water is also the gift of heaven, and meant for the use of all. We now come to the question how far the fish are your property. If the fish only bred on purpose to please you, and make you a present of their stock, it might then require a different line of argument; but as in breeding they only acted in obedience to an instinct with which they are endowed on purpose that they may supply man, I submit to you that you cannot prove these fish to be yours more than mine. As for feeding with the idea that they were your own, that is not an unusual case in this world, even when a man is giving bread and butter to his children. Further—but I have another bite—I beg your pardon, my dear sir. Ah! he's off again—"

"Then, Mr Easy, you mean to say that the world and its contents are made for all."

"Exactly, sir, that is my father's opinion, who is a very great philosopher."

"How then does your father account for some possessing property and others being without it?"

"Because those who are the strongest have deprived those who are weaker."

"But would not that be always the case even if we were in that state of general inheritance which you have supposed. For instance, allowing two men to chase the same animal, and both to come up to it at the same time, would not the strongest bear it off?"

"I grant that, sir."

"Well, then, where is your equality?"

"That does not disprove that men were not intended to be equal; it only proves that they are not so. Neither does it disprove that everything was not made for the benefit of all; it only proves that the strong will take advantage of the weak, which is very natural."

"Oh! you grant that to be very natural.—Well, Mr Easy, I am glad to perceive that we are of one mind, and I trust we shall continue so. You'll observe that I and my keepers being three, we are the strong party in this instance, and admitting your argument, that the fish are as much yours as mine, still I take advantage of my strength to repossess myself of them, which is, as you say, very natural.—James, take those fish."

"If you please," interrupted Jack, "we will argue that point—"

"Not at all; I will act according to your own arguments—I have the fish, but I now mean to have more—that fishing-rod is as much mine as yours, and being the stronger party, I will take possession of it.—James, William, take that fishing-rod—it is ours."

"I presume you will first allow me to observe," replied Jack, "that although I have expressed my opinion that the earth and the animals on it were made for us all, that I never yet have asserted that what a man creates by himself, or has created for him for a consideration, is not his own property."

"I beg your pardon; the trees that that rod was made from were made for us all, and if you, or any one for you, have thought proper to make it into a rod, it is no more my fault than it is that I have been feeding the fish with the supposition that they were my own. Everything being common, and it being but natural that the strong should take advantage of the weak, I must take that rod as my property, until I am dispossessed by one more powerful. Moreover, being the stronger party, and having possession of this land, which you say does not belong to me more than to you—I also shall direct my keepers to see you off this property. James, take the rod—see Mr Easy over the park palings. Mr Easy, I wish you a good morning."

"Sir, I beg your pardon, you have not yet heard all my arguments," replied Jack, who did not approve of the conclusions drawn.

"I have no time to hear more, Mr Easy: I wish you a good morning." And the proprietor departed, leaving Jack in company with the keepers.

"I'll trouble you for that rod, master," said William. James was very busy stringing the fish through the gills upon a piece of osier.

"At all events you will hear reason," said Jack. "I have arguments—"

"I never heard no good arguments in favour of poaching," interrupted the keeper.

"You're an insolent fellow," replied Jack. "It is by paying such vagabonds as you that people are able to be guilty of injustice."

"It's by paying us that the land an't poached—and if there be some excuse for a poor devil who is out of work, there be none for you, who call yourself a gentleman."

"According to his 'count, as we be all equal, he be no more a gentleman than we be."

"Silence, you blackguard, I shall not condescend to argue with such as you: if I did I could prove that you are a set of base slaves, who have just as much right to this property as your master or I have."

"As you have, I dare say, master."

"As I have, you scoundrel; this pond is as much my property, and so are the fish in it, as they are of your master, who has usurped the right."

"I say, James, what do you say, shall we put the young gentleman in possession of his property?" said William, winking to the other.

William took the hint; they seized Jack by the arms and legs, and soused him into the pond. Jack arose after a deep submersion, and floundered on shore blowing and spluttering. But in the meantime the keepers had walked away, carrying with them the rod and line, fish, and tin-can of bait, laughing loudly at the practical joke which they had played our hero.

"Well," thought Jack, "either here must be some mistake in my father's philosophy, or else this is a very wicked world. I shall submit this case to my father."

And Jack received this reply—"I have told you before, Jack, that these important truths will not at present be admitted—but it does not the less follow that they are true. This is the age of iron, in which might has become right—but the time will come when these truths will be admitted, and your father's name will be more celebrated than that of any philosopher of ancient days. Recollect, Jack, that although in preaching against wrong and advocating the rights of man, you will be treated as a martyr, it is still your duty to persevere; and if you are dragged through all the horse-ponds in the kingdom, never give up your argument."

"That I never will, sir," replied Jack; "but the next time I argue it shall be, if possible, with power on my side, and, at all events, not quite so near a pond."

"I think," said Mrs Easy, who had been a silent listener, "that Jack had better fish in the river, and then, if he catches no fish, at all events he will not be soused in the water, and spoil his clothes."

But Mrs Easy was no philosopher.

A few days afterwards, Jack discovered, one fine morning, on the other side of a hedge, a summer apple-tree bearing tempting fruit, and he immediately broke through the hedge, and climbing the tree, as our first mother did before him, he culled the fairest and did eat.

"I say, you sir, what are you doing there?" cried a rough voice.

Jack looked down, and perceived a stout, thick-set personage in grey coat and red waistcoat, standing underneath him.

"Don't you see what I'm about," replied Jack, "I'm eating apples—shall I throw you down a few?"

"Thank you kindly—the fewer that are pulled the better; perhaps, as you are so free to give them to others as well as to help yourself, you may think that they are your own property!"

"Not a bit more my property than they are yours, my good man."

"I guess that's something like the truth; but you are not quite at the truth yet, my lad; those apples are mine, and I'll trouble you to come down as fast as you please; when you're down we can then settle our accounts; and," continued the man, shaking his cudgel, "depend upon it you shall have your receipt in full."

Jack did not much like the appearance of things.

"My good man," said he, "it is quite a prejudice on your part to imagine that apples were not given, as well as all other fruit, for the benefit of us all—they are common property, believe me."

"That's a matter of opinion, my lad, and I may be allowed to have my own."

"You'll find it in the Bible," says Jack.

"I never did yet, and I've read it through and through all, bating the 'Pocryfar."

"Then," said Jack, "go home and fetch the Bible, and I'll prove it to you."

"I suspect you'll not wait till I come back again. No, no; I have lost plenty of apples, and have long wanted to find the robbers out; now I've caught one I'll take care that he don't 'scape without apple-sauce, at all events—so come down, you young thief, come down directly—or it will be all the worse for you."

"Thank you," said Jack, "but I am very well here. I will, if you please, argue the point from where I am."

"I've no time to argue the point, my lad; I've plenty to do, but do not think I'll let you off. If you don't choose to come down, why then you may stay there, and I'll answer for it, as soon as work is done I shall find you safe enough."

"What can be done," thought Jack, "with a man who will not listen to argument? What a world is this!—however, he'll not find me here when he comes back, I've a notion."

But in this Jack was mistaken. The farmer walked to the hedge, and called to a boy, who took his orders and ran to the farm-house. In a minute or two a large bull-dog was seen bounding along the orchard to his master. "Mark him, Caesar," said the farmer to the dog, "mark him." The dog crouched down on the grass, with his head up, and eyes glaring at Jack, showing a range of teeth, that drove all our hero's philosophy out of his head.

"I can't wait here, but Caesar can, and I will tell you, as a friend, that if he gets hold of you, he'll not leave a limb of you together—when work's done I'll come back." So saying, the farmer walked off, leaving Jack and the dog to argue the point, if so inclined. What a sad jade must philosophy be, to put her votaries in such predicaments!

After a while the dog laid his head down and closed his eyes as if asleep, but Jack observed, that at the least movement on his part one eye was seen to partially unclose; so Jack, like a prudent man, resolved to remain where he was. He picked a few more apples, for it was his dinner-time, and as he chewed he ruminated.

Jack had been but a few minutes ruminating before he was interrupted by another ruminating animal, no less a personage than a bull, who had been turned out with full possession of the orchard, and who now advanced, bellowing occasionally, and tossing his head at the sight of Caesar, whom he considered as much a trespasser as his master had our hero. Caesar started on his legs and faced the bull, who advanced pawing, with his tail up in the air. When within a few yards the bull made a rush at the dog, who evaded him and attacked him in return, and thus did the warfare continue until the opponents were already at some distance from the apple-tree. Jack prepared for immediate flight, but unfortunately the combat was carried on by the side of the hedge at which Jack had gained admission. Never mind, thought Jack, there are two sides to every field, and although the other hedge joined on to the garden near to the farm-house, there was no option. "At all events," said Jack, "I'll try it." Jack was slipping down the trunk, when he heard a tremendous roar; the bull-dog had been tossed by the bull; he was then high in the air, and Jack saw him fall on the other side of the hedge; and the bull was thus celebrating his victory with a flourish of trumpets. Upon which Jack, perceiving that he was relieved from his sentry, slipped down the rest of the tree and took to his heels. Unfortunately for Jack, the bull saw him, and, flushed with victory, he immediately set up another roar, and bounded after Jack. Jack perceived his danger, and fear gave him wings; he not only flew over the orchard, but he flew over the hedge, which was about five feet high, just as the bull drove his head into it. "Look before you leap," is an old proverb. Had Jack done so, he would have done better; but as there were cogent reasons to be offered in extenuation of our philosopher, we shall say no more, but merely state that Jack, when he got on the other side of the hedge, found that he had pitched into a small apiary, and had upset two hives of bees, who resented the intrusion; and Jack had hardly time to get upon his legs before he found them very busy stinging him in all quarters. All that Jack could do was to run for it, but the bees flew faster than he could run, and Jack was mad with pain, when he stumbled, half-blinded, over the brickwork of a well. Jack could not stop his pitching into the well, but he seized the iron chain as it struck him across the face. Down went Jack, and round went the windlass, and after a rapid descent of forty feet our hero found himself under water, and no longer troubled with the bees, who, whether they had lost scent of their prey from his rapid descent, or being notoriously clever insects, acknowledged the truth of the adage, "leave well alone," had certainly left Jack with no other companion than Truth. Jack rose from his immersion, and seized the rope to which the chain of the bucket was made fast—it had all of it been unwound from the windlass, and therefore it enabled Jack to keep his head above water. After a few seconds Jack felt something against his legs, it was the bucket, about two feet under the water; Jack put his feet into it and found himself pretty comfortable, for the water, after the sting of the bees and the heat he had been put into by the race with the bull, was quite cool and refreshing.

"At all events," thought Jack, "if it had not been for the bull, I should have been watched by the dog, and then thrashed by the farmer; but then again, if it had not been for the bull, I should not have tumbled among the bees; and if it had not been for the bees, I should not have tumbled into the well; and if it had not been for the chain, I should have been drowned. Such has been the chain of events, all because I wanted to eat an apple."

"However, I have got rid of the farmer, and the dog, and the bull, and the bees—all's well that ends well but how the devil am I to get out of the well?—All creation appears to have conspired against the rights of man. As my father said, this is an iron age, and here I am swinging to an iron chain."

We have given the whole of Jack's soliloquy, as it will prove that Jack was no fool, although he was a bit of a philosopher; and a man who could reason so well upon cause and effect, at the bottom of a well up to his neck in water, showed a good deal of presence of mind. But if Jack's mind had been a little twisted by his father's philosophy, it had still sufficient strength and elasticity to recover itself in due time. Had Jack been a common personage, we should never have selected him for our hero.

Chapter Seven.

In which Jack makes some very sage reflections, and comes to a very unwise decision.

After all, it must be acknowledged that although there are cases of distress in which a well may become a place of refuge, a well is not at all calculated for a prolonged residence—so thought Jack. After he had been there some fifteen minutes, his teeth chattered, and his limbs trembled; he felt a numbness all over, and he thought it high time to call for assistance, which at first he would not, as he was afraid he should be pulled up to encounter the indignation of the farmer and his family. Jack was arranging his jaws for a halloo, when he felt the chain pulled up, and he slowly emerged from the water. At first he heard complaints of the weight of the bucket, at which Jack was not surprised, then he heard a tittering and laughing between two parties, and soon afterwards he mounted up gaily. At last his head appeared above the low wall, and he was about to extend his arms so as to secure a position on it, when those who were working at the windlass beheld him. It was a heavy farming-man and a maid-servant.

"Thank you," said Jack.

One never should be too quick in returning thanks; the girl screamed and let go the winch; the man, frightened, did not hold it fast: it slipped from his grasp, whirled round, struck him under the chin and threw him over it headlong, and before the "Thank you" was fairly out of Jack's lips, down he went again like lightning to the bottom. Fortunately for Jack, he had not yet let go the chain, or he might have struck the sides and have been killed; as it was, he was merely soused a second time, and in a minute or two regained his former position.

"This is mighty pleasant," thought Jack, as he clapped his wet hat once more on his head: "at all events, they can't now plead ignoranc; they must know that I'm here."

In the meantime the girl ran into the kitchen, threw herself down on a stool, from which she reeled off in a fit upon sundry heaps of dough waiting to be baked in the oven, which were laid to rise on the floor before the fire.

"Mercy on me, what is the matter with Susan?" exclaimed the farmer's wife. "Here—where's Mary—where's John?—Deary me, if the bread won't all be turned to pancakes."

John soon followed, holding his under-jaw in his hand, looking very dismal and very frightened, for two reasons; one, because he thought that his jaw was broken, and the other, because he thought he had seen the devil.

"Mercy on us, what is the matter?" exclaimed the farmer's wife again. "Mary, Mary, Mary!" screamed she, beginning to be frightened herself, for with all her efforts she could not remove Susan from the bed of dough, where she lay senseless and heavy as lead. Mary answered to her mistress's loud appeal, and with her assistance they raised up Susan; but as for the bread, there was no hopes of it ever rising again. "Why don't you come here and help Susan, John?" cried Mary.

"Aw-yaw-aw!" was all the reply of John, who had had quite enough of helping Susan, and who continued to hold his head, as it were, in his hand.

"What's the matter here, missus?" exclaimed the farmer, coming in. "Highty-tighty, what ails Susan, and what ails you?" continued the farmer, turning to John. "Dang it, but everything seems to go wrong this blessed day. First there be all the apples stolen—then there be all the hives turned topsy-turvy in the garden—then there be Caesar with his flank opened by the bull—then there be the bull broken through the hedge and tumbled into the saw-pit—and now I come to get more help to drag him out, I find one woman dead like, and John looks as if he had seen the devil."

"Aw-yaw-aw!" replied John, nodding his head very significantly.

"One would think that the devil had broke loose to-day. What is it, John? Have you seen him, and has Susan seen him?"

"Aw-yaw."

"He's stopped your jaw, then, at all events, and I thought the devil himself wouldn't have done that—we shall get nothing of you. Is that wench coming to her senses?"

"Yes, yes, she's better now.—Susan, what's the matter?"

"Oh, oh, ma'am! the well, the well—"

"The well! Something wrong there, I suppose: well, I will go and see."

The farmer trotted off to the well; he perceived the bucket was at the bottom and all the rope out; he looked about him, and then he looked into the well. Jack, who had become very impatient, had been looking up some time for the assistance which he expected would have come sooner; the round face of the farmer occasioned a partial eclipse of the round disc which bounded his view, just as one of the satellites of Jupiter sometimes obscures the face of the planet round which he revolves.

"Here I am," cried Jack, "get me up quick, or I shall be dead;" and what Jack said was true, for he was quite done up by having been so long down, although his courage had not failed him.

"Dang it, but there be somebody fallen into the well," cried the farmer; "no end to mishaps this day. Well, we must get a Christian out of a well afore we get a bull out of a saw-pit, so I'll go call the men."

In a very short time the men who were assembled round the saw-pit were brought to the well.

"Down below there, hold on now."

"Never fear," cried Jack.

Away went the winch, and once more Jack had an extended horizon to survey. As soon as he was at the top, the men hauled him over the bricks and laid him down upon the ground, for Jack's strength had failed him.

"Dang it, if it bean't that chap who was on my apple-tree," cried the farmer—"howsomever, he must not die for stealing a few apples; lift him up, lads, and take him in—he is dead with cold—no wonder."

The farmer led the way, and the men carried Jack into the house, when the farmer gave him a glass of brandy; this restored Jack's circulation, and in a short time he was all right again.

After some previous conversation, in which Jack narrated all that had happened, "What may be your name?" inquired the farmer.

"My name is Easy," replied Jack.

"What, be you the son of Mr Easy, of Forest Hill?"

"Yes."

"Dang it, he be my landlord, and a right good landlord too—why didn't you say so when you were up in the apple-tree? You might have picked the whole orchard and welcome."

"My dear sir," replied Jack, who had taken a second glass of brandy, and was quite talkative again, "let this be a warning to you, and when a man proposes to argue the point, always, in future, listen. Had you waited, I would have proved to you most incontestably that you had no more right to the apples than I had; but you would not listen to argument, and without discussion we can never arrive at truth. You send for your dog, who is ripped up by the bull—the bull breaks his leg in a saw-pit—the bee-hives are overturned and you lose all your honey—your man John breaks his jaw—your maid Susan spoils all the bread—and why? because you would not allow me to argue the point."

"Well, Mr Easy, it be all true that all these mishaps have happened because I would not allow you to argue the point, perhaps, although, as I rent the orchard from your father, I cannot imagine how you could have proved to me that the apples were not mine; but now, let's take your side of the question, and I don't see how you be much better off. You get up in a tree for a few apples, with plenty of money to buy them if you like—you are kept there by a dog—you are nearly gored by a bull—you are stung by the bees, and you tumble souse into a well, and are nearly killed a dozen times, and all for a few apples not worth twopence."

"All very true, my good man," replied Jack; "but you forget that I, as a philosopher, was defending the rights of man."

"Well, I never knew before that a lad who stole apples was called a philosopher—we calls it petty larceny in the indictments; and as for your rights of man, I cannot see how they can be defended by doing what's wrong."

"You do not comprehend the matter, farmer."

"No, I don't—and I be too old to learn, Master Easy. All I have to say is this, you are welcome to all the apples in the orchard if you please, and if you prefers, as it seems you do, to steal them, instead of asking for them, which I only can account for by the reason that they say, that 'stolen fruit be sweetest,' I've only to say that I shall give orders that you be not interfered with. My chaise be at the door, Master Easy, and the man will drive you to your father's—make my compliments to him, and say that I'm very sorry that you tumbled into our well."

As Jack was much more inclined for bed than argument, he wished the farmer good-night, and allowed himself to be driven home.

The pain from the sting of the bees, now that his circulation had fully returned, was so great, that he was not sorry to find Dr Middleton taking his tea with his father and mother. Jack merely said that he had been so unfortunate as to upset a hive, and had been severely stung. He deferred the whole story till another opportunity. Dr Middleton prescribed for Jack, but on taking his hand found that he was in a high fever, which, after the events of the day, was not to be wondered at. Jack was bled, and kept his bed for a week, by which time he was restored; but during that time Jack had been thinking very seriously, and had made up his mind.

But we must explain a circumstance which had occurred, which was probably the cause of Jack's decision. When Jack returned on the evening in question, he found seated with his father and Dr Middleton, a Captain Wilson, a sort of cousin to the family, who but occasionally paid them a visit, for he lived at some distance; and having a wife and large family, with nothing but his half-pay for their support, he could not afford to expend even shoe-leather in compliments. The object of this visit on the part of Captain Wilson was to request the aid of Mr Easy. He had succeeded in obtaining his appointment to a sloop of war (for he was in the king's service), but was without the means of fitting himself out, without leaving his wife and family penniless. He therefore came to request Mr Easy to lend him a few hundred pounds, until he should be able, by his prize-money, to repay them. Mr Easy was not a man to refuse such a request, and, always having plenty of spare cash at his banker's, he drew a cheque for a thousand pounds, which he gave to Captain Wilson, requesting that he would only repay it at his convenience. Captain Wilson wrote an acknowledgment of the debt, promising to pay upon his first prize-money, which receipt, however binding it may be to a man of honour, was, in point of law, about as valuable as if he had agreed to pay as soon "as the cows came home." The affair had been just concluded, and Captain Wilson had returned into the parlour with Mr Easy, when Jack returned from his expedition.

Jack greeted Captain Wilson, whom he had long known; but, as we before observed, he suffered so much pain, that he soon retired with Dr Middleton, and went to bed.

During a week there is room for much reflection, even in a lad of fourteen, although at that age we are not much inclined to think. But Jack was in bed; his eyes were so swollen with the stings of the bees that he could neither read nor otherwise amuse himself; and he preferred his own thoughts to the gabble of Sarah, who attended him. So Jack thought, and the result of his cogitations we shall soon bring forward.

It was on the eighth day that Jack left his bed and came down into the drawing-room. He then detailed to his father the adventures which had taken place, which had obliged him to take to his bed.

"You see, Jack," replied his father, "it's just what I told you: the world is so utterly demoralised by what is called social compact, and the phalanx supporting it by contributing a portion of their unjust possessions for the security of the remainder, is so powerful, that any one who opposes it, must expect to pass the life of a martyr; but martyrs are always required previous to any truth, however sublime, being received, and, like Abraham, whom I have always considered as a great philosopher, I am willing to sacrifice my only son in so noble a cause."

"That's all very good on your part, father, but we must argue the point a little. If you are as great a philosopher as Abraham, I am not quite so dutiful a son as Isaac, whose blind obedience, in my opinion, is very contrary to your rights of man: but the fact, in few words, is simply this. In promulgating your philosophy, in the short space of two days, I have been robbed of the fish I caught, and my rod and line—I have been soused into a fish-pond—I have been frightened out of my wits by a bull-dog—been nearly killed by a bull—been stung to death by bees, and twice tumbled into a well. Now, if all that happens in two days, what must I expect to suffer in a whole year? It appears to be very unwise to attempt making further converts, for people on shore seem determined not to listen to reason or argument. But it has occurred to me, that although the whole earth has been so nefariously divided among the few, that the waters at least are the property of all. No man claims his share of the sea—every one may there plough as he pleases, without being taken up for a trespasser. Even war makes no difference; every one may go on as he pleases, and if they meet, it is nothing but a neutral ground on which the parties contend. It is, then, only upon the ocean that I am likely to find that equality and rights of man, which we are so anxious to establish on shore; and therefore I have resolved not to go to school again, which I detest, but to go to sea, and propagate our opinions as much as I can."

"I cannot listen to that, Jack. In the first place, you must return to school; in the next place, you shall not go to sea."

"Then, father, all I have to say is, that I swear by the rights of man I will not go back to school, and that I will go to sea. Who and what is to prevent me? Was not I born my own master?—has any one a right to dictate to me as if I were not his equal? Have I not as much right to my share of the sea as any other mortal? I stand upon perfect equality," continued Jack, stamping his right foot on the floor.

What had Mr Easy to offer in reply? He must either, as a philosopher, have sacrificed his hypothesis, or, as a father, have sacrificed his son. Like all philosophers, he preferred what he considered as the less important of the two, he sacrificed *his* son; but—we will do him justice—he did it with a sigh.

"Jack, you shall, if you wish it, go to sea."

"That, of course," replied Jack, with the air of a conqueror, "but the question is, with whom? Now it has occurred to me that Captain Wilson has just been appointed to a ship, and I should like to sail with him."

"I will write to him," said Mr Easy mournfully, "but I should have liked to have felt his head first;" and thus was the matter arranged.

The answer from Captain Wilson was, of course, in the affirmative, and he promised that he would treat Jack as his own son.

Our hero mounted his father's horse, and rode off to Mr Bonnycastle.

"I am going to sea, Mr Bonnycastle."

"The very best thing for you," replied Mr Bonnycastle.

Our hero met Dr Middleton.

"I am going to sea, Dr Middleton."

"The very best thing for you," replied the doctor.

"I am going to sea, mother," said John.

"To sea, John, to sea? no, no, dear John, you are not going to sea," replied Mrs Easy, with horror.

"Yes, I am; father has agreed, and says he will obtain your consent."

"My consent! Oh, my dear, dear boy!"—and Mrs Easy wept bitterly, as Rachel mourning for her children.

Chapter Eight.

In which Mr Easy has his first lesson as to zeal in His Majesty's Service.

As there was no time to lose, our hero very soon bade adieu to his paternal roof, as the phrase is, and found his way down to Portsmouth. As Jack had plenty of money, and was very much pleased at finding himself his own master, he was in no hurry to join his ship, and five or six companions not very creditable, whom either Jack had picked up, or had picked up Jack, and who lived upon him, strongly advised him to put it off until the very last moment. As this advice happened to coincide with Jack's opinion, our hero was three weeks at Portsmouth before any one knew of his arrival, but at last Captain Wilson received a letter from Mr Easy, by which he found that Jack had left home at the period we have mentioned, and he desired the first-lieutenant to make inquiries, as he was afraid that some accident might have happened to him. As Mr Sawbridge, the first-lieutenant, happened to be going on shore on the same evening for the last time previous to the ship's sailing, he looked into the Blue Posts, George, and Fountain Inns, to inquire if there was such a person arrived as Mr Easy. "Oh, yes," replied the waiter at the Fountain—"Mr Easy has been here these three weeks."

"The devil he has," roared Mr Sawbridge, with all the indignation of a first-lieutenant defrauded three weeks of a midshipman; "where is he; in the coffee-room?"

"Oh dear no, sir," replied the waiter, "Mr Easy has the front apartments on the first floor."

"Well, then, show me up to the first floor."

"May I request the pleasure of your name, sir?" said the waiter.

"First-lieutenants don't send up their names to midshipmen," replied Mr Sawbridge; "he shall soon know who I am."

At this reply the waiter walked upstairs, followed by Mr Sawbridge, and threw open the door.

"A gentleman wishes to see you, sir," said the waiter.

"Desire him to walk in," said Jack: "and, waiter, mind that the punch is a little better than it was yesterday; I have asked two more gentlemen to dine here."

In the meantime Mr Sawbridge, who was not in his uniform, had entered, and perceived Jack alone, with the dinner-table laid out in the best style for eight, a considerable show of plate for even the Fountain Inn, and everything, as well as the apartment itself, according to Mr Sawbridge's opinion, much more fit for a commander-in-chief than a midshipman of a sloop of war.

Now Mr Sawbridge was a good officer, one who had really worked his way up to the present rank, that is to say, that he had served seven-and-twenty years, and had nothing but his pay. He was a little soured in the service, and certainly had an aversion to the young men of family who were now fast crowding into it—and with some grounds, as he perceived his own chance of promotion decrease in the same ratio as the numbers increased. He considered that in proportion as midshipmen assumed a cleaner and more gentlemanly appearance, so did they become more useless, and it may therefore be easily imagined that his bile was raised by this parade and display in a lad, who was very shortly to be, and ought three weeks before to have been, shrinking from his frown. Nevertheless, Sawbridge was a good-hearted man, although a little envious of luxury, which he could not pretend to indulge in himself.

"May I beg to ask," said Jack, who was always remarkably polite and gentlemanly in his address, "in what manner I may be of service to you?"

"Yes, sir, you may—by joining your ship immediately. And may I beg to ask in return, sir, what is the reason you have stayed on shore three weeks without joining her?"

Hereupon Jack, who did not much admire the peremptory tone of Mr Sawbridge, and who during the answer had taken a seat, crossed his legs and played with the gold chain to which his watch was secured, after a pause very coolly replied:

"And pray, who are you?"

"Who am I, sir?" replied Sawbridge, jumping out of his chair—"my name is Sawbridge, sir, and I am the first-lieutenant of the *Harpy*. Now, sir, you have your answer."

Mr Sawbridge, who imagined that the name of the first-lieutenant would strike terror to a culprit midshipman, threw himself back in the chair, and assumed an air of importance.

"Really, sir," replied Jack, "what may be your exact situation on board, my ignorance of the service will not allow me to guess, but if I may judge from your behaviour, you have no small opinion of yourself."

"Look ye, young man, you may not know what a first-lieutenant is, and I take it for granted that you do not, by your behaviour; but depend upon it, I'll let you know very soon. In the meantime, sir, I insist upon it, that you go immediately on board."

"I'm sorry that I cannot comply with your very moderate request," replied Jack coolly. "I shall go on board when it suits my convenience, and I beg that you will give yourself no further trouble on my account."

Jack then rang the bell; the waiter, who had been listening outside, immediately entered, and before Mr Sawbridge, who was dumb with astonishment at Jack's impertinence, could have time to reply:

"Waiter," said Jack, "show this gentleman downstairs."

"By the god of war!" exclaimed the first-lieutenant, "but I'll soon show you down to the boat, my young bantam; and when once I get you safe on board, I'll make you know the difference between a midshipman and a first-lieutenant."

"I can only admit of *equality*, sir," replied Jack; "we are all born equal—I trust you'll allow that."

"Equality—damn it, I suppose you'll take the command of the ship. However, sir, your ignorance will be a little enlightened by-and-by. I shall now go and report your conduct to Captain Wilson; and I tell you plainly, that if you are not on board this evening, to-morrow morning, at daylight, I shall send a sergeant, and a file of marines, to fetch you."

"You may depend upon it, sir," replied Jack, "that I also shall not fail to mention to Captain Wilson that I consider you a very quarrelsome, impertinent fellow, and recommend him not to allow you to remain on board. It will be quite uncomfortable to be in the same ship with such an ungentlemanly bear."

"He must be mad—quite mad," exclaimed Sawbridge, whose astonishment even mastered his indignation. "Mad as a March hare—by God."

"No, sir," replied Jack, "I am not mad, but I am a philosopher."

"A *what*?" exclaimed Sawbridge, "damme, what next?—well, my joker, all the better for you; I shall put your philosophy to the proof."

"It is for that very reason, sir," replied Jack, "that I have decided upon going to sea: and if you do remain on board, I hope to argue the point with you, and make you a convert to the truth of equality and the rights of man."

"By the Lord that made us both, I'll soon make you a convert to the thirty-six articles of war—that is, if you remain on board; but I shall now go to the captain, and report your conduct, sir, and leave you to your dinner with what appetite you may."

"Sir, I am infinitely obliged to you; but you need not be afraid of my appetite; I am only sorry, as you happen to belong to the same ship, that I cannot, in justice to the gentlemanly young men whom I expect, ask you to join them. I wish you a very good morning, sir."

"Twenty years have I been in the service," roared Sawbridge, "and, damme,—but he's mad—downright, stark, staring mad." And the first-lieutenant bounced out of the room.

Jack was a little astonished himself. Had Mr Sawbridge made his appearance in uniform it might have been different, but that a plain-looking man, with black whiskers, shaggy hair, and old blue frock-coat and yellow casimere waistcoat, should venture to address him in such a manner, was quite incomprehensible;—he calls me mad, thought Jack, I shall tell Captain Wilson what is my opinion about his lieutenant. Shortly afterwards, the company arrived, and Jack soon forgot all about it.

In the meantime, Sawbridge called at the captain's lodgings, and found him at home: he made a very faithful report of all that had happened, and concluded his requests by demanding, in great wrath, either an instant dismissal or a court-martial on our hero, Jack.

"Stop, Sawbridge," replied Captain Wilson, "take a chair. As Mr Easy says, we must argue the point, and then I will leave it to your better feelings. As for the court-martial, it will not hold good, for Mr Easy, in the first place, has not yet joined the ship, and in the next place, could not be supposed to know that you were the first-lieutenant, or even an officer, for you went to him out of uniform."

"Very true, sir," replied Sawbridge, "I had forgotten that."

"Then, as for his dismissal, or rather, not allowing him to join, Mr Easy has been brought up in the country, and has never seen anything aquatic larger than a fish-pond, perhaps, in his life; and as for the service, or the nature of it, I believe he is as ignorant of it as a child not a year old—I doubt whether he knows the rank of a lieutenant; certainly, he can have no idea of the power of a first-lieutenant, by his treatment of you."

"I should think not," replied Sawbridge dryly.

"I do not think, therefore, that conduct which must have proceeded from sheer ignorance, should be so severely punished—I appeal to you, Sawbridge."

"Well, sir, perhaps you are right—but still he told me he was a philosopher, and talked about equality and rights of man. Told me that he could only admit of equality between us, and begged to argue the point. Now, sir, if a midshipman is to argue the point every time that an order is given, the service will come to a pretty pass."

"That is all very true, Sawbridge; and now you remind me of what never occurred to me at the time that I promised to take Mr Easy in the ship. I now recollect that his father, who is a distant relation of mine, has some very wild notions in his head, just like what have been repeated by his son on your interview with him. I have occasionally dined there, and Mr Easy has always been upholding the principles of natural equality and of the rights of man, much to the amusement of his guests, and I confess, at the time, of mine also. I recollect telling him that I trusted he would never be able to disseminate his opinions in the service to which I belonged, as we should have an end of all discipline. I little thought, at the time, that his only son, who has no more occasion to go to sea than the Archbishop of Canterbury, for his father has a very handsome property—I believe seven or eight thousand a year—would ever have sailed with me, and have brought these opinions with him into any ship that I commanded. It is a pity, a great pity—"

"He never could have brought his pigs to a worse market," observed Sawbridge.

"I agree with you, and, as a father myself, I cannot but help feeling how careful we should be how we inculcate anything like abstract and philosophical idea to youth. Allowing them to be in themselves correct, still they are dangerous as sharp instruments are in the hands of a child; allowing them to be erroneous, they are seized upon with an avidity by young and ardent minds, and are not to be eradicated without the greatest difficulty, and very often not until they have accomplished their ruin."

"Then you think, sir, that these ideas have taken deep root in this young man, and we shall not easily rid him of them."

"I do not say so; but still, recollect they have been instilled, perhaps, from the earliest period, by one from whom they must have been received with all confidence—from a father to a son; and that son has never yet been sufficiently in the world to have proved their fallacy."

"Well sir," replied Sawbridge, "if I may venture to offer an opinion on the subject, and in so doing I assure you that I only shall from a feeling for the service—if, as you say, these opinions will not easily be eradicated, as the young man is independent, would it not be both better for himself, as well as for the service, that he is sent home again? As an officer he will never do any good for himself, and he may do much harm to others. I submit this to you, Captain Wilson, with all respect; but as your first-lieutenant, I feel very jealous at any chance of the discipline of the ship being interfered with by the introduction of this young man, to whom it appears that a profession is no object."

"My dear Sawbridge," replied Captain Wilson, after taking one or two turns up and down the room, "we entered the service together, we were messmates for many years, and you must be aware that it is not only long friendship but an intimate knowledge of your unrewarded merit, which has induced me to request you to come with me as my first-lieutenant. Now, I will put a case to you, and you shall then decide the question—and, moreover, I will abide by your decision.

"Suppose that you were a commander like myself, with a wife and seven children, and that, struggling for many years to support them, you found yourself, notwithstanding the utmost parsimony, gradually running into debt. That, after many long applications, you had at last succeeded in obtaining employment by an appointment to a fine sloop, and there was every prospect, by prize-money and increased pay, of recovering yourself from your difficulties, if not realising a sufficient provision for your family. Then suppose that all this prospect and all these hopes were likely to be dashed to the ground by the fact of having no means of fitting yourself out, no credit, no means of paying debts you have contracted, for which you would have been arrested, or anything sufficient to leave for the support of your family during your absence, your agent only consenting to advance one-half of what you require. Now, suppose, in this awkward dilemma, without any one in this world upon whom you have any legitimate claim, as a last resource you were to apply to one with whom you have but a distant connection, and but an occasional acquaintance—and that when you had made your request for the loan of two or three hundred pounds, fully anticipating a refusal (from the feeling that he who goes a-borrowing goes a-sorrowing)—I say, suppose, to your astonishment, that this generous person was to present you with a cheque on his banker for one thousand pounds, demanding no interest, no legal security, and requests you only to pay it at your convenience—I ask you, Sawbridge, what would be your feelings towards such a man?"

"I would die for him," replied Sawbridge, with emotion.

"And suppose that, by the merest chance, or from a whim of the moment, the son of that man was to be placed under your protection?"

"I would be a father to him," replied Sawbridge.

"But we must proceed a little further: suppose that you were to find the lad was not all that you could wish—that he had imbibed erroneous doctrines, which would probably, if not eradicated, be attended with consequences fatal to his welfare and happiness, would you therefore, on that account, withdraw your protection, and leave him to the mercy of others, who had no claims of gratitude to sway them in his favour?"

"Most certainly not, sir," replied Sawbridge; "on the contrary, I would never part with the son until, by precept or otherwise, I had set him right again, and thus had, as far as it was possible, paid the debt of gratitude due to the generous father."

"I hardly need say to you, Sawbridge, after what has passed, that this lad you have just come from, is the son, and that Mr Easy of Forest Hill is the father."

"Then, sir, I can only say, that not only to please you, but also from respect to a man who has shown such goodwill towards one of our cloth, I shall most cheerfully forgive all that has passed between the lad and me, and all that may probably take place before we make him what he ought to be."

"Thank you, Sawbridge; I expected as much, and am not disappointed in my opinion of you."

"And now, Captain Wilson, pray what is to be done?"

"We must get him on board, but not with a file of marines—that will do more harm than good. I will send a note, requesting him to breakfast with me to-morrow morning, and have a little conversation with him. I do not wish to frighten him: he would not scruple to run back to Forest Hill—now I wish to keep him if I possibly can."

"You are right, sir; his father appears his greatest enemy. What a pity that a man with so good a heart should be so weak in the head! Then, sir, I shall take no notice of this at present, but leave the whole affair in your hands."

"Do, Sawbridge; you have obliged me very much by your kindness in this business."

Mr Sawbridge then took his leave, and Captain Wilson despatched a note to our hero, requesting the pleasure of his company to breakfast at nine o'clock the ensuing morning. The answer was in the affirmative, but verbal, for Jack had drunk too much champagne to trust his pen to paper.

Chapter Nine.

In which Mr Easy finds himself on the other side of the Bay of Biscay.

The next morning Jack Easy would have forgotten all about his engagement with the captain, had it not been for the waiter, who thought that, after the reception which our hero had given the first-lieutenant, it would be just as well that he should not be disrespectful to the captain. Now Jack had not, hitherto, put on his uniform, and he thought this a fitting occasion, particularly as the waiter suggested the propriety of his appearance in it. Whether it was from a presentiment of what he was to suffer, Jack was not at all pleased, as most lads are, with the change in his dress. It appeared to him that he was sacrificing his independence however, he did not follow his first impulse, which was to take it off again, but took his hat, which the waiter had brushed and handed to him, and then set off for the captain's lodgings. Captain Wilson received him as if he had not been aware of his delay in joining his ship, or his interview with his first-lieutenant, but before breakfast was over, Jack himself narrated the affair in a few words. Captain Wilson then entered into a detail of the duties and rank of every person on board of the ship, pointing out to Jack that where discipline was required, it was impossible, when duty was carried on, that more than one could command; and that that one was the captain, who represented the king in person, who represented the country; and that, as the orders were transmitted from the captain through the lieutenant, and from the lieutenant to the midshipmen, who, in their turn, communicated them to the whole ship's company, in fact, was the captain alone who gave the orders, and that every one was *equally* obliged to obey. Indeed, as the captain himself had to obey the orders of his superiors, the admiral and the admiralty, *all* on board might be said to be *equally* obliged to obey. Captain Wilson laid a strong emphasis on the word *equally*, as he cautiously administered his first dose; indeed, in the whole of his address, he made use of special pleading, which would have done credit to the Bar; for at the same time that he was explaining to Jack that he was entering a service in which *equality* could never for a moment exist, if the service was to exist, he contrived to show that all the grades were levelled, by all being equally bound to do their duty to their country, and that, in fact, whether a seaman obeyed *his* orders, or he obeyed the orders of *his* superior officer, they were in reality only obeying the orders of the country, which were administered through their channels.

Jack did not altogether dislike this view of the subject, and the captain took care not to dwell too long upon it. He then entered upon other details, which he was aware would be more agreeable to Jack. He pointed out that the articles of war were the rules by which the service was to be guided, and that everybody, from the captain to the least boy in the ship, was *equally* bound to adhere to them—that a certain allowance of provisions and wine was allowed to each person on board, and that this allowance was the same to all; the same to the captain as to the boy: the same in quantity as in quality; every one *equally* entitled to his allowance;—that, although there were, of necessity, various grades necessary in the service, and the captain's orders were obliged to be passed and obeyed by all, yet still, whatever was the grade of the officer, they were *equally* considered as gentlemen. In short, Captain Wilson, who told the truth, and nothing but the truth, without telling the whole truth, actually made Jack fancy that he had at last found out that equality he had been seeking for in vain on shore, when, at last, he recollected the language used by Mr Sawbridge the evening before, and asked the captain why that personage had so conducted himself. Now, as the language of Mr Sawbridge was very much at variance with equality, Captain Wilson was not a little puzzled. However, he first pointed out that the first-lieutenant was, at the time being, the captain, as he was the senior officer on board, as would Jack himself be if he were the senior officer on board; and that, as he before observed, the captain or senior officer represented the country. That in the articles of war, everybody who absented himself from the ship, committed an error, or breach of those articles; and if any error or breach of those articles was committed by any one belonging to the ship, if the senior officer did not take notice of it, he then himself committed a breach of those articles, and was liable himself to be punished, if he could not prove that he had noticed it; it was therefore to save himself that he was obliged to point out the error; and if he did it in strong language, it only proved his *zeal* for his country.

"Upon my honour, then," replied Jack, "there can be no doubt of his zeal; for if the whole country had been at stake, he could not have put himself in a greater passion."

"Then he did his duty; but depend upon it it was not a pleasant one to him: and I'll answer for it, when you meet him on board, he will be as friendly with you as if nothing had happened."

"He told me that he'd soon make me know what a first-lieutenant was: what did he mean by that?" inquired Jack.

"All zeal."

"Yes, but he said, that as soon as he got on board, he'd show me the difference between a first-lieutenant and a midshipman."

"All zeal."

"He said my ignorance should be a little enlightened by-and-by."

"All zeal."

"And that he'd send a sergeant and marines to fetch me."

"All zeal."

"That he would put my philosophy to the proof."

"All zeal, Mr Easy. Zeal will break out in this way; but we should do nothing in the service without it. Recollect that I hope and trust one day to see you also a zealous officer."

Here Jack cogitated considerably, and gave no answer.

"You will, I am sure," continued Captain Wilson, "find Mr Sawbridge one of your best friends."

"Perhaps so," replied Jack: "but I did not much admire our first acquaintance."

"It will perhaps be your unpleasant duty to find as much fault yourself; we are all equally bound to do our duty to our country. But, Mr Easy, I sent for you to say that we shall sail to-morrow: and, as I shall send my things off this afternoon by the launch, you had better send yours off also. At eight o'clock I shall go on board, and we can both go in the same boat."

To this Jack made no sort of objection, and having paid his bill at the Fountain, he sent his chest down to the boat by some of the crew who came up for it, and attended the summons of the captain to embark. By nine o'clock that evening, Mr Jack Easy was safe on board his Majesty's sloop *Harpy*.

When Jack arrived on board, it was dark, and he did not know what to do with himself. The captain was received by the officers on deck, who took off their hats to salute him. The captain returned the salute, and so did Jack very politely, after which the captain entered into conversation with the first-lieutenant, and for a while Jack was left to himself. It was too dark to distinguish faces, and to one who had never been on board of a ship, too dark to move, so Jack stood where he was, which was not far from the main bitts; but he did not stay long; the boat had been hooked on to the quarter davits, and the boatswain had called out:

"Set taut, my lads!"

And then with the shrill whistle, and "Away with her!" forward came galloping and bounding along the men with the tackles; and in the dark Jack was upset, and half a dozen marines fell upon him; the men, who had no idea that an officer was floored among the others, were pleased at the joke, and continued to dance over those who were down, until they rolled themselves out of the way. Jack, who did not understand this, fared badly, and it was not till the calls piped belay, that he could recover his legs, after having been trampled upon by half the starboard watch, and the breath completely jammed out of his body. Jack reeled to a carronade slide, when the officers, who had been laughing at the lark as well as the men, perceived his situation—among others, Mr Sawbridge, the first-lieutenant.

"Are you hurt, Mr Easy?" said he kindly.

"A little," replied Jack, catching his breath.

"You've had but a rough welcome," replied the first-lieutenant, "but at certain times, on board ship, it is every man for himself, and God for us all. Harpur," continued the first-lieutenant to the doctor, "take Mr Easy down in the gun-room with you, and I will be down myself as soon as I can. Where is Mr Jolliffe?"

"Here, sir," replied Mr Jolliffe, a master's mate, coming aft from the booms.

"There is a youngster come on board with the captain. Order one of the quartermasters to get a hammock slung."

In the meantime Jack went down into the gun-room, where a glass of wine somewhat recovered him. He did not stay there long, nor did he venture to talk much. As soon as his hammock was ready, Jack was glad to go to bed—and as he was much bruised he was not disturbed the next morning till past nine o'clock. He then dressed himself, went on deck, found that the sloop was just clear of the Needles, that he felt very queer, then very sick, and was conducted by a marine down below, put into his hammock, where he remained during a gale of wind of three days, bewildered, confused, puzzled, and every minute knocking his head against the beams with the pitching and tossing of the sloop.

"And this is going to sea," thought Jack; "no wonder that no one interferes with another here, or talks about a trespass; for I'm sure any one is welcome to my share of the ocean; and if I once get on shore again, the devil may have my portion if he chooses."

Captain Wilson and Mr Sawbridge had both allowed Jack more leisure than most midshipmen, during his illness. By the time that the gale was over, the sloop was off Cape Finisterre. The next morning the sea was nearly down, and there was but a slight breeze on the waters. The comparative quiet of the night before had very much recovered our hero, and when the hammocks were piped up, he was accosted by Mr Jolliffe, the master's mate, who asked, "whether he intended to rouse and bit, or whether he intended to sail to Gibraltar between his blankets."

Jack, who felt himself quite another person, turned out of his hammock and dressed himself. A marine had, by the captain's orders, attended Jack during his illness, and this man came to his assistance, opened his chest, and brought him all that he required, or Jack would have been in a sad dilemma.

Jack then inquired where he was to go, for he had not yet been in the midshipmen's berth, although five days on board. The marine pointed it out to him, and Jack, who felt excessively hungry, crawled over and between chests, until he found himself fairly in a hole infinitely inferior to the dog-kennels which received his father's pointers.

"I'd not only give up the ocean," thought Jack, "and my share of it, but also my share of the *Harpy*, unto any one who fancies it. Equality enough here! for every one appears equally miserably off."

As he thus gave vent to his thoughts, he perceived that there was another person in the berth—Mr Jolliffe, the master's mate, who had fixed his eye upon Jack, and to whom Jack returned the compliment. The first thing that Jack observed was, that Mr Jolliffe was very deeply pockmarked, and that he had but one eye, and that was a piercer; it appeared like a little ball of fire, and as if it reflected more light from the solitary candle than the candle gave.

"I don't like your looks," thought Jack—"we shall never be friends."

But here Jack fell into the common error of judging by appearances, as will be proved hereafter.

"I'm glad to see you up again, youngster," said Jolliffe; "you've been on your beam ends longer than usual, but those who are strongest suffer most—you made your mind up but late to come to sea. However, they say, 'Better late than never.'"

"I feel very much inclined to argue the truth of that saying," replied Jack; "but it's no use just now. I'm terribly hungry—when shall I get some breakfast?"

"To-morrow morning at half-past eight," replied Mr Jolliffe. "Breakfast for to-day has been over these two hours."

"But must I then go without?"

"No, I do not say that, as we must make allowances for your illness; but it will not be breakfast."

"Call it what you please," replied Jack. "Only pray desire the servants to give me something to eat. Dry toast or muffins—anything will do, but I should prefer coffee."

"You forget that you are off Finisterre, in a midshipman's berth: coffee we have none—muffins we never see—dry toast cannot be made, as we have no soft bread; but a cup of tea, and ship's biscuit and butter, I can desire the steward to get ready for you."

"Well then," replied Jack, "I will thank you to procure me that."

"Marine," cried Jolliffe, "call Mesty."

"Pass the word for Mesty," cried the marine—and the two syllables were handed forward until lost in the fore part of the vessel.

The person so named must be introduced to the reader. He was a curious anomaly—a black man who had been brought to America as a slave, and there sold.

He was a very tall, spare-built, yet muscular form, and had a face by no means common with his race. His head was long and narrow, high cheek-bones, from whence his face descended down to almost a point at the chin; his nose was very small, but it was straight and almost Roman; his mouth also was unusually small; and his lips thin for an African; his teeth very white, and filed to sharp points. He claimed the rank of prince in his own country, with what truth could not of course be substantiated. His master had settled at New York, and there Mesty had learned English, if it could be so called: the fact is, that all the emigrant labourers at New York being Irishmen, he had learned English with the strong brogue and peculiar phraseology of the sister kingdom dashed with a little Yankeeism.

Having been told that there was no slavery in England, Mesty had concealed himself on board an English merchant vessel, and escaped. On his arrival in England he had entered on board of a man-of-war. Having no name, it was necessary to christen him on the ship's books, and the first lieutenant, who had entered him, struck with his remarkable expression of countenance, and being a German scholar, had named him Mephistopheles Faust, from whence his Christian name had been razéed to Mesty. Mesty in other points was an eccentric character; at one moment, when he remembered his lineage, he was proud to excess, at others he was grave and almost sullen—but when nothing either in daily occurrences or in his mind ran contrary, he exhibited the drollery so often found in his nation, with a spice of Irish humour, as if he had caught up the latter with his Irish brogue.

Mesty was soon seen coming aft, but almost double as he couched under the beams, and taking large strides with his naked feet.

"By the powers, Massa Yolliffe, but it is not seasonable at all to send for me just now, anyhow, seeing how the praters are in the copper, and so many blackguard 'palpeens all ready to change net for net, and better themselves by the same mistake, 'dam um.'"

"Mesty, you know I never send for you myself, or allow others to do so, unless it is necessary," replied Jolliffe; "but this poor lad has eaten nothing since he has been on board, and is very hungry—you must get him a little tea."

"Is it tay you mane, sir?—I guess, to make tay, in the first place I must ab water, and in the next must ab room in the galley to put the kettle on—and 'pose you wanted to burn the tip of your little finger just now, it's not in the galley that you find a berth for it—and den the water before seven bells. I've a notion it's just impassible."

"But he must have something, Mesty."

"Never mind the tea, then," replied Jack, "I'll take some milk."

"Is it milk massa manes, and the bumboat woman on the oder side of the bay?"

"We have no milk, Mr Easy; you forget that we are on blue water," replied Jolliffe, "and I really am afraid that you'll have to wait till dinner-time. Mesty tells the truth."

"I tell you what, Massa Yolliffe, it just seven bells, and if the young gentleman would, instead of tay, try a little out of the copper, it might keep him asy. It but a little difference, *tay* soup and *pay* soup. Now a bowl of that, with some nuts and a flourish of pepper will do him good, anyhow."

"Perhaps the best thing he can take, Mesty; get it as fast as you can."

In a few minutes the black brought down a bowl of soup and whole peas swimming in it, put before our hero a tin bread-basket full of small biscuit, called midshipmen's nuts, and the pepper-castor. Jack's visions of tea, coffee, muffins, dry toast, and milk, vanished as he perceived the mess; but he was very hungry, and he found it much better than he expected; and he moreover found himself much the better after he had swallowed it. It struck seven bells, and he accompanied Mr Jolliffe on deck.

Chapter Ten.

Showing how Jack transgresses against his own philosophy.

When Jack Easy had gained the deck, he found the sun shining gaily, a soft air blowing from the shore, and the whole of the rigging and every part of the ship loaded with the shirts, trousers, and jackets of the seamen, which had been wetted during the heavy gale, and were now hanging up to dry; all the wet sails were also spread on the booms or triced up in the rigging, and the ship was slowly forging through the blue water. The captain and first lieutenant were standing on the gangway in converse, and the majority of the officers were with their quadrants and sextants ascertaining the latitude at noon. The decks were white and clean, the sweepers had just laid by their brooms, and the men were busy coiling down the ropes. It was a scene of cheerfulness, activity, and order, which lightened his heart after the four days of suffering, close air, and confinement, from which he had just emerged.

The captain, who perceived him, beckoned to him, asked him kindly how he felt: the first lieutenant also smiled upon him, and many of the officers, as well as his messmates, congratulated him upon his recovery.

The captain's steward came up to him, touched his hat, and requested the pleasure of his company to dinner in the cabin. Jack was the essence of politeness, took off his hat, and accepted the invitation. Jack was standing on a rope which a seaman was coiling down; the man touched his hat and requested he would be so kind as to take his foot off. Jack took his hat off his head in return, and his foot off the rope. The master touched his hat, and reported twelve o'clock to the first lieutenant—the first lieutenant touched his hat, and reported twelve o'clock to the captain—the captain touched his hat, and told the first lieutenant to make it so. The officer of the watch touched his hat, and asked the captain whether they should pipe to dinner—the captain touched his hat and said, "If you please."

The midshipman received his orders, and touched his hat, which he gave to the head boatswain's mate, who touched his hat, and then the calls whistled cheerily.

"Well," thought Jack, "politeness seems to be the order of the day, and every one has an equal respect for the other." Jack stayed on deck; he peeped through the ports, which were open, and looked down into the deep blue wave; he cast his eyes aloft, and watched the tall spars sweeping and tracing with their points, as it were, a small portion of the clear sky, as they acted in obedience to the motion of the vessel; he looked forward at the range of carronades which lined the sides of the deck, and then he proceeded to climb one of the carronades, and lean over the hammocks to gaze on the distant land.

"Young gentleman, get off those hammocks," cried the master, who was officer of the watch, in a surly tone.

Jack looked round.

"Do you hear me, sir? I'm speaking to you," said the master again.

Jack felt very indignant, and he thought that politeness was not quite so general as he supposed.

It happened that Captain Wilson was upon deck.

"Come here, Mr Easy," said the captain; "it is a rule in the service, that no one gets on the hammocks, unless in case of emergency—I never do—nor the first lieutenant—nor any of the officers or men—therefore, upon the principle of equality, you must not do it either."

"Cerainly not, sir," replied Jack, "but still I do not see why that officer in the shining hat should be so angry, and not speak to me as if I were a gentleman, as well as himself."

"I have already explained that to you, Mr Easy."

"Oh, yes, I recollect now, it's zeal; but this zeal appears to me to be the only unpleasant thing in the service. It's a pity, as you said, that the service cannot do without it."

Captain Wilson laughed, and walked away; and shortly afterwards, as he turned up and down the deck with the master, he hinted to him that he should not speak so sharply to a lad who had committed such a trifling error through ignorance. Now Mr Smallsole, the master, who was a surly sort of a personage, and did not like even a hint of disapprobation of his conduct, although very regardless of the feeling of others, determined to pay this off on Jack, the very first convenient opportunity. Jack dined in the cabin, and was very much pleased to find that every one drank wine with him, and that everybody at the captain's table appeared to be on an equality. Before the dessert had been on the table five minutes, Jack became loquacious on his favourite topic; all the company stared with surprise at such an unheard-of doctrine being broached on board of a man-of-war; the captain argued the point, so as to controvert, without too much offending, Jack's notions, laughing the whole time that the conversation was carried on.

It will be observed, that this day may be considered as the first in which Jack really made his appearance on board, and it also was on this first day that Jack made known, at the captain's table, his very peculiar notions. If the company at the captain's table, which consisted of the second lieutenant, purser, Mr Jolliffe, and one of the midshipmen, were astonished at such heterodox opinions being started in the presence of the captain, they were equally astonished at the cool, good-humoured ridicule with which they were received by Captain Wilson. The report of Jack's boldness, and every word and opinion that he had uttered (of course much magnified) was cirulated that evening through the whole ship; it was canvassed in the gun-room by the officers, it was descanted upon by the midshipmen as they walked the deck; the captain's steward held a levée abreast of the ship's funnel, in which he narrated this new doctrine. The sergeant of marines gave his opinion in his berth that it was damnable. The boatswain talked over the matter with the other warrant officers, till the grog was all gone, and then dismissed it as too dry a subject: and it was the general opinion of the ship's company, that as soon as they arrived at Gibraltar Bay, our hero would bid adieu to the service, either by being sentenced to death by a court-martial, or by being dismissed, and towed on shore on a grating. Others, who had more of the wisdom of the serpent, and who had been informed by Mr Sawbridge that our hero was a lad who would inherit a large property, argued differently, and considered that Captain Wilson had very good reason for being so lenient—and among them was the second lieutenant. There were but four who were well inclined towards Jack—to wit, the captain, the first lieutenant, Mr Jolliffe, the one-eyed master's mate, and Mephistopheles, the black, who, having heard that Jack had uttered such sentiments, loved him with all his heart and soul.

We have referred to the second lieutenant, Mr Asper. This young man had a very high respect for birth, and particularly for money, of which he had very little. He was the son of an eminent merchant who, during the time that he was a midshipman, had allowed him a much larger sum for his expenses than was necessary or proper; and, during his career, he found that his full pocket procured him consequence, not only among his own messmates, but also with many of the officers of the ships that he sailed in. A man who is able and willing to pay a large tavern bill will always find followers—that is, to the tavern; and lieutenants did not disdain to dine, walk arm in arm, and be "hail fellow well met" with a midshipman, at whose expense they lived during the time they were on shore. Mr Asper had just received his commission and appointment, when his father became a bankrupt, and the fountain was dried up from which he had drawn such liberal supplies. Since that, Mr Asper had felt that his consequence was gone: he could no longer talk about the service being a bore, or that he should give it up; he could no longer obtain that deference paid to his purse, and not to himself; and he had contracted very expensive habits, without having any longer the means of gratifying them. It was therefore no wonder that he imbibed a great respect for money; and, as he could no longer find the means himself, he was glad to pick up anybody else at whose cost he could indulge in that extravagance and expense to which he had been so long accustomed, and still sighed for. Now, Mr Asper knew that our hero was well supplied with money, as he had obtained from the waiter the amount of the bill paid at the Fountain, and he had been waiting for Jack's appearance on deck to become his very dearest and most intimate friend. The conversation in the cabin made him feel assured that Jack would require and be grateful for support, and he had taken the opportunity of a walk with Mr Sawbridge, to offer to take Jack in his watch. Whether it was that Mr Sawbridge saw through the design of Mr Asper, or whether he imagined that our hero would be better pleased with him than with the master, considering his harshness of deportment; or with himself, who could not, as first lieutenant, overlook any remission of duty, the offer was accepted, and Jack Easy was ordered, as he now entered upon his duties, to keep watch under Lieutenant Asper.

But not only was this the first day that Jack may be said to have appeared in the service, but it was the first day in which he had entered the midshipman's berth, and was made acquainted with his messmates.

We have already mentioned Mr Jolliffe, the master's mate, but we must introduce him more particularly. Nature is sometimes extremely arbitrary, and never did she show herself more so than in insisting that Mr Jolliffe should have the most sinister expression of countenance that ever had been looked upon.

He had suffered martyrdom with the small-pox, which probably had contracted his lineaments: his face was not only deeply pitted, but scarred, with this cruel disorder. One eye had been lost, and all eyebrows had disappeared—and the contrast between the dull, sightless opaque orb on one side of his face, and the brilliant, piercing little ball on the other, was almost terrifying. His nose had been eaten away by the disease till it formed a sharp but irregular point: part of the muscles of the chin were contracted, and it was drawn in with unnatural seams and puckers. He was tall, gaunt, and thin, seldom smiled, and when he did, the smile produced a still further distortion.

Mr Jolliffe was the son of a warrant officer. He did not contract this disease until he had been sent out to the West Indies, where it swept away hundreds. He had now been long in the service, with little or no chance of promotion. He had suffered from indigence, from reflections upon his humble birth, from sarcasms on his appearance. Every contumely had been heaped upon him at one time or another, in the ships in which he served; among a crowd he had found himself desolate—and now, although no one dared treat him to his face with disrespect, he was only respected in the service from a knowledge of his utility and exemplary performance of his duties—he had no friends or even companions. For many years he had retired within himself, he had improved by reading and study, had felt all the philanthropy of a Christian, and extended it towards others. Silent and reserved, he seldom spoke in the berth, unless his authority, as caterer, was called for; all respected Mr Jolliffe, but no one liked, as a companion, one at whose appearance the very dogs would bark. At the same time every one acknowledged his correct behaviour in every point, his sense of justice, his forbearance, his kindness, and his good sense. With him life was indeed a pilgrimage, and he wended his way in all Christian charity and all Christian zeal.

In all societies, however small they may be, provided that they do but amount to half a dozen, you will invariably meet with a bully. And it is also generally the case that you will find one of that society who is more or less the butt. You will discover this even in occasional meetings, such as a dinner-party, the major part of which have never met before.

Previous to the removal of the cloth, the bully will have shown himself by his dictatorial manner, and will also have selected the one upon whom he imagines that he can best practise. In a midshipman's berth this fact has become almost proverbial, although now perhaps it is not attended with that disagreeable despotism which was permitted at the time that our hero entered the service.

The bully of the midshipman's berth of H.M. sloop *Harpy* was a young man about seventeen, with light, curly hair, and florid countenance, the son of the clerk in the dockyard at Plymouth, and his name was Vigors.

The butt was a pudding-face Tartar-physiognomied boy of fifteen, whose intellects, with fostering, if not great, might at least have been respectable, had he not lost all confidence in his own powers from the constant jeers and mockeries of those who had a greater fluency of speech without perhaps so much real power of mind. Although slow, what he learned he invariably retained. This lad's name was Gossett. His father was a wealthy yeoman of Lynn, in Norfolk. There were at the time but three other midshipmen in the ship, of whom it can only be said that they were like midshipmen in general, with little appetite for learning, but good appetites for dinner, hating everything like work, fond of everything like fun, fighting *à l'outrance* one minute, and sworn friends the next—with general principles of honour and justice, but which were occasionally warped according to circumstances; with all the virtues and vices so heterogeneously jumbled and heaped together, that it was almost impossible to ascribe any action to its true motive, and to ascertain to what point their vice was softened down into almost a virtue, and their virtues from mere excess degenerated into vice. Their names were O'Connor, Mills, and Gascoigne. The other shipmates of our hero it will be better to introduce as they appear on the stage.

After Jack had dined in the cabin he followed his messmates Jolliffe and Gascoigne down into the midshipmen's berth.

"I say, Easy," observed Gascoigne, "you are a devilish free and easy sort of a fellow, to tell the captain that you considered yourself as great a man as he was."

"I beg your pardon," replied Jack, "I did not argue individually, but generally, upon the principles of the rights of man."

"Well," replied Gascoigne, "it's the first time I ever heard a middy do such a bold thing; take care your rights of man don't get you in the wrong box—there's no arguing on board of a man-of-war. The captain took it amazingly easy, but you'd better not broach that subject too often."

"Gascoigne gives you very good advice, Mr Easy," observed Jolliffe; "allowing that your ideas are correct, which it appears to me they are not, or at least impossible to be acted upon, there is such a thing as prudence, and however much this question may be canvassed on shore, in his Majesty's service it is not only dangerous in itself, but will be very prejudicial to you."

"Man is a free agent," replied Easy.

"I'll be shot if a midshipman is," replied Gascoigne, laughing, "and that you'll soon find."

"And yet it was the expectation of finding that equality that I was induced to come to sea."

"On the first of April, I presume," replied Gascoigne. "But are you really serious?"

Hereupon Jack entered into a long argument, to which Jolliffe and Gascoigne listened without interruption, and Mesty with admiration: at the end of it, Gascoigne laughed heartily and Jolliffe sighed.

"From whence did you learn all this?" inquired Jolliffe.

"From my father, who is a great philosopher, and has constantly upheld these opinions."

"And did your father wish you to go to sea?"

"No, he was opposed to it," replied Jack, "but of course he could not combat my rights and free-will."

"Mr Easy, as a friend," replied Jolliffe, "I request that you would as much as possible keep your opinions to yourself: I shall have an opportunity of talking to you on the subject, and will then explain to you my reasons."

As soon as Mr Jolliffe had ceased, down came Mr Vigors and O'Connor, who had heard the news of Jack's heresy.

"You do not know Mr Vigors and Mr O'Connor," said Jolliffe to Easy.

Jack, who was the essence of politeness, rose and bowed, at which the others took their seats, without returning the salutation. Vigors had, from what he had heard and now seen of Easy, thought he had somebody else to play upon, and without ceremony he commenced.

"So, my chap, you are come on board to raise a mutiny here with your equality—you came off scot free at the captain's table; but it won't do, I can tell you, even in the midshipman's berth some must knock under, and you are one of them."

"If, sir," replied Easy, "you mean by knock under, that I must submit, I can assure you that you are mistaken. Upon the same principle that I would never play the tyrant to those weaker than myself, so will I resent oppression if attempted."

"Damme, but he's a regular sea lawyer already: however, my boy, we'll soon put your mettle to the proof."

"Am I then to infer that I am not on an equality with my messmates?" replied Jack, looking at Jolliffe. The latter was about to answer him, but Vigors interrupted.

"Yes, you are on an equality as far as this—that you have an equal right to the berth, if you are not knocked out of it for insolence to your masters; that you have an equal share to pay for the things purchased for the mess, and an equal right to have your share, provided you can get it; you have an equal right to talk, provided you are not told to hold your tongue. The fact is, you have an equal right with every one else to do as you can, get what you can, and say what you can, always provided that you can do it; for here the weakest goes to the wall, and that is midshipmen's berth equality. Now, do you understand all that; or will you wait for a practical illustration?"

"I am then to infer that the equality here is as much destroyed as it even will be among savages, where the strong oppress the weak, and the only law is club law—in fact, much the same as it is at a public or large school on shore?"

"I suspect you are right for once. You were at a public school: how did they treat you there?"

"As you propose treating people here—'the weakest went to the wall.'"

"Well, then, a nod's as good as a wink to a blind horse, that's all, my hearty," said Vigors.

But the hands being turned up, "Shorten sail" put an end to the altercation for the present.

As our hero had not yet received orders to go to his duty, he remained below with Mesty.

"By de powers, Massa Easy, but I lub you with my hole soul," said Mesty. "By Jasus, you really tark fine, Massa Easy; dat Mr Vigor—nebber care for him, wouldn't you lik him—and sure you would," continued the black, feeling the muscle of Jack's arm. "By the soul of my fader, I'd bet my week's allowance on you anyhow. Nebber be 'fraid, Massa Easy."

"I am not afraid," replied Jack; "I've thrashed bigger fellows than he;" and Jack's assertion was true. Mr Bonnycastle never interfered in a fair fight, and took no notice of black eyes, provided the lessons were well said. Jack had fought and fought again, until he was a very good bruiser, and although not so tall as Vigors, he was much better built for fighting. A knowing Westminster boy would have bet his half-crown upon Jack, had he seen him and his anticipated adversary.

The constant battles which Jack was obliged to fight at school had been brought forward by Jack against his father's arguments in favour of equality, but they had been overruled by Mr Easy's pointing out that the combats of *boys* had nothing to do with the rights of man.

As soon as the watch was called, Vigors, O'Connor, Gossett, and Gascoigne, came down from the berth. Vigors, who was strongest in the berth, except Jolliffe, had successively had his superiority acknowledged, and, when on deck, he had talked of Easy's impertinence, and his intention of bringing him to his senses. The others, therefore, came down to see the fun.

"Well, Mr Easy," observed Vigors, as he came into the berth, "you take after your name, at all events; I suppose you intend to eat the king's provision, and do nothing."

Jack's mettle was already up.

"You will oblige me, sir, by minding your own business," replied Jack.

"You impudent blackguard, if you say another word I'll give you a good thrashing, and knock some of your equality out of you."

"Indeed," replied Jack, who almost fancied himself back at Mr Bonnycastle's; "we'll try that."

Whereupon Jack very coolly divested himself of his upper garments, neckerchief, and shirt, much to the surprise of Mr Vigors, who little contemplated such a proof of decision and confidence, and still more to the delight of the other midshipmen, who would have forfeited a week's allowance to see Vigors well thrashed. Vigors, however, knew that he had gone too far to retreat; he therefore prepared for action; and, when ready, the whole party went out into the steerage to settle the business.

Vigors had gained his assumed authority more by bullying than fighting; others had submitted to him without a sufficient trial; Jack, on the contrary, had won his way up in school by hard and scientific combat: the result, therefore, may easily be imagined. In less than a quarter of an hour Vigors, beaten dead, with his eyes closed, and three teeth out, gave in; while Jack, after a basin of water, looked as fresh as ever, with the exception of a few trifling scratches.

The news of this victory was soon through the ship; and before Jack had resumed his clothes, it had been told confidentially by Sawbridge to the captain.

"So soon!" said Captain Wilson, laughing; "I expected that a midshipman's berth would do wonders; but I did not expect this, yet awhile. This victory is the first severe blow to Mr Easy's equality, and will be more valuable than twenty defeats. Let him now go to his duty: he will soon find his level."

Chapter Eleven.

In which our hero proves that all on board should equally sacrifice decency to duty.

The success of any young man in a profession very much depends upon the occurrences at the commencement of his career, as from those is his character judged, and he is treated accordingly. Jack had chosen to enter the Service at a much later period than most lads; he was tall and manly for his age, and his countenance, if not strictly handsome, wore that expression of honesty and boldness which is sure to please. His spirit in not submitting to, and meeting Vigors when he had hardly recovered from his severe prostration of sea-sickness, had gained him with the many respect, and with all, except his antagonist and Mr Smallsole, goodwill. Instead of being laughed at by his messmates, he was played with; for Jolliffe smiled at his absurdities, and attempted to reason him out of them, and the others liked Jack for himself and his generosity, and, more over, because they looked up to him as a protector against Vigors, who had persecuted them all; for Jack had declared, that as might was right in a midshipman's berth, he would so far restore equality, that if he could not put down those who were the strongest, at all events he would protect the weak, and, let who would come into the berth, they must be his master before they should tyrannise over those weaker than he.

Thus did Jack Easy make the best use that he could of his strength, and become, as it were, the champion and security of those who, although much longer at sea and more experienced than he was, were glad to shelter themselves under his courage and skill, the latter of which had excited the admiration of the butcher of the ship, who had been a pugilist by profession. Thus did Jack at once take the rank of an oldster, and soon became the leader of all the mischief. We particularly observe this, because, had it so happened that our hero had succumbed to Vigors, the case would have been the very reverse. He then would have had to go through the ordeal to which most who enter the naval service are exposed, which cannot be better explained than by comparing it to the fagging carried to such an iniquitous extent in public schools.

Mr Asper, for his own reasons, made him his companion: they walked the night-watch together, and he listened to all Jack's nonsense about the rights of man. And here Mr Asper did good without intending it, for, at the same time that he appeared to agree with Jack, to secure his favour, he cautioned him, and pointed out why this equality could not exist altogether on board of a man-of-war.

As for himself, he said, he saw no difference between a lieutenant, or even a captain, and a midshipman, provided they were gentlemen: he should choose his friends where he liked, and despised that power of annoyance which the service permitted. Of course, Jack and Mr Asper were good friends, especially as, when half the watch was over, to conciliate his good will and to get rid of his eternal arguing, Mr Asper would send Jack down to bed.

They were now entering the Straits, and expected to anchor the next day at Gibraltar, and Jack was forward on the forecastle, talking with Mesty, with whom he had contracted a great friendship, for there was nothing that Mesty would not have done for Jack, although he had not been three weeks in the ship; but a little reflection will show that it was natural.

Mesty had been a great man in his own country; he had suffered all the horrors of a passage in a slave ship; he had been sold as a slave twice; he had escaped—but he found that the universal feeling was strong against his colour, and that on board of a man-of-war he was condemned, although free, to the humblest of offices.

He had never heard any one utter the sentiments, which *now* beat in his own heart, of liberty and equality—we say *now*, for when he was in his own country before his captivity, he had no ideas of equality; no one has who is in power: but he had been schooled; and although people talked of liberty and equality at New York, he found that what they preached for themselves, they did not practise towards others, and that, in the midst of liberty and equality, he and thousands more were enslaved and degraded beings.

Escaping to England, he had regained his liberty, but not his equality; his colour had prevented the latter, and in that feeling all the world appeared to conspire together against him, until, to his astonishment, he heard those sentiments boldly expressed from the lips of Jack, and that in a service where it was almost tantamount to mutiny. Mesty, whose character is not yet developed, immediately took a fondness for our hero, and in a hundred ways showed his attachment. Jack also liked Mesty, and was fond of talking with him, and every evening, since the combat with Vigors, they had generally met in the forecastle to discuss the principles of equality and the rights of man.

The boatswain, whose name was Biggs, was a slight, dapper, active little man, who, as captain of the foretop, had shown an uncommon degree of courage in a hurricane, so much so, as to recommend him to the admiral for promotion. It was given to him; and after the ship to which he had been appointed was paid off, he had been ordered to join H.M. sloop *Harpy*. Jack's conversation with Mesty was interrupted by the voice of the boatswain, who was haranguing his boy. "It's now ten minutes, sir, by my repeater," said the boatswain, "that I have sent for you;" and Mr Biggs pulled out a huge silver watch, almost as big as a Norfolk turnip. A Jew had sold him the watch; the boatswain had heard of repeaters, and wished to have one. Moses had only shown him watches with the hour and minute hands; he now produced one with a second hand, telling him it was a repeater.

"What makes it a repeater?" inquired the boatswain.

"Common watches," said the cunning Jew, "only tell the minutes and the hours; but all repeaters tell the seconds."

The boatswain was satisfied—bought the watch, and, although many had told him it was no repeater, he insisted that it *was*, and would call it so.

"I swear," continued the boatswain, "it's ten minutes and twenty seconds by my repeater."

"If you please, sir," said the boy, "I was changing my trousers when you sent for me, and then I had to stow away my bag again."

"Silence, sir; I'd have you to know that when you are sent for by your officer, trousers or no trousers, it is your duty to come up directly."

"Without trousers, sir!" replied the boy.

"Yes, sir, without trousers; if the captain required me, I should come without my shirt. Duty before decency." So saying, the boatswain lays hold of the boy.

"Surely, Mr Biggs," said Jack, "you are not going to punish that boy for not coming up without his trousers!"

"Yes, Mr Easy, I am—I must teach him a lesson. We are bound, now that newfangled ideas are brought into the ship, to uphold the dignity of the service; and the orders of an officer are not to be delayed ten minutes and twenty seconds because a boy has no trousers on." Whereupon the boatswain administered several smart cuts with his rattan upon the boy, proving that it was quite as well that he had put on his trousers before he came on deck. "There," said Mr Biggs, "is a lesson for you, you scamp—and, Mr Easy, it is a lesson for you also," continued the boatswain, walking away with a most consequential air.

"Murder Irish!" said Mesty—"how him cut caper. De oder day he hawl out de weather ear-ring, and touch him hat to a midshipman. Sure enough, make um cat laugh."

The next day, the *Harpy* was at anchor in Gibraltar Bay; the captain went on shore, directing the gig to be sent for him before nine o'clock; after which hour the sally-port is only opened by special permission. There happened to be a ball given by the officers of the garrison on that evening, and a polite invitation was sent to the officers of H.M. sloop *Harpy*. As those who accepted the invitation would be detained late, it was not possible for them to come off that night. And as their services were required for the next day, Captain Wilson allowed them to remain on shore until seven o'clock the next morning, at which hour, as there was a large party, there would be two boats sent for them.

Mr Asper obtained leave, and asked permission to take our hero with him; to which Mr Sawbridge consented. Many other officers obtained leave, and, among others, the boatswain, who, aware that his services would be in request as soon as the equipment commenced, asked permission for this evening. And Mr Sawbridge, feeling that he could be better spared at this than at any other time, consented. Asper and Jack went to an inn, dined, bespoke beds, and then dressed themselves for the ball, which was very brilliant, and, from the company of the officers, very pleasant. Captain Wilson looked on at the commencement, and then returned on board. Jack behaved with his usual politeness, danced till two o'clock, and then, as the ball thinned, Asper proposed that they should retire. Having once more applied to the refreshment-room, they had procured their hats, and were about to depart, when one of the officers of the garrison asked Jack if he would like to see a baboon, which had just been brought down from the rock; and, taking some of the cakes, they repaired to the court where the animal was chained down to a small tank. Jack fed the brute till all the cakes were gone, and then, because he had no more to give him, the baboon flew at Jack, who, in making his retreat, fell back into the tank, which was about two feet deep. This was a joke; and having laughed heartily, they wished the officer good-night, and went to the inn.

Now, what with the number of officers of the *Harpy* on shore, who had all put up at the same inn, and other occupants, the landlord was obliged to put his company into double and treble bedded rooms; but this was of little consequence. Jack was shown into a doubled-bedded room, and proceeded to undress; the other was evidently occupied, by the heavy breathing which saluted Jack's ear.

As Jack undressed, he recollected that his trousers were wet through, and to dry them he opened the window, hung them out, and then jammed down the window again upon them, to hold them in their position, after which he turned in and fell fast asleep. At six o'clock he was called, as he had requested, and proceeded to dress, but to his astonishment found the window thrown open and his trousers missing. It was evident that his partner in the room had thrown the window open during the night, and that his trousers, having fallen down into the street, had been walked off with by somebody or another. Jack looked out of the window once more, and perceived that whoever had thrown open the window had been unwell during the night. A nice drunken companion I have had, thought Jack; but what's to be done? And in saying this, he walked up to the other bed, and perceived that it was tenanted by the boatswain. Well, thought Jack, as Mr Biggs has thought proper to lose my trousers, I think I have a right to take his, or at least the wear of them, to go on board. It was but last night he declared that decency must give way to duty, and that the orders of a superior officer were to be obeyed, with or without garments. I know he is obliged to be on board, and now he shall try how he likes to obey orders in his shirt tails. So cogitating, Jack took the trousers of the boatswain, who still snored, although he had been called, and, putting them on, completed the rest of his dress, and quitted the room. He went to that of Mr Asper, where he found him just ready, and, having paid the bill—for Asper had forgotten his purse—they proceeded down to the sally-port, where they found other officers waiting, sufficient to load the first boat, which shoved off, and they went on board. As soon as he was down below, Jack hastened to change his trousers, and, unobserved by any one, threw those belonging to Mr Biggs on a chair in his cabin, and, having made a confidant of Mesty, who was delighted, he went on deck, and waited the issue of the affair.

Before Jack left the hotel, he had told the waiter that there was the boatswain still fast asleep, and that he must be roused up immediately; and this injunction was obeyed. The boatswain, who had drunk too much the night before, and, as Jack had truly imagined, had opened the window because he was unwell, was wakened up, and, hearing how late it was, hastened to dress himself. Not finding his trousers, he rang the bell, supposing that they had been taken down to be brushed, and, in the meantime, put on everything else, that he might lose no time: the waiter who answered the bell denied having taken the trousers out of the room, and poor Mr Biggs was in a sad quandary. What had become of them, he could not tell: he had no recollection of having gone to bed the night before; he inquired of the waiter, who said that he knew nothing about them—that he was very tipsy when he came home, and that when he called him, he had found the window open, and it appeared that he had been unwell—he supposed that he had thrown his trousers out of the window. Time flew, and the boatswain was in despair. "Could they lend him a pair?"

"He would call his master."

The master of the inn knew very well the difference of rank between officers, and those whom he could trust and those whom he could not. He sent up the bill by the waiter, and stated that, for a deposit, the gentleman might have a pair of trousers. The boatswain felt in his pockets and remembered that all his money was in his trousers' pocket. He could not only not leave a deposit, but could not pay his bill. The landlord was inexorable. It was bad enough to lose his money, but he could not lose more.

"I shall be tried by a court-martial, by heavens!" exclaimed the boatswain. "It's not far from the sally-port; I'll make a run for it, and I can slip into one of the boats and get another pair of trousers before I report myself as having come on board;" so, making up his mind, the boatswain took to his heels, and with his check shirt tails streaming in the wind, ran as hard as he could to where the boat was waiting to receive him. He was encountered by many, but he only ran the faster the more they jeered, and, at last, arrived breathless at his goal, flew down the steps, jumped into the boat, and squatted on the stern sheets, much to the surprise of the officers and men, who thought him mad. He stated in a few words that somebody had stolen his trousers during the night; and as it was already late, the boat shoved off, the men as well as the officers convulsed with laughter.

"Have any of you a pea-jacket?" inquired the boatswain of the men—but the weather was so warm that none of them had brought a pea-jacket. The boatswain looked round; he perceived that the officers were sitting on a boat-cloak.

"Whose boat-cloak is that?" inquired the boatswain.

"Mine," replied Gascoigne.

"I trust, Mr Gascoigne, you will have the kindness to lend it to me to go up the side with."

"Indeed I will not," replied Gascoigne, who would sooner have thrown it overboard and have lost it, than not beheld the anticipated fun; "recollect I asked you for a fishing-line, when we were becalmed off Cape St. Vincent, and you sent word that you'd see me damned first. Now I'll see you the same before you have my boat-cloak."

"Oh, Mr Gascoigne, I'll give you three lines, directly I get on board."

"I dare say you will, but that won't do now. 'Tit for tat,' Mr Boatswain, and hang all favours," replied Gascoigne, who was steering the boat, having been sent on shore for the others. "In bow—rowed of all." The boat was laid alongside—the relentless Gascoigne caught up his boat-cloak as the other officers rose to go on board, and rolling it up, in spite of the earnest entreaties of Mr Biggs, tossed it into the main chains to the man who had thrown the stern-fast, and to make the situation of Mr Biggs still more deplorable, the first lieutenant was standing looking into the boat, and Captain Wilson walking the quarter deck.

"Come, Mr Biggs, I expected you off in the first boat," cried Mr Sawbridge; "be as smart as you please, for the yards are not yet squared."

"Shall I go ahead in this boat, and square them, sir?"

"That boat, no; let her drop astern, jump up here and lower down the dinghy. What the devil do you sit there for, Mr Biggs?—you'll oblige me by showing a little more activity, or, by Jove, you may save yourself the trouble of asking to go on shore again. Are you sober, sir?"

The last observation decided Mr Biggs. He sprung up from the boat just as he was, and touched his hat as he passed the first lieutenant.

"Perfectly sober, sir, but I've lost my trousers."

"So it appears, sir," replied Mr Sawbridge, as Mr Biggs stood on the planeshear of the sloop where the hammock netting divides for an entrance, with his shirt tails fluttering in the sea breeze; but Mr Sawbridge could not contain himself any longer; he ran down the ship ladder which led on the quarter deck, choked with laughter. Mr Biggs could not descend until after Mr Sawbridge, and the conversation had attracted the notice of all, and every eye in the ship was on him.

"What's all this?" said Captain Wilson, coming to the gangway.

"Duty before decency," replied Jack, who stood by, enjoying the joke.

Mr Biggs recollected the day before—he cast a furious look at Jack, as he touched his hat to the captain, and then dived down to the lower deck.

If anything could add to the indignation of the boatswain, it was to find that his trousers had come on board before him. He now felt that a trick had been played him, and also that our hero must have been the party, but he could prove nothing; he could not say who slept in the same room, for he was fast asleep when Jack went to bed, and fast asleep when Jack quitted the room.

The truth of the story soon became known to all the ship, and "duty before decency" became a by-word. All that the boatswain could do he did, which was to revenge himself upon the poor boy—and Gascoigne and Jack never got any fishing-tackle. The boatswain was as obnoxious to the men as Vigors, and in consequence of Jack's known opinions upon the rights of man, and his having floored their two greatest enemies, he became a great favourite with the seamen, and, as all favourites are honoured by them with a sobriquet, our hero obtained that of *Equality Jack*.

Chapter Twelve.

In which our hero prefers going down to going up; a choice, it is to be hoped, he will reverse upon a more important occasion.

The next day being Sunday, the hands were turned up to divisions, and the weather not being favourable, instead of the Service, the articles of war were read with all due respect shown to the same, the captain, officers, and crew with their hats off in a mizzling rain. Jack, who had been told by the captain that these articles of war were the rules and regulations of the service, by which the captain, officers, and men were equally bound, listened to them as they were read by the clerk with the greatest attention. He little thought that there were about five hundred orders from the admiralty tacked on to them, which, like the numerous codicils of some wills, contained the most important matter, and to a certain degree make the will nugatory.

Jack listened very attentively, and, as each article was propounded, felt that he was not likely to commit himself in that point, and, although he was rather astonished to find such a positive injunction against swearing, considered quite a dead letter in the ship, he thought that, altogether, he saw his way very clear. But to make certain of it, as soon as the hands had been piped down he begged the clerk to let him have a copy of the articles.

Now the clerk had three, being the allowance of the ship, or at least all that he had in his possession, and made some demur at parting with one; but at last he proposed—"some rascal," as he said, "having stolen his tooth-brush"—that if Jack would give him one he would give him one of the copies of the articles of war. Jack replied that the one he had in use was very much worn, and that unfortunately he had but one new one, which he could not spare. Thereupon the clerk, who was a very clean personage, and could not bear that his teeth should be dirty, agreed to accept the one in use, as Jack could not part with the other. The exchange was made, and Jack read the articles of war over and over again, till he thought he was fully master of them.

"Now," says Jack, "I know what I am to do, and what I am to expect, and these articles of war I will carry in my pocket as long as I'm in the service; that is to say, if they last so long; and, provided they do not, I am able to replace them with another old tooth-brush, which appears to be the value attached to them."

The *Harpy* remained a fortnight in Gibraltar Bay, and Jack had occasionally a run on shore, and Mr Asper invariably went with him to keep him out of mischief; that is to say, he allowed him to throw his money away on nobody more worthless than himself.

One morning Jack went down in the berth, and found young Gossett blubbering.

"What's the matter, my dear Mr Gossett?" inquired Jack, who was just as polite to the youngster as he was to anybody else.

"Vigors has been thrashing me with a rope's end," replied Gossett, rubbing his arm and shoulders.

"What for?" inquired Jack.

"Because he says the service is going to hell—(I'm sure it's no fault of mine)—and that now all subordination is destroyed, and that upstarts join the ship who, because they have a five-pound note in their pocket, are allowed to do just as they please. He said he was determined to uphold the service, and then he knocked me down—and when I got up again he told me that I could stand a little more—and then he took out his colt, and said he was determined to ride the high horse—and that there should be no Equality Jack in future."

"Well," replied Jack.

"And then he colted me for half an hour, and that's all."

"By de soul of my fader, but it all for true, Massa Easy—he larrap, um, sure enough—all for noteing, bad luck to him—I tink," continued Mesty, "he hab debelish bad memory—and he want a little more of Equality Jack."

"And he shall have it too," replied our hero; "why, it's against the articles of war, 'all quarrelling, fighting, etc.' I say, Mr Gossett, have you got the spirit of a louse?"

"Yes," replied Gossett.

"Well, then, will you do what I tell you next time, and trust to me for protection?"

"I don't care what I do," replied the boy, "if you will back me against the cowardly tyrant."

"Do you refer to me?" cried Vigors, who had stopped at the door of the berth.

"Say yes," said Jack.

"Yes, I do," cried Gossett.

"You do, do you?—well then, my chick, I must trouble you with a little more of this," said Vigors, drawing out his colt.

"I think that you had better not, Mr Vigors," observed Jack.

"Mind your own business, if you please," returned Vigors, not much liking the interference. "I am not addressing my conversation to you, and I will thank you never to interfere with me. I presume I have a right to choose my own acquaintance, and, depend upon it, it will not be that of a leveller."

"All that is at your pleasure, Mr Vigors," replied Jack, "you have a right to choose your own acquaintance, and so have I a right to choose my own friends, and further, to support them. That lad is my friend, Mr Vigors."

"Then," replied Vigors, who could not help bullying even at the risk of another combat which he probably intended to stand, "I shall take the liberty of giving your friend a thrashing;" and he suited the action to the word.

"Then I shall take the liberty to defend my friend," replied Jack; "and as you call me a leveller, I'll try if I may not deserve the name"—whereupon Jack placed a blow so well under the ear, that Mr Vigors dropped on the deck, and was not in condition to come to the scratch, even if he had been inclined. "And now, youngster," said Jack, wresting the colt out of Vigors's hand, "do as I bid you—give him a good colting—if you don't I'll thrash you."

Gossett required no second threat—the pleasure of thrashing his enemy, if only for once, was quite enough—and he laid well on. Jack with his fists doubled ready to protect him if there was a show of resistance, but Vigors was half stupified with the blow under the ear, and quite cowed; he took his thrashing in the most passive manner.

"That will do," said Jack, "and now do not be afraid, Gossett; the very first time he offers to strike you when I am not present, I will pay him off for it as soon as you tell me. I won't be called Equality Jack for nothing."

When Jolliffe, who heard of this, met our hero alone, he said to him, "Take my advice, boy, and do not in future fight the battles of others, you'll find very soon that you will have enough to do to fight your own."

Whereupon Jack argued the point for half an hour, and then they separated. But Mr Jolliffe was right. Jack began to find himself constantly in hot water, and the captain and first lieutenant, although they did not really withdraw their protection, thought it high time that Jack should find out that, on board a man-of-war, everybody and everything must find its level.

There was on board of his Majesty's sloop *Harpy*, a man of the name of Easthupp, who did the duty of purser's steward; this was the second ship that he had served in; in the former he had been sent with a draft of men from the Tender lying off the Tower. How he had come into the service was not known in the present ship, but the fact was, that he had been one of the swell mob—and had been sent on board the Tender with a letter of recommendation from the magistrates to Captain Crouch. He was a cockney by birth, for he had been left at the workhouse of St. Mary Axe, where he had, been taught to read and write, and had afterwards made his escape. He joined the juvenile thieves of the metropolis, had been sent to Bridewell, obtained his liberty, and by degrees had risen from petty thieving of goods exposed outside of the shops and market-stalls, to the higher class of gentlemen pickpockets. His appearance was some what genteel, with a bullying sort of an impudent air, which is mistaken for fashion by those who know no better. A remarkable neat dresser, for that was part of his profession; a very plausible manner and address; a great fluency of language, although he clipped the king's English; and, as he had suffered more than once by the law, it is not to be wondered at that he was, as he called himself, a *hout-and-hout* radical. During the latter part of his service, in his last ship, he had been employed under the purser's steward, and having offered himself in this capacity to the purser of H.M. sloop *Harpy*, with one or two forged certificates, he had been accepted.

Now, when Mr Easthupp heard of Jack's opinions, he wished to cultivate his acquaintance, and with a bow and a flourish, introduced himself before they arrived at Gibraltar, but our hero took an immediate dislike to this fellow from his excessive and impertinent familiarity.

Jack knew a gentleman when he met one, and did not choose to be a companion to a man beneath him in every way, but who, upon the strength of Jack's liberal opinions, presumed to be his equal. Jack's equality did not go so far as that; in theory it was all very well, but in practice it was only when it suited his own purpose.

But the purser's steward was not to be checked—a man who has belonged to the swell mob is not easily repulsed; and although Jack would plainly show him that his company was not agreeable, Easthupp would constantly accost him familiarly on the forecastle and lower deck, with his arms folded, and with an air almost amounting to superiority. At last, Jack told him to go about his business, and not to presume to talk to him, whereupon Easthupp rejoined, and after an exchange of hard words, it ended by Jack kicking Mr Easthupp, as he called himself, down the after-lower-deck hatchway. This was but a sorry specimen of Jack's equality—and Mr Easthupp, who considered that his honour had been compromised, went up to the captain on the quarter-deck, and lodged his complaint—whereupon Captain Wilson desired that Mr Easy might be summoned.

As soon as Jack made his appearance, Captain Wilson called to Easthupp. "Now, purser's steward, what is this you have to say?"

"If you please, Captain Vilson, I am wery sorry to be obliged to make hany complaint of hany hofficer, but this Mr Heasy thought proper to make use of language quite hunbecoming of a gentleman, and then to kick me as I vent down the atchvay."

"Well, Mr Easy, is this true?"

"Yes, sir," replied Jack; "I have several times told the fellow not to address himself to me, and he will. I did tell him he was a radical blackguard, and I did kick him down the hatchway."

"You told him he was a radical blackguard, Mr Easy?"

"Yes, sir; he comes bothering me about his republic, and asserting that we have no want of a king and aristocracy."

Captain Wilson looked significantly at Mr Sawbridge.

"I crtainly did hoffer my political opinions, Captain Vilson; but you must be avare that ve hall ave an hequal stake in the country—and it's a Hinglishman's birthright."

"I'm not aware what your stake in the country may be, Mr Easthupp," observed Captain Wilson, "but I think that, if you used such expressions, Mr Easy was fully warranted in telling you his opinion."

"I ham villing, Captain Vilson, to make hany hallowance for the eat of political discussion—but that is not hall that I ave to complain hof. Mr Easy thought proper to say that I was a swindler and a liar."

"Did you make use of those expressions, Mr Easy?"

"Yes, sir, he did," continued the steward, "and, moreover, told me not to cheat the men, and not to cheat my master the purser. Now, Captain Vilson, is it not true that I am in a wery hostensible sitevation, but I flatter myself that I ave been vell edecated, and vos vonce moving in a wery different society—misfortains vill appin to us hall, and I feel my character has been severely injured by such impertations;" whereupon Mr Easthupp took out his handkerchief, flourished, and blew his nose. "I told Mr Heasy that I considered myself quite as much of a gentleman as himself, and at hall hewents did not keep company with a black feller (Mr Heasy will understand the insinevation), vereupon Mr Heasy, as I before said, your vorship, I mean you, Captain Vilson, thought proper to kick me down the atchvay."

"Very well, steward, I have heard your complaint, and now you may go."

Mr Easthupp took his hat off with an air, made his bow, and went down the main ladder.

"Mr Easy," said Captain Wilson, "you must be aware that, by the regulations of the service by which we are all equally bound, it is not permitted that any officer shall take the law into his own hands. Now, although I do not consider it necessary to make any remark as to your calling the man a radical blackguard, for I consider his impertinent intrusion of his opinions deserved it, still you have no right to attack any man's character without grounds—and as that man is in an office of trust, you were not at all warranted in asserting that he was a cheat. Will you explain to me why you made use of such language?"

Now our hero had no proofs against the man; he had nothing to offer in extenuation, until he recollected, all at once, the reason assigned by the captain for the language used by Mr Sawbridge. Jack had the wit to perceive that it would hit home, so he replied, very quietly and respectfully:

"If you please, Captain Wilson, that was all zeal."

"Zeal, Mr Easy? I think it but a bad excuse. But pray, then, why did you kick the man down the hatchway?—you must have known that that was contrary to the rules of the service."

"Yes, sir," replied Jack demurely, "but that was all zeal too."

"Then allow me to say," replied Captain Wilson, biting his lips, "that I think that your zeal has in this instance been very much misplaced, and I trust you will not show so much again."

"And yet, sir," replied Jack, aware that he was giving the captain a hard hit, and therefore looked proportionally humble, "we should do nothing in the service without it—and I trust one day, as you told me, to become a very zealous officer."

"I trust so too, Mr Easy," replied the captain. "There, you may go now, and let me hear no more of kicking people down the hatchway. That sort of zeal is misplaced."

"More than my foot was, at all events," muttered Jack, as he walked off.

Captain Wilson, as soon as our hero disappeared, laughed heartily, and told Mr Sawbridge "he had ascribed his language to our hero as all zeal. He has very cleverly given me it all back again; and really, Sawbridge, as it proves how weak was my defence of you, you may gain from this lesson."

Sawbridge thought so too—but both agreed that Jack's rights of man were in considerable danger.

The day before the ship sailed, the Captain and Mr Asper dined with the governor, and as there was little more to do, Mr Sawbridge, who had not quitted the ship since she had been in port, and had some few purchases to make, left her in the afternoon in the charge of Mr Smallsole, the master. Now, as we have observed, he was Jack's inveterate enemy—indeed Jack had already made three, Mr Smallsole, Mr Biggs the boatswain, and Easthupp, the purser's steward. Mr Smallsole was glad to be left in command, as he hoped to have an opportunity of punishing our hero, who certainly laid himself not a little open to it.

Like all those who are seldom in command, the master was proportionally tyrannical and abusive—he swore at the men, made them do the duty twice and thrice over on the pretence that it was not smartly done, and found fault with every officer remaining on board.

"Mr Biggs—by God, sir, you seem to be all asleep forward; I suppose you think that you are to do nothing, now the first lieutenant is out of the ship? How long will it be, sir, before you are ready to sway away?"

"By de holy poker, I tink he sway away finely, Massa Easy," observed Mesty, who was in converse with our hero on the forecastle.

Mr Smallsole's violence made Mr Biggs violent, which made the boatswain's mate violent—and the captain of the forecastle violent also; all which is practically exemplified by philosophy in the laws of motion, communicated from one body to another: and as Mr Smallsole swore, so did the boatswain swear—also the boatswain's mate, the captain of the forecastle, and all the men; showing the force of example.

Mr Smallsole came forward—"Damnation, Mr Biggs, what the devil are you about? can't you move here?"

"As much as we can, sir," replied the boatswain, "lumbered as the forecastle is with idlers;" and here Mr Biggs looked at our hero and Mesty, who were standing against the bulwark.

"What are you doing here, sir?" cried Mr Smallsole to our hero.

"Nothing at all, sir," replied Jack.

"Then I'll give you something to do, sir. Go up to the mast-head, and wait there till I call you down. Come, sir, I'll show you the way," continued the master, walking aft. Jack followed till they were on the quarter-deck.

"Now, sir, up to the main-top gallant mast-head; perch yourself upon the cross trees—up with you."

"What am I to go up there for, sir?" inquired Jack.

"For punishment, sir," replied the master.

"What have I done, sir?"

"No reply, sir—up with you."

"If you please, sir," replied Jack, "I should wish to argue this point a little."

"Argue the point," roared Mr Smallsole. "By Jove, I'll teach you to argue the point—away with you, sir."

"If you please, sir," continued Jack, "the captain told me that the articles of war were the rules and regulations by which every one in the service was to be guided. Now, sir," said Jack, "I have read them over till I know them by heart, and there is not one word of mast-heading in the whole of them." Here Jack took the articles out of his pocket, and unfolded them.

"Will you go to the mast-head, sir, or will you not?" said Mr Smallsole.

"Will you show me the mast-head in the articles of war, sir," replied Jack; "here they are."

"I tell you, sir, to go to the mast-head if not, I'll be damned if I don't hoist you up in a bread-bag."

"There's nothing about bread-bags in the articles of war," replied Jack; "but I'll tell you what there is, sir," and Jack commenced reading:

"All flag officers, and all persons in or belonging to his Majesty's ships or vessels of war, being guilty of profane oaths, execrations, drunkenness, uncleanness, or other scandalous actions, in derogation of God's honour, and corruption of good manners, shall incur such punishment as—"

"Damnation," cried the master, who was mad with rage, hearing that the whole ship's company were laughing.

"No, sir, not damnation," replied Jack, "that's when he's tried above; but according to the nature and degree of the offence—"

"Will you go to the mast-head, sir, or will you not?"

"If you please," replied Jack, "I'd rather not."

"Then, sir, consider yourself under an arrest—I'll try you by a court-martial, by God. Go down below, sir."

"With the greatest of pleasure, sir," replied Jack, "that's all right, and according to the articles of war, which are to guide us all." Jack folded up his articles of war, put them into his pocket, and went down into the berth.

Soon after Jack had gone down, Jolliffe, who had heard the whole of the altercation, followed him. "My lad," said Jolliffe, "I'm sorry for all this; you should have gone to the mast-head."

"I should like to argue that point a little," replied Jack.

"Yes, so would everybody; but if that were permitted, the service would be at a standstill—that would not do;—you must obey an order first, and then complain afterwards, if the order is unjust."

"It is not so in the articles of war."

"But it is so in the service."

"The captain told me that the articles of war were the guides of the service, and we were all equally bound to obey them."

"Well, but allowing that, I do not think your articles of war will bear you out. You observe, they say any officer, mariner, etcetera, guilty of disobedience to any lawful command. Now are you not guilty under that article?"

"That remains to be argued still," replied Jack. "A lawful command means an order established by law; now where is that law?—besides, the captain told me when I kicked that blackguard down the hatchway, that there was only the captain who could punish, and that officers could not take the law into their own hands; why then has the master?"

"His doing wrong as superior officer is no reason why you as an inferior should disobey him. If that were permitted—if every order were to be cavilled at and argued upon, as just or unjust, there would be an end of all discipline. Besides, recollect, that in the service there is custom, which is the same as law."

"That admits of a little argument," replied Jack.

"The service will admit of none, my dear boy: recollect that, even on shore, we have two laws, that which is written, and the *lex non scripta*, which is custom; of course we have it in the service, for the articles of war cannot provide for everything."

"They provide a court-martial for everything though," replied Jack.

"Yes, with death or dismissal from the service—neither of which would be very agreeable. You have got yourself into a scrape, and although the captain is evidently your friend, he cannot overlook it: fortunately, it is with the master, which is of less consequence than with the other officers; but still, you will have to submit, for the captain cannot overlook it."

"I'll tell you what, Jolliffe," replied Jack, "my eyes now begin to be opened to a great many things. The captain tells me, when I am astonished at bad language, that it is all zeal, and then I found out that what is all zeal in a superior to an inferior, is insolence when reversed. He tells me, that the articles of war are made to equally guide us all—the master breaks what is positively mentioned in the second article twenty times over, and goes scot free, while I am to be punished, because I do not comply with what the articles do not mention. How was I to know that I ought to go to the mast-head for punishment? particularly when the captain tells me that he alone is to punish in the ship. If I obey an order in opposition to the captain's order, is not that as bad as disobeying the captain? I think that I have made out a very strong case, and my arguments are not to be confuted."

"I'm afraid that the master will make out a very strong case, and that your arguments will never be heard."

"That will be contrary to all the rules of justice."

"But according to all the rules of service."

"I do believe that I am a great fool," observed Jack, after a pause. "What do you imagine made me come to sea, Jolliffe?"

"Because you did not know when you were well off," replied the mate dryly.

"That's true enough; but my reason was, because I thought I should find that equality here that I could not find on shore."

Jolliffe stared.

"My dear boy, I heard you say that you obtained those opinions from your father; I mean no disrespect to him, but he must be either mad or foolish, if at his age he has not yet discovered that there is no such thing in existence."

"I begin to think so," replied Jack; "but that does not prove that there ought not to be."

"I beg your pardon; the very non-existence proves that it ought not to be—'whatever is, is right'—you might as well expect to find perfect happiness or perfection in the individual. Your father must be a visionary."

"The best thing that I can do is to go home again."

"No, my dear Easy, the best thing that you can do is to stay in the service, for it will soon put an end to all such nonsensical ideas; and it will make you a clever, sensible fellow. The service is a rough, but a good school, where everybody finds his level—not the level of equality, but the level which his natural talent and acquirements will rise or sink him to, in proportion as they are plus or minus. It is a noble service, but has its imperfections, as everything in this world must have. I have little reason to speak in its favour, as far as I am concerned, for it has been hard bread to me, but there must be exceptions in every rule. Do not think of quitting the service until you have given it a fair trial. I am aware that you are an only son, and your father is a man of property, and, therefore, in the common parlance of the world, you are independent; but, believe me, no man, however rich, is independent, unless he has a profession, and you will find no better than this, notwithstanding—"

"What?"

"That you will be, most certainly, sent to the mast-head to-morrow."

"We'll argue that point," replied Jack; "at all events, I will go and turn in to-night."

Chapter Thirteen.

In which our hero begins to act and think for himself.

Whatever may have been Jack's thoughts, at all events they did not spoil his rest. He possessed in himself all the materials of a true philosopher, but there was a great deal of weeding still required. Jolliffe's arguments, sensible as they were, had very little effect upon him, for, strange to say, it is much more easy to shake a man's opinions when he is wrong than when he is right; proving that we are all of a very perverse nature. "Well," thought Jack, "if I am to go to the mast-head, I am, that's all; but it does not prove that my arguments are not good, only that they will not be listened to;" and then Jack shut his eyes, and in a few minutes was fast asleep.

The master had reported to the first lieutenant, and the first lieutenant to the captain, when he came on board the next morning, the conduct of Mr Easy, who was sent for in the cabin, to hear if he had any thing to offer in extenuation of his offence. Jack made an oration, which lasted more than half an hour, in which all the arguments he had brought forward to Jolliffe in the preceding chapter were entered fully into. Mr Jolliffe was then examined, and also Mr Smallsole was interrogated: after which the captain and the first lieutenant were left alone.

"Sawbridge," said Captain Wilson, "how true it is that any deviation from what is right invariably leads us into a scrape. I have done wrong: wishing to get this boy out of his father's hands, and fearful that he would not join the ship, and imagining him to be by no means the shrewd fellow that he is in reality, I represented the service in a much more favourable light than I should have done; all that he says I told him I did tell him, and it is I who really led the boy into error. Mr Smallsole has behaved tyrannically and unjustly; he punished the lad for no crime; so that what between the master and me, I am now on the horns of a dilemma. If I punish the boy, I feel that I am punishing him more for my own fault and the fault of others, than his own. If I do not punish him, I allow a flagrant and open violation of discipline to pass uncensured, which will be injurious to the service."

"He must be punished, sir," replied Sawbridge.

"Send for him," said the captain.

Jack made his appearance, with a very polite bow.

"Mr Easy, as you suppose that the articles of war contained all the rules and regulations of the service, I take it for granted that you have erred through ignorance. But recollect, that although you have erred through ignorance, such a violation of discipline, if passed unnoticed, will have a very injurious effect with the men, whose obedience is enforced by the example shown to them by the officers. I feel so convinced of your zeal, which you showed the other day in the case of Easthupp, that I am sure you will see the propriety of my proving to the men, by punishing you, that discipline must be enforced, and I shall therefore send for you on the quarter-deck, and order you to go to the mast-head in presence of the ship's company, as it was in the presence of the ship's company that you refused."

"With the greatest pleasure, Captain Wilson," replied Jack.

"And in future, Mr Easy, although I shall ever set my face against it, recollect that if any officer punishes you, and you imagine that you are unfairly treated, you will submit to the punishment, and then apply to me for redress."

"Certainly, sir," replied Jack, "now that I am aware of your wishes."

"You will oblige me, Mr Easy, by going on the quarter-deck, and wait there till I come up."

Jack made his best bow, and exit.

"Old Jolliffe told me that I should have to go," said Jack to himself, "and he was right, so far; but hang me if I hadn't the best of the argument, and that's all I care about."

Captain Wilson sent for the master, and reprimanded him for his oppression, as it was evident that there was no ground for punishment, and he forbade him ever to mast-head another midshipman, but to report his conduct to the first lieutenant or himself. He then proceeded to the quarter-deck, and, calling for Mr Easy, gave him what appeared to be a very severe reprimand, which Jack looked upon very quietly, because it was all *zeal* on the captain's part to give it, and all *zeal* on his own to take it. Our hero was then ordered up to the mast-head.

Jack took off his hat, and took three or four steps, in obedience to the order—and then returned and made his best bow—inquired of Captain Wilson whether he wished him to go to the fore or to the main-mast head.

"To the main, Mr Easy," replied the captain, biting his lips.

Jack ascended three spokes of the Jacob's ladder, when he again stopped, and took off his hat.

"I beg your pardon, Captain Wilson—you have not informed me whether it is your wish that I should go to the topmast, or the top-gallant cross-trees."

"To the top-gallant cross-trees, Mr Easy," replied the captain.

Jack ascended, taking it very easy: he stopped at the main-top for breath; at the main-topmast head, to look about him; and, at last, gained the spot agreed upon, where he seated himself, and, taking out the articles of war, commenced them again, to ascertain whether he could not have strengthened his arguments. He had not, however, read through the seventh article before the hands were turned up—"up anchor!" and Mr Sawbridge called, "All hands down from aloft!" Jack took the hint, folded up his documents, and came down as leisurely as he went up. Jack was a much better philosopher than his father.

The *Harpy* was soon under way, and made all sail, steering for Cape de Gatte, where Captain Wilson hoped to pick up a Spanish vessel or two, on his way to Toulon to receive the orders of the admiral.

A succession of light breezes and calms rendered the passage very tedious; but the boats were constantly out, chasing the vessels along shore, and Jack usually asked to be employed on this service: indeed, although so short a time afloat, he was, from his age and strength, one of the most effective midshipmen, and to be trusted, provided a whim did not come into his head; but hitherto Jack had always been under orders, and had always acquitted himself very well.

When the *Harpy* was off Tarragona, it so happened that there were several cases of dysentery in the ship, and Mr Asper and Mr Jolliffe were two of those who were suffering. This reduced the number of officers; and, at the same time, they had received information from the men of a fishing-boat, who, to obtain their own release, had given the intelligence, that a small convoy was coming down from Rosas as soon as the wind was fair, under the protection of two gun-boats.

Captain Wilson kept well off-shore until the wind changed, and then, allowing for the time that the vessels would take to run down the distance between Tarragona and Rosas, steered in the night, to intercept them; but it again fell calm, and the boats were therefore hoisted out, with directions to proceed along the shore, as it was supposed that the vessels could not now be far distant. Mr Sawbridge had the command of the expedition in the pinnace; the first cutter was in charge of the gunner, Mr Minus; and, as the other officers were sick, Mr Sawbridge, who liked Jack more and more every day, at his particular request gave him the command of the second cutter. As soon as he heard of it, Mesty declared to our hero that he would go with him; but without permission that was not possible. Jack obtained leave for Mesty to go in lieu of a marine: there were many men sick of the dysentery, and Mr Sawbridge was not sorry to take an idler out of the ship instead of a working man, especially as Mesty was known to be a good hand.

It was ten o'clock at night when the boats quitted the ship; and, as it was possible that they might not return till late the next day, one day's biscuit and rum were put on board each, that the crews might not suffer from exhaustion. The boats pulled in-shore, and then coasted for three hours, without seeing anything: the night was fine overhead, but there was no moon. It still continued calm, and the men began to feel fatigued, when, just as they were within a mile of a low point, they perceived the convoy over the land, coming down with their sails squared, before a light breeze.

Mr Sawbridge immediately ordered the boats to lie upon their oars, awaiting their coming, and arranging for the attack.

The white lateen sails of the gun-boat in advance were now plainly distinguishable from the rest, which were all huddled together in her wake. Down she came like a beautiful swan in the water, her sails just filled with the wind, and running about three knots an hour. Mr Sawbridge kept her three masts in one, that they might not be perceived, and winded the boats with their heads the same way, so that they might dash on board of her with a few strokes of the oars. So favourable was the course of the gun-boat, that she stood right between the launch on one bow and the two cutters on the other; and they were not perceived until they were actually alongside; the resistance was trifling, but some muskets and pistols had been fired, and the alarm was given. Mr Sawbridge took possession, with the crew of the launch, and brought the vessel to the wind, as he perceived that at the alarm all the convoy had done the same, directing the cutters to board the largest vessels, and secure as many as they could, while he would do the same with the launch, as he brought them to: but the other gun boat, which had not yet been seen, and had been forgotten, now made her appearance, and came down in a gallant manner to the support of her comrade.

Mr Sawbridge threw half his men into the launch, as she carried a heavy carronade, and sent her to assist the cutters, which had made right for the gun-boat. A smart firing of round and grape was opened upon the boats, which continued to advance upon her; but the officer commanding the gun-boat, finding that he had no support from his consort, and concluding that she had been captured, hauled his wind again, and stood out in the offing. Our hero pulled after her, although he could not see the other boats; but the breeze had freshened, and all pursuit was useless: he therefore directed his course to the convoy, and, after a hard pull, contrived to get on board of a one-masted xebeque, of about fifty tons. Mesty, who had eyes as sharp as a needle, had observed that when the alarm was given, several of the convoy had not rounded the point, and he therefore proposed, as this vessel was very light, that they should make short tacks with her, to weather the point, as if they were escaping, and by that means be able, particularly if it fell calm again, to capture some others. Jack thought this advice good. The convoy who had rounded the point had all stood out to seaward with the gun-boat, and had now a fresh breeze. To chase them was therefore useless; and the only chance was to do as Mesty had proposed. He therefore stood out into the breeze, and, after half an hour, tacked in shore, and fetched well to windward of the low point; but finding no vessels, he stood out again. Thus had he made three or four tacks, and had gained, perhaps, six or seven miles, when he perceived signals of recall made to leeward, enforced with guns.

"Mr Sawbridge wants us to come back, Mesty."

"Mr Sawbridge mind him own business," replied Mesty, "we nebber take all dis trubble to ply to windward for noting."

"But, Mesty, we must obey orders."

"Yes, sar, when he have him thumb upon you; but now, must do what tink most proper. By de powers, he catch me 'fore I go back."

"But we shall lose the ship."

"Find her again, by-and-bye, Massa Easy."

"But they will think that we are lost."

"So much the better, nebba look after us, Massa Easy; I guess we have a fine cruise anyhow. Morrow we take large vessel—make sail, take more, den we go to Toulon."

"But I don't know my way to Toulon; I know it lies up this way, and that's all."

"Dat enough, what you want more? Massa Easy, 'pose you not find fleet, fleet soon find you. By God, nobody nebba lost here. Now, Massa Easy, let um go 'bout gain. Somebody else burn biscuit and boil kettle to-morrow for de gentlemen. Murder Irish! only tink, Massa Easy—I boil kettle, and prince in my own country!"

Easy was very much of a mind with Mesty; "for," argued Jack, "if I go back now, I only bring a small vessel half full of beans, and I shall be ashamed to show my face. Now it is true, that they may suppose that we have been sunk by the fire of the gun-boat. Well, what then? they have a gun-boat to show for their night's work, and it will appear that there was harder fighting than there has been, and Mr Sawbridge may benefit by it." (Jack was a very knowing fellow to have learned so much about the service already.) "Well, and when they discover that we are not lost, how glad they will be to find us, especially if we bring some prizes—which I will do, or I'll not go back again. It's not often that one gets a command before being two months at sea, and, hang me, now I've got it if I won't keep it; and Mr Smallsole may mast-head whom he pleases. I'm sorry for poor Gossett though; if Vigors supposes me dead how he will murder the poor little fellow—however, it's all for the good of the service, and I'll revenge him when I come back. Hang me if I won't take a cruise."

"I talk to the men, they say thay all tick to you like leech. Now dat job settled, I tink we better go 'bout again."

A short time after this decision on the part of our hero, the day broke: Jack first looked to leeward, and perceived the gun-boat and convoy standing in for the shore about ten miles distant, followed by the *Harpy*, under all sail. He could also perceive the captured gun-boat lying to in-shore to prevent their escape.

"*Harpy* hab um all, by Gosh!" cried Mesty; "I ab notion dat she soon settle um hash."

They were so busy looking at the *Harpy* and the convoy, that, for some time, they quite forgot to look to windward. At last Mesty turned his eyes that way.

"Dam um, I see right last night; look, Massa Easy—one chip, one brig tree lateen—dem for us. By de power, but we make *bon*prize to-night."

The vessels found out by Mesty were not above three miles to windward; they were under all sail, beating up for the protection of a battery not far distant.

"Now, Massa, suppose dey see our boat, dey tink something; keep boat alongside, and shift her when we go 'bout every time: better not sail so fast now—keep further off till they drop anchor for de night; and den, when it dark, we take 'em."

All Mesty's advice was good, with the exception perhaps of advising our hero how to disobey orders and take a cruise. To prevent the vessel from approaching too near the others, and at the same time to let her have the appearance of doing her best, a sail was towed overboard under the bows, and after that they watched the motions of the *Harpy*.

The distance was too great to distinguish very clearly, but Mesty shinned up the mast of the vessel, and reported progress.

"By Jasus, dare one gun—two gun—go it, *Harpy*. Won't she ab um, sure enough. Now gun-boat fire—dat our gun-boat—no, dat not ours. Now our gun-boat fire—dat pretty—fire away. Ah, now de *Harpy* cum up. All 'mung 'em. Bung, bung, bung—rattle de grape, by gosh. I ab notion de Spaniard is very pretty considerable trouble just now, anyhow. All hove-to, so help me gosh—not more firing; *Harpy* take um all—dare gun boat hove-to, she strike um colours. By all powers, but suppose dey tink we no share prize-money—they find it not little mistake. Now, my lads, it all over, and," continued Mesty, sliding down the mast, "I tink you better not show yourself too much; only two men stay on deck, and dem two take off um jackets."

Mesty's report was correct; the *Harpy* had captured the other gun-boat, and the whole convoy. The only drawback to their good fortune was the disappearance of Mr Easy and the cutter: it was supposed that a shot from the gun-boat must have sunk her, and that the whole crew were drowned. Captain Wilson and Mr Sawbridge seriously regretted the loss of our hero, as they thought that he would have turned out a shining character as soon as he had sown his wild oats; so did Mr Asper, because our hero's purse went with him; so did Jolliffe, because he had taken an affection for him; so did little Gossett, because he anticipated no mercy from Vigors. On the other hand, there were some who were glad that he was gone; and as for the ship's company in general, they lamented the loss of the poor cutter's crew for twenty-four hours, which, in a man-of-war, is a very long while, and then they thought no more about them. We must leave the *Harpy* to make the best of her way to Toulon and now follow our hero.

The cutter's crew knew very well that Jack was acting contrary to orders, but anything was to them a change from the monotony of a man-of-war; and they, as well as Mesty, highly approved of a holiday.

It was, however, necessary that they should soon proceed to business, for they had but their allowance of bread and grog for one day, and in the vessel they found nothing except a few heads of garlic, for the Spaniards coasting down shore had purchased their provisions as they required them. There were only three prisoners on board, and they had been put down in the hold among the beans; a bag of which had been roused on deck, and a part put into the kettle to make soup. Jack did not much admire the fare of the first day—it was bean-soup for breakfast, bean-soup for dinner, and if you felt hungry during the intervals it was still bean-soup, and nothing else.

One of the men could speak a little Lingua Franca, and the prisoners were interrogated as to the vessels to windward. The ship was stated to be valuable, and also one of the brigs. The ship carried guns, and that was all that they knew about them. As the sun went down the vessels dropped their anchors off the battery. The breeze continued light, and the vessel which contained Jack and his fortunes was about four miles to leeward. As for the *Harpy*, they had long lost sight of her, and it was now time to proceed to some arrangement. As soon as it was dark Jack turned his hands up and made a very long speech. He pointed out to the men that his zeal had induced him not to return to the ship until he had brought something with him worth having—that they had had nothing but beans to eat during the whole day, which was anything but agreeable, and that, therefore, it was absolutely necessary that they should better their condition; and there was a large ship not four miles off, and that he intended to take her; and as soon as he had taken her he intended to take some more; that he trusted to their zeal to support him on this occasion, and that he expected to do a great deal during the cruise. He pointed out to them that they must consider themselves as on board of a man-of-war, and be guided by the articles of war, which were written for them all—and that in case they forgot them, he had a copy in his pocket, which he would read to them to morrow morning, as soon as they were comfortably settled on board of the ship. He then appointed Mesty as first lieutenant; the marine as sergeant; the coxswain as boatswain; two men as midshipmen to keep watch: two others as boatswain's mates, leaving two more for the ship's company, who were divided into the larboard and starboard watch. The cutter's crew were perfectly content with Jack's speech, and their brevet rank, and after that they commenced a more important topic, which was, how they were to take the ship. After some discussion, Mesty's advice was approved of; which was, that they should anchor not far ahead of the ship, and wait till about two o'clock in the morning, when they would drop silently down upon her in the cutter, and take possession.

About nine o'clock the vessel was anchored as they proposed, and Jack was a little astonished to find that the ship was much larger that he had any idea of; for, although polacca-rigged, she was nearly the same tonnage as the *Harpy*. The Spanish prisoners were first tied hand and foot, and laid upon the beans, that they might give no alarm, the sails were furled, and all was kept quiet.

On board of the ship, on the contrary, there was noise and revelry; and about half-past ten a boat was seen to leave her and pull for the shore; after which the noise gradually ceased, the lights one by one disappeared, and then all was silent.

"What do you think, Mesty?" said Jack; "do you think we shall take her?"

"It is take her, you mane; sure enough we'll take her, stop a bit—wait till um all fast asleep."

About twelve o'clock there came on a mizzling heavy rain, which was very favourable for our hero's operations. But as it promised soon to clear up, by Mesty's advice they did not delay any longer. They crept softly into the boat, and with two oars to steer her dropped under the bows of the vessel, climbed up the forechains, and found the deck empty. "Take care not fire pistol," said Mesty to the men as they came up, putting his finger to their lips to impress them with the necessity of silence, for Mesty had been an African warrior, and knew the advantage of surprise. All the men being on deck, and the boat made fast, Jack and Mesty led the way aft; not a soul was to be seen: indeed, it was too dark to see anybody unless they were walking the deck. The companion-hatch was secured, and the gratings laid on the after-hatch ways, and then they went aft to the binnacle again, where there was a light burning. Mesty ordered two of the men to go forward to secure the hatches, and then to remain there on guard—and then the rest of the men and our hero consulted at the wheel.

"By the power we ab the ship!" said Mesty, "but must manage plenty yet. I tink der some damn lazy rascal sleep 'tween the guns. A lilly while it no rain, and den we see better. Now keep all quiet."

"There must be a great many men in this ship," replied our hero; "she is very large, and has twelve or fourteen guns—how shall we manage to secure them?"

"All right," replied Mesty, "manage all dat by-and-bye. Don't care how soon daylight come."

"It has left off raining already," observed Easy; "there is a candle in the binnacle—suppose we light it and look round the decks."

"Yes," replied Mesty, "one man sentry over cabin hatch, and another over after-hatch. Now den we light candle, and all the rest go round the deck. Mind you leave all your pistols on capstern."

Jack lighted the candle, and they proceeded round the decks: they had not walked far, when, between two of the guns, they discovered a heap covered with gregos. "There de *watch*," whispered Mesty; "all fast—not ready for dem yet."

Mesty blew out the candle, and they all retreated to the binnacle, where Mesty took out a coil of the ropes about the mizzen-mast, and cutting it into lengths, gave them to the other men to unlay. In a few minutes they had prepared a great many seizings to tie the men with.

"Now den we light candle again, and make sure of them lazy hounds," said Mesty; "very much oblige to dem all de same; they let us take de ship—mind now, wake one at a time, and shut him mouth."

"But suppose they get their mouths free and cry out?" replied Jack.

"Den, Mr Easy," replied Mesty, changing his countenance to an expression almost demoniacal—"there no help for it"—and Mesty showed his knife which he held in his right hand.

"Oh, no! do not let us murder them."

"No, massa—suppose can help it; but suppose they get upper hand—what become of us? Spaniards hab knives, and use dem too, by de power!"

The observation of Mesty was correct, and the expression of his countenance when he showed his knife proved what a relentless enemy he could be, if his blood was once roused—but Mesty had figured in the Ashantee wars in former days, and after that the reader need not be surprised. They proceeded cautiously to where the Spaniards lay. The arrangements of Mesty were very good. There were two men to gag them while the others were to tie their limbs. Mesty and Easy were to kneel by them with the candle, with raised knives to awe them into silence, or to strike home, if their own safety required it.

The gregos were removed off the first man, who opened his eyes at the sight of the candle, but the coxswain's hand was on his mouth—he was secured in silence. The other two men were awaked, and threw off their coverings, but they were also secured without there being occasion to resort to bloodshed.

"What shall we do now, Mesty?"

"Now, sar," said Mesty, "open the after-hatch and watch—suppose more men come up, we make them fass; suppose no more come up, we wait till daylight—and see what take place."

Mesty then went forward to see if the men were watchful on the forecastle; and having again gone round the whole of the deck to see if there were any more men on it, he blew out the candle, and took his station with the others at the after-hatchway.

It was just at break of day that the Spaniards who had to keep the morning watch having woke up, as people generally do at that hour at which they expect to be called, dressed themselves and came on deck, imagining, and very truly, that those of the middle watch had fallen asleep, but little imagining that the deck was in possession of Englishmen. Mesty and the others retreated, to allow them all to come up before they could perceive them, and fortunately this was accomplished. Four men came on the deck, looked round them, and tried to make out in the dark where their shipmates might be. The grating was slapped on again by Jack, and before they could well gain their eyesight, they were seized and secured, not, however, without a scuffle and some noise.

By the time that these men were secured and laid between the guns it was daylight, and they now perceived what a fine vessel they had fairly taken possession of—but there was much to be done yet. There was, of course, a number of men in the ship, and, moreover, they were not a mile from a battery of ten guns. Mesty, who was foremost in everything, left four men abaft and went forward on the forecastle, examined the cable, which was *coir* rope, and therefore easily divided, and then directed the two men forward to coil a hawser upon the fore-grating, the weight of which would make all safe in that quarter, and afterwards to join them on the quarter-deck.

"Now, Mr Easy, the great ting will be to get hold of captain; we must get him on deck. Open cabin-hatch now, and keep the after-hatch fast. Two men stay there, the others all come aft."

"Yes," replied Jack, "it will be a great point to secure the captain—but how are we to get him up?"

"You no know how to get captain up? By de holy, I know very well."

And Mesty took up the coils of rope about the mizzen-mast, and threw them upon deck, one after another, making all the noise possible. In a short time there was a violent pull of a bell at the cabin door, and in a minute afterwards a man in his shirt came up the cabin-hatchway, who was immediately secured.

"Dis de captain's servant," said Mesty, "he come say no make such damned noise. Stop a little—captain get in passion, and come up himself."

And Mesty renewed the noise with the ropes over the cabin. Mesty was right; in a few minutes the captain himself came up, boiling with indignation. At the sound of the cabin door opening, the seamen and our hero concealed themselves behind the companion-hatch, which was very high, so as to give the captain time to get fairly on deck. The men already secured had been covered over with the gregos. The captain was a most powerful man, and it was with difficulty that he was pinioned, and then without his giving the alarm, had there been anyone to assist him, but as yet no one had turned out of his hammock.

"Now we all right," said Mesty, "and soon ab de ship; but I must make him 'fraid."

The captain was seated down on the deck against one of the guns, and Mesty, putting on the look of a demon, extended above him his long nervous arm, with the sharp knife clutched, as if ready every instant to strike it into his heart. The Spanish captain felt his situation anything but pleasant. He was then interrogated as to the number of men in the ship, officers, etcetera, to all which questions he answered truly: he cast his eyes at the firm and relentless countenance of Mesty, who appeared but to wait the signal.

"I tink all pretty safe now," said Mesty. "Mr Easy, we now go down below and beat all men into the hold."

Our hero approved of this suggestion. Taking their pistols from the capstern, they rushed down with their cutlasses, and leaving two men to guard the cabin door, they were soon among the crew, who were all naked in their hammocks: the resistance, although the numbers were more than double of the English, was of course trifling. In a few minutes, the Spaniards were all thrown down into the hold of the vessel, and the hatches placed over them. Every part of the ship was now in their possession except the cabin, and to that they all repaired. Our hero tried the door, and found it fast; they beat it open, and were received with loud screams from one side of the cabin, and the discharge of two pistols from the other, fortunately without injury: those who had fired the pistols were an elderly man and a lad about the age of our hero. They were thrown down and secured; the cabin was searched, and nobody else found in it but three women; one old and shrivelled, the other two, although with their countenances distorted with terror, were lovely as Houris. So thought Jack, as he took off his hat, and made them a very low bow with his usual politeness, as they crouched, half dressed, in a corner. He told them in English that they had nothing to fear, and begged that they would attend to their toilets. The ladies made no reply, because, in the first place, they did not know what Jack said, and in the next, they could not speak English.

Mesty interrupted Jack in his attentions, by pointing out that they must all go upon deck—so Jack again took off his hat and bowed, and then followed his men, who led away the two prisoners taken in the cabin. It was now five o'clock in the morning, and there was movement on board of the other vessels, which lay not far from the ship.

"Now then," said Jack, "what shall we do with the prisoners?—could we not send the boat and bring our own vessel alongside, and put them all in, tied as they are? We should then get rid of them."

"Massa Easy, you be one very fine officer one of dese days. Dat damn good idea, anyhow;—but suppose we send our own boat, what they *tink* on board of de oder vessel? Lower down lilly boat from stern, put in four men, and drop vessel 'longside—dat it."

This was done; the cutter was on the seaward side of the ship, and, as the ship was the outermost vessel, was concealed from the view of the Spaniards on board of the other vessels, and in the battery on shore. As soon as the lateen vessel was alongside, the men who had already been secured on deck, amounting to seven, were lowered into her, and laid upon the beans in the hold; all, except the captain, the two cabin prisoners, and the captain's servant. They then went down below, took off one part of the hatches, and ordered the Spaniards up from the hold: as they came on deck they were made fast and treated in the same manner. Mesty and the men went down to examine if there were any left concealed, and finding that they were all out, returned on deck. The men who had been beaten down in the hold were twenty-two in number, making the whole complement of thirty. As soon as they had all been put into the xebeque, she was again hauled off and anchored outside, and Jack found himself in possession of a fine ship of fourteen guns, with three prisoners male and three prisoners female.

When the men returned in the boat from the vessel in which the prisoners had been confined (the hatches having been secured over them, by way of further precaution), by the advice of Mesty they put on the jackets and caps of the Spanish seamen, of which there was a plentiful supply below.

"Now what's to be done, Mesty?" inquired Jack.

"Now, sar, we send some of the men aloft to get sails all ready, and while they do that I cast loose this fellow," pointing to the captain's servant, "and make him get some breakfast, for he know where to find it."

"Capital idea of yours, Mesty, for I'm tired of bean-soup already, and I will go down and pay my respects to the ladies."

Mesty looked over the counter.

"Yes, and be quick too, Massa Easy; damn the women, they toss their handkerchief in the air to people in the battery—quick, Massa Easy."

Mesty was right—the Spanish girls were waving their handkerchiefs for assistance; it was all that they could do, poor things. Jack hastened into the cabin, laid hold of the two young ladies, very politely pulled them out of the quarter gallery, and begged that they would not give themselves so much trouble. The young ladies looked very much confused, and as they could no longer wave their handkerchiefs, they put them up to their eyes and began to weep, while the elderly lady went on her knees, and held her hands up for mercy. Jack raised her up, and very politely handed her to one of the cabin lockers.

In the meantime Mesty, with his gleaming knife and expressive look, had done wonders with the captain's steward, for such the man was: and a breakfast of chocolate, salt meat, hams and sausages, white biscuit and red wine, had been spread on the quarter-deck. The men had come from aloft, and Jack was summoned on deck. Jack offered his hand to the two young ladies, and beckoned the old one to follow: the old lady did not think it advisable to refuse his courtesy, so they accompanied him.

As soon as the females came on deck, and found the two cabin prisoners bound, they ran to them and embraced them with tears. Jack's heart melted, and as there was now no fear, he asked Mesty for his knife, and cut loose the two Spaniards, pointing to the breakfast, and requesting that they would join them. The Spaniards made a bow, and the ladies thanked Jack with a sweet smile; and the captain of the vessel, who still lay pinioned against the gun, looked, as much as to say, Why the devil don't you ask me? but the fact was, they had had such trouble to secure him, that Jack did not much like the idea of letting him loose again. Jack and the seamen commenced their breakfast, and as the ladies and prisoners did not appear inclined to eat, they ate their share and their own too; during which the elderly man inquired of Jack if he could speak French.

Jack, with his mouth full of sausage, replied that he could; and then commenced a conversation, from which Jack learned as follows:—

The elderly gentleman was a passenger with the young man, who was his son, and the ladies, who were his wife and his two daughters, and they were proceeding to Tarragona. Whereupon Jack made a bow and thanked him; and then the gentleman, whose name was Don Cordova de Rimarosa, wished to know what Jack intended to do with them, hoping, as a gentleman, he would put them on shore with their effects, as they were non-combatants. Jack explained all this to Mesty and the men, and then finished his sausage. The men, who were a little elevated with the wine which they had been drinking, proposed that they should take the ladies a cruise, and Jack at first did not dislike the idea, but he said nothing; Mesty, however, opposed this, saying, that ladies only made a row in a ship, and the coxswain sided with him, saying, that they should all be at daggers drawn. Whereupon Jack pulled out the "articles of war," and informed the men, that there was no provision in them for women, and therefore the thing was impossible.

The next question was, as to the propriety of allowing them to take their effects; and it was agreed, at last, that they might take them. Jack desired the steward to feed his master the captain, and then told the Spanish Don the result of the consultation; further informing him, that as soon as it was dark, he intended to put them all on board the small vessel, when they could cast loose the men and do as they pleased. The Don and the ladies returned thanks, and went down to pack up their baggage; Mesty ordering two men to help them, but with a caution, that they were not to encumber themselves with any of the money, if there should happen to be any on board.

The crew were busy during the day making preparations for sailing. The coxswain had examined the provender in the ship, and found that there was enough for at least three months, of water, wine, and provisions, independent of luxuries for the cabin. All thoughts of taking any more of the vessels were abandoned, for their crew was but weak to manage the one which they had possession of. A fine breeze sprang up, and they dropped their fore-topsails, just as a boat was shoving off from the shore; but seeing the fore-topsails loosed, it put back again. This was fortunate, or all would have been discovered. The other vessels also loosed their sails, and the crews were heard weighing the anchors.

But the *Nostra Señora del Carmen*, which was Jack's prize, did not move. At last the sun went down, the baggage was placed in the cutter, the ladies and passengers went into the boat, thanking Jack for his kindness, who put his hand to his heart and bowed to the deck; and the captain was lowered down after them. Four men well armed pulled them alongside of the xebeque, put them and their trunks on deck, and returned to the ship. The cutter was then hoisted up, and as the anchor was too heavy to weigh, they cut the cable, and made sail. The other vessels followed their example. Mesty and the seamen cast longing eyes upon them, but it was of no use; so they sailed in company for about an hour, and then Jack hauled his wind for a cruise.

Chapter Fourteen.

In which our hero finds that disagreeable occurrences will take place on a cruise.

As soon as the ship had been hauled to the wind, Jack's ship's company seemed to think that there was nothing to do except to make merry, so they brought some earthen jars full of wine, and emptied them so fast that they were soon fast asleep on the deck, with the exception of the man at the helm, who, instead of thirty-two, could clearly make out sixty-four points in the compass, and of course was able to steer to a much greater nicety. Fortunately, the weather was fine, for when the man at the helm had steered till he could see no more, and requested to be released, he found that his shipmates were so overpowered with fatigue, that it was impossible to wake them. He kicked them one by one most unmercifully in the ribs, but it was of no use: under these circumstances, he did as they did, that is, lay down with them, and in ten minutes it would have taken as much kicking to awake him as he gave his shipmates.

In the meantime the ship had it all her own way, and not knowing where she was to go she went round and round the compass during the best part of the night. Mesty had arranged the watches, Jack had made a speech, and the men had promised everything, but the wine had got into their heads, and memory had taken that opportunity to take a stroll. Mesty had been down with Jack, examining the cabin, and in the captain's state-room they had found fourteen thousand dollars in bags: of this they determined not to tell the men, but locked up the money and every thing else of value, and took out the key. They then sat down at the cabin table, and after some conversation, it was no matter of surprise, after having been up all the night before, that Jack laid his head on the table and fell fast asleep. Mesty kept his eyes open for some time, but at last his head sank down upon his chest, and he also slumbered. Thus, about one o'clock in the morning, there was not a very good watch kept on board of the *Nostra Señora del Carmen*.

About four o'clock in the morning, Mesty tumbled forward, and he hit his head against the table, which roused him up.

"By de mass, I tink I almost fall asleep," cried he, and he went to the cabin window, which had been left open, and found that there was a strong breeze blowing in. "By de Lord, de wind ab come more aft," said Mesty, "why they not tell me?" So saying, he went on deck, where he found no one at the helm; every one drunk, and the ship with her yards braced up running before the wind, just by way of a change. Mesty growled, but there was no time to lose; the topsails only were set—these he lowered down, and then put the helm a-lee, and lashed it, while he went down to call our hero to his assistance. Jack roused up, and went on deck.

"This nebber do, Massa Easy; we all go to devil together—dam drunken dogs—I freshen um up any how." So Mesty drew some buckets of water, with which he soused the ship's company, who then appeared to be recovering their senses.

"By heavens!" says Jack, "but this is contrary to the 'articles of war'; I shall read them to them to-morrow morning."

"I tell what better ting, Massa Easy; we go lock up all de wine, and sarve out so much, and no more. I go do it at once, 'fore they wake up."

Mesty went down, leaving Jack on deck to his meditations.

"I am not sure," thought Jack, "that I have done a very wise thing. Here I am with a parcel of fellows who have no respect for the articles of war, and who get as drunk as David's sow. I have a large ship, but I have very few hands; and if it comes on bad weather, what shall I do?—for I know very little—hardly how to take in a sail. Then—as for where to steer, or how to steer, I know not—nor do any of my men; but, however, as it was very narrow when we came into the Mediterranean, through the straits, it is hardly possible to get out of them without perceiving it: besides, I should know the rock of Gibraltar again, if I saw it. I must talk to Mesty."

Mesty soon returned with the keys of the provision-room tied to his bandana.

"Now," says he, "they not get drunk again in a hurry."

A few more buckets of water soon brought the men to their senses: they again stood on their legs, and gradually recovered themselves. Daylight broke, and they found that the vessel had made an attempt for the Spanish coast, being within a mile of the beach, and facing a large battery *fleur d'eau*; fortunately they had time to square the yards, and steer the ship along shore under the top-sails, before they were perceived. Had they been seen at daylight in the position that they were in during the night, the suspicions of the Spaniards would have been awakened; and had a boat been sent off, while they were all drunk, they must have been recaptured.

The men, who perceived what danger they had been in, listened very penitently to Jack's remonstrances; and our hero, to impress them more strongly on their minds, took out the articles of war, and read that on drunkenness from beginning to end; but the men had heard it read so often at the gangway, that it did not make a due impression. As Mesty said, his plan was better, and so it proved; for as soon as Jack had done, the men went down to get another jug of wine, and found, to their disappointment, that it was all under lock and key.

In the meantime, Jack called Mesty aft, and asked him if he knew the way to Toulon. Mesty declared that he knew nothing about it.

"Then, Mesty, it appears to me that we have a better chance of finding our way back to Gibraltar; for you know the land was on our left side all the way coming up the Mediterranean; and if we keep it, as it is now, on our right, we shall get back again along the coast."

Mesty agreed with Jack that this was the *ne plus ultra* of navigation: and that old Smallsole could not do better with his "pig-yoke" and compasses. So they shook a reef out of the top-sails, set top-gallant-sails, and ran directly down the coast from point to point, keeping about five miles distant. The men prepared a good dinner; Mesty gave them their allowance of wine, which was just double what they had on board the *Harpy*—so they soon appeared to be content. One man, indeed, talked very big and very mutinously, swearing that if the others would join him, they would soon have liquor enough, but Mesty gave him his look, opened his knife, and swore that he would settle him, and Jack knocked him down with a handspike; so that, what with the punishment received, and that which was promised, the fellow thought he might as well say no more about it. The fact is, that had it not been from fear of Mesty, the whole of the men would, in all probability, have behaved equally as bad; nevertheless, they were a little staggered, it must be owned, at seeing Jack play so good a stick with the handspike.

After this night Jack and Mesty kept watch and watch, and everything went on very well until they were nearly abreast of Carthagena, when a gale came on from the northward, and drove them out of sight of land. Sail after sail was reduced with difficulty from their having so few hands, and the gale blew for three days with great fury. The men were tired out and discontented. It was Jack's misfortune that he had but one good man with him: even the coxswain of the boat, although a fine-looking man, was worth nothing. Mesty was Jack's sheet-anchor. The fourth day the gale moderated, but they had no idea where they were: they knew that they had been blown off, but how far they could not tell; and Jack now began to discover that a cruise at sea without a knowledge of navigation was a more nervous thing than he had contemplated. However, there was no help for it: at night they wore the ship, and stood on the other tack, and at daylight they perceived that they were close to some small islands, and much closer to some large rocks, against which the sea beat high, although the wind had subsided. Again was the helm put up, and they narrowly escaped. As soon as the sails were trimmed, the men came aft, and proposed that if they could find anchorage, they should run into it, for they were quite tired out. This was true; and Jack consulted with Mesty, who thought it advisable to agree to the proposal. That the islands were not inhabited was very evident. The only point to ascertain was if there were good anchorage. The coxswain offered to go in the boat and examine; and, with four men, he set off, and in about an hour returned, stating that there was plenty of water, and that it was as smooth as a mill-pond, being land-locked on every side. As they could not weigh the bower-anchor, they bent the kedge, and, running in without accident, came to in a small bay, between the islands, in seven fathoms water. The sails were furled, and everything put in order by the seamen, who then took the boat and pulled on shore. "They might as well have asked leave," thought Jack. In an hour they returned, and, after a short discussion, came aft to our hero in a body.

The coxswain was spokesman. He said that they had had hard work, and required now to have some rest,—that there were provisions on board for three months, so that there could not be any hurry,—and that they had found they could pitch a tent very well on shore, and live there for a short time,—and that as there was no harm in getting drunk on shore, they expected that they might be allowed to take provisions and plenty of wine with them; and that the men had desired him to ask leave, because they were determined to go, whether or no. Jack was about to answer with the handspike; but perceiving that the men had all put on their cutlasses, and had their pistols at their belts, he thought proper to consult Mesty, who, perceiving that resistance was useless, advised Jack to submit, observing, that the sooner all the wine was gone the better, as there would be nothing done while it lasted. Jack, therefore, very graciously told them, that they should have their own way, and he would stay there as long as they pleased. Mesty gave them the keys of the provision-hatch, and told them, with a grin, to help themselves. The men then informed Jack that he and Mesty should stay on board, and take care of the ship for them, and that they would take the Spaniard on shore to cook their victuals; but to this Jack observed, that if he had not two hands, he could not obey their orders, in case they wished him to come on shore for them. The men thought there was good argument in that observation, and therefore allowed Jack to retain the Spaniard, that he might be more prompt to their call from the beach: they then wished him good day, and begged that he would amuse himself with the "articles of war."

As soon as they had thrown a spare sail into the boat, with some spars to make a tent, and some bedding, they went down below, hoisted up two pipes of wine out of the three, a bag or two of biscuit, arms and ammunition, and as much of the salt provisions as they thought they might require. The boat being full, they shoved off, with three cheers of derision. Jack was sensible to the compliment: he stood at the gangway, took off his hat, and made them a polite bow.

As soon as they were gone, Mesty grinned with his sharp-filed teeth, and looking at our hero, said:

"I tink I make um pay for all dis—stop a little; by de piper as played before Moses, but our turn come by-and-by."

As for Jack, he said nothing, but he thought the more. In about an hour the men returned in the boat: they had forgotten many things they wanted—wood to make a fire, and several utensils; they helped themselves freely, and having now everything that they could think of, they again went on shore.

"How damn lucky we never tell dem about the dollars," said Mesty, as Jack and he were watching the motions of the men.

"It is, indeed," replied Jack, "not that they could spend them here."

"No, Massa Easy, but suppose they find all that money, they take boat and go away with it. Now, I hab them in my clutch—stop a little."

A narrow piece of salt pork had been left at the gangway: Jack, without knowing why, tossed it over board; being almost all fat it sank very gradually: Jack watched it as it disappeared, so did Mesty, both full of thought, when they perceived a dark object rising under it: it was a ground shark, who took it into his maw, sank down, and disappeared.

"What was that?" said Jack.

"That ground shark, Massa Easy,—worst shark of all; you neber see him till you feel him;" and Mesty's eyes sparkled with pleasure. "By de powers, they soon stop de mutiny; now I hab 'em."

Jack shuddered and walked away.

During the day, the men on shore were seen to work hard, and make all the preparations before they abandoned themselves to the sensual gratification of intemperance. The tent was pitched, the fire was lighted, and all the articles taken on shore rolled up and stowed away in their places; they were seen to sit down and dine, for they were within hail of the ship, and then one of the casks of wine was spiled. In the meantime the Spaniard, who was a quiet lad, had prepared the dinner for Easy and his now only companion. The evening closed, and all was noise and revelry on shore; and as they danced, and sung, and tossed off the cans of wine by the light of the fire, as they hallooed and screamed, and became more and more intoxicated, Mesty turned to Jack with his bitter smile, and only said:

"Stop a little."

At last the noise grew fainter, the fire died away, and gradually all was silent. Jack was still hanging over the gangway when Mesty came up to him. The new moon had just risen, and Jack's eyes were fixed upon it.

"Now, Massa Easy, please you come aft and lower down little boat; take your pistols and then we go on shore and bring off the cutter; they all asleep now."

"But why should we leave them without a boat, Mesty?" for Jack thought of the sharks, and the probability of the men attempting to swim off.

"I tell you, sar, this night they get drunk, to morrow they get drunk again, but drunken men never keep quiet—suppose one man say to others, 'Let's go aboard and kill officer, and then we do as we please,' they all say yes, and they all come and do it. No, sar—must have boat—if not for your sake, I must hab it, save my own life anyhow, for they hate me and kill me first;—by de powers, stop a little."

Jack felt the truth of Mesty's observation; he went aft with him, lowered down the small boat, and they hauled it alongside. Jack went down with Mesty into the cabin and fetched his pistols—"And the Spaniard, Mesty, can we leave him on board alone?"

"Yes, sar, he no got arms, and he see dat we have—but suppose he find arms he never dare do any thing—I know de man."

Our hero and Mesty went down into the boat and shoved off, pulling gently on shore; the men were in a state of intoxication, so as not to be able to move, much less hear. They cast off the cutter, towed her on board, and made her fast with the other boat astern.

"Now, sar, we may go to bed; to-morrow morning you will see."

"They have everything they require on shore," replied Easy; "all they could want with the cutter would be to molest us."

"Stop a little," replied Mesty.

Jack and Mesty went to bed, and as a precaution against the Spaniard, which was hardly necessary, Mesty locked the cabin door—but Mesty never forgot anything.

Jack slept little that night—had melancholy forebodings which he could not shake off; indeed, Jack had reflected so much since he had left the ship, he had had his eyes so much opened, and had felt what a responsibility he had taken by indulging himself in a whim of the moment, that it might be almost said that in the course of one fortnight he had at once from a boy sprung up into a man. He was mortified and angry, but he was chiefly so with himself.

Mesty was up at daylight and Jack soon followed him: they watched the party on shore, who had not yet left the tent. At last, just as Jack had finished his breakfast, one or two made their appearance: the men looked about them as if they were searching for something, and then walked down to the beach, to where the boat had been made fast. Jack looked at Mesty, who grinned, and answered with the words so often repeated:

"Stop a little."

The men then walked along the rocks until they were abreast of the ship.

"Ship ahoy!"

"Halloo," replied Mesty.

"Bring the boat ashore directly, with a breaker of water."

"I knew dat," cried Mesty, rubbing his hands with delight. "Massy Easy, you must tell them No."

"But why should I not give them water, Mesty?"

"Because, sar, den they take boat."

"Very true," replied Easy.

"Do you hear on board?" cried the coxswain, who was the man who hailed—"send the boat immediately, or we'll cut the throats of every mother's son of you, by God!"

"I shall not send the boat," replied Jack, who now thought Mesty was right.

"You won't—won't you?—then your doom's sealed," replied the man, walking up to the tent with the other. In a short time all the seamen turned out of the tent, bringing with them four muskets, which they had taken on shore with them.

"Good heavens! they are not, surely, going to fire at us, Mesty."

"Stop a little."

The men then came down abreast of the ship, and the coxswain again hailed, and asked if they would bring the boat on shore.

"You must say No, sar," replied Mesty.

"I feel I must," replied Jack, and then he answered the coxswain, "No."

The plan of the mutineers had been foreseen by the wily negro—it was to swim off to the boats which were riding astern, and to fire at him or Jack, if they attempted to haul them up alongside and defend them. To get into the boats, especially the smaller one, from out of the water, was easy enough. Some of the men examined their priming and held the muskets at their hips all ready, with the muzzles towards the ship, while the coxswain and two men were throwing off their clothes.

"Stop, for God's sake, stop!" cried Jack "The harbour is full of ground sharks—it is, upon my soul!"

"Do you think to frighten us with ground sharks?" replied the coxswain, "keep under cover, my lad; Jack, give him a shot to prove we are in earnest, and every time he or that nigger show their heads, give them another, my lads."

"For God's sake, don't attempt to swim," said Jack, in an agony; "I will try some means to give you water."

"Too late now—you're doomed;" and the coxswain sprang off the rock into the sea, and was followed by two other men: at the same moment a musket was discharged, and the bullet whistled close to our hero's ear.

Mesty dragged Jack from the gangway, who was now nearly fainting from agonising feelings. He sank on the deck for a moment, and then sprang up and ran to the port to look at the men in the water. He was just in time to see the coxswain raise himself with a loud yell out of the sea, and then disappear in a vortex, which was crimsoned with his blood.

Mesty threw down his musket in his hand, of which he had several all ready loaded, in case the men should have gained the boats.

"By the powers, dat no use now!"

Jack had covered his face with his hands. But the tragedy was now complete: the other men, who were in the water, had immediately turned and made for the shore; but before they could reach it, two more of those voracious monsters, attracted by the blood of the coxswain, had flown to the spot, and there was a contention for the fragments of their bodies.

Mesty, who had seen this catastrophe, turned towards our hero, who still hid his face.

"I'm glad he no see dat, anyhow," muttered Mesty.

"See what?" exclaimed Jack.

"Shark eat 'em all."

"Oh, horrid, horrid!" groaned our hero.

"Yes, sar, very horrid," replied Mesty, "and dat bullet at your head very horrid. Suppose the sharks no take them, what then? They kill us, and the sharks have our body. I think that more horrid still."

"Mesty," replied Jack, seizing the negro convulsively by the arm, "it was not the sharks—it was I—I who have murdered these men."

Mesty looked at Jack with surprise.

"How dat possible?"

"If I had not disobeyed orders," replied our hero, panting for breath, "if I had not shown them the example of disobedience, this would not have happened. How could I expect submission from them? It's all my fault—I see it now—and, O God! when will the sight be blotted from my memory?"

"Massa Easy, I not understand that," replied Mesty: "I think you talk foolish—might as well say, suppose Ashantee men not make war, this not happen; for suppose Ashantee not make war, I not slave—I not run away—I not come board *Harpy*—I not go in boat with you—I not hinder men from getting drunk—and that why they make mutiny—and the mutiny why the shark take um?"

Jack made no reply, but he felt some consolation from the counter-argument of the negro.

The dreadful death of the three mutineers appeared to have had a sensible effect upon their companions, who walked away from the beach with their heads down and with measured steps. They were now seen to be perambulating the island, probably in search of that water which they required. At noon, they returned to their tent, and soon afterwards were in a state of intoxication, hallooing and shouting as the day before. Towards the evening they came down to the beach abreast of the ship, each with a vessel in their hands, and perceiving that they had attracted the notice of our hero and Mesty, tossed the contents of the vessels up in the air to show that they had found water, and hooting and deriding, went back, dancing, leaping, and kicking up their heels, to renew their orgies, which continued till after mid night, when they were all stupified as before.

The next day Jack had recovered from the first shock which the catastrophe had given him, and he called Mesty into the cabin to hold a consultation.

"Mesty, how is this to end?"

"How do you mean, sar?—end here, or end on board of de *Harpy*?"

"The *Harpy*!—there appears little chance of our seeing her again—we are on a desolate island, or what is the same thing; but we will hope that it will be so: but how is this mutiny to end?"

"Massa Easy, suppose I please I make it end very soon, but I not in a hurry."

"How do you mean, Mesty, not in a hurry?"

"Look, Massa Easy, you wish take a cruise, and I wish the same ting: now because mutiny you want to go back—but, by all de powers, you tink that I, a prince in my own country, feel wish to go back and boil kettle for de young gentlemen. No, Massa Easy, gib me mutiny—gib me anyting—but—once I was prince," replied Mesty, lowering his voice at the last few emphatic words.

"You must one of these days tell me your history, Mesty," replied Jack; "but just now let us argue the point in question. How could you put an end to this mutiny?"

"By putting an end to all wine. Suppose I go shore after they all drunk, I spile the casks in three or four places, and in the morning all wine gone—den dey ab get sober, and beg pardon—we take dem on board, put away all arms 'cept yours and mine, and I like to see the mutiny after dat. Blood and 'ounds—but I settle um, anyhow."

"The idea is very good, Mesty—why should we not do so?"

"Because I not like run de risk to go ashore—all for what? to go back, boil de kettle for all gentlemans—I very happy here, Massa," replied Mesty carelessly.

"And I am very miserable," replied Jack; "but, however, I am completely in your power, Mesty, and I must, I suppose, submit."

"What you say, Massa Easy—submit to me?—no, sar, when you are on board *Harpy* as officer, you talk with me as a friend, and not treat me as negro servant. Massa Easy, I feel—I feel what I am," continued Mesty, striking his bosom, "I feel it here—for all first time since I leave my country, I feel dat I am someting; but, Massa Easy, I love my friend as much as I hate my enemy—and you neber submit to me—I too proud to allow dat, 'cause, Massa Easy—I am a man—and once I was a prince."

Although Mesty did not perhaps explain by words half so well as he did by his countenance, the full tide of feeling which was overflowing in his heart, Jack fully understood and felt it. He extended his hand to Mesty, and said:

"Mesty—that you have been a prince, I care little about, although I doubt it not, because you are incapable of a lie; but you are a man, and I respect you, nay, I love you as a friend—and with my will we never part again."

Mesty took the hand offered by Jack. It was the first peace-offering ever extended to him, since, he had been torn away from his native land—the first compliment, the first tribute, the first acknowledgment, perhaps, that he was not an inferior being; he pressed it in silence, for he could not speak; but could the feelings which were suffocating the negro but have been laid before sceptics, they must have acknowledged that at that moment they were all and only such as could do honour, not only to the prince, but even to the Christian. So much was Mesty affected with what had happened, that when he dropped the hand of our hero, he went down into the cabin, finding it impossible to continue the conversation, which was not renewed until the next morning.

"What is your opinion, Mesty?—tell me, and I will be governed by it."

"Den, sar, I tell you I tink it right that they first come and ask to come on board before you take them—and, sar, I tink it also right, as we are but two and they are five, dat they first eat all their provision—let 'em starve plenty, and den dey come on board tame enough."

"At all events," replied Jack, "the first overtures of some kind or another must come from them. I wish I had something to do—I do not much like this cooping up on board ship."

"Massa, why you no talk with Pedro?"

"Because I cannot speak Spanish."

"I know dat, and dat why I ask de question. You very sorry when you meet the two pretty women in the ship, you not able to talk with them—I guess that."

"I was very sorry, I grant," replied Jack.

"Well, Massa Easy, by-and-by we see more Spanish girl. Why not talk all day with Pedro, and den you able to talk with dem."

"Upon my word, Mesty, I never had an idea of your value. I will learn all the Spanish that I can," replied Jack, who was glad to have employment found for him, and was quite disgusted with the articles of war.

As for the men on shore, they continued the same course, if not as before, one day succeeded another, and without variety. It was, however, to be observed, that the fire was now seldomer lighted, which proved their fuel scarce, and the weather was not so warm as it had been, for it was now October. Jack learnt Spanish from Pedro for a month, during which there was no appearance of submission on the part of the mutineers, who, for the first fortnight, when intoxicated, used to come down and fire at Jack or Mesty, when they made their appearance. Fortunately drunken men are not good marksmen, but latterly this had been discontinued, because they had expended their ammunition—and they appeared to have almost forgotten that the ship was there, for they took no notice of her whatever.

On the other hand, Jack had decided that if he waited there a year, the overtures should come from them who had mutinied; and now, having an occupation, he passed his time very quietly, and the days flew so fast that two months had actually been run off the calendar, before he had an idea of it.

One evening, as they were down in the cabin, for the evenings had now become very cold, Jack asked Mesty whether he had any objection to give him a history of his life. Mesty replied, that if he wished he was ready to talk; and at a nod from our hero, Mesty commenced as follows.

Chapter Fifteen.

In which mutiny, like fire, is quenched for want of fuel and no want of water.

Although we have made the African negro hitherto talk in his own mixed jargon, yet, as we consider that, in a long narration, it will be tedious to the reader, we shall now translate the narrative part into good English, merely leaving the conversation with which it may be broken in its peculiar dialect.

"The first thing I recollect," said Mesty, "is that I was carried on the shoulders of a man with my legs hanging down before, and holding on by his head.

"Every one used to look at me, and get out of the way, as I rode through the town and market place, so loaded with heavy gold ornaments that I could not bear them, and was glad when the women took them off: but, as I grew older I became proud of them, because I knew that I was the son of a king—I lived happy, I did nothing but shoot my arrows, and I had a little sword which I was taught to handle, and the great captains who were about my father showed me how to kill my enemies. Some times I lay under the shady trees, sometimes I was with the women belonging to my father, sometimes I was with him and played with the skulls, and repeated the names of those to whom they had belonged, for in our country, when we kill our enemies, we keep their skulls as trophies.

"As I grew older, I did as I pleased; I beat the women and the slaves; I think I killed some of the latter—I know I did one, to try whether I could strike well with my two-handed sword made of hard and heavy wood—but that is nothing in our country. I longed to be a great captain, and I thought of nothing else but war and fighting, and how many skulls I should have in my possession when I had a house and wives of my own, and I was no longer a boy. I went out in the woods to hunt, and I stayed for weeks. And one day I saw a panther basking in the sun, waving his graceful tail. I crept up softly till I was behind a rock within three yards of it, and drawing my arrow to the head I pierced him through the body. The animal bounded up in the air, saw me, roared and made a spring, but I dropped behind the rock, and he passed over me. He turned again to me, but I had my knife ready, and, as he fixed his talons into my shoulder and breast, I pierced him to the heart. This was the happiest day of my life; I had killed a panther without assistance, and I had wounds to show. Although I was severely hurt, I thought nothing of it. I took off the skin as my blood dropped down and mixed with that of the beast—but I rejoiced in it. Proudly did I go into the town dripping with gore and smarting with pain. Every one extolled the feat, called me a hero and a great captain. I filed my teeth, and I became a man.

"From that day I ranked among the warriors, and, as soon as my wounds were healed, I went out to battle. In three fights I had gained five skulls, and when I returned they weighed me out gold. I then had a house and wives, and my father appointed me a Caboceer. I wore the plume of eagle and ostrich feathers, my dress was covered with fetishes, I pulled on the boots with bells, and with my bow and arrows slung on my back, my spear and blunderbuss, my knives and my double-handed sword, I led the men to battle and brought back skulls and slaves. Every one trembled at my name, and, if my father threatened to send me out, gold-dust covered the floor of his hall of council—Now, I boil the kettle for the young gentlemen.

"There was one man I liked. He was not a warrior, or I should have hated him, but he was brought up with me in my father's house, and was a near relative. I was grave and full of pride, he was gay and fond of music; and although there was no music to me equal to the tom-tom, yet I did not always wish for excitement. I often was melancholy, and then I liked to lay my head in the lap of one of my wives, under the shady forest behind my house, and listen to his soft music. At last he went to a town near us where his father lived, and as he departed I gave him gold-dust. He had been sent to my father to be formed into a warrior, but he had no strength of body, and he had no soul; still I loved him because he was not like myself. There was a girl in the town who was beautiful; many asked for her as their wife, but her father had long promised her to my friend; he refused even the greatest warrior of the place, who went away in wrath to the fetish-man, and throwing him his gold armlets asked for a fetish against his rival. It was given, and two days before he was to be married my friend died. His mother came to me, and it was enough. I put on my war dress, I seized my weapons, sat for a whole day with my skulls before me, working up my revenge, called out my men, and that night set off for the town where the warrior resided, killed two of his relatives and carried off ten of his slaves. When he heard what I had done, he trembled and sent gold; but I knew that he had taken the girl home as his wife, and I would not listen to the old man who sought to pacify me. Again I collected a larger force, and attacked him in the night: we fought, for he was prepared with his men, but after a struggle he was beaten back. I fired his house, wasted his provision ground, and taking away more slaves, I returned home with my men, intending soon to assault him again. The next day there came more messengers, who knelt in vain, so they went to my father, and many warriors begged him to interfere. My father sent for me, but I would not listen; the warriors spoke, and I turned my back: my father was wroth and threatened, the warriors brandished their two-handed swords—they dared to do it; I looked over my shoulder with contempt, and I returned to my house. I took down my skulls, and I planned. It was evening, and I was alone, when a woman covered up to the eyes approached; she fell down before me as she exposed her face.

"'I am the girl who was promised to your relation, and I am now the wife of your enemy. I shall be a mother. I could not love your relation, for he was no warrior. It is not true that my husband asked for a fetish—it was I who bought it, for I would not wed him. Kill me and be satisfied.'

"She was very beautiful, and I wondered not that my enemy loved her—and she was with child—it was his child, and she had fetished my friend to death. I raised my sword to strike, and she did not shrink: it saved her life. 'Thou art fit to be the mother of warriors,' said I, as I dropped my sword, 'and thou shalt be my wife, but first his child shall be born, and I will have thy husband's skull.'

"'No, no,' replied she, 'I will be the mother of no warriors but my present husband, whom I love; if you keep me as your slave I will die.'

"I told her she said foolish things, and sent her to the women's apartment, with orders to be watched—but she hardly had been locked up before she drew her knife, plunged it into her heart, and died.

"When the king my father heard this he sent me a message—'Be satisfied with the blood that has been shed, it is enough'—but I turned away, for I wished for mine enemy's skull. That night I attacked him again, and met him hand to hand; I killed him, and carried home his skull, and I was appeased.

"But all the great warriors were wroth, and my father could not restrain them. They called out their men, and I called out my men, and I had a large body, for my name was terrible. But the force raised against me was twice that of mine, and I retreated to the bush—after a while we met and fought and I killed many, but my men were too few and were overpowered—the fetish had been sent out against me, and their hearts melted; at last I sank down with my wounds, for I bled at every pore, and I told my men who were about me to take off my feathers, and my dress and boots, that my enemies might not have my skull: they did so, and I crawled into the bush to die. But I was not to die; I was recovering, when I was discovered by those who steal men to sell them: I was bound, and fastened to a chain with many more. I, a prince and a warrior, who could show the white skulls of his enemies—I offered to procure gold, but they derided me; they dragged me down to the coast, and sold me to the Whites. Little did I think, in my pride, that I should be a slave. I knew that I was to die, and hoped to die in battle: my skull would have been more prized than all the gold in the earth, and my skin would have been stuffed and hung up in a fetish-house—instead of which, I now boil the kettle for the young gentlemen."

"Well," replied Jack, "that's better than being killed and stuffed."

"Mayhap it is," replied Mesty, "I tink very different now dan I tink den—but still, its women's work and not suit me.

"They put me with others into a cave until the ship came, and then we were sent on board, put in irons, and down in the hold, where you could not sit upright—I wanted to die, but could not: others died every day, but I lived—I was landed in America, all bone, and I fetched very little money—they laughed at me as they bid their dollars: at last a man took me away, and I was on a plantation with hundreds more, but too ill to work, and not intending to work. The other slaves asked me if I was a fetish-man; I said yes, and I would fetish any man that I did not like: one man laughed, and I held up my finger; I was too weak to get up, for my blood had long boiled with fever, and I said to him, '*you shall die*;' for I meant to have killed him, as soon as I was well. He went away, and in three days he was dead. I don't know how, but all the slaves feared me, and my master feared me, for he had seen the man die, and he, although he was a white man, believed in fetish, and he wished to sell me again, but no one would buy a fetish-man, so he made friends with me; for I told him, if I was beat he should die, and he believed me. He took me into his house, and I was his chief man, and I would not let the other slaves steal, and he was content. He took me with him to New York, and there after two years, when I had learned English, I ran away, and got on board of an English ship—and they told me to cook. I left the ship as soon as I came to England, and offered myself to another, and they said they did not want a cook; and I went to another, and they asked me if I was a good cook: everybody seemed to think that a black man must be a cook, and nothing else. At last I starve, and I go on board man-of-war, and here I am, after having been a warrior and a prince, cook, steward and everyting else, boiling kettle for de young gentlemen."

"Well," replied Jack, "at all events that is better than being a slave."

Mesty made no reply: any one who knows the life of a midshipman's servant will not be surprised at his silence.

"Now, tell me, do you think you were right in being so revengeful, when you were in your own country?" inquired Jack.

"I tink so den, Massa Easy, sometimes when my blood boil, I tink so now—oder time, I no know what to tink—but when a man love very much, he hate very much."

"But you are now a Christian, Mesty."

"I hear all that your people say," replied the negro, "and it make me tink—I no longer believe in fetish, anyhow."

"Our religion tells us to love our enemies."

"Yes, I heard parson say dat—but den what we do with our friends, Massy Easy?"

"Love them too."

"I no understand dat, Massa Easy—I love you, because you good, and treat me well—Mr Vigors, he bully, and treat me ill—how possible to love him? By de power, I hate him, and wish I had him *skull*. You tink little Massa Gossett love him?"

"No," replied Jack, laughing, "I'm afraid that he would like to have his skull as well as you, Mesty—but at all events we must try and forgive those who injure us."

"Then, Massa Easy, I tink so too—too much revenge very bad—it very easy to hate, but not very easy to forgive—so I tink that if a man forgive he hab *more soul* in him, he more of a *man*."

"After all," thought Jack, "Mesty is about as good a Christian as most people."

"What that?" cried Mesty, looking out of the cabin window—"Ah! damn drunken dogs—they set fire to tent."

Jack looked, and perceived that the tent on shore was in flames.

"I tink these cold nights cool their courage any how," observed Mesty—"Massa Easy, you see they soon ask permission to come on board."

Jack thought so too, and was most anxious to be off, for, on looking into the lockers in the state-room, he had found a chart of the Mediterranean, which he had studied very attentively—he had found out the rock of Gibraltar, and had traced the *Harpy's* course up to Cape de Gatte, and thence to Tarragona—and, after a while, had summoned Mesty to a cabinet council.

"See, Mesty," said Jack, "I begin to make it out; here is Gibraltar, and Cape de Gatte, and Tarragona—it was hereabout we were when we took the ship, and, if you recollect, we had passed Cape de Gatte two days before we were blown off from the land, so that we had gone about twelve inches, and had only four more to go."

"Yes, Massa Easy, I see all dat."

"Well, then, we were blown off shore by the wind, and must of course have come down this way; and here you see are three little islands, called Zaffarine Islands, and with no names of towns upon them, and therefore uninhabited; and you see they lie just like the islands we are anchored among now—we must be at the Zaffarine Islands—and only six inches from Gibraltar."

"I see, Massa Easy, dat all right—but six debbelish long inches."

"Now, Mesty, you know the compass on the deck has a flourishing thing for the north point—and here is a compass with a north point also. Now the north point from the Zaffarine Islands leads out to the Spanish coast again, and Gibraltar lies five or six points of the compass to this side of it—if we steer that way we shall get to Gibraltar."

"All right, Massa Easy," replied Mesty; and Jack was right, with the exception of the variation, which he knew nothing about.

To make sure, Jack brought one of the compasses down from deck, and compared them. He then lifted off the glass, counted the points of the compass to the westward, and marked the corresponding one on the binnacle compass with his pen.

"There," said he, "that is the way to Gibraltar, and as soon as the mutiny is quelled, and the wind is fair, I'll be off."

Chapter Sixteen.

In which Jack's cruise is ended, and he regains the Harpy.

A few more days passed, and, as was expected, the mutineers could hold out no longer. In the first place, they had put in the spile of the second cask of wine so loosely when they were tipsy that it dropped out, and all the wine ran out, so that there had been none left for three or four days; in the next, their fuel had long been expended, and they had latterly eaten their meat raw the loss of their tent, which had been fired by their carelessness, had been followed by four days and nights of continual rain. Everything they had had been soaked through and through, and they were worn out, shivering with cold, and starving. Hanging they thought better than dying by inches from starvation; and, yielding to the imperious demands of hunger, they came down to the beach, abreast of the ship, and dropped down on their knees.

"I tell you so, Massa Easy," said Mesty: "damn rascals, they forget they come down fire musket at us every day: by all de powers, Mesty not forget it."

"Ship ahoy!" cried one of the men on shore.

"What do you want?" replied Jack.

"Have pity on us, sir—mercy!" exclaimed the other men, "we will return to our duty."

"Debbil doubt 'em!"

"What shall I say, Mesty?"

"Tell 'em no, first, Massa Easy—tell 'em to starve and be damned."

"I cannot take mutineers on board," replied Jack.

"Well, then, our blood be on your hands, Mr Easy," replied the first man who had spoken. "If we are to die, it must not be by inches—if you will not take us, the sharks shall—it is but a crunch, and all is over. What do you say, my lads? let's all rush in together: good-bye, Mr Easy, I hope you'll forgive us when we're dead it was all that rascal Johnson, the coxswain, who persuaded us. Come, my lads, it's no use thinking of it, the sooner done the better—let us shake hands, and then make one run of it."

It appeared that the poor fellows had already made up their minds to do this, if our hero, persuaded by Mesty, had refused to take them on board. They shook hands all round, and then walking a few yards from the beach, stood in a line while the man gave the signal—one—two.

"Stop," cried Jack, who had not forgotten the dreadful scene which had already taken place,—"stop."

The men paused.

"What will you promise if I take you on board?"

"To do our duty cheerfully till we join the ship, and then be hung as an example to all mutineers," replied the men.

"Dat very fair," replied Mesty; "take dem at their word, Massa Easy."

"Very well," replied Jack, "I accept your conditions; and we will come for you."

Jack and Mesty hauled up the boat, stuck their pistols in their belts, and pulled to the shore. The men, as they stepped in, touched their hats respectfully to our hero, but said nothing. On their arrival on board Jack read that part of the articles of war relative to mutiny, by which the men were reminded of the very satisfactory fact, "that they were to suffer death;" and then made a speech which, to men who were starving, appeared to be interminable. However, there is an end to everything in this world, and so there was to Jack's harangue; after which Mesty gave them some biscuit, which they devoured in thankfulness, until they could get something better. The next morning the wind was fair, they weighed their hedge with some difficulty, and ran out of the harbour: the men appeared very contrite, worked well, but in silence, for they had no very pleasant anticipations; but hope always remains with us; and each of the men, although he had no doubt but that the others would be hung, hoped that he would escape with a sound flogging. The wind, however, did not allow them to steer their course long; before night it was contrary, and they fell off three points to the northward. "However," as Jack observed, "at all events we shall make the Spanish coast, and then we must run down it to Gibraltar: I don't care—I under stand navigation much better than I did." The next morning they found themselves, with a very light breeze, under a high cape, and, as the sun rose, they observed a large vessel inshore, about two miles to the westward of them, and another outside, about four miles off. Mesty took the glass and examined the one outside, which, on a sudden, had let fall all her canvas, and was now running for the shore, steering for the cape under which Jack's vessel lay. Mesty put down the glass.

"Massa Easy—I tink dat de *Harpy*."

One of the seamen took the glass and examined her, while the others who stood by showed great agitation.

"Yes, it is the *Harpy*," said the seaman. "Oh Mr Easy, will you forgive us?" continued the man, and he and the others fell on their knees. "Do not tell all, for God's sake, Mr Easy."

Jack's heart melted; he looked at Mesty.

"I tink," said Mesty apart to our hero, "dat with what them hab suffer already, suppose they get *seven dozen apiece*, dat quite enough."

Jack thought that even half that punishment would suffice; so he told the men, that although he must state what had occurred, he would not tell all, and would contrive to get them off as well as he could. He was about to make a long speech, but a gun from the *Harpy*, which had now come up within range, made him defer it till a more convenient opportunity. At the same time the vessel in shore hoisted Spanish colours, and fired a gun.

"By de powers, but we got in the middle of it," cried Mesty; "*Harpy* tink us Spaniard. Now, my lads, get all gun ready, bring up powder and shot. Massa, now us fire at Spaniard—Harpy not fire at us—no ab English colours on board—dat all we must do."

The men set to with a will; the guns were all loaded, and were soon cast loose and primed, during which operations it fell calm, and the sails of all three vessels flapped against their masts. The *Harpy* was then about two miles from Jack's vessel, and the Spaniard about a mile from him, with all her boats ahead of her, towing towards him; Mesty examined the Spanish vessel.

"Dat man-o'-war, Massa Easy—what de debbil we do for colour? must hoist someting."

Mesty ran down below; he recollected that there was a very gay petticoat, which had been left by the old lady who was in the vessel when they captured her. It was of green silk, with yellow and blue flowers, but very faded, having probably been in the Don's family for a century. Mesty had found it under the mattress of one of the beds, and had put it into his bag, intending probably to cut it up into waistcoats. He soon appeared with this under his arm, made it fast to the peak halyards and hoisted it up.

"Dere, massa, dat do very well—dat what you call *all nation colour*. Everybody strike him flag to dat—men nebber pull it down," said Mesty, "anyhow. Now den, ab hoist colour, we fire away—mind you only fire one gun at a time, and point um well, den ab time to load again."

"She's hoisted her colours, sir," said Sawbridge, on board of the *Harpy*; "but they do not show out clear, and it's impossible to distinguish them; but there's a gun."

"It's not at us, sir," said Gascoigne, the midshipman; "its at the Spanish vessel—I saw the shot fall ahead of her."

"It must be a privateer," said Captain Wilson, "at all events, it is very fortunate, for the corvette would otherwise have towed into Carthagena. Another gun, round and grape, and well pointed too; she carries heavy metal, that craft; she must be a Maltese privateer."

"That's as much as to say that she's a pirate," replied Sawbridge; "I can make nothing of her colours—they appear to me to be green—she must be a Turk. Another gun—and devilish well aimed; it has hit the boats."

"Yes, they are all in confusion: we will have her now, if we can only get a trifle of wind. That is a breeze coming up in the offing. Trim the sails, Mr Sawbridge."

The yards were squared, and the *Harpy* soon had steerage way. In the meantime Jack and his few men had kept up a steady, well-directed, although slow, fire with their larboard guns upon the Spanish corvette; and two of her boats had been disabled. The *Harpy* brought the breeze up with her, and was soon within range; she steered to cut off the corvette, firing only her bow-chasers.

"We ab her now," cried Mesty, "fire away—men take good aim. Breeze come now; one man go to helm. By de power, what dat?"

The exclamation of Mesty was occasioned by a shot hulling the ship on the starboard side. Jack and he ran over, and perceived that three Spanish gun-boats had just made their appearance round the point, and had attacked them. The fact was, that on the other side of the cape was the port and town of Carthagena, and these gun-boats had been sent out to the assistance of the corvette. The ship had now caught the breeze, fortunately for Jack, or he would probably have been taken into Carthagena; and the corvette, finding herself cut off by both the *Harpy* and Jack's vessel, as soon as the breeze came up to her, put her head the other way, and tried to escape by running westward along the coast close in shore. Another shot, and then another, pierced the hull of the ship, and wounded two of Jack's men; but as the corvette had turned, and the *Harpy* followed her, of course Jack did the same, and in ten minutes he was clear of the gun-boats, which did not venture to make sail and stand after him. The wind now freshened fast, and blew out the green petticoat, but the *Harpy* was exchanging broadsides with the corvette, and too busy to look after Jack's ensign. The Spaniard defended himself well, and had the assistance of the batteries as he passed, but there was no anchorage until he had run many miles farther. About noon the wind died away, and at one o'clock it again fell nearly calm; but the *Harpy* had neared her distance, and was now within three cables' length of her antagonist, engaging her and a battery of four guns. Jack came up again, for he had the last of the breeze, and was about half a mile from the corvette when it fell calm. By the advice of Mesty, he did not fire any more, or otherwise the *Harpy* would not obtain so much credit, and it was evident that the fire of the Spaniard slackened fast. At three o'clock the Spanish colours were hauled down, and the *Harpy*, sending a boat on board and taking possession, directed her whole fire upon the battery, which was soon silenced.

The calm continued, and the *Harpy* was busy enough with the prize, shifting the prisoners and refitting both vessels, which had very much suffered in the sails and rigging. There was an occasional wonder on board the *Harpy* what that strange vessel might be which had turned the corvette and enabled them to capture her, but when people are all very busy, there is not much time for surmise.

Jack's crew, with himself, consisted but of eight, one of whom was a Spaniard, and two were wounded. It therefore left him but four, and he had also some thing to do, which was to assist his wounded men, and secure his guns. Moreover, Mesty did not think it prudent to leave the vessel a mile from the *Harpy* with only two on board; besides, as Jack said, he had had no dinner, and was not quite sure that he should find anything to eat when he went into the midshipmen's berth; he would therefore have some dinner cooked, and eat it before he went on board in the meantime, they would try and close with her. Jack took things always very easy, and he said he should report himself at sunset. There were other reasons which made Jack in no very great hurry to go on board; he wanted to have time to consider a little what he should say to excuse himself, and also how he should plead for the men. His natural correctness of feeling decided him, in the first place, to tell the whole truth, and in the next, his kind feelings determined him to tell only part of it. Jack need not have given himself this trouble, for, as far as regarded himself, he had fourteen thousand good excuses in the bags which lay in the state-room; and as for the men, after an action with the enemy, if they behave well, even mutiny is forgiven. At last Jack, who was tired with excitement and the hard work of the day, thought and thought till he fell fast asleep, and instead of waking at sunset did not wake till two hours afterwards; and Mesty did not call him, because he was in no hurry himself to go on board and *boil de kettle for de young gentlemen.*

When Jack woke up he was astonished to find that he had slept so long: he went on deck; it was dark and still calm, but he could easily perceive that the *Harpy* and corvette were still hove-to, repairing damages. He ordered the men to lower down the small boat, and leaving Mesty in charge, with two oars he pulled to the *Harpy*. What with wounded men, with prisoners, and boats going and coming between the vessels, every one on board the *Harpy* were well employed; and in the dark Jack's little boat came alongside without notice. This should not have been the case, but it was, and there was some excuse for it. Jack ascended the side, and pushed his way through the prisoners, who were being mustered to be victualled. He was wrapped up in one of the gregos, and many of the prisoners wore the same.

Jack was amused at not being recognised: he slipped down the main ladder, and had to stoop under the hammocks of the wounded men, and was about to go aft to the captain's cabin to report himself, when he heard young Gossett crying out, and the sound of the rope. "Hang me, if that brute Vigors an't thrashing young Gossett," thought Jack. "I dare say the poor fellow had had plenty of it since I have been away; I'll save him this time at least." Jack, wrapped up in his grego, went to the window of the berth, looked in, and found it was as he expected. He cried out in an angry voice, "*Mr Vigors, I'll thank you to leave Gossett alone.*" At the sound of the voice Vigors turned round with his colt in his hand, saw Jack's face at the window, and, impressed with the idea that the reappearance was supernatural, uttered a yell and fell down in a fit—little Gossett also trembling in every limb, stared with his mouth open. Jack was satisfied, and immediately disappeared. He then went aft to the cabin, pushed by the servant, who was giving some orders from the captain to the officer on deck, and entering the cabin, where the captain was seated with two Spanish officers, took off his hat and said:

"Come on board, Captain Wilson."

Captain Wilson did not fall down in a fit, but he jumped up and upset the glass before him.

"Merciful God! Mr Easy, where did you come from?"

"From that ship astern, sir," replied Jack.

"That ship astern! what is she?—where have you been so long?"

"It's a long story, sir," replied Jack.

Captain Wilson extended his hand and shook Jack's heartily.

"At all events, I'm delighted to see you, boy: now sit down and tell me your story in a few words; we will have it in detail by-and-bye."

"If you please, sir," said Jack, "we captured that ship with the cutter the night after we went away—I'm not a first-rate navigator, and I was blown to the Zaffarine Islands, where I remained two months for want of hands: as soon as I procured them I made sail again—I have lost three men by sharks, and I have two wounded in to-day's fight—the ship mounts twelve guns, is half laden with lead and cotton prints, has fourteen thousand dollars in the cabin, and three shot-holes right through her—and the sooner you send some people on board of her the better."

This was not very intelligible, but that there were fourteen thousand dollars, and that she required hands sent on board, was very satisfactorily explained. Captain Wilson rang the bell, sent for Mr Asper, who started back at the sight of our hero—desired him to order Mr Jolliffe to go on board with one of the cutters, send the wounded men on board, and take charge of the vessel, and then told Jack to accompany Mr Jolliffe, and to give him every information; telling him that he would hear his story to-morrow, when they were not so very busy.

Chapter Seventeen.

In which our hero finds out that trigonometry is not only necessary to navigation, but may be required in settling affairs of honour.

As Captain Wilson truly said, he was too busy even to hear Jack's story that night, for they were anxious to have both vessels ready to make sail as soon as a breeze should spring up, for the Spaniards had vessels of war at Carthagena, which was not ten miles off, and had known the result of the action: it was therefore necessary to change their position as soon as possible. Mr Sawbridge was on board the prize, which was a corvette mounting two guns more than the *Harpy*, and called the *Cacafuogo*.

She had escaped from Cadiz, run through the straits in the night, and was three miles from Carthagena when she was captured, which she certainly never would have been but for Jack's fortunately blundering against the cape with his armed vessel, so that Captain Wilson and Mr Sawbridge (both of whom were promoted, the first to the rank of post-captain, the second to that of commander), may be said to be indebted to Jack for their good fortune. The *Harpy* had lost nineteen men, killed and wounded, and the Spanish corvette forty-seven. Altogether, it was a very creditable affair.

At two o'clock in the morning, the vessels were ready, everything had been done that could be done in so short a time, and they stood under easy sail during the night for Gibraltar, the *Nostra Señora del Carmen*, under the charge of Jolliffe, keeping company. Jolliffe had the advantage over his shipmates, of first hearing Jack's adventures, with which he was much astonished as well as amused—even Captain Wilson was not more happy to see Jack than was the worthy master's mate. About nine o'clock the *Harpy* hove-to, and sent a boat on board for our hero and the men who had been so long with him in the prize, and then hoisted out the pinnace to fetch on board the dollars, which were of more importance. Jack, as he bade adieu to Jolliffe, took out of his pocket and presented him with the *articles of war*, which, as they had been so useful to him, he thought Jolliffe could not do without, and then went down the side: the men were already in the boat, casting imploring looks upon Jack, to raise feelings of compassion, and Mesty took his seat by our hero in a very sulky humour, probably because he did not like the idea of having again "to boil de kettle for de young gentlemen." Even Jack felt a little melancholy at resigning his command, and he looked back at the green petticoat, which blew out gracefully from the mast, for Jolliffe had determined that he would not haul down the colours under which Jack had fought so gallant an action.

Jack's narration, as may be imagined, occupied a large part of the forenoon; and, although Jack did not attempt to deny that he had seen the recall signal of Mr Sawbridge, yet, as his account went on, the captain became so interested that at the end of it he quite forgot to point out to Jack the impropriety of not obeying orders. He gave Jack great credit for his conduct, and was also much pleased with that of Mesty. Jack took the opportunity of stating

Mesty's aversion to his present employment, and his recommendation was graciously received. Jack also succeeded in obtaining the pardon of the men, in consideration of their subsequent good behaviour; but notwithstanding this promise on the part of Captain Wilson, they were ordered to be put in irons for the present. However, Jack told Mesty, and Mesty told the men, that they would be released with a reprimand when they arrived at Gibraltar, so all that the men cared for was a fair wind.

Captain Wilson informed Jack that after his joining the admiral he had been sent to Malta with the prizes, and that, supposing the cutter to have been sunk, he had written to his father, acquainting him with his son's death, at which our hero was much grieved, for he knew what sorrow it would occasion, particularly to his poor mother. "But," thought Jack, "if she is unhappy for three months, she will be overjoyed for three more when she hears that I am alive, so it will be all square at the end of the six; and as soon as I arrive at Gibraltar I will write, and, as the wind is fair, that will be to-morrow or next day."

After a long conversation Jack was graciously dismissed, Captain Wilson being satisfied from what he had heard that Jack would turn out a very good officer, and had already forgotten all about equality and the rights of man; but there Captain Wilson was mistaken—tares sown in infancy are not so soon rooted out.

Jack went on deck as soon as the captain had dismissed him, and found the captain and officers of the Spanish corvette standing aft, looking very seriously at the *Nostra Señora del Carmen*. When they saw our hero, who Captain Wilson had told them was the young officer who had barred their entrance into Carthagena, they turned their eyes upon him not quite so graciously as they might have done.

Jack, with his usual politeness, took off his hat to the Spanish captain, and, glad to have an opportunity of sporting his Spanish, expressed the usual wish that he might live a thousand years. The Spanish captain, who had reason to wish that Jack had gone to the devil at least twenty-four hours before, was equally complimentary, and then begged to be informed what the colours were that Jack had hoisted during the action. Jack replied that they were colours to which every Spanish gentleman considered it no disgrace to surrender, although always ready to engage, and frequently at tempting to board. Upon which the Spanish captain was very much puzzled. Captain Wilson, who under stood a little Spanish, then interrupted by observing:

"By-the-bye, Mr Easy, what colours did you hoist up? we could not make them out. I see Mr Jolliffe still keeps them up at the peak."

"Yes, sir," replied Jack, rather puzzled what to call them, but at last he replied that it was the banner of equality and the rights of man.

Captain Wilson frowned, and Jack, perceiving that he was displeased, then told him the whole story, whereupon Captain Wilson laughed, and Jack then also explained, in Spanish, to the officers of the corvette, who replied that it was not the first time, and would not be the last, that men had got into a scrape through a petticoat.

The Spanish captain complimented Jack on his Spanish, which was really very good (for in two months, with nothing else in the world to do, he had made great progress), and asked him where he had learned it.

Jack replied, "At the Zaffarine Islands."

"Zaffarine Isles," replied the Spanish captain; "they are not inhabited."

"Plenty of ground sharks," replied Jack.

The Spanish captain thought our hero a very strange fellow, to fight under a green silk petticoat, and to take lessons in Spanish from the ground sharks. However, being quite as polite as Jack, he did not contradict him, but took a huge pinch of snuff, wishing from the bottom of his heart that the ground sharks had taken Jack before he had hoisted that confounded green petticoat.

However, Jack was in high favour with the captain, and all the ship's company, with the exception of his four enemies—the master, Vigors, the boatswain, and the purser's steward. As for Mr Vigors, he had come to his senses again, and had put his colt in his chest until Jack should take another cruise. Little Gossett, at any insulting remark made by Vigors, pointed to the window of the berth and grinned; and the very recollection made Vigors turn pale, and awed him into silence.

In two days they arrived at Gibraltar—Mr Sawbridge rejoined the ship—so did Mr Jolliffe—they remained there a fortnight, during which Jack was permitted to be continually on shore—Mr Asper accompanied him, and Jack drew a heavy bill to prove to his father that he was still alive. Mr Sawbridge made our hero relate to him all his adventures, and was so pleased with the conduct of Mesty, that he appointed him to a situation which was particularly suited to him—that of ship's corporal. Mr Sawbridge knew that it was an office of trust, and provided that he could find a man fit for it, he was very indifferent about his colour. Mesty walked and strutted about, at least three inches taller than he was before. He was always clean, did his duty conscientiously, and seldom used his cane.

"I think, Mr Easy," said the first lieutenant, "that as you are so particularly fond of taking a cruise"—for Jack had told the whole truth—"it might be as well that you improve your navigation."

"I do think myself, sir," replied Jack, with great modesty, "that I am not yet quite perfect."

"Well, then, Mr Jolliffe will teach you; he is the most competent in this ship: the sooner you ask him the better, and if you learn it as fast as you have Spanish, it will not give you much trouble."

Jack thought the advice good: the next day he was very busy with his friend Jolliffe, and made the important discovery that two parallel lines continued to infinity would never meet.

It must not be supposed that Captain Wilson and Mr Sawbridge received their promotion instanter. Promotion is always attended with delay, as there is a certain routine in the service which must not be departed from. Captain Wilson had orders to return to Malta after his cruise. He therefore carried his own despatches away from England—from Malta the despatches had to be forwarded to Toulon to the admiral, and then the admiral had to send to England to the Admiralty, whose reply had to come out again. All this, with the delays arising from vessels not sailing immediately, occupied an interval of between five and six months—during which time there was no alteration in the officers and crew of his Majesty's sloop *Harpy*.

There had, however, been one alteration; the gunner, Mr Minus, who had charge of the first cutter in the night action in which our hero was separated from his ship, carelessly loading his musket, had found himself minus his right hand, which, upon the musket going off as he rammed down, had gone off too. He was invalided and sent home during Jack's absence, and another had been appointed, whose name was Tallboys. Mr Tallboys was a stout dumpy man, with red face, and still redder hands; he had red hair and red whiskers, and he had read a good deal—for Mr Tallboys considered that the gunner was the most important personage in the ship. He had once been a captain's clerk, and having distinguished himself very much in cutting-out service, had applied for and received his warrant as a gunner. He had studied the *Art of Gunnery*, a part of which he understood, but the remainder was above his comprehension: he continued, however, to read it as before, thinking that by constant reading he should understand it at last. He had gone through the work from the title-page to the finis at least forty times, and had just commenced it over again. He never came on deck without the gunner's vade-mecum in his pocket, with his hand always upon it to refer to it in a moment.

But Mr Tallboys had, as we observed before, a great idea of the importance of a gunner, and, among other qualifications, he considered it absolutely necessary that he should be a navigator. He had at least ten instances to bring forward of bloody actions, in which the captain and all the commissioned officers had been killed or wounded, and the command of the ship had devolved upon the gunner.

"Now, sir," would he say, "if the gunner is no navigator, he is not fit to take charge of his Majesty's ships. The boatswain and carpenter are merely practical men; but the gunner, sir, is, or ought to be, scientific. Gunnery, sir, is a science—we have our own disparts and our lines of sight—our windage and our parabolas and projectile forces—and our point blank, and our reduction of powder upon a graduated scale. Now, sir, there's no excuse for a gunner not being a navigator; for knowing his duty as a gunner, he has the same mathematical tools to work with." Upon this principle Mr Tallboys had added John Hamilton Moore to his library, and had advanced about as far into navigation as he had in gunnery, that is, to the threshold, where he stuck fast, with all his mathematical tools, which he did not know how to use. To do him justice, he studied for two or three hours everyday, and it was not his fault if he did not advance—but his head was confused with technical terms; he mixed all up together, and disparts, sines and cosines, parabolas, tangents, windage, seconds, lines of sight, logarithms, projectiles and traverse sailing, quadrature and Gunter's scales, were all crowded together, in a brain which had not capacity to receive the rule of three. "Too much learning," said Festus to the apostle, "hath made thee mad." Mr Tallboys had not wit enough to go mad, but his learning lay like lead upon his brain: the more he read, the less he understood, at the same time that he became more satisfied with his supposed acquirements, and could not speak but in "mathematical parables."

"I understand, Mr Easy," said the gunner to him one day, after they had sailed for Malta, "that you have entered into the science of navigation—at your age it was high time."

"Yes," replied Jack, "I can raise a perpendicular, at all events, and box the compass."

"Yes, but you have not yet arrived at the dispart of the compass."

"Not come to that yet," replied Jack.

"Are you aware that a ship sailing describes a parabola round the globe?"

"Not come to that yet," replied Jack.

"And that any propelled body striking against another flies off at a tangent?"

"Very likely," replied Jack, "that is a *sine* that he don't like it."

"You have not yet entered into *acute* trigonometry?"

"Not come to that yet," replied Jack.

"That will require very sharp attention."

"I should think so," replied Jack.

"You will then find out how your parallels of longitude and latitude meet."

"Two parallel lines, if continued to infinity, will never meet," replied Jack.

"I beg your pardon," said the gunner.

"I beg yours," said Jack.

Whereupon Mr Tallboys brought up a small map of the world, and showed Jack that all the parallels of latitude met at a point at the top and bottom.

"Parallel lines never meet," replied Jack, producing Hamilton Moore.

Whereupon Jack and the gunner argued the point, until it was agreed to refer the case to Mr Jolliffe, who asserted, with a smile, that those lines were parallels and not parallels.

As both were right, both were satisfied.

It was fortunate that Jack would argue in this instance: had he believed all the confused assertions of the gunner, he would have been as puzzled as the gunner himself. They never met without an argument and a reference, and as Jack was put right in the end, he only learned the faster. By the time that he did know something about navigation he discovered that his antagonist knew nothing. Before they arrived at Malta Jack could fudge a day's work.

But at Malta Jack got into another scrape. Although Mr Smallsole could not injure him, he was still Jack's enemy; the more so as Jack had become very popular: Vigors also submitted, planning revenge; but the parties in this instance were the boatswain and purser's steward. Jack still continued his forecastle conversation with Mesty; and the boatswain and purser's steward, probably from their respective ill-will towards our hero, had become great allies. Mr Easthupp now put on his best jacket to walk the dog-watches with Mr Biggs, and they took every opportunity to talk at our hero.

"It's my peculiar hopinion," said Mr Easthupp, one evening, pulling at the frill of his shirt, "that a gentleman should behave as a gentleman, and that if a gentleman professes hopinions of hequality and such liberal sentiments, that he is bound as a gentle man to hact up to them."

"Very true, Mr Easthupp; he is bound to act up to them; and not because a person, who was a gentleman as well as himself, happens not to be on the quarter-deck, to insult him because he only has perfessed opinions like his own."

Hereupon Mr Biggs struck his rattan against the funnel, and looked at our hero.

"Yes," continued the purser's steward, "I should like to see the fellow who would have done so on shore however, the time will come when I can hagain pull on my plain coat, and then the insult shall be vashed out in blood, Mr Biggs."

"And I'll be cursed if I don't some day teach a lesson to the blackguard who stole my trousers."

"Vas hall your money right, Mr Biggs?" inquired the purser's steward.

"I didn't count," replied the boatswain magnificently.

"No—gentlemen are above that," replied Easthupp; "but there are many light-fingered gentry habout. The quantity of vatches and harticles of value vich were lost ven I valked Bond Street in former times is incredible."

"I can say this, at all events," replied the boatswain, "that I should be always ready to give satisfaction to any person beneath me in rank, after I had insulted him. I don't stand upon my rank, although I don't talk about equality, damme—no, nor consort with niggers." All this was too plain for our hero not to understand, so Jack walked up to the boatswain, and taking his hat off, with the utmost politeness, said to him:

"If I mistake not, Mr Biggs, your conversation refers to me."

"Very likely it does," replied the boatswain. "Listeners hear no good of themselves."

"It appears that gentlemen can't converse without being vatched," continued Mr Easthupp, pulling up his shirt-collar.

"It is not the first time that you have thought proper to make very offensive remarks, Mr Biggs; and as you appear to consider yourself ill-treated in the affair of the trousers, for I tell you at once, that it was I who brought them on board, I can only say," continued our hero, with a very polite bow, "that I shall be most happy to give you satisfaction."

"I am your superior officer, Mr Easy," replied the boatswain.

"Yes, by the rules of the service; but you just now asserted that you would waive your rank—indeed, I dispute it on this occasion; I am on the quarter-deck, and you are not."

"This is the gentleman whom you have insulted, Mr Easy," replied the boatswain, pointing to the purser's steward.

"Yes, Mr Heasy, quite as good a gentleman as yourself, although I av ad misfortune—I ham of as hold a family as hany in the country," replied Mr Easthupp, now backed by the boatswain; "many the year did I valk Bond Street, and I ave as good blood in my weins as you, Mr Heasy, halthough I have been misfortunate—I've had hadmirals in my family."

"You have grossly insulted this gentleman," said Mr Biggs, in continuation; "and notwithstanding all your talk of equality, you are afraid to give him satisfaction—you shelter yourself under your quarter-deck."

"Mr Biggs," replied our hero, who was now very wroth, "I shall go on shore directly we arrive at Malta. Let you, and this fellow, put on plain clothes, and I will meet you both—and then I'll show you whether I am afraid to give satisfaction."

"One at a time," said the boatswain.

"No, sir, not one at a time, but both at the same time—I will fight both or none. If you are my superior officer, you must *descend*," replied Jack, with an ironical sneer, "to meet me, or I will not descend to meet that fellow, whom I believe to have been little better than a pickpocket."

This accidental hit of Jack's made the purser's steward turn pale as a sheet, and then equally red. He raved and foamed amazingly, although he could not meet Jack's indignant look, who then turned round again.

"Now, Mr Biggs, is this to be understood, or do you shelter yourself under your *forecastle*?"

"I'm no dodger," replied the boatswain, "and we will settle the affair at Malta."

At which reply Jack returned to Mesty.

"Massa Easy, I look at um face, dat feller, Eastop, he no like it. I go shore wid you, see fair play, anyhow—suppose I can?"

Mr Biggs having declared that he would fight, of course had to look out for a second, and he fixed upon Mr Tallboys, the gunner, and requested him to be his friend. Mr Tallboys, who had been latterly very much annoyed by Jack's victories over him in the science of navigation, and therefore felt ill-will towards him, consented; but he was very much puzzled how to arrange that *three* were to fight at the same time, for he had no idea of there being two duels; so he went to his cabin and commenced reading. Jack, on the other hand, dared not say a word to Jolliffe on the subject: indeed, there was no one in the ship to whom he could confide but Gascoigne: he therefore went to him, and although Gascoigne thought it was excessively *infra dig* of Jack to meet even the boatswain, as the challenge had been given there was no retracting: he therefore consented, like all midshipmen, anticipating fun, and quite thoughtless of the consequences.

The second day after they had been anchored in Vallette harbour, the boatswain and gunner, Jack and Gascoigne, obtained permission to go on shore. Mr Easthupp, the purser's steward, dressed in his best blue coat with brass buttons and velvet collar, the very one in which he had been taken up when he had been vowing and protesting that he was a gentleman, at the very time that his hand was abstracting a pocket book, went up on the quarter-deck, and requested the same indulgence, but Mr Sawbridge refused, as he required him to return staves and hoops at the cooperage. Mesty also, much to his mortification, was not to be spared.

This was awkward, but it was got over by proposing that the meeting should take place behind the cooperage at a certain hour, on which Mr Easthupp might slip out and borrow a portion of the time appropriated to his duty, to heal the breach in his wounded honour. So the parties all went on shore, and put up at one of the small inns to make the necessary arrangements.

Mr Tallboys then addressed Mr Gascoigne, taking him apart while the boatswain amused himself with a glass of grog, and our hero sat outside teasing a monkey.

"Mr Gascoigne," said the gunner, "I have been very much puzzled how this duel should be fought, but I have at last found it out. You see that there are *three* parties to fight; had there been two or four there would have been no difficulty, as the right line or square might guide us in that instance; but we must arrange it upon the *triangle* in this."

Gascoigne stared; he could not imagine what was coming.

"Are you aware, Mr Gascoigne, of the properties of an equilateral triangle?"

"Yes," replied the midshipman, "that it has three equal sides—but what the devil has that to do with the duel?"

"Everything, Mr Gascoigne," replied the gunner; "it has resolved the great difficulty: indeed, the duel between three can only be fought upon that principle. You observe," said the gunner, taking a piece of chalk out of his pocket, and making a triangle on the table, "in this figure we have three points, each equidistant from each other; and we have three combatants—so that placing one at each point, it is all fair play for the three: Mr Easy, for instance, stands here, the boatswain here, and the purser's steward at the third corner. Now, if the distance is fairly measured, it will be all right."

"But then," replied Gascoigne, delighted at the idea, "how are they to fire?"

"It certainly is not of much consequence," replied the gunner, "but still, as sailors, it appears to me that they should fire with the sun; that is, Mr Easy fires at Mr Biggs, Mr Biggs fires at Mr Easthupp, and Mr Easthupp fires at Mr Easy, so that you perceive that each party has his shot at one, and at the same time receives the fire of another."

Gascoigne was in ecstasies at the novelty of the proceeding, the more so as he perceived that Easy obtained every advantage by the arrangement.

"Upon my word, Mr Tallboys, I give you great credit; you have a profound mathematical head, and I am delighted with your arrangement. Of course, in these affairs, the principals are bound to comply with the arrangements of the seconds, and I shall insist upon Mr Easy consenting to your excellent and scientific proposal."

Gascoigne went out, and pulling Jack away from the monkey, told him what the gunner had proposed, at which Jack laughed heartily.

The gunner also explained it to the boatswain, who did not very well comprehend, but replied:

"I dare say it's all right—shot for shot, and damn all favours."

The parties then repaired to the spot with two pairs of ship's pistols, which Mr Tallboys had smuggled on shore; and, as soon as they were on the ground, the gunner called Mr Easthupp out of the cooperage. In the meantime, Gascoigne had been measuring an equilateral triangle of twelve paces—and marked it out. Mr Tallboys, on his return with the purser's steward, went over the ground, and finding that it was "equal angles subtended by equal sides," declared that it was all right. Easy took his station, the boatswain was put into his, and Mr Easthupp, who was quite in a mystery, was led by the gunner to the third position.

"But, Mr Tallboys," said the purser's steward, "I don't understand this. Mr Easy will first fight Mr Biggs, will he not?"

"No," replied the gunner, "this is a duel of three. You will fire at Mr Easy, Mr Easy will fire at Mr Biggs, and Mr Biggs will fire at you. It is all arranged, Mr Easthupp."

"But," said Mr Easthupp, "I do not understand it. Why is Mr Biggs to fire at me? I have no quarrel with Mr Biggs."

"Because Mr Easy fires at Mr Biggs, and Mr Biggs must have his shot as well."

"If you have ever been in the company of gentlemen, Mr Easthupp," observed Gascoigne, "you must know something about duelling."

"Yes, yes, I've kept the best company, Mr Gascoigne, and I can give a gentleman satisfaction; but—"

"Then, sir, if that is the case, you must know that your honour is in the hands of your second, and that no gentleman appeals."

"Yes, yes, I know that, Mr Gascoigne; but still I've no quarrel with Mr Biggs, and therefore, Mr Biggs, of course you will not aim at me."

"Why, you don't think that I'm going to be fired at for nothing," replied the boatswain; "no, no, I'll have my shot anyhow."

"But at your friend, Mr Biggs?"

"All the same, I shall fire at somebody; shot for shot, and hit the luckiest."

"Vel, gentlemen, I purtest against these proceedings," replied Mr Easthupp; "I came here to have satisfaction from Mr Easy, and not to be fired at by Mr Biggs."

"Don't you have satisfaction when you fire at Mr Easy," replied the gunner; "what more would you have?"

"I purtest against Mr Biggs firing at me."

"So you would have a shot without receiving one," cried Gascoigne: "the fact is, that this fellow's a confounded coward, and ought to be kicked into the cooperage again."

At this affront Mr Easthupp rallied, and accepted the pistol offered by the gunner.

"You ear those words, Mr Biggs; pretty language to use to a gentleman. You shall ear from me, sir, as soon as the ship is paid off. I purtest no longer, Mr Tallboys; death before dishonour. I'm a gentleman, damme!"

At all events, the swell was not a very courageous gentleman, for he trembled most exceedingly as he pointed his pistol.

The gunner gave the word, as if he were exercising the great guns on board ship.

"Cock your locks!"—"Take good aim at the object!"—"Fire!"—"Stop your vents!"

The only one of the combatants who appeared to comply with the latter supplementary order was Mr Easthupp, who clapped his hand to his trousers behind, gave a loud yell, and then dropped down: the bullet having passed clean through his seat of honour, from his having presented his broadside as a target to the boatswain as he faced towards our hero. Jack's shot had also taken effect, having passed through both the boatswain's cheeks, without further mischief than extracting two of his best upper double teeth, and forcing through the hole of the farther cheek the boatswain's own quid of tobacco. As for Mr Easthupp's ball, as he was very unsettled, and shut his eyes before he fired, it had gone the Lord knows where.

The purser's steward lay on the ground and screamed—the boatswain spit his double teeth and two or three mouthfuls of blood out, and then threw down his pistols in a rage.

"A pretty business, by God," sputtered he; "he's put my pipe out. How the devil am I to pipe to dinner when I'm ordered, all my wind 'scaping through the cheeks?"

In the meantime, the others had gone to the assistance of the purser's steward, who continued his vociferations. They examined him, and considered a wound in that part not to be dangerous.

"Hold your confounded bawling," cried the gunner, "or you'll have the guard down here: you're not hurt."

"Han't hi?" roared the steward. "Oh, let me die, let me die; don't move me!"

"Nonsense," cried the gunner, "you must get up and walk down to the boat; if you don't we'll leave you—hold your tongue, confound you. You won't? then I'll give you something to halloo for."

Whereupon Mr Tallboys commenced cuffing the poor wretch right and left, who received so many swinging boxes of the ear, that he was soon reduced to merely pitiful plaints of "Oh, dear!—such inhumanity—I purtest—oh, dear! must I get up? I can't, indeed."

"I do not think he can move, Mr Tallboys," said Gascoigne; "I should think the best plan would be to call up two of the men from the cooperage, and let them take him at once to the hospital."

The gunner went down to the cooperage to call the men. Mr Biggs, who had bound up his face as if he had a toothache for the bleeding had been very slight, came up to the purser's steward.

"What the hell are you making such a howling about? Look at me, with two shot-holes through my figure-head, while you have only got one in your stern: I wish I could change with you, by heavens, for I could use my whistle then—now if I attempt to pipe, there will be such a wasteful expenditure of his Majesty's stores of wind, that I never shall get out a note. A wicked shot of yours, Mr Easy."

"I really am very sorry," replied Jack, with a polite bow, "and I beg to offer my best apology."

During this conversation, the purser's steward felt very faint, and thought he was going to die.

"Oh, dear! oh, dear! what a fool I was; I never was a gentleman—only a swell: I shall die; I never will pick a pocket again—never—never—God forgive me!"

"Why, confound the fellow," cried Gascoigne, "so you were a pickpocket, were you?"

"I never will again," replied the fellow, in a faint voice: "Hi'll hamend and lead a good life—a drop of water—oh! *lagged* at last!"

Then the poor wretch fainted away: and Tallboys coming up with the men, he was taken on their shoulders and walked off to the hospital, attended by the gunner and also the boatswain, who thought he might as well have a little medical advice before he went on board.

"Well, Easy," said Gascoigne, collecting the pistols and tying them up in his handkerchief, "I'll be shot, but we're in a pretty scrape; there's no hushing this up. I'll be hanged if I care, it's the best piece of fun I ever met with." And at the remembrance of it Gascoigne laughed till the tears ran down his cheeks. Jack's mirth was not quite so excessive, as he was afraid that the purser's steward was severely hurt, and expressed his fears.

"At all events, you did not hit him," replied Gascoigne; "all you have to answer for is the boatswains's mug—I think you've stopped his jaw for the future."

"I'm afraid that our leave will be stopped for the future," replied Jack.

"That we may take our oaths of," replied Gascoigne.

"Then look you, Ned," said Easy; "I've lots of dollars; we may as well be hanged for a sheep as a lamb, as the saying is; I vote that we do not go on board."

"Sawbridge will send and fetch us," replied Ned; "but he must find us first."

"That won't take long, for the soldiers will soon have our description and rout us out—we shall be pinned in a couple of days."

"Confound it, and they say that the ship is to be hove down, and that we shall be here six weeks at least, cooped up on board in a broiling sun, and nothing to do but to watch the pilot fish playing round the rudder, and munch bad apricots. I won't go on board; look ye, Jack," said Gascoigne, "have you plenty of money?"

"I have twenty doubloons, besides dollars," replied Jack.

"Well, then we will pretend to be so much alarmed at the result of this duel, that we dare not show ourselves, lest we should be hung. I will write a note, and send it to Jolliffe, to say that we have hid ourselves until the affair is blown over, and beg him to intercede with the captain and first lieutenant. I will tell him all the particulars, and refer to the gunner for the truth of it; and then I know that, although we should be punished, they will only laugh; but I will pretend that Easthupp is killed, and we are frightened out of our lives. That will be it; and then let's get on board one of the speronares which come with fruit from Sicily, sail in the night for Palermo, and then we'll have a cruise for a fortnight, and when the money is all gone we'll come back."

"That's a capital idea, Ned, and the sooner we do it the better. I will write to the captain, begging him to get me off from being hung, and telling him where we have fled to, and that letter shall be given after we have sailed."

They were two very nice lads—our hero and Gascoigne.

Chapter Eighteen.

In which our hero sets off on another cruise, in which he is not blown off shore.

Gascoigne and our hero were neither of them in uniform, and they hastened to Nix Mangare stairs where they soon picked up the padrone of a speronare. They went with him into a wine-shop, and with the assistance of a little English from a Maltese boy, whose shirt hung out of his trousers, they made a bargain, by which it was agreed that, for the consideration of two doubloons, he would sail that evening and land them at Gergenti or some other town in Sicily, providing them with something to eat and gregos to sleep upon.

Our two midshipmen then went back to the tavern from which they had set off to fight the duel, and ordering a good dinner to be served in a back room, they amused themselves with killing flies, as they talked over the events of the day, and waited for their dinner.

As Mr Tallboys did not himself think proper to go on board till the evening, and Mr Biggs also wished it to be dark before he went up the ship's side, the events of the duel did not transpire till the next morning. Even then it was not known from the boatswain or gunner, but by a hospital mate coming on board to inform the surgeon that there was one of their men wounded under their charge, but that he was doing very well.

Mr Biggs had ascended the side with his face bound up.

"Confound that Jack Easy," said he, "I have only been on leave twice since I sailed from Portsmouth—once I was obliged to come up the side without my trousers, and show my bare stern to the whole ship's company, and now I am coming up, and dare not show my figure-head." He reported himself to the officer of the watch, and hasting to his cabin, went to bed, and lay the whole night awake from pain, thinking what excuse he could possibly make for not coming on deck next morning to his duty.

He was, however, saved this trouble, for Mr Jolliffe brought the letter of Gascoigne up to Mr Sawbridge, and the captain had received that of our hero.

Captain Wilson came on board, and found that Mr Sawbridge could communicate all the particulars of which he had not been acquainted by Jack; and after they had read over Gascoigne's letter in the cabin, and interrogated Mr Tallboys, who was sent down under an arrest, they gave free vent to their mirth.

"Upon my soul, there's no end to Mr Easy's adventures," said the captain. "I could laugh at the duel, for after all, it is nothing—and he would have been let off with a severe reprimand; but the foolish boys have set off in a speronare to Sicily, and how the devil are we to get them back again?"

"They'll come back, sir," replied Sawbridge, "when all their money's gone."

"Yes, if they do not get into any more scrapes—that young scamp Gascoigne is as bad as Easy, and now they are together there's no saying what may happen. I dine at the Governor's to-day; how he will laugh when I tell him of this new way of fighting a duel!"

"Yes, sir, it is just the thing that will tickle old Tom."

"We must find out if they have got off the island, Sawbridge, which may not be the case."

But it was the case. Jack and Gascoigne had eaten a very good dinner, sent for the monkey to amuse them till it was dark, and there had waited till the padrone came to them.

"What shall we do with the pistols, Easy?"

"Take them with us, and load them before we go—we may want them: who knows but there may be a mutiny on board of the speronare?—I wish we had Mesty with us."

They loaded the pistols, took a pair each and put them in their waists, concealed under their clothes—divided the ammunition between them, and soon afterwards the padrone came to tell them all was ready.

Whereupon Messrs Gascoigne and Easy paid their bill and rose to depart, but the padrone informed them that he should like to see the colour of their money before they went on board. Jack, very indignant at the insinuation that he had not sufficient cash, pulled out a handful of doubloons, and tossing two to the padrone, asked him if he was satisfied.

The padrone untied his sash, put in the money, and with many thanks and protestations of service, begged our young gentlemen to accompany him: they did so, and in a few minutes were clear of Nix Mangare stairs, and, passing close to his Majesty's ship *Harpy,* were soon out of the harbour of Vallette.

Of all the varieties of vessels which float upon the wave, there is not, perhaps, one that bounds over the water so gracefully or so lightly as a speronare, or any one so picturesque and beautiful to the eye of those who watch its progress.

The night was clear, and the stars shone out brilliantly as the light craft skimmed over the water, and a fragment of a descending and waning moon threw its soft beams upon the snow-white sail. The vessel, which had no neck, was full of baskets, which had contained grapes and various fruits brought from the ancient granary of Rome, still as fertile and as luxuriant as ever. The crew consisted of the padrone, two men and a boy; the three latter, with their gregos, or night greatcoats with hoods, sitting forward before the sail, with their eyes fixed on the land as they flew past point after point, thinking perhaps of their wives, or perhaps of their sweethearts, or perhaps not thinking at all.

The padrone remained aft at the helm, offering every politeness to our two young gentlemen, who only wished to be left alone. At last they requested the padrone to give them gregos to lie down upon, as they wished to go to sleep. He called the boy to take the helm, procured them all they required, and then went forward. And our two midshipmen laid down looking at the stars above them, for some minutes, without exchanging a word. At last Jack commenced.

"I have been thinking, Gascoigne, that this is very delightful. My heart bounds with the vessel, and it almost appears to me as if the vessel herself was rejoicing in her liberty. Here she is capering over the waves instead of being tied by the nose with a cable and anchor."

"That's a touch of the sentimental, Jack," replied Gascoigne; "but she is no more free than she was when at anchor, for she now is forced to act in obedience to her steersman, and go just where he pleases. You may just as well say that a horse, if taken out of the stable, is free, with the curb and his rider on his back."

"That's a touch of the rational, Ned, which destroys the illusion. Never mind, we are free, at all events. What machines we are on board of a man-of-war! We walk, talk, eat, drink, sleep, and get up, just like clock-work; we are wound up to go the twenty-four hours, and then wound up again; just like old Smallsole does the chronometers."

"Very true, Jack; but it does not appear to me, that, hitherto, you have kept very good time: you require a little more regulating," said Gascoigne.

"How can you expect any piece of machinery to go well, so damnably knocked about as a midshipman is?" replied our hero.

"Very true, Jack; but sometimes you don't keep any time, for you don't keep any watch. Mr Asper don't wind you up. You don't go at all."

"No; because he allows me to go *down;* but still I do *go,* Ned."

"Yes, to your hammock—but it's *no go* with old Smallsole, if I want a bit of *caulk*. But, Jack, what do you say—shall we keep watch to-night?"

"Why, to tell you the truth, I have been thinking the same thing—I don't much like the looks of the padrone—he squints."

"That's no proof of anything, Jack, except that his eyes are not straight; but if you do not like the look of him, I can tell you that he very much liked the look of your doubloons—I saw him start, and his eyes twinkled, and I thought at the time it was a pity you had not paid him in dollars."

"It was very foolish in me; but at all events he has not seen all."

"He saw quite enough, Ned."

"Very true, but you should have let him see the pistols, and not have let him see the doubloons."

"Well, if he wishes to take what he has seen, he shall receive what he has not seen—why, there are only four of them?"

"Oh, I have no fear of them, only it may be as well to sleep with one eye open."

"When shall we make the land?"

"To-morrow evening with this wind, and it appears to be steady. Suppose we keep watch and watch, and have our pistols out ready, with the greatcoats just turned over them, to keep them out of sight?"

"Agreed—it's about twelve o'clock now—who shall keep the middle watch?"

"I will, Jack, if you like it."

"Well, then, mind you kick me hard, for I sleep devilish sound. Good—night, and keep a sharp lookout."

Jack was fast asleep in less than ten minutes; and Gascoigne, with his pistols lying by him all ready for each hand, sat up at the bottom of the boat.

There certainly is a peculiar providence in favour of midshipmen compared with the rest of mankind; they have more lives than a cat—always in the greatest danger, but always escaping from it.

The padrone of the vessel had been captivated with the doubloons which Jack had so foolishly exposed to his view, and he had, moreover, resolved to obtain them. At the very time that our two lads were conversing aft, the padrone was talking the matter over with his two men forward, and it was agreed that they should murder, rifle, and then throw them overboard.

About two o'clock in the morning, the padrone came aft to see if they were asleep, but found Gascoigne watching. He returned aft again and again; but found the young man still sitting up. Tired of waiting, anxious to possess the money, and supposing that the lads were armed, he went once more forward and spoke to the men. Gascoigne had watched his motions; he thought it singular that, with three men in the vessel, the helm should be confided to the boy—and at last he saw them draw their knives. He pushed our hero, who woke immediately Gascoigne put his hand over Jack's mouth, that he might not speak, and then he whispered his suspicions. Jack seized his pistols—they both cocked them without noise, and then waited in silence, Jack still lying down while Gascoigne continued to sit up at the bottom of the boat. At last Gascoigne saw the three men coming aft—he dropped one of his pistols for a second to give Jack a squeeze of the hand, which was returned, and as Gascoigne watched them making their way through the piles of empty baskets he leaned back as if he was slumbering. The padrone, followed by the two men, was at last aft—they paused a moment before they stepped over the strengthening plank, which ran from side to side of the boat between them and the midshipmen, and as neither of them stirred they imagined that both were asleep—advanced and raised their knives, when Gascoigne and Jack, almost at the same moment, each discharged their pistols into the breast of the padrone and one of the men, who was with him in advance, who both fell with the send aft of the boat, so as to encumber the midshipmen with the weight of their bodies. The third man started back. Jack, who could not rise, from the padrone lying across his legs, took a steady aim with his second pistol, and the third man fell. The boy at the helm, who, it appeared, either was aware of what was to be done, or seeing the men advance with their knives, had acted upon what he saw, also drew his knife and struck at Gascoigne from behind. The knife fortunately, after slightly wounding Gascoigne on the shoulder, had shut on the boy's hand—Gascoigne sprang up with his other pistol, the boy started back at the sight of it, lost his balance, and fell overboard.

Our two midshipmen took a few seconds to breathe.

"I say, Jack," said Gascoigne at last, "did you ever—"

"No, I never—" replied Jack.

"What's to be done now?"

"Why, as we've got possession, Ned, we had better put a man at the helm—for the speronare is having it all her own way."

"Very true," replied Gascoigne; "and as I can steer better than you, I suppose it must be me."

Gascoigne went to the helm, brought the boat up to the wind, and then they resumed their conversation.

"That rascal of a boy gave me a devil of a lick on the shoulder; I don't know whether he has hurt me—at all events it's my left shoulder, so I can steer just as well. I wonder whether the fellows are dead."

"The padrone is, at all events," replied Jack. "It was as much as I could do to get my legs from under him—but we'll wait till daylight before we see to that—in the meantime, I'll load the pistols again."

"The day is breaking now—it will be light in half an hour or less. What a devil of a spree, Jack!"

"Yes, but how can one help it? We ran away because two men are wounded—and now we are obliged to kill four in self-defence."

"Yes, but that is not the end of it; when we get to Sicily what are we to do? we shall be imprisoned by the authorities—perhaps hung."

"We'll argue that point with them," replied Jack.

"We had better argue the point between ourselves, Jack, and see what will be the best plan to get out of our scrape."

"I think that we just have got out of it—never fear but we'll get out of the next. Do you know, Gascoigne, it appears to me very odd, but I can do nothing but there's a bobbery at the bottom of it."

"You certainly have a great talent that way, Jack. Don't I hear one of these poor fellows groan?"

"I should think that not impossible."

"What shall we do with them?"

"We will argue that point, Ned—we must either keep their bodies or we must throw them overboard. Either tell the whole story or say nothing about it."

"That's very evident; in short, we must do something, for your argument goes no further. But now let us take up one of your propositions."

"Well then, suppose we keep the bodies on board, run into a seaport, go to the authorities, and state all the facts, what then?"

"We shall prove, beyond all doubt, that we have killed three men, if not four; but we shall not prove that we were obliged so to do, Jack. And then we are heretics—we shall be put in prison till they are satisfied of our innocence, which we never can prove, and there we shall remain until we have written to Malta, and a man-of-war comes to redeem us, if we are not stabbed, or something else in the meantime."

"That will not be a very pleasant cruise," replied Jack. "Now let's argue the point on the other side."

"There is some difficulty there—suppose we throw their bodies overboard, toss the baskets after them, wash the boat clean, and make for the first port. We may chance to hit upon the very spot from which they sailed, and then there will be a pack of wives and children, and a populace with knives, asking us what has become of the men of the boat."

"I don't much like the idea of that," said Jack.

"And if we don't have such bad luck, still we shall be interrogated as to who we are, and how we were adrift by ourselves."

"There will be a difficulty about that again—we must swear that it is a party of pleasure, and that we are gentlemen yachting."

"Without a crew or provisions—yachts don't sail with a clean-swept hold, or gentlemen without a spare shirt—we have nothing but two gallons of water and two pairs of pistols."

"I have it," said Jack—"we are two young gentlemen in our own boat who went out to Gozo with pistols to shoot sea-mews, were caught in a gale, and blown down to Sicily—that will excite interest."

"That's the best idea yet, as it will account for our having nothing in the boat. Well then, at all events, we will get rid of the bodies; but suppose they are not dead—we cannot throw them overboard alive—that will be murder."

"Very true," replied Jack; "then we must shoot them first, and toss them overboard afterwards."

"Upon my soul, Easy, you are an odd fellow: however, go and examine the men, and we'll decide that point by-and-bye—you had better keep your pistol ready cocked for they may be shamming."

"Devil a bit of sham here, anyhow," replied Jack, pulling at the body of the padrone, "and as for this fellow you shot, you might put your fist into his chest. Now for the third," continued Jack, stepping over the strengthening piece—"he's all among the baskets. I say, my cock, are you dead?" and Jack enforced his question with a kick in the ribs. The man groaned. "That's unlucky, Gascoigne, but, however, I'll soon settle him," said Jack, pointing his pistol.

"Stop, Jack," cried Gascoigne, "it really will be murder."

"No such thing, Ned; I'll just blow his brains out, and then I'll come aft and argue the point with you."

"Now do oblige me by coming aft and arguing the point first. Do, Jack, I beg of you—I entreat you."

"With all my heart," replied Jack, resuming his seat by Gascoigne; "I assert, that in this instance killing's no murder. You will observe, Ned, that by the laws of society, any one who attempts the life of another has forfeited his own; at the same time, as it is necessary that the fact should be clearly proved and justice be duly administered, the parties are tried, convicted, and then are sentenced to the punishment."

"I grant all that."

"In this instance the attempt has been clearly proved; we are the witnesses, and are the judges and jury, and society in general, for the best of all possible reasons, because there is nobody else. These men's lives being therefore forfeited to society, belong to us; and it does not follow because they were not all killed in the attempt, that therefore they are not now to be brought out for punishment. And as there is no common hangman here, we, of course, must do this duty as well as every other. I have now clearly proved that I am justified in what I am about to do. But the argument does not stop there—self-preservation is the first law of nature, and if we do not get rid of this man, what is the consequence?—that we shall have to account for his being wounded, and then, instead of judges, we shall immediately be placed in the position of culprits, and have to defend ourselves without witnesses. We therefore risk our lives from a misplaced lenity towards a wretch unworthy to live."

"Your last argument is strong, Easy, but I cannot consent to your doing what may occasion you uneasiness hereafter when you think of it."

"Pooh! nonsense—I am a philosopher."

"Of what school, Jack? Oh, I presume you are a disciple of Mesty's. I do not mean to say that you are wrong, but still hear my proposition. Let us lower down the sail, and then I can leave the helm to assist you. We will clear the vessel of everything except the man who is still alive. At all events, we may wait a little, and if at last there is no help for it, I will then agree with you to launch him overboard, even if he is not quite dead."

"Agreed; even by your own making out, it will be no great sin. He is half dead already—I only do *half* the work of tossing him over, so it will be only *quarter* murder on my part, and he would have shown no quarter on his." Here Jack left off arguing and punning, and went forward and lowered down the sail. "I've half a mind to take my doubloons back," said Jack, as they launched over the body of the padrone, "but he may have them—I wonder whether they'll ever turn up again?"

"Not in our time, Jack," replied Gascoigne.

The other body, and all the basket lumber, etcetera, were then tossed over, and the boat was cleared of all but the man who was not yet dead.

"Now let's examine the fellow, and see if he has any chance of recovery," said Gascoigne.

The man lay on his side; Gascoigne turned him over, and found that he was dead.

"Over with him, quick," said Jack, "before he comes to life again."

The body disappeared under the wave—they again hoisted the sail, Gascoigne took the helm, and our hero proceeded to draw water and wash away the stains of blood; he then cleared the boat of vine-leaves and rubbish, with which it was strewed, swept it clean fore and aft, and resumed his seat by his comrade.

"There," said Jack, "now we've swept the decks, we may pipe to dinner. I wonder whether there is anything to eat in the locker?"

Jack opened it, and found some bread, garlic, sausages, a bottle of aquadente, and a jar of wine.

"So the padrone did keep his promise, after all."

"Yes, and had you not tempted him with the sight of so much gold, might now have been alive."

"To which I reply, that if you had not advised our going off in a speronare, he would now have been alive."

"And if you had not fought a duel, I should not have given the advice."

"And if the boatswain had not been obliged to come on board without his trousers, at Gibraltar, I should not have fought a duel."

"And if you had not joined the ship, the boatswain would have had his trousers on."

"And if my father had not been a philosopher, I should not have gone to sea; so that it is all my father's fault, and he has killed four men off the coast of Sicily, without knowing it—cause and effect. After all, there's nothing like argument; so having settled that point, let us go to dinner."

Having finished their meal, Jack went forward and observed the land ahead; they steered the same course for three or four hours.

"We must haul our wind more," said Gascoigne; "it will not do to put into any small town: we have now to choose, whether we shall land on the coast and sink the speronare, or land at some large town."

"We must argue that point," replied Jack.

"In the meantime, do you take the helm, for my arm is quite tired," replied Gascoigne: "you can steer well enough; by-the-bye, I may as well look at my shoulder, for it is quite stiff." Gascoigne pulled off his coat, and found his shirt bloody and sticking to the wound, which, as we before observed, was slight. He again took the helm, while Jack washed it clean and then bathed it with aquadente.

"Now take the helm again," said Gascoigne; "I'm on the sick list."

"And as surgeon—I'm an idler," replied Jack; "but what shall we do?" continued he; "abandon the speronare at night and sink her, or run in for a town?"

"We shall fall in with plenty of boats and vessels if we coast it up to Palermo, and they may overhaul us."

"We shall fall in with plenty of people if we go on shore, and they will overhaul us."

"Do you know, Jack, that I wish we were back and alongside of the *Harpy;* I've had cruising enough."

"My cruises are so unfortunate," replied Jack; "they are too full of adventure; but then, I have never yet had a cruise on shore. Now, if we could only get to Palermo, we should be out of all our difficulties."

"The breeze freshens, Jack," replied Gascoigne; "and it begins to look very dirty to windward. I think we shall have a gale."

"Pleasant—I know what it is to be short-handed in a gale; however, there's one comfort, we shall not be blown *off shore* this time."

"No, but we may be wrecked on a lee shore. She cannot carry her whole sail, Easy; we must lower it down, and take in a reef; the sooner the better, for it will be dark in an hour. Go forward and lower it down, and then I'll help you."

Jack did so, but the sail went into the water, and he could not drag it in.

"Avast heaving," said Gascoigne, "till I throw her up and take the wind out of it."

This was done; they reefed the sail, but could not hoist it up: if Gascoigne left the helm to help Jack, the sail filled; if he went to the helm and took the wind out of the sail, Jack was not strong enough to hoist it. The wind increased rapidly, and the sea got up; the sun went down, and with the sail half hoisted, they could not keep to the wind, but were obliged to run right for the land. The speronare flew, rising on the crest of the waves with half her keel clear of the water: the moon was already up, and gave them light enough to perceive that they were not five miles from the coast, which was lined with foam.

"At all events, they can't accuse us of running away with the boat," observed Jack; "for she's running away with us."

"Yes," replied Gascoigne, dragging at the tiller with all his strength; "she has taken the bit between her teeth."

"I wouldn't care if I had a bit between mine," replied Jack; "for I feel devilish hungry again. What do you say, Ned?"

"With all my heart," replied Gascoigne; "but, do you know, Easy, it may be the last meal we ever make."

"Then I vote it's a good one—but why so, Ned?"

"In half an hour, or thereabouts, we shall be on shore."

"Well, that's where we want to go."

"Yes, but the sea runs high, and the boat may be dashed to pieces on the rocks."

"Then we shall be asked no questions about her or the men."

"Very true, but a lee shore is no joke; we may be knocked to pieces, as well as the boat—even swimming may not help us. If we could find a cove or sandy beach, we might, perhaps, manage to get on shore."

"Well," replied Jack, "I have not been long at sea, and, of course, cannot know much about these things. I have been blown off shore, but I never have been blown on. It may be as you say, but I do not see the great danger—let's run her right up on the beach at once."

"That's what I shall try to do," replied Gascoigne, who had been four years at sea, and knew very well what he was about.

Jack handed him a huge piece of bread and sausage.

"Thank ye, I cannot eat."

"I can," replied Jack, with his mouth full.

Jack ate while Gascoigne steered; and the rapidity with which the speronare rushed to the beach was almost frightful. She darted like an arrow from wave to wave, and appeared as if mocking their attempts as they curled their summits almost over her narrow stern. They were within a mile of the beach, when Jack, who had finished his supper, and was looking at the foam boiling on the coast, exclaimed:

"That's very fine—very beautiful, upon my soul!"

"He cares for nothing," thought Gascoigne; "he appears to have no idea of danger."

"Now, my dear fellow," said Gascoigne, "in a few minutes we shall be on the rocks. I must continue at the helm, for the higher she is forced up the better chance for us; but we may not meet again, so if we do not, good-bye, and God bless you."

"Gascoigne," said Jack, "you are hurt and I am not; your shoulder is stiff, and you can hardly move your left arm. Now I can steer for the rocks as well as you. Do you go to the bow, and there you will have a better chance. By-the-bye," continued he, picking up his pistols, and sticking them into his waist, "I won't leave them, they've served us too good a turn already. Gascoigne, give me the helm."

"No, no, Easy."

"I say yes," replied Jack, in a loud, authoritative tone, "and what's more, I will be obeyed, Gascoigne. I have nerve, if I haven't knowledge, and at all events I can steer for the beach. I tell you, give me the helm. Well, then, if you won't—I must take it."

Easy wrested the tiller from Gascoigne's hand, and gave him a shove forward.

"Now do you look out ahead, and tell me how to steer."

Whatever may have been Gascoigne's feelings at this behaviour of our hero's, it immediately occurred to him that he could not do better than to run the speronare to the safest point, and that therefore he was probably more advantageously employed than if he were at the helm. He went forward and looked at the rocks, covered at one moment with the tumultuous waters, and then pouring down cascades from their sides as the waves recoiled. He perceived a chasm right ahead, and he thought if the boat was steered for that, she must be thrown up so as to enable them to get clear of her, for at every other part escape appeared impossible.

"Starboard a little—that'll do. Steady—port it is—port. Steer small, for your life, Easy. Steady now—mind the yard don't hit your head—hold on."

The speronare was at this moment thrown into a large cleft in a rock, the sides of which were nearly perpendicular; nothing else could have saved them, as, had they struck the rock outside, the boat would have been dashed to pieces, and its fragments have disappeared in the undertow. As it was, the cleft was not four feet more than the width of the boat, and as the waves hurled her up into it, the yard of the speronare was thrown fore and aft with great violence, and had not Jack been warned, he would have been struck overboard without a chance of being saved; but he crouched down and it passed over him. As the water receded, the boat struck, and was nearly dry between the rocks, but another wave followed, dashing the boat farther up, but, at the same time, filling it with water. The bow of the boat was now several feet higher than the stern, where Jack held on; and the weight of the water in her, with the force of the returning waves, separated her right across abaft the mast. Jack perceived that the after-part of the boat was going out again with the wave; he caught hold of the yard which had swung fore and aft, and as he clung to it, the part of the boat on which he had stood disappeared from under him, and was swept away by the returning current.

Jack required the utmost of his strength to maintain his position until another wave floated him, and dashed him higher up: but he knew his life depended on holding on to the yard, which he did, although under water, and advanced several feet. When the wave receded, he found footing on the rock, and still clinging, he walked till he had gained the fore-part of the boat, which was wedged firmly into a narrow part of the cleft. The next wave was not very large, and he had gained so much that it did not throw him off his legs. He reached the rock, and as he climbed up the side of the chasm to gain the ledge above, he perceived Gascoigne standing above him, and holding out his hand to his assistance.

"Well," says Jack, shaking himself to get rid of the water, "here we are, ashore at last—I had no idea of anything like this. The rush back of the water was so strong that it has almost torn my arms out of their sockets. How very lucky I sent you forward with your disabled shoulder. By-the-bye, now that it's all over, and you must see that I was right, I beg to apologise for my rudeness."

"There needs no apology for saving my life, Easy," replied Gascoigne, trembling with the cold; "and no one but you would ever have thought of making one at such a moment."

"I wonder whether the ammunition's dry," said Jack; "I put it all in my hat."

Jack took off his hat, and found the cartridges had not suffered.

"Now then, Gascoigne, what shall we do?"

"I hardly know," replied Gascoigne.

"Suppose, then, we sit down and argue the point."

"No, I thank you, there will be too much cold water thrown upon our arguments—I'm half dead; let us walk on."

"With all my heart," said Jack, "it's devilish steep, but I can argue up hill or down hill, wet or dry—I'm used to it—for, as I told you before, Ned, my father is a philosopher, and so am I."

"By the Lord! *you are*," replied Gascoigne, as he walked on.

Chapter Nineteen.

In which our hero follows his destiny and forms a tableau.

Our hero and his comrade climbed the precipice, and, after some minutes' severe toil, arrived at the summit, when they sat down to recover themselves. The sky was clear, although the gale blew strong. They had an extensive view of the coast, lashed by the angry waves.

"It's my opinion, Ned," said Jack, as he surveyed the expanse of troubled water, "that we're just as well out of that."

"I agree with you, Jack; but it's also my opinion that we should be just as well out of this, for the wind blows through one. Suppose we go a little farther inland, where we may find some shelter till the morning."

"It's rather dark to find anything," rejoined our hero; "but, however, a westerly gale on the top of a mountain with wet clothes in the middle of the night with nothing to eat or drink, is not the most comfortable position in the world, and we may change for the better."

They proceed over a flat of a hundred yards, and then descended—the change in the atmosphere was immediate. As they continued their march inland, they came to a high-road, which appeared to run along the shore, and they turned into it; for, as Jack said very truly, a road must lead to something. After a quarter of an hour's walk, they again heard the rolling of the surf, and perceived the white walls of houses.

"Here we are at last," said Jack. "I wonder if any one will turn out to take us in, or shall we stow away for the night in one of those vessels hauled up on the beach?"

"Recollect this time, Easy," said Gascoigne, "not to show your money; that is, show only a dollar, and say you have no more, or promise to pay when we arrive at Palermo; and if they will neither trust us, nor give to us, we must make it out as we can."

"How the cursed dogs bark! I think we shall do very well this time, Gascoigne: we do not look as if we were worth robbing, at all events, and we have the pistols to defend ourselves with if we are attacked. Depend upon it I will show no more gold. And now let us make our arrangements. Take you one pistol, and take half the gold—I have it all in my right-hand pocket—my dollars and pistarenes in my left. You shall take half of them too. We have silver enough to go on with till we are in a safe place."

Jack then divided the money in the dark, and also gave Gascoigne a pistol.

"Now then, shall we knock for admittance?—Let's first walk through the village, and see if there's anything like an inn. Those yelping curs will soon be at our heels; they come nearer and nearer every time. There's a cart, and it's full of straw—suppose we go to bed till to-morrow morning—we shall be warm, at all events."

"Yes," replied Gascoigne, "and sleep much better than in any of the cottages. I have been in Sicily before, and you have no idea how the fleas bite."

Our two midshipmen climbed up into the cart, nestled themselves into the straw, or rather Indian corn-leaves, and were soon fast asleep. As they had not slept for two nights, it is not to be wondered at that they slept soundly—so soundly, indeed, that about two hours after they had got into their comfortable bed, the peasant, who had brought to the village some casks of wine to be shipped and taken down the coast in a felucca, yoked his bullocks, and not being aware of his freight, drove off without, in any way, disturbing their repose, although the roads in Sicily are not yet macadamised.

The jolting of the roads rather increased than disturbed the sleep of our adventurers; and, although there were some rude shocks, it only had the effect of making them fancy in their dreams that they were again in the boat, and that she was still dashing against the rocks. In about two hours, the cart arrived at its destination—the peasant unyoked his bullocks and led them away. The same cause will often produce contrary effects: the stopping of the motion of the cart disturbed the rest of our two midshipmen; they turned round in the straw, yawned, spread out their arms, and then awoke. Gascoigne, who felt considerable pain in his shoulder, was the first to recall his scattered senses.

"Easy," cried he, as he sat up and shook off the corn-leaves.

"Port it is," said Jack, half dreaming.

"Come, Easy, you are not on board now. Rouse and bitt."

Jack then sat up and looked at Gascoigne. The forage in the cart was so high round them that they could not see above it; they rubbed their eyes, yawned, and looked at each other.

"Have you any faith in dreams," said Jack to Gascoigne, "because I had a very queer one last night."

"Well, so had I," replied Gascoigne. "I dreamt that the cart rolled by itself into the sea, and went away with us right in the wind's eye back to Malta; and, considering that it never was built for such service, she behaved uncommonly well. Now what was your dream?"

"Mine was, that we woke up and found ourselves in the very town from which the speronare had sailed, and that they had found the fore-part of the speronare among the rocks, and recognised her, and picked up one of our pistols. That they had laid hold of us, and had insisted that we had been thrown on shore in the boat, and asked us what had become of the crew—they were just seizing us, when I awoke."

"Your dream is more likely to come true than mine, Easy; but still I think we need not fear that. At the same time, we had better not remain here any longer; and it occurs to me, that if we tore our clothes more, it would be advisable—we shall, in the first place, look more wretched; and, in the next place, can replace them with the dress of the country, and so travel without exciting suspicion. You know that I can speak Italian pretty well."

"I have no objection to tear my clothes if you wish," replied Jack; "at the same time give me your pistol; I will draw the charges and load them again. They must be wet."

Having reloaded the pistols and rent their garments, the two midshipmen stood up in the cart and looked about them.

"Halloo!—why, how's this, Gascoigne? last night we were close to the beach, and among houses, and now—where the devil are we? You dreamt nearer the mark than I did, for the cart has certainly taken a cruise."

"We must have slept like midshipmen, then," replied Gascoigne: "surely it cannot have gone far."

"Here we are, surrounded by hills on every side, for at least a couple of miles. Surely some good genius has transported us into the interior, that we might escape from the relatives of the crew whom I dreamt about," said Jack, looking at Gascoigne.

As it afterwards was known to them, the speronare had sailed from the very seaport in which they had arrived that night, and where they had got into the cart. The wreck of the speronare had been found, and had been recognised, and it was considered by the inhabitants that the padrone and his crew had perished in the gale. Had they found our two midshipmen and questioned them, it is not improbable that suspicion might have been excited, and the results have been such as our hero had conjured up in his dream. But, as we said before, there is a peculiar providence for midshipmen.

On a minute survey, they found that they were in an open space which, apparently, had been used for thrashing and winnowing maize, and that the cart was standing under a clump of trees in the shade.

"There ought to be a house hereabouts," said Gascoigne; "I should think that behind the trees we shall find one. Come, Jack, you are as hungry as I am, I'll answer for it; we must look out for a breakfast somewhere."

"If they won't give us something to eat, or sell it," replied Jack, who was ravenous, clutching his pistol, "I shall take it—I consider it no robbery. The fruits of the earth were made for us all, and it never was intended that one man should have a superfluity and another starve. The laws of equality—"

"May appear very good arguments to a starving man, I grant, but still, won't prevent his fellow creatures from hanging him," replied Gascoigne. "None of your confounded nonsense, Jack; no man starves with money in his pocket, and as long as you have that, leave those that have none to talk about equality and the rights of man."

"I should like to argue that point with you, Gascoigne."

"Tell me, do you prefer sitting down here to argue, or to look out for some breakfast, Jack?"

"Oh, the argument may be put off, but hunger cannot."

"That's very good philosophy, Jack, so let's go on."

They went through the copse of wood, which was very thick, and soon discovered the wall of a large house on the other side.

"All right," said Jack; "but still let us reconnoitre. It's not a farm-house; it must belong to a person of some consequence—all the better—they will see that we are gentlemen, notwithstanding our tattered dress. I suppose we are to stick to the story of the sea-mews at Gozo?"

"Yes," replied Gascoigne; "I can think of nothing better. But the English are well received in this island; we have troops at Palermo."

"Have we? I wish I was sitting down at the mess-table—but what's that? a woman screaming?—Yes, by heavens!—come along, Ned." And away dashed Jack towards the house, followed by Gascoigne. As they advanced the screams redoubled; they entered the porch, burst into the room from whence they proceeded, and found an elderly gentleman defending himself against two young men, who were held back by an elderly and a young lady. Our hero and his comrade had both drawn their pistols, and just as they burst open the door, the old gentleman who defended himself against such odds had fallen down. The two others burst from the women, and were about to pierce him with their swords, when Jack seized one by the collar of his coat and held him fast, pointing the muzzle of the pistol to his ear: Gascoigne did the same to the other. It was a very dramatic tableau. The two women flew to the elderly gentleman and raised him up; the two assailants being held just as dogs hold pigs by the ear, trembling with fright, with the points of their rapiers dropped, looked at the midshipmen and the muzzles of their pistols with equal dismay; at the same time, the astonishment of the elderly gentleman and the women, at such an unexpected deliverance, was equally great. There was a silence for a few seconds.

"Ned," at last said Jack, "tell these chaps to drop their swords, or we fire."

Gascoigne gave the order in Italian, and it was complied with. The midshipmen then possessed themselves of the rapiers, and gave the young men their liberty.

The elderly gentleman at last broke the silence.

"It would appear, signors, that there was an especial interference of Providence, to prevent you from committing a foul and unjust murder. Who these are that have so opportunely come to my rescue, I know not, but thanking them as I do now, I think that you will yourselves, when you are calm, also thank them for having prevented you from committing an act which would have loaded you with remorse and embittered your future existence. Gentlemen, you are free to depart: you, Don Silvio, have indeed disappointed me; your gratitude should have rendered you incapable of such conduct: as for you, Don Scipio, you have been misled; but you both have, in one point, disgraced yourselves. Ten days back my sons were both here—why did you not come then? If you sought revenge on me, you could not have inflicted it deeper than through my children, and at least you would not have acted the part of assassins in attacking an old man. Take your swords, gentlemen, and use them better henceforth. Against future attacks I shall be well prepared."

Gascoigne, who perfectly understood what was said, presented the sword to the young gentleman from whom he had taken it—our hero did the same. The two young men returned them to their sheaths, and quitted the room without saying a word.

"Whoever you are, I owe to you and thank you for my life," said the elderly gentleman, scanning the outward appearance of our two midshipmen.

"We are," said Gascoigne, "officers in the English navy, and gentlemen; we were wrecked in our boat last night, and have wandered here in the dark, seeking for assistance, and food, and some conveyance to Palermo, where we shall find friends, and the means of appearing like gentlemen."

"Was your ship wrecked, gentlemen?" inquired the Sicilian, "and many lives lost?"

"No, our ship is at Malta; we were in a boat on a party of pleasure, were caught by a gale, and driven on the coast. To satisfy you of the truth, observe that our pistols have the king's mark, and that we are not paupers, we show you gold."

Gascoigne pulled out his doubloons—and Jack did the same, coolly observing:

"I thought we were only to show silver, Ned!"

"It needed not that," replied the gentleman; "your conduct in this affair, your manners and address, fully convince me that you are what you represent—but were you common peasants, I am equally indebted to you for my life, and you may command me. Tell me in what way I can be of service."

"In giving us something to eat, for we have had nothing for many, many hours. After that we may, perhaps, trespass a little more upon your kind offices."

"You must, of course, be surprised at what has passed, and curious to know the occasion," said the gentleman; "you have a right to be informed of it, and shall be, as soon as you are more comfortable; in the meantime, allow me to introduce myself as Don Rebiera de Silva."

"I wish," said Jack, who, from his knowledge of Spanish, could understand the whole of the last part of the Don's speech, "that he would introduce us to his breakfast."

"So do I," said Gascoigne; "but we must wait a little—he ordered the ladies to prepare something instantly."

"Your friend does not speak Italian," said Don Rebiera.

"No, Don Rebiera, he speaks French and Spanish."

"If he speaks Spanish my daughter can converse with him; she has but shortly arrived from Spain. We are closely united with a noble house in that country."

Don Rebiera then led the way to another room, and in a short time there was a repast brought in, to which our midshipmen did great justice.

"I will now," said the Don, "relate to you, sir, for the information of yourself and friend, the causes which produced this scene of violence, which you so opportunely defeated. But first, as it must be very tedious to your friend, I will send for Donna Clara and my daughter Agnes to talk to him; my wife understands a little Spanish, and my daughter, as I said before, has but just left the country, where, from circumstances, she remained some years."

As soon as Donna Clara and Donna Agnes made their appearance and were introduced, Jack, who had not before paid attention to them, said to himself, "I have seen a face like that girl's before." If so, he had never seen many like it, for it was the quintessence of brunette beauty, and her figure was equally perfect; although, not having yet completed her fifteenth year, it required still a little more development.

Donna Clara was extremely gracious, and as, perhaps, she was aware that her voice would drown that of her husband, she proposed to our hero to walk in the garden, and in a few minutes they took their seats in a pavilion at the end of it. The old lady did not talk much Spanish, but when at a loss for a word she put in an Italian one, and Jack understood her perfectly well. She told him her sister had married a Spanish nobleman many years since, and that before the war broke out between the Spanish and the English, they had gone over with all their children to see her; that when they wished to return, her daughter Agnes, then a child, was suffering under a lingering complaint, and it was thought advisable, as she was very weak, to leave her under the charge of her aunt, who had a little girl of nearly the same age; that they were educated together at a convent near Tarragona, and that she had only returned two months ago; that she had a very narrow escape, as the ship in which her uncle, and aunt, and cousins, as well as herself, were on board, returning from Genoa, where her brother-in-law had been obliged to go to secure a succession to some property bequeathed to him, had been captured in the night by the English; but the officer, who was very polite, had allowed them to go away next day, and very handsomely permitted them to take all their effects.

"Oh, oh," thought Jack; "I thought I had seen her face before; this then was one of the girls in the corner of the cabin—now, I'll have some fun."

During the conversation with the mother, Donna Agnes had remained some paces behind, picking now and then a flower, and not attending to what passed.

When our hero and her mother sat down in the pavilion she joined them, when Jack addressed her with his usual politeness.

"I am almost ashamed to be sitting by you, Donna Agnes, in this ragged dress—but the rocks of your coast have no respect for persons."

"We are under great obligations, signor, and do not regard such trifles."

"You are all kindness, signora," replied Jack; "I little thought this morning of my good fortune—I can tell the fortunes of others, but not of my own."

"You can tell fortunes!" replied the old lady.

"Yes, madam, I am famous for it—shall I tell your daughter hers?"

Donna Agnes looked at our hero, and smiled.

"I perceive that the young lady does not believe me; I must prove my art, by telling her of what has already happened to her. The signora will then give me credit."

"Certainly, if you do that," replied Agnes.

"Oblige me, by showing me the palm of your hand."

Agnes extended her little hand, and Jack felt so very polite, that he was nearly kissing it. However, he restrained himself, and examining the lines:

"That you were educated in Spain—that you arrived here but two months ago—that you were captured and released by the English, your mother has already told me; but to prove to you that I knew all that, I must now be more particular. You were in a ship mounting fourteen guns—was it not so?"

Donna Agnes nodded her head.

"I never told the signor that," cried Donna Clara. "She was taken by surprise in the night, and there was no fighting. The next morning the English burst open the cabin door; your uncle and your cousin fired their pistols."

"Holy Virgin!" cried Agnes, with surprise.

"The English officer was a young man, not very good-looking."

"There you are wrong, signor; he was very handsome."

"There is no accounting for taste, signora; you were frightened out of your wits, and with your cousin you crouched down in the corner of the cabin. Let me examine that little line closer—you had—yes, it's no mistake, you had very little clothes on."

Agnes tore away her hand and covered her face.

"E vero, è vero; Holy Jesus! how could you know that?"

Of a sudden Agnes looked at our hero, and after a minute appeared to recognise him.

"Oh, mother, 'tis he—I recollect now, 'tis he!"

"Who, my child?" replied Donna Clara, who had been struck dumb with Jack's astonishing power of fortune-telling.

"The officer who captured us, and was so kind."

Jack burst out into laughter, not to be controlled for some minutes, an then acknowledged that she had discovered him.

"At all events, Donna Agnes," said he at last, "acknowledge that, ragged as I am, I have seen you in a much greater deshabille."

Agnes sprang up and took to her heels, that she might hide her confusion, and at the same time go to her father and tell him who he had as his guest.

Although Don Rebiera had not yet finished his narrative, this announcement of Agnes, who ran in breathless to communicate it, immediately brought all the parties together, and Jack received their thanks.

"I little thought," said the Don, "that I should have been so doubly indebted to you, sir. Command my services as you please, both of you. My sons are at Palermo, and I trust you will allow them the pleasure of your friendship when you are tired of remaining with us."

Jack made his politest bow, and then with a shrug of his shoulders, looked down upon his habiliments, which, to please Gascoigne, he had torn into ribands, as much as to say, We are not provided for a lengthened stay.

"My brothers' clothes will fit them, I think," said Agnes to her father; "they have left plenty in their wardrobes."

"If the signors will condescend to wear them till they can replace their own."

Midshipmen are very condescending—they followed Don Rebiera, and condescended to put on clean shirts belonging to Don Philip and Don Martin; also to put on their trousers—to select their best waistcoats and coats—in short, they condescended to have a regular fit-out—and it so happened that the fit-out was not far from a regular *fit*.

Having condescended, they then descended, and the intimacy between all parties became so great that it appeared as if they not only wore the young men's clothes, but also stood in their shoes. Having thus made themselves presentable, Jack presented his hand to both ladies, and led them into the garden, that Don Rebiera might finish his long story to Gascoigne without further interruption, and resuming their seats in the pavilion, he entertained the ladies with a history of his cruise in the ship after her capture. Agnes soon recovered from her reserve, and Jack had the forbearance not to allude again to the scene in the cabin, which was the only thing she dreaded. After dinner, when the family, according to custom, had retired for the siesta, Gascoigne and Jack, who had slept enough in the cart to last for a week, went out together in the garden.

"Well, Ned," said Jack, "do you wish yourself on board the *Harpy* again?"

"No," replied Gascoigne; "we have fallen on our feet at last, but still not without first being knocked about like peas in a rattle. What a lovely little creature that Agnes is! How strange that you should fall in with her again! How odd that we should come here!"

"My good fellow, we did not come here. Destiny brought us in a cart. She may take us to Tyburn in the same way."

"Yes, if you sport your philosophy as you did when we awoke this morning."

"Nevertheless, I'll be hanged if I'm not right. Suppose we argue the point?"

"Right or wrong, you will be hanged, Jack; so instead of arguing the point, suppose I tell you what the Don made such a long story about."

"With all my heart; let us go to the pavilion."

Our hero and his friend took their seats, and Gascoigne then communicated the history of Don Rebiera, to which we shall dedicate the ensuing chapter.

Chapter Twenty.

A long story, which the reader must listen to, as well as our hero.

"I have already made you acquainted with my name, and I have only to add, that it is one of the most noble in Sicily, and that there are few families who possess such large estates. My father was a man who had no pleasure in the pursuits of most young men of his age; he was of a weakly constitution, and was with difficulty reared to manhood. When his studies were completed he retired to his country-seat, belonging to our family, which is about twenty miles from Palermo, and shutting himself up, devoted himself wholly to literary pursuits.

"As he was an only son, his parents were naturally very anxious that he should marry; the more so as his health did not promise him a very extended existence. Had he consulted his own inclinations he would have declined, but he felt that it was his duty to comply with their wishes; but he did not trouble himself with the choice, leaving it wholly to them. They selected a young lady of high family, and certainly of most exquisite beauty. I only wish I could say more in her favour, for she was my mother; but it is impossible to narrate the history without exposing her conduct. The marriage took place, and my father, having woke up as it were at the celebration, again returned to his closet, to occupy himself with abstruse studies; the results of which have been published, and have fully established his reputation as a man of superior talent and deep research. But, however much the public may appreciate the works of a man of genius, whether they be written to instruct or to amuse, certain it is that a literary man requires, in his wife, either a mind congenial to his own, or that pride in her husband's talents which induces her to sacrifice much of her own domestic enjoyment to the satisfaction of having his name extolled abroad. I mention this point as some extenuation of my mother's conduct. She was neglected most certainly, but not neglected for frivolous amusements, or because another form had more captivated his fancy; but, in his desire to instruct others, and I may add, his ambition for renown, he applied himself to his literary pursuits, became abstracted, answered without hearing, and left his wife to amuse herself in any way she might please. A literary husband is, without exception, although always at home, the least domestic husband in the world, and must try the best of tempers, not by unkindness, for my father was kind and indulgent to excess, but by that state of perfect abstraction and indifference which he showed to everything except the favourite pursuit which absorbed him. My mother had but to speak, and every wish was granted—a refusal was unknown. You may say, what could she want more; I reply, that anything to a woman is preferable to indifference. The immediate consent to every wish took away, in her opinion, all merit in the grant; the value of everything is only relative, and in proportion to the difficulty of obtaining it. The immediate assent to every opinion was tantamount to insult; it implied that he did not choose to argue with her.

"It is true that women like to have their own way; but they like, at the same time, to have difficulties to surmount and to conquer; otherwise, half the gratification is lost. Although tempests are to be deplored, still a certain degree of oscillation and motion are requisite to keep fresh and clear the lake of matrimony, the waters of which otherwise soon stagnate and become foul, and without some contrary currents of opinion between a married couple such a stagnation must take place.

"A woman permitted always and invariably to have her own way without control, is much in the same situation as the child who insists upon a whole instead of half a holiday, and before the evening closes is tired of himself and everything about him. In short, a little contradiction, like salt at dinner, seasons and appetises the repast; but too much, like the condiment in question, spoils the whole, and it becomes unpalatable in proportion to its excess.

"My mother was a vain woman in every sense of the word—vain of her birth and of her beauty, and accustomed to receive that homage to which she considered herself entitled. She had been spoiled in her infancy, and as she grew up had learned nothing, because she was permitted to do as she pleased; she was therefore frivolous, and could not appreciate what she could not comprehend. There never was a more ill-assorted union."

"I have always thought that such must be the case," replied Gascoigne, "in Catholic countries, where a young person is taken out of a convent and mated according to what her family or her wealth may consider as the most eligible connection."

"On that subject there are many opinions, my friend," replied Don Rebiera. "It is true, that when a marriage of convenience is arranged by the parents, the dispositions of the parties are made a secondary point; but then, again, it must be remembered, that when a choice is left to the parties themselves, it is at an age at which there is little worldly consideration: and, led away, in the first place, by their passions, they form connections with those inferior in their station, which are attended with eventual unhappiness; or, in the other, allowing that they do choose in their own rank of life, they make quite as bad or often a worse choice than if their partners were selected for them."

"I cannot understand that," replied Gascoigne.

"The reason is, because there are no means, or if means, no wish, to study each other's disposition. A young man is attracted by person, and he admires; the young woman is flattered by the admiration, and is agreeable; if she has any faults she is not likely to display them—not concealing them from hypocrisy, but because they are not called out. The young man falls in love, so does the young woman; and when once in love, they can no longer see faults; they marry, imagining that they have found perfection. In the blindness of love, each raises the other to a standard of perfection which human nature can never attain, and each becomes equally annoyed on finding, by degrees, that they were in error. The reaction takes place, and they then underrate, as much as before they had overrated, each other. Now, if two young people marry without this violence of passion, they do not expect to find each other perfect, and perhaps have a better chance of happiness."

"I don't agree with you," thought Gascoigne; "but as you appear to be as fond of argument as my friend Jack, I shall make no reply, lest there he no end to the story."

Don Rebiera proceeded.

"My mother, finding that my father preferred his closet and his books to gaiety and dissipation, soon left him to himself, and amused herself after her own fashion, but not until I was born, which was ten months after their marriage. My father was confiding, and, pleased that my mother should be amused, he indulged her in everything. Time flew on, and I had arrived at my fifteenth year, and came home from my studies, it being intended that I should enter the army, which you are aware is generally the only profession embraced in this country by the heirs of noble families. Of course, I knew little of what had passed at home, but still I had occasionally heard my mother spoken lightly of, when I was not supposed to be present, and I always heard my father's name mentioned with compassion, as if an ill-used man, but I knew nothing more: still this was quite sufficient for a young man, whose blood boiled at the idea of anything like a stigma being cast upon his family. I arrived at my father's—I found him at his books; I paid my respects to my mother—I found her with her confessor. I disliked the man at first sight; he was handsome, certainly: his forehead was high and white, his eyes large and fiery, and his figure commanding; but there was a dangerous, proud look about him which disgusted me—nothing like humility or devotion. I might have admired him as an officer commanding a regiment of cavalry, but as a churchman he appeared to be most misplaced. She named me with kindness, but he appeared to treat me with disdain; he spoke authoritatively to my mother, who appeared to yield implicitly, and I discovered that he was lord of the whole household. My mother, too, it was said, had given up gaieties and become devout. I soon perceived more than a common intelligence between them, and before I had been two months at home I had certain proofs of my father's dishonour; and what was still more unfortunate for me, they were aware that such was the case. My first impulse was to acquaint my father; but, on consideration, I thought it better to say nothing, provided I could persuade my mother to dismiss Father Ignatio. I took an opportunity when she was alone to express my indignation at her conduct, and to demand his immediate dismissal, as a condition of my not divulging her crime. She appeared frightened, and gave her consent; but I soon found that her confessor had more power with her than I had, and he remained. I now resolved to acquaint my father, and I roused him from his studies that he might listen to his shame. I imagined that he would have acted calmly and discreetly; but, on the contrary, his violence was without bounds, and I had the greatest difficulty from preventing his rushing with his sword to sacrifice them both. At last he contented himself by turning Father Ignatio out of the house in the most ignominious manner, and desiring my mother to prepare for seclusion in a convent for the remainder of her days. But he fell their victim; three days afterwards, as my mother was, by his directions, about to be removed, he was seized with convulsions and died. I need hardly say, that he was carried off by poison; this, however, could not be established till long afterwards. Before he died he seemed to be almost supernaturally prepared for an event which never came into my thoughts. He sent for another confessor, who drew up his confession in writing at his own request, and afterwards inserted it in his will. My mother remained in the house, and Father Ignatio had the insolence to return. I ordered him away, and he resisted. He was turned out by the servants. I had an interview with my mother, who defied me, and told me that I should soon have a brother to share in the succession. I felt that, if so, it would be the illegitimate progeny of her adultery, and told her my opinion. She expressed her rage in the bitterest curses, and I left her. Shortly afterwards she quitted the house and retired to another of our country-seats, where she lived with Father Ignatio as before. About four months afterwards, formal notice was sent to me of the birth of a brother; but as, when my father's will was opened, he there had inserted his confession, or the substance of it, in which he stated, that aware of my mother's guilt, and supposing that consequences might ensue, he solemnly declared before God that he had for years lived apart, I cared little for this communication. I contented myself with replying that as the child belonged to the church, it had better be dedicated to its service.

"I had, however, soon reason to acknowledge the vengeance of my mother and her paramour. One night I was attacked by bravos; and had I not fortunately received assistance, I should have forfeited my life; as it was, I received a severe wound.

"Against attempts of that kind I took every precaution in future, but still every attempt was made to ruin my character, as well as to take my life. A young sister disappeared from a convent in my neighbourhood, and on the ground near the window from which she descended, was found a hat, recognised to be mine. I was proceeded against, and notwithstanding the strongest interest, it was with difficulty that the affair was arranged, although I had incontestably proved an *alibi*.

"A young man of rank was found murdered, with a stiletto, known to be mine, buried in his bosom, and it was with difficulty that I could establish my innocence.

"Part of a banditti had been seized, and on being asked the name of their chief, when they received absolution, they confessed that I was the chief of the band.

"Everything that could be attempted was put into practice; and if I did not lose my life, at all events I was avoided by almost everybody as a dangerous and doubtful character.

"At last a nobleman of rank, the father of Don Scipio, whom you disarmed, was assassinated; the bravos were taken, and they acknowledged that I was the person who hired them. I defended myself, but the king imposed upon me a heavy fine and banishment. I had just received the order, and was crying out against the injustice, and lamenting my hard fate, as I sat down to dinner. Latterly, aware of what my enemies would attempt, I had been accustomed to live much alone. My faithful valet Pedro was my only attendant. I was eating my dinner with little appetite, and had asked for some wine. Pedro went to the beaufet behind him, to give me what I required. Accidentally I lifted up my head, and there being a large pier-glass opposite to me, I saw the figure of my valet, and that he was pouring a powder in the flagon of wine which he was about to present to me. I recollected the hat being found at the nunnery, and also the stiletto in the body of the young man.

"Like lightning it occurred to me that I had been fostering the viper who had assisted to destroy me. He brought me the flagon. I rose, locked the door, and drawing my sword, I addressed him:—

"'Villain; I know thee; down on your knees, for your life is forfeited.'

"He turned pale, trembled, and sank upon his knees.

"'Now, then,' continued I, 'you have but one chance—either drink off this flagon of wine, or I pass my sword through your body.' He hesitated, and I put the point to his breast—even pierced the flesh a quarter of an inch.

"'Drink,' cried I—'is it so very unjust an order to tell you to drink old wine? Drink,' continued I, 'or my sword does its duty.'

"He drank, and would then have quitted the room. 'No, no,' said I, 'you remain herd, and the wine must have its effect. If I have wronged you I will make amends to you—but I am suspicious.'

"In about a quarter of an hour, during which time I paced up and down the room, with my sword drawn, my servant fell down, and cried in mercy to let him have a priest. I sent for my own confessor, and he then acknowledged that he was an agent of my mother and Father Ignatio, and had been the means of making it appear that I was the committer of all the crimes and murders which had been perpetrated by them, with a view to my destruction. A strong emetic having been administered to him, he partially revived, and was taken to Palermo, where he gave his evidence before he expired.

"When this was made known, the king revoked his sentence, apologised to me, and I found that once more I was visited and courted by everybody. My mother was ordered to be shut up in a convent, where she died, I trust, in grace, and Father Ignatio fled to Italy, and I have been informed is since dead.

"Having thus rid myself of my principal enemies, I considered myself safe. I married the lady whom you have just seen, and before my eldest son was born, Don Silvio, for such was the name given to my asserted legitimate brother, came of age, and demanded his succession. Had he asked me for a proper support, as my uterine brother, I should not have refused; but that the son of Friar Ignatio, who had so often attempted my life, should, in case of my decease, succeed to the title and estates, was not to be borne. A lawsuit was immediately commenced, which lasted four or five years, during which Don Silvio married, and had a son, that young man whom you heard me address by the same name; but after much litigation, it was decided that my father's confessor and will had proved his illegitimacy, and the suit was in my favour. From that time to this there has been a constant enmity. Don Silvio refused all my offers of assistance, and followed me with a pertinacity which often endangered my life. At last he fell by the hands of his own agents, who mistook him for me. Don Silvio died without leaving any provision for his family; his widow I pensioned, and his son I have had carefully brought up, and have indeed treated most liberally, but he appears to have imbibed the spirit of his father, and no kindness has been able to imbue him with gratitude.

"He had lately been placed by me in the army, where he found out my two sons, and quarrelled with them both upon slight pretence; but, in both instances, he was wounded and carried off the field.

"My two sons have been staying with me these last two months, and did not leave till yesterday. This morning Don Silvio, accompanied by Don Scipio, came to the house, and after accusing me of being the murderer of both their parents, drew their rapiers to assassinate me. My wife and child, hearing the noise, came down to my assistance—you know the rest."

Chapter Twenty One.

In which our hero is brought up all standing under a press of sail.

Our limits will not permit us to relate all that passed during our hero's stay of a fortnight at Don Rebiera's. He and Gascoigne were treated as if they were his own sons, and the kindness of the female part of the family was equally remarkable. Agnes, naturally perhaps, showed a preference or partiality for Jack: to which Gascoigne willingly submitted, as he felt that our hero had a prior and stronger claim, and during the time that they remained a feeling of attachment was created between Agnes and the philosopher, which, if not love, was at least something very near akin to it; but the fact was, that they were both much too young to think of marriage; and, although they walked and talked, and laughed, and played together, they were always at home in time for their dinner. Still, the young lady thought she preferred our hero even to her brothers, and Jack thought that the young lady was the prettiest and kindest girl that he had ever met with. At the end of the fortnight our two midshipmen took their leave, furnished with letters of recommendation to many of the first nobility in Palermo, and mounted on two fine mules with bell bridles. The old Donna kissed them both—the Don showered down his blessings of good wishes, and Donna Agnes's lips trembled as she bade them adieu; and, as soon as they were gone, she went up to her chamber and wept. Jack also was very grave, and his eyes moistened at the thoughts of leaving Agnes. Neither of them were aware, until the hour of parting, how much they had wound themselves together.

The first quarter of an hour our two midshipmen followed their guide in silence. Jack wished to be left to his own thoughts, and Gascoigne perceived it.

"Well, Easy," said Gascoigne, at last, "if I had been in your place, constantly in company of, and loved by, that charming girl, I could never have torn myself away."

"Loved by her, Ned!" replied Jack; "what makes you say that?"

"Because I am sure it was the case; she lived but in your presence. Why, if you were out of the room, she never spoke a word, but sat there as melancholy as a sick monkey—the moment you came in again she beamed out as glorious as the sun, and was all life and spirit."

"I thought people were always melancholy when they were in love," replied Jack.

"When those that they love are out of their presence."

"Well, then, I am out of her presence, and I feel very melancholy, so I suppose, by your argument, I am in love. Can a man be in love without knowing it?"

"I really cannot say, Jack, I never was in love myself, but I've seen many others *spooney*. My time will come, I suppose, by-and-bye. They say that for every man made there is a woman also made to fit him, if he could only find her. Now, it's my opinion that you have found yours—I'll lay my life she's crying at this moment."

"Do you really think so, Ned? let's go back—poor little Agnes—let's go back; I feel I do love her, and I'll tell her so."

"Pooh, nonsense! it's too late now; you should have told her that before, when you walked with her in the garden."

"But I did not know it, Ned. However, as you say, it would be foolish to turn back, so I'll write to her from Palermo."

Here an argument ensued upon love, which we shall not trouble the reader with, as it was not very profound, both sides knowing very little on the subject. It did, however, end with our hero being convinced that he was desperately in love, and he talked about giving up the service as soon as he arrived at Malta. It is astonishing what sacrifices midshipmen will make for the objects of their adoration.

It was not until late in the evening that our adventurers arrived at Palermo. As soon as they were lodged at the hotel, Gascoigne sat down and wrote a letter in their joint names to Don Rebiera, returning him many thanks for his great kindness, informing him of their safe arrival, and trusting that they should soon meet again: and Jack took up his pen, and indited a letter in Spanish to Agnes, in which he swore that neither tide nor time, nor water, nor air, nor heaven, nor earth, nor the first lieutenant, nor his father, nor absence, nor death itself, should prevent him from coming back and marrying her, the first convenient opportunity, begging her to refuse a thousand offers, as come back he would, although there was no saying when. It was a perfect love-letter, that is to say, it was the essence of nonsense, but that made it perfect, for the greater the love the greater the folly.

These letters were consigned to the man who was sent as their guide, and also had to return with the mules. He was liberally rewarded; and, as Jack told him to be very careful of his letter, the Italian naturally concluded that it was to be delivered clandestinely, and he delivered it accordingly, at a time when Agnes was walking in the garden thinking of our hero. Nothing was more opportune than the arrival of the letter; Agnes ran to the pavilion, read it over twenty times, kissed it twenty times, and hid it in her bosom; sat for a few minutes in deep and placid thought, took the letter out of its receptacle, and read it over and over again. It was very bad Spanish and very absurd, but she thought it delightful, poetical, classical, sentimental, argumentative, convincing, incontrovertible, imaginative, and even grammatical, for if it was not good Spanish, there was no Spanish half so good. Alas! Agnes was, indeed, unsophisticated, to be in such ecstasies with a midshipman's love-letter. Once more she hastened to her room to weep, but it was from excess of joy and delight. The reader may think Agnes silly, but he must take into consideration the climate, and that she was not yet fifteen.

Our young gentlemen sent for a tailor and each ordered a new suit of clothes; they delivered their letters of recommendation, and went to the banker to whom they were addressed by Don Rebiera.

"I shall draw for ten pounds, Jack," said Gascoigne, "on the strength of the shipwreck; I shall tell the truth, all except that we forgot to ask for leave, which I shall leave out; and I am sure the story will be worth ten pounds. What shall you draw for, Jack?"

"I shall draw for two hundred pounds," replied Jack; "I mean to have a good cruise while I can."

"But will your governor stand that, Easy?"

"To be sure he will."

"Then you're right—he is a philosopher—I wish he'd teach mine, for he hates the sight of a bill."

"Then don't you draw, Ned—I have plenty for both. If every man had his equal share and rights in the world, you would be as able to draw as much as I; and, as you cannot, upon the principles of equality, you shall have half."

"I really shall become a convert to your philosophy, Jack; it does not appear to be so nonsensical as I thought it. At all events it has saved my old governor ten pounds, which he can ill afford, as a colonel on half-pay."

On their return to the inn, they found Don Philip and Don Martin, to whom Don Rebiera had written, who welcomed them with open arms. They were two very fine young men of eighteen and nineteen, who were finishing their education in the army. Jack asked them to dinner, and they and our hero soon became inseparable. They took him to all the theatres, the conversaziones of all the nobility, and, as Jack lost his money with good humour, and was a very handsome fellow, he was everywhere well received and was made much of: many ladies made love to him, but Jack was only very polite, because he thought more and more of Agnes every day. Three weeks passed away like lightning, and neither Jack nor Gascoigne thought of going back. At last, one fine day, H.M. frigate *Aurora* anchored in the bay, and Jack and Gascoigne, who were at a party at the Duke of Pentaro's, met with the captain of the *Aurora*, who was also invited. The duchess introduced them to Captain Tartar, who, imagining them, from their being in plain clothes, to be young Englishmen of fortune on their travels, was very gracious and condescending. Jack was so pleased with his urbanity that he requested the pleasure of his company to dinner the next day: Captain Tartar accepted the invitation, and they parted, shaking hands, with many expressions of pleasure in having made his acquaintance. Jack's party was rather large, and the dinner sumptuous. The Sicilian gentlemen did not drink much wine, but Captain Tartar liked his bottle, and although the rest of the company quitted the table to go to a ball given that evening by the Marquesa Novara, Jack was too polite not to sit it out with the captain: Gascoigne closed his chair to Jack's, who, he was afraid, being a little affected with the wine, would "let the cat out of the bag."

The captain was amazingly entertaining. Jack told him how happy he should be to see him at Forest Hill, which property the captain discovered to contain six thousand acres of land, and also that Jack was an only son; and Captain Tartar was quite respectful when he found that he was in such very excellent company. The captain of the frigate inquired of Jack what brought him out here, and Jack, whose prudence was departing, told him that he came in his Majesty's ship *Harpy*. Gascoigne gave Jack a nudge, but was of no use, for as the wine got into Jack's brain, so did his notions of equality.

"Oh! Wilson gave you a passage; he's an old friend of mine."

"So he is of ours," replied Jack; "he's a devilish good sort of a fellow, Wilson."

"But where have you been since you came out?" inquired Captain Tartar.

"In the *Harpy*," replied Jack, "to be sure, I belong to her."

"You belong to her! in what capacity may I ask?" inquired Captain Tartar, in a much less respectful and confidential tone.

"Midshipman," replied Jack; "so is Mr Gascoigne."

"Umph! you are on leave then."

"No, indeed," replied Jack; "I'll tell you how it is, my dear fellow."

"Excuse me for one moment," replied Captain Tartar, rising up; "I must give some directions to my servant which I forgot."

Captain Tartar hailed his coxswain out of the window, gave orders just outside of the door, and then returned to the table. In the meantime, Gascoigne, who expected a breeze, had been cautioning Jack, in a low tone, at intervals, when Captain Tartar's back was turned; but it was useless, the extra quantity of wine had got into Jack's head, and he cared nothing for Gascoigne's remonstrance. When the captain resumed his seat at the table, Jack gave him the true narrative of all that had passed, to which his guest paid the greatest attention. Jack wound up his confidence by saying that in a week or so he should go back to Don Rebiera and propose for Donna Agnes.

"Ah!" exclaimed Captain Tartar, drawing his breath with astonishment and compressing his lips.

"Tartar, the wine stands with you," said Jack, "allow me to help you."

Captain Tartar threw himself back in his chair, and let all the air out of his chest with a sort of whistle, as if he could hardly contain himself.

"Have you had wine enough?" said Jack, very politely; "if so, we will go to the Marquesa's."

The coxswain came to the door, touched his hat to the captain, and looked significantly.

"And so, sir," cried Captain Tartar, in a voice of thunder, rising from his chair, "you're a damned runaway midshipman, who, if you belonged to my ship, instead of marrying Donna Agnes, I would marry you to the gunner's daughter, by God! Two midshipmen sporting plain clothes in the best society in Palermo, and having the impudence to ask a post-captain to dine with them! To ask me, and address me as *Tartar*, and *my dear fellow*! you infernal young scamps!" continued Captain Tartar, now boiling with rage, and striking his fist on the table so as to set all the glasses waltzing.

"Allow me to observe, sir," said Jack, who was completely sobered by the address, "that we do not belong to your ship, and that we are in plain clothes."

"In plain clothes—midshipmen in mufti—yes, you are so: a couple of young swindlers, without a sixpence in your pocket, passing yourselves off as young men of fortune, and walking off through the window without paying your bill."

"Do you mean to call me a swindler, sir?" replied Jack.

"Yes, sir, you—"

"Then you lie," exclaimed our hero, in a rage. "I am a gentleman, sir—I am sorry I cannot pay you the same compliment."

The astonishment and rage of Captain Tartar took away his breath. He tried to speak, but could not—he gasped and gasped, and then sat or almost fell down in his chair—at last he recovered himself.

"Matthews—Matthews!"

"Sir," replied the coxswain, who had remained at the door.

"The sergeant of marines."

"Here he is, sir."

The sergeant entered, and raised the back of his hand to his hat.

"Bring your marines in—take charge of these two. Direct you are on board, put them both legs in irons."

The marines with their bayonets walked in and took possession of our hero and Gascoigne.

"Perhaps, sir," replied Jack, who was now cool again, "you will permit us to pay our bill before we go on board. We are no swindlers, and it is rather a heavy one—or, as you have taken possession of our persons, you will, perhaps, do us the favour to discharge it yourself;" and Jack threw on the table a heavy purse of dollars. "I have only to observe, Captain Tartar, that I wish to be very liberal to the waiters."

"Sergeant, let them pay their bill," said Captain Tartar, in a more subdued tone—taking his hat and sword, and walking out of the room.

"By heavens, Easy, what have you done?—you will be tried by a court-martial, and turned out of the service."

"I hope so," replied Jack; "I was a fool to come into it. But he called me a swindler, and I would give the same answer to-morrow."

"If you are ready, gentlemen," said the sergeant, who had been long enough with Captain Tartar to be aware that to be punished by him was no proof of fault having been committed.

"I will go and pack up our things, Easy, while you pay the bill," said Gascoigne. "Marine, you had better come with me."

In less than half an hour, our hero and his comrade, instead of finding themselves at the Marquesa's ball, found themselves very comfortably in irons under the half-deck of H.M. frigate *Aurora*.

We shall leave them, and return to Captain Tartar, who had proceeded to the ball, to which he had been invited. On his entering he was accosted by Don Martin and Don Philip, who inquired what had become of our hero and his friend. Captain Tartar, who was in no very good humour, replied briskly, "that they were on board his ship in irons."

"In irons! for what?" exclaimed Don Philip.

"Because, sir, they are a couple of young scamps who have introduced themselves into the best company, passing themselves off as people of consequence, when they are only a couple of midshipmen who have run away from their ship."

Now the Rebieras knew very well that Jack and his friend were midshipmen; but this did not appear to them any reason why they should not be considered as gentlemen, and treated accordingly.

"Do you mean to say, signor," said Don Philip, "that you have accepted their hospitality, laughed, talked, walked arm in arm with them, pledged them in wine, as we have seen you this evening, and after they have confided in you that you have put them in irons?"

"Yes, sir, I do," replied Captain Tartar.

"Then, by Heaven, you have my defiance, and you are no gentleman!" replied Don Philip, the elder.

"And I repeat my brother's words, sir," cried Don Martin.

The two brothers felt so much attachment for our hero, who had twice rendered such signal service to their family, that their anger was without bounds.

In every other service but the English navy there is not that power of grossly insulting and then sheltering yourself under your rank; nor is it necessary for the discipline of any service. To these young officers, if the power did exist, the use of such power under such circumstances appeared monstrous, and they were determined, at all events, to show to Captain Tartar, that in society, at least, it could be resented. They collected their friends, told them what had passed, and begged them to circulate it through the room. This was soon done, and Captain Tartar found himself avoided. He went up to the Marquesa and spoke to her—she turned her head the other way. He addressed a count he had been conversing with the night before—he turned short round upon his heel, while Don Philip and Don Martin walked up and down talking, so that he might hear what they said, and looking at him with eyes flashing with indignation. Captain Tartar left the ball-room and returned to the inn, more indignant than ever. When he rose the next morning he was informed that a gentleman wished to speak with him; he sent up his card as Don Ignatio Verez, colonel commanding the fourth regiment of infantry. On being admitted, he informed Captain Tartar that Don Philip de Rebiera wished to have the pleasure of crossing swords with him, and requested to know when it would be convenient for Captain Tartar to meet him.

It was not in Captain Tartar's nature to refuse a challenge; his courage was unquestionable, but he felt indignant that a midshipman should be the cause of his getting into such a scrape. He accepted the challenge, but having no knowledge of the small-sword, refused to fight unless with pistols. To this the colonel raised no objections, and Captain Tartar despatched his coxswain with a note to his second lieutenant, for he was not on good terms with his first. The meeting took place—at the first fire the ball of Don Philip passed through Captain Tartar's brain, and he instantly fell dead. The second lieutenant hastened on board to report the fatal result of the meeting, and shortly after, Don Philip and his brother, with many of their friends, went off in the Governor's barge to condole with our hero.

The first lieutenant, now captain *pro tempore*, received them graciously, and listened to their remonstrances relative to our hero and Gascoigne.

"I have never been informed by the captain of the grounds of complaint against the young gentlemen," replied he, "and have therefore no change to prefer against them. I shall therefore order them to be liberated. But, as I learn that they are officers belonging to one of his Majesty's ships lying at Malta, I feel it my duty, as I sail immediately, to take them there and send them on board of their own ship."

Jack and Gascoigne were then taken out of irons and permitted to see Don Philip, who informed him that he had revenged the insult, but Jack and Gascoigne did not wish to go on shore again after what had passed. After an hour's conversation, and assurances of continued friendship, Don Philip, his brother, and their friends, took leave of our two midshipmen, and rowed on shore.

And now we must be serious.

We do not write these novels merely to amuse,—we have always had it in our view to instruct, and it must not be supposed that we have no other end in view than to make the reader laugh. If we were to write an elaborate work, telling truths, and plain truths, confining ourselves only to point out errors and to demand reform, it would not be read; we have therefore selected this light and trifling species of writing, as it is by many denominated, as a channel through which we may convey wholesome advice a palatable shape. If we would point out an error, we draw a character, and although that character appears to weave naturally into the tale of fiction, it becomes as much a beacon, as is a vehicle of amusement. We consider this to be the true art of novel-writing, and that crime and folly and error can be as severely lashed, as virtue and morality can be upheld, by a series of amusing causes and effects, that entice the reader to take a medicine, which, although rendered agreeable to the palate, still produces the same internal benefit as if it had been presented to him in its crude state, in which it would either be refused or nauseated.

In our naval novels, we have often pointed out the errors which have existed, and still do exist, in a service which an honour to its country; for what institution is there on earth that is perfect, or into which, if it once was perfect, abuses will not creep? Unfortunately, others have written to decry the service, and many have raised up their voices against our writings, because they felt that, in exposing error, we were exposing them. But to this we have been indifferent; we felt that we were doing good, and we have continued. To prove that we are correct in asserting that we have done good, we will, out of several, state one single case.

In "The King's Own," a captain, when requested to punish a man *instanter* for a fault committed, replies that he never has and never will punish a man until twenty-four hours after the offence, that he may not be induced by the anger of the moment to award a severer punishment than in his cooler moments he might think commensurate—and that he wished that the Admiralty would give out an order to that effect.

Some time after the publication of that work, the order was given by the Admiralty, forbidding the punishment until a certain time had elapsed after the offence; and we had the pleasure of knowing from the First Lord of the Admiralty of the time, that it was in consequence of the suggestion in the novel.

If our writings had effected nothing else, we might still lay down our pen with pride and satisfaction; but they have done more, much more, and while they have amused the reader, they have improved the service; they have held up in their characters a mirror, in which those who have been in error may see their own deformity, and many hints which have been given, have afterwards returned to the thoughts of those who have had influence, have been considered as their own ideas, and have been acted upon. The conduct of Captain Tartar may be considered as a libel on the service—is it not? The fault of Captain Tartar was not in sending them on board, or even putting them in irons as deserters, although, under the circumstances, he might have shown more delicacy. The fault was in stigmatising a young man as a swindler, and the punishment awarded to the error is intended to point out the moral, that such an abuse of power should be severely visited. The greatest error now in our service, is the disregard shown to the feelings of the junior officers in the language of their superiors: that an improvement has taken place I grant, but that it still exists, to a degree injurious to the service, I know too well. The articles of war, as our hero was informed by his captain, were equally binding on officers and crew; but what a dead letter do they become if officers are permitted to break them with impunity! The captain of a ship will turn the hands up to punishment, read the article of war for the transgressing of which the punishment is inflicted, and to show at that time their high respect for the articles of war, the captain and every officer take off their hats. The moment the hands are piped down, the second article of war, which forbids all swearing, etcetera, in derogation of God's honour, is immediately disregarded. We are not strait-laced,—we care little about an oath as a mere *expletive*; we refer now to swearing at *others*, to insulting their feelings grossly by coarse and intemperate language. We would never interfere with a man for damning his *own* eyes, but we deny the right of his damning those of *another*.

The rank of a master in the service is above that of a midshipman, but still the midshipman is a gentleman by birth, and the master, generally speaking, is not. Even at this moment, in the service, if the master were to damn the eyes of a midshipman, and tell him that he was a liar, would there be any redress, or if so, would it be commensurate to the insult? If a midshipman were to request a court-martial, would it be granted?—certainly not: and yet this is a point of more importance than may be conceived. Our service has been wonderfully improved since the peace, and those who are now permitted to enter it must be gentlemen. We know that even now there are many who cry out against this as dangerous and injurious to the service; as if education spoiled an officer, and the scion of an illustrious house would not be more careful to uphold an escutcheon without blemish for centuries, than one who has little more than brute courage; but those who argue thus are the very people who are injurious to the service, for they can have no other reason, except that they wish that the juniors may be tyrannised over with impunity.

But it remembered that these are not the observations of a junior officer smarting under insult—they are the result of deep and calm reflection. We have arrived to that grade, that, although we have the power to inflict, we are too high to receive insult, but we have not forgotten how our young blood has boiled when wanton, reckless, and cruel torture has been heaped upon our feelings, merely because, as a junior officer, we were not in a position to retaliate, or even to reply. And another evil is, that this *great error* is *disseminated*. In observing on it, in one of our works, called *Peter Simple*, we have put the following true observation in the mouth of O'Brien. Peter observes, in his simple, right-minded way:

"I should think, O'Brien, that the very circumstance of having had your feelings so often wounded by such language when you were a junior officer would make you doubly careful not to use it towards others, when you had advanced in the service?"

"Peter, that's just the first feeling, which wears away after a time, till at last, your own sense of indignation becomes blunted, and becomes indifferent to it; you forget, also, that you wound the feelings of others, and carry the habit with, you, to the great injury and disgrace of the service."

Let it not be supposed that in making these remarks we want to cause litigation, or insubordination. On the contrary, we assert that this error is the cause, and eventually will be much more the cause, of insubordination; for as the junior officers who enter the service are improved, so will they resist it. The complaint here is more against the officers, than the captains, whose power has been perhaps already too much curtailed by late regulations: that power must remain, for although there may be some few who are so perverted as to make those whom they command uncomfortable, in justice to the service we are proud to assert that the majority acknowledge, by their conduct, that the greatest charm attached to power is to be able to make so many people happy.

Chapter Twenty Two.

Our hero is sick with the service, but recovers with proper medicine—an argument, ending, as most do, in a blow up—Mesty lectures upon craniology.

The day after the funeral, H.M. ship *Aurora* sailed for Malta, and on her arrival the acting captain sent our two midshipmen on board the *Harpy* without any remark, except "victualled the day discharged," as they had been borne on the ship's books as supernumeraries.

Mr James, who was acting in the *Aurora*, was anxious to join the admiral at Toulon, and intended to sail the next day. He met Captain Wilson at the Governor's table, and stated that Jack and Gascoigne had been put in irons by order of Captain Tartar; his suspicions, and the report that the duel had in consequence taken place; but Gascoigne and Jack had both agreed that they would not communicate the events of their cruise to anybody on board of the *Aurora*; and therefore nothing else was known, except that they must have made powerful friends somehow or another; and there appeared in the conduct of Captain Tartar, as well as in the whole transaction, somewhat of a mystery.

"I should like to know what happened to my friend Jack, who fought the duel," said the Governor, who had laughed at it till he held his sides; "Wilson, do bring him here to-morrow morning, and let us have his story."

"I am afraid of encouraging him, Sir Thomas—he is much too wild already. I told you of his first cruise. He has nothing but adventures, and they all end too favourably."

"Well, but you can send for him here and blow him up just as well as in your own cabin, and then we will have the truth out of him."

"That you certainly will," replied Captain Wilson, "for he tells it plainly enough."

"Well, to oblige me, send for him—I don't see he was much to blame in absconding, as it appears he thought he would be hung—I want to see the lad."

"Well, Governor, if you wish it," replied Captain Wilson, who wrote a note to Mr Sawbridge, requesting he would send Mr Easy to him at the Governor's house at ten o'clock in the morning.

Jack made his appearance in his uniform—he did not much care for what was said to him, as he was resolved to leave the service. He had been put in irons, and the iron had *entered into his soul*.

Mr Sawbridge had gone on shore about an hour before Jack had been sent on board, and he had remained on shore all the night. He did not therefore see Jack but for a few minutes, and thinking it his duty to say nothing to him at first, or to express his displeasure, he merely observed to him that the captain would speak to him as soon as he came on board. As Gascoigne and our hero did not know how far it might be safe, even at Malta, to acknowledge to what occurred on board the speronare, which might get wind, they did not even tell their messmates, resolving only to confide it to the captain.

When Jack was ushered into the presence of the captain, he found him sitting with the Governor, and the breakfast on the table ready for them. Jack walked in with courage, but respectfully. He was fond of Captain Wilson, and wished to show him respect. Captain Wilson addressed him, pointed out that he had committed a great error in fighting a duel, a greater error in demeaning himself by fighting the purser's steward, and still greater in running away from his ship. Jack looked respectfully to Captain Wilson, acknowledged that he had done wrong, and promised to be more careful another time, if Captain Wilson would look over it.

"Captain Wilson, allow me to plead for the young gentleman," said the Governor; "I am convinced that it has only been an error in judgment."

"Well, Mr Easy, as you express your contrition, and the Governor interferes in your behalf, I shall take no more notice of this; but recollect, Mr Easy, that you have occasioned me a great deal of anxiety by your mad pranks, and I trust another time you will remember that I am too anxious for your welfare not to be uncomfortable when you run such risks. You may now go on board to your duty, and tell Mr Gascoigne to do the same; and pray let us hear of no more duels or running away."

Jack, whose heart softened at this kind treatment, did not venture to speak; he made his bow, and was about to quit the room, when the Governor said:

"Mr Easy, you have not breakfasted."

"I have, sir," replied Jack, "before I came on shore."

"But a midshipman can always eat two breakfasts, particularly when his own comes first—so sit down and breakfast with us—it's all over now."

"Even if it was not," replied Captain Wilson, laughing, "I doubt whether it would spoil Mr Easy's breakfast;—come, Mr Easy, sit down."

Jack bowed, and took his chair, and proved that his lecture had not taken away his appetite. When breakfast was over, Captain Wilson observed:

"Mr Easy, you have generally a few adventures to speak of when you return; will you tell the Governor and me what has taken place since you left us."

"Certainly, sir," replied Jack; "but I venture to request that it may be under the promise of secrecy, for it's rather important to me and Gascoigne."

"Yes, if secrecy is really necessary, my boy; but I'm the best judge of that," replied the Governor.

Jack then entered into a detail of his adventures, which we have already described, much to the astonishment of the Governor and his captain, and concluded his narration by stating that he wanted to leave the service; he hoped that Captain Wilson would discharge him and send him home.

"Pooh, nonsense!" said the Governor, "you shan't leave the Mediterranean while I am here. No, no; you must have more adventures, and come back and tell them to me. And recollect, my lad, that whenever you come to Malta, there is a bed at the Governor's house, and a seat at his table, always ready for you."

"You are very kind, Sir Thomas," replied Jack, "but—"

"No buts at all, sir—you shan't leave the service; besides, recollect that I can ask for leave of absence for you to go and see Donna Agnes—ay, and send you there too."

Captain Wilson also remonstrated with our hero, and he gave up the point. It was harsh treatment which made him form the resolution, it was kindness which overcame it.

"With your permission, Captain Wilson, Mr Easy shall dine with us to-day, and bring Gascoigne with him; you shall first scold him, and I'll console him with a good dinner—and, boy, don't be afraid to tell your story everywhere: sit down and tell it at Nix Mangare stairs, if you please—I'm Governor here."

Jack made his obeisance, and departed.

"The lad must be treated kindly, Captain Wilson," said the Governor; "he would be a loss to the service. Good heavens, what adventures! and how honestly he tells everything. I shall ask him to stay with me for the time you are here, if you will allow me: I want to make friends with him; he must not leave the service."

Captain Wilson, who felt that kindness and attention would be more effectual with our hero than any other measures, gave his consent to the Governor's proposition. So Jack ate at the Governor's table, and took lessons in Spanish and Italian until the *Harpy* had been refitted, after heaving down. Before she was ready a vessel arrived from the fleet, directing Captain Wilson to repair to Mahon, and send a transport, lying there, to procure live bullocks for the fleet. Jack did not join his ship very willingly, but he had promised the Governor to remain in the service, and he went on board the evening before she sailed. He had been living so well that he had, at first, a horror of midshipman's fare, but a good appetite seasons everything, and Jack soon complained that there was not enough. He was delighted to see Jolliffe and Mesty after so long an absence; he laughed at the boatswain's cheeks, inquired after the purser's steward's shot-holes, shook hands with Gascoigne and his other mess-mates, gave Vigors a thrashing, and then sat down to supper.

"Ah, Massa Easy, why you take a cruise without me?" said Mesty; "dat very shabby—by de power, but I wish I was there; you ab too much danger, Massa Easy, without Mesty, anyhow."

The next day the *Harpy* sailed, and Jack went to his duty. Mr Asper borrowed ten pounds, and our hero kept as much watch as he pleased, which, as watching did not please him, was very little. Mr Sawbridge had long conversations with our hero, pointing out to him the necessity of discipline and obedience in the service, and that there was no such thing as equality, and that the rights of man secured to every one the property which he held in possession. "According to your ideas, Mr Easy, a man has no more right to his wife than anything else, and any other man may claim her." Jack thought of Agnes, and he made matrimony an exception, as he continued to argue the point; but although he argued, still his philosophy was almost upset at the idea of any one disputing with him the rights of man, with respect to Agnes.

The *Harpy* made the African coast, the wind continued contrary, and they were baffled for many days; at last they espied a brig under the land, about sixteen miles off; her rig and appearance made Captain Wilson suspect that she was a privateer of some description or another, but it was calm, and they could not approach her. Nevertheless, Captain Wilson thought it his duty to examine her; so at ten o'clock at night the boats were hoisted out: as this was merely intended for a reconnoitre, for there was no saying what she might be, Mr Sawbridge did not go. Mr Asper was on the sick-list, so Mr Smallsole the master had the command of the expedition. Jack asked Mr Sawbridge to let him have charge of one of the boats. Mr Jolliffe and Mr Vigors went in the pinnace with the master. The gunner had the charge of one cutter, and our hero had the command of the other. Jack, although not much more than seventeen, was very strong and tall for his age; indeed, he was a man grown, and shaved twice a week. His only object in going was to have a yarn for the Governor when he returned to Malta. Mesty went with him, and, as the boat shoved off, Gascoigne slipped in, telling Jack that he was come to take care of him, for which considerate kindness Jack expressed his warmest thanks. The orders to the master were very explicit; he was to reconnoitre the vessel, and if she proved heavily armed not to attack, for she was embayed, and could not escape the *Harpy* as soon as there was wind. If not armed he was to board her, but he was to do nothing till the morning: the reason for sending the boats away so soon was, that the men might not suffer from the heat of the sun during the day-time, which was excessive, and had already put many men on the sick-list. The boats were to pull to the bottom of the bay, not to go so near as to be discovered, and then drop their grapnels till daylight. The orders were given to Mr Smallsole in presence of, the other officers who were appointed to the boats, that there might be no mistake, and the boats then shoved off. After a three hours' pull, they arrived to where the brig lay becalmed, and as they saw no lights moving on board, they supposed they were not seen. They dropped their grapnels in about seven fathoms water and waited for daylight. When Jack heard Captain Wilson's orders that they were to lie at anchor till daylight he had sent down Mesty for fishing-lines, as fresh fish is always agreeable in a midshipman's berth: he and Gascoigne amused themselves this way, and as they pulled up the fish they entered into an argument, and Mr Smallsole ordered them to be silent. The point which they discussed was relative to boat service; Gascoigne insisted that the boats should all board at once—while our hero took it into his head that it was better they should come up one after another; a novel idea, but Jack's ideas on most points were singular.

"If you throw your whole force upon the decks at once, you overpower them," observed Gascoigne; "if you do not, you are beaten in detail."

"Very true," replied Jack, "supposing that you have an overpowering force, or they are not prepared; but recollect, that if they are, the case is altered; for instance, as to fire-arms—they fire theirs at the first boat, and they have not time to reload, when the second comes up with its fire reserved; every fresh boat arriving adds to the courage of those who have boarded, and to the alarm of those who defend; the men come on fresh and fresh. Depend upon it, Gascoigne, there is nothing like a *corps de reserve*."

"Will you keep silence in your boat, Mr Easy, or will you not?" cried the master; "you're a disgrace to the service, sir."

"Thank ye, sir," replied Jack, in a low tone. "I've another bite, Ned."

Jack and his comrade continued to fish in silence till the day broke. The mist rolled off the stagnant water, and discovered the brig, who, as soon as she perceived the boats, threw out the French tricolour and fired a gun of defiance. Mr Smallsole was undecided; the gun fired was not a heavy one, and so Mr Jolliffe remarked; the men, as usual, anxious for the attack, asserted the same, and Mr Smallsole, afraid of retreating from the enemy, and being afterwards despised by the ship's company, ordered the boats to weigh their grapnels.

"Stop a moment, my lads," said Jack to his men, "I've got a bite." The men laughed at Jack's taking it so easy, but he was their pet; and they did stop for him to pull up his fish, intending to pull up to the other boats and recover their loss of a few seconds.

"I've hooked him now," said Jack; "you may up with the grapnel while I up with the fish." But this delay gave the other boats a start of a dozen strokes of their oars, which was a distance not easy to be regained.

"They will be aboard before us, sir," said the coxswain.

"Never mind that," replied Jack; "some one must be last."

"But not the boat I am in," replied Gascoigne; "if I could help it."

"I tell you," replied Jack, "we shall be the *corps de reserve*, and have the honour of turning the scale in our favour."

"Give way, my lads," cried Gascoigne, perceiving the other boats still kept their distance ahead of them, which was about a cable's length.

"Gascoigne, I command the boat," said Jack, "and I do not wish my men to board without any breath in their bodies—that's a very unwise plan. A steady pull, my lads, and not too much exertion."

"By heavens, they'll take the vessel before we get alongside."

"Even if they should, I am right, am I not, Mesty?"

"Yes, Massa Easy, you are right—suppose they take vessel without you, they no want you—suppose they want you, you come." And the negro, who had thrown his jacket off, bared his arm, as if he intended mischief.

The first cutter, commanded by the gunner, now gained upon the launch, and was three boats'-lengths ahead of her when she came alongside. The brig poured in her broadside—it was well directed, and down went the boat.

"Cutter's sunk," exclaimed Gascoigne, "by heavens! Give way, my men."

"Now, don't you observe, that had we all three been pulling up together, the broadside would have sunk us all?" said Jack, very composedly.

"There's board in the launch—give way, my men, give way," said Gascoigne, stamping with impatience.

The reception was evidently warm; by the time that the launch had poured in her men, the second cutter was close under the brig's quarter—two more strokes and she was alongside; when of a sudden a tremendous explosion took place on the deck of the vessel, and bodies and fragments were hurled up in the air. So tremendous was the explosion, that the men of the second cutter, as if transfixed, simultaneously stopped pulling, their eyes directed to the volumes of smoke which poured through the ports, and hid the whole of the masts and rigging of the vessel.

"Now's your time, my lads, give way and alongside," cried our hero.

The men, reminded by his voice, obeyed—but the impetus already given to the boat was sufficient. Before they could drop their oars in the water they grazed against the vessel's sides, and, following Jack, were in a few seconds on the quarter-deck of the vessel. A dreadful sight presented itself—the whole deck was black, and corpses lay strewed; their clothes on them still burning, and among the bodies lay fragments of what once were men.

The capstern was unshipped and turned over on its side—the binnacles were in remnants, and many of the ropes ignited. There was not one person left on deck to oppose them.

As they afterwards learned from some of the men who had saved their lives by remaining below, the French captain had seen the boats before they anchored, and had made every preparation; he had filled a large ammunition chest with cartridges for the guns, that they might not have to hand them up. The conflict between the men of the pinnace and the crew of the vessel was carried on near the capstern, and a pistol fired had accidentally communicated with the powder, which blew up in the very centre of the dense and desperate struggle.

The first object was to draw water and extinguish the flames, which were spreading over the vessel; as soon as that was accomplished, our hero went aft to the taffrail, and looked for the cutter which had been sunk.—"Gascoigne, jump into the boat with four men—I see the cutter floats a quarter of a mile astern: there may be some one alive yet. I think now I see a head or two."

Gascoigne hastened away, and soon returned with three of the cutter's men; the rest had sunk, probably killed or wounded by the discharge of the broadside.

"Thank God, there's three saved!" said Jack, "for we have lost too many. We must now see if any of these poor fellows are yet alive, and clear the decks of the remnants of those who have been blown to pieces. I say, Ned, where should we have been if we had boarded with the pinnace?"

"You always fall upon your feet, Easy," replied Gascoigne; "but that does not prove that you are right."

"I see there's no convincing you, Ned, you are so confoundedly fond of argument. However, I've no time to argue now—we must look to these poor fellows; some are still alive."

Body after body was thrown through the ports, the habiliments, in most cases, enabling them to distinguish whether it was that of a departed friend or foe.

Jack turned round, and observed Mesty with his foot on a head which had been blown from the trunk.

"What are you about, Mesty?"

"Massa Easy, I look at dis, and I tink it Massa Vigor's head, and den I tink dis skull of his enemy nice present make to little Massa Gossett; and den I tink again, and I say, no, he dead and nebber thrash any more—so let him go overboard."

Jack turned away, forgiving Vigors in his heart, he thought of the petty animosities of a midshipman's berth, as he looked at the blackened portion of a body, half an hour before possessing intellect.

"Massy Easy," said Mesty, "I tink you say right, anyhow, when you say forgive: den, Massa Vigors," continued Mesty, taking up the head by the singed hair, and tossing it out of the port, "you really very bad man—but Ashantee forgive you."

"Here's somebody alive," said Gascoigne to Jack, examining a body, the face of which was black as a cinder and not to be recognised, "and he is one of our men too, by his dress."

Our hero went up to examine, and to assist Gascoigne in disengaging the body from a heap of ropes and half-burned tarpaulings with which it was entangled. Mesty followed, and looking at the lower extremities said, "Massa Easy, dat Massa Jolliffe, I know him trousers; marine tailor say he patch um for ever, and so old dat de thread no hold; yesterday he had dis patch put in, and marine tailor say he damn if he patch any more, please nobody."

Mesty was right; it was poor Jolliffe, whose face was burned as black as a coal by the explosion. He had also lost three fingers of the left hand, but as soon as he was brought out on the deck he appeared to recover, and pointed to his mouth for water, which was instantly procured.

"Mesty," said Jack, "I leave you in charge of Mr Jolliffe; take every care of him till I can come back."

The investigation was then continued, and four English sailors found who might be expected to recover, as well as about the same number of Frenchmen; the remainder of the bodies were then thrown overboard. The hat only of the master was picked up between the guns, and there were but eleven Frenchmen found below.

The vessel was the *Franklin*, a French privateer, of ten guns and sixty-five men, of which eight men were away in prizes. The loss on the part of the vessel was forty-six killed and wounded. On that of the *Harpy*, it was five drowned in the cutter, and eighteen blown up belonging to the pinnace, out of which total of twenty-three, they had only Mr Jolliffe and five seamen alive.

"The *Harpy* is standing in with a breeze from the offing," said Gascoigne to Easy.

"So much the better, for I am sick of this, Ned; there is something so horrible in it, and I wish I was on board again. I have just been to Jolliffe; he can speak a little; I think he will recover. I hope so, poor fellow; he will then obtain his promotion, for he is the commanding officer of all us who are left."

"And if he does," replied Gascoigne, "he can swear that it was by having been blown up which spoiled his beauty—but here comes the *Harpy*. I have been looking for an English ensign to hoist over the French, but cannot find one; so I hoist a wheft over it—that will do."

The *Harpy* was soon hove-to close to the brig, and Jack went on board in the cutter to report what had taken place. Captain Wilson was much vexed and grieved at the loss of so many men: fresh hands were put in the cutter to man the pinnace, and he and Sawbridge both went on board to witness the horrible effects of the explosion as described by our hero.

Jolliffe and the wounded men were taken on board, and all of them recovered. We have before stated how disfigured the countenance of poor Mr Jolliffe had been by the smallpox—so severely was it burned that the whole of the countenance came off in three weeks like a mask, and every one declared that, seamed as it still was, Mr Jolliffe was better looking than he was before. It may be as well here to state that Mr Jolliffe not only obtained his promotion, but a pension for his wounds, and retired from the service. He was still very plain, but as it was known that he had been blown up, the loss of his eye as well as the scars on his face were all put down to the same accident, and he excited interest as a gallant and maimed officer. He married, and lived contented and happy to a good old age.

The *Harpy* proceeded with her prize to Mahon. Jack, as usual, obtained a great deal of credit; whether he deserved it, or whether, as Gascoigne observed, he always fell upon his feet, the reader may decide from our narrative; perhaps there was a little of both. The seamen of the *Harpy*, if summoned in a hurry, used very often to reply, "Stop a minute, I've got a bite"—as for Jack, he often said to himself, "I have a famous good yarn for the Governor."

Chapter Twenty Three.

Jack goes on another cruise—love and diplomacy—Jack proves himself too clever for three, and upsets all the arrangements of the high contracting powers.

A few days after the arrival of the *Harpy* at Port Mahon, a Cutter came in with despatches from the admiral. Captain Wilson found that he was posted into the *Aurora* frigate, in which a vacancy had been made by the result of our hero's transgressions.

Mr Sawbridge was raised to the rank of commander, and appointed to the command of the *Harpy*. The admiral informed Captain Wilson that he must detain the *Aurora* until the arrival of another frigate, hourly expected, and then she would be sent down to Mahon for him to take the command of her. Further, he intimated that a supply of live bullocks would be very agreeable, and begged that he would send to Tetuan immediately.

Captain Wilson had lost so many officers that he knew not whom to send: indeed, now he was no longer in command of the *Harpy*, and there was but one lieutenant, and no master or master's mate. Gascoigne and Jack were the only two serviceable midshipmen, and he was afraid to trust them on any expedition in which expedition was required.

"What shall we do, Sawbridge? shall we send Easy or Gascoigne, or both, or neither?—for if the bullocks are not forthcoming, the admiral will not let them off as we do."

"We must send somebody, Wilson," replied Captain Sawbridge, "and it is the custom to send two officers, as one receives the bullocks on board, while the other attends to the embarkation."

"Well, then send both, Sawbridge, but lecture them well first."

"I don't think they can get into any mischief there," replied Sawbridge; "and it's such a hole that they will be glad to get away from it."

Easy and Gascoigne were summoned, listened very respectfully to all Captain Sawbridge said, promised to conduct themselves with the utmost propriety, received a letter to the vice-consul, and were sent with their hammocks and chests in the cabin on board the *Eliza Ann*, brig, of two hundred and sixteen tons, chartered by government—the master and crew of which were all busy forward heaving up their anchors.

The master of the transport came aft to receive them: he was a short red-haired young man, with hands as broad as the flappers of a turtle; he was broad-faced, broad-shouldered, well-freckled, pug-nosed; but if not very handsome he was remarkably good-humoured. As soon as the chests and hammocks were on the deck, he told them that when he could get the anchor up and make sail, he would give them some bottled porter. Jack proposed that he should get the porter up, and they would drink it while he got the anchor up, as it would save time.

"It may save time mayhap, but it won't save porter," replied the master; "however, you shall have it."

He called the boy, ordered him to bring up the porter, and then went forward. Jack made the boy bring up two chairs, put the porter on the companion hatch, and he and Gascoigne sat down. The anchor was weighed, and the transport ran out under her fore-topsail, as they were light-handed, and had to secure the anchor. The transport passed within ten yards of the *Harpy*, and Captain Sawbridge, when he perceived the two midshipmen taking it so very easy, sitting in their chairs with their legs crossed, arms folded, and their porter before them, had a very great mind to order the transport to heave-to, but he could spare no other officer, so he walked away, saying to himself, "There'll be another yarn for the Governor, or I'm mistaken."

As soon as sail was made on the transport, the master, whose name was Hogg, came up to our hero, and asked him how he found the porter. Jack declared that he never could venture an opinion upon the first bottle—"So, Captain Hogg, we'll trouble you for a second"—after which they troubled him for a third—begged for a fourth—must drink his health in a fifth, and finally, pointed out the propriety of making up the half-dozen. By this time they found themselves rather light-headed, so, desiring Captain Hogg to keep a sharp lookout, and not to call them on any account whatever, they retired to their hammocks.

The next morning they awoke late; the breeze was fresh and fair: they requested Captain Hogg not to consider the expense, as they would pay for all they ate and drank, and all he did, into the bargain, and promised him a fit-out when they got to Tetuan.

What with this promise and calling him captain, our hero and Gascoigne won the master's heart, and being a very good-tempered fellow, they did what they pleased. Jack also tossed a doubloon to the men for them to drink on their arrival, and all the men of the transport were in a transport, at Jack's coming to "reign over them." It must be acknowledged that Jack's reign was, for the most part of it, "happy and glorious." At last they arrived at Tetuan, and our Pylades and Orestes went on shore to call upon the vice-consul, accompanied by Captain Hogg. They produced their credentials and demanded bullocks. The vice-consul was a very young man, short and thin, and light-haired; his father had held the situation before him, and he had been appointed his successor because nobody else had thought the situation worth applying for. Nevertheless Mr Hicks was impressed with the immense responsibility of his office. It was, however, a place of some little emolument at this moment, and Mr Hicks had plenty on his hands besides his sister, who, being the only English lady there, set the fashion of the place, and usurped all the attention of the gentlemen mariners who occasionally came for bullocks. But Miss Hicks knew her own importance, and had successively refused three midshipmen, one master's mate, and an acting purser. African bullocks were plentiful at Tetuan, but English ladies were scarce; moreover, she had a pretty little fortune of her own, to wit, three hundred dollars in a canvas bag, left her by her father, and entirely at her own disposal. Miss Hicks was very like her brother, except that she was more dumpling in her figure, with flaxen hair; her features were rather pretty, and her skin very fair. As soon as the preliminaries had been entered into, and arrangements made in a small room with bare walls, which Mr Hicks denominated his office, they were asked to walk into the parlour to be introduced to the vice-consul's sister. Miss Hicks tossed her head at the two midshipmen, but smiled most graciously at Captain Hogg. She knew the relative ranks of midshipman and captain. After a short time she requested the honour of Captain Hogg's company to dinner, and begged that he would bring his midshipmen with him, at which Jack and Gascoigne looked at each other and burst out in a laugh, and Miss Hicks was very near rescinding the latter part of her invitation. As soon as they were out of the house, they told the captain to go on board and get all ready whilst they walked round the town. Having peeped into every part of it, and stared at Arabs, Moors, and Jews, till they were tired, they proceeded to the landing-place, where they met the captain, who informed them that he had done nothing, because the men were all drunk with Jack's doubloon. Jack replied that a doubloon would not last for ever, and that the sooner they drank it out the better. They then returned to the vice-consul's, whom they requested to procure for them fifty dozen of fowls, twenty sheep, and a great many other articles, which might be obtained at the place; for, as Jack said, they would live well going up to Toulon, and if there were any of the stock left, they would give them to the admiral, for Jack had taken the precaution to put his *father's philosophy* once more to the proof, before he quitted Mahon. As Jack gave such a liberal order, and the vice-consul cheated him out of at least one-third of what he paid, Mr Hicks thought he could do no less than offer beds to our midshipmen as well as to Captain Hogg; so, as soon as dinner was over, they ordered Captain Hogg to go on board and bring their things on shore, which he did. As the time usual for transports remaining at Tetuan before they could be completed with bullocks was three weeks, our midshipmen decided upon staying at least so long if they could find anything to do, or if they could not, doing nothing was infinitely preferable to doing duty. So they took up their quarters at the vice-consul's, sending for porter and other things which were not to be had but from the transport; and Jack, to prove that he was not a swindler, as Captain Tartar had called him, gave Captain Hogg a hundred dollars on account, for Captain Hogg had a large stock of porter and English luxuries, which he had brought out as a venture, and of which he had still a considerable portion left. As, therefore, our midshipmen not only were cheated by the vice-consul, but they also supplied his table, Mr Hicks was very hospitable, and everything was at their service except Miss Julia, who turned up her nose at a midshipman, even upon full pay; but she made great advances to the captain, who, on his part, was desperately in love: so the mate and the men made all ready for the bullocks, Jack and Gascoigne made themselves comfortable, and Captain Hogg made love, and thus passed the first week.

The chamber of Easy and Gascoigne was at the top of the house, and finding it excessively warm, Gascoigne had forced his way up to the flat roof above (for the houses are all built in that way in most Mahomedan countries, to enable the occupants to enjoy the cool of the evening, and sometimes to sleep there). Those roofs, where houses are built next to each other, are divided by a wall of several feet, to insure that privacy which the Mahomedan customs demand.

Gascoigne had not been long up there before he heard the voice of a female, singing a plaintive air in a low tone, on the other side of the wall. Gascoigne sang well himself, and having a very fine ear, he was pleased with the correctness of the notes, although he had never heard the air before. He leaned against the wall, smoked his cigar, and listened. It was repeated again and again at intervals; Gascoigne soon caught the notes, which sounded so clear and pure in the silence of the night.

At last they ceased, and having waited another half-hour in vain, our midshipman returned to his bed, humming the air which had so pleased his ear. It haunted him during his sleep, and rang in his ears when he awoke, as it is well known any new air that pleases us will do. Before breakfast was ready, Gascoigne had put English words to it, and sang them over and over again. He inquired of the vice-consul who lived in the next house, and was answered, that it was an old Moor, who was reported to be wealthy, and to have a daughter, whom many of the people had asked in marriage, but whether for her wealth or for her beauty he could not tell; he had, however, heard that she was very handsome. Gascoigne made no further inquiries, but went out with Jack and Captain Hogg, and on board to see the water got in for the bullocks.

"Where did you pick up that air, Gascoigne? it is very pretty, but I never heard you sing it before."

Gascoigne told him, and also what he had heard from Mr Hicks.

"I'm determined, Jack, to see that girl if I can. Hicks can talk Arabic fast enough; just ask him the Arabic for these words—'Don't be afraid—I love you—I cannot speak your tongue,'—and put them down on paper as they are pronounced."

Jack rallied Gascoigne upon his fancy, which could end in nothing.

"Perhaps not," replied Gascoigne; "and I should have cared nothing about it, if she had not sung so well. I really believe the way to my heart is through my ear;—however, I shall try to-night, and soon find if she has the feeling which I think she has. Now let us go back: I'm tired of looking at women in garments up to their eyes, and men in dirt up to their foreheads."

As they entered the house they heard an altercation between Mr and Miss Hicks.

"I shall never give my consent, Julia; one of those midshipmen you turn your nose up at is worth a dozen Hoggs."

"Now, if we only knew the price of a hog in this country," observed Easy, "we should be able to calculate our exact value, Ned."

"A hog, being an unclean animal, is not—"

"Hush," said Jack.

"Mr Hicks," replied Miss Julia, "I am mistress of myself and my fortune, and I shall do as I please."

"Depend upon it, you shall not, Julia. I consider it my duty to prevent you from making an improper match; and, as his Majesty's representative here, I cannot allow you to marry this young man."

"Mercy on us!" said Gascoigne, "his Majesty's representative!"

"I shall not ask your consent," replied the lady.

"Yes, but you shall not marry without my consent. I have, as you know, Julia, from my situation here, as one of his Majesty's *corps diplomatick*, great power, and I shall forbid the banns; in fact, it is only I who can marry you."

"Then I'll marry elsewhere."

"And what will you do on board of the transport until you are able to be married?"

"I shall do as I think proper," replied the lady; "and I'll thank you for none of your indelicate insinuations." So saying, the lady bounced out of the room into her own, and our midshipmen then made a noise in the passage, to intimate that they had come in. They found Mr Hicks looking very red and vice-consular indeed, but he recovered himself; and Captain Hogg making *his* appearance, they went to dinner; but Miss Julia would not make *her* appearance, and Mr Hicks was barely civil to the captain, but he was soon afterwards called out, and our midshipmen went into the office to enable the two lovers to meet. They were heard then talking together, and after a time they said less, and their language was more tender.

"Let us see what's going on, Jack," said Gascoigne; and they walked softly, so as to perceive the two lovers, who were too busy to be on the lookout.

Captain Hogg was requesting a lock of his mistress's hair. The plump Julia could deny him nothing; she let fall her flaxen tresses, and taking out the scissors cut off a thick bunch from her hair behind, which she presented to the captain: it was at least a foot and a half long and an inch in circumference. The Captain took it in his immense hand, and thrust it into his coat pocket behind, but one thrust down to the bottom would not get it in, so he thrust again and again, until it was all coiled away like a cable in a tier.

"That's a liberal girl," whispered Jack; "she gives by *wholesale* what it will take some time to *retail*. But here comes Mr Hicks, let's give them warning; I like Hogg and as she fancies pork, she shall have it, if I can contrive to help them."

That night Gascoigne went again on the roof, and after waiting some time, heard the same air repeated: he waited until it was concluded, and then, in a very low tone, sang it himself to the words he had arranged for it. For some time all was silent, and then the singing recommenced, but it was not to the same air. Gascoigne waited until the new air had been repeated several times, and then giving full scope to his fine tenor voice, sang the first air again. It echoed through the silence of the night air, and then he waited, but in vain; the soft voice of the female was heard no more, and Gascoigne retired to rest.

This continued for three or four nights, Gascoigne singing the same airs the ensuing night that he had heard the preceding, until at last it appeared that the female had no longer any fear, but changed the airs so as to be amused with the repetition of them next evening. On the fifth night she sang the first air, and our midshipman responding, she then sang another, until she had sung them all, waiting each time for the response. The wall was not more than eight feet high, and Gascoigne now determined, with the assistance of Jack, to have a sight of his unknown songstress. He asked Captain Hogg to bring on shore some inch line, and he contrived to make a ladder with three or four poles which were upstairs, used for drying linen. He fixed them against the wall without noise, all ready for the evening. It was a beautiful clear moonlight night, when he went up, accompanied by Jack. The air was again sung, and repeated by Gascoigne, who then softly mounted the ladder, held by Jack, and raised his head above the wall; he perceived a young Moorish girl, splendidly dressed, half lying on an ottoman, with her eyes fixed upon the moon, whose rays enabled him to observe that she was indeed beautiful. She appeared lost in contemplation; and Gascoigne would have given the world to have divined her thoughts. Satisfied with what he had seen, he descended, and singing one of the airs, he then repeated the words, "Do not be afraid—I love you—I cannot speak your language." He then sang another of the airs, and after he had finished he again repeated the words in Arabic; but there was no reply. He sang the third air, and again repeated the words, when, to his delight, he heard an answer in Lingua Franca.

"Can you speak in this tongue?"

"Yes," replied Gascoigne, "I can, Allah be praised. Be not afraid—I love you."

"I know you not; who are you? you are not of my people."

"No, but I will be anything that you wish. I am a Frank, and an English officer."

At this reply of Gascoigne there was a pause.

"Am I then despised?" said Gascoigne.

"No, not despised, but you are not of my people or of my land; speak no more, or you will be heard."

"I obey," replied Gascoigne, "since you wish it, but I shall pine till to-morrow's moon. I go to dream of you. Allah protect you!"

"How amazingly poetical you were in your language, Ned," said Easy, when they went into their room.

"To be sure, Jack, I've read the *Arabian Nights*. You never saw such eyes in your life: what a houri she is!"

"Is she as handsome as Agnes, Ned?"

"Twice as handsome by moonlight."

"That's all moonshine, and so will be your courting, for it will come to nothing."

"Not if I can help it."

"Why, Gascoigne, what would you do with a wife?"

"Just exactly what you would do, Jack."

"I mean, my dear Ned, can you afford to marry?"

"Not while the old governor lives, but I know he has some money in the funds. He told me one day that I could not expect more than three thousand pounds. You know I have sisters."

"And before you come into that you'll have three thousand children."

"That's a large family, Jack," replied Gascoigne, bursting out into laughter, in which our hero joined.

"Well, you know I only wanted to argue the point with you."

"I know that, Jack; but I think we're counting our chickens before they are hatched, which is foolish."

"In every other case except when we venture upon matrimony."

"Why, Jack, you're becoming quite sensible."

"My wisdom is for my friends, my folly for myself. Good-night."

But Jack did not go to sleep. "I must not allow Gascoigne to do such a foolish thing," thought he—"marry a dark girl on midshipman's pay, if he succeeds—get his throat cut if he does not." As Jack said, his wisdom was for his friends, and he was so generous that he reserved none for his own occasions.

Miss Julia Hicks, as we before observed, set the fashions at Tetuan, and her style of dress was not unbecoming. The Moorish women wore large veils, or they may be called what you will, for their head-dresses descend to their heels at times, and cover the whole body, leaving an eye to peep with, and hiding everything else. Now Miss Julia found this much more convenient than the bonnet, as she might walk out in the heat of the sun without burning her fair skin, and stare at everybody and everything without being stared at in return. She therefore never went out without one of these overalls, composed of several yards of fine muslin. Her dress in the house was usually of coloured sarcenet, for a small vessel came into the port one day during her father's lifetime, unloaded a great quantity of bales of goods with English marks; and as the vessel had gone out in ballast, there was a surmise on his part by what means they came into the captain's possession. He therefore cited the captain up to the Governor, but the affair was amicably arranged by the vice-consul receiving about one quarter of the cargo in bales of silks and muslins. Miss Hicks had therefore all her dresses of blue, green, and yellow sarcenet, which, with the white muslin overall, made her as conspicuous as the only Frankish lady in the town had a right to be, and there was not a dog which barked in Tetuan which did not know the sister of the vice-consul, although few had seen her face.

Now it occurred to Jack, as Gascoigne was determined to carry on his amour, that in case of surprise it would be as well if he dressed himself as Miss Hicks. He proposed it to Gascoigne the next morning, who approved of the idea, and in the course of the day, when Miss Hicks was busy with Captain Hogg, he contrived to abstract one of her dresses and muslin overalls—which he could do in safety, as there were plenty of them, for Miss Hicks was not troubled with mantua-maker's bills.

When Gascoigne went up on the roof the ensuing night, he put on the apparel of Miss Hicks, and looked very like her as far as figure went, although a little taller. He waited for the Moorish girl to sing, but she did not—so he crept up the ladder and looked over the wall—when he observed that she was reclining, as before, in deep thought. His head covered with the muslin caught her eye, and she gave a faint scream.

"Fear not, lady," said Gascoigne, "it is not the first time that I have beheld that sweet face. I sigh for a companion. What would I not give to be sitting by your side? I am not of your creed, 'tis true—but does it therefore follow that we should not love each other?"

The Moorish girl was about to reply, when Gascoigne received an answer from a quarter whence he little expected it. It was from the Moor himself, who, hearing his daughter scream, had come swiftly up to the roof.

"Does the Frankish lily wish to mingle her perfumes with the dark violet?" said he, for he had often seen the sister of the vice-consul, and he imagined it was she who had come on the roof and ascended the wall to speak with his daughter.

Gascoigne had presence of mind to avail himself of this fortunate mistake.

"I am alone, worthy Moor," replied he, pulling the muslin more over his face, "and I pine for a companion. I have been charmed by the nightingale on the roof of your dwelling; but I thought not to meet the face of a man, when I took courage to climb this ladder."

"If the Frankish lily will have courage to descend, she can sit by the side of the dark violet."

Gascoigne thought it advisable to make no reply.

"Fear not," said the old Moor; "what is an old man but a woman?" and the Moor brought a ladder, which he placed against the wall.

After a pause, Gascoigne said, "It is my fate;" and he then descended, and was led by the Moor to the mattress upon which his daughter reclined. The Moor then took his seat near them, and they entered into conversation. Gascoigne knew quite enough of the vice-consul and his sister to play his part—and he thought proper to tell the Moor that her brother wished to give her as wife to the captain of the ship, whom she abhorred, and would take her to a cold and foggy climate; that she had been born here, and wished to live and die here, and would prefer passing her life in his women's apartments, to leaving this country. At which Abdel Faza, for such was his name, felt very amorous; he put his hand to his forehead, salaamed, and told Gascoigne that his zenana, and all that were in it, were hers, as well as his house and himself. After an hour's conversation, in which Azar, his daughter, did not join, the old Moor asked Gascoigne to descend into the women's apartment; and observing his daughter's silence, said to her:

"Azar, you are angry that this Frankish houri should come to the apartments of which you have hitherto been sole mistress. Fear not, you will soon be another's, for Osman Ali has asked thee for his wife, and I have listened to his request."

Now Osman Ali was as old as her father, and Azar hated him. She offered her hand tremblingly, and led Gascoigne into the zenana. The Moor attended them to the threshold, bowed, and left them.

That Gascoigne had time to press his suit, and that he did not lose such a golden opportunity, may easily be imagined, and her father's communication relative to Osman Ali very much assisted our midshipman's cause.

He left the zenana, like most midshipmen, in love, that is, a little above quicksilver boiling heat. Jack, who had remained in a state of some suspense all this time, was not sorry to hear voices in an amicable tone, and in a few minutes afterwards he perceived that Gascoigne was ascending the ladder. It occurred to our hero that it was perhaps advisable that he should not be seen, as the Moor, in his gallantry, might come up the ladder with the supposed lady. He was right, for Abdel Faza not only followed her up the ladder on his side, but assisted her to descend on the other, and with great ceremony took his leave.

Gascoigne hastened to Jack, who had been peeping, and gave him a detail of what had passed, describing Azar as the most beautiful, fascinating, and fond creature that ever was created. After half an hour's relation he stopped short, because he discovered that Jack was fast asleep.

The visits of Gascoigne were repeated every night; old Abdel Faza became every time more gallant, and our midshipman was under the necessity of assuming a virtue if he had it not. He pretended to be very modest.

In the meantime Captain Hogg continued his attentions to the real Miss Hicks; the mate proceeded to get the bullocks on board, and as more than three weeks had already passed away, it was time to think of departing for Toulon; but Captain Hogg was too much in love, and as for Gascoigne, he intended, like all midshipmen in love, to give up the service. Jack reasoned with the Captain, who appeared to listen to reason, because Miss Hicks had agreed to follow his fortunes, and crown his transports in the transport *Mary Ann*. He therefore proposed that they should get away as fast as they could, and as soon as they had weighed the anchor, he would come on shore, take off Miss Hicks, and make all sail for Toulon.

Jack might have suffered this; the difficulty was with Gascoigne, who would not hear of going away without his lovely Azar. At last Jack planned a scheme, which he thought would succeed, and which would be a good joke to tell the Governor. He therefore appeared to consent to Gascoigne's carrying off his little Moor, and they canvassed how it was to be managed. Jack then told Gascoigne that he had hit upon a plan which would succeed. "I find," said he, "from Captain Hogg, that he has an intention of carrying off Miss Hicks, and when I sounded him as to his having a lady with him, he objected to it immediately, saying, that he must have all the cabin to himself and his intended. Now, in the first place, I have no notion of giving up the cabin to Miss Hicks or Mrs Hogg. It will be very uncomfortable to be shut out because he wishes to make love; I therefore am determined that he shall not take off Miss Hicks. He has proposed to me that he shall go on board, and get the brig under way, leaving me with a boat on shore to sign the vouchers, and that Miss Hicks shall slip into the boat when I go off at dusk. Now I will not bring off Miss Hicks; if he wants to marry her, let him do it when I am not on board. I have paid for everything, and I consider the cabin as mine."

"Look you, Ned, if you wish to carry off your little Moor, there is but one way, and that is a very simple one; leave her a dress of Miss Hicks's when you go there to-morrow night, and tell her to slip down at dusk, and come out of the house: all the danger will be in her own house, for as soon as she is out she will be supposed to be the vice-consul's sister, and will not be observed or questioned. I will look out for and bring her on board instead of Miss Hicks. Hogg will have the brig under way, and will be too happy to make all sail, and she shall lock the cabin inside, so that the mistake shall not be discovered till the next morning, and we shall have a good laugh at Captain Hogg."

Gascoigne pronounced that Jack's scheme was capital, and agreed to it, thanking him and declaring that he was the best friend that he ever had. "So I will be," thought Jack, "but you will not acknowledge it at first." Jack then went to Captain Hogg, and appeared to enter warmly into his views, but told him that Hicks suspected what was going on, and had told him so, at the same time declaring that he would not lose sight of his sister until after Hogg was on board.

"Now," says Jack, "you know you cannot do the thing by main force; so the best plan will be for you to go on board and get under way, leaving me to bring off Miss Hicks, when her brother will imagine all danger to be over."

"Many thanks, Mr Easy," replied Captain Hogg; "it will be capital, and I'll arrange it all with my Julia. How very kind of you!"

"But, Hogg, will you promise me secrecy?"

"Yes," replied the captain.

"That Gascoigne is a very silly fellow, and wants to run away with a girl he has made acquaintance with here; and what do you think he has proposed? that after the ship was under way, I should carry her off in the boat; and he has borrowed one of the dresses of Miss Hicks, that it may appear to be her. I have agreed to it, but as I am determined that he shall not commit such a folly, I shall bring off Miss Hicks instead; and observe, Hogg, he is that sort of wild fellow, that if he was to find that I had cheated him, he would immediately go on shore and be left behind; therefore we must hand Miss Hicks down in the cabin, and she will lock the door all night, so that he may not observe the trick till the next morning, and then we shall have a fine laugh at him."

Captain Hogg replied it would be an excellent joke, as Gascoigne did before him.

Now it must be observed, that the water and the bullocks, and the sheep and fowls, were all on board; and Mr Hicks, having received his money from Jack, had very much altered his manner; he was barely civil, for as he had got all he could out of our hero, he was anxious to get rid of him as well as of Captain Hogg. Our hero was very indignant at this, but as it would not suit his present views, pretended not to notice it—on the contrary, he professed the warmest friendship for the vice-consul, and took an opportunity of saying that he could not return his kindness in a better way than by informing him of the plot which had been arranged. He then told him of the intended escape of his sister, and that he was the person intended to bring her off.

"Infamous, by heavens!" cried the vice-consul; "I shall write to the Foreign Office on the subject."

"I think," said Jack, "it will be much better to do what I shall propose, which will end in a hearty laugh, and to the confusion of Captain Hogg. Do you dress yourself in your sister's clothes, and I will bring you off instead of her. Let him imagine that he has your sister secure; I will hand you down to the cabin, and do you lock yourself in. He cannot sail without my orders, and I will not sign the vouchers. The next morning we will open the cabin door and have a good laugh at him. Desire your boat to be off at daylight to take you on shore, and I will then make him proceed to Toulon forthwith. It will be a capital joke."

So thought the vice-consul, as well as Gascoigne and Captain Hogg. He shook hands with Jack, and was as civil to him as before.

That night Gascoigne left one of Miss Hicks's many dresses with Azar, who agreed to follow his fortunes, and who packed up all the jewels and money she could lay her hands upon. Poor little Child, she trembled with fear and delight. Miss Hicks smuggled, as she thought, a box of clothes on board, and in the box was her fortune of three hundred dollars. Mr Hicks laughed in his sleeve, so did Jack; and every one went to bed, with expectations that their wishes would be realised. After an early dinner, Captain Hogg and Gascoigne went on board, both squeezing Jack's hand as if they were never to see him again, and looks of intelligence passed between all the parties.

As soon as they were out of the door the vice-consul chuckled, and Miss Hicks, who thought he chuckled at the idea of having rid himself of Captain Hogg, chuckled still more as she looked at our hero, who was her confidant, and our hero, for reasons known to the reader, chuckled more than either of them.

A little before dark, the boat was sent on shore from the brig, which was now under way, and Mr Hicks, as had been agreed, said that he should go into the office and prepare the vouchers—that is, put on his sister's clothes. Miss Hicks immediately rose, and wishing our hero a pleasant voyage, as had been agreed, said that she should retire for the night, as she had a bad headache—she wished her brother good-night, and went into her room to wait another hour, when our hero, having shoved off the boat to deceive the vice-consul, was to return, meet her in the garden, and take her off to the brig. Our hero then went into the office and assisted the vice-consul, who took off all his own clothes and tied them up in a handkerchief, intending to resume them after he had gone into the cabin.

As soon as he was ready, Jack carried his bundle and led the supposed Miss Hicks down to the boat. They shoved off in a great hurry, and Jack took an opportunity of dropping Mr Hicks's bundle overboard. As soon as they arrived alongside, Mr Hicks ascended, and was handed by Jack down into the Cabin: he squeezed Jack's hand as he entered, saying in a whisper, "To-morrow morning what a laugh we shall have!" and then he locked the door. In the meantime the boat was hooked on and hoisted up, and Jack took the precaution to have the dead-lights lowered that Mr Hicks might not be able to ascertain what was going on. Gascoigne came up to our hero and squeezed his hand.

"I'm so much obliged to you, Jack. I say, tomorrow morning what a laugh we shall have!"

As soon as the boat was up, and the mainyard filled, Captain Hogg also came up to our hero, shaking him by the hand and thanking him; and he, too, concluded by saying, "I say, Mr Easy, to-morrow morning what a laugh we shall have!"

"Let those laugh who win," thought Jack.

The wind was fair, the watch was set, the course was steered, and all went down to their hammocks, and went to sleep, waiting for to-morrow morning. Mr Hicks, also, having nothing better to do, went to sleep, and by the morning dawn, the transport *Mary Ann* was more than a hundred miles from the African shore.

Chapter Twenty Four.

Our hero plays the very devil.

We must leave the reader to imagine the effect of the next morning's *dénouement*. Every one was in a fury except Jack, who did nothing but laugh. The captain wanted to return to obtain Miss Hicks, Gascoigne to obtain Azar, and the vice-consul to obtain his liberty—but the wind was foul for their return, and Jack soon gained the captain on his side. He pointed out to him that, in the first place, if he presumed to return, he would forfeit his charter bond; in the second, he would have to pay for all the bullocks which died; in the third, that if he wished to take Miss Hicks as his wife, he must not first injure her character by having her on board before the solemnity; and lastly, that he could always go and marry her whenever he pleased; the brother could not prevent him. All this was very good advice, and the captain became quite calm and rational, and set his studding-sails below and aloft.

As for Gascoigne, it was no use reasoning with him, so it was agreed that he should have satisfaction as soon as they could get on shore again. Mr Hicks was the most violent; he insisted that the vessel should return, while both Jack and the captain refused, although he threatened them with the whole Foreign Office. He insisted upon having his clothes, but Jack replied that they had tumbled overboard as they pulled from the shore. He then commanded the mate and men to take the vessel back, but they laughed at him and his woman's clothes. "At all events, I'll have you turned out of the service," said he to our hero, in his fury. "I shall be extremely obliged to you," said Jack—and Captain Hogg was so much amused with the vice-consul's appearance in his sister's clothes, that he quite forgot his own disappointment in laughing at his intended brother-in-law. He made friends again with Jack, who regained his ascendancy, and ordered out the porter on the capstern-head. They had an excellent dinner, but Mr Hicks refused to join them; which, however, did not spoil the appetite of Jack or the captain: as for Gascoigne, he could not eat a mouthful, but he drank to excess, looking over the rim of his tumbler as if he could devour our hero, who only laughed the more. Mr Hicks had applied to the men to lend him some clothes, but Jack had foreseen that, and he was omnipotent. There was not a jacket or a pair of trousers to be had for love or money. Mr Hicks then considered it advisable to lower his tone, and he applied to Captain Hogg, who begged to be excused without he consented to his marriage with his sister, to which Mr Hicks gave an indignant negative. He then applied to Gascoigne, who told him in a very surly tone to go to hell. At last he applied to our hero, who laughed, and said that he would see him damned first. So Mr Hicks sat down in his petticoats, and vowed revenge. Gascoigne, who had drunk much and eaten nothing, turned in and went to sleep—while Captain Hogg and our hero drank porter on the capstern. Thus passed the first day, and the wind was famously fair—the bullocks lowed, the cocks crew, the sheep baa'd, and the *Mary Ann* made upwards of two hundred miles. Jack took possession of the other berth in the cabin, and his Majesty's representative was obliged to lie down in his petticoats upon a topsail which lay between decks, with a bullock on each side of him, who every now and then made a dart at him with their horns, as if they knew that it was to him that they were indebted for their embarkation and being destined to drive the scurvy out of the Toulon fleet.

We cannot enter into the details of the passage, which, as the wind was fair, was accomplished in ten days without the loss of a bullock. During this time Mr Hicks condescended to eat without speaking, imagining that the hour of retribution would come when they joined the admiral. Gascoigne gradually recovered himself, but did not speak to our hero, who continued to laugh and drink porter. On the eleventh morning they were in the midst of the Toulon fleet, and Mr Hicks smiled exultingly as he passed our hero in his petticoats, and wondered that Jack showed no signs of trepidation.

The fleet hove-to, Jack ran under the admiral's stern, lowered down his boat, and went on board, showed his credentials, and reported his bullocks. The general signal was made, there was a fair division of the spoil, and then the admiral asked our hero whether the master of the transport had any other stock on board. Jack replied that he had not; but that having been told by the Governor of Malta that they might be acceptable, he had bought a few sheep and some dozen of fowls, which were much at his service, if he would accept of them. The admiral was much obliged to the Governor, and also to Jack, for thinking of him, but would not, of course, accept of the stock without paying for them. He requested him to send all of them on board that he could spare, and then asked Jack to dine with him, for Jack had put on his best attire, and looked very much of a gentleman.

"Mr Easy," said the flag-captain, who had been looking at the transport with his glass, "is that the master's wife on board?"

"No, sir," replied Jack; "it's the vice-consul."

"What, in petticoats! the vice-consul?"

"Yes, the vice-consul of Tetuan. He came on board in that dress when the brig was under way, and I considered it my duty not to delay, being aware how very important it was that the fleet should be provided with fresh beef."

"What is all this, Mr Easy?" said the admiral; "there has been some trick here. You will oblige me by coming into the cabin."

Easy followed the admiral and flag-captain into the cabin, and then boldly told the whole story how he tricked them all. It was impossible for either of them to help laughing, and when they began to laugh it was almost as impossible to stop.

"Mr Easy," said the admiral at last, "I do not altogether blame you; it appears that the captain of the transport would have delayed sailing because he was in love—and that Mr Gascoigne would have stayed behind because he was infatuated; independent of the ill-will against the English which would have been excited by the abduction of the girl. But I think you might have contrived to manage all that without putting the vice-consul in petticoats."

"I acted to the best of my judgment, sir," replied Jack, very humbly.

"And altogether you have done well. Captain Malcolm, send a boat for the vice-consul."

Mr Hicks was too impatient to tell his wrongs to care for his being in his sister's clothes: he came on board, and although the tittering was great, he imagined that it would soon be all in his favour, when it was known that he was a diplomatic. He told his story, and waited for the decision of the admiral, which was to crush our hero, who stood with the midshipmen on the lee-side of the deck; but the admiral replied, "Mr Hicks, in the first place, this appears to me to be a family affair concerning the marriage of your sister, with which I have nothing to do. You went on board of your own free will in woman's clothes. Mr Easy's orders were positive, and he obeyed them. It was his duty to sail as soon as the transport was ready. You may forward your complaint if you please, but, as a friend, I tell you that it will probably occasion your dismissal, for these kind of pranks are not understood at the Foreign Office. You may return to the transport, which, after she has touched at Mahon, will proceed again to Tetuan. The boat is alongside, sir."

Mr Hicks, astonished at the want of respect, paid to a vice-consul, shoved his petticoats between his legs and went down the side amidst the laughter of the whole of the ship's company. Our hero dined with the admiral, and was well received. He got his orders to sail that night for Minorca, and as soon as dinner was over he returned on board, where he found Captain Hogg very busy selling his porter—Gascoigne walking the deck in a brown study—and Mr Hicks *solus* abaft, sulking in his petticoats.

As soon as they were clear of the boats, the *Mary Ann* hoisted her ensign and made sail, and as all the porter was not yet sold, Jack ordered up a bottle.

Jack was much pleased with the result of his explanation with the admiral, and he felt that, for once, he had not only got into no scrape himself, but that he had prevented others. Gascoigne walked the deck gloomily; the fact was that he was very unhappy; he had had time to reflect, and now that the first violence had subsided, he felt that our hero had done him a real service, and had prevented him from committing an act of egregious folly; and yet he had summoned this friend to meet him in the field—and such had been his gratitude. He would have given the world to recall what had passed and to make friends, but he felt ashamed, as most people do, to acknowledge his error; he had, however, almost made up his mind to it, and was walking up and down thinking in what manner he might contrive it, when Jack, who was sitting, as usual, in a chair by the capstern, with his porter by him, said to himself, "Now I'll lay my life that Ned wants to make friends, and is ashamed to speak first; I may be mistaken, and he may fly off at a tangent, but even if I am, at all events it will not be I who am wrong—I'll try him." Jack waited till Gascoigne passed him again, and then said, looking kindly and knowingly in his face:

"I say, Ned, will you have a glass of porter?"

Gascoigne smiled, and Jack held out his hand; the reconciliation was effected in a moment, and the subject of quarrel was not canvassed by either party.

"We shall be at Minorca in a day or two," observed Jack, after a while; "now I shall be glad to get there. Do you know, Ned, that I feel very much satisfied with myself; I have got into no scrape this time, and I shall, notwithstanding, have a good story to tell the Governor when I go to Malta."

"Partly at my expense," replied Gascoigne.

"Why, you will figure a little in it, but others will figure much more."

"I wonder what has become of that poor girl," observed Gascoigne, who could not refrain from mentioning her; "what hurts me most is, that she must think me such a brute."

"No doubt of that, Ned—take another glass of porter."

"Her father gave me this large diamond."

"The old goat—sell it, and drink his health with it."

"No, I'll keep it in memory of his daughter."

Here Gascoigne fell into a melancholy reverie, and Jack thought of Agnes.

In two days they arrived at Mahon, and found the *Aurora* already there, in the command of Captain Wilson. Mr Hicks had persuaded Captain Hogg to furnish him with clothes, Jack having taken off the injunction as soon as he had quitted the admiral. Mr Hicks was aware that if the admiral would not listen to his complaint, it was no use speaking to a captain: so he remained on board a pensioner upon Captain Hogg, and after our midshipmen quitted the transport they became very good friends. Mr Hicks consented to the match, and Captain Hogg was made happy. As for poor Azar, she had wandered about until she was tired in Miss Hicks's dress, and at last returned broken-hearted to her father's, and was admitted by Abdel Faza himself; he imagined it was Miss Hicks, and was in transports—he discovered it was his daughter, and he was in a fury. The next day she went to the zenana of Osman Ali.

When Jack reported himself he did not tell the history of the elopements, that he might not hurt the feelings of Gascoigne. Captain Wilson was satisfied with the manner in which he had executed his orders, and asked him, "whether he preferred staying in the *Harpy* or following him into the *Aurora*."

Jack hesitated.

"Speak frankly, Mr Easy; if you prefer Captain Sawbridge to me I shall not be affronted."

"No, sir," replied Easy, "I do not prefer Captain Sawbridge to you; you have both been equally kind to me, but I prefer you. But the fact is, sir, that I do not much like to part with Gascoigne, or—"

"Or who?" said the captain, smiling.

"With Mesty, sir; you may think me very foolish—but I should not be alive at this moment, if it had not been for him."

"I do not consider gratitude to be foolish, Mr Easy," replied Captain Wilson. "Mr Gascoigne I intend to take with me, if he chooses to come, as I have a great respect for his father, and no fault to find with him, that is, generally speaking—but as for Mesty—why, he is a good man, and as you have behaved yourself very well, perhaps I may think of it."

The next day Mesty was included among the boat's crew taken with him by Captain Wilson, according to the regulations of the service, and appointed to the same situation under the master-at-arms of the *Aurora*. Gascoigne and our hero were also discharged into the frigate.

As our hero never has shown any remarkable predilection for duty, the reader will not be surprised at his requesting from Captain Wilson a few days on shore, previous to his going on board of the *Aurora*. Captain Wilson allowed the same licence to Gascoigne, as they had both been cooped up for some time on board of a transport. Our hero took up his quarters at the only respectable hotel in the town, and whenever he could meet an officer of the *Aurora*, he very politely begged the pleasure of his company to dinner. Jack's reputation had gone before him, and the midshipmen drank his wine and swore he was a trump. Not that Jack was to be deceived, but upon the principles of equality he argued that it was the duty of those who could afford dinners to give them to those who could not. This was a sad error on Jack's part; but he had not yet learned the value of money; he was such a fool as to think that the only real use of it was to make other people happy. It must, however, be offered in his extenuation that he was a midshipman and a philosopher, and not yet eighteen.

At last Jack had remained so long on shore, keeping open house, and the first lieutenant of the *Aurora* found the officers so much more anxious for leave, now that they were at little or no expense, that he sent him a very polite message, requesting the pleasure of his company on board that evening. Jack returned an equally polite answer, informing the first lieutenant that not being aware that he wished to see him, he had promised to accompany some friends to a masquerade that night, but that he would not fail to pay his respects to him the next day. The first lieutenant admitted the excuse, and our hero, after having entertained half a dozen of the *Auroras*, for the *Harpy* had sailed two days before, dressed himself for the masquerade, which was held in a church about two miles and a half from Mahon.

Jack had selected the costume of the *devil*, as being the most appropriate, and mounting a jackass, he rode down in his dress to the masquerade. But, as Jack was just going in, he perceived a yellow carriage, with two footmen in gaudy liveries, draw up, and, with his usual politeness, when the footmen opened the door, offered his arm to hand out a fat old dowager covered with diamonds; the lady looked up, and perceiving Jack covered with hair, with his trident and his horns and long tail, gave a loud scream, and would have fallen had it not been for Captain Wilson, who, in his full uniform, was coming in, and caught her in his arms: while the old lady thanked him, and Captain Wilson bowed, Jack hastily retreated. "I shall make no conquests to-night," thought he, so he entered the church, and joined the crowd; but it was so dense that it was hardly possible to move, and our hero soon got tired of flourishing his trident, and sticking it into people, who wondered what the devil he meant.

"This is stupid work," thought Jack, "I may have more fun outside:" so Jack put on his cloak, left the masquerade, and went out in search of adventures. He walked into the open country about half a mile, until he came to a splendid house, standing in a garden of orange-trees, which he determined to reconnoitre. He observed that a window was open and lights were in the room; and he climbed up to the window, and just opened the white curtain and looked in. On a bed lay an elderly person, evidently dying, and by the side of the bed were three priests, one of whom held the crucifix in his hand, another the censer, and a third was sitting at a table with a paper, pen, and ink. As Jack understood Spanish, he listened, and heard one of the priests say:

"Your sins have been enormous, my son, and I cannot give you extreme unction or absolution unless you make some amends."

"I have," answered the moribund, "left money for ten thousand masses to be said for my soul."

"Five hundred thousand masses are not sufficient: how have you gained your enormous wealth? by usury and robbing the poor."

"I have left a thousand dollars to be distributed among the poor on the day of my funeral."

"One thousand dollars is nothing—you must leave all your property to holy church."

"And my children!" replied the dying man faintly.

"What are your children compared to your salvation?—reply not: either consent, or not only do I refuse you the consolation of the dying, but I excommunicate—"

"Mercy, holy father—mercy!" said the old man, in a dying voice.

"There is no mercy, you are damned for ever and ever. Amen. Now hear: *excommunicabo te*—"

"Stop—stop—have you the paper ready?"

"'Tis here, all ready, by which you revoke all former wills, and endow the holy church with your property. We will read it, for God forbid that it should be said that the holy church received an involuntary gift."

"I will sign it," replied the dying man; "but my sight fails me; be quick, absolve me." And the paper was signed, with difficulty, as the priests supported the dying man. "And now—absolve me."

"I do absolve thee," replied the priest, who then went through the ceremony.

"Now this is a confounded rascally business," said Jack to himself; who then dropped his cloak, jumped upon the window-sill, opened wide the window-curtains with both hands, and uttered a yelling kind of "ha! ha! ha! ha!"

The priests turned round, saw the demon, as they imagined—dropped the paper on the table, and threw themselves with their faces on the floor.

"*Exorciso te*," stammered one.

"Ha! ha! ha! ha!" repeated Jack, entering the room, and taking up the paper, which he burned by the flame of the candle. Our hero looked at the old man on the bed; his jaw had fallen, his eyes were turned. He was dead. Jack then gave one more "ha! ha! ha! ha!" to keep the priests in their places, blew out the candles, made a spring out of the window, caught up his cloak, and disappeared as fast as his legs could carry him.

Jack ran until he was out of breath, and then he stopped, and sat down by the side of the road. It was broad moonlight, and Jack knew not where he was; "but Minorca has not many high-roads," thought Jack, "and I shall find my way home. Now let me see—I have done some good this evening. I have prevented those rogues from disinheriting a family. I wonder who they are; they ought to be infinitely obliged to me. But if the priests find me out, what shall I do? I never dare come on shore again—they'd have me in the inquisition. I wonder where I am," said Jack; "I will get on that hill, and see if I can take a departure."

The hill was formed by the road being cut perpendicularly almost through it, and was perhaps some twelve or fourteen feet high. Jack ascended it, and looked about him. "There is the sea, at all events, with the full moon silvering the waves," said Jack, turning from the road, "and here is the road; then that must be the way to Port Mahon. But what comes here?—it's a carriage. Why, it's the yellow carriage of that old lady with her diamonds, and her two splashy footmen!" Jack was watching it as it passed the road under him, when, of a sudden, he perceived about a dozen men rush out, and seize the horses' heads—a discharge of fire-arms, the coachman dropped off the box, and the two footmen dropped from behind. The robbers then opened the door, and were hauling out the fat old lady covered with diamonds. Jack thought a second—it occurred to him, that, although he could not cope with so many, he might frighten them, as he had frightened one set of robbers already that night. The old lady had just been tumbled out of the carriage door, like a large bundle of clothes tied up for the wash, when Jack, throwing off his cloak, and advancing to the edge of the precipice, with the full moon behind him throwing out his figure in strong relief, raised his trident, and just as they were raising their knives, yelled a most unearthly "ha! ha! ha! ha!" The robbers looked up, and forgetting the masquerade, for there is a double tremor in guilt, screamed with fear; most of them ran away, and dropped after a hundred yards; others remained paralysed and insensible. Jack descended the hill, went to the assistance of the old lady, who had swooned, and had to put her into the carriage; but although our hero was very strong, this was a work of no small difficulty. After one or two attempts, he lowered down the steps, and contrived to bump her on the first, from the first he purchased her on the second, and from the second he at last seated her at the door of the carriage. Jack had no time to be over-polite. He then threw her back into the bottom of the carriage, her heels went up to the top, Jack shoved in her petticoats as fast as he could, for decency, and then shutting the door seized the reins, and jumped upon the box. "I don't know the way," thought Jack, "but we must needs go when the *devil drives*;" so sticking his trident into the horses, they set off at a rattling pace, passing over the bodies of the two robbers, who had held the reins, and who both lay before him in a swoon. As soon as he had brought the horses into a trot, he slackened the reins, for, as Jack wisely argued, they will be certain to go home if I let them have their own way. The horses, before they arrived at the town, turned off, and stopped at a large country house. That he might not frighten the people, Jack had put on his cloak, and taken off his mask and head-piece, which he had laid beside him on the box. At the sound of the carriage wheels the servants came out, when Jack, in a few words, told them what had happened. Some of the servants ran in, and a young lady made her appearance, while the others were helping the old lady out of the carriage, who had recovered her senses, but had been so much frightened that she had remained in the posture in which Jack had put her.

As soon as she was out, Jack descended from the coach-box and entered the house. He stated to the young lady what had taken place, and how opportunely he had frightened away the robbers, just as they were about to murder her relation; and also suggested the propriety of sending after the servants who had fallen in the attack, which was immediately done by a strong and well-armed party collected for the occasion. Jack, having made his speech, made a very polite bow and took his leave, stating that he was an English officer belonging to a frigate in the harbour. He knew his way back, and in half an hour was again at the inn, and found his comrades. Jack thought it advisable to keep his own secret, and therefore merely said that he had taken a long walk in the country; and soon afterwards went to bed.

The next morning our hero, who was always a man of his word, packed up his portmanteau, and paid his bill. He had just completed this heavy operation, when somebody wanted to speak to him, and a sort of half-clerical, half-legal sort of looking gentleman was introduced, who, with a starched face and prim air, said that he came to request in writing the name of the officer who was dressed as a devil in the masquerade of the night before.

Jack looked at his interrogator, and thought of the priests and the inquisition. "No, no," thought he, "that won't do; a name I must give, but it shall be one that you dare not meddle with. A midshipman you might get hold of, but it's more than the whole island dare to touch a post-captain of one of his Majesty's frigates." So Jack took the paper and wrote Captain Henry Wilson, of his Majesty's ship *Aurora*.

The prim man made a prim bow, folded up the paper, and left the room.

Jack threw the waiter half a doubloon, lighted his cigar, and went on board.

Chapter Twenty Five.

In which the old proverb is illustrated, "that you must not count your chickens before they are hatched."

The first lieutenant of the *Aurora* was a very good officer in many respects, but, as a midshipman, he had contracted the habit of putting his hands in his pockets, and could never keep them out, even when the ship was in a gale of wind; and hands are of some use in a heavy lurch. He had more than once received serious injury from falling on these occasions, but habit was too powerful; and, although he had once broken his leg by falling down the hatchway, and had moreover a large scar on his forehead, received from being thrown to leeward against one of the guns, he still continued the practice; indeed, it was said that once, when it was necessary for him to go aloft, he had actually taken the two first rounds of the Jacob's ladder without withdrawing them, until, losing his balance, he discovered that it was not quite so easy to go aloft with his hands in his pockets. In fact, there was no getting up his hands, even when all hands were turned up. He had another peculiarity, which was, that he had taken a peculiar fancy to a quack medicine, called Enouy's Universal Medicine for all Mankind; and Mr Pottyfar was convinced in his own mind that the label was no libel, except from the greatness of its truth. In his opinion, it cured everything, and he spent one of his quarterly bills every year in bottles of this stuff; which he not only took himself every time he was unwell, but occasionally when quite well, to prevent his falling sick. He recommended it to everybody in the ship, and nothing pleased him so much as to give a dose of it to every one who could be persuaded to take it.

The officers laughed at him, but it was generally behind his back, for he became very angry if contradicted upon this one point, upon which he certainly might be considered to be a little cracked. He was indefatigable in making proselytes to his creed, and expatiated upon the virtues of the medicine for an hour running, proving the truth of his assertion by a pamphlet, which, with his hands, he always carried in his trousers pocket.

Jack reported himself when he came on board, and Mr Pottyfar, who was on the quarter-deck at the time, expressed a hope that Mr Easy would take his share of the duty, now that he had had such a spell on shore; to which Jack very graciously acceded, and then went down below, where he found Gascoigne and his new messmates, with most of whom he was already acquainted.

"Well, Easy," said Gascoigne, "have you had enough of the shore?"

"Quite," replied Jack, recollecting that after the events of the night before he was just as well on board; "I don't intend to ask for any more leave."

"Perhaps it's quite as well, for Mr Pottyfar is not very liberal on that score, I can tell you; there is but one way of getting leave from him."

"Indeed," replied Jack; "and what is that?"

"You must pretend that you are not well, take some of his quack medicine, and then he will allow you a run on shore to work it off."

"Oh! that's it, is it? well then, as soon as we anchor in Valette, I'll go through a regular course, but not till then."

"It ought to suit you, Jack; it's an equality medicine; cures one disorder just as well as the other."

"Or kills—which levels all the patients. You're right, Gascoigne, I must patronise that stuff—for more reasons than one. Who was that person on deck in mufti?"

"The mufti, Jack? in other words, the chaplain of the ship; but he's a prime sailor, nevertheless."

"How's that?"

"Why, he was brought up on the quarter-deck, served his time, was acting lieutenant for two years, and then, somehow or other, he bore up for the church."

"Indeed—what were his reasons?"

"No one knows—but they say he has been unhappy ever since."

"Why so?"

"Because he did a very foolish thing, which cannot now be remedied. He supposed at the time that he would make a good parson, and now that he has long got over his fit, he finds himself wholly unfit for it—he is still the officer in heart, and is always struggling with his natural bent, which is very contrary to what a parson should feel."

"Why don't they allow parsons to be broke by a court-martial, and turned out of the service, or to resign their commissions, like other people?"

"It won't do, Jack—they serve Heaven—there's a difference between that and serving his Majesty."

"Well, I don't understand these things. When do we sail?"

"The day after to-morrow."

"To join the fleet off Toulon?"

"Yes; but I suppose we shall be driven on the Spanish coast going there. I never knew a man-of-war that was not."

"No; wind always blows from the South going up the Mediterranean."

"Perhaps you'll take another prize, Jack—mind you don't go away without the articles of war."

"I won't go away without Mesty, if I can help it. Oh, dear, how abominable a midshipman's berth is after a long run on shore! I positively must go on deck and look at the shore, if I can do nothing else."

"Why, ten minutes ago you had had enough of it."

"Yes, but ten minutes here has made me feel quite sick. I shall go to the first lieutenant for a dose."

"I say, Easy, we must both be physicked on the same day."

"To be sure; but stop till we get to Malta."

Jack went on deck, made acquaintance with the chaplain and some of the officers whom he had not known, then climbed up into the maintop, where he took a seat on the armolest, and, as he looked at the shore, thought over the events that had passed, until Agnes came to his memory, and he thought only of her. When a mid is in love, he always goes aloft to think of the object of his affection; why, I don't know, except that his reverie is not so likely to be disturbed by an order from a superior officer.

The *Aurora* sailed on the second day, and with a fine breeze, stood across, making as much northing as easting; the consequence was, that one fine morning they saw the Spanish coast before they saw the Toulon fleet. Mr Pottyfar took his hands out of his pockets, because he could not examine the coast through a telescope without so doing; but this, it is said, was the first time that he had done so on the quarter-deck from the day that the ship had sailed from Port Mahon. Captain Wilson was also occupied with his telescope, so were many of the officers and midshipmen, and the men at the mast-heads used their eyes, but there was nothing but a few small fishing-boats to be seen. So they all went down to breakfast, as the ship was hove-to close in with the land.

"What will Easy bet," said one of the midshipmen, "that we don't see a prize to-day?"

"I will not bet that we do not see a vessel—but I'll bet you what you please, that we do not take one before twelve o'clock at night."

"No, no, that won't do—just let the teapot travel over this way, for it's my forenoon watch."

"It's a fine morning," observed one of the mates, of the name of Martin; "but I've a notion it won't be a fine evening."

"Why not?" inquired another.

"I've now been eight years in the Mediterranean, and know something about the weather. There's a watery sky, and the wind is very steady. If we are not under double-reefed topsails to-night, say I'm no conjuror."

"That you will be, all the same, if we are under bare poles," said another.

"You're devilish free with your tongue, my youngster. Easy, pull his ears for me."

"Pull them easy, Jack, then," said the boy, laughing.

"All hands make sail!" now resounded at the hatchways.

"There they are, depend upon it," cried Gascoigne, catching up his hat and bolting out of the berth, followed by all the others except Martin, who had just been relieved, and thought that his presence in the waist might be dispensed with for the short time, at least, which it took him to swallow a cup of tea.

It was very true; a galliot and four lateen vessels had just made their appearance round the easternmost point, and, as soon as they observed the frigate, had hauled their wind. In a minute the *Aurora* was under a press of canvas, and the telescopes were all directed to the vessels.

"All deeply laden, sir," observed Mr Hawkins, the chaplain; "how the topsail of the galliot is scored!"

"They have a fresh breeze just now," observed Captain Wilson to the first lieutenant.

"Yes, sir, and it's coming down fast."

"Hands by the royal halyards, there."

The *Aurora* careened with the canvas to the rapidly increasing breeze.

"Top-gallant sheet and halyards."

"Luff you may, quarter-master; luff, I tell you. A small pull of that weather maintop-gallant brace—that will do," said the master.

"Top-men aloft there;—stand by to clew up the royals—and, Captain Wilson, shall we take them in?—I'm afraid of that pole—it bends now like a coach-whip," said Mr Pottyfar, looking up aloft, with his hands in both pockets.

"In royals—lower away."

"They are going about, sir," said the second lieutenant, Mr Haswell.

"Look out," observed the chaplain, "it's coming." Again the breeze increased, and the frigate was borne down.

"Hands reef topsails in stays, Mr Pottyfar."

"Ay, ay, sir—'bout ship."

The helm was put down and the topsails lowered and reefed in stays.

"Very well, my lads, very well indeed," said Captain Wilson.

Again the topsails were hoisted and top-gallant sheets home. It was a strong breeze, although the water was smooth, and the *Aurora* dashed through at the rate of eight miles an hour, with her weather leeches lifting.

"Didn't I tell you so?" said Martin to his mess-mates on the gangway; "but there's more yet, my boys."

"We must take the top-gallant sails off her," said Captain Wilson, looking aloft—for the frigate now careened to her bearings, and the wind was increasing and squally. "Try them a little longer;" but another squall came suddenly—the halyards were lowered, and the sails clewed up and furled.

In the meantime the frigate had rapidly gained upon the vessels, which still carried on every stitch of canvas, making short tacks in-shore. The *Aurora* was again put about with her head towards them, and they were not two points on her weather bow. The sky, which had been clear in the morning, was now overcast, the sun was obscured with opaque white clouds, and the sea was rising fast. Another ten minutes, and then they were under double-reefed topsails, and the squalls were accompanied with heavy rain. The frigate now dashed through the waves, foaming in her course and straining under the press of sail. The horizon was so thick that the vessels ahead were no longer to be seen.

"We shall have it, I expect," said Captain Wilson.

"Didn't I say so?" observed Martin to Gascoigne. "We take no prizes this day, depend upon it."

"We must have another hand to the wheel, sir, if you please," said the quarter-master, who was assisting the helmsman.

Mr Pottyfar, with his hands concealed as usual, stood by the capstern. "I fear, sir, we cannot carry the mainsail much longer."

"No," observed the chaplain, "I was thinking so."

"Captain Wilson, if you please, we are very close in," said the master: "don't you think we had better go about?"

"Yes, Mr Jones. Hands about ship—and—yes, by heavens, we must!—up mainsail."

The mainsail was taken off, and the frigate appeared to be immediately relieved. She no longer jerked and plunged as before.

"We're very near the land, Captain Wilson; thick as it is, I think I can make out the loom of it—shall we wear round, sir?" continued the master.

"Yes—hands wear ship—put the helm up."

It was but just in time, for, as the frigate flew round, describing a circle, as she payed off before the wind, they could perceive the breakers lashing the precipitous coast not two cables' length from them.

"I had no idea we were so near," observed the captain, compressing his lips—"can they see anything of those vessels?"

"I have not seen them this quarter of an hour, sir," replied the signalman, protecting his glass from the rain under his jacket.

"How's her head now, quarter-master?"

"South south-east, sir."

The sky now assumed a different appearance—the white clouds had been exchanged for others dark and murky, the wind roared at intervals, and the rain came down in torrents. Captain Wilson went down into the cabin to examine the barometer.

"The barometer has risen," said he on his return on deck. "Is the wind steady?"

"No, sir, she's up and off three points."

"This will end in a south-wester."

The wet and heavy sails now flapped from the shifting of the wind.

"Up with the helm, quarter-master."

"Up it is—she's off to south-by-west."

The wind lulled, the rain came down in a deluge—for a minute it was quite calm, and the frigate was on an even keel.

"Man the braces. We shall be taken aback directly, depend upon it."

The braces were hardly stretched along before this was the case. The wind flew round to the south-west with a loud roar, and it was fortunate that they were prepared—the yards were braced round, and the master asked the captain what course they were to steer.

"We must give it up," observed Captain Wilson, holding on by the belaying pin. "Shape our course for Cape Sicie, Mr Jones."

And the *Aurora* flew before the gale, under her foresail and topsails close reefed. The weather was now so thick that nothing could be observed twenty yards from the vessel; the thunder pealed, and the lightning darted in every direction over the dark expanse. The watch was called as soon as the sails were trimmed, and all who could went below, wet, uncomfortable, and disappointed.

"What an old Jonah you are, Martin," said Gascoigne.

"Yes, I am," replied he; "but we have the worst to come yet, in my opinion. I recollect, not two hundred miles from where we are now, we had just such a gale in the *Favourite*, and we as nearly went down, when—"

At this moment a tremendous noise was heard above, a shock was felt throughout the whole ship, which trembled fore and aft as if it were about to fall into pieces; loud shrieks were followed by plaintive cries, the lower deck was filled with smoke, and the frigate was down on her beam ends. Without exchanging a word, the whole of the occupants of the berth flew out, and were up the hatchway, not knowing what to think, but convinced that some dreadful accident had taken place.

On their gaining the deck it was at once explained; the foremast of the frigate had been struck by lightning, had been riven into several pieces, and had fallen over the larboard bow, carrying with it the main topmast and jib-boom. The jagged stump of the foremast was in flames, and burned brightly, notwithstanding the rain fell in torrents. The ship, as soon as the foremast and main topmast had gone overboard, broached-to furiously, throwing the men over the wheel and dashing them senseless against the carronades; the forecastle, the fore part of the main deck, and even the lower deck, were spread with men, either killed or seriously wounded or insensible from the electric shock. The frigate was on her beam ends, and the sea broke furiously over her; all was dark as pitch, except the light from the blazing stump of the foremast, appearing like a torch, held up by the wild demons of the storm, or when occasionally the gleaming lightning cast a momentary glare, threatening every moment to repeat its attack upon the vessel, while the deafening thunder burst almost on their devoted heads. All was dismay and confusion for a minute or two: at last Captain Wilson, who had himself lost his sight for a short time, called for the carpenter and axes—they climbed up, that is, two or three of them, and he pointed to the mizzen-mast; the master was also there, and he cut loose the axes for the seamen to use; in a few minutes the mizzen-mast fell over the quarter, and the helm being put hard up, the frigate payed off and slowly righted. But the horror of the scene was not yet over. The boatswain, who had been on the forecastle, had been led below, for his vision was gone for ever. The men who lay scattered about had been examined, and they were assisting them down to the care of the surgeon, when the cry of "Fire!" issued from the lower deck. The ship had taken fire at the coal-hole and carpenter's storeroom, and the smoke that now ascended was intense.

"Call the drummer," said Captain Wilson, "and let him beat to quarters—all hands to their stations—let the pumps be rigged and the buckets passed along. Mr Martin, see that the wounded men are taken down below. Where's Mr Haswell? Mr Pottyfar, station the men to pass the water on by hand on the lower deck. I will go there myself. Mr Jones, take charge of the ship."

Pottyfar, who actually had taken his hands out of his pockets, hastened down to comply with the captain's orders on the main deck, as Captain Wilson descended to the deck below.

"I say, Jack, this is very different from this morning," observed Gascoigne.

"Yes," replied Jack, "so it is; but I say, Gascoigne, what's the best thing to do?—when the chimney's on fire on shore, they put a wet blanket over it."

"Yes," replied Gascoigne; "but when the coal-hole's on fire on board, they will not find that sufficient."

"At all events, wet blankets must be a good thing, Ned, so let us pull out the hammocks; cut the lanyards and get some out—we can but offer them, you know, and if they do no good, at least it will show our zeal."

"Yes, Jack, and I think when they turn in again, those whose blankets you take will agree with you that zeal makes the service very uncomfortable. However, I think you are right."

The two midshipmen collected three or four hands, and in a very short time they had more blankets than they could carry—there was no trouble in wetting them, for the main deck was afloat—and followed by the men they had collected, Easy and Gascoigne went down with large bundles in their arms to where Captain Wilson was giving directions to the men.

"Excellent, Mr Easy! excellent, Mr Gascoigne;" said Captain Wilson. "Come, my lads, throw them over now, and stamp upon them well;" the men's jackets and the captain's coat had already been sacrificed to the same object.

Easy called the other midshipmen, and they went up for a further supply; but there was no occasion, the fire had been smothered: still the danger had been so great that the fore magazine had been floated. During all this, which lasted perhaps a quarter of an hour, the frigate had rolled gunwale under, and many were the accidents which occurred. At last all danger from fire had ceased, and the men were ordered to return to their quarters, when three officers and forty-seven men were found absent—seven of them were dead—most of them were already under the care of the surgeon, but some were still lying in the scuppers.

No one had been more active or more brave during this time of danger than Mr Hawkins the chaplain. He was everywhere, and when Captain Wilson went down to put out the fire he was there, encouraging the men and exerting himself most gallantly. He and Mesty came aft when all was over, one just as black as the other. The chaplain sat down and wrung his hands—"God forgive me!" said he, "God forgive me!"

"Why so, sir?" said Easy, who stood near, "I am sure you need not be ashamed of what you have done."

"No, no, not ashamed of what I've done; but, Mr Easy—I have sworn so, sworn such oaths at the men in my haste—I, the chaplain! God forgive me!—I meant nothing." It was very true that Mr Hawkins had sworn a great deal during his exertions, but he was at that time the quarter-deck officer and not the chaplain; the example to the men and his gallantry had been most serviceable.

"Indeed, sir," said Easy, who saw that the chaplain was in great tribulation, and hoped to pacify him, "I was certainly not there all the time, but I only heard you say, 'God bless you, my men! be smart,' and so on; surely, that is not swearing."

"Was it *that* I said, Mr Easy, are you sure? I really had an idea that I had damned them all in heaps, as some of them deserved—no, no, not deserved. Did I really bless them—nothing but bless them?"

"Yes, sir," said Mesty, who perceived what Jack wanted; "it was nothing, I assure you, but 'God bless you, Captain Wilson!—Bless your heart, my good men!—Bless the king!' and so on. You do noting but shower down blessing and wet blanket."

"I told you so," said Jack.

"Well, Mr Easy, you've made me very happy," replied the chaplain; "I was afraid it was otherwise."

So indeed it was, for the chaplain had sworn like a boatswain; but, as Jack and Mesty had turned all his curses into blessings, the poor man gave himself absolution, and shaking hands with Jack, hoped he would come down into the gun-room and take a glass of grog; nor did he forget Mesty, who received a good allowance at the gun-room door, to which Jack gladly consented, as the rum in the middy's berth had all been exhausted after the rainy morning—but Jack was interrupted in his third glass, by somebody telling him the captain wanted to speak with Mr Hawkins and with him.

Jack went up and found the captain on the quarter-deck with the officers.

"Mr Easy," said Captain Wilson, "I have sent for you, Mr Hawkins, and Mr Gascoigne, to thank you on the quarter-deck, for your exertions and presence of mind on this trying occasion." Mr Hawkins made a bow. Gascoigne said nothing, but he thought of having extra leave when they arrived at Malta. Jack felt inclined to make a speech, and began something about when there was danger that it levelled every one to an equality even on board of a man-of-war.

"By no means, Mr Easy," replied Captain Wilson, "it does the very contrary, for it proves which is the best man, and those who are the best raise themselves at once above the rest."

Jack was very much inclined to argue the point, but he took the compliment and held his tongue, which was the wisest thing he could have done; so he made his bow, and was about to go down into the midshipmen's berth when the frigate was pooped by a tremendous sea, which washed all those who did not hold on down into the waist. Jack was among the number, and naturally catching at the first object which touched him, he caught hold of the chaplain by the leg, who commenced swearing most terribly, but before he could finish the oath, the water, which had burst into the cabin through the windows—for the dead-lights, in the confusion, had not yet been shipped—burst out the cross bulkheads, sweeping like a torrent the marine, the cabin-door, and everything else in its force, and floating Jack and the chaplain with several others down the main hatchway on to the lower deck. The lower deck being also full of water, men and chests were rolling and tossing about, and Jack was sometimes in company with the chaplain, and at other times separated; at last they both recovered their legs, and gained the midshipmen's berth, which, although afloat, was still a haven of security. Mr Hawkins spluttered and spit, and so did Jack, until he began to laugh.

"This is very trying, Mr Easy," said the chaplain: "very trying indeed to the temper. I hope I have not sworn—I hope not."

"Not a word," said Jack—"I was close to you all the time—you only said, 'God preserve us!'"

"Only that? I was afraid that I said 'God damn it!'"

"Quite a mistake, Mr Hawkins. Let's go into the gun-room, and try to wash this salt water out of our mouths, and then I will tell you all you said, as far as I could hear it, word for word."

So Jack by this means got another glass of grog, which was very acceptable in his wet condition, and made himself very comfortable, while those on deck were putting on the dead-lights, and very busy setting the goose-wings of the mainsail, to prevent the frigate from being pooped a second time.

Chapter Twenty Six.

In which our hero becomes excessively unwell, and agrees to go through a course of medicine.

The hammocks were not piped down that night: some were taken indiscriminately for the wounded, but the rest remained in the nettings, for all hands were busy preparing jury-masts and jury-rigging, and Mr Pottyfar was so well employed that, for twelve hours, his hands were not in his pockets. It was indeed a dreadful night: the waves were mountains high, and chased the frigate in their fury, cresting, breaking, and roaring at her taffrail; but she flew before them with the wings of the wind; four men at the helm assisted by others at the relieving tackles below. Jack, having been thanked on and washed off the quarter-deck, thought that he had done quite enough; he was as deep as he could swim before he had satisfied all the scruples of the chaplain, and stowing himself away on one of the lockers of the midshipmen's berth, was soon fast asleep, notwithstanding that the frigate rolled gunwale under. Gascoigne had done much better; he had taken down a hammock, as he said, for a poor wounded man, hung it up, and turned in himself. The consequence was, that the next morning the surgeon, who saw him lying in the hammock, had put him down in the report; but as Gascoigne had got up as well as ever, he laughed, and scratched his name out of the list of wounded.

Before morning, the ship had been pumped out dry, and all below made as secure and safe as circumstances would permit; but the gale still continued its violence, and there was anything but comfort on board.

"I say, Martin, you ought to be thrown overboard," said Gascoigne; "all this comes from your croaking you're a Mother Carey's chicken."

"I wish I had been any one's chicken," replied Martin; "but the devil a thing to nestle under have I had since I can well remember."

"What a bore to have no galley fire lighted," said one of the youngsters, "no tea, and not allowed any grog."

"The gale will last three days," replied Martin, "and by that time we shall not be far from the admiral; it won't blow home there."

"Well, then, we shall be ordered in directly, and I shall go on shore to-morrow," replied Easy.

"Yes, if you're ill," replied Gascoigne.

"Never fear, I shall be sick enough: we shall be there at least six weeks, and then we'll forget all this."

"Yes," replied Martin, "we may forget it, but will the poor fellows whose limbs are shrivelled forget it? and will poor Miles, the boatswain, who is blind for ever?"

"Very true, Martin, we are thinking about ourselves, not thankful for our escape, and not feeling for others," replied Gascoigne.

"Give us your hand, Ned," said Jack Easy. "And, Martin, we ought to thank you for telling us the truth—we are a selfish set of fellows."

"Still we took our share with the others," replied one of the midshipmen.

"That's more reason for us to be grateful and to pity them," replied Jack; "suppose you had lost your arm or your eyesight—we should have pitied you; so now pity others."

"Well, so I do, now I think of it."

"Think oftener, youngster," observed Martin, going on deck.

What a change from the morning of the day before!—but twenty-four hours had passed away, and the sea had been smooth, the frigate dashed through the blue water, proud in all her canvas, graceful as a swan. Since that, there had been fire, tempest, lightning, disaster, danger, and death; her masts were tossed about on the snowy waves hundreds of miles away from her—and she, a wreck, was rolling heavily, groaning and complaining in every timber as she urged her impetuous race with the furious-running sea.

How wrong are those on shore who assert that sailors are not religious!—how is it possible, supposing them to be possessed of feeling, to be otherwise? On shore, where you have nothing but the change of seasons, each in his own peculiar beauty—nothing but the blessings of the earth, its fruit, its flowers—nothing but the bounty, the comforts, the luxuries which have been invented, where you can rise in the morning in peace, and lay down your head at night in security—God may be neglected and forgotten for a long time; but at sea, when each gale is a warning, each disaster acts as a check, each escape as a homily upon the forbearance of Providence, that man must be indeed brutalised who does not feel that God is there. On shore we seldom view Him but in all His beauty and kindness; but at sea we are as often reminded how terrible He is in His wrath. Can it be supposed that the occurrences of the last twenty-four hours were lost upon the mind of any one man in that ship? No, no. In their courage and activity they might appear reckless, but in their hearts they acknowledged and bowed unto their God.

Before the day was over a jury-foremast had been got up, and sail having been put upon it, the ship was steered with greater ease and safety—the main brace had been spliced to cheer up the exhausted crew, and the hammocks were piped down.

As Gascoigne had observed, some of the men were not very much pleased to find that they were minus their blankets, but Captain Wilson ordered their losses to be supplied by the purser and expended by the master; this quite altered the case, as they obtained new blankets in most cases for old ones; but still it was impossible to light the galley fire, and the men sat on their chests and nibbled biscuit. By twelve o'clock that night the gale broke, and more sail was necessarily put on the scudding vessel, for the sea still ran fast and mountains high. At daylight the sun burst out and shone brightly on them, the sea went gradually down, the fire was lighted, and Mr Pottyfar, whose hands were again in his pockets, at twelve o'clock gave the welcome order to pipe to dinner. As soon as the men had eaten their dinner, the frigate was once more brought to the wind, her jury-mast forward improved upon, and more sail made upon it. The next morning there was nothing of the gale left except the dire effects which it had produced, the black and riven stump of the foremost still holding up a terrific warning of the power and fury of the elements.

Three days more, and the *Aurora* joined the Toulon fleet. When she was first seen it was imagined by those on board of the other ships that she had been in action; but they soon learned that the conflict had been against more direful weapons than any yet invented by mortal hands. Captain Wilson waited upon the admiral, and of course received immediate orders to repair to port and refit. In a few hours the *Aurora* had shaped her course for Malta, and by sunset the Toulon fleet were no longer in sight.

"By de holy poker, Massa Easy, but that terrible sort of gale the other day anyhow—I tink one time we all go to Davy Joney's lacker."

"Very true, Mesty; I hope never to meet with such another."

"Den, Massa Easy, why you go to sea? When man ab no money, noting to eat, den he go to sea, but everybody say you ab plenty money—why you come to sea?"

"I'm sure I don't know," replied Jack thoughtfully; "I came to sea on account of equality and the rights of man."

"Eh, Massa Easy, you come to wrong place anyhow; now I tink a good deal lately, and by all de power, I tink equality all stuff."

"All stuff, Mesty, why? you used to think otherwise."

"Yes, Massa Easy, but den I boil de kettle for all young gentleman. Now dat I ship's corporal and hab cane, I tink so no longer."

Jack made no reply, but he thought the more. The reader must have perceived that Jack's notions of equality were rapidly disappearing; he defended them more from habit, and perhaps a wilfulness which would not allow him to acknowledge himself wrong; to which may be added his love of argument. Already he had accustomed himself to obedience to his superiors, and, notwithstanding his arguments, he would admit of no resistance from those below him; not that it was hardly ever attempted, for Jack was anything but a tyrant, and was much beloved by all in the ship. Every day brought its lesson, and Captain Wilson was now satisfied that Jack had been almost cured of the effects of his father's ridiculous philosophy.

After a few minutes, Mesty tapped his cane on the funnel, and recommenced.

"Then why you stay at sea, Massa Easy?"

"I don't know, Mesty; I don't dislike it."

"But, Massa Easy, why you stay in midshipman berth—eat hard biscuit, salt pig, salt horse, when you can go shore, and live like gentleman? Dat very foolish! Why not be your own master? By all power! suppose I had money, catch me board ship. Little sea very good, Massa Easy—open one eyes; but tink of the lightning t'other night: poor massa boatswain, he shut um eyes for ebber!"

"Very true, Mesty."

"Me hope you tink of this, sar, and when you go on shore, you take Mesty wid you: he sarve you well, Massa Easy, long as he live, by de holy St. Patrick. And den, Massa Easy, you marry wife—hab pickaninny—lib like gentleman. You tink of this, Massa Easy."

The mention of the word marriage turned the thoughts of our hero to his Agnes, and he made no reply. Mesty walked away, leaving our hero in deep thought.

This conversation had more effect upon Jack than would have been imagined, and he very often found he was putting to himself the question of Mesty—"Why do you stay at sea?" He had not entered the service with any particular view, except to find equality; and he could not but acknowledge to himself that, as Mesty observed, he had come to the wrong place. He had never even thought of staying to serve his time, nor had he looked forward to promotion, and one day commanding a ship. He had only cared for the present, without indulging in a future anticipation of any reward, except in a union with Agnes. Mesty's observations occasioned Jack to reflect upon the future for the first time in his life; and he was always perplexed when he put the question of Mesty, and tried to answer to himself as to what were his intentions in remaining in the service.

Nevertheless, Jack did his duty very much to the satisfaction of Mr Pottyfar; and after a tedious passage, from baffling and light winds, the *Aurora* arrived at Malta. Our hero had had some conversation with his friend Gascoigne, in which he canvassed his future plans; all of which, however, ended in one settled point, which was that he was to marry Agnes. As for the rest, Gascoigne was of opinion that Jack ought to follow up the service, and become a captain, but there was plenty of time to think about that, as he observed, now all they had to consider was how to get on shore; for the refitting of the ship was an excuse for detaining them on board, which they knew Mr Pottyfar would avail himself of. Jack dined in the gun-room on the day of their arrival, and he resolved that he would ask that very evening. Captain Wilson was already on shore at the Governor's. Now, there had been a little difference of opinion between Mr Pottyfar and Mr Hawkins, the chaplain, on a point of seamanship; and most of the officers sided with the chaplain, who, as we have before observed, was a first-rate seaman. It had ended in high words, for Mr Hawkins had forgotten himself so far as to tell the first lieutenant that he had a great deal to learn, not having even got over the midshipman's trick of keeping his hands in his pockets; and Mr Pottyfar had replied that it was very well for him as chaplain to insult others, knowing that his cassock protected him. This was a bitter reply to Mr Hawkins, who at the very time that the insinuation made his blood boil, was also reminded that his profession forbade a retort: he rushed into his cabin, poor fellow, having no other method left, vented his indignation in tears, and then consoled himself by degrees with prayer. In the meantime, Mr Pottyfar had gone on deck, wroth with Hawkins and his messmates, as well as displeased with himself. He was, indeed, in a humour to be pleased with nobody, and in a most unfortunate humour to be asked leave by a midshipman. Nevertheless, Jack politely took off his hat, and requested leave to go on shore and see his friend the Governor. Upon which Mr Pottyfar turned round to him, with his feet spread wide open, and thrusting his hands to the very bottom of his pockets, as if in determination, said, "Mr Easy, you know the state of the ship; we have everything to do—new masts, new rigging, everything almost to refit—and yet you ask to go on shore! Now, sir, you may take this answer for yourself and all the other midshipmen in the ship, that not one soul of you puts his foot on shore until we are all a-taunto."

"Allow me to observe, sir," said our hero, "that it is very true that all our services may be required when the duty commences, but this being Saturday night, and to-morrow Sunday, the frigate will not be even moved till Monday morning; and as the work cannot begin before that, I trust you will permit leave until that time."

"My opinion is different, sir," replied the first lieutenant.

"Perhaps, sir, you will allow me to argue the point," replied Jack.

"No, sir, I never allow argument; walk over to the other side of the deck, if you please."

"Oh, certainly, sir," said Jack, "if you wish it."

Jack's first idea was to go on shore without leave, but from this he was persuaded by Gascoigne, who told him that it would displease Captain Wilson, and that old Tom, the Governor, would not receive him. Jack agreed to this, and then, after a flourish about the rights of man, tyranny, oppression, and so forth, he walked forward to the forecastle, where he found his friend Mesty, who had heard all that had passed, and who insidiously said to him in a low tone:

"Why you stay at sea, Massa Easy?"

"Why, indeed," thought Jack, boiling with indignation, "to be cooped up here at the will of another? I am a fool—Mesty is right—I'll ask for my discharge to-morrow." Jack went down below and told Gascoigne what he had determined to do.

"You'll do no such thing, Jack," replied Gascoigne "depend upon it, you'll have plenty of leave in a day or two. Pottyfar was in a pet with the chaplain, who was too much for him. Captain Wilson will be on board by nine o'clock."

Nevertheless, Jack walked his first watch in the *magnificents*, as all middies do when they cannot go on shore, and turned in at twelve o'clock, with the resolution of sticking to his purpose, and quitting his Majesty's service; in fact, of presenting his Majesty with his between two and three years' time, served as midshipman, all free, gratis, and for nothing, except his provisions and his pay, which some captains are bold enough to assert that they not only are not worth, but not even the salt that accompanies it; forgetting that they were once midshipmen themselves, and at the period were, of course, about the same value.

The next morning Captain Wilson came off; the ship's company were mustered, the service read by Mr Hawkins, and Jack, as soon as all the official duties were over, was about to go up to the captain, when the captain said to him:

"Mr Easy, the Governor desired me to bring you on shore to dine with him, and he has a bed at your service."

Jack touched his hat, and ran down below, to make his few preparations.

By the time that Mesty, who had taken charge of his chest, etcetera, had put his necessaries in the boat, Jack had almost made up his mind that his Majesty should not be deprived yet awhile of so valuable an officer. Jack returned on deck, and found that the captain was not yet ready; he went up to Mr Pottyfar, and told him that the captain had ordered him to go on shore with him; and Mr Pottyfar, who had quite got over his spleen, said:

"Very well, Mr Easy—I wish you a great deal of pleasure."

"This is very different from yesterday," thought Jack; "suppose I try the medicine?"

"I am not very well, Mr Pottyfar, and those pills of the doctor's don't agree with me—I always am ill if I am long without air and exercise."

"Very true," said the first lieutenant, "people require air and exercise. I've no opinion of the doctor's remedies; the only thing that is worth a farthing is the universal medicine."

"I should so long to try it, sir," replied Jack; "I read the book one day, and it said that if you took it daily for a fortnight or three weeks, and with plenty of air and exercise, it would do wonders."

"And it's very true," replied Mr Pottyfar, "and if you'd like to try it you shall—I have plenty—shall I give you a dose now?"

"If you please, sir," replied Jack; "and tell me how often I am to take it, for my head aches all day."

Mr Pottyfar took Jack down, and putting into his hand three or four bottles of the preparation, told him that he was to take thirty drops at night, when he went to bed, not to drink more than two glasses of wine, and to avoid the heat of the sun.

"But, sir," replied Jack, who had put the bottles in his pocket, "I am afraid that I cannot take it for long; for as the ship is ready for fitting, I shall be exposed to the sun all day."

"Yes, if you are wanted, Mr Easy; but we have plenty here without you; and when you are unwell you cannot be expected to work. Take care of your health; and I trust, indeed I am sure, that you will find this medicine wonderfully efficacious."

"I will begin to-night, sir, if you please," replied Jack, "and I am very much obliged to you. I sleep at the Governor's—shall I come on board to-morrow morning?"

"No, no; take care of yourself, and get well; I shall be glad to hear that you get better. Send me word how it acts."

"I will, sir, send you word by the boat every day," replied Jack, delighted; "I am very much obliged to you, sir. Gascoigne and I were thinking of asking you, but did not like to do so: he, poor fellow, suffers from headaches almost as bad as I do, and the doctor's pills are of no use to him."

"He shall have some, too, Mr Easy. I thought he looked pale. I'll see to it this afternoon. Recollect, moderate exercise, Mr Easy, and avoid the sun at midday."

"Yes, sir," replied Jack, "I'll not forget;" and off went Jack, delighted. He ordered Mesty to put up his whole portmanteau instead of the small bundle he put into the boat, and telling Gascoigne what a spoke he had put into his wheel, was soon in the boat with the captain, and went on shore, where he was cordially greeted by the Governor.

Chapter Twenty Seven.

In which Captain Wilson is repaid with interest for Jack's borrowing his name; proving that a good name is as good as a legacy.

"Well, Jack, my boy, have you any long story ready for me?" inquired the Governor.

"Yes, sir," replied Jack, "I have one or two very good ones."

"Very well, we'll hear them after dinner," replied old Tom. "In the meantime find out your room and take possession."

"That must not be for very long, Governor," observed Captain Wilson. "Mr Easy must learn his duty, and there is a good opportunity now."

"If you please, sir," replied Jack, "I'm on the sick-list."

"Sick-list," said Captain Wilson; "you were not in the report that Mr Wilson gave me this morning."

"No, I'm on Mr Pottyfar's list; and I'm going through a course of the universal medicine."

"What's all this, Jack—what's all this?—there's some story here—don't be afraid of the captain—you've me to back you," said the Governor.

Jack was not at all afraid of the captain, so he told him how the first-lieutenant had refused him leave the evening before, and how he had now given him permission to remain, and try the universal medicine, at which the Governor laughed heartily, nor could Captain Wilson refrain from joining.

"But, Mr Easy," replied the captain, after a pause, "if Mr Pottyfar will allow you to stay on shore, I cannot—you have your duty to learn. You must be aware that now is your time, and you must not lose opportunities that do not occur every day. You must acknowledge the truth of what I say."

"Yes, sir," replied Jack, "I admit it all, provided I do intend to follow the profession;" and so saying, our hero bowed, and left the veranda where they had been talking.

This hint of Jack's, thrown out by him more with the intention of preventing his being sent on board than with any definite idea, was not lost upon either the captain or the Governor.

"Does he jib, then?" observed the Governor.

"On the contrary, I never knew him more attentive and so entirely getting rid of his former notions. He has behaved most nobly in the gale, and there has not been one complaint against him—I never was more astonished—he must have meant something."

"I'll tell you what he means, Wilson—that he does not like to be sent on board, nothing more. He's not to be cooped up—you may lead him, but not drive him."

"Yes, but the service will not admit of it. I never could allow it—he must do his duty like the rest, and conform to the rules."

"Exactly, so he must; but look ye, Wilson, you must not lose him: it's all easily settled—appoint him your orderly midshipman to and from the ship; that will be employment, and he can always remain here at night. I will tell him that I have asked, as a favour, what I now do, and leave me to find out what he is thinking about."

"It may be done that way, certainly," replied Captain Wilson, musing; "and you are more likely to get his intentions from him than I am. I am afraid he has too great a command of money ever to be fond of the ship; it is the ruin of a junior officer to be so lavishly supplied."

"He's a long way from ruin yet, Wilson—he's a very fine fellow, even by your own acknowledgment. You humoured him out of gratitude to his father, when he first came into the service; humour him a little now to keep him in it. Besides, if your first lieutenant is such a fool with his universal medicine, can you wonder at a midshipman taking advantage of it?"

"No, but I ought not to allow him to do so with my eyes open."

"He has made it known to you upon honour, and you ought not to take advantage of his confidence: but still what I proposed would, I think, be the best, for then he will be at his duty in a way that will suit all parties. You, because you employ him on service—the first lieutenant, because Jack can take his medicine—and Jack, because he can dine with me every day."

"Well, I suppose it must be so," replied Captain Wilson, laughing; "but still, I trust, you will discover what is working in his mind to induce him to give me that answer, Governor."

"Never fear, Jack shall confess, and lay his soul as bare as that of a Catholic bigot before his padre."

The party sat down to dinner, and what with the Governor's aide-de-camp and those invited, it was pretty numerous. After the cloth had been removed, the Governor called upon Jack for his stories, whereupon, much to the surprise of Captain Wilson, who had never heard one word of it, for the admiral had not mentioned anything about it to him during the short time the *Aurora* was with the Toulon fleet, our hero gave the Governor and the company the narrative of all that happened in the *Mary Ann* transport—the loves of Captain Hogg and Miss Hicks—the adventures of Gascoigne—and his plan, by which he baulked them all. The Governor was delighted, and Captain Wilson not a little astonished.

"You prevented a very foolish thing, Mr Easy, and behaved very well," observed the captain, laughing again at the idea; "but you never told me of all this."

"No, sir," replied Jack, "I have always reserved my stories for the Governor's table, where I am sure to meet you, and then telling once does for all."

Jack received his appointment as orderly midshipman, and everything went on well; for, of his own accord, he stayed on board the major part of the day to learn his duty, which very much pleased the captain and Mr Pottyfar. In this Jack showed a great deal of good sense, and Captain Wilson did not repent of the indulgence he had shown him. Jack's health improved daily, much to Mr Pottyfar's satisfaction, who imagined that he took the universal medicine night and morning. Gascoigne also was a patient under the first lieutenant's hands, and often on shore with our hero, who thought no more of quitting the service.

For seven weeks they had now remained in harbour, for even the masts had to be made, when, one day, Captain Wilson opened a letter he received at breakfast-time, and having read it, laid it down with the greatest surprise depicted in his countenance. "Good heavens! what can this mean?" said he.

"What's the matter, Wilson?" said the Governor.

"Just hear its contents, Sir Thomas."

Captain Wilson then read in Spanish as follows:—

"*Honourable Sir*:—

"It is my duty to advise you that the Honourable Lady Signora Alforgas de Guzman, now deceased, has, in her testament, bequeathed to you the sum of one thousand doubloons in gold as a testimony of your kind services on the night of the 12th of August. If you will authorise any merchant here to receive the money, it shall be paid forthwith, or remitted in any way you please to appoint. May you live a thousand years.

"Your most obedient servant:—

"*Alfonzo Xerez*."

Jack heard the letter read, rose quietly, whistled low, as if not attending to it, and then slipped out of the room, unperceived by the Governor or Captain Wilson.

The fact was, that although Jack had longed to tell the Governor about his adventures after the masquerade, he did not like yet awhile, until he was sure that there were no consequences—because he had given the captain's name instead of his own. As soon as he heard the letter read, he at once perceived that it had been the old lady, and not the priests, who had made the inquiry, and that by giving Captain Wilson's name he had obtained for him this fine legacy. Jack was delighted, but still puzzled, so he walked out of the room to reflect a little.

"What can it mean?" said Captain Wilson. "I never rendered any services to any one on the 12th of August or after it. It is some mistake—12th of August—that was the day of the grand masquerade."

"A lucky one for you, at all events—for you know, mistake or not, no one else can touch the legacy. It can only be paid to you."

"I never heard of anything taking place at the masquerade—I was there, but I left early, for I was not very well. Mr Easy," said Captain Wilson, turning round, but Jack was gone.

"Was he at the masquerade?" asked the Governor.

"Yes, I know he was, for the first lieutenant told me that he requested not to come on board till the next day."

"Depend upon it," replied the Governor, striking his fist upon the table, "that Jack's at the bottom of it."

"I should not be surprised at his being at the bottom of anything," replied Captain Wilson, laughing.

"Leave it to me, Wilson, I'll find it out."

After a little more conversation, Captain Wilson went on board, leaving Jack on purpose that the Governor might pump him. But this Sir Thomas had no occasion to do, for Jack had made up his mind to make the Governor his confidant, and he immediately told him the whole story. The Governor held his sides at our hero's description, especially at his ruse of giving the captain's name instead of his own.

"You'll kill me, Jack, before you've done with me," said old Tom, at last; "but now what is to be done?"

Our hero now became grave; he pointed out to the Governor that he himself had plenty of money, and would come into a large fortune, and that Captain Wilson was poor, with a large family. All Jack wished the Governor to manage was, that Captain Wilson might consent to accept the legacy.

"Right, boy, right! you're my own boy," replied the Governor; "but we must think of this, for Wilson is the very soul of honour, and there may be some difficulty about it. You have told nobody?"

"Not a soul but you, Sir Thomas."

"It never will do to tell him all this, Jack, for he would insist that the legacy belonged to you."

"I have it, sir," replied Jack. "When I was going into the masquerade, I offered to hand this very old lady, who was covered with diamonds, out of her carriage, and she was so frightened at my dress of a devil, that she would have fallen down had it not been for Captain Wilson, who supported her, and she was very thankful to him."

"You are right, Jack," replied the Governor, after a short pause; "that will, I think, do. I must tell him the story of the friars, because I swore you had something to do with it—but I'll tell him no more: leave it all to me."

Captain Wilson returned in the afternoon, and found the Governor in the veranda.

"I have had some talk with young Easy," said the Governor, "and he has told me a strange story about that night, which he was afraid to tell to everybody."

The Governor then narrated the history of the friars and the will.

"Well, but," observed Captain Wilson, "the history of that will afford no clue to the legacy."

"No, it does not; but still, as I said, Jack had a hand in this. He frightened the old lady as a devil, and you caught her in your arms and saved her from falling, so he had a hand in it, you see."

"I do now remember that I did save a very dowager-like old personage from falling at the sight of a devil, who, of course, must have been our friend Easy."

"Well, and that accounts for the whole of it."

"A thousand doubloons for picking up an old lady!"

"Yes, why not?—have you not heard of a man having a fortune left him for merely opening the pew-door of a church to an old gentleman?"

"Yes, but it appears so strange."

"There's nothing strange in this world, Wilson, nothing at all—we may slave for years and get no reward, and do a trifle out of politeness and become independent. In my opinion, this mystery is unravelled. The old lady, for I knew the family, must have died immensely rich: she knew you in your full uniform, and she asked your name; a heavy fall would have been to one so fat a most serious affair; you saved her, and she has rewarded you handsomely."

"Well," replied Captain Wilson, "as I can give no other explanation, I suppose yours is the correct one; but it's hardly fair to take a thousand doubloons from her relations merely for an act of civility."

"You really are quite ridiculous; the old lady owned half Murcia, to my knowledge. It is no more to them than any one leaving you a suit of mourning in an English legacy. I wish you joy; it will help you with a large family, and in justice to them you are bound to take it. Everybody does as he pleases with his own money,—depend upon it, you saved her from breaking her leg short off at the hip joint."

"Upon that supposition I presume I must accept of the legacy," replied Captain Wilson, laughing.

"Of course, send for it at once. The rate of exchange is now high. I will give you government bills, which will make it nearly four thousand pounds."

"Four thousand pounds for preventing an old woman from falling," replied Captain Wilson.

"Devilish well paid, Wilson, and I congratulate you."

"For how much am I indebted to the father of young Easy!" observed Captain Wilson, after a silence of some minutes; "if he had not assisted me when I was appointed to a ship, I should not have gained my promotion—nor three thousand pounds I have made in prize-money—the command of a fine frigate—and now four thousand pounds in a windfall."

The Governor thought that he was more indebted to Jack than to his father for some of these advantages, but he was careful not to point them out.

"It's very true," observed the Governor, "that Mr Easy was of service to you when you were appointed; but allow me to observe that for your ship, your prize-money, and for your windfall, you have been wholly indebted to your own gallantry in both senses of the word; still Mr Easy is a fine generous fellow, and so is his son, I can tell you. By-the-bye, I had a long conversation with him the other day."

"About himself?"

"Yes, all about himself. He appears to me to have come into the service without any particular motive, and will be just as likely to leave it in the same way. He appears to be very much in love with that Sicilian nobleman's daughter. I find that he has written to her, and to her brother, since he has been here."

"That he came into the service in search of what he never will find in this world, I know very well; and I presume that he has found that out—and that he will follow up the service is also very doubtful; but I do not wish that he should leave it yet; it is doing him great good," replied Captain Wilson.

"I agree with you there—I have great influence with him, and he shall stay yet awhile. He is heir to a very large fortune, is he not?"

"A clear eight thousand pounds a year, if not more."

"If his father dies he must, of course, leave: a midshipman with eight thousand pounds a year would indeed be an anomaly."

"That the service could not permit. It would be as injurious to himself as it would to others about him. At present, he has almost, indeed I may say quite, an unlimited command of money."

"That's bad, very bad. I wonder he behaves so well as he does."

"And so do I: but he really is a very superior lad, with all his peculiarities, and a general favourite with those whose opinions and friendship are worth having."

"Well, don't curb him up too tight—for really he does not require it. He goes very well in a snaffle."

Chapter Twenty Eight.

"Philosophy made easy" upon agrarian principles, the subject of some uneasiness to our hero—the first appearance, but not the last, of an important personage.

The conversation was here interrupted by a mail from England which they had been expecting. Captain Wilson retired with his letters; the Governor remained equally occupied; and our hero received the first letter ever written to him by his father. It ran as follows:—

"***My Dear Son***:—

"I have many times taken up my pen with the intention of letting you know how things went on in this country. But as I can perceive around but one dark horizon of evil, I have as often laid it down again without venturing to make you unhappy with such bad intelligence.

"The account of your death, and also of your unexpectedly being yet spared to us, were duly received, and I trust, I mourned and rejoiced on each occasion with all the moderation characteristic of a philosopher. In the first instance I consoled myself with the reflection that the world you had left was in a state of slavery and pressed down by the iron arm of despotism, and that to die was gain, not only in all the parson tells us, but also in our liberty; and, at the second intelligence, I moderated my joy for nearly about the same reasons, resolving, notwithstanding what Dr Middleton may say, to die as I have lived, a true philosopher.

"The more I reflect the more am I convinced that there is nothing required to make this world happy but equality, and the rights of man being duly observed—in short, that everything and everybody should be reduced to one level. Do we not observe that it is the law of nature—do not brooks run into rivers—rivers into seas—mountains crumble down upon the plains?—are not the seasons contented to equalise the parts of the earth? Why does the sun run round the ecliptic, instead of the equator, but to give an equal share of his heat to both sides of the world? Are we not all equally born in misery? does not death level us all *aequo pede*, as the poet hath? are we not all equally hungry, thirsty, and sleepy, and thus levelled by our natural wants? And such being the case, ought we not to have our equal share of good things in this world, to which we have an undoubted equal right? Can any argument be more solid or more level than this, whatever nonsense Dr Middleton may talk?

"Yes, my son, if it were not that I still hope to see the sun of Justice arise, and disperse the manifold dark clouds which obscure the land—if I did not still hope, in my time, to see an equal distribution of property—an Agrarian law passed by the House of Commons, in which all should benefit alike—I would not care how soon I left this vale of tears, created by tyranny and injustice. At present, the same system is carried on; the nation is taxed for the benefit of the few, and it groans under oppression and despotism; but I still do think that there is, if I may fortunately express myself, a bright star in the west; and signs of the times which comfort me. Already we have had a good deal of incendiarism about the country, and some of the highest aristocracy have pledged themselves to raise the people above themselves, and have advised sedition and conspiracy; have shown to the debased and unenlightened multitude that their force is physically irresistible, and recommended them to make use of it, promising that if they hold in power, they will only use that power to the abolition of our farce of a constitution, of a church, and of a king; and that if the nation is to be governed at all, it shall only be governed by the many. This is cheering. Hail, patriot lords! all hail! I am in hopes yet the great work will be achieved, in spite of the laughs and sneers and shakes of the head which my arguments still meet with from that obstinate fellow Dr Middleton.

"Your mother is in a quiet way; she has given over reading and working, and even her knitting, as useless; and she now sits all day long at the chimney corner twiddling her thumbs, and waiting, as she says, for the millennium. Poor thing! she is very foolish with her ideas upon this matter, but as usual I let her have her own way in every thing, copying the philosopher of old, who was tied to his Xantippe.

"I trust, my dear son, that your principles have strengthened with your years and fortified with your growth, and that, if necessary, you will sacrifice all to obtain what in my opinion will prove to be the real millennium. Make all the converts you can, and believe me to be, your affectionate father and true guide:—

"*Nicodemus Easy*."

Jack, who was alone, shook his head as he read this letter, and then laid it down with a pish! He did it involuntarily, and was surprised at himself when he found that he had so done. "I should like to argue the point," thought Jack, in spite of himself; and then he threw the letter on the table, and went into Gascoigne's room, displeased with his father and with himself. He asked Ned whether he had received any letters from England, and it being dinner-time, went back to dress. On his coming down into the receiving-room with Gascoigne, the Governor said to them:

"As you two both speak Italian, you must take charge of a Sicilian officer who has come here with letters of introduction to me, and who dines here to-day."

Before dinner they were introduced to the party in question, a slight-made, well-looking young man, but still there was an expression in his countenance which was not agreeable. In compliance with the wishes of the Governor, Don Mathias, for so he was called, was placed between our two midshipmen, who immediately entered into conversation with him, being themselves anxious to make inquiries about their friends at Palermo. In the course of conversation Jack inquired of him whether he was acquainted with Don Rebiera, to which the Sicilian answered in the affirmative, and they talked about the different members of the family. Don Mathias, towards the close of the dinner, inquired of Jack by what means he had become acquainted with Don Rebiera, and Jack, in reply, narrated how he and his friend Gascoigne had saved him from being murdered by two villains; after this reply the young officer appeared to be less inclined for conversation, but before the party broke up requested to have the acquaintance of our two midshipmen. As soon as he was gone, Gascoigne observed in a reflective way, "I have seen that face before, but where I cannot exactly say; but you know, Jack, what a memory of people I have, and I have seen him before, I am sure."

"I can't recollect that ever I have," replied our hero, "but I never knew any one who could recollect in that way as you do."

The conversation was then dropped between them, and Jack was for some time listening to the Governor and Captain Wilson, for the whole party were gone away, when Gascoigne, who had been in deep thought since he had made the observation to Jack, sprang up.

"I have him at last!" cried he.

"Have who?" demanded Captain Wilson.

"That Sicilian officer—I could have sworn that I had seen him before."

"That Don Mathias?"

"No, Sir Thomas! He is not Don Mathias! He is the very Don Silvio who was murdering Don Rebiera, when we came to his assistance and saved him."

"I do believe you are right, Gascoigne."

"I'm positive of it," replied Gascoigne; "I never made a mistake in my life."

"Bring me those letters, Easy," said the Governor, "and let us see what they say of him. Here it is—Don Mathias de Alayeres. You may be mistaken, Gascoigne; it's a heavy charge you are making against this young man."

"Well, Sir Thomas, if that is not Don Silvio, I'd forfeit my commission if I had it here in my hand. Besides, I observed the change in his countenance when we told him it was Easy and I who had come to Don Rebiera's assistance; and did you observe after that, Easy, that he hardly said a word?"

"Very true," replied Jack.

"Well, well, we must see to this," observed the Governor; "if so, this letter of introduction must be a forgery."

The party then retired to bed, and the next morning, while Easy was in Gascoigne's room talking over their suspicions, letters from Palermo were brought up to him. They were in answer to those written by Jack on his arrival at Malta: a few lines from Don Rebiera, a small note from Agnes, and a voluminous detail from his friend Don Philip, who informed him of the good health of all parties and of their good-will towards him; of Agnes being as partial as ever; of his having spoken plainly, as he had promised Jack, to his father and mother relative to the mutual attachment; of their consent being given, and then withheld, because Father Thomas, their confessor, would not listen to the union of Agnes with a heretic; but, nevertheless, telling Jack this would be got over through the medium of his brother and himself, who were determined that their sister and he should not be made unhappy about such a trifle. But the latter part of the letter contained intelligence equally important, which was, that Don Silvio had again attempted the life of their father, and would have succeeded, had not Father Thomas, who happened to be there, thrown himself between them. That Don Silvio in his rage had actually stabbed the confessor, although the wound was not dangerous. That, in consequence of this, all further lenity was denied to him, and that the authorities were in search of him to award him the punishment due to murder and sacrilege. That up to the present they could not find him, and it was supposed that he had made his escape to Malta in one of the speronares.

Such were the contents of the letter, which were immediately communicated to the Governor and Captain Wilson, upon their meeting at breakfast.

"Very well, we must see to this," observed the Governor, who then made his inquiries as to the other intelligence contained in the letters.

Jack and Gascoigne were uneasy till the breakfast was over, when they made their escape: a few moments afterwards Captain Wilson rose to go on board, and sent for them, but they were not to be found.

"I understand it all, Wilson," said the Governor; "leave them to me; go on board and make yourself quite easy."

In the meantime our two midshipmen had taken their hats and walked away to the parapet of the battery, where they would not be interrupted.

"Now, Gascoigne," observed Jack, "you guess what I'm about—I must shoot that rascal this very morning, and that's why I came out with you."

"But, Easy, the only difference is this, that I must shoot him, and not you; he is my property, for I found him out."

"We'll argue that point," replied Jack: "he has attempted the life of my is-to-be, please God, father-in-law, and therefore I have the best claim to him."

"I beg your pardon, Jack, he is mine, for I discovered him. Now let me put a case: suppose one man walking several yards before another, picks up a purse, what claim has the other to it? I found him, and not you."

"That's all very well, Gascoigne; but suppose the purse you picked up to be mine, then I have a right to it, although you found it; he is my bird by right, and not yours."

"But I have another observation to make, which is very important: he is a blood relation of Agnes, and if his blood is on your hands, however much he may deserve it, depend upon it, it will be raised as an obstacle to your union; think of that."

Jack paused in thought.

"And let me induce you by another remark—you will confer on me a most particular favour."

"It will be the greatest I ever could," replied Jack, "and you ought to be eternally indebted to me."

"I trust to make him *eternally* indebted to me," replied Gascoigne.

Sailors, if going into action, always begin to reckon what their share of their prize-money may be, before a shot is fired—our two midshipmen appear in this instance to be doing the same.

The point having been conceded to Gascoigne, Jack went to the inn where Don Silvio had mentioned that he had taken up his quarters, and sending up his card, followed the waiter upstairs. The waiter opened the door, and presented the card.

"Very well," replied Don Silvio, "you can go down and show him up."

Jack, hearing these words, did not wait, but walked in, where he found Don Silvio very busy removing a hone upon which he had been whetting a sharp double-edged stiletto. The Sicilian walked up to him, offering his hand with apparent cordiality; but Jack with a look of defiance said, "Don Silvio, we know you; my object now is to demand, on the part of my friend, the satisfaction which you do not deserve, but which our indignation at your second attempt upon Don Rebiera induces us to offer; for if you escape from him you will have to do with me. On the whole, Don Silvio, you may think yourself fortunate, for it is better to die by the hands of a gentleman than by the gibbet."

Don Silvio turned deadly pale—his hand sought his stiletto in his bosom, but it was remaining on the table; at last he replied, "Be it so—I will meet you when and where you please, in an hour from this."

Jack mentioned the place of meeting, and then walked out of the room. He and Gascoigne then hastened to the quarters of an officer they were intimate with, and having provided themselves with the necessary fire-arms, were at the spot before the time. They waited for him till the exact time, yet no Don Silvio made his appearance.

"He's off," observed Gascoigne; "the villain has escaped us."

Half an hour over the time had passed, and still there was no sign of Gascoigne's antagonist, but one of the Governor's aides-de-camp was seen walking up to them.

"Here's Atkins," observed Jack; "that's unlucky, but he won't interfere."

"Gentlemen," said Atkins, taking off his hat with much solemnity, "the Governor particularly wishes to speak to you both."

"We can't come just now—we'll be there in half an hour."

"You must be there in three minutes, both of you. Excuse me, my orders are positive—and to see them duly executed I have a corporal and a file of men behind that wall—of course, if you walk with me quietly there will be no occasion to send for their assistance."

"This is confounded tyranny," cried Jack. "Well may they call him King Tom."

"Yes," replied Atkins, "and he governs here *in rey absoluto*—so come along."

Jack and Gascoigne, having no choice, walked up to the government-house, where they found Sir Thomas in the veranda, which commanded a view of the harbour and offing.

"Come here, young gentlemen," said the Governor, in a severe tone; "do you see that vessel about two miles clear of the port? Don Silvio is in it, going back to Sicily under a guard. And now remember what I say as a maxim through life. Fight with gentlemen, if you must fight, but not with villains and murderers. By *consenting* to fight with a *blackguard*, you as much disparage your cloth and compromise your own characters, as by refusing to give satisfaction to a *gentleman*. There, go away, for I'm angry with you, and don't let me see you till dinner-time."

Chapter Twenty Nine.

In which our hero sees a little more service, and is better employed than in fighting Don Silvio.

But before they met the Governor at his table, a sloop-of-war arrived from the fleet with despatches from the Commander-in-Chief. Those to Captain Wilson required him to make all possible haste in fitting, and then to proceed and cruise off Corsica, to fall in with a Russian frigate which was on that coast; if not there, to obtain intelligence, and to follow her wherever she might be.

All was now bustle and activity on board of the *Aurora*. Captain Wilson, with our hero and Gascoigne, quitted the Governor's house and repaired on board, where they remained day and night. On the third day the *Aurora* was complete and ready for sea, and about noon sailed out of Valette harbour.

In a week the *Aurora* had gained the coast of Corsica, and there was no need of sending look-out men to the mast-head, for one of the officers or midshipmen was there from daylight to dark. She ran up the coast to the northward without seeing the object of her pursuit, or obtaining any intelligence.

Calms and light airs detained them for a few days, when a northerly breeze enabled them to run down the eastern side of the island. It was on the eighteenth day after they had quitted Malta that a large vessel was seen ahead about eighteen miles off. The men were then at breakfast.

"A frigate, Captain Wilson, I'm sure of it," said Mr Hawkins the chaplain, whose anxiety induced him to go to the mast-head.

"How is she steering?"

"The same way as we are."

The *Aurora* was under all possible sail, and when the hands were piped to dinner, it was thought that they had neared the chase about two miles.

"This will be a long chase; a stern chase always is," observed Martin to Gascoigne.

"Yes, I'm afraid so—but I'm more afraid of her escaping."

"That's not unlikely either," replied the mate.

"You are one of Job's Comforters, Martin," replied Gascoigne.

"Then I'm not so often disappointed," replied the mate. "There are two points to be ascertained; the first is, whether we shall come up with the vessel or lose her—the next is, if we do come up with her, whether she is the vessel we are looking for."

"You seem very indifferent about it."

"Indeed I am not: I am the oldest passed midshipman in the ship, and the taking of the frigate will, if I live, give me my promotion, and if I'm killed, I shan't want it. But I've been so often disappointed, that I now make sure of nothing until I have it."

"Well, for your sake, Martin, I will still hope that the vessel is the one we seek, that we shall not be killed, and that you will gain your promotion."

"I thank you, Easy—I wish I was one that dared hope as you do."

Poor Martin! he had long felt how bitter it was to meet disappointment upon disappointment. How true it is that hope deferred maketh the heart sick! and his anticipations of early days, the buoyant calculations of youth, had been one by one crushed, and now, having served his time nearly three times over, the reaction had become too painful, and, as he truly said, he dared not hope: still his temper was not soured but chastened.

"She has hauled her wind, sir," hailed the second-lieutenant from the topmast cross-trees.

"What think you of that, Martin?" observed Jack.

"Either that she is an English frigate, or that she is a vessel commanded by a very brave fellow, and well manned."

It was sunset before the *Aurora* had arrived within two miles of the vessel; the private signal had been thrown out, but had not been answered, either because it was too dark to make out the colours of the flags, or that these were unknown to an enemy. The stranger had hoisted the English colours, but that was no satisfactory proof of her being a friend; and just before dark she had put her head towards the *Aurora*, who had now come stem down to her. The ship's company of the *Aurora* were all at their quarters, as a few minutes would now decide whether they had to deal with a friend or a foe.

There is no situation perhaps more difficult, and demanding so much caution, as the occasional meeting with a doubtful ship. On the one hand, it being necessary to be fully prepared and not allow the enemy the advantage which may be derived from your inaction; and on the other, the necessity of prudence, that you may not assault your friends and countrymen. Captain Wilson had hoisted the private night-signal, but here again it was difficult, from his sails intervening, for the other ship to make it out. Before the two frigates were within three cables length of each other, Captain Wilson, determined that there should be no mistake from any want of precaution on his part, hauled up his courses and brailed up his driver that the night-signal might be clearly seen.

Lights were seen abaft on the quarter-deck of the other vessel, as if they were about to answer, but she continued to keep the *Aurora* to leeward at about half a cable's length, and as the foremost guns of each vessel were abreast of each other, hailed in English—

"Ship ahoy; what ship's that?"

"His Majesty's ship *Aurora*," replied Captain Wilson, who stood on the hammocks. "What ship's that?"

By this time the other frigate had passed half her length clear of the beam of the *Aurora*, and at the same time that a pretended reply of "His Majesty's ship—" was heard, a broadside from her guns, which had been trained aft on purpose, was poured into the *Aurora* and, at so short a distance, doing considerable execution. The crew of the *Aurora*, hearing the hailing in English, and the vessel passing them apparently without firing, had imagined that she had been one of their own cruisers. The captains of the guns had dropped their lanyards in disappointment, and the silence which had been maintained as the two vessels met was just breaking up in various ways of lamentation at their bad luck, when the broadside was poured in, thundering in their ears, and the ripping and tearing of the beams and planks astonished their senses. Many were carried down below, but it was difficult to say whether indignation at the enemy's ruse, or satisfaction at discovering that they were not called to quarters in vain, most predominated. At all events it was answered by three voluntary cheers, which drowned the cries of those who were being assisted to the cockpit.

"Man the larboard-guns and about ship!" cried Captain Wilson, leaping off the hammocks. "Look out, my lads, and rake her in stays! We'll pay him off for that foul play before we've done with him. Look out, my lads, and take good aim as she pays round."

The *Aurora* was put about, and her broadside poured into the stern of the Russian frigate—for such she was. It was almost dark, but the enemy, who appeared as anxious as the *Aurora* to come to action, hauled up her courses to await her coming up. In five minutes the two vessels were alongside exchanging murderous broadsides at little more than pistol-shot—running slowly in for the land, than not more than five miles distant. The skin-clad mountaineers of Corsica were aroused by the furious cannonading, watching the incessant flashes of the guns, and listening to their reverberating roar.

After half an hour's fierce combat, during which the fire of both vessels was kept up with undiminished vigour, Captain Wilson went down on the main deck, and himself separately pointed each gun after it was loaded; those amidships being direct for the main-channels of the enemy's ship, while those abaft the beam were gradually trained more and more forward, and those before the beam more and more aft, so as to throw all their shot nearly into one focus, giving directions that they were all to be fired at once, at the word of command. The enemy, not aware of the cause of the delay, imagined that the fire of the *Aurora* had slackened, and loudly cheered. At the word given the broadside was poured in, and, dark as it was, the effects from it were evident. Two of the midship ports of the antagonist were blown into one, and her main-mast was seen to totter, and then to fall over the side. The *Aurora* then set her courses, which had been hauled up, and, shooting ahead, took up a raking position while the Russian was still hampered with her wreck, and poured in grape and cannister from her upper deck carronades to impede their labours on deck, while she continued her destructive fire upon the hull of the enemy from the main-deck battery.

The moon now burst out from a low bank of clouds, and enabled them to accomplish their work with more precision. In a quarter of an hour the Russian was totally dismasted, and Captain Wilson ordered half of his remaining ship's company to repair the damages, which had been most severe, whilst the larboard men at quarters continued the fire from the main deck. The enemy continued to return the fire from four guns, two on each of her decks, which she could still make bear upon the *Aurora*; but after some time even these ceased, either from the men having deserted them, or from their being dismounted. Observing that the fire from her antagonist had ceased, the *Aurora* also discontinued, and the jolly-boat astern being still uninjured, the second lieutenant was deputed to pull alongside of the frigate to ascertain if she had struck.

The beams of the bright moon silvered the rippling water as the boat shoved off; and Captain Wilson and his officers who were still unhurt, leant over the shattered sides of the *Aurora*, waiting for a reply: suddenly the silence of the night was broken upon by a loud splash from the bows of the Russian frigate, then about three cables' length distant.

"What could that be?" cried Captain Wilson. "Her anchor's down. Mr Jones, a lead over the side, and see what water we have."

Mr Jones had long been carried down below, severed in two with a round shot—but a man leaped into the chains, and lowering down the lead, sounded in seven fathoms.

"Then I suspect he will give us more trouble yet," observed Captain Wilson; and so indeed it proved, for the Russian captain, in reply to the second lieutenant, had told him in English, "that he would answer that question with his broadside," and before the boat was dropped astern, he had warped round with the springs on his cable, and had recommenced his fire upon the *Aurora*.

Captain Wilson made sail upon his ship, and sailed round and round the anchored vessel, so as to give her two broadsides to her one, and from the slowness with which she worked at her springs upon her cables, it was evident that she must be now very weak-handed. Still the pertinacity and decided courage of the Russian captain convinced Captain Wilson that, in all probability, he would sink at his anchor before he would haul down his colours; and not only would he lose more of the *Aurora's* men, but also the Russian vessel, without he took a more decided step. Captain Wilson, therefore, resolved to try her by the board. Having poured in a raking fire, he stood off for a few moments, during which he called the officers and men on deck, and stated his intention. He then went about, and himself conning the *Aurora*, ran her on board the Russian, pouring in his reserved broadside as the vessels came into collision, and heading his men as they leaped on the enemy's decks.

Although, as Captain Wilson had imagined, the Russian frigate had not many men to oppose to the *Aurora's*, the deck was obstinately defended, the voice and the arm of the Russian captain were to be heard and seen everywhere, and his men, encouraged by him, were cut down by numbers where they stood.

Our hero, who had the good fortune to be still unhurt, was for a little while close to Captain Wilson when he boarded, and was about to oppose his unequal force against that of the Russian captain, when he was pulled back by the collar by Mr Hawkins, the chaplain, who rushed in advance with a sabre in his hand. The opponents were well matched, and it may be said that, with little interruption, a hand-to-hand conflict ensued, for the moon lighted up the scene of carnage, and they were well able to distinguish each other's faces. At last, the chaplain's sword broke; he rushed in, drove the hilt into his antagonist's face, closed with him, and they both fell down the hatchway together. After this, the deck was gained, or rather cleared, by the crew of the *Aurora*, for few could be said to have resisted, and in a minute or two the frigate was in their possession. The chaplain and the Russian captain were hoisted up, still clinging to each other, both senseless from the fall, but neither of them dead; although bleeding from several wounds.

As soon as the main-deck had been cleared, Captain Wilson ordered the hatches to be put on, and left a party on board while he hastened to attend to the condition of his own ship and ship's company.

It was daylight before anything like order had been restored to the decks of the *Aurora*; the water was still smooth, and instead of letting go her own anchor, she had hung on with a hawser to the prize, but her sails had been furled, her decks cleared, guns secured, and the buckets were dashing away the blood from her planks and the carriages of the guns, when the sun rose and shone upon them. The numerous wounded had, by this time, been put into their hammocks, although there were still one or two cases of amputation to be performed.

The carpenter had repaired all shot-holes under or too near to the water-line, and then had proceeded to sound the well of the prize; but although her upper works had been dreadfully shattered, there was no reason to suppose that she had received any serious injury below, and therefore the hatches still remained on, although a few hands were put to the pumps to try if she made any water. It was not until the *Aurora* presented a more cheerful appearance that Captain Wilson went over to the other ship, whose deck, now that the light of heaven enabled them to witness all the horrors even to minuteness, presented a shocking spectacle of blood and carnage. Body after body was thrown over; the wounded were supplied with water and such assistance as could be rendered until the surgeons could attend them; the hatches were then taken off, and the remainder of her crew ordered on deck; about two hundred obeyed the summons, but the lower deck was as crowded with killed and wounded as was the upper. For the present the prisoners were handed over down into the forehold of the *Aurora*, which had been prepared for their reception, and the work of separation of the dead from the living then underwent. After this such repairs as were immediately necessary were made, and a portion of the *Aurora's* crew, under the orders of the second lieutenant, were sent on board to take charge of her. It was not till the evening of the day after this night-conflict that the *Aurora* was in a situation to make sail. All hands were then sent on board of the *Trident*, for such was the name of the Russian frigate, to fit her out as soon as possible. Before morning—for there was no relaxation from their fatigue, nor was there any wish for it—all was completed, and the two frigates, although in a shattered condition, were prepared to meet any common conflict with the elements. The *Aurora* made sail with the *Trident* in tow; the hammocks were allowed to be taken down, and the watch below permitted to repose.

In this murderous conflict the *Trident* had more than two hundred men killed and wounded. The *Aurora's* loss had not been so great, but still it was severe, having lost sixty-five men and officers. Among the fallen there were Mr Jones the master, the third lieutenant Mr Awkwright, and two midshipmen killed. Mr Pottyfar, the first lieutenant, severely wounded at the commencement of the action. Martin, the master's mate, and Gascoigne, the first mortally, and the second badly, wounded. Our hero had also received a slight cutlass wound, which obliged him to wear his arm, for a short time, in a sling.

Among the ship's company who were wounded was Mesty: he had been hurt with a splinter before the *Trident* was taken by the board, but had remained on deck, and had followed our hero, watching over him and protecting him as a father. He had done even more, for he had with Jack thrown himself before Captain Wilson, at a time that he had received such a blow with the flat of a sword as to stun him and bring him down on his knee. And Jack had taken good care that Captain Wilson should not be ignorant, as he really would have been, of this timely service on the part of Mesty, who certainly, although with a great deal of *sang-froid* in his composition when in repose, was a fiend incarnate when his blood was up.

"But you must have been with Mesty," observed Captain Wilson, "when he did me the service."

"I was with him, sir," replied Jack, with great modesty, "but was of very little service."

"How is your friend Gascoigne this evening?"

"Oh, not very bad, sir—he wants a glass of grog."

"And Mr Martin?"

Jack shook his head.

"Why, the surgeon thinks he will do well."

"Yes, sir, and so I told Martin; but he said that it was very well to give him hope—but that he thought otherwise."

"You must manage him, Mr Easy; tell him that he is sure of his promotion."

"I have, sir, but he won't believe it. He never will believe it till he has his commission signed. I really think that an acting order would do more than the doctor can."

"Well, Mr Easy, he shall have one to-morrow morning. Have you seen Mr Pottyfar? He, I am afraid, is very bad."

"Very bad, sir; and, they say, is worse every day, and yet his wound is healthy, and ought to be doing well."

Such was the conversation between Jack and his captain, as they sat at breakfast on the third morning after the action.

The next day Easy took down an acting order for Martin, and put it into his hands. The mate read it over as he lay bandaged in his hammock.

"It's only an acting order, Jack," said he; "it may not be confirmed."

Jack swore, by all the articles of war, that it would be; but Martin replied that he was sure it never would.

"No, no," said the mate, "I knew very well that I never should be made. If it is not confirmed, I may live; but if it is, I am sure to die."

Every one that went to Martin's hammock wished him joy of his promotion; but six days after the action poor Martin's remains were consigned to the deep.

The next person who followed him was Mr Pottyfar, the first lieutenant, who had contrived, wounded as he was, to reach a packet of the universal medicine, and had taken so many bottles before he was found out, that he was one morning found dead in his bed, with more than two dozen empty phials under his pillow, and by the side of his mattress. He was not buried with his hands in his pockets, but when sewed up in his hammock, they were, at all events, laid in the right position.

Chapter Thirty.

Modern philanthropy which, as usual, is the cause of much trouble and vexation.

In three weeks the *Aurora*, with her prize in tow, arrived at Malta. The wounded were sent to the hospital, and the gallant Russian captain recovered from his wounds about the same time as Mr Hawkins, the chaplain.

Jack, who constantly called to see the chaplain, had a great deal to do to console him. He would shake his hands as he lay in his bed, exclaiming against himself. "Oh," Would he say, "the spirit is willing, but the flesh is weak. That I, a man of God, as they term me, who ought to have been down with the surgeons, whispering comfort to the desponding, should have gone on deck (but I could not help it), and have mixed in such a scene of slaughter! What will become of me?"

Jack attempted to console him by pointing out that not only chaplains but bishops have been known to fight in armour from time immemorial. But Mr Hawkins's recovery was long doubtful, from the agitation of his mind. When he was able to walk, Jack introduced to him the Russian captain, who was also just out of his bed.

"I am most happy to embrace so gallant an officer," said the Russian, who recognised his antagonist, throwing his arms round the chaplain, and giving him a kiss on both cheeks. "What is his rank?" continued he, addressing himself to Jack, who replied, very quietly, "that he was the ship's padre."

"The padre!" replied the captain, with surprise, as Hawkins turned away with confusion. "The padre—par exemple! Well, I always had a great respect for the church. Pray sir," said he, turning to Easy, "do your padres always head your boarders?"

"Always, sir," replied Jack; "it's a rule of the service—and the duty of a padre to show the men the way to heaven. It's our ninety-ninth article of war."

"You are a fighting nation," replied the Russian, bowing to Hawkins, and continuing his walk, not exactly pleased that he had been floored by a parson.

Mr Hawkins continued very disconsolate for some time; he then invalided and applied himself to his duties on shore, where he would not be exposed to such temptations from his former habits.

As the *Aurora*, when she was last at Malta, had nearly exhausted the dockyard for her repairs, she was even longer fitting out this time, during which Captain Wilson's despatches had been received by the admiral, and had been acknowledged by a brig sent to Malta. The admiral, in reply, after complimenting him upon his gallantry and success, desired that, as soon as he was ready, he should proceed to Palermo with communications of importance to the authorities, and having remained there for an answer, was again to return to Malta to pick up such of his men as might be fit to leave the hospital, and then join the Toulon fleet. This intelligence was soon known to our hero, who was in ecstasies at the idea of again seeing Agnes and her brothers. Once more the *Aurora* sailed away from the high-crowned rocks of Valette, and with a fine breeze dashed through the deep blue waves.

But towards the evening the breeze increased, and they were under double-reefed topsails. On the second day they made the coast of Sicily, not far from where Easy and Gascoigne had been driven on shore; the weather was then more moderate, and the sea had, to a great degree, subsided. They therefore stood in close to the coast, as they had not a leading wind to Palermo. As they stood in, the glasses, as usual, were directed to land; observing the villas with which the hills and valleys were studded, with their white fronts embowered in orange groves.

"What is that, Gascoigne," said Easy, "under that precipice?—it looks like a vessel."

Gascoigne turned his glass in the direction—"Yes, it is a vessel on the rocks: by her prow she looks like a galley."

"It is a galley, sir—one of the row galleys—I can make out her bank of oars," observed the signal-man.

This was reported to Captain Wilson, who also examined her.

"She is on the rocks, certainly," observed he; "and I think I see people on board. Keep her away a point, quarter-master."

The *Aurora* was now steered right for the vessel, and in the course of an hour was not more than a mile from her. Their suppositions were correct—it was one of the Sicilian government galleys bilged on the rocks, and they now perceived that there were people on board of her, making signals with their shirts and pieces of linen.

"They must be the galley-slaves; for I perceive that they do not one of them change their positions: the galley must have been abandoned by the officers and seamen, and the slaves left to perish."

"That's very hard," observed Jack to Gascoigne; "they were condemned to the galleys, but not to death."

"They will not have much mercy from the waves," replied Gascoigne; "they will all be in kingdom come to-morrow morning, if the breeze comes more on the land. We have already come up two points this forenoon."

Although Captain Wilson did not join in this conversation, which he overheard as he stood on the forecastle gun, with his glass over the hammocks, it appears he was of the same opinion; but he demurred: he had to choose between allowing so many of his fellow-creatures to perish miserably, or to let loose upon society a set of miscreants, who would again enter a course of crime until they were recaptured, and by so doing probably displease the Sicilian authorities. After some little reflection he resolved that he would take his chance of the latter. The *Aurora* was hove-to in stays, and the two cutters ordered to be lowered down, and the boat's crew to be armed.

"Mr Easy, do you take one cutter and the armourers; pull on board of the galley, release those people, and land them in small divisions. Mr Gascoigne, you will take the other to assist Mr Easy, and when he lands them in his boat, you will pull by his side ready to act, in case of any hostile attempt on the part of the scoundrels; for we must not expect gratitude: of course, land them at the nearest safe spot for debarkation."

In pursuance of these orders, our two midshipmen pulled away to the vessel. They found her fixed hard upon the rocks, which had pierced her slight timbers, and, as they had supposed, the respectable part of her crew, with the commander, had taken to the boats, leaving the galley-slaves to their fate. She pulled fifty oars, but had only thirty-six manned. These oars were forty feet long, and ran in from the thole-pin with a loom six feet long, each manned by four slaves, who were chained to their seat before it, by a running chain made fast by a padlock in amidships. A plank, of two feet wide, ran fore and aft the vessel between the two banks of oars, for the boatswain to apply the lash to those who did not sufficiently exert themselves.

"Viva los Inglesos," cried the galley-slaves, as Easy climbed up over the quarter of the vessel.

"I say, Ned, did you ever see such a precious set of villains?" observed Easy, as he surveyed the faces of the men who were chained.

"No," replied Gascoigne; "and I think if the captain had seen them as we have, that he would have left them where they were."

"I don't know—but however, our orders are positive. Armourer, knock off all the padlocks, beginning aft; when we have a cargo we will land them. How many are there?—twelve dozen; twelve dozen villains to let loose upon society. I have a great mind to go on board again and report my opinion to the captain—one hundred and forty-four villains, who all deserve hanging—for drowning is too good for them."

"Our orders are to liberate them, Jack."

"Yes; but I should like to argue this point with Captain Wilson."

"They'll send after them fast enough, Jack, and they'll all be in limbo again before long," replied Gascoigne.

"Well, I suppose we must obey orders; but it goes against my conscience to save such villainous-looking rascals. Armourer, hammer away."

The armourer, who, with the seamen, appeared very much of Jack's opinion, and had not commenced his work, now struck off the padlocks, one by one, with his sledge-hammer. As soon as they were released the slaves were ordered into the cutter, and when it was sufficiently loaded Jack shoved off, followed by Gascoigne as guard, and landed them at the point about a cable's length distant. It required six trips before they were all landed: the last cargo were on shore, and Easy was desiring the men to shove off, when one of the galleriens turned round, and cried out to Jack in a mocking tone, "Addio signor, a reveder la." Jack started, stared, and in the squalid, naked wretch who addressed him, he recognised Don Silvio!

"I will acquaint Don Rebiera of your arrival, signor," said the miscreant, springing up the rocks, and mixing with the rest, who now commenced hooting and laughing at their preservers.

"Ned," observed Easy to Gascoigne, "we have let that rascal loose."

"More's the pity," replied Gascoigne; "but we have only obeyed orders."

"It can't be helped, but I've a notion there will be some mischief out of this."

"We obeyed orders," replied Gascoigne.

"We've let the rascals loose not ten miles from Don Rebiera's."

"Obeyed orders, Jack."

"With a whole gang to back him, if he goes there."

"Orders, Jack."

"Agnes at his mercy."

"Captain's orders, Jack."

"I shall argue this point when I go on board," replied Jack.

"Too late, Jack."

"Yes," replied Easy, sinking down on the stern sheets with a look of despair.

"Give way, my lads, give way."

Jack returned on board and reported what he had done; also that Don Silvio was among those liberated; and he ventured to mention his fears of what might take place from their contiguity to the house of Don Rebiera. Captain Wilson bit his lips: he felt that his philanthropy had induced him to act without his usual prudence.

"I have done a rash thing, Mr Easy, I am afraid. I should have taken them all on board and delivered them up to the authorities. I wish I had thought of that before. We must get to Palermo as fast as we can, and have the troops sent after these miscreants. Hands 'bout ship, fill the main-yard."

The wind had veered round, and the *Aurora* was now able to lay up clear of the island of Maritimo. The next morning she anchored in Palermo Roads—gave immediate notice to the authorities, who, wishing Captain Wilson's philanthropy at the devil, immediately dispatched a large body of troops in quest of the liberated malefactors. Captain Wilson, feeling for Jack's anxiety about his friends, called him over to him on deck, and gave him and Gascoigne permission to go on shore.

"Will you allow me to take Mesty with me, sir, if you please?" said Jack.

"Yes, Mr Easy: but recollect that, even with Mesty, you are no match for one hundred and fifty men, so be prudent. I send, you to relieve your anxiety, not to run into danger."

"Of course, sir," replied Jack, touching his hat, and walking away quietly till he came to the hatch-way, when he darted down like a shot, and was immediately occupied with his preparations.

In half an hour our two midshipmen, with Mesty, had landed, and proceeded to the inn where they had put up before: they were armed up to the teeth. Their first inquiries were for Don Philip and his brother.

"Both on leave of absence," replied the landlord, "and staying with Don Rebiera."

"That's some comfort," thought Jack. "Now we must get horses as fast as we can.—Mesty, can you ride?"

"By all de power can I ride, Massa Easy; suppose you ride Kentucky horse, you ride anyting."

In half an hour four horses and a guide were procured, and at eight o'clock in the morning the party set off in the direction of Don Rebiera's country-seat.

They had not ridden more than six miles when they came up with one of the detachments sent out in pursuit of the liberated criminals. Our hero recognised the commanding officer as an old acquaintance, and imparting to him the release of Don Silvio, and his fears upon Don Rebiera's account, begged him to direct his attention that way.

"Corpo di Bacco—you are right, Signor Mid," replied the officer, "but Don Philip is there, and his brother too, I believe. I will be there by ten o'clock to-morrow morning; we will march almost the whole night."

"They have no arms," observed Easy.

"No, but they will soon get them: they will go to some small town in a body, plunder it, and then seek the protection of the mountains. Your captain has given us a pretty job."

Jack exchanged a few more words, and then, excusing himself on account of his haste, put the spurs to his horse and regained his own party, who now proceeded at a rapid pace.

"O Signor!" said the guide, "we shall kill the horses."

"I'll pay for them," said Jack.

"Yes, but we shall kill them before we get there, Jack," replied Gascoigne, "and have to walk the rest of the way."

"Very true, Ned; let's pull up, and give them their wind."

"By de holy poker, Massa Easy, but my shirt stick to my ribs," cried Mesty, whose black face was hung with dewdrops from their rapid course.

"Never mind, Mesty."

It was about five o'clock in the afternoon when they arrived at the seat of Don Rebiera. Jack threw himself off his jaded steed, and hastened into the house, followed by Gascoigne. They found the whole family collected in the large sitting-room, quite ignorant of any danger threatening them, and equally astonished and pleased at the arrival of their old friends. Jack flew to Agnes, who screamed when she saw him, and felt so giddy afterwards that he was obliged to support her. Having seated her again, he was kindly greeted by the old people and the two young officers. After a few minutes dedicated to mutual inquiries, our hero stated the cause of their expeditious arrival.

"Don Silvio with one hundred and fifty galleriens, let loose on the coast yesterday afternoon!" exclaimed Don Rebiera; "you are right, I only wonder they were not here last night. But I expect Pedro from the town; he has gone down with a load of wine: he will bring us intelligence."

"At all events, we must be prepared," said Don Philip, "the troops you say will be here to-morrow morning."

"Holy Virgin!" exclaimed the ladies in a breath.

"How many can we muster?" said Gascoigne.

"We will have five men here, or we shall have by the evening," replied Don Philip—"all, I think, good men—my father, my brother and myself."

"We are three—four with the guide, whom I know nothing about."

"Twelve in all—not one too many; but I think that now we are prepared, if they attack, we can hold out till the morning."

"Had we not better send the ladies away?" said Jack.

"Who is to escort them?" replied Don Philip; "we shall only weaken our force: besides, they may fall into the miscreants' hands."

"Shall we all leave the house together? they can but plunder it," observed Don Rebiera.

"Still we may be intercepted by them, and our whole force will be nothing against so many," observed Don Philip, "if we are without defence, whereas in the house we shall have an advantage."

"E vero," replied Don Rebiera, thoughtfully; "then let us prepare, for depend upon it Don Silvio will not lose such an opportunity to wreak his vengeance. He will be here to-night: I only wonder he has not been here with his companions before. However, Pedro will arrive in two hours."

"We must now see what means we have of defence," said Philip. "Come, brother—will you come, sir?"

Chapter Thirty One.

A regular set-to, in which the parties beaten are not knocked down, but rise higher and higher at each discomfiture—nothing but the troops could have prevented them from going up to Heaven.

Don Rebiera and his two sons quitted the room, Gascoigne entered into conversation with the senora, while Easy took this opportunity of addressing Agnes. He had been too much occupied with the consultation to pay her much attention before. He had spoken, with his eyes fixed upon her, and had been surprised at the improvement which had taken place in less than a year. He now went to her, and asked her, in a low voice, "whether she had received his letter?"

"Oh, yes!" replied she, colouring.

"And were you angry with what I said, Agnes?" in a low tone.

"No," replied she, casting her eyes down on the floor.

"I repeat now what I said, Agnes—I have never forgotten you."

"But—"

"But what?"

"Father Thomaso."

"What of him?"

"He never will—"

"Will what?"

"You are a heretic," he says.

"Tell him to mind his own business."

"He has great influence with my father and mother."

"Your brothers are on our side."

"I know that, but there will be great difficulty. Our religion is not the same. He must talk to you—he will convert you."

"We'll argue that point, Agnes. I will convert him if he has common sense; if not, it's no use arguing with him. Where is he?"

"He will soon be at home."

"Tell me, Agnes, if you had your own will, would you marry me?"

"I don't know; I have never seen any one I liked so well."

"Is that all?"

"Is it not enough for a maiden to say?" replied Agnes, raising her eyes, and looking reproachfully. "Signor, let me go, here comes my father."

Notwithstanding, Jack cast his eyes to the window where Gascoigne and the senora were in converse, and perceiving that the old lady's back was turned, he pressed Agnes to his bosom before he released her. The gentlemen then returned with all the fire-arms and destructive weapons they could collect.

"We have enough," observed Don Philip, "to arm all the people we have with us."

"And we are all well armed," replied Jack, who had left Agnes standing alone. "What now are your plans?"

"Those we must now consult about. It appears"—but at this moment the conversation was interrupted by the sudden entrance of Pedro, who had been despatched to the town with the load of wine. He rushed in, flurried and heated, with his red cap in his hand.

"How now, Pedro, back so early!"

"O signor!" exclaimed the man—"they have taken the cart and the wine, and have drawn it away up to the mountains."

"Who?" inquired Don Rebiera.

"The galley-slaves who have been let loose—and by the body of our blessed saint, they have done pretty mischief—they have broken into the houses, robbed everything—murdered many—clothed themselves with the best—collected all the arms, provisions, and wine they could lay their hands on, and have marched away into the mountains. This took place last night. As I was coming down within a mile of the town, they met me with my loaded cart, and they turned the bullocks round and drove them away along with the rest. By the blessed Virgin! but they are stained with blood, but not altogether of men, for they have cut up some of the oxen. I heard this from one of the herdsmen, but he too fled and could not tell me more. But, signor, I heard them mention your name."

"I have no doubt of it," replied Don Rebiera. "As for the wine, I only hope they will drink too much of it to-night. But, Pedro, they will be here, and we must defend ourselves—so call the men together; I must speak to them."

"We shall never see the bullocks again," observed Pedro mournfully.

"No; but we shall never see one another again, if we do not take care. I have information they come here to-night."

"Holy Saint Francis! and they say there are a thousand of them."

"Not quite so many, to my knowledge," observed Jack.

"They told me that a great many were killed in their attack upon the town, before they mastered it."

"So much the better. Go now, Pedro, drink a cup of wine, and then call the other men."

The house was barricaded as well as circumstances would permit; the first story was also made a fortress by loading the landing-place with armoires and chests of drawers. The upper story, or attic, if it might be so called, was defended in the same way, that they might retreat from one to the other if the doors were forced.

It was eight o'clock in the evening before all was ready, and they were still occupied with the last defence, under the superintendence of Mesty, who showed himself an able engineer, when they heard the sound of an approaching multitude. They looked out of one of the windows and perceived the house surrounded by the galley-slaves, in number, apparently, about a hundred. They were all dressed in a most fantastic manner with whatever they could pick up: some had fire-arms, but the most of them were supplied with only swords or knives. With them came also their cortège of plunder: carts of various descriptions, loaded with provisions of all sorts, and wine; women lashed down with ropes, sails from the vessels and boats to supply them with covering in the mountains, hay and straw and mattresses. Their plunder appeared to be well chosen for their exigencies. To the carts were tied a variety of cattle, intended to accompany them to their retreat. They all appeared to be under a leader, who was issuing directions—that leader was soon recognised by those in the house to be Don Silvio.

"Massa Easy, you show me dat man?" said Mesty, when he heard the conversation between Easy and the Rebieras; "only let me know him."

"Do you see him there, Mesty, walking down in front of those men? he has a musket in his hand, a jacket with silver buttons, and white trousers."

"Yes, Massa Easy, me see him well—let me look little more—dat enough."

The galley slaves appeared to be very anxious to surround the house that no one should escape, and Don Silvio was arranging the men.

"Ned," said Jack, "let us show him that we are here. He said that he would acquaint Don Rebiera with our arrival—let us prove to him that he is too late."

"It would not be a bad plan," replied Gascoigne; "if it were possible that these fellows had any gratitude among them, some of them might relent at the idea of attacking those who saved them."

"Not a bit; but it will prove to them that there are more in the house than they think for; and we can frighten some of them by telling them that the soldiers are near at hand."

Jack immediately threw up the casement, and called out in a loud voice, "Don Silvio! galley-slave! Don Silvio!"

The party hailed turned round, and beheld Jack, Gascoigne, and Mesty, standing at the window of the upper floor.

"We have saved you the trouble of announcing us," called out Gascoigne. "We are here to receive you."

"And in three hours the troops will be here, so you must be quick, Don Silvio," continued Jack.

"*A reveder la,*" continued Gascoigne, letting fly his pistol at Don Silvio.

The window was then immediately closed. The appearance of our heroes, and their communication of the speedy arrival of the troops, was not without effect. The criminals trembled at the idea; Don Silvio was mad with rage—he pointed out to the men the necessity of immediate attack—the improbability of the troops arriving so soon, and the wealth which he expected was locked up by Don Rebiera in his mansion. This rallied them, and they advanced to the doors, which they attempted to force without success, losing several men by the occasional fire from those within the house. Finding their efforts, after half an hour's repeated attempts, to be useless, they retreated, and then bringing up a long piece of timber, which required sixty men to carry it, they ran with it against the door, and the weight and impetus of the timber drove it off its hinges, and an entrance was obtained. By this time it was dark, the lower story had been abandoned, but the barricade at the head of the stairs opposed their progress. Convenient loop-holes had been prepared by the defenders, who now opened a smart fire upon the assailants, the latter having no means of returning it effectually, had they had ammunition for their muskets, which fortunately they had not been able to procure. The combat now became fierce, and the galley-slaves were several times repulsed with great loss during a contest of two hours; but, encouraged by Don Silvio, and refreshed by repeated draughts of wine, they continued by degrees removing the barriers opposed to them.

"We shall have to retreat!" exclaimed Don Rebiera; "very soon they will have torn down all. What do you think, Signor Easy?"

"Hold this as long as we can. How are we off for ammunition?"

"Plenty as yet—plenty to last for six hours, I think."

"What do you say, Mesty?"

"By holy St. Patrig—I say hold out here—they got no fire-arms—and we ab um at arm-length."

This decision was the occasion of the first defence being held for two hours more, an occasional relief being afforded by the retreat of the convicts to the covered carts.

At last, it was evident that the barricade was no longer tenable, for the heavy pieces of furniture they had heaped up to oppose entrance were completely hammered to fragments by poles brought up by the assailants, and used as battering-rams. The retreat was sounded; they all hastened to the other story, where the ladies were already placed, and the galley-slaves were soon in possession of the first floor—exasperated by the defence, mad with wine and victory, but finding nothing.

Again was the attack made upon the second landing, but, as the stairs were now narrower, and their defences stronger in proportion, they for a long while gained no advantage. On the contrary, many of their men were wounded and taken down below.

The darkness of the night prevented both parties from seeing distinctly, which was rather in favour of the assailants. Many climbed over the fortress of piled-up furniture, and were killed as soon as they appeared on the other side, and, at last, the only ammunition used was against those who made this rash attempt. For four long hours did this assault and defence continue, until daylight came, and then the plan of assault was altered: they again brought up the poles, hammered the pieces of furniture into fragments, and gained ground. The defenders were worn out with fatigue, but flinched not; they knew that their lives, and the lives of those dearest to them, were at stake, and they never relaxed their exertions; still the criminals, with Silvio at their head, progressed, the distance between the parties gradually decreased, and there was but one massive chest of drawers now defending the landing-place, and over which there was a constant succession of blows from long poles and cutlasses, returned with the bullets from their pistols.

"We must now fight for our lives," exclaimed Gascoigne to Easy, "for what else can we do?"

"Do?—get on the roof and fight there, then," replied Jack.

"By-the-bye, that's well thought of, Jack," said Gascoigne. "Mesty, up and see if there is any place we can retreat to in case of need."

Mesty hastened to obey, and soon returned with a report that there was a trap-door leading into the loft under the roof, and that they could draw the ladder up after them.

"Then we may laugh at them," cried Jack. "Mesty, stay here while I and Gascoigne assist the ladies up," explaining to the Rebieras and to their domestics why they went.

Easy and Gascoigne hastened to the signora and Agnes, conducted them up the ladder into the loft, and requested them to have no fear; they then returned to the defences on the stairs, and joined their companions. They found them hard pressed, and that there was little chance of holding out much longer; but the stairs were narrow, and the assailants could not bring their force against them. But now, as the defences were nearly destroyed, although the convicts could not reach them with their knives, they brought up a large supply of heavy stones, which they threw with great force and execution. Two of Don Rebiera's men and Don Martin were struck down, and this new weapon proved most fatal.

"We must retreat, Jack," said Gascoigne, "the stones can do no harm where we are going to. What think you, Don Philip?"

"I agree with you; let those who are wounded be first carried up, and then we will follow."

This was effected, and as soon as the wounded men were carried up the ladder, and the arms taken up to prevent their falling into the hands of their assailants, for they were now of little use to them, the ammunition being exhausted, the whole body went into the large room which contained the trap-door of the loft, and, as soon as they were up, they drew the ladder after them. They had hardly effected this, when they were followed with the yells and shoutings of the galley-slaves, who had passed the last barriers, and thought themselves sure of their prey: but they were disappointed—they found them more secure than ever.

Nothing could exceed the rage of Don Silvio at the protracted resistance of the party, and the security of their retreat. To get at them was impossible, so he determined to set fire to the room, and suffocate them, if he could do no otherwise. He gave his directions to his men, who rushed down for straw, but in so doing he carelessly passed under the trap-door, and Mesty, who had carried up with him two or three of the stones, dashed one down on the head of Don Silvio, who fell immediately. He was carried away, but his orders were put in execution; the room was filled with straw and fodder, and lighted. The effects were soon felt. The trap-door had been shut, but the heat and smoke burst through; after a time, the planks and rafters took fire, and their situation was terrible. A small trap-window in the roof on the side of the house was knocked open, and gave them a temporary relief; but now the rafters burned and crackled, and the smoke burst on them in thick columns. They could not see and with difficulty could breathe. Fortunately the room below that which had been fired was but one out of four on the attics, and, as the loft they were in spread over the whole of the roof they were able to remove far from it. The house was slated with massive slate of some hundredweight each, and it was not found possible to remove them so as to give air, although frequent attempts were made. Donna Rebiera sank exhausted in the arms of her husband, and Agnes fell into those of our hero, who, enveloped in the smoke, kissed her again and again; and she, poor girl, thinking that they must all inevitably perish, made no scruple, in what she supposed her last moment, of returning these proofs of her ardent attachment.

"Massa Easy, help me here—Massa Gascoigne, come here. Now heab wid all your might: when we get one off we get plenty."

Summoned by Mesty, Jack and Gascoigne put their shoulders to one of the lower slates; it yielded—was disengaged, and slid down with a loud rattling below. The ladies were brought to it, and their heads put outside; they soon recovered; and now that they had removed one, they found no difficulty in removing others. In a few minutes they were all with their heads in the open air, but still the house was on fire below, and they had no chance of escape. It was while they were debating upon this point, and consulting as to their chance of safety, that a breeze of wind wafted the smoke that issued from the roof away from them, and they beheld the detachment of troops making up to the house; a loud cheer was given, and attracted the notice of the soldiers. They perceived Easy and his companions; the house was surrounded and entered in an instant.

The galley-slaves, who were in the house searching for the treasure reported by Don Silvio to be concealed, were captured or killed, and in five minutes the troops had possession. But how to assist those above was the difficulty. The room below was in flames, and burning fiercely. There were no ladders that could reach so high, and there were no means of getting to them. The commandant made signs from below, as if to ask what he was to do.

"I see no chance," observed Don Philip mournfully. "Easy, my dear fellow, and you, Gascoigne, I am sorry that the feuds of our family should have brought you to such a dreadful death; but what can be done?"

"I don't know," replied Jack, "unless we could get ropes."

"You quite sure, Massa Easy, that all galley-rascals below gone?" asked Mesty.

"Yes," replied Easy, "you may see that; look at some of them bound there, under charge of the soldiers."

"Den, sar, I tink it high time we go too."

"So do I, Mesty; but how?"

"How? stop a little."

"Come, help me, Massa Easy; dis board (for the loft was floored) is loose, come help, all of you."

They all went, and with united strength pulled up the board.

"Now strike like —!—and drive down de plaster," said Mesty, commencing the operation.

In a few minutes they had beaten an opening into one of the rooms below not on fire, pulled up another board, and Mesty having fetched the ladder, they all descended in safety, and, to the astonishment of the commandant of the troops, walked out of the door of the house, those who had been stunned with the stones having so far recovered as to require little assistance.

The soldiers shouted as they saw them appear, supporting the females. The commanding officer, who was an intimate friend of Don Philip, flew to his arms. The prisoners were carefully examined by Mesty, and Don Silvio was not among them. He might however, be among the dead who were left in the house, which now began to burn furiously. The galley-slaves who were captured amounted in number to forty-seven. Their dead they could not count. The major part of the plunder and the carts were still where they had been drawn up.

As soon as the culprits had been secured, the attention of the troops was directed to putting out the flames, but their attempts were ineffectual; the mansion was burned to the bare walls, and but little of the furniture saved; indeed, the major part of it had been destroyed in the attack made by Don Silvio and his adherents.

Leaving directions with Pedro and his people, that the property collected by the miscreants should be restored to the owners, Don Rebiera ordered the horses, and with the whole party put himself under the protection of the troops, who, as soon as they had been refreshed, and taken some repose, bent their way back to Palermo with the galley-slaves, bound and linked together in a long double row.

They halted when they had gone half-way, and remained for the night. The next day, at noon, Don Rebiera and his family were once more in their palazzo, and our two midshipmen and Mesty took their leave, and repaired on board to make themselves a little less like chimney-sweepers.

Captain Wilson was not out of the ship. Jack made his report, and then went down below, very much pleased at what had passed, especially as he would have another long yarn for the Governor on his return to Malta.

Chapter Thirty Two.

In which our hero and Gascoigne ought to be ashamed of themselves, and did feel what might be called midshipmite compunction.

The *Aurora* continued three weeks at Palermo, during which the most active search had been made for the remainder of the galley-slaves, and some few had been captured, but still Don Silvio, and a considerable number, were at large; and it was said that they had returned to the fastnesses in the mountains. Our hero was constantly on shore at Don Rebiera's house, and, after what had passed, he was now looked upon as soon to become a member of the family. The difference of religion was overlooked by Don Rebiera and the relations—by all but the confessor, Father Thomaso, who now began to agitate and fulminate into the ears of the Donna Rebiera all the pains and penalties attending heretical connection, such as excommunication and utter damnation. The effects of his remonstrances were soon visible, and Jack found that there was constraint on the part of the old lady, tears on the part of Agnes, and all father confessors heartily wished at the devil ten times a day on the part of Don Philip and his brother. At last he wormed the truth out of Agnes, who told her tale, and wept bitterly.

"Ned, I don't much like the appearance of things," observed Jack; "I must get rid of that Father Thomaso."

"You'll find that rather difficult," observed Gascoigne; "besides, if you get rid of him you would have his place filled up with another."

"He has frightened that poor old woman into the dismals, and she has the pains of purgatory on her already. I shall go and talk to Mesty."

"How can Mesty help you?"

"I don't know, but you can't; so, for want of better advice, I'll try the Ashantee."

Our hero went to Mesty, and laid the difficult affair open to him.

"I see," said Mesty, showing his filed teeth, "you want him skull."

"No, I don't, Mesty; but I want him out of the way."

"How dat possible, Massa Easy?—ship sail day after to-morrow. Now 'pose I ab time, I soon manage all dat. Stop a little."

"Confound it! but there's no stopping," replied Jack.

"Suppose, Massa Easy, you get leave go on shore—not come off again."

"That will be deserting, Mesty."

"By holy poker, I ab it—you go on shore and break your leg."

"Break my leg!—break my leave, you mean?"

"No, Massa Easy—you break your leg—den captain leave you shore, and leave me take care of you."

"But why should I break my leg, and how am I to break my leg?"

"Only pretend break leg, Massa Easy. Go talk Massa Don Philip, he manage all dat.—Suppose man break his leg in seven pieces, it is not possible to take him board."

"Seven pieces, Mesty! that's rather too many. However, I'll think of this."

Jack then went back and consulted Gascoigne, who approved of Mesty's advice, and thought the scheme feasible.

"If we could only pretend that we were thrown out of a caricola, you break your leg, a compound fracture of course—I break my arm—both left on shore at sick quarters, with Mesty to take care of us."

"Capital indeed," replied Jack; "I really would not mind it if it really took place; at all events we'll overturn the caricola."

"But shall we get leave the last day?"

"Yes, it's two days since I have been on shore, for I have not liked to go to Don Rebiera's since what Agnes told me. Besides, my clothes are all on shore, and that will be an excuse for a few hours."

Our two midshipmen applied for leave the next morning to be off in the afternoon. The first lieutenant gave them permission. They hastened to the hotel, sent for Don Philip, and made him a party to their plan. He readily promised his assistance, for he had resolved that our hero should marry his sister, and was fearful of the effect of his absence, coupled with Friar Thomaso's influence over his mother. He went to the surgeon of his regiment, who immediately entered into the scheme.

Our two midshipmen got into a caricola, rattled up and down the streets, and perceiving Captain Wilson at his window flogged the horse into a gallop: when abreast of the barracks Jack ran the wheel against a bank, and threw himself and Gascoigne out. Midshipmen are never hurt by these accidents, but fortunately for the success of the enterprise their faces were cut and bruised. Don Philip was standing by: he called the men to pick up our two scamps, carried them into the barracks, and sent for the surgeons, who undressed them, put Jack's left leg into a multitude of splints, and did the same to Gascoigne's arm. They were then put to bed, their contused faces with the blood, left *in statu quo*, while Don Philip sent an orderly, as from the commandant, to Captain Wilson, to acquaint him that two of his officers had been thrown out of a caricola, and were lying dangerously hurt at the barracks.

"Good heavens, it must be Mr Easy and Mr Gascoigne!" said Captain Wilson, when the intelligence was communicated; "I saw them galloping down the street like two madmen just now. Coxswain, take the gig on board and tell the surgeon to come on shore immediately, and bring him up to me at the barracks."

Captain Wilson then put on his hat, buckled on his sword, and hastened to ascertain the extent of the injury. Don Philip kept out of the way, but the captain was ushered into the room by one of the officers, where he found, in two beds, our two midshipmen stretched out, the surgeon of the forces and the regimental surgeon in consultation between them, while attendants were standing by each bed with restoratives. The medical gentlemen saluted Captain Wilson, and looked very grave, talked about fractures, contusions, injuries, in the most interminable manner—hoped that Mr Easy would recover—but had doubts. The other gentleman might do well with care; that is, as far as his arm was concerned, but there appeared to be a concussion of the brain. Captain Wilson looked at the cut and blood-smeared faces of the two young men, and waited with anxiety the arrival of his own surgeon, who came at last, puffing with the haste he had made, and received the report of the brothers of the faculty.

The leg of Mr Easy fractured in two places—had been set—bone protruding—impossible to move him. Gascoigne, arm, compound fracture—concussion of the brain not certain. Now, that all this would have been discovered to be false if the surgeon had been able to examine, is true; but how could he not credit the surgeon of the forces and the regimental surgeon, and how could he put the young men to fresh tortures by removing splints and unsetting limbs? Politeness, if nothing else, prevented his so doing, for it would have been as much as to say that either he did not credit their report, or that he doubted their skill. He looked at our hero and his companion, who kept their eyes closed, and breathed heavily with their mouths open, put on a grave face as well as his brothers in the art, and reported to Captain Wilson.

"But when can they be moved, Mr Daly?" inquired the latter; "I cannot wait; we must sail to-morrow, or the next day at the farthest."

The surgeon, as in duty bound, put the question to the others, who replied that there would be great risk in removing before the fever, which might be expected the next day, and which might last ten days; but that Captain Wilson had better not think of removing them, as they should have every care and attention where they were and could rejoin the ship at Malta. Mr Daly, the surgeon, agreed that this would be the most prudent step, and Captain Wilson then gave his consent.

That being settled, he walked up to the bed of Gascoigne, and spoke to him; but Gascoigne knew that he was to have a concussion of the brain, and he made no reply, nor gave any signs of knowing that Captain Wilson was near him. He then went to our hero, who, at the sound of Captain Wilson's voice, slowly opened his eyes without moving his head, and appeared to recognise him.

"Are you in much pain, Easy?" said the captain kindly.

Easy closed his eyes again, and murmured, "Mesty, Mesty!"

"He wants his servant, the ship's corporal, sir," said the surgeon.

"Well," replied Captain Wilson, "he had better have him: he is a faithful fellow, and will nurse him well. When you go on board, Mr Daly, desire the first lieutenant to send Mesty on shore with Mr Gascoigne's and Mr Easy's chests, and his own bag and hammock. Good heavens! I would not for a thousand pounds that this accident had occurred. Poor foolish boys—they run in couples, and if one's in a scrape the other is sure to share it. Gentlemen, I return you many thanks for your kindness, and I must accept of your promised care for my unfortunate officers. I sail to-morrow at daylight. You will oblige me by informing their friends, the Rebieras, of their mischance, as I am sure they will contribute all they can to their comfort." So saying, Captain Wilson bowed and quitted the room, followed by the surgeon.

As soon as the door was closed the two midshipmen turned their heads round and looked at each other, but they were afraid to speak at first, in case of the return of the surgeon. As soon as it was announced to them that Captain Wilson and Mr Daly were outside the barrack gates our hero commenced—"Do you know, Ned, that my conscience smites me, and if it had not been that I should have betrayed those who wish to oblige us, when poor Captain Wilson appeared so much hurt and annoyed at our accident, I was very near getting up and telling him of the imposition, to relieve his mind."

"I agree with you, Jack, and I felt much the same—but what's done cannot be undone. We must now keep up the imposition for the sake of those who, to help us, have deceived him."

"I don't think that you would find an English surgeon who would have consented to such an imposition."

"No, that is certain; but after all, it is an imposition that has hurt nobody."

"Oh, I do not wish to moralise—but I repent of my share in the deceit; and had it to be done over again I would not consent to it."

"Not even for —? but I won't mention her name in barracks."

"I don't know," replied Jack; "but let's say no more about it, and thank these gentlemen for their kindness."

"Yes, but we must keep it up until we see the *Aurora* under all sail."

"And longer too," replied Jack; "we must not let the affair get wind even on shore. We must not recover quickly, but still appear to recover. Don Rebiera and his wife must be deceived. I have a plot in my head, but I cannot work it out clear until I see Mesty."

Don Philip now came in. He had seen Captain Wilson, who had requested him to look after the two invalids, and stated his intention to sail the next morning. They consulted with him, and it was agreed that no one should be acquainted with the real fact but his brother Martin, and that all Palermo should be as much deceived as Captain Wilson, for if not, it would put Father Thomaso on the *qui vive*, and make him fulminate more than ever. Our midshipmen ate an excellent dinner, and then remained in bed conversing till it was time to go to sleep; but long before that, Mesty had made his appearance with their clothes. The eyes of the Ashantee said all that was necessary—he never spoke a word, but unlashed his hammock and lay down in a corner, and they were soon all three asleep.

The next morning Captain Wilson called to ascertain how our hero and his companion were, but the room had been darkened, and he could not see their faces plainly. Easy thanked him for his kindness in allowing Mesty to attend them, and having received his orders as to their joining the ship as soon as they recovered, and having promised to be very cautious in their behaviour and keep out of all scrapes, he wished them a speedy recovery, and departed.

In little more than half an hour afterwards, Mesty, who had been peeping out of the shutters, suddenly threw them open with a loud laugh.

The *Aurora* was under way, with studding sails below and aloft, standing out of the roads. Jack and Gascoigne got up, threw off the splints, and danced about in their shirts. As soon as they were quiet again, Mesty said in a grave tone, "Den why you stay at sea, Massa Easy?"

"Very true, Mesty, I've asked myself that question often enough lately; because I'm a fool, I suppose."

"And I, because I can't help it," replied Gascoigne; "never mind, we are on shore now, and I look for a famous cruise."

"But first we must see what the ground is we are to cruise on," replied Jack; "so, Mesty, let us have a palaver, as they say in your country."

The two midshipmen got into their beds, and Mesty sat on the chest between them, looking as grave as a judge. The question was, how to get rid of the padre Thomaso. Was he to be thrown over the molehead to the fishes—or his skull broke—was Mesty's knife to be resorted to—was he to be kidnapped or poisoned—or were fair means to be employed—persuasion, bribery? Every one knows how difficult it is to get rid of a priest.

As our hero and Gascoigne were not Italians, they thought that bribery would be the more English-like way of doing the thing; so they composed a letter, to be delivered by Mesty to the friar, in which Jack offered to Father Thomaso the moderate sum of one thousand dollars, provided he would allow the marriage to proceed, and not frighten the old lady with ecclesiastical squibs and crackers.

As Mesty was often on shore with Jack, and knew the friar very well by sight, it was agreed that the letter should be confided to his charge; but, as it was not consistent that a person in such a state as our hero was represented to be should sit up and write letters, the delivery was deferred for a few days, when, after waiting that time, Mesty delivered the letter to the friar, and made signs that he was to take back the answer. The friar beckoned him that he was to accompany him to his room, where he read the letter, and then again made signs to him to follow him. The friar led the way to his monastery, and as soon as Mesty was in his cell, he summoned another who could speak English to act as interpreter.

"Is your master recovering?"

"Yes," replied Mesty, "he is at present doing well."

"Have you served him long?"

"No," replied Mesty.

"Are you very fond of him? does he treat you well, give you plenty of money?"

At these questions, the artful black conceived that there was something in the wind, and he therefore very quietly replied, "I do not care much for him."

The friar fixed his keen eye upon Mesty, and perceived there was a savage look about the black, from which he augured that he was a man who would suit his purpose.

"Your master offers me a thousand dollars; would you wish to gain this money for yourself?"

Mesty grinned and showed his sharp-filed teeth.

"It would make me a rich man in my own country."

"It would," replied the friar; "now you shall have it, if you will only give your master a small powder."

"I understand," replied Mesty; "hab those things in my country."

"Well—do you consent?—if so, I will write the letter to get the money."

"Suppose they find me out?" replied Mesty.

"You will be safe, and you shall be sent away as soon as possible—say, will you consent?"

"The whole thousand dollars?"

"Every one of them."

"Den give me the powder?"

"Stay a little," replied the friar, who went out of the cell, and, in about ten minutes, returned with an answer to our hero's letter and a paper containing a grayish powder.

"Give him this in his soup or anything—spread it on his meat, or mix it up with his sugar if he eats an orange."

"I see," replied Mesty.

"The dollars shall be yours. I swear it on the holy cross."

Mesty grinned horribly, took his credentials, and then asked, "When I come again?"

"As soon as you have received the money bring it to me at Don Rebiera's—then give the powder: as soon as it is given you must let me know, for you must not remain in Palermo. I will myself conduct you to a place of safety."

Mesty then quitted the cell and was shown out of the monastery.

"By de holy poker he one damn rascal!" muttered Mesty, as he was once in the open air. "But stop a little."

The Ashantee soon arrived at the barracks, and repeated the whole of the conference between him and the Friar Thomaso.

"It must be poison, of course," observed Gascoigne; "suppose we try it upon some animal?"

"No, Massa Gascoigne," replied Mesty, "I try it myself, by-and-bye. Now what we do?"

"I must give you the order for the thousand dollars, Mesty," replied Jack. "The rascal here writes to me that for that sum he will consent not only not to oppose me, but agrees to assist my cause; but the great question is, whether he will keep his word with you, Mesty; if not, I shall lose my money. So therefore we must now have another palaver and argue the point."

The point was argued between Jack and Gascoigne. A thousand dollars was a large sum, but Jack's father was a philosopher. After many *pros* and *cons*, it was as last decided that the money should be given to Mesty; but that Mesty should state, when he took the money to the friar, that he had administered the powder, and claim it when he presented it.

The next day the order for the money was given to Mesty, and he went to the Friar Thomaso with it. The friar hastened with Mesty to the monastery and sent for the interpreter.

"You have given it?" inquired the friar.

"Yes—not one hour ago. Here de order for de money."

"You must run for the money before he is dead, for the powder is very rapid."

"And me," replied Mesty, apparently much alarmed, "where am I to go?"

"As soon as you bring the money here, you must go back to the barracks. Remain there till he is dead, and then return here. I will have all ready, and take you, as soon as it is dusk, to a monastery of our order in the mountains, where no one will think of looking for you till the affair is blown over; and then I will find you a passage in some vessel out of the island."

Mesty hastened for the money, and taking it in a large bag to the monastery, delivered it to the friar's charge, and then returned to the barracks to Easy and Gascoigne. It was agreed that he should go with the friar, who would probably remain away some time; indeed, Mesty insisted upon so doing. Mesty stayed two hours, and then returned about dusk to the monastery, and reported the death of our hero. He remained there until it was dark, and then the friar ordered him to tie the bag of dollars to his saddle-bow. They mounted two mules, which stood already caparisoned, and quitted Palermo.

In the morning, Don Philip, as usual, made his appearance, and told our hero that the friar had been summoned away by the abbot, and would not return for some time.

"I came to tell you this news," said Don Philip, "as I thought it would please you; the sooner you are now well, the better. I mean to propose your both being removed to my father's palazzo, and then you can recover your lost ground during the confessor's absence."

"And I have the means," replied Jack, showing the friar's letter. Don Philip read it with astonishment, but was still more surprised when he heard the whole story from Jack. He was for a time silent: at last he said:

"I am sorry for your poor black."

"Why so?" replied Jack.

"You will never see him again, depend upon it. A thousand dollars would sign the death-warrant of a thousand blacks; but there is another reason—they will put him out of the way that he may not give evidence. Where is the powder?"

"Mesty has it; he would not part with it."

"He is a shrewd fellow, that black; he may be too much for the friar," replied Don Philip.

"He means mischief, I'm sure," replied Gascoigne.

"Still I feel a great deal of alarm about him," replied Easy; "I wish now that I had not let him go."

"Are you sure that he went?"

"No, I am not; but the friar told him that he should take him to the mountains as soon as it was dark."

"And probably he will," replied Don Philip, "as the best place to get rid of him. However, the whole of this story must be told both to my father and my mother; to the former that he may take the right measures, and to my mother that it may open her eyes. Give me the copy of the letter you wrote to the friar, and then I shall have it all."

The report of the accident which had occurred to Easy and Gascoigne had been spread and fully believed throughout Palermo. Indeed, as usual, it had been magnified, and asserted that they could not recover. To Agnes only had the case been imparted in confidence by Don Philip, for her distress at the first intelligence had been so great that her brother could not conceal it.

Two days after Don Philip had made his parents acquainted with the villainy of the friar, the midshipmen were transported to the palazzo, much to the surprise of everybody, and much to the renown of the surgeons, who were indemnified for their duplicity and falsehood by an amazing extension of their credit as skilful men.

After their arrival at the palazzo, Don Rebiera was also entrusted with the secret, but it went no further. As now there was no particular hurry for our hero to get well, he was contented and happy in the society of Agnes and her parents; the old lady, after she had been informed of the conduct of Friar Thomaso, having turned round in our hero's favour, and made a vow never to have a confessor in the house again. Jack and Gascoigne were now as happy as could be; all their alarm was about Mesty, for whose return they were most anxious.

To Don Rebiera Jack made known formally his intentions with regard to Agnes. He fully satisfied him as to his qualifications and his property, and Don Rebiera was fully aware of his debt of gratitude to our hero. But all he required was the consent of Jack's father, and until this was obtained, he would not consent to the marriage taking place. Jack attempted to argue the point; his father, he said, had married without consulting him, and therefore he had a right to marry without consulting his father. But Don Rebiera, not having any acquaintance with the rights of man and equality, did not feel the full force of Jack's argument, and made it a *sine quâ non* that his parents should write and consent to the alliance before it took place.

Chapter Thirty Three.

In which Mesty should be called throughout Mephistopheles, for it abounds in black cloaks, disguises, daggers, and dark deeds.

On the fourth evening after the removal of our two midshipmen to the palazzo of Don Rebiera, as they were sitting in company with Agnes and Don Philip in their own room, a friar made his appearance at the door. They all started, for by his height they imagined him to be the Friar Thomaso, but no one addressed him. The friar shut the door without saying a word, and then lifting up his cowl, which had been drawn over it, discovered the black face of Mesty. Agnes screamed, and all sprang from their seats at this unusual and unexpected apparition. Mesty grinned, and there was that in his countenance which said that he had much to communicate.

"Where is the friar, Mesty?" inquired Easy.

"Stop a little, Massa—suppose we lock door first, and den I tell all."

Taking this precaution, Mesty threw off the friar's gown, and appeared in his own dress, with the bag of dollars slung round his body.

"Now, Massa Easy, I hab a long tory to tell—so I tink I better begin at the beginning."

"It is the most approved method," replied Jack; "but stop when I hold up my finger, that we may translate what you say to the lady and Don Philip."

"Dat all right, sar. Friar and I get on two mule as soon as it quite dark. He make me carry all tousand dollars—and we ride out of town. We go up mountain and mountain, but the moon get up shine and we go on cheek by jowl—he nebber say one word, and I nebber say one word, 'cause I no speak his lingo, and he no understand my English. About two o'clock in de morning, we stop at a house and stay dere till eight o'clock, and den we go on again all next day, up all mountain, only stop once, eat a bit bread and drink lilly wine. Second night come on, and den we stop again, and people bow very low to him, and woman bring in rabbit for make supper. I go in the kitchen, woman make stew smell very nice, so I nod my head, and I say very good, and she make a face, and throw on table black loaf of bread and garlic, and make sign dat for my supper; good enough for black fellow, and dat rabbit stew for friar. Den I say to myself, stop a little; suppose friar hab all de rabbit, I tink I give him a lilly powder."

"The powder, Mesty?" exclaimed Jack.

"What does he say?" inquired Don Philip.

Gascoigne translated all that Mesty had communicated. The interest of the narrative now became exciting. Mesty continued:

"Well, Massa Easy, den woman she go for dish to put stew in, and I take de powder and drop it in de pot, and den I sit down again and eat black bread, she say good enough for black man. She stir up de stew once more, and den she pour it out into dish, and take it to friar. He lick um chops, by all de powers, and he like um so well he pick all de bones, and wipe up gravy with him bread. You tink it very nice, Massa Friar, tink I; but stop a little. After he drink a whole bottle of wine he tell em bring mules to de door, and he put him hands on de woman head, and dat de way he pay for him supper.

"The moon shone bright, and we go up all mountain, always go up, and 'bout two hour, he got off him mule and he put him hand so, and set down on de rock. He twist, and he turn and he groan for half an hour, and den he look at me, as much as to say, you black villain, you do this? for he not able to speak, and den I pull out de paper of de powder, and I show him, and make him sign he swallow it: he look again, and I laugh at him—and he die."

"Oh Mesty, Mesty," exclaimed our hero; "you should not have done that—there will be mischief come from it."

"Now he dead, Massa Easy, so much less mischief."

Gascoigne then interpreted to Don Philip and Agnes, the former of whom looked very grave and the latter terrified.

"Let him go on," said Don Philip; "I am most anxious to hear what he did with the body."

Mesty, at the request of our hero, proceeded: "Den I thought what I should do, and I said I would hide him, and I tink I take his coat for myself—so I pull off him coat and I pull off all his oder clothes—he not wear many—and I take the body in my arm and carry him where I find a great split in de rock above all road. I throw him in, and den I throw plenty large pieces rock on him till I no see him any more; den I take de two mules and get on mine wid de dollars, and lead the other three four mile, till I come to a large wood—take off him saddle and bridle, turn him adrift. Den I tear up all clothes all in lilly bits, hide one piece here, noder piece dere, and de saddle and bridle in de bush. All right now, I say; so put on friar cloak, hide my face, get on my mule, and den I look where I shall go—so I say, I not be in dis road anyhow. I passed through wood till I find nother. I go 'bout two mile—moon go down, all dark, and five six men catch hold my bridle, and they all got arms, so I do nothing—they speak to me, but I no answer, and neber show my face. They find all dollars (damn um) fast enough, and they lead me away through the wood. Last we come to large fire in de wood, plenty of men lie 'bout, some eat and some drink. They pull me off, and I hold down my head and fold my arms, just like friar do. They bring me along to one man, and pour out all my dollar before him. He give some order, and they take me away, and I peep through the cloak, and I say to myself, he that damn galley—slave rascal Don Silvio."

"Don Silvio!" cried Jack.

"What does he say of Don Silvio?" demanded Don Philip.

Mesty's narrative was again translated, and he continued.

"Dey lead me away 'bout fifty yards, tie me to tree, and den dey leave me, and dey all drink and make merry, neber offer me anyting; so I hab noting den to eat. I eat de ropes and gnaw them through, and den I stay there two hour until all go asleep, and all quiet; for I say to myself, stop a little. Den when dey all fast asleep, I take out my knife and I crawl 'long de ground, as we do in our country sometime—and den I stop and look 'bout me; no man watch but two, and dey look out for squarl, not look in board where I was. I crawl 'gain till I lay down 'longside that damn galley-slave Don Silvio. He lie fast asleep with my bag thousand dollars under him head. So I tink, 'you not hab dem long, you rascal.' I look round—all right, and I drive my knife good aim into him heart, and press toder hand on him mouth, but he make no noise; he struggle little and look up, and den I throw off de head of de gown and show him my black face, and he look and he try to speak; but I stop dat, for down go my knife, again, and de damn galley-slave dead as herring."

"Stop, Mesty, we must tell this to Don Philip," said Gascoigne.

"Dead, Don Silvio dead! well, Mesty, we are eternally obliged to you, for there was no safety for my father while he was living. Let him go on."

"So when I put de knife through his body, I lie down by him, as if noting had happened, for ten minute, and den I take de bag of dollars from under him head, and den I feel him all over, and I find him pistols and him purse, which I hab here, all gold. So I take them and I look—all asleep, and I crawl back to de tree. Den I stay to tink a little; de man on watch come up and look at me, but he tink all right and he go away again. Lucky ting, by de power, dat I go back to tree. I wait again, and den I crawl and crawl till I clear of all, and den I take to my heel and run for um life, till daylight come, and den I so tired I lie down in bush: I stay in bush all day, and den I set off again back here, for I find road and know my way. I not eat den for one day and one night, and come to house where I put my head in and find woman there. I not able to speak, so I help myself, and not show my face. She not like dat and make a bobbery, but I lift up my cloak and show my black face and white teeth, and den she tink me de debil. She ran out of de house and I help myself very quick, and den set off and come close here yesterday morning. I hide myself all day and come in at night, and now, Massa Easy, you ab all de whole truth—and you ab your tousand dollars—and you ab got rid of de rascal friar and de damn galley-slave Don Silvio."

"Tell them all this, Ned," said Jack, who, whilst Gascoigne was so employed, talked with Mesty.

"I was very much frightened for you, Mesty," said Jack; "but still I thought you quite as cunning as the friar, and so it has turned out; but the thousand dollars ought to be yours."

"No, sar," replied Mesty, "the dollars not mine; but I hab plenty of gold in Don Silvio's purse—plenty, plenty of gold. I keep my property, Massa Easy, and you keep yours."

"I'm afraid that this affair may be found out, Mesty; the woman will spread the report of having been attacked by a black friar, and that will lead to suspicion, as the other friars of the convent knew that you left with Friar Thomaso."

"So I tink dat, but when a man starve, he quite forget his thought."

"I don't blame you; but now I must talk to Don Philip."

"Suppose you no objection, while you talk I eat something from the table then, Massa Easy; for I hungry enough to eat de friar, mule and all."

"Eat, my good fellow, and drink as much as you please."

The consultation between our two midshipmen and Don Philip was not long: they perceived the immediate necessity for the departure of Mesty, and the suspicion which would attach to themselves. Don Philip and Agnes left them, to go to Don Rebiera, and make him acquainted with what had passed, and to ask his advice.

When they went into the room, Don Rebiera immediately accosted his son.

"Have you heard, Philip, that Friar Thomaso has returned at last?—so the servants tell me."

"The report may be fortunate," replied Don Philip; "but I have another story to tell you."

He then sat down and imparted to Don Rebiera all the adventures of Mesty. Don Rebiera was for some time in deep thought; at last he replied:

"That Don Silvio is no more is fortunate, and the negro would be entitled to reward for his destruction—but for the friar, that is a bad business. The negro might remain and tell the whole story, and the facts might be proved by the evidence of Signor Easy and the letters; but what then? we should raise the whole host of the clergy against our house, and we have suffered too much from them already; the best plan would be the immediate departure, not only of the negro, but of our two young friends. The supposition of Friar Thomaso being here, and their departure with the negro servant to rejoin their ship, will remove much suspicion and destroy all inquiry. They must be off immediately. Go to them, Philip, and point out to them the absolute necessity of this measure, and tell our young friend that I rigidly adhere to my promise, and as soon as he has his father's sanction I will bestow upon him my daughter. In the meantime I will send down and see if a vessel can be chartered for Malta."

Our hero and Gascoigne fully admitted the wisdom of this measure, and prepared for their departure; indeed, now that Don Rebiera's resolution had been made known to our hero, he cared more for obtaining his father's consent than he did for remaining to enjoy himself at Palermo, and before noon of the next day all was ready, the vessel had been procured, Jack took his leave of Agnes and her mother, and accompanied by Don Rebiera and Don Philip (for Don Martin was on duty a few miles from Palermo), went down to the beach, and having bid them farewell embarked with Gascoigne and Mesty on board of the two-masted lateen which had been engaged, and before sunset not a steeple of Palermo was to be seen.

"What are you thinking of, Jack?" said Gascoigne, after our hero had been silent half an hour.

"I have been thinking, Ned, that we are well out of it."

"So do I," replied Gascoigne; and here the conversation dropped for a time.

"What are you thinking of now, Jack?" said Gascoigne after a long pause.

"I've been thinking that I've a good story for the old Governor."

"Very true," replied Gascoigne; and both were again silent for some time.

"What are you thinking of now, Jack?" said Gascoigne, after another long interval.

"I've been thinking that I shall leave the service," replied Jack.

"I wish you would take me with you," replied Gascoigne, with a sigh; and again they were both in deep contemplation.

"What are you thinking of now, Jack?" said Gascoigne again.

"Of Agnes," replied our hero.

"Well, if that's the case I'll call you when supper's ready. In the meantime I'll go and talk with Mesty."

Chapter Thirty Four.

Jack leaves the service, in which he had no business, and goes home to mind his own business.

On the fourth day they arrived at Malta, and our two midshipmen, as soon as they had settled with the padrone of the vessel, went up to the government-house. They found the Governor in the veranda, Who held out both his hands, one to each.

"Glad to see you, my lads. Well, Jack, how's the leg, all right? don't limp. And your arm, Gascoigne?"

"All right, sir, and as sound as ever it was," replied they both.

"Then you're in luck, and have made more baste than you deserve, after your mad pranks; but now sit down, and I suppose, my friend Jack, you have a story to tell me."

"Oh, yes, Sir Thomas, and a very long one."

"Then I won't have it now, for I expect people on business; we'll have it after dinner. Get your things up and take possession of your rooms. The *Aurora* sailed four days ago. You've had a wonderful recovery."

"Wonderful, sir!" replied our hero; "all Palermo rings with it."

"Well, you may go now—I shall see you at dinner. Wilson will be delighted when he hears that you have got round again, for he was low-spirited about it, I can tell you, which is more than you deserve."

"He's right there," said our hero to Gascoigne as they walked away.

When dinner was over, Jack narrated to the Governor the adventures of Mesty, with which he was much interested; but when they were quite alone in the evening, the Governor called our two midshipmen into the veranda, and said:

"Now, my lads, I'm not going to preach, as the saying is, but I've been long enough in the world to know that a compound fracture of the leg is not cured in fourteen or sixteen days. I ask you to tell me the truth. Did not you deceive Captain Wilson on this point?"

"I am ashamed to say that we did, sir," replied Easy.

"How did you manage that, and why?"

Jack then went into further details relative to himself and his amour, stating his wish to be left behind and all that had passed.

"Well, there's some excuse for you, but none for the surgeons. If any surgeon here had played such a trick, I would have hung him, as sure as I'm Governor. This affair of yours has become serious. Mr Easy, we must have some conversation on the matter to-morrow morning."

The next morning the packet from England was reported off the harbour's mouth. After breakfast the letters were brought on shore, and the Governor sent for our hero.

"Mr Easy, here are two letters for you, I am sorry to say with black seals. I trust that they do not bring the intelligence of the death of any very near relative."

Jack bowed without speaking, took the letters, and went to his room. The first he opened was from his father.

"My Dear John—

"You will be much grieved to hear that your poor mother, after sitting in the corner for nearly two years waiting for the millennium, appeared to pine away; whether from disappointment or not I do not know; but at last, in spite of all Dr Middleton could do, she departed this life; and, as the millennium would not come to her as she expected, it is to be hoped she is gone to the millennium. She was a good wife, and I always let her have her own way. Dr Middleton does not appear to be satisfied as to the cause of her death, and has wished to examine; but I said no, for I am a philosopher, and it is no use looking for causes after effects; but I have done since her death what she never would permit me to do during her life. I have had her head shaved, and examined it very carefully as a phrenologist, and most curiously has she proved the truth of the sublime science. I will give you the result. Determination, very prominent; Benevolence, small; Caution, extreme; Veneration, not very great; Philo-progenitiveness, strange to say, is very large, considering she has but one child; Imagination very strong: you know, my dear boy, she was always imagining some nonsense or another. Her other organs were all moderate. Poor dear creature! she is gone, and we may well wail, for a better mother or a better wife never existed. And now, my dear boy, I must request that you call for your discharge, and come home as soon as possible. I cannot exist without you, and I require your assistance in the grand work I have in contemplation. The time is at hand, the cause of equality will soon triumph; the abject slaves now hold up their heads; I have electrified them with my speeches, but I am getting old and feeble; I require my son to leave my mantle to, as one prophet did to another, and then I will, like him, ascend in glory.—Your affectionate Father:—

"*Nicodemus Easy.*"

From this it would appear, thought Jack, that my mother is dead, and that my father is mad. For some time our hero remained in a melancholy mood; he dropped many tears to the memory of his mother, whom, if he had never respected, he had much loved; and it was not till half an hour had elapsed, that he thought of opening the other letter. It was from Dr Middleton.

"My Dear Boy,—

"Although not a correspondent of yours, I take the right of having watched you through all your childhood, and from a knowledge of your disposition, to write you a few lines. That you have by this time discarded your father's foolish, nonsensical philosophy, I am very sure. It was I who advised your going away for that purpose, and I am sure that, as a young man of sense and the heir to a large property, you will before this have seen the fallacy of your father's doctrines. Your father tells me that he has requested you to come home, and allow me to add any weight I may have with you in persuading you to do the same. It is fortunate for you that the estate is entailed, or you might soon be a beggar, for there is no saying what debts he might, in his madness, be guilty of. He has already been dismissed from the magistracy by the lord lieutenant, in consequence of his haranguing the discontented peasantry, and, I may say, exciting them to acts of violence and insubordination. He has been seen dancing and hurrahing round a stack fired by an incendiary. He has turned away his keepers, and allowed all poachers to go over the manor. In short, he is not in his senses; and, although I am far from advising coercive measures, I do consider that it is absolutely necessary that you should immediately return home and look after what will one day be your property. You have no occasion to follow the profession with eight thousand pounds per annum. You have distinguished yourself—now make room for those who require it for their subsistence. God bless you. I shall soon hope to shake hands with you.

"Yours most truly:—

"G. Middleton."

There was matter for deep reflection in these two letters, and Jack never felt before how much his father had been in the wrong. That he had gradually been weaned from his ideas was true, but still he had, to a certain degree, clung to them, as we do to a habit; but now he felt that his eyes were opened; the silly, almost unfeeling, letter of his father upon the occasion of his mother's death opened his eyes. For a long while Jack was in a melancholy meditation, and then, casting his eyes upon his watch, he perceived that it was almost dinner-time. That he could eat his dinner was certain, and he scorned to pretend to feel what he did not. He therefore dressed himself and went down, grave, it is true, but not in tears. He spoke little at dinner, and retired as soon as it was over, presenting his two letters to the Governor, and asking his advice for the next morning. Gascoigne followed him, and to him he confided his trouble; and Ned, finding that Jack was very low-spirited, consoled him to the best of his power, and brought a bottle of wine which he procured from the butler. Before they retired to bed, Jack had given his ideas to his friend, which were approved of, and wishing him a good-night, he threw himself into bed, and was soon fast asleep.

"One thing is certain, my good fellow," observed the Governor to our hero, as he gave him back his letters at the breakfast table the next morning; "that your father is as mad as a March hare. I agree with that doctor, who appears a sensible man, that you had better go home immediately."

"And leave the service altogether, sir?" replied Jack.

"Why, I must say that I do not think you exactly fitted for it. I shall be sorry to lose you, as you have a wonderful talent for adventure, and I shall have no more yarns to hear when you return: but, if I understand right from Captain Wilson, you were brought into the profession because he thought that the service might be of use in eradicating false notions, rather than from any intention or necessity of your following it up as a profession."

"I suspect that was the case, sir," replied Jack; "as for my own part, I hardly know why I entered it."

"To find a mare's nest, my lad; I've heard all about it; but never mind that, the question is now about your leaving it to look after your own property, and I think I may venture to say that I can arrange all that matter at once, without referring to admiral or captain. I will be responsible for you, and you may go home in the packet which sails on Wednesday for England."

"Thank you, Sir Thomas, I am much obliged to you," replied Jack.

"You, Mr Gascoigne, I shall, of course, send out by the first opportunity to rejoin your ship."

"Thank you, Sir Thomas, I am much obliged to you," replied Gascoigne, making a bow.

"You'll break no more arms, if you please, sir," continued the Governor; "a man in love may have some excuse for breaking his leg, but you had none."

"I beg your pardon, sir; if Mr Easy was warranted in breaking his leg out of love, I submit that I could do no less than break my arm out of friendship."

"Hold your tongue, sir, or I'll break your head from the very opposite feeling," replied the Governor, good-humouredly. "But observe, young man, I shall keep this affair secret, as in honour bound; but let me advise you, as you have only your profession to look to, to follow it up steadily. It is high time that you and Mr Easy were separated. He is independent of the service, and you are not. A young man possessing such ample means will never be fitted for the duties of a junior officer. He can do no good for himself, and is certain to do much harm to others: a continuance of his friendship would probably end in your ruin, Mr Gascoigne. You must be aware that if the greatest indulgence had not been shown to Mr Easy by his captain and first lieutenant, he never could have remained in the service so long as he has done."

As the Governor made the last remark in rather a severe tone, our two midshipmen were silent for a minute. At last Jack observed, very quietly:

"And yet, sir, I think, considering all, I have behaved pretty well."

"You have behaved very well, my good lad, on all occasions in which your courage and conduct, as an officer, have been called forth. I admit it; and had you been sent to sea with a mind properly regulated, and without such an unlimited command of money, I have no doubt but that you would have proved an ornament to the service. Even now I think you would, if you were to remain in the service under proper guidance and necessary restrictions, for you have, at least, learned to obey, which is absolutely necessary before you are fit to command. But recollect, what would your conduct have brought upon you if you had not been under the parental care of Captain Wilson? But let us say no more about that: a midshipman with the prospect of eight thousand pounds a year is an anomaly which the service cannot admit, especially when that midshipman is resolved to take to himself a wife."

"I hope that you approve of that step, sir."

"That entirely depends upon the merit of the party, which I know nothing of, except that she has a pretty face, and is of one of the best Sicilian families. I think the difference of religion a ground of objection."

"We will argue that point, sir," replied Jack.

"Perhaps it will be the cause of more argument than you think for, Mr Easy; but every man makes his own bed, and as he makes it, so must he lie down in it."

"What am I to do about Mesty, sir? I cannot bear the idea of parting with him."

"I am afraid that you must; I cannot well interfere there."

"He is of little use to the service, sir; he has been sent to sick quarters as my servant: if he may be permitted to go home with me, I will procure his discharge as soon as I arrive, and send him on board the guard-ship till I obtain it."

"I think that, on the whole, he is as well out of the service as in it, and therefore I will, on consideration, take upon myself the responsibility, provided you do as you say."

The conversation was here ended, as the Governor had business to attend to, and Jack and Gascoigne went to their rooms to make their arrangements.

"The Governor is right," observed Gascoigne; "it is better that we part, Jack. You have half unfitted me for the service already; I have a disgust of the midshipmen's berth; the very smell of pitch and tar has become odious to me. This is all wrong; I must forget you and all our pleasant cruises on shore, and once more swelter in my greasy jacket. When I think that if our pretended accidents were discovered, I should be dismissed the service, and the misery which that would cause to my poor father, I tremble at my escape. The Governor is right, Jack: we must part, but I hope you never will forget me."

"My hand upon it, Ned. Command my interest, if ever I have any—my money—what I have, and the house, whether it belongs to me or my father—as far as you are concerned at least, I adhere to my notions of perfect equality."

"And abjure them, I trust, Jack, as a universal principle."

"I admit, as the Governor asserts, that my father is as mad as a March hare."

"That is sufficient; you don't know how glad it makes me to hear you say that."

The two friends were inseparable during the short time that they remained together. They talked over their future prospects, their hopes and anticipations, and when the conversation flagged, Gascoigne brought up the name of Agnes.

Mesty's delight at leaving the service, and going home with his patron, was indescribable. He laid out a portion of his gold in a suit of plain clothes, white linen shirts, and in every respect the wardrobe of a man of fashion; in fact, he was now a complete gentleman's gentleman; was very particular in frizzing his woolly hair—wore a white neckcloth, gloves, and cane. Every one felt inclined to laugh when he made his appearance; but there was some in Mesty's look, which, at all events, prevented their doing so before his face. The day for sailing arrived. Jack took leave of the Governor, thanking him for his great kindness, and stating his intention of taking Malta in his way out to Palermo in a month or two. Gascoigne went on board with him, and did not go down the vessel's side till it was more than a mile clear of the harbour.

Chapter Thirty Five.

Mr Easy's wonderful invention fully explained by himself—much to the satisfaction of our hero, and, it is to be presumed, to that also of the reader.

At last the packet anchored in Falmouth Roads. Jack, accompanied by Mesty, was soon on shore with his luggage, threw himself into the mail, arrived in London, and waiting there two or three days to obtain what he considered necessary from a fashionable tailor, ordered a chaise to Forest Hill. He had not written to his father to announce his arrival, and it was late in the morning when the chaise drew up at his father's door.

Jack stepped out and rang the bell. The servants who opened the door did not know him; they were not the same as those he left.

"Where is Mr Easy?" demanded Jack.

"Who are you?" replied one of the men, in a gruff tone.

"By de powers, you very soon find out who he is," observed Mesty.

"Stay here, and I'll see if he is at home."

"Stay here! stay in the hall like a footman? What do you mean, you rascal?" cried Jack, attempting to push by the man.

"Oh, that won't do here, master; this is Equality Hall; one man's as good as another."

"Not always," replied Jack knocking him down. "Take that for your insolence, pack up your traps, and walk out of the house to-morrow morning."

Mesty in the meantime, had seized the other by the throat.

"What I do with this fellow, Massa Easy?"

"Leave him now, Mesty; we'll settle their account to-morrow morning. I presume I shall find my father in the library."

"His father!" said one of the men to the other; "he's not exactly a chip of the old block."

"We shall have a change, I expect," replied the other, as they walked away.

"Mesty," cried Jack, in an authoritative tone, "bring those two rascals back to take the luggage out of the chaise; pay the postilion, and tell the housekeeper to show you my room and yours. Come to me for orders as soon as you have done this."

"Yes, sir," replied Mesty. "Now come here, you damn blackguard, and take tings out of chaise, or by de holy poker I choke your luff, both of you."

The filed teeth, the savage look, and determination of Mesty, had the due effect. The men sullenly returned and unloaded the chaise. In the meantime, Jack walked into his father's study; his father was there—the study was lighted up with argand lamps, and Jack looked with astonishment. Mr Easy was busy with a plaster cast of a human head, which he pored over, so that he did not perceive the entrance of his son. The cast of the skull was divided into many compartments, with writing on each; but what most astonished our hero was the alteration in the apartment. The book-cases and books had all been removed, and in the centre, suspended from the ceiling, was an apparatus which would have puzzled any one, composed of rods in every direction, with screws at the end of them, and also tubes in equal number, one of which communicated with a large air-pump, which stood on a table. Jack took a short survey, and then walked up to his father and accosted him.

"What!" exclaimed Mr Easy, "is it possible?—yes, it is my son John! I'm glad to see you, John—very glad indeed," continued the old gentleman, shaking him by both hands—"very glad that you have come home: I wanted you—wanted your assistance in my great and glorious project, which, I thank Heaven, is now advancing rapidly. Very soon shall equality and the rights of man be proclaimed everywhere. The pressure from without is enormous, and the bulwarks of our ridiculous and tyrannical constitution must give way. King, lords, and aristocrats; landholders, tithe-collectors, church and state, thank God, will soon be overthrown, and the golden age revived—the millennium, the true millennium—not what your poor mother talked about. I am at the head of twenty-nine societies, and if my health lasts, you will see what I will accomplish now that I have your assistance, Jack;" and Mr Easy's eyes sparkled and flashed in all the brilliancy of incipient insanity.

Jack sighed, and to turn the conversation he observed, "You have made a great change in this room, sir. What may all this be for? Is it a machine to improve equality and the rights of man?"

"My dear son," replied Mr Easy, sitting down, and crossing his legs complacently, with his two hands under his right thigh, according to his usual custom when much pleased with himself—"why, my dear son, that is not exactly the case, and yet you have shown some degree of perception even in your guess; for if my invention succeeds, and I have no doubt of it, I shall have discovered the great art of rectifying the mistakes of nature, and giving an equality of organisation to the whole species, of introducing all the finer organs of humanity, and of destroying the baser. It is a splendid invention, Jack, very splendid. They may talk of Gall and Spurzheim, and all those; but what have they done? nothing but divided the brain into sections, classed the organs, and discovered where they reside; but what good result has been gained from that? the murderer by nature remained a murderer—the benevolent man, a benevolent man—he could not alter his organisation. I have found out how to change all that."

"Surely, sir, you would not interfere with the organ of benevolence?"

"But indeed I must, Jack. I myself am suffering from my organ of benevolence being too large; I must reduce it, and then I shall be capable of greater things, shall not be so terrified by difficulties, shall overlook trifles, and only carry on great schemes for universal equality and the supreme rights of man. I have put myself into that machine every morning for two hours, for these last three months, and I feel now that I am daily losing a great portion."

"Will you do me the favour to explain an invention so extraordinary, sir," said our hero.

"Most willingly, my boy. You observe that in the centre there is a frame to confine the human head, somewhat larger than the head itself, and that the head rests upon the iron collar beneath. When the head is thus firmly fixed, suppose I want to reduce the size of any particular organ, I take the boss corresponding to where that organ is situated in the cranium, and fix it on it. For you will observe that all the bosses inside of the top of the frame correspond to the organs as described in this plaster-cast on the table. I then screw down pretty tight, and increase the pressure daily, until the organ disappears altogether, or is reduced to the size required."

"I comprehend that part perfectly, sir," replied Jack; "but now explain to me by what method you contrive to raise an organ which does not previously exist."

"That," replied Mr Easy, "is the greatest perfection of the whole invention, for without I could do that, I could have done little. I feel convinced that this invention of mine will immortalise me. Observe all these little bell-glasses which communicate with the air-pump. I shave my patient's head, grease it a little, and fix on the bell-glass, which is exactly shaped to fit the organ in length and breadth. I work the air-pump, and raise the organ by an exhausted receiver. It cannot fail. There is my butler, now; a man who escaped hanging last spring assizes on an undoubted charge of murder. I selected him on purpose; I have flattened down murder to nothing, and I have raised benevolence till it's like a wen."

"I am afraid my poor father's head is an exhausted receiver," thought Jack, who then replied, "Well, sir, if it succeeds it will be a good invention."

"If it succeeds!—why, it has succeeded!—it cannot fail. It has cost me near two thousand pounds. By-the-bye, Jack, you have drawn very liberally lately, and I had some trouble, with my own expenses, to meet your bills; not that I complain—but what with societies, and my machine, and tenants refusing to pay their rents on the principle that the farms are no more mine than theirs, which I admit to be true, I have had some difficulty in meeting all demands."

"The Governor was right," thought Jack, who now inquired after Dr Middleton.

"Ah, poor silly man! he's alive yet—I believe doing well. He is one who will interfere with the business of others, complains of my servants—very silly man indeed—but I let him have his own way. So I did your poor mother. Silly woman, Mrs Easy—but never mind that."

"If you please, sir, I have also a complaint to make of the servants for their insolence to me: but we will adjourn, if you please, as I wish to have some refreshment."

"Certainly, Jack, if you are hungry; I will go with you. Complain of my servants, say you?—there must be some mistake—they are all shaved, and wear wigs, and I put them in the machine every other morning; but I mean to make an alteration in one respect. You observe, Jack, it requires more dignity: we must raise the whole machinery some feet, ascend it with state as a throne, for it is the throne of reason, the victory of mind over nature."

"As you please, sir; but I am really hungry just now."

Jack and his father went into the drawing-room and rang the bell; not being answered, Jack rose and rang again.

"My dear sir," observed Mr Easy, "you must not be in a hurry; every man naturally provides for his own wants first, and afterwards for those of others. Now my servants—"

"Are a set of insolent scoundrels, sir, and insolence I never permit. I knocked one down as I entered your house, and, with your permission, I will discharge two, at least, to-morrow."

"My dear son," exclaimed Mr Easy, "you knocked my servant down!—are you not aware by the laws of equality—"

"I am aware of this, my dear father," replied Jack, "that by all the laws of society we have a right to expect civility and obedience from those we pay and feed."

"Pay and feed! Why, my dear son—my dear Jack—you must recollect—"

"I recollect, sir, very well; but if your servants do not come to their recollection in a very short time, either I or they must quit the house."

"But, my dear boy, have you forgotten the principles I instilled into you? Did you not go to sea to obtain that equality foiled by tyranny and despotism here on shore? Do you not acknowledge and support my philosophy?"

"We'll argue that point to-morrow, sir—at present I want to obtain my supper;" and Jack rang the bell furiously.

The butler made his appearance at this last summons, and he was followed by Mesty, who looked like a demon with anger.

"Mercy on me, whom have we here?"

"My servant, father," exclaimed Jack, starting up; "one that I can trust to, and who will obey me. Mesty, I wish some supper and wine to be brought immediately—see that scoundrel gets it ready in a moment. If he does not, throw him out of the door, and lock him out. You understand me."

"Yes, massa," grinned Mesty; "now you hab supper very quick, or Mesty know the reason why. Follow me, sar," cried Mesty, in an imperative tone to the butler; "quick, sar, or by de holy poker, I show you what Mesty can do;" and Mesty grinned in his wrath.

"Bring supper and wine immediately," said Mr Easy, giving an order such as the butler had never heard since he had been in the house.

The butler quitted the room, followed by the Ashantee.

"My dear boy—my Jack—I can make every allowance for hunger, it is often the cause of theft and crime in the present unnatural state of society—but really you are too violent. The principles—"

"Your principles are all confounded nonsense, father," cried Jack in a rage.

"What, Jack! my son—what do I hear? This from you—nonsense! Why, Jack, what has Captain Wilson been doing with you?"

"Bringing me to my senses, sir."

"Oh, dear, oh, dear! my dear Jack, you will certainly make me lose mine."

"Gone already," thought Jack.

"That you, my child, so carefully brought up in the great and glorious school of philosophy, should behave this way—should be so violent—forget your sublime philosophy, and all—just like Esau, selling your birthright for a mess of pottage. Oh, Jack, you'll kill me! and yet I love you, Jack—whom else have I to love in this world? Never mind, we'll argue the point, my boy—I'll convince you—in a week all will be right again."

"It shall, sir, if I can manage it," replied Jack.

"That's right, I love to hear you say so—that's consoling, very consoling—but I think now I was wrong to let you go to sea, Jack."

"Indeed you were not, father."

"Well, I'm glad to hear you say so; I thought they had ruined you, destroyed all your philosophy—but it will be all right again—you shall come to our societies, Jack—I am president—you shall hear me speak, Jack—you shall hear me thunder like Demosthenes—but here comes the tray."

The butler, followed by Mesty, who attended him as if he was his prisoner, now made his appearance with the tray—laid it down in a sulky manner and retired. Jack desired Mesty to remain.

"Well, Mesty, how are they getting on in the servants' hall?"

"Regular mutiny, sar—ab swear dat dey no stand our nonsense, and dat we both leave the house to-morrow."

"Do you hear, sir, your servants declare that I shall leave your house to-morrow."

"You leave my house, Jack, after four years' absence!—no, no. I'll reason with them—I'll make them a speech. You don't know how I can speak, Jack."

"Look you, father, I cannot stand this; either give me a carte-blanche to arrange this household as I please, or I shall quit it myself to-morrow morning."

"Quit my house, Jack! no, no—shake hands and make friends with them; be civil, and they will serve you—but you know upon the principles—"

"Principles of the devil!" cried Jack in a rage.

"Of the devil, Jack; dear me! I wish you had never gone to sea."

"In one word, sir, do you consent, or am I to leave the house?"

"Leave the house! Oh, no; not leave the house, Jack. I have no son but you. Then do as you please—but you must not send away my murderer, for I must have him cured, and shown as a proof of my wonderful invention."

"Mesty, get my pistols ready for to-morrow morning, and your own too—do ye hear?"

"All ready, massa," replied Mesty; "I tink dat right."

"Right!—pistols, Jack! What do you mean?"

"It is possible, father, that you may not have yet quite cured your murderer, and therefore it is as well to be prepared. I will now wish you goodnight; but before I go, you will be pleased to summon one of the servants that he may inform the others that the household is under my control for the future."

The bell was again rung, and was this time answered with more expedition. Jack told the servant, in the presence of his father, that, with the consent of the latter, he should hereafter take the whole control of the establishment, and that Mesty would be the major-domo from whom they would receive their orders. The man stared, and cast an appealing look to Mr Easy, who hesitated, and at last said:

"Yes, William; you'll apologise to all, and say that I have made the arrangement."

"You apologise to none, sir," cried Jack; "but tell them that I will arrange the whole business to-morrow morning. Tell the woman to come here and show me my bedroom. Mesty, get your supper and then come up to me; if they dare to refuse you, recollect who does, and point them out to-morrow morning. That will do, sir; away with you, and bring flat candlesticks."

Chapter Thirty Six.

In which Jack takes up the other side of the argument, and proves that he can argue as well on one side as the other.

This scene may give some idea of the state of Mr Easy's household upon our hero's arrival. The poor lunatic, for such we must call him, was at the mercy of his servants, who robbed, laughed at, and neglected him. The waste and expense were enormous. Our hero, who found how matters stood, went to bed, and lay the best part of the night revolving what to do. He determined to send for Dr Middleton, and consult him.

The next morning Jack rose early; Mesty was in the room, with warm water, as soon as he rang.

"By de power, Massa Easy, your fader very silly old man."

"I'm afraid so," replied Jack.

"He not right here," observed Mesty, putting his fingers to his head.

Jack sighed, and desired Mesty to send one of the grooms up to the door. When the man knocked he desired him to mount a horse and ride over to Dr Middleton, and request his immediate attendance.

The man, who was really a good servant, replied, "Yes, sir," very respectfully, and hastened away.

Jack went down to breakfast, and found it all ready, but his father was not in the room: he went to his study, and found him occupied with a carpenter who was making a sort of a frame as the model of the platform or daïs to be raised under the wonderful invention. Mr Easy was so busy that he could not come to breakfast, so Jack took his atone. An hour after this Dr Middleton's carriage drove up to the door. The doctor heartily greeted our hero.

"My dear sir—for so I suppose I must now call you—I am heartily glad that you have returned. I can assure you that it is not a moment too soon."

"I have found that out already, doctor," replied Jack: "sit down. Have you breakfasted?"

"No, I have not; for I was so anxious to see you, that I ordered my carriage at once."

"Then sit down, doctor, and we will talk over matters quietly."

"You, of course, perceive the state of your father. He has been some time quite unfit to manage his own affairs."

"So I am afraid."

"What do you intend to do then—put them in the hands of trustees?"

"I will be trustee for myself, Dr Middleton. I could not do the other without submitting my poor father to a process and confinement which I cannot think of."

"I can assure you that there are not many in Bedlam worse than he is; but I perfectly agree with you; that is, if he will consent to your taking charge of the property."

"A power of attorney will be all that is requisite," replied Jack; "that is, as soon as I have rid the house of the set of miscreants who are in it, and who are now in open mutiny."

"I think," replied the doctor, "that you will have some trouble. You know the character of the butler."

"Yes, I have it from my father's own mouth. I really should take it as a great favour, Dr Middleton, if you could stay here a day or two. I know that you have retired from practice."

"I would have made the same offer, my young friend. I will come here with two of my servants; for you must discharge these."

"I have one of my own who is worth his weight in gold—that will be sufficient. I will dismiss every man you think I ought, and as for the women, we can give them warning, and replace them at leisure."

"That is exactly what I should propose," replied the doctor. "I will now go, if you please, procure the assistance of a couple of constables, and also of your father's former, legal adviser, who shall prepare a power of attorney."

"Yes," replied Jack, "and we must then find out the tenants who refuse to pay upon the principles of equality, and he shall serve them with notice immediately."

"I am rejoiced, my dear young friend, to perceive that your father's absurd notions have not taken root."

"They lasted some time nevertheless, doctor," replied Jack, laughing.

"Well then, I will only quit you for an hour or two, and then, as you wish it, will take up my quarters here as long as you find me useful."

In the forenoon, Dr Middleton again made his appearance, accompanied by Mr Hanson, the solicitor, bringing with him his portmanteau and his servants. Mr Easy had come into the parlour, and was at breakfast when they entered. He received them very coolly; but a little judicious praise of the wonderful invention had its due effect; and after Jack had reminded him of his promise that in future he was to control the household, he was easily persuaded to sign the order for his so doing—that is, the power of attorney.

Mr Easy also gave up to Jack the key of his secretary, and Mr Hanson possessed himself of the books, papers, and receipts necessary to ascertain the state of his affairs, and the rents which had not yet been paid up. In the meantime the constables arrived. The servants were all summoned; Mr Hanson showed them the power of attorney empowering Jack to act for his father, and in less than half an hour afterwards all the men-servants, but two grooms, were dismissed: the presence of the constables and Mesty prevented any resistance, but not without various threats on the part of the butler, whose name was O'Rourke. Thus, in twenty-four hours, Jack had made a reformation in the household.

Mr Easy took no notice of anything; he returned to his study and his wonderful invention. Mesty had received the keys of the cellar, and had now complete control over those who remained. Dr Middleton, Mr Hanson, Mr Easy, and Jack, sat down to dinner, and everything wore the appearance of order and comfort. Mr Easy ate very heartily, but said nothing till after dinner, when, as was his usual custom, he commenced arguing upon the truth and soundness of his philosophy.

"By-the-bye, my dear son, if I recollect right, you told me last night that you were no longer of my opinion. Now, if you please, we will argue this point."

"I'll argue the point with all my heart, sir," replied Jack; "will you begin?"

"Let's fill our glasses," cried Mr Easy triumphantly; "let's fill our glasses, and then I will bring Jack back to the proper way of thinking. Now then, my son, I trust you will not deny that we were all born equal."

"I do deny it, sir," replied Jack; "I deny it *in toto*—I deny it from the evidence of our own senses, and from the authority of Scripture. To suppose all men were born equal is to suppose that they are equally endowed with the same strength and with the same capacity of mind, which we know is not the case. I deny it from Scripture, from which I could quote many passages; but I will restrict myself to one—the parable of the Talents: 'To one he gave five talents, to another but one,' holding them responsible for the trust reposed in them. We are all intended to fill various situations in society, and are provided by Heaven accordingly."

"That may be," replied Mr Easy; "but that does not prove that the earth was not intended to be equally distributed among all alike."

"I beg your pardon; the proof that that was not the intention of Providence is that that equality, allowing it to be put in practice, could never be maintained."

"Not maintained!—no, because the strong oppress the weak, tyrants rise up and conquer—men combine to do wrong."

"Not so, my dear father; I say it could not be maintained without the organisation of each individual had been equalised and several other points established. For instance, allowing that every man had, *ab origine*, a certain portion of ground, he who was the strongest or the cleverest would soon cause his to yield more than others would, and thus the equality be destroyed. Again, if one couple had ten children, and another had none, then again would equality be broken in upon, as the land that supports two in the one instance, would have to feed twelve in the other. You perceive, therefore, that without rapine or injustice your equality could not be preserved."

"But, Jack, allowing that there might be some diversity from such causes, that would be a very different thing from the present monstrous state of society, in which we have kings, and lords, and people, rolling in wealth, while others are in a state of pauperism, and obliged to steal for their daily bread."

"My dear father, I consider that it is to this inequality that society owes its firmest cementation, that we are enabled to live in peace and happiness, protected by just laws, each doing his duty in that state of life to which he is called, rising above or sinking in the scale of society according as he has been entrusted with the five talents or the one. Equality can and does exist nowhere. We are told that it does not exist in heaven itself—how can it exist upon earth?"

"But that is only asserted, Jack, and it is not proof that it ought not to exist."

"Let us argue the point, father, coolly. Let us examine a little what would be the effect if all was equality. Were all equal in beauty, there would be no beauty, for beauty is only by comparison—were all equal in strength, conflicts would be interminable—were all equal in rank, and power, and possessions, the greatest charms of existence would be destroyed—generosity, gratitude, and half the finer virtues would be unknown. The first principle of our religion, charity, could not be practised—pity would never be called forth—benevolence, your great organ, would be useless, and self-denial a blank letter. Were all equal in ability, there would be no instruction, no talent—no genius—nothing to admire, nothing to copy, to respect—nothing to rouse emulation or stimulate to praiseworthy ambition. Why, my dear father, what an idle, unprofitable, weary world would this be, if it were based on equality!"

"But, allowing all that, Jack," replied Mr Easy, "and I will say you argue well in a bad cause, why should the inequality be carried so far? king and lords, for instance."

"The most lasting and imperishable form of building is that of the pyramid, which defies ages, and to that may the most perfect form of society be compared. It is based upon the many, and rising by degrees, it becomes less as wealth, talent, and rank increase in the individual, until it ends at the apex, or monarch, above all. Yet each several stone from the apex to the base is necessary for the preservation of the structure, and fulfils its duty in its allotted place. Could you prove that those at the summit possess the greatest share of happiness in this world, then, indeed, you have a position to argue on; but it is well known that such is not the case; and, provided he is of a contented mind, the peasant is more happy than the king, surrounded as the latter is by cares and anxiety."

"Very well argued indeed, my dear sir," observed Dr Middleton.

"But, my dear boy, there are other states of society than monarchy; we have republics and despotisms."

"We have, but how long do they last, compared to the first? There is a cycle in the changes which never varies. A monarchy may be overthrown by a revolution, and republicanism succeed, but that is shortly followed by despotism, till, after a time, monarchy succeeds again by unanimous consent, as the most legitimate and equitable form of government; but in none of these do you find a single advance to equality. In a republic those who govern are more powerful than the rulers in a restricted monarchy—a president is greater than a king, and next to a despot, whose will is law. Even in small societies you find that some will naturally take the lead and assume domination. We commence the system at school, when we are first thrown into society, and there we are taught systems of petty tyranny. There are some few points in which we can obtain equality in this world, and that equality can only be obtained under a well-regulated form of society, and consists in an equal administration of justice and of laws to which we have agreed to submit for the benefit of the whole—the equal right to live and not be permitted to starve, which has been obtained in this country. And when we are all called to account, we shall have equal justice. Now, my dear father, you have my opinion."

"Yes, my dear, this is all very well in the abstract; but how does it work?"

"It works well. The luxury, the pampered state, the idleness—if you please, the wickedness of the rich, all contribute to the support, the comfort, and employment of the poor. You may behold extravagance—it is a vice; but that very extravagance circulates money, and the vice of one contributes to the happiness of many. The only vice which is not redeemed by producing commensurate good, is avarice. If all were equal there would be no arts, no manufactures, no industry, no employment. As it is, the inequality of the distribution of wealth may be compared to the heart, pouring forth the blood like a steam-engine through the human frame, the same blood returning from the extremities by the veins, to be again propelled, and keep up a healthy and vigorous circulation."

"Bravo, Jack!" said Dr Middleton. "Have you anything to reply, sir?" continued he, addressing Mr Easy.

"To reply, sir?" replied Mr Easy with scorn, "why, he has not given me half an argument yet—why, that black servant even laughs at him—look at him there, showing his teeth. Can he forget the horrors of slavery? can he forget the base unfeeling lash?—no, sir, he has suffered, and he can estimate the divine right of equality. Ask him now, ask him if you dare, Jack, whether he will admit the truth of your argument."

"Well, I'll ask him," replied Jack, "and I tell you candidly that he was once one of your disciples. Mesty, what's your opinion of equality?"

"Equality, Massa Easy?" replied Mesty, pulling up his cravat; "I say damn equality, now I major domo."

"The rascal deserves to be a slave all his life."

"True, I ab been slave—but I a prince in my own country—Massa Easy tell how many skulls I have."

"Skulls—skulls—do you know anything of the sublime science; are you a phrenologist?"

"I know man's skull very well in Ashantee country, anyhow."

"Then if you know that, you must be one. I had no idea that the science had extended so far—maybe it was brought from thence. I will have some talk with you to-morrow. This is very curious, Dr Middleton, is it not?"

"Very, indeed, Mr Easy."

"I shall feel his head to-morrow after breakfast, and if there is anything wrong I shall correct it with my machine. By-the-bye, I have quite forgot, gentlemen; you will excuse me, but I wish to see what the carpenter has done for me, and after that I shall attend the meeting of the society. Jack, my boy, won't you come and hear my speech."

"Thank you, sir, but I cannot well leave your friends."

Mr Easy quitted the room.

"Are you aware, my dear sir, that your father has opened his preserves to all the poachers?" said Mr Hanson.

"The devil he has!"

"Yes, he has allowed several gangs of gipsies to locate themselves in his woods, much to the annoyance of the neighbourhood, who suffer from their depredations," continued Dr Middleton.

"I find, by the receipts and books, that there is nearly two years' rental of the estate due; some tenants have paid up in full, others not for four years. I reckon fourteen thousand pounds still in arrear."

"You will oblige me by taking immediate steps, Mr Hanson, for the recovery of the sums due."

"Most certainly, Mr John. I trust your father will not commit himself to-night as he has done lately."

When they rose to retire Dr Middleton took our hero by the hand. "You do not know, my dear fellow, what pleasure it gives me to find that, in spite of the doting of your mother and the madness of your father, you have turned out so well. It is very fortunate that you have come home; I trust you will now give up the profession."

"I have given it up, sir; which, by-the-bye, reminds me that I have not applied for either my discharge or that of my servant; but I cannot spare time yet, so I shall not report myself."

Chapter Thirty Seven.

In which our hero finds himself an orphan, and resolves to go to sea again, without the smallest idea of equality.

The next morning, when they met at breakfast, Mr Easy did not make his appearance, and Jack inquired of Mesty where he was?

"They say down below that the old gentleman not come home last night."

"Did not come home!" said Dr Middleton, "this must be looked to."

"He great rascal dat butler man," said Mesty to Jack; "but de old gentleman not sleep in his bed, dat for sure."

"Make inquiries when he went out," said Jack.

"I hope no accident has happened," observed Mr Hanson; "but his company has lately been very strange."

"Nobody see him go out, sar, last night," reported Mesty.

"Very likely he is in his study," observed Dr Middleton; "he may have remained all night, fast asleep, by his wonderful invention."

"I'll go and see," replied Jack.

Dr Middleton accompanied him, and Mesty followed. They opened the door, and beheld a spectacle which made them recoil with horror. There was Mr Easy, with his head in the machine, the platform below fallen from under him, hanging, with his toes just touching the ground. Dr Middleton hastened to him, and, assisted by Mesty and our hero, took him out of the steel collar which was round his neck; but life had been extinct for many hours, and, on examination, it was found that the poor old gentleman's neck was dislocated.

It was surmised that the accident must have taken place the evening before, and it was easy to account for it. Mr Easy, who had had the machine raised four feet higher, for the platform and steps to be placed underneath, must have mounted on the frame modelled by the carpenter for his work, and have fixed his head in, for the knob was pressed on his bump of benevolence. The framework, hastily put together with a few short nails, had given way with his weight, and the sudden fall had dislocated his neck.

Mr Hanson led away our hero, who was much shocked at this unfortunate and tragical end of his poor father, while Dr Middleton ordered the body to be taken up into a bedroom, and immediately despatched a messenger to the coroner of the county. Poor Mr Easy had told his son but the day before that he felt convinced that this wonderful invention would immortalise him, and so it had, although not exactly in the sense that he anticipated.

We must pass over the few days of sorrow, and closed shutters, which always are given to these scenes. The coroner's inquest and the funeral over, daylight was again admitted, our hero's spirits revived, and he found himself in possession of a splendid property, and his own master.

He was not of age, it is true, for he wanted nine months; but on opening the will of his father, he found that Dr Middleton was his sole guardian. Mr Hanson, on examining and collecting the papers, which were in the greatest confusion, discovered bank-notes in different corners, and huddled up with bills and receipts, to the amount of two thousand pounds, and further, a cheque signed by Captain Wilson on his banker, for the thousand pounds advanced by Mr Easy, dated more than fifteen months back.

Dr Middleton wrote to the Admiralty, informing them that family affairs necessitated Mr John Easy, who had been left at sick quarters, to leave his Majesty's service, requesting his discharge from it forthwith. The Admiralty was graciously pleased to grant the request, and lose the services of a midshipman. The Admiralty were also pleased to grant the discharge of Mesty, on the sum required for a substitute being paid in.

The gipsies were routed out of their abodes, and sent once more to wander. The gamekeepers were restored, the preserves cleared of all poachers, and the gentry of the county were not a little pleased at Jack's succession, for they had wished that Mr Easy's neck had been broken long ago. The societies were dissolved, since, now that Mr Easy paid no longer for the beer, there was nothing to meet for. Cards and compliments were sent from all parts of the county, and every one was anxious that our hero should come of age, as then he would be able to marry, to give dinners, subscribe to the fox-hounds, and live as a gentleman ought to do.

But, during all these speculations, Jack had made Dr Middleton acquainted with the history of his amour with Agnes de Rebiera, and all particulars connected therewith, also with his determination to go out to bring her home as his wife. Dr Middleton saw no objection to the match, and he perceived that our hero was sincere. And Jack had made inquiries when the packet would sail for Malta, when Mesty, who stood behind his chair, observed:

"Packet bad vessel, Massa Easy. Why not go out in man-of-war?"

"Very true," replied Jack; "but you know, Mesty, that is not so easy."

"And den how come home, sar. Suppose you and Missy Agnes taken prisoner—put in prison?"

"Very true," replied Jack; "and as for a passage home in a man-of-war that will be more difficult still."

"Den I tink, sar, suppose you buy one fine vessel—plenty of guns—take out letter of marque—plenty of men, and bring Missy Agnes home like a lady. You captain of your own ship."

"That deserves consideration, Mesty," replied Jack, who thought of it during that night; and the next day resolved to follow Mesty's advice. The Portsmouth paper lay on the breakfast-table. Jack took it up, and his eye was caught by an advertisement for the sale of the *Joan d'Arc*, prize to H.M. ship *Thetis*, brigantine of 278 tons, copper-bottomed, armed *en flute*, with all her stores, spars, sails, running and standing rigging, then lying in the harbour of Portsmouth, to take place on the following Wednesday.

Jack rang the bell, and ordered post-horses.

"Where are you going, my dear boy?" inquired Dr Middleton.

"To Portsmouth, doctor."

"And pray what for, if not an impertinent question?"

Jack then gave Dr Middleton an insight into his plan, and requested that he would allow him to do so, as there was plenty of ready-money.

"But the expense will be enormous."

"It will be heavy, sir, I grant; but I have calculated it pretty nearly, and I shall not spend at the rate of more than my income. Besides, as letter of marque, I shall have the right of capture; in fact, I mean to take out a privateer's regular licence."

"But not to remain there and cruise?"

"No, upon my honour; I am too anxious to get home again. You must not refuse me, my dear guardian."

"As a lady is in the case, I will not, my dear boy; but be careful what you are about."

"Never fear, sir, I will be back in four months, at the furthest; but I must now set off and ascertain if the vessel answers the description given in the advertisement."

Jack threw himself into the chariot. Mesty mounted into the rumble, and in two hours they were at Portsmouth; went to the agent, viewed the vessel, which proved to be a very fine fast-sailing craft, well found, with six brass carronades on each side. The cabins were handsome, fitted up with bird's-eye maple and gilt mouldings.

This will do, thought Jack; a couple of long brass nines, forty men and six boys, and she will be just the thing we require. So Mesty and Jack went on shore again, and returned to Forest Hill to dinner, when he desired Mr Hanson to set off for Portsmouth, and bid at the sale for the vessel, as he wished to purchase her. This was Monday, and on Wednesday Mr Hanson purchased her, as she stood, for 1750 pounds, which was considered about half her value.

Dr Middleton had, in the meantime, been thinking very seriously of Jack's project. He could see no objection to it, provided that he was steady and prudent, but in both these qualities Jack had not exactly been tried. He therefore determined to look out for some steady naval lieutenant, and make it a *sine quâ non* that our hero should be accompanied by him, and that he should go out as sailing-master. Now that the vessel was purchased, he informed Jack of his wish; indeed, as Dr Middleton observed, his duty as guardian demanded this precaution, and our hero, who felt very grateful to Dr Middleton, immediately acquiesced.

"And, by-the-bye, doctor, see that he is a good navigator; for although I can fudge a day's work pretty well, latterly I have been out of practice."

Every one was now busy. Jack and Mesty at Portsmouth, fitting out the vessel, and offering three guineas a head to the crimps for every good able seaman—Mr Hanson obtaining the English register, and the letters of licence, and Dr Middleton in search of a good naval dry-nurse. Jack found time to write to Don Philip and Agnes, apprising them of the death of his father, and his intentions.

In about six weeks all was ready, and the brigantine, which had taken out her British register and licence under the name of the *Rebiera*, went out of harbour, and anchored at Spithead. Dr Middleton had procured, as he thought, a very fit person to sail with Jack, and our hero and Mesty embarked, wishing the doctor and solicitor good-bye, and leaving them nothing to do but to pay the bills.

The person selected by Dr Middleton, by the advice of an old friend of his, a purser in the navy who lived at Southsea, was a Lieutenant Oxbelly, who, with the ship's company, which had been collected, received our hero as their captain and owner upon his arrival on board. There certainly was no small contrast between our hero's active slight figure and handsome person, set-off with a blue coat, something like the present yacht-club uniform, and that of his second in command, who waddled to the side to receive him. He was a very short man, with an uncommon protuberance of stomach, with shoulders and arms too short for his body, and hands much too large, more like the paws of a Polar bear than anything else. He wore trousers, shoes, and buckles. On his head was a foraging cap, which, when he took it off, showed that he was quite bald. His age might be about fifty-five or sixty; his complexion florid, no whiskers and little beard, nose straight, lips thin, teeth black with chewing, and always a little brown dribble from the left corner of his mouth (there was a leak there, he said). Altogether his countenance was prepossessing, for it was honest and manly, but his waist was preposterous.

"Steady enough," thought Jack, as he returned Mr Oxbelly's salute.

"How do you do, sir?" said Jack, "I trust we shall be good shipmates," for Jack had not seen him before.

"Mr Easy," replied the lieutenant, "I never quarrel with any one, except (I won't tell a story) with my wife."

"I am sorry that you have ever domestic dissensions, Mr Oxbelly."

"And I only quarrel with her at night, sir. She will take up more than her share of the bed, and won't allow me to sleep single; but never mind that, sir; now will you please to muster the men?"

"If you please, Mr Oxbelly."

The men were mustered, and Jack made them a long speech upon subordination, discipline, activity, duty, and so forth.

"A very good speech, Mr Easy," said Mr Oxbelly, as the men went forward; "I wish my wife had heard it. But, sir, if you please, we'll now get under way as fast as we can, for there is a Channel cruiser working up at St. Helen's, and we may give him the go-by by running through the Needles."

"But what need we care for the Channel cruiser?"

"You forget, sir, that as soon as she drops her anchor she will come on board and take a fancy to at least ten of our men."

"But they are protected."

"Yes, sir, but that's no protection nowadays. I have sailed in a privateer at least three years, and I know that they have no respect for letters of marque or for privateers."

"I believe you are right, Mr Oxbelly, so if you please we will up with the anchor at once."

The crew of the *Rebiera* had been well chosen; they were prime men-of-war's men, most of whom had deserted from the various ships on the station, and, of course, were most anxious to be off. In a few minutes the *Rebiera* was under way with all sail set below and aloft. She was in excellent trim, and flew through the water; the wind was fair, and by night they had passed Portland Lights, and the next morning were steering a course for the Bay of Biscay without having encountered what they feared more than an enemy—a British cruiser to overhaul them.

"I think we shall do now, sir," observed Mr Oxbelly to our hero; "we have made a famous run. It's twelve o'clock, and if you please I'll work the latitude and let you know what it is. We must shape our course so as not to run in with the Brest squadron. A little more westing, sir. I'll be up in one minute. My wife—but I'll tell you about that when I come up.

"Latitude 41 degrees 12 minutes, sir. I was about to say that my wife, when she was on board of the privateer that I commanded—"

"Board of the privateer, Mr Oxbelly?"

"Yes, sir, would go; told her it was impossible, but she wouldn't listen to reason—came on board, flopped herself into the standing bed-place, and said that there she was for the cruise—little Billy with her—"

"What! your child, too?"

"Yes, two years old—fine boy—always laughed when the guns were fired, while his mother stood on the ladder and held him on the top of the booby-hatch."

"I wonder that Mrs Oxbelly let you come here now?"

"So you would, sir, but I'll explain that—she thinks I'm in London about my half-pay. She knows all by this time, and frets, I don't doubt; but that will make her thin, and then there will be more room in the bed. Mrs Oxbelly is a very stout woman."

"Why you are not a little man!"

"No, not little—tending to be lusty, as the saying is—that is, in good condition. It's very strange that Mrs Oxbelly has an idea that she is not large. I cannot persuade her to it. That's the reason we always spar in bed. She says it is I, and I know that it is she, who takes the largest share of it."

"Perhaps you may both be right."

"No, no, it is she who creates all the disturbance. If I get nearer to the wall she jams me up till I am as thin as a thread-paper. If I put her inside and stay outside, she cuts me out as you do a cask, by the chine, till I tumble out of bed."

"Why don't you make your bed larger, Mr Oxbelly?"

"Sir, I have proposed, but my wife will have it that the bed is large enough if I would not toss in my sleep. I can't convince her. However, she'll have it all to herself now. I slept well last night, for the first time since I left the *Boadicea*."

"The *Boadicea*?"

"Yes, sir, I was second lieutenant of the *Boadicea* for three years."

"She's a fine frigate, I'm told."

"On the contrary, such a pinched-up little craft below I never saw. Why, Mr Easy, I could hardly get into the door of my cabin—and yet, as you must see, I'm not a large man."

"Good heavens! is it possible," thought Jack, "that this man does not really know that he is monstrous?"

Yet such was the case. Mr Oxbelly had no idea that he was otherwise than in good condition, although he had probably not seen his knees for years. It was his obesity that was the great objection to him, for in every other point there was nothing against him. He had, upon one pretence and another, been shifted, by the manoeuvres of the captains, out of different ships, until he went up to the Admiralty to know if there was any charge against him. The First Lord at once perceived the charge to be preferred, and made a mark against his name as not fit for anything but harbour duty. Out of employment, he had taken the command of a privateer cutter, when his wife who was excessively fond, would, as he said, follow him with little Billy. He was sober, steady, knew his duty well; but he weighed twenty-six stone, and his weight had swamped him in the service.

His wish, long indulged, had become, as Shakespeare says, the father of his thought, and he had really at last brought himself to think that he was not by any means what could be considered a fat man. His wife, as he said, was also a very stout woman, and this exuberance of flesh on both sides, was the only, but continual, ground of dispute.

Chapter Thirty Eight.

In which our hero, as usual, gets into the very middle of it.

On the eleventh day the Rebiera entered the Straits, and the Rock of Gibraltar was in sight as the sun went down; after which the wind fell light, and about midnight it became calm, and they drifted up. At sunrise they were roused by the report of heavy guns, and perceived an English frigate about eight miles farther up the Straits, and more in the mid-channel, engaging nine or ten Spanish gunboats, which had come out from Algesiras to attack her. It still continued a dead calm, and the boats of the frigate were all ahead towing her, so as to bring her broadside to bear upon the Spanish flotilla. The reverberating of the heavy cannon on both sides over the placid surface of the water—the white smoke ascending as the sun rose in brilliancy in a clear blue sky—the distant echoes repeated from the high hills—had a very beautiful effect for those who are partial to the picturesque. But Jack thought it advisable to prepare for action instead of watching for tints—and in a short time all was ready.

"They'll not come to us, Mr Easy, as long as they have the frigate to hammer at; but still we had better be prepared, for we cannot well pass them without having a few shot. When I came up the Straits in the privateer we were attacked by two, and fought them for three hours; their shot dashed the water over our decks till they were wet fore and aft, but somehow or another they never hit us—we were as low as they were. I'll be bound but they'll hull the frigate though. Mrs Oxbelly and Billy were on deck the whole time—and Billy was quite delighted, and cried when they took him down to breakfast."

"Why, Mrs Oxbelly must be very courageous."

"Cares neither for shot nor shell, sir, laughs when they whiz over her head, and tells Billy to hark. But, sir, it's not surprising; her father is a major, and her two brothers are lieutenants in the bombardiers."

"That, indeed," replied Jack—"but see, there is a breeze springing up from the westward."

"Very true, Mr Easy, and a steady one it will be, for it comes up dark and slow; so much the better for the frigate, for she'll get little honour and plenty of mauling at this work."

"I hope we shall take it up with us," observed Jack; "how far do you reckon the gun-boats from the shore?"

"I should think about five miles, or rather less."

"Trim sails, Mr Oxbelly—perhaps we may cut one or two of these off—steer inshore of them."

"Exactly. Up there, my lads, set top-gallant studding sails, top-mast studdings to hand-rig out the booms—keep as you go now, my lad—we shall be well inshore of them, and out of the range of the batteries."

The breeze came down fresh, and all sail was set upon the *Rebiera*. She took the wind down with her, and it passed her but little—half a mile ahead of them all was still and smooth as a glass mirror, and they neared and gained inshore at the same time. The gun-boats were still engaging the frigate, and did not appear to pay any attention to the *Rebiera* coming down. At last the breeze reached them and the frigate, light at first and then gradually increasing, while the *Rebiera* foamed through the water and had now every chance of cutting off some of the gun-boats. The frigate trimmed her sails and steered towards the flotilla, which now thought proper to haul off and put their heads inshore, followed by the frigate firing her bow-chasers. But the *Rebiera* was now within half gun-shot, inshore, and steering so as to intercept them. As she rapidly closed, the flotilla scarcely knew how to act; to attack her would be to lose time, and allow the frigate to come up and occasion their own capture; so they satisfied themselves with firing at her as she continued to run down between them and the land. As they neared, Jack opened his fire with his eighteen-pound carronades and long nines. The gun-boats returned his fire, and they were within a quarter of a mile, when Jack shortened sail to his top-sails, and a warm engagement took place, which ended in one of the gun-boats being in a few minutes dismasted. The frigate, under all canvas, came rapidly up, and her shot now fell thick. The flotilla then ceased firing, passing about two cables' lengths ahead of the *Rebiera*, and making all possible sail for the land. Jack now fired at the flotilla as they passed, with his larboard broadside, while with his starboard he poured in grape and canister upon the unfortunate gun-boat which was dismasted, and which soon hauled down her colours. In a few minutes more the remainder were too far distant for the carronades, and, as they did not fire, Jack turned his attention to take possession of his prize, sending a boat with ten men on board, and heaving-to close to her to take her in tow. Ten minutes more and the frigate was hove-to a cable's length from the *Rebiera*, and our hero lowered down his other quarter boat to go on board.

"Have we any men hurt, Mr Oxbelly?" inquired Jack.

"Only two; Spearling has lost his thumb with a piece of langrage, and James has a bad wound in the thigh."

"Very well; I will ask for the surgeon to come on board."

Jack pulled to the frigate and went up the side, touched his hat in due form, and was introduced by the midshipmen to the other side, where the captain stood.

"Mr Easy!" exclaimed the captain.

"Captain Sawbridge?" replied our hero with surprise.

"Good heavens! what brought you here!" said the captain; "and what vessel is that?"

"The *Rebiera*, letter of marque, commanded and owned by Mr Easy," replied Jack, laughing.

Captain Sawbridge gave him his hand. "Come down with me in the cabin, Mr Easy; I am very glad to see you. Give you great credit for your conduct, and am still more anxious to know what has induced you to come out again. I knew that you had left the service."

Jack, in a very few words, told his object in fitting out the *Rebiera*; "but," continued Jack, "allow me to congratulate you upon your promotion, which I was not aware of. May I ask where you left the *Harpy*, and what is the name of your frigate?"

"The *Latona*! I have only been appointed to her one month, after an action in which the *Harpy* took a large corvette, and am ordered home with despatches to England. We sailed yesterday evening from Gibraltar, were becalmed the whole night, and attacked this morning by the gun-boats."

"How is Captain Wilson, sir?"

"I believe he is very well, but I have not seen him."

"How did you know, then, that I had left the service, Captain Sawbridge?"

"From Mr Gascoigne, who is now on board."

"Gascoigne!" exclaimed our hero.

"Yes, he was sent up to join the *Aurora* by the Governor, but she had left the fleet, and having served his time, and a passing day being ordered, he passed, and thought he might as well go home with me and see if he could make any interest for his promotion."

"Pray, Captain Sawbridge, is the gun-boat our prize or yours?"

"It ought to be wholly yours; but the fact is, by the regulations, we share."

"With all my heart, sir. Will you send an assistant-surgeon on board to look after two of my men who are hurt?"

"Yes, directly; now send your boat away, Easy, with directions to your officer in command. We must go back to Gibraltar, for we have received some injury, and, I am sorry to say, lost some men. You are going then, I presume, to stay on board and dine with me: we shall be at anchor before night."

"I will, with pleasure, sir. But now I will send my boat away and shake hands with Gascoigne."

Gascoigne was under the half-deck waiting to receive his friend, for he had seen him come up the side from his station on the forecastle. A hurried conversation took place, after our hero had dismissed his boat with the assistant-surgeon in it to dress the two wounded men. Jack then went on deck, talked with the officers, looked with pleasure at the *Rebiera* with the gun-boat in tow, keeping company with the frigate, although only under the same canvas— promised Gascoigne to spend the next day with him either on shore or on board of the *Rebiera*, and then returned to the cabin, where he had a long conference with Captain Sawbridge.

"When you first entered the service, Easy," said Captain Sawbridge, "I thought that the sooner the service was rid of you the better; now that you have left it, I feel that it has lost one, who, in all probability, would have proved a credit to it."

"Many thanks, sir," replied Jack; "but how can I be a midshipman with eight thousand pounds a year?"

"I agree with you that it is impossible:— but dinner is serving; go into the after-cabin and the steward will give you all you require."

Our hero, whose face and hands were not a little grimed with the gunpowder, washed himself, combed out his curly black hair, and found all the party in the fore-cabin. Gascoigne, who had not been asked in the forenoon, was, by the consideration of Captain Sawbridge, added to the number. Before dinner was long off the table, the first lieutenant reported that it was necessary to turn the hands up, as they were close to the anchorage. The party, therefore, broke up sooner than otherwise would have been the case; and as soon as the *Latona's* sails were furled Captain Sawbridge went on shore to acquaint the Governor with the results of the action. He asked Jack to accompany him, but our hero, wishing to be with Gascoigne, excused himself until the next day.

"And now, Easy," said Gascoigne, as soon as the captain had gone over the side, "I will ask permission to go on board with you—or will you ask?"

"I will ask," replied Jack; "a gentleman of fortune has more weight with a first lieutenant than a midshipman."

So Jack went up to the first lieutenant, and with one of his polite bows hoped, "if duty would permit, he would honour him by coming on board that evening with some of his officers, to see the *Rebiera* and to drink a bottle or two of champagne."

The first lieutenant, as the *Rebiera* was anchored not two cables' lengths from him, replied, "that as soon as he had shifted the prisoners and secured the gun-boat, he would be very glad;" so did three or four more of the officers, and then Jack begged as a favour that his old friend, Mr Gascoigne, might be permitted to go with him now, as he had important packages to entrust to his care to England. The first lieutenant was very willing, and Gascoigne and our hero jumped into the boat, and were once more in all the confidence of tried and deserved friendship.

"Jack, I've been thinking of it, and I've made up my mind," said Gascoigne. "I shall gain little or nothing by going home for my promotion: I may as well stay here, and as I have served my time and passed, my pay is now of little consequence. Will you take me with you?"

"It is exactly what I was thinking of, Ned. Do you think that Captain Sawbridge will consent?"

"I do; he knows how I am circumstanced, and that my going home was merely because I was tired of looking after the *Aurora*."

"We'll go together and ask him to-morrow," replied Jack.

"At all events, you'll have a more gentlemanly companion than Mr Oxbelly."

"But not so steady, Ned."

The first lieutenant and officers came on board, and passed a merry evening. There's nothing passes time more agreeably away than champagne, and if you do not affront this regal wine by mixing him with any other, he never punishes you next morning.

Chapter Thirty Nine.

A council of war, in which Jack decides that he will have one more cruise.

As Captain Sawbridge did not return on board that evening, Easy went on shore and called upon him at the Governor's, to whom he was introduced, and received an invitation to dine with him. As Gascoigne could not come on shore, our hero took this opportunity of making his request to Captain Sawbridge, stating that the person he had with him was not such as he wished and could confide everything to; that is, not one to whom he could talk to about Agnes. Jack, as he found that Captain Sawbridge did not immediately assent, pressed the matter hard; at last Captain Sawbridge, who reflected that Gascoigne's interest hereafter would be much greater through his friend Easy than any other quarter, and that the more the friendship was cemented the more advantageous it might prove to Gascoigne, gave his consent to our hero's wish, who called on board the *Latona* to acquaint Gascoigne and the first lieutenant of Captain Sawbridge's intentions, and then went on board of *Rebiera* and ordered Mesty to come with his portmanteau on shore to the inn, that he might dress for dinner. Gascoigne, now considered as not belonging to the *Latona*, was permitted to accompany him; and Jack found himself looking out of the window at which he had hung out his trousers upon the memorable occasion when the boatswain had to follow his own precept, of duty before decency.

"What scenes of adventure I have passed through since that," thought Jack; "not much more than four years ago, then not three weeks in the service." Whereupon Jack fell into a deep reverie, and thought of the baboon and of Agnes.

The repairs of the *Latona* were all made good by the next day, and Gascoigne, having received his discharge-ticket, went on board the *Rebiera*. The gun-boat was put into the hands of the agent, and shortly afterwards purchased by Government. The *Rebiera's* crew did not, however, obtain their prize-money and share of the head-money, for she had seventy men on board, until their return, but, as they did, they had broken the ice, and that was everything. Moreover, it gave them confidence in themselves, in their vessel, and in their commander. Our hero weighed a short time after the *Latona*, having first taken leave of Captain Sawbridge, and committed to his care a letter to Dr Middleton.

Once more behold the trio together—the two midshipmen hanging over the taffrail, and Mesty standing by them. They had rounded Europa Point, and with a fine breeze off the land, were lying close-hauled along the Spanish shore. Mr Oxbelly was also walking near them.

"When I was cruising here it was very different," observed Jack; "I had a vessel which I did not know how to manage, a crew which I could not command, and had it not been for Mesty, what would have become of me?"

"Massa Easy, you know very well how to get out of scrapes, anyhow."

"Yes, and how to get into them," continued Gascoigne.

"And how to get others out of them, too, Ned."

"'No more of that Hal, an thou lovest me,'" quoted Gascoigne. "I have often wondered what has been the lot of poor Azar."

"The lot of most women, Ned, in every country—prized at first, neglected afterwards—the lot she might have had with you."

"Perhaps so," replied Ned, with a sigh.

"Massa Easy, you get eberybody out of scrape; you get me out of scrape."

"I do not recollect how, Mesty."

"You get me out from boil kettle for young gentlemen—dat devil of scrape."

"And I'm sure I've got you out of a scrape, Mr Oxbelly."

"How so, Mr Easy?"

"How so!—have I not prevented your quarrelling with your wife every night?"

"Certainly, sir, you have been the means. But, do you know, when we were engaging the other day, I could not help saying to myself, 'I wish my wife was here now, holding little Billy at the hatchway.'"

"But at night, Mr Oxbelly."

"At night!—why, then I'm afraid I should have wished her home again—it's astonishing how comfortable I sleep now every night. Besides, in this climate it would be intolerable. Mrs Oxbelly is a very large woman—very large indeed."

"Well, but now we must hold a council of war. Are we to run up the coast, or to shape our course direct for Palermo?"

"Course direct, and we shall take nothing, that is certain," said Gascoigne.

"If we take nothing we shall make no prize-money," continued Oxbelly.

"If we make no prize-money the men will be discontented," said Easy.

"If no ab noting to do—it will be damned 'tupid," continued Mesty.

"Now then the other side of the question. If we steer for Palermo, we shall be sooner there and sooner home."

"To which I reply," said Gascoigne, "that the shorter the cruise is, the less I shall have of your company."

"And I shall have to sleep with Mrs Oxbelly," continued Oxbelly.

"Hab fine ship, fine gun, fine men, and do noting," cried Mesty. "By de power, I no like dat, Massa Easy."

"You want eight months of coming of age, Jack," observed Gascoigne.

"It won't make a difference of more than three or four weeks," said Mr Oxbelly; "and the expenses have been very great."

"But—"

"But what, Jack?"

"Agnes."

"Agnes will be better defended going home by men who have been accustomed to be in action. And, as for her waiting a little longer, it will only make her love you a little more."

"Sleep single a little longer, Mr Easy, it's very pleasant," said Mr Oxbelly.

"That's not very bad advice of yours," observed Gascoigne.

"*Stop a little*, Massa Easy," said Mesty, "you know dat very good advice."

"Well, then," replied Jack, "I will, as I am quite in the minority. We will work up the whole coast—up to Toulon. After all, there's something very pleasant in commanding your own ship, and I'm not in a hurry to resign it—so that point's decided."

The *Rebiera* was steered in to the land, and at sunset they were not four miles from the lofty blue mountains which overhang the town of Malaga. There were many vessels lying at the bottom of the bay, close in with the town; the wind now fell light, and the *Rebiera*, as she could not fetch the town, tacked as if she were a merchant vessel standing in, and showed American colours, a hint which they took from perceiving three or four large vessels lying in the outer roads, with the colours of that nation hoisted at the peak.

"What is your intention, Jack?" said Gascoigne.

"I'll be hanged if I know yet. I think of working up to the outer roads, and anchoring at night—boarding the American vessels, and gaining intelligence."

"Not a bad idea; we shall then learn if there is anything to be done, and if not, we may be off at daylight."

"The pratique boat will not come off after sunset."

"And if they did, we could pass for an American, bound to Barcelona or anywhere else—the outer roads where the vessels lie are hardly within gun-shot."

Mesty, who had resumed his sailor's clothes, now observed, "What we do, Massa Easy, we do quickly—time for all ting, time for show face and fight—time for hide face, crawl, and steal."

"Very true, Mesty, we'll crawl this time, and steal if we can. It's not the warfare I like best of the two."

"Both good, Massa Easy; suppose you no steal board of polacca ship, you not see Missy Agnes."

"Very true, Mesty. 'Bout ship, Mr Oxbelly."

"Mr Oxbelly not good for boat sarvice," observed Mesty, showing his teeth.

It was dark before the *Rebiera* was anchored in the outer roads, a cable's length astern of the outermost American vessel. One of her quarter-boats was lowered down, and Gascoigne and our hero pulled alongside, and, lying on their oars, hailed, and asked the name of the vessel.

"So help me Gad, just now I forget her name," replied a negro, looking over the gangway.

"Who's the captain?"

"So help me Gad, he gone on shore."

"Is the mate on board?"

"No, so help me Gad—he gone shore too."

"Who is aboard then?"

"So help me Gad, nobody on board but Pompey—and dat me."

"Good ship-keepers, at all events," said Jack. "A ship in the outer roads with only a black fellow on board! I say, Pompey, do they always leave you in charge of the vessel?"

"No, sar; but to-night great pleasure on shore. Eberybody dance and sing, get drunk, kick up bobbery, and all dat."

"What, is it a festival?"

"So help me Gad, I no know, sar."

"Is there any one on board of the other vessels?"

"Eberybody gone on shore. Suppose they have black man, he stay on board."

"Good-night, Pompey."

"Good-night, sar. Who I say call when captain come on board?"

"Captain Easy."

"Captain He-see, very well, sar."

Our hero pulled to another ship, and found it equally deserted; but at the third he found the second mate, with his arm in a sling, and from him they gained the information that it was a great festival, being the last day of the carnival; and that every one was thinking of nothing but amusement.

"I've a notion," said the mate, in reply, "that you're American."

"You've guessed right," replied Jack.

"What ship, and from what port?"

"Rhode Island, the *Susan and Mary*," replied Gascoigne.

"I thought you were north. We're of New York. What news do you bring?"

"Nothing," replied he, "we are from Liverpool last."

A succession of questions was now put by the American mate, and answered very skilfully by Gascoigne, who then inquired how the market was?

It was necessary to make and reply to all these inquiries before they could ask apparently indifferent questions of American traders; at last Gascoigne inquired:

"Do you think they would allow us to go on shore? the pratique boat has not been on board."

"They'll never find you out if you are off before daylight; I doubt if they know that you are anchored. Besides, from Liverpool you would have a clean bill of health, and if they found it out, they would not say much; they're not over-particular, I've a notion."

"What are those vessels lying inshore?"

"I guess, they have olive oil on board, the chief on 'em. But there are two double lateens come in from Valparaiso the day before yesterday, with hides and copper. How they 'scaped the British, I can't tell, but they did, that's sure enough."

"Good-night, then."

"You won't take a glass of sling this fine night, with a countryman?"

"To-morrow, my good fellow, to-morrow; we must go on shore now."

Our hero and Gascoigne returned on board the *Rebiera*, consulted with Oxbelly and Mesty, and then manned and armed the two quarter and stern boats. They thought it advisable not to hoist out their long-boat; no fire-arms were permitted to be taken lest, going off by accident or otherwise, an alarm should be given. Our hero and Mesty proceeded in the first boat, and pulled in for the town; Gascoigne shortly after in the second, and the boatswain, in the jolly-boat, followed at some distance.

There was no notice taken of them; they pulled gently down to the landing-place, which was deserted. There was a blaze of light, and the sounds of revelry in every quarter on shore; but the vessels appeared equally deserted as the American ones in the offing.

Finding themselves unobserved, for they had taken the precaution to pull only two oars in each boat, they dropped gently alongside one of the double-masted lateen vessels, and Mesty stepped on board. He peeped down in the cabin, and perceived a man lying on the lockers; he came up in his stealthy manner, closed the hatch softly, and said, "all right." Jack left Gascoigne to take out this vessel, which he did very successfully, for it was very dark; and although there were sentries posted not far off, their eyes and ears were turned towards the town, listening to the music.

A second vessel, her consort, was boarded in the same way, but here they found a man on deck, whom they were obliged to seize and gag. They put him down in the cabin, and Mesty, with another boat's crew, cut her cables and swept her gently out towards the American vessels. One more vessel was required, and Jack, pulling two oars as usual, saluted a galliot heavily laden, but of what her cargo consisted was not known. In this vessel they found two men in the cabin playing cards, whom they seized and bound, and cutting her cables were obliged to make sail upon her, as she was much too large to sweep out. As they were making sail they, however, met with an interruption which they did not expect. The crew belonging to the vessel, having had enough amusement for the evening, and intending to sail the next morning, had thought it right to come off sooner than the others: it was then about midnight or a little later, and while some of Jack's men were aloft, for he had six with him, Jack, to his annoyance, heard a boat coming off from the shore, the men in her singing a chorus. The galliot was at that time just under steerage way, her topsail had been loosed and her jib hoisted, but the former had not been sheeted home, for the three men below could not, in the dark, find the ropes. The other three men were on the foreyard loosing the foresail, and Jack was undetermined whether to call them down immediately or to allow them to loose the sail, and thus get good way on the vessel, so as to prevent the boat, which was loaded with men, from overtaking them. The boat was not more than twenty yards from the galliot, when, not finding her where they left her, they pulled to the right and lay on their oars. This gave a moment of time, but they very soon spied her out. "Carambo!" was the exclamation—and the head of the boat was pulled round.

"Down, my lads, in a moment by the swifters," cried Jack. "Here's a boat on board of us."

The men were in a few seconds on deck, and the others, who had now sheeted home the topsails, hastened aft. The vessel soon gathered way, but before that her way was sufficient, the boat had pulled under the counter, and the Spaniards, letting their oars swing fore and aft, were climbing up, their knives in their teeth. A scuffle ensued, and they were thrown down again, but they renewed their attempt. Our hero, perceiving a small water or wine cask lashed to the gunwale, cut it loose with his cutlass, and, with one of the men who was by his side, pushed it over, and dropped it into the boat. It struck the gunwale, stove a plank, and the boat began to fill rapidly; in the meantime the galliot had gained way—the boat could not longer be held on, from its weight, and dropped astern with the men in it. Those who were half in and half out were left clinging to the gunwale of the vessel, and as they climbed up were secured and put down in the cabin. Fortunately, no fire-arms having been used on either side, the alarm was not given generally, but the sentry reported fighting on board one of the vessels, and the people of the guard-boat were collected, and pulled out; but they only arrived in time to see that the galliot was under way, and that the two other vessels from Valparaiso were not in their berths.

They hastened on shore, gave the alarm; the gunboats, of which there were three at the mole, were ordered out, but half the crew and all the officers were on shore, some at balls, others drinking at taverns or posadas; before they could be collected all three vessels were alongside of the *Rebiera*; and not aware that anything had been discovered, our hero and his crew were lulled in security. Jack had gone on board, leaving fourteen of his men on board the galliot—Gascoigne had done the same—Mesty still remained on board his vessel; and they were congratulating themselves, and ordering the men on board to the windlass, when they heard the sound of oars.

"Silence!—what is that?" exclaimed Oxbelly. "The gun-boats or row-boats, as sure as I'm alive!"

At this moment Mesty jumped up the side.

"Massa Easy, I hear row-boat not far off."

"So do we, Mesty. Gascoigne, jump into the boat—tell the men in the prizes to make all sail right out, and leave us to defend their retreat—stay on board of one and divide your men."

"Dat all right, Massa Easy.—Mr Gascoigne, be smart—and now, sar, cut cable and make sail; no time get up anchor."

This order was given, but although the men were aloft in a moment, and very expeditious, as the *Rebiera* payed her head round and the jib was hoisted, they could perceive the boom of the three gun-boats pulling and sailing not five cables' length from them. Although rather short-handed, topsails, courses, and top-gallant sails were soon set, the men down to their quarters, and the guns cast loose, before the gun-boats were close under their stern. Then Jack rounded to, braced up, and the *Rebiera* stood across them to the westward.

"Why the devil don't they fire?" said Jack.

"I tink because they no ab powder," said Mesty.

Mesty was right—the ammunition chests of the gun-boats were always landed when they were at the mole, in case of accidents, which might arise from the crew being continually with cigars in their mouths, and in the hurry they had quite forgotten to put them on board.

"At all events, we have powder," said Jack, "and now we'll prove it. Grape and canister, my lads, and take good aim."

The commanders of the gun-boats had hailed each other, and agreed to board the *Rebiera*, but she now had good way on her, and sailed faster than they pulled. A well-directed broadside astonished them—they had no idea of her force; and the execution done was so great, that they first lay on their oars and then pulled back to the mole with all speed, leaving the *Rebiera* in quiet possession of her prizes, which had already gained two miles in the offing.

The *Rebiera*, as soon as Jack perceived that the gun-boats had retreated, was put before the wind, and soon closed with her captures, when she was hove-to till daylight with the three vessels in company. Gascoigne returned on board, prize-masters were selected, and Jack determined to keep them all with him, and take them to Palermo.

Chapter Forty.

In which there is another slight difference of opinion between those who should be friends.

The two lateen vessels proved of considerable value, being laden with copper, hides, and cochineal. The galliot was laden with sweet oil, and was also no despicable prize. At daylight they were all ready, and, to the mortification of the good people of Malaga, sailed away to the eastward without interruption.

"Me tink we do dat job pretty well, Massa Easy," observed Mesty, as he laid the breakfast table.

"Nothing like trying," replied Gascoigne; "I'm sure when we stood into the bay I would have sold all my prize-money for a doubloon. How do I share, Jack?"

"Only as one of the crew, Ned, for you are a supernumerary, and our articles and agreement for prize-money were signed previous to our sailing."

"I ought to share with Mr Oxbelly's class by rights," replied Gascoigne. "That would be to take half my prize-money away. I shall want it all, Mr Gascoigne, to pacify my wife for giving her the slip."

"Ah, very well; I'll get all I can."

For ten days they ran down the coast, going much too fast for the wishes of the crew, who were anxious to make more money. They seized a fishing boat and put on board of her the four prisoners, whom they had found in the vessels, and arrived off Barcelona, without falling in with friend or foe. The next morning, the wind being very light, they discovered a large vessel at daylight astern of them to the westward, and soon made her out to be a frigate. She made all sail in chase, but that gave them very little uneasiness, as they felt assured that she was a British cruiser. One fear, however, came over them, that she would, if she came up with them, impress a portion of their men.

"As certainly as I'm here, and Mrs Oxbelly's at Southsea," said Oxbelly, "they'll take some of the men—the more so as, supposing us to be a Spanish convoy, they will be disappointed."

"They will hardly take them out of the prizes," observed Easy.

"I don't know that; men must be had for his Majesty's service somehow. It's not their fault, Mr Easy—the navy must be manned, and as things are so, so things must be. It's the king's prerogative, Mr Easy, and we cannot fight the battles of the country without it."

"Yes," replied Gascoigne, "and although, as soon as the services of seamen are no longer wanted, you find that there are demagogues on shore who exclaim against impressment, they are quiet enough on the point when they know that their lives and property depend upon sailors' exertions."

"Very true, Mr Gascoigne, but it's not our fault if we are obliged to take men by force; it's the fault of those who do not legislate so as to prevent the necessity. Mrs Oxbelly used to say that she would easily manage the matter if she were Chancellor of the Exchequer."

"I dare say Mrs Oxbelly would make a very good Chancellor of the Exchequer," replied Gascoigne, smiling; "one thing is certain, that if they gave the subject half the consideration they have others of less magnitude, an arrangement might be made by which his Majesty's navy would never be short of men."

"No doubt, no doubt, Mr Gascoigne; but nevertheless, the king's prerogative must never be given up."

"Then I agree with you, Mr Oxbelly; it *must be held* in case of sudden emergency and absolute need."

"We'll argue that point by-and-bye," replied Jack; "now let us consult as to our measures. My opinion is, that if I made more sail we should beat the frigate, but she would come up with the prizes."

"That's the best thing we can do, Mr Easy; but let us send a boat on board of them, and take out all the men that can possibly be spared, that there may be no excuse for impressing them."

"Yes," replied Gascoigne; "and as the wind is falling it is possible it may fall calm, and they may send their boats; suppose we separate a mile or two from each other."

"Dat very good advice, Massa Gascoigne," observed Mesty.

This plan was acted upon; only three men were left in the lateens, and four in the galliot, and the vessels, in obedience to the orders, sheered off on both sides of the *Rebiera*, who made all sail and started ahead of the prizes. This manoeuvre was perceived on board of the frigate, and made them sure that it was a Spanish convoy attempting to escape. The fire-engine was got on deck, sails wetted, and every exertion made to come up. But about four o'clock in the afternoon, when the frigate was eight or nine miles off, it fell calm, as Gascoigne had predicted, and the heads of all the vessels, as well as the frigate, were now round the compass.

"There's out boats," said Mr Oxbelly; "they will have a long pull, and all for nothing."

"How savage they will be!" observed Gascoigne.

"Never mind that," replied Jack; "Mesty says that dinner is ready."

After dinner, they all went on deck, and found that the boats had separated, one pulling for each of the prizes, and two for the *Rebiera*. In less than an hour they would probably be alongside.

"And now let us decide how we are to act. We must not resist, if they attempt to impress the men?"

"I've been thinking upon that matter, Mr Easy, and it appears to me that the men must be permitted to act as they please, and that we must be neuter. I, as a lieutenant in his Majesty's service, cannot of course act, neither can Mr Gascoigne. You are not in the service, but I should recommend you to do the same. That the men have a right to resist, if possible, is admitted; they always do so, and never are punished for so doing. Under the guns of the frigate, of course, we should only have to submit; but those two boats do not contain more than twenty-five men, I should think, and our men are the stronger party. We had better leave it to them, and stand neuter."

"Dat very good advice," said Mesty; "leab it to us;" and Mesty walked away forward where the seamen were already in consultation.

Jack also agreed to the prudence of this measure, and he perceived that the seamen, after a consultation with Mesty, were all arming themselves for resistance.

The boats were now close on board, and English colours were hoisted at the gaff. This did not, however, check the impetus of the boats, which, with their ensigns trailing in the still water astern of them, dashed alongside, and an officer leaped on board, cutlass in hand, followed by the seamen of the frigate. The men of the *Rebiera* remained collected forward—Easy, Gascoigne, and Oxbelly aft.

"What vessel is this?" cried the lieutenant who commanded the boats.

Jack, with the greatest politeness, took off his hat, and told him that it was the *Rebiera* letter of marque, and that the papers were ready for his inspection.

"And the other vessels?"

"Prizes to the *Rebiera*, cut out of Malaga Bay," replied Jack.

"Then you are a privateer," observed the disappointed officer. "Where are your papers?"

"Mr Oxbelly, oblige me by bringing them up," said Jack.

"Fat Jack of the bone house," observed the lieutenant, looking at Oxbelly.

"A lieutenant in his Majesty's service, of longer standing than yourself, young man," replied Oxbelly firmly;—"and who, if he ever meets you in any other situation—will make you answer for your insolent remark."

"Indeed!" observed the lieutenant ironically; "now, if you had said you were once a boatswain or gunner."

"Consider yourself kicked," roared Oxbelly, losing his temper.

"Hey day! why, you old porpoise!"

"Sir," observed Jack, who listened with indignation, "Mr Oxbelly is a lieutenant in his Majesty's service, and you have no right to insult him, even if he were not."

"I presume you are all officers," replied the lieutenant.

"I am, sir," retorted Gascoigne, "an officer in his Majesty's service, and on board of this vessel by permission of Captain Sawbridge of the *Latona*."

"And I was, until a few months ago, sir," continued Jack; "at present I am captain and owner of this vessel—but here are the papers. You will have no obstruction from us in the execution of your duty—at the same time, I call upon the two young gentlemen by your side, and your own men, to bear witness to what takes place."

"Oh, very well, sir—just as you please. Your papers I perceive are all right. Now you will oblige me by mustering your men."

"Certainly, sir," replied Jack; "send all the men aft to muster, Mr Oxbelly."

The men came aft to the mainmast, with Mesty at their head, and answered to their names. As the men passed over, the lieutenant made a pencil-mark against ten of them, who appeared the finest seamen; and, when the roll had been called, he ordered those men to get their bags and go into the boat.

"Sir, as you must observe, I am short-handed, with my men away in prizes; and I, as commander of this vessel, protest against this proceeding: if you insist upon taking them, of course I can do nothing," observed Jack.

"I do insist, sir; I'm not going on board empty-handed, at all events."

"Well, sir, I can say no more," said Jack, walking aft to the taffrail, to which Oxbelly and Gascoigne had retreated.

"Come, my lads, get those men in the boat," said the lieutenant.

But the men had all retreated forward in a body, with Mesty at their head, and had armed themselves. Some of the seamen of the frigate had gone forward, in obedience to their officer, to lead the men selected into the boat; but they were immediately desired to keep back. The scuffle forward attracted the notice of the lieutenant, who immediately summoned all his men out of the boats.

"Mutiny, by heavens! Come up, all of you, my lads."

Mesty then came forward, with a sabre in one hand and a pistol in the other, and thus addressed the seamen of the frigate:

"I tell you dis, my lads—you not so strong as we—you not got better arms—we not under gun of frigate now, and we ab determination not to go board. 'Pose you want us, come take us—'pose you can. By all de power, but we make mince-meat of you, anyhow."

The seamen paused—they were ready to fight for their country, but not to be killed by or kill those who were their own countrymen, and who were doing exactly what they would have done themselves. The lieutenant thought otherwise; he was exasperated at this sensation.

"You black scoundrel, I left you out because I thought you not worth having, but now I'll add you to the number."

"Stop a little," replied Mesty.

The lieutenant would not take the Ashantee's very prudent advice; he flew forward to seize Mesty, who striking him a blow with the flat of his sabre, almost levelled him to the deck. At this the men and other officers of the frigate darted forward; but after a short scuffle, in which a few wounds were received, were beaten back into the boats. The lieutenant was thrown in after them, by the nervous arm of Mesty—and, assailed by cold shot and other missiles, they sheered off with precipitation, and pulled back in the direction of the frigate.

"There will be a row about this," said Oxbelly, "as soon as they come clear of the vessel. If the frigate gets hold of us she will show us no mercy. There is a breeze coming from the north-west. How fortunate! we shall be three leagues to windward, and may escape."

"I doubt if she could catch us at any point of sailing: they may come up with the prizes, but can do nothing with them."

"No, the boats which boarded them are already returned to the frigate; she must wait for them, and that will give us a start and it will be night before they can even make sail."

"Fire a gun for the prizes to close," said Jack; "we will put the men on board again, and then be off to Palermo as fast as we can."

"We can do no better," said Oxbelly. "If ever I chance to meet that fellow again, I will trouble him to repeat his words. Trim the sails, my lads."

"His language was unpardonable," observed Jack.

"Since I've been in the service, Mr Easy, I have always observed that some officers appear to imagine that, because they are under the king's pennant, they are warranted in insulting and tyrannising over all those who have not the honour to hoist it; whereas the very fact of their being king's officers should be an inducement to them to show an example of courtesy and gentlemanly conduct in the execution of their duty, however unpleasant it may be."

"It is only those who, insignificant themselves, want to make themselves of importance by the pennant they serve under," replied our hero.

"Very true, Mr Easy; but you are not aware that a great part of the ill-will shown to the service, is owing to the insolence of those young men in office. The king's name is a warrant for every species of tyranny and unwarrantable conduct. I remember Mrs Oxbelly telling one of them, when—"

"I beg your pardon, Mr Oxbelly," interrupted Jack, "but we have no time to chat now; the breeze is coming down fast, and I perceive the prizes are closing. Let us lower down the boat, send the men on board again, and give them their orders—which I will do in writing, in case they part company."

"Very true, sir. It will be dark in half an hour, and as we are now standing inshore, they will think that we intend to remain on the coast. As soon as it is quite dark we will shape our course for Palermo. I will go down and look at the chart."

Chapter Forty One.

Which winds up the Nautical Adventures of Mr Midshipman Easy.

In half an hour the prizes were again alongside, the men put on board, and the boat hoisted up. The frigate still remained becalmed to leeward, and hoisted in her boats. They watched until she was hid by the shades of night, and then wearing round stood away, with the wind two points free, for the coast of Sicily. The next morning when the sun rose there was nothing in sight. Strange anomaly, in a state of high civilisation, where you find your own countrymen avoided and more dreaded than even your foes!

The run was prosperous, the weather was fine, and the prizes did not part company.

On the sixteenth day the *Rebiera* and her convoy anchored in Palermo Bay. The wind was light in the morning that they stood in, and as Jack had a large blue flag with *Rebiera* in white letters hoisted at the main, Don Philip and

Don Martin were on board and greeting our hero, before the *Rebiera's* anchor had plunged into the clear blue water.

The information which our hero received, after having been assured of the health of Agnes and her parents, was satisfactory. The disappearance of the friar had, at first, occasioned much surprise;—but as the servants of Don Rebiera swore to his return without the black, and the letter of Don Rebiera, sent to the convent, requesting his presence, was opened and read, there was no suspicion against the family. A hundred conjectures had been afloat, but gradually they had subsided, and it was at last supposed that he had been carried off by the banditti, some of whom had been taken, and acknowledged that they had seized a friar on a day which they could not recollect. The reader will remember that it was Mesty.

The *Rebiera* received pratique, and Jack hastened on shore with Don Philip and his brother, and was once more in company of Agnes, who, in our hero's opinion, had improved since his departure. Most young men in love think the same after an absence, provided it is not too long. The prizes were sold and the money distributed, and every man was satisfied, as the cargoes fetched a larger sum than they had anticipated.

We must pass over the *pros* and *cons* of Don Rebiera and his lady, the pleading of Jack for immediate nuptials, the unwillingness of the mother to part with her only daughter, the family consultation, the dowry, and all these particulars. A month after his arrival Jack was married, and was, of course, as happy as the day was long.

A few days afterwards, Mr Oxbelly advised departure, as the expenses of the vessel were heavy, and it was his duty so to do. Don Philip and Don Martin obtained leave to go to England, with their sister and her husband. Nevertheless, Jack, who found Palermo a very pleasant residence, was persuaded by the Don and his wife to remain there a month, and then there was crying and sobbing, and embracing, and embarking; and at last the *Rebiera*, whose cabins had been arranged for the reception of the party, weighed and made sail for Malta, Jack having promised to call upon the Governor.

In four days they anchored in Valette harbour, and Jack paid his respects to his old friend, who was very glad to see him. The Governor sent his own barge for Mrs Easy, and she was installed in the state apartments, which were acknowledged to be very comfortable. Our hero had, as usual, a long story to tell the Governor, and the Governor listened to it very attentively, probably because he thought it would be the last, which opportunity Jack employed to narrate the unfortunate end of his father.

"I would not have said so at the time, Mr Easy, but now the wound is healed, I tell you that it is the best thing that could have happened—poor old gentleman! he was mad, indeed."

Our hero remained a fortnight at Malta, and then Signora Easy was re-embarked, and once more the *Rebiera* made sail.

"Fare you well, my lad; what I have seen of your brothers-in-law pleases me much; and as for your wife, it will be your own fault if she is not all that you would wish. If ever I come to England again, I will pay my first visit to Forest Hill. God bless you!"

But Sir Thomas never did go back to England, and this was their final adieu. Once more the *Rebiera* pursued her course, stopped a day or two at Gibraltar, shared the proceeds of the captured gun-boat, and then made sail for England, where she arrived without adventure or accident in three weeks.

Thus ended the last cruise of Mr Midshipman Easy. As soon as their quarantine at the Mother-bank was over, they disembarked, and found Dr Middleton and Mr Hanson waiting for them at the George Hotel. Our hero had scarcely time to introduce his wife, when the waiter said that a lady wished to speak to him. She did not wait to know if Jack was visible, but forced her way past him. Jack looked at her large proportions, and decided at once that it must be Mrs Oxbelly, in which conjecture he was right.

"Pray, sir, what do you mean by carrying off my husband in that way?" exclaimed the lady, red with anger.

"God forbid that I should have to carry your husband, Mrs Oxbelly; he is rather too heavy."

"Yes, sir, but it's little better than kidnapping, and there's a law for kidnapping children at all events. I shall send my lawyer to you, that you may depend upon."

"You hardly can consider your husband as a child, Mrs Oxbelly," replied Jack, laughing.

"Very well, sir, we shall see. Pray, where is he now?"

"He is on board, Mrs Oxbelly, and will be delighted to see you."

"I'm not quite so sure of that."

"He's very anxious to see little Billy," said Gascoigne.

"What do you know of little Billy, young man?"

"And more than anxious to be on shore again. He's quite tired of sleeping single, Mrs Oxbelly."

"Ah, very well, he has been talking, has he? very well," exclaimed the lady in a rage.

"But," said Easy, "I am happy to say that, with pay and prize-money, during his short absence, he has brought home nearly five hundred pounds."

"Five hundred pounds—you don't say so, sir?" exclaimed Mrs Oxbelly; "are you sure of that?"

"Quite sure," rejoined Gascoigne.

"Five hundred pounds!—Well, that is comfortable—dear me! how glad I shall be to see him! Well, Mr Easy, it was hard to part with him in so unhandsome a way—but all's for the best in this world. What a dear, nice lady your wife is, Mr Easy—but I won't intrude—I beg pardon. Where is the brig, Mr Easy?"

"Now coming into the harbour," replied Gascoigne: "if you bargain you can get off for twopence."

"Five hundred pounds!" exclaimed Mrs Oxbelly, whose wrath was now appeased.

"By all power, she no fool of a woman dat," said Mesty, as she retreated curtseying; "I tink Mr Oxbelly very right sleep tingle."

We have now come to the end of our hero's adventures; that afternoon they all started for Forest Hill, where everything was ready for their reception. The *Rebiera's* men were paid off, and were soon distributed on board of his Majesty's ships; the vessel was sold, and Mr Oxbelly retired to Southsea, to the society of his wife and little Billy. Whether he obtained from his wife a divorce *de thoro*, is not handed down.

Our hero, who was now of age, invited all within twenty miles of home to balls and dinners; became a great favourite, kept a pack of hounds, rode with the foremost, received a deputation to stand for the county on the conservative interest, was elected without much expense, which was very wonderful, and took his seat in parliament. Don Philip and Don Martin, after two months' stay, took their passage back to Palermo, fully satisfied with the prospects of their sister as to competence and happiness. Jack had no occasion to argue the point with Agnes; she conformed at once to the religion of her husband, proved an excellent and affectionate wife, and eventually the mother of four children, three boys and a girl.

Mesty held his post with dignity, and proved himself trustworthy. Gascoigne, by the interest of the conservative member, soon obtained the rank of post-captain, and was always his devoted and sincere friend. And thus ends the history of Mr Midshipman Easy.

Peter Simple and The Three Cutters, Vol. 1-2

Chapter I

The great advantage of being the fool of the family—My destiny is decided, and I am consigned to a stockbroker as part of His Majesty's sea stock—Unfortunately for me Mr Handycock is a bear, and I get very little dinner.

If I cannot narrate a life of adventurous and daring exploits, fortunately I have no heavy crimes to confess; and, if I do not rise in the estimation of the reader for acts of gallantry and devotion in my country's cause, at least I may claim the merit of zealous and persevering continuance in my vocation. We are all of us variously gifted from Above, and he who is content to walk, instead of to run, on his allotted path through life, although he may not so rapidly attain the goal, has the advantage of not being out of breath upon his arrival. Not that I mean to infer that my life has not been one of adventure. I only mean to say that, in all which has occurred, I have been a passive, rather than an active, personage; and, if events of interest are to be recorded, they certainly have not been sought by me.

As well as I can recollect and analyze my early propensities, I think that, had I been permitted to select my own profession, I should in all probability have bound myself apprentice to a tailor; for I always envied the comfortable seat which they appeared to enjoy upon the shopboard, and their elevated position, which enabled them to look down upon the constant succession of the idle or the busy, who passed in review before them in the main street of the country town, near to which I passed the first fourteen years of my existence.

But my father, who was a clergyman of the Church of England, and the youngest brother of a noble family, had a lucrative living, and a "soul above buttons," if his son had not. It has been from time immemorial the heathenish custom to sacrifice the greatest fool of the family to the prosperity and naval superiority of the country, and, at the age of fourteen, I was selected as the victim. If the custom be judicious, I had no reason to complain. There was not one dissentient voice, when it was proposed before all the varieties of my aunts and cousins, invited to partake of our new-year's festival. I was selected by general acclamation. Flattered by such an unanimous acknowledgment of my qualification, and a stroke of my father's hand down my head which accompanied it, I felt as proud, and, alas! as unconscious as the calf with gilded horns, who plays and mumbles with the flowers of the garland which designates his fate to every one but himself. I even felt, or thought I felt, a slight degree of military ardour, and a sort of vision of future grandeur passed before me, in the distant vista of which I perceived a coach with four horses and a service of plate. It was, however, driven away before I could decipher it, by positive bodily pain, occasioned by my elder brother Tom, who, having been directed by my father to snuff the candles, took the opportunity of my abstraction to insert a piece of the still ignited cotton into my left ear. But as my story is not a very short one, I must not dwell too long on its commencement. I shall therefore inform the reader, that my father, who lived in the north of England, did not think it right to fit me out at the country town, near to which we resided; but about a fortnight after the decision which I have referred to, he forwarded me to London, on the outside of the coach, with my best suit of bottle-green and six shirts. To prevent mistakes, I was booked in the way-bill "to be delivered to Mr Thomas Handycock, No. 14, Saint Clement's Lane—carriage paid." My parting with the family was very affecting; my mother cried bitterly, for, like all mothers, she liked the greatest fool which she had presented to my father, better than all the rest; my sisters cried because my mother cried; Tom roared for a short time more loudly than all the rest, having been chastised by my father for breaking his fourth window in that week;—during all which my father walked up and down the room with impatience, because he was kept from his dinner, and, like all orthodox divines, he was tenacious of the only sensual enjoyment permitted to his cloth.

At last I tore myself away. I had blubbered till my eyes were so red and swollen, that the pupils were scarcely to be distinguished, and tears and dirt had veined my cheeks like the marble of the chimney-piece. My handkerchief was soaked through with wiping my eyes and blowing my nose, before the scene was over. My brother Tom, with a kindness which did honour to his heart, exchanged his for mine, saying, with fraternal regard, "Here, Peter, take mine, it's as dry as a bone." But my father would not wait for a second handkerchief to perform its duty. He led me away through the hall, when, having shaken hands with all the men and kissed all the maids, who stood in a row with their aprons to their eyes, I quitted my paternal roof.

The coachman accompanied me to the place from whence the stage was to start. Having seen me securely wedged between two fat old women, and having put my parcel inside, he took his leave, and in a few minutes I was on my road to London.

I was too much depressed to take notice of anything during my journey. When we arrived in London, they drove to the Blue Boar (in a street, the name of which I have forgotten). I had never seen or heard of such an animal, and certainly it did appear very formidable; its mouth was open and teeth very large. What surprised me still more was to observe that its teeth and hoofs were of pure gold. Who knows, thought I, that in some of the strange countries which I am doomed to visit, but that I may fall in with, and shoot one of these terrific monsters? with what haste shall I select those precious parts, and with what joy should I, on my return, pour them as an offering of filial affection into my mother's lap!—and then, as I thought of my mother, the tears again gushed into my eyes.

The coachman threw his whip to the ostler, and the reins upon the horses' backs; he then dismounted, and calling to me, "Now, young gentleman, I'se a-waiting," he put a ladder up for me to get down by; then turning to a porter, he said to him, "Bill, you must take this here young gem'man and that ere parcel to this here direction.—Please to remember the coachman, sir." I replied that I certainly would, if he wished it, and walked off with the porter; the coachman observing, as I went away, "Well, he is a fool—that's sartain." I arrived quite safe at St Clement's-lane, when the porter received a shilling for his trouble from the maid who let me in, and I was shown up into a parlour, where I found myself in company with Mrs Handycock.

Mrs Handycock was a little meagre woman, who did not speak very good English, and who appeared to me to employ the major part of her time in bawling out from the top of the stairs to the servants below. I never saw her either read a book or occupy herself with needlework, during the whole time I was in the house. She had a large grey parrot, and I really cannot tell which screamed the worse of the two—but she was very civil and kind to me, and asked me ten times a day when I had last heard of my grandfather, Lord Privilege. I observed that she always did so if any company happened to call in during my stay at her house. Before I had been there ten minutes, she told me that she "hadored sailors—they were the defendiours and preserviours of their kings and countries," and that "Mr Handycock would be home by four o'clock, and then we should go to dinner." Then she jumped off her chair to bawl to the cook from the head of the stairs—"Jemima, Jemima!—ve'll ha'e the viting biled instead of fried." "Can't, marm," replied Jemima, "they be all begged and crumbed, with their tails in their mouths." "Vell, then, never mind, Jemima," replied the lady.—"Don't put your finger into the parrot's cage, my love—he's apt to be cross with strangers. Mr Handycock will be home at four o'clock, and then we shall have our dinner. Are you fond of viting?"

As I was very anxious to see Mr Handycock, and very anxious to have my dinner, I was not sorry to hear the clock on the stairs strike four, when Mrs Handycock again jumped up, and put her head over the banisters, "Jemima, Jemima, it's four o'clock!" "I hear it, marm," replied the cook; and she gave the frying-pan a twist, which made the hissing and the smell come flying up into the parlour, and made me more hungry than ever.

Rap, tap, tap! "There's your master, Jemima," screamed the lady. "I hear him, marm," replied the cook. "Run down, my dear, and let Mr Handycock in," said his wife. "He'll be so surprised at seeing you open the door."

I ran down, as Mrs Handycock desired me, and opened the street-door. "Who the devil are you?" in a gruff voice, cried Mr Handycock; a man about six feet high, dressed in blue cotton-net pantaloons and Hessian boots, with a black coat and waistcoat. I was a little rebuffed, I must own, but I replied that I was Mr Simple. "And pray, Mr Simple, what would your grandfather say if he saw you now? I have servants in plenty to open my door, and the parlour is the proper place for young gentlemen."

"Law, Mr Handycock," said his wife, from the top of the stairs, "how can you be so cross? I told him to open the door to surprise you."

"And you have surprised me," replied he, "with your cursed folly."

While Mr Handycock was rubbing his boots on the mat, I went upstairs rather mortified, I must own, as my father had told me that Mr Handycock was his stockbroker, and would do all he could to make me comfortable: indeed, he had written to that effect in a letter, which my father showed to me before I left home. When I returned to the parlour, Mrs Handycock whispered to me, "Never mind, my dear, it's only because there's something wrong on 'Change. Mr Handycock is a *bear* just now." I thought so too, but I made no answer, for Mr Handycock came upstairs, and walking with two strides from the door of the parlour to the fire-place, turned his back to it, and lifting up his coat-tails, began to whistle.

"Are you ready for your dinner, my dear?" said the lady, almost trembling.

"If the dinner is ready for me. I believe we usually dine at four," answered her husband, gruffly.

"Jemima, Jemima, dish up! do you hear, Jemima?" "Yes, marm," replied the cook, "directly I've thickened the butter;" and Mrs Handycock resumed her seat, with, "Well, Mr Simple, and how is your grandfather, Lord Privilege?" "He is quite well, ma'am," answered I, for the fifteenth time at least. But dinner put an end to the silence which followed this remark. Mr Handycock lowered his coat-tails and walked downstairs, leaving his wife and me to follow at our leisure.

"Pray, ma'am," inquired I, as soon as he was out of hearing, "what is the matter with Mr Handycock, that he is so cross to you?"

"Vy, my dear, it is one of the misfortunes of mater-mony, that ven the husband's put out, the vife is sure to have her share of it. Mr Handycock must have lost money on 'Change, and then he always comes home cross. Ven he vins, then he is as merry as a cricket."

"Are you people coming down to dinner?" roared Mr Handycock from below. "Yes, my dear," replied the lady, "I thought that you were washing your hands." We descended into the dining-room, where we found that Mr Handycock had already devoured two of the whitings, leaving only one on the dish for his wife and me. "Vould you like a little bit of viting, my dear?" said the lady to me. "It's not worth halving," observed the gentleman, in a surly tone, taking up the fish with his own knife and fork, and putting it on his plate.

"Well, I'm so glad you like them, my dear," replied the lady meekly; then turning to me, "there's some nice roast *weal* coming, my dear."

The veal made its appearance, and fortunately for us, Mr Handycock could not devour it all. He took the lion's share, nevertheless, cutting off all the brown, and then shoving the dish over to his wife to help herself and me. I had not put two pieces in my mouth before Mr Handycock desired me to get up and hand him the porter-pot, which stood on the sideboard. I thought that if it was not right for me to open a door, neither was it for me to wait at table—but I obeyed him without making a remark.

After dinner, Mr Handycock went down to the cellar for a bottle of wine. "O deary me!" exclaimed his wife, "he must have lost a mint of money—we had better go up stairs and leave him alone; he'll be better after a bottle of port, perhaps." I was very glad to go away, and being very tired, I went to bed without any tea, for Mrs Handycock dared not venture to make it before her husband came up stairs.

Chapter II

Fitting out on the shortest notice—Fortunately for me, this day Mr
Handycock is a bear, and I fare very well—I set off for Portsmouth—
Behind the coach I meet a man before the mast—He is disguised with
liquor, but is not the only disguise I fall in with in my journey.

The next morning Mr Handycock appeared to be in somewhat better humour. One of the linendrapers who fitted out cadets, &c, "on the shortest notice," was sent for, and orders given for my equipment, which Mr Handycock insisted should be ready on the day afterwards, or the articles would be left on his hands; adding, that my place was already taken in the Portsmouth coach.

"Really, sir," observed the man, "I'm afraid—on such very short notice—"

"Your card says, 'the shortest notice,'" rejoined Mr Handycock, with the confidence and authority of a man who is enabled to correct another by his own assertions. "If you do not choose to undertake the work, another will."

This silenced the man, who made his promise, took my measure, and departed; and soon afterwards Mr Handycock also quitted the house.

What with my grandfather and the parrot, and Mrs Handycock wondering how much money her husband had lost, running to the head of the stairs and talking to the cook, the day passed away pretty well till four o'clock; when, as before, Mrs Handycock screamed, the cook screamed, the parrot screamed, and Mr Handycock rapped at the door, and was let in—but not by me. He ascended the stair swith [sic] three bounds, and coming into the parlour, cried, "Well, Nancy, my love, how are you?" Then stooping over her, "Give me a kiss, old girl. I'm as hungry as a hunter. Mr Simple, how do you do? I hope you have passed the morning agreeably. I must wash my hands and change my boots, my love; I am not fit to sit down to table with you in this pickle. Well, Polly, how are you?"

"I'm glad you're hungry, my dear, I've such a nice dinner for you," replied the wife, all smiles. "Jemima, be quick and dish up—Mr Handycock is so hungry."

"Yes, marm," replied the cook; and Mrs Handycock followed her husband into his bedroom on the same floor, to assist him at his toilet.

"By Jove, Nancy, the *bulls* have been nicely taken in," said Mr
Handycock, as we sat down to dinner.

"O, I am so glad!" replied his wife, giggling; and so I believe she was, but why I did not understand.

"Mr Simple," said he, "will you allow me to offer you a little fish?"

"If you do not want it all yourself, sir," replied I politely.

Mrs Handycock frowned and shook her head at me, while her husband helped me. "My dove, a bit of fish?"

We both had our share to-day, and I never saw a man more polite than Mr Handycock. He joked with his wife, asked me to drink wine with him two or three times, talked about my grandfather; and, in short, we had a very pleasant evening.

The next morning all my clothes came home, but Mr Handycock, who still continued in good humour, said that he would not allow me to travel by night, that I should sleep there and set off the next morning; which I did at six o'clock, and before eight I had arrived at the Elephant and Castle, where we stopped for a quarter of an hour. I was looking at the painting representing this animal with a castle on its back; and assuming that of Alnwick, which I had seen, as a fair estimate of the size and weight of that which he carried, was attempting to enlarge my ideas so as to comprehend the stupendous bulk of the elephant, when I observed a crowd assembled at the corner; and asking a gentleman who sat by me in a plaid cloak, whether there was not something very uncommon to attract so many people, he replied, "Not very, for it is only a drunken sailor."

I rose from my seat, which was on the hinder part of the coach, that I might see him, for it was a new sight to me, and excited my curiosity, when to my astonishment, he staggered from the crowd, and swore that he'd go to Portsmouth. He climbed up by the wheel of the coach, and sat down by me. I believe that I stared at him very much, for he said to me, "What are you gaping at, you young sculping? Do you want to catch flies? or did you never see a chap half-seas-over before?"

I replied, "That I had never been at sea in my life, but that I was going."

"Well, then, you're like a young bear, all your sorrows to come—that's all, my hearty," replied he. "When you get on board, you'll find monkey's allowance—more kicks than half-pence. I say, you pewter-carrier, bring us another pint of ale."

The waiter of the inn, who was attending the coach, brought out the ale, half of which the sailor drank, and the other half threw into the waiter's face, telling him that was his "allowance: and now," said he, "what's to pay?" The waiter, who looked very angry, but appeared too much afraid of the sailor to say anything, answered fourpence; and the sailor pulled out a handful of banknotes, mixed up with gold, silver, and coppers, and was picking out the money to pay for his beer, when the coachman, who was impatient, drove off.

"There's cut and run," cried the sailor, thrusting all the money into his breeches pocket. "That's what you'll learn to do, my joker, before you've been two cruises to sea."

In the meantime the gentleman in the plaid cloak, who was seated by me, smoked his cigar without saying a word. I commenced a conversation with him relative to my profession, and asked him whether it was not very difficult to learn. "Larn," cried the sailor, interrupting us, "no; it may be difficult for such chaps as me before the mast to larn; but you, I presume, is a reefer, and they an't got much to larn, 'cause why, they pipe-clays their weekly accounts, and walks up and down with their hands in their pockets. You must larn to chaw baccy, drink grog, and call the cat a beggar, and then you knows all a midshipman's expected to know nowadays. Ar'n't I right, sir?" said the sailor, appealing to the gentleman in a plaid cloak. "I axes you, because I see you're a sailor by the cut of your jib. Beg pardon, sir," continued he, touching his hat, "hope no offence."

"I am afraid that you have nearly hit the mark, my good fellow," replied the gentleman.

The drunken fellow then entered into conversation with him, stating that he had been paid off from the *Audacious* at Portsmouth, and had come up to London to spend his money with his messmates, but that yesterday he had discovered that a Jew at Portsmouth had sold him a seal as gold, for fifteen shillings, which proved to be copper, and that he was going back to Portsmouth to give the Jew a couple of black eyes for his rascality, and that when he had done that he was to return to his messmates, who had promised to drink success to the expedition at the Cock and Bottle, St Martin's Lane, until he should return.

The gentleman in the plaid cloak commended him very much for his resolution; for he said, "that although the journey to and from Portsmouth would cost twice the value of a gold seal, yet, that in the end it might be worth a *Jew's Eye*." What he meant I did not comprehend.

Whenever the coach stopped, the sailor called for more ale, and always threw the remainder which he could not drink into the face of the man who brought it out for him, just as the coach was starting off, and then tossed the pewter pot on the ground for him to pick up. He became more tipsy every stage, and the last from Portsmouth, when he pulled out his money, he could find no silver, so he handed down a note, and desired the waiter to change it. The waiter crumpled it up and put it into his pocket, and then returned the sailor the change for a one-pound note; but the gentleman in the plaid had observed that it was a five-pound note which the sailor had given, and insisted upon the waiter producing it, and giving the proper change. The sailor took his money, which the waiter handed to him, begging pardon for the mistake, although he coloured up very much at being detected. "I really beg your pardon," said he again, "it was quite a mistake;" whereupon the sailor threw the pewter pot at the waiter, saying, "I really beg your pardon, too,"—and with such force, that it flattened upon the man's head, who fell senseless on the road. The coachman drove off, and I never heard whether the man was killed or not.

After the coach had driven off, the sailor eyed the gentleman in the plaid cloak for a minute or two, and then said, "When I first looked at you I took you for some officer in mufti; but now that I see you look so sharp after the rhino, it's my idea that you're some poor devil of a Scotchman, mayhap second mate of a marchant vessel—there's half a crown for your services—I'd give you more if I thought you would spend it."

The gentleman laughed, and took the half-crown, which I afterwards observed that he gave to a grey-headed beggar at the bottom of Portsdown Hill. I inquired of him how soon we should be at Portsmouth; he answered that we were passing the lines; but I saw no lines, and I was ashamed to show my ignorance. He asked me what ship I was going to join. I could not recollect her name, but I told him it was painted on the outside of my chest, which was coming down by the waggon; all that I could recollect was that it was a French name.

"Have you no letter of introduction to the captain?" said he.

"Yes I have," replied I; and I pulled out my pocket-book in which the letter was. "Captain Savage, H.M. ship *Diomede*," continued I, reading to him.

To my surprise he very coolly proceeded to open the letter, which, when I perceived what he was doing, occasioned me immediately to snatch the letter from him, stating my opinion at the same time that it was a breach of honour, and that in my opinion he was no gentleman.

"Just as you please, youngster," replied he. "Recollect, you have told me I am no gentleman."

He wrapped his plaid around him, and said no more; and I was not a little pleased at having silenced him by my resolute behaviour.

Chapter III

I am made to look very blue at the Blue Posts—Find wild spirits around, and, soon after, hot spirits within me; at length my spirits overcome me Call to pay my respects to the Captain, and find that I had had the pleasure of meeting him before—No sooner out of one scrape than into another.

When we stopped, I inquired of the coachman which was the best inn. He answered "that it was the Blue Postesses, where the midshipmen leave their chestesses, call for tea and toastesses, and sometimes forget to pay for their breakfastesses." He laughed when he said it, and I thought that he was joking with me; but he pointed out two large blue posts at the door next the coach-office, and told me that all the midshipmen resorted to that hotel. He then asked me to remember the coachman, which, by this time I had found out implied that I was not to forget to give him a shilling, which I did, and then went into the inn. The coffee-room was full of midshipmen, and, as I was anxious about my chest, I inquired of one of them if he knew when the waggon would come in.

"Do you expect your mother by it?" replied he.

"Oh no! but I expect my uniforms—I only wear these bottle-greens until they come."

"And pray what ship are you going to join?"

"The *Die-a-maid*—Captain Thomas Kirkwall Savage."

"The *Diomede*—I say, Robinson, a'n't that the frigate in which the midshipmen had four dozen apiece for not having pipe-clayed their weekly accounts on the Saturday?"

"To be sure it is," replied the other; "why the captain gave a youngster five dozen the other day for wearing a scarlet watch-riband."

"He's the greatest Tartar in the service," continued the other; "he flogged the whole starboard watch the last time that he was on a cruise, because the ship would only sail nine knots upon a bowline."

"Oh dear," said I, "then I'm very sorry that I am going to join him."

"'Pon my soul I pity you: you'll be fagged to death: for there's only three midshipmen in the ship now—all the rest ran away. Didn't they, Robinson?"

"There's only two left now; for poor Matthews died of fatigue. He was worked all day, and kept watch all night for six weeks, and one morning he was found dead upon his chest."

"God bless my soul!" cried I; "and yet, on shore, they say he is such a kind man to his midshipmen."

"Yes," replied Robinson, "he spreads that report every where. Now, observe, when you first call upon him, and report your having come to join his ship, he'll tell you that he is very happy to see you, and that he hopes your family are well—then he'll recommend you to go on board and learn your duty. After that, stand clear. Now, recollect what I have said, and see if it does not prove true. Come, sit down with us and take a glass of grog; it will keep your spirits up."

These midshipmen told me so much about my captain, and the horrid cruelties which he had practised, that I had some doubts whether I had not better set off home again. When I asked their opinion, they said, that if I did, I should be taken up as a deserter and hanged; that my best plan was to beg his acceptance of a few gallons of rum, for he was very fond of grog, and that then I might perhaps be in his good graces, as long as the rum might last.

I am sorry to state that the midshipmen made me very tipsy that evening. I don't recollect being put to bed, but I found myself there the next morning, with a dreadful headache, and a very confused recollection of what had passed. I was very much shocked at my having so soon forgotten the injunctions of my parents, and was making vows never to be so foolish again, when in came the midshipman who had been so kind to me the night before. "Come, Mr Bottlegreen," he bawled out, alluding, I suppose, to the colour of my clothes, "rouse and bitt. There's the captain's coxswain waiting for you below. By the powers, you're in a pretty scrape for what you did last night!"

"Did last night!" replied I, astonished. "Why, does the captain know that I was tipsy?"

"I think you took devilish good care to let him know it when you were at the theatre."

"At the theatre! was I at the theatre?"

"To be sure you were. You would go, do all we could to prevent you, though you were as drunk as David's sow. Your captain was there with the admiral's daughters. You called him a tyrant and snapped your fingers at him. Why, don't you recollect? You told him that you did not care a fig for him."

"Oh dear! oh dear! what shall I do? what shall I do?" cried I: "My mother cautioned me so about drinking and bad company."

"Bad company, you whelp—what do you mean by that?"

"O, I did not particularly refer to you."

"I should hope not! However, I recommend you, as a friend, to go to the George Inn as fast as you can, and see your captain, for the longer you stay away, the worse it will be for you. At all events, it will be decided whether he receives you or not. It is fortunate for you that you are not on the ship's books. Come, be quick, the coxswain is gone back."

"Not on the ship's books," replied I sorrowfully. "Now I recollect there was a letter from the captain to my father, stating that he had put me on the books."

"Upon my honour, I'm sorry—very sorry indeed," replied the midshipman; —and he quitted the room, looking as grave as if the misfortune had happened to himself. I got up with a heavy head, and heavier heart, and as soon as I was dressed, I asked the way to the George Inn. I took my letter of introduction with me, although I was afraid it would be of little service. When I arrived, I asked, with a trembling voice, whether Captain Thomas Kirkwall Savage, of H.M. ship *Diomede*, was staying there. The waiter replied, that he was at breakfast with Captain Courtney, but that he would take up my name. I gave it him, and in a minute the waiter returned, and desired that I would walk up. O how my heart beat!—I never was so frightened—I thought I should have dropped on the stairs. Twice I attempted to walk into the room, and each time my legs failed me; at last I wiped the perspiration from my forehead, and with a desperate effort I went into the room.

"Mr Simple, I am glad to see you," said a voice. I had held my head down, for I was afraid to look at him, but the voice was so kind that I mustered up courage; and, when I did look up, there sat with his uniform and epaulets, and his sword by his side, the passenger in the plaid cloak, who wanted to open my letter, and whom I had told to his face, that he was *no gentleman*.

I thought I should have died as the other midshipman did upon his chest. I was just sinking down upon my knees to beg for mercy, when the captain perceiving my confusion, burst out into a laugh, and said, "So you know me again, Mr Simple? Well, don't be alarmed, you did your duty in not permitting me to open the letter, supposing me, as you did, to be some other person, and you were perfectly right, under that supposition, to tell me that I was not a gentleman. I give you credit for your conduct. Now sit down and take some breakfast."

"Captain Courtney," said he to the other captain, who was at the table, "this is one of my youngsters just entering the service. We were passengers yesterday by the same coach." He then told him the circumstance which occurred, at which they laughed heartily.

I now recovered my spirits a little—but still there was the affair at the theatre, and I thought that perhaps he did not recognize me. I was, however, soon relieved from my anxiety by the other captain inquiring, "Were you at the theatre last night, Savage?"

"No; I dined at the admiral's; there's no getting away from those girls, they are so pleasant."

"I rather think you are a little—*taken* in that quarter."

"No, on my word! I might be if I had time to discover which I liked best; but my ship is at present my wife, and the only wife I intend to have until I am laid on the shelf."

Well, thought I, if he was not at the theatre, it could not have been him that I insulted. Now if I can only give him the rum, and make friends with him.

"Pray, Mr Simple, how are your father and mother?" said the captain.

"Very well, I thank you, sir, and desire me to present their compliments."

"I am obliged to them. Now I think the sooner you go on board and learn your duty the better." (Just what the midshipman told me—the very words, thought I—then it's all true—and I began to tremble again.)

"I have a little advice to offer you," continued the captain. "In the first place, obey your superior officers without hesitation; it is for me, not you, to decide whether an order is unjust or not. In the next place, never swear or drink spirits. The first is immoral and ungentleman-like, the second is a vile habit which will grow upon you. I never touch spirit myself, and I expect that my young gentlemen will refrain from it also. Now you may go, and as soon as your uniforms arrive, you will repair on board. In the meantime, as I had some little insight into your character when we travelled together, let me recommend you not to be too intimate at first sight with those you meet, or you may be led into indiscretions. Good morning."

I quitted the room with a low bow, glad to have surmounted so easily what appeared to be a chaos of difficulty; but my mind was confused with the testimony of the midshipman, so much at variance with the language and behaviour of the captain. When I arrived at the Blue Posts, I found all the midshipmen in the coffee-room, and I repeated to them all that had passed. When I had finished, they burst out laughing, and said that they had only been joking with me. "Well," said I to the one who had called me up in the morning, "you may call it joking, but I call it lying."

"Pray, Mr Bottlegreen, do you refer to me?"

"Yes, I do," replied I.

"Then, sir, as a gentleman, I demand satisfaction. Slugs in a saw-pit. Death before dishonour, d——e!"

"I shall not refuse you," replied I, "although I had rather not fight a duel; my father cautioned me on the subject, desiring me, if possible, to avoid it, as it was flying in the face of my Creator; but aware that I must uphold my character as an officer, he left me to my own discretion, should I ever be so unfortunate as to be in such a dilemma."

"Well, we don't want one of your father's sermons at second-hand," replied the midshipman, (for I had told them that my father was a clergyman); "the plain question is, will you fight, or will you not?"

"Could not the affair be arranged otherwise?" interrupted another. "Will not Mr Bottlegreen retract?"

"My name is Simple, sir, and not Bottlegreen," replied I; "and as he did tell a falsehood, I will not retract."

"Then the affair must go on," said the midshipman. "Robinson, will you oblige me by acting as my second?"

"It's an unpleasant business," replied the other; "you are so good a shot; but as you request it, I shall not refuse. Mr Simple is not, I believe, provided with a friend."

"Yes, he is," replied another of the midshipmen. "He is a spunky fellow, and I'll be his second."

It was then arranged that we should meet the next morning, with pistols. I considered that as an officer and a gentleman, I could not well refuse; but I was very unhappy. Not three days left to my own guidance, and I had become intoxicated, and was now to fight a duel. I went up into my room and wrote a long letter to my mother, enclosing a lock of my hair; and having shed a few tears at the idea of how sorry she would be if I were killed, I borrowed a bible from the waiter, and read it during the remainder of the day.

Chapter IV

I am taught on a cold morning, before breakfast, how to stand fire, and thus prove my courage—After breakfast I also prove my gallantry—My proof meets reproof—Woman at the bottom of all mischief—By one I lose my liberty, and, by another, my money.

When I began to wake the next morning I could not think what it was that felt like a weight upon my chest, but as I roused and recalled my scattered thoughts, I remembered that in an hour or two it would be decided whether I were to exist another day. I prayed fervently, and made a resolution in my own mind that I would not have the blood of another upon my conscience, and would fire my pistol up in the air. And after I had made that resolution, I no longer felt the alarm which I did before. Before I was dressed, the midshipman who had volunteered to be my second, came into my room, and informed me that the affair was to be decided in the garden behind the inn; that my adversary was a very good shot, and that I must expect to be winged if not drilled.

"And what is winged and drilled?" inquired I. "I have not only never fought a duel, but I have not even fired a pistol in my life."

He explained what he meant, which was, that being winged implied being shot through the arm or leg, whereas being drilled was to be shot through the body. "But," continued he, "is it possible that you have never fought a duel?"

"No," replied I; "I am not yet fifteen years old."

"Not fifteen! why I thought you were eighteen at the least." (But I was very tall and stout for my age, and people generally thought me older than I actually was.)

I dressed myself and followed my second into the garden, where I found all the midshipmen and some of the waiters of the inn. They all seemed very merry, as if the life of a fellow-creature was of no consequence. The seconds talked apart for a little while, and then measured the ground, which was twelve paces; we then took our stations. I believe that I turned pale, for my second came to my side and whispered that I must not be frightened. I replied, that I was not frightened, but that I considered that it was an awful moment. The second to my adversary then came up and asked me whether I would make an apology, which I refused to do as before: they handed a pistol to each of us, and my second showed me how I was to pull the trigger. It was arranged that at the word given, we were to fire at the same time. I made sure that I should be wounded, if not killed, and I shut my eyes as I fired my pistol in the air. I felt my head swim, and thought I was hurt, but fortunately I was not. The pistols were loaded again, and we fired a second time. The seconds then interfered, and it was proposed that we should shake hands, which I was very glad to do, for I considered my life to have been saved by a miracle. We all went back to the coffee-room, and sat down to breakfast. They then told me that they all belonged to the same ship that I did, and that they were glad to see that I could stand fire, for the captain was a terrible fellow for cutting-out and running under the enemy's batteries.

The next day my chest arrived by the waggon, and I threw off my "bottle-greens" and put on my uniform. I had no cocked hat, or dirk, as the warehouse people employed by Mr Handycock did not supply those articles, and it was arranged that I should procure them at Portsmouth. When I inquired the price, I found that they cost more money than I had in my pocket, so I tore up the letter I had written to my mother before the duel, and wrote another asking for a remittance, to purchase my dirk and cocked hat. I then walked out in my uniform, not a little proud, I must confess. I was now an officer in his Majesty's service, not very high in rank, certainly, but still an officer and a gentleman, and I made a vow that I would support the character, although I was considered the greatest fool of the family.

I had arrived opposite a place called Sally Port, when a young lady, very nicely dressed, looked at me very hard and said, "Well, Reefer, how are you off for soap?" I was astonished at the question, and more so at the interest which she seemed to take in my affairs. I answered, "Thank you, I am very well off; I have four cakes of Windsor, and two bars of yellow for washing." She laughed at my reply, and asked me whether I would walk home and take a bit of dinner with her. I was astonished at this polite offer, which my modesty induced me to ascribe more to my uniform than to my own merits, and, as I felt no inclination to refuse the compliment, I said that I should be most happy. I thought I might venture to offer my arm, which she accepted, and we proceeded up High Street on our way to her home.

Just as we passed the admiral's house, I perceived my captain walking with two of the admiral's daughters. I was not a little proud to let him see that I had female acquaintances as well as he had, and, as I passed him with the young lady under my protection, I took off my hat, and made him a low bow. To my surprise, not only did he not return the salute, but he looked at me with a very stern countenance. I concluded that he was a very proud man, and did not wish the admiral's daughters to suppose that he knew midshipmen by sight; but I had not exactly made up my mind on the subject, when the captain, having seen the ladies into the admiral's house, sent one of the messengers after me to desire that I would immediately come to him at the George Inn, which was nearly opposite.

I apologised to the young lady, and promised to return immediately if she would wait for me; but she replied, if that was my captain, it was her idea that I should have a confounded wigging and be sent on board. So, wishing me good-bye, she left me and continued her way home. I could as little comprehend all this as why the captain looked so black when I passed him; but it was soon explained when I went up to him in the parlour at the George Inn. "I am sorry, Mr Simple," said the captain, when I entered, "that a lad like you should show such early symptoms of depravity; still more so, that he should not have the grace which even the most hardened are not wholly destitute of—I mean to practise immorality in secret, and not degrade themselves and insult their captain by unblushingly avowing (I may say glorying in) their iniquity, by exposing it in broad day, and in the most frequented street of the town."

"Sir," replied I with astonishment, "O dear! O dear! what have I done?"

The captain fixed his keen eyes upon me, so that they appeared to pierce me through, and nail me to the wall. "Do you pretend to say, sir, that you were not aware of the character of the person with whom you were walking just now?"

"No, sir," replied I; "except that she was very kind and good-natured;" and then I told him how she had addressed me, and what subsequently took place.

"And is it possible, Mr Simple, that you are so great a fool?" I replied that I certainly was considered the greatest fool of our family. "I should think you were," replied he, drily. He then explained to me who the person was with whom I was in company, and how any association with her would inevitably lead to my ruin and disgrace.

I cried very much, for I was shocked at the narrow escape which I had had, and mortified at having fallen in his good opinion. He asked me how I had employed my time since I had been at Portsmouth, and I made an acknowledgment of having been made tipsy, related all that the midshipmen had told me, and how I had that morning fought a duel.

He listened to my whole story very attentively, and I thought that occasionally there was a smile upon his face, although he bit his lips to prevent it. When I had finished, he said, "Mr Simple, I can no longer trust you on shore until you are more experienced in the world. I shall desire my coxswain not to lose sight of you until you are safe on board of the frigate. When you have sailed a few months with me, you will then be able to decide whether I deserve the character which the young gentlemen have painted, with, I must say, I believe, the sole intention of practising upon your inexperience."

Altogether I did not feel sorry when it was over. I saw that the captain believed what I had stated, and that he was disposed to be kind to me, although he thought me very silly. The coxswain, in obedience to his orders, accompanied me to the Blue Posts. I packed up my clothes, paid my bill, and the porter wheeled my chest down to the Sally Port, where the boat was waiting.

"Come, heave a-head, my lads, be smart. The captain says we are to take the young gentleman on board directly. His liberty's stopped for getting drunk and running after the Dolly Mops!"

"I should thank you to be more respectful in your remarks, Mr Coxswain," said I with displeasure.

"Mister Coxswain! thanky, sir, for giving me a handle to my name," replied he. "Come, be smart with your oars, my lads!"

"La, Bill Freeman," said a young woman on the beach, "what a nice young gentleman you have there! He looks like a sucking Nelson. I say, my pretty young officer, could you lend me a shilling?"

I was so pleased at the woman calling me a young Nelson, that I immediately complied with her request. "I have not a shilling in my pocket," said I, "but here is half-a-crown, and you can change it and bring me back the eighteen pence."

"Well, you are a nice young man," replied she, taking the half-crown;
"I'll be back directly, my dear."

The men in the boat laughed, and the coxswain desired them to shove off.

"No," observed I, "you must wait for my eighteen pence."

"We shall wait a devilish long while then, I suspect. I know that girl, and she has a very bad memory."

"She cannot be so dishonest or ungrateful," replied I. "Coxswain, I order you to stay—I am an officer."

"I know you are, sir, about six hours old: well, then, I must go up and tell the captain that you have another girl in tow, and that you won't go on board."

"Oh no, Mr Coxswain, pray don't; shove off as soon as you please, and never mind the eighteen pence."

The boat then shoved off, and pulled towards the ship, which lay at
Spithead.

Chapter V

I am introduced to the quarter-deck and first lieutenant, who pronounces me very clever—Trotted below to Mrs Trotter—Connubial bliss in a cock-pit—Mr Trotter takes me in as a mess-mate—Feel very much surprised that so many people know that I am the son of—my father.

On our arrival on board, the coxswain gave a note from the captain to the first lieutenant, who happened to be on deck. He read the note, looked at me earnestly, and then I overheard him say to another lieutenant, "The service is going to the devil. As long as it was not popular, if we had not much education, we at least had the chance that natural abilities gave us; but now that great people send their sons for a provision into the navy, we have all the refuse of their families, as if anything was good enough to make a captain of a man-of-war, who has occasionally more responsibility on his shoulders, and is placed in situations requiring more judgment, than any other people in existence. Here's another of the fools of a family made a present of to the country—another cub for me to lick into shape. Well, I never saw the one yet I did not make something of. Where's Mr Simple?"

"I am Mr Simple, sir," replied I, very much frightened at what I had overheard.

"Now, Mr Simple," said the first lieutenant, "observe, and pay particular attention to what I say. The captain tells me in this note that you have been shamming stupid. Now, sir, I am not to be taken in that way. You're something like the monkeys, who won't speak because they are afraid they will be made to work. I have looked attentively at your face, and I see at once that you are *very clever*, and if you do not prove so in a very short time, why—you had better jump overboard, that's all. Perfectly understand me. I know that you are a very clever fellow, and having told you so, don't you pretend to impose upon me, for it won't do."

I was very much terrified at this speech, but at the same time I was pleased to hear that he thought me clever, and I determined to do all in my power to keep up such an unexpected reputation.

"Quarter-master," said the first lieutenant, "tell Mr Trotter to come on deck."

The quarter-master brought up Mr Trotter, who apologized for being so dirty, as he was breaking casks out of the hold. He was a short, thick-set man, about thirty years of age, with a nose which had a red club to it, very dirty teeth, and large black whiskers.

"Mr Trotter," said the first lieutenant, "here is a young gentleman who has joined the ship. Introduce him into the berth, and see his hammock slung. You must look after him a little."

"I really have very little time to look after any of them, sir," replied Mr Trotter; "but I will do what I can. Follow me, youngster." Accordingly, I descended the ladder after him; then I went down another, and then to my surprise I was desired by him to go down a third, which when I had done, he informed me that I was in the cock-pit.

"Now, youngster," said Mr Trotter, seating himself upon a large chest, "you may do as you please. The midshipmen's mess is on the deck above this, and if you like to join, why you can; but this I will tell you as a friend, that you will be thrashed all day long, and fare very badly; the weakest always goes to the wall there, but perhaps you do not mind that. Now that we are in harbour, I mess here, because Mrs Trotter is on board. She is a very charming woman, I can assure you, and will be here directly; she has just gone up into the galley to look after a net of potatoes in the copper. If you like it better, I will ask her permission for you to mess with us. You will then be away from the midshipmen, who are a sad set, and will teach you nothing but what is immoral and improper, and you will have the advantage of being in good society, for Mrs Trotter has kept the very best in England. I make you this offer because I want to oblige the first lieutenant, who appears to take an interest about you, otherwise I am not very fond of having any intrusion upon my domestic happiness."

I replied that I was much obliged to him for his kindness, and that if it would not put Mrs Trotter to an inconvenience, I should be happy to accept of his offer; indeed, I thought myself very fortunate in having met with such a friend. I had scarcely time to reply, when I perceived a pair of legs, cased in black cotton stockings, on the ladder above us, and it proved that they belonged to Mrs Trotter, who came down the ladder with a net full of smoking potatoes.

"Upon my word, Mrs Trotter, you must be conscious of having a very pretty ankle, or you would not venture to display it, as you have to Mr Simple, a young gentleman whom I beg to introduce to you, and who, with your permission, will join our mess."

"My dear Trotter, how cruel of you not to give me warning; I thought that nobody was below. I declare I'm so ashamed," continued the lady, simpering, and covering her face with the hand which was unemployed.

"It can't be helped now, my love, neither was there anything to be ashamed of. I trust Mr Simple and you will be very good friends. I believe I mentioned his desire to join our mess."

"I am sure I shall be very happy in his company. This is a strange place for me to live in, Mr Simple, after the society to which I have been accustomed; but affection can make any sacrifice; and rather than lose the company of my dear Trotter, who has been unfortunate in pecuniary matters—"

"Say no more about it, my love. Domestic happiness is everything, and will enliven even the gloom of a cock-pit."

"And yet," continued Mrs Trotter, "when I think of the time when we used to live in London, and keep our carriage. Have you ever been in London, Mr Simple?" I answered that I had.

"Then, probably, you may have been acquainted with, or have heard of, the Smiths?"

I replied that the only people that I knew there were a Mr and Mrs Handycock.

"Well, if I had known that you were in London, I should have been very glad to have given you a letter of introduction to the Smiths. They are quite the topping people of the place."

"But, my dear," interrupted Mr Trotter, "is it not time to look after our dinner?"

"Yes; I am going forward for it now. We have skewer pieces to-day. Mr Simple, will you excuse me?" and then, with a great deal of flirtation and laughing about her ankles, and requesting me, as a favour, to turn my face away, Mrs Trotter ascended the ladder.

As the reader may wish to know what sort of looking personage she was, I will take this opportunity to describe her. Her figure was very good, and at one period of her life I thought her face must have been very handsome; at the time I was introduced to her, it showed the ravages of time or hardship very distinctly; in short, she might be termed a faded beauty, flaunting in her dress, and not very clean in her person.

"Charming woman, Mrs Trotter, is she not, Mr Simple?" said the master's mate; to which, of course, I immediately acquiesced. "Now, Mr Simple," continued he, "there are a few arrangements which I had better mention while Mrs Trotter is away, for she would be shocked at our talking about such things. Of course, the style of living which we indulge in is rather expensive. Mrs Trotter cannot dispense with her tea and her other little comforts; at the same time I must put you to no extra expense—I had rather be out of pocket myself. I propose that during the time you mess with us you shall only pay one guinea per week; and as for entrance money, why I think I must not charge you more than a couple of guineas. Have you any money?"

"Yes," I replied, "I have three guineas and a half left."

"Well, then, give me the three guineas, and the half-guinea you can reserve for pocket-money. You must write to your friends immediately for a further supply."

I handed him the money, which he put in his pocket. "Your chest," continued he, "you shall bring down here, for Mrs Trotter will, I am sure, if I request it, not only keep it in order for you, but see that your clothes are properly mended. She is a charming woman, Mrs Trotter, and very fond of young gentlemen. How old are you?"

I replied that I was fifteen.

"No more! well, I am glad of that, for Mrs Trotter is very particular after a certain age. I should recommend you on no account to associate with the other midshipmen. They are very angry with me, because I would not permit Mrs Trotter to join their mess, and they are sad story-tellers."

"That they certainly are," replied I; but here we were interrupted by Mrs Trotter coming down with a piece of stick in her hand upon which were skewered about a dozen small pieces of beef and pork, which she first laid on a plate, and then began to lay the cloth and prepare for dinner.

"Mr Simple is only fifteen, my dear," observed Mr Trotter.

"Dear me!" replied Mrs Trotter, "why, how tall he is! He is quite as tall for his age as young Lord Foutretown, whom you used to take out with you in the *chay*. Do you know Lord Foutretown, Mr Simple?"

"No, I do not, ma'am," replied I; but wishing to let them know that I was well connected, I continued, "but I dare say that my grandfather, Lord Privilege, does."

"God bless me! is Lord Privilege your grandfather? Well, I thought I saw a likeness somewhere. Don't you recollect Lord Privilege, my dear Trotter, that we met at Lady Scamp's—an elderly person? It's very ungrateful of you not to recollect him, for he sent you a very fine haunch of venison."

"Privilege—bless me, yes. Oh, yes! an old gentleman, is he not?" said
Mr Trotter, appealing to me.

"Yes, sir," replied I, quite delighted to find myself among those who were acquainted with my family.

"Well, then, Mr Simple," said Mrs Trotter, "since we have the pleasure of being acquainted with your family, I shall now take you under my own charge, and I shall be so fond of you that Trotter shall become quite jealous," added she, laughing. "We have but a poor dinner to-day, for the bumboat woman disappointed me. I particularly requested her to bring me off a leg of lamb, but she says that there was none in the market. It is rather early for it, that's true; but Trotter is very nice in his eating. Now, let us sit down to dinner."

I felt very sick, indeed, and could eat nothing. Our dinner consisted of the pieces of beef and pork, the potatoes, and a baked pudding in a tin dish. Mr Trotter went up to serve the spirits out to the ship's company, and returned with a bottle of rum.

"Have you got Mr Simple's allowance, my love?" inquired Mrs Trotter.

"Yes; he is victualled to-day, as he came on board before twelve o'clock. Do you drink spirits, Mr Simple?"

"No, I thank you," replied I; for I remembered the captain's injunction.

"Taking, as I do, such an interest in your welfare, I must earnestly recommend you to abstain from them," said Mr Trotter. "It is a very bad habit, and once acquired, not easy to be left off. I am obliged to drink them, that I may not check the perspiration after working in the hold; I have, nevertheless, a natural abhorrence of them; but my champagne and claret days are gone by, and I must submit to circumstances."

"My poor Trotter!" said the lady.

"Well," continued he, "it's a poor heart that never rejoiceth." He then poured out half a tumbler of rum, and filled the glass up with water.

"My love, will you taste it?"

"Now, Trotter, you know that I never touch it, except when the water is so bad that I must have the taste taken away. How is the water to-day?"

"As usual, my dear, not drinkable." After much persuasion Mrs Trotter agreed to sip a little out of his glass. I thought that she took it pretty often, considering that she did not like it, but I felt so unwell that I was obliged to go on the main-deck. There I was met by a midshipman whom I had not seen before. He looked very earnestly in my face, and then asked my name. "Simple," said he. "What, are you the son of old Simple?"

"Yes, sir," replied I, astonished that so many should know my family.

"Well, I thought so by the likeness. And how is your father?"

"Very well, I thank you, sir."

"When you write to him, make my compliments, and tell him that I desired to be particularly remembered to him;" and he walked forward, but as he forgot to mention his own name, I could not do it.

I went to bed very tired; Mr Trotter had my hammock hung up in the cock-pit, separated by a canvas-screen from the cot in which he slept with his wife. I thought this very odd, but they told me it was the general custom on board ship, although Mrs Trotter's delicacy was very much shocked by it. I was very sick, but Mrs Trotter was very kind. When I was in bed she kissed me, and wished me good night, and very soon afterwards I fell fast asleep.

Chapter VI

Puzzled with very common words—Mrs Trotter takes care of my wardrobe—A matrimonial duet, ending *con strepito*.

I awoke the next morning at daylight with a noise over my head which sounded like thunder; I found it proceeded from holystoning and washing down the main-deck. I was very much refreshed nevertheless, and did not feel the least sick or giddy. Mr Trotter, who had been up at four o'clock, came down, and directed one of the marines to fetch me some water. I washed myself on my chest, and then went on the main-deck, which they were swabbing dry. Standing by the sentry at the cabin-door, I met one of the midshipmen with whom I had been in company at the Blue Posts.

"So, Master Simple, old Trotter and his faggot of a wife have got hold of you—have they?" said he. I replied, that I did not know the meaning of faggot, but that I considered Mrs Trotter a very charming woman. At which he burst into a loud laugh. "Well," said he, "I'll just give you a caution. Take care, or they'll make a clean sweep. Has Mrs Trotter shown you her ankle yet?"

"Yes," I replied, "and a very pretty one it is."

"Ah! she's at her old tricks. You had much better have joined our mess at once. You're not the first greenhorn that they have plucked. Well," said he, as he walked away, "keep the key of your own chest—that's all."

But as Mr Trotter had warned me that the midshipmen would abuse them, I paid very little attention to what he said. When he left me I went on the quarter-deck. All the sailors were busy at work, and the first lieutenant cried out to the gunner, "Now, Mr Dispart, if you are ready, we'll breech these guns."

"Now, my lads," said the first lieutenant, "we must slue (the part that breeches cover) more forward." As I never heard of a gun having breeches, I was very anxious to see what was going on, and went up close to the first lieutenant, who said to me, "Youngster, hand me that *monkey's tail*." I saw nothing like a *monkey's tail*, but I was so frightened that I snatched up the first thing that I saw, which was a short bar of iron, and it so happened that it was the very article which he wanted. When I gave it to him, the first lieutenant looked at me, and said, "So you know what a monkey's tail is already, do you? Now don't you ever sham stupid after that."

Thought I to myself, I'm very lucky, but if that's a monkey's tail it's a very stiff one!

I resolved to learn the names of everything as fast as I could, that I might be prepared; so I listened attentively to what was said; but I soon became quite confused, and despaired of remembering anything.

"How is this to be finished off, sir?" inquired a sailor of the boatswain.

"Why, I beg leave to hint to you, sir, in the most delicate manner in the world," replied the boatswain, "that it must be with a *double-wall*—and be d——d to you—don't you know that yet? Captain of the foretop," said he, "up on your *horses*, and take your *stirrups* up three inches."—"Ay, ay, sir." (I looked and looked, but I could see no horses.)

"Mr Chucks," said the first lieutenant to the boatswain, "what blocks have we below—not on charge?"

"Let me see, sir, I've one *sister*, t'other we split in half the other day, and I think I have a couple of *monkeys* down in the store-room.—I say, you Smith, pass that brace through the *bull's eye,* and take the *sheepshank* out before you come down."

And then he asked the first lieutenant whether something should not be fitted with a *mouse* or only a *Turk's head*—told him the *goose-neck* must be spread out by the armourer as soon as the forge was up. In short, what with *dead eyes* and *shrouds, cats* and *cat-blocks, dolphins* and *dolphin-strikers, whips* and *puddings*, I was so puzzled with what I heard, that I was about to leave the deck in absolute despair.

"And, Mr Chucks, recollect this afternoon that you *bleed* all the *buoys*."

Bleed the boys, thought I, what can that be for? at all events, the surgeon appears to be the proper person to perform that operation.

This last incomprehensible remark drove me off the deck, and I retreated to the cock-pit, where I found Mrs Trotter. "Oh, my dear!" said she, "I am glad you are come, as I wish to put your clothes in order. Have you a list of them—where is your key?" I replied that I had not a list, and I handed her the key, although I did not forget the caution of the midshipman; yet I considered that there could be no harm in her looking over my clothes when I was present. She unlocked my chest, and pulled everything out, and then commenced telling me what were likely to be useful and what were not.

"Now these worsted stockings," she said, "will be very comfortable in cold weather, and in the summer time these brown cotton socks will be delightfully cool, and you have enough of each to last you till you outgrow them; but as for these fine cotton stockings, they are of no use—only catch the dirt when the decks are swept, and always look untidy. I wonder how they could be so foolish as to send them; nobody wears them on board ship nowadays. They are only fit for women—I wonder if they would fit me."

She turned her chair away, and put on one of my stockings, laughing the whole of the time. Then she turned round to me and showed me how nicely they fitted her. "Bless you, Mr Simple, it's well that Trotter is in the hold, he'd be so jealous—do you know what these stockings cost? They are of no use to you, and they fit me. I will speak to Trotter, and take them off your hands." I replied, that I could not think of selling them, and as they were of no use to me and fitted her, I begged that she would accept of the dozen pairs. At first she positively refused, but as I pressed her, she at last consented, and I was very happy to give them to her as she was very kind to me, and I thought, with her husband, that she was a very charming woman.

We had beef-steaks and onions for dinner that day, but I could not bear the smell of the onions. Mr Trotter came down very cross, because the first lieutenant had found fault with him. He swore that he would cut the service—that he had only remained to oblige the captain, who said that he would sooner part with his right arm, and that he would demand satisfaction of the first lieutenant as soon as he could obtain his discharge. Mrs Trotter did all she could to pacify him, reminded him that he had the protection of Lord this and Sir Thomas that, who would see him righted; but in vain. The first lieutenant had told him, he said, that he was not worth his salt, and blood only could wipe away the insult. He drank glass of grog after glass of grog, and at each glass became more violent, and Mrs Trotter drank also, I observed, a great deal more than I thought she ought to have done; but she whispered to me, that she drank it that Trotter might not, as he would certainly be tipsy. I thought this very devoted on her part; but they sat so late that I went to bed and left them—he still drinking and vowing vengeance against the first lieutenant. I had not been asleep above two or three hours when I was awakened by a great noise and quarrelling, and I discovered that Mr Trotter was drunk and beating his wife. Very much shocked that such a charming woman should be beaten and ill-used, I scrambled out of my hammock to see if I could be of any assistance, but it was dark, although they scuffled as much as before. I asked the marine, who was sentry at the gun-room door above, to bring his lantern, and was very much shocked at his replying that I had better go to bed and let them fight it out.

Shortly afterwards Mrs Trotter, who had not taken off her clothes, came from behind the screen. I perceived at once that the poor woman could hardly stand; she reeled to my chest, where she sat down and cried. I pulled on my clothes as fast as I could, and then went up to her to console her, but she could not speak intelligibly. After attempting in vain to comfort her, she made me no answer, but staggered to my hammock, and, after several attempts, succeeded in getting into it. I cannot say that I much liked that, but what could I do? So I finished dressing myself, and went up on the quarter-deck.

The midshipman who had the watch was the one who had cautioned me against the Trotters; he was very friendly to me. "Well, Simple," said he, "what brings you on deck?" I told him how ill Mr Trotter had behaved to his wife, and how she had turned into my hammock.

"The cursed drunken old catamaran," cried he; "I'll go and cut her down by the head;" but I requested he would not, as she was a lady.

"A lady!" replied he; "yes, there's plenty of ladies of her description;" and then he informed me that she had many years ago been the mistress of a man of fortune who kept a carriage for her; but that he grew tired of her, and had given Trotter £200 to marry her, and that now they did nothing but get drunk together and fight with each other.

I was very much annoyed to hear all this; but as I perceived that Mrs Trotter was not sober, I began to think that what the midshipman said was true. "I hope," added he, "that she has not had time to wheedle you out of any of your clothes."

I told him that I had given her a dozen pairs of stockings, and had paid Mr Trotter three guineas for my mess. "This must be looked to," replied he; "I shall speak to the first lieutenant to-morrow. In the mean time, I shall get your hammock for you. Quarter-master, keep a good look-out." He then went below, and I followed him, to see what he would do. He went to my hammock and lowered it down at one end, so that Mrs Trotter lay with her head on the deck in a very uncomfortable position. To my astonishment, she swore at him in a dreadful manner, but refused to turn out. He was abusing her, and shaking her in the hammock, when Mr Trotter, who had been roused at the noise, rushed from behind the screen. "You villain! what are you doing with my wife?" cried he, pommelling at him as well as he could, for he was so tipsy that he could hardly stand.

I thought the midshipman able to take care of himself, and did not wish to interfere; so I remained above, looking on—the sentry standing by me with his lantern over the coombings of the hatchway to give light to the midshipman, and to witness the fray. Mr Trotter was soon knocked down, when all of a sudden Mrs Trotter jumped up from the hammock, and caught the midshipman by the hair, and pulled at him. Then the sentry thought right to interfere; he called out for the master-at-arms, and went down himself to help the midshipman, who was faring badly between the two. But Mrs Trotter snatched the lantern out of his hand and smashed it all to pieces, and then we were all left in darkness, and I could not see what took place, although the scuffling continued. Such was the posture of affairs when the master-at-arms came up with his light. The midshipman and sentry went up the ladder, and Mr and Mrs Trotter continued beating each other. To this, none of them paid any attention, saying, as the sentry had said before, "Let them fight it out."

After they had fought some time, they retired behind the screen, and I followed the advice of the midshipman, and got into my hammock, which the master-at-arms hung up again for me. I heard Mr and Mrs Trotter both crying and kissing each other. "Cruel, cruel, Mr Trotter," said she, blubbering.

"My life, my love, I was so jealous!" replied he.

"D—n and blast your jealousy," replied the lady; "I've two nice black eyes for the galley to-morrow." After about an hour of kissing and scolding, they both fell asleep again.

The next morning before breakfast, the midshipman reported to the first lieutenant the conduct of Mr Trotter and his wife. I was sent for and obliged to acknowledge that it was all true. He sent for Mr Trotter, who replied that he was not well, and could not come on deck. Upon which the first lieutenant ordered the sergeant of marines to bring him up directly. Mr Trotter made his appearance, with one eye closed, and his face very much scratched.

"Did not I desire you, sir," said the first lieutenant, "to introduce this young gentleman into the midshipmen's berth? instead of which you have introduced him to that disgraceful wife of yours, and have swindled him out of his property. I order you immediately to return the three guineas which you received as mess-money, and also that your wife give back the stockings which she cajoled him out of."

But then I interposed, and told the first lieutenant that the stockings had been a free gift on my part and that, although I had been very foolish, yet that I considered that I could not in honour demand them back again.

"Well, youngster," replied the first lieutenant, "perhaps your ideas are correct, and if you wish it, I will not enforce that part of my order; but," continued he to Mr Trotter, "I desire, sir, that your wife leave the ship immediately; and I trust that when I have reported your conduct to the captain, he will serve you in the same manner. In the meantime, you will consider yourself under an arrest for drunkenness."

Chapter VII

Scandalum magnatum clearly proved—I prove to the captain that I consider him a gentleman, although I had told him the contrary, and I prove to the midshipmen that I am a gentleman myself—They prove their gratitude by practising upon me, because practice makes perfect.

The captain came on board about twelve o'clock, and ordered the discharge of Mr Trotter to be made out, as soon as the first lieutenant had reported what had occurred. He then sent for all the midshipmen on the quarter-deck.

"Gentlemen," said the captain to them, with a stern countenance, "I feel very much indebted to some of you for the character which you have been pleased to give of me to Mr Simple. I must now request that you will answer a few questions which I am about to put in his presence. Did I ever flog the whole starboard watch because the ship would only sail nine knots on a bowline?"

"No, sir, no!" replied they all, very much frightened.

"Did I ever give a midshipman four dozen for not having his weekly accounts pipe-clayed; or another five dozen for wearing a scarlet watch ribbon?"

"No, sir," replied they all together.

"Did any midshipman ever die on his chest from fatigue?"

They again replied in the negative.

"Then, gentlemen, you will oblige me by stating which of you thought proper to assert these falsehoods in a public coffee-room; and further, which of you obliged this youngster to risk his life in a duel?"

They were all silent.

"Will you answer me, gentlemen?"

"With respect to the duel, sir," replied the midshipman who had fought me, "I *heard* say, that the pistols were only charged with powder. It was a joke."

"Well, sir, we'll allow that the duel was only a joke, (and I hope and trust that your report is correct); is the reputation of your captain only a joke, allow me to ask? I request to know who of you dared to propagate such injurious slander?" (Here there was a dead pause.) "Well, then, gentlemen, since you will not confess yourselves, I must refer to my authority. Mr Simple, have the goodness to point out the person or persons who gave you the information."

But I thought this would not be fair; and as they had all treated me very kindly after the duel, I resolved not to tell; so I answered, "If you please, sir, I consider that I told you all that in confidence."

"Confidence, sir!" replied the captain; "who ever heard of confidence between a post-captain and a midshipman?"

"No, sir," replied I, "not between a post-captain and a midshipman, but between two gentlemen."

The first lieutenant, who stood by the captain, put his hand before his face to hide a laugh. "He may be a fool, sir," observed he to the captain, aside; "but I can assure you he is a very straight, forward one."

The captain bit his lip, and then turning to the midshipmen, said, "You may thank Mr Simple, gentlemen, that I do not press this matter further. I do believe that you were not serious when you calumniated me; but recollect, that what is said in joke is too often repeated in earnest. I trust that Mr Simple's conduct will have its effect, and that you leave off practising upon him, who has saved you from a very severe punishment."

When the midshipmen went down below, they all shook hands with me, and said that I was a good fellow for not peaching; but, as for the advice of the captain that they should not practise upon me, as he termed it, they forgot that, for they commenced again immediately, and never left off until they found that I was not to be deceived any longer.

I had not been ten minutes in the berth, before they began their remarks upon me. One said that I looked like a hardy fellow, and asked me whether I could not bear a great deal of sleep.

I replied that I could, I dare say, if it was necessary for the good of the service; at which they laughed, and I supposed that I had said a good thing.

"Why here's Tomkins," said the midshipman; "he'll show you how to perform that part of your duty. He inherits it from his father, who was a marine officer. He can snore for fourteen hours on a stretch without once turning round in his hammock, and finish his nap on the chest during the whole of the day, except meal-times."

But Tomkins defended himself, by saying, that "some people were very quick in doing things, and others were very slow; that he was one of the slow ones, and that he did not in reality obtain more refreshment from his long naps than other people did in short ones, because he slept much slower than they did."

This ingenious argument was, however, overruled *nem. con.*, as it was proved that he ate pudding faster than any one in the mess.

The postman came on board with the letters, and put his head into the midshipman's berth. I was very anxious to have one from home, but I was disappointed. Some had letters and some had not. Those who had not, declared that their parents were very undutiful, and that they would cut them off with a shilling; and those who had letters, after they had read them, offered them for sale to the others, usually at half-price. I could not imagine why they sold, or why the others bought them; but they did do so; and one that was full of good advice was sold three times, from which circumstance I was inclined to form a better opinion of the morals of my companions. The lowest-priced letters sold, were those written by sisters. I was offered one for a penny, but I declined buying, as I had plenty of sisters of my own. Directly I made that observation, they immediately inquired all their names and ages, and whether they were pretty or not. When I had informed them, they quarrelled to whom they should belong. One would have Lucy, and another took Mary; but there was a great dispute about Ellen, as I had said that she was the prettiest of the whole. At last they agreed to put her up to auction, and she was knocked down to a master's mate of the name of O'Brien, who bid seventeen shillings and a bottle of rum. They requested that I would write home to give their love to my sisters, and tell them how they had been disposed of, which I thought very strange; but I ought to have been flattered at the price bid for Ellen, as I repeatedly have since been witness to a very pretty sister being sold for a glass of grog.

I mentioned the reason why I was so anxious for a letter, viz., because I wanted to buy my dirk and cocked hat; upon which they told me that there was no occasion for my spending my money, as, by the regulations of the service, the purser's steward served them out to all the officers who applied for them. As I knew where the purser's steward's room was, having seen it when down in the cock-pit with the Trotters, I went down immediately. "Mr Purser's Steward," said I, "let me have a cocked hat and a dirk immediately."

"Very good, sir," replied he, and he wrote an order upon a slip of paper, which he handed to me. "There is the order for it, sir; but the cocked hats are kept in the chest up in the main-top; and as for the dirk, you must apply to the butcher, who has them under his charge."

I went up with the order, and thought I would first apply for the dirk; so I inquired for the butcher, whom I found sitting in the sheep-pen with the sheep, mending his trousers. In reply to my demand, he told me that he had not the key of the store-room, which was under the charge of one of the corporals of marines.

I inquired who, and he said, "Cheeks [1] the marine."

I went everywhere about the ship, inquiring for Cheeks the marine, but could not find him. Some said that they believed he was in the fore-top, standing sentry over the wind, that it might not change; others, that he was in the galley, to prevent the midshipmen from soaking their biscuit in the captain's dripping-pan. At last, I inquired of some of the women who were standing between the guns on the main-deck, and one of them answered that it was no use looking for him among them, as they all had husbands, and Cheeks was a *widows man.*[2]

As I could not find the marine, I thought I might as well go for my cocked hat, and get my dirk afterwards. I did not much like going up the rigging, because I was afraid of turning giddy, and if I fell overboard I could not swim; but one of the midshipmen offered to accompany me, stating that I need not be afraid, if I fell overboard, of sinking to the bottom, as if I was giddy, my head, at all events, *would swim;* so I determined to venture. I climbed up very near to the main-top, but not without missing the little ropes very often, and grazing the skin of my shins. Then I came to large ropes stretched out from the mast, so that you must climb them with your head backwards. The midshipman told me these were called the cat-harpings, because they were so difficult to climb, that a cat would expostulate if ordered to go out by them. I was afraid to venture, and then he proposed that I should go through lubber's hole, which he said had been made for people like me. I agreed to attempt it, as it appeared more easy, and at last arrived, quite out of breath, and very happy to find myself in the main-top.

The captain of the main-top was there with two other sailors. The midshipman introduced me very politely:— "Mr Jenkins—Mr Simple, midshipman,—Mr Simple, Mr Jenkins, captain of the main-top. Mr Jenkins, Mr Simple has come up with an order for a cocked hat." The captain of the top replied that he was very sorry that he had not one in store, but the last had been served out to the captain's monkey. This was very provoking. The captain of the top then asked me if I was ready with my *footing*.

I replied, "Not very, for I had lost it two or three times when coming up." He laughed and replied, that I should lose it altogether before I went down; and that I must *hand* it out. "*Hand* out my *footing!*" said I, puzzled, and appealing to the midshipman; "what does he mean?" "He means that you must fork out a seven-shilling bit." I was just as wise as ever, and stared very much; when Mr Jenkins desired the other men to get half a dozen *foxes* and make a *spread eagle* of me, unless he had his parkisite. I never should have found out what it all meant, had not the midshipman, who laughed till he cried, at last informed me that it was the custom to give the men something to drink the first time that I came aloft, and that if I did not, they would tie me up to the rigging.

Having no money in my pocket, I promised to pay them as soon as I went below; but Mr Jenkins would not trust me. I then became very angry, and inquired of him "if he doubted my honour." He replied, "Not in the least, but that he must have the seven shillings before I went below." "Why, sir," said I, "do you know whom you are speaking to? I am an officer and a gentleman. Do you know who my grandfather is?"

"O yes," replied he, "very well."

"Then, who is he, sir?" replied I very angrily.

"Who is he! why he's the *Lord knows who*."

"No," replied I, "that's not his name; he is Lord Privilege." (I was very much surprised that he knew that my grandfather was a lord.) "And do you suppose," continued I, "that I would forfeit the honour of my family for a paltry seven shillings?"

This observation of mine, and a promise on the part of the midshipman, who said he would be bail for me, satisfied Mr Jenkins, and he allowed me to go down the rigging. I went to my chest, and paid the seven shillings to one of the top-men who followed me, and then went up on the main-deck, to learn as much as I could of my profession. I asked a great many questions of the midshipmen relative to the guns, and they crowded round me to answer them. One told me they were called the frigate's *teeth*, because they stopped the Frenchman's *jaw*. Another midshipman said that he had been so often in action, that he was called the *Fire-eater*. I asked him how it was that he escaped being killed. He replied that he always made it a rule, upon the first cannon-ball coming through the ship's side, to put his head into the hole which it had made; as, by a calculation made by Professor Innman, the odds were 32,647, and some decimals to boot, that another ball would not come in at the same hole. That's what I never should have thought of.

FOOTNOTES: [1] This celebrated personage is the prototype of Mr Nobody on board of a man-of-war.

[B] Widows' men are imaginary sailors, borne on the books, and receiving pay and prize-money, which is appropriated to Greenwich Hospital.

Chapter VIII

My messmates show me the folly of running in debt—Duty carried on politely—I become acquainted with some gentlemen of the home department—The episode of Sholto M'Foy.

Now that I have been on board about a month, I find that my life is not disagreeable. I don't smell the pitch and tar, and I can get into my hammock without tumbling out on the other side. My messmates are good-tempered, although they laugh at me very much; but I must say that they are not very nice in their ideas of honour They appear to consider that to take you in is a capital joke; and that because they laugh at the time that they are cheating you, it then becomes no cheating at all. Now I cannot think otherwise than that cheating is cheating, and that a person is not a bit more honest, because he laughs at you in the bargain. A few days after I came on board, I purchased some tarts of the bumboat woman, as she is called; I wished to pay for them, but she had no change, and very civilly told me she would trust me. She produced a narrow book, and said that she would open an account with me, and I could pay her when I thought proper. To this arrangement I had no objection, and I sent up for different things until I thought that my account must have amounted to eleven or twelve shillings. As I promised my father that I never would run in debt, I considered that it was then time that it should be settled. When I asked for it, what was my surprise to find that it amounted to £2 14s. 6d. I declared that it was impossible, and requested that she would allow me to look at the items, when I found that I was booked for at least three or four dozen tarts every day, ordered by the young gentlemen, "to be put down to Mr Simple's account." I was very much shocked, not only at the sum of money which I had to pay, but also at the want of honesty on the part of my messmates; but when I complained of it in the berth, they all laughed at me.

At last one of them said, "Peter, tell the truth; did not your father caution you not to run in debt?"

"Yes, he did," replied I.

"I know that very well," replied he; "all fathers do the same when their sons leave them; it's a matter of course. Now observe, Peter; it is out of regard to you, that your messmates have been eating tarts at your expense You disobeyed your father's injunctions before you had been a month from home; and it is to give you a lesson that may be useful in after-life, that they have considered it their duty to order the tarts. I trust that it will not be thrown away upon you. Go to the woman, pay your bill, and never run up another."

"That I certainly shall not," replied I; but as I could not prove who ordered the tarts, and did not think it fair that the woman should lose her money, I went up and paid the bill with a determination never to open an account with anybody again.

But this left my pockets quite empty, so I wrote to my father, stating the whole transaction, and the consequent state of my finances. My father, in his answer, observed that whatever might have been their motives, my messmates had done me a friendly act; and that as I had lost my money by my own carelessness, I must not expect that he would allow me any more pocket-money. But my mother, who added a postscript to his letter, slipped in a five-pound note, and I do believe that it was with my father's sanction, although he pretended to be very angry at my forgetting his injunctions. This timely relief made me quite comfortable again. What a pleasure it is to receive a letter from one's friends when far away, especially when there is same money in it!

A few days before this, Mr Falcon, the first lieutenant, ordered me to put on my side-arms to go away on duty. I replied that I had neither dirk nor cocked hat, although I had applied for them. He laughed at my story, and sent me on shore with the master, who bought them, and the first lieutenant sent up the bill to my father, who paid it, and wrote to thank him for his trouble. That morning, the first lieutenant said to me, "Now, Mr Simple, we'll take the shine off that cocked hat and dirk of yours. You will go in the boat with Mr O'Brien, and take care that none of the men slip away from it, and get drunk at the tap."

This was the first time that I had ever been sent away on duty, and I was very proud of being an officer in charge. I put on my full uniform, and was ready at the gangway a quarter of an hour before the men were piped away. We were ordered to the dockyard to draw sea stores. When we arrived there, I was quite astonished at the piles of timber, the ranges of storehouses, and the immense anchors which lay on the wharf. There was such a bustle, every body appeared to be so busy, that I wanted to look every way at once. Close to where the boat landed, they were hauling a large frigate out of what they called the basin; and I was so interested with the sight, that I am sorry to say I quite forgot all about the boat's crew, and my orders to look after them. What surprised me most was, that although the men employed appeared to be sailors, their language was very different from what I had been lately accustomed to on board of the frigate. Instead of damning and swearing, everybody was so polite. "Oblige me with a pull of the starboard bow hawser, Mr Jones."—"Ease off the larboard hawser, Mr Jenkins, if you please."— "Side her over, gentlemen, side her over."—"My compliments to Mr Tompkins, and request that he will cast off the quarter-check."—"Side her over, gentlemen, side her over, if you please."—"In the boat there, pull to Mr Simmons, and beg he'll do me the favour to check her as she swings. What's the matter, Mr Johnson?"—"Vy, there's one of them ere midshipmites has thrown a red hot tater out of the stern-port, and hit our officer in the eye."—"Report him to the commissioner, Mr Wiggins; and oblige me by under-running the guess-warp. Tell Mr Simkins, with my compliments, to coil away upon the jetty. Side her over, side her over, gentlemen, if you please."

I asked of a bystander who these people were, and he told me that they were dockyard mateys. I certainly thought that it appeared to be quite as easy to say "If you please," as "D——n your eyes," and that it sounded much more agreeable.

During the time that I was looking at the frigate being hauled out, two of the men belonging to the boat slipped away, and on my return they were not to be seen. I was very much frightened, for I knew that I had neglected my duty, and that on the first occasion on which I had been intrusted with a responsible service. What to do I did not know I ran up and down every part of the dockyard until I was quite out of breath, asking everybody I met whether they had seen my two men. Many of them said that they had seen plenty of men, but did not exactly know mine; some laughed, and called me a greenhorn. At last I met a midshipman, who told me that he had seen two men answering to my description on the roof of the coach starting for London, and that I must be quick if I wished to catch them; but he would not stop to answer any more questions. I continued walking about the yard until I met twenty or thirty men with grey jackets and breeches, to whom I applied for information: they told me that they had seen two sailors skulking behind the piles of timber. They crowded round me, and appeared very anxious to assist me, when they were summoned away to carry down a cable. I observed that they all had numbers on their jackets, and either one or two bright iron rings on their legs. I could not help inquiring, although I was in such a hurry, why the rings were worn. One of them replied that they were orders of merit, given to them for their good behaviour.

I was proceeding on very disconsolately, when, as I turned a corner, to my great delight, I met my two men, who touched their hats and said that they had been looking for me. I did not believe that they told the truth, but I was so glad to recover them that I did not scold, but went with them down to the boat, which had been waiting some time for us. O'Brien, the master's mate, called me a young sculping,[1] a word I never heard before. When we arrived on board, the first lieutenant asked O'Brien why he had remained so long. He answered that two of the men had left the boat, but that I had found them. The first lieutenant appeared to be pleased with me, observing, as he had said before, that I was no fool, and I went down below, overjoyed at my good fortune, and very much obliged to O'Brien for not telling the whole truth. After I had taken off my dirk and cocked hat, I felt for my pocket-handkerchief, and found that it was not in my pocket, having in all probability been taken out by the men in grey jackets, whom, in conversation with my messmates, I discovered to be convicts condemned to hard labour for stealing and picking pockets.

A day or two afterwards, we had a new messmate of the name of M'Foy. I was on the quarter-deck when he came on board and presented a letter to the captain, inquiring first if his name was "Captain Sauvage." He was a florid young man, nearly six feet high, with sandy hair, yet very good-looking. As his career in the service was very short, I will tell at once, what I did not find out till some time afterwards. The captain had agreed to receive him to oblige a brother officer, who had retired from the service, and lived in the Highlands of Scotland. The first notice which the captain had of the arrival of Mr M'Foy, was from a letter written to him by the young man's uncle. This amused him so much, that he gave it to the first lieutenant to read: it ran as follows:—

"Glasgow, April 25, 1——

"Sir,—Our much esteemed and mutual friend, Captain M'Alpine, having communicated by letter, dated the 14th inst., your kind intentions relative to my nephew Sholto M'Foy, (for which you will be pleased to accept my best thanks), I write to acquaint you that he is now on his way to join your ship, the *Diomede*, and will arrive, God willing, twenty-six hours after the receipt of this letter.

"As I have been given to understand by those who have some acquaintance with the service of the king, that his equipment as an officer will be somewhat expensive, I have considered it but fair to ease your mind as to any responsibility on that score, and have therefore enclosed the half of a Bank of England note for ten pounds sterling, No. 3742, the other half of which will be duly forwarded in a frank promised to me the day after to-morrow. I beg you will make the necessary purchases, and apply the balance, should there be any, to his mess account, or any other expenses which you may consider warrantable or justifiable.

"It is at the same time proper to inform you, that Sholto had ten shillings in his pocket at the time of his leaving Glasgow; the satisfactory expenditure of which I have no doubt you will inquire into, as it is a large sum to be placed at the discretion of a youth only fourteen years and five months old. I mention his age, as Sholto is so tall that you might be deceived by his appearance, and be induced to trust to his prudence in affairs of this serious nature. Should he at any time require further assistance beyond his pay, which I am told is extremely handsome to all king's officers, I beg you to consider that any draught of yours, at ten days' sight, to the amount of five pounds sterling English, will be duly honoured by the firm of Monteith, M'Killop, and Company, of Glasgow. Sir, with many thanks for your kindness and consideration,

"I remain, your most obedient,

"WALTER MONTEITH."

The letter brought on board by M'Foy was to prove his identity. While the captain read it, M'Foy stared about him like a wild stag. The captain welcomed him to the ship, asked him one or two questions, introduced him to the first lieutenant, and then went on shore. The first lieutenant had asked me to dine in the gun-room; I supposed that he was pleased with me because I had found the men; and when the captain pulled on shore, he also invited Mr M'Foy, when the following conversation took place.

"Well, Mr M'Foy, you have had a long journey; I presume it is the first that you have ever made."

"Indeed it is, sir," replied M'Foy; "and sorely I've been pestered. Had I minded all they whispered in my lug as I came along, I had need been made of money—sax-pence here, sax-pence there, sax-pence every where. Sich extortion I ne'er dreamt of."

"How did you come from Glasgow?"

"By the wheelboat, or steamboat, as they ca'd it, to Lunnon: where they charged me sax-pence for taking my baggage on shore—a wee boxy nae bigger than yon cocked-up hat. I would fain carry it mysel', but they wadna let me."

"Well, where did you go to when you arrived in London?"

"I went to a place ca'd Chichester Rents, to the house of Storm and Mainwaring, Warehousemen, and they must have another sax-pence for showing me the way. There I waited half-an-hour in the counting-house, till they took me to a place ca'd Bull and Mouth, and put me into a coach, paying my whole fare: nevertheless they must din me for money the whole of the way down. There was first the guard, and then the coachman, and another guard, and another coachman; but I wudna listen to them, and so they growled and abused me."

"And when did you arrive?"

"I came here last night; and I only had a bed and a breakfast at the twa Blue Pillars' house, for which they extortioned me three shillings and sax-pence, as I sit here. And then there was the chambermaid hussy and waiter loon axed me to remember them, and wanted more siller; but I told them as I told the guard and coachman, that I had none for them."

"How much of your ten shillings have you left?" inquired the first lieutenant, smiling.

"Hoot, sir lieutenant, how came you for to ken that? Eh! it's my uncle Monteith at Glasgow. Why, as I sit here, I've but three shillings and a penny of it lift. But there's a smell here that's no canny; so I'll just go up again into the fresh air."

When Mr M'Foy quitted the gun-room they all laughed very much. After he had been a short time on deck he went down into the midshipmen's berth; but he made himself very unpleasant, quarrelling and wrangling with everybody. It did not, however, last very long; for he would not obey any orders that were given to him. On the third day, he quitted the ship without asking the permission of the first lieutenant; when he returned on board the following day, the first lieutenant put him under an arrest, and in charge of the sentry at the cabin door. During the afternoon I was under the half-deck, and perceived that he was sharpening a long clasp-knife upon the after-truck of the gun. I went up to him, and asked him why he was doing so, and he replied, as his eyes flashed fire, that it was to revenge the insult offered to the bluid of M'Foy. His look told me that he was in earnest. "But what do you mean?" inquired I. "I mean," said he, drawing the edge and feeling the point of his weapon, "to put it into the weam of that man with the gold podge on his shoulder, who has dared to place me here."

I was very much alarmed, and thought it my duty to state his murderous intentions, or worse might happen; so I walked up on deck and told the first lieutenant what M'Foy was intending to do, and how his life was in danger. Mr Falcon laughed, and shortly afterwards went down on the main-deck. M'Foy's eyes glistened, and he walked forward to where the first lieutenant was standing; but the sentry, who had been cautioned by me, kept him back with his bayonet. The first lieutenant turned round, and perceiving what was going on, desired the sentry to see if Mr M'Foy had a knife in his hand; and he had it sure enough, open, and held behind his back. He was disarmed, and the first lieutenant, perceiving that the lad meant mischief, reported his conduct to the captain, on his arrival on board. The captain sent for M'Foy, who was very obstinate, and when taxed with his intention would not deny it, or even say that he would not again attempt it; so he was sent on shore immediately, and returned to his friends in the Highlands. We never saw any more of him; but I heard that he obtained a commission in the army, and three months after he had joined his regiment, was killed in a duel, resenting some fancied affront offered to the bluid of M'Foy.

[Footnote 1: Peter's memory is short, p. 9.—ED.]

Chapter IX

We post up to Portsdown Fair—Consequence of disturbing a lady at supper —Natural affection of the pelican, proved at my expense—Spontaneous combustion at Ranelagh Gardens—Pastry *versus* Piety—Many are bid to the feast; but not the halt, the lame, or the blind.

A few days after M'Foy quitted the ship, we all had leave from the first lieutenant to go to Portsdown fair, but he would only allow the oldsters to sleep on shore. We anticipated so much pleasure from our excursion, that some of us were up early enough to go away in the boat sent for fresh beef. This was very foolish. There were no carriages to take us to the fair, nor indeed any fair so early in the morning; the shops were all shut, and the Blue Posts, where we always rendezvoused, was hardly opened. We waited there in the coffee-room, until we were driven out by the maid sweeping away the dirt, and were forced to walk about until she had finished, and lighted the fire, when we ordered our breakfast; but how much better would it have been to have taken our breakfast comfortably on board, and then to have come on shore, especially as we had no money to spare. Next to being too late, being too soon is the worst plan in the world. However, we had our breakfast, and paid the bill; then we sallied forth, and went up George-street, where we found all sorts of vehicles ready to take us to the fair. We got into one which they called a dilly. I asked the man who drove it why it was so called, and he replied, because he only charged a shilling. O'Brien, who had joined us after breakfasting on board, said that this answer reminded him of one given to him by a man who attended the hackney-coach stands in London. "Pray," said he, "why are you called Waterman?" "Waterman," replied the man, "vy, sir, 'cause we opens the hackney-coach doors." At last, with plenty of whipping, and plenty of swearing, and a great deal of laughing, the old horse, whose back curved upwards like a bow, from the difficulty of dragging so many, arrived at the bottom of Portsdown hill, where we got out, and walked up to the fair. It really was a most beautiful sight. The bright blue sky, and the coloured flags flapping about in all directions, the grass so green, and the white tents and booths, the sun shining so bright, and the shining gilt gingerbread, the variety of toys and the variety of noise, the quantity of people and the quantity of sweetmeats; little boys so happy, and shop-people so polite, the music at the booths, and the bustle and eagerness of the people outside, made my heart quite jump. There was Richardson, with a clown and harlequin, and such beautiful women, dressed in clothes all over gold spangles, dancing reels and waltzes, and looking so happy! There was Flint and Gyngell, with fellows tumbling over head and heels, playing such tricks—eating fire, and drawing yards of tape out of their mouths. Then there was the Royal Circus, all the horses standing in a line, with men and women standing on their backs, waving flags, while the trumpeters blew their trumpets. And the largest giant in the world, and Mr Paap, the smallest dwarf in the world, and a female dwarf, who was smaller still, and Miss Biffin, who did everything without legs or arms. There was also the learned pig, and the Herefordshire ox, and a hundred other sights which I cannot now remember. We walked about for an hour or two seeing the outside of every thing: we determined to go and see the inside. First we went into Richardson's, where we saw a bloody tragedy, with a ghost and thunder, and afterwards a pantomime, full of tricks, and tumbling over one another. Then we saw one or two other things, I forget what; but this I know, that, generally speaking, the outside was better, than the inside. After this, feeling very hungry, we agreed to go into a booth and have something to eat. The tables were ranged all round, and in the centre there was a boarded platform for dancing. The ladies were there all ready dressed for partners; and the music was so lively, that I felt very much inclined to dance, but we had agreed to go and see the wild beasts fed at Mr Polito's menagerie, and as it was now almost eight o'clock, we paid our bill and set off. It was a very curious sight, and better worth seeing than any thing in the fair; I never had an idea that there were so many strange animals in existence. They were all secured in iron cages, and a large chandelier with twenty lights, hung in the centre of the booth, and lighted them up, while the keeper went round and stirred them up with his long pole; at the same time he gave us their histories, which were very interesting. I recollect a few of them. There was the tapir, a great pig with a long nose, a variety of the hiptostamass, which the keeper said was an amphibilious animal, as couldn't live on land, and *dies* in the water—however, it seemed to live very well in a cage. Then there was the kangaroo with its young ones peeping out of it—a most astonishing animal. The keeper said that it brought forth two young ones at a birth, and then took them into its stomach again, until they arrived at years of discretion. Then there was the pelican of the wilderness, (I shall not forget him), with a large bag under his throat, which the man put on his head as a night-cap: this bird feeds its young with its own blood—when fish are scarce. And there was the laughing hyæna, who cries in the wood like a human being in distress, and devours those who come to his assistance—a sad instance of the depravity of human nature, as the keeper observed. There was a beautiful creature, the royal Bengal tiger, only three years old, what growed ten inches every year, and never arrived at its full growth. The one we saw, measured, as the keeper told us, sixteen feet from the snout to the tail, and seventeen from the tail to the snout: but there must have been some mistake there. There was a young elephant and three lions, and several other animals which I forget now, so I shall go on to describe the tragical scene which occurred. The keeper had poked up all the animals, and had commenced feeding them. The great lion was growling and snarling over the shin-bone of an ox, cracking it like a nut, when, by some mismanagement, one end of the pole upon which the chandelier was suspended fell down, striking the door of the cage in which the lioness was at supper, and bursting it open. It was all done in a second; the chandelier fell, the cage opened, and the lioness sprang out. I remember to this moment seeing the body of the lioness in the air, and then all was dark as pitch. What a change! not a moment before all of us staring with delight and curiosity, and then to be left in darkness, horror, and dismay! There was such screaming and shrieking, such crying, and fighting, and pushing, and fainting, nobody knew where to go, or how to find their way out. The people crowded first on one side, and then on the other, as their fears instigated them. I was very soon jammed up with my back against the bars of one of the cages, and feeling some beast lay hold of me behind, made a desperate effort, and succeeded in climbing up to the cage above, not however without losing the seat of my trowsers, which the laughing hyæna would not let go. I hardly knew where I was when I climbed up; but I knew the birds were mostly stationed above. However, that I might not have the front of my trowsers torn as well as the behind, as soon as I gained my footing I turned round, with my back to the bars of the cage, but I had not been there a minute before I was attacked by something which digged into me like a pickaxe, and as the hyæna had torn my clothes, I had no defence against it. To turn round would have been worse still; so, after having received above a dozen stabs, I contrived by degrees to shift my position until I was opposite to another cage, but not until the pelican, for it was that brute, had drawn as much blood from me as would have fed his young for a week. I was surmising what danger I should next encounter, when to my joy I discovered that I had gained the open door from which the lioness had escaped. I crawled in, and pulled the door to after me, thinking myself very fortunate: and there I sat very quietly in a corner during the remainder of the noise and confusion. I had been there but a few minutes, when the beef-eaters, as they were called, who played the music outside, came in with torches and loaded muskets. The sight which presented itself was truly shocking, twenty or thirty men, women, and children, lay on the ground, and I thought at first the lioness had killed them all, but they were only in fits, or had been trampled down by the crowd. No one was seriously hurt. As for the lioness, she was not to be found: and as soon as it was ascertained that she had escaped, there was as much terror and scampering away outside as there had been in the menagerie. It appeared afterwards, that the animal had been as much frightened as we had been, and had secreted herself under one of the waggons. It was some time before she could be found. At last O'Brien, who was a very brave fellow, went a-head of the beef-eaters, and saw her eyes glaring. They borrowed a net or two from the carts which had brought calves to the fair, and threw them over her. When she was fairly entangled, they dragged her by the tail into the menagerie. All this while I had remained very quietly in the den, but when I perceived that its lawful owner had come back to retake possession, I thought it was time to come out; so I called to my messmates, who, with O'Brien were assisting the beef-eaters. They had not discovered me, and laughed very much when they saw where I was. One of the midshipmen shot the bolt of the door, so that I could not jump out, and then stirred me up with a long pole. At last I contrived to unbolt it again, and got out, when they laughed still more, at the seat of my trowsers being torn off. It was not exactly a laughing matter to me, although I had to congratulate myself upon a very lucky escape; and so did my messmates think, when I narrated my adventures. The pelican was the worst part of the business. O'Brien lent me a dark silk handkerchief, which I tied round my waist, and let drop behind, so that my misfortunes might not attract any notice, and then we quitted the menagerie; but I was so stiff that I could scarcely walk.

   We then went to what they called the Ranelagh Gardens, to see the fireworks, which were to be let off at ten o'clock. It was exactly ten when we paid for our admission, and we waited very patiently for a quarter of an hour, but there were no signs of the fireworks being displayed. The fact was, that the man to whom the gardens belonged waited until more company should arrive, although the place was already very full of people. Now the first lieutenant had ordered the boat to wait for us until twelve o'clock, and then return on board; and, as we were seven miles from Portsmouth, we had not much time to spare. We waited another quarter of an hour, and then it was agreed that as the fireworks were stated in the handbill to commence precisely at ten o'clock, we were fully justified in letting them off ourselves. O'Brien went out, and returned with a dozen penny rattans, which he notched in the end. The fireworks were on the posts and stages, all ready, and it was agreed that we should light them all at once, and then mix with the crowd. The oldsters lighted cigars, and fixing them in the notched end of the canes, continued to puff them until they were all well lighted. They handed one to each of us, and at a signal we all applied them to the match papers, and as soon as the fire communicated we threw down our canes and ran in among the crowd. In about half a minute, off they all went, in a most beautiful confusion; there were silver stars and golden stars, blue lights and Catherine-wheels, mines and bombs, Grecian-fires and Roman-candles, Chinese-trees, rockets and illuminated mottoes, all firing away, cracking, popping, and fizzing, at the same time. It was unanimously agreed that it was a great improvement upon the intended show. The man to whom the gardens belonged ran out of a booth, where he had been drinking beer at his ease, while his company were waiting, swearing vengeance against the perpetrators; indeed, the next day he offered fifty pounds reward for the discovery of the offenders. But I think that he was treated very properly. He was, in his situation, a servant of the public, and he had behaved as if he was their master. We all escaped very cleverly, and taking another dilly, arrived at Portsmouth, and were down to the boat in good time. The next day I was so stiff and in such pain, that I was obliged to go to the doctor, who put me on the list, where I remained a week before I could return to my duty. So much for Portsdown fair.

It was on a Saturday that I returned to my duty, and Sunday being a fine day, we all went on shore to church with Mr Falcon, the first lieutenant. We liked going to church very much, not, I am sorry to say, from religious feelings, but for the following reason:—The first lieutenant sat in a pew below, and we were placed in the gallery above, where he could not see us, nor indeed could we see him. We all remained very quiet, and I may say very devout, during the time of the service; but the clergyman who delivered the sermon was so tedious, and had such a bad voice, that we generally slipped out as soon as he went up into the pulpit, and adjourned to a pastry-cook's opposite, to eat cakes and tarts and drink cherry-brandy, which we infinitely preferred to hearing a sermon. Somehow or other, the first lieutenant had scent of our proceedings: we believed that the marine officer informed against us, and this Sunday he served us a pretty trick. We had been at the pastry-cook's as usual, and as soon as we perceived the people coming out of church, we put all our tarts and sweetmeats into our hats, which we then slipped on our heads, and took our station at the church-door, as if we had just come down from the gallery, and had been waiting for him. Instead, however, of appearing at the church-door, he walked up the street, and desired us to follow him to the boat. The fact was, he had been in the back-room at the pastry-cook's watching our motions through the green blinds. We had no suspicion, but thought that he had come out of church a little sooner than usual. When we arrived on board and followed him up the side, he said to us as we came on deck,—"Walk aft, young gentlemen." We did; and he desired us to "toe a line," which means to stand in a row. "Now, Mr Dixon," said he, "what was the text to-day?" As he very often asked us that question, we always left one in the church until the text was given out, who brought it to us in the pastry-cook's shop, when we all marked it in our Bibles, to be ready if he asked us. Dixon immediately pulled out his Bible where he had marked down the leaf, and read it. "O! that was it," said Mr Falcon; "you must have remarkably good ears, Mr Dixon, to have heard the clergyman from the pastry-cook's shop. Now, gentlemen, hats off, if you please." We all slided off our hats, which, as he expected, were full of pastry. "Really, gentlemen," said he, feeling the different papers of pastry and sweetmeats, "I am quite delighted to perceive that you have not been to church for nothing. Few come away with so many good things pressed upon their seat of memory. Master-at-arms, send all the ship's boys aft."

The boys all came tumbling up the ladders, and the first lieutenant desired each of them to take a seat upon the carronade slides. When they were all stationed, he ordered us to go round with our hats, and request of each his acceptance of a tart, which we were obliged to do, handing first to one and then to another, until the hats were all empty. What annoyed me more than all, was the grinning of the boys at their being served by us like foot-men, as well as the ridicule and laughter of the whole ship's company, who had assembled at the gangways.

When all the pastry was devoured, the first lieutenant said,

"There, gentlemen, now that you have had your lesson for the day, you may go below." We could not help laughing ourselves, when we went down into the berth; Mr Falcon always punished us good-humouredly, and, in some way or other, his punishments were severally connected with the description of the offence. He always had a remedy for every thing that he disapproved of, and the ship's company used to call him "Remedy Jack." I ought to observe that some of my messmates were very severe upon the ship's boys after that circumstance, always giving them a kick or a cuff on the head whenever they could, telling them at the same time, "There's another tart for you, you whelp." I believe, if the boys had known what was in reserve for them, they would much rather have left the pastry alone.

Chapter X

A pressgang; beaten off by one woman—Dangers at Spithead and Point—A treat for both parties, of *pulled chicken*, at my expense—Also gin for twenty—I am made a prisoner: escape and rejoin my ship.

I must now relate what occurred to me a few days before the ship sailed, which will prove that it is not necessary to encounter the winds and waves, or the cannon of the enemy, to be in danger, when you have entered his Majesty's service: on the contrary, I have been in action since, and I declare, without hesitation, that I did not feel so much alarm on that occasion, as I did on the one of which I am about to give the history. We were reported ready for sea, and the Admiralty was anxious that we should proceed. The only obstacle to our sailing was, that we had not yet completed our complement of men. The captain applied to the port-admiral, and obtained permission to send parties on shore to impress seamen. The second and third lieutenants, and the oldest midshipman, were despatched on shore every night, with some of the most trustworthy men, and generally brought on board in the morning about half a dozen men, whom they had picked up in the different alehouses, or grog-shops, as the sailors call them. Some of them were retained, but most of them sent on shore as unserviceable; for it is the custom, when a man either enters or is impressed, to send him down to the surgeon in the cockpit, where he is stripped and examined all over, to see if he be sound and fit for his majesty's service; and if not, he is sent on shore again. Impressing appeared to be rather serious work, as far as I could judge from the accounts which I heard, and from the way in which our sailors, who were employed on the service, were occasionally beaten and wounded; the seamen who were impressed appearing to fight as hard not to be forced into the service, as they did for the honour of the country, after they were fairly embarked in it. I had a great wish to be one of the party before the ship sailed, and asked O'Brien, who was very kind to me in general, and allowed nobody to thrash me but himself, if he would take me with him, which he did on the night after I had made the request. I put on my dirk, that they might know I was an officer, as well as for my protection. About dusk we rowed on shore, and landed on the Gosport side: the men were all armed with cutlasses, and wore pea jackets, which are very short great-coats made of what they call Flushing. We did not stop to look at any of the grog-shops in the town, as it was too early, but walked out about three miles in the suburbs, and went to a house, the door of which was locked, but we forced it open in a minute, and hastened to enter the passage, where we found the landlady standing to defend the entrance. The passage was long and narrow, and she was a very tall corpulent woman, so that her body nearly filled it up, and in her hands she held a long spit pointed at us, with which she kept us at bay. The officers, who were the foremost, did not like to attack a woman, and she made such drives at them with her spit, that had they not retreated, some of them would soon have been ready for roasting. The sailors laughed and stood outside, leaving the officers to settle the business how they could. At last, the landlady called out to her husband, "Be they all out, Jem?" "Yes," replied the husband, "they be all safe gone." "Well, then," replied she, "I'll soon have all these gone too;" and with these words she made such a rush forward upon us with her spit, that had we not fallen back and tumbled one over another, she certainly would have run it through the second lieutenant, who commanded the party. The passage was cleared in an instant, and as soon as we were all in the street she bolted us out: so there we were, three officers and fifteen armed men, fairly beat off by a fat old woman; the sailors who had been drinking in the house having made their escape to some other place. But I do not well see how it could be otherwise; either we must have killed or wounded the woman, or she would have run us through, she was so resolute. Had her husband been in the passage, he would have been settled in a very short time; but what can you do with a woman who fights like a devil, and yet claims all the rights and immunities of the softer sex? We all walked away, looking very foolish; and O'Brien observed that the next time he called at that house he would weather the old cat, for he would take her ladyship in the rear.

We then called at other houses, where we picked up one or two men, but most of them escaped, by getting out at the windows or the back doors, as we entered the front. Now there was a grog-shop which was a very favourite rendezvous of the seamen belonging to the merchant vessels, and to which they were accustomed to retreat when they heard that the pressgangs were out. Our officers were aware of this, and were therefore indifferent as to the escape of the men, as they knew that they would all go to that place, and confide in their numbers for beating us off. As it was then one o'clock, they thought it time to go there; we proceeded without any noise, but they had people on the look-out, and as soon as we turned the corner of the lane the alarm was given. I was afraid that they would all run away, and we should lose them; but, on the contrary, they mustered very strong on that night, and had resolved to "give fight." The men remained in the house, but an advanced guard of about thirty of their wives saluted us with a shower of stones and mud. Some of our sailors were hurt, but they did not appear to mind what the women did. They rushed on, and then they were attacked by the women with their fists and nails. Notwithstanding this, the sailors only laughed, pushing the women on one side, and saying, "Be quiet, Poll;"—"Don't be foolish, Molly;"—"Out of the way, Sukey; we a'n't come to take away your fancy man;" with expressions of that sort, although the blood trickled down many of their faces, from the way in which they had been clawed. Thus we attempted to force our way through them, but I had a very narrow escape even in this instance. A woman seized me by the arm, and pulled me towards her; had it not been for one of the quarter-masters I should have been separated from my party; but, just as they dragged me away, she caught hold of me by the leg, and stopped them. "Clap on here, Peg," cried the woman to another, "and let's have this little midshipmite; I wants a baby to dry nurse." Two more women came to her assistance, catching hold of my other arm, and they would have dragged me out of the grasp of the quarter-master, had he not called out for more help on his side, upon which two of the seamen laid hold of my other leg, and there was such a tussle (all at my expense), such pulling and hauling; sometimes the women gained an inch or two of me, then the sailors got it back again. At one moment I thought it was all over with me, and in the next I was with my own men. "Pull devil; pull baker!" cried the women, and then they laughed, although I did not, I can assure you, for I really think that I was pulled out an inch taller, and my knees and shoulders pained me very much indeed. At last the women laughed so much that they could not hold on, so I was dragged into the middle of our own sailors, where I took care to remain; and, after a little more squeezing and fighting, was carried by the crowd into the house. The seamen of the merchant ships had armed themselves with bludgeons and other weapons, and had taken a position on the tables. They were more than two to one against us, and there was a dreadful fight, as their resistance was very desperate. Our sailors were obliged to use their cutlasses, and for a few minutes I was quite bewildered with the shouting and swearing, pushing and scuffling, collaring and fighting, together with the dust raised up, which not only blinded, but nearly choked me. By the time that my breath was nearly squeezed out of my body, our sailors got the best of it, which the landlady and women of the house perceiving, they put out all the lights, so that I could not tell where I was; but our sailors had every one seized his man, and contrived to haul him out of the street door, where they were collected together, and secured.

Now again I was in great difficulty; I had been knocked down and trod upon, and when I did contrive to get up again, I did not know the direction in which the door lay. I felt about by the wall, and at last came to a door, for the room was at that time nearly empty, the women having followed the men out of the house. I opened it, and found that it was not the right one, but led into a little side parlour, where there was a fire, but no lights. I had just discovered my mistake, and was about to retreat, when I was shoved in from behind, and the key turned upon me: there I was all alone, and, I must acknowledge, very much frightened, as I thought that the vengeance of the women would be wreaked upon me. I considered that my death was certain, and that, like the man Orpheus I had read of in my books, I should be torn to pieces by these Bacchanals. However, I reflected that I was an officer in his Majesty's service, and that it was my duty, if necessary, to sacrifice my life for my king and country. I thought of my poor mother; but as it made me unhappy, I tried to forget her, and call to my memory all I had read of the fortitude and courage of various brave men, when death stared them in the face. I peeped through the key-hole, and perceived that the candles were re-lighted, and that there were only women in the room, who were talking all at once, and not thinking about me. But in a minute or two, a woman came in from the street, with her long black hair hanging about her shoulders, and her cap in her hand. "Well," cried she, "they've nabbed my husband; but I'll be dished if I hav'n't boxed up the midshipmite in that parlour, and he shall take his place." I thought I should have died when I looked at the woman, and perceived her coming up to the door, followed by some others, to unlock it. As the door opened, I drew my dirk, resolving to die like an officer, and as they advanced I retreated to a corner, brandishing my dirk, without saying a word. "Vell," cried the woman who had made me a prisoner, "I do declare I likes to see a puddle in a storm—only look at the little biscuit-nibbler showing fight! Come, my lovey, you belongs to me."

"Never!" exclaimed I with indignation. "Keep off, I shall do you mischief" (and I raised my dirk in advance); "I am an officer and a gentleman."

"Sall," cried the odious woman, "fetch a mop and a pail of dirty water, and I'll trundle that dirk out of his fist."

"No, no," replied another rather good-looking young woman, "leave him to me—don't hurt him—he really is a very nice little man. What's your name, my dear?"

"Peter Simple is my name," replied I; "and I am a king's officer, so be careful what you are about."

"Don't be afraid, Peter, nobody shall hurt you; but you must not draw your dirk before ladies, that's not like an officer and a gentleman—so put up your dirk, that's a good boy."

"I will not," replied I, "unless you promise me that I shall go away unmolested."

"I do promise you that you shall, upon my word, Peter—upon my honour— will that content you?"

"Yes," replied I, "if every one else will promise the same."

"Upon our honours," they all cried together; upon which I was satisfied, and putting my dirk into its sheath, was about to quit the room.

"Stop, Peter," said the young woman who had taken my part; "I must have a kiss before you go." "And so must I; and so must we all," cried the other women.

I was very much shocked, and attempted to draw my dirk again, but they had closed in with me, and prevented me. "Recollect your honour," cried I to the young woman, as I struggled.

"My honour!—Lord bless you, Peter, the less we say about that the better."

"But you promised that I should go away quietly," said I, appealing to them.

"Well, and so you shall; but recollect, Peter, that you are an officer and a gentleman—you surely would not be so shabby as to go away without treating us. What money have you got in your pocket?" and, without giving me time to answer, she felt in my pocket, and pulled out my purse, which she opened. "Why, Peter, you are as rich as a Jew," said she, as they counted thirty shillings on the table. "Now, what shall we have?"

"Anything you please," said I, "provided that you will let me go."

"Well, then, it shall be a gallon of gin. Sall, call Mrs Flanagan. Mrs Flanagan, we want a gallon of gin, and clean glasses."

Mrs Flanagan received the major part of my money, and in a minute returned with the gin and wine-glasses.

"Now, Peter, my cove, let's all draw round the table, and make ourselves cosy."

"O no," replied I, "take my money, drink the gin, but pray let me go;" but they wouldn't listen to me. Then I was obliged to sit down with them, the gin was poured out, and they made me drink a glass, which nearly choked me. It had, however, one good effect, it gave me courage, and in a minute or two, I felt as if I could fight them all. The door of the room was on the same side as the fire-place, and I perceived that the poker was between the bars, and red hot. I complained that I was cold, although I was in a burning fever; and they allowed me to get up to warm my hands. As soon as I reached the fire-place, I snatched out the red-hot poker, and, brandishing it over my head, made for the door. They all jumped up to detain me, but I made a poke at the foremost, which made her run back with a shriek, (I do believe that I burnt her nose.) I seized my opportunity, and escaped into the street, whirling the poker round my head, while all the women followed, hooting and shouting after me. I never stopped running and whirling my poker until I was reeking with perspiration, and the poker was quite cold. Then I looked back, and found that I was alone. It was very dark; every house was shut up, and not a light to be seen anywhere. I stopped at the corner, not knowing where I was, or what I was to do. I felt very miserable indeed, and was reflecting on my wisest plan, when who should turn the corner, but one of the quarter-masters who had been left on shore by accident. I knew him by his pea-jacket and straw hat to be one of our men, and I was delighted to see him. I told him what had happened, and he replied that he was going to a house where the people knew him and would let him in. When we arrived there, the people of the house were very civil; the landlady made us some purl, which the quarter-master ordered, and which I thought very good indeed. After we had finished the jug, we both fell asleep in our chairs. I did not awaken until I was roused by the quarter-master, at past seven o'clock, when we took a wherry, and went off to the ship.

Chapter XI

O'Brien takes me under his protection—The ship's company are paid, so are the bumboat-women, the Jews, and the emancipationist after a fashion—We go to sea—*Doctor* O'Brien's cure for sea-sickness—One pill of the doctor's more than a dose.

When we arrived, I reported myself to the first lieutenant, and told him the whole story of the manner in which I had been treated, showing him the poker, which I brought on board with me. He heard me very patiently, and then said, "Well, Mr Simple, you may be the greatest fool of your family for all I know to the contrary, but never pretend to be a fool with me. That poker proves the contrary: and if your wit can serve you upon your own emergency, I expect that it will be employed for the benefit of the service." He then sent for O'Brien, and gave him a lecture for allowing me to go with the pressgang, pointing out, what was very true, that I could have been of no service, and might have met with a serious accident. I went down on the main deck, and O'Brien came to me. "Peter," said he, "I have been jawed for letting you go, so it is but fair that you should be thrashed for having asked me." I wished to argue the point, but he cut all argument short, by kicking me down the hatchway; and thus ended my zealous attempt to procure seamen for his majesty's service.

At last the frigate was full manned; and, as we had received drafts of men from other ships, we were ordered to be paid previously to our going to sea. The people on shore always find out when a ship is to be paid, and very early in the morning we were surrounded with wherries, laden with Jews and other people, some requesting admittance to sell their goods, others to get paid for what they had allowed the sailors to take up upon credit. But the first lieutenant would not allow any of them to come on board until after the ship was paid; although they were so urgent that he was forced to place sentries in the chains with cold shot, to stave the boats if they came alongside. I was standing at the gangway, looking at the crowd of boats, when a black-looking fellow in one of the wherries said to me, "I say, sir, let me slip in at the port, and I have a very nice present to make you;" and he displayed a gold seal, which he held up to me. I immediately ordered the sentry to keep him further off, for I was very much affronted at his supposing me capable of being bribed to disobey my orders. About eleven o'clock the dockyard boat, with all the pay-clerks, and the cashier, with his chest of money, came on board, and was shown into the fore-cabin, where the captain attended the pay-table. The men were called in, one by one, and, as the amount of the wages due had been previously calculated, they were paid; very fast. The money was always received in their hats, after it had been counted out in the presence of the officers and captain. Outside the cabin door there stood a tall man in black, with hair straight combed, who had obtained an order from the Port Admiral to be permitted to come on board. He attacked every sailor as he came out; with his money in his hat, for a subscription to emancipate the slaves in the West Indies; but the sailors would not give him anything, swearing that the niggers were better off than they were; for they did not work harder by day, and had no watch and watch to keep during the night. "Sarvitude is sarvitude all over the world, my old psalmsinger," replied one. "They sarve their masters, as in duty bound; we sarve the king, 'cause he can't do without us—and he never axes our leave, but helps himself."

"Yes," replied the straight-haired gentleman; "but slavery is a very different thing."

"Can't say that I see any difference; do you, Bill?"

"Not I: and I suppose as if they didn't like it they'd run away."

"Run away! poor creatures," said the black gentleman. "Why, if they did, they would be flogged."

"Flogged—heh; well, and if we run away we are to be hanged. The nigger's better off nor we: ar'n't he, Tom?" Then the purser's steward came out: he was what they call a bit of a lawyer,—that is, had received more education than the seamen in general.

"I trust, sir," said the man in black, "that you will contribute something."

"Not I, my hearty: I owe every farthing of my money, and more too, I'm afraid."

"Still, sir, a small trifle."

"Why, what an infernal rascal you must be, to ask a man to give away what is not his own property! Did I not tell you that I owed it all? There's an old proverb—be just before you're generous. Now, it's my opinion that, you are a methodistical, good-for-nothing blackguard; and if any one is such a fool as to give you money, you will keep it for yourself."

When the man found that he could obtain nothing at the door, he went down on the lower deck, in which he did not act very wisely; for now that the men were paid, the boats were permitted to come alongside, and so much spirits were smuggled in, that most of the seamen were more or less intoxicated. As soon as he went below, he commenced distributing prints of a black man kneeling in chains, and saying, "Am not I your brother?" Some of the men laughed, and swore that they would paste their brother up in the mess, to say prayers for the ship's company; but others were very angry, and abused him. At last, one man, who was tipsy, came up to him. "Do you pretend for to insinivate that this crying black thief is my brother?"

"To be sure I do," replied the methodist.

"Then take that for your infernal lie," said the sailor, hitting him in the face right and left, and knocking the man down into the cable tier, from whence he climbed up, and made his escape out of the frigate as soon as he was able.

The ship was now in a state of confusion and uproar; there were Jews trying to sell clothes, or to obtain money for clothes which they had sold; bumboat-men and bumboat-women showing their long bills, and demanding or coaxing for payment; other people from the shore, with hundreds of small debts; and the sailors' wives, sticking close to them, and disputing every bill presented, as an extortion or a robbery. There was such bawling and threatening, laughing and crying—for the women were all to quit the ship before sunset—at one moment a Jew was upset, and all his hamper of clothes tossed into the hold; at another, a sailor was seen hunting everywhere for a Jew who had cheated him,—all squabbling or skylarking, and many of them very drunk. It appeared to me that the sailors had rather a difficult point to settle. They had three claimants upon them, the Jew for clothes, the bumboat-men for their mess in harbour, and their wives for their support during their absence; and the money which they received was, generally speaking, not more than sufficient to meet one of the demands. As it may be supposed, the women had the best of it; the others were paid a trifle, and promised the remainder when they came back from their cruise; and although, as the case stood then, it might appear that two of the parties were ill-used, yet in the long run they were more than indemnified, for their charges were so extravagant, that if one-third of their bills were paid, there would still remain a profit. About five o'clock the orders were given for the ship to be cleared. All disputed points were settled by the sergeant of marines with a party, who divided their antagonists from the Jews; and every description of persons not belonging to the ship, whether male or female, was dismissed over the side. The hammocks were piped down, those who were intoxicated were put to bed, and the ship was once more quiet. Nobody was punished for having been tipsy, as pay-day is considered, on board a man-of-war, as the winding-up of all incorrect behaviour, and from that day the sailors turn over a new leaf; for, although some latitude is permitted, and the seamen are seldom flogged in harbour, yet the moment that the anchor is at the bows, strict discipline is exacted, and intoxication must no longer hope to be forgiven.

The next day everything was prepared for sea, and no leave was permitted to the officers. Stock of every kind was brought on board, and the large boats hoisted and secured. On the morning after, at daylight, a signal from the flag-ship in harbour was made for us to unmoor; our orders had come down to cruise in the Bay of Biscay. The captain came on board, the anchor weighed, and we ran through the Needles with a fine N.E. breeze. I admired the scenery of the Isle of Wight, looked with admiration at Alum Bay, was astonished at the Needle rocks, and then felt so very ill that I went down below. What occurred for the next six days I cannot tell. I thought that I should die every moment, and lay in my hammock or on the chests for the whole of that time, incapable of eating, drinking, or walking about. O'Brien came to me on the seventh morning, and said, that if I did not exert myself I never should get well; that he was very fond of me and had taken me under his protection, and, to prove his regard, he would do for me what he would not take the trouble to do for any other youngster in the ship, which was, to give me a good basting, which was a sovereign remedy for sea-sickness. He suited the action to the word, and drubbed me on the ribs without mercy, until I thought the breath was out of my body, and then he took out a rope's end and thrashed me until I obeyed his orders to go on deck immediately. Before he came to me, I could never have believed it possible that I could have obeyed him; but somehow or other I did contrive to crawl up the ladder to the main-deck, where I sat down on the shot-racks and cried bitterly. What would I have given to have been at home again! It was not my fault that I was the greatest fool in the family, yet how was I punished for it! If this was kindness from O'Brien, what had I to expect from those who were not partial to me? But, by degrees, I recovered myself, and certainly felt a great deal better, and that night I slept very soundly. The next morning O'Brien came to me again. "It's a nasty slow fever, that sea-sickness, my Peter, and we must drive it out of you;" and then he commenced a repetition of yesterday's remedy until I was almost a jelly. Whether the fear of being thrashed drove away my sea-sickness, or whatever might be the real cause of it, I do not know, but this is certain, that I felt no more of it after the second beating, and the next morning when I awoke I was very hungry. I hastened to dress myself before O'Brien came to me, and did not see him until we met at breakfast.

"Pater," said he, "let me feel your pulse."

"Oh no!" replied I, "indeed I'm quite well."

"Quite well! Can you eat biscuit and salt butter?"

"Yes, I can."

"And a piece of fat pork?"

"Yes, that I can."

"It's thanks to me then, Pater," replied he; "so you'll have no more of my medicine until you fall sick again."

"I hope not," replied I, "for it was not very pleasant."

"Pleasant! you simple Simple, when did you ever hear of physic being pleasant, unless a man prescribe for himself? I suppose you'd be after lollipops for the yellow fever. Live and larn, boy, and thank Heaven that you've found somebody who loves you well enough to baste you when it's good for your health."

I replied, "that I certainly hoped that much as I felt obliged to him, I should not require any more proofs of his regard."

"Any more such *striking* proofs, you mean, Pater; but let me tell you that they were sincere proofs, for since you've been ill I've been eating your pork and drinking your grog, which latter can't be too plentiful in the Bay of Biscay. And now that I've cured you, you'll be tucking all that into your own little breadbasket, so that I'm no gainer, and I think that you may be convinced that you never had or will have two more disinterested thumpings in all your born days. However, you're very welcome, so say no more about it."

I held my tongue and ate a very hearty breakfast. From that day I returned to my duty, and was put into the same watch with O'Brien, who spoke to the first lieutenant, and told him that he had taken me under his charge.

Chapter XII

New theory of Mr Muddle remarkable for having no end to it—Novel practice of Mr Chucks—O'Brien commences his history—There were giants in those days—I bring up the master's *night-glass*.

As I have already mentioned sufficient of the captain and the first lieutenant to enable the reader to gain an insight into their characters, I shall now mention two very odd personages who were my shipmates, the carpenter and the boatswain. The carpenter, whose name was Muddle, used to go by the appellation of Philosopher Chips, not that he followed any particular school, but had formed a theory of his own, from which he was not to be dissuaded. This was, that the universe had its cycle of events turned round, so that in a certain period of time everything was to happen over again. I never could make him explain upon what data his calculations were founded; he said, that if he explained it, I was too young to comprehend it; but the fact was this, "that in 27,672 years everything that was going on now would be going on again, with the same people as were existing at this present time." He very seldom ventured to make the remark to Captain Savage, but to the first lieutenant he did very often. "I've been as close to it as possible, sir, I do assure you, although you find fault; but 27,672 years ago you were first lieutenant of this ship, and I was carpenter, although we recollect nothing about it; and 27,672 years hence we shall both be standing by this boat, talking about the repairs, as we are now."

"I do not doubt it, Mr Muddle," replied the first lieutenant; "I dare say that it is all very true, but the repairs must be finished this night, and 27,672 years hence you will have the order just as positive as you have it now, so let it be done."

This theory made him very indifferent as to danger, or indeed as to anything. It was of no consequence, the affair took its station in the course of time. It had happened at the above period, and would happen again. Fate was fate. But the boatswain was a more amusing personage. He was considered to be the *taughtest* (that is, the most active and severe) boatswain in the service. He went by the name of "Gentleman Chucks"—the latter was his surname. He appeared to have received half an education; sometimes his language was for a few sentences remarkably well chosen, but, all of a sudden, he would break down at a hard word; but I shall be able to let the reader into more of his history as I go on with my adventures. He had a very handsome person, inclined to be stout, keen eyes, and hair curling in ringlets. He held his head up, and strutted as he walked. He declared "that an officer should look like an officer, and *comport* himself accordingly." In his person he was very clean, wore rings on his great fingers, and a large frill to his bosom, which stuck out like the back fin of a perch, and the collar of his shirt was always pulled up to a level with his cheek-bones. He never appeared on deck without his "persuader," which was three rattans twisted into one, like a cable; sometimes he called it his Order of the Bath, or his Tri_o_ junct_o_ in Uno; and this persuader was seldom idle. He attempted to be very polite, even when addressing the common seamen, and, certainly, he always commenced his observations to them in a very gracious manner, but, as he continued, he became less choice in his phraseology. O'Brien said that his speeches were like the Sin of the poet, very fair at the upper part of them, but shocking at the lower extremities. As a specimen of them, he would say to the man on the forecastle, "Allow me to observe, my dear man, in the most delicate way in the world, that you are spilling that tar upon the deck—a deck, sir, if I may venture to make the observation, I had the duty of seeing holystoned this morning. You understand me, sir, you have defiled his majesty's forecastle. I must do my duty, sir, if you neglect yours; so take that—and that—and that—(thrashing the man with his rattan)—you d—d hay-making son of a sea-cook. Do it again, d—n your eyes, and I'll cut your liver out."

I remember one of the ship's boys going forward with a kid of dirty water to empty in the head, without putting his hand up to his hat as he passed the boatswain. "Stop, my little friend," said the boatswain, pulling out his frill, and raising up both sides of his shirt-collar. "Are you aware, sir, of my rank and station in society?"

"Yes, sir," replied the boy, trembling, and eyeing the rattan.

"Oh, you are!" replied Mr Chucks. "Had you not been aware of it, I should have considered a gentle correction necessary, that you might have avoided such an error in future; but, as you *were* aware of it, why then, d—n you, you have no excuse, so take that—and that—you yelping, half-starved abortion. I really beg your pardon, Mr Simple," said he to me, as the boy went howling forward, for I was walking with him at the time; "but really the service makes brutes of us all. It is hard to sacrifice our health, our night's rest, and our comforts; but still more so, that in my responsible situation, I am obliged too often to sacrifice my gentility."

The master was the officer who had charge of the watch to which I was stationed; he was a very rough sailor, who had been brought up in the merchant service, not much of a gentleman in his appearance, very good-tempered, and very fond of grog. He always quarrelled with the boatswain, and declared that the service was going to the devil, now that warrant officers put on white shirts, and wore frills to them. But the boatswain did not care for him; he knew his duty, he did his duty, and if the captain was satisfied, he said, that the whole ship's company might grumble. As for the master, he said, the man was very well, but having been brought up in a collier, he could not be expected to be very refined; in fact, he observed, pulling up his shirt-collar—"it was impossible to make a silk purse out of a sow's ear." The master was very kind to me, and used to send me down to my hammock before my watch was half over. Until that time, I walked the deck with O'Brien, who was a very pleasant companion, and taught me everything that he could, connected with my profession. One night, when he had the middle watch, I told him I should like very much if he would give me the history of his life. "That I will, my honey," replied he, "all that I can remember of it, though I have no doubt but that I've forgotten the best part of it. It's now within five minutes of two bells, so we'll heave the log and mark the board, and then I'll spin you a yarn, which will keep us both from going to sleep." O'Brien reported the rate of sailing to the master, marked it down on the log-board, and then returned.

"So now, my boy, I'll come to an anchor on the topsail halyard rack, and you may squeeze your thread-paper little carcass under my lee, and then I'll tell you all about it. First and foremost, you must know that I am descended from the great O'Brien Borru, who was king in his time, as the great Fingal was before him. Of course you've heard of Fingal?"

"I can't say that I ever did," replied I.

"Never heard of Fingal!—murder! Where must you have been all your life? Well, then, to give you some notion of Fingal, I will first tell you how Fingal bothered the great Scotch giant, and then I'll go on with my own story. Fingal, you must know, was a giant himself, and no fool of one, and any one that affronted him was as sure of a bating, as I am to keep the middle watch to-night. But there was a giant in Scotland as tall as the mainmast, more or less, as we say when we a'n't quite sure, as it saves telling more lies than there's occasion for. Well, this Scotch giant heard of Fingal, and how he had beaten everybody, and he said, 'Who is this Fingal? By Jasus,' says he in Scotch, 'I'll just walk over and see what he's made of.' So he walked across the Irish Channel, and landed within half-a-mile of Belfast, but whether he was out of his depth or not I can't tell, although I suspect that he was not dry-footed. When Fingal heard that this great chap was coming over, he was in a devil of a fright, for they told him that the Scotchman was taller by a few feet or so. Giants, you know, measure by feet, and don't bother themselves about the inches, as we little devils are obliged to do. So Fingal kept a sharp look-out for the Scotchman, and one fine morning, there he was, sure enough, coming up the hill to Fingal's house. If Fingal was afraid before, he had more reason to be afraid when he saw the fellow, for he looked for all the world like the Monument upon a voyage of discovery. So Fingal ran into his house, and called to his wife Shaya, 'My vourneen,' says he, 'be quick now; there's that big bully of a Scotchman coming up the hill. Kiver me up with the blankets, and if he asks who is in bed, tell him it's the child.' So Fingal laid down on the bed, and his wife had just time to cover him up, when in comes the Scotchman, and though he stooped low, he broke his head against the portal. 'Where's that baste Fingal?' says he, rubbing his forehead; 'show him to me, that I may give him a bating.' 'Whisht, whisht!' cries Shaya, 'you'll wake the babby, and then him that you talk of bating will be the death of you, if he comes in.' 'Is that the babby?' cried the Scotchman with surprise, looking at the great carcass muffled up in the blankets. 'Sure it is,' replied Shaya, 'and Fingal's babby too; so don't you wake him, or Fingal will twist your neck in a minute.' 'By the cross of St Andrew,' replied the giant, 'then it's time for me to be off; for if that's his babby, I'll be but a mouthful to the fellow himself. Good morning to ye.' So the Scotch giant ran out of the house, and never stopped to eat or drink until he got back to his own hills, foreby he was nearly drowned in having mistaken his passage across the Channel in his great hurry. Then Fingal got up and laughed, as well he might, at his own 'cuteness; and so ends my story about Fingal. And now I'll begin about myself. As I said before, I am descended from the great O'Brien, who was a king in his time, but that time's past. I suppose, as the world turns round, my children's children's posterity may be kings again, although there seems but little chance of it just now; but there's ups and downs on a grand scale, as well as in a man's own history, and the wheel of fortune keeps turning for the comfort of those who are at the lowest spoke, as I may be just now. To cut the story a little shorter, I skip down to my great-grandfather, who lived like a real gentleman, as he was, upon his ten thousand a year. At last he died, and eight thousand of the ten was buried with him. My grandfather followed his father all in good course of time, and only left my father about one hundred acres of bog, to keep up the dignity of the family. I am the youngest of ten, and devil a copper have I but my pay, or am I likely to have. You may talk about *descent*, but a more *descending* family than mine was never in existence, for here am I with twenty-five pounds a-year, and a half-pay of 'nothing a day, and find myself,' when my great ancestor did just what he pleased with all Ireland, and everybody in it. But this is all nothing, except to prove satisfactorily that I am not worth a skillagalee, and that is the reason which induces me to condescend to serve his Majesty. Father M'Grath, the priest, who lived with my father, taught me the elements, as they call them. I thought I had enough of the elements then, but I've seen a deal more of them since. 'Terence,' says my father to me one day, 'what do you mane to do?' 'To get my dinner, sure,' replied I, for I was not a little hungry. 'And so you shall to-day, my vourneen,' replied my father, 'but in future you must do something to get your own dinner: there's not praties enow for the whole of ye. Will you go to the *say*?' 'I'll just step down and look at it,' says I, for we lived but sixteen Irish miles from the coast; so when I had finished my meal, which did not take long, for want of ammunition, I trotted down to the Cove to see what a ship might be like, and I happened upon a large one sure enough, for there lay a three-decker with an admiral's flag at the fore. 'May be you'll be so civil as to tell me what ship that is,' said I to a sailor on the pier. 'It's the Queen Charlotte,' replied he, 'of one hundred and twenty guns.' Now when I looked at her size, and compared her with all the little smacks and hoys lying about her, I very naturally asked how old she was; he replied, that she was no more than three years old. 'But three years old!' thought I to myself, 'it's a fine vessel you'll be when you'll come of age, if you grow at that rate: you'll be as tall as the top of Bencrow,'(that's a mountain we have in our parts). You see, Peter, I was a fool at that time, just as you are now; but by-and-by, when you've had as many thrashings as I have had, you may chance to be as clever. I went back to my father, and told him all I had seen, and he replied, that if I liked it I might be a midshipman on board of her, with nine hundred men under my command. He forgot to say how many I should have over me, but I found that out afterwards. I agreed, and my father ordered his pony and went to the lord-lieutenant, for he had interest enough for that. The lord-lieutenant spoke to the admiral, who was staying at the palace, and I was ordered on board as midshipman. My father fitted me out pretty handsomely, telling all the tradesmen that their bills should be paid with my first prize-money, and thus, by promises and blarney, he got credit for all I wanted. At last all was ready: Father M'Grath gave me his blessing, and told me that if I died like an O'Brien, he would say a power of masses for the good of my soul. 'May you never have the trouble, sir,' said I. 'Och, trouble! a pleasure, my dear boy,' replied he, for he was a very polite man; so off I went with my big chest, not quite so full as it ought to have been, for my mother cribbed one half of my stock for my brothers and sisters. 'I hope to be back again soon, father,' said I as I took my leave. 'I hope not, my dear boy,' replied he: 'a'n't you provided for, and what more would you have?' So, after a deal of bother, I was fairly on board, and I parted company with my chest, for I stayed on deck, and that went down below. I stared about with all my eyes for some time, when who should be coming off but the captain, and the officers were ordered on deck to receive him. I wanted to have a quiet survey of him, so I took up my station on one of the guns, that I might examine him at my leisure. The boatswain whistled, the marines presented arms, and the officers all took off their hats as the captain came on the deck, and then the guard was dismissed, and they all walked about the deck as before; but I found it very pleasant to be astride on the gun, so I remained where I was. 'What do you mane by that, you big young scoundrel?' says he, when he saw me. 'It's nothing at all I mane,' replied I; 'but what do you mane by calling an O'Brien a scoundrel?' 'Who is he?' said the captain to the first lieutenant. 'Mr O'Brien, who joined the ship about an hour since.' 'Don't you know better than to sit upon a gun?' said the captain. 'To be sure I do,' replied I, 'when there's anything better to sit upon.' 'He knows no better, sir,' observed the first lieutenant. 'Then he must be taught,' replied the captain. 'Mr O'Brien, since you have perched yourself on that gun to please yourself, you will now continue there for two hours to please me. Do you understand, sir?—you'll ride on that gun for two hours.' 'I understand, sir,' replied I; 'but I am afraid that he won't move without spurs, although there's plenty of *metal* in him.' The captain turned away and laughed as he went into his cabin, and all the officers laughed, and I laughed too, for I perceived no great hardship in sitting down an hour or two, any more than I do now. Well, I soon found that, like a young bear, all my troubles were to come. The first month was nothing but fighting and squabbling with my messmates; they called me a *raw* Irishman, and *raw* I was, sure enough, from the constant thrashings and coltings I received from those who were bigger and stronger than myself; but nothing lasts for ever—as they discovered that whenever they found blows I could find back, they got tired of it, and left me and my brogue alone. We sailed for the Toolong fleet."

"What fleet?" inquired I.

"Why, the Toolong fleet, so called, I thought, because they remained too long in harbour, bad luck to them; and then we were off Cape See-see (devil a bit could we see of them except their mast-heads) for I don't know how many months. But I forgot to say that I got into another scrape just before we left harbour. It was my watch when they piped to dinner, and I took the liberty to run below, as my messmates had a knack of forgetting absent friends. Well, the captain came on board, and there were no side boys, no side ropes, and no officers to receive him. He came on deck foaming with rage, for his dignity was hurt, and he inquired who was the midshipman of the watch. 'Mr O'Brien,' said they all. 'Devil a bit,' replied I, 'it was my forenoon watch.' 'Who relieved you, sir?' said the first lieutenant. 'Devil a soul, sir,' replied I; 'for they were all too busy with their pork and beef.' 'Then why did you leave the deck without relief?' 'Because, sir, my stomach would have had but little relief if I had remained.' The captain, who stood by, said, 'Do you see those cross-trees, sir?' 'Is it those little bits of wood that you mane, on the top there, captain?' 'Yes, sir; now just go up there, and stay until I call you down. You must be brought to your senses, young man, or you'll have but little prospect in the service.' 'I've an idea that I'll have plenty of prospect when I get up there,' replied I, 'but it's all to please you.' So up I went, as I have many a time since, and as you often will, Peter, just to enjoy the fresh air and your own pleasant thoughts, all at one and the same time.

"At last I became much more used to the manners and customs of *say*-going people, and by the time that I had been fourteen months off Cape See-see, I was considered a very genteel young midshipman, and my messmates (that is, all that I could thrash, which didn't leave out many) had a very great respect for me.

"The first time that I put my foot on shore was at Minorca, and then I put my foot into it (as we say), for I was nearly killed for a heretic, and only saved by proving myself a true Catholic, which proves that religion is a great comfort in distress, as Father M'Grath used to say. Several of us went on shore, and having dined upon a roast turkey, stuffed with plum-pudding (for everything else was cooked in oil, and we could not eat it), and having drunk as much wine as would float a jolly-boat, we ordered donkeys, to take a little equestrian exercise. Some went off tail on end, some with their hind-quarters uppermost, and then the riders went off instead of the donkeys; some wouldn't go off at all; as for mine he would go—and where the devil do you think he went? Why, into the church where all the people were at mass; the poor brute was dying with thirst, and smelt water. As soon as he was in, notwithstanding all my tugging and hauling, he ran his nose into the holy-water font, and drank it all up. Although I thought, that seeing how few Christians have any religion, you could not expect much from a donkey, yet I was very much shocked at the sacrilege, and fearful of the consequences. Nor was it without reason, for the people in the church were quite horrified, as well they might be, for the brute drank as much holy-water as would have purified the whole town of Port Mahon, suburbs and all to boot. They rose up from their knees and seized me, calling upon all the saints in the calendar. Although I knew what they meant, not a word of their lingo could I speak, to plead for my life, and I was almost torn to pieces before the priest came up. Perceiving the danger I was in, I wiped my finger across the wet nose of the donkey, crossed myself, and then went down on my knees to the priests, crying out *Culpa mea*, as all good Catholics do—though 'twas no fault of mine, as I said before, for I tried all I could, and tugged at the brute till my strength was gone. The priests perceived by the manner in which I crossed myself that I was a good Catholic, and guessed that it was all a mistake of the donkey's. They ordered the crowd to be quiet, and sent for an interpreter, when I explained the whole story. They gave me absolution for what the donkey had done, and after that, as it was very rare to meet an English officer who was a good Christian, I was in great favour during my stay at Minorca, and was living in plenty, paying for nothing, and as happy as a cricket. So the jackass proved a very good friend, and, to reward him, I hired him every day, and galloped him all over the island. But, at last, it occurred to me that I had broken my leave, for I was so happy on shore that I quite forgot that I had only permission for twenty-four hours, and I should not have remembered it so soon, had it not been for a party of marines, headed by a sergeant, who took me by the collar, and dragged me off my donkey. I was taken on board, and put under an arrest for my misconduct. Now, Peter, I don't know anything more agreeable than being put under an arrest. Nothing to do all day but eat and drink, and please yourself, only forbid to appear on the quarter-deck, the only place that a midshipman wishes to avoid. Whether it was to punish me more severely, or whether he forgot all about me, I can't tell, but it was nearly two months before I was sent for to the cabin; and the captain, with a most terrible frown, said, that he trusted that my punishment would be a warning to me, and that now I might return to my duty. 'Plase your honour,' said I, 'I don't think that I've been punished enough yet.' 'I am glad to find that you are so penitent, but you are forgiven, so take care that you do not oblige me to put you again in confinement.' So, as there was no persuading him, I was obliged to return to my duty again; but I made a resolution that I would get into another scrape again as soon as I dared—"

"Sail on the starboard bow!" cried the look-out man.

"Very well," replied the master; "Mr O'Brien—where's Mr O'Brien?"

"Is it me you mane, sir?" said O'Brien, walking up to the master, for he had sat down so long in the topsail-halyard rack, that he was wedged in and could not get out immediately.

"Yes, sir; go forward, and see what that vessel is."

"Aye, aye, sir," said O'Brien. "And Mr Simple," continued the master, "go down and bring me up my night-glass."

"Yes, sir," replied I. I had no idea of a night-glass; and as I observed that about this time his servant brought him up a glass of grog, I thought it very lucky that I knew what he meant. "Take care that you don't break it, Mr Simple." "Oh, then, I'm all right," thought I; "he means the tumbler." So down I went, called up the gunroom steward, and desired him to give me a glass of grog for Mr Doball. The steward tumbled out in his shirt, mixed the grog, and gave it to me, and I carried it up very carefully to the quarter-deck.

During my absence, the master had called the captain, and in pursuance of his orders, O'Brien had called the first lieutenant, and when I came up the ladder, they were both on deck. As I was ascending, I heard the master say, "I have sent young Simple down for my night-glass, but he is so long, that I suppose he has made some mistake. He's but half a fool." "That I deny," replied Mr Falcon, the first lieutenant, just as I put my foot on the quarter-deck; "he's no fool." "Perhaps not," replied the master. "Oh, here he is. What made you so long, Mr Simple—where is my night-glass?"

"Here it is, sir," replied I, handing him the tumbler of grog; "I told the steward to make it stiff." The captain and the first lieutenant burst out into a laugh for Mr Doball was known to be very fond of grog; the former walked aft to conceal his mirth; but the latter remained. Mr Doball was in a great rage. "Did not I say that the boy was half a fool?" cried he to the first lieutenant. "At all events, I'll not allow that he has proved himself so in this instance," replied Mr Falcon, "for he has hit the right nail on the head." Then the first lieutenant joined the captain, and they both went off laughing. "Put it on the capstan, sir," said Mr Doball to me, in an angry voice. "I'll punish you by-and-by." I was very much astonished; hardly knew whether I had done right or wrong; at all events, thought I to myself, I did for the best; so I put it on the capstan and walked to my own side of the deck. The captain and first lieutenant then went below, and O'Brien came aft. "What vessel is it?" said I.

"To the best of my belief, it's one of your bathing-machines going home with despatches," replied he.

"A bathing machine," said I; "why I thought that they were hauled up on the beach." "That's the Brighton sort; but these are made not to go up at all."

"What then?"

"Why, to *go down*, to be sure; and remarkably well they answer their purpose. I won't puzzle you any more, my Peter—I'm spaking helligorically, which I believe means telling a hell of a lie. It's one of your ten-gun brigs, to the best of my knowledge."

I then told O'Brien what had occurred, and how the master was angry with me. O'Brien laughed very heartily, and told me never to mind, but to keep in the lee-scuppers and watch him. "A glass of grog is a bait that he'll play round till he gorges. When you see it to his lips, go up to him boldly, and ask his pardon, if you have offended him, and then, if he's a good Christian, as I believe him to be, he'll not refuse it."

I thought this was very good advice, and I waited under the bulwark on the lee-side. I observed that the master made shorter and shorter turns every time, till at last he stopped at the capstan and looked at the grog. He waited about half a minute, and then he took up the tumbler, and drank about half of it. It was very strong, and he stopped to take breath. I thought this was the right time, and I went up to him. The tumbler was again to his lips, and before he saw me, I said, "I hope, sir, you'll forgive me; I never heard of a night telescope, and knowing that you had walked so long, I thought you were tired, and wanted something to drink to refresh you." "Well, Mr Simple," said he, after he had finished the glass, with a deep sigh of pleasure, "as you meant kindly, I shall let you off this time; but recollect, that whenever you bring me a glass of grog again, it must not be in the presence of the captain or first lieutenant." I promised him very faithfully, and went away quite delighted with my having made my peace with him, and more so, that the first lieutenant had said that I was no fool for what I had done.

At last our watch was over, and about two bells I was relieved by the midshipmen of the next watch. It is very unfair not to relieve in time, but if I said a word I was certain to be thrashed the next day upon some pretence or other. On the other hand, the midshipman whom I relieved was also much bigger than I was, and if I was not up before one bell, I was cut down and thrashed by him: so that between the two I kept much more than my share of the watch, except when the master sent me to bed before it was over.

Chapter XIII

The first lieutenant prescribes for one of his patients, his prescriptions consisting of *draughts* only—O'Brien finishes the history of his life, in which the proverb of "the more the merrier" is sadly disproved—*Shipping* a new pair of boots causes the *unshipping* of their owner—Walking home after a ball, O'Brien meets with an accident.

The next morning I was on deck at seven bells, to see the hammocks stowed, when I was witness to Mr Falcon, the first lieutenant, having recourse to one of his remedies to cure a mizen-top-boy of smoking, a practice to which he had a great aversion. He never interfered with the men smoking in the galley, or chewing tobacco; but he prevented the boys, that is, lads under twenty or there-abouts, from indulging in the habit too early. The first lieutenant smelt the tobacco as the boy passed him on the quarter-deck. "Why, Neill, you have been smoking," said the first lieutenant. "I thought you were aware that I did not permit such lads as you to use tobacco."

"If you please, sir," replied the mizen-top-man, touching his hat, "I'se got worms, and they say that smoking be good for them."

"Good for them!" said the first lieutenant; "yes, very good for them, but very bad for you. Why, my good fellow, they'll thrive upon tobacco until they grow as large as conger eels. Heat is what the worms are fond of; but cold—cold will kill them. Now I'll cure you. Quarter-master, come here. Walk this boy up and down the weather-gangway, and every time you get forward abreast of the main-tack block, put his mouth to windward, squeeze him sharp by the nape of the neck until he opens his mouth wide, and there keep him and let the cold air blow down his throat, while you count ten; then walk him aft, and when you are forward again, proceed as before.—Cold kills worms, my poor boy, not tobacco—I wonder that you are not dead by this time."

The quarter-master, who liked the joke, as did all the seamen, seized hold of the lad, and as soon as they arrived forward, gave him such a squeeze of the neck as to force him to open his mouth, if it were only to cry with pain. The wind was very fresh, and blew into his mouth so strong, that it actually whistled while he was forced to keep it open; and thus, he was obliged to walk up and down, cooling his inside, for nearly two hours, when the first lieutenant sent for him, and told him, that he thought all the worms must be dead by that time; but if they were not, the lad was not to apply his own remedies, but come to him for another dose. However, the boy was of the same opinion as the first lieutenant, and never complained of worms again.

A few nights afterwards, when we had the middle watch, O'Brien proceeded with his story.

"Where was it that I left off?"

"You left off at the time that you were taken out of confinement."

"So I did, sure enough; and it was with no good-will that I went to my duty. However, as there was no help for it, I walked up and down the deck as before, with my hands in my pockets, thinking of old Ireland, and my great ancestor, Brien Borru. And so I went on behaving myself like a real gentleman, and getting into no more scrapes, until the fleet put into the Cove of Cork, and I found myself within a few miles of my father's house. You may suppose that the anchor had hardly kissed the mud, before I went to the first lieutenant, and asked leave to go on shore. Now the first lieutenant was not in the sweetest of tempers, seeing as how the captain had been hauling him over the coals for not carrying on the duty according to his satisfaction. So he answered me very gruffly, that I should not leave the ship. 'Oh, bother!' said I to myself, 'this will never do.' So up I walked to the captain, and touching my hat, reminded him that 'I had a father and mother, and a pretty sprinkling of brothers and sisters, who were dying to see me, and that I hoped that he would give me leave.' 'Ax the first lieutenant,' said he, turning away. 'I have, sir,' replied I, 'and he says that the devil a bit shall I put my foot on shore.' 'Then you have misbehaved yourself,' said the captain. 'Not a bit of it, Captain Willis,' replied I; 'it's the first lieutenant who has misbehaved.' 'How, sir?' answered he, in an angry tone. 'Why, sir, didn't he misbehave just now in not carrying on the duty according to your will and pleasure? and didn't you serve him out just as he deserved—and isn't he sulky because you did— and arn't that the reason why I am not to go on shore? You see, your honour, it's all true as I said; and the first lieutenant has misbehaved and not I. I hope you will allow me to go on shore, captain, God bless you! and make some allowance for my parental feelings towards the arthers of my existence.' 'Have you any fault to find with Mr O'Brien?' said the captain to the first lieutenant, as he came aft. 'No more than I have with midshipmen in general; but I believe it is not the custom for officers to ask leave to go on shore before the sails are furled and the yards squared.' 'Very true,' replied the captain; 'therefore, Mr O'Brien, you must wait until the watch is called, and then, if you ask the first lieutenant, I have no doubt but you will have leave granted to you to go and see your friends.' 'Thank'e kindly, sir,' replied I; and I hoped that the yards and sails would be finished off as soon as possible, for my heart was in my mouth, and I felt that if I had been kept much longer, it would have flown on shore before me.

"I thought myself very clever in this business, but I was never a greater fool in my life; for there was no such hurry to have gone on shore, and the first lieutenant never forgave me for appealing to the captain—but of that by-and-by, and all in good time. At last I obtained a grumbling assent to my going on shore, and off I went like a sky-rocket. Being in a desperate hurry, I hired a jaunting-car to take me to my father's house. 'Is it the O'Brien of Ballyhinch that you mane?' inquired the spalpeen who drove the horse. 'Sure it is,' replied I; 'and how is he, and all the noble family of the O'Briens?" 'All well enough, bating the boy Tim, who caught a bit of confusion in his head the other night at the fair, and now lies at home in bed quite insensible to mate or drink; but the doctors give hopes of his recovery, as all the O'Briens are known to have such thick heads.' 'What do you mane by that, bad manners to you?' said I, 'but poor Tim—how did it happen—was there a fight?' 'Not much of a fight—only a bit of a skrummage—three crowners' inquests, no more.' 'But you are not going the straight road, you thief,' said I, seeing that he had turned off to the left. 'I've my reasons for that, your honour,' replied he; 'I always turn away from the Castle out of principle—I lost a friend there, and it makes me melancholy.' 'How came that for to happen?' 'All by accident, your honour; they hung my poor brother Patrick there, because he was a bad hand at arithmetic.' 'He should have gone to a better school then,' said I. 'I've an idea that it was a bad school that he was brought up in,' replied he, with a sigh. 'He was a cattle-dealer, your honour, and one day, somehow or another, he'd a cow too much—all for not knowing how to count, your honour,—bad luck to his school-master.' 'All that may be very true,' said I, 'and pace be to his soul; but I don't see why you are to drag me, that's in such a hurry, two miles out of my way, out of principle.' 'Is your honour in a hurry to get home? Then I'll be thinking they'll not be in such a hurry to see you.' 'And who told you that my name was O'Brien, you baste?—and do you dare to say that my friends won't be glad to see me?' 'Plase your honour, it's all an idea of mine—so say no more about it. Only this I know: Father M'Grath, who gives me absolution, tould me the other day that I ought to pay him, and not run in debt, and then run away like Terence O'Brien, who went to say without paying for his shirts, and his shoes, and his stockings, nor anything else, and who would live to be hanged as sure as St Patrick swam over the Liffey with his head under his arm.' 'Bad luck to that Father McGrath,' cried I; 'devil burn me, but I'll be revenged upon him!'

"By that time we had arrived at the door of my father's house. I paid the rapparee, and in I popped. There was my father and mother, and all my brothers and sisters (bating Tim, who was in bed sure enough, and died next day), and that baste Father McGrath to boot. When my mother saw me she ran to me and hugged me as she wept on my neck, and then she wiped her eyes and sat down again; but nobody else said 'How d'ye do?' or opened their mouths to me. I said to myself, 'Sure there's some trifling mistake here,' but I held my tongue. At last they all opened their mouths with a vengeance. My father commenced—'Ar'n't you ashamed on yourself, Terence O'Brien?' 'Ar'n't you ashamed on yourself, Terence O'Brien?' cried Father M'Grath. 'Ar'n't you ashamed on yourself?' cried out all my brothers and sisters in full chorus, whilst my poor mother put her apron to her eyes and said nothing. 'The devil a bit for myself, but very much ashamed for you all,' replied I, 'to treat me in this manner. What's the meaning of all this?' 'Haven't they seized my two cows to pay for your toggery, you spalpeen?' cried my father. 'Haven't they taken the hay to pay for your shoes and stockings?' cried Father M'Grath. 'Haven't they taken the pig to pay for that ugly hat of yours?' cried my eldest sister. 'And haven't they taken my hens to pay for that dirk of yours?' cried another. 'And all our best furniture to pay for your white shirts and black cravats?' cried Murdock, my brother. 'And haven't we been starved to death ever since?' cried they all. 'Och hone!' said my mother. 'The devil they have!' said I, when they'd all done. 'Sure I'm sorry enough, but it's no fault of mine. Father, didn't you send me to say?' 'Yes, you rapparee; but didn't you promise—or didn't I promise for you, which is all one and the same thing—that you'd pay it all back with your prize-money—and where is it? answer that, Terence O'Brien.' 'Where is it, father? I'll tell you; it's where next Christmas is—coming, but not come yet.' 'Spake to him, Father M'Grath,' said my father. 'Is not that a lie of yours, Terence O'Brien, that you're after telling now?' said Father McGrath; 'give me the money.' 'It's no lie, Father McGrath; if it pleased you to die to-morrow, the devil of a shilling have I to jingle on your tombstone for good luck, bating those three or four, which you may divide between you, and I threw them on the floor.

"'Terence O'Brien,' said Father McGrath, 'its absolution that you'll be wanting to-morrow, after all your sins and enormities; and the devil a bit shall you have—take that now.'

"'Father M'Grath,' replied I very angrily, 'it's no absolution that I'll want from you, any how—take that now.'

"'Then you have had your share of heaven; for I'll keep you out of it, you wicked monster,' said Father M'Grath—'take that now.'

"'If it's no better than a midshipman's berth,' replied I, 'I'd just as soon stay out; but I'll creep in in spite of you—take that now, Father M'Grath.'

"'And who's to save your soul, and send you to heaven, if I don't, you wicked wretch? but I'll see you d——d first—so take that now, Terence O'Brien.'

"'Then I'll turn Protestant, and damn the Pope—take that now, Father M'Grath.'

"At this last broadside of mine, my father and all my brothers and sisters raised a cry of horror, and my mother burst into tears. Father M'Grath seized hold of the pot of holy water, and dipping in the little whisk, began to sprinkle the room, saying a Latin prayer, while they all went on squalling at me. At last, my father seized the stool, which he had been seated upon, and threw it at my head. I dodged, and it knocked down Father M'Grath, who had just walked behind me in full song. I knew that it was all over after that, so I sprang over his carcass, and gained the door. 'Good morning to ye all, and better manners to you next time we meet,' cried I, and off I set as fast as I could for the ship.

"I was melancholy enough as I walked back, and thought of what had passed. 'I need not have been in such a confounded hurry,' said I to myself, 'to ask leave, thereby affronting the first lieutenant;' and I was very sorry for what I had said to the priest, for my conscience thumped me very hard at having even pretended that I'd turn Protestant, which I never intended to do, nor never will, but live and die a good Catholic, as all my posterity have done before me, and, as I trust, all my ancestors will for generations to come. Well, I arrived on board, and the first lieutenant was very savage. I hoped he would get over it, but he never did; and he continued to treat me so ill that I determined to quit the ship, which I did as soon as we arrived in Cawsand Bay. The captain allowed me to go, for I told him the whole truth of the matter, and he saw that it was true; so he recommended me to the captain of a jackass frigate, who was in want of midshipmen."

"What do you mean by a jackass frigate?" inquired I.

"I mean one of your twenty-eight gun-ships, so called, because there is as much difference between them and a real frigate, like the one we are sailing in, as there is between a donkey and a racehorse. Well, the ship was no sooner brought down to the dock-yard to have her ballast taken in, than our captain came down to her—a little, thin, spare man, but a man of weight nevertheless, for he brought a great pair of scales with him, and weighed everything that was put on board. I forget his real name, but the sailors christened him Captain Avoirdupois. He had a large book, and in it he inserted the weight of the ballast, and of the shot, water, provisions, coals, standing and running rigging, cables, and everything else. Then he weighed all the men, and all the midshipmen, and all the midshipmen's chests, and all the officers, with everything belonging to them: lastly, he weighed himself, which did not add much to the sum total. I don't exactly know what this was for; but he was always talking about centres of gravity, displacement of fluid, and Lord knows what. I believe it was to find out the longitude, somehow or other, but I didn't remain long enough in her to know the end of it, for one day I brought on board a pair of new boots, which I forgot to report that they might be put into the scales, which swang on the gangway; and whether the captain thought that they would sink his ship, or for what I can not tell, but he ordered me to quit her immediately—so, there I was adrift again. I packed up my traps and went on shore, putting on my new boots out of spite, and trod into all the mud and mire I could meet, and walked up and down from Plymouth to Dock until I was tired, as a punishment to them, until I wore the scoundrels out in a fortnight.

"One day I was in the dockyard, looking at a two-decker in the basin, just brought forward for service, and I inquired who was to be the captain. They told me that his name was O'Connor. Then's he's a countryman of mine, thought I, and I'll try my luck. So I called at Goud's Hotel, where he was lodging, and requested to speak with him. I was admitted, and I told him, with my best bow, that I had come as a volunteer for his ship, and that my name was O'Brien. As it happened, he had some vacancies, and liking my brogue, he asked me in what ships I had served. I told him, and also my reason for quitting my last—which was, because I was turned out of it. I explained the story of the boots, and he made inquiries, and found that it was all true; and then he gave me a vacancy as master's mate. We were ordered to South America, and the trade winds took us there in a jiffey. I liked my captain and officers very much; and what was better, we took some good prizes. But somehow or other, I never had the luck to remain long in one ship, and that by no fault of mine; at least, not in this instance. All went on as smooth as possible, until one day the captain took us on shore to a ball, at one of the peaceable districts. We had a very merry night of it; but as luck would have it, I had the morning watch to keep, and see the decks cleaned, and as I never neglected my duty, I set off about three o'clock in the morning, just at break of day, to go on board of the ship. I was walking along the sands, thinking of the pretty girl that I'd been dancing with, and had got about half way to the ship, when three rapparees of Spanish soldiers came from behind a rock and attacked me with their swords and bayonets. I had only my dirk, but I was not to be run through for nothing, so I fought them as long as I could. I finished one fellow, but at last they finished me; for a bayonet passed through my body, and I forgot all about it. Well, it appears—for I can only say to the best of my knowledge and belief—that after they had killed me, they stripped me naked and buried me in the sand, carrying away with them the body of their comrade. So there I was—dead and buried."

"But, O'Brien," said I

"Whist—hold your tongue—you've not heard the end of it. Well, I had been buried about an hour—but not very deep it appears, for they were in too great a hurry—when a fisherman and his daughter came along the beach, on their way to the boat; and the daughter, God bless her! did me the favour to tread upon my nose. It was clear that she had never trod upon an Irishman's nose before, for it surprised her, and she looked down to see what was there, and not seeing anything, she tried it again with her foot, and then she scraped off the sand, and discovered my pretty face. I was quite warm and still breathing, for the sand had stopped the blood, and prevented my bleeding to death. The fisherman pulled me out, and took me on his back to the house where the captain and officers were still dancing. When he brought me in, there was a great cry from the ladies, not because I was murdered, for they are used to it in those countries, but because I was naked, which they considered a much more serious affair. I was put to bed and a boat despatched on board for our doctor; and in a few hours I was able to speak, and tell them how it happened. But I was too ill to move when the ship sailed, which she was obliged to do in a day or two afterwards, so the captain made out my discharge, and left me there. The family were French, and I remained with them for six months before I could obtain a passage home, during which I learnt their language, and a very fair allowance of Spanish to boot. When I arrived in England, I found that the prizes had been sold, and that the money was ready for distribution. I produced my certificate, and received £167 for my share. So it's come at last, thought I.

"I never had such a handful of money in my life; but I hope I shall again very soon. I spread it out on the table as soon as I got home, and looked at it, and then I said to myself, 'Now, Terence O'Brien, will you keep this money to yourself, or send it home?' Then I thought of Father M'Grath, and the stool that was thrown at my head, and I was very near sweeping it all back into my pocket. But then I thought of my mother, and of the cows, and the pig, and the furniture, all gone; and of my brothers and sisters wanting praties, and I made a vow that I'd send every farthing of it to them, after which Father M'Grath would no longer think of not giving me absolution. So I sent them every doit, only reserving for myself the pay which I had received, amounting to about £30: and I never felt more happy in my life than when it was safe in the post-office, and fairly out of my hands. I wrote a bit of a letter to my father at the time, which was to this purpose:—

"'HONOURED FATHER,—
Since our last pleasant meeting, at which you threw the stool at my head, missing the pigeon and hitting the crow, I have been dead and buried, but am now quite well, thank God, and want no absolution from Father M'Grath, bad luck to him. And what's more to the point, I have just received a batch of prize-money, the first I have handled since I have served his Majesty, and every farthing of which I now send to you, that you may get back your old cows, and the pig, and all the rest of the articles seized to pay for my fitting out; so never again ask me whether I am not ashamed of myself; more shame to you for abusing a dutiful son like myself, who went to sea at your bidding, and has never had a real good potato down his throat ever since. I'm a true O'Brien, tell my mother, and don't mane to turn Protestant, but uphold the religion of my country; although the devil may take Father M'Grath and his holy water to boot. I sha'n't come and see you, as perhaps you may have another stool ready for my head, and may take better aim next time.
So no more at present from your affectionate son, 'TERENCE O'BRIEN.'"

"About three weeks afterwards I received a letter from my father, telling me that I was a real O'Brien, and that if any one dared hint to the contrary, he would break every bone in his body; that they had received the money, and thanked me for a real gentleman as I was; that I should have the best stool in the house next time I came, not for my head, but for my tail; that Father M'Grath sent me his blessing, and had given me absolution for all I had done, or should do for the next ten years to come; that my mother had cried with joy at my dutiful behaviour; and that all my brothers and sisters (bating Tim, who had died the day after I left them) wished me good luck, and plenty more prize-money to send home to them.

"This was all very pleasant; and I had nothing left on my mind but to get another ship; so I went to the port-admiral, and told him how it was that I left my last: and he said, 'that being dead and buried was quite sufficient reason for any one leaving his ship, and that he would procure me another, now that I had come to life again.' I was sent on board of the guard-ship, where I remained about ten days, and then was sent round to join this frigate—and so my story's ended; and there's eight bells striking—so the watch is ended too; jump down, Peter, and call

Robinson, and tell him that I'll trouble him to forget to go to sleep again as he did last time, and leave me here kicking my heels, contrary to the rules and regulations of the service."

Chapter XIV

The first lieutenant has more patients—Mr Chucks the Boatswain, lets me into the secret of his gentility.

Before I proceed with my narrative, I wish to explain to the reader that my history was not written in after-life, when I had obtained a greater knowledge of the world. When I first went to sea, I promised my mother that I would keep a journal of what passed, with my reflections upon it. To this promise I rigidly adhered, and since I have been my own master, these journals have remained in my possession. In writing, therefore, the early part of my adventures, everything is stated as it was impressed on my mind at the time. Upon many points I have since had reason to form a different opinion from that which is recorded, and upon many others I have since laughed heartily at my folly and simplicity; but still, I have thought it advisable to let the ideas of the period remain, rather than correct them by those of dear-bought experience. A boy of fifteen, brought up in a secluded country town, cannot be expected to reason and judge as a young man who has seen much of life, and passed through a variety of adventures. The reader must therefore remember, that I have referred to my journal for the opinions and feelings which guided me between each distinct anniversary of my existence.

We had now been cruising for six weeks, and I found that my profession was much more agreeable than I had anticipated. My desire to please was taken for the deed; and, although I occasionally made a blunder, yet the captain and first lieutenant seemed to think that I was attentive to my duty to the best of my ability, and only smiled at my mistakes. I also discovered, that, however my natural capacity may have been estimated by my family, that it was not so depreciated here; and every day I felt more confidence in myself, and hoped, by attention and diligence, to make up for a want of natural endowment. There certainly is something in the life of a sailor which enlarges the mind. When I was at home six months before, I allowed other people to think for me, and acted wholly on the leading-strings of their suggestions; on board, to the best of my ability, I thought for myself. I became happy with my messmates—those who were harsh upon me left off, because I never resented their conduct, and those who were kind to me were even kinder than before. The time flew away quickly, I suppose, because I knew exactly what I had to do, and each day was the forerunner of the ensuing. The first lieutenant was one of the most amusing men I ever knew, yet he never relaxed from the discipline of the service, or took the least liberty with either his superiors or inferiors. His humour was principally shown in his various modes of punishment; and, however severe the punishment was to the party, the manner of inflicting it was invariably a source of amusement to the remainder of the ship's company. I often thought, that although no individual liked being punished, yet, that all the ship's company were quite pleased when a punishment took place. He was very particular about his decks; they were always as white as snow, and nothing displeased him so much as their being soiled. It was for that reason that he had such an objection to the use of tobacco. There were spitting-pans placed in different parts of the decks for the use of the men, that they might not dirty the planks with the tobacco-juice. Sometimes a man in his hurry forgot to use these pans, but, as the mess to which the stain might be opposite had their grog stopped if the party were not found out, they took good care not only to keep a look-out, but to inform against the offender. Now the punishment for the offence was as follows—the man's hands were tied behind his back, and a large tin spitting-box fixed to his chest by a strap over the shoulders. All the other boxes on the lower deck were taken away, and he was obliged to walk there, ready to attend the summons of any man who might wish to empty his mouth of the tobacco-juice. The other men were so pleased at the fancy, that they spat twice as much as before, for the pleasure of making him run about. Mr Chucks, the boatswain, called it "the first lieutenant's *perambulating* spitting-pan." He observed to me one day, "that really Mr Falcon was such an *epicure* about his decks, that he was afraid to pudding an anchor on the forecastle."

I was much amused one morning watch that I kept. We were stowing the hammocks in the quarter-deck nettings, when one of the boys came up with his hammock on his shoulder, and as he passed the first lieutenant, the latter perceived that he had a quid of tobacco in his cheek. "What have you got there, my good lad—a gum-boil?—your cheek is very much swelled." "No, sir," replied the boy, "there's nothing at all the matter." "O there must be; it is a bad tooth, then. Open your mouth, and let me see." Very reluctantly the boy opened his mouth, and discovered a large roll of tobacco-leaf. "I see, I see," said the first lieutenant, "your mouth wants overhauling, and your teeth cleaning. I wish we had a dentist on board; but as we have not, I will operate as well as I can. Send the armourer up here with his tongs." When the armourer made his appearance, the boy was made to open his mouth, while the chaw of tobacco was extracted with his rough instrument. "There now," said the first lieutenant, "I'm sure that you must feel better already; you never could have had any appetite. Now, captain of the afterguard, bring a piece of old canvas and some sand here, and clean his teeth nicely." The captain of the afterguard came forward, and putting the boy's head between his knees, scrubbed his teeth well with the sand and canvas for two or three minutes. "There, that will do," said the first lieutenant. "Now, my little fellow, your mouth is nice and clean, and you'll enjoy your breakfast. It was impossible for you to have eaten anything with your mouth in such a nasty state. When it's dirty again, come to me, and I'll be your dentist."

One day I was on the forecastle with Mr Chucks, the boatswain, who was very kind to me. He had been showing me how to make the various knots and bends of rope which are used in our service. I am afraid that I was very stupid, but he showed me over and over again, until I learnt how to make them. Amongst others, he taught me a fisherman's bend, which he pronounced to be the *king* of all knots; "and, Mr Simple," continued he, "there is a moral in that knot. You observe, that when the parts are drawn the right way, and together, the more you pull the faster they hold, and the more impossible to untie them; but see, by hauling them apart, how a little difference, a pull the other way, immediately disunites them, and then how easy they cast off in a moment. That points out the necessity of pulling together in this world, Mr Simple, when we wish to hold on, and that's a piece of philosophy worth all the twenty-six thousand and odd years of my friend the carpenter, which leads to nothing but a brown study, when he ought to be attending to his duty."

"Very true, Mr Chucks, you are the better philosopher of the two."

"I am the better educated, Mr Simple, and I trust, more of a gentleman. I consider a gentleman to be, to a certain degree, a philosopher, for very often he is obliged, to support his character as such, to put up with what another person may very properly fly in a passion about. I think coolness is the great character-stick of a gentleman. In the service, Mr Simple, one is obliged to appear angry without indulging the sentiment. I can assure you, that I never lose my temper, even when I use my rattan."

"Why, then, Mr Chucks, do you swear so much at the men? Surely that is not gentlemanly?"

"Most certainly not, sir. But I must defend myself by observing the very artificial state in which we live on board of a man-of-war. Necessity, my dear Mr Simple, has no law. You must observe how gently I always commence when I have to find fault. I do that to prove my gentility; but, sir, my zeal for the service obliges me to alter my language, to prove in the end that I am in earnest. Nothing would afford me more pleasure than to be able to carry on the duty as a gentleman, but that's impossible."

"I really cannot see why."

"Perhaps, then, Mr Simple, you will explain to me why the captain and first lieutenant swear."

"That I do not pretend to answer, but they only do so upon an emergency."

"Exactly so; but, sir, their 'mergency is my daily and hourly duty. In the continual working of the ship I am answerable for all that goes amiss. The life of a boatswain is a life of 'mergency, and therefore I swear."

"I still cannot allow it to be requisite, and certainly it is sinful."

"Excuse me, my dear sir; it is absolutely requisite, and not at all sinful. There is one language for the pulpit, and another for on board ship, and, in either situation, a man must make use of those terms most likely to produce the necessary effect upon his listeners. Whether it is from long custom of the service, or from the indifference of a sailor to all common things and language (I can't exactly explain myself, Mr Simple, but I know what I mean), perhaps constant excitement may do, and therefore he requires more 'stimilis,' as they call it, to make him move. Certain it is, that common parlancy won't do with a common seaman. It is not here as in the scriptures, 'Do this, and he doeth it' (by the bye, that chap must have had his soldiers in tight order); but it is, 'Do this, d—n your eyes,' and then it is done directly. The order to *do* just carries the weight of a cannon-shot, but it wants the perpelling power—the d—n is the gunpowder which sets it flying in the execution of its duty. Do you comprehend me, Mr Simple?"

"I perfectly understand you, Mr Chucks, and I cannot help remarking, and that without flattery, that you are very different from the rest of the warrant officers. Where did you receive your education?"

"Mr Simple, I am here a boatswain with a clean shirt, and, I say it myself, and no one dare gainsay it, also with a thorough knowledge of my duty. But although I do not say that I ever was better off, I can say this, that I've been in the best society, in the company of lords and ladies. I once dined with your grandfather."

"That's more than ever I did, for he never asked me, nor took the least notice of me," replied I.

"What I state is true. I did not know that he was your grandfather until yesterday, when I was talking with Mr O'Brien; but I perfectly recollect him, although I was very young at that time. Now, Mr Simple, if you will promise me as a gentleman (and I know you are one), that you will not repeat what I tell you, then I'll let you into the history of my life."

"Mr Chucks, as I am a gentleman I never will divulge it until you are dead and buried, and not then if you do not wish it."

"When I am dead and buried, you may do as you please; it may then be of service to other people, although my story is not a very long one."

Mr Chucks then sat down upon the fore-end of the booms by the funnel, and I took my place by his side, when he commenced as follows:—

"My father was a boatswain before me—one of the old school, rough as a bear, and drunken as a Gosport fiddler. My mother was—my mother, and I shall say no more. My father was invalided for harbour duty after a life of intoxication, and died shortly afterwards. In the meantime I had been, by the kindness of the port-admiral's wife, educated at a foundation school. I was thirteen when my father died, and my mother, not knowing what to do with me, wished to bind me apprentice to a merchant vessel; but this I refused, and, after six months' quarrelling on the subject, I decided the point by volunteering in the *Narcissus* frigate. I believe that my gentlemanly ideas were innate, Mr Simple; I never, as a child, could bear the idea of the merchant service. After I had been a week on board, I was appointed servant to the purser, where I gave such satisfaction by my alertness and dexterity, that the first lieutenant took me away from the purser to attend upon himself, so that in two months I was a person of such consequence as to create a disturbance in the gunroom, for the purser was very angry, and many of the officers took his part. It was whispered that I was the son of the first lieutenant, and that he was aware of it. How far that may be true I know not, but there was a likeness between us; and my mother, who was a very pretty woman, attended his ship many years before as a bumboat girl. I can't pretend to say anything about it, but this I do say, Mr Simple—and many will blame me for it, but I can't help my natural feelings—that I had rather be the bye-blow of a gentleman, than the 'gitimate offspring of a boatswain and his wife. There's no chance of good blood in your veins in the latter instance, whereas, in the former you may have stolen a drop or two. It so happened, that after I had served the first lieutenant for about a year, a young lord (I must not mention his name, Mr Simple) was sent to sea by his friends, or by his own choice, I don't know which, but I was told that his uncle, who was 'zeckative, and had an interest in his death, persuaded him to go. A lord at that period, some twenty-five years ago, was a rarity in the service, and they used to salute him when he came on board. The consequence was, that the young lord must have a servant to himself, although all the rest of the midshipmen had but one servant between them. The captain inquired who was the best boy in the ship, and the purser, to whom he appealed, recommended me. Accordingly, much to the annoyance of the first lieutenant (for first lieutenants in those days did not assume as they do now, not that I refer to Mr Falcon, who is a gentleman), I was immediately surrendered to his lordship. I had a very easy, comfortable life of it—I did little or nothing; if inquired for when all hands were turned up, I was cleaning his lordship's boots, or brushing his lordship's clothes, and there was nothing to be said when his lordship's name was mentioned. We went to the Mediterranean (because his lordship's mamma wished it), and we had been there about a year, when his lordship ate so many grapes that he was seized with a dysentery. He was ill for three weeks, and then he requested to be sent to Malta in a transport going to Gibraltar, or rather to the Barbary coast, for bullocks. He became worse every day, and made his will, leaving me all his effects on board, which I certainly deserved for the kindness with which I had nursed him. Off Malta we fell in with a xebeque, bound to Civita Vecchia, and the captain of the transport, anxious to proceed, advised our going on board of her, as the wind was light and contrary, and these Mediterranean vessels sailed better on a wind than the transport. My master, who was now sinking fast, consented, and we changed our ships. The next day he died, and a gale of wind came on, which prevented us from gaining the port for several days, and the body of his lordship not only became so offensive, but affected the superstition of the Catholic sailors so much, that it was hove overboard. None of the people could speak English, nor could I speak Maltese; they had no idea who we were, and I had plenty of time for cogitation. I had often thought what a fine thing it was to be a lord, and as often wished that I had been born one. The wind was still against us, when a merchant vessel ran down to us, that had left Civita Vecchia for Gibraltar. I desired the captain of the xebeque to make a signal of distress, or rather I did myself, and the vessel, which proved to be English, bore down to us.

"I manned the boat to go on board, and the idea came into my head, that, although they might refuse to take me, they would not refuse a lord. I put on the midshipman's uniform belonging to his lordship (but then certainly belonging to me), and went alongside of the merchant vessel; I told them that I had left my ship for the benefit of my health, and wanted a passage to Gibraltar, on my way home. My title, and immediate acceptance of the terms demanded for my passage, was sufficient. My property was brought from the xebeque; and, of course, as they could not speak English, they could not contradict, even if they suspected. Here, Mr Simple, I must acknowledge a slight flaw in my early history, which I impart to you in confidence; or otherwise I should not have been able to prove that I was correct in asserting that I had dined with your grandfather. But the temptation was too strong, and I could not resist. Think yourself, Mr Simple, after having served as a ship's boy clouted here, kicked there, damned by one, and sent to hell by another—to find myself treated with such respect and deference, and my lorded this and my lorded that, every minute of the day. During my passage to Gibraltar, I had plenty of time for arranging my plans. I hardly need say that my lord's *kit* was valuable; and what was better, they exactly fitted me. I also had his watches and trinkets, and many other things, besides a bag of dollars. However, they were honestly mine; the only thing that I took was his name, which he had no further occasion for, poor fellow! But it's no use defending what was wrong—it was dishonest, and there's an end of it.

"Now observe, Mr Simple, how one thing leads to another. I declare to you, that my first idea of making use of his lordship's name, was to procure a passage to Gibraltar. I then was undecided how to act; but, as I had charge of his papers and letters to his mother and guardian, I think—indeed I am almost sure—that I should have laid aside my dignity and midshipman's dress, and applied for a passage home to the commissioner of the yard. But it was fated to be otherwise; for the master of the transport went on shore to report and obtain pratique, and he told them everywhere that young Lord A—— was a passenger with him, going to England for the benefit of his health. In less than half-an-hour, off came the commissioner's boat, and another boat from the governor, requesting the honour of my company, and that I would take a bed at their houses during my stay. What could I do? I began to be frightened; but I was more afraid to confess that I was an impostor, for I am sure the master of the transport alone would have kicked me overboard, if I had let him know that he had been so confounded polite to a ship's boy. So I blushed half from modesty and half from guilt, and accepted the invitation of the governor; sending a polite verbal refusal to the commissioner, upon the plea of there being no paper or pens on board. I had so often accompanied my late master, that I knew very well how to conduct myself, and had borrowed a good deal of his air and appearance—indeed, I had a natural taste for gentility. I could write and read; not perhaps so well as I ought to have done, considering the education I had received, but still quite well enough for a lord, and indeed much better than my late master. I knew his signature well enough, although the very idea of being forced to use it made me tremble. However, the die was cast. I ought to observe, that in one point we were not unlike—both had curly light hair and blue eyes; in other points there was no resemblance. I was by far the better-looking chap of the two; and as we had been up the Mediterranean for two years, I had no fear of any doubt as to my identity until I arrived in England. Well, Mr Simple, I dressed myself very carefully, put on my chains and rings, and a little perfume on my handkerchief, and accompanied the aide-de-camp to the governor's, where I was asked after my mother, Lady ——, and my uncle, my guardian, and a hundred other questions. At first I was much confused, which was attributed to bashfulness; and so it was, but not of the right sort. But before the day was over, I had become so accustomed to be called 'my lord,' and to my situation, that I was quite at my ease, and began to watch the motions and behaviour of the company, that I might regulate my comportment by that of good society. I remained at Gibraltar for a fortnight, and then was offered a passage in a transport ordered to Portsmouth. Being an officer, of course it was free to a certain extent. On my passage to England, I again made up my mind that I would put off my dress and title as soon as I could escape from observation; but I was prevented as before. The port-admiral sent off to request the pleasure of my company to dinner. I dared not refuse; and there I was, my lord, as before, courted and feasted by everybody. Tradesmen called to request the honour of my lordship's custom; my table at the hotel was covered with cards of all descriptions; and, to confess the truth, I liked my situation so much, and had been so accustomed to it, that I now began to dislike the idea that one day or other I must resign it, which I determined to do as soon as I quitted the place. My bill at the hotel was very extravagant, and more than I could pay: but the master said it was not of the least consequence; that of course his lordship had not provided himself with cash, just coming from foreign parts, and offered to supply me with money if I required it. This, I will say, I was honest enough to refuse. I left my cards, P.P.C., as they do, Mr Simple, in all well-regulated society, and set off in the mail for London, where I fully resolved to drop my title, and to proceed to Scotland to his lordship's mother, with the mournful intelligence of his death—for you see, Mr Simple, no one knew that his lordship was dead. The captain of the transport had put him into the xebeque alive, and the vessel bound to Gibraltar had received him, as they imagined. The captain of the frigate had very soon afterwards advices from Gibraltar, stating his lordship's recovery and return to England. Well, I had not been in the coach more than five minutes, when who should get in but a gentleman whom I had met at the port-admiral's; besides which the coachman and others knew me very well. When I arrived in London (I still wore my midshipman's uniform), I went to an hotel recommended to me, as I afterwards found out, the most fashionable in town, my title still following me. I now determined to put off my uniform, and dress in plain clothes—my farce was over. I went to bed that night, and the next morning made my appearance in a suit of mufti, making inquiry of the waiter which was the best conveyance to Scotland.

"'Post chay and four, my lord. At what time shall I order it?'

"'O,' replied I, 'I am not sure that I shall go tomorrow.'

"Just at this moment in came the master of the hotel, with the *Morning Post* in his hand, making me a low bow, and pointing to the insertion of my arrival at his hotel among the fashionables. This annoyed me; and now that I found how difficult it was to get rid of my title, I became particularly anxious to be William Chucks, as before. Before twelve o'clock, three or four gentlemen were ushered into my sitting-room, who observing my arrival in that damn'd *Morning Post*, came to pay their respects; and before the day was over I was invited and re-invited by a dozen people. I found that I could not retreat, and I went away with the stream, as I did before at Gibraltar and Portsmouth. For three weeks I was everywhere; and if I found it agreeable at Portsmouth, how much more so in London! But I was not happy, Mr Simple, because I was a cheat, every moment expecting to be found out. But it really was a nice thing to be a lord.

"At last the play was over. I had been enticed by some young men into a gambling-house, where they intended to fleece me; but, for the first night, they allowed me to win, I think, about £300. I was quite delighted with my success, and had agreed to meet them the next evening; but when I was at breakfast, with my legs crossed, reading the *Morning Post*, who should come to see me but my guardian uncle. He knew his nephew's features too well to be deceived; and my not recognising him proved at once that I was an impostor. You must allow me to hasten over the scene which took place—the wrath of the uncle, the confusion in the hotel, the abuse of the waiters, the police officer, and being dragged into a hackney coach to Bow-street. There I was examined and confessed all. The uncle was so glad to find that his nephew was really dead, that he felt no resentment towards me; and as, after all, I had only assumed a name, but had cheated nobody, except the landlord at Portsmouth, I was sent on board the tender off the Tower, to be drafted into a man-of-war. As for my £300, my clothes, &c., I never heard any more of them; they were seized, I presume, by the landlord of the hotel for my bill, and very handsomely he must have paid himself. I had two rings on my fingers, and a watch in my pocket, when I was sent on board the tender, and I stowed them away very carefully. I had also a few pounds in my purse. I was sent round to Plymouth, where I was drafted into a frigate. After I had been there some time, I turned the watch and rings into money, and bought myself a good kit of clothes; for I could not bear to be dirty. I was put into the mizen-top, and no one knew that I had been a lord."

"You found some difference, I should think, in your situation?"

"Yes, I did, Mr Simple; but I was much happier. I could not forget the ladies, and the dinners, and the opera, and all the delights of London, beside the respect paid to my title, and I often sighed for them; but the police officer and Bow-street also came to my recollection, and I shuddered at the remembrance. It had, however, one good effect; I determined to be an officer if I could, and learnt my duty, and worked my way up to quarter-master, and thence to boatswain—and I know my duty, Mr Simple. But I've been punished for my folly ever since. I formed ideas above my station in life, and cannot help longing to be a gentleman. It's a bad thing for a man to have ideas above his station."

"You certainly must find some difference between the company in London and that of the warrant officers."

"It's many years back now, sir; but I can't get over the feeling. I can't 'sociate with them at all. A man may have the feelings of a gentleman, although in a humble capacity; but how can I be intimate with such people as Mr Dispart or Mr Muddle, the carpenter? All very well in their way, Mr Simple, but what can you expect from officers who boil their 'tators in a cabbage-net hanging in the ship's coppers, when they know that there is one-third of a stove allowed them to cook their victuals on?"

Chapter XV

I go on service and am made prisoner by an old lady, who, not able to obtain my hand, takes part of my finger as a token—O'Brien rescues me— A lee shore and narrow escape.

Two or three days after this conversation with Mr Chucks, the captain ran the frigate in shore, and when within five miles we discovered two vessels under the land. We made all sail in chase, and cut them off from escaping round a sandy point which they attempted to weather. Finding that they could not effect their purpose, they ran on shore under a small battery of two guns, which commenced firing upon us. The first shot which whizzed between the masts had to me a most terrific sound, but the officers and men laughed at it, so of course I pretended to do the same, but in reality I could see nothing to laugh at. The captain ordered the starboard watch to be piped to quarters, and the boats to be cleared, ready for hoisting out; we then anchored within a mile of the battery, and returned the fire. In the meantime, the remainder of the ship's company hoisted out and lowered down four boats, which were manned and armed to storm the battery. I was very anxious to go on service, and O'Brien, who had command of the first cutter, allowed me to go with him, on condition that I stowed myself away under the foresheets, that the captain might not see me before the boats had shoved off. This I did, and was not discovered. We pulled in abreast towards the battery, and in less than ten minutes the boats were run on the beach, and we jumped out. The Frenchmen fired a gun at us as we pulled close to the shore, and then ran away, so that we took possession without any fighting, which, to confess the truth, I was not sorry for, as I did not think that I was old or strong enough to cope hand to hand with a grown-up man. There were a few fishermen's huts close to the battery, and while two of the boats went on board of the vessels, to see if they could be got off, and others were spiking the guns and destroying the carriages, I went with O'Brien to examine them: they were deserted by the people, as might have been supposed, but there was a great quantity of fish in them, apparently caught that morning. O'Brien pointed to a very large skate—"Murder in Irish!" cried he, "it's the very ghost of my grandmother! we'll have her if it's only for the family likeness. Peter, put your finger into the gills, and drag her down to the boat." I could not force my finger into the gills, and as the animal appeared quite dead, I hooked my finger into its mouth; but I made a sad mistake, for the animal was alive, and immediately closed its jaws, nipping my finger to the bone, and holding it so tight that I could not withdraw it, and the pain was too great to allow me to pull it away by main force, and tear my finger, which it held so fast. There I was, caught in a trap, and made a prisoner by a flat-fish. Fortunately, I hallooed loud enough to make O'Brien, who was close down to the boats, with a large codfish under each arm, turn round and come to my assistance. At first he could not help me, from laughing so much; but at last he forced open the jaw of the fish with his cutlass, and I got my finger out, but very badly torn indeed. I then took off my garter, tied it round the tail of the skate, and dragged it to the boat, which was all ready to shove off. The other boats had found it impossible to get the vessels off without unloading—so, in pursuance of the captain's orders, they were set on fire, and before we lost sight of them, had burnt down to the water's edge. My finger was very bad for three weeks, and the officers laughed at me very much, saying that I narrowly escaped being made a prisoner of by an "old maid."

We continued our cruise along the coast, until we had run down into the Bay of Arcason, where we captured two or three vessels, and obliged many more to run on shore. And here we had an instance showing, how very important it is that a captain of a man-of-war should be a good sailor, and have his ship in such discipline as to be strictly obeyed by his ship's company. I heard the officers unanimously assert, after the danger was over, that nothing but the presence of mind which was shown by Captain Savage could have saved the ship and her crew. We had chased a convoy of vessels to the bottom of the bay: the wind was very fresh when we hauled off, after running them on shore, and the surf on the beach even at that time was so great, that they were certain to go to pieces before they could be got afloat again. We were obliged to double-reef the topsails as soon as we hauled to the wind, and the weather looked very threatening. In an hour afterwards, the whole sky was covered with one black cloud, which sank so low as nearly to touch our mast-heads, and a tremendous sea, which appeared to have risen up almost by magic, rolled in upon us, setting the vessel on a dead lee shore. As the night closed in, it blew a dreadful gale, and the ship was nearly buried with the press of canvas which she was obliged to carry; for had we sea-room, we should have been lying-to under storm staysails; but we were forced to carry on at all risks, that we might claw off shore. The sea broke over as we lay in the trough, deluging us with water from the forecastle, aft to the binnacles; and very often as the ship descended with a plunge, it was with such force that I really thought she would divide in half with the violence of the shock. Double breechings were rove on the guns, and they were further secured with tackles, and strong cleats nailed behind the trunnions, for we heeled over so much when we lurched, that the guns were wholly supported by the breechings and tackles, and had one of them broken loose, it must have burst right through the lee side of the ship, and she must have foundered. The captain, first lieutenant, and most of the officers, remained on deck during the whole of the night; and really, what with the howling of the wind, the violence of the rain, the washing of the water about the decks, the working of the chain-pumps, and the creaking and groaning of the timbers, I thought that we must inevitably have been lost; and I said my prayers at least a dozen times during the night, for I felt it impossible to go to bed. I had often wished, out of curiosity, that I might be in a gale of wind, but I little thought it was to have been a scene of this description, or anything half so dreadful. What made it more appalling was, that we were on a lee shore, and the consultations of the captain and officers, and the eagerness with which they looked out for daylight, told us that we had other dangers to encounter besides the storm. At last the morning broke, and the look-out man upon the gangway called out, "Land on the lee beam." I perceived the master dash his fist against the hammock-rails, as if with vexation, and walk away without saying a word, and looking very grave.

"Up, there, Mr Wilson," said the captain, to the second lieutenant, "and see how far the land trends forward, and whether you can distinguish the point." The second lieutenant went up the main-rigging, and pointed with his hand to about two points before the beam.

"Do you see two hillocks inland?"

"Yes, sir," replied the second lieutenant.

"Then it is so," observed the captain to the master, "and if we weather it, we shall have more sea-room. Keep her full, and let her go through the water; do you hear, quarter-master?"

"Ay, ay, sir."

"Thus, and no nearer, my man. Ease her with a spoke or two when she sends; but be careful, or she'll take the wheel out of your hands."

It really was a very awful sight. When the ship was in the trough of the sea, you could distinguish nothing but a waste of tumultuous water; but when she was borne up on the summit of the enormous waves, you then looked down, as it were, upon a low, sandy coast, close to you, and covered with foam and breakers. "She behaves nobly," observed the captain, stepping aft to the binnacle, and looking at the compass; "if the wind does not baffle us, we shall weather." The captain had scarcely time to make the observation, when the sails shivered and flapped like thunder. "Up with the helm; what are you about, quarter-master?"

"The wind has headed us, sir," replied the quarter-master, coolly.

The captain and master remained at the binnacle watching the compass, and when the sails were again full, she had broken off two points, and the point of land was only a little on the lee bow.

"We must wear her round, Mr Falcon. Hands, wear ship—ready, oh, ready."

"She has come up again," cried the master, who was at the binnacle.

"Hold fast there a minute. How's her head now?"

"N.N.E., as she was before she broke off, sir."

"Pipe belay," said the captain. "Falcon," continued he, "if she breaks off again we may have no room to wear; indeed there is so little room now, that I must run the risk. Which cable was ranged last night—the best bower?"

"Yes, sir."

"Jump down, then, and see it double-bitted and stoppered at thirty fathoms. See it well done—our lives may depend upon it."

The ship continued to hold her course good; and we were within half a mile of the point, and fully expected to weather it, when again the wet and heavy sails flapped in the wind, and the ship broke off two points as before. The officers and seamen were aghast, for the ship's head was right on to the breakers. "Luff now, all you can, quarter-master," cried the captain. "Send the men aft directly. My lads, there is no time for words—I am going to *club-haul* the ship, for there is no room to wear. The only chance you have of safety is to be cool, watch my eye, and execute my orders with precision. Away to your stations for tacking ship. Hands by the best bower anchor. Mr Wilson, attend below with the carpenter and his mates, ready to cut away the cable at the moment that I give the order. Silence, there, fore and aft. Quarter-master, keep her full again for stays. Mind you ease the helm down when I tell you." About a minute passed before the captain gave any further orders. The ship had closed—to within a quarter of a mile of the beach, and the waves curled and topped around us, bearing us down upon the shore, which presented one continued surface of foam, extending to within half a cable's length of our position. The captain waved his hand in silence to the quarter-master at the wheel, and the helm was put down. The ship turned slowly to the wind, pitching and chopping as the sails were spilling. When she had lost her way, the captain gave the order, "Let go the anchor. We will haul all at once, Mr Falcon," said the captain. Not a word was spoken, the men went to the fore brace, which had not been manned; most of them knew, although I did not, that if the ship's head did not go round the other way, we should be on shore, and among the breakers in half a minute. I thought at the time that the captain had said that he would haul all the yards at once, there appeared to be doubt or dissent on the countenance of Mr Falcon; and I was afterwards told that he had not agreed with the captain, but he was too good an officer, and knew that there was no time for discussion, to make any remark; and the event proved that the captain was right. At last the ship was head to wind, and the captain gave the signal. The yards flew round with such a creaking noise, that I thought the masts had gone over the side, and the next moment the wind had caught the sails, and the ship, which for a moment or two had been on an even keel, careened over to her gunnel with its force. The captain, who stood upon the weather-hammock rails, holding by the main-rigging, ordered the helm amidships, looked full at the sails, and then at the cable, which grew broad upon the weather bow, and held the ship from nearing the shore. At last he cried, "Cut away the cable!" A few strokes of the axes were heard, and then the cable flew out of the hawsehole in a blaze of fire, from the violence of the friction, and disappeared under a huge wave, which struck us on the chess-tree, and deluged us with water fore and aft. But we were now on the other tack, and the ship regained her way and we had evidently increased our distance from the land. "My lads," said the captain to the ship's company, "you have behaved well, and I thank you; but I must tell you honestly that we have more difficulties to get through. We have to weather a point of the bay on this tack. Mr Falcon, splice the main-brace, and call the watch. How's her head, quarter-master?"

"S.W. by S. Southerly, sir."

"Very well; let her go through the water;" and the captain, beckoning to the master to follow him, went down into the cabin. As our immediate danger was over, I went down into the berth to see if I could get anything for breakfast, where I found O'Brien and two or three more.

"By the powers, it was as nate a thing as ever I saw done," observed O'Brien: "the slightest mistake as to time or management, and at this moment the flatfish would have been dubbing at our ugly carcases. Peter, you're not fond of flatfish, are you, my boy? We may thank Heaven and the captain, I can tell you that, my lads; but now, where's the chart, Robinson? Hand me down the parallel rules and compasses, Peter; they are in the corner of the shelf. Here we are now, a devilish sight too near this infernal point. Who knows how her head is?"

"I do, O'Brien: I heard the quarter-master tell the captain S.W. by S. Southerly."

"Let me see," continued O'Brien, "variation 2 1/4 lee way—rather too large an allowance of that, I'm afraid; but, however, we'll give her 2 1/2 points; the *Diomede* would blush to make any more, under any circumstances. Here—the compass—now we'll see;" and O'Brien advanced the parallel rule from the compass to the spot where the ship was placed on the chart. "Bother! you see it's as much as she'll do to weather the other point now, on this tack, and that's what the captain meant, when he told us we had more difficulty. I could have taken my Bible oath that we were clear of everything, if the wind held."

"See what the distance is, O'Brien," said Robinson. It was measured, and proved to be thirteen miles. "Only thirteen miles; and if we do weather, we shall do very well, for the bay is deep beyond. It's a rocky point, you see, just by way of variety. Well, my lads, I've a piece of comfort for you, anyhow. It's not long that you'll be kept in suspense, for by one o'clock this day, you'll either be congratulating each other upon your good luck, or you'll be past praying for. Come, put up the chart, for I hate to look at melancholy prospects; and, steward, see what you can find in the way of comfort." Some bread and cheese, with the remains of yesterday's boiled pork, were put on the table, with a bottle of rum, procured at the time they "spliced the mainbrace;" but we were all too anxious to eat much, and one by one returned on deck to see how the weather was, and if the wind at all favoured us. On deck the superior officers were in conversation with the captain, who had expressed the same fear that O'Brien had in our berth. The men, who knew what they had to expect—for this sort of intelligence is soon communicated through a ship—were assembled in knots, looking very grave, but at the same time not wanting in confidence. They knew that they could trust to the captain, as far as skill or courage could avail them, and sailors are too sanguine to despair, even at the last moment. As for myself, I felt such admiration for the captain, after what I had witnessed that morning, that, whenever the idea came over me, that in all probability I should be lost in a few hours, I could not help acknowledging how much more serious it was that such a man should be lost to his country. I do not intend to say that it consoled me; but it certainly made me still more regret the chances with which we were threatened.

Before twelve o'clock, the rocky point which we so much dreaded was in sight, broad on the lee-bow; and if the low sandy coast appeared terrible, how much more did this, even at a distance: the black masses of rock, covered with foam, which each minute dashed up in the air, higher than our lower mast-heads. The captain eyed it for some minutes in silence, as if in calculation.

"Mr Falcon," said he at last, "we must put the mainsail on her."

"She never can bear it, sir."

"She *must* bear it," was the reply. "Send the men aft to the mainsheet.
See that careful men attend the buntlines."

The mainsail was set, and the effect of it upon the ship was tremendous. She careened over so that her lee channels were under the water, and when pressed by a sea, the lee-side of the quarter-deck and gangway were afloat. She now reminded me of a goaded and fiery horse, mad with the stimulus applied; not rising as before, but forcing herself through whole seas, and dividing the waves, which poured in one continual torrent from the forecastle down upon the decks below. Four men were secured to the wheel—the sailors were obliged to cling, to prevent being washed away—the ropes were thrown in confusion to leeward, the shot rolled out of the lockers, and every eye was fixed aloft, watching the masts, which were expected every moment to go over the side. A heavy sea struck us on the broadside, and it was some moments before the ship appeared to recover herself; she reeled, trembled, and stopped her way, as if it had stupefied her. The first lieutenant looked at the captain, as if to say, "This will not do." "It is our only chance," answered the captain to the appeal. That the ship went faster through the water, and held a better wind, was certain; but just before we arrived at the point the gale increased in force. "If anything starts, we are lost, sir," observed the first lieutenant again.

"I am perfectly aware of it," replied the captain, in a calm tone; "but, as I said before, and you must now be aware, it is our only chance. The consequence of any carelessness or neglect in the fitting and securing of the rigging, will be felt now; and this danger, if we escape it, ought to remind us how much we have to answer for if we neglect our duty. The lives of a whole ship's company may be sacrificed by the neglect or incompetence of an officer when in harbour. I will pay you the compliment, Falcon, to say, that I feel convinced that the masts of the ship are as secure as knowledge and attention can make them."

The first lieutenant thanked the captain for his good opinion, and hoped it would not be the last compliment which he paid him.

"I hope not too; but a few minutes will decide the point."

The ship was now within two cables' lengths of the rocky point; some few of the men I observed to clasp their hands, but most of them were silently taking off their jackets, and kicking off their shoes, that they might not lose a chance of escape provided the ship struck.

"'Twill be touch and go indeed, Falcon," observed the captain (for I had clung to the belaying-pins, close to them, for the last half-hour that the mainsail had been set). "Come aft, you and I must take the helm. We shall want *nerve* there, and only there, now."

The captain and first lieutenant went aft, and took the forespokes of the wheel, and O'Brien, at a sign made by the captain, laid hold of the spokes behind him. An old quarter-master kept his station at the fourth. The roaring of the seas on the rocks, with the howling of the wind, were dreadful; but the sight was more dreadful than the noise. For a few moments I shut my eyes, but anxiety forced me to open them again. As near as I could judge, we were not twenty yards from the rocks, at the time that the ship passed abreast of them. We were in the midst of the foam, which boiled around us; and as the ship was driven nearer to them, and careened with the wave, I thought that our main-yard-arm would have touched the rock; and at this moment a gust of wind came on, which laid the ship on her beam-ends, and checked her progress through the water, while the accumulated noise was deafening. A few moments more the ship dragged on, another wave dashed over her and spent itself upon the rocks, while the spray was dashed back from them, and returned upon the decks. The main rock was within ten yards of her counter, when another gust of wind laid us on our beam-ends, the foresail and mainsail split, and were blown clean out of the bolt-ropes—the ship righted, trembling fore and aft. I looked astern: the rocks were to windward on our quarter, and we were safe. I thought at the time, that the ship, relieved of her courses, and again lifting over the waves, was not a bad similitude of the relief felt by us all at that moment; and, like her, we trembled as we panted with the sudden reaction, and felt the removal of the intense anxiety which oppressed our breasts.

The captain resigned the helm, and walked aft to look at the point, which was now broad on the weather quarter. In a minute or two, he desired Mr Falcon to get new sails up and bend them, and then went below to his cabin. I am sure it was to thank God for our deliverance: I did most fervently, not only then, but when I went to my hammock at night. We were now comparatively safe—in a few hours completely so; for strange to say, immediately after we had weathered the rocks, the gale abated, and before morning we had a reef out of the topsails. It was my afternoon watch, and perceiving Mr Chucks on the forecastle, I went forward to him, and asked him what he thought of it.

"Thought of it, sir!" replied he; "why, I always think bad of it when the elements won't allow my whistle to be heard; and I consider it hardly fair play. I never care if we are left to our own exertions; but how is it possible for a ship's company to do their best, when they cannot hear the boatswain's pipe? However, God be thanked, nevertheless, and make better Christians of us all! As for that carpenter, he is mad. Just before we weathered the point, he told me that it was just the same 27,600 and odd years ago. I do believe that on his death-bed (and he was not far from a very hard one yesterday), he will tell us how he died so many thousand years ago, of the same complaint. And that gunner of ours is a fool. Would you believe it, Mr Simple, he went crying about the decks, 'O my poor guns, what will become of them if they break loose?' He appeared to consider it of no consequence if the ship and ship's company were all lost, provided that his guns were safely landed on the beach.

"'Mr Dispart,' said I, at last, 'allow me to observe, in the most delicate way in the world, that you're a d——d old fool.' You see, Mr Simple, it's the duty of an officer to generalise, and be attentive to parts, only in consideration of the safety of the whole. I look after my anchors and cables, as I do after the rigging; not that I care for any of them in particular, but because the safety of a ship depends upon her being well found. I might just as well cry because we sacrificed an anchor and cable yesterday morning, to save the ship from going on shore."

"Very true, Mr Chucks," replied I.

"Private feelings," continued he, "must always be sacrificed for the public service. As you know, the lower deck was full of water, and all our cabins and chests were afloat; but I did not think then about my shirts, and look at them now, all blowing out in the forerigging, without a particle of starch left in the collars or the frills. I shall not be able to appear as an officer ought to do for the whole of the cruise."

As he said this, the cooper, going forward, passed by him, and jostled him in passing. "Beg pardon, sir," said the man, "but the ship lurched."

"The ship lurched, did it?" replied the boatswain, who, I am afraid, was not in the best of humours about his wardrobe. "And pray, Mr Cooper, why has heaven granted you two legs, with joints at the knees, except to enable you to counteract the horizontal deviation? Do you suppose they were meant for nothing but to work round a cask with? Hark, sir, did you take me for a post to scrub your pig's hide against? Allow me just to observe, Mr Cooper—just to insinuate, that when you pass an officer, it is your duty to keep at a respectable distance, and not to soil his clothes with your rusty iron jacket. Do you comprehend me, sir; or will this make you recollect in future?" The rattan was raised, and descended in a shower of blows, until the cooper made his escape into the head. "There, take that, you contaminating, stave-dubbing, gimlet-carrying, quintessence of a bung-hole! I beg your pardon, Mr Simple, for interrupting the conversation, but when duty calls, we must obey."

"Very true, Mr Chucks. It's now striking seven bells, and I must call the master—so good-by."

Chapter XVI

News from home—A *fatigue* party employed at Gibraltar—More particulars in the life of Mr Chucks—A brush with the enemy—A court-martial and a lasting impression.

A few days afterwards, a cutter joined us from Plymouth, with orders for the frigate to proceed forthwith to Gibraltar, where we should learn our destination. We were all very glad of this: for we had had quite enough of cruising in the Bay of Biscay; and, as we understood that we were to be stationed in the Mediterranean, we hoped to exchange gales of wind and severe weather, for fine breezes and a bright sky. The cutter brought out our letters and newspapers. I never felt more happy than I did when I found one put into my hands. It is necessary to be far from home and friends, to feel the real delight of receiving a letter. I went down into the most solitary place in the steerage, that I might enjoy it without interruption. I cried with pleasure before I opened it, but I cried a great deal more with grief, after I had read the contents—for my eldest brother Tom was dead of a typhus fever. Poor Tom! when I called to mind what tricks he used to play me—how he used to borrow my money and never pay me—and how he used to thrash me and make me obey him, because he was my eldest brother—I shed a torrent of tears at his loss; and then I reflected how miserable my poor mother must be, and I cried still more.

"What's the matter, spooney?" said O'Brien, coming up to me. "Who has been licking you now?"

"O, nobody," replied I; "but my eldest brother Tom is dead, and I have no other."

"Well, Peter, I dare say that your brother was a very good brother; but I'll tell you a secret. When you've lived long enough to have a beard to scrape at, you'll know better than to make a fuss about an elder brother. But you're a good, innocent boy just now, so I won't thrash you for it. Come, dry your eyes, Peter, and never mind it. We'll drink his health and long life to him, after supper, and then never think any more about it."

I was very melancholy for a few days; but it was so delightful running down the Portuguese and Spanish coasts, the weather was so warm, and the sea so smooth, that I am afraid I forgot my brother's death sooner than I ought to have done; but my spirits were cheered up, and the novelty of the scene prevented me from thinking. Every one, too, was so gay and happy, that I could not well be otherwise. In a fortnight, we anchored in Gibraltar Bay, and the ship was stripped to refit. There was so much duty to be done, that I did not like to go on shore. Indeed, Mr Falcon had refused some of my messmates, and I thought it better not to ask, although I was very anxious to see a place which was considered so extraordinary. One afternoon, I was looking over the gangway as the people were at supper, and Mr Falcon came up to me and said, "Well, Mr Simple, what are you thinking of?" I replied, touching my hat, that I was wondering how they had cut out the solid rock into galleries, and that they must be very curious.

"That is to say, that you are very curious to see them. Well, then, since you have been very attentive to your duty, and have not asked to go on shore, I will give you leave to go to-morrow morning and stay till gun-fire."

I was very much pleased at this, as the officers had a general invitation to dine with the mess, and all who could obtain leave being requested to come, I was enabled to join the party. The first lieutenant had excused himself on the plea of there being so much to attend to on board; but most of the gun-room officers and some of the midshipmen obtained leave. We walked about the town and fortifications until dinner-time, and then we proceeded to the barracks. The dinner was very good, and we were all very merry; but after the dessert had been brought in, I slipped away with a young ensign, who took me all over the galleries, and explained everything to me, which was a much better way of employing my time than doing as the others did, which the reader will acknowledge. I was at the sally-port before gun-fire—the boat was there, but no officers made their appearance. The gun fired, the drawbridge was hauled up, and I was afraid that I should be blamed; but the boat was not ordered to shove off, as it was waiting for commissioned officers. About an hour afterwards, when it was quite dark, the sentry pointed his arms and challenged a person advancing with, "Who comes there?"—"Naval officer, drunk on a wheelbarrow," was the reply, in a loud singing voice. Upon which, the sentry recovered his arms, singing in return, "Pass naval officer, drunk on a wheelbarrow—and all's well!" and then appeared a soldier in his fatigue dress, wheeling down the third lieutenant in a wheelbarrow, so tipsy that he could not stand or speak. Then the sentry challenged again, and the answer was, "Another naval officer, drunk on a wheelbarrow;" upon which the sentry replied as before, "Pass, another naval officer, drunk on a wheelbarrow —and all's well." This was my friend O'Brien, almost as bad as the third lieutenant; and so they continued for ten minutes, challenging and passing, until they wheeled down the remainder of the party, with the exception of the second lieutenant, who walked arm and arm with the officer who brought down the order for lowering the drawbridge. I was much shocked, for I considered it very disgraceful; but I afterwards was told, which certainly admitted of some excuse, that the mess were notorious for never permitting any of their guests to leave the table sober. They were all safely put into the boat, and I am glad to say, the first lieutenant was in bed and did not see them; but I could not help acknowledging the truth of an observation made by one of the men as the officers were handed into the boat, "I say, Bill, if *them* were *we*, what a precious twisting we should get to-morrow at six bells!"

The ship remained in Gibraltar Bay about three weeks, during which time we had refitted the rigging fore and aft, restowed and cleaned the hold, and painted outside. She never looked more beautiful than she did when, in obedience to our orders, we made sail to join the admiral. We passed Europa Point with a fair wind, and at sunset we were sixty miles from the Rock, yet it was distinctly to be seen, like a blue cloud, but the outline perfectly correct. I mention this, as perhaps my reader would not have believed that it was possible to see land at such a distance. We steered for Cape de Gatte, and we were next day close in shore. I was very much delighted with the Spanish coast, mountain upon mountain, hill upon hill, covered with vines nearly to their summits. We might have gone on shore at some places, for at that time we were friendly with the Spaniards, but the captain was in too great a hurry to join the admiral. We had very light winds, and a day or two afterwards we were off Valencia, nearly becalmed. I was on the gangway, looking through a telescope at the houses and gardens round the city, when Mr Chucks, the boatswain, came up to me. "Mr Simple, oblige me with that glass a moment; I wish to see if a building remains there, which I have some reason to remember."

"What, were you ever on shore there?"

"Yes I was, Mr Simple, and nearly *stranded*, but I got off again without much damage."

"How do you mean—were you wrecked, then?"

"Not my ship, Mr Simple, but my peace of mind was for some time; but it's many years ago, when I was first made boatswain of a corvette (during this conversation he was looking through the telescope); yes, there it is," said he; "I have it in the field. Look, Mr Simple, do you see a small church, with a spire of glazed tiles, shining like a needle?"

"Yes, I do."

"Well, then, just above it, a little to the right, there is a long white house, with four small windows—below the grove of orange-trees."

"I see it," replied I; "but what about that house, Mr Chucks?"

"Why, thereby hangs a tale," replied he, giving a sigh, which raised and then lowered the frill of his shirt at least six inches.

"Why, what is the mystery, Mr Chucks?"

"I'll tell you, Mr Simple. With one who lived in that house, I was for the first, and for the last time, in love."

"Indeed! I should like very much to hear the story."

"So you shall, Mr Simple, but I must beg that you will not mention it, as young gentlemen are apt to quiz; and I think that being quizzed hurts my authority with the men. It is now about sixteen years back—we were then on good terms with the Spaniards, as we are now. I was then little more than thirty years old, and had just received my warrant as boatswain. I was considered a well-looking young man at that time, although lately I have, to a certain degree, got the better of that."

"Well, I consider you a remarkably good-looking man now, Mr Chucks."

"Thank you, Mr Simple, but nothing improves by age, that I know of, except rum. I used to dress very smart, and 'cut the boatswain' when I was on shore: and perhaps I had not lost so much of the polish I had picked up in good society. One evening, I was walking in the Plaza, when I saw a female ahead, who appeared to be the prettiest moulded little vessel that I ever cast my eyes on. I followed in her wake, and examined her: such a clean run I never beheld—so neat, too, in all her rigging— everything so nicely stowed under hatches. And then, she sailed along in such a style, at one moment lifting so lightly, just like a frigate, with her topsails on the caps, that can't help going along. At another time, as she turned a corner sharp up in the wind—wake as straight as an arrow—no leeway—I made all sail to sheer alongside of her, and, when under quarter, examined her close. Never saw such a fine swell in the counter, and all so trim—no ropes towing overboard. Well, Mr Simple, I said to myself, 'D—n it, if her figurehead and bows be finished off by the same builder, she's perfect.' So I shot ahead, and yawed a little—caught a peep at her through her veil, and saw two black eyes—as bright as beads, and as large as damsons. I saw quite enough, and not wishing to frighten her, I dropped astern. Shortly afterwards she altered her course, steering for that white house. Just as she was abreast of it, and I playing about her weather quarter, the priests came by in procession, taking the *host* to somebody who was dying. My little frigate lowered her top-gallant sails out of respect, as other nations used to do, and ought now, and be d——d to them, whenever they pass the flag of old England—"

"How do you mean?" inquired I.

"I mean that she spread her white handkerchief, which fluttered in her hand as she went along, and knelt down upon it on one knee. I did the same, because I was obliged to heave-to to keep my station, and I thought, that if she saw me, it would please her. When she got up, I was on my legs also; but in my hurry I had not chosen a very clean place, and I found out, when I got up again, that my white jean trousers were in a shocking mess. The young lady turned round, and seeing my misfortune, laughed, and then went into the white house, while I stood there like a fool, first looking at the door of the house, and then at my trousers. However, I thought that I might make it the means of being acquainted with her, so I went to the door and knocked. An old gentleman in a large cloak, who was her father, came out; I pointed to my trousers, and requested him in Spanish to allow me a little water to clean them. The daughter then came from within, and told her father how the accident had happened. The old gentleman was surprised that an English officer was so good a Christian, and appeared to be pleased. He asked me very politely to come in, and sent an old woman for some water. I observed that he was smoking a bit of paper, and having very fortunately about a couple of dozen of real Havannahs in my pocket (for I never smoke anything else, Mr Simple, it being my opinion that no gentleman can), I took them out, and begged his acceptance of them. His eyes glistened at the sight of them, but he refused to take more than one; however, I insisted upon his taking the whole bundle, telling him that I had plenty more on board, reserving one for myself, that I might smoke it with him. He then requested me to sit down, and the old woman brought some sour wine, which I declared was very good, although it made me quite ill afterwards. He inquired of me whether I was a good Christian. I replied that I was. I knew that he meant a Catholic, for they call us heretics, Mr Simple. The daughter then came in without her veil, and she was perfection; but I did not look at her, or pay her any attention after the first salutation, I was so afraid of making the old gentleman suspicious. He then asked what I was—what sort of officer— was I captain? I replied that I was not. Was I 'tenente? which means lieutenant; I answered that I was not, again, but with an air of contempt, as if I was something better. What was I, then? I did not know the Spanish for boatswain, and, to tell the truth, I was ashamed of my condition. I knew that there was an officer in Spain called corregidor, which means a corrector in English, or one who punishes. Now I thought that quite near enough for my purpose, and I replied that I was the corregidor. Now, Mr Simple, a corregidor in Spain is a person of rank and consequence, so they imagined that I must be the same, and they appeared to be pleased. The young lady then inquired if I was of good family—whether I was a gentleman or not. I replied that I hoped so. I remained with them for half-an-hour more, when my segar was finished; I then rose, and thanking the old gentleman for his civility, begged that I might be allowed to bring him a few more segars, and took my leave. The daughter opened the street door, and I could not refrain from taking her hand and kissing it—"

"Where's Mr Chucks? call the boatswain there forward," hallooed out the lieutenant.

"Here I am, sir," replied Mr Chucks, hastening aft, and leaving me and his story.

"The captain of the maintop reports the breast backstay much chafed in the serving. Go up and examine it," said the first lieutenant.

"Yes, sir," replied the boatswain, who immediately went up the rigging.

"And, Mr Simple, attend to the men scraping the spots off the quarter-deck."

"Yes, sir," replied I; and thus our conversation was broken up.

The weather changed that night, and we had a succession of rain and baffling winds for six or seven days, during which I had no opportunity of hearing the remainder of the boatswain's history. We joined the fleet off Toulon, closed the admiral's ship, and the captain went on board to pay his respects. When he returned, we found out, through the first lieutenant, that we were to remain with the fleet until the arrival of another frigate, expected in about a fortnight, and then the admiral had promised that we should have a cruise. The second day after we had joined, we were ordered to form part of the in-shore squadron, consisting of two line-of-battle ships and four frigates. The French fleet used to come out and manoeuvre within range of their batteries, or, if they proceeded further from the shore, they took good care that they had a leading wind to return again into port. We had been in-shore about a week, every day running close in, and counting the French fleet in the harbour, to see that they were all safe, and reporting it to the admiral by signal, when one fine morning, the whole of the French vessels were perceived to hoist their topsails, and in less than an hour they were under weigh, and came out of the harbour. We were always prepared for action, night and day, and, indeed, often exchanged a shot or two with the batteries when we reconnoitred; the in-shore squadron could not, of course, cope with the whole French fleet, and our own was about twelve miles in the offing, but the captain of the line-of-battle ship who commanded us, hove-to, as if in defiance, hoping to entice them further out. This was not very easy to do, as the French knew that a shift of wind might put it out of their power to refuse an action, which was what they would avoid, and what we were so anxious to bring about. I say we, speaking of the English, not of myself, for to tell the truth, I was not so very anxious. I was not exactly afraid, but I had an unpleasant sensation at the noise of a cannon-ball, which I had not as yet got over. However, four of the French frigates made sail towards us, and hove-to, when within four miles, three or four line-of-battle ships following them as if to support them. Our captain made signal for permission to close the enemy, which was granted, with our pennants, and those of another frigate. We immediately made all sail, beat to quarters, put out the fires, and opened the magazines. The French line-of-battle ships perceiving that only two of our frigates were sent against their four, hove-to at about the same distance from their frigates, as our line-of-battle ships and other frigates were from us. In the meantime our main fleet continued to work in shore under a press of sail, and the French main fleet also gradually approached the detached ships. The whole scene reminded me of the tournaments I had read of; it was a challenge in the lists, only that the enemy were two to one; a fair acknowledgment on their parts of our superiority. In about an hour we closed so near, that the French frigates made sail and commenced firing. We reserved our fire until within a quarter of a mile, when we poured our broadside into the headmost frigate, exchanging with her on opposite tacks. The *Sea-horse*, who followed, also gave her a broadside. In this way we exchanged broadsides with the whole four, and we had the best of it, for they could not load so fast as we could. We were both ready again for the frigates as they passed us, but they were not ready with their broadside for the *Sea-horse*, who followed us very closely, so that they had two broadsides each, and we had only four in the *Diomede*, the *Sea-horse* not having one. Our rigging was cut up a great deal, and we had six or seven men wounded, but none killed. The French frigates suffered more, and their admiral perceiving that they were cut up a good deal, made a signal of recall. In the meantime we had both tacked, and were ranging up on the weather quarter of the sternmost frigate: the line-of-battle ships perceiving this, ran down with the wind, two points free, to support their frigates, and our in-shore squadron made all sail to support us, nearly laying up for where we were. But the wind was what is called at sea a soldier's wind, that is, blowing so that the ships could lie either way, so as to run out or into the harbour, and the French frigates, in obedience to their orders, made sail for their fleet in-shore, the line-of-battle ships coming out to support them. But our captain would not give it up, although we all continued to near the French line-of-battle ships every minute—we ran in with the frigates, exchanging broadsides with them as fast as we could. One of them lost her foretopmast, and dropped astern, and we hoped to cut her off, but the others shortened sail to support her. This continued for about twenty minutes, when the French line-of-battle ships were not more than a mile from us, and our own commodore had made the signal of our recall, for he thought that we should be overpowered and taken. But the *Sea-horse*, who saw the recall up, did not repeat it, and our captain was determined not to see it, and ordered the signal-man not to look that way. The action continued, two of the French frigates were cut to pieces, and complete wrecks, when the French line-of-battle ships commenced firing. It was then high time to be off. We each of us poured in another broadside, and then wore round for our own squadron, which was about four miles off, and rather to leeward, standing in to our assistance. As we wore round, our main-topmast, which had been badly wounded, fell over the side, and the French perceiving this, made all sail, with the hope of capturing us; but the *Sea-horse* remained with us, and we threw up in the wind, and raked them until they were within two cables' lengths of us. Then we stood on for our own ships; at last one of the line-of-battle ships, which sailed as well as the frigates, came abreast of us, and poured in a broadside, which brought everything about our ears, and I thought we must be taken; but on the contrary, although we lost several men, the captain said to the first lieutenant, "Now, if they only wait a little longer, they are nabbed, as sure as fate." Just at this moment, our own line-of-battle ships opened their fire, and then the tables were turned. The French tacked, and stood in as fast as they could, followed by the in-shore squadron, with the exception of our ship, which was too much crippled to chase them. One of their frigates had taken in tow the other, who had lost her top-mast, and our squadron came up with her very fast. The English fleet were also within three miles, standing in, and the French fleet standing out, to the assistance of the other ships which had been engaged. I thought, and so did everybody, that there would be a general action, but we were disappointed; the frigate which towed the other, finding that she could not escape, cast her off, and left her to her fate, which was to haul down her colours to the commodore of the in-shore squadron. The chase was continued until the whole of the French vessels were close under their batteries, and then our fleet returned to its station with the prize, which proved to be the *Narcisse*, of thirty-six guns, Captain Le Pelleteon. Our captain obtained a great deal of credit for his gallant behaviour. We had three men killed, and Robinson, the midshipman, and ten men wounded, some of them severely. I think this action cured me of my fear of a cannon-ball, for during the few days we remained with the fleet, we often were fired at when we reconnoitred, but I did not care anything for them. About the time she was expected, the frigate joined, and we had permission to part company. But before I proceed with the history of our cruise, I shall mention the circumstances attending a court-martial, which took place during the time that we were with the fleet, our captain having been recalled from the in-shore squadron to sit as one of the members. I was the midshipman appointed to the captain's gig, and remained on board of the admiral's ship during the whole of the time that the court was sitting. Two seamen, one an Englishman, and the other a Frenchman, were tried for desertion from one of our frigates. They had left their ship about three months, when the frigate captured a French privateer, and found them on board as part of her crew. For the Englishman, of course, there was no defence; he merited the punishment of death, to which he was immediately sentenced. There may be some excuse for desertion, when we consider that the seamen are taken into the service by force, but there could be none for fighting against his country. But the case of the Frenchman was different. He was born and bred in France, had been one of the crew of the French gunboats at Cadiz, where he had been made a prisoner by the Spaniards, and expecting his throat to be cut every day, had contrived to escape on board of the frigate lying in the harbour, and entered into our service, I really believe to save his life. He was nearly two years in the frigate before he could find an opportunity of deserting from her, and returning to France, when he joined the French privateer. During the time that he was in the frigate, he bore an excellent character. The greatest point against him was, that on his arrival at Gibraltar he had been offered, and had received the bounty. When the

Englishman was asked what he had to say in his defence, he replied that he had been pressed out of an American ship, that he was an American born, and that he had never taken the bounty. But this was not true. The defence of the Frenchman was considered so very good for a person in his station of life, that I obtained a copy of it, which ran as follows:—

"Mr President, and Officers of the Honourable Court;—It is with the greatest humility that I venture to address you. I shall be very brief, nor shall I attempt to disprove the charges which have been made against me, but confine myself to a few facts, the consideration of which will, I trust, operate upon your feelings in mitigation of the punishment to which I may be sentenced for my fault—a fault which proceeded, not from any evil motive, but from an ardent love for my country. I am by birth a Frenchman; my life has been spent in the service of France until a few months after the revolution in Spain, when I, together with those who composed the French squadron at Cadiz, was made a prisoner. The hardships and cruel usage which I endured became insupportable. I effected my escape, and after wandering about the town for two or three days, in hourly expectation of being assassinated, the fate of too many of my unfortunate countrymen; desperate from famine, and perceiving no other chance of escaping from the town, I was reduced to the necessity of offering myself as a volunteer on board of an English frigate. I dared not, as I ought to have done, acknowledge myself to have been a prisoner, from the dread of being delivered up to the Spaniards. During the period that I served on board of your frigate, I confidently rely upon the captain and the officers for my character.

"The love of our country, although dormant for a time, will ultimately be roused, and peculiar circumstances occurred which rendered the feeling irresistible. I returned to my duty, and for having so done, am I to be debarred from again returning to that country so dear to me— from again beholding my aged parents, who bless me in my absence—from again embracing my brothers and sisters—to end my days upon a scaffold; not for the crime which I did commit in entering into your service, but for an act of duty and repentance—that of returning to my own? Allow me to observe, that the charge against me is not for entering your service, but for having deserted from it. For the former, not even my misery can be brought forward but in extenuation; for the latter I have a proud consciousness, which will, I trust, be my support in my extremity.

"Gentlemen, I earnestly entreat you to consider my situation, and I am sure that your generous hearts will pity me. Let that love of your country, which now animates your breasts, and induces you to risk your lives and your all, now plead for me. Already has British humanity saved thousands of my countrymen from the rage of the Spaniards; let that same humanity be extended now, and induce my judges to add one more to the list of those who, although our nations are at war, if they are endowed with feeling, can have but one sentiment towards their generous enemy—a sentiment overpowering all other, that of a deep-felt gratitude."[1]

Whatever may have been the effect of the address upon the court individually, it appeared at the time to have none upon them as a body. Both the men were condemned to death, and the day after the morrow was fixed for their execution. I watched the two prisoners as they went down the side, to be conducted on board of their own ship. The Englishman threw himself down in the stern sheets of the boat, every minor consideration apparently swallowed up in the thought of his approaching end; but the Frenchman, before he sat down, observing that the seat was a little dirty, took out his silk handkerchief, and spread it on the seat, that he might not soil his nankeen trowsers.

I was ordered to attend the punishment on the day appointed. The sun shone so brightly, and the sky was so clear, the wind so gentle and mild, that it appeared hardly possible that it was to be a day of such awe and misery to the two poor men, or of such melancholy to the fleet in general. I pulled up my boat with the others belonging to the ships of the fleet, in obedience to the orders of the officer superintending, close to the fore-chains of the ship. In about half-an-hour afterwards, the prisoners made their appearance on the scaffold, the caps were pulled over their eyes, and the gun fired underneath them. When the smoke rolled away, the Englishman was swinging at the yard-arm, but the Frenchman was not; he had made a spring when the gun fired, hoping to break his neck at once, and put an end to his misery; but he fell on the edge of the scaffold, where he lay. We thought that his rope had given way, and it appeared that he did the same, for he made an enquiry, but they returned him no answer. He was kept on the scaffold during the whole hour that the Englishman remained suspended; his cap had been removed, and he looked occasionally at his fellow-sufferer. When the body was lowered down, he considered that his time was come, and attempted to leap overboard. He was restrained and led aft, where his reprieve was read to him and his arms were unbound. But the effect of the shock was too much for his mind; he fell down in a swoon, and when he recovered, his senses had left him, and I heard that he never recovered them, but was sent home to be confined as a maniac. I thought, and the result proved, that it was carried too far. It is not the custom, when a man is reprieved, to tell him so, until after he is on the scaffold, with the intention that his awful situation at the time may make a lasting impression upon him during the remainder of his life; but, as a foreigner, he was not aware of our customs, and the hour of intense feeling which he underwent was too much for his reason. I must say, that this circumstance was always a source of deep regret in the whole fleet, and that his being a Frenchman, instead of an Englishman, increased the feeling of commiseration.

[Footnote 1: This is fact.—AUTHOR.]

Chapter XVII

Mr Chucks's opinion on proper names—He finishes his Spanish tale—March of intellect among the Warrant Officers.

We were all delighted when our signal was hoisted to "part company," as we anticipated plenty of prize-money under such an enterprising captain. We steered for the French coast, near to its junction with Spain, the captain having orders to intercept any convoys sent to supply the French army with stores and provisions.

The day after we parted company with the fleet, Mr Chucks finished his story.

"Where was I, Mr Simple, when I left off?" said he, as we took a seat upon the long eighteen.

"You had just left the house after having told them that you were a corregidor, and had kissed the lady's hand."

"Very true. Well, Mr Simple, I did not call there for two or three days afterwards; I did not like to go too soon, especially as I saw the young lady every day in the Plaza. She would not speak to me, but, to make use of their expression, 'she gave me her eyes,' and sometimes a sweet smile. I recollect I was so busy looking at her one day, that I tripped over my sword, and nearly fell on my nose, at which she burst out a laughing."

"Your sword, Mr Chucks? I thought boatswains never wore swords."

"Mr Simple, a boatswain is an officer, and is entitled to a sword as well as the captain, although we have been laughed out of it by a set of midshipman monkeys. I always wore my sword at that time; but now-a-days, a boatswain is counted as nobody, unless there is hard work to do, and then it's Mr Chucks this, and Mr Chucks that. But I'll explain to you how it is, Mr Simple, that we boatswains have lost so much of consequence and dignity. The first lieutenants are made to do the boatswain's duty now-a-days, and if they could only wind the call, they might scratch the boatswain's name off half the ships' books in his Majesty's service. But to go on with my yarn. On the fourth day, I called with my handkerchief full of segars for the father, but he was at siesta, as they called it. The old serving-woman would not let me in at first; but I shoved a dollar between her skinny old fingers, and that altered her note. She put her old head out, and looked round to see if there was anybody in the street to watch us, and then she let me in and shut the door. I walked into the room, and found myself alone with Seraphina."

"Seraphina!—what a fine name!"

"No name can be too fine for a pretty girl, or a good frigate, Mr Simple; for my part, I'm very fond of these hard names. Your Bess, and Poll, and Sue, do very well for the Point, or Castle Rag; but in my opinion, they degrade a lady. Don't you observe, Mr Simple, that all our gun-brigs, a sort of vessel that will certainly d———n the inventor to all eternity, have nothing but low common names, such as Pincher, Thrasher, Boxer, Badger, and all that sort, which are quite good enough for them; whereas all our dashing saucy frigates have names as long as the main-top bowling, and hard enough to break your jaw—such as Melpomeny, Terpsichory, Arethusy, Bacchanty—fine flourishers, as long as their pennants which dip alongside in a calm."

"Very true," replied I; "but do you think, then, it is the same with family names?"

"Most certainly, Mr Simple. When I was in good society, I rarely fell in with such names as Potts or Bell, or Smith or Hodges; it was always Mr Fortescue, or Mr Fitzgerald, or Mr Fitzherbert—seldom bowed, sir, to anything under *three* syllables."

"Then I presume, Mr Chucks, you are not fond of your own name?"

"There you touch me, Mr Simple; but it is quite good enough for a boatswain," replied Mr Chucks, with a sigh. "I certainly did very wrong to impose upon people as I did, but I've been severely punished for it— it has made me discontented and unhappy ever since. Dearly have I paid for my spree; for there is nothing so miserable as to have ideas above your station in life, Mr Simple. But I must make sail again. I was three hours with Seraphina before her father came home, and during that time I never was quietly at an anchor for above a minute. I was on my knees, vowing and swearing, kissing her feet and kissing her hand, till at last I got to her lips, working my way up as regularly as one who gets in at the hawsehole and crawls aft to the cabin windows. She was very kind, and she smiled, and sighed, and pushed me off, and squeezed my hand, and was angry—frowning till I was in despair, and then making me happy again with her melting dark eyes beaming kindly, till at last she said that she would try to love me, and asked me whether I would marry her and live in Spain. I replied that I would; and, indeed, I felt as if I could, only at the time the thought occurred to me where the rhino was to come from, for I could not live, as her father did, upon a paper segar and a piece of melon per day. At all events, as far as words went, it was a settled thing. When her father came home, the old servant told him that I had just at that moment arrived, and that, his daughter was in her own room; so she was, for she ran away as soon as she heard her father knock. I made my bow to the old gentleman, and gave him the segars. He was serious at first, but the sight of them put him into good humour, and in a few minutes Donna Seraphina (they call a lady a Donna in Spain) came in, saluting me ceremoniously, as if we had not been kissing for the hour together. I did not remain long, as it was getting late, so I took a glass of the old gentleman's sour wine, and walked off, with a request from him to call again, the young lady paying me little or no attention during the time that I remained, or at my departure."

"Well, Mr Chucks," observed I, "it appears to me that she was a very deceitful young person."

"So she was, Mr Simple; but a man in love can't see, and I'll tell you why. If he wins the lady, he is as much in love with himself as with her, because he is so proud of his conquest. That was my case. If I had had my eyes, I might have seen that she who could cheat her old father for a mere stranger, would certainly deceive him in his turn. But if love makes a man blind, vanity, Mr Simple, makes him blinder. In short, I was an ass."

"Never mind, Mr Chucks, there was a good excuse for it."

"Well, Mr Simple, I met her again and again, until I was madly in love, and the father appeared to be aware of what was going on, and to have no objection. However, he sent for a priest to talk with me, and I again said that I was a good Catholic. I told him that I was in love with the young lady, and would marry her. The father made no objection on my promising to remain in Spain, for he would not part with his only daughter. And there again I was guilty of deceit, first, in making a promise I did not intend to keep, and then in pretending that I was a Catholic. Honesty is the best policy, Mr Simple, in the long run, you may depend upon it."

"So my father has always told me, and I have believed him," replied I.

"Well, sir, I am ashamed to say that I did worse; for the priest, after the thing was settled, asked me whether I had confessed lately. I knew what he meant, and answered that I had not. He motioned me down on my knees; but, as I could not speak Spanish enough for that, I mumbled-jumbled something or another, half Spanish and half English, and ended with putting four dollars in his hand for *carita*, which means charity. He was satisfied at the end of my confession, whatever he might have been at the beginning, and gave me absolution, although he could not have understood what my crimes were; but four dollars, Mr Simple, will pay for a deal of crime in that country. And now, sir, comes the winding up of this business. Seraphina told me that she was going to the opera with some of her relations, and asked me if I would be there; that the captain of the frigate, and all the other officers were going, and that she wished me to go with her. You see, Mr Simple, although Seraphina's father was so poor, that a mouse would have starved in his house, still he was of good family, and connected with those who were much better off. He was a Don himself, and had fourteen or fifteen long names, which I forget now. I refused to go with her, as I knew that the service would not permit a boatswain to sit in an opera-box, when the captain and first lieutenant were there. I told her that I had promised to go on board and look after the men while the captain went on shore; thus, as you'll see, Mr Simple, making myself a man of consequence, only to be more mortified in the end. After she had gone to the opera, I was very uncomfortable: I was afraid that the captain would see her, and take a fancy to her. I walked up and down, outside, until I was so full of love and jealousy that I determined to go into the pit and see what she was about. I soon discovered her in a box, with some other ladies, and with them were my captain and first lieutenant. The captain, who spoke the language well, was leaning over her, talking and laughing, and she was smiling at what he said. I resolved to leave immediately, lest she should see me and discover that I had told her a falsehood; but they appeared so intimate that I became so jealous I could not quit the theatre. At last she perceived me, and beckoned her hand; I looked very angry, and left the theatre cursing like a madman. It appeared that she pointed me out to the captain, and asked him who I was; he told her my real situation on board, and spoke of me with contempt. She asked whether I was not a man of family; at this the captain and first lieutenant both burst out laughing, and said that I was a common sailor who had been promoted to a higher rank for good behaviour—not exactly an officer, and anything but a gentleman. In short, Mr Simple, I was *blown upon*, and, although the captain said more than was correct, as I learnt afterwards through the officers, still I deserved it. Determined to know the worst, I remained outside till the opera was over, when I saw her come out, the captain and first lieutenant walking with the party—so that I could not speak with her. I walked to a posada (that's an inn), and drank seven bottles of rosolio to keep myself quiet; then I went on board, and the second lieutenant, who was commanding officer, put me under arrest for being intoxicated. It was a week before I was released; and you can't imagine what I suffered, Mr Simple. At last, I obtained leave to go on shore, and I went to the house to decide my fate. The old woman opened the door, and then calling me a thief, slammed it in my face; as I retreated, Donna Seraphina came to the window, and, waving her hand with a contemptuous look, said, 'Go, and God be with you, Mr Gentleman.' I returned on board in such a rage, that if I could have persuaded the gunner to have given me a ball cartridge, I should have shot myself through the head. What made the matter worse, I was laughed at by everybody in the ship, for the captain and first lieutenant had made the story public."

"Well, Mr Chucks," replied I, "I cannot help being sorry for you, although you certainly deserved to be punished for your dishonesty. Was that the end of the affair?"

"As far as I was concerned it was, Mr Simple; but not as respected others. The captain took my place, but without the knowledge of the father. After all, they neither had great reason to rejoice at the exchange."

"How so, Mr Chucks—what do you mean?"

"Why, Mr Simple, the captain did not make an honest woman of her, as I would have done; and the father discovered what was going on, and one night the captain was brought on board run through the body. We sailed immediately for Gibraltar, and it was a long while before he got round again: and then he had another misfortune."

"What was that?"

"Why he lost his boatswain, Mr Simple; for I could not bear the sight of him—and then he lost (as you must know, not from your own knowledge, but from that of others) a boatswain who knows his duty."

"Every one says so, Mr Chucks. I'm sure that our captain would be very sorry to part with you."

"I trust that every captain has been with whom I've sailed, Mr Simple. But that was not all he lost, Mr Simple; for the next cruise he lost his masts; and the loss of his masts occasioned the loss of his ship, since which he has never been trusted with another, but is laid on the shelf. Now he never carried away a spar of any consequence during the whole time that I was with him. A mast itself is nothing, Mr Simple—only a piece of wood—but fit your rigging properly, and then a mast is strong as a rock. Only ask Mr Faulkner, and he'll tell you the same; and I never met an officer who knew better how to support a mast."

"Did you ever hear any more of the young lady?"

"Yes; about a year afterwards I returned there in another ship. She had been shut up in a convent, and forced to take the veil. Oh, Mr Simple! if you knew how I loved that girl! I have never been more than polite to a woman since, and shall die a bachelor. You can't think how I was capsized the other day, when I looked at the house; I have hardly touched beef or pork since, and am in debt two quarts of rum more than my allowance. But, Mr Simple, I have told you this in confidence, and I trust you are too much of a gentleman to repeat it; for I cannot bear quizzing from young midshipmen."

I promised that I would not mention it, and I kept my word; but circumstances which the reader will learn in the sequel have freed me from the condition. Nobody can quiz him now.

We gained our station off the coast of Perpignan; and as soon as we made the land, we were most provokingly driven off by a severe gale. I am not about to make any remarks about the gale, for one storm is so like another; but I mention it, to account for a conversation which took place, and with which I was very much amused. I was near to the captain when he sent for Mr Muddle, the carpenter, who had been up to examine the main-topsail yard, which had been reported as sprung.

"Well, Mr Muddle," said the captain.

"Sprung, sir, most decidedly; but I think we'll be able to *mitigate* it."

"Will you be able to secure it for the present, Mr Muddle?" replied the captain, rather sharply.

"We'll *mitigate* it, sir, in half an hour."

"I wish that you would use common phrases when you speak to me, Mr Muddle. I presume, by mitigate, you mean to say that you can secure it. Do you mean so, sir, or do you not?"

"Yes, sir, that is what I mean, most decidedly. I hope no offence, Captain Savage; but I did not intend to displease you by my language."

"Very good, Mr Muddle," replied the captain; "it's the first time that I have spoken to you on the subject, recollect that it will be the last."

"The first time!" replied the carpenter, who could not forget his philosophy; "I beg your pardon, Captain Savage, you found just the same fault with me on this quarter-deck 27,672 years ago, and—"

"If I did, Mr Muddle," interrupted the captain, very angrily, "depend upon it that at the same time I ordered you to go aloft, and attend to your duty, instead of talking nonsense on the quarter-deck; and, although, as you say, you and I cannot recollect it, if you did not obey that order instantaneously, I also put you in confinement, and obliged you to leave the ship as soon as she returned to port. Do you understand me, sir?"

"I rather think, sir," replied the carpenter, humbly touching his hat, and walking to the main rigging, "that no such thing took place, for I went up immediately, as I do now; and," continued the carpenter, who was incurable, as he ascended the rigging, "as I shall again in another 27,672 years."

"That man is incorrigible with his confounded nonsense," observed the captain to the first lieutenant. "Every mast in the ship would go over the side, provided he could get any one to listen to his ridiculous theory."

"He is not a bad carpenter, sir," replied the first lieutenant.

"He is not," rejoined the captain; "but there is a time for all things."

Just at this moment, the boatswain came down the rigging.

"Well, Mr Chucks, what do you think of the yard? Must we shift it?" inquired the captain.

"At present, Captain Savage," replied the boatswain, "I consider it to be in a state which may be called precarious, and not at all permanent; but, with a little human exertion, four fathom of three-inch, and half-a-dozen tenpenny nails, it may last, for all I know, until it is time for it to be sprung again."

"I do not understand you, Mr Chucks. I know no time when a yard ought to be sprung."

"I did not refer to our time, sir," replied the boatswain, "but to the 27,672 years of Mr Muddle, when—"

"Go forward immediately, sir, and attend to your duty," cried the captain, in a very angry voice; and then he said to the first lieutenant, "I believe the warrant officers are going mad. Who ever heard a boatswain use such language—'precarious and not at all permanent?' His stay in the ship will become so, if he does not mind what he is about."

"He is a very odd character, sir," replied the first lieutenant; "but I have no hesitation in saying that he is the best boatswain in his majesty's service."

"I believe so too," replied the captain; "but—well, every one has his faults. Mr Simple, what are you about sir?"

"I was listening to what you said," replied I, touching my hat.

"I admire your candour, sir," replied he, "but advise you to discontinue the practice. Walk over to leeward, sir, and attend to your duty."

When I was on the other side of the deck, I looked round, and saw the captain and first lieutenant both laughing.

Chapter XVIII

I go away on service, am wounded and taken prisoner with O'Brien—
Diamond cut diamond between the O'Briens—Get into comfortable quarters
—My first interview with Celeste.

And now I have to relate an event, which, young as I was at the time, will be found to have seriously affected me in after life. How little do we know what to-morrow may bring forth! We had regained our station, and for some days had been standing off and on the coast, when one morning at daybreak, we found ourselves about four miles from the town of Cette, and a large convoy of vessels coming round a point. We made all sail in chase, and they anchored close in shore, under a battery, which we did not discover until it opened fire upon us. The shot struck the frigate two or three times, for the water was smooth, and the battery nearly level with it. The captain tacked the ship, and stood out again, until the boats were hoisted out, and all ready to pull on shore and storm the battery. O'Brien, who was the officer commanding the first cutter on service, was in his boat, and I again obtained permission from him to smuggle myself into it.

"Now, Peter, let's see what kind of a fish you'll bring on board this time," said he, after we had shoved off: "or may be, the fish will not let you off quite so easy." The men in the boat all laughed at this, and I replied, "That I must be more seriously wounded than I was last time, to be made a prisoner." We ran on shore, amidst the fire of the gunboats, who protected the convoy, by which we lost three men, and made for the battery, which we took without opposition, the French artillery-men running out as we ran in. The directions of the captain were very positive, not to remain in the battery a minute after it was taken, but to board the gunboats, leaving only one of the small boats, with the armourer to spike the guns, for the captain was aware that there were troops stationed along the coast, who might come down upon us and beat us off. The first lieutenant, who commanded, desired O'Brien to remain with the first cutter, and after the armourer had spiked the guns, as officer of the boat he was to shove off immediately. O'Brien and I remained in the battery with the armourer, the boat's crew being ordered down to the boat, to keep her afloat, and ready to shove off at a moment's warning. We had spiked all the guns but one, when all of a sudden a volley of musketry was poured upon us, which killed the armourer, and wounded me in the leg above the knee. I fell down by O'Brien, who cried out, "By the powers! here they are, and one gun not spiked." He jumped down, wrenched the hammer from the armourer's hand, and seizing a nail from the bag, in a few moments he had spiked the gun. At this time I heard the tramping of the French soldiers advancing, when O'Brien threw away the hammer, and lifting me upon his shoulders, cried, "Come along, Peter, my boy," and made for the boat as fast as he could; but he was too late; he had not got half way to the boat, before he was collared by two French soldiers, and dragged back into the battery. The French troops then advanced, and kept up a smart fire: our cutter escaped, and joined the other boat, who had captured the gun-boats and convoy with little opposition. Our large boats had carronades mounted in their bows, and soon returned the fire with round and grape, which drove the French troops back into the battery, where they remained, popping at our men under cover, until most of the vessels were taken out; those which they could not man were burnt.

In the meantime, O'Brien had been taken into the battery, with me on his back; but as soon as he was there, he laid me gently down, saying, "Peter, my boy, as long as you were under my charge, I'd carry you through thick and thin; but now that you are under the charge of these French beggars, why let them carry you. Every man his own bundle, Peter, that's fair play, so if they think you're worth the carrying, let them bear the weight of ye."

"And suppose they do not, O'Brien, will you leave me here?"

"Will I lave you, Peter! not if I can help it, my boy; but they won't leave you, never fear them; prisoners are so scarce with them, that they would not leave the captain's monkey, if he were taken."

As soon as our boats were clear of their musketry, the commanding officer of the French troops examined the guns in the battery, with the hope of reaching them, and was very much annoyed to find that every one of them was spiked. "He'll look sharper than a magpie before he finds a clear touch-hole, I expect," said O'Brien, as he watched the officer. And here I must observe, that O'Brien showed great presence of mind in spiking the last gun; for had they had one gun to fire at our boats towing out the prizes, they must have done a great deal of mischief to them, and we should have lost a great many men; but in so doing, and in the attempt to save me, he sacrificed himself, and was taken prisoner. When the troops ceased firing, the commanding officer came up to O'Brien, and looking at him, said, "Officer?" to which O'Brien nodded his head. He then pointed to me—"Officer?" O'Brien nodded his head again, at which the French troops laughed, as O'Brien told me afterwards, because I was what they called an *enfant*, which means an infant. I was very stiff, and faint, and could not walk. The officer who commanded the troops left a detachment in the battery, and prepared to return to Cette, from whence they came. O'Brien walked, and I was carried on three muskets by six of the French soldiers—not a very pleasant conveyance at any time, but in my state excessively painful. However, I must say, that they were very kind to me, and put a great coat or something under my wounded leg, for I was in an agony, and fainted several times. At last they brought me some water to drink. O how delicious it was! I have often thought since, when I have been in company, where people fond of good living have smacked their lips at their claret, that if they could only be wounded, and taste a cup of water, they would then know what it was to feel a beverage grateful. In about an hour and a half, which appeared to me to be five days at the least, we arrived at the town of Cette, and I was taken up to the house of the officer who commanded the troops, and who had often looked at me as I was carried there from the battery, saying, "*Pauvre enfant!*" I was put on a bed, where I again fainted away. When I came to my senses, I found a surgeon had bandaged my leg, and that I had been undressed. O'Brien was standing by me, and I believe that he had been crying, for he thought that I was dead. When I looked him in the face, he said, "Pater, you baste, how you frightened me: bad luck to me if ever I take charge of another youngster. What did you sham dead for?"

"I am better now, O'Brien," replied I, "how much I am indebted to you: you have been made prisoner in trying to save me."

"I have been made prisoner in doing my duty, in one shape or another. If that fool of an armourer hadn't held his hammer so tight, after he was dead, and it was of no use to him, I should have been clear enough, and so would you have been! but, however, all this is nothing at all, Peter; as far as I can see, the life of a man consists in getting into scrapes, and getting out of them. By the blessing of God, we've managed the first, and by the blessing of God we'll manage the second also; so be smart, my honey, and get well, for although a man may escape by running away on two legs, I never heard of a boy who hopped out of a French prison upon one."

I squeezed the offered hand of O'Brien, and looked round me; the surgeon stood at one side of the bed, and the officer who commanded the troops at the other. At the head of the bed was a little girl about twelve years old, who held a cup in her hand, out of which something had been poured down my throat. I looked at her, and she had such pity in her face, which was remarkably handsome, that she appeared to me as an angel, and I turned round as well as I could, that I might look at her alone. She offered me the cup, which I should have refused from any one but her, and I drank a little. Another person then came into the room, and a conversation took place in French.

"I wonder what they mean to do with us," said I to O'Brien.

"Whist, hold your tongue," replied he; and then he leaned over me, and said in a whisper, "I understand all they say; don't you recollect, I told you that I learnt the language after I was kilt and buried in the sand, in South America?" After a little more conversation, the officer and the others retired, leaving nobody but the little girl and O'Brien in the room.

"It's a message from the governor," said O'Brien, as soon as they were gone, "wishing the prisoners to be sent to the gaol in the citadel, to be examined; and the officer says (and he's a real gentleman, as far as I can judge) that you're but a baby, and badly wounded in the bargain, and that it would be a shame not to leave you to die in peace; so I presume that I'll part company from you very soon."

"I hope not, O'Brien," replied I; "if you go to prison, I will go also, for I will not leave you, who are my best friend, to remain with strangers; I should not be half so happy, although I might have more comforts in my present situation."

"Pater, my boy, I am glad to see that your heart is in the right place, as I always thought it was, or I wouldn't have taken you under my protection. We'll go together to prison, my jewel, and I'll fish at the bars with a bag and a long string, just by way of recreation, and to pick up a little money to buy you all manner of nice things; and when you get well, you shall do it yourself, mayhap you'll have better luck, as Peter your namesake had, who was a fisherman before you. There's twice as much room in one of the cells as there is in a midshipman's berth, my boy; and the prison yards, where you are allowed to walk, will make a dozen quarter-decks, and no need of touching your hat out of respect when you go into it. When a man has been cramped up on board of a man-of-war, where midshipmen are stowed away like pilchards in a cask, he finds himself quite at liberty in a prison, Peter. But somehow or another, I think we mayn't be parted yet, for I heard the officer (who appears to be a real gentleman, and worthy to have been an Irishman born) say to the other, that he'd ask the governor for me to stay with you on parole, until you are well again." The little girl handed me the lemonade, of which I drank a little, and then I felt very faint again. I laid my head on the pillow, and O'Brien having left off talking, I was soon in a comfortable sleep. In an hour I was awakened by the return of the officer, who was accompanied by the surgeon. The officer addressed O'Brien in French who shook his head as before.

"Why don't you answer, O'Brien," said I, "since you understand him?"

"Peter, recollect that I cannot speak a word of their lingo; then I shall know what they say before us, and they won't mind what they say, supposing I do not understand them."

"But is that honest, O'Brien?"

"Is it honest you mean? If I had a five-pound note in my pocket, and don't choose to show it to every fellow that I meet—is that dishonest?"

"To be sure it's not."

"And a'n't that what the lawyers call a case in pint?"

"Well," replied I, "if you wish it, I shall of course say nothing; but I think that I should tell them, especially as they are so kind to us."

During this conversation, the officer occasionally spoke to the surgeon, at the same time eyeing us, I thought, very hard. Two other persons then came into the room; one of them addressed O'Brien in very bad English, saying, that he was interpreter, and would beg him to answer a few questions. He then inquired the name of our ship, number of guns, and how long we had been cruising. After that, the force of the English fleet, and a great many other questions relative to them; all of which were put in French by the person who came with him, and the answer translated, and taken down in a book. Some of the questions O'Brien answered correctly, to others he pleaded ignorance; and to some, he asserted what was not true. But I did not blame him for that, as it was his duty not to give information to the enemy. At last they asked my name, and rank, which O'Brien told them. "Was I noble?"

"Yes," replied O'Brien.

"Don't say so, O'Brien," interrupted I.

"Peter, you know nothing about it, you are grandson to a lord."

"I know that, but still I am not noble myself, although descended from him; therefore pray don't say so."

"Bother! Pater, I have said it, and I won't unsay it; besides, Pater, recollect it's a French question, and in France you would be considered noble. At all events, it can do no harm."

"I feel too ill to talk, O'Brien; but I wish you had not said so."

They then inquired O'Brien's name, which he told them; his rank in the service, and also, whether he was noble.

"I am an O'Brien," replied he; "and pray what's the meaning of the O before my name, if I'm not noble? However, Mr Interpreter, you may add, that we have dropped our title because it's not convanient." The French officer burst out into a loud laugh, which surprised us very much. The interpreter had great difficulty in explaining what O'Brien said; but as O'Brien told me afterwards, the answer was put down *doubtful*.

They all left the room except the officer, who then, to our astonishment, addressed us in good English. "Gentlemen, I have obtained permission from the governor for you to remain in my house, until Mr Simple is recovered. Mr O'Brien, it is necessary that I should receive your parole of honour that you will not attempt to escape. Are you willing to give it?"

O'Brien was quite amazed; "Murder an' Irish," cried he; "so you speak English, colonel. It was not very genteel of you not to say so, considering how we've been talking our little secrets together."

"Certainly, Mr O'Brien, not more necessary," replied the officer, smiling, "than for you to tell me that you understood French."

"O, bother!" cried O'Brien, "how nicely I'm caught in my own trap! You're an Irishman, sure?"

"I'm of Irish descent," replied the officer, "and my name, as well as yours, is O'Brien. I was brought up in this country, not being permitted to serve my own, and retain the religion of my forefathers. I may now be considered as a Frenchman, retaining nothing of my original country, except the language, which my mother taught me, and a warm feeling towards the English wherever I meet them. But to the question, Mr O'Brien, will you give your parole?"

"The word of an Irishman, and the hand to boot," replied O'Brien, shaking the colonel by the hand; "and you're more than doubly sure, for I'll never go away and leave little Peter here; and as for carrying him on my back, I've had enough of that already."

"It is sufficient," replied the colonel. "Mr O'Brien, I will make you as comfortable as I can; and when you are tired of attending your friend, my little daughter shall take your place. You'll find her a kind little nurse, Mr Simple."

I could not refrain from tears at the colonel's kindness: he shook me by the hand; and telling O'Brien that dinner was ready, he called up his daughter, the little girl who had attended me before; and desired her to remain in the room. "Celeste," said he, "you understand a little English; quite enough to find out what he is in want of. Go and fetch your work, to amuse yourself when he is asleep." Celeste went out, and returning with her embroidery, sat down by the head of the bed: the colonel and O'Brien then quitted the room. Celeste then commenced her embroidery, and as her eyes were cast down upon her work, I was able to look at her without her observing it. As I said before, she was a very beautiful little girl; her hair was light brown, eyes very large, and eyebrows drawn as with a pair of compasses; her nose and mouth were also very pretty; but it was not so much her features as the expression of her countenance, which was so beautiful, so modest, so sweet, and so intelligent. When she smiled, which she almost always did when she spoke, her teeth were like two rows of little pearls.

I had not looked at her long, before she raised her eyes from her work, and perceiving that I was looking at her, said, "You want—something— want drink—I speak very little English."

"Nothing, I thank ye," replied I; "I only want to go to sleep."

"Then—shut—your—eye," replied she smiling; and she went to the window, and drew down the blinds to darken the room. But I could not sleep; the remembrance of what had occurred—in a few hours wounded, and a prisoner—the thought of my father and mother's anxiety; with the prospect of going to a prison and close confinement, as soon as I was recovered, passed in succession in my mind, and, together with the actual pain of my wound, prevented me from obtaining any rest. The little girl several times opened the curtain to ascertain whether I slept or wanted anything, and then as softly retired. In the evening, the surgeon called again; he felt my pulse, and directing cold applications to my leg, which had swelled considerably, and was becoming very painful, told Colonel O'Brien, that, although I had considerable fever, I was doing as well as could be expected under the circumstances.

But I shall not dwell upon my severe sufferings for a fortnight, after which the ball was extracted; nor upon how carefully I was watched by O'Brien, the colonel, and little Celeste, during my peevishness and irritation, arising from pain and fever. I feel grateful to them, but partiqularly [sic] to Celeste, who seldom quitted me for more than half-an-hour, and, as I gradually recovered, tried all she could to amuse me.

Chapter XIX

We remove to very unpleasant quarters—Birds of a feather won't always flock together—O'Brien cuts a cutter midshipman, and gets a taste of French steel—Altogether *flat* work—A walk into the interior.

As soon as I was well enough to attend to my little nurse, we became very intimate, as might be expected. Our chief employment was teaching each other French and English. Having the advantage of me in knowing a little before we met, and also being much quicker of apprehension, she very soon began to speak English fluently, long before I could make out a short sentence in French. However, as it was our chief employment, and both were anxious to communicate with each other, I learnt it very fast. In five weeks I was out of bed, and could limp about the room; and before two months were over, I was quite recovered. The colonel, however, would not report me to the governor; I remained on a sofa during the day, but at dusk I stole out of the house, and walked about with Celeste. I never passed such a happy time as the last fortnight; the only drawback was the remembrance that I should soon have to exchange it for a prison. I was more easy about my father and mother, as O'Brien had written to them, assuring them that I was doing well; and besides, a few days after our capture, the frigate had run in, and sent a flag of truce to inquire if we were alive or made prisoners; at the same time Captain Savage sent on shore all our clothes, and two hundred dollars in cash for our use. I knew that even if O'Brien's letter did not reach them, they were sure to hear from Captain Savage that I was doing well. But the idea of parting with Celeste, towards whom I felt such gratitude and affection, was most painful; and when I talked about it, poor Celeste would cry so much, that I could not help joining her, although I kissed away her tears. At the end of twelve weeks, the surgeon could no longer withhold his report, and we were ordered to be ready in two days to march to Toulon, where we were to join another party of prisoners, to proceed with them into the interior. I must pass over our parting, which the reader may imagine was very painful. I promised to write to Celeste, and she promised that she would answer my letters, if it were permitted. We shook hands with Colonel O'Brien, thanking him for his kindness, and, much to his regret, we were taken in charge by two French cuirassiers, who were waiting at the door. As we preferred being continued on parole until our arrival at Toulon, the soldiers were not at all particular about watching us; and we set off on horseback, O'Brien and I going first, and the French cuirassiers following us in the rear.

We trotted or walked along the road very comfortably. The weather was delightful: we were in high spirits, and almost forgot that we were prisoners. The cuirassiers followed us at a distance of twenty yards, conversing with each other, and O'Brien observed that it was amazingly genteel of the French governor to provide us with two servants in such handsome liveries. The evening of the second day we arrived at Toulon, and as soon as we entered the gates, we were delivered into the custody of an officer with a very sinister cast of countenance, who, after some conversation with the cuirassiers, told us in a surly tone that our parole was at an end, and gave us in charge of a corporal's guard, with directions to conduct us to the prison near the Arsenal. We presented the cuirassiers with four dollars each, for their civility, and were then hurried away to our place of captivity. I observed to O'Brien, that I was afraid that we must now bid farewell to anything like pleasure. "You're right there, Peter," replied he: "but there's a certain jewel called Hope, that somebody found at the bottom of his chest, when it was clean empty, and so we must not lose sight of it, but try and escape as soon as we can; but the less we talk about it the better." In a few minutes we arrived at our destination: the door was opened, ourselves and our bundles (for we had only selected a few things for our march, the colonel promising to forward the remainder as soon as we wrote to inform him to which depot we were consigned), were rudely shoved in; and as the doors again closed, and the heavy bolts were shot, I felt a creeping, chilly sensation pass through my whole body.

As soon as we could see—for although the prison was not very dark, yet so suddenly thrown in, after the glare of a bright sunshiny day, at first we could distinguish nothing—we found ourselves in company with about thirty English sailors. Most of them were sitting down on the pavement, or on boxes, or bundles containing their clothes that they had secured, conversing with each other, or playing at cards or draughts. Our entrance appeared to excite little attention; after having raised their eyes to indulge their curiosity, they continued their pursuits. I have often thought what a feeling of selfishness appeared to pervade the whole of them. At the time I was shocked, as I expected immediate sympathy and commiseration; but afterwards I was not surprised. Many of these poor fellows had been months in the prison, and a short confinement will produce that indifference to the misfortunes of others, which I then observed. Indeed, one man, who was playing at cards, looked up for a moment as we came in, and cried out, "Hurrah, my lads! the more the merrier," as if he really was pleased to find that there were others who were as unfortunate as himself. We stood looking at the groups for about ten minutes, when O'Brien observed, "that we might as well come to an anchor, foul ground being better than no bottom;" so we sat down in a corner, upon our bundles, where we remained for more than an hour, surveying the scene, without speaking a word to each other. I could not speak—I felt so very miserable. I thought of my father and mother in England, of my captain and my messmates, who were sailing about so happily in the frigate, of the kind Colonel O'Brien, and dear little Celeste, and the tears trickled down my cheeks as these scenes of former happiness passed through my mind in quick succession. O'Brien did not speak but once, and then he only said, "This is dull work, Peter."

We had been in the prison about two hours, when a lad in a very greasy, ragged jacket, with a pale emaciated face, came up to us, and said, "I perceive by your uniforms that you are both officers, as well as myself."

O'Brien stared at him for a little while, and then answered, "Upon my soul and honour, then, you've the advantage of us, for it's more than I could perceive in you; but I'll take your word for it. Pray what ship may have had the misfortune of losing such a credit to the service?"

"Why, I belonged to the *Snapper* cutter," replied the young lad; "I was taken in a prize, which the commanding officer had given in my charge to take to Gibraltar: but they won't believe that I'm an officer. I have applied for officer's allowance and rations, and they won't give them to me."

"Well, but they know that we are officers," replied O'Brien; "why do they shove us in here, with the common seamen?"

"I suppose you are only put in here for the present," replied the cutter's midshipman; "but why I cannot tell."

Nor could we, until afterwards, when we found out, as our narrative will show, that the officer who received us from the cuirassiers had once quarrelled with Colonel O'Brien, who first pulled his nose, and afterwards ran him through the body. Being told by the cuirassiers that we were much esteemed by Colonel O'Brien, he resolved to annoy us as much as he could; and when he sent up the document announcing our arrival, he left out the word "Officers," and put us in confinement with the common seamen. "It's very hard upon me not to have my regular allowance as an officer," continued the midshipman. "They only give me a black loaf and three sous a day. If I had

had my best uniform on, they never would have disputed my being an officer; but the scoundrels who retook the prize stole all my traps, and I have nothing but this old jacket."

"Why, then," replied O'Brien, "you'll know the value of dress for the future. You cutter and gun-brig midshipmen go about in such a dirty state, that you are hardly acknowledged by us who belong to frigates to be officers, much less gentlemen. You look so dirty, and so slovenly when we pass you in the dockyard, that we give you a wide berth; how then can you suppose strangers to believe that you are either officers or gentlemen? Upon my conscience, I absolve the Frenchmen from all prejudice, for, as to, your being an officer, we, as Englishmen have nothing but your bare word for it."

"Well, it's very hard," replied the lad, "to be attacked this way by a brother officer; your coat will be as shabby as mine, before you have been here long."

"That's very true, my darling," returned O'Brien: "but at least I shall have the pleasant reflection that I came in as a gentleman, although I may not exactly go out under the same appearance. Good night, and pleasant dreams to you!" I thought O'Brien rather cross in speaking in such a way, but he was himself always as remarkably neat and well dressed, as he was handsome and well made.

Fortunately we were not destined to remain long in this detestable hole. After a night of misery, during which we remained sitting on our bundles, and sleeping how we could, leaning with our backs against the damp wall, we were roused, at daybreak by the unbarring of the prison doors, followed up with an order to go into the prison yard. We were huddled out like a flock of sheep, by a file of soldiers with loaded muskets; and, as we went into the yard, were ranged two and two. The same officer who ordered us into prison, commanded the detachment of soldiers who had us in charge. O'Brien stepped out of the ranks, and, addressing them, stated that we were officers, and had no right to be treated like common sailors. The French officer replied, that he had better information, and that we wore coats which did not belong to us; upon which O'Brien was in a great rage, calling the officer a liar, and demanding satisfaction for the insult, appealing to the French soldiers, and stating, that Colonel O'Brien, who was at Cette, was his countryman, and had received him for two months into his house upon parole, which was quite sufficient to establish his being an officer. The French soldiers appeared to side with O'Brien after they had heard this explanation, stating that no common English sailor could speak such good French, and that they were present when we were sent in on parole, and they asked the officer whether he intended to give satisfaction. The officer stormed, and drawing his sword out of the scabbard, struck O'Brien with the flat of the blade, looking at him with contempt, and ordering him into the ranks. I could not help observing that, during this scene, the men-of-war sailors who were among the prisoners, were very indignant, while, on the contrary, those captured in merchant vessels appeared to be pleased with the insult offered to O'Brien. One of the French soldiers then made a sarcastic remark, that the French officer did not much like the name of O'Brien. This so enraged the officer, that he flew at O'Brien, pushed him back into the ranks, and taking out a pistol, threatened to shoot him through the head. I must do the justice to the French soldiers, that they all cried out "Shame!" They did not appear to have the same discipline, or the same respect for an officer, as the soldiers have in our service, or they would not have been so free in their language; yet, at the same time, they obeyed all his orders on service very implicitly.

When O'Brien returned to the ranks, he looked defiance at the officer, telling him, "That he would pocket the affront very carefully, as he intended to bring it out again upon a future and more suitable occasion." We were then marched out in ranks, two and two, being met at the street by two drummers, and a crowd of people, who had gathered to witness our departure. The drums beat, and away we went. The officer who had charge of us mounted a small horse, galloping up and down from one end of the ranks to the other, with his sword drawn, bullying, swearing, and striking with the flat of the blade at any one of the prisoners who was not in his proper place. When we were close to the gates, we were joined by another detachment of prisoners: we were then ordered to halt, and were informed, through an interpreter, that any one attempting to escape would immediately be shot, after which information we once more proceeded on our route.

Nothing remarkable occurred during our first day's march, except perhaps a curious conversation between O'Brien and one of the French soldiers, in which they disputed about the comparative bravery of the two nations. O'Brien, in his argument, told the Frenchman that his countrymen could not stand a charge of English bayonets. The Frenchman replied that there was no doubt but the French were quite as brave as the English—even more so; and that, as for not standing the charge of bayonets, it was not because they were less brave; but the fact was, that they were most excessively *ticklish*. We had black bread and sour wine served out to us this day, when we halted to refresh. O'Brien persuaded a soldier to purchase something for us more eatable; but the French officer heard of it, and was very angry, ordering the soldier to the rear.

Chapter XX

O'Brien fights a duel with a French officer, and proves that the great art of fencing is knowing nothing about it— We arrive at our new quarters, which we find very secure.

At night we arrived at a small town, the name of which I forget. Here we were all put into an old church for the night, and a very bad night we passed. They did not even give us a little straw to lie down upon: the roof of the church had partly fallen in, and the moon shone through very brightly. This was some comfort; for to have been shut up in the dark, seventy-five in number, would have been very miserable. We were afraid to lie down anywhere, as, like all ruined buildings in France, the ground was covered with filth, and the smell was shocking. O'Brien was very thoughtful, and would hardly answer any question that I put to him; it was evident that he was brooding over the affront which he had received from the French officer. At daybreak, the door of the church was again opened by the French soldiers, and we were conducted to the square of the town, where we found the troops quartered, drawn up with their officers, to receive us from the detachment who had escorted us from Toulon. We were very much pleased with this, as we knew that we should be forwarded by another detachment, and thus be rid of the brutal officer who had hitherto had charge of the prisoners. But we were rid of him in another way. As the French officers walked along our ranks to look at us, I perceived among them a captain, whom we had known very intimately when we were living at Cette with Colonel O'Brien. I cried out his name immediately; he turned round, and seeing O'Brien and me, he came up to us, shaking us by the hand, and expressing his surprise at finding us in such a situation. O'Brien explained to him how we had been treated, at which he expressed his indignation, as did the other officers who had collected round us. The major who commanded the troops in the town turned to the French officer (he was only a lieutenant) who had conducted us from Toulon, and demanded of him his reason for behaving to us in such an unworthy manner. He denied having treated us ill, and said that he had been informed that we had put on officers' dresses which did not belong to us. At this O'Brien declared that he was a liar, and a cowardly *foutre*, that he had struck him with the back of his sabre, which he would not have dared do if he had not been a prisoner; adding, that all he requested was satisfaction for the insult offered to him, and appealed to the officers whether, if it were refused, the lieutenant's epaulets ought not to be cut off his shoulders. The major commandant and the officers retired to consult, and, after a few minutes, they agreed that the lieutenant was bound to give the satisfaction required. The lieutenant replied that he was ready; but, at the same time, did not appear to be very willing. The prisoners were left in charge of the soldiers, under a junior officer, while the others, accompanied by O'Brien, myself, and the lieutenant, walked to a short distance outside the town. As we proceeded there, I asked O'Brien with what weapons they would fight.

"I take it for granted," replied he, "that it will be with the small sword."

"But," said I, "do you know anything about fencing?"

"Devil a bit, Peter; but that's all in my favour."

"How can that be?" replied I.

"I'll tell you, Peter. If one man fences well, and another is but an indifferent hand at it, it is clear that the first will run the other through the body; but, if the other knows nothing at all about it, why then, Peter, the case is not quite so clear: because the good fencer is almost as much puzzled by your ignorance as you are by his skill, and you become on more equal terms. Now, Peter, I've made up my mind that I'll run that fellow through the body, and so I will, as sure as I am an O'Brien."

"Well, I hope you will; but pray do not be too sure."

"It's feeling sure that will make me able to do it, Peter. By the blood of the O'Briens! didn't he slap me with his sword, as if I were a clown in the pantomime. Peter, I'll kill the harlequin scoundrel, and my word's as good as my bond!"

By this time we had arrived at the ground. The French lieutenant stripped to his shirt and trousers; O'Brien did the same, kicking his boots off, and standing upon the wet grass in his stockings. The swords were measured, and handed to them; they took their distance, and set to. I must say, that I was breathless with anxiety; the idea of losing O'Brien struck me with grief and terror. I then felt the value of all his kindness to me, and would have taken his place, and have been run through the body, rather than he should have been hurt. At first, O'Brien put himself in the correct attitude of defence, in imitation of the lieutenant, but this was for a very few seconds; he suddenly made a spring, and rushed on to his adversary, stabbing at him with a velocity quite astonishing, the lieutenant parrying in his defence, until at last he had an opportunity of lungeing at O'Brien. O'Brien, who no longer kept his left arm raised in equipoise, caught the sword of the lieutenant at within six inches of the point, and directing it under his left arm, as he rushed in, passed his own through the lieutenant's body. It was all over in less than a minute—the lieutenant did not live half an hour afterwards. The French officers were very much surprised at the result, for they perceived at once that O'Brien knew nothing of fencing. O'Brien gathered a tuft of grass, wiped the sword, which he presented to the officer to whom it belonged, and thanking the major and the whole of them for their impartiality and gentlemanlike conduct, led the way to the square, where he again took his station in the ranks of the prisoners.

Shortly after, the major commandant came up to us, and asked whether we would accept of our parole, as, in that case, we might travel as we pleased. We consented, with many thanks for his civility and kindness; but I could not help thinking at the time, that the French officers were a little mortified at O'Brien's success, although they were too honourable to express the feeling. O'Brien told me, after we had quitted the town, that had it not been for the handsome conduct of the officers, he would not have accepted our parole, as he felt convinced that we could have easily made our escape. We talked over the matter a long while, and at last agreed that there would be a better chance of success by and by, when more closely guarded, than there would be now, under consideration of all circumstances, as it required previously concerted arrangements to get out of the country.

I had almost forgotten to say, that on our return after the duel the cutter's midshipman called out to O'Brien, requesting him to state to the commandant that he was also an officer; but O'Brien replied, that there was no evidence for it but his bare word. If he was an officer he must prove it himself, as everything in his appearance flatly contradicted his assertion.

"It's very hard," replied the midshipman, "that because my jacket's a little tarry or so I must lose my rank."

"My dear fellow," replied O'Brien, "it's not because your jacket's a little tarry; it is because what the Frenchmen call your *tout ensemble* is quite disgraceful in an officer. Look at your face in the first puddle, and you'll find that it would dirty the water you look into. Look at your shoulders above your ears, and your back with a bow like a *kink* in a cable. Your trowsers, sir, you have pulled your legs too far through, showing a foot and a half of worsted stockings. In short, look at yourself altogether, and then tell me, provided you be an officer, whether, from respect to the service, it would not be my duty to contradict it. It goes against my conscience, my dear fellow; but recollect that when we arrive at the depot, you will be able to prove it, so it's only waiting a little while, until the captains will pass their word for you, which is more than I will."

"Well, it's very hard," replied the midshipman, "that I must go on eating this black rye bread; and very unkind of you."

"It's very kind of me, you spalpeen of the Snapper. Prison will be a paradise to you, when you get into good commons. How you'll relish your grub by-and-by! So now shut your pan, or by the tail of Jonah's whale, I'll swear you're a Spaniard."

I could not help thinking that O'Brien was very severe upon the poor lad, and I expostulated with him afterwards. He replied, "Peter, if, as a cutter's midshipman, he is a bit of an officer, the devil a bit is he of a gentleman, either born or bred: and I'm not bound to bail every blackguard-looking chap that I meet. By the head of St Peter, I would blush to be seen in his company, if I were in the wildest bog in Ireland, with nothing but an old crow as spectator."

We were now again permitted to be on our parole, and received every attention and kindness from the different officers who commanded the detachments which passed the prisoners from one town to another. In a few days we arrived at Montpelier, where we had orders to remain a short time until directions were received from Government as to the depots for prisoners to which we were to be sent. At this delightful town, we had unlimited parole, not even a gendarme accompanying us. We lived at the table d'hote, were permitted to walk about where we pleased, and amused ourselves every evening at the theatre. During our stay there we wrote to Colonel O'Brien at Cette, thanking him for his kindness, and narrating what had occurred since we parted. I also wrote to Celeste, inclosing my letter unsealed in the one to Colonel O'Brien. I told her the history of O'Brien's duel, and all I could think would interest her; how sorry I was to have parted from her; that I never would forget her; and trusted that some day, as she was only half a Frenchwoman, we should meet again. Before we left Montpelier, we had the pleasure of receiving answers to our letters: the colonel's letters were very kind, particularly the one to me, in which he called me his dear boy, and hoped that I should soon rejoin my friends, and prove an ornament to my country. In his letter to O'Brien, he requested him not to run me into useless danger—to recollect that I was not so well able to undergo extreme hardship. I have no doubt but that this caution referred to O'Brien's intention to escape from prison, which he had not concealed from the colonel, and the probability that I would be a partner in the attempt. The answer from Celeste was written in English; but she must have had assistance from her father, or she could not have succeeded so well. It was like herself, very kind and affectionate; and also ended with wishing me a speedy return to my friends, who must (she said) be so fond of me, that she despaired of ever seeing me more, but that she consoled herself as well as she could with the assurance that I should be happy. I forgot to say, that Colonel O'Brien, in his letter to me, stated that he expected immediate orders to leave Cette, and take the command of some military post in the interior, or join the army, but which, he could not tell; that they had packed up everything, and he was afraid that our correspondence must cease, as he could not state to what place we should direct our letters. I could not help thinking at the time, that it was a delicate way of pointing out to us that it was not right that he should correspond with us in our relative situations; but still, I was sure that he was about to leave Cette, for he never would have made use of a subterfuge. I must here acquaint the reader with a circumstance which I forgot to mention, which was that when Captain Savage sent in a flag of truce with our clothes and money, I thought that it was but justice to O'Brien that they should know on board of the frigate the gallant manner in which he had behaved. I knew that he would never tell himself, so, ill as I was at the time, I sent for Colonel O'Brien, and requested him to write down my statement of the affair, in which I mentioned how O'Brien had spiked the last gun, and had been taken prisoner by so doing, together with his attempting to save me. When the colonel had written all down, I requested that he would send for the major, who first entered the fort with the troops, and translate it to him in French. This he did in my presence, and the major declared every word to be true. "Will he attest it, colonel, as it may be of great service to O'Brien?" The major immediately assented. Colonel O'Brien then enclosed my letter, with a short note from himself, to Captain Savage, paying him a compliment, and assuring him that his gallant young officers should be treated with every attention, and all the kindness which the rules of war would admit of. O'Brien never knew that I had sent that letter, as the colonel, at my request, kept the secret.

In ten days we received an order to march on the following morning. The sailors, among whom was our poor friend the midshipman of the Snapper cutter, were ordered to Verdun; O'Brien and I, with eight masters of merchant vessels, who joined us at Montpelier, were directed by the Government to be sent to Givet, a fortified town in the department of Ardennes. But, at the same time, orders arrived from Government to treat the prisoners with great strictness, and not to allow any parole; the reason of this, we were informed, was that accounts had been sent to Government of the death of the French officer in the duel with O'Brien, and they had expressed their dissatisfaction at its having been permitted. Indeed, I very much doubt whether it would have been permitted in our country, but the French officers are almost romantically chivalrous in their ideas of honour; in fact, as enemies, I have always considered them as worthy antagonists to the English, and they appear more respectable in themselves, and more demanding our goodwill in that situation, than they do when we meet them as friends, and are acquainted with the other points of their character, which lessen them in our estimation.

I shall not dwell upon a march of three weeks, during which we alternately received kind or unhandsome treatment, according to the dispositions of those who had us in charge; but I must observe, that it was invariably the case, that officers who were gentlemen by birth treated us with consideration, while those who had sprung from nothing during the Revolution, were harsh, and sometimes even brutal. It was exactly four months from the time of our capture that we arrived at our destined prison at Givet.

"Peter," said O'Brien, as he looked hastily at the fortifications, and the river which divided the two towns, "I see no reason, either English or French, that we should not eat our Christmas dinner in England. I've a bird's eye view of the outside, and now, have only to find out where-abouts we may be in the inside."

I must say that, when I looked at the ditches and high ramparts, I had a different opinion; so had a gendarme who was walking by our side, and who had observed O'Brien's scrutiny, and who quietly said to him in French, "*Vous le croyez possible!*"

"Everything is possible to a brave man—the French armies have proved that," answered O'Brien.

"You are right," replied the gendarme, pleased with the compliment to his nation; "I wish you success, you will deserve it; but—" and he shook his head.

"If I could but obtain a plan of the fortress," said O'Brien, "I would give five Napoleons for one," and he looked at the gendarme.

"I cannot see any objection to an officer, although a prisoner, studying fortification," replied the gendarme. "In two hours you will be within the walls; and now I recollect, in the map of the two towns, the fortress is laid down sufficiently accurately to give you an idea of it. But we have conversed too long." So saying, the gendarme dropped into the rear.

In a quarter of an hour, we arrived at the Place d'Armes, where we were met, as usual, by another detachment of troops, and drummers, who paraded us through the town previous to our being drawn up before the governor's house. This, I ought to have observed, was, by order of Government, done at every town we passed through; it was very contemptible, but prisoners were so scarce, that they made all the display of us that they could. As we stopped at the governor's house, the gendarme, who had left us in the square, made a sign to O'Brien, as much as to say, I have it. O'Brien took out five Napoleons, which he wrapped in paper, and held in his hand. In a minute or two, the gendarme came up and presented O'Brien with an old silk handkerchief, saying, "*Votre mouchoir, monsieur.*"

"*Merci,*" replied O'Brien, putting the handkerchief which contained the map into his pocket, "*voici à boire, mon ami;*" and he slipped the paper with the five Napoleons into the hand of the gendarme, who immediately retreated.

This was very fortunate for us, as we afterwards discovered that a mark had been put against O'Brien's and my name, not to allow parole or permission to leave the fortress, even under surveillance. Indeed, even if it had not been so, we never should have obtained it, as the lieutenant killed by O'Brien was nearly related to the commandant of the fortress, who was as much a *mauvais sujet* as his kinsman. Having waited the usual hour before the governor's house, to answer to our muster-roll, and to be stared at, we were dismissed; and in a few minutes, found ourselves shut up in one of the strongest fortresses in France.

Chapter XXI

O'Brien receives his commission as lieutenant, and then we take French leave of Givet.

If I doubted the practicability of escape when I examined the exterior, when we were ushered into the interior of the fortress, I felt that it was impossible, and I stated my opinion to O'Brien. We were conducted into a yard surrounded by a high wall; the buildings appropriated for the prisoners were built with *lean-to* roofs on one side, and at each side of the square was a sentry looking down upon us. It was very much like the dens which they now build for bears, only so much larger. O'Brien answered me with a "Pish! Peter, it's the very security of the place which will enable us to get out of it. But don't talk, as there are always spies about who understand English."

We were shown into a room allotted to six of us; our baggage was examined, and then delivered over to us. "Better and better, Peter," observed O'Brien, "they've not found it out!"

"What?" inquired I.

"Oh, only a little selection of articles, which might be useful to us by-and-by."

He then showed me what I never before was aware of: that he had a false bottom to his trunk; but it was papered over like the rest, and very ingeniously concealed. "And what is there, O'Brien?" inquired I.

"Never mind; I had them made at Montpelier. You'll see by-and-by."

The others, who were lodged in the same room, then came in, and after staying a quarter of an hour, went away at the sound of the dinner-bell. "Now, Peter," said O'Brien, "I must get rid of my load. Turn the key."

O'Brien then undressed himself, and when he threw off his shirt and drawers, showed me a rope of silk, with a knot at every two feet, about half-an-inch in size, wound round and round his body. There were about sixty feet of it altogether. As I unwound it, he, turning round and round, observed, "Peter, I've worn this rope ever since I left Montpelier, and you've no idea of the pain I have suffered; but we must go to England, that's decided upon."

When I looked at O'Brien, as the rope was wound off, I could easily imagine that he had really been in great pain; in several places his flesh was quite raw from the continual friction, and after it was all unwound, and he had put on his clothes, he fainted away. I was very much alarmed, but I recollected to put the rope into the trunk, and take out the key, before I called for assistance. He soon came to, and on being asked what was the matter, said that he was subject to fits from his infancy. He looked earnestly at me, and I showed him the key, which was sufficient.

For some days O'Brien, who really was not very well, kept to his room. During this time, he often examined the map given him by the gendarme. One day he said to me, "Peter, can you swim?"

"No," replied I; "but never mind that."

"But I must mind it, Peter; for observe, we shall have to cross the river Meuse, and boats are not always to be had. You observe, that this fortress is washed by the river on one side: and as it is the strongest side, it is the least guarded—we must escape by it. I can see my way clear enough till we get to the second rampart on the river, but when we drop into the river, if you cannot swim, I must contrive to hold you up, somehow or another."

"Are you then determined to escape, O'Brien? I cannot perceive how we are even to get up this wall, with four sentries staring us in the face."

"Never do you mind that, Peter, mind your own business; and first tell me, do you intend to try your luck with me?"

"Yes," replied I, "most certainly; if you have sufficient confidence in me to take me as your companion."

"To tell you the truth, Peter, I would not give a farthing to escape without you. We were taken together, and, please God, we'll take ourselves off together; but that must not be for this month; our greatest help will be the dark nights and foul weather."

The prison was by all accounts very different from Verdun and some others. We had no parole, and but little communication with the townspeople. Some were permitted to come in and supply us with various articles; but their baskets were searched to see that they contained nothing that might lead to an escape on the part of the prisoners. Without the precautions that O'Brien had taken, any attempt would have been useless. Still, O'Brien, as soon as he left his room, did obtain several little articles—especially balls of twine—for one of the amusements of the prisoners was flying kites. This, however, was put a stop to, in consequence of one of the strings, whether purposely or not, I cannot say, catching the lock of the musket carried by one of the sentries who looked down upon us, and twitching it out of his hand; after which an order was given by the commandant for no kites to be permitted. This was fortunate for us, as O'Brien, by degrees, purchased all the twine belonging to the other prisoners; and, as we were more than three hundred in number, it amounted to sufficient to enable him, by stealth, to lay it up into very strong cord, or rather, into a sort of square plait, known only to sailors. "Now, Peter," said he one day, "I want nothing more than an umbrella for you."

"Why an umbrella for me?"

"To keep you from being drowned with too much water, that's all."

"Rain won't drown me."

"No, no, Peter; but buy a new one as soon as you can."

I did so. O'Brien boiled up a quantity of bees' wax and oil, and gave it several coats of this preparation. He then put it carefully away in the ticking of his bed. I asked him whether he intended to make known his plan to any of the other prisoners; he replied in the negative, saying, that there were so many of them who could not be trusted, that he would trust no one. We had been now about two months in Givet, when a Steel's List was sent to a lieutenant, who was confined there. The lieutenant came up to O'Brien, and asked him his Christian name.

"Terence, to be sure," replied O'Brien.

"Then," answered the lieutenant, "I may congratulate you on your promotion, for here you are upon the list of August."

"Sure there must be some trifling mistake; let me look at it. Terence O'Brien, sure enough; but now the question is, has any other fellow robbed me of my name and promotion at the same time? Bother, what can it mane? I won't belave it—not a word of it. I've no more interest than a dog who drags cats'-meat."

"Really, O'Brien," observed I, "I cannot see why you should not be made; I am sure you deserve your promotion for your conduct when you were taken prisoner."

"And what did I do then, you simple Peter, but put you on my back as the men do their hammocks when they are piped down; but, barring all claim, how could any one know what took place in the battery, except you, and I, and the armourer, who lay dead? So explain that, Peter, if you can."

"I think I can," replied I, after the lieutenant had left us. And I then told O'Brien how I had written to Captain Savage, and had had the fact attested by the major who had made us prisoners.

"Well, Peter," said O'Brien, after a pause, "there's a fable about a lion and a mouse. If, by your means, I have obtained my promotion, why then the mouse is a finer baste than the lion; but instead of being happy, I shall now be miserable until the truth is ascertained one way or the other, and that's another reason why I must set off to England as fast as I can."

For a few days after this O'Brien was very uneasy; but fortunately letters arrived by that time; one to me from my father, in which he requested me to draw for whatever money I might require, saying that the whole family would retrench in every way to give me all the comfort which might be obtained in my unfortunate situation. I wept at his kindness, and more than ever longed to throw myself in his arms, and thank him. He also told me that my uncle William was dead, and that there was only one between him and the title, but that my grandfather was in good health, and had been very kind to him lately. My mother was much afflicted at my having been made a prisoner, and requested I would write as often as I could. O'Brien's letter was from Captain Savage; the frigate had been sent home with despatches, and O'Brien's conduct represented to the Admiralty, which had, in consequence, promoted him to the rank of lieutenant. O'Brien came to me with the letter, his countenance radiant with joy as he put it into my hands. In return I put mine into his, and he read it over.

"Peter, my boy, I'm under great obligations to you. When you were wounded and feverish, you thought of me at a time when you had quite enough to think of yourself; but I never thank in words. I see your uncle William is dead. How many more uncles have you?"

"My uncle John, who is married, and has already two daughters."

"Blessings on him; may he stick to the female line of business! Peter, my boy, you shall be a lord before you die."

"Nonsense, O'Brien; I have no chance. Don't put such foolish ideas in my head."

"What chance had I of being a lieutenant, and am I not one? Well, Peter, you've helped to make a lieutenant of me, but I'll make a *man* of you, and that's better. Peter, I perceive, with all your simplicity, that you're not over and above simple, and that, with all your asking for advice, you can think and act for yourself on an emergency. Now, Peter, these are talents that must not be thrown away in this cursed hole, and therefore, my boy, prepare yourself to quit this place in a week, wind and weather permitting; that is to say, not fair wind and weather, but the fouler the better. Will you be ready at any hour of any night that I call you up?"

"Yes, O'Brien, I will, and do my best."

"No man can do much more that ever I heard of. But, Peter, do me one favour, as I am really a lieutenant, just touch your hat to me only once, that's all; but I wish the compliment, just to see how it looks."

"Lieutenant O'Brien," said I, touching my hat, "have you any further orders?"

"Yes, sir," replied he; "that you never presume to touch your hat to me again, unless we sail together, and then that's a different sort of thing."

About a week afterwards, O'Brien came to me, and said, "The new moon's quartered in with foul weather; if it holds, prepare for a start. I have put what is necessary in your little haversack; it may be to-night. Go to bed now, and sleep for a week if you can, for you'll get but little sleep, if we succeed, for the week to come."

This was about eight o'clock. I went to bed, and about twelve I was roused by O'Brien, who told me to dress myself carefully, and come down to him in the yard. I did so without disturbing any body, and found the night as dark as pitch (it was then November), and raining in torrents; the wind was high, howling round the yard, and sweeping in the rain in every direction as it eddied to and fro. It was some time before I could find O'Brien, who was hard at work; and, as I had already been made acquainted with all his plans, I will now explain them. At Montpelier he had procured six large pieces of iron, about eighteen inches long, with a gimlet at one end of each, and a square at the other, which fitted to a handle which unshipped. For precaution he had a spare handle, but each handle fitted to all the irons. O'Brien had screwed one of these pieces of iron between the interstices of the stones of which the wall was built, and sitting astride on that, was fixing another about three feet above. When he had accomplished this, he stood upon the lower iron, and supporting himself by the second, which about met his hip, he screwed in a third, always fixing them about six inches on one side of the other, and not one above the other. When he had screwed in his six irons, he was about half up the wall, and then he fastened his rope, which he had carried round his neck, to the upper iron, and lowering himself down, unscrewed the four lower irons: then ascending by the rope, he stood upon the fifth iron, and supporting himself by the upper iron, recommenced his task. By these means he arrived in the course of an hour and a half to the top of the wall, where he fixed his last iron, and making his rope fast, he came down again. "Now, Peter," said he, "there is no fear of the sentries seeing us; if they had the eyes of cats, they could not until we were on the top of the wall; but then we arrive at the glacis, and we must creep to the ramparts on our bellies. I am going up with all the materials. Give me your haversack—you will go up lighter; and recollect, should any accident happen to me, you run to bed again. If, on the contrary, I pull the rope up and down three or four times, you may sheer up it as fast as you can." O'Brien then loaded himself with the other rope, the two knapsacks, iron crows, and other implements he had procured; and, last of all, with the umbrella. "Peter, if the rope bears me with all this, it is clear it will bear such a creature as you are, therefore don't be afraid." So whispering, he commenced his ascent; in about three minutes he was up, and the rope pulled. I immediately followed him, and found the rope very easy to climb, from the knots at every two feet, which gave me a hold for my feet, and I was up in as short a time as he was. He caught me by the collar, putting his wet hand on my mouth, and I lay down beside him while he pulled up the rope. We then crawled on our stomachs across the glacis till we arrived at the rampart. The wind blew tremendously, and the rain pattered down so fast, that the sentries did not perceive us; indeed, it was no fault of theirs, for it was impossible to have made us out. It was some time before O'Brien could find out the point exactly above the drawbridge of the first ditch; at last he did—he fixed his crow-bar in, and lowered down the rope. "Now, Peter, I had better go first again; when I shake the rope from below, all's right." O'Brien descended, and in a few minutes the rope again shook; I followed him, and found myself received in his arms upon the meeting of the drawbridge; but the drawbridge itself was up. O'Brien led the way across the chains, and I followed him. When we had crossed the moat, we found a barrier gate locked; this puzzled us. O'Brien pulled out his picklocks to pick it, but without success; here we were fast. "We must undermine the gate, O'Brien; we must pull up the pavement until we can creep under." "Peter, you are a fine fellow; I never thought of that." We worked very hard until the hole was large enough, using the crow-bar which was left, and a little wrench which O'Brien had with him. By these means we got under the gate in the course of an hour or more. This gate led to the lower rampart, but we had a covered way to pass through before we arrived at it. We proceeded very cautiously, when we heard a noise: we stopped, and found that it was a sentry, who was fast asleep, and snoring. Little expecting to find one here, we were puzzled; pass him we could not well, as he was stationed on the very spot where we required to place our crow-bar to descend the lower rampart into the river. O'Brien thought for a moment. "Peter," said he, "now is the time for you to prove yourself a man. He is fast asleep, but his noise must be stopped. I will stop his mouth, but at the very moment that I do so you must throw open the pan of his musket, and then he cannot fire it." "I will, O'Brien; don't fear me." We crept cautiously up to him, and O'Brien motioning to me to put my thumb upon the pan, I did so, and the moment that O'Brien put his hand upon the soldier's mouth, I threw open the pan. The fellow struggled, and snapped his lock as a signal, but of course without discharging his musket, and in a minute he was not only gagged but bound by O'Brien, with my assistance. Leaving him there, we proceeded to the rampart, and fixing the crow-bar again, O'Brien descended; I followed him, and found him in the river, hanging on to the rope; the umbrella was opened and turned upwards; the preparation made it resist the water, and, as previously explained to me by O'Brien, I had only to hold on at arm's length to two beckets which he had affixed to the point of the umbrella, which was under water. To the same part O'Brien had a tow-line, which taking in his teeth, he towed me down with the stream to about a hundred yards clear of the fortress, where we landed. O'Brien was so exhausted that for a few minutes he remained quite motionless; I also was benumbed with the cold. "Peter," said he, "thank God we have succeeded so far; now must we push on as far as we can, for we shall have daylight in two hours." O'Brien took out his flask of spirits, and we both drank a half tumbler at least, but we should not in our state have been affected with a bottle. We now walked along the river-side till we fell in with a small craft, with a boat towing astern: O'Brien swam to it, and cutting the painter without getting in, towed it on shore. The oars were fortunately in the boat. I got in, we shoved off, and rowed away down the stream till the dawn of day. "All's right, Peter; now we'll land. This is the Forest of Ardennes." We landed, replaced the oars in the boat, and pushed her off into the stream, to induce people to suppose that she had broken adrift, and then hastened into the thickest of the wood. It still rained hard; I shivered, and my teeth chattered with the cold, but there was no help for it. We again took a dram of spirits, and, worn out with fatigue and excitement, soon fell fast asleep upon a bed of leaves which we had collected together.

Chapter XXII

Grave consequences of gravitation—O'Brien enlists himself as a gendarme, and takes charge of me—We are discovered, and obliged to run for it—The pleasures of a winter bivouac.

It was not until noon that I awoke, when I found that O'Brien had covered me more than a foot deep with leaves to protect me from the weather. I felt quite warm and comfortable; my clothes had dried on me, but without giving me cold. "How very kind of you, O'Brien!" said I.

"Not a bit, Peter: you have hard work to go through yet, and I must take care of you. You're but a bud, and I'm a full-blown rose." So saying, he put the spirit-flask to his mouth, and then handed it to me. "Now, Peter, we must make a start, for depend upon it they will scour the country for us; but this is a large wood, and they may as well attempt to find a needle in a bundle of hay, if we once get into the heart of it."

"I think," said I, "that this forest is mentioned by Shakespeare, in one of his plays."

"Very likely, Peter," replied O'Brien; "but we are at no playwork now; and what reads amazing prettily, is no joke in reality. I've often observed, that your writers never take the weather into consideration."

"I beg your pardon, O'Brien; in King Lear the weather was tremendous."

"Very likely; but who was the king that went out in such weather?"

"King Lear did, when he was mad."

"So he was, that's certain, Peter; but runaway prisoners have some excuse; so now for a start."

We set off, forcing our way through the thicket, for about three hours, O'Brien looking occasionally at his pocket compass; it then was again nearly dark, and O'Brien proposed a halt. We made up a bed of leaves for the night, and slept much more comfortably than we had the night before. All our bread was wet, but as we had no water, it was rather a relief; the meat we had with us was sufficient for a week. Once more we laid down and fell fast asleep. About five o'clock in the morning I was roused by O'Brien, who at the same time put his hand gently over my mouth. I sat up, and perceived a large fire not far from us. "The Philistines are upon us, Peter," said he; "I have reconnoitred, and they are the gendarmes. I'm fearful of going away, as we may stumble upon some more of them. I've been thinking what's best before I waked you; and it appears to me, that we had better get up the tree, and lie there."

At that time we were hidden in a copse of underwood, with a large oak in the centre, covered with ivy. "I think so too, O'Brien; shall we go up now, or wait a little?"

"Now, to be sure, that they're eating their prog. Mount you, Peter, and
I'll help you."

O'Brien shoved me up the tree, and then waiting a little while to bury our haversacks among the leaves, he followed me. He desired me to remain in a very snug position, on the first fork of the tree, while he took another, amongst a bunch of ivy, on the largest bough. There we remained for about an hour, when day dawned. We observed the gendarmes mustered at the break of day, by the corporal, and then they all separated in different directions, to scour the wood. We were delighted to perceive this, as we hoped soon to be able to get away; but there was one gendarme who remained. He walked to and fro, looking everywhere, until he came directly under the tree in which we were concealed. He poked about, until at last he came to the bed of leaves upon which we had slept; these he turned over and over with his bayonet, until he routed out our haversacks. "Pardi!" exclaimed he, "where the nest and eggs are, the birds are near." He then walked round the tree, looking up into every part, but we were well concealed, and he did not discover us for some time. At last he saw me, and ordered me to come down. I paid no attention to him, as I had no signal from O'Brien. He walked round a little farther, until he was directly under the branch on which O'Brien lay. Taking up this position, he had a fairer aim at me, and levelled his musket, saying, "*Descendez, ou je tire*." Still I continued immoveable, for I knew not what to do. I shut my eyes, however; the musket shortly afterwards was discharged, and, whether from fear or not I can hardly tell, I lost my hold of a sudden, and down I came. I was stunned with the fall, and thought that I must have been wounded, and was very much surprised, when, instead of the gendarme, O'Brien came up to me, and asked whether I was hurt. I answered, I believed not, and got upon my legs, when I found the gendarme lying on the ground, breathing heavily, but insensible. When O'Brien perceived the gendarme level his musket at me, he immediately dropped from the bough, right upon his head; this occasioned the musket to go off, without hitting me, and at the same time, the weight of O'Brien's body from such a height killed the gendarme, for he expired before we left him. "Now, Peter," said O'Brien, "this is the most fortunate thing in the world, and will take us half through the country; but we have no time to lose." He then stripped the gendarme, who still breathed heavily, and dragging him to our bed of leaves, covered him up, threw off his own clothes, which he tied in a bundle, and gave to me to carry, and put on those of the gendarme. I could not help laughing at the metamorphosis, and asked O'Brien what he intended. "Sure, I'm a gendarme, bringing with me a prisoner, who has escaped." He then tied my hands with a cord, shouldered his musket, and off we set. We now quitted the wood as soon as we could; for O'Brien said that he had no fear for the next ten days; and so it proved. We had one difficulty, which was, that we were going the wrong way; but that was obviated by travelling mostly at night, when no questions were asked, except at the cabarets, where we lodged, and they did not know which way we came. When we stopped at night, my youth excited a great deal of commiseration, especially from the females; and in one instance I was offered assistance to escape. I consented to it, but at the same time informed O'Brien of the plan proposed. O'Brien kept watch—I dressed myself, and was at the open window, when he rushed in, seizing me, and declaring that he would inform the Government of the conduct of the parties. Their confusion and distress were very great. They offered O'Brien twenty, thirty, forty Napoleons, if he would hush it up, for they were aware of the penalty and imprisonment. O'Brien replied that he would not accept of any money in compromise of his duty; that after he had given me into the charge of the gendarme of the next post, his business was at an end, and he must return to Flushing, where he was stationed.

"I have a sister there," replied the hostess, "who keeps an inn. You'll want good quarters, and a friendly cup; do not denounce us, and I'll give you a letter to her, which, if it does not prove of service, you can then return and give the information."

O'Brien consented; the letter was delivered, and read to him, in which the sister was requested, by the love she bore to the writer, to do all she could for the bearer, who had the power of making the whole family miserable, but had refused so to do. O'Brien pocketed the letter, filled his brandy-flask, and saluting all the women, left the cabaret, dragging me after him with a cord. The only difference, as O'Brien observed after he went out, was, that he (O'Brien) kissed all the women, and all the women kissed me. In this way, we had proceeded by Charleroy and Louvain, and were within a few miles of Malines, when a circumstance occurred which embarrassed us not a little. We were following our route, avoiding Malines, which was a fortified town, and at the time were in a narrow lane, with wide ditches, full of water, on each side. At the turning of a sharp corner, we met the gendarme who had supplied O'Brien with a map of the town of Givet. "Good morning, comrade," said he to O'Brien, looking earnestly at him, "whom have we here?"

"A young Englishman, whom I picked up close by, escaped from prison."

"Where from?"

"He will not say; but I suspect from Givet."

"There are two who have escaped from Givet," replied he: "how they escaped no one can imagine; but," continued he, again looking at O'Brien, "*avec les braves, il n'y a rien d'impossible*."

"That is true," replied O'Brien; "I have taken one, the other cannot be far off. You had better look for him."

"I should like to find him," replied the gendarme, "for you know that to retake a runaway prisoner is certain promotion. You will be made a corporal."

"So much the better," replied O'Brien; "*adieu, mon ami*."

"Nay, I merely came for a walk, and will return with you to Malines, where of course you are bound."

"We shall not get there to-night," said O'Brien, "my prisoner is too much fatigued."

"Well, then, we will go as far as we can; and I will assist you. Perhaps we may find the second, who, I understand, obtained a map of the fortress by some means or other."

We at once perceived that we were discovered. He afterwards told us that the body of a gendarme had been found in the wood, no doubt murdered by the prisoners, and that the body was stripped naked. "I wonder," continued he, "whether one of the prisoners put on his clothes, and passed as a gendarme."

"Peter," said O'Brien, "are we to murder this man or not?"

"I should say not: pretend to trust him, and then we may give him the slip." This was said during the time that the gendarme stopped a moment behind us.

"Well, we'll try; but first I'll put him off his guard." When the gendarme came up with us, O'Brien observed, that the English prisoners were very liberal; that he knew that a hundred Napoleons were often paid for assistance, and he thought that no corporal's rank was equal to a sum that would in France make a man happy and independent for life.

"Very true," replied the gendarme; "and let me only look upon that sum, and I will guarantee a positive safety out of France."

"Then we understand each other," replied O'Brien; "this boy will give two hundred—one half shall be yours, if you will assist."

"I will think of it," replied the gendarme, who then talked about indifferent subjects, until we arrived at a small town, called Acarchot, where we proceeded to a cabaret. The usual curiosity passed over we were left alone, O'Brien telling the gendarme that he would expect his reply that night or to-morrow morning. The gendarme said, to-morrow morning. O'Brien requesting him to take charge of me, he called the woman of the cabaret to show him a room; she showed him one or two, which he refused, as not sufficiently safe for the prisoner. The woman laughed at the idea, observing, "What had he to fear from a *pauvre enfant* like me?"

"Yet this *pauvre enfant* escaped from Givet," replied O'Brien; "these Englishmen are devils from their birth." The last room showed to O'Brien suited him, and he chose it—the woman not presuming to contradict a gendarme. As soon as they came down again, O'Brien ordered me to bed, and went up-stairs with me. He bolted the door, and pulling me to the large chimney, we put our heads up, and whispered, that our conversation should not be heard. "This man is not to be trusted," said O'Brien, "and we must give him the slip. I know my way out of the inn, and we must return the way we came, and then strike off in another direction."

"But will he permit us?"

"Not if he can help it; but I shall soon find out his manoeuvres."

O'Brien then went and stopped the key-hole, by hanging his handkerchief across it, and stripping himself of his gendarme uniform, put on his own clothes; then he stuffed the blankets and pillow into the gendarme's dress, and laid it down on the outside of the bed, as if it were a man sleeping in his clothes—indeed, it was an admirable deception. He laid his musket by the side of the image, and then did the same to my bed, making it appear as if there was a person asleep in it, of my size, and putting my cap on the pillow. "Now, Peter, we'll see if he is watching us. He will wait till he thinks we are asleep." The light still remained in the room, and about an hour afterwards we heard a noise of one treading on the stairs, upon which, as agreed, we crept under the bed. The latch of our door was tried, and finding it open, which he did not expect, the gendarme entered, and looking at both beds, went away. "Now," said I, after the gendarme had gone down-stairs, "O'Brien, ought we not to escape?"

"I've been thinking of it, Peter, and I have come to a resolution that we can manage it better. He is certain to come again in an hour or two. It is only eleven. Now I'll play him a trick." O'Brien then took one of the blankets, make it fast to the window, which he left wide open, and at the same time disarranged the images he had made up, so as to let the gendarme perceive that they were counterfeit. We again crept under the bed, and as O'Brien foretold, in about an hour more the gendarme returned; our lamp was still burning, but he had a light of his own. He looked at the beds, perceived at once that he had been duped, went to the open window, and then exclaimed, "*Sacre Dieu! ils m'ont echappés et je ne suis plus caporal. F——tre! à la chasse!*" He rushed out of the room, and in a minute afterwards we heard him open the street door, and go away.

"That will do, Peter," said O'Brien, laughing; "now we'll be off also, although there's no great hurry." O'Brien then resumed his dress of a gendarme; and about an hour afterwards we went down, and wishing the hostess all happiness, quitted the cabaret, returning the same road by which we had come. "Now, Peter," said O'Brien, "we're in a bit of a puzzle. This dress won't do any more, still there's a respectability about it, which will not allow me to put it off till the last moment." We walked on till daylight, when we hid ourselves in a copse of trees. At night we again started for the forest of Ardennes, for O'Brien said our best chance was to return, until they supposed that we had had time to effect our escape; but we never reached the forest, for on the next day a violent snowstorm came on; it continued without intermission for four days, during which we suffered much. Our money was not exhausted, as I had drawn upon my father for £60, which, with the disadvantageous exchange, had given me fifty Napoleons. Occasionally O'Brien crept into a cabaret, and obtained provisions; but, as we dared not be seen together as before, we were always obliged to sleep in the open air, the ground being covered more than three feet with snow. On the fifth day, being then six days from the forest of Ardennes, we hid ourselves in a small wood, about a quarter of a mile from the road. I remained there while O'Brien, as a gendarme, went to obtain provisions. As usual, I looked out for the best shelter during his absence, and what was my horror at falling in with a man and woman who lay dead in the snow, having evidently perished from the weather. Just as I discovered them, O'Brien returned, and I told him; he went with me to view the bodies. They were dressed in a strange attire, ribands pinned upon their clothes, and two pairs of very high stilts lying by their sides. O'Brien surveyed them, and then said, "Peter, this is the very best thing that could have happened to us. We may now walk through France without soiling our feet with the cursed country."

"How do you mean?"

"I mean," said he, "that these are the people that we met near Montpelier, who come from the Landes, walking about on their stilts for the amusement of others, to obtain money. In their own country they are obliged to walk so. Now, Peter, it appears to me that the man's clothes will fit me, and the girl's (poor creature, how pretty she looks, cold in death!) will fit you. All we have to do is to practise a little, and then away we start."

O'Brien then, with some difficulty, pulled off the man's jacket and trowsers, and having so done, buried him in the snow. The poor girl was despoiled of her gown and upper petticoat, with every decency, and also buried. We collected the clothes and stilts, and removed to another quarter of the wood, where we found a well-sheltered spot, and took our meal. As we did not travel that night as usual, we had to prepare our own bed. We scraped away the snow, and made ourselves as comfortable as we could without a fire, but the weather was dreadful.

"Peter," said O'Brien, "I'm melancholy. Here, drink plenty;" and he handed me the flask of spirits, which had never been empty.

"Drink more, Peter."

"I cannot, O'Brien, without being tipsy."

"Never mind that, drink more; see how these two poor devils lost their lives by falling asleep in the snow. Peter," said O'Brien, starting up, "you sha'n't sleep here—follow me."

I expostulated in vain. It was almost dark, and he led me to the village, near which he pitched upon a hovel (a sort of out-house). "Peter, here is shelter; lie down and sleep, and I'll keep the watch. Not a word, I will have it—down at once."

I did so, and in a very few minutes was fast asleep, for I was worn out with cold and fatigue. For several days we had walked all night, and the rest we gained by day was trifling. Oh how I longed for a warm bed with four or five blankets! Just as the day broke, O'Brien roused me; he had stood sentry all night, and looked very haggard.

"O'Brien, you are ill," said I.

"Not a bit; but I've emptied the brandy-flask; and that's a bad job. However, it is to be remedied."

We then returned to the wood in a mizzling rain and fog, for the weather had changed, and the frost had broken up. The thaw was even worse than the frost, and we felt the cold more. O'Brien again insisted upon my sleeping in the out-house, but this time I positively refused without he would also sleep there, pointing out to him, that we ran no more risk, and perhaps not so much, as if he stayed outside. Finding I was positive, he at last consented, and we both gained it unperceived. We lay down, but I did not go to sleep for some time, I was so anxious to see O'Brien fast asleep. He went in and out several times, during which I pretended to be fast asleep; at last it rained in torrents, and then he lay down again, and in a few minutes, overpowered by nature, he fell fast asleep, snoring so loudly, that I was afraid some one would hear us. I then got up and watched, occasionally lying down and slumbering awhile, and then going to the door.

Chapter XXIII

Exalted with our success, we march through France without touching the ground—I become feminine—We are voluntary conscripts.

At day-break I called O'Brien, who jumped up in a great hurry.

"Sure I've been asleep, Peter."

"Yes, you have," replied I, "and I thank Heaven that you have, for no one could stand such fatigue as you have, much longer; and if you fall ill, what would become of me?" This was touching him on the right point.

"Well, Peter, since there's no harm come of it, there's no harm done. I've had sleep enough for the next week, that's certain."

We returned to the wood; the snow had disappeared, and the rain ceased; the sun shone out from between the clouds, and we felt warm.

"Don't pass so near that way," said O'Brien, "we shall see the poor creatures, now that the snow is gone. Peter, we must shift our quarters to-night, for I have been to every cabaret in the village, and I cannot go there any more without suspicion, although I am a gendarme."

We remained there till the evening, and then set off, still returning towards Givet. About an hour before daylight we arrived at a copse of trees, close to the road-side, and surrounded by a ditch, not above a quarter of a mile from a village. "It appears to me," said O'Brien, "that this will do: I will now put you there, and then go boldly to the village and see what I can get, for here we must stay at least a week."

We walked to the copse, and the ditch being rather too wide for me to leap, O'Brien laid the four stilts together so as to form a bridge, over which I contrived to walk. Tossing to me all the bundles, and desiring me to leave the stilts as a bridge for him on his return, he set off to the village with his musket on his shoulder. He was away two hours, when he returned with a large supply of provisions, the best we had ever had. French saucissons, seasoned with garlic, which I thought delightful; four bottles of brandy, besides his flask; a piece of hung beef and six loaves of bread, besides half a baked goose and part of a large pie.

"There," said he, "we have enough for a good week; and look here, Peter, this is better than all." And he showed me two large horse-rugs.

"Excellent," replied I; "now we shall be comfortable."

"I paid honestly for all but these rugs," observed O'Brien; "but I was afraid to buy them, so I stole them. However, we'll leave them here for those they belong to—it's only borrowing, after all."

We now prepared a very comfortable shelter with branches, which we wove together, and laying the leaves in the sun to dry, soon obtained a soft bed to put one horse-rug on, while we covered ourselves up with the other. Our bridge of stilts we had removed, so that we felt ourselves quite secure from surprise. That evening we did nothing but carouse—the goose, the pie, the saucissons as big as my arm, were alternately attacked, and we went to the ditch to drink water, and then ate again. This was quite happiness to what we had suffered, especially with the prospect of a good bed. At dark, to bed we went, and slept soundly; I never felt more refreshed during our wanderings. At daylight O'Brien got up.

"Now, Peter, a little practice before breakfast."

"What practice do you mean?"

"Mean! why on the stilts. I expect in a week that you'll be able to dance a gavotte at least; for mind me, Peter, you travel out of France upon these stilts, depend upon it."

O'Brien then took the stilts belonging to the man, giving, me those of the woman. We strapped them to our thighs, and by fixing our backs to a tree, contrived to get upright upon them; but, at the first attempt to walk, O'Brien fell to the right, and I fell to the left. O'Brien fell against a tree, but I fell on my nose, and made it bleed very much; however, we laughed and got up again, and although we had several falls, at last we made a better hand of them. We then had some difficulty in getting down again, but we found out how, by again resorting to a tree. After breakfast we strapped them on again, and practised, and so we continued to do for the whole day, when we again attacked our provisions, and fell asleep under our horse-rug. This continued for five days, by which time, being constantly on the stilts, we became very expert; and although I could not dance a gavotte—for I did not know what that was—I could hop about with them with the greatest ease.

"One day's more practice," said O'Brien, "for our provisions will last one day more, and then we start; but this time we must rehearse in costume."

O'Brien then dressed me in the poor girl's clothes, and himself in the man's; they fitted very well, and the last day we practised as man and woman.

"Peter, you make a very pretty girl," said O'Brien. "Now, don't you allow the men to take liberties."

"Never fear," replied I. "But, O'Brien, as these petticoats are not very warm, I mean to cut off my trowsers up to my knees, and wear them underneath."

"That's all right," said O'Brien, "for you may have a tumble, and then they may find out that you're not a lady."

The next morning we made use of our stilts to cross the ditch, and carrying them in our hands we boldly set off on the high road to Malines. We met several people, gens-d'armes and others, but with the exception of some remarks upon my good looks, we passed unnoticed. Towards the evening we arrived at the village where we had slept in the outhouse, and as soon as we entered it we put on our stilts, and commenced a march. When the crowd had gathered we held out our caps, and receiving nine or ten sous, we entered a cabaret. Many questions were asked us, as to where we came from, and O'Brien answered, telling lies innumerable. I played the modest girl, and O'Brien, who stated I was his sister, appeared very careful and jealous of any attention. We slept well, and the next morning continued our route to Malines. We very often put on our stilts for practice on the road, which detained us very much, and it was not until the eighth day, without any variety or any interruption, that we arrived at Malines. As we entered the barriers we put on our stilts, and marched boldly on. The guard at the gate stopped us, not from suspicion, but to amuse themselves, and I was forced to submit to several kisses from their garlic lips, before we were allowed to enter the town. We again mounted on our stilts, for the guard had forced us to dismount, or they could not have kissed me, every now and then imitating a dance, until we arrived at the *Grande Place*, where we stopped opposite the hotel, and commenced a sort of waltz which we had practised. The people in the hotel looked out of the window to see our exhibition, and when we had finished I went up to the windows with O'Brien's cap to collect money. What was my surprise to perceive Colonel O'Brien looking full in my face, and staring very hard at me;—what was my greater astonishment at seeing Celeste, who immediately recognised me, and ran back to the sofa in the room, putting her hands up to her eyes, and crying out "*C'est lui, c'est lui!*" Fortunately O'Brien was close to me, or I should have fallen, but he supported me. "Peter, ask the crowd for money, or you are lost." I did so, and collecting some pence, then asked him what I should do. "Go back to the window—you can then judge of what will happen." I returned to the window; Colonel O'Brien had disappeared, but Celeste was there, as if waiting for me. I held out the cap to her, and she thrust her hand into it. The cap sank with the weight. I took out a purse, which

I kept closed in my hand, and put it into my bosom. Celeste then retired from the window, and when she had gone to the back of the room kissed her hand to me, and went out at the door. I remained stupefied for a moment, but O'Brien roused me, and we quitted the *Grande Place*, taking up our quarters at a little cabaret. On examining the purse, I found fifty Napoleons in it: these must have been, obtained from her father. I cried over them with delight. O'Brien was also much affected at the kindness of the colonel. "He's a real O'Brien, every inch of him," said he: "even this cursed country can't spoil the breed."

At the cabaret where we stopped, we were informed, that the officer who was at the hotel had been appointed to the command of the strong fort of Bergen-op-Zoom, and was proceeding thither.

"We must not chance to meet him again, if possible," said O'Brien; "it would be treading too close upon the heels of his duty. Neither will it do to appear on stilts among the dikes; so, Peter, we'll just jump on clear of this town and then we'll trust to our wits."

We walked out of the town early in the morning, after O'Brien had made purchases of some of the clothes usually worn by the peasantry. When within a few miles of St Nicholas, we threw away our stilts and the clothes which we had on, and dressed ourselves in those O'Brien had purchased. O'Brien had not forgotten to provide us with two large brown-coloured blankets, which we strapped on to our shoulders, as the soldiers do their coats.

"But what are we to pass for now, O'Brien?"

"Peter, I will settle that point before night. My wits are working, but I like to trust to chance for a stray idea or so; we must walk fast, or we shall be smothered with the snow."

It was bitter cold weather, and the snow had fallen heavily during the whole day; but although nearly dusk, there was a bright moon ready for us. We walked very fast, and soon observed persons ahead of us. "Let us overtake them, we may obtain some information." As we came up with them, one of them (they were both lads of seventeen to eighteen) said to O'Brien, "I thought we were the last, but I was mistaken. How far is it now to St Nicholas?"

"How should I know?" replied O'Brien, "I am a stranger in these parts as well as yourself."

"From what part of France do you come?" demanded the other, his teeth chattering with the cold, for he was badly clothed, and with little defence from the inclement weather.

"From Montpelier," replied O'Brien.

"And I from Toulouse. A sad change, comrade, from olives and vines to such a climate as this. Curse the conscription: I intended to have taken a little wife next year."

O'Brien gave me a push, as if to say, "Here's something that will do," and then continued,—

"And curse the conscription I say too, for I had just married, and now my wife is left to be annoyed by the attention of the *fermier général*. But it can't be helped. *C'est pour la France et pour la gloire*."

"We shall be too late to get a billet," replied the other, "and not a sou have I in my pocket. I doubt if I get up with the main body till they are at Flushing. By our route, they are at Axel to-day."

"If we arrive at St Nicholas, we shall do well," replied O'Brien; "but I have a little money left, and I'll not see a comrade want a supper or a bed who is going to serve his country. You can repay me when we meet at Flushing."

"That I will with thanks," replied the Frenchman; "and so will Jacques here, if you will trust him."

"With pleasure," replied O'Brien, who then entered into a long conversation, by which he drew out from the Frenchmen that a party of conscripts had been ordered to Flushing, and that they had dropped behind the main body. O'Brien passed himself off as a conscript belonging to the party, and me as his brother, who had resolved to join the army as a drummer, rather than part with him. In about an hour we arrived at St Nicholas, and after some difficulty obtained entrance into a cabaret. "*Vive la France!*" said O'Brien, going up to the fire, and throwing the snow off his hat. In a short time we were seated to a good supper and very tolerable wine, the hostess sitting down by us, and listening to the true narratives of the real conscripts, and the false one of O'Brien. After supper the conscript who first addressed us pulled out his printed paper, with the route laid down, and observed that we were two days behind the others. O'Brien read it over, and laid it on the table, at the same time calling for more wine, having already pushed it round very freely. We did not drink much ourselves, but plied them hard, and at last the conscript commenced the whole history of his intended marriage and his disappointment, tearing his hair, and crying now and then. "Never mind," interrupted O'Brien, every two or three minutes, "*buvons un autre coup pour la gloire!*" and thus he continued to make them both drink until they reeled away to bed, forgetting their printed paper, which O'Brien had some time before slipped away from the table. We also retired to our room, when O'Brien observed to me. "Peter, this description is as much like me as I am to Old Nick; but that's of no consequence, as nobody goes willingly as a conscript, and therefore they will never have a doubt but that it is all right. We must be off early to-morrow, while these good people are in bed, and steal a long march upon them. I consider that we are now safe as far as Flushing."

Chapter XXIV

What occurred at Flushing, and what occurred when we got out of Flushing.

An hour before daybreak we started; the snow was thick on the ground, but the sky was clear, and without any difficulty or interruption we passed through the towns of Axel and Halst, arrived at Terneuse on the fourth day, and went over to Flushing in company with about a dozen more stragglers from the main body. As we landed, the guard asked us whether we were conscripts. O'Brien replied that he was, and held out his paper. They took his name, or rather that of the person it belonged to, down in a book, and told him that he must apply to the *état major* before three o'clock. We passed on delighted with our success, and then O'Brien pulled out the letter which had been given to him by the woman of the cabaret, who had offered to assist me to escape, when O'Brien passed off as a gendarme, and reading the address, demanded his way to the street. We soon found out the house, and entered.

"Conscripts!" said the woman of the house, looking at O'Brien; "I am billeted full already. It must be a mistake. Where is your order?"

"Read," said O'Brien, handing her the letter.

She read the letter, and putting it into her neckerchief, desired him to follow her. O'Brien beckoned me to come, and we went into a small room. "What can I do for you?" said the woman; "I will do all in my power: but, alas! you will march from here in two or three days."

"Never mind," replied O'Brien, "we will talk the matter over by-and-by, but at present only oblige us by letting us remain in this little room; we do not wish to be seen."

"*Comment done*!—you a conscript, and not wish to be seen! Are you, then, intending to desert?"

"Answer me one question; you have read that letter, do you intend to act up to its purport, as your sister requests?"

"As I hope for mercy I will, if I suffer everything. She is a dear sister, and would not write so earnestly if she had not strong reason. My house and everything you command are yours—can I say more?"

"But," continued O'Brien, "suppose I did intend to desert, would you then assist me?"

"At my peril," replied the woman: "have you not assisted my family when in difficulty?"

"Well, then, I will not at present detain you from your business; I have heard you called several times. Let us have dinner when convenient, and we will remain here."

"If I have any knowledge of phiz—*what d'ye call it*," observed O'Brien, after she left us, "there is honesty in that woman, and I must trust her, but not yet; we must wait till the conscripts have gone." I agreed with O'Brien, and we remained talking until an hour afterwards, when the woman brought us our dinner.

"What is your name?" inquired O'Brien.

"Louise Eustache; you might have read it on the letter."

"Are you married?"

"Oh yes, these six years. My husband is seldom at home; he is a Flushing pilot. A hard life, harder even than that of a soldier. Who is this lad?"

"He is my brother, who, if I go as a soldier, intends to volunteer as a drummer."

"*Pauvre enfant! c'est dommage.*"

The cabaret was full of conscripts and other people, so that the hostess had enough to do. At night, we were shown by her into a small bed-room, adjoining the room we occupied. "You are quite alone here; the conscripts are to muster to-morrow, I find, in the *Place d'Armes*, at two o'clock; do you intend to go?"

"No," replied O'Brien: "they will think that I am behind. It is of no consequence."

"Well," replied the woman, "do as you please, you may trust me: but I am so busy, without any one to assist me, that until they leave the town, I can hardly find time to speak to you."

"That will be soon enough, my good hostess," replied O'Brien: "*au revoir*."

The next evening, the woman came in, in some alarm, stating that a conscript had arrived whose name had been given in before, and that the person who had given it in, had not mustered at the place. That the conscript had declared, that his pass had been stolen from him by a person with whom he had stopped at St Nicholas, and that there were orders for a strict search to be made through the town, as it was known that some English officers had escaped, and it was supposed that one of them had obtained the pass. "Surely you're not English?" inquired the woman, looking earnestly at O'Brien.

"Indeed, but I am, my dear," replied O'Brien: "and so is this lad with me: and the favour which your sister requires is, that you help us over the water, for which service there are one hundred louis ready to be paid upon delivery of us."

"*Oh, mon Dieu! mais c'est impossible.*"

"Impossible!" replied O'Brien; "was that the answer I gave your sister in her trouble?"

"*Au moins c'est fort difficile.*"

"That's quite another concern; but with your husband a pilot, I should think a great part of the difficulty removed."

"My husband! I've no power over him," replied the woman, putting the apron up to her eyes.

"But one hundred louis may have," replied O'Brien.

"There is truth in that," observed the woman, after a pause, "but what am I to do, if they come to search the house?"

"Send us out of it, until you can find an opportunity to send us to England. I leave it all to you—your sister expects it from you."

"And she shall not be disappointed, if God helps us," replied the woman, after a short pause: "but I fear you must leave this house and the town also to-night."

"How are we to leave the town?"

"I will arrange that; be ready at four o'clock, for the gates are shut at dusk. I must go now, for there is no time to be lost."

"We are in a nice mess now, O'Brien," observed I, after the woman had quitted the room.

"Devil a bit, Peter; I feel no anxiety whatever, except at leaving such good quarters."

We packed up all our effects, not forgetting our two blankets, and waited the return of the hostess. In about an hour she entered the room. "I have spoken to my husband's sister, who lives about two miles on the road to Middelburg. She is in town now, for it is market-day, and you will be safe where she hides you. I told her, it was by my husband's request, or she would not have consented. Here, boy, put on these clothes; I will assist you." Once more I was dressed as a girl, and when my clothes were on, O'Brien burst out into laughter at my blue stockings and short petticoats. "*Il n'est pas mal,*" observed the hostess, as she fixed a small cap on my head, and then tied a kerchief under my chin, which partly hid my face. O'Brien put on a greatcoat, which the woman handed to him, with a wide-brimmed hat. "Now follow me!" She led us into the street, which was thronged, till we arrived at the market-place, when she met another woman, who joined her. At the end of the market-place stood a small horse and cart, into which the strange woman and I mounted, while O'Brien, by the directions of the landlady, led the horse through the crowd until we arrived at the barriers, when she wished us good day in a loud voice before the guard. The guard took no notice of us, and we passed safely through, and found ourselves upon a neatly-paved road, as straight as an arrow, and lined on each side with high trees and a ditch. In about an hour, we stopped near to the farmhouse of the woman who was in charge of us. "Do you observe that wood?" said she to O'Brien, pointing to one about half a mile from the road. "I dare not take you into the house, my husband is so violent against the English, who captured his schuyt, and made him a poor man, that he would inform against you immediately; but go you there, make yourselves as comfortable as you can to-night, and to-morrow I will send you what you want. *Adieu! Je vous plains, pauvre enfant.*" said she, looking at me, as she drove off in the cart towards her own house.

"Peter," said O'Brien, "I think that her kicking us out of her house is a proof of her sincerity, and therefore I say no more about it; we have the brandy-flask to keep up our spirits. Now then for the wood, though, by the powers, I shall have no relish for any of your pic-nic parties, as they call them, for the next twelve years."

"But, O'Brien, how can I get over this ditch in petticoats? I could hardly leap it in my own clothes."

"You must tie your petticoats round your waist and make a good run; get over as far as you can, and I will drag you through the rest."

"But you forget that we are to sleep in the wood, and that it's no laughing matter to get wet through, freezing so hard as it does now."

"Very true, Peter; but as the snow lies so deep upon the ditch, perhaps the ice may bear. I'll try; if it bears me, it will not condescend to bend at your shrimp of a carcass."

O'Brien tried the ice, which was firm, and we both walked over, and making all the haste we could, arrived at the wood, as the woman called it, but which was not more than a clump of trees of about half an acre. We cleared away the snow for about six feet round a very hollow part, and then O'Brien cut stakes and fixed them in the earth, to which we stretched one blanket. The snow being about two feet deep, there was plenty of room to creep underneath the blanket. We then collected all the leaves we could, beating the snow off them, and laid them at the bottom of the hole; over the leaves we spread the other blanket, and taking our bundles in, we then stopped up with snow every side of the upper blanket, except the hole to creep in at. It was quite astonishing what a warm place this became in a short time after we had remained in it. It was almost too warm, although the weather outside was piercingly cold. After a good meal and a dose of brandy, we both fell fast asleep, but not until I had taken off my woman's attire and resumed my own clothes. We never slept better or more warmly than we did in this hole which we had made on the ground, covered with ice and snow.

Chapter XXV

O'Brien parts company to hunt for provisions, and I have other company in consequence of another hunt—O'Brien pathetically mourns my death and finds me alive—We escape.

The ensuing morning we looked out anxiously for the promised assistance, for we were not very rich in provisions, although what we had were of a very good quality. It was not until three o'clock in the afternoon that we perceived a little girl coming towards us, escorted by a large mastiff. When she arrived at the copse of trees where we lay concealed, she cried out to the dog in Dutch, who immediately scoured the wood until he came to our hiding-place, when he crouched down at the entrance, barking furiously, and putting us in no small dread, lest he should attack us; but the little girl spoke to him again, and he remained in the same position, looking at us, wagging his tail, with his under jaw lying on the snow. She soon came up, and looking underneath, put a basket in, and nodded her head. We emptied the basket. O'Brien took out a napoleon and offered it to her; she refused it, but O'Brien forced it into her hand, upon which she again spoke to the dog, who commenced barking so furiously at us, that we expected every moment he would fly upon us. The girl at the same time presented the napoleon, and pointing to the dog, I went forward and took the napoleon from her, at which she immediately silenced the enormous brute, and laughing at us, hastened away.

"By the powers, that's a fine little girl!" said O'Brien; "I'll back her and her dog against any man. Well, I never had a dog set at me for giving money before, but we live and learn, Peter; now let's see what she brought in the basket." We found hard-boiled eggs, bread, and a smoked mutton ham, with a large bottle of gin. "What a nice little girl! I hope she will often favour us with her company. I've been thinking, Peter, that we're quite as well off here, as in a midshipman's berth."

"You forget you are a lieutenant."

"Well, so I did, Peter, and that's the truth, but it's the force of habit. Now let's make our dinner. It's a new-fashioned way though, of making a meal, lying down; but however, it's economical, for it must take longer to swallow the victuals."

"The Romans used to eat their meals lying down, so I have read, O'Brien."

"I can't say that I ever heard it mentioned in Ireland, but that don't prove that it was not the case; so, Peter, I'll take your word for it. Murder! how fast it snows again! I wonder what my father's thinking on just at this moment."

This observation of O'Brien induced us to talk about our friends and relations in England, and after much conversation we fell fast asleep. The next morning we found the snow had fallen about eight inches, and weighed down our upper blanket so much, that we were obliged to go out and cut stakes to support it up from the inside. While we were thus employed, we heard a loud noise and shouting, and perceived several men, apparently armed and accompanied with dogs, running straight in the direction of the wood where we were encamped. We were much alarmed, thinking that they were in search of us, but on a sudden they turned off in another direction, continuing with the same speed as before. "What could it be?" said I, to O'Brien. "I can't exactly say, Peter; but I should think that they were hunting something, and the only game that I think likely to be in such a place as this are otters." I was of the same opinion. We expected the little girl, but she did not come, and after looking out for her till dark, we crawled into our hole and supped upon the remainder of our provisions.

The next day, as may be supposed, we were very anxious for her arrival, but she did not appear at the time expected. Night again came on, and we went to bed without having any sustenance, except a small piece of bread that was left, and some gin which was remaining in the flask. "Peter," said O'Brien, "if she don't come again to-morrow, I'll try what I can do; for I've no idea of our dying of hunger here, like the two babes in the wood, and being found covered up with dead leaves. If she does not appear at three o'clock, I'm off for provisions, and I don't see much danger, for in this dress I look as much of a boor as any man in Holland."

We passed an uneasy night, as we felt convinced, either that the danger was so great that they dared not venture to assist us, or, that being over-ruled, they had betrayed us, and left us to manage how we could. The next morning I climbed up the only large tree in the copse and looked round, especially in the direction of the farm-house belonging to the woman who had pointed out to us our place of concealment; but nothing was to be seen but one vast tract of flat country covered with snow, and now and then a vehicle passing at a distance on the Middelburg road. I descended, and found O'Brien preparing for a start. He was very melancholy, and said to me, "Peter, if I am taken, you must, at all risks, put on your girl's clothes and go to Flushing to the cabaret. The women there, I am sure, will protect you, and send you back to England. I only want two napoleons; take all the rest, you will require them. If I am not back by to-night, set off for Flushing to-morrow morning." O'Brien waited some time longer, talking with me, and it then being past four o'clock, he shook me by the hand, and, without speaking, left the wood. I never felt more miserable during the whole time since we were first put into prison at Toulon, till that moment, and, when he was a hundred yards off, I knelt down and prayed. He had been absent two hours, and it was quite dusk, when I heard a noise at a distance: it advanced every moment nearer and nearer. On a sudden, I heard a rustling of the bushes, and hastened under the blanket, which was covered with snow, in hopes that they might not perceive the entrance; but I was hardly there before in dashed after me an enormous wolf. I cried out, expecting to be torn to pieces every moment, but the creature lay on his belly, his mouth wide open, his eyes glaring, and his long tongue hanging out of his mouth, and although he touched me, he was so exhausted that he did not attack me. The noise increased, and I immediately perceived that it was the hunters in pursuit of him. I had crawled in feet first, the wolf ran in head foremost, so that we lay head and tail. I crept out as fast as I could, and perceived men and dogs not two hundred yards off in full chase. I hastened to the large tree, and had not ascended six feet when they came up; the dogs flew to the hole, and in a very short time the wolf was killed. The hunters being too busy to observe me, I had in the meantime climbed up the trunk of the tree, and hidden myself as well as I could. Being not fifteen yards from them, I heard their expressions of surprise as they lifted up the blanket and dragged out the dead wolf, which they carried away with them; their conversation being in Dutch, I could not understand it, but I was certain that they made use of the word "*English*." The hunters and dogs quitted the copse, and I was about to descend, when one of them returned, and pulling up the blankets, rolled them together and walked away with them. Fortunately he did not perceive our bundles by the little light given by the moon. I waited a short time and then came down. What to do I knew not. If I did not remain and O'Brien returned, what would he think? If I did, I should be dead with cold before the morning. I looked for our bundles, and found that in the conflict between the dogs and the wolf, they had been buried among the leaves. I recollected O'Brien's advice, and dressed myself in the girl's clothes, but I could not make up my mind to go to Flushing. So I resolved to walk towards the farmhouse, which, being close to the road, would give me a chance of meeting with O'Brien. I soon arrived there and prowled round it for some time, but the doors and windows were all fast, and I dared not knock, after what the woman had said about her husband's inveteracy to the English. At last, as I looked round and round, quite at a loss what to do, I thought I saw a figure at a distance proceeding in the direction of the copse. I hastened after it and saw it enter. I then advanced very cautiously, for although I thought it might be O'Brien, yet it was possible that it was one of the men who chased the wolf in search of more plunder. But I soon heard O'Brien's voice, and I hastened towards him. I was close to him without his perceiving me, and found him sitting down with his face covered up in his two hands. At last he cried, "O Pater! my poor Pater! are you taken at last? Could I not leave you for one hour in safety? Ochone! why did I leave you? My poor, poor Pater! simple you were, sure enough, and that's why I loved you; but, Pater, I would have made a man of you, for you'd all the materials, that's the truth—and a fine man, too. Where am I to look for you, Pater? Where am I to find you, Pater? You're fast locked up by this time, and all my trouble's gone for nothing. But I'll be locked up too, Pater. Where you are, will I be; and if we can't go to England together, why then we'll go back to that blackguard hole at Givet together. Ochone! Ochone!" O'Brien spoke no more, but burst into tears. I was much affected with this proof of O'Brien's sincere regard, and I came to his side and clasped him in my arms. O'Brien stared at me, "Who are you, you ugly Dutch frow?" (for he had quite forgotten the woman's dress at the moment), but recollecting himself, he hugged me in his arms. "Pater, you come as near to an angel's shape as you can, for you come in that of a woman, to comfort me; for, to tell the truth, I was very much distressed at not finding you here; and all the blankets gone to boot. What has been the matter?" I explained in as few words as I could.

"Well, Peter, I'm happy to find you all safe, and much happier to find that you can be trusted when I leave you, for you could not have behaved more prudently; now I'll tell you what I did, which was not much, as it happened. I knew that there was no cabaret between us and Flushing, for I took particular notice as I came along; so I took the road to Middelburg, and found but one, which was full of soldiers. I passed it, and found no other. As I came back past the same cabaret, one of the soldiers came out to me, but I walked along the road. He quickened his pace, and so did I mine, for I expected mischief. At last he came up to me, and spoke to me in Dutch, to which I gave him no answer. He collared me, and then I thought it convenient to pretend that I was deaf and dumb. I pointed to my mouth with an Au—au—and then to my ears, and shook my head; but he would not be convinced, and I heard him say something about English. I then knew that there was no time to be lost, so I first burst out into a loud laugh and stopped; and on his attempting to force me, I kicked up his heels, and he fell on the ice with such a rap on the pate, that I doubt if he has recovered it by this time. There I left him, and have run back as hard as I could, without anything for Peter to fill his little hungry inside with. Now, Peter, what's your opinion? for they say that out of the mouth of babes there is wisdom; and although I never saw anything come out of their mouths but sour milk, yet perhaps I may be more fortunate this time, for, Peter, you're but a baby."

"Not a small one, O'Brien, although not quite so large as Fingal's *babby* that you told me the story of. My idea is this.—Let us, at all hazards, go to the farmhouse. They have assisted us, and may be inclined to do so again; if they refuse, we must push on to Flushing and take our chance."

"Well," observed O'Brien, after a pause, "I think we can do no better, so let's be off." We went to the farmhouse, and, as we approached the door, were met by the great mastiff. I started back, O'Brien boldly advanced. "He's a clever dog, and may know us again. I'll go up," said O'Brien, not stopping while he spoke, "and pat his head: if he flies at me, I shall be no worse than I was before, for depend upon it he will not allow us to go back again." O'Brien by this time had advanced to the dog, who looked earnestly and angrily at him. He patted his head, the dog growled, but O'Brien put his arm round his neck, and patting him again, whistled to him, and went to the door of the farmhouse. The dog followed him silently but closely. O'Brien knocked, and the door was opened by the little girl: the mastiff advanced to the girl, and then turned round, facing O'Brien, as much as to say, "Is he to come in?" The girl spoke to the dog, and went indoors. During her absence the mastiff lay down at the threshold. In a few seconds the woman who had brought us from Flushing, came out, and desired us to enter. She spoke very good French, and told us that fortunately her husband was absent; that the reason why we had not been supplied was, that a wolf had met her little girl returning the other day, but had been beaten off by the mastiff, and that she was afraid to allow her to go again; that she heard the wolf had been killed this evening, and had intended her girl to have gone to us early to-morrow morning; that wolves were hardly known in that country, but that the severe winter had brought them down to the lowlands, a very rare circumstance, occurring perhaps not once in twenty years. "But how did you pass the mastiff?" said she; "that has surprised my daughter and me." O'Brien told her, upon which she said "that the English were really '*des braves*.' No other man had ever done the same." So I thought, for nothing would have induced me to do it. O'Brien then told the history of the death of the wolf, with all particulars, and our intention, if we could not do better, of returning to Flushing.

"I heard that Pierre Eustache came home yesterday," replied the woman; "and I do think that you will be safer there than here, for they will never think of looking for you among the *casernes*, which join their cabaret."

"Will you lend us your assistance to get in?"

"I will see what I can do. But are you not hungry?"

"About as hungry as men who have eaten nothing for two days."

"*Mon Dieu! c'est vrai.* I never thought it was so long, but those whose stomachs are filled forget those who are empty. God make us better and more charitable!"

She spoke to the little girl in Dutch, who hastened to load the table, which we hastened to empty. The little girl stared at our voracity; but at last she laughed out, and clapped her hands at every fresh mouthful which we took, and pressed us to eat more. She allowed me to kiss her, until her mother told her that I was not a woman, when she pouted at me, and beat me off. Before midnight we were fast asleep upon the benches before the kitchen fire, and at daybreak were roused up by the woman, who offered us some bread and spirits, and then we went out to the door, where we found the horse and cart all ready, and loaded with vegetables for the market. The woman, the little girl, and myself got in, O'Brien leading as before, and the mastiff following. We had learnt the dog's name, which was "*Achille*," and he seemed to be quite fond of us. We passed the dreaded barriers without interruption, and in ten minutes entered the cabaret of Eustache; and immediately walked into the little room through a crowd of soldiers, two of whom chucked me under the chin. Whom should we find there but Eustache, the pilot himself, in conversation with his wife, and it appeared that they were talking about us, she insisting, and he unwilling to have any hand in the business. "Well, here they are themselves, Eustache; the soldiers who have seen them come in will never believe that this is their first entry if you give them up. I leave them to make their own bargain; but mark me, Eustache, I have slaved night and day in this cabaret for your profit; if you do not oblige me and my family, I no longer keep a cabaret for you."

Madame Eustache then quitted the room with her husband's sister and little girl, and O'Brien immediately accosted him. "I promise you," said he to Eustache, "one hundred louis if you put us on shore at any part of England, or on board of any English man-of-war; and if you do it within a week, I will make it twenty louis more." O'Brien then pulled out the fifty napoleons given us by Celeste, for our own were not yet expended, and laid them on the table. "Here is this in advance, to prove my sincerity. Say, is it a bargain or not?"

"I never yet heard of a poor man who could withstand his wife's arguments, backed with one hundred and twenty louis," said Eustache smiling, and sweeping the money off the table.

"I presume you have no objection to start to-night? That will be ten louis more in your favour," replied O'Brien.

"I shall earn them," replied Eustache. "The sooner I am off the better, for I could not long conceal you here. The young frow with you is, I suppose, your companion that my wife mentioned. He has begun to suffer hardships early. Come, now, sit down and talk, for nothing can be done till dark."

O'Brien narrated the adventures attending our escape, at which Eustache laughed heartily; the more so, at the mistake which his wife was under, as to the obligations of the family. "If I did not feel inclined to assist you before, I do now, just for the laugh I shall have at her when I come back, and if she wants any more assistance for the sake of her relations, I shall remind her of this anecdote; but she's a good woman and a good wife to boot, only too fond of her sisters." At dusk he equipped us both in sailor's jackets and trowsers, and desired us to follow him boldly. He passed the guard, who knew him well. "What, to sea already?" said one. "You have quarrelled with your wife." At which they all laughed, and we joined. We gained the beach, jumped into his little boat, pulled off to his vessel, and, in a few minutes, were under weigh. With a strong tide and a fair wind we were soon clear of the Scheldt, and the next morning a cutter hove in sight. We steered for her, ran under her lee, O'Brien hailed for a boat, and Eustache, receiving my bill for the remainder of his money, wished us success; we shook hands, and in a few minutes found ourselves once more under the British pennant.

Chapter XXVI

Adventures at home—I am introduced to my grandfather—He obtains employment for O'Brien and myself, and we join a frigate.

As soon as we were on the deck of the cutter, the lieutenant commanding her inquired of us, in a consequential manner, who we were. O'Brien replied that we were English prisoners who had escaped. "Oh, midshipmen, I presume," replied the lieutenant; "I heard that some had contrived to get away."

"My name, sir," said O'Brien, "is Lieutenant O'Brien; and if you'll send for a 'Steel's List,' I will have the honour of pointing it out to you. This young gentleman is Mr Peter Simple, midshipman, and grandson to the Right Honourable Lord Viscount Privilege."

The lieutenant, who was a little snub-nosed man, with a pimply face, then altered his manner towards us, and begged we would step down into the cabin, where he offered, what perhaps was the greatest of all luxuries to us, some English cheese and bottled porter. "Pray," said he, "did you see anything of one of my officers, who was taken prisoner when I was sent with despatches to the Mediterranean fleet?"

"May I first ask the name of your lively little craft?" said O'Brien.

"'The Snapper,'" replied the lieutenant.

"Och, murder; sure enough we met him. He was sent to Verdun, but we had the pleasure of his company *en route* as far as Montpelier. A remarkably genteel, well-dressed young man, was he not?"

"Why, I can't say much about his gentility; indeed, I am not much of a judge. As for his dress, he ought to have dressed well, but he never did when on board of me. His father is my tailor, and I took him as midshipman, just to square an account between us."

"That's exactly what I thought," replied O'Brien.

He did not say any more, which I was glad of, as the lieutenant might not have been pleased at what had occurred.

"When do you expect to run into port?" demanded O'Brien; for we were rather anxious to put our feet ashore again in old England. The lieutenant replied that his cruise was nearly up; and he considered our arrival quite sufficient reason for him to run in directly, and that he intended to put his helm up after the people had had their dinner. We were much delighted with this intelligence, and still more to see the intention put into execution half an hour afterwards.

In three days we anchored at Spithead, and went on shore with the lieutenant to report ourselves to the admiral. Oh! with what joy did I first put my foot on the shingle beach at Sallyport, and then hasten to the post-office to put in a long letter which I had written to my mother. We did not go to the admiral's, but merely reported ourselves at the admiral's office; for we had no clothes fit to appear in. But we called at Meredith's the tailor, and he promised that, by the next morning, we should be fitted complete. We then ordered new hats, and everything we required, and went to the Fountain inn. O'Brien refused to go to the Blue Posts, as being only a receptacle for midshipmen. By eleven o'clock the next morning, we were fit to appear before the admiral, who received us very kindly, and requested our company to dinner. As I did not intend setting off for home until I had received an answer from my mother, we, of course, accepted the invitation.

There was a large party of naval officers and ladies, and O'Brien amused them very much during dinner. When the ladies left the room, the admiral's wife told me to come up with them; and when we arrived at the drawing-room, the ladies all gathered round me, and I had to narrate the whole of my adventures, which very much entertained and interested them. The next morning I received a letter from my mother—such a kind one! entreating me to come home as fast as I could, and bring my *preserver* O'Brien with me. I showed it to O'Brien, and asked him whether he would accompany me.

"Why, Peter, my boy, I have a little business of some importance to transact; which is, to obtain my arrears of pay, and some prize-money which I find due. When I have settled that point, I will go to town to pay my respects to the First Lord of the Admiralty, and then I think I will go and see your father and mother: for, until I know how matters stand, and whether I shall be able to go with spare cash in my pocket, I do not wish to see my own family;

so write down your address here, and you'll be sure I'll come, if it is only to square my accounts with you, for I am not a little in your debt."

I cashed a cheque sent by my father, and set off in the mail that night; the next evening I arrived safe home. But I shall leave the reader to imagine the scene: to my mother I was always dear, and circumstances had rendered me of some importance to my father; for I was now an only son, and his prospects were very different from what they were when I left home. About a week afterwards, O'Brien joined us, having got through all his business. His first act was to account with my father for his share of the expenses; and he even insisted upon paying his half of the fifty napoleons given me by Celeste, which had been remitted to a banker at Paris before O'Brien's arrival, with a guarded letter of thanks from my father to Colonel O'Brien, and another from me to dear little Celeste. When O'Brien had remained with us about a week, he told me that he had about one hundred and sixty pounds in his pocket, and that he intended to go and see his friends, as he was sure that he would be welcome even to Father M'Grath. "I mean to stay with them about a fortnight, and shall then return and apply for employment. Now, Peter, will you like to be again under my protection?"

"O'Brien, I will never quit you or your ship, if I can help it."

"Spoken like a sensible Peter. Well, then, I was promised immediate employment, and I will let you know as soon as the promise is performed."

O'Brien took his leave of my family, who were already very partial to him, and left that afternoon for Holyhead. My father no longer treated me as a child; indeed, it would have been an injustice if he had. I do not mean to say that I was a clever boy; but I had seen much of the world in a short time, and could act and think for myself. He often talked to me about his prospects, which were very different from what they were when I left him. My two uncles, his elder brothers, had died, the third was married and had two daughters. If he had no son, my father would succeed to the title. The death of my elder brother Tom had brought me next in succession. My grandfather, Lord Privilege, who had taken no more notice of my father than occasionally sending him a basket of game, had latterly often invited him to the house, and had even requested, *some day or another*, to see his wife and family. He had also made a handsome addition to my father's income, which the death of my two uncles had enabled him to do. Against all this, my uncle's wife was reported to be again in the family way. I cannot say that I was pleased when my father used to speculate upon these chances so often as he did. I thought, not only as a man, but more particularly as a clergyman, he was much to blame; but I did not know then so much of the world. We had not heard from O'Brien for two months, when a letter arrived, stating that he had seen his family, and bought a few acres of land, which had made them all quite happy, and had quitted with Father M'Grath's double blessing, with unlimited absolution; that he had now been a month in town trying for employment, but found that he could not obtain it, although one promise was backed up by another.

A few days after this, my father received a note from Lord Privilege, requesting he would come and spend a few days with him, and bring his son Peter who had escaped from the French prison. Of course this was an invitation not to be neglected, and we accepted it forthwith. I must say, I felt rather in awe of my grandfather; he had kept the family at such a distance, that I had always heard his name mentioned more with reverence than with any feeling of kindred, but I was a little wiser now. We arrived at Eagle Park, a splendid estate, where he resided, and were received by a dozen servants in and out of livery, and ushered into his presence. He was in his library, a large room, surrounded with handsome bookcases, sitting on an easy chair. A more venerable, placid old gentleman I never beheld; his grey hairs hung down on each side of his temples, and were collected in a small *queue* behind. He rose and bowed, as we were announced; to my father he held out *two* fingers in salutation, to me only *one*, but there was an elegance in the manner in which it was done which was indescribable. He waved his hand to chairs, placed by the *gentleman* out of livery, and requested we would be seated. I could not, at the time, help thinking of Mr Chucks, the boatswain, and his remarks upon high breeding, which were so true: and I laughed to myself when I recollected that Mr Chucks had once dined with him. As soon as the servants had quitted the room, the distance on the part of my grandfather appeared to wear off. He interrogated me on several points, and seemed pleased with my replies; but he always called me "child." After a conversation of half an hour, my father rose, saying that his lordship must be busy, and that we would go over the grounds till dinner-time. My grandfather rose, and we took a sort of formal leave; but it was not a formal leave, after all, it was high breeding, respecting yourself and respecting others. For my part, I was pleased with the first interview, and so I told my father after we had left the room. "My dear Peter," replied he, "your grandfather has one idea which absorbs most others—the peerage, the estate, and the descent of it in the right line. As long as your uncles were alive, we were not thought of, as not being in the line of descent; nor should we now, but that your uncle William has only daughters. Still we are not looked upon as actual, but only contingent, inheritors of the title. Were your uncle to die to-morrow, the difference in his behaviour would be manifested immediately."

"That is to say, instead of *two fingers* you would receive the *whole* hand, and instead of *one* finger, I should obtain promotion to *two*."

At this my father laughed heartily, saying, "Peter, you have exactly hit the mark. I cannot imagine how we ever could have been so blind as to call you the fool of the family."

To this I made no reply, for it was difficult so to do without depreciating others or depreciating myself; but I changed the subject by commenting on the beauties of the park, and the splendid timber with which it was adorned. "Yes, Peter," replied my father, with a sigh, "thirty-five thousand a year in land, money in the funds, and timber worth at least forty thousand more, are not to be despised. But God wills everything." After this remark, my father appeared to be in deep thought, and I did not interrupt him.

We stayed ten days with my grandfather, during which he would often detain me for two hours after breakfast, listening to my adventures, and I really believe was very partial to me. The day before I went away he said, "Child, you are going to-morrow; now tell me what you would like, as I wish to give you a token of regard. Don't be afraid; what shall it be—a watch and seals, or—anything you most fancy?"

"My lord," replied I, "if you wish to do me a favour, it is, that you will apply to the First Lord of the Admiralty to appoint Lieutenant O'Brien to a fine frigate, and, at the same time, ask for a vacancy as midshipman for me."

"O'Brien!" replied his lordship; "I recollect it was he who accompanied you from France, and appears, by your account, to have been a true friend. I am pleased with your request, my child, and it shall be granted."

His lordship then desired me to hand him the paper and ink-standish, wrote by my directions, sealed the letter, and told me he would send me the answer. The next day we quitted Eagle Park, his lordship wishing my father good-bye with *two* fingers, and to me extending *one*, as before; but he said, "I am pleased with you, child; you may write occasionally."

When we were on our route home, my father observed that "I had made more progress with my grandfather than he had known anyone to do, since he could recollect. His saying that you might write to him is at least ten thousand pounds to you in his will, for he never deceives any one, or changes his mind." My reply was, that I should like to see the ten thousand pounds, but that I was not so sanguine.

A few days after our return home, I received a letter and enclosure from Lord Privilege, the contents of which were as follow:—

"My dear Child,—I send you Lord——'s answer, which I trust will prove satisfactory. My compliments to your family.—Yours, &c., PRIVILEGE."

The inclosure was a handsome letter from the First Lord, stating that he had appointed O'Brien to the *Sanglier* frigate, and had ordered me to be received on board as midshipman. I was delighted to forward this letter to O'Brien's address, who, in a few days sent me an answer, thanking me, and stating that he had received his 'appointment, and that I need not join for a month, which was quite time enough, as the ship was refitting; but, that if my family were tired of me, which was sometimes the case in the best regulated families, why, then I should learn something of my duty by coming to Portsmouth. He concluded by sending his kind regards to all the family, and his *love* to my grandfather, which last I certainly did not forward in my letter of thanks. About a month afterwards I received a letter from O'Brien, stating that the ship was ready to go out of harbour, and would be anchored off Spithead in a few days.

Chapter XXVII

Captain and Mrs To—Pork—We go to Plymouth, and fall in with our old Captain.

I immediately took leave of my family, and set off for Portsmouth, and in two days arrived at the Fountain inn, where O'Brien was waiting to receive me. "Peter, my boy, I feel so much obliged to you, that if your uncle won't go out of the world by fair means, I'll pick a quarrel with him, and shoot him, on purpose that you may be a lord, as I am determined you shall be. Now come up into my room, where we'll be all alone, and I'll tell you all about the ship and our new captain. In the first place, we'll begin with the ship, as the most important personage of the two: she's a beauty, I forget her name before she was taken, but the French know how to build ships better than keep them. She's now called the *Sanglier*, which means a wild pig, and, by the powers! a *pig* ship she is, as you will hear directly. The captain's name is a very short one, and wouldn't please Mr Chucks, consisting only of two letters, T and O, which makes To; his whole title is Captain John To. It would almost appear as if somebody had broken off the better half of his name, and only left him the commencement of it; but, however, it's a handy name to sign when he pays off his ship. And now I'll tell you what sort of a looking craft he is. He's built like a Dutch schuyt, great breadth of beam, and very square tuck. He applied to have the quarter galleries enlarged in the two last ships he commanded. He weighs about eighteen stone, rather more than less. He is a good-natured sort of a chap, amazingly ungenteel, not much of an officer, not much of a sailor, but a devilish good hand at the trencher. But he's only part of the concern; he has his wife on board, who is a red-herring sort of a lady, and very troublesome to boot. What makes her still more annoying is, that she has a *piano* on board, very much out of *tune*, on which she plays very much out of *time*. Holystoning is music compared with her playing: even the captain's spaniel howls when she comes to the high notes; but she affects the fine lady, and always treats the officers with music when they dine in the cabin, which makes them very glad to get out of it."

"But, O'Brien, I thought wives were not permitted on board."

"Very true, but there's the worst part in the man's character: he knows that he is not allowed to take his wife to sea, and, in consequence, he never says she *is* his wife, or presents her on shore to anybody. If any of the other captains ask how Mrs To is to-day? 'Why,' he replies, 'pretty well, I thank you;' but at the same time he gives a kind of smirk, as if to say, 'She is not my wife;' and although everybody knows that she is, yet he prefers that they should think otherwise, rather than be at the expense of keeping her on shore; for you know, Peter, that although there are regulations about wives, there are none with regard to other women."

"But does his wife know this?" inquired I.

"I believe, from my heart, she is a party to the whole transaction, for report says, that she would skin a flint if she could. She's always trying for presents from the officers, and, in fact, she commands the ship."

"Really, O'Brien, this is not a very pleasant prospect."

"Whist! wait a little; now I come to the wind-up. This Captain To is very partial to pig's *mate*, and we have as many live pigs on board as we have pigs of ballast. The first lieutenant is right mad about them. At the same time he allows no pigs but his own on board, that there may be no confusion. The manger is full of pigs; there are two cow-pens between the main-deck guns, drawn from the dock-yard, and converted into pig-pens. The two sheep-pens amidships are full of pigs, and the geese and turkey-coops are divided off into apartments for four *sows* in the *family way*. Now, Peter, you see there's little or no expense in keeping pigs on board of a large frigate, with so much *pay*-soup and whole peas for them to eat, and this is the reason why he keeps them, for the devil a bit of any other stock has he on board. I presume he means to *milk* one of the *old sows* for breakfast when the ship sails. The first thing that he does in the morning, is to go round to his pigs with the butcher, feeling one, scratching the dirty ears of another, and then he classes them—his *bacon* pigs, his *porkers*, his *breeding* sows, and so on. The old boar is still at the stables of this inn, but I hear he is to come on board with the sailing orders: but he is very savage, and is therefore left on shore to the very last moment. Now really, Peter, what with the squealing of the pigs and his wife's piano, we are almost driven mad. I don't know which is the worse of the two; if you go aft you hear the one, if you go forward you hear the other, by way of variety, and that, they say, is charming. But, is it not shocking that such a beautiful frigate should be turned into a pig-sty, and that her main-deck should smell worse than a muckheap?"

"But how does his wife like the idea of living only upon hog's flesh?"

"She! Lord bless you, Peter! why, she looks as spare as a shark, and she has just the appetite of one, for she'll *bolt* a four-pound piece of pork before it's well put on her plate."

"Have you any more such pleasant intelligence to communicate, O'Brien?"

"No, Peter; you have the worst of it. The lieutenants are good officers and pleasant messmates: the doctor is a little queer, and the purser thinks himself a wag; the master, an old north-countryman, who knows his duty, and takes his glass of grog. The midshipmen are a very genteel set of young men, and full of fun and frolic. I'll bet a wager there'll be a bobbery in the pig-sty before long, for they are ripe for mischief. Now, Peter, I hardly need say that my cabin and everything I have is at your service; and I think if we could only have a devil of a gale of wind, or a hard-fought action, to send the *pigs* overboard and smash the *piano*, we should do very well."

The next day I went on board, and was shown down into the cabin, to report my having joined. Mrs To, a tall thin woman, was at her piano; she rose, and asked me several questions—who my friends were—how much they allowed me a year, and many other questions, which I thought impertinent: but a captain's wife is allowed to take liberties. She then asked me if I was fond of music? That was a difficult question, as, if I said that I was, I should in all probability be obliged to hear it: if I said that I was not, I might have created a dislike in her. So I replied, that I was very fond of music on shore, when it was not interrupted by other noise. "Ah! then I perceive you are a real amateur, Mr Simple," replied the lady.

Captain To then came out of the after-cabin, half-dressed. "Well, youngster, so you've joined us at last. Come and dine with us to-day? and, as you go down to your berth, desire the sentry to pass the word for the butcher; I want to speak with him."

I bowed and retired. I was met in the most friendly manner by the officers and by my own messmates, who had been prepossessed in my favour by O'Brien, previous to my arrival. In our service you always find young men of the best families on board large frigates, they being considered the most eligible class of vessels; I found my messmates to be gentlemen, with one or two exceptions, but I never met so many wild young lads together. I sat down and ate some dinner with them, although I was to dine in the cabin, for the sea air made me hungry.

"Don't you dine in the cabin, Simple?" said the caterer.

"Yes," replied I.

"Then don't eat any pork, my boy, now, for you'll have plenty there. Come, gentlemen, fill your glasses; we'll drink happiness to our new messmate, and pledging him, we pledge ourselves to try to promote it."

"I'll just join you in that toast," said O'Brien, walking into the midshipmen's berth. "What is it you're drinking it in?"

"Some of Collier's port, sir. Boy, bring a glass for Mr O'Brien."

"Here's your health, Peter, and wishing you may keep out of a French prison this cruise. Mr Montague, as caterer, I will beg you will order another candle, that I may see what's on the table, and then perhaps I may find something I should like to pick a bit off."

"Here's the fag end of a leg of mutton, Mr O'Brien, and there's a piece of boiled pork."

"Then I'll just trouble you for a bit close to the knuckle. Peter, you dine in the cabin, so do I—the doctor refused."

"Have you heard when we sail, Mr O'Brien?" inquired one of my messmates.

"I heard at the admiral's office, that we were expected to be ordered round to Plymouth, and receive our orders there, either for the East or West Indies, they thought; and, indeed, the stores we have taken on board indicate that we are going foreign, but the captain's signal is just made, and probably the admiral has intelligence to communicate."

In about an hour afterwards, the captain returned, looking very red and hot. He called the first lieutenant aside from the rest of the officers, who were on deck to receive him, and told him, that we were to start for Plymouth next morning; and the admiral had told him confidentially, that we were to proceed to the West Indies with a convoy, which was then collecting. He appeared to be very much alarmed at the idea of going to make a feast for the land crabs; and certainly, his gross habit of body rendered him very unfit for the climate. This news was soon spread through the ship, and there was of course no little bustle and preparation. The doctor, who had refused to dine in the cabin upon plea of being unwell, sent up to say, that he felt himself so much better, that he should have great pleasure to attend the summons, and he joined the first lieutenant, O'Brien, and me, as we walked in. We sat down to table; the covers were removed, and as the midshipmen prophesied, there was plenty of *pork*—mock-turtle soup, made out of a pig's head—a boiled leg of pork and peas-pudding—a roast spare-rib, with the crackling on—sausages and potatoes, and pig's pettitoes. I cannot say that I disliked my dinner, and I ate very heartily; but a roast sucking-pig came on as a second course, which rather surprised me; but what surprised me more, was the quantity devoured by Mrs To. She handed her plate from the boiled pork to the roast, asked for some pettitoes, tried the sausages, and finished with a whole plateful of sucking-pig and stuffing. We had an apple pie at the end, but as we had already eaten apple sauce with the roast pork, we did not care for it. The doctor, who abominated pork, ate pretty well, and was excessively attentive to Mrs To.

"Will you not take a piece of the roast pig, doctor?" said the captain.

"Why, really Captain To, as we are bound, by all reports, to a station where we must not venture upon pork, I think I will not refuse to take a piece, for I am very fond of it."

"How do you mean?" inquired the captain and his lady, both in a breath.

"Perhaps I may be wrongly informed," replied the doctor, "but I have heard that we were ordered to the West Indies; now, if so, everyone knows, that although you may eat salt pork there occasionally without danger, in all tropical climates, and especially the West Indies, two or three days' living upon this meat will immediately produce dysentery, which is always fatal in that climate."

"Indeed!" exclaimed the captain.

"You don't say so!" rejoined the lady.

"I do indeed: and have always avoided the West Indies for that very reason—I am so fond of pork."

The doctor then proceeded to give nearly one hundred instances of messmates and shipmen who had been attacked with dysentery, from the eating of fresh pork in the West Indies; and O'Brien, perceiving the doctor's drift, joined him, telling some most astonishing accounts of the dreadful effects of pork in a hot country. I think he said, that when the French were blockaded, previous to the surrender of Martinique, that, having nothing but pigs to eat, thirteen hundred out of seventeen hundred soldiers and officers died in the course of three weeks, and the others were so reduced by disease, that they were obliged to capitulate. The doctor then changed the subject, and talked about the yellow fever, and other diseases of the climate, so that, by his account, the West India islands were but hospitals to die in. Those most likely to be attacked, were men in full strong health. The spare men stood a better chance. This conversation was carried on until it was time to leave—Mrs To at last quite silent, and the captain gulping down his wine with a sigh. When we rose from the table, Mrs To did not ask us, as usual, to stay and hear a little music; she was, like her piano, not a little out of tune.

"By the powers, doctor, you did that nately," said O'Brien, as we left the cabin.

"O'Brien," said the doctor, "oblige me, and you, Mr Simple, oblige me also, by not saying a word in the ship about what I have said; if it once gets wind, I shall have done no good, but if you both hold your tongues for a short time, I think I may promise you to get rid of Captain To, his wife, and his pigs." We perceived the justice of his observation, and promised secrecy. The next morning the ship sailed for Plymouth, and Mrs To sent for the doctor, not being very well. The doctor prescribed for her, and I believe, on my conscience, made her worse on purpose. The illness of his wife, and his own fears, brought Captain To more than usual in contact with the doctor, of whom he frequently asked his candid opinion, as to his own chance in a hot country.

"Captain To," said the doctor, "*I* never would have given my opinion, if you had not asked it, for I am aware, that, as an officer, you would never flinch from your duty, to whatever quarter of the globe you may be ordered; but, as you have asked the question, I must say, with your full habit of body, I think you would not stand a chance of living for more than two months. At the same time, sir, I may be mistaken; but, at all events, I must point out that Mrs To is of a very bilious habit, and I trust you will not do such an injustice to an amiable woman, as to permit her to accompany you."

"Thanky, doctor, I'm much obliged to you," replied the captain, turning round and going down the ladder to his cabin. We were then beating down the channel; for, although we ran through the Needles with a fair wind, it fell calm, and shifted to the westward, when we were abreast of Portland. The next day the captain gave an order for a very fine pig to be killed, for he was out of provisions. Mrs To still kept her bed, and he therefore directed that a part should be salted, as he could have no company. I was in the midshipman's berth, when some of them proposed that we should get possession of the pig; and the plan they agreed upon was as follows:—they were to go to the pen that night, and with a needle stuck in a piece of wood, to prick the pig all over, and then rub gunpowder into the parts wounded. This was done, and although the butcher was up a dozen times during the night to ascertain what made the pigs so uneasy, the midshipmen passed the needle from watch to watch, until the pig was well tattooed in all parts. In the morning watch it was killed, and when it had been scalded in the tub, and the hair taken off, it appeared covered with blue spots. The midshipman of the morning watch, who was on the main-deck, took care to point out to the butcher, that the pork was *measly*, to which the man unwillingly assented, stating, at the same time, that he could not imagine how it could be, for a finer pig he had never put a knife into. The circumstance was reported to the captain, who was much astonished. The doctor came in to visit Mrs To, and the captain requested the doctor to examine the pig, and give his opinion. Although this was not the doctor's province, yet, as he had great reason for keeping intimate with the captain, he immediately consented. Going forward, he met me, and I told him the secret. "That will do," replied he; "it all tends to what we wish." The doctor returned to the captain, and said, "that there was no doubt but that the pig was measly, which was a complaint very frequent on board ships, particularly in hot climates, where all pork became *measly*—one great reason for its there proving so unwholesome." The captain sent for the first lieutenant, and, with a deep sigh, ordered him to throw the pig overboard; but the first lieutenant, who knew what had been done from O'Brien, ordered the *master's mate* to throw it overboard: the master's mate, touching his hat, said, "Ay, ay, sir," and took it down into the berth, where we cut it up, salted one half, and the other we finished before we arrived at Plymouth, which was six days from the time we left Portsmouth. On our arrival, we found part of the convoy lying there, but no orders for us; and, to my great delight, on the following day the *Diomede* arrived, from a cruise off the Western Islands. I obtained permission to go on board with O'Brien, and we once more greeted our messmates. Mr Falcon, the first lieutenant, went down to Captain Savage, to say we were on board, and he requested us to come into the cabin. He greeted us warmly, and gave us great credit for the manner in which we had effected our escape. When we left the cabin, I found Mr Chucks, the boatswain, waiting outside.

"My dear Mr Simple, extend your flapper to me, for I'm delighted to see you. I long to have a long talk with you."

"And I should like it also, Mr Chucks, but I'm afraid we have not time; I dine with Captain Savage to-day, and it only wants an hour of dinner-time."

"Well, Mr Simple, I've been looking at your frigate, and she's a beauty —much larger than the *Diomede*."

"And she behaves quite as well," replied I. "I think we are two hundred tons larger. You've no idea of her size until you are on her decks."

"I should like to be boatswain of her, Mr Simple; that is, with Captain Savage, for I will not part with him." I had some more conversation with Mr Chucks, but I was obliged to attend to others, who interrupted us. We had a very pleasant dinner with our old captain, to whom we gave a history of our adventures, and then we returned on board.

Chapter XXVIII

We get rid of the pigs and piano-forte—The last boat on shore before sailing—The First Lieutenant too hasty, and the consequences to me.

We waited three days, at the expiration of which, we heard that Captain To was about to exchange with Captain Savage. We could not believe such good news to be true, and we could not ascertain the truth of the report, as the captain had gone on shore with Mrs To, who recovered fast after she was out of our doctor's hands; so fast, indeed, that a week afterwards, on questioning the steward, upon his return on board, how Mrs To was, he replied, "O charming well again, sir, she has eaten a *whole pig*, since she left the ship." But the report was true: Captain To, afraid to go to the West Indies, had effected an exchange with Captain Savage. Captain Savage was permitted, as was the custom of the service, to bring his first lieutenant, his boatswain, and his barge's crew with him. He joined a day or two before we sailed, and never was there more joy on board: the only people miserable were the first lieutenant, and those belonging to the *Sanglier* who were obliged to follow Captain To; who, with his wife, his pigs, and her piano, were all got rid of in the course of one forenoon.

I have already described pay-day on board of a man-of-war, but I think that the two days before sailing are even more unpleasant; although, generally speaking, all our money being spent, we are not sorry when we once are fairly out of harbour, and find ourselves in *blue water*. The men never work well on those days: they are thinking of their wives and sweethearts, of the pleasure they had when at liberty on shore, where they might get drunk without punishment; and many of them are either half drunk at the time, or suffering from the effects of previous intoxication. The ship is in disorder, and crowded with the variety of stock and spare stores which are obliged to be taken on board in a hurry, and have not yet been properly secured in their places. The first lieutenant is cross, the officers are grave, and the poor midshipmen, with all their own little comforts to attend to, are harassed and driven about like post-horses. "Mr Simple," inquired the first lieutenant, "where do you come from?"

"From the gun wharf, sir, with the gunner's spare blocks, and breechings."

"Very well—send the marines aft to clear the boat, and pipe away the first putter. Mr Simple, jump into the first cutter, and go to Mount Wise for the officers. Be careful that none of your men leave the boat. Come, be smart."

Now, I had been away the whole morning, and it was then half-past one, and I had had no dinner: but I said nothing, and went into the boat. As soon as I was off, O'Brien, who stood by Mr Falcon, said, "Peter was thinking of his dinner, poor fellow!"

"I really quite forgot it," replied the first lieutenant, "there is so much to do. He is a willing boy, and he shall dine in the gun-room when he comes back." And so I did—so I lost nothing by not expostulating, and gained more of the favour of the first lieutenant, who never forgot what he called *zeal*. But the hardest trial of the whole, is to the midshipman who is sent with the boat to purchase the supplies for the cabin and gun-room on the day before the ship's sailing. It was my misfortune to be ordered upon that service this time, and that very unexpectedly. I had been ordered to dress myself to take the gig on shore for the captain's orders, and was walking the deck with my very best uniform and side arms, when the marine officer, who was the gun-room caterer, came up to the first lieutenant, and asked him for a boat. The boat was manned, and a midshipman ordered to take charge of it; but when he came up, the first lieutenant recollecting that he had come off two days before with only half his boat's crew, would not trust him, and called out to me, "Here, Mr Simple, I must send you in this boat; mind you are careful that none of the men leave it; and bring off the sergeant of marines, who is on shore looking for the men who have broken their liberty." Although I could not but feel proud of the compliment, yet I did not much like going in my very best uniform, and would have run down and changed it, but the marine officer and all the people were in the boat, and I could not keep it waiting, so down the side I went, and we shoved off. We had, besides the boat's crew, the marine officer, the purser, the gun-room steward, the captain's steward, and the purser's steward; so that we were pretty full. It blew hard from the S.E., and there was a sea running, but as the tide was flowing into the harbour there was not much bubble. We hoisted the foresail, flew before the wind and tide, and in a quarter of an hour we were at Mutton Cove, when the marine officer expressed his wish to land. The landing-place was crowded with boats, and it was not without sundry exchanges of foul words and oaths, and the bow-men dashing the point of their boat-hooks into the shore-boats, to make them keep clear of us, that we forced our way to the beach. The marine officer and all the stewards then left the boat, and I had to look after the men. I had not been there three minutes before the bow-man said that his wife was on the wharf with his clothes from the wash, and begged leave to go and fetch them. I refused, telling him that she could bring them to him. "Vy now, Mr Simple," said the woman, "ar'n't you a nice lady's man, to go for to ax me to muddle my way through all the dead dogs, cabbage-stalks, and stinking hakes' heads, with my bran new shoes and clean stockings?" I looked at her, and sure enough she was, as they say in France, *bien chaussée*. "Come, Mr Simple, let him out to come for his clothes, and you'll see that he's back in a moment." I did not like to refuse her, as it was very dirty and wet, and the shingle was strewed with all that she had mentioned. The bow-man made a spring out with his boat-hook, threw it back, went up to his wife, and commenced talking with her, while I watched him. "If you please, sir, there's my young woman come down, mayn't I speak to her?" said another of the men. I turned round, and refused him. He expostulated, and begged very hard, but I was resolute; however, when I again turned my eyes to watch the bow-man, he and his wife were gone. "There," says I to the coxswain, "I knew it would be so; you see Hickman is off."

"Only gone to take a parting glass, sir," replied the coxswain; "he'll be here directly."

"I hope so; but I'm afraid not." After this, I refused all the solicitations of the men to be allowed to leave the boat, but I permitted them to have some beer brought down to them. The gun-room steward then came back with a basket of *soft-tack*, *i.e.* loaves of bread, and told me that the marine officer requested I would allow two of the men to go up with him to Glencross's shop, to bring down some of the stores. Of course, I sent two of the men, and told the steward if he saw Hickman, to bring him down to the boat.

By this time many of the women belonging to the ship had assembled, and commenced a noisy conversation with the boat's crew. One brought an article for Jim, another some clothes for Bill; some of them climbed into the boat, and sat with the men; others came and went, bringing beer and tobacco, which the men desired them to purchase. The crowd, the noise, and confusion were so great, that it was with the utmost difficulty that I could keep my eyes on all my men, who, one after another, made an attempt to leave the boat. Just at that time came down the sergeant of the marines, with three of our men whom he had picked up, *roaring drunk*. They were tumbled into the boat, and increased the difficulty, as in looking after those who were riotous, and would try to leave the boat by force, I was not so well able to keep my eyes on those who were sober. The sergeant then went up after another man, and I told him also about Hickman. About half an hour afterwards the steward came down with the two men, loaded with cabbages, baskets of eggs, strings of onions, crockery of all descriptions, paper parcels of groceries, legs and shoulders of mutton, which were crowded in, until not only the stern-sheets, but all under the thwarts of the boat were also crammed full. They told me that they had a few more things to bring down, and that the marine officer had gone to Stonehouse to see his wife, so that they should be down long before him. In half an hour more, during which I had the greatest difficulty to manage the boat's crew, they returned with a dozen geese and two ducks, tied by the legs, but without the two men, who had given them the slip, so that there were now three men gone, and I knew Mr Falcon would be very angry, for they were three of the smartest men in the ship. I was now determined not to run the risk of losing more men, and I ordered the boat's crew to shove off, that I might lie at the wharf, where they could not climb up. They were very mutinous, grumbled very much, and would hardly obey me; the fact is, they had drunk a great deal, and some of them were more than half tipsy. However, at last I was obeyed, but not without being saluted with a shower of invectives from the women, and the execrations of the men belonging to the wherries and *shore* boats which were washed against our sides by the swell. The weather had become much worse, and looked very threatening. I waited an hour more, when the sergeant of marines came down with two more men, one of whom, to my great joy, was Hickman. This made me more comfortable, as I was not answerable for the other two; still I was in great trouble from the riotous and insolent behaviour of the boat's crew, and the other men brought down by the sergeant of marines. One of them fell back into a basket of eggs, and smashed them all to atoms; still the marine officer did not come down, and it was getting late. The tide being now at the ebb, running out against the wind, there was a heavy sea, and I had to go off to the ship with a boat deeply laden, and most of the people in her in a state of intoxication. The coxswain, who was the only one who was sober, recommended our shoving off, as it would soon be dark, and some accident would happen. I reflected a minute, and agreeing with him, I ordered the oars to be got out, and we shoved off, the sergeant of marines and the gun-room steward perched up in the bows—drunken men, ducks and geese, lying together at the bottom of the boat—the stern sheets loaded up to the gunwale, and the other passengers and myself sitting how we could among the crockery and a variety of other articles with which the boat was crowded. It was a scene of much confusion—the half-drunken boat's crew *catching crabs*, and falling forward upon the others—those who were quite drunk swearing they *would* pull. "Lay on your oar, Sullivan; you are doing more harm than good. You drunken rascal, I'll report you as soon as we get on board."

"How the divil can I pull, your honour, when there's that fellow Jones breaking the very back o' me with his oar, and he never touching the water all the while?"

"You lie," cried Jones; "I'm pulling the boat by myself against the whole of the larbard oars."

"He's rowing *dry*, your honour—only making bilave."

"Do you call this rowing dry?" cried another, as a sea swept over the boat, fore and aft, wetting everybody to the skin.

"Now, your honour, just look and see if I ain't pulling the very arms off me?" cried Sullivan.

"Is there water enough to cross the bridge, Swinburne?" said I to the coxswain.

"Plenty, Mr Simple; it is but quarter ebb, and the sooner we are on board the better."

We were now past Devil's Point, and the sea was very heavy: the boat plunged in the trough, so that I was afraid that she would break her back. She was soon half full of water, and the two after-oars were laid in for the men to bale. "Plase your honour, hadn't I better cut free the legs of them ducks and geese, and allow them to swim for their lives?" cried Sullivan, resting on his oar; "the poor birds will be drowned else in their own *iliment*."

"No, no—pull away as hard as you can."

By this time the drunken men in the bottom of the boat began to be very uneasy, from the quantity of water which washed about them, and made several staggering attempts to get on their legs. They fell down again upon the ducks and geese, the major part of which were saved from being drowned by being suffocated. The sea on the bridge was very heavy; and although the tide swept us out, we were nearly swamped. Soft bread was washing about the bottom of the boat; the parcels of sugar, pepper, and salt, were wet through with the salt water, and a sudden jerk threw the captain's steward, who was seated upon the gunwale close to the after-oar, right upon the whole of the crockery and eggs, which added to the mass of destruction. A few more seas shipped completed the job, and the gun-room steward was in despair. "That's a darling," cried Sullivan: "the politest boat in the whole fleet. She makes more bows and curtseys than the finest couple in the land. Give way, my lads, and work the crater stuff out of your elbows, and the first lieutenant will see us all so sober, and so wet in the bargain, and think we're all so dry, that perhaps he'll be after giving us a raw nip when we get on board."

In a quarter of an hour we were nearly alongside, but the men pulled so badly, and the sea was so great, that we missed the ship and went astern. They veered out a buoy with a line, which we got hold of, and were hauled up by the marines and after-guard, the boat plunging bows under, and drenching us through and through. At last we got under the counter, and I climbed up by the stern ladder. Mr Falcon was on deck, and very angry at the boat not coming alongside properly. "I thought, Mr Simple, that you knew by this time how to bring a boat alongside."

"So I do, sir, I hope," replied I; "but the boat was so full of water, and the men would not give way."

"What men has the sergeant brought on board?"

"Three, sir," replied I, shivering with the cold, and unhappy at my very best uniform being spoiled.

"Are all your boat's crew with you, sir?"

"No sir; there are two left on shore; they—"

"Not a word, sir. Up to the mast-head, and stay there till I call you down. If it were not so late, I would send you on shore, and not receive you on board again without the men. Up, sir, immediately."

I did not venture to explain, but up I went. It was very cold, blowing hard from the S.E., with heavy squalls; I was so wet that the wind appeared to blow through me, and it was now nearly dark. I reached the cross-trees, and when I was seated there, I felt that I had done my duty, and had not been fairly treated. During this time, the boat had been hauled up alongside to clear, and a pretty clearance there was. All the ducks and geese were dead, the eggs and crockery all broke, the grocery almost all washed away; in short, as O'Brien observed, there was "a very pretty general average." Mr Falcon was still very angry. "Who are the men missing?" inquired he, of Swinburne, the coxswain, as he came up the side.

"Williams and Sweetman, sir."

"Two of the smartest topmen, I am told. It really is too provoking; there is not a midshipman in the ship I can trust. I must work all day, and get no assistance. The service is really going to the devil now, with the young men who are sent on board to be brought up as officers, and who are above doing their duty. What made you so late, Swinburne?"

"Waiting for the marine officer, who went to Stonehouse to see his wife; but Mr Simple would not wait any longer, as it was getting dark, and we had so many drunken men in the boat."

"Mr Simple did right. I wish Mr Harrison would stay on shore with his wife altogether—it's really trifling with the service. Pray, Mr Swinburne, why had you not your eyes about you if Mr Simple was so careless? How came you to allow these men to leave the boat?"

"The men were ordered up by the marine officer to bring down your stores, sir, and they gave the steward the slip. It was no fault of Mr Simple's, nor of mine either. We lay off at the wharf for two hours before we started, or we should have lost more; for what can a poor lad do, when he has charge of drunken men who *will not* obey orders?" And the coxswain looked up at the mast-head, as much as to say, Why is he sent there? "I'll take my oath, sir," continued Swinburne, "that Mr Simple never put his foot out of the boat, from the time that he went over the side until he came on board, and that no young gentleman could have done his duty more strictly."

Mr Falcon looked very angry at first at the coxswain speaking so freely, but he said nothing. He took one or two turns on the deck, and then hailing the mast-head, desired me to come down. But I *could not*; my limbs were so cramped with the wind blowing upon my wet clothes, that I could not move. He hailed again; I heard him, but was not able to answer. One of the topmen then came up, and perceiving my condition, hailed the deck, and said he believed I was dying, for I could not move, and that he dared not leave me for fear I should fall. O'Brien, who had been on deck all the while, jumped up the rigging, and was soon at the cross-trees where I was. He sent the topman down into the top for a tail-block and the studding-sail haulyards, made a whip, and lowered me on deck. I was immediately put into my hammock; and the surgeon ordering me some hot brandy-and-water, and plenty of blankets, in a few hours I was quite restored.

O'Brien, who was at my bedside, said, "Never mind, Peter, and don't be angry with Mr Falcon, for he is very sorry."

"I am not angry, O'Brien; for Mr Falcon has been too kind to me not to make me forgive him for being once hasty."

The surgeon came to my hammock, gave me some more hot drink, desired me to go to sleep, and I woke the next morning quite well.

When I came into the berth, my messmates asked me how I was, and many of them railed against the tyranny of Mr Falcon; but I took his part, saying, that he was hasty in this instance, perhaps, but that, generally speaking, he was an excellent and very just officer. Some agreed with me, but others did not. One of them, who was always in disgrace, sneered at me, and said, "Peter reads the Bible, and knows that if you smite one cheek, he must offer the other. Now, I'll answer for it, if I pull his right ear he will offer me his left." So saying, he lugged me by the ear, upon which I knocked him down for his trouble. The berth was then cleared away for a fight, and in a quarter of an hour my opponent gave in; but I suffered a little, and had a very black eye. I had hardly time to wash myself and change my shirt, which was bloody, when I was summoned on the quarter-deck. When I arrived, I found Mr Falcon walking up and down. He looked very hard at me, but did not ask me any questions as to the cause of my unusual appearance.

"Mr Simple," said he, "I sent for you to beg your pardon for my behaviour to you last night, which was not only very hasty but very unjust. I find that you were not to blame for the loss of the men."

I felt very sorry for him when I heard him speak so handsomely; and, to make his mind more easy, I told him that, although I certainly was not to blame for the loss of those two men, still I had done wrong in permitting Hickman to leave the boat; and that had not the sergeant picked him up, I should have come off without him, and therefore I *did* deserve the punishment which I had received.

"Mr Simple," replied Mr Falcon, "I respect you, and admire your feelings; still, I was to blame, and it is my duty to apologise. Now go down below. I would have requested the pleasure of your company to dinner, but I perceive that something else has occurred, which, under any other circumstances, I would have inquired into, but at present I shall not."

I touched my hat and went below. In the meantime, O'Brien had been made acquainted with the occasion of the quarrel, which he did not fail to explain to Mr Falcon, who, O'Brien declared, "was not the least bit in the world angry with me for what had occurred." Indeed, after that, Mr Falcon always treated me with the greatest kindness, and employed me on every duty which he considered of consequence. He was a sincere friend; for he did not allow me to neglect my duty, but, at the same time, treated me with consideration and confidence.

The marine officer came on board very angry at being left behind, and talked about a court-martial on me for disrespect, and neglect of stores entrusted to my charge; but O'Brien told me not to mind him, or what he said. "It's my opinion, Peter, that the gentleman has eaten no small quantity of *flap-doodle* in his lifetime."

"What's that, O'Brien?" replied I; "I never heard of it."

"Why, Peter," rejoined he, "it's the stuff they *feed fools on.*"

Chapter XXIX

A long conversation with Mr Chucks—The advantage of having a prayer-book in your pocket—We run down the trades—Swinburne, the quartermaster, and his yarns—The Captain falls sick.

The next day the captain came on board with sealed orders, with directions not to open them until off Ushant. In the afternoon, we weighed and made sail. It was a fine northerly wind, and the Bay of Biscay was smooth. We bore up, set all the studding-sails, and ran along at the rate of eleven miles an hour. As I could not appear on the quarter-deck, I was put down on the sick-list. Captain Savage, who was very particular, asked what was the matter with me. The surgeon replied, "An inflamed eye." The captain asked no more questions; and I took care to keep out of his way. I walked in the evening on the forecastle, when I renewed my intimacy with Mr Chucks, the boatswain, to whom I gave a full narrative of all my adventures in France. "I have been ruminating, Mr Simple," said he, "how such a stripling as you could have gone through so much fatigue, and now I know how it is. It is *blood*, Mr Simple—all blood—you are descended from good blood; and there's as much difference between nobility and the lower classes, as there is between a racer and a cart-horse."

"I cannot agree with you, Mr Chucks. Common people are quite as brave as those who are well-born. You do not mean to say that you are not brave— that the seamen on board this ship are not brave?"

"No, no, Mr Simple; but as I observed about myself, my mother was a woman who could not be trusted, and there is no saying who was my father; and she was a very pretty woman to boot, which levels all distinctions for the moment. As for the seamen, God knows, I should do them an injustice if I did not acknowledge that they were as brave as lions. But there are two kinds of bravery, Mr Simple—the bravery of the moment, and the courage of bearing up for a long while. Do you understand me?"

"I think I do; but still do not agree with you. Who will bear more fatigue than our sailors?"

"Yes, yes, Mr Simple, that is because they are *endured* to it from their hard life: but if the common sailors were all such little thread-papers as you, and had been brought up so carefully, they would not have gone through all you have. That's my opinion, Mr Simple— there's nothing like *blood*."

"I think, Mr Chucks, you carry your ideas on that subject too far."

"I do not, Mr Simple; and I think, moreover, that he who has more to lose than another will always strive more. Now a common man only fights for his own credit; but when a man is descended from a long line of people famous in history, and has a coat *in* arms, criss-crossed, and stuck all over with lions and unicorns to support the dignity of—why, has he not to fight for the credit of all his ancestors, whose names would be disgraced if he didn't behave well?"

"I agree with you, Mr Chucks, in the latter remark, to a certain extent."

"Ah! Mr Simple, we never know the value of good descent when we have it, but it's when we cannot get it that we can *'preciate* it. I wish I had been born a nobleman—I do, by heavens!" and Mr Chucks slapped his fist against the funnel, so as to make it ring again. "Well, Mr Simple," continued he, after a pause, "it is, however, a great comfort to me that I have parted company with that fool, Mr Muddle, with his twenty-six thousand and odd years, and that old woman, Dispart, the gunner. You don't know how those two men used to fret me; it was very silly, but I couldn't help it. Now the warrant officers of this ship appear to be very respectable, quiet men, who know their duty and attend to it, and are not too familiar, which I hate and detest. You went home to your friends, of course, when you arrived in England?"

"I did, Mr Chucks, and spent some days with my grandfather, Lord Privilege, whom you say you once met at dinner."

"Well, and how was the old gentleman?" inquired the boatswain, with a sigh.

"Very well, considering his age."

"Now do, pray, Mr Simple, tell me all about it; from the time that the servants met you at the door until you went away. Describe to me the house and all the rooms, for I like to hear of all these things, although I can never see them again."

To please Mr Chucks, I entered into a full detail, which he listened to very attentively, until it was late, and then with difficulty would he permit me to leave off, and go down to my hammock. The next day, rather a singular circumstance occurred. One of the midshipmen was mast-headed by the second lieutenant, for not waiting on deck until he was relieved. He was down below when he was sent for, and expecting to be punished from what the quarter-master told him, he thrust the first book into his jacket-pocket which he could lay his hand on, to amuse himself at the mast-head, and then ran on deck. As he surmised, he was immediately ordered aloft. He had not been there more than five minutes, when a sudden squall carried away the main-top-gallant mast, and away he went flying over to leeward (for the wind had shifted, and the yards were now braced up). Had he gone overboard, as he could not swim, he would, in all probability, have been drowned; but the book in his pocket brought him up in the jaws of the fore-brace block, where he hung until taken out by the main-topmen. Now it so happened that it was a prayer-book which he had laid hold of in his hurry, and those who were superstitious declared it was all owing to his having taken a religious book with him. I did not think so, as any other book would have answered the purpose quite as well: still the midshipman himself thought so, and it was productive of good, as he was a sad scamp, and behaved much better afterwards. But I had nearly forgotten to mention a circumstance which occurred on the day of our sailing, which will be eventually found to have had a great influence upon my after life. It was this. I received a letter from my father, evidently written in great vexation and annoyance, informing me that my uncle, whose wife I have already mentioned had two daughters, and was again expected to be confined, had suddenly broken up his housekeeping, discharged every servant, and proceeded to Ireland under an assumed name. No reason had been given for this unaccountable proceeding; and not even my grandfather, or any of the members of the family, had had notice of his intention. Indeed, it was by mere accident that his departure was discovered, about a fortnight after it had taken place. My father had taken a great deal of pains to find out where he was residing; but although my uncle was traced to Cork, from that town all clue was lost, but still it was supposed, from inquiries, that he was not very far from thence. "Now," observed my father, in his letter, "I cannot help surmising, that my brother, in his anxiety to retain the advantages of the title to his own family, has resolved to produce to the world a spurious child as his own, by some contrivance or other. His wife's health is very bad, and she is not likely to have a large family. Should the one now expected prove a daughter, there is little chance of his ever having another; and I have no hesitation in declaring my conviction that the measure has been taken with a view of defrauding you of your chance of eventually being called to the House of Lords."

I showed this letter to O'Brien, who, after reading it over two or three times, gave his opinion that my father was right in his conjectures "Depend upon it, Peter, there's foul play intended, that is, if foul play is rendered necessary."

"But, O'Brien, I cannot imagine why, if my uncle has no son of his own, he should prefer acknowledging a son of any other person's, instead of his own nephew."

"But I can, Peter: your uncle is not a man likely to live very long, as you know. The doctors say that, with his short neck, his life is not worth two years' purchase. Now if he had a son, consider that his daughters would be much better off, and much more likely to get married; besides, there are many reasons which I won't talk about now, because it's no use making you think your uncle to be a scoundrel. But I'll tell you what I'll do. I'll go down to my cabin directly, and write to Father M'Grath, telling him the whole affair, and desiring him to ferret him out, and watch him narrowly, and I'll bet you a dozen of claret, that in less than a week he'll find him out, and will dog him to the last. He'll get hold of his Irish servants, and you little know the power that a priest has in our country. Now give the description as well as you can of your uncle's appearance, also of that of his wife, and the number of their family, and their ages. Father M'Grath must have all particulars, and then let him alone for doing what is needful."

I complied with O'Brien's directions as well as I could, and he wrote a very long letter to Father M'Grath, which was sent on shore by a careful hand. I answered my father's letter, and then thought no more about the matter.

Our sealed orders were opened, and proved our destination to be the West Indies, as we expected. We touched at Madeira to take in some wine for the ship's company; but as we only remained one day, we were not permitted to go on shore. Fortunate indeed would it have been if we had never gone there; for the day after, our captain, who had dined with the consul, was taken alarmingly ill. From the symptoms, the surgeon dreaded that he had been poisoned by something which he had eaten, and which most probably had been cooked in a copper vessel not properly tinned. We were all very anxious that he should recover; but, on the contrary, he appeared to grow worse and worse every day, wasting away, and dying, as they say, by inches. At last he was put into his cot, and never rose from it again. This melancholy circumstance, added to the knowledge that we were proceeding to an unhealthy climate, caused a gloom throughout the ship; and, although the trade wind carried us along bounding over the bright blue sea—although the weather was now warm, yet not too warm—although the sun rose in splendour, and all was beautiful and cheering, the state of the captain's health was a check to all mirth. Every one trod the deck softly, and spoke in a low voice, that he might not be disturbed; all were anxious to have the morning report of the surgeon, and our conversation was generally upon the sickly climate, the yellow fever, of death, and the palisades where they buried us. Swinburne, the quarter-master, was in my watch, and as he had been long in the West Indies, I used to obtain all the information from him that I could. The old fellow had a secret pleasure in frightening me as much as he could. "Really, Mr Simple, you ax so many questions," he would say, as I accosted him while he was at his station at the *conn*, "I wish you wouldn't ax so many questions, and make yourself uncomfortable —'steady so'—'steady it is;'—with regard to Yellow Jack, as we calls the yellow fever, it's a devil incarnate, that's sartain—you're well and able to take your allowance in the morning, and dead as a herring 'fore night. First comes a bit of a head-ache—you goes to the doctor, who bleeds you like a pig—then you go out of your senses—then up comes the black vomit, and then it's all over with you, and you go to the land crabs, who pick your bones as clean and as white as a sea elephant's tooth. But there be one thing to be said in favour of Yellow Jack, a'ter all. You dies *straight,* like a gentleman—not cribbled up like a snow-fish, chucked out on the ice of the river St Lawrence, with your knees up to your nose, or your toes stuck into your arm-pits, as does take place in some of your foreign complaints; but straight, quite straight, and limber, like a *gentleman.* Still Jack is a little mischievous, that's sartain. In the Euridiscy we had as fine a ship's company as was ever piped aloft—'Steady, starboard, my man, you're half-a-pint off your course;'—we dropped our anchor in Port Royal, and we thought that there was mischief brewing, for thirty-eight sharks followed the ship into the harbour, and played about us day and night. I used to watch them during the night watch, as their fins, above water, skimmed along, leaving a trail of light behind them; and the second night I said to the sentry abaft, as I was looking at them smelling under the counter—'Soldier,' says I, 'them sharks are mustering under the orders of Yellow Jack,' and I no sooner mentioned Yellow Jack, than the sharks gave a frisky plunge, every one of them, as much as to say, 'Yes, so we are, d———n your eyes.' The soldier was so frightened that he would have fallen overboard, if I hadn't caught him by the scruff of the neck, for he was standing on the top of the taffrail. As it was, he dropped his musket over the stern, which the sharks dashed at from every quarter, making the sea look like fire—and he had it charged to his wages, £1 16s. I think. However, the fate of his musket gave him an idea of what would have happened to him if he had fallen in instead of it— and he never got on the taffrail again. 'Steady, port—mind your helm, Smith—you can listen to my yarn all the same.' Well, Mr Simple, Yellow Jack came, sure enough. First the purser was called to account for all his roguery. We didn't care much about the land crabs eating him, who had made so many poor dead men chew tobacco, cheating their wives and relations, or Greenwich Hospital, as it might happen. Then went two of the middies, just about your age, Mr Simple: they, poor fellows, went off in a sad hurry; then went the master—and so it went on, till at last we had no more nor sixty men left in the ship. The captain died last, and then Yellow Jack had filled his maw, and left the rest of us alone. As soon as the captain died, all the sharks left the ship, and we never saw any more of them."

Such were the yarns told to me and the other midshipmen during the night watches; and I can assure the reader, that they gave us no small alarm. Every day that we worked our day's work, and found ourselves so much nearer to the islands, did we feel as if we were so much nearer to our graves. I once spoke to O'Brien about it, and he laughed. "Peter," says he, "fear kills more people than the yellow fever, or any other complaint, in the West Indies. Swinburne is an old rogue, and only laughing at you. The devil's not half so black as he's painted—nor the yellow fever half so yellow, I presume." We were now fast nearing the island of Barbadoes, the weather was beautiful, the wind always fair; the flying fish rose in shoals, startled by the foaming seas, which rolled away, and roared from the bows as our swift frigate cleaved through the water; the porpoises played about us in thousands—the bonetas and dolphins at one time chased the flying fish, and at others, appeared to be delighted in keeping company with the rapid vessel. Everything was beautiful, and we all should have been happy, had it not been for the state of Captain Savage, in the first place, who daily became worse and worse, and from the dread of the hell, which we were about to enter through such a watery paradise. Mr Falcon, who was in command, was grave and thoughtful; he appeared indeed to be quite miserable at the chance which would insure his own promotion. In every attention, and every care that could be taken to insure quiet and afford relief to the captain, he was unremitting; the offence of making a noise was now, with him, a greater crime than drunkenness, or even mutiny. When within three days' sail of Barbadoes, it fell almost calm, and the captain became much worse; and now for the first time did we behold the great white shark of the Atlantic. There are several kinds of sharks, but the most dangerous are the great white shark and the ground shark. The former grows to an enormous length—the latter is seldom very long, not more than twelve feet, but spreads to a great breadth. We could not hook the sharks as they played around us, for Mr Falcon would not permit it, lest the noise of hauling them on board should disturb the captain. A breeze again sprang up. In two days we were close to the island, and the men were desired to look out for the land.

Chapter XXX

Death of Captain Savage—His funeral—Specimen of true Barbadian born—Sucking the monkey—Effects of a hurricane.

The next morning, having hove-to part of the night, land was discovered on the bow, and was reported by the mast-head man at the same moment that the surgeon came up and announced the death of our noble captain. Although it had been expected for the last two or three days, the intelligence created a heavy gloom throughout the ship; the men worked in silence, and spoke to one another in whispers. Mr Falcon was deeply affected, and so were we all. In the course of the morning, we ran in to the island, and unhappy as I was, I never can forget the sensation of admiration which I felt on closing with Needham Point to enter Carlisle Bay. The beach of such a pure dazzling white, backed by the tall, green cocoa-nut trees, waving their spreading heads to the fresh breeze, the dark blue of the sky, and the deeper blue of the transparent sea, occasionally varied into green as we passed by the coral rocks which threw their branches out from the bottom—the town opening to our view by degrees, houses after houses, so neat, with their green jalousies, dotting the landscape, the fort with the colours flying, troops of officers riding down, a busy population of all colours, relieved by the whiteness of their dress. Altogether the scene realised my first ideas of Fairyland, for I thought I had never witnessed anything so beautiful. "And can this be such a dreadful place as it is described?" thought I. The sails were clewed up, the anchor was dropped to the bottom, and a salute from the ship, answered by the forts, added to the effect of the scene. The sails were furled, the boats lowered down, the boatswain squared the yards from the jolly-boat ahead. Mr Falcon dressed, and his boat being manned, went on shore with the despatches. Then, as soon as the work was over, a new scene of delight presented itself to the sight of midshipmen who had been so long upon his Majesty's allowance. These were the boats, which crowded round the ship, loaded with baskets of bananas, oranges, shaddocks, soursops, and every other kind of tropical fruit, fried flying fish, eggs, fowls, milk, and everything which could tempt a poor boy after a long sea voyage. The watch being called, down we all hastened into the boats, and returned loaded with treasures, which we soon contrived to make disappear. After stowing away as much fruit as would have sufficed for a dessert to a dinner given to twenty people in England, I returned on deck.

There was no other man-of-war in the bay; but my attention was directed to a beautiful little vessel, a schooner, whose fairy form contrasted strongly with a West India trader which lay close to her. All of a sudden, as I was looking at her beautiful outline, a yell rose from her which quite startled me, and immediately afterwards her deck was covered with nearly two hundred naked figures with woolly heads, chattering and grinning at each other. She was a Spanish slaver, which had been captured, and had arrived the evening before. The slaves were still on board, waiting the orders of the governor. They had been on deck about ten minutes, when three or four men, with large panama straw hats on their heads, and long rattans in their hands, jumped upon the gunnel, and in a few seconds drove them all down below. I then turned round, and observed a black woman who had just climbed up the side of the frigate. O'Brien was on deck, and she walked up to him in the most consequential manner.

"How do you do, sar? Very happy you com back again," said she to O'Brien.

"I'm very well, I thank you, ma'am," replied O'Brien, "and I hope to go back the same; but never having put my foot into this bay before, you have the advantage of me."

"Nebber here before, so help me Gad! me tink I know you—me tink I recollect your handsome face—I Lady Rodney, sar. Ah, piccaninny buccra! how you do?" said she, turning round to me. "Me hope to hab the honour to wash for you, sar," courtesying to O'Brien.

"What do you charge in this place?"

"All the same price, one bit a piece."

"What do you call a bit?" inquired I.

"A bit, lilly massa?—what you call um *bit*? Dem four _sharp shins_ to a pictareen."

Our deck was now enlivened by several army officers, besides gentlemen residents, who came off to hear the news. Invitations to the mess and to the houses of the gentlemen followed, and as they departed Mr Falcon returned on board. He told O'Brien and the other officers, that the admiral and squadron were expected in a few days, and that we were to remain in Carlisle Bay and refit immediately. But although the fright about the yellow fever had considerably subsided in our breasts, the remembrance that our poor captain was lying dead in the cabin was constantly obtruding. All that night the carpenters were up making up his coffin, for he was to be buried the next day. The body is never allowed to remain many hours unburied in the tropical climates, where putrefaction is so rapid. The following morning the men were up at daylight, washing the decks and putting the ship in order; they worked willingly, and yet with a silent decorum which showed what their feelings were. Never were the decks better cleaned, never were the ropes more carefully *flemished* down; the hammocks were stowed in their white cloths, the yards carefully squared, and the ropes hauled taut. At eight o'clock, the colours and pennant were hoisted half-mast high. The men were then ordered down to breakfast, and to clean themselves. During the time that the men were at breakfast, all the officers went into the cabin to take a last farewell look at our gallant captain. He appeared to have died without pain, and there was a beautiful tranquillity in his face; but even already a change had taken place, and we perceived the necessity of his being buried so soon. We saw him placed in his coffin, and then quitted the cabin without speaking to each other. When the coffin was nailed down, it was brought up by the barge's crew to the quarter-deck, and laid upon the gratings amidships, covered over with the Union Jack. The men came up from below without waiting for the pipe, and a solemnity appeared to pervade every motion. Order and quiet were universal, out of respect to the deceased. When the boats were ordered to be manned, the men almost appeared to steal into them. The barge received the coffin, which was placed in the stern sheets. The other boats then hauled up, and received the officers, marines, and sailors, who were to follow the procession. When all was ready, the barge was shoved off by the bow-men, the crew dropped their oars into the water without a splash and pulled the _minute stroke:_ the other boats followed, and as soon as they were clear of the ship, the minute guns boomed along the smooth surface of the bay from the opposite side of the ship, while the yards were topped to starboard and to port, the ropes were slackened and hung in bights, so as to give the idea of distress and neglect. At the same time, a dozen or more of the men who had been ready, dropped over the sides of the ship in differents [sic] parts, and with their cans of paint and brushes in a few minutes effaced the whole of the broad white riband which marked the beautiful run of the frigate, and left her all black and in deep mourning. The guns from the forts now responded to our own. The merchant ships lowered their colours, and the men stood up respectfully with their hats off, as the procession moved slowly to the landing-place. The coffin was borne to the burial-ground by the crew of the barge, followed by Mr Falcon as chief mourner, all the officers of the ship who could be spared, one hundred of the seamen walking two and two, and the marines with their arms reversed. The *cortege* was joined by the army officers, while the troops lined the streets, and the bands played the Dead March. The service was read, the volleys were fired over the grave, and with oppressed feelings we returned to the boats, and pulled on board. It then appeared to me, and to a certain degree I was correct, that as soon as we had paid our last respect to his remains, we had also forgotten our grief. The yards were again squared, the ropes hauled taut, working dresses resumed, and all was activity and bustle. The fact is, that sailors and soldiers have no time for lamentation, and running as they do from clime to clime, so does scene follow scene in the same variety and quickness. In a day or two, the captain appeared to be, although he was not, forgotten. Our first business was to *water* the ship by rafting and towing off the casks. I was in charge of the boat again, with Swinburne as coxswain. As we pulled in, there were a number of negroes bathing in the surf, bobbing their woolly heads under it, as it rolled into the beach. "Now, Mr Simple," said Swinburne, "see how I'll make them *niggers* scamper." He then stood up in the stern sheets, and pointing with his finger, roared out, "A shark! a shark!" Away started all the bathers for the beach, puffing and blowing, from their dreaded enemy; nor did they stop to look for him until they were high and dry out of his reach. Then, when we all laughed, they called us "*all the hangman tiefs*," and every other opprobrious name which they could select from their vocabulary. I was very much amused with this scene, and as much afterwards with the negroes who crowded round us when we landed. They appeared such merry fellows, always laughing, chattering, singing, and showing their white teeth. One fellow danced round us, snapping his fingers, and singing songs without beginning or end. "Eh, massa, what you say now? Me no slave—true Barbadian born, sir. Eh!

"Nebba see de day
Dat Rodney run away,
Nebba see um night
Dat Rodney cannot fight.

Massa me free man, sar. Suppose you give me pictareen, drink massa health.

"Nebba see de day, boy,
Pompey lickum de Caesar.

Eh! and you nebba see de day dat de Grasshopper run on de Warrington."

"Out of the way, you nigger," cried one of the men who was rolling down a cask.

"Eh! who you call nigger? Me free man, and true Barbadian born. Go along you man-of-war man.

"Man-of-war, buccra,
Man-of-war, buccra,
He de boy for me;
Sodger, buccra,
Sodger, buccra,
Nebba, nebba do,
Nebba, nebba do for me;
Sodger give me one shilling,
Sailor give me two.

Massa, now suppose you give me only one pictareen now. You really handsome young gentleman."

"Now, just walk off," said Swinburne, lifting up a stick he found on the beach.

"Eh! walk off.

"Nebba see de day, boy,
'Badian run away, boy.

Go, do your work, sar. Why you talk to me? Go, work, sar. I free man, and real Barbadian born.

"Negro on de shore
See de ship come in,
De buccra come on shore,
Wid de hand up to the chin;
Man-of-war buccra,
Man-of-war buccra,
He de boy for me,
Man-of-war, buccra,
Man-of-war, buccra,
Gib pictareen to me."

At this moment my attention was directed to another negro, who lay on the beach rolling and foaming at the mouth, apparently in a fit. "What's the matter with that fellow?" said I to the same negro who continued close to me, notwithstanding Swinburne's stick. "Eh! call him Sam Slack, massa. He ab um *tic tic* fit." And such was apparently the case. "Stop, me cure him;" and he snatched the stick out of Swinburne's hand, and running up to the man, who continued to roll on the beach, commenced belabouring him without mercy. "Eh, Sambo!" cried he at last, quite out of breath, "you no better yet—try again." He recommenced, until at last the man got up and ran away as fast as he could. Now, whether the man was shamming, or whether it was real *tic tic*, or epileptic fit, I know not; but I never heard of such a cure for it before. I threw the fellow half a pictareen, as much for the amusement he had afforded me as to get rid of him. "Tanky, massa; now man-of-war man, here de tick for you again to keep off all the dam niggers." So saying, he handed the stick to Swinburne, made a polite bow, and departed. We were, however, soon surrounded by others, particularly some dingy ladies with baskets of fruit, and who, as they said, "sell ebery ting." I perceived that my sailors were very fond of cocoa-nut milk, which, being a harmless beverage, I did not object to their purchasing from these ladies, who had chiefly cocoa-nuts in their baskets. As I had never tasted it, I asked them what it was, and bought a cocoa-nut. I selected the largest. "No, massa, dat not good for you. Better one for buccra officer." I then selected another, but the same objection was made. "No, massa, dis very fine milk. Very good for de tomac." I drank off the milk from the holes on the top of the cocoa-nut, and found it very refreshing. As for the sailors, they appeared very fond of it indeed. But I very soon found that if good for de tomac, it was not very good for the head, as my men, instead of rolling the casks, began to roll themselves in all directions, and when it was time to go off to dinner, most of them were dead drunk at the bottom of the boat. They insisted that it was the *sun* which affected them. Very hot it certainly was, and I believed them at first, when they were only giddy; but I was convinced to the contrary when I found that they became insensible; yet how they had procured the liquor was to me a mystery. When I came on board, Mr Falcon, who, although acting captain, continued his duties as first lieutenant almost as punctually as before, asked how it was that I had allowed my men to get so tipsy. I assured him that I could not tell, that I had never allowed one to leave the watering-place, or to buy any liquor: the only thing that they had to drink was a little cocoa-nut milk, which, as it was so very hot, I thought there could be no objection to. Mr Falcon smiled and said, "Mr Simple, I'm an old stager in the West Indies, and I'll let you into a secret. Do you know what '*sucking the monkey*' means?" "No, sir." "Well, then, I'll tell you; it is a term used among seamen for drinking *rum* out of _cocoa-nuts, _the milk having been poured out, and the liquor substituted. Now do you comprehend why your men are tipsy?" I stared with all my eyes, for it never would have entered into my head; and I then perceived why it was that the black woman would not give me the first cocoa-nuts which I selected. I told Mr Falcon of this circumstance, who replied, "Well, it was not your fault, only you must not forget it another time."

It was my first watch that night, and Swinburne was quarter-master on deck. "Swinburne," said I, "you have often been in the West Indies before, why did you not tell me that the men were '*sucking the monkey*' when I thought that they were only drinking cocoa-nut milk?"

Swinburne chuckled, and answered, "Why, Mr Simple, d'ye see, it didn't become me as a ship-mate to peach. It's but seldom that a poor fellow has an opportunity of making himself a 'little happy,' and it would not be fair to take away the chance. I suppose you'll never let them have cocoa-nut milk again?"

"No, that I will not; but I cannot imagine what pleasure they can find in getting so tipsy."

"It's merely because they are not allowed to be so, sir. That's the whole story in few words."

"Well, I think I could cure them if I were permitted to try."

"I should like to hear how you'd manage that, Mr Simple."

"Why, I would oblige a man to drink off a half pint of liquor, and then put him by himself. I would not allow him companions to make merry with so as to make a pleasure of intoxication. I would then wait until next morning when he was sober, and leave him alone with a racking headache until the evening, when I would give him another dose, and so on, forcing him to get drunk until he hated the smell of liquor."

"Well, Mr Simple, it might do with some, but many of our chaps would require the dose you mention to be repeated pretty often before it would effect a cure; and what's more, they'd be very willing patients, and make no wry faces at their physic."

"Well, that might be, but it would cure them at last. But tell me,
Swinburne, were you ever in a hurricane?"

"I've been in everything, Mr Simple, I believe, except at school, and I never had no time to go there. Do you see that battery at Needham Point? Well, in the hurricane of '82, them same guns were whirled away by the wind, right over to this point here on the opposite side, the sentries in their sentry-boxes after them. Some of the soldiers who faced the wind had their teeth blown down their throats like broken 'baccy-pipes, others had their heads turned round like dog vanes, 'cause they waited for orders to the '*right about face*,' and the whole air was full of young *niggers* blowing about like peelings of *ingons*."

"You don't suppose I believe all this, Swinburne?"

"That's as may be, Mr Simple, but I've told the story so often, that I believe it myself."

"What ship were you in?"

"In the *Blanche*, Captain Faulkner, who was as fine a fellow as poor Captain Savage, whom we buried yesterday; there could not be a finer than either of them. I was at the taking of the Pique, and carried him down below after he had received his mortal wound. We did a pretty thing out here when we took Fort Royal by a coup-de-*main*, which means, boarding from the *main*-yard of the frigate, and dropping from it into the fort. But what's that under the moon?—there's a sail in the offing."

Swinburne fetched the glass and directed it to the spot. "One, two, three, four. It's the admiral, sir, and the squadron hove-to for the night. One's a line-of-battle ship, I'll swear." I examined the vessels, and agreeing with

Swinburne, reported them to Mr Falcon. My watch was then over, and as soon as I was released I went to my hammock.

END OF VOL. I.

Peter Simple and The Three Cutters, Vol. 2

Chapter XXXI

Captain Kearney—The dignity ball.

The next morning at daylight we exchanged numbers, and saluted the flag, and by eight o'clock they all anchored. Mr Falcon went on board the admiral's ship with despatches, and to report the death of Captain Savage. In about half an hour he returned, and we were glad to perceive, with a smile upon his face, from which we argued that he would receive his acting order as commander, which was a question of some doubt, as the admiral had the power to give the vacancy to whom he pleased, although it would not have been fair if he had not given it to Mr Falcon; not that Mr Falcon would not have received his commission, as Captain Savage dying when the ship was under no admiral's command, he *made himself*; but still the admiral might have sent him home, and not have given him a ship. But this he did, the captain of the *Minerve* being appointed to the *Sanglier*, the captain of the *Opossum* to the *Minerve*, and Captain Falcon taking command of the *Opossum*. He received his commission that evening, and the next day the exchanges were made. Captain Falcon would have taken me with him, and offered so to do; but I could not leave O'Brien, so I preferred remaining in the *Sanglier*.

We were all anxious to know what sort of a person our new captain was, whose name was Kearney; but we had no time to ask the midshipmen, except when they came in charge of the boats which brought his luggage; they replied generally, that he was a very good sort of fellow, and there was no harm in him. But when I had the night watch with Swinburne, he came up to me, and said, "Well, Mr Simple, so we have a new captain. I sailed with him for two years in a brig."

"And pray, Swinburne, what sort of a person is he?"

"Why, I'll tell you, Mr Simple: he's a good-tempered, kind fellow enough, but—"

"But what?"

"Such a *bouncer*!!"

"How do you mean? He's not a very stout man."

"Bless you, Mr Simple, why you don't understand English. I mean that he's the greatest liar that ever walked a deck. Now, Mr Simple, you know I can spin a yarn occasionally."

"Yes, that you can, witness the hurricane the other night."

"Well, Mr Simple, I cannot *hold a candle* to him. It a'n't that I might not stretch now and then, just for fun, as far as he can, but, d——n it, he's always on the stretch. In fact, Mr Simple, he never tells the truth except *by mistake*. He's as poor as a rat, and has nothing but his pay; yet to believe him, he is worth at least as much as Greenwich Hospital. But you'll soon find him out, and he'll sarve to laugh at behind his back, you know, Mr Simple, for that's *no go* before his face."

Captain Kearney made his appearance on board the next day. The men were mustered to receive him, and all the officers were on the quarter-deck. "You've a fine set of marines here, Captain Falcon," observed he; "those I left on board of the *Minerve* were only fit to be *hung*; and you have a good show of reefers too—those I left in the *Minerve* were not *worth hanging*. If you please, I'll read my commission, if you'll order the men aft." His commission was read, all hands with their hats off from respect to the authority from which it proceeded. "Now, my lads," said Captain Kearney, addressing the ship's company, "I've but few words to say to you. I am appointed to command this ship, and you appear to have a very good character from your late first lieutenant. All I request of you is this: be smart, keep sober, and always *tell the truth*—that's enough. Pipe down. Gentlemen," continued he, addressing the officers, "I trust that we shall be good friends; and I see no reason that it should be otherwise." He then turned away with a bow, and called his coxswain—"Williams, you'll go on board, and tell my steward that I have promised to dine with the governor to-day, and that he must come to dress me; and, coxswain, recollect to put the sheepskin mat on the stern gratings of my gig—not the one I used to have when I was on shore in my *carriage*, but the blue one which was used for the *chariot*—you know which I mean." I happened to look Swinburne in the face, who cocked his eye at me, as much as to say—"There he goes." We afterwards met the officers of the *Minerve*, who corroborated all that Swinburne had said, although it was quite unnecessary, as we had the captain's own words every minute to satisfy us of the fact.

Dinner parties were now very numerous, and the hospitality of the island is but too well known. The invitations extended to the midshipmen, and many was the good dinner and kind reception which I had during my stay. There was, however, one thing I had heard so much of, that I was anxious to witness it, which was a *dignity ball*. But I must enter a little into explanation, or my readers will not understand me. The coloured people of Barbadoes, for reasons best known to themselves, are immoderately proud, and look upon all the negroes who are born on other islands as *niggers*; they have also an extraordinary idea of their own bravery, although I never heard that it has ever been put to the proof. The free Barbadians are, most of them, very rich, and hold up their heads as they walk with an air quite ridiculous. They ape the manners of the Europeans, at the same time that they appear to consider them as almost their inferiors. Now, a *dignity* ball is a ball given by the most consequential of their coloured people, and from the amusement and various other reasons, is generally well attended by the officers both on shore and afloat. The price of the tickets of admission was high—I think they were half a joe, or eight dollars each.

The governor sent out cards for a grand ball and supper for the ensuing week, and Miss Betsy Austin, a quadroon woman, ascertaining the fact, sent out her cards for the same evening. This was not altogether in *rivalry*, but for another reason, which was, that she was aware that most of the officers and midshipmen of the ships would obtain permission to go to the governor's ball, and, preferring hers, would slip away and join the party, by which means she ensured a full attendance.

On the day of invitation our captain came on board, and told our new first lieutenant (of whom I shall say more hereafter) that the governor insisted that all *his* officers should go—that he would take no denial, and, therefore, he presumed, go they must; that the fact was, that the governor was a *relation* of his wife, and under some trifling obligations to him in obtaining for him his present command. He certainly had spoken to the *prime minister*, and he thought it not impossible, considering the intimate terms which the minister and he had been on from childhood, that his solicitation might have had some effect; at all events, it was pleasant to find that there was some little gratitude left in this world. After this, of course, every officer went, with the exception of the master, who said that he'd as soon have two round turns in his hawse as go to see people kick their legs about like fools, and that he'd take care of the ship.

The governor's ball was very splendid, but the ladies were rather sallow, from the effects of the climate. However, there were exceptions, and on the whole it was a very gay affair; but we were all anxious to go to the *dignity* ball of Miss Betsy Austin. I slipped away with three other midshipmen, and we soon arrived there. A crowd of negroes were outside of the house; but the ball had not yet commenced, from the want of gentlemen, the ball being very correct, nothing under mulatto in colour being admitted. Perhaps I ought to say here, that the progeny of a white and a negro is a mulatto, or half and half—of a white and mulatto, a *quadroon*, or one-quarter black, and of this class the company were chiefly composed. I believe a quadroon and white make the *mustee* or one-eighth black, and the mustee and white the mustafina, or one-sixteenth black. After that, they are *whitewashed*, and considered as Europeans. The pride of colour is very great in the West Indies, and they have as many quarterings as a German prince in his coat of arms; a quadroon looks down upon a mulatto, while a mulatto looks down upon a *sambo*, that is, half mulatto half negro, while a sambo in his turn looks down upon a *nigger*. The quadroons are certainly the handsomest race of the whole, some of the women are really beautiful; their hair is long and perfectly straight, their eyes large and black, their figures perfection, and you can see the colour mantle in their cheeks quite as plainly, and with as much effect, as in those of a European. We found the door of Miss Austin's house open, and ornamented with orange branches, and on our presenting ourselves were accosted by a mulatto gentleman, who was, we presumed, "usher of the black rod." His head was well powdered, he was dressed in white jean trousers, a waistcoat not six inches long, and a half-worn post-captain's coat on, as a livery, With a low bow, he "took de liberty to trouble de gentlemen for de card for de ball," which being produced, we were ushered on by him to the ball-room, at the door of which Miss Austin was waiting to receive her company. She made us a low courtesy, observing, "She really happy to see de *gentlemen* of de ship, but hoped to see de *officers* also at her *dignity*."

This remark touched our *dignity*, and one of my companions replied, "That we midshipmen considered ourselves officers, and no *small* ones either, and that if she waited for the lieutenants she must wait until they were tired of the governor's ball, we having given the preference to hers." This remark set all to rights; sangaree was handed about, and I looked around at the company. I must acknowledge, at the risk of losing the good opinion of my fair countrywomen, that I never saw before so many pretty figures and faces. The *officers* not having yet arrived, we received all the attention, and I was successively presented to Miss Eurydice, Miss Minerva, Miss Sylvia, Miss Aspasia, Miss Euterpe, and many others, evidently borrowed from the different men-of-war which had been on the station. All these young ladies gave themselves all the airs of Almack's. Their dresses I cannot pretend to describe—jewels of value were not wanting, but their drapery was slight; they appeared neither to wear nor to require stays, and on the whole, their figures were so perfect that they could only be ill dressed by having on too much dress. A few more midshipmen and some lieutenants (O'Brien among the number) having made their appearance, Miss Austin directed that the ball should commence. I requested the honour of Miss Eurydice's hand in a cotillon, which was to open the ball. At this moment stepped forth the premier violin, master of the ceremonies and ballet-master, Massa Johnson, really a very smart man, who gave lessons in dancing to all the "'Badian ladies." He was a dark quadroon, his hair slightly powdered, dressed in a light blue coat thrown well back, to show his lily-white waistcoat, only one button of which he could afford to button to make full room for the pride of his heart, the frill of his shirt, which really was *un Jabot superb*, four inches wide, and extending from his collar to the waistband of his nankeen tights, which were finished off at his knees with huge bunches of ribbon; his legs were encased in silk stockings, which, however, was not very good taste on his part, as they showed the manifest advantage which an European has over a coloured man in the formation of the leg: instead of being straight, his shins curved like a cheese-knife, and, moreover, his leg was planted into his foot like the handle into a broom or scrubbing-brush, there being quite as much of the foot on the heel side as on the toe side. Such was the appearance of Mr Apollo Johnson, whom the ladies considered as the _ne plus ultra_ of fashion, and the *arbiter elegantiarum*. His *bow-tick*, or fiddle-stick, was his wand, whose magic rap on the fiddle produced immediate obedience to his mandates. "Ladies and gentle, take your seats." All started up. "Miss Eurydice, you open de ball."

Miss Eurydice had but a sorry partner, but she undertook to instruct me. O'Brien was our *vis-à-vis* with Miss Euterpe. The other gentlemen were officers from the ships, and we stood up twelve, checkered brown and white, like a chess-board. All eyes were fixed upon Mr Apollo Johnson, who first looked at the couples, then at his fiddle, and lastly, at the other musicians, to see if all was right, and then with a wave of his *bow-tick* the music began. "Massa lieutenant," cried Apollo to O'Brien, "cross over to opposite lady, right hand and left, den figure to Miss Eurydice—dat right; now four hand round. You lilly midshipman, set your partner, sir; den twist her round; dat do; now stop. First figure all over."

At this time I thought I might venture to talk a little with my partner, and I ventured a remark; to my surprise she answered very sharply, "I come here for dance, sar, and not for chatter; look, Massa Johnson, he tap um bow-tick."

The second figure commenced, and I made a sad bungle; so I did of the third, and fourth, and fifth, for I never had danced a cotillon. When I handed my partner to her place, who certainly was the prettiest girl in the room, she looked rather contemptuously at me, and observed to a neighbour, "I really pity de gentleman as come from England dat no know how to dance nor nothing at all, until em hab instruction at Barbadoes."

A country dance was now called for, which was more acceptable to all parties, as none of Mr Apollo Johnson's pupils were very perfect in their cotillon, and none of the officers, except O'Brien, knew anything about them. O'Brien's superior education on this point, added to his lieutenant's epaulet and handsome person, made him much courted; but he took up with Miss Eurydice after I had left her, and remained with her the whole evening; thereby exciting the jealousy of Mr Apollo Johnson, who, it appears, was amorous in that direction. Our party increased every minute; all the officers of the garrison, and, finally, as soon as they could get away, the governor's aid-de-camps, all dressed in *mufti* (i.e., plain clothes). The dancing continued until three o'clock in the morning, when it was quite a squeeze, from the constant arrival of fresh recruits from all the houses of Barbadoes. I must say, that a few bottles of eau de Cologne thrown about the room would have improved the atmosphere. By this time the heat was terrible, and the *mopping* of the ladies' faces everlasting. I would recommend a DIGNITY ball to all stout gentlemen who wish to be reduced a stone or two. Supper was now announced, and having danced the last country dance with Miss Minerva, I of course had the pleasure of handing her into the supper-room. It was my fate to sit opposite to a fine turkey, and I asked my partner if I should have the pleasure of helping her to a piece of the breast. She looked at me very indignantly, and said, "Curse your impudence, sar, I wonder where you larn manners. Sar, I take a lilly turkey *bosom*, if you please. Talk of *breast* to a lady, sar;—really quite *horrid*." I made two or three more barbarous mistakes before the supper was finished. At last the eating was over, and I must say a better supper I never sat down to. "Silence, gentlemen and ladies," cried Mr Apollo Johnson. "Wid the permission of our amiable hostess, I will propose a toast. Gentlemen and ladies—You all know, and if be so you don't, I say that there no place in the world like Barbadoes. All de world fight against England, but England nebber fear; King George nebber fear, while *Barbadoes 'tand 'tiff*. 'Badian fight for King George to last drop of him blood. Nebber see the day 'Badian run away; you all know dem Frenchmans at San Lucee, give up Morne Fortunee, when he hear de 'Badian volunteer come against him. I hope no 'fence present company, but um sorry to say English come here too jealous of 'Badians. Gentlemen and lady—Barbadian born ab only one fault—he *really too brave*. I propose health of 'Island of Barbadoes.'" Acclamations from all quarters followed this truly modest speech, and the toast was drunk with rapture; the ladies were delighted with Mr Apollo's eloquence, and the lead which he took in the company.

O'Brien then rose and addressed the company as follows:—

"Ladies and gentlemen—Mr Poll has spoken better than the best parrot I ever met with in this country, but as he has thought proper to drink the 'Island of Barbadoes,' I mean to be a little more particular. I wish, with him, all good health to the island; but there is a charm without which the island would be a desert—that is, the society of the lovely girls which now surround us, and take our hearts by storm—" (here O'Brien put his arm gently round Miss Eurydice's waist, and Mr Apollo ground his teeth so as to be heard at the furthest end of the room)"— therefore, gentlemen, with your permission, I will propose the health of the "Badian Ladies.'" This speech of O'Brien's was declared, by the females at least, to be infinitely superior to Mr Apollo Johnson's. Miss Eurydice was even more gracious, and the other ladies were more envious.

Many other toasts and much more wine was drunk, until the male part of the company appeared to be rather riotous. Mr Apollo, however, had to regain his superiority, and after some hems and hahs, begged permission to give a sentiment. "Gentlemen and ladies, I beg then to say—

"Here's to de cock who make lub to de hen,
Crow till he hoarse and make lub again."

This *sentiment* was received with rapture; and after silence was obtained, Miss Betsy Austin rose and said—"Unaccustomed as she was to public 'peaking, she must not sit 'till and not tank de gentleman for his very fine toast, and in de name of de ladies she begged to propose another sentimen', which was—

"Here to de hen what nebber refuses,
Let cock pay compliment whenebber he chooses."

If the first toast was received with applause, this was with enthusiasm; but we received a damper after it was subsided, by the lady of the house getting up and saying—"Now, gentlemen and ladies, me tink it right to say dat it time to go home; I nebber allow people get drunk or kick up bobbery in my house, so now I tink we better take parting-glass, and very much obliged to you for your company."

As O'Brien said, this was a broad hint to be off, so we all now took our parting-glass, in compliance with her request, and our own wishes, and proceeded to escort our partners on their way home. While I was assisting Miss Minerva to her red crape shawl, a storm was brewing in another quarter, to wit, between Mr Apollo Johnson and O'Brien. O'Brien was assiduously attending to Miss Eurydice, whispering what he called soft blarney in her ear, when Mr Apollo, who was above spirit-boiling heat with jealousy, came up, and told Miss Eurydice that he would have the honour of escorting her home.

"You may save yourself the trouble, you dingy gut-scraper," replied O'Brien; "the lady is under my protection, so take your ugly black face out of the way, or I'll show you how I treat a "Badian who is really too brave.'"

"So 'elp me Gad, Massa Lieutenant, 'pose you put finger on me, I show you what 'Badian can do."

Apollo then attempted to insert himself between O'Brien and his lady, upon which O'Brien shoved him back with great violence, and continued his course towards the door. They were in the passage when I came up, for hearing O'Brien's voice in anger, I left Miss Minerva to shift for herself.

Miss Eurydice had now left O'Brien's arm, at his request, and he and Mr Apollo were standing in the passage, O'Brien close to the door, which was shut, and Apollo swaggering up to him. O'Brien, who knew the tender part of a black, saluted Apollo with a kick on the shins which would have broken my leg. Massa Johnson roared with pain, and recoiled two or three paces, parting the crowd away behind him. The blacks never fight with fists, but butt with their heads like rams, and with quite as much force. When Mr Apollo had retreated, he gave his shin one more rub, uttered a loud yell, and started at O'Brien, with his head aimed at O'Brien's chest, like a battering-ram. O'Brien, who was aware of this plan of fighting, stepped dexterously on one side, and allowed Mr Apollo to pass by him, which he did with such force, that his head went clean through the panel of the door behind O'Brien, and there he stuck as fast as if in a pillory, squeaking like a pig for assistance, and foaming with rage. After some difficulty he was released, and presented a very melancholy figure. His face was much cut, and his superb *Jabot* all in tatters; he appeared, however, to have had quite enough of it, as he retreated to the supper-room, followed by some of his admirers, without asking or looking after O'Brien.

But if Mr Apollo had had enough of it, his friends were too indignant to allow us to go off scot free. A large mob was collected in the street, vowing vengeance on us for our treatment of their flash man, and a row was to be expected. Miss Eurydice had escaped, so that O'Brien had his hands free. "Cam out, you hangman tiefs, cam out; only wish had rock stones, to mash your heads with," cried the mob of negroes. The officers now sallied out in a body, and were saluted with every variety of missile, such as rotten oranges, cabbage-stalks, mud, and cocoa-nut shells. We fought our way manfully, but as we neared the beach the mob increased to hundreds, and at last we could proceed no further, being completely jammed up by the niggers, upon whose heads we could make no more impression than upon blocks of marble. "We must draw our swords," observed an officer. "No, no," replied O'Brien, "that will not do; if once we shed blood, they will never let us get on board with our lives. The boat's crew by this time must be aware that there is a row." O'Brien was right. He had hardly spoken, before a lane was observed to be made through the crowd in the distance, which in two minutes was open to us. Swinburne appeared in the middle of it, followed by the rest of the boat's crew, armed with the boat's stretchers, which they did not aim at the *heads* of the blacks, but swept them like scythes against their *shins*. This they continued to do, right and left of us, as we walked through and went down to the boats, the seamen closing up the rear with their stretchers, with which they ever and anon made a sweep at the black fellows if they approached too near. It was now broad daylight, and in a few minutes we were again safely on board the frigate. Thus ended the first and last dignity ball that I attended.

Chapter XXXII

I am claimed by Captain Kearney as a relation—Trial of skill between first lieutenant and captain with the long bow—The shark, the pug-dog, and the will—A quarter-deck picture.

As the admiral was not one who would permit the ships under his command to lie idle in port, in a very few days after the dignity ball which I have described, all the squadron sailed on their various destinations. I was not sorry to leave the bay, for one soon becomes tired of profusion, and cared nothing for either oranges, bananas, or shaddocks, nor even for, the good dinners and claret at the tables of the army mess and gentlemen of the island. The sea breeze soon became more precious to us than anything else, and if we could have bathed without the fear of a shark, we should have equally appreciated that most refreshing of all luxuries under the torrid zone. It was therefore with pleasure that we received the information that we were to sail the next day to cruise off the French island of Martinique. Captain Kearney had been so much on shore that we saw but little of him, and the ship was entirely under the control of the first lieutenant, of whom I have hitherto not spoken. He was a very short, pock-marked man, with red hair and whiskers, a good sailor, and not a bad officer; that is, he was a practical sailor, and could show any foremast man his duty in any department—and this seamen very much appreciate, as it is not very common; but I never yet knew an officer who prided himself upon his practical knowledge, who was at the same time a good navigator, and too often, by assuming the Jack Tar, they lower the respect due to them, and become coarse and vulgar in their manners and language. This was the case with Mr Phillott, who prided himself upon his slang, and who was at one time "hail fellow well met" with the seamen, talking to them, and being answered as familiarly as if they were equals, and at another, knocking the very same men down with a handspike if he was displeased. He was not bad-tempered, but very hasty; and his language to the officers was occasionally very incorrect; to the midshipmen invariably so. However, on the whole, he was not disliked, although he was certainly not respected as a first lieutenant should have been. It is but fair to say, that he was the same to his superiors as he was to his inferiors, and the bluntness with which he used to contradict and assert his disbelief of Captain Kearney's narratives often produced a coolness between them for some days.

The day after we sailed from Carlisle Bay I was asked to dine in the cabin. The dinner was served upon plated dishes, which looked very grand, but there was not much in them. "This plate," observed the captain, "was presented to me by some merchants for my exertions in saving their property from the Danes when I was cruising off Heligoland."

"Why, that lying steward of yours told me that you bought it at Portsmouth," replied the first lieutenant: "I asked him in the galley this morning."

"How came you to assert such a confounded falsehood, sir?" said the captain to the man who stood behind his chair.

"I only said that I thought so," replied the steward.

"Why, didn't you say that the bill had been sent in, through you, seven or eight times, and that the captain had paid it with a flowing sheet?"

"Did you dare say that, sir?" interrogated the captain, very angrily.

"Mr Phillott mistook me, sir?" replied the steward. "He was so busy damning the sweepers, that he did not hear me right. I said, the midshipmen had paid their crockery bill with the fore-topsail."

"Ay! ay!" replied the captain, "that's much more likely."

"Well, Mr Steward," replied Mr Phillott, "I'll be d——d if you ar'n't as big a liar as your—" (master, he was going to plump out, but fortunately the first lieutenant checked himself, and added)—"as your father was before you."

The captain changed the conversation by asking me whether I would take a slice of ham. "It's real Westphalia, Mr Simple; I have them sent me direct by Count Troningsken, an intimate friend of mine, who kills his own wild boars in the Hartz mountains."

"How the devil do you get them over, Captain Kearney?"

"There are ways and means of doing everything, Mr Phillott, and the First Consul is not quite so bad as he is represented. The first batch was sent over with a very handsome letter to me, written in his own hand, which I will show you some of these days. I wrote to him in return, and sent to him two Cheshire cheeses by a smuggler, and since that they came regularly. Did you ever eat Westphalia ham, Mr Simple?"

"Yes," replied I; "once I partook of one at Lord Privilege's."

"Lord Privilege! why he's a distant relation of mine, a sort of fifth cousin," replied Captain Kearney.

"Indeed, sir!" replied I.

"Then you must allow me to introduce you to a relation, Captain Kearney," said the first lieutenant; "for Mr Simple is his grandson."

"Is it possible? I can only say, Mr Simple, that I shall be most happy to show you every attention, and am very glad that I have you as one of my officers."

Now although this was all false, for Captain Kearney was not in the remotest manner connected with my family, yet having once asserted it, he could not retract, and the consequence was, that I was much the gainer by his falsehood, as he treated me very kindly afterwards, always calling me *cousin*.

The first lieutenant smiled and gave me a wink, when the captain had finished his speech to me, as much as to say, "You're in luck," and then the conversation changed. Captain Kearney certainly dealt in the marvellous to admiration, and really told his stories with such earnestness, that I actually believe that he thought he was telling the truth. Never was there such an instance of confirmed habit. Telling a story of a cutting-out expedition, he said, "The French captain would have fallen by my hand, but just as I levelled my musket, a ball came, and cut off the cock of the lock as clean as if it was done with a knife—a very remarkable instance," observed he.

"Not equal to what occurred in a ship I was in," replied the first lieutenant, "when the second lieutenant was grazed by a grape-shot, which cut off one of his whiskers, and turning round his head to ascertain what was the matter, another grape-shot came and took off the other. Now that's what I call a *close shave*."

"Yes," replied Captain Kearney, "very close, indeed, if it were true; but you'll excuse me, Mr Phillott, but you sometimes tell strange stories. I do not mind it myself, but the example is not good to my young relation here, Mr Simple."

"Captain Kearney," replied the first lieutenant, laughing very immoderately, "do you know what the pot called the kettle?"

"No, sir, I do not," retorted the captain, with offended dignity. "Mr Simple, will you take a glass of wine?"

I thought that this little *brouillerie* would have checked the captain; it did so, but only for a few minutes, when he again commenced. The first lieutenant observed that it would be necessary to let water into the ship every morning, and pump it out, to avoid the smell of the bilge-water. "There are worse smells than bilge-water," replied the captain. "What do you think of a whole ship's company being nearly poisoned with otto of roses? Yet that occurred to me when in the Mediterranean. I was off Smyrna, cruising for a French ship, that was to sail to France, with a pasha on board, as an ambassador. I knew she would be a good prize, and was looking sharp out, when one morning we discovered her on the lee bow. We made all sail, but she walked away from us, bearing away gradually till we were both before the wind, and at night we lost sight of her. As I knew that she was bound to Marseilles, I made all sail to fall in with her again. The wind was light and variable; but five days afterwards, as I lay in my cot, just before daylight, I smelt a very strong smell, blowing in at the weather port, and coming down the skylight, which was open; and after sniffing at it two or three times, I knew it to be otto of roses. I sent for the officer of the watch, and asked him if there was anything in sight. He replied 'that there was not;' and I ordered him to sweep the horizon with his glass, and look well out to windward. As the wind freshened, the smell became more powerful. I ordered him to get the royal yards across, and all ready to make sail, for I knew that the Turk must be near us. At daylight there he was, just three miles ahead in the wind's eye. But although he beat us going free, he was no match for us, on a wind, and before noon we had possession of him and all his harem. By-the-by, I could tell you a good story about the ladies. She was a very valuable prize, and among other things, she had a *puncheon* of otto of roses on board—."

"Whew!" cried the first lieutenant. "What! a whole puncheon?"

"Yes," replied the captain, "a Turkish puncheon—not quite so large, perhaps, as ours on board; their weights and measures are different. I took out most of the valuables into the brig I commanded—about 20,000 sequins—carpets—and among the rest, this cask of otto of roses, which we had smelt three miles off. We had it safe on board, when the mate of the hold, not slinging it properly, it fell into the spirit-room with a run, and was stove to pieces. Never was such a scene; my first lieutenant and several men on deck fainted; and the men in the hold were brought up lifeless; it was some time before they were recovered. We let the water into the brig, and pumped it out, but nothing would take away the smell, which was so overpowering, that before I could get to Malta I had forty men on the sick list. When I arrived there, I turned the mate out of the service for his carelessness. It was not until after having smoked the brig, and finding that of little use, after having sunk her for three weeks, that the smell was at all bearable; but even then it could never be eradicated, and the admiral sent the brig home, and she was sold out of the service. They could do nothing with her at the dockyards. She was broken up, and bought by the people at Brighton and Tunbridge Wells, who used her timbers for turning fancy articles, which, smelling as they did, so strongly of otto of roses, proved very profitable. Were you ever at Brighton, Mr Simple?"

"Never, sir."

Just at this moment, the officer of the watch came down to say that there was a very large shark under the counter, and wished to know if the captain had any objection to the officers attempting to catch it.

"By no means," replied Captain Kearney; "I hate sharks as I do the devil. I nearly lost £14,000 by one, when I was in the Mediterranean."

"May I inquire how, Captain Kearney?" said the first lieutenant, with a demure face; "I'm very anxious to know."

"Why the story is simply this," replied the captain. "I had an old relation at Malta, whom I found out by accident—an old maid of sixty, who had lived all her life on the island. It was by mere accident that I knew of her existence. I was walking upon Strada Reale, when I saw a large baboon that was kept there, who had a little fat pug-dog by the tail, which he was pulling away with him, while an old lady was screaming out for help: for whenever she ran to assist her dog, the baboon made at her as if he would have ravished her, and caught her by the petticoats with one hand, while he held the pug-dog fast by the other. I owed that brute a spite for having attacked me one night when I passed him, and perceiving what was going on, I drew my sword and gave Mr Jacko such a clip as sent him away howling, and bleeding like a pig, leaving me in possession of the little pug, which I took up and handed to his mistress. The old lady trembled very much, and begged me to see her safe home. She had a very fine house, and after she was seated on the sofa, thanked me very much for my gallant assistance, as she termed it, and told me her name was Kearney: upon this I very soon proved my relationship with her, at which she was much delighted, requesting me to consider her house as my home. I was for two years afterwards on that station, and played my cards very well; and the old lady gave me a hint that I should be her heir, as she had no other relations that she knew anything of. At last I was ordered home, and not wishing to leave her, I begged her to accompany me, offering her my cabin. She was taken very ill a fortnight before we sailed, and made a will, leaving me her sole heir; but she recovered, and got as fat as ever. Mr Simple, the wine stands with you. I doubt if Lord Privilege gave you better claret than there is in that bottle; I imported it myself ten years ago, when I commanded the *Coquette*."

"Very odd," observed the first lieutenant—"we bought some at Barbadoes with the same mark on the bottles and cork."

"That may be," replied the captain; "old-established houses all keep up the same marks; but I doubt if your wine can be compared to this."

As Mr Phillott wished to hear the end of the captain's story, he would not contradict him this time, by stating what he knew to be the case, that the captain had sent it on board at Barbadoes; and the captain proceeded.

"Well, I gave up my cabin to the old lady, and hung up my cot in the gun-room during the passage home.

"We were becalmed abreast of Ceuta for two days. The old lady was very particular about her pug-dog, and I superintended the washing of the little brute twice a week; but at last I was tired of it, and gave him to my coxswain to bathe. My coxswain, who was a lazy fellow, without my knowledge, used to put the little beast into the bight of a rope, and tow him overboard for a minute or so. It was during this calm that he had him overboard in this way, when a confounded shark rose from under the counter, and took in the pug-dog at one mouthful. The coxswain reported the loss as a thing of no consequence; but I knew better, and put the fellow in irons. I then went down and broke the melancholy fact to Miss Kearney, stating that I had put the man in irons, and would flog him well. The old lady broke out into a most violent passion at the intelligence, declared that it was my fault, that I was jealous of the dog, and had done it on purpose. The more I protested, the more she raved; and at last I was obliged to go on deck to avoid her abuse and keep my temper. I had not been on deck five minutes before she came up— that is, was shoved up—for she was so heavy that she could not get up without assistance. You know how elephants in India push the cannon through a morass with their heads from behind; well, my steward used to shove her up the companion-ladder just in the same way, with his head completely buried in her petticoats. As soon as she was up, he used to pull his head out, looking as red and hot as a fresh-boiled lobster. Well, up she came, with her will in her hand, and, looking at me very fiercely, she said, 'Since the shark has taken my dear dog, he may have my will also,' and, throwing it overboard, she plumped down on the carronade slide. 'It's very well, madam,' said I, 'but you'll be cool by-and-by, and then you'll make another will.' 'I swear by all the hopes that I have of going to heaven that I never will!' she replied. 'Yes, you will, madam,' replied I. 'Never, so help me God! Captain Kearney; my money may now go to my next heir, and that, you know, will not be you.' Now, as I knew very well that the old lady was very positive and as good as her word, my object was to recover the will, which was floating about fifty yards astern, without her knowledge. I thought a moment, and then I called the boatswain's mate to *pipe all hands to bathe*. 'You'll excuse me, Miss Kearney,' said I, 'but the men are going to bathe, and I do not think you would like to see them all naked. If you would, you can stay on deck.' She looked daggers at me, and, rising from the carronade slide, hobbled to the ladder, saying, 'that the insult was another proof of how little I deserved any kindness from her.' As soon as she was below, the quarter-boats were lowered down, and I went in one of them and picked up the will, which still floated. Brigs having no stern-windows, of course she could not see my manoeuvre, but thought that the will was lost for ever. We had very bad weather after that, owing to which, with the loss of her favourite pug, and constant quarrelling with me—for I did all I could to annoy her afterwards—she fell ill, and was buried a fortnight after she was landed at Plymouth. The old lady kept her word; she never made another will. I proved the one I had recovered at Doctors' Commons, and touched the whole of her money."

As neither the first lieutenant nor I could prove whether the story was true or not, of course we expressed our congratulations at his good fortune, and soon afterwards left the cabin to report his marvellous story to our messmates. When I went on deck, I found that the shark had just been hooked, and was hauling on board. Mr Phillott had also come on deck. The officers were all eager about the shark, and were looking over the side, calling to each other, and giving directions to the men. Now, although certainly there was a want of decorum on the quarter-deck, still, the captain having given permission, it was to be excused; but Mr Phillott thought otherwise, and commenced in his usual style, beginning with the marine officer.

"Mr Westley, I'll trouble you not to be getting upon the hammocks. You'll get off directly, sir. If one of your fellows were to do so, I'd stop his grog for a month, and I don't see why you are to set a bad example; you've been too long in barracks, sir, by half. Who is that? Mr Williams and Mr Moore—both on the hammocks, too. Up to the foretopmast head, both of you, directly. Mr Thomas, up to the main; and I say, you youngster, stealing off, perch yourself upon the spanker-boom, and let me know when you've rode to London. By God! the service is going to hell! I don't know what officers are made of now-a-days. I'll marry some of you young gentlemen to the gunner's daughter before long. Quarter-deck's no better than a bear-garden. No wonder, when lieutenants set the example."

This latter remark could only be applied to O'Brien, who stood in the quarter-boat giving directions, before the tirade of Mr Phillott stopped the amusement of the party. O'Brien immediately stepped out of the boat, and going up to Mr Phillott, touched his hat, and said, "Mr Phillott, we had the captain's permission to catch the shark, and a shark is not to be got on board by walking up and down on the quarter-deck. As regards myself, as long as the captain is on board, I hold myself responsible to him alone for my conduct; and if you think I have done wrong, forward your complaint; but if you pretend to use such language to me, as you have to others, I shall hold you responsible. I am here, sir, as an officer and a gentleman, and will be treated as such; and allow me to observe, that I consider the quarter-deck more disgraced by foul and ungentlemanly language, than I do by an officer accidentally standing upon the hammocks. However, as you have thought proper to interfere, you may now get the shark on board yourself."

Mr Phillott turned very red, for he never had come in contact in this way with O'Brien. All the other officers had submitted quietly to his unpleasant manner of speaking to them. "Very well, Mr O'Brien; I shall hold you answerable for this language," replied he, "and shall most certainly report your conduct to the captain."

"I will save you the trouble; Captain Kearney is now coming up, and I will report it myself."

This O'Brien did, upon the captain's putting his foot on the quarter-deck.

"Well," observed the captain to Mr Phillott, "what is it you complain of?"

"Mr O'Brien's language, sir. Am I to be addressed on the quarter-deck in that manner?"

"I really must say, Mr Phillott," replied Captain Kearney, "that I do not perceive anything in what Mr O'Brien said, but what is correct. I command here; and if an officer so nearly equal in rank to yourself has committed himself, you are not to take the law into your own hands. The fact is, Mr Phillott, your language is not quite so correct as I could wish it. I overheard every word that passed, and I consider that *you* have treated *your superior* officer with disrespect—that is, *me*. I gave permission that the shark should be caught, and with that permission, I consequently allowed those little deviations from the discipline of the service which must inevitably take place. Yet you have thought proper to interfere with my permission, which is tantamount to an order, and have made use of harsh language, and punished the young gentlemen for obeying my injunctions. You will oblige me, sir, by calling them all down, and in restraining your petulance for the future. I will always support your authority when you are correct; but I regret that in this instance you have necessitated me to weaken it."

This was a most severe check to Mr Phillott, who immediately went below, after hailing the mastheads and calling down the midshipmen. As soon as he was gone we were all on the hammocks again; the shark was hauled forward, hoisted on board, and every frying-pan in the ship was in requisition. We were all much pleased with Captain Kearney's conduct on this occasion; and, as O'Brien observed to me, "He really is a good fellow and clever officer. What a thousand pities it is, that he is such a confounded liar!" I must do Mr Phillott the justice to say that he bore no malice on this occasion, but treated us as before, which is saying a great deal in his favour, when it is considered what power a first lieutenant has of annoying and punishing his inferiors.

Chapter XXXIII

Another set-to between the captain and first lieutenant—Cutting-out expedition—Mr Chucks mistaken—He dies like a gentleman—Swinburne begins his account of the battle off St Vincent.

We had not been more than a week under the Danish island of St Thomas when we discovered a brig close inshore. We made all sail in chase, and soon came within a mile and a half of the shore, when she anchored under a battery, which opened its fire upon us. Their elevation was too great, and several shots passed over us and between our masts.

"I once met with a very remarkable circumstance," observed Captain Kearney. "Three guns were fired at a frigate I was on board of from a battery, all at the same time. The three shots cut away the three topsail ties, and down came all our topsail yards upon the cap at the same time. That the Frenchmen might not suppose that they had taken such good aim, we turned up our hands to reef topsails; and by the time that the men were off the yards the ties were spliced and the topsails run up again."

Mr Phillott could not stand this most enormous fib, and he replied, "Very odd, indeed, Captain Kearney; but I have known a stranger circumstance. We had put in the powder to the four guns on the main deck when we were fighting the Danish gun-boats in a frigate I was in, and, as the men withdrew the rammer, a shot from the enemy entered the muzzle, and completed the loading of each gun. We fired their own shot back upon them, and this occurred three times running."

"Upon my word," replied Captain Kearney, who had his glass upon the battery, "I think you must have dreamt that circumstance, Mr Phillott."

"Not more than you did about the topsail ties, Captain Kearney."

Captain Kearney at that time had the long glass in his hand, holding it up over his shoulder. A shot from the battery whizzed over his head, and took the glass out of his hand, shivering it to pieces. "That's once," said Captain Kearney, very coolly; "but will you pretend that that could ever happen three times running? They might take my head off, or my arm, next time, but not another glass; whereas the topsail ties might be cut by three different shot. But give me another glass, Mr Simple: I am certain that this vessel is a privateer. What think you, Mr O'Brien?"

"I am every bit of your opinion, Captain Kearney," replied O'Brien; "and I think it would be a very pretty bit of practice to the ship's company to take her out from under that footy battery."

"Starboard the helm, Mr Phillott; keep away four points, and then we will think of it to-night."

The frigate was now kept away, and ran out of the fire of the battery. It was then about an hour before sunset, and in the West Indies the sun does not set as it does in the northern latitudes. There is no twilight: he descends in glory, surrounded with clouds of gold and rubies in their gorgeous tints; and once below the horizon, all is dark. As soon as it was dark, we hauled our wind off shore; and a consultation being held between the captain, Mr Phillott, and O'Brien, the captain at last decided that the attempt should be made. Indeed, although cutting-out is a very serious affair, as you combat under every disadvantage, still the mischief done to our trade by the fast-sailing privateers was so great in the West Indies, that almost every sacrifice was warrantable for the interests of the country. Still, Captain Kearney, although a brave and prudent officer—one who calculated chances, and who would not risk his men without he deemed that necessity imperiously demanded that such should be done—was averse to this attack, from his knowledge of the bay in which the brig was anchored; and although Mr Phillott and O'Brien both were of opinion that it should be a night attack, Captain Kearney decided otherwise. He considered, that although the risk might be greater, yet the force employed would be more consolidated, and that those who would hold back in the night dare not do so during the day. Moreover, that the people on shore in the battery, as well as those in the privateer, would be on the alert all night, and not expecting an attack during the day, would be taken off their guard. It was therefore directed that everything should be in preparation during the night, and that the boats should shove off before daylight, and row in-shore, concealing themselves behind some rocks under the cliffs which formed the cape upon one side of the harbour; and, if not discovered, remain there till noon, at which time it was probable that the privateer's men would be on shore, and the vessel might be captured without difficulty.

It is always a scene of much interest on board a man-of-war when preparations are made for an expedition of this description; and, as the reader may not have been witness to them, it may perhaps be interesting to describe them. The boats of men-of-war have generally two crews; the common boats' crews, which are selected so as not to take away the most useful men from the ship; and the service, or fighting boats' crews, which are selected from the very best men on board. The coxswains of the boats are the most trustworthy men in the ship, and, on this occasion, have to see that their boats are properly equipped. The launch, yawl, first and second cutters, were the boats appointed for the expedition. They all carried guns mounted upon slides, which ran fore and aft between the men. After the boats were hoisted out, the guns were lowered down into them and shipped in the bows of the boats. The arm-chests were next handed in, which contain the cartridges and ammunition. The shot were put into the bottom of the boats; and so far they were all ready. The oars of the boats were fitted to pull with grummets upon iron thole-pins, that they might make little noise, and might swing fore and aft without falling overboard when the boats pulled alongside the privateer. A breaker or two (that is, small casks holding about seven gallons each) of water was put into each boat, and also the men's allowance of spirits, in case they should be detained by any unforeseen circumstances. The men belonging to the boats were fully employed in looking after their arms; some fitting their flints to their pistols, others, and the major part of them, sharpening their cutlasses at the grindstone, or with a file borrowed from the armourer,—all were busy and all merry. The very idea of going into action is a source of joy to an English sailor, and more jokes are made, more merriment excited, at that time than at any other. Then, as it often happens that one or two of the service boats' crews may be on the sick list, urgent solicitations are made by others that they may supply their places. The only parties who appear at all grave are those who are to remain in the frigate, and not share in the expedition. There is no occasion to order the boats to be manned, for the men are generally in long before they are piped away. Indeed, one would think that it was a party of pleasure, instead of danger and of death, upon which they were about to proceed.

Captain Kearney selected the officers who were to have the charge of the boats. He would not trust any of the midshipmen on so dangerous a service. He said that he had known so many occasions in which their rashness and foolhardiness had spoilt an expedition; he therefore appointed Mr Phillott, the first lieutenant, to the launch; O'Brien to the yawl; the master to the first, and Mr Chucks, the boatswain, to the second cutter. Mr Chucks was much pleased with the idea of having the command of a boat, and asked me to come with him, to which I consented, although I had intended, as usual, to have gone with O'Brien.

About an hour before daylight we ran the frigate to within a mile and a half of the shore, and the boats shoved off; the frigate then wore round, and stood out in the offing, that she might at daylight be at such a distance as not to excite any suspicion that our boats were sent away, while we in the boats pulled quietly in-shore. We were not a quarter of an hour before we arrived at the cape forming one side of the bay, and were well secreted among the cluster of rocks which were underneath. Our oars were laid in; the boats' painters made fast; and orders given for the strictest silence. The rocks were very high, and the boats were not to be seen without any one should come to the edge of the precipice; and even then they would, in all probability, have been supposed to have been rocks. The water was as smooth as glass, and when it was broad daylight, the men hung listlessly over the sides of the boats, looking at the corals below, and watching the fish as they glided between.

"I can't say, Mr Simple," said Mr Chucks to me in an under tone, "that I think well of this expedition; and I have an idea that some of us will lose the number of our mess. After a calm comes a storm; and how quiet is everything now! But I'll take off my great coat, for the sun is hot already. Coxswain, give me my jacket."

Mr Chucks had put on his great coat, but not his jacket underneath, which he had left on one of the guns on the main deck, all ready to change as soon as the heavy dew had gone off. The coxswain handed him the jacket, and Mr Chucks threw off his great coat to put it on; but when it was opened it proved, that by mistake he had taken away the jacket, surmounted by two small epaulettes, belonging to Captain Kearney, which the captain's steward, who had taken it out to brush, had also laid upon the same gun.

"By all the nobility of England!" cried Mr Chucks, "I have taken away the captain's jacket by mistake. Here's a pretty mess! if I put on my great coat I shall be dead with sweating; if I put on no jacket I shall be roasted brown; but if I put on the captain's jacket I shall be considered disrespectful."

The men in the boats tittered; and Mr Phillott, who was in the launch next to us, turned round to see what was the matter; O'Brien was sitting in the stern-sheets of the launch with the first lieutenant, and I leaned over and told them.

"By the powers! I don't see why the captain's jacket will be at all hurt by Mr Chucks putting it on," replied O'Brien; "unless, indeed, a bullet were to go through it, and then it won't be any fault of Mr Chucks."

"No," replied the first lieutenant; "and if one did, the captain might keep the jacket, and swear that the bullet went round his body without wounding him. He'll have a good yarn to spin. So put it on, Mr Chucks; you'll make a good mark for the enemy."

"That I will stand the risk of with pleasure," observed the boatswain to me, "for the sake of being considered a gentleman. So here's on with it."

There was a general laugh when Mr Chucks pulled on the captain's jacket, and sank down in the stern-sheets of the cutter, with great complacency of countenance. One of the men in the boat that we were in thought proper, however, to continue his laugh a little longer than Mr Chucks considered necessary, who, leaning forward, thus addressed him: "I say, Mr Webber, I beg leave to observe to you, in the most delicate manner in the world—just to hint to you—that it is not the custom to laugh at your superior officer. I mean just to insinuate, that you are a d———d impudent son of a sea cook; and if we both live and do well, I will prove to you, that if I am to be laughed at in a boat with the captain's jacket on, that I am not to be laughed at on board the frigate with the boatswain's rattan in my fist; and so look out, my hearty, for squalls, when you come on the forecastle; for I'll be d———d if I don't make you see more stars than God Almighty ever made, and cut more capers than all the dancing-masters in France. Mark my words, you burgoo-eating, pea-soup-swilling, trowsers-scrubbing son of a bitch."

Mr Chucks, having at the end of this oration raised his voice above the pitch required by the exigency of the service, was called to order by the first lieutenant, and again sank back into the stern-sheets with all the importance and authoritative show peculiarly appertaining to a pair of epaulettes.

We waited behind the rocks until noonday, without being discovered by the enemy; so well were we concealed. We had already sent an officer, who, carefully hiding himself by lying down on the rocks, had several times reconnoitred the enemy. Boats were passing and repassing continually from the privateer to the shore; and it appeared that they went on shore full of men, and returned with only one or two; so that we were in great hopes that we should find but few men to defend the vessel. Mr Phillott looked at his watch, held it up to O'Brien, to prove that he had complied exactly with the orders he had received from the captain, and then gave the word to get the boats under weigh. The painters were cast off by the bowmen, the guns were loaded and primed, the men seized their oars, and in two minutes we were clear of the rocks, and drawn up in a line within a quarter of a mile from the harbour's mouth, and not half a mile from the privateer brig. We rowed as quickly as possible, but we did not cheer until the enemy fired the first gun; which he did from a quarter unexpected, as we entered the mouth of the harbour, with our union jack trailing in the water over our stern, for it was a dead calm. It appeared, that at the low point under the cliffs, at each side of the little bay, they had raised a water battery of two guns each. One of these guns, laden with grape shot, was now fired at the boats, but the elevation was too low, and although the water was ploughed up to within five yards of the launch, no injury was received. We were equally fortunate in the discharge of the other three guns; two of which we passed so quickly, that they were not aimed sufficiently forward, so that their shot fell astern; and the other, although the shot fell among us, did no further injury than cutting in half two of the oars of the first cutter.

In the meantime, we had observed that the boats had shoved off from the privateer as soon as they had perceived us, and had returned to her laden with men; the boats had been despatched a second time, but had not yet returned. They were now about the same distance from the privateer as were our boats, and it was quite undecided which of us would be first on board. O'Brien perceiving this, painted out to Mr Phillott that we should first attack the boats, and afterwards board on the side to which they pulled; as, in all probability, there would be an opening left in the boarding nettings, which were tied up to the yard-arms, and presented a formidable obstacle to our success. Mr Phillott agreed with O'Brien: he ordered the bowmen to lay in their oars and keep the guns pointed ready to fire at the word given, and desiring the other men to pull their best. Every nerve, every muscle was brought into play by our anxious and intrepid seamen. When within about twenty yards of the vessel, and also of the boats, the orders were given to fire—the carronade of the launch poured out round and grape so well directed, that one of the French boats sunk immediately; and the musket balls with which our other smaller guns were loaded, did great execution among their men. In one minute more, with three cheers from our sailors, we were all alongside together, English and French boats pell-mell, and a most determined close conflict took place. The French fought desperately, and as they were overpowered, they were reinforced by those from the privateer, who could not look on and behold their companions requiring their assistance, without coming to their aid. Some jumped down into our boats from the chains, into the midst of our men; others darted cold shot at us, either to kill us or to sink our boats; and thus did one of the most desperate hand-to-hand conflicts take place that ever was witnessed. But it was soon decided in our favour, for we were the stronger party and the better armed; and when all opposition was over, we jumped into the privateer, and found not a man left on board, only a large dog, who flew at O'Brien's throat as he entered the port.

"Don't kill him," said O'Brien, as the sailors hastened to his assistance; "only take away his gripe."

The sailors disengaged the dog, and O'Brien led him up to a gun, saying,
"By Jasus, my boy, you are my prisoner."

But although we had possession of the privateer, our difficulties, as it will prove, were by no means over. We were now exposed not only to the fire of the two batteries at the harbour-mouth which we had to pass, but also to that of the battery at the bottom of the bay, which had fired at the frigate. In the meantime, we were very busy in cutting the cable, lowering the topsails, and taking the wounded men on board the privateer, from out of the boats. All this was, however, but the work of a few minutes. Most of the Frenchmen were killed; our own wounded amounted to only nine seamen and Mr Chucks, the boatswain, who was shot through the body, apparently with little chance of surviving. As Mr Phillott observed, the captain's epaulettes had made him a mark for the enemy, and he had fallen in his borrowed plumes.

As soon as they were all on board, and laid on the deck—for there were, as near as I can recollect, about fourteen wounded Frenchmen as well as our own—tow-ropes were got out forwards, the boats were manned, and we proceeded to tow the brig out of the harbour.

It was a dead calm, and we made but little way, but our boat's crew, flushed with victory, cheered, and rallied, and pulled with all their strength. The enemy perceiving that the privateer was taken, and the French boats drifting empty up the harbour, now opened their fire upon us, and with great effect. Before we had towed abreast of the two water batteries, we had received three-shots between wind and water from the other batteries, and the sea was pouring fast into the vessel. I had been attending to poor Mr Chucks, who lay on the starboard side, near the wheel, the blood flowing from his wound, and tracing its course down the planks of the deck, to a distance of some feet from where he lay. He appeared very faint, and I tied my handkerchief round his body, so as to stop the effusion of blood, and brought him some water, with which I bathed his face, and poured some into his mouth. He opened his eyes wide, and looked at me.

"Ah, Mr Simple," said he, faintly, "is it you? It's all over with me; but it could not be better—could it?"

"How do you mean?" inquired I.

"Why, have I not fallen dressed like an officer and a gentleman?" said he, referring to the captain's jacket and epaulettes. "I'd sooner die now with this dress on, than recover to put on the boatswain's uniform. I feel quite happy."

He pressed my hand, and then closed his eyes again, from weakness. We were now nearly abreast of the two batteries on the points, the guns of which had been trained so as to bear upon our boats that were towing out the brig. The first shot went through the bottom of the launch, and sank her; fortunately, all the men were saved; but as she was the boat that towed next to the brig, great delay occurred in getting the others clear of her, and taking the brig again in tow. The shot now poured in thick, and the grape became very annoying. Still our men gave way, cheering at every shot fired, and we had nearly passed the batteries, with trifling loss, when we perceived that the brig was so full of water that she could not swim many minutes longer, and that it would be impossible to tow her alongside of the frigate. Mr Phillott, under these circumstances, decided that it would be useless to risk more lives, and that the wounded should be taken out of the brig, and the boats should pull away for the ship. He desired me to get the wounded men into the cutter, which he sent alongside, and then to follow the other boats. I made all the haste I could, not wishing to be left behind; and as soon as all our wounded men were in the boats, I went to Mr Chucks, to remove him. He appeared somewhat revived, but would not allow us to remove him.

"My dear Mr Simple," said he, "it is of no use; I never can recover it, and I prefer dying here. I entreat you not to move me. If the enemy take possession of the brig before she sinks, I shall be buried with military honours; if they do not, I shall at least die in the dress of a gentleman. Hasten away as fast as you can, before you lose more men. Here I stay—that's decided."

I expostulated with him, but at that time two boats full of men appeared, pulling out of the harbour to the brig. The enemy had perceived that our boats had deserted her, and were coming to take possession. I had therefore no time to urge Mr Chucks to change his resolution, and not wishing to force a dying man, I shook his hand and left him. It was with some difficulty I escaped, for the boats had come up close to the brig; they chased me a little while, but the yawl and the cutter turning back to my assistance, they gave up the pursuit. On the whole, this was a very well arranged and well conducted expedition. The only man lost was Mr Chucks, for the wounds of the others were none of them mortal. Captain Kearney was quite satisfied with our conduct, and so was the admiral, when it was reported to him. Captain Kearney did indeed grumble a little about his jacket, and sent for me to inquire why I had not taken it off Mr Chucks, and brought it on board. As I did not choose to tell him the exact truth, I replied, "That I could not disturb a dying man, and that the jacket was so saturated with blood, that he never could have worn it again," which was the case.

"At all events, you might have brought away my epaulettes," replied he; "but you youngsters think of nothing but gormandizing."

I had the first watch that night, when Swinburne, the quarter-master, came up to me, and asked me all the particulars of the affair, for he was not in the boats. "Well," said he, "that Mr Chucks appeared to be a very good boatswain in his way, if he could only have kept his rattan a little quiet. He was a smart fellow, and knew his duty. We had just such another killed in our ship, in the action off Cape St Vincent."

"What! were you in that action?" replied I.

"Yes, I was, and belonged to the *Captain*, Lord Nelson's ship."

"Well, then, suppose you tell me all about it."

"Why, Mr Simple, d'ye see, I've no objection to spin you a yarn, now and then," replied Swinburne, "but, as Mr Chucks used to say, allow me to observe, in the most delicate manner in the world, that I perceive that the man who has charge of your hammock, and slings you a clean one now and then, has very often a good glass of grog for his *yarns*, and I do not see but that mine are as well worth a glass of grog as his."

"So they are, Swinburne, and better too, and I promise you a good stiff one to-morrow evening."

"That will do, sir: now then, I'll tell you all about it, and more about it too than most can, for I know how the action was brought about."

I have the log, marked the board, and then sat down abaft on the signal chest with Swinburne, who commenced his narrative as follows:—

"You must know, Mr Simple, that when the English fleet came down the Mediterranean, after the 'vackyation of Corsica, they did not muster more than seventeen sail of the line, while the Spanish fleet from Ferrol and Carthagena had joined company at Cadiz, and 'mounted to near thirty. Sir John Jervis had the command of our fleet at the time, but as the Dons did not seem at all inclined to come out and have a brush with us, almost two to one, Sir John left Sir Hyde Parker, with six sail of the line, to watch the Spanish beggars, while he went in to Lisbon with the remainder of the fleet, to water and refit. Now, you see, Mr Simple, Portugal was at that time what they calls neutral, that is to say, she didn't meddle at all in the affair, being friends with both parties, and just as willing to supply fresh beef and water to the Spaniards as to the English, if so be the Spaniards had come out to ax for it, which they dar'n't. The Portuguese and the English have always been the best of friends, because we can't get no port wine anywhere else, and they can't get nobody else to buy it of them; so the Portuguese gave up their arsenal at Lisbon, for the use of the English, and there we kept all our stores, under the charge of that old dare-devil, Sir Isaac Coffin. Now it so happened, that one of the clerks in old Sir Isaac's *office*, a Portuguese chap, had been some time before that in the office of the Spanish ambassador; he was a very smart sort of a chap, and sarved as interpreter, and the old commissioner put great faith in him."

"But how did you learn all this, Swinburne?"

"Why, I'll tell you, Mr Simple. I steered the yawl as coxswain, and when admirals and captains talk in the stern-sheets, they very often forget that the coxswain is close behind them. I only learnt half of it that way; the rest I put together when I compared logs with the admiral's steward, who, of course, heard a great deal now and then. The first I heard of it was when old Sir John called out to Sir Isaac, after the second bottle, 'I say, Sir Isaac, who killed the Spanish messenger?' 'Not I, by God!' replied Sir Isaac; 'I only left him for dead;' and then they both laughed, and so did Nelson, who was sitting with them. Well, Mr Simple, it was reported to Sir Isaac that his clerk was often seen taking memorandums of the different orders given to the fleet, particularly those as to there being no wasteful expenditure of his Majesty's stores. Upon which, Sir Isaac goes to the admiral, and requests that the man might be discharged. Now, old Sir John was a sly old fox, and he answered, 'Not so, commissioner; perhaps we may catch them in their own trap.' So the admiral sits down, and calls for pen and ink, and he flourishes out a long letter to the commissioner, stating that all the stores of the fleet were expended, representing as how it would be impossible to go to sea without a supply, and wishing to know when the commissioner expected more transports from England. He also said that if the Spanish fleet were now to come out from Cadiz, it would be impossible for him to protect Sir H. Parker with his six sail of the line, who was watching the Spanish fleet, as he could not quit the port in his present condition. To this letter the commissioner answered that, from the last accounts, he thought that in the course of six weeks or two months they might receive supplies from England, but that sooner than that was impossible. These letters were put in the way of the d——d Portuguese spy-clerk, who copied them, and was seen that evening to go into the house of the Spanish ambassador. Sir John then sent a message to Ferro—that's a small town on the Portuguese coast to the southward—with a despatch to Sir Hyde Parker, desiring him to run away to Cape St Vincent, and decoy the Spanish fleet there, in case they should come out after him. Well, Mr Simple, so far d'ye see the train was well laid. The next thing to do was to watch the Spanish ambassador's house, and see if he sent away any despatches. Two days after the letters had been taken to him by this rascal of a clerk, the Spanish ambassador sent away two messengers—one for Cadiz and the other for Madrid, which is the town where the King of Spain lives. The one to Cadiz was permitted to go, but the one to Madrid was stopped by the directions of the admiral, and this job was confided to the commissioner, Sir Isaac, who settled it somehow or another; and this was the reason why the admiral called out to him, 'I say, Sir Isaac, who killed the messenger?' They brought back his despatches, by which they found out that advice had been sent to the Spanish admiral—I forget his name, something like *Magazine*—informing him of the supposed crippled state of our squadron. Sir John, taking it for granted that the Spaniards would not lose an opportunity of taking six sail of the line— more English ships than they have ever taken in their lives—waited a few days to give them time, and then sailed from Lisbon for Cape St Vincent, where he joined Sir Hyde Parker, and fell in with the Spaniards sure enough, and a pretty drubbing we gave them. Now, it's not everybody that could tell you all that, Mr Simple."

"Well, but now for the action, Swinburne."

"Lord bless you, Mr Simple! it's now past seven bells, and I can't fight the battle of St Vincent in half an hour; besides which, it's well worth another glass of grog to hear all about that battle."

"Well, you shall have one, Swinburne; only don't forget to tell it to me."

Swinburne and I then separated, and in less than an hour afterwards I was dreaming of despatches—Sir John Jervis—Sir Isaac Coffin—and Spanish messengers.

Chapter XXXIV

O'Brien's good advice—Captain Kearney again deals in the marvellous.

I do not remember any circumstance in my life which, at that time, lay so heavily on my mind as the loss of poor Mr Chucks, the boatswain, who, of course, I took it for granted I should never see again. I believe that the chief cause was that at the time I entered the service, and every one considered me to be the fool of the family, Mr Chucks and O'Brien were the only two who thought of and treated me differently; and it was their conduct which induced me to apply myself and encouraged me to exertion. I believe that many a boy, who, if properly patronized, would turn out well, is, by the injudicious system of browbeating and ridicule, forced into the wrong path, and, in his despair, throws away all self-confidence, and allows himself to be carried away by the stream to perdition. O'Brien was not very partial to reading himself. He played the German flute remarkably well, and had a very good voice. His chief amusement was practising, or rather playing, which is a very different thing; but although he did not study himself, he always made me come into his cabin for an hour or two every day, and, after I had read, repeat to him the contents of the book. By this method he not only instructed me, but gained a great deal of information himself; for he made so many remarks upon what I had read, that it was impressed upon both our memories.

"Well, Peter," he would say, as he came into the cabin, "what have you to tell me this morning? Sure it's you that's the schoolmaster, and not me—for I learn from you every day."

"I have not read much, O'Brien, to-day, for I have been thinking of poor Mr Chucks."

"Very right for you so to do, Peter. Never forget your friends in a hurry. You'll not find too many of them as you trot along the highway of life."

"I wonder whether he is dead?"

"Why, that's a question I cannot answer. A bullet through the chest don't lengthen a man's days, that's certain; but this I know, that he'll not die if he can help it, now that he's got the captain's jacket on."

"Yes; he always aspired to be a gentleman, which was absurd enough in a boatswain."

"Not at all absurd, Peter, but very absurd of you to talk without thinking. When did any one of his shipmates ever know Mr Chucks to do an unhandsome or mean action? Never; and why? Because he aspired to be a gentleman, and that feeling kept him above it. Vanity's a confounded donkey, very apt to put his head between his legs, and chuck us over; but pride's a fine horse, who will carry us over the ground, and enable us to distance our fellow-travellers. Mr Chucks has pride, and that's always commendable, even in a boatswain. How often have you read of people rising from nothing, and becoming great men? This was from talent, sure enough; but it was talent with pride to force it onward, not talent with vanity to check it."

"You are very right, O'Brien; I spoke foolishly."

"Never mind, Peter, nobody heard you but me; so it's of no consequence. Don't you dine in the cabin to-day?"

"Yes."

"So do I. The captain is in a most marvellous humour this morning. He told me one or two yarns that quite staggered my politeness and my respect for him on the quarter-deck. What a pity it is that a man should have gained such a bad habit!"

"He's quite incurable, I'm afraid," replied I; "but, certainly, his fibs do no harm; they are what they call white lies. I do not think he would really tell a lie—that is, a lie which would be considered to disgrace a gentleman."

"Peter, *all* lies disgrace a gentleman, white or black, although I grant there is a difference. To say the least of it, it is a dangerous habit; for white lies are but the gentlemen ushers to black ones. I know but of one point on which a lie is excusable, and that is, when you wish to deceive the enemy. Then your duty to your country warrants your lying till you're black in the face; and, for the very reason that it goes against your grain, it becomes, as it were, a sort of virtue."

"What was the difference between the marine officer and Mr Phillott that occurred this morning?"

"Nothing at all in itself. The marine officer is a bit of a gaby, and takes offence where none is meant. Mr Phillott has a foul tongue; but he has a good heart."

"What a pity it is!"

"It is a pity, for he's a smart officer; but the fact is, Peter, that junior officers are too apt to copy their superiors, and that makes it very important that a young gentleman should sail with a captain who is a gentleman. Now, Phillott served the best of his time with Captain Ballover, who is notorious in the service for foul and abusive language. What is the consequence? That Phillott and many others who have served under him have learnt his bad habit."

"I should think, O'Brien, that the very circumstance of having had your feelings so often wounded by such language when you were a junior officer, would make you doubly careful not to make use of it to others, when you had advanced in the service."

"Peter, that's just the *first* feeling, which wears away after a time; but at last, your own sense of indignation becomes blunted, and becoming indifferent to it, you forget also that you wound the feelings of others, and carry the habit with you, to the great injury and disgrace of the service. But it's time to dress for dinner, so you'd better make yourself scarce, Peter, while I tidivate myself off a little, according to the rules and regulations of His Majesty's service, when you are asked to dine with the skipper."

We met at the captain's table, where we found, as usual, a great display of plate, but very little else, except the ship's allowance. We certainly had now been cruising some time, and there was some excuse for it; but still, few captains would have been so unprovided. "I'm afraid, gentlemen, you will not have a very grand dinner," observed the captain, as the steward removed the plated covers of the dishes; "but when on service we must rough it out how we can. Mr O'Brien, pea-soup? I recollect faring harder than this through one cruise in a flush vessel. We were thirteen weeks up to our knees in water, and living the whole time upon raw pork—not being able to light a fire during the cruise."

"Pray, Captain Kearney, may I ask where this happened?"

"To be sure. It was off Bermudas: we cruised for seven weeks before we could find the Islands, and began verily to think that the Bermudas were themselves on a cruise."

"I presume, sir, you were not so sorry to have a fire to cook your provisions when you came to an anchor?" said O'Brien.

"I beg your pardon," replied Captain Kearney; "we had become so accustomed to raw provisions and wet feet, that we could not eat our meals cooked, or help dipping our legs over the side, for a long while afterwards. I saw one of the boat-keepers astern catch a large barracouta and eat it alive—indeed, if I had not given the strictest orders, and flogged half-a-dozen of them, I doubt whether they would not have eaten their victuals raw to this day. The force of habit is tremendous."

"It is, indeed," observed Mr Phillott, drily, and winking to us, referring to the captain's incredible stories.

"It is, indeed," repeated O'Brien; "we see the ditch in our neighbour's eye, and cannot observe the log of wood in our own;" and O'Brien winked at me, referring to Phillott's habit of bad language.

"I once knew a married man," observed the captain, "who had been always accustomed to go to sleep with his hand upon his wife's head, and would not allow her to wear a nightcap in consequence. Well, she caught cold and died, and he never could sleep at night until he took a clothes-brush to bed with him, and laid his hand upon that, which answered the purpose—such was the force of habit."

"I once saw a dead body galvanized," observed Mr Phillott: "it was the body of a man who had taken a great deal of snuff during his lifetime, and as soon as the battery was applied to his spine, the body very gently raised its arm, and put its fingers to its nose, as if it was taking a pinch."

"You saw that yourself, Mr Phillott?" observed the captain, looking at the first lieutenant earnestly in the face.

"Yes, sir," replied Mr Phillott, coolly.

"Have you told that story often?"

"Very often, sir."

"Because I know that some people, by constantly telling a story, at last believe it to be true; not that I refer to you, Mr Phillott; but still, I should recommend you not to tell that story where you are not well known, or people may doubt your credibility."

"I make it a rule to believe everything myself," observed Mr Phillott, "out of politeness, and I expect the same courtesy from others."

"Then, upon my soul! when you tell that story, you trespass very much upon our good manners. Talking of courtesy, you must meet a friend of mine, who has been a courtier all his life; he cannot help bowing, I have seen him bow to his horse and thank him after he had dismounted— beg pardon of a puppy for treading on his tail; and one day, when he fell over a scraper, he took his hat off, and made it a thousand apologies for his inattention."

"Force of habit again," said O'Brien.

"Exactly so. Mr Simple, will you take a slice of this pork? and perhaps you'll do me the honour to take a glass of wine? Lord Privilege would not much admire our dinner to-day, would he, Mr Simple?"

"As a variety he might, sir, but not for a continuance."

"Very truly said. Variety is charming. The negroes here get so tired of salt fish and occra broth, that they eat dirt by way of a relish. Mr O'Brien, how remarkably well you played that sonata of Pleydel's this morning."

"I am happy that I did not annoy you, Captain Kearney, at all events," replied O'Brien.

"On the contrary, I am very partial to good music. My mother was a great performer. I recollect once, she was performing a piece on the piano in which she had to imitate a *thunderstorm*. So admirably did she hit it off, that when we went to tea all the cream was *turned sour*, as well as three casks of *beer* in the cellar."

At this assertion Mr Phillott could contain himself no longer; he burst out into a loud laugh, and having a glass of wine to his lips, spattered it all over the table, and over me, who unfortunately was opposite to him.

"I really beg pardon, Captain Kearney, but the idea of such an expensive talent was too amusing. Will you permit me to ask you a question? As there could not have been thunder without lightning, were any people killed at the same time by the electric fluid of the piano?"

"No sir," replied Captain Kearney, very angrily; "but her performance *electrified* us, which was something like it. Perhaps, Mr Phillott, as you lost your last glass of wine, you will allow me to take another with you?"

"With great pleasure," replied the first lieutenant, who perceived that he had gone far enough.

"Well, gentlemen," said the captain, "we shall soon be in the land of plenty. I shall cruise a fortnight more, and then join the admiral at Jamaica. We must make out our despatch relative to the cutting out of the *Sylvia* (that was the name of the privateer brig), and I am happy to say that I shall feel it my duty to make honourable mention of all the party present. Steward, coffee."

The first lieutenant, O'Brien, and I, bowed to this flattering avowal on the part of the captain; as for me, I felt delighted. The idea of my name being mentioned in the "Gazette," and the pleasure that it would give to my father and mother, mantled the blood in my cheeks till I was as red as a turkey-cock.

"*Cousin* Simple," said the captain, good-naturedly, "you have no occasion to blush; your conduct deserves it; and you are indebted to Mr Phillott for having made me acquainted with your gallantry."

Coffee was soon over, and I was glad to leave the cabin, and be alone, that I might compose my perturbed mind. I felt too happy. I did not, however, say a word to my messmates, as it might have created feelings of envy or ill-will. O'Brien gave me a caution not to do so, when I met him afterwards, so that I was very glad that I had been so circumspect.

Chapter XXXV

Swinburne continues his narrative of the battle off Cape St Vincent.

The second night after this, we had the middle watch, and I claimed Swinburne's promise that he would spin his yarn, relative to the battle of St Vincent. "Well, Mr Simple, so I will; but I require a little priming, or I shall never go off."

"Will you have your glass of grog before or after?"

"Before, by all means, if you please, sir. Run down and get it, and I'll heave the log for you in the meantime, when we shall have a good hour without interruption, for the sea-breeze will be steady, and we are under easy sail." I brought up a stiff glass of grog, which Swinburne tossed off, and as he finished it, sighed deeply as if in sorrow that there was no more. Having stowed away the tumbler in one of the capstern holes for the present, we sat down upon a coil of ropes under the weather bulwarks, and Swinburne, replacing his quid of tobacco, commenced as follows—

"Well, Mr Simple, as I told you before, old Jervis started with all his fleet for Cape St Vincent. We lost one of our fleet—and a three-decker too—the *St George*; she took the ground, and was obliged to go back to Lisbon; but we soon afterwards were joined by five sail of the line, sent out from England, so that we mustered fifteen sail in all. We had like to lose another of our mess, for d'ye see, the old *Culloden* and *Colossus* fell foul of each other, and the *Culloden* had the worst on it; but Troubridge, who commanded her, was not a man to shy his work, and ax to go in to refit, when there was a chance of meeting the enemy— so he patched her up somehow or another, and reported himself ready for action the very next day. Ready for action he always was, that's sure enough, but whether his ship was in a fit state to go into action is quite another thing. But as the sailors used to say in joking, he was a *true bridge*, and you might trust to him; which meant as much as to say, that he knew how to take his ship into action, and how to fight her when he was fairly in it. I think it was the next day that Cockburn joined us in the *Minerve*, and he brought Nelson along with him with the intelligence that the Dons had chased him, and that the whole Spanish fleet was out in pursuit of us. Well, Mr Simple, you may guess we were not a little happy in the *Captain*, when Nelson joined us, as we knew that if he fell in with the Spaniards our ship would cut a figure— and so she did sure enough. That was on the morning of the 13th, and old Jervis made the signal to prepare for action, and keep close order, which means, to have your flying jib-boom in at the starn windows of the ship ahead of you; and we did keep close order, for a man might have walked right round from one ship to the other, either lee or weather line of the fleet. I sha'n't forget that night, Mr Simple, as long as I live and breathe. Every now and then we heard the signal guns of the Spanish fleet booming at a distance to windward of us, and you may guess how our hearts leaped at the sound, and how we watched with all our ears for the next gun that was fired, trying to make out their bearings and distance, as we assembled in little knots upon the booms and weather-gangway. It was my middle watch, and I was signalman at the time, so of course I had no time to take a caulk if I was inclined. When my watch was over I could not go down to my hammock, so I kept the morning watch too, as did most of the men on board: as for Nelson, he walked the deck the whole night, quite in a fever. At daylight it was thick and hazy weather, and we could not make them out; but, about five bells, the old *Culloden*, who, if she had broke her nose, had not lost the use of her eyes, made the signal for a part of the Spanish fleet in sight. Old Jervis repeated the signal to prepare for action, but he might have saved the wear and tear of the bunting, for we were all ready, bulk-heads down, screens up, guns shotted, tackles rove, yards slung, powder filled, shot on deck, and fire out—and what's more, Mr Simple, I'll be d——d if we weren't all willing too. About six bells in the forenoon, the fog and haze all cleared away at once, just like the raising of the foresail that they lower down at the Portsmouth theatre, and discovered the whole of the Spanish fleet. I counted them all. 'How many, Swinburne?' cries Nelson. 'Twenty-six sail, sir,' answered I. Nelson walked the quarter-deck backwards and forwards, rubbing his hands, and laughing to himself, and then he called for his glass, and went to the gangway with Captain Miller. 'Swinburne, keep a good look upon the admiral,' says he. 'Ay, ay, sir,' says I. Now you see, Mr Simple, twenty-six sail against fifteen were great odds upon paper; but we didn't think so, because we know'd the difference between the two fleets. There was our fifteen sail of the line, all in apple-pie order, packed up as close as dominoes, and every man on board of them longing to come to the scratch; while there was their twenty-six, all *somehow nohow*, two lines here and *no lines* there, with a great gap of water in the middle of them. For this gap between their ships we all steered, with all the sail we could carry because, d'ye see, Mr Simple, by getting them on both sides of us, we had the advantage of fighting both broadsides, which is just as easy as fighting one, and makes shorter work of it. Just as it struck seven bells, Troubridge opened the ball *setting* to half a dozen of the Spaniards, and making them *reel* 'Tom Collins' whether or no. Bang—bang—bang, bang! Oh, Mr Simple, it's a beautiful sight to see the first guns fired that are to bring on a general action. He's the luckiest dog, that Troubridge,' said Nelson, stamping with impatience. Our ships were soon hard at it, hammer and tongs (my eyes, how they did pelt it in!), and old Sir John, in the *Victory*, smashed the cabin windows of the Spanish admiral, with such a hell of a raking broadside, that the fellow bore up as if the devil kicked him. Lord a mercy, you might have drove a Portsmouth waggon into his starn—the broadside of the *Victory* had made room enough. However, they were soon all smothered up in smoke, and we could not make out how things were going on—but we made a pretty good guess. Well, Mr Simple, as they say at the play, that was act the first, scene the first; and now we had to make our appearance, and I'll leave you to judge, after I've told my tale, whether the old*Captain* wasn't principal performer, and *top sawyer* over them all. But stop a moment, I'll just look at the binnacle, for that young topman's nodding at the wheel.—I say, Mr Smith, are you shutting your eyes to keep them warm, and letting the ship run half a point out of her course? Take care I don't send for another helmsman, that's all, and give the reason why. You'll make a wry face upon six-water grog to-morrow, at seven bells. D——n your eyes, keep them open—can't you?"

Swinburne, after this genteel admonition to the man at the wheel, reseated himself and continued his narrative.

"All this while, Mr Simple, we in the *Captain* had not fired a gun; but were ranging up as fast as we could to where the enemy lay in a heap. There were plenty to pick and choose from; and Nelson looked out sharp for a big one, as little boys do when they have to choose an apple; and, by the piper that played before Moses! it was a big one that he ordered the master to put him alongside of. She was a four-decker, called the *Santissima Trinidad*. We had to pass some whoppers, which would have satisfied any reasonable man; for there was the *San Josef*, and *Salvador del Mondo* and *San Nicolas*: but nothing would suit Nelson but this four-decked ship; so we crossed the hawse of about six of them, and as soon as we were abreast of her, and at the word 'Fire!' every gun went off at once, slap into her, and the old *Captain* reeled at the discharge, as if she was drunk. I wish you'd only seen how we pitched it into this *Holy Trinity*; she was *holy* enough before we had done with her, riddled like a sieve, several of her ports knocked into one, and every scupper of her running blood and water. Not but what she stood to it as bold as brass, and gave us nearly gun for gun, and made a very pretty general average in our ship's company. Many of the old captains went to kingdom-come in that business, and many more were obliged to bear up for Greenwich Hospital.

"'Fire away, my lads—steady aim!' cries Nelson. 'Jump down there, Mr Thomas; pass the word to reduce the cartridges, the shot go clean through her. Double shot the guns there, fore and aft.'

"So we were at it for about half an hour, when our guns became so hot from quick firing, that they bounced up to the beams overhead, tearing away their ringbolts, and snapping their breechings like rope-yarns. By this time we were almost as much unrigged as if we had been two days paying off in Portsmouth harbour. The four-decker forged ahead, and Troubridge, in the jolly old *Culloden*, came between us and two other Spanish ships, who were playing into us. She was as fresh as a daisy, and gave them a dose which quite astonished them. They shook their ears, and fell astern, when the *Blenheim* laid hold of them, and mauled them so that they went astern again. But it was out of the frying-pan into, the fire: for the *Orion, Prince George*, and one or two others, were coming up, and knocked the very guts out of them. I'll be d——d if they forget the 14th of April, and sarve them right, too. Wasn't a four-decker enough for any two-decker, without any more coming on us? and couldn't the beggars have matched themselves like gentlemen? Well, Mr Simple, this gave us a minute or two to fetch, our breath, let the guns cool, and repair damages, and swab the blood from the decks; but we lost our four-decker, for we could not get near her again."

"What odd names the Spaniards give to their ships, Swinburne?"

"Why yes, they do; it would almost appear wicked to belabour the *Holy Trinity* as we did. But why they should call a four-decked ship the *Holy Trinity*, seeing as how there's only three of them, Father, Son, and Holy Ghost, I can't tell. Bill Saunders said that the fourth deck was for the Pope, who was as great a personage as the others; but I can't understand how that can be. Well, Mr Simple, as I was head signalman, I was perched on the poop, and didn't serve at a gun. I had to report all I could see, which was not much, the smoke was so thick; but now and then I could get a peep, as it were through the holes in the blanket. Of course I was obliged to keep my eye as much as possible upon the admiral, not to make out his signals, for Commodore Nelson wouldn't thank me for that; I knew he hated a signal when in action, so I never took no notice of the bunting, but just watched to see what he was about. So while we are repairing damages, I'll just tell you what I saw of the rest of the fleet. As soon as old Jervis had done for the Spanish admiral, he hauled his wind on the larboard tack, and followed by four or five other ships, weathered the Spanish line, and joined Collingwood in the *Excellent*. Then they all dashed through the line; the *Excellent* was the leading ship, and she first took the shine out of the *Salvador del Mondo*, and then left her to be picked up by the other ships, while she attacked a two-decker, who hauled down her colours—I forget her name just now. As soon as the *Victory* ran alongside of the *Salvador del Mondo*, down went her colours, and *excellent* reasons had she for striking her flag. And now, Mr Simple. The old *Captain* comes into play again. Having parted company with the four-decker, we had recommenced action with the *San Nicolas*, a Spanish eighty, and while we were hard at it, old Collingwood comes up in the *Excellent*. The *San Nicolas*, knowing that the *Excellent's* broadside would send her to old Nick, put her helm up to avoid being raked: in so doing, she fell foul of the *San Josef*, a Spanish three-decker, and we being all cut to pieces and unmanageable—all of us indeed reeling about like drunken men—Nelson ordered his helm a-starboard, and in a jiffy there we were, all three hugging each other, running in one another's guns, smashing our chain-plates, and poking our yard-arms through each other's canvas.

"'All hands to board!' roared Nelson, leaping on the hammocks and waving his sword.

"'Hurrah! hurrah!' echoed through the decks, and up flew the men, like as many angry bees out of a bee-hive. In a moment pikes, tomahawks, cutlasses, and pistols were seized (for it was quite unexpected, Mr Simple), and our men poured into the eighty-gun ship, and in two minutes the decks were cleared and all the Dons pitched below. I joined the boarders and was on the main deck when Captain Miller came down, and cried out 'On deck again immediately.' Up we went, and what do you think it was for, Mr Simple? Why to board a second time; for Nelson having taken the two-decker, swore that he'd have the three-decker as well. So away we went again, clambering up her lofty sides how we could, and dropping down on her decks like hailstones. We all made for the quarter-deck, beat down every Spanish beggar that showed fight, and in five minutes more we had hauled down the colours of two of the finest ships in the Spanish navy. If that wasn't taking the shine out of the Dons, I should like to know what is. And didn't the old captains cheer and shake hands, as Commodore Nelson stood on the deck of the *San Josef*, and received the swords of the Spanish officers! There was enough of them to go right round the capstern, and plenty to spare. Now, Mr Simple, what do you think of that for a spree?"

"Why, Swinburne, I can only say that I wish I had been there."

"So did every man in the fleet, Mr Simple, I can tell you."

"But what became of the *Santissima Trinidad*?"

"Upon my word, she behaved one *deck* better than all the others. She held out against four of our ships for a long while, and then hauled down her colours, and no disgrace to her, considering what a precious hammering she had taken first. But the lee division of the Spanish weather fleet, if I may so call it, consisting of eleven sail of the line, came up to her assistance, and surrounded her, so that they got her off. Our ships were too much cut up to commence a new action, and the admiral made the signal to secure the prizes. The Spanish fleet then did what they should have done before—got into line; and we lost no time in doing the same. But we both had had fighting enough."

"But do you think, Swinburne, that the Spaniards fought well?"

"They'd have fought better, if they'd only have known how. There's no want of courage in the Dons, Mr Simple, but they did not support each other. Only observe how Troubridge supported us. By God, Mr Simple, he was the *real fellow*, and Nelson knew it well. He was Nelson's right-hand man; but you know, there wasn't room for *two* Nelsons. Their ships engaged held out well, it must be acknowledged, but why weren't they all in their proper berths? Had they kept close order of sailing, and had all fought as well as those who were captured, it would not have been a very easy matter for fifteen ships to gain a victory over twenty-six. That's long odds, even when backed with British seamen."

"Well, how did you separate?"

"Why, the next morning the Spaniards had the weathergage, so they had the option whether to fight or not. At one time they had half a mind, for they bore down to us; upon which we hauled our wind to show them we were all ready to meet them, and then they thought better of it, and rounded-to again. So as they wouldn't fight, and we didn't wish it, we parted company in the night; and two days afterwards we anchored, with our four prizes, in Lagos Bay. So now you have the whole of it, Mr Simple, and I've talked till I'm quite hoarse. You haven't by chance another drop of the stuff left to clear my throat? It would be quite a charity."

"I think I have, Swinburne; and as you deserve it, I will go and fetch it."

Chapter XXXVI

A letter from Father M'Grath, who diplomatizes—When priest meets priest, then comes the tug of war—Father O'Toole not to be made a tool of.

We continued our cruise for a fortnight, and then made sail for Jamaica, where we found the admiral at anchor at Port Royal, but our signal was made to keep under weigh, and Captain Kearney, having paid his respects to the admiral, received orders to carry despatches to Halifax. Water and provisions were sent on board by the boats of the admiral's ships, and, to our great disappointment, as the evening closed in, we were again standing out to sea, instead of, as we had anticipated, enjoying ourselves on shore; but the fact was, that orders had arrived from England to send a frigate immediately up to the admiral at Halifax, to be at his disposal.

I had, however, the satisfaction to know that Captain Kearney had been true to his word in making mention of my name in the despatch, for the clerk showed me a copy of it. Nothing occurred worth mentioning during our passage, except that Captain Kearney was very unwell nearly the whole of the time, and seldom quitted his cabin. It was in October that we anchored in Halifax harbour, and the Admiralty, expecting our arrival there, had forwarded our letters. There were none for me, but there was one for O'Brien, from Father M'Grath, the contents of which were as follows:—

"MY DEAR SON,—And a good son you are, and that's the truth on it, or devil a bit should you be a son of mine. You've made your family quite contented and peaceable, and they never fight for the *praties* now— good reason why they shouldn't, seeing that there's a plenty for all of them, and the pig craturs into the bargain. Your father and your mother, and your brother, and your three sisters, send their duty to you, and their blessings too—and you may add my blessing, Terence, which is worth them all; for won't I get you out of purgatory in the twinkling of a bed-post? Make yourself quite aisy on that score, and lave it all to me; only just say a *pater* now and then, that when St Peter lets you in, he mayn't throw it in your teeth, that you've saved your soul by contract, which is the only way by which emperors and kings ever get to heaven. Your letter from Plymouth came safe to hand: Barney, the post-boy, having dropped it under foot, close to our door, the big pig took it into his mouth and ran away with it; but I caught sight of him, and *speaking* to him, he let it go, knowing (the 'cute cratur!) that I could read it better than him. As soon as I had digested the contents, which it was lucky the pig did not instead of me, I just took my meal and my big stick, and then set off for Ballycleuch.

"Now you know, Terence, if you haven't forgot—and if you have, I'll just remind you—that there's a flaunty sort of young woman at the poteen shop there, who calls herself Mrs O'Rourke, wife to a Corporal O'Rourke, who was kilt or died one day, I don't know which, but that's not of much consequence. The devil a bit do I think the priest ever gave the marriage-blessing to that same; although she swears that she was married on the rock of Gibraltar—it may be a strong rock fore I know, but it's not the rock of salvation like the seven sacraments, of which marriage is one. *Benedicite*! Mrs O'Rourke is a little too apt to fleer and jeer at the priests; and if it were not that she softens down her pertinent remarks with a glass or two of the real poteen, which proves some respect for the church, I'd excommunicate her body and soul, and every body and every soul that put their lips to the cratur at her door. But she must leave that off, as I tell her, when she gets old and ugly, for then all the whisky in the world sha'n't save her. But she's a fine woman now, and it goes agin my conscience to help the devil to a fine woman. Now this Mrs O'Rourke knows everybody and everything that's going on in the country about; and she has a tongue which has never had a holiday since it was let loose.

"'Good morning to ye, Mrs O'Rourke,' says I.

"'An' the top of the morning to you, Father M'Grath,' says she, with a smile; 'what brings you here? Is it a journey that you're taking to buy the true wood of the cross? or is it a purty girl that you wish to confess, Father M'Grath? or is it only that you're come for a drop of poteen, and a little bit of chat with Mrs O'Rourke?'

"'Sure it's I who'd be glad to find the same true wood of the cross, Mrs O'Rourke, but it's not grown, I suspect, at your town of Ballycleuch; and it's no objection I'd have to confess a purty girl like yourself, Mrs O'Rourke, who'll only tell me half her sins, and give me no trouble; but it's the truth, that I'm here for nothing else but to have a bit of chat with yourself, dainty dear, and taste your poteen, just by way of keeping my mouth nate and clane.'

"So Mrs O'Rourke poured out the real stuff, which I drank to her health; and then says I, putting down the bit of a glass, 'So you've a stranger come, I find, in your parts, Mrs O'Rourke.'

"'I've heard the same,' replied she. So you observe, Terence, I came to the fact all at once by a guess.

"'I am tould,' says I, 'that he's a Scotchman, and spakes what nobody can understand.'

"'Devil a bit,' says she, 'he's an Englishman, and speaks plain enough.'

"'But what can a man mane, to come here and sit down all alone?' says I.

"'All alone, Father M'Grath!' replied she; 'is a man all alone when he's got his wife and childer, and more coming, with the blessing of God?'

"'But those boys are not his own childer, I believe,' says I.

"'There again you're all in a mistake, Father M'Grath,' rejoins she. 'The childer are all his own, and all girls to boot. It appears that it's just as well that you come down, now and then, for information, to our town of Ballycleuch.'

"'Very true, Mrs O'Rourke,' says I; 'and who is it that knows everything so well as yourself?' You observe, Terence, that I just said everything contrary and *arce versa*, as they call it, to the contents of your letter; for always recollect, my son, that if you would worm a secret out of a woman, you'll do more by contradiction than you ever will by coaxing—so I went on: 'Anyhow, I think it's a burning shame, Mrs O'Rourke, for a gentleman to bring over with him here from England a parcel of lazy English servants, when there's so many nice boys and girls here to attind upon them.'

"'Now there you're all wrong again, Father M'Grath,' says she. 'Devil a soul has he brought from the other country, but has hired them all here. Arn't there Ella Flanagan for one maid, and Terence Driscol for a footman? and it's well that he looks in his new uniform, when he comes down for the newspapers; and arn't Moggy Cala there to cook the dinner, and pretty Mary Sullivan for a nurse for the babby as soon as it comes into the world?'

"'Is it Mary Sullivan you mane?' says I; 'she that was married about three months back, and is so quick in child-getting, that she's all but ready to fall to pieces in this same time?'

"'It's exactly she,' says Mrs O'Rourke; 'and do you know the reason?'

"'Devil a bit,' says I; 'how should I?'

"'Then it's just that she may send her own child away, and give her milk to the English babby that's coming; because the lady is too much of a lady to have a child hanging to her breast.'

"'But suppose Mary Sullivan's child ar'n't born till afterwards, how then?" says I. 'Speak, Mrs O'Rourke, for you're a sensible woman.'

"'How then?' says she. 'Och! that's all arranged; for Mary says that she'll be in bed a week before the lady, so that's all right, you'll perceive, Father M'Grath.'

"'But don't you perceive, sensible woman as you are, that a young woman, who is so much out of her reckoning as to have a child three months after her marriage, may make a little mistake in her lying-in arithmetic, Mrs O'Rourke.'

"'Never fear, Father M'Grath, Mary Sullivan will keep her word; and sooner than disappoint the lady, and lose her place, she'll just tumble down-stairs, and won't that put her to bed fast enough?'

"'Well, that's what I call a faithful good servant that earns her wages,' says I; 'so now I'll just take another glass, Mrs O'Rourke, and thank you too. Sure you're the woman that knows everything, and a mighty pretty woman into the bargain.'

"'Let me alone now, Father M'Grath, and don't be pinching me that way, anyhow.'

"'It was only a big flea that I perceived hopping on your gown, my darling, devil anything else.'

"'Many thanks to you, father, for that same; but the next time you'd kill my fleas, just wait until they're in a *more dacent* situation.'

"'Fleas are fleas, Mrs O'Rourke, and we must catch 'em when we can, and how we can, and as we can, so no offence. A good night's rest to you, Mrs O'Rourke—when do you mean to confess?'

"'I've an idea that I've too many fleas about me to confess to you just now, Father M'Grath, and that's the truth on it. So a pleasant walk back to you.'

"So you'll perceive, my son, that having got all the information from Mrs O'Rourke, it's back I went to Ballyhinch, till I heard it whispered that there were doings down at the old house at Ballycleuch. Off I set, and went to the house itself, as priests always ought to be welcomed at births, and marriages, and deaths, being, as you know, of great use on such occasions—when who should open the door but Father O'Toole, the biggest rapparee of a priest in the whole of Ireland. Didn't he steal a horse, and only save his neck by benefit of clergy? and did he ever give absolution to a young woman without making her sin over again? 'What may be your pleasure here, Father M'Grath?' says he, holding the door with his hand.

"'Only just to call and hear what's going on.'

"'For the matter of that,' says he, 'I'll just tell you that we're all going on very well; but ar'n't you ashamed of yourself, Father M'Grath, to come here to interfere with my flock, knowing that I confess the house altogether?'

"'That's as may be,' says I; 'but I only wanted to know what the lady had brought into the world.'

"'It's a *child*' says he.

"'Indeed!' says I; 'many thanks for the information; and pray what is it that Mary Sullivan has brought into the world?'

"'That's a *child* too,' says he; 'and now that you know all about it, good evening to you, Father M'Grath.' And the ugly brute slammed the door right in my face.

"'Who stole a horse?' cries I; but he didn't hear me—more's the pity.

"So you'll perceive, my dear boy, that I have found out something, at all events, but not so much as I intended; for I'll prove to Father O'Toole that he's no match for Father M'Grath. But what I find out must be reserved for another letter, seeing that it's not possible to tell it to you in this same. Praties look well, but somehow or another, *clothes* don't grow upon trees in ould Ireland; and one of your half-quarterly bills, or a little prize-money, if it found its way here, would add not a little to the respectability of the family appearance. Even my cassock is becoming too *holy* for a parish priest; not that I care about it so much, only Father O'Toole, the baste! had on a bran new one—not that I believe that he ever came honestly by it, as I have by mine—but, get it how you may, a new gown always looks better than an old one, that's certain. So no more at present from your loving friend and confessor,

"URTAGH M'GRATH."

"Now, you'll observe, Peter," said O'Brien, after I had read the letter, "that, as I supposed, your uncle meant mischief when he went over to Ireland. Whether the children are both boys or both girls, or your uncle's is a boy, and the other is a girl, there is no knowing at present. If an exchange was required, it's made, that's certain; but I will write again to Father M'Grath, and insist upon his finding out the truth, if possible. Have you any letter from your father?"

"None, I am sorry to say. I wish I had, for he would not have failed to speak on the subject."

"Well, never mind, it's no use dreaming over the matter; we must do our best when we get to England ourselves, and in the meantime trust to Father M'Grath. I'll go and write to him while my mind's full of it."

O'Brien wrote his letter, and the subject was not started again.

Chapter XXXVII

Captain Kearney's illness—He makes his will, and devises sundry châteaux en Espagne for the benefit of those concerned—The legacy duty in this instance not ruinous—He signs, seals, and dies.

The captain, as was his custom, went on shore, and took up his quarters at a friend's house; that is to say, the house of an acquaintance, or any polite gentleman who would ask him to take a dinner and a bed. This was quite sufficient for Captain Kearney, who would fill his portmanteau, and take up his quarters, without thinking of leaving them until the ship sailed, or some more advantageous invitation was given. This conduct in England would have very much trespassed on our ideas of hospitality; but in our foreign settlements and colonies, where the society is confined and novelty is desirable, a person who could amuse like Captain Kearney was generally welcome, let him stay as long as he pleased. All sailors agree in asserting that Halifax is one of the most delightful ports in which a ship can anchor. Everybody is hospitable, cheerful, and willing to amuse and be amused. It is, therefore, a very bad place to send a ship to if you wish her to refit in a hurry; unless, indeed, the admiral is there to watch over your daily progress, and a sharp commissioner to expedite your motions in the dockyard. The admiral was there when we arrived, and we should not have lain there long, had not the health of Captain Kearney, by the time that we were ready for sea, been so seriously affected, that the doctor was of opinion that he could not sail. Another frigate was sent to our intended cruising-ground, and we lay idle in port. But we consoled ourselves: if we did not make prize-money, at all events, we were very happy, and the major part of the officers very much in love.

We had remained in Halifax harbour about three weeks, when a very great change for the worse took place in Captain Kearney's disease. Disease, indeed, it could hardly be called. He had been long suffering from the insidious attacks of a hot climate, and though repeatedly advised to invalid, he never would consent. His constitution appeared now to be breaking up. In a few days he was so ill, that, at the request of the naval surgeons, he consented to be removed to the hospital, where he could command more comforts than in any private house. He had not been at the hospital more than two days, when he sent for me, and stated his wish that I should remain with him. "You know, Peter, that you are a cousin of mine, and one likes to have one's relations near one when we are sick, so bring your traps on shore. The doctor has promised me a nice little room for yourself, and you shall come and sit with me all day." I certainly had no objection to remain with him, because I considered it my duty so to do, and I must say that there was no occasion for me to make any effort to entertain him, as he always entertained me; but I could not help seriously reflecting, and feeling much shocked, at a man, lying in so dangerous a state—for the doctors had pronounced his recovery to be impossible—still continuing a system of falsehood during the whole day, without intermission. But it really appeared in him to be innate; and, as Swinburne said, "if he told truth, it was entirely by mistake."

"Peter," said he, one day, "there's a great draught. Shut the door, and put on some more coals."

"The fire does not draw well, sir," replied I, "without the door is open."

"It's astonishing how little people understand the nature of these things. When I built my house, called Walcot Abbey, there was not a chimney would draw; I sent for the architect and abused him, but he could not manage it: I was obliged to do it myself."

"Did you manage it, sir?"

"Manage it—I think I did. The first time I lighted the fire, I opened the door, and the draught was so great, that my little boy, William, who was standing in the current of air, would have gone right up the chimney, if I had not caught him by the petticoats; as it was, his frock was on fire."

"Why sir, it must have been as bad as a hurricane!"

"No, no, not quite so bad—but it showed what a little knowledge of philosophical arrangement could effect. We have no hurricanes in England, Peter; but I have seen a very pretty whirlwind when I was at Walcot Abbey."

"Indeed, sir."

"Yes; it cut four square haystacks quite round, and I lost twenty tons of hay; it twisted the iron lamp-post at the entrance just as a porpoise twists a harpoon, and took up a sow and her litter of pigs, that were about a hundred yards from the back of the house, and landed them safe over the house to the front, with the exception of the old sow putting her shoulder out."

"Indeed, sir."

"Yes, but what was strange, there were a great many rats in the hayrick, and up they went with the hay. Now, Peter, by the laws of gravitation, they naturally come down before the hay, and I was walking with my greyhound, or rather terrier, and after one coming down close to her, which she killed, it was quite ridiculous to witness her looking up in the air, and watching for the others."

"A greyhound did you say, sir, or a terrier?"

"Both, Peter; the fact is, she had been a greyhound, but breaking her foreleg against a stump, when coursing, I had the other three amputated as well, and then she made a capital terrier. She was a great favourite of mine."

"Well," observed I, "I have read something like that in Baron Munchausen."

"Mr Simple," said the captain, turning on his elbow and looking me severely in the face, "what do you mean to imply?"

"Oh, nothing, sir, but I have read a story of that kind."

"Most probably; the great art of invention is to found it upon facts. There are some people who out of a mole-hill will make a mountain; and facts and fiction become so blended nowadays, that even truth becomes a matter of doubt."

"Very true, sir," replied I; and as he did not speak for some minutes, I ventured to bring my Bible to his bedside, as if I was reading it to myself.

"What are you reading, Peter?" said he.

"Only a chapter in the Bible, sir," said I. "Would you like that I should read aloud?"

"Yes, I'm very fond of the Bible—it's the book of *truth*. Peter, read me about Jacob, and his weathering Esau with a mess of pottage, and obtaining his father's blessing." I could not help thinking it singular that he should select a portion in which, for divine reasons, a lie was crowned with success and reward.

When I had finished it, he asked me to read something more; I turned over to the Acts of the Apostles, and commenced the chapter in which Ananias and Sapphira were struck dead. When I had finished, he observed very seriously, "That is a very good lesson for young people, Peter, and points out that you never should swerve from the truth. Recollect, as your motto, Peter, to 'tell truth and shame the devil.'"

After this observation I laid down the book, as it appeared to me that he was quite unaware of his propensity; and without a sense of your fault, how can repentance and amendment be expected? He became more feeble and exhausted every day, and, at last, was so weak that he could scarcely raise himself in his bed. One afternoon he said, "Peter, I shall make my will, not that I am going to kick the bucket just yet; but still it is every man's duty to set his house in order, and it will amuse me; so fetch pen and paper, and come and sit down by me."

I did as he requested.

"Write, Peter, that I, Anthony George William Charles Huskisson Kearney (my father's name was Anthony, Peter; I was christened George, after the present Regent, William and Charles after Mr Pitt and Mr Fox, who were my sponsors; Huskisson is the name of my great uncle, whose property devolves to me; he's eighty-three now, so he can't last long)—have you written down that?"

"Yes, sir."

"Being in sound mind, do hereby make my last will and testament, revoking all former wills."

"Yes, sir."

"I bequeath to my dearly beloved wife, Augusta Charlotte Kearney (she was named after the Queen and Princess Augusta, who held her at the baptismal font), all my household furniture, books, pictures, plate, and houses, for her own free use and will, and to dispose of at her pleasure upon her demise. Is that down?"

"Yes, sir."

"Also, the interest of all my money in the three percents, reduced, and in the long annuities, and the balance in my agent's hands, for her natural life. At her death to be divided into equal portions between my two children, William Mohamed Potemkin Kearney, and Caroline Anastasia Kearney. Is that down?"

"Yes, sir."

"Well, then, Peter, now for my real property. My estate in Kent (let me see, what is the name of it?)—Walcot Abbey, my three farms in the Vale of Aylesbury, and the marsh lands in Norfolk, I bequeath to my two children aforenamed, the proceeds of the same to be laid up, deducting all necessary expenses for their education, for their sole use and benefit. Is that down?"

"Not yet, sir—'use and benefit.' Now it is, sir."

"Until they come to the age of twenty-one years; or in case of my daughter, until she marries with the consent of my executors, then to be equally and fairly valued and divided between them. You observe, Peter, I never make any difference between girls and boys—a good father will leave one child as much as another. Now, I'll take my breath a little."

I was really astonished. It was well known that Captain Kearney had nothing but his pay, and that it was the hopes of prize-money to support his family, which had induced him to stay out so long in the West Indies. It was laughable; yet I could not laugh: there was a melancholy feeling at such a specimen of insanity, which prevented me.

"Now, Peter, we'll go on," said Captain Kearney, after a pause of a few minutes. "I have a few legacies to bequeath. First, to all my servants £50 each, and two suits of mourning; to my nephew, Thomas Kearney, of Kearney Hall, Yorkshire, I bequeath the sword presented me by the Grand Sultan. I promised it to him, and although we have quarrelled, and not spoken for years, I always keep my word. The plate presented me by the merchants and underwriters of Lloyd's, I leave to my worthy friend, the Duke of Newcastle. Is that down?"

"Yes, sir."

"Well; my snuff-box, presented me by Prince Potemkin, I bequeath to Admiral Sir Isaac Coffin; and, also, I release him from the mortgage which I hold over his property of the Madeline Islands, in North America. By-the-bye, say, and further, I bequeath to him the bag of snuff presented to me by the Dey of Algiers; he may as well have the snuff as he has the snuff-box. Is that down?"

"Yes, sir."

"Well then, now, Peter, I must leave you something."

"Oh, never mind me," replied I.

"No, no, Peter, I must not forget my cousin. Let me see; you shall have my fighting sword. A real good one, I can tell you. I once fought a duel with it at Palermo, and ran a Sicilian prince so clean through the body, and it held so tight, that we were obliged to send for a pair of post-horses to pull it out again. Put that down as a legacy for my cousin, Peter Simple. I believe that is all. Now for my executors; and I request my particular friends, the Earl of Londonderry, the Marquis of Chandos, and Mr John Lubbock, banker, to be my executors, and leave each of them the sum of one thousand pounds for their trouble, and in token of regard. That will do, Peter. Now, as I have left so much real property, it is necessary that there should be three witnesses; so call in two more, and let me sign in your presence."

This order was obeyed, and this strange will duly attested, for I hardly need say, that even the presents he had pretended to receive were purchased by himself at different times; but such was the force of his ruling passion even to the last. Mr Phillott and O'Brien used to come and see him, as did occasionally some of the other officers, and he was always cheerful and merry, and seemed to be quite indifferent about his situation, although fully aware of it. His stories, if anything, became more marvellous, as no one ventured to express a doubt as to their credibility.

I had remained in the hospital about a week, when Captain Kearney was evidently dying: the doctor came, felt his pulse, and gave it as his opinion that he could not outlive the day. This was on a Friday, and there certainly was every symptom of dissolution. He was so exhausted that he could scarcely articulate; his feet were cold, and his eyes appeared glazed, and turned upwards. The doctor remained an hour, felt his pulse again, shook his head, and said to me, in a low voice, "He is quite gone." As soon as the doctor quitted the room, Captain Kearney opened his eyes, and beckoned me to him. "He's a confounded fool, Peter," said he: "he thinks I am slipping my wind now—but I know better; going I am, 'tis true—but I shan't die till next Thursday." Strange to say, from that moment he rallied; and although it was reported that he was dead, and the admiral had signed the acting order for his successor, the next morning, to the astonishment of everybody, Captain Kearney was still alive. He continued in this state, between life and death, until the Thursday next, the day on which he asserted that he would die—and, on that morning, he was evidently sinking fast. Towards noon, his breathing became much oppressed and irregular, and he was evidently dying; the rattle in his throat commenced; and I watched at his bedside, waiting for his last gasp, when he again opened his eyes, and beckoning me, with an effort, to put my head close to him to hear what he had to say, he contrived, in a sort of gurgling whisper, and with much difficulty, to utter—"Peter, I'm going now—not that the rattle—in my throat—is a sign of death: for I once knew a man—to *live*with—*the rattle in his throat*—for *six weeks*." He fell back and expired, having, perhaps, at his last gasp, told the greatest lie of his whole life.

Thus died this most extraordinary character, who, in most other points, commanded respect: he was a kind man and a good officer; but from the idiosyncrasy of his disposition, whether from habit or from nature, could not speak the truth. I say from *nature*, because I have witnessed the vice of stealing equally strong, and never to be eradicated. It was in a young messmate of good family, and who was supplied with money to almost any extent: he was one of the most generous, open-hearted lads that I ever knew; he would offer his purse, or the contents of his chest, to any of his messmates, and, at the same time, would steal everything that he could lay his hands upon. I have known him watch for hours, to steal what could be of no use to him, as, for instance, an *odd* shoe, and that much too small for his foot. What he stole he would give away the very next day; but to check it was impossible. It was so well known, that if anything was missed, we used first to apply to his chest to see if it was there, and usually found the article in question. He appeared to be wholly insensible to shame upon this subject, though in every other he showed no want of feeling or of honour; and, strange to say, he never covered his theft with a lie. After vain attempts to cure him of this propensity, he was dismissed the service as incorrigible.

Captain Kearney was buried in the churchyard with the usual military honours. In his desk we found directions, in his own hand, relative to his funeral, and the engraving on his tombstone. In these, he stated his aged to be thirty-one years. If this was correct, Captain Kearney, from the time that he had been in the service of his country, must have entered the navy just *four months before* he was born. It was unfortunate that he commenced the inscription with "Here lies Captain Kearney," &c. &c. His tombstone had not been set up twenty-four hours before somebody, who knew his character, put a dash under one word, as emphatic as it was true of the living man,
"Here *lies* Captain."

Chapter XXXVIII

Captain Horton—Gloomy news from home—Get over head and ears in the water, and find myself afterwards growing one way, and my clothes another—Though neither as rich as a Jew, nor as large as a camel, I pass through my examination, which my brother candidates think passing strange.

The day after Captain Kearney's decease, his acting successor made his appearance on board. The character of Captain Horton was well known to us from the complaints made by the officers belonging to his ship, of his apathy and indolence; indeed, he went by the *soubriquet* of "the Sloth." It certainly was very annoying to his officers to witness so many opportunities of prize-money and distinction thrown away through the indolence of his disposition. Captain Horton was a young man of family who had advanced rapidly in the service from interest, and from occasionally distinguishing himself. In the several cutting-out expeditions, on which he had not volunteered but had been ordered, he had shown, not only courage, but a remarkable degree of coolness in danger and difficulty, which had gained him much approbation: but it was said that this coolness arose from his very fault—an unaccountable laziness. He would walk away, as it were, from the enemy's fire, when others would hasten, merely because he was so apathetic that he would not exert himself to run. In one cutting-out expedition in which he distinguished himself, it is said that having to board a very high vessel, and that in a shower of grape and musketry, when the boat dashed alongside, and the men were springing up, he looked up at the height of the vessel's sides, and exclaimed, with a look of despair, "My God! must we really climb up that vessel's decks?" When he had gained the deck, and became excited, he then proved how little fear had to do with the remark, the captain of the ship falling by his hand, as he fought in advance on his own men. But this peculiarity, which in a junior officer was of little consequence, and a subject of mirth, in a captain became of a very serious nature. The admiral was aware how often he had neglected to annoy or capture the enemy when he might have done it; and, by such neglect, Captain Horton infringed one of the articles of war, the punishment awarded to which infringement is *death*. His appointment, therefore, to the *Sanglier* was as annoying to us as his quitting his former ship was agreeable to those on board of her.

As it happened, it proved of little consequence: the admiral had instructions from home to advance Captain Horton to the first vacancy, which of course he was obliged to comply with; but not wishing to keep on the station an officer who would not exert himself, he resolved to send her to England with despatches and retain the other frigate which had been ordered home, and which we had been sent up to replace. We therefore heard it announced with feelings of joy, mingled with regret, that we were immediately to proceed to England. For my part, I was glad of it. I had now served my time as midshipman, to within five months, and I thought that I had a better chance of being made in England than abroad. I was also very anxious to go home, for family reasons, which I have already explained. In a fortnight we sailed with several vessels, and directions to take charge of a large convoy from Quebec, which was to meet us off the island of St John's. In a few days we joined our convoy, and with a fair wind bore up for England. The weather soon became very bad, and we were scudding before a heavy gale, under bare poles. Our captain seldom quitted the cabin, but remained there on a sofa, stretched at his length, reading a novel, or dozing, as he found most agreeable.

I recollect a circumstance which occurred, which will prove the apathy of his disposition, and how unfit he was to command so fine a frigate. We had been scudding three days, when the weather became much worse.

O'Brien, who had the middle watch, went down to report that "it blew very hard."

"Very well," said the captain; "let me know if it blows harder."

In about an hour more the gale increased, and O'Brien went down again.
"It blows much harder, Captain Horton."

"Very well," answered Captain Horton, turning in his cot; "you may call me again when it *blows harder*."

At about six bells the gale was at its height, and the wind roared in its fury. Down went O'Brien again. "It blows tremendous hard now, Captain Horton."

"Well, well, if the weather becomes worse—"

"It can't be worse," interrupted O'Brien; "it's impossible to blow harder."

"Indeed! Well, then," replied the captain, "let me know when *it lulls*."

In the morning watch a similar circumstance took place. Mr Phillott went down, and said that several of the convoy were out of sight astern. "Shall we heave-to, Captain Horton?"

"Oh, no," replied he, "she will be so uneasy. Let me know if you lose sight of any more."

In another hour the first lieutenant reported that "there were very few to be seen."

"Very well, Mr Phillott," replied the captain, turning round to sleep; "let me know if you lose any more."

Some time elapsed, and the first lieutenant reported "that they were all out of sight."

"Very well, then," said the captain; "call me when you see them again."

This was not very likely to take place, as we were going twelve knots an hour, and running away from them as fast as we could; so the captain remained undisturbed until he thought proper to get up to breakfast. Indeed, we never saw any more of our convoy, but taking the gale with us, in fifteen days anchored in Plymouth Sound. The orders came down for the frigate to be paid off, all standing, and recommissioned. I received letters from my father, in which he congratulated me at my name being mentioned in Captain Kearney's despatches, and requested me to come home as soon as I could. The admiral allowed my name to be put down on the books of the guard-ship, that I might not lose my time, and then gave me two months' leave of absence. I bade farewell to my shipmates, shook hands with O'Brien, who proposed to go over to Ireland previous to his applying for another ship, and, with my pay in my pocket, set off in the Plymouth mail, and in three days was once more in the arms of my affectionate mother, and warmly greeted by my father and the remainder of my family.

Once more with my family, I must acquaint the reader with what had occurred since my departure. My eldest sister, Lucy, had married an officer in the army, a Captain Fielding, and his regiment having been ordered out to India, had accompanied her husband, and letters had been received, just before my return announcing their safe arrival at Ceylon. My second sister, Mary, had also been engaged to be married, and from her infancy was of extremely delicate health. She was very handsome, and much admired. Her intended husband was a baronet of good family; but unfortunately, she caught a cold at the assize ball and went off in a decline. She died about two months before my arrival, and the family were in deep mourning. My third sister, Ellen, was still unmarried; she also was a very beautiful girl, and now seventeen. My mother's constitution was much shaken by the loss of my sister Mary, and the separation from her eldest child. As for my father, even the loss of his daughter appeared to be wholly forgotten in the unwelcome intelligence which he had received, that my uncle's wife had been safely delivered of a *son*, which threw him out of the anticipated titles and estates of my grandfather. It was indeed a house of mourning. My mother's grief I respected, and tried all I could to console her; that of my father was so evidently worldly, and so at variance with his clerical profession, that I must acknowledge I felt more of anger at it than sorrow. He had become morose and sullen, harsh to those around him, and not so kind to my mother as her state of mind and health made it his duty to be, even if inclination were wanted. He seldom passed any portion of the day with her, and in the evening she went to bed very early, so that there was little communication between them. My sister was a great consolation to her, and so I hope was I; she often said so as she embraced me, and the tears rolled down her cheeks, and I could not help surmising that those tears were doubled from the coolness and indifference, if not unkindness, with which my father behaved to her. As for my sister, she was an angel; and as I witnessed her considerate attentions to my mother, and the total forgetfulness of self which she displayed (so different from my father, who was all self), I often thought what a treasure she would prove to any man who was fortunate enough to win her love. Such was the state of my family when I returned to it.

I had been at home about a week, when one evening, after dinner, I submitted to my father the propriety of trying to obtain my promotion.

"I can do nothing for you, Peter; I have no interest whatever," replied he, moodily.

"I do not think that much is required, sir," replied I; "my time will be served on the 20th of next month. If I pass, which I trust I shall be able to do, my name having been mentioned in the public despatches will render it a point of no very great difficulty to obtain my commission at the request of my grandfather."

"Yes, your grandfather might succeed, I have no doubt; but I think you have little chance now in that quarter. My brother has a son, and we are thrown out. You are not aware, Peter, how selfish people are, and how little they will exert themselves for their relations. Your grandfather has never invited me since the announcement of my brother's increase to his family. Indeed, I have never been near him, for I know that it is of no use."

"I must think otherwise of Lord Privilege, my dear father, until your opinion is confirmed by his own conduct. That I am not so much an object of interest, I grant; but still he was very kind, and appeared to be partial to me."

"Well, well, you can try all you can, but you'll soon see of what stuff this world is made; I am sure I hope it will be so, for what is to become of you children if I die, I do not know;—I have saved little or nothing. And now all my prospects are blasted by this—" and my father dashed his fist upon the table in a manner by no means clerical, and with a look very unworthy of an apostle.

I am sorry that I must thus speak of my father, but I must not disguise the truth. Still, I must say, there was much in extenuation of his conduct. He had always a dislike to the profession of the church: his ambition, as a young man, had been to enter the army, for which service he was much better qualified; but, as it has been the custom for centuries to entail all the property of the aristocracy upon the eldest son, and leave the other brothers to be supported by the state, or rather by the people, who are taxed for their provision, my father was not permitted to follow the bent of his own inclination. An elder brother had already selected the army as his profession, and it was therefore decided that my father should enter the church; and thus it is that we have had, and still have, so many people in that profession, who are not only totally unfit for, but who actually disgrace, their calling. The law of primogeniture is beset with evils and injustice; yet without it, the aristocracy of a country must sink into insignificance. It appears to me, that as long as the people of a country are content to support the younger sons of the nobility, it is well that the aristocracy should be held up as a third estate, and a link between the sovereign and the people; but that if the people are either too poor, or are unwilling to be so taxed, they have a right to refuse taxation for such purposes, and to demand that the law of primogeniture should be abolished.

I remained at home until my time was complete, and then set off for Plymouth to undergo my examination. The passing-day had been fixed by the admiral for the Friday, and, as I arrived on Wednesday, I amused myself during the day, walking about the dockyard, and trying all I could to obtain further information in my profession. On the Thursday, a party of soldiers from the depot were embarking at the landing-place in men-of-war boats, and, as I understood, were about to proceed to India. I witnessed the embarkation, and waited till they shoved off, and then walked to the anchor wharf to ascertain the weights of the respective anchors of the different classes of vessels in the King's service.

I had not been there long, when I was attracted by the squabbling created by a soldier, who, it appeared, had quitted the ranks to run up to the tap in the dockyard to obtain liquor. He was very drunk, and was followed by a young woman with a child in her arms, who was endeavouring to pacify him.

"Now be quiet, Patrick, jewel," said she, clinging to him; "sure it's enough that you've left the ranks, and will come to disgrace when you get on board. Now be quiet, Patrick, and let us ask for a boat, and then perhaps the officer will think it was all a mistake, and let you off aisy; and sure I'll speak to Mr O'Rourke, and he's a kind man."

"Out wid you, you cratur, it is Mr O'Rourke you'd be having a conversation wid, and he be chucking you under that chin of yours. Out wid you, Mary, and lave me to find my way on board. Is it a boat I want, when I can swim like St Patrick, wid my head under my arm, if it wasn't on my shoulders? At all events, I can wid my nappersack and musket to boot."

The young woman cried, and tried to restrain him, but he broke from her, and running down to the wharf, dashed off into the water. The young woman ran to the edge of the wharf, perceived him sinking, and shrieking with despair, threw up her arms in her agony. The child fell, struck on the edge of the piles, turned over, and before I could catch hold of it, sank into the sea. "The child! the child!" burst forth in another wild scream, and the poor creature lay at my feet in violent fits. I looked over, the child had disappeared; but the soldier was still struggling with his head above water. He sank and rose again—a boat was pulling towards him, but he was quite exhausted. He threw back his arms as if in despair, and was about disappearing under a wave, when, no longer able to restrain myself, I leaped off the high wharf, and swam to his assistance, just in time to lay hold of him as he was sinking for the last time. I had not been in the water a quarter of a minute before the boat came up to us, and dragged us on board. The soldier was exhausted and speechless. I, of course, was only very wet. The boat rowed to the landing-place at my request, and we were both put on shore. The knapsack which was fixed on the soldier's back, and his regimentals, indicated that he belonged to the regiment just embarked; and I stated my opinion that, as soon as he was a little recovered, he had better be taken on board. As the boat which picked us up was one of the men-of-war boats, the officer who had been embarking the troops, and had been sent on shore again to know if there were any yet left behind, consented. In a few minutes the soldier recovered, and was able to sit up and speak, and I only waited to ascertain the state of the poor young woman whom I had left on the wharf. In a few minutes she was led to us by the warder, and the scene between her and her husband was most affecting. When she had become a little composed, she turned round to me, where I stood dripping wet, and, intermingled with lamentation for the child, showering down emphatic blessings on my head, inquired my name. "Give it to me!" she cried; "give it to me on paper, in writing, that I may wear it next my heart, read and kiss it every day of my life, and never forget to pray for you, and to bless you!"

"I'll tell it you. My name—"

"Nay, write it down for me—write it down. Sure you'll not refuse me. All the saints bless you, dear young man, for saving a poor woman from despair!"

The officer commanding the boat handed me a pencil and a card; I wrote my name and gave it to the poor woman; she took my hand as I gave it, kissed the card repeatedly, and put it into her bosom. The officer, impatient to shove off, ordered her husband into the boat—she followed, clinging to him, wet as he was—the boat shoved off, and I hastened up to the inn to dry my clothes. I could not help observing, at the time, how the fear of a greater evil will absorb all consideration for a minor. Satisfied that her husband had not perished, she had hardly once appeared to remember that she had lost her child.

I had only brought one suit of clothes with me: they were in very good condition when I arrived, but salt water plays the devil with a uniform. I laid in bed until they were dry; but when I put them on again, not being before too large for me, for I grew very fast, they were now shrunk and shrivelled up, so as to be much too small. My wrists appeared below the sleeves of my coat—my trousers had shrunk half way up to my knees—the buttons were all tarnished, and altogether I certainly did not wear the appearance of a gentlemanly, smart midshipman. I would have ordered another suit, but the examination was to take place at ten o'clock the next morning, and there was no time. I was therefore obliged to appear as I was, on the quarter-deck of the line-of-battle ship, on board of which the passing was to take place. Many others were there to undergo the same ordeal, all strangers to me, and as I perceived by their nods and winks to each other, as they walked up and down in their smart clothes, not at all inclined to make my acquaintance.

There were many before me on the list, and our hearts beat every time that a name was called, and the owner of it walked aft into the cabin. Some returned with jocund faces, and our hopes mounted with the anticipation of similar good fortune; others came out melancholy and crest-fallen, and then the expression of their countenances was communicated to our own, and we quailed with fear and apprehension. I have no hesitation in asserting, that although "passing" may be a proof of being qualified, "not passing" is certainly no proof to the contrary. I have known many of the cleverest young men turned back (while others of inferior abilities have succeeded), merely from the feeling of awe occasioned by the peculiarity of the situation: and it is not to be wondered at, when it is considered that all the labour and exertion of six years are at stake at this appalling moment. At last my name was called, and almost breathless from anxiety, I entered the cabin, where I found myself in presence of the three captains who were to decide whether I were fit to hold a commission in His Majesty's service. My logs and certificates were examined and approved; my time calculated and allowed to be correct. The questions in navigation which were put to me were very few, for the best of all possible reasons, that most captains in His Majesty's service know little or nothing of navigation. During their servitude as midshipmen, they learn it by *rote*, without being aware of the principles upon which the calculations they use are founded. As lieutenants, their services as to navigation are seldom required, and they rapidly forget all about it. As captains, their whole remnant of mathematical knowledge consists in being able to set down the ship's position on the chart. As for navigating the ship, the master is answerable; and the captains not being responsible themselves, they trust entirely to his reckoning. Of course there are exceptions, but what I state is the fact; and if an order from the Admiralty was given, that all captains should pass again, although they might acquit themselves very well in seamanship, nineteen out of twenty would be turned back when they were questioned in navigation. It is from the knowledge of this fact that I think the service is injured by the present system, and the captain should be held _wholly _responsible for the navigation of his ship. It has been long known that the officers of every other maritime state are more scientific than our own, which is easily explained, from the responsibility not being invested in our captains. The origin of masters in our service is singular. When England first became a maritime power, ships for the King's service were found by the Cinque Ports and other parties—the fighting part of the crew was composed of soldiers sent on board. All the vessels at that time had a crew of sailors, with a master to navigate the vessel. During our bloody naval engagements with the Dutch, the same system was acted upon. I think it was the Earl of Sandwich, of whom it is stated, that his ship being in a sinking state, he took a boat to hoist his flag on board of another vessel in the fleet, but a shot cutting the boat in two, and the *weight of his armour* bearing him down, the Earl of Sandwich perished. But to proceed.

As soon as I had answered several questions satisfactorily, I was desired to stand up. The captain who had interrogated me on navigation, was very grave in his demeanour towards me, but at the same time not uncivil. During his examination, he was not interfered with by the other two, who only undertook the examination in "seamanship." The captain, who now desired me to stand up, spoke in a very harsh tone, and quite frightened me. I stood up pale and trembling, for I augured no good from this commencement. Several questions in seamanship were put to me, which I have no doubt I answered in a very lame way, for I cannot even now recollect what I said.

"I thought so," observed the captain; "I judged as much from your appearance. An officer who is so careless of his dress, as not even to put on a decent coat when he appears at his examination, generally turns out an idle fellow, and no seaman. One would think you had served all your time in a cutter, or a ten-gun brig, instead of dashing frigates. Come, sir, I'll give you one more chance."

I was so hurt at what the captain said, that I could not control my feelings. I replied, with a quivering lip, "that I had had no time to order another uniform,"—and I burst into tears.

"Indeed, Burrows, you are rather too harsh," said the third captain; "the lad is frightened. Let him sit down and compose himself for a little while. Sit down, Mr Simple, and we will try you again directly."

I sat down, checking my grief and trying to recall my scattered senses. The captains, in the meantime, turning over the logs to pass away the time; the one who had questioned me in navigation reading the Plymouth newspaper, which had a few minutes before been brought on board and sent into the cabin. "Heh! what's this? I say Burrows—Keats, look here," and he pointed to a paragraph. "Mr Simple, may I ask whether it was you who saved the soldier who leaped off the wharf yesterday?"

"Yes, sir," replied I; "and that's the reason why my uniforms are so shabby. I spoilt them then, and had no time to order others. I did not like to say why they were spoilt." I saw a change in the countenances of all the three, and it gave me courage. Indeed, now that my feelings had found vent, I was no longer under any apprehension.

"Come, Mr Simple, stand up again," said the captain, kindly, "that is, if you feel sufficiently composed; if not, we will wait a little longer. Don't be afraid, we *wish* to pass you."

I was not afraid, and stood up immediately. I answered every question satisfactorily; and finding that I did so, they put more difficult ones. "Very good, very good indeed, Mr Simple; now let me ask you one more; it's seldom done in the service, and perhaps you may not be able to answer it. Do you know how to *club-haul* a ship?"

"Yes, sir," replied I, having, as the reader may recollect, witnessed the manoeuvre when serving under poor Captain Savage, and I immediately stated how it was to be done.

"That is sufficient, Mr Simple. I wish to ask you no more questions. I thought at first you were a careless officer and no seaman: I now find that you are a good seaman and a gallant young man. Do you wish to ask any more questions?" continued he, turning to the two others.

They replied in the negative; my passing certificate was signed, and the captains did me the honour to shake hands with me, and wish me speedy promotion. Thus ended happily this severe trial to my poor nerves; and, as I came out of the cabin, no one could have imagined that I had been in such distress within, when they beheld the joy that irradiated my countenance.

Chapter XXXIX

Is a chapter of plots—Catholic casuistry in a new cassock—Plotting promotes promotion—A peasant's love and a peer's peevishness—Prospects of prosperity.

As soon as I arrived at the hotel, I sent for a Plymouth paper, and cut out the paragraph which had been of such importance to me in my emergency, and the next morning returned home to receive the congratulations of my family. I found a letter from O'Brien, which had arrived the day before. It was as follows:—

"MY DEAR PETER,—Some people, they say, are lucky to 'have a father born before them,' because they are helped on in the world—upon which principle, mine was born *after* me, that's certain; however, that can't be helped. I found all my family well and hearty; but they all shook a cloth in the wind with respect to toggery. As for Father M'Grath's cassock, he didn't complain of it without reason. It was the ghost of a garment; but, however, with the blessing of God, my last quarterly bill, and the help of a tailor, we have had a regular refit, and the ancient family of the O'Briens of Ballyhinch are now rigged from stem to starn. My two sisters are both to be spliced to young squireens in the neighbourhood; it appears that they only wanted for a dacent town gown to go to the church in. They will be turned off next Friday, and I only wish, Peter, you were here to dance at the weddings. Never mind, I'll dance for you and for myself too. In the meantime, I'll just tell you what Father M'Grath and I have been doing, all about and consarning that thief of an uncle of yours.

"It's very little or nothing at all that Father M'Grath did before I came back, seeing as how Father O'Toole had a new cassock, and Father M'Grath's was so shabby that he couldn't face him under such a disadvantage; but still Father M'Grath spied about him, and had several hints from here and from there, all of which, when I came to add them up, amounted to just nothing at all.

"But since I came home, we have been busy. Father M'Grath went down to Ballycleuch, as bold as a lion in his new clothing, swearing that he'd lead Father O'Toole by the nose for slamming the door in his face, and so he would have done, if he could have found him; but as he wasn't to be found, Father M'Grath came back again just as wise, and quite as brave, as he went out.

"So, Peter, I just took a walk that way myself, and, as I surrounded the old house where your uncle had taken up his quarters, who should I meet but the little girl, Ella Flanagan, who was in his service; and I said to myself, 'There's two ways of obtaining things in this world, one is for love, and the other is for money.' The O'Briens are better off in the first article than in the last, as most of their countrymen are, so I've been spending it very freely in your service, Peter.

"'Sure,' says I, 'you are the little girl that my eyes were ever looking upon when last I was in this way.'

"'And who are you?' says she.

"'Lieutenant O'Brien, of his Majesty's service, just come home for a minute to look out for a wife,' says I; 'and it's one about your make, and shape, and discretion that would please my fancy.'

"And then I praised her eyes, and her nose, and her forehead, and so downwards, until I came to the soles of her feet; and asked her leave to see her again, and when she would meet me in the wood and tell me her mind. At first, she thought (sure enough) that I couldn't be in earnest, but I swore by all the saints that she was the prettiest girl in the parts—and so she is altogether—and then she listened to my blarney. The devil a word did I say about your uncle, or your aunt, or Father M'Grath, that she might not suspect for I've an idea that they're all in the story. I only talked about my love for her pretty self, and that blinded her, as it will all women, 'cute as they may be.

"And now, Peter, it's three weeks last Sunday, that I've been bespeaking this poor girl for your sake, and my conscience tells me that it's not right to make the poor crature fond of me, seeing as how that I don't care a fig for her in the way of a wife, and in any other way it would be the ruin of the poor thing. I have spoken to Father M'Grath on the subject, who says, 'that we may do evil that good may come, and that, if she has been a party to the deceit, it's nothing but proper that she should be punished in this world, and that will, perhaps, save her in the next;' still I don't like it, Peter, and it's only for you among the living that I'd do such a thing; for the poor creature now hangs upon me so fondly, and talks about the wedding-day; and tells me long stories about the connections which have taken place between the O'Flanagans and the O'Briens, times bygone, when they were all in their glory. Yesterday, as we sat in the wood, with her arm round my waist, 'Ella, dear,' says I, 'who are these people that you stay with?' And then she told me all she knew about their history, and how Mary Sullivan was a nurse to the baby.

"'And what is the baby?' says I.

"'A boy, sure,' says she.

"'And Sullivan's baby?'

"'That's a girl.'

"'And is Mary Sullivan there now?'

"'No' says she; 'it's yestreen she left with her husband and baby, to join the regiment that's going out to Ingy.'

"'Yesterday she left?' says I, starting up.

"'Yes,' replies she, 'and what do you care about them?'

"'It's very much I care,' replied I, 'for a little bird has whispered a secret to me.'

"'And what may that be?' says she.

"'Only that the childer were changed, and you know it as well as I do.' But she swore that she knew nothing about it, and that she was not there when either of the children was born, and I believe that she told the truth. 'Well,' says I, 'who tended the lady?'

"'My own mother,' says Ella. 'And if it was so, who can know but she?'

"Then,' says I, 'Ella, jewel, I've made a vow that I'll never marry till I find out the truth of this matter; so the sooner you get it out of your mother the better.' Then she cried very much, and I was almost ready to cry too, to see how the poor thing was vexed at the idea of not being married. After a while, she swabbed up her cheeks, and kissing me, wished me good-by, swearing by all the saints that the truth should come out, somehow or another.

"It's this morning that I saw her again, as agreed upon yesterday, and red her eyes were with weeping, poor thing; and she clung to me, and begged me to forgive her, and not to leave her; and then she told me that her mother was startled when she put the question to her, and chewed it, and cursed her when she insisted upon the truth; and how she had fallen on her knees, and begged her mother not to stand in the way of her happiness, as she would die if she did (I leave you to guess if my heart didn't smite me when she said that, Peter, but the mischief was done), and how her mother had talked about her oath and Father O'Toole, and said that she would speak to him.

"Now, Peter, I'm sure that the childer have been changed, and that the nurse has been sent to the Indies to be out of the way. They say they were to go to Plymouth. The husband's name is, of course, O'Sullivan; so I'd recommend you to take a coach and see what you can do in that quarter; in the meantime I'll try all I can for the truth in this, and will write again as soon as I can find out anything more. All I want to do is to get Father M'Grath to go to the old devil of a mother, and I'll answer for it, he'll frighten her into swearing anything. God bless you, Peter, and give my love to all the family.

"Yours ever,

"TERENCE O'BRIEN."

This letter of O'Brien was the subject of much meditation. The advice to go to Plymouth was too late, the troops having sailed some time; and I had no doubt but that Mary Sullivan and her husband were among those who had embarked at the time that I was at that port to pass my examination. Show the letter to my father I would not, as it would only have put him in a fever, and his interference would, in all probability, have done more harm than good. I therefore waited quietly for more intelligence, and resolved to apply to my grandfather to obtain my promotion.

A few days afterwards I set off for Eagle Park, and arrived about eleven o'clock in the morning. I sent in my name, and was admitted into the library, where I found Lord Privilege in his easy chair as usual.

"Well, child," said he, remaining on his chair, and not offering even *one* finger to me, "what do you want, that you come here without an invitation?"

"Only, my lord, to inquire after your health, and to thank you for your kindness to me in procuring me and Mr O'Brien the appointment to a fine frigate."

"Yes," replied his lordship, "I recollect—I think I did so, at your request, and I think I heard some one say that you have behaved well, and had been mentioned in the despatches."

"Yes, my lord," replied I, "and I have since passed my examination for lieutenant."

"Well, child, I'm glad to hear it. Remember me to your father and family." And his lordship cast his eyes down upon the book which he had been reading.

My father's observations appeared to be well grounded, but I would not leave the room until I had made some further attempt.

"Has your lordship heard from my uncle?"

"Yes," replied he, "I had a letter from him yesterday. The child is quite well. I expect them all here in a fortnight or three weeks, to live with me altogether. I am old—getting very old, and I shall have much to arrange with your uncle before I die."

"If I might request a favour of your lordship, it would be to beg that you would interest yourself a little in obtaining my promotion. A letter from your lordship to the First Lord—only a few lines—"

"Well, child, I see no objection—only—I am very old, too old to write now." And his lordship again commenced reading.

I must do Lord Privilege the justice to state that he evidently was fast verging to a state of second childhood. He was much bowed down since I had last seen him, and appeared infirm in body as well as mind.

I waited at least a quarter of an hour before his lordship looked up.

"What, not gone yet, child? I thought you had gone home."

"Your lordship was kind enough to say that you had no objection to write a few lines to the First Lord in my behalf. I trust your lordship will not refuse me."

"Well," replied he, peevishly, "so I did—but I am too old, too old to write—I cannot see—I can hardly hold a pen."

"Will your lordship allow me the honour of writing the letter for your lordship's signature?"

"Well, child—yes—I've no objection. Write as follows—no—write anything you please—and I'll sign it. I wish your uncle William were come."

This was more than I did. I had a great mind to show him O'Brien's letter, but I thought it would be cruel to raise doubts, and harass the mind of a person so close to the brink of the grave. The truth would never be ascertained during his life, I thought, and why, therefore, should I give him pain? At all events, although I had the letter in my pocket, I resolved not to make use of it except as a *dernier* resort.

I went to another table, and sat down to write the letter. As his lordship had said that I might write what I pleased, it occurred to me that I might assist O'Brien, and I felt sure that his lordship would not take the trouble to read the letter. I therefore wrote as follows, while Lord Privilege continued to read his book:—

"MY LORD,—You will confer a very great favour upon me, if you will hasten the commission which, I have no doubt, is in preparation for my nephew, Mr Simple, who has passed his examination, and has been mentioned in the public despatches, and also that you will not lose sight of Lieutenant O'Brien, who has so distinguished himself by his gallantry in the various cutting-out expeditions in the West Indies. Trusting that your lordship will not fail to comply with my earnest request, I have the honour to be, your lordship's very obedient humble servant."

I brought this letter, with a pen full of ink, and the noise of my approach induced his lordship to look up. He stared at first, as having forgotten the whole circumstance—then said—"Oh yes! I recollect, so I did—give me the pen." With a trembling hand he signed his name, and gave me back the letter without reading it, as I expected.

"There, child, don't tease me any more. Good-bye; remember me to your father."

I wished his lordship a good morning, and went away well satisfied with the result of my expedition. On my arrival I showed the letter to my father, who was much surprised at my success, and he assured me that my grandfather's interest was so great with the administration, that I might consider my promotion as certain. That no accident might happen, I immediately set off for London, and delivered the letter at the door of the First Lord with my own hands, leaving my address with the porter.

Chapter XL

O'Brien and myself take a step each, *pari passu*—A family reunion productive of anything but unity—My uncle not always the best friend.

A few days afterwards I left my card with my address with the First Lord, and the next day received a letter from his secretary, which, to my delight, informed me that my commission had been made out some days before. I hardly need say that I hastened to take it up, and when paying my fee to the clerk, I ventured, at a hazard, to inquire whether he knew the address of Lieutenant O'Brien.

"No," replied he, "I wish to find it out, for he has this day been promoted to the rank of Commander."

I almost leaped with joy when I heard this good news. I gave O'Brien's address to the clerk, hastened away with my invaluable piece of parchment in my hand, and set off immediately for my father's house.

But I was met with sorrow. My mother had been taken severely ill, and I found the house in commotion—doctors, and apothecaries, and nurses, running to and fro, my father in a state of excitement, and my dear sister in tears. Spasm succeeded spasm; and although every remedy was applied, the next evening she breathed her last. I will not attempt to describe the grief of my father, who appeared to feel remorse at his late unkind treatment of her, my sister, and myself. These scenes must be imagined by those who have suffered under similar bereavements. I exerted myself to console my poor sister, who appeared to cling to me as to her only support, and, after the funeral was over, we recovered our tranquillity, although the mourning was still deeper in our hearts than in our outward dress. I had written to O'Brien to announce the mournful intelligence, and, like a true friend, he immediately made his appearance to console me.

O'Brien had received the letter from the Admiralty, acquainting him with his promotion; and, two days after he arrived, went to take up his commission. I told him frankly by what means he had obtained it, and he again concluded his thanks by a reference to the mistake of the former supposition, that of my being "the fool of the family."

"By the powers, it would be well for any man if he had a few of such foolish friends about him," continued he; "but I won't blarney you, Peter; you know what my opinion always has been, so we'll say no more about it."

When he came back, we had a long consultation as to the best method of proceeding to obtain employment, for O'Brien was anxious to be again afloat, and so was I. I regretted parting with my sister, but my father was so morose and ill-tempered, that I had no pleasure at home, except in her company. Indeed, my sister was of opinion, that it would be better if I were away, as my father's misanthropy, now unchecked by my mother, appeared to have increased, and he seemed to view me with positive dislike. It was, therefore, agreed unanimously between my sister, and me, and O'Brien, who was always of our councils, that it would be advisable that I should be again afloat.

"I can manage him much better when alone, Peter; I shall have nothing to occupy me, and take me away from him, as your presence does now; and, painful as it is to part with you, my duty to my father, and my wish for your advancement, induce me to request that you will, if possible, find some means of obtaining employment."

"Spoken like a hero, as ye are, Miss Ellen, notwithstanding your pretty face and soft eyes," said O'Brien. "And now, Peter, for the means to bring it about. If I can get a ship, there is no fear for you, as I shall choose you for my lieutenant; but how is that to be managed? Do you think that you can come over the old gentleman at Eagle Park?"

"At all events, I'll try," replied I; "I can but be floored, O'Brien."

Accordingly, the next day I set off for my grandfather's, and was put down at the lodge, at the usual hour, about eleven o'clock. I walked up the avenue, and knocked at the door: when it was opened, I perceived a hesitation among the servants, and a constrained air, which I did not like. I inquired after Lord Privilege—the answer was, that he was pretty well, but did not see *any* body.

"Is my uncle here?" said I.

"Yes, sir," replied the servant, with a significant look, "and all his family are here too."

"Are you sure that I cannot see my *grandfather*" said I, laying a stress upon the word.

"I will tell him that you are here, sir," replied the man, "but even that is against orders."

I had never seen my uncle since I was a child, and could not even recollect him—my cousins, or my aunt, I had never met with. In a minute an answer was brought, requesting that I would walk into the library. When I was ushered in, I found myself in the presence of Lord Privilege, who sat in his usual place, and a tall gentleman, whom I knew at once to be my uncle, from his likeness to my father.

"Here is the young gentleman, my lord," said my uncle, looking at me sternly.

"Heh! what—oh? I recollect. Well, child, so you've been behaving very ill—sorry to hear it. Good-bye."

"Behaving ill, my lord!" replied I. "I am not aware of having so done."

"Reports are certainly very much against you, nephew," observed my uncle, drily. "Some one has told your grandfather what has much displeased him. I know nothing about it myself."

"Then some rascal has slandered me, sir," replied I.

My uncle started at the word rascal; and then recovering himself, replied, "Well, nephew, what is it that you require of Lord Privilege, for I presume this visit is not without a cause?"

"Sir," replied I, "my visit to Lord Privilege was, first to thank him for having procured me my commission as lieutenant, and to request the favour that he would obtain me active employment, which a line from him will effect immediately."

"I was not aware, nephew, that you had been made lieutenant; but I agree with you, that the more you are at sea the better. His lordship shall sign the letter. Sit down."

"Shall I write it, sir?" said I to my uncle: "I know what to say."

"Yes; and bring it to me when it is written."

I felt convinced that the only reason which induced my uncle to obtain me employment was the idea that I should be better out of the way, and that there was more risk at sea than on shore. I took a sheet of paper, and wrote as follows:—

"My LORD,—May I request that your lordship will be pleased to appoint the bearer of this to a ship, as soon as convenient, as I wish him to be actively employed.

"I am, my lord, &c, &c."

"Why not mention your name?"

"It is of no consequence," replied I, "as it will be delivered in person, and that will insure my speedy appointment."

The letter was placed before his lordship for signature. It was with some difficulty that he was made to understand that he was to sign it. The old gentleman appeared much more imbecile than when I last saw him. I thanked him, folded up the letter, and put it in my pocket. At last he looked at me, and a sudden flash of recollection appeared to come across his mind.

"Well child so you escaped from the French prison—heh! and how's your friend—what is his name, heh?"

"O'Brien, my lord."

"O'Brien!" cried my uncle, "he is *your* friend; then, sir, I presume it is to you that I am indebted for all the inquiries and reports which are so industriously circulated in Ireland—the tampering with my servants— and other impertinences?"

I did not choose to deny the truth, although I was a little fluttered by the sudden manner in which it came to light. I replied, "I never tamper with any people's servants, sir."

"No," said he, "but you employ others so to do. I discovered the whole of your proceedings after the scoundrel left for England."

"If you apply the word scoundrel *to* Captain O'Brien, sir, in his name I contradict it."

"As you please, sir," replied my uncle, in a passion; "but you will oblige me by quitting this house immediately, and expect nothing more, either from the present or the future Lord Privilege, except that retaliation which your infamous conduct has deserved."

I felt much irritated, and replied very sharply, "From the present Lord Privilege I certainly expect nothing more, neither do I from his successor; but after your death, uncle, I expect that the person who succeeds to the title will do all he can for your humble servant. I wish you a good morning, uncle."

My uncle's eyes flashed fire as I finished my speech, which indeed was a very bold, and a very foolish one too, as it afterwards proved. I hastened out of the room, not only from the fear of being turned out of the house before all the servants, but also from the dread that my letter to the First Lord might be taken from me by force; but I shall never forget the scowl of vengeance which crossed my uncle's brows, as I turned round and looked at him as I shut the door. I found my way out without the assistance of the servants, and hastened home as fast as I could.

"O'Brien," said I, on my return, "there is no time to be lost; the sooner you hasten to town with this letter of introduction, the better it will be, for depend upon it my uncle will do me all the harm that he can." I then repeated to him all that had passed, and it was agreed that O'Brien should take the letter, which, having reference to the bearer, would do as well for him as for me; and, if O'Brien obtained an appointment, I was sure not only of being one of his lieutenants, but also of sailing with a dear friend. The next morning O'Brien set off for London, and fortunately saw the First Lord the day after his arrival, which was a levee day. The First Lord received the letter from O'Brien, and requested him to sit down. He then read it, inquired after his lordship, asked whether his health was good, &c.

O'Brien replied, "that with the blessing of God, his lordship might live many years: that he had never heard him complain of ill health." All which was not false, if not true. I could not help observing to O'Brien, when he returned home and told me what had passed, "that I thought, considering what he had expressed with respect to white lies and black lies, that he had not latterly adhered to his own creed."

"That's very true, Peter; and I've thought of it myself, but it is my creed nevertheless. We all know what's right, but we don't always follow it. The fact is, I begin to think that it is absolutely necessary to fight the world with its own weapons. I spoke to Father M'Grath on the subject, and he replied—'That if anyone, by doing wrong, necessitated another to do wrong to circumvent him, that the first party was answerable, not only for his own sin, but also for the sin committed in self-defence."

"But, O'Brien, I do not fix my faith so implicitly upon Father M'Grath; and I do not much admire many of his directions."

"No more do I, Peter, when I think upon them; but how am I to puzzle my head upon these points? All I know is, that when you are divided between your inclination and your duty, it's mighty convenient to have a priest like Father M'Grath to decide for you, and to look after your soul into the bargain."

It occurred to me that I myself, when finding fault with O'Brien, had, in the instance of both the letters from Lord Privilege, been also guilty of deceit. I was therefore blaming him for the same fault committed by myself; and I am afraid that I was too ready in consoling myself with Father M'Grath's maxim, "that one might do evil that good might come." But to return to O'Brien's interview.

After some little conversation, the First Lord said, "Captain O'Brien, I am always very ready to oblige Lord Privilege, and the more so as his recommendation is of an officer of your merit. In a day or two, if you call at the Admiralty, you will hear further." O'Brien wrote to us immediately, and we waited with impatience for his next letter: but, instead of the letter, he made his appearance on the third day, and first hugged me in his arms, he then came to my sister, embraced her, and skipped and danced about the room.

"What is the matter, O'Brien?" said I, while Ellen retreated in confusion.

O'Brien pulled a parchment out of his pocket. "Here, Peter, my dear Peter; now for honour and glory. An eighteen-gun brig, Peter. The *Rattlesnake*—Captain O'Brien—West India station. By the holy father! my heart's bursting with joy!" and down he sank into an easy chair. "A'n't I almost beside myself?" inquired he, after a short pause.

"Ellen thinks so, I dare say," replied I, looking at my sister, who stood in the corner of the room, thinking O'Brien was really out of his senses, and still red with confusion.

O'Brien, who then called to mind what a slip of decorum he had been guilty of, immediately rose, and resuming his usual unsophisticated politeness, as he walked up to my sister, took her hand, and said, "Excuse me, my dear Miss Ellen; I must apologize for my rudeness; but my delight was so great, and my gratitude to your brother so intense, that I am afraid that in my warmth I allowed the expression of my feelings to extend to one so dear to him, and so like him in person and in mind. Will you only consider that you received the overflowings of a grateful heart towards your brother, and for his sake pardon my indiscretion?"

Ellen smiled, and held out her hand to O'Brien, who led her to the sofa, where we all three sat down: and he then commenced a more intelligible narrative of what had passed. He had called on the day appointed, and sent up his card. The First Lord could not see him, but referred him to the private secretary, who presented him with his commission to the *Rattlesnake*, eighteen-gun brig. The secretary smiled most graciously, and told O'Brien in confidence that he would proceed to the West India station as soon as his vessel was manned and ready for sea. He inquired of O'Brien whom he wished as his first lieutenant. O'Brien replied that he wished for me; but as, in all probability, I should not be of sufficient standing to be first lieutenant, that the Admiralty might appoint any other to the duty, provided I joined the ship. The secretary made a minute of O'Brien's wish, and requested him, if he had a vacancy to spare as midshipman, to allow him to send one on board; to which O'Brien willingly acceded, shook hands with him, and O'Brien quitted the Admiralty to hasten down to us with the pleasing intelligence.

"And now," said O'Brien, "I have made up my mind how to proceed. I shall first run down to Plymouth and hoist my pennant; then I shall ask for a fortnight's leave, and go to Ireland to see how they get on, and what Father M'Grath may be about. So, Peter, let's pass this evening as happily as we can; for though you and I shall soon meet again, yet it may be years, or perhaps never, that we three shall sit down on the same sofa as we do now."

Ellen, who was still nervous, from the late death of my mother, looked down, and I perceived the tears start in her eyes at the remark of O'Brien, that perhaps we should never meet again. And I did pass a happy evening. I had a dear sister on one side of me, and a sincere friend on the other. How few situations more enviable!

O'Brien left us early the next morning; and at breakfast-time a letter was handed to my father. It was from my uncle, coldly communicating to him that Lord Privilege had died the night before, very suddenly, and informing him that the burial would take place on that day week, and that the will would be opened immediately after the funeral. My father handed the letter over to me without saying a word, and sipped his tea with his tea-spoon. I cannot say that I felt very much on the occasion; but I did feel, because he had been kind to me at one time: as for my father's feelings, I could not—or rather I should say, I did not wish to analyze them. As soon as he had finished his cup of tea, he left the breakfast-table, and went into his study. I then communicated the intelligence to my sister Ellen.

"My God!" said she, after a pause, putting her hand up to her eyes; "what a strange unnatural state of society must we have arrived at, when my father can thus receive the intelligence of a parent's death! Is it not dreadful?"

"It is, my dearest girl," replied I; "but every feeling has been sacrificed to worldly considerations and an empty name. The younger sons have been neglected, if not deserted. Virtue, talent, everything set at naught—intrinsic value despised—and the only claim to consideration admitted, that of being the heir entail. When all the ties of nature are cast loose by the parents, can you be surprised if the children are no longer bound by them? Most truly do you observe, that it is a detestable state of society."

"I did not say detestable, brother; I said strange and unnatural."

"Had you said what I said, Ellen, you would not have been wrong. I would not for the title and wealth which it brings, be the heartless, isolated, I may say neglected being that my grandfather was; were it offered now, I would not barter for it Ellen's love."

Ellen threw herself in my arms; we then walked into the garden, where we had a long conversation relative to our future wishes, hopes, and prospects.

Chapter XLI

Pompous obsequies—The reading of the will, not exactly after Wilkie—I am left a legacy—What becomes of it—My father, very warm, writes a sermon to cool himself—I join O'Brien's brig, and fall in with Swinburne.

On that day week I accompanied my father to Eagle Park, to assist at the burial of Lord Privilege. We were ushered into the room where the body had laid in state for three days. The black hangings, the lofty plumes, the rich ornaments on the coffin, and the number of wax candles with which the room was lighted, produced a solemn and grand effect. I could not help, as I leaned against the balustrade before the coffin and thought of its contents, calling to mind when my poor grandfather's feelings seemed, as it were, inclined to thaw in my favour, when he called me "his child," and, in all probability, had not my uncle had a son, would have died in my arms, fond and attached to me for my own sake, independently of worldly considerations. I felt that had I known him longer, I could have loved him, and that he would have loved me; and I thought to myself, how little all these empty honours, after his decease, could compensate for the loss of those reciprocal feelings, which would have so added to his happiness during his existence. But he had lived for pomp and vanity; and pomp and vanity attended him to his grave. I thought of my sister Ellen, and of O'Brien, and walked away with the conviction that Peter Simple might have been an object of envy to the late Right Honourable Lord Viscount Privilege, Baron Corston, Lord Lieutenant of the county, and one of His Majesty's Most Honourable Privy Councillors.

When the funeral, which was very tedious and very splendid, was over, we all returned in the carriages to Eagle Park, when my uncle, who had of course assumed the title, and who had attended as chief mourner, was in waiting to receive us. We were shown into the library, and in the chair so lately and constantly occupied by my grandfather, sat the new lord. Near to him were the lawyers, with parchments lying before them. As we severally entered, he waved his hand to unoccupied chairs, intimating to us to sit down; but no words were exchanged, except an occasional whisper between him and the lawyers. When all the branches of the family were present, down to the fourth and fifth cousins, the lawyer on the right of my uncle put on his spectacles, and unrolling the parchment commenced reading the will. I paid attention to it at first; but the legal technicalities puzzled me, and I was soon thinking of other matters, until after half an hour's reading, I was startled at the sound of my own name. It was a bequest by codicil to me, of the sum of ten thousand pounds. My father who sat by me, gave me a slight push, to attract my attention; and I perceived that his face was not quite so mournful as before. I was rejoicing at this unexpected intelligence. I called to mind what my father had said to me when we were returning from Eagle Park, "that my grandfather's attentions to me were as good as ten thousand pounds in his will," and was reflecting how strange it was that he had hit upon the exact sum. I also thought of what my father had said of his own affairs, and his not having saved anything for his children, and congratulated myself that I should now be able to support my dear sister Ellen, in case of any accident happening to my father, when I was roused by another mention of my name. It was a codicil dated about a week back, in which my grandfather, not pleased at my conduct, revoked the former codicil, and left me nothing. I knew where the blow came from, and I looked my uncle in the face; a gleam of malignant pleasure was in his eyes, which had been fixed on me, waiting to receive my glance. I returned it with a smile expressive of scorn and contempt, and then looked at my father, who appeared to be in a state of misery. His head had fallen upon his breast, and his hands were clasped. Although I was shocked at the blow, for I knew how much the money was required, I felt too proud to show it; indeed, I felt that I would not for worlds have exchanged situations with my uncle, much less feelings; for when those who remain meet to ascertain the disposition made, by one who is summoned away to the tribunal of his Maker, of those worldly and perishable things which he must leave behind him, feelings of rancour and ill-will might, for the time, be permitted to subside, and the memory of a "departed brother" be productive of charity and good-will. After a little reflection, I felt that I could forgive my uncle.

Not so my father; the codicil which deprived me of my inheritance, was the last of the will, and the lawyer rolled up the parchment and took off his spectacles. Everybody rose; my father seized his hat, and telling me in a harsh voice to follow him, tore off the crape weepers, and then threw them on the floor as he walked away. I also took off mine, and laid them on the table, and followed him. My father called his carriage, waited in the hall till it was driven up, and jumped into it. I followed him; he drew up the blind, and desired them to drive home.

"Not a sixpence! By the God of heaven, not a sixpence! My name not even mentioned, except for a paltry mourning ring! And yours—pray sir, what have you been about, after having such a sum left you, to forfeit your grandfather's good opinion? Heh! sir—tell me directly," continued he, turning round to me in a rage.

"Nothing, my dear father, that I'm aware of. My uncle is evidently my enemy."

"And why should he be particularly your enemy? Peter, there must be some reason for his having induced your grandfather to alter his bequest in your favour. I insist upon it, sir, that you tell me immediately."

"My dear father, when you are more calm, I will talk this matter over with you. I hope I shall not be considered wanting in respect, when I say, that as a clergyman of the church of England—"

"D—n the church of England, and those that put me into it!" replied my father, maddened with rage.

I was shocked, and held my tongue. My father appeared also to be confused at his hasty expressions. He sank back in his carriage, and preserved a gloomy silence until we arrived at our own door. As soon as we entered, my father hastened to his own room, and I went up to my sister Ellen, who was in her bed room. I revealed to her all that had passed, and advised with her on the propriety of my communicating to my father the reasons which had occasioned my uncle's extreme aversion towards me. After much argument, she agreed with me, that the disclosure had now become necessary.

After the dinner-cloth had been removed, I then communicated to my father the circumstances which had come to our knowledge relative to my uncle's establishment in Ireland. He heard me very attentively, took out tablets, and made notes.

"Well, Peter," said he, after a few minutes' silence, when I had finished, "I see clearly through this whole business. I have no doubt but that a child has been substituted to defraud you and me of our just inheritance of the title and estates; but I will now set to work and try if I cannot find out the secret; and, with the help of Captain O'Brien and Father M'Grath, I think it is not at all impossible."

"O'Brien will do all that he can, sir," replied I; "and I expect soon to hear from him. He must have now been a week in Ireland."

"I shall go there myself," replied my father; "and there are no means that I will not resort to, to discover this infamous plot. No," exclaimed he, striking his fist on the table, so as to shiver two of the wine-glasses into fragments—"no means but I will resort to."

"That is," replied I, "my dear father, no means which may be legitimately employed by one of your profession."

"I tell you, no means that can be used by *man* to recover his defrauded rights! Tell me not of legitimate means, when I am to lose a title and property by a spurious and illegitimate substitution! By the God of heaven, I will meet them with fraud for fraud, with false swearing for false swearing, and with blood for blood, if it should be necessary! My brother has dissolved all ties, and I will have my right, even if I demand it with a pistol at his ear."

"For Heaven's sake, my dear father, do not be so violent—recollect your profession."

"I do," replied he, bitterly; "and how I was forced into it against my will. I recollect my father's words, the solemn coolness with which he told me, 'I had my choice of the church, or—to starve.'—But I have my sermon to prepare for to-morrow, and I can sit here no longer. Tell Ellen to send me in some tea."

I did not think my father was in a very fit state of mind to write a sermon, but I held my tongue. My sister joined me, and we saw no more of him till breakfast the next day. Before we met, I received a letter from O'Brien.

"MY DEAR PETER,—I ran down to Plymouth, hoisted my pennant, drew my jollies from the dockyard, and set my first lieutenant to work getting in the ballast and water-tanks. I then set off for Ireland, and was very well received as Captain O'Brien by my family, who were all flourishing.

"Now that my two sisters are so well married off, my father and mother are very comfortable, but rather lonely; for I believe I told you long before, that it had pleased Heaven to take all the rest of my brothers and sisters, except the two now married, and one who bore up for a nunnery, dedicating her service to God, after she was scarred with the small-pox, and no man would look at her. Ever since the family have been grown up, my father and mother have been lamenting and sorrowing that none of them would go off; and now that they're all gone off one way or another, they cry all day because they are left all alone with no one to keep company with them, except Father M'Grath and the pigs. We never are to be contented in this world, that's sartain; and now that they are comfortable in every respect, they find that they are very uncomfortable, and having obtained all their wishes, they wish everything back again; but as old Maddocks used to say, 'A good growl is better than a bad dinner' with some people; and the greatest pleasure that they now have is to grumble; and if that makes them happy, they must be happy all day long—for the devil a bit do they leave off from morning till night.

"The first thing that I did was to send for Father M'Grath, who had been more away from home than usual—I presume, not finding things quite so comfortable as they used to be. He told me that he had met with Father O'Toole, and had a bit of a dialogue with him, which had ended in a bit of a row, and that he had cudgelled Father O'Toole well, and tore his gown off his back, and then tore it into shivers,— that Father O'Toole had referred the case to the bishop, and that was how the matter stood just then. 'But,' says he, 'the spalpeen has left this part of the country, and, what is more, has taken Ella and her mother with him; and what is still worse, no one could find out where they were gone; but it was believed that they had all been sent over the water.' So you see, Peter, that this is a bad job in one point, which is, that we have no chance of getting the truth out of the old woman; for now that we have war with France, who is to follow them? On the other hand, it is good news; for it prevents me from decoying that poor young girl, and making her believe what will never come to pass; and I am not a little glad on that score, for Father M'Grath was told by those who were about her, that she did nothing but weep and moan for two days before she went away, scolded as she was by her mother, and threatened by that blackguard O'Toole. It appears to me, that all our hopes now are in finding out the soldier, and his wife the wet-nurse, who were sent to India—no doubt with the hope that the climate and the fevers may carry them off. That uncle of yours is a great blackguard, every bit of him. I shall leave here in three days, and you must join me at Plymouth. Make my compliments to your father, and my regards to your sister, whom may all the saints preserve! God bless her, for ever and ever. Amen.

"Yours ever,

"TERENCE O'BRIEN."

I put this letter into my father's hands when he came out of his room. "This is a deep-laid plot," said he, "and I think we must immediately do as O'Brien states—look after the nurse who was sent to India. Do you know the regiment to which her husband belongs?"

"Yes, sir," replied I; "it is the 33rd, and she sailed for India about three months back."

"The name, you say, I think, is O'Sullivan," said he, pulling out his tablets. "Well, I will write immediately to Captain Fielding, and beg him to make the minutest inquiries. I will also write to your sister Lucy, for women are much keener than men in affairs of this sort. If the regiment is ordered to Ceylon, all the better: if not, he must obtain furlough to prosecute his inquiries. When that is done, I will go myself to Ireland, and try if we cannot trace the other parties."

My father then left the room, and I retired with Ellen to make preparations for joining my ship at Plymouth. A letter announcing my appointment had come down, and I had written to request my commission to be forwarded to the clerk of the cheque at Plymouth, that I might save a useless journey to London. On the following day I parted with my father and my dear sister, and, without any adventure, arrived at Plymouth Dock, where I met with O'Brien. The same day I reported myself to the admiral, and joined my brig, which was lying alongside the hulk with her topmasts pointed through. Returning from the brig, as I was walking up Fore-street, I observed a fine stout sailor, whose back was turned to me, reading the handbill which had been posted up everywhere announcing that the *Rattlesnake*, Captain O'Brien (about to proceed to the West India station, where *doubloons* were so plentiful that dollars were only used for ballast), was in want of a *few* stout hands. It might have been said, of a great many: for we had not entered six men, and were doing all the work with the marines and riggers of the dockyard; but it is not the custom to show your poverty in this world either with regard to men or money. I stopped, and overheard him say, "Ay, as for the doubloons, that cock won't fight. I've served long enough in the West Indies not to be humbugged; but I wonder whether Captain O'Brien was the second lieutenant of the *Sanglier*. If so, I shouldn't mind trying a cruise with him." I thought that I recollected the voice, and touching him on the shoulder, he turned round, and it proved to be Swinburne. "What, Swinburne!" said I, shaking him by the hand, for I was delighted to see him, "is it you?"

"Why, Mr Simple! Well, then, I expect that I'm right, and that Mr O'Brien is made, and commands this craft. When you meet the pilot-fish, the shark arn't far off, you know."

"You're very right, Swinburne," said I, "in all except calling Captain O'Brien a shark. He's no shark."

"No, that he arn't, except in one way; that is, that I expect he'll soon show his teeth to the Frenchmen. But I beg your pardon, sir;" and Swinburne took off his hat.

"Oh! I understand; you did not perceive before that I had shipped the swab. Yes, I'm lieutenant of the *Rattlesnake*, Swinburne, and hope you'll join us."

"There's my hand upon it, Mr Simple," said he, smacking his great fist into mine so as to make it tingle. "I'm content if I know that the captain's a good officer; but when there's two, I think myself lucky. I'll just take a boat, and put my name on the books, and then I'll be on shore again to spend the rest of my money, and try if I can't pick up a few hands as volunteers, for I know where they all be stowed away. I was looking at the craft this morning, and rather took a fancy to her. She has a d—d pretty run; but I hope Captain O'Brien will take off her fiddle-head, and get one carved: I never knew a vessel do much with a *fiddle*-head."

"I rather think that Captain O'Brien has already applied to the Commissioner on the subject," replied I; "at all events, it won't be very difficult to make the alteration ourselves."

"To be sure not," replied Swinburne; "a coil of four-inch will make the body of the snake; I can carve out the head; and as for a *rattle*, I be blessed if I don't rob one of those beggars of watchmen this very night. So good-bye, Mr Simple, till we meet again."

Swinburne kept his word; he joined the ship that afternoon, and the next day came off with six good hands, who had been induced from his representations to join the brig. "Tell Captain O'Brien," said he to me, "not to be in too great a hurry to man his ship. I know where there are plenty to be had; but I'll try fair means first." This he did, and every day, almost, he brought off a man, and all he did bring off were good able seamen. Others volunteered, and we were now more than half-manned, and ready for sea. The admiral then gave us permission to send pressgangs on shore.

"Mr Simple," said Swinburne, "I've tried all I can to persuade a lot of fine chaps to enter, but they won't. Now I'm resolved that my brig shall be well manned; and if they don't know what's good for them, I do, and I'm sure that they will thank me for it afterwards; so I'm determined to take every mother's son of them."

The same night we mustered all Swinburne's men and went on shore to a crimp's house which they knew, surrounded it with our marines in blue jackets, and took out of it twenty-three fine able seamen, which nearly filled up our complement. The remainder we obtained by a draft from the admiral's ship; and I do not believe that there was a vessel that left Plymouth harbour and anchored in the Sound, better manned than the *Rattlesnake*. So much for good character, which is never lost upon seamen O'Brien was universally liked by those who had sailed with him, and Swinburne, who knew him well persuaded many, and forced the others, to enter with him, whether they liked it or not. This they in the event did, and, with the exception of those drafted from the flag-ship, we had no desertions. Indeed, none deserted whom we would have wished to retain, and their vacancies were soon filled up with better men.

Chapter XLII

We sail for the West Indies—A volunteer for the ship refused and set on shore again, for reasons which the chapter will satisfactorily explain to the reader.

We were very glad when the master-attendant came on board to take us into the Sound; and still more glad to perceive that the brig, which had just been launched before O'Brien was appointed to her, appeared to sail very fast as she ran out. So it proved after we went to sea; she sailed wonderfully well, beating every vessel that she met, and overhauling in a very short time everything that we chased; turning to windward like magic, and tacking in a moment. Three days after we anchored in the Sound the ship's company were paid, and our sailing orders came down to proceed with despatches, by next evening's post, to the island of Jamaica. We started with a fair wind, and were soon clear of the channel. Our whole time was now occupied in training our new ship's company at the guns, and learning them *to pull together;* and by the time that we had run down the trades, we were in a very fair state of discipline. The first lieutenant was rather an odd character; his brother was a sporting man of large property, and he had contracted, from his example, a great partiality for such pursuits. He knew the winning horses of the Derby and the Oaks for twenty years back, was an adept at all athletic exercises, a capital shot, and had his pointer on board. In other respects, he was a great dandy in his person, always wore gloves, even on service, very gentlemanlike and handsome, and not a very bad sailor; that is, he knew enough to carry on his duty very creditably, and evidently, now that he was the first lieutenant, and obliged to work, learnt more of his duty every day. I never met a more pleasant messmate or a more honourable young man. A brig is only allowed two lieutenants. The master was a rough, kind-hearted, intelligent young man, always in good humour. The surgeon and purser completed our mess; they were men of no character at all, except, perhaps, that the surgeon was too much of a courtier, and the purser too much of a skin-flint; but pursers are, generally speaking, more sinned against than sinning.

But I have been led away, while talking of the brig and the officers, and had almost forgotten to narrate a circumstance which occurred two days before we sailed. I was with O'Brien in the cabin, when Mr Osbaldistone, the first lieutenant, came in, and reported that a boy had come on board to volunteer for the ship.

"What sort of a lad is he?" said O'Brien.

"A very nice lad—very slight, sir," replied the first lieutenant. "We have two vacancies."

"Well, see what you make of him; and if you think he will do, you may put him on the books."

"I have tried him, sir. He says that he has been a short time at sea. I made him mount the main-rigging, but he did not much like it."

"Well, do as you please, Osbaldistone," replied O'Brien; and the first lieutenant quitted the cabin.

In about a quarter of an hour he returned. "If you please, sir," said he, laughing, "I sent the boy down to the surgeon to be examined, and he refused to strip. The surgeon says that he thinks she is a woman. I have had her up on the quarter-deck, and she refuses to answer any questions, and requires to speak with you."

"With me!" said O'Brien, with surprise. "Oh! one of the men's wives, I suppose, trying to steal a march upon us. Well, send her down here, Osbaldistone, and I'll prove to her the moral impossibility of her sailing in his Majesty's brig *Rattlesnake*."

In a few minutes the first lieutenant sent her down to the cabin door, and I was about to retire as she entered; but O'Brien stopped me. "Stay, Peter: my reputation will be at stake if I'm left all alone," said he, laughing.

The sentry opened the door, and whether boy or girl, a more interesting face I never beheld; the hair was cut close, and I could not tell whether the surgeon's suspicions were correct.

"You wish to speak—holy St Patrick!" cried O'Brien, looking earnestly at her features; and O'Brien covered his face and bent over the table, exclaiming, "My God, my God!"

In the meantime the colour of the young person fled from her countenance, and then rushed into it again, alternately leaving it pale and suffused with blushes. I perceived a trembling over the frame, the knees shook and knocked together, and had I not hastened, she—for a female it was—would have fallen on the deck. I perceived that she had fainted; I therefore laid her down on the deck, and hastened to obtain some water. O'Brien ran up and went to her.

"My poor, poor girl!" said he, sorrowfully. "Oh! Peter, this is all your fault."

"All my fault! how could she have come here?"

"By all the saints who pray for us—dearly as I prize them, I would give up my ship and my commission, that this could be undone."

As O'Brien hung over her, the tears from his eyes fell upon her face, while I bathed it with the water I had brought from the dressing-room. I knew who it must be, although I had never seen her. It was the girl to whom O'Brien had professed love, to worm out the secret of the exchange of my uncle's child; and as I beheld the scene I could not help saying to myself, "Who now will assert that evil may be done that good may come?" The poor girl showed symptoms of recovering, and O'Brien waved his hand to me, saying, "Leave us, Peter, and see that no one comes in."

I remained nearly an hour at the cabin-door, by the sentry, and prevented many from entering, when O'Brien opened the door, and requested me to order his gig to be manned and then to come in. The poor girl had evidently been weeping bitterly, and O'Brien was much affected.

"All is arranged, Peter; you must go on shore with her, and not leave her till you see her safe off by the night coach. Do me that favour, Peter—you ought indeed," continued he, in a low voice, "for you have been partly the occasion of this."

I shook O'Brien's hand and made no answer—the boat was reported ready, and the girl followed me with a firm step. I pulled on shore, saw her safe in the coach without asking her any question, and then returned on board.

"Come on board, sir," said I, entering the cabin with my hat in my hand, and reporting myself according to the regulations of the service.

"Thank you," replied O'Brien: "shut the door, Peter. Tell me, how did she behave? What did she say?"

"She never spoke, and I never asked her a question. She seemed to be willing to do as you had arranged."

"Sit down, Peter. I never felt more unhappy, or more disgusted with myself in all my life. I feel as if I never could be happy again. A sailor's life mixes him up with the worst part of the female sex, and we do not know the real value of the better. I little thought when I was talking nonsense to that poor girl, that I was breaking one of the kindest hearts in the world, and sacrificing the happiness of one who would lay down her existence for me, Peter. Since you have been gone, it's twenty times that I've looked in the glass just to see whether I don't look like a villain. But, by the blood of St Patrick! I thought woman's *love* was just like our own, and that a three months' cruise would set all to rights again."

"I thought she had gone over to France."

"So did I; but now she has told me all about it. Father M'Dermot[1] and her mother brought her down to the coast near here to embark in a smuggling boat for Dieppe. When the boat pulled in-shore in the night to take them in, the mother and the rascally priest got in, but she felt as if it was leaving the whole world to leave the country I was in, and she held back. The officers came down, one or two pistols were fired, and the boat shoved off without her, and she, with their luggage, was left on the beach. She went back to the next town with the officers, where she told the truth of the story, and they let her go. In Father M'Dermot's luggage she found letters, which she read, and found out that she and her mother were to have been placed in a convent at Dieppe; and, as the convent was named in the letters,—which she says are very important, but I have not had courage to read them yet,—she went to the people from whose house they had embarked, requesting them to forward the luggage and a letter to her mother—sending everything but the letters, which she reserved for me. She has since received a letter from her mother, telling her that she is safe and well in the convent, and begging her to come over to her as soon as possible. The mother took the vows a week after she arrived there, so we know where to find her, Peter."

"And where is the poor girl going to stay now, O'Brien?"

"That's all the worst part of it. It appears that she hoped not to be found out till after we had sailed, and then to have, as she said, poor thing! to have laid at my feet and watched over me in the storms; but I pointed out to her that it was not permitted, and that I would not be allowed to marry her. O Peter! this is a very sad business," continued O'Brien, passing his hand across his eyes.

"Well, but, O'Brien, what is to become of the poor girl?"

"She is going home to be with my father and mother, hoping one day that I shall come back and marry her. I have written to Father M'Grath, to see what he can do."

"Have you then not undeceived her?"

"Father M'Grath must do that, I could not. It would have been the death of her. It would have stabbed her to the heart, and it's not for me to give that blow. I'd sooner have died—sooner have married her, than have done it, Peter. Perhaps when I'm far away she'll bear it better. Father M'Grath will manage it."

"O'Brien, I don't like that Father M'Grath."

"Well, Peter, you may be right; I don't exactly like all he says myself; but what is a man to do?—either he is a Catholic, and believes as a Catholic, or he is not one. Will I abandon my religion, now that it is persecuted? Never,

Peter: I hope not, without I find a much better, at all events. Still I do not like to feel that this advice of my confessor is at variance with my own conscience. Father M'Grath is a worldly man; but that only proves that he is wrong, not that our religion is—and I don't mind speaking to you on this subject. No one knows that I'm a Catholic except yourself: and at the Admiralty they never asked me to take that oath which I never would have taken, although Father M'Grath says I may take any oath I please with what he calls heretics, and he will grant me absolution. Peter, my dear fellow, say no more about it."

I did not; but I may as well end the history of poor Ella Flanagan at once, as she will not appear again. About three months afterwards, we received a letter from Father M'Grath, stating that the girl had arrived safe, and had been a great comfort to O'Brien's father and mother, who wished her to remain with them altogether; that Father M'Grath, had told her that when a man took his commission as captain it was all the same as going into a monastery as a monk, for he never could marry. The poor girl believed him, and thinking that O'Brien was lost to her for ever, with the advice of Father M'Grath, had entered as a nun in one of the religious houses in Ireland, that, as she said, she might pray for him night and day.

Many years afterwards, we heard of her—she was well, and not unhappy; but O'Brien never forgot his behaviour to this poor girl. It was a source of continual regret; and I believe, until the last day of his existence, his heart smote him for his inconsiderate conduct towards her. But I must leave this distressing topic, and return to the *Rattlesnake*, which had now arrived at the West Indies, and joined the Admiral at Jamaica.

[Footnote 1: The worthy priest formerly called Father O'Toole.—ED.]

Chapter XLIII

Description of the Coast of Martinique—Popped at for peeping—No heroism in making oneself a target—Board a miniature Noah's Ark, under Yankee colours—Capture a French slaver—Parrot soup in lieu of mock turtle.

We found orders at Barbadoes to cruise off Martinique, to prevent supplies being furnished to the garrison of the island, and we proceeded there immediately. I do not know anything more picturesque than running down the east side of this beautiful island—the ridges of hill spreading down to the water's edge, covered with the freshest verdure, divided at the base by small bays, with the beach of dazzling white sand, and where the little coasting vessels employed to bring the sugar from the neighbouring estates were riding at anchor. Each hill, at its adjutment towards the sea, crowned with a fort, on which waved the tri-colour—certainly, in appearance, one of the most warlike flags in the world.

On the third morning we had rounded the Diamond Rock, and were scudding along the lee-side of the island just opening Fort Royal bay, when hauling rather too close round its eastern entrance, formed by a promontory called Solomon's Point, which was covered with brush-wood, we found ourselves nearer than agreeable to a newly constructed battery. A column of smoke was poured along the blue water, and it was followed by the whizzing of a shot, which passed through our boom main sail, first cutting away the dog-vane, which was close to old Swinburne's head, as he stood on the carronade, conning the brig. I was at dinner in the cabin with O'Brien and the first lieutenant.

"Where the devil have they got the brig now?" said O'Brien, rising from his chair, and going on deck.

We both followed; but before we were on deck, three or four more shot passed between the masts. "If you please, sir," said the master's mate in charge of the deck, whose name was O'Farrell, "the battery has opened upon us."

"Thank you very much for your information, Mr O'Farrell," replied O'Brien; "but the French have reported it before you. May I ask if you've any particular fancy to be made a target of, or if you think that His Majesty's brig *Rattlesnake* was sent here to be riddled for nothing at all? Starboard the helm, quartermaster."

The helm was put up, and the brig was soon run out of the fire; not, however, until a few more shot were pitched close to us, and one carried away the foretopmast backstay.

"Now, Mr O'Farrell," replied O'Brien, "I only wish to point out to you that I trust neither I nor any one in this ship cares a fig about the whizzing of a shot or two about our ears when there is anything to be gained for it, either for ourselves or for our country; but I do care a great deal about losing even the leg or the arm, much more the life of any of my men, when there's no occasion for it; so, in future, recollect it's no disgrace to keep out of the way of a battery when all the advantage is on their side. I've always observed that chance shots pick out the best men. Lower down the mainsail, and send the sailmakers aft to repair it."

When O'Brien returned to the cabin I remained on deck, for it was my afternoon watch; and although O'Farrell had permission to look out for me, I did not choose to go down again. The bay of Fort Royal was now opened, and the view was extremely beautiful. Swinburne was still on the carronade; and as I knew he had been there before, I applied to him for information as to the *locale*. He told me the names of the batteries above the town, pointed out Fort Edward and Negro Point, and particularly Pigeon Island, the battery at the top of which wore the appearance of a mural crown.

"It's well I remember that place, Mr Simple," said he. "It was in '94 when I was last here. The sodgers had 'sieged it for a whole month, and were about to give it up, 'cause they couldn't get a gun up on that 'ere hill you see there. So poor Captain Faulkner says, 'There's many a clear head under a tarpaulin hat, and I'll give any chap five doubloons that will hitch up a twenty-four pounder to the top of that hill.' Not quite so easy a matter, as you may perceive from here, Mr Simple."

"It certainly appears to me to have been almost impossible, Swinburne," replied I.

"And so it did to most of us, Mr Simple; but there was one Dick Smith, mate of a transport, who had come on shore, and he steps out, saying, 'I've been looking at your men handling that gun, and my opinion is, that if you gets a butt, crams in a carronade, well woulded up, and fill it with old junk and rope yarns, you might parbuckle it up to the very top.' So Captain Faulkner pulls out five doubloons, and gives them to him, saying, 'You deserve the money for the hint, even if it don't succeed.' But it did succeed, Mr Simple; and the next day, to their surprise, we opened fire on the French beggars, and soon brought their boasting down. One of the French officers, after he was taken prisoner, axed me how we had managed to get the gun up there; but I wasn't going to blow the gaff, so I told him, as a great secret, that we got it up with a kite, upon which he opened all his eyes, and crying '*sacre bleu!*' walked away, believing all I said was true; but a'n't that a sail we have opened with the point, Mr Simple?"

It was so, and I reported it to O'Brien, who came up and gave chase. In half an hour we were alongside of her, when she hoisted American colours, and proved to be a brigantine laden up to her gunwale, which was not above a foot out of the water. Her cargo consisted of what the Americans called *notions*; that is, in English, an assorted cargo. Half-way up her masts down to the deck were hung up baskets containing apples, potatoes, onions, and nuts of various kinds. Her deck was crowded with cattle, sheep, pigs, and donkeys. Below was full of shingle, lumber, and a variety of different articles too numerous to mention. I boarded her, and asked the master whither he was bound?

"Why," replied he, "I am bound for a market—nowise particular; and I guess you won't stop me."

"Not if all's right," replied I; "but I must look at your log."

"Well, I've a notion there's no great objection to that," replied he; and he brought it up on deck.

I had no great time to examine it, but I could not help being amused at the little I did read, such as—"Horse latitudes—water very short— killed white-faced bullock—caught a dolphin, and ate him for dinner— broached molasses cask No. I, letter A. Fine night—saw little round things floating on the water—took up a bucket full—guessed they were pearls—judge I guessed wrong, only little Portuguese men-of-war—threw them overboard again—heard a scream, guessed it was a mermaid—looked out, saw nothing. Witnessed a very strange rippling ahead—calculated it might be the sea-serpent—stood on to see him plain, and nearly ran on Barbuda. Hauled off again—met a Britisher—treated *politely*."

Having overhauled his log, I then begged to overhaul his men to ascertain if there were any Englishmen among his crew. This was not pleasing, and he grumbled very much; but they were ordered aft. One man I was satisfied was an Englishman, and told him so; but the man as well as the master persisted to the contrary. Nevertheless, I resolved to take him on board for O'Brien to decide, and ordered him into the boat.

"Well, if you will use force, I can't help it. My decks an't clear as you see, or else—I tell you what, Mr Lieutenant, your vessel there will be another *Hermione*, I've a notion, if you presses true-blooded Yankees; and, what's more, the States will take it up, as sure as there's snakes in Virginny."

Notwithstanding this remonstrance, I took them on board to O'Brien, who had a long conversation with the American in the cabin. When they returned on deck he was allowed to depart with his man, and we again made sail. I had the first watch that night, and as we ran along the coast I perceived a vessel under the high land in what the sailors called the *doldrums*; that is, almost becalmed, or her sails flapping about in every direction with the eddying winds. We steered for her, and were very soon in the same situation, not more than a quarter of a mile from her. The quarter-boat was lowered down, and I proceeded to board her; but as she was large and rakish, O'Brien desired me to be careful, and if there was the least show of resistance to return. As I pulled up to her bows they hailed me in French, and desired me to keep off, or they would fire. This was quite sufficient; and, in obedience to my orders, I returned to the brig and reported to O'Brien. We lowered down all the quarter-boats, and towed round the brig's broadside to her, and then gave her half a dozen carronades of round and grape. Hearing great noise and confusion on board after we had ceased firing, O'Brien again sent me to know if they had surrendered. They replied in the affirmative, and I boarded her. She proved to be the *Commerce de Bordeaux*, with three hundred and thirty slaves on board, out of five hundred embarked from the coast, bound to Martinique. The crew were very sickly, and were most of them in their hammocks. Latterly, they had been killing parrots to make soup for them; a few that were left, of the grey species, spoke remarkably well. When they left the coast they had nearly one thousand parrots on board.

O'Brien perceiving that I had taken possession, sent another boat to know what the vessel was. I desired the surgeon to be sent on board, as some of the men and many of the poor slaves were wounded by our shot. Of all the miserable objects, I know of none to be compared to the poor devils of slaves on board of a slave vessel: the state of suffocation between decks—the dreadful stench arising from their filth, which is hardly ever cleared away—the sick lying without help, and looked upon by those who are stronger with the utmost indifference—men, women, and children, all huddled and crowded together in a state of nudity, worn to skin and bone from stench, starvation, and living in an atmosphere that none but a negro could exist in. If all that occurs in a slave-ship were really known, I think it would be acknowledged that to make the slave-trade piracy would be nothing more than a just retribution; and this is certain, that unless it be made piracy, it never will be discontinued.

By daylight the vessel was ready, and O'Brien determined to take her to Dominica, so that the poor devils might be immediately sent on shore. We anchored with her, in a few days, in Prince Rupert's Bay, where we only had twenty-four hours to obtain some refreshments and arrange about our prize, which I hardly need say was of some value.

During the short time that I was on shore, purchasing some fowls and vegetables for O'Brien and our own mess, I was amused at witnessing a black serjeant drilling some of his regiment of free negroes and mulattoes. He appeared resolved to make the best appearance that he could, for he began by saying, "You hab shoe and 'tocking, stand in front—you hab shoe no 'tocking, stand in centre—you hab no shoe no 'tocking, stand in um rear. Face to mountain—back to sea-beach. Why you no 'tep out, sar?—you hangman!"

I was curious to count the numbers qualified for the front rank: there were only two mulattoes. In the second rank there were also only two. No shoe and no 'tocking appeared to be the fashion. As usual, we were surrounded by the negroes; and although we had been there but a few hours, they had a song composed for us, which they constantly repeated:—

"Don't you see the *Rattlesnake*
Coming under sail?
Don't you see the *Rattlesnake*
With prizes at um tail?—'
Rattlesnake hab all the money—ding, ding—
She shall have all that's funny, ding, ding!"

Chapter XLIV

Money can purchase anything in the new country—American information not always to be depended upon—A night attack; we are beaten off—It proves a *cut up*, instead of a *cut out*—After all, we save something out of the fire.

The next morning we weighed anchor, and returned to our station off Martinique. We had run within three miles of St Pierre's when we discovered a vessel coming out under jury-masts. She steered directly for us, and we made her out to be the American brigantine which we had boarded some time before. O'Brien sent a boat to bring the master of her on board.

"Well, captain," said he, "so you met with a squall?"

"I calculate not," replied he.

"Why, then, what the devil have you been about?"

"Why, I guess I sold all my cargo, and, what's more, I've sold my masts."

"Sold your masts! who did you sell them to?"

"To an almighty pretty French privateer lying in St Pierre's, which had lost her spars when she was chased by one of your brass-bottomed sarpents; and I've a notion they paid pretty handsomely too."

"But how do you mean to get home again?"

"I calculate to get into the *stream*, and then I'll do very well. If I meet a nor-wester, why then I'll make a signal of distress, and some one will tow me in, I guess."

"Well," replied O'Brien, "but step down into the cabin and take something, captain."

"With particular pleasure," replied this strange mortal; and down they went.

In about half an hour they returned on deck, and the boat took the American on board. Soon afterwards, O'Brien desired Osbaldistone and myself to step down into the cabin. The chart of the harbour of St Pierre's lay on the table, and O'Brien said, "I have had a long conversation with the American, and he states that the privateer is at anchor in this spot" (pointing to a pencil-mark on the chart). "If so, she is well out; and I see no difficulty in capturing her. You see that she lays in four fathoms water, and so close under the outer battery, that the guns could not be pointed down upon the boats. I have also inquired if they keep a good look-out, and the American says that they feel so secure that they keep no look-out at all; that the captain and officers belonging to her are on shore all night, drinking, smoking, and boasting of what they will do. Now the question is, whether this report be correct. The American has been well-treated by us, and I see no reason to doubt him; indeed, he gave the information voluntarily, as if he wished to serve us."

I allowed Osbaldistone to speak first: he coincided with O'Brien. I did not: the very circumstance of her requiring new masts made me doubt the truth of his assertion as to where she lay; and if one part of his story was false, why not the whole? O'Brien appeared struck with my argument, and it was agreed that if the boats did go away, it should be for a reconnoissance, and that the attempt should only be made, provided it was found that the privateer laid in the same spot pointed out by the American master. It was, however, decided that the reconnoissance should take place that very night, as, allowing the privateer to be anchored on the spot supposed, there was every probability that she would not remain there, but haul further in, to take in her new masts. The news that an expedition was at hand was soon circulated through the ship, and all the men had taken their cutlasses from the capstern to get them ready for action. The lighting boats' crews, without orders, were busy with their boats, some cutting up old blankets to muffle the oars, other making new grummets. The ship's company were as busy as bees, bustling and buzzing about the decks, and reminding you of the agitation which takes place in a hive previous to a swarm. At last, Osbaldistone came on deck, and ordered the boats' crews to be piped away, and prepare for service. He was to have the command of the expedition in the launch—I had charge of the first cutter—O'Farrell of the second, and Swinburne had the charge of the jolly-boat. At dusk, the head of the brig was again turned towards St Pierre's, and we ran slowly in. At ten we hove-to, and about eleven the boats were ordered to haul up, O'Brien repeating his orders to Mr Osbaldistone, not to make the attempt if the privateer were found to be anchored close to the town. The men were all mustered on the quarter-deck, to ascertain if they had the distinguishing mark on their jackets, that is, square patches of canvas sewed on the left arm, so that we might recognize friend from foe—a very necessary precaution in a night expedition; and then they were manned, and ordered to shove off. The oars were dropped in the water, throwing out a phosphorescent light, so common in that climate, and away we went. After an hour's pulling, Osbaldistone lay on his oars in the launch, and we closed with him.

"We are now at the mouth of the harbour," said he, "and the most perfect silence must be observed."

"At the mouth of the harbour, sir!" said Swinburne; "I reckon we are more than half way in; we passed the point at least ten minutes ago, and this is the second battery we are now abreast of."

To this Osbaldistone did not agree, nor indeed did I think that Swinburne was right; but he persisted in it, and pointed out to us the lights in the town, which were now all open to us, and which would not be the case if we were only at the mouth of the harbour. Still we were of a different opinion, and Swinburne, out of respect to his officers, said no more.

We resumed our oars, pulling with the greatest caution; the night was intensely dark, and we could distinguish nothing. After pulling ten minutes more, we appeared to be close to the lights in the town; still we could see no privateer or any other vessel. Again we lay upon our oars, and held a consultation. Swinburne declared that if the privateer laid where we supposed, we had passed her long ago; but while we were debating, O'Farrell cried out, "I see her," and he was right—she was not more than a cable's length from us. Without waiting for orders, O'Farrell desired his men to give way, and dashed alongside of the privateer. Before he was half-way on board of her, lights flew about in every direction, and a dozen muskets were discharged. We had nothing to do but to follow him, and in a few seconds we were all alongside of her; but she was well prepared, and on the alert. Boarding nettings were triced up all round, every gun had been depressed as much as possible, and she appeared to be full of men. A scene of confusion and slaughter now occurred, which I trust never again to witness. All our attempts to get on board were unavailing; if we tried at a port, a dozen pikes thrust us back; if we attempted the boarding nettings, we were thrown down, killed or wounded, into the boats. From every port, and from the decks of the privateer, the discharge of musketry was incessant. Pistols were protruded and fired in our faces, while occasionally her carronades went off, stunning us with their deafening noise, and rocking the boats in the disturbed water, if they had no other effect. For ten minutes our exertions never ceased; at last, with half our numbers lying killed and wounded in the bottom of the boats, the men, worn out and dispirited at their unavailing attempts, sat down most of them on the boats' thwarts, loading their muskets, and discharging them into the ports. Osbaldistone was among the wounded; and perceiving that he was not in the launch, of whose crew not six remained, I called to Swinburne, who was alongside of me, and desired him to tell the other boats to make the best of their way out of the harbour. This was soon communicated to the survivors, who would have continued the unequal contest to the last man, if I had not given the order. The launch and second cutter shoved off—O'Farrell also having fallen; and, as soon as they were clear of the privateer, and had got their oars to pass, I proceeded to do the same, amidst the shouts and yells of the Frenchmen, who now jumped on their gunwale and pelted us with their musketry, cheering, and mocking us.

"Stop, sir," cried Swinburne, "we'll have a bit of revenge;" so saying, he hauled-to the launch, and wending her bow to the privateer, directed her carronade—which they had no idea that we had on board, as we had not fired it—to where the Frenchmen were crowded the thickest.

"Stop one moment, Swinburne; put another dose of canister in." We did so, and then discharged the gun, which had the most murderous effect, bringing the major part of them down upon the deck. I feel convinced, from the cries and groans which followed, that if we had had a few more men, we might have returned and captured the privateer; but it was too late. The batteries were all lighted up, and although they could not see the boats, fired in the direction where they supposed us to be; for they were aware, from the shouting on board the vessel, that we had been beaten off. The launch had but six hands capable of taking an oar; the first cutter had but four. In my own boat I had five. Swinburne had two besides himself in the jolly-boat.

"This is a sorry business, sir," said Swinburne; "now, what's best to be done? My idea is, that we had better put all the wounded men into the launch, man the two cutters and jolly-boat, and tow her off. And, Mr Simple, instead of keeping on this side, as they will expect in the batteries, let us keep close in-shore, upon the near side, and their shot will pass over us."

This advice was too good not to be followed. It was now two o'clock, and we had a long pull before us, and no time to lose: we lifted the dead bodies and the wounded men out of the two cutters and jolly-boat into the launch. I had no time for examination, but I perceived that O'Farrell was quite dead, and also a youngster of the name of Pepper, who must have smuggled himself into the boats. I did, however, look for Osbaldistone, and found him in the stern sheets of the launch. He had received a deep wound in the breast, apparently with a pike. He was sensible, and asked me for a little water, which I procured from the breaker which was in the launch, and gave it to him. At the word water, and hearing it poured out from the breaker, many of the wounded men faintly called out for some. Having no time to spare, I left two men in the launch, one to steer and the other to give them water, and then taking her in tow, pulled directly in for the batteries, as advised by Swinburne, who now sat alongside of me.

As soon as we were well in-shore, I pulled out of the harbour, with feelings not by any means enviable. Swinburne said to me in a low voice, "This will be a hard blow for the captain, Mr Simple. I've always been told, that a young captain losing his men without bringing any dollars to his admiral, is not very well received."

"I am more sorry for him than I can well express, Swinburne," replied I; "but—what is that a-head—a vessel under weigh?"

Swinburne stood up in the stern of the cutter, and looked for a few seconds. "Yes, a large ship standing in under royals—she must be a Frenchman. Now's our time, sir; so long as we don't go out empty-handed, all will be well. Oars, all of you. Shall we cast off the launch, sir?"

"Yes," replied I; "and now, my lads, let us only have the vessel, and we shall do. She is a merchantman, that's clear (not that I was sure of it). Swinburne, I think it will be better to let her pass us in-shore; they will all be looking out of the other side, for they must have seen the firing."

"Well thought of, sir," replied Swinburne.

We laid on our oars, and let her pass us, which she did, creeping in at the rate of two miles an hour. We then pulled for her quarter in the three boats, leaving the launch behind us, and boarded. As we premised, the crew were on deck, and all on the other side of the vessel, so anxiously looking at the batteries, which were still firing occasional random shot, that they did not perceive us until we were close to them, and then they had no time to seize their arms. There were several ladies on board; some of the people protected them, others ran below. In two minutes we had possession of her, and had put her head the other way. To our surprise we found that she mounted fourteen guns. One hatch we left open for the ladies, some of whom had fainted, to be taken down below; the others were fastened down by Swinburne. As soon as we had the deck to ourselves, we manned one of the cutters, and sent it for the launch; and as soon as she was made fast alongside, we had time to look about us. The breeze freshened, and, in half an hour, we were out of gun-shot of all the batteries. I then had the wounded men taken out of the launch, and Swinburne and the other men bound up their wounds, and made them as comfortable as they could.

Chapter XLV

Some remarkable occurrences take place in the letter of marque—Old friends with improved faces—The captor a captive; but not carried away, though the captive is, by the ship's boat—The whole chapter a mixture of love, war, and merchandise.

We had had possession of the vessel about an hour, when the man who was sentry over the hatchway told me that one or the prisoners wished to speak with the English commanding officer, and asked leave to come on deck. I gave permission, and a gentleman came up, stating that he was a passenger; that the ship was a letter of marque, from Bordeaux; that there were seven lady passengers on board, who had come out to join their husbands and families; and that he trusted I would have no objection to put them on shore, as women could hardly be considered as objects of warfare. As I knew that O'Brien would have done so, and that he would be glad to get rid of both women and prisoners if he could, I replied "Most certainly;" that I would heave-to, that they might not have so far to pull on shore, and that I would permit the ladies and other passengers to go on shore. I begged that they would be as quick as possible in getting their packages ready, and that I would give them two of the boats belonging to the ship, with a sufficient number of French seamen belonging to her to man the boats. The Frenchman was very grateful, thanked me in the name of the ladies, and went down below to impart the intelligence. I then hove-to, lowered down the boats from the quarters, and waited for them to come up. It was daylight before they were ready, but that I did not care about; I saw the brig in the offing about seven miles off, and I was well clear of the batteries. At last they made their appearance, one by one coming up the ladder, escorted by French gentlemen. They had to wait while the packages and bundles were put into the boats. The first sight which struck them with horror was the many dead and wounded Englishmen lying on the decks. Expressing their commiseration, I told them that we had attempted to take the privateer, and had been repulsed, and that it was coming out of the harbour that I had fallen in with their ship and captured it. All the ladies had severally thanked me for my kindness in giving them their liberty, except one, whose eyes were fixed upon the wounded men, when the French gentleman went up to her, and reminded her that she had not expressed her thanks to the commanding officer.

She turned round to me—I started back. I certainly had seen that face before—I could not be mistaken; yet she had now grown up into a beautiful young woman. "Celeste," said I, trembling. "Are you not Celeste?"

"Yes," replied she, looking earnestly at me, as if she would discover who I was, but which it was not very easy to do, begrimed as my face was with dust and gunpowder.

"Have you forgotten Peter Simple?"

"Oh! no—no—never forgot you!" cried Celeste, bursting into tears, and holding out her hands.

This scene occasioned no small astonishment to the parties on deck, who could not comprehend it. She smiled through her tears, as I told her how happy I was to have the means of being of service to her. "And where is the colonel?" said I.

"There," replied she, pointing to the island; "he is now general, and commands the force in the garrison. And where is Mr O'Brien?" interrogated Celeste.

"There," replied I; "he commands that man-of-war, of which I am the second lieutenant."

A rapid exchange of inquiries took place, and the boats were stopped while we were in conversation. Swinburne reported that the brig was standing in for us, and I felt that in justice to the wounded I could no longer delay. Still I found time to press her hand, to thank her for the purse she had given me when I was on the stilts, and to tell her that I had never forgotten her, and never would. With many remembrances to her father, I was handing her into the boat, when she said, "I don't know whether I am right to ask it, but you could do me such a favour."

"What is it, Celeste?"

"You have allowed more than one-half of the men to pull us on shore; some must remain, and they are so miserable—indeed it is hardly yet decided which of them are to go. Could you let them all go?"

"That I will, for your sake, Celeste. As soon as your two boats have shoved off, I will lower down the boat astern, and send the rest after you; but I must make sail now—God bless you!"

The boats then shoved off, the passengers waving their handkerchiefs to us, and I made sail for the brig. As soon as the stern-boat was alongside, the rest of the crew were called up and put into her, and followed their companions. I felt that O'Brien would not be angry with me for letting them all go: and especially when I told him who begged for them. The vessel's name was the *Victorine*, mounting fourteen guns, and twenty-four men, with eleven passengers. She was chiefly laden with silks and wine, and was a very valuable prize. Celeste had time to tell me that her father had been four years in Martinique, and had left her at home for her education; and that she was then coming out to join him. The other ladies were all wives or daughters of officers of the French garrison on the island, and the gentlemen passengers were some of them French officers; but as this was told me in secrecy, of course I was not bound to know it, as they were not in uniform.

As soon as we had closed with the brig, I hastened on board to O'Brien; and as soon as a fresh supply of hands to man the boats, and the surgeon had been despatched on board of the prize, to superintend the removal of the wounded, I went down with him into the cabin, and narrated what had occurred.

"Well," said O'Brien, "all's well that ends well; but this is not the luckiest hit in the world. Your taking the ship has saved me, Peter; and I must make as flourishing a despatch as I can. By the powers but it's very lucky that she has fourteen guns—it sounds grand. I must muddle it all up together, so that the admiral must think we intended to cut them both out—and so we did, sure enough, if we had known she had been there. But I am most anxious to hear the surgeon's report, and whether poor Osbaldistone will do well. Peter, oblige me by going on board, and put two marines sentry over the hatchway, so that no one goes down and pulls the traps about; for I'll send on shore everything belonging to the passengers, for Colonel O'Brien's sake."

The surgeon's report was made—six killed and sixteen wounded. The killed were, O'Farren and Pepper, midshipmen, two seamen and two marines. The first lieutenant, Osbaldistone, was severely wounded in three places, but likely to do well; five other men were dangerously wounded: the other ten would, in all probability, return to their duty in less than a month. As soon as the wounded were on board, O'Brien returned with me to the prize, and we went down into the cabin. All the passengers' effects were collected; the trunks which had been left open were nailed down: and O'Brien wrote a handsome letter to General O'Brien, containing a list of the packages sent on shore. We sent the launch with a flag of truce to the nearest battery; after some demur it was accepted, and effects landed. We did not wait for an answer, but made all sail to join the admiral at Barbadoes.

The next morning we buried those who had fallen. O'Farrell was a fine young man, brave as a lion, but very hot in his temper. He would have made a good officer had he been spared. Poor little Pepper was also much regretted. He was but twelve years old. He had bribed the bowman of the second cutter to allow him to conceal himself under the fore-sheets of the boat. His day's allowance of spirits had purchased him this object of his ambition, which ended so fatally. But as soon as the bodies had disappeared under the wave, and the service was over, we all felt happier. There is something very unpleasant, particularly to sailors, in having a corpse on board.

We now sailed merrily along, the prize keeping company with us; and, before we reached Barbadoes, most of the men were convalescent. Osbaldistone's wounds, were, however, very severe; and he was recommended to return home, which he did, and obtained his promotion as soon as he arrived. He was a pleasant messmate, and I was sorry to lose him; although, the lieutenant appointed in his room being junior to me, I was promoted to be first lieutenant of the brig. Soon after Osbaldistone went home, his brother broke his neck when hunting, and Osbaldistone came into the property. He then quitted the service.

We found the admiral at Barbadoes, who received O'Brien and his despatch very well. O'Brien had taken two good prizes, and that was sufficient to cover a multitude of sins, even if he had committed any; but the despatch was admirably written, and the admiral, in his letter to the Admiralty, commented upon Captain O'Brien's successful and daring attack; whereas, if the truth had been known, it was Swinburne's advice of pulling up the weather shore, which was the occasion of our capturing the *Victorine*; but it is very hard to come at the real truth of these sort of things, as I found out during the time that I was in His Majesty's service.

Chapter XLVI

O'Brien tells his crew that one Englishman is as good as three Frenchmen on salt water—They prove it—We fall in with an old acquaintance, although she could not be considered as a friend.

Our next cruise was on the coast of Guinea and Gulf of Mexico, where we were running up and down for three months, without falling in with anything but West Indiamen bound to Demerara, Berbice, and Surinam, and occasionally chasing a privateer; but in the light winds they were too fast for us. Still we were useful in protecting the trade, and O'Brien had a letter of thanks from the merchants, and a handsome piece of plate upon his quitting the station. We had made sail for Barbadoes two days, and were within sight of the island of Trinidad, when we perceived six sail on the lee-bow. We soon made them out to be three large ships and three schooners; and immediately guessed, which afterwards proved to be correct, that they were three privateers, with West India ships which they had captured. We made all sail, and at first the three privateers did the same; but afterwards, having made out our force, and not liking to abandon their prizes, they resolved to fight. The West Indiamen hauled to the wind on the other tack, and the three privateers shortened sail and awaited our coming. We beat to quarters, and when everything was ready, and we were within a mile of the enemy, who had now thrown out the tri-coloured flag, O'Brien ordered all the men aft on the quarter-deck, and addressed them: "Now, my men, you see that there are three privateers, and you also see that there are three West Indiamen, which they have captured. As for the privateers, it's just a fair match for you one Englishman can always beat three Frenchmen. We must lick the privateers for honour and glory, and we must re-capture the ships for profit, because you'll all want some money when you get on shore again. So you've just half-a-dozen things to do, and then we'll pipe to dinner."

This harangue suited the sailors very well, and they returned to their guns. "Now, Peter," said O'Brien, "just call away the sail-trimmers from the guns, for I mean to fight these fellows under sail, and out-manoeuvre them, if I can. Tell Mr Webster I want to speak with him."

Mr Webster was the second lieutenant, a very steady, quiet young man, and a good officer.

"Mr Webster," said O'Brien, "remember that all the foremost guns must be very much depressed. I prefer that the shot should strike the water before it reaches them, rather than it should go over them. See that your screws are run up at once, and I will take care that no broadside is thrown away. Starboard, Swinburne."

"Starboard it is, sir."

"Steady; so—that's right for the stern of the leeward vessel."

We were within two cable lengths of the privateers, who still remained hove-to within half a cable's length of each other. They were very large schooners, full of men, with their boarding netting triced up, and showing a very good set of teeth: as it afterwards proved, one mounted sixteen, and the other two fourteen, guns.

"Now, my lads, over to the lee guns, and fire as they bear, when we round to. Hands by the lee head-braces, and jib-sheet, stretch along the weather braces. Quarter-master abaft, tend the boom-sheet. Port hard, Swinburne."

"Port it is, sir," replied Swinburne; and the brig rounded up on the wind, shooting up under the sterns of the two weathermost schooners, and discharging the broadsides into them as the guns bore.

"Be smart and load, my lads, and stand by the same guns. Round in the weather head-braces. Peter, I don't want her to go about. Stand by to haul over the boom-sheet, when she pays off. Swinburne, helm amidships."

By this time another broadside was poured into the schooner, who had not yet returned our fire, which, having foolishly remained hove to the wind, they could not do. The brig had now stern way, and O'Brien then executed a very skilful manoeuvre: he shifted the helm, and made a stern board, so as to back in between the two weather schooners and the one to leeward, bracing round at the same time on the other tack.

"Man both sides, my lads, and give them your broadsides as we pass."

The men stationed at the starboard guns flew over, and the other side being again loaded, we exchanged broadsides with the leeward and one of the windward schooners, the brig continuing her stern way until we passed ahead of them. By the time that we had re-loaded, the brig had gathered headway, and again passed between the same two schooners, exchanging broadsides, and then passing astern of them.

"Capital, my lads—capital!" said O'Brien; "this is what I call good fighting." And so it was; for O'Brien had given two raking broadsides, and four others, receiving only two in return, for the schooners were not ready for us when we passed between them the last time.

The smoke had now rolled away to leeward, and we were able to see the effect of our broadsides. The middle schooner had lost her main-boom, and appeared very much cut up in the hull. The schooner to leeward did not appear to have suffered much; but they now perceived their error, and made sail. They had expected that we should have run in between them, and fought broadside to broadside, by which means the weathermost schooner would have taken a raking position, while the others engaged us to windward and to leeward. Our own damages were trifling—two men slightly wounded, and one main shroud cut away. We ran about half a mile astern from them; then with both broadsides ready, we tacked, and found that, as we expected, we could weather the whole of them. This we did; O'Brien running the brig within biscuit-throw of the weather schooner, engaging him broadside to broadside, with the advantage that the other two could not fire a shot into us without standing a chance of striking their consort. If he made more sail, so did we; if he shortened, so did we; so as to keep our position with little variation. The schooner fought well; but her metal was not to be compared with our thirty-two pound carronades, which ploughed up her sides at so short a distance, driving two ports into one. At last her foremast went by the board, and she dropped astern. In the meantime the other schooners had both tacked, and were coming up under our stern to rake us, but the accident which happened to the one we had engaged left us at liberty. We knew that she could not escape, so we tacked and engaged the other two, nearing them as fast as we could. The breeze now sprang up fast, and O'Brien put up the helm and passed between them, giving them both a raking broadside of grape and cannister, which brought the sticks about their ears. This sickened them; the smallest schooner, which had been the leewardmost at the commencement of the action, made all sail on a wind. We clapped on the royals to follow her, when we perceived that the other schooner, which had been in the middle, and whose main-boom we had shot away, had put her helm up, and was crowding all sail before the wind. O'Brien then said, "Must not try for too much, or we shall lose all. Put her about, Peter, we must be content with the one that is left us."

We went about, and ranged up to the schooner which had lost her foremast; but she, finding that her consort had deserted her, hauled down her colours just as we were about to pour in our broadside. Our men gave three cheers;

and it was pleasant to see them all shaking hands with each other, congratulating and laughing at the successful result of our action.

"Now, my lads, be smart;—we've done enough for honour, now for profit. Peter, take the two cutters full of men, and go on board of the schooner, while I get hold of the three West Indiamen. Rig something jury forward, and follow me."

In a minute the cutters were down and full of men. I took possession of the schooner, while the brig again tacked, and crowding all sail stood after the captured vessels. The schooner, which was the largest of the three, was called the *Jean d'Arc*, mounting sixteen guns, and had fifty-three men on board, the remainder being away in the prizes. The captain was wounded very badly, and one officer killed. Out of her ship's company, she had but eight killed and five wounded. They informed me, that they had sailed three months ago from St Pierre's, Martinique, and had fallen in with the other two privateers, and cruised in company, having taken nine West Indiamen since they had come out. "Pray," said I to the officer who gave the information, "were you ever attacked by boats when you laid at St Pierre's?" He replied, yes; and that they had beaten them off. "Did you purchase these masts of an American?" He replied in the affirmative; so that we had captured the very vessel, in attempting to cut out which, we had lost so many men.

We were all very glad of this, and Swinburne said, "Well, hang me if I didn't think that I had seen that port-hole before; there it was that I wrenched a pike out of one of the rascal's hands, who tried to stab me, and into that port-hole I fired at least a dozen muskets. Well, I'm d———d glad we've got hold of the beggar at last."

We secured the prisoners below, and commenced putting the schooner in order. In half an hour, we had completed our knotting and splicing, and having two of the carpenters with us, in an hour we had got up a small jury mast forward, sufficient for the present. We lowered the mainsail, put try-sails on her, and stood after the brig, which was now close to the prizes; but they separated, and it was not till dark that she had possession of two. The third was then hull down on the other tack, with the brig in chase. We followed the brig, as did the two re-captured vessels, and even with our jury up, we found that we could sail as fast as they. The next morning, we saw the brig hove-to, and about three miles a-head, with the three vessels in her possession. We closed, and I went on board. Webster was put in charge of the privateer; and, after lying-to for that day to send our prize-masters and men on board to remove the prisoners, we got up a proper jury-mast, and all made sail together for Barbadoes. On my return on board, I found that we had but one man and one boy killed and six wounded, which I was not aware of. I forgot to say that the names of the other two privateers were *L'Etoile* and *La Madeleine*.

In a fortnight we arrived with all our prizes safe in Carlisle Bay, where we found the admiral, who had anchored but two days before. I hardly need say that O'Brien was well received, and gained a great deal of credit for the action. I found several letters from my sister, the contents of which gave me much pain. My father had been some months in Ireland, and returned without gaining any information. My sister said that he was very unhappy, paid no attention to his clerical duties, and would sit for days without speaking. That he was very much altered in his appearance, and had grown thin and care-worn. "In short," said she "my dear Peter, I am afraid that he is fretting himself to death. Of course, I am very lonely and melancholy. I cannot help reflecting upon what will be my situation if any accident should happen to my father. Accept my uncle's protection I will not; yet, how am I to live, for my father has saved nothing? I have been very busy lately, trying to qualify myself for a governess, and practise the harp and piano for several hours every day. I shall be very, very glad when you come home again." I showed the letters to O'Brien, who read them with much attention. I perceived the colour mount into his cheeks, when he read those parts of her letters in which she mentioned his name, and expressed her gratitude for his kindness towards me.

"Never mind, Peter," said O'Brien, returning me the letters; "to whom is it that I am indebted for my promotion, and this brig, but to you—and for all the prize-money which I have made, and which, by the head of St Patrick, comes to a very dacent sum, but to you? Make yourself quite easy about your dear little sister. We'll club your prize-money and mine together, and she shall marry a duke, if there is one in England deserving her; and it's the French that shall furnish her dowry, as sure as the *Rattlesnake* carries a tail."

Chapter XLVII

I am sent away after prizes, and meet with a hurricane—Am driven on shore, with the loss of more than half my men—Where is the *Rattlesnake?*

In three weeks we were again ready for sea, and the admiral ordered us to our old station off Martinique. We had cruised about a fortnight off St Pierre's, and, as I walked the deck at night, often did I look at the lights in the town, and wonder whether any of them were in the presence of Celeste, when, one evening, being about six miles off shore, we observed two vessels rounding Negro Point, close in-shore. It was quite calm, and the boats were towing ahead.

"It will be dark in half-an-hour, Peter," said O'Brien, "and I think we might get them before they anchor, or, if they do anchor, it will be well outside. What do you think?"

I agreed with him, for in fact, I always seemed to be happier when the brig was close in-shore, as I felt as if I was nearer to Celeste, and the further we were off, the more melancholy I became. Continually thinking of her, and the sight of her after so many years' separation, had changed my youthful attachment into strong affection. I may say that I was deeply in love. The very idea of going into the harbour, therefore, gave me pleasure, and there was no mad or foolish thing that I would not have done, only to gaze upon the walls which contained the constant object of my thoughts. These were wild and visionary notions, and with little chance of ever arriving to any successful issue; but at one or two-and-twenty we are fond of building castles, and very apt to fall in love, without considering our prospect of success. I replied, that I thought it very possible, and wished he would permit me to make the attempt, as, if I found there was much risk, I would return.

"I know that I can trust you, Peter," replied O'Brien, "and it's a great pleasure to know that you have an officer you can trust: but haven't I brought you up myself, and made a man of you, as I promised I would, when you were a little spalpeen, with a sniffling nose, and legs in the shape of two carrots? So hoist out the launch, and get the boats ready— the sooner the better. What a hot day this has been—not a cat's-paw on the water, and the sky all of a mist. Only look at the sun, how he goes down, puffed out to three times his size, as if he were in a terrible passion. I suspect we shall have the land breeze off strong."

In half an hour I shoved off with the boats. It was now quite dark, and I pulled towards the harbour of St Pierre. The heat was excessive and unaccountable; not the slightest breath of wind moved in the heavens or below; no clouds to be seen, and the stars were obscured by a sort of mist: there appeared a total stagnation in the elements. The men in the boats pulled off their jackets, for, after a few moments' pulling, they could bear them no longer. As we pulled in, the atmosphere became more opaque, and the darkness more intense. We supposed ourselves to be at the mouth of the harbour, but could see nothing—not three yards ahead of the boat. Swinburne, who always went with me, was steering the boat, and I observed to him the unusual appearance of the night.

"I've been watching it, sir," replied Swinburne, "and I tell you, Mr Simple, that if we only know how to find the brig, that I would advise you to get on board of her immediately. She'll want all her hands this night, or I'm much mistaken."

"Why do you say so?" replied I.

"Because I think, nay, I may say that I'm sartin, we'll have a hurricane afore morning. It's not the first time I've cruised in these latitudes. I recollect in '94—"

But I interrupted him: "Swinburne, I believe that you are right. At all events, I'll turn back: perhaps we may reach the brig before it comes on. She carries a light, and we can find her out." I then turned the boat round, and steered, as near as I could guess, for where the brig was lying. But we had not pulled out more than two minutes before a low moaning was heard in the atmosphere—now here, now there—and we appeared to be pulling through solid darkness, if I may use the expression. Swinburne looked around him and pointed out on the starboard bow.

"It's a-coming, Mr Simple, sure enough; many's the living being that will not rise on its legs to-morrow. See, sir."

I looked, and dark as it was, it appeared as if a sort of black wall was sweeping along the water right towards us. The moaning gradually increased to a stunning roar, and then at once it broke upon us with a noise to which no thunder can bear a comparison. The oars were caught by the wind with such force that the men were dashed forward under the thwarts, many of them severely hurt. Fortunately we pulled with tholes and pins, or the gunwale and planks of the boat would have been wrenched off, and we should have foundered. The wind soon caught the boat on her broadside, and, had there been the least sea, would have inevitably thrown her over; but Swinburne put the helm down, and she fell off before the hurricane, darting through the boiling water at the rate of ten miles an hour. All hands were aghast; they had recovered their seats, but were obliged to relinquish them and sit down at the bottom, holding on by the thwarts. The terrific roaring of the hurricane prevented any communication, except by gesture. The other boats had disappeared; lighter than ours, they had flown away faster before the sweeping element; but we had not been a minute before the wind before the sea rose in a most unaccountable manner—it appeared to be by magic. Of all the horrors that ever I witnessed, nothing could be compared to the scene of this night. We could see nothing, and heard only the wind, before which we were darting like an arrow—to where we knew not, unless it was to certain death. Swinburne steered the boat, every now and then looking back as the waves increased. In a few minutes we were in a heavy swell, that at one minute bore us all aloft, and at the next almost sheltered us from the hurricane; and now the atmosphere was charged with showers of spray, the wind cutting off the summits of the waves, as if with a knife, and carrying them along with it, as it were, in its arms. The boat was filling with water, and appeared to settle down fast. The men baled with their hats in silence, when a large wave culminated over the stern, filling us up to our thwarts. The next moment we all received a shock so violent, that we were jerked from our seats. Swinburne was thrown over my head. Every timber of the boat separated at once, and she appeared to crumble from under us, leaving us floating on the raging waters. We all struck out for our lives, but with little hope of preserving them; but the next wave dashed us on the rocks, against which the boat had already been hurled. That wave gave life to some and death to others. Me, in Heaven's mercy, it preserved: I was thrown so high up that I merely scraped against the top of the rock, breaking two of my ribs. Swinburne, and eight more, escaped with me, but not unhurt: two had their legs broken, three had broken arms, and the others were more or less contused. Swinburne miraculously received no injury. We had been eighteen in the boat, of which ten escaped: the others were hurled up at our feet; and the next morning we found them dreadfully mangled. One or two had their skulls literally shattered to pieces against the rocks. I felt that I was saved, and was grateful; but still the hurricane howled —still the waves were washing over us. I crawled further up upon the beach, and found Swinburne sitting down with his eyes directed seaward. He knew me, took my hand, squeezed it, and then held it in his. For some moments we remained in this position, when the waves, which every moment increased in volume, washed up to us, and obliged us to crawl further up. I then looked around me; the hurricane continued in its fury, but the atmosphere was not so dark. I could trace, for some distance, the line of the harbour, from the ridge of foam upon the shore; and, for the first time, I thought of O'Brien and the brig. I put my mouth close to Swinburne's ear, and cried out, "O'Brien!" Swinburne shook his head, and looked up again at the offing. I thought whether there was any chance of the brig's escape. She was certainly six, if not seven miles off, and the hurricane was not direct on the shore. She might have a drift of ten miles, perhaps; but what was that against such tremendous power? I prayed for those on board of the brig, and returned thanks for my own preservation. I was, or soon should be, a prisoner, no doubt; but what was that? I thought of Celeste, and felt almost happy.

In about three hours the force of the wind subsided. It still blew a heavy gale, but the sky cleared up, the stars again twinkled in the heavens, and we could see to a considerable distance.

"It's breaking now, sir," said Swinburne, at last; "satisfied with the injury it has done—and that's no little. This is worse than '94."

"Now, I'd give all my pay and prize-money if it were only daylight, and
I could know the fate of the poor *Rattlesnake*. What do you think,
Swinburne?"

"All depends upon whether they were taken unprepared, sir. Captain O'Brien is as good a seaman as ever trod a plank; but he never has been in a hurricane, and may not have known, the signs and warnings which God in His mercy has vouchsafed to us. Your flush vessels fill easily—but we must hope for the best."

Most anxiously did we look out for the day, which appeared to us as if it never would break. At last the dawn appeared, and we stretched our eyes to every part of the offing as it was lighted up, but we could not see the brig. The sun rose, and all was bright and clear; but we looked not around us, our eyes were directed to where we had left the brig. The sea was still running high, but the wind abated fast.

"Thank God!" ejaculated Swinburne, when he had directed his eyes along the coast, "she is above water, at all events!" and looking in the direction where he pointed, I perceived the brig within two miles of the shore, dismantled, and tossing in the waves.

"I see her," replied I, catching my breath with joy; "but—still—I think she must go on shore."

"All depends upon whether she can get a little bit of sail up to weather the point," replied Swinburne; "and depend upon it, Captain O'Brien knows that as well as we do."

We were now joined by the other men who were saved. We all shook hands. They pointed out to me the bodies of our shipmates who had perished. I directed them to haul them further up, and put them all together; and continued, with Swinburne, to watch the brig. In about half an hour we perceived a triangle raised, and in ten minutes afterwards a jury-mast abaft—a try-sail was hoisted and set. Then the shears were seen forward, and in as short a time another try-sail and a storm-jib were expanded to the wind.

"That's all he can do now, Mr Simple," observed Swinburne; "he must trust to them and Providence. They are not more than a mile from the beach—it will be touch and go."

Anxiously did we watch for more than half an hour; the other men returned to us, and joined in our speculations. At one time we thought it impossible—at another, we were certain that she would weather the point. At last, as she neared us, she warped ahead: my anxiety became almost insupportable. I stood first on one leg, and then on the other, breathless with suspense. She appeared to be on the point—actually touching the rocks—"God! she's struck!" said I.

"No!" replied Swinburne;—and then we saw her pass on the other side of the outermost rock and disappear.

"Safe, Mr Simple!—weathered, by God!" cried Swinburne, waving his hat with joy.

"God be thanked!" replied I, overcome with delight.

Chapter XLVIII

The devastation of the hurricane—Peter makes friends—At destroying or saving, nothing like British seamen—Peter meets with General O'Brien, much to his satisfaction—Has another meeting still more so—A great deal of pressing of hands, "and all that," as Pope says.

Now that the brig was safe, we thought of ourselves. My first attention was directed to the dead bodies, and as I looked at their mangled limbs, I felt grateful to Heaven that I had been so miraculously spared. We then cast our eyes along the beach to see if we could trace any remnants of the other boats, but in vain. We were about three miles from the town, which we could perceive had received considerable damage, and the beach below it was strewed with wrecks and fragments. I told the men that we might as well walk into the town and deliver ourselves up as prisoners; to which they agreed, and we set forward, promising to send for the poor fellows who were too much hurt to accompany us.

As soon as we climbed up the rocks, and gained the inland, what a sight presented itself to us! Trees torn up by the roots in every direction— cattle lying dead—here and there the remains of a house, of which the other parts had been swept away for miles. Everything not built of solid masonry had disappeared. We passed what had been a range of negro huts, but they were levelled to the ground. The negroes were busily searching for their property among the ruins, while the women held their infants in their arms, and the other children by their sides. Here and there was the mother wailing over the dead body of some poor little thing which had been crushed to death. They took no notice of us. About half a mile further on, to our great delight, we fell in with the crews of the other boats, who were sitting by the side of the road. They had all escaped unhurt; their boats, being so much more buoyant than ours, had been thrown up high and dry. They joined us, and we proceeded on our way. On our road we fell in with a cart blown over, under the wheel of which was the leg of the negro who conducted it. We released the poor fellow; his leg was fractured. We laid him by the side of the road in the shade, and continued our march. Our whole route was one scene of desolation and distress; but when we arrived at the town, we found that there it was indeed accumulated. There was not one house in three standing entire— the beach was covered with remnants of bodies and fragments of vessels, whose masts lay forced several feet into the sand, and broken into four or five pieces. Parties of soldiers were busy taking away the bodies, and removing what few valuables had been saved. We turned up into the town, for no one accosted us or even noticed us; and here the scene was even more dreadful. In some streets they were digging out those who were still alive, and whose cries were heard among the ruins; in others they were carrying away the dead bodies. The lamentations of the relatives— the howling of the negroes—the cries of the wounded—the cursing and swearing of the French soldiers, and the orders delivered continually by officers on horseback, with all the confusion arising from crowds of spectators, mingling their voices together, formed a scene as dreadful as it was novel. After surveying it for a few minutes, I went up to an officer on horseback, and told him in French, that I wished to surrender myself as a prisoner.

"We have no time to take prisoners now," replied he; "hundreds are buried in the ruins, and we must try to save them. We must now attend to the claims of humanity."

"Will you allow my men to assist you, sir?" replied I. "They are active and strong fellows."

"Sir," said he, taking off his hat, "I thank you in the name of my unfortunate countrymen."

"Show us, then, where we may be most useful."

He turned and pointed to a house higher up, the offices of which were blown down. "There are living beings under those ruins."

"Come, my lads," said I; and sore as they were, my men hastened with alacrity to perform their task. I could not help them myself, my side was so painful; but I stood by giving them directions. In half an hour we had cleared away, so as to arrive at a poor negro girl, whose cries we had distinctly heard. We released her and laid her down in the street, but she fainted. Her left hand was dreadfully shattered. I was giving what assistance I could, and the men were busy clearing away, throwing on one side the beams and rafters, when an officer on horseback rode up. He stood and asked me who we were. I told him that we belonged to the brig, and had been wrecked; and that we were giving what assistance we could until they were at leisure to send us to prison.

"You English are fine brave fellows," replied he, and he rode on.

Another unfortunate object had been recovered by our men, an old white-headed negro, but he was too much mangled to live. We brought him out, and were laying him beside the negro girl, when several officers on horseback rode down the street. The one who was foremost, in a general's uniform, I immediately recognized as my former friend, then Colonel O'Brien. They all stopped and looked at us. I told who we were. General O'Brien took off his hat to the sailors, and thanked them. He did not recognize me, and he was passing on, when I said to him in English, "General O'Brien, you have forgotten me, but I shall never forget your kindness."

"My God!" said he, "is it you, my dear fellow?" and he sprang from his horse and shook me warmly by the hand. "No wonder that I did not know you; you are a very different person from little Peter Simple, who dressed up as a girl and danced on stilts. But I have to thank you, and so has Celeste for your kindness to her. I will not ask you to leave your work of charity and kindness, but when you have done what you can, come up to my house. Anyone will show it to you; and if you do not find me you will find Celeste, as you must be aware cannot leave this melancholy employment. God bless you!" He then rode off, followed by his staff.

"Come, my lads," said I, "depend upon it we shall not be very cruelly treated. Let us work hard, and do all the good we can, and the Frenchmen won't forget it."

We had cleared that house, and went back to where the other people were working under the orders of the officer on horseback. I went up to him, and told him we had saved two, and if he had no objection, would assist his party. He thankfully accepted our services.

"And now, my lads," said Swinburne, "let us forget all our bruises, and show these French fellows how to work."

And they did so: they tossed away the beams and rafters right and left with a quickness and dexterity which quite astonished the officer and other inhabitants who were looking on, and in half an hour had done more work than could have been possibly expected. Several lives were saved, and the French expressed their admiration at our sailors' conduct, and brought them something to drink, which they stood much in need of, poor fellows. After that they worked double tides, as we say, and certainly were the means of saving many lives which otherwise would have been sacrificed.

The disasters occasioned by this hurricane were very great, owing to its having taken place at night, when the chief of the inhabitants were in bed and asleep. I was told that most of the wood houses were down five minutes after the hurricane burst upon them. About noon there was no more work for us to do, and I was not sorry that it was over. My side was very painful, and the burning heat of the sun made me feel giddy and sick at the stomach. I inquired of a respectable looking old Frenchman which was the General's house. He directed me to it, and I proceeded there, followed by my men. When I arrived, I found the orderly leading away the horse of General O'Brien, who had just returned. I desired a sergeant, who was in attendance at the door, to acquaint the general that I was below. He returned, and desired me to follow him. I was conducted into a large room, where I found him in company with several officers. He again greeted me warmly, and introduced me to the company as the officer who had permitted the ladies who had been taken prisoners to come on shore.

"I have to thank you, then, for my wife," said an officer, coming up, and offering his hand.

Another came up, and told me that I had also released his. We then entered into a conversation, in which I stated, the occasion of my having been wrecked, and all the particulars; also, that I had seen the brig in the morning dismasted, but that she had weathered the point, and was safe.

"That brig of yours, I must pay you the compliment to say, has been very troublesome; and my namesake keeps the batteries more upon the alert than ever I could have done," said General O'Brien. "I don't believe there is a negro five years old upon the island who does not know your brig."

We then talked over the attack of the privateer, in which we were beaten off. "Ah!" replied the aide-de-camp, "you made a mess of that. He has been gone these four months. Captain Carnot swears that he'll fight you if he falls in with you."

"He has kept his word," replied I; and then I narrated our action with the three French privateers, and the capture of the vessel; which surprised and, I think, annoyed them very much.

"Well, my friend," said General O'Brien, "you must stay with me while you are on the island; if you want anything, let me know."

"I am afraid that I want a surgeon," replied I; "for my side is so painful that I can scarcely breathe."

"Are you hurt then?" said General O'Brien, with an anxious look.

"Not dangerously, I believe," said I, "but rather painfully."

"Let me see," said an officer, who stepped forward; "I am surgeon to the forces here, and perhaps you will trust yourself in my hands. Take off your coat."

I did so with difficulty. "You have two ribs broken," said he, "and a very severe contusion. You must go to bed, or lie on a sofa, for a few days. In a quarter of an hour I will come and dress you, and promise you to make you all well in ten days, in return for your having given me my daughter, who was on board of the *Victorine* with the other ladies." The officers now made their bows, and left me alone with General O'Brien.

"Recollect," said he, "that I tell it you once for all, that my purse, and everything, is at your command. If you do not accept them freely, I shall think you do not love us. It is not the first time, Peter, and you repaid me honourably. However, of course, I was no party to that affair; it was Celeste's doing," continued he, laughing. "Of course, I could not imagine that it was you who was dressed up as a woman, and so impudently danced through France on stilts. But I must hear all your adventures by-and-by, Celeste is most anxious to see you. Will you go now, or wait till after the surgeon comes?"

"Oh, now, if you please, general. May I first beg that some care may be taken of my poor men; they have had nothing to eat since yesterday, are very much bruised, and have worked hard; and that a cart may be sent for those who lie maimed on the beach?"

"I should have thought of them before," replied he: "and I will also order the same party to bury the other poor fellows who are lying on the beach. Come, now—will take you to Celeste."

Chapter XLIX

Broken ribs not likely to produce broken hearts—O'Brien makes something very like a declaration of peace—Peter Simple actually makes a declaration of love—Rash proceedings on all sides.

I followed the general into a handsomely furnished apartment, where I found Celeste waiting to receive me. She ran to me as soon as I entered; and with what pleasure did I take her hand, and look on her beautiful expressive countenance! I could not say a word—neither did Celeste. For a minute I held her hand in mine, looking at her; the general stood by regarding us alternately. He then turned round, and walked to the window. I lifted the hand to my lips, and then released it.

"It appears to be a dream, almost," said Celeste.

I could not make any reply, but continued to gaze upon her—she had grown up into such a beautiful creature. Her figure was perfect, and the expression of her countenance was so varied—so full of intellect and feeling—it was angelic. Her eyes, suffused with tears, beamed so softly, so kindly on me, I could have fallen down and worshipped her.

"Come," said General O'Brien; "come, my dear friend, now that you have seen Celeste, the surgeon must see you."

"The surgeon," cried Celeste, with alarm.

"Yes, my love; it is of no consequence—only a couple of ribs broken."

I followed General O'Brien out of the room, and as I came to the door I turned round to look at Celeste. She had retreated to the sofa, and her handkerchief was up to her eyes. The surgeon was waiting for me; he bandaged me, and applied some cooling lotion to my side, which made me feel quite comfortable.

"I must now leave you," said General O'Brien; "you had better lie down for an hour or two, and then, if I am not back, you know your way to Celeste."

I lay down as he requested; but as soon as I heard the clatter of the horse's hoofs, as he rode off, I left the room, and hurried to the drawing-room. Celeste was there, and hastened to inquire if I was much hurt. I replied in the negative, and told her that I had come down to prove it to her; and we then sat down on the sofa together.

"I have the misfortune never to appear before you, Celeste, except in a very unprepossessing state. When you first saw me I was wounded; at our next meeting I was in woman's clothes; the last time we met I was covered with dirt and gunpowder; and now I return to you wounded and in rags. I wonder whether I shall ever appear before you as a gentleman?"

"It is not the clothes which make the gentleman, Peter. I am too happy to see you to think of how you are dressed. I have never yet thanked you for your kindness to us when we last met. My father will never forget it."

"Nor have I thanked you, Celeste, for your kindness in dropping the purse into the hat, when you met me, trying to escape from France. I have never forgotten you, and since we met the last time, you have hardly ever been out of my thoughts. You don't know how thankful I am to the hurricane for having blown me into your presence. When we cruised in the brig, I have often examined the town with my glass, trying to fancy that I had my eye upon the house you were in; and have felt so happy when we were close in shore, because I knew that I was nearer to you."

"And, Peter, I have often watched the brig, and have been so glad to see it come nearer, and then so afraid that the batteries would fire at you. What a pity it is that my father and you should be opposed to each other—we might be so happy!"

"And may be yet, Celeste," replied I.

We conversed for two hours, which appeared to be but ten minutes. I felt that I was in love, but I do not think that Celeste had any idea at the time that she was—but I leave the reader to judge from the little conversation I have quoted, whether she was not, or something very much approaching to it.

The next morning I went out early to look for the brig, and, to my great delight, saw her about six miles off the harbour's mouth, standing in for the land. She had now got up very respectable jury-masts, with topgallants for topsails, and appeared to be well under command. When she was within three miles of the harbour she lowered the jolly-boat, the only one she had left, and it pulled in-shore with a flag of truce hoisted at the bows. I immediately returned to my room, and wrote a detailed account of what had taken place, ready to send to O'Brien when the boat returned, and I, of course, requested him to send me my effects, as I had nothing but what I stood in. I had just completed my letter when General O'Brien came in.

"My dear friend," said he, "I have just received a flag of truce from Captain O'Brien, requesting to know the fate of his boats' crews, and permission to send in return the clothes and effects of the survivors."

"I have written down the whole circumstances for him, and made the same request to him," replied I; and I handed him my letter. He read it over and returned it.

"But, my dear lad, you must think very poorly of us Frenchmen, if you imagine that we intend to detain you here as a prisoner. In the first place, your liberation of so many French subjects, when you captured the *Victorine*, would entitle you to a similar act of kindness; and, in the next place, you have not been fairly captured, but by a visitation of Providence, which, by the means of the late storm, must destroy all national antipathies, and promote that universal philanthropy between all men, which your brave fellows proved that they possess. You are, therefore, free to depart with all your men, and we shall still hold ourselves your debtors. How is your side to-day?"

"Oh, very bad, indeed," replied I; for I could not bear the idea of returning to the brig so soon, for I had been obliged to quit Celeste very soon after dinner the day before, and go to bed. I had not yet had much conversation with her, nor had I told General O'Brien how it was that we escaped from France. "I don't think I can possibly go on board to-day, but I feel very grateful to you for your kindness."

"Well, well," replied the general, who observed my feelings, "I do not think it is necessary that you should go on board to-day. I will send the men and your letter, and I will write to Captain O'Brien, to say that you are in bed, and will not bear moving until the day after tomorrow. Will that do?"

I thought it but a very short time, but I saw that the general looked as if he expected me to consent; so I did.

"The boat can come and return again with some of your clothes," continued the general, "and I will tell Captain O'Brien that if he comes off the mouth of the harbour the day after to-morrow, I will send you on board in one of our boats."

He then took my letter and quitted the room. As soon as he was gone I found myself quite well enough to go to Celeste, who waited for me, and I told her what had passed. That morning I sat with her and the general, and narrated all my adventures, which amused the general very much. I did not conceal the conduct of my uncle, and the hopes which I faintly entertained of being able, some day or another, to discover the fraud which had been practised, or how very unfavourable were my future prospects if I did not succeed. At this portion of my narrative the general appeared very thoughtful and grave. When I had finished, it was near dinner time, and I found that my clothes had arrived with a letter from O'Brien, who stated how miserable he had been at the supposition of my loss, and his delight at my escape. He stated that on going down into the cabin, after I had shoved off, he, by chance, cast his eyes on the barometer, and, to his surprise, found that it had fallen two inches, which he had been told was the case previous to a hurricane. This, combined with the peculiar state of the atmosphere, had induced him to make every preparation, and that they had just completed their work when it came on. The brig was thrown on her beam ends, and lay there for half an hour, when they were forced to cut away the masts to right her. That they did not weather the point the next morning by more than half a cable's length; and concluded by saying, that the idea of my death had made him so unhappy that, if it had not been for the sake of the men, it was almost a matter of indifference to him whether he had been lost or not. He had written to General O'Brien, thanking him for his kindness; and that, if fifty vessels should pass the brig, he would not capture one of them, until I was on board again, even if he were dismissed the service for neglect of duty. He said, that the brig sailed almost as fast under jury-masts as she did before, and that, as soon as I came on board, he should go back to Barbadoes. "As for your ribs being so bad, Peter, that's all bother," continued he; "I know that you are making arrangements for another sort of *rib*, as soon as you can manage it; but you must stop a little, my boy. You shall be a lord yet, as I always promised you that you should. It's a long lane that has no turning—so good-bye."

When I was alone with Celeste, I showed her O'Brien's letter. I had read the part of it relative to his not intending to make any capture while I was on shore to General O'Brien, who replied, "that under such circumstances he thought' he should do right to detain me a little longer but," said he, "O'Brien is a man of honour, and worthy of his name."

When Celeste came to that part of the letter in which O'Brien stated that I was looking after another rib, and which I had quite forgotten, she asked me to explain it; for, although she could read and speak English very well, she had not been sufficiently accustomed to it to comprehend the play upon words. I translated, and then said, "Indeed, Celeste, I had forgotten that observation of O'Brien's, or I should not have shown you the letter; but he has stated the truth. After all your kindness to me, how can I help being in love with you? and need I add, that I should consider it the greatest blessing which Heaven could grant me, if you could feel so much regard for me as one day to become my wife! Don't be angry with me for telling you the truth," continued I, for Celeste coloured up as I spoke to her.

"Oh, no! I am not angry with you, Peter; far from it. It is very complimentary to me—what you have just said."

"I am aware," continued I, "that at present I have little to offer you— indeed, nothing. I am not even such a match as your father might approve of; but you know my whole history, and what my desires are."

"My dear father loves me, Peter, and he loves you too, very much—he always did, from the hour he saw you—he was so pleased with your candour and honesty of character. He has often told me so, and very often talked of you."

"Well, Celeste, tell me,—may I when far away, be permitted to think of you, and indulge a hope, that some day we may meet never to part again?" And I took Celeste by the hand, and put my arm round her waist.

"I don't know what to say," replied she; "I will speak to my father, or perhaps you will; but I will never marry anybody else, if I can help it."

I drew her close to me, and kissed her. Celeste burst into tears, and laid her head upon my shoulder. When General O'Brien came I did not attempt to move, nor did Celeste.

"General," said I, "you may think me to blame, but I have not been able to conceal what I feel for Celeste. You may think that I am imprudent, and that I am wrong in thus divulging what I ought to have concealed, until I was in a situation to warrant my aspiring to your daughter's hand; but the short time allowed me to be in her company, the fear of losing her, and my devoted attachment, will, I trust, plead my excuse."

The general took one or two turns up and down the room, and then replied, "What says Celeste?"

"Celeste will never do anything to make her father unhappy," replied she, going up to him and hiding her face in his breast, with her arm round his neck.

The general kissed his daughter, and then said, "I will be frank with you, Mr Simple. I do not know any man whom I would prefer to you as a son-in-law; but there are many considerations which young people are very apt to forget. I do not interfere in your attachment, which appears to be mutual; but, at the same time, I will have no promise and no engagement, you may never meet again. However, Celeste is very young, and I shall not put any constraint upon her; and at the same time you are equally free, if time and circumstances should alter your present feelings."

"I can ask no more, my dear sir," replied I, taking the general by the hand; "it is candid—more than I had any reason to expect. I shall now leave you with a contented mind, and the hopes of one day claiming Celeste shall spur me to exertion."

"Now, if you please, we will drop the subject," said the general. "Celeste, my dear, we have a large party to dinner, as you know. You had better retire to your room and get ready. I have asked all the ladies that you liberated, Peter, and all their husbands and fathers; so you will have the pleasure of witnessing how many people you made happy by your gallantry. Now that Celeste has left the room, Peter, I must beg that, as a man of honour, you do not exact from her any more promises, or induce her to tie herself down to you by oaths. Her attachment to you has grown up with her unaccountably, and she is already too fond of you for her peace of mind, should accident or circumstances part you for ever. Let us hope for the best, and depend upon it that it shall be no trifling obstacle which will hinder me from seeing you one day united."

I thanked the general with tears; he shook me warmly by the hand as I gave my promise, and we separated.

How happy did I feel when I went into my room, and sat down to compose my mind and think over what had happened. True, at one moment the thought of my dependent situation threw a damp over my joy; but in the next I was building castles, inventing a discovery of my uncle's plot, fancying myself in possession of the title and property, and laying it at the feet of my dear Celeste. Hope sustained my spirits, and I felt satisfied for the present with the consideration that Celeste returned my love. I decked myself carefully, and went down, where I found all the company assembled. We had a very pleasant, happy party, and the ladies entreated General O'Brien to detain me as a prisoner—very kind of them —and I felt very much disposed to join in their request.

Chapter L

Peter Simple first takes a command, then three West Indiamen, and twenty prisoners—One good turn deserves another—The prisoners endeavour to take him, but are themselves taken in.

The next day I was very unhappy. The brig was in the offing waiting for me to come on hoard. I pointed her out to Celeste as we were at the window, and her eyes met mine. An hour's conversation could not have said more. General O'Brien showed that he had perfect confidence in me for he left us together.

"Celeste," said I, "I have promised your father—"

"I know what has passed," interrupted she; "he told me everything."

"How kind he is! But I did not say that I would not bind myself, Celeste."

"No! but my father made me promise that you should not—that if you attempted, I was immediately to prevent you—and so I shall."

"Then you shall keep your word, Celeste. Imagine everything that can be said in this—" and I kissed her.

"Don't think me forward, Peter, but I wish you to go away happy," said Celeste; "and therefore, in return, imagine all I could say in this" and she returned my salute.

After this we had a conversation of two hours; but what lovers say is very silly, except to themselves, and the reader need not be troubled with it. General O'Brien came in and told me the boat was ready. I rose up—I was satisfied with what had passed, and with a firm voice I said, "Good-bye, Celeste; God bless you!" and followed the general, who, with some of his officers, walked down with me to the beach. I thanked the general, who embraced me, paid my adieus to the officers, and stepped into the boat. In half an hour I was on board of the brig, and in O'Brien's arms. We put the helm up, and in a short time the town of St Pierre was shut out from my longing sight, and we were on our way to Barbadoes. That day was passed in the cabin with O'Brien, giving him a minute detail of all that had passed.

When we anchored once more in Carlisle Bay, we found that the hurricane had been much more extensive in the Windward Islands than we had imagined. Several men of war were lying there, having lost one or more of their masts, and there was great difficulty in supplying the wants of so many. As we arrived the last, of course we were last served; and, there being no boats left in store, there was no chance of our being ready for sea under two or three months. The *Joan d' Arc* schooner privateer was still lying there, but had not been fitted out for want of men; and the admiral proposed to O'Brien that he should man her with a part of his ship's company, and send one of his lieutenants out to cruise in her. This was gladly assented to by O'Brien, who came on board and asked me whether I should like to have her, which I agreed to, as I was quite tired of Barbadoes and fried flying fish.

I selected two midshipmen, Swinburne, and twenty men, and having taken on board provisions and water for three months, I received my written instructions from O'Brien, and made sail. We soon discovered that the masts which the American had sold to the schooner, were much too large for her; she was considerably overmasted, and we were obliged to be very careful. I stood for Trinidad, off which island was to be my cruising ground, and in three weeks had recaptured three West Indiamen, when I found myself so short of hands, that I was obliged to return to Barbadoes. I had put four hands into the first vessel, which, with the Englishmen, prisoners, were sufficient, and, three hands into the two others; but I was very much embarrassed with my prisoners, who amounted to nearly double my ship's company remaining on board. Both the midshipmen I had sent away, and I consulted with Swinburne as to what was best to be done.

"Why, the fact is, Mr Simple, Captain O'Brien ought to have given us more hands; twenty men are little enough for a vessel with a boom mainsail like the one we have here; and now we have only ten left; but I suppose he did not expect us to be so lucky, and it's true enough that he has plenty of work for the ship's company, now that he has to turn everything in afresh. As for the prisoners, I think we had better run close in, and give them two of our boats to take them on shore. At all events, we must be rid of them, and not be obliged to have one eye aloft, and the other down the hatchway, as we must now."

This advice corresponded with my own ideas, and I ran in-shore, gave them the stern boat, and one of the larger ones, which held them all, and sent them away, leaving only one boat for the schooner, which we hoisted up in the star-board chess-tree. It fell a dead calm as we sent away the prisoners; we saw them land and disappear over the rocks, and thought ourselves well rid of them, as they were twenty-two in number, most of them Spaniards, and very stout ferocious-looking fellows. It continued calm during the whole day, much to our annoyance, as I was very anxious to get away as soon as I could; still I could not help admiring the beauty of the scenery—the lofty mountains rising abruptly from the ocean, and towering in the clouds, reflected on the smooth water, as clear as in a looking-glass, every colour, every tint, beautifully distinct. The schooner gradually drifted close in-shore, and we could perceive the rocks at the bottom, many fathoms deep. Not a breath of wind was to be seen on the surface of the water for several miles round, although the horizon in the offing showed that there was a smart breeze outside.

Night came on, and we still lay becalmed. I gave my orders to Swinburne, who had the first watch, and retired to my standing bed-place in the cabin. I was dreaming, and I hardly need say who was the object of my visions. I thought I was in Eagle Park, sitting down with her under one of the large chestnut trees, which formed the avenue, when I felt my shoulder roughly pushed. I started up—"What is the matter? Who's that— Swinburne?"

"Yes, sir. On with your clothes immediately, as we have work on hand, I expect." And Swinburne left the cabin, and I heard him calling the other men who were below. I knew that Swinburne would not give a false alarm. In a minute I was on deck, and was looking at the stern of the schooner. "What is that, Swinburne?" said I.

"Silence, sir. Hark! don't you hear them?"

"Yes," replied I; "the sound of oars."

"Exactly, sir; depend upon it, those Spaniards have got more help, and are coming back to take the vessel; they know we have only ten hands on board."

By this time the men were all on deck. I directed Swinburne to see all the muskets loaded, and ran down for my own sword and pistols. The water was so smooth, and the silence so profound, that Swinburne had heard the sound of the oars at a considerable distance. Fortunate it was, that I had such a trusty follower. Another might have slumbered, and the schooner have been boarded and captured without our being prepared. When I came on deck again, I spoke to the men, exhorted them to do their duty, and pointed out to them that these cut-throat villains would certainly murder us all if we were taken, which I firmly believe would have been the case. The men declared that they would sell their lives as dearly as they could. We had twenty muskets, and the same number of pistols, all of which were now loaded. Our guns were also ready, but of no use, now that the schooner had not steerage-way.

The boats were in sight, about a quarter of a mile astern, when Swinburne said, "There's a cat's-paw flying along the water, Mr Simple; if we could only have a little wind, how we would laugh at them; but I'm afraid there's no such luck. Shall we let them know that we are ready?"

"Let every one of us take two muskets," said I: "when the first boat is under the counter, take good aim, and discharge into one of the boats; then seize the other musket, and discharge it at the other boat. After that we must trust to our cutlasses and pistols; for if they come on, there will be no time to load again. Keep silence, all of you."

The boats now came up full of men; but as we remained perfectly quiet, they pulled up gently, hoping to surprise us. Fortunately, one was a little in advance of the other; upon which I altered my directions, and desired my men to fire their second musket into the first boat, as, if we could disable her, we were an equal match for those in the other. When the boat was within six yards of the schooner's counter, "Now!" said I, and all the muskets were discharged at once, and my men cheered. Several of the oars dropped, and I was sure we had done great execution; but they were laid hold of by the other men, who had not been pulling, and again the boat advanced to the counter.

"Good aim, my lads, this time," cried Swinburne; "the other boat will be alongside as soon as you have fired. Mr Simple, the schooner has headway, and there's a strong breeze coming up."

Again we discharged our ten muskets into the boat, but this time we waited until the bow-man had hooked on the planeshear with his boat-hook, and our fire was very effective. I was surprised to find that the other boat was not on board of us; but a light breeze had come up, and the schooner glided through the water. Still she was close under our counter, and would have been aboard in a minute. In the meantime, the Spaniards who were in the first boat were climbing up the side, and were repulsed by my men with great success. The breeze freshened, and Swinburne ran to the helm. I perceived the schooner was going fast through the water, and the second boat could hardly hold her course. I ran to where the boat-hook was fixed on the planeshear, and unhooked it; the boat fell astern, leaving two Spaniards clinging to the side, who were cut down, and they fell into the water. "Hurrah! all safe!" cried Swinburne; "and now to punish them."

The schooner was now darting along at the rate of five miles, with an increasing breeze. We stood in for two minutes, then tacked, and ran for the boats. Swinburne steered, and I continued standing in the bows, surrounded by the rest of the men. "Starboard a little, Swinburne."— "Starboard it is."

"Steady—steady: I see the first boat, she is close under our bows. Steady—port—port—port a little—port. Look out, my lads, and cut down all who climb up."

Crash went the schooner on to the boat, the men in her in vain endeavouring to escape us. For a second or two she appeared to right, until her further gunwale was borne down under the water; she turned up, and the schooner went over her, sending every soul in her to their account. One man clung on to a rope, and was towed for a few seconds, but a cutlass divided the rope at the gunwale, and with a faint shriek he disappeared. The other boat was close to us, and perceived what had been done. They remained with their oars poised, all ready to pull so as to evade the schooner. We steered for her, and the schooner was now running at the rate of seven miles an hour. When close under our bows, by very dexterously pulling short round with their starboard oars, we only struck her with our bow; and before she went down many of the Spaniards had gained the deck, or were clinging to the side of the vessel. They fought with desperation, but we were too strong for them. It was only those who had gained the deck which we had to contend with. The others clung for a time, and, unable to get up the sides, one by one dropped into the water and went astern. In a minute, those on deck were lying at our feet, and in a minute more they were tossed overboard after their companions; not, however, until one of them struck me through the calf of the leg with his knife as we were lifting him over the gunwale. I do not mean to say that the Spaniards were not justified in attempting to take the schooner; but still, as we had liberated them but a few hours before, we felt that it was unhandsome and treacherous on their part, and therefore showed them no quarter. There were two of my men wounded as well as myself, but not severely, which was fortunate, as we had no surgeon on board, and only about half a yard of a diachylum plaster in the vessel.

"Well out of that, sir," said Swinburne, as I limped aft. "By the Lord Harry! it might have been a *pretty go*."

Having shaped our course for Barbadoes, I dressed my leg and went down to sleep. This time I did not dream of Celeste, but fought the Spaniards over again, thought I was wounded, and awoke with the pain of my leg.

Chapter LI

Peter turned out of his command by his vessel turning bottom up—A cruise on a main-boom, with sharks *en attendant*—Self and crew, with several flying fish, taken on board a negro boat—Peter regenerates by putting on a new outward man.

We made Barbadoes without any further adventure, and were about ten miles off the bay, steering with a very light breeze, and I went down into the cabin, expecting to be at anchor before breakfast the next morning. It was just daylight, when I found myself thrown out of my bed-place on the deck, on the other side of the cabin, and heard the rushing of water. I sprang up, I knew the schooner was on her beam ends, and gained the deck. I was correct in my supposition: she had been upset by what is called a white squall, and in two minutes would be down. All the men were up on deck, some dressed, others, like myself, in their shirts. Swinburne was aft; he had an axe in his hand, cutting away the rigging of the main-boom. I saw what he was about; I seized another, and disengaged the jaw-rope and small gear about the mast. We had no other chance; our boat was under the water, being hoisted up on the side to leeward. All this, however, was but the work of two minutes; and I could not help observing by what trifles lives are lost or saved. Had the axe not been fortunately at the capstern, I should not have been able to cut the jaw-rope, Swinburne would not have had time, and the main-boom would have gone down with the schooner. Fortunately we had cleared it; the schooner filled, righted a little, and then sank, dragging us and the main-boom for a few seconds down in its vortex, and then we rose to the surface.

The squall still continued, but the water was smooth. It soon passed over, and again it was nearly calm. I counted the men clinging to the boom, and found that they were all there. Swinburne was next to me. He was holding with one hand, while with the other he felt in his pocket for a quid of tobacco, which he thrust into his cheek. "I wasn't on deck at the time, Mr Simple," said he, "or this wouldn't have happened. I had just been relieved, and I told Collins to look out sharp for squalls. I only mention it, that if you are saved, and I am not, you mayn't think I was neglectful of my duty. We arn't far from the land, but still we are more likely to fall in with a shark than a friend, I'm thinking."

These, indeed, had been my thoughts, but I had concealed them; but after Swinburne had mentioned the shark, I very often looked along the water for their fins, and down below to see if they were coming up to tear us to pieces. It was a dreadful feeling.

"It was not your fault, Swinburne, I am sure. I ought to have relieved you myself, but I kept the first watch, and was tired. We must put our trust in God; perhaps, we may yet be spared."

It was now almost calm, and the sun had mounted in the heavens: the scorching rays were intolerable upon our heads, for we had not the defence of hats. I felt my brain on fire, and was inclined to drop into the water, to screen myself from the intolerable heat. As the day advanced so did our sufferings increase. It was a dead calm, the sun perpendicular over us, actually burning that part of our bodies which rose clear of the water. I could have welcomed even a shark to relieve me of my torment; but I thought of Celeste, and I clung to life. Towards the afternoon I felt sick and dizzy; my resolution failed me; my vision was imperfect; but I was roused by Swinburne, who cried out, "A boat, by all that's gracious! Hang on a little longer, my men, and you are saved."

It was a boat full of negroes, who had come out to catch flying-fish. They had perceived the spar on the water, and hastened to secure the prize. They dragged us all in, gave us water, which appeared like nectar, and restored us to our fleeting senses. They made fast the boom, and towed it in-shore. We had not been ten minutes on our way, when Swinburne pointed to the fin of a large shark above the water. "Look there, Mr Simple." I shuddered, and made no answer; but I thanked God in my heart.

In two hours we were landed, but were too ill to walk. We were carried up to the hospital, bled, and put into cots. I had a brain fever, which lasted six or seven days, during which O'Brien never left my bedside. My head was shaved, all the skin came off my face like a mask, as well as off my back and shoulders. We were put into baths of brandy and water, and in three weeks were all recovered.

"That was but an unlucky schooner from beginning to end," observed O'Brien, after I had narrated the events of my cruise. "We had a bad beginning with her, and we had a bad ending. She's gone to the bottom, and the devil go with her; however, all's well that ends well, and, Peter, you're worth a dozen dead men yet; but you occasion me a great deal of trouble and anxiety, that's the truth of it, and I doubt if I shall ever rear you, after all."

I returned to my duty on board of the brig, which was now nearly ready for sea. One morning O'Brien came on board and said, "Peter, I've a piece of news for you. Our gunner is appointed to the *Araxes*, and the admiral has given me a gunner's warrant for old Swinburne. Send for him on deck."

Swinburne was summoned, and came rolling up the hatchway. "Swinburne," said O'Brien, "you have done your duty well, and you are now gunner of the *Rattlesnake*. Here is your warrant, and I've great pleasure in getting it for you."

Swinburne turned the quid in his cheek, and then replied, "May I be so bold as to ax, Captain O'Brien, whether I must wear one of them long tog, swallow-tailed coats—because, if so, I'd prefer being a quarter-master?"

"A gunner may wear a jacket, Swinburne, if he likes; when you go on shore you may bend the swallow-tail, if you please."

"Well, sir, then if that's the case, I'll take the warrant, because I know it will please the old woman."

So saying, Swinburne hitched up his trousers, and went down below. I may here observe that Swinburne kept his round jacket until our arrival in England, when the "old woman," his wife, who thought her dignity at stake, soon made him ship the swallow-tail; and, after it was once on, Swinburne took a fancy to it, and always wore it, except when he was at sea.

The same evening, as I was coming with O'Brien from the governor's house, where I had dined, we passed a building, lighted up. "What can that be?" observed O'Brien; "not a dignity ball—there is no music." Our curiosity induced us to enter, and we found it to be fitted up as a temporary chapel, filled with black and coloured people, who were ranged on the forms, and waiting for the preacher.

"It is a Methodist meeting," said I to O'Brien.

"Never mind," said he, "let us hear what is going on."

In a moment afterwards the pulpit was filled, not by a white man, as we had anticipated, but by a tall negro. He was dressed in black, and his hair, which it was impossible to comb down straight, was plaited into fifty little tails, well tied at the end of them, like you sometimes see the mane of a horse; this produced a somewhat more clerical appearance. His throat was open and collar laid back; the wristbands of his shirt very large and white, and he flourished a white cambric handkerchief.

"What a dandy he is!" whispered O'Brien.

I thought it almost too absurd when he said he would take the liberty to praise God in the 17th hymn, and beg all the company to join chorus. He then gave out the stanzas in the most strange pronunciation.

"Gentle Jesus, God um lub," &c.

When the hymn was finished, which was sung by the whole congregation, in the most delightful discord,—everyone chose his own key—he gave an extempore prayer, which was most unfortunately incomprehensible, and then commenced his discourse, which was on *Faith*. I shall omit the head and front of his offending, which would, perhaps, hardly be gratifying although ludicrous. He reminded me of a monkey imitating a man; but what amused me most was his finale, in which he told his audience that there could be no faith without charity. For a little while he descanted upon this generally, and at last became personal. His words were, as well as I can recollect, nearly as follows:—

"And now you see, my dear bredren, how unpossible to go to heaven, with all the faith in the world, without charity. Charity mean, give away. Suppose you no give—you no ab charity; suppose you no ab charity—you no ab faith; suppose you no ab faith—you all go to hell and be damned. Now den, let me see if you ab charity. Here, you see, I come to save all your soul from hell-fire; and hell-fire dam hot, I can tell you. Dere you all burn like coal, till you turn white powder, and den burn on till you come black again; and so you go on, burn, burn, sometime white, sometime black, for ebber and ebber. The debil never allow Sangoree to cool tongue. No, no cocoa-nut milk,—not a lilly drap of water; debil see you damned first. Suppose you ask, he poke um fire, and laugh. Well, den, ab you charity? No, you ab not. You, Quashee, how you dare look me in the face? You keep shop—you sell egg—you sell yam—you sell pepper hot—but when you give to me? Eh! nebber, so help me God. Suppose you no send—you no ab charity, and you go to hell. You black Sambo," continued he, pointing to a man in the corner, "ab very fine boat, go out all day, catch fly-fish, bring um back, fry um, and sell for money; but when you send to me? not one little fish ebber find way to my mouth. What I tell you 'bout Peter and 'postles—all fishermen; good men, give 'way to poor. Sambo, you no ab charity; and 'spose you no repent this week, and send one very fine fish in plantain leaf, you go to hell, and burn for ebber and ebber. Eh! so you will run away, Massa Johnson," cried he out to another, who was edging to the door; "but you no run away from hell-fire: when debil catch you, he hold dam tight. You know you kill sheep and goat ebery day. You send bell ring all 'bout town for people to come buy; but when you send to me? nebber, 'cept once, you gave me lilly bit of libber. That not do, Massa Johnson; you no ab charity; and suppose you no send me sheep's head to-morrow morning, dam you libber, that's all. I see many more, but I see um all very sorry, and dat they mean to sin no more, so dis time I let um off, and say noting about it, because I know plenty of plantain and banana (pointing to one) and oranges and shaddock (pointing to another), and salt fish (pointing to a fourth), and ginger-pop and spruce beer (pointing to a fifth), and a straw hat (pointing to a sixth), and eberything else, come to my house to-morrow. So I say no more 'bout it; I see you all very sorry—you only forget. You all ab charity, and all ab faith; so now, my dear bredren, we go down on our knees, and thank God for all this, and more especially that I save all your souls from going to the debil, who run about Barbadoes like one roaring lion, seeking what he may lay hold of, and cram into his dam fiery jaw."

"That will do, Peter," said O'Brien; "we have the cream of it, I think."

We left the house, and walked down to the boat. "Surely, O'Brien," said I, "this should not be permitted?"

"He's no worse than his neighbours," replied O'Brien, "and perhaps does less harm. I admire the rascal's ingenuity; he gave his flock what, in Ireland, we should call a pretty broad hint."

"Yes, there was no mistaking him: but is he a licensed preacher?"

"Very little licence in his preaching, I take it; no, I suppose he has had a *call*."

"A call!—what do you mean?"

"I mean that he wants to fill his belly. Hunger is a call of nature, Peter."

"He seems to want a good many things, if we were to judge by his catalogue; what a pity it is that these poor people are not better instructed."

"That they never will be, Peter, while there is what may be called free trade in religion."

"You speak like a Catholic, O'Brien."

"I am one," replied he. And here our conversation ended, for we were close to the boat, which was waiting for us on the beach.

The next day a man-of-war brig arrived from England, bringing letters for the squadron on the station. I had two from my sister Ellen which made me very uncomfortable. She stated that my father had seen my uncle, Lord Privilege, and had had high words with him; indeed, as far as she could ascertan of the facts, my father had struck my uncle, and had been turned out of the house by the servants; that he had returned in a state of great excitement, and was very ill ever since; that there was a great deal of talk in the neighbourhood on the subject, people generally highly blaming my father's conduct, thinking that he was deranged in his intellect—a supposition very much encouraged by my uncle. She again expressed her hopes of my speedy return. I had now been absent nearly three years, and she had been so uncomfortable that she felt as if it had been at least ten. O'Brien also received a letter from Father M'Grath, which I shall lay before the reader:—

"MY DEAR SON,—Long life, and all the blessings of all the saints be upon you now and for evermore! Amen. And may you live to be married, and may I dance at your wedding, and may you never want children, and may they grow up as handsome as their father and their mother (whoever she may hereafter be), and may you die of a good old age, and in the true faith, and be waked handsomely, as your own father was last Friday s'ennight, seeing as how he took it into his head to leave this world for a better. It was a very dacent funeral-procession, my dear Terence, and your father must have been delighted to see himself so well attinded. No man ever made a more handsome corpse, considering how old, and thin, and haggard he had grown of late, and how gray his hair had turned. He held the nosegay between his fingers, across his breast as natural as life, and reminded us all of the blessed saint, Pope Gregory, who was called to glory some hundred years before either you or I was born.

"Your mother's quite comfortable; and there she sits in her ould chair, rocking to and fro all day long, and never speaking a word to nobody, thinking about heaven, I dare to say; which is just what she ought to do, seeing that she stands a very pretty chance of going there in the course of a month or so. Divil a word has she ever said since your father's departure, but then she screamed and yelled enough to last for seven years at the least. She screamed away all her senses anyhow, for she has done nothing since but cough, cough, and fumble at her pater-nosters—a very blessed way to pass the remainder of her days, seeing that I expect her to drop every minute like an over-ripe sleepy pear. So don't think any more about her, my son, for without you are back in a jiffy, her body will be laid in consecrated ground, and her happy, blessed soul in purgatory. *Pax vobiscum.* Amen! amen!

"And now having disposed of your father and your mother so much to your satisfaction, I'll just tell you that Ella's mother died in the convent at Dieppe, but whether she kept her secret or not I do not know; but this I do know, that if she didn't relieve her soul by confession, she's damned to all eternity. Thanks be to God for all his mercies. Amen! Ella Flanagan is still alive, and, for a nun, is as well as can be expected. I find that she knows nothing at all about the matter of the exchanging the genders of the babbies—only that her mother was on oath to Father M'Dermot, who ought to be hanged, drawn, and quartered instead of those poor fellows whom the government called rebels, but who were no more rebels than Father M'Grath himself, who'll uphold the Pretender, as they call our true Catholic king, as long as there's life in his body or a drop of whiskey left in ould Ireland to drink his health wid.—

"Talking about Father M'Dermot puts me in mind that the bishop has not yet decided our little bit of a dispute, saying that he must take time to think about it. Now, considering that it's just three years since the row took place, the old gentleman must be a very slow thinker not to have found out by this time that I was in the right, and that Father M'Dermot, the baste, is not good enough to be hanged.

"Your two married sisters are steady and diligent young women, having each made three children since you last saw them. Fine boys, every mother's son of them, with elegant spacious features, and famous mouths for taking in whole potatoes. By the powers, but the offsets of the tree of the O'Briens begin to make a noise in the land, anyhow, as you would say if you only heard them roaring for their bit of suppers.

"And now, my dear son Terence, the real purport of this letter, which is just to put to your soul's conscience, as a dutiful son, whether you ought not to send me a small matter of money to save your poor father's soul from pain and anguish—for it's no joke that being in purgatory, I can tell you; and you wouldn't care how soon you were tripped out of it yourself. I only wish you had but your little toe in it, and then you'd burn with impatience to have it out again. But you're a dutiful son, so I'll say no more about it—a nod's as good as a wink to a blind horse.

"When your mother goes, which, with the blessing of God, will be in a very little while, seeing that she has only to follow her senses, which are gone already, I'll take upon myself to sell everything, as worldly goods and chattels are of no use to dead people; and I have no doubt but that, what with the furniture and the two cows, and the pigs, and the crops in the ground, there will be enough to save her soul from the flames, and bury her dacently into the bargain. However, as you are the heir-at-law, seeing that the property is all your own, I'll keep a debtor and creditor account of the whole; and should there be any over, I'll use it all out in masses, so as to send her up to heaven by express; and if there's not sufficient, she must remain where she is till you come back and make up the deficiency. In the meanwhile I am your loving father in the faith,

"URTAGH M'GRATH."

Chapter LII

Good sense in Swinburne—No man a hero to his valet de chambre, or a prophet in his own country—O'Brien takes a step by strategy—O'Brien parts with his friend, and Peter's star no longer in the ascendant.

O'Brien was sorry for the death of his father, but he could not feel as most people would have done, as his father had certainly never been a father to him. He was sent to sea to be got rid of, and ever since he had been there, had been the chief support of his family; his father was very fond of whiskey, and not very fond of exertion. He was too proud of the true Milesian blood in his veins to do anything to support himself, but not too proud to live upon his son's hard-earned gains. For his mother O'Brien felt very much; she had always been kind and affectionate, and was very fond of him. Sailors, however, are so estranged from their families when they have been long in their profession and so accustomed to vicissitudes, that no grief for the loss of a relation lasts very long, and in a week O'Brien had recovered his usual spirits, when a vessel brought us the intelligence that a French squadron had been seen off St Domingo. This put us all on the *qui vive*. O'Brien was sent for by the admiral, and ordered to hasten his brig for sea with all possible despatch, as he was to proceed with despatches to England forthwith. In three days we were reported ready, received our orders, and at eight o'clock in the evening made sail from Carlisle Bay. "Well, Mr Swinburne," said I, "how do you like your new situation?"

"Why, Mr Simple, I like it well enough; and it's not disagreeable to be an officer, and sit in your own cabin; but still I feel that I should get on better if I were in another ship. I've been hail-fellow well met with the ship's company so long, that I can't top the officer over them, and we can't get the duty done as smart as I could wish: and then at night I find it very lonely stuck up in my cabin like a parson's clerk, and nobody to talk to; for the other warrants are particular, and say that I'm only acting, and may not be confirmed, so they hold aloof. I don't much like being answerable for all that lot of gunpowder—it's queer stuff to handle."

"Very true, Swinburne; but still, if there were no responsibility, we should require no officers. You recollect that you are now provided for life, and will have half-pay."

"That's what made me bite, Mr Simple. I thought of the old woman, and how comfortable it would make her in her old age; and so, d'ye see, I sacrificed myself."

"How long have you been married, Swinburne?"

"Ever since Christmas '94. I wasn't going to be hooked carelessly, so I nibbled afore I took the bait. Had four years' trial of her first, and, finding that she had plenty of ballast, I sailed her as my own."

"How do you mean by plenty of ballast?"

"I don't mean, Mr Simple, a broad bow and square hulk. You know very well that if a vessel has not ballast, she's bottom up in no time. Now, what keeps a woman stiff under her canvas is her modesty."

"Very true; but it's a rare commodity on the beach."

"And why, Mr Simple? because liquor is more valued. Many a good man has found it to be his bane; and as for a woman, when once she takes to it, she's like a ship without a rudder, and goes right before the wind to the devil. Not that I think a man ought not to take a nor-wester or two, when he can get them. Rum was not given by God Almighty only to make the niggers dance, but to make all our hearts glad; neither do I see why a woman is to stand out neither; what's good for Jack can't hurt Poll; only there is a medium, as they say, in all things, and half-an-half is quite strong enough."

"I should think it was," replied I, laughing.

"But don't be letting me prevent you from keeping a look-out, Mr Simple.—You, Hoskins, you're half a point off the wind. Luff you may.— I think, Mr Simple, that Captain O'Brien didn't pick out the best man, when he made Tom Alsop a quarter-master in my place."

"Why, he is a very steady, good man, Swinburne."

"Yes, so he is; but he has natural defects, which shouldn't be overlooked. I doubt if he can see so far as the head of the mainsail."

"I was not aware of that."

"No, but I was. Alsop wants to sarve out his time for his pension, and when he has sarved, you see if, when the surgeons examine him, they don't invalid him, as blind as a bat. I should like to have him as gunner's mate, and that's just what he's fit for. But, Mr Simple, I think we shall have some bad weather. The moon looks greasy, and the stars want snuffing. You'll have two reefs in the topsails afore morning. There's five bells striking. Now I'll turn in; if I didn't keep half the first, and half the morning watch, I shouldn't sleep all the night. I miss my regular watch very much, Mr Simple—habit's everything —and I don't much fancy a standing bed-place, it's so large, and I feel so cold of my sides. Nothing like a hammock, after all. Good-night, Mr Simple."

Our orders were to proceed with all *possible* despatch; and O'Brien carried on day and night, generally remaining up himself till one or two o'clock in the morning. We had very favourable weather, and in a little more than a month we passed the Lizard. The wind being fair, we passed Plymouth, ran up Channel, and anchored at Spithead.

After calling upon the admiral, O'Brien set off for town with his despatches, and left me in command of the ship. In three days I received a letter from him, informing me that he had seen the First Lord, who had asked him a great many questions concerning the station he had quitted; that he had also complimented O'Brien on his services. "On that hint I spake," continued O'Brien; "I ventured to insinuate to his lordship, that I had hoped I had earned my promotion; and as there is nothing like *quartering on the enemy*, I observed that I had not applied to Lord Privilege, as I considered my services would have been sufficient, without any application on his part. His lordship returned a very gracious answer: said that my Lord Privilege was a great ally of his, and very friendly to the government; and inquired when I was going to see him. I replied, that I certainly should not pay my respects to his lordship at present, unless there was occasion for it, as I must take a more favourable opportunity. So I hope that good may come from the great lord's error, which, of course, I shall not correct, as I feel I deserve my promotion—and you know, Peter, if you can't gain it by *hook*, you must by *crook*." He then concluded his letter; but there was a postscript as follows:

"Wish me joy, my dear Peter. I have this moment received a letter from the private secretary, to say that I am *posted*, and appointed to the *Semiramis* frigate, about to set sail for the East Indies. She is all ready to start; and now I must try to get you with me, of which I have no doubt; as, although her officers have been long appointed there will be little difficulty of success, when I mention your relationship to Lord Privilege, and while they remain in error as to his taking an interest in my behalf." I rejoiced at O'Brien's good fortune. His promotion I had considered certain, as his services had entitled him to it; but the command of so fine a frigate must have been given upon the supposition that it would be agreeable to my uncle, who was not only a prime supporter, but a very useful member, of the Tory Government. I could not help laughing to myself, at the idea of O'Brien obtaining his wishes from the influence of a person who probably detested him as much as one man could detest another; and I impatiently waited for O'Brien's next letter, by which I hoped to find myself appointed to the *Semiramis*; but a sad *contretemps* took place.

O'Brien did not write; but came down two days afterwards, hastened on board the *Semiramis*, read his commission, and assumed the command before even he had seen me; he then sent his gig on board of the *Rattlesnake* to desire me to come to him directly. I did so, and we went down into the cabin of the frigate. "Peter," said he, "I was obliged to hasten down and read myself captain of this ship, as I am in fear that things are not going on well. I had called to pay my respects at the Admiralty, previous to joining, and was kicking my heels in the waiting-room, when who should walk up the passage, as if he were a captain on his own quarter-deck, but your uncle, Lord Privilege. His eye met mine—he recognised me immediately—and, if it did not flash fire, it did something very like it. He asked a few questions of one of the porters, and was giving his card, when my name was called for. I passed him, and up I went to the First Lord, thanked him for the frigate; and having received a great many compliments upon my exertions in the West India station, made my bow and retired. I had intended to have requested your appointment, but I knew that your name would bring up Lord Privilege's; and, moreover, your uncle's card was brought up and laid upon the table while I was sitting there. The First Lord, I presume, thought that his lordship was come to thank him for his kindness to me, which only made him more civil. I made my bow and went down, when I met the eye of Lord Privilege; who looked daggers at me as he walked up stairs—for, of course, he was admitted immediately after my audience was finished. Instead of waiting to hear the result of the explanation, I took a post-chaise, and have come down here as fast as four horses can bring me, and have read myself in—for, Peter, I feel sure, that if not on board, my commission will be cancelled; and I know that if once in command, as I am now, I can call for a court-martial, to clear my character if I am superseded. I know that the Admiralty *can* do anything, but still they will be cautious in departing from the rules of the service, to please even Lord Privilege. I looked up at the sky as soon as I left the Admiralty portico, and was glad to see that the weather was so thick, and the telegraph not at work, or I might have been too late. Now I'll go on shore, and report myself to the admiral, as having taken the command of the *Semiramis*."

O'Brien went on shore to report himself, was well received by the admiral, who informed him, that if he had any arrangements to make, he could not be too soon, as he should not be surprised if his sailing orders came down the next morning. This was very annoying, as I could not see how I should be able to join O'Brien's ship, even if I could effect an exchange, in so short a time. I therefore hastened on board of the *Semiramis*, and applied to the officers to know if any of them were willing to exchange into the *Rattlesnake*; but, although they did not much like going to the East Indies, they would not exchange into a brig, and I returned disappointed. The next morning, the admiral sent for O'Brien, and told him confidentially, for he was the same admiral who had received O'Brien when he had escaped from prison with me, and was very kind to him, that there was some *hitch* about his having the *Semiramis*, and that orders had come down to pay her off, all standing, and examine her bottom, if Captain O'Brien had not joined her. "Do you understand what this means?" said the admiral, who was anxious to know the reason.

O'Brien answered frankly, that Lord Privilege, by whose interest he had obtained his former command, was displeased with him; and that, as he saw him go up to the First Lord, he had no doubt but that his lordship had said something to his disadvantage, as he was a very vindictive man.

"Well," said the admiral, "it's lucky that you have taken the command, as they cannot well displace you, or send her into dock without a survey, and upon your representation."

And so it proved; the First Lord, when he found that O'Brien had joined, took no further steps, but allowed the frigate to proceed to her intended destination. But all chance of my sailing with him was done away, and now, for the first time, I had to part with O'Brien. I remained with him the whole time that I could be spared from my duties. O'Brien was very much annoyed, but there was no help. "Never mind, Peter," said he, "I've been thinking that perhaps it's all for the best. You will see more of the world, and be no longer in leading-strings. You are now a fine man grown up, big enough and ugly enough, as they say, to take care of yourself. We shall meet again; and if we don't, why then, God bless you, my boy, and don't forget O'Brien."

Three days afterwards, O'Brien's orders came down. I accompanied him on board; and it was not until the ship was under weigh, and running towards the Needles with a fair wind, that I shook hands with him, and shoved off. Parting with O'Brien was a heavy blow to me; but I little knew how much I was to suffer before I saw him again.

Chapter LIII

I am pleased with my new captain—Obtain leave to go home—Find my father afflicted with a very strange disease, and prove myself a very good doctor, although the disorder always breaks out in a fresh place.

The day after O'Brien had sailed for the East Indies, the dockyard men came on board to survey the brig, and she was found so defective as to be ordered into dock. I had received letters from my sister, who was overjoyed at the intelligence of my safe return, and the anticipation of seeing me. The accounts of my father were, however, very unsatisfactory. My sister wrote, that disappointment and anxiety had had such an effect upon him, that he was deranged in his intellects. Our new captain came down to join us. He was a very young man, and had never before commanded a ship. His character as lieutenant was well known, and not very satisfactory, being that of a harsh, unpleasant officer; but, as he had never been first lieutenant, it was impossible to say what he might prove when in command of a ship. Still we were a little anxious about it, and severely regretted the loss of O'Brien. He came on board the hulk to which the ship's company's had been turned over, and read his commission. He proved to be all affability, condescension, and good-nature. To me, he was particularly polite, stating that he should not interfere with me in carrying on the duty, as I must be so well acquainted with the ship's company. We thought that those who gave us the information must have been prejudiced or mistaken in his character. During the half hour that he remained on board, I stated, that now that the brig was in dock, I should like very much to have an opportunity of seeing my friends, if he would sanction my asking for leave. To this he cheerfully consented, adding, that he would extend it upon his own responsibility. My letter to the Admiralty was therefore forwarded through him, and was answered in the affirmative. The day afterwards, I set off by the coach, and once more embraced my dear sister.

After the first congratulations were over, I inquired about my father; she replied, that he was so wild that nobody could manage him. That he was melancholy and irritable at the same time, and was certainly deranged, fancying himself to be made of various substances, or to be in a certain trade or capacity. That he generally remained in this way four or five days, when he went to bed, and slept for twenty-four hours, or more, and awoke with some new strange imagination in his head. His language was violent, but that, in other respects, he seemed to be more afraid of other people, than inclined to be mischievous, and that every day he was getting more strange and ridiculous. He had now just risen from one of his long naps, and was in his study; that before he had fallen asleep he had fancied himself to be a carpenter, and had sawed and chopped up several articles of furniture in the house.

I quitted my sister to see my father, whom I found in his easy-chair. I was much shocked at his appearance. He was thin and haggard, his eye was wild, and he remained with his mouth constantly open. A sick-nurse, who had been hired by my sister, was standing by him.

"Pish, pish, pish, pish!" cried my father; "what can you, a stupid old woman, know about my inside? I tell you the gas is generating fast, and even now I can hardly keep on my chair. I'm lifting—lifting now; and if you don't tie me down with cords, I shall go up like a balloon."

"Indeed, sir," replied the woman, "it's only the wind in your stomach.
You'll break it off directly."

"It's inflammable gas, you old Hecate!—I know it is. Tell me, will you get a cord, or will you not? Hah! who's that—Peter? Why you've dropped from the clouds, just in time to see me mount up to them."

"I hope you feel yourself better, sir," said I.

"I feel myself a great deal lighter every minute. Get a cord, Peter, and tie me to the leg of the table."

I tried to persuade him that he was under a mistake; but it was useless. He became excessively violent, and said I wished him in heaven. As I had heard that it was better to humour people afflicted with hypochondriacism, which was evidently the disease under which my father laboured, I tried that method. "It appears to me, sir," said I, "that if we could remove the gas every ten minutes, it would be a good plan."

"Yes—but how?" replied he, shaking his head mournfully.

"Why, with a syringe, sir," said I; "which will, if empty, of course draw out the gas, when inserted into your mouth."

"My dear Peter, you have saved my life: be quick, though, or I shall go up, right through the ceiling."

Fortunately, there was an instrument of that description in the house. I applied it to his mouth, drew up the piston, and then ejected the air, and re-applied it. In two minutes he pronounced himself better, and I left the old nurse hard at work, and my father very considerably pacified. I returned to my sister, to whom I recounted what had passed; but it was no source of mirth to us, although, had it happened to an indifferent person, I might have been amused. The idea of leaving her, as I must soon do—having only a fortnight's leave—to be worried by my father's unfortunate malady, was very distressing. But we entered into a long conversation, in which I recounted the adventures that had taken place since I had left her, and for the time forgot our source of annoyance and regret. For three days my father insisted upon the old woman pumping the gas out of his body; after that, he again fell into one of his sleeps, which lasted nearly thirty hours.

When he arose, I went again to see him. It was eight o'clock in the evening, and I entered with a candle. "Take it away—quick, take it away; put it out carefully."

"Why, what's the matter, sir?"

"Don't come near me, if you love me; don't come near me. Put it out, I say—put it out."

I obeyed his orders, and then asked him the reason. "Reason!" said he, now that we were in the dark; "can't you see?"

"No, father; I can see nothing in the dark."

"Well, then, Peter, I'm a magazine, full of gunpowder; the least spark in the world, and I am blown up. Consider the danger. You surely would not be the destruction of your father, Peter?" and the poor old gentleman burst into tears, and wept like a child.

I knew that it was in vain to reason with him. "My dear father," said I, "on board ship, when there is any danger of this kind, we always *float* the magazine. Now, if you were to drink a good deal of water, the powder would be spoiled, and there would be no danger." My father was satisfied with my proposal, and drank a tumbler of water every half-hour, which the old nurse was obliged to supply as fast as he called for it; and this satisfied him for three or four days, and I was again left to the company of my dear Ellen, when my father again fell into his stupor, and we wondered what would be his next fancy. I was hastily summoned by the nurse, and found my poor father lying in bed, and breathing in a very strange manner. "What is the matter, my dear sir?" inquired I.

"Why don't you see what is the matter? How is a poor little infant, just born, to live, unless its mother is near to suckle it, and take care of it?"

"Indeed, sir, do you mean to say that you are just born?"

"To be sure I do. I'm dying for the breast."

This was almost too absurd; but I gravely observed, "That it was all very true, but unfortunately his mother had died in childbirth, and the only remedy was to bring him up by hand."

He agreed with me. I desired the nurse to make some gruel with brandy, and feed him; which she did, and he took the gruel just as if he were a baby. I was about to wish him goodnight, when he beckoned to me, and said, "Peter, she hasn't changed my napkin." This was too much, and I could not help laughing. I told the nurse what he said, and she replied, "Lord bless you, sir, what matter? if the old gentleman takes a fancy, why not indulge him? I'll fetch the kitchen table-cloth." This fit lasted about six days; for he went to sleep, because a baby always slept much: and I was in hopes it would last much longer: but he again went off into his lethargic fit, and, after a long sleep, awoke with a new fancy. My time had nearly expired, and I had written to my new captain, requesting an extension of leave, but I received an answer stating that it could not be granted, and requesting me to join the brig immediately. I was rather surprised at this, but of course was compelled to obey; and, embracing my dear sister once more, set off for Portsmouth. I advised her to humour my father, and this advice she followed; but his fancies were such, occasionally, as would have puzzled the most inventive genius to combat, or to find the remedy which he might acknowledge to be requisite. His health became certainly worse and worse, and his constitution was evidently destroyed by a slow, undermining, bodily and mental fever. The situation of my poor sister was very distressing; and I quitted her with melancholy forebodings.

I ought here to observe that I received all my prize-money, amounting to £1560, a large sum for a lieutenant. I put it into the funds, and gave a power of attorney to Ellen, requesting her to use it as her own. We consulted as to what she should do if my father should die, and agreed that all his debts, which we knew to amount to three or four hundred pounds, should be paid, and that she should manage how she could upon what was left of my father's property, and the interest of my prize-money.

Chapter LIV

We receive our sailing orders, and orders of every description—A quarter-deck conversation—Listeners never hear any good of themselves.

When I arrived at Portsmouth, I reported myself to the captain, who lived at the hotel. I was ushered into his room to wait for him, as he was dressing to dine with the admiral. My eyes naturally turned to what lay on the table, merely from the feeling which one has to pass away the time, not from curiosity; and I was much surprised to see a pile of letters, the uppermost of which was franked by Lord Privilege. This, however, might be merely accidental; but my curiosity was excited, and I lifted up the letter, and found that the second, the third, and indeed at least ten of these were franked by my uncle. I could not imagine how there could be any intimacy between him and my uncle, and was reflecting upon it when Captain Hawkins, for that was his name, entered the room. He was very kind and civil, apologized for not being able to extend my leave, which, he said, was because he had consulted the admiral, who would not sanction the absence of the first lieutenant, and had very peremptorily desired he would recall me immediately. I was satisfied: he shook my hand, and we parted. On my arrival on board the hulk, for the brig was still in dock, I was warmly received by my messmates. They told me that the captain had, generally speaking, been very civil, but that, occasionally, the marks of the cloven foot appeared.

"Webster," said I, to the second lieutenant, "do you know anything about his family or connections?"

"It is a question I have asked of those who have sailed with him, and they all say that he never speaks of his own family, but very often boasts of his intimacy with the nobility. Some say that he is a *bye-blow* of some great man."

I reflected very much upon this, and connecting it with the numerous franks of Lord Privilege, which I saw on the table, had my misgivings; but then I knew that I could do my duty, and had no reason to fear any man. I resolved, in my own mind, to be very correct, and put it out of the power of any one to lay hold of me, and then dismissed the subject. The brig was repaired and out of dock, and for some days I was very busy getting her ready for sea. I never quitted her; in fact, I had no wish. I never had any taste for bad company and midnight orgies, and I had no acquaintance with the respectable portion of the inhabitants of Portsmouth. At last the ship's company were removed into the brig: we went out of harbour, and anchored at Spithead.

Captain Hawkins came on board and gave me an order-book, saying, "Mr Simple, I have a great objection to written orders, as I consider that the articles of war are quite sufficient to regulate any ship. Still, a captain is in a very responsible situation, and if any accident occurs he is held amenable. I therefore have framed a few orders of my own for the interior discipline of the vessel, which may probably save me harmless, in case of being *hauled over the coals*; but not with any wish that they should interfere with the comforts of the officers, only to guard against any mischance, of which the *onus* may fall upon myself."

I received the order-book, and the captain went ashore. When I went down into the gun-room, to look through it, I at once perceived that if rigidly conformed to, every officer in the ship would be rendered uncomfortable; and if not conformed to, I should be the party that was answerable. I showed it to Webster, who agreed with me, and gave it as his opinion that the captain's good nature and amiability were all a blind, and that he was intending to lay hold of us as soon as it was in his power. I therefore called all the officers together, and told them my opinion. Webster supported me, and it was unanimously agreed that the orders should be obeyed, although not without remonstrance. The major part of the orders, however, only referred to the time that the brig was in harbour; and, as we were about to proceed to sea, it was hardly worth while saying anything at present. The orders for the sailing of the brig came down, and by the same post I received a letter from my sister Ellen, stating that they had heard from Captain Fielding, who had immediately written to Bombay, where the regiment was stationed, and had received an answer, informing him that there was no married man in the regiment of the name of Sullivan, and no woman who had followed that regiment of that name. This at once put an end to all our researches after the wet-nurse, who had been confined in my uncle's house. Where she had been sent, it was of course impossible to say; but I gave up all chance of discovering my uncle's treachery; and, as I thought of Celeste, sighed at the little hope I had of ever being united to her. I wrote a long letter to O'Brien, and the next day we sailed for our station in the North Sea.

The captain added a night order-book to the other, and sent it up every evening, to be returned in the morning, with the signature of every officer of the night watches. He also required all our signatures to his general order-book, that we might not say we had not read them. I had the first watch, when Swinburne came up to me. "Well, Mr Simple, I do not think we have made much by our exchange of captains; and I have a shrewd suspicion we shall have squalls ere long."

"We must not judge too hastily, Swinburne," replied I.

"No, no—I don't say that we should; but still, one must go a little by looks in the world, and I'm sure his looks wouldn't help him much. He's just like a winter's day, short and dirty; and he walks the deck as if planks were not good enough for his feet. Mr Williams says, he looks as if he were 'big with the fate of Cato and of Rome:' what that means, I don't know—some joke, I suppose, for the youngsters are always joking. Were you ever up the Baltic, Mr Simple? Now I think of it, I know you never were. I've seen some tight work up there with the gun-boats; and so we should now with Captain O'Brien; but as for this little man, I've an idea 'twill be more talk than work."

"You appear to have taken a great dislike to the captain, Swinburne. I do not know whether, as first lieutenant, I ought to listen to you."

"It's because you're first lieutenant that I tell it you, Mr Simple. I never was mistaken, in the main, of an officer's character, when I could look him in the face, and hear him talk for half an hour; and I came up on purpose to put you on your guard: for I feel convinced, that towards you he means mischief. What does he mean by having the greasy-faced serjeant of marines in his cabin for half an hour every morning? His reports as master of arms ought to come through you, as first lieutenant; but he means him as a spy upon all, and upon you in particular. The fellow has begun to give himself airs already, and speaks to the young gentlemen as if they were beneath him. I thought you might not know it, Mr Simple, so I thought it right to tell you."

"I am much obliged to you, Swinburne, for your good wishes; but I can do my duty, and why should I fear anything?"

"A man may do his duty, Mr Simple; but if a captain is determined to ruin him, he has the power. I have been longer in the service than you have, and have been wide awake: only be careful of one thing, Mr Simple; I beg your pardon for being so free, but in no case lose your temper."

"No fear of that, Swinburne," replied I.

"It's very easy to say 'no fear of that,' Mr Simple; but recollect, you have not yet had your temper tried as some officers have. You have always been treated like a gentleman; but should you find yourself treated otherwise, you have too good blood in your veins not to speak—I am sure of that. I've seen officers insulted and irritated, till no angel could put up with the treatment—and then for an unguarded word, which they would have been *swabs* not to have made use of, sent out of the service to the devil."

"But you forget, Swinburne, that the articles of war are made for the captain as well as for everybody else in the ship."

"I know that; but still, at court-martials captains make a great distinction between what a superior says to an inferior, and what an inferior says to a superior."

"True," replied I, quoting Shakespeare:

"'That's in the captain but a choleric word, Which in the soldier is
rank blasphemy.'"

"Exactly my meaning—I rather think," said Swinburne, "if a captain calls you no gentleman, you mus'n't say the same to him."

"Certainly not, but I can demand a court-martial."

"Yes; and it will be granted: but what do you gain by that? It's like beating against a heavy gale and a lee tide—thousand to one if you fetch your port; and if you do, your vessel is strained to pieces, sails worn as thin as a newspaper, and rigging chafed half through, wanting fresh serving: no orders for a re-fit, and laid up in ordinary for the rest of your life. No, no, Mr Simple, the best plan is to grin and bear it, and keep a sharp look-out; for depend upon it, Mr Simple, in the best ship's company in the world, a spy captain will always find spy followers."

"Do you refer that observation to me, Mr Swinburne?" said a voice from under the bulwark. I started round, and found the captain, who had crept upon deck, unperceived by us, during our conversation. Swinburne made no reply; but touched his hat and walked over to leeward. "I presume, Mr Simple," said the captain, turning to me, "that you consider yourself justified in finding fault, and abusing your captain, to an inferior officer, on His Majesty's quarter-deck."

"If you heard the previous conversation, sir," replied I, "you must be aware that we were speaking generally about court-martials. I do not imagine that I have been guilty of any impropriety in conversing with an officer upon points connected with the service."

"You mean then to assert, sir, that the gunner did not refer to me when he said the words, 'spy captain.'"

"I acknowledge, sir, that as you were listening unperceived, the term might appear to refer to you; but the gunner had no idea, at the time, that you were listening. His observation was, that a spy captain would always find spy followers. This I take to be a general observation; and I am sorry that you think otherwise."

"Very well, Mr Simple," said Captain Hawkins—and he walked down the companion ladder into his cabin.

"Now a'n't it odd, Mr Simple, that I should come up with the intention of being of service to you, and yet get you into such a scrape? However, perhaps it is all for the best; open war is preferable to watching in the dark, and stabbing in the back. He never meant to have shown his colours; but I hit him so hard, that he forgot himself."

"I suspect that to be the case, Swinburne; but I think that you had better not talk any more with me to-night."

"Wish I hadn't talked quite so much, as things have turned out," replied
Swinburne. "Good-night, sir."

I reflected upon what had passed, and felt convinced that Swinburne was right in saying that it was better this had occurred than otherwise. I now knew the ground which I stood upon; and forewarned was being forearmed.

Chapter LV

We encounter a Dutch brig of war—Captain Hawkins very contemplative near the capstan—Hard knocks, and no thanks for it—Who's afraid?—Men will talk—The brig goes about on the wrong tack.

At daylight the next morning we were off the Texel, and could see the low sand-hills; but we had scarcely made them out, when the fog in the offing cleared up, and we made a strange vessel. The hands were turned up, and all sail made in chase. We made her out to be a brig of war; and as she altered her course considerably, we had an idea that she was an enemy. We made the private signal, which was unanswered, and we cleared for action; the brig making all sail on the starboard tack, and we following her—she bearing about two miles on our weather bow. The breeze was not steady; at one time the brig was staggering under her top-gallant sails, while we had our royals set; at another we would have hands by the top-gallant sheets and topsail halyards, while she expanded every stitch of canvas. On the whole, however, in an hour we had neared about half a mile. Our men were all at their quarters, happy to be so soon at their old work. Their jackets and hats were thrown off, a bandana handkerchief tied round their heads, and another, or else their black silk handkerchiefs, tied round their waists. Every gun was ready, everything was in its place, and every soul, I was going to say, was anxious for the set-to; but I rather think I must not include the captain, who from the commencement, showed no signs of pleasure, and anything but presence of mind. When we first chased the vessel, it was reported that it was a merchantman; and it was not until we had broad daylight, that we discovered her to be a man-of-war. There was one thing to be said in his favour—he had never been in action in his life.

The breeze now fell light, and we were both with our sails set, when a thick fog obscured her from our sight. The fog rolled on till we met it, and then we could not see ten yards from the brig. This was a source of great mortification, as we had every chance of losing her. Fortunately, the wind was settling down fast into a calm, and about twelve o'clock the sails flapped against the mast. I reported twelve o'clock, and asked the captain whether we should pipe to dinner.

"Not yet," replied he; "we will put her head about."

"Go about, sir?" replied I, with surprise.

"Yes;" said he, "I'm convinced that the chase is on the other tack at this moment; and if we do not, we shall lose her."

"If she goes about, sir," said I, "she must get among the sands, and we shall be sure of her."

"Sir," replied he, "when I ask your advice, you will be pleased to give it. I command this vessel."

I touched my hat, and turned the hands up about ship, convinced that the captain wished to avoid the action, as the only chance of escape for the brig was her keeping her wind in the tack she was on. "'Bout ship—'bout ship!" cried the men. "What the hell are we going about for?" inquired they of one another, as they came up the ladder. "Silence there, fore and aft!" cried I. "Captain Hawkins, I do not think we can get her round, unless we wear—the wind is very light."

"Then wear ship, Mr Simple."

There are times when grumbling and discontent among the seamen is so participated by the officers, although they do not show it, that the expressions made use of are passed unheeded. Such was the case at present. The officers looked at each other, and said nothing; but the men were unguarded in their expressions. The brig wore gradually round; and when the men were bracing up the yards, sharp on the other tack, instead of the "Hurrah!" and "Down with the mark!" they fell back with a groan.

"Brace up those yards in silence, there," said I to the men.

The ropes were coiled down, and we piped to dinner. The captain, who continued on deck, could not fail to hear the discontented expressions which occasionally were made use of on the lower deck. He made no observation, but occasionally looked over the side, to see whether the brig went through the water. This she did slowly for about ten minutes, when it fell a perfect calm—so that, to use a common sea phrase, he gained little by his motion. About half-past one, a slight breeze from the opposite quarter sprung up—we turned round to it—it increased—the fog blew away, and, in a quarter of an hour, the chase was again visible, now upon our lee beam. The men gave three cheers.

"Silence there, fore and aft," cried the captain, angrily. "Mr Simple, is this the way that the ship's company have been disciplined under their late commander, to halloo and bawl whenever they think proper?"

I was irritated at any reflection upon O'Brien, and I replied, "Yes, sir; they have been always accustomed to express their joy at the prospect of engaging the enemy."

"Very well, Mr Simple," replied he.

"How are we to shift her head?" inquired the master, touching his hat: "for the chase?"

"Of course," replied the captain, who then descended into his cabin.

"Come, my lads," said Swinburne, as soon as the captain was below, "I have been going round, and I find that your *pets* are all in good fighting order. I promise ye, you sha'n't wait for powder. They'll find that the *Rattlesnake* can bite devilish hard yet, I expect."—"Aye, and without its *head*, too," replied one of the men, who was the Joe Miller of the brig. The chase, perceiving that she could not escape—for we were coming up with her, hand over hand, now shortened sail for action, hoisting Dutch colours. Captain Hawkins again made his appearance on the quarter-deck, when we were within half a mile of her.

"Are we to run alongside of her or how?" inquired I.

"Mr Simple, I command her," replied he, "and want no interference whatever."

"Very well, sir," replied I, and I walked to the gangway.

"Mr Thompson," cried the captain, who appeared to have screwed up his courage to the right pitch, and had now taken his position for a moment on one of the carronades; "you will lay the brig right—"

Bang, bang—whiz, whiz—bang—whiz, came three shots from the enemy, cleaving the air between our masts. The captain jumped down from the carronade, and hastened to the capstern, without finishing his sentence. "Shall we fire when we are ready, sir?" said I; for I perceived that he was not capable of giving correct orders.

"Yes—yes, to be sure," replied he, remaining where he was.

"Thompson," said I to the master, "I think we can manage, in our present commanding position, to get foul of him, so as to knock away his jib-boom and fore topmast, and then she can't escape. We have good way on her."

"I'll manage it, Simple, or my name's not Thompson," replied the master, jumping into the quarter-boat, conning the vessel in that exposed situation, as we received the enemy's fire.

"Look out, my lads, and pour it into her now, just as you please," said I to the men.

The seamen were, however, too well disciplined to take immediate advantage of my permission; they waited until we passed her, and just as the master put up his helm, so as to catch her jib-boom between our masts, the whole broadside was poured into his bow and chess-tree. Her jib-boom and fore-topgallant went down, and she had so much way through the water, that we tore clear from her, and rounding to the wind shot a-head. The enemy, although in confusion from the effects of our broadside, put up his helm to rake us; we perceived his manoeuvre, and did the same, and then, squaring our sails, we ran with him before the wind, engaging broadside to broadside. This continued about half an hour, and we soon found that we had no fool to play with. The brig was well fought, and her guns well directed. We had several men taken down below, and I thought it would be better to engage her even closer. There was about a cable's length between both vessels, as we ran before the wind, at about six miles an hour, with a slight rolling motion.

"Thompson," said I, "let us see if we cannot beat them from their guns. Let's port the helm and close her, till we can shy a biscuit on board."

"Just my opinion, Simple; we'll see if they won't make another sort of running fight of it."

In a few minutes we were so close on board of her, that the men who loaded the guns could touch each other with their rammers and sponges. The men cheered; it was gallantly returned by the enemy, and havoc was now commenced by the musketry on both sides. The French captain, who appeared as brave a fellow as ever stepped, stood for some minutes on the hammocks; I was also holding on by the swifter of the main rigging, when he took off his hat and politely saluted me. I returned the compliment; but the fire became too hot, and I wished to get under the shelter of the bulwark. Still I would not go down first, and the French captain appeared determined not to be the first either to quit the post of honour. At last one of our marines hit him in the right arm: he clapped his hand to the part, as if to point it out to me, nodded, and was assisted down from the hammocks. I immediately quitted my post, for I thought it foolish to stand as a mark for forty or fifty soldiers. I had already received a bullet through the small of my leg. But the effects of such close fire now became apparent: our guns were only half manned, our sides terribly cut up, and our sails and rigging in tatters. The enemy was even worse off, and two broadsides more brought her mainmast by the board. Our men cheered, and threw in another broadside. The enemy dropped astern; we rounded to rake her; she also attempted to round to, but could not until she had cleared away her wreck, and taken in her foresail, and lowered her topsail. She then continued the action with as much spirit as ever.

"He's a fine fellow, by God!" exclaimed Thompson; "I never saw a man fight his ship better: but we have him. Webster's down, poor fellow!"

"I'm sorry for it," replied I; "but I'm afraid that there are many poor fellows who have lost the number of their mess. I think it useless throwing away the advantage which we now have. He can't escape, and he'll fight this way for ever. We had better run a-head, repair damages, and then he must surrender, in his crippled state, when we attack him again."

"I agree with you," said Thompson; "the only point is, that it will soon be dark."

"I'll not lose sight of him, and he cannot get away. If he puts before the wind, then we will be at him again."

We gave him the loaded guns as we forged a-head, and when we were about half a mile from him, hove-to to repair damages.

The reader may now ask, "But where was the captain all this time?" My answer is, that he was at the capstern, where he stood in silence, not once interfering during the whole action, which was fought by Thompson, the master, and myself. How he looked, or how he behaved in other points during the engagement, I cannot pretend to say, for I had no time to observe him. Even now I was busy knotting the rigging, rousing up new sails to bend, and getting everything in order, and I should not have observed him, had he not come up to me; for as soon as we had ceased firing he appeared to recover himself. He did not, however, first address me; he commenced speaking to the men.

"Come, be smart, my lads; send a hand here to swab up the blood. Here, youngster, run down to the surgeon, and let him know that I wish a report of the killed and wounded."

By degrees he talked more, and at last came up to me, "This has been rather smartish, Mr Simple."

"Very smart indeed, sir," replied I, and then turned away to give directions. "Maintop there, send down the hauling line on the starboard side."

"Ay, ay, sir."

"Now then, my lads, clap on, and run it up at once."

"Maintop, there," hailed the captain, "be a little smarter, or by G——d, I'll call you down for something." This did not come with a good grace from one who had done nothing, to those who were working with all their energy. "Mr Simple," said the captain, "I wish you would carry on duty with less noise."

"At all events, he set us that example during the action," muttered the Joe Miller; and the other men laughed heartily at the implication. In two hours, during which we had carefully watched the enemy, who still lay where we left him, we were again ready for action.

"Shall I give the men their grog now, sir?" said I to the captain; "they must want it."

"No, no," replied the captain; "no, no, Mr Simple, I don't like what you call *Dutch* courage."

"I don't think he much does; and this fellow has shown plenty of it," said the Joe Miller, softly; and the men about him laughed heartily.

"I think, sir," observed I, "that it is an injustice to this fine ship's company to hint at their requiring Dutch courage." (Dutch courage is a term for courage screwed up by drinking freely.) "And I most respectfully beg leave to observe, that the men have not had their afternoon's allowance; and, after the fatigues they have undergone, really require it."

"I command this ship, sir," replied he.

"Certainly, sir, I am aware of it," rejoined I. "She is now all ready for action again, and I wait your orders. The enemy is two miles on the lee quarter."

The surgeon here came up with his report.

"Good heavens!" said the captain, "forty-seven men killed and wounded, Mr Webster dangerously. Why, the brig is crippled. We can do no more— positively, we can do no more."

"*We can take that brig, anyhow*," cried one of the seamen from a dozen of the men who were to leeward, expecting orders to renew the attack.

"What man was that?" cried the captain.

No one answered.

"By G——d! this ship is in a state of mutiny, Mr Simple."

"Will *soon* be, I think," said a voice from the crowd, which I knew very well; but the captain, having been but a short time with us, did not know it.

"Do you hear that, Mr Simple?" cried the captain.

"I regret to say that I did hear it, sir; I little thought that ever such an expression would have been made use of on board of the *Rattlesnake*." Then, fearing he would ask me the man's name, and to pretend not to have recognised it, I said, "Who was that who made use of that expression?" But no one answered; and it was so dark, that it was impossible to distinguish the men.

"After such mutinous expressions," observed the captain, "I certainly will not risk His Majesty's brig under my command, as I should have wished to have done, even in her crippled state, by again engaging the enemy. I can only regret that the officers appear as insolent as the men."

"Perhaps, Captain Hawkins, you will state in what, and when, I have proved myself insolent. I cannot accuse myself."

"I hope the expression was not applied to me, sir," said Thompson, the master, touching his hat.

"Silence, gentlemen, if you please. Mr Simple, wear round the ship."

Whether the captain intended to attack the enemy or not, we could not tell, but we were soon undeceived; for when we were round, he ordered her to be kept away until the Dutch brig was on our lee quarter: then ordering the master to shape his course for Yarmouth, he went down into the cabin, and sent up word that I might pipe to supper and serve out the spirits.

The rage and indignation of the men could not be withheld. After they went down to supper they gave three heavy groans in concert; indeed, during the whole of that night, the officers who kept the watches had great difficulty in keeping the men from venting their feeling, in what might be almost termed justifiable mutiny. As for myself, I could hardly control my vexation. The brig was our certain prize; and this was proved, for the next day she hauled down her colours immediately to a much smaller man-of-war, which fell in with her, still lying in the same crippled state; the captain and first lieutenant killed, and nearly two-thirds of her ship's company either killed or wounded. Had we attacked her, she would have hauled down her colours immediately, for it was our last broadside which had killed the captain. As first lieutenant, I should have received my promotion, which was now lost. I cried for vexation when I thought of it as I lay in bed. That his conduct was severely commented upon by the officers in the gun-room, as well as by the whole ship's company, I hardly need say. Thompson was for bringing him to a court-martial, which I would most gladly have done, if it only were to get rid of him; but I had a long conversation with old Swinburne on the subject, and he proved to me that I had better not attempt it. "For, d'ye see, Mr Simple, you have no proof. He did not run down below; he stood his ground on deck, although he did nothing. You can't *prove* cowardice, then, although there can be no great doubt of it. Again, with regard to his not renewing the attack, why, is not a captain at liberty to decide what is the best for His Majesty's service? And if he thought, in the crippled state of the brig, so close to the enemy's coast, that it wasn't advisable, why, it could only be brought in as an error in judgment. Then there's another thing which must be remembered, Mr Simple, which is, that no captains sitting on a court-martial will, if it be possible to extricate him, ever prove *cowardice* against a brother captain, because they feel that it's a disgrace to the whole cloth."

Swinburne's advice was good, and I gave up all thoughts of proceeding; still it appeared to me, that the captain was very much afraid that I would, he was so extremely amiable and polite during our run home. He said, that he had watched how well I had behaved in the action, and would not fail to notice it. This was something, but he did not keep his word: for his despatch was published before we quitted the roadstead, and not the name of one officer mentioned, only generally saying, that they conducted themselves to his satisfaction. He called the enemy a corvette, not specifying whether she was a brig or ship corvette; and the whole was written in such a bombastic style, that any one would have imagined that he had fought a vessel of superior force. He stated, at the end, that as soon as he repaired damages, he wore round, but that the enemy declined further action. So she did—certainly—for the best of all possible reasons, that she was too disabled to come down to us. All this might have been contested; but the enormous list of killed and wounded proved that we had had a hard fight, and the capture of the brig afterwards, that we had really overpowered her. So that, on the whole, Captain Hawkins gained a great deal of credit with some; although whispers were afloat which came to the ears of the Admiralty, and prevented him from being posted—the more so, as he had the modesty not to apply for it.

Chapter LVI

Consequences of the action—A ship without a fighting captain is like a thing without a head—So do the sailors think—A mutiny, and the loss of our famous ship's company.

During our stay at Yarmouth, we were not allowed to put our foot on shore, upon the plea that we must repair damages, and proceed immediately to our station; but the real fact was, that Captain Hawkins was very anxious that we should not be able to talk about the action. Finding no charges preferred against him, he re-commenced his system of annoyance. His apartments had windows which looked out upon where the brig lay at anchor, and he constantly watched all our motions with his spy-glass, noting down if I did not hoist up boats, &c., exactly at the hour prescribed in his book of orders, so as to gather a list of charges against me if he could. This we did not find out until afterwards.

I mentioned before, that when Swinburne joined us at Plymouth, he had recommended a figure-head being put on the brig. This had been done at O'Brien's expense—not in the cheap way recommended by Swinburne, but in a very handsome manner. It was a large snake coiled up in folds, with its head darting out in a menacing attitude, and the tail, with its rattle appeared below. The whole was gilded, and had a very good effect; but after the dock-yard men had completed the repairs, and the brig was painted, one night the head of the rattlesnake disappeared. It had been sawed off by some malicious and evil disposed persons, and no traces of it were to be found. I was obliged to report this to the captain, who was very indignant, and offered twenty pounds for the discovery of the offender; but had he offered twenty thousand he never would have found out the delinquent. It was, however, never forgotten; for he understood what was implied by these manoeuvres. A new head was carved, but disappeared the night after it was fixed on.

The rage of the captain was without bounds: he turned the hands up, and declared that if the offender was not given up, he would flog every hand on board. He gave the ship's company ten minutes, and then prepared to execute his threat. "Mr Paul, turn the hands up for punishment," said the captain, in a rage, and descended to his cabin for the articles of war. When he was down below, the officers talked over the matter. To flog every man for the crime of one was the height of injustice, but it was not for us to oppose him; still the ship's company must have seen, in our countenances, that we shared their feelings. The men were talking with each other in groups, until they all appeared to have communicated their ideas on the subject. The carpenters, who had been slowly bringing aft the gratings, left off the job; the boatswain's mates, who had came aft, rolled the tails of their cats round the red handles; and every man walked down below. No one was left on the quarter-deck but the marines under arms, and the officers. Perceiving this, I desired Mr Paul, the boatswain, to send the men up to rig the gratings, and the quartermasters with their seizings. He came up, and said that he had called them, but that they did not answer. Perceiving that the ship's company would break out into open mutiny, if the captain persisted in his intention, I went down into the cabin, and told the captain the state of things, and wished for his orders or presence on deck.

The captain, whose wrath appeared incapable of reflection, immediately proceeded on deck, and ordered the marines to load with ball-cartridge. This was done; but, as I was afterwards told by Thompson, who was standing aft, the marines loaded with powder, and put the balls into their pockets. They wished to keep up the character of their corps for fidelity, and at the same time not fire upon men whom they loved as brothers, and with whom they coincided in opinion. Indeed, we afterwards discovered that it was a *marine* who had taken off the *head* of the snake a second time.

The captain then ordered the boatswain to turn the hands up. The boatswain made his appearance with his right arm in a sling.—"What's the matter with your arm, Mr Paul?" said I, as he passed me.

"Tumbled down the hatchway just now—can't move my arm; I must go to the surgeon as soon as this is over."

The hands were piped up again, but no one obeyed the order. Thus was the brig in a state of mutiny. "Mr Simple, go forward to the main hatchway with the marines, and fire on the lower deck," cried the captain.

"Sir," said I, "there are two frigates within a cable's length of us; and would it not be better to send for assistance, without shedding blood? Besides, sir, you have not yet tried the effect of calling up the carpenter's and boatswain's mates by name. Will you allow me to go down first, and bring them to a sense of their duty?"

"Yes, I presume you know your power; but of this hereafter."

I went down below and called the men by name.

"Sir," said one of the boatswain's mates, "the ship's company say that they will not submit to be flogged."

"I do not speak to the ship's company generally, Collins," replied I; "but you are now ordered to rig the gratings, and come on deck. It is an order that you cannot refuse. Go up directly, and obey it. Quarter-masters, go on deck with your seizings. When all is ready, you can then expostulate." The men obeyed my orders; they crawled on deck, rigged the gratings, and stood by. "All is ready, sir," said I, touching my hat to the captain.

"Send the ship's company aft, Mr Paul."

"Aft, then, all of you, for punishment," cried the boatswain.

"Yes, it is *all of us for punishment*," cried one voice. "We're all to flog one another, and then pay off the *jollies*."[1]

This time the men obeyed the order; they all appeared on the quarter-deck. "The men are all aft, sir," reported the boatswain.

"And now, my lads," said the captain, "I'll teach you what mutiny is. You see the two frigates alongside of us. You had forgotten them, I suppose, but I hadn't. Here, you scoundrel, Mr Jones"—(this was the Joe Miller)—"strip, sir. If ever there was mischief in a ship, you are at the head."

"Head, sir," said the man, assuming a vacant look; "what head, sir? Do you mean the snake's head? I don't know anything about it, sir."— "Strip, sir!" cried the captain in a rage; "I'll soon bring you to your senses."

"If you please, your honour, what have I done to be tied up?" said the man.

"Strip, you scoundrel!"—"Well, sir, if you please, it's hard to be flogged for nothing." The man pulled off his clothes, and walked up to the grating. The quarter-masters seized him up.

"Seized up, sir," reported the scoundrel of a sergeant of marines who acted as the captain's spy.

The captain looked for the articles of war to read, as is necessary previous to punishing a man, and was a little puzzled to find one, where no positive offence had been committed. At last, he pitched upon the one which refers to combination and conspiracy, and creating discontent. We all took off our hats as he read it, and he then called Mr Paul, the boatswain, and ordered him to give the man a dozen. "Please, sir," said the boatswain, pointing to his arm in a sling, "I can't flog—I can't lift up my arm."—"Your arm was well enough when I came on board, sir," cried the captain.

"Yes, sir; but in hurrying the men up, I slipped down the ladder, and
I'm afraid I've put my shoulder out."

The captain bit his lips; he fully believed it was a sham on the part of the boatswain (which indeed it was) to get off flogging the men. "Well, then, where is the chief boatswain's mate, Miller?"

"Here, sir," said Miller, coming forward: a stout, muscular man, nearly six feet high, with a pig-tail nearly four feet long, and his open breast covered with black, shaggy hair.

"Give that man a dozen, sir," said the captain.

The man looked at the captain, then at the ship's company, and then at the man seized up, but did not commence the punishment.

"Do you hear me, sir?" roared the captain.

"If you please, your honour, I'd rather take my disrating—I—don't wish to be chief boatswain's mate in this here business."

"Obey your orders, immediately, sir," cried the captain; "or, by God,
I'll try you for mutiny."

"Well, sir, I beg your pardon; but what must be, must be. I mean no disrespect, Captain Hawkins, but I cannot flog that man—my conscience won't let me."

"Your *conscience*, sir!"

"Beg your pardon, Captain Hawkins, I've always done my duty, foul weather or fair; and I've been eighteen years in His Majesty's service, without ever being brought to punishment; but if I am to be hung now, saving your pleasure, and with all respect, I can't help it."

"I give you but one moment more, sir," cried the captain; "do your duty." The man looked at the captain, and then eyed the yard-arm. "Captain Hawkins, I will *do my duty*, although I must swing for it." So saying he threw his cat down on the quarter-deck, and fell back among the ship's company.

The captain was now confounded, and hardly knew how to act: to persevere appeared useless—to fall back was almost as impossible. A dead silence of a minute ensued. Every one was breathless with impatience, to know what would be done next. The silence was, however, first broken by Jones, the Joe Miller, who was seized up. "Beg your honour's pardon, sir," said he, turning his head round; "but if I am to be flogged, will you be pleased to let me have it over? I shall catch my death a-cold, naked here all day." This was decided mockery, on the part of the man, and roused the captain.

"Sergeant of marines, put Miller and that man Collins, both legs in irons, for mutiny. My men, I perceive that there is a conspiracy in the ship, but I shall very soon put an end to it: I know the men, and, by God, they shall repent it. Mr Paul, pipe down. Mr Simple, man my gig; and recollect, it's my positive orders that no boat goes on shore." The captain left the brig, looking daggers at me as he went over the side; but I had done my duty, and cared little for that; indeed, I was now watching his conduct as carefully as he did mine.

"The captain wishes to tell his own story first," said Thompson, coming up to me. "Now, if I were you, Simple, I would take care that the real facts should be known."

"How's that to be done," replied I; "he has ordered no communication with the shore."

"Simply by sending an officer on board of each of the frigates to state that the brig is in a state of mutiny, and request that they will keep a look-out upon her. This is no more than your duty as commanding officer; you only send the message, leave me to state the facts of my own accord. Recollect that the captains of these frigates will be summoned, if there is a court of inquiry, which I expect will take place."

I considered a little, and thought the advice good. I despatched Thompson first to one frigate, and then to the other. The next day the captain came on board. As soon as he stepped on the quarter-deck he inquired how I dare disobey his orders in sending the boats away. My reply was that his orders were, not to communicate with the shore, but that, as commanding officer, I considered it my duty to make known to the other ships that the men were in a state of insubordination, that they might keep their eyes upon us. He *kept his eyes* upon me for some time, and then turned away without reply. As we expected, a court of inquiry was called, upon his representations to the admiral. About twenty of the men were examined, but so much came out as to the *reason why* the head of the snake had been removed—for the sailors spoke boldly—that the admiral and officers who were appointed strongly recommended Captain Hawkins not to proceed further than to state that there were some disaffected characters in the ship, and move the admiral to have them exchanged into others. This was done, and the captains of the frigates, who immediately gave their advice, divided all our best men between them. They spoke very freely to me, and asked me who were the best men, which I told them honestly, for I was glad to be able to get them out of the power of Captain Hawkins; these they marked as disaffected, and exchanged them for all the worst they had on board. The few that were left ran away, and thus, from having one of the finest and best organised ship's companies in the service, we were now one of the very worst. Miller was sent on board of the frigate, and under surveillance: he soon proved that his character was as good as I stated it to be, and two years afterwards was promoted to the rank of boatswain. Webster, the second lieutenant, would not rejoin us, and another was appointed. I must here remark, that there is hardly any degree of severity which a captain may not exert towards his seamen, provided they are confident of, or he has proved to them, his courage; but if there be a doubt, or a confirmation to the contrary, all discipline is destroyed by contempt, and the ship's company mutiny, either directly or indirectly. There is an old saying, that all tyrants are cowards; that tyranny is in itself a species of meanness, I acknowledge: but still the saying ought to be modified. If it is asserted that all mean tyrants are cowards, I agree; but I have known in the service most special tyrants, who were not cowards: their tyranny was excessive, but there was no meanness in their dispositions. On the contrary, they were generous, open-hearted, and, occasionally, when not influenced by anger, proved that their hearts, if not quite right, were not very much out of their places. Yet they were tyrants; but, although tyrants, the men forgave them, and one kind act, when they were not led away by the impetuosity of their feelings, obliterated a hundred acts of tyranny. But such is not the case in our service with men who, in their tyranny, are mean; the seamen show no quarter to them, and will undergo all the risk which the severity of the articles of war renders them liable to, rather than not express their opinion of a man whom they despise. I do not like to mention names, but I could point out specimens of brave tyrants, and of cowardly tyrants who have existed, and do even now exist in our service. The present regulations have limited tyranny to a certain degree, but it cannot check the *mean* tyrant; for it is not in points of consequence, likely to be brought before the notice of his superiors, that he effects his purpose. He resorts to paltry measures—he smiles that he may betray—he confines himself within the limit that may protect him; and he is never exposed, unless by his courage being called in question, which but rarely occurs; and when it does occur it is most difficult, as well as most dangerous, to attempt to prove it. It may be asked why I did not quit the ship, after having been aware of the character of the captain, and the enmity which he bore to me. In reply, I can only say that I did often think of it, talked over the subject with my messmates, but they persuaded me to remain, and, as I was a first lieutenant, and knew that any successful action would, in all probability, insure my promotion, I determined, to use a nautical expression, to rough it out, and not throw away the only chance which I now had of obtaining my rank as commander.

[Footnote 1: Marines.]

Chapter LVII

News from home not very agreeable, although the reader may laugh—We arrive at Portsmouth, where I fall in with my old acquaintance, Mrs Trotter—We sail with a convoy for the Baltic.

I had written to my sister Ellen, giving her an account of all that had passed, and mentioning the character of the captain, and his apparent intimacy with my uncle. I received an answer from her, telling me that she had discovered, from a very communicative old maiden lady, that Captain Hawkins was an illegitimate son of my uncle, by a lady with whom he had been acquainted about the time that he was in the army. I immediately conceived the truth, that my uncle had pointed me out to him as an object of his vengeance, and that Captain Hawkins was too dutiful and too dependent a son not to obey him. The state of my father was more distressing than ever, but there was something very ludicrous in his fancies. He had fancied himself a jackass, and had brayed for a week, kicking the old nurse in the stomach, so as to double her up like a hedgehog. He had taken it into his head that he was a pump; and, with one arm held out as a spout, he had obliged the poor old nurse to work the other up and down for hours together. At another time, he had an idea that he was a woman in labour, and they were obliged to give him a strong dose of calomel, and borrow a child of six years old from a neighbour, to make him believe that he was delivered. He was perfectly satisfied, although the child was born to him in cloth trousers, and a jacket with three rows of sugar-loaf buttons. Aye, said he, it was those buttons which hurt my side so much. In fact, there was a string of strange conceptions of this kind that had accumulated, so as to drive my poor sister almost mad; and sometimes his ideas would be attended with a very heavy expense, as he would send for architects, make contracts, &c., for building, supposing himself to have come to the title and property of his brother. This, being the basis of his disease, occurred frequently. I wrote to poor Ellen, giving her my best advice, and by this time the brig was again ready for sea, and we expected to sail immediately. I did not forget to write to O'Brien, but the distance between us was so great that I knew I could not obtain his answer probably for a year, and I felt a melancholy foreboding how much I required his advice.

Our orders were to proceed to Portsmouth, and join a convoy collected there, bound up the Baltic, under the charge of the *Acasta* frigate, and two other vessels. We did not sail with any pleasure, or hopes of gaining much in the way of prize-money. Our captain was enough to make any ship a hell; and our ship's company were composed of a mutinous and incorrigible set of scoundrels, with, of course, a few exceptions. How different did the officers find the brig after losing such a captain as O'Brien, and so fine a ship's company! But there was no help for it, and all we had to do was to make the best of it, and hope for better times. The cat was at work nearly every day, and I must acknowledge that, generally speaking, it was deserved; although sometimes a report from the sergeant of marines of any good man favoured by me, was certain to be attended to. This system of receiving reports direct from an inferior officer, instead of through me, as first lieutenant, became so annoying, that I resolved, at all risk, to expostulate. I soon had an opportunity, for one morning the captain said to me, "Mr Simple, I understand that you had a fire in the galley last night after hours."

"It is very true, sir, that I did order a stove to be lighted; but may I inquire whether the first lieutenant has not a discretionary power in that point? and further, how it is that I am reported to you by other people? The discipline of this ship is carried on by me, under your directions, and all reports ought to come through me; and I cannot understand upon what grounds you permit them through any other channel."

"I command my own ship, sir, and shall do as I please in that respect. When I have officers I can confide in, I shall, in all probability, allow them to report to me."

"If there is anything in my conduct which has proved to you that I am incapable, or not trustworthy, I would feel obliged to you, sir, if you would, in the first place, point it out;—and, in the next, bring me to a court-martial if I do not correct it."

"I am no court-martial man, sir," replied he, "but I am not to be dictated to by an inferior officer, so you'll oblige me by holding your tongue. The sergeant of marines, as master-at-arms, is bound to report to me any deviation from the regulations I have laid down for the discipline of the ship."

"Granted, sir; but that report, according to the custom of the service, should come through the first lieutenant."

"I prefer it coming direct, sir;—it stands less chance of being garbled."

"Thank you, Captain Hawkins, for the compliment." The captain walked away without further reply, and shortly after went down below. Swinburne ranged up alongside of me as soon as the captain disappeared.

"Well, Mr Simple, so I hear we are bound to the Baltic. Why couldn't they have ordered us to pick up the convoy off Yarmouth, instead of coming all the way to Portsmouth? We shall be in to-morrow with this slant of wind."

"I suppose the convoy are not yet collected, Swinburne; and you recollect there's no want of French privateers in the channel."

"Very true, sir."

"When were you up the Baltic, Swinburne?"

"I was in the old *St George*, a regular old ninety-eight; she sailed just like a hay-stack, one mile ahead and three to leeward. Lord bless you, Mr Simple, the Cattegat wasn't wide enough for her; but she was a comfortable sort of vessel after all, excepting on a lee-shore, so we used always to give the land a wide berth, I recollect. By the bye, Mr Simple, do you recollect how angry you were because I didn't peach at Barbadoes, when the men *sucked the monkey?*"

"To be sure I do."

"Well, then, I didn't think it fair then, as I was one of them. But now that I'm a bit of an officer, I just tell you that when we get to Carlscrona there's a method of *sucking the monkey* there, which, as first lieutenant, with such a queer sort of captain, it is just as well that you should be up to. In the old *St George* we had seventy men drunk one afternoon, and the first lieutenant couldn't find it out nohow."

"Indeed, Swinburne, you must let me into that secret."

"So I will, Mr Simple. Don't you know there's a famous stuff for cuts and wounds, called balsam?"

"What, Riga balsam?"

"Yes, that's it; well, all the boats will bring that for sale, as they did to us in the old *St George*. Devilish good stuff it is for wounds, I believe; but it's not bad to drink, and it's very strong. We used to take it *inwardly*, Mr Simple, and the first lieutenant never guessed it."

"What! you all got tipsy upon Riga balsam?"

"All that could; so I just give you a hint."

"I'm much obliged to you, Swinburne; I certainly never should have suspected it. I believe seamen would get drunk upon anything."

The next morning we anchored at Spithead, and found the convoy ready for sea. The captain went on shore to report himself to the admiral, and, as usual, the brig was surrounded with bumboats and wherries, with people who wished to come on board. As we were not known on the Portsmouth station, and had no acquaintance with the people, all the bumboats were very anxious to supply the ship: and, as this is at the option of the first lieutenant, he is very much persecuted until he has made his decision. Certificates of good conduct from other officers were handed up the side from all of them; and I looked over the books at the capstern. In the second book the name struck me; it was that of Mrs Trotter, and I walked to the gangway out of curiosity, to ascertain whether it was the same personage who, when I was a youngster, had taken such care of my shirts. As I looked at the boats, a voice cried out, "O, Mr Simple, have you forgot your old friend? don't you recollect Mrs Trotter?" I certainly did not recollect her; she had grown very fat, and, although more advanced in years, was a better-looking woman than when I had first seen her, for she looked healthy and fresh.

"Indeed, I hardly did recollect you, Mrs Trotter."

"I've so much to tell you, Mr Simple," replied she, ordering the boat to pull alongside; and, as she was coming up, desired the man to get the things in, as if permission was quite unnecessary. I did not counter-order it, as I knew none of the others, and, as far as honesty was concerned, believed them all to be much on a par. On the strength, then, of old acquaintance, Mrs Trotter was admitted.

"Well, I'm sure, Mr Simple," cried Mrs Trotter, out of breath with climbing up the brig's side; "what a man you've grown,—and such a handsome man, too! Dear, dear, it makes me feel quite old to look at you, when I call to mind the little boy whom I had charge of in the cockpit. Don't you think I look very old and ugly, Mr Simple?" continued she, smiling and smirking.

"Indeed, Mrs Trotter, I think you wear very well. Pray, how is your husband?"

"Ah, Mr Simple, poor dear Mr Trotter—he's gone. Poor fellow! no wonder; what with his drinking, and his love for me—and his jealousy—(do you recollect how jealous he was, Mr Simple?)—he wore himself out at last. No wonder, considering what he had been accustomed to, after keeping his carriage and dogs with everybody, to be reduced to see his wife go a *bumming*. It broke his heart, poor fellow! and, Mr Simple, I've been much happier ever since, for I could not bear to see him fretting. Lord, how jealous he was—and all about nothing! Don't you want some fresh meat for the gun-room? I've a nice leg of mutton in the boat, and some milk for tea."

"Recollect, Mrs Trotter, I shall not overlook your bringing spirits on board."

"Lord, Mr Simple, how could you think of such a thing? It's very true that these common people do it, but the company I have kept, the society I have been in, Mr Simple! Besides, you must recollect that I never drank anything but water."

I could not exactly coincide with her, but I did not contradict her.

"Would you like the Portsmouth paper, Mr Simple?" taking one out of her pocket; "I know gentlemen are fond of the news. Poor Trotter used never to stir from the breakfast table until he had finished the daily paper— but that was when we lived in very different style. Have you any clothes to wash, Mr Simple,—or have any of the gentlemen?"

"I fear we have no time, we sail too soon," replied I; "we go with the convoy."

"Indeed!" cried Mrs Trotter, who walked to the main hatchway and called to her man Bill. I heard her give him directions to sell nothing upon trust, in consequence of the intelligence of our immediate sailing.

"I beg your pardon, Mr Simple, I was only desiring my head man to send for your steward, that he might be supplied with the best, and to save some milk for the gun-room."

"And I must beg your pardon, Mrs Trotter, for I must attend to my duty." Mrs Trotter made her courtesy and walked down the main ladder to attend to *her duty*, and we separated. I was informed that she had a great deal of custom, as she understood how to manage the officers, and made herself generally useful to them. She had been a bumboat woman for six years, and had made a great deal of money. Indeed, it was reported, that if a _first lieutenant _wanted forty or fifty pounds, Mrs Trotter would always lend it to him, without requiring his promissory note.

The captain came on board in the evening, having dined with the admiral, and left directions for having all ready for unmooring and heaving short at daylight. The signal was made from the frigate at sunrise, and before twelve o'clock we were all under weigh, and running past St Helen's with a favourable wind. Our force consisted of the *Acasta* frigate, the *Isis* ship, sloop, mounting twenty guns, the *Reindeer*, eighteen, and our own brig. The convoy amounted to nearly two hundred. Although the wind was fair, and the water smooth, we were more than a week before we made Anholt light, owing *to* the bad sailing and inattention of many of the vessels belonging to the convoy. We were constantly employed repeating signals, firing guns, and often sent back to tow up the sternmost vessels. At last we passed the Anholt light, with a light breeze; and the next morning the main land was to be distinguished on both bows.

Chapter LVIII

How we passed the Sound, and what passed in the Sound The Captain overhears again a conversation between Swinburne and me.

I was on the signal-chest abaft, counting the convoy, when Swinburne came up to me. "There's a little difference between this part of the world and the West Indies, Mr Simple," observed he. "Black rocks and fir woods don't remind us of the Blue Mountains of Jamaica, or the cocoa-nut waving to the sea-breeze."

"Indeed not, Swinburne," replied I.

"We shall have plenty of calms here, without panting with the heat, although we may find the gun-boats a little too warm for us; for, depend upon it, the very moment the wind goes down, they will come out from every nook and corner, and annoy us not a little."

"Have you been here before, with a convoy, Swinburne?"

"To be sure I have; and it's sharp work that I've seen here, Mr Simple— work that I've an idea our captain won't have much stomach for."

"Swinburne, I beg you will keep your thoughts relative to the captain to yourself; recollect the last time. It is my duty not to listen to them."

"And I should rather think to report them also, Mr Simple," said Captain
Hawkins, who had crept up to us, and overheard our conversation.

"In this instance there is no occasion for my reporting them, sir," replied I, "for you have heard what has passed."

"I have, sir," replied he; "and I shall not forget the conversation."

I turned forward. Swinburne had made his retreat the moment that he heard the voice of the captain. "How many sails are there in sight, sir?" inquired the captain.

"One hundred and sixty-three, sir," replied I.

"Signal for convoy to close from the *Acasta*" reported the midshipman of the watch.

We repeated it, and the captain descended to his cabin. We were then running about four miles an hour, the water very smooth, and Anholt lighthouse hardly visible on deck, bearing N.N.W. about twenty miles. In fact, we were near the entrance of the Sound, which, the reader may be aware, is a narrow passage leading into the Baltic Sea. We ran on, followed by the convoy, some of which were eight or ten miles astern of us, and we were well into the Sound, when the wind gradually died away, until it fell quite calm, and the heads of the vessels were laid round the compass.

My watch was nearly out, when the midshipman, who was looking round with his glass on the Copenhagen side, reported three gun-boats, sweeping out from behind a point. I examined them and went down to report them to the captain. When I came on deck, more were reported, until we counted ten, two of them large vessels, called praams. The captain now came on deck, and I reported them. We made the signal of enemy in sight, to the *Acasta*, which was answered. They divided—six of them pulling along shore towards the convoy in the rear, and four coming out right for the brig. The *Acasta* now made the signal for "Boats manned and armed to be held in readiness." We hoisted out our pinnace, and lowered down our cutters—the other men-of-war doing the same. In about a quarter of an hour the gun-boats opened their fire with their long thirty-two pounders, and their first shot went right through the hull of the brig, just abaft the fore-bits; fortunately, no one was hurt. I turned round to look at the captain; he was as white as a sheet. He caught my eye, and turned aft, when he was met by Swinburne's eye, steadily fixed upon him. He then walked to the other side of the deck. Another shot ploughed up the water close to us, rose, and came through the hammock-netting, tearing out two of the hammocks, and throwing them on the quarter-deck, when the *Acasta* hoisted out pennants, and made the signal to send our pinnace and cutter to the assistance of vessels astern. The signal was also made to the *Isis* and *Reindeer*. I reported the signal, and inquired who was to take the command.

"You, Mr Simple, will take the pinnace, and order Mr Swinburne into the cutter."

"Mr Swinburne, sir!" replied I; "the brig will, in all probability, be in action soon, and his services as a gunner will be required."

"Well, then, Mr Hilton may go. Beat to quarters. Where is Mr Webster?"[1] The second lieutenant was close to us, and he was ordered to take the duty during my absence.

I jumped into the pinnace, and shoved off; ten other boats from the *Acasta* and the other men-of-war were pulling in the same direction, and I joined them. The gun-boats had now opened fire upon the convoy astern, and were sweeping out to capture them, dividing themselves into two parts, and pulling towards different portions of the convoy. In half an hour we were within gunshot of the nearest, which directed its fire at us; but the lieutenant of the *Acasta*, who commanded the detachment, ordered us to lie on our oars for a minute, while he divided his force in three divisions, of four boats each, with instructions that we should each oppose a division of two gun-boats, by pulling to the outermost vessel of the convoy, and securing ourselves as much as possible from the fire, by remaining under her lee, and be in readiness to take them by boarding, if they approached to capture any of our vessels.

This was well arranged. I had the command of one division, for the first lieutenants had not been sent away from the *Isis* and *Reindeer*, and having inquired which of the divisions of gun-boats I was to oppose, I pulled for them. In the meantime, we observed that the two praams, and two gun-boats, which had remained behind us, and had been firing at the *Racehorse*, had also divided—one praam attacking the *Acasta*, the two gun-boats playing upon the *Isis*, and the other praam engaging the _Rattlesnake _and *Reindeer*; the latter vessel being in a line with us, and about half a mile further out, so that she could not return any effectual fire, or, indeed, receive much damage.

The *Rattlesnake* had the worst of it, the fire of the praam being chiefly directed to her. At the distance chosen by the enemy, the frigate's guns reached, but the other men-of-war, having only two long guns, were not able to return the fire but with their two, the carronades being useless.

One of the praams mounted ten guns, and the other eight. The last was opposed to the *Rattlesnake*, and the fire was kept up very smartly, particularly by the *Acasta* and the enemy. In about a quarter of an hour I arrived with my division close to the vessel which was nearest to the enemy. It was a large Sunderland-built ship. The gun-boats, which were within a quarter of a mile of her, sweeping to her as fast as they could, as soon as they perceived our approach, directed their fire upon us, but without success, except the last discharge, in which, we being near enough, they had loaded with grape. The shot fell a little short, but one piece of grape struck one of the bowmen of the pinnace, taking off three fingers of his right hand as he was pulling his oar. Before they could fire again, we were sheltered by the vessel, pulling close to her side, hid from the enemy. My boat was the only one in the division which carried a gun, and I now loaded, waiting for the discharge of the gun-boats, and then, pulling a little ahead of the ship, fired at them, and then returned under cover to load. This continued for some time, the enemy not advancing nearer, but now firing into the Sunderland ship, which protected us. At last the master of the ship looked over the side, and said to me, "I say, my joker, do you call this *giving me assistance?* I think I was better off before you came. Then I had only my share of the enemy's fire, but now that you have come, I have it all. I'm riddled like a sieve, and have lost four men already. Suppose you give me a spell now—pull behind the vessel ahead of us. I'll take my chance."

I thought this request very reasonable, and as I should be really nearer to the enemy if I pulled to the next vessel, and all ready to support him if attacked, I complied with his wish. I had positive orders not to board with so small a force (the four boats containing but forty men, and each gun-boat having at least seventy), unless they advanced to capture, and then I was to run all risks.

I pulled up to the other vessel, a large brig, and the captain, as soon as we came alongside, said, "I see what you're about, and I'll just leave you my vessel to take care of. No use losing my men, or being knocked on the head."

"All's right—you can't do better, and we can't do better either."

His boat was lowered down, and getting in with his men, he pulled to another vessel, and lay behind it, all ready to pull back if a breeze sprang up.

As was to be expected, the gun-boats shifted their fire to the deserted vessel, which our boat lay behind; and thus did the action in our quarter continue until it was dark, the gun-boats not choosing to advance, and we restricted from pulling out to attack them. There was no moon, and, as daylight disappeared, the effect was very beautiful. In the distance, the cannonading of the frigate, and other men-of-war, answered by the praams and gunboats, reinforced by six more, as we afterwards found out—the vivid flashing of the guns, reflected by the water, as smooth as glass—the dark outlines of the numerous convoy, with their sails hanging down the masts, one portion of the convoy appearing for a moment, as the guns were discharged in that direction, and then disappearing, while others were momentarily seen—the roar of the heavy guns opposed to us—the crashing of the timbers of the brig, which was struck at every discharge, and very often perforated—with the whizzing of the shot as it passed by;—all this in a dark yet clear night, with every star in the heavens twinkling, and, as it were, looking down upon us, was interesting as well as awful. But I soon perceived that the gun-boats were nearing us every time that they fired, and I now discharged grape alone, waiting for the flash of the fire to ascertain their direction. At last I could perceive their long, low hulls, not two cables' length from us, and their sweeps lifting from the water. It was plain that they were advancing to board, and I resolved to anticipate them if possible. I had fired ahead of the brig, and I now pulled with all my boats astern, giving my orders to the officers, and laying on our oars in readiness. The gun-boats were about half a cable's length from each other, pulling up abreast, and passing us at about the same distance, when I directed the men to give way. I had determined to throw all my force upon the nearest boat, and in half a minute our bows were forced between their sweeps, which we caught hold of to force our way alongside.

The resistance of the Danes was very determined. Three times did I obtain a footing on the deck, and three times was I thrown back into the boats. At last we had fairly obtained our ground, and were driving them gradually forward, when, as I ran on the gunwale to obtain a position more in advance of my men, I received a blow with the butt end of a musket—I believe on the shoulder—which knocked me overboard, and I fell between the sweeps, and sunk under the vessel's bottom. I rose under her stern; but I was so shook with the violence of the blow, that I was for some time confused; still I had strength to keep myself above water, and paddled, as it appeared, away from the vessel, until I hit against a sweep which had fallen overboard. This supported me, and I gradually recovered myself. The loud report of a gun close to me startled me, and I perceived that it was from the gun-boat which I had boarded, and that her head was turned in the direction of the other gun-boat. From this, with the noise of the sweeps pulling, I knew that my men had succeeded in capturing her. I hallooed, but they did not hear me, and I soon lost sight of her. Another gun was now fired; it was from the other gun-boat retreating, and I perceived her pulling in-shore, for she passed me not twenty yards off. I now held the sweep with my hands, and struck out off the shore, in the direction of the convoy.

A light breeze rippled the water, and I knew that I had no time to lose. In about five minutes I heard the sound of oars, and perceived a boat crossing me. I hailed as loud as I could—they heard me, laid on their oars—and I hailed again—they pulled to me, and took me in. It was the master of the brig, who, aware of the capture of one gun-boat, and the retreat of the other, was looking for his vessel; or, as he told me, for what was left of her. In a short time we found her, and, although very much cut up, she had received no shot under water. In an hour the breeze was strong, the cannonading had ceased in every direction, and we had repaired her damages, so as to be able to make sail, and continue our course through the Sound.

Here I may as well relate the events of the action. One of the other divisions of gun-boats had retreated when attacked by the boats. The other had beaten off the boats, and killed many of the men, but had suffered so much themselves, as to retreat without making any capture. The *Acasta* lost four men killed, and seven wounded; the *Isis*, three men wounded; the *Reindeer* had nobody hurt; the *Rattlesnake* had six men killed, and two wounded, including the captain; but of that I shall speak hereafter.

I found that I was by no means seriously hurt by the blow I had received: my shoulder was stiff for a week, and very much discoloured, but nothing more. When I fell overboard I had struck against a sweep, which had cut my ear half off. The captain of the brig gave me dry clothes, and in a few hours I was very comfortably asleep, hoping to join my ship the next day; but in this I was disappointed. The breeze was favourable and fresh, and we were clear of the Sound, but a long way astern of the convoy, and none of the headmost men-of-war to be seen. I dressed and went on deck, and immediately perceived that I had little chance of joining my ship until we arrived at Carlscrona, which proved to be the case. About ten o'clock, the wind died away, and we had from that time such baffling light winds, that it was six days before we dropped our anchor, every vessel of the convoy having arrived before us.

[Footnote 1: Webster, however, had left the ship at Yarmouth. See p. 202.—ED.]

Chapter LIX

The dead man attends at the auction of his own effects, and bids the sale to stop—One more than was wanted—Peter steps into his shoes again—Captain Hawkins takes a friendly interest in Peter's papers— Riga Balsam sternly refused to be admitted for the relief of the ship's company.

As soon as the sails were furled, I thanked the master of the vessel for his kindness, and requested the boat. He ordered it to be manned, saying, "How glad your captain will be to see you!" I doubted that. We shook hands, and I pulled to the *Rattlesnake*, which lay about two cables' length astern of us. I had put on a jacket, when I left the brig on service, and coming in a merchantman's boat, no attention was paid to me; indeed, owing to circumstances, no one was on the look-out, and I ascended the side unperceived. The men and officers were on the quarter-deck, attending the sale of dead men's effects before the mast; and every eye was fixed upon six pair of nankeen trousers exposed by the purser's steward which I recognized as my own. "Nine shillings for six pair of nankeen trousers," cried the purser's steward.

"Come, my men, they're worth more than that," observed the captain, who appeared to be very facetious. "It's better to be in his trousers than in his shoes." This brutal remark created a silence for a moment. "Well, then, steward, let them go. One would think that pulling on his trousers would make you as afraid as he was," continued the captain, laughing.

"Shame!" was cried out by one or two of the officers, and I recognised
Swinburne's voice as one.

"More likely if they put on yours," cried I, in a loud, indignant tone.

Everybody started, and turned round; Captain Hawkins staggered to a carronade: "I beg to report myself as having rejoined my ship, sir," continued I.

"Hurrah, my lads! three cheers for Mr Simple!" said Swinburne.

The men gave them with emphasis. The captain looked at me, and without saying a word, hastily retreated to his cabin. I perceived, as he went down, that he had his arm in a sling. I thanked the men for their kind feeling towards me, shook hands with Thompson and Webster, who warmly congratulated me, and then with old Swinburne, (who nearly wrung my arm off, and gave my shoulder such pain as to make me cry out,) and with the others who extended theirs. I desired the sale of my effects to be stopped; fortunately for me, it had but just begun, and the articles were all returned. Thompson had informed the captain that he knew my father's address, and would take charge of my clothes, and send them home, but the captain would not allow him.

In a few minutes, I received a letter from the captain, desiring me to acquaint him in writing, for the information of the senior officer, in what manner I had escaped. I went down below, when I found one very melancholy face, that of the passed midshipman of the *Acasta*, who had received an acting order in my place. When I went to my desk, I found two important articles missing; one, my private letter-book, and the other, the journal which I kept of what passed, and from which this narrative has been compiled. I inquired of my messmates, who stated that the desk had not been looked into by any one but the captain, who, of course, must have possessed himself of those important documents.

I wrote a letter containing a short narrative of what had happened, and, at the same time, another on service to the captain, requesting that he would deliver up my property, the private journal, and letter-book in his possession. The captain, as soon as he received my letters, sent up word for his boat to be manned. As soon as it was manned, I reported it, and then begged to know whether he intended to comply with my request. He answered that he should not, and then went on deck, and quitted the brig to pull on board of the senior officer. I therefore determined immediately to write to the captain of the *Acasta*, acquainting him with the conduct of Captain Hawkins, and requesting his interference. This I did immediately, and the boat that had brought me on board not having left the brig, I sent the letter by it, requesting them to put it into the hands of one of the officers. The letter was received previous to Captain Hawkins' visit being over, and the Captain of the *Acasta* put it into his hands, inquiring if the statement were correct. Captain Hawkins replied that it was true that he had detained these papers, as there was so much mutiny and disaffection in them, and that he should not return them to me.

"That I cannot permit," replied the captain of the *Acasta*, who was aware of the character of Captain Hawkins; "if, by mistake, you have been put in possession of any of Mr Simple's secrets, you are bound in honour not to make use of them; neither can you retain property not your own." But Captain Hawkins was determined, and refused to give them to me.

"Well, then, Captain Hawkins," replied the captain of the *Acasta*, "you will oblige me by remaining on my quarter-deck till I come out of the cabin."

The captain of the *Acasta* then wrote an order, directing Captain Hawkins immediately to deliver up *to him* the papers of mine in his possession; and coming out of the cabin, put it into Captain Hawkins' hands, saying, "Now, sir, here is a written order from your superior officer. Disobey it, if you dare. If you do, I will put you under arrest, and try you by a court-martial. I can only regret, that any captain in His Majesty's service should be forced in this way to do his duty as a gentleman and a man of honour."

Captain Hawkins bit his lip at the order, and the cutting remarks accompanying it. "Your boat is manned, sir," said the captain of the *Acasta*, in a severe tone. Captain Hawkins came on board, sealed up the books, and sent them to the captain of the *Acasta*, who re-directed them to me, on His Majesty's service, and returned them by the same boat. The public may therefore thank the captain of the *Acasta* for the memoirs which they are now reading.

From my messmates I gained the following intelligence of what had passed after I had quitted the brig. The fire of the praam had cut them up severely, and Captain Hawkins had been struck in the arm with a piece of the hammock-rail, which had been shot away shortly after I left. Although the skin only was razed, he thought proper to consider himself badly wounded; and giving up the command to Mr Webster, the second lieutenant, had retreated below, where he remained until the action was over. When Mr Webster reported the return of the boats, with the capture of the gun-boat, and my supposed death, he was so delighted, that he quite forgot his wound, and ran on deck, rubbing his hands as he walked up and down. At last, he recollected himself, went down into his cabin, and came up again with his arm in a sling.

The next morning he went on board of the *Acasta*, and made his report to the senior officer, bringing back with him the disappointed passed-midshipman as my successor. He had also stated on the quarter-deck, that if I had not been killed, he intended to have tried me by a court-martial, and have turned me out of the service; that he had quite enough charges to ruin me, for he had been collecting them ever since I had been under his command; and that now he would make that old scoundrel of a gunner repent his intimacy with me. All this was confided to the surgeon, who, as I before observed, was very much of a courtier; but the surgeon had repeated it to Thompson, the master, who now gave me the information. There was one advantage in all this, which was that I knew exactly the position in which I stood, and what I had to expect.

During the short time that we remained in port, I took care that *Riga balsam* should not be allowed to come alongside, and the men were all sober. We received orders from the captain of the *Acasta* to join the admiral, who was off the Texel in pursuance of directions he had received from the Admiralty to despatch one of the squadron, and we were selected, from the dislike which he had taken to Captain Hawkins.

Chapter LX

An old friend in a new case—Heart of oak in Swedish fur—A man's a man all the world over, and something more in many parts of it—Peter gets reprimanded for being dilatory, but proves a title to a defence— Allowed.

When we were about forty miles off the harbour, a frigate hove in sight. We made the private signal: she hoisted Swedish colours, and kept away a couple of points to close with us.

We were within two miles of her when she up courses and took in her topgallant sails. As we closed to within two cables' lengths, she hove-to. We did the same; and the captain desired me to lower down the boat, and board her, ask her name, by whom she was commanded, and offer any assistance if the captain required it. This was the usual custom of the service, and I went on board in obedience to my orders. When I arrived on the quarter-deck, I asked in French, whether there was any one who spoke it. The first lieutenant came forward, and took off his hat: I stated that I was requested to ask the name of the vessel and the commanding officer, to insert it in our log, and to offer any service that we could command. He replied that the captain was on deck, and turned round, but the captain had gone down below. "I will inform him of your message—I had no idea that he had quitted the deck;" and the first lieutenant left me. I exchanged a few compliments and a little news with the officers on deck, who appeared to be very gentlemanlike fellows, when the first lieutenant requested my presence in the cabin. I descended—the door was opened—I was announced by the first lieutenant, and he quitted the cabin. I looked at the captain, who was sitting at the table: he was a fine, stout man, with two or three ribands at his button-hole, and a large pair of moustachios. I thought that I had seen him before, but I could not recollect when: his face was certainly familiar to me, but, as I had been informed by the officers on deck, that the captain was a Count Shucksen, a person I had never heard of, I thought that I must be mistaken. I therefore addressed him in French, paying him a long compliment, with all the necessary *et ceteras*.

The captain turned round to me, took his hand away from his forehead, which it had shaded, and looking me full in the face, replied, "Mr Simple, I don't understand but very little French. Spin your yarn in plain English."

I started—"I thought that I knew your face," replied I; "am I mistaken?—no, it must be—Mr Chucks!"

"You are right, my dear Mr Simple: it is your old friend, Chucks, the boatswain, whom you now see. I knew you as soon as you came up the side, and I was afraid that you would immediately recognize me, and I slipped down into the cabin (for which apparent rudeness allow me to apologise), that you might not explain before the officers."

We shook hands heartily, and then he requested me to sit down. "But," said I, "they told me on deck that the frigate was commanded by a Count Shucksen."

"That is my present rank, my dear Peter," said he; "but as you have no time to lose, I will explain all. I know I can trust to your honour. You remember that you left me, as you and I supposed, dying in the privateer, with the captain's jacket and epaulettes on my shoulders. When the boats came out, and you left the vessel, they boarded and found me. I was still breathing; and judging of my rank by the coat, they put me into the boat, and pushed on shore. The privateer sank very shortly after. I was not expected to live, but in a few days a change took place, and I was better. They asked me my name, and I gave my own, which they lengthened into Shucksen, somehow or another. I recovered by a miracle, and am now as well as ever I was in my life. They were not a little proud of having captured a captain in the British service, as they supposed, for they never questioned me as to my real rank. After some weeks I was sent home to Denmark in a running vessel; but it so happened, that we met with a gale, and were wrecked on the Swedish coast, close to Carlscrona. The Danes were at that time at war, having joined the Russians; and they were made prisoners, while I was of course liberated, and treated with great distinction; but as I could not speak either French or their own language, I could not get on very well. However, I had a handsome allowance, and permission to go to England as soon as I pleased. The Swedes were then at war with the Russians, and were fitting out their fleet; but, Lord bless them! they didn't know much about it. I amused myself walking in the dockyard, and looking at their motions; but they had not thirty men in the fleet who knew what they were about, and, as for a man to set them going, there wasn't one. Well, Peter, you know I could not be idle, and so by degrees I told one, and then told another—until they went the right way to work; and the captains and officers were very much obliged to me. At last, they all came to me, and if they did not understand me entirely, I showed them how to do it with my own hands; and the fleet began to make a show with their rigging. The admiral who commanded was very much obliged, and I seemed to come as regularly to my work as if I was paid for it. At last, the admiral came with an English interpreter, and asked me whether I was anxious to go back to England, or would I like to join their service. I saw what they wanted, and I replied that I had neither wife nor child in England, and that I liked their country very much; but I must take time to consider of it, and must also know what they had to propose. I went home to my lodgings, and, to make them more anxious, I did not make my appearance at the dockyard for three or four days, when a letter came from the admiral, offering me the command of a frigate if I would join their service. I replied, (for I knew how much they wanted me,) that I would prefer an English frigate to a Swedish one, and that I would not consent unless they offered something more; and then, with the express stipulation that I should not take arms against my own country. They then waited for a week, when they offered to make me a *Count*, and give me the command of a frigate. This suited me, as you may suppose, Peter; it was the darling wish of my heart—I was to be made a gentleman. I consented, and was made Count Shucksen, and had a fine large frigate under my command. I then set to work with a will, superintended the fitting out of the whole fleet, and showed them what an Englishman could do. We sailed, and you of course know the brush we had with the Russians, which, I must say, did us no discredit. I was fortunate to distinguish myself, for I exchanged several broadsides with a Russian two-deck ship, and came off with honour. When we went into port I got this riband. I was out afterwards, and fell in with a Russian frigate, and captured her, for which I received this other riband. Since that I have been in high favour, and now that I speak the languages, I like the people very much. I am often at court when I am in harbour; and, Peter, I am *married*."

"I wish you joy, count, with all my heart."

"Yes, and well married too—to a Swedish countess of very high family, and I expect that I have a little boy or girl by this time. So you observe, Peter, that I am at last a gentleman, and, what is more, my children will be noble by two descents. Who would have thought that this would have been occasioned by my throwing the captain's jacket into the boat instead of my own? And now, my dear Mr Simple, that I have made you my confidant, I need not say, do not say a word about it to anybody. They certainly could not do me much harm, but still, they might do me some; and although I am not likely to meet any one who may recognize me in this uniform and these moustachios, it's just as well to keep the secret, which to you and O'Brien only would I have confided."

"My dear count," replied I, "your secret is safe with me. You have come to your title before me, at all events; and I sincerely wish you joy, for you have obtained it honourably; but, although I would like to talk with you for days, I must return on board, for I am now sailing with a very unpleasant captain."

I then, in a few words, stated where O'Brien was; and when we parted, I went with him on deck, Count Shucksen taking my arm, and introducing me as an old shipmate to his officers. "I hope we may meet again," said I, "but I am afraid there is little chance."

"Who knows?" replied he; "see what chance has done for me. My dear Peter, God bless you! You are one of the very few whom I always loved. God bless you, my boy! and never forget that all I have is at your command if you come my way."

I thanked him, and saluting the officers, went down the side. As I expected, when I came on board, the captain demanded, in an angry tone, why I had stayed so long. I replied, that I was shown down into Count Shucksen's cabin, and he conversed so long, that I could not get away sooner, as it would not have been polite to have left him before he had finished his questions. I then gave a very civil message, and the captain said no more; the very name of a great man always silenced him.

Chapter LXI

Bad news from home, and worse on board—Notwithstanding his previous trials, Peter forced to prepare for another—Mrs Trotter again; improves as she grows old—Captain Hawkins and his twelve charges.

No other event of consequence occurred until we joined the admiral, who only detained us three hours with the fleet, and then sent us home with his despatches. We arrived, after a quiet passage, at Portsmouth, where I wrote immediately to my sister Ellen, requesting to know the state of my father's health. I waited impatiently for an answer, and by return of post received one with a black seal. My father had died the day before from a brain fever; and Ellen conjured me to obtain leave of absence, to come to her in her state of distress. The captain came on board the next morning, and I had a letter ready written on service to the admiral, stating the circumstances, and requesting leave of absence. I presented it to him, and entreated him to forward it. At any other time I would not have condescended, but the thoughts of my poor sister, unprotected and alone, with my father lying dead in the house, made me humble and submissive. Captain Hawkins read the letter, and very coolly replied, "that it was very easy to say that my father was dead, but he required proofs." Even this insult did not affect me; I put my sister's letter into his hand—he read it, and as he returned it to me, he smiled maliciously. "It is impossible for me to forward your letter, Mr Simple, as I have one to deliver to you."

He put a large folio packet into my hand, and went below. I opened it: it was a copy of a letter demanding a court-martial upon me, with a long list of the charges preferred by him. I was stupefied, not so much at his asking for a court-martial, but at the conviction of the impossibility of my now being able to go to the assistance of my poor sister. I went down into the gunroom and threw myself on a chair, at the same time tossing the letter to Thompson, the master. He read it over carefully, and folded it up.

"Upon my word, Simple, I do not see that you have much to fear. These charges are very frivolous."

"No, no—that I care little about; but it is my poor sister. I had written for leave of absence, and now she is left, God knows how long, in such distressing circumstances."

Thompson looked grave. "I had forgotten your father's death, Simple: it is indeed cruel. I would offer to go myself, but you will want my evidence at the court-martial. It can't be helped. Write to your sister, and keep up her spirits. Tell her why you cannot come, and that it will all end well."

I did so, and went early to bed, for I was really ill. The next morning, the official letter from the port-admiral came off, acquainting me that a court-martial had been ordered upon me, and that it would take place that day week. I immediately resigned the command to the second lieutenant, and commenced an examination into the charges preferred. They were very numerous, and dated back almost to the very day that he had joined the ship.

There were twelve in all. I shall not trouble the reader with the whole of them, as many were very frivolous. The principal charges were—

1. For mutinous and disrespectful conduct to Captain Hawkins, on such a date, having, in a conversation with an inferior officer on the quarter-deck, stated that Captain Hawkins was a spy, and had spies in the ship.

2. For neglect of duty, in disobeying the orders of Captain Hawkins on the night of the —— of ——.

3. For having, on the —— of ——, sent away two boats from the ship, in direct opposition to the orders of Captain Hawkins.

4. For having again, on the morning of the —— of ——, held mutinous and disrespectful conversation relative to Captain Hawkins with the gunner of the ship, allowing the latter to accuse Captain Hawkins of cowardice, without reporting the same.

5. For insulting expressions on the quarter-deck to Captain Hawkins on his rejoining the brig on the morning of the —— of ——.

6. For not causing the orders of Captain Hawkins to be put in force on several occasions, &c. &c. &c.

And further, as Captain Hawkins' testimony was necessary in two of the charges, the king, on _those charges,_ was the prosecutor. Although most of these charges were frivolous, yet I at once perceived my danger. Some were dated back many months, to the time before our ship's company had been changed: and I could not find the necessary witnesses. Indeed, in all but the recent charges, not expecting to be called to a court-martial, I had serious difficulties to contend with. But the most serious was the first charge, which I knew not how to get over. Swinburne had most decidedly referred to the captain when he talked of spy captains. However, with the assistance of Thompson, I made the best defence I could, ready for my trial.

Two days before my court-martial I received a letter from Ellen, who appeared in a state of distraction from this accumulation of misfortune. She told me that my father was to be buried the next day, and that the new rector had written to her, to know when it would be convenient for the vicarage to be given up. That my father's bills had been sent in, and amounted to twelve hundred pounds already; and that she knew not the extent of the whole claims. There appeared to be nothing left but the furniture of the house; and she wanted to know whether the debts were to be paid with the money I had left in the funds for her use. I wrote immediately, requesting her to liquidate every claim, as far as my money went, sending her an order upon my agent to draw for the whole amount, and a power of attorney to him to sell out the stock.

I had just sealed the letter, when Mrs Trotter, who had attended the ship since our return to Portsmouth, begged to speak with me, and walked in after her message, without waiting for an answer. "My dear Mr Simple," said she, "I know all that is going on, and I find that you have no lawyer to assist you. Now I know that it is necessary, and will very probably be of great service in your defence—for when people are in distress and anxiety, they have not their wits about them; so I have brought a friend of mine from Portsea, a very clever man, who, for my sake, will undertake your cause, and I hope you will not refuse him. You recollect giving me a dozen pair of stockings. I did not refuse them, nor shall you refuse me now. I always said to Mr Trotter, 'Go to a lawyer;' and if he had taken my advice he would have done well. I recollect, when a hackney-coachman smashed the panel of our carriage—'Trotter,' says I, 'go to a lawyer;' and he very politely answered, 'Go to the devil!' But what was the consequence!—he's dead and I'm bumming. Now, Mr Simple, will you oblige me?—it's all free gratis for nothing—not for nothing, for it's for my sake. You see, Mr Simple, I have admirers yet," concluded she, smiling.

Mrs Trotter's advice was good; and although I would not listen to receiving his services gratuitously, I agreed to employ him; and very useful did he prove against such charges, and such a man as Captain Hawkins. He came on board that afternoon, carefully examined into all the documents and the witnesses whom I could bring forward, showed me the weak side of my defence, and took the papers on shore with him. Every day he came on board to collect fresh evidence and examine into my case.

At last the day arrived. I dressed myself in my best uniform. The gun fired from the admiral's ship, with the signal for a court-martial at nine o'clock; and I went on board in a boat, with all the witnesses. On my arrival, I was put under the custody of the provost-marshal. The captains ordered to attend pulled alongside one after another, and were received by a party of marines, presenting their arms.

At half-past nine the court was all assembled, and I was ushered in. Courts-martial are open courts, although no one is permitted to print the evidence. At the head of the long table was the admiral, as president; on his right hand, standing, was Captain Hawkins, as prosecutor. On each side of the table were six captains, sitting near to the admiral, according to their seniority. At the bottom, facing the admiral, was the judge-advocate, on whose left hand I stood, as prisoner. The witnesses called in to be examined were stationed on his right; and behind him, by the indulgence of the court, was a small table, at which sat my legal adviser, so close as to be able to communicate with me. The court were all sworn, and then took their seats. Stauncheons, with ropes covered with green baize, passed along, were behind the chairs of the captains who composed the court, so that they might not be crowded upon by those who came in to listen to what passed. The charges were then read, as well as the letters to and from the admiral, by which the court-martial was demanded and granted: and then Captain Hawkins was desired to open his prosecution. He commenced with observing his great regret that he had been forced to a measure so repugnant to his feelings; his frequent cautions to me, and the indifference with which I treated them; and, after a preamble composed of every falsity that could be devised, he commenced with the first charge, and stating himself to be the witness, gave his evidence. When it was finished, I was asked if I had any questions to put. By the advice of my lawyer, I replied, "No." The president then asked the captains composing the court-martial, commencing according to their seniority, whether they wished to ask any questions.

"I wish," said the second captain who was addressed, "to ask Captain Hawkins whether, when he came on deck, he came up in the usual way in which a captain of a man-of-war comes on his quarter-deck, or whether he slipped up without noise?"

Captain Hawkins declared that he came up as he *usually did.* This was true enough, for he invariably came up by stealth.

"Pray, Captain Hawkins, as you have repeated a good deal of conversation which passed between the first lieutenant and the gunner, may I ask you how long you were by their side without their perceiving you?"

"A very short time," was the answer.

"But, Captain Hawkins, do you not think, allowing that you came up on deck in your *usual* way, as you term it, that you would have done better to have hemmed or hawed, so as to let your officers know that you were present? I should be very sorry to hear all that might be said of me in my supposed absence."

To this observation Captain Hawkins replied, that he was so astonished at the conversation, that he was quite breathless, having, till then, had the highest opinion of me.

No more questions were asked, and they proceeded to the second charge. This was a very trifling one—for lighting a stove, contrary to orders; the evidence brought forward was the sergeant of marines. When his evidence in favour of the charge had been given, I was asked by the president if I had any questions to put to the witness. I put the following:—

"Did you repeat to Captain Hawkins that I had ordered the stove to be lighted?"—"I did."

"Are you not in the custom of reporting, direct to the captain, any negligence, or disobedience of orders, you may witness in the ship?"—"I am."

"Did you ever report anything of the sort to me, as first lieutenant, or do you always report direct to the captain?" "I always report direct to the captain."

"By the captain's orders?"—"Yes."

The following questions were then put by some of the members of the court:—

"You have served in other ships before?"—"Yes."

"Did you ever, sailing with other captains, receive an order from them to report direct to them, and not through the first lieutenant?" The witness here prevaricated.

"Answer directly, yes or no."—"No."

The third charge was then brought forward—for sending away boats contrary to express orders. This was substantiated by Captain Hawkins' own evidence, the order having been verbal. By the advice of my counsel, I put no questions to Captain Hawkins, neither did the court.

The fourth charge—that of holding mutinous conversation with the gunner, and allowing him to accuse the captain of unwillingness to engage the enemy—was then again substantiated by Captain Hawkins, as the only witness. I again left my reply for my defence; and only one question was put by one of the members, which was, to inquire of Captain Hawkins, as he appeared peculiarly unfortunate in overhearing conversations, whether he walked up as usual to the taffrail, or whether he *crept up.* Captain Hawkins gave the same answer as before.

The fifth charge—for insulting expressions to Captain Hawkins, on my rejoining the brig at Carlscrona—was then brought forward, and the sergeant of marines and one of the seamen appeared as witnesses. This charge excited a great deal of amusement. In the cross-examination by the members of the court, Captain Hawkins was asked what he meant by the expression, when disposing of the clothes of an officer who was killed in action, that the men appeared to think that his trousers would instil fear.

"Nothing more, upon my honour, sir," replied Captain Hawkins, "than an implication that they were alarmed lest they should be haunted by his ghost."

"Then, of course, Mr Simple meant the same in his reply," observed the captain sarcastically.

The remainder of the charges were then brought forward, but they were of little consequence. The witnesses were chiefly the sergeant of marines, and the spy-glass of Captain Hawkins, who had been watching me from the shore.

It was late in the afternoon before they were all gone through; and the president then adjourned the court, that I might bring forward my own witnesses, in my defence, on the following day, and I returned on board the *Rattlesnake*.

Chapter LXII

A good defence not always good against a bad accusation—Peter wins the heart of his judges, yet loses his cause, and is dismissed his ship.

The next day I commenced my defence, and I preferred calling my own witnesses first, and, by the advice of my counsel, and at the request of Swinburne, I called him. I put the following questions:—"When we were talking on the quarter-deck, was it fine weather?"—"Yes, it was."

"Do you think that you might have heard any one coming on deck, in the usual way, up the companion ladder?" "Sure of it."

"Do you mean, then, to imply that Captain Hawkins came up stealthily?"

"I have an idea he pounced upon us as a cat does on a mouse."

"What were the expressions made use of?"

"I said that a spy captain would always find spy followers."

"In that remark were you and Mr Simple referring to your own captain?"—

"The remark was mine. What Mr Simple was thinking of, I can't tell; but I *did* refer to the captain, and he has proved that I was right." This bold answer of Swinburne's rather astonished the court, who commenced cross-questioning him; but he kept to his original assertion—that I had only answered generally. To repel the second charge I produced no witnesses; but to the third charge I brought forward three witnesses to prove that Captain Hawkins's orders were that I should send no boats on shore, not that I should not send them on board of the men-of-war close to us. In answer to the fourth charge, I called Swinburne, who stated that if I did not, he would come forward. Swinburne acknowledged that he accused the captain of being shy, and that I reprimanded him for so doing. "Did he say that he would report you?" inquired one of the captains. "No, sir," replied Swinburne, "'cause he never meant to do it." This was an unfortunate answer.

To the fifth charge, I brought several witnesses to prove the words of Captain Hawkins, and the sense in which they were taken by the ship's company, and the men calling out "Shame!" when he used the expression.

To refute the other charges I called one or two witnesses, and the court then adjourned, inquiring of me when I would be ready to commence my defence. I requested a day to prepare, which was readily granted; and the ensuing day the court did not sit. I hardly need say that I was busily employed, arranging my defence with my counsel. At last all was done, and I went to bed tired and unhappy; but I slept soundly, which could not be said of my counsel, for he went on shore at eleven o'clock, and sat up all night making a fair copy. After all, the fairest court of justice is a naval court-martial—no brow-beating of witnesses, an evident inclination towards the prisoner—every allowance and every favour granted him, and no legal quibbles attended to. It is a court of equity, with very few exceptions; and the humbler the individual, the greater the chance in his favour.

I was awoke the following morning by my counsel, who had not gone to bed the previous night, and who had come off at seven o'clock to read over with me my defence. At nine o'clock I again proceeded on board, and in a short time the court was sitting. I came in, handed my defence to the judge-advocate, who read it aloud to the court. I have a copy still by me, and will give the whole of it to the reader.

"Mr President and Gentlemen,—After nearly fourteen years' service in his Majesty's navy, during which I have been twice made prisoner, twice wounded, and once wrecked; and, as I trust I shall prove to you, by certificates and the public despatches, I have done my duty with zeal and honour; I now find myself in a situation in which I never expected to be placed—that of being arraigned before and brought to a court-martial for charges of mutiny, disaffection, and disrespect towards my superior officer. If the honourable court will examine the certificates I am about to produce, they will find that, until I sailed with Captain Hawkins, my conduct has always been supposed to have been diametrically opposite to that which is now imputed to me. I have always been diligent and obedient to command; and I have only to regret that the captains with whom I have had the honour to sail are not now present to corroborate by their oral evidence the truth of these documents. Allow me, in the first place, to point out to the court, that the charges against me are spread over a large space of time, amounting to nearly eighteen months, during the whole of which period Captain Hawkins never stated to me that it was his intention to try me by a court-martial; and, although repeatedly in the presence of a senior officer, has never preferred any charge against me. The articles of war state expressly that if any officer, soldier, or marine has any complaint to make he is to do so upon his arrival at any port or fleet where he may fall in with a superior officer. I admit that this article of war refers to complaints to be made by inferiors against superiors; but, at the same time, I venture to submit to the honourable court that a superior is equally bound to prefer a charge, or to give notice that the charge will be preferred, on the first seasonable opportunity, instead of lulling the offender into security, and disarming him in his defence, by allowing the time to run on so long as to render him incapable of bringing forward his witnesses. I take the liberty of calling this to your attention, and shall now proceed to answer the charges which have been brought against me.

"I am accused of having held a conversation with an inferior officer on the quarter-deck of his Majesty's brig *Rattlesnake*, in which my captain was treated with contempt. That it may not be supposed that Mr Swinburne was a new acquaintance, made upon my joining the brig, I must observe that he was an old shipmate, with whom I had served many years, and with whose worth I was well acquainted. He was my instructor in my more youthful days, and has been rewarded for his merit, with the warrant which he now holds as gunner of His Majesty's brig *Rattlesnake*. The offensive observation, in the first place, was not mine; and, in the second, it was couched in general terms. Here Mr Swinburne has pointedly confessed that *he* did refer to the captain, although the observation was in the plural; but that does not prove the charge against me—on the contrary, adds weight to the assertion of Mr Swinburne, that I was guiltless of the present charge. That Captain Hawkins has acted as a spy, his own evidence on this charge, as well as that brought forward by other witnesses, will decidedly prove; but as the truth of the observation does not warrant the utterance, I am glad that no such expression escaped my lips.

"Upon the second charge I shall dwell but a short time. It is true that there is a general order that no stoves shall be alight after a certain hour; but I will appeal to the honourable court, whether a first lieutenant is not considered to have a degree of licence of judgment in all that concerns the interior discipline of the ship. The surgeon sent to say that a stove was required for one of the sick. I was in bed at the time, and replied immediately in the affirmative. Does Captain Hawkins mean to assert to the honourable court, that he would have refused the request of the surgeon? Most certainly not. The only error I committed, if it were an error, was not going through the form of awaking Captain Hawkins, to ask the permission, which, as first lieutenant, I thought myself authorized to give.

"The charge against me, of having sent away two boats, contrary to his order, I have already disproved by witnesses. The order of Captain Hawkins was, not to communicate with the shore. My reasons for sending away the boats"—(Here Captain Hawkins interposed, and stated to the president that my reasons were not necessary to be received. The court was cleared, and, on our return, the court had decided, that my reasons ought to be given, and I continued.) "My reasons for sending away these boats, or rather it was one boat which was despatched to the two frigates, if I remember well, were, that the brig was in a state of mutiny. The captain had tied up one of the men, and the ship's company refused to be flogged. Captain Hawkins then went on shore to the admiral, to report the situation of his ship, and I conceived it my duty to make it known to the men-of-war anchored close to us. I shall not enter into further particulars, as they will only detain the honourable court; and I am aware that this court-martial is held upon my conduct, and not upon that of Captain Hawkins. To the charge of again holding disrespectful language on the quarter-deck, as overheard by Captain. Hawkins, I must refer the honourable court to the evidence, in which it is plainly proved that the remarks upon him were not mine, but those of Mr Swinburne, and that I remonstrated with Mr Swinburne for using such unguarded expressions. The only point of difficulty is, whether it was not my duty to have reported such language. I reply, that there is no proof that I did not intend to report it; but the presence of Captain Hawkins, who heard what was said, rendered such report unnecessary.

"On the fifth charge, I must beg that the court will be pleased to consider that some allowance ought to be made for a moment of irritation. My character was traduced by Captain Hawkins, supposing that I was dead; so much so, that even the ship's company cried out *shame*. I am aware, that no language of a superior officer can warrant a retort from an inferior; but, as what I intended to imply by that language is not yet known, although Captain Hawkins has given an explanation to his, I shall merely say, that I meant no more by my insinuations, than Captain Hawkins did at the time, by those which he made use of with respect to me.

"Upon the other trifling charges brought forward, I lay no stress, as I consider them fully refuted by the evidence which has been already adduced; and I shall merely observe, that, for reasons best known to himself, I have been met with a most decided hostility on the part of Captain Hawkins, from the time that he first joined the ship; that, on every occasion, he has used all his efforts to render me uncomfortable, and embroil me with others; that, not content with narrowly watching my conduct on board, he has resorted to his spy-glass from the shore; and, instead of assisting me in the execution of a duty sufficiently arduous, he has thrown every obstacle in my way, placed inferior officers as spies over my conduct, and made me feel so humiliated in the presence of the ship's company, over which I have had to superintend, and in the disciplining of which I had a right to look to him for support, that, were it not that some odium would necessarily be attached to the sentence, I should feel it as one of the happiest events of my life that I were dismissed from the situation which I now hold under his command. I now beg that the honourable court will allow the documents I lay upon the table to be read in support of my character."

When this was over, the court was cleared, that they might decide upon the sentence. I waited about half an hour in the greatest anxiety, when I was again summoned to attend. The usual forms of reading the papers were gone through, and then came the sentence, which was read by the president, he and the whole court standing up with their cocked hats on their heads. After the preamble, it concluded with saying, "that it was the opinion of that court that the charges had been *partly* proved, and therefore, that Lieutenant Peter Simple was dismissed his ship; but, in consideration of his good character and services, his case was strongly recommended to the consideration of the Lords Commissioners of the Admiralty."

Chapter LXIII

Peter looks upon his loss as something gained—Goes on board the Rattlesnake *to pack up, and is ordered to pack off—Polite leave-taking between relations. Mrs Trotter better and better—Goes to London, and afterwards falls into all manner of misfortunes by the hands of robbers, and of his own uncle.*

I hardly knew whether I felt glad or sorry at this sentence. On the one hand, it was almost a deathblow to my future advancement or employment in the service; on the other, the recommendation very much softened down the sentence, and I was quite happy to be quit of Captain Hawkins, and free to hasten to my poor sister. I bowed respectfully to the court, which immediately adjourned. Captain Hawkins followed the captains on the quarter-deck, but none of them would speak to him—so much to his disadvantage had come out during the trial.

About ten minutes afterwards, one of the elder captains composing the court called me into the cabin. "Mr Simple," said he, "we are all very sorry for you. Our sentence could not be more lenient, under the circumstances: it was that conversation with the gunner at the taffrail which floored you. It must be a warning to you to be more careful in future, how you permit any one to speak of the conduct of your superiors on the quarter-deck. I am desired by the president to let you know that it is our intention to express ourselves very strongly to the admiral in your behalf; so much so, that if another captain applies for you, you will have no difficulty in being appointed to a ship; and as for leaving your present ship, under any other circumstances I should consider it a matter of congratulation."

I returned my sincere thanks, and soon afterwards quitted the guard-ship, and went on board of the brig to pack up my clothes, and take leave of my messmates. On my arrival, I found that Captain Hawkins had preceded me, and he was on deck when I came up the side. I hastened down into the gun-room, where I received the condolements of my messmates.

"Simple, I wish you joy," cried Thompson, loud enough for the captain to hear on deck. "I wish I had your luck; I wish somebody would try me by a court-martial."

"As it has turned out," replied I, in a loud voice, "and after the communication made to me by the captains composing the court, of what they intend to say to the Admiralty, I agree with you, Thompson, that it is a very kind act on the part of Captain Hawkins, and I feel quite grateful to them."

"Steward, come—glasses," cried Thompson, "and let us drink success to
Mr Simple."

All this was very annoying to Captain Hawkins, who overheard every word. When our glasses were filled—"Simple, your good health, and may I meet with as good a messmate," said Thompson.

At this moment, the sergeant of marines put his head in at the gun-room door, and said, in a most insolent tone, that I was to leave the ship immediately. I was so irritated, that I threw my glass of grog in his face, and he ran up to the captain to make the complaint; but I did not belong to the ship, and even if I had, I would have resented such impertinence.

Captain Hawkins was in a great rage, and I believe would have written for another court-martial, but he had had enough of them. He inquired very particularly of the sergeant whether he had told me that I was to leave the ship directly, or whether, that Captain Hawkins desired that I should leave the ship immediately; and finding that he had not given the latter message (which I was aware of, for had he given it, I dare not have acted as I did); he then sent down again by one of the midshipmen, desiring me to leave the ship immediately. My reply was, that I should certainly obey his orders with the greatest pleasure. I hastened to pack up my clothes, reported myself ready to the second lieutenant, who went up for permission to man a boat, which was refused by Captain Hawkins, who said I might go on shore in a shore-boat. I called one alongside, shook hands with all my messmates, and when I arrived on the quarter-deck, with Swinburne, and some of the best men, who came forward; Captain Hawkins stood by the binnacle, bursting with rage. As I went over the planeshear, I took my hat off to him, and wished him good-morning very respectfully, adding, "If you have any commands for my *uncle*, Captain Hawkins, I shall be glad to execute them."

This observation, which showed him that I knew the connection and correspondence between them, made him gasp with emotion. "Leave the ship, sir, or by God I'll put you in irons for mutiny," cried he. I again took off my hat, and went down the side, and shoved off.

As soon as I was a few yards distant, the men jumped on the carronades and cheered, and I perceived Captain Hawkins order them down, and before I was a cable's length from her, the pipe "all hands to punishment;" so I presume some of the poor fellows suffered for their insubordination in showing their good will. I acknowledge that I might have left the ship in a more dignified manner, and that my conduct was not altogether correct; but still, I state what I really did do, and some allowance must be made for my feelings. This is certain, that my conduct after the court-martial, was more deserving of punishment, than that for which I had been tried. But I was in a state of feverish excitement, and hardly knew what I did.

When I arrived at Sally Port, I had my effects wheeled up to the Blue Posts, and packing up those which I most required, I threw off my uniform, and was once more a gentleman at large. I took my place in the mail for that evening, sent a letter of thanks, with a few bank notes, to my counsel, and then sat down and wrote a long letter to O'Brien, acquainting him with the events which had taken place.

I had just finished, and sealed it up, when in came Mrs Trotter. "Oh my dear Mr Simple! I'm so sorry, and I have come to console you. There's nothing like women when men are in affliction, as poor Trotter used to say, as he laid his head in my lap. When do you go to town?"

"This evening, Mrs Trotter."

"I hope I am to continue to attend the ship?"

"I hope so too, Mrs Trotter, I have no doubt but you will."

"Now, Mr Simple, how are you off for money? Do you want a little? You can pay me by-and-by. Don't be afraid. I'm not quite so poor as I was when you came down to mess with Trotter and me, and when you gave me the dozen pair of stockings. I know what it is to want money, and what it is to want friends."

"Many thanks to you, Mrs Trotter," replied I; "but I have sufficient to take me home, and then I can obtain more."

"Well, I'm glad of it, but it was offered in earnest. Good-bye, God bless you! Come, Mr Simple, give me a kiss; it won't be the first time."

I kissed her, for I felt grateful for her kindness; and with a little smirking and ogling she quitted the room. I could not help thinking, after she was gone, how little we know the hearts of others. If I had been asked if Mrs Trotter was a person to have done a generous action, from what I had seen of her in adversity, I should have decidedly said, No. Yet in this offer she was disinterested, for she knew the service well enough to be aware that I had little chance of being a first lieutenant again, and of being of service to her. And how often does it also occur, that those who ought, from gratitude or long friendship, to do all they can to assist you, turn from you in your necessity, and prove false and treacherous! It is God alone who knows our hearts. I sent my letter to O'Brien to the admiral's office, sat down to a dinner which I could not taste, and at seven o'clock got into the mail.

When I arrived in town I was much worse, but I did not wait more than an hour. I took my place in a coach which did not go to the town near which we resided; for I had inquired and found that coach was full, and I did not choose to wait another day. The coach in which I took my place went within forty miles of the vicarage, and I intended to post across the country. The next evening I arrived at the point of separation, and taking out my portmanteau, ordered a chaise, and set off for what had once been my home. I could hardly hold my head up, I was so ill, and I lay in a corner of the chaise in a sort of dream, kept from sleeping from intense pain in the forehead and temples. It was about nine o'clock at night, when we were in a dreadful jolting road, the shocks proceeding from which gave me agonizing pain, that the chaise was stopped by two men, who dragged me out on the grass. One stood over me, while the other rifled the chaise. The post-boy, who appeared a party to the transaction, remained quietly on his horse, and as soon as they had taken my effects, turned round and drove off. They then rifled my person, taking away everything that I had, leaving me nothing but my trousers and shirt. After a short consultation, they ordered me to walk on in the direction in which we had been proceeding in the chaise, and to hasten as fast as I could, or they would blow my brains out. I complied with their request, thinking myself fortunate to have escaped so well. I knew that I was still thirty miles at least from the vicarage; but ill as I was, I hoped to be able to reach it on foot. I walked during the remainder of the night, but I got on but slowly. I reeled from one side of the road to the other, and occasionally sat down to rest. Morning dawned, and I perceived habitations not far from me. I staggered on in my course.

The fever now raged in me, my head was splitting with agony, and I tottered to a bank near a small neat cottage, on the side of the road. I have a faint recollection of some one coming to me and taking my hand, but nothing further; and it was not till many months afterwards, that I became acquainted with the circumstances which I now relate. It appears that the owner of the cottage was a half-pay lieutenant in the army, who had sold-out on account of his wounds. I was humanely taken into his house, laid on a bed, and a surgeon requested to come to me immediately. I had now lost all recollection, and who I was they could not ascertain. My pockets were empty, and it was only by the mark on my linen that they found that my name was Simple. For three weeks I remained in a state of alternate stupor and delirium. When the latter came on, I raved of Lord Privilege, O'Brien, and Celeste. Mr Selwin, the officer who had so kindly assisted me, knew that Simple was the patronymic name of Lord Privilege, and he immediately wrote to his lordship, stating that a young man of the name of Simple, who, in his delirium called upon him and Captain O'Brien, was lying in a most dangerous state in his house, and, that as he presumed I was a relative of his lordship's he had deemed it right to apprise him of the fact.

My uncle, who knew that it must be me, thought this too favourable an opportunity, provided I should live, not to have me in his power. He wrote to say that he would be there in a day or two; at the same time thanking Mr Selwin for his kind attention to his poor nephew, and requesting that no expense might be spared. When my uncle arrived, which he did in his own chariot, the crisis of the fever was over, but I was still in a state of stupor, arising from extreme debility. He thanked Mr Selwin for his attention, which he said he was afraid was of little avail, as I was every year becoming more deranged; and he expressed his fears that it would terminate in chronic lunacy. "His poor father died in the same state," continued my uncle, passing his hand across his eyes, as if much affected. "I have brought my physician with me, to see if he can be moved. I shall not be satisfied unless I am with him night and day."

The physician (who was my uncle's valet) took me by the hand, felt my pulse, examined my eyes, and pronounced that it would be very easy to move me, and that I should recover sooner in a more airy room. Of course, Mr Selwin raised no objections, putting down all to my uncle's regard for me; and my clothes were put on me, as I lay in a state of insensibility, and I was lifted into the chariot. It is most wonderful that I did not die from being thus taken out of my bed in such a state, but it pleased Heaven that it should be otherwise. Had such an event taken place, it would probably have pleased my uncle much better than my surviving. When I was in the carriage, supported by the pseudo-physician, my uncle again thanked Mr Selwin, begged that he would command his interest, wrote a handsome cheque for the surgeon who had attended me, and getting into the carriage, drove off with me still in a state of insensibility—that is, I was not so insensible, but I think I felt I had been removed, and I heard the rattling of the wheels; but my mind was so uncollected, and I was in a state of such weakness, that I could not feel assured of it for a minute.

For some days afterwards, for I recollect nothing about the journey, I found myself in bed in a dark room and my arms confined. I recalled my senses, and by degrees was able to recollect all that had occurred, until I laid down by the roadside. Where was I? The room was dark, I could distinguish nothing; that I had attempted to do myself some injury, I took for granted, or my arms would not have been secured. I had been in a fever and delirious, I supposed, and had now recovered. I had been in a reverie for more than an hour, wondering why I was left alone, when the door of the apartment opened. "Who is there?" inquired I.

"Oh! you've come to yourself again," said a gruff voice; "then I'll give you a little daylight."

He took down a shutter which covered the whole of the window, and a flood of light poured in, which blinded me. I shut my eyes, and by degrees admitted the light until I could bear it. I looked at the apartment: the walls were bare and whitewashed. I was on a truckle-bed. I looked at the window—it was closed up with iron bars.—"Why, where am I?" inquired I of the man, with alarm.

"Where are you?" replied he; "why, in Bedlam!"

Chapter LXIV

As O'Brien said; it's a long lane that has no turning—I am rescued, and happiness pours in upon me as fast as misery before overwhelmed me.

The shock was too great—I fell back on my pillow insensible. How long I laid, I know not, but when I recovered the keeper was gone, and I found a jug of water and some bread by the side of the bed, I drank the water, and the effect it had upon me was surprising. I felt that I could get up, and I rose: my arms had been unpinioned during my swoon. I got on my feet, and staggered to the window. I looked out, saw the bright sun, the passers-by, the houses opposite—all looked cheerful and gay, but I was a prisoner in a madhouse. Had I been mad? I reflected, and supposed that I had been, and had been confined by those who knew nothing of me. It never came into my head that my uncle had been a party to it. I threw myself on the bed, and relieved myself with tears. It was about noon that the medical people, attended by the keepers and others, came into my apartment. "Is he quite quiet?" "O Lord! yes, sir, as quiet as a lamb," replied the man who had before entered. I then spoke to the medical gentleman, begging him to tell why, and how, I had been brought here. He answered mildly and soothingly, saying that I was there at the wish of my friends, and that every care would be taken of me; that he was aware that my paroxysms were only occasional, and that, during the time I was quiet, I should have every indulgence that could be granted, and that he hoped that I soon should be perfectly well, and be permitted to leave the hospital. I replied by stating who I was, and how I had been taken ill. The doctor shook his head, advised me to lie down as much as possible, and then quitted me to visit the other patients.

As I afterwards discovered, my uncle had had me confined upon the plea that I was a young man who was deranged with an idea that his name was Simple, and that he was the heir to the title and estates; that I was very troublesome at times, forcing my way into his house and insulting the servants, but in every other respect was harmless; that my paroxysms generally ended in a violent fever, and it was more from the fear of my coming to some harm, than from any ill-will towards the poor young man, that he wished me to remain in the hospital, and be taken care of. The reader may at once perceive the art of this communication: I, having no idea why I was confined, would of course continue to style myself by my true name; and as long as I did this, so long would I be considered in a deranged state. The reader must not therefore be surprised when I tell him that I remained in Bedlam for one year and eight months. The doctor called upon me for two or three days, and finding me quiet, ordered me to be allowed books, paper, and ink, to amuse myself; but every attempt at explanation was certain to be the signal for him to leave my apartment. I found, therefore, not only by him, but from the keeper, who paid no attention to anything I said, that I had no chance of being listened to, or of obtaining my release.

After the first month, the doctor came to me no more: I was a quiet patient, and he received the report of the keeper. I was sent there with every necessary document to prove that I was mad; and, although a very little may establish a case of lunacy, it requires something very strong indeed to prove that you are in your right senses. In Bedlam I found it impossible. At the same time I was well treated, was allowed all necessary comforts, and such amusement as could be obtained from books, &c. I had no reason to complain of the keeper—except that he was too much employed to waste his time in listening to what he did not believe. I wrote several letters to my sister and to O'Brien, during the first two or three months, and requested the keeper to put them in the post. This he promised to do, never refusing to take the letters; but, as I afterwards found out, they were invariably destroyed. Yet I still bore up with the hopes of release for some time; but the anxiety relative to my sister, when I thought of her situation, my thoughts of Celeste and of O'Brien, sometimes quite overcame me; then, indeed, I would almost become frantic, and the keeper would report that I had had a paroxysm. After six months I became melancholy, and I wasted away. I no longer attempted to amuse myself, but sat all day with my eyes fixed upon vacancy. I no longer attended to my person; I allowed my beard to grow— my face was never washed, unless mechanically, when ordered by the keeper; and if I was not mad, there was every prospect of my soon becoming so. Life passed away as a blank—I had become indifferent to everything—I noted time no more—the change of seasons was unperceived —even the day and the night followed without my regarding them.

I was in this unfortunate situation, when one day the door was opened, and, as had been often the custom during my imprisonment, visitors were going round the establishment, to indulge their curiosity, in witnessing the degradation of their fellow-creatures, or to offer their commiseration. I paid no heed to them, not even casting up my eyes. "This young man," said the medical gentleman who accompanied the party, "has entertained the strange idea that his name is Simple, and that he is the rightful heir to the title and property of Lord Privilege."

One of the visitors came up to me, and looked me in the face. "And so he is," cried he to the doctor, who looked with astonishment. "Peter, don't you know me?" I started up. It was General O'Brien. I flew into his arms, and burst into tears.

"Sir," said General O'Brien, leading me to the chair, and seating me upon it, "I tell you that *is* Mr Simple, the nephew of Lord Privilege; and I believe, the heir to the title. If, therefore, his assertion of such being the case is the only proof of his insanity, he is illegally confined. I am here, a foreigner, and a prisoner on parole; but I am not without friends. My Lord Belmore," said he, turning to another of the visitors who had accompanied him, "I pledge you my honour that what I state is true; and I request that you will immediately demand the release of this poor young man."

"I assure you, sir, that I have Lord Privilege's letter," observed the doctor.

"Lord Privilege is a scoundrel," replied General O'Brien. "But there is justice to be obtained in this country, and he shall pay dearly for his *lettre de cachet*. My dear Peter, how fortunate was my visit to this horrid place! I had heard so much of the excellent arrangements of this establishment, that I agreed to walk round with Lord Belmore; but I find that it is abused."

"Indeed, General O'Brien, I have been treated with kindness," replied I; "and particularly by this gentleman. It was not his fault."

General O'Brien and Lord Belmore then inquired of the doctor if he had any objection to my release.

"None whatever, my lord, even if he were insane; although I now see how I have been imposed upon. We allow the friends of any patient to remove him, if they think that they can pay him more attention. He may leave with you this moment."

I now did feel my brain turn with the revulsion from despair to hope, and I fell back in my seat. The doctor, perceiving my condition, bled me copiously, and laid me on the bed, where I remained more than an hour, watched by General O'Brien. I then got up, calm and thankful. I was shaved by the barber of the establishment, washed and dressed myself, and, leaning on the general's arm, was let out. I cast my eyes upon the two celebrated stone figures of Melancholy and Raving Madness, as I passed them; I trembled, and clung more tightly to the general's arm, was assisted into the carriage, and bade farewell to madness and misery. The general said nothing until we approached the hotel where he resided, in Dover-street, and then he inquired, in a low voice, whether I could bear more excitement.

"It is Celeste you mean, general?"

"It is, my dear boy; she is here;" and he squeezed my hand.

"Alas!" cried I, "what hopes have I now of Celeste?"

"More than you had before," replied the general. "She lives but for you; and if you are a beggar, I have a competence to make you sufficiently comfortable."

I returned the general's pressure of the hand, but could not speak. We descended, and in a minute I was led by the father into the arms of the astonished daughter.

I must pass over a few days, during which I had almost recovered my health and spirits, and had narrated my adventures to General O'Brien and Celeste. My first object was to discover my sister. What had become of poor Ellen, in the destitute condition in which she had been left I knew not; and I resolved to go down to the vicarage, and make inquiries. I did not, however, set off until a legal adviser had been sent for by General O'Brien, and due notice given to Lord Privilege of an action to be immediately brought against him for false imprisonment.

I set off in the mail, and the next evening arrived at the town of———. I hastened to the parsonage, and the tears stood in my eyes as I thought of my mother, my poor father, and the peculiar and doubtful situation of my dear sister. I was answered by a boy in livery, and found the present incumbent at home. He received me politely, listened to my story, and then replied that my sister had set off for London on the day of his arrival, and that she had not communicated her intentions to any one. Here, then, was all clue lost, and I was in despair. I walked to the town in time to throw myself into the mail, and the next evening joined Celeste and the general, to whom I communicated the intelligence, and requested advice how to proceed.

Lord Belmore called the next morning, and the general consulted him. His lordship took great interest in my concerns, and, previous to any further steps, advised me to step into his carriage, and allow him to relate my case to the First Lord of the Admiralty. This was done immediately; and, as I had now an opportunity of speaking freely to his lordship, I explained to him the conduct of Captain Hawkins, and his connection with my uncle; also the reason of my uncle's persecution. His lordship, finding me under such powerful protection as Lord Belmore's, and having an eye to my future claims, which my uncle's conduct gave him reason to suppose were well founded, was extremely gracious, and said that I should hear from him in a day or two. He kept his word, and, on the third day after my interview, I received a note, announcing my promotion to the rank of commander. I was delighted with this good fortune, as was General O'Brien and Celeste.

When at the Admiralty, I inquired about O'Brien, and found that he was expected home every day. He had gained great reputation in the East Indies, was chief in command at the taking of some of the islands, and, it was said, was to be created a baronet for his services. Everything wore a favourable aspect, excepting the disappearance of my sister. This was a weight on my mind I could not remove.

But I have forgotten to inform the reader by what means General O'Brien and Celeste arrived so opportunely in England. Martinique had been captured by our forces about six months before, and the whole of the garrison surrendered as prisoners of war. General O'Brien was sent home, and allowed to be on parole; although born a Frenchman, he had very high connections in Ireland, of whom Lord Belmore was one. When they arrived, they had made every inquiry for me without success; they knew that I had been tried by a court-martial, and dismissed my ship, but after that, no clue could be found for my discovery.

Celeste, who was fearful that some dreadful accident had occurred to me, had suffered very much in health; and General O'Brien, perceiving how much his daughter's happiness depended upon her attachment for me, had made up his mind that if I were found we should be united. I hardly need say how delighted he was when he discovered me, though in a situation so little to be envied.

The story of my incarceration, of the action to be brought against my uncle, and the reports of foul play relative to the succession, had in the meantime been widely circulated among the nobility; and I found that every attention was paid me, and I was repeatedly invited out as an object of curiosity and speculation. The loss of my sister also was a subject of much interest, and many people, from goodwill, made every inquiry to discover her. I had returned one day from the solicitor's, who had advertised for her in the newspapers without success, when I found a letter for me on the table, in an Admiralty enclosure. I opened it—the enclosure was one from O'Brien, who had just cast anchor at Spithead, and who had requested that the letter should be forwarded to me, if any one could tell my address. I tore it open.

"My dear Peter,—Where are, and what has become of, you? I have received no letters for these two years, and I have fretted myself to death. I received your letter about the rascally court-martial; but perhaps you have not heard that the little scoundrel is dead. Yes, Peter; he brought your letter out in his own ship, and that was his death-warrant. I met him at a private party. He brought up your name— I allowed him to abuse you, and then told him he was a liar and a scoundrel; upon which he challenged me, very much against his will; but the affront was so public, that he couldn't help himself. Upon which I shot him, with all the good-will in the world, and could he have jumped up again twenty times, like Jack-in-the-Box, I would have shot him every time. The dirty scoundrel! but there's an end of him. Nobody pitied him, for every one hated him; and the admiral only looked grave, and then was very much obliged to me for giving him a vacancy for his nephew. By-the-bye, from some unknown hand, but I presume from the officers of his ship, I received a packet of correspondence between him and your worthy uncle, which is about as elegant a piece of rascality as ever was carried on between two scoundrels; but that's not all, Peter. I've got a young woman for you who will make your heart glad—not Mademoiselle Celeste, for I don't know where she is—but the wet-nurse who went out to India. Her husband was sent home as an invalid, and she was allowed her passage home with him in my frigate. Finding that he belonged to the regiment, I talked to him about one O'Sullivan, who married in Ireland, and mentioned the girl's name, and when he discovered that he was a countryman of mine he told me that his real name was O'Sullivan, sure enough, but that he had always served as O'Connell, and that his wife on board was the young woman in question. Upon which I sent to speak to her, and telling her that I knew all about it, and mentioning the names of Ella Flanagan and her mother, who had given me the information, she was quite astonished; and when I asked her what had become of the child which she took in place of her own, she told me that it had been drowned at Plymouth, and that her husband was saved at the same time by a young officer, 'whose name I have here,' says she; and then she pulled out of her neck your card, with Peter Simple on it. 'Now,' says I, 'do you know, good woman, that in helping on the rascally exchange of children, you ruin that very young man who saved your husband, for you deprive him of his title and property?" She stared like a stuck pig, when I said so, and then cursed and blamed herself, and declared she'd right you as soon as we came home; and most anxious she is still to do so, for she loves the very name of you; so you see, Peter, a good action has its reward sometimes in this world, and a bad action also, seeing as how I've shot that confounded villain who dared to ill-use you. I have plenty more to say to you, Peter; but I don't like writing what, perhaps, may never be read, so I'll wait till I hear from you; and then, as soon as I get through my business, we will set to and trounce that scoundrel of an uncle. I have twenty thousand pounds jammed together in the Consolidated, besides the Spice Islands, which will be a pretty penny; and every farthing of it shall go to right you, Peter, and make a lord of you, as I promised you often that you should be; and if you win you shall pay, and if you don't then d—n the luck and d—n the money too. I beg you will offer my best regards to Miss Ellen, and say how happy I shall be to hear that she is well; but it has always been on my mind, Peter, that your father did not leave too much behind him, and I wish to know how you both get on. I left you a _carte blanche_ at my agent's, and I only hope that you have taken advantage of it, if required; if not, you're not the Peter that I left behind me. So now, farewell, and don't forget to answer my letter in no time. Ever yours,

"Terence O'Brien."

This was indeed joyful intelligence. I handed the letter to General O'Brien, who read it, Celeste hanging over his shoulder, and perusing it at the same time.

"This is well," said the General. "Peter, I wish you joy, and Celeste, I ought to wish you joy also at your future prospects. It will indeed be a gratification if ever I hail you as Lady Privilege."

"Celeste," said I, "you did not reject me when I was pennyless, and in disgrace. O my poor sister Ellen! If I could but find you, how happy should I be!"

I sat down to write to O'Brien, acquainting him with all that had occurred, and the loss of my dear sister. The day after the receipt of my letter, O'Brien burst into the room. After the first moments of congratulation were past, he said, "My heart's broke, Peter, about your sister Ellen: find her I must. I shall give up my ship, for I'll never give up the search as long as I live. I must find her."

"Do, pray, my dear O'Brien, and I only wish—"

"Wish what, Peter? shall I tell you what I wish?—that if I find her, you'll give her to me for my trouble."

"As far as I am concerned, O'Brien, nothing would give me greater pleasure; but God knows to what wretchedness and want may have compelled her."

"Shame on you, Peter, to think so of your sister. I pledge my honour for her. Poor, miserable, and unhappy she may be—but no—no, Peter. You don't know—you don't love her as I do, if you can allow such thoughts to enter your mind."

This conversation took place at the window: we then turned round to General O'Brien and Celeste.

"Captain O'Brien," said the general.

"Sir Terence O'Brien, if you please, general. His Majesty has given me a handle to my name."

"I congratulate you, Sir Terence," said the general, shaking him by the hand: "what I was about to say is, that I hope you will take up your quarters at this hotel, and we will all live together. I trust that we shall soon find Ellen: in the meanwhile we have no time to lose, in our exposure of Lord Privilege. Is the woman in town?"

"Yes, and under lock and key; but the devil a fear of her. Millions would not bribe her to wrong him who risked his life for her husband. She's Irish, general, to the back bone. Nevertheless, Peter, we must go to our solicitor, to give the intelligence, that he may take the necessary steps."

For three weeks, O'Brien was diligent in his search for Ellen, employing every description of emissary without success. In the meanwhile, the general and I were prosecuting our cause against Lord Privilege. One morning, Lord

Belmore called upon us, and asked the general if we would accompany him to the theatre, to see two celebrated pieces performed. In the latter, which was a musical farce, a new performer was to come out, of whom report spoke highly. Celeste consented, and after an early dinner, we joined his lordship in his private box, which was above the stage, on the first tier. The first piece was played, and Celeste, who had never seen the performance of Young, was delighted. The curtain then drew up for the second piece. In the second act, the new performer, a Miss Henderson, was led by the manager on the stage; she was apparently much frightened and excited, but three rounds of applause gave her courage, and she proceeded. At the very first notes of her voice I was startled, and O'Brien, who was behind, threw himself forward to look at her; but as we were almost directly above, and her head was turned the other way, we could not distinguish her features. As she proceeded in her song, she gained courage, and her face was turned towards us, and she cast her eyes up—saw me—the recognition was mutual—I held out my arm, but could not speak—she staggered, and fell down in a swoon.

"'Tis Ellen!" cried O'Brien, rushing past me; and making one spring down on the stage, he carried her off, before any other person could come to her assistance. I followed him, and found him with Ellen still in his arms, and the actresses assisting in her recovery. The manager came forward to apologize, stating that the young lady was too ill to proceed, and the audience, who had witnessed the behaviour of O'Brien and myself, were satisfied with the romance in real life which had been exhibited. Her part was read by another, but the piece was little attended to, every one trying to find out the occasion of this uncommon occurrence. In the meantime, Ellen was put into a hackney-coach by O'Brien and me, and we drove to the hotel, where we were soon joined by the general and Celeste.

Chapter LXV

It never rains but it pours, whether it be good or bad news—I succeed in everything, and to everything, my wife, my title, and estate—And "All's well that ends well."

I shall pass over the scenes which followed, and give my sister's history in her own words.

"I wrote to you, my dear Peter, to tell you that I considered it my duty to pay all my father's debts with your money, and that there were but sixty pounds left when every claim had been satisfied; and I requested you to come to me as soon as you could, that I might have your counsel and assistance as to my future arrangements."

"I received your letter, Ellen, and was hastening to you, when—but no matter, I will tell my story afterwards."

"Day after day I waited with anxiety for a letter, and then wrote to the officers of the ship to know if any accident had occurred. I received an answer from the surgeon, informing me that you had quitted Portsmouth to join me, and had not since been heard of. You may imagine my distress at this communication, as I did not doubt but that something dreadful had occurred, as I knew, too well, that nothing would have detained you from me at such a time. The new vicar appointed had come down to look over the house, and to make arrangements for bringing in his family. The furniture he had previously agreed to take at a valuation, and the sum had been appropriated in liquidation of your father's debts. I had already been permitted to remain longer than was usual, and had no alternative but to quit, which I did not do until the last moment. I could not leave my address, for I knew not where I was to go. I took my place in the coach, and arrived in London. My first object was to secure the means of livelihood, by offering myself as a governess; but I found great difficulties from not being able to procure a good reference, and from not having already served in that capacity. At last I was taken into a family to bring up three little girls; but I soon found out how little chance I had of comfort. The lady had objected to me as too good-looking—for this same reason the gentleman insisted upon my being engaged.

"Thus was I a source of disunion; the lady treated me with harshness, and the gentleman with too much attention. At last her ill-treatment and his persecution, were both so intolerable, that I gave notice that I should leave my situation."

"I beg pardon, Miss Ellen, but you will oblige me with the name and residence of that gentleman?" said O'Brien.

"Indeed, Ellen, do no such thing," replied I; "continue your story."

"I could not obtain another situation as governess; for, as I always stated where I had been, and did not choose to give the precise reason for quitting, merely stating that I was not comfortable, whenever the lady was called upon for my character, she invariably spoke of me so as to prevent my obtaining a situation. At last I was engaged as teacher to a school. I had better have taken a situation as housemaid. I was expected to be everywhere, to do everything; was up at daylight, and never in bed till past midnight; fared very badly, and was equally ill paid; but still it was honest employment, and I remained there for more than a year; but, though as economical as possible, my salary would not maintain me in clothes and washing, which was all I required. There was a master of elocution, who came every week, and whose wife was the teacher of music. They took a great liking to me, and pointed out how much better I should be off if I could succeed on the stage, of which they had no doubt. For months I refused, hoping still to have some tidings of you; but at last my drudgery became so insupportable, and my means so decreased, that I unwillingly consented. It was then nineteen months since I had heard of you, and I mourned you as dead. I had no relations except my uncle, and I was unknown even to him. I quitted the situation, and took up my abode with the teacher of elocution and his wife, who treated me with every kindness, and prepared me for my new career. Neither at the school, which was three miles from London, nor at my new residence, which was over Westminster-bridge, did I ever see a newspaper. It was no wonder, therefore, that I did not know of your advertisements. After three months' preparation I was recommended and introduced to the manager by my kind friends, and accepted. You know the rest."

"Well, Miss Ellen, if any one ever tells you that you were on the stage, at all events you may reply that you wasn't there long."

"I trust not long enough to be recognised," replied she. "I recollect how often I have expressed my disgust at those who would thus consent to exhibit themselves; but circumstances strangely alter our feelings. I do, however, trust that I should have been respectable, even as an actress."

"That you would, Miss Ellen," replied O'Brien. "What did I tell you, Peter?"

"You pledged your honour that nothing would induce Ellen to disgrace her family, I recollect, O'Brien."

"Thank you, Sir Terence, for your good opinion," replied Ellen.

My sister had been with us about three days, during which I had informed her of all that had taken place, when, one evening, finding myself alone with her, I candidly stated to her what were O'Brien's feelings towards her, and pleaded his cause with all the earnestness in my power.

"My dear brother," she replied, "I have always admired Captain O'Brien's character, and always have felt grateful to him for his kindness and attachment to you; but I cannot say that I love him. I have never thought about him except as one to whom we are both much indebted."

"But do you mean to say that you could not love him?"

"No, I do not; and I will do all I can, Peter—I will try. I never will, if possible, make him unhappy who has been so kind to you."

"Depend upon it, Ellen, that with your knowledge of O'Brien, and with feelings of gratitude to him, you will soon love him, if once you accept him as a suitor. May I tell him—"

"You may tell him that he may plead his own cause, my dear brother; and, at all events, I will listen to no other until he has had fair play; but recollect that at present I only *like* him—like him _very much, _it is true; but still I only *like* him."

I was quite satisfied with my success, and so was O'Brien, when I told him. "By the powers, Peter, she's an angel, and I can't expect her to love an inferior being like myself; but if she'll only like me well enough to marry me, I'll trust to after-marriage for the rest. Love comes with the children, Peter. Well, but you need not say that to her—divil a bit—they shall come upon her like old age, without her perceiving it."

O'Brien having thus obtained permission, certainly lost no time in taking advantage of it. Celeste and I were more fondly attached every day. The solicitor declared my case so good, that he could raise fifty thousand pounds upon it. In short, all our causes were prosperous, when an event occurred, the details of which, of course, I did not obtain until some time afterwards, but which I shall narrate here.

My uncle was very much alarmed when he discovered that I had been released from Bedlam—still more so, when he had notice given him of a suit, relative to the succession to the title. His emissaries had discovered that the wet-nurse had been brought home in O'Brien's frigate, and was kept so close that they could not communicate with her. He now felt that all his schemes would prove abortive. His legal adviser was with him, and they had been walking in the garden, talking over the contingencies, when they stopped close to the drawing-room windows of the mansion at Eagle Park.

"But, sir," observed the lawyer, "if you will not confide in me, I cannot act for your benefit. You still assert that nothing of the kind has taken place?"

"I do," replied his lordship. "It is a foul invention."

"Then, my lord, may I ask you why you considered it advisable to imprison Mr Simple in Bedlam?"

"Because I hate him," retorted his lordship,—"detest him."

"And for what reason, my lord? his character is unimpeached, and he is your near relative."

"I tell you, sir, that I hate him—would that he were now lying dead at my feet!"

Hardly were the words out of my uncle's mouth, when a whizzing was heard for a second, and then something fell down within a foot of where they stood, with a heavy crash. They started—turned round—the adopted heir lay lifeless at their feet, and their legs were bespattered with his blood and his brains. The poor boy, seeing his lordship below, had leaned out of one of the upper windows to call to him, but lost his balance, and had fallen head foremost upon the wide stone pavement which surrounded the mansion. For a few seconds the lawyer and my uncle looked upon each other with horror.

"A judgment!—a judgment!" cried the lawyer, looking at his client. My uncle covered his face with his hands, and fell. Assistance now came out, but there was more than one to help up. The violence of his emotion had brought on an apoplectic fit, and my uncle, although he breathed, never spoke again.

It was in consequence of this tragical event, of which we did not know the particulars until afterwards, that the next morning my solicitor called upon me, and put a letter into my hand, saying, "Allow me to congratulate your lordship." We were all at breakfast at the time, and the general, O'Brien, and myself jumped up, all in such astonishment at this unexpected title being so soon conferred upon me, that we had a heavy bill for damages to pay; and had not Ellen caught the tea-urn, as it was tipping over, there would, in all probability, have been a doctor's bill into the bargain. The letter was eagerly read—it was from my uncle's legal adviser, who had witnessed the catastrophe, informing me, that all dispute as to the succession was at an end by the tragical event that had taken place, and that he had put seals upon everything, awaiting my arrival or instructions. The solicitor, as he presented the letter, said that he would take his leave, and call again in an hour or two, when I was more composed. My first movement, when I had read the letter aloud, was to throw my arms round Celeste, and embrace her—and O'Brien, taking the hint, did the same to Ellen, and was excused in consideration of circumstances; but, as soon as she could disengage herself, her arms were entwined round my neck, while Celeste was hanging on her father's. Having disposed of the ladies, the gentlemen now shook hands, and though we had not all appetites to finish our breakfasts, never was there a happier quintette.

In about an hour my solicitor returned, and congratulated me, and immediately set about the necessary preparations. I desired him to go down immediately to Eagle Park, attend to the funeral of my uncle, and the poor little boy who had paid so dearly for his intended advancement, and take charge from my uncle's legal adviser, who remained in the house. The "dreadful accident in high life" found its way into the papers of the day, and before dinner time a pile of visiting cards was poured in, which covered the table. The next day a letter arrived from the First Lord, announcing that he had made out my commission as post-captain, and trusted that I would allow him the pleasure of presenting it himself at his dinner hour, at half-past seven. Very much obliged to him, the "fool of the family" might have waited a long while for it.

While I was reading this letter, the waiter came up to say that a young woman below wanted to speak to me. I desired her to be shown up. As soon as she came in, she burst into tears, knelt down, and kissed my hand.

"Sure, it's you—oh! yes—it's you that saved my poor husband when I was assisting to your ruin. And an't I punished for my wicked doings—an't my poor boy dead?"

She said no more, but remained on her knees, sobbing bitterly. Of course, the reader recognises in her the wet-nurse who had exchanged her child. I raised her up, and desired her to apply to my solicitor to pay her expenses, and leave her address.

"But do you forgive me, Mr Simple? It's not that I have forgiven myself."

"I do forgive you with all my heart, my good woman. You have been punished enough."

"I have, indeed," replied she, sobbing; "but don't I deserve it all, and more too? God's blessing, and all the saints' too, upon your head, for your kind forgiveness, anyhow. My heart is lighter." And she quitted the room.

She had scarcely quitted the hotel, when the waiter came up again. "Another lady, my lord, wishes to speak with you, but she won't give her name."

"Really, my lord, you seem to have an extensive female acquaintance," said the general.

"At all events, I am not aware of any that I need be ashamed of. Show the lady up, waiter."

In a moment entered a fat, unwieldly little mortal, very warm from walking; she sat down in a chair, threw back her tippet, and then exclaimed, "Lord bless you, how you have grown! Gemini, if I can hardly believe my eyes; and I declare he don't know me."

"I really cannot exactly recollect where I had the pleasure of seeing you before, madam."

"Well, that's what I said to Jemima, when I went down in the kitchen.
'Jemima,' says I, 'I wonder if little Peter Simple will know me.' And
Jemima says, 'I think he would the parrot, marm.'"

"Mrs Handycock, I believe," said I, recollecting Jemima and the parrot, although, from a little thin woman, she had grown so fat as not to be recognisable.

"Oh! so you've found me out, Mr Simple—my lord, I ought to say. Well, I need not ask after your grandfather now, for I know he's dead; but as I was coming this way for orders, I thought I would just step in and see how you looked."

"I trust Mr Handycock is well, ma'am. Pray is he a bull or a bear?"

"Lord bless you, Mr Simple, my lord, I should say, he's been neither bull nor bear for this three years. He was obliged to *waddle*. If I didn't know much about bulls and bears, I know very well what a *lame duck* is, to my cost. We're off the Stock Exchange, and Mr Handycock is set up as a coal merchant."

"Indeed!"

"Yes; that is, we have no coals, but we take orders, and have half-a-crown a chaldron for our trouble. As Mr Handycock says, it's a very good business, if you only had enough of it. Perhaps your lordship may be able to give us an order. It's nothing out of your pocket, and something into ours."

"I shall be very happy, when I return again to town, Mrs Handycock. I hope the parrot is quite well."

"Oh! my lord, that's a sore subject; only think of Mr Handycock, when we retired from the 'Change, taking my parrot one day and selling it for five guineas, saying, five guineas were better than a nasty squalling bird. To be sure, there was nothing for dinner that day; but, as Jemima agreed with me, we'd rather have gone without a dinner for a month, than have parted with Poll. Since we've looked up a little in the world, I saved up five guineas, by hook or by crook, and tried to get Poll back again, but the lady said she wouldn't take fifty guineas for him."

Mrs Handycock then jumped from her chair, saying, "Good morning, my lord; I'll leave one of Mr Handycock's cards. Jemima would be so glad to see you."

As she left the room, Celeste laughingly asked me whether I had any more such acquaintances. I replied, that I believed not; but I must acknowledge that Mrs Trotter was brought to my recollection, and I was under some alarm, lest she should also come and pay me her respects.

The next day I had another unexpected visit. We had just sat down to dinner, when we heard a disturbance below; and, shortly after, the general's French servant came up in great haste, saying that there was a foreigner below, who wished to see me: and that he had been caning one of the waiters of the hotel, for not paying him proper respect.

"Who can that be?" thought I: and I went out of the door, and looked over the banisters, as the noise continued.

"You must not come here to beat Englishmen, I can tell you," roared one of the waiters. "What do we care for your foreign counts?"

"Sacre, canaille?" cried the other party, in a contemptuous voice, which I well knew.

"Ay, canal!—we'll duck you in the canal, if you don't mind."

"You will!" said the stranger, who had hitherto spoken French. "Allow me to observe—in the most delicate manner in the world—just to hint, that you are a d——d trencher-scraping, napkin-carrying, shilling-seeking, up-and-down-stairs son of a bitch—and take this for your impudence!"

The noise of the cane was again heard; and I hastened downstairs, where I found Count Shucksen thrashing two or three of the waiters without mercy. At my appearance, the waiters, who were showing fight, retreated to a short distance, out of reach of the cane.

"My dear count," exclaimed I, "is it you?"

"My dear Lord Privilege, will you excuse me? but these fellows are saucy."

"Then I'll have them discharged," replied I. "If a friend of mine, and an officer of your rank and distinction, cannot come to see me without insult, I will seek another hotel."

This threat of mine, and the reception I gave the count, put all to rights. The waiters sneaked off, and the master of the hotel apologised. It appeared that they had desired him to wait in the coffee-room until they could announce him, which had hurt the count's dignity.

"We are just sitting down to dinner, count; will you join us?"

"As soon as I have improved my toilet, my dear lord," replied he; "you must perceive that I am off a journey."

The master of the hotel bowed, and proceeded to show the count to a dressing-room. When I returned upstairs—"What was the matter?" inquired O'Brien.

"Oh, nothing!—a little disturbance in consequence of a foreigner not understanding English."

In about five minutes the waiter opened the door, and announced Count Shucksen.

"Now, O'Brien, you'll be puzzled," said I; and in came the count.

"My dear Lord Privilege," said he, coming up and taking me by the hand, "let me not be the last to congratulate you upon your accession. I was running up the channel in my frigate when a pilot-boat gave me a newspaper, in which I saw your unexpected change of circumstances. I made an excuse for dropping my anchor at Spithead this morning, and I have come up post, to express how sincerely I participate in your good fortune." Count Shucksen then politely saluted the ladies and the general, and turned round to O'Brien, who had been staring at him with astonishment. "Count Shucksen, allow me to introduce Sir Terence O'Brien."

"By the piper that played before Moses, but it's a puzzle," said O'Brien. "Blood and thunder! if it a'n't Chucks!—my dear fellow, when did you rise from your grave?"

"Fortunately," replied the count, as they shook each other's hands for some time, "I never went into it, Sir Terence. But now, with your permission, my lord, I'll take some food, as I really am not a little hungry. After dinner, Captain O'Brien, you shall hear my history."

His secret was confided to the whole party, upon my pledging myself for their keeping it locked up in their own breasts, which was a bold thing on my part, considering that two of them were ladies. The count stayed with us for some time, and was introduced everywhere. It was impossible to discover that he had not been bred up in a court, his manners were so good. He was a great favourite with the ladies; and his moustachios, bad French, and waltzing—an accomplishment he had picked up in Sweden—were quite the vogue. All the ladies were sorry when the Swedish count announced his departure by a P.P.C.

Before I left town I called upon the First Lord of the Admiralty, and procured for Swinburne a first-rate building—that is to say, ordered to be built. This he had often said he wished, as he was tired of the sea, after a service of forty-five years. Subsequently I obtained leave of absence for him every year, and he used to make himself very happy at Eagle Park. Most of his time was, however, passed on the lake, either fishing or rowing about; telling long stories to all who would join him in his water excursions.

A fortnight after my assuming my title, we set off for Eagle Park, and Celeste consented to my entreaties that the wedding should take place that day month. Upon this hint O'Brien spake; and, to oblige *me*, Ellen consented that we should be united on the same day.

O'Brien wrote to Father M'Grath; but the letter was returned by post, with "*dead*" marked upon the outside. O'Brien then wrote to one of his sisters, who informed him that Father M'Grath would cross the bog one evening when he had taken a very large proportion of whisky; and that he was seen out of the right path, and had never been heard of afterwards.

On the day appointed we were all united, and both unions have been attended with as much happiness as this world can afford. Both O'Brien and I are blessed with children, which, as O'Brien observed, have come upon us like old age, until we now can muster a large Christmas party in the two families. The general's head is white, and he sits and smiles, happy in his daughter's happiness, and in the gambols of his grandchildren.

Such, reader, is the history of Peter Simple, Viscount Privilege, no longer the fool, but the head of the family, who now bids you farewell.

THE END.

The Three Cutters

Chapter I

CUTTER THE FIRST

Reader, have you ever been at Plymouth? If you have, your eye must have dwelt with ecstasy upon the beautiful property of the Earl of Mount Edgcumbe: if you have not been at Plymouth, the sooner that you go there, the better. At Mount Edgcumbe you will behold the finest timber in existence, towering up to the summits of the hills, and feathering down to the shingle on the beach. And from this lovely spot you will witness one of the most splendid panoramas in the world. You will see—I hardly know what you will not see—you will see Ram Head, and Cawsand Bay; and then you will see the Breakwater, and Drake's Island, and the Devil's Bridge below you; and the town of Plymouth and its fortifications, and the Hoe; and then you will come to the Devil's Point, round which the tide runs devilish strong; and then you will see the New Victualling Office,—about which Sir James Gordon used to stump all day, and take a pinch of snuff from every man who carried a box, which all were delighted to give, and he was delighted to receive, proving how much pleasure may be communicated merely by a pinch of snuff—and then you will see Mount Wise and Mutton Cove; the town of Devonport, with its magnificent dockyard and arsenals, North Corner, and the way which leads to Saltash. And you will see ships building and ships in ordinary; and ships repairing and ships fitting; and hulks and convict ships, and the guardship; ships ready to sail and ships under sail; besides lighters, men-of-war's boats, dockyard-boats, bumboats, and shore-boats. In short, there is a great deal to see at Plymouth besides the sea itself: but what I particularly wish now, is, that you will stand at the battery of Mount Edgecumbe and look into Barn Pool below you, and there you will see, lying at single anchor, a cutter; and you may also see, by her pendant and ensign, that she is a yacht.

Of all the amusements entered into by the nobility and gentry of our island there is not one so manly, so exciting, so patriotic, or so national, as yacht-sailing. It is peculiar to England, not only from our insular position and our fine harbours, but because it requires a certain degree of energy and a certain amount of income rarely to be found elsewhere. It has been wisely fostered by our sovereigns, who have felt that the security of the kingdom is increased by every man being more or less a sailor, or connected with the nautical profession. It is an amusement of the greatest importance to the country; as it has much improved our ship-building and our ship-fitting, while it affords employment to our seamen and shipwrights. But if I were to say all that I could say in praise of yachts, I should never advance with my narrative. I shall therefore drink a bumper to the health of Admiral Lord Yarborough and the Yacht Club, and proceed.

You observe that this yacht is cutter-rigged, and that she sits gracefully on the smooth water. She is just heaving up her anchor; her foresail is loose, all ready to cast her—in a few minutes she will be under weigh. You see that there are some ladies sitting at the taffrail; and there are five haunches of venison hanging over the stern. Of all amusements, give me yachting. But we must go on board. The deck, you observe, is of narrow deal planks as white as snow; the guns are of polished brass; the bitts and binnacles of mahogany; she is painted with taste; and all the mouldings are gilded. There is nothing wanting; and yet how clear and unencumbered are her decks! Let us go below. This is the ladies' cabin: can anything be more tasteful or elegant? is it not luxurious? and, although so small, does not its very confined space astonish you, when you view so many comforts so beautifully arranged? This is the dining-room, and where the gentlemen repair. What can be more complete or *recherché*? and just peep into their state-rooms and bed-places. Here is the steward's room and the beaufet: the steward is squeezing lemons for the punch, and there is the champagne in ice; and by the side of the pail the long-corks are ranged up, all ready. Now, let us go forwards: here are the men's berths, not confined as in a man-of-war. No! luxury starts from abaft, and is not wholly lost, even at the fore-peak. This is the kitchen: is it not admirably arranged? What a *multum in parvo*! And how delightful are the fumes of the turtle-soup! At sea we do meet with rough weather at times; but, for roughing it out, give me a *yacht*. Now that I have shown you round the vessel, I must introduce the parties on board.

You observe that florid, handsome man in white trousers and blue jacket, who has a telescope in one hand, and is sipping a glass of brandy and water which he has just taken off the skylight. That is the owner of the vessel, and a member of the Yacht Club. It is Lord B—: he looks like a sailor, and he does not much belie his looks; yet I have seen him in his robes of state at the opening of the House of Lords. The one near to him is Mr Stewart, a lieutenant in the navy. He holds on by the rigging with one hand, because, having been actively employed all his life, he does not know what to do with hands which have nothing in them. He is *protégé* of Lord B., and is now on board as sailing-master of the yacht.

That handsome, well-built man who is standing by the binnacle, is a Mr Hautaine. He served six years as midshipman in the navy, and did not like it. He then served six years in a cavalry regiment, and did not like it. He then married, and in a much shorter probation, found that he did not like that. But he is very fond of yachts and other men's wives, if he does not like his own; and wherever he goes, he is welcome.

That young man with an embroidered silk waistcoat and white gloves, bending to talk to one of the ladies, is a Mr Vaughan. He is to be seen at Almack's, at Crockford's, and everywhere else. Everybody knows him, and he knows everybody. He is a little in debt, and yachting is convenient.

The one who sits by the lady is a relation of Lord B.; you see at once what he is. He apes the sailor; he has not shaved, because sailors have no time to shave every day; he has not changed his linen, because sailors cannot change every day. He has a cigar in his mouth, which makes him half sick and annoys his company. He talks of the pleasure of a rough sea, which will drive all the ladies below—and then they will not perceive that he is more sick than themselves. He has the misfortune to be born to a large estate, and to be a *fool*. His name is Ossulton.

The last of the gentlemen on board whom I have to introduce, is Mr Seagrove. He is slightly made, with marked features full of intelligence. He has been brought up to the bar; and has every qualification but application. He has never had a brief, nor has he a chance of one. He is the fiddler of the company, and he has locked up his chambers, and come, by invitation of his lordship, to play on board of his yacht.

I have yet to describe the ladies—perhaps I should have commenced with them—I must excuse myself upon the principle of reserving the best to the last. All puppet-showmen do so: and what is this but the first scene in my puppet-show?

We will describe them according to seniority. That tall, thin, cross-looking lady of forty-five is a spinster, and sister to Lord B. She has been persuaded very much against her will to come on board; but her notions of propriety would not permit her niece to embark under the protection of *only* her father. She is frightened at everything: if a rope is thrown down on the deck, up she starts, and cries, "Oh!" if on the deck, she thinks the water is rushing in below; if down below, and there is a noise, she is convinced there is danger; and, if it be perfectly still, she is sure there is something wrong. She fidgets herself and everybody, and is quite a nuisance with her pride and ill-humour; but she has strict notions of propriety, and sacrifices herself as a martyr. She is the Hon. Miss Ossulton.

The lady who, when she smiles, shows so many dimples in her pretty oval face, is a young widow of the name of Lascelles. She married an old man to please her father and mother, which was very dutiful on her part. She was rewarded by finding herself a widow with a large fortune. Having married the first time to please her parents, she intends now to marry to please herself; but she is very young, and is in no hurry.

The young lady with such a sweet expression of countenance is the Hon. Miss Cecilia Ossulton. She is lively, witty, and has no fear in her composition; but she is very young yet, not more than seventeen—and nobody knows what she really is—she does not know herself. These are the parties who meet in the cabin of the yacht. The crew consists of ten fine seamen, the steward, and the cook. There is also Lord B.'s valet, Mr Ossulton's gentleman, and the lady's maid of Miss Ossulton. There not being accommodation for them, the other servants have been left on shore.

The yacht is now under weigh, and her sails are all set. She is running between Drake's Island and the main. Dinner has been announced. As the reader has learnt something about the preparations, I leave him to judge whether it be not very pleasant to sit down to dinner in a yacht. The air has given everybody an appetite; and it was not until the cloth was removed that the conversation became general.

"Mr Seagrove," said his lordship, "you very nearly lost your passage; I expected you last Thursday."

"I am sorry, my lord, that business prevented my sooner attending to your lordship's kind summons."

"Come, Seagrove, don't be nonsensical," said Hautaine; "you told me yourself, the other evening, when you were talkative, that you had never had a brief in your life."

"And a very fortunate circumstance," replied Seagrove; "for if I had had a brief I should not have known what to have done with it. It is not my fault; I am fit for nothing but a commissioner. But still I had business, and very important business, too; I was summoned by Ponsonby to go with him to Tattersall's, to give my opinion about a horse he wishes to purchase, and then to attend him to Forest Wild to plead his cause with his uncle."

"It appears, then, that you were retained," replied Lord B.; "may I ask you whether your friend gained his cause?"

"No, my lord, he lost his cause, but he gained a suit."

"Expound your riddle, sir," said Cecilia Ossulton.

"The fact is, that old Ponsonby is very anxious that William should marry Miss Percival, whose estates join on to Forest Wild. Now, my friend William is about as fond of marriage as I am of law, and thereby issue was joined."

"But why were you to be called in?" inquired Mrs Lascelles.

"Because, madam, as Ponsonby never buys a horse without consulting me—"

"I cannot see the analogy, sir," observed Miss Ossulton, senior, bridling up.

"Pardon me, madam: the fact is," continued Seagrove, "that, as I always have to back Ponsonby's horses, he thought it right that, in this instance, I should back him: he required special pleading, but his uncle tried him for the capital offence, and he was not allowed counsel. As soon as we arrived, and I had bowed myself into the room, Mr Ponsonby bowed me out again—which would have been infinitely more jarring to my feelings, had not the door been left a-jar."

"Do anything but pun, Seagrove," interrupted Hautaine.

"Well, then, I will take a glass of wine."

"Do so," said his lordship; "but, recollect, the whole company are impatient for your story."

"I can assure you, my lord, that it was equal to any scene in a comedy."

Now be it observed that Mr Seagrove had a great deal of comic talent; he was an excellent mimic, and could alter his voice almost as he pleased. It was a custom of his to act a scene as between other people, and he performed it remarkably well. Whenever he said that anything he was going to narrate was "as good as a comedy," it was generally understood by those who were acquainted with him, that he was to be asked so to do. Cecilia Ossulton therefore immediately said, "Pray act it, Mr Seagrove."

Upon which, Mr Seagrove—premising that he had not only heard, but also seen all that passed—changing his voice, and suiting the action to the word, commenced.

"It may," said he, "be called

"FIVE THOUSAND ACRES IN A RING-FENCE."

We shall not describe Mr Seagrove's motions; they must be inferred from his words.

"'It will, then, William,' observed Mr Ponsonby, stopping, and turning to his nephew, after a rapid walk up and down the room with his hands behind him under his coat, so as to allow the tails to drop their perpendicular about three inches clear of his body, 'I may say, without contradiction, be the finest property in the county—five thousand acres in a ring-fence.'

"'I dare say it will, uncle,' replied William, tapping his foot as he lounged in a green morocco easy-chair; 'and so, because you have set your fancy upon having these two estates enclosed together in a ring-fence, you wish that I should also be enclosed in a *ring*-fence.'

"'And a beautiful property it will be,' replied Mr Ponsonby.

"'Which, uncle?—the estate, or the wife?'

"'Both, nephew, both; and I expect your consent.'

"'Uncle, I am not avaricious. Your present property is sufficient for me. With your permission, instead of doubling the property, and doubling myself, I will remain your sole heir, and single.'

"'Observe, William, such an opportunity may not occur again for centuries. We shall restore Forest Wild to its ancient boundaries. You know it has been divided nearly two hundred years. We now have a glorious, golden opportunity of re-uniting the two properties; and when joined, the estate will be exactly what it was when granted to our ancestors by Henry the Eighth, at the period of the Reformation. This house must be pulled down, and the monastery left standing. Then we shall have our own again, and the property without encumbrance.'

"'Without encumbrance, uncle! You forget that there will be a wife.'

"'And you forget that there will be five thousand acres in a ring-fence.'

"'Indeed, uncle, you ring it too often in my ears that I should forget it; but much as I should like to be the happy possessor of such a property, I do not feel inclined to be the happy possessor of Miss Percival; and the more so, as I have never seen the property.'

"'We will ride over it to-morrow, William."

"'Ride over Miss Percival, uncle! That will not be very gallant. I will, however, one of these days, ride over the property with you, which, as well as Miss Percival, I have not as yet seen.'

"'Then I can tell you, she is a very pretty property.'

"'If she were not in a ring-fence.'

"'In good heart, William. That is, I mean an excellent disposition.'

"'Valuable in matrimony.'

"'And well tilled—I should say well-educated, by her three maiden aunts, who are the patterns of propriety.'

"'Does any one follow the fashion?'

"'In a high state of cultivation; that is, her mind highly cultivated, and according to the last new system—what is it?'

"'A four-course shift, I presume,' replied William, laughing; 'that is, dancing, singing, music, and drawing.'

"'And only seventeen! Capital soil, promising good crops. What would you have more?'

"'A very pretty estate, uncle, if it were not the estate of matrimony. I am sorry, very sorry, to disappoint you; but I must decline taking a lease of it for life.'

"'Then, sir, allow me to hint to you that in my testament you are only tenant-at-will. I consider it a duty that I owe to the family, that the estate should be re-united. That can only be done by one of our family marrying Miss Percival; and, as you will not, I shall now write to your cousin James, and if he accept my proposal, shall make *him* my heir. Probably he will more fully appreciate the advantages of five thousand acres in a ring-fence.'

"And Mr Ponsonby directed his steps towards the door.

"'Stop, my dear uncle,' cried William, rising up from his easy-chair; 'we do not quite understand one another. It is very true that I would prefer half the property and remaining single to the two estates and the estate of marriage; but, at the same time I did not tell you that I would prefer beggary to a wife and five thousand acres in a ring-fence. I know you to be a man of your word;—I accept your proposal, and you need not put my cousin James to the expense of postage.'

"'Very good, William; I require no more: and as I know you to be a man of your word, I shall consider this match as settled. It was on this account only that I sent for you, and now you may go back again as soon as you please. I will let you know when all is ready.'

"'I must be at Tattersall's on Monday, uncle; there is a horse I must have for next season. Pray, uncle, may I ask when you are likely to want me?'

"'Let me see—this is May—about July, I should think.'

"'July, uncle! Spare me—I cannot marry in the dog-days. No, hang it, not July.'

"'Well, William, perhaps, as you must come down once or twice to see the property—Miss Percival, I should say—it may be too soon—suppose we put it off till October.'

"'October—I shall be down at Melton.'

"'Pray, sir, may I then inquire what portion of the year is not, with you, *dog*-days?'

"'Why, uncle, next April, now—I think that would do.'

"'Next April. Eleven months, and a winter between. Suppose Miss Percival was to take a cold, and die.'

"'I should be excessively obliged to her,' thought William.

"'No! no!' continued Mr Ponsonby: 'there is nothing certain in this world, William.'

"'Well, then, uncle, suppose we arrange it for the first *hard frost*.'

"'We have had no hard frosts lately, William.—We may wait for years.— The sooner it is over the better.—Go back to town, buy your horse, and then come down here—my dear William, to oblige your uncle—never mind the dog-days.'

"'Well, sir, if I am to make a sacrifice, it shall not be done by halves; out of respect for you I will even marry in July, without any regard to the thermometer.'

"'You are a good boy, William.—Do you want a cheque?'

"'I have had one to-day,' thought William, and was almost at fault. 'I shall be most thankful, sir—they sell horse-flesh by the ounce now-a-days.'

"'And you pay in pounds.—There, William.'

"'Thank you, sir, I'm all obedience; and I'll keep my word, even if there should be a comet. I'll go and buy the horse, and then I shall be ready to take the ring-fence as soon as you please.'

"'Yes, and you'll get over it cleverly, I've no doubt.—Five thousand acres, William, and—a pretty wife!'

"'Have you any further commands, uncle?' said William, depositing the cheque in his pocket-book.

"'Now, my dear boy, are you going?'

"'Yes, sir; I dine at the Clarendon.'

"'Well, then, good-bye.—Make my compliments and excuses to your friend Seagrove.—You will come on Tuesday or Wednesday.'

"Thus was concluded the marriage between William Ponsonby and Emily Percival, and the junction of the two estates, which formed together the great desideratum,—*five thousand acres in a ring-fence*."

Mr Seagrove finished, and he looked round for approbation.

"Very good, indeed, Seagrove," said his lordship, "you must take a glass of wine after that."

"I would not give much for Miss Percival's chance of happiness," observed the elder Miss Ossulton.

"Of two evils choose the least, they say," observed Mr Hautaine. "Poor Ponsonby could not help himself."

"That's a very polite observation of yours, Mr Hautaine—I thank you in the name of the sex," replied Cecilia Ossulton.

"Nay, Miss Ossulton; would you like to marry a person whom you never saw?"

"Most certainly not; but when you mentioned the two evils, Mr Hautaine, I appeal to your honour, did you not refer to marriage or beggary?"

"I must confess it, Miss Ossulton; but it is hardly fair to call on my honour to get me into a scrape."

"I only wish that the offer had been made to me," observed Vaughan; "I should not have hesitated as Ponsonby did."

"Then I beg you will not think of proposing for me," said Mrs Lascelles, laughing;—for Mr Vaughan had been excessively attentive.

"It appears to me, Vaughan," observed Seagrove, "that you have slightly committed yourself by that remark."

Vaughan, who thought so too, replied: "Mrs Lascelles must be aware that I was only joking."

"Fie! Mr Vaughan," cried Cecilia Ossulton; "you know it came from your heart."

"My dear Cecilia," said the elder Miss Ossulton, "you forget yourself— what can you possibly know about gentlemen's hearts?"

"The Bible says, 'that they are deceitful and desperately wicked,' aunt."

"And cannot we also quote the Bible against your sex, Miss Ossulton?" replied Seagrove.

"Yes, you could, perhaps, if any of you had ever read it," replied Miss Ossulton, carelessly.

"Upon my word, Cissy, you are throwing the gauntlet down to the gentlemen," observed Lord B.; "but I shall throw my warder down, and not permit this combat *à l'outrance*.—I perceive you drink no more wine, gentlemen, we will take our coffee on deck."

"We were just about to retire, my lord," observed the elder Miss Ossulton, with great asperity: "I have been trying to catch the eye of Mrs Lascelles for some time, but—"

"I was looking another way, I presume," interrupted Mrs Lascelles, smiling.

"I am afraid that I am the unfortunate culprit," said Mr Seagrove. "I was telling a little anecdote to Mrs Lascelles—"

"Which, of course, from its being communicated in an undertone, was not proper for all the company to hear," replied the elder Miss Ossulton; "but if Mrs Lascelles is now ready—" continued she, bridling up, as she rose from her chair. "At all events, I can hear the remainder of it on deck," replied Mrs Lascelles. The ladies rose, and went into the cabin, Cecilia and Mrs Lascelles exchanging very significant smiles, as they followed the precise spinster, who did not choose that Mrs Lascelles should take the lead, merely because she had once happened to have been married.—The gentlemen also broke up, and went on deck.

"We have a nice breeze now, my lord," observed Mr Stewart, who had remained on deck, "and we lie right up Channel."

"So much the better," replied his lordship; "we ought to have been anchored at Cowes a week ago. They will all be there before us."

"Tell Mr Simpson to bring me a light for my cigar," said Mr Ossulton to one of the men.

Mr Stewart went down to his dinner; the ladies and the coffee came on deck; the breeze was fine, the weather (it was April) almost warm; and the yacht, whose name was the *Arrow*, assisted by the tide, soon left the Mewstone far astern.

Chapter II

CUTTER THE SECOND

Reader, have you ever been at Portsmouth? If you have, you must have been delighted with the view from the saluting battery; and, if you have not, you had better go there as soon as you can. From the saluting battery you may look up the harbour, and see much of what I have described at Plymouth; the scenery is different; but similar arsenals and dockyards, and an equal portion of our stupendous navy, are to be found there.—And you will see Gosport on the other side of the harbour, and Sally Port close to you; besides a great many other places, which, from the saluting battery, you cannot see. And then there is Southsea Beach to your left. Before you, Spithead, with the men-of-war, and the Motherbank, crowded with merchant vessels;—and there is the buoy where the *Royal George* was wrecked, and where she still lies, the fish swimming in and out of her cabin windows; but that is not all; you can also see the Isle of Wight,—Ryde, with its long wooden pier, and Cowes, where the yachts lie. In fact, there is a great deal to be seen at Portsmouth as well as at Plymouth; but what I wish you particularly to see, just now, is a vessel holding fast to the buoy, just off the saluting battery. She is a cutter; and you may know that she belongs to the Preventive Service by the number of gigs and galleys which she has hoisted up all round her. She looks like a vessel that was about to sail with a cargo of boats. Two on deck, one astern, one on each side of her. You observe that she is painted black, and all her boats are white. She is not such an elegant vessel as the yacht, and she is much more lumbered up. She has no haunches of venison over the stern; but I think there is a leg of mutton, and some cabbages hanging by their stalks. But revenue-cutters are not yachts.—You will find no turtle or champagne; but, nevertheless, you will, perhaps, find a joint to carve at, a good glass of grog, and a hearty welcome.

Let us go on board.—You observe the guns are iron, and painted black, and her bulwarks are painted red; it is not a very becoming colour; but then it lasts a long while, and the dock-yard is not very generous on the score of paint—or lieutenants of the navy troubled with much spare cash. She has plenty of men, and fine men they are; all dressed in red flannel shirts, and blue trousers; some of them have not taken off their canvas or tarpaulin petticoats, which are very useful to them, as they are in the boats night and day, and in all weathers. But we will at once go down into the cabin, where we shall find the lieutenant who commands her, a master's mate, and a midshipman. They have each their tumbler before them, and are drinking gin-toddy, hot, with sugar—capital gin, too, 'bove proof; it is from that small anker, standing under the table. It was one that they forgot to return to the custom-house when they made their last seizure. We must introduce them.

The elderly personage, with grizzly hair and whiskers, a round pale face, and a somewhat red nose (being too much in the wind will make the nose red, and this old officer is very often "in the wind," of course, from the very nature of his profession), is a Lieutenant Appleboy. He has served in every class of vessel in the service, and done the duty of first lieutenant for twenty years; he is now on promotion—that is to say, after he has taken a certain number of tubs of gin, he will be rewarded with his rank as commander. It is a pity that what he takes inside of him does not count, for he takes it morning, noon, and night. —He is just filling his fourteenth glass: he always keeps a regular account, as he never exceeds his limited number, which is seventeen; then he is exactly down to his bearings.

The master's mate's name is Tomkins; he has served his six years three times over, and has now outgrown his ambition; which is fortunate for him, as his chances of promotion are small. He prefers a small vessel to a large one, because he is not obliged to be so particular in his dress —and looks for his lieutenancy whenever there shall be another charity promotion. He is fond of soft bread, for his teeth are all absent without leave; he prefers porter to any other liquor, but he can drink his glass of grog, whether it be based upon rum, brandy, or the liquor now before him.

Mr Smith is the name of that young gentleman, whose jacket is so out at the elbows; he has been intending to mend it these last two months, but is too lazy to go to his chest for another. He has been turned out of half the ships in the service for laziness; but he was born so—and therefore it is not his fault.—A revenue-cutter suits him, she is half her time hove to; and he has no objection to boat-service, as he sits down always in the stern-sheets, which is not fatiguing. Creeping for tubs is his delight, as he gets over so little ground. He is fond of grog, but there is some trouble in carrying the tumbler so often to his mouth; so he looks at it, and lets it stand. He says little, because he is too lazy to speak. He has served more than _eight years; _but as for passing—it has never come into his head. Such are the three persons who are now sitting in the cabin of the revenue-cutter, drinking hot gin-toddy.

"Let me see, it was, I think, in ninety-three or ninety-four. Before you were in the service, Tomkins.—"

"Maybe, sir; it's so long ago since I entered, that I can't recollect dates,—but this I know, that my aunt died three days before."

"Then the question is, when did your aunt die?"

"Oh! she died about a year after my uncle."

"And when did your uncle die?"

"I'll be hanged if I know!"

"Then, d'ye see, you've no departure to work from. However, I think you cannot have been in the service at that time. We were not quite so particular about uniform as we are now."

"Then I think the service was all the better for it. Now-a-days, in your crack ships, a mate has to go down in the hold or spirit-room, and after whipping up fifty empty casks, and breaking out twenty full ones, he is expected to come on quarter-deck as clean as if he was just come out of a band-box."

"Well, there's plenty of water alongside, as far as the outward man goes, and iron dust is soon brushed off. However, as you say, perhaps a little too much is expected; at least, in five of the ships in which I was first-lieutenant, the captain was always hauling me over the coals about the midshipmen not dressing properly, as if I was their dry-nurse. I wonder what Captain Prigg would have said, if he had seen such a turn-out as you, Mr Smith, on his quarter-deck."

"I should have had one turn-out more," drawled Smith.

"With your out-at-elbows jacket, there, heh!" continued Mr Appleboy.

Smith turned up his elbows, looked at one and then at the other: after so fatiguing an operation, he was silent.

"Well, where was I? Oh! it was about ninety-three or ninety-four, as I said, that it happened—Tomkins, fill your glass, and hand me the sugar —how do I get on? This is No. 15," said Appleboy, counting some white lines on the table by him; and taking up a piece of chalk, he marked one more line on his tally. "I don't think this is so good a tub as the last, Tomkins, there's a twang about it—a want of juniper—however, I hope we shall have better luck this time. Of course, you know we sail to-morrow?"

"I presume so, by the leg of mutton coming on board."

"True—true—I'm regular—as clock-work.—After being twenty years a first-lieutenant, one gets a little method—I like regularity. Now the admiral has never omitted asking me to dinner once, every time I have come into harbour, except this time—I was so certain of it, that I never expected to sail; and I have but two shirts clean in consequence."

"That's odd, isn't it? and the more so, because he has had such great people down here, and has been giving large parties every day."

"And yet I made three seizures, besides sweeping up those thirty-seven tubs."

"I swept them up," observed Smith.

"That's all the same thing, *younker*.—When you've been a little longer in the service, you'll find out that the commanding officer has the merit of all that is done—but you're *green* yet. Let me see, where was I? Oh!—It was about ninety-three or ninety-four, as I said. At that time I was in the Channel fleet—Tomkins, I'll trouble you for the hot water; this water's cold.—Mr Smith, do me the favour to ring the bell. —Jem, some more hot water."

"Please, sir," said Jem, who was barefooted as well as bare-headed, touching the lock of hair on his forehead, "the cook has capsized the kettle—but he has put more on."

"Capsized the kettle! Ha!—very well—we'll talk about that to-morrow. Mr Tomkins, do me the favour to put him in the report, I may forget it. And pray, sir, how long is it since he has put more on?"

"Just this moment, sir, as I came aft."

"Very well, we'll see to that to-morrow:—You bring the kettle aft as soon as it is ready. I say, Mr Jem, is that fellow sober?"

"Yees, sir, he be sober as you be."

"It's quite astonishing what a propensity the common sailors have to liquor. Forty odd years have I been in the service, and I've never found any difference: I only wish I had a guinea for every time that I have given a fellow seven-water grog during my servitude as first-lieutenant, I wouldn't call the king my cousin. Well, if there's no hot water, we must take lukewarm—it won't do to heave to. By the Lord Harry! who would have thought it?—I'm at number sixteen! Let me count—yes!— surely I must have made a mistake. A fact, by Heaven!" continued Mr Appleboy, throwing the chalk down on the table. "Only one more glass, after this—that is, if I have counted right—I may have seen double."

"Yes," drawled Smith.

"Well, never mind—let's go on with my story.—It was either in the year ninety-three or ninety-four, that I was in the Channel fleet—we were then abreast of Torbay—"

"Here be the hot water, sir," cried Jem, putting the kettle down on the deck.

"Very well, boy—by-the-bye, has the jar of butter come on board?"

"Yes, but it broke all down the middle; I tied him up with a ropeyarn."

"Who broke it, sir?"

"Coxswain says as how he didn't."

"But who did, sir?"

"Coxswain handed it up to Bill Jones, and he says as how he didn't."

"But who did, sir?"

"Bill Jones gave it to me, and I'm sure as how I didn't."

"Then who did, sir, I ask you?"

"I think it be Bill Jones, sir, 'cause he's fond of butter, I know, and there be very little left in the jar."

"Very *well*, we'll see to that to-morrow morning. Mr Tomkins, you'll oblige me by putting the butter-jar down in the report, in case it should slip my memory. Bill Jones, indeed, looks as if butter wouldn't melt in his mouth—never mind. Well, it was, as I said before—it was in the year ninety-three or ninety-four, when I was in the Channel fleet; we were then off Torbay, and had just taken two reefs in the top-sails. Stop, before I go on with my story, I'll take my last glass—I think it's the last: let me count—yes, by heavens I make out sixteen, well told. Never mind, it shall be a stiff one. Boy, bring the kettle, and mind you don't pour the hot water into my shoes, as you did the other night. There, that will do. Now, Tomkins, fill up yours; and you, Mr Smith: let us all start fair, and then you shall have my story—and a very curious one it is, I can tell you; I wouldn't have believed it myself if I hadn't seen it. Hilloa! what's this? confound it! what's the matter with the toddy? Heh, Mr Tomkins?"

Mr Tomkins tasted, but, like the lieutenant, he had made it very stiff; and, as he had also taken largely before, he was, like him, not quite so clear in his discrimination: "It has a queer *twang*, sir: Smith, what is it?"

Smith took up his glass, tasted the contents.

"*Salt water*" *drawled the midshipman.

"Salt water! so it is, by heavens!" cried Mr Appleboy.

"Salt as Lot's wife!—by all that's infamous!" cried the master's mate.

"Salt water, sir!" cried Jem in a fright, expecting a *salt* eel for supper.

"Yes, sir," replied Mr Appleboy, tossing the contents of the tumbler in the boy's face, "salt water. Very well, sir,—very well!"

"It warn't me, sir," replied the boy, making up a piteous look.

"No, sir, but you said the cook was sober."

"He was not so *very* much disguised, sir," replied Jem.

"Oh! very well—never mind. Mr Tomkins, in case I should forget it, do me the favour to put the kettle of salt water down in the report. The scoundrel! I'm very sorry, gentlemen, but there's no means of having any more gin-toddy,—but never mind, we'll see to this to-morrow. Two can play at this; and if I don't salt-water their grog, and make them drink it, too, I have been twenty years a first-lieutenant for nothing—that's all. Good night, gentlemen; and," continued the lieutenant, in a severe tone, "you'll keep a sharp look-out, Mr Smith—do you hear, sir?"

"Yes," drawled Smith, "but it's not my watch; it was my first watch, and, just now, it struck one bell."

"You'll keep the middle watch, then, Mr Smith," said Mr Appleboy, who was not a little put out; "and, Mr Tomkins, let me know as soon as it's daylight. Boy, get my bed made. Salt water, by all that's blue! However, we'll see to that to-morrow morning."

Mr Appleboy then turned in; so did Mr Tomkins; and so did Mr Smith, who had no idea of keeping the middle watch because the cook was drunk and had filled up the kettle with salt water. As for what happened in ninety-three or ninety-four, I really would inform the reader if I knew, but I am afraid that that most curious story is never to be handed down to posterity.

The next morning, Mr Tomkins, as usual, forgot to report the cook, the jar of butter, and the kettle of salt water; and Mr Appleboy's wrath had long been appeased before he remembered them. At daylight the lieutenant came on deck, having only slept away half of the sixteen, and a taste of the seventeenth salt-water glass of gin-toddy. He rubbed his grey eyes, that he might peer through the grey of the morning; the fresh breeze blew about his grizzly locks, and cooled his rubicund nose. The revenue-cutter, whose name was the *Active*, cast off from the buoy; and, with a fresh breeze, steered her course for the Needles' passage.

Chapter III

CUTTER THE THIRD

Reader! have you been to St Maloes? If you have, you were glad enough to leave the hole; and, if you have not, take my advice, and do not give yourself the trouble to go and see that, or any other French port in the Channel. There is not one worth looking at. They have made one or two artificial ports, and they are no great things; there is no getting out, or getting in. In fact, they have no harbours in the Channel, while we have the finest in the world; a peculiar dispensation of Providence, because it knew that we should want them, and France would not. In France, what are called ports are all alike, nasty narrow holes, only to be entered at certain times of tide and certain winds; made up of basins and back-waters, custom-houses, and cabarets; just fit for smugglers to run into, and nothing more; and, therefore, they are used for very little else.

Now, in the dog-hole called St Maloes there is some pretty land, although a great deficiency of marine scenery. But never mind that: stay at home, and don't go abroad to drink sour wine, because they call it Bordeaux, and eat villanous trash, so disguised by cooking that you cannot possibly tell which of the birds of the air, or beasts of the field, or fishes of the sea, you are cramming down your throat. "If all is right, there is no occasion for disguise," is an old saying; so depend upon it, that there is something wrong, and that you are eating offal, under a grand French name. They eat everything in France, and would serve you up the head of a monkey who has died of the smallpox, as *singe au petite vérole*—that is, if you did not understand French; if you did, they would call it, *Tête d'amour a l'Ethiopique*, and then you would be even more puzzled. As for their wine, there is no disguise in that—it's half vinegar. No, no! stay at home; you can live just as cheaply, if you choose; and then you will have good meat, good vegetables, good ale, good beer, and a good glass of grog—and what is of more importance, you will be in good company. Live with your friends, and don't make a fool of yourself.

I would not have condescended to have noticed this place, had it not been that I wish you to observe a vessel which is lying along the pier-wharf, with a plank from the shore to her gunnel. It is low water, and she is aground, and the plank dips down at such an angle that it is a work of danger to go either in or out of her. You observe that there is nothing very remarkable in her. She is a cutter, and a good sea-boat, and sails well before the wind. She is short for her breadth of beam, and is not armed. Smugglers do not arm now—the service is too dangerous; they effect their purpose by cunning, not by force. Nevertheless, it requires that smugglers should be good seamen, smart, active fellows, and keen-witted, or they can do nothing. This vessel has not a large cargo in her, but it is valuable. She has some thousand yards of lace, a few hundred pounds of tea, a few bales of silk, and about forty ankers of brandy—just as much as they can land in one boat. All they ask is a heavy gale or a thick fog, and they trust to themselves for success.

There is nobody on board except a boy; the crew are all up at the cabaret, settling their little accounts of every description—for they smuggle both ways, and every man has his own private venture. There they are all, fifteen of them, and fine-looking fellows, too, sitting at that long table. They are very merry, but quite sober, as they are to sail to-night.

The captain of the vessel (whose name, by-the-bye is the "*Happy-go-lucky*,"—the captain christened her himself) is that fine-looking young man, with dark whiskers, meeting under his throat. His name is Jack Pickersgill. You perceive, at once, that he is much above a common sailor in appearance. His manners are good, he is remarkably handsome, very clean, and rather a dandy in his dress. Observe, how very politely he takes off his hat to that Frenchman, with whom he has just settled accounts; he beats Johnny Crapeau at his own weapons. And then there is an air of command, a feeling of conscious superiority about Jack; see how he treats the landlord, *de haut en bas*, at the same time that he is very civil. The fact is, that Jack is of a very good, old family, and received a very excellent education; but he was an orphan, his friends were poor, and could do but little for him: he went out to India as a cadet, ran away, and served in a schooner which smuggled opium into China, and then came home. He took a liking to the employment, and is now laying up a very pretty little sum: not that he intends to stop: no, as soon as he has enough to fit out a vessel for himself, he intends to start again for India, and with two cargoes of opium, he will return, he trusts, with a handsome fortune, and re-assume his family name. Such are Jack's intentions; and, as he eventually means to reappear as a gentleman, he preserves his gentlemanly habits: he neither drinks, nor chews, nor smokes. He keeps his hands clean, wears rings, and sports a gold snuff-box; notwithstanding which, Jack is one of the boldest and best of sailors, and the men know it. He is full of fun, and as keen as a razor. Jack has a very heavy venture this time— all the lace is his own speculation, and if he gets it in safe, he will clear some thousands of pounds. A certain fashionable shop in London has already agreed to take the whole off his hands.

That short, neatly-made young man is the second in command, and the companion of the captain. He is clever, and always has a remedy to propose when there is a difficulty, which is a great quality in a second in command. His name is Corbett. He is always merry—half-sailor, half-tradesman; knows the markets, runs up to London, and does business as well as a chapman—lives for the day, and laughs at to-morrow.

That little punchy old man, with long gray hair and fat face, with a nose like a note of interrogation, is the next personage of importance. He ought to be called the sailing-master, for, although he goes on shore in France, off the English coast he never quits the vessel. When they leave her with the goods, he remains on board; he is always to be found off any part of the coast where he may be ordered; holding his position in defiance of gales, and tides, and fogs: as for the revenue-vessels, they all know him well enough, but they cannot touch a vessel in ballast, if she has no more men on board than allowed by her tonnage. He knows every creek, and hole, and corner, of the coast; how the tide runs in—tide, half-tide, eddy, or current. That is his value. His name is Morrison.

You observe that Jack Pickersgill has two excellent supporters in Corbett and Morrison; his other men are good seamen, active, and obedient, which is all that he requires. I shall not particularly introduce them.

"Now you may call for another *litre*, my lads, and that must be the last; the tide is flowing fast, and we shall be afloat in half an hour, and we have just the breeze we want. What d'ye think, Morrison, shall we have dirt?"

"I've been looking just now, and if it were any other month in the year I should say, yes; but there's no trusting April, captain. Howsomever, if it does blow off, I'll promise you a fog in three hours afterwards."

"That will do as well. Corbett, have you settled with Duval?"

"Yes, after more noise and *charivari* than a panic in the Stock Exchange would make in England. He fought and squabbled for an hour, and I found that, without some abatement, I never should have settled the affair."

"What did you let him off?"

"Seventeen sous," replied Corbett, laughing.

"And that satisfied him?" inquired Pickersgill.

"Yes—it was all he could prove to be a *surfaire*: two of the knives were a little rusty. But he will always have something off; he could not be happy without it. I really think he would commit suicide, if he had to pay a bill without a deduction."

"Let him live," replied Pickersgill. "Jeannette, a bottle of Volnay, of 1811, and three glasses."

Jeannette, who was the *fille de cabaret*, soon appeared with a bottle of wine, seldom called for, except by the captain of the *Happy-go-lucky*.

"You sail to-night?" said she, as she placed the bottle before him.

Pickersgill nodded his head.

"I had a strange dream," said Jeannette; "I thought you were all taken by a revenue cutter, and put in a *cachot*. I went to see you, and I did not know one of you again—you were all changed."

"Very likely, Jeannette—you would not be the first who did not know their friends again when in misfortune. There was nothing strange in your dream."

"*Mais, mon Dieu! je ne suis pas comme ça moi.*"

"No, that you are not, Jeannette; you are a good girl, and some of these fine days I'll marry you," said Corbett.

"*Doit être bien beau ce jour là, par exemple*," replied Jeannette, laughing; "you have promised to marry me every time you have come in, these last three years."

"Well, that proves I keep to my promise, any how."

"Yes; but you never go any further."

"I can't spare him, Jeannette, that is the real truth," said the captain: "but wait a little—in the meantime, here is a five-franc piece to add to your *petite fortune*."

"*Merci bien, monsieur le capitaine; bon voyage!*" Jeannette held her finger up to Corbett, saying, with a smile, "*méchant!*" and then quitted the room.

"Come, Morrison, help us to empty this bottle, and then we will all go on board."

"I wish that girl wouldn't come here with her nonsensical dreams," said Morrison, taking his seat; "I don't like it. When she said that we should be taken by a revenue cutter, I was looking at a blue and a white pigeon sitting on the wall opposite; and I said to myself, now, if that be a warning, I will see: if the *blue* pigeon flies away first, I shall be in jail in a week; if the *white,* I shall be back here."

"Well?" said Pickersgill, laughing.

"It wasn't well," answered Morrison, tossing off his wine, and putting the glass down with a deep sigh; "for the cursed *blue* pigeon flew away immediately."

"Why, Morrison, you must have a chicken-heart to be frightened at a blue pigeon," said Corbett, laughing, and looking out of the window; "at all events, he has come back again, and there he is sitting by the white one."

"It's the first time that ever I was called chicken-hearted," replied Morrison, in wrath.

"Nor do you deserve it, Morrison," replied Pickersgill; "but Corbett is only joking."

"Well, at all events, I'll try my luck in the same way, and see whether I am to be in jail: I shall take the blue pigeon as my bad omen, as you did."

The sailors and Captain Pickersgill all rose and went to the window, to ascertain Corbett's fortune by this new species of augury. The blue pigeon flapped his wings, and then he sidled up to the white one; at last, the white pigeon flew off the wall and settled on the roof of the adjacent house. "Bravo, white pigeon!" said Corbett; "I shall be here again in a week." The whole party, laughing, then resumed their seats; and Morrison's countenance brightened up. As he took the glass of wine poured out by Pickersgill, he said, "Here's your health, Corbett; it was all nonsense, after all—for, d'ye see, I can't be put in jail without you are. We all sail in the same boat, and when you leave me, you take with you everything that can condemn the vessel—so here's success to our trip."

"We will all drink that toast, my lads, and then on board," said the captain; "here's success to our trip."

The captain rose, as did the mates and men, drank the toast, turned down the drinking-vessels on the table, hastened to the wharf, and, in half an hour, the *Happy-go-lucky* was clear of the port of St Maloes.

Chapter IV

PORTLAND BILL

The *Happy-go-lucky* sailed with a fresh breeze and a flowing sheet from St Maloes, the evening before the *Arrow* sailed from Barn Pool. The *Active* sailed from Portsmouth the morning after.

The yacht, as we before observed, was bound to Cowes, in the Isle of Wight. The *Active* had orders to cruise wherever she pleased within the limits of the admiral's station; and she ran for West Bay, on the other side of the Bill of Portland. The *Happy-go-lucky* was also bound for that bay to land her cargo.

The wind was light, and there was every appearance of fine weather, when the *Happy-go-lucky*, at ten o'clock on the Tuesday night, made the Portland lights; as it was impossible to run her cargo that night, she hove to.

At eleven o'clock, the Portland lights were made by the revenue cutter *Active*. Mr Appleboy went up to have a look at them, ordered the cutter to be hove to, and then went down to finish his allowance of gin-toddy. At twelve o'clock, the yacht *Arrow* made the Portland lights, and continued her course, hardly stemming the ebb tide.

Day broke, and the horizon was clear. The first on the look-out were, of course, the smugglers; they, and those on board the revenue cutter, were the only two interested parties—the yacht was neuter.

"There are two cutters in sight, sir," said Corbett, who had the watch; for Pickersgill, having been up the whole night, had thrown himself down on the bed with his clothes on.

"What do they look like?" said Pickersgill, who was up in a moment.

"One is a yacht, and the other may be; but I rather think, as far as I can judge in the gray, that it is our old friend off here."

"What! old Appleboy?"

"Yes, it looks like him; but the day has scarcely broke yet."

"Well, he can do nothing in a light wind like this; and before the wind we can show him our heels; but are you sure the other is a yacht?" said Pickersgill, coming on deck.

"Yes; the king is more careful of his canvas."

"You're right," said Pickersgill, "that is a yacht; and you're right there again in your guess—that is the stupid old *Active*, which creeps about creeping for tubs. Well, I see nothing to alarm us at present, provided it don't fall a dead calm, and then we must take to our boat as soon as he takes to his; we are four miles from him at least. Watch his motions, Corbett, and see if he lowers a boat. What does she go now? Four knots?—that will soon tire their men."

The positions of the three cutters were as follows:—

The *Happy-go-lucky* was about four miles off Portland Head, and well into West Bay. The revenue cutter was close to the Head. The yacht was outside of the smuggler, about two miles to the westward, and about five or six miles from the revenue cutter.

"Two vessels in sight, sir," said Mr Smith, coming down into the cabin to Mr Appleboy.

"Very well," replied the lieutenant, who was *lying* down in his *standing* bed-place.

"The people say one is the *Happy-go-lucky*, sir," drawled Smith.

"Heh? what! *Happy-go-lucky*? Yes, I recollect; I've boarded her twenty times—always empty. How's she standing?"

"She stands to the westward now, sir; but she was hove to, they say, when they first saw her."

"Then she has a cargo in her;" and Mr Appleboy shaved himself, dressed, and went on deck.

"Yes," said the lieutenant, rubbing his eyes again and again, and then looking through the glass, "it is her sure enough. Let draw the fore sheet—hands make sail. What vessel's the other?"

"Don't know, sir,—she's a cutter."

"A cutter? yes; may be a yacht, or may be the new cutter ordered on the station. Make all sail, Mr Tomkins; hoist our pendant, and fire a gun— they will understand what we mean then; they don't know the *Happy-go-lucky* as well as we do."

In a few minutes the *Active* was under a press of sail; she hoisted her pendant, and fired a gun. The smuggler perceived that the *Active* had recognised her, and she also threw out more canvas, and ran off more to the westward.

"There's a gun, sir," reported one of the men to Mr Stewart, on board of the yacht.

"Yes; give me the glass—a revenue cutter; then this vessel in shore, running towards us, must be a smuggler."

"She has just now made all sail, sir."

"Yes, there's no doubt of it; I will go down to his lordship—keep her as she goes."

Mr Stewart then went down to inform Lord B. of the circumstance. Not only Lord B., but most of the gentlemen came on deck; as did soon afterwards the ladies, who had received the intelligence from Lord B., who spoke to them through the door of the cabin.

But the smuggler had more wind than the revenue cutter, and increased her distance.

"If we were to wear round now, my lord," observed Mr Stewart, "she is just abreast of us and in shore, we could prevent her escape."

"Round with her, Mr Stewart," said Lord B.; "we must do our duty, and protect the laws."

"That will not be fair, papa," said Cecilia Ossulton; "we have no quarrel with the smugglers: I'm sure the ladies have not, for they bring us beautiful things."

"Miss Ossulton," observed her aunt, "it is not proper for you to offer an opinion."

The yacht wore round, and, sailing so fast, the smuggler had little chance of escaping her; but to chase is one thing—to capture, another.

"Let us give her a gun," said Lord B., "that will frighten her; and he dare not cross our hawse."

The gun was loaded, and not being more than a mile from the smuggler, actually threw the ball almost a quarter of the way.

The gentlemen, as well as Lord B., were equally excited by the ardour of pursuit; but the wind died away, and at last it was nearly calm. The revenue cutter's boats were out, and coming up fast.

"Let us get our boat out, Stewart," said his lordship; "and help them; it is quite calm now."

The boat was soon out: it was a very large one, usually stowed on, and occupied a large portion of, the deck. It pulled six oars; and when it was manned, Mr Stewart jumped in, and Lord B. followed him.

"But you have no arms," said Mr Hautaine.

"The smugglers never resist now," observed Stewart.

"Then you are going on a very gallant expedition, indeed," observed Cecilia Ossulton; "I wish you joy."

But Lord B. was too much excited to pay attention. They shoved off, and pulled towards the smuggler.

At this time, the revenue boats were about five miles astern of the *Happy-go-lucky*, and the yacht about three-quarters of a mile from her in the offing. Pickersgill had, of course, observed the motions of the yacht; had seen her wear on chase, hoist her ensign and pendant, and fire her gun.

"Well," said he, "this is the blackest ingratitude; to be attacked by the very people whom we smuggle for. I only wish she may come up with us; and, let her attempt to interfere, she shall rue the day: I don't much like this, though."

As we before observed, it fell nearly calm, and the revenue boats were in chase. Pickersgill watched them as they came up.

"What shall we do," said Corbett,—"get the boat out?"

"Yes," replied Pickersgill, "we will get the boat out, and have the goods in her all ready; but we can pull faster than they do, in the first place; and, in the next, they will be pretty well tired before they come up to us. We are fresh, and shall soon walk away from them; so I shall not leave the vessel till they are within half a mile. We must sink the ankers, that they may not seize the vessel, for it is not worth while taking them with us. Pass them along ready to run them over the bows, that they may not see us and swear to it. But we have a good half hour, and more."

"Ay, and you may hold all fast if you choose," said Morrison, "although it's better to be on the right side and get ready; otherwise, before half an hour, I'll swear that we are out of their sight. Look there," said he, pointing to the eastward at a heavy bank, "it's coming right down upon us, as I said it would."

"True enough; but still there is no saying which will come first, Morrison; the boats or the fog, so we must be prepared."

"Hilloa! what's this? why, there's a boat coming from the yacht!"

Pickersgill took out his glass.

"Yes, and the yacht's own boat, with the name painted on her bows. Well, let them come—we will have no ceremony in resisting them; they are not in the Act of Parliament, and must take the consequences. We have nought to fear. Get stretchers, my lads, and hand-spikes; they row six oars, and are three in the stern sheets—they must be good men if they take us."

In a few minutes Lord B. was close to the smuggler.

"Boat, ahoy! what do you want?"

"Surrender in the king's name."

"To what, and to whom, and what are we to surrender? We are an English vessel coasting along shore."

"Pull on board, my lads," cried Stewart; "I am a king's officer—we know her."

The boat darted alongside, and Stewart and Lord B., followed by the men, jumped on the deck.

"Well, gentlemen, what do you want?" said Pickersgill.

"We seize you—you are a smuggler; there's no denying it: look at the casks of spirits stretched along the deck."

"We never said that we were not smugglers," replied Pickersgill; "but what is that to you? You are not a king's ship, or employed by the revenue."

"No, but we carry a pendant, and it is our duty to protect the laws."

"And who are you?" said Pickersgill.

"I am Lord B."

"Then, my lord, allow me to say that you would do much better to attend to the framing of laws, and leave people of less consequence, like those astern of me, to execute them. 'Mind your own business,' is an old adage. We shall not hurt you, my lord, as you have only employed words, but we shall put it out of your power to hurt us. Come aft, my lads. Now, my lord, resistance is useless; we are double your numbers, and you have caught a Tartar."

Lord B. and Mr Stewart perceived that they were in an awkward predicament.

"You may do what you please," observed Mr Stewart, "but the revenue boats are coming up, recollect."

"Look you, sir, do you see the revenue cutter?" said Pickersgill.

Stewart looked in that direction, and saw that she was hidden in the fog.

"In five minutes, sir, the boats will be out of sight also, and so will your vessel; we have nothing to fear from them."

"Indeed, my lord, we had better return," said Mr Stewart, who perceived that Pickersgill was right.

"I beg your pardon, you will not go on board your yacht so soon as you expect. Take the oars out of the boat, my lads, two or three of you, and throw in a couple of our paddles for them to reach the shore with. The rest of you knock down the first man who offers to resist. You are not aware, perhaps, my lord, that you have attempted *piracy* on the high seas?"

Stewart looked at Lord B. It was true enough. The men of the yacht could offer no resistance; the oars were taken out of the boat, and the men put in again.

"My lord," said Pickersgill, "your boat is manned—do me the favour to step into it; and you, sir, do the same. I should be sorry to lay my hands upon a peer of the realm, or a king's officer even on half pay."

Remonstrance was vain; his lordship was led to the boat by two of the smugglers, and Stewart followed.

"I will leave your oars, my lord, at the Weymouth Custom-house; and I trust this will be a lesson to you in future to 'mind your own business.'"

The boat was shoved off from the sloop by the smugglers, and was soon lost sight of in the fog, which had now covered the revenue boats as well as the yacht; at the same time, it brought down a breeze from the eastward.

"Haul to the wind, Morrison," said Pickersgill, "we will stand out to get rid of the boats; if they pull on, they will take it for granted that we shall run into the bay, as will the revenue cutter."

Pickersgill and Corbett were in conversation abaft for a short time, when the former desired the course to be altered two points.

"Keep silence all of you, my lads, and let me know if you hear a gun or a bell from the yacht," said Pickersgill.

"There is a gun, sir, close to us," said one of the men; "the sound was right ahead."

"That will do, keep her as she goes. Aft here, my lads; we cannot run our cargo in the bay, for the cutter has been seen to chase us, and they will all be on the look-out at the preventive stations for us on shore. Now, my lads, I have made up my mind that, as these yacht gentlemen have thought proper to interfere, I will take possession of the yacht for a few days. We shall then out-sail everything, go where we like unsuspected, and land our cargo with ease. I shall run alongside of her—she can have but few hands on board; and mind, do not hurt anybody, but be civil and obey my orders. Morrison, you and your four men and the boy will remain on board as before, and take the vessel to Cherbourg, where we will join you."

In a short time another gun was fired from the yacht.

Those on board, particularly the ladies, were alarmed; the fog was very thick, and they could not distinguish the length of the vessel. They had seen the boat board, but had not seen her turned adrift without oars, as the fog came on just at that time. The yacht was left with only three seamen on board, and, should it come on bad weather, they were in an awkward predicament. Mr Hautaine had taken the command, and ordered the guns to be fired that the boat might be enabled to find them. The fourth gun was loading, when they perceived the smuggler's cutter close to them looming through the fog.

"Here they are," cried the seamen; "and they have brought the prize along with them! Three cheers for the *Arrow*!"

"Hilloa! you'll be on board of us?" cried Hautaine.

"That's exactly what I intended to be, sir," replied Pickersgill, jumping on the quarter-deck, followed by his men.

"Who the devil are you?"

"That's exactly the same question that I asked Lord B. when he boarded us," replied Pickersgill, taking off his hat to the ladies.

"Well, but what business have you here?"

"Exactly the same question which I put to Lord B.," replied Pickersgill.

"Where is Lord B., sir?" said Cecilia Ossulton, going up to the smuggler; "is he safe?"

"Yes, madam, he is safe; at least he is in his boat with all his men, and unhurt: but you must excuse me if I request you and the other ladies to go down below while I speak to these gentlemen. Be under no alarm, miss; you will receive neither insult nor ill-treatment—I have only taken possession of this vessel for the present."

"Take possession," cried Hautaine, "of a yacht."

"Yes, sir, since the owner of the yacht thought proper to attempt to take possession of me. I always thought that yachts were pleasure-vessels, sailing about for amusement, respected themselves, and not interfering with others; but it appears that such is not the case. The owner of this yacht has thought proper to break through the neutrality, and commence aggression, and under such circumstances I have now, in retaliation, taken possession of her."

"And, pray, what do you mean to do, sir?"

"Simply for a few days to make an exchange. I shall send you on board of my vessel as smugglers, while I remain here with the ladies and amuse myself with yachting."

"Why, sir, you cannot mean—"

"I have said, gentlemen, and that is enough; I should be sorry to resort to violence, but I must be obeyed. You have, I perceive, three seamen only left: they are not sufficient to take charge of the vessel, and Lord B. and the others you will not meet for several days. My regard for the ladies, even common humanity, points out to me that I cannot leave the vessel in this crippled condition. At the same time, as I must have hands on board of my own, you will oblige me by going on board and taking her safely into port. It is the least return you can make for my kindness. In those dresses, gentlemen, you will not be able to do your duty; oblige me by shifting, and putting on these." Corbett handed a flannel shirt, a rough jacket and trousers, to Messrs Hautaine, Ossulton, Vaughan, and Seagrove. After some useless resistance they were stripped, and having put on the smugglers' attire, they were handed on board of the *Happy-go-lucky*.

The three English seamen were also sent on board and confined below, as well as Ossulton's servant, who was also equipped like his master, and confined below with the seamen. Corbett and the men then handed up all the smuggled goods into the yacht, dropped the boat, and made it fast astern; and, Morrison having received his directions, the vessels separated—Morrison running for Cherbourg, and Pickersgill steering the yacht along shore to the westward. About an hour after this exchange had been effected, the fog cleared up, and showed the revenue cutter hove to for her boats, which had pulled back and were close on board of her; and the *Happy-go-lucky*, about three miles in the offing. Lord B. and his boat's crew were about four miles in shore, paddling and drifting with the tide towards Portland. As soon as the boats were on board, the revenue cutter made all sail after the smuggler, paying no attention to the yacht, and either not seeing or not caring about the boat which was drifting about in West Bay.

Chapter V

THE TRAVESTIE

"Here we are, Corbett, and now I only wish my venture had been double," observed Pickersgill; "but I shall not allow business to absorb me wholly—we must add a little amusement. It appears to me, Corbett, that the gentleman's clothes which lie there will fit you, and those of the good-looking fellow who was spokesman will, I am sure, suit me well. Now, let us dress ourselves, and then for breakfast."

Pickersgill then exchanged his clothes for those of Mr Hautaine, and Corbett fitted on those of Mr Ossulton. The steward was summoned up, and he dared not disobey; he appeared on deck, trembling.

"Steward—you will take these clothes below," said Pickersgill, "and, observe, I now command this yacht; and, during the time that I am on board, you will pay me the same respect as you did Lord B.: nay, more, you will always address me as Lord B. You will prepare dinner and breakfast, and do your duty just as if his lordship was on board, and take care that you feed us well, for I will not allow the ladies to be entertained in a less sumptuous manner than before.—You will tell the cook what I say,—and now that you have heard me, take care that you obey; if not, recollect that I have my own men here, and if I but point with my finger, *overboard you go*.—Do you perfectly comprehend me?"

"Yes,—sir," stammered the steward.

"Yes, *sir*!—What did I tell you, sirrah?—Yes, my lord.—Do you understand me?"

"Yes—my lord."

"Pray, steward, whose clothes has this gentleman put on?"

"Mr—Mr Ossulton's, I think—sir—my lord, I mean."

"Very well, steward; then recollect, in future you always address that gentleman as *Mr Ossulton*."

"Yes, my lord," and the steward went down below, and was obliged to take a couple of glasses of brandy, to keep himself from fainting.

"Who are they, and what are they! Mr Maddox?" cried the lady's-maid, who had been weeping.

"Pirates!—*bloody, murderous, stick-at-nothing* pirates!" replied the steward.

"Oh!" screamed the lady's-maid, "what will become of us, poor unprotected females?" And she hastened into the cabin, to impart this dreadful intelligence.

The ladies in the cabin were not in a very enviable situation. As for the elder Miss Ossulton (but, perhaps, it will be better in future to distinguish the two ladies, by calling the elder simply Miss Ossulton, and her niece, Cecilia), she was sitting with her salts to her nose, agonised with a mixture of trepidation and wounded pride. Mrs Lascelles was weeping, but weeping gently. Cecilia was sad, and her heart was beating with anxiety and suspense—when the maid rushed in.

"O madam! O miss! O Mrs Lascelles! I have found it all out!—they are murderous, bloody, do-everything pirates!!!"

"Mercy on us!" exclaimed Miss Ossulton; "surely they will never dare—?"

"Oh, ma'am, they dare anything!—they just now were throwing the steward overboard—and they have rummaged all the portmanteaus, and dressed themselves in the gentlemen's best clothes—the captain of them told the steward that he was Lord B.—and that if he dared to call him anything else, he would cut his throat from ear to ear—and if the cook don't give them a good dinner, they swear that they'll chop his right hand off, and make him eat it, without pepper or salt!"

Miss Ossulton screamed, and went off into hysterics. Mrs Lascelles and Cecilia went to her assistance; but the latter had not forgotten the very different behaviour of Jack Pickersgill, and his polite manners, when he boarded the vessel. She did not, therefore, believe what the maid had reported, but still her anxiety and suspense were great, especially about her father. After having restored her aunt, she put on her bonnet, which was lying on the sofa.

"Where are you going, dear?" said Mrs Lascelles.

"On deck," replied Cecilia. "I must and will speak to these men."

"Gracious heaven, Miss Ossulton going on deck! have you heard what Phoebe says?"

"Yes, aunt, I have; but I can wait here no longer."

"Stop her! stop her!—she will be murdered!—she will be—she is mad!" screamed Miss Ossulton; but no one attempted to stop Cecilia, and on deck she went. On her arrival, she found Jack Pickersgill and Corbett walking the deck; one of the smugglers at the helm, and the rest forward, and as quiet as the crew of the yacht. As soon as she made her appearance, Jack took off his hat, and made her a bow.

"I do not know whom I have the honour of addressing, young lady! but I am flattered with this mark of confidence. You feel, and I assure you, you feel correctly, that you are not exactly in lawless hands."

Cecilia looked with more surprise than fear at Pickersgill; Mr Hautaine's dress became him, he was a handsome, fine-looking man, and had nothing of the ruffian in his appearance; unless, like Byron's Corsair, he was *half savage, half soft*. She could not help thinking that she had met many with less pretensions, as far as appearance went, to the claims of a gentleman, at Almack's, and other fashionable circles.

"I have ventured on deck, sir," said Cecilia, with a little tremulousness in her voice, "to request, as a favour, that you will inform me what your intentions may be, with regard to the vessel, and with regard to the ladies!"

"And I feel much obliged to you, for so doing, and I assure you, I will, as far as I have made up my own mind, answer you candidly: but you tremble—allow me to conduct you to a seat. In few words, then, to remove your present alarm, I intend that the vessel shall be returned to its owner, with every article in it, as religiously respected as if they were church property. With respect to you, and the other ladies on board, I pledge you my honour, that you have nothing to fear; that you shall be treated with every respect; your privacy never invaded; and that, in a few days, you will be restored to your friends. Young lady, I pledge my hopes of future salvation to the truth of this; but, at the same time, I must make a few conditions, which, however, will not be very severe."

"But, sir," replied Cecilia, much relieved, for Pickersgill had stood by her in the most respectful manner, "you are, I presume, the captain of the smuggler? Pray, answer me one question more—What became of the boat, with Lord B.,—he is my father?"

"I left him in his boat, without a hair of his head touched, young lady; but I took away the oars."

"Then he will perish!" cried Cecilia, putting her handkerchief to her eyes.

"No, young lady, he is on shore probably by this time; although I took away his means of assisting to capture us, I left him the means of gaining the land. It is not every one who would have done that, after his conduct to us."

"I begged him not to go," said Cecilia; "I told him that it was not fair, and that he had no quarrel with the smugglers."

"I thank you even for that," replied Pickersgill. "And now, Miss—I have not the pleasure of recollecting his lordship's family name—"

"Ossulton, sir," said Cecilia, looking at Pickersgill with surprise.

"Then, with your permission, Miss Ossulton, I will now make you my confidant: excuse my using so free a term, but it is because I wish to relieve your fears; at the same time, I cannot permit you to divulge all my intentions to the whole party on board; I feel that I may trust you, for you have courage, and where there is courage, there generally is truth; but you must first tell me whether you will condescend to accept these terms?"

Cecilia demurred a moment—the idea of being the confidant of a smuggler rather startled her; but still, her knowledge of what his intentions were, if she might not reveal them, might be important; as, perhaps, she might dissuade him. She could be in no worse position than she was now, and she might be in a much better. The conduct of Pickersgill had been such, up to the present, as to inspire confidence; and, although he defied the laws, he appeared to regard the courtesies of life. Cecilia was a courageous girl, and at length she replied:—

"Provided what you desire me to keep secret will not be injurious to any one, or compromise me, in my peculiar situation, I consent."

"I would not hurt a fly, Miss Ossulton, but in self-defence, and I have too much respect for you, from your conduct during our short meeting, to compromise you. Allow me now to be very candid; and then, perhaps, you will acknowledge that, in my situation, others would do the same; and, perhaps, not show half so much forbearance. Your father, without any right whatever, interferes with me, and my calling: he attempts to make me a prisoner, to have me thrown in jail; heavily fined, and, perhaps, sent out of the country. I will not enter into any defence of smuggling, it is sufficient to say, that there are pains and penalties attached to the infraction of certain laws, and that I choose to risk them—but Lord B. was not empowered by Government to attack me; it was a gratuitous act—and had I thrown him, and all his crew into the sea, I should have been justified, for it was in short, an act of piracy on their part. Now, as your father has thought to turn a yacht into a revenue cutter, you cannot be surprised at my retaliating, in turning her into a smuggler; and as he has mixed up looking after the revenue with yachting, he cannot be surprised if I retaliate, by mixing up a little yachting with smuggling. I have dressed your male companions as smugglers, and have sent them in the smuggling vessel to Cherbourg, where they will be safely landed; and I have dressed myself, and the only person whom I could join with me in this frolic, as gentlemen, in their places. My object is twofold: one is, to land my cargo, which I have now on board, and which is very valuable; the other is, to retaliate upon your father and his companions, for their attempt upon me, by stepping into their shoes, and enjoying, for a day or two, their luxuries. It is my intention to make free with nothing, but his lordship's wine and eatables,—that you may be assured of; but I shall have no pleasure, if the ladies do not sit down to the dinner-table with us, as they did before with your father and his friends."

"You can hardly expect that, sir," said Cecilia.

"Yes, I do; and that will be not only the price of the early release of the yacht and themselves, but it will also be the only means by which they will obtain anything to eat. You observe, Miss Ossulton, the sins of the fathers are visited on the children. I have now told you what I mean to do, and what I wish. I leave you to think of it, and decide whether it will not be the best for all parties to consent. You have my permission to tell the other ladies, that whatever may be their conduct, they are as secure from ill-treatment or rudeness, as if they were in Grosvenor Square; but I cannot answer that they will not be hungry, if, after such forbearance in every point, they show so little gratitude, as not to honour me with their company."

"Then I am to understand that we are to be starved into submission?"

"No, not starved, Miss Ossulton; but recollect that you will be on bread and water, and detained until you do consent, and your detention will increase the anxiety of your father."

"You know how to persuade, sir," said Cecilia. "As far as I am concerned, I trust I shall ever be ready to sacrifice any feelings of pride, to spare my father so much uneasiness. With your permission, I will now go down into the cabin, and relieve my companions from the worst of their fears. As for obtaining what you wish, I can only say, that, as a young person, I am not likely to have much influence with those older than myself, and must inevitably be overruled, as I have not permission to point out to them reasons which might avail. Would you so far allow me to be relieved from my promise, as to communicate all you have said to me, to the only married woman on board? I think I then might obtain your wishes, which, I must candidly tell you, I shall attempt to effect, *only* because I am most anxious to rejoin my friends."

"And be relieved of my company," replied Pickersgill, smiling, ironically,—"of course you are; but I must and will have my petty revenge: and although you may, and probably will detest me, at all events you shall not have any very formidable charge to make against me Before you go below, Miss Ossulton, I give you my permission to add the married lady to the number of my confidants; and you must permit me to introduce my friend, Mr Ossulton;" and Pickersgill waved his hand in the direction of Corbett, who took off his hat, and made a low obeisance.

It was impossible for Cecilia Ossulton to help smiling.

"And," continued Pickersgill, "having taking the command of this yacht, instead of his lordship, it is absolutely necessary that I also take his lordship's name. While on board I am Lord B.; and allow me to introduce myself under that name—I cannot be addressed otherwise. Depend upon it, Miss Ossulton, that I shall have a most paternal solicitude to make you happy and comfortable."

Had Cecilia Ossulton dared to have given vent to her real feelings at that time, she would have burst into a fit of laughter, it was too ludicrous. At the same time, the very burlesque reassured her still more. She went into the cabin with a heavy weight removed from her heart.

In the meantime, Miss Ossulton and Mrs Lascelles remained below, in the greatest anxiety at Cecilia's prolonged stay; they knew not what to think, and dared not go on deck. Mrs Lascelles had once determined at all risks to go up; but Miss Ossulton and Phoebe had screamed, and implored her so fervently not to leave them, that she unwillingly consented to remain. Cecilia's countenance, when she entered the cabin, reassured Mrs Lascelles, but not her aunt, who ran to her, crying and sobbing, and clinging to her, saying, "What have they done to you, my poor, poor Cecilia?"

"Nothing at all, aunt," replied Cecilia, "the captain speaks very fairly, and says he shall respect us in every possible way, provided that we obey his orders, but if not—"

"If not—what, Cecilia?" said Miss Ossulton, grasping her niece's arm.

"He will starve us, and not let us go!"

"God have mercy on us!"—cried Miss Ossulton, renewing her sobs.

Cecilia then went to Mrs Lascelles, and communicated to her, apart, all that had passed. Mrs Lascelles agreed with Cecilia, that they were in no danger of insult; and as they talked over the matter, they at last began to laugh; there was a novelty in it, and there was something so ridiculous in all the gentlemen being turned into smugglers. Cecilia was glad that she could not tell her aunt, as she wished her to be so frightened, as never to have her company on board of the yacht again; and Mrs Lascelles was too glad to annoy her for many and various insults received. The matter was, therefore, canvassed over very satisfactorily, and Mrs Lascelles felt a natural curiosity to see this new Lord B. and the second Mr Ossulton. But they had had no breakfast and were feeling very hungry, now that their alarm was over. They desired Phoebe to ask the steward for some tea or coffee. The reply was, that, "Breakfast was laid in the cabin, and Lord B. trusted that the ladies would come to partake of it."

"No, no," replied Mrs Lascelles, "I never can, without being introduced to them first."

"Nor will I go," replied Cecilia, "but I will write a note, and we will have our breakfast here." Cecilia wrote a note in pencil as follows:—

"Miss Ossulton's compliments to Lord B., and, as the ladies feel rather indisposed after the alarm of this morning, they trust that his lordship will excuse their coming to breakfast; but hope to meet his lordship at dinner, if not before that time, on deck."

The answer was propitious, and the steward soon appeared with the breakfast in the ladies' cabin.

"Well Maddox," said Cecilia, "how do you get on with your new master?"

The steward looked at the door to see if it was closed, shook his head, and then said with a look of despair, "He has ordered a haunch of venison for dinner, miss, and he has twice threatened to toss me overboard."

"You must obey him, Maddox, or he certainly will. These pirates are dreadful fellows; be attentive, and serve him just as if he was my father."

"Yes, yes, ma'am, I will, but our time may come; it's *burglary* on the high seas, and I'll go fifty miles to see him hanged."

"Steward!" cried Pickersgill, from the cabin.

"O lord! he can't have heard me—d'ye-think he did, miss?"

"The partitions are very thin, and you spoke very loud," said Mrs Lascelles; "at all events, go to him quickly."

"Good-bye, miss; good-bye, ma'am; if I shouldn't see you any more," said Maddox, trembling with fear, as he obeyed the awful summons—which was to demand a tooth-pick.

Miss Ossulton would not touch the breakfast; not so Mrs Lascelles and Cecilia, who ate very heartily.

"It's very dull to be shut up in this cabin," said Mrs Lascelles; "come, Cecilia, let's go on deck."

"And leave me," cried Miss Ossulton.

"There is Phoebe here, aunt; we are going up to persuade the pirates to put us all on shore."

Mrs Lascelles and Cecilia put on their bonnets and went up. Lord B. took off his hat, and begged the honour of being introduced to the pretty widow. He handed the ladies to a seat, and then commenced conversing upon various subjects, which, at the same time, possessed great novelty. His lordship talked about France, and described its ports; told now and then a good anecdote; pointed out the different headlands, bays, towns, and villages, which they were passing rapidly, and always had some little story connected with each. Before the ladies had been two hours on deck, they found themselves, to their infinite surprise, not only interested, but in conversation with the captain of the smuggler, and more than once they laughed outright. But the *soi-disant* Lord B. had inspired them with confidence; they fully believed that what he had told them was true, and that he had taken possession of the yacht to smuggle his goods, to be revenged, and to have a laugh. Now none of these three offences are capital in the eyes of the fair sex; and Jack was a handsome, fine-looking fellow, of excellent manners, and very agreeable conversation, at the same time, neither he nor his friend were in their general deportment and behaviour otherwise than most respectful.

"Ladies, as you are not afraid of me, which is a greater happiness than I had reason to expect, I think you may be amused to witness the fear of those who accuse your sex of cowardice. With your permission, I will send for the cook and steward, and inquire about the dinner."

"I should like to know what there is for dinner," observed Mrs Lascelles demurely; "wouldn't you, Cecilia?"

Cecilia put her handkerchief to her mouth.

"Tell the steward and the cook both to come aft immediately," cried Pickersgill.

In a few seconds they both made their appearance.

"Steward!" cried Pickersgill, with a loud voice.

"Yes, my lord," replied Maddox, with his hat in his hand.

"What wines have you put out for dinner?"

"Champagne, my lord; and claret, my lord; and Madeira and sherry, my lord."

"No Burgundy, sir?"

"No, my lord; there is no Burgundy on board."

"No Burgundy, sir! do you dare to tell me that?"

"Upon my soul, my lord," cried Maddox, dropping on his knees, "there is no Burgundy on board—ask the ladies."

"Very well, sir; you may go."

"Cook, what have you got for dinner?"

"Sir, a haunch of mutt—of venison, my lord," replied the cook, with his white night-cap in his hand.

"What else, sirrah?"

"A boiled calf's head, my lord."

"A boiled calf's head! Let it be roasted, or I'll roast you, sir!" cried Pickersgill in an angry tone.

"Yes, my lord; I'll roast it."

"And what else, sir?"

"Maintenon cutlets, my lord."

"Maintenon cutlets! I hate them—I won't have them, sir. Let them be dressed *à l'ombre Chinoise*."

"I don't know what that is, my lord."

"I don't care for that, sirrah; if you don't find out by dinner-time, you're food for fishes—that's all; you may go."

The cook walked off wringing his hands and his night-cap as well—for he still held it in his right hand—and disappeared down the fore-hatchway.

"I have done this to pay you a deserved compliment, ladies; you have more courage than the other sex."

"Recollect that we have had confidence given to us in consequence of your pledging your word, my lord."

"You do me, then, the honour of believing me?"

"I did not until I saw you," replied Mrs Lascelles; "but now I am convinced that you will perform your promise."

"You do, indeed, encourage me, madam, to pursue what is right," said Pickersgill, bowing; "for your approbation I should be most sorry to lose, still more sorry to prove myself unworthy of it."

As the reader will observe, everything was going on remarkably well.

Chapter VI

THE SMUGGLING YACHT

Cecilia returned to the cabin, to ascertain whether her aunt was more composed; but Mrs Lascelles remained on deck. She was much pleased with Pickersgill; and they continued their conversation. Pickersgill entered into a defence of his conduct to Lord B.; and Mrs Lascelles could not but admit the provocation. After a long conversation, she hinted at his profession, and how superior he appeared to be to such a lawless life.

"You may be incredulous, madam," replied Pickersgill, "if I tell you that I have as good a right to quarter my arms as Lord B. himself; and that I am not under my real name. Smuggling is, at all events, no crime; and I infinitely prefer the wild life I lead at the head of my men, to being spurned by society because I am poor. The greatest crime in this country is poverty. I may, if I am fortunate, some day resume my name. You may, perhaps, meet me, and, if you please, you may expose me."

"That I should not be likely to do," replied the widow; "but still I regret to see a person, evidently intended for better things, employed in so disreputable a profession."

"I hardly know, madam, what is and what is not disreputable in this conventional world. It is not considered disreputable to cringe to the vices of a court, or to accept a pension wrung from the industry of the nation, in return for base servility. It is not considered disreputable to take tithes, intended for the service of God, and lavish them away at watering-places or elsewhere, seeking pleasure instead of doing God service. It is not considered disreputable to take fee after fee to uphold injustice, to plead against innocence, to pervert truth, and to aid the devil. It is not considered disreputable to gamble on the Stock Exchange, or to corrupt the honesty of electors by bribes, to doing which the penalty attached is equal to that decreed to the offence of which I am guilty. All these, and much more, are not considered disreputable; yet, by all these are the moral bonds of society loosened, while in mine we cause no guilt in others—"

"But still it is a crime."

"A violation of the revenue laws, and no more. Observe, madam, the English Government encourage the smuggling of our manufactures to the Continent, at the same time that they take every step to prevent articles being smuggled into this country. Now, madam, can that be a *crime*, when the head of the vessel is turned north, which becomes *no crime* when she steers the opposite way?"

"There is a stigma attached to it, you must allow."

"That I grant you, madam; and as soon as I can quit the profession I shall. No captive ever sighed more to be released from his chains; but I will not leave it, till I find that I am in a situation not to be spurned and neglected by those with whom I have a right to associate."

At this moment, the steward was seen forward making signs to Mrs Lascelles, who excused herself, and went to him.

"For the love of God, madam," said Maddox, "as he appears to be friendly with you, do pray find out how these cutlets are to be dressed; the cook is tearing his hair, and we shall never have any dinner; and then it will all fall upon me, and I—shall be tossed overboard."

Mrs Lascelles desired poor Maddox to wait there while she obtained the desired information. In a few minutes she returned to him.

"I have found it out. They are first to be boiled in vinegar; then fried in batter, and served up with a sauce of anchovy and Malaga raisins!"

"First fried in vinegar; then boiled in batter, and served up with almonds and raisins!"

"No—no!" Mrs Lascelles repeated the injunction to the frightened steward; and then returned aft, and re-entered into a conversation with Pickersgill, in which for the first time, Corbett now joined. Corbett had sense enough to feel, that the less he came forward until his superior had established himself in the good graces of the ladies, the more favourable would be the result.

In the mean time Cecilia had gone down to her aunt, who still continued to wail and lament. The young lady tried all she could to console her, and to persuade her that if they were civil and obedient they had nothing to fear.

"Civil and obedient, indeed!" cried Miss Ossulton, "to a fellow who is a smuggler and a pirate! I, the sister of Lord B.! Never! The presumption of the wretch!"

"That is all very well, aunt; but recollect, we must submit to circumstances. These men insist upon our dining with them; and we must go, or we shall have no dinner."

"I sit down with a pirate! Never! I'll have no dinner—I'll starve—I'll die!"

"But, my dear aunt, it's the only chance we have of obtaining our release; and if you do not do it Mrs Lascelles will think that you wish to remain with them."

"Mrs Lascelles judges of other people by herself."

"The captain is certainly a very well-behaved, handsome man. He looks like a nobleman in disguise. What an odd thing it would be, aunt, if this should be all a hoax!"

"A hoax, child?" replied Miss Ossulton, sitting up on the sofa.

Cecilia found that she had hit the right nail, as the saying is; and she brought forward so many arguments to prove that she thought it was a hoax to frighten them, and that the gentleman above was a man of consequence, that her aunt began to listen to reason, and at last consented to join the dinner-party. Mrs Lascelles now came down below; and when dinner was announced they repaired to the large cabin, where they found Pickersgill and Corbett waiting for them.

Miss Ossulton did not venture to look up, until she heard Pickersgill say to Mrs Lascelles, "Perhaps, madam, you will do me the favour to introduce me to that lady, whom I have not had the honour of seeing before?"

"Certainly, my lord," replied Mrs Lascelles. "Miss Ossulton, the aunt of this young lady."

Mrs Lascelles purposely did not introduce *his lordship* in return, that she might mystify the old spinster.

"I feel highly honoured in finding myself in the company of Miss Ossulton," said Pickersgill. "Ladies, we wait but for you to sit down. Ossulton, take the head of the table and serve the soup."

Miss Ossulton was astonished; she looked at the smugglers, and perceived two well-dressed gentlemanly men, one of whom was apparently a lord, and the other having the same family name.

"It must be all a hoax," thought she; and she very quietly took to her soup.

The dinner passed off very pleasantly; Pickersgill was agreeable, Corbett funny, and Miss Ossulton so far recovered herself as to drink wine with his lordship, and to ask Corbett what branch of their family he belonged to.

"I presume it's the Irish branch," said Mrs Lascelles, prompting him.

"Exactly, madam," replied Corbett.

"Have you ever been to Torquay, ladies?" inquired Pickersgill.

"No, my lord," answered Mrs Lascelles.

"We shall anchor there in the course of an hour, and probably remain there till to-morrow. Steward, bring coffee. Tell the cook these cutlets were remarkably well dressed."

The ladies retired to the cabin. Miss Ossulton was now convinced that it was all a hoax; but said she, "I shall tell Lord B. my opinion of their practical jokes when he returns. What is his lordship's name who is on board?"

"He won't tell us," replied Mrs Lascelles; "but I think I know; it is Lord Blarney."

"Lord Blaney you mean, I presume," said Miss Ossulton; "however, the thing is carried too far. Cecilia, we will go on shore at Torquay, and wait till the yacht returns with Lord B. I don't like these jokes; they may do very well for widows, and people of no rank."

Now, Mrs Lascelles was sorry to find Miss Ossulton so much at her ease. She owed her no little spite, and wished for revenge. Ladies will go very far to obtain this. How far Mrs Lascelles would have gone, I will not pretend to say; but this is certain, that the last innuendo of Miss Ossulton very much added to her determination. She took her bonnet and went on deck, at once told Pickersgill that he could not please her or Cecilia more than by frightening Miss Ossulton, who, under the idea that it was all a hoax, had quite recovered her spirits; talked of her pride and ill-nature, and wished her to receive a useful lesson. Thus, to follow up her revenge, did Mrs Lascelles commit herself so far, as to be confidential with the smuggler in return.

"Mrs Lascelles, I shall be able to obey you, and, at the same time, to combine business with pleasure."

After a short conversation, the yacht dropped her anchor at Torquay. It was then about two hours before sunset. As soon as the sails were furled, one or two gentlemen, who resided there, came on board to pay their respects to Lord B.; and, as Pickersgill had found out from Cecilia that her father was acquainted with no one there, he received them in person; asked them down in the cabin; called for wine; and desired them to send their boat away, as his own was going on shore. The smugglers took great care, that the steward, cook, and lady's maid, should have no communication with the guests; one of them, by Corbett's direction, being a sentinel over each individual. The gentlemen remained about half-an-hour on board, during which Corbett and the smugglers had filled the portmanteaus found in the cabin with the lace, and they were put in the boat. Corbett then landed the gentlemen in the same boat, and went up to the hotel, the smugglers following him with the portmanteaus, without any suspicion or interruption. As soon as he was there, he ordered post-horses, and set off for a town close by, where he had correspondents; and thus the major part of the cargo was secured. Corbett then returned in the night, bringing with him people to receive the goods; and the smugglers landed the silks, teas, &c., with the same good fortune. Everything was out of the yacht except a portion of the lace, which the portmanteaus would not hold. Pickersgill might easily have sent this on shore; but, to please Mrs Lascelles, he arranged otherwise.

The next morning, about an hour after breakfast was finished, Mrs Lascelles entered the cabin pretending to be in the greatest consternation, and fell on the sofa as if she were going to faint.

"Good heavens! what is the matter?" exclaimed Cecilia, who knew very well what was coming.

"Oh, the wretch! he has made such proposals!"

"Proposals! what proposals? what! Lord Blaney?" cried Miss Ossulton.

"Oh, he's no lord! he's a villain and a smuggler! and he insists that we shall both fill our pockets full of lace, and go on shore with him."

"Mercy on me! Then it is no hoax after all; and I've been sitting down to dinner with a smuggler!"

"Sitting down, madam!—if it were to be no more than that—but we are to take his arm up to the hotel. Oh, dear! Cecilia, I am ordered on deck, pray come with me!"

Miss Ossulton rolled on the sofa, and rang for Phoebe; she was in a state of great alarm.

A knock at the door.

"Come in," said Miss Ossulton, thinking it was Phoebe; when Pickersgill made his appearance.

"What do you want, sir? Go out, sir! go out directly, or I'll scream!"

"It is no use screaming, madam; recollect that all on board are at my service. You will oblige me by listening to me, Miss Ossulton. I am, as you know, a smuggler, and I must send this lace on shore. You will oblige me by putting it into your pockets, or about your person, and prepare to go on shore with me. As soon as we arrive at the hotel, you will deliver it to me, and I then shall reconduct you on board of the yacht. You are not the first lady who has gone on shore with contraband articles about her person."

"Me, sir! go on shore in that way? No, sir, never! What will the world say? the Hon. Miss Ossulton walking with a smuggler! No, sir, never!"

"Yes, madam, walking arm-in-arm with a smuggler: I shall have you on one arm, and Mrs Lascelles on the other; and I would advise you to take it very quietly; for, in the first place, it will be you who smuggle, as the goods will be found on your person, and you will certainly be put in prison, for, at the least appearance of insubordination, we run and inform against you; and, further, your niece will remain on board as a hostage for your good behaviour, and if you have any regard for her liberty, you will consent immediately."

Pickersgill left the cabin, and shortly afterwards Cecilia and Mrs Lascelles entered, apparently much distressed. They had been informed of all, and Mrs Lascelles declared, that, for her part, sooner than leave her poor Cecilia to the mercy of such people, she had made up her mind to submit to the smuggler's demands. Cecilia also begged so earnestly, that Miss Ossulton, who had no idea that it was a trick, with much sobbing and blubbering, consented.

When all was ready, Cecilia left the cabin; Pickersgill came down, handed up the two ladies, who had not exchanged a word with each other during Cecilia's absence; the boat was ready alongside—they went in, and pulled on shore. Everything succeeded to the smuggler's satisfaction. Miss Ossulton, frightened out of her wits, took his arm; and, with Mrs Lascelles on the other, they went up to the hotel, followed by four of his boat's crew. As soon as they were shown into a room, Corbett, who was already on shore, asked for Lord B., and joined them. The ladies retired to another apartment, divested themselves of their contraband goods, and, after calling for some sandwiches and wine, Pickersgill waited an hour, and then returned on board. Mrs Lascelles was triumphant; and she rewarded her new ally, the smuggler, with one of her sweetest smiles. Community of interest will sometimes make strange friendships.

Chapter VII

CONCLUSION

We must now return to the other parties who have assisted in the acts of this little drama. Lord B., after paddling and paddling, the men relieving each other in order to make head against the wind which was off shore, arrived about midnight at a small town in West Bay, from whence he took a chaise on to Portsmouth, taking it for granted that his yacht would arrive as soon as, if not before himself, little imagining that it was in possession of the smugglers. There he remained three or four days, when, becoming impatient, he applied to one of his friends who had a yacht at Cowes, and sailed with him to look after his own.

We left the *Happy-go-lucky* chased by the revenue cutter. At first the smuggler had the advantage before the wind; but, by degrees, the wind went round with the sun, and brought the revenue cutter to leeward: it was then a chase on a wind, and the revenue cutter came fast up with her.

Morrison, perceiving that he had no chance of escape, let run the ankers of brandy that he might not be condemned; but still he was in an awkward situation, as he had more men on board than allowed by Act of Parliament. He therefore stood on, notwithstanding the shot of the cutter went over and over him, hoping that a fog or night might enable him to escape; but he had no such good fortune,—one of the shot carried away the head of his mast, and the *Happy-go-lucky's* luck was all over. He was boarded and taken possession of; he asserted that the extra men were only passengers; but, in the first place, they were dressed in seamen's clothes; and, in the second, as soon as the boat was aboard of her, Appleboy had gone down to his gin-toddy, and was not to be disturbed. The gentlemen smugglers therefore passed an uncomfortable night; and the cutter going to Portland by daylight before Appleboy was out of bed, they were taken on shore to the magistrate. Hautaine explained the whole affair, and they were immediately released and treated with respect; but they were not permitted to depart until they were bound over to appear against the smugglers, and prove the brandy having been on board. They then set off for Portsmouth in the seamen's clothes, having had quite enough of yachting for that season, Mr Ossulton declaring that he only wanted to get his luggage, and then he would take care how he put himself again in the way of the shot of a revenue cruiser, or of sleeping a night on her decks.

In the mean time Morrison and his men were locked up in the jail, the old man, as the key was turned on him, exclaiming, as he raised his foot in vexation, "That cursed blue pigeon!"

We will now return to the yacht.

About an hour after Pickersgill had come on board, Corbett had made all his arrangements and followed him. It was not advisable to remain at Torquay any longer, through fear of discovery; he, therefore, weighed the anchor before dinner, and made sail.

"What do you intend to do now, my lord?" said Mrs Lascelles.

"I intend to run down to Cowes, anchor the yacht in the night; and an hour before daylight have you in my boat with all my men. I will take care that you are in perfect safety, depend upon it, even if I run a risk. I should, indeed, be miserable, if, through my wild freaks, any accident should happen to Mrs Lascelles or Miss Ossulton."

"I am very anxious about my father," observed Cecilia. "I trust that you will keep your promise."

"I always have hitherto, Miss Ossulton; have I not?"

"Ours is but a short and strange acquaintance."

"I grant it; but it will serve for you to talk about long after. I shall disappear as suddenly as I have come—you will neither of you, in all probability, ever see me again."

The dinner was announced, and they sat down to table as before; but the elderly spinster refused to make her appearance; and Mrs Lascelles and Cecilia, who thought she had been frightened enough, did not attempt to force her. Pickersgill immediately yielded to these remonstrances, and, from that time she remained undisturbed in the ladies' cabin, meditating over the indignity of having sat down to table, having drank wine, and been obliged to walk on shore, taking the arm of a smuggler, and appear in such a humiliating situation.

The wind was light, and they made but little progress, and were not abreast of Portland till the second day, when another yacht appeared in sight, and the two vessels slowly neared until in the afternoon they were within four miles of each other. It then fell a dead calm—signals were thrown out by the other yacht, but could not be distinguished, and, for the last time, they sat down to dinner. Three days' companionship on board of a vessel, cooped up together, and having no one else to converse with, will produce intimacy; and Pickersgill was a young man of so much originality and information, that he was listened to with pleasure. He never attempted to advance beyond the line of strict decorum and politeness; and his companion was equally unpresuming. Situated as they were, and feeling what must have been the case had they fallen into other hands, both Cecilia and Mrs Lascelles felt some degree of gratitude towards him; and, although anxious to be relieved from so strange a position, they had gradually acquired a perfect confidence in him, and this had produced a degree of familiarity, on their parts, although never ventured upon by the smuggler. As Corbett was at the table, one of the men came down and made a sign. Corbett shortly after quitted the table and went on deck. "I wish, my lord, you would come up a moment, and see if you can make this flag out," said Corbett, giving a significant nod to Pickersgill. "Excuse me, ladies, one moment," said Pickersgill, who went on deck.

"It is the boat of the yacht coming on board," said Corbett; "and Lord B. is in the stern-sheets with the gentleman who was with him."

"And how many men in the boat?—let me see—only four. Well, let his lordship and his friend come: when they are on the deck, have the men ready in case of accident; but if you can manage to tell the boat's crew that they are to go on board again, and get rid of them that way, so much the better. Arrange this with Adams, and then come down again—his lordship must see us all at dinner."

Pickersgill then descended, and Corbett had hardly time to give his directions and to resume his seat, before his lordship and Mr Stewart pulled up alongside and jumped on deck. There was no one to receive them but the seamen, and those whom they did not know. They looked round in amazement; at last his lordship said to Adams, who stood forward,

"What men are you?"

"Belong to the yacht, ye'r honour."

Lord B. heard laughing in the cabin; he would not wait to interrogate the men; he walked aft, followed by Mr Stewart, looked down the skylight, and perceived his daughter and Mrs Lascelles with, as he supposed, Hautaine and Ossulton.

Pickersgill had heard the boat rub the side, and the sound of the feet on deck, and he talked the more loudly, that the ladies might be caught by Lord B. as they were. He heard their feet at the skylight, and knew that they could hear what passed; and at that moment he proposed to the ladies that as this was their last meeting at table they should all take a glass of champagne to drink to "their happy meeting with Lord B." This was a toast which they did not refuse. Maddox poured out the wine, and they were all bowing to each other, when his lordship, who had come down the ladder, walked into the cabin, followed by Mr Stewart. Cecilia perceived her father; the champagne-glass dropped from her hand—she flew into his arms, and burst into tears.

"Who would not be a father, Mrs Lascelles?" said Pickersgill, quietly seating himself, after having first risen to receive Lord B.

"And pray, whom may I have the honour of finding established here?" said Lord B., in an angry tone, speaking over his daughter's head, who still lay in his arms. "By heavens, yes?—Stewart, it is the smuggling captain dressed out."

"Even so, my lord," replied Pickersgill. "You abandoned your yacht to capture me; you left these ladies in a vessel crippled for want of men; they might have been lost. I have returned good for evil by coming on board with my own people, and taking charge of them. This night, I expected to have anchored your vessel in Cowes, and have left them in safety."

"By the—" cried Stewart.

"Stop, sir, if you please!" cried Pickersgill; "recollect you have once already attacked one who never offended. Oblige me by refraining from intemperate language; for I tell you I will not put up with it. Recollect, sir, that I have refrained from that, and also from taking advantage of you when you were in my power. Recollect, sir, also, that the yacht is still in possession of the smugglers, and that you are in no condition to insult with impunity. My lord, allow me to observe, that we men are too hot of temperament to argue, or listen coolly. With your permission, your friend, and my friend, and I, will repair on deck, leaving you to hear from your daughter and that lady all that has passed. After that, my lord, I shall be most happy to hear anything which your lordship may please to say."

"Upon my word—" commenced Mr Stewart.

"Mr Stewart," interrupted Cecilia Ossulton, "I request your silence; nay, more, if ever we are again to sail in the same vessel together, I *insist* upon it."

"Your lordship will oblige me by enforcing Miss Ossulton's request," said Mrs Lascelles.

Mr Stewart was dumbfounded, no wonder, to find the ladies siding with the smuggler.

"I am obliged to you ladies for your interference," said Pickersgill; "for, although I have the means of enforcing conditions, I should be sorry to avail myself of them. I wait for his lordship's reply."

Lord B. was very much surprised. He wished for an explanation; he bowed with *hauteur*. Everybody appeared to be in a false position; even he, Lord B., somehow or another had bowed to a smuggler.

Pickersgill and Stewart went on deck, walking up and down, crossing each other without speaking, but reminding you of two dogs who both are anxious to fight, but have been restrained by the voice of their masters. Corbett followed, and talked in a low tone to Pickersgill; Stewart went over to leeward to see if the boat was still alongside, but it had long before returned to the yacht. Miss Ossulton had heard her brother's voice, but did not come out of the after-cabin; she wished to be magnificent and, at the same time, she was not sure whether all was right, Phoebe having informed her that there was nobody with her brother and Mr Stewart, and that the smugglers still had the command of the vessel. After a while, Pickersgill and Corbett went down forward, and returned dressed in the smuggler's clothes, when they resumed their walk on the deck.

In the mean time, it was dark; the cutter flew along the coast; and the Needles' lights were on the larboard bow. The conversation between Cecilia, Mrs Lascelles, and her father, was long. When all had been detailed, and the conduct of Pickersgill duly represented, Lord B. acknowledged that, by attacking the smuggler, he had laid himself open to retaliation; that Pickersgill had shown a great deal of forbearance in every instance; and, after all, had he not gone on board the yacht she might have been lost, with only three seamen on board. He was amused with the smuggling and the fright of his sister; still more with the gentlemen being sent to Cherbourg, and much consoled that he was not the only one to be laughed at. He was also much pleased with Pickersgill's intention of leaving the yacht safe in Cowes harbour, his respect to the property on board, and his conduct to the ladies. On the whole, he felt grateful to Pickersgill; and where there is gratitude there is always good will.

"But who can he be?" said Mrs Lascelles; "his name he acknowledges not to be Pickersgill; and he told me confidentially that he was of good family."

"Confidentially, my dear Mrs Lascelles!" said Lord B.

"Oh, yes! we are both his confidants. Are we not, Cecilia?"

"Upon my honour, Mrs Lascelles, this smuggler appears to have made an impression which many have attempted in vain."

Mrs Lascelles did not reply to that remark, but said, "Now, my lord, you must decide—and I trust you will to oblige us—treat him as he has treated us, with the greatest respect and kindness."

"Why should you suppose otherwise?" replied Lord B.; "it is not only my wish but my interest so to do. He may take us over to France to-night, or anywhere else. Has he not possession of the vessel?"

"Yes," replied Cecilia; "but we flatter ourselves that we have *the command*. Shall we call him down, papa?"

"Ring for Maddox. Maddox, tell Mr Pickersgill, who is on deck, that I wish to speak with him, and shall be obliged by his stepping down into the cabin."

"Who, my lord? What? *Him*?"

"Yes, *him*," replied Cecilia, laughing.

"Must I call him, my lord, now, miss?"

"You may do as you please, Maddox; but recollect, he is still in possession of the vessel," replied Cecilia.

"Then, with your lordship's permission, I will; it's the safest way."

The smuggler entered the cabin; the ladies started as he appeared in his rough costume, with his throat open, and his loose black handkerchief. He was the *beau idéal* of a handsome sailor.

"Your lordship wishes to communicate with me?"

"Mr Pickersgill, I feel that you have had cause of enmity against me, and that you have behaved with forbearance. I thank you for your considerate treatment of the ladies; and I assure you, that I feel no resentment for what has passed."

"My lord, I am quite satisfied with what you have said; and I only hope that, in future, you will not interfere with a poor smuggler, who may be striving, by a life of danger and privation, to procure subsistence for himself and, perhaps, his family. I stated to these ladies my intention of anchoring the yacht this night at Cowes, and leaving her as soon as she was in safety. Your unexpected presence will only make this difference, which is, that I must previously obtain your lordship's assurance that those with you will allow me and my men to quit her without molestation, after we have performed this service."

"I pledge you my word, Mr Pickersgill, and I thank you into the bargain.
I trust you will allow me to offer some remuneration."

"Most certainly not, my lord."

"At all events, Mr Pickersgill, if, at any other time, I can be of service, you may command me."

Pickersgill made no reply.

"Surely, Mr Pickersgill,—"

"Pickersgill! how I hate that name!" said the smuggler, musing. "I beg your lordship's pardon—if I may require your assistance for any of my unfortunate companions—"

"Not for yourself, Mr Pickersgill?" said Mrs Lascelles.

"Madam, I smuggle no more."

"For the pleasure I feel in hearing that resolution, Mr Pickersgill," said Cecilia, "take my hand and thanks."

"And mine," said Mrs Lascelles, half crying.

"And mine, too," said Lord B., rising up.

Pickersgill passed the back of his hand across his eyes, turned round, and left the cabin.

"I'm so happy!" said Mrs Lascelles, bursting into tears.

"He's a magnificent fellow," observed Lord B. "Come, let us all go on deck."

"You have not seen my aunt, papa."

"True; I'll go in to her, and then follow you."

The ladies went upon deck. Cecilia entered into conversation with Mr Stewart, giving him a narrative of what had happened. Mrs Lascelles sat abaft at the taffrail, with her pretty hand supporting her cheek, looking very much *à la Juliette*.

"Mrs Lascelles," said Pickersgill, "before we part, allow me to observe, that it is *you* who have induced me to give up my profession—"

"Why me, Mr Pickersgill?"

"You said that you did not like it."

Mrs Lascelles felt the force of the compliment. "You said, just now, that you hated the name of Pickersgill: why do you call yourself so?"

"It was my smuggling name, Mrs Lascelles."

"And now, that you have left off smuggling, pray what may be the name we are to call you by?"

"I cannot resume it till I have not only left this vessel, but shaken hands with, and bid farewell to, my companions; and by that time, Mrs Lascelles, I shall be away from you."

"But I've a great curiosity to know it, and a lady's curiosity must be gratified. You must call upon me some day, and tell it me. Here is my address."

Pickersgill received the card with a low bow: and Lord B. coming on deck, Mrs Lascelles hastened to meet him.

The vessel was now passing the Bridge at the Needles, and the smuggler piloted her on. As soon as they were clear and well inside, the whole party went down into the cabin, Lord B. requesting Pickersgill and Corbett to join him in a parting glass. Mr Stewart, who had received the account of what had passed from Cecilia, was very attentive to Pickersgill, and took an opportunity of saying, that he was sorry that he had said or done anything to annoy him. Every one recovered his spirits; and all was good humour and mirth, because Miss Ossulton adhered to her resolution of not quitting the cabin till she could quit the yacht. At ten o'clock the yacht was anchored. Pickersgill took his leave of the honourable company, and went in his boat with his men; and Lord B. was again in possession of his vessel, although he had not a ship's company. Maddox recovered his usual tone; and the cook flourished his knife, swearing that he should like to see the smuggler who would again order him to dress cutlets *à l'ombre Chinoise*.

The yacht had remained three days at Cowes, when Lord B. received a letter from Pickersgill, stating that the men of his vessel had been captured, and would be condemned, in consequence of their having the gentlemen on board, who were bound to appear against them, to prove that they had sunk the brandy. Lord B. paid all the recognisances, and the men were liberated for want of evidence.

It was about two years after this that Cecilia Ossulton, who was sitting at her work-table in deep mourning for her aunt, was presented with a letter by the butler. It was from her friend Mrs Lascelles, informing her that she was married again to a Mr Davenant, and intended to pay her a short visit on her way to the Continent. Mr and Mrs Davenant arrived the next day; and when the latter introduced her husband, she said to Miss Ossulton, "Look, Cecilia, dear, and tell me if you have ever seen Davenant before."

Cecilia looked earnestly: "I have, indeed," cried she at last, extending her hand with warmth; "and happy am I to meet with him again."

For in Mr Davenant she recognised her old acquaintance, the captain of the *Happy-go-lucky*, Jack Pickersgill, the smuggler.

Printed in Great Britain
by Amazon.co.uk, Ltd.,
Marston Gate.

Greek Civilization
Through the Eyes of
Travellers and Scholars

GREEK CIVILIZATION THROUGH THE EYES OF TRAVELLERS AND SCHOLARS

From the Collection of Dimitris Contominas

Compiled by
LEONORA NAVARI

Preface by
HÉLÈNE AHRWEILER

Historical Introduction by
IOLI VINGOPOULOU

Designed by
KONSTANTINOS SP. STAIKOS

OAK KNOLL PRESS
HES & DE GRAAF Publishers BV
KOTINOS
2004

First English Edition, 2004

Published by **OAK KNOLL PRESS**
310 Delaware Street, New Castle, Delaware, USA
Web:http://www.oakknoll.com
and
HES & DE GRAAF Publishers BV
Tuurdijk 16, 3997 MS 't Goy-Houten, The Netherlands
Web:http://www.hesdegraaf.com
and
KOTINOS PUBLICATIONS, Panou Aravantinou 10, Athens, Greece
e-mail: kotinos@libraries.gr

ISBN: 1-58456-134-3 (USA)
ISBN: 90-6194-269-1 (EUROPE)

Title: Greek Civilization Through the Eyes of Travellers and Scholars
Author: Leonora Navari
Editor: Konstantinos Sp. Staikos
Typographer: Petros Balidis, Athens, Greece
Photographic Editor: Socrates Mavrommatis
Proof Reading: Olga Papakosta
English Translations of Greek Prefaces: Timothy Cullen
English Translation of Historical Introduction: David Hardy
Publishing Director: J. Lewis von Hoelle

Copyright © KOTINOS, D. CONTOMINAS, 2003

CIP Available Upon Request from the Publisher

Greek Civilization Through the Eyes of Travellers and Scholars. From the Collection of Dimitris
    Contominas /
Compiled by Leonora Navari
    p. cm.
    Includes bibliographical references and index.
    ISBN 1-58456-134-3; ISBN 90-6194-269-1

ALL RIGHTS RESERVED:
No part of this book may be reproduced in any manner without the express written consent of the
publisher, except in the case of brief excerpts in critical reviews
and articles. All inquiries should be addressed to:
Oak Knoll Press, 310 Delaware Street, New Castle, DE 19720, USA.
Web: http://www.oakknoll.com

This work was printed and bound in Athens, Greece in 2004 on
archival, acid-free paper meeting the requirements of the American
Standard for Permanence of Paper for Printed Library Materials.

Contents

FOREWORD by Hélène Glykatzi-Ahrweiler	IX-X
TO THE READER by Konstantinos Sp. Staikos	XI-XII
INTRODUCTION by Leonora Navari	XIII-XV
DIMITRIS CONTOMINAS AND VIEWS OF HIS LIBRARY	XVI-XIX
HISTORICAL INTRODUCTION by Ioli Vingopoulou	XXI-XXXIX
BOOKS AND COMMENTARIES	3-481
REFERENCES CITED AND BIBLIOGRAPHY	485-489
ABBREVIATIONS	490
INDEX OF NAMES	491-511
INDEX OF PRINTERS, PUBLISHERS, BOOKSELLERS AND BOOKBINDERS	512-521
INDEX OF PROVENANCES	522-525
CORRIGENDA	526

Foreword

If you live with books, if books are your best friends, if your house is full of books by authors old and new, whether in *éditions de luxe* or cheap editions, then you simply cannot help wanting to see and learn new things from those well-travelled, knowledgeable writers; you cannot help feeling an urge for self-improvement. It is hard to be interested in the doings of your fellow human beings and in their thoughts, their dreams and their cares, without wanting to know what they have written and said. Books, then, are not only sources of knowledge, scholarship and culture but also – and perhaps most of all – a palpable proof of a humanistic outlook.

'Tell me which books you possess and have enjoyed and I will tell you who you are.' There must be countless people who, when they enter a house for the first time, discreetly (or not so discreetly) take a look at the books on the shelves. Every book – be it a reference book or manual for one's work, a book bought for edification or something shared by the whole family, be it sumptuously bound or dog-eared from constant rereading – is perhaps the nearest thing to an infallible mirror of its owner's character. How much more, then, is this true of a person's private library, a product of persistent effort, time, money and, above all, love of books, whose very presence attests to a cultural achievement.

It is no accident that in nearly all languages the word for a library is the Greek word, *bibliotheke*, nor that the holy book of the Christian faith containing the corpus of revealed truth is called the Bible: *the* Book, the book *par excellence*. Nor is it a coincidence that European civilization has so often been described as a library shared by the European peoples. Pride of place in this imaginary library has always belonged to the works of ancient Greek literature. That cultural heritage bequeathed by Greece to the world has numerous offshoots and ramifications that have provided a stimulus for the Greek mind down through the ages to our own time, either as a Byzantine intellectual byway, or as fictional reading through the centuries of slavery, or as a clarion-call for national regeneration during the Neohellenic Enlightenment. Our knowledge of this Greek continuity comes not only from Greek literature and books about Greek literature, but also, and more especially, from foreign men of letters, scientists, artists, antiquarians and scholars in every branch of learning – those persons, in fact, who have never ceased to take an interest in the country and the people who have striven to preserve the spark of their ancestral anthropocentric idea.

We therefore owe a debt of gratitude to men and women like Dimitris Contominas, who have devoted their energies to forming libraries that testify to the Greek way of life through the ages, collecting books regarded by modern scholars as valuable sources because the information they provide about different periods of history is extremely interesting: I am referring to books by foreign travellers who toured Greece. Mr. Contominas's collection contains primary sources of this kind as well as the other material required for an 'ideal' library: studies and reviews by Greek and foreign specialists in every period covered by the age-old history of Greece.

It is greatly to be hoped that this most laudable achievement of Mr. Contominas will be imitated both by other members of the world of business, in which he himself has earned such distinction, and by others who, like him, combine wealth with breadth of learning and a concern for the welfare of posterity. To conclude this brief note on a significant achievement, I should like to stress that the only precepts offering hope for a better tomorrow are those that express universal values. And our only sources for the knowledge of those eternal values, that ever-necessary succour, have always been and still are books: books in whatever form.

Today, when so much is heard about universal public resources, it is time for us to view books as a resource for all members of the human race, to fight to make books accessible to all and to hail as benefactors all those who strive to perform this service for the intellectual community in a spirit of altruism.

Hélène Glykatzi-Ahrweiler
President of the European University

To the Reader

The formation of any library at any given moment encapsulates not only the life and work of its creator but also, in one way or another, a whole outlook on life.

In the early 1980s the library of Dimitris Contominas was no more than a collection of books intended for his own general edification or on specialized subjects connected with his work; but within the next ten years or so, by about 1992, it had been enriched by the acquisition of an extremely fine collection of at least four hundred titles. Most of these were books by travellers, with a relatively small number of works by ancient Greek and Byzantine writers and standard works on the history of Byzantine civilization by scholars like Charles Diehl and Gustave Schlumberger.

This marked the beginning of my own involvement with that section of Mr. Contominas's library, as I would browse through those books one by one and form an opinion of each. At the same time the friendship that grew up between us – mainly through our collaboration in another field, architecture – gradually gave me an insight into his firmly-held beliefs on the role of education in the formation of a person's character. And so, appreciating the value of every item of written and visual evidence concerning the Greece that is steadily disappearing, and of the buildings and monuments that stand witness to her civilization all round the Mediterranean basin, we made unobtrusive but rapid progress in enlarging the main body of the library, that is the travel literature section. The breadth and multiplicity of Mr. Contominas's interests over so wide a geographical area may perhaps have prevented him from perusing every new acquisition thoroughly, but there were periods when we would meet every morning and I would tell him about every new 'member' of his collection, its distinguishing characteristics and its subject matter.

Our intention was not to build up a purely bibliophilic collection consisting entirely of rare books printed in special editions with bindings by great artists, but rather to search out and acquire every book that paints a picture of one or other aspect of Greek civilization from the fifteenth to the mid twentieth century. With its memoirs by scholars, poets, antiquarians, epigrammatists, travellers, diplomats, naturalists, pilgrims, archaeologists and historians, not to mention a mass of pictorial material, most of it in the form of illustrations to those books, Mr. Contominas's library presents a vivid panorama of the life and times of Greeks living in the West as well as the East.

Besides the classic works of travel literature by Clarke, Dodwell, Haygarth, Pococke, Drummond, Spon and Wheler, Koberger, Dapper, de Bruyn and others, this fine collection includes books by and about philhellenes, books about classical geography and books about travellers' writings on Greece. Among them are Fénelon's *Télémaque*, the Abbé Barthélemy's *Jeune Anacharsis*, the *Description of the Inhabited Earth* by Dionysius Periegetes, Strabo's *Geography* (in several rare editions), the *Anaplus* by Nearchus, the commander of Alexander the Great's fleet, and the poem *De Situ Orbis* by Marcian of Heraclea, some of them in two or more editions. One of the most interesting sections of the library contains memoirs by twentieth-century French politicians reflecting the shift of French policy towards Greece during the run-up to the First World War. Then there are booklets and pamphlets written by philhellenes before and during the Greek War of Independence and books from the heyday of nineteenth-century romanticism, such as Ernest Renan's *Prière sur l'Acropole*.

The library as it is today, with its 900 titles and 1,500 volumes, is one of the most important of the well-known private collections, containing a large number of books that are here classified thematically in this way for the first time. Yet this treasure-house of books cannot be described as just another library, because the manner of its formation reflects a long, well-tried, unbroken friendship between Dimitris Contominas and myself. When I look at the present volume, I am irresistibly reminded of the dictum of the philosopher Archytas of Tarentum as recorded by Cicero in his *De Amicitia*: that if a man could ascend to heaven and view the natural order of the universe and the beauty of the heavenly bodies, he would get no pleasure from that wonderful spectacle if there were no one to whom he could tell what he had seen.

Konstantinos Sp. Staikos

Introduction

I am glad to have had the opportunity to catalogue the Contominas collection. It is a pleasure as well as a challenge to catalogue new material, to add to one's store of knowledge, and to expand the jigsaw puzzle which makes up a picture of travel in the Levant. The Contominas collection is rich in books which I have not encountered before; in fact about half of the books in the library were new to me.

The Contominas library is a Greek library in the sense that the Gennadius Library is a 'Greek' library. As Gennadius said of his own library, it is "composed of works referring to Greece and its people of all epochs and in every aspect". This includes books which describe its relations with other nations. In his prologue Constantinos Staikos has mentioned a number of the subject categories and books which go to make up the collection, so I will content myself with references to a very few of the particularly rare or unusual items. These include Le Huen's adaptation of Breydenbach's pilgrimage to Jerusalem, constituting the first illustrated French book; the first printed account of Cyriac of Ancona's travels in the East; Carlo Widmann's extremely scarce account of the Ionian Islands; Pomardi's uncommon description of his travels with Dodwell; and Prejelan's album illustrating air combat and aviation in northern Greece and Thasos during the First World War.

Some of the books in the collection are old friends which I first encountered in the Blackmer or Atabey libraries, but even then there is something new to be learned: an unsuspected issue point, an unexpected variant in an imprint, a different state. In fact, these books, familiar though they are, are sometimes the most problematic. Among these we may number Clark's *Peloponnesus*, hardly an uncommon book, but the Contominas copy is unusual, with a variant title added to the original edition. Another example is George Rose's account of his travels on leave. This is not a common work, but the only copy I was able to locate, in the Gennadius Library, was also issued with a variant title added to the original sheets.

The catalogue is arranged alphabetically by author. If a number of works by the same author are listed, they will be in chronological order of publication, then each by date of publication of the individual work. Translations follow all publications of the editions in the original language. There are a number of duplicate copies of specific titles; these are mentioned at the end of the entry. The entry is made up of four parts: the title with its heading, the bibliographical description, the note, and the bibliographical references.

The Heading. The headings are formed either by the names of the author or authors, or by the first word of the title of an anonymous work. If the name of the author of an anonymously published book is known, the author's name is used in the heading, and the title of the book is cross-referenced in the index. There are a very few entries in which the name of a publisher or concerned person is used. In some cases the dates of birth and death of an author are given in parentheses, if I happened to come across this information in the course of research, but not otherwise. Thus the addition of this information is purely arbitrary, since I was not searching for it on a regular basis. In the case of several books by the same author, the dates are added only to the first entry.

The Title. The titles have not been recorded in semi-facsimile form, as they were in the Blackmer catalogue, in which words printed in upper case in the title began with a capital letter, and the diacritical marks, or lack of them, were preserved. In the Contominas catalogue titles for the most part have been transcribed as if they formed a sentence, so that normally only the significant words, or words that indicate the start of a subtitle, begin with a capital letter. Spelling is preserved, especially for early works. As far as diacritical marks are concerned, they are supplied if necessary. This is particularly true of the French titles, in which words printed in upper case are normally unaccented. However, when these titles are transcribed in lower case, accents have been added in accordance with French usage. Apart from the titles, the use of accents or other diacritical marks for words in upper case is arbitrary. My rule of thumb is to use diacritical marks in an English text only if the pronunciation is seriously affected.

The Imprint. The imprint is composed of the place of publication, the name of the publisher as it appears on the title, and the date. Dates in roman numerals or according to the French Revolutionary Calendar are followed by the date in arabic numerals within parentheses, introduced by an equal (=) sign. Dates attributed by myself or according to a bibliography or library citation are within brackets.

The Bibliographical Description. The description of the book includes the size of the book expressed according to format, and the collation given in pagination form. Unpaginated preliminary leaves are recorded in lower case roman numerals within brackets, for example the frequently used 'pp. [iii]' usually indicates the half title and title. A blank page between two pages of text is assigned a page number, but final blank pages are not numbered, so pp. [iii] means half title, blank page, title page. If there is text on the verso of the title, the indication would be pp. [iiii]. If a final page with letterpress is not paginated, it is assigned a new page number in brackets thus: [1]. So a familiar type of collation may be pp. [iii] 1-457 [1]. The use of a plus sign between segments of pagination means that the new section of pagination begins on a recto, and not on the verso of the previous page, for example pp. [iii] 1-457 + [1]. I enter into these details because collation by pagination can be very complicated if we want to present the actual state of the book and its composition, and to distinguish between pages with letterpress and those without. There follow the number and description of the illustrations, including the type of reproduction (woodcut, engraving, lithograph, etc.), a description of the binding and a note of any provenance. A collation of signatures is given at the end of the entry for certain rare or problematic books. In the collations, π indicates an unsigned preliminary leaf, while χ indicates an inserted, unsigned, leaf in the text. Blank leaves are expressed by the sign [ ].

The Note. The bibliographical description is followed by a note which contains varied information. This may concern the printing history of the book, information about the author, an account of the illustrations or any other material which is considered appropriate.

Bibliographical References. A location is given for each book; ideally this would be the national library of the place where it was published. In many cases this is not possible, and other libraries may be cited. For the Contominas catalogue I have used the world wide web to search library catalogues in order to cite other locations of books in the collection. This has produced some interesting results, with previously unknown editions coming to light. However, one has to be careful in the interpretation of library cataloguing information. For example, the French and English systems of translating the Revolutionary calendar sometimes differ, so the dates of a specific edition can vary by one year, depending on which library catalogue is being consulted, and it sometimes seems that another edition exists. With regard to locations, the first and sometimes only reference is usually to the library which would normally have a copy of the book, depending on the place and language in which it was printed. Other locations may follow, depending on the nature of the book described, its rarity, and other factors. Bibliographies are cited when appropriate. Note that the Gennadius Library will not always be cited if a Weber reference is given.

With reference to the transliteration of Greek into English, note that the British Library system is generally used, with the Greek H (ēta) is transliterated as e, not i; B (vēta) is transliterated as b, not v. However, Y (ēpsilon) is usually transliterated as y, not u. Greek names which occur as captions to illustrations are usually given as they appear on the plate, which may give rise to two forms of a name in the index.

In many cases the publication of a catalogue signifies that the collector has come to the end of his collecting activities, but we hope that this is not the case with the Contominas collection. In fact this catalogue describes only a part of the Contominas 'Greek Library', that is, the travel books, together with some geographical and historical works. There is another side to the collection which includes early editions of the classical authors, and of the Byzantine historians. Perhaps these collections will produce a catalogue some day. Many people cannot understand the purpose of making a catalogue, particularly a catalogue of a library which has been dispersed. In his *Book Catalogues, their Varieties and Uses*, Archer Taylor comments on the salient fact concerning the catalogue of a private library: "These catalogues are lists of books which actually exist, or once existed, and have been seen by the maker of the catalogue. This fact gives them a peculiar value as reference works. However obscure and confusing an entry in one of these catalogues may be, it concerns a book that was once in existence." These books continue to live, to exist, to be known, in catalogues such as this. We congratulate Mr. Dimitris Contominas on his decision to produce a catalogue of his library.

Leonora Navari

DIMITRIS CONTOMINAS
AND
VIEWS OF HIS LIBRARY
IN THE HOUSE IN
MELEAGER STREET, ATHENS

The Greek world as seen by Travellers
15th-20th centuries

Historical Introduction

Travel. Enchanting in both word and practice. A transition from the familiar to the unfamiliar, from the search for something different to the inner journey involved in every transition, from the exciting planet life to the process of storing up its fruits. Travel is an age-old story: a personal adventure, the need for movement, escape, curiosity; it is knowledge, material benefit, an end in itself or the result of necessity, it is an obligation, a way of life. It is the story of a condition that has existed ever since ancient times, whose face and style change, but which always remains the same in essence: the transition from one world to another. From the land of origin to another land, which is new, unknown and therefore attractive.

In the Middle Ages, journeys were undertaken purely for commercial purposes or as pilgrimages to the Holy Sepulchre and other sacred shrines. Gradually, with the first portents of modern times and the major realignments in the balances of the world, new roads opened up for Western European travellers. Political, ideological, religious or personal reasons determined their journey, their route, their observations, their writings, and the expediency of their work.

The material. The term 'travel writing' may be considered to apply to any text recording experience or knowledge, or a vision of a place, bequeathed to us by any traveller or non-traveller, whether or not he visited and stayed in the place in question. The list contains a crowded host of travellers and scholar geographers, cartographers, humanists, diplomats and pilgrims, spies and naturalists, soldiers and sailors, doctors and priests, theoreticians and experts, painters, topographers, architects and engineers, archaeologists, romantic writers, merchants and missionaries, monks, scientists and pirates, prisoners-of-war, men of letters and adventurers.

The travel writings of the 15th-19th century form a rich body of material of value to the study of the modern history of Hellenism, in which eye-witness evidence, as well as theories, visions, and ideologies that conflicted with experience, formed stereotypes which fed back into the travel literature. The multi-faceted nature of the subject, with the subjective views of writers, whether travellers or not, most of whom represented political positions, ideologies with horizons wider than national frontiers, and even the more objective formations of applied science, have determined my approach to these sources. By separating the subjective from the objective and by reconstitution the actual or imagined reality of places and people of modern history, I reject the use of them simply as sources of information.

The approach. For some time researchers have sought to establish an intellectual approach to travel writing that goes beyond simply quarrying it for information. Given the subjective nature of these sources, the material naturally needs to be studied with some caution and accompanied by full investigation of the validity both of events and of the interpretation given to them by the authors themselves. Distinctions are drawn between accounts deriving from theoretical knowledge and those deriving from personal experience of events. Sometimes instances of copying or plagiarism are encountered. The more remote, less obvious reasons for the visit and the gathering of information are analysed. The self-serving or random testimony. The classification of the material is accompanied by in-depth analysis of the traveller's world. The difference between scholar-traveller and traveller-tourist is defined. We concentrate on the human being-traveller and attempt to establish the difference between him and the later traveller-author. Groupings are made on the basis of the destinations or purposes of travel, and on the basis of the traveller's intellectual or cultural baggage. They are also grouped according to their participation in and influence on the major intellectual and cultural currents of the period to which they belonged or to which they have been assigned.

The Greek world and its perception. When we consider the Greek world through travel writing, it should be made clear first and foremost that we are referring not only to Greeks as people, but also to their geographical space. We are speaking of a spatial reality, of factual evidence (daily life, customs), of subjects that exist in space and aroused their interest (antiquities, monuments), of subjects that develop in space and aroused their interest (political ambitions and expediency, wars). Space, then, people, everything in space, people in space, and also the non-factual of travellers: ideology and how it is expressed, the individual or collective dream, personal myths, perseverance, needs, the existential trend, even when memories, eloquent ruins, forgotten secrets, hidden correspondences are expressed in an artful literary style in a dimension that may even ignore the actual of the Greek world altogether.

Between the European West and the Greeks and the powers that dominated them at different periods and to different geographical extents (Ottoman Turks,

Venetians, Genoese, French, British) intervenes an element of communication: the traveller and the product of his journey. The tissue created by the traveller, as needle, and his journey, as thread, combines the individual elements of these worlds at the practical and symbolic level. Even if the discovery/rediscovery of Greece through their travels is now a commonplace. The traveller-subject finds himself confronted with a reality-object different from the one he knows. At first, the perception seems clear enough, but the recording of reality is by no means self-evident. The traveller and later his account are two different aspects of the two or more worlds that meet. Accordingly, the approach to the sources has two aspects: analysis of the traveller and analysis of the product of his journey. But which truth did the travellers choose to record or to ignore, to transmit, to embellish, or to distort? The *other*, the '*over there*', depends, quite apart from the symbolic, which may be a mirror, and the actual, on what one *considers* to be 'over there', and what one *sees* in the mirror. Sight is thus almost invariably identified with insight.

Travel and 'the Greek tour'. Travel requires theoretical knowledge of the land and the people. Next comes the encounter with knowledge, through the experience of the journey. This is followed by the synthesis of the two, with the requisite documentation. The first component – theoretical knowledge – thus depends on the 'whom' of the traveller; our education helps us to judge his substance both with regard to his attitude to the journey he is undertaking, and, above all, how he defines the events, he 'sees' and perceives or 'doesn't see', and the stance he adopts with regard to them and the comments he makes on them. The second component –personal inspection – depends on the aims for the journey and the experience of it, while the purpose of the journey becomes a guide as to the kind of details he records, the kind of information he himself seeks and writes down. The third component – the synthesis – is again stamped by the environment in which the traveller-author writes, while the date at which his chronicle is published determines the way in which the knowledge and the experience culled from his journey are handed on.

So, the reading of and search for the Greek world through their works demands a critique of the substance of the traveller-author, a critique of his information, a critique of the way in which it is handed down to us. The perception of the land and the people followed the ebb and flow of all the intellectual, political and cultural currents that swept Europeans along in the grand game of history from the 15th to the 20th centuries. For the "western traveller, then, whether actual or a traveller in the imagination, the *Greek tour* was from the very beginning a long journey of the memory. Memory that halted here and there, depending on junctures, motives and interests. Looking upon themselves as heirs to and participants in the Greek spirit, they approach the land with their own personal baggage, their own version of Greece, steeped predominantly in historical memory".

Travel, then, that personal adventure, is also a mirror of the reciprocal relationship between the traveller and the land/people visited. A relationship that was gradually nourished from the 15th to the early 20th century and projected an escalating knowledge that evolved as a chain reaction. At the beginning of the trend for foreign travel, the traveller himself created dim islands of reality relating to the land and people, for, simply put, "he looks but does not see." He still cannot see anything beyond what he carries inside him (16th-early 17th c.). Gradually, western man began to approach both the past and the new with greater sensitivity and knowledge. Objectives and directions were clarified through various processes and experience was enriched beyond expectation (late 17th-18th c.). Unprecedented experiences and an unexpected enrichment intrude, either at the ideological or the pragmatic level (18th c.). With the advent of the 19th century, however, "something overtakes them": the variety and numbers of people, situations, events and ideas that move and are transported, meet and are exchanged, are evidence that the increasing intensity and breadth of the current to Greece does not simply mean traveller-author and the theoretical-historical past of the Greeks, or their monumental present. From the 19th century on, the traveller-author also met his public: the predominantly human dynamic, while at the same time the transformation of the journey into written form expressed in a uniquely charming manner the eternal conflict between the objective and the subjective.

The naïvety of the early. From as early as the Middle Ages, journeys were embarked upon that brought wealth, power or even immortality of the soul, for the pilgrimage to the Holy Sepulchre was an obligation for all Christians. The spirit of renewal that enraptured Europe from the 15th century, interwoven with the revival of Classical studies, created a fertile climate in which to review and study the ancient Greek world. The dialogue between the West and Greece had begun.

Interest in the ancient Greek world began and ended for the 15th century with Ciriaco Pizzecolli Anconitano, that "meteorite" of ancient scholarship. An isolated instance of a traveller, more a travelling humanist, despite all his mainly commercial activity, this pioneering, inspired, perceptive 'collector of ancient inscriptions' made many visits to greek space and bequeathed a six-volume ms. account of his travels in Latin, which was burned in 1514, though fragments of it that had already been copied were later published.

The Greek archipelago entered the sphere of literature and the geographical spirit through the pioneering work, that was destined to serve as a model, of the restless Florentine monk Chr. Buondelmonti, who travelled amongst the islands for many years meticulously collecting information and gleaning material from ancient Greek and Latin authors. His manuscript was composed about 1420 and enjoyed an unprecedented dissemination, since it was to be regurgitated, used unmodified, enriched and recycled over the following centuries.

The fragmentary picture. In the 16th century, the great discoveries, the spread of the printing press, and humanism changed the face of the inhabited world and brought a fresh breath to society and the intellectual world. The new political-economic balance between East and West, both in the diplomatic field and in the struggle for commercial which went along with the religious reforms, swept along to the East the first significant current of travellers, which gradually disentangled itself from its intellectual relationship with the Greeks and became more or less embroiled in their ordinary life.

In the early centuries of foreign travel, the term Greek included all the Orthodox Christians of the East (Greeks, Serbs, Bulgarians, Orthodox Arabs, etc.) in the eyes of the travellers. In the European languages, the Latin name for the Greeks distinguished them from the ancient Greeks and identified them with the Christians of the East. The travellers, exponents of the ideas of a different Christian reality, perceived and commented on deviations from the Christian dogma, common law, and religious habits of the Greeks in general chapters dealing with 'the customs of the peoples of the East'. The Greek Orthodox were in their eyes 'schismatic infidels' who had departed from the proper, *'orthodoxe catholique'* faith, and who therefore suffered subjugation, debasement, abandonment, etc., and they contrasted them with the ancient Greeks or even, more generally, with the brilliance of the ancient Greek civilisation. They looked upon them with pity and sympathy as poor slaves, in a wretched condition, with all their rights infringed upon only on Ottoman territory!

With a fragmentary, deficient picture, they recorded the behaviour of Greek women and their dress preferences (N. Nicolay, J. Palerne). In Constantinople, they brought to the learned public the Byzantine monuments (P. Gilles), the active involvement of Greek merchants, and the notable hospitality extended to them by figures in the circle of the Ecumenical Patriarchate (Ph. du Fresne-Canaye, St. Gerlach). In the islands of the Archipelago, their comments on the inhabitants were simple impressions and naïve opinions occasioned by fortuitous events (J. le Saige, G. Giraudet, S. Kiechel, J. Zuallardo). They vented their rage – the Catholics – on the clergy and deluded themselves, persisting in their extreme theoretical positions (A. Thevet), while others – the reformers – dwelt determinedly on the rapprochement of the two creeds (S. Schweigger). Those of these journeys that remained unpublished until the 19th-20th c. do not contain unfavourable criticisms, but only comments occasioned by chance encounters between the foreigners and Greeks (H. Derschwam). By contrast, the works that were included in the competitive publishing programmes of their time invariably contain opinions that do not represent assessments made on the basis of personal experience, but are criticisms that reflect the perceptions of the period and the intellectual environment from which they come (O.G. Busbecq).

The 16th-century travellers voyaged or journeyed blinkered by their intellectual cargo and the aim of their travel. They thus saw through the filter of their desire to know the Ottoman empire and to discharge their Christian debt. They formed no opinion of the Greeks beyond those that arose from their theoretical knowledge, with the exception of Pierre Belon (1553). He travelled with the passion of the humanist naturalist who abandons the theoretical environment of knowledge, puts on the garb of the *aventurier* and fanatically parades his scientific, inveterate way of thought and life. He was, on the one hand, the first who ventured to decipher, albeit not consciously, an entire world – the Greek – to separate it from the fairytale of ancient Greece, from the shelter of foreign domination, and from the fanatical religious prejudices of his contemporaries; on the other hand he was the harbinger of the very large group of later travellers who were to inundate Greece and compile the corpus of writings that became extremely valuable sources for many subjects connected with modern Hellenism.

Anxiety and discovery. The 17th century was the century of the final turbulent Turko-Venetian wars – twenty-five years' siege and fall of Crete (1669) – resulting in a fresh overturning of the balance of power in the carrying trade – with the discovery of the Cape of Good Hope by the Portuguese, and the direct procurement by the Europeans of luxury goods from the Orient, dispensing with the intervention of the Moslems; the century of the birth of archaeology, during which pilgrims to the Holy Land and emissaries to Constantinople were transformed mainly into merchants and 'pilgrims of knowledge': experienced observers who gradually penetrated Greece (J.B. Tavernier, H. Chardin, H. Thevenot), signalling a more systematic form of travel in which local observations were combined with a healthy criticism of the ancient texts. Another factor that determined the presence and movement of foreigners in Greece was the permanent settlement here of missionaries – Jesuits in Athens in 1645 – and Capuchin monks, who facilitated communication, assembled information of an archaeological nature and devoted themselves to the struggle to convert the Greek population. The dynamic penetration of the Eastern Mediterranean by British travellers in the 17th century was due partly to the tardy (compared with other countries) establishment of a British embassy in Constantinople at the end of the 16th century, and, of course, to the foundation of the Levant Company. The stream of merchants now travelled in the islands, gradually also entering their hinterland (B. Randolph, C. de Bruyn).

The 17th-century writings constitute the long transitional period that takes us from the pilgrimages and diplomatic reports that dominated the 16th century to the systematic scientism of the 18th century, when the traveller's eye became more penetrating and interpretative. They still hovered on the fringes of geography, history and the autobiographical travel journal, with a fluid and contradictory character – an anxious desire to transmit knowledge – geographical, anthropological, original, unique – which, precisely because it could not easily be cross-checked, degenerated into the repetition of an unchanged and unchecked picture of the countries visited, as a guarantee of their authenticity. The writings of the last twenty-five years of the century, however, attest unequivocally to the new demands of the readers. The traveller-writer not only persists in giving a descriptive account of countries, but is distinguished by a logical, critical and systematic way of thought, and strives by all means possible – drawings, visual arts – to guarantee the validity of his information. G.J. Grelot (1680), who was the first to draw plans of Aghia Sophia in Constantinople – the crowning glory of Byzantine artistic and religious expression which, like the Parthenon, condensed the spiritual and intellectual expression of the period in an architectural masterpiece – commented that he had brought back to Louis XIV "drawings, instead of pearls and diamonds".

Amongst the important representatives of the British presence in the Eastern Mediterranean in the 16th century were P. Rycaut, consul in Smyrna for sixteen years, who wrote, in addition to his famous history of the Ottoman empire, an essay on the Greek Church, and the English cleric and Hellenist J. Covel, who composed a treatise on Orthodox doctrine and a travel chronicle containing many strands of meaning, in which knowledge of the situation went hand in hand with a new, rationalist interpretation.

Down to the 17th century, Athens continued to be a hazy place, more alive in the thought of the scholars of the West who, from the Renaissance onwards, turned more to ancient Greek literature, philosophy and later Greco-Roman art. About 1674-75, the city of Athens suddenly entered European awareness through the first detailed topographical plans of the city and through an increasing interest fed by related publications. A group of travellers, scholars, writers, Jesuits, historians and consuls (P. Babin, J. Spon, G. Wheler, A. Guillet, R. de Dreux, G. Nointel) became involved in debate and recording and specified the new definitive symbolic link between Athens and Europe and the "new imperious attitude" of the latter to "the Greek historical and geographical space", which was not completely divorced from contemporary reality.

The bombardment of the Parthenon in 1687 during campaign against the Turks by the Venetian Morosini; the measured drawings of the monuments by the travellers who brought the neoclassical style to Europe; the 'rescue' of sculptures from possible acts of vandalism by the Turks; and the systematic recording, measuring and study of antiquities are some of the most important chapters in the modern history of Athens, which were to determine the city's future. The elevation of the city both at the symbolic level and in practical terms into an archaeological site of the greatest interest attracted hundreds of visitors over the following centuries: experts and specialists, writers and painters, romantics and politicians, on a pilgrimage mainly to the Acropolis and its monuments but also to other sites of archaeological interest. At the same time, the forming of remarkable collections of ancient objects from this land of light, mainly by private individuals – many of which ultimately came into the possession of the great museums of the European cities – was a phenomenon that formed part of the general spirit of the retrieval of the ancient Greek past. From the beginning of the 17th century, it assumed the dimensions of a social phenomenon, an epidemic of 'antiquity hunting', with the 'end' of the Classical ideal as a model for the new philosophical view of the world 'justifying' the means – the acquisition of the artefacts.

The tradition of including learned geographical-historical writings in the travel literature culminated towards the end of the 17th century in the mapping activities of the Venetians, due in the main to V. M. Coronelli, the founder of the Geographical Academy. The measured drawings that appeared in his books, of ports, fortified sites and coastlines in areas where the *Serenissima Republica* had established its presence after its long wars with the Sublime Porte, served for many years as models that were reproduced and saw several later editions, and not only in Italy. These modern texts, that accompanied the entire drawing output of the Academy, mostly scholar and displaying superiority and disdain, incorporate a liberal, obscure blend of details about the lands and the peoples: mythology, contemporary geographical or demographic factors, literary narratives, in a style thoroughly versed at this period. Henceforth these drawings accompanied many further editions or translations of Coronelli's work, and also illustrated later traveller's chronicles, historical writing and even books on geography. At the same period and down to the middle of the 18th century, the Flemish cartographers and publishers copied and edited the same subjects with their expert techniques (O. Dapper, Peeters, Enderlin).

Insatiability and disdain for knowledge. The entry of the 18th century – the century of the Enlightenment, or rationalism, and systematic travel – is marked by the travels and ground-breaking work (1717) of J. Pitton de Tournefort, who was famous in his own time as a doctor and botanist and was sent by Louis XIV as an envoy to study the history, geography, and natural sciences along with the social condition and methods of administration of the regions he visited. Tournefort followed a specific method in describing the states he visited, giving details of the topography, economy, administration, ethnological composition, customs and daily habits, and demonstrated that true knowledge is approached through research, systematic study, classification and generalisation. He thus recorded and successfully conveyed a panorama of the ancient world and the first systematic, analytical account of modern Greek society and a lucid picture of the personality of the Greek landscape, and became a model for travellers throughout the 18th century.

The dream had need of stimuli, sometimes resulting from the intellectual process and sometimes stemming from the environment. The tour of Greece was now undertaken by scholars, with the prospect of acquainting themselves with the

Greek world through its monuments (P. Lucas, R. Pococke). The intellectual world of Europe began to look with suspicion on the affectation of rococo, represented in the visual travel literature by the French architect J.D. Le Roy; in his work, in the imaginary kingdom in which the European dream of Greece was set, anything was permissible, the subject was greater than the image and emotion was more important than the impression. However, the austerity of the Doric vocabulary was discovered, and the dialogue with Greek antiquity was redefined. The lead was taken in the projection this sensitivity to things Greek by the Society of Dilettanti –a learned travel club founded in London in 1732– by a club of aristocratic British art-lovers, and by the German classicist J.J. Winckelmann (1755), who proclaimed in his writings "the supreme humanism of the Greeks". The process of idealising the ancient Greek world thus began with the high belief that "the only source of models for life and education was ancient Greece". This generation of architects, archaeologists and philologists raised the fundamental questions relating to the study of Greek archaeology, which was fuelled by the monumental publication of J. Stuart and N. Revett, completed several years after their journey in 1751; this preserved the *Antiquities of Athens* in tasteful plates with very accurate measurements and was greeted with enthusiasm by the European public.

The ancient world was a model of life, education, ethics, and it was sought amongst the ruins. The archaeological missions, however, concealed an impassioned desire to plunder antiquities and enrich the collections of private individuals and rulers in the West, which went as far as the looting and destruction of ancient monuments. R. Chandler, an envoy of the Society, was charged in 1764 with the recording of monuments in the general area of ancient Greek civilisation, but diffidently developed an unprecedented interest in modern Hellenism, stemming from the conviction that modern Greeks were living monuments of the civilisation that had shone in these same areas in ancient times. This perception was launched by the work of P.A. Guys (1771), the product of Classical dreams and long experience of Greece. Beginning with his profound knowledge of ancient Greece and the ideals of the grandeur of antiquity, he embarked upon an impassioned investigation of modern Hellenism and arrived at the indisputable conclusion that modern Greeks were the descendants of the ancient Greeks. Similarities and analogies had been preserved over the centuries in their character, occupations, behaviour, music, houses, dress, and major occasions of life. But how had this come about, through so many historical transformations? Guys did not stop to ask himself. The ancient light, the light of modern Greece had blinded him completely. Religious customs and practices, beliefs and rituals remained in the sphere of the new anthropological investigation or even more originally, as expressed by Guys, were traced back to antiquity. The dynamic invasion of 18th century travel writing by interest in anthropology led to detailed descriptions, though always involving a prolix presentation of the historical past, inextricably linked with their preferences as collectors and their missions –

Lady Montagu, C. Savary, C. S. Sonnini, G. A. Olivier, whose works summarise this entire period in which the ancient world overpowered all other stimuli from the environment with Guys' also comparative critical method on modern life; gradually they were concentrated as studies in economy, institutions, society or the natural sciences (X. Scrofani, F. de Beaujour, N. & D. Stefanopoli, Sibthorp). The much-debated question of religion, doctrine, and beliefs always had its place, but now it was either presented as part of the everyday life described, or was used as visual material to illustrate to related subjects.

The reading public's knowledge of the ancient world was fuelled by publications in which artists projected the historical reshaping of the ancient Greek world, literature was nourished by sentimental treatises inspired by mythology, and the best seller of the period proved to be the *Voyage du jeune Anacharsis en Grèce*, 1788, by the Abbé Barthélemy, a work that presents a very idyllic panorama of the ancient world. Western European travellers were thus blinded by the ancient light. They turned passionately to archaeological investigation, searched for ancient testimonia, carried off souvenirs. The reading public was captivated. Ever-increasing numbers of journeys, ever-increasing numbers of chronicles in a fine literary style, material for reflection, study, ideas and research. First it had been religion, then the monuments, now it was turn of the people to invade the travel accounts, mainly through illustrated publications.

Towards the end of the century, the monumental work by M.G.A.F. Choiseul-Gouffier, the major innovation of which was that it was illustrated, brought the magical world of the Levant to European readers. The French noble was impulsively enthusiastic as a young man in his first journey (1776), but in his second (1784), now an established diplomat guided by the texts of ancient Greek and Latin literature, he viewed life as a piece of ancient Greek land on which, as in a stage-set with ruins, people were still a fount of authentic and true sentiments of hospitality, courtesy and honesty; he produced a valuable corpus of work (1782, 1809, 1822) that betrays a multi-faceted talent, with archaeological interests, curiosity, a critical mind, artistic sensitivity and information drawn from his direct contacts with Greek reality. In his monumental work, Choiseul-Gouffier expressed the love of the ancient world and the new, diffident philhellene spirit of his time in a new and original manner; an unprecedented interest, still hesitant in the face of the awakening of Greek nationalism.

For the 18th century was also the period of the Greek renaissance, perceptible to foreign visitors, who did not cease to speak of the 'Greek revival' and to believe in the reconstitution of Hellenism. Greek society was formed with new, sturdy rhythms, an admirable variety of structures, institutions and activity in centres scattered throughout the south-east Balkans and the Eastern Mediterranean, cultivating common characteristics that tended towards the liberation of the nation and independence.

The tremors of the French revolution, felt in many ways by Hellenism, and the decline of the Ottoman empire proved favourable to the Greek cause. Systematic observation of the modern Greek cultural and national personality, and the informing of the European public regarding the radical processes which were taking place in Greek society, leading to liberty, are due in large measure to the travellers. Their experience in the first two decades of the 19th century followed the forging of the national consciousness, which played a catalytic role in the reconstruction of the Greeks and culminated in the Greek Revolution.

A narrative which takes many forms*. The 19th is the most troubled of centuries: the last years of Ottoman rule and the sensitive years of the pre-revolutionary period, Philhellenism, Romanticism, the awakening, the revolution, the decade of the 1820s as a new rich source of inspiration, reconstruction, the new reality, the newly formed Greek state, the inclusion of Greece in the Grand Tour, the new Kingdom of Greece with its varied internal alterations, foreign interests, and cultural changes. Technicians, archaeologists, architects, diplomats, journalists, artists, litterateurs, have a road open to them for every sort of investigation and specialization. Mass travel begins, and the personal experience is lost; the wisdom of the ancients disappears in the grind of daily life and the Orient becomes entertainment. Thus with the gradual but vehement penetration of travellers into the eastern Mediterranean and to the lands, not only of the new Greece, but to wherever Greeks coexisted with other peoples and national groups, we have inherited a huge number of works from the 19th century which cannot be easily categorized in terms of goals or grouped into collective portraits. In fact the charm of these works is to be found in their authors' individuality, in their tales of personal experience, in the lack of confidence with which they explore the area, and the events, and share in the various example of public, political, and private life of the Greek world.

The beginning of the century is stamped with the seal of Chateaubriand. The traveller and litterateur, deeply religious and progressive beyond the reach of classical tradition, meditates, inspired by the land of his ideals, and his scientific and intellectual curiosity is expressed in the new romantic literary style, rich in ideas and dreams.

Never were so many important and active travellers found at one time in Greece and Asia Minor as in the first quarter of the 19th century, which is also reflected in the many facets of the travel phenomenon. Among the innumerable richness of travellers' narratives, poetry, novels, graphic works, scientific descriptions and every sort of product of a journey, we note: Ed. Dodwell (1801, 1805-6) where landscape for the most part regenerates historical memory, travel into the interior presents contemporary Greek reality, and scientific investigation defines the knowledge of the place; in

---

* Dates in brackets which accompany travellers' names indicate mostly dates of travel and not dates of publications.

his work J. Bartholdy (1803-1804) touched on certain reorientations of European cultural approaches and was attacked by the deeper thinkers of Hellenism, armed with arguments for the other side. There is also the mineralogist and cleric E. D. Clarke (1801), who spent a long period in the Levant, with his interesting pages on the social and educational level of the Greeks; the tireless topographer and archaeologist W. Gell (1801, ...1811); the smooth-tongued merchant J. Galt (1809-10); searchers after antiquities, C. R. Cockerell who admired, described and made familiar valuable architectural and sculptural ancient structures, and the Count Marcellus (1820) who struggled to obtain at any cost the famous Venus de Milo; T. S. Hughes (1812-1814) with his valuable information about Ali Pasha; Byron's fellow travellers H. Holland (1812-1813) who provides the fullest account of daily life in Greece before the Revolution, J.C. Hobhouse, social analyst of town life in continental Greece and warm supporter of the Revolution, and O. M. von Stackelberg (1810-1813), the 'amateur' of antiquity filled with the romantic idea of the unity of nature, life and art, who recorded pictorially the conceptions of the period about the monuments of antiquity and the contemporary population. The voice of the philhellene A. F. Didot, son of the famous printer, the student of Korais, who studied at the famous School of Kydonies in 1816, proclaimed "Greece today lies on the ruins of the splendor of Byzantium... ."

The fan of this travel phenomenon contains two figures in strong opposition. On the one hand Thomas Bruce, Lord Elgin (1799-1803) who emerged the victor in the hunt for Greek antiquities, with his rival the Frenchman Choiseul-Gouffier. The Lord and his 'gang' secured a special firman and organized the largest (in terms of number of pieces) violent uprooting and pillaging of ancient sculpture and architectural segments from Athens, the Peloponnesus and the Cyclades. The Elgin marbles, as they are known, were sold to the British Museum: a valuable bequest, yet a melancholy reminder of the hunt for antiquities in the early decades of the 19th century.

On the other hand, in the person of Lord Byron we find the most impressive portrait of the European traveller. This disputed personality, already recognized by English society, dismissed the prejudices of his contemporaries, and he journeyed through the 'land of the sun' with poetic sensibility, with neither hostility nor credulousness, and sincerity won the sympathy of local people. His poetry and his personal involvement in Greek affairs have transformed him into "hero of modern Greece".

The work of F.C.H.L. Pouqueville forms a valuable guide for all later travellers. The French doctor and consul knew Greece in depth and brought it to light in a thoughtful and considered manner; he perhaps has given us the most complete and well-organized text as far as the geomorphology of the country is concerned. With his identifications of places based on ancient texts, on eccesiastical bishoprics and the Ottoman registers, his objective descriptions of the events of the Revolution and the very clear picture of the economic strengths of the various parts of the country, he became the most in depth analyst of the historic continental area of Greece.

The work of the topographer Colonel W. M. Leake, products of his mission to the provinces of European Turkey (1794-1815) in the service of future English political and strategic interests, are in strong contrast to the brief but vaguely antiquarian investigations which precede them; they record with specific observations and detailed style whatever these areas have to demonstrate, and they always contain related evidence from classical texts.

The travellers who followed after the men mentioned here were deeply influenced by their works. From this point on we acknowledge the real discovery of a 'place': a journey becomes a way of recognizing and reading the landscape, in which the monuments, the history, the local inhabitants, and proven information are recorded. Travel, whether by land or sea, allows for reminiscences, cultivates curiosity, enriches knowledge, while the sentiments which are brought away set their mark on the experience.

The changes in administration which occurred as a result of the Revolution (1821-1827) and the newly established Greek state brought a new wave of travellers to Greece. Until the end of the century is marked by fully developed accounts of voyages. We are confronted by works in which the literary presentation rivals the complexities of the political and cultural phenomena of the period, where the travellers' knowledge is in conflict with experiences enriched by graphic pictures of the daily life of the local population, while their reactions to the varied stimuli they receive are revealed in their text. These pictures take the form of living dialogues, and often the reader is not certain whether the opinions expressed are those of the author or of the local population.

The number of visitors, and their spontaneous need to describe in as much detail as possible the new picture which the country presented, is indeed impressive. Their works are marked by a boundless chattering which struggles to develop into a personal literary style, while they attempt to bring to the surface pictures of their surroundings as well as their emotional world. Life in the new capital, first Nauplion and then Athens (1834), is revealed in penetrating detail: litterateurs and soldiers meet, talk with, and compose sketches of the politicians and personalities of Athens society (Davesies de Pontes, 1833; Malherbe, 1843; Grenier, c.1863). These sketches occupy large portions of these works, and the need for pictorial material introduces the first portraits of the chieftains of the Revolution and of political figures (Hervé, 1833). The political events of Otho's arrival or of the anarchic period following his abdication are discussed (Cornille, 1833; Tilley, 1861-63), while the court environment and its visitors (Christiana Lüth, 1839-1852; H.C. Andersen, 1841; Th. Hansen, 1864-65) mentioned in journals, bare of literary elements, simply sketches of the people. Writers with new ideas and well-intentioned objectivity talk clearly about land and human beings (J.Th. Bent, 1885). The archaeological sites, mainly of the Peloponnesus, attract visitors. The descriptions of different types of behaviour mix up politics and ethnography, while at times the physical environment dominates their impressions (Barres). German and Danish scientists and artists, their first goal the inspiration and study of ancient Greek art, particularly as it ornamented Athens, also entered the simple daily life of contemporary Greeks; the Prussian engineer Aldenhoven had a topographical map of the capital printed by an Athenian printer, as well as an *Itinéraire* (1841) which goes beyond its title and forms a revealing record of demographic measurements and social data in Athens and the Peloponnesus.

The introduction of steam transport gradually transforms the wandering traveller into the shifting tourist. This dynamic change was signalled by the grand entrance of the first steam-powered ship in the Eastern Mediterranean, organized by Marchebeus and described by himself and well as by Giraudeau (1833). Mass movement enters the picture, personal adventure is lost, the wisdom of the ancients is refracted negatively within daily life, and the Orient becomes a form of entertainment.

Dynamic and much discussed writers of the 19th century, echoes of Romanticism (Nerval, 1843; Lamartine, 1831; Gautier, 1851; Renan; Maurras) travel in search of the charm of the East and of their dreams in its reality, - which, however, remains a literary dream (Flaubert; Du Camp, 1850), or is successfully transformed into the category of 'personal narrative' (Kinglake, 1834), or else the impressions gained on the journey are embodied in mythic or fabulous texts, and transform the journey itself into literature (Gobineau, 1864-68).

Archaeological investigations (Ulrichs, 1843; Witte, 1841; Chase, 1853; Burnouf, 1856; Breton, 1856) are accompanied by an interest in the social and human landscape, the political situation and its fluctuations (Ross, 1832-45; Beule, 1851), while comparative research into the ancient and modern cultures allows the writer to combine accounts of journeys with recent historical events and characterizing approaches to the Greek people (Brandis, 1837-39; Curtius, 1852). The contribution of Buchon (1840-41) to the historiography of medieval Hellenism does not invalidate his interest in the organization, the economy, and the community system, however outstanding his ethnographic records. And Byzantine archaeology begins to appear, timidly but steadily (Godard-Faultrier, 1855-56; G. L. Schlumberger). However, when the ideas of Voltaire displace archaeological study and bring the democratic wind of liberalism, as expressed by European satire, to look directly at the reality of Greece and to cauterize it, albeit generously affirming popular culture and the character of the Greek, then the politico-social problems which bedevil Otho's Greece are marvelously mirrored in the much-discussed works of Edmond About (1852).

We owe valuable works to clerics, with the return of illustration together with narrative (Wordsworth, 1830-32), or books in which travel, botanical observation, and discussions relating to the union of the western and eastern Churches are joined together (Michon, 1850). American travellers – clerics, politicians, teachers, or journalists – enter the picture strongly, following their first philhellenic compatriots, and quickly achieve publishing successes which their European counterparts never managed (Stephens, 1835; Colton, 1835). A noteworthy example is Perdicaris (1837-43), a Greek from Veroia, a teacher and the first American consul in Athens, before the arrival of the first official ambassador Tuckerman (1867), whose book is full of social and political commentary.

Britain's interest in the Ionian Islands under her rule is expressed with studies of an anthropo-historico-geographical nature (Ansted, 1863), while travellers produce simultaneously archaeological questions and outstanding records of an economic and ethnographical nature (Vischer, 1857; Buchon, 1841; L. Salvator, 1876). Travel narratives in which critical essays co-exist with philosophical discussion are provoked by a stay in Corfu, although these narratives are unconnected with their authors' professional activities (Ferrer, 1841; Gregorovius, c.1864).

As the Cretan revolution approached (1866-69), the result of a desire for union with Greece, travellers, as well as missions (Scott, 1833-34) and journalistic dashes (Taylor, 1851-52) from the American continent, have left us an inheritance of chorographic studies enriched with linguistic appendix (Spratt, 1851-c.1860), archaeological and epigraphic researches (Perrot, 1857; Thenon, 1857), the botany of the island (Raulin, 1845), and of course the work of the economist R. Pashley, 1834, which constitutes the most complete and fullest narrative about the island, with illustrations, the product of a journey which omitted nothing concerning the island and its people.

Northern Greece and Hellenism under Ottoman rule allowed for indeterminate views, nostalgic responses to the declining picture of the East, and with its population of mixed ethnic groups, it formed most fruitful area for travellers in the 19th century, who, under the cloak of the traveller, extended their interference in archaeological, political, religious, and anthropological questions, and in the emerging political aims in the southern Balkans. with the consequent nationalistic antagonisms (G. Deschamps, Bérard, R. Puaux). They visit monastic centers (Athos, Meteora) with undiminished interest, as of old, but with renewed interest in manuscripts and ecclesiastical heirlooms (Curzon, 1827-41; Burgess, 1834; Best, 1838-39). A notable example is Urquhart (1827-29, 1830, 1834), a former philhellene who participated in the Revolution, represented British interests in the fragile post-revolutionary period and became a turcophile diplomat after his journey through Epirus, Thessaly, Macedonia and Mt. Athos, and who failed completely in his attempt to analyze the relations between the eastern and western way of life. The new field of archaeological investigation with its established methods of research continues: the archaeological journey emerges in the new unknown areas of northern Greece and curiosity about antiquity is joined to a lively interest and deep sympathy for the Greeks who desire union with Greece (Heuzey, 1855-58; Perrot, 1856; Conze, 1858; Dumont, 1868).

Of the hundreds of travellers of the 19th century, all, with very few exceptions, visited or spent considerable periods of time in Constantinople, that city of wonders and political machinations. In a place where Europeans felt like Easterners and where Easterners felt Europeans, the presence of foreigners in the life of the community was as much a matter of course as Islam itself. Foreign observers, in text and illustrations, describe with wonder and penetration the active participation of the non-Muslim populations in the life of the city, particularly that of the Greeks, with their renaissance in the quarter of the Fanar. And this without neglecting the fact of their being impressed by all which characterizes the Orient, especially within the beat of a cosmopolitan city: the various nations, the bazaars, the caiques and boatmen, the places of worship, the monuments, the women, and so forth (Walsh, 1830-35 and Allom, 1836-c.1837; Marchebeus, 1833; MacFarlane, 1847-1848; Auldjo, 1833-35; Miss Pardoe, 1835; Slade, 1849-1866). The extremely important political reforms, the decrees of Sultan Abdul Medjid known as 'tanzimat', promulgated to modernize the empire and to forestall foreign intervention, the modernization of the city which co-existed with the traditional way of life, the multi-coloured and multi-cultural population, the unique co-existence of liveliness and suspicion, indolence and activity, which always characterized the life of the city, is displayed in texts which are transformed into pictures (Walsh, 1830-35; Pardoe, 1835-36; Du Camp, 1844; Marmier, 1846; Tchihatcheff, ed. 1866; Slade, 1849-1866; Gautier, 1852; De Amicis, ed. 1877).

During the decade of the 1830s the archaeologist Charles Texier elaborates his *Description géographique, historique et archéologique d'Asie Mineure*, in which all previous comparable but simpler studies culminate. Thus began the gradual advance of travellers into the vast hinterland, journeying at first through the ancient Greek coasts which revealed their secrets, and which are more strongly connected with the search for antiquities rather than with romantic journeys, attracting travellers both for their Hellenistic-Roman past and for their Christian present, expressed by the Seven Churches of Apocalypse (Walsh, 1830-35, and Allom 1936-c.1837; Michaud, 1830-31, and Poujoulat, 1836-38; Arundell, 1833; Marmont, 1835; Carne, 1834; Elliott, 1834-35).

Sir Charles Fellows was more daring and explored Lycia four times (1838, 39, 41, 44), carrying away yet again a large number of antiquities on behalf of the British nation. From this period on travel guides, the most important products of the English conception of travel, helped visitors to the wider areas of the Eastern Mediterranean to orient themselves in the region, explaining how to move about, with pre-selected choices and a ready-made interpretive form (Murray, 1840, 1845, 1854; Baedeker, 1839 et al.).

The discourse and the light of a picture. A historical narrative has no meaning if it simply is limited to a chronicle of events. An image, a means of communication and revelation, a part of the external printed world, as well as the inner world of the artist, is memory's tool for every epoch. Thus History must have its appropriate illustrators. Thus the engraving is brought in to the sphere of the idealistic, and at the same time opportunistic, conception of the world where publishing strategy and convenience, the fashion of the period, and the cultural or artistic trend, are paramount. Pictures were regarded as unique evidence for the history of the area, as well as for evidence of an anthropological nature.

The reconstruction of the place, the chief product of travel, developed from the early panoramic views of cities, with elements of the fantastic (end of the 15th-16th centuries), to illustrations of a cartographic and yet artistic character, a conception which projects brings forth a topographical description and which serves chiefly military occupations of areas (17th c.). Gradually travel by western Europeans assumes a variety of reasons and purposes, and this occurs with the methods of reproduction as well (18th- beginning of the 19th c.). Modern methods of engraving, new artistic conceptions, the publisher's need for enriching his text with illustrations, the need to provide evidence for excavations and other geophysical studies, and detailed mapping all to supply the rich illustrative treasure which this long period has bequeathed us.

The contributions of the artist-travellers of the 19th century, who at first depict a Greece which forms a timeless, intelligible world, and then slowly begin to impress reality on it – for example the combination of heroic and religious, of the classic and oriental element of the Greek Revolution – and who reveal at last the most impressive pictures of every day life, are very important. The same trend is dominant in the late 19th century, whether the subject of the work focuses on anthropology, philhellenism, orientalism, or that romanticism which prefers tragedy to victory, all subjects which richly nourished the eyes and spirit of the viewer. Europeans owe to these artists the most penetrating display of human behaviour. All the trends and movements of European art are revealed in these works, as well as the generally wider cultural framework.

Artists, at the same time architects or university professors, each with his special art and his preferred subject (buildings, political events, physical environment, human types, excavation finds, and so forth) enriched the iconic representation of the Hellenic world (W. Williams, 1829; Chenavard and Rey, 1843-44; Rottmann, 1834; Latour and de Sinety, 1845; Du Moncel, 1843; Wordsworth, 1840; F. Perilla). Works in which descriptions of monuments are accompanied by drawings look towards the same publishing success, with similar works for ancient Italian cities (Breton, 1859; J. P. Mahaffy).

Constantinople, its charismatic scenic landscape with its physical graces and its monuments, remains, together with the newly emerging areas of Asia Minor, a source of pictorial inspiration, and a place where panoramic views are juxtaposed to themes from the life of the city (Allom, 1836-c.1837; Bartlett, 1836-c.1837; MacFarlane, c.1840; De Amicis, 1877). The Ionian islands, blessed by nature with superbly alternating light, were a rich source of inspiration for artist-travellers. The figure of the much-discussed and productive landscape painter Edward Lear, with his long residence in Greece in mid-century, depicted the Greek landscape with his personal painterly idiom. Without prejudice and with a real interest, he renders the historicity of the place during the post-revolutionary period, combing it with a intense feeling for light.

At this same time, with improvements in chemistry combined with knowledge of physical phenomena, photography enters the picture. In the hands of the user it becomes a gentle weapon – the philosopher's stone of memory – at the moment when illustration is being produced with whatever misleading attitude / position. Only two months after the official birth of photography, in October, 1839, the Acropolis will become the first subject of photographs from Greece, taken by the traveller Lotbinière.

In 1851 Maxime Du Camp embraces the new tool and brings back the first calotypes from his journey to the Levant. The new method of reproduction with its significant contribution of reading the truth and its recognition of an historic moment, co-exists with the 19th c. romantic, neo-classical and graphic compositions produced by lithography. At first the techniques of photography also form the method of lithography reproduction, unavoidably bowing to the weakness of engraving. With surprising speed with foretells the future of this art, there begin to creep into this dry objective picture taking which was introduced as an unexpectedly valuable heirloom of history, prototype subjects: antiquities, landscapes, human types, all products of travels (Gautier, 1854; Normand, 1852; Bedford, 1862; Bayet, c.1870; Bonfils, c.1870; Fr. Boissonnas).

Having in fact travelled in lands which carry the burden of their past, the wreckage of so many wars, and yet filled with the unbelievable reanimating force of redefinition, the travellers of the 19th and the beginning of the 20th centuries try to remain optimistic, responsible, vindicatory, with impressive knowledge of their contemporary subjects, little politicians who discuss and listen, write and publish. They mix simple views with mature deductions, political positions with dreamy narratives. Their books are full of unanswered questions, mostly due to the incapacity of man to accept the power of nature, as well as the unbelievably destructive or self-interested dynamic of war. They penetrate nature or they allow nature to penetrate their thoughts and feelings, to cross through them until they can render it not only with pictures, but with words. The deep need for approximation is overshadowed by the weight of the historic past. Previous books shaped Antiquity, now the archaeological areas and locations exist, each with its own special quality. The complexity of politics and diplomacy is deceptive as protection, while daily life is rendered almost in relief, with innumerable pragmatic elements. At last both personal vision and recreation are expressed within the concept of travelling.

The phenomenon of travel. Travel towards the Greek world, following its 'simplicity' in the 15th century, moved through the 'confusion' of theoretical knowledge and the bombardment of ideas of the 16th century to the 'anxiety' and the promised wealth of the 17th century. The 18th century is signalized by the greed and the strivings which the search for antiquities launched on the one hand and by the 'arrogance' of the Enlightenment on the other. The travel phenomenon of the 19th century leads to scientific and specialized classification and culminates in political involvement, the cost of which is born solely by the human element and its creations, and which of course marks the physical landscape itself.

The factors. Let us note some of the factors which in the end shaped the long journey of Europe towards the Greek world. One of these factors is diachronic with variations: the reality of Orthodoxy. At first this disturbs European travellers, and they consider it to be a cause of evil, then they subject it to theological analysis, link it to antiquity, merge it with the population and the landscape, and finally they slowly conclude that they must confront it as an object of scientific study which leads them in the end to the Byzantine monuments.

The second factor emerges and expands, at some times with catastrophic, and at others, with positive results: the worship, the mania, and the search for antiquities affected every area of the Greek world under the constellations of glory, of memory, of the mirage, as from an unending Pandora's box, in which the final hope was that all this was in aid of independence and emancipation.

We perceive daily Greek life as a third factor which follows a course parallel with each of the movements of the travellers: at first it appears only as 'religious diversity', then as a form of peculiarity, focusing mainly on female costume and behaviour. Afterwards these formless attitudes began to take on shape, and contemporary Greeks, after their vague connection with their classic ancestors, took their place in the course of events with all their surrounding tragedies and hopes.

Finally, with the constantly interfering attitudes and the political rivalries of Europe with regard to the Eastern question, the involvement and participation of travellers in the diplomatic arena constitutes them also responsible for the course of contemporary Hellenism and wherever it runs aground.

After the monuments and the people, which move together through travel literature, the essence of the place stands out, the grandeur of the Aegean Archipelago and the variegated hinterland, the unhealed wounded landscape. However, the most valuable charm of Greekness is that primordial beauty of absolute necessities, and the harmonious co-existence of opposites: reality and dream in a magical and unrivalled proportion which real travellers still search for.

Ioli Vingopoulou, Ph.D.

The Library
of
Dimitris Contominas

BOOKS and COMMENTARIES

1. ABBOTT, G.F. *Under the Turk in Constantinople A Record of Sir John Finch's Embassy 1674-1681. With a foreword by Viscount Bryce, O.M.* London: MacMillan, 1920.

Lge 8vo, pp. XV, 418 (pp.I=ht, 409-418=index). With 5 photographic plates of portraits. Original red cloth. Bookplate of Alfred Thomlinson.

First and apparently only edition. The portraits include Finch, Rycaut, and Covel. This is an early work on Finch's embassy to the Porte.

BL 9134.g.6.

1

2. ABOUT, Edmond François Valentin (1828-1885). *La Grèce contemporaine. Deuxième édition.* Paris: Ch. Lahure for L. Hachette et Cie, 1855.

8vo, pp. [iii] 1-474 + [1] (p.[i]=ht, [1]=colophon). Quarter red morocco gilt over red marbled paper boards.

Second edition, first published in 1854. About's picture of Greece was a great success. Twelve editions had appeared by 1907, and an English translation was published in 1855. About was a student at the newly established French Archaeological School in Athens from 1851 to 1853, but his interest in modern Greek life and manners was grounded in his belief that he had a special mission to propagate French ideas among

the Greeks. The success of this work led About to a career in literature rather than archaeology. The first edition was reprinted in 1996 with notes and introduction by Jean Tucoo-Chala.

BNF 30001262. This edition not in BLC.

3. ABOUT, Edmond François Valentin. ***La Grèce contemporaine. Troisième édition.*** Paris: L. Hachette et Cie, 1858.

8vo, pp. [iii] 1-474 + [1] + 4 (p.[i]=ht, pp.465-74=contents, p.[1]=imprint, pp.1-4=adverts). Uncut in old half red polished calf, back gilt in romantique style, original yellow printed paper wrappers bound in.

Third edition, first published in 1854.

BNF 30001263; Blackmer 1; Weber 471. This edition not in BL.

4. ABOUT, Edmond François Valentin. ***Nouvelles et Souvenirs. Édition illustrée de 13 gravures.*** Paris: Hachette, 1885.

Lge 8vo, pp. 331 (pp.1=ht, 2=fp, 3=t). With 13 full-page wood engravings in the text. Recent calf, back ruled gilt, brown leather labels.

First collected edition, part of the series 'Bibliothèque des Écoles et des Familles', and edited by E.F., 'un ancien camarade et ami', probably to commemorate About in the year of his death. Seven editions had appeared by 1913. This is a garland of selections from About's various works, including the first chapter of *La Grèce Contemporaine*, three chapters from *Le Roi des Montagnes*, About's novel about brigands in Greece, and selections from *De Pontoise á Stamboul*, and chapters from 'Le Fellah' and 'La mort du Turco' from About's *Recits et Nouvelles*.

BNF 3001347. Not in Blackmer or Atabey.

5. ABOUT, Edmond François Valentin. ***Le Roi des Montagnes Nouvelle Edition illustrée de 158 dessins par Gustave Doré.*** Paris: Hachette, 1927.

Lge 8vo, pp. [iii] 297 [2] (pp.[i]=ht, [1-2]=conts). Numerous wood engravings in the text, some full-page. Original red decorated cloth gilt.

A late edition of About's famous tale, based on the kidnapping of the Duchesse de Plaisance by the brigand Bibichi, which was first published in 1857. The first edition with illustrations by Doré seems to be that of 1861. *Le Roi des Montagnes* was also illustrated by Charles Delort, first edition 1883.

This edition not in BNF, but several editions with this format are listed, the earliest of which seems to be 1898; the edition published in 1910 has the same pagination.

6. ADELPHUS, i.e. Johann Adolph MEULICH. *Die Türckisch Chronica von irem Vrsprung anefang und Regiment/ bisz vff dise Zeit/ sampt yre kriegen und streyten mit den christen begangen/ Erbämrklich zü lesen. [colophon: Getruckt zü Stassburg [sic] durch den fürsichtigen Martin flach/ im iar des herre[n]. M.CCCC.XIII [sic].]* [Strasbourg: Martin Flach, 1513.]

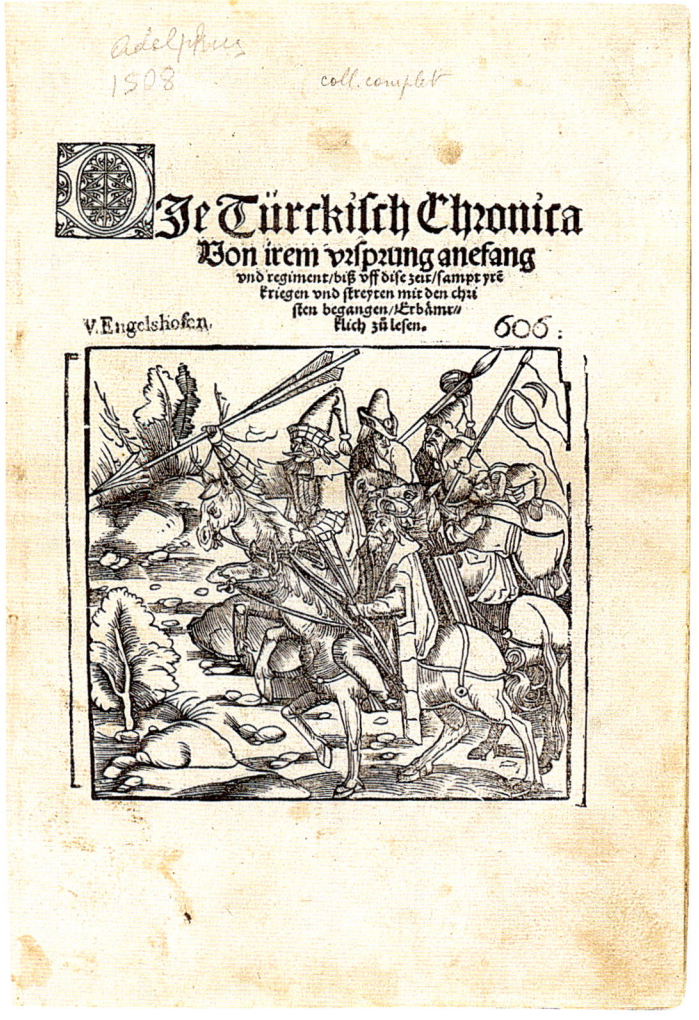

4to, 48 unnumbered leaves. With large woodcut on title and a number of large cuts in the letterpress. 19th c. calf, sides panelled in blind with fleurons in corners, back gilt with tulips. Red leather book label of G.J. Arvanitides mounted on front pastedown, bookstamp of V. Engelshofen with no. 606 on title.

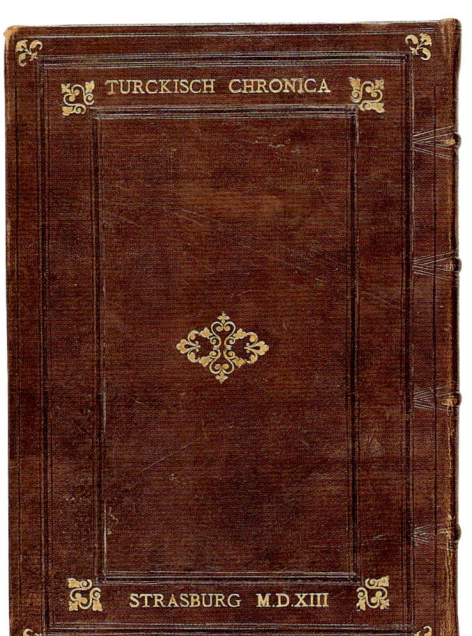

Third edition of this chronicle of the Turks. Three editions appeared the same year; the first was printed in Strasbourg by Knobloch, the other two by Martin Flach. Göllner cites 25 woodcuts in the first or Knobloch edition, 23 in the first Flach edition/issue, and 24 in the second Flach edition/issue. Adelphus, who also translated the *Historia von Rhodis*, discusses Rhodes among the other topics related to the Turks, mentioning Guillaume Caoursin. The numerous woodcuts include views of Modon (Methoni) and Constantinople; these are conventional cuts which are used several times.

BL 799.n.14 (as ours, with 'Stassburg' in the colophon and the misprint 1413 for 1513); Göllner 57. Not in Blackmer or Atabey; Karlsruhe cites 4 copies.

7. ALDENHOVEN, Ferdinand. *Itinéraire descriptif de l'Attique et du Péloponèse, avec cartes et plans topographiques.* Athens: Imprimerie de l'Ami du Peuple for Adolph Nast, Rodolphe Bund and the Author, 1841.

8vo, pp. [viii] XXVIII, 436 (p.[i]=t). With 20 lithographed plans/maps (out of 21; this copy lacks the large folding map). Old three-quarter polished calf, back panelled in blind.

First edition. The plates include views of some unusual subjects: Sicyon, Zarex, Ira, Gortys, Stobitzi and others. An enlarged German version appeared in 1842 under the title *Handbuch für Reisende in Griechenland* in 2 vols, edited by J.F. Neigebaur with a biographical notice of Aldenhoven. He was a resident of Cologne who arrived in Greece at about the same time as King Otho. He was connected with the Bavarian establishment and prepared several maps for the government, including a large map of the new Greek Kingdom in 1838, and a plan of Athens lithographed by A. Forster in 1837 and published in 1841 in J.A. Sommer's *Repertoire analytique et descriptif pour la Carte d'Athenes et des Environs*.

BNF 30008800; Blackmer 15.

ALGEMEENE HISTORI. See UNIVERSAL HISTORY

8. ALIGNY, Théodore Caruelle d' (1798-1871). *Vues des Sites les plus célèbres de la Grèce Antique dessinées sur Nature et gravées à l'eau forte par Théodore Aligny.* A Paris 1845 [Athens: Commercial Bank of Greece, 1971.]

Folio, pp. [vi] and pp. [12] (p.[i]-[iv]=prefaces, [v]-[vi]=biographical note on Aligny, pp.1-12=title to Aligny's work and descriptive text). With ten facsimile plates, with the blindstamp of the Commercial Bank on each leaf (an antique head). Modern Greek calf with raised architectural design on upper cover, unsigned.

This facsimile reprint of the first edition of 1845 was produced by the Commercial Bank of Greece to celebrate the 150th anniversary of the Greek War of Independence. The original edition is now very scarce. Aligny travelled in Greece in 1843 for the French government. After his return he exhibited at the Salons, usually pictures evocative of Greece. He etched the plates for this work himself. We have seen some of Aligny's etchings reproduced from the original plates by the Bibliothèque Nationale in the 1950s. They were still for sale until fairly recently.

BNF 35621153; Blackmer 19; Paris-Rome-Athènes, p. 422.

9. ALLAN, John Harrison. *A Pictorial Tour in the Mediterranean: Including Malta - Dalmatia - Turkey - Asia Minor - Grecian Archipelago - Egypt - Nubia - Greece - Ionian Islands - Sicily - Italy - and Spain.* London: Longman, Brown... [etc.], 1843.

Folip, pp. [viii] 1-96 (p.[i]=ht, [viii]=list of plates). With chromolithographed title and 40 tinted lithographic plates. Numerous wood engravings in the text. Rough cut in half calf, red leather label.

First edition. Later editions appeared in 1845 and 1846. Allan travelled through the Mediterranean from April 1841 to June 1842. The lithographs are after drawings by the author and include mostly sites in Egypt, but also in Cos, Rhodes, Asia Minor and Greece. A useful work.

BL 1263.g.16; Blackmer 24; Weber 1143.

ALLOM. See WALSH

ALQUIE. See SAVINIEN D'ALQUIÉ

10. ANCEL, Jacques. *La Macédoine Son évolution contemporaine.* Paris: Delagrave, 1930.

4to, pp.[iii] 352 (p.[i]=ht, pp.349-52=contents, errata leaf tipped in between pp.348 and 349). With a large folding map and 64 photographic plates. Illustrations and sketch maps in the text. Uncut and unopened in the original printed paper wrappers.

First published edition. This work appeared the same year in thesis form as *La Macédoine. Étude de colonisation contemporaine Thèse...*, without the errata.

BNF 31718290; BL 10127.h.4.

11. ANDERSON, R.C. *Naval Wars in the Levant 1559-1853.* Liverpool: University Press, 1952.

8vo, pp. ix, 619 (p.i=ht). 10 no'd photographic illustrations, and a folding sketch map of the Aegean. Sketch plans in the text. Original cloth, in a dust jacket.

First and only edition of this basic reference work which discusses naval battles in the Levant from the Battle of Lepanto to that of Navarino.

BL 09136.bb.36.

12. ANDREOSSY, Antoine François, *Count. Voyage à l'embouchure de la Mer-Noire, ou Essai sur le Bosphore et la partie du delta de Thrace comprenant le système des eaux qui abreuvent Constantinople... Avec un atlas composé d'une carte nouvelle du Bosphore et du Canal de la Mer Noire.* Paris: Denugon for Plancher, 1818.

8vo, pp. lxiv, 1-334 (p.i=ht, ii=colophon, iii=t). Without the 9 folding plates. Contemporary quarter calf over paper boards marbled to resemble tree calf, sides with crowned cypher AE or EA, back ruled gilt, black leather label.

First and only edition, uncommon. The plates in this work are sometimes found bound separately, but despite the reference on the title there is no separate atlas title. Andréossy, who had served in Egypt with Napoleon, was French ambassador to the Porte, 1811-1814. He had always had an interest in waterworks and hydraulics, being descended from an Italian family that had constructed the grand canal of Languedoc. In this work he has described the hydraulic systems of Constantinople.

Apparently not in BNF on line. BL 151.c.1, 3.Tab.67 (plates bound separately). Not in Blackmer; Weber 51; Atabey 21; Brunet I, 276.

13. ANSTED, David Thomas. *The Ionian Islands in the year 1863.* London: Wm. H. Allen, 1863.

8vo, pp. xi [i] 1-480 (p.i=t, [i]=list of ills). With four maps and a lithographed frontispiece, and wood engravings in the letterpress. Uncut and partly unopened in contemporary red embossed cloth gilt.

First edition. Ansted made this visit to the Islands especially because he believed they would soon be ceded to Greece. He was a geologist and engineer who wrote many books on geology and geography.

BL 2360.f.1; Blackmer 35; Weber 607; Bib. Ionienne 2399.

14. [ANTONOPOULOU, Maria G.] *Οἱ τελευταῖες μέρες τῆς Χριστιανικῆς Καισαρείας (Εἰκόνες ἀπὸ μακρινὸ ταξίδι).* Athens: A. Th. Lampropoulos [1925].

Sm. 4to, pp. 1-92 (p.1=t). With 8 photographic illustrations. Modern leather, original decorated stiff paper wrappers bound in.

First and apparently only edition. Maria Antonopoulou was a member of the 12th Committee for the Exchange of Populations between Greece and Turkey. Her account, published under the initials M.G.A., describes the Committee's journey through Asia Minor, mainly in Kaisareia, from June to October, 1924.

GL GT1538.

15. APPERT, Benjamin Nicolas Marie. *Voyage en Grèce dedié au Roi… Se vend au profit des prisonniers.* Athens: Imprimerie Royale, 1856.

8vo, pp. [i], VIII, 1-194 (p.[i]=t). Quarter cloth over marbled paper boards.

First and apparently only edition. This work by the philanthropist Appert discusses the prisons, hospitals and schools of the young Greek state. Appert travelled in Greece from July, 1855, to January, 1856. The work is dedicated to King Otho, and the subscribers include Mavrocordatos, Kountouriotis, Delighiannis, Typaldos, Kriezis, Plapoutas, Terzetis and other members of the government, important figures of the Greek revolution and Greek litterateurs. Appert also wrote *Voyages dans les Principautés Danubiennes*, Mayence, 1854, and *Conseils d'un veritable Ami de la Grèce*, Athens, 1860, as well as many works of a philanthropic, educational and sociological nature on prisons and hospitals in Germany and other parts of Europe.

BNF 30023876; GL Spentsas p. 40. Not in BLC, Blackmer or Atabey.

16. ARGENTI, Philip P. *The Costumes of Chios Their development from the XVth to the XXth century.* London: B.T. Batsford [1953].

Lge thick 8vo, pp. xiii, [i], 1-338 (p.i=ht, [I]=st, 303-38=index). With 111 plates, the majority printed in colour. Original blue cloth, gilt medallion on upper cover.

16

First edition of this important work, limited to 500 copies. Argenti, a member of a family (Ἀργέντης) long established on Chios, with its roots in the island's Genoese past, devoted his life to studies of its history and its political and cultural life. Although the scope of this work may appear to be restricted, it is based on a thorough understanding of the travellers and visitors to the island who produced illustrated accounts of their travels.

BL 7744.d.37.

16

11

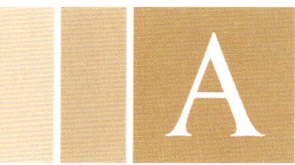

17. ARMSTRONG, Isabel Julien. *Two roving Englishwomen in Greece.* London: Sampson Low, Marston & Co., 1893.

8vo, pp. XI [1] 1-300 (p.I=ht, [1]=list of ills). With a lithographed frontispiece and a photographic portrait. Numerous illustrations in the text. Uncut in modern leather.

First and apparently only edition.

BL 10125.aaa.21; Weber 956.

18. ARUNDELL, Francis Vyvyan Jago. *A visit to the seven Churches of Asia; with an excursion into Pisidia...* London: John Rodwell, 1828.

8vo, pp. iv, 1-339 [1] (p.i=t, [1]=errata). With 22 lithographed plates of inscriptions, some folding, on 13 sheets. Modern half calf, panelled back gilt, red and green leather labels.

First edition. A second edition appeared in 1842. Arundell was the chaplain to the British factory at Smyrna from 1822 to 1836; he was married to the sister of James Morier, explorer of Persia. This tour of the Seven Churches of Asia Minor was made in 1826. In 1833 he made another long tour of Asia Minor and wrote up the results in *Discoveries in Asia Minor*, 1834.

BL 487.d.23; Blackmer 48; Weber 159; Atabey 36.

19. ARUNDELL, Francis Vyvyan Jago. *Discoveries in Asia Minor: including a description of the ruins of several ancient cities, and especially Antioch of Pisidia.* London: Richard Bentley, 1834.

2 vols., 8vo, pp. xxii, 1-358; vii, 1-439 (p.i=ht in v.1, p.i=t in v.2, pp.429-439= index). With a folding map by J. Arrowsmith and two plates. Half brown morocco gilt. With library stamp of the Relief Synod on both titles.

First and only edition.

BL 1046.f.8-9; Blackmer 49; Weber 216; Atabey 37.

20. ASPIOTIS, Marie, and René PUAUX. *Corfou Préface de Sir James Rennel [sic] Rodd Trente-Deux eaux-fortes originales de Lyc. Kogévinas et quinze reproductions en taille-douce de cartes et gravures anciennes.* Paris: [Coulouma and Padovani for] L'Art Grec [1930].

4to, pp.[v] I-VII, 1-[119] (pp.[i]=ht, [iv]=fp, [v]=t, [119]=colophon). With 10 plates hors texte. 37 etchings and engravings in text, some full-page. Original decorative paper wrappers, in a blue marbled paper folder with printed paper label, in a blue marbled paper slip case.

First and only edition, printed in 570 copies of which this is no. 177. Forty-five copies no'd 1-45 were printed on handmade Montval paper, each with a suite of the ten plates hors texte. Twenty-five copies marked A-Z were issued for the people who collaborated on the publication. The ten hors texte plates include reproductions of plates by Joseph Cartwright. The work contains 32 etchings by Kogevinas in the text.

BNF 31157303; GL Spentsas p. 49.

21. AULDJO, John. *Journal of a visit to Constantinople, and some of the Greek islands, in the spring and summer of 1833*. London: Longman, Rees... [et al.], 1835.

8vo, pp. xii, 1-259 [1] (p.i=ht, p.259=note, [1]=colophon). With seven plates drawn and etched by Cruikshank. Wood engravings on the title and p. 203 after Gell. Contemporary embossed red cloth, back ornately gilt and stamped 'Voyages and Travels', gilt edges.

First and apparently only edition, dedicated to Sir William Gell, whom Auldjo knew in Naples where he was resident for some years. Auldjo made his name with his ascent of Mt. Blanc, and he continued this tradition with Mt. Vesuvius. He was also a friend of Bulwer Lytton and contributed to *The Last Days of Pompeii*. His *Journal* is a lively account of several months' visit to the Levant, with interesting descriptions of all sorts of manufactures. The binding is contemporary, possibly made especially for someone who collected voyages and travels and wanted a uniform binding for them, or for a bookseller who specialized in the subject.

BL 1047.c.18; Blackmer 56; Weber 225; Atabey 42.

22. AVELOT, Henri. *Croquis de Grèce et de Turquie 1896-1897 Autour de l'Archipel.* Tours: Alfred Mame et Fils, 1897.

Lge 8vo, pp. 1-208 (p.1=ht, 4=fp, 5=t). Numerous full-page wood-engraved illustrations in the letterpress, including the frontispiece, although the versos are blank; vignettes in the text, some coloured. Modern cloth.

First edition. A second edition appeared in 1899, and a third in 1919. Brief sketches of Athens, the Argolid, Meteora, Volos, Larissa, Chania and Smyrna. Avelot published *Montenegro, Bosnie Herzegovine* in 1895.

BNF 30041528; Weber 1034 (2nd ed.); Atabey 43. Not in BLC.

B

23. BACHEVILLE, Barthélemy. ***Voyages des Frères Bacheville, Capitaines de l'Ex-Garde, Chevaliers de la Légion d'Honneur, en Europe et en Asie, après leur condamnation par la Cour Prévôtale du Rhône, en 1816.*** Paris: Imprimerie David for Bacheville, and for Corréard and Ponthieu, 1822.

8vo, pp. VIII, [5]-401 [1] (pp.I=ht, III=t, V-VIII=avis, p.[5]=first leaf of text, [1]=table of conts.). Lithographic portrait frontispiece of Antoine Bacheville. Modern leather.

First edition, uncommon, printed by David for Bacheville. This edition was edited from Bacheville's notes by two of his friends, and it was sold out within two months. The second edition appeared the same year, published by Bechet ainé, with a preface by Bacheville. The frontispiece in the second edition differs from that in the first edition and depicts the brothers' separation. The restoration of the monarchy in France in 1816 led to the brothers' condemnation and subsequent exile; they travelled in Europe and overland to Constantinople where they separated. Antoine travelled as far as Syria, Persia, and Muscat, where he died. Barthélemy journeyed to Athens via Smyrna and the Aegean. He reached Ioannina in July 1818 where he took service with Ali Pasha.

BNF (2nd ed only); BL 932.d.16; Blackmer 60 (2nd ed); Weber 105 (2nd ed); Atabey 45.

24. BAEDEKER, Karl. ***Ἑλλὰς ἤτοι ἱστορική, γεωγραφικὴ καὶ τοπογραφικὴ περιγραφὴ τῆς Ἑλλάδος καὶ ὁδηγὸς τῶν ταξειδιωτῶν καὶ περιηγητῶν κατὰ τὸ Γερμανικὸν τοῦ Καρόλου Μπαίδεκερ μετὰ χαρτῶν καὶ πινάκων ὑπὸ Τρ. Ε. Εὐαγγελίδου καὶ Γ. Σ. Μαυρογένους.*** Athens: D.G. Eustratios, 1901.

Sm. 8vo, pp. [i] 598 [4] + 88 + [3] pp. of adverts (pp.[i]=advert, 1=t, [1-4]=index). With 27 maps of which 9=dp. Modern tan morocco gilt.

First edition in Greek of Baedeker's guide to Greece translated and edited by T.E. Evangelides and G.S. Mavrogenes. The German edition was published in 1878. The adverts in the Greek edition are very interesting and give a good picture of Greek bourgeois life. In this copy the index has been bound in after the first group of adverts.

This edition not in BL or GL. Not cited on line in Karlsruhe. There is a copy in the German Archaeological School in Athens.

25. BAEDEKER, Karl. ***Konstantinopel und das westliche Kleinasien. Handbuch für Reisende von Karl Baedeker. Mit 9 Karten, 29 Planen und 5 Grundrissen.*** Leipzig: Baedeker, 1905.

Sm. 8vo, pp. XXIV, 275 (p.I=ht, lacking). With a large folding map of Greece, coloured in outline, and 24 plates of maps/plans. Numerous plans in text. Modern brown morocco gilt.

First edition of this guide to Constantinople and the western portion of Asia Minor, together with Cyprus. A later edition appeared in 1914 which included the Aegean islands and the Balkans. Baedeker's guides to the Levant began to appear in the 1870s. As they developed new editions appeared, and the guides changed, with the descriptions of large areas broken up into various editions, as more information on each area became available, or as new tourist areas opened up.

BL 10108.dg.2. Not in Blackmer or Atabey.

26. BALTHASARD DE LA FERRIÈRE, *Mme de la*. *La Grèce ancienne et moderne, depuis les temps primitifs jusqu'au Regne du Roi Othon, actuellement régnant, en 1844. A l'usage de la jeunesse.* Tours: R. Pornin et Cie, 1845.

8vo, pp. [iii] ii [1] 1-367 (pp.[i]=ht, [1]=st, 353-67=conts). With an engraved frontispiece and title, and two engraved maps. Original embossed black decorative cloth gilt, gilt edges. From the library of Panos Gratsos, with his 'Skinos' bookplate.

First edition. There seem to be two issues of this work, depending on the imprint on the engraved title. This copy has the imprint of P.C. Lehuby, Paris, on the engraved title, although the printed title bears the Pornin Tours imprint. The other issue bears the Pornin imprint on the engraved title as well. This work is also to be found in a number of variants of what seem to be original cloth bindings, but with variations in the gilt stamped designs on upper and lower sides. Thus far we have noted four different bindings on this work: one of gilt and colours on black cloth, one of gilt on brown cloth, and two of gilt on black cloth. Each of the gilt stamps is different, both on upper and lower sides. Two of these bindings are to be found in the Spentsas collection in the Gennadius Library, one of which was executed by or for Lehuby. However, there does not seem to be any specific relationship between the binding and the issue. The frontispiece depicts the battle of Navarino.

BNF 30713762 cites only one edition, with the Pornin imprint. BL 1560/2255 is as ours and contains the Lehuby imprint on the engraved title; GL Spentsas, p. 44. Not in Blackmer.

27. BARRÈS, Maurice. *Le Voyage de Sparte.* Paris: Félix Juven [1906].

8vo, pp. VIII, [9]-300 [1] + [1] (p.I=ht, [1]=contents, [1]=colophon). half calf gilt, red and green leather labels.

First edition of the novelist and politician's account of his sojourn in Greece; the title contains a conscious reference to Chateaubriand. A second edition appeared in 1910 and a third in 1922. The work was reprinted as recently as 1987. This is an account of Barrès' first trip to Greece, c. 1896, where he spent about two years. The first chapter contains a very interesting account of the circle of Leconte de Lisle and in particular Louis Menard who was the spiritual instigator of Barrès' journey. Much of his sojourn in Greece was spent in company with the Abbe Bremond (q.v.) who in fact dedicated his own account of this journey to Barrès.

BNF 31766464; BL 10126.df.6. Not in Weber. See Basch, pp. 378-384.

28. BARROWS, Samuel June (1845-1909). *The Isles and Shrines of Greece.* Boston: Roberts Bros., 1898.

8vo, pp. xii + [i] 389 +[1] (pp.i=ht, v=ded to Dorpfeld, [i]=list of plates, [1]=Greek index). With 19 photographic illustrations, including frontispiece. Uncut in the original green decorated cloth.

First edition of this undated journey which presumably took place c. 1895. An English edition was also published in 1898. Barrows was a miscellaneous writer who was particularly interested in penology and prison reform. This work and his *Shaybacks in Camp, ten summers under canvas*, are his only works of travel.

LoC DF725.B27; Weber 1022 (Engl. ed). Not in Blackmer.

29. BARTHELEMY, Jean Jacques. *[Voyage du jeune Anacharsis en Grèce, dans le milieu du quatrième siècle avant l'ère vulgaire. Troisième édition.] – Receuil de cartes géographiques, plans, vues et médailles de l'Ancienne Grèce, relatifs au Voyage du jeune Anacharsis. Troisième édition.* Paris: de Bure l'aîné, 1790.

4to, pp. xxxii (p.i=t). With 31 engraved plates of maps, views, coins, no'd I-IV, 1-27. Contemporary half calf gilt over speckled paper boards. Library stamp of the Lyceum of Constanz on the title.

Atlas only from the third edition. This famous and influential work was first published in 1788 by de Bure. He published second and third editions in 1790. Numerous editions and translations appeared throughout the 19th century. Although there had been earlier attempts to popularize what was known of Greek antiquity, none was so immediately successful and influential as Barthélemy's 'Anacharsis', which played an important part in the development both of neo-classicism and of philhellenic sentiment in France. The atlas contains maps after Barbié du Bocage. The text contains Barbié's analysis of the maps with notices of the cartographers he used and important information supplied by Laurent Truguet, Foucherot and Choiseul-Gouffier who had all done research on the ground during their sojourn in Constantinople during Choiseul-Gouffier's embassy, as well as information supplied by the hydrographer Beauchamp.

BNF 31768712, cites 42 plates, but several plates contain more than one engraving. Note that plate 27 is marked '27 et dernier'.

30. BARTHELEMY, Jean Jacques. *Voyage du jeune Anacharsis en Grèce, vers le milieu du quatrième siècle avant l'ère vulgaire. Quatrième édition. – Receuil de cartes géographiques, plans, vues et médailles de l'Ancienne Grèce, relatifs au Voyage du Jeune Anacharsis; précédé d'une Analyse critique des cartes. Nouvelle édition.* Paris: Didot le jeune, An Septième. [=1799]

7 vols, lge 4to and 1 vol, folio. pp. viii, cxxxij, 1-352; viii, 1-494; [v] 1-479; viii, 1-483; [v] 1-471; [v] 1-469; viii, 1-422 (pp.i,[i]=hts, cxv=st). With an engraved portrait frontispiece of Barthélemy. The atlas: pp. [iv] 5-56 + [1] (p.[i]=t, [1]=explanation of the unn. plate). With 39 (out of 40) plates no'd 2-38 + 19b and 1 unn. plate (médailles grecques), of which 11 coloured in outline and 1 double-page. This copy lacks plate 1, the map of Greece with its colonies. A large paper copy in contemporary quarter red roan over red paper boards, flat backs gilt in compartments with urns and diapering.

Fourth edition, the important edition by Didot, with a new edition of the Atlas. The maps in the atlas have been newly engraved by Tardieu after Barbié du Bocage. Didot also produced an octavo edition in 1799 with the atlas in quarto.

BNF 30061983; BL 12514.m.11.

30

31. BARTHELEMY, Jean Jacques. *[Voyage du jeune Anacharsis en Grèce, dans le milieu du quatrième siècle avant l'ère vulgaire –]. Atlas du voyage du jeune Anacharsis.* Paris: Menard and Desenne, 1821.

8vo, engraved title and two leaves(=list of plates). With 35 no'd engraved plates of maps and views (nos 1 and 2=large folding) by Giraldon-Bovinet. Uncut, in half vellum over marbled paper boards, red leather label.

Another edition of the atlas, possibly the first in 8vo format, uncommon, published to accompany Menard and Desenne's edition of the text which seems never to have appeared. Ledoux also brought out an octavo edition in 1821, but with the atlas in quarto.

Not in BNF or COPAC on line. Karlsruhe cites 2 copies of the Atlas only. See Atabey 67 for the Ledoux edition.

32. BARTHELEMY, Jean Jacques. ***Voyage du jeune Anacharsis en Grèce, vers le milieu du quatrième siècle avant l'ère vulgaire. Tome premier [... Tome Second... Troisième... Quatrième... Cinquième... Sixième... Septième.]*** Paris: [Imprimerie Stereotype de Tremblay for the] Veuve Dabo, Librairie Stereotype, 1822.

7 vols, sm. 8vo, pp. [iii], 555; [iii] ii, 603; [iii] ii, 571; [iii] ii, 578; [iii] ii, 566; [iii] [i] 522; [iii] ii, 514 (pp.[i]=hts, pp.ii, and p.[i] in vol.6=conts). Quarter roan faded to brown, rebacked and repaired, over green marbled paper boards.

There was a new spurt of interest in Barthélemy's work in the years 1821 and 1822, probably due to the outbreak of the Greek revolution. Six editions appeared during these two years, including an edition dated 1821 published by Gueffier jeune and Dabo. As St. Clair points out, Barthélemy's work, even though it concerned ancient Greece, was very important during these years because it spread information about Greece and strengthened the identification of modern and ancient Greece which was so necessary to the philhellenic movement. The edition published by the Veuve Dabo in 1822 is of interest because it is one of the earliest works to be printed by the stereotype process, so new as to require the advert 'faite au moyen de matrices mobiles en cuivre d'après le Procédé d'Herhan'. There is apparently no atlas to this edition, which is uncommon, nor any illustrations in the text.

Not in BNF or BLC on line. Karlsruhe cites 1 copy. St. Clair, p. 368.

33. BARTHELEMY, Jean Jacques. ***Voyage du jeune Anacharsis en Grèce, vers le milieu du quatrième siècle avant l'ère vulgaire. – Atlas.*** Paris: Abel Ledoux fils, 1832.

5 vols, 8vo and 1 vol. 4to, pp. [iii] 1-451 [1]; [iii] 1-462 [1]; [iii] 1-448 [1]; [iii] 1-434 [1]; [iii] 1-449 + [1]; pp. 7 (pp.[i]=hts, [iii]=ts, [1]=contents, pp.443-449=general index, pp.1=ht, 3=t in atlas). With an engraved portrait frontispiece in volume 1, and 44 plates numbered 1-43 + 1b in the atlas. This copy lacks plate 1, the folding map. A fine copy, uncut and partly unopened in contemporary blue-green speckled paper boards, red leather labels.

Barthélemy's work seemed to take on a new lease of life in the 1830s. Armand Aubrée and E. Ledoux both published 8vo editions in 5 vols in 1830 and Rolland also published an edition in 1830. The atlas is based on Didot's atlas of 1799, with the plates engraved by Ambroise Tardieu. The atlas published under Tardieu's name was first printed in this form (oblong 4to format) possibly as early as 1822, and reprinted in 1824, 1825 and 1826 ('atlas sur un plan neuf'). An new atlas was prepared by C.V. Monin and engraved by the Malo Brothers in 1830.

This edition not in BNF or BLC on line.

34. BARTHELEMY, Jean Jacques. *Voyage du jeune Anacharsis en Grèce, vers le milieu du quatrième siècle avant l'ère vulgaire.* Paris: Lebigre Frères, 1834.

5 vols, 8vo, pp.[iii] 407 [1]; [iii] 397 + [1]; [iii] 388 [1]; [iii] 382 [1]; [iii] 404 (pp.[i]=hts, pp.[1], pp.403-4=conts). Old half leather gilt, not en suite, over marbled paper boards.

One of the several editions of Barthélemy's work published in the 1830s. Apparently an atlas was not published with this edition; certainly one is not cited with the BNF copy. It is possible that the atlas prepared by Monin in 1830 could be purchased separately, so that some publishers did not bother to print an atlas. Although the binding of this copy is half leather, it is not uniform: vols 1 and 2 are in faded burgundy morocco, vols 3-5 in burgundy roan gilt.

BNF 37509367.

35

35. BARTHELEMY, Jean Jacques. *Voyage du jeune Anacharsis en Grèce.* Paris: A. Hiard, MDCCCXXXV. [=1835]

Lge 8vo, pp. [iii] 566 + [1] xxxviii + [1] (pp.i=ht, [1]=st, [1]=conts). With engraved portrait frontispiece and 34 engraved plates and maps no'd 1-40, mostly coloured in outine, see below. 19th c. orange paper boards marbled to imitate tree calf, red leather label.

An abridged edition. The plates in this work are numbered 1-10, 13-14, 13-15, 17, 20-26 +23b, 25b, 25c, 28, 33-35 + 34b, 35b, 38, 40. Hiard also produced a pocket edition the same year in 8 vols in 24mo.

BNF 30062011. This edition not in BLC or GL.

36. [BARTHELEMY, Jean Jacques.] *Viaggio d'Anacarsi il giovine nella Grecia verso la meta' del quarto secolo avanti l'era volgare. Tradotto dal Francese. Tomo Primo. [... Tomo XII ed ultimo.]* Venezia: Antonio Zatta e Figli. MDCCXCI. Con Approvazione e Privilegio. [... MDCCXCIII.] [Venice: 1791-1793].

12 vols, sm. 8vo, pp. XVI, 1-307; 304; 288; 296; 311; [iii] 332; [vi] 304; [vi] 312; [vi] 344; [vi] 360; [vi] 359; VIII, 384 (pp.I, 1, [i]=hts, final pages of vols. 1, 4, 5, 6= privilege; adverts form final leaves of vols. 2, 3, 7, 9, 10; vols 8 and 11 end with notes; v. 12 contains index). With 31 engraved folding plates, of which several coloured. Old vellum. Small armorial bookstamp on titles, notes in a contemporary hand on final leaf of volume 1.

?First edition in Italian. What appears to be an abridged version, *Compendio dell' opera... voyage du jeune Anacharsis*, with the translation attributed to Angelo Fabroni by the Bibliothèque Nationale, was published at Pisa in 1791. This 12 volume edition was reprinted in 1825-6 by Antonelli, with the text corrected by Spyridon Blantes.

Marcian Library, 83.D.155-166. Not in BLC on line.

37. BARTHELEMY, Jean Jacques. *Travels of Anacharsis the Younger in Greece, during the middle of the Fourth Century before the Christian Aera... In Seven Volumes, and an eighth in Quarto. — Maps, Plans, Views and Coins, illustrative of the Travels of Anacharsis the younger in Greece.* London: for G.G. and J. Robinson, 1796 — M.DCC.XCVI. [=1796]

7 vols, 8vo, and 1 vol, 4to, pp. [iii] 1-474; [vii] [i] 1-503; [vi] 1-490; vi + [i] 1-501; [vi 1-490; vi + [i] 1-446; vi, 1-401; pp. 1-28 in the atlas (pp.[i]=hts, pp.[i] in vols 2, 4, 6=errata, p.1 in atlas=t). With 29 no'd plates (out of 31) plus a large folding map. Lacking plates 9 and 18, pl. 5 unnumbered. Contemporary calf, atlas in mottled calf, flat backs gilt in compartments, red and black leather labels. With the 19th c. armorial bookplate of E.W. Wynne Pendarves with his motto 'Nec Timeo Nec Tumeo' in the text vols.

Third edition in English issued by the Robinsons, translated by William Beaumont of Hoxton. They published the first English editon in 1791, second edition 1793/4, all in the same format. Apparently Robinson gave the rights to L. White of Dublin for the Irish editions.

BL 1609/4506, 4 vols only. This edition not in Blackmer but see 84 for the fourth English edition issued by J. Johnson, 1806.

38. BARTHELEMY, Jean Jacques. *Ἐπιτομὴ τῆς περιηγήσεως τοῦ Νέου Ἀναχάρσιδος... μεταφρασθεῖσα ὑπὸ Σ. Σκούφου καὶ ἐκδοθεῖσα δαπάνῃ τοῦ Β. Βιβλιοπωλείου.* Athens: Royal Printing Office, 1838.

8vo, pp. [vii] λα´, 450 (p.[i]=t). Old quarter black roan over marbled paper boards, worn.

Apparently first abridged edition in Greek. The translator is Spyridon Skouphos. A Greek translation of the entire work was published in 1819.

GL MGL366.

39. BARTHOLDY, Jakob Ludwig Salomon. *Voyage en Grèce fait dans les années 1803 et 1804... Contenant les details sur la maniere de voyages dans la Grèce et l'Archipel; la descrition de la vallée de Tempé; un tableau pittoresqe des sites les plus remarquables de la Grèce et du Levant.* Paris: Dentu, 1807.

2 vols in 1, 8vo, pp. [iv] i-[xii], 1-272; 1-[296] (pp.[i]=hts, [iii]=titles, missing in volume 2, p.[xii]=dir to the binder, p.[296]=advert). With a large folding map (no'd XVI) and fifteen engraved plates no'd I-V, VII-XV + 1 unn. plate (of which 10=hand coloured costume plates). Lacking the two plates (or plate?, see below) of music. Contemporary tree calf, sides bordered in gilt, flat back gilt in compartments, green leather labels. From the library of K.Th. Dimaras, with his bookstamp on the lower fly-leaf, Βιβλιοθήκη Κ.Θ. ΔΗΜΑΡΑ.

First edition in French, translated by Auguste Du Coudray from the first edition published at Berlin in 1805. Bartholdy spent the years 1803 and 1804 travelling in Greece and the Aegean; his work is of especial interest for its discussions of contemporary Greek culture; the plates depict contemporary costume, icons and folk music. The costume plates are after drawings by George Gropius, who accompanied Bartholdy on his journey. Gropius later became Austrian consul in Athens, where he spent the rest of his life; he was instrumental in assisting many travellers, archaeologists and collectors. Bartholdy himself settled in Rome as the Prussian consul-general, and his collection of antiquities was catalogued by Theodor Panofka, who was secretary to the German Archaeological Institute there. There is a problem relating to the plate of music. According to the list of plates, the plate of music is no. 6. But in the GL copy this plate is no'd VII and in fact is made up of two sections. In some copies this plate is separated; one section is numbered VII, while the other is unnumbered. The music plate was probably numbered VII in error for VI and was intended to form one double-page plate. The pieces of music contained therein are numbered 1-4. The unnumbered plate (Vases Thessaliens) at p. 225 is not on the list of plates. In the Contominas copy the map is no'd XVI. If we count the music plate as two plates there should be 18 plates: a map, plates I-V, VII-XV, 1 unn. plate and two plates of music. The French edition has more plates than the German edition.

BNF 30366107; Blackmer 87; Weber 12; Atabey 68.

40. BARTLETT, Sir Ellis Ashmead (1848-1902). *The Battlefields of Thessaly. With personal experiences in Turkey and Greece.* London: John Murray, 1897.

8vo, pp. ix + [iii], 1-412 (pp.i=ht, [i]-[iii]=conts and list of plates, 401-12=index). With photographic portrait frontispiece and 6 photographic illustrations, 2 folding maps and 3 sketch maps. Rough cut in the original red cloth.

First and apparently only edition. E.A. Bartlett, M.P., accompanied by his son, travelled with the Turkish army in Thessaly. Bartlett, who visited Serbia and Bulgaria in 1877-78, supported Britain's turcophile policy. This is one of the many works written on the Turkish-Greek war of 1897. Bartlett's son later wrote on the Balkan Wars, see below.

BL 9136.ee.8; GL HG 690A82. Not in Weber.

41. BARTLETT, Ellis Ashmead, *the younger* (1881-1931). **With the Turks in Thrace**. London: William Heinemann, MCMXIII. [=1913]

Lge 8vo, pp. x, 355 [1] (i=ht, [1]=colophon). Errata slip tipped in at vol. 1, p. 1. With photographic frontispiece and 34 photographic illustrations. Half brown morocco, back gilt.

First edition. Bartlett, son of Sir Edward Ashmead Bartlett, M.P., wrote this account in collaboration with his brother Seabury. It describes their travels with the Turkish Army during the Balkan Wars. Bartlett later wrote *Despatches from the Dardanelles*, 1916, and *The Uncensored Dardanelles*, 1928.

BL 9136.aa.4

42. BARUFFI, Giuseppe Filippo (1800-1875). *Pellegrinazioni autunnali ed Opuscoli. Il presente Volume contiene il viaggio da Torino a Costantinopoli attraverso la Grecia, nell' autunno 1841.* Torino: Cassone and Marzorati, 1842.

8vo, pp. 1-301 + [2] (p.1=t, pp.[1]=contents, [2]=errata). Uncut in three-quarter brown morocco.

First edition, fascicule eleven only of *Pellegrinazioni autunnali ed Opuscoli*, an eventual four volume work, published in Torino from 1840-43. The *Viaggio da Torino à Costantinopoli* seems to form the entire volume for 1842. This fascicule was reprinted in small format as *Viaggio à Costantinopoli*, Milan, 1847. The *Pellegrinazioni* is the first collected edition of Baruffi's articles which were originally published in various journals in Italy and abroad. It was published in parts, since Baruffi was still engaged on his travels during the four or five years of the publication of the entire work. Every autumn for fifteen years Baruffi undertook a journey to some part of the world. He also published separate accounts of some of the other voyages, as he did for the voyage to Constantinople. For example, in 1848 he produced *Viaggio da Torino alle piramide fatto nell' autunno del 1843*.

BL 795.k.33. Not in Blackmer, Weber or Atabey. The on line Italian union catalogue cites copies in Torino.

B

43. BATTYE, Aubyn Bernard Rochford Trevor. ***Camping in Crete with notes upon the animal and plant life of the Island. Including a Description of certain Caves and their ancient deposits by Dorothea M. A. Bate.*** London: Witherby & Co., 1913.

Lge 8vo, pp. XXI, 1-308 (p.I=ht). With a folding map and 34 photographic plates (including frontispiece). Rough cut in the original blue cloth.

First and only edition.

BL 10126.d.34.

44. BAUDIER, Michel. ***Inventaire de l'Histoire generale des Turcs ou sont descriptes les Guerres de Turcs, leurs conquestes, seditions, & choses remarquables, tant aux affairs qu'ils ont eu contre les Chrestiens, comme Grecs, Hongres, Polonois, Bulgares, Moldaves, Transilvains, Valaques, Sclavons, Venitiens, Espagnols, Chevaliers de Rhodes, & de Malte, que contre les infidelles, comme Tartares, Perses, Egyptiens, Arabes, & autres, depuis l'an mil trois cens, iusques en l'année 1640. Quatriesme edition reveue et augmentee.*** Rouen: chez Clement Malassis, Lovys Oursel, Jacques Besongne, MDCXLI. [=1641]

Thick large 8vo, pp. [lxv] 1-886 [52] (p.i=t). Title in red and black, gauzed. Contemporary ownership signature of the Abbé de Montenai and faded ownership stamps on title. Modern vellum.

Fourth edition, first published in 1617. Baudier was a popularizer of general knowledge on Turkey and the Ottoman empire. His works, which included a history of the Serail, were very popular and appeared in multiple editions. It is possible that this work should contain eighteen plates of portraits of the Sultans. These plates occur in the first edition.

BNF 30066733; BL 802.i.15 cites 4th edition with the imprint 'Rouen, I. Berthelin, 1642'. This edition not in Blackmer or Atabey, but see Blackmer 93 and Atabey 69 (1st eds). See Rouillard, pp. 250-53.

45. [BEAUCHAMP, Alphonse.] ***The life of Ali Pacha, of Jannina, late Vizier of Epirus.*** London: for Lupton Relfe, 1823.

8vo, pp. xii, 368 (p.i=t, pp.357-68=notes). With 2 lithographed portraits (1=fp), a folding panoramic view of 'Yannina' engraved by I. Clarke after Theophilus Richards, and a folding map of Greece by Neele and Son with an inset of the environs of 'Janina'. Old half calf over worn paper boards. With the bookplate of A. Hatzidemou.

Second edition in English. The first English edition appeared in 1822, the same year as the French edition. The English translation has been attributed to R.A. Davenport who published his own biography of Ali in 1837; he has added more information, much of it supplied by Theophilus Richards who drew the panoramic sketch of Ioannina. Davenport may well be connected with the W. Davenport who produced the well-known illustrated work, *Historical portraiture of leading events in the life of Ali Pacha*, London, 1823.

BL 1452.i.1; Blackmer 100, see also 454.

There is another copy in the Contominas collection, in quarter black leather, ruled gilt.

45

46. BEAUFORT, Emily Anne, *Viscountess Strangford*. **The Eastern Shores of the Adriatic in 1863. With a visit to Montenegro.** London: Richard Bentley, 1864.

8vo, pp. [vii] 386 + 2 pp. of adverts (pp.[i]=t, [vii]=list of plates). With 4 lithographed plates printed in colour and a mounted photograph. Original brown cloth gilt.

First edition of this very interesting work. This may be a second issue, with the title in black only, not in red and black as the Blackmer copy. Emily Beaufort was the daughter of Sir Francis Beaufort of Caramania fame. She visited the Dalmatian coast, Montenegro and Albania in 1863. Her book includes much political discussion of panslavism and the problems in the Balkans at that period. The plates include views of Ioannina, Suli, Setinje and Almissa in Albania. In 1861 she produced *Egyptian Sepulchres and Syrian Shrines*.

BL 10126.d.32; Blackmer 102; Weber 626; Atabey 80.

46

47. BEAUJOUR, Louis Auguste Félix de (1765-1836). ***Tableau du Commerce de la Grèce, formé d'après une année moyenne, depuis 1787 jusqu'en 1797; par Félix-Beaujour, ex-Consul en Grèce. Tome Premier.*** Paris: [Crapelet for] A.A. Renouard, 1800.

8vo, pp.[iii] 1-331 (p.[i]=ht, 330-31=conts). Marbled paper boards, back ruled gilt, red leather label, ochre number label.

First edition, first volume only of two volumes. There are two issues of this work, differing only in imprint: ours as above, and an issue with the imprint of Crapelet and the date 'an VIII'. It is clear that Crapelet printed the work for Renouard and also issued copies with his own imprint. An English translation was produced by Thomas Hartwell Horne in 1800 as *View of the Commerce of Greece*. Beaujour, a member of the French diplomatic service, was consul in Thessaloniki from 1787 to 1797. He also served in Sweden and the United States. Beaujour returned to the Levant in 1816 where he served as French consul in Smyrna, later being appointed inspector general of all French diplomatic establishments in the Levant. In 1829 he produced *Voyage militaire dans l'Empire Othoman*.

BNF 33985942; BL also has two issues:1029.d.18, 280.h.30; Atabey 82.

 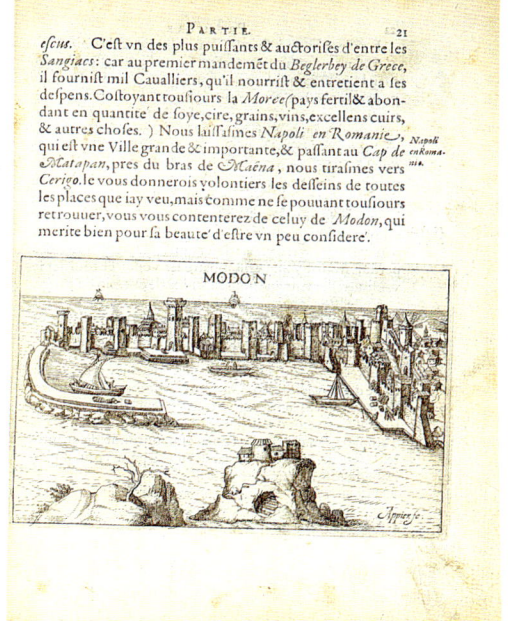

48

48. BEAUVAU, Henri de. *Relation Iournalière du Voyage du Levant faict & descrit... Reveu augmenté et enrichy par l'Autheur de pourtraicts des lieux les plus remarquables.* Nancy: Jacob Garnich, 1615.

4to, pp.[viii] 1-181 (p.[i]=engr. t). 48 maps in the letterpress. Contemporary mottled calf, back gilt in compartments, leather label. Ownership inscription 'Museo S.D. Daudat' dated 1807 on front pastedown, with a few notes.

First illustrated edition; a second illustrated edition appeared in 1619. The first edition, in 12mo, was published at Toul in 1608. Beauvau undertook the journey described here in 1604, during his service with de Salignac, French ambassador to the Porte. The plates, engraved by J. Appier Hanzelet, are in the style of Camocio and depict sites in the Levant, mainly of the Greek islands, Malta, Alexandria and Cairo.

BNF 30074256; BN also cites unillustrated eds. of 1608, 1609, 1610; Blackmer 106; Atabey 85, see also 84 for 2nd ed; Zacharakis 136-153. Not in Weber but see 237 for 1st ed;

49. BELABRE, F. de, *Baron*. **Rhodes of the Knights.** Oxford: Clarendon Press, MCMVIII. [=1908]

4to, pp. 196 (p.1=t). With a coloured frontispiece. Numerous photographic illustrations (of sketch maps/plans) in the text. Original black decorative cloth gilt. From the library of Christopher Tower, with his bookplate.

Only edition and apparently the author's only work. Belabre was resident on Rhodes for six years apparently as French consul. The photographic illustrations are the work of Belabre. This copy belonged to the bibliophile Christopher Tower who was resident in Athens for many years after his retirement from diplomatic life. At one time he was adviser to King Idris of Libya. A portion of his library was sold at Sotheby's in 1997.

BNF 31787664; BL 10125.ff.20.

50. BELLAIRE, J.P. **Précis des opérations générales de la division française du Levant chargée, pendant les années V, VI et VII, de la défence des îles et possessions ex-vénitiennes de la mer Ionienne, formant aujourd'hui la République des Sept-Isles.** Paris: for Magimel Libraire pour l'Art Militaire, and Humbert Libraire, An XIII, 1805.

8vo, pp. viii, 1-486 + [2] (p.i=ht, [2]=errata). With a folding map of Corfu. Uncut in half red morocco.

First and apparently only edition. The author Bellaire must have served in the Ionian Islands; this work was written while the islands were still under French rule. They had been acquired by the French after the fall of the Venetian Republic to Napoleon in 1797.

BNF 36380087; Blackmer 112 (misprint XII instead of XIII in imprint); Bib. Ionienne 720.

51. BELLE, Henri. **Trois années en Grèce.** Paris: Hachette, 1881.

8vo, pp. VII, 1-413 (p.I=ht, pp.409-13=contents). With an engraved folding map, and 32 wood-engraved plates. Modern calf gilt, original pictorial yellow and brown printed paper wrappers bound in.

First edition. Belle was a secretary in the French embassy, probably in Constantinople. This is an account of several undated journeys made during the late 1870s when Belle was travelling through Greece with a party of French naval officers. Note a detailed account of the Dilessi murders in 1870. The map is entitled 'Carte de la Grèce pour servir au voyage de M. Henri Belle'. Belle is well known to Greek travel literature because he published a series of articles under the general title 'Voyage en Grèce' de-

51

scribing his travels from 1861 to 1874 in the periodical *Tour du Monde* (vols. 32-35). These were collected and printed in one volume by Hachette in 1893.

BNF 31789084; Blackmer 113.

There is another copy in the Contominas collection, in what appears to be the original red cloth.

52. BELLIN, Jacques Nicolas. ***Description Géographique du Golfe de Venise et de la Morée. Avec des Remarques pour la Navigation, & des cartes & plans des Cotes, Villes, Ports & Mouillages.*** Paris: Didot, M.DCC.LXXI. [=1771]

4to, pp. xii, 1-235 (p.i=t). Engraved title after Arrivet and 49 no'd plates. Contemporary mottled calf, back gilt in compartments with daffodils, black leather label.

First edition of this work by Bellin, French naval engineer and map-maker. Many of the maps in this work were published in his *Le Petit Atlas Maritime*, 1764. He published several collections of maps, including the *Atlas Maritime*, 1751 and the *Neptune Français*, 1753.

BNF 30080706; Weber 765. Not in Atabey or Blackmer.

B

53. BENJAMIN, Samuel Green Wheeler. *The Turk and the Greek; or, Creeds, Races, Society, and Scenery in Turkey, Greece, and the Isles of Greece*. New York: Hurd and Houghton, 1867.

Sm. 8vo, pp. [v] v-vii (recte ix), 1-268 (pp.[i]=t, [iii]=ded., [v]=conts, v-vii=preface). Modern blue-green leather.

Apparently first edition. Several chapters had been published in periodicals, mainly *The Century* and *Harper's Magazine*. The preliminary leaves have either been paginated incorrectly, or else an extra leaf, possibly the dedication, was inserted after the work had been type-set. The work is dedicated to Benjamin's father, who was a missionary in the Levant. He died in the East and was buried at Constantinople. Benjamin himself spent some years in the Levant; he was in Athens in 1843 and he lived in Chios for two months with a family whose son had studied in the United States.

BL 10125.aaa.40. Not in Blackmer or GL. Not in LoC on line.

54. BENT, James Theodore. *The Cyclades or Life among the insular Greeks*. London: Spottiswoode and Co. for Longmans, Green, and Co., 1885.

8vo, pp. xx, 1-501 + [6] + 12 (p.i=ht, pp.[6], 12=adverts). With a folding map. Original green cloth, faded.

First edition, reprinted in 1966 with an introduction and bibliography by A.N. Oikonomides. Bent visited each of the Cyclades between 1883 and 1889; this work contains much detailed information on the islands. Bent was the editor of *Early voyages and travels in the Levant*, 1893, and he also wrote 'Modern life and thought amongst the Greeks' in Magnussen's *National Life and Thought*, 1891, a work connected with the development of nationalist thought at that period. Archaeological finds made by Bent during his travels are in the British Museum.

BL 10126.b.7; Blackmer 123. Not in Weber.

55. BERARD, Victor (1864-1932). *La Turquie et l'Hellénisme Contemporain. La Macédoine... La lutte des races*. Paris: Félix Alcan, ancienne librairie Germer Baillière et Cie, 1893.

8vo, pp.[iv] i-[vi], 1-352, + adverts, pp.1-3, 1-16 (pp.[i]=t, [iii]=ded, p.[vi]=map of Macedonia, pp.351-2= conts). Modern half calf gilt.

First edition. A second edition appeared in 1896. This is an account of a journey through Macedonia in August, 1890. Berard, who wrote a good deal on the Eastern Question, defines Macedonia as the area west of the river Vardar as far south as Thessaly and as far north as Pristina. He discusses the Albanians at length, as well as the 'Megali Idea'. Berard also produced *La Macédoine*, 1897 and *Les Affaires de Crète*, 1898. For some years director of the *Revue de Paris*, he published a number of articles on Greece and the Eastern Question in his journal.

BNF 30086146. See Basch, pp. 250-253.

56. BERARD, Victor. *Dans le Sillage d'Ulysse Photographies de Fred. Boissonnas.* Paris: Librarie Armand Colin, 1933.

4to, pp. 9 + [1], [11] + [1] (p.1=ht, [1]=st, [1]=colophon). With a folding map of Odysseus' voyages and 165 no'd photographic illustrations. Original printed paper wrappers.

First edition, reprinted in 1973. A Greek translation appeared in 1991. This work was published posthumously by Jean Berard. Victor Berard studied at the French School of Archaeology in Athens in 1887. He published a whole series of works on the Odyssey, and this album was to have formed part of the 'Navigations d'Ulysse'.

BNF 31795862; GL GC530.2; Radet, pp. 454-6.

57. BERGERON, Pierre (15..-1637). *Voyages faits principalement en Asie dans les XII, XIII, XIV, et XV siècles, par Benjamin de Tudele, Jean du Plan-Carpin, N. Ascelin, Guillaume de Rubruquis, Marc Paul Venetien, Haiton, Jean de Mandeville, et Ambroise Contarini: accompagnés de l'Histoire des Sarasins et des Tartares, et precedez d'une Introduction concernant les voyages et les nouvelles découvertes des principaux voyageurs, par Pierre Bergeron.* Tome Premier. [... Second.] The Hague: Jean Neaulme, M.DCC.XXXV. [=1735]

2 vols in 1, 4to, pp. [viii] 161, [vi] 67 + 2, [iii] 82 + [1], [iii] 161 [4], [i] 44, 186; [i] 96 +[2], 26 +[1], 62 [2], [4] 69 [4], 136, 38 [1] (pp.[i]=ts and subtitles). Titles in red and black. With 5 folding maps. Eight engraved plates in letterpress in the sections on Jean du Plan-Carpin and Rubruquis. Contemporary mottled calf, back gilt, red leather label.

First collected edition, first edited and published by Pierre Bergeron in 1634. The earlier collected edition did not include all the works which are contained in this edition, e.g. the account by Marco Polo and that by Ambroise Contarini. There is a leaf following the title in vol. 1 which is entitled 'Avertissement concernant ce Recueil'. Each voyage is preceded by a subtitle and followed by an index. Several of the later voyages are edited by Andre Muller Griffenhag, who may have been the general editor. Vander Aa, well-known publisher of engravings and maps, assisted in the publication. The

maps occur in the narratives of Benjamin of Tudela, Rubruquis, Jean Carpin, Marco Polo and Haython the Armenian.

BNF 30088211; Weber 41; Gay 2948; see Cordier, 1941-42. Not in Blackmer or Atabey. Collation: π^1 $2*^2)(^{42}$ A-E^4 F^1 A-E^4 F^3 [a]-[l]^4 *-3*^{4} (A)-(N)^4; π^1 (a)-(e)^4 (f)^6 ¶-2¶^{4} †-4†^{4} *^{2} ∇^{18} *^{2} o^{35} *-2*^{4} 3*^{2}

58. BERNARD, Marius. *Autour de la Méditerranée - Les Côtes Orientales - L'Autriche et la Grèce (De Venise à Salonique).* Paris: Henri Laurens, [c. 1900].

Lge 8vo, pp. [v] 388 (p.i=ht, iv=fp, v=t, 387-88=conts). With numerous illustrations in the text, some full-page, including a frontispiece map of the route, coloured in outline. Contemporary red cloth gilt, black leather label.

First edition. Bernard produced a series of works under the title *Autour de la Mediterranée* in nine volumes from 1895 to 1901. The section 'Les Côtes Orientales' includes 3 volumes: 'De Venise à Salonique', 'De Salonique à Jerusalem', and 'De Jerusalem à Tripoli'. 'De Venise à Salonique' includes Crete and the Cyclades, but not Cyprus or the islands of the eastern Aegean. The illustrations are after Avelot (q.v.).

BNF 30091015, citing copies both in wrappers and cloth.

59. BERTON, Charles. *Quatre Années en Orient et en Italie ou Constantinople, Jérusalem et Rome en 1848, 1849, 1850, 1851.* Paris: Louis Vivès, 1854.

8vo, pp. 1-472 (p.1=ht, pp.469-472=conts). Uncut in recent brown morocco gilt, central gilt stamp of Contominas bookplate on upper cover, original blue printed paper wrappers bound in.

First and apparently only edition, and the author's only work.

BNF35000564.

60. BESOLD, Christopher. *Historia Constantinopolitana post avulsum à Carolo Magno occidentem, ad nostra usque tempora deducta: et ex variorum historicorum collatione, ac ipsorum verbis formalibus repraesentata.* Argentorati sumptibus Haeredum Lazari Zetzneri. M.D.CXXXIV. [Strasbourg: heirs of L. Zetzner, 1634.]

Thick sm. 8vo, pp.[xlvi] 1371 (pp.[i]=engraved t, [xiii-xlvi]=index, usually bound at the end). Engraved title page in letterpress. Contemporary vellum. 18th c. armorial bookplate of (-) Nordkirchen.

First and only edition. Besold's history of Byzantium begins in 802, after the conquest of the West by Charlemagne, and continues through the Turkish conquest to 1623.

BL 1194.a.23; Blackmer 129.

61. BEST, James John. *Excursions in Albania; comprising a description of the wild boar, deer, and woodcock shooting in that country; and a journey from thence to Thessalonica & Constantinople, and up the Danube to Pest.* London: Wm. H. Allen, 1842.

12mo, pp. xii, 1-359 [1] (pp.i=ht, [1]=errata and directions to binder). With a folding map and an engraved plate. Blue cloth.

Apparently only edition and apparently Best's only work.

BL 1426.f.14; GL NH224.

62. BEULÉ, Charles Ernest (1826-1874). *L'Acropole d'Athènes. Tome premier. [... Tome second.]* Paris: Firmin Didot Frères, 1853-54.

2 vols, lge 8vo, pp.356; 392 (pp.1=hts, 335-6, 391-2=conts). With eight engraved plates (4=dp) by A.F. Lemaitre after Lebouteux. Half black morocco over marbled paper boards, backs ruled gilt, original beige printed paper wrappers bound in. Stamp of the Grand Seminaire de Versailles on wrappers. A Presentation copy, signed on the wrappers to M. Rossignol by Beulé.

First edition. A one volume 'nouvelle édition' was issued in 1862. The young Beulé discovered the propylaea of the Acropolis during his sojourn in Athens as one of the professors at the newly established French School of Archaeology. The archaeologist and later politician also wrote popular works on artistic and historical subjects and contributed articles on modern Greece to the *Revue des Deux Mondes*. His funeral eulogy, 'Monsieur Beulé, souvenirs personnels', was pronounced by Ideville (q.v.)

BNF 30101071; BL 560.b.14.

63. BEULÉ, Charles Ernest. *L'Acropole d'Athènes. Nouvelle édition.* Paris: Firmin Didot Frères, 1862.

Lge 8vo, pp. v, 1-400 (p.i=ht, v=ded.). With 5 engraved plates (3 folding) by A.E. Lemaitre after Lebouteux, Paccard, Tetaz, and Desbuisson. Quarter red morocco over red cloth, gilt wreath of the Lycee de Moulins on upper cover, back ruled gilt.

Second edition.

BNF 36575383; Blackmer 135.

64. BEULÉ, Charles Ernest. *Études sur la Péloponnèse [sic] publié sous les auspices du Ministère de l'Instruction Publique et des Cultes.* Paris: Firmin-Didot, 1875.

Sm. 8vo, pp. vi, 1-432 (pp.i=ht, 430-32=conts). Old quarter red morocco, back gilt in compartments, gilt arms of the College Stanislas on upper cover.

Second edition, first published in 1855. Essays connected with various sites in the Peloponnesus which Beulé visited during his travels.

This edition not in GL or NBF on line. See Blackmer 133 for first edition.

65. BIANCONI, F. *La Question d'Orient dévoilée ou La Verité sur la Turquie Musulmans, Raias Slaves et Grecs Tcherkess et Tziganes.* Paris: [Alcan-Levy for] Librairie Générale, 1876.

8vo, pp. 1-208 (pp.1=ht, 207-8=conts). Quarter roan over green marbled paper boards. Book label of the Nikolaevsky Academy, with its library stamp on the title.

First edition. Bianconi worked in the Balkans in the early 1870s. This period was one of turbulence in the area, and 1876 in particular was the year which included the massacres in Bulgaria. Bianconi produced a number of works which reflect his experiences in the Balkans, including *La Menées de M. de Bismark en Orient*, 1882, *Ethnographie et Statistique de la Turquie d'Europe et de la Grèce*, 1887, and *La Russie au point de vue commercial*, 1893. He also produced *Cartes Commerciales*, 1885, a series of maps in 16 volumes, 4to; the first series contains the maps of the Balkans.

BNF 30102775.

66. BIBLE. NEW TESTAMENT. Ἡ Καινή Διαθήκη. *Novum Testamentum. Post priores Steph. Curcellaei, tum & DD. Oxoniensium labores... Editio Milliana... examinat G.D.T.M.D.* Amsterdam: J. Wetstein and G. [i.e. W.] Smith, 1735.

8vo, pp. [viii] 112, 560, 38 (p.[i]=t). Title in red and black. With engraved title and four engraved folding plans/maps. Old calf, rubbed. Contemporary ownership signatures of E. Latham, and J. White-Newton of Norfolk dated 1755 on the engraved title, 18th c. ownership signature of G. White Legg on the fly-leaf.

Edited by Gerhard von Mastricht (G.D.T.M.D.). The maps include Palestine, the travels of the Apostles in the Mediterranean, a plan of Jerusalem and a plan of the temple.

KB Amsterdam, 0080a.

67. BIKELAS, Demetrios (1835-1908). *Louki Laras traduit du Grec par le Mis De Queux de Saint-Hilaire. Nouvelle édition illustrée par M. Ralli.* Paris: Firmin Didot, 1892.

Lge 8vo, pp. [iii] VI, [1] 1-244 + [3] (p.[i]=ht, [1]=st, pp.[1-3]=note and map). Title in red and black. Numerous illustrations in text. Uncut in original coloured pictorial wrappers.

Second edition in French, but the first to be illustrated. The first French edition was published by Auguste Henri Queux de St. Hilaire in 1879, in 16mo format without illustrations. This very successful novel of the Greek Revolution, in the form of the autobiographical memoirs of an elderly Chiote, was Bikelas's best known work; it was produced in numerous editions and translations. The first edition was published in Greek in 1879, followed by French and German translations the same year. Danish and Italian editions appeared in 1880. An English edition appeared in 1881, translated by Ioannes Gennadius. A Swedish edition appeared in 1883 and a Russian in 1888.

BNF 30105169; GL IND107.3.

68. BIKELAS, Demetrios. *La Grèce avant la révolution de 1821. Extrait de la Nouvelle Revue du 1er Janvier 1884.* Paris: G. Chamerot, 1884.

Lge 8vo, pp.30 (p.1=ht). Uncut in the original blue printed paper wrappers. A presentation copy from Bikelas to M. Weil, with the inscription 'hommage de l'auteur' on the printed wrapper.

First separate edition, an offprint from the *Nouvelle Revue* for January, 1884. The presentation inscription is probably to M. Henri Weil, classicist and editor of Euripides, Demosthenes and Aeschylus. Bikelas, who spent much of his adult life in Paris, is probably best known for his novel of the Greek Revolution, *Loukis Laras*, which was published in 1879. He produced many works on Greece, including *La Grèce byzantine et moderne*, 1893, and *Le role et les aspirations de la Grèce dans la question d'orient*, 1885.

GL KG133. Not in BL or BNF as a separate entry.

69. BILIOTTI, Edouard, and the Abbé COTTRET. *L'Ile de Rhodes.* Rhodes: for the Authors; Campiegne: for Cottret, 1881.

Lge 8vo, pp. [vii], VII, +[2], 1-722 (pp.[i]=t, [vii]=st, [1-2]=blank). Title in red and black. With a folding map, a folding plan and six plates. Illustrations in the text. Old quarter morocco, upper blue printed paper wrapper bound in.

First edition. A Greek translation by M. Malliarakis and S. Karavokyros also appeared in 1881. Biliotti was Italian consul on Rhodes. According to the introduction his relative Alfred Biliotti conducted excavations on Rhodes.

BNF 30867988.

70. BINOS, Marie Dominique de, *Abbé* (1730?-1804). ***Voyage par l'Italie, en Egypte au Mont-Liban et en Palestine ou Terre Sainte. Tome Second.*** Paris: [J.Ch. Desaint for] the Author and Boudet, Libraire, M.DCC.LXXXVII. [=1787]

Vol. 2 only, of 2 vols, sm. 8vo, pp. [iii] 1-167 (recte 367) [1] (pp.[i]=ht, [1]=errata and colophon). With 6 engraved plates on pale blue tinted paper. Old quarter calf over blue marbled paper boards, back ruled gilt.

Volume two only. Lacking the first volume. This is a variant issue of the first edition. The title does not contain a reference to the dedication of the work to Madame Elisabeth of France, and the imprint contains the words 'chez l'auteur'. Ordinary copies include only the reference to the bookseller Boudet. Volume two includes two letters on Zakynthos, three on Cephalonia and two on Cyprus before the text on Palestine. The costume plates are after Grasset St. Sauveur.

BNF 36023324 and GL GT699 (both apparently this issue). The other issue is cited in BNF 36575418; Atabey 107; Weber 570; Blackmer 144 (other issue); Tobler, p. 134. Collation agrees with Atabey 107 and Weber 570.

Collation: π^2 (π1=ht) A-P^{12} Q^4 (Q4v=errata).

71. [BISANI, Alessandro]. ***A picturesque tour through part of Europe, Asia, and Africa: containing many new remarks on the present state of society, remains of ancient edifices, &c. With plates, after designs by James Stuart... Written by an Italian gentleman.*** London: J. Davis for R. Faulder, 1793.

Sm. 4to, pp. xiv, 1-241 (p.i=ht). With six folding plates. Contemporary tree calf, sides framed gilt, flat back gilt in compartments with sunbursts. With the bookplate of Christopher Tower.

First edition in English. The first edition seems to be that of 1791, in French under the title *Lettres sur divers endroits*, but published in London and with Bisani's name on the title. A German edition appeared in 1798. The work does not seem to have appeared in Italian. It consists of 29 letters describing Bisani's travels in the Levant dated from 29 April 1788 to 7 October 1789, the majority from Thessaloniki, Athens,

71

71

37

Smyrna and Constantinople, and including descriptions of Myconos, Zea, and Skiathos. The English edition contains six plates (of which five are after drawings by James Stuart, q.v.); these plates do not appear in the earlier edition. This copy comes from the library of Christopher Tower. The diplomat Christopher Tower served in the British Embassy in Teheran and was special advisor to King Abdallah of Jordan and King Idris of Libya; he retired to Athens where he lived for many years. A portion of his library was sold at Sotheby's the 19th of May 1997.

BL 303.k.20; Blackmer 145 and 146; Weber 620.

72

72. BISHOP, Henry Halsall. *Pictorial Architecture of Greece and Italy. Second edition.* London: Society for the Propagation of Christian Knowledge, 1890.

Oblong folio, pp. [iii] 135 [1] (pp.[i]=[ ], [ii]=fp, [iii]=t, [iv]=colophon, [1]=advert). Numerous illustrations in text, including full-page frontispiece. Original pictorial brown cloth.

Second edition. Apparently the first edition was published in 1887.

This edition not in BLC.

73. BLAQUIERE, Edward. *Narrative of a second visit to Greece, including facts connected with the last days of Lord Byron.* London: G.B. Whittaker, 1825.

2 parts in 1, 8vo, pp. [iv] iv, 1-167, 1-175 (p.[i]=ht, missing here). With a lithographed frontispiece, mounted, and a folding facsimile. In half green calf, back gilt in compartments with flowers and fleurons, red leather label. 19th c. booksellers' ticket of Charles Hutt of London. With the bookplates of the Denham Court Library and of A.D. Hatzidemos.

73

First edition. Blaquiere was one of the instrumental figures in the development of British philhellenism; together with John Bowring he set up the London Greek Committee, and he also played a role in the proposals for the second Greek loan. Blaquiere's connection with Byron is also significant. He visited him in Genoa in 1823, and it was Blaquiere who persuaded Byron to go to Greece. The second part of this work is concerned with Byron's activities in Greece; it was originally published in the *Westminster Review* in 1824.

BL 790.h.17; Blackmer 150; Droulia 822.

74. BODIN, Félix. *Jubilé des Grecs, et jubilé de la Civilisation. Nouvel Appel en faveur des Grecs... Se vend au profit des Grecs. 25 centimes. Seconde édition.* Paris: Touquet, 1826.

32mo, pp. 1-64 (pp.1=ht, 2=note, 3=t). Old quarter maroon roan gilt. From the library of K.Th. Dimaras. (bound with Pouqueville, Paganel, Fabvier and other philhellenic items.)

Second edition, rare, issued by the Comité des Grecs de la Société de la Morale Chrétienne. The president of the committee was General Sebastiani, and the members included Benjamin Constant, A. de Laborde, Cost, Douin, Guizot, Lasteyrie, Rostan and the Baron Ternaux. Bodin was a miscellaneous writer who specialized in historical resumés. The first edition also appeared in 1826, with the same format.

BNF 30117978; Droulia 1075 (second edition, citing this copy). Not in GL;

75. BOETTICHER, Adolf. *Olympia Das Fest und seine Stätte nach den Berichten der Alten und den Ergebnissen der Deutschen Ausgrabungen.* Berlin: [Gustav Schade for] Julius Springer, 1883.

Lge 8vo, pp. XII, 407 [1] (pp.I=ht, V=verse, [1]=colophon). With 13 lithographed or engraved plates no'd I-XV (nos. VII-VIII and XIII-XIV together). Numerous wood engravings in text. Original black pictorial cloth gilt, red edges.

First edition. A second edition appeared in 1886. The German School had been excavating at Olympia since 1875. The first stage of excavation had been completed by 1881, and the official publication was completed then. Boetticher's account may be one of the earliest popular works on Olympia. He later produced an account of the Acropolis, as well as an account of an undated journey in Greece, *Auf griechischen Landstrassen*, 1883. In 1881 he produced an account of the excavations carried out by the Greek Archaeological Society, *Die neuesten Ausgraben der Griechischen Archäologischen Gesellschaft*.

BL 7706.c.28; GL A340.

76. BOETTICHER, Adolf. *Die Akropolis von Athen nach den Berichten der Alten und den neusten Erforschungen. Mit 132 Textfiguren und 36 Tafeln.* Berlin: Julius Springer, 1888.

Lge 8vo, pp. XV, 295 [1] (pp.I=ht, XI=list of plates, [1]=colophon). With 35 plates no'd 1-36 (19-20 on 1 d-p plate), and illustrations in the letterpress. Original pictorial brown cloth.

First and apparently only edition. Boetticher produced a number of works on Greece.

BL 7704.g.37; GL A291.

77. [BOISSONNAS, Frederic]. *La Grèce Immortelle.* Geneva: A. Kundig for Editions d'Art Boissonnas, 1919.

Sm. 4to, pp. XII, 1-259 [5] (p.I=ht, pp.[2]=list of plates, [4]=conts, [5]=colophon). With eight photographic illustrations. Quarter mottled calf, original printed paper wrappers bound in.

First edition of this collection of seven talks delivered in Paris during February and March, 1919, in conjunction with an exhibition of over 500 photographs taken by Fred Boissonnas during the course of his many journeys in Greece. The authors include G. Deschamps, Charles Diehl, A. Croiset, D. Baud-Bovy, L. Bertrand, and A. Andreades. There may have been some connection with Greece's political aims after the War, since the talk by Andreades is entitled 'La Grèce devant le Congres'.

BNF 33408786.

78. BOISSONNAS, Frederic. *L'Image de la Grèce Smyrne. Photographies de Edmond Boissonnas Introduction de Ed. Chapuisat.* Geneva: Boissonnas, 1919.

Lge 8vo, pp. [viii] + [1] (pp.[i]=ht, [viii]=list of plates, [1]=advert). With 48 photographic plates. Quarter calf over marbled paper boards, uncut, original decorative paper wrappers bound in.

First edition. This interesting album contains photographs depicting Smyrna before the great fire of 1922. This series, under the same general title, included *L'Epire, berceau des Grecs*, and *Salonique et ses basiliques*; forthcoming were *La Macédoine occidentale*, *Athènes ancienne*, and *Athènes moderne*.

BNF 33425315, containing all three sections. Not in BLC on line. Not in Weber.

79. BOISSONNAS, Frederic. *L'Image de la Grèce et de la Serbie. Photos Boissonnas.* Paris: Jean Budry [c. 1935].

5 parts in 1, 4to. pp. [viii], [v], [vi], iv (recte vi), [vi], ([i], i=ts). With a map and 192 plates of photographs. Red cloth, in a dust jacket.

Second editions, and first collected edition. Apparently Boissonnas published these texts separately but under the general title *L'Image de la Grèce*; the series also included 'Salonique' and 'Smyrne'. The five sections in this reprint include ancient Athens (text by W. Deonna), modern Athens, Epirus, western Macedonia (G. Arvanitakis), and Skopje and environs (by D. Baud-Bovy), which Boissonnas refers to as 'le berceau des Serbs'. *Epirus* was originally issued in 1915, *Athènes moderne* in 1920, *Athènes ancienne* in 1921 and *Macédoine occidentale* in 1921. Boissonnas'

In Greece, journeys by mountain and valley, Geneva, 1920, may be a translation of part of the work.

BNF cites *Image de la Grece*, 1919, with the sections on Epirus, Smyrna and Salonica.

80. BON, Antoine, and Fernand CHAPOUTIER (1899-1953). *Retour en Grèce. Cent trente-quatre photographies par Antoine Bon Introduction de Fernand Chapouthier.* Paris: Paul Hartmann [1934].

4to, pp. [vi] [112] [8] (p.[iv]=ht, [1-112]=photographs [1-8]=index). With 134 photographs on 112 pages. Blue cloth.

First edition. A 'nouvelle édition' was published under the date 1938, actually January 1940. Bon and Chapoutier were both members of the French Archaeological School in Athens.

This edition not in BNF or BL on line.

81. BOOTH, C.D., and Isabelle Bridge BOOTH. *Italy's Aegean Possessions.* London: Arrowsmith [1928].

8vo, pp. 323 [1] (p.1=ht, [1]=last page of index). With a photographic frontispiece and 15 plates of illustrations. Original blue coth, with a dust jacket, worn.

First edition. Interesting description of the Dodecanese shortly after the islands came under Italian rule, with an account of the political and cultural efforts to bring the population under Italian influence.

BL 08157.f.43.

82. BORCHGRAVE, Emile de. *Croquis d'Orient. Patras et l'Achaie.* Brussels: G. Van Oest & Co., 1908.

Lge 8vo, pp. [i] I-XVI, 1-430 (pp.[i]=t, 425-30=conts). With 24 photographic plates. Half leather over red pebbled cloth.

First and apparently only edition of this account of the Frankish kingdom in Achaia, continuing on to the reign of George I of the Hellenes. Borchgrave also discusses the 'Societe de l'Orient Latin' and the works of Buchon, Riant, and Hoepf. Borchgrave's interests were on the Flemish and the Franks in the Levant and the Belgians in Hungary and Transylvania in the 11th and 13th centures; he also wrote *La Serbie, administrative, economique et commerciale*, Brussels, 1883.

BNF 31844070.

83. BOSANQUET, Ellen Sophia, Mrs. R.C. *Days in Attica.* London: Methuen [1914].

8vo, pp. xiv [i] 1-348 (pp.i=ht, [i]=st). With a coloured frontispiece and 16 photographic illustrations, 2 plans and a folding map, partly coloured in outline. Original red cloth.

First edition. The frontispiece is a reproduction of a drawing by Lucy Violet Hodgkin. Mrs. Bosanquet was the wife of the archaeologist Robert Carr Bosanquet, director of the British School at Athens. She also wrote *The Tale of Athens*, 1932.

BL 10126.dd.28; GL GT1433. Not in Weber.

84. BOUHOURS, Dominique. *Histoire de Pierre d'Aubusson Grand Maistre de Rhodes. Seconde Edition.* Paris: Estienne Michallet... M.DC.XCI. [=1691]

Sm. 8vo, pp. [xvi] 1-471 + [42] (pp.i=t, [1-42]=indexes, license and privilege on p.[42]). Engraved view of Rhodes in the text. Contemporary calf, gilt back. Blindstamp of the Rhodocanakis Library on title, book label of H.M. Blackmer.

Second edition, second issue, apparently unrecorded. The first issue of the second edition appeared in 1677, published by E. Marbre-Cramoisy who also published the first edition (in 4to) in 1676. According to the BNF entry the pagination of both issues is the same. Only the date and imprint on the title have been changed. Presumably Michallet bought the unsold sheets and altered the title to name himself as printer. An English translation appeared in 1679 with additional material by the translator. Bouhours was tutor to Colbert's son. His work on Aubusson is mainly concerned with the latter's valour as grand master of the Knights of Rhodes during the unsuccessful Turkish siege of 1480.

BNF 30140436 (2nd ed, first issue.) Blackmer 180, this copy. This issue not in BNF, GL or BLC; Atabey 142 (1st ed), 143 (English ed.).

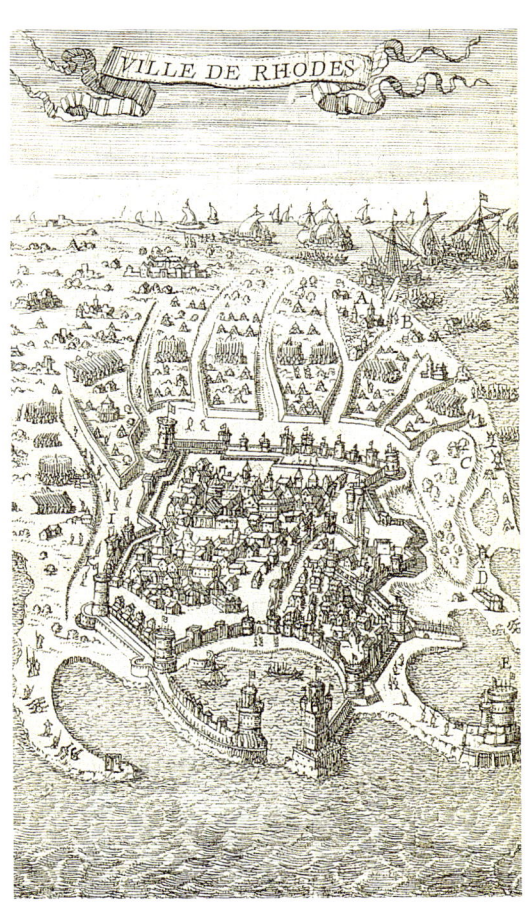

85. BOULANGER, François Louis Florimond (1807-1875). ***Ambélakia ou les Associations et les Municipalités Helléniques avec documents confirmatifs recueillis et mis en ordre.*** Paris: Librairie de Guillaumin et Cie, 1875.

8vo, pp. XXIII, 1-264 (p.I=ht, 263-4=conts). Old half calf gilt.

First and only edition of this interesting work, published posthumously. Boulanger studied at the French Academy at Rome and spent 30 years working in Athens as an architect, where he was involved mostly in restoration work. His study of Ambelakia was a product of his interest in François Fourier's social theory of society, the 'Theory of Associations'. He consulted Beaujour and Urquhart, but the most important part of the work is his collection of documents and the statistics which accompany them. This may be one of the earliest works of its kind.

BNF 30141883.

86. BOVET, Marie Anne de. ***La jeune Grèce.*** Paris: Société française d'Editions d'Art L.-Henry May [1897].

8vo, pp. XIV, 1-299 + [1] (p.I=ht, V=ded. to King Otho of Greece, [1]=conts). Quarter calf, original beige decorative wrappers bound in.

First edition. This journey took place in late 1896, and the preface is dated from Rome, May, 1897. Marie Bovet travelled through Corfu, the Peloponnese, Athens, Meteora and Thessaly.

BNF 31861707; Weber 1005.

87. BOWEN, George Ferguson. ***Ithaca in 1850. Third edition, revised.*** London: James Ridgway, 1854.

8vo, pp. [1]-70 (p.[1]=t). Modern cloth.

Third edition, first published in 1850 at Corfu and dedicated to Gladstone. The second edition appeared in 1851. A Greek translation appeared in 1859. Bowen was resident in Corfu for four years as president of the Ionian University. This third edition may have been issued in the wake of the Crimean War, or more probably with Bowen's appointment as Chief Secretary of Government in the Ionian Islands in 1854. His topographical description of Ithaca is considered to have established its identity with the Homeric island.

BL 10125.b.7; Blackmer 186 (2nd ed). Not in Weber.

88. BOYIAJIAN, Zabelle C. *In Greece with pen and palette. Illustrated by the author and with a preface by Sir Frederic Kenyon, G.B.E., K.C.B, F.B.A.* London: J.M. Dent [1938].

Sm. 4to, pp. xi + [i] 205 + [1] (pp.i=ht, [i]=st, [1]=colophon). With a frontispiece and 15 plates printed in colour. Half green morocco gilt.

First and apparently only edition. Zabelle Boyiazian travelled in Greece in 1928 and 1930. The plates are reproductions of her paintings. She also produced *Armenian Legends*, 1916 and *Gilgamesh*, 1924.

BL 2360.d.19 (under Poyacean, Zapel C.)

89. BRANDSTÄTER, Franz August. *Die Geschichten des Aetolischen Landes, Volkes und Bundes, in drei Büchern... nebst einer historiographischen Abhandlung über Polybius.* Berlin: G. Reimer, 1844.

8vo, pp. VIII, 1-513 (pp.I=t, 511-13=errata). Quarter calf, back ruled gilt.

Apparently first and only edition. Brandstäter had previously published *Bemerkungen uber das Geschichtswerk des Polybius*, Danzig, 1843. He was especially interested in language, literature and linguistics.

BL 1306.f.13. Karlsruhe cites only this edition.

90. BRASSEY, Annie, *Baroness*. *Sunshine and Storm in the East, or Cruises to Cyprus and Constantinople.* London: Longmans, Green and Co., 1880.

8vo, pp. xiii, 1-448 (p.i=ht, p.v=ded). With a wood-engraved frontispiece, 2 folding maps and 8 engraved plates. Quarter calf. With the ticket of the Alford Library.

First edition. A second edition appeared in 1881, and another in 1886. This work was still being advertised in 1886 in both the 'library edition, 8vo, 21 shillings' and the 'cabinet edition, crown 8vo, seven shillings and sixpence' (advert in Bent's *Cyclades*); it contains accounts of two separate cruises, the first to Constantinople in 1874, and the second to Cyprus in 1878. These accounts were composed from the long letter-journals which Mrs. Brassey sent to her friends and family. Note that the engraved title page, although conjugate with the frontispiece, is included in the pagination. One of the maps depicts Cyprus. The plates are mostly after drawings by A.Y. Bingham, engraved by Pearson.

BL 10126.f.8; Blackmer 195; Weber 807.

91. BRASSEY, Annie, *Baroness*. *Voyages d'une famille à travers la Méditerranée à bord de son yacht Le Sunbeam racontes par la Mère. Traduits de l'anglais par Jehan de Bouteiller. Ouvrage illustré de 127 dessins, par A. Y. Bingham.* Paris: Maurice Dreyfous, [before 1900].

Lge 8vo, pp. [ix] 10-304 (pp.[i]=ht, [iii]=fp, 303-4=conts). Numerous illustrations in the letterpress, several full-page, including frontispiece and portrait of Lady Brassey. Original red decorative cloth gilt. An ex-dono inscription appears on the fly-leaf dated 1900.

A late French edition of *Sunshine and Storm in the East*. The first French edition appeared in 1880, translated by Jean C.J.F.H. Bouteiller, dit Jehan, who used the pseudonym 'Butler'. The first English edition appeared in 1880. The Bibliothèque Nationale cites an edition with the name 'Butler' on the title, and attributes the date [1890], but pagination and publisher are the same as in our edition.

BNF 30155993; Weber 808.

92. BREMOND, Henri, *Abbé*. *Le Charme d'Athènes*. Paris: E. Sansot, 1905.

12mo, pp. [vi], 7-48 (p.[i]=ht). Quarter burgundy leather, original grey printed paper wrappers bound in. Ex-dono bookstamp of Amilka S. Alivizatou on title.

First edition, dedicated to Maurice Barrès, whom Bremond met in Greece c. 1896, and with whom he explored Athens and Daphni. A new edition appeared in 1924 and a collected edition in 1925 as *Charme d'Athènes et autres essais*.

BNF 31869409. Not in Blackmer or Weber. Basch, pp. 382-9, cites the first edition as 1902; this is a misprint for 1905.

93. BRETON, Ernest François Pierre Hippolyte. *Athènes décrite et dessinée suivie d'un voyage dans le Péloponèse*. Paris: Gide, 1862.

Lge 8vo, pp. [v] 3-374 + [5] (pp.[i]=ht, [1-5]=conts). With wood-engraved frontispiece and 8 no'd plates. Illustrations in the text. Quarter brown morocco over original brown cloth, sides framed in gilt, romantique.

First edition. A second edition appeared in 1868. The account of the journey to the Peloponnesus first appeared in the periodical *Investigateur* in 1860. Breton travelled in Greece in 1858-59. His other works on the Levant include the articles *Du Pirée à la Corne d'or*, 1862, and *Un Dimanche à Constantinople*, 1863. Breton was a popular writer on art, ancient history and archaeology.

BNF 30159355; Blackmer 199. Not in Weber.

93

94. BROFFERIO, Angelo. *Antica e Nuova Grecia Scene Elleniche... con cenni ed illustrazioni sull'Antica Grecia del Cav. Professore Amedeo Peyron.* Torino: Fontana, 1844-46.

2 vols, 4to, pp.XII, 1-139 [2], 1-425 [2]; [iii] 1-488 (pp.I, [i]=hts, pp.[1-2] in vol.1 =[], in vol.2 p.[1]=conts, p.[2]=list of plates). With ten woodcut portraits and 39 engraved plates (out of 40). Numerous wood engravings in the letterpress. 19th c. quarter calf gilt over red cloth.

First edition, ordinary format; there is another format with the text within ornamental rules. A second edition appeared in 1863. The work was translated into modern Greek in 1851 by Spiridon York. Note that there are two plates extra to the list of plates: Aegina and the Theseion. This copy lacks the plate opposite page 1 in vol. 2, 'Promontorio'. Brofferio was a Piedmontese litterateur and poet. The long introduction on ancient Greece in vol. 1 is by Vittorio Amedeo Peyron.

BL 790.m.17-18. See Blackmer 211 and GL IND237 for the special format. On Brofferio see Enzo Botasso, ed., *Angelo Brofferio. Mostra bibliografica nel centenario della morte.* Torino, 1966.

95. BRÖNDSTED, Peter Oluf. *Reisen und Untersuchungen in Griechenland, nebst Darstellung und Erklärung vieler neuentdeckten Denkmäler griechischen Styls, und einer kritischen Übersicht aller Unternehmungen dieser Art, von Pausanias bis auf unsere Zeiten. In act Büchern. Sr M. Dem Könige von Dänemank gewidmet von Dr P. O. Bröndsted. Erstes Buch. [... Zweites Buch.]* Paris: Firmin Didot, 1826-1830.

2 vols, 4to, pp. XX, 129 [1]; XXII, 131-318 + [2] (pp.I=hts, p.[1]in v.1=errata, p.[1]in v.2=illus, p. LXII, pp.[2]=errata). With 27 engraved plates no'd together 1-72 together with the letterpress vignettes. A number of plates coloured, or partly so. Uncut and partly unopened in the original printed paper boards, with the binder's ticket of Bauzonnet of the Maison Purgold of Paris. With ex-dono inscription of Ole Hastvig Nissen to Christian Larssen.

First edition in German. A French version was published simultaneously. According to F. K. Plesner (see Blackmer) a total of 555 copies of part 1 were printed of which 500 were in German, the remainder in French. The German edition was produced in two states, on ordinary paper and on vellum paper. This copy is on ordinary paper. According to the printed boards, copies were issued 'auf sehr guten Schreibpapier' and 'auf velinpapier mit den ersten abdrücken'. Book 1, on the antiquities of Keos (Zeà), is dedicated to Frederik VI of Denmark; book 2, containing studies of various parts of the Parthenon, is dedicated to the sculptor Thorwaldsen and to the architect Robert Cockerell (q.v.). Bröndsted travelled in Greece with various members of the group of painters, architects and amateurs who carried out excavations at Aegina and Bassae. This informal group, which numbered among its members Jakob Linckh, Baron Stackelberg (q.v.), Cockerell, and Haller von Hallerstein, was active in Greece from about 1810 to 1814. Bröndsted revisted Italy and the Ionian Islands in 1820-21, when he had the plates for this work engraved in Rome, and he visited England in 1826.

Blackmer 214; Weber 138. Karlsruhe cites many copies in German libraries. On Brönsted see N. V. Dorph, *Reise i Graekenland i Aarene 1810-1813*, Copenhagen, 1844.

96. BROWN, Adna. *From Vermont to Damascus returning by way of Beyrout, Smyrna, Ephesus, Athens, Constantinople, Budapest, Vienna, Paris, Scotland, England.* Boston: G. H. Ellis, 1895.

8vo, pp. viii, 1-209 (p.i=t, vii=list of plates). With a photographic portrait frontispiece and 15 photographic plates. Original green decorative cloth gilt, gilt edges.

Apparently first edition, uncommon. Note that the frontispiece is not the same as that listed in the illustrations, which is 'two Vermont ladies'.

GL GT1653.5. Not in LoC or BLC on line. Not in Weber.

97. BROWNE, Edward. *A brief Account of some Travels in Hungaria, Servia, Bulgaria, Macedonia, Thessaly... as also some Observations on the gold, silver, copper, quick-silver Mines, Baths, and mineral Waters in those parts: With the figures of some habits and remarkable places.* London: T. R. for Benjamin Tooke, 1673.

Sm. 4to, pp. [x] 1-144 [3] (pp.[i]=t, vii-x=pref.[1]-[2]=advert, [3]=errata). With 8 plates (of 9), of which 4 are folding. Contemporary calf, back ruled gilt, red leather label. Later ownership signature of F. Deane of Colchester on the title.

First edition. A second edition in folio was published in 1685 with additional material and 12 new plates. A French translation appeared in 1674. Browne, son of Sir Thomas Browne, travelled in Germany and through Hungary and the Balkans to Macedonia and Thessaly from 1668-1673. He was particularly interested in mining, and there is a great deal of important information on mines and early mining techniques in this book. The plates include a view of the mosque in Larissa. Browne's account of his travels in Germany was published in a separate work in 1677 with two folding plates, and the two works are occasionally found together. The Contominas copy also contains the German travels.

BL 982.d.14; Blackmer 217; Weber 353; Wing B5110; Spencer, p. 119.

98. BRUNET DE PRESLE, Charles Marie Wladimir (1809-1875), and Alexandre BLANCHET. *Grèce depuis la conquête romaine jusqu'à nos jours.* Paris: Firmin Didot, 1860.

2 parts in 1, 8vo, pp. [iv] 320 + 58 + [1] + 321-589 (p.[i]=ht, p.[1]=ht to part 2). With 36 no'd plates (out of 40, lacking nos. 5, 25, 26 and 40). Half calf, back panelled in blind with red and black leather labels.

First edition, uncommon. A second edition appeared in 1869. Blackmer 224 incorrectly states that the 1869 edition is the first; the same sheets have been used with a new title page. Part I (to 1453) was written by Brunet de Presle, part II (after 1453) by Blanchet. This appeared as part of the series 'L'Univers'. The second edition was also issued as part of that series. Brunet de Presle was a friend and student of Fauriel and was strongly influenced by the philhellenic climate in France in the 1820s. He studied modern Greek at a young age, and later published Korais's letters to Chardon de la Rochette, as well as producing an anonymous translation of Christopoulos's poems into French in 1831. Brunet de Presle wrote a great deal on Egyptian antiquities, as well as on other archaeological subjects.

BNF 30169911. This edition not in GL or BL.

99. BRUYN, Cornelis de (1652-1727). *Reizen... door de vermaardste Deelen van Klein Asia, de Eylanden Scio, Rhodus, Cyprus, Metelino, Stanchio, &c. Mitsgaders de voornaamste Steden van Aegypten, Syrien en Palestina.* Delft: Henrik van Krooneveld, MDCXCVIII. [=1698]

Folio, pp.[xviii] 1-398 + [8] (pp.[i]=t, [vi-ix]=list of subscribers, pp.[1-7]=index and errata on p.[7], [8]=list of plates). With engraved title, portrait of de Bruyn, map and 214 engravings numbered 1-210 (-5, -199, + A, A-B, 22b, 22c, 125b, 170b). The hors texte plates (100) and the engravings in the letterpress are numbered consecutively. A large paper copy in contemporary mottled calf, rebacked, original spine preserved, sides framed in gilt, back gilt in compartments, red leather label.

First edition of this impressive work. The artist-traveller Bruyn spent a number of years in the Levant, from 1678 until 1685, when he returned to Venice, where he settled for eight years. It is possible that during this period he was working on his illustrations. According to Benezit, de Bruyn probably engraved his own drawings, but many are also

99

the work of Jan and Caspar Luyken. He returned to Holland in 1693 and began to prepare his work for the press. Its many fine plates, including panoramic views of Smyrna, Alexandria, Jerusalem and Contstantinople, make this book the 'most beautifully illustrated travel account of its age' (-Koster). The portrait of de Bruyn is by G. Valck after Godfrey Kneller, the engraved title by J. Mulder after R. de Val.

GL GT563.1q; UBA 294.A.3; Atabey 159; Tiele 207; Koster 34. This edition not in BL, Blackmer or Weber.

100

51

100. BRUYN, Cornelis de. ***Voyage au Levant, c'est-à-dire, dans les principaux endroits de l'Asie Mineure, dans les isles de Chio, Rhodes, & Chypre &c. De même que dans les plus considerables villes d'Egypte, de Syrie, et de la Terre Sainte; enrichi de plus de deux cens tailles-douces, où sont représentées les plus célèbres villes, pais, bourgs, & autres choses dignes de remarque, le tout dessiné d'après nature.*** Paris: Guillaume Cavelier, 1714.

Folio, pp. [xii] 1-408 [6] (pp.[i]=t, [iii-iv]=ded, [v]-[xi]=preface, commend. verse and letters, [xii]=directions to the binder, pp.[1-6]=index). Title in red and black. With engraved title, engraved portrait of de Bruyn, a folding map and 98 plates no'd A, A+B, 1-210. Numerous engravings in the letterpress which are included in the plate numbers. Plates 151/152 reproduced in facsimile from what appear to be the original drawings. Contemporary calf, sides framed in gilt with palmetto pattern, gilt edges. Ownership signature of Nicolas François Vander Cruysen of Antwerp dated 1730. (Ownership stamp deleted from title causing wear and small hole, repaired.)

Second French edition. Brunet also cites an issue of this edition with Amsterdam in the imprint instead of Paris. The first French edition was printed at Delft in 1700, two years after the first edition, in Dutch, printed at Delft in 1698. Plates 151-2 depict the 'Marina di Tripoli' and 'Tripoli'.

BNF 30168069; Brunet III, 911; Blackmer 225; Weber 402; Cohen-De Ricci 610. This edition not in Atabey.

101. BRUYN, Cornelis de. ***Voyages de Corneille le Brun par la Moscovie, en Perse, et aux Indes Orientales. Ouvrage enrichi de plus de 320. Tailles douces, des plus curieuses, representant les plus belles vuës de ces Païs; leurs principales Villes... [etc] & particulièrement celles du fameux Palais de Persepolis... On y a ajouté la route qu'a suivie Mr. Isbrants, ambassadeur de Moscovie, en traversant la Russie & la Tartarie, pour se rendre à la Chine. Et quelques remarques contre Mrs Chardin et Kempfer. Avec un lettre escrite à l'auteur, sur ce sujet. Tome I. [... Tome II.]*** Amsterdam: Frères Wetstein, 1718.

2 vols, folio, pp. [viii] 1-252; [i] 253-469 (pp.[i]=ht in vol.1, t in vol.2, pp.[iii]=t, [v-vi]=ded, [vii-viii]=pref.) Titles in red and black. With an engraved frontispiece after Bernard Picart, a portrait frontispiece of the author by G. Valck after Kneller, and 261 (out of 262) no'd engraved plates. Numerous engravings in the letterpress. 19th c. vellum. With the gilt booklabel of 'Lowther' with his crest, a winged griffon.

First edition in French. These travels also were published in a collected edition with the travels in the Levant in 1725. Bruyn undertook a long journey to Persia and India via Moscow in 1701. He published an account of these travels in Dutch in 1711. The hors-texte plates are numbered separately from the plates in the text, which are unnumbered. This is distinct from the system employed in Bruyn's earlier work on the Levant.

BNF 30168071; BL 455.e.6,7; Weber 463. Brunet III, 911 states that large paper copies are known.

102

102. BRUYN, Cornelis de. *Voyage au Levant, c'est-à-dire, dans les principaux endroits de l'Asie Mineure, dans les Isles de Chio, Rhodes, & Chypre &c... Nouvelle edition... Tome Premier. [... Second... Voyages... par la Moscovie, en Perse, et aux Indes Orientales Tome Troisième... Quatrième... Cinquième.]* Rouen: Charles Ferrand, M.DCC.XXV. [=1725]

5 vols, 4to, pp. [xvi] 648 + [12]; [i] 565 + [10]; [i] 520 + [16]; [i] 522 + [12]; [i] 498 + [14] (pp.[i]=ts). Titles in red and black. With an engraved portrait, 5 folding maps and 84 plates. Contemporary calf, backs gilt in compartments. Contemporary large armorial bookplate with the cypher FCM in vols 3-5.

First collected edition, edited by Antoine Banier. The work appears with both Rouen and Paris (J.-B.-C. Bauche) imprints. The plates have been reduced from those in the first editions. The first two volumes contain the voyage to the Levant; vols 3-5 contain the voyage to Persia and India via Russia. The Levant travels were first published in Dutch in 1698, with French editions in 1700 and 1714. The Persian travels were first published in Dutch in 1711, with a French edition in 1718.

BNF 30168072; Atabey 161 (Paris imprint). This edition not in Blackmer or Weber.

103. BUCHON, Jean Alexandre C., *editor and translator*. ***Chroniques étrangères relatives aux expéditions françaises pendant le XIIIe siècle, publiées pour la première fois, élucidées et traduites par J.A.C. Buchon. Anonyme Grec. – Chronique de la Principauté Française d'Achaie... Ramon Muntaner. – Chronique d'Aragon, de Sicile et de Grèce.*** Paris: Mairet, 1841.

Sm. folio, pp. [viii] LXXII [3] XV, 1-802 (pp.[i]=series t, iii=ht, v=t, vii-viii=ded, pp.I-XV= tables, pp.753-802=contents, indexes). Quarter red morocco, panelled back.

First edition, second issue, published as part of the series 'Pantheon Litteraire'. The first edition appeared in 1840 under the imprint of A. Desrez. Presumably in the second issue the same sheets have been used, with a new title, since the pagination in both issues is the same. BNF also cites editions of 1860 and 1875. In this collection Buchon has edited and translated several important texts, including the chronicle of the Morea by the 'anonyme Grec', with the Greek text below the French translation. He has also produced a new translation of Ramon Muntaner's chronicle of the Grand Catalan Company's expedition to the Levant. Buchon's objective was to record the history of the Frankish domination of the Levant following the fourth Crusade. In 1840 he produced *Recherches et matériaux pour servir à une histoire de la domination française ... dans les provinces démembrées de la empire grec*, and in 1843 *Nouvelles recherches historiques sur la principauté française de Morée*. The series 'Pantheon litteraire' was to serve as a framework for collections of chronicles and memoirs on this subject.

BNF 30172639. GL, BL, LoC all cite Desrez issue which is the more common. Not in Blackmer.

104. BUCHON, Jean Alexandre C. ***La Grèce continentale et la Morée. Voyage, séjour et études historiques en 1840 et 1841.*** Paris: Charles Gosselin, 1843.

Sm. 8vo, pp. VII, 1-567, [1] (pp.I=ht, V-VII=ded to Duchesse d'Orleans, p.[1]=errata). Uncut in modern calf, original yellow printed paper wrappers bound in. Ownership signature of C.G. de Bellevine on upper wrapper.

First edition. The printed wrappers are dated 1844. After a gap of 200 years Buchon re-introduced the study of medieval Greece to French historiography as part of the reawakening of interest in French medieval history and its chronicles. During his travels in Greece and Italy in 1840 and 1841 he searched archives for source materials, and in 1843 he also published the important *Nouvelles Recherches sur la principauté francaise de Morée*, as well as 'La Grèce, Les Cyclades et les Iles Ioniennes' in the journal *Revue de Paris*, the issue for March 12th 'Melanges de Litterature', 18.

BNF 30172585; Blackmer 230.

There is another copy in the Contominas Collection, in quarter red morocco, back panelled gilt, over red embossed cloth.

105. BUCHON, Jean Alexandre C. *Voyage dans l'Eubée, les Iles Ioniennes et les Cyclades en 1841 publié pour la première fois... par Jean Longnon. Préface de Maurice Barrès.* Paris: Emile-Paul, 1911.

Lge 8vo, pp. LXIII, 1-291 + [1] (pp.I=ht, 277-91=index, [1]=conts). With a portrait frontispiece of Buchon. Uncut in recent red morocco gilt by Ch. Leggas, with his blindstamp on a fly-leaf, original beige printed paper wrappers bound in.

First complete edition, edited by Jean Longnon from Buchon's journals and from the articles published in 1843 in the *Revue de Paris*. Buchon had visited Euboea and the Cyclades in 1841 but he published only his account of the Morea and Continental Greece at the time, since that was where the majority of Frankish antiquities were located. His work is remarkably thorough, particularly on Euboea. The work includes a biographical notice of Buchon and a preface by Maurice Barrès.

BNF 31885781.

106. BUDRY, Claude, and Paul BUDRY. *ΗΛΙΟΣ La Croisière en Hellade.* Lausanne: Les Amitiés Gréco-Suisses, 1935.

4to, pp. [16] (p.[1]=ht, [3]=t, [13]=contents, [16]=colophon). With 40 no'd photographic plates by Claude Budry. In modern paper wrappers, in a fold-down box of black morocco. No. 847 of 1000 copies, numbered 1-90 and A-J on Holland Van Gelder paper, and 900 on ordinary paper.

First and apparently only edition. This was published by the Greco-Swiss Friendship League under the presidency of Pierre Cailler. About half the subjects are of Athens, with some uncommon subjects such as Braurona.

BNF 31886517. Not in BL.

107. BUONDELMONTI, Cristoforo. *Christoph. Bondelmontii, Florentini, Librum Insularum Archipelagi. E Codicibus Parisinis ... edidit, praefatione et annotatione instruxit Gabr. Rud. Ludovicus de Sinner, Helveto-Bernas.* Leipzig and Berlin: G. Reimer, 1824.

8vo, pp. 263 (pp.1=t, 263=errata). With 2 folding woodcut plans, hand coloured in pink and green. Contemporary paper boards. Contemporary book label of I.T. Voemel of Frankfurt.

First edition of Buondelmonti's 'Liber Insularum', edited by Gabriel Sinner. According to Legrand, Buondelmonti, a monk from Florence, took up residence in Rhodes in 1406 and lived there for eight years; he then spent the next six years travelling through the Aegean. He wrote his account of his travels in about 1420, describing all the islands he had visited. For over 400 years Buondelmonti's work circulated only in manuscript. It was the prototype for the isolario, that literary product which was so popular in 16th and 17th century Italy, and which formed the basis for the later encyclopaedic collections of Coronelli, Dapper, Mallet and others.

BL 794.g.33; Weber 95. Not in Blackmer or Atabey. See E. Legrand's edition of a Greek manuscript of Buondelmonti's 'Liber Insularum' with a parallel French translation, *Description des Iles de l'Archipel*, Paris, 1897.

108. BURGESS, Richard. *Greece and the Levant; or, Diary of a summer's excursion in 1834: With epistolary supplements.* London: for Longman, Rees... [et al.], 1835.

2 vols, 8vo, pp. xiii (-p.i), 1-312; vii, 1-311 [1] (p.i in v.1=ht, missing here, p.i in v.2=t, [1]=advert). With a folding plan of Constantinople. Modern tree calf. With an ownership note on the fly-leaf, possibly in the hand of Ioannes Gennadius.

First and apparently only edition. Burgess made this journey during the time he was the Anglican chaplain at Rome, 1831-6. His book is a combination of journal entries interspersed with letters to the missionary John Hartley, to Richard Ingram at Athens, Alexander Woodford at Corfu and Frances Ingram at Rome. The work contains interesting information on missions. This copy may have belonged to Ioannes Gennadius; the style and the hand of the note on the fly-leaf: 'Salkeld 15 8´ 19' strongly resembles similar notes in books in the Gennadius Library.

BL 790.d.2; Blackmer 242; Weber 227.

109. BURNELL, Frederic Spencer. *Wanderings in Greece.* London: Edward Arnold, 1931.

8vo, pp. 253 (p.1=ht). Photographic frontispiece and 15 plates of photographic illustrations. Original blue cloth.

First and apparently only edition. Burnell has tried to produce a guide book to Greece combined with a history or what he refers to as a 'compressed reference library'.

BL 10127.df.9.

110. BURR, A.M., *Mrs. Hickford*. **Sketches.** [London: n.d. but c. 1850.]

Folio, no title, one leaf of descriptive text. With 14 tinted lithographed plates on 12 sheets. Contemporary cloth, gilt title on upper cover 'Mrs. Burr's Sketches'.

Apparently first and only edition. The plates depict scenes in Egypt, Greece, Palestine and Spain and probably represent the souvenirs of a journey in the East made c. 1844. Plates 9-10 and 12-13 are printed together on two sheets. Many of the lithographs are signed by a picture of an owl in the lower corners, and nos. 1 and 6 are signed on the plate surface 'A.M. Burr' and no. 6 is dated 1844. Apparently the work was issued without a a general title. There is a copy in the National Art Library, catalogued as 'Sketches, a portfolio of chromo-lithographs'. In the NAL copy the plates are printed on card, hand coloured, and mounted on thick paper.

Not in BLC, not in Abbey. NAL 110.D.8.

List of plates:
1. Street leading to the mosk of El Azhar
2. Gateway of a Bazaar - Cairo
3. Court of the Mosk of Soltan Hassan
4. The Interior of a Harem
5. The Great Pyramid With the Sphynx
6. Our Room in the Armenian Convent
7. Court in front of the Holy Sepulchre
8. The Misr Tcharsky, (Egyptian Market) - Constantinople
9. From the Parthenon - Athens
10. Fountain in the Plain of Sharon
11. Hall of the Ambassadors in the Alcazar - Spain
12. Patio de la Alberca
13. Entrance to the Cathedral Seville
14. Chapter House of the Convent of St. Jeronimo - Belem nr. Lisbon

111. BYRON, George Gordon Noel, *Lord*. **The Poetical Works of Lord Byron. In Eight Volumes.** London: John Murray, 1839.

8 vols, 4to, pp. [iii] 475 [1]; [iii] 462; viii 471 [1]; vii, 510; [iii] 453 [1]; [iii] 451; [iii] 448; [iii] 512 (pp.[i], i=hts, 1=sts, [1]=colophons, 445-512=index). Portrait frontispiece in volume 1 dated 1839. Extra-illustrated with engraved titles (vols. 1-3) and plates, all on india paper and mounted, from Finden's Illustrations to Lord Byron's works, first published 1832-33. 19th c. full ochre morocco, sides with wide dentelle borders enclosing central ornament, backs gilt in compartments with red leather labels, all edges gilt. Ex-dono inscription on the fly-leaf of volume I from Lord Saye and Seale to the Reverend Edward Coleridge, and his inscription to his son Francis Edward Coleridge.

Murray had already published several editions of Byron's works, the earliest dated 1815. This edition in 8 volumes, possibly because of its size, is frequently found extra-illustrated; e.g. both the GL copy and the BL copy; the BL copy has been expanded to 44 volumes because of the extra illustrations.

BL C.44.e-g; GL BY1.

111

112. BYRON, George Gordon Noel, *Lord*. ***The Poetical Works of Lord Byron. With notes, and a memoir of the author. Pictorial edition.*** London: George Henry and Co. [1849].

Lge 8vo, pp. [viii] cliv [6], 1-344 (p.[i]=t, [viii]=dir to the binder). With engraved title and frontispiece and 30 engraved plates (out of 31). Contemporary calf, back blindstamped in compartments.

This edition was published in parts; the publisher's note to the reader is dated 1849. The work includes an anonymous biographical sketch of Byron on pp. i-cliv. This copy lacks the plate of Lara.

Not in BLC on line. Not in GL.

111

59

113. BYRON, George Gordon Noel, *Lord*. ***The Poetical Works of Lord Byron: with a life of the author and copious notes. Beautifully illustrated. Family Edition.*** Halifax: Milner and Sowerby, 1865.

8vo, pp. xv, 702 + 2 pp. of adverts (pp.i=ht, iii=t). With a wood-engraved title and frontispiece, and 6 wood-engraved plates. Original black decorated cloth gilt, gilt edges.

A late illustrated edition of Byron's works with wood engravings by T.G. Flowers, printed by W. Bank of Edinburgh. This illustrated edition was first issued by Milner and Sowerby in 1863.

BL 11661.ee.10.

114. BYRON, George Gordon Noel, *Lord*. ***Letters written by Lord Byron during his residence at Missolonghi January to April 1824, to Mr. Samuel Barff at Zante. Printed solely for the members of Mr. Barff's family.*** Naples: Desanctis, MDCCCLXXXIV. [=1884]

Sm. 4to, pp. [i], 1-26 (p.[i]=t). Original grey paper wrappers, printed in red. With the ownership signature 'Sargint' on upper cover.

Only edition, uncommon. Samuel Barff, a steadfast philhellene, was a banker resident in Zakynthos from 1816. Byron used Barff as his banker while he was in Greece, up until two weeks before his death in Missolonghi. Barff died in 1880, and his family arranged to print Byron's correspondence with him. The letters contain interesting glimpses of Byron's financial dealings with the Greek government, and provide some information about his relations with Leicester Stanhope and Johann Meyer, the printer of Missolonghi. This copy may have belonged to Vivian Sargint, great-grandchild of Samuel Barff, whose family tree is detailed in manuscript on the inner lower wrapper. Some of these letters are reproduced by Marchand in his collected letters of Byron; he states that the originals are in the Benaki Museum.

Blackmer 1936. Not in GL or BLC.

115. BYRON, Robert. ***The Station Athos: Treasures and Men. With an introduction by Christopher Sykes.*** London: John Lehman, 1949.

8vo, pp. 163 (p.1=ht). With photographic frontispiece and 32 photographic illustratons. Original blue cloth, back gilt. Bookplate of E. Caffery.

Second edition, first published in 1928.

BL W.P.13755/2.

116. BYZANTIOS, Skarlatos D. *Ἡ Κωνσταντινούπολις. Περιγραφὴ τοπογραφική, ἀρχαιολογικὴ καὶ ἱστορικὴ τῆς περιωνύμου ταύτης μεγαλοπόλεως καὶ τῶν ἑκατέρωθεν τοῦ κόλπου καὶ τοῦ Βοσπόρου προαστείων αὐτῆς... Τόμος Α΄ περιέχων τὴν ἐντὸς καὶ πέριξ τειχῶν Κωνσταντινούπολιν. [... Τόμος Β΄ περιέχων τὴν ἐπὶ τοῦ κόλπου περαίαν καὶ τὸ ἑκατέρωθεν τοῦ Βοσπόρου... Τόμος Γ΄ περιέχων τὰ πάλαι καὶ νῦν ἤθη καὶ ἔθη τῶν τῆς Κωνσταντινουπόλεως κατοίκων.]* Athens: Andreas Koromilas and Ch. N. Philadelpheus, 1851-1862-1869.

3 vols, lge 8vo, pp. [iii] [20] 616 + [2]; [iv] [12] 556; [i] [14] + [1] + [1] 656 (pp.[i]=ts, [1-2]=errata, list of plates, [1]=errata, [1]=subscribers). With 56 engraved plates, 2 maps and a table. Recent panelled red morocco.

First edition of this valuable description and history of Constantinople, together with an account of the customs and habits of its inhabitants.

BL 10125.e.20 (under Buzantios); GL GT2429.

117. CABROL, Elie (1829-1905). ***Voyage en Grèce 1889 Notes et Impressions. Vingt et une planches en héliogravure et cinq plans lithographiés tirés hors texte.*** Paris: [D. Jouast for] Librairie des Bibliophiles, 1890.

4to, pp. [iii] 156 + [3] (pp.[i]=ht, [1-3]=list of illustrations and colophon). With 21 plates of heliogravures and 5 lithographed plans. Uncut in half red morocco, original beige printed paper wrappers bound in.

First and only edition of Cabrol's account of Athens and an excursion to the Argolid, printed in only 500 copies of which 50 were on Holland paper. The heliogravures were taken according to the Dujardin process. Cabrol, litterateur, playwright, and novelist, also produced *Notes de Voyage*, 1883, an account of a sojourn in Italy.

BNF 30182706; Weber 925. Not in Blackmer.

117

118. CAIGNART DE SAULCY, Lucien F. ***Carnets de voyage en orient (1845-1869) publiés avec une introduction, des notes critiques et des appendices par Fernande Bassan.*** Paris: Presses Universitaires de France, 1955.

8vo, pp. VIII, 248 (p.I=ht, 247-8=conts). With a folding map. Uncut in modern half leather gilt, original printed pale green paper wrappers bound in. From the library of K.Th. Dimaras, with his library stamp on the last page and the verso of the folding map.

First edition of de Saulcy's travel diaries, covering a period of many years. Caignart de Saulcy was a numismatist and archaeologist best known for his travels in the Holy Land in 1850-51.

BNF 31770933.

119. CALAS, Theophile. *La Grèce de Toujours. Douze conférences.* Paris: Librairie Fischbacher, 1911.

8vo, pp. [vi], 1-343 + [1] (p.[i]=ht, p.[1]=contents). Quarter black roan, rubbed. With the bookplate of Shirley Atchley. Bound with Gomez-Carrillo.

First edition. Twelve accounts of various locations, e.g. Athens, Meteora, Argolid, Peloponnesus, etc. Calas also wrote *En terre désolée, au pays des Croisés*, 1900, and *En voyage avec Saint Paul*, 1903. This copy belonged to Shirley Atchley, attached to the British embassy and resident in Athens for many years. He is best known for his account of the wild-flowers of Attica.

GL GT1348.1. Not in BL, BNF or LoC on line..

CAMPAGNES de Monsieur le Prince Eugène. See TRICAUD

120. CANAYE, Philippe, *Seigneur de Fresne* (1551-1610). *Le Voyage du Levant de Philippe du Fresne-Canaye (1573) publié et annoté par M. H. Hauser.* Paris: Ernest Leroux, M.D.CCC.XCVII. [=1897]

Sm. folio, pp. XXXVII [1] 333 + [1] (pp.I=ht, III=ded, V=t, [1]=st, p.333=errata, [1]=conts). With frontispiece, plate and folding map. Uncut in new leather, original printed paper wrappers bound in.

First edition, edited by Henri Hauser, and reprinted in 1980. This was no. 16 in the series 'Recueil de voyage et de Documents pour servir a l'histoire de la Géographie' directed by Charles Schefer and H. Cordier. The folding map is a reprint of part of Sophianos's map of Greece.

BNF 30369175; Weber 193.

121. CARAYON, Auguste, *editor. Relations inédites des missions de la Compagnie de Jésus a Constantinople et dans le Levant au XVIIe siècle.* Poitiers: Henri Oudin; Paris: Ch. Douniol, 1864.

8vo, pp. [ii] III-XX, 1-288 (pp.[i-ii]=blank, p.III=ht, 285-88=conts). Quarter red roan. From the library of Şefik Atabey, with his book label.

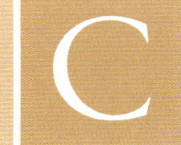

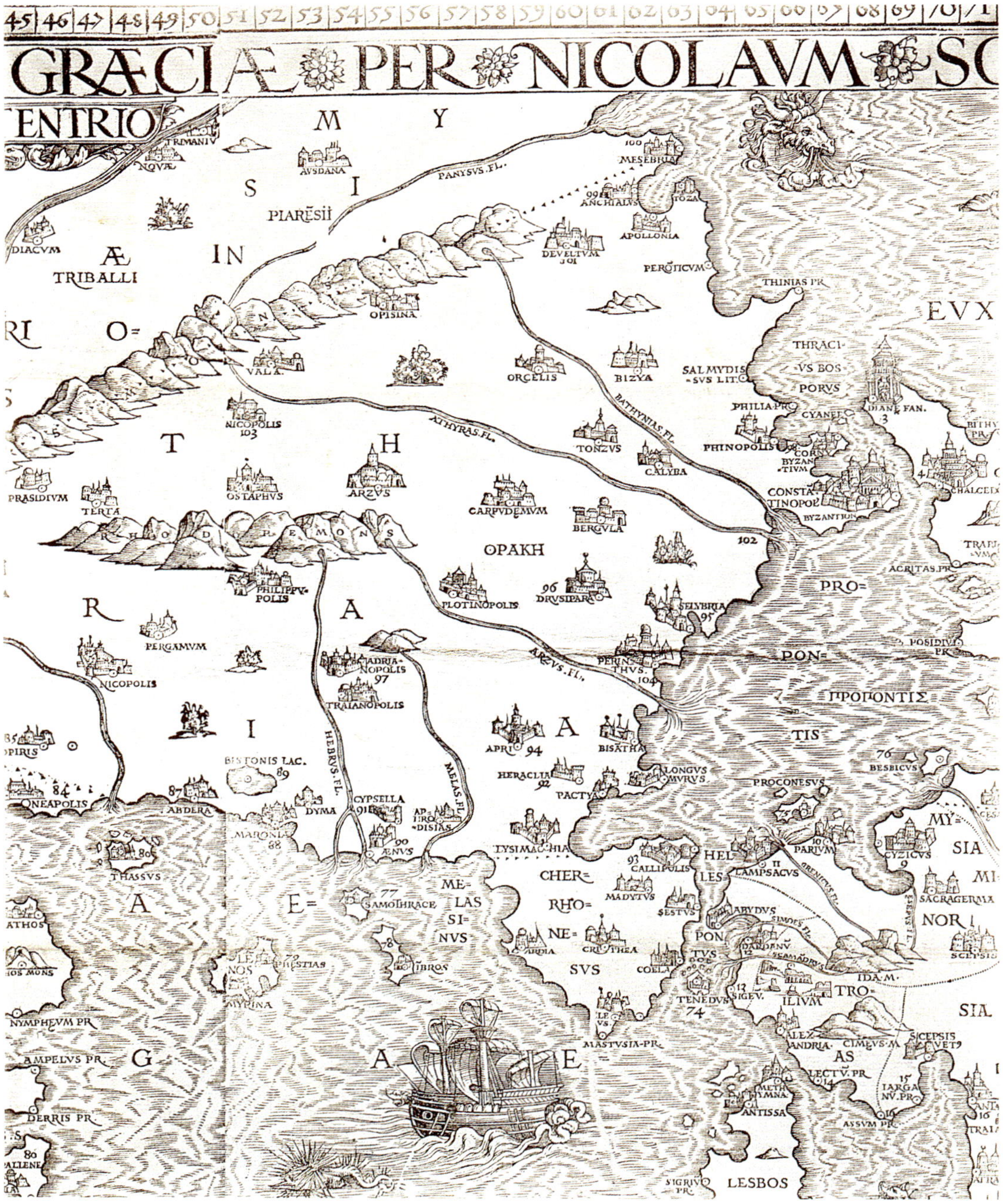
GRÆCIÆ PER NICOLAVM
ENTRIO
MESEBRIA
ANCHIALVS
APOLLONIA
DEVELTVM
TRIBALLI
OPISINA
THINIAS PR.
EVX
THRACI-
VS BOS-
PORVS
SALMYDIS-
SVS LIT.
ORCELIS
BIZYA
NICOPOLIS
TONZVS
CALYBA
PHINOPOLIS
ARZVS
OSTAPHVS
PRASIDIVM
CARPVDEMVM
BERGVLA
CONSTA-
TINOPOL
ΘΡΑΚΗ
PHILIPPV-
POLIS
PLOTINOPOLIS
DRVSIPARA
SELYBRIA
PRO-
PON-
ΠΡΟΠΟΝΤΙΣ
TIS
PERGAMVM
ADRIA-
NOPOLIS
TRAIANOPOLIS
NICOPOLIS
HEBRVS FL.
MELAS FL.
BISATHA
HERACLIA
PACTYA
PROCONESVS
BESBICVS
NEAPOLIS
ABDERA
MARONIA
DYMA
CYPSELLA
ÆNVS
LYSIMACHIA
CALLIPOLIS
LAMPSACVS
PARIVM
CYZICVS
THASSVS
SAMOTHRACE
ME-
LAS
SI-
NVS
CHER-
RHO-
NE-
SVS
MADYTVS
SESTVS
ABYDVS
IMBROS
TENEDVS
SIGEV.
ILIVM
TRO-
SIA
IDA M.
NYMPHEVM PR.
AMPELVS PR.
MYRINA
MASTVSIA PR.
ANTISSA
LESBOS
ASSVM PR.
DERRIS PR.

120

First edition of this selection of letters and reports from the Jesuit establishments in Turkey and the Aegean, which forms volume 11 in the collection of documents published by Carayon. The earliest report among the relations is dated 1609, from Constantinople; other reports from Naxos, Paros, Athens, Nauplion and Patras are dated from the 1640s. Reports from Smyrna and Thyatira (Ak-Hissar) are dated 1656-58. Carayon, librarian of the Jesuit order, also edited many other works connected with the order.

BNF 33579733; Blackmer 284; Atabey 197 (this copy); Sommervogel II, 716.

122. CARLISLE, George William Frederick Howard, *7th Earl of*. *Diary in Turkish and Greek waters. Second Edition.* London: Longman, Brown, et al., 1854.

8vo, pp. xi, 1-353 [1] + [2] + 24 (pp.i=ht, [1]=imprint, pp.[1-2], 24=adverts). Half calf, back gilt with stars, red leather label.

Second edition, first published the same year. Five editions had appeared by 1855, as well as an American edition with notes by C.C. Felton and engraved plates. An account of travels from June 1853 to May 1854.

This edition not in BLC on line. This edition not in Weber or Blackmer.

123. CARNARVON, Henry J.G. Herbert, *3rd Earl of*. *Reminiscences of Athens and the Morea Extracts from a Journal of Travels in Greece in 1839.* London: John Murray, 1869.

8vo, pp. XXIX + [1] 1-230 + [2] (pp.I=ht, [1]=conts, [1-2]=advts. Title and letterpress within rules. With an engraved folding map. A fine copy, uncut and unopened in the original embossed green cloth by Edmonds and Remnants, London, with their ticket. Bookplate of J.C. Eliasco.

First and only edition, published posthumously from Carnarvon's journal, edited by his son. Carnarvon travelled in Greece in 1839. His travels in Portugal in 1820 were published during his lifetime.

BL 10126.b.22; Blackmer 806; Weber 683.

124. CARNE, John. *Syria, The Holy Land, Asia Minor, &c. Illustrated. In a series of views, drawn from nature by W. H. Bartlett, William Purser, &c. First [... Second... Third]* London: Fisher, Son & Co., 1836-1838.

3 vols, 4to, pp. [iv] ii, 80; 76; 100 [4] (pp.[i], 1, 1=ts, [1-4]=index). With 45 engraved plates in vol. 1, 37 in vol. 2 and 37 in vol. 3 (including 3 engraved titles and 2 maps). Contemporary polished green calf, sides framed in gilt with central decorative gilt panel, flat backs gilt, romantique.

First edition. The engraved titles are dated 1836, 1837 and 1838. A later edition was produced in about 1853 by Peter Jackson, and another edition appeared c. 1860-1863 with an appendix by W. Cooke Stafford on the massacres in Syria in the early 1860s. This work formed the first part of Fisher's 'The Turkish Empire Illustrated' which also included Walsh's *Constantinople and the Scenery of the Seven Churches of Asia Minor* (q.v.). John Carne produced the text to accompany these illustrations by W.H. Bartlett, William Purser and Thomas Allom. Bartlett's illustrations were taken during his first voyage to the Levant, 1834-35; Allom's drawing were made c. 1836-37; he was hired by Fisher to travel in the East and make drawings especially for the completion of this work.

BL 563.d.21; Blackmer 291; Atabey 199; Weber 1125. Tobler cites a French edition.

125. CARREL, Armand. *Résumé de l'Histoire des Grecs Modernes, depuis l'envahissement de la Grèce par les Turcs jusqu'aux derniers événemens de la Révolution actuelle.* Paris: [Lebel for] Lecointe et Durey, 1825.

12mo, pp. XII, 1-468 (p.I=ht). Old half mottled calf gilt, red roan label. Presentation inscription on the verso of the title dated 3 June 1829 in Greek to George Ghinis from K. Aristeias.

First edition. A second edition appeared in 1829. A Greek translation appeared in 1838. This was published as part of a series: 'Collection de résumés de l'histoire de tous les peuples anciens et modernes'. Both Droulia and the BNF call for 498 pages. The extra 30 pages may be some sort of appendix. This copy ends at p. 368, finishing with a rule at the bottom of the page.

BNF 36576259; GL HG532 C31; Droulia 854. Not in Blackmer.

126. CASTELA, Henri (1570?-16..). [*Le Sainct Voyage de Hierusalem et Mont Sinay, faict en lan du Grand Iubilé 1600.* Bordeaux: P. A. Du Brel, 1603.]

8vo, pp. [x] 502 + [17] (p.[i]=t, pp.[ix]=conts, p.[x]=anagram, p.[17]=errata). With 5 engraved plates. Contemporary calf.

First edition. The Bibliothèque Nationale cites another issue with the imprint 'Paris, L. Sonnius, 1603'. A second edition was published by Sonnius in 1612. This copy lacks

124

126

the title page and at least one preliminary leaf. We have not been able to see another copy, so the collation of the preliminary leaves is from the description in the Bibliothèque Nationale. Castela made a pilgrimage to the Holy Land in 1600, the year of Jubilee. He compares the work of writing this book to the labours of Hercules, anticipating the criticisms of historians, cosmographers and architects. The five plates illustrate the Church of the Holy Sepulchre with its ground plan and its various sections.

BNF 30204154; BL 1570/2716. This edition not in Weber but see 235. Not in Blackmer.

127

127. CASTELLAN, Antoine Laurent (1772-1838). *Lettres sur la Morée, et les Iles de Cerigo, Hydra et Zante; ... avec vingt-trois Dessins de l' auteur, gravés par lui-même, et trois plans. Première partie. [... Deuxième partie.]* Paris: H. Agasse, 1808.

2 parts in 1 vol., 8vo, pp. [iii] 112; [iii] 156 + [1] (pp.[i]=hts, [1]=errata). With 23 etched plates and 3 plans no'd 1-24 (+5b,7b). Quarter red roan over red paper boards, back gilt with sunbursts and lozenges.

First edition. A further selection of letters appeared in 1811 under the title Lettres sur la Grèce, and a second edition of both works appeared in 1820 as a collected edition. A German translation of the Lettres sur la Morée appeared at Weimar in 1809. Castellan travelled to the East in 1796 as a draughtsman with an abortive French engineering mission to Turkey. He spent several years in the Levant, returning to Paris in 1804.

The *Lettres sur la Morée* describe the first six months of Castellan's travels through Greece on his way to Turkey. The *Lettres sur la Grèce, l'Hellespont*, etc. is mostly an account of his sojourn in Turkey. He himself engraved all the plates with which his works are illustrated. In 1812 Castellan's letters on Constantinople were adapted to form the text to a 6-volume set of Ottoman costumes published by Nepveu, which were reduced versions of Dalvimart's costume plates first published in 1802. This costume book was published in English by Shoberl for his 'World in Miniature' series, and it is likely that these costume books are probably the best known of Castellan's works at large, though not the most important. His work is one of the cornerstones of French philhellenism.

BNF 30204309; Blackmer 298; Weber 637; Malakis pp. 56-58.

128. CASTELLAN, Antoine Laurent. ***Lettres sur la Grèce, l'Hellespont et Constantinople, faisant suite aux lettres sur la Morée. Avec vingt dessins de l'auteur, gravés par lui même, et deux plans. [... Deuxième partie.]*** Paris: H. Agasse, 1811.

2 vols in 1, 8vo, pp. [iii] 171; [iii] 235 (pp.[i]=hts). With 22 no'd engraved plates. Contemporary half calf over marbled paper boards, back gilt with stars.

First edition. In 1811 Castellan published a further selection of his letters on Greece and the Levant, describing mostly Constantinople. The work forms a continuation of the *Lettres sur la Morée*.

BNF 30204310; Blackmer 299; Malakis pp. 56-57. Not in Weber.

129. CASTELLAN, Antoine Laurent. ***Lettres sur l'Italie, faisant suite aux lettres sur la Morée, l'Hellespont et Constantinople. Tome Premier. [... Tome II ... Tome III.]*** Paris: [Le Normant for] A. Nepveu, MDCCCXIX. [=1819]

3 vols, 8vo, pp. [iii] 367; [iii] 307; [iii] 365 (pp.[i]=hts). With 50 no'd plates of etchings, including a frontispiece, and 4 pp. of engraved music. Contemporary vellum, tan and black leather labels.

Only edition. This work describes Castellan's return to France via Corfu and Italy. The first chapter is on Corfu. It was published a year before the collected edition of the *Lettres sur la Morée* and the *Lettres sur la Grèce, l'Hellespont* etc., which appeared in 1820 under the title *Lettres sur la Morée, l'Hellespont et Constantinople*.

BNF 30204312. Not in Blackmer or Weber.

130. CASTELLAN, Antoine Laurent. *Lettres sur la Morée, l'Hellespont et Constantinople... Seconde édition, ornée de soixante-trois planches dessinées et gravées par l'Auteur. Tome Premier. [... Tome Second... Troisième.]* Paris: A. Nepveu, MDCCCXX. [=1820]

3 vols, 8vo, pp. xvi, 1-288; [iv] 1-298; [iv] 1-313 [2] (pp.i, [i]=hts, pp.[1-2]=directions to the binder). With 63 plates engraved by Castellan after his drawings. Old polished green calf, sides framed by a blindstamped palmetto border within four gilt filets, flat backs gilt, black leather labels.

First collected edition, containing the second editions of both the *Lettres sur la Morée*, 1808, and the *Lettres sur la Grèce, l'Hellespont et Constantinople*, 1811. This edition contains many more plates than both the earlier editions together, all etched by Castellan after his own drawings.

BNF 30204311; Atabey 207; Weber 639; Malakis, pp. 56-8. This edition not in Blackmer.

130

131. CAVAN, Frederick Edward Gould Lambart, *9th Earl of*. **With the Yacht, Camera, and Cycle in the Mediterranean.** London: Sampson Low, Marston & Co., 1895.

8vo, pp. xv, 1-94 +[2] (p.i=ht, iii=ded, v=t, pp.[1]=[ ], [2]=colophon). With a photographic frontispiece and 94 photomezzotype illustrations. Uncut in the original brown cloth gilt, uncut.

First edition. Dedicated to Edward, Prince of Wales.

BL 10107.bb.3 (BL cites type of photo). Not in GL.

CAZZAITI, Marco Antonio. See KATSAITES

132. CELLARIUS, Christopher. ***Christophori Cellarii Smalcaldensis Geographia Antiqua recognita denuo, & ad veterum novorumque scriptorum fidem, historicum maxime, identidem castigata, &c. ... Huic demum sextae editioni tot Chartas ex majori auctoris Geographia antiqua quot ad minorem hanc illustrandam requirebantur, duplicemque indicem ... addidit, totam recensuit, & scholarum usui accomodavit Samuel Patrick.*** London: S. Ballard, J. Senex, G. Innys, J. Osborn & T. Longman, 1731.

8vo, pp. viii, 1-180 (p.i=t, p.[128]=errata, pp.129-180=indexes). Title in red and black. With 27 engraved plates, mostly folding. A crisp copy in modern calf, back ruled gilt.

Sixth edition, for the use of schools, edited by Samuel Patrick who added the indexes. The first edition appeared in 1686. This edition also contains a preface by Cellarius dated 1691.

BL 10005.c.24; Zacharakis 575-589. Not in GL.

133. CELLARIUS, Christopher. ***Christophori Cellarii Smalcaldensis Geographia Antiqua recognita denuo, & ad veterum novorumque scriptorum fidem, historicum maxime, identidem castigata... Addidit, totam recensuit & Scholarum usui accomodavit, Samuel Patrick, L.L.D. Editio altera & castigatior.*** London: for J. & T. Pote, E. Ballard, C. Bathurst et al., M.DCC.LXXXVI. [=1786]

8vo, pp. [viii] 1-168 (pp.[i]=ht, [viii]=list of plates). Title in red and black. With 27 folding maps. Calf antique, back gilt. Contemporary ownership signatures of S. Skerrett dated 1789 on title, and of I. Skerret on lower edges.

A late edition of this very successful publication. The previous edition appeared in 1782.

BL 10005.cc.15.

134. CEREMONIES. *The Ceremonies and Religious Customs of the various Nations of the known World.* Vol. I. [... Vol. II... III... IV... V... VI... VII.] London: William Jackson for Claude du Bosc, 1733-1739.

7 vols in 6, folio, pp. [xxxvi] viii, 1-450; [xxiii] 1-364; [xi] 1-495 [26+1]; [xii] 1-514 + [13] + ix; [iv] 1-470 + [26]; [iii] 1-228 + [8]; [iii] 1-164 + [12] (pp.[i]=hts). With an engraved dedication leaf to Richard Boyle by Claude du Bosc, and 202 engraved plates by Bernard Picart (out of 208; lacks 1 plate from vol.2, 2 plates from vol.3, 2 from vol.4, and 1 from vol.5). Modern vellum, final leaves in several volumes washed.

First English edition, probably based on the Amsterdam edition of 1733-39. This work is sometimes catalogued under the name of Bernard Picart, the engraver of the plates. The original work was edited by J.B. Bernard and Bruzen de la Martiniere and published at Amsterdam in eleven volumes from 1723 to 1743; vols. 10 and 11 'Superstitions ancienne et moderne' are by J.B. Thiers and P. Le Brun; they form an appendix to the 'Ceremonies'.

BL 878.l.2 calls for 7 vols, 1733-39.

135. [CERFBERR, Alphonse.] *Mémoires sur la Grèce et l'Albanie, pendant le gouvernement d'Ali-Pacha; par Ibrahim-Manzour-Efendi, commandant du génie, au service de ce visir, ouvrage pouvant servir de complément à celui de M. de Pouqueville. Seconde édition.* Paris: Paul Ledoux, Ponthieu and H. Langlois, 1827.

8vo, pp. [iii] lxxvi, XXXIX + [2] 1-415 (p.[i]=ht, pp.[1-2]=corrections and errata). With lithographed portrait frontispiece of Ali Pasha. Rough cut in half red morocco gilt over marbled paper boards, original upper red printed paper wrapper bound in.

Second edition, first published by Ledoux in the same year. According to the Bibliothèque Nationale, the first edition is in 16mo and does not contain the first preface (pp. lxxvi). This edition contains two prefaces, the first providing information on the author Cerfberr, who used the pseudonym Ibrahim Manzour Effendi, and the second on Albania. A third edition appeared in 1828 under the imprint of J.N. Barba, also marked 'seconde edition'. A German translation by E. Schult appeared in [1913]. Cerfberr seems to have been a picaresque character who travelled to Constantinople in 1803, took service under the Sultan and married a Turkish woman. He returned to France in 1809 and then set out again on his travels through Scandinavia and Russia, ending up in the Balkans where he sought service as a mercenary; according to Larousse Cerfberr offered to carry despatches to Napoleon in Egypt, where he was taken prisoner by the English.

BNF 30632501; GL BG211; Droulia 1332. See Blackmer 304 (3rd ed). NUC attributes this to Samson Cerfberr.

136. CHALCOCONDYLAS, Laonicus. *Λαόνικου Χαλκοκονδύλου Ἀθηναίου... Laonici Chalcondylae Atheniensis Historiarum libri decem. Interprete Conrado Clausero Tigurino. Parisiis, e Typographia Regia. M.DC.L.* [Paris: Sebastian Cramoisy, 1650.]

Folio, pp. [xii] 1-506 + [28] (p.[i]=t, p.[28]=colophon). Contemporary calf, red leather label.

Second edition in Greek. The first edition in Greek appeared in 1615. This edition of Chalcocondylas's history was published as part of the Corpus Byzantinae historiae. His work is often referred to as the 'Turkish History', although it covers the period 1298-1463, and describes the fall of Constantinople in detail, because for the first time in Byzantine historiography the real center of the work is not Byzantium but the Ottoman empire; the section on the annals of the Ottoman sultans begins on p. 303. The work was first printed in 1556, in a Latin translation by Conrad Clauser, and several Latin editions were published during the 16th century.

BNF 34006680; Hoffmann II, 509. Not in Blackmer. This edition not in Atabey.
Collation: $a^4 e^4 A-3X^4 (3X4=[\,])$.

137. CHALCOCONDYLAS, Laonicus. *L'Histoire de la Decadence de l'Empire Grec et Establissement de celuy des Turcs; comprise en dix livres... De la traduction de Blaise De Vigenère. A Paris, chez Nicolas Chesneau... M.D.LXXVII. Avec Privilege du Roy.* [Paris: Claude Bruneval for Nicolas Chesneau, 1577.]

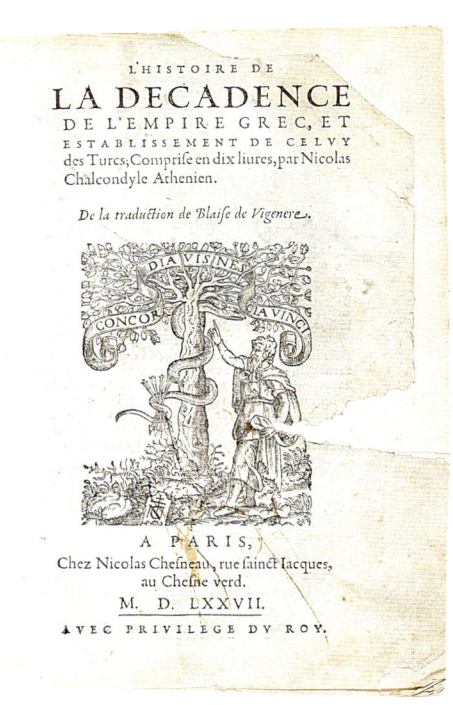

Lge 8vo, pp. [lxvi] 1-734 + [1] + [40] (pp.[i]=t, [1]=colophon, [1-38]=index, [39]=[], [40]=printer's device). Old vellum.

First edition in French, translated by Blaise de Vigenère. It was through this edition that Chalcocondylas's history was introduced to French historiography. A second edition in French was published in 1584 by A. L'Angelier, who also published Vigenère's history of Villehardouin the same year. The editions from 1612 to 1662 contain the various continuations, see below.

BNF 30216407; Hoffmann II, 509. Not in Blackmer. This edition not in Atabey.
Collation: A-H⁴ I² A-Z⁴, 2a-2z⁴ 3A-3Z, 4A-4Z⁴, a-e⁴.

138. CHALCOCONDYLAS, Laonicus. *L'Histoire de la Decadence de l'Empire Grec et Establissement de celuy des Turcs par Chalcondile Athenien De la traduction de B. De Vigenere Bourbonois et illustrée par luy de curieuse recherche trouvées depuis son deces Avec la continuation de la mesme histoire depuis la ruine du Peloponese iusques a l'an 1612 par Thomas Artus Et en cette edition, par le Sieur de Mezeray, jusques en l'année 1661. Tome I. [... Histoire des Turcs Second Tome. Contenant ce qui est passé dans cet Empire iusqu'a lannée presente 1649. Par Franc. De Mezeray Avec l'Histoire du Serrail par le S.ʳ Baudier.]* Paris: chez Augustin Courbé, 1662.

2 vols, folio, pp. [xxii] 1-907; [vii] 1-204 (recte 228) + [12], [iv] 1-89 [3], folios 1-64, [1] pp. 67-116 + [3], 1-85 [10], columns 1-239 [27] (p.[i] in v.1=ht, in v.2=t, pp.[3], [27]=indexes, p.[iv], [i]=st and contents). Titles in red and black. With two engraved titles, a double-page plate of the Turkish army, and a double-page folding plan of Constantinople. Numerous en-

gravings in the letterpress including portraits of the sultans, emblem plates (in the prophecy in v.2), and costume plates after Nicolay (v.2, 'plusieurs descriptions des accoustremens'). Marbled paper boards, brown leather labels. Ownership inscription of the Bibliotheca Hippolytana on printed title dated 1763.

A late French collected edition. This edition also appears under the variant title *Histoire générale des Turcs contenant l'histoire de Chalcondyle* (see Atabey 214 and BLC). Chalcocondylas's history was first translated into French by Blaise de Vigenère in 1577. It was published with Thomas Artus's continuation in 1612, with further editions in 1616, 1620, and 1632. In 1650 the work was published with Mezeray's additions bringing it up to date to 1649. Apparently the first Courbé edition appeared in 1660, possibly shared with the publisher Jean Berthelin, under whose name a 1660 edition also appears. For some reason this collected edition was reprinted several times between 1660 and 1662, possibly because of the Nicolay plates.

This edition not in BNF, which cites Courbe's 1660 edition. BLC cites issue with variant title; Atabey 214 (variant issue. In the Atabey copy the sections of the book are bound differently, e.g. the index of 27 pages occurs at the end of vol. 1 in the Atabey copy, not at the end of vol. 2). Not in Blackmer.

139. CHANDLER, Richard (1738-1810). *Travels in Asia Minor: Or an account of a Tour made at the Expense of the Society of Dilettanti.* Oxford: Clarendon Press, M.DCC.LXX.V. [=1775]

4to, pp. xiv, xiii [i] 1-283 [1] (pp.i=t, [i]=errata, [1]=advert). With a large folding map of the Aegean by T. Kitchin. Contemporary calf, back ruled gilt with roundels. 19th c. armorial bookplate of Sir John Tilley.

First edition. According to Carter, only 500 copies were printed. A Dublin edition in 8vo also appeared in 1775; a second edition appeared in 1776; a collected edition appeared in 1817 (with the Greek travels) and a new collected edition was issued in 1825 with posthumous notes by Nicholas Revett. The Society of Dilettanti commissioned Chandler to undertake a tour of exploration in Asia Minor; this was the first mission organized by the Society, and the other members of the party included the architect Nicholas Revett, who had already worked in Athens with Chandler, and the artist William Pars. The party spent two years in the East, from 1764 to 1766. Two other works connected with these travels were to appear: Chandler's *Travels in Greece*, 1776, and the very important *Ionian Antiquities* (1769-1797). The *Travels* are based on Chandler's journals and contain an account of the travellers' day to day experiences. The *Ionian Antiquities*, which took many years to produce, was the result of their researches on the ground.

BL 148.b.1; Blackmer 318; Weber 552; Atabey 215; Spencer pp. 163-169.

140. CHANDLER, Richard. *Voyages dans l'Asie Mineure et en Grèce, faits aux dépens de la Société des Dilettanti, dans les années 1764, 1765 et 1766. Traduits de l'anglais, et accompagnés de notes géographiques, historiques et critiques, par MM. J.P. Servois et Barbié du Bocage. Tome I.er [... Tome II... III.]* Paris: Arthus-Bertrand, and Buisson, 1806.

3 vols, 8vo, pp. XXX + [1] 1-458; [iv] 1-573; [iii] 513 + [2] (pp.I, [i]=hts, [1]=st, pp.457-8, 571=3=errata; pp.[1-2]=additions and corrections). With a large folding map of the Aegean (of 2), a folding map of the Peloponnese engraved by Doudan after Thomas Kitchin, and a folding plan of Athens. Contemporary quarter calf over marbled boards, back gilt with red and black leather labels.

First edition in French of Chandler's *Travels in Greece* (1776), and *Travels in Asia Minor* (1775). This edition also forms the first collected edition. It was distributed at twelve other towns besides Paris, and the imprints may contain such diverse places as Riom, Lyon, etc. The English collected edition did not appear until 1817. The French edition was edited by J.P. Servois and J.D. Barbié du Bocage, and it contains important notes by Louis Fauvel, Choiseul-Gouffier and others. The maps of the northern and southern Aegean are by T. Kitchin. Only the map of the northern Aegean is present in this copy.

BNF 30219858; BL 1046.f.5-7; Weber 558. This edition not in Blackmer but see 318-19 and 321. This edition not in Atabey.

141. CHATEAUBRIAND, François René. *Itinéraire de Paris à Jerusalem illustré de gravures sur acier. I [... II].* Paris: Gabriel Roux and Arnauld de Vresse [c. 1860].

2 vols, 12mo, pp. [iii] 1-266; [iii] 1-240 (pp.[i]=hts). With two steel-engraved frontispieces. In a prize binding of contemporary embossed cloth, rebacked, central gilt wreath enclosing 'Maison d'Education de Mlle Caignaire' on upper cover. With the prize bookplate to Marie Charrin, dated 1863, and with the ownership stamp of Justin Godart of Lyon and the later library stamp of K.Th. Dimaras on the lower fly-leaf. Bookseller's ticket of H. Samuelian.

A late edition of Chateaubriand's *Itinéraire*, first published in 1811. BNF cites an edition by A. de Vresse dated [1860]; there is also an edition by G. Roux dated 1855.

This edition/issue not in BNF. This edition not in COPAC. See Blackmer 328 (first ed.).

142. CHATEAUBRIAND, François René. *Itinéraire de Paris à Jerusalem et de Jerusalem à Paris Précedé d'une étude par M. A. de Pontmartin. I. [... II.].* Paris: Calmann Levy, 1881.

2 vols in 1, sm. 8vo, pp.[iv] 1-315 [1]; [iv] XII, 1-265 + [1] (pp.[iv]=hts, [1]=tables of contents). Uncut in half brown morocco gilt, original blue printed paper wrappers bound in. Presentation inscription of I. Papatheodorou to 'Zitsa' dated 1883 on half title.

A late edition of Chateaubriand's *Itinéraire*, which was first published in 1811. This edition is accompanied by three essays by Armand de Pontmartin. The first consists of a rapid review of previous travellers, the second of an examination of Christian traditions in Jerusalem, and the third is an account of Chateaubriand as seen by his secretary M. de Marcellus. Other important editions of Chateaubriand's work include that by Didot with his own notes, 1856.

BNF 30227857. This edition not in BLC. Not in Weber.

143. [CHAUSSARD, Pierre Jean Baptiste (1766-1823).] ***Fêtes et Courtisanes de la Grèce. Supplément aux Voyages d'Anacharsis et d'Antenor... Troisième édition, revue, corrigée avec soin; presentée sous une forme dramatique; augmentée de notes piquantes... Tome Premier. [... Second... Troisième... Quatrième.]*** Paris: Barba, M.DCCC.III. [=1803]

4 vols, 8vo, pp. [iii] civ, 444; [iii] 438; [iii] 382; xii, 466 (pp.[i]=hts). With 4 frontispieces and 4 folding plates (of 6?), and a folding table. Lacking the plates of engraved music. Contemporary half calf over marbled paper boards, back gilt with sunbursts. Verse ownership inscriptions of Pietro Baggi dated 1853 in each volume.

Third edition, first published in 1801. The second edition also appeared in 1803. Chaussard took advantage of the interest in the ancient world aroused by the success of Barthélemy's *Anacharsis* and Lantier's *Antenor* to produce a salacious account of ancient Greek customs and religion.

BNF 31230022; Atabey 227 (1st ed.); see Cohen-de Ricci 231-32. Not in Blackmer.

144. CHENAVARD, Antoine Marie. ***Voyage en Grèce et dans le Levant fait en 1843-44 par A. M. Chenavard, Architecte, E. Rey, peintre, Professeurs à l'Ecole des Beaux Arts de Lyon, et J. M. Dalgabio, Architecte. Relation par A. M. Chenavard.*** Lyon: Léon Boitel, 1849.

8vo, pp. [vii] 9-272 (p.[i]=ht, [vii]=st, pp.271-2=list of plates). Folding map and 12 engraved plates on india paper, mounted, by Louvier and Dubouchet after Chenavard. Uncut in modern calf gilt. Original printed paper wrappers bound in.

Second edition of Chenavard's *Relation*, but the first to be illustrated. The first edition appeared in 1846. The *Relation* contains a full account of Rey and Chenavard's travels in the Levant in 1843 and 1844. Chenavard's *Voyage* below is in fact a collection of plates with only a summary account of the journey and is sometimes referred to as the 'atlas' to the *Relation*.

BNF 30232539; Weber 378. This edition not in Blackmer but see 332 (1st ed.).

There is another copy of the *Relation* in the Contominas collection, in calf with the original beige wrappers bound in.

145. CHENAVARD, Antoine Marie. *Voyage en Grèce et dans le Levant fait en MDCCCXLIII et MDCCCLIV.* Lyon: Louis Perrin, 1858.

Large folio, pp. 27 [79] [2], (p.1=ht, pp.[1-2]=list of plates). With 81 plates no'd 1-75, + 0, 00, 28b, 48b, 56b and 57b. Both the text and plates are on stubs. Quarter brown roan over brown marbled paper boards, back panelled in blind, top edge gilt.

145

First and only edition. Brunet states that only 200 copies were printed. The plates are engraved after drawings by Chenavard and Rey taken during their travels with Dalgabio. There are many plates of Athens. Note that plates 28b and 48b are not called for in the list of plates. In 1867 Rey produced his own collection of plates lithographed after his drawings. The titles are similar and the two works are often confused; but they are totally dissimilar in style and content.

BNF 30232540; Blackmer 334; Weber 379; Atabey 230; Brunet I, 1831.

146. CHENNECHOT, L.E., and F.C.H.L. POUQUEVILLE. *Histoire de la régénération de la Grèce, résumée d'après M. Poucqueville [sic], et continuée jusqu'aux événemens le plus récemment connus.* Paris: [Casimir] for the Author and Dauthereau, 1826.

32mo, pp. [iii] i-iv, 1-182 + [2] (p.[i]=ht, pp.181-2=glossary, pp.[1-2]=adverts 'Librairie au rabais'. Old quarter maroon roan gilt, from the library of K.Th.Dimaras, with his bookstamp on the lower fly-leaf.

First and only edition. Chennechot was a miscellaneous writer who produced a number of historical resumés. He also wrote on the Algerian campaign. This is Chennechot's only philhellenic work.

BNF 30233036; Droulia 1065. Not in BLC on line. Bound with Paganel and others.

147. CHOISEUL-GOUFFIER, Marie G.A. Florent de. *Voyage pittoresque de la Grèce. Planches. A Bruxelles. [vignette imprint:] Bruxelles: Calcographie Royale de J. Goubaud.* [Brussels: c. 1830.]

Folio, no letterpress. With a lithographed title, folding map and 174 lithographed plates on 128 sheets, as follows: 98 plates on 76 sheets no'd 1-100 (nos. 14, 30, 31, 53, 61, 71 and 91 not used, +12a, 55a and 3 unn. plates), 13 sheets with 36 plates, + 40 unnumbered plates. The plates are also numbered in a contemporary hand up to 138, but these numbers cannot be trusted: e.g. 101 is used twice, nos. 102-105 missing. Modern half calf, back ruled gilt.

A pirated Brussels edition of the atlas of plates only from Choiseul-Gouffier's monumental *Voyage pittoresque de la Grèce*. The text of this edition (edited by Lesbroussart) was printed by Auguste Wahlen at Brussels in 1823-5, and is relatively uncommon. This undated atlas of lithographed plates was produced around 1830 to accompany the text. It was issued in parts, and it is possible that it began printing in about 1825. The entire work may have been completed c. 1830. The lithographed plates bear the imprint 'Lemonnier et Plou del' or 'Plou et Michelot del'. Wahlen had also produced an edition of Melling's *Constantinople* in 1829, and the atlas also contains lithographed versions of some of the plates from Melling's work. The numbered plates, together with the 36 unnumbered plates on 13 leaves represent the plates from volumes I and II of Choiseul-Gouffier's work. The 40 unnumbered plates beginning with the portrait of Selim III are lithographed versions of plates from Melling's *Voyage Pittoresque de Constantinople*, 1819. These plates depict sites in the environs of Constantinople, and they are mostly signed by Peetermanns, Lauters, Delpierre or Lemonnier. The Brussels atlas of plates does not reproduce all the plates from either of these works, and some plates have been altered. Most of the costume plates from Choiseul-Gouffier (four to a page in the original work) have been omitted. The maps of Delos, Santorini, etc. are not present. Comparison with the copy of this atlas in the Gennadius Library indicates that the Choiseul-Gouffier section should consist of 106 plates (on 82 sheets) no'd 1-100. In the GL copy nos. 14, 30, 31, 61, 71, 96 and 96 are not used, plus 12b, and 12 unn. plates. Certain plates which are numbered in the Contominas copy are unnumbered in the Gennadius copy, and vice-versa. The Contominas copy lacks 10 of the 12 unnumbered plates in the Gennadius copy, but has the 36 plates on 13 sheets not in the Gennadius copy. It is possible that plates 61 and 71, which are missing in both copies, may not have been published, or the numbers not used; the other unused numbers can be related to the unnumbered plates. In the first edition the plates are engraved, not lithographed.

Weber 573. This edition not in Blackmer or Atabey, or BNF and BL on line.

148. CHOISEUL-GOUFFIER, Marie G. A. Florent de. *Voyage pittoresque dans l'empire Ottoman, en Grèce, dans la Troade, les îles de l'Archipel et sur les côtes de l'Asie-Mineure... Seconde édition, augmentée de notices historiques d'après les voyageurs modernes les plus célèbres. Redigées avec le concours et les observations inédites de M. Hase... et de M. Miller. Tome Premier. [... Deuxième... Troisième... Quatrième.] – Atlas. 1ʳᵉ Partie [... 2ᵐᵉ Partie].* Paris: J.-P. Aillaud, 1842.

4 vols in 2, 8vo, and folio atlas, pp. xvi, 1-347; vi, 1-398; vi, 1-390; x, 1-240; no letterpress in atlas (pp.i=ht, missing in vols 1 and 4, pp.v-x=table of contents, bound at the end of vol.4.) With a folding table in vol. 2. The atlas in two parts in 1, part I with an engraved portrait of Choiseul-Gouffier, and 126 plates on 100 leaves, no'd 1-124, 126 and 126b, + 2 unn. folding maps and 12 plates of culs-de-lampe; part II with 163 plates no'd 1-159 + 8b, 33b, 33c, and 76b on 70 leaves, + 2 plates of culs-de-lampe. The text in 19th c. quarter blue calf gilt over marbled boards, uncut, the atlas in new green quarter morocco gilt in romantique style, with the initials JFV at the foot of the spine, in a box.

Second edition, produced in 8vo format for wider distribution, although the atlas of plates remained in folio format. The first edition appeared between 1782 and 1822; Choiseul-Gouffier died in 1817 and the first edition was completed by the publication of the second part of volume II by Barbié du Bocage in 1822; this edition, published twenty years after the first, has been edited by Hase and Miller. The preliminary material contains a long account of Choiseul-Gouffier by Dacier. The change of title from *Voyage pittoresque de la Grèce* to *Voyage pittoresque dans l'empire Ottoman* may be significant of a change in attitudes, not only towards Greece and Turkey, but particularly from that of sentimental philhellenism to scientific observation. A Brussels piracy of the first edition was published in 1823-5.

BNF 30239256; Atabey 242. This edition not in Weber or in Blackmer.

VOYAGE PITTORESQUE
DANS L'EMPIRE OTTOMAN.
ATLAS.
I.re PARTIE.

A LA LIBRAIRIE DE J.-P. AILLAUD, QUAI VOLTAIRE, N° 11.

1842.

There is another copy in the Contominas collection, in 4 vols in 2, in 19th c. quarter blue calf gilt over marbled boards, uncut.

149. CHRISTOPHER OF GREECE, Prince. *Le Monde et les Cours. Mémoires de S.A.R. le Prince Christophe de Grèce. Traduction Française de Henri Delgove.* Paris: Plon, 1939.

Sm. 4to, pp. [vi] 1-310 (p.[i]=ht, p.[v]=avis au lecteur). With 17 photographic plates. Half blue cloth.

First edition in French. Prince Christopher was the youngest child of George I. His brother Prince Constantine, heir to the throne, was 20 years older than he. The photographs include pictures of the French, Russian and English Royal families. A curious feature of the Greek royal family was the fact that the younger children of George I spent their adult lives outside Greece, possibly as a result of the struggles between Venizelos and Constantine, viz. Prince Peter (q.v.) and Prince Philip. Princess Marina of Kent was Christopher's niece, the child of his brother Nicholas.

BNF 31945828. Not in GL.

CHRISTOPHOROS, Ierodidaskalos. See PROSKYNETARION

CHRYSANTHOS Kamarases of Proussa. See PROSKYNETARION

150. CHURCH, Alfred John. *Stories of the East from Herodotus. With illustrations from ancient frescoes and sculptures.* London: Seeley, Jackson, & Halliday, MDCCCLXXXI. [=1881]

8vo, pp. xii, 299 (p.i=ht, ix=ded). With lithographed frontispece and 15 lithographed plates all printed in colour. Contemporary tree calf, back gilt in compartments, a prize binding from Alderley Edge High School dated 1885, with gilt cypher on upper cover.

First edition. Church was a prolific writer who adapted tales from ancient authors for school children. His many works include *Stories from Homer*, 1878, *The fall of Athens, a story of the Peloponnesian War*, 1895, the *Story of the Iliad*, 1902, and *Greek Story and Song*, 1903. He also produced a story of modern Greece, *Three Greek Children*, and tales from Lucretius and Ovid.

BL 09055.aa.18.

151. CLAPARÈDE, Arthur de. *Corfou et les Corfiotes.* Geneva: H. Kündig, and Paris: Fischbacher, 1900.

Sm. 8vo, pp. x, 1-177 (p.i=ht, 173-77=conts). Uncut in the original printed paper wrappers.

Apparently only edition. Claparède mentions several Corfiots who helped him with information: N. G. Catsakis, Alexandros Mouzzachy, Constantinos Eleftherioannou, Jean Marmora and Marini. Claparède was a balloonist and miscellaneous writer with a general interest in geography and travel. He also wrote on Malta, Algeria and Geneva, where he may have lived.

BNF 30246264; GL GT3335.

152. CLARK, William George. *Greece and the Greeks. Peloponnesus: Notes of Study and Travel.* London: John W. Parker and Son, [after 1858].

8vo, pp. xiv [i] 1-344 (p.i=ht, missing here; p.iii=t). With 5 no'd maps/plans (of which 1 folding). Extra-illustrated with lithographed frontispiece not called for in the list of plates. Decorative embossed purple cloth gilt, gilt edges.

First edition, second issue? The first issue appeared the same year. The pagination and the collation of this issue are the same as that of the first issue, but the title page is a variant; it has been cancelled and replaced. The words 'Greece and the Greeks' do not occur on the first edition title. Clark has dedicated this account of an excursion to the Peloponnesus in 1856 to George Finlay, historian of Greece. The lithographed frontispiece, a view of St. Paul's Bay, Malta, is not called for in the list of plates. Note that the Blackmer copy of the first issue also had a frontispiece (not described) which may have been an extra-illustration, but the Atabey and GL copies (both first issue) do not have one.

BL 10125.dd.23; Blackmer 361; Weber 554; Atabey 252 (all=1st issue).

153. CLARKE, Edward Daniel (1769-1822). *Travels in various countries of Europe Asia and Africa. Part the Second Greece Egypt and the Holy Land Section the First. [... the Second.]* London: R. Watts for T. Cadell and W. Davies, MDCCCXIII [... MDCCCXIV.] [=1813,1814]

2 vols, thick 4to, pp. [i] xix [xiii] 720; [i] xv + [xii] (1)-(20) 822 (pp.[i]=ts). With 33 plates in section one and 28 in section two. Contemporary tree calf, backs ruled gilt, red and black leather labels.

153

This set consists of the first two sections of part two of Clarke's travels, on Greece, Egypt and Palestine. Section one is of the second edition, section two is of the first edition. The first edition of Clarke's travels was published in six volumes from 1810 to 1823 as follows: v.1 (Russia, Tartary, Turkey) 1810; vols 2-4 (Greece, Egypt, Palestine) 1812 (2nd ed. 1813), 1814, 1816; vols. 5-6 (Scandinavia) 1819-1823. The entire publication contains 185 plates. Clarke's travels may be regarded as one of the high points in the history of travel in the Levant. This encyclopaedic account of his journey, 1799-1801, with John Marten Cripps to Scandinavia and thence overland via Moscow to Constantinople, Syria and Egypt encompasses many of the most significant happenings of the period. In the Troad Clarke met Lusieri and Preaux who were working for Lord Elgin; he travelled overland to Egypt with the Anglo-Turkish expeditionary force under Abercromby; in Egypt he joined W.R. Hamilton, Elgin's secretary, in a campaign to prevent Egyptian antiquities from being carried off by the French Napoleonic forces. From Egypt he went to Greece where he secured many antiquities, including the colossal statue of the Kistophors, the so-called Ceres, from Eleusis, which he deposited in Cambridge.

BL 231.b.5-10; Weber 19; Atabey 253. This edition not in Blackmer.

154. CLARKE, Edward Daniel. *Travels in various countries of Europe Asia and Africa. Part the First Russia Tahtary [sic] and Turkey. [... Part the Second Greece Egypt and the Holy Land... Part the Third Scandinavia] Fourth Edition. Volume the First. [... Volume the Second ... Volume the third. Section the second. ... Volume the Fourth... the Fifth... the Sixth. ... the Seventh... the Eighth... Volume the Ninth. Section the third... Volume the Tenth... Volume the Eleventh.]* London: R. Watts for Cadell and Davies, MDCCCXVI. [MDCCCXVII … MDCCCXVIII … MDCCCXXIV.] [=1816, 1817, 1818, 1824]

11 vols, 8vo, pp. [xvii] xi + [xi] 533; [x] 524 + [22]; xxvii [ix] 453; [x] 463; xxvii + [viii] 460; [xiii] 647; [iv] xxvi [xi] 481; [xvi] 462 [62]; xvii [xiii] 571 [1]; [xii] 580; [xiv] 492 (pp.[i]=ts, pp.[22]=index to pt 1, [62]=index to pt 2, [1]=colophon). With an engraved portrait of Clarke in v.1, and 37 engraved maps and plates (of 42). Contemporary calf, rebacked, backs ruled gilt, red and black leather labels. With the 18th c. book stamp of Carlow College library on titles.

Fourth edition of volumes 1-8, second edition of vols 9-11. The section on Scandinavia was first published in 1823. Section two, on Greece and Turkey, occupies volumes three to eight. The octavo edition contains only a selection of the 185 plates which were issued with the quarto edition.

BL 1048.g.1-8; Blackmer 365; Atabey 254 (without colophon leaf). This edition not in Weber.

155. COCHRANE, George. *Wanderings in Greece.* London: Henry Colburn, 1837.

2 vols, 8vo, pp. xii, 1-322; vii, 1-382 (p.i=ht in vol.1, t in vol.2). With two lithographed frontispieces, coloured, a folding plan of Athens, 5 lithographed plates with modern colour, a folding map of Greece and a folding map of Athens and environs. Uncut in the original mauve embossed cloth, skilfully rebacked. With an ex-dono inscription from Mrs. William Shedden to John Shedden, stating that Cochrane was a friend of hers. Modern bookplate obscured.

First edition. Cochrane first visited Greece in 1827 with his uncle (actually first cousin) Admiral Thomas Cochrane who was attempting to bring two steamships to the assistance of the Greeks. He returned to Greece in 1834 and 1835-6 in an attempt to establish a steamship line. This very interesting work throws light on an important period in Greek history. The lithographs are by A. Picken after drawings by Cochrane, printed by Day and Haghe.

BL 790.i.27; Blackmer 373; Weber 250. Not in Abbey.

156. COLLAS, Bernard Camille. *La Turquie en 1861.* Paris: A. Franck, 1861.

8vo, pp. [iii] VII, 1-399 (pp.[i]=ht, I-VII=pref., 397-99=index). Quarter red russia over maroon marbled paper boards, back gilt with star and crescents, signed by E. Marchall at foot of spine.

First and apparently only edition. Collas followed this with *La Turquie en 1864*. A captain in the French merchant marine, he was interested in various projects connected with the French colonies. He wrote on the pack-boat services and the postal services in the Mediterranean, as well as on shipping in general, telegraph lines and related subjects.

BNF 30256970; Atabey 262; Bengesco 1144. Not in Blackmer.

157. COLLAS, Bernard Camille. *La Turchia nel 1864. Traduzione dal Francese.* Milan: [Tip. Guglielmini for] Corona and Caimi, 1865.

8vo, pp. 495 (pp.1=ht, 5-16, pref. to Italian edition). Three quarter calf, back embossed in blind, painted red. Ticket of Mantzakos of Athens.

First edition in Italian, published in the series 'Collana di Storie e Memoria contemporanee diretta da Cesare Cantu', vol. 12. The first edition was published in French in 1864. Note Collas' name is spelled Colas on Italian title page.

BL 9077.cc. This edition not in Atabey but see 263. Not in Blackmer.

158. COLLEGNO, Giacinto Provana di. ***Diario dell' Assedio di Navarino Memorie di Giacinto Collegno precedute da un ricordo biografico dell' autore, scritta da Massimo d'Azeglio.*** Torino: Pelazza, 1857.

8vo, pp. 136 (p.1=ht). Half tan morocco, back ruled black, original yellow printed paper wrappers bound in.

First edition. This account of the siege of Navarino by by the forces of Ibrahim Pasha in 1825 was first printed in the newpaper *Il Cronista*. The Bonapartist Collegno, who accompanied the philhellene Santa Rosa to Greece, wrote it originally in French. Santa Rosa was killed during the course of the siege; Collegno dedicated the *Diario* to him. The French text has been reprinted in L. Ottolenghi's *La Vita e i tempi di Giacinto Provana di Collegno*, Torino, 1882.

BNF 30257162; BL 9135.b.9; Blackmer 378. Not in Atabey.

159. COLTON, Walter (1797-1851). ***Land and Lee in the Bosphorus and Aegean; or Views of Athens and Constantinople. By Rev. Walter Colton... Edited from the notes and manuscripts of the Author. By Rev. Henry T. Cheever.*** New York: D. W. Evans & Co., 1860.

8vo, pp. 366, + 6 pp. of adverts (p.1=ht). Wood-engraved frontispiece of Constantinople by Jocelyn and Purcell and 1 plate. Modern green morocco panelled in blind.

Third edition. The first edition was published in 1836 as *A Visit to Constantinople and Athens*. The second edition appeared in 1851. Note that a Dublin edition was printed in 1849 under the original title. In 1832 Colton was appointed chaplain to the 'Constellation' which sailed from Virginia to Smyrna. The 'Constellation' remained in the Mediterranean for three years. Colton produced an account of this journey in *Ship and Shore, or leaves from the journal of a cruise to the Levant*, New York, 1835. *Land and Lee* contains an account of his travels on the return cruise when he visited mainland Greece and the Argolid.

LoC DR721.C724 1860; GL GT1139.5; this edition not in Blackmer but see 382 (2nd edition). This edition not in Atabey but see 265 (1st edition).

160. COMBES, Edmond. ***Voyage en Égypte, en Nubie dans les déserts de Beyouda, des Bicharys, et sur les cotes de la Mer Rouge.*** Paris: Desessart, 1846.

2 vols, 8vo, pp. [vi] I-XVI, 1-376 + [1]; [iii] 1-484 (pp.[i]=hts, [1]=errata, pp.1 in both vols=chapter sts). With a large folding map of Egypt by A. Vuillemin, engraved by Schwaer. Old quarter brown roan, gilt panelled backs.

First edition. Combes, French vice-consul at Scala Nuova (Kusadasi), travelled in Egypt and Nubia in 1841. He had previously written *Voyage en Abyssinie*, 1838.

Not in BNF on line. Blackmer 385; Hilmy I, 141; Carre I, 272.

161. COMSTOCK, John Lee. *History of the Greek Revolution; compiled from official documents of the Greek Government; Sketches of the War in Greece, by Philip James Green, Esq... and the recent publications of Mr. Blaquiere, Mr. Humphrey, Mr. Emerson, Count Pecchio, Rt. Hon. Col. Stanhope, The Modern Traveller, and other authentic sources.* New York: William W. Reed, 1828.

Sm. 8vo, pp. Iv, 5-503 (p.i=t). With a folding frontispiece and a folding engraved plate. Contemporary tree calf, back gilt in compartments.

First edition, first issue. There is an issue with the date 1829 on the title. A second edition appeared in 1853 with an appendix on Byron and events up to 1851. The plates depict the fall of Missolonghi and the battle of Navarino. A map is mentioned on the title; this map is missing in almost all copies of the book. However, according to NUC it is present in one of the Library of Congress copies.

LoC DF805.C73; Blackmer 388; Droulia 1529.

162. CONDER, Josiah. *A Popular Description of Greece. Geographical, historical and topographical. Illustrated by Maps and Plates. By Josiah Conder. In Two Volumes. Vol. I. [... Vol. II.]* London: James Duncan and Thomas Tegg [?1827].

2 vols in 1, 12mo, pp. [i] iv, 1-375; [i] iv, 1-336 (pp.[i]=hts, i=ts). With frontispiece map of Greece (missing in this copy) and 7 engraved plates (1 in v.1, 6 in v.2). Original red cloth, rebacked, red pictorial gilt spine laid down.

Second edition of *The Modern Traveller*, with the title beginning 'A popular Description of...' followed by the name of the country described, and with Conder's name on the title. The original series was published anonymously in parts beginning in 1826. The parts on Greece formed volumes 15 and 16 of the original series; it is debatable whether they appeared in 1826 or 1827. The series had a considerable success and the work immediately began reprinting. The appearance of Conder's name on the title in subsequent editions probably resulted from the general acclaim which the work received on its publication. The series was reprinted in 1830-31 under its original title, which does not include the name of country described, this appearing on the half title only. *The Modern Traveller* was a very successful encyclopaedic work on the different

countries of the globe. The plates, after L. Vulliamy, T.L. Donaldson and J. Wolfe, depict Argos, Corinth, Patras, Eleutherai, Athens and Aegina (v.2) while v.1 contains a folding map of Greece and a plate of Mistra.

Droulia 1144. This edition not in BLC. See Blackmer 394.

163. CONDER, Josiah. *The Modern Traveller. A Descripton, geographical, historical and topographical, of the various Countries of the Globe. In thirty Volumes. By Josiah Conder. Volume the Fifteenth [...the Sixteenth].* London: James Duncan, MDCCCXXX. [=1830]

2 vols, 12mo, pp. iv (recte vi) 1-375 [1]; iv (recte vi) 1-336 (pp.i=hts, v-vi=conts, [1]=colophon). With an engraved map and 6 (of 7) plates; this copy lacks the plate of Argos. 19th c. polished calf, back gilt in compartments, red leather labels. Later ownership signature of Clarentia Chichester on fly-leaf.

Third edition of this account of Greece, first published anonymously in 1826, the name of the country described appearing not on the title, but on the half title. The work was reprinted between 1830 and 1831 with its original title, but with Conder's name added to it, as above. However, there is a variant issue, see below.

BL 566.a.1-30; Droulia 1856. See Blackmer 393, 394.

164. [CONDER, Josiah.] *The Modern Traveller. A Popular Descripton, geographical, historical and topographical, of the various Countries of the Globe. Greece. Vol. II.* London: James Duncan, MDCCCXXX. [=1830]

Vol. 2 only, of 2, pp. iv, 1-336 (p.i=t, iii-iv=conts). With 6 (of 7) engraved plates. Uncut in the original cloth, printed paper title label on back. Upper joint split.

?Third edition, another issue, with a variant title and without Conder's name on the title. The title and contents pages have been reprinted, while the rest of the sheets are the same as the edition above. The second volume only. This appears to be a variant of the third edition of this very successful series. Titles of third edition copies normally contain only the volume number of the entire series, without reference to the country described, and also include Conder's name on the title, as the copy above. And normally the words 'Popular Description' without reference to the 'Modern Traveller' occur on second edition titles. Apparently there is no real chronological distinction between these editions or issues. The original volumes were produced anonymously; possibly when the work became successful Conder wished his name to appear on the title. The original format without country name on title could have been the result of the work being printed in parts, the title being supplied at the end of each complete part with volume number only for the sake of convenience, and then new titles supplied with the country name. This volume contains 6 of the 7 plates.

This edition not in BLC. See Blackmer 393 and 394.

165. COOK, Joel (1842-1910). *The Mediterranean and its Borderlands. Illustrated in two volumes Vol. I Western Countries [... Vol. II Eastern Countries].* Philadelphia: John C. Winston, 1910.

2 vols, 8vo, pp. vii, 609; [v] 648 (p.i, [i]=ts). Titles in red and black. With 2 photographic frontispieces and 48 plates. Original blue decorative cloth gilt, upper edge gilt.

First and apparently only edition. Cook was a miscellaneous travel writer who also produced Holiday Tour in Europe, 1870, and America, picturesque and Descriptive, 1900.

LoC D973.C75. Not in BL on line.

CORDELLAS. See KORDELLAS

166. CORNILLE, Henri. *Souvenirs d'Orient... Constantinople.– Grèce.– Jérusalem.– Égypte. 1831.– 1832.– 1833. Deuxième édition. Avec vignettes.* Paris: Arthus Bertrand, MD.CCC.XXXVI. [=1836]

8vo, pp. [iii] ii, 416 (p.[i]=ht, pp.i-ii=avant propos, 415-16=conts). With woodcut frontispiece and title and 1 woodcut plate. Quarter vellum over green marbled paper boards.

Second edition, first published in 1833. An interesting account of life and manners in the Levant. Cornille, who travelled in the Levant from 1831-1833 was in touch with Ottoman political functionaries. In Greece he visited the Argolid, which was the first seat of Otho's government, and he discusses the political questions connected with the arrival of King Otho in Greece.

BNF 30273117; Weber 238. See Blackmer 406 and Atabey 284 for 1st edition.

167. CORONELLI, Vincenzo (1650-1718). *Memorie Istoriografiche delli Regni della Morea, e Negroponte e Luoghi adiacenti descritte e consecrate all' Altezza Serenissima del Sig.ʳ Principe Masssimiliano Guglielmo Duca di Brunsuich, Luneburgo, &c. Generale dell' Armi Venete dal P. Mro. Moro Min. Conv. nel Laboratorio del P.M. Coronelli Cosmografo della Sereniss. Republica di Venezia.* [Venice: Coronelli, 1686.]

Folio, [i] + [88] (?of 110 or 98, see below); (p.i=ded, pp.[1-88]=text). With an engraved half title, engraved title, engraved plate of arms, and 15 (of 16) engraved double-page plates (lacking the plate 'Battaglia sotto Calamata'). Extra-illustrated with 8 vignette plates. Vignettes in letterpress. Contemporary pasteboards, vellum back.

First edition of this important work, the best-known of all Coronelli's productions, although the first edition is relatively uncommon. Coronelli had been asked by the Venetian Senate to prepare a publication on the Venetian conquests in the Morea during the war of the Holy League (Venice, Poland, Austria) against the Turks in 1685 and 1686. He began by producing the *Conquiste della Ser[enissima] Republica di Venezia nella Dalmazia, Epiro et Morea durante la Guerra intrapresa contro Meemet IV*, 1686. This work, dedicated to four Venetian generals and their conquests in specific geographical areas (lower Hungary, Dalmatia, Epirus and the Morea), included eleven plates which Coronelli used in the *Memorie Istoriografiche*, 1686, his second production connected with the Venetian-Turkish conflict, which describes only the action in the Morea. The text is by Padre Moro, and Coronelli prepared five additional plates of views. The vignettes include sites not connected with the Morea; what Coronelli's purpose was in preparing these plates is not clear. Perhaps he already envisioned future publications in which he would use these plates. As we know, Coronelli continued to produce collections of various plates under different titles up to 1707. We include below a list of the double-page plates in this copy, as well as the hors texte vignette plates which may be regarded as extra-illustrations. Armao does not call for hors texte vignettes in this edition, but copies do occur with differing numbers of hors texte vignette plates; this is probably due to the fact that the small edition of the *Memorie* was being prepared in Coronelli's laboratory at roughly the same time as the folio edition, and copies seem to have been made up at random.

This edition not in BLC; this edition not in Blackmer; not in Weber; Armao 33, pp. 79-80. See L. Navari, 'Vincenzo Coronelli and the Iconography of the Morea' in *Annual of the British School at Athens*, v. 90, 1995. COPAC cites copies at Oxford and Edinburgh which call for 98 pp.; Atabey 286 calls for 110 pp. but the collation and pagination do not agree, so this number may be incorrect. The Contominas copy must lack 2 or 3 leaves, because there are only 11 text vignettes instead of the 15 which are called for by Armao.

DOUBLE-PAGE PLATES:
Patrasso; Navarino citta e fortezza; Citta e fort: di Coron; Coron; [Turkish standard]; Citta... di Coron battuta; Piazza di Calamata; Zarnata; Fort: di Chielafa; Passava; Napoli di Romania; Fortezza della Prevesa e Santa Maura; Fort: di S. Maura; Santa Maura; Cerigo. Lacking Battaglia sotto Calamata.

HORS TEXTE VIGNETTES:
Golfo d'Engia; Megara; Citta di Atene; Negroponte; Prospecto di Volo; Della Fort: di Volo; Dardanelli di Lepanto; Lepanto.

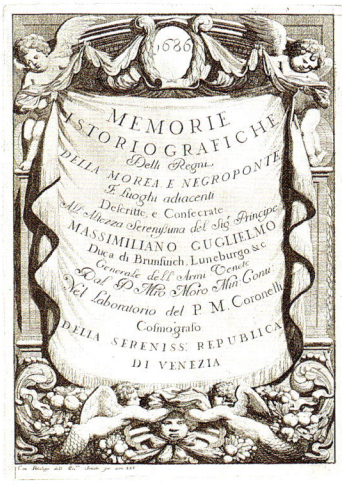

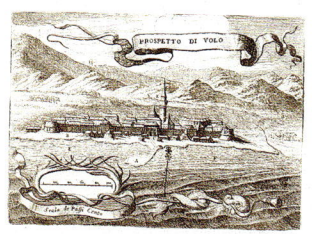

DICHIARATIONE
Delle lettere poste nel presente
DISEGNO DEL
Del prospetto della Fortezza
DI VOLO

A. Molo
B. Magazzini
C. Porta dalla parte di Mare
D. Torrioni intorno la Fortezza
E. Moschea
F. Vltimo reccesso del Golfo di Volo

167

TEXT VIGNETTES:

Allegorical plate (Venice triumphant); Modone; Veduta di Zarnata dalla parte di Greco; Sparta; Maina; Malvasia; Isola di Corfu, Cefalonia, Fortezza di Assos; Isola di Zante; Porto di Cerigo.

168. CORONELLI, Vincenzo. *Memorie Istoriografiche de' Regni della Morea, Negroponte e Littorali fin' a Salonichi Accresciute in questa seconda edizione. Nel Laboratorio del P. M. Coronelli Cosmog[rafo] della Ser. Republica di Venezia. Con Privilegio dell' Ecc. Senato per anni XXV Se vende alla Libraria del Colosso sul Ponte di Rialto.* [Venice: 1686.]

8vo, pp. [xii] 1-237 (p.[i]=engraved t). With 43 engraved double-page plates. Vellum antique.

First octavo edition. This small edition is referred to as the second on the title because Coronelli regarded the folio edition of 1686 as the first edition. Although undated, this edition probably appeared in the late summer of 1686. It includes all the plates which appeared in the folio edition as well as the hors texte vignette plates listed above: the 16 double-page plates from the large edition were re-engraved in reduced versions and the 15 vignettes which originally were printed in the letterpress are printed in the octavo edition as separate plates. This edition also includes a map of the Morea, an allegorical plate of Venice, and a plate of the Turkish horse tails which accompanied the standard. It was this edition of Coronelli's *Memorie della Morea* which exercized such influence throughout Europe. Translations appeared at London, Frankfurt, Paris, Amsterdam and Antwerp, and Coronelli's plates were used as the basis for many illustrated works, such as that of Dapper's *Morea*, Tebaldi's *Morea Rediviva*, and the many works produced by Johann Hoffmann or Jacob Enderlin. A second octavo edition appeared in 1687 with some new plates.

168

BL 10125.a.35; Weber 806. This edition not in Blackmer or Atabey. See L. Navari, 'Vincenzo Coronelli and the Iconography of the Morea' in *Annual of the British School at Athens*, v. 90, 1995.

169. CORONELLI, Vincenzo. *An Historical and Geographical Account of the Morea, Negropont, and the Maritime places, as far as Thessalonica. Illustrated with 42 maps of the countries, plains, and draughts of the Cities, Towns and Fortifications. Written in Italian by P. M. Coronelli, Geographer to the Republick of Venice. Englished by R. W. Gent.* London: for Matthew Gillyflower and W. Canning, 1687.

Sm. 8vo, pp. [viii] 1-230 + [1] (p.[i]=t, [vi-vii]=list of plates, [1]=advert). With 40 (of 42) maps, plans, views, mostly folding. Lacking the views of Coroni and Negropont, and the flow of Evripus. Old calf, red leather label gilt, upper joint cracked. With the Hopetoun bookplate.

169

First edition in English of Coronelli's *Memorie istoriografiche della Morea*, 1686. The translator R.W. has not been identified. The English edition is among the scarcest of the editions of Coronelli's Morea. Note that the view of Volos is not in the list of plates; whether this should be considered an extra-illustration is debatable. It would seem likely that the full complement of plates from the Italian edition (43) should be present, but note that the Amsterdam edition, from which the English edition plates are taken, also has only 42 plates.

BL 572.a.16. This edition not in Blackmer but see 407 for the Dutch edition. This edition not in Atabey.

170. CORONELLI, Vincenzo, and Andrea PARISOTTI. *Isola di Rodi geografica-storica, antica e moderna coll' altre adiacenti, già possedute da Cavalieri Hospitalieri di S. Giovanni di Gerusalemme. Dedicate all' Eminentissimo, e Reverendissimo Principe il Signore Cardinale Panfilio Gran Priore di Roma dell' Ordine Gerosolim, &c.* Venice: [Coronelli], 1695.

8vo, pp. [i] 1-430+ [2] (p.[i]=t, [1-2]=errata). With 15 engraved plates (out of 21). Half mottled calf, back gilt in compartments. Bookstamp of W. B. Chorley on title. From the library of Şefik Atabey, with his book label.

170

Second edition, reprinted from the first edition of 1688. The first edition has an engraved title instead of a printed title, and it also contains a 30-page appendix of the members of the Academy of Argonauts, the earliest geographical society to have been founded in Europe. This work on Rhodes and its neighbouring islands is dedicated to the Knights of St. John of Jerusalem, also known as the Knights of Rhodes, and later as the Knights of Malta; the dedicatee Panfilio was Grand Prior of the Order at Rome. This copy lacks six plates: the frontispiece, the large folding map of the Archipelago, the two maps of Caloiero, the plate of the ruins of Scoglio Capra, and the plate of the arms of the Knights of Rhodes.

Blackmer 411; Atabey 289 (this copy); Armao 95. This edition not in GL or BLC.

171. CORSINI, Edoardo. *Notae Graecorum sive vocum et numerorum Compendia. Quae in aereis atque marmoreis Graecorum tabulis observantur... accedent dissertationes sex quibis marmora quaedam tum sacra tum profana exponuntur ac emendantur.* Florence: 'Typographio Imperiali', MDCCIL. [=1749]

2 parts in 1, folio, pp. XXXXVIII, 1-92, CXXXII (I=ht, III=title in red and black, I=st to appendix). With a folding woodcut of an inscription. Contemporary speckled calf, back ruled gilt. Ownership inscription of Cambridge School Library dated 1758 on both titles.

First edition. Corsini also wrote *Inscriptiones Atticae*, 1752. He was especially interested in the ancient games, and in inscriptions as a historical source. He maintained a correspondence with the antiquarian Paciaudi (q.v.). This work is dedicated to Angelo Maria Quirini.

BL 145.g.1; Brunet II, 309.

172. COVEL, John. *Some Account of the present Greek Church, with reflections on their present Doctrine and Discipline; particularly in the Eucharist, and the rest of their seven pretended Sacraments; compared with Jac. Goar's Notes upon the Greek Ritual, or Ευχολόγιον.* Cambridge: for Cornelius Crownfield, and sold by James Knapton, Robert Knaplock, and William Taylor in London, MDCCXXII. [=1722]

Folio, pp. [xiv] 1-400 + [10] (pp.[i]=ht, [xi-xiii]=list of subscribers, pp.[1-10]=index). With 3 (of 4) engraved plates. Contemporary Cambridge calf, rebacked.

First and only edition. Extracts from Covel's diaries were published by Theodore Bent in his *Early Voyages and Travels in the Levant*, 1893. Covel spent seven years in Constantinople (1670-1676) as chaplain to the embassies of Sir Daniel Harvey and his successor Sir John Finch. There was a great deal of interest in the doctrines of the Orthodox Church at that time in England, and he was asked by several English bishops to investigate the tenets of the Church, particularly the doctrine of Transubstantiation. The subscribers include George Wheler and the botanist John Ray. The plates illustrate priestly robes and other accoutrements.

BL 487.k.3; Blackmer 420; Spencer pp. 96, 99, 108.

173. CRAVEN, Elizabeth, *Lady*. *A Journey through the Crimea to Constantinople. In a Series of Letters from the Right Honourable Elizabeth Lady Craven, to His Serene Highness the Margrave of Brandebourg*

C

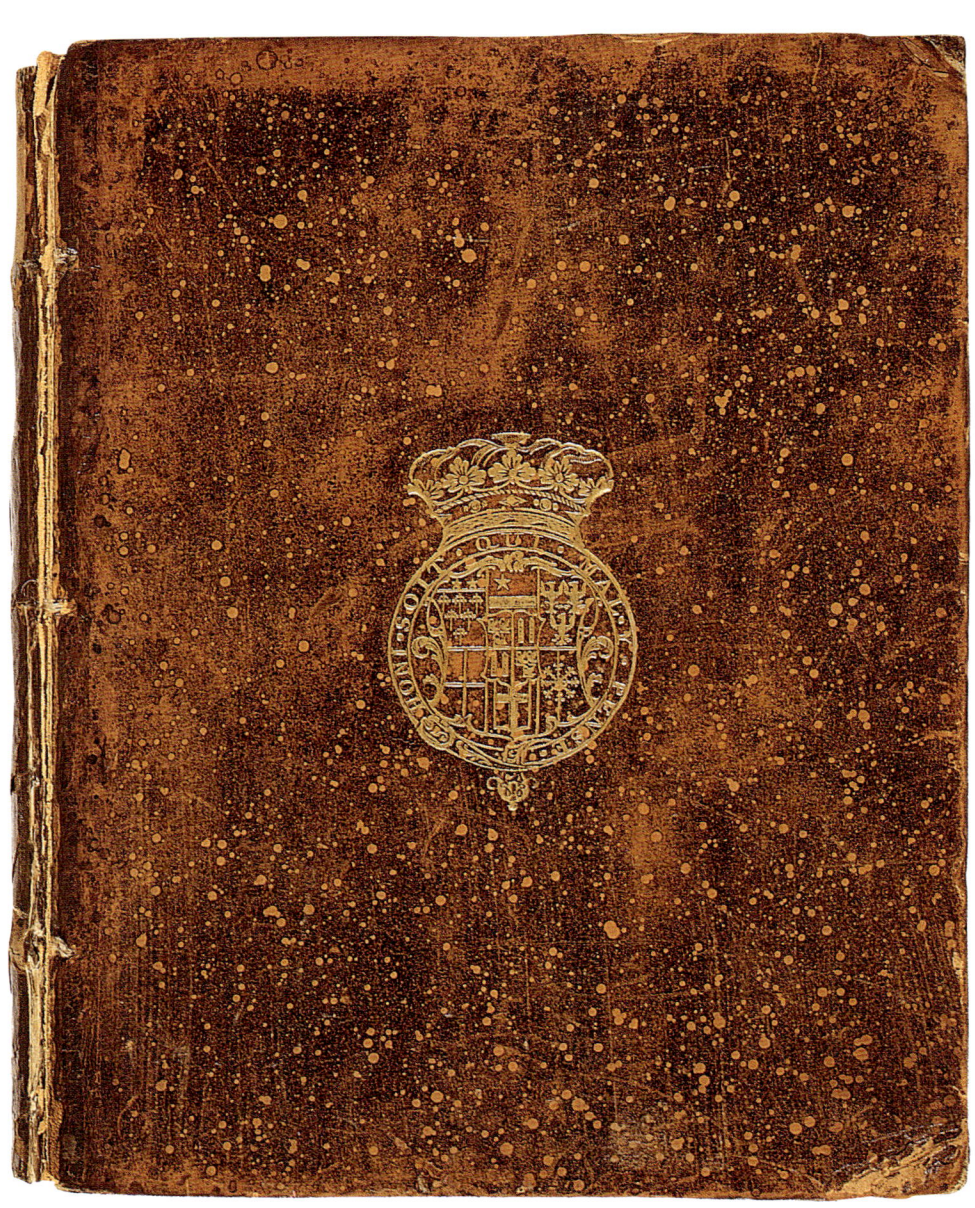

173

[sic], Anspach, and Bareith. Written in the year M DCC LXXXVI. London: for G.G.J. and J. Robinson, MDCCLXXXIX. [=1789]

4to, pp. [viii] 327 [1] (pp.[i]=ht, [1]=dir. to the binder). With an engraved map of the Crimea and 6 plates. Contemporary calf, central gilt arms on both sides.

First edition. The British Library also cites a second edition dated 1789 which appears to be a reprint of the first. A Dublin edition in 8vo also appeared in 1789 and a 'second edition' in folio appeared in 1814 under the imprint of Colburn. An English edition also appeared at Vienna in 1800. The popularity of this work may be due to the fact that it is connected with the journeys made by Lady Craven after she separated from her husband in 1783; in fact it is composed of letters written between June 1785 and August 1786 to the man she eventually married after her divorce. Among the most interesting letters is her account of Choiseul-Gouffier, whom she visited during her sojourn in Constantinople; she discusses many details of his activities as a collector. The plates include views of Gavrion in Andros, Siphnos and the Grotto of Antiparos.

BL 149.h.15; Blackmer 424; Weber 614; Atabey 297.

174. CRAVEN, Elizabeth, *Lady*. **Voyage de Milady Craven à Constantinople, par la Crimée, en 1786. Traduit de l'Anglois, par M. D***.** Paris: Durand Père & Fils, MDCC.LXXXIX. [=1789]

8vo, pp. [iii] 1-306 + [2] (pp.[i]=ht, ii=advert, iii=t, p.[1-2]=privilege). Folding map of the Crimea engraved by P.F. Tardieu, and six no'd engraved plates. Modern red leather gilt.

First edition of this French translation of Lady Craven's voyage by P.-Noel Durand, son of the publisher of the work. The plates include views of Andros, Siphnos and the Grotto of Antiparos. Another translation, by Pierre Guedon de la Berchere appeared the same year. A German translation also appeared at Leipzig in 1789.

BNF 30284980; Atabey 298. This edition not in Weber, but see Weber 616.

175. CUNLIFFE-OWEN, E. Betty. **Silhouettes of Republican Greece (Romances and Refugees). Foreword by Mr. H. Morgenthau, Chairman of the Refugee Settlement Commission, formerly Ambassador to the United States in Constantinople.** London: Hutchinson & Co. [1927].

8vo, pp. 278 (p.1=ht). With photographic frontispiece and 23 plates of photographic illustrations. Half green morocco over marbled paper boards, back gilt with meander pattern.

First edition. This very interesting work gives an account of the Settlement Commission inaugurated under the auspices of the League of Nations to deal with the prob-

lems of the exchange of populations between Greece and Turkey following the Asia Minor catastrophe. Mrs. Cunliffe-Owen's husband was employed by the Commission; she spent two years with him in Greece in the early 1920s. There is a long discussion of the Refugee Loan. Mrs. Cunliffe-Owen also wrote *Thro' the Gates of Memory From the Bosphorus to Baghdad*, c. 1925.

BL 10127.g.8; GL GT2104.2.

176. CURIO, Caelius Augustinus. ***Sarracenische Geschichte und Schröckliche Kriegsrüstung, welche die Sarracenen von ihrem ersten Auffgang an, bisz zu ihres Reichs Abgang, auff den Ersten Türckischen Keyser Othoman siebenhundert Jar lang, wider das Römisch Reich, und die Christen ... haben begangen... Von dem Hochgelehrten Herrn Coelio Augustino Curione... in Latinischer Sprach beschrieben... in das Teutsch gebracht, durch Nicolaum Höniger von Tauber Königshofen. Mit Röm. Key. May. Gnad und freyheit. Getruckt zu Basel, Durch Sebastian Henricpetri.*** [Basle: Henricpetri, 1580.]

Sm. folio, pp. [xx], 215 [1] (p.[i]=t, [1]=printer's device). With 10 woodcut illustrations in the letterpress of which 5=double-page maps and views. Modern vellum.

First edition in German. The first edition appeared at Basle in 1567, in Latin. An English translation was published in 1575 by Abraham Veale. The German translation has been dedicated by Höniger to Philip Elech von Schwartzenberg. The maps and views include the Arabian peninsula, Africa, the Holy Land, Constantinople and Cairo. The text consists of the three books of the Saracen History, and book 3 includes Giovio's history of the Turks.

GL TH13 C97qB; Göllner 1720. This edition not in BL on line.

177. CURTIUS, Ernst (1814-96), and J.A. KAUPERT. ***Atlas von Athen. Im Auftrage des Kaiserlich Deutschen Archäologischen Instituts.*** Berlin: Dietrich Reimer, 1878.

Sm. folio, pp. 35 (p.1=t and conts, 3-4=introduction, 5-35=explanation of the plates). With 12 no'd large folding plates. Original mauve cloth gilt, faded.

First edition. An important work, published on behalf of the German Archaeological School in Athens. The plates include both lithographs and engravings. The lithographs of views are by C. Unte after Peltz, printed by Leopold Kraatz. The engraved maps/plans, by Kaupert, were printed by H. Petters of Hildburghause. The great Ger-

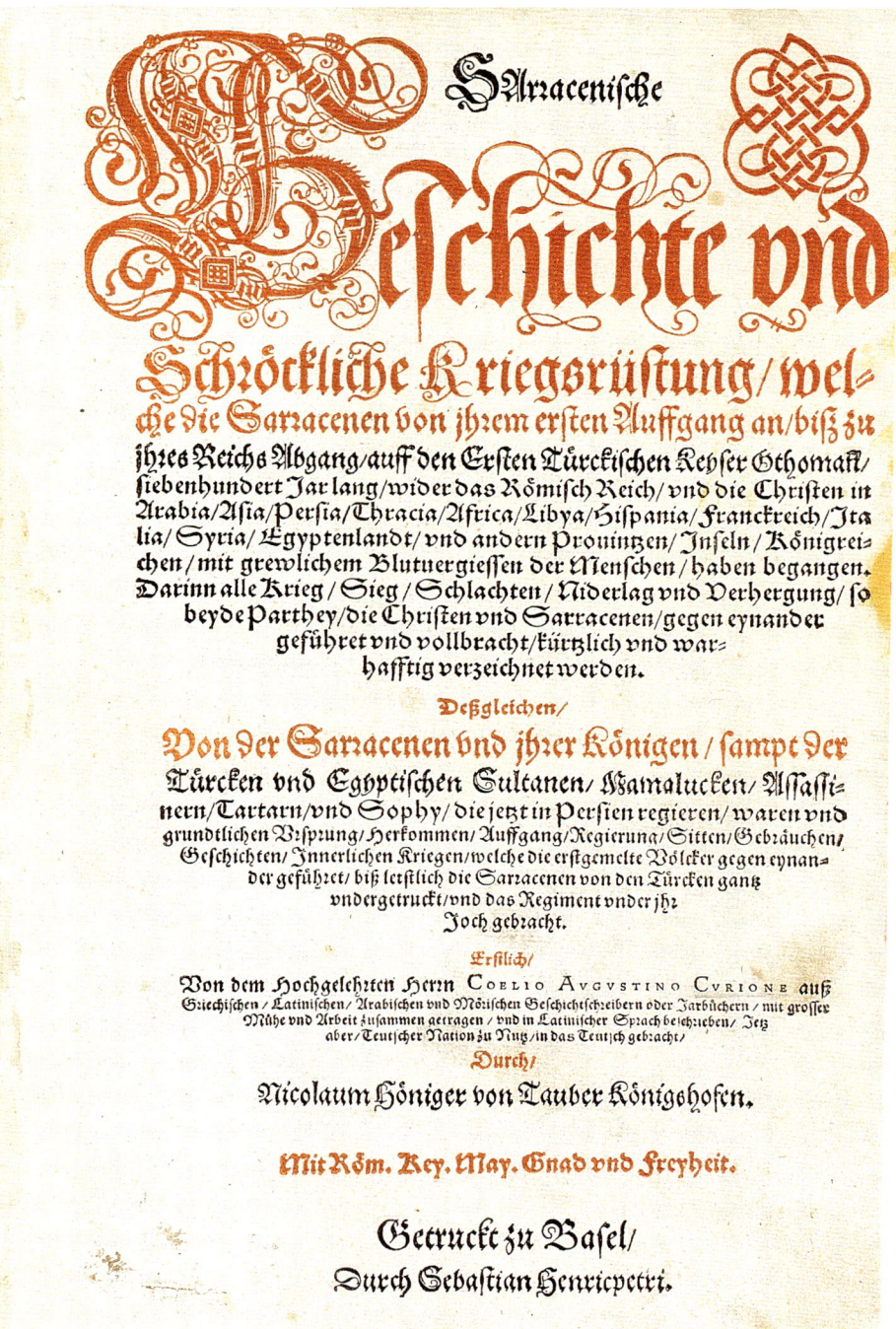

Sarracenische Geschichte vnd

Schröckliche Kriegsrüstung/ welche die Sarracenen von jhrem ersten Auffgang an/ biß zu jhres Reichs Abgang/auff den Ersten Türckischen Keyser Othomann/ siebenhundert Jar lang/wider das Römisch Reich/ vnd die Christen in Arabia/Asia/Persia/Thracia/Africa/Libya/Hispania/Franckreich/Italia/Syria/Egyptenlandt/ vnd andern Prouintzen/ Inseln/ Königreichen/ mit grewlichem Blutuergiessen der Menschen/ haben begangen. Darinn alle Krieg/ Sieg/ Schlachten/ Niderlag vnd Verhergung/ so beyde Parthey/die Christen vnd Sarracenen/gegen eynander geführet vnd vollbracht/kürtzlich vnd warhafftig verzeichnet werden.

Deßgleichen/

Von der Sarracenen vnd jhrer Königen/ sampt der Türcken vnd Egyptischen Sultanen/ Mamalucken/ Assassinern/Tartarn/vnd Sophy/ die jetzt in Persien regieren/ waren vnd grundtlichen Vrsprung/ Herkommen/ Auffgang/Regierung/ Sitten/ Gebräuchen/ Geschichten/ Innerlichen Kriegen/ welche die erstgemelte Völcker gegen eynander geführet/ biß letstlich die Sarracenen von den Türcken gantz vndergetruckt/vnd das Regiment vnder jhr Joch gebracht.

Erstlich/

Von dem Hochgelehrten Herrn COELIO AVGVSTINO CVRIONE auß Griechischen / Lateinischen/ Arabischen vnd Mösischen Geschichtschreibern oder Jarbüchern / mit grosser Mühe vnd Arbeit zusammen getragen / vnd in Lateinischer Sprach beschrieben/ Jetz aber/ Teutscher Nation zu Nutz/in das Teutsch gebracht/

Durch/

Nicolaum Höniger von Tauber Königshofen.

Mit Röm. Key. May. Gnad vnd Freyheit.

Getruckt zu Basel/
Durch Sebastian Henricpetri.

man archaeologist Curtius carried out many excavations in Greece, mainly at Olympia. He produced many books; one of his earliest works is *Peloponnesos eine historisch-geographische Beschreibung.*

BL MAPS 5.d.27; GL GT2168.5q.

178. CURZON, Robert, *Baron Zouche*. Visits to Monasteries in the Levant. Second Edition. London: John Murray, 1849.

8vo, pp. lv, 420 + 40 pp. + pp. 461-500 (p.i=ht, xix=list of plates, lv=st). With a wood-engraved frontispiece and title and 15 wood-engraved plates. Contemporary panelled calf gilt, sides panelled in gilt and blind with central gilt arms of 'G.B.', upper edge gilt. Armorial bookplate of Henry White, J.P., F.S.A.

Second edition, published the same year as the first edition, with an appendix which does not appear in the earlier edition. Curzon is one of the most interesting travellers of this period. He spent a long time in the Levant, beginning with his travels in 1833 which took him to Mt. Athos in 1837. In 1841 he was appointed attaché to the British embassy in Constantinople, and he later served as secretary to Sir Stratford Canning. In 1843-4 he was a member of the joint commission to determine the borders between Turkey and Persia. Curzon's account of his travels is considered 'a worthy companion even to *Eothen*', and many editions have appeared, with three editions in 1849, and a fourth in 1851. Numerous editions followed, including one with an introduction by D.G. Hogarth published in 1916. The work is illustrated by wood engravings after Preziosi, the originals of which Curzon had commissioned during his sojourn in Constantinople. This set of drawings, known as the 'Curzon Album', is now in the British Museum.

This edition not in BLC, but COPAC cites four copies; the Birmingham and University of London Library copies call for a folding plan. See Blackmer 436, Weber 415 and Atabey 301 for the first edition.

179. CURZON, Robert, *Baron Zouche*. Visits to Monasteries in the Levant. London: George Newnes, 1897.

8vo, pp. xxiv, 307 (p.i=ht). Title in red and black. With a frontispiece. Quarter leather, back gilt with black leather labels.

A late edition. The frontispiece depicts the Abyssinian library of the Monastery of Souriani. Part of Newnes' 'The New Library'.

BL 10076.bbb.28.

180. CUSANI, Francesco. ***La Dalmazia Le Isole Ionie e la Grecia (visitate nel 1840) Memorie Storico-Statistiche.*** Milan: Pirotta, 1846-47.

2 vols in 1, 8vo, pp. 1-320; 1-324 (pp.1=hts). With a large folding map of Dalmatia in vol. 1 and a folding map of Greece and the Ionian Islands in vol. 2. Quarter brown roan gilt over marbled paper boards, with the initials MB.

First and apparently only edition. The preface is dated 1845, but Cusani began his travels in 1840. The map of Greece is titled 'Nuova Carta itineraria della Grecia e delle Isole Ionie/ 1847/ F. Naymiller Inc.'; it contains a vignette of Athens in the lower left hand corner. Cusani was a prolific miscellaneous writer; among many other works he produced Italian translations of Bulwer Lytton and Walter Scott.

BNF 30292562; GL GT1110.38; Bib Ionienne 1494; Papadopoulos IB 3061.

181. CYRIAC, *of Ancona*. ***Kyriaci Anconitani Itinerarium nunc primum ex ms. cod. in lucem erutum ex bibl. illus. clarissimique Baronis Philippi Stosch. Editionem recensuit... [etc.] Laurentius Mehus. Florentiae MDCCXLII. Ex novo typographio Joannis Pauli Giovannelli ad Insigne Palmae Sumptibus Typographi. Praesidum Permissu.*** Florence: G.P. Giovannelli, MDCCXLII. [=1742]

Sm. 8vo, pp. lxxii, 1-80 (p.i=ht). Modern vellum, red leather label. Ownership signature of J.B. Van de Mortel dated 1800-1801.

First edition of the itinerary of Cyriac of Ancona. This is the earliest published account of Cyriac's travels in the Levant in the 15th century. Cyriac was born c. 1391 in Ancona and died some years before 1457; he is considered the founding father of modern classical archaeology. (According to the BLC some of his fragments or epigrams on Illyria were found and published c. 1664.) Cyriac made a number of journeys to the Levant beginning in 1412 with visits to Rhodes, Chios, Cyprus and Asia Minor. He travelled to Constantinople in 1418 and 1419 and visited many ports in the Aegean and eastern Mediterranean between 1425 and 1431; his visit to Athens took place in about 1450. The Itinerary was edited by Laurence Mehus from a manuscript in the possession of the antiquary and book collector Baron Philipp von Stosch, who had studied Greek with Bentley in England and knew the orientalists Banduri and Galland in Paris. Stosch's main interest was numismatics; his fine collection of gems was catalogued by Winckelmann in 1760. The catalogue of his important library was published at Florence in 1759.

BL 1046.b.29 calls for 86 pages; GL copy as ours with 80 pages; Weber 97.

182. DALLAWAY, James. *Constantinople ancient and modern, with excursions to the shores and islands of the Archipelago and to the Troad.* London: T. Bensley for T. Cadell Jr. and W. Davies, 1797.

4to, pp. xi [1] 415 + [6] + 1 p. advert (pp.i=t, [i]=dir to binder). With engraved title, 9 aquatinted plates, and an engraved map. Contemporary tree calf, back gilt, black leather label.

First edition, ordinary state. Large paper copies with coloured plates are also known. A French edition appeared in 1799, followed by German editions in 1800 (Chemnitz) and 1804 (Giessen). Dallaway spent 18 months in Constantinople as chaplain to Liston's embassy, 1794-96, having travelled overland with his entourage, which included the botanist Sibthorp and Gaetano Mercati, Liston's draughtsman. Dallaway travelled in the Troad in November, 1794, with Mercati and J.B.S. Morritt. The plates are by Bovinet after Mercati. Morritt's *Vindication of Homer* also used Mercati's plates.

BL 148.h.5; Blackmer 441; Weber 640; Abbey 392 (coloured copy); Lascarides 72; Atabey 308.

183. DALLAWAY, James. *Constantinople ancienne et moderne, et description des côtes et isles de l'Archipel et de la Troade... Traduit de l'Anglais par André Morellet.* Paris: Denné jeune, An VII. [=1799]

2 vols, 8vo, pp. viii, 1-371 [1]; [iii] 1-292 (pp.i=hts, [1]=advert, pp.365-71, 287-92=conts). With two engraved folding plates, a folding map of the plain of Troy and a folding table. Half red morocco gilt.

First edition in French, translated by André Morellet. A large paper edition in 4to is also known. The English edition was published in 1797 with nine plates. A German edition appeared at Giessen in 1804. Dallaway spent 18 months in Constantinople as chaplain to Liston's embassy, 1794-96. He travelled in the Troad in November, 1794, with J.B.S. Morritt and the draughtman Gaetano Mercati. The plates are by Bovinet after Mercati. Note that the French edition has fewer plates than the English.

BNF 33989598; GL GT709.2; Brunet II, 473. Not in BLC but COPAC cites one copy, at Leeds. See Blackmer 441 (English edition).

184. DALLAWAY, James. *Constantinople ancienne et moderne, et description des côtes et isles de l'Archipel et de la Troade... Traduit de l'Anglais par André Morellet. Tome Premier. [... Tome Second.]* Paris: Denné jeune, An VII. [=1799]

2 vols in 1, 4to, pp. viii, 371 [1]; [iii] 292 (pp.[i]=hts, [1]=advert). With 2 aquatinted frontispieces before letters by Bovinet after Mercati, a folding map and a folding table. Quarter green calf, green leather label.

First edition in French, translated by André Morellet. This is one of the large paper copies.

BNF cites 8vo issue only. GL GT709.2.

184

185. DALLAWAY, James. **Reise in die Levante. Mit Kupfern.** Giesen: Tasché and Müller, 1804.

Sm. 8vo, pp. 1-462 (p.1=first p. of text). Gothic letter. With an engraved title and frontispiece. Old marbled paper boards, ms. paper label.

Third edition in German. The first German edition was published by Tasché in 1800 at Chemnitz in 2 vols, 8vo, with a second at Berlin in 1801 under the title *Reise nach Constantinopel, der Ebene von Troja und in die Levante*. These may be different translations from our edition, but we have been unable to determine this. A fourth edition appeared at Giesen in 1806, also published by Tasché, with a preface by Dr. Crome and with the words 'Zweite Auflage' on the title, presumably the second publication of our edition.

This edition not in BLC on line. Weber 641. Karlsruhe cites copies at Friburg and Augsburg, but collations of text and plates do not agree. Not in Blackmer or Atabey.

186. DALTON, Richard. [*Antiquities and views in Greece and Egypt*. London: for Richard Dalton, 1751-1752.]

Folio, no title or letterpress. With 42 (of 43) engraved plates, numbered in manuscript. Full blue morocco, sides gilt with double filets, fleurons in the corners, back ruled gilt with fleurons, white silk liners.

The first state of these plates, before numbers, engraved for a projected work by Dalton which he intended to publish under the title 'Musaeum Graecum'. A prospectus for this work is preserved in the British Library. Present in this copy are the 23 plates of views and antiquities in Athens, together with the plate of Mt. Aetna in Sicily, engraved in 1751, and the additional views of Egypt (15), the Archipelago (2) and Constantinople (1), engraved in 1752. The plates are numbered in manuscript and plate 25 has been removed (one of the views of Constantinople). The work was never issued

186

as Dalton intended, although sometime after 1771 he published nine plates depicting the bas-reliefs from Halicarnassus, and in 1781 he published the 27 costume plates of Egypt. After Dalton's death in 1791 the entire series appeared with a general title page: *Antiquities and views in Greece and Egypt: with the manners and customs of the inhabitants: from Drawings made on the spot, A.D. 1749*, London, 1791, published by Thomas King and Henry Chapman. Dalton made the drawings during an excursion in the eastern Mediterranean in company with James Caulfeild, Earl of Charlemont, who had chartered a frigate in Italy in the spring of 1749 to tour the Levant. His party included his tutor Edward Murphy, Frances Pierpoint Burton, afterwards Baron Conyngham, and his friend Alexander Scott. Dalton was not a member of the original group, but met with Charlemont's party in Sicily, and in Malta he was persuaded to join it as resident artist. He left the party abruptly in 1750, presumably as the result of a quarrel with Charlemont. The engravings he published in 1751-52 appeared without Charlemont's support, and perhaps this is the reason for what seems to be a relative lack of success, despite the fact that they were the first engravings of many Greek monuments to be published in England. Not all of the drawings made by Dalton have been published; some are in the possession of the Royal Library at Windsor Castle. Dalton was later librarian and eventually keeper of pictures for George III.

BL 149.i.14(1); Weber 825; Colas 779; Brunet II, 475; Atabey 310. For the 1791 edition see Blackmer 443; See *The Travels of Lord Charlemont in Greece & Turkey*, edited by W. J. Stanford and E. J. Finopoulos, London, 1984.

187. [DALVIMART, Octavien.] *The Costume of Turkey, illustrated by a Series of Engravings; with Descriptions in English and French.* London: W. Bulmer for William Miller, 1804.

Folio, pp. [xiv] [120] (pp.[i]=English t, [iii]=French t). With 60 aquatinted plates, hand coloured. 19th c. green straight-grained morocco, sides framed in gilt and blind, with central blindstamp of eagle within a wreath, back diapered gilt.

Second edition, first published in 1802. This copy appears to be of the genuine 1804 edition, although the paper of this copy is not watermarked. According to Abbey, p. 370... "the first impression of this second edition, 1804, is on paper watermarked prior to 1804". There is a later reprint of this edition on paper watermarked 1818 for the text and 1820 for the plates. Although this work was issued anonymously, presumably because the text is edited from Tott, Dallaway, d'Ohsson and others, Dalvimart's name occurs on the plate imprints. According to the preface, he travelled in Turkey c. 1798 and took drawings on the spot. This information is confirmed by a letter of Fauvel's to Cousinery in which he mentions that Dalvimart was in Athens in 1797. Dalvimart's illustrations form the prototype for many collections of Ottoman costume, both

printed and manuscript. In particular they were used by William Alexander for his *Picturesque representations of the dress and manners of the Turks*, London, c. 1830. Reduced versions of the plates were used for Castellan's *Moeurs, usages, costumes des Othomans*, Paris, 1812.

This edition not in BLC, GL, Blackmer or Atabey. Not in Weber, but the GL has an 1804 edition which is also a late reprint. See Abbey 370 and 533 for an account of these reprints. See Blackmer 444 and Atabey 312-314 for other editions.

187

188. DAMER, Mary Georgina Emma, *Mrs. G.L. Dawson*. **Diary of a Tour in Greece, Turkey, Egypt, and the Holy Land. Second edition.** London: Henry Colburn, 1842.

2 vols in 1, 8vo, pp. [i] XII, 324; [i] VII, 335 (pp.[i]=hts, XII=list of ills. With 13 lithographed plates. Half green roan gilt.

Second edition, first published in 1841. The second edition is uncommon; it includes five appendices: one by Colonel Damer and four with reprints of letters from various newspapers on the return of the Jews to the Holy Land. The lithographs are after drawings by M. Chacaton, a French artist who accompanied the Damer party on its tour to the East during the winter of 1839-40.

BL T38540 OIOC. This edition not in Blackmer, Atabey, or Weber.

187

189. [DANIELO, Julien.] *Itinéraire de Paris à Jerusalem par Julien Domestique de M. de Chateaubriand publié d'après le manuscrit original appartenant à M. Lesouëf avec introduction et notes par Edouard Champion.* Paris: H. Champion, 1904.

8vo, pp. VIII, 1-127 [1] + 6 (pp.I=ht, [1]=imprint, 1-6=adverts). With a facsimile of the title of the journal and two folding facsimiles. Modern cloth, leather labels. Presentation copy from the editor Edouard Champion to his uncle, M. Lecheval[ier].

First edition, edited by Edouard Champion. Apparently three editions appeared in 1904, probably the same sheets with altered title pages. The Bibliothèque Nationale attributes the work to Julien Danielo, Chateaubriand's manservant. This work was published semi-privately and 27 copies were printed which were numbered; nos. 1 and 2 were printed on Japanese vellum and nos. 3-27 were printed on papier d'Arches. This copy is not numbered.

BNF 36565018; GL GT1004 is the 3rd edition, 1904.

190

190. DAPPER, Olfert. *Naukeurige Beschryving der Eilanden in de Archipel der Middelantsche Zee, en ontrent dezelve, gelegen: Waer onder de voornaemste Cyprus, Rhodes, Kandien, Samos, Scio, Negroponte, Lemnos, Paros, Delos, Patmos, en andere, in groten getale...* Amsterdam: Wolfgangh, Waesbergen, Boom, Someren, and Goethals, 1688.

Folio, pp.[xii] 1-24, 17-92, 1-84, 33-200, 1-152, 145-150, 143-200, 153-320, 40 (p.[i]=engr. t, p.[iii]=t, p.[xii]=dir to binder). Title in red and black. With 31 (of 32) engraved plates of maps, plans, and views of which 17=dp (some of the double-page engravings contain 4 maps and the single-page engravings 2 maps). Contemporary Dutch vellum, sides panelled in blind with central ornament.

First edition of Dapper's description of the Aegean Archipelago. A French edition was published in 1703, with a later French edition in 1730. The section on Crete was translated into Greek in 1836 by Manuel Bernardos. The pagination in the Dutch edition is not continuous: UBA, Koster and BL give various collations of the pagination; for this reason we give the collation of signatures below. Our copy contains 6 preliminary leaves, i.e. 12 unpaginated pages. The two-leaf 'Blatwyzer', A1-2, which normally occurs after p. 320, forms pp. x-xii in this copy. This collation of the preliminary leaves agrees with Koster. Dapper, a Dutch physician and scholar, was devoted to geographical studies. He himself did not travel in the Levant, but his encyclopaedic works are based on material collected from earlier sources. In the case of the *Archipel* he has used material from Boschini and Coronelli, as well as reduced versions of maps by Blaeu and other well-known cartographers and map publishers. The list of plates does not include all the hors texte plates in this work. This copy lacks the chart of the Archipelago.

BL 147.h.3; GL GT2591; UBA also cites a copy; Koster 36. This edition not in Weber, Blackmer or Atabey.
Collation: *^{4} A^2 A-C^4 ^{2}C^4 D-K^4 L^6 A-K^4 L^2 E-T^4 t^4 ^{2}t^4 v-2b^4 V-Z^4 2A-2R^4 A-E^4

191. DARCHINI, Gaetano. *Ellade (Note di Viaggio, 1909)*. Milan: Fratelli Treves, 1912.

8vo, pp.[vi], 1-23 (p.[i]=ht). Modern calf.

Apparently first and only edition. This is a mixture of sentimental thoughts on ancient Greece with some political discussion on the Young Turks, the Megali Idea, Garibaldi, etc. Darchini wrote on language questions; he is best known for his French-Italian dictionary. He also wrote *Alla ricerca di Gesu (note di un viaggio in Oriente 1906)*, Rome, 1910.

Not in GL. Not in BL or BNF on line. The Italian Union Catalogue on line cites three copies.

192. DAVESIÈS DE PONTÈS, Lucien (1806-1859). *Études sur l'Orient et l'Égypte. Seconde édition revue et corrigée.* Paris: Amyot, 1869.

8vo, pp.[iii] 1-480 (pp.[i]=ht, 479-80=conts). Brown morocco, back ruled gilt, original grey printed paper wrappers bound in.

Second edition, second issue. The first issue of the second edition is dated 1865. Davesiès de Pontès died in December, 1859. His widow arranged for the publication of a number of his works. The *Études* first appeared in 1864, edited from the author's manuscripts and with a biographical notice by Paul Lacroix ('P.L. Jacob', also known as 'bibliophile Jacob'). It includes 'Itinéraire de Navarin à Messéne 1831', 'Nauplie et l'Argolid', and 'Egypte en 1838'. The philhellene Davesiès de Pontès spent some years in Greece and the Levant. From 1828-30 he sailed with the 'Conquerant' in Greek waters, and he travelled in Greece in 1831 and 1833. He was in Egypt in 1838. His translation of Byron's *Childe Harold* appeared in 1862, and his *Notes sur la Grèce* in 1864.

BNF 30304401 (2nd edition 1865, but same pagination as our edition).

193. DAVY, John. *Notes and Observations on the Ionian Islands and Malta: With some remarks on Constantinople and Turkey... In two volumes, Vol. I. [... Vol. II.]* London: Smith, Elder & Co., MDCCCXLII. [=1842]

2 vols, 8vo, pp. 1-436 + adverts; xi, 1-500 (pp.1, i=hts). Lacking the folding map, 6 plates, folding table and the list of plates. Original embossed brown cloth. Ownership signature of Thomas Sherlock dated 1874 on fly-leaves.

First edition. The author was the younger brother of Sir Humphry Davy; he spent 11 years with the Army Medical Staff in the Mediterranean and as inspector general of Army Hospitals was in charge of the quarantine arrangements.

BL 1299.c.11-12; GL GT3309; Blackmer 460; Bib. Ionienne 1394; Papadopoulos IB 2815.

194. DE AMICIS, Edmondo. *Constantinople ouvrage traduit de l'Italien avec l'autorisation de l'Auteur par Mme J. Colomb et illustré de 183 dessins pris sur nature par C. Biseo.* Paris: Hachette, 1883.

Sm. folio, pp. [iv] 452 (pp.[i]=ht, [ii]=portrait of the author). Title in red and black. Numerous wood engravings in the text, some full-page, with versos blank, but still included in the pagination. Old three-quarter calf, green leather label.

First folio edition in French. The work was first published in Italian in 1877 and was frequently reprinted. At least fifteen Italian editions were produced. The first French edition was published in 1878 in 18mo and small editions also appeared in 1883, 1885, and 1892. The translator is Josephine Blanche Bouchet Colomb, i.e. Mme. Louis Casimir Colomb.

BNF 36574579; Weber 842. Atabey 19 (under Amicis) incorrectly states that this is the first French edition.

195. DELL, Anthony. *Isles of Greece. With a map and illustrations from photographs by the author and M. Roger Dell.* London: Geoffrey Bles [1926].

4to, pp. ix + [1] 226 (pp.i=ht, [i]=st). With 24 plates. Original quarter white buckram over blue cloth.

First edition of this tour of the Ionian and Aegean seas from May to June, c. 1925, including descriptions of Rhodes and Corfu. Dell, a dramatist, also wrote *Llama Land*, an account of travels in Peru.

BL 10125.f.4.

196. DEMETRIADES, Phokion. *Shadow over Athens.* New York: Rinehart [1946].

4to, pp. xiii, 1-155 (p.i=ht). Numerous full-page illustrations in text. Original grey cloth, with a dust jacket. Ownership signature of Julian S. Huxley on front fly-leaf.

First edition. A Greek translation appeared in 1970 as Σκιὰ πάνω ἀπ' τὴν Ἀθήνα. The illustrations are reproductions of monotone watercolour drawings depicting scenes of daily life in Athens under the German occupation, 1941-1945. The drawings include, among other subjects, the strike of 1943, Haidari concentration camp, and a mass execution in 1944. In 1947 Demetriades produced Τὸ παρδαλὸ καὶ ἡ ἐποχή του, a book of cartoons.

BL X.805/6564; GL HG810.D37.

197. DESCHAMPS, Gaston. *La Grèce d'aujourd'hui.* Paris: Armand Colin, 1892.

8vo, pp. [iii] 1-388 (p.[i]=ht, 387-8=conts). Uncut in quarter calf, with the original yellow printed paper wrappers bound in.

First edition. There were ten numbered copies on Holland Paper. A second edition appeared in 1897. The archaeologist turned journalist Deschamps travelled extensively in the Levant in the late 1880's, and his book reflects life in Greece and especially Athens at that period, with discussions of the politics, life and society of the capitol, and with accounts of literary personalities like Sourris and Psycharis. Interesting descriptions include Amorgos, Volos, Locris (Amphissa, Lidoriki and Mt. Othrys) and Thessaly. Deschamps was a member of the Committe of the French League for the Rights of Hellenism. He also produced *À Constantinople* and *Sur les routes d'Asie*, 1894, and he published an account of Amorgos in the *Revue des Deux Mondes*.

BNF 36577511. This edition not in Weber. Basch, pp. 242-46.

198. DESCHAMPS, Gaston. *La Grèce d'aujourd'hui. Quinzième édition.* Paris: Armand Colin, 1930.

8vo, pp. [iv] 1-408 (p.[i]=ht, 407-8=contents). Uncut in half calf gilt, original yellow printed paper wrappers bound in.

A late edition. This work was first printed in 1892.

Not in BNF on line.

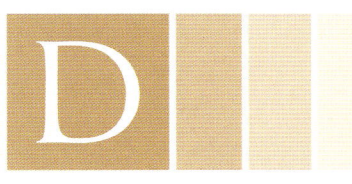

199. DESCHAMPS, Philippe. *De Saint-Petersbourg à Constantinople, recits de voyage.* Paris: E. Leroux, 1896.

Sm. 8vo, pp. 214 [1] (pp.1=ht, [1]=conts). Uncut in modern leather, original tan printed paper wrappers bound in.

?Fourth edition, so stated on the wrappers. It could be that the first edition also appeared in 1896. Deschamps was a prolific miscellaneous writer on travel and politics. In 1896 he also produced *A travers l'Égypte, le Nil, la Palestine*, and he wrote on Montenegro in 1902. A general collection of his voyages was published in 1900 as *Vingt mille lieues à travers le monde*.

BNF 30329062 (note BNF has only the fourth edition). Not in BLC on line.

200. [DESHAYES, Louis, *Baron de Courmenin.*] *Voiage de Levant fait par le commandement du Roy en lannée 1621 par le Sr. D. C.* A Paris. Chez Adrian Taupinart Rue S.ᵗ Iacques a la Sphere. 1624. [Paris: Taupinart, 1624.]

4to, pp. [vi] 1-404 [20] (p.[i]=t, pp.[1-19]=index, p.[20]=errata). With an engraved title and six engraved maps of which 4=dp and 2=folding. Four full-page woodcut views in the letterpress and a woodcut of the tugra on pp. 214 and 381. Old speckled red paper boards, with the shelf label of Count Schönborn-Buchheim on the upper cover. Large armorial bookplate of Michel d'Asquier de Ialion (with the motto 'Salus morientibus una') mounted on the verso of the title.

First edition, with a leaf of errata (3G4). A second edition was published in 1629 (2nd issue 1632) and a third in 1645. Deshayes de Courmenin was sent to the Levant in 1621 to establish a French consulate at Jerusalem, and he spent six weeks at Constantinople in order to obtain the necessary papers. Deshayes showed an unusual understanding of the Turkish political and military organization for this period. The plates: 'Bosfore', 'Constantinople qui est appellée par les turcs Stambol', 'Helespont a present Destroit de Galipoli', 'Plan de la Ville de Rode', 'Hierusalem', and a map of the coast of Asia Minor with the Hellespont and the Bosphorus.

This edition not in BNF on line. BL 790.i.22; Blackmer 479 (2nd ed.); Rouillard, pp. 243-8. Collation: a⁴ A-3G⁴ (a1=engr. t).

201. DE VERE, Aubrey Thomas. *Picturesque Sketches of Greece and Turkey. In Two Volumes. Vol. I. [... Vol. II.]* London: Richard Bentley, 1850.

2 vols, 8vo, p. viii, 306 + [1]; viii, 283 (pp.i=hts, [1]=advert). Original red embossed publishers' cloth, rebacked, original back preserved. With the endpapers composed of adverts.

First edition of this very interesting account of the young Greek state. De Vere, a poet and man of letters, friend of Coleridge, Wordsworth and Carlyle, discusses Greek politics, education and language. The date of this journey is unknown but in 1839 De Vere travelled in Italy; he may have continued on to the Levant in 1840. In 1843 he wrote *Search after Proserpine Recollections of Greece and other poems*.

BL 10125.b.15; Blackmer 481; Weber 432.

202. DIDON, Henri Louis (1840-1900). *La Dix-neuvième Caravane des Dominicains d'Arcueil [Constantinople Le Mt. Athos La Grèce. 19th Caravane d'Arcueil]* Paris: J. Mersch [1895].

Lge 8vo, pp. viii, 298 + [1] (p.i=[], [1]=colophon). With 27 photographic plates. Numerous illustrations in the text. Half calf, original wrappers bound in, uncut.

Apparently first edition. There is another issue of this work published under the subtitle, see below. The title of the work is unclear; the BNF lists it as 'Aux Jeunes'. The work seems to form part of a series published under the title of 'Caravane des Dominicains d'Arcueil' and apparently addressed to the Catholic youth of France.

BNF 30341128 attributes the date 1895; BL 10125.ee.34.

203. [DIDON, Henri Louis.] *Constantinople Le Mt. Athos La Grèce Épisodes d'un voyage en Orient.* [Paris: J. Briguet, c. 1895.]

Lge 8vo, pp. [viii] 298 + [1] (pp.[i]=[], [1]=colophon). With 27 photographic plates. Numerous illustrations in the text. Uncut in olive morocco gilt, original pale blue printed paper wrappers bound in.

Another issue, published by Briguet. The issue above was published by Mersch. The sheets are the same, but the printed wrappers differ.

Not in BNF or COPAC under this title.

204. [DIDOT, Ambroise Firmin (1790-1876).] *Notes d'un Voyage fait dans le Levant en 1816 et 1817.* Paris: Firmin Didot [1826].

8vo, pp. [vii] 1-403 (pp.[i]=ht, vi-vii=ded to Korais). Old quarter calf over marbled paper boards, back gilt with black leather label.

First and only edition, all published. The last leaf reads 'fin de la première partie', but the second part was never published. Only a small number of copies was published as the work was not intended as a commercial venture. It records Firmin Didot's experiences in Greece and Turkey in 1816 and 1817. He studied Greek with Korais in Paris and then went to Kydonies in Asia Minor to finish his studies. He was later attached to the French embassy in Constantinople. Didot was a devoted philhellene and became one of the principal founders of the Paris Greek Committee. He was also interested in promoting the cause of Greek letters and sent printing presses to Greece. The date of publication is interesting; 1826 saw the peak of French philhellenic publications.

BNF 30437592; Blackmer 485; Weber 142; Droulia 1123.

205. DIEHL, Charles (1859-1944). *Excursions archéologiques en Grèce Mycène – Délos – Athènes Olympie – Éleusis – Épidore – Dodone Tyrinthe – Tanagra.* Paris: Armand Colin, 1897.

8vo, pp. X, 1-386 + 2 (p.I=ht, 381-6=contents, pp.1-2=adverts). With eight numbered plans, several folding. Half brown leather over brown cloth, original yellow printed paper wrappers bound in.

Fourth edition, first printed in 1890. Note second edition also appeared in 1890. This work was translated into English in 1893 by Emma Perkins and into Greek in 1896 by Alexandros Karales. It is especially useful for tracing the early history of the excavations of important archaeological sites.

BNF 30341454. This edition not in BLC. Not in Weber.

206. DIEHL, Charles. *Excursions archéologiques en Grèce Mycène – Délos – Athènes Olympie – Éleusis – Épidore – Dodone Tyrinthe – Tanagra. Ouvrage couronné par l'Académie Française.* Paris: Armand Colin, 1921.

8vo, pp. X, 1-386 (p.I=ht). Uncut in half leather, faded, original yellow printed paper wrappers bound in.

A late edition, the tenth, first published in 1890. Two editions appeared in 1890 and a fourth in 1897.

207. DIEHL, Charles. *Excursions in Greece to recently explored sites of classical interest... translated by Emma R. Perkins. With an introduction by Reginald Stuart Poole.* London: [Hazell Watson and Viney for] H. Grevel, 1893; New York: B. Westermann.

8vo, pp. xxiv, 1-408 + 12 pp. of Grevel adverts (pp.i=ht, 403-8=index). Plans and illustrations in the text, some full-page. Half tan calf over marbled paper boards, uncut.

First edition in English, translated from Diehl's *Excursions archéologiques en Grèce* by Emma Read Perkins. The British Library Catalogue attributes the date [1892] to this edition and also cites what appears to be a later issue, dated 1893, under the imprint of Grevel only. The work was in fact printed by Hazell Watson and Viney in England. The preface is by Reginald Stuart Poole, son of Sophia Lane Poole, sister of the arabist Edward Lane. Poole was professor of archaeology at University College, London, and later Keeper of Coins at the British Museum.

BL 2258.b.17 (BLC entry cites 9 plates; this is a misprint for 9 plans). BLC attributes date [1892] to Grevel and Westerman issue.

208. DIEHL, Charles. *Justinien et la civilisation byzantine au VIe siècle.* Paris: Ernest Leroux, 1901.

Lge 8vo, pp. XL, 1-695 [1] (p.I=ht, [1]=errata). With nine photographic plates. Numerous illustrations in letterpress. Half black leather gilt over red marbled cloth, by Tourian Brothers of Cairo, with their ticket on front pastedown.

Apparently first and only edition. The work contains an extensive bibliography. The preliminaries in this copy have been misbound.

BNF 30341459.

209. DIEHL, Charles. *En Méditerranée Promenades d'histoire et d'art Spalato et Salone En Bosnie-Herzegovine Delphes - L'Athos Constantinople – Chypre et Rhodes Jerusalem. Quatrième édition.* Paris: Armand Colin, 1912.

8vo, pp. [v] 1-286 + [2] (p.[i]=ht, [v]=ded, [1-2]=adverts). Quarter red roan gilt over cloth, with the original yellow printed paper wrappers bound in. From the library of K.Th. Dimaras, with his stamp on p. 286 and p. [2].

Fourth edition, apparently first published in 1901. A later edition appeared in 1933.

This ed not in GL (1st and 2nd eds) or BNF (1st, 2nd, 3rd eds).

210. DIONYSIUS, *Periegetes.* **Dionysii Alexandrini Opus de Situ Orbis. Cum commentariis Eustathii Thessalonices Archiepiscopi. Abele Matthaeo Iurisconsulto interprete. Ad Principem clarissimum et lectissimum Cardinalem Carolum Lotaringum. Cum privilegio Regis. Parisiis, apud Poncetum le preux, via Iacobea, sub insigni Lupi.** [Paris: Poncet le Preux, 1556.]

4to, pp. [iv] + 2 unn. leaves + fol. 1-79 (recte 87), [27] (p.[i]=t, [iii-iv]=ded). Old sprinkled calf, rebacked, back ruled gilt, red leather label.

First and only edition of this Latin translation of Dionysius Periegetes by Abel Matthieu. There are numerous editions of the work, especially as a school text. This was also the case during antiquity, when the book enjoyed a high degree of popularity as a school book. Little or nothing is known of Dionysius, though there is some reason for believing that he was from Alexandria and worked during the Hadrianic period.

BNF 30324550; BL 304.k.16(2); Hoffmann I, 591; Brunet II, 781.

211. DIONYSIUS, *Periegetes.* **Dionysii Orbis Descriptio; cum commentariis Eustathii Archiepiscopi Thessalonicensis.** Oxford: Sheldonian, 1710.

8vo, pp. [iii], II-XIII, 2-199 (p.[i]=t, II=first leaf of Eustathios letter; n.b. p. 2 is on the verso of p. XIII). With four folding engraved maps by - Harris. Old polished calf. Ownership inscription of T.R. Salweg (?Salwey) dated 1772.

Edited by J. Hudson. This edition was first published in 1704 at Oxford; many editions followed. BLC cites an edition printed at Oxford in 1718 as the third edition. The four maps: 'Libyae seu Africae tabula', 'Europae tabula antiqua', 'Graeciae tabula antiqua', 'Asiae tabula antiqua'. There is a leaf missing before the text begins, possibly a subtitle, see collation below. The text is in Greek and Latin on facing pages. The pagination is determined by the placing of the Greek and Latin. The first Greek page=p. 2, the first Latin page=p. 3.

BL 999.f.9; Hoffmann I, 593.
Collation: π⁴ b⁴ A⁴ (–A1=?st) B-2B⁴

212. DIONYSIUS, *Periegetes.* **Διονυσίου Οἰκουμένης Περιήγησις. Dionysii Orbis Terrarum Descriptio. Recensuit et adnotatione critica instruxit Franciscus Passow. Accessit Tabula Geographica Lapidi Inscripta.** Leipzig: B.G. Teubner, MDCCCXXV. [=1825]

12mo, pp. XV, 1-104 (p.I=t). Greek letter. With an engraved frontispiece by Albert Wachler. Half vellum over red marbled paper boards.

A late edition of Dionysius Perigetes's description of the world, edited by Passow and dedicated to Johann Heinrich Vossius, through whom he had access to the geographical table illustrated in the frontispiece. Wachler was Passow's brother-in-law.

BL 11335.aaa.23; Hoffmann I, 593. Karlsruhe also cites a London edition dated 1825.

213. DIXON, William MacNeile. *Hellas Revisited. With illustrations by Mary R.L. Bryce.* London: Edwin Arnold [1930].

8vo, pp. xi, 1-209 + 2 pp. of adverts (pp.i=ht, xi=list of plates). With sixteen plates and two folding maps. Original blue cloth.

Second edition, first published in 1929. This is an account of a six-week journey in the spring of 1928. Dixon visited some relatively unusual places for this period: Mt. Helicon, Hippocrene, Osios Loukas, and the Ladon Gorge in Arcadia. The plates are pencil drawings by Mary Bryce made from photographs by the travellers, who included Captain and Mrs. Brodie, and Mr. and Mrs. Cecil Harmsworth. The dragoman was Constantinos Bizanis.

BL 10127.

214. DODWELL, Edward. *A classical and topographical tour through Greece, during the years 1801, 1805, and 1806.* London: Rodwell and Martin, 1819.

2 vols, quarto, pp.xii, 587 [1]; vii, 537 [1] + [2], (pp.i=ts, pp.[1]=imprints, pp.[1-2] in vol.2=errata). With a folding map and 66 engraved plates of which 6 double-page and 2 coloured. In contemporary speckled calf, sides gilt, backs pointillé gilt in compartments with fleurons and lozenges, brown leather labels. Armorial bookplate of Snelston Hall.

First edition of this important account of travels in Greece. The work was translated into German in 1821-2 at Meiningen. A rare *tirage à part* is also known (GL) in which india paper proofs of the plates are mounted on folio leaves. Dodwell's travels in Greece fall into two periods: in 1801 he toured the Ionian Islands and the Troad with Gell; in 1805, officially a French prisoner-of-war, he travelled in mainland Greece accompanied by the artist Simone Pomardi. During their travels Dodwell and Pomardi made upwards of a thousand drawings. Dodwell's *Views in Greece* are based on his own drawings, while most of the plates in the *Tour* are the work of Pomardi. Pomardi also produced his own account of this journey, *Viaggio nella Grecia*, 1820 (q.v.).

BL 148.h.16; Blackmer 492; Weber 62; Brunet II, 788.

214

121

215. DODWELL, Edward. [*Views and Descriptions of Cyclopian, or, Pelasgic Remains, in Greece and Italy; with Constructions of a later period; from drawings by the late Edward Dodwell.* London: Adolphus Richter, 1834.]

Folio, pp.[2]=list of plates. With 131 lithographed plates no'd 1-127 (+ 2b, 12b, 25b, 25c). Old half blue roan gilt, gilt edges.

First and only edition. This copy lacks the title page and all the text, with the exception of the last leaf, the list of plates. This is Dodwell's last work, published posthumously. He prepared the text for the Greek section only (plates 1-71). The work was edited by an anonymous friend of Dodwell's to whom he had bequeathed the plates, with instructions for publication. They were printed by the lithographic printer Hullmandel. Apparently a French edition was published simultaneously at Paris. This interesting work depicts many sites little-known at the time: Orchomenos, Aliartos, Salona (Amphissa) and so forth.

BL 762.h.9; Blackmer 494; Brunet II, 788. Not in Abbey or Weber.

216. DOUGLAS, Frederick Sylvester North. *An Essay on Certain points of Resemblance between the Ancient and Modern Greeks. Third edition, corrected.* London: C. Roworth and T. Davison for John Murray, 1813.

8vo, pp.[vii] 1-198 + [1] (pp.[i]=ht, [1]=imprint). Contemporary tree calf, back defective. Bookplate of M. Eardley with his motto 'Non Nobis Solum' and his crest, a deer.

Third edition, first published in 1813. In fact all three editions appeared the same year, and they are all scarce, especially the first. Douglas travelled in Greece in April, 1811, with his uncle, the philhellene Frederick North, Lord Guilford. Spencer (pp. 242-244) regards Douglas's work as the most accurate and balanced book about Greece published before the revolution. Douglas died in 1819.

This edition not in GL or BL (2nd editions only). Not in Blackmer.

217. DREUX, Robert de. *Voyage en Turquie et en Grèce du R.P. Robert de Dreux aumonier de l'Ambassadeur de France (1665-1669) publié et annoté par Hubert Pernot.* Paris: Société d'Edition "Les Belles Lettres", 1925.

8vo, pp. XI [1] 1-202 + [2] (I=ht, V=ded to Penelope Delta, [1]= acknowledgements, pp.[1-2]=adverts). Modern cloth, original printed paper wrapper bound in.

First edition. Pernot has edited Dreux's journal; he was a Capuchin priest and the uncle by marriage of the ambassador to Constantinople Haye-Vantelet. The original manuscript may be in the library of the Institut Neo-hellénique. This is part of the series 'Collections de l'Institut Neo-hellénique de l'Université de Paris', Fasc. 3.

BL Ac.442/4.(3.); BNF 31226170, giving preliminary pagination as XL, a misprint; comparison with the GL copy, GT 797.2, confirms the correct pagination as XI.

218. DRIAULT, Edouard (1864-1947). *La Question d'Orient depuis ses origines jusqu'à nos jours. Troisième édition revue.* Paris: Félix Alcan, 1905.

Lge 8vo, pp. XV, 407 (p.I=ht). Uncut in half red calf gilt over red marbled paper boards, black leather label, original rust printed paper wrappers bound in.

Third edition, first published in 1898, with a preface by Gabriel Monod. Driault kept revising this work and bringing it up to date. For example, the seventh edition appeared in 1917 as *La question d'orient depuis ses origines jusqu'à la Grand Guerre*; in 1921 he published *La question d'orient jusqu'à la Paix des Sèvres*; in 1938 appeared *La question d'orient 1918-1937*. Driault was a diplomatic historian who wrote many books on different aspects of the history of the Levant. Among his most important is the five volume *Histoire diplomatique de la Grèce*, 1925-26.

This edition not in BNF.

219. DRIAULT, Edouard. *La Grand Idée La renaissance de l'Hellénisme Préface de M. Politis Ministre [sic] des Affaires Étrangères de Grèce.* Paris: Félix Alcan, 1920.

8vo, pp. [v] VI, 1-242 + [1] (pp.[i]=ht, [ii]=advert, VI=pref. [1]=conts). Quarter black roan, back worn and defective.

First and apparently only edition, issued in the series 'Bibliothèque d'histoire contemporaine'. The preface is by Nikolaos E. Politis, minister of foreign affairs under the Venizelos government. It is interesting to note that this work was written just as Greece was drawn into the disastrous Asia Minor expedition which brought the Grand Idea to a halt in 1922.

BNF 31130882.

220. DRIAULT, Edouard, *editor*. *L'Expedition de Crète et de Morée (1823-1828) Correspondance des Consuls de France en Égypte et en*

Crète. [Cairo:] Institute Français de Archéologie Orientale, MCMXXX. [=1930]

Lge 8vo, pp. XXIII, 354 (I=[ ], III=ht, 315-54=conts). With two illustrations. Half blue leather.

First and only edition of this very important collection of documents covering most of the period of the Greek Revolution up to the Battle of Navarino.

BNF 32044741; GL IND162.17.

221. DRUMMOND, Alexander. *Travels through different Cities of Germany, Italy, Greece, and several parts of Asia, as far as the banks of the Euphrates: In a Series of Letters. Containing, an account of what is most remarkable in their present state, as well as in their monuments of antiquity.* London: W. Strahan for the author, 1754.

folio, pp. [iii], 1-311 (pp.[i]=t, [iii]=table of the Greek alphabet). With a large folding frontispiece and 34 engraved plates of which 15=folding. Contemporary calf, rebacked. Bookplate of Maud Hodgson.

First and only edition. Some sections were reprinted in J.H. Moore's *A New Collection of Voyages*, vol. 2, 1780. Drummond travelled in the Levant from 1744-1750. He was resident in Cyprus for some time, where he stayed with the British consul, George Wakeman. Drummond was himself appointed consul in Aleppo from 1754-56. This important work contains much information on Cyprus.

BL 457.e.2; Blackmer 497; Weber 524; Atabey 363; Spencer, p. 153,"... an impressive work, based unquestionably on intimate knowledge of Cyprus".

222. DU CHOUL, Guillaume. *Discorso... sopra la castrametatione, & bagni antichi de i Greci, & Romani. Con l'aggiunta della figura del Campo Romano. Et una informatione della militia Turchesca, & de gli habiti de soldati Turchi, scritta da M. Francesco Sansovino. In Vinegia, presso Altobello Salicato. MDLXXXII.* Venice: Altobello Salicato, 1582.

2 parts in 1, sm. 8vo, ff. 1-80 [4], 1-28 (p.1=t, pp.[1-4]=index). With a large woodcut folding plate. Numerous woodcut costume illustrations in the letterpress of both parts. Contemporary limp vellum.

Third Italian edition, but the first collected edition, with the additional material from Sansovino's *Historia dell'origine de Turchi*. Du Choul's French text was translated into Italian by Gabriel Simeoni. The first edition was printed by Rouille at Lyon in 1555; other French editions were published at Lyon in 1567 and 1581; a Spanish edi-

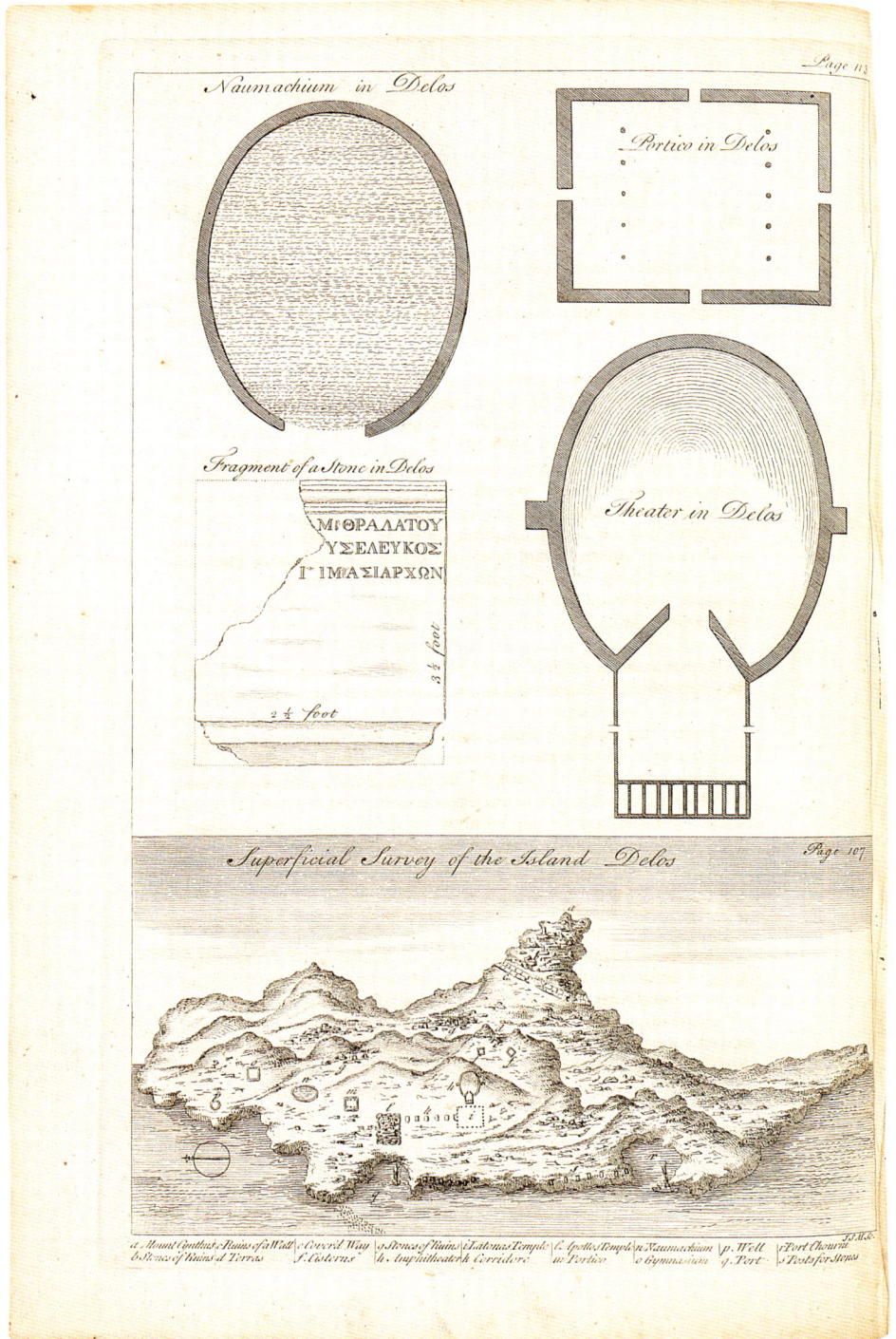

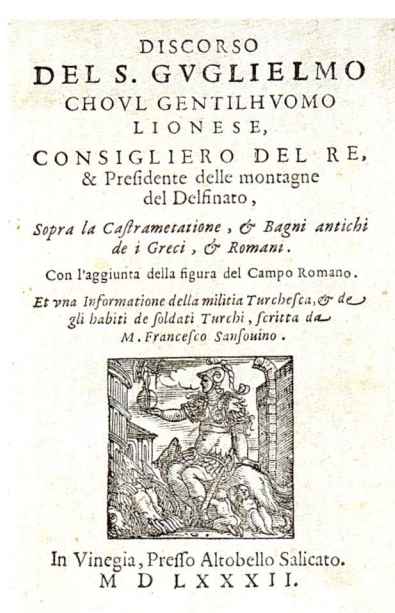

222

tion also appeared there in 1579. The first edition in Italian was printed at Padua in 1558/9 by the Olmo family, and the second Italian edition appeared at Lyon in 1559. This work, which may be one of the earliest on the subject of ancient baths, had a continuous success: Dutch and Latin editions were printed at Amsterdam in 1684 and 1685. Du Choul was a French antiquary from Lyon; he was one of the first Frenchmen to study medals, seals, bas-reliefs and other monuments of antiquity. He travelled to Italy in about 1550, and on his return he wrote the *Discorsi*. The costume plates in part two are after Nicolay. The plates in part one include Greek and Roman military costume figures, those in part two illustrate the use of baths, their structure, and bathing implements. The large woodcut plate 'Figura del Campo de Romani' first appears in this edition.

BL Cup. 402.k.27; GL A1116; Atabey 246.

223. DU CROS, Joseph. *Histoire des voyages de Monsieur le Marquis Ville en Levant, et du Siège de Candie; Ecrite par L. P. Ioseph Du Cros, D.* Lyon: Veuve Guill. Barbier and François Barbier. M.DC.LXIX. [=1669]

12mo, pp. [xii] 1-418 + [4] (pp.[i]=ht,[1-4]=privilege). 19th c. quarter brown roan, back gilt in compartments with thistles. From the library of Şefik Atabey, with his book label.

First edition. Another edition appeared at Paris in 1669 anonymously, under the imprint of François Clousier and Pierre Aubouyn, and with an undated privilege signed by De la Reynie. Ours is the edition/issue with the privilege ceded to Barbier and dated 20 August 1669. Cioranescu 26842 cites an issue with the privilege dated 8 October 1669. BNF cites the Clousier issue, with preliminaries and 286 pages, but does not cite the Lyon edition.

BL 149.A.27. This edition not in BNF. Blackmer 505 (Clousier issue); Atabey 370 (this copy); Weber 346; Brunet V, 1222.

224. DUFRENOY, Adelaide Gillete Billet. *Beautés de l'Histoire de la Grèce Moderne, ou récit des faits mémorables des Hellènes, depuis 1770 jusqu'à ce jour.* Paris: Alexis Eymery, 1825.

2 vols, 8vo, pp. xliv, 1-488; [iii] 1-520 (pp.i, [i]=ht, ii=adverts, iii=ts, pp.482-8= table of contents). Titles within a border of type ornaments. Two engraved frontispieces and 9 (of 10) engraved plates. Lacking the map. Vol. I in contemporary vellum boards, vol. II in old calf, back gilt with leather labels. With an ex-dono inscription in vol. I from S. Mendonides to Spyridon Carayannopoulos dated 1850, and with the bookplate of A. Hatzidemos in vol. 2.

First edition. The work consists of a series of short articles on various Greek topics: Ali Pasha, Greek superstitions, topographical descriptions, etc., from well-known books. The news from the Greek Revolution comes from various unknown correspondents. Mme. Dufrénoy also produced a French edition of Lady Mary Wortley Montagu's letters which was published together with Berton's *Les Turcs dans la balance politique de l'Europe*, Paris, 1822.

BNF 30369026; Blackmer 509; Droulia 689-90.

224

225. DU GABÉ, —, Baron. *Échelles du Levant. Impressions d'un Français.* Paris: Th. J. Plange, 1902.

Sm. 8vo, pp. VIII, 1-293 + [1] (p.I=ht, [1]=colophon). Modern calf, back ruled black.

First and only edition. The Baron du Gabé spent the winter and spring of 1901-2 in the Levant, visiting the main ports. He spent March in Athens, and also visited Egypt, Jerusalem, Smyrna, Syria and Constantinople. He was interested in advancing French

interests in the Levant, and his work gives information about individual Frenchmen in key positions, e.g. the head of the Asia Minor railway. He also visited Homolle, the director of the French School in Athens, and Guillois, consul general in Smyrna.

BNF 30369323. Not in GL.

226. DUHN, Friedrich von, and Louis JACOBI. *Der griechische Tempel in Pompeji... nebst einem Anhang: über Schornsteinanlagen und eine Badeeinrichtung im Frauenbad der Stabianer Thermen in Pompeji. Zur Erinnerung an die Studienriese Badischer Gymnasiallehrer nach Italien im Frühjahr 1889.* Heidelberg: Carl Winter, 1890.

Folio, pp. [iii] 36 + [1] (p.[i]=t, [1]=list of plates). Without the 9 plates. Half calf over brown cloth, original printed paper wrapper bound in.

First and only edition. This publication, an account of the so-called Greek temple in Pompeii, commemorates the study excursion made by the professors of the Baden Gymnasium to Italy in 1889. Duhn, who carried out most of his archaeological researches in Italy, continued his work in Pompeii and later produced *Pompeji eine hellenische Stadt in Italien*. Jacobi was an architect. The plates are lacking in this copy; note that plate nine was published in the Anhang, not in the main section.

BL D-7703.b.27. Karlsruhe cites several copies.

227. DU MONCEL, Théodose. *Athènes monumentale et pittoresque. Collection composée de quatorze planches lithographiées d'un panorama de la ville et d'un texte explicatif avec gravures sur bois. Par le Vte Th. Du Moncel Correspondant des Comités Historiques, Membre de plusieurs sociétés savants.* Paris: chez Gide et Cie, Libraires-Editeurs, Rue des Petits Augustins, 5. Imprimé par H. Fournier et Cie, 7 Rue Saint-Benoit MDCCCXLVI. [=1846]

Oblong folio, pp. [1] 1-9 [1] (pp.[1]=t, [1]=list of pls). With 14 no'd tinted lithographed plates and a folding unnumbered lithographed panorama. Half black roan over blue pebbled cloth, with the gilt initials M.T. on upper cover.

First separate edition. This collection of plates seems to predate Du Moncel's *De Venise à Constantinople*, with its 54 plates, but in fact it appeared after the publication of the latter. Another part collection published by Du Moncel is entitled *Excursion par terre d'Athènes à Nauplie*; the plates in that work also occur in *De Venise à Constantinople*, but they bear different plate numbers. It is clear from the text in the

Excursion that the part collections were issued after the publication of the larger work. It is likely that both sets were published in parts, possibly produced simultaneously, and customers could purchase the plates they wished. Occasionally this collection of the Athens plates is cited as *Vues pittoresques des monuments d'Athènes. Collection composée de quatorze grandes planches*: this is the title on the wrappers. The plates are by Du Moncel, possibly his earliest publication. He travelled in Greece and Turkey from November 1843 to the spring of 1844. Later he wrote a great deal on electricity, telephones, and electro-magnetism.

BNF 30375457, under the title 'Vues pittoresques des monuments d'Athènes', Paris, Gide, 1846, this is from the lithographed title wrapper. BL 648.a.28 gives date 1845 (under Theodore Du Moncel); Adhemar 644 cites a copy with the imprint of Delarue, 1845; Not in Blackmer. Weber1147, with date 1845 and publisher Delarue.

228. DUMONT, Albert. *Le Balkan et l'Adriatique. Les Bulgares et les Albanais - L'Administration en Turquie - La Vie des Campagnes - Le Panslavisme et l'Hellénisme.* Paris: Didier, 1873.

8vo, pp. [iii] IV, 1-411 + [1] (p.[i]=ht) + 56 pp. of adverts. Quarter black roan gilt. With notes on the fly-leaf in the hand of K.Th.Dimaras.

Apparently first edition. A second edition also appeared in 1873 in 18mo. Dumont was head of the French School of Archaeology at Athens. The work consists of articles originally printed in the *Revue des Deux Mondes*. Dumont also wrote *Voyage archéologique en Thrace*, 1871, and he was the editor of Benjamin Brue's *Journal de la Campagne que le Grand Visir Ali Pacha a faite en 1715 pour la conquête de la Morée*, which he published in 1870.

BNF 30375549.

229. DUPONCHEL, Augustin Amedée. *Histoires de Grèce et d'Italie, depuis les temps les plus reculés jusqu'à nos jours... Ouvrage orné d'environ 33 belles planches gravées sur acier.* Paris: Librairie Universelle, 1846.

8vo, pp. vii [i], 1-575 [1] (p.i=ht, [i]=errata). With 33 engraved plates no'd 1-8, 1-25. Old marbled boards, calf back strip.

Apparently second edition. The first edition formed volume five of *Le Monde, histoire de tous les peuples et des revolutions du Monde*, Paris, 1840. This edition consists of the sheets of the first edition with a new title; the avant propos and errata are from the original edition. The half title is missing, probably because it was the original half title to 'Le Monde'. The 1846 edition was probably prepared for sale to Spain since the

plates have an additional caption in Spanish. The entire set of 'Le Monde' was reprinted in 1858-59, edited by Lostalot-Bachoué (q.v.). The first part of the work deals with Greece. Many of the Greek plates, composite costume figures, are after Stackelberg.

See Colas 1452. This edition not in BNF on line, which cites editions of 1840 and 1858.

230. DUPRE. VLACHOS, Manolis. *Louis Dupré Ταξίδι στην Αθήνα και την Κωνσταντινούπολη.* Athens: Olkos, 1994.

Folio, pp. 287 (p.1=ht, 287=colophon). Numerous illustrations in the text, many full-page. There are several folding plates. Original blue cloth, in a dust jacket.

First edition. Vlachos examines Dupré as an artist, not as a traveller, and includes other examples of his work from various sources. The illustrations are taken not only from the *Voyage à Athènes* but from other artist-travellers working in Greece at the same period.

231. DURAND DE FONTMAGNE, Marie Caroline, *née Drummond de Melfort. Un Séjour à l'Ambassade de France à Constantinople sous le Second Empire.* Paris: Plon-Nourrit, 1902.

8vo, pp. [iii] III, 316 (pp.[i]=ht, I-III=avant propos). Half blue morocco. Bookplate of Count F. de Rohan Chabot.

First and apparently only edition. The Baroness de Fontmagne as Mademoiselle de Melfort accompanied the family of ambassador Edouard Thouvenel (q.v.) to Constantinople in 1856. Thouvenel had previously served as French ambassador in Athens, and an account of his sojourn there was published by his son Louis Thouvenel in 1890. Louis Thouvenel continued to publish his father's papers through the 1890s. It is possible that the Baroness was persuaded to publish her account because of the interest in Thouvenel and this period of French politics aroused by these publications.

BNF 30385450; BL 09077.ee.5. Not in Atabey.

232. DURUY, Victor. *Histoire des Grecs depuis les temps les plus reculés jusq'à la reduction de la Grèce en province romaine. Nouvelle édition revue, augmentée et enrichie d'environ 2000 gravures... et 50 cartes ou plans.* Paris: Hachette, 1887-89.

3 vols, 4to, pp. [iii] 822 [1]; [iii] 749 [1]; [iii] 740 (pp.[i]=hts, [ii]=fps, pp.[1] and 669-770 in v.3=errata, 671-740=indexes). With 33 plates (14=chromolithographs). Numerous illustra-

230

135

tions in the text, many full-page with versos blank. Old quarter burgundy morocco over marbled paper boards.

First edition with these illustrations. Duruy's history of Greece was a standard reference work for many years. It first appeared in 1862 in two volumes and was reprinted several times in this format up to 1883. In 1887 the work was revised and augemented and published with illustrations.

BNF 36578017.

233. DUVAL, Amaury, *the younger*. **Amaury-Duval. Souvenirs (1829-1830) Intérieur de ma famille – Salon de Charles Nodier Soirées du Quai Conti – Voyage en Morée Lettres du Maréchal Pélissier – Retour en France Révolution de Juillet.** Paris: E. Plon, Nourrit et Cie [1885].

Sm. 8vo, pp. [iii] VI, 256 (p.[i]=ht, I-VI=preface). Quarter maroon morocco over marbled paper boards, uncut. From the library of K.Th. Dimaras, with his bookstamp on title and on lower fly-leaf.

First edition. The date 1885 is attributed by the BNF. Most of the work concerns Duval's sojourn in Greece with the French expeditionary force and its accompanying Commission Scientifique in 1829-30; it includes letters from Aimable Pélissier, who was later to distinguish himself in the Crimea. Duval was a student of Ingres, which brought him to the attention of Dubois, one of the leaders of the Commission, who offered him a place as draughtsman in the archaeological section. Amaury Duval signed himself Amaury-Duval to distinguish himself from his father, the litterateur Amaury Duval, secretary to Talleyrand-Perigord before the Revolution. Duval père edited Moustoxydes' work on Parga, *Exposé des faits qui ont précédé et suivi la cession de Parga*, 1820.

BNF 34159360; GL IND367.2.

234. DYER, Thomas Henry. **Ancient Athens: Its History, Topography, and Remains.** London: Bell and Daldy, 1873.

Lge 8vo, pp. xii [i] 553 [1] (pp.i=ht, [i]=list of plates, [1]=colophon). With engraved frontispiece and 10 wood-engraved plates. Several wood-engraved vignettes in text. Slightly later polished calf, back gilt in compartments, black leather label.

First edition. This comprehensive account includes the first description of the theatre of Dionysus which was discovered in 1862. Dyer travelled in Greece a number of times, notably in 1869.

BL 560.b.4; Blackmer 525. Not in Weber.

230

D

137

235. ELLIOTT, Charles Boileau. *Travels in the three great empires of Austria, Russia, and Turkey. In two volumes. Vol. I. [... Vol. II.]* London: Richard Bentley, 1838.

2 vols, 8vo, pp. 497 [1]; 517 [1] (pp.1=ts, unn. leaf after p.24=list of plates, p.24=errata, pp.[1]=colophons). With 2 lithographed frontispieces and 2 maps. Contemporary calf, re-backed, red and black leather labels.

First edition of this very interesting work. An American edition appeared in 1839 at Philadelphia. Volume one ends with a description of Constantinople. Volume two is dedicated to the Aegean islands and Asia Minor. Elliott, a member of the well-known Elliott family which included his brothers Edward Bishop Elliott and Henry Venn Eliott, travelled in the Levant after 1826, and possibly c. 1834-35, according to internal evidence. The plates have been lithographed by Auguste Hervieu after drawings by E.G. Eliott. The Contominas collection also includes Elliott's *Letters from the North of Europe*, 1832, bound en suite to the set above.

BL 791.e.21; Blackmer 541; Weber 271; Abbey 31.

236. EMERSON, James, Giuseppe PECCHIO, and W.H. HUMPHREYS. *A Picture of Greece in 1825; as exhibited in the personal Narratives of James Emerson, Esq., Count Pecchio, and W.H. Humphreys, Esq. Comprising a detailed Account of the Events of the late Campaign, and Sketches of the principal military, naval and political Chiefs. In Two Volumes.* London: Henry Colburn, 1826.

2 vols in 1, pp. xii, 1-359; viii, 1-344 + 4 pp. of adverts (p.i=ht in v.1, t in v.2, colophon on p. 359 of v.1). With a portrait frontispiece in v.1 of Miaoulis. Modern calf. Library stamp of the Russell Institution on the title.

First edition, apparently edited by Emerson. An American edition appeared at New York in 1826. The engraved portrait frontispiece depicts Miaoulis after a drawing by Emerson, engraved by Henry Meyer. This work contains three separate accounts: Emerson's *Journal of a residence among the Greeks in 1825*, Pecchio's *A Visit to Greece in the Spring of 1825* and Humphreys' *Journal of a visit to Greece*. Humphrey, one of the first English volunteers, went out to Greece in 1821 with Gordon; he died on Aegina in 1826. Emerson first went out to Greece at the end of 1823 and left after Byron's death in 1824; he returned to Greece in 1825 as correspondent for the *Times* and fought alongside Miaoulis and Makriyannis. The Italian revolutionary Pecchio's narrative is of particular interest despite the fact that he spent only a few weeks in

Greece. He has included three letters from the Italian philhellene Santa Rosa in his account.

BL 790.h.20; Blackmer 548; Droulia 1138-39. See St. Clair, pp. 253-5.

237. EMERSON, James, and Giuseppe PECCHIO. *Tableau de la Grèce en 1825, ou récit des voyages de M. J. Emerson et du Cte Pecchio, traduit de l'anglais... par Jean Cohen.* Paris: Alexis Eymery, 1826.

8vo, pp. xvi, 1-464 (p.i=ht). With an engraved frontispiece of Miaoulis. Old quarter maroon morocco, panelled back faded, over maroon cloth. From the library of K.Th.Dimaras, with his stamp on lower fly-leaf.

First edition in French, translated from the English edition of *A Picture of Greece in 1825* by Jean Cohen. The French edition does not include the account by W.H. Humphreys which appears in the English edition, but Cohen has brought the work up to date.

BNF 31442711; Blackmer 549; Droulia 1180.

238. EMERSON, James. *The History of Modern Greece, from its conquest by the Romans B.C. 146, to the present time. In two volumes. Vol. I. [... Vol. II.]* London: Henry Colburn and Richard Bentley, 1830.

2 vols, 8vo, pp. cxxiii, 446 + [2]; xxii, 579 [1] (pp.i=ts, [1-2]=adverts, [1]=errata). Uncut in the original boards, quarter cream cloth backs, red leather labels. A presentation copy from Emerson to Viscount Mahon, signed on both titles. With a 19th c. armorial bookplate, presumably that of Mahon.

First edition. A second edition appeared in 1845 under the name Emerson Tennent. Interestingly enough, Emerson has added the name Tennent, which he adopted in 1832, in manuscript to both titles of this copy, which he presented to Lord Viscount Mahon. Emerson, who had already published his *Letters from the Aegean* and his *Picture of Greece in 1825*, has prefaced the work by a long section on the Greek Revolution at the beginning of volume one.

BL 1053.g.1; Blackmer 551; Droulia 1843-44.

239. ENDERLIN, Jacob, *publisher. Die hoche Stein-Klippen und Gebürge Cyaneae, Olympus und Athos. Von welchen zu sehen seyn: Die grosse Welt=Beruffene zwischen dem Schwarzen und Weissen Meer,*

E *am Bosphoro-Thracico in Europa ligende, desz Griechischen Reichs haubt=und der Ottomannischen Porten dermahlige Residentz=Stadt Byzantz, Roma Nova, Stampol oder Constantinopel. Augspurg, in Verlag Jacob Enderlins, Buchhandlers. Druckts Anthonius Nepperschmidt. M.DC.LXXXVIII.* [Augsburg: A. Nepperschmidt for Jacob Enderlin, 1688.]

Sm. folio, pp. 72 (p.1=t, p.72=index). Title in red and black. With engraved frontispiece of Sultan Soliman, and 33 plates containing 87 engravings. New brown morocco by Koutsiaftis, in a red marbled paper box.

239

First edition, first issue. Another issue appeared in 1689, the only difference being the date on the title. Examination of the 1689 issue indicates that the same sheets were used, even perhaps the same title, in the date of which an extra 'I' was squeezed to change 'MDCLXXXVIII' to 'MDCLXXXVIIII'. Some of the plates in this work also appear in other publications by Enderlin. He began publishing collections of plates and text inspired by the campaigns of the Holy League (Venice, Austria Poland) against Turkey, 1684-1690. Many of these plates are based on engravings from Coronelli's

Memorie Istoriografiche della Morea. Enderlin's first publication, in 1685, was *Die Grosse Welt-Beruffene in Thracien oder Romanien am Hellespont Ligende Haup-Stadt Bisanz, Neu Rom, Constantinopel, oder nach Turckischer Benennung Stampol*. All these Enderlin publications are related, and they make use of many of the same plates. There was one publication a year from 1685 to at least 1693.

BL 10125.f.1; Weber 748; Atabey 402, but see also 401 and 403 for other publications by Enderlin. Not in Blackmer but see 42 and 1303 for other publications by Enderlin.

240. ESTOURMEL, Joseph d', *Count*, (1783-1853). *Album du Journal d'un Voyage en Orient.* Paris: [Comon for] Imprimeurs Unis, 1848.

Lge 8vo, pp. 4 = list of plates. With 80 lithographed plates. Half calf over marbled paper boards, original cream printed paper wrappers bound in.

The plates only from Estourmel's *Journal d'un voyage en Orient*, first published in 1844. Normally the plates are bound in with the text, but what appears to be a *tirage à part* is known dated 1844, with the imprint of Crapelet, who published the first edition (EJF collection). It is possible that our work is a second edition of this *tirage à part*, but it was more probably issued to accompany the text, since there is also an edition of the text dated 1848 which was issued without plates. Thus it is likely that this album was intended to accompany the text, and was not issued separately as a *tirage à part*. Estourmel travelled in the Levant from June 1832 to September 1833. The plates are after drawings by Estourmel, although he travelled with the Swiss artist Wolfensberger, many of whose drawings have been engraved for various travel books.

This issue not in BNF or COPAC on line; the BNF has three copies of this work, all with the Crapelet imprint. This edition not in Blackmer or Atabey, but see Blackmer 557 and Atabey 408 for the earlier edition.

241. EXAMEN. *Examen Critique de l'Ouvrage: "De l'état actuel de la Grèce et des moyens d'arriver à sa restauration, par M. Frédéric Thiersch."* Leipzig: F.A. Brockhaus, 1835.

8vo, pp. [i] 1-100 (p.[i]=t). Half green calf, original beige printed stiff paper wrappers bound in.

First and only edition. An anonymous reply to Frederick Thiersch's *De l'état actuel de la Grèce*, 1833. The writer was a supporter of Capodistrias. The publisher Brockhaus published both works. In her entry on Thiersch, Droulia mentions that this work was attributed to Viaro Capodistrias.

BNF 33378744. See Droulia 2021-22.

242. FABVIER. *Fabvier. Chant lyrique sur la Grèce. (Au profit des Grecs.)* Paris: [Selligue for] Touquet et Compagnie, 1826.

32mo, pp. [viii] 9-24 + 4 (p.[i]=t, pp.1-4=adverts). Old quarter maroon roan gilt, bound with Boudin, Pouqueville and other philhellenic items. Ownership stamp of Konstantinos Th. Dimaras.

First and apparently only edition, rare. The preface is signed 'A. Th.'. The adverts are dated July 1826 and are for the 'Bibliothèque Populaire'.

BNF 33387816; Droulia 1021, citing this copy.

243. FALKE, Jakob von. *Hellas und Rom Eine Culturgeschichte des classischen Alterthums.* Stuttgart: W. Spemann [1880].

Folio, pp. XII, 1-344 [2] (p.I=ht, III=decorative title, V=title). Title in red and black. With 45 (out of 51) full-page wood engravings. Numerous woodcuts in the text. Half cloth over marbled paper boards.

?Second edition or issue. First published in 1878. There is also a dated edition of 1880, with the same pagination as our undated edition.

BL 1704.b.7.

244. FALLS, Cyril Bentham. *Military Operations Macedonia from the outbreak of war to the spring of 1917. [... From the spring of 1917 to the end of the war.]* London: HMSO, 1933-35.

2 vols, 8vo, pp. xvi, 1-409; svi, 1-365 (pp.i=hts, 393-409, 353-65=indexes). With fifteen no'd sketch maps/plans and five illustrations in vol. 1, and ten sketch maps, 6 illustrations in vol. 2. Map in lower cover pocket in vol. 2, lacking map in vol. 1. Original red cloth.

First edition of this account of the Macedonia campaign. The maps have been compiled by Major Archibald Frank Becke. The 21 maps in a separate slip case are not present with this copy.

BL B.S. 68/101.

245. FANELLI, Francesco. *Atene Attica Descritta da suoi Principii sino all' acquisto fatto dall' Armi Venete nel 1687... Divisa in quattro parti. Con varieta di medaglie, ritratti, e dissegni.* Venice: Antonio Bortoli, 1707.

4to, pp. [vi] 1-386 [2] (p.[i]=t, [iii-iv]=ded., [vi]=license, [2]=errata). With an engraved frontispiece, 8 engraved portraits and 5 (out of 6) folding plates. Uncut, in modern brown goatskin, panelled and diapered in blind.

First and only edition of this important work which describes the explosion which partially destroyed the Parthenon during the Venetian siege of the Acropolis in 1687. There are two issues of this work, depending on the length of the errata. In this issue the errata consist of 64 corrections.

BL 796.ff.23; Blackmer 573; Weber 756. See Laborde II, pp. 112-3.

245

246. FAROCHON, Paul Auguste. *Chypre et Lépante Saint Pie V et Don Juan d'Autriche.* Paris: Firmin Didot [1894].

Lge 8vo, pp. 320 (pp.1=[ ], 3=ht, 6=fp, 7=t, pp.319-20=conts). Title in red and black. Numerous wood engravings in letterpress, including frontispiece. Contemporary red decorative cloth gilt and black, a school prize binding.

Apparently only edition. BNF notes a work with a similar title, dated [1892], under the title *La Bataille de Lépante, Saint Pie V et Don Juan d'Autriche*. Farochon, a professor of history, also used the pseudonym P. de Hazel. He wrote on subjects connected with religious history, especially the Knights of St. John of Jerusalem.

BNF 30419111.

344.

Franciscus Maurocenus Peloponenacus
Expugnatis Athenis
Marmorea Leonum Simulacra
Triumphali Manu E Pireo Direpta
In Patriam Transtulit Futura Veneti Leonis
Quę fuerant Minervę Atticę Ornamenta

247. FARRER, Richard Ridley. *A Tour in Greece 1880.* Edinburgh: William Blackwood, 1882.

Lge 8vo, pp. vii + [iv] 1-216 (pp.[i]=ht, [iv]=conts and list of plates.). With a large folding engraved map and 27 wood-engraved plates. Half calf gilt.

First edition. The wood-engraved plates are after drawings by Lord Windsor. The map is titled 'Greece by T.B. Johnston, Geographer to the Queen', imprint: 'Engraved and printed by W. & A.K. Johnson, Edinburgh'. It contains an inset map of the Cyclades and Corfu.

BL 10125.ee.14; Blackmer 575; Weber 833.

247

248. [FAUVEL, Robert, and Vincent STOCHOVE.] *Le Voyage d'Italie et du Levant, de Messieurs Fermanel... Fauvel... Baudouin... et de Stochove... contenant la description des royaumes, provinces, gouvernemens, villes, bourgs... [etc.] vies, moeurs, actions tant des Italiens que des Turcs, Juifs, Grecs, Arabes, Armeniens, Mores, Negres, & autres nations... qui habitent dans ... tout le païs du Levant.* A Rouen, chez la Veuve de Louis Behourt... MDC.LXXXVII. [Rouen: Veuve Behourt, 1687.]

12mo, pp. vii 1-481 [2] (pp.[i]=t, [1-2]=conts). Vellum antique, in a green marbled paper box. Contemporary ownership signature of Jan, Baron de Roly, dated 1690.

Third edition, uncommon. This work was first published in 1664, second edition 1670. According to the editor's preface, he collated this text from a manuscript by Robert Fauvel and from the printed account of the same journey by Vincent Stochove (*Voyage*, editions of 1643, 1650 and 1662, Flemish editions 1680 and 1681). Fauvel, Fermanel and Baudouin were from Rouen; together with the Belgian Stochove they travelled in the Levant in the 1630s, exploring the Aegean islands and the coast Asia Minor in detail. Stochove published an account of this journey as early as 1643. The editor, commenting that three of the travellers were from Rouen, felt that a Rouen version of the journey was desirable. He published the first edition in 1664. Editions of the *Voyage de l'Italie et du Levant* may be found catalogued under the names of any of the four travellers.

This edition not in BNF or BLC on line. Not cited in Karlsruhe. This edition not in Weber but see 266 for the second edition; see also 265-269a for related works. Not in Blackmer or Atabey, but see Blackmer 576 for related works.
Collation: a^4 A-V^{12} X^2

There is another copy in the Contominas collection, in quarter red roan, blindstamped back. Bookplate of George Martakis with his motto «ἐκ μελέτης πλείους ἢ φύσεως ἀγαθοί».

249. FEBURE, Michele, *Marquis*. *Theatre de la Turquie ou sont representéees les choses les plus remarquables, qui s'y passent aujourd'hui. Avec les moeurs, le gouvernement, les coutumes, & la religion des Turcs, & de treize autres sortes de Nations qui habitent dans l'Empire Ottoman... Traduit de l'Italien par le sieur Michel Le Févre.* Paris: Jacques Le Febvre, M.DC.LXXXVIII. [=1688]

Sm. 4to, pp. [xx] 558 + [11] (p.[i]=t, [1-11]=index). Contemporary calf, worn. Booklabel on title obscuring part of the imprint.

Third edition in French, first printed in 1682. Karlsruhe cites a 1686 French edition. Febure, a Capuchin missionary and orientalist, spent eighteen years in the Levant. He wrote this work in Italian in 1681 and translated it himself into French. He took the name Giustiniano when he entered religious life. His previous work was *Specchio overo descrittione della Turchia*, 1674, published in French in 1675 as *L'Etat present de la Turquie*.

This edition not in BNF or BLC on line. Weber 730. This edition not in Blackmer but see 577. This edition not in Atabey but see 420-423 for other editions and works.
Collation: a^4 e^4 i^2 A-$4B^4$ $4C^2$ ($4C2$=[ ])

250. FEITHIUS, Everhardus. *Antiquitatum Homericarum Libri IV. Editio accuratior.* Amsterdam: Salomon Schouten, M.DCC.XXVI. [=1726]

Sm. 8vo, pp. [xx] 404 + [43] (pp.[i]=t, [1-42]=index, [43]=addenda). Contemporary marbled paper pasteboards.

Second edition edited by H. Brumanus, first published in Leiden in 1677. This work was reprinted in Gronovius's *Thesaurus* in 1699.

BL 237.i.16; Karlsruhe cites a number of copies.

251. FELLOWS, Sir Charles. ***A Journal written during an excursion in Asia Minor.*** London: John Murray, 1839.

8vo, pp. xi, 1-347 (p.i=t, 341-7=index). With an etched frontispiece by W.H. Brooke, double-page map coloured in outline, and 20 lithographed plates (of which 1=dp). Wood engravings in the letterpress. Quarter calf.

First edition of Fellows' account of his first journey in Lycia, February to May, 1838. A collected edition appeared in 1852 as *Travels and Researches in Asia Minor, more particularly in the province of Lycia*, together with Fellows' account of his second journey, 1839-40, made on behalf of the British Museum. The *Journal* created a good deal of interest when it appeared, since the monuments Fellows described and illustrated, thought to be examples of 'Graeco-Persian' art, were unknown in Europe. The Trustees of the British Museum asked Fellows to undertake an expedition to recover some of these works of art. These are now known by the general name of the Xanthian marbles.

BL 560.b.16; Blackmer 578; Weber 291.

252. FENELON, François de Salignac de la Mothe (1651-1715). ***Les Avantures de Télémaque, fils d'Ulysse. Composées par feu Messire François de Salignac, De la Motte Fenelon. Auquelles on a joints des remarques nécessaires pour la facilité des jeunes Gens. Nouvelle Edition corrigée plus exactement que toutes les précedentes. Avec Privilége de sa Majesté Imperiale & enrichie de figures en taille-douce. à Ulm 1761 chez Daniel Barthélemy & Fils.*** [Ulm: D. Barthélemy, 1761.]

Sm. 8vo, pp. [viii] XXXIII [7] 1-505 [45] (p.[i]=t, p.[1]= approbation, p.[2]=testimony, p.[3-5]=genealogy of Telemachus, [6-7]=st and summary to book I, first five pages of pp.[1-45]=laudatory odes, rest=index). With engraved portrait, engraved frontispiece, folding map and 24 engraved plates. Title in red and black. Contemporary calf, panelled back gilt, red and green leather labels.

A late edition. This work was first published in 1699, and literally hundreds of editions followed. The year 1761 saw several editions of Fenelon: this edition was specifically prepared as a school book. Wetstein published a deluxe edition with engravings at Amsterdam in 1761, a folio edition appeared at Leiden, and J.C. Wohler produced an edition in 2 vols with plates and notes by J.A. d'Ehrenreichat at Augsburg. Fenelon's account of the adventures of Telemachus during his search for his father Ulysses is a political novel with a purpose: each adventure has a hidden moral, and the entire work forms a sort of Utopia in which man and society would be reformed. It was the last of three works composed as moral guides for the Duke of Burgundy, grandson of Louis XIV, and thus the future King of France, to whom Fenelon had been appointed tutor in 1689. Fenelon's early grounding in classical studies gave the work 'the very essence of the antique', and although it was published long before the development of philhellenic sentiment in France, it may be considered a precursor of the sorts of books represented by Barthélemy's *Anacharsis*.

This ed. not in GL, BNF or COPAC on line. Karlsruhe cites several copies.
Collation: *⁷ 2*⁸ 3*⁸ A-2L⁸ 2M⁴.

253. FENELON, François de Salignac de la Mothe. *Les Aventures de Télémaque, fils d'Ulysse. Tome Premier [... Tome Second.]* Paris: Mame Frères, 1810.

2 vols, 8vo, pp. [iv] [1]-292; [iv] [1]-297 (pp.[i]=hts, pp.[1]=sts). With 24 engraved plates by Godefroy, after Lefebvre, J.B. Simonet, Dambrun, Cony and others. Contemporary half calf over marbled boards, back ruled gilt. Booklabel and stamp of Dr. J.G. Sleeswijk of Amsterdam on front pastedown and fly-leaf.

A late edition, but apparently the first to be printed in stereotype. This must be one of the first books to be printed by this method, because each volume contains an 'Avis sur la Stereotypie' on the verso of the half title, as well as a note on the half title referring to this method as the Herhan process (le procédé d'Herhan). The plates occur at the beginning of each book. Again this same year saw several editions of Fenelon's work, including two editions published at Lyon in 2 volumes each in 12mo and 18mo by Blanche and Boget, and a 2 volume edition in 4to at Paris.

This edition not in BNF on line.

254. FENELON, François de Salignac de la Mothe. *Les Aventures de Télémaque. Avec des notes géographiques et littéraires. Tome premier [... second.]* Paris: Lefevre, MDCCCXXIV. [=1824]

2 vols, 8vo, pp. [iii] lix, 1-322; [iii] 1-49 (p.[i]=series ts, [iii]=ts). With a folding map and 24 no'd plates by Pauquet and Langlois after Marillier and others. Half red roan, faded, over red marbled paper boards, backs panelled gilt.

A late edition, but the first with the notes by the literary critic Jean François Boissonade. The map, dated 1824, has been engraved by Pierre Tardieu.

BNF 30426395.

255. FENELON, François de Salignac de la Mothe. ***Aventures de Télémaque, précédées du Discours sur le poésie épique et sur l'excellence du poëme de Télémaque par Ramsai [sic]. Tome premier [... second.]*** Paris: Froment and Lequien, 1828.

2 vols, 8vo, pp. [iii] xl, 1-318; [iii] 1-424 (pp.[i]=hts, pp.401-424='aventures d'Aristonoüs'). With engraved portrait frontispiece in v. 1. Contemporary quarter calf over marbled paper boards, back ruled gilt.

A late edition. For some reason several editions of *Télémaque* were published in 1828.

BNF 30426422.

256. FENELON, François de Salignac de la Mothe. ***Le Avventure di Telemaco figlio di Ulisse. Prima Versione Italiana. Tomo I.*** Livorno: Gio. Mazzajoli, 1850.

12mo, pp. XI, 13-502 (p.I=t, 13=first page of book I). With 24 wood-engraved plates. Red leather gilt.

?Third edition of this format, all published, complete with the 24 books. An edition which appears to be in the same format, 'nuova versione Italiana', was printed at Livorno by the Vignozze Brothers in 1833 with the same pagination, with another edition in 1844. Despite the claim on the title, this is not the first edition of *Télémaque* in Italian. An Italian translation by B. Moretti appeared at least as early as 1704. There was a revival of interest in Fenelon's work in the mid-19th century; Spanish and Italian editions were published in Paris in 1850 and 1847 respectively.

This edition not in the Italian Union Catalogue on line, not in Karlsruhe.

257. FENELON, François de Salignac de la Mothe. ***Τύχαι τοῦ Τηλεμάχου... μεταφρασθεῖσαι... ὑπὸ Κωνσταντίνου Σταματιάδου Καθηγη-***

τοῦ τοῦ ἐν Τριπόλει Γυμνασίου καὶ ἐκδοθεῖσαι δαπάνῃ Ν.Β. Νάκη Βιβλιοπώλου. Athens: Z. Grypares and A. Kanariotes, 1864.

8vo, pp. [xvii] 1-408 (p.[i]=t). Contemporary green half calf over green paper boards, central gilt wreath enclosing title, back ruled gilt.

A late Greek translation of *Télémaque* by K. Stamatiades. The first Greek translation, by A. Skiadas, was published in 1742 at Venice by Bortoli. The first 19th century edition in Greek was published at Budapest in 1801, translated by Demetrios Panaghiotis Govdelas. The binding on this copy is rather curious. The green paper has been added to the existing boards at an apparently later date, although it is contemporary.

This edition not in GL or Polemis.

258. FERMOR, Patrick Leigh. *Roumeli. Travels in Northern Greece.* [London:] John Murray [1966].

8vo, pp. viii, 248 (p.i=ht). With a double-page sketch map by John Craxton and 20 photographic illustrations. Original blue cloth.

First edition. This work with reissued with the same pagination in 1973, but the first edition is distinguished by the absence of an international standard book number (isbn). Reprinted in 1983 and 1988.

BL X.800/1220.

259. FERRARI, Pompeo. *Venezia in Oriente La "Relatione dell' Isola et Città di Tine di Pompeo Ferrari Gentil'huomo piacentino".* Rome: G. Bardi, 1938.

8vo, pp. 138 (p.1=[], 3=t). With three folding maps/plans, a plan and a photograph mounted in letterpress. Three-quarter calf, original printed paper wrappers bound in.

First edition, edited and with an introduction by Ermanno Armao, the commentator on Coronelli. This account of Tinos was written in 1623. Ferrari's manuscript was deposited in the National Library of Piacenza after the death of its owner, the Count Pallastrelli. Armao published this in a series called 'Venezia in Oriente'; it contains a useful bibliography on Tinos.

BL 10125.ccc.38.

260. FERRER, Giuseppe di, *Count. Mémoires critiques sur l'Orient, suivis de réflexions politiques et essai sur l'Ile de Corfou, et d'un petit*

aperçu de sort des officiers de l'armée napolitaine, après les événements de 1821 ... Traduit de l'Italien par l'Auteur lui-même. Paris: for the Author, 1845.

8vo, pp. [iv] i-iv, 1-213 (p.[i]=ht). With a lithographed portrait frontispiece. Uncut, with wide margins, in half red morocco with the original blue decorative printed paper wrappers bound in.

First collected edition in French, but second edition of the *Mémoires*. The first French edition of the *Mémoires* appeared in 1844, without the essay on Corfu. There is another issue of the 1845 edition without the words 'Traduit... lui-même' on the title, but there is no difference between the issues except for the existence of an extra portrait, lithographed by S. Come after Pauthier, which is a reverse of the portrait in our edition; this may be an extra-illustration. Firmin Didot published another edition in 1847. This work was translated by Ferrer himself from the original Italian edition which appeared in 1842, apparently without the essay on Corfu.

This issue not in BNF on line. See Weber 365 for the other 1845 issue. Blackmer 589. Not in Bibliographie Ionienne; Papadopoulos IB 3019;

261. FERRIÈRES-SAUVEBOEUF, Louis Francois, *Count*. *Mémoires historiques, politiques et géographiques des Voyages du Comte de Ferrières Sauveboeuf, faits en Turquie, en Perse et en Arabie depuis 1782, jusqu' en 1789... Tome Premier. [... Tome Second.]* Paris: [Veuve Delaguette for] Buisson, 1790.

2 vols in 1, 8vo, pp. [iii] xxiv, 298 + [1]; [iii] x, 303 [1] (pp.[i]=hts, pp.[1]=errata). Contemporary mottled calf, backs gilt in compartments with acorns, red leather labels. From the library of K.Th. Dimaras, with his bookstamp on final leaves.

First edition. Another edition was published at Maestricht in 1790 by J.P. Roux. An abridged edition in Swedish appeared at Stockholm in 1794. Volume one is concerned mainly with the Russo-Turkish war of 1788-1789; volume two gives an account of the author's travels in Greece, Egypt, Syria and Palestine. Ferrières seems to have been something of an adventurer. He was in Aleppo in 1783; he travelled to Persia where he represented himself to the Shah as a precursor of the French envoy; later he undertook missions on behalf of Vergennes, French ambassador at Constantinople prior to Choiseul-Gouffier. Either his loyalty to Vergennes or his Republican politics prompted his severe criticism of Choiseul-Gouffier's *Voyage Pittoresque*, the first volume of which had appeared in 1782, and of Volney's work on the Russo-Turkish war, *Sur la Guerre actuelle des Turcs*, 1788. Choiseul-Gouffier replied in his *Observations sur les mémoires de ...Ferrières Sauveboeuf*, Paris, 1790.

BNF 30431301; Blackmer 590; Weber 598; Pingaud, pp. 125-127; Atabey 428 (2nd edition).

262. FINDEN, William, and Edward Francis FINDEN. *Finden's Byron Beauties: or, the principal female characters in Lord Byron's Poems. Engraved from original paintings under the superintendence of W. and E. Finden.* London: Charles Tilt, MDCCCXXXVI. [=1836]

Sm. 4to, pp. [vi] 36 (of 39) leaves of text (p.[i]=t). With 34 (of 39) no'd plates. Old polished blue calf, back gilt in compartments with fleurons, red leather label.

First edition. Tilt also published an undated edition of this work under the title *Le Byron des Dames; or Portraits of the principal female characters in Lord Byron's Poems.* Ullmann published a German edition in 1845 as *Lord Byron's Frauenkranz.* The work consists of portraits of the Maid of Athens, Laura, Haidee, and other heroines of Byron's poems, engraved after portraits commissioned by artists including Henry Corbould and Charles Cockerell.

This edition not in BLC. Not in Blackmer or Atabey.

263. FINLAY, George. *A History of Greece from its conquest by the Romans to the present time B.C. 146 to A.D. 1864. A new edition, revised throughout, and in part re-written, with considerable Additions, by the author, and edited by the Rev. H. F. Tozer, M. A. Tutor and late fellow of Exeter College, Oxford. In Seven Volumes.* Oxford: Clarendon Press, MDCCCLXXVII. [=1877]

7 vols, 8vo, pp. [iii] iii-xlix 483; xi 460; xii 526; ix + [1] 439; xii 295; xii 438; viii 431 + 8 pp. of adverts (pp.[i], 1=hts, [1]=ded. to Leake). With an engraved portrait of Finlay in vol. 1. The title is printed on special paper. Original brown cloth gilt, rough cut. With the bookplate of Dr. Ernst Garland and his ownership signature in each volume.

First collected edition, with additions, published posthumously, with a biographical sketch of the author, and with letters from C.C. Felton and others. Finlay had considerably revised and rewritten much of this work, which was originally published over a number of years, with separate titles for each chronological period; some of these individual works appeared in second editions, e.g. *The History of the Byzantine empire from DCCVI to MLVII,* which was first published in 1853, second edition 1856. In the collected edition the work was reorganized. Finlay, who took part in the Greek war of independence, lived most of his life in Greece. The most salient feature of his character was his disappointment as a philhellene. Tozer, who had travelled extensively in Greece and Turkey and wrote several accounts of his journeys (q.v.), undertook to finish the work.

BL 1570/267. Not in Blackmer or Atabey.

264. FISCHER, Max. *Rendez-vous avec l'Acropole Pages d'un Carnet de Notes. Couverture et presentation de Renefer.* [Paris: E. Grevin for] Ernest Flammarion [1929].

8vo, pp. [i] 1-140 + [1] (pp.[i], [1]=colophons). Uncut in polished blue calf, sides framed in gilt with fleurons, back gilt in compartments with red and green leather labels, inner gilt dentelles, by Riviere and Son, with their stamp on fly-leaf, original white printed paper wrappers bound in.

Apparently first and only edition. 100 copies were printed on special papers. This is one of 25 on Holland paper no'd 11-35; it is numbered 33. Ten copies were printed on Madagascar paper (nos. 1-10) and 65 copies on Lafuma paper, no'd 36-100.

BNF 32108211.

265. FLANDIN, Eugène Napoleon. *Histoire des Chevaliers de Rhodes depuis la création de l'ordre à Jérusalem jusqu'à se capitulation à Rhodes.* Tours: Alfred Mame, 1864.

Lge 8vo, pp. [iii] VIII, 328 (p.[i]=ht). With 4 steel-engraved plates. Illustrations in the text. Contemporary quarter calf over embossed green cloth, back gilt in compartments, gilt edges.

265

First edition. A second edition appeared in 1867, a third in 1873 and a fourth in 1879. Flandin is best known for his elaborately produced *L'Orient*, of which volume two is entirely devoted to Rhodes. Flandin, artist and antiquary, was attached to the French embassy in Persia from 1839 to 1841. In 1843 he was sent to assist Botta at the excavations in Nineveh. On his way out he spent some time in Rhodes.

BNF 30441052. This edition not in Blackmer but see 600.

266. FLAUBERT, Gustave. *Oeuvres complètes illustrées de Gustave Flaubert. Voyage en Orient (1849-1851). Édition du Centenaire.* Paris: Librairie de France, 1925.

4to, pp. [vii] 5-400 (p.[i]=ht). Uncut in quarter tan morocco over marbled paper boards, original printed paper wrappers bound in.

First edition of Flaubert's account of his travels in the Levant, edited from his journals. The text is in the form of notes. Flaubert travelled in the East from October 1849 to February 1851 with Maxime Du Camp. There is a long section on Egypt. The text of this work was established in 1948 by Rene Dumesnil when a second volume was published concerning Flaubert's journey to North Africa in 1858.

BNF 35460710.

267. FLAXMAN, John (1755-1826). *John Flaxman's Umrisse zu Homer's Ilias und Odysee. Gestochen von E. Riepenhausen. Mit erläuterndem Texte.* Berlin: [Gustav Schaele for] Th. Chr. Fr. Enslin and Adolph Enslin [after 1852].

Oblong folio, pp. [i] [12] (pp.[i]=t, [1-12]=explanations of the plates). With 62 engraved plates no'd 1-34 and 1-28. Quarter cloth-backed boards, original decorative paper wrappers mounted on upper cover. Bookstamps of H. Hallensleben with his signature on the title page.

This is a late German edition of Flaxman's designs for Homer, engraved by Ernst Ludwig Riepenhuasen in 1817 and frequently reprinted. An earlier German edition of Flaxman's compositions is known, dated 1805, but this is by a different engraver. The date [after 1852] has been assigned on the basis of the short introduction which states that the verses in the text are translated from E. Wiedasch's edition of Homer, Stuttgart, 1852. It is possible that ours is the edition cited by the HBZ as [1865]. Editions also appeared in 1870 and 1875. Flaxman's compositions to Homer were first published in Rome in 1793. They exercised a great influence on his contemporaries and on the development of neo-classical art, especially in Germany, where Flaxman's

work attracted the attention of Friedrich Schlegel as early as 1799, when he wrote a long critique of the artist's work in the magazine *Athenaeum*, published in Berlin.

Karlsruhe cites several editions on line. See Blackmer 602-603. See also David Irwin, *John Flaxman 1755-1826*, London, 1979, and David Bindman, editor, *John Flaxman, R.A.* [Catalogue of the John Flaxman exhibition], Royal Academy of Arts, London,1979.

268. FORBIN, Louis Nicolas Philippe Auguste de, *Count*. Voyage dans le Levant en 1817 et 1818 par M. le Comte de Forbin. Tom. I. [... Tom. II.] Torino: Alliana, 1830.

2 vols in 1, 16mo, pp. 223; 223 + [1] (pp.1 = ?hts, missing here, p.3=ts, p.[1]=privilege). Contemporary quarter green roan, flat back ruled gilt with ornaments, lettered on the spine 'Viaggi'.

A small format version of Forbin's folio work describing his travels in the Levant, and uncommon. The work first appeared in large folio in 1819.

Not in BNF, BL or LoC on line. Apparently not in the Italian Union Catalogue on line.

269. FRANCE. Ministry of Foreign Affairs. Ministère des Affaires Étrangères. Documents diplomatiques Arrangement financier avec la Grèce Travaux de la Commission Internationale chargée de la préparation du projet. Paris: Imprimerie Nationale, MDCCCXCVIII. [=1898]

Folio, pp. VI, 1-206 (p.I=ht). With 3 tables (2=folding). Original printed paper wrappers.

?Only edition. A detailed account of the financial state of Greece in 1897 in preparation for the allied loan to Greece- the indemnity for the war with Turkey in 1897. This document was prepared after the preliminaries of the Peace of Constantinople, 18 Sept., 1897. It includes an account of the meetings of the 12th and 21st of January 1898. The allied commission was composed of Charles Testa, Alexandre de Suzzara, Etienne Dubois de l'Estang, Edward Fitzgerald Lane, Luigi Bodio, Alexis Smirnow and Wilhelm Kaufmann.

BNF 33877388.

270. FRANÇOIS, Achille. Précis d'Histoire Universelle. Édition augmentée par M. Dareste. Lyon: A. Brun et Cie, 1850.

Sm. 8vo, pp. [iv] 1-168 (p.[i]=ht). Several pages with small defects. Quarter calf over brown marbled paper boards. Bookstamp of the Bibliothèque Militaire of N.D. De Fourvieres on title. Bound with Savary and others.

Second edition, revised by Antoine Dareste de la Chavanne. The first edition was published at Paris in 1839. François was doyen of the Faculty of Letters at Lyon. This is a brief ancient history up to the period of the Arrian heresy. i.e. to about 325 A.D.

BNF 30459195.

271. FROMMEL, Carl. ***Ansichten aus Griechenland gestochen unter der Leitung von C. Frommel. Vues de la Grèce. Gravées sous la direction de C. Frommel.*** [Karlsruhe: Scotzniovsky, 1830.]

Oblong 8vo. Engraved title and 30 engraved plates, with thirty leaves of facing text, unpaginated and printed on versos only. Text within rules. Contemporary half calf gilt over brown speckled paper boards, imitating leather.

First edition. Special format copies are known with the plates on india paper, mounted. The plates are reduced versions of Williams' views of Greece (q.v.). Frommel chose to reproduce 30 of the 64 plates and added his own descriptive text. The plates are engraved by Schütze, Pöppel and others. This work appeared in printed paper wrappers with the title *Dreissig Ansichten Griechenlands...*, in three parts.

BL W1/6603; Blackmer 636 (on india paper); Weber 1118; Droulia 1823.

271

GABÉ. See DU GABÉ

272. GADSBY, John (1809-1893). *My Wanderings: being Travels in the East 1846-1847, 1850-1851, 1852-1853. Twenty-fifth Thousand.— Revised. [... Volume II. Stereotyped Edition. Revised.]* London: Gadsby, 1883 [... 1885].

2 vols, 8vo, pp. 594 [29] +[1]; [xi] 5-546 [6] 10 + 2 pp. of adverts (p.1=t, [i]=ht, [1]=advert, pp.1-10=scripture index). With portrait frontispiece and a folding map, coloured in outline in volume 1. Wood engravings in the text. Old half calf, red and black leather labels.

A late edition, apparently the sixth. In 1855 Gadsby, who called himself a biblical and oriental lecturer, first published his *Wanderings*, or the account of his travels from 1846 to 1853, with a second volume or appendix published in 1860 containing the journeys from 1855 to 1860. The subsequent publishing history of these two volumes is rather confused, because it seems that Gadsby continued to publish them separately. Thus a second edition of volume one appeared in 1858. Another edition appeared in 1862, but possibly of volume 1 only. An edition of volume two (?second) appeared in 1865; a third edition of both volumes appeared in 1868-69, with a fourth in 1872 and a fifth in 1876. The map is entitled 'Lands of the Bible with countries adjacent' and contains an inset of the Holy Land.

This edition not in BLC or COPAC. This edition not in Blackmer, Weber or Atabey.

273. GALLAND, Julien Claude. *Recueil des rits et cérémonies du pelerinage de la Mecque, auquel on a joint divers écrits relatifs à la religion, aux sciences & aux moeurs des Turcs.* Amsterdam and Paris: Desaint and Saillant, 1754.

Sm. 8vo, pp. viii, 1-215 (p.=t). Contemporary marbled calf, back gilt in compartments with carnations, Dutch marbled endpapers.

First edition, and the only edition in French. A German edition appeared in 1757. This work contains five essays; the first three are translations from Arabic and Turkish. The last two are eye-witness accounts; the one a long description of Chios and the other an account of the wedding of Sultana Esma with Yakub Pasha, governor of Silistria. Galland, an interpreter who probably worked for the French embassy, was the nephew of the orientalist Antoine Galland. He also produced *Relation de l'ambassade de Mehemet Effendi, à la cour de France*, 1757.

BNF 30476466; Blackmer 643; Atabey 470.

274. GALT, John. *Letters from the Levant; containing views of the state of society, manners, opinions, and commerce, in Greece, and several of the principal islands of the Archipelago.* London: for T. Cadell and W. Davies, 1813.

8vo, pp. XV [i] 1-386 (p.I=t, [i]=advert, 349-386=appendix). With engraved frontispiece map. Old red paper wrappers, gilt edges, back missing. Ownership signature of John Caley, F.R.S., dated 1821 on front fly-leaf.

First edition. Following the relative success of Galt's *Voyages and Travels* in 1812, he published this second work consisting of the letters actually written by him during his travels in the Levant from 1809-1811, many of which contain accounts of his meetings with Byron. Galt travelled in the Levant in the hope of discovering commercial opportunities.

BL 10125.bb.6; Blackmer 645; Weber 32; Moore, pp. 255-70.

275. GAMBA, Pietro. *Relation de l'expédition de Lord Byron en Grèce. Traduite de l'Anglais par J.T. Parisot, ancien officier de marine, traducteur des Lettres de Junius.* Paris: Peytieux, Galerie Delorme, 1825.

8vo, pp. xii, 1-307 (pp.i=ht, 303-7=conts). Uncut in quarter red morocco gilt. Bookplate of A.D. Hatzidemos.

First edition in French, translated by Jacques Parisot from the first edition, in English, published the same year. Pietro Gamba was the brother of Byron's mistress Theresa Guiccioli; he became Byron's secretary and accompanied him to Greece, where he was with him to the end. He wrote this account of Byron's last days with Hobhouse's approval and assistance; after its publication he returned to Greece where he died at Methana in 1826.

BNF 36564241; GL BY246; Blackmer 646 (Engl. ed.); Droulia 849. Bound with *La Mort de Napoleon. Dithyrambe traduit de l'anglais de Lord Byron*, 3rd ed. Paris: Charles Painparré, 1821. 8vo, pp. iv, 1-31. (BNF 30258601, attributing the poem to J.A.S. Collin de Plancy).

There is another copy in the Contominas collection, uncut, in old marbled paper boards, paper label with title in ms.

276. GARDNER, Ernest Arthur. *Greece and the Aegean. With a preface by Sir Rennell Rodd G.C.B. and a chapter on Constantinople by S. Casson.* London: George G. Harrap [1933].

8vo, pp. [v] 5-253 [1] (pp.[i]=ht, [v]=ded, p.5=first leaf of text). With a coloured frontispiece, 32 photographic illustrations (on 16 leaves), and 4 maps/plans of which 2 hors texte and folding. Modern tan leather.

First edition. A second edition appeared in 1938, revised by Stanley Casson. The frontispiece is a reproduction of a watercolour by George Grahame. Gardner, archaeologist and classicist, also produced *Ancient Athens*, 1902, *Poet and Artist in Greece*, 1933, and *Religion and Art in ancient Greece*, 1910, among many other works on Greek art and archaeology. The anomaly in pagination could be caused by dedication (p.[v]) to Sir Henry Lunn being added after printing had begun.

GL GT2083.67; BL 10127.de.24.

276

277. [GASPARIN, Valerie de, *Countess*.] ***Journal d'un Voyage au Levant par l'Auteur des Horizons Prochains Tome Premier - La Grèce - Deuxième édition.*** Paris: Michel Lévy Frères, 1866.

Volume 1 only (of 3), 8vo, pp. [iii] III, XVIII, 1-224 + 72 pp. of adverts pag. 36 + 36 (pp.[i]=ht, [ii]=advert, I-III=conts, I-XVIII=prefaces to first and second eds). Quarter blue roan, original yellow printed paper wrappers bound in. From the library of K.Th. Dimaras, with his library stamp on lower fly-leaf.

Third edition despite the information on the title, volume one only, previously published in 1848 and in 1850 in three volumes under the pseudonym 'auteur de Mariage au point de vue Chrétien'. This third edition was issued after the success of *Horizons Prochains*, published in 1858. The Countess Gasparin travelled in the Levant from September 1847 to May, 1848. Her work is full of religious and philosophical observations. In 1867 she wrote an account of a later journey entitled *À Constantinople*.

This edition not in BNF or COPAC. Karlsruhe cites 1 copy. This edition not in Blackmer but see 654 for first edition. This edition not in Weber.

278. GAUTHEY, Leon (1848-1918). *L'Orient notes de Voyage et études de Moeurs. L'Egypte. – La Palestine. – La Syrie. – L'Asie Mineure. – Constantinople. – La Grèce. – Les Iles Ioniennes.* Charolles: Veuve Lamborot, A. Chavet successeur, 1886.

Lge 8vo, pp. [vii] 5-414 (pp.[i]=ht, 413-4=conts). Title in red and black. Uncut in maroon calf, red leather label, original printed paper wrappers bound in. A presentation copy, signed by Gauthey to 'Monsieur Barnaud'.

First edition. 153 copies were printed of which only 78 contain the entire work. 75 copies contain only part 1, Egypt and Palestine. This is copy 53. This work consists of articles first published in the parish magazine *Le Pelerin de Paray-Le-Monial* from 1884-1886. Gauthey was a Catholic missionary, and there is an interesting chapter on the oriental churches.

BNF 30488849. Not in Blackmer, Weber or Atabey.

279. GAZES, Anthimos (1758-1828). *Μελετίου Γεωγραφία παλαιὰ καὶ νέα συλλεχθεῖσα ἐκ διαφόρων συγγραφέων παλαιῶν τε καὶ νέων. Τόμος Α [... Β ... Γ ... Δ].* Venice: Panos Theodosios, 1807.

4 vols in 3, 8vo, pp. [20] 512; 475; 412; 384 (pp.[1], 1=hts). Lacking the 5 maps. Half green roan, backs gilt, over marbled paper boards.

First and apparently only edition of Gazes's reworking of Meletius's 'Geography'. Meletius, Bishop of Athens, wrote this work at the end of the 17th century, but it was first printed posthumously at Venice in 1728. Gazes edited Meletius's text and added

important new material in order to bring the work into line with modern knowledge of geography, particularly in those sections dealing with Greece. He also edited for the press several scientific works translated into Greek, including Fourcroy's philosophy of chemistry, 1802, and Lalande's astronomy, 1803. According to T. Papoutsanis (*Brief Account of the Cartography of the shores and islands of Greece*, Athens, 1989) Gazes produced his 'Geographic Table of Greece with ancient and modern names' in 1800, and in 1810 he published a map of Greece engraved by Schindelmayer.

BL G.7775; GL F70.2; Iliou 1807.44-47.

280. GEIL, William Edgar (1865-1925). *The Isle that is called Patmos.* London: Marshall Brothers [1904].

8vo, pp. xiv, 1-341 [1] (p.i=ht, [1]=colophon). With photographic frontispiece and 103 photographic illustrations. Original blue cloth.

Second edition. One of the few books devoted exclusively to Patmos. The first edition, 1897, was published at Philadelphia by A.J. Rowland. Geil was a travel writer who produced several books on China and Africa.

BL 10077.dd.19; GL GT2720; LoC cites 1897 edition only.

281. GELL, Sir William. *The Geography and Antiquities of Ithaca.* London: J. Wright for Longman, Hurst, Rees, and Orme, 1807.

4to, pp. [iii] 1-119 [1] (pp.[i]=t, [ii-iii]=dedication to King George III, [1]=errata). With 11 engraved plates, mostly aquatints (of 13). Lacking the two maps. Half calf.

First and only edition. Gell visited Ithaca in the spring of 1806 in the company of Edward Dodwell. He was the first to study the island seriously for its Homeric associations.

BL 569.g.24; Blackmer 661; Weber 13; Abbey, 133; Spencer pp. 208-9.

282. GELL, Sir William. *Narrative of a Journey in the Morea.* London: [A. and R. Spottiswoode] for Longman, Hurst, Rees, Orme, and Brown, 1823.

8vo, pp. ix, 1-411 [1] (pp.[i]=t, [1]=colophon; lacking the leaf of directions to the binder). With frontispiece and 8 plates lithographed by T.M. Baynes after Gell and printed by Hullmandel. Wood engravings in the text. Half polished green calf gilt.

First edition. This very interesting work is dedicated to Lady Drummond of Logie Almond who was Gell's Maecenas. Gell travelled through the Peloponnesus in 1805-6, at the same period that he visited Ithaca. In 1823 he decided to publish his account of the Morea in order to combat the growing philhellenic sentimentality which was being created by the Greek war of independence. Gell's *Itinerary of the Morea*, 1817, is also based on this same journey, but the *Itinerary* is not a connected narrative, rather a collection of information organized along plotted routes. Gell's connection with Greece began in about 1800 when he was sent to the Ionian Islands on a diplomatic mission. It was on his return to England in 1803 that he was knighted. He visited Greece again in 1805-1806. Gell did not travel as extensively in the country as

282

one would suppose, considering the number of his literary productions. His reputation began to grow after the publication of the *Topography of Troy*, 1804, *Ithaca*, 1807, and the *Itinerary of Greece*, 1810 (on the Argolid), which Byron reviewed in *The Monthly Review* for August, 1811. It was Byron who first referred to him as 'classic Gell' and later as 'rapid Gell'.

BL 1047.l.8; Blackmer 665; Weber 119; Droulia 434; St. Clair p. 192; Spencer pp. 208-9, p. 241. Blackmer refers to the possible existence of a half title, due to the fact that the dedication leaf (pp. ii-iii) is signed A3 instead of A2. This is unlikely; it is more probable that the signature is an error.

283. GENOUDE, Antoine Eugène de (1792-1849). *Considérations sur les Grecs et les Turcs, suivies de Mélanges religieux, politiques et littéraires.* Paris: L.T. Cellot for Méquignon, and Lyon: Périsse Frères, 1821.

8vo, pp. [iii] II, 1-302 (p.[i]=ht, 300-2=conts). Prize binding of contemporary tree calf, gilt bordered sides, central medallion 'College Royal de Limoges', back panelled gilt, green leather label.

First edition. The 'Considerations' is one of a number of essays on religious and political themes contained in this volume, and the only one with a philhellenic interest. A second, but first separate, edition of the 'Considerations' only was published by Mequignon-Havard in 1824. Genoude was a politician who was also involved in the Oratory Movement; he was particularly interested in religious questions and also produced a French translation of the Bible.

BNF 30495873; GL IND760; Droulia 30.

284. GEORGIRENES, Joseph. *A description of the present state of Samos, Nicaria, Patmos, and Mount Athos...* London: W.G. for Moses Pitt, 1678. [Athens: Karavias, 1967.]

Lge 8vo, pp. [xx] 112 (p.[i]=). New half brown morocco.

A photographic reprint of the first edition. This work was first published in English in 1678, translated by Henry Denton from Georgirenes' manuscript. Georgirenes, archbishop of Samos from 1666 to 1671, travelled to London in 1676 to have a book printed for the use of the Orthodox Church. There he met Henry Denton whom he had known in Constantinople when Denton was chaplain to the English embassy. Denton added a dedication to James, Duke of York, in both Greek and English. A German translation appeared in 1689. This reprint was issued by the Athens bookseller Notis Karavias in the series 'Βιβλιοθήκη Ἱστορικῶν Μελετῶν'; it formed no. 23 in this reprint series.

See Blackmer 672; Weber 727; Wing G536; Legrand 17th c. II, 539; Spencer pp. 103-104.

285. GERBELIUS, Nicolas. *Nicolai Gerbelij in descriptionem Graeciae Sophiani, Praefatio. In qua docetur, quem fructum, quamque voluptatem allatura fit haec pictura studiosis, si diligenter eam cum historicum, poëtarum, geographorumque scriptis contulerint. Eiusdem de situ, nominibus & regionibus Graeciae perbrevis in picturam Sophiani introductio.* Basileae. [Colophon: ... ex officina Ioannis Oporini, Anno Salutis Humanae MD.XLV. Mense Septembri.] [Basle: Oporinus, 1545.]

Sm. folio, pp. [vii] 1-80 + [13] (p.[i]=t, [13]=colophon). 21 large woodcuts in the letterpress. Contemporary panelled and embossed vellum, a remboitage.

First edition. The work was reprinted in volume four of Gronovius's *Thesaurus Graecarum antiquitatum*, 1697. The *Praefatio* was written to accompany the map of Greece by Nikolaos Sophianos, which was first printed in 1538, and reprinted in 1543 and 1552. It is especially important since copies of the first and second editions of the map have disappeared and only a few copies of the 1552 edition are known today. Gerbelius, editor of Erasmus, classicist, historian and professor of law at Vienna, has provided what are essentially notes and a commentary on the map. He was probably working from the 1543 edition. The woodcuts include Gothic city views of Athens, Amphilochia, Amphissa, Actium, Argos, Corinth, Delphi, Dodona, Lamia, Larissa, Lacedemon, Megara, Messene, Megalopolis, Olympia, Pella, Tempe, Thebes, and Thessaloniki. The vellum binding is actually formed from one cover of a large folio volume, turned crosswise and used for both sides of the small folio volume. This is clear from the position of the embossed ornament which is positioned over the spine and inner sides of both covers. In the binding's original form this ornament would have been positioned in the center of the upper cover. Gerbelius also edited Jacob Moltzer's lives of the Sultans, 1544, and Callimachus Buonaccorsi's *De Bello Turcis*.

BL 794.i.23; Blackmer 676; Adams G479; Legrand 16th c. III, 466; Papadopoulos IB 23; Bib. Ionienne 35.
Collation: a^4 A-M^4 (M4=[ ]).

286. GERVINUS, Georg Gottfried (1805-1871). *Risorgimento della Grecia. Traduzione dal Tedesco. [... Volume Terzo. Coi fatti posteriori della Grecia e delle Isole Jonie.]* Milan: Corona e Caimi Editori, 1863-64.

3 vols. in 1, 8vo, pp. 1-327; 1-378; 1-412, + errata slip tipped in at end of vol. 3 (pp.1=series half titles, 3=ts, 411-12=conts). 19th c. quarter dark blue calf gilt over paper marbled in imitation of tree calf.

First edition in Italian, forming vols 3-5 of the series 'Collana di storie et memorie contemporanee diretta da Cesare Cantu'. A later Italian edition appeared at Milan in 1871. The work first appeared in German as part of Gervinus's history of the 19th Century, 1855-66. The first separate edition is the French translation by J.F. Minssen and Leonidas Sgoutas, *Insurrection et régénération de la Grèce*, Paris, 1863, see below. The material in volume 3 of the Italian edition is new, possibly because of the union of the Ionian islands with Greece in 1864. The original work ends in 1829, as does the French edition. The work was also translated into Greek in 1864.

This edition not in GL or BLC. Italian Union Catalogue cites 6 copies. Not in Papadopoulos IB.

287. GERVINUS, Georg Gottfried. *Insurrection et régénération de la Grèce. Traduction française par J. F. Minssen... Léonidas Sgouta.* Paris: A. Durand, 1863.

2 vols, 8vo, pp.[iii] 1-618; [iii] XVI, 1-704 (pp.[i]=hts, pp.617-8, 703-4=errata). Uncut in old three-quarter vellum over blue cloth.

First separate edition and first edition in French, translated from volumes five and six of Gervinus's *Geschichte des neunzehn Jahrhunderts*. The preface by Sgoutas and Minssen contains an interesting critique of the histories of Gordon, Trikoupis and Finlay.

BNF 33992620; GL IND226.

288. GIFFARD, Edward. *A short visit to the Ionian Islands, Athens, and the Morea.* London: John Murray, 1837.

8vo, pp. vi + [ii] 1-399 [1] + 4 pp. of adverts. (p.i=t, [i]=list of plates, [ii]=errata, [1]=colophon). With a lithographed frontispiece, a map, and 5 lithographed plates. Modern panelled calf gilt.

First edition. A later edition was published at Paris in 1838 without the plates of views. Giffard spent three months (January-March) in Greece and the Ionian Islands in 1836 with his travelling companion F. W. Newton, whose sketches provided the prototypes for the lithographed views.

BL 1047.e.6; Blackmer 683; Weber 252.

289. GILLES, Pierre (1490-1555). *Petri Gylii De Topographia Constantinopoleos, et de illius Antiquitatibus Libri quatuor. Ad Reverendiss. & illustriss. D. Georgium Cardinalem Armaignacum. Lugduni, apud Gulielmum Rovillium... M.D.LXII. Cum privilegio Regis.* [Lyon: Rouille, 1562.]

4to, pp. [viii] 1-245 (p.[i]=t). Recent blindstamped brown morocco.

First edition, second issue, published posthumously. The first issue is dated 1561; this is the only difference between the issues. Pierre Gilles died at Rome in 1555; this work, together with Gilles' account of the Thracian Bosphorus, (*De Bosphoro Thracio lib.III*, Lyon, 1561/2) was edited by his nephew Antoine Gilles. These two volumes are among the earliest to describe Constantinople and its environs. Gilles accompanied d'Aramon's embassy to the Porte in 1547; he was charged with searching for antiquities on behalf of François I. This work and its companion volume are not accounts of

Gilles' travels, but describe the antiquities and archaeology of the places he visited. An English translation by John Ball appeared in 1729.

BNF 30506990; Blackmer 685; Adams G1613; Göllner 1023 (1st issue). This edition not in Weber.

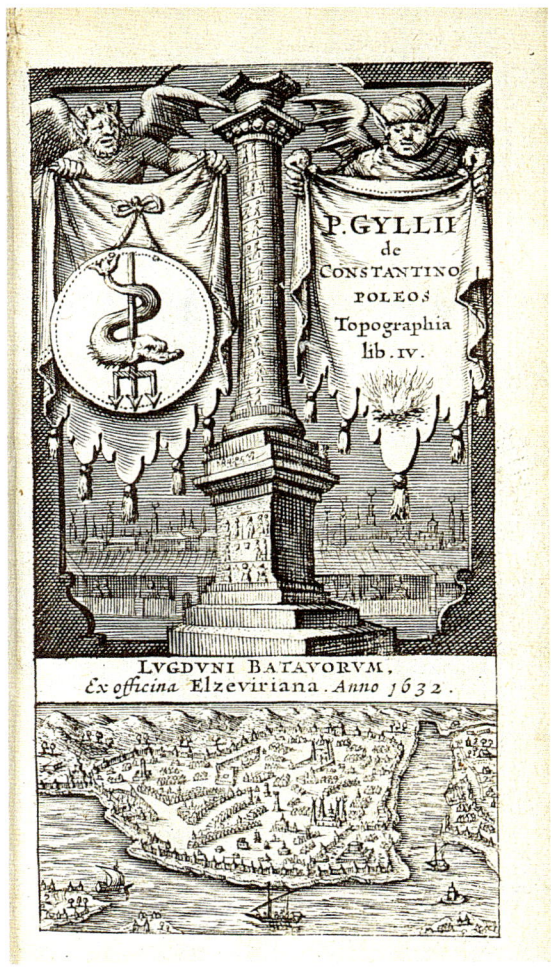

290

290. GILLES, Pierre. *P. Gyllii de Constantinopoleos Topographia lib. iv.* Leiden: Elzevir, 1632.

18mo, pp. [xx] 21-428 (p.[i]=engr. title, [pp.[iii]-[iv]=pref). Contemporary vellum.

Second edition. The first edition was published in 4to in 1561/62. Elzevir also published the companion volume on the Thracian Bosphorus the same year.

BNF 36173268; Blackmer 687; Weber 678; Willems 367.

291. GOBINEAU, Joseph Arthur, *Count de* (1816-1882). ***Souvenirs de Voyage Céphalonie Naxie et Terre-Neuve. Le Mouchoir rouge Akrivie Phrangopoulo La chasse au caribou.*** Paris: Henri Plon, MDCCCLXXII. [=1872]

8vo, pp. [iii] 222 + [1] (p.[i]=ht, p.[1]=conts). Quarter blue morocco, original mauve printed paper wrapper bound in.

First edition. This charming work by the Count Gobineau contains three novelettes, two of which, *Le Mouchoir rouge* and *Akrivie Phrangopoulo*, are the product of his travels through the Cyclades. *Akrivie Phrangopoulo* was re-issued in 1924 with etchings by the Greek artist Demetris Galanis. Gobineau, diplomat and amateur archaeologist, spent three years in the Levant, 1855-1858, during which time he served as French ambassador in Athens. He published an account of his experiences as *Trois Ans en Asie*, 1859. He was a prolific writer of both tales and political works and used the pseudonym 'Comte Ariel des Faux'. He contributed many articles to the *Revue des Deux Mondes*, but many of his works connected with Greece were published posthumously. Gobineau engaged in a long correspondence with Alexis de Tocqueville, and his papers and correspondence were edited by J.F. de Raymond and published in 1985. His daughter, Diane de Guldencrone (q.v.), also wrote on Greece.

BNF 30515892; GL V166.3. Not in Blackmer or Weber.

292. GOBINEAU, Joseph Arthur, *Count de*. ***Deux Études sur la Grèce Moderne Capodistrias Le Royaume des Hellènes.*** Paris: Plon-Nourrit, 1905.

8vo, pp. [iii] IV, 325 + [1] (pp.[i]=ht, [ii]=advert, [1]=conts). Uncut in green paper boards, original blue printed paper wrappers bound in.

First edition, published posthumously. According to the Bibliothèque Nationale this work was edited by L. Schemann.

BNF 30515875; GL HG672G57. Not in Blackmer or Atabey.

293. GODARD-FAULTRIER, Victor. ***D'Angers au Bosphore pendant la Guerre d'Orient. Constantinople, Athènes, Rome. Impressions, curiosités, archéologie, art et histoire, établissements chrétiens, monuments byzantins. Souvenirs d'Anjou à Malte, Naples...*** Angers: Cosnier and Lachèse, 1857.

Lge 8vo, pp. [iii] (p.[i]=ht). No letterpress. With 30 lithographed plates. Half red cloth over red and black marbled paper boards.

First edition, first issue. These plates were republished in Paris in 1858 under the imprint of L. Maison together with a text of 559 pages. There are 32 plates in the 1858 edition. This collection of 30 plates was published in Angers in 1857, printed at E. Barasse's lithographic press; they are lithographed by H.L. after the traveller-artist H.G. It is possible that this issue forms either a separate atlas of plates, or a *tirage à part*. Godard-Faultrier had the entire work printed in Angers but distributed by a Paris publisher. All copies cited bear the Paris imprint and date. Godard-Faultrier, who wrote on subjects connected with Angers, set out from Marseille in August 1855.

BL 10107.h.1 (1858 issue); BNF 30516577 (1858 issue); Weber 556 (1858 issue).

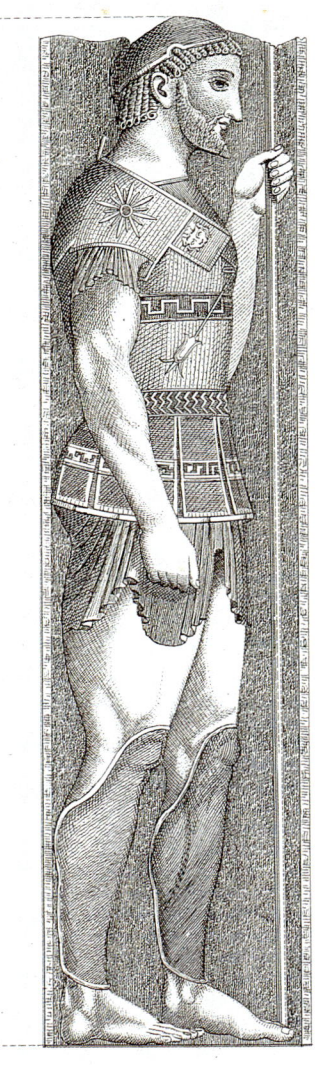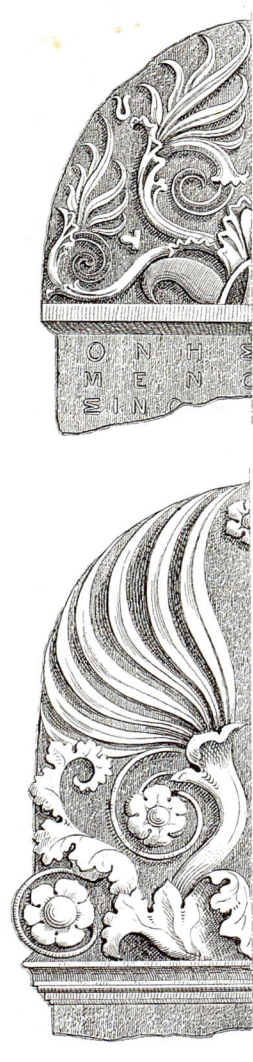

294. GOMEZ-CARRILLO, Enrique (1873-1927). *La Grèce Éternelle Traduit de l'Espagnol par Ch. Barthez. Préface de Jean Moréas.* Paris: Perrin, 1909.

8vo, pp. XIX, 1-328 + [2] (p.I=ht, V=ded, [1]=table of contents [2]=colophon). Half black roan gilt, rubbed. With the bookplate of Shirley Atchley. Bound with Calas.

First edition in French, translated by Charles Barthez, possibly from the Spanish edition of 1906 entitled *Grecia*. This is basically an account of an undated cruise to Greece which has been treated in an expansive poetical manner. The preface is by Jean Moréas, i.e. Yannis Papadiamantopoulos (q.v.), a member of the circle around Barrès and other French hellenists of the early 20th century. This preface was translated into Spanish and published separately in 1908. Gomez-Carrillo was a miscellaneous and travel writer who also produced accounts of the Holy Land, Japan, North Africa and so forth. This copy comes from the library of Shirley Atchley, attached to the British Embassy and resident in Athens in the 50's. Atchley produced one of the earliest accounts of the wild flowers of Attica.

BNF 32179289.

295. GOODISSON, William. *A Historical and Topographical Essay upon the Islands of Corfù, Leucadia, Cephalonia, Ithaca and Zante: with remarks upon the character, manners, and customs of the Ionian Greeks.* London: for Thomas and George Underwood, 1822.

Lge 8vo, pp. xxiv, 267 + [1] (pp.[i]=t, [1]=binder's directions and errata). With 4 maps and 8 no'd plates lithographed by George Scharf after Goodisson. Contemporary diced calf, gilt framed sides, back gilt in compartments with bird and branch, gilt crest of chained cat at top of spine.

First and apparently only edition. The author spent five years in the Ionian Islands as a medical officer with the British army, and he has written a detailed work on the political and social life of the islands. The artist George Scharf worked with a number of travellers and scholars, among whom were Charles Fellows, Theodor Panofka and Christopher Wordsworth.

BL 572.g.27 (under Goodison); Blackmer 705; Droulia 245; Bib. Ionienne 1008. Not in Weber.

296. [GOODRICH, Samuel Griswold]. *Tales about Greece. By Peter Parley. The third edition. With numerous engravings.* London: for Thomas Tegg et al., 1845.

16mo, pp. viii, 1-349 [3] (pp.i=[ ], ii=map, iii=t, pp.[1-3]=adverts). Numerous wood engravings in text. Original decorative blue coth gilt, gilt edges.

Apparently second edition. The first edition was published in 1837. Another edition was published at Philadelphia in 1845. This is a collection of historical stories about Greece for children. Peter Parley was a pseudonym used by several people, including the American author Nathaniel Hawthorne. Goodrich, himself an American, travelled in Europe in 1823 and was appointed U.S. consul in Paris from 1851-53. He also employed a staff of writers who produced many of the Peter Parley stories under his direction.

This edition not in BLC or COPAC. LoC cites 2nd London edition only.

297. GOODRICH, Samuel Griswold. *A Pictorial History of Greece; ancient and Modern. By S. G. Goodrich, author of Peter Parley's Tales. For the use of Schools.* New York: Huntington and Savage, 1849.

8vo, pp. viii, 9-371 + 1 p. of adverts (p.i=[ ], ii=fp). Frontispiece and numerous vignettes in letterpress. Original embossed black roan over black cloth.

Apparently first edition. Goodrich also used the pseudonym 'Peter Parley', but in addition to the books published under the name of Peter Parley, a pseudonym used by several writers, Goodrich also produced schoolbooks under his own name.

This edition not in COPAC or LoC. Both BL and LoC cite Philadelphia, 1855.

298. GOSSELIN, Pascal François Joseph. *Géographie des grecs analysée; ou les systêmes d'Eratosthenes, de Strabon et de Ptolémée comparés entre eux et avec nos connoissances modernes.* Paris: Didot l'ainé, M.DCC.LXXXX. [=1790]

4to, pp. [viii] 1-148 + VIII + xxvii + [1] + 1 (pp.[i]=ht, I-VIII=tables, i-xxvii=index, [1]=errata, 1=privilege). With ten no'd maps (9 folding). Uncut in contemporary marbled paper boards, brown leather label gilt. With the booksellers' ticket of J. Mongenet, Geneva.

First edition. The privilege was issued by the Academy of Inscriptions and Belles Lettres. Gosselin had previously produced a catalogue of the medals in the Ennery collection, 1788. After his analysis of Greek geography appeared, he continued to work in this field, publishing *Recherches sur la géographie systematique des Anciens*, 4 vols, 1797-1813, and contributing the notes to the French translation of Strabo by Korais and La Porte du Theil, 1805-1819.

BNF 30524636; BL 456.b.18; GL GT5.

299. GOUIN, Gustave. *L'Armée d'Orient Des Dardanelles au Danube... Illustrations de F. Detaille.* Marseille: Rotogravure S.A.; Geneva: for F. Detaille, 1931.

4to, pp. [xvii] 1-286 [1] (p.[i]=advt, [iii]=ht, [vii-ix=portraits, [1]=colophon). Numerous illustrations in the text, including many full-page portraits. Original coloured pictorial wrappers.

First edition of this account of the Balkan campaign of 1916, with discussions of activity in Thessaloniki and Monastir. The photographs are the work of Fernand Detaille. GL cites *L'Armée d'Orient aux Dardanelles, en Serbie en Macedoine, à Monastir*, [Marseille], 1928, by Gouin. Although the advert on p.[i] announces the publication of several other works by Gouin connected with the Army of the Orient, none of them, including the above, are listed in the on line catalogue of the Bibliothèque Nationale.

BL 9085.cc.16.

300. GOUPIL-FESQUET, Frederic Auguste Antoine. *Voyage d'Horace Vernet en Orient rédigé par M. Goupil Fesquet.* Paris: Challamel [1843].

8vo, pp. [iii] 1-328 (recte 228), (p.[i]=ht, ii=list of plates, 22-28=conts). With 16 coloured lithographic plates. Contemporary quarter red roan over original lithographed cream paper boards with a design in red and blue.

300

First edition, first issue, published in 20 livraisons. There is another issue with the variant title 'Voyage en orient fait avec Horace Vernet'. Goupil Fesquet travelled in the Levant from October 1830 to February 1840 in company with the artist Horace Vernet. They visited Egypt, Palestine and Syria, stopping at Syros, Santorini, Crete and Smyrna on the way. One of the objects of their journey was to take daguerreotypes for the photographic incunable *Les Excursions Daguerriennes* projected by the publisher Lerebours. Apparently the cream paper boards are made up of the decorative paper wrappers mentioned by Carteret.

BNF 30528112, attributing date [1843], with plates uncoloured, but with coloured title (?perhaps referring to coloured title wrappers.); Blackmer 718; Atabey 511; Carteret III, 594.

301. GRAND-CARTERET, John. *La Crète devant l'image. 150 Reproductions de caricatures grecques, françaises, allemandes, anglaises... [etc.].* Paris: L.-Henry May [1897].

8vo, pp. 1-144 (p.1=ht). Numerous illustrations in the letterpress. Uncut in the original beige pictorial printed wrappers.

First edition. This is a collection of cartoons concerning Greece, Turkey, the war in Crete, and the Greco-Turkish war of 1897, together with European reactions as seen in cartoons and caricatures. Grand-Carteret produced many works in this mode, among them *Les moeurs et caricatures en France*, 1888, *La Turquie en image*, 1909, *Les Images galantes*, 1907, and *Wagner en caricatures*, 1891.

BNF 30532437; BL 8027.b.14 attributes the date 1897; GL HG87.7G75.

302. GRASSET DE SAINT SAUVEUR, André. *Voyage historique, littéraire et pittoresque dans les isles et possessions ci-devant Vénitiennes du Levant: savoir: Corfou, Paxo, Bucintro, Parga, Prevesa, Vonizza, Sainte-Maure, Thiaqui, Céphalonie, Zante, Strophades, Cérigo et Cérigotte.* Paris: Tavernier, An VIII. [=1800]

3 vols, 8vo, pp. [iii] XVI, 407; [iii] 358; [iii] 383 (pp.[i]=hts). With 30 engraved plates in the atlas, lacking in this copy. Old half leather, backs gilt in compartments, red and brown leather labels.

First edition. This copy lacks the atlas of plates. A German translation appeared in 1801 at Weimar, and an abridged edition at Vienna in 1806. Grasset was resident in the Ionian Islands from 1781 until 1798; when the Islands came into French possession in 1797 he acted as commissioner of commercial relations for Napoleon. This important and detailed work was probably prompted by the French acquisition of the Islands. Grasset de Saint Sauveur must have been related to Jacques Grasset de Saint Sauveur, French diplomat, who produced the important *Costumes Civils de tous les Peuples connus*, 1784-1787.

BNF 33993075; Blackmer 722; Weber 593; Bib. Ionienne 582.

303. GRASSI, Alfio. *Charte Turque, ou organisation religieuse, civile et militaire de l'Empire Ottoman: suivie de quelques réflexions sur la guerre des Grecs contre les Turcs. Tome premier. [... Tome deuxième.]* Paris: P. Mongie ainé, 1825.

2 vols, 8vo, pp. [iii] 1-439; [iii] 468 (pp.[i]=hts, pp.437-39, 465-68=conts). Without the lithographed frontispiece of the prophet Mohammed. This copy not bound en suite; vol 1 uncut in old half tree calf, red and green leather labels, with the book stamp of the Nicolaevsky Academy, vol 2 uncut in green morocco, back ruled gilt, original blue printed paper wrappers bound in.

First edition. Grassi himself published another issue the same year, under the title *Charte Ottomane* which does not contain the section on the Greek revolution. It is possible that the *Charte Ottomane* is in fact the earlier issue, and that Grassi added the section on the Greek revolution to make the work more saleable and of more interest to a commercial publisher. A second edition appeared in 1826 under the imprint of A. Dupont. Grassi's earliest work appears to be *Extrait historique sur la milice romain et sur la phalange grecque*, Paris, 1815. He also wrote *La Sainte Alliance les Anglais et les Jesuites leur système politique a l'égard de la Grèce*, 1827.

BNF 30535580; Atabey 520 (2nd ed); Droulia 710-11. See Blackmer 724 for an account of the *Charte Ottomane*.

304. GREECE. [*A Collection of Watercolour Drawings*].

8vo, no title page. 19 watercolour drawings, uncaptioned and unsigned. Old red morocco, gilt fanfare border, rebacked, back gilt.

Leaves have been removed both from the front and back of this album; the entire work probably included views of a journey in the Levant which have been excised. Although the work is unsigned and undated, it most likely was executed in the late 19th century, since the depiction of the 'lantern of Demosthenes' shows it cleared of the buildings around it. The binding may be a remboitage since it unlikely that a collection of drawings would have been bound in such a way.

List of Drawings: our captions. In some cases the drawings can not be clearly identified.

Corfu? or Igoumenitsa?, 4; Philopappous; Ioannina or Kastoria 2; Costumes, 4; Acropolis; Hadrian's gate; Temple of Zeus; Caryatid porch; Lantern of Demosthenes; Missolonghi?; Phaleron; Vari.

305. GREGOROVIUS, Ferdinand. *Geschichte der Stadt Athen im Mittelalter. Von der Zeit Justinian's bis zur türkischen Eroberung. Erster Band. [... Zweiter Band.]* Stuttgart: Kröner Brothers for J.B. Cotta, 1889.

2 vols, 8vo, pp. XII, 1-490; X, 1-477 (pp.I=hts). Contemporary half russia, backs gilt over green marbled paper boards, original grey printed paper wrappers bound in. Bookplate of Dr. Moriz Grolig of Vienna, with his cypher bookstamp on the last page of each volume.

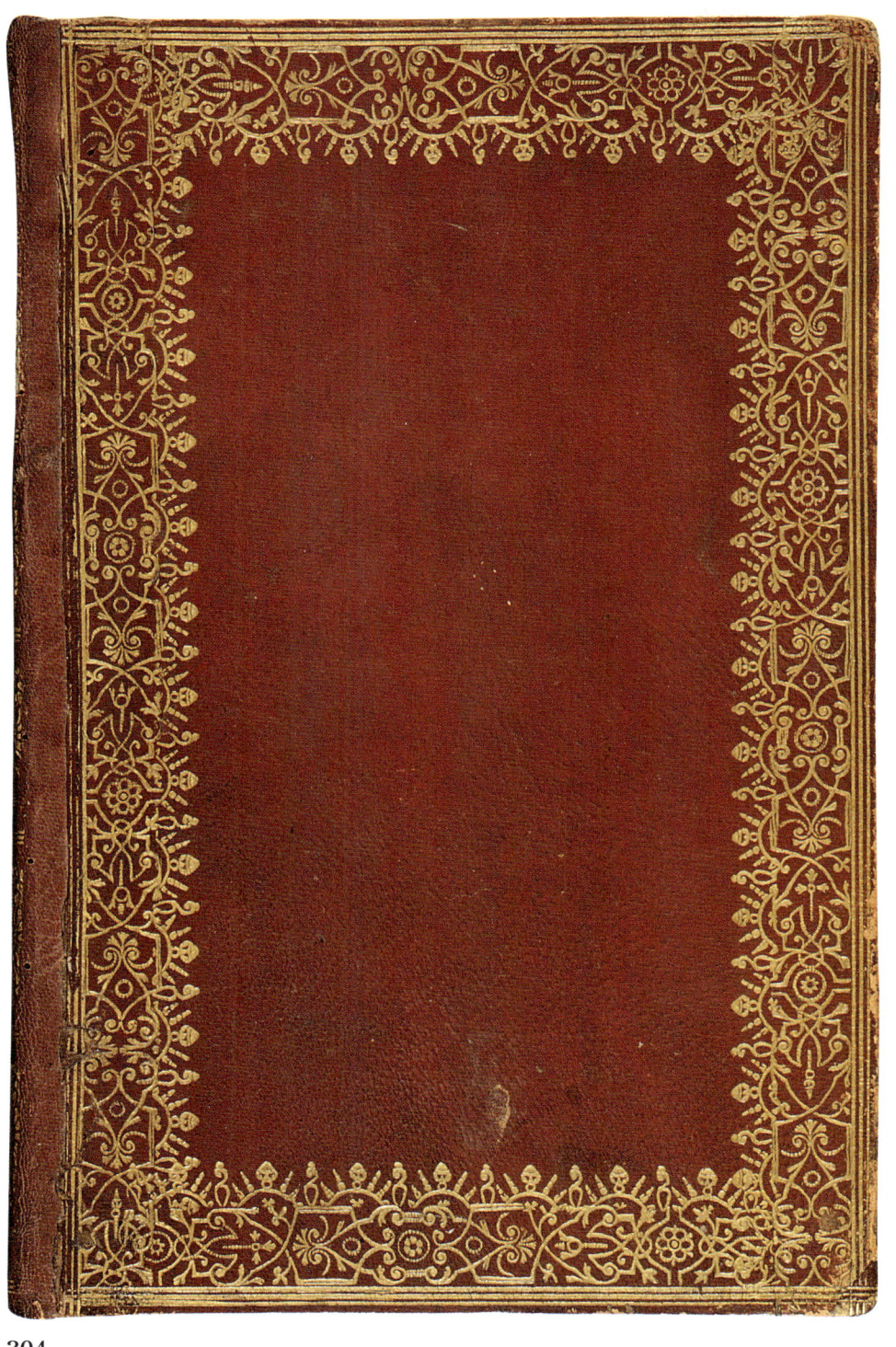

304

First edition of this important history of Athens during the medieval period, up to the Turkish conquest. The work was translated into modern Greek by Spyridon Lampros in 1904-6. With bibliographical notes in Grolig's hand on the preliminary leaves and with catalogue cuttings of books on Athens mounted on a preliminary leaf. Gregorovius also wrote *Korfu. Ein jonische Idylle*, Leipzig, 1882.

BL 9136.f.16.

306. GRELOT, Guillaume Joseph. *Relation nouvelle d'un voyage de Constantinople. Enrichie de plans levez par l'auteur sur les lieux, & des figures de tout ce qu'il y a de plus remarquable dans cette ville. Presentée au Roy. A Paris, en la boutique de Pierre Rocolet, chez la veuve de Damien Foucault... M.DC.LXXX. Avec privilège du Roy.* [Paris: Veuve Damien Foucault for Pierre Rocolet, 1680.]

4to, pp. [xii] 1-306 + [1] (pp.[i]=t, [1]=privilege). With 13 engraved plates (10 folding). 4 engravings of costume in the text. Contemporary calf, rebacked, original gilt back preserved, red leather label, central gilt arms of the Dugue de Bagnoll family of Lyon.

First edition. A 12mo edition appeared in 1681 and another 4to edition in 1689. An English translation appeared in 1683. This work contains the first detailed plans of St. Sophia and other monuments in Constantinople, which Grelot prepared during his long sojourn in the city. These plans were the only reasonably accurate drawings of St. Sophia extant until the mid-19th century. According to the attestations of Galland, Covel and others which Grelot included in his work to prove the veracity of his plans, he seems to have been resident in Constantinople for some time previous to 1671, when he left for Persia with Chardin.

BNF 30539578; Blackmer 750; Weber 369. Brunet II, 1733, cites a pirated edition, Amsterdam, 1681.

307. GRELOT, Guillaume Joseph. *A late voyage to Constantinople: containing an exact description of the Propontis and Hellespont, with the Dardanels, and what else is remarkable in those Seas; as also of the city of Constantinople... Likewise an account of the ancient and present state of the Greek Church... Made English by J. Philips.* London: John Playford for Henry Bonwicke, 1683.

8vo, pp. [xiv] 1-243 [13] (pp.[i]=[ ], [ii]=frontispiece, [iii]=t, [xiii-xiv]=attestations). With three plates (out of 8); frontispiece and six plans in the letterpress. This copy lacks the folding plans of St. Sophia. Modern ochre leather.

First English edition, translated by John Philips from the French edition published at Paris in 1680. This important work contains the first detailed description of Saint Sophia, with ground plans and facades. Grelot spent some years in Constantinople before 1671, and the attestations in the preliminary leaves, signed by Covel (q.v.) and Antoine Galland who knew Grelot, bear witness to the veracity of these plans. There should be eight folding engraved plates in this edition, numbered consecutively 1-14 with the 6 plans in the letterpress, plus a frontispiece of Mahomet IV. The first two plates in this copy are out of order and not numbered.

Blackmer 751; Weber 371; Wing G1934.

308. GUER, Jean Antoine. *Moeurs et usages des Turcs, leur religion, leur Gouvernement civil, militaire et politique, Avec un abrégé de l'Histoire Ottomane. Tome Premier. [... Tome Second.]* Paris: Veuve Delatour for Coustelier, 1746-47.

2 vols, 4to, pp. [v] XXIV, 1-453 [17]; [i] viii [2] 1-537 [2] (pp.[i]=ts, p.[v]=list of plates, vol. 1, pp.[1-17]=tables of sovereigns; pp.[1-2]=list of plates vol. 2, [1]-[2]=privilege and approbation). With two engraved frontispieces and 28 engraved plates (of which 6 folding and one panoramic). Titles in red and black. Contemporary mottled calf, worn, red and green leather labels, red edges. Ownership signatures cut from both titles.

First edition. The privilege was granted only to Antoine Coustelier, but a second issue of the work appeared in 1747 with the name of Merigot and Piget on the titles. A Dutch issue also appeared in 1747 under the name of Pierre Mortier, again the original sheets with a new title. On occasion copies of this work are found made up of mixed issues. The 'avertissement' on the list of plates in vol. 1 states that the work was printed by subscription; perhaps the subscriptions did not cover the cost of the publication and the privilege was ceded to other publishers. This work is especially valued for its engravings of Turkish costume figures and genre scenes by Duflos after Boucher and Hallé. According to the list of plates the panoramic view of the serail was originally intended to face p. 404 in vol. 1, but when vol. 2 was published its place was changed to p. 47 in vol. 2. In this copy the plate is still in vol. 1.

BL 149.h.12-13; BNF 30550511; Blackmer 762; Weber 761 (2nd ed.); Atabey 534; Brunet II, 1783; Colas 1348-49; Cohen-De Ricci 465.
Collation: $\pi^2 \chi^1$ a-c^4 A-3N^4; π^1 a^4 χ^1 A-3X^4 3Y^2. Note that the Blackmer and Atabey copies did not contain χ1 (list of plates) in either volume.

309. GUERIN, Victor Honoré (1821-1891). *Description de l'Ile de Patmos et de l'Ile de Samos.* Paris: Auguste Durand, 1856.

8vo, pp. [iii] III, 326 (pp.[i]=ht). With 2 folding maps/plans. Fine in the original printed grey paper wrappers, uncut.

Apparently only edition. Guerin visited Patmos and Samos c. 1853. He was a member of the French School of Archaeology in Athens from 1852, and was the first student to widen its field of activities to include Asia Minor and Syria. He also produced *Étude sur l'Ile de Rhodes*, 1856. Most of his archaeological work was concerned with Palestine, and in 1868 he produced *Description géographique, historique et archéologique de la Palestine*. In 1862 he produced *Voyage archéologique dans la Régence de Tunis*.

BNF 30551672; Blackmer 763. Not in Weber.

310. GUILLERAGUES. *Rélation veritable de ce qui s'est passé à Constantinople avec Monsieur de Guilleragues ambassadeur de France. Où on montre clairemont les bévuës de la Gazette de Paris. A Chio, chez Pierre de Touche, à l'Enseigne de Monsieur du Quene.* [Paris: publisher unidentified], 1682.

12mo, pp. [iv] 1-109 [2] (pp.[i]=t, pp.[2]=blank). Contemporary vellum boards. With the armorial bookplate of Nordkirchen.

First edition. Gabriel Joseph de Lavergne, Count de Guilleragues, took up the post of French ambassador to the Porte in 1679. In 1682 Abraham Du Quesne pursued and attacked Barbary pirates in the port of Chios, causing damage to the city. The Porte demanded damages from Guilleragues, who refused to pay and was thrown into prison. This caused a sensation in Paris, and several anonymous pamphlets were produced discussing the case: first the above, and then *Substance d'une lettre... touchant l'expedition de Monsr. du Quesne a Chio* (Ville Franche, 1683, translated into English as *Account of Monsieur de Quesne's late expediton at Chio*, London, 1683), and later *Ambassades de M. le Comte de Guilleragues et de M. Girardin aupres du Grand Seigneur* (Paris, 1687)

BL 1193.b.34. Not in Atabey or Blackmer but see Atabey 382, 537, 538 and Blackmer 1620. Collation: a^2 A-D^{12} E^8 (E8=[ ])

311. GUILLET, André Georges, *dit de La Guilletière* (1624-1705). *Athènes ancienne et nouvelle. Et l'estat present de l'empire des Turcs, contenant la vie du Sultan Mahomet IV. Le ministere de Coprogli Achmet Pacha, Grand Vizir. Ce qui s'est passé dans la camp des Turcs au siège de Candie. Et plusieurs autres particularitez des affaires de la Porte.*

Avec le plan de la ville d'Athènes, par le Sr. de la Guilletière. Paris: Estienne Michallet, 1675.

8vo, pp. [xxiv] 1-446 [32] (p.[i]=t, p.[xx]=errata, pp.[1-32]=index). With an engraved plan of Athens. Without the engraved plate of the theatre of Herodes Atticus. Contemporary calf, worn.

First edition. The second edition also appeared in 1675, but with the errata corrected. A third edition appeared in 1676. An English edition also appeared in 1676. The second half of the 17th century saw a growth of interest in Greece and the Levant. Apparently Guillet decided to capitalize on this interest, and although he had never visited Greece, he wrote a book in which he claimed that his brother had visited Athens and had sent him the information which he used to write this very successful description of the city. This information was in fact sent to him by the French consul Giraud and the Capuchin monks settled in the monastery built around the so-called lantern of Demosthenes, and the plan of Athens is also based on the map constructed by the Capuchin monks. Guillet's grasp of the antique was such that the work achieved a remarkable success despite the fact that Spon, who visited Athens in 1675 and realized that neither Guillet nor his brother could ever have actually seen the city, wrote a critique of the work in his own account of his travels in Greece (q.v.). Guillet replied in *Lettres écrites sur un dissertation d'un voyage de Grèce publié par Mr. Spon*, 1679.

BL 978.b.3; Blackmer 766; Weber 364; Atabey 539, 540. This edition not in BNF on line. Laborde I, pp. 214-45, says that Guillet had an '...intelligence remarquable des choses de l'antiquité'.

312. GUILLET, André Georges, *dit de La Guilletière*. **Lettres écrites sur une Dissertation d'un voyage de Grèce, publié par Mr. Spon, medecin antiquaire. Avec des remarques sur les medailles, les inscriptions... [etc.]** Paris: Estienne Michallet... M.DC.LXXIX. [=1679]

12mo, pp. [x] 1-288 (p.[i]=t). With an engraved map. Contemporary calf, back gilt. With an 18th c. armorial bookplate. From the library of K.Th. Dimaras, with his bookstamp on lower pastedown.

First and only edition of Guillet's reply to Spon's accusation that neither Guillet nor his supposed brother had ever visited Athens. Spon made this claim in his *Voyage* of 1678. Guillet countered at once with the *Lettres*, in answer to which Spon made a formal accusation in his *Reponse à la critique publiée par M. Guillet*, 1679. Guillet also included a map of the Bosphorus and the Hellespont in his work: 'Carte destroits du Bosphore de Thrace et de l'Hellespont selon Mr. Spon/ Carte veritable des Destroits...', in order to point out Spon's errors with regard to the geography of this area.

BNF 32642839; Blackmer 768; Laborde II, p. 31.

313. GULDENCRONE, Diane de, *Baroness, née Gobineau*. ***L'Achaïe féodale Étude sur le Moyen Age en Grèce (1205-1456)***. Paris: Ernest Leroux, 1886.

8vo, pp. [v] 1-393 (p.[i]=ht, [v]=ded, 391-93=conts). Quarter black roan over marbled paper boards. A presentation copy from the author to the Count Bandini Piccolomini dated 1899. Ownership stamp of George A. Zervas, later ownership inscription of Michael Stewart dated 1928.

First and apparently only edition. Diane de Guldencrone was the daughter of the Count de Gobineau, diplomat, amateur archaeologist, and author of *Trois ans en Asie*, 1859; *Souvenirs de Voyage*, 1872; *Deux études sur la Grèce moderne*. The work is dedicated to her father. She also wrote *Abrégé d' histoire ancienne*, 1896, and *Italie Byzantine*, 1914.

BNF 30562222; GL HG407.

314. GUY, Noël. ***Athènes Illustrations en couleurs de Marilac ouvrage orné de 148 photographies***. Paris: Fernand Nathan [1934].

Sm. 4to, pp. 158 + [1] (pp.1=ht, [1]=colophon). With 4 colour plates. Numerous photographs in text. Original cream boards, coloured illustration of the Acropolis mounted on upper cover.

First edition, uncommon. The date is attributed by the BNF. Noël produced similar works on Rome (1934) and Prague (1938). He worked with a number of artists including Marilac, Zenker, and Camoreyt. Karlsruhe cites a second edition, 1945.

BNF 32211575. Not in COPAC. Karlsruhe cites editions/issues with the dates 1936 and 1939.

315. GUYS, Pierre Augustin (1721-1799). ***Voyage littéraire de la Grèce, ou lettres sur les Grecs, anciens et modernes, avec un parallel de leurs moeurs. Nouvelle édition revue, corrigée, & considerablement augmentée. On y a joint un voyage de Sophie à Constantinople, un voyage d'Italie, et quelques opuscules du même***. Paris: Veuve Duchesne, 1776.

2 vols, 8vo, pp. [iv] IV, 1-540; [iv] 1-558 + [2] (pp.[i]=hts, [1]=conts, [2]=approbation). With 7 engraved plates. Contemporary mottled calf, backs gilt with thistles in compartments, black leather labels.

Second edition, enlarged. The first edition appeared in 1771 without illustrations. The second edition is uncommon in the market. This edition includes a contribution by Madame Chenier on Greek dances.

BNF 30565627; BL 1047.d.1-2. This edition not in Blackmer, Weber or Atabey.

316. GUYS, Pierre Augustin. *Voyage littéraire de la Grèce, ou lettres sur les Grecs, anciens et modernes, avec un parallel de leurs moeurs. Troisième edition revue, corrigée, considerablement augmentée.* Paris: Veuve Duchesne, 1783.

4 vols, 8vo, pp. [iv] i-viii, 1-527; [iv] 1-382 [2]; [iv] 1-373 [2]; [iv] 1-140 [3] (p.[i]=hts [lacking in vol 1], pp.[1-2]=errata, in vols.2 and 3, pp.[1-3] in vol.4=adverts). With eight (of 10) plates of which 4 folding. (This copy lacks the plate of the 'Branle Grec' and the plate of the Baths). Contemporary mottled calf, backs gilt, red edges. Contemporary ownership inscription in vol. I, with a reference to the Correspondence of La Harpe, vol. 2, p. 67, which contains a reference to Guys' work.

Third edition, with new material and plates, including 'Lettres sur les Turcs' by Guys' son. This edition was also produced in quarto format (GL copy). The first edition appeared in 1771 in 2 vols, 12mo, without illustrations. The second edition appeared in 1776 in 2 vols, 8vo, with seven plates. Guys was established in Constantinople from 1739, when he went there to work in his uncle's business establishment. He spent more than thirty years in the Levant, and his son continued the family tradition by serving as French consul in Zakynthos. Guys' work, in which he compares the ancient and modern Greeks, forms an important stage in the development of French philhellenism. The plates are engraved by Laurent mostly after drawings by Antoine Favray. They include: 2 plates of female costume, a wedding, a funeral, a fountain, a fishery, an aqueduct, a Greek dance, and a scene in a bath house.

BNF 36579319; GL GT655.2; Blackmer 169; Weber 529.

317. GUYS, Pierre Augustin. *A sentimental journey through Greece. In a series of letters, written from Constantinople... to M. Bourlat de Montredon, at Paris. Translated from the French. In three volumes.* London: for T. Cadell, 1772.

3 vols, 8vo, pp. [ii] x, 1-250; [vi] 1-231; [vi] 1-236 (pp.[i]=hts, pp.i-x=preface). Slightly later polished calf, joints broken. Early 19th c. booklabel of E.W. Leyborne Popham.

First edition in English, uncommon, published a year after the original French edition, which was unillustrated, consequently this translation does not contain any engravings. There is no indication of the translator's name. Apparently a Dublin edition appeared in 1773 in 16mo. The collation of gathering b in vol. 1 should probably be b^2; something is missing, possibly a contents leaf, because the catchword has been defaced.

BL 10126.h.3.; Weber 531. This edition not in Blackmer or Atabey.
Collation: (a)^6 b^1 A^{10} B-K^{12} L^6 M^1; (a)^3 A-T^6 U^2; (a)^3 A-I^{12} K^{10}.

318. HANSON, Charles Henry. *The Land of Greece described and illustrated.* London: T. Nelson and Sons, 1886.

Lge 8vo, pp. xii [13]-400 (pp.i=[], ii=fp, iii=vignette title, iv=printed title, xi=list of plates). With three double-page maps (1 printed in colour). Forty-two plates in the letterpress (versos blank). Original green pictorial cloth.

Apparently only edition.

BL 10125.ee.21 attributes the date 1886 [1885]; GL GT2083 with the date 1886.

318

319. HAYGARTH, William. *Greece, a Poem, in three parts; with notes, classical illustrations, and sketches of the scenery.* London: W. Bulmer for G. and W. Nicol, 1814.

4to, pp. viii + [4] 1-304 (p.i=ht, missing here, pp.[1-4]=contents, list of ills, st to pt. 1 and contents to pt 1). With 9 aquatinted plates in sepia. Half calf over marbled paper boards. With the armorial bookplate of George Head Head of Rickerby.

First edition. A French edition appeared in 1827. The aquatinted plates by Charles Turner are after drawings by Haygarth who spent the years 1810-1811 in Greece. He was an accomplished draughtsman, and a large set of his drawings is in the possession of the Gennadius Library. Gennadius himself regarded Haygarth's work as the best depiction of the countryside of pre-revolutionary Greece. The aquatinted plates were reproduced as lithographs by A. Joly in *Vues de la Grece Moderne*, Paris, 1824. Haygarth also contributed some drawings and notes to Walpole's *Memoirs*, 1817; his notes to *Greece, a poem* refer to his experiences during his sojourn in Greece.

BL 840.m.10; Blackmer 797; Weber 35.

319

320. HELLWALD, Friedrich von, and L.C. BECK. *Turkiet i våra Dagar. Bilder och Skildringar från alla Delar af det Osmaniska Riket. Förra Delen Osmaniska Riket i Europa. Öfversättning af O.W. Ålund. [... Senare Delen. Det Asiatiska Turkiet. Öfversättning af P.W. Thunman.]* Stockholm: E.T. Bergegrens Boekhandel [1878].

2 vols, 8vo, pp. V + [1] 440; IV, 441-952 (pp.I=ts, II=colophons, [1],441=sts, 941=st to index). With a double-page map printed in colour. Numerous wood engravings in the text, some full-page. Original publisher's binding of quarter red roan over red pictorial cloth gilt, back gilt.

Apparently first and only edition, uncommon. This is not an account of a journey, but contains information resulting from a journey. Volume one is an account of the coun-

tries of Turkey in Europe, i.e. Serbia, Albania, Bulgaria etc.; volume two deals with Turkey in Asia, and includes accounts of Cyprus, Rhodes, Thessaly, Macedonia, Mt. Athos, Smyrna, and the islands of the northern and eastern Aegean. The plates are reminiscent of those in the *Tour du Monde*.

Not in BL, Weber, Blackmer or Atabey. Karlsruhe cites 1 copy, in the Norwegian Union Catalogue.

321

321. HELYOT, Pierre Hippolyte. ***P. Hippolyt Helyots ausführliche Geschichte aller geistlichen und weltlichen Kloster= und Ritterorden für beyderley Geschlecht, in welcher deren Ursprung, Stiftung, Regeln, Anwachs, und merkwürdigste Begebenheiten, die aus ihnen entstandenen oder auch nach ihren Mustern gebildeten Brüderschaften und Congregationen ... Aus dem Französischen übersetzet. Erster Band. [... Siebenter Band.]*** Leipzig: Arkstee and Merkus, 1753-1756.

7 vols (of 8), 4to, pp. [xxiv] LXXXVIII, 486 + [28]; XXIV, 516 + [20]; [xii] 542 + [30]; [xii] 542 + [18]; [viii] 566 + [26]; [viii] 522 + [22]; [viii] 572 + [28] (pp.[i], I=ts). With 610 engraved *plates no'd 102; 119; 117 + 29*, 29**; 112; 87; 100; 71. Contemporary half brown calf over marbled paper boards, red edges.*

First edition in German, translated by J.J. Schwabe. This copy lacks volume 8. The first edition, in French, appeared in 1714-1719 in eight quarto volumes, with a second edition in 1721. This very interesting work illustrates the costume of all the religious orders of the middle ages, including that of the Greek priests and monks.

BL 1299.dd.4; Karlsruhe cites several copies.

322. HENRIQUEL-DUPONT, Louis Pierre, editor. Bas-Reliefs du Parthénon et du Temple de Phigalie disposés suivant l'ordre de la compostion originale et gravés par les procedés de M. Achille Collas sous la direction de M. Paul Delaroche... M. Henriquel Dupont... M. Charles Lenormant. Nouvelle édition. Paris: Didier, 1860.

Oblong folio, pp. [iii] 1-39 (pp.[i]=ht, [ii]=series title, [iii]=t, 39=errata). With 20 no'd engraved plates. Original embossed red cloth gilt, dampstained.

?Third edition. The first edition was published in 1834 as part of the series 'Tresor de Numismatique et de Glyptique' in 20 volumes, edited by Henriquel-Dupont, of which the 'Bas Reliefs' formed the third volume. The BNF also cites an edition dated 1838 published by Rittner and Goupil. According to an advert in Dumont's *Le Balkan* (q.v.), also published by Didier, this work was still available in 1873.

This edition not in BNF or BLC on line. This edition not in GL, which has the first edition.

323. HERODOTUS. Ἡροδότου Ἁλικαρνασσῆος Ἱστοριῶν Λόγοι Θ΄. Herodoti Halecarnassei Historiarum Libri IX novem musarum nominibus inscripti. London: E. Horton and J. Grover for John Dunmore, Richard Chiswell, Benj. Tooke and Thomas Sawbridge, MDCLXXIX. [=1679]

Sm. folio, pp. [lxxii] 1-708 + [41] + 33 + [35] (p.[i]=t, pp.[1-41]=Estienne on Herodotus, 1-33=notes by T. Gale, [1-35]=index). Double columns of Greek and Latin. With a large folding map. Contemporary panelled calf, rebacked. 19th c. bookseller's ticket of R. Saywell, London, on front pastedown.

First edition to be printed in England. This edition is based on Estienne's edition of Herodotus which first appeared almost a century earlier, and it includes Estienne's 'apologia' concerning Herodotus's accuracy. The map is captioned 'Tabula Geographica ad Herodotum illustrandum concin[n]ata', engraved by F. Lamb.

BL 585.k.4; Hoffmann II, 230.

324. HEROLD, Gottfried. *Beiträge zur Kenntniss des griechischen Landes und Volkes in Briefen.* Ansbach: Karl Brügel, 1839.

12mo, pp.[viii] 1-167 (p.[i]=t). Green paper boards. With notes on the front and back fly-leaves in the hand of a contemporary owner.

First edition of these letters written by Gottfried Herold, interpreter for the Bavarian Regency in Greece. Herold travelled to Greece as a member of the young King Otho's entourage, and the first letter is dated March, 1833, from Nauplion. Other letters are written from Milos, Naxos, Santorini, Myconos and Tinos in the summer of 1834. In 1847 Herold became professor at the Gymnasium in Nuremberg, and he began to produce school texts for classical studies. In 1870 he published *Die klassischen Studien im Gymnasium*. This work is uncommon; Karlsruhe V.K. cites only two copies.

BL 10126.A.12. Not in Weber or Blackmer.

325. HERRIOT, Edouard (1872-1957). *Sous l'Olivier.* [Paris:] Librairie Hachette [1930].

8vo, pp.[vi] [7]-324 + [1] + [1] (pp.[i]=ht, [iii]=ded., pp.[1]=conts, [1]=colophon). Woodcut vignette on title. Quarter leather, original grey pictorial paper wrappers bound in. A presentation copy signed on the fly-leaf 'A Monsieur et Madame Thomson hommage cordial Herriot'.

First edition. The work was reprinted in 1932 with dry-point illustrations by Mme. Bardey. The politician Herriot has dedicated his account of a journey through Greece in August of 1929 to Venizelos. His guide in 1929 was the young George Seferis. According to the colophon, ten numbered copies were produced on Jap vellum, 20 numbered copies on Holland paper, 75 numbered copies on Madagascar paper, and 800 numbered copies on ordinary paper. The Contominas copy is unnumbered. Herriot's presentation inscription may be to G.D. Thomson, the editor of Aeschylus. In 1917 Herriot edited *La France en Macédoine* and in 1934 he wrote *Orient*, in which he dedicates a chapter to the refugees of Asia Minor.

BNF 32241648; BL 10127.de.18; GL GT1435.7. See Basch, p. 422.

326. HERZOG & Cie. *M.L. Herzog & Cie. Fournisseurs de S.M.I. Le Sultan. Budapest (Hongrie) Cavalla (Turquie) Xanthi (Turquie) Drama (Turquie) Pravista (Turquie) Smyrne (Asie Mineure) Salonique (Turquie) New-York (États-Unis) Samsoun (Asie Mineure) Haskovo (Bulgarie).* [Budapest: Gelléri & Szekely, c. 1902.]

Oblong sm. folio, 2 leaves (title and 1 leaf resume of figures). With a folding panoramic pho-

tograph of Cavalla and eleven photographic plates, several with 3 or 4 photographs. Original grey cloth gilt.

Apparently only edition. The one leaf resume contains the turnover figures for the period 1890-1901. It seems likely that the date of publication would have been quite soon after this period. This publication is a form of trade catalogue, possibly an advert for stockholders, since it includes the turnover figures for ten years, but it does not include photographs of products or packaging. Herzog was a tobacco merchant who supplied the Turkish Sultan; the photographs illustrate tobacco workers, offices and warehouses in Cavalla, Drama, Xanthi, and Pravasti.

327. HEUZEY, Leon. *Excursion dans la Thessalie Turque en 1858.* Paris: "Les Belles-Lettres", 1927.

8vo, pp. [v] 191 + [1] (p.[i]=ht, v=avis [1]=conts). With a photographic frontispiece. Half blue cloth gilt over marbled paper boards.

First edition, published posthumously, although the preface was written by Heuzey in 1918. As he contemplated the problems of the Balkans as background to the War and the problems of peace, he recovered the notes of a journey he had made in 1858 through Thessaly and other parts of European Turkey. Hubert Pernot and Heuzey's grandson decided to publish the manuscript as no. 5 in the series of the 'Collection de l'Institut Néo-Hellénique'.

BNF 32244999.

328. HICHENS, Robert Smythe (1864-1950). *The Near East Dalmatia, Greece and Constantinople.* New York: The Century Co., 1913.

Lge 8vo, pp. x, 1-268 (p.i=ht). With a coloured frontispiece and 49 plates, many coloured. Uncut in the original blue decorative cloth gilt.

First edition. An English edition was also published in 1913 (q.v. below). The coloured plates are photographs of paintings by Jules Guerin (1866-1946), with captions on guard leaves. Note that the plates are hors texte, but are included in the pagination. Hichens and Guerin apparently travelled in the Levant in about 1908. Several works resulted from this journey: *Egypt and its monuments*, 1908; *The Holy Land*, 1910; *The Spell of Egypt*, 1911; and *The Near East*, 1913. Hichens also contributed travel articles to the *Pall Mall Magazine* from as early as 1894, and to the *Century Magazine* (with illustrations by Guerin). Hichens, an American, later developed as a novelist; perhaps his best known work is *The Paradine Case*.

LoC D972.H6.

329. HICHENS, Robert Smythe. *The Near East Dalmatia, Greece and Constantinople.* London: Hodder and Stoughton, 1913.

Lge 8vo, pp. x, 1-268 (p.i=ht). With a coloured frontispiece and 49 plates, many coloured. On thick paper, with headlines and page numbers printed in beige. Rough cut in the original red decorative cloth gilt and turquoise, top edge gilt.

First English edition. This is a more luxurious format than that of the American edition. BL 10125.ff.22.

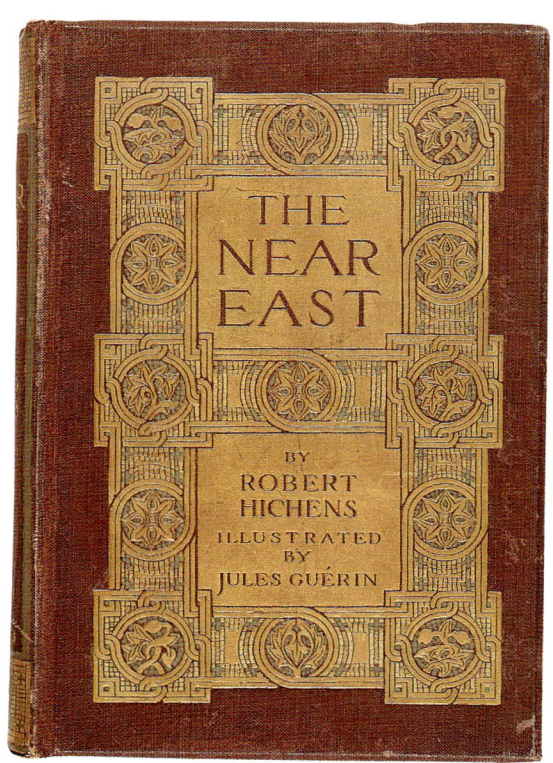

329

330. HOBHOUSE, John Cam, *Lord Broughton*. *A Journey through Albania, and other provinces of Turkey in Europe and Asia, to Constantinople, during the years 1809 and 1810... Second Edition. Vol. I. [... Vol. II.]* London: for James Cawthorn, 1813.

2 vols, 4to, pp. xv, 1-518; [i] 519-1152 + [2] (pp.i,[i]=ts, [1]=list of pls, [2]=advert). With a large folding map of Albania and Epirus, a frontispiece, 21 engraved plates (of which 17= coloured aquatints), 2 facsimiles and 2 leaves of engraved music. Uncut in three-quarter red morocco gilt.

329

A COLONEL OF THE JANISSARIES.

London, Published by James Cawthorn, 24, Cockspur Street, 1812.

Second edition, produced in the same year as the first. The second edition appeared in two issues, one in two volumes, with continuous pagination but with separate titles, as above, and the other in one volume. There is also a third issue, undated, and with uncoloured plates. Hobhouse travelled in the Levant with Byron; this may have given a special cachet to his work, which was extremely successful. Numerous editions appeared, and the work was reprinted in 1855 in 2 vols, 8vo, under Hobhouse's title as Baron Broughton, with the addition of important notes, and with new plates. Hobhouse's long and intimate relationship with Byron undoubtedly gave value to this account of their travels together, and it is possible that Hobhouse's membership of the London Greek Committee in 1823 had some influence on Byron's decision to go to Greece in 1824. Hobhouse spent some time with Byron in Italy in 1816-1817, and he wrote the notes to the 4th canto of *Childe Harold* which was published in 1818. He met Byron for the last time at Pisa in 1822. The work is also of great value for its detailed ethnographical and topographical accounts and for its description of the court of Ali Pasha. The coloured aquatints depict costumes (7) and views (10); the views are of particular interest for their depictions of Athens.

BL 568.f.21,22; Blackmer 821 (first ed); Weber 33; Abbey 202.

331. HOLDT, Hanns, and Hugo von HOFMANNSTHAL. *Griechenland Baukunst Landschaft Volksleben*. Berlin: Ernst Wasmuth [1923].

4to, pp. XIV, + [2] (p.I=ht, p.[1]=[], [2]=colophon). With 176 pages of photographic illustrations. Recent blue-green morocco.

First edition, reprinted in 1928. The text is by Hofmannsthal, the photographs mostly by Holdt. There is no indication of the date of the journey but they probably travelled c. 1920. The captions are in French, German and English. Hofmannsthal's text is limited to the introduction which accompanies the photographs and includes some interesting remarks on the ideals of German classicism. What appears to be an abridged edition appeared in 1924 under the title *Augenblicke in Griechenland*, edited by Alfred Happ.

BL 07705.cc.19.

332. HOLDT, Hanns, and Hugo von HOFMANNSTHAL. *Greece. Architecture Landscape Life of the People*. Berlin: Ernst Wasmuth [1928].

4to, pp. XXI (p.I=ht). With map and 304 pp. of photographic illustrations. Original green decorative cloth gilt.

First edition in English, published for *The Studio*.

BL L.R.51.e.7.

333. HOLLAND, Sir Henry (1773-1840). *Travels in the Ionian Isles, Albania, Thessaly, Macedonia, &c. during the years 1812 and 1813.* London: for Longman, Hurst, Rees, Orme, and Brown, 1815.

4to, pp. x + [i], 1-551 + [1] (p.i=t, [i]=list of plates, [1]=errata). With an engraved map by M. Thomson, and 12 engraved plates by Elizabeth and J. Byrne, R. Sands, John LeKeux, and G. Cooke. Contemporary half calf over paper boards. 19th c. armorial bookplate of John Nicol Fergusson Pixley on lower pastedown, 19th c. ownership inscription of Rathbone Greenbank on front fly-leaf.

333

First edition. A second edition appeared in 2 volumes, octavo, in 1819. Holland, a medical man, spent two months in Albania in 1812 as physician to Ali Pasha, and most of the plates are connected with Thessaly and Epirus: Argyrokastro, Metzovo, Larissa, Meteora, Souli, Ioannina. He travelled back to England in 1813 with Frederick North, Lord Guilford.

BL 148.h.14; Blackmer 825; Weber 37; Bib. Ionienne 880.

There is another copy in the Contominas collection, in contemporary half calf over marbled paper boards. Atabey 589.

334. HOPE, Thomas (?1770-1831). *Anastase, ou mémoires d'un Grec, écrits à la fin du XVIII.e siècle; traduits de l'Anglais par l'auteur de Lon-*

332

dres en 1819. Tome Premier. [... Tome Deuxième.] Paris: [J. Smith for] Gide fils and H. Nicolle, 1820

2 vols, 8vo, pp.[iii] 1-499; 1-525 (pp.[i],1=hts),+ 14 pp. of adverts and a 4-page prospectus for Moliere's Works. With a folding map. Contemporary half blue roan, backs gilt with sunburst. Bookplate of the Bibliothèque de Lancut.

First French edition, translated by Auguste J.-B. Defauconpret. Hope published *Anastasius, or memoirs of a Greek* anonymously in 1819 in London. Although *Anastasius* is a novel, it reflects Hope's travels in the Balkans and the Levant in the late 18th century (1787-1795) on which he embarked when he was eighteen years old. Buchon, who edited the second French edition (q.v.), regarded the work as 'le portrait le plus fidèle de l'état politique et social de l'empire ottoman et des éléments si divers qui le composent...'. The map is entitled 'Carte de l'Empire Ottoman, pour servir aux Mémoires d' Anastase. 1820. Gravé par G. Lemaitre'. *Anastasius* is a fascinating work, a form of picaresque novel in which Hope seems to have captured many of the facets of the Greek character.

BNF 30615959. This edition not in Blackmer but see 827. See David Watkin, *Thomas Hope*, London,1968, and *Pictures from 18th century Greece*, Athens, 1985, an album containing reproductions of drawings of the Greek subjects taken from Hope's original volumes of drawings in the possession of the Benaki Museum, with a long introduction by Fani-Maria Tsigakou.

335. HOPE, Thomas. *Anastase, ou mémoires d'un Grec. Traduits par M. Defauconpret. Précédés d'une notice sur l'auteur et de notes par J.-A. Buchon.* Paris: Charles Gosselin, 1844.

8vo, pp. [iii] I-VII [1] 1-650 (pp.[i]=ht, [1]=Hope's dedication to his wife, pp.643-50=conts). With a folding map. Old quarter green calf.

Second edition in French. The first French edition was published in 1820, translated by A. J.-B. Defauconpret. This second French edition contains an introduction by the medievalist J.A. Buchon (q.v.), who also provides a brief biographical notice of Hope and a list of his other works. An abridged French version was published in 1837 entitled *Anastase et Euphrosyne*. The folding map depicts Greece and the eastern Mediterranean (this edition of the map without imprint).

BNF 30615960. This edition not in Blackmer but see 827 (first edition).

336. HOPE, Thomas. *Anastasius, or memoirs of a Greek; written at the close of the Eighteenth Century. Vol. I. [... Vol. II.]* Paris: Baudry's Foreign Library, 1831.

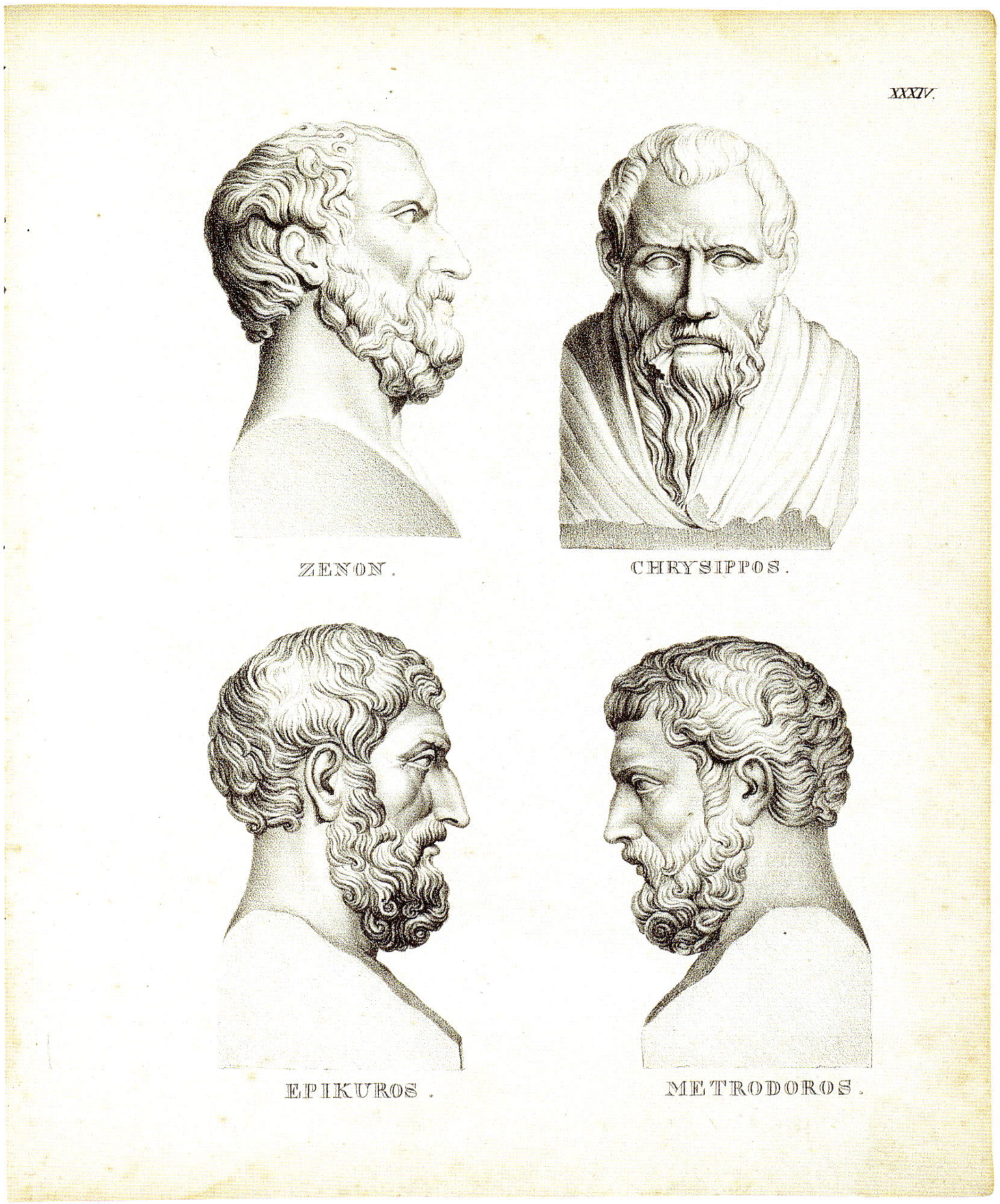

XXXIV.

ZENON. CHRYSIPPOS.

EPIKUROS. METRODOROS.

2 vols, 8vo, pp.[i] xv, iii, 4-430; [i] 442 (pp.[i]=t). With a folding map. Contemporary half calf, panelled backs gilt romantique.

First English edition to be published in France, in the series 'British Authors ancient and modern'. Hope published *Anastasius, or memoirs of a Greek* anonymously in 1819 in London. The second English edition appeared in 1820 with a preface signed by the author. Many still thought Byron had written *Anastasius*, and in 1821 Hope wrote to the editor of *Blackwood's Edinburgh Magazine* claiming authorship (vol. X, October 1821, p. 312). The work had an immediate success, and on reading it Byron is said to have wept twice: once because he had not written it, and twice because Hope had. Although *Anastasius* is a novel, it reflects Hope's travels in the Balkans and the Levant in the late 18th century (1787-1795) on which he embarked when he was eighteen years old.

BNF 30615958; Blackmer 827 (2nd edition). See David Watkin, *Thomas Hope*, London,1968, and *Pictures from 18th century Greece*, Athens, 1985, an album containing reproductions of drawings of the Greek subjects taken from Hope's original volumes of drawings in the possession of the Benaki Museum, with a long introduction by Fani-Maria Tsigakou.

337. HORNBY, Emily Bithynia, *Lady*. **Constantinople during the Crimean War. With illustrations in Chromo-lithography.** London: Richard Bentley, 1863.

Lge 8vo, pp. xvi + [1] 500 (p.i=ht, [1]=publisher's advert). Title in red and black. With 5 lithographed plates printed in colour. Recent ochre morocco, back gilt.

First edition, based on Lady Hornby's *In and Around Stamboul* published in a limited edition in 1858, but considerably enlarged and revised. Lady Hornby was resident in Constantinople for three years, 1855-1858, while her husband assisted in the administration of the British Government Loan to Turkey. The plates are after drawings by the artist Mary Walker, who spent over 40 years in the Levant. Her brother was chaplain to the English community at Constantinople and then was sent to Thessaloniki. She produced several illustrated books including *Through Macedonia to the Albanian Lakes*, 1864, *Eastern Life and Scenery*, 1886, and *Old Tracks and new Landmarks Wayside Sketches in Crete, Macedonia, Mitylene*, 1897.

BL 10126.e.8; Blackmer 829; Weber 615; Atabey 594.

338. HORNER, Johann Jakob. *Bilder des griechischen Alterthums oder Darstellung der berühmtesten Gegenden und der wichtigsten Kunstwerke des alten Griechenlandes.* Zurich: Orell, Füssli and Co., M.D.CCC.XXIII. [=1823]

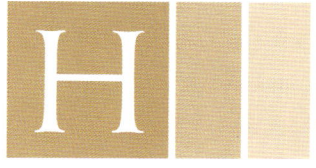

4to, pp. IV, 1-178 (pp. I=t, III-IV=pref., 177-8=conts). Lithographed title and 71 lithographed plates no'd 1-72 (14-15 used together on the view of Athens). Contemporary black marbled paper boards, defective. 19th c. ownership signature of (-) Wachler on front pastedown.

First edition, uncommon. A French edition appeared in 1824-5 in apparently only two livraisons with 35 plates. Horner's work consists of a series of articles on various aspects of ancient Greek life, each accompanied by a plate. The plates, many signed J. Brodtmann, are after plates from the works of Stuart and Revett, Leake, Visconti, Gell, and the *Unedited Antiquities of Attica*.

Not in BLC or LoC. Blackmer 830. Karlsruhe cites 6 copies.

339. HUGHES, Thomas Smart. *Travels in Sicily Greece and Albania... Illustrated with engravings of maps scenery plans &c. In two volumes Vol. I. [... Vol. II.]* London: for J. Mawman, 1820.

2 vols, 4to, pp. xii [i] 532; viii, 393 + 2 pp. of adverts (pp.i=ts, [1]=list of plates). With 15 engraved plates (of which 2=aquatints, 3=maps/plans). Half leather, lower edges rough cut.

First edition. A second edition, enlarged, appeared in 2 vols, 8vo, in 1830. The work was translated into French in 1821. Hughes undertook a long journey in the Mediterranean and Greece in 1813 and 1814 as tutor to Richard Townley Parker who was engaged on the Grand Tour. Hughes and Parker arrived in Preveza in late 1813 where they met C.R. Cockerell, who spent about two months with them on their Albanian tour. Most of the views are after Cockerell's drawings of Epirus, engraved by J. Smith, with the aquatints by F.C. Lewis. Hughes' work is devoted for the most part to a description of Epirus and southern Albania, and it is a major source of information about Ali Pasha. Hughes was a fervent philhellene, an early member of the Philomuse Society which he probably joined when he was in Athens in 1814. He later became a member of the London Greek Committee and published several pamphlets on the massacre of Chios in 1822.

BL 528.f.18; Blackmer 842; Weber 86; Atabey 599 (the Blackmer copy); Abbey 203.

340. HUGHES, Thomas Smart. *Voyage à Janina en Albanie, par la Sicile et la Grèce. Traduit de l'Anglais... par l'auteur de Londres en 1819.* Paris: Gide fils, 1821.

2 vols in 1, 8vo, pp. 1-326; 1-351 (pp.1=hts, 2=adverts). Lithographed frontispiece of Ali Pacha in vol. 1. Old polished calf gilt, back defective, red leather label.

First edition in French, translated by A.J.B. Defauconpret, who had translated Hope's *Anastasius* (q.v.) the previous year. This work was published in the series 'Collection des meilleurs voyages modernes', vols 34 and 35.

BNF 30624868; Weber 88; Atabey 600; Droulia 121-122. This edition not in Blackmer.

341. HUNTER, Isobel L. *This is Greece.* London: Evans Brothers [1947].

8vo, pp. viii, 9-102 (p.i=ht). With a coloured frontispiece and 16 photographic plates. Original blue cloth, faded.

First and only edition, and the author's only work. The frontispiece is a photograph of a painting of windmills on Chios from the Argentis collection. The endpapers form maps of Greece and the Aegean.

BL 10127.ee.17.

342. HUNTER, Mary. *Εὐχαριστήρια τοῦ Μετώπου πρὸς τὴν φιλέλληνα Ἀγγλίδα Κυρίαν Μαίρην Χοῦντερ παρ' ὅλων τῶν στρατηγῶν, μεράρχων καὶ διοικητῶν τῆς Στρατιᾶς Μικρᾶς Ἀσίας.* Athens: Typografia 'Kallitechnia', 1922.

Oblong 8vo, pp. 1-79 (p.1=t). Photographic illustrations in text. Original printed blue paper title wrappers.

Apparently only edition. This album is a memento from all the Greek battalions in Asia Minor to Mary Hunter and the White Cross Nurses. Mary Hunter, who had worked in Macedonia (perhaps during the Balkan Wars), founded a White Cross nursing group in Constantinople. Her nurses served in Greek hospitals in Asia Minor. Many of the photographs illustrate the army hospital 'Aghios Charalampos' in Smyrna. The wrapper bears the title: 'Λεύκωμα τοῦ Μικρασιατικοῦ μετώπου τῆς φιλέλληνος Ἀγγλίδος Κ. Μαίρης Χοῦντερ'. The White Cross movement was an organization active in the late 19th and early 20th century; grounded in the temperance movement and supported by a number of Anglican clergy, it embraced many forms of charitable work.

Apparently not in GL or BLC on line.

343. HUTTON, Edward (1875-). **A glimpse of Greece.** New York: MacMillan [1929].

8vo, pp. xii, 1-324 (pp.[i]=ht, ix-xii=list of ills, 321-4=index). With a large folding map printed in colour and 43 photographic illustrations. Modern brown morocco, back gilt.

First American edition. The first edition was published in London in 1928 by the Medici Society. Hutton travelled in Greece in company with the writer Norman Douglas. He was a litterateur and miscellaneous writer who edited Crashaw, wrote the introduction to an edition of the Decameron, produced guides to various Italian cities and to the English counties, edited Palgraves' *Golden Treasury*, produced a memoir of the Dukes of Urbino, etc. etc.

LoC DF726.HB. See Dennis Rhodes, *The writings of Edward Hutton A Bibliographical Tribute*, London, 1955.

344. IDEVILLE, Henri Amédée Lelorgne de, *Count*. **Journal d'un diplomate en Allemagne et en Grèce Notes intimes pouvant servir à l'histoire du Second Empire. Dresde-Athènes 1867-1868.** Paris: Hachette et Cie, 1875.

2 parts in 1, 8vo, pp. viii, 1-371 (p.i=ht, p.187=st to Greek section). Half green cloth gilt. From the library of K.Th. Dimaras, with his stamp on the lower pastedown.

First edition; a second edition appeared the same year. Ideville left for Athens in December 1866; he was stationed there about six months. Although his assignment in Athens was previous to that in Dresden, the Greek material follows his German experiences. Ideville produced *Journal d'un diplomate en Italie* in two volumes, 1872-3, and he also wrote a personal memoir of the archaeologist Beulé.

BNF 30632822; BL 10662.cc.1 (2nd ed). This edition not in GL which has the 2nd ed. Not in Atabey or Blackmer.

345. INWOOD, Henry William. **The Erechtheion At Athens. Fragments of Athenian Architecture and a few Remains in Attica Megara and Epirus. Illustrated with outline plates and a descriptive historical view combining also under the divisions Cadmeia Homeros and Herodotos the origin of Temples and of Grecian Art of the periods preceding.** London: William Nicol for James Carpenter and Son, Josiah Taylor, and Priestley and Weale. M.DCCC.XXVII. [=1827]

Folio, pp. [vii] 1-161 [1] and with 3 additional 2-page dedications (unpaginated) between pp. 90-91, 123-125, and 153-155 (pp.[i]=t, vii=ded., [1]=notes and colophon). With 35 engraved plates on 34 sheets, no'd 1-39 (nos. 6, 7, 13 and 18 not published; engravings 8 + 9 on same plate). Modern panelled calf.

First edition. A German version was published at Berlin in 1840 with a text on the history of Greek architecture by A. F. von Quast, and in 1843 at Potsdam, with Quast's text in 8vo and the plates in folio. This copy is complete with the four dedications: the chief dedication to Lord Colchester, and the other three to W. J. Bankes, the Duke of Bedford and Thomas Hope (q.v.). Inwood, who travelled in Greece in 1819, was one of the architects of the church of St. Pancras, one of the chief monuments of the neo-classical style in London, which includes a caryatid porch in the manner of the Erechtheion. This important work provided the theoretical basis for much of Inwood's architectural practice. The list of subscribers includes the names of most of the architects who were working in the neo-classical style in the early 19th century.

BL 745.e.10; GL A26q; Blackmer 856.

346. IORGA, Nicolas. *Brève Histoire des Croisades et de leurs fondations en Terre Sainte.* Paris: J. Gamber, 1924.

8vo, pp. xix, 194 [1] (pp.1=ht, [1]=conts). Half brown morocco gilt, original stiff printed paper wrapper bound in.

First edition.

BNF 32270944.

347. IORGA, Nicolas. ***Les Voyageurs Français dans l'Orient Européen. Conferences faites en Sorbonne. Extraites de la Revue des Cours et Conferences.*** Paris: Boivin & Cie, and J. Gamber [1928]. – ***Une vingtaine de voyageurs dans l'Orient Européen. Pour faire suite aux "Voyageurs Français dans l'Orient Européen".*** Paris: J. Gamber, 1928. – ***Les Voyageurs orientaux en France.*** Paris: J. Gamber, 1927.

3 works in 1 volume, 8vo, pp. 128 (p.1=ht); pp. 86 [1] (p.1=t, [1]=conts); pp. [i] 105 +[1] (p.[i]=t, [1]=table of conts). Uncut in quarter turquoise calf, all three works bound in with their original printed paper wrappers. From the library of K. Th. Dimaras, with his stamp on the lower paste-down.

First editions. Iorga was a prolific historian and bibliographer of travel in the Levant. The last work, *Voyageurs orientaux en France*, includes Greek, Turkish and Romanian travellers. This collection is bound together with two other pamphlets, by Emile Malakis and Panos Morphopoulos (see descriptions under separate entries). This collection comes from the library of K. Th. Dimaras, who may have known Iorga personally.

BNF 35818786 and 32271020.

348. IPSARIOTE. ***L'Ipsariote, ou La Grèce vengée. Tome Premier [... Tome Deuxième].*** Paris: [Huzard-Courcier for] Boulland, 1825.

2 vols in 1, 12mo, pp. [iii] 1-195; [iii] 1-196 (p.[i]=hts). Uncut in calf antique, back gilt with meander design. From the library of K. Th. Dimaras.

Apparently only edition, rare. The author is unknown. This work may consist of four volumes. Droulia, citing only this copy which belonged to Dimaras, calls for two volumes, but the BNF catalogue calls for four volumes. We have not been able to confirm this.

BNF 33438617; Droulia 784-785. Not in GL or Blackmer, not in BLC on line.

349. JACOPI, Giulio. *Rodi Con 193 illustrazioni e 2 tavole di cui una in colori.* Bergamo: Istituto Italiano d'arti grafiche [1933].

Lge 8vo, pp. 1-134 (pp.1-2=adverts, 3=ht, 5=t). Two plates hors texte (1 folding, 1 in colour). Numerous illustrations in the text. Original stiff green and white paper wrappers gilt.

First and apparently only edition. Part of the series 'Collezione di Monografie Illustrate'.

BL D-7824.gg.37.

350. [JOLY, Alexis Victor], and E.L. *Vues de la Grèce Moderne, lithographiées par A.J., Accompagnées d'un texte descriptif par E.L.* Paris: C. de Lasteyrie for Dondey-Dupre and Treuttel and Würtz, MDCCCXXIV. [=1824]

Oblong folio, pp. 22 (p.1=first p. of text). Lithographed title and ten lithographed plates. Contemporary green boards, upper joint broken.

First and only edition, rare. Nine of the lithographs have been adapted from the aquatints in Haygarth's *Greece*, 1814. However, the text, by E.L. (? Emilie de L., a miscellaneous and travel writer) is markedly philhellenic and has no connection with Haygarth.

350

BNF 33650024; Blackmer 881; Droulia 676. Not in BLC or LoC on line. NUC cites two copies. Adhemar 91 identifies Joly as a prolific lithographer who was working up until at least 1839.

351. JOURDAIN, Jean Philippe Paul. *Mémoires historiques et militaires sur les événements de la Grèce, depuis 1822, jusqu'au combat de Navarin: par Jourdain, Capitaine de Frégate ... Tome Premier. [... Second.]* Paris: Brissot-Thivars, 1828.

2 vols, 8vo, pp. li, 1-316; [iii] 1-464 (pp.i, [i]=ht). With a folding map, coloured in outline, 2 lithographed portraits (Miaoulis and Mavrocordatos), and a folding plate (of 3). Vol. 1 in contemporary tree calf, back gilt with title 'Tableau de la Grèce', red and black leather labels; vol. 2 not ensuite, in slightly later quarter calf, flat back gilt in compartments.

First and only edition. The long preface contains biographical details of Jourdain by the unknown editor. The philhellene Jourdain was apparently settled in Siphnos in 1826. He became involved in the Knights of Malta scandal, whereby the Knights, in return for assisting the Greeks, would regain possession of Rhodes and other parts of the Ottoman empire. The map is entitled 'Carte de la Grèce moderne donnant le détail pour suivre le theatre de la guerre avec les frontières de la Turquie et de la Russie à Paris chez H. Langlois fils et cie (1826)'. The two missing plates depict the female costume of Siphos. The GL copy contains an extra-illustration, an uncaptioned portrait which resembles Canaris.

BNF 30663481; BL 9135.bb.1; Blackmer 890; Droulia 1557-58. GL IND274.

JULIEN, *domestique*. See DANIELO

352. JURIEN DE LA GRAVIÈRE, Jean Baptiste Edmond. *La Station du Levant. Tome Premier. [... Second.]* Paris: E. Plon, 1876.

2 vols in 1, sm. 8vo, pp. [iii] 356; [iii] 345 (pp.[i]=hts). With a large folding map. Half brown morocco, back ruled gilt.

First edition. This important work first appeared in parts in the *Revue des Deux Mondes* in 1872-1874 as 'Les Missions de la Marine III. La Station du Levant'. A Greek translation was published in 1894. The work provides source material on the activities of the French navy in the eastern Mediterranean from 1816-1830. Jurien based much of his work on the papers of Admiral de Rigny, French naval commander and philhellene. There is a short appendix on Montenegro.

BNF 30669339; Blackmer 895.

353. KAMBOUROGLOUS, D.G. *Mémoires du Prince Nicolas Ypsilanti d'après le manuscrit n° 2144 de la Bibliothèque Nationale de Grèce.* Athens and Paris: Meissner and Kargadouris (Estia) for Eleutheroudakis and Nilsson, n.d.

8vo, pp.[iii] 132 [1] (pp.[i]=t, [iii]=st, [1]=errata). With 2 preliminary leaves of notes in Greek. Recent leather, original printed paper wrappers bound in.

First edition, printed in 1000 copies. This is copy no. 880.

BL 1609/3653.

354. KATSAITES, Marco Antonio. *Δύο ταξίδια στὴ Σμύρνη 1740 καὶ 1742. Εἰσαγωγή, κείμενο, μετάφραση-σχόλια, πίνακες.* Athens: Myrtides Bros., 1972.

8vo, pp.[x] 13-205 [6]; (pp.[i]=ht, [v]=ded. [1-6]=list of plates, conts, errata, colophon). With 3 folding illustrations. Half calf, red leather label, back ruled gilt and embossed in black. Bound with the Journey to Constantinople, below.

First edition, edited by Philippos K. Phalbos from Katsaites' manuscript in the Sorbonne, in the library of the Institute for Modern Greek Studies. This manuscript contains the text of three journeys, in Italian. Phalbos has provided a Greek translation and notes. The first part, published here, is an account of travels in the Ionian Islands and the Aegean to Smyrna; the second part, below, describes a journey from Smyrna to Constantinople. The third part of the manuscript, giving an account of Moldovlachia, was published in 1979 (q.v.). Katsaites (also spelled Cazzaiti) was an Ionian Greek who studied in Venice. Papadopoulos records his *Geografia in Dialogo*, Venice, Lazzaroni, 1738, but has no record of the journey to Smyrna.

BL X.702/15564. See Legrand 18th c. I, 269-70 for information on Katsaites.

There is another copy in the Contominas collection, with a presentation inscription from the editor to K.Th. Dimaras, in the original wrappers.

355. KATSAITES, Marco Antonio. *Ταξίδια τοῦ 1742 Βορειοδυτικὴ Παραλία Μικρᾶς Ἀσίας. Προποντίδα. Κωνσταντινούπολη. Εἰσαγωγή, κείμενο, μετάφραση-σχόλια, πίνακες.* Athens: Myrtides Bros. [for the Enosis Smyrnaion], 1974.

8vo, pp.[x] 13-329 [6] (pp.[i]=ht, [v]=ded. [1-6]=list of plates, conts, errata, colophon). Half calf, red leather label, back ruled gilt and embossed in black. Bound with the Journeys to Smyrna.

First edition, edited by Philippos K. Phalbos from Katsaites' manuscript in the Sorbonne, in the library of the Institute for Modern Greek Studies. This second work records Katsaites' travels through Asia Minor to Constantinople, and his return to the Ionian Islands in 1743.

Not in BLC.

356. KATSAITES, Marco Antonio. *Ταξίδι στὴ Μολδοβλαχία τὸ ἔτος 1742.* Athens: Myrtides, 1979.

8vo, pp. [xii] 13-176 [3] (p.[i]=ht, [3]=colophon). With 8 illustrations. Original printed paper wrappers, uncut.

First edition, edited by Philippos Phalbos with an introduction, notes and translation into Greek. The manuscript, in Italian, is an account of Katsaites' journey in 1742 through the Danubian principalities from Jassy to Constantinople.

357. KING, Francis Henry, *editor.* **Introducing Greece.** London: Methuen [1956].

8vo, pp. 264 (p.1=ht). With 18 plates of photographs. Original cloth, worn.

First edition. A revised edition appeared in [1967]. This very good picture of Greece before the advent of mass tourism contains articles by Ian Scott-Kilvert, Robert Liddel and others, including King. All three were connected with the British Council which was established in Athens after the war. It is possible that this publication was part of an official effort to encourage British involvement in Greece.

BL 10127.eee.48.

358. KINGLAKE, Alexander William (1809-1891). **Eothen, or Traces of travel brought home from the East. Fourth Edition.** London: John Ollivier, 1845.

8vo, pp. xi, 1-423 (p.i=t). With a tinted lithographed frontispiece and 1 lithographed plate. Original green embossed and pictorial cloth gilt, rough cut.

Fourth edition. The second and third editions also appeared in 1845. There is another edition marked 'fourth edition' dated 1846 and published as vol. 105 in the series 'Collection of British Authors' with a different collation (pp. xii, 308). This famous book of travels was first published anonymously by Ollivier in 1844. It has been reprinted innumerable times; later editions have appeared with notes by D.G. Hogarth, A.T.

Quiller-Couch and W. H. Rouse. Kinglake travelled in the East in about 1835. His most important work is his history of the Crimean war in eight volumes, 1863-87.

BL 108.pp.2. This edition not in Blackmer but see 911 (1st ed.).

359. KINGLAKE, Alexander William. *Eothen, or traces of travel brought home from the East. Fifth Edition.* London: John Ollivier, 1847.

Sm. 8vo, pp. xii, 1-306 (p.i=t). With a wood-engraved frontispiece captioned 'Eastern Travel' and 3 wood-engraved plates. Old half calf, back gilt in compartments.

Fifth edition.

360. KINGLAKE, Alexander William. *Eothen, or traces of travel brought home from the East. New Edition.* Edinburgh and London: Blackwood & Son, 1885.

Sm. 8vo, pp. xiv, 1-371 [1] (p.i=ht, [1]=imprint). 19th c. half red morocco over red marbled paper boards.

A late edition.

361. KINGLAKE, Alexander William. *Eothen Relation d'un voyage en orient Traduit de l'Anglais sur la cinquième édition.* Paris: Amyot, 1847.

8vo, pp. xvi, 1-350 (p.i=ht). Quarter green morocco over green cloth, back gilt romantique.

First edition in French, translated by Pierre-Gustave Brunet.

BNF 30681890; Weber 371; Atabey 635.

362. KITTO, Humphrey Davy Findley. *In the mountains of Greece.* London: Methuen [1933].

8vo, pp. x, 1-150 (pp.i=ht, x=map). With photographic frontispiece and three photographic illustrations. Original orange cloth, uncut.

First and apparently only edition, uncommon. An account of two months in Greece in the summer of 1931 or 1932 by the classicist H.D.F. Kitto. He and his wife set out for Euboea with Mr. and Mrs. Heurtley and Miss Negroponte of the British School at Athens and continued on their own to Aetolia and on through the Peloponnesus, where Kitto gives some splendid descriptions of encounters on the way.

BL 10125.df.30

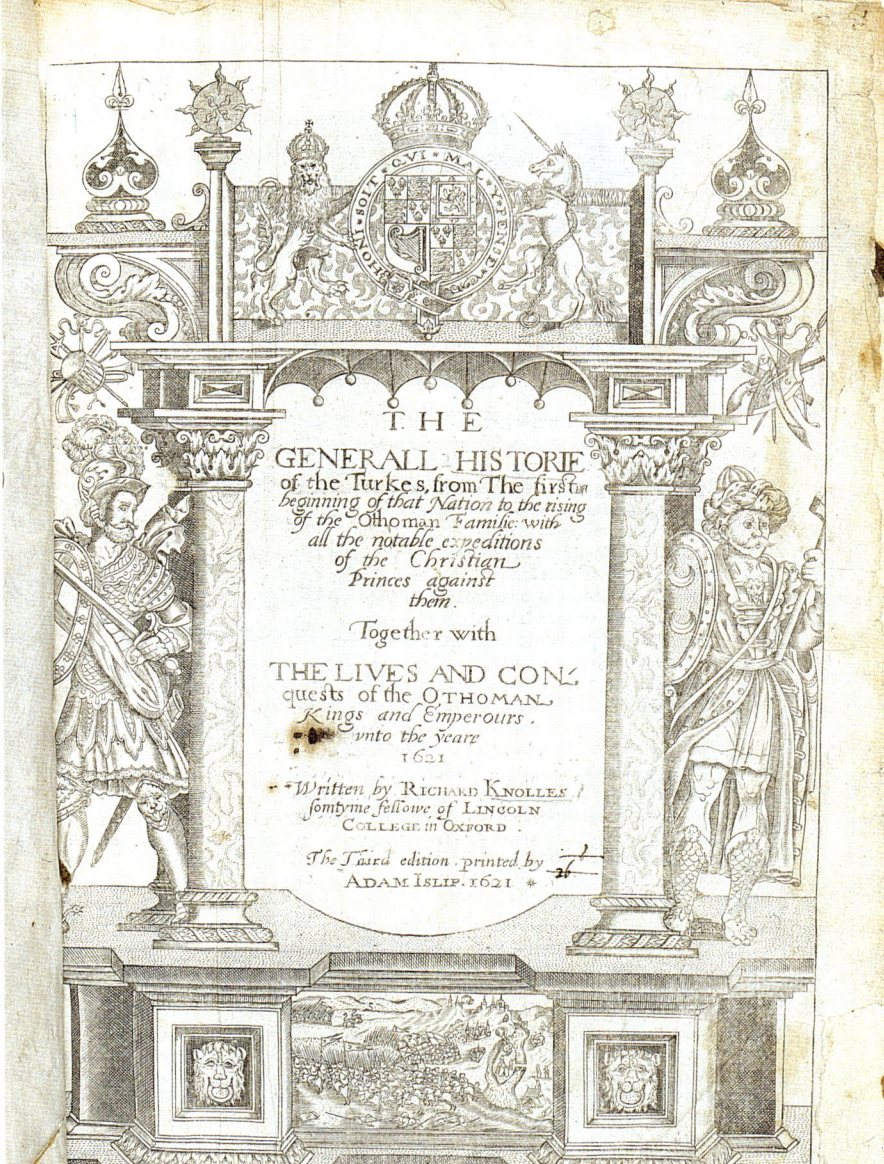

363

363. KNOLLES, Richard. *The Generall Historie of the Turkes, from the first beginning of that Nation to the rising of the Othoman Familie: with all the notable expeditions of the Christian Princes against them... The Third edition, printed by Adam Islip. 1621.* [London: Islip, 1621.]

Folio, pp. [viii] 1-1396 + [15] + [23] (p.[i]=dedication, pp.[1-23]=index). With an engraved title. Contemporary calf, rebacked, black leather labels. 18th c. bookplate of Beilby Thompson of Escrick.

Third edition of the most important early English work on the Turks, first published in 1603. The work went through many editions; the fifth edition was edited by Thomas Nabbe, and a sixth edition appeared between 1687 and 1700, completely revised by Paul Rycaut, with many additions from his own works. Knolles spent twelve years compiling his great history; it was praised by Dr. Johnson and its influence was acknowledged by Byron.

BL 9135.h.5; Blackmer 919 (1st ed) and 920 (5th ed); Atabey 1076 (6th ed, under Rycaut). See Samuel C. Chew, *The crescent and the rose, Islam and England during the Renaissance*, New York, 1937, pp. 111-115.

364. KONSTANTIOS, Byzantios, *Archbishop of Mt. Sinai, Patriarch of Constantinople*. Ἀρχαία Ἀλεξάνδρεια. Περιγραφὴ τῆς πόλεως ταύτης ἐν τῇ κατὰ πάροδον περιηγήσσι τοῦ Κιαιβο-Αικατερινο-Γραικικοῦ Μοναστιρίου Ἀρχιμανδρίτου Κωνσταντίου, καλλωπισθεῖσα μετὰ εἰκονογραφικῶν καὶ ἰχνογραφικῶν σχεδίων... Μόσκβα 1803. Ἐν τῇ Ἐλευθέρα Τυπογραφία Γαρίου καὶ Κομπανίας. [Moscow: Garios and Co., 1803.]

4to, pp. [viii] [i]-vii [1], 1-67 + [3] (pp.[i]=ht, [ii]=Russian title, [iii]=Greek title, [iv]=ded in Russian, [v]=ded in Greek, [vi]-[i]=ep. ded. to Alexander I, [ii]-vii=preface in Russian and Greek on facing pages, p.[1]=quotation from Herodotus, pp.[1-3]=errata, p.1=st). With four folding plates. Three large half-page vignettes in letterpress. Modern red leather gilt.

First edition. Konstantios was peculiarly fitted to write this description of Alexandria. For many years he was abbot of the monastery of St. Catharine on Mt. Sinai. This may be Konstantios's earliest work. His descriptions of Constantinople and of the Monastery of Kykkou in Cyprus were published in 1819. The plates include a map of Alexandria and its harbour; a panoramic view of the new harbour; the obelisk of Cleopatra; and Pompey's column. Note that the prefaces in Russian and Greek do not consist of the same text. In 1841 Konstantios produced *Aegyptiaca*.

BL 793.l.34; GL GT2569.7; Iliou 1803.17. Not in Blackmer or Atabey.
Collation: π⁸ А⁴ Б⁴ В⁴ Г⁴ Д⁴ Е⁴ Ж⁴ З⁴ И⁴

365. Konstantios, Byzantios, *Archbishop of Mt. Sinai, Patriarch of Constantinople, editor.* **Περιγραφὴ Ἱερὰ τοῦ ἁγίου καὶ Θεοβαδίστου Ὄρους Σινᾶ, περιέχουσα ἐν πρώτοις μὲν τὴν Ἀκολουθίαν τοῦ Ἁγίου καὶ Ἐνδόξου Μεγάλου προφήτου Μωϋσέως τοῦ Θεόπτου. Δεύτερον δὲ τὴν Ἀκολουθίαν τῆς Ἁγίας Ἐνδόξου Μεγαλομάρτυρος Χριστονύμφης, παρθένου καὶ πανσόφου Αἰκατερίνης, ἑπομένως δὲ ἐξιστοροῦσα συ-**

ντόμως καὶ περιληπτικῶς τὰ τοῦ Θεοβαδίστου τούτου Ὄρους... Τυπωθεῖσα νῦν πέμπτον διὰ δαπάνης τῆς ἱερᾶς καὶ Βασιλικῆς μονῆς τοῦ Ἁγίου καὶ Θεοβαδίστου Ὄρους Σινᾶ. Venice: Nikolaos Glykys, 1817.

4to, pp. 1-219 (p.1=t, p.219=conts). With 4 engraved plates. Woodcut head- and tailpieces and capitals. Contemporary marbled pasteboards. Ownership inscription cut away from the corner of the front fly-leaf.

Fifth Venice edition, first published in Venice in 1727. Apparently an earlier edition appeared at Tergovisti in 1710. The fifth edition was prepared by Konstantios the Sinaite and was seen through the press by Spyridon Blantes. This is not a proskynetarion in the ordinary sense, but a brief description of the monastery of St. Catherine at Mount Sinai with liturgies. The plates include 1) Moses receiving the ten commandments 2) St. Catherine with the monastery at her feet 3) the Virgin 4) Holy Saints.

GL T1683.4; Ghinis-Mexas 994; Iliou 1817.88 calls for an extra leaf at the end.

366. KORDELLAS, Andreas. *Le Laurium par André Cordella Ingénieur des Mines.* Marseille: Cayer & Co., 1869. [Athens: 1874.]

8vo, pp. [i], I-VIII [1], IX, 10-120 (pp.[i]=ht, I-VIII=preface, [1]=ded; there is no printed title). With a lithographed title, five lithographed plates (4 double-page) and a large folding map. Several diagrams in the letterpress. Old quarter leather over paper boards.

Second edition, first published in 1869. In fact the original sheets of the first edition have been reissued to form this second edition with a new preface dated 1874. The dedication to King George I is dated 1870; the GL copy of the first edition is in a wrapper dated 1871. The 1869 edition probably actually appeared in 1870. This very interesting work was first published on the occasion of the Greek Government decision to reopen the silver mines of Lavrion. Kordellas was the engineer appointed by the Government to determine whether the ancient silver mines were still worth exploiting. The double-page plates are especially interesting; they include a view of Lavrion and the works, a tinted view of the works, a geological profile of Lavrion, and a view of the area where the minerals were washed in large basins. The lithographed title contains a vignette of the furnaces which is repeated on a separate plate. The large folding map depicts the bay of Lavrion. This is Kordellas's earliest work. He was a prolific writer on mineralogy and related subjects, with many pamphlets on Lavrion and its products.

BNF 30269403; BL 7106.g.25.

367. KUPFER, Grace H. *Legends of Greece and Rome Stories of Long Ago. Third edition revised and enlarged.* London: D.C. Heath, 1907.

8vo, pp. 220 [1] + 2 pp. of adverts (pp.1=ht, [1]=glossary of names). With 16 photographic illustrations. Original quarter calf gilt over green decorative cloth gilt, upper edge gilt.

Third editon, first published in 1898, with a second edition in 1900. This account of classical myths and legends is illustrated with photographs of classical statues and archaeological sites.

BL 12411.p.1/20.

368. KUYPERS, Franz. *Griechenland. Mit 96 Bildtafeln nach Originalaufnahmen von Charlotte von Gwinner.* Munich: F. Bruckmann [1935].

4to, pp. xx, 199 (pp.i=ht, 195-99=index). With photographic frontispiece, 95 photographic illustrations, and a folding map. Original blue cloth.

First and apparently only edition. The photographs are very fine.

BL 10127.h.9.

369. LABORDE, Leon Emmanuel S.J. de, *Marquis*. **Athènes aux XVe, XVIe et XVIIe siècles.** Paris: Jules Renouard, 1854.

2 vols, lge 8vo, pp. XVIII [viii] 1-276; [vi] 1-392 + [1] (pp.I, [i]=hts, [i-viii]=facsimiles, [1]=advert). With nine (of 10) engraved plates (4 folding) in vol. 1, and twelve (1 =folding, 4=dp) in vol. 2. Old cloth, original blue printed paper wrappers mounted on both sides.

First edition of this important work on early modern Athens, as seen through the eyes of travellers, containing previously unpublished drawings and sketches of the Acropolis and other monuments. It remains an essential biographical and historical reference work. Laborde made his first journey to the Levant in 1825; in 1826-7 he travelled in Asia Minor and Syria, and in 1828 he explored Egypt and Arabia Petraea (Petra and Mt. Sinai). Both of these journeys produced important publications: *Voyage de l'Arabie Petrée*, 1830 and *Voyage de l'Asie Mineure* which appeared in parts from 1838 to 1862. When Laborde retired from his diplomatic career in 1845 he was appointed keeper of antiquities at the Louvre. He also produced *Documents inédits ou peu connus sur l'histoire et les antiquités d'Athènes*, and in 1854 he reprinted J.P. Babin's rare 1674 account of Athens. The etching of the Lantern of Demosthenes by Charles Meryon is not present, as is frequently the case since work by this engraver is sought after.

BNF 30704073; Blackmer 932.

370. LACRETELLE, Jacques de (1888-1985). **Le Demi-Dieu ou le Voyage en Grèce avec des gravures au burin de G. Gallibert.** Paris: Société d'Édition "Le Livre", 1930.

4to, pp. [v] 1-203 + [3] (p.[i]=ht, [v]=ded, pp.[1]=conts, [3]=colophon). With an engraved frontispiece. Engravings in the letterpess. Uncut and partly unopened in half calf gilt, original printed paper wrappers bound in. This copy is numbered 146 (out of 600 on vellum paper). A presentation copy, signed on the half title to 'Irene' by the editor 'Ramond'.

First edition, with engravings by Gallibert. This edition was produced in several formats: 30 copies were produced on Jap vellum with a double suite of engravings, no'd 1-30. Nos. 31-630 were produced on vellum paper d'Arches. Ten copies were produced on Holland paper for Kaufmann of Athens, marked A-J, and thirty copies were produced on various papers for the collaborators on the work, no'd I-XXX. A second edition came out in 1937 with woodcuts by Serveau and a third in 1944 (q.v.). Lacretelle also wrote *Images de Grèce, Notes de Voyage*, 1947, and he produced a study on Count Gobineau, *Quatre Études sur Gobineau*, Liege, 1926. In 1939 Lacretelle was to produce *Croisières en eaux troubles*, which deals with the Greece of Metaxas.

BNF 32335191. See Basch, pp. 438-39, 445-48.

371. LACRETELLE, Jacques de. *Le Demi-Dieu ou le Voyage de Grèce illustré de photographies de Emmanuel Boudot-Lamotte.* Paris: Bernard Grasset [1944].

4to, pp. [vii] 13-231 [4] (pp.[i]=ht, [v]=ded, [vii]=st, pp.[1]=list of ills, [4]=colophon). 48 no'd photographic illustrations in the text. Half calf gilt, green and red leather labels, original decorative paper wrappers bound in.

Third edition, but the first with these illustrations.

BNF 32335194.

372. LACROIX, Pierre Louis. *Iles de la Grèce.* Paris: Firmin Didot Frères, 1853.

8vo, pp. [iii] IV, 1-644 (pp.[i]=ht, 643-4=conts). With 31 maps/views/plans no'd 1-32 (pl. 1, folding map of the Archipelago no'd 1-2). Old quarter calf over marbled paper boards.

First edition. A second edition appeared in 1881. This forms vol. 38 of the series 'L'Univers'. The plates include views of Cyprus, Rhodes, Crete and Antiparos. Lacroix had already produced *Souvenirs d' un Voyage en Égypte*, 1847.

BNF 3071117; Blackmer 939. This edition not in GL or BLC.

373. LACROIX, Pierre Louis. *Iles de la Grèce.* Paris: Firmin Didot et Cie, 1881.

8vo, pp. [iv] IV, 1-644 (p.[i]=ht, pp.643-4=contents, gathering 32 (pp.497-512) bound in upside down). With 31 engraved plates no'd 1-32 (nos 1+2 together on folding map of the Aegean). Quarter calf gilt, green leather label.

Second edition, uncommon, first published in 1853. The work was originally published as part of the series 'L'Univers'.

This edition not in BNF on line. This edition not in Blackmer, but see 939.

374. LACROIX DE MARLÈS, J. de. *Tableau de la Grèce ancienne et moderne. 3e Édition.* Tours: A. Mame et Cie, 1850.

Sm. 8vo, pp. 1-234 [1] (p.1=t, p.[1]=table of contents). With an engraved frontispiece and engraved title. Quarter calf over brown marbled paper boards, back ruled gilt. Bound with Savary and François.

Third edition; apparently the first edition was printed by Mame in 1845, with six editions appearing by 1869. La Croix de Marlès was an historian who produced similar works on India, Russia, England etc., as well as *Histoire de la domination des Arabes et des Maures en Espagne et en Portugal*, 1825.

This edition not in BNF, but a 5th edition is cited with the same pagination. Not in BLC. This edition not in GL, but see GL Spentsas catalogue, p. 132.

375. LAMARTINE, Marie Louis Alphonse de. *Souvenirs, impressions, pensées et paysages, pendant un voyage en Orient (1832-1833), ou Notes d'un voyageur.* Paris: Librairie de Charles Gosselin and Librairie de Furne, 1835.

4 vols, 8vo, pp. [i] XIII + [1] 1-340; [i] 1-429; [i] 1-388; [i] 1-395 (pp.[i]=ts, hts missing in all vols, [1]=st). With an engraved portrait frontispiece, two folding maps and a folding table. 19th c. polished quarter green calf, backs gilt with red and black leather labels. Ownership signature of E.H. Coles.

First edition of this classic of travel literature. The half titles, missing in this copy, usually bear the words 'Oeuvres Complètes...Voyage en Orient'. Gosselin also produced a 16mo edition in 1835. Numerous editions and translations were produced in 1835, including English, German, and Dutch translations, and several Brussels editions. A Spanish translation appeared in 1846. Lamartine left France in 1832 with his wife and his daughter Julie, who was suffering from consumption and later died in Beirut. He spent 16 months in the Levant and was known in the East as the 'Emir Français' because of the luxurious style in which he travelled.

BNF 30725870; Blackmer 942; Weber 232.

376. LAMARTINE, Marie Louis Alphonse de. *Souvenirs, impressions, pensées et paysages, pendant un voyage en Orient (1832-1833), ou Notes d'un voyageur.* Leipzig and Stuttgart: J. Scheible, 1835.

4 vols.in 2, sm. 8vo, pp. X, 1-285; 1-360; 1-333; 1-317 (pp.I, 1=ts, 289-314 in v.4=index, 315-17=table of tribes). With an engraved portrait frontispiece and 2 folding maps. Contemporary quarter calf, back ruled gilt, green leather labels.

A German reprint of the first edition, in a smaller format. When Lamartine's work first appeared in 1835 it achieved an immediate success. This edition may be modeled on Gosselin's small edition.

BNF 35180881. The Gesamtkatalog GBV cites four copies. This edition not in Weber.

377. LAMARTINE, Marie Louis Alphonse de. *Oeuvres de Lamartine. Voyage en Orient.* Paris: Hachette, 1876-78.

2 vols, 8vo, pp. [iii] 484 + [3]; [iii] 574 [1] (pp.[i]=hts, [1]=conts, [3]=colophon, pp.1 in both vols=sts). Old half vellum gilt, red and blue leather labels.

A late edition. In most editions after that of 1835, Lamartine's *Souvenirs* was published under the title 'Voyage en Orient' as part of his collected works.

BNF 30725874 gives the date 1875 for this edition, which probably represents the date of the first volume of this edition of the collected works. Weber 725 cites an 1875 edition, 2 vols, 12mo, imp. of Hachette, & Furne, Jouvet et Cie.

378. LAMARTINE, Marie Louis Alphonse de. *Oeuvres de Lamartine. Voyage en Orient Tome Premier.* Paris: Hachette, 1913.

Volume 1 (of 2), 8vo, pp. [iii] 484 + [1] + 4 pp. of adverts (pp.[i]=ht, [1]=conts). Rough cut in quarter brown morocco over tan marbled paper boards, original yellow printed paper wrappers bound in. From the library of K.Th. Dimaras, with his bookstamp on lower fly-leaf.

A late edition, volume one only. This work was first published in 1835 in four volumes under the title *Souvenirs, impressions, pensées et paysages, pendant un voyage en Orient (1832-33), ou Notes d'un Voyageur*. This volume includes an account of Lamartine's visit to Athens. The first edition under the title *Voyage en Orient* seems to have appeared in 1841.

Not in BNF on line.

379. LA MOTTRAYE, Aubry de (1674?-1743). *Voyages du Sr A. de La Motraye, en Europe, Asie & Afrique. Où l'on trouve une grande varieté de Recherches géographiques, historiques & politiques, sur l'Italie, la Grèce, la Turquie, la Tartarie Crimée, & Nogaye, la Circassie ... comme aussi des relations fidelles des evenemens considerables arrivées pendant plus de xxvi. années qui l'auteur a employées dans ses voyages; comme de la Révolution en Turquie... Tome Premier. [... Tome Second.]* The Hague: T. Johnson and J. van Duren, M.DCC.XXVII. [=1727]

2 vols, folio, pp. [xiv] 1-472 + 23; [vi] 1-496 + 39 (pp.[i]=hts). Titles in red and black. With 2 engraved titles and 29 plates no'd I-XXVIII + VIIb and maps A+B, and 18 plates no'd I-XVII + IXb and maps C+D. Contemporary calf, backs gilt in compartments with fleurons, red and black leather labels, red edges.

First edition in French, first issue. There are two issues of the French edition. The second issue preliminaries have been reset and contain La Mottraye's 'avis' referring to the long delay in producing volume two. The first edition was printed in London in 1723, second edition 1732, where the Huguenot La Mottraye had established himself. The subscribers to the English edition include many notables such as Richard Steele, Isaac Newton, and others. This important work describes La Mottraye's travels over a period of 26 years beginning in 1696, through northern Europe to Tartary and the Levant. Many of the plates are signed by Hogarth and represent his early work. The plates depicting scenes from eastern life are especially interesting. The French edition contains four plates which do not appear in the English edition, and conversely lacks three plates from the English edition. Prospectuses for La Mottraye's *Voyages* appeared in English (London, G. & J. Innys, n.d.) and in French (Johnson and van Duren, 1724). A separate work describing La Mottraye's travels through Russia, Prussia and Poland was published in French in 1732. Its English title contains a reference to 'Voyages and Travels vol. III', but it is not a continuation of the earlier work.

Note: subscribers in this copy also include Bonneval, Thomas Brereton, Alexander Drummond, Fabrice, Kalkoens, Richard Mead, Hans Sloane, Jacob Tindal.

BNF 30730313; Blackmer 946 (1st issue); Weber 443; Atabey 661 (1st issue).

There is another copy in the Contominas collection, tall, in contemporary half calf gilt over speckled paper boards, uncut.

380. LANTIER, Etienne François de (1734-1826). *Voyages d'Antenor en Grèce et en Asie, avec de notions sur l'Égypte; manuscript grec trouvé à Herculanum. Traduit par E.-F. Lantier. Tome premier [... deuxième... troisième.]* Paris: Belin and Bernard, An VI. [=1798]

3 vols, 8vo, pp. xvi, 1-348; [i] 1-350; [i] 5-378 (pp.i, [i]=ts). With three engraved frontispieces. Contemporary half calf over blue marbled paper boards, backs ruled gilt and with crowned cypher AML, red leather labels.

First edition, uncommon. The second edition appeared the same year with some corrections. A third editon appeared in 'An VIII'. Many editions followed, at least 17 by 1836. Numerous translations were also produced, including English, Italian, Spanish, German, and Modern Greek. Lantier's work was known as the 'Anacharsis of the boudoir'; it is an imitation of Anacharsis but without Barthelemy's detailed knowledge of ancient Greek history and customs. However, it was very influential in spreading popular knowledge of ancient Greece.

BNF 30737523 (vol. 2 only); Blackmer 950; Atabey 667 (3rd ed). COPAC cites only 1 copy.

381. LANTIER, Etienne François de. ***Voyages d'Antenor en Grèce et en Asie, avec de notions sur l'Égypte; manuscript grec trouvé à Herculanum. Traduit par E.-F. Lantier. Avec Figures. Seconde édition, revue, corrigée et augmentée par l'Auteur. Tome premier [... deuxième... troisième.]*** Paris: Belin and Bernard, An VI. [=1798]

3 vols, 8vo, pp. xvi, 1-348; [iv] 1-350; 378 (pp.i, [i], 1=hts, pp.345-438, 346-350, 374-48=conts). With three engraved frontispieces. Contemporary mottled calf.

Second edition, first published the same year. Note the name Bernard in the imprint of this edition and the previous one; none of the copies cited in the references contain this name. Could this be another issue? In this copy the title pages to vols 1 and 2 have been reversed in the binding.

BNF 30737524; GL SPE L29v.

382. LANTIER, Etienne François de. ***Voyages d'Antenor en Grèce et en Asie, avec de notions sur l'Égypte; manuscript grec trouvé à Herculanum. Traduit par E.-F. Lantier. Avec Figures. Tome premier [... second... troisième.]*** Paris: F. Buisson, An X (1802).

3 vols, 8vo, pp. [iii] XIV, 15-372; [iii] 1-390; [iii] 1-362 + [2] (pp.[i]=hts, [2]=adverts). With 3 frontispieces and 2 plates. Contemporary mottled calf, flat backs gilt, black leather labels. Bookseller's ticket of F. Riss of Moscow.

Fifth edition. In the same year Buisson also brought out an edition in 5 vols, 16mo. The third and fourth editions appeared in 'An VIII' and 1801. Lantier's *Antenor* had a tremendous popular success.

BNF 30737527.

383. LAROCHE, Charles. ***La Crète ancienne et moderne.*** Paris: L-Henry May [1898].

Sm. 8vo, pp. 312 (p.1=ht, pp. 311-12=list of plates). Three maps and numerous illustrations in the text. Uncut and mostly unopened in the original decorative green paper wrappers.

Apparently only edition. Laroche was a travel writer who also translated Mikkelson's adventures in the Arctic into French. He can also possibly be identified with the engineer Charles Laroche who wrote on public works, ports and naval installations, including a description of the port of Casablanca.

BNF 30742117; BL 10125.b.41; GL HG87.6C35 attributes the date [1897].

384. LARROUMET, Gustave (1852-1902). *Vers Athènes et Jérusalem Journal de Voyage en Grèce et en Syrie. Troisième édition.* Paris: [Paul Brodard for] Hachette, 1898.

8vo, pp. x, 1-354 (pp.I=ht). Uncut and mostly unopened in quarter calf, original blue printed paper wrappers bound in.

Third collected edition. First and second collected editions also appeared in 1898. This account of two separate excursions consists of two series of letters; those on Greece were first published in *Le Temps* in 1896 and those on Syria in *Figaro* in 1897. The Blackmer collection included a rare separate account of the first part, the excursion to Greece in the spring of 1896, also published by Hachette as *Quinze Jours en Grèce Lettres adressées au Journal "Le Temps" Croisière du Sénégal Voyage organisé par le "Tour du Monde"— Mars-Avril 1896.* The cruise was organized by the *Tour du Monde* in view of the approach of the first Olympic Games, and the group included Salomon Reinach, Homolle (q.v.) and the hellenist Monceaux. The second, to Syria in September of 1897, was organized by the *Revue Générale des Sciences*. Larroumet was a litterateur and philologist. These excursions were organized by the publishers of periodicals, understandable in the case of the *Tour du Monde*. Several publications appeared in consequence of the tours organized by the *Revue Générale des Sciences* (q.v.).

BNF 36565930; Weber 1029. See Basch, pp. 258-60.

There is another copy in the Contominas collection, in half tan roan gilt, original grey-green printed paper wrappers bound in, uncut.

385. [LA SOLAYE, L. de]. *Memoires ou relation militaire; contenant ce qui s'est passé de plus considerable dans les attaques, & dans la deffence de la ville de Candie depuis l'année 1645, qu'elle fut bloquée des Turcs, iusques au iour de sa reduction...* Paris: chez Claude Barbin... M.DC.LXX. [=1670]

12mo, pp. [xxiv] 1-345 [4] (p.[i]=t, [1-4]=privilege). Tree calf antique. An ownership signature has been deleted from a preliminary leaf.

First and apparently only edition. The dedication is signed L. de la Solaye. He claimed to be a captain in the infantry who accompanied Montbrun, Marquis de Saint André to Crete. Montbrun replaced Francesco Ghiron Villa as head of the Venetian forces in Crete. This is a description of the last phase of the Veneto-Turkish war in Crete, from May 1668 to the fall of Crete in 1669.

BNF 30746039; Blackmer 951; Atabey 675; Barbier III, 232.

386. LAURENBERG, Johann (1590-1658). *V. Cl. Joannis Laurenbergi Graecia Antiqua. Edidit Samuel Pufendorf.* Amsterdam: Jan Janssonius, MDC LX. [=1660]

Oblong small quarto, pp. [viii] 1-62 +[1] (pp.[i]=t, [1]=list of maps). With 31 engraved maps. Contemporary vellum boards. Old bookplate of Gavin Elliot of Melross on front pastedown defaced, ownership signature 'Scholae Regiae Edinensis' on title.

First edition, uncommon. An edition in 8vo format appeared in 1661, with the maps folded. Laurenberg was a mathematician and historical cartographer from Rostock in

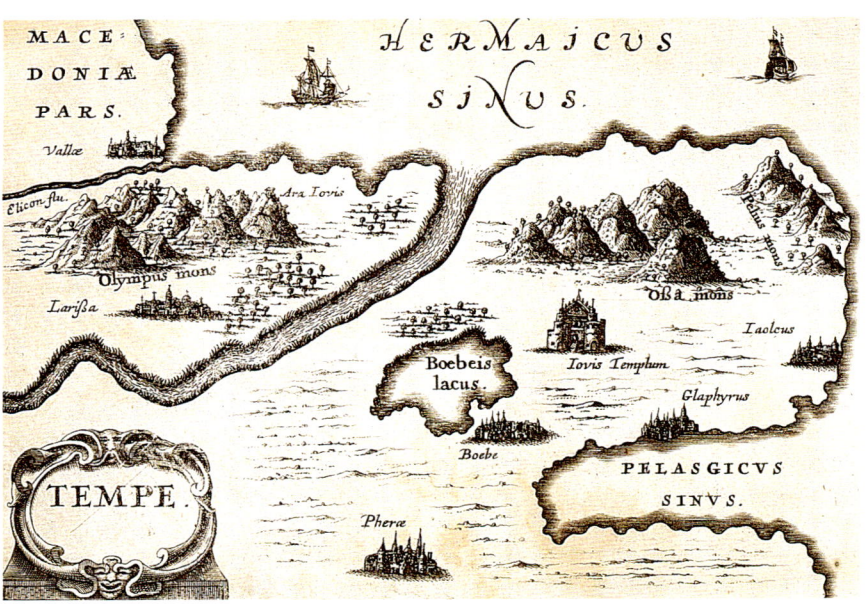

386

Germany. His cartographical productions were concerned almost exclusively with Greece, and he constructed many maps of special Greek interest.

This edition not in BLC. Karlsruhe cites six copies.
Collation: *^{4} A-H^4

387. LEAKE, William Martin. *The Topography of Athens with some Remarks on its Antiquities.* London: John Murray, MDCCCXXI. [=1821]

8vo, pp. [v] CXIV [1] 435 [1] (p.[i]=t, [v]=errata, [1]=st, [1]=colophon). With a frontispiece and 8 plates. Half tan polished calf, back gilt in compartments, brown leather label. An A.L.s. from Leake tipped in.

First edition. This work is sometimes found with the plates bound separately. A second edition appeared in 1841. The work was translated into French in 1849 and into German in 1823. Leake's work on Athens is the basis for modern topographical and archaeological studies of the city. The unaddressed letter is a formal reply from Leake refusing an invitation.

BL 572.g.31; Blackmer 971; Brunet III, 895.

388. LEAKE, William Martin. *Journal of a tour in Asia Minor, with comparative remarks on the ancient and modern geography of that country... Accompanied by a map.* London: John Murray, 1824.

8vo, pp. [i] XXVII [2] 1-362 + 2 pp. adverts (p.[i]=ht, [2]=conts). With a large folding map, a plate of inscriptions, and 2 plans of the Troad. Half calf, back gilt in compartments, brown leather label. With the 19th c. armorial bookplate of Sir Archibald Edmonstone of Duntreath.

First edition. Leake's account of Asia Minor is the first complete and systematic description of the country, although he traversed the area many years before he wrote this account. Leake's map is very interesting as it traces earlier travellers' routes. It also includes the Peutinger table of Asia Minor as an inset at the top of a page. This is an interesting association copy; it belonged to Archibald Edmonstone who travelled in the Levant in 1818-1819. He was in Egypt in January 1819 where he met Belzoni who encouraged him to visit the oases of Upper Egypt, and his account of these travels was published by John Murray in 1822; in fact his book is advertised in the advert attached to Leake's work.

BL 1046.f.2; Blackmer 972; Weber 127.

389. LEAKE, William Martin. *Travels in the Morea. With a map and plans. In three volumes. Vol. I. [... Vol. II ... Vol. III.]* London: John Murray, MDCCCXXX. [=1830]

3 vols, 8vo, pp. xvii [1] 513; viii, 534 + [2]; vii, 478 (pp.i=hts, missing in this copy, p.[1]=directions to binder, pp.[1-2]=corrections). With 17 engraved maps/plans including a large folding map; 12 lithographed plates of inscriptions. Old half black roan, ruled gilt. Bookplate of the Union Club with its stamp on title.

First edition, describing Leake's travels in the Morea in 1805 and 1806. A supplement was published in 1846 as *Peloponnesiaca* (q.v.). Leake of course is the topographer *par excellence* of Greece. His actual journeys through Greece took place over a period of years, not always continuous. His earliest journey to the Levant occurred in 1799 when he was seconded to teach gunnery to the new Turkish army. He took part in the combined Anglo-Turkish expedition to Egypt in 1800, returning to England via Greece in 1802. He again travelled in Greece from 1804 to 1807 and from 1808 to 1810; for part of the latter period he was official resident at the court of Ali Pasha in Ioannina.

BL 1047.d.1-9; Blackmer 974 (Leake's own copy); Weber 189; Droulia 1884-86; Atabey 691.

390. LEAKE, William Martin. *Peloponnesiaca: a Supplement to Travels in the Morea.* London: J. Rodwell, 1846.

8vo, pp. xv, 1-432 (p.i=ht, errata to 'Travels in the Morea' on pp.411-12). With a large folding map, 3 folding plans and an engraved view. New half green morocco, gilt stamped back 'Travels in the Morea'.

First edition. This is a true supplement, with additional information organized according to the sections in Leake's earlier three-volume work, *Travels in the Morea*, 1830.

BL 1047.d.23; Atabey 693; Weber 190. Not in Blackmer.
Collation: π^1 B-2E^8.

391. LEAKE, William Martin. *Travels in Northern Greece.* Amsterdam: A.M. Hakkert, 1967. [Reprint of the 1835 edition.]

4 vols, pp. xii [3] 527; vii, 643; vii, 578˙ vi 588 + [41] (p.i=ts in all vols except v. 1=[ ], pp.[1-3]=errata and list of plates, [1-41]=st to index and index). With 10 engraved maps/plans and 44 plates of inscriptions, plus 10 facsimiles of leaves from Leake's original journal. Half ochre morocco gilt.

This is a facsimile reprint of the first edition, 1835. It reproduces all the material from the first edition, plus ten leaves from Leake's journals.

392. LEAR, Edward. *Journals of a Landscape Painter in Albania, &c.* London: [Schulze for] Richard Bentley, M.D.CCC.LI. [=1851]

Lge 8vo, pp.[iii] 1-428 (pp.[i]=t, [iii]=list of pls, 428=colophon). With a map and 20 no'd lithographed plates printed in 3 tints, ochre, grey, and blue. Uncut in half polished maroon calf, back gilt.

First edition; a second edition, enlarged, appeared in 1852. Lear collected the notes for this work during two journeys. In 1848 he visited Corfu, where he stayed with George Bowen of the Ionian University. He travelled to Constantinople with Sir Stratford Canning, and on his return to Corfu he travelled overland through Macedonia and Albania. In 1849 he travelled through Albania, Epirus and Thessaly. According to Field, the text of this work is extremely detailed as far as Lear's life at this period is concerned. The charming plates depict some little known sites, including Berat, Khimara, Avlona, and Argyrokastro.

BL 2360.g.4; Blackmer 986; Abbey 45. W.B.O. Field, *Edward Lear on my shelves*, New York, 1933, p. 148. The growth of Lear's reputation in the 20th century has made up for the lack of interest in the 19th. Many new studies and reference works have appeared in the last thirty years.

393

393. LEAR, Edward. *Journals of a Landscape Painter in Albania, Illyria &c. Second edition*. London: Richard Bentley, M.D.CCC.LII. [=1852]

Lge 8vo, pp. xiii + [1] 1-418 (p.i=ht, missing, p.[1]=list of plates, pp.417-418=index). With a map and 20 no'd lithographed plates printed in 3 tints, ochre, grey, and blue. Uncut in half polished maroon calf, back gilt.

Second edition, first published in 1851. The second edition includes additional material. There are several 20th c. reprints.

BL 1572/642.

394. LEAR, Edward. *Views in the Seven Ionian Islands by Edward Lear. A facsimile of the original edition published in 1863 by the Artist.* Oldham: Hugh Broadbent [1979].

Folio, pp. [x], 1-20 (p.i=t, p.iii=facsimile lith. title, p.v=preface, p.vii=list of plates, pp.ix-x=explanation of the lithographed title). With twenty leaves of explanation, 20 tinted lithographed plates and a list of subscribers produced in photographic facsimile. Green cloth, in a slip case. No. 630 of 1000 numbered copies.

A facsimile of the original edition published in 1863. There is a second copy in the Contominas collection, no'd 801.

395. LE CHEVALIER, Jean Baptiste (1752-1836). *Voyage dans la Troade, ou Tableau de la Plaine de Troie dans son état actuel. Seconde Édition.* Paris: Laran, An VII. [=1799]

8vo, pp. [iii] 1-269 + [2] (pp. [i]=ht, [1]=errata, [2]=directions to the binder). With a large folding map of the Troad and 8 engraved plates no'd 1-5 + 3 unnumbered. Contemporary quarter calf, back gilt over blue marbled paper boards, blindstamped arms on both sides.

Second edition in French, actually the first separate French edition, uncommon. The first French edition appeared in vol. III of the *Transactions of the Royal Society of Edinburgh*, 1794, with four plates. The first edition appeared in English; Le Chevalier spent six months in Edinburgh, 1790-91, where he read his memoir on the Troad at three sessions of the meetings of the Royal Society. Andrew Dalzel quickly produced a translation of Le Chevalier's memoir which he had printed in 1791. Note that this edition does not contain the account of Le Chevalier's journey to the Troad via Venice and the Ionian islands and Athens which was published in the third edition.

BNF 30764815. This edition not in COPAC. Not in Blackmer but see 993 for 1st ed.

396. LE CHEVALIER, Jean Baptiste. *Voyage de la Troade, fait dans les années 1785 et 1786 ... Troisième édition, revue, corrigée et considérablement augmentée. Tome premier. [... Tome second... troisième.]* Paris: Dentu, An. X.-1802.

3 vols, 8vo, and 4to atlas (described below), pp. xviii, 1-303; [iii] 1-332; [iii] 1-315 [1] + 16 pp. of adverts (pp.i, [i]=hts, [1]=errata). Contemporary speckled calf, backs gilt with fleurons, green leather labels, central gilt arms on both sides.

Third and definitive edition in French of Le Chevalier's work on Troy. This is actually the second separate edition; the first French edition appeared in volume III of the *Transactions of the Royal Society of Edinburgh*, 1794. Le Chevalier visited the Troad on three separate occasions between 1785 and 1787, each visit apparently financed by Choiseul-Gouffier. In fact there is some suggestion that the ideas put forward by Le Chevalier were not entirely his own, and that Choiseul-Gouffier also made some contributions to his theory. In the aftermath of the French revolution, Le Chevalier spent six months in Edinburgh in 1791, where he read his memoir to the Royal Society. The first edition appeared in English in 1791, translated by Andrew Dalzel as *Description of the Plain of Troy*. A German translation was produced in 1792 by C.G. Heyne. This edition also includes an account of Le Chevalier's voyage out to Constantinople in 1785 via the Ionian Islands, Athens and Skyros, as well as a French translation of Morritt's *Vindication of Homer*, and of Heyne's *Pretended Tomb of Homer*.

BNF 30764816; Weber 608; Atabey 698; Lascarides 107; Spencer pp. 202-3. This edition not in Blackmer but see 993 and 994.

397. LE CHEVALIER, Jean Baptiste. *Recueil des Cartes, Plans, Vues et Médailles pour servir au Voyage de la Troade*. Paris: Dentu, An X. (1802).

4to, pp. [i], 1-14 (p.[i]=t). With 37 no'd plates of maps and views of which several folding or double-page (nos. 11-12 and 24-37 are two to a leaf). Contemporary tree calf over marbled paper boards, red leather label.

The atlas to the third edition (i.e. second separate edition) of Le Chevalier's *Voyage de la Troade*. The third edition, with its atlas, contains many plates, especially of the Ionian islands, which do not occur in the earlier editions.

BNF 33996151, atlas only (the Bibliothèque Nationale also cites an edition dated (1801). This may be a variant issue, without a date in parentheses on the title, since the date on the title normally reads 'An X-(1802)', otherwise both imprints are exactly the same). Blackmer 994; Atabey 698; Lascarides 107.

398. LE CHEVALIER, Jean Baptiste. *Voyage de la Propontide et du Pont-Euxin; avec la carte générale de ces deux mers, la description topographique de leurs rivages... [etc.]* Paris: Dentu, An VIII (1800).

2 vols in 1, 8vo, pp. xii, 1-168, 169-416 (pp.i, 169=hts, pp.iii, 171=ts). With six folding maps/plans. Old calf, panelled back gilt.

First and only edition, first issue, with the separate title and half title to volume two. Second issue copies do not have a separate title and half title to vol. two, and are without plates. Le Chevalier left Constantinople and Choiseul-Gouffier's embassy in 1787 to join Alexander Ypsilantis, Hospodar of Moldavia, at Jassy. It was during this sojourn that he became interested in exploring the shores of the Black Sea.

BNF 30764819; Blackmer 995; Weber 649; Atabey 697.

399. [LE CHEVALIER, Jean Baptiste.] *Ulysse-Homère, ou Du véritable Auteur de l'Iliade et de l'Odyssée. Par Constantin Koliades, professeur dans l'Université Ionienne.* Paris: [Crapelet for] de Bure Frères, M.D.CCC.XXIX. [=1829]

Folio, pp. [iii] viii, 1-100, 3 + [3] (p.[i]=ht, pp.1-3=supplement, [1-2]=conts [3]=list of plates and errata). With engraved portrait frontispiece of Koliades and 19 lithographed plates. Uncut in the original beige printed paper wrappers.

First and only edition of this curious work. Le Chevalier, known for his work on Troy, argues that the true author of the Iliad and the Odyssey is Odysseus himself. The illustrations include maps and views connected with Troy. Le Chevalier must also have known something of the Ionian Academy and Lord Guilford's injunction that the students and professors wear ancient Greek costume, because the frontispiece shows the supposed professor Koliades wearing such a costume. Because of the scarcity of this work we append a list of the plates, which are unnumbered.

BNF 30764813. Not in Blackmer.

List of plates (our numbers and captions):
 1. Portrait frontispiece of Koliades in Greek costume, uniform of the Ionian Academy
 2. Map of the Greek Confederation [Greece]
 3. Map of the Trojan Confederation [Asia Minor]
 4. Philoctetes [2 views of Lemnos on 1 sheet]
 5. Gardens of Laertius
 6. Map of Ulysses' voyages [Mediterranean and Western Europe]
 7. Map of Ithaca
 8. Fountain of Arethusa
 9. Plan of Ulysses' palace on Ithaca
 10. School of Homer on Ithaca
 11. Coins
 12. Hellespont
 13. Map of the plain of Troy
 14. Source of the Scamandre (hot)

399

15. Source of the Scamandre (cold)
16. Temple of Minerva, Sunium
17. Trezene, Egine, Tempe, Orchomene. 4 views on 1 plate
18. Mycenae, Tiryns, Lac Stymphale, fountain of Hyperia. 4 views on 1 plate
19. Alpheus
20. View of the port of Ithaca

Collation: π^2 a-b^2, 1-25^2 χ^2 26^2

400. LECONTE, Casimir. *Étude économique de la Grèce, de sa position actuelle, de son avenir; suivie de documents sur le commerce de l'Orient, sur l'Égypte, etc., avec une carte de la Grèce.* Paris: Firmin Didot Frères for Didot and Guillaumin, 1847.

8vo, pp. [iii] 1-452 + 1 (pp.i=ht, 1=conts). With a large folding map and four folding tables. Half brown roan over brown marbled paper boards. A presentation copy signed by Leconte to N. Copineau.

Apparently first and only edition. The map of Greece is entitled 'Carte du Royaume Hellénique. 1847. Lith. Kaeppelin'. Leconte was a writer on economics and railways. He also produced *Promenade dans l'Isthme de Suez*, 1864.

BNF 30767937; BL 8032.f.39.

401. LEGRAND, Emile, *editor.* [Drophead title:] ***Voyages de Basile Vatace en Europe et en Asie.*** [Paris: École des Langues Orientales Vivantes, 1886.]

Lge 8vo, pp. [185]-295 (p.[185]=first leaf of text with drophead title). With a folding facsimile map. Uncut and unopened in three-quarter brown morocco, back gilt.

First edition, extracted from the journal *Nouveaux Mélanges Orientaux*. This section, lacking the half title, p. 183, was removed and bound separately. Legrand was very active in publishing forgotten works by Greek litterateurs. The map is a facsimile of the map Vatazes had engraved in London depicting his travels; it has been reproduced from a copy in the Bibliothèque Nationale.

Not in BNF as a separate entry. BL 14003.k.18.

402. LEGRAND, Emile, *editor.* ***Morceaux choisis en Grec savant des XIXe siècle réunis et publiés par Émile Legrand. Textes en prose.*** Paris: Imprimerie Nationale for Ernest Leroux, MDCCCCIII. [=1903]

8vo, pp. XI, 448 (p.I=ht, 447-8=index). Uncut and unopened in the original grey printed paper wrappers.

First and only edition, volume three in the series 'Bibliothèque de l'Ecole des Langues orientales vivantes'. 'Grec savant' is Legrand's label for Katharevousa, the formal language introduced by Korais and his supporters, to which he was wholly opposed. But he felt that his students needed to know what constituted 'Grec savant'. So he produced this collection of essays, news stories and novellas, many taken from the *Estia* newspaper and published during the 1890s. The excerpts are by such writers as Xenopoulos, Bikelas, Skarlatos Byzantios, Angelos Blachos, Alexandros Rangabes, and Spyridon Trikoupis.

BNF 36588106.

403. LEGRAND, Jacques Guillaume. ***Monumens de la Grèce, ou Collection des Chefs-d'Oeuvre d'Architecture, de Sculpture et de Peinture antiques. Tome I.*** Paris: Treuttel & Würtz, MDCCCVIII. [=1808]

Folio, pp. [iii] 1-183 [1] (p.[i]=ht, [1]=conts). With 97 engraved plates no'd 1-93 + A, B, 13b, and 13c. Modern buckram.

First edition, all published. This is the first part of the proposed 'Galerie Antique, ou Collection des chefs-d'oeuvre d'Architecture, de Sculpture et de Peinture antiques', planned as a supplement to Stuart and Revett, under the direction of L. F. Cassas and the architect Legrand. However, Legrand died in 1807 and the work was stopped. The first part, on Greece, which had already been printed, was issued in 1808 with a new title page, but it retained the original half title, which refers to the Galerie Antique. A second edition appeared in 1842.

BNF 30778309; Blackmer 1000; Brunet III, 946. This issue not in GL or BLC.

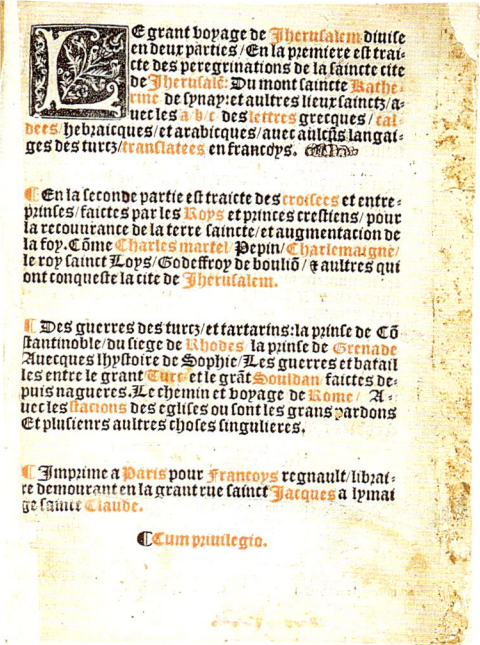
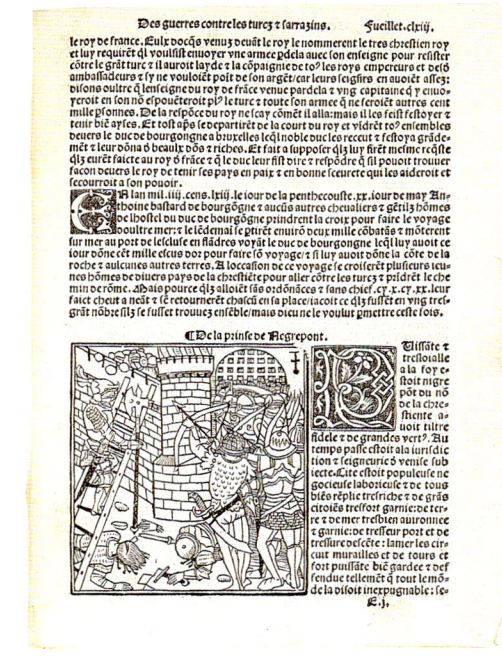

404

404. [LE HUEN, Nicolas]. *Le grant voyage de Jherusalem divise en deux parties. En la premiere est traicte des peregrinations de la saincte cite de Jherusale[m]: Du mont saincte Katherine de Synay: et aultres lieux sainctz, avec les a,b,c des lettres grecques... [etc] translatees en francoys. En la seconde partie est traicte des croisees et entreprinses, faicts par les Roys et princes crestiens... Des guerres des turcz, et tartarins: la prinse de Co[n]stantinoble, du siege de Rhodes, la prinse de Grenade... Imprime a Paris pour Francoys regnault, libraire demourant e la grant rue sainct Jacques a lymaige saincte Claude. Cum privilegio. [colophon: ... le douzieme jour de octobre lan mil cinq cens et dix sept.]* [Paris: François Regnault, 1517.]

2 parts in 1, 4to, ff. [iv] 3-90, [16] 91-197 (f.[i]=t, f.[1]=t to part 2). Gothic letter. Title in red and black. With many woodcuts in the letterpress. Lacking the woodcut plate of Jerusalem and the plan of the Holy Land. Modern vellum.

Second edition, first printed in 1488. A third edition appeared in 1522. The very rare first edition includes folding views of Venice, Corfu, Candia, Modon, Rhodes and Jerusalem. It constitutes the first French book to be issued with copperplates. Le Huen has produced a not very literal translation of Breydenbach's journey. Some early scholars thought him an original traveller.

BL C.32.M.13; BNF 30160148.
Collation: a^4 $a-c^6$ $d-p^{8.4}$ $2p-3p^8$ $q-z^{8.4}$, $A-F^{8.4}$ G^4 H^8 $I-K^6$ ($-K6=[\ ]$).

405. LEMAITRE, Alfred. *Musulmans et Chrétiens Notes sur la Guerre de l'Indépendance Grecque.* Paris: [E. Plon for] G. Martin, 1895.

8vo, pp. VII, 120 + [1] + [1] (pp.I=ht, [1]=conts, [1]=colophon). Uncut in half blue cloth over marbled paper boards, red leather label, original blue-grey printed paper wrappers bound in. Bookplate of A.D. Hatzidemos.

First and only edition. Lemaitre also edited an account of a journey which took place in 1308, *Abou Naddara à Stamboul*, 1892.

BNF 30784903. Not in Atabey. There was a copy in the Blackmer Collection, but not in the Catalogue.

406. LENORMANT, François (1837-1883). *La Grèce et les Iles Ioniennes Études de Politique et d'Histoire Contemporaine.* Paris: Michel Levy, 1865.

8vo, pp. [iii] 368 (p.[i]=ht). Quarter calf gilt, original yellow printed paper wrappers bound in. From the library of K.Th. Dimaras, with his bookstamp on p. 368 and on the lower wrapper, and with notes in his hand on the verso of the fly-leaf and the half title.

Apparently first and only edition. Lenormant was the son of the archaeologist Charles Lenormant. He was a polymath with an extraordinary breadth of interests. In addition to his archaeological work, especially on the civilisations of Mesopotamia, he also wrote on political and historical subjects. He had previously written *Le Gouvernement des Iles Ioniennes*, 1861, and he later produced *Histoire de massacres en Syrie en 1860*, 1861, and *Turcs et Montenegrins*, 1866. His publications on archaeological subjects are innumerable, despite the fact that he died at the early age of 46, of a disease contracted during an expedition to Calabria. Neverthe-

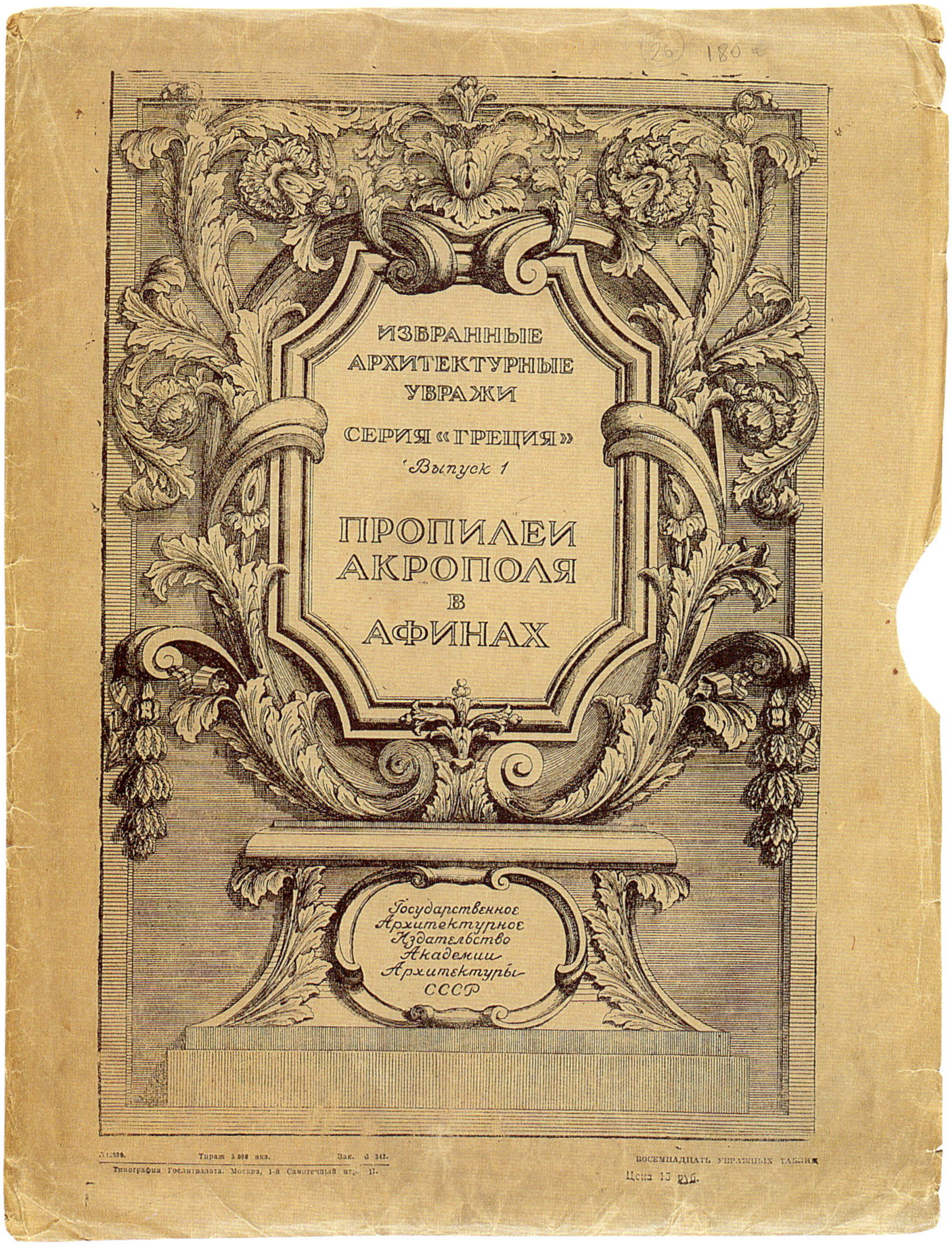
ИЗБРАННЫЕ
АРХИТЕКТУРНЫЕ
УВРАЖИ
СЕРИЯ «ГРЕЦИЯ»
Выпуск 1
ПРОПИЛЕИ
АКРОПОЛЯ
В
АФИНАХ
Государственное
Архитектурное
Издательство
Академии
Архитектуры
СССР
Тираж 5 000 экз.
Типография Гослитиздата. Москва, 1-й Самотечный пер., 17.
ВОСЕМНАДЦАТЬ УВРАЖНЫХ ТАБЛИЦ
Цена 15 руб.

407

less, he managed to finish the book connected with this expedition, *La Grand Grèce, paysages et histoire*, 1881-1884.

BNF 30791201. Not in Blackmer.

407. LEONIDOV, Ivan, *editor*. **Propilei Akropolya v Afinach** [Cyrillic]. [Moscow: Russian Academy of Architecture, 1940.]

Folio, pp. 8 (p.1=first p. of text, 8=list of plates and colophon). Drophead title. With 18 no'd plates, several double-page. Loose in a printed decorative paper envelope.

First edition. Apparently an offprint from a periodical publication entitled 'Grecia' published by the Russian Academy of Architecture. This study of the Propylea consists of text and tables of measurements by the architect N. E. Rosobuna, edited by I. E. Leonidov.

408. LE ROY, Julien David. [subtitle:] **Les Ruines des plus beaux Monumens de la Grèce. Seconde Partie.** [Paris: H. L. Guerin and L. F. Delatour, 1758.]

Part 2 only, folio, pp. [i] i-vi, 1-28 (pp.[i]=st, 28=privilege and approbation and directions to the binder for both parts). With 32 no'd plates. Quarter calf, panelled back gilt with fleurons over cloth boards.

This is part two only of the complete work which was published in two parts. Part one contains 28 plates, many of which are views. Part two contains mostly plates of architectural details with measurements. The engravers include Patte and Deneufforge. Le Roy was a pensionner at the French Academy in Rome in 1748 when the prospectus for Stuart and Revett's *Antiquities of Athens* was published. He visited Greece in 1754, and decided to publish his own work on Greek architecture, anticipating by four years the first volume of Stuart and Revett's own publication, which did not appear until 1762. There has always been some rivalry between the supporters of these two works, which both claim to be the first to reintroduce Greek architecture to western Europe and thus to play a significant role in the development of neo-classical architecture. Le Roy's work is not as thorough and detailed as Stuart and Revett's. This is clear especially from the plates of views which are decidedly romantic in spirit. Stuart in fact wrote a critique of Le Roy's publication in the first volume of the *Antiquities*, to which Le Roy replied in *Observations sur les édifices... précédés de Réflexions sur la critique des Ruines de la Grèce, publiée dans un ouvrage anglais*, Paris, 1767

BNF 30799260; Blackmer 1009; Brunet III, 1003; Cohen de Ricci 627. For a long discussion of the part played by Le Roy in neo-classical architecture, see Dora Wiebenson, *Sources of Greek Revival Architecture*, London, 1969.

409. LESTER, E. *Costumes Grecs.* [Collection of Greek costume plates, c. 1930.]

47 plates of watercolour drawings on paper, mounted on gilt paper, then mounted on card. Each plate signed 'E. Lester, Athens', in red ink. In a folder, in a box of half red cloth over marbled paper boards, gilt title on back 'Costumes Grecs', ex-dono stamp on box 'Δωρεὰ Βιβλιοθήκη Σπ. Λοβέρδου'.

This collection, possibly made circa 1930 judging from the style of the work and certain of the plates (Monastir in southern Yugoslavia, Argyrokastro in Albania), is of some interest because of the subjects depicted. The portrait details on several of the plates seem to indicate that at least some were taken from life. Note that there are two plates each of the Amalia costume, Suli, Corfu and Cyprus; this second plate is a close-up of the face of the model wearing the costume. The costume of local areas in or near Attica (Salamina, Keratea, Marathon) is also of interest. The nature of the signature and some of the spellings indicates that the artist is probably a Greek, possibly a Greek woman married to a foreigner named Lester. The plates depict the costume of Amorgos, Arachova, Argyrokastro (2), Astypalia (2), Chios, Corfu (2), Crete, Cyprus (2), Epirus (3), Epirus-Ziza, Ioannina (sp. Janina), Kalymnos, Kea, Kastelorizo (4), Keratea, Kuluri (Salamina), Lefkas, Lemnos, Marathon, Megara, Mitylene (sp. 'Metelene'), Myconos, Monastir, Nisyros (sp. 'Nisseris'), Psara, Rhodes (2), Siphnos (sp. 'Syfnos'), Skyros (sp. 'Skiros') Suli (2), Thessalia, Trapezunda (sp. 'Trapesont'), and Trikkeri (sp. 'Trykeri'). There are three additional subjects: Otho, Amalia (2) and a female figure in classical dress.

410. LETHABY, William Richard, and Harold SWAINSON. *The Church of Sancta Sophia Constantinople A Study of Byzantine building.* London and New York: Richard Clay & Sons for MacMillan & Co., 1894.

Lge 8vo, pp. viii, 308 (p.i=ht, pp.291-307=index, 308=colophon). Woodcut illustrations in letterpress. Uncut in the original tan buckram. Pencil notes in a contemporary hand on margins of several pages regarding the marble masonry used in the church. From the library of H.M. Blackmer, with his book label.

First and apparently only edition. In this very interesting work Lethaby and Swainson discuss every aspect of the building of Saint Sophia, from furnishings to mosaics to glass to plaster, and so forth. They also use information supplied by travellers. Lethaby was an architect, and first professor of design at the Royal College of Art; he was much influenced by William Morris and Philip Webb, and exercised an important influence on later architects. This copy comes from the library of Henry Myron Blackmer, but it was not included in the Blackmer Catalogue.

BL 7814.g.4.

411. LEUNE, Jean. *Une revanche une étape Avec les Grecs, de Paris à Salonique par Athènes et la Macédoine. – Campagne de 1912. Préface de M. Gaston Deschamps.* Paris: Chapelot, 1914.

8vo, pp. [viii] ix-xvi, 1-499 (pp.[i]=ht, 495-499=conts and list of ills). With photographic portrait of Prince Constantine, 104 photographic illustrations and 3 folding plans/maps. Half red cloth, original beige printed paper wrappers bound in.

First and apparently only edition of this account of the first Balkan War. The preface is by the philhellene and archaeologist Deschamps (q.v.). The journalist Leune, who may have been working for the periodical *L'Illustration*, followed the Greek army in Epirus and Macedonia with his wife, who was Greek. The maps illustrate the battles of Sarantoporon and Yenitza. The third map, showing the action near Deskati from 8-21 October, is not in the list of plates. Leune contributed articles on Greece to a number of French reviews, including 'Les Iles de la Mer Egée' (*Revue de Paris*, 1912), 'Grèce et Albanie' (*Grand Revue*, 1913), 'L'Effort militaire de la Grèce' (*Nouvelle Revue*, 1912). He later wrote *L'eternel Ulysse, ou la vie aventureuse d'un Grec d'aujourdhui*, 1923. Mme. Leune was a member of the Red Cross during World War I.

BNF 30807490; BL 9136.k.6; GL HG699L65.

412. LEVKOMA. *Λεύκωμα τῶν ἐν Κωνσταντινουπόλει ἐθνικῶν Φιλανθρωπικῶν Καταστημάτων.* Constantinople: A. Koromelas, 1904.

Oblong lge 8vo, title leaf, one leaf and 26 leaves of photographs. Original decorative paper boards, gilt, gilt edges.

?Only edition. A committee was established to produce this album; it included I. Sioutes, L.D. Kazanoba, S. Karatheodores, S. Narles and K. Spanoudes. Members of the general committee for 1904 which oversaw the Greek philanthropic institutions in Constantinople included Syggros, Bernoudakis, and Mavrokordatos. Many of the photographs are of hospitals and clinics, as well as the orphanage and the psychiatric clinic.

Not in GL, but see GL Per 455 for a similar work.

413. LEWIS, John Frederick. *Lewis's Illustrations of Constantinople, made during a Residence in that City &c. in the years 1835-36. Arranged and drawn on stone from the original sketches of Coke Smyth, by John F. Lewis.* London: G. Hullmandel's Lithographic press for T. McLean, D. & P. Colnaghi, and John F. Lewis [1838].

Folio, no letterpress. Lithographed title and dedication (list of plates on verso). With 22 litho-

graphed plates (of 28) on 20 sheets (i.e. 20 plates with 22 views, nos. 10-11 and 21-22 printed together on two sheets). Plates [8] and [16] in this copy lithographed in two tints, beige and grey. Red morocco, sides ruled gilt, upper cover titled 'Lewis's Constantinople', back ruled gilt with fleurons.

First edition, ordinary state. There is a deluxe state in which the plates are printed on card. The prospectus for this work was issued in 1837. Although this is the work for which Lewis is most famous and which associates him with the East, he did not produced the drawings for this book. Lewis travelled in the Levant, but after the publication of this work, c. 1839-1851. He later exhibited at the Royal Academy, often works with an oriental flavour. Nothing is known of Coke Smyth, who travelled in the East in the mid-1830s, and whose drawings Lewis used for this publication. Some years later Smyth travelled in North America and produced *Sketches in Canada* (1839).

BL 744.e.18; Blackmer 1015 (deluxe state); Weber 1126a; Abbey 394.

414. LIGHT, Sir Henry. *Travels in Egypt, Nubia, Holy Land, Mount Libanon, and Cyprus, in the year 1814.* London: for Rodwell and Martin, 1818.

4to, pp.xvi, 1-279 + [2] (pp.[i]=ht, missing, 1=st, pp.[1-2]=list of ills). With 20 engraved plates of views, maps and inscriptions. Contemporary calf, sides framed in gilt with palmettos, rebacked, original gilt spine preserved, red leather label.

First edition. A German translation was produced in 1820. Light, a captain in the Royal Artillery stationed in Malta, obtained leave in 1814 to explore Egypt and Palestine. He was one of the first travellers to visit Nubia, and the illustrations in this book are among the earliest to depict the Nubian temples.

BL 212.c.1; Blackmer 1018; Weber 56. Not in Atabey.

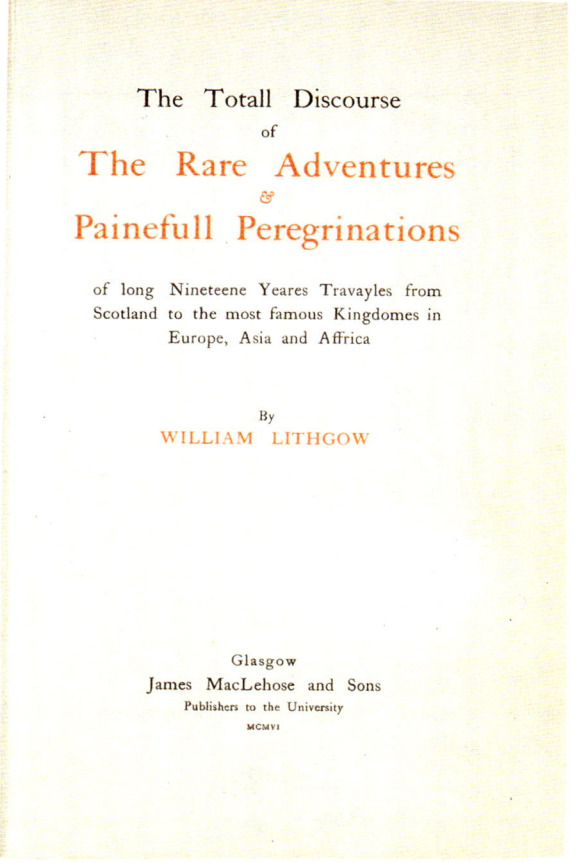

415

415. LITHGOW, William. *The Totall Discourse of the rare Adventures & painefull Peregrinations of long nineteene yeares travayles from Scotland to the most famous Kingdomes in Europe, Asia and Affrica.* Glasgow: James MacLehose and Sons, 1906.

Loe here's mine Effigie, and Turkish suite;
My Staffe, my Shasse, as I did Asia foote:
Plac'd in old Ilium; Priams Scepter thralles:
The Grecian Campe design'd; lost Dardan falles
Gird'd with small Simois: Idaes tops, a Gate;
Two fatall Tombes, an Eagle, sackt Troyes State.

8vo, pp. xxxi, 1-449 [1] (p.i=ht, [1]=printer's device). Title in red and black. With 11 facsimile plates. Uncut in the original quarter vellum gilt over red pictorial cloth gilt. Number 78 of 100 copies printed on handmade paper.

This is a reprint of the text of the first collected edition of Lithgow's travels, London, 1632, an account of three journeys made between 1610 and 1622. It includes a biographical notice of Lithgow and an index. The plates are for the most part facsimiles of those in the first collected edition. A first account of Lithgow's travels in the Levant appeared in 1614 as *Delectable and true Discourse of a... Peregrination*, second edition 1616. Lithgow travelled mostly on foot, and in general he had a greater knowledge of the interior of the countries he visited than most travellers of this period. The *Totall Discourse* includes journeys to North Africa, Italy and Spain, in addition to descriptions of Greece, Constantinople and the eastern Mediterranean.

BL 10024.k.4.

416. LÖFFLER, August, and Julius Hermann Moritz BUSCH. *L'Orient Pittoresque Publication artistique dessinée d'après Nature par A. Löffler et accompagnée du Texte descriptif du D.ʳ Maurice Busch. Avec 32 gravures en acier.* Trieste: Lloyd Autrichien, 1865.

Folio, pp. [iv] 108 (p.[i]=t, iv=list of plates). With 32 plates of steel engravings on thick paper. Original embossed black cloth, back gilt.

First edition in French, published originally as *Bilder aus dem Orient*, in parts from 1864-65. An Italian edition appeared in 1871. Most of the plates depict views in Syria and the Holy Land, but there are some interesting plates of Smyrna, Rhodes and Alexandria. Löffler was a landscape painter from Munich who travelled extensively. He visited Egypt and Palestine in 1849. Moritz travelled in the Levant for about three years c. 1855 to collect material for the Austrian Lloyd guidebook. He also wrote on Bismarck.

Not in BNF or BL on line. Weber 1184. See Blackmer 1025 for the Italian edition.

417. LÖHER, Franz von. *Kretische Gestade.* Bielefeld and Leipzig: [Breitkopf and Härtel for] Velhagen and Klasing, 1877.

12mo, pp. VIII 1-363 [1] (p.I=[ ], II=printers' device, III=title, [1]=colophon). Title in red and black, title and letterpress within decorative rules. Half black morocco over brown marbled paper boards, back gilt.

Apparently only edition. Löher is best known for his work on Cyprus, which includes and 'Cypern in der Geschichte' 1878, and *Cypern, Reiseberichte...* Stuttgart, 1878. He also produced *Griechische Küstenfahrten*, 1876.

GL GT2843; Weber 769. Not in BLC. Karlsruhe cites 3 entries.

418. LOSTALOT-BACHOUÉ, E. de, editor. **Le Monde Histoire de tous les Peuples depuis les Temps les plus reculés jusqu'à nos jours... Tome Huitième 1re et 2e parties.** Paris: Lebigre-Duquesne Frères, 1859.

8vo, pp. [iii] 1-579 (p.[i]=ht). With 33 engraved plates no'd 1-8 and 1-25. Contemporary green embossed cloth.

?Third edition, edited by Lostalot-Bachoué, volume eight only. This edition of *Le Monde* was published in ten volumes, 1858-59. Note that in this edition there is no separate part title page for the country described. The first edition appeared from 1838 to 1840, possibly in parts, edited by A. Houzé, and accompanied by an atlas of maps. The original editors also included Cassé de Saint-Prosper and André Augustin. In 1846 some or all of the volumes were published separately under the individual authors' names, e.g. Duponchel, *Histoires de Grèce et d'Italie*, by the Librairie Universelle (q.v.).

BL 9008.f.5; BNF 30380778, under Duponchel.

419. LOTI, Pierre, i.e. Louis Marie Julien VIAUD. **Constantinople (Aziyadé). Translated by Marjorie Laurie.** London: T. Werner Laurie Ltd. [1927].

8vo, pp. 266 + 4 pp. of adverts (p.1=ht). With a coloured frontispiece. Half red leather.

Apparently first English edition. This edition also includes *Phantom of the East*, a sort of sequel to *Aziyadé* which was first published in 1892 as *Fantome d'Orient*. The first edition of *Aziyadé* seems to be that of Paris, 1879. The French title is *Aziyadé.- Stamboul 1876-77. Extrait des notes et lettres d'un lieutenant de la Marine Anglaise entré au service de la Turquie le 10 mai 1876 tué dans le Murs de Kars le 27 Octobre 1877.* This was Loti's first novel; he was himself a naval officer, and the novel is an account of some curious experiences at Constantinople. The work is semi-autobiographical and is set during the Russo-Turkish war of 1877-78.

BL 10127.eee.18.

420. LOVINESCO, Eugène (1881-1943). **Les Voyageurs Français en Grèce au XIXe siècle (1800-1900). Thèse presentée à la Faculté des Lettres pour le Doctorat ès Lettres.** Paris: Henri Jouve, 1909.

8vo, pp. 1-228 (p.1=ht, 221-8=conts). Red cloth, original grey printed paper wrappers bound in.

First edition, doctoral thesis. The thesis was published the same year, 1909, by H. Champion, with a preface by Gustave Fougères.

This edition not in BL or BNF on line. GL has published edition.

421. LUCAS, Paul (1664-1737). ***Voyage du sieur Paul Lucas fait par ordre du Roi dans la Grèce, l'Asie Mineure, la Macédoine, et l'Afrique. Tome Premier. [... Tome Second. Contenant la description de Jerusalem, de l'Égypte, & du Fioume: avec un Mémoire pour servir à l'histoire de Tunis, depuis l'année 1684.]*** Amsterdam: Aux dépens de la Compagnie, M.DCC.XIV. [=1714]

2 vols in 1, 12mo, pp. [xxx] 1-323; [x] 1-328 (pp.[i]=ts). Titles in red and black. With two engraved frontispieces and 18 engraved plates (10 folding). Lacking the 2 maps. Contemporary calf, back blindstamped with lozenges in compartments.

Second edition of Lucas's second voyage to the Levant, 1705-08, when he visited Greece, the most uncommon of his three voyages. The first edition appeared at Paris in 1712. The work was edited by Etienne Fourmont from Lucas's notebooks. Lucas, a true adventurer, merchant, doctor and antiquary, served with the Venetians at the siege of Negroponte in 1688. On his return to France in 1696 he sold a large collection of medals and other antiquities to the Cabinet du Roi. This brought him to the attention of the court, and he then began the series of voyages for which he is famous. All three of Lucas's accounts were edited by others from his journals.

BL 978.a.3,4; GL GT624; Weber 466. This edition not in BNF on line , but see 30842438 for 1712 ed. Atabey 732 (1st ed) calls for 2 folding maps, 17 plates and 1 folding plate in the l-p (this is the inscription Lapis Ancyranus, the monumentum ancyranum). Not in Blackmer.

422. [LUDWIG Salvator, *Archduke of Austria.*] ***Eine Spazierfahrt im Golfe von Korinth.*** Prague: Heinrich Mercy, 1876.

Thick 4to, pp. [xi] XII-XXVII, 1-291 (p.[i]=t). Title in red and black. With 60 engraved plates on india paper, mounted. Numerous wood engravings in the letterpress. Lacking the two maps in the inner pockets. Quarter red roan.

First edition. Ludwig Salvator made the drawings for this work during cruises through the Gulf of Corinth made over a period of years. It includes a great deal of material on the coastal regions as well as some explorations of the coastal hinterland. He travelled extensively in the Ionian Islands, the Aegean and the Eastern Mediterranean, and he produced books on places in all these areas. These include *Einige Worte über die Kaymenen*, 1875, and *Levkosia die Hauptstadt von Cypern*, 1873. His work on the Gulf of Corinth is uncommon, e.g. Karlruhe cites only the Austrian National Library and Bavarian National Library copies. A reprint was published at Athens in 1983.

BL 10125.ff.1; Weber 750.

423. [LUDWIG Salvator, *Archduke of Austria*.] **Paxos und Antipaxos**. Würzburg and Vienna: [H. Stürtz for] Leo Woerl, 1887.

Thick 4to, pp. XV [1] 1-480 (pp.I=ht, [1]=st, 477-480=index). Title in red and black. With a folding frontispiece and 99 plates (of which 2=plans). Numerous illustrations in the letterpress. Original red decorative cloth gilt, gilt edges.

First edition. A second edition appeared in 1889, and the work was translated into Greek in 1905. Ludwig Salvator spent a year on Paxos from 1884-1885. The plates are especially interesting for their depictions of everyday life on the island. They were photographed from Ludwig Salvator's original drawings and engraved on zinc by Winwurm and Haffner in Stuttgart. His works on the Ionian islands include *Parga*, 1907, *Anmerkungen über Levkas*, 1908, *Sommertage auf Ithaka*, 1903, and *Wintertage auf Ithaka*, 1905.

BL 10125.ff.3; Blackmer 1940; Weber 897 (bound in shiny white diced paper with red lettering; this is also an original binding and may signal a special copy or issue)

424. LYSIMACHUS, Stanislaus, *pseud*. **Stanislai Lysimachi, equitis poloni, Epistola ad Claudium Lentulum nobilem marchiacum. In qua Tectae Gallorum, Pacis Bellive, artes; ac cum Turcis & seditiosis Hungaris Conspirationes, reteguntur. Christianopoli. M.DC.LXXXIII.** [?Paris: printer unknown, 1683.]

12mo, pp. 1-78 (p.1=t). Contemporary vellum boards. With the armorial bookplate of Nordkirchen.

Apparently first and only edition. The second part of this work refers to the battle at Presburg between the Turks, the Hungarian rebels under Tekely, and the Poles. It contains letters written in code connected with the Austrian-Turkish wars. Bound with Guilleragues.

BNF 30850190. Not in Barbier.
Collation: A-C^{12} D^4 (A1=t, D4=[ ]).

425. MACBEAN, Forbes. [*Sketches of Character & Costume in Constantinople, Ionian Islands &c. From the original drawings made on the spot by Capt.ⁿ Forbes Mac Bean...* London: T. McLean, 1854].

Lge folio, pp. [x] (pp.[i-x]=description of plates). Lacks both printed and lithographed titles. With 23 (of 25) lithographed plates by J. Sutcliffe, printed in colour (lacking pls. 2 and 18). Modern calf, stamped on upper cover 'Eastern Costumes'.

Apparently only edition. The Atabey Collection included two copies of this work, one with a printed title only, the other with a lithographed title only. MacBean, a member of the 92nd Highlanders, was probably stationed in the Levant and may have seen action in the Crimean War. The plates include standard Levantine characters: dervish, watercarrier, letter writer, and so forth. Plate 2 depicts 'Priests of the Greek Church, Corfu'; plate 18 is 'Coffee House, Constantinople'.

BL 650.a.13; Benaki Museum Library; Blackmer 1045; Atabey 740; Colas 1923. Not in GL.

426. MACCAS, Léon. *Ainsi parla Venizélos... Études de politique extérieure grecque.* Paris: Plon-Nourrit, 1916.

8vo, pp. [iii] IX, 319 (pp.[i]=ht, I-IX=pref. 317-19=conts). Uncut and partly unopened in half brown morocco, back gilt with cannons in compartments, red, green and ochre leather labels, gilt edges, original blue printed paper wrappers bound in.

First and apparently only edition. Maccas (Μακκᾶς), Greek politician and journalist, wrote a number of studies on Greek political questions, including *Constantin Ier, Roi des Hellènes*, 1917, *L'Hellénisme de l'Asie Mineure*, 1919, and *La Question gréco-albanaise*, 1921. He settled in Paris in 1914, where he wrote for the *Revue des Deux Mondes*; he also represented Greece at several international conferences.

BNF 30851479; GL HG716.5M12.

427. MACCLYMONT, James Alexander and John FULLEYLOVE. *Greece painted by John Fulleylove R.I. Described by Right Rev. J.A. McClymont C.B.E.V.D. D.D.* London: A. & C. Black [1924].

8vo, pp. [i] viii [1] 1-234 [1] + 4 pp. adverts (p.[1]=advert, [1]=map, [1]=sketch map). With coloured frontispiece and 31 coloured plates. Sketchmap in letterpess. Original blue embossed cloth.

Second edition, first published in 1906. The plates are coloured reproductions of Fulleylove's paintings. Fulleylove visited Greece in 1895 and exhibited paintings with Greek themes at the Royal Academy. See *Catalogue of the Work by the late J. Ful-*

leylove, R.I., London, 1908. MacClymont's text includes some interesting remarks on the language problem in Greece.

BL 010028.de.1/16; Tsigakou, 113 and 200c.

428. MACFARLANE, Charles. *Constantinople in 1828. A residence of sixteen months in the Turkish Capital and Provinces: With an account of the present state of the naval and military power, and of the resources of the Ottoman Empire.* London: Saunders and Otley, MDCCCXXIX. [=1829]

4to, pp. xix [i] 1-406 (p.i=ht, missing, xii-xix=conts, [i]=list of plates). With five lithographed plates of which 3=hand coloured, 1 printed in sepia, and 1=dp on india paper, mounted. Red leather gilt.

First edition. A second edition in 2 volumes, 8vo, with an appendix, was published the same year. The appendix was also issued separately in 4to, and some copies of the first edition have it bound in. There is also an issue of the second edition without the double-page view of Constantinople and an altered list of plates. MacFarlane spent the years 1827-28 in Constantinople and Asia Minor. His work on Turkey is valuable for his lengthy descriptions and his discussions of recent political history. MacFarlane also wrote novels with an eastern setting. He returned to Turkey in 1847.

GL GT1473; Blackmer 1047; Weber 175; Abbey 393; Droulia 1669.

There is another copy of MacFarlane in the Contominas collection, in three-quarter leather, back ruled gilt, with the contemporary ownership signature of Jane Collins, and the later ownership signature of A. Shirreff of Kensington on the title.

429. MACKENZIE, Georgina Mary Muir, and Adelina Paulina IRBY. *Travels in the Slavonic Provinces of Turkey-in-Europe. With nineteen illustrations by F. Kanitz.* London and New York: [Bradbury Evans and Co., Whitefriars, for] Alexander Strahan, 1866.

Lge 8vo, pp. [i] xxii, 687 [1] (p.[i]=ht, i=t, [1]=glossary). With wood-engraved frontispiece and 22 plates (of which 4=maps) after F.Kanitz. Uncut in the original publisher's binding of mauve pictorial cloth gilt, by Burn of Kirby Street, with his ticket on lower pastedown.

First edition, first issue, rare, with a variant title dated 1866. The second and more common issue is dated 1867 with the title beginning *The Turks, the Greeks, & the Slavons. Travels...*, and with the imprint of Bell and Daldy. However, comparison of

the gatherings and signatures of both issues indicates that the same sheets were used by both publishers. It is possible that the change of title occurred to make the work more saleable. This first issue is very uncommon, with no copies recorded by COPAC. The Blackmer copy was of the second issue, in green cloth. A second edition, revised and augmented, appeared in 1877. The work was translated into Serbo-Croatian in 1868. The Misses Irby and Mackenzie travelled in the Balkans from 1861 to 1864 and established a teacher-training school in Sarajevo. Their other works include *Across the Carpathians*, 1862, and *Notes on the South Slavonic Countries in Austria and Turkey*, 1865. *Travels in the Slavonic Provinces* is an important work which provides valuable information on the peoples of the former Yugoslavia, i.e. Slovenia, Bosnia, Croatia, Serbia and Montenegro, and helps to explain some of the conflicts in those areas today. The text begins with descriptions of Volos and Thessaloniki.

This issue not in BLC or COPAC. Blackmer 1051 (second issue). This edition not in Atabey, but see 746 for the second ed.

430. MACLAREN, Charles. *The Plain of Troy Described: and the identity of the Ilium of Homer with the New Ilium of Strabo proved, by comparing the Poet's narrative with the present topography.* Edinburgh: Adam and Charles Black, MDCCCLXIII. [=1863]

8vo, pp. xviii [2] 1-224 (p.i=ht, pp.[1]=errata, [2]=distance scales). With three no'd folding topgraphical sketches and a folding map of the plain of Troy (=fp). Contemporary calf, back gilt in compartments, brown leather label, sides gilt with the arms of the James VI School in Edinburgh, signed by Thomson of Edinburgh on fly-leaf.

Second edition, heavily revised with new material. The work was first published in 1822 as *A dissertation on the topography of the Plain of Troy*. The map of the plain of Troy is dated 1840; it was constructed by Thomas Graves and T.A.B. Spratt (q.v.) of the Royal Navy Hydrographic Survey which was being carried out in the Aegean during the late 1830s. MacLaren was editor of the newspaper the *Scotsman*.

Not in BLC on line. GL A391.1.

431. MADDEN, Richard Robert. *Travels in Turkey, Egypt, Nubia, and Palestine, in 1824, 1825, 1826, and 1827.* In Two Volumes. Vol. I. [... Vol. II.] London: Henry Colburn, 1829.

2 vols, 8vo, pp. xvi, 401 [1]; viii, 398 (p.i=ht in v.1, t in v.2, [1]=errata and colophon). With lithographed portrait frontispiece. Recent red morocco.

First edition. A second edition appeared in 1833. The text is in the form of letters, each chapter forming a letter addressed to a specific person, e.g. Garston, Quin, several medical men, and the Earl and Countess of Blessington. Madden travelled from 1824-27; his training as a doctor enabled him to enter areas closed to most Europeans. The frontispiece portrait, from a drawing by Henry Salt, British consul in Egypt, depicts Madden in Syrian costume, taking the pulse of a female patient. Madden later produced *Egypt and Mohammed Ali*, 1841. This copy lacks the half title in v.1.

BL 1047.d. 17,18; Blackmer 1056; Weber 178.

432

432. MAHAFFY, John Pentland. *Greek Pictures drawn with Pen and Pencil.* London: [W. Clowes for] Religious Tract Society, 1890.

4to, pp. 223 [1] + 8 pp. of adverts (pp.1=[ ], 2=fp, 3=t, [1]=index). Full-page wood engravings and a map in the text, versos blank, but included in the pagination. Original green pictorial cloth gilt, gilt edges.

First edition. Mahaffy, Irish classical scholar, published numerous works on the silver age of Greek history and literature; he was also Oscar Wilde's tutor. The wood engravings in this work are after photographs by Malcolm Macmillan and the Rev. W. Covington, and some are taken from the *Tour du Monde*. There was a copy of this work in the Blackmer collection, not included in the printed catalogue, in original brown cloth.

BL 10125.ff.7; Weber 1199.

433. MAHAFFY, John Pentland. *Rambles and Studies in Greece.* Phildelphia: Henry T. Coates & Co., 1900.

8vo, pp. xviii, 1-535 (p.i=ht, p.v=ded, pp.xvii-xviii=list of plates). Title in red and black. With a photographic frontispiece and 29 photographic plates with guards carrying the captions in red. Original red pictorial cloth gilt, top edge gilt.

Apparently first American edition. The preface has been supplied from the 'new edition', 1892. The first edition was published in 1876 with 12 plates. A reprint was produced in 1973 with a bibliography. Mahaffy produced a number of works on Greece, e.g. *Greek pictures drawn with Pen and Pencil*, *Social life in Greece*, etc. He also translated Duruy's history of Greece into English.

LoC 7263912. This ed. not in GL.

433

434. MALAKIS, Emile. *French travellers in Greece (1770-1820) An early phase of French Philhellenism. A Thesis presented to the Faculty of the Graduate School of the University of Pennsylvania.* Philadelphia: 1925.

8vo, pp. 90 [1] (pp.1=t, 89-90=bibliography, p.[1]=advert). Quarter turquoise calf, original grey printed paper wrappers preserved. A presentation copy to Professor A. Andreades, signed on the title by Malakis. And with an A.L.S. from Malakis to Andreades mounted on the verso of the advert. From the library of K.Th. Dimaras, with his stamp on lower paste-down. (Bound with Iorga.)

First edition of this useful work. Malakis was especially interested in Chateaubriand, whose *Itinéraire* he edited in 1946 with notes and a bibliography.

BNF 30864599.

435. MALTEZOS, Georgios Themistokles. *Μνημεῖα Τουρκοκρατίας Ἀθηνῶν. Εἰκονογράφησις Βασ. Γερμενῆ.* Athens: Ch. Spanos, 1960.

Lge 8vo, pp. 117 + [1] (p.1-2=[], p.3=t, [1]=colophon). Sketches in text. Half tan morocco over marbled paper boards, original orange printed upper wrapper bound in.

First edition. Without contents or index, but this work contains useful information on Turkish buildings in Athens.

GL A1508.38

436. MANDAT-GRANCEY, Edmond de, *Baron* (1842-1911). *Aux Pays d'Homère... Orné de gravures d'après des photographies de M. Anisson du Perron.* Paris: Plon-Nourrit et Cie., 1902.

8vo, pp. [iii] 1-381 + [1] + [1] (pp.[i]=ht, [1]=list of plates, [1]=conts). With eleven photographic illustrations. Quarter cloth over marbled paper boards. Library stamp of the 'Societe de Géographie Commerciale de Paris' on half title.

First edition of this account of a two-month cruise in 1901 to Greece and the islands, as far north as Mount Athos. The work was re-issued in 1904. Mandat-Grancey travelled with Anisson du Perron who took the photographs, all of sites in Greece. The work includes interesting photographs of Santorini and the excavations undertaken by Hiller van Gaertringen.

BNF 30870470; GL GT1414. Not in Weber.

437. MANDEVILLE, John. *The Voiage and Travaile of Sir John Maundevile, K'. Which treateth of the Way to Hierusalem; and of Marvayles of Inde, with other Ilands and Countryes. Now Publish'd entire from an Original Ms. in the Cotton Library.* London: for Woodman and Lyon, and C. Davis, 1727.

8vo, pp. XVI [viii] 1-384 + [7] (p.I=t, [i]-[viii]=conts, [1]=note on ms, [2]-[7]=index). Title in red and black. Contemporary calf, rebacked, back gilt with fleurons, red leather label. Contemporary armorial bookplate of Michael Kearney of Trinity College, Dublin. 19th c. booklabel of George Harwood.

First edition, second issue, of this manuscript of Mandeville's travels, describing a journey made from 1322-1356. There is an earlier issue with the date 1725 on the title. Copies are known with both titles. The earliest printed editions of Mandeville's travels seem to be in Italian (1567) and German (1692), under the names Mandavilla and Mantevilla. Accounts of Mandeville's journeys have also been published in several collected editions, one as early as 1584 (Frankfurt, Feyerabendt). Sir John Mandeville is considered to be an imaginary traveller. The earliest known manuscript of his travels, written in French, circulated in 1371, and the work, through translations into many other languages, gained extraordinary popularity. It has now been determined that these travels were in large part compiled from the works of genuine travellers of the 13th and 14th centuries by a Liège physician called Jehan à la Barbe.

This issue not in BLC on line. COPAC cites 4 copies. Weber 79. Not in Blackmer.
Collation: A^8 a^4 $B-Z^8$ $2A-B^8$, $2C^4$

438. MANDEVILLE, John. *The Marvellous Adventures of Sir John Maundevile Kt. being his voyage and travel which treateth of the way to Jerusalem... Edited and profusely illustrated by Arthur Layard. With a preface by John Cameron Grant.* [London:] Archibald Constable, 1895.

8vo, pp. xxx, 413 + 8 pp. of adverts (p.i=ht, pp.xxviii-xxx=list of ills). With a frontispiece and 25 full-page illustrations (versos blank but included in pagination). Numerous tail-pieces, vignettes and initials. Uncut in tan buckram, printed paper label. Bookplates of J. Timothy Kenrick and Thomas Middlemore of Hawkes Bay.

Only edition with Layard's illustrations.

BL 10025.cc.31.

439. MARCELLUS, Marie-Louis J.A.C. de Martin du Tyrac, Comte de. *Souvenirs de l'Orient.* Paris: Debecourt, 1839.

2 vols, 8vo, pp. [iii] VIII 1-464; [iii] 1-558 + [1] (pp.[i]=hts, pp.459, 461-64, [1]=errata, p.1=sts in both vols). With a folding map and 2 engraved plates. Uncut in contemporary quarter green roan gilt over marbled paper boards.

First edition. A second edition appeared in 1854 and a third in 1861. A Brussels edition was published in 3 vols, 16mo, in 1840. The plates depict the Venus de Milo, which Marcellus acquired for France, and a portrait of Pierre Gary, a renegade in the service of Mehmet Ali. This work is an account of Marcellus's early travels in the Levant, written twenty years after the events it describes. Marcellus was secretary to the French embassy at Constantinople, 1815-1820. In 1820 he was ordered to visit the important ports and harbours in the Aegean and the Eastern Mediterranean. During this mission he arranged for the purchase and transport of the Venus de Milo to France. Marcellus wrote all of his works in his retirement from the diplomatic corps; these include *Chants du Peuple en Grèce*, 1857, *Episodes Littéraires en Orient*, 1859, *Chants populaires de la Grèce Moderne*, 1860, *Les Grecs anciens et les Grecs modernes*, 1861; he also produced an edition of Nonnos's *Dionysiacs* in 1856. Marcellus was the son-in-law of the Comte de Forbin and among his many other works he edited the *Portefeuille de Comte de Forbin*, 1843.

BNF 30877511; BL 790.e.8; Blackmer 1097; Weber 296.

440. MARCELLUS, Marie-Louis J.A.C. de Martin du Tyrac, Comte de. *Souvenirs de l'Orient... Troisième édition.* Paris: Garnier Frères, 1861.

Sm. 8vo, pp. XII, 1-600 + [1] (pp.I=ht, [1]=errata). Quarter cloth, gilt ruled back.

Third edition, uncommon. This work was first printed in 1839 in two volumes, see above.

This edition not in BLC or BNF on line. This edition not in Blackmer but see 1087.

441. MARCELLUS, Marie-Louis J.A.C. de Martin du Tyrac, Comte de. *Les Grecs anciens et les Grecs modernes.* Paris: Michel Levy Frères, 1861.

8vo, pp. VI, 1-444 + [2] (pp.I=ht, V-VI=Avis, p.[1]=contents, [2]=errata). Blue cloth. Bookseller's stamp of Charles Wilberg of Athens on preliminary leaf.

First edition. The Count Marcellus spent over five years in the Levant as secretary of the French embassy at the Porte, 1815-1820. He retired from public life after the July Revolution and in later years he became an intimate of Chateaubriand; this work may reflect some of the latter's philhellenic fervour. It contains essays on ancient and modern Greek literature, comparing them in style and spirit, for example, 'Les Perses d'Eschyle à Constantinople', 'Medée et Nausicaé sur le Bosphore', and an essay on Villemain's translation of Pindar.

BNF 30877507; GL V93.5. Not in Blackmer.

442. MARCHEBEUS, (-). *Voyage de Paris à Constantinople par bateau à vapeur. Nouvel itinéraire orné d'une carte et de cinquante vues et vignettes sur acier, avec tableaux indiquant les lieux desservis par les paquebots à vapeur, sur la Méditerrranée, l'Adriatique et le Danube, le prix des places et des marchandises, les distances et la valeur des monnaies.* Paris: A. Bertrand, and the Author, 1839.

8vo, pp. i-xvi, 1-291 [1] (p.i=[], iii=ht, viii=errata [1]=table). With a double-page folding map and 24 lithographed plates. Illustrations in text. Original pictorial cloth gilt, badly faded, gilt edges.

First and apparently only edition of this account of the first organized steamer cruise in the Levant, April-August 1833. Other passengers included Maximilian of Bavaria (brother of King Otho of Greece) and the Duchesse de Berry. Marchebeus was an ar-

442

chitect who published several works on architectural and town planning projects. The plates include views of Hydra, Aegina, Syros and Tinos, among others. A description of this same cruise was produced by Giraudeau in 1835.

BNF 30879162; Blackmer 1075; Weber 297; Atabey 765.

There is another copy in the Contominas collection, in 19th c. quarter red roan, back ruled gilt.

443. MARCIAN, of Heracleia. Μαρκιανοῦ Ἡρακλεώτου Περιήγησις. *Marciani Heracleotae Poema de situ orbis. Fed. Morellus Profess. & Interpres Reg. Graeca recensuit, & Latine eodem genere versuum expressit. Cum notis & indice duplici.* Lutetiae, apud Federicum Morellum Architypographum Regium. M.DCVI. [Paris: F. Morel, 1606.]

Sm. 8vo, pp. [viii] 1-62 [8] (p.[i]=t). Greek and Latin text on facing pages. 19th c. red morocco, back ruled gilt, inner gilt dentelle, gilt edges. Ownership signature of M. Mnvās in red on title. Bound with Tzetzes and Morel.

First separate edition of the poem *De Situ Orbis*. The date on the title has been altered in ms. to 1615. This edition was produced by Fédéric Morel the younger, one of the greatest Greek scholars of his time. In addition to running his father's printing business he held the professorship of eloquence at the Collège de France. He edited Aristotle, Dio Chrysostom and Strabo, as well as producing translations and commentaries. Marcian lived c. 400 A.D.; he studied the works of Ptolemy, Protagoras, and Artemidorus. The surviving fragments of his own works indicate that he was one of the great geographers. His poem was first printed in David Hoeschell's *Geographica*, Augsburg, 1600. The ownership signature on the title may be that of Minoides Mynas (or Minas), collector of Greek manuscripts. At the instance of M. Villemain, Minister of Public Instruction, he explored the libraries of the Levant, particularly those of Mt. Athos.

BNF 30879738; BL 996.c.14(2); GL GC2888B; Hoffmann II, 580.
Collation: π⁴ A-H⁴)(⁴. Note that)(1 is signed)(4.

444. MARIGNAC, Aloys de. *Cyclades. Gouaches et dessins de M.E. Wrede Avant-Propos de Paul Valéry.* Athens: Librairie Kaufmann [1935].

Sm. 4to, pp. XI, 1-155 [4] (pp. I-IV=[ ], V=ht, VII=t, IX-XI=pref by Valery, pp.[1]=st to table of conts, [3]=conts, [4]=colophon). With four colour illustrations of paintings, mounted in the letterpress, and numerous illustrations in the text. Quarter red cloth, original beige printed paper wrappers bound in.

First edition, published in 1550 copies, with the first 50 copies 'hors de commerce'. This copy is no. 573. A second edition appeared at Athens in 1936 under the imprint of Castalie. The four colour reproductions depict Andros, Myconos, Delos and Santorini, paintings by Maria Elisabeth Wrede. The Contominas Collection also includes a portfolio of watercolours by M.E. Wrede illustrating daily life on Rhodes. Maria Elisabeth Wrede could be connected with the family of Walther Wrede who was at the German Archaeological Institute in Athens in the 1930s.

BNF 31521218; GL GT2662.9.

ΜΑΡΚΙΑΝΟΥ ΗΡΑΚΛΕΩΤΟΥ ΠΕΡΙΗΓΗΣΙΣ.
MARCIANI HERACLEOTÆ POEMA DE SITV ORBIS.

FED. MORELLVS *Profeff. & Interpres Reg.*
Græca recensuit, & Latinè eodem
genere versuum expressit.

Cum notis & Indice duplici.

Βασιλεῖ τ' ἀγαθῷ, κρατερῷ τ' αἰχμητῇ.

LVTETIÆ,
Apud FEDERICVM MORELLVM
Architypographum Regium.

cIɔ. Iɔcxx.

445. MARITI, Giovanni (1736-1806). *Voyages dans l'isle de Chypre, la Syrie et la Palestine, avec l'histoire generale du Levant. Tome Premier. [... Tome Second.]* Paris: Belin, 1791.

2 vols, sm. 8vo, pp. viii, 1-327; [iv] 1-416 (p.i, [i]=hts, pp.308-327, 392-416=tables of contents). Woodcut head- and tailpieces. Quarter brown leather antique, backs panelled with fleurons, red and green leather labels, pale blue edges.

First edition in French, translated by J. B. R. Robinet and/or J. Castilhon, from the Italian edition *Viaggi per l'Isola di Cipro, e per la Soria e Palestina*, published in 9 volumes between 1769 and 1776. The French edition is a translation of only a portion of the Italian work, but it also includes Mariti's essay on the wines of Cyprus, published separately in Italian in 1772. A Dutch piracy also appeared the same year at Neuwied. Mariti spent seven years in Cyprus, part of the time as vice-consul under Turner, the British consul at Larnaca. His work contains the most complete description of Cyprus up to his time. Mariti travelled in Egypt before his return to Florence. He also wrote on the rebellion of Ali Bey and on Fakhr-ed-Din, emir of the Druses.

BNF 33997823, citing Castilhon as the translator in the title entry, but also attributing the translation to Robinet. This edition not in Blackmer or Atabey, but see Blackmer 1079 for the Neuwied edition. Weber 543.

MARLÈS. See LACROIX DE MARLÈS

446. MARMIER, Xavier (1808-1892). *Du Rhin au Nil - De Constantinople au Caire 1845-1846. Nouvelle édition.* Paris: Librairie Victor Lecoffre, 1887.

8vo, pp. [iv] 1-439 + [1] (p.[i]=ht). Partly uncut and with wide margins, in half calf gilt over marbled boards.

A late edition of *Du Rhin au Nil*, part two only, on the Levant, entitled in this edition 'De Constantinople au Caire'. The first part, entitled in this edition 'Du Rhin au Constantinople' was published in a separate volume; apparently the two parts were issued separately in this edition. The original work first appeared in two volumes in 1846 and also included accounts of the Tyrol and Hungary. This work was very successful; five editions had appeared by 1877. Marmier was a well-known litterateur and travel writer. He also worked as a translator, especially of accounts of travels. He was asked to undertake this journey by the Minister of Public Instruction. In 1853 he produced *Lettres sur l'Adriatique et Montenegro*.

GL GT1114.1. The Gennadius Library catalogues the two parts separately. Not in Weber. This edition not in BLC or BNF on line. This edition not in Blackmer but see 1080 (1st ed.). Not in Atabey.

447. MARMONT, August-Frederic Louise Wiesse de, *Duc de Raguse*. *Voyage du Maréchal Duc de Raguse en Hongrie, en Transylvania... à Constantinople... et en Égypte. Tome Premier [... Deuxième ... Troisième ... Quatrième.]* Paris: Ladvocat, 1839 — *[Voyage en Sicile... Troisième édition.]* Paris: Ladvocat, 1838. — *[Atlas]*.

5 vols, 8vo, and 1 vol, 4to (atlas), pp. [iii] 402; [iii] 396; [iii] 406 [1]; [iii] 384; [iii] 372; no letterpress in atlas (pp.[i]=hts, p.1 in vols 2,3 5=sts, [1]=table of conts, pp.383-4 in vol. 4=errata to vols. 1 and 2, pp.351-72=conts and index). With a lithographed portrait, 12 engraved plates no'd at random, and 8 no'd maps (all either double-page or large folding). Half green calf gilt romantique, atlas in half red calf over red pebbled cloth.

Third editions? The first and second editions of the voyage to Constantinople and Egypt were both issued in 1837. The voyage to Sicily was apparently first issued in 1838. Although published separately, it was envisaged as the fifth volume of the set, and is so marked on the half title; in some editions the volume number appears on the half title only, in others on the title. The atlas issued with this work is scarce; it is untitled and the plates have been adapted from Finden's engravings for the travels of Baron Taylor, which accounts for the random numbers on the plates. Five of the maps are of sites in Egypt, three of Sicily. Marmont carried out these travels in 1834 and 1835. Vol. 3 contains documents relating to the Expedition de l'Égypte.

BNF 35976588; BL 1045.i.5, neither with atlas. BLC attributes the work to Anne Marie Hortense Viesse de Marmont, Duchesse de Raguse. This edition not in Blackmer but see 1638-39. Atabey 772; GL Spentsas, p. 132-3; Weber 256 cites the second edition.

448. MARMORA, Andrea. *Della Istoria di Corfu descritta da Andrea Marmora nobile Corcirese. Libri Otto. Al Serenissimo Principe ed eccellentiss.^{mo} Senato di Venetia.* Venice: Curti, M.DC.LXXII. [=1672]

4to, pp. [xxxii] 1-456 + [11] (pp.[i]=engraved t, [iii]=printed title, [11]=index). Printed title within rules. Engraved title, repaired, engraved portrait of Marmora, five plates of coins, and 3 double-page maps/plans, all in the letterpress. Modern quarter blue morocco. 17th c. ownership signature of Peter Burmann II on title.

First edition of the early standard history of Corfu. Marmora was a member of an old Corfiot family; one of the interesting features of the work is his list of the prominent

Greek families living in Corfu at that time. The three maps depict the island of Corfu, a plan of Corfu town, and a plan of Palaeopolis.

BL 657.c.24; Blackmer 1082; Bib. Ionienne 203; Papadopoulos IB 95 cites many copies.

449. [MARTIN, Guillaume.] *Voyage à Constantinople, fait à l'occasion de l'ambassade de M. le Comte de Choiseul-Gouffier à la Porte Ottomane. Par un ancien aumônier de la Marine Royale.* Paris: François and Louis Janet, 1819.

Sm. 8vo, pp. VIII, 256 (p.I=ht). With a lithographed frontispiece of Abdul Hamid. Quarter polished calf, back gilt in compartments, red leather label. With the ticket of the German binder Hutter.

First edition. A second edition appeared in 1821, and Barbier also cites an edition of 1824. Martin accompanied Choiseul-Gouffier on his second journey to the Levant, when he took up the post of ambassador to the Porte in 1784. Abdul Hamid reigned as sultan during the embassy of Choiseul-Gouffier.

449

BNF 30895094; Barbier IV, 1056; Weber 602; Atabey 778. Not in Blackmer.

450. MARTIN, Percy Falcke. *La Grèce Nouvelle. Adapté de l'anglais par Th. Pontsevrez.* Paris: E. Guilmoto (Librairie Orientale-Américaine) [1917].

8vo, pp. XVI, 1-294 (p.I=[ ], III=ht, 289-94=conts). Photographic portrait frontispiece of Venizelos and 5 photographic illustrations. Uncut and unopened in recent brown morocco gilt by Leggas, central gilt bookstamp of Contominas on upper cover, original beige printed paper wrappers bound in.

First edition in French of Martin's *Greece of the 20th Century*, London, 1913, with a preface by Andreas Andreades, translated by Pontsevrez. The date [1917] is attributed by the Bibliothèque Nationale. This appears to be Pontsevrez' only work. Martin produced a number of historical and descriptive works on Egypt, the Sudan, Mexico and places in South America.

BNF 30896370; GL GT2083.43.

451. MATHESON, William. *Auf den Götterbergen Griechenlands (Griechenlandfahrt des S.A.C.) Mit einem Beitrag von Franz Carl Endres und sechsundzwanzig Bildern.* Basle: Benno Schwabe, 1936.

Sm. 4to, pp. 118 (p.1=[ ], 3=ornament, 5=t). With photographic frontispece and 25 photographic plates. Original beige cloth.

First and apparently only edition of this account of an excursion to Greece in 1934 made by a party from the Swiss Alpine Club. Matheson was a member of the Welsh Climbing Group and seems to have been invited to join the excursion. The Swiss group was hosted by the Greek Mountaineering Society (EOS), and they climbed a number of mountain peaks on Olympus and other ranges, including Skala, Skolion, the Throne of Zeus, and others. The very interesting photographs are of these mountain ranges. This is one of fifty copies on Echt Bütten paper, signed by Matheson and Endres. We were not able to ascertain the number of ordinary copies. The work is uncommon and may have been produced for private circulation.

Not in COPAC. Karlsruhe cites seven copies.

452. MATHIEU, Henri. *La Turquie et ses différents Peuples. Tome premier. [... deuxième.]* Paris: E. Dentu [1857].

2 vols, sm. 8vo, pp. [iii] xxiv, 364; [iii] 396 (pp.[i]=hts, pp.357-64 and 391-96=conts). Full red morocco, sides panelled gilt with fleurons in corners, panelled backs gilt with stars, gilt edges.

First and only edition. The introduction is dated 1857.

BNF 30906135 attributes the date 1857. Not in Blackmer or Atabey.

453. MAUCLAIR, Camille. *Athènes Trente planches en couleur d'après les tableaux de Paul Bret.* Paris: Henri Laurens, 1935.

Sm. 4to, pp. [iv] 1-171 [2] (p.[i]=ht, p.[2]=colophon dated 1946). Title in red and black. With 30 mounted colour reproductions. Original quarter ivory cloth over paper boards, uncut.

First edition, second issue? The title page is dated 1935, but the colophon bears the date 1946. The charming plates by Paul Bret (1902-1956) include views of Eleusis, Aegina, Myconos and Megara (depicting the 'Trata', traditionally danced on the first Tuesday after Easter). The symbolist and art critic Mauclair produced similar works on Bruges, Brittany, etc. He also wrote *Le Pur Visage de La Grèce*, 1934, and *De Jerusalem à Istanbul*, 1939.

BNF 32431073; GL GT2161.35.

453

454. MAURRAS, Charles (1868-1952). *Anthinéa D'Athènes à Florence. Le Voyage d'Athènes – Une Ville Grecque et Française...* Paris: Ernest Flammarion and Honoré and Edouard Champion, 1923.

8vo, pp. [vi] XI, 304 (pp.[i]=ht, 303-4=conts). Quarter red calf gilt over red cloth.

A late edition, the 23rd. The first edition of this very successful work appeared in 1901, published by Juven. A fifth edition had appeared by 1912, and there were several illustrated editions. Maurras' journey to Athens took place in 1896, on the occasion of the first Olympic games. The work includes 'Lettres des jeux Olympiques', and an essay on the Greek settlement in Corsica. Maurras, litterateur and politician, wrote on George Sand and Anatole France; his political writings included the Dreyfus case and socialism during the First World War. He later produced *Athènes antique*, 1918.

BNF 30912695.

455. MAURRAS, Charles. *Anthinéa D'Athènes à Florence. Le Voyage d' Athènes – Une Ville Grecque et Française... [etc.] Nouvelle Édition.* Paris: [E. Grevin for] Ernest Flammarion and Edouard Champion [1927].

Sm. 8vo, pp. XVI, 17-284 (p.I=ht, 284=colophon). Old half vellum, brown leather labels.

A late edition, first published in 1901. According to the half title verso, this edition was published in 1000 copies, of which 1-100 were printed on 'papier vergé d'Arches', and 101-500 on 'papier vergé pur fil Lafuma'. BNF cites a quarto edition with coloured plates by Renefer published by Lapina the same year, 1927.

BNF 37168222.

456. MELETIOS, *Bishop of Athens* (1661-1714). *Γεωγραφία Παλαιὰ καὶ Νέα Συλλεχθεῖσα ἐκ διαφόρων Συγγραφέων Παλαιῶντε καὶ Νέων, καὶ ἐκ διαφόρων Ἐπιγραφῶν, τῶν ἐν λίθοις, καὶ εἰς κοινὴν Διάλεκτον ἐκτεθεῖσα χάριν τῶν πολλῶν τοῦ ἡμετέρου Γένους.* Venice: Nikolaos Glykys, 1728.

Folio, pp. [vi] 1-620 + [86] (p.[i]=t, [1-86]=index). With an engraved frontispiece. Old quarter calf over red marbled paper boards.

First edition, published posthumously. This work was later edited and greatly amplified by Anthimos Gazes in 1807 (q.v.).

BL 569.h.11; Legrand 18th c. I, 179; Papadopoulos 3830.

456

265

457. MELLING, Antoine Ignace (1763-1831). *Vue générale de Constantinople, prise du Chemin de Buyuk-Déré. Dessiné par Melling. Gravé à l'eau-forte par Schroeder & Le Rouge. Terminé par Schroeder. N.º 8.*

Engraving, 48 x 90.5 cms. As issued.

First edition, from Melling's *Voyage pittoresque de Constantinople et des rives du Bosphore*, Paris, 1819. This important work began publishing in 1809 and was completed in 1819, issued in 13 livraisons. Melling, who set out on his travels at the age of 19, became the architect to Hatice, sister of the Sultan Selim III. Trained as an architect and artist, he began to work on the renovation of her property at Ortakoy in 1795. As an employee of the Sultan's family he had access to the inner apartments of the palace at Topkapi, and thus Melling has provided us with the earliest interior views of the harem and several of the Sultan's palaces, as well as beautiful views of Constantinople and its environs. He returned to Paris in 1803, and in 1804 he published a prospectus for his proposed work.

BNF 30710213; Blackmer 1105; Weber 77; Atabey 799; Brunet III, 1591; Boppe, pp. 164-181, 198-200.

458. MELOT, Joseph. *Entre l'Olympe et le Taygète.* Paris: Plon-Nourrit, 1913.

Sm. 8vo, pp. [iii] II, 309 + [1] (pp.[i]=ht, [1]=colophon). With 6 photographic illustrations. Uncut in three-quarter calf gilt, originalblue printed paper wrappers bound in.

Only edition, and Melot's only work on Greece.

BNF 30923349.

459. MEURS, Jan (1579-1639). *Ioannis Meursi Regnum Atticum. Sive, De Regibus Atheniensium, eorumque rebus gestis, libri III.* Amsterdam: Jan Janssonius. M.DC.XXXIII. [=1633]

Sm. 4to, pp. 1-238 + [25] (p.1=t, pp.[1-25]=indexes). Contemporary vellum.

First edition. Meurs or Meursius, Dutch classical scholar and antiquary, was appointed professor of Greek and history at the University of Leiden in 1610. He produced many treatises on classical subjects, a number of which have been reprinted in Gronovius's *Thesaurus Graecarum antiquitatum*, 1697. Some of these treatises were printed posthumously, edited by Graevius and others. *Regnum Atticum* was reprinted in vol. 4 of Gronovius's *Thesaurus*.

BL 802.f.10; BNF 30936985; GL HG130M594.

460. MEURS, Jan. *Rhodus, Sive, De illius insulae, atque urbis, rebus memoratu dignis, Liber I.* Amsterdam: Abraham Wolfgang, 1675.

Sm. 4to, pp. [i] 1-124 + [68] (p.[i]=t). Half calf gilt antique.

First edition, edited by J.G. Graevius and published posthumously. Part three only. This is one of three works printed together under the title *Creta, Cyprus, Rhodus sive de nobilissimarum harum insularum rebus & antiquitatibus Commentarii postumi.* Each of the works, *Creta, Cyprus, Rhodus*, has a separate title page. However, the index at the end of *Rhodus* (pp.[1]=[68]) also includes the index to Crete and Cyprus, an indication that these three texts were intended to be published together, albeit with separate title pages.

BL 795.g.20 (3 works together); GL A381; Blackmer 1121 (3 works).

461. MEURS, Jan. *Theseus sive De ejus vita rebusque gestis Liber postumus. Accedunt Ejusdem Paralipomena de Pagis Atticis, et excerpta ex V. Cl. Jacobi Sponii Itinerario de Iisdem Pagis.* Utrecht: Franciscus Halma, MDCLXXXIV. [=1684] — *Reliqua Attica; sive, Ad Librum De Populis Atticae, Paralipomena. Liber singularis. Cui accedit Auctarium ex itinerario Jacobii Sponii V. C.* Utrecht: Franciscus Halma, MDCLXXXIV. [=1684]

2 works in 1, 2 parts in the first work, sm. 4to, pp. [viii] 1-136 + [12], 1-40; 1-52 + [8] (p.[i]=t, p.1=st to part 2; p.1=t to second work). Titles in red and black. Old vellum. Contemporary ownership signature of John Venables on title.

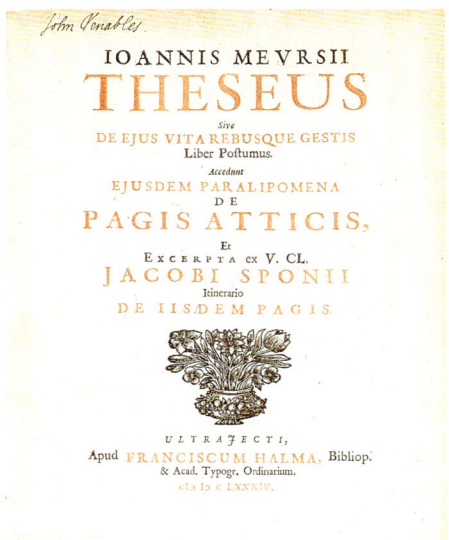

First editions, possibly edited by Graevius, who edited many of Meurs' works, and published posthumously. These two works may have been published separately; certainly the signatures are not continuous, and they are found separately as well as bound together. The editor has also included material from Spon's voyage, first published in 1678, in the first work, *Theseus*. According to the Gennadius Library catalogue, the additions from Spon in the *Reliqua Attica* are not actually included in the work, despite the information on the title.

BL 585.c.33 (*Theseus* only); GL A264.11 (*Reliqua Attica* only).

Collation: *⁴ A-S⁴ 2S², A-E⁴; A-G⁴ H².

462. MEURS, Jan. *Joanni Meursi De Regno Laconico Libri II. De Piraeeo [sic] Liber Singularis. Et in Helladii Chrestomathiam Animadversiones. Omnia nunc primum prodeunt.* Utrecht: Guiljelmus van de Water, MDCLXXXVII. [=1687]

3 parts in 1, sm. 4to, pp. [vii] 1-108 + [12], 1-51 [7], 1-71 [6] (p.[i]=gen title, pp.1=part titles; pages [1-12], [1-6]=indexes). Contemporary vellum, red leather label gilt. With the Chatsworth library label.

First edition, edited by Joannes Graevius, and published posthumously. These three work were reprinted in Gronovius's *Thesaurus* in 1697. The three parts have separate part titles (titles to pts 2 and 3 dated 1686) but the general title clearly indicates that the three sections were issued together.

BL 802.f.12; GL A262; Blackmer 1945.

463. MEYER. *Meyers Reisebücher. Türkei und Untere Donauländer. Vierte Auflage. Mit 5 Karten, 19 Plänen und Grundrissen und 1 Panorama.* Leipzig and Vienna: Bibliographisches Institut, 1892.

Sm. 8vo, pp. XII, X, 399 [1] + 64 + [3] (p.1-XII=adverts and timetable, pp.I=t, [1]=colophon, pp.64, [1-3]=adverts). With 4 (of 5) maps, 19 plans (of which several in text), and a folding lithographed panorama of Constantinople. Brown morocco, back ruled gilt.

Fourth edition, edited by K. Mühl. The general title of this work is *Türkei und Griechenland*; it appeared in two volumes; the title above is the title of the first volume. Greece is described in volume two. It is unclear when the first and third editions appeared. A second edition of both volumes was published in 1888. It is possible that, as with the case of the Baedeker and Murray guides, the material in these guides is divided into separate volumes as more information becomes available. In the fifth edition, 1898, the work is arranged with the volumes entitled *Unter Donauländer und Türkei*, and *Türkei, Rumanien, Serbien, Bulgarien*. Greece is not included in the fifth edition.

Not in BLC. Karlsruhe cites 2 copies

464. MEZZANOTTE, Antonio. *Fasti della Grecia nel XIX Secolo Poesie Liriche.* Pisa: N. Capurro e Comp., MDCCCXXXII. [=1832]

8vo, pp. [ix] 11-252 [2] (p.[i]=t, [iii]=ded, [1-2]=errata). Quarter calf gilt over marbled paper boards. Indecipherable ownership stamp on title.

First edition. A second edition was published at Bologna in 1836. A collection of poems, philhellenic in character which concern Greek victories and events connected with the Revolution — the death of Gregory V, the siege of Missolonghi, the battle of Navarino, Botsaris, etc. Mezzanotte was a professor at the University of Perugia.

BL 11436.f.44; GL IND752; Droulia 1977.

465. MICHAUD, Joseph François, and Jean J.F. POUJOULAT. *Correspondance d'Orient 1830-1831... I [... II... III... IV... V... VI... VII.]* Paris: Ducollet, 1833 [...1834 ... 1835.]

7 vols, 8vo, pp. [iii] IV, 468; [iii] VIII, 416; [iii] 503; [iii] 440; [iii] 543; [iii] 478; [iii] 612 (pp.[i]=hts). With a large folding map. Uncut in half tan morocco, backs panelled gilt, black leather labels, original printed paper wrappers bound in. With the red and white cypher booklabel of A.M. or M.A. mounted on title of v.1 and the preliminary leaves of some of the other volumes.

First edition. A Brussels edition appeared in 9 vols, 12mo, in 1835-36. In 1830 Michaud and his secretary Poujoulat travelled to the Levant to collect additional material for the *Histoire des Croisades*. After arriving in Jerusalem via Greece, Constantinople and the Archipelago they separated, Michaud going to Egypt and Poujoulat to Syria. The majority of the letters were written during this period. The first three volumes, mostly containing letters from Michaud, deal with Greece and Turkey. Poujoulat's letters constitute the major portion of volumes four to seven. In addition to accounts of their travels, the letters contain discussions of points in the *Histoire*. There are also letters from other contributors, including Gillot de Kerhardene, Camille Callier, and Victor de la Boulaye, with an account of Otho's court in Greece in 1834. Poujoulat's brother Baptistin also wrote an account of his travels in the East (q.v.).

BNF 31142507; Blackmer 1122; Weber 211; Atabey 807.

466. MICHAUD, Joseph François (1767-1839). *Histoire de Croisades ... Septième édition augmentée d'un Appendice par M. Huillard Bréholles. Tome I. [... Tome II... III... IV.]* Paris: Furne, and Dezobry and E. Magdeleine, 1849.

4 vols, 8vo, pp. [iii] VII, 528; [iii] 502; [iii] 510; [iii] 494 (pp.[i]=hts, pp.457-94=index). With 4 engraved frontispieces and a folding map in v.4, coloured in outline. 19th c. quarter green calf, backs gilt in compartments. Prize bookplate of the College de Roanne for 1853 to Louis Labrosse.

Seventh edition of this important work, which brought the Crusades back into French historiography, but the first with Bréholles' appendix. Part I, on the first Crusade, was published in 1812. Michaud's history of the Crusades took its final form in 1838, in six volumes, just before his death in 1839. The sixth edition, 1841, was edited by his secretary and travelling companion Poujoulat (q.v.). Michaud also produced *Bibliothèque des Croisades*, 1829, which contains European and Arabic sources on the Crusades.

This edition not in BNF on line.

467. MICHON, Jean Hippolyte (1806-1881). *Voyage religieux en Orient. Tome premier [... Tome deuxième].* Paris: Veuve Comon, 1853.

2 vols, 8vo, pp. XII, 1-308, 28; [iii] 1-393, 10 (pp.I, [i]=hts, pp.1-28 and 1-10=documents, errata on p.10). With six engraved plates by J. Penel after Ichon. 19th c. dark green roan, backs ruled gilt, over green cloth. Contemporary book label of M. Pairier.

First edition. A second edition appeared in 1854. The work was translated into English in 1853 as *Narrative of a religious journey in the East*. Michon accompanied Caignart de Saulcy (q.v.) on his scientific mission to the Dead Sea as botanist, and he wrote the introduction to the Catalogue of Plants in de Saulcy's work. The plates consist of ground plans of churches including the monastery of Daphne, Aghioi Theodori in Athens, Aghia Sophia in Leondari (?Leonidion) and others. Michon was a writer on religious questions; he also wrote novels with religious themes and was interested in graphology. This work contains many questions and discussions on the possibility of the reunification of the eastern and western Churches. The bookplate could belong to Henri, Louis or J. Pairier.

BNF 30944184; Weber 462. See Blackmer 1123 for English edition.

468. MIGNOT, Vincent. *Histoire de l'empire Ottoman, depuis son origine jusqu'à la paix de Belgrade en 1740.* Paris: Le Clerc, 1771.

4 vols, 12mo, pp. xii, 1-531; [iii] 1-517; [iii] 1-503; [iii] 1-500 + [3] (pp.i, [i]=ts, [iii]=conts and errata, [3]=privilege and approbation). Contemporary polished calf ruled gilt, backs gilt in compartments, green and red leather labels, several missing or defective. 18th c. bookplates of William Beauchamp Lygon with his motto 'Ex Fide Fortis', and of the Lansdowne family, with the motto 'Virtute non Verbis'.

First edition. A second edition appeared in 1773, also in four volumes. The work was translated into English in 1787. Mignot was Voltaire's nephew.

BNF 30946012; Blackmer 1124; GL Spentsas p. 135.

469. MILITARY COSTUME. *The Military Costume of Turkey; illustrated by a Series of Engravings from Drawings made on the spot. Dedicated, by permission, to His Excellency the Minister of the Ottoman Porte to His Brittannic Majesty.* London: W. Lewis for Thomas MacLean [c. 1820].

folio, pp. [v] viii + [i], [30] (pp.[i]=t, [iii]=ded, pp.i-viii=preface, p.[i]=list of plates, pp.[1]-[30]=descriptions of the plates; this copy lacks the subtitle (p.[v]) before the preface). With engraved title, engraved portrait frontispiece and 27(of 29)aquatinted plates (lacking pl. 2, the Grand Vizier, and pl. 18, a cavalry officer). Contemporary red straight-grained morocco, sides framed in gilt and blind, gilt edges.

Second edition, completely reset and more imposing than the first, with a larger typeface. The first edition appeared in 1818 (on paper watermarked 1817) with the imprint 'Published by T. M'Lean... B.R. Howlett Printer'. A later edition exists with the plates on paper watermarked 1822. MacLean probably produced this work as a companion to his reprint of Dalvimart's *Costume of Turkey*. The artist who produced the drawings for the *Military Costume* is unknown, but several of the plates are based on the same prototypes used for a few plates (Mameluke, Dehli, Arnaout) in Wittman's *Travels in Turkey*, 1803. The portrait frontispiece is of Antonaki Ramadani, Turkish minister in London.

Not in BLC on line. Blackmer 1125; Atabey 813 (see 812 for first ed.); Colas 2059; Abbey 373.

470. MILLE, Pierre (1864-1941). *De Thessalie en Crète Impressions de Campagne Avril-Mai 1897. Avec 16 gravures hors texte.* Paris and Nancy: Berger Levrault, 1898.

Sm. 8vo, pp. [v] 246 + [2] (pp.[i]=ht, [1-2]=contents and list of plates). With 16 photographic plates. Old half tan morocco over brown and yellow marbled paper boards.

First and apparently only edition. This is one of Mille's earlier works. His later work included novels and essays, as well as fantasy.

BNF 30947413. Not in Blackmer, Weber or Atabey.

471. MILLER, Emmanuel Clement Benigne. *Le Mont Athos Vatopédi L'Ile de Thasos. Avec une notice sur la vie et les travaux de M. Emm. Miller par Le Mis Quex de Saint Hilaire.* Paris: Ernest Leroux, 1889.

Lge 8vo, pp. XCIII [1] 409 (pp.I=t, [1]=st, 407-409=conts). With 2 maps. Uncut in new half calf, remains of original printed paper wrappers bound in.

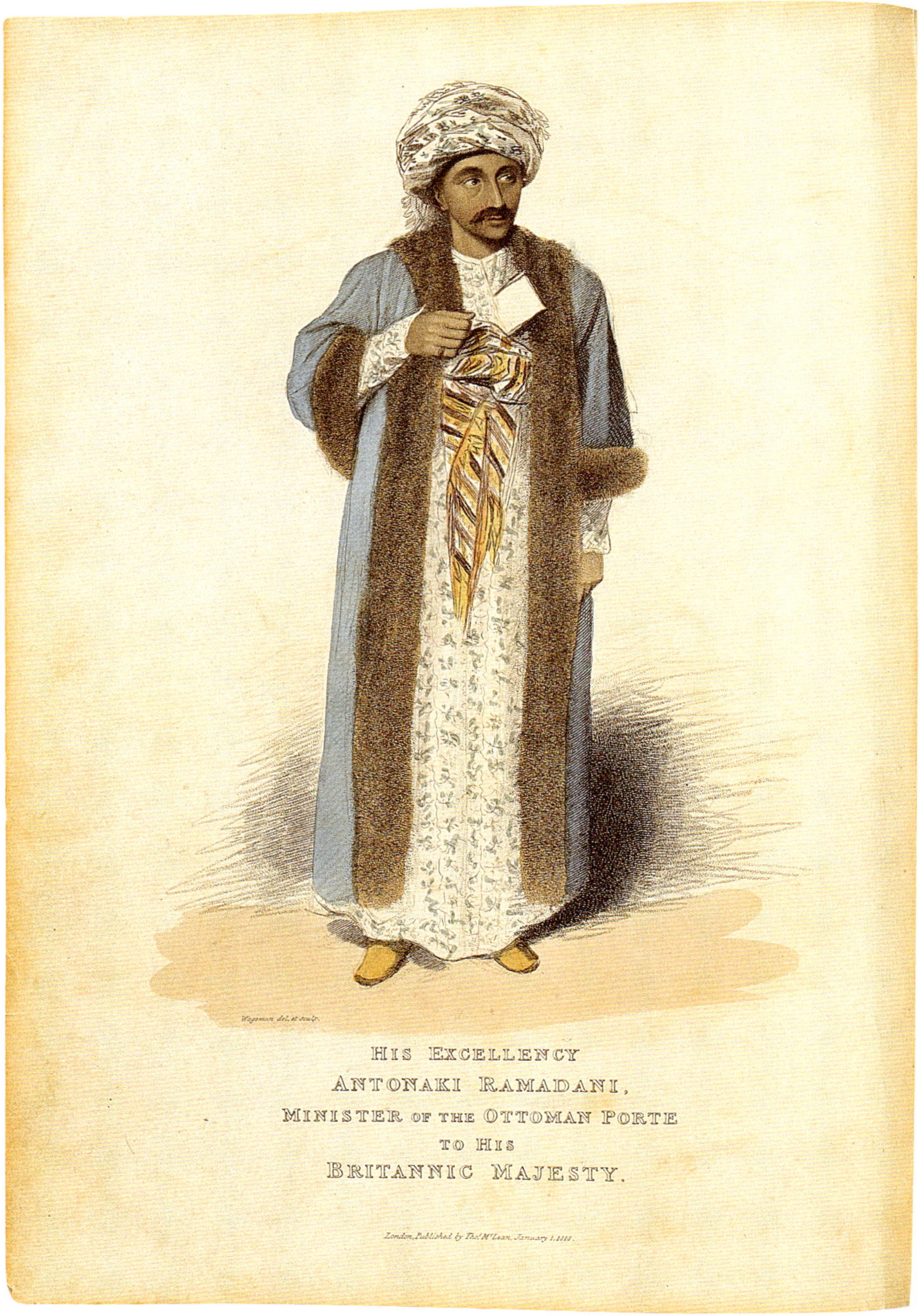
Wageman del. et sculp.
HIS EXCELLENCY
ANTONAKI RAMADANI,
MINISTER OF THE OTTOMAN PORTE
TO HIS
BRITANNIC MAJESTY.
London, Published by Thos. M'Lean, January 1, 1818.

469

First edition, published posthumously, and with a biographical notice by Quex de St. Hilaire. In addition to his work as an archaeologist, Miller was a prolific editor of texts and cataloguer of Greek manuscripts. This posthumous work consists of a series of letters in three parts: the first part, 'Souvenirs de Mont Athos', was published in the *Correspondant* 25 April 1866. These letters were written by Miller during his missions to Mount Athos and Thasos in 1863 and 1864. The work ends with a list of finds made during Miller's missions which are now in the Louvre.

BNF 30947554; Weber 918; Doens 1075. Not in Blackmer.

472. MILLINGEN, Julius. *Memoirs of the affairs of Greece; containing an account of the military and political events, which occurred in 1823 and following years. With various anecdotes relating to Lord Byron, and an account of his last illness and death.* London: for John Rodwell, 1831.

8vo, pp. xi, 1-338 (p.i=t). Extra-illustrated with an engraved portrait of Lord Byron tipped in. Uncut in modern red cloth.

First and only edition. Millingen, son of the antiquary James V. Millingen, was sent to Greece by the London Greek Committee where he served as Byron's doctor at Missolonghi. Later he entered the Turkish service under Ibrahim Pasha; he eventually settled in Constantinople where he served as doctor to the Sultan.

BL 1053.g.12; Blackmer 1136; Droulia 1938; Wise II, 97; St. Clair, pp. 236-7.

473. MILLS, Charles. *The Travels of Theodore Ducas, in various countries in Europe, at the Revival of Letters and Art. Part the First. Italy.* London: Longman, Hurst, Rees, Orme & Brown, 1822.

2 vols, 8vo, pp. viii, 1-388; vii, 1-399 + [1] (pp.i=hts, missing, [1]=advert). 19th c. half blue roan, back gilt romantique over marbled paper boards. 19th c. bookplate with the crowned cypher GO within a wreath of olive leaves, and the motto '+L'Olivette+'.

First edition, all published. This very interesting work describes the travels of the mythical Ducas, a Greek who fled to the West on the fall of Constantinople. In essence Mills is describing the contribution of the Greek refugees of the 15th century to the revival of letters during the Renaissance. He was a miscellaneous writer who wrote mainly on historical subjects, including *History of Muhamedanism*, and *History of the Crusades*.

BL 635.g.27; GL GT632M65. Not in Blackmer. On Mills see A. Skollowe, *Memoir*, 1828.

474. MILLS, John Saxon, and Matthew George CHRUSSACHI. *La Question de Thrace. Grecs, Bulgares et Turcs.* London: Edward Stanford, 1919.

2 parts in 1, oblong 4to, pp. [46] (p.1=t). Nineteen maps in the text no'd 1-18 + 8a. Original printed blue paper wrappers.

First edition in French. This work was published simultaneously in English. It seems likely that its appearance was connected with the Congress of Versailles and the peace treaty of World War I. The first part contains historic maps from the works of Freeman and Zlatarski. The authors state that the maps were taken from Dimitri Rizoff's *Les Bulgares dans leurs frontieres historiques*, 1917, but the work itself supports Greek claims in Thrace.

Not in BNF on line. This edition not in GL, which has the English edition, 1919.

475. MINERVINO, Ciro Saverio. *Origine, e Corso del Fiume Meandro in occasione di un luogo di Plinio. Lettera al Signor Conte Anton Gioseffo della Torre Rezzonico di Ciro Saverio Minervo.* Naples: Stamperia Simoniana MDCCLXVIII. [=1768]

8vo, pp. 1-115 (p.1=ht, 114-5=license). With a folding engraved map and an engraved plate of variations of the design known as the meander or Greek key. Contemporary vellum, ownership stamp on title of CVPF and of BMPF on p. 23.

First and apparently only edition of this charming work. The issuer of the license quotes the Greek tag 'whoever has a suffiency of pepper also puts it on cabbage', presumably as a compliment to Minervino on his knowledge.

BL 234.h.59. Not in GL.

476. MONCADA, Francisco de. *Expedicion de los Catalanes y Aragoneses contra Turcos y Griegos, dirigida a D. Juan de Moncada, Arzobispo de Tarragona.* Madrid: Imprenta de Sancha, MDCCV. [=1805]

8vo, pp. XVI, 1-384 (pp.I=t, 375-84=conts). A fine copy, uncut and unopened in contemporary marbled paper wrappers, printed paper label. Bookseller's ticket of V. Salva of Regent Street.

Third edition of this chronicle of the Catalan expedition to the Levant (1302-1388), first published in 1623, with a second edition in 1777. Both a French and a German translation appeared in 1828. Moncada has re-written the last part of Ramon Muntaner's history, which deals with his experiences with the Catalan Grand Company, a mercenary band which was brought to the East by the Byzantine emperors to fight against the Turks; they turned against the Byzantines and then ravaged the Frankish settlements in Greece, wreaking havoc wherever they went and bringing a virtual end to the Latin empire in the East. The work was reprinted in 1906 with notes and introduction by Samuel Gili y Gaya.

Not in BLC on line. GL HG435M731. See Blackmer 1144 (1st ed). COPAC cites 2 copies.

477. MONTAGU, John, *4th Earl of Sandwich*. *A voyage performed by the late Earl of Sandwich round the Mediterranean in the years 1738 and 1739. Written by himself... To which are prefixed, memoirs of the noble author's life, by John Cooke.* London: for T. Cadell, Jr. and W. Davies, MDCCXCIX. [=1799]

4to, pp.[iii] xl, 539 [1] (pp.[i]=t, [1]=list of plates). With an engraved portrait frontispiece, 21 engraved plates, and engraved folding map, coloured, and 4 plates of inscriptions. Contemporary calf, repaired, back gilt with ships, red leather label.

First edition. A second edition appeared in 1808; this is probably the edition referred to by Brunet and Graesse as dated 1807. This work purports to be the journal which Montagu kept during a cruise in the Mediterranean in 1738. However, the work was produced so many years later than the actual events that it is not clear what is Montagu's and what is Cooke's. The party, which included the artist Jean Etienne Liotard, visited Athens, the islands of the Archipelago, Smyrna, Constantinople, Egypt and Malta. The plates for the most part consist of floor plans and diagrams. None are after Liotard, who produced many paintings during his sojourn in the Levant. Montagu was instrumental in forming the Society of Dilettanti.

BL 983.f.4; Blackmer 1149; Weber 522; Atabey 828; Brunet V, 125; Spencer, pp. 157-58.

478. MONTAGU, Lady Mary Wortley. *Letters of the right honourable Lady M---y W----y M-----e: Written, during her travels in Europe, Asia and Africa, to Persons of distinction, Men of Letters, &c. in different parts of Europe. Which contain, among other curious relations, accounts of the policy and manners of the Turks... The third edition. In three volumes. Vol. I. [...II ...III.]* London: for T. Becket and P.A. de Hondt, 1763.

3 vols in 1, sm. 8vo, pp. i-xii [3] 1-165 + 1 blank leaf; p.[iii] 167 + 1 blank leaf; p.[iii] 1-134 + 1 blank leaf (pp.i,[i]=hts, pp.[1-3]=adverts). Contemporary quarter calf gilt over marbled boards, red and green leather labels.

Third edition, published the same year as the first two editions, which appeared a year after Lady Mary's death in August, 1762. Apparently the second and third editions are made up of the same sheets as the first. The preface is signed M.A., i.e. Mary Astell, a close friend of Lady Mary and a champion of women's rights. Both second and third editions were pirated, with a word-for-word copy of the titles, in Dublin versions in one volume in 1763 and 1765, but the English editions have a much longer text than the Dublin editions. An additional volume of letters, spurious, was published in 1767. Lady Mary accompanied her husband to Turkey when he was appointed English ambassador to the Porte in 1716 and remained in Constantinople until 1718. One of her letters was published in 1719 as *The Genuine Copy of a Letter written from Constantinople by an English Lady, who was lately in Turkey...* London, J. Roberts, 1719. Apparently the Turkish letters were composed some years after her return to England; although based on her journal they are headed and dated close to the dates of actual letters. They circulated in manuscript for some years before their unauthorized publication in 1763.

BL 1486.de.12. This edition not in GL. This edition not in Blackmer but see 1150 for the Dublin edition of 1765.
Collation: A-L^8 M^4; A^2 B-L^8 M^4; A^2 B-I^8 K^4 (M4 in v.1=[ ]; K4 in v.3=[ ]). With thanks to Ilia Chatzipanaghiotou for information on the editions of Lady Mary Wortley Montagu's letters.

479. MONTAGU, Lady Mary Wortley. *Lettres... écrites pendant ses voyages en Europe, en Asie et in Afrique, à plusieurs personnes de distinction, gens de lettres &c. en differens pays; ou l'on trouve, entr'autres relations intérresantes, des Anecdotes sur les moeurs & le gouvernemens des Turcs... Traduit de l'Anglois. Nouvelle édition. [... Troisième partie pour servir de supplement aux deux premieres. On y joint une Reponse à la critique... par M. G... de Marseille.]* Rotterdam: Henri Beman, 1764-68.

3 vols, 12mo, pp. xvi, 1-238; [i] 1-222; [x] 11-174 (pp.i, [i]=hts). *Contemporary quarter calf, backs gilt, red and blue labels, over printed beige paper boards. A very pretty copy.*

Second Beman edition of vols 1-2, first edition of vol. 3. The first Beman edition appeared in 1763 in 2 volumes, without the supplement. The author of the 'Reponse' was Guys (q.v.), who replied to de Tott's criticisms of the Lady Mary's Letters published in the *Journal Encyclopédique*. Beman produced another edition in 1764 of vols 1 and 2 only. A French edition was first published at Amsterdam in 1763 in 1 volume by J.F. Boite. The translation is by Jean Brunet and - Suard. Presumably this translation was made for the French edition published at Paris in 1763 in 3 vols, translated from the second English edition. However, the history of the French editions of Lady Mary's letters is rather complex, since French editions were published simultaneously in Berlin, Amsterdam and Paris in 1763. We might assume the Paris edition to be the first, but it appeared in 3 volumes, while the Amsterdam and Berlin editions appeared in only 1 volume.

This edition not in BNF on line. This edition not in BLC or GL. There is a copy in the KB, Amsterdam. See Atabey 830 for the other Beman 1764 edition.
Collation: *⁸ A-P⁸; π¹ A-O⁸; A-L⁸ (final leaf in each vol=[ ])

480. MOREAS, Jean, *pseud.*, i.e. Ioannis PAPADIAMANTOPOULOS (1856-1910). *Le Voyage de Grèce.* Paris: La Plume, MCMII. [=1902]

8vo, pp. 150 + [5] (p.1=ht, pp.[1]=st, [5]=colophon). Quarter red roan gilt, original olive green printed paper wrappers bound in. From the library of K.Th. Dimaras, with his library stamp on the verso of the last leaf and on the lower wrapper.

First edition. This is one of 500 copies printed on ordinary paper; 25 numbered copies were issued, signed by the author, of which 3 are on China paper, 7 on Jap vellum, and 15 on Hollande Van Gelder paper. Although the statement of editions states 'Cette édition ne sera jamais reimprimée', a facsimile edition was issued at Paris in 1975. Moréas, poet and litterateur, was born Ioannis Papadiamantopoulos in 1856; he settled in Paris in the late 1870s. The *Voyage*, which Basch refers to as 'ce petit texte étonnant' is not an account of a journey but a miscellany of articles and poems about Greece, including a few soliloquies on the Greco-Turkish war of 1897, songs and tales with a Greek setting, and some samples of the works of Palamas, Kalvos, Malakassis and Stephanos, translated into French. Many of these articles were were first published in the journal *La Plume*. Moréas also wrote the preface to Gomez-Carillo's work on Greece (q.v.).

BNF 36567361; GL MGL732.8. Basch, pp. 300-305. On Moreas see Robert Jouanny, *Jean Moréas, écrivain français*, Paris, 1969.

MOREL, Frédéric. See MARCIAN

481. MOREL, Frédéric (1552-1630). *[De numerorum historia carmen φιλοσοφοθεολογοποιητικοον. F. Morellus... collegit, recensavit, composuit, digessit.] M. Antonii Mureti, Renati Pincaei, et Fed. Morelli Nomismatographia.* [Paris: Morel, 1609.]

Sm. 8vo, pp. [8] (p.[1]=?st see below). 19th c. red morocco, back ruled gilt, inner gilt dentelle, gilt edges. Bound with Marcian of Heraclea.

Only edition of this work on numismatics from the collections of Antonio Mureto, Renato Pinceo and Morel himself. The title is cited from the British Library copy. It is possible that what appears to be the title in our copy is in fact a subtitle.

BNF 31113971; BL 1213.f.11. Not in GL.
Collation: A^4.

482. MORELL, Thomas. *Studies in history; containing the history of Greece, from its earliest period, to its final subjugation by the Romans; in a series of essays, accompanied with reflections, references to original authorities, and historical questions. Fourth edition, embellished with a map.* London: for James Black, 1820.

Sm. 8vo, pp. xii, 1-334 (p.i=t, iii=ded to Samuel Whitbread, 328-334=index). With a folding map. Contemporary calf, back ruled gilt, red leather label. Bookstamp of the booksellers Sotheran on the front paste-down.

Fourth edition, augmented. A sixth edition appeared in 1827. Could the first appearance of the map have been in the 3rd edition, ?1817. The first edition seems to have been produced before 1814, since an edition in 2 vols dated St. Neots, 1814 is recorded as the second. The preface to our edition is dated from St. Neots, Nov. 28, 1820. The imprint on the map reads 'Nov 12 1817 by Black & Son'. Morell was a minister and musicologist, and principal of Coward College.

BL cites 2nd and 6th eds only. Not in GL. LoC cites an edition dated 1824 with a folding map.

483. [MORENO, José.] *Viage à Constantinopla, en el Año de 1784, escrito de orden superior.* Madrid. MDCCCXC. [Madrid: Lazaro Gayguer, 1790.]

4to, pp. [xvi] 360 + XXXIII (p.[i]=t). With a double-page engraved map and 24 no'd engraved plates. Contemporary calf, rebacked, original spine preserved, back gilt with fleurons, red leather label.

First edition. A *tirage à part* is also known. Moreno, who did not accompany the fleet, has produced an account of the Spanish naval mission to the Levant in 1784, based on the manuscript prepared by Don Gabriel de Aristizabal, commander of the mission. Aristizabal's original manuscript formed part of the Atabey Collection. There is an appendix containing an account of a second mission in 1788 which Moreno accompanied. The very attractive plates are engraved after drawings by A. Aguadro and J. Velasquez; some of them are based costume plates by van Mour.

[? Jos. Moreno]

VIAGE

Á CONSTANTINOPLA,

EN EL AÑO DE 1784,

ESCRITO DE ORDEN SUPERIOR.

MADRID. MDCCXC.

BL 149.h.14; Weber 603; Brunet V, 1166; Blackmer 1152, see 1153 for the *tirage à part*; Atabey 835, see also 31 (Aristizabal).

484. MOROSINI, Antonio. ***Chronique d'Antonio Morosini extraits relatifs a l'histoire de France publiés pour la Société de l'histoire de France... Introduction et commentaire par Germain Lefèvre-Pontalis. Texte établi et traduit par Léon Dorez.*** Paris: Renouard and H. Laurens, 1898-1902.

4 vols, 8vo, pp.[v] 1-327; [v] 1-355; [v] 1-392; [v] 1-460 (p.[i]=hts). Quarter maroon roan over marbled paper boards. Bookplate removed from front pastedowns, but with cypher 'TS' and crest (jester) at foot of spine.

First edition. This chronicle, written between c. 1400 and 1434, contains important source material on such events as the fall of Thessaloniki to the Turks. Excerpts from Morosini's chronicle occupy volumes 1-3. Volume 4 includes historical and biographical information on Morosini, patrician and rich merchant of Venice. The Morosini family had a factory at Aleppo. Much of the chronicle concerns the struggles between the Venetians and Genoese for commercial supremacy in the Levant between 1396 and 1433. The entire text has not yet been published.

BNF 34019054; BL Ac.6884/92. Not in GL.

485. MORPHOPOULOS, Panos. ***L'image de la Grèce chez les voyageurs français (du XVIe au début du XVIIIe siècles).*** Baltimore: [J.H. Furst & Co.], 1947.

8vo, pp. viii, 1-45 (p.i=t). Quarter turquoise calf, original printed paper wrappers bound in. From the library of K.Th. Dimaras, with his stamp on lower paste-down. (Bound with Iorga.)

Only edition. Morphopoulos also wrote on Byron. He also used the name Morphos.

GL GT812.33 under Morphos. BNF 32467891 calls for 47 pp., but GL calls for 45 pp. as ours.

486. MORRITT, John Bacon Sawrey. ***A Vindication of Homer and of the ancient Poets and Historians, who have recorded the Siege and Fall of Troy. In Answer to two late Publicatons of Mr. Bryant.*** York: W. Blanchard for T. Cadell, Jr. and W. Davies, London, 1798.

4to, pp. [i] 1-124 (p.[i]=t, errata on p.124). With five aquatinted plates. Lacking the map. Contemporary half calf.

First edition. Morritt travelled in the Levant from 1794-1796. The journey to the Troad was made in company with James Dallaway and Gaetano Mercati in November 1794. The artist Mercati was in the employ of Sir Robert Liston, ambassador in Constantinople, and Dallaway was chaplain to the mission. Both Dallaway and Morritt used Mercati's drawings in their books, but only one in common. Morritt wrote this account of his travels in answer to Jacob Bryant's two works on Troy published in 1796, *Dissertation concerning the War of Troy*, and *Observations upon a Treatise, entitled a Description of the Plain of Troy*, which was an attack on Le Chevalier. Morritt travelled extensively in Greece, especially in the Mani, which was little visited at this time. His letters, published by C.E. Marindin in 1914, provide a great deal of information, especially on his Greek travels.

BL 673.g.10; Blackmer 1157; Lascarides 65; Spencer 202-3, 225-6.

487. MOUNT ATHOS. *Vidy Monastyrei i Skitov' svyatoi Athonskoi Gory* [Cyrillic]. Ἐνθύμιον τοῦ Ἁγίου Ὄρους. *Souvenir du Mont Athos.* N.p., n.d. [after 1900].

Oblong 12mo, 3 leaves=list of plates. With a sketch map of Mylopotamos and 45 (? of 47) photographic plates. Original green decorative paper boards gilt. Ownership label of St. Panteleimon Monastery.

?Only edition. This little album could be missing the title page and two plates of photographs. It was published during the patriarchate of Joachim III, resident at Mylopotamos. There are many illustrations of St. Panteleimon Monastery.

Apparently not in Doens.

488. MOÜY, Charles de, *Count*. *Lettres Athéniennes Dessins de Hubert Clerget et gravures sur bois de Farlet.* Paris: E. Plon Nourrit [1887].

8vo, pp. [iii] III, 326 + [1] (pp.[i]=ht, [1]=list of plates). With 8 wood-engraved plates. Half brown morocco, back ruled gilt, original grey printed paper wrappers bound in.

First edition. Moüy was French ambassador in Athens from 1880 to 1886, a sensitive period in Greek history which involved the annexation of Thessaly and the blocade of Athens in April, 1886. In 1879 he published *Lettres du Bosphore*, an account of his sojourn in Constantinople as ambassador to the Porte. In 1909 his *Souvenirs et causeries d'un diplomate* appeared. Moüy was a talented amateur artist; an album of sketches made during his residence in Greece formed part of the Blackmer Collection.

NBF 30990453; Weber 892. Not in Blackmer but see 1915. Not in Atabey.

MUELICH, Johann Adolph. See ADELPHUS

489. MÜLLER, Christian. *Journey through Greece and the Ionian Islands, in June, July, and August, 1821.* London: [W. Lewis for] Sir Richard Phillips, 1822.

8vo, pp. [i] 1-72 (p.[i]=t). Modern brown morocco.

First and only edition in English, abridged, an extract from Sir Richard Phillips' periodical *New Voyages and Travels*, vol. 8. The first edition was published at Leipzig in 1822 in German; a French edition appeared the same year, published by Leon Astoin. Müller's was one of the earliest publications by a philhellene. Müller and three friends set off from Zakynthos to join the Greek 'army' at Kalamata in the summer of 1821.

Blackmer 1168; Weber 114. See Droulia 295.

490. MÜLLER, Elisabeth, i.e. Leonie BEDELET. *Les Annales de l' Antiquité illustrées Tableaux de l'Histoire Universelle depuis la Création jusqu' à l' Ère Chrètienne... Dessins de M. Fossey, peintre d'Histoire, Second Grand Prix de Rome.* Paris: Amédée Bedelet [1868].

Oblong folio, pp. 1-68 (p.1=ht, 3=t). With 18 plates lithographed in red and beige. Original red cloth, gilt title on upper cover, red morocco backstrip gilt, gilt edges. Bookplate of Prince Antoine d' Orleans.

First edition. According to the Bibliothèque Nationale, Elisabeth Müller is a pseudonym for Leonie Bedelet, presumably a relative of the publisher. She had previously co-operated with Fossey on *La Monarchie française en estampes*, 1861, and had also produced *Le Monde en estampes, géographie pittoresque, types et costumes*, 1858, after works by Leloir and Fossey. The date [1868] is attributed by the Bibliothèque Nationale.

BNF 30076603. Not in COPAC or GL.

491. MÜLLER, Hans (1854-1897). *Griechische Reisen und Studien. Erster theil. [... Zweiter Theil.]* Leipzig: Wilhelm Friedrich, 1887.

2 parts in 1, 8vo, pp. XI, 244; VI [1] 209 [1] (pp.I=ts, [1]=st, [1]=colophon). Half red roan. Bookplate of Thomas Day Seymor.

Apparently first edition. Volume one is an account of Müller's journey to Greece in January, 1881, via Trieste and Corfu. He reached Athens after travelling through the northern Peloponnesus, Delphi and Thebes; he also journeyed through Euboea, and visited the Noel family in Achmet Aga. Volume two contains a collection of modern Greek songs with German translations on facing pages. The former owner Seymor may have had some connection with Greece; his bookplate contains a view of the Acropolis.

Not in BLC. Weber 893. Not in Blackmer. Karlsruhe cites several copies.

492. MÜLLER, Karl Otfried. *Geschichten hellenischer Stämme und Städte. Erster Band Orchomenos und die Minyer. Mit einer Karte. [... Zweiter Band. Die Dorier, erste Abtheilung.. Dritter Band. Die Dorier, zweite Abtheilung.]* Breslau: Josef Max, 1820-24.

3 vols, 8vo, pp. [vii] 8-512; XXIV, 1-458; [v] 6-578 + [1] (pp.[i] in v.1, II, [ii] in v.2-3 = ts, pp.III, [iii] in v.2-3 = part titles, p.510 = errata, 511-12 = adverts, [1] = errata). With a folding map of Boeotia in v.1 and a large folding engraved map of the Peloponnesus by K. Kolbe, coloured in outline, in v.2. Old half calf over marbled paper boards.

First edition. Some bibliographies give the date 1819-24. In vols two and three the general title, 'Hellenischen Stämme', occurs on the verso of the first leaf, i.e. p. II, while the part title, 'Die Dorier', is on the title page. Volumes two and three came to be considered a separate work from volume one, and a translation of *Die Dorier* was produced in 1839 by Henry Tufnel and G.C. Lewis as *History and antiquities of the Doric Race*. A second edition of the entire work appeared in 1844, corrected and enlarged, edited by F. W. Schneidewin. Müller also wrote a history of ancient Greek literature, on Greek sculpture, and on the archaeology of Aegina.

BL 584.g.24. This edition not in GL.

493. MURALT, Edward von. *Lexidion der morgenländischen Kirche nach den besten schriftlichen und mündlichen Quellen mit 5 Abbildungen.* Leipzig: Weygand'sche Buchhandlung, 1838.

Sm. 8vo, pp. VIII, 95 [1] (pp.I = t, [1] = colophon). With 5 plates, (1 = folding). Old quarter calf gilt. Bound with 'Athen im Jahre 1844'.

?Second edition. The BLC cites an edition of 1835 (3476.c.52), but all the copies cited by Karlsruhe are dated 1838. It may be that the 1835 edition is exceeding scarce, or the BLC date could be a misprint; we have not been able to see this copy to confirm it. The *Lexidion* was published as a supplement to A.N. Muraviev's *Briefe über den Gotterdienst der Morgenländischen Kirche*, 1838, 2 vols. The wrapper of the GL copy

makes this clear: 'Erklärender Anhang zu den Briefen'. Muralt produced a catalogue of the Greek manuscripts in St. Petersburg in 1804.

BNF 30997139; BL 3478.b.18; GL T461.1. Not in Blackmer or Atabey.

494. MURALT, Edward von. *Athen im Jahre 1844.* St. Petersburg: 1847.

8vo, pp. [i] 16 (pp.[i]=t). Old quarter calf gilt. With a presentation inscription from the author to Heinrich Schliemann on the title: Τῷ ἐν τοῖς ἐμπόροις καὶ εὐπόροις μόνῳ φιλέλληνι καὶ φιλομουσοτάτῳ Κυρίῳ Σχλείμαν. Ταῦτα τὰ μικρὰ τῆς κλεινοτάτης ἐν Ἑλλάδι πόλεως ἀπομνημονεύματα ἀνατίθησιν ὁ Συγγραφεύς. ΑΩΝΖ'. Bound with 'Lexidion'.

First separate edition, a reprint of four articles from the St. Petersburg *Zeitung*, nos. 78, 80, 81 and 82. Muralt's presentation inscription to Schliemann, excavator of Troy and Mycenae, is dated 1857.

BNF 30997136; BL 10125.bb.28. Not in Weber or GL.

495

495. MURE, William. *Journal of a Tour in Greece and the Ionian Islands, with Remarks on the Recent History – Present State – And Classical Antiquities of those Countries. In two Volumes. Vol. 1. [... Vol. II.]* Edinburgh: William Blackwood, M.DCCC.XLII. [=1842]

2 vols., 12mo: pp. [i] xiii + [iii] 291 + 4 pp. of adverts; [i] v, 327 [1] (pp.[i]=hts, pp.[i]=errata, [iii]=list of plates). Illus: 8 maps and 7 lithographed plates. Uncut, in the original embossed green cloth.

First edition. Mure travelled from February to April, 1838. An interesting work, with a particularly long chapter on Ithaca. Mure was a classical scholar whose principal work was *A Critical History of the Language and Literature of Ancient Greece*, 1850-57.

BL 1426.f.10; Blackmer 1170; Weber, 343; Bib. Ionienne, 1389. Not in Abbey.

496. MUSPRATT, Eric. *Greek Seas.* London: Duckworth [1933].

8vo, pp. 190 + [2] (p.1=ht, pp.[2]=adverts). Sketch map in the text. Original green cloth, faded.

Apparently first and only edition. Muspratt, a curious character, rather cynical and bitter, had worked at many jobs; he spent six months cruising in the Aegean from November 1932 to April 1933 on a boat which he had himself hired and outfitted in the most economic way possible.

BL 10125.ccc.30; GL GT1436.

497. MYSTAKIDES, Basileios. *Notes sur Martin Crusius ses livres, ses ouvrages et ses manuscrits. Extrait de la Revue des Études Grecques Juillet-Septembre 1898.* Paris: Ernest Leroux, 1898.

8vo, pp. [iii] 1-28 (p.[i]=t). Old half black cloth over borwn marbled paper boards. Presentaton copy, inscribed by Mystakides to Anthimos, Bishop of Amaseia.

An offprint from the *Revue des Études Grecques*. Bound with Wächter, *Der Verfall des Griechentums in Kleinasien*.

498. MYSTAKIDES, Basileios. *Byzantinisch-Deutsche Beziehungen zur Zeit des Ottonen.* Stuttgart: Alfred Müller, 1891.

8vo, pp. XVIII, 1-99 (p.I=t in red and black). Old half black cloth over brown marbled paper boards.

Only edition. Bound with Wächter, *Der Verfall des Griechentums in Kleinasien*.

499. NAHMER, Ernst von der. *Vom Mittelmeer zum Pontus. Mit 20 Abbildungen und einer Karte. 2. Auflage.* Berlin: Allgemeiner Verein für Deutsche Litteratur, 1904.

8vo, pp. [iv] 1-324 (pp.[i]=t, [iv]=notice). With a folding map and 20 photographic illustrations. Original red cloth gilt.

Second edition, first published the same year, 1904. This work consists of articles first published in the *Kölnischen Zeitung*. The illustrations include views of Amasia, Sivas, Caesarea, Tarsus, Mersina, Priene, and so forth.

BL 12249.ccc.40. Not in GL.

500. NAPIER, Charles James. *The Colonies: treating of their value generally – Of the Ionian Islands in particular; the importance of the latter in war and commerce – As regards Russian policy – Their finances – Why an expense to Great Britain – Detailed proofs that they ought not to be so – Turkish government – Battle of Navarino – Ali Pacha – Sir Thomas Maitland – Strictures on the administration of Sir Frederick Adam.* London: T. and W. Boone, MDCCCXXXIII. [=1833]

8vo, pp. xv + [1] 1-608 (pp.i=t, [1]=errata). With 16 no'd lithographed plates and 2 unn. plans. Contemporary polished panelled calf, back gilt with red leather labels, marbled edges. Armorial bookplate of Richard Gregory of Coole, Ireland, on front pastedown, and bookplate of Richard Gregory, F.R.S., F.A.S., of Trinity College, Cambridge on lower pastedown.

First and only edition of this important work. Napier was sent to the Ionian Islands in 1819 and carried out several special assignments, including a secret meeting with Ali Pasha. In 1822 he was appointed resident of Cephalonia, and he remained there until 1830 when he left Greece for other duties. Napier's book is informed by an understanding of Greek politics and by his accounts of his contacts with Maitland, Ali Pasha, Byron, and the philhellene Lord Guilford. Byron in particular spent several months in Cephalonia. Napier also wrote *The war in Greece*, 1821, *Greece in 1824*, 1824, and *The roads of Cephalonia*, 1825. Napier's official biography was written by his brother William and appeared in 1857.

BL 1053.g.20; Blackmer 1181; Droulia 2018; Bibl Ionienne 1201.

501. NERVAL, Gérard Labrunie de. *Voyage en Orient suivi d'Isis. Texte intégral, établi avec ses appendices, une introduction, une biblio-*

graphie et des notes par Jean Chuzeville. Orné, en gravures originales au burin, d'un frontispice [sic] par Gandon et d'une portrait par Ouvré. Premier Volume. Paris: [F. Paillart for] Éditions Bossard, 1927.

Volume 1 only, of three, 8vo, pp. XVII, 1-344 + [1] (p.I=wrapper, III=[ ], V=ht, 343-4=conts, [1]=colophon). With an engraved portrait frontispiece and an engraved plate. Title in red and black. Uncut in quarter red morocco gilt, original brown printed paper wrappers bound in. From the library of K.Th. Dimaras, with his bookstamp on the lower fly-leaf.

A late edition, edited by Jean Chuzeville. Another edition appeared the same year, edited by Henri Clouard. This volume contains *Les Femmes du Caire*, first published in 1848. Volumes two and three contain the rest of the *Voyage en Orient*, and *Isis*. There is also a bibliography of Nerval's works in volume 3. The work known as the 'Voyage en Orient' consists of several works: *Les Femmes du Caire*, 1848, and *Les Femmes du Liban*, which was first published in 1850, issued together with *Les Femmes du Caire* under the general title *Scenes de la Vie Orientale*. The two were then republished together with *Les Nuits de Ramazan* in 1851 as *Voyage en Orient*. *Isis* first appeared in 1854 as a novelette in *Les Filles du Feu, nouvelles*. A section entitled 'Vers l'Orient', which contains segments from Nerval's travels in Greece, extracted from his journal, completes the first volume. Volume three contains a bibliography. Nerval's travels took place in 1843; he spent most of his time in the Levant in Egypt. The various episodes which form the work first appeared as articles in the *Revue des Deux Mondes* in 1846 and 1847.

BNF 31009549, 31946648. See Blackmer 1190.

502. NERVAL, Gérard Labrunie de. *Voyage en Orient suivi d'Isis. Tome premier. [... Volume Second.]* Paris: Club des Libraires de France [1955].

2 vols, 8vo, pp. XXIII 382 [15]; [iv] 1-404 [1] + [13] (pp.I=[ ], III=t, p.[15]=colophon; pp.[i]=prelim page with facsimile of Nerval's signature, iii=t, [1]=last leaf of text pp.[13]= tables). Illustrations in the text. Original pictorial green cloth gilt, a presentation copy to K.Th. Dimaras from Gilbert Rouger, the author of the preface.

A late edition, edited with preface and notes by Gilbert Rouger, published for the French book club, 'Club des Libraires de France'. The *Femmes du Caire* forms volume one; *Les Femmes du Liban* (subtitle *Druses et Maronites*) together with *Isis*, forms vol. 2. Five thousand copies were printed: this is no. 4372. In 1950 Rouger published a critical text of the *Voyage en Orient* with notes, and with woodcuts by Henri Renand after Yves Trevedy.

BNF 32482424.

503. NEWTON, Charles Thomas. *Travels & Discoveries in the Levant ... With numerous illustrations.* London: Day and Son, 1865.

2 vols, pp. xiv [ii] 360; xiv [ii] 275 (p.[i]=hts). With 41 lithographed plates. A prize binding in full red polished calf, flat backs gilt in compartments, arms of the Western College, Brighton, on upper covers.

First editon. A variant issue exists in which some of the lithographs are replaced by mounted photographs of drawings. Newton, vice-consul at Mitylene, carried out excavations in the Levant between 1852 and 1859. It was at this time that he explored Mitylene and Rhodes, Kalymnos, and the shores of Asia Minor, especially at Halicarnassus. The plates include views of Mitylene, Rhodes, Cos and Kalymnos, as well as illustrations of the sculptures from the Mausoleum at Halicarnassus after photographs by Francis Bedford and others. The work includes D.E. Colnaghi's account of his tour in Lycia and Mitylene in 1854.

BL 560.b.3; Blackmer 1193; Weber 636.

504. NEYRAT, Alexandre Stanislas. *L'Athos Notes d'une excursion à la presqu'île et à la Montagne des Moines.* Paris: E. Plon, and Lyon: Briday, 1880.

12mo, pp. [iii] 1-246 + [2] (pp.[i]=ht, [ii]=imprimatur, [1]=conts, [2]=list of plates). With 11 heliogravures and a folding facsimile of a patriarchal letter. Half red roan over red marbled paper boards.

First edition. According to Doens a second edition appeared in 1884. Neyrat wrote on religious subjects, especially on church music.

BNF 31012855; Doens 1177.

505. NICOLAY, Nicolas de. *Discours et histoire veritable des navigations, pérégrinations et voyages, faicts en la Turquie.* Antwerp: Arnould Coninx, M.D.LXXXVI. [=1586]

4to, pp. [xvi] 1-209 + [13] (p.[i]=t, [pp.1-13]=conts and index). 61 full-page woodcuts in text, within woodcut borders. Recent half calf.

Third edition in French, with one more plate that the earlier editions, the 'Delly à pied'. Nicolay's costume book was first published in folio at Lyon in 1567/68 with 60 engraved plates. The second edition was published at Antwerp in 1576 in 4to, with 60 woodcut plates by A. Londerseel or Antony van Leest. Nicolay, royal geographer,

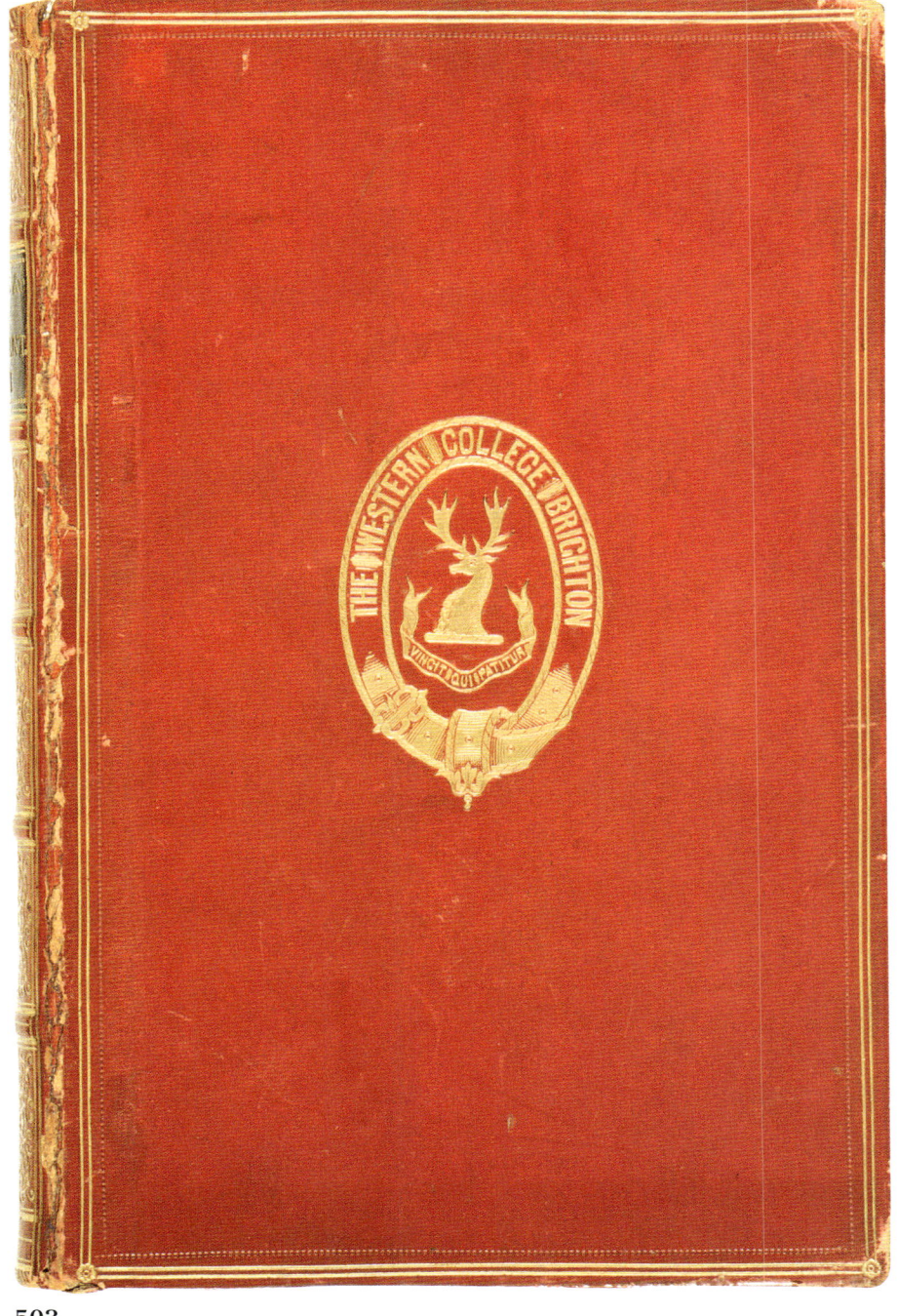

503

travelled to Constantinople in 1551 to join d'Aramon's embassy. Nicolay claimed these drawings as his own, but modern authorities believe that many of his drawings are taken from other sources. Certainly his work was probably the most influential pictorial description of Turkish costume of the 16th century. In addition to the French editions, Dutch, German, and Italian editions were printed at Antwerp in 1576, and there is also an English edition printed in London in 1585. Nicolay's plates were also used in other works, mainly in the 17th century French editions of Chalcocondylas's history. They were also the source for many manuscript albums of the period.

BNF 31016286; Atabey 872; Colas 2002; Göllner 1798. This edition not in Blackmer.

505

506. NICOLAY, Nicolas de. *Le Navigationi et viaggi, fatti nella Turchia ... Novamente tradotto di Francese in Italiano da Francesco Flori da Lilla, Aritmetico. Con sessantasette figure naturali, si d' huomini come di donne, secondo la varietà delle nationi...* Venice: Francesco Ziletti, MDLXXX. [=1580]

Sm. folio, pp.[xxiv] 1-191 [1] (pp.[i]=t, [1]=engraving). 67 full-page engravings in text. Old vellum. With contemporary ownership inscription of Bartolomeo Piacenza.

506

First edition to be printed in Italy, third edition in Italian. This work was first translated into Italian and published in Antwerp in 1576, second edition 1577. The Antwerp edition contains woodcut plates. The copper engravings in this edition are reminiscent of the copper plates of the first edition, in French, published at Lyon in 1567. This edition contains seven more costume plates than any of the earlier editions.

BL C.82.h.2; Blackmer 1196; Weber 168; Adams N253; Colas 2204; Göllner 1723.

507. NOE BIANCHI, *attributed to*. ***Viaggio da Venezia al S. Sepolcro, ed al Monte Sinai, col disegno delle città, castelli, ville, chiese, monasteri, isole, porti, e fiumi, che sin là si ritrovano, Ed una breve regola di quanto si deve osservare nel detto viaggio... Composto dal R. Padre Fr. Noe dell' Ordine di S. Francesco. Aggiuntovi il modo di pigliar le sante indulgenze, ed a quali chiese, monasterj et altri luoghi siano concesse. Bassano, MDCCXCI. A Spese Remondini di Venezia. Con licenza de' Superiori.***
[Bassano: for Remondini of Venice, 1791.]

Sm. 4to, pp. 1-136 (p.1=t, license on p.136). With woodcuts in the letterpress. Quarter calf over marbled paper boards. Bookplate of Nathan Schur.

A late edition. This little book is one of the earliest Italian guides for pilgrims to the Holy Land. It was first printed anonymously at Bologna in 1500 as *Viazo da Venesia al Santo Iherusale[m] et al Monte Sinai*. The second edition, with the addition of the woodcuts, appeared in 1518/19 in small octavo format, which was much more convenient for travellers, and it was reprinted in this format many times during the 16th, 17th and 18th centuries; the late editions were produced mainly in Venice and Bassano. The name of Noe Bianchi was attached to the work in 1600, in an edition printed at Lucca. In fact it was not until 1566 that Noe's own account of his travels (a journey which took place in 1527) appeared as *Viaggio ...fatto in Terra Santa, & descritto per benificio de' Pellegrini*. Although both works describe roughly the same places, a direct comparison of the texts clearly indicates the different authorship, as does the fact that Noe's text was not published until 1566. The first edition of the *Viaggio di Santa Sepolcra* which occurs with Noe Bianchi's name on the title is that of Lucca, 1600, and all subsequent editions (including 1610, 1640, 1647, 1680, 1700, 1728, 1800) follow suit. (Editions examined include those of 1500, 1519, 1546, 1555, 1563 and 1587; there are others which we could not see. See Blackmer note). The woodcuts include views of Corfu, Methoni (Modone), Crete, Rhodes, Jerusalem and other sites in the Holy Land. It is possible that the inspiration for the anonymous *Viaggio* was Breydenbach's *Peregrinato in Terram Sanctam*, which includes cuts of

AL S. SEPOLCRO.

to, e copiosissimo vivere: in terra ferma ha per trenta miglia di Territorio, con molti Castelli, Isole, e Scogli più di quattro cento; delle quali Isole alcuna gira sessanta miglia; ed è fertile. Vi sono pascoli grandi, e vi è copia di bestiame, ed abbondanza di ogni sorte di Pesce; vestono pomposamente, sono dediti molto all'armi, e prima agli studj di umanità; hanno molti Maestri di scuola, e ha dei Mercanti assai; il popolo è amico de' Veneziani, e universalmente sono amici de' Forestieri; vi sono reliquie di Giulio Cesare, come si giudica per lo suo nome, che appare in una Torre da lui fatta appresso la porta di Terra ferma, e sonovi molte altre cose, ec.

Questi sono gli Uomini di CORFU'
ritratti al suo naturale.

the same Greek towns as the *Viaggio*. These were the harbours where pilgrim ships normally stopped on the way to the Holy Land.

This edition not in BLC or GL. Blackmer 1206; Brunet V, 1166-67; Tobler p. 63. See the Exhibition Catalogue *Navigare et Descrivare, Isolari e portolani di Museo Correr di Venezia*, Venice 2001, no. 15 (p. 86), for an account of this travel guide.

508. NOEL, Frank. *Letters of Mr. Frank Noel respecting the murder by brigands of the captives of Marathon and his prosecution by the Greek Government. With an Introduction by his Father.* London: Williams and Norgate, 1871.

8vo, pp. [iii] 1-103 (p.[i]=t). Quarter black roan over black cloth.

First edition. Letters from Frank Noel to his father Edward H. Noel (a cousin of Isabella Milbanke, Lady Byron) who settled in Greece after the Revolution and purchased the property of Achmet Aga in northern Euboea. Frank Noel attempted to assist in the negotiations between the Greek Government and the brigands to ransom the British party who had been taken captive during an excursion to Marathon in 1869, an event which came to be known as the 'Dilessi Murders'.

BL 8028.bb.51 (an undated edition [1871]); GL KG744.

509. NOLAU, J.F. *Les Antiquités d'Athènes, et autres monumens Grecs, d'après les mesures de Stuart et Revett: enrichis des nouvelles découvertes. Édition portative.* Paris: Audot, 1835.

Sm. 4to, pp. 62 +[1] (pp.1=ht, [1]=conts). With 71 engraved plates no'd I-LXX + XXXIIb; plate XII forms the frontispiece. Old half red calf, back gilt romantique, over black cloth.

First edition, and apparently Nolau's only work. An English version appeared in 1837 under the imprint of Charles Tilt without Nolau's name on the title, and a later French edition was published in Athens in 1850. The plates are engraved by Hibon and Reveil. In the Blackmer copy the extra plate was numbered XXXIX bis.

BNF 31023222; BL 811.b.13; Blackmer 1207.

510. NOLHAC, Stanislas de. *La Dalmatie les Iles Ioniennes Athènes et le Mont Athos.* Paris: E. Plon, 1882.

Sm. 8vo, pp. [vi] 314 + [1] (pp.[i]=ht, [1]=conts). Rough cut in half calf, panelled back gilt, original grey printed paper wrappers bound in.

First and apparently only edition. These travels are undated, but the journey to Mount Athos may have taken place c. 1879-80, since Nolhac contributed an account of his visit to the monasteries to the journal *Correspondant* in 1880, in two numbers.

NBF 31023513; Blackmer 1208; Weber 838; Bib. Ionienne 3315; Doens 1201.

511. NOUKIOS, Nicandros, i.e. Andronikos. *The second book of the Travels of Nicander Nucius, of Corcyra. Edited from the original Greek ms. in the Bodleian Library, with an English translation, by the Rev. J. A. Cramer.* London: John Bowyer for the Camden Society, M.DCCC.XLI. [=1841]

4to, pp. xxvii, 1-126 + [1] (pp.i=t, [1]=colophon). Original embossed green cloth gilt, rough cut. With the 19th c. bookplate of the Vernon family on front pastedown. Binder's ticket of Remnant and Edwards.

First edition. Number 17 of the Camden Society series. This is an account of Nucius's travels to England in 1545-46. The Bodleian library manuscript of his travels consists of three books describing the entire account of his journey from Corfu to England, but only the section dealing with England was translated by Cramer. Various fragments have also been published from a manuscript in the Ambrosiana Library, including an account of the siege of Corfu by the Turks in 1537, edited by Moustoxydes. There is a French edition of Nucius's text edited by J.A. de Foucault and published in 1962.

BL G.13323; Weber 150; Bib. Ionienne 1380. See Spencer, p. 21.

512. NOUVEL ANTENOR. *Le Nouvel Anténor, ou voyages et aventures de Trasybulle en Grèce; ouvrage pouvant faire suite aux Voyage d'Anténor par Lantier; orné de quatre gravures et de notes historiques, critiques et littéraires.* Paris: Mayeur and Capelle, M.DCCC.III. [=1803]

8vo, pp. xi, 1-272 [recte 372] (pp.i=ht, 361-272=conts). With four engraved plates. Mottled leather, back gilt.

First edition under this title, uncommon. According to Barbier, this is a translation of Achilles Tatius's novel 'Leucippe and Clitophon', by L. A. Du Perron de Castera, first published in 1797 as *Les Amours de Leucippe et Clitophon, traduites du Grec d'Achilles Tatius*. The publisher of the 1803 edition wanted to take advantage of the enormous success of Lantier's *Anténor*.

Not in BLC or BNF on line. Not in GL. We have traced one copy, at Leipzig University Library, catalogued under Lantier. Barbier III, 539.

513. O'CONNOR, Vincent Clarence Scott. *Isles of the Aegean.* London: Hutchinson & Co. [1929].

Lge 8vo, pp. 1-384 (p.1=ht, 5=acknowledgements, pp.7-10=introduction by Prince Nicholas of Greece). With a coloured frontispiece and 7 coloured photographic illustrations of paintings by N. Cheimonas, and 75 photographic illustrations on 64 plates. Original blue cloth.

First edition. Many of the photographs are by Fred Boissonas, who made his first journey to Greece in 1903. O'Connor was a travel writer who also produced works on Morocco, Kashmir and Burma.

BL 10127.g.18. Not in GL.

514. OLIN, Stephen (1797-1851). *Greece, and the Golden Horn. With an introduction, by Rev. John M' Clintock, D.D. Third Thousand.* New York: J.C. Derby, Boston: Phillips, Sampson & Co., Cincinnati: H.W. Derby, 1854.

8vo, pp. xii [i] 13-323 (pp.i=ht, [i]=st). With woodcut frontispiece and title by N. Orr. Lacking the three engraved plates. Original mauve cloth, back gilt, faded.

First edition, second issue, published posthumously. The first issue has the imprint of Carlton & Phillips. Olin spent three years in Europe and the Levant from 1837-1840. He travelled in the Levant from November 1839 to June 1840. This work is an account of a portion of the last months of this tour. Olin describes in detail his sojourn in Greece in November and December, 1839, and his residence in Constantinople in June, 1840, where he stayed with the missionary Cyrus Hamlin. The rest of his travels in the Levant were published in 1843 in *Travels in Egypt, Arabia Petraea and the Holy Land.*

LoC DF725.046 calls for a map; Blackmer 1219; Weber 491.

515. OLIVIER, Guillaume Antoine (1756-1814). *Voyage dans l'Empire Othoman, l'Égypte et la Perse, fait par ordre du Gouvernement, pendant les six premières années de la Republique... Avec Atlas. Tome Premier. [...Second ...Troisième ...Quatrième ...Cinquième ...Sixième.]* Paris: H. Agasse, An 9. [...An12...1807.] [=1801-1804-1807]

6 vols, 8vo, pp.xx, 392 +[1]; [iii] 377 = [1]; [ii] iv, 359 + [1]; [iii] 456 [1]; [iii] xv, 485 + [1]; [iii] 522 + [1] (pp.[i]=hts, [1]=errata, pp.i-iv, i-xv=avis). 19th c. quarter black roan, backs gilt, over pink marbled paper boards, red leather labels.

First 8vo edition. A quarto edition in three volumes also appeared the same year. The same atlas was sold with both editions. An English edition of the first two volumes appeared in 1801 with the first livraison of the atlas. A German edition of the complete work appeared at Vienna in 1809 in three illustrated volumes. Olivier, a naturalist and entomologist, travelled in the Levant from 1792 to 1799 during the course of a French government mission to Persia. He spent a considerable period of time in Constantinople and travelled to Egypt via the Archipelago. He did not reach Persia until 1795. This important work contains a great deal of information on the Aegean islands.

BNF 36582614; BL 978.k.7; Blackmer 1220; Weber 627; Atabey 887.

516. OLIVIER, Guillaume Antoine. *Atlas pour servir au Voyage dans l'Empire Othoman, l'Égypte et la Perse, fait par ordre du Gouvernement...* Paris: H. Agasse, An IX [... An XII... 1807.] [=1801-1804-1807]

4to, pp. vii, vii, viii (pp.i=hts). With 50 engraved plates, many folding. Uncut in contemporary quarter calf gilt, red leather label, over brown marbled paper boards.

First edition, published in three livraisons. These fine plates include costumes, maps, plans and natural history plates. The genre plates are after Horace Vernet; some of the natural history plates are by P.J. Redouté. The explications of the plates are by A. Dezauche.

BNF 33999886 (4to format); BL 456.e.18; Blackmer 1220; Weber 628; Atabey 886 and 887.

517. ORTELIUS, Abraham. *Abrahami Ortelii Antverpiani Thesaurus Geographicus recognitus et auctus. In quo omnium totius Terrae regionum ... nomina & appellationes veteres; additis magna ex parte etiam recentioribus ... emendantur, arguuntur, enodantur & conciliantur.* Antwerp: Officina Plantiniana, M.D.XCVI. [=1596]

Folio, ff. [364] (f.1=t). Engraved title page in text. Contemporary vellum, flat back gilt in compartments, red leather label.

Second edition, first published in 1587. Ortelius, the renowned cartographer and map publisher, was particularly interested in historical geography, as demonstrated in his *Parergon*, an atlas of historical maps illustrating the voyage of Aeneas, the journey of the Ten Thousand, the voyages of St. Paul, the wanderings of Odysseus, and other historical or mythical events. In this work, which forms a type of geographical diction-

ary, he provides a list of the ancient names of all the places on the earth, in many cases with the contemporary equivalents.

BL 569.h.13.

Collation: †⁶ *⁴ 2*⁴ A-Z⁴, a-z⁴, 2A-2Z⁴, 2a-2r⁴ 2s⁶.

518. OUKHTOMSKY, Esper Esperovich. *Voyage en Orient - 1890 - Grèce Égypte Inde - 1891. Traduction de Louis Leger... Préface de A. Le Roy-Beaulieu... Illustré de 178 compositions de N.N. Karazine.* Paris: Charles Delagrave, 1893.

Folio, volume one only (of 2), pp. [iv] i-xvi, 1-388, [5] (p.[i]=ht, pp.[3-4]=list of plates, [5]=colophon). Title in red and black. With a coloured lithographed map of Egypt. The portrait frontispiece is in the second volume. Numerous illustrations in the letterpress, many full-page and with versos blank, but still included in the pagination. Quarter red roan gilt over red cloth, a prize binding with the arms of the city of Paris on the upper cover, gilt edges.

Volume one only of the first edition in French of this account of the Czarevitch Nicolas II's tour of the Levant and the Far East from November 1890 to August 1891, translated by Louis Leger. Nicolas travelled from Trieste through the Ionian Islands to mainland Greece, and there is a substantial account of his visit to Athens, but the emphasis of the work is on Egypt, with an account of the journey through the Suez canal to India. The second volume was published in 1898 and included the continuation of his journey from India to Japan and China. The French edition appeared with 75 copies numbered: 25 were on Japanese vellum, 25 on Holland Paper, and 25 on French Paper. The original Russian edition appeared in 1893-96. This work was also translated into English and Greek.

BNF 30776591; BL 1787.d.1; Blackmer 1230; Weber 960.

519. OWEN, Harry Collinson. *Salonica and After The Sideshow that ended the War.* London: Hodder and Stoughton, MCMXIX. [=1919]

8vo, pp. viii, 1-295 + [1] (p.i=t, [1]=colophon). With photographic frontispiece and 12 photographic illustrations. Map on back endpapers. Original red cloth, faded.

First and apparently only edition. Owen was editor of *The Balkan News* and later worked for the *Evening Standard*. He was also a writer of drama and thrillers. This is an account of the Salonica campaign which also includes anecdotes of military and social life, Venizelos in Thessaloniki, etc. With an introduction by General Sir George Milne, commander in chief of the British Salonica Force.

BL 09082.c.42.

520. PACIAUDI, Paolo Maria. *Monumenta Peloponnesia Commentariis Explicata a Paullo M. Paciaudio. Volumen Secundum.* Rome: Typographia Palladis for Nicolo and Marco Palearino, MDCCLXI. [=1761]

Vol. 2 only, of 2, 14to: pp. XXV [i] 311 [1] (pp.I=ht, [i]=imprimatur, [1]=errata). Illus: engraved title, engraved frontispiece and numerous engravings, all in the letterpress. Title page in red and black. Contemporary vellum.

First edition. Paciaudi's work is a description of, and annotations to, part of the collection of antiquities formed by the Nani family of Venice, specifically that part of the collection brought from the Peloponnesus during the Venetian conquests against the Turks in the 1680s.

BL 678.f.16; Blackmer 1232.

520

521. PAGANEL, Camille Pierre Alexis. *Missolonghi n'est plus! Appel aux Amis des Grecs.* Paris: [du Breuil for] Achille Désanges, 1826.

32mo, pp. 40 (p.1=ht). Old quarter maroon roan gilt, from the library of K.Th. Dimaras, with his ownership stamp on the lower fly leaf. Bound with three other philhellenic items.

First and only edition, uncommon. This philhellenic pamphlet was published after the fall of Missolonghi. On the half title: 'Se vend au profit des Grecs'. Paganel, a writer on politics and history, also produced in the same year *Le Tombeau de Marcos Botzaris*. The year 1826 saw the height of French philhellenism. Paganel also wrote about Scanderbeg.

BNF 31048956; GL IND647B; Droulia 1107.

522. PAGANELIS, Spyridon. Ἀπὸ τῆς Ἀκροπόλεως εἰς τὴν Ἄλτιν.
New York: Atlantis, 1908.

Sm. 4to, pp. 102 [3] (p.1=t, pp.[2-3]=adverts). With 11 photographic illustrations. Original cloth gilt, ownership signature on title of E. Boïou.

First and apparently only edition of this account of an excursion from Athens to Olympia. It is curious that it should have been printed in New York. Paganelis wrote a descriptive account of the Peloponnesus, Πέραν τοῦ Ἰσθμοῦ, 1891, and accounts of the other parts of Greece. He also wrote Ἀθηναϊκαὶ Νύχτες.

GL GT1763.

523. PALMER, Roger, *Earl of Castlemaine*. **Das von den Türcken auffs äusserst bedrangte, Aber: Durch die Christliche Waffen der heroischen Republic Venedig auffs tapfferst beschützte Candia, vorgestellt in einer auszführlichen Beschreibung desz heutigen Kriegs-und Regiments-Staats der Venetianer, in dem Königreich Candia und in der Levante; auffgesetzt in Venedig, an den König in Engelland, durch den Graffen von Castlemaine, und in unsere hoch-Teutsche Sprache gebracht...**
Frankfurt: Wilhelm Serlin, 1669.

2 parts in 1, 4to, pp. [vi] 1-118, 1-27 (p.[i]=t, [iii-v]=ded, [vi]=expl. of plan of Candia, pp.1-27='Aussführliche' continuation). Gothic letter. With engraved title and 7 (out of 8) engraved plates. Contemporary vellum. Ownership inscription on engraved title: 'Ad usum Wendelini praeterii'.

Second separate German edition, with additional material, i.e. the continuation by the Marquis Porroni. The first separate edition appeared the same year (see Blackmer 1240). The first German edition appeared as a segment in a Frankfurt periodical: *Diarium Europaeum*, edited by Martin Mayer under the pseudonym 'Philemerus Irenicus Elisius'. Note that in both German editions the letter from the Earl of Castlemaine is the same, but the continuations differ. These editions were published to track the day-

to-day development of the war. The collation of the continuation in the Contominas copy differs from that described in the Blackmer catalogue. In addition to the continuation, the prelims have been reset, and leaf):(3r contains an explanation of the plan of Candia, without any directions to the binder.

Not in GL or BLC. Atabey 919. See Blackmer 1240 for the first separate German edition. The on line catalogue of the Bavarian National Library cites 5 copies.

Collation:):(^{3} A-O^4 P^3, A-C^4 D^2 (A-C^4 D^2=drophead title 'Ausführliche continuation', a description of the war by the Marchese Porroni, 1669). The letter by the officer of the Comte de St. Pol is on O1v to P3v. The Blackmer collation:):(^{3} A-O^4)(- 2)(^{4} 3)(^{2}. The prelims and last sections differ in the two editions.

List of plates, our numbers:

1. Plan of Candia and environs
2. De Middelantsche Zee
3. Candia [view of Candia]
4. Genuina delineatio insulae Cretae / quam moderni Candiam appellant (first half)
5. Genuina delineatio insulae Cretae (second half 'Eigentlicher Abrisz der vornehmen Insul Creta so heut zu tag Candia genemet wird')
6. Candia per la terza volta attacatta (plan of the city)
7. Disegno del combattimento
8. Map of Greece, missing in this copy

524. PAPADOPOULOS BRETOS, Andreas. *Su le tre Città conosciute anticamente sotto il nome di Leucade Ricerche storico-critiche di Andrea Papadopulo-Vretò Leucadio Dottore in Medicina Socio correspondente estero del Reale Istituto d'Incoraggiamento, e della Società Pontaniana di Napoli, e fu bibliotecario dell' Università Ionia.* Venice: Alvisopoli, 1830.

8vo, pp. [v] 6-15 (p.[i]=t). Marbled paper boards.

First and only edition. Bretos was librarian to the philhellene Frederick North, Earl of Guildford. Although Guilford died in 1827, Bretos was resident in Corfu until about 1830. Many of his works were printed in Italy, until the establishment of the Greek printers and publishers in Athens and other parts of Greece after the Revolution. Bretos later produced a biography of Capodistrias. He has dedicated this work to Emilio Typaldo.

BL 1299.c.20; GL HG107.59; Bibliographie Ionienne 1160; Papadopoulos 1968. Not in Blackmer.

523

525. PARDIEU, Charles, *Count de*. ***Excursion en Orient. L'Égypte, le Mont Sinaï, l'Arabie, la Palestine, la Syrie, le Liban.*** Paris: Garnier Frères, 1851.

8vo, pp. [vi] 400 (p.[i]=ht, 391-400=conts). Three-quarter maroon morocco. With a 19th c. armorial bookplate with the motto 'Lucem Amare Amore Lucere'.

First and apparently only edition, and the author's only work.

BNF 31058035; BL 10011.r.12. Not in Blackmer, Atabey or Weber.

526. PARDOE, Julia (1806-1862). ***The City of the Sultan; and domestic manners of the Turks, in 1836. In two volumes.*** London: Henry Colburn, 1837.

2 vols, 8vo, pp. xix [1], 1-514; x, 1-500 (pp.i=ts, [1]=list of ills). With 9 lithographed plates (including 2 fps). Wood-engraved vignettes on title and in letterpress. Three-quarter morocco, faded, gilt edges.

First edition. Later editions apeared in 1838 (3 vols, 12mo), 1845 (3 vols, 16mo) and 1854. An American edition also appeared in 1837, without plates, at Philadelphia. The list of plates includes 16 illustrations, but this includes the vignettes. Miss Pardoe spent almost the whole of 1836 in Constantinople and Asia Minor, and she has written a very interesting and detailed account of Turkish life, full of anecdotes concerning all the 'nations' in the Ottoman empire. 'Since Lady Mary Wortley Montague no woman has acquired so intimate a knowledge of Turkey' (-DNB). Miss Pardoe also wrote novels, biography, and historical fiction. In 1839 she produced *Romance of the Harem*.

BL 1047.k.9; Weber 257; Blackmer 1253 (n.b. the Blackmer copy contained an advert before the title of volume 2).

527. PARDOE, Julia. ***The Beauties of the Bosphorus; ... Illustrated in a series of views of Constantinople and its environs, from original drawings by W.H. Bartlett.*** London: for the Proprietors by George Virtue, 1838.

4to, pp. [vi] 3-164 (pp.[i]=t, [iii]=ded to Mustafa Rechid Pasha, v-vi=conts and list of plates). With engraved portrait frontispiece (Miss Pardoe) and engraved title, a map and 78 engraved plates. Contemporary half red roan gilt, romantique, over blue embossed cloth, pink endpapers, by W. Warne of Newport, Isle of Wight, with his ticket. Ownership signature of Elizabeth Lydia Brigstocke on front pastedown and title.

First edition. A second edition, enlarged, appeared in 1854-5. A French edition appeared in 1838 translated by L. de Bauclas, printed in London by Virtue. Miss Pardoe had already produced the extremely popular *City of the Sultan* (1837) and the 'Bosphorus' was planned to take advantage of the former's success. It is one of the earliest works to contain engraved views after drawings by W.H. Bartlett, and it reflects the fruits of his second journey to the Levant in 1837. He had already produced the drawings for Carne's *Syria and the Holy Land* which were made during his first journey in 1834. Miss Pardoe was a miscellaneous writer; she produced a similar book on Hungary, *City of the Magyars*, and also wrote historical works.

BL L.R.177.d.9; Blackmer 1254; Atabey 922.

528. PARDOE, Julia. *The Beauties of the Bosphorus ... Illustrated in a series of views of Constantinople and its environs, from original drawings by W.H. Bartlett.* London: Virtue and Co. [c. 1854-55.]

4to, pp. [iv] xii 1-172 (pp.[i]=t, xii=intro, 165-72=appendix). With an engraved title, 85 engraved plates, and two portraits (Miss Pardoe and Sultan Abdul Medjid). Original red pictorial cloth gilt, rebacked, gilt edges.

Second edition, produced in view of the Crimean War. Six new plates were added depicting Varna, Gallipoli, Smyrna, Odessa, the Dardanelles, and Sebastopol. Three of these are by W.H. Bartlett and are among the last works produced before he died at sea in 1854.

This edition not in BLC. Weber 1151. This edition not in Blackmer.

PARLEY, Peter. See GOODRICH

529. PARTSCH, Joseph. *Die Insel Korfu. Eine geographische Monographie. (Ergänzungsheft No. 88 zu "Petermanns Mitteilungen").* Gotha: Justus Perthes, 1887.

4to, pp. [v] 1-97 (pp.[i]=t, [v]=ded). Large folding map of Corfu with three insets, lithographed in colour. Quarter green cloth over paper boards.

Only edition. The map title is 'Originalkarte der Insel Korfu'; the insets are 'Zunahme der Bevölkerung von 1766-1879', 'Korfu und Korkyra', and 'Geologische Skizze'. Partch wrote a great deal on the geography of Greece, including *Physikalische Geographie von Griechenland*, 1885, *Die Insel Leukas*, 1889, and *Kephallenia und Ithaka*, 1890.

BL P.P. 3946/2. Karlsruhe cites many copies.

530. PASHLEY, Robert. *Travels in Crete.* Cambridge: J.W. Parker (Pitt Press, Cambridge) for John Murray, 1837.

2 vols, 8vo, pp. XL, 1-321; ix [2] 1-326 + [1] (pp.I, i=hts, missing here, [1-2]=list of ills, [1] in v.2=errata). With ten lithographed plates (6 in v.1 and 4 in v.2) and a map of Crete at the end of v. 2. Numerous wood engravings in the letterpress. Title pages damaged in an attempt to remove ownership inscriptions. 19th c. half calf, red leather labels. Bookplate of John L. Middleton on front pastedown.

First and apparently only edition of this important work. Large paper copies are also known with the plates and vignettes on india paper. Pashley spent most of 1834 in Crete, exploring it in detail. He was accompanied by Antonio Schranz, of the Maltese family of artists. The two men visited almost every village, monastery, and ancient site on the island.

BL 1045.k.7; Blackmer 1263; Weber 258.

531. PATON, William, editor. *Inscriptiones Insularum Maris Aegaei Fasciculus II Inscriptiones Lesbi Nesi Tenedi. Consilio et auctoritate Academiae Litterarum Regiae Borussicae edidit Guilelmus Paton.* Berlin: Georg Reimer, 1899.

Folio, pp. [vii] 1-156 (p.i=[], ii=series title, iii=t, v=pref, vii=conts). With a folding map of Lesbos and a coloured plan of Mitylene. Original boards, cloth backstrip, remains of printed paper label.

First edition. This is the second fascicule of volume XII of the *Corpus Inscriptionum Graecarum*, published under the auspices of the Royal Prussian Academy; the entire series was edited by Hiller von Gaertringen and the work began printing in 1873. The general title of Volume XII is *Inscriptiones Graecae Insularum Maris Aegaei praeter Delum*, on the Greek inscriptions to be found in the Aegean islands except for those on Delos; it appeared in several fascicules and continued printing up to at least 1915. Paton spent ten months in Mitylene working on the inscriptions of Lesbos and Tenedos; his preface is dated from Kalymnos, January, 1899. The maps of Lesbos and the town of Mitylene are by Richard Kiepert. Paton was also the editor of the Greek Anthology.

BL L.R.300.b.1/12.

532. PAUSANIAS. Παυσανίου τῆς Ἑλλάδος Περιήγησις. *Hoc est Pausaniae accurata Graeciae descriptio, qua Lector ceu manu per eam regionem circumducitur: A Guilelmo Xylandro Augustano diligenter recogni-*

ta, & ab innumeris mendis repurgata... Francofurti Apud haeredes Andreae Wecheli, Anno MDLXXXIII. – Pausaniae de veteris Graecia regionibus Commentarii... A Romulo Amasaeo illustrati. Francofurti Apud haeredes Andreae Wecheli, Anno MDLXXXIII. [Frankfurt: Heirs of Andreas Wechel, 1583]

2 volumes in 1, sm. folio, pp. [xii] 1-508 + [56], [xii] 1-352 [1] (pp.[i]=ts, [1]=printer's device). Contemporary calf, repaired, central gilt bishop's arms. Ownership inscription of Richard Lelorier dated 1709.

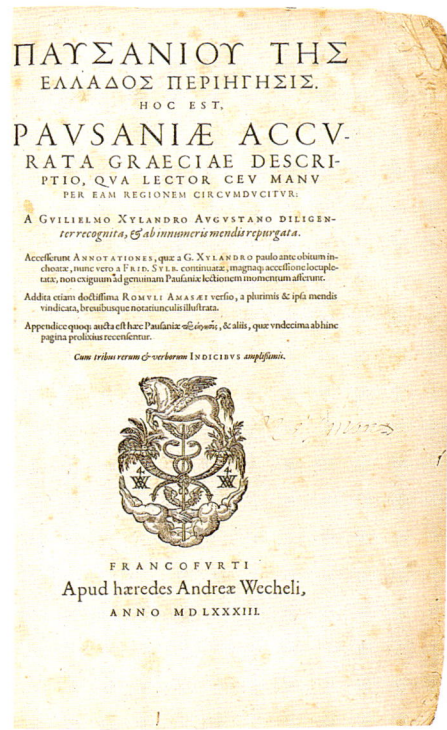

532

First Xylander edition of Pausanias, the second edition of the Greek text. The first edition of Pausanias's description of Greece was published by Aldus in 1516. This edition was corrected by the German classical scholar Gulielmus Xylander (Wilhelm Holtzman), the editor of Strabo, Plutarch and Dio Cassius. The work was completed by Friedrich Sylburg after Xylander's death. In this edition the Latin translation by Romulus Amasaeus, who first translated the work into Latin, is printed separately, but it is bound together with the Pausanias in this copy.

BL C.73.g.3; Hoffmann III, 48-49.

533. PAUSANIAS. Παυσανίου τῆς Ἑλλάδος Περιήγησις. Hoc est Pausaniae Graeciae descriptio accurata, qua Lector ceu manu per eam regionem circumducitur: cum Latina Romuli Amasaei Interpretatione. Acceserunt Gul. Xylandri & Frid. Sylburgii Annotationes, ac Novae Notae Ioachimi Kuhnii. Leipzig: Thomas Fritsch, M.DC.XCVI. [=1696]

Folio, pp. [xxv] 1-943 [37] (p.[i]=ht, [iii]=t, [xxv]=st, pp.[1]-[37]=index). Greek and Latin letter in double columns. Full blue morocco, sides framed in narrow meander border, back gilt in compartments with diamond pattern, possibly by Derome. Bookplate of Charles W.G. Howard, ex dono Sir David Dundas of Ochtertyne.

Fritsch's edition is the fourth of the Greek text. The first edition in Greek was printed by Aldus in 1516. The Latin translation is by Romulus Amasaeus. The Greek text has been edited by Kühn from a manuscript annotated by Casaubon. Brunet cites copies on large paper but notes they are rare.

BL 678.h.10; Blackmer 1273; Hoffmann III, 49; Brunet IV, 355-'édition estimé'.

534. PAUSANIAS. *Pausanias, ou voyage historique de la Grèce, Traduit en François, avec des remarques. Par M. l'Abbé Gedoyn.* Paris: F.G. Quillau, 1731.

2 vols, 4to, pp.[i] xxiv, 1-478 + [4] + viii; [i] 1-523 [1] vi (pp.[i]=ts, missing in vol. 1, pp.[4]=errata and privilege, [1]=errata, pp.i-xxiv and i-viii=observations by Follart; the notes in vol. 2 are incorrectly paginated 481-86 instead of 410-16). Title in red and black. With 4 folding plates in vol. 1 and 3 folding plates in vol. 2. Old calf, back gilt in compartments.

Apparently the first edition in French of Pausanias's travels in Greece. The work appears either with the imprint of Quillau or of Nyon. Both are associated in the privilege. However, Hoffmann attributes the publication to Didot, who may have been the printer. There may be another issue; we have been unable to confirm this. The work was reprinted in Amsterdam in 1733 in 4 vols, 12mo, and in Paris in 1793 in 4 vols, 8vo.

BL 200.d.11; BNF 34000346 citing the Nyon imprint; Hoffmann III, 51; Brunet III, 456.

List of plates (our captions and numbers):

1. Map of Peloponnesus and Aegean
2. Map of Greece and coast of Asia Minor
3. Battle of Mt. Ithome
4. Battle of the Messenians and Spartans
5. Olympia

6. Battle of Mantinea
7. Map of Northern and Continental Greece, by Buache after Delisle

535. PAUSANIAS. *Pausanias, ou voyage historique de la Grèce, Traduit en François, avec des remarques. Par M. l'Abbé Gedoyn.* Tome premier [... second ... troisième... quatrième.] Amsterdam: aux dépens de la Compagnie, 1733.

4 vols in 2, 12mo, pp. LX, 1-376; [iii] 1-359; [iii] 1-368; [iii] 1-475 (pp.I, [i]=hts). Title in red and black. With three folding maps and four engraved plates. Slightly later half calf, backs gilt with ochre and green leather labels over speckled paper boards. Ownership signatures of A.V. Lassòe and C. Molvais (?).

Second edition in French, probably a Dutch piracy. The plates are the same as in the Paris edition.

BNF 31069286; Hoffman III, p. 50.

There is another copy in the Contominas collection, in contemporary speckled calf, backs heavily gilt in compartments with fleuron lozenges, red leather labels, red edges.

536. PAUSANIAS. Παυσανίου Ἑλλάδος Περιήγησις. *Description de la Grèce de Pausanias. Traduction nouvelle avec le texte grec collationné sur les manuscrits de la bibliothèque du Roi, par M. Clavier.* Paris: J.-M. Eberhart and A. Bobée, 1814-1823.

7 vols, 8vo, pp. [iv] XV, 1-599; [iii] 1-497; vii 1-429 [3]; [iii] 1-585 + vi + [4]; [iii] 1-449; [iii] 449-551 + xxiii [5] + 1-258; [iii] 1-246 (pp.[i]=hts; pp.[3], [4], [5]=errata; pp.vi in vol. 4 and xxiii in vol. 6=notes by Koraïs, pp.1-258 in v.6=indexes). Greek and French text on facing pages. Contemporary quarter green polished calf gilt, romantique, over green marbled paper boards.

First edition of this translation by Etienne Clavier, published together with the Greek text. Clavier died after the publication of the second volume and the rest of the work was edited by Pierre C.F. Dannou and seen through the press by Adamantios Koraïs and P.L. Courier. This is also reflected in the imprint: Volumes 1 and 2 were published by Eberhart, while the rest were published by Bobée. Sometimes volume seven, the supplement with notes, is found bound with volume six. Hoffmann cites this edition as the best of the French translations.

BNF 31069267; Hoffmann III, 49; Brunet III, 456.

537. PAUW, Cornelius de. **Recherches philosophiques sur les Grecs.** Berlin: George Jacques Decker & Fils, 1788.

2 vols, 12mo, pp. XXII [2] 395; [i] 452 [1] (pp.I, [i]=ts, [2]=blank leaf, pp.1=sts in both vols, [1]=errata). Old half calf over speckled paper boards, imitating calf, back ruled gilt with lighter brown leather labels. 19th c. bookplate of Giovanni Francesco Bertalazoni, 20th c. bookplate of Leonardo Piemonte. Bookstamp of K.Th. Dimaras on lower pastedown.

Second edition. The first edition appeared in 1787-88 in 8vo, and there is another issue of the first edition with the imprint of Onfroy of Paris joined with the Decker imprint. This second edition has been reset, and the collation is not the same as that of the first edition. An English translation appeared in 1793. De Pauw's work is of particular interest because it is contrary to the philhellenic conventions of the period. He is very critical of Greece and the Greeks although he never visited Greece and had no personal experience of the place or the people. He wrote similar works on the Chinese, the Americans and the Egyptians.

BNF 36582815, BN also cites an edition of Berlin and Liege, G.J. Decker and C. Plomtaux, 1788. We have not been able to examine this to confirm the edition. See Blackmer 1275 for the first ed.
Collation: $*^{12}$ A-Q^{12} R^6; π^1 A-T^{12}.

538. PECCHIO, Giuseppe. **Relazione degli Avvenimenti della Grecia nella primavera del 1825 del Signor Giuseppe Pecchio Prima edizione Italiana tratta dal manoscritto originale.** Lugano: Vanelli, M.D.CCC.XXVI. [=1826]

8vo, pp. VII 9-150 [1] (p.I=ht, [1]=conts). Uncut in half brown morocco over embossed paper boards, back ruled in black.

First separate edition, and first edition in Italian. Uncommon. Pecchio's account appeared the same year in English, edited by James Emerson (q.v.), and it is that edition which is the more familiar. It is likely that the Italian edition was being printed either at the same time, or slightly previously to Emerson's English edition, since it contains only one of the three letters from Santa Rosa to Pecchio. The two latter were only received by Pecchio in London. Lugano was his native place, so it is not unlikely that he left his manuscript there with a friend or relative for publication; but the editor is unknown. German and French editions exist, based on Emerson's work. A Greek translation was produced by S.A. Antonopoulos in 1855. Pecchio also wrote a life of Ugo Foscolo.

BL 1053.d.22; GL IND301. Not in Blackmer or Atabey.

539. PENDLEBURY, John Dewitt Stringfellow. *John Pendlebury in Crete Comprising his Travelling Hints and his First Trip to Eastern Crete (1928) together with appreciations by Nicholas Hammond and T.J. Dunbabin and a prefatory note by S.C. Roberts.* Cambridge: University Press, for private circulation, 1948.

8vo, pp. x [i] 1-67 [1] (p.i=ht). With two photographic illustrations. Original quarter buckram. Presentation inscription to Mrs. Davies-Evans by H.S. Pendlebury.

First and only edition. Only 250 copies were printed, as a memorial to Pendlebury who was killed in Crete in 1941. He studied at the British School of Archaeology in Athens, and in 1930 he worked at Tell-el-Amarna as director of excavations. He was curator of excavations at Knossos in Crete, and his *Archaeology of Crete*, 1939, is a standard work. Pendlebury returned to Crete as a captain in the British Army and was killed there in 1941. The presentation inscription is signed by Pendlebury's father. An exhibition to commemorate Pendlebury and the fall of Crete was held at the British School in 2001.

BL X.429/5123.

539

540. PENNELL, Joseph. *Joseph Pennell's Pictures in the Land of Temples. Reproductions of a series of Lithographs made by him... March-June 1913, together with impressions and notes by the artist.* London: William Heinemann; Phildelphia: J.B. Lippincott [1915].

Lge 8vo, pp. [xxix] [160], i.e. 40 leaves of plates with 40 leaves of facing text, see below (pp.[i]=[], [ii]=st, note of edition, [iii]=ht, [v]=t, [ix-x]=Pennell's note, pp.[xiii-xxix]=Rouse's introduction). 40 plates of reproductions in the text. Original decorated cloth.

This is the Student's Edition of the work, with an introduction by W.H.D. Rouse. The first edition appeared the same year, without Rouse's introduction. The only difference between the two issues consists of variant preliminaries. This book is not paginated: it consists of 160 pages divided into 40 units of four pages each, organized as follows: first page: caption, second page: text, third page: illustration, fourth page blank. It is dedicated to R.M. Dawkins, then head of the British School at Athens.

This edition not in BL on line, see BL 10106.I.16 for the first edition. GL GT1352.1.

541. PERDICARIS, Gregory A. *The Greece of the Greeks. In two volumes.* New York: Paine and Burgess, 1845.

2 vols, 8vo, pp. vi, 7-293; 1-300 + [2] (pp.i, 1=ts, [1-2]=errata). With two lithographed portrait frontispieces (Amalia and Otho), 2 maps, and 8 lithographed plates of views. Original brown embossed cloth. Ownership signature of Jesse Kinsey on front fly-leaves.

First edition, first issue. The second issue is dated 1846 on volume 1. Perdicaris, from Verroia in northern Greece, arrived in the United States in 1826. He may have had some connection with Amherst College (where many missionaries to the Levant were trained) since he taught at the Mt. Pleasant Seminary in Amherst. In 1838 Perdicaris was the first American consul to be appointed to Athens and he remained in the post until c. 1843. His work includes accounts of his travels in Greece as well as political and social commentary.

LoC DF725.P43 (dated as Blackmer copy); BL 1426.g.3 (dated as Contominas copy); Blackmer 1284; Larrabee pp. 247-49; Weber 375;.

542. PERILLA, Francesco (1874-?). *Chio, l'Ile heureuse Ses Légendes, son Histoire, ses Tragédies, ses Beautés naturelles, ses Moeurs, ses Richesses. Aquarelles Dessins Photographies de l'auteur.* Athens: [Paris: A. Lahure for] Perilla, 1928.

4to, pp. 121 + [1] (p.1=ht, [1]=colophon). With 32 plates of which 16 = mounted reproductions of watercolours on stiff brown paper. Illustrations in text. Original blue pictorial wrappers, uncut.

First and only edition, uncommon. Very little is known of Perilla beyond the fact that he lived in Athens and produced a number of beautiful books on various parts of Greece.

BNF 31082168; BL 10127.h.17; GL GT3261.17. Karlsruhe cites 1 copy.

543. PERILLA, Francesco. *Mistra. Histoires Franques - Byzantines - Catalanes en Grèce = Notes d'Arte et de Voyages Dessins - Aquarelles - Photographies de l'Auteur.* Athens: [Paris: A. Lahure for] Perilla [1929].

4to, pp. 184 + [5] (pp.1-4=[], 5=ht, 7=t, 183-4=plan and map, [5]=colophon). With 28 plates of photographs and reproductions of watercolours. Recent quarter calf over marbled paper boards, original decorative paper wrappers bound in.

Only edition, uncommon. A beautifully produced work.

BNF 33132630; GL A1528. Not in BLC. Karlsruhe cites 2 copies.

542

544. PERILLA, Francesco. [*Grèce*]. [Athens: c. 1930-40.]

Sm. 4to, 12 unn. leaves, each with a reproduction of a painting by Perilla. Lacks title page. Original paper boards, upper board embossed gilt with title 'Grèce'. Bookstamp of Ep. N. Liokes.

Only edition, possibly a form of *tirage à part* using some photographs and ornaments which first appeared in 1930 in *Grèce: Routes de Croquis*, which was published under the auspices of the Greek Automobile Touring Club (ELPA). A version of the latter was reissued in 1943 as *Aquarelles de Grèce*. Our work is related to both publications: the shadow vignettes in the letterpress, plus a photograph of Delphi, come from the 1930 edition, and four of the photographs appear in a different form in the 1943 edition. The plates include one each of Sounion, Eleusis, Corinth, Bourzi (Nauplion), Tiryns, and Delphi. There are two photographs of Mycenae. Perilla produced many illustrated books on Greece based on his paintings. Possibly his best known are on Chios (1928) and Mount Athos (1927), but he also produced albums on Mistra, Daphne, Pelion, and Athens, as well as *Promenades Attiques*, 1944.

Not in BNF or BL on line. Not in GL, but see GT2004.23 and 2004.24.

545. PERILLA, Francesco. *Les Iles de la Grèce.* [Athens: Pyrsos for Editions Perilla, 1935.]

3 parts in 1, folio, pp. 130 [5] (p.1=t, pp.[4]=list of plates, [5]=list of wood engravings). With 24 plates of which 9 are reproductions of watercolours, mounted on thick brown paper. Numerous wood engravings in text. Uncut in half brown morocco, back gilt in compartments, black leather label, original blue pictorial printed wrappers bound in.

First and apparently only edition of this attractive work, uncommon. Despite the format in parts, the pagination is continuous. Part two begins with Naxos and part three with Folegandros. The imprint information comes from the wrappers, of which parts one and three are present; only the lower wrapper of part two is present.

Not in BNF, BLC or GL.

546. PERROT, Georges. *L'Ile de Crète Souvenirs de voyage.* Paris: L. Hachette, 1867.

8vo, pp. [v] XXXI, 1-278 + [1] + 4 pp. of adverts (p.[i]=ht, [1]=conts). Original yellow printed paper wrappers, uncut.

First separate edition. The preface is dated November, 1866. The material first appeared in two issues of the *Revue des Deux Mondes* in 1864. Its publication in book form was probably influenced by the Cretan revolution of 1867. Perrot was a member

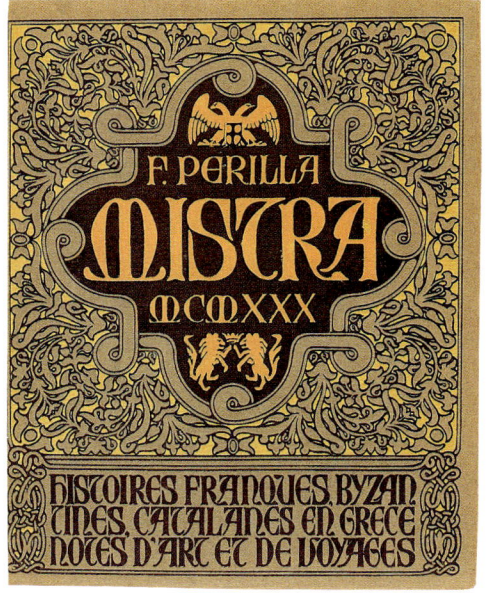

543

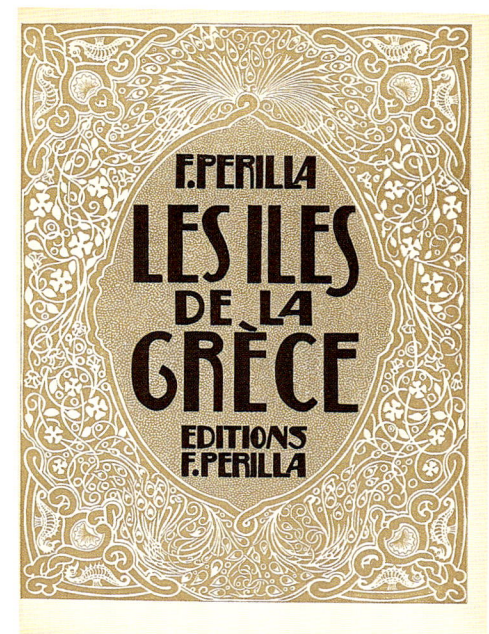

545

544

545

315

of the French School of Archaeology in Athens, 1855-58. He visited Crete for two months in 1857. He also carried out important excavations in Asia Minor and published *Souvenirs d'un voyage en Asie Mineure*, 1864, having already published *Catalogue de la mission d'Asie Mineure*, 1862. He later collaborated with Charles Chipiez on an important series of histories of eastern art which included Persia, Phrygia, Lydia, Assyria and so on. In 1897 he published 'La Crète, son passé, son present, son avenir', an article in the *Bulletin de la Société Normande de Géographie*.

BNF 31087972; Blackmer 1290.

547. PERRY, Charles. *A view of the Levant: particularly of Constantinople, Syria, Egypt and Greece. In which their antiquities, government, politics, maxims, manners and customs... are attempted to be described and treated on.* London: for T. Woodward and C. Davis, and J. Shuckburgh, M.DCC.XLIII. [=1743]

Folio, pp. xviii [8] -524 + [4] (p.i=t, pp.[1-8]=list of subscribers, [1-4]=index). With 20 plates engraved plates no'd 1-33 (1-4, 5-8, 9-12, 13-15, 16-17, 26-27 together on 6 plates. Later half calf over old marbled paper boards, red leather label.

First edition. A second edition appeared in 1770. German editions appeared in 1754 and 1765. Perry, a doctor who wrote on treatises on spa waters and an essay on the small-pox, travelled in the Levant from 1739 to 1732; he amassed a great deal of information, especially on Egypt. Most of the plates in the book illustrate Egyptian antiquities. The list of subscribers includes Dr. Mead, Francis Godolphin and the Earl of Sandwich, as well as Richard Pococke and Horace Walpole.

BL 455.e.3; Blackmer 1291; Weber 523; Atabey 940.

548. PERTUSIER, Charles. *Promenades pittoresques dans Constantinople et sur les rives du Bosphore, suivies d'une notice sur la Dalmatie. Tome premier. [... Tome second ... Tome troisième.]* Paris: H. Nicolle, 1815.

3 vols, 8vo, pp.[iii] 1-438; [iii] 1-467; [iii] 1-476 (pp.[i]=hts). Old half calf gilt over brown marbled paper boards.

First edition. The folio atlas which was published in 1817 for Nicolle by Didot is not present; it contains 25 aquatinted plates after Michel François Preault (or Preaux). An abridged English version was published by Sir Richard Phillips in 1820. Pertusier, an officer in the French artillery, spent some time in Constantinople as aide-de-campe to General Andréossy (q.v.), French ambassador to the Porte, 1811-1814, and before

1811 he was stationed in Dalmatia. He also produced *La fortification ordonée d'après les principes de la strategie et de balistiques modernes*, 1820, *La Bosnie*, 1822, and *La Valachie... et de l'influence politique du Grecs du fanal*, 1822.

BNF 34000562 (without atlas), 31089461 (with atlas); Blackmer 1292; Weber 39; Brunet IV, 524 states that copies on vellum paper, before letters, are known.

549. PETER OF GREECE, Prince. Ἀπ' Ἀθηνῶν εἰς Καλκούτταν (ταξιδιωτικαὶ Ἐντυπώσεις). Ἐπιμέλεια Α. Σκανδάμη. Athens: 1941.

8vo, pp. 111 (p.1=t). With a photographic illustration of Peter and a map. Quarter morocco, brown leather label. A presentation copy to the editor from Prince Peter, signed on the title 'Πέτρος', signed on the photograph 'Πέτρος Π 1940 Πρὸς τὸν κ. Α. Σκανδάμην ἐνθύμιον τῆς συνεργασίας μας'.

Second edition. Prince Peter, grandson of George I, and son of Prince George and Marie Bonaparte, was brought up in France. He returned to Greece in 1937. A new Greek edition was published in 1997. Prince Peter also wrote on sociology and anthropology.

Not in GL or BLC.

550. PEYTIER, Eugène. *Liberated Greece and the Morea Scientific Expedition. The Peytier Album in the Stephen Vagliano Collection.* Athens: National Bank of Greece, 1971.

Oblong folio, pp. 107 (pp.1=ht, p.105=list of plates, 106=contents, 107=colophon). Numerous coloured illustrations in the text. Original buckram, with a dust jacket, defective.

First edition in English, translated by Timothy Cullen. A Greek edition was published at the same time. Only four hundred numbered copies of the English edition were printed. Peytier was a member of the Scientific Expedition to the Morea, 1829-33. This expedition was an adjunct to the French military mission in the Peloponnesus, just as the French expedition to Egypt was an adjunct to Napoleon's invasion of that country. The object of the mission was to force Ibrahim Pasha to evacuate his forces from the Morea. Peytier was a member of the geographical section. The album contains sketches of views and costumes which Peytier made during his time in Greece. The work contains a useful introduction by S. A. Papadopoulos and notes by Agape Karakatsanis, as well as an excellent bibliography. The original manuscript belonged to Stephen Vagliano of Zakynthos.

BL Cup.1261.aa.11.

551. PHILIPPSON, Alfred. *Beitrage zur Kenntnis der griechischen Inselwelt. Mit 4 Karten. (Ergänzungsheft No. 134 zu "Petermanns Mitteilungen".)* Gotha: Justus Perthes, 1901.

Lge 8vo, pp.[iv] 1-172 (p.[i]=t). With four large folding maps, coloured. As issued, paper backstrip.

A supplement to *A. Petermanns Geographische Mitteilungen*, no. 134 from volume 29. The four maps include two of Skyros and the Northern Sporades and two of the Cyclades. The second map in both cases is a geological map. Philippson produced many works on Greek geography and geology, including *Über den Schnee in Griechenland*.

BL P.P. 3946/2; GL GT2626.

552. PHILLIPS, Walter Alison. *The War of Greek Independence 1821-1833.* London: Smith Elder & Co., 1897.

8vo, pp. xvi, 1-424 + 8 pp. of adverts (p.i=ht). With a large folding map, partly coloured. Original green cloth. Bookplate of Newnham College Library (Cambridge), cancelled.

Apparently only edition, possibly inspired by the Greco-Turkish war of 1897. Phillips used Finlay, Gordon and Prokesch-Osten for some of his sources.

BL 9136.de.6.

553. PHOTOGRAPHS. [*Collection of Photographs mainly of Athens, with some views of other archaeological sites, c. 1880.*]

Oblong sm. folio, 42 photographs within mounts, with ms. captions in French. Old green cloth.

Unsigned photographs by an unknown photographer, after 1876. The attribution of this date is based on the fact that one of the photographs depicts Schliemann's excavations at Mycenae, which he undertook in 1876. Thirteen of the photographs depict sites outside Athens: these include the temple at Corinth, the theatre at Epidaurus, the ramparts of Tiryns, Piraeus, the Dardanelles, sites at Delphi, the fortress of Palamede, and the excavations at Mycenae. It is possible that some of these photographs are the work of the Romaïdis brothers, who were commissioned to photograph Schliemann's excavations at Mycenae. They established a studio in Athens in 1876 and came to specialize in archaeological photography. They were used by the foreign archaeological schools in Athens almost to the exclusion of other photographers during the late 19th century. This album was probably prepared for sale to a tourist, and sold together with the photographs because the mounts, with printed red borders, are the correct size for the photos. Five of the mounts are empty.

See Alkis Xanthakis, *History of Greek Photography*, Athens, E.L.I.A., 1988, pp. 98-100.

554. PHOTOGRAPHS. [*Collection of Photographs of Syria and Greece, mostly by the photographer Bonfils, c. 1880.*]

4to, 61 mounted photographs, most signed and numbered on the negative by Bonfils. Quarter black roan over cloth, gilt stamped title on upper cover 'Syrie et Grèce'.

A collection of 17 photographs (albumen prints) of Syria and Lebanon, and 44 photographs of Greece and Asia Minor, including a photograph of Vathy in Samos, Rhodes, Ephesus, and Piraeus, as well as many photographs of sites and antiquities in Athens. Most of the photographs of sites in Lebanon and Syria are signed by Bonfils on the negative. Félix Bonfils established a studio in Beirut in 1867 and became one of the most prolific photographers of the 19th century. According to Xanthakis, Bonfils visited Athens between 1876 and again in 1878-82; he photographed the best-known archaeological sites and also took photographs of Greek costume.

Xanthakis, pp. 86-88.

555. PHOTOGRAPHS. [*Collection of Photographs of Athens, after 1896.*]

Oblong folio, 67 mounted photographs, unsigned but captioned in English or English and Greek, and numbered on the negative. In a black roan album, inner gilt dentelle, gilt letter 'S' on upper cover.

A collection of 67 photographs, mostly of sites in Athens and Delphi, and of sculptures from museums in both places. The numbers indicate that they have been selected from a larger series, and mounted as a souvenir of a visit to Greece. This visit may have taken place in the 1930s, since a pamphlet is enclosed in a blue roan envelope inset into the lower cover: Alexander Philadelpheus, *The Museums of Athens. Archaeological, historical and artistic guide book. Fifth Editon. Translated by Miss R. Rigidis*. Athens, 1935. This very interesting account of the museums in Athens, apparently published privately, includes at the end a brief list of private collections mostly of Byzantine interest. The author mentions the Loverdos Museum, and the collections of Stathatos, Lappas, Stringos, Lambikes, Vlastos and others.

556. PHOTOGRAPHS. *Eine Reise nach Griechenland am 30 Mai 1928... und Constantinople am 5 Juni 1928.*

Folio album of mounted photographs, mostly amateur snapshots, without captions. In modern brown morocco, back ruled gilt.

This is a souvenir photograph album recording the visit of two German ladies to Greece and Turkey. Some of the photographs have been purchased, but most are snapshots.

PICART, Bernard. See CEREMONIES

557. PICQUENARD, J.-B. *Victoires et conquêtes des Grecs Modernes, depuis leurs premières hostilités contre les Turcs jusqu'à la fin de l'année 1824; précédées d'une introduction historique contenant l'histoire abrégée de la Grèce; depuis la revolution de 1740 jusq'à nos jours. Seconde édition revue et corrigée.* Paris: Henry for Lelong, 1826.

2 vols, 12mo, pp. [iii] iii, 1-363; [iii] 1-306 (pp.[i]=hts). With two engraved portrait frontispieces and a folding map. Original embossed brown cloth gilt.

Second edition, first published in 1825. A German translation appeared at Leipzig in 1827. The portraits depict Mavrocordatos and Odysseus Androutsos and resemble the portraits in Pouqueville's work. The map is entitled 'Carte de la Grèce Moderne', 1825, engraved by Bonnet. Picquenard was a miscellaneous writer and 'romancier'.

BNF 31106727; GL IND209; Droulia 1200-1201. Not in Blackmer.

558. [PIERI, Mario (1776-1852).] *Compendio della Storia del Risorgimento della Grecia dal 1740 al 1824 Compilato da M.P.C. Vol. I [... Vol. II.]* Naples: Marotta and Vanspandoch, 1832.

2 vols in 1, 12mo, pp. 252; 252 (pp.1=[ ], 3=ts). Contemporary quarter calf over orange marbled paper boards, back ruled gilt, brown leather label.

Second edition, first published in 1825, also anonymously. Pieri (Greek form Πιερῆς) was of a well-known Corfu family which included the poet Antonios Trivoli Pieri and the botanist Michele Trivoli Pieri. The initials M.P.C. indicate 'Mario Pieri Corcirese'. Pieri was a litterateur who collaborated on several publications, including translations of Goldsmith and Horace into Italian. His correspondence with the Corfu poetess Maria Pettretini was published in 1852 by A. Pasquale Pettretini.

GL IND186.4; Droulia 1969-70; Papadopoulos IB 2016. This edition not in BLC. Not in Blackmer or Atabey. The Italian Union Catalogue on line cites 2 copies.

559. PIERI, Mario. *Storia del Risorgimento della Grecia dal 1740 al 1824.* Milan: Ronchetti for R. Marazzani and F. Legros, 1858.

8vo, pp. 1-640 (p.1=ht). Text within a border of type ornaments. With a lithographed title, partly in colour. Quarter maroon roan gilt. Bookplate of P.T. with the motto 'Dio mi concesse questi ozi'.

?Fourth edition. This work was first published anonymously in 1825 as *Compendio della storia del Risorgimento della Grecia dal 1740 al 1824*, and it was reprinted under this title at Naples in 1832. The British Library Catalogue cites a Torino edition dated 1853. Marazzani and Legros, the editors and publishers, may have edited the text either from another manuscript or from Pieri's collected works published at Florence in 1850.

GL IND186.42 (with imprint Milan, n.d.); BL 9135.b.4 (1853 ed). This edition not in Droulia.

560. PINGAUD, Léonce (1841-1923). *Choiseul-Gouffier. La France en Orient sous Louis XVI.* Paris: Alphonse Picard, 1887.

8vo, pp. IX, 1-297 (p.I=ht). Quarter blue roan gilt, original grey printed paper wrappers bound in. From the library of K.Th. Dimaras with his library stamp on the verso of the last leaf and on the lower wrapper.

Only edition of this important account of French diplomatic history in the Levant in the late 18th century, and of the role played by Choiseul-Gouffier. It includes a long discussion of the Russo-Turkish war of 1787-8, as well as an account of Choiseul-Gouffier's work on the *Voyage Pittoresque* (q.v.). Pingaud was a prolific biographical and historical writer; he also used the pseudonym Pierre Philibert.

BNF 31114881.

PITTON DE TOURNEFORT, Joseph. See TOURNEFORT

561. POCOCKE, Richard (1704-1765). *A Description of the East, and Some other Countries. Volume the First. Observations on Egypt. [Vol. II. Part I. Observations on Palestine... Cyprus and Candia. Vol. II. Part II. Observations on the Islands of the Archipelago, Asia Minor, Thrace, Greece...].* London: W. Bowyer for the Author and sold by J. and P. Knapton, W. Innys, W. Meadows, G. Hawkins, S. Birt, T. Longman, C. Hitch, R. Dodsley, J. Nourse and J. Rivington. MDCCXLIII [... MDCCXLV.] [=1743-45]

2 vols, folio, pp.[i] vi [viii] 1-310; xi [1] 1-268, vii [1] 1-308 (pp.[i], i, i=ts, pp.[viii], [1],[1]=errata, pp.[iii-vii], x=xi, iii-vii=conts and lists of plates). With an engraved dedication to Philip Stanhope, Earl of Chesterfield, in vol. 2, and 75 engraved plates no'd 1-76 in vol. 1 (no. 33 not used), and 103 plates in vol. 2. In 18th c. red morocco, wide dentelle borders on both sides enclosing painted cardinal's arms. Maroon leather booklabel with crest and cypher DMR. Book stamp on titles with the arms depicted on the covers and the cypher BA. Contemporary ownership signature of W. Grylle (?).

An ANCIENT MARBLE CHAIR at MYTILENE.

First edition of this important work of travels. Pococke travelled in the Levant for three years; his first port of call was Alexandria, where he arrived in September, 1737. He visited Egypt, Palestine, Asia Minor and Greece, which he describes in his work, not necessarily in the order in which he visited them. The plates of antiquities are after drawings by Pococke, but the plates of the Athenian antiquities were not drawn on the spot. The plates also include a map of Cyprus. The work was very popular during Pococke's lifetime and translations appeared in French (Paris and Neuchatel), German (Erlangen, 1754-55), and Dutch (Utrecht, 1776-78, 6 vols). Apparently the English edition was never reprinted in its entirety. In 1752 Pococke published the inscriptions he collected during his travels: *Inscriptionum Antiquarum Graec. et Latin. Liber.* He also produced a catalogue of his antiquities which were sold in June, 1766.

BL 457.f.8; Blackmer 1323; Weber 513; Atabey 965.

562. POCOCKE, Richard. ***Voyages... en Orient, dans l'Égypte, l'Arabie, la Palestine, la Syrie, la Grèce, la Thrace, &c. &c. Contenant une description exacte de l'Orient... Traduits de l'Anglois sur la seconde Édition, par une Société de Gens de Lettres. Tome Premier. [...Second ...Troisième ...Quatrième ...Cinquième ...Sixième.]*** Paris: J. P. Costard, 1772.

6 vols in 4, sm. 8vo, pp. [iii] viii, 485; [iii] 500; [iii] 501; viii, 479; [iii] 456; [iii] 466 (pp.[i], iii in v.4=ts, p.i in v.4=ht, missing). Half red morocco gilt over blue marbled paper boards. Book stamp of the Neustrelitz Library on verso of title.

First edition in French, translated by de la Flotte. The BNF cites a seventh volume issued in 1773.

BNF 33995321; Brunet IV, 750. This edition not in BLC or Weber. This edition not in Blackmer or Atabey.

563. POCOCKE, Richard. ***Voyages... en Orient, dans l'Egypte, l'Arabie, la Palestine, la Syrie, la Grèce, la Thrace, &c. &c. Contenant une descrip-***

561

tion exacte de l'Orient... Traduits de l'Anglois sur la seconde Édition. par une Société de Gens de Lettres. Tome premier. [... Par M. Eydous. Nouvelle édition soigneusement corrigée & augmentée de quelque notes. Tome Second ... Troisième... Quatrième... Cinquième... Sixième.] Neuchatel: aux dépens de la Société Typographique, 1772-1773.

Six volumes, sm. 8vo, pp. [iii] 556; [iii] viii, 485; 1-444; 1-502; 1-468; 1-431; 1-448 (pp.[i], 1=ts, missing in vol. 3). Contemporary boards, ms. paper labels. Volume 1 (of the first edition) uncut in faded red cloth, paper labels.

Second edition in French, published at Neuchatel in Switzerland, translated and with corrections by Emmanuel(?) Eydous, who based his translation on La Flotte's. This copy is of a mixed edition, with volume one from the first French edition of Paris. This edition is in six volumes only, with vols 1 and 2 dated 1772, and vols 3-6 dated 1773.

BL 10077.b.34; Weber 514. This edition not in BNF. Karlsruhe cites 1 copy, in the Westschweizer Union Catalogue. This edition not in Blackmer or Atabey.

564. POCOCKE, Richard. ***Richard Pocockes Beschreibung des Morgenlandes und einiger anderer Länder Der erste Theil von Egypten [... Der zweite Theil von Palästina, Syrien... Cypern und Candie... Der dritte Theil von den Inseln des Archipelagus, Kleinasien, Thracien, Griechenland...] Aus dem Englischen übersetzet durch Christian Ernst von Windheim.*** Erlanden: Stiftshaus, and Leipzig: Tetschner und Breitkopf, 1754-1755.

3 vols in 1, thick 4to, pp. [xxxiv] 1-457 [1]; [xlvi] 1-374; [xxii] 1-428 + [18] (pp.[i]=ts, 1=sts, [1]=errata, [xlvi]=list of plates, pp.[1=18]=index). With 3 engraved titles and 76 plates in v. 1, 36 in v. 2, 103 in v. 3. Contemporary calf, backs gilt, tan leather number labels.

First edition in German, translated by Christian von Windheim. A second German edition appeared in 1773 at Erlangen, and a 'neue ausgabe' in 1791-92.

BL 10076.g.12; Weber 516. Not in Blackmer or Atabey.

565. [POISSON DE GOMEZ, Madeleine Angelique]. ***Anecdoti o sia la storia segreta della famiglia ottomana tradotta dal Franzese, e divisa in dieci libri, de' quali il IX. e 'l X. sono del traduttore, e contengono gl' avvenimenti più rimarchevoli del Regno di Mustafa' II., e di Acmet III., che regna oggidì nell' Imperio de' Turchi con l'ultime guerre d'Ungheria, e della Morea...*** Naples: Francesco Ricciardi, 1729.

564

4to, pp. [xvi] 1-594 + [8] (p.[i]=t, [1-8]=conts). Lacks portrait frontispiece of dedicatee Savelli. Contemporary vellum boards. Ownership inscription on title.

First edition in Italian, with two supplementary books by the translator, possibly the Giusero Dasippe who signed the dedication, on the wars in Hungary and the Morea. The original French text, published at Amsterdam in 1722, ends with the events of 1699, but the Italian translator has brought the history up to date.

Not in BLC on line. Blackmer 1326. Karlsruhe cites two copies.

566. POMARDI, Simone. *Viaggio nella Grecia fatto negli anni 1804, 1805, e 1806. Arricchito di tavole in rame. Tomo I. [... Tomo II.]* Rome: Vincenzo Poggioli, 1820.

2 vols, 8vo, pp. VII, 1-183; pp.1-171 (p.I=t, p.1=t). With a folding map, coloured in outline, and 87 engraved plates of which 9=folding panoramas. In old half calf gilt over green paper boards.

First and only edition, uncommon. The artist Simone Pomardi accompanied Dodwell on his travels in Greece in 1805-6 and made many of the drawings which Dodwell used in his illustrated works. The plates in the present work are engraved by P. Parboni after Pomardi's drawings; note the captions are in both French and Italian. The nine folding plates depict a folding plan of Athens and a folding panorama of Athens in volume I, and volume II contains panoramas of the Plain of Thebes, Argos, two panoramas of Methana, Santa Maura, Corfu, and Attica in the environs of Sunion. This work is surprisingly rare, considering its date of publication. It is possible that Dodwell, whose own travels in Greece were published in London in 1819 and who was resident in Italy, objected to Pomardi's publication and made some attempt to suppress it.

BL 10126.bb.28; Weber 90. Not in Blackmer or Atabey. Not in Italian Union Catalogue on line. Kalsruhe cites 4 copies.
Collation: π^4 1-11^8 12^4; 1-10^4 11^6

567. PONTEN, Josef (1883-1940), and Julia PONTEN VON BROICH. *Griechische Landschäften ein Versuch künstlerischen Erdsbeschreibens. Text [... Bilder].* Stuttgart and Berlin: Deutsche Verlags-Anstalt, 1914.

2 vols, lge 8vo, pp. [v] 253 [2] + 1 p. advert [4] (pp.[i]=ht, pp.[4]=adverts). With a folding map in the text vol. and 124 photographic illustrations, and 8 colour reproductions of paintings mounted on stiff paper in the volume of illustrations. Original quarter cream buckram over brown paper boards.

566

567

First edition. A second edition appeared in 1924, reprinted in 1933. Ponten was a poet, novelist, and essayist; his long correspondence with Thomas Mann, 1919-1930 was published by Hans Wysling in Berne, c. 1988. The illustrations are by Julia Ponten von Broich. Ponten also wrote *Hertige Berge Griechenlands*, 1936.

This edition not in BLC. Not in Weber. Karlsruhe cites several copies, but the second edition is the more common.

568. PONTREMOLI, Emmanuel (1865-1956), and Bernard HAUSSOULLIER (1853-1926). *Didymes Fouilles de 1895 et 1896.* Paris: Ernest Leroux, 1904.

Folio, pp. VIII, 1-212 (pp.I=ht, 211-212=conts). Title in red and black. With 20 heliogravure plates of which 9=double-page. Numerous illustrations in the text, some full-page and with blank versos, but included in the pagination. Original green cloth, uncut. Booklabel of the architect Charles Edouard Ese, see below.

First and only edition. The heliogravures include photographs of drawings. Pontremoli also worked on the excavations at Pergamus. Haussoullier wrote a general work on Greece which was published by Hachette in 2 vols, 1888-1891, in their Guides Joanne series. He also wrote many essays connected with Asia Minor and with Greek history generally. This copy belonged to the architect Charles Edouard Ese or Wese; his booklabel is in the form of a cypher and it is difficult to decipher correctly. Two of his books were in the Blackmer Collection (466, Delagardette, and 650, Garnier).

BNF 31135676; BL 7701.ccc.4.

569. POST, Henry A.V. *A visit to Greece and Constantinople, in the year 1827-8.* New York: [Sleight and Robinson for] G.C. and H. Carvill; White, Gallaher and White; E. Bliss, et al., 1830.

8vo, pp. vii, 1-367 (pp.i=t, 359-67=appendix). Three-quarter green morocco over marbled paper boards, by N. Mantzakos of Athens, with his ticket.

First and apparently only edition, uncommon. The appendix contains material on modern Greek literature. Post was an agent of the New York Greek Committee.

LoC DF723.P8; BL 1426.f.4; Droulia 1888, citing BNG copy. Not in Weber.

570. POTTER, John. **Archaeologia Graeca, or the Antiquities of Greece. A new Edition. To which is added, An Appendix, containing a**

concise history of the Grecian States, and a short account of the lives and writings of the most celebrated Greek authors. by G. Dunbar, F.R.S.E. and professor of Greek in the University of Edinburgh. In two volumes. Vol. I. [... Vol. II.] Edinburgh: for Stirling and Slade, 1818.

2 vols, 8vo, pp. xiv, 1-527 + [16]; viii, 1-422, 1-112 + [21] (pp.i=ts, pp.[1-16] and [1-21]=indexes). With an engraved folding map of Greece and 32 plates. Contemporary embossed polished calf gilt, rebacked, original back laid down. 19th c. bookplate of John A. Irving.

First edition with Dunbar's appendix. Potter was Bishop of Oxford and later Archbishop of Canterbury. His work on Greece was first published in 1697-9; many editions followed throughout the 18th and into the 19th century, including one in Latin which was published in 1702. The map is entitled 'Grecia Antiqua', engraved by W. and D. Lizars of Edinburgh, with the imprint of Doig, Stirling and Slade, 1818.

BL 1560/1378.

571. POTTER, John. *Archaeologia Graeca, or the Antiquities of Greece... A new edition; with a life of the Author, by Robert Anderson, M.D. and an appendix, containing a concise history of the Grecian States... by George Dunbar, F.R.S.E... In two volumes. Vol. I. [... Vol. II.]* Edinburgh: for Stirling and Kenney, et al., 1824.

2 vols, 8vo, pp. [i] xv + [1] 1-527 + [16]; vi, 1-422 + 1-112 + [21] (pp.[i], i=ts, [1]=list of pls, pp.[1-16], [1-21]=index). With a folding map and 32 plates. Old polished calf. Ownership signatures of Stanley, dated 1826, and of St. John.

?Third edition with the appendix by Dunbar, which was first published at Edinburgh in 1818. The second Dunbar edition appeared in 1820. This is the first appearance of the biographical notice by Anderson. It is possible that this 1824 edition may have been issued to take advantage of the interest aroused by the Greek revolution, but it is not listed in Droulia. The map of Greece, 'Grecia Antiqua', bears the imprint 'W. & D. Lizars Edinburgh, Stirling and Slade, 1824'.

BL 1560/3815. See Blackmer 1338 (1795 ed.).

572. POTTER, John. *Archaeologia Graeca, or the Antiquities of Greece... A new edition; with a life of the Author, by Robert Anderson, M.D. and an appendix, containing a concise history of the Grecian States... by George Dunbar, F.R.S.E... In two volumes. Vol. I. [... Vol. II.]* Edinburgh: for Stirling and Kenney, et al., 1832.

2 vols, 8vo, pp.[iii] xv + [1] 1-544; [iii] iv, 1-555 (pp.[i]=hts, [1]=list of pls). With 32 engraved plates. Contemporary calf, brown leather labels.

A late edition. Without the map.

BL 07702.aaa.2.

573. POUJOULAT, Baptistin. *Voyage à Constantinople, dans l'Asie Mineure, en Mésopotamie, à Palmyre, en Syrie, en Palestine, et en Égypte. Faisant suite à la Correspondance d'Orient.* Brussels: N.-J. Gregoir, V. Wouters, 1841.

2 vols in 1, 8vo, pp. 1-234; 1-304 (pp.1=hts, 233-4, 298-304=conts). Contemporary half red roan, back gilt, black leather label.

Second edition, ?a piracy. This work was first published by Ducollet of Paris in 1840-41, under two titles, one as above, and another beginning 'Voyage dans l'Asie Mineure...', and omitting the reference to Constantinople. However, the text is exactly the same. This work consists of the letters Poujoulat wrote to his brother, Jean Poujoulat, and to Joseph Michaud, the authors of the *Correspondance d'Orient*, 1833-35. He envisaged his work as a sort of continuation. Poujoulat was a penetrating observer and his work is a fitting successor to the *Correspondance*.

This edition not in BLC or BNF on line. Blackmer 1341. See Atabey 981-82. This edition not in Weber but see 313.

There is another copy in the Contominas collection, in red morocco, back ruled gilt.

574. POUJOULAT, Baptistin. *Récits et Souvenirs d'un Voyage en Orient. Cinquième édition.* Tours: A. Mame, 1859.

8vo, pp.[iv], 1-284 (p.[i]=ht, pp.283-4=table of contents). With an engraved frontispiece and 5 engraved plates. Contemporary embossed brown cloth gilt, back gilt in compartments. A prize copy with the label of the School of the Sacre-Coeur de Jesus at Layrac.

Fifth Mame edition, an abridged version of Poujoulat's *Voyage dans l'Asie Mineure, en Mesopotamie*, etc. which was first published by Ducollet at Paris in 1840-41. Mame then took up the work and issued this abridged version with a new title; he published a 'third edition' in 1852 and a fourth in 1854. This forms part of his 'Bibliothèque de la Jeunesse chrétienne', which included a large number of accounts of travel. Note that another abridged version appeared as *Voyage à Constantinople*, Paris, 1860.

This edition not in BNF, which cites an edition dated 1848 which is probably the first Mame edition. This edition not in GL. This edition not in Atabey or Blackmer but see Atabey 981-3.

POUQUEVILLE. See CHENNECHOT and ROVANI

575. POUQUEVILLE, François Charles Hugues Laurent (1770-1838). *Voyage en Morée, à Constantinople, en Albanie, et dans plusieurs autres parties de l'empire Othoman, pendant les années 1798, 1799, 1800 et 1801. Comprenant la description de ces pays, leurs productions, les moeurs, les usages, les maladies et le commerce de leurs habitans; avec des rapprochemens entre l'état actuel de la Grèce, et ce qu'elle fut dans l'antiquité.* Paris: [Marchant for] Gabon and Co., M.DCCC.V. [=1805]

3 vols, 8vo, pp. [v] VII, 542; [v] XV, 287; [v] XXI, 344; (pp.[i]=hts, lacking p.[v] in vols 2 and 3, and pp.XVII-XXI in vol. 3). With 2 lithographed maps and 1 plate (out of 3) and a folding table. Contemporary tree calf, backs gilt in compartments with stars, red leather labels.

First edition of this important work which was a tremendous success in France and gained for Pouqueville his appointment as French consul to the court of Ali Pasha in 1805. The first volume contains the account of the Morea; volume two contains the description of Constantinople, volume three the 'Voyage en Albanie'. Translations were published in German (Leipzig, 1805, and Vienna, 1807), Dutch (The Hague, 1808), Swedish (Örebro, 1807), and Italian (Milan, 1816). An abridged English edition was published by Sir Richard Phillips in 1806; the complete work was translated into English by Ann Plumptre in 1813. The plate in volume two depicts the fortress of the Seven Towers, where Pouqueville was imprisoned in Constantinople. A doctor, Pouqueville was a member of the Scientific Commission attached to Napoleon's expedition to Egypt. His adventures began when he was captured by privateers and landed in Greece; he was declared a prisoner of war by the Turks and spent about a year in Greece before being taken to Constantinople where he spent two years.

BNF 36029440-441; Blackmer 1344; Weber 5; Atabey 988 (with an advert in vol. 3 which stated that copies were also issued on 'papier carre fin').

576. POUQUEVILLE, François Charles Hugues Laurent. *Travels through the Morea, Albania, and several other Parts of the Ottoman Empire, to Constantinople, during the years 1798, 1799, 1800, and 1801. Translated from the French.* London: Barnard and Sultzer for Richard Phillips, 1806.

8vo, pp. vi, 7-192 [4] (p.i=t, pp.[1-4]=index). With one plate, a plan and a table, all folding. Three-quarter brown morocco, back gilt.

First edition in English of Pouqueville's *Voyage en Morée*, Paris, 1805. This is an abridged version published by Sir Richard Phillips in vol. 3 of his *Collections of Modern Voyages*. (In 1820 and 1822 Phillips published two installments from Pouqueville's *Voyage dans la Grèce*, 1820-21, see below.) The entire *Voyage en Morée* was translated into English by Anne Plumptre and published in 1813. It is the earliest and best of all of Pouqueville's works on Greece. Dedicated to Napoleon, it attracted a good deal of attention which influenced the appointment of Pouqueville as French consul at the court of Ali Pasha in Ioannina, a post he held for ten years.

BL P.P. 3904.h. This edition not in Weber, Blackmer or Atabey.

577

577. POUQUEVILLE, François Charles Hugues Laurent. *Travels in the Morea, Albania, and several other Parts of the Ottoman Empire, comprehending a general description of those countries... and an historical and geographical description of the ancient Epirus. Translated from the French by Anne Plumptre.* London: for Henry Colburn, 1813.

4to, pp. xii, 1-482 + 2 pp. of adverts (p.i=ht). With a folding map and 7 engraved plates. Contemporary sprinkled calf, rebacked, back gilt in compartments, red leather labels. 19th c. ownership signature of H. MacNeal on title.

First complete edition in English. This is a handsome work; the frontispiece depicts Navarino and there is also an illustration of Hydra. An abridged edition was published in 1806 in volume three of Sir Richard Phillips' 'Collection of Modern Voyages'. Anne Plumptre also published translations of Musaeus's *Physiognomical Travels*, 1800, and Lichtenstein's *Travels in Southern Africa*, 1812-1815.

BL 10125.f.24; Atabey 989. This edition not in Blackmer or Weber.

578. POUQUEVILLE, François Charles Hugues Laurent. *Voyage dans la Grèce... Tome premier [... cinquième].* Paris: Firmin Didot Père et Fils, 1820-21.

5 vols, 8vo, pp. [iii] XLVII, 510 + [1]; [iii] 624 + [1]; [iii] 576 + [1]; [iii] 462 + [1]; [iii], (3), 630 (pp.[i]=hts, pp.[1]=errata in vols. 1-4, (3)=advertissement, pp.499-630=index). With five lithographed frontispieces and 3 folding maps. Contemporary black roan gilt, red leather labels. Ownership signature of Charles des Moulins on titles.

First edition. This work was re-issued in 1826, much augmented and corrected. This is Pouqueville's second work on Greece; it contains an account of his experiences of Greek life as French consul at Ioannina where he spent the years from 1805 to 1815. The two years before his return to France in 1817 he spent as consul at Patras. Two English versions exist: in 1820 and 1822 Phillips published two installments in his series of abridged travel accounts, and in 1820 an English version of the first part was published by Henry Colburn as *Travels in Greece and Turkey*.

BNF 31143909. This edition not in Blackmer but see 1346 (2nd ed.).

There is another copy in the Contominas collection, in half green roan, back ruled gilt, over green marbled paper boards. 19th c. ownership signature of Lady Georgiana Codrington, 20th c. booklabel of Edward Hutton. Lady Georgiana may be related to Admiral Edward Codrington, commander of the British fleet at Navarino.

579. POUQUEVILLE, François Charles Hugues Laurent. *Voyage de la Grèce... Tome premier [... sixième]. Deuxième édition.* Paris: Firmin Didot, Père et Fils, 1826-27.

6 vols, 8vo, pp. [iii] lxxviii, 1-418; [iii] 1-524; [iii] 1-552; [iii] 1-511; [iii] 1-624; [iii] 1-481 (p.[i]=hts; there is a blank leaf before page 1 in vol. 1). With 10 lithographed maps/views (out of 38) and extra-illustrated with three portraits (Mavrocordatos, Colocotronis, Ali Pasha) from the first edition. Quarter calf, back ruled gilt, black leather labels over marbled paper boards simulating tree calf, gilt arms on both sides.

Second edition, much augmented and corrected from the first edition of 1820-21. The are many differences between the two editions with regard to both text and illustrations. For example, the history of Epirus by Michael Nepotas, in Greek with a French translation on facing pages by Pouqueville, was removed from the second edition. The

579

map of Greece in the first edition, by Barbié du Bocage, was replaced in the second by two maps by Lapie. In fact, the illustrations in the second edition are entirely different from those in the first edition. In this copy only 10 of the second edition illustrations are present, but three portraits from the first edition have been bound in.

BNF 31143910; Blackmer 1346 (with list of plates).

There is another copy in the Contominas collection, in quarter green calf over embossed green cloth panelled in blind, single gilt filet enclosing gilt wreath with stamp of the Lycee Imperial d'Avignon, back gilt in compartments.

580. POUQUEVILLE, François Charles Hugues Laurent. *Histoire de la régénération de la Grèce, comprenant le précis de événements depuis 1740 jusqu'en 1824.* Paris: Firmin Didot, MDCCCXXV. [=1825]

4 vols, 8vo, pp. [iii] 1-538; [iii] 1-594; [iii] 1-586; [iii] 1-552 (pp.[i]=hts). With a frontispiece (Grec soldat), five engraved portraits, and six folding maps. Slightly later polished calf, sides embossed in romantique style, backs gilt, brown leather labels. Booksellers' tickets of Edet Jeune and of Vallee-Edet, both of Rouen, on the front pastedowns and the versos of the half-titles of all volumes.

Second edition, first published in 1824. The second edition is much more common than the first. A third edition appeared in 1826. This work achieved an amazing success throughout Europe. Many Italian editions were produced: two in 1825 with only the imprint 'Italia'; in 1833 at Palermo; in 1837-40 at Naples; and in 1854 at Milan. A German edition appeared in 1824-5 at Heidelberg and another at Halberstadt in 1827. Apparently the work did not appear in English. It gives full expression to Pouqueville's philhellenic sentiments, which developed during the ten years he spent as French consul at Ioannina with Ali Pasha.

BNF 31143903; Blackmer 1245 (first ed.).

581. POUQUEVILLE, François Charles Hugues Laurent. *Histoire de la régénératon de la Grèce contenant le précis de événements depuis 1740 jusqu'en 1824.* Brussels: Wouters, 1843.

6 vols in 3, 8vo, pp. 1-238; 1-230; 1-234; 1-228; 1-228; 1-212 (pp.1=hts). With six lithographed portrait frontispieces (including one of Pouqueville), mounted. Half calf gilt over marbled paper boards, faded.

First Brussels edition. The first edition appeared in 1824 in five volumes, with portraits and maps. A second edition appeared in 1825 (q.v.) and a third in 1826.

This edition not in BNF. This edition not in Blackmer but see 1345 (first ed.). This edition not in GL.

582. POUQUEVILLE, François Charles Hugues Laurent. *Grèce.* Paris: Firmin Didot, MDCCCXXXV. [=1835]

8vo, pp. [iii] 1-447 [1] (p.[i]=ht, p.[1]=dir. to binder). With 2 folding maps of Greece and 113 engraved plates. Uncut in half calf, blue leather labels, by A. Sangrouber of Vevey, with his ticket, original red and blue engraved paper wrappers bound in.

First edition, part of the series 'L'Univers'. Note that the name of the country described is not on the wrappers. Pouqueville's description of Greece was very successful and was translated into German and Italian in 1836, and possibly into Spanish. The format of the plates was such that they could be used in multiple editions. We have seen plates from this work with captions in French, German and Russian on the same plate. Didot reprinted the work in 1843, 1859 and 1865.

BNF 31143901; Blackmer 1348; BNF also cites an edition dated 1861.

583

583. PRÉJELAN, René. *Croquis d'Aviation en Macédoine. Dessins, Croquis & Aquarelles par René Préjelan.* Paris: Devambez [1917].

Oblong folio, title page and colophon, printed in red, and 28 mounted reproductions of watercolours. In a green cloth portfolio, ties.

Only edition of this very interesting album. Ten copies, unnumbered, on Jap vellum imperial were issued with an original watercolour signed by the artist, as well as 25 numbered copies on vellum paper, also with an original watercolour signed by the artist. There were also 250 numbered copies issued on vellum paper; this is number 161. Préjelan was active as an artist and caricaturist from as early as 1903, and at least up to 1952. He spent some time during World War I with the French Air Force in the Balkans; most of the plates illustrate scenes in Thassos island and give a very good idea of aviation at that early period.

BNF 35818897.

584. PRIDEAUX, Humphrey (1648-1724). *Histoire des Juifs et des Peuples voisins. Depuis la décadence des Royaumes d'Israël & de Juda jusqu' à la mort de Jesus-Christ. Traduite de l'Anglois. Nouvelle Edition corrigée & augmentée. Tome Premier. [... Second ... Troisième ... Quatrième ... Cinquième ... Sixième.]* Amsterdam: Henri du Sauzet, M.DCC.XXVIII. [=1728]

6 vols in 3, 12mo, pp. [iv] CVIII, 362; [i] 424; [i] 368; [i] 408; [i] 404; [i] 256 + LXVI [1] + [72] + [1] CXXXIX-CXCII + [8] (pp.[i]=ts, pp.LXVI=chronological tables, [72]=index, [8]=adverts). Titles in red and black. With frontispieces in vols 1-5, 9 maps/plans (mostly folding), and 2 folding plates. Contemporary Cambridge calf, backs painted blue, red leather labels. Ownership signature of Eric von Roland on the title of volume one.

?Fourth edition in French, translated by J.B. Brutel de la Rivière and Moïse Du Sou from the first edition, London, 1716, published under the title *The Old and New Testament connected in the History of the Jews*. Prideaux's work appeared in numerous editions up to the 19th century. The first French edition appeared in 1722 in 5 vols, 12mo; a second edition appeared in 1725 and a third in 1726. Prideaux, English divine and oriental scholar, had just taken his M.A. when he produced his earliest publication, *Marmora Oxoniensia*, 1676, a description of the Arundel marbles given to the University of Oxford. His *Old and New Testament* received a great deal of critical acclaim and stimulated further research.

BNF 31151082; BL 4520.bb.13; Brunet IV, 872, citing this as the best of the 12mo editions.

585. PROSKYNETARION. KOMNENOS, Ioannis. *Προσκυνητάριον τοῦ Ἁγίου Ὄρους τοῦ Ἄθωνος, πρότερον μὲν, παρὰ τοῦ Ἐξοχωτάτου Ἰατροῦ Κυρίου Ἰωάννου τοῦ Κομνηνοῦ, καὶ συγγραφέν, καὶ εἰς τύπους ἐκδοθὲν, νῦν δὲ, πόνῳ, καὶ ἐπιμελείᾳ Ἰγνατίου Ἱεροδιακόνου Κεμίζου, τοῦ ἐκ Μονεμβασίας ... Δαπάνῃ ... Χριστοφόρου, τοῦ ἐξ Ἰωαννίνων.* Venice: Nikolaos Glykys, 1745.

Sm. 8vo, pp. [xxiv] 1-110 [8] (p.[i]=t, [xxiv]=license). Greek letter. A fine copy in quarter vellum, black leather labels. Ownership stamp of Ioannis G.Ch. Konstas on title page.

Second edition, first printed at the Monastery of Sigovo in 1701. The author is Ioannis Komnenos.

GL T1687.21; Papadopoulos 3143; Legrand 18th c. I, 334.

586. PROSKYNETARION. SYMEON, *Archimandrite*. *Προσκυνητάριον τῆς ἁγίας πόλεως Ἰερουσαλὴμ καὶ πάσης Παλαιστίνης νῦν πρῶτον προτροπῇ... Τύποις μετὰ σχεδίων ἐκδοθέν... παρὰ τοῦ πανοσιωτάτου ἀρχιμανδρίτου τοῦ... ἁγίου τάφου κυρίου Συμεὼν τυπωθέν. ἵνα παρέχηται τοῖς εὐσεβέσι χάριν. Ἐν Βιέννε τῆς Ἀουστρίας 1749. παρὰ τῷ ἱεροδιακόνῳ Χριστοφόρῳ Ζεφάρ, καὶ τῶν ἰλλυρικο-σερβῶν κοινῷ ζωγράφῳ.* Vienna: Christophoros Zephar, 1749.

Sm. 4to, no letterpress. Entirely engraved in 56 pages (p.1=t). With a large folding engraved plan of the church of the Holy Sepulchre. Numerous engravings in the text. Recent brown morocco.

First edition in Greek, rare, based on a proskynetarion in Slavonic which appeared in 1748. Note that this proskynetarion is engraved, not printed. Both the Greek and Slavonic prokynetaria were entirely engraved, both text and illustrations, by the Serbian engraver and icon painter Christophoros Zephar. Zephar was commissioned by the Serbian archbishop Arsenios IV to produce religious works and engravings. One of the earliest of these works was the 'Stemmatographia', printed at the press of Thomas Mesmer in Vienna in 1741. Zephar was born in Doirani at the end of the 17th century; brought up in Macedonia, he studied art in a Greek environment, possibly in Thessaloniki or perhaps in Mount Athos. In 1745-46 he made the pilgrimage to the Holy Land, and it was after his return that he began to prepare the engravings for the Proskynetarion, as well as a great deal of other material, including paper icons with dual language texts in Greek and Slavonic. Many of these paper icons have been preserved, and thus we know that Zephar was active in Vienna between 1741 and 1752.

GL T1678; Weber 845; Legrand 18th c. I, 376, cites two copies, the Gennadius copy and one in the Bibliothèque Nationale. See also the article on Zephar's proskynetarion in K. Sp. Staikos, *Die in Wien gedruckten griechischen Bücher 1749-1800*, Athens, 1995, pp. 2-6.

587. PROSKYNETARION. *Ρισαλέγι Σερρίῳ Μεσλὲκ Οὐλλὰχ Μουκαττὲς Τζεπέλη Σινανὴν Πεγιανηντέτουρ. Σιναΐτη Πρωτοσύγκελος*

※ 23 ※

Εἰς τὰ δώματα ἔχει κὶ τρία παραθύρια ὁπȣ βλέπȣν μέσα εἰς τὸν ἅγιον τάφον. Ἅπτȣσι κὶ αὐτȣ κανδυλία δεκαοκτώ, τὰ ἕξη ἀκοίμητα, αὐτȣ μέσα εἶναι καὶ ἡ ἐκκλησία τῆς ἁγίας πρωτομάρτυρος Θέκλης.

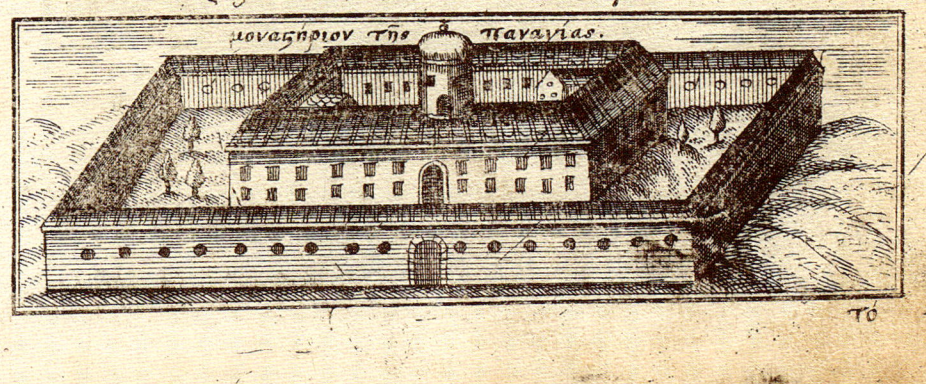

Καὶ ὡς δοξαρȣ βολή εἶναι καὶ ἡ παναγία.

Ἰσταμπολλοῦ Βελιουλὰχ Φαξιζετλοῦ Δανιὴλ Ἱερομόναχοζοῦν ... Ἰγνάτιος Ἱερομόναχοσταν.. Venice: Demetrios Theodosios, 1784.

4to, pp. α´-ϑ´ (recte η´, i.e. viii), 1-148 (p.α´=t). Woodcut on title, full-page woodcut of St. Katharine on title verso, woodcut headpiece on page one. Modern half ochre morocco over marbled paper boards.

First edition in Karamanlidika, that is, Turkish written in Greek characters. Rare. Proskynetaria of the Monastery of St. Katharine on Mount Sinai were published a number of times in the 18th century, under the title *Περιγραφὴ ἱερὰ τοῦ θεοβαδίστου ὄρους Σινᾶ*. The Turkish translation from the Greek is by Ignatius Saraphoglou.

Not in GL. Papadopoulos 4778 (citing no copies). Legrand 18th c. II, 1145, cites two copies, one at the Monastery of Iviron on Mount Athos, the other at the Greek Institute in Venice. Papadopoulos Athos, p. 194, cites one more copy, at the Skete of the Holy Apostles on Mt. Athos. Salaville 20, gives 9, 148, a correct translation of ϑ´, but the pages have been incorrectly numbered by the printer.
Collation: *⁴ A-R⁴ S⁶.

588. PROSKYNETARION. CHRYSANTHOS Kamarases, *of Proussa*.

Προσκυνητάριον τῆς Ἁγίας Πόλεως Ἱερουσαλὴμ καὶ Πάσης Παλαιστίνης. Συντεθὲν μὲν παρὰ τοῦ Πανοσιωλογιωτάτου (sic) Ἁγίου Καμαράσπ τοῦ Παναγίου, καὶ Ζωοδόχου Τάφου Κυρίου Χρύσανθου τοῦ ἐκ Προύσπς. Ἀφιερωθὲν δὲ παρ' αὐτοῦ τῷ μακαριωτάτῳ... πατριάρχῃ, τῆς ἁγίας πόλεως Ἱερουσαλήμ, καὶ πάσης Παλαιστίνης Κυρίῳ Κυρίῳ Ἀβραμίῳ οὗ τοῖς ἀναλώμασιν ἐξεδόθη. Ἐπιστασίᾳ Δημητρίου Φρονίμου. Vienna: Josef Baumeister, 1787.

Sm. folio, pp. δ´, 1-104 (pp.α´=t, 104=conts). Text within narrow woodcut borders. With an engraved portrait frontispiece of Abramios and 51 plates, mostly folding. Note that many plates contain more than one engraving. Recent red morocco.

Second edition. An earlier edition was printed in 1728. A fourth edition was printed in Moscow in 1837. The engravings of sites in the Holy Land are very fine.

GL T1679.B; Weber 842. Not in Legrand or Papadopoulos.

589. PROSKYNETARION. CHRYSANTHOS Kamarases, *of Proussa*.

Προσκυνητάριον τῆς Ἁγίας Πόλεως Ἱερουσαλὴμ καὶ Πάσης Παλαιστίνης. Συντεθὲν μὲν παρὰ τοῦ Πανοσιωλογιωτάτου Ἁγίου Καμαράσπ τοῦ Παναγίου, καὶ Ζωοδόχου Τάφου Κυρίου Χρυσάνθου τοῦ ἐκ Πρού-

σης. *Αφιερωθὲν δὲ παρ' αὐτοῦ τῷ μακαριωτάτῳ... πατριάρχῃ, τῆς ἁγίας πόλεως Ἰερουσαλήμ, καὶ πάσης Παλαιστίνης Κυρίῳ Κυρίῳ Ἀνθίμῳ οὗ τοῖς ἀνααώμασιν [sic] ἐξεδόθη εἰς διανομὴν τῶν εὐσεβῶν Χριστιανῶν. Ἐπιστασίᾳ, Ἀποστόλου Μπόρα.* Vienna: Joanna Schraembl, 1807.

Sm. folio, pp. [iv] 1-104 (pp.[i]=t, 104=conts). Text within narrow woodcut borders. With an engraved portrait frontispiece of Anthimos and 51 no'd plates, mostly folding (nos. 7 and 3 bound out of order). Note that many plates contain more than one engraving and that all the plates bear two other numbers, one of which refers to the page where the plate should be bound, and the other to the total number of engravings (85). The plate number itself is engraved below the lower right hand corner. New brown morocco, upper cover panelled in gilt and blind with fleurons in corners enclosing gilt title.

Third edition, first printed in 1728. A second edition was printed at Vienna in 1787 by Baumeister.

GL T1679.2B; Iliou 1807.51; Weber 843.

590. PROSKYNETARION. CHRISTOPHOROS *Ierodidaskalos.* **Προσκυνητάριον τῆς ἐν Μακεδονίᾳ παρὰ τῇ πόλει Σερρῶν Σταυροπηγιακῆς ἱερᾶς μονῆς τοῦ Ἁγίου Ἰωάννου τοῦ Προδρόμου συνταχθὲν παρὰ τοῦ Χριστοφόρου Ἱεροδιδασκάλου καὶ ἡγουμέμου [sic] αὐτῆς.** Leipzig: [1904].

Sm. folio, pp. 1-113 (p.1=t, 109-10=conts, 111-113=subscribers). New limp vellum, ties. A presentation copy to Ioannes Mavrokordatos, with a long inscription on the title signed by Christophoros and dated 1912.

Apparently only edition of this description of the Monastery of St. John Prodromos (the Baptist) outside the town of Serres in northern Greece. The subscribers include the monasteries of Mount Athos and residents of Serres and Alistratios.

GL T1688.4.

PROSKYNETARION. See KONSTANTIOS

591. PTOLEMAEUS, Claudius. **Κλαυδίου Πτολεμαίου Ἀλεξανδρέως φιλοσόφου... περὶ τῆς γεωγραφίας βιβλία ὀκτώ...** *Claudii Ptolemaei Alexandrini Philosophis cum primis eruditi, de geographia libri octo, summa cum vigilantia excusi.* Paris: Christian Wechel, M.D.XLVI. [=1546]

4to, pp. [viii] 1-435 [1] (pp.[i]=t, [1]=printer's device). Greek letter. Title page margins repaired. Modern vellum. With a note in a 16th c. hand on p. v, discussing Ptolemy as the author of the Almagest, and a few side notes in the same hand.

Second edition, of some rarity, of the text of the *Geographia* in Greek. It is essentially a reprint of the first edition in Greek, edited by Erasmus and published at Basle in 1533. These two editions have been printed without any maps. The first published appearance of the *Geographia* was in the Latin translation by Jacopo d'Angelo printed at Vicenza in 1475. The first illustrated edition was that of Bologna, 1477.

BL C.79.b.21; Hoffmann III, 308; Adams P2229; Brunet IV, 450 -'belle édition'.
Collation: a^4 A-$3G^4$ $3H^6$.

592. PUAUX, René (1878-1937). *La malheureuse Épire. Ouvrage illustré de nombreuses gravures d'après les photographies de l'auteur.* Paris: Perrin, 1914.

Sm. 8vo, pp. [iv] I-VII, 1-198 + [1] (pp.[i]=ht, 197-8=conts, [1]=colophon). With 18 leaves of photographic illustrations. Uncut in the original brown printed paper wrappers.

First edition. Several photographs are printed on both rectos and versos of the plates. The philhellene and journalist Puaux wrote on many issues connected with Greece, both literary and political. In 1922 he produced *La Question d'Orient devant le Parlement*, as well as pamphlets on the exchange of populations and the fall of Smyrna. He co-authored a work on Corfu with Marie Aspiotis (q.v.); his last work was *Revenons en Grèce*, 1932. Puaux had a large collection of philhellenic material including pamphlets; some of these have been deposited in Pylos. Some of his papers are held in the Historical Archive of the Benaki Museum.

BNF 31157320.

593. PUAUX, René. *Grèce Terre aimée des Dieux.* Paris: [G. de Maleherbe] MCMXXXII. [=1932]

Folio, pp. [vi] 122 + [2] (pp.[i]=ht, [v-vi]=dedication, [2]=colophon). Title in blue and black. With a frontispiece and 39 plates of which many printed in colour. Three-quarter blue calf over marbled paper boards, back gilt, original decorative paper wrappers bound in. A presentation copy by the dedicatee, A. Michalopoulos, to G. Bastianini, Italian ambassador to Greece.

Apparently first edition, uncommon. The work was translated into Greek in 1995 by Ch. Baltas.

GL GT2030.2. Not in BNF or BL on line.

THERESA MACRI, « *LA VIERGE D'ATHENES* » *(plus tard Madame Black).*
1. - Le portrait traditionnel par Alloson (1812). 2. - Portrait inédit appartenant à la famille Black. 3. - Le faire-part mortuaire de Thérésa (1875). 4. - Autographe de Thérésa « *Je reste avec votre vieux souvenir* ». 5. - Le bonnet de Thérésa.

594. QUELQUES. *Quelques Témoignages sur l'Hellénisme de la Thrace.* Geneva: Imprimerie Jent, 1919.

Lge 8vo, pp. 175 [2] (pp.1=t, [2]=list of authors cited). Woodcut map of Northern Greece and Bulgaria. Quarter brown roan gilt. 20th c. ownership signature of Peter Zervudachi.

Only edition, rare. This work has been attributed to G. Arvanitakis, cited on line at Orpheus.ee.duth.gr, with a variant title: *Quelques témoignages sur l'hellénisme de la Thrace recueillis par A.G.* This may represent another issue of the work, but we cannot confirm this information. The 'témoignages' consist of quotations from various publications from the 16th to the 19th centuries, including Villehardouin, Nicolay, de Bruyn, Marcellus, Albert Dumont, etc., etc. An interesting collection of materials.

Not in BNF, BL, or Karlsruhe on line. Not in GL.

595. QUINET, Edgar (1803-1875). *De la Grèce Moderne et de de [sic] ses rapports avec l'antiquité.* Paris and Strasbourg: F.G. Levrault, 1830.

8vo, pp. xii, 1-445 (p.i=ht). New tan morocco gilt.

First edition, reprinted in Quinet's collected works in 1857, and reprinted again in 1984, edited by Jean Tucoo-Chala and Willy Aeschimann. Quinet was a member of the archaeological section of the French expedition to the Morea, which disbanded after two months in the country, but Quinet remained in Greece, travelling on his own in the early months of 1829. In 1895 he produced *Vie et Mort du Génie Grec.* See also George Zioutos, *L'expedition scientifique en Morée et la 'relation' de Edgar Quinet*, 1951.

BNF 31165165; GL GT1310.1; Blackmer 1372; Droulia 1817; Weber 191.

596. RAFFENEL, Claude Denis. *Histoire des Grecs Modernes, depuis la prise de Constantinople par Mahomet II, jusqu'à ce jour.* Paris: Raymond, 1825.

Sm. 8vo, pp. [i] 1-332 (pp.[i]=t, 331-2=conts). Uncut in modern half brown morocco gilt.

First edition. A translation into Greek appeared in 1861. Raffenel was established at Smyrna at the beginning of the Greek Revolution where he edited the pro-Turkish newspaper, *Spectateur Oriental*. In 1822 he began publication of his important account of the Revolution, the *Histoire des Événemens de la Grèce.* In 1826 he went to Greece under the auspices of the Paris Greek Committee and was killed in Athens in 1827. He also wrote *Resumé de l'histoire du Bas Empire*, 1826.

BNF 31171249; Blackmer 1377; Droulia 778.

597. [RAICEVICH, Stefano.] *Voyage en Valachie et en Moldavie, avec des observations sur l'histoire, la physique et la politique: Augmenté de notes et additions pour l'intelligence de divers points essentiels. Traduit de l'Italien par M. J. M. Lejeune, professeur de littérature, ex-professeur particulier de son Altesse le Prince de Moldavie.* Paris: Masson and Son, 1822.

8vo, pp. [xxix] 1-187 (p.[i]=ht). Quarter green calf gilt, original green wrappers bound in. Ownership inscription of Guy Henri on half title. Library stamp of K. Th. Dimaras on p. 186.

First edition in French, translated by Lejeune from the Italian edition, first printed at Naples in 1788 and reprinted at Milan in 1822. A German translation appeared at Vienna in 1789, second edition Strasbourg, 1790. It is possible that interest was revived in the work (note Italian reprint and French translation both appeared in 1822) because of the interest aroused by the revolt of Ypsilantis in 1821. This work has been attributed to Raicevich of Ragusa by (-) Benjescu.

NBF 31172435. This edition not in GL, but see Italian edition. This edition not in BLC. Not in Droulia. Note that the author's first name appears in different forms: GL has F. Rajcevic, BNF has J. Raicevich, BLC and Karlsruhe have Stefano Raicevich.

598. RÅLAMB, Claes (1622-1698). *Kort Beskriffning om thet som wid then Constantinopolitaniske resan år föreluppit/ huruledes Kongl. May:tz auförtrodde åhrender åro förrättade/ sampt uthi hwad wilkor then Turkiske Staten widh samma Tijdh befans... Tilskyldigh underrättelse, aff thezs troo=och underdånige tienare til Portam Ottomannicam extraordinarie affskickader Clas Rålamb, anno 1658.* Stockholm: Henrich Keyser, 1679.

4to, pp. [v] 6-93 [11] (pp.[i]=t, [1-11]=register of names). Gothic letter. Woodcut printer's device on verso of last leaf. 18th c. half calf over speckled paper boards, red leather label. With the ownership cypher stamp ACG on the title page, and the signature P. Borüth on the preface.

First edition of the first printed account of Swedish travels in the Levant. Apparently this account was also issued the same year together with Rålamb's *Observationes juris Practicae*. An English version was published in volume four of Awnsham Churchill's *Collection of Voyages*, 1745. This is an account of the embassy of Claes Rålamb to the Porte in 1657-8. The preface is signed I. H. It includes a letter from Carl Gustavus of Sweden to Mehmet IV introducing his ambassador and discussing Swedish interests in Poland. Rålamb's diary of his journey to Constantinople (with a portrait) was published at Stockholm in 1963 by J. A. C. Callmer (Historiska Handlingar dl. 37, no. 3).

BL 1197.d.14 (13); Weber 320; Atabey 1010. Not in Blackmer. See T.J. Arne, *Svenskarna och Osterlandet*, 1952, pp. 67-70.

599. RAMSAY, William Mitchell. *Impressions of Turkey during twelve years' Wanderings.* New York and London: [Aberdeen University Press for] G.P. Putnam's Sons and Hodder and Stoughton, 1897.

8vo, pp. xvi, 1-296 + [2] (p.i=ht, x-xiii=preface to American edition, xv-xvi=conts, [2]=adverts). New brown morocco, back ruled gilt.

First American edition, with an additional preface which discusses American missionary work in Turkey. This edition includes a very interesting chapter on the American missionaries and the Armenian Protestants. The first edition was published in London the same year. Ramsay lived in Asia Minor continuously from 1880 to 1884 and from then until 1912 he made short journeys in the country every year. The English preface includes information on the men with whom Ramsay travelled during his long sojourn in the Levant. His understanding of Asia Minor was unparalleled, and his *Historical Geography of Asia Minor*, 1890, is considered the basic work on the area. Ramsay's *Impressions* contains a fascinating account of his contacts with the native populations during his archaeological expeditions. The last chapter is entitled 'Tips to Archaeological Travellers'.

LoC DS48.3.R2; BL 10076.ee.24. There was a copy of the English edition in the Blackmer collection, but not in the printed catalogue.

600. RANDOLPH, Bernard. *The present state of the Morea, called anciently Peloponnesus: Which hath been near two hunded years under the dominion of the Turks; and is now very much depopulated. Together with a Description of the city of Athens, islands of Zant, Strafades, and Serigo. Faithfully described by Bernard Randolph, who resided in those parts from 1671 to 1679. By his Majesties Special Licence.* London: Printed for the Author, and are to be sold by Tho. Basset... John Penn... and John Hill... 1686.

4to, pp. [i] 1-26 (pp.[i]=t). With five engraved plates. Lacking the map of the Morea which should be present. Panelled calf antique, back ruled gilt, bound with 'Archipelago'.

Second edition. The first edition was printed at Oxford the same year with the map of the Morea only. A third edition appeared in 1689 with the map of the Morea re-engraved (with two insets) and a double-page plate of the Seraglio, as well as at least two other plates. The Blackmer catalogue, 1384, states that the 1686 editions should not have plates, but only the map. This theory is based on a comparison of the titles of the three editions of the work. However, the GL copy and the Contominas copy agree with regard to the plates: engravings of AcroCorinth, Mistra, Navarino, Modon, and Napoli di Romania are present in both copies. Thus Blackmer may be incorrect in stating that both 1686 editions should have the map only. However, copies of the three editions of this work are found with varying numbers of plates, and several copies seen have different numbers of the plates, or none, or they are bound at random in both the Morea and the Archipelago. Little is known of Randolph, who was a merchant engaged in the Levant trade; he spent about nine years in the Peloponnesus and the Archipelago, according to his statement on the title, and may have had some connection with Heneage Finch, English ambassador at Constantinople, to whom his map of Greece is dedicated.

BL 568.d.27; Weber 387. This edition not in Blackmer, but see 1384 (1st ed).
Collation: A-C^4 D^2.

601. RANDOLPH, Bernard. *The present state of the islands in the Archipelago, (or Arches) Sea of Constantinople, and Gulph of Smyrna; With the islands of Candia, and Rhodes. Faithfully describ'd by Ber. Randolph. To which is annexed an Index, shewing the longitude and latitude of all the places in the New Map of Greece lately published by the same author. Printed at the Theater in Oxford, 1687.* [Oxford: Sheldonian Theatre, 1687.]

4to, pp. [i] 1-108 + [9] (pp.[i]=t, [1-9]=index and errata on p.[9]). With two engraved plates (out of 3, lacks plate of Tenedos, but with the plate of Negroponte and costume plate). Extra-illustrated with a large folding map of Greece. Panelled calf antique, back ruled gilt, bound with 'Morea'.

First edition. Randolph's map of Greece, dedicated to Heneage Finch, Earl of Winchelsea, ambassador to the Porte, is frequently found bound into this work because of the reference to it on the title page, but it was printed before the book was published, as is clear from the title. There are three issues of the map, although changes to the map surface occur only on the third; they are distinguished by the imprint: 1)Barnard Randolph Author sold by Richard Palmer... 2)Barnard Randolph Author sold by Richard Palmer... and Thos. Terrey... 3) London Printed and Sold by Christop.^{r} Browne.

BL 568.d.28; Blackmer 1386; Weber 389.
Collation: A-P^4.

A. Terra ferma d' Achaja.
B. Citta di Negroponte.
C. Borghi.
D. Castello del Scoglio.

A. Part of Achaja.
B. City of Negroponte.
C. Suburbs or new Town.
D. Castle on the Islet.

NEGROPONTE.

LA Citta di Negroponte Capitale dell' Isola di quel nome, La quale hà doi miglia di Circuito senza li Borghi.

Dalli Greci fu chiamata Calcis & è devisa dalla Terra ferma della Provincia d' Achaja di un braccio di Mare nominato L' Euripo ò vero il Stretto di Negroponte. Un Imperatore di Costantinopoli la donò con tutta L' Isola alli Signori Venetiani; L' Anno 1204 per li Grandi Servitii che quella Republica hà resi al Imperio. Diverse volte li Turchi minacciorono di pigliarla, mà in riguardo della Fortezza del Sito differirono fin all' Anno 1469. E Mahometto il Grande mandò una Armata di più di 300. Navi, Gallere, & altri bastimenti sottili Comparendo poi Lui in Persona alla Testa di Cento e vinti mille huomini Assediò la Citta per Mare e per Terra più d'un mese di continuo, travagliandola in più forme, & Gli furono dati più di vinti Assalti Generali. Di Presedio è Guarniggione vi erano più di vinti quatro mille huomini che valorosamente resisterono al Nemico, Sprezzando L' Offerte fattegli per rendere La Piazza. La Citta fù presa per Assalto Generale & a puochissimi del Presidio fù data La Vita. Un Nobile Venetiano di Casa Erizzo con una picciola parte de suoi se retirò nel Castello del Scoglietto mà non poteva resistere a tante Forze, & havendo il Gran Signore promesso di donargli la vita, si rese, & dopo fù per ordine suo segato per mezzo. Una figlia toltagli fù tagliata in pezzi per non volere assentire alla volontà libidinosa del Tiranno. In questa Speditione il Turco hà perduta più di quaranta mille huomini. La Citta per hora è ben fortificata con Fortezze nove, Le Fosse sono fatte più fonde & più Larghe di quel che erano.

NEGROPONTE.

THE City of *Negroponte*, Capital of the Island of that Name, is two miles in Circuit, without the Suburbs.

By the *Greeks* it was called *Calcis*, and is devided from the main Land of the Province *Achaja* by an Arm of the Sea called the *Euripo*, or Streight of *Negroponte*. An Emperour of *Constantinople* gave it, with the whole Island, to the *Venetian* Lords, *Anno* 1204. for the great Services that that Republick had render'd to the Empire. Diverse times the *Turks* threatned to take it, but in regard of the strength of its scituation they desisted, till the year 1469. *Mahomet the Great* sent a Fleet of above 300 Ships, Gallys, and smaller Vessels; he in Person appeared at the Head of above One hundred and twenty thousand men, besieging the City by Sea and Land above a month, in which time above twenty assaults were given. The Garrison were above twenty four thousand, who Valiantly resisted the Enemy, despising the offers made them to surrender the place. The City was taken by General Storm; very few of the Besieged were spared alive. A Noble *Venetian*, of the Family of *Erizzo*, with a small Party of his, retir'd into the Island Castle, but could not resist so great a Power: And the *Grand Signior* having promised to spare his life, surrender'd himself. He was afterwards sawn asunder by the *Grand Signiors* command, and his Daughter cut in pieces for refusing to yield to the lustful will of that Tyrant. The *Turks* lost above forty thousand men in this Siege: The City is now well fortified with new fortifications, and the Ditches made deeper and wider than they formerly were.

Sold by Mr. *Nott* in the *Pall-Mall*, Mr. *Basset* at the *George* in *Fleet-street*, Mr. *Bennet* at the *Half-Moon* in St. *Paul's Church-yard*, Mr. *John Hill* in *Exchange-Alley*, and Mr. *Terry*, at the *Red-Lyon*, without *Newgate*.

602. RATCLIFFE, Dorothy, afterwards Dorothy Una MacGrigor PHILLIPS. *News of Persephone Impressions in Northern and Southern Greece with a car, a kettle and cameras.* London: Eyre and Spottiswoode, 1939.

Lge 8vo, pp. x, 1-224 (p.i=ht). With a photographic frontispiece and 45 photographic illustrations on 27 plates (mostly back to back). Original blue cloth, in a dust jacket.

First edition. An interesting account of a journey made in 1938.

BL 10127.ff.29.

603. RAULIN, Félix Victor. *Description physique de l'Ile de Créte... Extrait.* Bordeaux: Th. Lafargue, MDCCCLVIII. [=1858]

Lge 8vo, pp. [iv] 292 + [3] (pp.[i]=t, [3]=conts). 19th c. three-quarter vellum, back gilt, red leather labels, original tan printed paper wrappers bound in. A presentation copy, with Raulin's inscription 'A Monsieur Geoffroy St. Hilaire hommage respectuaux V. Raulin. Book stamp of Geoffroy Saint-Hilaire on title.

First edition, an offprint from the *Actes de la Societe Linnéene de Bordeaux*. This is the first part of Raulin's important work on the natural history of Crete, which appeared in three volumes in 1869. It was first published in the transactions of the Linnean Society of Bordeaux in 1858. Note that the offprint wrapper is dated 1859.

BL X20/6158. Not in BNF as a separate entry but see 31180249 for the 1869 edition. See Blackmer 1394 for complete edition.

604. RAY, John, editor. *A Collection of Curious Travels and Voyages. In Two Parts. Part I. Containing, Dr. Leonhard Rauwolf's Journey into the Eastern Countries... translated from the original High Dutch, by Nicholas Staphorst. Part II. Containing Travels into Greece, Asia minor, Egypt, Arabia felix... collected from the Observations of Mons. Belon, Mr. Vernon, Dr. Spon... [etc.]. To which are added, Three catalogues of such trees, shrubs, and herbs, as grow in the Levant. The Second edition corrected and improved.* London: for Oliver Payne, Thomas Woodman, and William Shropshire. MDCCXXXVIII. [=1738]

2 parts in 1, 8vo, pp. [x] 1-489 +[1] +44 (pp.[i]=tp, [ii-x]=conts, [1]=st to catalogue; p.339=st to part 2, no imprint, but marked 'Vol. II'). Title in red and black. Old green cloth gilt, recased.

Third edition of this collected work, despite the claim on the title. In fact this work forms the second volume of Ray's *Travels through the Low Countries* which appeared in 1738 in two volumes. The first edition of the *Collection of Curious Travels* appeared in 1693, with a second in 1705. Ray, the great naturalist, was the editor of this work: he revised Staphorst's translation of the botanist Rauwolf's travels which first appeared in 1582-83 as *Aigentliche Beschreibung der Raisz... gegen Auffgang inn die Morgenländer* and published it first in the 1693 edition; he also added selections, some presumably translated by himself, from the works of other naturalists who travelled in the Levant, e.g. Belon, Alpinus, Spon.

BLC 1509/1083. See Blackmer 1397 for the first edition. Not in Atabey.

605

605. REISINGER, Ernst. *Griechenland Schilderungen deutscher Reisender In zweiter, veränderter Auflage herausgegeben. Mit 90 Bildtafeln, davon 62 nach Aufnahmen der Preussischen Messbildanstalt.* Leipzig: Insel-Verlag, 1923.

4to, pp. 109 + [1] (p.1=[], [1]=colophon). With 90 no'd photographic plates. Original quarter cloth over grey pictorial paper boards.

Second edition, first published in 1916 with 88 plates under the title *Griechenland Landschaften und Bauten Schilderungen*.

This edition not in BLC or Weber. Karlsruhe cites a number of copies.

606. REMERAND, Gabriel. *Ali de Tébélen Pacha de Janina (1744-1822)*. Paris: Librairie Orientaliste Paul Geuthner, 1928.

Sm. 4to, pp. 290 (pp.1=[ ], 3=ht). With a frontispiece and a folding map. Uncut and unopened in the original grey printed paper wrappers, upper wrapper defective.

First and apparently only edition, published in the series 'Les Grandes Figures de l'Orient'.

BNF 31194479.

607. RENAN, Ernest. *La prière sur l'Acropole et ses mystères. Par Henriette Psichari*. Paris: CNRS, 1956.

8vo, pp. 175 (p.1=ht). Original yellow cloth. From the library of K.Th.Dimaras, with his stamp on the fly-leaf and the lower pastedown.

This is a study of the philosopher Ernest Renan's 'Prière sur l'Acropole' by his granddaughter, Henriette Psichari. Renan visited Athens in 1865; while on the Acropolis he recited this prayer. The 'Prière' was published in Renan's *Souvenirs d'enfance et de jeunesse*, 1883, but it must have been known at large before its publication, and it aroused a great deal of discussion in French intellectual circles. It has been published several times in illustrated versions. In 1910 Anatole France wrote a response: *Réponse de Pallas Athéne à la Prière sur l'Acropole*.

BNF 33871479. See Basch, pp. 146-155, for a long discussion of the 'Prière sur l'Acropole' and its influence on French letters.

608. REVELLI, Paolo. *L'Egeo (Dall' Eta' Micenea ai Tempi Nostri) con 179 illustrazioni, 3 tavole a colori fuori lesto e 4 carte geografiche colorate*. Bergamo: Istituto Italiano d'Arti Grafiche, 1912.

Lge 8vo, pp. 167 (p.1=t, 161-7=index). With 4 plates of maps (1=lge folding) and 3 coloured plates. Many illustrations in the text. Original pictorial stiff paper wrappers.

First edition, published in the series 'Collezione di monografie illustrate', series 5, Viaggi, no. 12. Revelli wrote a great deal on cartography and geography. The maps number six, with four maps on two pages (including two maps of Santorini), and a folding map of Rhodes. The large folding map is entitled 'Il Mare Egeo (Arcipelago) Eugenio Heberdis/ Prof. Revelli dir/ Istituto Ital.° d'Arti Grafiche Bergamo'. It contains an inset: Il Mare di Siria.

BL 7814.ccc.5/12.

609. [REVICZKY, Karoly Imre Sander, *translator.*] *Traité de Tactique, ou Méthode Artificielle pour l'Ordonnance des Troupes. Ouvrage publié & imprimé à Constantinople, par Ibrahim Effendi, Officier Mutteferrika de la Porte Ottomane, l'an de l'Hégire 1144, qui est la premiere année après la derniere rébellion & la déposition du Sultan Ichmet [sic], arrivée l'an 1730, de l'Ere Chrétienne, traduit du Turc. A Vienne, chez Jean-Thom. de Trattnern... M.D.CC.LXIX.* [?Paris: 1769].

8vo, pp. xliv, 1-224 (p.i=t). Contemporary tree calf, back ruled gilt, ochre leather label, marbled edges. Bookplate of the Nikolaevsky Academy.

Second edition in French, translated from Ottoman Turkish by Baron Reviczky from Ibrahim Effendi's work *Usul ul-hikem fi nizam il-ümem*, an account of European military strategy, printed in 1732 at the first Ottoman press to be established in Turkey, by its author, the Hungarian Ibrahim Effendi Müteferrika, founder of printing in Turkey. The first edition was printed at Vienna by Trattnern; it includes a Turkish heading on the title and the information that the work was first printed at the French embassy press at Constantinople, which was incorrect. Ibrahim Effendi printed the work at his own press. According to Brunet the title without the Turkish heading is a piracy printed at Paris. However, Brunet cites the piracy as being in 12mo format, while our edition is in octavo. Certainly our edition, without the Turkish heading, has been reset, as can be seen from the comparisons of the collations below. The translator Reviczky owned an important collection of books. He edited Petronius, translated the poems of Hafiz into Latin and also wrote on Persian literature and history.

BNF 30632506; BL OR.70.a.13; Atabey 603 (first edition); Brunet III, 400.
Collation: *^{8} 2*^{8} 3*^{8} A-O^8 (O7,8=[ ]). The Atabey edition collates *^{8} A-H^8.

610. REVUE GENERALE des SCIENCES. *Aux Sanctuaires Grecs. Paques 1912. XLVIIme Croisière de la "Revue Générale des Sciences".* [Paris: A. Faucheux, 1912.]

Folio, pp. 76 (p.1=t). Title and p. 75 in red and black. A map of the route and 58 plates of photographs in the text. Original decorated wrappers, uncut.

Only edition of this interesting work, of which only 130 copies were printed. This is a souvenir of a cruise made in 1912 under the auspices of the *Revue Générale des Sciences*. The text consists of talks given at several archaeological sites. The photographs were taken by the passengers. The directors of the cruise were Gustave Fougères and Charles Diehl. Maxime Collignon, E. Rhodocanachi and the archaeologist Charles Waddington were among the passengers. The wrappers are decorated with paintings by Louise Brouardel, one of the passengers. Several accounts of cruises sponsored by the *Revue Générale* are known, including *Cerigo-Lo!*, an account of a cruise made in 1904.

Not in BNF or BLC on line.

611

611. REY, Etienne. *Voyage pittoresque en Grèce et dans le Levant fait en 1843-1844. Journal de Voyage Dessins et planches lithgraphiées par Etienne Rey. Tome Premier. [... Tome Deuxième.]* Lyon: Louis Perrin, 1867.

2 vols in 1, lge folio, pp. [iii] XI [II] 1-82 [2]; [iii] 1-148 [2] (pp.[i]=hts, [I-II]=list of plates, [1-2]=errata in both vols). With 55 lithographed plates no'd 1-35 and 1-20 of which 52 on india paper, mounted, and 3=maps. Numerous lithographed vignettes in letterpress. Panelled brown morocco. A presentation copy from Rey to the historian Duruy (q.v.), signed on the verso of the fly-leaf.

First and only edition. A charming and lively work. Because of the similarity of title, this work is sometimes confused with Chenavard's folio description of the same journey published in 1858, but Chenavard's work contains engraved plates, while Rey's consists of lithographs. Rey, Chenavard and the architect Dalgabio travelled in Greece and Asia Minor from September 1843 to the early spring of 1844. Rey later became director of the Museum of Vienne in Isère.

BNF 31203836; Blackmer 1412. Not in Weber. See the biographical notice of Rey by E.C. Martin Daussigny.

RICAUT. See RYCAUT

612. RICHARDSON, Rufus Byam. *Greece through the Stereoscope. A Tour conducted by Rufus B. Richardson, Ph.D.* New York: Underwood & Underwood [1907].

8vo, pp. 1-363 + [4] (p.1=t, pp.[1-4]=adverts). With a booklet of 15 folding maps on onion skin paper in a pocket in the lower cover. Original brown cloth gilt.

Apparently first edition. A German edition translated by Aloys Weiss appeared in 1908. The work must have been accompanied by a set of slides for the stereoscope. Richardson may have been connected with the American School of Classical Studies in Athens. He also wrote *Vacation Days in Greece*, 1903.

LoC DF726.R6, cites only this edition. BL 10126.df.18. Not in Weber.

613. RICHIER, Christophe. [*De rebus Turcaru[m] ad Franciscum Gallorum Regem Christianiss. libri quinque: Christophoro Richerio Thorigneo Senone, Cubiculario Regio, & Cancellario Franciae à secretis, authore. De origine Turcaru[m], & Ottomanni imperio. De moribus & institutis illius gentis. De Tammerlanis Parthi rebus gestis. De expugnata à Maomethe Consta[n]tinopoli. De Castellinoui Dalmatiae oppidi recenti direptione. Cum Privilegio Regis. Parisiis. Ex officina Rob. Stephani... M.D.XL.*] [*Colophon: Excudebat Rob. Stephanus... Ann. M.D.XL. III. Non. Martii.*] [Paris: Robert Estienne, 1540.]

Sm. 4to, pp. 1-115 (-pp.1-2) + [12] (p.1=title, missing, p.3=first page of text, pp.[1-11]=index, p.[12]=colophon). Title page lacking. Embossed calf antique.

First edition. The preface occupies a2-3a, with the text beginning on a3a. Note that the first gathering of the Contominas copy is signed a, not ā as in the Blackmer copy. Richier, diplomat and political figure, was a member of the circle around Etienne Dolet and Lazarus Baifius; he and Baifius in particular were close to Charles Estienne. Elizabeth Armstrong, in her book on Estienne, suggests that one of the reasons for the printing of this book was connected with the daring Franco-Turkish treaty signed in 1536. This was the first time a Christian power signed a treaty of cooperation with the Ottoman Empire, and the whole of Europe was shocked. Robert Estienne supported François I by printing books which explained and examined Turkish life and customs. Richier carried out several diplomatic missions to Turkey as secretary to Chancellor Poyet, valet du chambre to François I. Later he was appointed French ambassador to Denmark and Sweden.

BNF 31213222; BLC C.46.d.5.(2); GL TH20R52. Blackmer 1418; Atabey 1043; Göllner 672; Brunet IV, 1294. See E. Armstrong, *Robert Estienne Royal Printer*. Cambridge, 1954, pp. 144, 149.

Collation: a⁴ (-a1) b-h⁸ i⁴ (i4v=colophon)

613

614. RICKETTS, Clemuel Green, *of Pennsylvania*. *Notes of Travel, in Europe, Egypt, and the Holy Land, including a visit to the city of Constantinople, in 1841 and 1842.* Philadelphia: C. Sherman, 1844.

8vo, pp. xii, [13]-319 (p.i=[], p.iii=t). With an engraved portrait frontispiece. Modern panelled green morocco.

First and apparently only edition and Ricketts' only work. Uncommon. Ricketts travelled for his own amusement from October 1841 to September 1842. There were many travellers in the Holy Land in 1842, including W.H. Bartlett, the Ewalds, the Americans David Millard and Samuel Wolcott.

LoC D975.R53. Not in BLC on line. Not in GL, Blackmer or Atabey. Not in Tobler. Larrabee, p. 329, cites Ricketts in the notes only.

615. RIEDL, J. *Carte de la Turquie Européenne ou la Presqu'il entre la Save, le Danube et la Mediterranée par J. Riedl [cartouche:] General Charte von Rumeli nebst Morea und Bosnia nach allen vorhandenen Ortsbestimmungen Seecharten, Reisen, Aufnahmen, Nachrichten und dem Geographischchen Werke des Hadschi Chalfa kritisch bearbeitet and gezeichnet und dem hochgebornen herrn Grafen Wenzeslaus Severin Rzewusky... gewidmet von J. Riedl. Wien MDCCCXII Im Kunst und Industrie Comptoir. Gestochen von Carl Stein. Pesth, im Industrie Comptoir.* Berlin: S. Schropp & Co. [Vienna: Riedl, 1812.]

Map, 55.5x62 cms, folding to 8vo. With an inset of a view of the Serai at Edirne (Adrianopolis), a plan of Edirne, and a plan of the Golden Horn in a circular inset at the lower right hand corner. Gauzed. In a folder of grey marbled paper boards, in a matching box.

A very interesting map of European Turkey constructed by J. Riedl after information from various sources, including the geographical work by Hadschi Chalfa, and dedicated by him to Count Wenceslaus Rzewusky.

BL Maps 43920.(1).

616. RIO Y CORONEL, Marcos Manuel. *Compendio histórico del origen y progresos de la insurrección de los Griegos contra los Turcos desde el año de 1821 hasta la Llegada a Egina del Presidente actual de la Grecia, Conde de Capo de Istria. Tomo I. [... Tomo II.]* Madrid: Ramos y Compañia, 1828.

2 vols, pp.1-314 [3]; 1-352 [3] (pp.1=ts, pp.347-52=list of subscribers, pp.[3], [3]=conts; in v.1 the contents bound between pages 2 and 3). Engraved portrait of Canaris in vol. 2. Contemporary tree calf, backs ruled gilt, red leather labels.

First edition. Another edition/issue also appeared in 1828 under a slightly different title. Spanish philhellenic material is uncommon.

BL 9135.A.24; Droulia 1450-51. Not in BNF on line. Not in GL, Blackmer or Atabey.

617. ROBERTS, David. *Sketches in the Holy Land. Introduction and commentary by Dr. C.H.J. de Geus.* Aalsmeer: Pulchri Press, n.d.

Folio, pp. 383 +[1] (p.1=ht, [1]=colophon). Half modern green morocco gilt, gilt edges.

This work is a reprint of the plates from Roberts's *Holy Land, Syria, Idumea*, London, 1842-49, published in 1000 copies. Geus has provided notes to each plate and a biographical notice of Roberts.

See Blackmer 1432 (first ed). Many reprints have been produced of Roberts' work.

618. RODD, James Rennell, *Baron Rennell*. **The Customs and Lore of Modern Greece.** London: David Stott, 1892.

Sm. 4to, pp. xvi, 1-294 (p.i=t, p.iii=ded). With wood-engraved frontispiece and six engraved plates by Tristram Ellis. In the original rust cloth.

First and apparently only edition. Rodd, the grandson of the geographer James Rennell, spent two years in Greece in about 1888, much of the time with the Noel family at Achmet Aga. This very interesting work may be one of the earliest books in English which deals consciously with Greek ethnography. In 1888 Lucy M. J. Garnett and G. S. Stuart-Glennie had published their work *Greek Folk Songs*, which connected folk songs with anthropological material. Rodd's work is illustrated by Tristram Ellis who had previously produced *On a raft and through the Desert*, 1881. He also produced illustrations to Homer. Rodd later produced *Princes of Achaia and the Chronicle of Morea*, 1907, and *Homer's Ithaca*, 1927. In his *Social and Diplomatic Memories*, 1925, Rodd discusses many of the political problems in the Balkans which affected Europe and Greece in particular.

BL 2346.e.4; Blackmer 1441.

619. RONART, Stephan. **Griechenland von Heute.** Amsterdam: [Athens: G. E. Calergis] for Steenuil [1935].

Lge 8vo, pp. 348 (pp.1=t, 346=st, 347-8=bibliography). With a photographic frontispiece and 2 chromolithographed folding maps. Numerous photographic illustrations and several coloured statistical tables in text. Recent brown morocco gilt, original white printed paper wrappers bound in.

First edition. The preface, by the Greek foreign minister D. Maximos, is dated December 1934. The two maps depict the transport system and the locations of mineral waters or spas. Ronart wrote a series of these 'Today' books on the Balkans, including *Albanien von Heute*, Vienna 1933, *Bulgarien von Heute*, Amsterdam, 1935, and *Die Turkei von Heute*, Amsterdam, 1936.

Not in BLC on line. Karlsruhe cites 1 copy.

620. ROQUE, Phocion. *Athènes d'après le Colonel Leake Ouvrage mis au courant des découvertes les plus récentes... Introduction de M.C. Wescher. Dessins de L. Breton, d'après des photographies. Deuxième édition.* Paris: E. Plon, 1876.

8vo, pp. [iv] XX, I-III, [5]-336 (p.[i]=ht, pp.335-6=conts). With eight plates and a folding plan. Uncut in quarter calf, the original blue printed paper wrappers bound in.

Second edition, first printed in 1869 under the title *Topographie d'Athènes*. With an introduction by Carl Wescher. This work describes the Athenian monuments in the wake of the archaeological work undertaken after the establishment of the Greek state.

620

Leake's original work describes Athens as he saw it previous to the Revolution. Roque also produced a French abridged translation of Leake which was printed at Malta in 1849. According to Thouvenel (q.v.), Roque came from a Franco-Greek family long established in Athens. He was an official with the Ministry of Foreign Affairs and served as Secretary of Legation in Paris and London. He died in 1870.

BL 10125.cc.2; BNF 30788058. This edition not in GL.

There is another copy in Contominas collection, in quarter green panelled calf gilt.

621. ROSE, William George. ***Three months' leave.*** London: Richard Bentley, 1838.

8vo, pp. V, 1-346 (p.I=t). 19th c. half calf rebacked, gilt arms of the Signet Library on both sides.

First edition of this account of Rose's travels during his army service in the Levant. Weber cites what appears to be another issue, with the same pagination, published in 1838 under the title *Three months' leave or military reminiscences*. Rose's journal begins with an account of Paxos and Santa Maura. He visited Patras four times in seven months. The journal also includes an account of a journey through Greece to Constantinople and through the Black Sea to the Danube, with an interesting description of the Balkan, and Rose's route to Vienna through Galatz, Orsova, Temesvar and other cities in Hungary.

BL 1047.d.24; Weber 283. Not in Blackmer or Atabey.

622. ROSS, Ludwig. ***Reisen des Königs Otto und der Königinn Amalia in Griechenland. Aufgezeichnet und gesammelt von Ludwig Ross. Erster Band. [... Zweiter Band. Mit einer Karte.]*** Halle: C.A. Schwetschke and Son, 1848.

2 vols in 1, 8vo, pp. XIX, 1-256; VIII, 1-256 (pp.I=hts). With a folding map, coloured in outline, in back pocket. Half brown leather gilt.

First edition. A second edition appeared under the title *Wanderungen in Griechenland im Gefolge des König Otto und der Königinn Amalia*, Halle, 1851. The map is entitled 'Übersichts Karte des Konigreichs Griechenland zu L. Ross Griechischen Konigsreisen'.

BL 10125.d.21. This edition not in GL. Not in Blackmer. Karlsruhe cites several copies.

623. ROSS, Ludwig. ***Erinnerungen und Mittheilungen aus Griechenland... Mit einem Vorwort von Otto Jahn.*** Berlin: Rudolph Gaertner, 1863.

8vo, pp. XXX [1] 1-313 [1] (pp.i=t, [1]=conts, [1]=imprint). Quarter brown morocco over marbled paper boards.

?First collected edition, published posthumously. It may be that this edition was published as a memorial to Ross. According to the introduction by Jahn, a personal friend of Ross, the first part was first published as *Erinnerungen aus Griechenland* in 1853, and Ross himself saw the work through the press. This work contains letters about social and political events in Greece during a residence from 1832 to

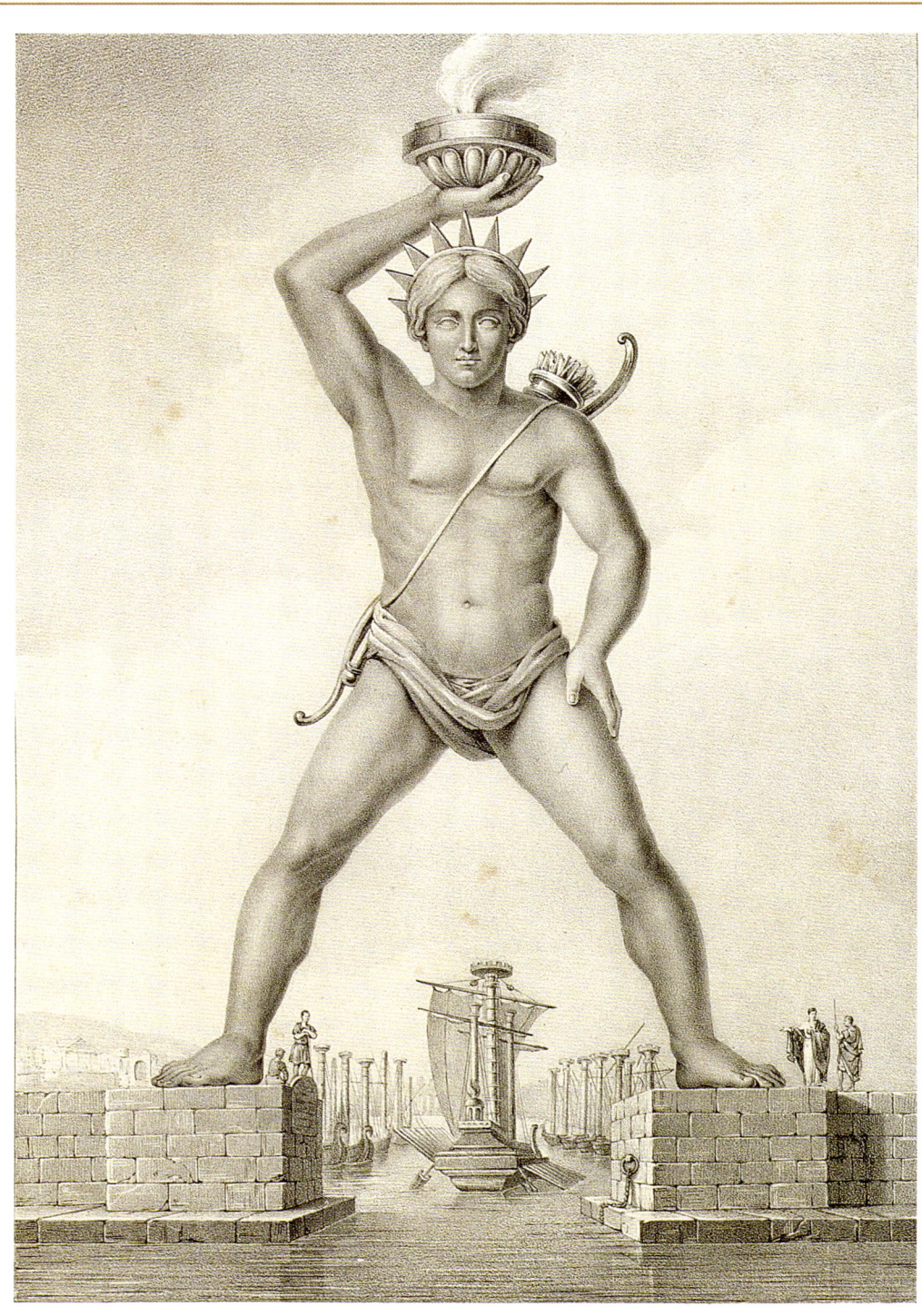
624

1836, as well as a good deal of information on archaeological remains. Ross seems to have come to Greece with the Bavarians; certainly he was close to King Otho, as demonstrated by his *Reisen*, above. He travelled extensively and carried out archaeological excavations.

BL 10126.b.15; GL GT1316. Not in Blackmer. Karlsruhe cites several copies.

624. ROTTIERS, Bernard Eugène Antoine. ***Description des monumens de Rhodes, dédiée à sa Majesté le Roi des Pays-Bas.*** Brussels: Mme. Ve A. Colinez, 1830. — ***Monumens de Rhodes [Atlas].*** Brussels: Lith. Belge. de H. Delpierre, 1828.

1 vol., 4to, and 1 vol., oblong folio, pp. [ix] 10-426 [1] (p.[i]=ht, [1]=errata); no letterpress in atlas volume. With a lithographed portrait frontispiece of Rottiers by Van Genk after a portrait by Sir Thomas Lawrence. With a lithographed title and a lithographed list of plates (1 lf.), and 62 lithographed plates out of 75 (lacking plates 2-7, 30, 34, 42, 48, 54, 56 and 72; nos. 28, 41 and 61-66 coloured; note that some plates are numbered 25a, 60b etc. This does not mean that there is an extra plate 25 or 60). Text volume with wide margins in 19th c. quarter calf gilt over marbled paper boards, original lithographed decorative paper wrapper bound in, bearing the title 'Monumenta Rhodiana'; the atlas volume in contemporary marbled paper boards, cloth backstrip.

First edition, second issue of text. The first issue was published in 1828 under the imprint of Tencé Frères. The only difference in the issues is the imprint on the title. Blackmer incorrectly states that the portrait only occurs in the 1828 issue. The Bibliothèque Nationale copy, with Colinez imprint, includes a prospectus issued by Tencé; it is possible that Colinez took over the publication in 1830. The atlas was printed at the lithographic press of H. Delpierre under the direction of Rottiers; the imprint 'Veuve Colinez' appears at the lower margin of the list of plates. Rottiers, accompanied by the artist P. J. Witdoeck, spent some time in Rhodes in 1826. He had travelled in the Levant before 1819 and set out again in 1825 to carry out an archaeological mission for the King of the Netherlands. He settled on Rhodes because it was still under Turkish rule and he could freely carry out excavatons there.

BNF 31252113 (Colinez, 1830); BL 745.b.3; Blackmer 1450; Weber 163 (first issue); Droulia 1474 (first issue); Brunet IV, 1415 - Brunet also cites Colinez, 1828.

625. ROUS, Francis, and Zachary BOGAN. *Archaeologiae Atticae libri septem Seven books of the Attick Antiquities... The sixt [sic] edition corrected and enlarged.* Oxford: William Hall for John Adams and Edward Forrest, 1667.

8vo, pp. [xii] 1-374 [10] (p.[i]=t, pp.[1-2]=commend. verse, [3-10]=index). Old half calf, black leather label.

Sixth edition, first published in 1637. The first three books are by Rous, while books 4-7 are by Zachary Bogan.

BL 590.b.12.(3.). This edition not in Blackmer but see 1453. This edition not in GL, which has 5th.

626. ROUX, Joseph. *Recueil des principaux plans, des ports, et rades de la Mer Méditerranée estraits de ma Carte en Douze Feüilles dediée à Mons.^{gr} Le Duc de Choiseul Ministre de la Guerre et de la Marine gravée avec privilege du Roy. Par son tres humble serviteur Joseph Roux Hidrographe du Roy.* Marseille: Roux, 1764.

Oblong lge 8vo, pp. [2] + [2] (pp.[1]-[2]=text on Alexandria, pp.[1-2]=table of conts). With engraved title and 170 no'd plates of harbour guides. Old quarter calf ruled gilt over paper boards, worn, black leather label.

This is the most complete issue of Roux's *Recueil*, with 170 plans. There are three issues known dated 1764, one with 65 plans, one with 121, and this with 170 plans. The other issues do not seem to have the two-page text on Alexandria. This text occurs in another copy of the 170-plate issue known to us (EJF copy), but not in the other issues and editions we have seen. It is possible that more text was published, but we cannot confirm this. Several later editions are known: Genoa, 1779 and Livorno, 1795, both with 121 plans and Genoa, 1804, with 163 plans. Roux's work was continued by Allezard who published several editions under his own name. The hydrographer Roux also produced *Directions pour l'usage de l'octant*, Marseille, n.d. and *Carte de la Mer Mediterranée en douze feuilles*, Marseille, 1764, a map of the entire Mediterranean basin printed on twelve separate sheets.

BNF 32590191 and Benaki Museum, 1764 edition (121-plate issue); GL, editions of 1779 and 1804; Harvard Library, 1764 edition (65-plate issue). The most complete collection of Roux's harbour guide is to be found in the Peabody Museum, Salem, Massachusetts.

627. ROVANI, Giuseppe. *Storia della Grecia negli ultimi trent' anni 1824-1854 in continuazione a quella di Pouqueville.* Milan: Libreria Ferrario, 1854.

8vo, pp. [iv] 1-360 (p.[i]=ht, p.1=ded/st to 'i Greci', pp.358-60=index; errata slip mounted on p.360). Lithographed frontispiece and 7 woodcut portraits (out of ?9). Old quarter green cloth over red marbled paper boards, paper label.

First edition. The Gennadius Library copy contains the frontispiece and 8 portraits but does not contain the portrait of Gouras which is present in this copy and also in the Blackmer copy. The portraits in this copy are: Gouras, Collettis, Sakturis, Karaiskakis, Capodistrias, Ibrahim pasha, Miaulis.

BL 1053.d.20; GL IND187; Blackmer 1456.

628. ROY, Just-Jean-Etienne (1794-1871?). *Illustrations de l' Histoire de la Grèce.* Paris and Limoges: Martial Ardant Frères, 1845.

12mo, pp. 312 (p.1=ht, missing). Engraved frontispiece and title. Publisher's binding of blue paper boards, gilt embossed plaquette on both sides, signed 'Martial' on the spine.

First edition. A second edition appeared in 1852.

BNF 31264507.

629. RUSSELL, William Howard. *The Prince of Wales' Tour: A Diary in India; with some account of the visits of His Royal Highness to the Courts of Greece, Egypt, Spain and Portugal. In Two Volumes. Vol. I. [... Vol. II.]* London: [W. Clowes for] Sampson Low, Marston, Searle & Rivington, 1877.

2 vols, lge 8vo, pp. xxxix, 1-292; [i] 293-617 [1] (p.i, [i]=t, [1]=colophon). With portrait frontispiece (missing), lithographed map and 30 wood-engraved plates. Numerous illustrations in text. Half leather, back gilt.

First edition. The Prince of Wales visited Greece and Egypt on his tour to India in 1875. Russell, journalist and war correspondent especially known for his reporting of the Crimean war, acted as his honorary secretary and produced this official account of the journey. This was the third time that the Prince of Wales toured the Levant. The first tour, its major purpose being a visit to Palestine, took place in 1862; during this journey he was accompanied by the photographer Francis Bedford. In 1869 he visited the East again, mainly Egypt. Several works connected with this second tour were

630

published, including Russell's account of 1869 which was more or less an official account of the journey.

BL V10440.OIOC. Not in Weber.

630. RYCAUT, Paul (1628-1700). *Histoire de l'État present de l'empire Ottoman: contenant les maximes politiques des Turcs; les principaux points de la religion Mahometane, ses sectes, ses Héresies, & ses diverses sortes de Religieux... Traduite de l'Anglois de Monsieur Ricaut... par Monsieur Briot.* Amsterdam: Abraham Wolfgank, MDCLXX. [=1670]

12mo, pp. [viii] 9-498 + [6] (pp.[i]=engr t, [iii]=t, [1-6]=conts). With 17 (of 18) double-page engraved plates. Contemporary vellum.

Third edition in French, first issue. The second issue has the date 1671 on the title. Briot's translation first appeared Paris in 1670 in both 4to and 12mo editions. The 12mo edition is referred to as 'seconde édition' on the title. Our edition is probably a Dutch piracy of the second Paris edition.

BNF 31272639; Blackmer 1464 (2nd issue); Atabey 1069; Weber 331.

631. RYCAUT, Paul. *Histoire de l'État present de l'empire Ottoman: contenant les maximes politiques des Turcs... Traduite de l'Anglois de Monsieur Ricaut... par Monsieur Briot.* Amsterdam: Abraham Wolfgank, 1686.

12mo, pp. [viii] 9-498 [6] (pp.[i]=engr. t, [iii]=t, [v-viii]=preface, pp.[1-6]=table of contents). With 18 engraved plates of Turkish characters. The engraved title page is in the letterpress. Contemporary calf, back gilt in compartments with daffodils and fleurons. 18th c. ownership inscription of J.C.de Majo on a preliminary leaf: '1730 Vienna...', and on an end leaf: '1735.Decembre a Vienne. C'est le meilleur livre, qu'en peux des mots donne l'État Del' Empire Ottoman, et est très instructif touchant cette matières. J. Chr. de Majo'.

A late edition of the small format version of Pierre Briot's translation of Rycaut's *Present State of the Ottoman Empire*, first published in English in 1666/7. Editions of this small format appeared in 1670 both at Paris and Amsterdam, the same year in which the first edition in 4to appeared. It is possible that the sheets of the 1670/71 Amsterdam edition have been used with a new title page, since the collation is the same. The Austrian-Turkish wars beginning with the Turkish siege of Vienna in 1683 may have inspired this new edition.

This edition not in COPAC or BNF on line. This edition not in GL, but see TH4R486 which is another translation of Rycaut's work by - Bespier. Blackmer 1464 (1671 edition).

632. RYCAUT, Paul. *Histoire des trois derniers Empereurs des Turcs. Depuis 1623 jusqu' à 1677. Traduite de l'Anglois du S.ʳ Ricaut. Tome Premier. Seconde édition reveuë & corrigée. [... Tome Second... Troisième... Quatrième.] Suivie la copie imprimée à Paris chez la Veuve Louis Billaine, MDCLXXXIV.* [=1684]

4 vols in 1, 12mo, pp. [i] 162; [i] 165-352; 1-224; [i] 227-412 (pp.[i], 1=ts). Contemporary vellum.

Second edition, place of publication unknown, possibly Amsterdam. This work was first published by the Widow Billaine in 1682. BNF cites another issue/edition dated 1684. The work is a translation of Rycaut's *History of the Turkish Empire*, 1680, by Jean Baptiste de Rosemond, 'le Sieur de Rozemont', who is mentioned in the privilege as the translator.

BNF 31272628. BN also cites a 1682 edition with the imprint of Claude Barbin. Not in BLC. This edition not in Atabey but see 1075 (1st ed).

633. RYCAUT, Paul. *Warhaffte und eigentliche Beschreibung dess gegenwärtigen Zustandes deren unter der Türckischen Tyrraney seuffzenden Griechisch und Armenischen Kirchen durch Herrn von Ricaut in Englischer Sprach gesetzet. Welchem beygefüget, was der Herr de la Croix von der Maronitischen Kirchen observirt; nebst einem Anhang, von der Standhafftigkeit und Marter eines griechischen Knabens, Nicolaus genant; Aus der französischen in die hoch-Teutsche Sprache überbracht. ...].* Frankfurt and Leipzig: Kroniger and Göbel [c. 1699].

Sm. folio, pp. [x] 1-116 (p.[i]=st). Contemporary vellum.

Apparently first edition in German, a translation of Rycaut's *Present State of the Greek and Armenian Churches*, 1679. This material also forms the appendix to *Der Neueröffneten Ottomanischen Pforten Fortsetzung*, Augsburg, 1700. This was a continuation to the *Die Neu-Eröffnete Ottomannische Pforte*, 1694, a translaton of Rycaut's *Present state of the Ottoman Empire*. The *Fortsetzung* includes Rycaut's *Present state of the Greek and Armenian Churches* and other material on the churches of the East. Rycaut's important work on the Orthodox church was first published in London in 1679, written at the request of Charles II. There was a good deal of interest in England at this time about the doctrines of the Orthodox church.

Not in BLC as a separate entry but see BL 149.f.5. Karlsruhe cites 7 copies. See Atabey 1072. Collation: π¹ (o)² 2(o)² A-O⁴ P² geregter massen/ in Italien der Grund und die Hauptstücke ihres Glaubens eingepflantzet werden; gestalten sich daselbsten eigentlich ihre Collegia und Bibliothecken/ wie auch die Quelle findet/ woraus sie ihre Wissenschafft und Gelehrtheit schöpffen: Dahero es dann kommet/ daß/ was die Stritt-Puncten anlanget/ die Latinisirte Griechen fast durchgehends mit denen Schulen der Röm. Gemeinde einstimmig seynd: Und ereignet sich zwischen beyden der gröste Unterscheid bloß darinnen/ das die Lateinische Missalia und Rosaria mit lauter Gebeten/ so sich zu denen Heiligen und den Englen richten/ angefüllet/ die Griechische Breviers hergegen darmit gantz gesparsam sind/ in dem man dergleichen nur von Zeiten zu Zeiten einige darinnen antrifft; unter die auch die Nachgesetzte gehören:

Extract aus den Gebeten/ so an die Heilige gerichtet seyn.

Ἅγιοι Μάρτυρες οἱ καλῶς ἀθλήσαντες πρεσβεύσατε πρὸς Κύριον ἐλεηθῆναι ψύχας ἡμῶν.

Ἀπόστολοι ἅγιοι πρεσβεύσατε τῷ ἐλεήμονι Θεῷ, ἵνα πταισμάτων ἄφεσιν παράσχη ταῖς ψυχαῖς ἡμῶν.

Heilige Martyrer/ die ihr so tapffer gekämpffet/ und auch gekrönt worden seynd/ bittet den HERRN/ daß er unsern Seelen gnädig und barmhertzig seye.

Heilige Apostel/ bittet die Göttliche Barmhertzigkeit/ daß sie unseren Seelen die Vergebung unserer Sünden wiederfahren lasse.

Die Kinder lernen sonsten auch nachfolgendes Gebet auswendig/ so ebenfalls für einen Morgen- und Abendsegen gebraucht wird:

Παναγία Δέσποινα Θεοτόκε πρέσβευε ὑπὲρ ἡμῶν ἁμαρτολῶν.

Πᾶσαι αἱ Οὐράνιαι δυνάμεις, τῶν ἁγίων Ἀγγέλων καὶ Ἀρχαγγέλων πρεσβεύσατε ὑπὲρ ἡμῶν ἁμαρτολῶν.

Ἅγιε Ἰωάννη προφῆτα καὶ πρόδρομε καὶ βαπτιστὰ τοῦ Κυρίου ἡμῶν Ἰησοῦ Χριστοῦ, πρέσβευε ὑπὲρ ἡμῶν τῶν ἁμαρτολῶν.

Ἅγιοι ἔνδοξοι Ἀπόστολοι προφῆται καὶ μάρτυρες καὶ πάντες ἅγιοι πρεσβεύσατε ὑπὲρ ἡμῶν τῶν ἁμαρτολῶν.

Ὅσιοι Θεοφόροι πατέρες ἡμῶν, ποιμένες, καὶ διδάσκαλοι τῆς οἰκουμένης, πρεσβεύσατε ὑπὲρ ἡμῶν τῶν ἁμαρτολῶν.

Ἡ ἀήττητος, καὶ ἀκατάλυτος καὶ θεία δύναμις τοῦ τιμίου, καὶ ζωοποιοῦ σταυροῦ, μὴ ἐγκαταλίπῃς ἡμᾶς τοὺς ἁμαρτολούς.

Heilige Frau und Mutter GOttes/ bitte für uns Sünder.

Alle Himmlische Herrschafften der Engel und Ertz-Engel/ bittet für uns Sünder.

Heiliger Johannes/ Prophet/ Vorlauffer und Tauffer unsers HERRN JESU Christi/ bitte für uns Sünder.

Heilige GOttes Diener/ unsere Vätter/ Priester und Lehrer der Welt/ bittet für uns Sünder.

Unüberwindliche/ unzertrennliche und Göttliche Gewalt deß würdigen und lebendigmachenden Kreutzes/ weiche nicht von uns Sündern.

Hieraus nun zeiget sich genugsam/ daß in der Griechischen gleich wie in der Römischen Kirchen die Heilige und die Engel angeruffen werden/ ꝛc.

Cap. XIX.

S

634. SAGREDO, Giovanni. *Histoire de l'Empire Ottoman, traduite de l'Italien de Sagredo. Par Monsieur Laurent. Tomes II. & III. [... IV.]* Paris: François Barois, 1724.

3 vols in 1 (of 7), 12mo, pp. [i] 157; 294; [i] 416 (pp.[i]=ts, lacking in v. 2). Contemporary speckled calf, back gilt with fleuron lozenges.

First edition in French of Sagredo's history of the Ottoman empire, translated by Jacques Laurent. The first edition of Sagredo's history was printed in Venice in 1673. Sagredo was a Venetian diplomat; his most important mission was a diplomatic visit to Oliver Cromwell. Several volumes of the 7-volume work were printed together. This copy does not have a title page in volume 3, and it is possible that some material is lacking at the end of the volume, since there is no indication that the volume is complete, as is the case with volumes 2 and 4 which bear the statement 'fin' on the final pages of text.

BNF 31277384; BL 280.c.19.

SANDWICH, *Earl of*. See MONTAGU, John

635. SAINT JOHN, James Augustus. *Egypt and Nubia, their scenery and their people. Being incidents of history and travel, from the best and most recent authorities, including J.L. Burckhardt and Lord Lindsay.* London: Chapman and Hall [1845].

8vo, pp. viii, 1-472 (p.i=ht, missing). Numerous wood-engraved vignettes in letterpress. Contemporary russia, double gilt filets on side, back panelled gilt. Ex-dono inscription to William Morris, presented to him on his leaving Eton in 1863 by Edward Joseph Hartnell.

First edition, another issue, with the title undated. The collation is the same in both issues. St. John was a very interesting and prolific miscellaneous and travel writer who lived on the Continent for many years. He travelled extensively in Egypt and Nubia, mostly on foot, in 1832 and 1833, and used the experiences gained during this period in several books, including *Egypt and Mohammed Ali*, 1834, his novel *Tales of the Ramad'han*, 1835, as well as his edition of Mary Wortley Montagu's *Letters from the Levant*, 1838, with notes and an introduction, and the *Oriental Album*, 1848 (with the plates by Prisse d'Avennes), as well as *Isis*, 1853. Previous to his Levantine travels St. John had written *Lives and exploits of the most distinguished travellers*, 1831. He also cooperated with James Silk Buckingham on his journal, *The Oriental Herald*.

BL 1424.f.3; Blackmer 1471. Not in GL.

636. SAINT-SYLVESTRE, P. de, *pseud.*, (i.e. PARENT-DESBARRES). *Chefs-d'oeuvre de l'art antique avec un texte explicatif en regard. Album.* Paris: Parent-Desbarres [1859].

Folio, pp. [iii] I-XLVI [1] (pp.[i]=ht, [1]=list of plates). With 46 engraved plates by Bouillon. Original red embossed pictorial cloth, back gilt with stars, gilt stamped title on upper cover.

First and only edition of this collection of engravings of antique statuary. The date 1859 is attributed by the Bibliothèque Nationale. Apparently Parent-Desbarres used the nom-de-plume 'Saint-Sylvestre' for works written by himself which he also published. These include several historical works: *Abrégé d'histoire d'Espagne*, 1839, *Abrégé d'histoire de Pologne*, 1842, etc.

BNF 31285395. Not in BLC on line. Not in GL.

637. [SALABERRY, Charles Marie d'Irumberry, *Count*]. *Voyage à Constantinople, en Italie, et aux Iles de l'Archipel par l'Allemagne et la Hongrie.* Paris: Crapelet for Maradan, 7. [=1799]

8vo, pp. [iii] 1-331 + [1] (pp.[i]=ht, [1]=conts). Uncut in the original pink paper wrappers, upper wrapper defective, original printed paper label.

First edition, first issue. The first issue has no errata, and the contents are on p. [1]. In the second issue the contents are on p. 332 and the errata are on p. [1]. Salaberry, political pamphleteer and French deputy, travelled in the Levant from 1790-91; he developed into a firm Turcophile. He later produced *Histoire de l'Empire Ottoman*, 1813 (2nd ed. 1817) and *Essais sur la Valachie et la Moldavie, theatre de l'insurrection dite Ypsilanti*, 1821.

BNF 31286246; Blackmer 863; Weber 625.

638. SANDYS, George (1578-1644). *Relation of a Iourney begun An: Dom: 1610. Foure Bookes. Containing a description of the Turkish Empire, of Aegypt, of the Holy Land, of the Remote parts of Italy, and Ilands adioyning.* London: for W. Barrett, 1615.

Sm. folio, pp. [iv] 1-309 (pp.[i]=engr t, [iv]=ded). Engraved title and numerous engravings in the letterpress. Without the double-page map or the plate of the seraglio. Old panelled calf, central blindstamped ornament on upper cover. Contemporary ownership signature of Edward Frauncys on dedication dated March 1616, long note on lower end leaf in a contemporary hand signed Thorlock Honour, 18th c. ownership signature of Sir William Goring on engraved title, 20th c. bookplate of Robert Edward Way.

First edition, first issue, without the errata. There are two issues of this edition, one with and one without errata. The Gennadius Library has a copy of the 1615 edition with errata on the verso of 2D5, i.e. on the verso of p. 309; the pagination in the second issue is [iv] 1-309 [1]. These errata also occur in the second edition, 1621, also on the verso of p. 309. The second edition seems to be made up of first edition sheets with a new title. This was the most elaborately illustrated English book on the Levant of its time, and Sandys, who travelled in the east from 1610 to 1611, was regarded as a special authority throughout the seventeenth century. Numerous editions were published, up to a seventh in 1673. The work was translated into German in 1669 and into Dutch in 1653.

BL 679.h.16; GL GT504. See Blackmer 1484 for the 2nd ed. This edition not in Weber or Atabey.
Collation: A^2 B-$2C^5$ $2B^5$.

639. SANDYS, John Edwin. *An Easter Vacation in Greece*. London: MacMillan and Co., 1887.

Sm. 8vo, pp. xvi, 1-175 [1] (p.i=ht, [1]=colophon). With a folding map, coloured in outline, and a folding plan of Olympia. Original green cloth gilt.

First edition. This account of a tour made in 1886 by the author of *A History of Classical Scholarship*, with an interesting appendix of books on Greek travel and topography, is probably the lightest work among Sandys' many studies of classical literature and philosophy. In addition to his editions of Aristotle, Isocrates, Demosthenes, and Euripides, Sandys produced his useful *Companion to Latin Studies*, and his *Dictionary of Classical Antiquities*. He also took an interest in modern Greece and wrote an article for the *Cambridge Review* for October, 1913, entitled 'The University of Athens and the Balkan Wars'.

BL 10126.aaa.24; GL GT1389; Blackmer 1485.

640. SATHAS, Constantinos N. *Μνημεία Ἑλληνικῆς Ἱστορίας. Documents inédits relatifs à l'Histoire de la Grèce au Moyen Âge. Première Série Documents tirés des Archives de Venise (1400-1500) Tome I*. [Venice: by M. Visentini for] Paris: Maisonneuve; London: B. Quaritch; Athens: A. Coromilas; Leipzig and Vienna: F.A. Brockhaus MDCCCLXXX. [=1880]

Sm. folio, pp. XXXIX, 1-344 (p.I=t). Title in red and black. With a coloured lithographed folding map of the Morea. Quarter brown roan over marbled paper boards.

First and only edition. Volume I only of the eventual nine volumes which make up the series, published between 1880 and 1890. Sathas, historian and byzantinist, was a prolific editor of documents and source material on the medieval history of Greece. He published an earlier collection of documents entitled Μεσαιωνικὴ Βιβλιοθήκη in 7 volumes, Venice, 1872-74.

BNF 33489721; BL 9135.f.6.

641. SAVARY, Claude Etienne. *Lettres sur la Grèce, faisant suite de celles sur l'Égypte.* Paris: Onfroi, M.DCC.LXXXVIII. [=1788]

8vo, pp. [iii] 1-632 (recte 362) + [1] (pp.[i]=ht, [ii]=advert, p.'632'=errata, [1]=privilege). With a folding map, and an engraved plate of the Labyrinth. Contemporary green paper boards, red vellum label.

First edition, first issue. Another issue appeared in 1788, mostly a page-for-page reprint, but with the errata corrected and with the map re-engraved. Two English translations also appeared the same year. A 'nouvelle' edition appeared in 1798 (q.v.). Savary produced his *Lettres sur l'Egypte* in 1785-86, and this work is seen as a continuation of the earlier. Savary spent about three years in Egypt; in September 1779 he left Alexandria for a sojourn in Asia Minor and the islands of the Aegean, returning to France in 1780. He spent a considerable period of time in Crete and also visited some of the islands of the Dodecanese (Simi, Kastelorizo, Cos, Cassos), as well as Kimolos and other islands of the Cyclades. His information on Rhodes was supplied by the French consul Pontier. The map depicts Crete and the southern Aegean. Savary's letters describe actual conditions in the Greek islands rather than dealing with archaeological and antiquarian subjects. In 1783 Savary produced a translation of the Koran; he also wrote an Arabic grammar and a life of Mohammed. According to Carré he was the first Frenchman to cite Arab texts.

BNF 31305396; Blackmer 1493; Malakis pp. 41-42; Spencer p. 219. This edition not in Weber but see GL GT6743B. This edition not in Atabey. Carre I, pp. 80-90.

642. SAVARY, Claude Etienne. *Lettres sur la Grèce, faisant suite de celles sur l'Égypte.* Paris: Onfroi, M.DCC.LXXXVIII. [=1788]

8vo, pp. [iii] 1-362 + [2] (pp.[i]=ht, [ii]=advert, [1-2]=privilege). With a folding map, and an engraved plate of the Labyrinth. Quarter calf, back gilt, red leather labels.

First edition, second issue, sometimes referred to as a second edition. In this issue the errata have been corrected, including the error in pagination on p. 362, and the map has been re-engraved.

643. SAVARY, Claude Etienne. *Lettres sur la Grèce, pour servir de suite à celles sur l'Égypte. Nouvelle Édition. Ornée de cartes géographiques.* Paris: Bleuet jeune, An VII. (1798.).

8vo, pp.[iii] 1-382 (p.[i]=ht). Engraved map and folding plate of the labyrinth. Old quarter calf gilt over marbled paper boards, red edges.

Third edition; Bleuet jeune also produced a reprint of Savary's *Lettres sur l'Egypte* the same year.

BNF 31305398; Weber 584; Atabey 1092. This edition not in Blackmer but see 1493 (1st edition).
Collation: π² A-Z⁸ 2A⁷

644. SAVARY, Claude Etienne. *Voyages en Grèce. Édition revue et corrigée par René d'Isle.* Paris and Limoges: Martial Ardant Frères, 1853.

Sm. 8vo, pp. 1-211 (p.1= ?ht, missing, p.3=t). With a wood-engraved frontispiece of Alexandria and a woodcut title page. Quarter calf over brown marbled paper boards, back ruled gilt.

A late edition of Savary's *Lettres sur la Grèce*, but the first to appear under this title, which was issued again in 1881 and 1883 by Ardant. The work focuses on actual conditions in the places Savary visited, rather than on antiquities and historical anecdote. The woodcut title reads 'Voyages dans les Iles de la Grèce' and occasionally the work is catalogued under this title.

BNF 31305399 notes that the work was issued in pictorial wrappers: 'couv. ill. en coul.'. Not in GL or BLC.

645. SAVINIEN D'ALQUIE, François. *Les mémoires du voyage de Monsieur le Marquis de Ville au Levant, ou l'histoire curieuse du siège de Candie comprenant en trois parties tout ce qui s'est passé tant avant l'arrivée & sous le commandement de ce General que sous celuy de Mr. le Marquis de S. André Montbrun ... Le tout tiré des Mémoires de J.B. Rostagne... par François Savinien d'Alquié.* Amsterdam: Henry & Theodore Boom, MDCLXXI. [=1671]

Vol. 1 only (of 2), 12mo, pp. [xii] 1-60, 1-153 [recte 453] (p.[i]=engr t, [iii]=t). Engraved title in letterpress. Contemporary vellum boards.

Part one only of the first complete edition in French, translated by Savinien de Alquié from Rostagno's *Viaggi di Ghiron Francesco Villa in Dalmatia e Levante*, Torino,

1668. The second volume, containing parts 2 and 3, was published in 1670. Part 3 is a continuation of the history of the siege of Candia which prefaces part one. These two sections were reprinted and issued separately under the title *Histoire curieuse du Siège de Candie* by Boom in 1671, but they do not form a separate volume as part of the larger work. Savinien's work is not to be confused with that by Joseph Du Cros, who produced an abridged account of Rostagno's work, mainly on the siege of Candia, *Le Histoire des voyages de Monsieur le Marquis Ville en Levant, et du siège de Candie*, Lyon and Paris, 1669. Villa died of his wounds in Crete. The original work by Rostagno is relatively rare.

BNF 36379754; BL 150.a.32; Weber 347; Atabey 17.

646. SAYER, Robert. *Ruins of Athens, with Remains and other valuable Antiquities in Greece.* London: Robert Sayer, 1759.

Tall folio, pp. ii, 1-31 [1] (p.i=t, [1]=list of plates). With an engraved frontispiece, no'd 'pl. 1', and with 26 plates no'd 1-26, of which the views are coloured by a modern hand. In late 18th c. red straight-grained morocco, sides framed in gilt with gilt ornaments in corners, back gilt in compartments, green leather label, gilt edges. With the 19th c. bookplate of Marie Elizabeth Hope-Vere.

First edition of Sayer's adaptation of Le Roy's *Ruines des plus beaux monumens de la Grèce*, Paris, 1758. The text is Sayer's own; he has adapted Le Roy's text to such an extent that it has little in common with the French original, and he has re-engraved the plates. Sayer's plates were reprinted in the 19th century: engravings are known with the watermark 'Pine and Thomas' dated 1814. At least one of the watermarks in the 1759 edition is a fleur-de-lys within a shield. A reprint was published in 1969. The first edition is surprisingly uncommon in the market, despite the fact that Copac cites five copies.

GL Spentsas p. 125. This edition not in BLC. There a copy in the library of the Royal Institute of British Architects (RIBA). Not in Brunet.
Collation: π^2 B-R^1.

647. SCHARLING, Henrik. *Graekenland. En Reisebeskrivelse.* Copenhagen: P. S. Wibes for Gyldendalske Boghandel (F. Hegel), 1866.

8vo, pp. [iii] 1-291 (p.[i]=t). With a lithgraphed frontispiece of Athens and a folding plan of the Acropolis. Wood-engraved vignettes in the text. Three-quarter brown cloth.

First and apparently only edition. Scandinavian accounts of travels in Greece are uncommon.

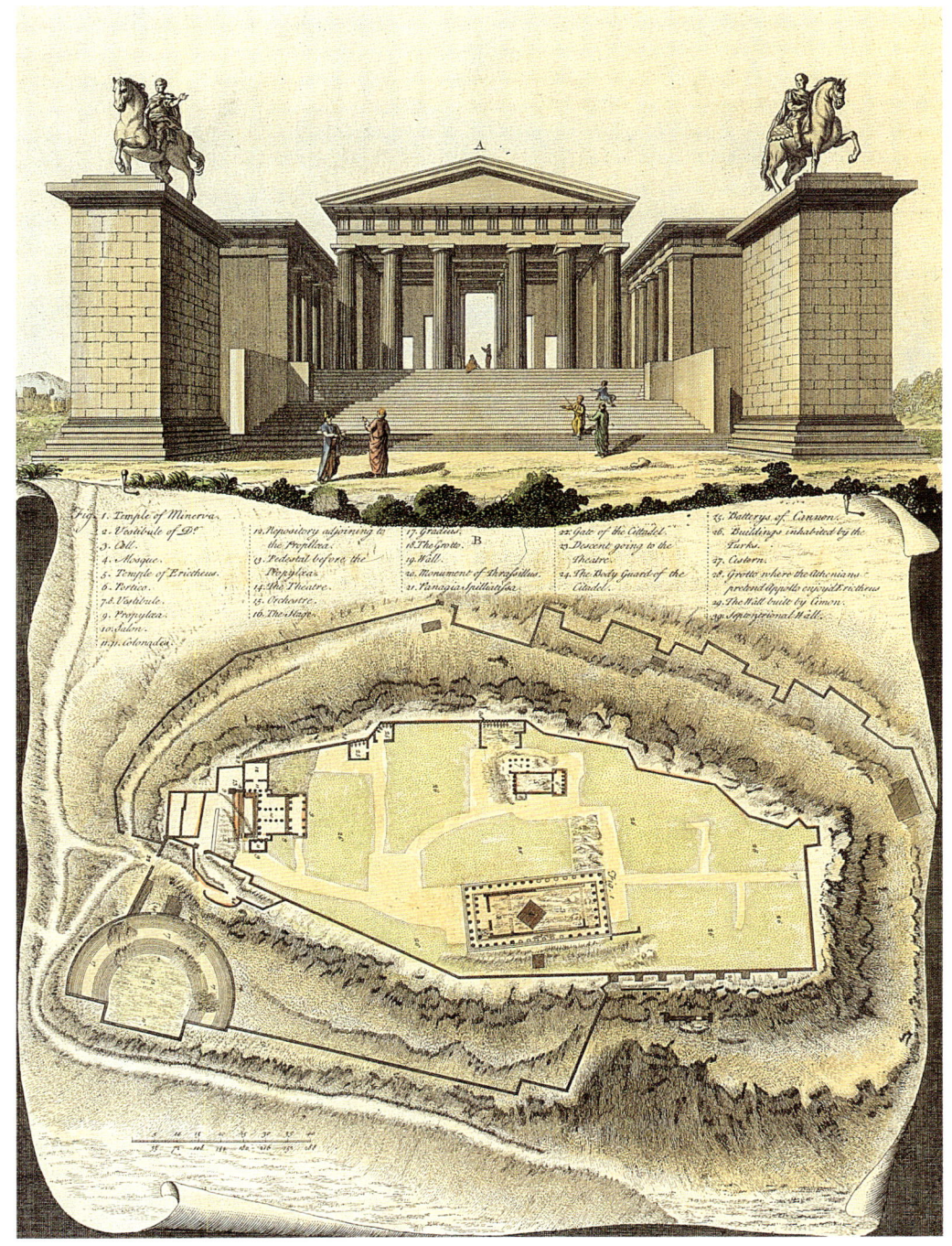

646

BL 10126.bb.30. Not in Weber or Blackmer. Karlsruhe cites two copies in Sweden and four in Norway.

648. [SCHAUB, Charles.] *Excursion en Morée en 1840.* Geneva: Ch. Gruaz, 1859.

8vo, pp. 1-49 (p.1=t). Quarter red roan, lower beige printed paper wrapper preserved. From the library of K.Th. Dimaras, with his book stamp.

First and only edition, uncommon. During this same visit to Greece Schaub also visited Delphi. He produced an account of that excursion for the *Bibliothèque Universelle de Genève*, 1841, as *Les Thermopyles et Delphes en 1840* which was also produced in offprint form. He also published *Poèmes grecs modernes traduits par C. Schaub*, and a small pamphlet, *Comment l'esprit rude de la langue grecque est il représenté en Latin*, Geneva, 1875.

BL 10126.bb.25; GL GT1324.3. Not in BNF on line. Not in Blackmer. Karlsruhe cites 1 copy.

649. SCHAUB, Charles. *Excursion en Grèce au printemps de 1862.* Geneva: Joel Cherbuliez, 1863.

8vo, pp. [iii] 1-266 [1] (p.[i]=ht). Uncut and unopened in recent brown morocco, central gilt bookstamp, original green printed paper wrappers bound in, by Ch. Leggas, with his blindstamp.

First and apparently only edition.

BL 10125.c.10; Weber 640. Not in BNF on line. Not in Blackmer.

There is another copy in the Contominas collection, in quarter red roan, bound with *Excursion en Morée*.

650. SCHEDA, Josef, *Ritter von. General-karte der Europaeischen Turkei und des Konigreiches Griechenland.* [?Vienna: 1869].

Engraved map folding to 8vo, in 9 parts (out of at least 13). Sheets gauzed, in a folder, in a quarter red roan box gilt, with initials A.N. Bookseller's ticket of S.H. Weiss of Constantinople.

There is an earlier version of this map dated 1860; in 1880 Scheda published 'General-Karte der Balkan Lander'. Scheda produced many maps of central Europe and the Balkans, including maps of Bosnia and Herzegovina, the Austro-Hungarian empire, Greece and the Aegean, as well as *Hand-Atlas der neuesten Geographie*.

BL MAPS 26.d.29; GL GT272.33.

651. SCHEDEL, Hartmann (1440-1514). *Liber Cronicarum*. Nuremberg: Anton Koberg for Sebald Schreyer and Sebastian Kammermeister, 12 July 1493.

Folio, 325 leaves foliated as follows: [xx] I-CCLXVI [5] CCLXVII-CCXCIX + [1]. Folio [i]=title, folios 259-261 are blank but for the foliations, f.229 is incorrectly no'd 231, f.299v and f.[1]r form the map of northern Europe at the end, f.[1]v= colophon. Woodcut title and numerous woodcuts in the letterpress by Michael Wolgemut and Wilhelm Pleydenwurff, including views of Greek cities and provinces. In fine state in early 18th c. red morocco, sides framed in gilt with wide composite gilt tooled border of rolls and rules with fleurons and lozenges,

651

back gilt in compartments, gilt edges. With stamped cypher at foot of the 'tabula operis', the armorial bookplate of Sir Thomas Brand dated 1735 on the verso of the first leaf, the 19th c. bookplate of James Norman on front pastedown, and the ownership signature of Leonard Woodeson on a preliminary leaf.

First edition of the *Nuremberg Chronicle*, the most extensively illustrated book of the 15th century. It is the woodcuts which give it its significance. The text is mainly based on the chronicle of Jacobus Phillipus Foresti de Bergamo, the *Supplementum Chronicarum*. Complete copies of the *Chronicle* contain more that 1800 woodcuts, of which 1164 are repeats. The views of Greek towns and provinces include Athens, Corinth, Rhodes, Lacedemonia, Troy, Alexandria, Constantinople, Achaia, Macedonia, Thrace, plus two views: 'Expugnatione Constantinopolis' and 'De Turcis'. The first leaf forms the title to the Register: 'Registrum huius operis libri cronicarum cum figuris et ymagibus ab initio mundi'. The five unnumbered leaves following leaf CCLXVI are often found after the colophon; they deal with Poland. A German edition was published in December, 1493, and a second Latin edition in 1497.

BL 187.h.1; Goff S307.

652. SCHERZER, Carl von. *Smyrna. Mit Besonderer Rücksicht auf die geographischen, wirthschaftlichen und intellectuellen Verhältnisse von Vorder-Kleinasien.* Vienna: Alfred Hölder, 1873.

8vo, pp. [vii] 1-273 (pp.[i]=t, [v]=conts, [vii]=st). With folding map by Humann, lithographed in colour, a map of minerals, a folding plan of Smyrna and 2 folding plans of water levels, and 5 folding tables. Half green morocco over marbled paper boards, back ruled gilt.

First edition. A French edition appeared simultaneously. Scherzer was the Austrian consul in Smyrna. In 1872 all the Austrian consulates were asked to prepare a detailed report on the economic conditions in their areas. In response, Scherzer produced this work with the assistance of the civil engineer C. Humann and the merchant J. F. Stöckel. Other contributors include Dr. Carrer, Dr. Diamantopoulos, the Lehmann brothers, Dr. Leoni, S. Stab and W. Fürst, all members or friends of the Austrian colony in Smyrna. The folding tables record the prices of commodities, including cotton, acorns, opium and wool, for the ten year period 1863-1872. There is an appendix on Mitylene by Dr. Bargiglio, the consul there.

BL 10077.f.3; GL GT2553; Blackmer 1497 (French ed.). Not in Atabey.

653. SCHILDT, Göran. *The Sea of Icarus. Translated from the Swedish by Alan Blair.* London: Staples Press, 1959.

8vo, pp. 239 [1] (p.1=ht, [1]=last page of text). With 8 plates of photographic illustrations. Original red cloth.

First edition in English, translated from the Swedish edition of 1957, *Ikaros' Hav*.

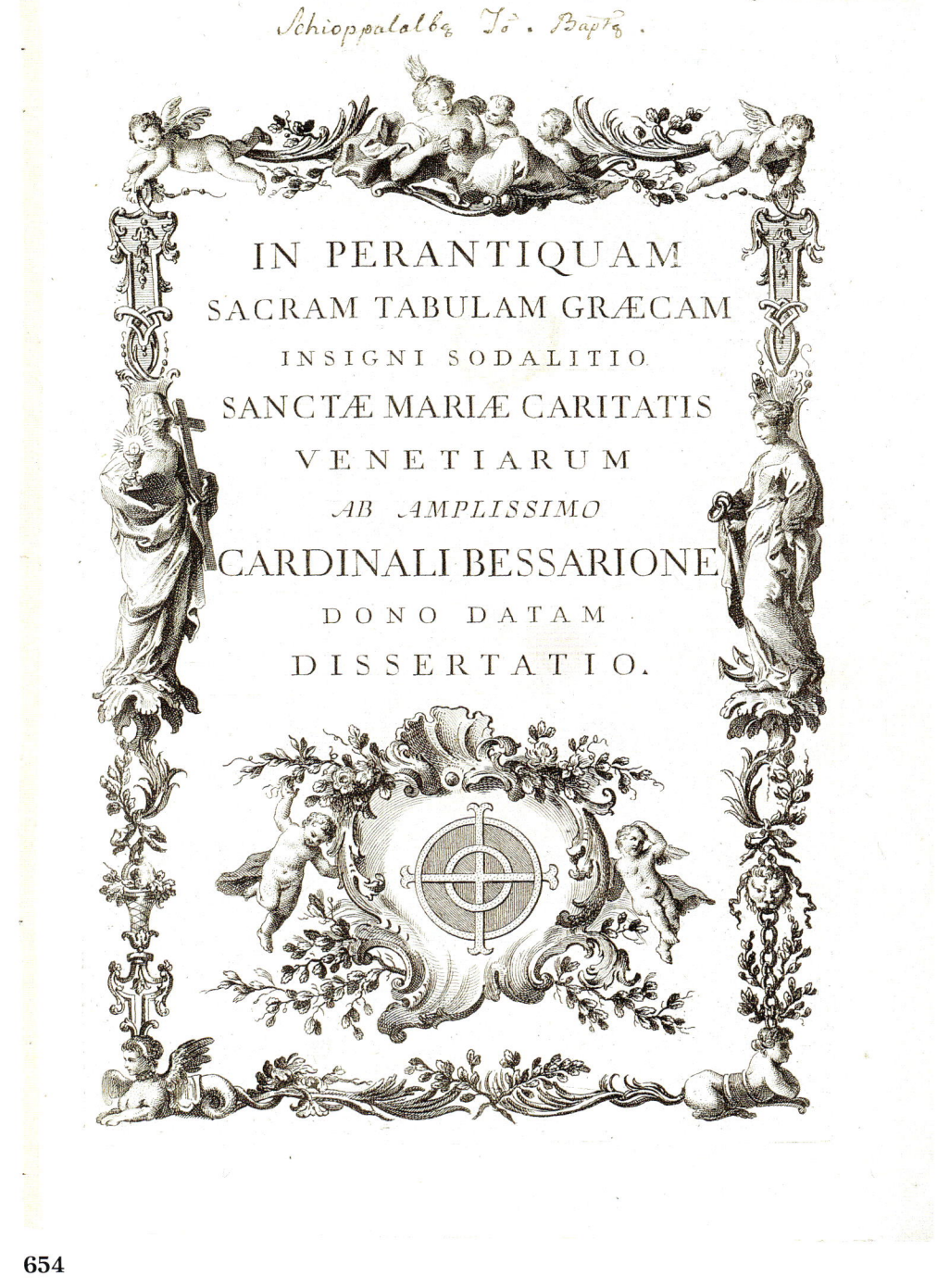

This is a description of a cruise on the yacht 'Daphne' from Venice to Beirut through the Aegean, via Istanbul and Cyprus. An English edition of Schildt's earlier account of sailing in the Mediterranean was published in c. 1953 as *In the Wake of Ulysses*.

BLC 10110.c.49; GL GT1441.17.

654. [SCHIOPPALALBA, Giovanni Battista.] *In perantiquam sacram tabulam Graecam insigni sodalitio Sanctae Mariae Caritatis Venetiarum ab amplissimo Cardinali Bessarione dono datam Dissertatio. [Colophon: Venetiis MDCCLXVII typis Modesti Fentii, superioroum permissu].* [Venice: M. Fenzo, 1767.]

Sm. folio, pp. [3]-154 (p.[3]=first leaf of text). With an engraved frontispiece and title, and four large folding plates. Half old vellum over red and white decorative paper boards.

Apparently only edition, of Schioppalalba's dissertation on a Greek icon given to the order of St. Mary of Charity in Venice by Cardinal Bessarion. A handsome work. The frontispiece depicts Bessarion holding the icon; the folding plates illustrate details of the icon, which is still in the possession of the church of Santa Maria della Carità.

BL 662.g.11; GL A1290. There is a copy in the Marcian Library but it is not listed on line.

655. SCHLIEMANN, Heinrich. *Ilios: The city and country of the Trojans: The results of researches and discoveries on the site of Troy and throughout the Troad in the years 1871-72-73-78-79. Including an autobiography of the author... With a preface, appendices, and notes.* London: John Murray, 1880.

Lge 8vo, pp. xvi, 1-800 (p.i=t, 752-800=index). With a frontispiece, a folding map of the Troad by Emile Burnouf dated 1879, 6 no'd folding plans and 32 lithographic illustrations on 16 pages no'd consecutively with the numerous illustrations in the letterpress. Original blue pictorial cloth gilt, top edge gilt. A presentation copy signed by Sophia Schliemann to (-) Kasdagles and dated 1914.

First edition. A French translation appeared in 1885. *Ilios*, Schliemann's second work on Troy, contains accounts of his researches in the years 1871-73 and 1878-79. On the latter occasion Schliemann was joined in his excavations by professional archaeologists, mainly Rudolf Virchow of Berlin and Emile Burnouf of the French School in Athens, but also including Max Müller, A. H. Sayce, J. P. Mahaffy, F. Calvert and others. Two of the folding plans are not listed in the list of plates. Schliemann's first

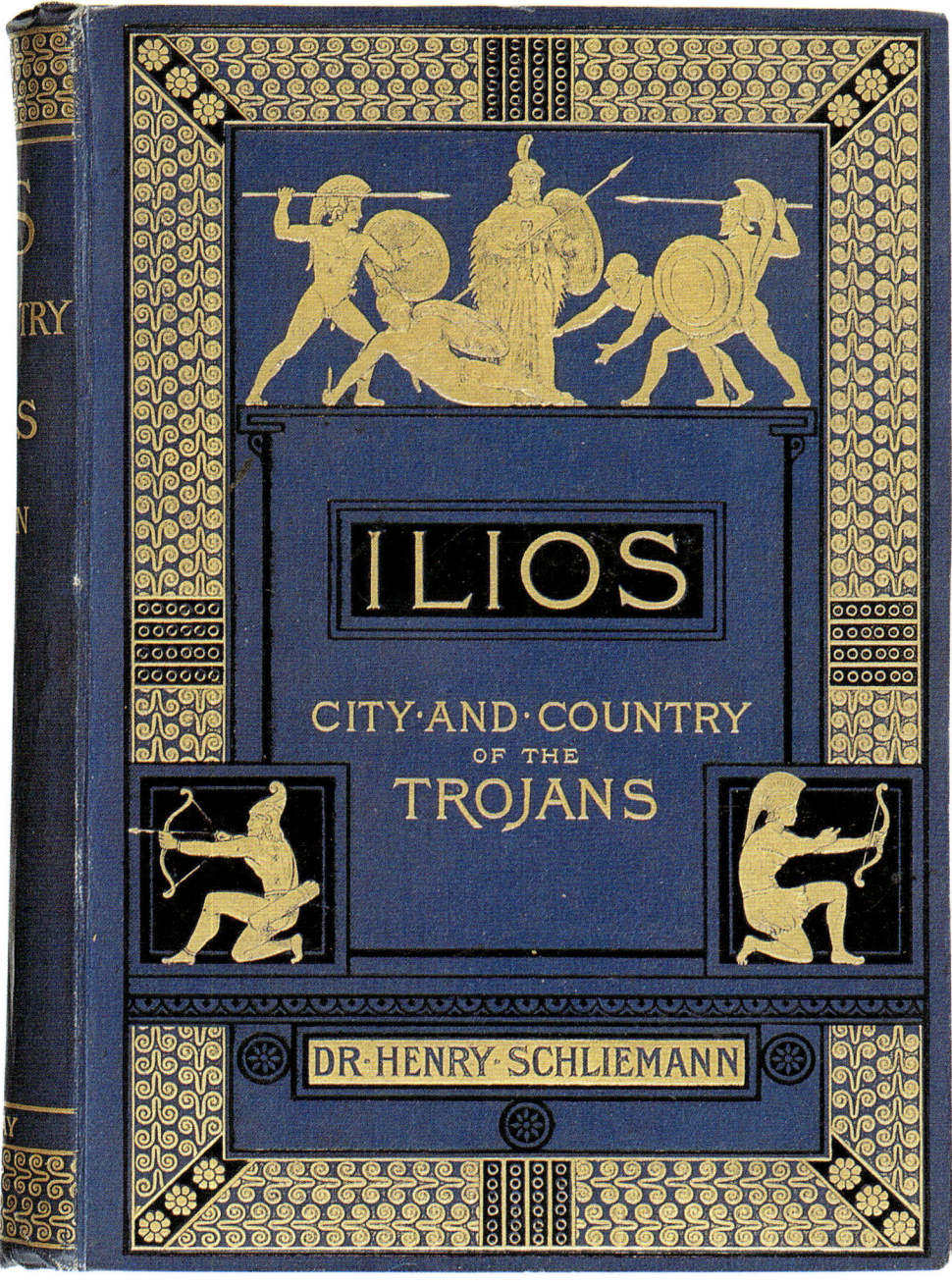

655

work on Troy was published in 1874 as *Trojanische Alterthümer*. An English edition was published in 1875 as *Troy and its Remains*. In 1884 Schliemann published *Troja, results of the latest researches*.

BL 07703.i.12. This edition not in Blackmer but see 1499 for the French edition.

656. SCHLUMBERGER, Gustave Léon (1844-1929). *Les Principautés franques du Levant d'après les plus récentes découvertes de la numismatique.* Paris: D. Bardin for Ernest Leroux, 1877.

8vo, pp. [iv] 1-123 [1] (pp.[i]=ht, [iv]=note, [1]=conts). Numismatical illustrations in the text. Quarter green roan over marbled eau-de-nil paper boards.

First edition. The first four chapters were produced originally as articles in the *Revue des Deux Mondes*. Schlumberger, archeologue and historian of Byzantium, produced many works on Byzantine art and history. His correspondence with Penelope Delta, the Greek writer of children's books, was published in 1962.

BNF 36569568; GL H155S34.

657. SCHLUMBERGER, Gustave Léon. *Les Iles des Princes Le Palais et l'Église des Blachernes La Grand Muraille de Byzance Souvenirs d'Orient.* Paris: Calmann Levy, 1884.

Sm. 8vo, pp. [iv] 1-425 + [1] (p.[i]=ht, p.[1]=table of contents). Old half cream morocco gilt, brown leather labels. Ownership initials O.I.X. stamped in gilt at foot of spine and in pencil on the title.

First edition. A second edition was published in 1925.

BNF 31318410; GL GT2464.

658. SCHLUMBERGER, Gustave Léon. *Les Iles des Princes Le Palais et l'Église des Blachernes La Grand Muraille de Byzance. Deuxième édition.* Paris: A. de Boccard, 1925.

Sm. 8vo, pp. [v] 395 [1] (p.[i]=ht, [1]=conts). 20th c. brown quarter roan gilt, with the initials J.C.P. at the foot of the spine.

Second edition.

BNF 31318411.

659. SCHLUMBERGER, Gustave Léon. *L' Epopée Byzantine à la fin du dixième Siècle. Guerres contre les Russes Les Arabes Les Allemands Les Bulgares Luttes Civiles Contre les Deux Bardas... (969-989).* Paris: Hachette, MCCCXCVI. [=1896]

Lge thick 8vo, pp.[iii] VI, 799 [1] (pp.[i]=ht, [1]=list of plates). Title in red and green. With a coloured map and ten plates. Numerous illustrations in the text. Original green cloth, top edge gilt.

First edition. This work appeared in three volumes. We have described each volume separately since the title and binding of each is different. A second edition of volume one appeared in 1925. Schlumberger, the French historian of Byzantium *par excellence*, entered into a long correspondence with Penelope Delta, writer of many Greek children's books and sister of Antonis Benakis, founder of the Benaki Museum in Athens. He was in some sort her mentor, and her first novel, Γιὰ τὴν Πατρίδα, London, 1909, set in the Byzantine period, was inspired by Schlumberger's *Epopée* and was based on an episode described by Kedrinos.

BNF 36569565.

660. SCHLUMBERGER, Gustave Léon. *L' Epopée Byzantine à la fin du dixième Siècle. Seconde Partie Basile II le tueur de Bulgares.* Paris: Hachette, M.D.CD. [=1900]

Lge thick 8vo, pp.[iii] VI, 653 + [1] (pp.[i]=ht, [1]=errata). Title in ochre, green and blue. With ten no'd plates. Numerous illustrations in the text. Original blue cloth, top edge gilt.

First edition.

BNF 36569565.

661. SCHLUMBERGER, Gustave Léon. *L' Epopée Byzantine à la fin du dixième Siècle. Troisième Partie Les Porphyrogénètes Zoe et Théodora... 1025-1057.* Paris: Hachette, M.D.CCCC.V. [=1905]

Lge thick 8vo, pp.[iii] VIII, 846 + [1] + [1] (pp.[i]=ht, [1]=list of plates, [1]=errata). Title in maroon and green. With frontispiece and ten plates. Numerous illustrations in the text. Original red cloth, top edge gilt.

First edition.

BNF 36569565.

662. SCHWEIGER-LERCHENFELD, Amand. *Griechenland in Wort und Bild. Eine Schilderung des Hellenischen Königreiches.* Leipzig: Heinrich Schmidt and Carl Günther, 1882.

Folio, pp. XIV, 1-224 (pp.I=ht, XIII-XIV=list of ills). With 59 full-page wood engravings, and numerous illustrations in the text. Contemporary half black roan gilt, gilt stamped title on upper cover, by Kaspar Egelsehr of Schweinfurt, with his embossed stamp on a preliminary leaf.

First edition. The illustrations in this work are taken from the sections on Greece in the *Tour du Monde*, the French periodical which contained many accounts of travels in different parts of Greece. Schweiger-Lerchenfeld also wrote *Zwischen Donau und Kaukasus*, 1887, and *Die Frauen des Orients*, 1904.

GL GT2019.

663. SCROFANI, Saverio (1756-1835). *Viaggio in Grecia. Vol. I. [... Vol. II.]* Palermo: [Abbate Heirs for] Gio. Battista Ferrari, 1831.

2 vols in 1, 8vo, pp. 192; [i] VII, 3-178 (p.1, [i]=ts). With two engraved frontispieces. Quarter calf over pasteboards, remains of paper marbled to resemble tree calf. Notes in a contemporary hand on both titles.

Late edition of this important work, but apparently the first to be printed in Italy, uncommon. It was first printed in 1799 at London, in Italian. A French edition appeared at Paris in 1800 in three volumes. The work was also translated into German (1801) and Swedish (1806). An abridged French version was published at Lyon in 1834 by Joachim Campe for his travel series. Scrofani, economist and historian, later became director of Agriculture and Commerce for the Venetian Republic. This important work is the result of his travels in the Ionian Islands, Morea and southern Roumeli on behalf of the Republic, in order to examine the state of commerce and to give exact information on the economic life of these areas.

Not in BLC or Karlsruhe. This edition not in Weber. This edition not in Blackmer but see 1517. The Italian Union Catalogue cites 1 copy, at Catania. There are three 20th. c. editions: Milan 1945, Rome 1965 with an introduction by Carlo Mutini, and Venice 1988.

664. SCYLAX, of *Caryander. Periplus Scylacis Caryandensis, cum tralatione, & castigationibus Isaaci Vossii. Accedit Anonymi Periplus Ponti Euxini, è Bibliotheca Claudii Salmasii, cum ejusdem Is. Vossii versione, ac notis. Amstelodami, Apud Ioh. & Cornel. Blaeu, MDCXXXIX.* [Amsterdam: Jan and Cornelis Blaeu, 1639.]

3 parts in 1, sm. 4to, pp. [viii] 1-54, [1] 1-16, [1] 1-38 [3] (p.[i]=t, [1]=st, [1]=st to Vossius's notes, pp.[1]=addendum and errata, [2-3]=refs). Greek letter. Greek and Latin text in double columns. Contemporary calf, both sides with central gilt stamped arms of Jacques de Thou. Armorial bookplate of Charles W. G. Howard, with ex-dono inscription, the gift of Sir David Dundas of Ochtertyne, dated 1877. Black leather book label of G. J. Arvanitidis, book label of Giannalisa Feltrinelli.

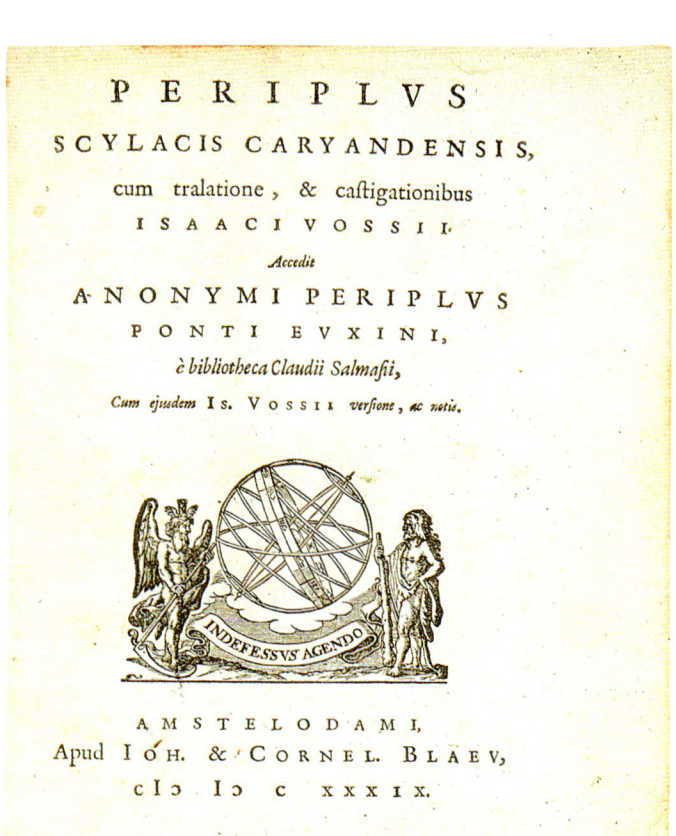

664

First separate edition, and first edition with Vossius's notes. The first edition of the text of Scylax was published in David Hoeschl's editon of the Scriptores Geographici, *Geographica Marciani...* et al., Augsburg, 1600. This material was reprinted in Gronovius's *Thesaurus Antiquitatum Graecarum* in 1697. Although this copy bears the de Thou arms, they must represent another branch of the family, perhaps one of his brothers who acted as his librarians, since de Thou himself died in 1617.

BL 569.D.31; Hoffmann III, 392. This edition not in Brunet.

665. SERGEANT, Lewis. *Greece in the nineteenth century A record of Hellenic emancipation and progress: 1821-1897.* London: T. Fisher Unwin, 1897.

8vo, pp. x, 1-400 (p.i=ht, ix-x=list of ills, 397-400=index). With a frontispiece, folding map and 23 plates. Original blue decorative cloth gilt.

First edition. A very interesting work, full of statistics and political and economic information; it also includes a chapter on modern Greek literature. Much of the material has been reprinted from Sergeant's *New Greece*, 1878. He also wrote an article on English Philhellenism which was published in the Πανελλνικὸν Ἡμερολόγιον for 1880. Sergeant was an educationist and miscellaneous writer.

BL 9136.ff.3; GL GT2083.2

666. SESTINI, Domenico (1732-1850). *Viaggio di ritorno da Bassora à Costantinopoli fatto dall' Abate Domenico Sestini.* [Yverdun:] 1788.

8vo, pp. XII, 1-196 (p.I=t). Quarter green morocco over green marbled paper boards.

First edition. This is the second part of Sestini's *Viaggio da Costantinopoli à Bassora*, 1786, describing the return journey to Constantinople, but it is the more uncommon. It may have been published privately, since none of the bibliographical references give the name of the printer or publisher. A French translation attributed to the Count de Fleury appeared in 1797/98. In later editions the two works are printed together. Sestini made this journey in company with John Sullivan, East India Company resident at Golconda. On the outward journey the travellers reached Diarbekir via Nicomedia and Tokat, and from Diarbekir they descended the Tigris and the Euphrates to Bassora via Bagdad. The return, described in this work, was from Alexandria via Cyprus and Aleppo.

BNF 31357132; BL 280.e.22, both citing a 4to format. Karlsruhe cites 2 copies in 8vo. This edition not in Weber. This edition not in Blackmer or Atabey but see Blackmer 1530, and see Atabey 1126 for the outward journey.

667. SESTINI, Domenico. *Voyage dans la Grèce Asiatique, à la péninsule de Cyzique, à Brusse et à Nicée; avec des détails sur l'histoire naturelle de ces contrées. A Londres. Et se trouve à Paris, chez Leroy... M.DCC.LXXXIX.* [Paris: Leroy, 1789.]

8vo, pp. [iii] viii, 1-252 (p.[i]=ht, pp.238-52=flora of the Asian Olympus). Old quarter green morocco over green paper boards, back ruled gilt with red leather labels.

First French edition, translated by Jean Claude Pingeron from the first edition: *Lettere odeporiche o sia viaggio... di Cizico per Brussa*, 2 vols, Livorno, 1785. Pingeron's translation of Sestini's letters into French also appeared in 1789. Sestini, tutor to the family of Count Ludolf, ambassador of the Two Sicilies in Constantinople, travelled extensively with Ludolf; the journey described in this work, from Brussa to Nicomedia, took place in 1779. Sestini is one of the most interesting of those who lived in Constantinople in the late 18th century. He was a polymath who served several important families: from 1774-1778 he acted as librarian to the Prince Biscari in Sicily; in mid-1778 he took service with Count Ludolf and remained with him until 1780, when he joined the entourage of Robert Ainslie, English ambassador to the Porte, to whom he acted as numismatist, and whose fine collection of coins he catalogued. Sestini, who was particularly interested in medals and coins, followed his own interests and wrote many important books based on his experiences in his various posts: *Lettere... dalla Sicilia e dalla Turchia*, 1779-1784, *Viaggio da Costantinopoli à Bassora*, 1786, *Viaggio di ritorna da Bassora*, 1788, *Viaggio da Costantinopoli à Bukoresti*, 1794, and *Viaggio curioso-scientifico-antiquario per la Valachia, Transilvania e Ungherio fino à Vienna*.

BNF 34003729; BL 1047.d.4; Blackmer 1529; Weber 587.

668. SESTINI, Domenico. *Viaggi e Opusculi diversi.* Berlin: Carlo Quien, MDCCCVII. [=1807]

8vo, pp. xiii [1] 1-313 (pp.i=t, [1]=conts). With 2 folding plates. Contemporary speckled paper boards, black leather label.

First edition, second issue? The Gennadius Library has an edition dated 1806, with the same pagination. There is also an edition of *Opusculi* published at Florence in 1785, but the contents may not be the same as our work. This Berlin edition may have been published as an appendix to Sestini's *Lettere e dissertazione numismatiche*, published at Berlin in nine volumes, 1789-1806. Whatever the circumstances of its publication, it is very uncommon. The work includes three accounts of Sestini's travels: a journey from Vienna to Constantinople via Rustchuk, Varna and the Black Sea, travels in various parts of Asia Minor, and a journey from Constantinople to Angora via Brussa and the Asian Olympus. There is also an essay on the cultivation of sesame.

GL GT627; Weber 592. Not in BLC or BNF on line. Not in Karlsruhe. Not in Blackmer or Atabey.

669. SHAW, Thomas (1694-1751). *Travels, or Observations, relating to several parts of Barbary and the Levant. Illustrated with Copper plates.*

The Third Edition, corrected, with some account of the Author. In two volumes. Volume I. [... II.] Edinburgh: J. Ritchie for A. Johnstone, J. Ogle, A. Black, et al., 1808.

2 vols, 8vo, pp. xxxiv, 29-462; vi (out of viii), 9-440 (pp.i=t; 2 pp. missing between pp. vi and 9 in v.2, pp. 439-440=list of pls). With 39 engraved plates. Woodcut plan in text. Old half calf over marbled paper boards, black leather label.

Third edition, first published in 1738; a second edition appeared in 1757. Shaw's work is very important for the history and topography of North Africa in the 18th century, and it had a considerable success; it was translated into German (Leipzig 1765), Dutch (Utrecht 1773) and French (The Hague, 1743 and Paris, 1830). This third edition includes the material from the *Supplement*, Shaw's reply to Pococke's criticisms of his work, which was published in 1746. Shaw was chaplain to the English factory at Algiers from 1720-1733. During this period he visited most of North Africa, Egypt, Cyprus, and Palestine. The plates, engraved by R. Scott, include botanical and zoological specimens, as well as many maps.

BL 010094.h.1.; Blackmer 1535; Weber 499. Playfair 247 (— This is one of the most valuable works ever written on North Africa). Not in Atabey.

670. SHAW, Thomas. *Voyages de Monsr Shaw, M.D. dans plusieurs provinces de la Barbarie et du Levant: Contenant des observations géographiques, physiques, philologiques et melées sur les Royaumes d'Alger et de Tunis, sur la Syrie, l'Egypte et l'Arabie Petrée. Tome Premier [... Second.]* The Hague: Jean Neaulme, M.DCC.XLIII. [=1743]

2 vols, 4to, pp. [iv] III-xliv, 1-414 (-p.1); iv, 1-192 + 172 (pp.[i], i=ts, pp. 161-172=adverts). Title in red and black. With 33 plates. Old quarter calf over paper boards.

First edition in French. This edition, which precedes the second English edition published posthumously, contains corrections and notes by Shaw sent to the translator, Etienne Bordeaux, who has signed the dedication to Frederick II of Prussia. This copy lacks the final two pages of the introduction.

BNF 30144293; Blackmer 1536; Weber 500; Brunet V, 362. Not in Atabey.

671. SIEBER, Rudolf. *Führer durch Griechenland und Albanien nebst einem kleinen Sprachführer: Deutsch-Albanisch und Deutsch-Neugriechisch. Mit 2 karten und 18 Plänen.* Dresden: Ilf-Verlag, 1931-32.

Sm. 8vo, pp. [2] 223 + 10 pp. of adverts (pp.[1-2]=adverts, 1=t). With 2 maps, 8 photographic illustrations and 18 plans/maps. Modern red leather gilt, original stiff printed paper wrappers bound in.

First edition. Apparently the section on Greece was reissued in 1954.

Not in BLC on line. Karlsruhe cites several copies.

672. SIMONELLI, Vittorio. *Candia ricordi di escursione. Illustrati con fotografie e disegni dell'autore.* Parma: L. Battei, 1897.

Sm. 4to, pp. vii, 1-180 (p.i=[ ], iii=t, 179-80=conts and list of plates). With 18 photographic illustrations and a map of Crete. Cloth.

First and only edition of this account of an excursion made in the summer of 1893. Simonelli was a natural historian and geologist and the work contains notes on the flora, fauna and geology of Crete.

BL 10126.g.25; BNF 31371177. Italian Union Catalogue cites 3 copies.

673. SIRMOND, Jacques, *editor. Idatii Episcopi Chronicon et fasti consulares. Opera & studio Iac. Sirmondi Societatis Iesu Presbyteri.* Paris: S. Cramoisy for the Officina Nivelliana, 1619.

8vo, pp. [viii] 1-64; [iv] 1-78 [2] (pp.[i]=t, pp.[1]=[ ], [2]=privilege, d. 1619). Woodcut printer's device on title. Modern vellum, red leather label. Remains of contemporary ownership signature on title.

This chronicle by Idatius, bishop of Chaves, and the one below, both edited by Jacques Sirmond, may have been published as one work; the privilege was issued for both works together, but in the catalogue of the Bibliothèque Nationale they are listed separately.

BNF 30632760; BL 580.c.12(3.). Not in GL.

674. SIRMOND, Jacques, *editor. Marcellini V.C. Comitis Illyriciani Chronicon.* Paris: S. Cramoisy for the Officina Nivelliana, 1619.

8vo, pp. [iv] 1-78 [2] (p.[i]=t, pp.[1]=[ ], [2]=privilege, d. 1619). Woodcut printer's device on title. Modern vellum, red leather label.

First edition of the chronicle of Marcellinus, which contains information on the Eastern Orthodox Church, Constantinople, Bulgaria etc.

BNF 30877276; BL 580.c.12(4.). Not in GL.

S

675. SLADE, Sir Adolphus. ***Records of Travels in Turkey, Greece, &c. And of a Cruise in the Black Sea, with the Capitan Pasha, in the years 1829, 1830, and 1831. In Two Volumes. Vol. I. [... Vol. II.] Second edition.*** London: [B. Bensley for] Saunders and Otley, 1833.

2 vols, 8vo, pp. xiv, 519; viii, 513 (pp.i=hts). Lacking the plates (2 frontispieces, map, plate and facsimile). Contemporary polished green calf, sides ruled gilt, backs gilt in compartments with red leather labels.

Second edition, first published in 1832, but first edition copies are also known with the date 1833 on the title. A third edition appeared in 1854. Slade spent over 40 years in the navy, much of this time in the Levant. He was present at the battle of Navarino, and from 1828 to 1831 he travelled extensively in Greece and Turkey. He visited Constantinople in 1829 where he became friendly with the Capitan Pasha, the head of the Turkish navy, who invited him on a cruise of the Black Sea at a time when Turkey was at war with Russia (Russo-Turkish War 1828-29). From 1834 to 1836 Slade was attached to the British Mediterranean Squadron and was employed on several missions in Greece and Constantinople. In 1849 he was seconded to the Porte for service in the Turkish fleet; Slade served under the name Mushaver Pasha, and was administrative head of the Turkish navy until 1866. As a confirmed Turcophile he was very concerned with Russian policy in the Levant.

This edition apparently not in BLC on line. Blackmer 1549; Atabey 1143. For the first edition see Weber 205 and Droulia 1997-98.

676. SLADE, Sir Adolphus. ***Turkey Greece and Malta. In two volumes. Vol. I. [... Vol. II.]*** London: Saunders and Otley, 1837.

2 vols, 8vo, pp. xvi, 1-504; vii [i], 1-538 [2] (pp.i=ts, [i]=erratum, [2]=adverts). Lacking the two aquatinted frontispieces. Three-quarter brown morocco gilt, uncut and partly unopened.

First and apparently only edition. Slade's naval career spanned over 40 years, most of it in the Levant. He was present at the battle of Navarino in 1827, and from 1828 to 1831 he travelled extensively in Greece and Turkey. His book *Records of Travels in Turkey, Greece, &c. and of a cruise in the Black Sea*, 1832, describes this period of his life.

BL 1046.k.12; Blackmer 1550; Weber 264.

677. SMYRNAKES, Gerasimos. ***Τὸ Ἅγιον Ὄρος... Μετὰ 66 καλλιτεχνικῶν εἰκόνων καὶ χρωμολιθογραφικοῦ χάρτου τοῦ Ἁγίου Ὄρους καὶ τῆς Χαλκιδικῆς.*** Athens: Anestes Konstantinides, 1903.

Thoricus. London: W. Bulmer and Co. for Longman, Hurst, Rees, Orme, and Brown, and John Murray, MDCCCXVII. [=1817]

Folio, pp. [vii] 1-59 (p.[i]=ht, [vii]=conts). With 78 engraved plates distributed and numbered as follows: 8 pls in ch. 1, 16 pls in ch. 2, 8 in ch. 3, 7 in ch. 4, 8 in ch. 5, 13 in ch. 6, 5 in ch. 7, 10 in ch. 8, and 3 in ch. 9 (pl. 3 misno'd 5). Half calf, with the red bookseller's ticket of Priestley and Weale of London. Bookplate of Francis Palmer.

First edition. A French translation appeared in 1832, see below. This work was the result of the second Ionian expediton sent by the Society of Dilettanti to the Levant in 1812-13; its members included William Gell, Francis Bedford and John Gandy. On their return from Asia Minor they stopped in Athens to examine the remains of antiquities in Attica. Although much work was done in Asia Minor, the material on Attica alone was sufficient for a complete volume and it was undertaken immediately. The list of members of the Society (p.[v]) includes many of the major travellers and writers on Greece, including Leake, Aberdeen, Morritt, John Hawkins, Frederick North, William Hamilton, Gell himself, Thomas Legh, Charlemont and so on. This volume is of particular interest since it describes and illustrates some areas of Attica which were not very well known. Rhamnus and Thoricus are on the eastern shore of the Attic peninsula, facing the island of Euboea. The engravers for this work included J. Walker and S. Porter. Note that the plates on Sunium had already been published in *Ionian Antiquities*, but were re-engraved to match the other plates in *Attica*. In additon to *Attica* and the *Ionian Antiquities*, the Society of Dilettanti published several other works, including Penrose's *Principles of Athenian Architecture*, 1851, and Bröndsted's *The Bronzes of Siris*, 1836.

BL 745.e.13; Blackmer 1569; Cust, pp. 149-164.

There is another copy in the Contominas collection, in contemporary calf panelled in blind with triple gilt filets, rebacked. This copy is printed on thinner paper than the one above.

681. SOCIETY OF DILETTANTI. ***L'Antiquités inédites de l'Attique, contenant les restes d'architecture d'Éleusis, de Rhamnus, de Sunium et de Thoricus, par la Société des Dilettanti; ouvrage traduit de l'anglais, augmenté de notes et de plusiers dessins, par J. J. Hittorff, Architecte... La gravure des planches a été exécutée par E. Olivier.*** Paris: Firmin Didot Frères, MDCCCXXXII. [=1832]

Tall folio, pp. xi [i], 1-63 + [i] +[i] (p.i=ht, p.v=ded, p.[i]=table, the last two leaves, [i]+[i]=list of members of the society and table of contents). With sixty engraved plates no'd, according to chapters, I-VIII, I-XII, I-VI, I-V, I-VI, I-XI, I-III, I-VII, I-II. In quarter reddish brown roan gilt, back gilt in compartments, bound en suite to the French edition of Stuart and Revett below, and numbered 5 on the spine.

First edition in French, translated and with notes by the architect J.J. Hittorff who travelled in Italy and Sicily from 1822 to 1824. It was Hittorff who pioneered research on the use of colour in ancient architecture. The plates have been engraved by Emile Edmond Olivier. The English edition, published in 1817, gives an account of the second Ionian mission sent to Greece by the Society of Dilettanti in 1812-13 under the leadership of Sir William Gell. This French edition of *Attica* was published by Didot some years after he had issued the French edition of Stuart and Revett; a later owner viewed it as an adjunct to the other publication and had it bound en suite, although the English editions were published entirely independently of each other.

BNF 31651283; BL Cup. 652.dd.8; Cust, pp. 149-164. Not in Harris. This edition not in Blackmer but see 1569.

682. SONNINI DE MANONCOURT, Charles Nicolas Sigisbert. *Voyage dans la Haute et Basse Égypte, fait par ordre de l'Ancien Gouvernement, et contenant des observations de tous genres... Avec une collection de 40 planches... Tome Premier. [...Second ...Troisième.]* Paris: F. Buisson, An 7. [=1799]

3 vols, 8vo, pp. [iv] (viii) 1-425 [3]; [iii] 1-417; [iii] 1-424 (pp.[i]=hts, errata on p.(viii), pp.[1-3]=adverts, pp. 409-410 and 411-412 in v.2=folding). Contemporary quarter red roan gilt over red paper boards. Bookplate of George Martakis.

First edition. English translations appeared in 1799 and 1800, and a German in 1800. Sonnini, a member of de Tott's mission to the Levant, embarked for Alexandria in 1777. He received orders from Louis XVI to explore Egypt and spent three years travelling through the country. He returned to France in 1780 via Greece and Turkey. This important work contains much information on the natural history of Egypt.

BNF 31384066; Blackmer 1572; Weber 579. This edition not in Atabey.

683. SONNINI DE MANONCOURT, Charles Nicolas Sigisbert. *Voyage dans la Haute et Basse Égypte... Collection de Planches.* Paris: F. Buisson, An VII. [=1799]

4to, pp. [i] 1-2 (p.[i]=t, pp.1-2=list of plates). With an engraved portrait and 39 engraved plates no'd 1-38 + 23b. Recent tan morocco gilt.

Only edition of the atlas to Sonnini's travels in Egypt. The plates illustrate views,

botanical and zoological specimens and antiquities, and have been engraved by Tardieu after drawings made under the supervision of the author.

BNF 36584538; Blackmer 1572; Weber 579. This edition not in Atabey.

684. SORIA, Diego. *Istoria della Grecia dal 1824 in poi per servire di continuazione a quella del Signor Pouqueville. Volume I. [... II ... III.]* Naples: Tipografia all' Insegna del Diogene, 1840-41.

3 vols, 8vo, pp. 527; 526; 349, recte 449 (p.1=ts). With 12 lithographed portraits and 2 folding maps (out of 4). Contemporary quarter black roan gilt.

First edition. The portraits depict the heroes of the Greek revolution. Soria also wrote an historical novel based on the life of Ali Pasha. He was a novelist and historian who produced several works on the history of Italy. The two maps present are the map of Greece and the plan of Ioannina and environs.

BL 1053.f.22; Blackmer 1576. Not in the Italian Union Catalogue on line.

685. [SPANDONES, -]. *Πανόραμα τοῦ Πολέμου 1912-1913.* Athens: A. Konstantinides, 1913.

Oblong folio, pp. XXVIII, pp. 1-152 [1] (pp.I=t, [1]=colophon). With numerous illustrations in the text. Original grey pictorial cloth gilt.

First edition. This album was reprinted in 1992. It is concerned with the Balkan wars of 1912-1913, when Greece gained possession of Thessaloniki.

This edition not in GL.

686. SPON, Jacob. *Voyage d'Italie, de Dalmatie, de Grèce, et du Levant, fait aux années 1675 & 1676.* The Hague: Rutgert Alberts, 1724.

2 vols, sm. 8vo, pp. [xvi], 1-367; [i] 1-405 (pp.[i]=ts). Titles in red and black. With 2 engraved titles, a portrait of Spon, and 33 plates. Contemporary speckled calf, back gilt, red leather label. 19th c. bookplate of Westport House Library.

?Third edition in French. Spon's work originally appeared in three volumes at Lyon in 1678, second edition Amsterdam, 1679. Spon travelled with the Englishman George Wheler (q.v.) whom he met in Italy in 1675; they journeyed together with Francis Vernon to Zakynthos, where the two groups separated, Spon and Wheler continuing on to Constantinople by sea. Spon's is one of the most important 17th c. travel accounts of Greece, and especially Athens. He was a careful and systematic observer, combining a

knowledgeable interest in classical antiquity with an accurate and detailed observation of men and manners in modern Greece. The whole of volume two is devoted to Greece. Before setting out on his own travels, Spon had edited and published the Père Babin's account of Athens (1672), which had been communicated to him by a fellow Lyonnaise, the Abbé Pecoil. Despite the appearance of Wheler's name, the work is Spon's own.

BNF 31395305. This edition not in BLC. This edition not in Blackmer but see 1586 (2nd ed). This edition not in Weber or Atabey.

687. SPRATT, Thomas Abel Brimage. *Travels and Researches in Crete... In Two Volumes. Vol. I. [... Vol. II.].* London: John Van Voorst, 1865.

2 vols., 8vo, pp. [i] xii [1] 387; ix + [1] 435 + [1] (p.[i]=advert, i=ts, pp.[1]=list of plates, p.[1] at end of vol.2=advert). With 14 tinted lithographed plates (of which 2=frontispieces), 2 folding coloured maps (eastern and western Crete), and 3 engraved plates (inscriptions and coins). 26 lithographed illustrations on india paper, mounted in letterpress. Advert tipped in to volume 1. Half morocco gilt. A doubtful presentation copy, inscribed on the title to volume 1 "With the author's compliments", but probably not in the author's hand.

First edition of this important work. The plate which should be at p. 263 in volume 2 is facing p. 259. The plan of Arkadia is mounted on p. 325. Spratt, author of *Travels in Lycia*, 1847, became director of the Mediterranean Survey in 1851 at which time he began the survey of Crete. The survey work was interrupted by the Crimean War and was not finished until about 1860. The survey information was printed in 1861 as *Sailing Directions for the Island of Candia*. Spratt's archaeological and topographical interests were recorded in the important *Travels in Crete*, which also contains an account of the Cretan dialect by Viscount Strangford. The plates are by J. Schranz, probably Giovanni, i.e. Jean, a member of the Maltese family of artists; it was his brother Antonio who accompanied Pashley to Crete. Joseph Schranz, another brother, and probably the best known, worked in Constantinople. Spratt's work on the inscriptions in Crete was edited in a pamphlet by C. Babington as *Greek inscriptions found in Crete*, 1865.

BL 10126.bb.17; Blackmer 1590; Weber 641.

688. STACKELBERG, Otto Magnus von. *Costumes & Usages des Peuples de la Grèce Moderne dessinés sur les lieux par le Baron O. M. De Stackelberg, lithographiés par Levilly & publiés par P. Marino, Editeur de la Collection des Costumes de l'Italie, Rue Montmorency, N.° 13. A Paris Sr. e Ml. scr. & lith. Imprimerie de Senefelder.* [Paris: Senefelder and Formentin for Marino, c. 1828.]

Paysan des environs d'Athènes
en habit de fête
dessiné par le Baron de Stackelberg

Folio, lithographed title and 30 no'd lithographed plates, hand coloured as issued by the publisher. Loose in a blue cloth wrapper, in a box of quarter blue morocco, back gilt with red leather label.

First French lithographed edition, very uncommon in its entirety. It was produced in livraisons of 5 plates each. Although undated, it must have appeared before 1831 (with the first livraison possibly as early as 1826), since it does not contain the plate of the Woman of Missolonghi which was first published in the German edition of 1831. Stackelberg's plates first appeared as engravings, published at Rome in 1825, with captions in French. These costume plates attracted a great deal of attention, and they were immediately taken up by other publishers in England, France and Italy. Thomas McLean, the London publisher of many costume albums and other illustrated works, issued a lithographed version. Cuccinielli and Bianchi of Naples also issued a lithographed version. The French edition was produced with the plates lithographed by Levilly and printed mostly at Mlle. Formentin's lithographic press. We have given the title in its entirety, because of the information contained therein. It looks like an engraving, but the imprint indicates that it is a lithograph. It was printed by Senefelder, who introduced the practical application of lithography to printing. See the article on Levilly in the *Inventaire des fonds français*. Although the article in the *Fonds Français* does not mention Senefelder, the presence of this title proves his involvement in the publication. Perhaps he printed the title, while the plates were printed at the Formentin press. We have gone into these details because without being able to see an actual copy of the work in its entirety, it has been assumed that there were two editions of Levilly's costume plates, one printed c. 1826-27, the other either printed c. 1835 by Senefelder or produced by Marino in an undated version.

BNF, Dept. des Estampes. *Inventaire des fonds français après 1800*, vol. 14, pp. 252-268. Colas 2790-91 and 3027; Adhemar 146, citing the Senefelder edition with the date 1826. On the German and Italian Stackelberg editions see Blackmer 1591 and 1592.

689. STADEMANN, Ferdinand. *Panorama von Athen. An Ort und Stelle aufgenommen und herausgegeben von Ferdinand Stademann... Deponirt... 15 April, 1840 bei dem Koniglichen bayerischen Ministerium des Innern.* Munich: J.B. Kuhn, Franz Wild'schen Buchdruckerey, for the Author, and for R. Weigel, Leipzig, and Artaria & Fontaine, Mannheim, 1841.

Oblong large folio, pp. [vi] [8] (pp.[i]=title, [iii]=dedication to King Otho, [v]=list of subscribers, [vi]=preface; pp.[1]-[8]=list and explanation of the plates). With 9 lithographed plates (of 10, no. 7 missing, supplied in photocopy) and 6 onion skin overlays (of 10, nos. 1, 4, 7-8 missing), a map of Athens and environs, and with an unnumbered plate 'Supplementblatt' on india paper, mounted. Five vignettes (of 6, no. 3 'Nympheion' missing and supplied in photo-

copy, nos. 4-6 on india paper, mounted, nos. 1 and 2 printed with letterpress). In a portfolio of three-quarter cloth over marbled paper, table of contents/advert (possibly cut from wrappers) mounted on front pastedown of portfolio.

First edition. A reprint was issued at Mainz in 1977. According to the mounted contents the text was published also in French, and copies are known which contain both texts together, e.g. Blackmer copy. We cannot confirm if copies exist with only the French text; certainly the title exists only in German. Stademann was secretary to the regency which governed Greece during King Otho's minority. The list of subscribers reflects this, and includes the names of many persons resident in Athens at that period, or connected with the Bavarian court: J. H. Hill, Mr. Bracebridge, Gustave Eichthal, Lord Erskine, Heideck, Hess, Thiersch, Klenze, Moltke, Falbe, etc. etc. The map is by J. A. Sommer, Stademann's brother-in-law, who also published *Repertoire analytique et descriptif pour la carte d'Athènes*, Munich, 1841.

BL Tab.1238.a; Blackmer 1595 with vignette no. 2 on india paper, mounted; Weber 1142. Karlsruhe cites a number of copies.

690. STAI, Niccolo. *Raccolta di antiche autorità, e di monumenti storici riguardanti l'Isola di Citera oggidì Cerigo in senso fisico, morale, e politico fatta dal Citereo nobil. Sig. Dottore Niccolò Stai.* Pisa: Tipografia Pieraccini, 1847.

8vo, pp. 1-62 (p.1=t). Half brown morocco over marbled paper boards.

Only edition, uncommon. Stai may also be the author of Διάλεξις περὶ τῆς ἀρχαίας σοφῆς Ἑλληνικῆς Γλώσσης, Athens, 1849. Stai (Greek form Στάης) was a native of Kythera, i.e. Cerigo.

GL HG116S78; Bibliographie Ionienne 1533; Papadopoulos IB 3119 cites 3 copies. Not in BLC on line. Not in Blackmer. Not in the Italian Union Catalogue on line.

691. STANHOPE, John Spencer. *Olympia; or, Topography illustrative of the Actual State of the Plain of Olympia, and of the Ruins of the City of Elis.* London: Thomas Davison for Rodwell and Martin, MDCCCXXIV. [=1824]

Folio, pp. [v] 1-63 (p.[i]=t, [v]=list of pls). With 14 engraved plates. Three engravings in letterpress. Three-quarter brown morocco over brown cloth. A presentation copy, singed on the flyleaf, 'From John Spencer Stanhope Esq to Francis Blaikie'. With the ownership inscription, 'Purchased at Mr. Blaikie's sale in 1875 by A. Sutherland'.

First edition, uncommon. A second edition appeared in 1835 with the text in 8vo and the plates in folio. Stanhope carried out his examination of Olympia under the aegis of the French Institute while still technically a prisoner of war. In 1813 he visited Greece in company with the architect Thomas Allason (refered to thus on plate 1) who produced the drawings from which the engravings have been made. They spent about two years in Greece, where Stanhope also travelled with the architect Robert Cockerell. One of the letterpress engravings is a map of Elis. The engravers include E. Finden, G. Hollis, George Cooke, W. Cooke Jr., Josiah Cross, and I. Pye.

BL 744.f.15; Blackmer 1596; Droulia 600.

There is another copy in the Contominas collection, in modern panelled calf. The engravings in this copy are on india paper, mounted, except for 3 letterpress engravings.

692. STANHOPE, Leicester Fitzgerald Charter. *Greece, in 1823 and 1824; being a series of letters, and other documents, on the Greek Revolution, written during a visit to that country... Illustrated with several curious fac similes. To which is added, the life of Mustapha Ali.* London: for Sherwood, Jones, and Co., 1824.

8vo, pp.xiii + [1] 1-368 (pp.i=t, [1]=letter from S. to the editor, Richard Ryan). With a coloured aquatinted frontispiece of Mustapha Ali by T.L. Busby after Wageman, and 6 double-page or folding facsimiles of letters. Original cloth, remains of black leather label.

First edition. Several editions appeared in 1825 with reminiscences of Lord Byron and different plates. Mustapha Ali was a Turkish child whose parents were killed during the taking of Argos.

BL 790.h.15; Droulia 551. This edition not in Blackmer but see 1598 (2nd English ed.)

There is another copy in the Contominas collection, in old half calf worn, black leather label.

693. STEPHANI, Ludolf. *Reise durch einige Gegenden des nördlichen Griechenlandes. Mit sechs Steindrucktafeln.* Leipzig: Breitkopf and Härtel, 1843.

8vo, pp. iv, 1-107 (p.i=t). With six lithographed plates, of which the first is a map and the remaining five=plates of inscriptions. Modern calf gilt, original printed paper wrappers bound in.

Apparently first edition. Stephani travelled in Greece in July, 1842. Most of the time he spent in the area around Lamia (Hypati, Stylida, Chaeronaea, Orchomenos, Skripou) but he also visited Kifissia, crossed to Chalkida from Oropos and travelled through northern Euboea, crossing back to the mainland by boat to Stylida. Stephani wrote on Greek art and archaeology.

BL 1426.f.12; Weber 352. Not in Blackmer.

694. STEPHANOPOLI, Dimo and Nicolo. *Voyage ...en Grèce, pendant les années V et VI (1797 et 1798 v. st.) D'après deux missions, dont l'une du Gouvernement français, et l'autre du général en chef Buonaparte. Rédigé par un des professeurs du Prytanée. Avec figures, plans et vues levés sur les lieux. Tome premier. [... Tome second.]* Paris: Guilleminet, An VIII. [=1800]

2 vols, pp. xvi, 1-303; [iii] 1-319 (pp.i, [i]=hts; lacks pp.3-14 in vol.1). Six engraved plates (out of 8, missing the 2 plates in vol.2). Not bound en suite: vol. 1 in quarter roan over embossed cloth, vol. 2 in new mottled calf. Notes in a contemporary hand tipped in at p. 2 in vol. 1.

First edition. Volume two is of the first issue, but volume one may be of a later issue. Note both volumes have the date of the journey in both old style and Revolutionary style on the title; note also that volume one is undated: the imprint reads 'A Paris, de l'imprimerie de Guilleminet, rue de la Harpe au ci-devant College d'Harcourt, n.º 117'. The Blackmer order of issues, i.e. that the 'Londres 1800' is first, is incorrect in view of later findings. The Stephanopoli, uncle and nephew, were descended from the Maniotes who had established a colony at Corsica. On their way to the Ionian islands in 1797 to search for medicinal plants, they were introduced to Napoleon at Milan, who apparently suggested that they contact the Maniot chieftains who had written to Napoleon for help against the Turks. Their account of their mission was edited by Antoine Serieys, who later produced *Voyage en Orient*, 1801.

BNF 34003698; Blackmer 1606; Weber 642; Bib. Ionienne 581.

695. STEPHANOPOLI, Dimo and Nicolo. *Voyage ...en Grèce, pendant les années 1797 et 1798, D'après deux missions, dont l'un du Gouvernement français, et l'autre du général en chef Buonaparte. Rédigé par un des professeurs du Prytanée. Avec figures, plans et vues levés sur les lieux. Tome premier. [... Tome second.] A Londres. 1800.* [Paris: Guilleminet, 1800.]

2 vols, 8vo, pp. [xvi] 1-303; [iii] 1-319 (pp.[i]=hts). Lacking the eight plates. Not bound en suite: volume 1 in new mottled calf, vol. 2 in contemporary tree calf, back gilt with red leather labels.

First edition, second issue. There is no publisher's name on the title, but despite the fact that Guilleminet's name is not present, his printer's device still appears on the title, and the same booksellers are mentioned on the half title versos. Note that this issue contains the date of the journey on the title in old style only; this seems to indicate that it was printed after the issue in which both types of date are included on the title. Could this issue have been produced for the English market?

BL 979.g.15. This issue not in BNF on line.

696. STEPHANOPOLI, Dimo and Nicolo. ***Voyage ...en Grèce, pendant les années 1797 et 1798, D'après deux missions, dont l'un du Gouvernement français, et l'autre du général en chef Buonaparte. Rédigé par un des professeurs du Prytanée. Avec figures, plans et vues levés sur les lieux. Tome premier. [... Tome second.] A Londres. 1800. [... Paris, A la Librairie Économique, Rue Du Hurepoix, No. 11.]*** [Paris: Guilleminet, 1800.]

2 vols, 8vo, pp. xvi 1-303; [iii] 1-319 (pp.i, [i]=hts, missing in vol.1, pp. 299-303 and 316-319=conts). With 8 engraved plates in v.1 (2=folding). Uncut in half calf gilt antique, original blue printed paper wrappers, defective, bound in.

A mixed edition. Volume 2 is undated in the imprint. Note that on the title of volume 2 the journey date is given in years of the Republic, i.e. in Roman numerals, V et VI and in arabic numerals ('1797 et 1798 v.st.') which would imply an earlier date of printing. For some reason this work appeared in several issues with variant imprints

697

and titles, presumably all in the same year. The first edition, first issue, is probably that of Paris, Guilleminet, An VIII, the issue in which the dates of the journey are also given on the title in Years of the Republic, V and VI.

The Bibliothèque Nationale cites the issue with the imprint 'Paris, Guilleminet, An VIII'. The British Library cites the issue with the imprint 'Londres, 1800'. Gennadius Library cites the 'Guilleminet, An VIII' issue. No copies with the imprint of the Librairie Économique (v. 2) have been located.

697. STEPHANOS, *Ieromonachos Kelliotes*. *Λεύκωμα τοῦ Ἁγίου Ὄρους Ἄθω ... Album du Mont-Athos par Stephâne Ieromonache Celule Apôtre Thoma à Karyes.* N.p., 1913.

Oblong lge 8vo, pp. [iii] (p.[i]=t, [iii]=approbation). With 36 leaves of photographic illustrations on thick paper. Original blue pictorial cloth.

Only edition. Stephanos brought out another album, with 52 photographs, in 1928. This could be an enlarged version of the 1913 album, or it could contain all new photographs.

Doens 698. Not in BL or BNF on line.

698. STEPHENS, John Lloyd (1805-1852). *Incidents of Travel in Egypt, Arabia Petraea, and the Holy Land.* Edinburgh: William and Robert Chambers, 1839. — *Incidents of Travel in Greece Turkey Russia and Poland.* Edinburgh: William and Robert Chambers, 1839.

2 parts in 1, lge 8vo, pp. 120; 114 (pp.1=t, p.120=note). In double columns. Quarter calf, worn, leather label.

Published a year after the first English edition of both works. Stephens' *Incidents of Travel*, the two accounts of his travels, were first published in 1837 (Egypt and the Holy Land) and 1838 (Greece and Turkey). They both achieved a great success, especially the travels in the Holy Land. Van Wyck Brooks has called Stephens 'the greatest of American travel writers'. The Chambers edition is a cheap edition in a popular format.

This edition not in BLC.

699. STEPHENS, John Lloyd. *Incidents of travel in Egypt, Arabia Petraea, and the Holy Land. With a map and engravings. Eleventh Edition. In two volumes.* New York: Harper & Brothers, 1855.

2 vols, 8vo, pp. i-v [ii] v-vii (recte ix) [13]-240; v [7]-286 (pp.i=ts, ppp.283-286=notes). With two frontispieces, a folding map, and 16 plates. Modern red leather.

A late edition of Stephens' account of his travels in Egypt and Palestine. This work, which first appeared anonymously in 1837, was very successful, with eight editions in that year. The tenth edition was published in 1839. Stephens' account of his travels in Greece, Russia, and Turkey first appeared in 1838. The two works were published in collected editions under the title *Travels in the Russian and Turkish empires*.

Loc DS48.5841860 cites an 11th edition by Harper dated 1860. Blackmer 1607 (8th edition); Weber 302 (10th edition).

700. STEUB, Ludwig. *Bilder aus Griechenland. Altes und Neues.* Leipzig: S. Herzel, 1885.

2 parts in 1, 8vo, pp. iv, 1-386 (p.i=t, pp.385-6=contents). Uncut in the original blue-grey printed paper wrappers. 20th c. bookplate of Arthur Wickelmann of Berlin, printed in colour.

First edition and first collected edition. First edition of part 2, an account of Steub's travels to Greece in 1884. Part 1, 'Bilder aus Griechenland', an account of Steub's journey from Athens to Corfu, was first published in 1841. Steub was resident in Greece from May 1834 to February 1836; he was one of the many young Bavarians who followed King Otho to Greece. On his return to Munich in 1836 he became a journalist and travel writer; many of his works concern the Tyrol.

BL 10126.c.5; Weber 332.

701. STOBART, J. C. *The Glory that was Greece A Survey of Hellenic Culture and Civilisation.* London: Sidgwick & Jackson [1918].

Lge 8vo, pp. [xxxvii] 292 (pp.[ii-iii]=adverts, [v]=ht, [vii]=t). Title in red and black. With 2 plates in photogravure and 91 photographic plates. Illustrations in text. Maps form the endpapers. Original red embossed cloth gilt.

This is a reprint of the second edition, which appeared in 1915. The first edition appeared in 1911, and the third in 1933. Stobart's work was extremely successful and was reprinted as recently as the 1960s. An abridged version was produced by Elsie Herron as *Teach yourself about the Greeks*. Stobart wrote popularizing works on ancient history which were very well received; another of his successful publications was *The Grandeur that was Rome*. The adverts on pp. [ii-iii] include press reviews.

This issue not in BLC, but see 07703.l.28 for the 1915 ed.

702. STRABO. *Strabonis de Situ Orbis Libri XVII... Tomus Primus [... Tomus Secundus.]* Amsterdam: Joannes Janssonius, 1652.

2 vols in 1, 12mo, pp. 809 + 41; 670 + [23] (p.1 in v.1=engraved t, pp.1-41=index; p.1 in v.2=printed t, pp.[1-23]=index). With a folding map. Contemporary vellum.

First Janssonius edition. The folding map is of France. It is likely that there should be more maps, but we have not been able to confirm this.

UBA UBM684F36; Hoffmann III, 458—'nette ausgabe'. This edition not in BLC.

703. STRABO. *Γεωγραφικῶν Βίβλοι ιζ. Strabonis rerum geographicarum libri XVII. Accedunt huic editioni, ad Casaubonianam III expressae, notae integrae G. Xylandri, Is. Casauboni, F. Morellii, Jac. Palmerii... Subjiciuntur Chrestomathiae Graec. & Lat.* Amsterdam: Jan Wolters, M.DCCVII. [=1707]

2 vols in 1, folio, pp. [xliv] 1-677; 679-1329 [98] (p.[i]=ht, 679=st). With engraved title. Engravings in letterpress. Contemporary Dutch vellum, sides panelled in blind enclosing central blindstamped ornament. Bookplate of J.A. van Praag.

This edition of Strabo, with the text in double columns of Greek and Latin, is edited by Theodoor Jansson van Almeloven.

BL 215.f.11; Hoffmann III, 454-55 (... 'Eine gute ausgabe, die das früher über Strabo bekannt Gewordene enthalt').

704. STRABO. *Rerum Geographicarum libri XVII. Graeca ad optimos codices manuscriptos recensuit, varietate lectionis, adnotationibusque illustravit, Xylandri versionem emendavit Ioannes Philippus Siebenkees. Tomus Primus. [... Secundus... Tertius... Quartus... Quintus.. Sextus.... Septimus.]* Leipzig: [B.G. Teubner for] Weidmann, 1796-1818.

7 vols, 8vo, pp. XLII, 470; XVI, 495; XI, 677; VI, 602; [i] 752 + 6 pp. of adverts; VI, 709 + 4 pp. of adverts; XLVI, 777 [1] (pp.I, [i]=ts in vols 1-6; p.I=[] in v.7, III=t, [1]=colophon). Quarter roan over marbled paper boards, backs ruled gilt with sunbursts. 18th c. bookplate of the Roslebischen School library.

Siebenkees's edition of Strabo was unfinished. Volume 7 forms the first volume of the notes and commentaries.

BL 793.f.2; Hoffmann III, 455.

705. STRAHLHEIM, C., *pseud.*, i.e. Johann Konrad FRIEDRICH (1798-1858). *Die Wundermappe oder sämmtliche Kunst= und Natur= Wunder des ganzen Erdballs. Treu nach der natur abgebildet und topographisch-historisch beschrieben. Sechster Band. Die Türkei.* Frankfurt: Comptoir für Literatur und Kunst, 1837.

Lge 8vo, pp. V, 1-176 (pp.I=t, V=list of plates). With an engraved frontispiece and 30 engraved plates. Quarter calf gilt over brown marbled paper boards, maroon leather label.

Second issue, apparently first published in 1833. Strahlheim, a pseudonym for J.K. Friedrich, began publishing his *Wundermappe* in 1832, with a first volume on Italy. The first issue seems to have appeared between 1832 and 1836, with the second issue appearing between 1834 and 1837. These issue points could simply reflect a new date on the title pages. The work apparently was issued in parts and was intended to be formed of two 'abtheilungs', the first on Europe and the second on Asia. For this reason the volumes on Europe are sometimes referred to as parts, and it is difficult to get a clear idea of the composition of the work. The section on Asia seems never to have appeared. So far eleven volumes in this series have been traced: Greece is described in volume nine, 1833, while the eleventh volume, which appeared in 1835-37, is on Russia, Poland and Scandinavia. The plates in *Türkei* include views of Chania, Adrianople, Ioannina, Constantinople, and the Dardanelles, among others less familiar, e.g. Berat. A true second edition seems to have appeared in 1862; Weber 1182 cites *Griechenland, treu nach der natur abgebildet... Zweite Ausgabe, 1862*.

BL 740.f.1 cites 15 vols which are not described individually. Karlsruhe cites two series, 1832-36 and 1834-37. Atabey 179. See Weber 1182 for second edition.

STRANGFORD, *Viscountess*. See BEAUFORT, Emily Anne

706. STRUTZ, George, *editor*. *Herbstschlacht in Macedonien Cernabogen 1916 Unter Benutzung der amtlichen Quellen des Reichsarchivs, persönlicher Aufzeichnungen von Mitkämpfern und einer Darstellung des Majors Liebmann, s. Z in Genst. der 11 Armee. Mit 6 Karten, 2 Textskizzen, 2 Anlagen, 15 Abbildungen. 2. Auflage.* Oldenburg and Berlin: Gerhard Stalling, 1925.

Sm. 4to, pp. 117 [3] (pp.2=series title, 3=t, [1-3]=index). With 3 plates of photographic illustrations and 6 maps on 3 sheets loose in lower inner cover. Original quarter green cloth over green paper boards gilt.

Second edition. There is also a second edition dated 1824, possibly an earlier issue. The first edition appeared in 1921, where it formed volume 3 in the series. In the second edition this volume forms volume five in the series 'Schlachten des Weltkrieges in Einzeldarstellungen bearbeitet und herausgegeben in Auftrage des Reichsarchivs'. The work is mostly concerned with the campaign in Cernaboga in 1916. The area described is south of Monastir, near Florina, and is referred to as the south-eastern front. A Bulgarian division under German command was fighting a combined force of Russians, French and Serbs. The interesting photographs depict Ochrid as well as the Bulgarian columns. There is an index of names of the mostly German officers who took part in the campaign.

BL 9086.e.1/3. Karlsruhe cites several copies.

707. STRUYS, Jan (c. 1630-1694). *Les Voyages de Jean Struys, en Moscovie, en Tartarie, en Perse, aux Indes, & en plusieurs autres païs étrangers; Accompagnés de remarques particulières sur la qualité, la religion, le gouvernement, les coutumes & la négoce des lieux qu'il a vus... A quoi l'on a ajouté comme une chose digne d'etre suë, la Rélation d'un naufrage... par Monsieur Glanius.* Amsterdam: Veuve de Jacob van Meurs, M.DC.LXXXI. [=1681]

2 parts in 1, sm. 4to, pp. [xvi] 1-360 + [14], [vi] 80 (pp.[i]=engr ts, [iii]=ts, [1-14]=index). Titles in red and black. With 18 (of 19) folding or double-page engraved plates. Contemporary calf.

First edition in French, apparently translated by Glanius. The work was first published in Dutch in 1676. Later French editions appeared at Amsterdam in 1718 and 1720. An English translation by John Morrison was published in 1684. Struys travelled extensively over a period of many years, taking employment with various foreign services to support himself. In 1656-57 he travelled in the Mediterranean and the Levant and was in the Venetian service for a while. The plates of Patmos, Tenos (?Tenedos) and Delos-Delphi refer to this section of his journeys. He set out on a second journey to the East in 1668 and apparently reached India; in Persia he was taken prisoner and wrote to the Dutch consul in Smyrna to secure his release. There are 4 plates (3 before letters) which are not included in the list of plates at p. 337. These are: Massacre at Siam, at p. 51; Pirates abducting a Persian princess, at p. 174; the author at the foot of Mt. Ararat, at p. 207; and the punishment for adulterous wives, at p. 266. This copy lacks pp. 345-352, and the plate at p. 349.

BNF 34004270; BL G.7194; UBA 180C2. This edition not in Blackmer but see 1616. This edition not in Weber but see 357-58. This edition not in Koster but see 24. Not in Atabey.

708. STUART, James, (1713-1788) and Nicholas REVETT (1720-1804). *Les Antiquités d'Athènes, mesurées et dessinées par J. Stuart and N. Revett, peintres et architectes. Ouvrage traduit de l'Anglais, par L.F.F. et publié par C.P. Landon, peintre.* Paris: Firmin Didot, 1808-1810-1812, and Bance ainé, 1822.

Four vols, folio, pp xviii, 1-75 [1]; [iv] 1-54 [1]; [iv] 1-89 [1]; x, 11-78, 2 (p.[i], i=hts, p.[iii], iii=ts, pp.[1], 1-2=contents). With 139 plates no'd 1-36 (pl. 32=dp); 1-49 (pls. 2, 43=dp); 1-54 (pls. 1, 2, 38=dp). Uncut in quarter reddish brown roan gilt, backs gilt in compartments.

First edition to be published in France, translated by Laurent François Feuillet. Apparently a French edition was published by John Nichols (London, 1793, apparently vol. 1 only). The plates are numbered consecutively in each volume, not by chapters as they are in the English edition, and they have been re-engraved to half or quarter scale.

BNF 31415770; Harris p. 449.

709. STUART, James, and Nicholas REVETT. *The Antiquities of Athens and other monuments of Greece.* London: Bell & Daldy, 1873.

Sm. 8vo, pp. [6] viii, 149 + [2] + 4 (pp.[1-6]=adverts, p.i=t, p.[2]=colophon, pp.1-4=adverts). With 71 engraved plates no'd I-LXX + XXXIIbis. Blue cloth, red leather labels.

?First Bell edition of this abridgement. Following the publication of Nolau's 1835 abridgement of Stuart and Revett for the use of architectural students, a number of English editions were produced on his plan. Copac cites editions of 1837, 1841, 1858, 1881, 1889, 1892 and 1898 which appeared under various imprints. There is probably some connection between the Bohn and Bell editions, since this edition contains Bohn adverts. Bohn brought out an edition in 1858 which states 'third' on the title; he also brought out a 'third edition, enlarged' in 1881. Bell brought out a 'third edition' in 1892, followed by a 'new' edition in 1893. The first English edition of the abridgement seems to be that of 1837, but the sequences with regard to the publishers are difficult to follow.

This edition not in BLC or COPAC.

710. STUART, James, and Nicholas REVETT. *The Antiquities of Athens and other monuments of Greece. New Edition.* London: George Bell & Sons, 1893.

Sm. 8vo, pp. viii, 1-149 + [2] + 12 pp. of adverts (p.i=t, p.[2]=colophon). With 71 no'd plates.

original green cloth. Bookplate of P.G. Overall, with his ownership signature on the title. Presentation letter to him from E. Lawrence Hall, architect, mounted on front fly-leaf.

?Fourth Bell edition. Bell brought out a 'third' edition of this abridgement, enlarged, in 1892.

This edition not in BLC or COPAC.

STUART, James, and Nicholas REVETT. See NOLAU

711. SUARÈS, André (1868-1948). ***Temples Grecs Maisons des Dieux. Illustré de quatorze eaux-fortes originales par Pierre Matossy.*** [Paris: André Dantan, 1937.]

Folio, pp.[iv] 44.(p.[i]=ht). With 14 etchings. Modern quarter morocco over brown cloth, original decorative stiff paper wrappers bound in.

First and only edition. A very attractive work. It was printed in 1000 copies of which 50 were produced on velin d'Arches, no'd 911-960, 10 on Japon imperial no'd 961-970, 30 no'd 1-30 and 910 no'd 1-910. This is copy 880. The etchings illustrate the Greek temples in Sicily. Suares' interest in Greece was longstanding. In 1915 he discussed the problem of Greece, the War, Venizelos and King Constantine in his work *Occident*.

BNF 31417465. Basch, pp. 322-23.

712. SWAN, Charles. ***Journal of a voyage up the Mediterranean; principally among the Islands of the Archipelago, and in Asia Minor: including many interesting particulars relative to the Greek Revolution, especially a journey through Maina to the camp of Ibrahim Pasha... To which is added An Essay on the Fanariotes, translated from the French of Mark Philip Zallony, a Greek. In Two Volumes. Vol. I. [... Vol. II.]*** London: [R. Gilbert] for C. and J. Rivington, 1826.

2 vols, 8vo, pp. xvi, 366; [ii] 423 [1] (pp.i, [i]=ts, p.[ii]=colophon, p.xvi=errata, p.[1]=advert). 19th c. half calf, backs ruled gilt, black leather labels.

First and only edition. Swan was chaplain aboard H.M.S. Cambrian which cruised for a year in the Mediterranean from October 1824 to September 1825. His journal contains many interesting details of events in Greece in 1825. The 'Essay' by Zallony was published in French in 1824.

BL 1049.h.25; Blackmer 1625; Weber 144; Droulia 1072-73; Atabey 1187.

ANDRÉ SUARÈS

TEMPLES GRECS MAISONS DES DIEUX

ILLUSTRÉ
DE
QUATORZE EAUX-FORTES ORIGINALES
PAR
PIERRE MATOSSY

713. TAFRALI, Oreste (1876-?). ***Thessalonique au Quatorzième Siècle. Préface de Ch. Diehl.*** Paris: Paul Geuthner, 1913.

8vo, pp. [vii] A-G, XXVI, 1-312 (pp.[i]=ht, 311-312=errata). With a folding table, and a few figures in the text. Half blue cloth over blue marbled paper boards.

First edition. This work was reprinted in 1993. Tafrali, a Romanian, also wrote *Topographie de Thessalonique*, 1913, *Thessalonique des origines au XIVe siècle*, 1919, and *Mélanges d'Archéologie et d'Epigraphie Byzantines*, 1918.

BL 9136.cc.9. Not in BNF on line.

714. TANCOIGNE, J. M. ***Voyage à Smyrne, dans l'Archipel et l'Ile de Candie, en 1811, 1812, 1813 et 1814; suivie d'une notice sur Péra et d'une description de la marche du Sultan.*** Paris: Bethune and Plon for Nepveu, 1817.

2 vols, 12mo, pp. viii, 9-176 + 4; [iv] 5-147 [1] (pp.i, [i]=hts, 175-6=conts, 1-4=adverts, [1]=conts). With two folding frontispieces. Uncut in the original printed pale blue paper wrappers, faded.

First edition. The two folding frontispieces depict the procession of the Sultan and his entourage at Bairam. The work exists in three states: uncoloured plates, with hand coloured plates, and with hand coloured plates on vellum paper. In 1807 Tancoigne was appointed attaché at the French embassy in Persia; during his sojourn there he made three trips to Constantinople. From 1812-14 he was attached to the French consulate in Crete. Tancoigne also wrote *Lettres sur la Perse et la Turquie d'Asie*, 1819, translated into English in 1820 as *Journey to Persia*.

BNF 31431685; Blackmer 1628; Weber 50; Atabey 1192.

715. TAVERNIER, Jean Baptiste (1605-1689). ***Nouvelle Relation de l'intérieur du Serrail du Grand Seigneur. Contenant plusieurs singularitez qui jusq' icy n'ont point esté mises en lumière.*** Cologne: Corneille Egmon, & ses associez. M.DC.LXXV. [=1675]

12mo, pp. 1-386 (p.1=t). Contemporary calf.

First pocket edition, probably a piracy. The first edition was published in Paris under the imprint of Gervaise Clouzier or Olivier de Varennes in quarto format the same year, together with an octavo edition. This was the first work to appear under the name of the celebrated traveller, and it achieved an immediate popularity. Later editions appeared in Amsterdam in 1678 and in Paris in 1680; the work was translated into English (1677), Italian (Milan, 1687) and German (1789). Tavernier's notes on the Serail were edited by La Chapelle, who also edited portions of the *Six Voyages*. Tavernier spent almost a year in Constantinople previous to his voyage to Persia in 1638, perhaps as early as 1631. His account, which is based on information supplied by two Europeans, an Italian and a Frenchman, who worked for the Sultan, may be one of the earliest description of the Serail, or the palace of Topkapi.

GL GT585; Weber 271. This edition not in BNF, BLC, COPAC or Karlsruhe on line. This edition not in Blackmer or Atabey.

716. TAVERNIER, Jean Baptiste. *Nova, ed esatta descrizione del Seraglio del Gran Turco con tutte le sue parti interiori, minutamente distinte, e spiegate secondo lo stato presente in cui si trova sotto l'Imperio di Mahomet IV. hoggidì regnante ... Publicata già in lingua Francese dal Sig. Tavernier, e trasportata novamente nell' Italiana dal Sig. Filippo Bagliotti Nob. Patrizio Novarese.* Milan: Ambrogio Ramellati, 1687.

12mo, pp. [xxiv] 1-330 + [16] (pp.[i]=ht, [1-16]=conts). Contemporary vellum.

Apparently first edition in Italian of Tavernier's description of the Serail, translated by Filippo Bagliotti. The first edition appeared in 1675.

GL GT587; Weber 274. Not in BLC, Atabey or Blackmer. Not in Italian Union Catalogue on line. Collation: †^{12} A-O^{12} P^6 (P6=[])

717. TAVERNIER, Jean Baptiste. *Les six voyages ... en Turquie, en Perse, et aux Indes, pendant l'espace de quarante ans, & par toutes les routes qui l'on peut tenir: accompagnez d'observations particulières sur la qualité, la religion, le gouvernement, les coutumes & le commerce de chaque païs, avec les figures, le poids, & la valeur des monnoyes qui y ont cours. Première Partie, où il n'est parlé que de la Turquie & de la Perse.* Paris: Gervaise Clouzier and Claude Barbin, M.D.C.LXXVII. [=1677]

4to, pp. 1-698 + [2] + 8 (p.1=t, pp.[1-2]=privilege, pp.1-8=account of the burning of the King of England in effigy by the Dutch in Persia). With 7 plates (of 8) of which 4 folding. Contemporary calf, back faintly gilt.

First edition, second issue, of the first part only of Tavernier's voyages, concerning his travels in Turkey and Persia. This important work appeared in two volumes in 1676/77, edited from Tavernier's notes by Samuel Chappuzeau and C.E. La Chapelle.

Copies are known with either date on the title. Some copies of the 1677 issue are titled in error 'Première partie où il est parlé des Indes et des isles voisines'; the section on India forms the second part and constitutes volume two of the work, which is complete in 3 volumes. The third volume forms the supplement published in 1679 describing Tavernier's travels to the Far East and Japan. A second 4to edition appeared in 1681. The plates include plans of Bagdad, of Erivan, of Kandahar, of the island of Ormuz, and of a Kalmuk village, a plate of Persian coins, and a plate of the Fer de Lance. The Persian Passport is missing in this copy. Tavernier began his long series of voyages to the East in the 1630s. He is an important figure in the history of travel, because he was the first French traveller to trace out trade routes to the east; he was granted a patent of nobility for his contributions to the establishment of French trade in Asia.

BNF 31437440. This edition not in Blackmer but see 1631. This edition not in Atabey or Weber.

718. TAVERNIER, Jean Baptiste. *Les six voyages... Qu'il a fait en Turquie, en Perse, et aux Indes... Première Partie, où il n'est parlé que de la Turquie & de la Perse. [... Seconde Partie, où il est parlé des Indes, & des isles voisines.] Suivant la Copie, imprimée à Paris. M.DC.LXXIX. [... M.DCC.III.]* [Brussels: Eugène Henry Fricx, 1679-1703.]

2 vols, sm. 8vo, pp. [xxxvi] 1-782 + [10]; [viii] 1-616 (p.[i] in v.1=engraved t, [xxxvi]=list of ills in v.1, [10]=conts and errata; [i] in v.2=printed t). With an engraved portrait and 7 engraved plates in v.1 and 27 plates in v.2. Volume 1 in old vellum, volume 2 in contemporary calf, panelled back gilt with lozenges, black leather label.

Pocket edition, mixed, of this important collection of Travels, ?second issue of volume one, second edition of volume two. The bibliography of Tavernier is complex, since accounts of his voyages appeared over a number of years in various formats. The two volumes of Tavernier's account of his six voyages were first published in quarto format in 1676-77, with the third 4to volume, or appendix, appearing in 1679 under the title *Receuil de plusieurs Relations*, which also included the text of the Serail. Following the appearance of the supplement the entire work was issued in small fomat without imprint in a pirated version. According to the on line catalogue of the University of Amsterdam library, it was printed by Fricx of Brussels. The Bibliothèque Nationale attributes the work to Jan van Someren of Amsterdam, with the dates 1678-79. Weber attributes the work to van Someren with the date 1678. However, the pagination of the body of the text is the same in all these variants. Volume one is of the first edition, 1678/9; volume two must be of the second edition, but we have been unable to trace this edition in any major library. The appendix, mainly on Japan, was also reprinted in pocket format. However, it does not form an integral part of the six voyages and is not included with the copies cited in BNF or in Weber, but it is described as a separate work. The copy in the Atabey collection included all three volumes, dated 1679 (Atabey 1201). The pocket edition was reissued at Rouen in 1713 and in 1724. The quarto format edition was reprinted in 1681 (Atabey 1200).

BL G.15607-8; Weber 277; Atabey 1201. Not in BNF but see 36028382 (attributed to van Someren of Amsterdam). See Weber 276 for van Someren edition dated 1678.

719. TAVERNIER, Jean Baptiste. *Les six voyages... en Turquie, en Perse, et aux Indes. Nouvelle édition. Revue, corrigée par un des amis de l'Autheur, compagnon de ses voyages, & augmentée de cartes & d'estampes curieuses. Tome I – Suite de Voyages... en Turquie, en Perse et aux Indes. [... Tome II ... III ... IV.] – Recueil de plusieurs relations et traitez singuliers & curieux... qui n'ont point été mis dans ses six premiers voyages. Tome V. – Nouvelle Relation de l'intérieur du Serrail du Grand Seigneur ... Tome VI.* Rouen: Pierre Le Boucher, 1713.

Six vols, sm. 8vo, pp. [lii] 1-501 [3]; [i] 1-465 [3]; [i] 1-402 [5]; [i] 1-367 [5]; [vi] 1-467 + [4]; [i] [8] 9-244 [4] (pp.[i]=ts, pp.[3], [3], [5], [5]=conts, pp.[3-4]=privilege and approbation. Titles in red and black. With engraved title and portrait frontispiece of Tavernier in eastern costume in vol.I, and 61 engraved plates, most folding, as follows: 10 in vol.I, 14 in vol.II, 4 in vol.III, 23 in vol.IV, and 10 in vol.V. Titles in red and black. Calf gilt antique.

Second pocket edition. This edition was printed at Rouen for P. Ribou and the privilege was issued in his name, but he allowed Jean-Baptiste Machuel père, Eustache Herault, Pierre le Boucher (as here) and J.-B. Machuel fils to share it. Thus this edition is found under all these imprints. References are occasionally found to copies dated 1712; this date appears on the engraved title in volume I. Tavernier began his long series of voyages in Turkey and Persia in 1638; subsequent voyages were made in 1643, 1651, 1657, 1663 and 1668, when he reached Japan.

NBF cites two issues, 31437446 (Paris, Ribou), and 31437447 (Rouen, Ribou). The latter, as ours, does not contain the separate section at the end of vol. I, 'Suite de l'avis du libraire au lecteur' and the corrections and notes, all with separate pagination. BL T13224 (OIOC). This edition not in Weber.

720. TAYLOR, Bayard. *Travels in Greece and Russia, with an excursion to Crete.* New York: G.P. Putnam, 1859.

Sm. 8vo, pp. vii, 1-426 (p.i=t). With a wood-engraved title and frontispiece. Original black cloth, back gilt, lettered 'Bayard Taylor's Works. Greece & Russia'.

First edition, but without the four leaves of added adverts. A second edition appeared in 1889. The greater part of the work deals with Greece. The frontispiece depicts Delphi. This edition was published as part of Bayard Taylor's works, as is clear from the lettering on the binding. An English edition also appeared in 1859; the work was translated into German in 1862 by Marie Hanson-Taylor. Taylor travelled in the Levant in 1851-2.

LoC DR14.T23. This edition not in Blackmer but see 1636 for English edition. This edition not in Weber.

721. TAYLOR, Bayard. *Travels in Greece and Russia, with an excursion to Crete.* New York: G.P. Putnam, 1859.

Sm. 8vo, pp. vii, 1-426 + 8 pp. of adverts (p.i=t). With a wood-engraved title and frontispiece. Original grey cloth.

First edition. This copy is in the same cloth binding as the copy above, but this binding is lettered 'Bayard Taylor's Travels'.

722. TCHIHATCHEFF, Peter Alexandrovitch (1808-1890). *Le Bosphore et Constantinople avec perspectives des pays limitrophes. Troisième édition.* Paris, London, Madrid: J.-B. Baillière, Baillière, Tindal and Cox, Carlos Bailly-Baillière, 1877.

Lge 8vo, pp. [iii] XII, 1-589 + [1] (p.[i]=ht, pp.I-XII=preface, [1]=list of pls). With nine engraved plates and two folding maps. Old half leather over brown marbled paper boards. Library stamp of the Nikolaevsky Academy on the title, and its bookplate on front pastedown. Bookseller's ticket of Lorentz & Keil, Constantinople.

Third edition, first published in 1864. A second edition appeared in 1866. The plates are engraved by - Sauvage and A. Guillaumot after Tchihatcheff's drawings. Tchihatcheff (modern spelling Chikhachev) spent over 17 years in Turkey and the Crimea. His great work is his description of Asia Minor which was published in five parts from 1853 to 1869 (Geography, 1853, in 1 vol and atlas; Climatology and Zoology, 1856, 1 vol; Botany, 1860, 2 vols and atlas; Geology, 1866-69, 3 vols; and Palaeontology, 1866, 1 vol and atlas). *Le Bosphore* contains material collected during his sojourn in Asia Minor, but of a more popular nature.

Not in BNF on line. Atabey 1205 (2nd ed). This edition not in GL or BLC on line, which have the first edition.

723. TEBALDI, Pio. *La Morea Compendiata... in cui si descrivono le città principali costumi, e riti di quei popoli, da quanti, & da chi fù dominata, con altre notabili curiosità. Annessovi le vittorie ultimamente ottenute dalla Sereniss. Republica di Venetia. All' illustriss. & eccell. Sig. Gio: Domenico Tiepolo, nobile Veneto.* Venice: Leonardo Pittoni, M.DC.LXXXVI. [=1686]

Sm. 8vo, pp. [viii] 9-92 + [2] (pp.[i]=t, [1]=dir to binder, [2]=license). With a folding map and ten folding plates. A fine uncut copy in contemporary marbled paper boards. Old library stamps on title of the Biblioteca Pontificia Leontina.

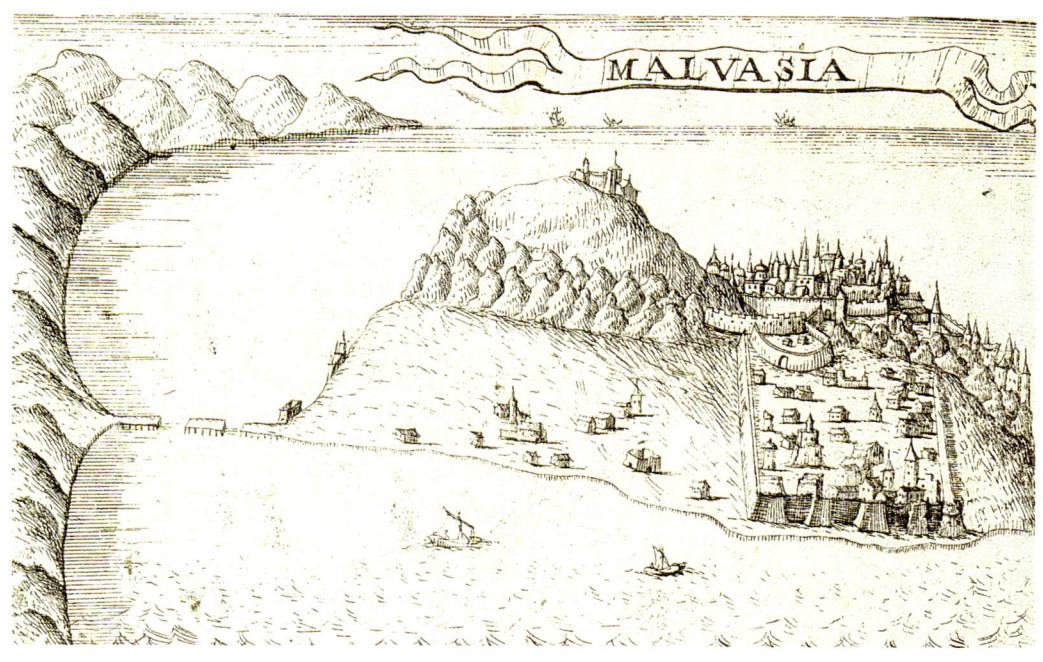

723

First and only edition, uncommon, and Tebaldi's only work, inspired by the Venetian conquests in the Morea in 1685-6. The folding map is entitled 'Arcipelago con la Morea sino à Costantinopoli'. The Coronelli-type cuts depict the principal cities of the Morea. Note that twelve plates are mentioned on the title but the directions to the binder list only ten.

GL GT2243B; Blackmer 1642; Weber 739. Not in BLC or Karlsruhe on line. The Italian Union Catalogue on line cites only the Querini Stampalia copy.

T

724. TEONGE, Henry. *The Diary of Henry Teonge, chaplain on board His Majesty's Ships Assistance, Bristol, and Royal Oak, anno 1675 to 1679. Now first published from the original Ms. with biographical and historical notes.* London: [S. & R. Bentley] for Charles Knight, 1825.

8vo, pp. xviii [i] 327 (pp.[i]=ht, [i]=st). With an engraved title and folding facsimile. Half calf gilt, red leather label. With the armorial bookplate of J.W.G. Spicer of Spye Park.

First edition, reprinted in 1927. The editor is unknown. Teonge, a naval chaplain, served with Sir John Narborough's squadron sent to the Mediterranean to subdue the Barbary pirates. Teonge made two voyages, first entering Greek waters in September, 1675. The facsimile is of a page from the original manuscript.

BL 1202.k.12; Blackmer 1644; Weber 412; Spencer, p. 128.

725. TEXIER, Charles Félix Marie. *Asie Mineure. Description géographique, historique et archéologique des provinces et des villes de la Chersonnèse d'Asie.* Paris: Firmin-Didot, 1882.

Thick 8vo, pp. [iii] 1-757 (pp.[i]=ht, 733=list of plates). In double columns. With 64 engraved plates and 5 double-page maps no'd 1-4, 6 (plate 5 on the list of plates is no'd 6 on the plate surface). Old red cloth, ownership initials S.D.M. stamped in gilt at foot of spine.

Second edition, first published in 1862 as part of the series 'L'Univers'. This is an abridged popular version of Texier's monumental work *Description de l'Asie Mineure fait par ordre du Gouvernement Français*, published from 1839 to 1849 in three large folio volumes. Texier made three journeys to the Levant between 1834 and 1836, collecting and amassing information on the art, architecture and antiquities of Asia Minor. This was probably the greatest work of exploration made by a single traveller.

Not in BNF on line. This edition not in BLC or GL. This edition not in Blackmer but see 1646 (1st ed.).

726. TEXIER, Edmond. *La Grèce et ses insurrections.* Paris: Librarie Nouvelle, 1855.

Sm. 8vo, pp. [iv] X [11]-319 + [4] (p.[i]=ht, [4]=adverts). Folding map by L. Sagansan. Modern quarter red morocco gilt, remains of original blue printed paper wrappers bound in.

First edition, second issue? The first edition/issue was printed in 1854. The pagination in both issues is the same. This is an historical overview of modern Greek history, probably produced in view of the Crimean War. The map depicts Greece and the coast of Asia Minor. Sagansan was geographer to the emperor Napoleon III. Texier also used the pseudonyms 'Kel-Kun', 'Peregrinus', and 'Sylvius'.

BNF 31448010 (1854); BL 9135.b.8 (1854). Not in Blackmer.

There is another copy in the Contominas collection, in quarter blue polished calf, back ruled gilt.

727. THACKERAY, William Makepeace. *Notes of a Journey from Cornhill to Grand Cairo, by way of Lisbon, Athens, Constantinople, and Jerusalem: performed in the steamers of the Peninsular and Oriental Company. Third edition.* London: Smith, Elder and Co., 1865.

8vo, pp. viii, 1-208 (p.i=t). Wood engravings in the letterpress. Half ochre morocco.

Third edition. The first edition appeared anonymously in 1846. This work, an account of a cruise in the Mediterranean in 1844, was printed numerous times during the 19th century in both separate and collected editions. The vignettes are after sketches by Thackeray himself.

BL 010028.p.30. This edition not in Blackmer but see 1649 (first ed).

728. THEVENOT, Jean. *Relation d'un voyage fait au Levant. Dans la quelle il est curieusement traité des Estats sujets au Grand Seigneur, des Moeurs, Religions, Forces, Gouvernemens, Politiques, Langues, & Coustumes des Habitans de ce grand Empire... A Paris, chez Louis Billaine... M.DC.LXV. Avec Privilège du Roy.* [Paris: Louis Billaine, 1665.]

4to, pp. [xviii] 1-576 (p.[i]=t, [xviii]=privilege). With an engraved portrait frontispiece of Thevenot. Contemporary calf, back gilt in compartments.

Second edition of the first part of Thevenot's voyages, the section on Greece and Turkey. This includes descriptions of the Archipelago, Constantinople, and Asia Minor. Thevenot's travels were first published between 1664 and 1684. The first part, the travels to the Levant, appeared in 1663/4. Most first edition copies are dated 1664, but a very few, the earliest printed, are dated 1663. The travels in Persia were published posthumously in 1674 and the travels in India in 1684, both volumes edited by Petis de la Croix and the Sieur de Luisandre. This second edition of part one appears to be composed of the same sheets as the first edition, with a new title. There are two Paris issues and yet another issue with the imprint 'A Rouen et se vend à Paris', which appears either under the name of Joly or of Billaine. Thomas Joly, Louis Billaine and Claude Barbin all shared in the privilege, and issues of this work appear under the im-

728

print of all three. The work was printed in Rouen, and in one issue this is indicated in the imprint; in the other only Paris is mentioned. Thevenot's travels were not continuous, and this is reflected in his work, which is complete in three separate volumes published many years apart. Thevenot set out on his travels in 1655 and returned to Paris in 1659, when he began to prepare the text of his first voyage. In 1663 he set out again and journeyed through Syria and Persia to India; he died at Tabriz in 1667.

BNF 31453983. This issue not in Weber but see 309. This edition not in Blackmer but see 1650.

729. THEVENOT, Jean. *Relation d'un voyage fait au Levant. Dans la quelle il est curieusement traité des Estats sujets au Grand Seigneur, des Moeurs, Religions, Forces, Gouvernemens, Politiques, Langues, & Coustumes des Habitans de ce grand Empire... A Paris, chez Thomas Iolly... M.DC.LXV. Avec Privilège du Roy.* [Paris: Thomas Joly, 1665.]

729

4to, pp. [xviii] 1-576 (p.[i]=t, [xviii]=privilege). Lacking the engraved portrait frontispiece. Contemporary calf, central gilt arms.

Second edition, the Paris issue with the imprint of Thomas Joly.

BNF 31453984; Weber 309. This edition not in Blackmer but see 1650. Atabey 1215, citing Rouen and Paris issue.

730. THEVENOT, Jean. *Voyages de M^r. De Thevenot en Europe, Asie & Afrique, divisez in trois parties, contenant cinq tomes. Première Partie Contenant le Voyage du Levant – Suite du Voyage... – Les voyages aux Indes Orientales. Troisième édition.* Amsterdam: Michel Charles le Céne, 1727.

5 vols, sm. 8vo, pp. [xiv] 1-378; [viii] 381-939 [38]; [xlii] 1-414; [vi] 415-709 [28]; [xii] 1-344 [22] (pp.[i]=ts in red and black). With engraved titles in volumes 1 and 3, and 50 engraved plates distributed as follows: engraved portrait and 8 plates in v. 1, 10 plates in v. 2, 14 plates in v. 3, 4 plates in v. 4, and 13 plates in v. 5. Calf antique, backs gilt in compartments.

Despite the statement on the title this appears to be the second French collected edition. The first French collected edition seems to be that published by Angot in 1689. The first collected edition seems to be an English edition of 1687. In this edition the travels to the Levant form volumes 1 and 2 (note continuous pagination and engraved title to vol. 1), the travels in Persia, 'Suite de Voyage', form volumes 3 and 4 (continuous pagination and engraved title to vol. 3), and the travels in India form volume 5. The first editions contained only a very few illustrations; the many illustrations to be found in later editions seem to have first appeared in the small collected editions printed in the late 1680s.

BNF 31453988; Weber 312 and 313; Atabey 1216, citing 48 plates and 2 engraved titles.

731. THIBAUDET, Albert. *Les Images de Grèce.* Paris: Albert Messein, 1926.

Sm. 4to, pp. XII, [13]-200 (p.I=ht). Uncut, in quarter red roan, original orange printed paper wrappers bound in. From the library of K.Th. Dimaras, with his library stamp.

First separate edition, published in the series 'Collection La Phalange'. The work was issued in 1535 copies, with numbers 1-10 on China paper and numbers 11-35 on Vergè d'Arches paper. This is one of the copies on Vergè d'Arches paper, no. 22. This account was first published in the early volumes of the *Phalange*, the avant-garde magazine published by Royère from 1906 to 1914. Thibaudet, the editor of Montaigne and Flaubert, and part of the circle of Barrès and Maurras, spent a winter and spring in Greece in about 1906. His interesting introduction concerns the 'image of Greece' as a literary vogue brought to an end by Charles Maurras with his *Anthinea* (q.v.), and he discusses the two types of French travellers who approached Greece during the 19th century. In 1913 Thibaudet wrote *Les Heurs de L'Acropole*, and in 1929 he produced *L'Acropole*, with photographs by Boissonas.

BNF 31454434. Basch discusses Thibaudet's ideas and reactions to other writers and travellers at length; of *Les Images* she says '... petit livre moins célèbre que ses *Heures de l'Acropole*, mais carnet de voyage d'un ton bien plus vif, d'une émotion bien plus précieuse...' (p. 382).

730

732. THIERSCH, Friedrich Wilhelm von. *De l'état actuel de la Grèce et des moyens d'arriver à sa restauration. En deux volumes. Premier volume. De l'état politique et de la pacification de la Grèce. [... Second Volume. Des moyens d'arriver à la restauration de la Grèce.]* Leipzig: F.A. Brockhaus, 1833.

2 vols, 8vo, pp. XXIV [1] 1-464 + [2]; XVII + [1] 1-325 + [1] (pp.I=hts, [1]=st, [2]=errata; [1]=st, [1]=errata). Old grey mottled paper boards, remains of ms. paper labels.

First edition of this important work by the German litterateur and philhellene. Thiersch went to Greece in 1831 on behalf of Ludwig of Bavaria to promote the nomination of Otho as king of Greece. He produced many works on Greek archaeology and philology, including *Über die neugriechische Poesie*, Munich, 1828. His work on Greece was replied to by the anonymous *Examen critique*, published by Brockhaus in 1835 (q.v.).

BNF 31457204; Blackmer 1652; Droulia 2021-22.

733. THORNTON, Thomas (?-1814). *The present state of Turkey; or a description of the political, civil, and religious constitution, government, and laws of the Ottoman Empire... From observations made, during a residence of fifteen years in Constantinople and the Turkish provinces.* London: for Joseph Mawman, 1807.

4to, pp. xxi [i] 436 (pp.i=t, [i]=errata). Old half calf, back ruled gilt. Armorial bookplate of Sir George Strickland.

First edition. A second edition appeared in 1809 in two volumes, octavo. The work was translated into German in 1808 and into French in 1812. Thornton was connected with the English Factory at Constantinople for fourteen years and spent over a year at Odessa. He had connections with Pola in Istria and travelled frequently in Asia Minor and the Archipelago in the course of his commercial activities. Thornton returned to England in 1805 and immediately began to work on his book. It is a valuable study of the contemporary situation in the Levant despite its markedly pro-Turkish tone. Thornton was hostile to Eton and Pouqueville, as well as Elgin. Eton immediately replied with *A Letter... in regard to Turkey, Greece, and France ... with strictures on Mr. Thornton's Present State of Turkey*, London, 1807. This copy contains a long note in a contemporary hand quoting from a review in the *Gentleman's Magazine* for April 1814.

BL V9751OIOC; Blackmer 1655; Spencer pp. 237-38; Atabey 1219.

734. THOUVENEL, Edouard Antoine. *La Grèce du Roi Othon Correspondance du M. Thouvenel avec sa famille et ses amis recueillie et publiée avec notes et index biographique par L. Thouvenel.* Paris: Calmann Lévy, 1890.

8vo, pp. [iii] V, 1-465 (pp.[i]=ht, 461-65=conts). Quarter brown roan gilt, original upper yellow-beige printed paper wrapper bound in.

First and only edition. Edouard Thouvenel was a career diplomat and later Minister of Foreign Affairs. He was French ambassador to Greece from about 1845 to 1850, and later became ambassador to Constantinople. His correspondence, which consists of letters written during his sojourn in Athens, dated from December 1845 to 1850, to Desages, Cuvillier-Fleury and the Prince de Broglie, has been edited by his son Louis, who has also added very useful biographical notes on the people discussed in the letters, e.g. Wyse, Trikoupis, Stratford Canning, Jurien de la Gravière, Phocion Roque, Prokesch-Osten, and many Greek statesmen such as Kriezis, Deliyannis, Colokotronis, Koundouriotis, and Colletis. Louis Thouvenel edited many of his father's papers and his correspondence, including *Trois années de la question d'Orient, 1856-59, d'apres les papiers inedits de M. Thouvenel*, 1897. Thouvenel himself published *L'Hongrie et la Valachie. Souvenirs de voyage et notices historiques*, Paris, 1840.

BNF 31466285; BL 8028.de.25; GL HG670T52.

735. THUCYDIDES. *The History of the Grecian War: in Eight Books. Written by Thucydides. Faithfully translated from the Original by Thomas Hobbes of Malmsbury. With maps describing the countrey. The second edition, much corrected and amended.* London: Andrew Clark for Charles Harper, MDCLXXVI. [=1676]

Folio, pp.[xlvi] 357 [1] + [10] (pp.[i]=t, [1]=advert, [1-10]=index). Title in red and black. With an engraved title and 5 engraved maps/plans. Contemporary panelled calf. Contemporary ownership signature of Thomas Pope Blount dated 6 May 1676 on title and with a long note in his hand in Latin on a preliminary leaf. Ownership inscription of the Tittenhanger Library on front pastedown.

Second edition. The first edition of Hobbes' translation of Thucydides was published in 1629, with a second issue in 1634. This is the second translation of Thucydides in English; the first translation, by Thomas Nicolls, was made in 1550 from a French translation. Hobbes translated from the Greek text. He has dedicated the work to his patron, William Cavendish, Earl of Devonshire. The maps are very interesting and include a large folding map of Greece, double-page maps of Sicily and Syracuse, and

735

plans of Sphacteria and Plataea. This copy comes from the library of Thomas Pope Blount, the author of *De Re Poetica*, 1694, and Essays on Several Subjects, 1692. He inherited the Tittenhanger estate in 1678.

BL 585.k.8; Hoffmann III, 560.

736. THUCYDIDES. *The History of the Peloponnesian War, translated from the Greek of Thucydides... by William Smith, A. M.* London: John Watts, MDCCLIII. [=1753]

2 vols, 4to, pp. [xxiii] lxxxiii, 1-308; [i] 1-484 + [12] (pp.[i]=ts, 1=sts, [12]=errata). With a folding map, 'Ancient Greece', engraved by R.W. Seale. Contemporary calf, rebacked. Book label of Philip G. Matthews of Christ College, Cambridge.

First edition of the third English translation of Thucydides, by William Smith; a second edition appeared in 1892 as part of the series of Sir John Lubbock's Hundred Books. The first translation of Thucydides, by Thomas Nicolls, was published in 1550. The second translation, by the philosopher Thomas Hobbes, first appeared in 1629 and was many times reprinted.

BL 1306.k.4,5; Hoffmann III, 560.

737. THUCYDIDES. *Thucydidis De Bello Peloponnesiaco libri octo. Ad optimorum librorum fidem... adiecit atque de vita auctoris praefatus est Franciscus Goeller. Vol. I. Libri I-IV. [... Vol II. Libri V-VIII.]* Leipzig: Karl Knobloch, MDCCCXXXVI. [=1836]

2 vols, 8vo, pp. XVI, 1-676; [i] 1-620 + [2] (p.I, [i]=ts, p.[1]=index orationum, [2]=errata). Pages 613-615 + [2] misbound at the beginning of vol. 2 instead of at the end in the index. With eleven maps/plans, plus duplicates of two maps from vol. 1 (Portus Navarini and Phea) bound in vol. 2. Later polished calf, backs gilt in compartments, black leather labels, by Riviere, signed on the fly-leaf.

Edited by Franz Joseph Goeller. The first Goeller edition was published at Leipzig in 1826.

BL 1306.e.16; Hoffmann III, 556.

738. TILLEY, Henry Arthur. *Eastern Europe and Western Asia Political and Social Sketches on Russia, Greece, and Syria in 1861-2-3.* London: Longman, Green, et al., 1864.

8vo, pp. xi, 1-374 (pp.i=ht, v=ded). With a lithographed frontispiece of the Greek royal palace (now the Parliament building). Purple polished calf, upper cover gilt with a wreath, back gilt in compartments with fleurons, a prize binding of the Brunswick School, Leamington, dated 1869. With the ownership signature of Charles Wincote dated 1869.

First edition. Tilley was in Greece for over a year, a period which included the forced abdication of Otho and Amalia in 1862. He must have had some connection with the Russian service since he was travelling aboard a Russian frigate and his previous journeys had been on Russian ships.

BL 10027.cc.13; Weber 627.

738

739. TORRES Y RIBERA, Antonio de. *Insulae Augustae Cretae Periplus, Prodromus Antiquitatum Cretensium.* Venice: Francesco Andreola, MDCCCV. [=1805]

Folio, pp. XII, 1-351 (p.III=t, missing pp.I-II, probably half title). With 3 folding plates. Uncut in quarter leather, back ruled gilt, contemporary blue-grey wrappers bound in.

First edition, rare. This is the introduction to Torres y Ribera's *Antiquitates Cretenses*, which was published at Venice in 1808. According to Sommervogel, Torres died in 1805, and the *Antiquitates Cretenses* appeared in only a few copies.

GL GT2766. Not in BNF, COPAC or LoC on line. Karlsruhe cites 2 copies. Not in Italian Union Catalogue on line. Palau 337228. Sommervogel VIII, 111.

740. TOTT, François de, *Baron*. ***Mémoires du Baron de Tott, sur les Turcs et les Tartares. Première Partie. [... Second Partie ... Troisième Partie ... Quatrième Partie.]*** Amsterdam: M.DCC.LXXXIV. [=1784]

4 parts in 4 vols, 8vo, pp. lvi, 1-274; [1]-301; [1]-252; [1]-208 (pp.i, [1]=hts, pp.188-208 in v.4=index). Contemporary mottled calf, flat backs diapered gilt with cloverleaves, red and green leather labels.

First edition of this important work. A quarto edition in two volumes appeared at Amsterdam in 1785 with 16 aquatinted plates and critical material. Later octavo editions appeared at Maestricht and Paris in 1785. The French octavo editions do not contain the plates or the additional critical material by Ruffin, consul at Constantinople. Two English editions also appeared in 1785. A German translation appeared at Vienna in 1788, with plates. De Tott, a Hungarian in the French service, travelled to the Levant in 1755 in the entourage of Vergennes, French ambassador to Constantinople, where he remained until 1763. He was appointed French consul in the Crimea in 1767. In about 1769 he returned to Constantinople with orders to reorganize the Turkish army and navy. One of his jobs was to fortify the shores of the Black Sea. On his return to France in 1776 he was appointed inspector general of the Levant consulates, and accompanied by Sonnini (q.v.) he departed immediately for a tour of inspection which lasted until 1778. His memoirs had an immediate success. The plates in the quarto editions are after drawings by 'C.V.'; according to Boppe many of the plates are in fact after drawings by de Tott himself.

BNF 31482987; BL 1053.i.12-13; Atabey 1227; Boppe p. 231; Brunet V, 901. This edition not in Weber. This edition not in Blackmer but see 1667 for the 4to ed.

741. TOTT, François de, *Baron*. ***Mémoires du Baron de Tott, sur les Turcs et les Tartares. Première Partie. [... Second Partie ... Troisième Partie ... Quatrième Partie.]*** Maestricht: J.E. Dufour & Ph. Roux, M.DCC.LXXXV. [=1785]

4 parts in 2 vols, 12mo, pp.xxxv, 195; [iii] 204; [iii] 173; [iii] 143 (pp.i, [i]=hts). Quarter brown calf, ruled gilt, blindstamped in compartments, over brown marbled paper boards.

Second octavo edition? Dufour and Roux also published an edition/issue in 1786 which had a fifth part in 176 pages (Weber 535). The first edition was published at Amsterdam in 1784 in octavo. The quarto format edition appeared a year later. An octavo edition also appeared at Paris in 1785.

BNF 31482990. This edition not in Weber but see 535. This edition not in Atabey or Blackmer. COPAC cites a copy in Trinity College, Dublin.

742. TOUDOUZE, Edouard Henri Georges, *dit Georges Goustave-Toudouze*. ***La Dernière des Spartiates (1821).*** Paris: Hachette, [c. 1920].

Lge 8vo, pp. [iv] 1-322 + [1] (pp.[i]=ht, [1]=conts). Full-page illustrations in the letterpress, versos blank. Original red decorative cloth gilt. A school prize, with a prize bookplate to Lucienne Martin dated 1929.

Toudouze has written a novel of the Greek War of Independence. Editions of 1909 and 1910 are recorded. This may be a later edition, undated, c. 1920.

Not in BLC. This edition not in BNF.

743

743. TOURNEFORT, Joseph Pitton de. ***Relation d'un Voyage du Levant, fait par ordre du Roy. Contenant l'histoire ancienne & moderne de plusieurs Isles de l'Archipel, de Constantinople, des côtes de la Mer Noire, de l'Armenie, de la Georgie, des frontières de Perse & de l'Asie Mineure. Avec les plans des villes & des lieux considérables... Tome Premier. [... Tome Second.]*** Paris: Imprimerie Royale, M.DCCXVII. [=1717]

2 vols, 4to, pp. [xviii] 1-544; [iv] 1-526 + [37] (pp.[i]=ts, [1-37]=index). With 152 engraved plates. Calf antique, backs gilt with stars, blue leather labels.

First edition. Copies are known on *papier fin*; these are distinguished by a stop before the signature of each gathering. An octavo edition appeared the same year at Lyon in

3 vols. A second quarto edition in one volume appeared at Amsterdam in 1718. A second octavo edition appeared at Lyon in 1727. The work was translated into English in 1718, into Dutch in 1737, and into German in 1777. This is one of the most important accounts of travel in the East; Pitton de Tournefort was sent on a mission to the Levant by Louis XIV in 1700. He was a botanist, a careful and trustworthy observer who recorded what he saw and learned with accuracy. He was accompanied by the artist Claude Aubriet. They returned to Paris in 1702, and Tournefort began to prepare his work for the press. But he died in 1708, after volume one was printed. Volume two was published posthumously; the unknown editor kept back volume one until the entire work was completed, and both volumes appeared in 1717. The plates depict botanical specimens, views and many costumes, especially of the islands of the Greek archipelago. There is some variation in the arrangement of the plates depending on the edition.

BNF 32116387; Weber 458; Blackmer 1318; Brunet V, 903; Atabey 959-960.

744. TOURNEFORT, Joseph Pitton de. ***A voyage into the Levant: perform'd by command of the late French King. Containing the antient and modern state of the islands of the Archipelago; as also of Constantinople, the coasts of the Black Sea, Armenia, Georgia, the frontiers of Persia, and Asia Minor... To which is prefix'd, the author's life, in a letter to M. Begon: As also his elogium, pronounc'd by M. Fontenelle, before a publick assembly of the Academy of Sciences... In two volumes.*** London: for D. Browne, A. Bell, J. Darby, A. Bettesworth... [et al.], M.DCC.XVIII. [=1718]

2 vols, 4to, pp. xliii, 1-402; [iv] 1-398 [18] (pp.i, [i]=ts, [1-18]=index). With a folding map in vol. 1 and 152 engraved plates, many folding. Contemporary panelled calf, rebacked, original back preserved. Ownership signature of W. Sturge (?) dated 1862.

First English edition, translated by J. Ozell. A second English edition appeared in 1741 in 3 vols, 8vo. The first edition appeared at Paris in 1717. The map by John Senex was produced for the English edition. Pitton's biographical notice is by H.M. Lantier.

BL 796.ff.25; Weber 460. This edition not in Atabey but see 961 (2nd English ed.).

745. TOWNSHEND, Frederick Trench. ***A Cruise in Greek Waters with a hunting excursion in Tunis.*** London: Hurst and Blackett, 1870.

8vo, pp. XV, 1-286 + [1] (p.I=[ ], III=ht, [1]=advert). Wood-engraved title and frontispiece. Old half calf, repaired. 19th c. bookplate of Alexander Allan.

First and only edition. This excursion took place from August to December, 1869. Townshend was a military man and sportsman who wrote several other accounts of his sporting excursions. He had travelled in the Levant ten years earlier, and in addition to hunting anecdotes he discusses the changes which had taken place during this period.

BL 10125.dd.9; Blackmer 1668. Not in Weber.

746. TOZER, Henry Fanshawe. *The Islands of the Aegean. With maps.* Oxford: Clarendon Press, 1890.

8vo, pp. xii, 362 + [1] (p.i=ht, [1]=advert). With a folding coloured map. Original blue cloth gilt.

First edition. This interesting work contains accounts of three separate journeys made in 1874, 1886 and 1889.

BL 10126.aa.18; Blackmer 1670; Weber 934.

747. TRANT, Thomas Abercromby. *Narrative of a journey through Greece, in 1830. With remarks upon the actual state of the naval and military power of the Ottoman Empire.* London: Henry Colburn and Richard Bentley, 1830.

8vo, pp. X [i] 1-435. (pp.I=t, [i]=list of plates). With an engraved frontispiece and five plates. Quarter calf over marbled paper boards, back gilt romantique.

First and apparently only edition. Trant, an army officer, began this journey in October, 1829. He travelled extensively through Greece to Constantinople. There is a great deal of discussion of Greek politics and social life. The plates depict Karitena, Mistra, Bassae, Argos and Megaspileon. Trant, of whom not much is known, also visited Ava, the capital of Burma, and published an account of it in 1827; on the title of that work he describes himself as 'Officer on the staff of the Quarter-Master General's Department'.

BL 1047.d.6; Blackmer 1671; Weber 192; Droulia 1859.

748. [TRICAUD, Anthelme de]. *Campagnes de Monsieur le Prince Eugène en Hongrie, et des Generaux Venitiens dans la Morée pendant les Années 1716. & 1717. Tome Premier. A Lyon, chez Thomas Amaulry, rue Merciere, & sur le Quay de S. Antoine, au Mercure Galant. M.DCC.XVIII. Avec Privilège du Roy.* [Lyon: T. Amaulry, 1718.]

8vo, pp. [vi] i-lxx, 1-444 (p.[i]=t, pp.440-444=adverts). Contemporary calf, back gilt, red leather label.

Volume one only, of two. First and apparently only edition. Tricaud, prior of the Abbey of Belmont, was a litterateur and historian. Most of the work is concerned with the Turco-Venetian campaign in the Morea; the campaign of 1716 occupies approximately half of volume 1, while the campaign of 1717 takes up most of volume 2.

BNF 31495079; Barbier I, 487; GL HG50A48. Not in Atabey or Blackmer. Not in BLC on line. See B. Boehm, *Bibliographie zur Geschichte des Prinzen Eugens*. Vienna, 1943. Collation: a-f⁶ g² A-2N⁶ 2O⁴.

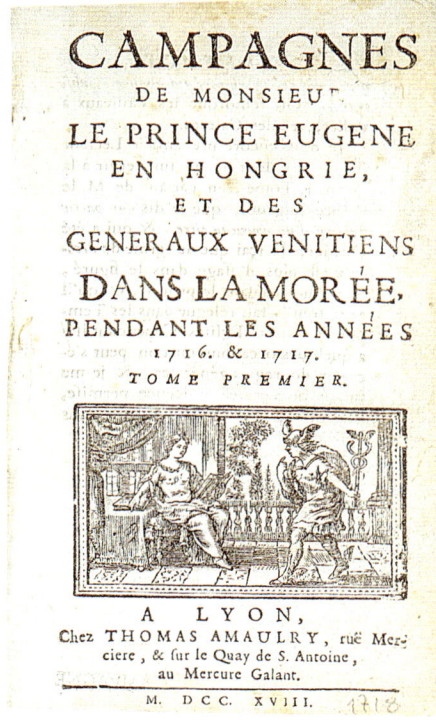

748

749. TSIMAS, Georgios, and Pericles PAPACHATZIDAKIS. *Χιακόν Λεύκωμα*. [Athens: B. Papayiannopoulos, 1930.]

Oblong sm. folio, pp. 8 (pp.1=st, 2=imprint, 3='notice'). With 20 plates of photographic illustrations (of which 7 on darker paper contain mounted photographs). Original decorative paper title wrappers.

?Only edition. This scarce album is concerned with the village of Pyrgi in Chios. In 1931 Tsimas and Papachatzidakis produced another work on Chios, *Ψηφιδωτὰ Νέας Μονῆς Χίου*.

Not in GL.

750. TUMIATI, Domenico (1874-1943). *Una primavera in Grecia*. Milan: Fratelli Treves, 1907.

8vo, pp. [iv] 1-332+[1]+[5] (pp.[i]=ht, [1]=conts, [1-5]=adverts). Original printed wrappers, uncut.

First edition. This is an account of a journey undertaken from March through May of 1906, starting with a description of Corfu. Tumiati visited the Peloponnese, Athens, Thebes, Mount Parnassus, Thessaloniki, Mt. Athos and Constantinople. He was a dramatist and poet.

BL 10126.df.17. Not in Blackmer or Weber. The on line Italian Union Catalogue cites four copies.

751. TURCICI. *Turcici imperii Status seu Discursus varii de Rebus Turcarum*. Leiden: Elzevir, 1630.

16mo, pp. [viii] 1-314 [5] (pp.[i]=engr. t, [iii]=t, pp.[1-5]=index. Engraved title in letterpress. Contemporary limp vellum pasteboards. Contemporary ownership signature on the title of the monastery of S. Maria Magdalena Rothoma[gensis]

First edition. A second, enlarged edition appeared in 1634. This work consists of excerpts and in some cases whole treatises by well-known writers on the Turks, including Busbecq, Soranzo, Malaguzzi, Montalbano, Leunclavius and others. It was probably edited by the Elzevirs themselves, as they have signed the preface to the reader.

BL 166.a.14; Blackmer 1685.

There is another copy in the Contominas collection, also in contemporary vellum boards.

752. TURNER, William. *Journal of a tour in the Levant... In Three Volumes. Vol. I. [... Vol. II... III.]* London: John Murray, 1820.

3 vols, 8vo, pp. xxiii + [3] 480; vi + [1] 608; vi + [1] 546 + [1] (pp.[i]=hts, [1]=list of plates, [3]=st; [1]=sts; [1] at end of vol.3=errata; half titles missing in vols. 1 and 3, errata missing). With 2 maps and 20 (out of 22) engraved plates, see below. Quarter calf gilt, black leather labels. 19th c. ownership signature of W. Gilmore of Brooklyn, Long Island.

First edition. This copy lacks the plate of the Araba and the view of Zakynthos. Of the 22 plates, 6 are coloured aquatints and 1 is a facsimile. Turner, attached to the British embassy in Constantinople, spent five years in the Levant, 1812-16. This interesting work contains accounts of various tours in Greece and Asia Minor, not con-

751

secutive, which include Zakynthos, Rhodes and Simi, Albania, Patmos, Samos, Ephesus, etc. The maps ('Greece and the Archipelago', and 'Countries on the East Coast of the Mediterranean Sea') bear the imprint 'Drawn by J. Walker for the Journal of W. Turner, published by J. Murray, 1820'.

Bl 1047.e.3-5; Blackmer 1687; Weber 94; Abbey 375.

752

753. TUROT, Henri (1865-19..). *L'Insurrection Crétoise et la Guerre Gréco-Turque Ouvrage contenant soixante-quatorze illustrations d'après les photographies de l'auteur.* Paris: Hachette, 1898.

8vo, pp. [v] IV, 1-224 + [1] + [1] (pp.[i]=ht, IV=preface, [1]=contents, [1]=colophon). Two folding maps and numerous photographic illustrations in the text. Uncut in the original yellow decorative paper wrappers with red and black ornamental borders.

First edition. This interesting work discusses the Cretan war of 1896-1897 and the Greek-Turkish war of 1897. Turot was a miscellaneous writer who produced books on politics and travel.

BNF 31506425; GL HG690T95.

754. TWEDDELL, John. *Remains of the late John Tweddell Fellow of Trinity College Cambridge being a selection of his letters written from*

various parts of the Continent together with a republication of his Prolusiones Juveniles To which is adjoined an appendix containing some account of the author's Journals Mss. Collections Drawings &c. and of their extraordinary disappearance. Prefixed is a brief biographical memoir by the editor the Rev. Robert Tweddell A. M. London: Joyce Gold for J. Mawman, 1815.

2 parts in 1, 4to, pp. [iii] 1-479, 1-179 [1] (pp.[i]=t, iii=ded to the Levant Company, [1]=advert). With engraved frontispiece and eleven engraved plates. Half cloth over marbled paper boards, calf cornerpieces, rubbed. With two inscriptions mounted on the front pastedown referring to Robert Walpole's inscription on Tweddell's tomb. Early 20th c. memorial booklabel of Sir William Harcourt.

First edition, edited by Robert Tweddell fifteen years after his brother John's death in Greece. This work is part memorial to Tweddell and part vicious attack on Elgin at the time when he was trying to arrange the sale of the Marbles to the nation. The attack concerned John Tweddell's manuscripts and journals which disappeared after they were sent to the British embassy in Constantinople. A second edition appeared in 1816 with an addenda replying to a letter of Elgin's which had appeared in the *Edinburgh Review*. This addenda was also published separately in 1816 and is sometimes found bound into the 1815 edition. Philip Hunt, chaplain to Elgin's embassy, replied to Tweddell's attack in *Narrative of what is known respecting the literary remains of the late John Tweddell*, 1816.

BL 615.k.6; Blackmer 1690; St. Clair Elgin, pp. 230-41.

755. [TZETZES, Joannes]. *Iliacum Carmen Epici Poetae Graeci, cuius nomen ignoratur, ingenium proditur hoc eleganti Fragmento. Nunc primum prodit cum scholiis ex vet. mss. membranis biblioth. v.c. Isaaci Casauboni. Fed. Morellus... latinis heroicis expressit & notis illustravit.* Paris: F. Morel [1616].

Sm. 8vo, pp. 6, 2, 8, 8, (p.1=t, pp.1-2=[]). Modern vellum. Bound with Marcian of Heraclea and Morel.

First edition. Attributed by Hoffmann and Brunet to Joannes Tzetzes, with the date 1616. The *Carmen* consists of verses 147-295 of the 'Antehomerica', a part of Tzetzes' *Iliaca*, a long hexameter poem containing a supplement to the *Iliad*.

BL 832.d.18, under Antehomerica, attributing the date 1610. BNF 31508743; Hoffmann III, 570; Brunet IV, 996.
Collation: a^4 A^4 A^4.

UKHTOMSKY. See OUKHTOMSKY

756. UNGER, Franz. *Wissenschaftliche Ergebnisse einer Reise in Griechenland und in den jonischen Inseln.* Vienna: Wilhelm Braumüller, 1862.

8vo, pp. XII [1] 1-213 (pp.I=t, 212-213=bibliography). With a double-page folding map and three plates of wood engravings. Illustrations in the letterpress, several of which are nature-printed. Modern calf gilt, original yellow paper wrappers bound in.

First and apparently only edition. Unger, Austrian botanist and geologist, travelled in Greece and the Ionian Islands in 1860. The work contains a flora of Corfu. The plates illustrate Steni (Euboea), Bragagniotica, and the Casa Inglese on Monte Nero. Unger later produced Die Insel Cypern, 1865, and Die fossile flora von Kumi, 1867.

BL 10126.dd.8; ÖNB 107.533-b; Blackmer 1694; Stafleu 15. 624.

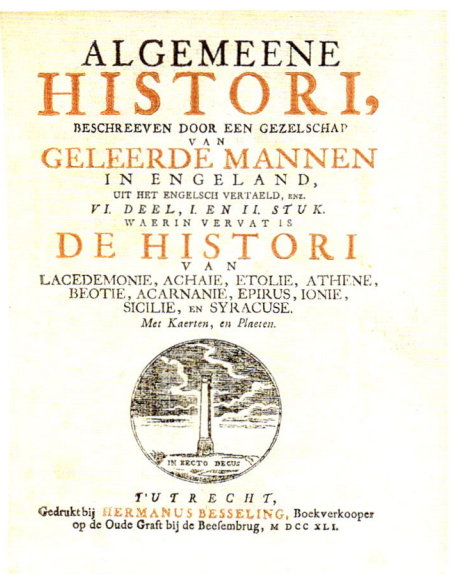 

757

757. UNIVERSAL HISTORY. *Algemeene Histori van het begin der Wereld af tot de Tegenwoordigen tijd toe: getrokken uit Oorsprongelijke Schrijveren: en opgehelderd met Landkaerten ... en andere Tafelen ... Beschreeven door een Gezelschap van geleerde Mannen in Engeland. Uit het Engelsch vertaeld, en met eenige Aentekeningen vermeerderd door Kornelis Westerbaen.* Utrecht: Herman Besseling, 1736-1755.

17 vols (out of 19, lacking vols 11 and 19), 8vo. Titles in red and black. With 6 plates and a folding table in v.1, 8 plates in v.2, 5 plates in v.3, 5 plates in v.4, 5 plates in v.5, 3 maps/plans in v.6, 3 maps and a portrait in v.7, 2 maps and a portrait in v.8, 5 maps/plans in v.9, 12 maps and plans in v.10, v.11 missing, 23 plates of maps, portraits, plans in v.12, 6 plates in v.13, 3 plates and a folding table in v.14, 8 maps in v.15, 10 plates in v.16, and 2 maps in v.17. Contemporary Dutch vellum.

?First edition in Dutch, translated from the English compilation *An Universal History, from the earliest account of time to the present*, London, 1736-65, completed in 23 volumes. The authors included A. Bower, G. Sale, J. Campbell, J. Swinton, G. Shelrocke, among others. Leiben and UBA refer to this edition as the second, but we cannot locate an earlier Dutch edition. It is complete in 19 volumes, with vol. 19 dated 1755 and forming the index. Volumes 5 and 7 deal with Asia Minor and Greece.

UB Leiden THYS 2508; UBA UBM282B1-16.

758. URQUHART, David. *The Spirit of the East, illustrated in a journal of travels through Roumeli during an eventful period.* London: Henry Colburn, 1838.

2 vols, lge 8vo, pp. xxxi, 1-456; vii, 1-443 (pp.i=hts). With an engraved plan. Contemporary calf, rebacked, brown leather labels.

First edition of this important work. The first edition does not contain the map of Greece which was issued with the second edition, 1839. Urquhart is one of the most interesting of the travellers to the East. He took part in the Greek Revolution and spent three years in Greece and Turkey, including time on the staff of the English embassy in Constantinople; on his way back to England he was seconded to survey the Greek frontier in 1830. He developed into a Turcophile, maintaining a life-long interest in Turkey; he always supported Turkey against Russia and carried on a long correspondence with Karl Marx on the subject. Urquhart was one of the few travellers of his time who attempted to analyze the differences in ways of thought between East and West.

BL 1047.l.3. This edition not in Blackmer but see 1707 (2nd ed). Atabey 1262.

There is another copy in the Contominas collection, in three-quarter brown morocco.

759. USSING, Johan Ludwig. *Griechische Reisen und Studien... Mit 3 Tafeln.* Copenhagen: Thieles Buchdruckerei for Gyldendalschen Buchhandlung (F. Hegel), 1857.

760

2 parts in 1, 8vo, pp. VIII, 1-200 (p.I=t). With 3 no'd folding plates. Original blue cloth, back gilt.

First edition in German of articles originally published in Danish. Part one, 'Thessalien', describes a journey in Thessaly in 1846; part two 'Attische Studien' consists of architectural and archaeological studies. The three plates include a folding map, a diagram of the Parthenon, and a piece of sculpture.

BL 10126.c.20; Weber 547. Not in Blackmer.

760. VALIERO, Andrea. *Historia della Guerra di Candia.* Venice: Paolo Baglioni, M.DC.LXXIX. [=1679]

Thick 4to, pp. [viii] 1-751 [1] + [24] (pp.[i]=t, viii=approbation, [1]=woodcut arms, [1-24]=index). Contemporary quarter calf, ruled gilt.

First edition of this account of the Turkish-Venetian wars in Crete from 1644 to 1669. In 1646 Valiero took part in a sea battle against the Turks off the Dardanelles. In 1667 he was elected Provveditore Generale of Corfu, Zakynthos, and Cefalonia. This work was reprinted at Trieste in 1859.

BL 665.f.17; Blackmer 1710; Atabey 1268.

761. VALON, Alexis de. *Une Année dans le Levant Voyage en Sicile, en Grèce et en Turquie.* Paris: Dauvin and Fontaine, 1850.

2 parts in 1, 8vo, pp. [iii] 1-347, 1-270 + [1] (p.[i]=ht, [1]=conts and colophon). 19th c. quarter calf, back ruled gilt, with cypher DcS.

Second edition. The first edition appeared in 1846 in two volumes, with a variant title: *Une Année dans le Levant. Tome Premier. La Sicile sous Ferdinand II et la Grèce sous Othon I, Tome Second. La Turquie sous Abdul-Medjid.* In the second edition the two volumes have been bound together with a new title and no separate title to the second part. This undated journey took place c. 1845. Valon gives a long account of Tinos in the section on Greece, as well as an account of the Greek state expenses for 1843.

BL 10127.ee.38; Blackmer 1713. This edition not in GL. This edition not in BNF on line.

762. VAN DEN BRULE, Alfred. *L'Orient Hellène. Grèce - Crète - Macédoine.* Paris: Félix Juven [1907].

Lge 8vo, pp. 320 (1=ht, 315-20=conts). With 55 plates of photographic illustrations (6=dp). Quarter roan over marbled paper boards, worn.

First and apparently only edition. Van den Brule gives an account of the Greco-Turkish war of 1897 in some detail. The photographs include many of Crete, with the young Venizelos, and some little photographed streets in Athens. Van den Brule also produced *Le Bluff Macedonien*, 1904, and he may also be connected with the pseudonymous Varino (q.v.).

BNF 31530033; BL 10127.h.7; GL GT1423; Basch, 254-55.

763. VARINO, *pseudonym* [? S. VAN DEN BRULE]. *Au pied de l'Acropole par Varino.* Bucharest: 1895.

12mo, pp. 116 + 1 blank leaf + [1] (pp.1=ht, [1]=conts). Red cloth. A presentation copy signed on the title 'au notre ami Monsieur Raetivand S. van den Brule Varino'.

Apparently only edition of this account of travels in Greece starting from Patras, extremely uncommon. We were unable to trace this work in any major library. It also contains four Greek tales: 'Le fou d'amour', 'Le Serment', 'La légende du Lac', and 'Thais'. The inscription on the title would seem to indicate that the author is in fact S. Van den Brule, who probably has some connection with Alfred Van den Brule. Karlsruhe cites a work by A. Varino, *Le Pays du Bey*, Paris, Juven, 1903, at Tübingen.

Not in BNF or BLC on line. Not in GL. Not cited in Karlsruhe.

764. VAUDOYER, Jean Louis (1883-1963). *D'Athènes à la Havane via Berlin.* Paris: Plon [1931].

8vo, pp. vi, 262 + [1] (p.[i]=[ ], ii=statement of edition, [iii]=ht, [v]=t). Quarter red roan gilt.

First and only edition. The first part is on Greece. A certain number of copies were printed on special papers: 12 copies on Hollande van Gelder paper numbered 1-12, 30 copies on Lafuma paper numbered 13-42, and 25 copies on Madagascar paper numbered I-XXV. Ordinary copies were not numbered. Vaudoyer was a novelist and prolific writer of essays on art and applied art. He became director of the Musèe Carnavalet and future director of the Comédie Française.

BNF 31548811.

765. VECELLIO, Cesare. *Costumes anciens et modernes Habiti antichi et moderni di tutto il Mondo di Cesare Vecellio précédés d'un essai sur la gravure sur bois par M. Amb. Firmin Didot.* Paris: Firmin Didot Frères Fils & Cie, M.DCCC.LIX. [=1859-60]

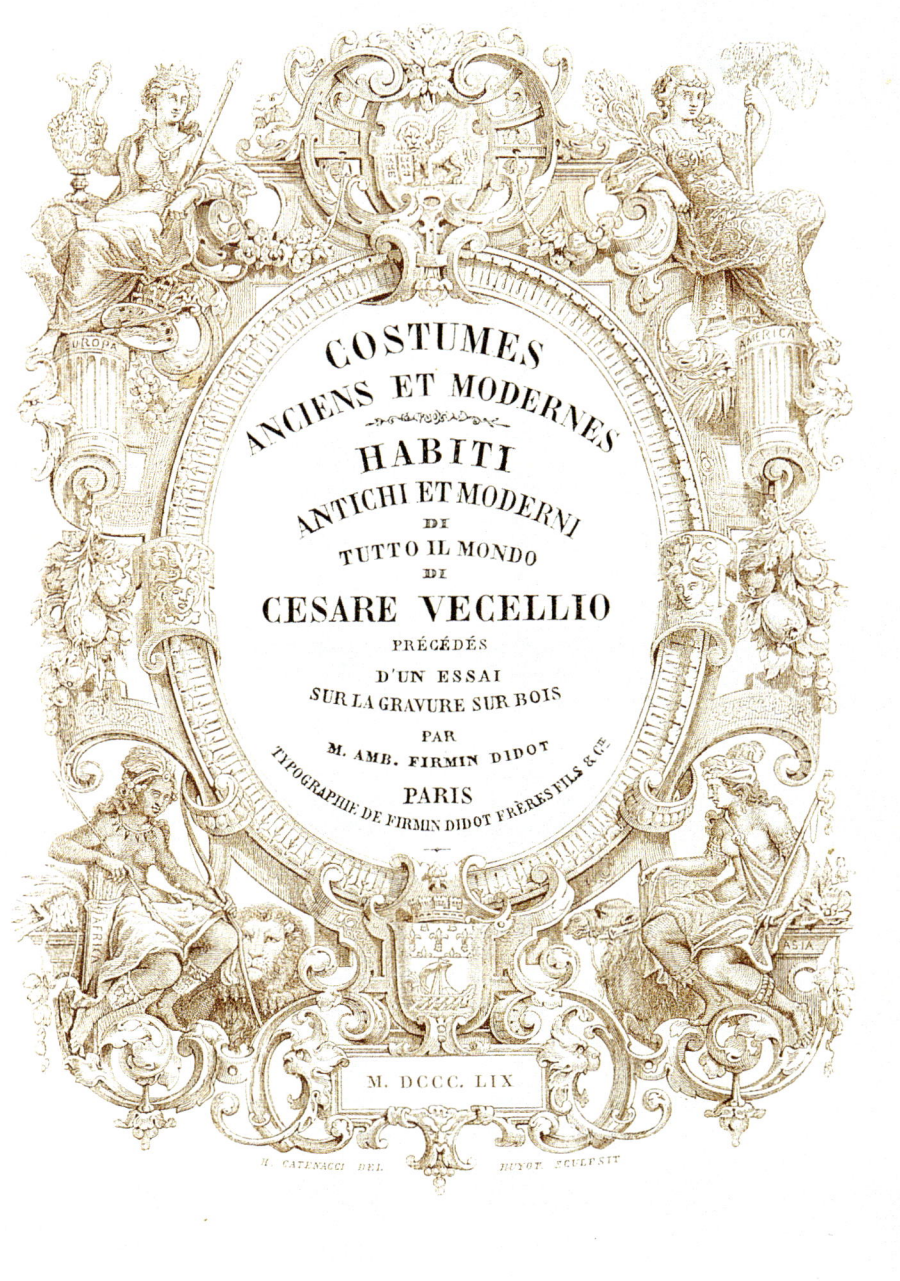

2 vols, pp. 9 [1]-[469], 1-18; [iii] [559] (p.1=ht, 3=engr. t., pp.1-18=conts). With 513 wood-engraved plates in the text. Full blue morocco, sides panelled blind with ivy-leaves in the corners, backs gilt, gilt edges. 19th c. booklabel of CM [Charlotte M...].

Fourth edition in French. The title is followed by an 'Avis sur la IVe édition'. The first French edition appeared under the same date, translated by Armand Lacombe. There is a small variation in title: in earlier editions the title reads 'Costumes... suivis d'un essai'; in our edition the title reads 'précédés d'un essai'. In this copy the Avis forms a brief summary of the *Essai sur la gravure sur Bois*, which was published separately in 1863. Vecellio's work was first published in Venice by Giovanni Sessa in 1590. Didot's reprint has the French and Italian text together on the same page. The wood engravings are by Gerard Seguin and E. F. Huyot, the borders designed by Catenacci and Fellmann.

BNF 31551932.

There is another copy of the fourth edition in the Contominas collection, in three-quarter beige calf, red and black leather labels.

766. VELLAY, Charles. *L'Irrédentisme hellénique.* Paris: Perrin et Cie, 1913.

8vo, pp. VIII, 1-329 (p.I=ht). Modern calf.

First edition. Six numbered copies were printed on Hollande Van Gelder paper. This work contains descriptions of Macedonia, Epirus, Thrace and several of the Aegean islands in the wake of the Balkan wars of 1912-13, with numerous documents and statistical information, and petitions by the populations of Koritsa, Tepeleni, Chimarra, Arta, Patmos, Rhodes and Nissyros, etc. etc. It addresses itself to the questions: 'Y-at-il des grecs hors de Grèce? Veulent ils être réunis à la mère patrie?'. Vellay also wrote *La Guerre Européene et la Question de l'Adriatique*, 1915, *Dans l'enfer Bulgare*, 1919, and 'Smyrna, a Greek City', in *Hellas and unredeemed Hellenism*, New York, 1920, published by the American Hellenic Society. Vellay, historian and archeologue, was interested in political questions which concerned Greece.

BNF 31554310; BL 8028.aaa.45; GL EQ1701.

767. VICTOIRES. *Victoires conquêtes désastres, revers et guerres civiles des Français par Une Société de Militaires et de Gens de Lettres. Tome vingt-neuvième 1827-1832.* Paris: C. L. F. Pancoucke, MDCCCXXXIII. [=1833]

8vo, pp. [vii] 1-130 + (4), (p.[i]=avis, [iii]=ht, [vii]=st, pp.(1-4)=adverts). With an engraved portrait frontispiece of de Rigny and an engraved folding plan of the battle of Navarino. Uncut in half tan morocco, original ochre printed paper wrappers bound in.

First edition, volume 29 of this periodical or encyclopaedic work, edited by General Charles Beauvais and P.F. Tissot. The 'Victoires' is a history of the period 1789 to 1815, i.e. from the French Revolution to the Congress of Vienna, published in 28 volumes from 1818 to 1825. A second edition of the set appeared in 34 volumes in 8vo from 1828 to 1831. This volume forms a supplement and is often catalogued separately from the earlier volumes. According to the BNF it was written by Beauvais, although according to the 'avis', much of the material on the battle of Navarino was written by Parisot.

BNF 34080999 (this volume only). This volume apparently not in BLC. Not in GL.

768. VILLEHARDOUIN, Geoffroy de. ***Histoire de la Conquête de Constantinople par Geoffroi de Ville-Hardouin avec la continuation de Henri de Valenciennes Texte rapproché du français moderne et mis a la portée de tous par M. Natalis de Wailly.*** Paris: [Paul Brodard for] Hachette, 1909.

Sm. 8vo, pp. XIII, 287 (pp.I=ht, 281-87=index). Quarter calf gilt. With the bookplate of J.C. Eliasco.

769

A late edition of Villehardouin's chronicle of the 4th crusade, but with the text adapted to modern French. The first edition of the chronicle was published in 1577 by Blaise de Vigenère.

BNF 31581617.

769. VIMERCATI, Cesare. *Constantinople et l'Égypte. Sixième édition revue et corrigée par Charles Hertz.* Paris: Henri and Charles Noblet, 1858.

8vo, pp.[iii] 1-371 + [1] (p.[i]=ht, [1]=conts). With engraved frontispiece of Vimercati by G. de Montant and a plate (massacre of the Janissaries). Modern brown morocco.

Sixth edition in French. The first French edition appeared in 1852, translated by Hertz and the author himself from the Italian edition published in 1849 as *Costantinopoli e l'Egitto* by Alberghetti at Prato. The French translation of this work was extraordinarily successful, and reached seven editions by 1859; what is especially curious is that different publishers produced these editions. This may have been due in part to the Crimean War, which provoked new interest in the Levant in the 1850s. Vimercati took part in the combined compaign against Mehmet Ali in Syria in 1840. He later wrote on the Isthmus of Suez and produced a history of Italy.

BNF 31585614; Hilmy II, 310. See Blackmer 1739 (2nd ed) and Weber 451(1st) and 540(3rd).

770. VINCENT, William. *The Voyage of Nearchus from the Indus to the Euphrates, collected from the original journal preserved by Arrian, and illustrated by authorities ancient and modern; Containing an account of the first navigation attempted by Europeans in the Indian Ocean.* London: for T. Cadell Jr. and W. Davies, 1797.

4to, pp. xv, 1-530+[2] (pp.i=ht, [1]=errata, [2]=list of plates). With an engraved frontispiece and six maps (of which 4 folding). Contemporary tree calf, skilfully rebacked.

First edition. A second edition appeared in 2 vols, 8vo, in 1807. This is not a translation of Arrian, but an account of Nearchus's voyage. Nearchus, an officer of Alexander the Great, was charged with the task of reaching the Indus river from the mouth of the Euphrates; this involved the navigation of the Arabian or Persian gulf. Nearchus's narrative of this expedition is preserved in its entirety in Arrian's 'Indica'. Vincent's edition is of great importance for the study of the geography of the ancients; he includes as one of his authorities Dalrymple's survey of the coast between the Indus and the gulf of Persia. He later translated both Nearchus's text and the Periplus of the Erythrean Sea into English; the work appeared with parallel texts in Greek and English in 1809 in 4to. Vincent also produced *Commerce and Navigation of the Ancients in the Indian Ocean*, 1807. He was the dean of Westminster Cathedral.

BL 214.c.19; Hoffmann II, 619. This edition not in GL.

771. VINCENT, William. ***Voyage de Néarque, des bouches de l'Indus jusqu'à l'Euphrate, ou Journal de l'Expédition de la flotte d'Alexandre, rédigé sur le journal original de Néarque conservé par Arrien... et contenant l'histoire de la première navigation que des Européens aient tentée dans la Mer des Indes.*** Paris: Imprimerie de la Republique, An VIII. [=1800]

4to, pp. [iii] XX, 1-661 (pp.[i]=ht, I=avis au relieur). With 6 maps/plans (out of 7, lacking the map to book III). Without the frontispiece portrait of Alexander the Great. Contemporary speckled calf gilt, back gilt with urns and flowers, marbled edges.

First edition in French, translated by J.B.L.J. Billecocq from Vincent's English text. An 8vo edition appeared the same year published by Maradan. The first edition appeared in 1797 (see above). The maps are engraved by P.F. Tardieu after L. Aubert.

BNF 31587633; Hoffmann II, 614. Brunet V, 1252-53 cites copies on vellum paper.

772. VIVES, Juan Luis. ***Wie der Türck die Christen haltet so un-der im leben, Johannis Ludovici Vivis Valentini gschrifft [sic]. Sampt der Türcken Ursprung fürgang und erweiterung biss auff den heüttigen tag. Neülich durch D. Caspar Hedion verteütscht in disen schweren sorgklichen leüffen, allen liebhabern Christlicher religion und Teütscher nation wolzülesen. MDXXXii. Strassburg.*** [Strasbourg: Balthazar Becken, 1532.]

Sm. 4to, 40 pages, unpaginated (p.[1]=t). Gothic letter. Marbled paper boards, green leather label gilt mounted on upper cover. With the red leather book label of G.J. ArvanitidIs.

First German edition of Vives's 'Quam misera esset vita Christianorum sub Turca' from *De Concordia & Discordia in humano genere*, first printed in 1529, and translated into German by Caspar Hedio from Vives' Latin text. Hedio, who also translated Barletius's work on Scanderbeg into German, has dedicated the work to Martin Seyler Schultheisen. A Latin edition also appeared in 1532.

Not in BLC. Göllner 448. Karlsruhe cites 4 copies.
Collation: A-E^4 (A1=t)

773. VOGUÉ, Marie Eugène Melchior de, *Viscount*. **Syrie Palestine, Mont Athos Voyage aux pays du passé. Troisième édition.** Paris: Plon Nourrit, 1887.

8vo, pp. XII, 1-333 + [1] (pp.I=ht, [1]=conts). Wood-engraved frontispiece and 6 plates. Old half calf, back gilt, red leather label.

773

Third edition, first published in 1876. Many of the chapters first appeared in the *Revue des deux Mondes*. This work describes travels from 1872-75. The section on Mount Athos describes the major monasteries. The engravings are by Smeeton-Tilley after J. Pelcoq. One is a double-page plate of the Monastery of Vatopedi on Mt. Athos.

BNF 31598961; Blackmer 1746.

774. VOGUÉ, Marie Eugène Melchior de, *Viscount*. **Syrie Palestine, Mont Athos Voyage aux pays du passé. Quatrième édition.** Paris: Plon Nourrit, 1894.

8vo, pp.XII, 1-333 + [1] (pp.I=ht, [1]=conts). Wood-engraved frontispiece and 6 plates. Uncut in the original grey paper wrappers printed in red and black. Ownership signature of 'Mossat' on the title. Bookseller's ticket of H. Samuelian of Paris, 'Librairie Orientale'.

Fourth edition, first published in 1876, with later editions in 1878 and 1887.

This edition not in BNF on line.

There is another copy of the fourth edition in the Contominas collection, in old half blue cloth over marbled boards, blue grey printed paper wrappers bound in.

775. VOLNEY, Constantin François de. *Voyage en Syrie et en Égypte, pendant les années 1783, 1784 et 1785, avec deux cartes géographiques et deux planches gravées, représentant les ruines du Temple du Soleil à Balbek, et celles de la ville de Palmyre, dans le désert de Syrie... Seconde édition revue et corrigée. Tome Premier. [... Second.]* Paris: Desenne and Volland, 1787.

2 vols, 8vo, pp. xvi, 1-383; viii 1-458 + [4] (pp.i=hts, ii=dir to binder, [1-4]=privilege and approbation). With two folding maps (Syria and Egypt) and three engraved plates (of which 1=folding). Uncut in modern half leather gilt. 18th c. ownership stamp of the ducal library of Neustrelitz on title versos.

Second edition. The first edition also appeared in 1787, apparently under the imprint of Volland only. Apparently these editions also appeared in 4to format. A third edition appeared in 1799 with 3 maps and 6 plates. A fourth edition appeared in 1807. The three plates include a view of Palmyra, a view of Baalbec, and a plan of the temple of the sun at Baalbec. Volney set out for the Levant at the end of 1782. He spent three years travelling through Syria and Egypt, mostly on foot. He travelled with Cassas in Syria in 1785. This important work constitutes the one of the best exposés of Ottoman Egypt. 'One of the most exact and valuable works of the kind ever published' (–Cox, p. 235).

BNF 31601986; Blackmer 1748.

776. VOUTIER, Olivier. *Mémoires du Colonel Voutier sur la Guerre actuelle des Grecs.* Paris: Bossange Frères, 1823.

8vo, pp. xiv, 1-396 (p.i=ht, 382-396=index). With an engraved frontispiece and 4 portraits. Contemporary quarter calf, back ruled gilt, blue bookseller's ticket of H. Samuelian of Paris.

First edition. Two German translations appeared in 1824, one at Stuttgart translated by F. Ritter, with a preface by Schott, and the other translated by Heidemann and published at Ilmenau. Voutier went to Greece in 1821 and became A.D.C. to Mavrocordatos. He returned to Paris in 1823 and quickly produced this flamboyant work. Its fables were exposed by Maxime Raybaud. Voutier produced *Lettres sur la Grèce* in 1826.

BNF 31608778; Blackmer 1750; Droulia 429; St. Clair pp. 116 and 228.

777. WÄCHTER, Albert. *Der Verfall des Griechentums in Kleinasien im XIV. Jahrhundert.* Leipzig: B.G. Teubner, 1903.

8vo, pp. [iv] 1-70 (p.[i]=t). Old half black cloth over brown marbled paper boards. Book label of Anthimos Alexoudes, Bishop of Amaseia. Bound with two works by Mystakides.

First edition of this account of the conquest of Asia Minor by the Turks.

BLC 09004.b.9.

778. WÄGNER, Wilhelm. *Hellas. Das Land und Volk der alten Griechen. Bearbeitet für Freunde des klassischen Alterthums, insbesondere für die deutsche Jugend. Erster Band [... Zweiter Band.] Dritte vermehrte und verbesserte Auflage.* Leipzig: Otto Spamer, 1873.

2 vols, 8vo, pp. x, 1-364 + [2]; vi, 1-321 [1] (pp.i=hts, ii=series titles, iii=part titles, pp.[1]=advert, [2]=illus., p.[1]=errata). With wood-engraved title (vol. 1) and two wood-engraved frontispieces and a folding map. Numerous illustrations in the text, some full-page. Original maroon pictorial cloth gilt. Ownership signature of M. Locher on fly-leaves.

Third edition, first published in 1859, second edition 1867. This work was published in the series 'Neue Jugend und Hausbibliothek' issued by Spamer. Later editions appeared in 1886 and 1902 (ninth), and a modern reprint appeared in 1997. Wägner translated Bikelas into German and edited a number of medieval Greek texts.

Not in GL. BLC cites 1902 ed only. Karlsruhe cites up to nine editions.

779. WALKER, Mary Adelaide. *Through Macedonia to the Albanian lakes.* London: Chapman and Hall, 1864.

Lge 8vo, pp. xi [i] 1-274 (pp.i=ht, [i]=list of ills). With 12 lithographed plates of which 8 tinted and 4 printed in colour. Old polished green calf, back gilt with fleurons in compartments. A school prize book, with presentation inscription dated 1870.

First and apparently only edition. Mary Walker was the sister of the English chaplain at Constantinople, whom she joined c. 1856, and she spent many years in the Levant. In about 1860 she was resident with her brother in Thessaloniki; *Through Macedonia* is an account of her travels in northern Greece and along the borders of Albania and Yugoslavia. Mrs. Walker wrote a number of works describing her travels in Greece and the Levant: *Old Tracks and New Landmarks*, 1897; *Eastern Life and Scenery*, 1886; *Brousse, Album historique*, 1866. She also produced the illustrations for Lady Hornby's book, *Constantinople during the Crimean War*, 1863.

BL 10125.e.22; Blackmer 1757; Weber 628.

780. WALPOLE, Frederick. *The Ansayrii, and the Assassins, with Travels in the Further East in 1850-51. Including a visit to Nineveh. In Three Volumes. Vol. I. [... Vol. II. ... III.]* London: Richard Bentley, 1851.

3 vols, 8vo, pp. xv, 402; xi, 378; viii, 458 + [1] (pp.i=ts in vols. 1 and 3, [ ] or ht in v.2, p.[1]=prayer). Mounted portrait frontispiece of the author. Old calf, backs gilt in compartments, red and black leather labels.

First and apparently only edition, dedicated to Warburton, author of *The Crescent and the Cross*. Walpole was an army officer; his journey began from Malta. He travelled through most of Asia Minor, and as far as Lebanon and Syria, and he also visited Chios, Cos and Rhodes. A few remnants of the Ismaelite sect of the Assassins, who were active in Syria in the 12th and 13th centuries, were still to be found in northern Syria in the 19th century.

BL 10075.d.17; Weber 443. Not in Blackmer or Atabey.

781. WALPOLE, Robert, *editor*. *Memoirs relating to European and Asiatic Turkey; edited from Manuscript journals, by Robert Walpole, M.A. The Second Edition.* London: for Longman, Hurst... [et al.], 1818.

4to, pp. xxii, 1-611 (p.i=t). With 4 maps, 9 plates and a folding inscription. Calf antique, back gilt, red leather label.

Second edition, with some new material, first published in 1817. Walpole, the grandson of Horatio Walpole, travelled extensively in the Levant at some time between 1803 and 1808. He began to compile the *Memoirs* from his own and other travellers' papers and journals. This valuable collection of materials includes contributions by Haygarth, Sibthorp, Morritt, W.G. Browne, Leake, and many others. Many of these contributions are to be found only in Walpole's work.

BL 1298.m.12; Weber 60. This edition not in Blackmer or Atabey but see Blackmer 1762 and Atabey 1310. Spencer p. 209.

782. WALPOLE, Robert, *editor*. *Travels in various countries of the East; being a Continuation of Memoirs relating to European and Asiatic Turkey, &c.* London: for Longman, Hurst, Rees, Orme and Brown, 1820.

4to, pp. xxi +[ii] 1-603 + 8 (pp.i=t, [i]=directions to the binder, [ii]=errata, pp.1-8=appendix). With 2 maps and 11 plates (1=dp, 1=folding). Contemporary polished calf gilt, rebacked, original back preserved, red leather label, gilt edges.

First and only edition of this continuation to Walpole's *Memoirs*. The contributors in-

453

clude John Hawkins, Hunt, W.G. Browne, Leake and Clarke. Much of Sibthorp's material was published posthumously in this collection. There is also an account by Colonel Squires, who travelled in Syria with Leake and William Hamilton.

BL 982.i.7; Weber 97; Blackmer 1763.

783. WALSH, Robert (1772-1852). *Narrative of a Journey from Constantinople to England.* Philadelphia: Carey, Lea & Carey, 1828.

8vo, pp. iv, 1-270 (p.i=t). Uncut in modern quarter calf gilt, red leather labels.

First American edition. The first edition was published in London in 1828, and three editions had appeared by 1829. This is an account of Walsh's return to England in 1824/5 after having served as chaplain to Lord Strangford's embassy to the Porte from 1821. Walsh later produced *A Residence at Constantinople*, 1836, and he wrote the text to accompany Thomas Allom's plates in *Constantinople and the Scenery of the seven Churches of Asia Minor*, 1838.

This ed. not in LoC. Harvard, Houghton Library cites 1 copy. Not in BLC or GL.

784. WALSH, Robert. *A Residence at Constantinople, during a period including the commencement, progress, and termination of the Greek and Turkish Revolutions.* London: Frederick Westley and A.H. Davis, MDCCCXXXVI. [=1836]

2 vols, 8vo, pp. xv, 1-412; viii [2] 1-542 + [1] (pp.i=ts, pp.[1-2]=lists of plates, p.[1]=errata). With a folding map, 11 engraved plates and an inserted woodcut. Four leaves of woodcut inscriptions, and illustrations in the letterpress. Rough cut in the original mauve cloth, rebacked, original spine laid down.

784

First edition. A second edition appeared in 1838. Walsh spent two periods in Constantinople, 1821-24 and 1830-35. Thus he was resident in Turkey on the outbreak of the Greek revolution, and he returned to Turkey after the destruction of the Janissaries by Mahmoud II. Confusion may occur with regard to the number of plates in this work. The four leaves of woodcut inscriptions form part of the letterpress and are not hors texte, but occasionally are described as so. There are eleven engraved plates and an inserted woodcut.

BL 1047.k.8; Blackmer 1765; Weber 247.

785. WALSH, Robert, and Thomas ALLOM. *Constantinople and the Scenery of the Seven Churches of Asia Minor illustrated. In a Series of Drawings from Nature by Thomas Allom. With an historical account of Constantinople, and descriptions of the plates, by the Rev. Robert Walsh... First Series. [... Second Series.]* London and Paris: Fisher, Son & Co. [1836-38].

2 vols, 4to, pp. [iv] xxxvi, 1-84; [iv] 1-100 (pp.[i]=ts, [iv]=lists of plates, pp.95-100=index). With 2 engraved titles, a double-page map of the Mediterranean, and 93 engraved plates. Contemporary half calf, backs gilt in compartments, black leather labels.

First edition, issued in parts. This work forms the second part of Fisher's series 'The Turkish Empire Illustrated', and the engraved title reads 'Fisher's Illustrations of Constantinople'. The first part of the series is formed by Carne's *Syria and Asia Minor*. Walsh's text was translated into German in 1841, but the plates, by Thomas Allom, have been used in many other publications. Allom spent about nine months in Turkey in 1836-37. He lithographed ten of the plates from this work for Emma Reeve's *Character and Costume in Turkey*.

BL 562.*d.26, suggesting the date [1839?]; Weber 1150; Blackmer 1766; Atabey 1316.

786. WARBURTON, Bartholomew Eliot George. *The Crescent and the Cross; or, Romance and Realities of Eastern Travel. In two volumes. Seventh Edition.* London: Henry Colburn, 1848.

2 vols, 8vo, pp. xii, 1-326; pp. viii, 1-322 (pp.i=hts). With lithographed frontispieces to each volume. Wood-engraved vignettes in the letterpress. Three-quarter red morocco, back gilt in compartments with fleurons, circles etc., top edge gilt by Burrel, with his stamp on the fly-leaf. 20th c. bookplate of Arthur G. Soames.

Seventh edition, first published in 1845. Warburton's account of his experiences in the East can be compared to Kinglake's *Eothen*, which in fact Kinglake had dedicated to him. His work rivalled Kinglake's in popularity: seventeen editions had appeared by 1880. Warburton also wrote *Zoe, an episode of the Greek War*, London, 1847.

This edition not in Blackmer but see 1771. This edition not in BLC on line.

787. WARSBERG, Alexander, *Freiherr von. Ithaka. Mit 5 Aquarellfarbendrucken, 1 Karte und 40 Phototypien nach originalen von Ludwig Hans Fischer.* Vienna: Carl Gerold's Sohn, 1887.

785

4to, pp. V, 144 (p.I=t, 142-44=list of ills). Mounted frontispiece, four mounted colour plates and a map. Letterpress within decorative sepia border. Vignettes in the text. Original decorative brown cloth gilt, red edges. Bookplate of Paul Landauer.

First edition.

BL 10125.f.12; Weber 903.

788. WEBSTER, Daniel. *Mr. Webster's Speech on the Greek Revolution.* Washington, D.C.: John S. Meehan, 1824.

8vo, pp. 1-50 (p.1=t). Disbound, in a quarter buckram box. Presentation inscription of Dr. Sewall on title.

First edition. A second edition was published at Boston the same year. Webster, a strong supporter of the Greek war of independence, made this decisive speech in the House of Representatives the 8th of December 1823. It indicated moral support for the Greek Revolution and influenced the American philhellenic movement. Webster's resolution led to a lengthy debate on the Greek question which began January 19, 1824 and lasted several days. A number of pamphlets appeared in connection with the debate, see Blackmer 1695 and 1696.

LoC DF814.W4; Blackmer 1777; Droulia 592.

789. WHELER, George. *A Journey into Greece... In Company of Dr Spon Of Lyons. In six books. Containing I. A Voyage from Venice to Constantinople. II. An Account of Constantinople and the adjacent places. III. A voyage through the Lesser Asia. IV. A Voyage from Zant through several parts of Greece to Athens. V. An Account of Athens. VI. Several journeys from Athens, into Attica, Corinth, Boeotia, &c...* London: for William Cademan, Robert Kettlewell, and Awnsham Churchill, MDCLXXXII. [=1682]

Folio, pp. [xiv] 1-80, 177-483 (p.[i]=t). With a large folding map, 4 plates of coins and 3 small plates tipped in (in some copies the 3 small plates are printed on 1 leaf). Engravings in the letterpress. Calf, back gilt, black leather label.

First and only edition. The work was translated into French in 1689. Wheler had been on the grand tour since 1673; he met Spon in Italy in 1675 and the two decided to travel to Greece and Turkey. Spon's account of this same journey appeared four years earlier, in 1678. It is interesting to compare the two texts. Spon is an antiquarian, while Wheler is especially interested in botany and topography. Wheler only brought

out this work when he learned that an English translation of Spon's work was being contemplated. In the event Spon's text was never translated into English, and Wheler's account became the standard English book on Greece for many years. The gap in the pagination occurs in all copies seen. It is probably due to two compositors working at the same time.

BL 567.i.1; Weber 413; Blackmer 1786; Atabey 1328;

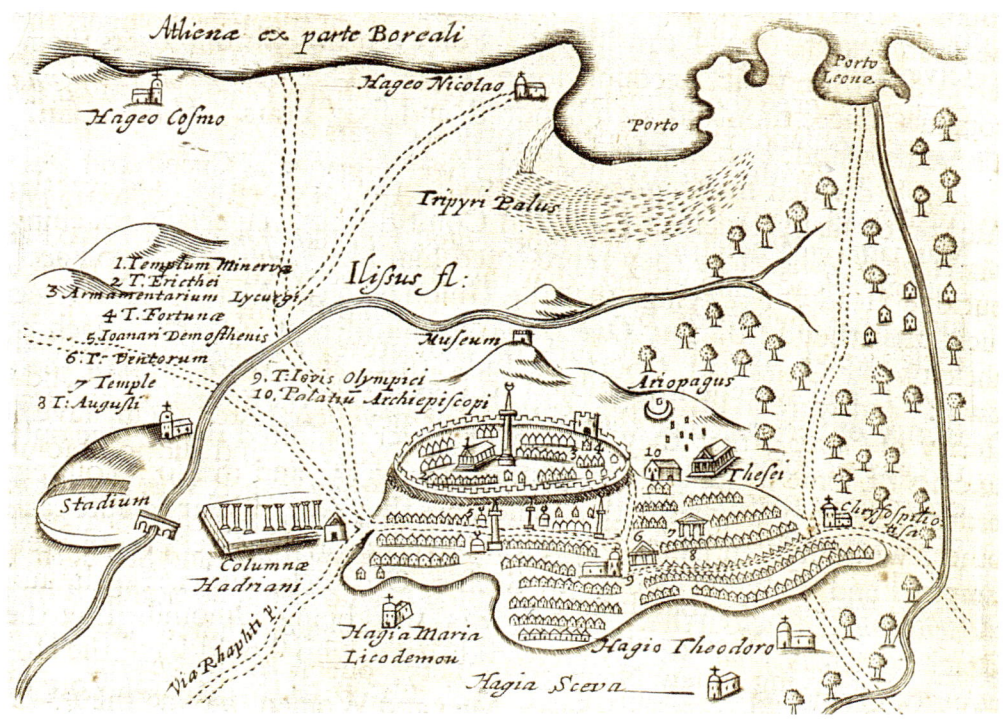

789

790. WHELER, George. *Voyage de Dalmatie, de Grèce, et du Levant. Enrichi de médailles, & de figures des principales antiquitez qui se trouvent dans ces lieux... Traduit de l'Anglois. Tome Premier. [... Second.]* Amsterdam: Jean Wolters, MDCLXXXIX. [=1689]

2 vols, sm. 8vo, pp. [xvi] 1-301; [i] 302-607 + 1 blank + [8] (p.[i]=engr t, [iii]=t; p.[i]=t, p.[8]=dir. to binder). With 72 engraved plates, 8 double-page plates of coins on stubs, 5 plates of inscriptions (4 folding) and a folding map. Contemporary calf, backs gilt in compartments with fleurons.

First edition in French. There are three issues, the second with the name Dunewald in the imprint. Wolters apparently produced this in cooperation with the Widow Dunewald of Antwerp. The same sheets were also published under the imprint of Horthmels of Antwerp. A second French edition was published at The Hague in 1723. Wheler's account of his travels in the Levant in 1675-76 with Jacob Spon first appeared in London in 1682. Wheler also wrote an account of the architectural structure and fittings of Byzantine churches, *An account of the churches, or places of assembly of the primitive Christians*.

BNF 31643323; GL Spentsas p. 188; Blackmer 1787; Atabey 1329; Weber 415 is a copy of the 1723 edition.

 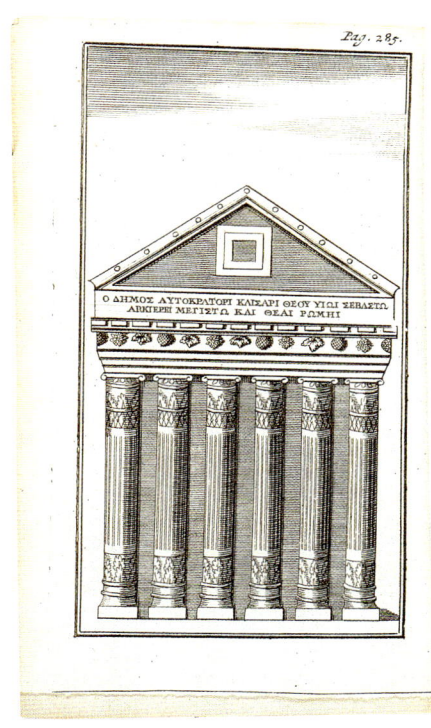

790

791. WIDMANN, Carolo Aurelio. *Discorso apologetico scritto dal nobil Uomo E. Co: Carlo Aurelio Widmann Provveditore Generale da Mar nell' Isole del Veneto Levante con l'aggiunta di alcune illustrazioni e documenti relativi. Lugli 1799.* [?Venice: 1799].

Lge 8vo, pp. XIV, 1-480 (p.I=t, pp.XIII-IV=errata). Modern quarter calf over decorated paper boards.

Apparently first and only edition of this extremely rare work on affairs in the Ionian islands up to the arrival of the French in 1797. Widmann, 'provveditore generale da mar', also produced *Dispacci da Corfu*, and *La Nave ben manovrata ossia Trattato di Manovra*; these two works were published in Venice in 1995.

We have been unable to locate a copy in any major library. See Bib. Ionienne 564 (– 'tres rare'). Papadopoulos BI 658 cites a copy in the Loverdos Library, Athens. Not in GL, BNF or BL. Not in Italian Union Catalogue on line. Not in COPAC, ARGOS or Karlsruhe.
Collation: *^{7} A-2G^8.

792. WILDE, William Robert Wills. *Narrative of a Voyage to Madeira, Teneriffe, and along the Shores of the Mediterranean, Including a visit to Algiers, Egypt, Palestine, Tyre, Rhodes, Telmessus, Cyprus, and Greece... In Two Volumes. Vol. I. [... Vol. II.]* Dublin: William Curry, and London: Longman, Orme... [et al.], 1840.

2 vols, 8vo, pp. xiv + [i] 1-464; viii, 1-495 (pp.i=ts, [1]=list of illustrations). With 4 lithographed plates and 2 plans. Numerous wood engravings in the text. Contemporary polished calf by Thomas Gaw of Coleraine, with his ticket. Ownership signature of Thomas McGea on the lower pastedown of vol. 2.

First edition. A second edition appeared in 1844 in one volume. This is an account of a nine month tour in the Mediterranean. The plates are after drawings by Robert Meiklam, Wilde's patient and travelling companion. This copy lacks two of the plates and a plan.

BL 791.k.10; Blackmer 1795. This edition not in Weber but see 359; Abbey 199.

793. WILHELM II, *Emperor of Germany* (1859-1941). *Erinnerungen an Korfu.* Berlin and Leipzig: Walter de Gruyter, 1924.

8vo, pp. 143 [2] (pp.1=[ ], 2=fp, 3=t, p.[2]=cul-de-lampe). With 2 folding maps and a folding plan. Original green cloth, faded.

First and only edition. With a description of the Achilleion, built for Elizabeth of Austria and later sold to Wilhelm II.

GL GT3314.1. Not in BLC on line.

794. WILKINS, William. *Atheniensia, or Remarks on the Topography and Buildings of Athens.* London: W. Bulmer for John Murray, 1816.

8vo, pp. viii + [3] 218 (pp.i=t, [1]=conts, [2]=errata, [3]=st). With a folding plan of Athens; without the double-page plate of the Erechtheum which should be present. Contemporary tree calf, back gilt in compartments, olive leather label, by Nettleton & Son, Plymouth, with their ticket.

First and only edition. The architect Wilkins was the prime exponent of the Greek revival style in England. Setting out in 1801, he travelled in the Levant for four years and was resident in Athens for some period in 1802. In 1807 he published *The Antiquities of Magna Graecia*, a work on the Greek buildings in southern Italy which was well received; the list of subscribers included many travellers such as Gell, Aberdeen, Hope, Elgin, Clarke and others.

BL 560.a.5; Blackmer 1798.

795. WILKINSON, Charles, *editor.* ***A Tour through Asia Minor and the Greek Islands. With an account of the Inhabitants, Natural Productions and Curiosities. For the Instruction and Amusement of Youth.*** London: Darton & Harvey, 1806.

Sm. 8vo, pp. iv [4] 424 (pp.i=t, [1-3]=conts, [4]=errata + list of plates). With a large folding map and 3 folding engraved plates. Contemporary half calf gilt over marbled paper boards, red leather label.

First and apparently only edition. This is a children's book compiled from the narratives of many travellers, in the form of a tour made by an uncle and his two nephews.

BL 794.b.7; Blackmer 1799; Weber 11.

796. WILLEMIN, Nicolas Xavier, and Charles Phillippe CAMPION DE TERSAN. ***Choix de Costumes civils et militaires des peuples de l'antiquité, leurs instrumens de musique, leurs meubles, et les décorations intérieurs de leurs maisons, d'après les monumens antiques, avec un texte tiré des anciens Auteurs... Tome Premier. [... Tome Second.]*** Paris: Pierre Plassan for the Author, An VI. 1798-[1802].

2 vols in 1, folio, pp. [iii] 5-108; 19 [1] (pp.[i]=ht, [iii]=t, pp.106-108=directions to binder and first list of subscribers, [1]=second list of subscribers). With 2 engraved titles and 77 plates in v.1 no'd 2-78, and 101 plates in v.2 no'd 2-102. Contemporary calf, sides framed in gilt with grape vine.

First and only edition, printed in 30 livraisons. The text was edited by Campion de Tersan, the plates drawn and engraved by Willemin, antiquary and engraver. The subscribers included Elgin and David. This work was used as a pattern book by many craftsmen whose names appear in the lists of subscribers, with jewellers, embroiderers, and wall-paper manufacturers among them. There is no printed title in volume two, only the engraved title..

BNF 31652097; Blackmer 1810. Colas 3085 also cites large paper copies without letterpress; Brunet V, 1453.

797. WILLIAMS, Hugh William. *Travels in Italy, Greece, and the Ionian Islands, in a series of letters descriptive of manners, scenery, and the fine arts.* Edinburgh: Archibald Constable, 1820.

2 vols, 8vo, pp. xxii [i] 1-399 + [1] + [1]; xiv [i] 437 + [1] (pp.i=hts, pp.[i]=sts, [1]=errata, p.[1] in v.1=list of plates, p.[1] in v.2=advert). With 18 engraved plates. Recent quarter tan morocco gilt.

First and only edition. This was the first work Williams published connected with his travels in 1816-17. Volume two is wholly devoted to Greece.

BL 1047.e.1-2; Weber 98. Not in Blackmer.

798. WILLIAMS, Hugh William. *Select Views in Greece with Classical Illustrations.* London: Longman, Rees... [et al.], and Edinburgh: Adam Black, M.DCCC.XXIX. [=1829]

2 vols, lge 8vo, pp. [vii] [64]; [ii], [64] [1] (pp.[i]=hts, [vii]=list of plates; [1]=verse). With 64 engraved plates. Half red morocco.

First edition, ordinary format. Note that the descriptive text, which consists of a page of text opposite each plate, is unpaginated except when the text continues onto a second page. This work was published in parts between 1824 and 1827. A 4to format is known, and also a large paper format with proof plates on india paper. Plates before letters are also known. Williams travelled in Greece and Italy before 1818 and made many paintings during these travels which earned him the sobriquet 'Grecian Williams'. On his return he published *Travels in Italy, Greece and the Ionian Islands, in a series of Letters.* In 1822 he exhibited his Greek paintings in Edinbugh, together with a catalogue: *Views in Greece... painted in watercolours.*

BL 653.d.20; Blackmer 1811; Weber 1116; Brunet V, 1455.

799. WILLIAMS, Hugh William. *Select Views in Greece with Classical Illustrations. Two volumes in One.* London: Longman, Rees... [et al.], and Edinburgh: Adam Black, M.DCCC.XXIX. [Reprinted from the Original Plates. 1892.]

Sm. folio, pp. [x] 63 (p.[i]=engr t). With 64 engraved plates by J. Horsborough after H. W. Williams. Old brown morocco gilt, top edge gilt.

Second edition, a reprint of the first edition of 1829.

This edition not in BLC; this edition not in Blackmer, but see 1811 for the first edition; see Atabey 1337.

798

799

800. WILLIS, Nathaniel Parker (1806-1867). *Summer Cruise in the Mediterranean on board an American Frigate.* London: T. Bosworth, 1853.

Sm. 8vo, pp. Xvi, 1-283 [1] + [2] (p.i=ht, missing, [1]=colophon, [1-2]=adverts). Half brown morocco over marbled paper boards.

First abridged English edition. Apparently another edition was published the same year by T. Nelson and Sons. American abridged editions were published the same year in New York, and in Rochester and Auburn in 1856, from Parker's original account of his experiences abroad, *Pencillings by the Way* (first edition London, 1835, first American edition Philadelphia, 1836). The work was reprinted in 1942 with a portrait and introduction. Willis was a prolific humourist, writer and journalist. He became foreign correspondent for the *New York Mirror* in 1831 and remained abroad for five years, sending weekly reports to the journal. In 1833 he was invited to join the U.S. Mediterranean Squadron aboard the frigate 'United States' on its summer tour. The reports describing this tour were published in the *Mirror* in 1834. Parker was one of the first American literary figures to travel in the Levant; an enthusiastic philhellene, he met Solomos in Corfu, and in Athens he met Otho, Pittakis, Trikoupis, Mavrocordatos and the Maid of Athens, Theresa Black. Parker later edited Poe's works and Bartlett's *American Scenery*.

BL 10027.c.27; Blackmer 1812; Weber 470; Larrabee, pp. 221-7.

801. WILLOUGHBY, Vera. *A Vision of Greece described and painted by Vera Willoughby.* London: Philip Allan, 1925.

4to, pp. viii, 1-197 + [1] (pp.i=ht, [1]=colophon). With 16 plates of colour reproductions of paintings. Half calf over marbled paper boards, back panelled gilt with tan leather labels, outer and lower edges uncut.

First edition. Five hundred copies were printed; this is copy no. 489. The plates include landscapes in watercolours and genre scenes in pastels. The latter include many art deco elements. A very attractive work. Vera Willoughby illustrated books by various authors, including Laurence Sterne, Jane Austen, Farquhar, Horace, and Catullus, among others.

BL L.R.41.c.4; GL GT1332.

802. WILSON, Charles William, *editor. Picturesque Palestine Sinai and Egypt.* London: Virtue and Co. [1881-1884].

4 vols in 2, thick 4to, pp.X, 1-240; VI, 1-240; VI, 1-240; VI, 1-236 (pp.I=ts, III=tables of contents, V-VI=lists of plates). Titles in red and black. With engraved frontispiece and title in each

801

volume, 2 double-page maps and 34 plates of steel engravings (no'd in the list of plates 1-8, 1-10, 1-9, 1-7). Numerous wood engravings in the letterpress, some full-page. A very good large copy in half maroon morocco gilt.

First edition, with a later issue of vol. 1; it also appears with the date 1880. A supplement, sometimes referred to as vol. 5, was published in 1884 entitled *Social Life in Egypt* by Stanley Lane-Pool which contains an additional four plates. The contributors to these volumes include C.R. Conder, Selah Merrill and E.H. Palmer, among others. The plates are after J.D. Woodward, C. Werner, H. Fenn, R. Beavis, and H.A. Harper, engraved by S. Bradshaw, E. Brandard, C. Cousen, J.C. Armytage, A. Willmore, J. Godfrey, W. French, C. Bertrand, J.J. Crew, and J. Saddler.

BL 1785.a.17 gives 1880-1884; Blackmer 1817 calls for 38 plates for the five volumes.

803. WILSON, Samuel Sheridan. ***A Narrative of the Greek Mission; or, Sixteen years in Malta and Greece: including tours in the Peloponnesus, in the Aegean and Ionian Isles; with Remarks on the religious opinions, moral state, social habits, politics, language, history, and lazarettos of Malta and Greece. With engravings by G. Baxter.*** London: John Snow, 1839.

8vo, pp. [i] i-ii, v-xiii, 1-596 + 2 pp. of adverts (pp.[i]=t on thick paper, ii=ded to Queen Adelaide). The vignette title is printed on thick paper. With a woodcut frontispiece printed in colour. Original embossed green cloth.

First edition, first issue. The work was reissued c. 1850 using the same sheets, but with an undated title, printed, and without the vignette. Wilson, who arrived in Malta in 1819, went to Greece in 1824, where he was the first missionary to be employed full-time in Greece, by Leicester Stanhope (q.v.). His description of Greece contains some account of the revolution and its aftermath. On his return to Malta he established the Mission Press, where he published tales and moral tracts in modern Greek for children, many composed or translated by himself. He also published an Anglo-Greek primer in 1829. The frontispiece is an early example of printing in colours by George Baxter's process of wood engraving.

BL 790.h.24; Blackmer 1820 (2nd issue); Weber 305; St. Clair pp. 199-201. See Abbey I, p. 136 for a general note on Baxter's process.

804. WILSON, William Rae. ***Travels in the Holy Land, Egypt, &c. &c. Third edition. In Two Volumes. Vol. II.*** London: for Longman, Rees, Orme... [et al.], 1831.

2 vols, 8vo, pp. xviii + [4] 1-404; viii 1-440 (pp.i=ts, missing in vol. 1, p.[1]=list of plates, pp.[2-4]=reviews. With 11 aquatinted plates (of 13) by J. Clark. Old half calf. Old ownership signature of James McCheyne of Woodhall House.

Third edition, with additional material. The first two editions (1823, 1824) each appeared in one volume only. A fourth edition appeared in 1847.

BL 1046.k.3-4. This edition not in Blackmer but see 1822 (first ed.). This edition not in GL.

805. WIMMER, Gottlieb August. *Neuestes Gemälde der europäischen Türkei und Griechenlands.* Vienna: Anton Doll, 1833.

8vo, pp. [iv] 1-425 [1] (p.[i]=[], [ii]=series title, [iii]=t, [1]=advert). Lacks the 6 engravings (Adrianople, Acheron, Berat, Ioannina, Megaspileon, Mistras). 19th c. quarter calf over marbled paper boards.

?First edition. This forms volume 29 of Schutz's 'Allgemeine Erdkunde, oder Beschreibung aller Länder'.

GL GT2422.5. Not in BLC. Karlsruhe cites several copies. Not in Blackmer.

806. WISKOTT, Carl T. *Griechenland im Auto erlebt.* Munich: F. Bruckmann, 1936.

Sm. 4to, pp. 165 + [1] (p.1=t, [1]=st). With 3 sketch maps at the end. Numerous photographic illustrations in the text. Original blue cloth.

First edition. Four friends from Berlin travel to Olympia to accompany the 'Fackelstaffellauf' or the transport of the Olympic flame to Berlin for the 1936 Olympics. The Greek marathon runner Spyros Louis, who won the gold medal in the first Olympic games in Athens in 1896, carried the flame into the Olympic stadium in Berlin. The locations of the interesting photographs, taken by Dr. Paul Wolff and - Tritschler, are not always indicated.

BL 10125.ccc.35.

807. WITTMAN, William. *Travels in Turkey, Asia-Minor, Syria, and across the desert into Egypt during the years 1799, 1800, and 1801, in company with the Turkish Army, and the British Military Mission. To which are annexed, observations on the plague and on the diseases prevalent in Turkey, and a meteorological Journal.* London: T. Gillet for Richard Phillips, 1803.

A Greek Lady

Published March 1 1803 by R.Phillips 71 St Pauls Church Yard

807

4to, pp. xvi, 1-595 [1] (p.i=t, [1]=advert). With a folding engraved frontispiece, a folding map, folding facsimile of the Firman, and 21 plates no'd I-XX + 1 unnumbered plate. Of the numbered plates 16 are printed in sanguine and hand coloured. Recent panelled red morocco.

First edition. A German translation was published at Leipzig in 1804. Wittman accompanied the British Military Mission which, together with the Turkish Army, travelled overland from Constantinople through Asia Minor and Syria in 1799 to fight Napoleon's forces in Egypt. Other members of the Mission included Leake, E.D. Clarke, Elgin's secretary William Hamilton, and Hammer-Purgstall, interpreter at the Austrian embassy to the Porte and future historian of the Ottoman Empire. The coloured plates are costume figures of military functionaries; some of these plates were later used in MacLean's *Military Costume of Turkey*.

BL 148.d.5; Blackmer 1832; Weber 647; Atabey 1344.

There is another copy in the Contominas collection, in contemporary calf, rebacked, gilt ruled sides. 19th c. ownership signature of John Hosken Harper.

808. WOOD, John Turtle. ***Discoveries at Ephesus Including the Site and Remains of the Great Temple of Diana.*** London: Longmans, Green, and Co., 1877.

Lge 8vo, pp. xviii [2] 1-285, 42, 20, 12, 10, 74, 20, 44 (p.i=ht, [2]=errata, pp.42 and following are transcriptions of inscriptions). With lithographed frontispiece, a folding plan of the site and 33 lithographed plates of which 4 are coloured and 5 double-page. Numerous wood engravings in the text. Old green calf, sides panelled in gilt with acorns in corners, back gilt in compartments, red leather label, inner gilt dentelles, gilt edges.

First edition. Wood, an architect, was the first excavator of Ephesus, and he undertook the initial excavations at his own expense in 1863. As his theories proved correct he continued his excavations, under the auspices of the British Museum, until 1874.

BL 07704.h.28. Not in Blackmer or Atabey.

808

809. WORDSWORTH, Christopher (1807-1885). *Athens and Attica: Journal of a Residence there.* London: John Murray, M.DCCC.XXXVI. [=1836]

8vo, pp. xii, 1-285 (p.i=ht). With frontispiece and 2 plates lithographed by Louis Haghe after Robert Cockerell, a folding plan of Athens, a folding map of Attica and a folding plate of inscriptions. Uncut, in the original green cloth.

First edition. A second edition appeared in 1837. Wordsworth, who is best known for his encyclopaedic work, *Greece, Pictorial, Descriptive and Historical*, was the nephew of the poet and his literary executor. He travelled extensively in Greece in 1832-3 and in fact discovered the location of the oracle of Zeus at Dodona, but the only part of his journal to be published was this detailed account of Athens and Attica, although Wordsworth's knowledge of Greece was displayed in his encyclopaedic work.

BL 1047.d.15; Blackmer 1839. This edition not in Weber.

There is another copy of the first edition in the Contominas collection, in half brown morocco, panelled back gilt, book label of 'Hoar Cross, Burton on Trent'.

810. WORDSWORTH, Christopher. *Athens and Attica: Journal of a Residence there.* London: John Murray, M.DCCC.XXXVII. [=1837]

8vo, pp. xx, 1-297 + 8 pp. of adverts (p.i=ht). With frontispiece and 2 plates lithographed by Louis Haghe after Robert Cockerell, hand coloured, a folding plan of Athens and a folding map of Attica, plus a folding plate of inscriptions. Uncut, in the original green cloth. Contemporary ownership signature of Montague Williams dated from Corfu, 1844, on title. Bookplate of Errol Graham Sebastian.

Second edition, revised by John Wordsworth. The appendix contains an additional letter from Bracebridge concerning the new excavation on the Acropolis and developments in Athens. This copy comes from the library of Errol Graham Sebastian, British consular official in Thessaloniki c. 1955. His fine collection of travel books was dispersed in the 1960s, and books from his library are to be found in the Blackmer and Atabey catalogues.

BL 1560/2865; Weber 266.

811. WORDSWORTH, Christopher. *Athens and Attica: Notes of a Tour. Third edition, revised.* London: John Murray, 1855.

Sm. 8vo, pp. xviii [i] 1-251 [1] (pp.i=ht, [i]=list of ills, [1]=colophon). Title printed on thick paper. With a wood-engraved frontispiece and two plates, a folding map, two folding plans and a folding inscription. Wood engravings in the text. New brown cloth, gilt edges. Ownership stamp of St. Aloysius College, Glasgow, ex-dono inscription of the Rev. F. de Zulueta on a preliminary leaf dated 1884.

Third edition, completely revised by John Wordsworth from the first edition of 1836. The plates of views in this edition, by the Maltese artist George Scharf, are not the same as those in the earlier editions after Cockerell. The list of plates includes the wood engravings in the text.

BL 10125.c.; Weber 267. This edition not in Blackmer.

812. WORDSWORTH, Christopher. *Greece, Pictorial, Descriptive and Historical. A New Edition, carefully revised. With numerous engravings ... And a History of the characteristics of Greek Art by George Scharf.* London: John Murray, 1859.

809

810

Lge 8vo, pp. xxiv, 452 (p.i=t). Text within rules. With 21 engraved plates (including frontispiece, engraved title and 2 maps). 19th c. decorative red morocco gilt, back gilt with palmettos in circles, gilt edges, by R. and A. Suttaby of London, signed on inner dentelle. Armorial bookpalte of Harry Chester Goodheart with his motto 'A Deo Omnia'.

Third edition of this very successful encyclopaedic work. The first edition was published in 1839/40. There is a so-called second edition dated 1844, but this is an issue of the first edition with the text printed within borders. The true second edition appeared in 1853, with the addition of George Scharf's essay on Greek art. This 'new edition' contains only 21 plates, as opposed to the 28 plates of the earlier editions. Wordsworth's *Greece* is a purely descriptive work, although based on his travels in Greece in 1832 and 1833.

BL 10125.e.24;. This edition not in Blackmer but see 1841-1842. This edition not in Weber.

812

813. WORDSWORTH, Christopher. ***Greece, Pictorial, Descriptive, and Historical... And a History of the characteristics of Greek Art by George Scharf, F.S.A. Fifth Edition.*** London: John Murray, 1868.

Lge 8vo, pp. xxiv, 452 (p.=t, pp.1-87=Scharf essay). With 21 steel engravings (including engraved title, frontispiece and 2 maps). Numerous wood engravings in text. Contemporary pol-

812

473

ished calf, back gilt in compartments with fleurons, brown leather label, a prize binding from the Middlesex Hospital School of Medicine, with its arms on both sides.

Fifth edition, first published in 1839. The fourth edition was published in 1862.

This edition not in BLC. This edition not in Blackmer or Weber.

813

814. WORDSWORTH, Christopher. *La Grèce pittoresque et historique ... traduction de M. E. Regnault.* Paris: L. Curmer, 1841.

Lge 8vo, pp. [iii] 1-372 (p.[i]=t, pp.364-72=list of plates). Without the 28 hors texte plates. Contemporary half red roan over embossed cloth, back gilt romantique, with the intials CJV and the date 1849 stamped at the foot of the spine.

First edition in French, translated by Elias George Regnault.

BNF 36585568; Weber 1140. This edition not in Blackmer.

815. WORSLEY, Sir Richard. *Museum Worsleyanum. Eine Sammlung von antiken Basreliefs, Büsten, Statuen und Gemmen, nebst Ansichten aus der Levante. Herausgegeben von Heinrich Wilhelm Eberhard, Architect, und Heinrich Schaefer, Secretair der Grossherzoglich*

813

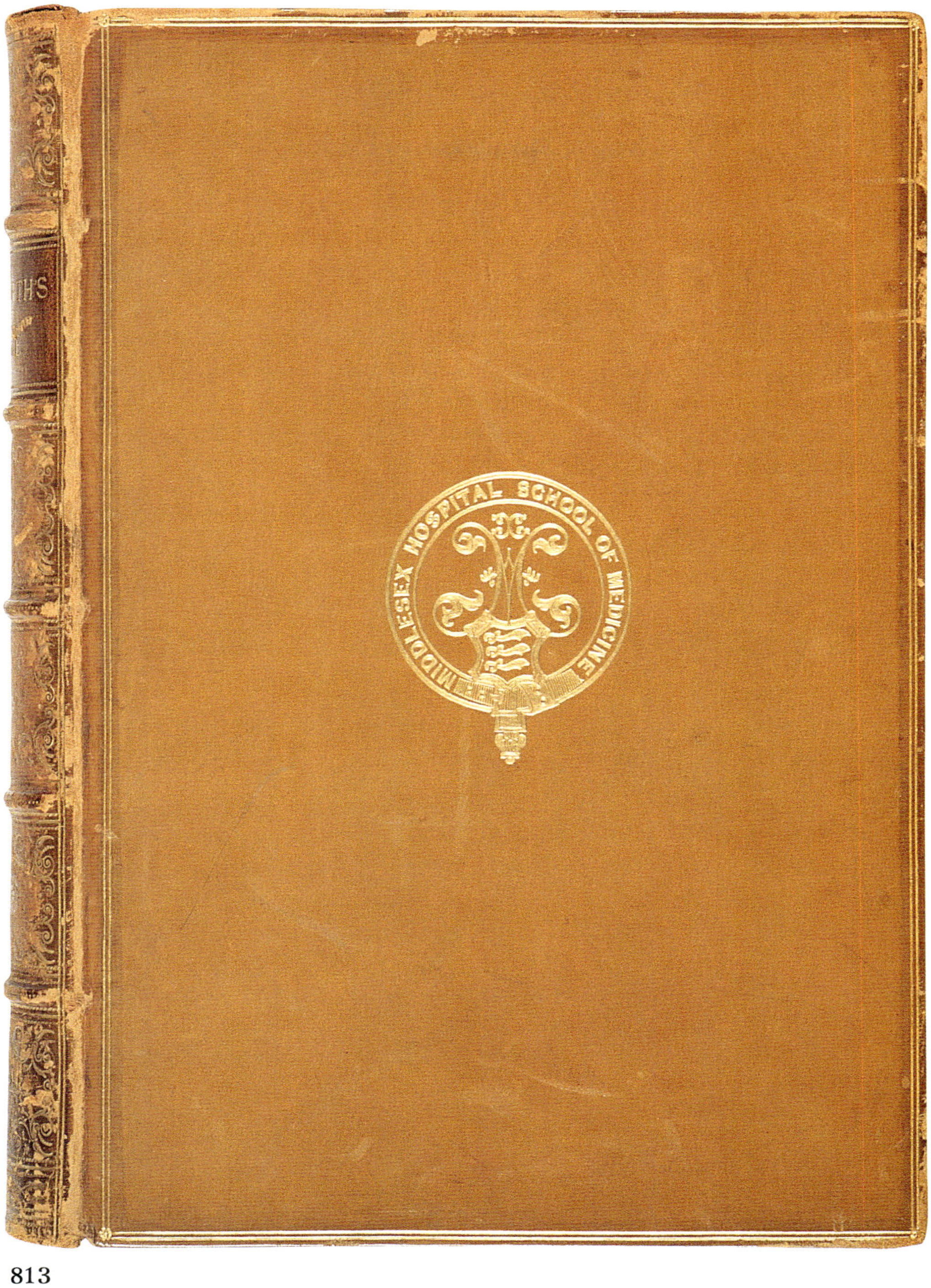

475

Hessischen Hofbibliothek. Leipzig and Darmstadt: Carl Wilhelm Leske [1826-29].

6 parts, sm. folio. no letterpress. 53 plates containing 69 engravings (29 in part 1, 10 in part 2, 13 in part 3, 9 in part 4 and 8 in part 5). Loose in the original printed paper wrappers.

First German edition, all published, edited by H. Schaefer and H.W. Eberhard. This, the only German edition of the *Museum Worsleyanum*, was published in six livraisons between 1826 and 1829. At about the same time Leske also published the German edition of Stuart and Revett. The *Museum Worsleyanum* was first published in two volumes, 1794-1803, second edition in 1824. The German edition is uncommon, especially in this state. Worsley, British Resident at Venice, toured the Levant between 1785 and 1787, accompanied by the architect Willy Reveley. The views have been engraved after drawings by Reveley and William Pars, who contributed to the *Ionian Antiquities*. Worsley is of special interest as being the first British traveller to bring back antiquities from Greece itself.

Karlsruhe cites 6 copies in German libraries. This edition not in Blackmer but see 1842 (English ed.) This ed. not in COPAC.

816. WREDE, Maria Elisabeth. [*Views from Rhodes. 1918.*]

Lge folio, no letterpress. With 15 pencil, pen and watercolour drawings, on india paper, mounted, most signed M.E. Wrede, one dated from Rhodes, 1918. Quarter brown morocco gilt, red leather title label, incorrectly stamped 'E.M.' Wrede. From the library of Şefik Atabey, with his book label.

This charming collection of drawings depicts daily life in Rhodes, with views and costumes. The drawings were probably removed from Wrede's original sketchbook, possibly dated 1918, and mounted in this format, between two leaves of mounting paper with a window in the upper leaf. We have been unable to discover anything about the artist, but she may be connected with Walther Wrede, a member of the German Archaeological Institute in Athens in the 1930s. M.E. Wrede also contributed illustrations to Marignac's *Cyclades*, q.v.

Atabey 1349.

817. WRIGHT, George Newenham. *The Rhine, Italy, and Greece. In a series of drawings from nature by Colonel Cockburn, Major Irton; Messrs. Bartlett, Leitch and Wolfensberger. With historical and legendary descriptions by the Rev. G.N. Wright, MA.* London and Paris: Fisher, Son & Co. [c. 1842].

2 vols, 4to, pp.[iv] 5-76; [iv] 5-90 + [2] (pp.[i]=ts?, [1-2]=index). *With two engraved titles and 71 (32, 39) steel-engraved plates, including frontispieces. Half brown morocco.*

First edition. Wright had previously produced the text for *The Shores and Islands of the Mediterranean*, published by Fisher c. 1840. A collected edition of these two works was published c. 1851 as *Belgium, the Rhine, Italy, Greece and the Shores and Islands of the Mediterranean*. Wright was a prolific miscellaneous writer who produced school books, and dictionaries and grammars, and provided the texts for illustrated works on China, France, etc. as well as for a series of guides to English topography.

BL 789.e.20; Weber 1152. See Blackmer 1845.

817

818. WYON, Reginald. ***The Balkans from within.*** London: James Finch & Co., 1904.

Lge 8vo, pp. xviii [1] 1-475 (p.i=ht, p.v=ded. [1]=st). With photographic frontispiece, folding map, a folding plan of the area around Kastoria, and 103 photographic illustrations on 75 plates. Original red cloth, photographic illustration mounted on upper cover, top edge gilt.

Apparently first edition. Wyon was a journalist who travelled extensively in the Balkans. He contributed articles to *Blackwood's, Chambers* and other magazines. He blamed the state of the Balkans in 1904 on the consequences of the Treaty of Berlin, which

followed the Russian-Turkish war of 1877-78. The various chapters represent travels over a period of several years previous to 1904.

BL 10126.ee.37.

819. WYSE, Sir Thomas. *An Excursion in the Peloponnesus in the year 1858... With numerous illustrations.* London: Day & Son, 1865.

2 vols, lge 8vo, pp. xii + [2] 314; ix [iii] 243 (recte 343) (pp.i=hts, [1-2]=list of illustrations). With 2 frontispieces, a folding map and 22 etched plates. Recent brown buckram, tan leather labels.

First edition, published posthumously and edited by Wyse's niece Winifrede M. Wyse from the journals kept by Wyse during this excursion. Wyse, British ambassador in Athens from 1849 to 1862, first travelled in the Levant 1818-1820. On the outbreak of the Crimean War, Greece attempted to assist Russia, thus drawing down on her head the wrath of the allies. Wyse suggested a Franco-British occupation of Piraeus, and for nearly three years he virtually ruled Greece together with the French envoy. In 1857 the commission formed to look into the still outstanding Greek loan of 1833 had requested a report on the Greek economy. Wyse travelled all over the country in order to gather the information necessary for the report. The plates are lithographed by A. Severn after drawings by Wyse himself, and the artist Vincenzo Lanza, who accompanied the party. Lanza probably came to Greece c. 1848 when he was exiled from Venice by the Austrians. These drawings may be some of the earliest of Lanza's published work; he later produced oil paintings of Greek scenes.

BL 10125.e.19; Blackmer 1847; Weber 646.

820. WYSE, Sir Thomas. *Impressions of Greece... With an introduction by his Niece, Miss Wyse, and Letters from Greece to Friends at Home by Arthur Penrhyn Stanley, Dean of Westminter.* London: Hurst and Blackett, 1871.

8vo, pp. vii [i] 332 (pp.i=ht, [i]=errata). Three-quarter red morocco, back gilt in compartments with fleurons, tan and black leather labels.

First edition. This account of an excursion in Boeotia, Euboea and Roumeli c. 1859 was edited by Miss Wyse from her uncle's journals. Her introduction gives an interesting picture of the political situation in Greece during the period of her uncle's ambassadorship. The three letters by Dean Stanley describe an excursion to Delphi which he made with Wyse.

BL 10126.d.16; Blackmer 1848; Weber 703.

821. YONGE, Charlotte Mary (1823-1901). *Young Folks' History of Greece.* Boston: [Rockwell Churchill for] Estes & Lauriat [1879].

8vo, pp. 427 (p.1=[ ], 2=fp, 3=t). Illustrations in text, some full-page with versos blank, but included in pagination. Original tan decorative cloth gilt.

First edition, second issue. The first issue seems to be that of 1878; in that year the work was published in Boston, Cincinnati and New York by three different publishers. According to the title verso of this copy Estes and Lauriat shared the edition with the Boston publisher D. Lothrop under whose imprint the work had appeared in 1878. All these copies have the same pagination. According to the Library of Congress this work was originally published as *Aunt Charlotte' Stories of Greek History for the Little Ones*, London, 1876. In 1879 it was published by Estes and Lauriat as *A Popular History of Greece*. Mrs. Yonge is best known for her novels of Victorian family life, in particular the *Heir of Redclyffe*. She was also a prolific writer of tales and popular histories for children.

This issue not in LoC. Not in BLC or COPAC.

822. [YORKE, Philip, 2nd Earl of Hardwicke, Charles YORKE and others.] *Lettres Athéniennes, ou correspondance d'un agent du Roi de Perse, à Athènes, pendant la guerre du Péloponèse; traduites de l'Anglais, par Alexandre-Louis Villeterque.* Paris: Dentu, 1803.

3 vols, 8vo, pp. (31) 1-396; [iii] 1-408; [iii] 1-385 [1] (pp.(1), [i]=hts; [1]=list of plates; the errata appear on the verso of the half title of vol.1). With twelve engraved plates (including frontispieces in each vol.). Without the map of Greece at the end. Old calf, rubbed, blue endpapers.

First edition in French, translated from the *Athenian Letters*. According to the BNF, a second edition in 4 vols, 12mo appeared the same year under Dentu's imprint, while another French translation, by Mathieu Christophe, also appeared in 4 vols in 12mo the same year published by Ouvrier. A later edition appeared in 1805 in 3 volumes. The *Letters*, fictitious letters describing Athens during the Peloponnesian War written by a group of Cambridge dons and students, circulated in literary circles for many years, but the first edition appeared in only twelve copies in 1741-3, edited by Thomas Birch; a second edition of only 100 copies appeared in 1781; this edition was pirated and appeared in 1792 in 2 vols, 8vo (London and Dublin issues). The first authorized public edition appeared in 1798. This work is often compared to *Anacharsis*, and Barthélemy admired it greatly: 'si j'avois en ce modele devant les yeux on n'aurois pas commencé mon ouvrage...'. The translator Villeterque was a miscellaneous writer. The engravings are by Adam and may have been produced for the 1798 edition.

BNF 36587744; GL V4.2q. This edition not in Blackmer but see 1859.

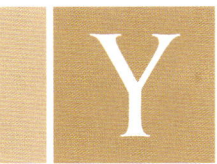

823. YOUNG, James Foster. *Five Weeks in Greece.* London: Sampson Low, Marston, Searle & Rivington, 1876.

8vo, pp. xvi, 1-299 (p.i=ht, 295-99=appendix). With an engraved frontispiece. Original embossed green cloth gilt.

First and only edition, and apparently the author's only work. The excursion took place in May and June, 1875, through the Peloponnesus, Attica and Boeotia. It was written after the Dilessi murders and the preface discusses the question of brigandage in Greece. The appendix includes the War Song of Rhigas, with a version by Byron.

BL 10125.aa.5; Blackmer 1862; Weber 754.

823

824. YOUNG, Sir William. *The History of Athens; including a commentary on the principles, policy, and practice, of Republican Government; and on the causes of elevation and of decline, which operate in every free and commercial State. The Third Edition, corrected and enlarged.* London: W. Bulmer for Robson, Payne, and White, and Prince, Oxford, and Deighton, Cambridge, 1804.

8vo, pp. xxiv, 1-475 [1] (pp.i=t, [1]=errata). Old three-quarter polished green calf, red leather labels, by Zaehnsdorf, with his stamp on the fly-leaf.

Third edition, enlarged. First published in 1777 as *The Spirit of Athens*; a second edition appeared in 1786 under the new title *The History of Athens*. A prospectus to the third edition was issued in 1803 which included the preface to the work. Young was a political and economic writer who wrote on the West Indies; he edited Hornemann's travel writings, but he was interested in Athens essentially as an example of a type of government.

BLC 584.f.19. Not in GL.

824

825. ZERVOS, Skevos George. **Rhodes Capitale du Dodécanèse**. Paris: [Ernest Flammarion], 1920.

4to, pp. [vii] 11-377 [1] + [1] (pp.[i]=ht, [1]=colophon). Numerous illustrations in the text, of which a number are coloured, with versos blank, but included in the pagination. Half red roan.

First edition.

BNF 36571251.

REFERENCES CITED AND BIBLIOGRAPHY

ABBREVIATIONS

INDEX OF NAMES

INDEX OF PRINTERS, PUBLISHERS, BOOKSELLERS
AND BOOKBINDERS

INDEX OF PROVENANCES

CORRIGENDA

REFERENCES CITED AND BIBLIOGRAPHY

Note: Much of the research work for the Contominas Catalogue has been done on line, searching catalogues of the major rare book and university libraries. The libraries which have been searched on line include, for the most part, the British Library, the Bibliothèque Nationale, the University of Amsterdam Library, the Bavarian State Library and other German libraries, the Marcian Library, Venice, and the Italian Union Catalogue. These references are given in the relative entries.

Abbey = *Travel in aquatint and lithography, 1770-1860 from the library of J.R. Abbey. A bibliographical catalogue.* 2 vols. London, 1956-1957.

Adams = H.M. Adams. *Catalogue of books printed on the continent of Europe, 1501-1600, in Cambridge libraries.* 2 vols. Cambridge, 1967.

Adhemar = J. Adhemar. 'Les lithographies de paysage en France à l'époque romantique' in *Archives de l'art française.* Vol. 19, pp. 189-367. Paris, 1938.

Amat di S. Filippo = P. Amat di S. Filippo. *Biografia dei viaggiatori italiani.* Rome, 1882. (Vol. I of *Studi biografici e bibliografici sulla storia della geografia in Italia.*)

Anderson = S. Anderson. *An English consul in Turkey, Paul Rycaut at Smyrna.* Oxford, 1989.

Armao = E. Armao. *Vincenzo Coronelli: cenni sul'uomo e la sua vita, catalogo ragionato delle sue opere...* Florence, 1944.

Atabey = *The Şefik E. Atabey Collection Books Manuscripts and Maps The Ottoman World Text by Leonora Navari.* [London, Istanbul printed, 1998.]

Barbier = A.A. Barbier. *Bibliographie des ouvrages anonymes.* 4 vols. Paris, 1872-3 (reprint, 1964).

Basch = Sophie Basch. *Le Mirage Grec La Grèce moderne devant l'opinion Française depuis la Creation de l'École d'Athènes jusqu'à la Guerre Civile Grecque (1846-1946).* [Athens, 1995.]

Bengesco = G. Bengesco. *Essai d'une notice bibliographique sur la question d'orient. Orient Européen, 1821-1897.* Brussels, 1897.

Bib. Ionienne = E. Legrand and H. Pernot. *Bibliographie Ionienne description raisonnée des ouvrages publiés par les Grecs des Sept-Iles du quinzième siècles à l'année 1900.* 2 vols. Paris, 1910.

References Cited and Bibliography

Blackmer = Leonora Navari. *Greece and the Levant The Catalogue of the Henry Myron Blackmer Collection of Books and Manuscripts.* London, 1989.

BLC = *British Museum general catalogue of printed books to 1955.* Compact edition. New York, Readex Microprint Corporation, 1967.

BL Maps = British Library. *Catalogue of printed maps.* 15 vols. London, 1967. Supplements 1978, 1989.

BNF = *Catalogue general des livres imprimés de la Bibliothèque Nationale.* Paris, 1897-1981.

Boppe = A. Boppe. *Les peintres du Bosphore au dix-huitième siècle.* Paris, 1911. Second, illustrated, edition, Paris, 1989.

Brunet = J.C. Brunet. *Manuel du libraire et de l'amateur de livres.* 6 vols. Paris, 1860-65 (reprint Berlin, 1922). Supplement. Paris 1878-80.

Carré = J.M. Carré. *Voyageurs et écrivains français en Egypte.* 2 vols. Cairo, 1932.

Carteret = L. Carteret. *Le trésor du bibliophile romantique et moderne 1801-1875.* 3 vols. Paris, 1924-1927.

Chew = Samuel C. Chew. *Byron in England, his fame and afterfame.* London, 1924.

Chew = Samuel C. Chew. *The crescent and the rose: Islam and England during the renaissance.* New York, 1937.

Cicogna = E.A. Cicogna. *Saggio de bibliografia veneziana.* Venice, 1847.

Cohen-De Ricci = H. Cohen. *Guide de livres à gravures du XVIIIe siècle.* Sixième édition revue... par Seymour de Ricci. Paris, 1912.

Colas = R.J. Colas. *Bibliographie du costume et de la mode.* 2 vols. Paris, 1933 (reprint New York, 1963).

Cordier = H. Cordier. *Bibliotheca Sinica. Dictionnaire bibliographique des ouvrages relatifs à l'empire chinois.* 5 vols. Paris, 1904-1924.

Cox = E.G. Cox. *A Reference Guide to the Literature of Travel.* Seattle, 1935-1938.

Cust = *History of the Society of Dilettanti,* compiled by L. Cust and edited by Sir Sidney Colvin. London, 1914.

Dakin = D. Dakin. *The unification of Greece, 1770-1923.* London, [1972].

Doens = Irénée Doens. *Bibliographie de la Sainte Montagne de l'Athos.* Mount Athos, 2001 (reprint of the 1964 edition).

Droulia = L. Droulia. *Philhellénisme, ouvrages inspirés par la guerre de l'independance grecque 1821-1833 Repertoire Bibliographique.* Athens, 1974.

Fairfax Murray = H.W. Davies. *Catalogue of a collection of early German books in the library of C. Fairfax Murray.* 2 vols. London, 1961-1962.

Gernsheim = H. Gernsheim. *The History of Photography.* London, 1969.

GL Spentsas = *Books from the Collection of Damianos Kyriazis donated to the Gennadius Library by Maria Kyriazis-Spentsas.* Athens, 2001.

Göllner = C. Göllner. *Turcica: die europäischen Türkendrucke des XVI. Jahrhunderts.* 2 vols. Berlin 1961-1968.

Graesse = J.G. Graesse. *Trésor de livres rares et precieux.* 7 vols in 8. Berlin, 1922.

Guigard = J. Guigard. *Armorial du bibliophile.* 2 vols. Paris, 1870-1873.

GV 1700-1910 = *Gesamtverzeichnis des deutschsprachigen Schrifttums 1700-1910.* Munich, 1979-1987.

Halkett and Laing = S. Halkett and J. Laing. *Dictionary of anonymous and pseudonymous English literature.* 9 vols. London, 1926.

Hamilton = A. Hamilton, *Europe and the Arab World.* London, 1994.

Harris = Eileen Harris, assisted by Nicholas Savage. *British architectural books and writers 1556-1785.* London, 1980.

Hilmy = Prince Ibrahim Hilmy. *The literature of Egypt and the Sudan.* 2 vols. London, 1886-1887.

Hoffman = S.F.W. Hoffman. *Bibliographisches Lexicon der gesammten Literatur der Griechen.* 3 vols. Amsterdam, 1961.

Iliou, P. = ʽΕλληνικὴ Βιβλιογραφία τοῦ 19ου Αἰώνα. Τόμος πρῶτος 1801-1818. Athens, 1997.

Karlsruhe = On line Catalogue of libraries in Germany, Norway, Sweden, Switzerland and Austria.

Koster = Daniël Koster. *To Hellen's Noble Land. Dutch Accounts of travellers, geographers and historians on Greece (1488-1854).* Athens, 1995.

Laborde = L.E.S.J. de Laborde. *Athènes aux XVe, XVIe, et XVIIe siècles.* 2 vols. Paris, 1854.

Larrabee = S.A. Larrabee. *Hellas observed: the American experience of Greece, 1775-1865.* New York, 1957.

Lascarides = A.K. Lascarides. *The search for Troy, 1553-1865.* [Indianapolis] Lilly Library, 1977.

Legrand = E. Legrand. *Bibliographie hellenique ou description des ouvrages publiés en Grec par des Grecs aux XVe et XVIe siècles [... 17e siècle ... 18e siècle].* 11 vols. Paris, 1885-1928.

Legrand albanaise = E. Legrand. *Bibliographie albanaise; description raisonnée des ouvrages publiés en albanais ou relatifs a l'Albanie du quinzième siècle à l'année 1900.* Paris, 1912.

Lowndes = W.T. Lowndes. *The bibliographer's manual of English literature.* New edition revised by H.G. Bohn. 4 vols. London, 1864.

Lumsden = H. Lumsden. *Bibliography of John Galt.* Glasgow, 1931.

Madan = F. Madan. *Oxford Books. A bibliography of printed works.* 3 vols. Oxford, 1895-1931.

REFERENCES CITED AND BIBLIOGRAPHY

Malakis = E. Malakis. *French travellers in Greece (1770-1820)*. Philadelphia, 1925.

Marchand = L. A. Marchand, ed. *Byron's letters and Journals*. 11 vols. London, 1973-1981.

Martin = J. Martin. *Bibliographical catalogue of privately printed books*. London, 1854 (reprint, New York, 1968).

Melzi = G. Melzi. *Dizionario di opere anonime e pseudonime di scrittori italiani*. Milan, 1848.

Moore = D. L. Moore. *The late Lord Byron; posthumous dramas*. London, [1961].

Mortimer = R. Mortimer. *Harvard College Library Dept. of printing and graphic arts. Catalogue of Books and Manuscripts. Part I French 16th century books. Part II Italian 16th century books.* Cambridge, Mass. 1964-1974.

NUC = *The National Union Catalog. Pre-1956 Imprints. A cumulative author list...* 685 vols. [London] 1968-1980.

Olivier = E. Olivier. *Manual de l'amateur de reliures armoriées françaises.* Paris, 1924-1938.

Palau = A. Palau y Dulcet. *Manuel del librero Hispano-Americano Bibliografia general Espanola e Hispano-Americana.* 28 vols. Barcelona, 1948-1977.

Papadopoulos = Thomas Papadopoulos Ἑλληνικὴ Βιβλιογραφία *(1466-1800)*. 2 vols. Athens, 1984-1986.

Papadopoulos IB. = Thomas Papadopoulos. Ἰονικὴ Βιβλιογραφία *Bibiliographie Ionienne*. 3 vols. Athens, 1998-2002.

Penrose = B. Penrose. *Travel and discovery in the renaissance 1420-1620*. Cambridge, Mass., 1955.

Penzer = N. M. Penzer. *An annotated bibliography of Sir Richard Francis Burton*. London, 1923.

Playfair = Sir R. Lambert Playfair. *The Bibliography of the Barbary States*. Farnborough, 1971 (a reprint of the separate bibliographies published 1888-1898).

Polemis = P. Polemis. Ἡ βιβλιοθήκη τοῦ ΕΛΙΑ. Athens, 1995.

Querard = J. M. Querard. *La France littéraire*. 12 vols. Paris, 1827-39 (reprint 1967).

St. Clair = W. St. Clair. *That Greece might still be free; the philhellenes in the war of independence*. London, 1972.

St. Clair Elgin = W. St. Clair. *Lord Elgin and the marbles*. London, 1967.

Sommervogel = A. de Backer and C. Sommervogel. *Bibliothèque de la Compagnie de Jesus*. 10 vols. Paris, 1890-1910.

Soranzo = G. Soranzo. *Bibliografia veneziana*. Venice, 1885.

Spencer = T. Spencer. *Fair Greece, Sad Relic literary philhellenism from Shakespeare to Byron*. London, 1954 (reprint Bath, 1974).

Stafleu = F. A. Stafleu and R. S. Cowan. *Taxonomic literature. A selective guide to botanic publications*. Second edition. 7 vols. Utrecht, 1976-1988.

STC = A.W. Pollard and G.R. Redgrave. *Short-title catalogue of books printed in England, Scotland & Ireland 1475-1640.* 3 vols. Second edition, ed. by W.A. Jackson, F.S. Ferguson and K. Pantzer. London, 1976-1991.

Tchemerzine = F. Tchemerzine. *Bibliographie d'editions originales et rares d'auteurs français des XVe, XVIe, XVIIe et XVIIIe siècles.* 10 vols. Paris, 1927-1933.

Tobler = T. Tobler. *Bibliographia geographica Palaestinae.* Leipzig, 1867.

VD16 = *Verzeichnis der im Deutschen Sprachbereich erscheinen Drucke des XVI Jahrhunderts.* Stuttgart, 1989.

Weber = S.H. Weber. *Voyages and travels in the Near East during the XIX century. — Voyages and Travels in Greece, the Near East and adjacent regions made previous to the year 1801.* 2 vols. Princeton, N.J., 1952-1953.

Willems = A. Willems. *Les Elzevier, histoire et annales typographiques.* Brussels, 1880.

Wing = D. Wing. *Short title catalogue of books printed in England... and of English books printed in other countries 1641-1700.* 3 vols. Second edition, revised. New York, 1972-1988.

Wise = T.J. Wise. *A bibliography of the writings of George Gordon Noel, Baron Byron.* 2 vols. London, 1932-1933.

Xanthakis. = A. Xanthakis. *History of Greek Photography 1839-1960. Translated by John Solman and Geoffroy Cox.* Athens, 1988.

Zacharakis = C.G. Zacharakis. *A Catalogue of printed maps of Greece and Greek regions, 1477-1800.* Second edition. Athens, 1982.

The standard biographical references have not been listed separately in the bibliography. These include the *Dictionary of National Biography*, the *Dictionary of American Biography*, Hoefer's *Nouvelle Biographie Generale*, Michaud's *Biographie Universelle*, the *Dizionario biografico degli Italiani*, Benezit's dictionary of artists, the *Allgemeines Biographisches Lexikon*, and the *Encyclopaedia Britannica*, eleventh edition.

ABBREVIATIONS

π	unsigned preliminary leaf or leaves
χ	unsigned leaf or leaves
[]	blank leaf
advert	advertising matter normally extra to the letterpress
ARGOS	On line Union Catalogue of the libraries of the Archaeological Schools, Athens, on going.
BL	British Library, London
BL Maps	British Map Library, London
BNF	Bibliotheque Nationale, Paris
conts	contents
COPAC	On line Union Catalogue of libraries in the UK and Ireland
ded	dedication
dir	directions
d-p	double-page
engr	engraved
f. fo	folio
fp, f-piece	frontispiece
GL	Gennadius Library, Athens
ht, hts	half title, half titles
illus	illustrations
intro	introduction
l., lvs	leaf, leaves
ms	manuscript
NAL	National Art Library, Victoria and Albert Museum, London
no	number
no'd, nos	numbered, numbers
pl, pls	plate, plates
pref	preface
priv	privilege
r	recto
st, sts	subtitle, subtitles
subscr	subscribers
t, ts	title, titles
unn	unnumbered
v	verso
vol, vols	volume, volumes

INDEX OF NAMES

This index contains the names of authors and editors, artists, engravers and lithographers, and other persons mentioned in the notes, as well as selected places and subjects. There are separate indexes of provenances, and of printers, publishers, booksellers and bookbinders. The references are to page numbers. ∗ The introductory texts are not included in the index.

A

A., M.G., see Antonopoulou
Abbott, G.F. 3
Abdul Hamid 261
Abdul Medjid 305
Abercromby, Sir R. 86
Aberdeen 461
About, Edmond François Valentin 3, 4
Acheron 467
Achilleion 460
Achmet Aga 294
AcroCorinth 347
Actium 167
Adam, engraver 479
Adam, Sir Frederick 286
Adelphus 5
Adrianople 467
Aegina 90, 256, 262
Aeneas 297
Aeschimann, Willy 344
Aetolia 210
Aghia Sophia, Leondari 270
Aghioi Theodori, Athens 270
Ak-Hissar, see Thyatira
Albania 25, 227, 438, 452
Aldenhoven, Ferdinand 6
Alexander the Great 448
Alexander, William 108
Alexandria 27, 212, 244, 322
Algemeene Histori 440
Ali Bey 259
Ali Pasha 14, 73, 129, 193, 194, 202, 226, 286, 331, 332, 333, 335, 351
Aliartos 124
Aligny, Théodore Caruelle d' 7
Allan, John Harrison 7

Allezard, Jean Joseph 362
Allgemeine Erdkunde, oder Beschreibung aller Länder 467
Allom, Thomas 7, 66, 454, 455
Almissa 26
Alpinus, R. 350
Alquie, see Savinien d'Alquié 7
Alund, O.W. 185
Amalia 359, 430
Amasaeus, Romulus 307, 308
Amasia 286
Amaury-Duval, see Duval
Ambelakia 44
American School of Classical Studies, Athens 354
Amicis, see De Amicis
Amorgos 114
Amours de Leucippe et Clitophon 295
Amphilochia 167
Amphissa 114, 124, 167
Anastase et Euphrosyne 196
Ancel, Jacques 8
Anderson, R.C. 8
Anderson, Robert 329
Andreades, Andreas 41, 261
Andreossy, Antoine François, Count 8, 316
Andros 99, 257
Androutsos, Odysseus 320
Anecdoti o sia la storia segreta 324
Angelo, Jacopo d' 342
Anisson du Perron 253
Ansted, David Thomas 9
Antiparos 99, 217
Antonopoulos, S.A. 310
Antonopoulou, Maria G. 9
Appert, Benjamin Nicolas Marie 9
Arachova 239

491

INDEX

Aramon 168, 290
Argenti, Philip P. 10
Αργέντης 10
Argolid 13, 63
Argos 90, 167, 326, 434
Argyrokastro 194, 227, 239
Ariel des Feux 170
Aristonoüs 150
Armao, Ermanno 151
Armstrong, Isabel Julien 12
Armytage, J.C. 466
Arrowsmith, J. 12
Arta 446
Artus, Thomas 74
Arundel Marbles 337
Arundell, Francis Vyvyan Jago 12
Arvanitakis, G. 41, 344
Asia Minor 7, 12, 15, 209, 225, 346, 418, 420, 452, 453
Aspiotis, Marie 12, 342
Assassins 453
Astell, Mary 276
Astypalia 239
Athens 13, 14, 44, 63, 65, 90, 129, 167, 168, 170, 178, 181, 182, 210, 219, 224, 253, 262, 264, 275, 282, 294, 298, 319, 322, 326, 421, 436, 444, 457, 460, 469, 470, 480
Athos, Mt. 116, 166, 271, 281, 288, 294, 436, 450
Attica 326, 457, 469, 470, 480
Aubert, L. 449
Aubriet, Claude 433
Aubusson, Pierre d' 43
Augustin, André 245
Auldjo, John 13
Auteur de Mariage au point de vue Chrétien, see Gasparin
Avelot, Henri 13, 32
Aviation 336
Avlona 227
Azeglio, Massimo d' 88
Aziyadé 245

B

Babin, J.P. 216
Bacheville, Antoine 14
Bacheville, Barthélemy 14
Baedeker, Karl 14, 268
Bagdad 416
Bagliotti, Filippo 415

Baifius, Lazarus 355
Balkan Wars 240
Balkans 477
Ball, John 169
Baltas, Ch. 342
Balthasard de la Ferriere, Mme de la 15
Banduri, A. 103
Banier, Antoine 53
Bank, W. 60
Bankes, W.J. 204
Barbié du Bocage, J.D. 17, 18, 77, 81, 334
Bardey, Mme. 188
Barff, Samuel 60
Barrès, Maurice 16, 46, 55, 424
Barrows, Samuel June 16
Barthelemy, Jean Jacques 17, 18, 19, 20, 21, 78, 149, 221, 479
Barthez, Charles 172
Bartholdy, Jakob Ludwig Salomon 22
Bartlett, Ellis Ashmead the younger 23
Bartlett, Sir Ellis Ashmead 22
Bartlett, Seabury 23
Bartlett, W.H. 65, 304, 305, 355, 476
Baruffi, Giuseppe Filippo 23
Bassae 434
Bassan, Fernande 62
Bate, Dorothea 24
Battye, Aubyn Bernard Rochford Trevor 24
Bauclas, L. de 305
Baud-Bovy, D. 41
Baudier, Michel 24, 74
Baudouin de Launay 146
Baxter, George 466
Baynes, T.M. 164
Beauchamp, Alphonse 24
Beaufort, Emily Anne 25
Beaufort, Sir Francis 25
Beaujour, Louis Auguste Félix de 26
Beaumont, William 21
Beauvais, General Charles 447
Beauvau, Henri de 27
Beavis, R. 466
Beck, L.C. 185
Becke, Archibald Frank 142
Bedelet, Leonie, see Müller, Elisabeth
Bedford, Duke of, see Russel, J.
Bedford, Francis 288, 363
Belabre, F. de, Baron 28
Bellaire, J.P. 28

INDEX

Belle, Henri 28
Bellin, Jacques Nicolas 29
Belon, Pierre 349
Belzoni, G.B. 225
Benjamin of Tudela 32
Benjamin, Samuel Green Wheeler 30
Bent, James Theodore 30
Bentley, R. 103
Berard, Jean 31
Berard, Victor 30, 31
Berat 227, 467
Berchere, see Guedon de la Berchere
Bergeron, Pierre 31
Bernard, J.B. 72
Bernard, Marius 32
Bernardos, Manuel 111
Bernoudakis 240
Berry, Duchesse de 256
Berton, Charles 32
Bertrand, C. 466
Bertrand, L. 41
Besold, Christopher 32
Best, James John 33
Beulé, Charles Ernest 33, 34, 204
Bianconi, F. 34
Bibichi 4
Bible, New Testament 34
Bibliothèque de la Jeunesse chrétienne 330
Bikelas, Demetrios 35, 452
Biliotti, Alfred 36
Biliotti, Edouard 35
Billecocq, J.B.L.J. 449
Bingham, A.Y. 45, 46
Binos, Marie Dominique de 36
Birch, Thomas 479
Bisani, Alessandro 36
Biseo, C. 112
Bishop, Henry Halsall 38
Bizanis, Constantinos 120
Blachos, Angelos 234
Black, Theresa 464
Black Sea 8, 231
Blanchet, Alexandre 49
Blantes, Spyridon 21, 214
Blaquiere, Edward 39, 89
Blessington, Earl and Countess of 251
Bodin, Félix 40
Bodio, Luigi 156
Boeotia 457, 478, 480

Boetticher, Adolf 40
Bogan, Zachary 362
Boissonade, Jean François 150
Boissonnas, Edmond 41
Boissonnas, Frederic 41, 296, 424, 526
Bon, Antoine 42
Bonaparte, Marie 317
Bonfils, Félix 319
Bonnet, engraver 320
Bonneval, C.A., Count 221
Booth, C.D. 42
Booth, Isabelle Bridge 42
Borchgrave, Emile de 42
Bosanquet, Ellen Sophia, Mrs. R.C. 43
Bosanquet, Robert Carr 43
Boschini, Marco 111
Bosnia 250
Bosphorus 115
Botsaris 269
Botta, E. 155
Boucher, F. 179
Boudot-Lamotte, Emmanuel 217
Bouhours, Dominique 43
Boulanger, François Louis Florimond 44
Boulaye, Victor de la 269
Bourlat de Montredon 183
Bouteiller, Jehan de 46
Bovet, Marie Anne de 44
Bovinet, engraver 104, 105
Bowen, George Ferguson 44, 226
Bower, A. 441
Bowring, John 39
Boyiajian, Zabelle C. 45
Boyle, Richard 72
Bracebridge, C.H. 470
Bradshaw, S. 466
Brandard, E. 466
Brandstäter, Franz August 45
Brassey, Annie, Baroness 45, 46
Braurona 55
Bréholles, Huillard 269
Bremond, Henri, Abbé 16, 46
Brereton, Thomas 221
Bret, Paul 262
Breton, E.F.P.H. 46
Breton, L. 358
Breydenbach 292
Briot, Pierre 365
British Council, Athens 209

493

INDEX

British Military Mission to Egypt 468
British School of Archaeology, Athens 210, 311
Brodie, Captain and Mrs. 120
Brodtmann, J. 199
Brofferio, Angelo 47
Broglie, Prince de 427
Brönsted, Peter Oluf 47
Brooke, W.H. 148
Brouardel, Louise 353
Brown, Adna 48
Browne, Thomas Sir 49
Browne, Edward 48
Browne, W.G. 453, 454
Brue, Benjamin 131
Brumanus, H. 148
Brunet de Presle, C.M.W. 49
Brunet, Jean 276
Brunet, Pierre-Gustave 210
Brutel de la Rivière, J.B. 337
Bruyn, Cornelis de 49, 52, 53, 344
Bruzen de la Martiniere, A.A. 72
Bryant, Jacob 281
Bryce, Mary R.L. 120
Bryce, James, Viscount 3
Buchon, Jean Alexandre C. 42, 54, 55, 196
Budry, Claude 55
Budry, Paul 55
Bulwer Lytton, E.G.E. 13
Buonaccorsi, Callimachus 167
Buondelmonti, Cristoforo 55
Burgess, Richard 56
Burgundy, Duke of 149
Burnell, Frederic Spencer 56
Burr, A.M., Mrs. Hickford 57
Burton, Francis Pierpoint 107
Busbecq, O.G. de 436
Busch, J.H.M. 244
Byrne, Elizabeth 194
Byrne, J. 194
Byron, George Gordon Noel, Lord 39, 57, 58, 60, 89, 112, 153, 159, 165, 193, 198, 212, 273, 286, 480
Byron, Isabella Milbanke, Lady 294
Byron, Robert 60
Byzantios, Skarlatos 61, 234

C

Cabrol, Elie 62
Caesarea 286
Caesarea, see also Kaisareia
Caignart de Saulcy, Lucien F. 62, 270
Cailler, Pierre 55
Cairo 27
Calas, Theophile 63
Calcoens, see Kalkoens
Callier, Camille 269
Callmer, J.A.C. 345
Camden Society 295
Camoreyt, artist 182
Campagnes de Monsieur Prince Eugène 434
Campbell, J. 441
Campion de Tersan, Charles Phillippe 461
Canaris 207, 356
Canaye, Philippe, Seigneur de Fresne 63
Candia 236, 321, 347, 414
Canning, Sir Stratford 102, 226, 427
Cantu, Cesare 87, 167
Caoursin, Guillaume 6
Capodistrias, Ioannes 170, 302, 363
Capodistrias, Viaro 141
Carayon, Auguste 63
Carl Gustavus, of Sweden 345
Carlisle, George William Frederick Howard, 7th Earl of 65
Carlyle, T. 116
Carnarvon, Henry J.G. Herbert, 3rd Earl of 65
Carne, John 65, 305, 455
Carpin, Jean du Plan 31, 32
Carrel, Armand 66
Cartwright, Joseph 13
Casaubon, I. 308, 439
Cassas, L.F. 235, 451
Cassé de Saint-Prosper 245
Casson, Stanley 159, 160
Castela, Henri 66
Castellan, Antoine Laurent 68, 69, 70, 108
Castilhon, J. 259
Catalan Grand Company 274
Catenacci, designer 446
Catsakis, N.G. 84
Caulfeild, James, Earl of Charlemont 107
Cavalla 189
Cavan, F.E.G. Lambart, 9th Earl of 70
Cavendish, William, Earl of Devonshire 427
Cazzaiti, see Katsaites
Cellarius, Christopher 71
Cephalonia 286
Ceremonies and Religious Customs 72

INDEX

Cerfberr, Alphonse 73
Cerigo-Lo! 353
Chacaton, J.N.H. de 108
Chalcocondylas, Laonicus 73, 74, 290
Chalfa, Hadschi 356
Champion, Edouard 110
Chandler, Richard 76, 77
Chania 13
Chapoutier, Fernand 42
Chappuzeau, Samuel 415
Chardin, Sir J. 178Charlemont, Earl of, See Caulfeild
Charles II 366
Chateaubriand, François René 16, 77, 110, 253, 255
Chaussard, Pierre Jean Baptiste 78
Chavanne, see Dareste de la Chavanne
Cheever, Henry T. 88
Chenavard, Antoine Marie 78, 79, 354
Chenier, E., Madame Louis 182
Chennechot, L.E. 80
Chikhachev, see Tchihatcheff
Chimarra 227, 446
Chios 158, 180, 239, 312, 435, 453
Chipiez, Charles 316
Choiseul-Gouffier, M.G.A.F. de 17, 77, 80, 81, 99, 152, 231, 232, 261, 321
Christophe, Mathieu 479
Christopher, of Greece, Prince 83
Christophoros, Ierodidaskalos 341
Christopoulos, A. 49
Chrussachi, Matthew George 274
Chrysanthos Kamarases 340
Church, Alfred John 83
Churchill, Awnsham 345
Chuzeville, Jean 287
Claparede, Arthur de 84
Clark, J. 467
Clark, William George 84
Clarke, Edward Daniel 84, 86, 454, 461, 468
Clarke, I. 24
Clauser, Conrad 73
Clavier, Etienne 309
Clerget, Hubert 281
Clouard, Henri 287
Cochrane, Thomas 87
Cochrane, George 87
Cockburn, Colonel 476
Cockerell, Charles Robert 48, 153, 202, 469, 470

Codrington, Edward 333
Cohen, Jean 139
Colas, see Collas, Bernard Camille
Colchester, Lord 204
Coleridge 116
Collas, Achille 187
Collas, Bernard Camille 87
Collegno, Giacinto Provana di 88
Colletis 363, 427
Collignon, Maxime 352
Colnaghi, D.E. 288
Colocotronis 333, 427
Colomb, Josephine B.B. 112
Colton, Walter 88
Combes, Edmond 88
Come, S. 152
Comité des Grecs de la Société de la Morale Chrétienne 40
Compendio della Storia del Risorgimento della Grecia 320
Comstock, John Lee 89
Conder, C.R. 466
Conder, Josiah 89, 90
Constant, Benjamin 40
Constantine I, King of Greece 83
Constantinople 6, 8, 14, 15, 23, 45, 115, 116, 129, 168, 170, 178, 198, 209, 240, 245, 249, 259, 268, 275, 297, 316, 319, 328, 330, 331, 418, 421, 426, 436, 454, 455, 457
Constantinople Le Mt. Athos La Grèce Épisodes d'un voyage en Orient 116
Cony, artist 149
Cook, Joel 91
Cooke, John 275
Cooke, G. 194
Corbould, Henry 153
Cordella, see Kordellas
Corfu 28, 44, 84, 227, 236, 239, 260, 282, 292, 305, 326, 436, 440, 460
Corinth 90, 167, 246, 314, 318, 457
Cornille, Henri 91
Coronelli, Vincenzo 56, 91, 94, 95, 96, 111, 419
Corsini, Edoardo 97
Cos 7, 288, 453
Cost 40
Cottret, Abbé 35
Coudray, Auguste Du 22
Courier, P.L. 309
Cousen, C. 466

495

INDEX

Cousinery, E.M. 107
Covel, John 3, 97, 178, 179
Covington, Rev. W. 251
Cramer, J.A. 295
Craven, Elizabeth, Lady 97, 99
Craxton, John 151
Crete 174, 175, 217, 239, 244, 271, 292, 306, 314, 316, 349, 414, 417, 418, 430, 438
Crew, J.J. 466
Cripps, John Martin 86
Croatia 250
Croiset, A. 41
Crome, Dr. 105
Cruikshank, G. 13
Crusius, Martin 285
Cullen, Timothy 317
Cunliffe-Owen, E. Betty 99
Curio, Caelius Augustinus 100
Curtius, Ernst 100
Curzon, Robert, Baron Zouche 102
Cusani, Francesco 103
Cuvillier-Fleury 427
Cyclades 170, 318
Cyprus 15, 45, 217, 239, 244, 259, 321, 322, 460
Cyriac, of Ancona 103

D

D.C., see Deshayes 115
Dacier, B.J., Baron 81
Dalgabio, J.M. 354
Dallaway, James 104, 105, 107, 281
Dalmatia 25, 294
Dalrymple, A. 448
Dalton, Richard 106
Dalvimart, Octavien 107, 271
Dalzel, Andrew 230, 231
Dambrun, artist 149
Damer, Colonel G.L. Dawson 108
Damer, Mary Georgina Emma, Mrs. G.L. Dawson 108
Danielo, Julien 110
Dannou, Pierre C.F. 309
Danubian principalities 209
Daphne Monastery 270
Dapper, Olfert 56, 94, 110
Darchini, Gaetano 111
Dardanelles 305, 318
Dareste de la Chavanne, Antoine 156, 157
Davenport, R.A. 25
Davenport, W. 25
Davesies de Pontes, Lucien 111
David, J.L. 461
Davy, Sir Humphry 112
Davy, John 112
Dawkins, R.M. 311
De Amicis, Edmondo 112
De la Reynie 128
De Vere, Aubrey Thomas 116
Defauconpret, Auguste J.-B. 196, 202
Delaroche, Paul 187
Delgove, Henri 83
Delighiannis, see Deliyannis
Deliyannis 9, 427
Dell, Anthony 114
Dell, Roger M. 114
Delort, Charles 4
Delos 257
Delphi 167, 283, 314, 318, 319, 418, 478
Delpierre, engraver 80
Delta, Penelope 124
Demetriades, Phokion 114
Denton, Henry 166
Deonna, W. 41
Desages 427
Desbuisson, artist 33
Deschamps, Gaston 41, 114, 115, 240
Deschamps, Philippe 115
Deshayes, Louis, Baron de Courmenin 115
Deskati 240
Detaille, Fernand 174
Dezauche, A. 297
Diana, Temple of 468
Diarium Europaeum 301
Didon, Henri Louis 116
Didot, Ambroise Firmin 78, 117, 444
Didymes 328
Diehl, Charles 41, 117, 118, 352, 414
Dilessi murders 28, 294, 480
Dionysius, Periegetes 119
Dixon, William MacNeile 120
Dodona 167, 469
Dodwell, Edward 120, 124, 164, 326
Dolet, Etienne 355
Dominicains d'Arcueil 116
Don John of Austria, see John
Donaldson, T.L. 90
Doré, Gustave 4
Dorez, Léon 280

Doudan, engraver 77
Douglas, Frederick Sylvester North 124
Douglas, Norman 203
Douin, G. 40
Dreux, Robert de 124
Driault, Edouard 125
Drummond de Melfort, see Durand de Fontmagne
Drummond, Alexander 126, 221
Drummond, Lady, of Logie Almond 165
Druses et Maronites 287
Du Bosc, Claude 72
Du Camp, Maxime 155
Du Choul, Guillaume 126
Du Cros, Joseph 128
Du Gabé 129
Du Moncel, Théodose 130
Du Perron de Castera, L.A. 295
Du Quesne, Abraham 180
Du Sou, Moïse 337
Dubois, J.J. 136
Dubois de l'Estang, Etienne 156
Dubouchet, engraver 78
Ducas, Theodore 273
Duflos, engraver 179
Dufrenoy, Adelaide Gillete Billet 128
Duhn, Friedrich von 130
Dumesnil, Rene 155
Dumont, Albert 131, 187, 344
Dunbar, George 329
Duponchel, Augustin Amedée 131, 245
Dupré, Louis 134
Durand de Fontmagne, Marie Caroline 134
Durand, P.-Noel 99
Duruy, Victor 134, 252
Duval, Amaury, the younger 136
Dyer, Thomas Henry 136

E

Eberhard, Heinrich Wilhelm 474
Edward, Prince of Wales 71, 363
Egypt 275, 316
Ehrenreichat, J.A. d' 149
Eleftherioannou, Constantinos 84
Eleusis 262, 314
Eleutherai 90
Elgin, Lord 86, 426, 439, 461, 468
Elizabeth of Austria 460
Elliott, Charles Boileau 138

Elliott, E.G. 138
Elliott, Edward Bishop 138
Elliott, Henry Venn 138
Ellis, Tristram 357
ELPA 314
Emerson, James 89, 138, 139, 310
Enderlin, Jacob 94, 139
Endres, Franz Carl 262
Ephesus 319, 438, 468
Epidaurus 318
Epirus 194, 202, 227, 239, 342
Erasmus 342
Eratosthenes 173
Erivan 416
Estang, see Doubois de l'Estang
Estienne, Charles 187, 355
Estourmel, Joseph d' 141
Eton 426
Euboea 210, 283, 294, 478
Evangelides, T.E. 14
Ewald, Mr. and Mrs. 355
Examen Critique 141, 426
Excursions Daguerriennes 174
Expedition Scientifique de Moree 317, 331, 344
Eydous, ?Emmanuel 324

F

Fabrice 221
Fabroni, Angelo 21
Fabvier. Chant lyrique sur la Grèce 142
Fakhr-ed-Din, emir of the Druses 259
Falke, Jakob von 142
Falls, Cyril Bentham 142
Fanelli, Francesco 142
Fantome d'Orient 245
Farlet, engraver 281
Farochon, Paul Auguste 144
Farrer, Richard Ridley 146
Fauriel, C.C. 49
Fauvel, Louis 77
Fauvel, Robert 107, 146
Favray, Antoine 183
Febure, Michele 147
Feithius, Everhardus 148
Fellmann, designer 446
Fellows, Sir Charles 148, 172
Felton, C.C. 65, 153
Femmes du Caire 287
Femmes du Liban 287

INDEX

Fenelon, François de Salignac de la Mothe 148, 149, 150
Fenn, H. 466
Fermanel, G. 146
Fermor, Patrick Leigh 151
Ferrari, Pompeo 151
Ferrer, Giuseppe di, Count 151
Ferriere, see Balthasard de la Ferriere
Ferrieres-Sauveboeuf, Louis François, Count 152
Fêtes et Courtisanes de la Grèce 78
Filles du Feu 287
Finch, Heneage 347
Finch, Sir John 3, 97
Finden, Edward Francis 57, 153, 260
Finden, William 57, 153
Finlay, George 84, 168, 153, 318
Fischer, Ludwig Hans 455
Fischer, Max 154
Fisher's Illustrations of Constantinople 455
Flach, Martin 6
Flandin, Eugene Napoleon 154
Flaubert, Gustave 155
Flaxman, John 155
Flori, Francesco 290
Flowers, T.G. 60
Folegandros 314
Fontenelle, B. le Boyer de 433
Forbin, L.N.P.A. de, Count 156, 255
Forster, A. 6
Foscolo, Ugo 310
Fossey, artist 282
Foucault, J.A. de 295
Foucherot 17
Fougeres, Gustave 246, 352
Fourcroy, A.F. 164
Fourier, François 44
Fourmont, Etienne 246
France, Anatole 351
France. Ministry of Foreign Affairs 156
François I 355
François, Achille 156
Freeman, E.A. 274
French navy 207
French School of Archaeology, Athens 131, 180, 316
French, W. 466
Frommel, Carl 157
Fulleylove, John 248

G

G., H. 171
Gabé, see Du Gabé
Gadsby, John 158
Gaertringen, see Hiller von Gaertringen
Galanis, Demetris 170
Galatz 359
Galland, Antoine 103, 158, 179
Galland, Julien Claude 158
Gallibert, G. 216
Gallipoli 115, 305
Galt, John 159
Gamba, Pietro 159
Gandon, engraver 287
Gardner, Ernest Arthur 159
Garibaldi, G. 111
Garnett, Lucy M.J. 357
Garston, E. 251
Gary, Pierre 255
Gasparin, Valerie de, Countess 160
Gauthey, Leon 161
Gavrion 99
Gazes, Anthimos 161, 264
Gedoyn, Nicolas, Abbé 308, 309
Geil, William Edgar 164
Gell, Sir William 13, 120, 164, 199, 461
Gennadius, Ioannes 35, 56, 185
Genoude, Antoine Eugène de 166
George I, of Greece 83
George, of Greece, Prince 317
Georgirenes, Joseph 166
Gerbelius, Nicolas 166
Gervinus, Georg Gottfried 167, 168
Geus, C.H.J. de 356
Giffard, Edward 168
Gili y Gaya, Samuel 275
Gilles, Antoine 168
Gilles, Pierre 168, 169
Gillot de Kerhardene 269
Giraud, J. 181
Giraudeau de St. Gervaise, J. 256
Giustiniano, see Febure
Gladstone, W.E. 44
Gobineau, Joseph Arthur, Count de 170, 182, 216
Godard-Faultrier, Victor 170
Godefroy, engraver 149
Godfrey, J. 466
Godolphin, Francis 316
Goeller, Franz Joseph 429

Gomez-Carrillo, Enrique 172, 277
Goodisson, William 172
Goodrich, Samuel Griswold 172, 173
Gordon, Thomas 138, 168, 318
Gortys 6
Gosselin, Pascal François Joseph 173
Gouin, Gustave 174
Goupil-Fesquet, Frederic Auguste Antoine 174
Gouras 363
Goustave-Toudouze, see Toudouze
Govdelas, Panaghiotis Demetrios 151
Graevius, J.G. 267, 268
Grahame, George 160
Grand Catalan Company 54
Grand-Carteret, John 175
Grant voyage de Jherusalem 235
Grant, John Cameron 254
Grasset de Saint Sauveur, Andre 175
Grasset de Saint Sauveur, Jacques 175
Grassi, Alfio 175
Graves, Thomas 250
Grèce Immortelle, La 41
Greco-Swiss Friendship League 55
Greco-Turkish war of 1897 175, 277, 438
Greek Automobile Touring Club 314
Green, Philip James 89
Gregorovius, Ferdinand 176
Gregory V 269
Grelot, Guillaume Joseph 178
Griffenhag, Andre Muller 31
Gronovius, J. 167, 266, 268
Gropius, George 22
Guedon de la Berchere, Pierre 99
Guer, Jean Antoine 179
Guerin, Jules 189
Guerin, Victor Honoré 179
Guiccioli, Theresa 159
Guides Joanne 328
Guilford, Lord, see North, Frederick, Earl of
Guillaumot, A. 418
Guilleragues, see Lavergne
Guillet, Andre Georges 180, 181
Guilletière, see Guillet
Guillois, consul 130
Guizot, F.P.G. 40
Guldencrone, Diane de 170, 182
Guy, Noël 182
Guys, Pierre Augustin 182, 183, 276
Gwinner, Charlotte von 215

H

H., I. 345
Haffner, engraver 247
Haghe, Louis 469, 470
Halicarnassus 288
Hallé, engraver 179
Haller von Hallerstein 48
Hamilton, William 454, 468
Hamilton, W.R. 86
Hamlin, Cyrus 296
Hammer-Purgstall, J. von 468
Hanson, Charles Henry 184
Hanson-Taylor, Marie 418
Hanzelet, J. Appier 27
Happ, Alfred 193
Harmsworth, Cecil 120
Harper, H.A. 466
Harris, engraver 119
Hartley, John 56
Harvey, Sir Daniel 97
Hase, C.B. 81
Hatice, sister of the Sultan Selim III 266
Hauser, Henri 63
Haussollier, Bernard 328
Hawkins, John 454
Hawthorne, Nathaniel 173
Haye-Vantelet 125
Haygarth, William 184, 206, 453
Haython the Armenian 32
Hedio, Caspar 449
Heidemann, translator 451
Helicon, Mt. 120
Hellespont 115
Hellwald, Friedrich von 185
Helyot, Pierre Hippolyte 186
Henriquel-Dupont, Louis Pierre 187
Herbert, Henry J.G., see Carnarvon, 3rd Earl of
Herhan process 149
Herodotus 187
Herold, Gottfried 188
Herriot, Edouard 188
Hertz, Charles 448
Hervieu, Auguste 138
Herzog, L., & Cie 188
Heurtley, Mr. and Mrs. 210
Heuzey, Leon 189
Heyne, C.G. 231
Hibon, engraver 294
Hichens, Robert Smythe 189, 190

INDEX

Hiller von Gaertringen, J., Baron 253
Hippocrene 120
Hobbes, Thomas 427, 429
Hobhouse, John Cam, Lord Broughton, 159,190
Hoepf 42
Hoffmann, Johann 94
Hofmannsthal, Hugo von 193, 526
Hogarth, D.G. 102, 209
Holdt, Hanns 193, 526
Holland, Sir Henry 194
Holtzman, Wilhelm, see Xylander
Holy Land 68
Holy League 140
Homer 357
Homolle, T. 130, 223
Höniger, Nicolaus 100
Hope, Thomas 194, 196, 204, 461
Hornby, Emily Bithynia, Lady 198, 452
Horne, Thomas Hartwell 26
Horner, Johann Jakob 198
Horsborough, J. 462
Houzé, A. 245
Howard, George William Frederick, see Carlisle, 7th Earl of
Hudson, J. 119
Hughes, Thomas Smart 202
Humphrey, see Humphreys
Humphreys, W.H. 89, 138, 139
Hunt, Philip 439, 454
Hunter, Isobel L. 202
Hunter, Mary 203
Hutton, Edward 203
Huyot, E.F. 446
Hydra 256, 333

I

Ibrahim Effendi Müteferrika 352
Ibrahim Manzour Effendi 73
Ibrahim Pasha 88, 317, 363
Icaria 166
Ichon, artist 270
Ideville, Henri Amédée Lelorgne de, Count 33, 204
Iliacum Carmen 439
Ingram, Frances 56
Ingram, Richard 56
Ingres 136
Inwood, Henry William 204
Ioannina 14, 26, 194, 239, 333, 467

Ionian Islands 9, 28,103, 112, 167, 168, 172, 175, 230, 236, 285, 286, 294, 298, 459
Iorga, Nicolas 205
Ipsariote, ou La Grèce vengée 205
Ira 6
Irby, Adelina Paulina 249
Irton, Major 476
Irumberry, see Salaberry
Isis 287
Ithaca 44, 164, 285

J

Jacob, bibliophile, see Lacroix, Paul
Jacob, P.L., see Lacroix, Paul
Jacobi, Louis 130
Jacopi, Giulio 206
Jahn, Otto 359
Janissaries 454
Jassy 209
Jehan à la Barbe 254
Jerusalem 34, 115, 129, 236, 292
Jesuit Order 65
Joachim III 281
Jocelyn, engraver 88
John, Don John, of Austria 144
Johnson, A.K. 146
Johnson, Dr. 212
Johnson, W. 146
Johnston, T.B. 146
Joly, Alexis Victor 185, 206
Jourdain, Jean Philippe Paul 207
Journal d'un Voyage au Levant 160
Julien, domestique, see Danielo
Jurien de la Gravière, Jean Baptiste Edmond 207, 427

K

Kaeppelin, lithographer 233
Kaisareia 9
Kalkoens 221
Kalvos, A. 277
Kalymnos 239, 288, 306
Kambouroglous, D.G. 208
Kandahar 416
Kanitz, F. 249
Karaiskakis 363
Karakatsanis, Agape 317
Karales, Alexandros 117
Karamanlidika 340

Karatheodores, S.S. 240
Karavokyros, S. 36
Karazine, N.N. 298
Karitena 434
Kastelorizo 239
Kastoria 477
Katsaites, Marc Antonio 208, 209
Kaufmann, Wilhelm 156
Kaupert, J.A. 100
Kazanoba, L.G. 240
Kea, see Keos
Kel-Kun, see Texier, Edmond
Kenyon, Sir Frederic 45
Keos 48, 239
Keratea 239
Kiepert, Richard 306
King, Francis Henry 209
Kinglake, Alexander William 209, 210
Kitchin, Thomas 76, 77
Kitto, Humphrey Davy Findley 210
Kneller, Godfrey 50, 52
Knolles, Richard 212
Kogevinas, Lycourgos 12
Kolbe, K. 283
Koliades, Constantin 232
Komnenos, Ioannis 337
Konstantios, Byzantios 212, 213
Koraïs, Adamantios 49, 117, 173, 234, 309
Kordellas, Andreas 214
Koritsa 446
Koundouriotis 9, 427
Kriezis 9, 427
Kühn, J. 308
Kupers, Franz 215
Kupfer, Grace H. 215

L

L., E., see Emilie de L.
L., Emilie de 206
L., H. 171
La Chapelle, C.E. 415
La Flotte 322, 324
La Guilletière, see Guillet
La Mottraye, Aubry de 219
La Porte du Theil 173
La Solaye, L. de 223
Laborde, A. de 40
Laborde, L.E.S.J. de, Marquis 216
Lacedemon 167
Lacombe, Armand 446
Lacretelle, Jacques de 216, 217
Lacroix de Marlès, J. de 217
Lacroix, Paul 112
Lacroix, Pierre Louis 217
Ladon Gorge 120
Lalande 164
Lamartine, M.L.A. de 218, 219
Lamb, F. 187
Lambart, F.E.G., see Cavan, Earl of
Lambikes Collection 319
Lamia 167
Lamotte, see Boudot-Lamotte
Lampros, Spyridon 178
Lane, Edward 118
Lane, Edward Fitzgerald 156
Lane-Poole, see Poole, Stanley Lane
Langlois, engraver 150
Lantier, H.M. 433
Lantier, Etienne François de 78, 221, 222, 295
Lanza, Vincenzo 478
Lapie 334
Lappas Collection 319
Larissa 13, 49, 167, 194
Laroche, Charles 222
Larroumet, Gustave 223
Lasteyrie, C.P. 40
Laurenberg, Johann 224
Laurent, engraver 183
Lauters, engraver 80
Lavergne, Gabriel Joseph de, Count de Guilleragues 180
Lavrion 215
Lawrence, Sir Thomas 361
Layard, Arthur 254
Le Brun, P. 72
Le Chevalier, Jean Baptiste 230, 231, 232, 281
Le Févre, Michel 147
Le Huen, Nicolas 235
Le Rouge, engraver 266
Le Roy, Julien David 238
Le Roy-Beaulieu, A. 298
Leake, William Martin 199, 224, 225, 226, 358, 453, 454, 468
Lear, Edward 226, 227, 230
Lebouteux, artist 33
Leconte de Lisle, C.M. 16
Leconte, Casimir 233
Leest, Antony van 288

Lefèvre-Pontalis, Germain 280
Lefkas, see Leucada
Leger, Louis 298
Legrand, Emile 234
Legrand, Jacques Guillaume 234
Leitch, artist 476
Lejeune, J. M. 345
LeKeux, John 194
Leloir, Auguste 282
Lemaitre, A. F. 33
Lemaitre, Alfred 236
Lemaitre, G. 196
Lemnos 239
Lemonnier 80
Lenormant, Charles 187, 236
Lenormant, François 236
Leonidov, Ivan 238
Lepanto 144
Lesbos 306
Lesbroussart, editor 80
Lesouëf, 110
Lester, E. 239
Lethaby, William Richard 239
Letters written by Lord Byron 60
Lettres Athéniennes 479
Lettres sur divers endroits 36
Leucada 239, 302,
Leucippe and Clitophon 295
Λεύκωμα τῶν ἐν Κωνσταντινουπόλει ἐθνικῶν Φιλανθρωπικῶν Καταστημάτων 240
Leunclavius 436
Leune, Jean 240
Lewis, F. C., engraver 202
Lewis, G. C. 283
Lewis, John Frederick 240
Liddel, Robert 209
Lidoriki 114
Life of Ali Pacha 24
Light, Sir Henry 241
Linckh, Jakob 48
Liotard, Jean Etienne 275
Liston, Sir Robert 104, 281
Lithgow, William 242
Lizars, W. and D. 329
Locris 114
Löffler, August 244
Löher, Franz von 244
Londerseel, A. 288
London Greek Committee 193, 202, 273

Longnon, Jean 55
Lostalot-Bachoué, E. de 245
Loti, Pierre 245
Louis, Spyros 467
Louis XIV 433
Louvier, engraver 78
Loverdos Museum 319
Lovinesco, Eugène 245
Lubbock, Sir John 429
Lucas, Paul 246
Ludwig of Bavaria 426
Ludwig Salvator 246, 247
Luisandre, Sieur de 421
Lunn, Sir Henry 160
Lusieri 86
Luyken, Jan and Caspar 50
Lycia 288
Lysimachus, Stanislaus 247
Lytton, see Bulwer Lytton

M
M.G.A., see Antonopoulou
M.P.C., see Pieri
MacBean, Forbes. 248
Maccas, Léon 248
M'Clintock, John 296
MacClymont, James Alexander 248
Macedonia 49, 227
MacFarlane, Charles 249
MacKenzie, Georgina Mary Muir 249
MacLaren, Charles 250
Macmillan, Malcolm 251
Madden, Richard Robert 250
Mahaffy, John Pentland 251, 252
Mahmoud II 454
Maid of Athens, see Black, Theresa
Maitland, Thomas 286
Malaguzzi, O. 436
Malakassis, M. 277
Malakis, Emile 205, 252
Mallet, Alain Manesson 56
Malliarakis, M. 36
Malo Brothers 19
Malta 27, 84, 275
Malta, Knights of, see St. John of Jerusalem, Knights of
Maltezos, Georgios Themistokles 253
Mandat-Grancey, Edmond de, Baron 253
Mandavilla, see Mandeville, John

Mandeville, John 253, 254
Mann, Thomas 328
Mantevilla, see Mandeville, John
Manzour Effendi, see Ibrahim Manzour
Marathon 239
Marcellus, M.-L. J.A.C. de Martin du Tyrac, Comte de 78, 254, 255, 344
Marchebeus 256
Marcian, of Heracleia 257
Marignac, Aloys de 257, 476
Marilac, artist 182
Marillier, artist 150
Marina of Kent 83
Marindin, C.E. 281
Marini, of Corfu 84
Mariti, Giovanni 259
Marlès, see Lacroix de Marlès 259
Marmier, Xavier 259
Marmont, A.-F. L. Wiesse de, Duc de Raguse 260
Marmora, Andrea 260
Marmora, Jean 84
Martin du Tyrac, see Marcellus
Martin, Percy Falcke 261
Martine, Guillaume 261
Marx, Karl 441
Mastricht, Gerhard von 34
Matheson, William 262
Mathieu, Henri 262
Matthieu, Abel 119
Mauclair, Camille 262
Maundeville, see Mandeville
Maurras, Charles 264, 424
Mavrocordatos 9, 207, 240, 320, 333, 451, 464
Mavrogenes, G.S. 14
Maximilian, of Bavaria 256
Maximos, D. 357
Mayer, Martin 301
Mead, Richard 221, 316
Megalopolis 167
Megara 167, 239, 262
Megaspileon 434, 467
Mehmet Ali 255, 448
Mehmet IV 345
Mehus, Laurence 103
Meiklam, Robert 460
Meletios, see Meletius
Meletius, Bishop of Athens, 161, 264
Melling, Antoine Ignace 80, 266

Melot, Joseph 266
Memoires ou relation militaire 223
Mémoires sur la Grèce et l'Albanie 73
Menard, Louis 16
Mercati, Gaetano 104, 105, 281
Merrill, Selah 466
Mersina 286
Meryon, Charles 216
Messene 167
Metaxas, Ioannes 216
Meteora 13, 44, 63, 194
Methana 326
Methoni, see Modon
Metzovo 194
Meulich, Johann Adolph, see Adelphus
Meurs, Jan 266, 267, 268
Meursius, see Meurs
Meyer, Henry 138
Meyers Reisebücher 268
Mezeray, F. de 74
Mezzanotte, Antonio 268
Miaoulis 138, 207, 363
Michalopoulos, A. 342
Michaud, Joseph François 269, 330
Michelot, engraver 80
Michon, Jean Hippolyte 270
Mignot, Vincent 270
Milbanke, Isabella, Lady Byron 294
Military Costume of Turkey 271, 468
Millard, David 355
Mille, Pierre 271
Miller, E.C.B. 81, 271
Millingen, James V. 273
Millingen, Julius 273
Mills, Charles 273
Mills, John Saxon 274
Milne, General Sir George 298
Milos 188
Minervino, Ciro Saverio 274
Minssen, J.F. 167, 168
Mission Press 466
Missionaries 346, 466
Missolonghi 89, 269, 301
Mistra 90, 312, 347, 434, 467
Mitylene 239, 288, 306
Modern Traveller 89, 90
Modon 6, 236, 292, 347
Moltzer, Jacob 167
Monastir 174, 239

Moncada, Francisco de 274
Moncada, Juan 274
Monceaux, P. 223
Monin, C.V. 19, 20
Monod, Gabriel 125
Montagu, John, 4th Earl of Sandwich 275
Montagu, Lady Mary Wortley 129, 275, 276
Montalbano, I.B. 436
Montant, G. de 448
Montbrun, A. du Puy, Marquis de Saint André 223
Montenegro 25, 207, 250
Moore, J.H. 126
Morea 168, 225, 226, 331, 346, 419, 435
Moreas, Jean 172, 277
Morel, Federic 277, 439
Morell, Thomas 278
Morellet, André 104, 105
Morellus, F., see Morel
Moreno, Jose 278
Moretti, B. 150
Morgenthau, H. 99
Morier, James 12
Moro, Padre 92
Morosini, Antonio 280
Morphopoulos, Panos 205, 280
Morphos, see Morphopoulos
Morris, William 239
Morritt, J.B.S. 104, 231, 280, 453
Mt. Athos, see Athos
Mt. Helicon, see Helicon
Mt. Othrys, see Othrys
Mt. Parnassus, see Parnassus
Mt. Sinai, see Sinai
Moustoxydes, A. 295
Moüy, Charles de, Count 281
Mouzzachy, Alexandros 84
Muelich, Johann Adolph 282
Mühl, K. 268
Mulder, J. 50
Müller, Christian 282
Müller, Elisabeth 282
Müller, Hans 282
Müller, Karl Otfried 283
Muntaner Ramon 54, 274
Muralt, Edward von 283, 284
Muraviev, A.N. 283
Mure, William 285
Mureto, Antonio 278
Murphy, Edward 107

Murray Guides 268
Muspratt, Eric 285
Mustafa Rechid Pasha 304
Mycenae 318
Myconos 188, 239, 257, 262
Mystakides, Basileios 285

N
Nabbe, Thomas 212
Nahmer, Ernst von der 286
Nani Family 300
Napier, Charles James 286
Napoleon 73, 175, 332, 468
Napoli di Romania, see Nauplion
Narborough, Sir John 420
Narles, S. 240
Nauplion 65, 188, 314, 347
Navarino 89, 269, 333, 347, 447
Naxos 65, 188, 314
Naymiller, F. 103
Nearchus 449
Neele and Son, engravers 25
Negroponte 347
Negroponte, Miss 210
Neigebaur, J.F. 6
Nepotas, Michael 334
Nerval, Gerard Labrunie de 286, 287
New York Greek Committee 328
Newton, Charles Thomas 288
Newton, F.W. 168
Newton, Isaac 221
Neyrat, Alexandre Stanislas 288
Nicholas, of Greece, Prince 296
Nicolas II, of Russia 298
Nicolay, Nicolas de 76, 288, 290, 344
Nicolls, Thomas 427, 429
Nissyros 239, 446
Noe Bianchi 292
Noel, Edward H. 293, 294
Noel, Frank 294
Nolau, J.F. 294
Nolhac, Stanislas de 294
North, Frederick, Earl of Guilford 124, 194, 232, 286, 302
Notes d'un Voyage fait dans le Levant 117
Noukios, Nicandros 295
Nouvel Antenor 295
Nucius, see Noukios
Nuits de Ramazan 287

O

O'Connor, V.C.S. 296
Odessa 305
Odysseus 297
Ohsson, I. Mouradga d' 107
Οἱ τελευταῖες μέρες τῆς Χριστιανικῆς Καισαρείας 9
Oikonomides, A.N. 30
Olin, Stephen 296
Olivier, Guillaume Antoine 296, 297
Olympia 167, 301, 467
Olympic Games of 1936 467
Orchomenos 124
Ormuz 416
Orr, N. 296
Orsova 359
Ortelius, Abraham 297
Orthodox Church 366
Osios Loukas 120
Otho, King of Greece 188, 256, 359, 361 426, 430, 464
Othrys, Mt. 114
Ottolenghi, L. 88
Oukhtomsky, Esper Esperovich 298
Ouvré, engraver 287
Owen, Harry Collinson 298
Owen, see Cunliffe-Owen
Ozell, J. 433

P

Paccard, artist 33
Paciaudi, Paolo Maria 300
Paganel, Camille Pierre Alexis 300
Paganelis, Spyridon 301
Palamas, Kostis 277
Palamede 318
Palestine 34, 464
Palmer, E.H. 466
Palmer, Roger, Earl of Castlemaine 301
Panfilio, Cardinal 96
Panofka, Theodor 22, 172
Papachatzidakis, Pericles 435
Papadiamantopoulos, Yannis, see Moreas, Jean
Papadopoulos Bretos, Andreas 302
Papadopoulos, S.A. 317
Parboni, P. 326
Pardieu, Charles, Count de 304
Pardoe, Julia 304, 305
Paris Greek Committee 117, 344
Parisot, Jacques 159, 447
Parisotti, Andrea 96
Parker, Richard Townley 202
Parley, Peter, see Goodrich
Parnassus 436
Paros 65
Pars, William 76, 476
Partsch, Joseph 305
Pashley, Robert 306
Passow, F. 120
Patmos 164, 166, 180, 438, 446
Paton, William 306
Patras 65, 90, 333, 359
Patrick, Samuel 71
Pauquet, engraver 150
Pausanias 306, 308, 309
Pauthier, artist 152
Pauw, Cornelius de 310
Paxos 359
Pearson, engraver 45
Pecchio, Giuseppe 89, 138, 139, 310
Peetermanns, engraver 80
Pelcoq, J. 450
Pelissier, General Aimable 136
Pella 167
Peloponnesus 63, 210, 283, 300, 301, 317, 436, 478, 480
Peloponnesus, see also Morea
Peltz, artist 100
Pencillings by the Way 464
Pendlebury, H.S. 311
Pendlebury, John Dewitt Stringfellow 311
Penel, J. 270
Pennell, Joseph 311
Perdicaris, Gregory A. 312
Peregrinus, see Texier, Edmond
Pergamus 328
Perilla, Francesco 312, 314
Periplus of the Erythrean Sea 448
Perkins, Emma Read 117, 118
Pernot, Hubert 124, 189
Perrot, Georges 314
Perry, Charles 316
Pertusier, Charles 316
Peter, of Greece, Prince 317
Peter Parley, see Goodrich 173
Petermanns Geographische Mitteilungen 305, 318
Petis de la Croix, F. 421
Petrettini, A. Pasquale 320

INDEX

Petrettini, Maria 320
Peutinger Table 225
Peyron, Vittorio Amedeo 47
Peytier, Eugene 317
Phalbos, Philippos K. 208 209
Philadelpheus, Alexander 319
Philemerus Irenicus Elisius 301
Philhellenism, American 457
Philibert, Pierre 321
Philippson, Alfred 318
Philips, John 179
Phillips, Dorothy Una MacGrigor, see Ratcliffe
Phillips, Walter Alison 318
Philomuse Society 202
Picart, Bernard 52, 72
Picken, A. 87
Picquenard, J.-B. 320
Picturesque tour through part of Europe 36
Pieri, Mario 320
ΠιερÉs 320
Pinceo, Renato 278
Pingaud, Leonce 321
Piraeus 318, 319
Piraeus, Franco-British occupation of 478
Pisidia 12
Pittakis, K. 464
Pitton de Tournefort, see Tournefort
Plaisance, Sophie de Marbois Lebrun, Duchesse de 4
Plapoutas 9
Plesner, F. K. 48
Plou, engraver 80
Plumptre, Anne 332
Pococke, Richard 316, 321, 322, 324
Poisson de Gomez, Madeleine Angelique 324
Politis, Nikolaos E. 126
Polo, Marco 31
Polybius 45
Pomardi, Simone 120, 326
Pompeii 130
Ponten von Broich, Julia 326
Ponten, Josef 326
Pontmartin, Armand 77, 78
Pontremoli, Emmanuel 328
Pontsevrez, Th. 261
Poole, Reginald Stuart 118
Poole, Sophia Lane 118
Poole, Stanley Lane 466
Pöppel, engraver 157

Porroni, Marquis 301
Post, Henry A.V. 328
Potter, John 328, 329
Poujoulat, Baptistin 269, 330
Poujoulat, Jean J. F. 269, 330
Pouqueville, F. C. H. L. 80, 73, 331, 332, 333, 335, 426
Poyet, Chancellor 355
Pravasti 189
Preault, Michel François 86, 316
Preaux, see Preault
Prejelan, René 336
Preussischen Messbildanstalt 350
Preziosi, A. 102
Prideaux, Humphrey 337
Priene 286
Prokesch-Osten 318, 427
Proskynetarion 338, 339, 340, 341,
Psara 239
Psichari, Henriette 351
Ptolemaeus, Claudius 173, 341
Puaux, René 12, 342
Pufendorf, Samuel 224
Purcell, engraver 88
Purser, William 65

Q

Quast, A. F. von 204
Quelques Témoignages sur l'Hellénisme de la Thrace 344
Queux de Saint Hilaire, Auguste Henri, Marquis de 35, 271
Quiller-Couch, A.T. 209
Quin, M.J. 251
Quinet, Edgar 344
Quirini, Angelo Maria 97

R

Raffenel, Claude Denis 344
Raicevich, J. 345
Raicevich, Stefano 345
Rajcevic, F. 345
Rålamb, Claes 345
Ralli, artist 35
Ramadani, Antonaki 271
Ramsay, Patrick 150
Ramsay, William Mitchell 346
Randolph, Bernard 346, 347
Rangabes, Alexandros 234

Ratcliffe, Dorothy 349
Raulin, Félix Victor 349
Rauwolf, Leonhard 349
Ray, John 97, 349
Raybaud, Maxime 451
Raymond, J.F. de 170
Redouté, P.J. 297
Reeve, Emma 455
Ρήγας Βελεστινλής, see Rhigas
Regnault, Elias George 474
Reinach, Salomon 223
Reisinger, Ernst 350
Remerand, Gabriel 351
Renan, Ernest 351
Renand, Henri 287
Renefer, Jean Constant 154, 264
Rennell, James 357
Reveil, engraver 294
Reveley, Willy 476
Revelli, Paolo 351
Revett, Nicholas 76, 199, 235, 238, 294
Reviczky, Karoly Imre Sander 352
Revue des deux Mondes 450
Revue Générale des Sciences 223, 352
Rey, Etienne 78, 79, 353
Rhigas 480
Rhodes 7, 115, 180, 206, 217, 236, 239, 244, 288, 292, 319, 347, 351, 438, 446, 453, 460, 476, 481
Rhodes, Knights of, see St. John of Jerusalem, Knights of
Rhodocanachi, E. 352
Riant, Paul Edouard Didier, Comte de 42
Ricaut, see Rycaut
Richards, Theophilus 24
Richardson, Rufus Byam 354
Richier, Christophe 354
Ricketts, Clemuel Green 355
Riedl, J. 356
Riepenhausen, Ernst Ludwig 155
Rigidis, R. 319
Rigny, Admiral de 207
Rio y Coronel, Marcos Manuel 356
Rizoff, Dimitri 274
Roberts, David 356
Robinet, J.B.R. 259
Rodd, Sir James Rennell 12, 159, 357
Romaïdis Brothers 318
Ronart, Stephan 357
Roque, Phocion 358, 427

Rose, William George 359
Rosemond, Jean Baptiste de 366
Rosobuna, N.E. 238
Ross, Ludwig 359
Rostan 40
Rottiers, Bernard Eugène Antoine 361
Rouger, Gilbert 287
Roumeli 478
Rous, Francis 362
Rouse, W.H.D. 210, 311
Roux, Joseph 362
Rovani, Giuseppe 363
Roy, Just-Jean-Etienne 363
Royère, Jean 424
Rozemont, Sieur de, see Rosemond
Rubruquis, G. de 31, 32
Ruffin, consul 431
Russel, J., Duke of Bedford, 204
Russell, William Howard 363
Russo-Turkish war of 1787-8 321
Rycaut, Paul 3, 212, 365, 366
Rzewusky, Wenceslaus 356

S

Saddler, J. 466
Sagansan, L. 420, 421
St. John of Jerusalem, Knights of 43, 96, 144, 207
St. Paul 297
Saint Sophia 239
Sakturis 363
Salaberry, C.M. Irumberry, Count 369
Salamina 239
Sale, G. 441
Salignac, J. de Gontaut Biron, Baron de 27
Salmasius, Claudius 384
Salona 124
Salonica Campaign 298
Salt, Henry 251
Samos 166, 180, 319, 438
Sands, R. 194
Sandwich, Earl of, see Montagu, John
Sansovino, F. 126
Santa Maura 326, 359
Santa Maura, see also Leucada
Santa Rosa, A., Santorre di 88, 139, 310
Santorini 174, 188, 257, 351
Sarantoporon 240
Saraphoglou, Ignatius 340
Sauvage, engraver 418

INDEX

Savelli 326
Scanderbeg 301
Schaefer, Heinrich 474
Scharf, George 172, 470, 472
Schemann, L. 170
Schindelmayer, engraver 164
Schlegel, Friedrich 156
Schliemann, Heinrich 318
Schneidewin, F.W. 283
Schott, Dr. A. 451
Schranz, Antonio 306
Schroeder, engraver 266
Schult, E. 73
Schultheisen, Martin Seyler 449
Schütz, H. 467
Schütze, engraver 157
Schwabe, J.J. 187
Schwaer, engraver 88
Schwartzenberg, Philip Elech von 100
Scott, Alexander 107
Scott-Kilvert, Ian 209
Seale, R.W. 429
Sebastiani, General 40
Sebastopol 305
Seferis, George 188
Seguin, Gerard 446
Sénégal, Croisière du 223
Senex, John 433
Serbia 250
Serres 341
Serveau, engraver 216
Servois, J.P. 77
Setinje 26
Seven Churches of Asia Minor 455
Severn, A. 478
Sgoutas, Leonidas 167, 168
Shelrocke, G. 441
Shores and Islands of the Mediterranean 477
Sibthorp, John 104, 453, 454
Sicyon 6
Simeoni, Gabriel 126
Simi 438
Simonet, J.B. 149
Sinai, Mt. 212, 214, 340, 464
Sinner, Gabriel 56
Sioutes, I. 240
Siphnos 99, 207, 239
Sivas 286
Σκανδάμης, A. 317

Skiadas, A. 151
Skouphos, Spyridon 21
Skyros 239, 318
Sloane, Hans 221
Slovenia 250
Smeeton-Tilley, engraver 450
Smirnow, Alexis 156
Smith, J. 202
Smith, William 429
Smyrna 13, 14, 65, 129, 174, 208, 244, 275, 305, 414, 446
Smyth, Coke 240
Society of Dilettanti 76, 275
Sommer, J.A. 6
Sonnini, C.N.S. 431
Sophianos, Nikolaos 63, 167
Soranzo, G. 436
Spanoudes, K. 240
Spectateur Oriental 344
Spon, Jacob 181, 267, 349, 457
Sporades islands, northern 318
Spratt, T.A.B. 250
Squires, Colonel 454
Stackelberg, O.M., Baron 48
Stafford, W. Cooke 66
Σταματιάδης, Κωνσταντίνος 150
Stanhope, Leicester 89, 466
Stanhope, Philip, Earl of Chesterfield 321
Stanley, Arthur Penrhyn 478
Staphorst, Nicholas 349
Stathatos Collection 319
Steele, Richard 221
Stein, Carl 356
Steni (Euboea) 440
Stephanos, K. 277
Stereotype process 149
Stereotype process, see also Herhan process
Stobitzi 6
Stochove, Vincent 146
Stosch, Philipp von, Baron 103
Strabo 173
Strangford, Lord 454
Strangford, Viscountess, see Beaufort, Emily Anne 25
Stringos Collection 319
Stuart, James 38, 199, 235, 238, 294
Stuart-Glennie, G.S. 357
Suard, translator 276
Suli 26, 194, 239

Sunion 314, 326
Sutcliffe, J. 248
Suzzara, Alexandre de 156
Swainson, Harold 239
Swinton, J. 441
Swiss Alpine Club 262
Syggros, A. 240
Sylburg, Friedrich 307, 308
Sylvius, see Texier, Edmond
Symeon, Archimandrite 338
Syria 174
Syros 174, 256

T

Tafrali, Oreste 414
Tancoigne, J. M. 414
Tardieu, engraver 18
Tardieu, P. F. 99, 449
Tardieu, Ambroise 19
Tardieu, Pierre 150
Tarsus 286
Tatius, Achilles 295
Tavernier, Jean Baptiste 414, 415, 416, 417
Taylor, I.J.S., Baron 260
Taylor, Bayard 417, 418
Tchihatcheff, Peter Alexandrovitch 418
Tebaldi, Pio 94, 419
Tekely 247
Telmessus 460
Temesvar 359
Tempe 167
Tenedos 306, 347
Tennent, see Emerson, James
Teonge, Henry 420
Tepeleni 446
Ternaux, Baron 40
Terzetis, G. 9
Testa, Charles 156
Tetaz, artist 33
Texier, Charles Félix Marie 420
Texier, Edmond 420
Thackeray, William Makepeace 421
Thasos 271, 337
Thebes 167, 283, 326, 436
Thessaloniki 167, 174, 250, 436, 452
Thessaly 23, 44, 49, 114, 194, 227, 239, 443
Thevenot, Jean 421, 423, 424
Thibaudet, Albert 424
Thiers, J. B. 72

Thiersch, Friedrich Wilhelm von 141, 426
Thornton, Thomas 426
Thorwaldsen, B. 48
Thouvenel, Edouard Antoine 134, 427
Thouvenel, Louis 134, 358, 427
Thrace 8, 274
Thucydides 427, 429
Thunman, P.W. 185
Thyatira 65
Tilley, Henry Arthur 429
Tindal, Jacob 221
Tinos 188, 256, 443
Tiryns 314, 318
Tissot, P. F. 447
Tobacco 189
Tocqueville, Alexis de 170
Tököly, see Tekely
Torres y Ribera, Antonio de 430
Tott, François de, Baron 107, 276, 431
Toudouze, Edouard Henri Georges 432
Tour du Monde 29, 223, 251
Tournefort, Joseph Pitton de 432, 433
Townshend, Frederick Trench 433
Tozer, Henry Fanshawe 153, 434
Trant, Thomas Abercromby 434
Trebisond 239
Treaty of Berlin 477
Trevedy, Yves 287
Tricaud, Anthelme de 434
Trikkeri 239
Trikoupis, Spyridon 168, 234, 427, 464
Tritschler, photographer 467
Troad 230
Troy 250
Truguet, Laurent 17
Tsimas, Georgios 435
Tucoo-Chala, Jean 4, 344
Tufnel, Henry 283
Tumiati, Domenico 436
Turcici imperii Status 436
Turkish Empire Illustrated 455
Turner, consul at Larnaca 259
Turner, Charles 184
Turner, William 436
Turot, Henri 438
Tweddell, Robert 439
Tweddell, John 438
Typaldos, Emilio 9, 302
Tzetzes, Joannes 439

INDEX

U

Ukthomsky, see Oukthomsky
Unedited Antiquities of Attica 199
Unger, Franz 440
U.S. Mediterranean Squadron 464
Univers, L' 336
Unte, C. 100
Urquhart, David 441
Ussing, Johan Ludvig 441

V

V., C., artist 431
Vagliano, Stephen 317
Val, R. de 50
Valck, G. 50, 52
Valery, Paul 257
Valiero, Andrea 443
Valon, Alexis de 443
Van den Brule, Alfred 443
Van den Brule, S. 444
Van Genk, engraver 361
Varino, 444
Varna 305
Vatazes, Basileios 234
Vathy 319
Vaudoyer, Jean Louis 444
Vecellio, Cesare 444
Vellay, Charles 446
Venice 236
Venizelos, Eleutherios 83, 188, 444
Venus de Milo 255
Vergennes, C.G., Comte de 152, 431
Vernet, Horace 174, 297
Vernon, Francis 349
Viage à Constantinopla 278
Viaggio d'Anacarsi 20
Viaggio da Venezia al S. Sepolcro 292
Viaud, Louis Marie Julien, see Loti, Pierre
Victoires conquêtes désastres 446
Vigenere, Blaise de 74, 448
Villa, Francesco Ghiron 128, 223
Villehardouin, Geoffroy de 344, 447
Villemain, A.F. 257
Villeterque, Alexandre-Louis 479
Vimercati, Cesare 448
Vincent, William 449
Visconti, E.Q. 199
Vives, Juan Luis 449
Vlachos, Manolis 134
Vlastos Collection 319
Vogue, Marie Eugène Melchior de 450
Volney, Constantin François de 152, 451
Volos 13, 114, 250
Voltaire 270
Vossius, Johann Heinrich 120
Voutier, Olivier 451
Voyage à Constantinople, fait à l' occasion de l' ambassade de M. le Comte de Choiseul-Gouffier 261
Voyage en Valachie et en Moldavie 345
Vulliamy, L. 90

W

Wachler, Albert 120
Wächter, Albert 452
Waddington, Charles 352
Wägner, Wilhelm 452
Wailly, Natalis de 447
Wakeman, George 126
Wales, Prince of, see Edward, Prince of Wales
Walker, J. 438
Walker, Mary Adelaide 198, 45
Walpole, Frederick 453
Walpole, Horace 316
Walpole, Horatio 453
Walpole, Robert 185, 439, 453
Walsh, Robert 66, 454, 455
Warburton, Bartholomew Eliot George 453, 455
Warsberg, Alexander, Freiherr von 455
Webb, Philip 239
Webster, Daniel 457
Weiss, Aloys 354
Werner, C. 466
Wescher, Carl 358
Westerbaen, Kornelis 440
Wheeler, G., see Wheler
Wheler, George 97, 457, 458
White Cross Movement 203
Widmann, Carolo Aurelio 459
Wiedasch, E. 155
Wilde, Oscar 251
Wilde, William Robert Wills 460
Wilhelm II, Emperor of Germany 460
Wilkins, William 460
Wilkinson, Charles 461
Willemin, Nicolas Xavier 461
Williams, Hugh William 157, 462
Willis, Nathaniel Parker 464

Willmore, A. 466
Willoughby, Vera 464
Wilson, Charles William 464
Wilson, Samuel Sheridan 466
Wilson, William Rae 466
Wimmer, Gottlieb August 467
Winckelmann, J.J. 103
Windheim, Christian von 324
Winwurm, engraver 247
Wiskott, Carl T. 467
Witdoeck, P.J. 361
Wittman, William 271, 467
Wolcott, Samuel 355
Wolfe, J. 90
Wolfensberger, J.J. 141, 476
Wolff, Dr. Paul 467
Wood, John Turtle 468
Woodford, Alexander 56
Woodward, J.D. 466
Wordsworth, Christopher 116, 172, 469, 470, 472, 474
Worsley, Sir Richard 474
Wrede, Walther 257, 476
Wrede, Maria Elisabeth 257, 476
Wright, George Newenham 476
Wyon, Reginald 477
Wyse, Sir Thomas 427, 478
Wyse, Winifrede M. 478

Wysling, Hans 328

X
Xanthi 189
Xenopon's Ten Thousand 297
Xenopoulos, G. 234
Xylander, Gulielmus 307

Y
Yenitza 240
Yonge, Charlotte Mary 479
York, Spiridon 47
Yorke, Charles 479
Yorke, Philip, 2nd Earl of Hardwicke 479
Young, James Foster 480
Young, Sir William 480
Ypsilantis, Dimitrios 345
Ypsilantis, Alexander 232
Ypsilantis, Nicolas 208

Z
Zakynthos 438
Zarex 6
Zeà, see Keos
Zenker, artist 182
Zephar, Christophoros 338
Zervos, Skevos George 481
Zlatarski, V.N. 274

INDEX OF PRINTERS, PUBLISHERS, BOOKSELLERS AND BOOKBINDERS

A

Adams, John 362
Agasse, H. 68, 69, 296, 297
Aillaud, J.-P. 81
Alcan, Félix 30, 125
Alcan-Levy 34
Aldus 307, 308
Allan, Philip 464
Allen, Wm. H. 9, 33
Allgemeiner Verein für Deutsche Litteratur 286
Alliana 156
Altobello, Salicato 126
Alvisopoli 302
Amaulry, T. 434
Ami du Peuple, Imprimerie de l' 6
Amitiés Gréco-Suisses 55
Amyot 111, 210
Andreola, Francesco 430
Angot 424
Ardant, see Martial Ardant
Arkstee 186
Arnold, Edward 56, 120
Arrowsmith 42
Art Grec 12
Artaria and Fontaine 400
Arthus-Bertrand 77, 91
Astoin, Leon 282
Athens, Imprimerie Royale 9, 21
Atlantis 301
Aubouyn, Pierre 128
Audot 294
Autrichien Lloyd 244

B

Baedeker 14
Baglioni, Paolo 443
Baillière, see also Germer Baillière
Baillière, J. B. 418
Bailly-Baillière, Carlos 418
Ballard, E. 71
Ballard, S. 71
Bance ainé 411
Barasse, E. 171
Barba 78
Barbier, François 128
Barbier, Veuve Guill. 128
Barbin, Claude 223, 415, 421
Bardi, G. 151
Bardin, D. 382
Barnard and Sultzer 331
Barois, François 368
Barrett, W. 369
Barthélemy, D. 148
Basset, Thomas 346
Bathurst, C. 71
Batsford, B. T. 10
Battei, L. 389
Baudry 196
Baumeister, Josef 340
Bauzonnet, bookbinder 48
Becken, Balthazar 449
Becket, T. 275
Bedelet, Amédée 282
Behourt, Louis 146
Behourt, Veuve 146
Belin 221, 222, 259
Bell, A. 433
Bell, George, & Sons 411
Bell and Daldy 136, 249, 411
Beman, Henri 276
Bensley, B. 390
Bensley, T. 104
Bentley, Richard 12, 25, 116, 138, 139, 198, 226, 227, 359, 434, 453
Bentley, S. and R. 420
Bergegrens, E. T. 185
Berger Levrault 271
Bernard, 221, 222
Bertrand, A. 256
Bertrand, see Arthus-Bertrand

INDEX

Besongne, Jacques 24
Bethune 414
Bettesworth, A. 433
Bianchi, see Cuccinielli and Bianchi
Bibliographisches Institut 268
Billaine, Louis 421
Billaine, Veuve Louis 366
Birt, S. 321
Black & Son 278
Black, Adam 388, 462
Black, Adam and Charles 248, 250
Black, James 278
Blackett, see Hurst and Blackett
Blackwood & Son 210
Blackwood, William 146, 285
Blaeu, Jan and Cornelis 384
Blanchard, W. 280
Blanche 149
Bleuet jeune 373
Bliss, E. 328
Bobée, A. 309
Boccard, A. de 382
Boget 149
Bohn 411
Boissonnas, F. 41
Boite, J. F. 276
Boitel, Léon 78
Bonwicke, Henry 178
Boom, Henry and Theodore 110, 373
Boone, T. and W. 286
Boras, Apostolos 341
Bortoli, Antonio 142
Bossange Frères 451
Bossard 287
Bosworth, T. 464
Boudet, – 36
Boulland 205
Bowyer, John 295
Braumüller, Wilhelm 440
Breitkopf and Härtel 244, 402
Breitkopf, see Tetschner and Breitkopf
Briday 288
Briguet, J. 116
Brissot-Thivars 207
Broadbent, Hugh 230
Brockhaus, F. A. 141, 371, 426
Brodard, Paul 223, 447
Brown, see Longman
Browne, Christopher 347
Browne, D. 433
Bruckmann, F. 215, 467
Brügel, Karl 188
Brun, A., et Cie 156
Bruneval, Claude 74
Budry, Jean 41
Buisson, F. 77, 152, 222, 394
Bulmer W. 107, 184, 392, 393, 460, 480
Bund, Rodolphe 6
Burgess, see Paine and Burgess
Burn, of Kirby Street 249
Burrel 455

C

Cadell, T. 183
Cadell, T. and W. Davies 84, 86, 104, 159, 275, 280, 448
Cademan, William 457
Caimi, see Corona and Caimi
Calergis, G. E. 357
Calmann Levy 382, 427
Cambridge University Press 311
Camden Society 295
Canning, W. 95
Capelle, see Mayeur and Capelle
Capurro, N., e Comp. 268
Carey, see Lea and Carey
Carl Gerold's Sohn 455
Carpenter, James, and Son 204
Carvill, G.C. and H. 328
Casimir 80
Cassone 23
Castalie 257
Cavelier, Guillaume 52
Cawthorn, James 190
Cayer & Co. 214
Cellot, L. T. 166
Céne, Michel Charles le 424
Century Co. 189
Challamel 174
Chambers, William and Robert 405
Chamerot, G. 35
Champion, H. 110
Champion, Honoré and Edouard 264
Chapelot 240
Chapman and Hall 368, 452
Chapman, Henry 107
Chavet, A. 161
Cherbuliez, Joel 376

INDEX

Chesneau, Nicolas 74
Chiswell, Richard 187
Churchill, Awnsham 457
Churchill, Rockwell 479
Clarendon Press 28, 76, 153, 434
Clark, Andrew 427
Clay, Richard & Sons 239
Clousier, François 128
Clouzier, Gervaise 414, 415
Clowes, W. 251, 363
Club des Libraires de France 287
CNRS 351
Coates, Henry T. & Co. 252
Colburn, Henry 87, 99, 108, 138, 139, 250, 304, 332, 333, 434, 441, 455
Colin, Armand 31, 114, 115, 117, 118
Colinez, Veuve A. 361
Colnaghi, D. & P. 240
Commercial Bank of Greece 7
Comon 141
Comon, Veuve 270
Compagnie des Libraires, Amsterdam 246, 309
Comptoir für Literatur und Kunst 409
Coninx, Arnould 288
Constable, Archibald 254, 462
Coromilas, A. see Koromelas
Corona and Caimi 87, 167
Coronelli 91
Corréard and Ponthieu 14
Cosnier and Lachèse 170
Costard, J.P. 322
Cotta, J.B. 176
Cottret 35
Coulouma and Padovani 12
Courbé, Augustin 74
Coustelier, Antoine 179
Cox, see Tindal and Cox
Cramoisy, Sebastian 73, 389
Crapelet 26, 232, 369
Crownfield, Cornelius 97
Cuccinielli and Bianchi 400
Curmer, L. 474
Curry, William 460
Curti 260

D

Dabo, Veuve 19
Daldy, see Bell and Daldy
Dantan, André 412
Darby, J. 433
Darton and Harvey 461
Dauthereau 80
Dauvin and Fontaine 443
David, Imprimerie 14
Davies, W., see Cadell and Davies
Davis, A.H. 454
Davis, C. 253, 316
Davis, J. 36
Davison, Thomas 124, 401
Day and Son 288, 478
De Bure 17
De Bure Frères 232
Debecourt 254
Decker, George Jacques, & Fils 310
Deighton 480
Delagrave, Charles 8, 298
Delaguette, Veuve 152
Delatour, L.F. 238
Delatour, Veuve 179
Delpierre, H. 361
Denné jeune 104
Dent, J.M. 45
Dentu, E. 22, 230, 231, 262, 479
Denugon 8
Derby, H.W. 296
Derby, J.C. 296
Derome 308
Desaint, J.Ch. 36, 158
Desanctis 60
Désanges, Achille 300
Desenne 18
Desenne and Volland 451
Desessart 88
Desrez, A. 54
Detaille, F. 174
Deutsche Verlags-Anstalt 326
Devambez 336
Dezobry 269
Didier 131, 187
Didot, see also Firmin Didot
Didot 17, 29, 173, 233, 308
Dodsley, R. 321
Doig, Stirling and Slade 329
Doll, Anton 467
Dondey-Dupre 206
Douniol, Ch. 63

INDEX

Dreyfous, Maurice 46
Du Bosc, Claude 72
Du Brel, P. A. 66
Du Breuil 300
Duchesne, Veuve 182, 183
Duckworth 285
Ducollet 269
Dufour, J. E. 431
Duncan, James 89, 90
Dunewald, Veuve 458
Dunmore, John 187
Dupont, A. 176
Durand, Auguste 168 179
Durand Père & Fils 99
Duren, J. van, see Van Duren
Durey, see Lecointe et Durey

E

Eberhart, J.-M. 309
Ecole des Langues Orientales Vivantes 234
Edet Jeune, of Rouen 335
Edmonds and Remnants 65
Egelsehr, Kaspar, of Schweinfurt 384
Egmon, Corneille 414
Eleutheroudakis 208
Ellis, G. H. 48
Elzevir 169, 436
Emile-Paul 55
Enderlin, Jacob 140
Enosis Smyrnaion 208
Enslin, Adolph 155
Enslin, Th.Chr.Fr. 155
Estes and Lauriat 479
Estienne, Robert 354
Eustratios, D.G. 14
Evans Brothers 202
Evans, Bradbury and Co. 249
Evans, D.W. & Co. 88
Eymery, Alexis 128, 139
Eyre and Spottiswoode 349

F

Faucheux, A. 352
Faulder, R. 36
Fentius, see Fenzo
Fenzo, Modesto 380
Ferrand, Charles 53
Ferrario, Libreria 363
Feyerabendt 254
Finch, James, & Co. 477
Firmin Didot 33, 34, 35, 47, 49, 117, 144, 335, 411, 420
Firmin Didot et Cie 217
Firmin Didot Frères 217, 233, 393
Firmin Didot Frères Fils & Cie 444
Firmin Didot Père et Fils 333
Fischbacher 63, 84
Fisher, Son & Co. 65, 455, 476
Flach, Martin 5
Flammarion, Ernest 154, 264, 481
Florence, 'Typographio Imperiali' 97
Fontaine, see Dauvin and Fontaine
Fontaine, see Artaria and Fontaine
Fontana 47
Formentin 398
Forrest, Edward 362
Foss, see Payne and Foss
Foucault, Veuve Damien 178
Fournier, H. 130
Franck, A. 87
Fricx, Eugène Henry 416
Friedrich, Wilhelm 282
Fritsch, Thomas 308
Froment and Lequien 150
Furne 269
Furne, Jouvet et Cie 219
Furst, J.H., & Co. 280

G

Gabon and Co. 331
Gadsby 158
Gaertner, Rudolph 359
Galerie Delorme 159
Gallaher, see White, Gallaher and White
Gamber, J. 205
Garios and Co. 212
Garnich, Jacob 27
Garnier Frères 255, 304
Gaw, Thomas of Coleraine 460
Gayguer, Lazaro 278
Gelléri and Szekely 188
Générale, Librairie 34
Germer, Baillière et Cie 30
Gerold, see Carl Gerold's Sohn
Geuthner, Paul 351, 414
Gide 46, 130

515

INDEX

Gide fils 196, 202
Gilbert, R. 412
Gillet, T. 467
Gillyflower, Matthew 95
Giovannelli, G.P. 103
Glykys, Nikolaos 214, 264, 337
Goethals 110
Gold, Joyce 439
Gosselin, Charles 54, 196, 218
Goubaud, J. 80
Grasset, Bernard 217
Gregoir, N.-J. 330
Grevel, H. 118
Grevin, E. 154, 264
Grover, J. 187
Gruaz, Ch. 376
Gruyter, Walter de 460
Grypares, Z. 151
Guerin, H.L. 238
Guglielmini 87
Guillaumin 44, 233
Guilleminet 403, 404
Guilmoto, E. 261
Günther, Carl 384
Gyldendalschen, see Gyldendalske
Gyldendalske Boghandel (F. Hegel) 374, 441

H

Hachette 4, 28, 112, 134, 188, 204, 219, 223, 383, 432, 438, 447
Hachette, L. 3, 4, 314
Hakkert, A.M. 226
Hall, see Chapman and Hall
Hall, William 362
Halliday, see Seeley
Halma, Franciscus 267
Harper & Brothers 405
Harper, Charles 427
Harrap, George G. 159
Härtel, see Breitkopf and Härtel
Hartmann, Paul 42
Harvey, see Darton and Harvey
Haskell, W. 391
Hawkins, G. 321
Hazell, Watson and Viney 118
Heath, D.C. 215
Hegel, F., see Gyldendalske Boghandel
Heinemann, William 23, 311
Henricpetri, Sebastian 100

Henry 320
Henry, George, and Co. 58
Herault, Eustache 417
Herhan 19
Herzel, S. 407
Hiard, A. 20
Hill, John 346
Hitch, C. 321
HMSO 142
Hodder and Stoughton 190, 298, 346
Hölder, Alfred 378
Hondt, P.A. de 275
Horthmels 458
Horton, E. 187
Houghton, see Hurd and Houghton
Howlett, B.R. 271
Hullmandel, G. 164, 240
Humbert 28
Huntington and Savage 173
Hurd and Houghton 30
Hurst, see Longman, Hurst
Hurst and Blackett 433
Hutchinson & Co. 99, 296
Hutter, binder 261
Huzard-Courcier 205

I

Ilf-Verlag 388
Imprimeurs Unis 141
Innys, G. & J. 221
Innys, G. 71
Innys, W. 321
Insegna del Diogene, Tipografia all' 396
Insel-Verlag 350
Institut Français de Archéologie Orientale 126
Islip, Adam 212
Istituto Italiano d'arti grafiche 206, 351

J

Jackson, see Seeley
Jackson, see Sidgwick and Jackson
Jackson, William 72
Janet, François and Louis 261
Janssonius, J. 224, 266, 408
Jent 344
Johnson, T. 219
Johnstone, A. 388
Joly, Thomas 421, 423
Jouast, D. 62

Jouve, Henri 245
Jouvet, see Furne
Juven, Félix 16, 443

K

Kallitechnia 203
Kammermeister, Sebastian 377
Kanariotes, A. 151
Karavias, Notis 166
Kargadouris, see Meissner
Kaufmann 216, 257
Kenney, see Stirling and Kenney
Kettlewell, Robert 457
Keyser, Henrich 345
King, Thomas 107
Klasing 244
Knaplock, Robert 97
Knapton, J. and P. 321
Knight, Charles 420
Knobloch, Johann 6
Knobloch, Karl 429
Koberg, Anton 377
Konstantinides, A. 390, 396
Koromelas, A. 61, 240, 371
Koutsiaftis 140
Kröner Brothers 176
Krooneveld, Henrik van 49
Kuhn, J.B. 400
Kündig, H. 84
Kundig, A. 41

L

L'Angelier A. 74
La Plume 277
Lachèse, see Cosnier and Lachèse
Ladvocat 260
Lafargue, Th. 349
Lahure, A. 312
Lahure, Ch. 3
Lamborot, Veuve 161
Lampropoulos, A.Th. 9
Langlois, H. 73
Langlois, H. fils et cie 207
Laran 230
Lasteyrie, C. de 206
Laurens, Henri 32, 262, 280
Lauriat, see Estes and Lauriat
Laurie, T. Werner, Ltd. 245
Le Boucher, Pierre 417

Le Clerc 270
Le Febvre, Jacques 147
Le Normant 69
Lea and Carey 454
Lebel 66
Lebigre Frères 20
Lebigre-Duquesne Frères 245
Lecoffre, Victor 259
Lecointe et Durey 66
Ledoux, Abel, fils 18, 19
Ledoux, Paul 73
Lefevre 149
Leggas Ch. 55, 261, 376
Legros, F. 320
Lehman, John 60
Lehuby, P.C. 16
Lelong 320
Lequien, see Froment and Lequien
Lerebours 174
Leroux, Ernest 63, 115, 118, 182, 234, 271, 285, 328, 382
Leroy 386
Leske, Carl Wilhelm 476
Levrault, see Berger Levrault
Levrault, F.G. 344
Levy, Michel 236
Levy, Michel, see also Michel Levy Frères
Levy, see Alcan-Levy
Levy, see Calmann Levy
Lewis W. 271, 282
Librairie de France 155
Librairie des Bibliophiles 62
Librairie Nouvelle 420
Librairie Orientale 450
Librairie Orientale-Américaine 261
Librairie Universelle 131, 245
Lippincott, J.B. 311
Liverpool University Press 8
Longman & Co. 392
Longman, Brown, et al. 7, 65
Longman, Green, et al. 429
Longman, Hurst et al. 164, 194, 273, 393, 453
Longman, Orme et al. 460
Longman, Rees et al. 13, 56, 462, 466
Longman, T. 71, 321
Longmans, Green and Co. 30, 45, 468
Lorentz & Keil, Constantinople 418
Lothrop, D. 479
Lyon, see Woodman and Lyon

INDEX

M

Machuel, Jean-Baptiste 417
MacLean, Thomas 271
MacLean, see also McLean
MacLehose, James and Sons 242
MacMillan & Co. 3, 203, 239, 371
Magdeleine, E. 269
Magimel 28
Mairet 54
Maison, L. 171
Maisonneuve 371
Malassis, Clement 24
Maleherbe, G. de 342
Mame, Alfred 13, 154, 217, 330
Mame Frères 149
Mantzakos, N., of Athens 87, 328
Maradan 369
Marazzani, R. 320
Marbre-Cramoisy, E. 43
Marchant, 331
Marino, P. 398
Marotta and Vanspandoch 320
Marshall Brothers 164
Marston, see Sampson Low
Martial Ardant Frères 363, 373
Martin, G. 236
Martin, see Rodwell and Martin
Marzorati 23
Masson and Son 345
Mawman, Joseph 202, 426, 439
Max, Josef 283
May, L.-Henry 44, 175, 222
Mayeur and Capelle 295
Mazzajoli, Gio. 150
McLean, Thomas 240, 248, 400
Meadows, W. 321
Meehan, John S. 457
Meissner and Kargadouris 208
Menard 18
Méquignon 166
Mercy, Heinrich 246
Merigot 179
Merkus 186
Mersch, J. 116
Messein, Albert 424
Methuen 43, 209, 210
Meurs, Veuve Jacob van 410
Michallet, Estienne 43, 181
Michel Levy Frères 160, 255
Miller, William 107
Milner and Sowerby 60
Mongenet, J. 173
Mongie, P., aîné 175
Morel, Fédéric 257, 439
Mortier, Pierre 179
Μπόρα, Αποστόλου 341
Müller, Alfred 285
Müller, see Tasché and Müller
Murray John 22, 57, 65, 102 124, 151, 168, 224, 225, 306, 380, 393, 436, 460, 469, 470, 472
Myrtides Bros. 208, 209

N

Nast, Adolph 6
Nathan, Fernand 182
National Bank of Greece 317
Neaulme, Jean 31, 388
Nelson, T. 184
Nelson, T., and Sons 464
Nepperschmidt, A. 140
Nepveu A. 69, 70, 414
Nettleton and Son, Plymouth 460
Nicol, G. and W. 184
Nicol, George 392
Nicol, William 204, 392
Nicolle, H. 196, 316
Nilsson 208
Nivelliana, Officina 389
Noblet, Henri and Charles 448
Norgate, see Williams and Norgate
Nourrit, see Plon-Nourrit
Nourse, J. 321
Nyon 308

O

Ogle, J. 388
Olkos 134
Ollivier, John 209, 210
Onfroi 310, 372
Onfroy, see Onfroi
Oporinus, Joannes 166
Orell, Füssli and Co. 198
Orme, see Longman
Osborn, J. 71
Otley, see Saunders and Otley
Oudin, Henri 63
Oursel, Lovys 24
Ouvrier 479

P

Padovani, see Coulouma and Padovani
Paine and Burgess 312
Palearino, Nicolo and Marco 300
Palmer, Richard 347
Pancoucke, C.L.F. 446
Papayiannopoulos, B. 435
Parent-Desbarres 369
Paris, Imprimerie de la Republique 449
Paris, Imprimerie Nationale 156, 234
Paris, Imprimerie Royale 432
Parker, J.W. 306
Parker, John W. and Son 84
Payne 480
Payne and Foss 392
Payne, Oliver 349
Pelazza 88
Penn, John 346
Perilla 312, 314
Périsse Frères 166
Perrin 172, 342, 446
Perrin, Louis 79, 353
Perthes, Justus 305, 318
Petters, H. 100
Peytieux 159
Philadelpheus, Ch.N. 61
Phillips, Sir Richard 282, 331, 467
Phillips, Sampson & Co. 296
Φρόνιμος, Δημήτριος 340
Picard, Alphonse 321
Pieraccini, Tipografia 401
Piget 179
Pine and Thomas 374
Pirotta 103
Pitt Press, Cambridge 306
Pittoni, Leonardo 419
Plancher 8
Plange, Th.J. 129
Plantiniana, Officina 297
Plassan, Pierre 461
Playford, John 178
Plon 83, 414, 444
Plon, E. 207, 236, 358
Plon, Henri 170
Plon-Nourrit 134, 136, 170, 248, 253, 266, 281, 288, 294, 450
Poggioli, Vincenzo 326
Poncet le Preux 119
Ponthieu, see Corréard and Ponthieu
Pornin, R. 15
Pote, J. & T. 71
Presses Universitaires de France 62
Priestley and Weale 204, 393
Prince 480
Pulchri Press 356
Purgold, Maison 48
Putnam, G.P. 346, 417, 418
Pyrsos 314

Q

Quaritch, B. 371
Quien, Carlo 387
Quillau, F.G. 308

R

Ramellati, Ambrogio 415
Ramos y Compañia 356
Raymond 344
Reed, William W. 89
Rees, see Longman
Regnault, François 235
Reimer, Dietrich 100
Reimer, Georg 45, 55, 306
Relfe, Lupton 24
Religious Tract Society 251
Remnant and Edwards 295
Remondini of Venice 292
Renouard 280
Renouard, A.A. 26
Renouard, Jules 216
Ribou, P. 417
Ricciardi, Francesco 324
Richter, Adolphus 124
Ridgway, James 44
Riedl 356
Rinehart 114
Riss, F. 222
Ritchie, J. 388
Riviere and Son 154, 429
Rivington, see Sampson Low
Rivington, C. and J. 321, 412
Roberts Bros. 16
Roberts, J. 276
Robinson, G.G. and J. 21
Robinson, G.G.J. and J. 99
Robinson, see Sleight and Robinson

INDEX

Robson 480
Rocolet, Pierre 178
Rodwell and Martin 120, 241, 392, 401
Rodwell, John 12, 226, 273
Ronchetti 320
Rotogravure S. A. 174
Rouille 168
Roux, Gabriel 77
Roux, Ph. 431
Rowland, A. J. 164
Roworth, C. 124
Russian Academy of Architecture 238
Rutgert, Alberts 396

S

Saillant 158
Salva, V., of Regent Street 274
Sampson Low, Marston & Co. 12, 70, 363, 480
Samuelian, H., of Paris 77, 451
Sancha, Imprenta de 274
Sangrouber, A., of Vevey 336
Sansot, E. 46
Saunders and Otley 249, 390
Sauzet, Henri du 337
Savage, see Huntington and Savage
Sawbridge, Thomas 187
Sayer, Robert 374
Saywell, R. 187
Schade, Gustav 40
Schaele, Gustav 155
Scheible, J. 218
Schmidt, Heinrich 384
Schouten, Salomon 148
Schraembl, Joanna 341
Schreyer, Sebald 377
Schropp, S. 356
Schulze 226
Schwabe, Benno 262
Schwetschke, C. A., and Son 359
Scotzniovsky 157
Searle, see Sampson Low
Seeley, Jackson, & Halliday 83
Selligue 142
Senefelder 398
Senex, J. 71
Serlin, Wilhelm 301
Sessa, Giovanni 446
Sheldonian Theatre 119, 347

Sherman, C. 355
Sherwood, Jones, and Co. 402
Shoberl 69
Shropshire, William 349
Shuckburgh, J. 316
Sidgwick and Jackson 407
Simoniana, Stamperia 274
Slade, see Doig
Sleight and Robinson 328
Smith, Elder & Co. 112, 318, 421
Smith, G. [i.e. W.] 34
Smith, J. 196
Snow, John 466
Société d' Édition "Le Livre" 216
Société Typographique, Neuchatel 324
Society for the Propagation of Christian Knowledge 38
Someren, Jan van 110, 416
Sonnius, L. 66
Sotheran 278
Sowerby, see Milner
Spamer, Otto 452
Spanos, Ch. 253
Spemann, W. 142
Spilsbury, T. 391
Spottiswoode, A. and R. 164
Spottiswoode, see Eyre and Spottiswoode
Springer, Julius 40
Stalling, Gerhard 409
Stanford, Edward 274
Staples Press 378
Steenuil 357
Stiftshaus 324
Stirling and Kenney 329
Stirling, see Doig
Stott, David 357
Stoughton, see Hodder and Stoughton
Strahan, Alexander 249
Strahan, W. 126
Stürtz, H. 247
Sultzer, see Barnard and Sultzer
Suttaby, R. and A., of London 472
Szekely, see Gelléri and Szekely

T

T. R. 48
Tasché and Müller 105
Taupinart, Adrian 115

Tavernier 175
Taylor, Josiah 204
Taylor, William 97
Tegg, Thomas 89, 172
Tencé Frères 361
Terrey, Thos. 347
Tetschner and Breitkopf 324
Teubner, B.G. 119, 408, 452
Theodosios, Demetrios 340
Theodosios, Panos 161
Thieles Buchdruckerei 441
Thomas, see Pine and Thomas
Thomson of Edinburgh 250
Tilt, Charles 153
Tindal and Cox 418
Tooke, Benjamin 48, 187
Touquet 40, 142
Tourian Brothers 118
Trattnern, Jean Thomas 352
Tremblay 19
Treuttel and Würtz 206, 234
Treves, Fratelli 111, 436
Typographia Palladis 300

U

Underwood & Underwood 354
Underwood, Thomas and George 172
Unwin, T. Fisher 386

V

Vallee-Edet, of Rouen 335
Van de Water, Guiljelmus 268
Van Duren, J. 219, 221
Van Oest, G., & Co. 42
Van Voorst, John 398
Vanelli 310
Vanspandoch, see Marotta and Vanspandoch
Varennes, Olivier de 414
Veale, Abraham 100
Velhagen 244
Viney, see Hazell
Virtue and Co. 305, 464
Virtue, George 304
Visentini, M. 371
Vivès, Louis 32
Volland, see Desenne and Volland
Vresse, Arnauld de 77

W

Waesbergen 110
Wahlen, Auguste 80
Warne, W., of Newport, Isle of Wight 304
Wasmuth, Ernst 193
Watson, see Hazell
Watts, John 429
Watts, R. 84, 86
Weale, see Priestley and Weale
Wechel, Andreas, Heirs of 307
Wechel, Christian 341
Weidmann 408
Weigel, R. 400
Weiss, S.H., of Constantinople 376
Westermann, B. 118
Westley, Frederick 454
Wetstein Frères 52
Wetstein J. 34, 149
Weygand'sche Buchhandlung 283
White 480
White, Gallaher and White 328
White, L. 21
Whittaker, G.B. 39
Wibes, P.S. 374
Wilberg, Charles, of Athens 255
Wild'schen Buchdruckerey, Franz 400
Williams and Norgate 294
Winston, John C. 91
Witherby & Co. 24
Woerl, Leo 247
Wohler, J.C. 149
Wolfgang, Abraham 110, 267, 365
Wolfgangh, see Wolfgang
Wolfgank, see Wolfgang
Wolters, Jan 408, 458
Woodman and Lyon 253
Woodman, Thomas 349
Woodward, T. 316
Wouters, V. 330, 335
Wright, J. 164
Würtz, see Treuttel and Würtz

Z

Zaehnsdorf 481
Zatta, Antonio 20
Zephar, Christophoros 338
Zetzner, L. 32
Ziletti, Francesco 290

INDEX OF PROVENANCES

Included in the index of provenances are mottos and cyphers. In many cases it is difficult to interpret the cypher correctly, so the letters of the cypher may be listed in several ways.

A
'A Deo Omnia' 472
A.M. 269
A.N. 376
ACG 345
'Ad usum Wendelini praeterii' 301
Alderley Edge High School 83
Alexoudes, Anthimos, Bishop of Amaseia 285, 452
Alford Library 45
Alivizatou, Amilka S. 44
Allan, Alexander 433
AML 221
Andreades, A., professor 252
Anthimos, Bishop of Amaseia, see Alexoudes
Aristeias, K. 66
Arvanitidis, G.J. 6, 385, 449
Asquier de Ialion, Michel d' 115
Atabey, Şefik 63, 96, 128, 476
Atchley, Shirley 63, 172
Avignon, Lycée Imperial d' 335

B
BA 321
Baggi, Pietro 78
Bandini Piccolomini, Count 182
Barnaud, – 161
Bastianini, G. 342
Beauchamp, William Lygon 270
Bellevine, C.G. de 52
Bertalazoni, Giovanni Francesco 310
Blackmer, H.M. 41, 239
Blaikie, Francis 401
Blount, Thomas Pope 427
BMPF 274
Boïou, E. 301
Borüth, P. 345
Brand, Sir Thomas 377
Brigstocke, Elizabeth Lydia 304
Brunswick School, Leamington 430
Burmann, Peter II 260

C
Caffery, E. 60
Caignaire, Maison d'Education de 77
Caley, John 159
Cambridge School Library 97
Carayannopoulos, Spyridon 129
Carlow College 86
Chabot, see Rohan de Chabot
Charrin, Marie 77
Chatsworth Library 268
Chichester, Clarentia 90
Chorley, W.B. 96
CJV 474
CM, see M., Charlotte
Codrington, Lady Georgiana 333
Coleridge, Francis Edward 57
Coleridge, Rev. Edward 57
Coles, E.H. 218
Collins, Jane 249
Constanz, Lyceum of 17
Copineau, N. 233
Cruysen, see Vander Cruysen
CVPF 274

D
Daudat, S.D. 27
Davies-Evans, Mrs. 311
DcS 443
De Fourvieres, N.D. 156
Deane, F., of Colchester 49
Denham Court Library 39
Dimaras K.Th. 22, 60, 62, 77, 80 118, 131, 136, 139, 142 152, 161, 181, 204, 205, 219, 236, 253, 277, 280, 287, 300, 310, 321, 345, 351, 376, 424

'Dio mi concesse questi ozi' 320
DMR 321
Dugue de Bagnoll, family of 178
Dundas, Sir David, of Ochtertyne 308, 385
Duruy, Victor 353

E
Edinburgh, Royal School 224
Edmonstone, Sir Archibald, of Duntreath 225
Eliasco, J.C. 65, 447
Elliot, Gavin, of Melross 224
Engelshofen, V. 6
Ese, Charles Edouard 328
'Ex Fide Fortis' 270

F
FCM 53
Feltrinelli, Giannalisa 385
Fraunceys, Edward 369

G
Garland, Ernst, Dr. 153
Gennadius, Ioannes 56
Geoffroy Saint-Hilaire, E. 349
Ghinis, George 66
Gilmore, W., of Brooklyn 436
GO 273
Godart, Justin 77
Goodheart, Harry Chester 472
Goring, Sir William 369
Gratsos, Panos 15
Greenbank, Rathbone 194
Gregory, Richard, F.A.S. of Trinity College, Dublin 286
Gregory, Richard, of Coole, Ireland 286
Grolig, Moriz 176
Grylle, W. 321

H
Hall, E. Lawrence 412
Hallensleben, H. 155
Harcourt, Sir William 439
Hartnell, Edward Joseph 368
Hatzidemos, A. 25, 39, 129, 159, 236
Head, George Head, of Rickerby 184
Henri, Guy 345
Hippolytana, Bibliotheca 76
Hoar Cross, Burton on Trent 470, 526
Hodgson, Maud 126

Hopetoun, Earl of 95
Hope-Vere, Marie Elizabeth 374
Howard, Charles W.G. 308, 385
Hutt, Charles 39
Hutton, Edward 333
Huxley, Julian S. 114

I
Irving, John A. 329

J
J.C.P. 382
James VI School, Edinburgh 250
Jan, Baron de Roly 146
Jester (crest) 280
JFV 81

K
Kasdagles, – 380
Kearney, Michael, of Trinity College, Dublin 254
Kenrick, J. Timothy 254
Kinsey, Jesse 312
Konstas, Ioannis G.Ch. 338

L
Labrosse, Louis 269
Lancut, Bibliothèque de 196
Landauer, Paul 457
Lansdowne family 270
Larssen, Christian 48
Lassee, A.V. 309
Latham, E. 34
Layrac, School of the Sacre-Coeur de Jesus 330
Lechevalier 110
Legg, G. White 34
Lelorier, Richard 307
Leontina, Biblioteca Pontificia 419
Limoges, College Royal de 166
Lingard, Charles 392
Liokes, Ep. N. 314
Locher, M. 452
'L' Olivette' 273
Loverdos Library 239
Lowther 52
'Lucem Amare Amore Lucere' 304

M
M.A. 269
M., Charlotte 446

INDEX

McCheyne, James, of Woodhall House 467
McGea, Thomas 460
MacNeal, H. 332
Mahon, Viscount 139
Majo, J. Chr. de 365
Martakis, George 394
Martin, Lucienne 432
Matthews, Philip G., of Christ College, Cambridge 429
Mavrokordatos, Ioannes 341
MB 103
Mηνας, see Mynas
Mendonides, S. 129
Middlemore, Thomas, of Hawkes Bay 254
Middlesex Hospital School of Medicine 474
Middleton, John L. 306
Minoides Mynas, see Mynas
Molvais, C. 309
Montenai, Abbé de 24
Morris, William 368
Mortel, see Van de Mortel
Moulins, Charles des 333
Moulins, Lycée de 33
Mynas, Constantinos Minoides 257

N

N. A. 376
Neustrelitz Library 322, 451
Newnham College Library 318
Nicolaevsky Academy 34, 176, 352, 418
Nissen, Ole Hastvig 48
'Non Nobis Solum' 124
Nordkirchen, – 32, 180, 247
Norman, James 377

O

O. I. X. 382
Orléans, Antoine, d', Duc de Montpensier 282
Overall, P. G. 412

P

P. T. 320
Pairier 270
Palmer, Francis 393
Papatheodorou, I. 78
Paris, city of 298
Pendarves, E. W. Wynne 21
Piacenza, Bartolomeo 290
Piccolomini, see Bandini
Piemonte, Leonardo 310
Pixley, John Nicol Fergusson 194
Popham, E. W. Leyborne 183
Praag, J. A. van 408

R

Raetivand 444
Ramond 216
Raulin, V. 349
Relief Synod 12
Rey, E. 353
Rhodocanakis Library 41
Roanne, College de 269
Rohan Chabot, F. de, Count 134
Roland, Eric von 337
Roslebischen School library 408
Rossignol, – 33
Rouger, Gilbert 287
Russell Institution 138

S

S. D. M. 420
'Salus morientibus una' 115
Salweg, T. R. (?Salwey) 119
Santa Maria Magdalena Rothomagensis 436
Saye and Seale, Lord 57
Schliemann, Heinrich 284
Schliemann, Sophia 380
Schönborn-Buchheim, Count 115
Schur, Nathan 292
Sebastian, Errol Graham 470
Sewall, Dr. 457
Seymor, Thomas Day 282
Shedden, John 87
Shedden, William, Mrs. 87
Sherlock, Thomas 112
Shirreff, A. 249
Signet Library 359
Σκανδάμης, A. 317
Skerret, I. 71
Skerrett, S. 71
'Skinos', see Gratsos
Sleeswijk, J. G. Dr. 149
Snelston Hall 120
Soames, Arthur G. 455
Société de Géographie Commerciale de Paris 253
Spicer, J. W. G., of Spye Park 420
St. Aloysius College 470
St. John, – 329

St. Panteleimon Monastery 281
Stanhope, John Spencer 401
Stanley, – 329
Stewart, Michael 182
Strickland, Sir George 426
Sturge, W. 433
Sutherland, A. 401

T
Thomlinson, Alfred 3
Thompson, Beilby, of Escrick 212
Thomson, G.D. 188
Thorlock, Honour 369
Thou, Jacques de 385
Tilley, Sir John 76
Tittenhanger Library 427
Tower, Christopher 28, 36
TS 280

U
Union Club 225

V
Van de Mortel, J.B. 103

Vander Cruysen, Nicolas François 52
Venables, John 267
Vernon family 295
Versailles, Grand Seminaire de 33
'Virtute non Verbis' 270
Voemel, I.T. 56

W
Wachler, – 199
Way, Robert Edward 369
Wese 328
Western College, Brighton 288
Westport House Library 396
White, Henry 102
White-Newton, J. 34
Wickelmann, Arthur, of Berlin 407
Williams, Montague 470
Wincote, Charles 430
Woodeson, Leonard 377

Z
Zervas, George A. 182
Zervudachi, Peter 344
Zulueta, Rev. F. de 470

CORRIGENDA

The references are to entry numbers.

6. for Arvanitides read Arvanitidis
63. for A. E. Lemaitre read A. F. Lemaitre
77. Fred Boissonnas made his first trip to Greece in 1903, in company with Daniel Baud-Bovy, head of the School of Fine Arts in Geneva. During the ensuing years from 1903 to 1930 he photographed many places in Greece and Asia Minor and published a number of albums of his Greek photographs, including several books which appeared under the general title *L'Image de la Grèce*, with subtitles citing the areas described. An English edition of his photographs with text by Baud-Bovy is the large folio *In Greece: Journeys by mountain and valley*, 1920. In 1913 he and Baud-Bovy, in company with a local climber, made the first ascent of Mt. Olympus.
116. heading imprint: for Koromilas read Koromelas
153. line 8: for John Marten Cripps read John Martin Cripps
186. line 9: for Frances Pierpoint Burton read Francis Pierpoint Burton
213. heading imprint: for Edwin Arnold read Edward Arnold
235. lines 5 and 7: for Eliott read Elliott
261. heading: for Francois read François
267. line 2 of note: for Riepenhuasen read Riepenhausen
291. line 8 of note: for Ariel des Faux read Ariel des Feux
331. The poet, novelist, and dramatist Hofmannsthal used themes from ancient Greek literature for many of his works. His dramatic poem *Elektra* was set to music by Richard Strauss, and the two men also produced *Ariadne auf Naxos*. Hofmannsthal's introductory text to Holdt's photographs reflects his feelings about classical antiquity as a background to a journey in Greece, and the spiritual quality with which he regards such a journey.
365. heading imprint: for Glykes read Glykys
436. last line of note: for Hiller van Gaertringen read Hiller von Gaertringen
456. heading: for Meletios read Meletius
558. last line of note: for Pettretini read Petrettini
726. heading imprint: for Librarie read Librairie
802. line 3 of the note: for Lane-Pool read Lane-Poole
805. line 1 of the note: for Schutz read Schütz
809. Hoar Cross Hall in Staffordshire belonged to the Meynell family until the middle of the 20th century.

The Catalogue of the Library of Dimitris Contominas, compiled and edited by Leonora Navari, and designed by Konstantinos Sp. Staikos, was typeset and electronically paginated by Mary Karava in Apollonia fonts. Preparation of the illustrations, colour separations, computer aided stripping and films by Diagramma - Ch. Koutrouditsos. Lay-out by Anna Hadjiantoniou. The book was printed by Petros Ballides in 1000 copies for Kotinos S.A., on 135 gram Garda matt paper in January 2004. Bookbinding by Vassilis Kypraios.